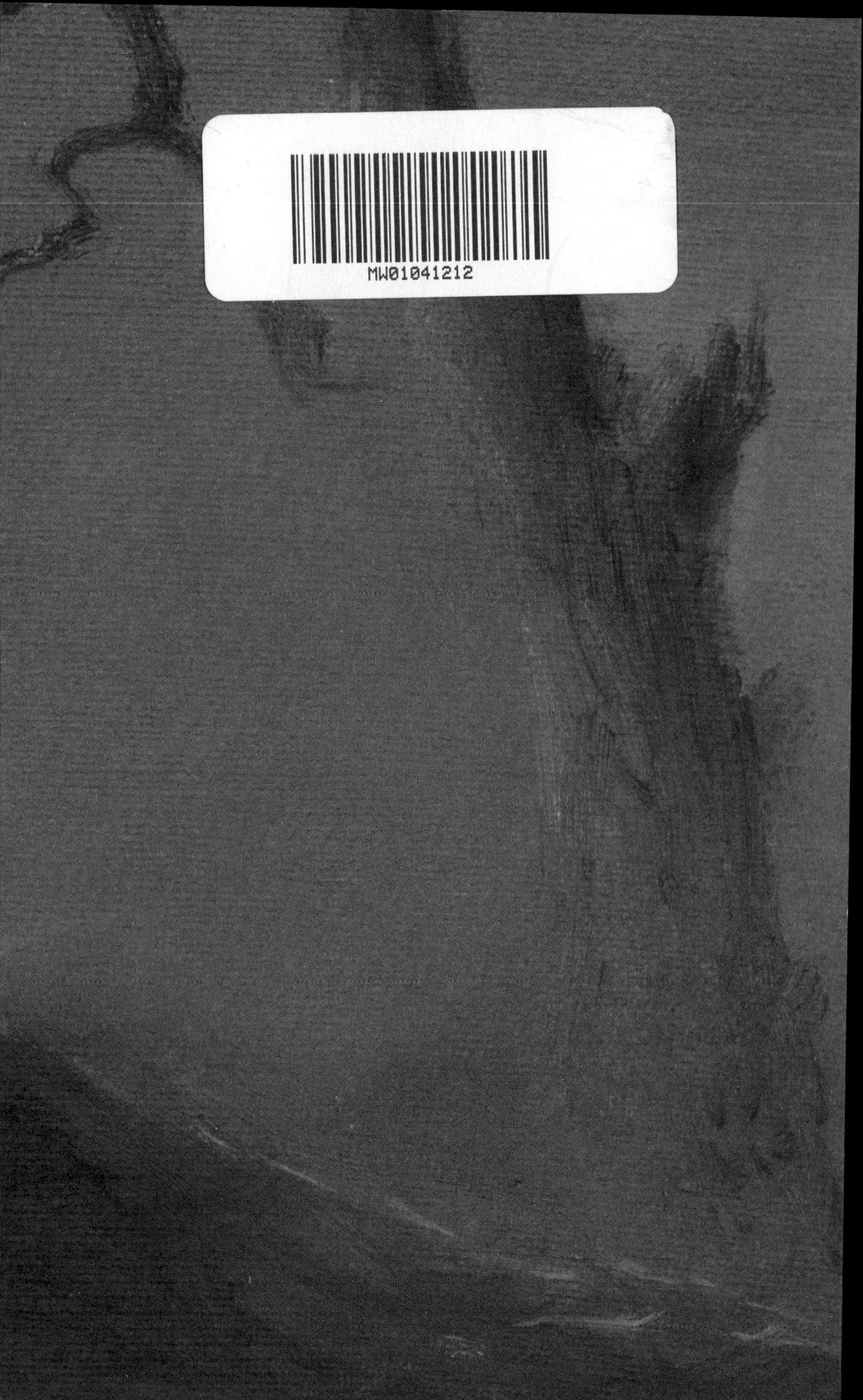

Selected Works of Edgar Allan Poe

Selected Works of Edgar Allan Poe

Word Cloud Classics
San Diego

Canterbury Classics
An imprint of Printers Row Publishing Group
9717 Pacific Heights Blvd, San Diego, CA 92121
www.canterburyclassicsbooks.com • mail@canterburyclassicsbooks.com

Correspondence concerning the content of this book should be sent to Canterbury Classics, Editorial Department, at the above address.

Publisher: Peter Norton • Associate Publisher: Ana Parker
Art Director: Charles McStravick
Senior Developmental Editor: April Graham
Editorial Team: Stephanie Romero Gamboa, Angela Garcia, Traci Douglas
Production/Design Team: Jonathan Lopes, Rusty von Dyl, Beno Chan, Julie Greene, Rosemary Rae

Cover design: Jeanette Barroso at J20Graphics
Image credits: gio_banfi/DigitalVision Vectors via Getty Images, alexblacksea/Shutterstock.com; Campwillowlake via Getty Images; DenisKrivoy via Getty Images; FORGEM via Getty Images; Vectorig via Getty Images; Tuleedin via Getty Images
Endpapers: Pobytov/DigitalVision Vectors via Getty Images

ISBN: 978-1-6672-0318-8

MIX
Paper | Supporting responsible forestry
FSC www.fsc.org FSC® C144853

Printed in China
27 26 25 24 23 2 3 4 5 6

Editor's Note: These works have been published in their original form to preserve the author's intent and style.

CONTENTS

Poems

Stories

MS. Found in a Bottle

Qui n'a plus qu'un moment à vivre
N'a plus rien a dissimuler.
—*Quinault*—*Atys*

Of my country and of my family I have little to say. Ill usage and length of years have driven me from the one, and estranged me from the other. Hereditary wealth afforded me an education of no common order, and a contemplative turn of mind enabled me to methodize the stores which early study very diligently garnered up.—Beyond all things, the study of the German moralists gave me great delight; not from any ill-advised admiration of their eloquent madness, but from the ease with which my habits of rigid thought enabled me to detect their falsities. I have often been reproached with the aridity of my genius; a deficiency of imagination has been imputed to me as a crime; and the Pyrrhonism of my opinions has at all times rendered me notorious. Indeed, a strong relish for physical philosophy has, I fear, tinctured my mind with a very common error of this age—I mean the habit of referring occurrences, even the least susceptible of such reference, to the principles of that science. Upon the whole, no person could be less liable than myself to be led away from the severe precincts of truth by the *ignes fatui* of superstition. I have thought proper to premise thus much, lest the incredible tale I have to tell should be considered rather the raving of a crude imagination, than the positive experience of a mind to which the reveries of fancy have been a dead letter and a nullity.

After many years spent in foreign travel, I sailed in the year 18—, from the port of Batavia, in the rich and populous island of Java, on a voyage to the Archipelago of the Sunda islands. I went as passenger—having no other inducement than a kind of nervous restlessness which haunted me as a fiend.

Our vessel was a beautiful ship of about four hundred tons, copper-fastened, and built at Bombay of Malabar teak. She was freighted with cotton-wool and oil, from the Lachadive islands. We had also on board coir, jaggeree, ghee, cocoa-nuts, and a few cases of opium. The stowage was clumsily done, and the vessel consequently crank.

We got under way with a mere breath of wind, and for many days stood along the eastern coast of Java, without any other incident to beguile the monotony of our course than the occasional meeting with some of the small grabs of the Archipelago to which we were bound.

One evening, leaning over the taffrail, I observed a very singular, isolated cloud, to the N.W. It was remarkable, as well for its color, as from its being the first we had seen since our departure from Batavia. I watched it attentively until sunset, when it spread all at once to the eastward and westward, girting in the horizon with a narrow strip of vapor, and looking like a long line of low beach. My notice was soon afterwards attracted by the dusky-red appearance of the moon, and the peculiar character of the sea. The latter was undergoing a rapid change, and the water seemed more than usually transparent. Although I could distinctly see the bottom, yet, heaving the lead, I found the ship in fifteen fathoms. The air now became intolerably hot, and was loaded with spiral exhalations similar to those arising from heat iron. As night came on, every breath of wind died away, and more entire calm it is impossible to conceive. The flame of a candle burned upon the poop without the least perceptible motion, and a long hair, held between the finger and thumb, hung without the possibility of detecting a vibration. However, as the captain said he could perceive no indication of danger, and as we were drifting in bodily to shore, he ordered the sails to be furled, and the anchor let go. No watch was set, and the crew, consisting principally of Malays, stretched themselves deliberately upon deck. I went below—not without a full presentiment of evil. Indeed, every appearance warranted me in apprehending a Simoom. I told the captain my fears; but he paid no attention to what I said, and left me without deigning to give a reply. My uneasiness, however, prevented me from sleeping, and about midnight I went upon deck. As I placed my foot upon the upper step of the companion-ladder,

I was startled by a loud, humming noise, like that occasioned by the rapid revolution of a mill-wheel, and before I could ascertain its meaning, I found the ship quivering to its centre. In the next instant, a wilderness of foam hurled us upon our beam-ends, and, rushing over us fore and aft, swept the entire decks from stem to stern.

The extreme fury of the blast proved, in a great measure, the salvation of the ship. Although completely water-logged, yet, as her masts had gone by the board, she rose, after a minute, heavily from the sea, and, staggering awhile beneath the immense pressure of the tempest, finally righted.

By what miracle I escaped destruction, it is impossible to say. Stunned by the shock of the water, I found myself, upon recovery, jammed in between the stern-post and rudder. With great difficulty I gained my feet, and looking dizzily around, was, at first, struck with the idea of our being among breakers; so terrific, beyond the wildest imagination, was the whirlpool of mountainous and foaming ocean within which we were engulfed. After a while, I heard the voice of an old Swede, who had shipped with us at the moment of our leaving port. I hallooed to him with all my strength, and presently he came reeling aft. We soon discovered that we were the sole survivors of the accident. All on deck, with the exception of ourselves, had been swept overboard;—the captain and mates must have perished as they slept, for the cabins were deluged with water. Without assistance, we could expect to do little for the security of the ship, and our exertions were at first paralyzed by the momentary expectation of going down. Our cable had, of course, parted like pack-thread, at the first breath of the hurricane, or we should have been instantaneously overwhelmed. We scudded with frightful velocity before the sea, and the water made clear breaches over us. The frame-work of our stern was shattered excessively, and, in almost every respect, we had received considerable injury; but to our extreme joy we found the pumps unchoked, and that we had made no great shifting of our ballast. The main fury of the blast had already blown over, and we apprehended little danger from the violence of the wind; but we looked forward to its total cessation with dismay; well believing, that, in our shattered condition, we should inevitably perish in the tremendous swell which would ensue. But this very just apprehension seemed by no means likely to be soon verified. For five entire days and nights—during which our only subsistence was a small quantity of jaggeree, procured with great difficulty from the forecastle—the hulk flew at a rate defying computation, before rapidly succeeding flaws of wind, which, without equalling the first violence of the Simoom, were still more terrific than any tempest I had before encountered. Our course for the first four days was, with trifling variations, S.E. and by S.; and we must have run down the coast of New Holland.—On the fifth day the cold became extreme, although the wind had hauled round a point more to the northward.—The sun arose with a sickly yellow lustre, and clambered a very few degrees above the horizon—emitting no decisive light.—There were no clouds apparent, yet the wind was upon the increase, and blew with a fitful and unsteady fury. About noon, as nearly as we could guess, our attention was again arrested by the appearance of the sun. It gave out no light, properly so called, but a dull and sullen glow without reflection, as if all its rays were polarized. Just before sinking within the turgid sea, its central fires suddenly went out, as if hurriedly extinguished by some unaccountable power. It was a dim, sliver-like rim, alone, as it rushed down the unfathomable ocean.

We waited in vain for the arrival of the sixth day—that day to me has not arrived—to the Swede, never did arrive. Thenceforward we were enshrouded in patchy darkness, so that we could not have seen an object at twenty paces from the ship. Eternal night continued to envelop us, all unrelieved by the phosphoric sea-brilliancy to which we had been accustomed in the tropics. We observed too, that, although the tempest continued to rage with unabated violence, there was no longer to be discovered the usual appearance of surf, or foam, which had hitherto attended us. All around were horror, and thick gloom, and a black sweltering desert of ebony.—Superstitious terror crept by degrees into the spirit of the old Swede, and my own soul was wrapped up in silent wonder. We neglected all care of the ship, as worse than useless, and securing ourselves, as well as possible, to the stump of the mizen-mast, looked out bitterly into the world of ocean. We had no means of calculating time, nor could we form any guess of our situation. We were, however, well aware of having made farther to the southward than any previous navigators, and felt great amazement at not meeting with the usual impediments of ice. In the meantime every moment threatened to be our last—every mountainous billow hurried to overwhelm us. The swell surpassed anything I had imagined possible, and that we were not instantly buried is a miracle. My companion spoke of the lightness of our cargo, and reminded me of the excellent qualities of our ship; but I could not help feeling the utter hopelessness of hope itself, and prepared myself gloomily for that death which I thought nothing could defer beyond an hour, as, with every knot of way the ship made, the swelling of the black stupendous seas became more dismally appalling. At times we gasped for breath at an elevation beyond the albatross—at times became dizzy with the velocity of our descent into some watery hell, where the air grew stagnant, and no sound disturbed the slumbers of the kraken.

We were at the bottom of one of these abysses, when a quick scream from my companion broke fearfully upon the night. "See! see!" cried he, shrieking in my ears, "Almighty God! see! see!" As he spoke, I became aware of a dull, sullen glare of red light which streamed down the sides of the vast chasm where we lay, and threw a fitful brilliancy upon our deck. Casting my eyes upwards, I beheld a spectacle which froze the current of my blood. At a terrific height directly above us, and upon the very verge of the precipitous descent, hovered a gigantic ship of, perhaps, four thousand tons. Although upreared upon the summit of a wave more than a hundred times her own altitude, her apparent size exceeded that of any ship of the line or East Indiaman in existence. Her huge hull was of a deep dingy black, unrelieved by any of the customary carvings of a ship. A single row of brass cannon protruded from her open ports, and dashed from their polished surfaces the fires of innumerable battle-lanterns, which swung to and fro about her rigging. But what mainly inspired us with horror and astonishment, was that she bore up under a press of sail in the very teeth of that supernatural sea, and of that ungovernable hurricane. When we first discovered her, her bows were alone to be seen, as she rose slowly from the dim and horrible gulf beyond her. For a moment of intense terror she paused upon the giddy pinnacle, as if in contemplation of her own sublimity, then trembled and tottered, and—came down.

At this instant, I know not what sudden self-possession came over my spirit. Staggering as far aft as I could, I awaited fearlessly the ruin that was to overwhelm. Our own vessel was at length ceasing from her struggles, and sinking with her head to the sea. The shock of the descending mass struck her, consequently, in that portion of her frame which was already under water, and the inevitable result was to hurl me, with irresistible violence, upon the rigging of the stranger.

As I fell, the ship hove in stays, and went about; and to the confusion ensuing I attributed my escape from the notice of the crew. With little difficulty I made my way unperceived to the main hatchway, which was partially open, and soon found an opportunity of secreting myself in the hold. Why I did so I can hardly tell. An indefinite sense of awe, which at first sight of the navigators of the ship had taken hold of my mind, was perhaps the principle of my concealment. I was unwilling to trust myself with a race of people who had offered, to the cursory glance I had taken, so many points of vague novelty, doubt, and apprehension. I therefore thought proper to contrive a hiding-place in the hold. This I did by removing a small portion of the shifting-boards, in such a manner as to afford me a convenient retreat between the huge timbers of the ship.

I had scarcely completed my work, when a footstep in the hold forced me to make use of it. A man passed by my place of concealment with a feeble and unsteady gait. I could not see his face, but had an opportunity of observing his general appearance. There was about it an evidence of great age and infirmity. His knees tottered beneath a load of years, and his entire frame quivered under the burthen. He muttered to himself, in a low broken tone, some words of a language which I could not understand, and groped in a corner among a pile of singular-looking instruments, and decayed charts of navigation. His manner was a wild mixture of the peevishness of second childhood, and the solemn dignity of a God. He at length went on deck, and I saw him no more.

* * * * *

A feeling, for which I have no name, has taken possession of my soul—a sensation which will admit of no analysis, to which the lessons of bygone times are inadequate, and for which I fear futurity itself will offer me no key. To a mind constituted like my own, the latter consideration is an evil. I shall never—I know that I shall never—be satisfied with regard to the nature of my conceptions. Yet it is not wonderful that these conceptions are indefinite, since they have their origin in sources so utterly novel. A new sense—a new entity is added to my soul.

* * * * *

It is long since I first trod the deck of this terrible ship, and the rays of my destiny are, I think, gathering to a focus. Incomprehensible men! Wrapped up in meditations of a kind which I cannot divine, they pass me by unnoticed. Concealment is utter folly on my part, for the people *will not see*. It was but just now that I passed directly before the eyes of the mate—it was no long while ago that I ventured into the captain's own private cabin, and took thence the materials with which I write, and have written. I shall from time to time continue this Journal. It is true that I may not find an opportunity of transmitting it to the world, but I will not fail to make the endeavour. At the last moment I will enclose the MS. in a bottle, and cast it within the sea.

* * * * *

An incident has occurred which has given me new room for meditation. Are such things the operation of ungoverned Chance? I had ventured upon deck and thrown myself down, without attracting any notice, among a pile of ratlin-stuff and old sails in the bottom of the yawl. While musing upon the singularity of my fate, I unwittingly daubed with a tar-brush the edges of a neatly-folded studding-sail which lay near me on a barrel. The studding-sail is now bent upon the ship, and the thoughtless touches of the brush are spread out into the word DISCOVERY.

I have made many observations lately upon the structure of the vessel. Although well armed, she is not, I think, a ship of war. Her rigging, build, and general equipment, all negative a supposition of this kind. What she *is not*, I can easily perceive—what she is I fear it is impossible to say. I know not how it is, but in scrutinizing her strange model and singular cast of spars, her huge size and overgrown suits of canvas, her severely simple bow and antiquated stern, there will occasionally flash across my mind a sensation of familiar things, and there is always mixed up with such indistinct shadows of recollection, an unaccountable memory of old foreign chronicles and ages long ago.

* * * * *

I have been looking at the timbers of the ship. She is built of a material to which I am a stranger. There is a peculiar character about the wood which strikes me as rendering it unfit for the purpose to which it has been applied. I mean its extreme *porousness*, considered independently by the worm-eaten condition which is a consequence of navigation in these seas, and apart from the rottenness attendant upon age. It will appear perhaps an observation somewhat over-curious, but this wood would have every characteristic of Spanish oak, if Spanish oak were distended by any unnatural means.

In reading the above sentence a curious apothegm of an old weather-beaten Dutch navigator comes full upon my recollection. "It is as sure," he was wont to say, when any doubt was entertained of his veracity, "as sure as there is a sea where the ship itself will grow in bulk like the living body of the seaman."

* * * * *

About an hour ago, I made bold to thrust myself among a group of the crew. They paid me no manner of attention, and, although I stood in the very midst of them all, seemed utterly unconscious of my presence. Like the one I had at first seen in the hold, they all bore about them the marks of a hoary old age. Their knees trembled with infirmity; their shoulders were bent double with decrepitude; their shrivelled skins rattled in the wind; their voices were low, tremulous and broken; their eyes glistened with the rheum of years; and their gray hairs streamed terribly in the tempest. Around them, on every part of the deck, lay scattered mathematical instruments of the most quaint and obsolete construction.

* * * * *

I mentioned some time ago the bending of a studding-sail. From that period the ship, being thrown dead off the wind, has continued her terrific course due south, with every rag of canvas packed upon her, from her trucks to her lower studding-sail booms, and rolling every moment her top-gallant yard-arms into the most appalling hell of water which it can enter into the mind of a man to imagine. I have just left the deck, where I find it impossible to maintain a footing, although the crew seem to experience little inconvenience. It appears to me a miracle of miracles that our enormous bulk is not swallowed up at once and forever. We are surely doomed to hover continually upon the brink of Eternity, without taking a final plunge into the abyss. From billows a thousand times more stupendous than any I have ever seen, we glide away with the facility of the arrowy sea-gull; and the colossal waters rear their heads above us like demons of the deep, but like demons confined to simple threats and forbidden to destroy. I am led to attribute these frequent escapes to the only natural cause which can account for such effect.—I must suppose the ship to be within the influence of some strong current, or impetuous under-tow.

* * * * *

I have seen the captain face to face, and in his own cabin—but, as I expected, he paid me no attention. Although in his appearance there is, to a casual observer, nothing which might bespeak him more or less than man, still a feeling of irrepressible reverence and awe mingled with the sensation of wonder with which I regarded him. In stature he is nearly my own height; that is, about five feet eight inches. He is of a well-knit and compact frame of body, neither robust nor remarkably otherwise. But it is the singularity of the expression which reigns upon the face—it is the intense, the wonderful, the thrilling evidence of old age, so utter, so extreme, which excites within my spirit a sense—a sentiment ineffable. His forehead, although little wrinkled, seems to bear upon it the stamp of a myriad of years.—His gray hairs are records of the past, and his grayer eyes are Sybils of the future. The cabin floor was thickly strewn with strange, iron-clasped folios, and mouldering instruments of science, and obsolete long-forgotten charts. His head was bowed down upon his hands, and he pored, with a fiery unquiet eye, over a paper which I took to be a commission, and which, at all events, bore the signature of a monarch. He muttered to himself, as did the first seaman whom I saw in the hold, some low peevish syllables of a foreign tongue, and although the speaker was close at my elbow, his voice seemed to reach my ears from the distance of a mile.

* * * * *

The ship and all in it are imbued with the spirit of Eld. The crew glide to and fro like the ghosts of buried centuries; their eyes have an eager and uneasy meaning; and when their fingers fall athwart my path in the wild glare of the battle-lanterns, I feel as I have never felt before, although I have been all my life a dealer in antiquities, and have imbibed the shadows of fallen columns at Balbec, and Tadmor, and Persepolis, until my very soul has become a ruin.

* * * * *

When I look around me, I feel ashamed of my former apprehensions. If I trembled at the blast which has hitherto attended us, shall I not stand aghast at a warring of wind and ocean, to convey any idea of which the words tornado and simoom are trivial and ineffective? All in the immediate vicinity of the ship is the blackness of eternal night, and a chaos of foamless water; but, about a league on either side of us, may be seen, indistinctly and at intervals, stupendous ramparts of ice, towering away into the desolate sky, and looking like the walls of the universe.

* * * * *

As I imagined, the ship proves to be in a current; if that appellation can properly be given to a tide which, howling and shrieking by the white ice, thunders on to the southward with a velocity like the headlong dashing of a cataract.

* * * * *

To conceive the horror of my sensations is, I presume, utterly impossible; yet a curiosity to penetrate the mysteries of these awful regions, predominates even over my despair, and will reconcile me to the most hideous aspect of death. It is evident that we are hurrying onwards to some exciting knowledge—some never-to-be-imparted secret, whose attainment is destruction. Perhaps this current leads us to the southern pole itself. It must be confessed that a supposition apparently so wild has every probability in its favor.

* * * * *

The crew pace the deck with unquiet and tremulous step; but there is upon their countenances an expression more of the eagerness of hope than of the apathy of despair.

In the meantime the wind is still in our poop, and, as we carry a crowd of canvas, the ship is at times lifted bodily from out the sea—Oh, horror upon horror! The ice opens suddenly to the right, and to the left, and we are whirling dizzily, in immense concentric circles, round and round the borders of a gigantic amphitheatre, the summit of whose walls is lost in the darkness and the distance. But little time will be left me to ponder upon my destiny—the circles rapidly grow small—we are plunging madly within the grasp of the whirlpool—and amid a roaring, and bellowing, and thundering of ocean and of tempest, the ship is quivering, oh God! and—going down.

Note

The "MS. Found in a Bottle," was originally published in 1831, and it was not until many years afterwards that I became acquainted with the maps of Mercator, in which the ocean is represented as rushing, by four mouths, into the (northern) Polar Gulf, to be absorbed into the bowels of the earth; the Pole itself being represented by a black rock, towering to a prodigious height.

The Assignation (The Visionary)

Stay for me there! I will not fail.
To meet thee in that hollow vale.

—*Exequy on the death of his wife, by Henry King, Bishop of Chichester*

Ill-fated and mysterious man!—bewildered in the brilliancy of thine own imagination, and fallen in the flames of thine own youth! Again in fancy I behold thee! Once more thy form hath risen before me!—not—oh not as thou art—in the cold valley and shadow—but as thou *shouldst be*—squandering away a life of magnificent meditation in that city of dim visions, thine own Venice—which is a star-beloved Elysium of the sea, and the wide windows of whose Palladian palaces look down with a deep and bitter meaning upon the secrets of her silent waters. Yes! I repeat it—as thou *shouldst be*. There are surely other worlds than this—other thoughts than the thoughts of the multitude—other speculations than the speculations of the sophist. Who then shall call thy conduct into question? who blame thee for thy visionary hours, or denounce those occupations as a wasting away of life, which were but the overflowings of thine everlasting energies?

It was at Venice, beneath the covered archway there called the *Ponte di Sospiri*, that I met for the third or fourth time the person of whom I speak. It is with a confused recollection that I bring to mind the circumstances of that meeting. Yet I remember—ah! how should I forget?—the deep midnight, the Bridge of Sighs, the beauty of woman, and the Genius of Romance that stalked up and down the narrow canal.

It was a night of unusual gloom. The great clock of the Piazza had sounded the fifth hour of the Italian evening. The square of the Campanile lay silent and deserted, and the lights in the old Ducal Palace were dying fast away. I was returning home from the Piazetta, by way of the Grand Canal. But as my gondola arrived opposite the mouth of the canal San Marco, a female voice from its recesses broke suddenly upon the night, in one wild, hysterical, and long continued shriek. Startled at the sound, I sprang upon my feet: while the gondolier, letting slip his single oar, lost it in the pitchy darkness beyond a chance of recovery, and we were consequently left to the guidance of the current which here sets from the greater into the smaller channel. Like some huge and sable-feathered condor, we were slowly drifting down towards the Bridge of Sighs, when a thousand flambeaux flashing from the windows, and down the staircases of the Ducal Palace, turned all at once that deep gloom into a livid and preternatural day.

A child, slipping from the arms of its own mother, had fallen from an upper window of the lofty structure into the deep and dim canal. The quiet waters had closed placidly over their victim; and, although my own gondola was the only one in sight, many a stout swimmer, already in the stream, was seeking in vain upon the surface, the treasure which was to be found, alas! only within the abyss. Upon the broad black marble flagstones at the entrance of the palace, and a few steps above the water, stood a figure which none who then saw can have ever since forgotten. It was the Marchesa Aphrodite—the adoration of all Venice—the gayest of the gay—the most lovely where all were beautiful—but still the young wife of the old and intriguing Mentoni, and the mother of that fair child, her first and only one, who now, deep beneath the murky water, was thinking in bitterness of heart upon her sweet caresses, and exhausting its little life in struggles to call upon her name.

She stood alone. Her small, bare, and silvery feet gleamed in the black mirror of marble beneath her. Her hair, not as yet more than half loosened for the night from its ball-room array, clustered, amid a shower of diamonds, round and round her classical head, in curls like those of the young hyacinth. A snowy-white and gauze-like drapery seemed to be nearly the sole covering to her delicate form; but the mid-summer and midnight air was hot, sullen, and still, and no motion in the statue-like form itself, stirred even the folds of that raiment of very vapor which hung around it as the heavy marble hangs around the Niobe. Yet—strange to say!—her large lustrous eyes were not turned downwards upon that grave wherein her brightest hope lay buried—but riveted in a widely different direction! The prison of the Old Republic is, I think, the stateliest building in all Venice—but how could that lady gaze so fixedly upon it, when beneath her lay stifling her only child? Yon dark, gloomy niche, too, yawns right opposite her chamber window—what, then, *could* there be in its shadows—in its architecture—in its ivy-wreathed and solemn cornices—that the Marchesa di Mentoni had not wondered at a thousand times before? Nonsense!—Who does not remember that, at such a time as this, the eye, like a shattered mirror, multiplies the images of its sorrow, and sees in innumerable far-off places, the wo which is close at hand?

Many steps above the Marchesa, and within the arch of the water-gate, stood, in full dress, the Satyr-like figure of Mentoni himself. He was occasionally occupied in thrumming a guitar, and seemed *ennuye* to the very death, as at intervals he gave directions for the recovery of his child. Stupefied and aghast, I had myself no power to move from the upright position I had assumed upon first hearing the shriek, and must have presented to the eyes of the agitated group a spectral and ominous appearance, as with pale countenance and rigid limbs, I floated down among them in that funereal gondola.

All efforts proved in vain. Many of the most energetic in the search were relaxing their exertions, and yielding to a gloomy sorrow. There seemed but little hope for the child; (how much less than for the mother!) but now, from the interior of that dark niche which has been already mentioned as forming a part of the Old Republican prison, and as fronting the lattice of the Marchesa, a figure muffled in a cloak, stepped out within reach of the light, and, pausing a moment upon the verge of the giddy descent, plunged headlong into the canal. As, in an instant afterwards, he stood with the still living and breathing child within his grasp, upon the marble flagstones by the side of the Marchesa, his cloak, heavy with the drenching water, became unfastened, and, falling in folds about his feet, discovered to the wonder-stricken spectators the graceful person of a very young man, with the sound of whose name the greater part of Europe was then ringing.

No word spoke the deliverer. But the Marchesa! She will now receive her child—she will press it to her heart—she will cling to its little form, and smother it with her caresses. Alas! *another's* arms have taken it from the stranger—*another's* arms have taken it away, and borne it afar off, unnoticed, into the palace! And the Marchesa! Her lip—her beautiful lip trembles: tears are gathering in her eyes—those eyes which, like Pliny's acanthus, are "soft and almost liquid." Yes! tears are gathering in those eyes—and see! the entire woman thrills throughout the soul, and the statue has started into life! The pallor of the marble countenance, the swelling of the marble bosom, the very purity of the marble feet, we behold suddenly flushed over with a tide of ungovernable crimson; and a slight shudder quivers about her delicate frame, as a gentle air at Napoli about the rich silver lilies in the grass.

Why *should* that lady blush! To this demand there is no answer—except that, having left, in the eager haste and terror of a mother's heart, the privacy of her own boudoir, she has neglected to enthral her tiny feet in their slippers, and utterly forgotten to throw over her Venetian shoulders that drapery which is their due. What other possible reason could there have been for her so blushing?—for the glance of those wild appealing eyes? for the unusual tumult of that throbbing bosom?—for the convulsive pressure of that trembling hand?—that hand which fell, as Mentoni turned into the palace, accidentally, upon the hand of the stranger. What reason could there have been for the low—the singularly low tone of those unmeaning words which the lady uttered hurriedly in bidding him adieu? "Thou hast conquered," she said, or the murmurs of the water deceived me; "thou hast conquered—one hour after sunrise—we shall meet—so let it be!"

* * * * *

The tumult had subsided, the lights had died away within the palace, and the stranger, whom I now recognized, stood alone upon the flags. He shook with inconceivable agitation, and his eye glanced around in search of a gondola. I could not do less than offer him the service of my own; and he accepted the civility. Having obtained an oar at the water-gate, we proceeded together to his residence, while he rapidly recovered his self-possession, and spoke of our former slight acquaintance in terms of great apparent cordiality.

There are some subjects upon which I take pleasure in being minute. The person of the stranger—let me call him by this title, who to all the world was still a stranger—the person of the stranger is one of these subjects. In height he might have been below rather than above the medium size: although there were moments of intense passion when his frame actually *expanded* and belied the assertion. The light, almost slender symmetry of his figure, promised more of that ready activity which he evinced at the Bridge of Sighs, than of that Herculean strength which he has been known to wield without an effort, upon occasions of more dangerous emergency. With the mouth and chin of a deity—singular, wild, full, liquid eyes, whose shadows varied from pure hazel to intense and brilliant jet—and a profusion of curling, black hair, from which a forehead of unusual breadth gleamed forth at intervals all light and ivory—his were features than which I have seen none more classically regular, except, perhaps, the marble ones of the Emperor Commodus. Yet his countenance was, nevertheless, one of those which all men have seen at some period of their lives, and have never afterwards seen again. It had no peculiar—it had no settled predominant expression to be fastened upon the memory; a countenance seen and instantly forgotten—but forgotten with a vague and never-ceasing desire of recalling it to mind. Not that the spirit of each rapid passion failed, at any time, to throw its own distinct image upon the mirror of that face—but that the mirror, mirror-like, retained no vestige of the passion, when the passion had departed.

Upon leaving him on the night of our adventure, he solicited me, in what I thought an urgent manner, to call upon him *very* early the next morning. Shortly after sunrise, I found myself accordingly at his Palazzo, one of those huge structures of gloomy, yet fantastic pomp, which tower above the waters of the Grand Canal in the vicinity of the Rialto. I was shown up a broad winding staircase of mosaics, into an apartment whose unparalleled splendor burst through the opening door with an actual glare, making me blind and dizzy with luxuriousness.

I knew my acquaintance to be wealthy. Report had spoken of his possessions in terms which I had even ventured to call terms of ridiculous exaggeration. But as I gazed about me, I could not bring myself to believe that the wealth of any subject in Europe could have supplied the princely magnificence which burned and blazed around.

Although, as I say, the sun had arisen, yet the room was still brilliantly lighted up. I judge from this circumstance, as well as from an air of exhaustion in the countenance of my friend, that he had not retired to bed during the whole of the preceding night. In the architecture and embellishments of the chamber, the evident design had been to dazzle and astound. Little attention had been paid to the *decora* of what is technically called *keeping*, or to the proprieties of nationality. The eye wandered from object to object, and rested upon none—neither the *grotesques* of the Greek painters, nor the sculptures of the best Italian days, nor the huge carvings of untutored Egypt. Rich draperies in every part of the room trembled to the vibration of low, melancholy music, whose origin was not to be discovered. The senses were oppressed by mingled and conflicting perfumes, reeking up from strange convolute censers, together with multitudinous flaring and flickering tongues of emerald and violet fire. The rays of the newly risen sun poured in upon the whole, through windows, formed each of a single pane of crimson-tinted glass. Glancing to and fro, in a thousand reflections, from curtains which rolled from their cornices like cataracts of molten silver, the beams of natural glory mingled at length fitfully with the artificial light, and lay weltering in subdued masses upon a carpet of rich, liquid-looking cloth of Chili gold.

"Ha! ha! ha!—ha! ha! ha!"—laughed the proprietor, motioning me to a seat as I entered the room, and throwing himself back at full-length upon an ottoman. "I see," said he, perceiving that I could not immediately reconcile myself to the *bienséance* of so singular a welcome—"I see you are astonished at my apartment—at my statues—my pictures—my originality of conception in architecture and upholstery! absolutely drunk, eh, with my magnificence? But pardon me, my dear sir (here his tone of voice dropped to the very spirit of cordiality), pardon me for my uncharitable laughter. You appeared so *utterly* astonished. Besides, some things are so completely ludicrous, that a man *must* laugh or die. To die laughing, must be the most glorious of all glorious deaths! Sir Thomas More—a very fine man was Sir Thomas More—Sir Thomas More died laughing, you remember. Also in the *Absurdities* of Ravisius Textor, there is a long list of characters who came to the same magnificent end. Do you know, however," continued he musingly, "that at Sparta (which is now Palae; ochori), at Sparta, I say, to the west of the citadel, among a chaos of scarcely visible ruins, is a kind of *socle*, upon which are still legible the letters ΛΑΞΜ. They are undoubtedly part of ΓΕΛΑΞΜΑ. Now, at Sparta were a thousand temples and shrines to a thousand different divinities. How exceedingly strange that the altar of Laughter should have survived all the others! But in the present instance," he resumed, with a singular alteration of voice and manner, "I have no right to be merry at your expense. You might well have been amazed. Europe cannot produce anything so fine as this, my little regal cabinet. My other apartments are by no means of the same order—mere *ultras* of fashionable insipidity. This is better than fashion—is it not? Yet this has but to be seen to become the rage—that is, with those who could afford it at the cost of their entire patrimony. I have guarded, however, against any such profanation. With one exception, you are the only human being besides myself and my *valet*, who has been admitted within the mysteries of these imperial precincts, since they have been bedizzened as you see!"

I bowed in acknowledgment—for the overpowering sense of splendor and perfume, and music, together with the unexpected eccentricity of his address and manner, prevented me from expressing, in words, my appreciation of what I might have construed into a compliment.

"Here," he resumed, arising and leaning on my arm as he sauntered around the apartment, "here are paintings from the Greeks to Cimabue, and from Cimabue to the present hour. Many are chosen, as you see, with little deference to the opinions of Virtu. They are all, however, fitting tapestry for a chamber such as this. Here, too, are some *chefs d'oeuvre* of the unknown great; and here, unfinished designs by men, celebrated in their day, whose very names the perspicacity of the academies has left to silence and to me. What think you," said he, turning abruptly as he spoke—"what think you of this Madonna della Pieta?"

"It is Guido's own!" I said, with all the enthusiasm of my nature, for I had been poring intently over its surpassing loveliness. "It is Guido's own!—how *could* you have obtained it?—she is undoubtedly in painting what the Venus is in sculpture."

"Ha!" said he thoughtfully, "the Venus—the beautiful Venus?—the Venus of the Medici?—she of the diminutive head and the gilded hair? Part of the left arm (here his voice dropped so as to be heard with difficulty) and all the right, are restorations; and in the coquetry of that right arm lies, I think, the quintessence of all affectation. Give *me* the Canova! The Apollo, too, is a copy—there can be no doubt of it—blind fool that I am, who cannot behold the boasted inspiration of the Apollo! I cannot help—pity me!—I cannot help preferring the Antinous. Was it not Socrates who said that the statuary found his statue in the block of marble? Then Michael Angelo was by no means original in his couplet—

'Non ha l'ottimo artista alcun concetto
Che un marmo solo in se non circunscriva.'"

It has been, or should be remarked, that, in the manner of the true gentleman, we are always aware of a difference from the bearing of the vulgar, without being at once precisely able to determine in what such difference consists. Allowing the remark to have applied in its full force to the outward demeanor of my acquaintance, I felt it, on that eventful morning, still more fully applicable to his moral temperament and character. Nor can I better define that peculiarity of spirit which seemed to place him so essentially apart from all other human beings, than by calling it a *habit* of intense and continual thought, pervading even his most trivial actions—intruding upon his moments of dalliance—and interweaving itself with his very flashes of merriment—like adders which writhe from out the eyes of the grinning masks in the cornices around the temples of Persepolis.

I could not help, however, repeatedly observing, through the mingled tone of levity and solemnity with which he rapidly descanted upon matters of little importance, a certain air of trepidation—a degree of nervous *unction* in action and in speech—an unquiet excitability of manner which appeared to me at all times unaccountable, and upon some occasions even filled me with alarm. Frequently, too, pausing in the middle of a sentence whose commencement he had apparently forgotten, he seemed to be listening in the deepest attention, as if either in momentary expectation of a visiter, or to sounds which must have had existence in his imagination alone.

It was during one of these reveries or pauses of apparent abstraction, that, in turning over a page of the poet and scholar Politian's beautiful tragedy *The Orfeo* (the first native Italian tragedy), which lay near me upon an ottoman, I discovered a passage underlined in pencil. It was a passage towards the end of the third act—a passage of the most heart-stirring excitement—a passage which, although tainted with impurity, no man shall read without a thrill of novel emotion—no woman without a sigh. The whole page was blotted with fresh tears; and, upon the opposite interleaf, were the following English lines, written in a hand so very different from the peculiar characters of my acquaintance, that I had some difficulty in recognising it as his own:

Thou wast that all to me, love,
For which my soul did pine—
A green isle in the sea, love,
A fountain and a shrine,
All wreathed with fairy fruits and flowers;
And all the flowers were mine.

Ah, dream too bright to last!
Ah, starry Hope, that didst arise
But to be overcast!
A voice from out the Future cries,
"Onward! "—but o'er the Past
(Dim gulf!) my spirit hovering lies,
Mute—motionless—aghast!

For alas! alas! with me
The light of life is o'er.
"No more—no more—no more,"
(Such language holds the solemn sea
To the sands upon the shore),
Shall bloom the thunder-blasted tree,

Or the stricken eagle soar!
Now all my hours are trances;
And all my nightly dreams
Are where the dark eye glances,
And where thy footstep gleams,
In what ethereal dances,
By what Italian streams.

Alas! for that accursed time
They bore thee o'er the billow,
From Love to titled age and crime,
And an unholy pillow!—
From me, and from our misty clime,
Where weeps the silver willow!

That these lines were written in English—a language with which I had not believed their author acquainted—afforded me little matter for surprise. I was too well aware of the extent of his acquirements, and of the singular pleasure he took in concealing them from observation, to be astonished at any similar discovery; but the place of date, I must confess, occasioned me no little amazement. It had been originally written London, and afterwards carefully overscored—not, however, so effectually as to conceal the word from a scrutinizing eye. I say, this occasioned me no little amazement; for I well remember that, in a former conversation with a friend, I particularly inquired if he had at any time met in *London* the Marchesa di Mentoni (who for some years previous to her marriage had resided in that city), when his answer, if I mistake not, gave me to understand that he had never visited the metropolis of Great Britain. I might as (without, of course, giving credit to a report involving so many improbabilities), that the person of whom I speak, was not only by birth, but in education, an *Englishman*.

* * * * *

"There is one painting," said he, without being aware of my notice of the tragedy—"there is still one painting which you have not seen." And throwing aside a drapery, he discovered a full-length portrait of the Marchesa Aphrodite.

Human art could have done no more in the delineation of her superhuman beauty. The same ethereal figure which stood before me the preceding night upon the steps of the Ducal Palace, stood before me once again. But in the expression of the countenance, which was beaming all over with smiles, there still lurked (incomprehensible anomaly!) that fitful stain of melancholy which will ever be found inseparable from the perfection of the beautiful. Her right arm lay folded over her bosom. With her left she pointed downward to a curiously fashioned vase. One small, fairy foot, alone visible, barely touched the earth; and, scarcely discernible in the brilliant atmosphere which seemed to encircle and enshrine her loveliness, floated a pair of the most delicately imagined wings. My glance fell from the painting to the figure of my friend, and the vigorous words of Chapman's *Bussy D'Ambois*, quivered instinctively upon my lips:

"He is up
There like a Roman statue! He will stand
Till Death hath made him marble!"

"Come," he said at length, turning towards a table of richly enamelled and massive silver, upon which were a few goblets fantastically stained, together with two large Etruscan vases, fashioned in the same extraordinary model as that in the foreground of the portrait, and filled with what I supposed to be Johannisberger. "Come," he said, abruptly, "let us drink! It is early—but let us drink. It is *indeed* early," he continued, musingly, as a cherub with a heavy golden hammer made the apartment ring with the first hour after sunrise: "It is *indeed* early—but what matters it? let us drink! Let us pour out an offering to yon solemn sun which these gaudy lamps and censers are so eager to subdue!" And, having made me pledge him in a bumper, he swallowed in rapid succession several goblets of the wine.

"To dream," he continued, resuming the tone of his desultory conversation, as he held up to the rich light of a censer one of the magnificent vases—"to dream has been the business of my life. I have therefore framed for myself, as you see, a bower of dreams. In the heart of Venice could I have erected a better? You behold around you, it is true, a medley of architectural embellishments.

The chastity of Ionia is offended by antediluvian devices, and the sphynxes of Egypt are outstretched upon carpets of gold. Yet the effect is incongruous to the timid alone. Proprieties of place, and especially of time, are the bugbears which terrify mankind from the contemplation of the magnificent. Once I was myself a decorist; but that sublimation of folly has palled upon my soul. All this is now the fitter for my purpose. Like these arabesque censers, my spirit is writhing in fire, and the delirium of this scene is fashioning me for the wilder visions of that land of real dreams whither I am now rapidly departing." He here paused abruptly, bent his head to his bosom, and seemed to listen to a sound which I could not hear. At length, erecting his frame, he looked upwards, and ejaculated the lines of the Bishop of Chichester:

"Stay for me there! I will not fail
To meet thee in that hollow vale."

In the next instant, confessing the power of the wine, he threw himself at full-length upon an ottoman.

A quick step was now heard upon the staircase, and a loud knock at the door rapidly succeeded. I was hastening to anticipate a second disturbance, when a page of Mentoni's household burst into the room, and faltered out, in a voice choking with emotion, the incoherent words, "My mistress!—my mistress!—Poisoned!—poisoned! Oh, beautiful—oh, beautiful Aphrodite!"

Bewildered, I flew to the ottoman, and endeavored to arouse the sleeper to a sense of the startling intelligence. But his limbs were rigid—his lips were livid—his lately beaming eyes were riveted in *death*. I staggered back towards the table—my hand fell upon a cracked and blackened goblet—and a consciousness of the entire and terrible truth flashed suddenly over my soul.

Berenice

> Dicebant mihi sodales, si sepulchrum amicae visitarem, curas meas aliquantulum forelevatas.
>
> —*Ebn Zaiat*

Misery is manifold. The wretchedness of earth is multiform. Overreaching the wide horizon as the rainbow, its hues are as various as the hues of that arch—as distinct too, yet as intimately blended. Overreaching the wide horizon as the rainbow! How is it that from beauty I have derived a type of unloveliness?—from the covenant of peace, a simile of sorrow? But as, in ethics, evil is a consequence of good, so, in fact, out of joy is sorrow born. Either the memory of past bliss is the anguish of today, or the agonies which *are*, have their origin in the ecstasies which *might have been.*

My baptismal name is Egaeus; that of my family I will not mention. Yet there are no towers in the land more time-honored than my gloomy, gray, hereditary halls. Our line has been called a race of visionaries; and in many striking particulars—in the character of the family mansion—in the frescos of the chief saloon—in the tapestries of the dormitories—in the chiselling of some buttresses in the armory—but more especially in the gallery of antique paintings—in the fashion of the library chamber—and, lastly, in the very peculiar nature of the library's contents—there is more than sufficient evidence to warrant the belief.

The recollections of my earliest years are connected with that chamber, and with its volumes—of which latter I will say no more. Here died my mother. Herein was I born. But it is mere idleness to say that I had not lived before—that the soul has no previous existence. You deny it?—let us not argue the matter. Convinced myself, I seek not to convince. There is, however, a remembrance of aerial forms—of spiritual and meaning eyes—of sounds, musical yet sad—a remembrance which will not be excluded; a memory like a shadow—vague, variable, indefinite, unsteady; and like a shadow, too, in the impossibility of my getting rid of it while the sunlight of my reason shall exist.

In that chamber was I born. Thus awaking from the long night of what seemed, but was not, nonentity, at once into the very regions of fairy land—into a palace of imagination—into the wild dominions of monastic thought and erudition—it is not singular that I gazed around me with a startled and ardent eye—that I loitered away my boyhood in books, and dissipated my youth in reverie; but it *is* singular that as years rolled away, and the noon of manhood found me still in the mansion of my fathers—it *is* wonderful what stagnation there fell upon the springs of my life—wonderful how total an inversion took place in the character of my commonest thought. The realities of the world affected me as visions, and as visions only, while the wild ideas of the land of dreams became, in turn, not the material of my every-day existence, but in very deed that existence utterly and solely in itself.

* * * * *

Berenice and I were cousins, and we grew up together in my paternal halls. Yet differently we grew—I, ill of health, and buried in gloom—she, agile, graceful, and overflowing with energy; hers, the ramble on the hill-side—mine the studies of the cloister; I, living within my own heart, and addicted, body and soul, to the most intense and painful meditation—she, roaming carelessly through life, with no thought of the shadows in her path, or the silent flight of the raven-winged hours. Berenice!—I call upon her name—Berenice!—and from the gray ruins of memory a thousand tumultuous recollections are startled at the sound! Ah, vividly is her image before me now, as in the early days of her light-heartedness and joy! Oh, gorgeous yet fantastic beauty! Oh, sylph amid the shrubberies of Arnheim! Oh, Naiad among its fountains! And then—then all is mystery and terror, and a tale which should not be told. Disease—a fatal disease, fell like the simoon upon her frame; and, even while I gazed upon her, the spirit of change swept over her, pervading her mind, her habits, and her character, and, in a manner the most subtle and terrible, disturbing even the identity of her person! Alas! the destroyer came and went!—and the victim—where is she? I knew her not—or knew her no longer as Berenice.

Among the numerous train of maladies superinduced by that fatal and primary one which effected a revolution of so horrible a kind in the moral and physical being of my cousin, may be mentioned as the most distressing and obstinate in its nature, a species of epilepsy not unfrequently terminating in *trance* itself—trance very nearly resembling positive dissolution, and from which her manner of recovery was in most instances, startlingly abrupt. In the meantime my own disease—for I have been told that I should call it by no other appellation—my own disease, then, grew rapidly upon me, and assumed finally a monomaniac character of a novel and extraordinary form—hourly and momently gaining vigor—and at length obtaining over me the most incomprehensible ascendancy. This monomania, if I must so term it, consisted in a morbid irritability of those properties of the mind in metaphysical science termed the *attentive*. It is more than probable that I am not understood; but I fear, indeed, that it is in no manner possible to convey to the mind of the merely general reader, an adequate idea of that nervous *intensity of interest* with which, in my case, the powers of meditation (not to speak technically) busied and buried themselves, in the contemplation of even the most ordinary objects of the universe.

To muse for long unwearied hours, with my attention riveted to some frivolous device on the margin, or in the typography of a book; to become absorbed, for the better part of a summer's day, in a quaint shadow falling aslant upon the tapestry or upon the floor; to lose myself, for an entire night, in watching the steady flame of a lamp, or the embers of a fire; to dream away whole days over the perfume of a flower; to repeat, monotonously, some common word, until the sound, by dint of frequent repetition, ceased to convey any idea whatever to the mind; to lose all sense of motion or physical existence, by means of absolute bodily quiescence long and obstinately persevered in: such were a few of the most common and least pernicious vagaries induced by a condition of the mental faculties, not, indeed, altogether unparalleled, but certainly bidding defiance to anything like analysis or explanation.

Yet let me not be misapprehended. The undue, earnest, and morbid attention thus excited by objects in their own nature frivolous, must not be confounded in character with that ruminating propensity common to all mankind, and more especially indulged in by persons of ardent imagination. It was not even, as might be at first supposed, an extreme condition, or exaggeration of such propensity, but primarily and essentially distinct and different. In the one instance, the dreamer, or enthusiast, being interested by an object usually *not* frivolous, imperceptibly loses sight of this object in a wilderness of deductions and suggestions issuing therefrom, until, at the conclusion of a day dream *often replete with luxury*, he finds the *incitamentum*, or first cause of his musings, entirely vanished and forgotten. In my case, the primary object was *invariably frivolous*, although assuming, through the medium of my distempered vision, a refracted and unreal importance. Few deductions, if any, were made; and those few pertinaciously returning in upon the original object as a centre. The meditations were *never* pleasurable; and, at the termination of the reverie, the first cause, so far from being out of sight, had attained that supernaturally exaggerated interest which was the prevailing feature of the disease. In a word, the powers of mind more particularly exercised were, with me, as I have said before, the *attentive*, and are, with the day-dreamer, the *speculative*.

My books, at this epoch, if they did not actually serve to irritate the disorder, partook, it will be perceived, largely, in their imaginative and inconsequential nature, of the characteristic qualities of the disorder itself. I well remember, among others, the treatise of the noble Italian, Coelius Secundus Curio, "*De Amplitudine Beati Regni Dei;*" St. Austin's great work, the "City of God;" and Tertullian's "*De Carne Christi*," in which the paradoxical sentence "*Mortuus est Dei filius; credible est quia ineptum est: et sepultus resurrexit; certum est quia impossibile est,*" occupied my undivided time, for many weeks of laborious and fruitless investigation.

Thus it will appear that, shaken from its balance only by trivial things, my reason bore resemblance to that ocean-crag spoken of by Ptolemy Hephestion, which steadily resisting the attacks of human violence, and the fiercer fury of the waters and the winds, trembled only to the touch of the flower called Asphodel. And although, to a careless thinker, it might appear a matter beyond doubt, that the alteration produced by her unhappy malady, in the *moral* condition of Berenice, would afford me many objects for the exercise of that intense and abnormal meditation whose nature I have been at some trouble in explaining, yet such was not in any degree the case. In the lucid intervals of my infirmity, her calamity, indeed, gave me pain, and, taking deeply to heart that total wreck of her fair and gentle life, I did not fall to ponder, frequently and bitterly, upon the wonder-working means by which so strange a revolution had been so suddenly brought to pass. But these reflections partook not of the idiosyncrasy of my disease, and were such as would have occurred, under similar circumstances, to the ordinary mass of mankind. True to its own character, my disorder revelled in the less important but more startling changes wrought in the *physical* frame of Berenice—in the singular and most appalling distortion of her personal identity.

During the brightest days of her unparalleled beauty, most surely I had never loved her. In the strange anomaly of my existence, feelings with me, *had never been* of the heart, and my passions *always were* of the mind. Through the gray of the early morning—among the trellised shadows of the forest at noonday—and in the silence of my library at night—she had flitted by my eyes, and I had seen her—not as the living and breathing Berenice, but as the Berenice of a dream; not as a being of the earth, earthy, but as the abstraction of such a being; not as a thing to admire, but to analyze; not as an object of love, but as the theme of the most abstruse although desultory speculation. And *now*—now I shuddered in her presence, and grew pale at her approach; yet, bitterly lamenting her fallen and desolate condition, I called to mind that she had loved me long, and, in an evil moment, I spoke to her of marriage.

And at length the period of our nuptials was approaching, when, upon an afternoon in the winter of the year—one of those unseasonably warm, calm, and misty days which are the nurse of the beautiful Halcyon[1],—I sat (and sat, as I thought, alone), in the inner apartment of the library. But, uplifting my eyes, I saw that Berenice stood before me.

Was it my own excited imagination—or the misty influence of the atmosphere—or the uncertain twilight of the chamber—or the gray draperies which fell around her figure—that caused in it so vacillating and indistinct an outline? I could not tell. She spoke no word; and I—not for worlds could I have uttered a syllable. An icy chill ran through my frame; a sense of insufferable anxiety oppressed me; a consuming curiosity pervaded my soul; and sinking back upon the chair, I remained for some time breathless and motionless, with my eyes riveted upon her person. Alas! its emaciation was excessive, and not one vestige of the former being lurked in any single line of the contour. My burning glances at length fell upon the face.

The forehead was high, and very pale, and singularly placid; and the once jetty hair fell partially over it, and overshadowed the hollow temples with innumerable ringlets, now of a vivid yellow, and jarring discordantly, in their fantastic character, with the reigning melancholy of the countenance. The eyes were lifeless, and lustreless, and seemingly pupilless, and I shrank involuntarily from their glassy stare to he contemplation of the thin and shrunken lips. They parted; and in a smile of peculiar meaning, *the teeth* of the changed Berenice disclosed themselves slowly to my view. Would to God that I had never beheld them, or that, having done so, I had died!

* * * * *

The shutting of a door disturbed me, and, looking up, I found that my cousin had departed from the chamber. But from the disordered chamber of my brain, had not, alas! departed, and would not be driven away, the white and ghastly *spectrum* of the teeth. Not a speck on their surface—not a shade on their enamel—not an indenture in their edges—but what that period of her smile had sufficed to brand in upon my memory. I saw them *now* even more unequivocally than I beheld them *then*. The teeth!—the teeth!—they were here, and there, and everywhere, and visibly and palpably before me; long, narrow, and excessively white, with the pale lips writhing about them, as in the very moment of their first terrible development. Then came the full fury of my *monomania*, and I struggled in vain against its strange and irresistible influence. In the multiplied objects of the external world I had no thoughts but for the teeth. For these I longed with a phrenzied desire. All other matters and all different interests became absorbed in their single contemplation. They—they alone were present to the mental eye, and they, in their sole individuality, became the essence of my mental life. I held them in every light. I turned them in every attitude. I surveyed their characteristics. I dwelt upon their peculiarities. I pondered upon their conformation. I mused upon the alteration in their nature. I shuddered as I assigned to them in imagination a sensitive and sentient power, and even when unassisted by the lips, a capability of moral expression. Of Mademoiselle Salle it has been well said, "*Que tous ses pas étaient des sentiments*," and of Berenice I more seriously believed *que toutes ses dents étaient des idées. Des idées!*—ah here was the idiotic thought that destroyed me! *Des idées!*—ah *therefore* it was that I coveted them so madly! I felt that their possession could alone ever restore me to peace, in giving me back to reason.

And the evening closed in upon me thus—and then the darkness came, and tarried, and went—and the day again dawned—and the mists of a second night were now gathering around—and still I sat motionless in that solitary room—and still I sat buried in meditation—and still the *phantasma* of the teeth maintained its terrible ascendancy, as, with the most vivid hideous distinctness, it floated about amid the changing lights and shadows of the chamber. At length there broke in upon my dreams a cry as of horror and dismay; and thereunto, after a pause, succeeded the sound of troubled voices, intermingled with many low moanings of sorrow or of pain. I arose from my seat, and throwing open one of the doors of the library, saw standing out in the ante-chamber a servant maiden, all in tears, who told me that Berenice was—no more! She had been seized with epilepsy in the early morning, and now, at the closing in of the night, the grave was ready for its tenant, and all the preparations for the burial were completed.

* * * * *

I found myself sitting in the library, and again sitting there alone. It seemed that I had newly awakened from a confused and exciting dream. I knew that it was now midnight, and I was well aware, that since the setting of the sun, Berenice had been interred. But of that dreary period which intervened I had no positive, at least no definite comprehension. Yet its memory was replete with horror—horror more horrible from being vague, and terror more terrible from ambiguity. It was a fearful page in the record my existence, written all over with dim, and hideous, and unintelligible recollections. I strived to decypher them, but in vain; while ever and anon, like the spirit of a departed sound, the shrill and piercing shriek of a female voice seemed to be ringing in my ears. I had done a deed—what was it? I asked myself the question aloud, and the whispering echoes of the chamber answered me,—"*what was it?*"

On the table beside me burned a lamp, and near it lay a little box. It was of no remarkable character, and I had seen it frequently before, for it was the property of the family physician; but how came it *there*, upon my table, and why did I shudder in regarding it? These things were in no manner to be accounted for, and my eyes at length dropped to the open pages of a book, and to a sentence underscored therein. The words were the singular but simple ones of the poet Ebn Zaiat:—"*Dicebant mihi sodales si sepulchrum amicae visitarem, curas meas aliquantulum fore levatas.*" Why then, as I perused them, did the hairs of my head erect themselves on end, and the blood of my body become congealed within my veins?

There came a light tap at the library door—and, pale as the tenant of a tomb, a menial entered upon tiptoe. His looks were wild with terror, and he spoke to me in a voice tremulous, husky, and very low. What said he?—some broken sentences I heard. He told of a wild cry disturbing the silence of the night—of the gathering together of the household—of a search in the direction of the sound; and then his tones grew thrillingly distinct as he whispered me of a violated grave—of a disfigured body enshrouded, yet still breathing—still palpitating—*still alive*!

He pointed to garments;—they were muddy and clotted with gore. I spoke not, and he took me gently by the hand; it was indented with the impress of human nails. He directed my attention to some object against the wall. I looked at it for some minutes: it was a spade. With a shriek I bounded to the table, and grasped the box that lay upon it. But I could not force it open; and in my tremor, it slipped from my hands, and fell heavily, and burst into pieces; and from it, with a rattling sound, there rolled out some instruments of dental surgery, intermingled with thirty-two small, white and ivory-looking substances that were scattered to and fro about the floor.

Note

[1] For as Jove, during the winter season, gives twice seven days of warmth, men have called this element and temperate time the nurse of the beautiful Halcyon—*Simonides.*

The Unparalleled Adventure of One Hans Pfaall[1]

With a heart of furious fancies,
   Whereof I am commander,
With a burning spear *and a horse of air*,
To the wilderness I wander.
Tom O'Bedlam's Song

By late accounts from Rotterdam, that city seems to be in a high state of philosophical excitement. Indeed, phenomena have there occurred of a nature so completely unexpected—so entirely novel—so utterly at variance with preconceived opinions—as to leave no doubt on my mind that long ere this all Europe is in an uproar, all physics in a ferment, all reason and astronomy together by the ears.

It appears that on the—day of—(I am not positive about the date), a vast crowd of people, for purposes not specifically mentioned, were assembled in the great square of the Exchange in the well-conditioned city of Rotterdam. The day was warm—unusually so for the season—there was hardly a breath of air stirring; and the multitude were in no bad humor at being now and then besprinkled with friendly showers of momentary duration, that fell from large white masses of cloud which chequered in a fitful manner the blue vault of the firmament. Nevertheless, about noon, a slight but remarkable agitation became apparent in the assembly: the clattering of ten thousand tongues succeeded; and, in an instant afterward, ten thousand faces were upturned toward the heavens, ten thousand pipes descended simultaneously from the corners of ten thousand mouths, and a shout, which could be compared to nothing but the roaring of Niagara, resounded long, loudly, and furiously, through all the environs of Rotterdam.

The origin of this hubbub soon became sufficiently evident. From behind the huge bulk of one of those sharply defined masses of cloud already mentioned, was seen slowly to emerge into an open area of blue space, a queer, heterogeneous, but apparently solid substance, so oddly shaped, so whimsically put together, as not to be in any manner comprehended, and never to be sufficiently admired, by the host of sturdy burghers who stood open-mouthed below. What could it be? In the name of all the vrows and devils in Rotterdam, what could it possibly portend? No one knew, no one could imagine; no one—not even the burgomaster Mynheer Superbus Von Underduk—had the slightest clew by which to unravel the mystery; so, as nothing more reasonable could be done, every one to a man replaced his pipe carefully in the corner of his mouth, and cocking up his right eye towards the phenomenon, puffed, paused, waddled about, and grunted significantly—then waddled back, grunted, paused, and finally—puffed again.

In the meantime, however, lower and still lower toward the goodly city, came the object of so much curiosity, and the cause of so much smoke. In a very few minutes it arrived near enough to be accurately discerned. It appeared to be—yes! it *was* undoubtedly a species of balloon; but surely no *such* balloon had ever been seen in Rotterdam before. For who, let me ask, ever heard of a balloon manufactured entirely of dirty newspapers? No man in Holland certainly; yet here, under the very noses of the people, or rather at some distance *above* their noses was the identical thing in question, and composed, I have it on the best authority, of the precise material which no one had ever before known to be used for a similar purpose. It was an egregious insult to the good sense of the burghers of Rotterdam. As to the shape of the phenomenon, it was even still more reprehensible. Being little or nothing better than a huge fools-cap turned upside down. And this similitude was regarded as by no means lessened when, upon nearer inspection, there was perceived a large tassel depending from its apex, and, around the upper rim or base of the cone, a circle of little instruments, resembling sheep-bells, which kept up a continual tinkling to the tune of Betty Martin. But still worse. Suspended by blue ribbons to the end of this fantastic machine, there hung, by way of car, an enormous drab beaver hat, with a brim superlatively broad, and a hemispherical crown with a black band and a silver buckle. It is, however, somewhat remarkable that many citizens of Rotterdam swore to having seen the same hat repeatedly before; and indeed the whole assembly seemed to regard it with eyes of familiarity; while the vrow Grettel Pfaall, upon sight of it, uttered an exclamation of joyful surprise, and declared it to be the identical hat of her good man himself. Now this was a circumstance the more to be observed, as Pfaall, with three companions, had actually disappeared from Rotterdam about five years before, in a very sudden and unaccountable manner, and up to the date of this narrative all attempts had failed of obtaining any intelligence concerning them whatsoever. To be sure, some bones which were thought to be human, mixed up with a quantity of odd-looking rubbish, had been lately discovered in a retired situation to the east of Rotterdam, and some people went so far as to imagine that in this spot a foul murder had been committed, and that the sufferers were in all probability Hans Pfaall and his associates. But to return.

The balloon (for such no doubt it was) had now descended to within a hundred feet of the earth, allowing the crowd below a sufficiently distinct view of the person of its occupant. This was in truth a very droll little somebody. He could not have been more than two feet in height; but this altitude, little as it was, would have been sufficient to destroy his *equilibrium*, and tilt him over the edge of his tiny car, but for the intervention of a circular rim reaching as high as the breast, and rigged on to the cords of the balloon. The body of the little man was more than proportionately broad, giving to his entire figure a rotundity highly absurd. His feet, of course, could not be seen at all, although a horny substance of suspicious nature was occasionally protruded through a rent in the bottom of the car, or to speak more properly, in the top of the hat. His hands were enormously large. His hair was extremely gray, and collected in a queue behind. His nose was prodigiously long, crooked, and inflammatory; his eyes full, brilliant, and acute; his chin and cheeks, although wrinkled with age, were broad, puffy, and double; but of ears of any kind or character there was not a semblance to be discovered upon any portion of his head. This odd little gentleman was dressed in a loose surtout of sky-blue satin, with tight breeches to match, fastened with silver buckles at the knees. His vest was of some bright yellow material; a white taffety cap was set jauntily on one side of his head; and, to complete his equipment, a blood-red silk handkerchief enveloped his throat, and fell down, in a dainty manner, upon his bosom, in a fantastic bow-knot of super-eminent dimensions.

Having descended, as I said before, to about one hundred feet from the surface of the earth, the little old gentleman was suddenly seized with a fit of trepidation, and appeared disinclined to make any nearer approach to *terra firma*. Throwing out, therefore, a quantity of sand from a canvas bag, which, he lifted with great difficulty, he became stationary in an instant. He then proceeded, in a hurried and agitated manner, to extract from a side-pocket in his surtout a large morocco pocket-book. This he poised suspiciously in his hand, then eyed it with an air of extreme surprise, and was evidently astonished at its weight. He at length opened it, and drawing there from a huge letter sealed with red sealing-wax and tied carefully with red tape, let it fall precisely at the feet of the burgomaster, Superbus Von Underduk. His Excellency stooped to take it up. But the aeronaut, still greatly discomposed, and having apparently no farther business to detain him in Rotterdam, began at this moment to make busy preparations for departure; and it being necessary to discharge a portion of ballast to enable him to reascend, the half dozen bags which he threw out, one after another, without taking the trouble to empty their contents, tumbled, every one of them, most unfortunately upon the back of the burgomaster, and rolled him over and over no less than one-and-twenty times, in the face of every man in Rotterdam. It is not to be supposed, however, that the great Underduk suffered this impertinence on the part of the little old man to pass off with impunity. It is said, on the contrary, that during each and every one of his one-and twenty circumvolutions he emitted no less than one-and-twenty distinct and furious whiffs from his pipe, to which he held fast the whole time with all his might, and to which he intends holding fast until the day of his death.

In the meantime the balloon arose like a lark, and, soaring far away above the city, at length drifted quietly behind a cloud similar to that from which it had so oddly emerged, and was thus lost forever to the wondering eyes of the good citizens of Rotterdam. All attention was now directed to the letter, the descent of which, and the consequences attending thereupon, had proved so fatally subversive of both person and personal dignity to his Excellency, the illustrious Burgomaster Mynheer Superbus Von Underduk. That functionary, however, had not failed, during his circumgyratory movements, to bestow a thought upon the important subject of securing the packet in question, which was seen, upon inspection, to have fallen into the most proper hands, being actually addressed to himself and Professor Rub-a-dub, in their official capacities of President and Vice-President of the Rotterdam College of Astronomy. It was accordingly opened by those dignitaries upon the spot, and found to contain the following extraordinary, and indeed very serious, communication:

TO THEIR EXCELLENCIES VON UNDERDUK AND RUBADUB, PRESIDENT AND VICE-PRESIDENT OF THE STATES' COLLEGE OF ASTRONOMERS, IN THE CITY OF ROTTERDAM.

"Your Excellencies may perhaps be able to remember an humble artizan, by name Hans Pfaall, and by occupation a mender of bellows, who, with three others, disappeared from Rotterdam, about five years ago, in a manner which must have been considered by all parties at once sudden, and extremely unaccountable. If, however, it so please your Excellencies, I, the writer of this communication, am the identical Hans Pfaall himself. It is well known to most of my fellow citizens, that for the period of forty years I continued to occupy the little square brick building, at the head of the alley called Sauerkraut, in which I resided at the time of my disappearance. My ancestors have also resided therein time out of mind—they, as well as myself, steadily following the respectable and indeed lucrative profession of mending of bellows. For, to speak the truth, until of late years, that the heads of all the people have been set agog with politics, no better business than my own could an honest citizen of Rotterdam either desire or deserve. Credit was good, employment was never wanting, and on all hands there was no lack of either money or good-will. But, as I was saying, we soon began to feel the effects of liberty and long speeches, and radicalism, and all that sort of thing. People who were formerly, the very best customers in the world, had now not a moment of time to think of us at all.

They had, so they said, as much as they could do to read about the revolutions, and keep up with the march of intellect and the spirit of the age. If a fire wanted fanning, it could readily be fanned with a newspaper, and as the government grew weaker, I have no doubt that leather and iron acquired durability in proportion, for, in a very short time, there was not a pair of bellows in all Rotterdam that ever stood in need of a stitch or required the assistance of a hammer. This was a state of things not to be endured. I soon grew as poor as a rat, and, having a wife and children to provide for, my burdens at length became intolerable, and I spent hour after hour in reflecting upon the most convenient method of putting an end to my life. Duns, in the meantime, left me little leisure for contemplation. My house was literally besieged from morning till night, so that I began to rave, and foam, and fret like a caged tiger against the bars of his enclosure. There were three fellows in particular who worried me beyond endurance, keeping watch continually about my door, and threatening me with the law. Upon these three I internally vowed the bitterest revenge, if ever I should be so happy as to get them within my clutches; and I believe nothing in the world but the pleasure of this anticipation prevented me from putting my plan of suicide into immediate execution, by blowing my brains out with a blunderbuss. I thought it best, however, to dissemble my wrath, and to treat them with promises and fair words, until, by some good turn of fate, an opportunity of vengeance should be afforded me.

"One day, having given my creditors the slip, and feeling more than usually dejected, I continued for a long time to wander about the most obscure streets without object whatever, until at length I chanced to stumble against the corner of a bookseller's stall. Seeing a chair close at hand, for the use of customers, I threw myself doggedly into it, and, hardly knowing why, opened the pages of the first volume which came within my reach. It proved to be a small pamphlet treatise on Speculative Astronomy, written either by Professor Encke of Berlin or by a Frenchman of somewhat similar name. I had some little tincture of information on matters of this nature, and soon became more and more absorbed in the contents of the book, reading it actually through twice before I awoke to a recollection of what was passing around me. By this time it began to grow dark, and I directed my steps toward home. But the treatise had made an indelible impression on my mind, and, as I sauntered along the dusky streets, I revolved carefully over in my memory the wild and sometimes unintelligible reasonings of the writer. There are some particular passages which affected my imagination in a powerful and extraordinary manner. The longer I meditated upon these the more intense grew the interest which had been excited within me. The limited nature of my education in general, and more especially my ignorance on subjects connected with natural philosophy, so far from rendering me diffident of my own ability to comprehend what I had read, or inducing me to mistrust the many vague notions which had arisen in consequence, merely served as a farther stimulus to imagination; and I was vain enough, or perhaps reasonable enough, to doubt whether those crude ideas which, arising in ill-regulated minds, have all the appearance, may not often in effect possess all the force, the reality, and other inherent properties, of instinct or intuition; whether, to proceed a step farther, profundity itself might not, in matters of a purely speculative nature, be detected as a legitimate source of falsity and error. In other words, I believed, and still do believe, that truth, is frequently of its own essence, superficial, and that, in many cases, the depth lies more in the abysses where we seek her, than in the actual situations wherein she may be found. Nature herself seemed to afford me corroboration of these ideas. In the contemplation of the heavenly bodies it struck me forcibly that I could not distinguish a star with nearly as much precision, when I gazed on it with earnest, direct and undeviating attention, as when I suffered my eye only to glance in its vicinity alone. I was not, of course, at that time aware that this apparent paradox was occasioned by the center of the visual area being less susceptible of feeble impressions of light than the exterior portions of the retina. This knowledge, and some of another kind, came afterwards in the course of an eventful five years, during which I have dropped the prejudices of my former humble situation in life, and forgotten the bellows-mender in far different occupations. But at the epoch of which I speak, the analogy which a casual observation of a star offered to the conclusions I had already drawn, struck me with the force of positive conformation, and I then finally made up my mind to the course which I afterwards pursued.

"It was late when I reached home, and I went immediately to bed. My mind, however, was too much occupied to sleep, and I lay the whole night buried in meditation. Arising early in the morning, and contriving again to escape the vigilance of my creditors, I repaired eagerly to the bookseller's stall, and laid out what little ready money I possessed, in the purchase of some volumes of Mechanics and Practical Astronomy. Having arrived at home safely with these, I devoted every spare moment to their perusal, and soon made such proficiency in studies of this nature as I thought sufficient for the execution of my plan. In the intervals of this period, I made every endeavor to conciliate the three creditors who had given me so much annoyance. In this I finally succeeded—partly by selling enough of my household furniture to satisfy a moiety of their claim, and partly by a promise of paying the balance upon completion of a little project which I told them I had in view, and for assistance in which I solicited their services. By these means—for they were ignorant men—I found little difficulty in gaining them over to my purpose.

"Matters being thus arranged, I contrived, by the aid of my wife and with the greatest secrecy and caution, to dispose of what property I had remaining, and to borrow, in small sums, under various pretences, and without paying any attention to my future means of repayment, no inconsiderable quantity of ready money. With the means thus accruing I proceeded to procure at intervals, cambric muslin, very fine, in pieces of twelve yards each; twine; a lot of the varnish of caoutchouc; a large and deep basket of wicker-work, made to order; and several other articles necessary in the construction and equipment of a balloon of extraordinary dimensions. This I directed my wife to make up as soon as possible, and gave her all requisite information as to the particular method of proceeding. In the meantime I worked up the twine into a net-work of sufficient dimensions; rigged it with a hoop and the necessary cords; bought a quadrant, a compass, a spy-glass, a common barometer with some important modifications, and two astronomical instruments not so generally known. I then took opportunities of conveying by night, to a retired situation east of Rotterdam, five iron-bound casks, to contain about fifty gallons each, and one of a larger size; six tinned ware tubes, three inches in diameter, properly shaped, and ten feet in length; a quantity of a *particular metallic substance, or semi-metal,* which I shall not name, and a dozen demijohns of *a very common acid*. The gas to be formed from these latter materials is a gas never yet generated by any other person than myself—or at least never applied to any similar purpose. The secret I would make no difficulty in disclosing, but that it of right belongs to a citizen of Nantz, in France, by whom it was conditionally communicated to myself. The same individual submitted to me, without being at all aware of my intentions, a method of constructing balloons from the membrane of a certain animal, through which substance any escape of gas was nearly an impossibility. I found it, however, altogether too expensive, and was not sure, upon the whole, whether cambric muslin with a coating of gum caoutchouc, was not equally as good. I mention this circumstance, because I think it probable that hereafter the individual in question may attempt a balloon ascension with the novel gas and material I have spoken of, and I do not wish to deprive him of the honor of a very singular invention.

"On the spot which I intended each of the smaller casks to occupy respectively during the inflation of the balloon, I privately dug a hole two feet deep; the holes forming in this manner a circle twenty-five feet in diameter. In the centre of this circle, being the station designed for the large cask, I also dug a hole three feet in depth. In each of the five smaller holes, I deposited a canister containing fifty pounds, and in the larger one a keg holding one hundred and fifty pounds, of cannon powder. These—the keg and canisters—I connected in a proper manner with covered trains; and having let into one of the canisters the end of about four feet of slow match, I covered up the hole, and placed the cask over it, leaving the other end of the match protruding about an inch, and barely visible beyond the cask. I then filled up the remaining holes, and placed the barrels over them in their destined situation.

"Besides the articles above enumerated, I conveyed to the *dépôt*, and there secreted, one of M. Grimm's improvements upon the apparatus for condensation of the atmospheric air. I found this machine, however, to require considerable alteration before it could be adapted to the purposes to which I intended making it applicable. But, with severe labor and unremitting perseverance, I at length met with entire success in all my preparations. My balloon was soon completed. It would contain more than forty thousand cubic feet of gas; would take me up easily, I calculated, with all my implements, and, if I managed rightly, with one hundred and seventy-five pounds of ballast into the bargain. It had received three coats of varnish, and I found the cambric muslin to answer all the purposes of silk itself, quite as strong and a good deal less expensive.

"Everything being now ready, I exacted from my wife an oath of secrecy in relation to all my actions from the day of my first visit to the bookseller's stall; and promising, on my part, to return as soon as circumstances would permit, I gave her what little money I had left, and bade her farewell. Indeed I had no fear on her account. She was what people call a notable woman, and could manage matters in the world without my assistance. I believe, to tell the truth, she always looked upon me as an idle boy, a mere make-weight, good for nothing but building castles in the air, and was rather glad to get rid of me. It was a dark night when I bade her good-bye, and taking with me, as *aides-de-camp*, the three creditors who had given me so much trouble, we carried the balloon, with the car and accoutrements, by a roundabout way, to the station where the other articles were deposited. We there found them all unmolested, and I proceeded immediately to business.

"It was the first of April. The night, as I said before, was dark; there was not a star to be seen; and a drizzling rain, falling at intervals, rendered us very uncomfortable. But my chief anxiety was concerning the balloon, which, in spite of the varnish with which it was defended, began to grow rather heavy with the moisture; the powder also was liable to damage. I therefore kept my three duns working with great diligence, pounding down ice around the central cask, and stirring the acid in the others. They did not cease, however, importuning me with questions as to what I intended to do with all this apparatus, and expressed much dissatisfaction at the terrible labor I made them undergo. They could not perceive, so they said, what good was likely to result from their getting wet to the skin, merely to take a part in such horrible incantations. I began to get uneasy, and worked away with all my might, for I verily believe the idiots supposed that I had entered into a compact with the devil, and that, in short, what I was now doing was nothing better than it should be. I was, therefore, in great fear of their leaving me altogether. I contrived, however, to pacify them by promises of payment of all scores in full, as soon as I could bring the present business to a termination. To these speeches they gave, of course, their own interpretation; fancying, no doubt, that at all events I should come into possession of vast quantities of ready money; and provided I paid them all I owed, and a trifle more, in consideration of their services, I dare say they cared very little what became of either my soul or my carcass.

"In about four hours and a half I found the balloon sufficiently inflated. I attached the car, therefore, and put all my implements in it—not forgetting the condensing apparatus, a copious supply of water, and a large quantity of provisions, such as pemmican, in which much nutriment is contained in comparatively little bulk. I also secured in the car a pair of pigeons and a cat. It was now nearly daybreak, and I thought it high time to take my departure. Dropping a lighted cigar on the ground, as if by accident, I took the opportunity, in stooping to pick it up, of igniting privately the piece of slow match, whose end, as I said before, protruded a very little beyond the lower rim of one of the smaller casks. This manoeuvre was totally unperceived on the part of the three duns; and, jumping into the car, I immediately cut the single cord which held me to the earth, and was pleased to find that I shot upward, carrying with all ease one hundred and seventy-five pounds of leaden ballast, and able to have carried up as many more.

"Scarcely, however, had I attained the height of fifty yards, when, roaring and rumbling up after me in the most horrible and tumultuous manner, came so dense a hurricane of fire, and smoke, and sulphur, and legs and arms, and gravel, and burning wood, and blazing metal, that my very heart sunk within me, and I fell down in the bottom of the car, trembling with unmitigated terror. Indeed, I now perceived that I had entirely overdone the business, and that the main consequences of the shock were yet to be experienced. Accordingly, in less than a second, I felt all the blood in my body rushing to my temples, and immediately thereupon, a concussion, which I shall never forget, burst abruptly through the night and seemed to rip the very firmament asunder. When I afterward had time for reflection, I did not fail to attribute the extreme violence of the explosion, as regarded myself, to its proper cause—my situation directly above it, and in the line of its greatest power. But at the time, I thought only of preserving my life. The balloon at first collapsed, then furiously expanded, then whirled round and round with horrible velocity, and finally, reeling and staggering like a drunken man, hurled me with great force over the rim of the car, and left me dangling, at a terrific height, with my head downward, and my face outwards, by a piece of slender cord about three feet in length, which hung accidentally through a crevice near the bottom of the wicker-work, and in which, as I fell, my left foot became most providentially entangled. It is impossible—utterly impossible—to form any adequate idea of the horror of my situation. I gasped convulsively for breath—a shudder resembling a fit of the ague agitated every nerve and muscle of my frame—I felt my eyes starting from their sockets—a horrible nausea overwhelmed me—and at length I fainted away.

"How long I remained in this state it is impossible to say. It must, however, have been no inconsiderable time, for when I partially recovered the sense of existence, I found the day breaking, the balloon at a prodigious height over a wilderness of ocean, and not a trace of land to be discovered far and wide within the limits of the vast horizon. My sensations, however, upon thus recovering, were by no means so rife with agony as might have been anticipated. Indeed, there was much of incipient madness in the calm survey which I began to take of my situation. I drew up to my eyes each of my hands, one after the other, and wondered what occurrence could have given rise to the swelling of the veins, and the horrible blackness of the fingernails. I afterward carefully examined my head, shaking it repeatedly, and feeling it with minute attention, until I succeeded in satisfying myself that it was not, as I had more than half suspected, larger than my balloon. Then, in a knowing manner, I felt in both my breeches pockets, and, missing therefrom a set of tablets and a toothpick case, endeavored to account for their disappearance, and not being able to do so, felt inexpressibly chagrined. It now occurred to me that I suffered great uneasiness in the joint of my left ankle, and a dim consciousness of my situation began to glimmer through my mind. But, strange to say! I was neither astonished nor horror-stricken. If I felt any emotion at all, it was a kind of chuckling satisfaction at the cleverness I was about to display in extricating myself from this dilemma; and I never, for a moment, looked upon my ultimate safety as a question susceptible of doubt. For a few minutes I remained wrapped in the profoundest meditation. I have a distinct recollection of frequently compressing my lips, putting my forefinger to the side of my nose, and making use of other gesticulations and grimaces common to men who, at ease in their arm-chairs, meditate upon matters of intricacy or importance. Having, as I thought, sufficiently collected my ideas, I now, with great caution and deliberation, put my hands behind my back, and unfastened the large iron buckle which belonged to the waistband of my inexpressibles. This buckle had three teeth, which, being somewhat rusty, turned with great difficulty on their axis. I brought them, however, after some trouble, at right angles to the body of the buckle, and was glad to find them remain firm in that position. Holding the instrument thus obtained within my teeth, I now proceeded to untie the knot of my cravat. I had to rest several times before I could accomplish this manoeuvre, but it was at length accomplished. To one end of the cravat I then made fast the buckle, and the other end I tied, for greater security, tightly around my wrist. Drawing now my body upwards, with a prodigious exertion of muscular force, I succeeded, at the very first trial, in throwing the buckle over the car, and entangling it, as I had anticipated, in the circular rim of the wicker-work.

"My body was now inclined towards the side of the car, at an angle of about forty-five degrees; but it must not be understood that I was therefore only forty-five degrees below the perpendicular. So far from it, I still lay nearly level with the plane of the horizon; for the change of situation which I had acquired, had forced the bottom of the car considerably outwards from my position, which was accordingly one of the most imminent and deadly peril. It should be remembered, however, that when I fell in the first instance, from the car, if I had fallen with my face turned toward the balloon, instead of turned outwardly from it, as it actually was; or if, in the second place, the cord by which I was suspended had chanced to hang over the upper edge, instead of through a crevice near the bottom of the car,—I say it may be readily conceived that, in either of these supposed cases, I should have been unable to accomplish even as much as I had now accomplished, and the wonderful adventures of Hans Pfaall would have been utterly lost to posterity, I had therefore every reason to be grateful; although, in point of fact, I was still too stupid to be anything at all, and hung for, perhaps, a quarter of an hour in that extraordinary manner, without making the slightest farther exertion whatsoever, and in a singularly tranquil state of idiotic enjoyment. But this feeling did not fail to die rapidly away, and thereunto succeeded horror, and dismay, and a chilling sense of utter helplessness and ruin. In fact, the blood so long accumulating in the vessels of my head and throat, and which had hitherto buoyed up my spirits with madness and delirium, had now begun to retire within their proper channels, and the distinctness which was thus added to my perception of the danger, merely served to deprive me of the self-possession and courage to encounter it. But this weakness was, luckily for me, of no very long duration. In good time came to my rescue the spirit of despair, and, with frantic cries and struggles, I jerked my way bodily upwards, till at length, clutching with a vise-like grip the long-desired rim, I writhed my person over it, and fell headlong and shuddering within the car.

"It was not until some time afterward that I recovered myself sufficiently to attend to the ordinary cares of the balloon. I then, however, examined it with attention, and found it, to my great relief, uninjured. My implements were all safe, and, fortunately, I had lost neither ballast nor provisions. Indeed, I had so well secured them in their places, that such an accident was entirely out of the question. Looking at my watch, I found it six o'clock. I was still rapidly ascending, and my barometer gave a present altitude of three and three-quarter miles. Immediately beneath me in the ocean, lay a small black object, slightly oblong in shape, seemingly about the size, and in every way bearing a great resemblance to one of those childish toys called a domino. Bringing my telescope to bear upon it, I plainly discerned it to be a British ninety four-gun ship, close-hauled, and pitching heavily in the sea with her head to the W.S.W. Besides this ship, I saw nothing but the ocean and the sky, and the sun, which had long arisen.

"It is now high time that I should explain to your Excellencies the object of my perilous voyage. Your Excellencies will bear in mind that distressed circumstances in Rotterdam had at length driven me to the resolution of committing suicide. It was not, however, that to life itself I had any, positive disgust, but that I was harassed beyond endurance by the adventitious miseries attending my situation. In this state of mind, wishing to live, yet wearied with life, the treatise at the stall of the bookseller opened a resource to my imagination. I then finally made up my mind. I determined to depart, yet live—to leave the world, yet continue to exist—in short, to drop enigmas, I resolved, let what would ensue, to force a passage, if I could, to the moon. Now, lest I should be supposed more of a madman than I actually am, I will detail, as well as I am able, the considerations which led me to believe that an achievement of this nature, although without doubt difficult, and incontestably full of danger, was not absolutely, to a bold spirit, beyond the confines of the possible.

"The moon's actual distance from the earth was the first thing to be attended to. Now, the mean or average interval between the centres of the two planets is 59.9643 of the earth's equatorial *radii*, or only about 237,000 miles. I say the mean or average interval. But it must be borne in mind that the form of the moon's orbit being an ellipse of eccentricity amounting to no less than 0.05484 of the major semi-axis of the ellipse itself, and the earth's centre being situated in its focus, if I could, in any manner, contrive to meet the moon, as it were, in its perigee, the above mentioned distance would be materially diminished. But, to say nothing at present of this possibility, it was very certain that, at all events, from the 237,000 miles I would have to deduct the *radius* of the earth, say 4,000, and the radius of the moon, say 1,080, in all 5,080, leaving an actual interval to be traversed, under average circumstances, of 231,920 miles. Now this, I reflected, was no very extraordinary distance. Travelling on land has been repeatedly accomplished at the rate of thirty miles per hour, and indeed a much greater speed may be anticipated. But even at this velocity, it would take me no more than 322 days to reach the surface of the moon. There were, however, many particulars inducing me to believe that my average rate of travelling might possibly very much exceed that of thirty miles per hour, and, as these considerations did not fail to make a deep impression upon my mind, I will mention them more fully hereafter.

"The next point to be regarded was a matter of far greater importance. From indications afforded by the barometer, we find that, in ascensions from the surface of the earth we have, at the height of 1,000 feet, left below us about one-thirtieth of the entire mass of atmospheric air, that at 10,600 we have ascended through nearly one-third; and that at 18,000, which is not far from the elevation of Cotopaxi, we have surmounted one-half the material, or, at all events, one-half the *ponderable*, body of air incumbent upon our globe. It is also calculated that at an altitude not exceeding the hundredth part of the earth's diameter—that is, not exceeding eighty miles—the rarefaction would be so excessive that animal life could in no manner be sustained, and, moreover, that the most delicate means we possess of ascertaining the presence of the atmosphere would be inadequate to assure us of its existence. But I did not fail to perceive that these latter calculations are founded altogether on our experimental knowledge of the properties of air, and the mechanical laws regulating its dilation and compression, in what may be called, comparatively speaking, the *immediate vicinity* of the earth itself; and, at the same time, it is taken for granted that animal life is and must be essentially *incapable of modification* at any given unattainable distance from the surface. Now, all such reasoning and from such data must, of course, be simply analogical. The greatest height ever reached by man was that of 25,000 feet, attained in the aeronautic expedition of Messieurs Gay-Lussac and Biot. This is a moderate altitude, even when compared with the eighty miles in question; and I could not help thinking that the subject admitted room for doubt and great latitude for speculation.

"But, in point of fact, an ascension being made to any given altitude, the ponderable quantity of air surmounted in any *farther* ascension is by no means in proportion to the additional height ascended (as may be plainly seen from what has been stated before), but in a ratio constantly decreasing. It is therefore evident that, ascend as high as we may, we cannot, literally speaking, arrive at a limit beyond which no atmosphere is to be found. It *must exist*, I argued; although it *may* exist in a state of infinite rarefaction.

"On the other hand, I was aware that arguments have not been wanting to prove the existence of a real and definite limit to the atmosphere, beyond which there is absolutely no air whatsoever. But a circumstance which has been left out of view by those who contend for such a limit seemed to me, although no positive refutation of their creed, still a point worthy very serious investigation. On comparing the intervals between the successive arrivals of Encke's comet at its perihelion, after giving credit, in the most exact manner, for all the disturbances due to the attractions of the planets, it appears that the periods are gradually diminishing; that is to say, the major axis of the comet's ellipse is growing shorter, in a slow but perfectly regular decrease. Now, this is precisely what ought to be the case, if we suppose a resistance experienced from the comet from an extremely *rare ethereal medium* pervading the regions of its orbit. For it is evident that such a medium must, in retarding the comet's velocity, increase its centripetal, by weakening its centrifugal force. In other words, the sun's attraction would be constantly attaining greater power, and the comet would be drawn nearer at every revolution. Indeed, there is no other way of accounting for the variation in question. But again. The real diameter of the same comet's nebulosity is observed to contract rapidly as it approaches the sun, and dilate with equal rapidity in its departure towards its aphelion. Was I not justifiable in supposing with M. Valz, that this apparent condensation of volume has its origin in the compression of the same ethereal medium I have spoken of before, and which is only denser in proportion to its solar vicinity? The lenticular-shaped phenomenon, also called the zodiacal light, was a matter worthy of attention. This radiance, so apparent in the tropics, and which cannot be mistaken for any meteoric lustre, extends from the horizon obliquely upward, and follows generally the direction of the sun's equator. It appeared to me evidently in the nature of a rare atmosphere extending from the sun outward, beyond the orbit of Venus at least, and I believed indefinitely farther.[2] Indeed, this medium I could not suppose confined to the path of the comet's ellipse, or to the immediate neighborhood of the sun. It was easy, on the contrary, to imagine it pervading the entire regions of our planetary system, condensed into what we call atmosphere at the planets themselves, and perhaps at some of them modified by considerations, so to speak, purely geological.

"Having adopted this view of the subject, I had little further hesitation. Granting that on my passage I should meet with atmosphere *essentially* the same as at the surface of the earth, I conceived that, by means of the very ingenious apparatus of M. Grimm, I should readily be enabled to condense it in sufficient quantity for the purposes of respiration. This would remove the chief obstacle in a journey to the moon. I had indeed spent some money and great labor in adapting the apparatus to the object intended, and confidently looked forward to its successful application, if I could manage to complete the voyage within any reasonable period. This brings me back to the *rate* at which it might be possible to travel.

"It is true that balloons, in the first stage of their ascensions from the earth, are known to rise with a velocity comparatively moderate. Now, the power of elevation lies altogether in the superior lightness of the gas in the balloon compared with the atmospheric air; and, at first sight, it does not appear probable that, as the balloon acquires altitude, and consequently arrives successively in atmospheric strata of densities rapidly diminishing—I say, it does not appear at all reasonable that, in this its progress upwards, the original velocity should be accelerated. On the other hand, I was not aware that, in any recorded ascension, a diminution was apparent in the absolute rate of ascent; although such should have been the case, if on account of nothing else, on account of the escape of gas through balloons ill-constructed, and varnished with no better material than the ordinary varnish. It seemed, therefore, that the effect of such escape was only sufficient to counterbalance the effect of some accelerating power. I now considered that, provided in my passage I found the medium I had imagined, and provided that it should prove to be actually and *essentially* what we denominate atmospheric air, it could make comparatively little difference at what extreme state of rarefaction I should discover it—that is to say, in regard to my power of ascending—for the gas in the balloon would not only be itself subject to rarefaction partially similar (in proportion to the occurrence of which, I could suffer an escape of so much as would be requisite to prevent explosion), but, *being what it was*, would, at all events, continue specifically lighter than any compound whatever of mere nitrogen and oxygen. In the meantime, the force of gravitation would be constantly diminishing, in proportion to the squares of the distances, and thus, with a velocity prodigiously accelerating, I should at length arrive in those distant regions where the force of the earth's attraction would be superseded by that of the moon. In accordance with these ideas, I did not think it worth while to encumber myself with more provisions than would be sufficient for a period of forty days.

"There was still, however, another difficulty, which occasioned me some little disquietude. It has been observed, that, in balloon ascensions to any considerable height, besides the pain attending respiration, great uneasiness is experienced about the head and body, often accompanied with bleeding at the nose, and other symptoms of an alarming kind, and growing more and more inconvenient in proportion to the altitude attained.[3] This was a reflection of a nature somewhat startling. Was it not probable that these symptoms would increase indefinitely, or at least until terminated by death itself? I finally thought not. Their origin was to be looked for in the progressive removal of the *customary* atmospheric pressure upon the surface of the body, and consequent distention of the superficial blood-vessels—not in any positive disorganization of the animal system, as in the case of difficulty in breathing, where the atmospheric density is *chemically insufficient* for the due renovation of blood in a ventricle of the heart. Unless for default of this renovation, I could see no reason, therefore, why life could not be sustained even in a vacuum; for the expansion and compression of chest, commonly called breathing, is action purely muscular, and the *cause*, not the *effect*, of respiration. In a word, I conceived that, as the body should become habituated to the want of atmospheric pressure, the sensations of pain would gradually diminish—and to endure them while they continued, I relied with confidence upon the iron hardihood of my constitution.

"Thus, may it please your Excellencies, I have detailed some, though by no means all, the considerations which led me to form the project of a lunar voyage. I shall now proceed to lay before you the result of an attempt so apparently audacious in conception, and, at all events, so utterly unparalleled in the annals of mankind.

"Having attained the altitude before mentioned, that is to say three miles and three-quarters, I threw out from the car a quantity of feathers, and found that I still ascended with sufficient rapidity; there was, therefore, no necessity for discharging any ballast. I was glad of this, for I wished to retain with me as much weight as I could carry, for reasons which will be explained in the sequel. I as yet suffered no bodily inconvenience, breathing with great freedom, and feeling no pain whatever in the head. The cat was lying very demurely upon my coat, which I had taken off, and eyeing the pigeons with an air of *nonchalance*. These latter being tied by the leg, to prevent their escape, were busily employed in picking up some grains of rice scattered for them in the bottom of the car.

"At twenty minutes past six o'clock, the barometer showed an elevation of 26,400 feet, or five miles to a fraction. The prospect seemed unbounded. Indeed, it is very easily calculated by means of spherical geometry, what a great extent of the earth's area I beheld. The convex surface of any segment of a sphere is, to the entire surface of the sphere itself, as the versed sine of the segment to the diameter of the sphere. Now, in my case, the versed sine—that is to say, the *thickness* of the segment beneath me—was about equal to my elevation, or the elevation of the point of sight above the surface. 'As five miles, then, to eight thousand,' would express the proportion of the earth's area seen by me. In other words, I beheld as much as a sixteen-hundredth part of the whole surface of the globe. The sea appeared unruffled as a mirror, although, by means of the spy-glass, I could perceive it to be in a state of violent agitation. The ship was no longer visible, having drifted away, apparently to the eastward. I now began to experience, at intervals, severe pain in the head, especially about the ears—still, however, breathing with tolerable freedom. The cat and pigeons seemed to suffer no inconvenience whatsoever.

"At twenty minutes before seven, the balloon entered a long series of dense cloud, which put me to great trouble, by damaging my condensing apparatus and wetting me to the skin. This was, to be sure, a singular *recontre*, for I had not believed it possible that a cloud of this nature could be sustained at so great an elevation. I thought it best, however, to throw out two five-pound pieces of ballast, reserving still a weight of one hundred and sixty-five pounds. Upon so doing, I soon rose above the difficulty, and perceived immediately, that I had obtained a great increase in my rate of ascent. In a few seconds after my leaving the cloud, a flash of vivid lightning shot from one end of it to the other, and caused it to kindle up, throughout its vast extent, like a mass of ignited and glowing charcoal. This, it must be remembered, was in the broad light of day. No fancy may picture the sublimity which might have been exhibited by a similar phenomenon taking place amid the darkness of the night. Hell itself might have been found a fitting image. Even as it was, my hair stood on end, while I gazed afar down within the yawning abysses, letting imagination descend, as it were, and stalk about in the strange vaulted halls, and ruddy gulfs, and red ghastly chasms of the hideous and unfathomable fire. I had indeed made a narrow escape. Had the balloon remained a very short while longer within the cloud—that is to say—had not the inconvenience of getting wet, determined me to discharge the ballast, inevitable ruin would have been the consequence. Such perils, although little considered, are perhaps the greatest which must be encountered in balloons. I had by this time, however, attained too great an elevation to be any longer uneasy on this head.

"I was now rising rapidly, and by seven o'clock the barometer indicated an altitude of no less than nine miles and a half. I began to find great difficulty in drawing my breath. My head, too, was excessively painful; and, having felt for some time a moisture about my cheeks, I at length discovered it to be blood, which was oozing quite fast from the drums of my ears. My eyes, also, gave me great uneasiness. Upon passing the hand over them they seemed to have protruded from their sockets in no inconsiderable degree; and all objects in the car, and even the balloon itself, appeared distorted to my vision. These symptoms were more than I had expected, and occasioned me some alarm. At this juncture, very imprudently, and without consideration, I threw out from the car three five-pound pieces of ballast. The accelerated rate of ascent thus obtained, carried me too rapidly, and without sufficient gradation, into a highly rarefied stratum of the atmosphere, and the result had nearly proved fatal to my expedition and to myself. I was suddenly seized with a spasm which lasted for more than five minutes, and even when this, in a measure, ceased, I could catch my breath only at long intervals, and in a gasping manner—bleeding all the while copiously at the nose and ears, and even slightly at the eyes. The pigeons appeared distressed in the extreme, and struggled to escape; while the cat mewed piteously, and, with her tongue hanging out of her mouth, staggered to and fro in the car as if under the influence of poison. I now too late discovered the great rashness of which I had been guilty in discharging the ballast, and my agitation was excessive. I anticipated nothing less than death, and death in a few minutes. The physical suffering I underwent contributed also to render me nearly incapable of making any exertion for the preservation of my life. I had, indeed, little power of reflection left, and the violence of the pain in my head seemed to be greatly on the increase. Thus I found that my senses would shortly give way altogether, and I had already clutched one of the valve ropes with the view of attempting a descent, when the recollection of the trick I had played the three creditors, and the possible consequences to myself, should I return, operated to deter me for the moment. I lay down in the bottom of the car, and endeavored to collect my faculties. In this I so far succeeded as to determine upon the experiment of losing blood. Having no lancet, however, I was constrained to perform the operation in the best manner I was able, and finally succeeded in opening a vein in my right arm, with the blade of my penknife. The blood had hardly commenced flowing when I experienced a sensible relief, and by the time I had lost about half a moderate basin full, most of the worst symptoms had abandoned me entirely. I nevertheless did not think it expedient to attempt getting on my feet immediately; but, having tied up my arm as well as I could, I lay still for about a quarter of an hour. At the end of this time I arose, and found myself freer from absolute *pain* of any kind than I had been during the last hour and a quarter of my ascension. The difficulty of breathing, however, was diminished in a very slight degree, and I found that it would soon be positively necessary to make use of my condenser. In the meantime, looking toward the cat, who was again snugly stowed away upon my coat, I discovered to my infinite surprise, that she had taken the opportunity of my indisposition to bring into light a litter of three little kittens. This was an addition to the number of passengers on my part altogether unexpected; but I was pleased at the occurrence. It would afford me a chance of bringing to a kind of test the truth of a surmise, which, more than anything else, had influenced me in attempting this ascension. I had imagined that the *habitual* endurance of the atmospheric pressure at the surface of the earth was the cause, or nearly so, of the pain attending animal existence at a distance above the surface. Should the kittens be found to suffer uneasiness *in an equal degree with their mother*, I must consider my theory in fault, but a failure to do so I should look upon as a strong confirmation of my idea.

"By eight o'clock I had actually attained an elevation of seventeen miles above the surface of the earth. Thus it seemed to me evident that my rate of ascent was not only on the increase, but that the progression would have been apparent in a slight degree even had I not discharged the ballast which I did. The pains in my head and ears returned, at intervals, with violence, and I still continued to bleed occasionally at the nose; but, upon the whole, I suffered much less than might have been expected. I breathed, however, at every moment, with more and more difficulty, and each inhalation was attended with a troublesome spasmodic action of the chest. I now unpacked the condensing apparatus, and got it ready for immediate use.

"The view of the earth, at this period of my ascension, was beautiful indeed. To the westward, the northward, and the southward, as far as I could see, lay a boundless sheet of apparently unruffled ocean, which every moment gained a deeper and a deeper tint of blue and began already to assume a slight appearance of convexity. At a vast distance to the eastward, although perfectly discernible, extended the islands of Great Britain, the entire Atlantic coasts of France and Spain, with a small portion of the northern part of the continent of Africa. Of individual edifices not a trace could be discovered, and the proudest cities of mankind had utterly faded away from the face of the earth. From the rock of Gibraltar, now dwindled into a dim speck, the dark Mediterranean sea, dotted with shining islands as the heaven is dotted with stars, spread itself out to the eastward as far as my vision extended, until its entire mass of waters seemed at length to tumble headlong over the abyss of the horizon, and I found myself listening on tiptoe for the echoes of the mighty cataract. Overhead, the sky was of a jetty black, and the stars were brilliantly visible.

"The pigeons about this time seeming to undergo much suffering, I determined upon giving them their liberty. I first untied one of them, a beautiful gray-mottled pigeon, and placed him upon the rim of the wicker-work. He appeared extremely uneasy, looking anxiously around him, fluttering his wings, and making a loud cooing noise, but could not be persuaded to trust himself from off the car. I took him up at last, and threw him to about half a dozen yards from the balloon. He made, however, no attempt to descend as I had expected, but struggled with great vehemence to get back, uttering at the same time very shrill and piercing cries. He at length succeeded in regaining his former station on the rim, but had hardly done so when his head dropped upon his breast, and he fell dead within the car. The other one did not prove so unfortunate. To prevent his following the example of his companion, and accomplishing a return, I threw him downward with all my force, and was pleased to find him continue his descent, with great velocity, making use of his wings with ease, and in a perfectly natural manner. In a very short time he was out of sight, and I have no doubt he reached home in safety. Puss, who seemed in a great measure recovered from her illness, now made a hearty meal of the dead bird and then went to sleep with much apparent satisfaction. Her kittens were quite lively, and so far evinced not the slightest sign of any uneasiness whatever.

"At a quarter-past eight, being no longer able to draw breath without the most intolerable pain, I proceeded forthwith to adjust around the car the apparatus belonging to the condenser. This apparatus will require some little explanation, and your Excellencies will please to bear in mind that my object, in the first place, was to surround myself and cat entirely with a barricade against the highly rarefied atmosphere in which I was existing, with the intention of introducing within this barricade, by means of my condenser, a quantity of this same atmosphere sufficiently condensed for the purposes of respiration. With this object in view I had prepared a very strong perfectly air-tight, but flexible gum-elastic bag. In this bag, which was of sufficient dimensions, the entire car was in a manner placed. That is to say, it (the bag) was drawn over the whole bottom of the car, up its sides, and so on, along the outside of the ropes, to the upper rim or hoop where the net-work is attached. Having pulled the bag up in this way, and formed a complete enclosure on all sides, and at bottom, it was now necessary to fasten up its top or mouth, by passing its material over the hoop of the net-work—in other words, between the net-work and the hoop. But if the net-work were separated from the hoop to admit this passage, what was to sustain the car in the meantime? Now the net-work was not permanently fastened to the hoop, but attached by a series of running loops or nooses. I therefore undid only a few of these loops at one time, leaving the car suspended by the remainder. Having thus inserted a portion of the cloth forming the upper part of the bag, I refastened the loops—not to the hoop, for that would have been impossible, since the cloth now intervened—but to a series of large buttons, affixed to the cloth itself, about three feet below the mouth of the bag, the intervals between the buttons having been made to correspond to the intervals between the loops. This done, a few more of the loops were unfastened from the rim, a farther portion of the cloth introduced, and the disengaged loops then connected with their proper buttons. In this way it was possible to insert the whole upper part of the bag between the net-work and the hoop. It is evident that the hoop would now drop down within the car, while the whole weight of the car itself, with all its contents, would be held up merely by the strength of the buttons. This, at first sight, would seem an inadequate dependence; but it was by no means so, for the buttons were not only very strong in themselves, but so close together that a very slight portion of the whole weight was supported by any one of them. Indeed, had the car and contents been three times heavier than they were, I should not have been at all uneasy. I now raised up the hoop again within the covering of gum-elastic, and propped it at nearly its former height by means of three light poles prepared for the occasion. This was done, of course, to keep the bag distended at the top, and to preserve the lower part of the net-work in its proper situation. All that now remained was to fasten up the mouth of the enclosure; and this was readily accomplished by gathering the folds of the material together, and twisting them up very tightly on the inside by means of a kind of stationary tourniquet.

"In the sides of the covering thus adjusted round the car, had been inserted three circular panes of thick but clear glass, through which I could see without difficulty around me in every horizontal direction. In that portion of the cloth forming the bottom, was likewise, a fourth window, of the same kind, and corresponding with a small aperture in the floor of the car itself. This enabled me to see perpendicularly down, but having found it impossible to place any similar contrivance overhead, on account of the peculiar manner of closing up the opening there, and the consequent wrinkles in the cloth, I could expect to see no objects situated directly in my zenith. This, of course, was a matter of little consequence; for had I even been able to place a window at top, the balloon itself would have prevented my making any use of it.

"About a foot below one of the side windows was a circular opening, eight inches in diameter, and fitted with a brass rim adapted in its inner edge to the windings of a screw. In this rim was screwed the large tube of the condenser, the body of the machine being, of course, within the chamber of gum-elastic. Through this tube a quantity of the rare atmosphere circumjacent being drawn by means of a vacuum created in the body of the machine, was thence discharged, in a state of condensation, to mingle with the thin air already in the chamber. This operation being repeated several times, at length filled the chamber with atmosphere proper for all the purposes of respiration. But in so confined a space it would, in a short time, necessarily become foul, and unfit for use from frequent contact with the lungs. It was then ejected by a small valve at the bottom of the car—the dense air readily sinking into the thinner atmosphere below. To avoid the inconvenience of making a total *vacuum* at any moment within the chamber, this purification was never accomplished all at once, but in a gradual manner—the valve being opened only for a few seconds, then closed again, until one or two strokes from the pump of the condenser had supplied the place of the atmosphere ejected. For the sake of experiment I had put the cat and kittens in a small basket, and suspended it outside the car to a button at the bottom, close by the valve, through which I could feed them at any moment when necessary. I did this at some little risk, and before closing the mouth of the chamber, by reaching under the car with one of the poles before mentioned to which a hook had been attached.

"By the time I had fully completed these arrangements and filled the chamber as explained, it wanted only ten minutes of nine o'clock. During the whole period of my being thus employed, I endured the most terrible distress from difficulty of respiration, and bitterly did I repent the negligence or rather fool-hardiness, of which I had been guilty, of putting off to the last moment a matter of so much importance. But having at length accomplished it, I soon began to reap the benefit of my invention. Once again I breathed with perfect freedom and ease—and indeed why should I not? I was also agreeably surprised to find myself, in a great measure, relieved from the violent pains which had hitherto tormented me. A slight headache, accompanied with a sensation of fullness or distention about the wrists, the ankles, and the throat, was nearly all of which I had now to complain. Thus it seemed evident that a greater part of the uneasiness attending the removal of atmospheric pressure had actually *worn off*, as I had expected, and that much of the pain endured for the last two hours should have been attributed altogether to the effects of a deficient respiration.

"At twenty minutes before nine o'clock—that is to say, a short time prior to my closing up the mouth of the chamber, the mercury attained its limit, or ran down, in the barometer, which, as I mentioned before, was one of an extended construction. It then indicated an altitude on my part of 132,000 feet, or five-and-twenty miles, and I consequently surveyed at that time an extent of the earth's area amounting to no less than the three hundred-and-twentieth part of its entire superficies. At nine o'clock I had again lost sight of land to the eastward, but not before I became aware that the balloon was drifting rapidly to the N. N. W. The convexity of the ocean beneath me was very evident indeed, although my view was often interrupted by the masses of cloud which floated to and fro. I observed now that even the lightest vapors never rose to more than ten miles above the level of the sea.

"At half past nine I tried the experiment of throwing out a handful of feathers through the valve. They did not float as I had expected; but dropped down perpendicularly, like a bullet, *en masse*, and with the greatest velocity—being out of sight in a very few seconds. I did not at first know what to make of this extraordinary phenomenon; not being able to believe that my rate of ascent had, of a sudden, met with so prodigious an acceleration. But it soon occurred to me that the atmosphere was now far too rare to sustain even the feathers; that they actually fell, as they appeared to do, with great rapidity; and that I had been surprised by the united velocities of their descent and my own elevation.

"By ten o'clock I found that I had very little to occupy my immediate attention. Affairs went swimmingly, and I believed the balloon to be going upward with a speed increasing momently although I had no longer any means of ascertaining the progression of the increase. I suffered no pain or uneasiness of any kind, and enjoyed better spirits than I had at any period since my departure from Rotterdam, busying myself now in examining the state of my various apparatus, and now in regenerating the atmosphere within the chamber. This latter point I determined to attend to at regular intervals of forty minutes, more on account of the preservation of my health, than from so frequent a renovation being absolutely necessary. In the meanwhile I could not help making anticipations. Fancy revelled in the wild and dreamy regions of the moon. Imagination, feeling herself for once unshackled, roamed at will among the ever-changing wonders of a shadowy and unstable land. Now there were hoary and time-honored forests, and craggy precipices, and waterfalls tumbling with a loud noise into abysses without a bottom. Then I came suddenly into still noonday solitudes, where no wind of heaven ever intruded, and where vast meadows of poppies, and slender, lily-looking flowers spread themselves out a weary distance, all silent and motionless forever. Then again I journeyed far down away into another country where it was all one dim and vague lake, with a boundary line of clouds. And out of this melancholy water arose a forest of tall eastern trees, like a wilderness of dreams. And I have in mind that the shadows of the trees which fell upon the lake remained not on the surface where they fell, but sunk slowly and steadily down, and commingled with the waves, while from the trunks of the trees other shadows were continually coming out, and taking the place of their brothers thus entombed. 'This then,' I said thoughtfully, 'is the very reason why the waters of this lake grow blacker with age, and more melancholy as the hours run on.' But fancies such as these were not the sole possessors of my brain. Horrors of a nature most stern and most appalling would too frequently obtrude themselves upon my mind, and shake the innermost depths of my soul with the bare supposition of their possibility. Yet I would not suffer my thoughts for any length of time to dwell upon these latter speculations, rightly judging the real and palpable dangers of the voyage sufficient for my undivided attention.

"At five o'clock, p.m., being engaged in regenerating the atmosphere within the chamber, I took that opportunity of observing the cat and kittens through the valve. The cat herself appeared to suffer again very much, and I had no hesitation in attributing her uneasiness chiefly to a difficulty in breathing; but my experiment with the kittens had resulted very strangely. I had expected, of course, to see them betray a sense of pain, although in a less degree than their mother, and this would have been sufficient to confirm my opinion concerning the habitual endurance of atmospheric pressure. But I was not prepared to find them, upon close examination, evidently enjoying a high degree of health, breathing with the greatest ease and perfect regularity, and evincing not the slightest sign of any uneasiness whatever. I could only account for all this by extending my theory, and supposing that the highly rarefied atmosphere around might perhaps not be, as I had taken for granted, chemically insufficient for the purposes of life, and that a person born in such a medium might, possibly, be unaware of any inconvenience attending its inhalation, while, upon removal to the denser strata near the earth, he might endure tortures of a similar nature to those I had so lately experienced. It has since been to me a matter of deep regret that an awkward accident, at this time, occasioned me the loss of my little family of cats, and deprived me of the insight into this matter which a continued experiment might have afforded. In passing my hand through the valve, with a cup of water for the old puss, the sleeves of my shirt became entangled in the loop which sustained the basket, and thus, in a moment, loosened it from the bottom. Had the whole actually vanished into air, it could not have shot from my sight in a more abrupt and instantaneous manner. Positively, there could not have intervened the tenth part of a second between the disengagement of the basket and its absolute and total disappearance with all that it contained. My good wishes followed it to the earth, but of course, I had no hope that either cat or kittens would ever live to tell the tale of their misfortune.

"At six o'clock, I perceived a great portion of the earth's visible area to the eastward involved in thick shadow, which continued to advance with great rapidity, until, at five minutes before seven, the whole surface in view was enveloped in the darkness of night. It was not, however, until long after this time that the rays of the setting sun ceased to illumine the balloon; and this circumstance, although of course fully anticipated, did not fail to give me an infinite deal of pleasure. It was evident that, in the morning, I should behold the rising luminary many hours at least before the citizens of Rotterdam, in spite of their situation so much farther to the eastward, and thus, day after day, in proportion to the height ascended, would I enjoy the light of the sun for a longer and a longer period. I now determined to keep a journal of my passage, reckoning the days from one to twenty-four hours continuously, without taking into consideration the intervals of darkness.

"At ten o'clock, feeling sleepy, I determined to lie down for the rest of the night; but here a difficulty presented itself, which, obvious as it may appear, had escaped my attention up to the very moment of which I am now speaking. If I went to sleep as I proposed, how could the atmosphere in the chamber be regenerated in the interim? To breathe it for more than an hour, at the farthest, would be a matter of impossibility, or, if even this term could be extended to an hour and a quarter, the most ruinous consequences might ensue. The consideration of this dilemma gave me no little disquietude; and it will hardly be believed, that, after the dangers I had undergone, I should look upon this business in so serious a light, as to give up all hope of accomplishing my ultimate design, and finally make up my mind to the necessity of a descent. But this hesitation was only momentary. I reflected that man is the veriest slave of custom, and that many points in the routine of his existence are deemed essentially important, which are only so *at all* by his having rendered them habitual. It was very certain that I could not do without sleep; but I might easily bring myself to feel no inconvenience from being awakened at intervals of an hour during the whole period of my repose. It would require but five minutes at most to regenerate the atmosphere in the fullest manner, and the only real difficulty was to contrive a method of arousing myself at the proper moment for so doing. But this was a question which, I am willing to confess, occasioned me no little trouble in its solution. To be sure, I had heard of the student who, to prevent his falling asleep over his books, held in one hand a ball of copper, the din of whose descent into a basin of the same metal on the floor beside his chair, served effectually to startle him up, if, at any moment, he should be overcome with drowsiness. My own case, however, was very different indeed, and left me no room for any similar idea; for I did not wish to keep awake, but to be aroused from slumber at regular intervals of time. I at length hit upon the following expedient, which, simple as it may seem, was hailed by me, at the moment of discovery, as an invention fully equal to that of the telescope, the steam-engine, or the art of printing itself.

"It is necessary to premise, that the balloon, at the elevation now attained, continued its course upward with an even and undeviating ascent, and the car consequently followed with a steadiness so perfect that it would have been impossible to detect in it the slightest vacillation whatever. This circumstance favored me greatly in the project I now determined to adopt. My supply of water had been put on board in kegs containing five gallons each, and ranged very securely around the interior of the car. I unfastened one of these, and taking two ropes tied them tightly across the rim of the wicker-work from one side to the other; placing them about a foot apart and parallel so as to form a kind of shelf, upon which I placed the keg, and steadied it in a horizontal position. About eight inches immediately below these ropes, and four feet from the bottom of the car I fastened another shelf—but made of thin plank, being the only similar piece of wood I had. Upon this latter shelf, and exactly beneath one of the rims of the keg, a small earthern pitcher was deposited. I now bored a hole in the end of the keg over the pitcher, and fitted in a plug of soft wood, cut in a tapering or conical shape. This plug I pushed in or pulled out, as might happen, until, after a few experiments, it arrived at that exact degree of tightness, at which the water, oozing from the hole, and falling into the pitcher below, would fill the latter to the brim in the period of sixty minutes. This, of course, was a matter briefly and easily ascertained, by noticing the proportion of the pitcher filled in any given time. Having arranged all this, the rest of the plan is obvious. My bed was so contrived upon the floor of the car, as to bring my head, in lying down, immediately below the mouth of the pitcher. It was evident, that, at the expiration of an hour, the pitcher, getting full, would be forced to run over, and to run over at the mouth, which was somewhat lower than the rim. It was also evident, that the water thus falling from a height of more than four feet, could not do otherwise than fall upon my face, and that the sure consequences would be, to waken me up instantaneously, even from the soundest slumber in the world.

"It was fully eleven by the time I had completed these arrangements, and I immediately betook myself to bed, with full confidence in the efficiency of my invention. Nor in this matter was

I disappointed. Punctually every sixty minutes was I aroused by my trusty chronometer, when, having emptied the pitcher into the bung-hole of the keg, and performed the duties of the condenser, I retired again to bed. These regular interruptions to my slumber caused me even less discomfort than I had anticipated; and when I finally arose for the day, it was seven o'clock, and the sun had attained many degrees above the line of my horizon.

"*April 3rd.* I found the balloon at an immense height indeed, and the earth's apparent convexity increased in a material degree. Below me in the ocean lay a cluster of black specks, which undoubtedly were islands. Far away to the northward I perceived a thin, white, and exceedingly brilliant line, or streak, on the edge of the horizon, and I had no hesitation in supposing it to be the southern disk of the ices of the Polar Sea. My curiosity was greatly excited, for I had hopes of passing on much farther to the north, and might possibly, at some period, find myself placed directly above the Pole itself. I now lamented that my great elevation would, in this case, prevent my taking as accurate a survey as I could wish. Much, however, might be ascertained. Nothing else of an extraordinary nature occurred during the day. My apparatus all continued in good order, and the balloon still ascended without any perceptible vacillation. The cold was intense, and obliged me to wrap up closely in an overcoat. When darkness came over the earth, I betook myself to bed, although it was for many hours afterward broad daylight all around my immediate situation. The water-clock was punctual in its duty, and I slept until next morning soundly, with the exception of the periodical interruption.

"*April 4th.* Arose in good health and spirits, and was astonished at the singular change which had taken place in the appearance of the sea. It had lost, in a great measure, the deep tint of blue it had hitherto worn, being now of a grayish-white, and of a lustre dazzling to the eye. The islands were no longer visible; whether they had passed down the horizon to the southeast, or whether my increasing elevation had left them out of sight, it is impossible to say. I was inclined, however, to the latter opinion. The rim of ice to the northward was growing more and more apparent. Cold by no means so intense. Nothing of importance occurred, and I passed the day in reading, having taken care to supply myself with books.

"*April 5th.* Beheld the singular phenomenon of the sun rising while nearly the whole visible surface of the earth continued to be involved in darkness. In time, however, the light spread itself over all, and I again saw the line of ice to the northward. It was now very distinct, and appeared of a much darker hue than the waters of the ocean. I was evidently approaching it, and with great rapidity. Fancied I could again distinguish a strip of land to the eastward, and one also to the westward, but could not be certain. Weather moderate. Nothing of any consequence happened during the day. Went early to bed.

"*April 6th.* Was surprised at finding the rim of ice at a very moderate distance, and an immense field of the same material stretching away off to the horizon in the north. It was evident that if the balloon held its present course, it would soon arrive above the Frozen Ocean, and I had now little doubt of ultimately seeing the Pole. During the whole of the day I continued to near the ice. Toward night the limits of my horizon very suddenly and materially increased, owing undoubtedly to the earth's form being that of an oblate spheroid, and my arriving above the flattened regions in the vicinity of the Arctic circle. When darkness at length overtook me, I went to bed in great anxiety, fearing to pass over the object of so much curiosity when I should have no opportunity of observing it.

"*April 7th.* Arose early, and, to my great joy, at length beheld what there could be no hesitation in supposing the northern Pole itself. It was there, beyond a doubt, and immediately beneath my feet; but, alas! I had now ascended to so vast a distance, that nothing could with accuracy be discerned. Indeed, to judge from the progression of the numbers indicating my various altitudes, respectively, at different periods, between six A.M. on the second of April, and twenty minutes before nine A.M. of the same day (at which time the barometer ran down), it might be fairly inferred that the balloon had now, at four o'clock in the morning of April the seventh, reached a height of *not less*, certainly, than 7,254 miles above the surface of the sea. This elevation may appear immense, but the estimate upon which it is calculated gave a result in all probability far inferior to the truth. At all events I undoubtedly beheld the whole of the earth's major diameter; the entire northern hemisphere lay beneath me like a chart orthographically projected:

and the great circle of the equator itself formed the boundary line of my horizon. Your Excellencies may, however, readily imagine that the confined regions hitherto unexplored within the limits of the Arctic circle, although situated directly beneath me, and therefore seen without any appearance of being foreshortened, were still, in themselves, comparatively too diminutive, and at too great a distance from the point of sight, to admit of any very accurate examination. Nevertheless, what could be seen was of a nature singular and exciting. Northwardly from that huge rim before mentioned, and which, with slight qualification, may be called the limit of human discovery in these regions, one unbroken, or nearly unbroken, sheet of ice continues to extend. In the first few degrees of this its progress, its surface is very sensibly flattened, farther on depressed into a plane, and finally, becoming *not a little concave*, it terminates, at the Pole itself, in a circular centre, sharply defined, whose apparent diameter subtended at the balloon an angle of about sixty-five seconds, and whose dusky hue, varying in intensity, was, at all times, darker than any other spot upon the visible hemisphere, and occasionally deepened into the most absolute and impenetrable blackness. Farther than this, little could be ascertained. By twelve o'clock the circular centre had materially decreased in circumference, and by seven P.M. I lost sight of it entirely; the balloon passing over the western limb of the ice, and floating away rapidly in the direction of the equator.

"*April 8th.* Found a sensible diminution in the earth's apparent diameter, besides a material alteration in its general color and appearance. The whole visible area partook in different degrees of a tint of pale yellow, and in some portions had acquired a brilliancy even painful to the eye. My view downward was also considerably impeded by the dense atmosphere in the vicinity of the surface being loaded with clouds, between whose masses I could only now and then obtain a glimpse of the earth itself. This difficulty of direct vision had troubled me more or less for the last forty-eight hours; but my present enormous elevation brought closer together, as it were, the floating bodies of vapor, and the inconvenience became, of course, more and more palpable in proportion to my ascent. Nevertheless, I could easily perceive that the balloon now hovered above the range of great lakes in the continent of North America, and was holding a course, due south, which would bring me to the tropics. This circumstance did not fail to give me the most heartful satisfaction, and I hailed it as a happy omen of ultimate success. Indeed, the direction I had hitherto taken, had filled me with uneasiness; for it was evident that, had I continued it much longer, there would have been no possibility of my arriving at the moon at all, whose orbit is inclined to the ecliptic at only the small angle of 5° 8' 48".

"*April 9th.* Today the earth's diameter was greatly diminished, and the color of the surface assumed hourly a deeper tint of yellow. The balloon kept steadily on her course to the southward, and arrived, at nine P.M., over the northern edge of the Mexican Gulf.

"*April 10th.* I was suddenly aroused from slumber, about five o'clock this morning, by a loud, crackling, and terrific sound, for which I could in no manner account. It was of very brief duration, but, while it lasted resembled nothing in the world of which I had any previous experience. It is needless to say that I became excessively alarmed, having, in the first instance, attributed the noise to the bursting of the balloon. I examined all my apparatus, however, with great attention, and could discover nothing out of order. Spent a great part of the day in meditating upon an occurrence so extraordinary, but could find no means whatever of accounting for it. Went to bed dissatisfied, and in a state of great anxiety and agitation.

"*April 11th.* Found a startling diminution in the apparent diameter of the earth, and a considerable increase, now observable for the first time, in that of the moon itself, which wanted only a few days of being full. It now required long and excessive labor to condense within the chamber sufficient atmospheric air for the sustenance of life.

"*April 12th.* A singular alteration took place in regard to the direction of the balloon, and although fully anticipated, afforded me the most unequivocal delight. Having reached, in its former course, about the twentieth parallel of southern latitude, it turned off suddenly, at an acute angle, to the eastward, and thus proceeded throughout the day, keeping nearly, if not altogether, *in the exact plane of the lunar ellipse*. What was worthy of remark, a very perceptible vacillation in the car was a consequence of this change of route—a vacillation which prevailed, in a more or less degree, for a period of many hours.

"*April 13th.* Was again very much alarmed by a repetition of the loud, crackling noise which terrified me on the tenth. Thought long upon the subject, but was unable to form any satisfactory conclusion. Great decrease in the earth's apparent diameter, which now subtended from the balloon an angle of very little more than twenty-five degrees. The moon could not be seen at all, being nearly in my zenith. I still continued in the plane of the ellipse, but made little progress to the eastward.

"*April 14th.* Extremely rapid decrease in the diameter of the earth. Today I became strongly impressed with the idea, that the balloon was now actually running up the line of apsides to the point of perigee—in other words, holding the direct course which would bring it immediately to the moon in that part of its orbit the nearest to the earth. The moon itself was directly overhead, and consequently hidden from my view. Great and long-continued labor necessary for the condensation of the atmosphere.

"*April 15th.* Not even the outlines of continents and seas could now be traced upon the earth with anything approaching distinctness. About twelve o'clock I became aware, for the third time, of that appalling sound which had so astonished me before. It now, however, continued for some moments, and gathered intensity as it continued. At length, while, stupefied and terror-stricken, I stood in expectation of I knew not what hideous destruction, the car vibrated with excessive violence, and a gigantic and flaming mass of some material which I could not distinguish, came with a voice of a thousand thunders, roaring and booming by the balloon. When my fears and astonishment had in some degree subsided, I had little difficulty in supposing it to be some mighty volcanic fragment ejected from that world to which I was so rapidly approaching, and, in all probability, one of that singular class of substances occasionally picked up on the earth, and termed meteoric stones for want of a better appellation.

"*April 16th.* Today, looking upward as well as I could, through each of the side windows alternately, I beheld, to my great delight, a very small portion of the moon's disk protruding, as it were, on all sides beyond the huge circumference of the balloon. My agitation was extreme; for I had now little doubt of soon reaching the end of my perilous voyage. Indeed, the labor now required by the condenser had increased to a most oppressive degree, and allowed me scarcely any respite from exertion. Sleep was a matter nearly out of the question. I became quite ill, and my frame trembled with exhaustion. It was impossible that human nature could endure this state of intense suffering much longer. During the now brief interval of darkness a meteoric stone again passed in my vicinity, and the frequency of these phenomena began to occasion me much apprehension.

"*April 17th.* This morning proved an epoch in my voyage. It will be remembered that, on the thirteenth, the earth subtended an angular breadth of twenty-five degrees. On the fourteenth this had greatly diminished; on the fifteenth a still more remarkable decrease was observable; and, on retiring on the night of the sixteenth, I had noticed an angle of no more than about seven degrees and fifteen minutes. What, therefore, must have been my amazement, on awakening from a brief and disturbed slumber, on the morning of this day, the seventeenth, at finding the surface beneath me so suddenly and wonderfully *augmented* in volume, as to subtend no less than thirty-nine degrees in apparent angular diameter! I was thunderstruck! No words can give any adequate idea of the extreme, the absolute horror and astonishment, with which I was seized possessed, and altogether overwhelmed. My knees tottered beneath me—my teeth chattered—my hair started up on end. 'The balloon, then, had actually burst!' These were the first tumultuous ideas that hurried through my mind: 'The balloon had positively burst!—I was falling—falling with the most impetuous, the most unparalleled velocity! To judge by the immense distance already so quickly passed over, it could not be more than ten minutes, at the farthest, before I should meet the surface of the earth, and be hurled into annihilation!' But at length reflection came to my relief. I paused; I considered; and I began to doubt. The matter was impossible. I could not in any reason have so rapidly come down. Besides, although I was evidently approaching the surface below me, it was with a speed by no means commensurate with the velocity I had at first so horribly conceived. This consideration served to calm the perturbation of my mind, and I finally succeeded in regarding the phenomenon in its proper point of view. In fact, amazement must have fairly deprived me of my senses, when I could not see the vast difference, in appearance, between the surface below me, and the surface of my mother earth. The latter was indeed over my head, and completely hidden by the balloon, while the moon—the moon itself in all its glory—lay beneath me, and at my feet.

"The stupor and surprise produced in my mind by this extraordinary change in the posture of affairs was perhaps, after all, that part of the adventure least susceptible of explanation. For the *bouleversement* in itself was not only natural and inevitable, but had been long actually anticipated as a circumstance to be expected whenever I should arrive at that exact point of my voyage where the attraction of the planet should be superseded by the attraction of the satellite—or, more precisely, where the gravitation of the balloon toward the earth should be less powerful than its gravitation toward the moon. To be sure I arose from a sound slumber, with all my senses in confusion, to the contemplation of a very startling phenomenon, and one which, although expected, was not expected at the moment. The revolution itself must, of course, have taken place in an easy and gradual manner, and it is by no means clear that, had I even been awake at the time of the occurrence, I should have been made aware of it by any *internal* evidence of an inversion—that is to say, by any inconvenience or disarrangement, either about my person or about my apparatus.

"It is almost needless to say that, upon coming to a due sense of my situation, and emerging from the terror which had absorbed every faculty of my soul, my attention was, in the first place, wholly directed to the contemplation of the general physical appearance of the moon. It lay beneath me like a chart—and although I judged it to be still at no inconsiderable distance, the indentures of its surface were defined to my vision with a most striking and altogether unaccountable distinctness. The entire absence of ocean or sea, and indeed of any lake or river, or body of water whatsoever, struck me, at first glance, as the most extraordinary feature in its geological condition. Yet, strange to say, I beheld vast level regions of a character decidedly alluvial, although by far the greater portion of the hemisphere in sight was covered with innumerable volcanic mountains, conical in shape, and having more the appearance of artificial than of natural protuberance. The highest among them does not exceed three and three-quarter miles in perpendicular elevation;

but a map of the volcanic districts of the Campi Phlegraei would afford to your Excellencies a better idea of their general surface than any unworthy description I might think proper to attempt. The greater part of them were in a state of evident eruption, and gave me fearfully to understand their fury and their power, by the repeated thunders of the miscalled meteoric stones, which now rushed upward by the balloon with a frequency more and more appalling.

"*April 18th.* Today I found an enormous increase in the moon's apparent bulk—and the evidently accelerated velocity of my descent began to fill me with alarm. It will be remembered, that, in the earliest stage of my speculations upon the possibility of a passage to the moon, the existence, in its vicinity, of an atmosphere, dense in proportion to the bulk of the planet, had entered largely into my calculations; this too in spite of many theories to the contrary, and, it may be added, in spite of a general disbelief in the existence of any lunar atmosphere at all. But, in addition to what I have already urged in regard to Encke's comet and the zodiacal light, I had been strengthened in my opinion by certain observations of Mr. Schroeter, of Lilienthal. He observed the moon when two days and a half old, in the evening soon after sunset, before the dark part was visible, and continued to watch it until it became visible. The two cusps appeared tapering in a very sharp faint prolongation, each exhibiting its farthest extremity faintly illuminated by the solar rays, before any part of the dark hemisphere was visible. Soon afterward, the whole dark limb became illuminated. This prolongation of the cusps beyond the semicircle, I thought, must have arisen from the refraction of the sun's rays by the moon's atmosphere. I computed, also, the height of the atmosphere (which could refract light enough into its dark hemisphere to produce a twilight more luminous than the light reflected from the earth when the moon is about 32° from the new) to be 1,356 Paris feet; in this view, I supposed the greatest height capable of refracting the solar ray, to be 5,376 feet. My ideas on this topic had also received confirmation by a passage in the eighty-second volume of the Philosophical Transactions, in which it is stated that at an occultation of Jupiter's satellites, the third disappeared after having been about 1' or 2" of time indistinct, and the fourth became indiscernible near the limb.[4]

"Upon the resistance or, more properly, upon the support of an atmosphere, existing in the state of density imagined, I had, of course, entirely depended for the safety of my ultimate descent. Should I then, after all, prove to have been mistaken, I had in consequence nothing better to expect, as a *finale* to my adventure, than being dashed into atoms against the rugged surface of the satellite. And, indeed, I had now every reason to be terrified. My distance from the moon was comparatively trifling, while the labor required by the condenser was diminished not at all, and I could discover no indication whatever of a decreasing rarity in the air.

"*April 19th.* This morning, to my great joy, about nine o'clock, the surface of the moon being frightfully near, and my apprehensions excited to the utmost, the pump of my condenser at length gave evident tokens of an alteration in the atmosphere. By ten, I had reason to believe its density considerably increased. By eleven, very little labor was necessary at the apparatus; and at twelve o'clock, with some hesitation, I ventured to unscrew the *tourniquet*, when, finding no inconvenience from having done so, I finally threw open the gum-elastic chamber, and unrigged it from around the car. As might have been expected, spasms and violent headache were the immediate consequences of an experiment so precipitate and full of danger. But these and other difficulties attending respiration, as they were by no means so great as to put me in peril of my life, I determined to endure as I best could, in consideration of my leaving them behind me momently in my approach to the denser strata near the moon. This approach, however, was still impetuous in the extreme; and it soon became alarmingly certain that, although I had probably not been deceived in the expectation of an atmosphere dense in proportion to the mass of the satellite, still I had been wrong in supposing this density, even at the surface, at all adequate to the support of the great weight contained in the car of my balloon. Yet this *should* have been the case, and in an equal degree as at the surface of the earth, the actual gravity of bodies at either planet supposed in the ratio of the atmospheric condensation. That it *was not* the case, however, my precipitous downfall gave testimony enough; why it was not so, can only be explained by a reference to those possible geological disturbances to which I have formerly alluded. At all events I was now close upon the planet, and coming down with the most terrible impetuosity. I lost not a moment, accordingly, in throwing overboard first my ballast, then my water-kegs, then my condensing apparatus and gum-elastic chamber, and finally every article within the car. But it was all to no purpose. I still fell with horrible rapidity, and was now not more than half a mile from the surface. As a last resource, therefore, having got rid of my coat, hat, and boots, I cut loose from the balloon *the car itself*, which was of no inconsiderable weight, and thus, clinging with both hands to the net-work, I had barely time to observe that the whole country, as far as the eye could reach, was thickly interspersed with diminutive habitations, ere I tumbled headlong into the very heart of a fantastical-looking city, and into the middle of a vast crowd of ugly little people, who none of them uttered a single syllable, or gave themselves the least trouble to render me assistance, but stood, like a parcel of idiots, grinning in a ludicrous manner, and eyeing me and my balloon askant, with their arms set akimbo. I turned from them in contempt, and, gazing upward at the earth so lately left, and left perhaps for ever, beheld it like a huge, dull, copper shield, about two degrees in diameter, fixed immovably in the heavens overhead, and tipped on one of its edges with a crescent border of the most brilliant gold. No traces of land or water could be discovered, and the whole was clouded with variable spots, and belted with tropical and equatorial zones.

"Thus, may it please your Excellencies, after a series of great anxieties, unheard of dangers, and unparalleled escapes, I had, at length, on the nineteenth day of my departure from Rotterdam, arrived in safety at the conclusion of a voyage undoubtedly the most extraordinary, and the most momentous, ever accomplished, undertaken, or conceived by any denizen of earth. But my adventures yet remain to be related. And indeed your Excellencies may well imagine that, after a residence of five years upon a planet not only deeply interesting in its own peculiar character, but rendered doubly so by its intimate connection, in capacity of satellite, with the world inhabited by man, I may have intelligence for the private ear of the States' College of Astronomers of far more importance than the details, however wonderful, of the mere voyage which so happily concluded. This is, in fact, the case. I have much—very much which it would give me the greatest pleasure to communicate. I have much to say of the climate of the planet; of its wonderful alternations of heat and cold, of unmitigated and burning sunshine for one fortnight, and more than polar frigidity for the next; of a constant transfer of moisture, by distillation like that *in vacuo*, from the point beneath the sun to the point the farthest from it; of a variable zone of running water, of the people themselves; of their manners, customs, and political institutions; of their peculiar physical construction; of their ugliness; of their want of ears, those useless appendages in an atmosphere so peculiarly modified; of their consequent ignorance of the use and properties of speech; of their substitute for speech in a singular method of intercommunication; of the incomprehensible connection between each particular individual in the moon with some particular individual on the earth—a connection analogous with, and depending upon, that of the orbs of the planet and the satellites, and by means of which the lives and destinies of the inhabitants of the one are interwoven with the lives and destinies of the inhabitants of the other; and above all, if it so please your Excellencies—above all, of those dark and hideous mysteries which lie in the outer regions of the moon—regions which, owing to the almost miraculous accordance of the satellite's rotation on its own axis with its sidereal revolution about the earth, have never yet been turned, and, by God's mercy, never shall be turned, to the scrutiny of the telescopes of man. All this, and more—much more—would I most willingly detail. But, to be brief, I must have my reward. I am pining for a return to my family and to my home, and as the price of any farther communication on my part—in consideration of the light which I have it in my power to throw upon many very important branches of physical and metaphysical science—I must solicit, through the influence of your honorable body, a pardon for the crime of which I have been guilty in the death of the creditors upon my departure from Rotterdam. This, then, is the object of the present paper. Its bearer, an inhabitant of the moon, whom I have prevailed upon, and properly instructed, to be my messenger to the earth, will await your Excellencies' pleasure, and return to me with the pardon in question, if it can, in any manner, be obtained.

"I have the honor to be, etc., your Excellencies' very humble servant,

"HANS PFAALL."

Upon finishing the perusal of this very extraordinary document, Professor Rub-a-dub, it is said, dropped his pipe upon the ground in the extremity of his surprise, and Mynheer Superbus Von Underduk having taken off his spectacles, wiped them, and deposited them in his pocket, so far forgot both himself and his dignity, as to turn round three times upon his heel in the quintessence of astonishment and admiration. There was no doubt about the matter—the pardon should be obtained. So at least swore, with a round oath, Professor Rub-a-dub, and so finally thought the illustrious Von Underduk, as he took the arm of his brother in science, and without saying a word, began to make the best of his way home to deliberate upon the measures to be adopted. Having reached the door, however, of the burgomaster's dwelling, the professor ventured to suggest that as the messenger had thought proper to disappear—no doubt frightened to death by the savage appearance of the burghers of Rotterdam—the pardon would be of little use, as no one but a man of the moon would undertake a voyage to so vast a distance. To the truth of this observation the burgomaster assented, and the matter was therefore at an end. Not so, however, rumors and speculations. The letter, having been published, gave rise to a variety of gossip and opinion. Some of the over-wise even made themselves ridiculous by decrying the whole business; as nothing better than a hoax. But hoax, with these sort of people, is, I believe, a general term for all matters above their comprehension. For my part, I cannot conceive upon what data they have founded such an accusation. Let us see what they say:

Imprimus. That certain wags in Rotterdam have certain especial antipathies to certain burgomasters and astronomers.

Don't understand at all.

Secondly. That an odd little dwarf and bottle conjurer, both of whose ears, for some misdemeanor, have been cut off close to his head, has been missing for several days from the neighboring city of Bruges.

Well—what of that?

Thirdly. That the newspapers which were stuck all over the little balloon were newspapers of Holland, and therefore could not have been made in the moon. They were dirty papers—very dirty—and Gluck, the printer, would take his Bible oath to their having been printed in Rotterdam.

He was mistaken—undoubtedly—mistaken.

Fourthly. That Hans Pfaall himself, the drunken villain, and the three very idle gentlemen styled his creditors, were all seen, no longer than two or three days ago, in a tippling house in the suburbs, having just returned, with money in their pockets, from a trip beyond the sea.

Don't believe it—don't believe a word of it.

Lastly. That it is an opinion very generally received, or which ought to be generally received, that the College of Astronomers in the city of Rotterdam, as well as other colleges in all other parts of the world,—not to mention colleges and astronomers in general,—are, to say the least of the matter, not a whit better, nor greater, nor wiser than they ought to be.

Notes

1 NOTE—Strictly speaking, there is but little similarity between the above sketchy trifle and the celebrated "Moon-Story" of Mr. Locke; but as both have the character of *hoaxes* (although the one is in a tone of banter, the other of downright earnest), and as both hoaxes are on the same subject, the moon—moreover, as both attempt to give plausibility by scientific detail—the author of "Hans Pfaall" thinks it necessary to say, in *self-defence*, that his own *jeu d'esprit* was published in the "Southern Literary Messenger" about three weeks before the commencement of Mr. L's in the "New York Sun." Fancying a likeness which, perhaps, does not exist, some of the New York papers copied "Hans Pfaall," and collated it with the "Moon-Hoax," by way of detecting the writer of the one in the writer of the other.

As many more persons were actually gulled by the "Moon-Hoax" than would be willing to acknowledge the fact, it may here afford some little amusement to show why no one should have been deceived—to point out those particulars of the story which should have been sufficient to establish its real character. Indeed, however rich the imagination displayed in this ingenious fiction, it wanted much of the force which might have been given it by a more scrupulous attention to facts and to general analogy. That the public were misled, even for an instant, merely proves the gross ignorance which is so generally prevalent upon subjects of an astronomical nature.

The moon's distance from the earth is, in round numbers, 240,000 miles. If we desire to ascertain how near, apparently, a lens would bring the satellite (or any distant object), we, of course, have but to divide the distance by the magnifying or, more strictly, by the space-penetrating power of the glass. Mr. L. makes his lens have a power of 42,000 times. By this divide 240,000 (the moon's real distance), and we have five miles and five sevenths, as the apparent distance. No animal at all could be seen so far; much less the minute points particularized in the story. Mr. L. speaks about Sir John Herschel's perceiving flowers (the Papaver rheas, etc.), and even detecting the color and the shape of the eyes of small birds. Shortly before, too, he has himself observed that the lens would not render perceptible objects of less than eighteen inches in diameter; but even this, as I have said, is giving the glass by far too great power. It may be observed, in passing, that this prodigious glass is said to have been molded at the glasshouse of Messrs. Hartley and Grant, in Dumbarton; but Messrs. H. and G.'s establishment had ceased operations for many years previous to the publication of the hoax.

On page 13, pamphlet edition, speaking of "a hairy veil" over the eyes of a species of bison, the author says: "It immediately occurred to the acute mind of Dr. Herschel that this was a providential contrivance to protect the eyes of the animal from the great extremes of light and darkness to which all the inhabitants of our side of the moon are periodically subjected." But this cannot be thought a very "acute" observation of the Doctor's. The inhabitants of our side of the moon have, evidently, no darkness at all, so there can be nothing of the "extremes" mentioned. In the absence of the sun they have a light from the earth equal to that of thirteen full unclouded moons.

The topography throughout, even when professing to accord with Blunt's Lunar Chart, is entirely at variance with that or any other lunar chart, and even grossly at variance with itself. The points of the compass, too, are in inextricable confusion; the writer appearing to be ignorant that, on a lunar map, these are not in accordance with terrestrial points; the east being to the left, etc.

Deceived, perhaps, by the vague titles, *Mare Nubium*, *Mare Tranquillitatis*, *Mare Faecunditatis*, etc., given to the dark spots by former astronomers, Mr. L. has entered into details regarding oceans and other large bodies of water in the moon; whereas there is no astronomical point more positively ascertained than that no such bodies exist there. In examining the boundary between light and darkness (in the crescent or gibbous moon) where this boundary crosses any of the dark places, the line of division is found to be rough and jagged; but, were these dark places liquid, it would evidently be even.

The description of the wings of the man-bat, on page 21, is but a literal copy of Peter Wilkins' account of the wings of his flying islanders. This simple fact should have induced suspicion, at least, it might be thought.

On page 23, we have the following: "What a prodigious influence must our thirteen times larger globe have exercised upon this satellite when an embryo in the womb of time, the passive subject of chemical affinity!" This is very fine; but it should be observed that no astronomer would have made such remark, especially to any Journal of Science; for the earth, in the sense intended, is not only thirteen, but forty-nine times *larger* than the moon. A similar objection applies to the whole of the concluding pages, where, by way of introduction to some discoveries in Saturn, the philosophical correspondent enters into a minute schoolboy account of that planet—this to the "Edinburgh Journal of Science!"

But there is one point, in particular, which should have betrayed the fiction. Let us imagine the power actually possessed of seeing animals upon the moon's surface—what would first arrest the attention of an observer from the earth? Certainly neither their shape, size, nor any other such peculiarity, so soon as their remarkable *situation*. They would appear to be walking, with heels up and head down, in the manner of flies on a ceiling. The *real* observer would have uttered an instant ejaculation of surprise (however prepared by previous knowledge) at the singularity of their position; the *fictitious* observer has not even mentioned the subject, but speaks of seeing the entire bodies of such creatures, when it is demonstrable that he could have seen only the diameter of their heads!

It might as well be remarked, in conclusion, that the size, and particularly the powers of the man-bats (for example, their ability to fly in so rare an atmosphere—if, indeed, the moon have any)—with most of the other fancies in regard to animal and vegetable existence, are at variance, generally, with all analogical reasoning on these themes; and that analogy here will often amount to conclusive demonstration. It is, perhaps, scarcely necessary to add, that all the suggestions attributed to Brewster and Herschel, in the beginning of the article, about "a transfusion of artificial light through the focal object of vision," etc., etc., belong to that species of figurative writing which comes, most properly, under the denomination of rigmarole.

There is a real and very definite limit to optical discovery among the stars—a limit whose nature need only be stated to be understood. If, indeed, the casting of large lenses were all that is required, man's ingenuity would ultimately prove equal to the task, and we might have them of any size demanded. But, unhappily, in proportion to the increase of size in the lens, and consequently of space-penetrating power, is the diminution of light from the object, by diffusion of its rays. And for this evil there is no remedy within human ability; for an object is seen by means of that light alone which proceeds from itself, whether direct or reflected. Thus the only "*artificial*" light which could avail Mr. Locke, would be some artificial light which he should be able to throw—not upon the "focal object of vision," but upon the real object to be viewed—to wit: *upon the moon*. It has been easily calculated that, when the light proceeding from a star becomes so diffused as to be as weak as the natural light proceeding from the whole of the stars, in a clear and moonless night, then the star is no longer visible for any practical purpose.

The Earl of Ross' telescope, lately constructed in England, has a *speculum* with a reflecting surface of 4,071 square inches; the Herschel telescope having one of only 1,811. The metal of the Earl of Ross's is 6 feet diameter; it is 5½ inches thick at the edges, and 5 at the centre. The weight is 3 tons. The focal length is 50 feet.

I have lately read a singular and somewhat ingenious little book, whose title-page runs thus: —"L'Homme dans la lvne, ou le Voyage Chimerique fait au Monde de la Lvne, nouvellement decouvert par Dominique Gonzales, Aduanturier Espagnol, autremèt dit le Courier volant. Mis en notre langve par J. B. D. A. Paris, chez Francois Piot, pres la Fontaine de Saint Benoist. Et chez J. Goignard, au premier pilier de la grand' salle du Palais, proche les Consultations, MDCXLVII." pp. 176.

The writer professes to have translated his work from the English of one Mr. D'Avisson (Davidson?) although there is a terrible ambiguity in the statement. "J'en ai eu," says he "l'original de Monsieur D'Avisson, medecin des mieux versez qui soient aujourd'huy dans la cònoissance des Belles Lettres, et sur tout de la Philosophic Naturelle. Je lui ai cette obligation entre les autres, de m'auoir non seulement mis en main ce Livre en anglois, mais encore le Manuscrit du Sieur Thomas D'Anan, gentilhomme Eccossois, recommandable pour sa vertu, sur la version duquel j'advoue que j'ay tiré le plan de la mienne."

After some irrelevant adventures, much in the manner of Gil Blas, and which occupy the first thirty pages, the author relates that, being ill during a sea voyage, the crew abandoned him, together with a negro servant, on the island of St. Helena. To increase the chances of obtaining food, the two separate, and live as far apart as possible. This brings about a training of birds, to serve the purpose of carrier-pigeons between them. By and by these are taught to carry parcels of some weight—and this weight is gradually increased. At length the idea is entertained of uniting the force of a great number of the birds, with a view to raising the author himself. A machine is contrived for the purpose, and we have a minute description of it, which is materially helped out by a steel engraving. Here we perceive the Signor Gonzales, with point ruffles and a huge periwig, seated astride something which resembles very closely a broomstick, and borne aloft by a multitude of wild swans *(ganzas)* who had strings reaching from their tails to the machine.

The main event detailed in the Signor's narrative depends upon a very important fact, of which the reader is kept in ignorance until near the end of the book. The *ganzas,* with whom he had become so familiar, were not really denizens of St. Helena, but of the moon. Thence it had been their custom, time out of mind, to migrate annually to some portion of the earth. In proper season, of course, they would return home; and the author, happening, one day, to require their services for a short voyage, is unexpectedly carried straight up, and in a very brief period arrives at the satellite. Here he finds, among other odd things, that the people enjoy extreme happiness; that they have no *law;* that they die without pain; that they are from ten to thirty feet in height; that they live five thousand years; that they have an emperor called Irdonozur; and that they can jump sixty feet high, when, being out of the gravitating influence, they fly about with fans.

I cannot forbear giving a specimen of the general *philosophy* of the volume.

"I must now declare to you," says the Signor Gonzales, "the nature of the place in which I found myself. All the clouds were beneath my feet, or, if you please, spread between me and the earth. As to the stars, *since there was no night where I was, they always had the same appearance; not brilliant, as usual, but pale, and very nearly like the moon of a morning*. But few of them were visible, and these ten times larger (as well as I could judge) than they seem to the inhabitants of the earth. The moon, which wanted two days of being full, was a terrible bigness.

"I must not forget here, that the stars appeared only on that side of the globe turned towards the moon, and that the closer they were to it the larger they seemed. I have also to inform you that, whether it was calm weather or stormy, I found myself *always immediately between the moon and the earth*. I was convinced of this for two reasons—because my birds always flew in a straight line; and because whenever we attempted to rest, *we were carried insensibly around the globe of the earth*. For I admit the opinion of Copernicus, who maintains that it never ceases to revolve *from the east to the west*, not upon the poles of the Equinoctial, commonly called the poles of the world, but upon those of the Zodiac, a question of which I propose to speak more at length hereafter, when I shall have leisure to refresh my memory in regard to the astrology which I learned at Salamanca when young, and have since forgotten."

Notwithstanding the blunders italicized, the book is not without some claim to attention, as affording a naive specimen of the current astronomical notions of the time. One of these assumed, that the "gravitating power" extended but a short distance from the earth's surface, and, accordingly, we find our voyager "carried insensibly around the globe," etc.

There have been other "voyages to the moon," but none of higher merit than the one just mentioned. That of Bergerac is utterly meaningless. In the third volume of the "American Quarterly Review" will be found quite an elaborate criticism upon a certain "journey" of the kind in question—a criticism in which it is difficult to say whether the critic most exposes the stupidity of the book, or his own absurd ignorance of astronomy. I forget the title of the work; but the *means* of the voyage are more deplorably ill conceived than are even the *ganzas* of our friend the Signor Gonzales. The adventurer, in digging the earth, happens to discover a peculiar metal for which the moon has a strong attraction, and straightway constructs of it a box, which, when cast loose from its terrestrial fastenings, flies with him, forthwith, to the satellite. The "Flight of Thomas O'Rourke," is a *jeu d' esprit* not altogether contemptible, and has been translated into German. Thomas, the hero, was, in fact, the gamekeeper of an Irish peer, whose eccentricities gave rise to the tale. The "flight" is made on an eagle's back, from Hungry Hill, a lofty mountain at the end of Bantry Bay.

In these various *brochures* the aim is always satirical; the theme being a description of Lunarian customs as compared with ours. In none is there any effort at *plausibility* in the details of the voyage itself. The writers seem, in each instance, to be utterly uninformed in respect to astronomy. In "Hans Pfaall" the design is original, inasmuch as regards an attempt at *verisimilitude,* in the application of scientific principles (so far as the whimsical nature of the subject would permit), to the actual passage between the earth and the moon.

[2] The zodiacal light is probably what the ancients called Trabes. *Emicantet trabes quas docos vocant.*—Pliny, lib. 2, p. 26.

[3] Since the original publication of Hans Pfaall, I find that Mr. Green, of Nassau—balloon notoriety, and other late aeronauts, deny the assertions of Humboldt, in this respect, and speak of a *decreasing* inconvenience—precisely in accordance with the theory here urged in a mere spirit of banter.

[4] Hevelius writes that he has several times found, in skies perfectly clear, when even stars of the sixth and seventh magnitude were conspicuous, that, at the same altitude of the moon, at the same elongation from the earth, and with one and the same excellent telescope, the moon and its maculae did not appear equally lucid at all times. From the circumstances of the observation, it is evident that the cause of this phenomenon is not either in our air, in the tube, in the moon, or in the eye of the spectator, but must be looked for in something (an atmosphere?) existing about the moon.

Cassini frequently observed Saturn, Jupiter, and the fixed stars, when approaching the moon to occultation, to have their circular figure changed into an oval one; and, in other occultations, he found no alteration of figure at all. Hence it might be supposed, that at some times and not at others, there is a dense matter encompassing the moon wherein the rays of the stars are refracted.

Ligeia

And the will therein lieth, which dieth not. Who knoweth the mysteries of the will, with its vigor? For God is but a great will pervading all things by nature of its intentness. Man doth not yield himself to the angels, nor unto death utterly, save only through the weakness of his feeble will.

—*Joseph Glanvill*

I cannot, for my soul, remember how, when, or even precisely where, I first became acquainted with the Lady Ligeia. Long years have since elapsed, and my memory is feeble through much suffering. Or, perhaps, I cannot *now* bring these points to mind, because, in truth, the character of my beloved, her rare learning, her singular yet placid cast of beauty, and the thrilling and enthralling eloquence of her low musical language, made their way into my heart by paces so steadily and stealthily progressive that they have been unnoticed and unknown. Yet I believe that I met her first and most frequently in some large, old, decaying city near the Rhine. Of her family—I have surely heard her speak. That it is of a remotely ancient date cannot be doubted. Ligeia! Ligeia! Buried in studies of a nature more than all else adapted to deaden impressions of the outward world, it is by that sweet word alone—by Ligeia—that I bring before mine eyes in fancy the image of her who is no more. And now, while I write, a recollection flashes upon me that I have *never known* the paternal name of her who was my friend and my betrothed, and who became the partner of my studies, and finally the wife of my bosom. Was it a playful charge on the part of my

Ligeia? Or was it a test of my strength of affection, that I should institute no inquiries upon this point? Or was it rather a caprice of my own—a wildly romantic offering on the shrine of the most passionate devotion? I but indistinctly recall the fact itself—what wonder that I have utterly forgotten the circumstances which originated or attended it? And, indeed, if ever that spirit which is entitled *Romance*—if ever she, the wan and the misty-winged *Ashtophet* of idolatrous Egypt, presided, as they tell, over marriages ill-omened, then most surely she presided over mine.

There is one dear topic, however, on which my memory falls me not. It is the *person* of Ligeia. In stature she was tall, somewhat slender, and, in her latter days, even emaciated. I would in vain attempt to portray the majesty, the quiet ease, of her demeanor, or the incomprehensible lightness and elasticity of her footfall. She came and departed as a shadow. I was never made aware of her entrance into my closed study save by the dear music of her low sweet voice, as she placed her marble hand upon my shoulder. In beauty of face no maiden ever equalled her. It was the radiance of an opium-dream—an airy and spirit-lifting vision more wildly divine than the phantasies which hovered vision about the slumbering souls of the daughters of Delos. Yet her features were not of that regular mould which we have been falsely taught to worship in the classical labors of the heathen. "There is no exquisite beauty," says Bacon, Lord Verulam, speaking truly of all the forms and *genera* of beauty, "without some *strangeness* in the proportion." Yet, although I saw that the features of Ligeia were not of a classic regularity—although I perceived that her loveliness was indeed "exquisite," and felt that there was much of "strangeness" pervading it, yet I have tried in vain to detect the irregularity and to trace home my own perception of "the strange." I examined the contour of the lofty and pale forehead—it was faultless—how cold indeed that word when applied to a majesty so divine!—the skin rivalling the purest ivory, the commanding extent and repose, the gentle prominence of the regions above the temples; and then the raven-black, the glossy, the luxuriant and naturally-curling tresses, setting forth the full force of the Homeric epithet, "hyacinthine!" I looked at the delicate outlines of the nose—and nowhere but in the graceful medallions of the Hebrews had I beheld a similar perfection. There were the same luxurious smoothness of surface, the same scarcely perceptible tendency to the aquiline, the same harmoniously curved nostrils speaking the free spirit. I regarded the sweet mouth. Here was indeed the triumph of all things heavenly—the magnificent turn of the short upper lip—the soft, voluptuous slumber of the under—the dimples which sported, and the color which spoke—the teeth glancing back, with a brilliancy almost startling, every ray of the holy light which fell upon them in her serene and placid, yet most exultingly radiant of all smiles. I scrutinized the formation of the chin—and here, too, I found the gentleness of breadth, the softness and the majesty, the fullness and the spirituality, of the Greek—the contour which the god Apollo revealed but in a dream, to Cleomenes, the son of the Athenian. And then I peered into the large eyes of Ligeia.

For eyes we have no models in the remotely antique. It might have been, too, that in these eyes of my beloved lay the secret to which Lord Verulam alludes. They were, I must believe, far larger than the ordinary eyes of our own race. They were even fuller than the fullest of the gazelle eyes of the tribe of the valley of Nourjahad. Yet it was only at intervals—in moments of intense excitement—that this peculiarity became more than slightly noticeable in Ligeia. And at such moments was her beauty—in my heated fancy thus it appeared perhaps—the beauty of beings either above or apart from the earth—the beauty of the fabulous Houri of the Turk. The hue of the orbs was the most brilliant of black, and, far over them, hung jetty lashes of great length. The brows, slightly irregular in outline, had the same tint. The "strangeness," however, which I found in the eyes, was of a nature distinct from the formation, or the color, or the brilliancy of the features, and must, after all, be referred to the *expression*. Ah, word of no meaning! behind whose vast latitude of mere sound we intrench our ignorance of so much of the spiritual. The expression of the eyes of Ligeia! How for long hours have I pondered upon it! How have I, through the whole of a midsummer night, struggled to fathom it! What was it—that something more profound than the well of Democritus—which lay far within the pupils of my beloved? What *was* it? I was possessed with a passion to discover. Those eyes! those large, those shining, those divine orbs! they became to me twin stars of Leda, and I to them devoutest of astrologers.

There is no point, among the many incomprehensible anomalies of the science of mind, more thrillingly exciting than the fact—never, I believe, noticed in the schools—that, in our endeavors to recall to memory something long forgotten, we often find ourselves *upon the very verge* of remembrance, without being able, in the end, to remember. And thus how frequently, in my intense scrutiny of Ligeia's eyes, have I felt approaching the full knowledge of their expression—felt it approaching—yet not quite be mine—and so at length entirely depart! And (strange, oh strangest mystery of all!) I found, in the commonest objects of the universe, a circle of analogies to theat expression. I mean to say that, subsequently to the period when Ligeia's beauty passed into my spirit, there dwelling as in a shrine, I derived, from many existences in the material world, a sentiment such as I felt always aroused within me by her large and luminous orbs. Yet not the more could I define that sentiment, or analyze, or even steadily view it. I recognized it, let me repeat, sometimes in the survey of a rapidly-growing vine—in the contemplation of a moth, a butterfly, a chrysalis, a stream of running water. I have felt it in the ocean; in the falling of a meteor. I have felt it in the glances of unusually aged people. And there are one or two stars in heaven—(one especially, a star of the sixth magnitude, double and changeable, to be found near the large star in Lyra) in a telescopic scrutiny of which I have been made aware of the feeling. I have been filled with it by certain sounds from stringed instruments, and not unfrequently by passages from books. Among innumerable other instances, I well remember something in a volume of Joseph Glanvill, which (perhaps merely from its quaintness—who shall say?) never failed to inspire me with the sentiment—"And the will therein lieth, which dieth not. Who knoweth the mysteries of the will, with its vigor? For God is but a great will pervading all things by nature of its intentness. Man doth not yield him to the angels, nor unto death utterly, save only through the weakness of his feeble will."

Length of years, and subsequent reflection, have enabled me to trace, indeed, some remote connection between this passage in the English moralist and a portion of the character of Ligeia. An *intensity* in thought, action, or speech, was possibly, in her, a result, or at least an index, of that gigantic volition which, during our long intercourse, failed to give other and more immediate evidence of its existence. Of all the women whom I have ever known, she, the outwardly calm, the ever-placid Ligeia, was the most violently a prey to the tumultuous vultures of stern passion. And of such passion I could form no estimate, save by the miraculous expansion of those eyes which at once so delighted and appalled me—by the almost magical melody, modulation, distinctness and placidity of her very low voice—and by the fierce energy (rendered doubly effective by contrast with her manner of utterance) of the wild words which she habitually uttered.

I have spoken of the learning of Ligeia: it was immense—such as I have never known in woman. In the classical tongues was she deeply proficient, and as far as my own acquaintance extended in regard to the modern dialects of Europe, I have never known her at fault. Indeed upon any theme of the most admired, because simply the most abstruse of the boasted erudition of the academy, have I *ever* found Ligeia at fault? How singularly—how thrillingly, this one point in the nature of my wife has forced itself, at this late period only, upon my attention! I said her knowledge was such as I have never known in woman—but where breathes the man who has traversed, and successfully, *all* the wide areas of moral, physical, and mathematical science? I saw not then what I now clearly perceive, that the acquisitions of Ligeia were gigantic, were astounding; yet I was sufficiently aware of her infinite supremacy to resign myself, with a child-like confidence, to her guidance through the chaotic world of metaphysical investigation at which I was most busily occupied during the earlier years of our marriage. With how vast a triumph—with how vivid a delight—with how much of all that is ethereal in hope—did I *feel*, as she bent over me in studies but little sought—but less known—that delicious vista by slow degrees expanding before me, down whose long, gorgeous, and all untrodden path, I might at length pass onward to the goal of a wisdom too divinely precious not to be forbidden!

How poignant, then, must have been the grief with which, after some years, I beheld my well-grounded expectations take wings to themselves and fly away! Without Ligeia I was but as a child groping benighted. Her presence, her readings alone, rendered vividly luminous the many mysteries of the transcendentalism in which we were immersed. Wanting the radiant lustre of her eyes, letters, lambent and golden, grew duller than Saturnian lead. And now those eyes shone less and less frequently upon the pages over which I pored. Ligeia grew ill. The wild eyes blazed with a too—too glorious effulgence; the pale fingers became of the transparent waxen hue of the grave, and the blue veins upon the lofty forehead swelled and sank impetuously with the tides of the gentle emotion. I saw that she must die—and I struggled desperately in spirit with the grim Azrael. And the struggles of the passionate wife were, to my astonishment, even more energetic than my own. There had been much in her stern nature to impress me with the belief that, to her, death would have come without its terrors;—but not so. Words are impotent to convey any just idea of the fierceness of resistance with which she wrestled with the Shadow. I groaned in anguish at the pitiable spectacle. I would have soothed—I would have reasoned; but, in the intensity of her wild desire for life—for life—*but* for life—solace and reason were the uttermost folly. Yet not until the last instance, amid the most convulsive writhings of her fierce spirit, was shaken the external placidity of her demeanor. Her voice grew more gentle—grew more low—yet I would not wish to dwell upon the wild meaning of the quietly uttered words. My brain reeled as I hearkened entranced, to a melody more than mortal—to assumptions and aspirations which mortality had never before known.

That she loved me I should not have doubted; and I might have been easily aware that, in a bosom such as hers, love would have reigned no ordinary passion. But in death only, was I fully impressed with the strength of her affection. For long hours, detaining my hand, would she pour out before me the overflowing of a heart whose more than passionate devotion amounted to idolatry. How had I deserved to be so blessed by such confessions?—how had I deserved to be so cursed with the removal of my beloved in the hour of her making them, But upon this subject I cannot bear to dilate. Let me say only, that in Ligeia's more than womanly abandonment to a love, alas! all unmerited, all unworthily bestowed, I at length recognized the principle of her longing with so wildly earnest a desire for the life which was now fleeing so rapidly away. It is this wild longing—it is this eager vehemence of desire for life—*but* for life—that I have no power to portray—no utterance capable of expressing.

At high noon of the night in which she departed, beckoning me, peremptorily, to her side, she bade me repeat certain verses composed by herself not many days before. I obeyed her. They were these:

Lo! 'tis a gala night
 Within the lonesome latter years!
An angel throng, bewinged, bedight
 In veils, and drowned in tears,
Sit in a theatre, to see
 A play of hopes and fears,
While the orchestra breathes fitfully
 The music of the spheres.

Mimes, in the form of God on high,
 Mutter and mumble low,
And hither and thither fly;
 Mere puppets they, who come and go
At bidding of vast formless things
 That shift the scenery to and fro,
Flapping from out their Condor wings
 Invisible Woe!

That motley drama!—oh, be sure
 It shall not be forgot!
With its Phantom chased forever more,
 By a crowd that seize it not,
Through a circle that ever returneth in
 To the self-same spot,
And much of Madness and more of Sin
 And Horror the soul of the plot.

But see, amid the mimic rout,
 A crawling shape intrude!
A blood-red thing that writhes from out
 The scenic solitude!
It writhes!—it writhes!—with mortal pangs
 The mimes become its food,

And the seraphs sob at vermin fangs
 In human gore imbued.

Out—out are the lights—out all!
 And over each quivering form,
The curtain, a funeral pall,
 Comes down with the rush of a storm,
And the angels, all pallid and wan,
 Uprising, unveiling, affirm
That the play is the tragedy, "Man,"
 And its hero the Conqueror Worm.

"O God!" half shrieked Ligeia, leaping to her feet and extending her arms aloft with a spasmodic movement, as I made an end of these lines—"O God! O Divine Father!—shall these things be undeviatingly so?—shall this Conqueror be not once conquered? Are we not part and parcel in Thee? Who—who knoweth the mysteries of the will with its vigor? Man doth not yield him to the angels, *nor unto death utterly*, save only through the weakness of his feeble will."

And now, as if exhausted with emotion, she suffered her white arms to fall, and returned solemnly to her bed of death. And as she breathed her last sighs, there came mingled with them a low murmur from her lips. I bent to them my ear and distinguished, again, the concluding words of the passage in Glanvill—"*Man doth not yield him to the angels, nor unto death utterly, save only through the weakness of his feeble will.*"

She died—and I, crushed into the very dust with sorrow, could no longer endure the lonely desolation of my dwelling in the dim and decaying city by the Rhine. I had no lack of what the world calls wealth. Ligeia had brought me far more, very far more than ordinarily falls to the lot of mortals. After a few months, therefore, of weary and aimless wandering, I purchased, and put in some repair, an abbey, which I shall not name, in one of the wildest and least frequented portions of fair England. The gloomy and dreary grandeur of the building, the almost savage aspect of the domain, the many melancholy and time-honored memories connected with both, had much in unison with the feelings of utter abandonment which had driven me into that remote and unsocial region of the country. Yet although the external abbey, with its verdant decay hanging about it, suffered but little alteration, I gave way, with a child-like perversity, and perchance with a faint hope of alleviating my sorrows, to a display of more than regal magnificence within.—For such follies, even in childhood, I had imbibed a taste and now they came back to me as if in the dotage of grief. Alas, I feel how much even of incipient madness might have been discovered in the gorgeous and fantastic draperies, in the solemn carvings of Egypt, in the wild cornices and furniture, in the Bedlam patterns of the carpets of tufted gold! I had become a bounden slave in the trammels of opium, and my labors and my orders had taken a coloring from my dreams. But these absurdities must not pause to detail. Let me speak only of that one chamber, ever accursed, whither in a moment of mental alienation, I led from the altar as my bride—as the successor of the unforgotten Ligeia—the fair-haired and blue-eyed Lady Rowena Trevanion, of Tremaine.

There is no individual portion of the architecture and decoration of that bridal chamber which is not now visibly before me. Where were the souls of the haughty family of the bride, when, through thirst of gold, they permitted to pass the threshold of an apartment *so* bedecked, a maiden and a daughter so beloved? I have said that I minutely remember the details of the chamber—yet I am sadly forgetful on topics of deep moment—and here there was no system, no keeping, in the fantastic display, to take hold upon the memory. The room lay in a high turret of the castellated abbey, was pentagonal in shape, and of capacious size. Occupying the whole southern face of the pentagon was the sole window—an immense sheet of unbroken glass from Venice—a single pane, and tinted of a leaden hue, so that the rays of either the sun or moon, passing through it, fell with a ghastly lustre on the objects within. Over the upper portion of this huge window, extended the trellice-work of an aged vine, which clambered up the massy walls of the turret. The ceiling, of gloomy-looking oak, was excessively lofty, vaulted, and elaborately fretted with the wildest and most grotesque specimens of a semi-Gothic, semi-Druidical device. From out the most central recess of this melancholy vaulting, depended, by a single chain of gold with long links, a huge censer of the same metal, Saracenic in pattern, and with many perforations so contrived that there writhed in and out of them, as if endued with a serpent vitality, a continual succession of parti-colored fires.

Some few ottomans and golden candelabra, of Eastern figure, were in various stations about—and there was the couch, too—bridal couch—of an Indian model, and low, and sculptured of solid ebony, with a pall-like canopy above. In each of the angles of the chamber stood on end a gigantic sarcophagus of black granite, from the tombs of the kings over against Luxor, with their aged lids full of immemorial sculpture. But in the draping of the apartment lay, alas! the chief phantasy of all. The lofty walls, gigantic in height—even unproportionably so—were hung from summit to foot, in vast folds, with a heavy and massive-looking tapestry—tapestry of a material which was found alike as a carpet on the floor, as a covering for the ottomans and the ebony bed, as a canopy for the bed, and as the gorgeous volutes of the curtains which partially shaded the window. The material was the richest cloth of gold. It was spotted all over, at irregular intervals, with arabesque figures, about a foot in diameter, and wrought upon the cloth in patterns of the most jetty black. But these figures partook of the true character of the arabesque only when regarded from a single point of view. By a contrivance now common, and indeed traceable to a very remote period of antiquity, they were made changeable in aspect. To one entering the room, they bore the appearance of simple monstrosities; but upon a farther advance, this appearance gradually departed; and step by step, as the visitor moved his station in the chamber, he saw himself surrounded by an endless succession of the ghastly forms which belong to the superstition of the Norman, or arise in the guilty slumbers of the monk. The phantasmagoric effect was vastly heightened by the artificial introduction of a strong continual current of wind behind the draperies—giving a hideous and uneasy animation to the whole.

In halls such as these—in a bridal chamber such as this—I passed, with the Lady of Tremaine, the unhallowed hours of the first month of our marriage—passed them with but little disquietude. That my wife dreaded the fierce moodiness of my temper—that she shunned me and loved me but little—I could not help perceiving; but it gave me rather pleasure than otherwise. I loathed her with a hatred belonging more to demon than to man. My memory flew back (oh, with what intensity of regret!), to Ligeia, the beloved, the august, the beautiful, the entombed. I revelled in recollections of her purity, of her wisdom, of her lofty, her ethereal nature, of her passionate, her idolatrous love. Now, then, did my spirit fully and freely burn with more than all the fires of her own. In the excitement of my opium dreams (for I was habitually fettered in the shackles of the drug) I would call aloud upon her name, during the silence of the night, or among the sheltered recesses of the glens by day, as if, through the wild eagerness, the solemn passion, the consuming ardor of my longing for the departed, I could restore her to the pathway she had abandoned—ah, *could* it be forever?—upon the earth.

About the commencement of the second month of the marriage, the Lady Rowena was attacked with sudden illness, from which her recovery was slow. The fever which consumed her rendered her nights uneasy; and in her perturbed state of half-slumber, she spoke of sounds, and of motions, in and about the chamber of the turret, which I concluded had no origin save in the distemper of her fancy, or perhaps in the phantasmagoric influences of the chamber itself. She became at length convalescent—finally well. Yet but a brief period elapsed, ere a second more violent disorder again threw her upon a bed of suffering; and from this attack her frame, at all times feeble, never altogether recovered. Her illnesses were, after this epoch, of alarming character, and of more alarming recurrence, defying alike the knowledge and the great exertions of her physicians. With the increase of the chronic disease which had thus, apparently, taken too sure hold upon her constitution to be eradicated by human means, I could not fall to observe a similar increase in the nervous irritation of her temperament, and in her excitability by trivial causes of fear. She spoke again, and now more frequently and pertinaciously, of the sounds—of the slight sounds—and of the unusual motions among the tapestries, to which she had formerly alluded.

One night, near the closing in of September, she pressed this distressing subject with more than usual emphasis upon my attention. She had just awakened from an unquiet slumber, and I had been watching, with feelings half of anxiety, half of vague terror, the workings of her emaciated countenance. I sat by the side of her ebony bed, upon one of the ottomans of India. She partly arose, and spoke, in an earnest low whisper, of sounds which she then heard, but which I could not hear—of motions which she then saw, but which I could not perceive. The wind was rushing hurriedly behind the tapestries, and I wished to show her (what, let me confess it, I could not all believe) that those almost inarticulate breathings, and those very gentle variations of the figures upon the wall, were but the natural effects of that customary rushing of the wind. But a deadly pallor, overspreading her face, had proved to me that my exertions to reassure her would be fruitless. She appeared to be fainting, and no attendants were within call. I remembered where was deposited a decanter of light wine which had been ordered by her physicians, and hastened across the chamber to procure it. But, as I stepped beneath the light of the censer, two circumstances of a startling nature attracted my attention. I had felt that some palpable although invisible object had passed lightly by my person; and I saw that there lay upon the golden carpet, in the very middle of the rich lustre thrown from the censer, a shadow—a faint, indefinite shadow of angelic aspect—such as might be fancied for the shadow of a shade. But I was wild with the excitement of an immoderate dose of opium, and heeded these things but little, nor spoke of them to Rowena. Having found the wine, I recrossed the chamber, and poured out a gobletful, which I held to the lips of the fainting lady. She had now partially recovered, however, and took the vessel herself, while I sank upon an ottoman near me, with my eyes fastened upon her person. It was then that I became distinctly aware of a gentle footfall upon the carpet, and near the couch; and in a second thereafter, as Rowena was in the act of raising the wine to her lips, I saw, or may have dreamed that I saw, fall within the goblet, as if from some invisible spring in the atmosphere of the room, three or four large drops of a brilliant and ruby colored fluid. If this I saw—not so Rowena. She swallowed the wine unhesitatingly, and I forbore to speak to her of a circumstance which must, after all, I considered, have been but the suggestion of a vivid imagination, rendered morbidly active by the terror of the lady, by the opium, and by the hour.

Yet I cannot conceal it from my own perception that, immediately subsequent to the fall of the ruby-drops, a rapid change for the worse took place in the disorder of my wife; so that, on the third subsequent night, the hands of her menials prepared her for the tomb, and on the fourth, I sat alone, with her shrouded body, in that fantastic chamber which had received her as my bride. Wild visions, opium-engendered, flitted, shadow-like, before me. I gazed with unquiet eye upon the sarcophagi in the angles of the room, upon the varying figures of the drapery, and upon the writhing of the parti-colored fires in the censer overhead. My eyes then fell, as I called to mind the circumstances of a former night, to the spot beneath the glare of the censer where I had seen the faint traces of the shadow. It was there, however, no longer; and breathing with greater freedom, I turned my glances to the pallid and rigid figure upon the bed. Then rushed upon me a thousand memories of Ligeia—and then came back upon my heart, with the turbulent violence of a flood, the whole of that unutterable wo with which I had regarded her thus enshrouded. The night waned; and still, with a bosom full of bitter thoughts of the one only and supremely beloved, I remained gazing upon the body of Rowena.

It might have been midnight, or perhaps earlier, or later, for I had taken no note of time, when a sob, low, gentle, but very distinct, startled me from my revery. I felt that it came from the bed of ebony—the bed of death. I listened in an agony of superstitious terror—but there was no repetition of the sound. I strained my vision to detect any motion in the corpse—but there was not the slightest perceptible. Yet I could not have been deceived. I *had* heard the noise, however faint, and my soul was awakened within me. I resolutely and perseveringly kept my attention riveted upon the body. Many minutes elapsed before any circumstance occurred tending to throw light upon the mystery. At length it became evident that a slight, a very feeble, and barely noticeable tinge of color had flushed up within the cheeks, and along the sunken small veins of the eyelids. Through a species of unutterable horror and awe, for which the language of mortality has no sufficiently energetic expression, I felt my heart cease to beat, my limbs grow rigid where I sat. Yet a sense of duty finally operated to restore my self-possession. I could no longer doubt that we had been precipitate in our preparations—that Rowena still lived. It was necessary that some immediate exertion be made; yet turret was altogether apart from the portion of the abbey tenanted by the servants—there were none within call—I had no means of summoning them to my aid without leaving the room for many minutes—and this I could not venture to do. I therefore struggled alone in my endeavors to call back the spirit ill hovering. In a short period it was certain, however, that a relapse had taken place; the color disappeared from both eyelid and cheek, leaving a wanness even more than that of marble; the lips became doubly shrivelled and pinched up in the ghastly expression of death; a repulsive clamminess and coldness overspread rapidly the surface of the body; and all the usual rigorous illness immediately supervened. I fell back with a shudder upon the couch from which I had been so startlingly aroused, and again gave myself up to passionate waking visions of Ligeia.

An hour thus elapsed when (could it be possible?) I was a second time aware of some vague sound issuing from the region of the bed. I listened—in extremity of horror. The sound came again—it was a sigh. Rushing to the corpse, I saw—distinctly saw—a tremor upon the lips. In a minute afterward they relaxed, disclosing a bright line of the pearly teeth. Amazement now struggled in my bosom with the profound awe which had hitherto reigned there alone. I felt that my vision grew dim, that my reason wandered; and it was only by a violent effort that I at length succeeded in nerving myself to the task which duty thus once more had pointed out. There was now a partial glow upon the forehead and upon the cheek and throat; a perceptible warmth pervaded the whole frame; there was even a slight pulsation at the heart. The lady *lived*; and with redoubled ardor I betook myself to the task of restoration. I chafed and bathed the temples and the hands, and used every exertion which experience, and no little medical reading, could suggest. But in vain. Suddenly, the color fled, the pulsation ceased, the lips resumed the expression of the dead, and, in an instant afterward, the whole body took upon itself the icy chilliness, the livid hue, the intense rigidity, the sunken outline, and all the loathsome peculiarities of that which has been, for many days, a tenant of the tomb.

And again I sunk into visions of Ligeia—and again (what marvel that I shudder while I write), *again* there reached my ears a low sob from the region of the ebony bed. But why shall I minutely detail the unspeakable horrors of that night? Why shall I pause to relate how, time after time, until near the period of the gray dawn, this hideous drama of revivification was repeated; how each terrific relapse was only into a sterner and apparently more irredeemable death; how each agony wore the aspect of a struggle with some invisible foe; and how each struggle was succeeded by I know not what of wild change in the personal appearance of the corpse? Let me hurry to a conclusion.

The greater part of the fearful night had worn away, and she who had been dead, once again stirred—and now more vigorously than hitherto, although arousing from a dissolution more appalling in its utter hopelessness than any. I had long ceased to struggle or to move, and remained sitting rigidly upon the ottoman, a helpless prey to a whirl of violent emotions, of which extreme awe was perhaps the least terrible, the least consuming. The corpse, I repeat, stirred, and now more vigorously than before. The hues of life flushed up with unwonted energy into the countenance—the limbs relaxed—and, save that the eyelids were yet pressed heavily together, and that the bandages and draperies of the grave still imparted their charnel character to the figure, I might have dreamed that Rowena had indeed shaken off, utterly, the fetters of Death. But if this idea was not, even then, altogether adopted, I could at least doubt no longer, when, arising from the bed, tottering, with feeble steps, with closed eyes, and with the manner of one bewildered in a dream, the thing that was enshrouded advanced boldly and palpably into the middle of the apartment.

I trembled not—I stirred not—for a crowd of unutterable fancies connected with the air, the stature, the demeanor of the figure, rushing hurriedly through my brain, had paralyzed—had chilled me into stone. I stirred not—but gazed upon the apparition. There was a mad disorder in my thoughts—a tumult unappeasable. Could it, indeed, be the *living* Rowena who confronted me? Could it indeed be Rowena *at all*—the fair-haired, the blue-eyed Lady Rowena Trevanion of Tremaine? Why, *why* should I doubt it? The bandage lay heavily about the mouth—but then might it not be the mouth of the breathing Lady of Tremaine? And the cheeks—there were the roses as in her noon of life—yes, these might indeed be the fair cheeks of the living Lady of Tremaine. And the chin, with its dimples, as in health, might it not be hers?—but *had she then grown taller since her malady*? What inexpressible madness seized me with that thought? One bound, and I had reached her feet! Shrinking from my touch, she let fall from her head, unloosened, the ghastly ceremements which had confined it, and there streamed forth, into the rushing atmosphere of the chamber, huge masses of long and dishevelled hair; *it was blacker than the raven wings of the midnight!* And now slowly opened *the eyes* of the figure which stood before me. "Here then, at least," I shrieked aloud, "can I never—can I never be mistaken—these are the full, and the black, and the wild eyes—of my lost love—of the lady—of the *Lady Ligeia*."

William Wilson

What say of it? what say *CONSCIENCE*
grim, That spectre in my path?
Chamberlayne's
PHARRONIDA

Let me call myself, for the present, William Wilson. The fair page now lying before me need not be sullied with my real appellation. This has been already too much an object for the scorn—for the horror—for the detestation of my race. To the uttermost regions of the globe have not the indignant winds bruited its unparalleled infamy? Oh, outcast of all outcasts most abandoned!—to the earth art thou not forever dead? to its honors, to its flowers, to its golden aspirations?—and a cloud, dense, dismal, and limitless, does it not hang eternally between thy hopes and heaven?

I would not, if I could, here or to-day, embody a record of my later years of unspeakable misery, and unpardonable crime. This epoch—these later years—took unto themselves a sudden elevation in turpitude, whose origin alone it is my present purpose to assign. Men usually grow base by degrees. From me, in an instant, all virtue dropped bodily as a mantle. From comparatively trivial wickedness I passed, with the stride of a giant, into more than the enormities of an Elah-Gabalus. What chance—what one event brought this evil thing to pass, bear with me while I relate. Death approaches; and the shadow which foreruns him has thrown a softening influence over my spirit. I long, in passing through the dim valley, for the sympathy—I had nearly said for the pity—of my fellow men. I would fain have them believe that I have been, in some measure, the slave of circumstances beyond human control. I would wish them to seek out for me, in the details I am about to give, some little oasis of *fatality* amid a wilderness of error. I would have them allow—what they cannot refrain from allowing—that, although temptation may have erewhile existed as great, man was never *thus*, at least, tempted before—certainly, never *thus* fell. And is it therefore that he has never thus suffered? Have I not indeed been living in a dream? And am I not now dying a victim to the horror and the mystery of the wildest of all sublunary visions?

I am the descendant of a race whose imaginative and easily excitable temperament has at all times rendered them remarkable; and, in my earliest infancy, I gave evidence of having fully inherited the family character. As I advanced in years it was more strongly developed; becoming, for many reasons, a cause of serious disquietude to my friends, and of positive injury to myself. I grew self-willed, addicted to the wildest caprices, and a prey to the most ungovernable passions. Weak-minded, and beset with constitutional infirmities akin to my own, my parents could do but little to check the evil propensities which distinguished me. Some feeble and ill-directed efforts resulted in complete failure on their part, and, of course, in total triumph on mine. Thenceforward my voice was a household law; and at an age when few children have abandoned their leading-strings, I was left to the guidance of my own will, and became, in all but name, the master of my own actions.

My earliest recollections of a school-life, are connected with a large, rambling, Elizabethan house, in a misty-looking village of England, where were a vast number of gigantic and gnarled trees, and where all the houses were excessively ancient. In truth, it was a dream-like and spirit-soothing place, that venerable old town. At this moment, in fancy, I feel the refreshing chilliness of its deeply-shadowed avenues, inhale the fragrance of its thousand shrubberies, and thrill anew with undefinable delight, at the deep hollow note of the church-bell, breaking, each hour, with sullen and sudden roar, upon the stillness of the dusky atmosphere in which the fretted Gothic steeple lay imbedded and asleep.

It gives me, perhaps, as much of pleasure as I can now in any manner experience, to dwell upon minute recollections of the school and its concerns. Steeped in misery as I am—misery, alas! only too real—I shall be pardoned for seeking relief, however slight and temporary, in the weakness of a few rambling details. These, moreover, utterly trivial, and even ridiculous in themselves, assume, to my fancy, adventitious importance, as connected with a period and a locality when and where I recognise the first ambiguous monitions of the destiny which afterwards so fully overshadowed me. Let me then remember.

The house, I have said, was old and irregular. The grounds were extensive, and a high and solid brick wall, topped with a bed of mortar and broken glass, encompassed the whole. This prison-like rampart formed the limit of our domain; beyond it we saw but thrice a week—once every Saturday afternoon, when, attended by two ushers, we were permitted to take brief walks in a body through some of the neighbouring fields—and twice during Sunday, when we were paraded in the same formal manner to the morning and evening service in the one church of the village. Of this church the principal of our school was pastor. With how deep a spirit of wonder and perplexity was I wont to regard him from our remote pew in the gallery, as, with step solemn and slow, he ascended the pulpit! This reverend man, with countenance so demurely benign, with robes so glossy and so clerically flowing, with wig so minutely powdered, so rigid and so vast—could this be he who, of late, with sour visage, and in snuffy habiliments, administered, ferule in hand, the Draconian laws of the academy? Oh, gigantic paradox, too utterly monstrous for solution!

At an angle of the ponderous wall frowned a more ponderous gate. It was riveted and studded with iron bolts, and surmounted with jagged iron spikes. What impressions of deep awe did it inspire! It was never opened save for the three periodical egressions and ingressions already mentioned; then, in every creak of its mighty hinges, we found a plenitude of mystery—a world of matter for solemn remark, or for more solemn meditation.

The extensive enclosure was irregular in form, having many capacious recesses. Of these, three or four of the largest constituted the playground. It was level, and covered with fine hard gravel. I well remember it had no trees, nor benches, nor anything similar within it. Of course it was in the rear of the house. In front lay a small parterre, planted with box and other shrubs; but through this sacred division we passed only upon rare occasions indeed—such as a first advent to school or final departure thence, or perhaps, when a parent or friend having called for us, we joyfully took our way home for the Christmas or Midsummer holy-days.

But the house!—how quaint an old building was this!—to me how veritably a palace of enchantment! There was really no end to its windings—to its incomprehensible subdivisions. It was difficult, at any given time, to say with certainty upon which of its two stories one happened to be. From each room to every other there were sure to be found three or four steps either in ascent or descent. Then the lateral branches were innumerable—inconceivable—and so returning in upon themselves, that our most exact ideas in regard to the whole mansion were not very far different from those with which we pondered upon infinity. During the five years of my residence here, I was never able to ascertain with precision, in what remote locality lay the little sleeping apartment assigned to myself and some eighteen or twenty other scholars.

The school-room was the largest in the house—I could not help thinking, in the world. It was very long, narrow, and dismally low, with pointed Gothic windows and a ceiling of oak. In a remote and terror-inspiring angle was a square enclosure of eight or ten feet, comprising the *sanctum*, "during hours," of our principal, the Reverend Dr. Bransby. It was a solid structure, with massy door, sooner than open which in the absence of the "Dominic," we would all have willingly perished by the *peine forte et dure*. In other angles were two other similar boxes, far less reverenced, indeed, but still greatly matters of awe. One of these was the pulpit of the "classical" usher, one of the "English and mathematical." Interspersed about the room, crossing and recrossing in endless irregularity, were innumerable benches and desks, black, ancient, and time-worn, piled desperately with much-bethumbed books, and so beseamed with initial letters, names at full length, grotesque figures, and other multiplied efforts of the knife, as to have entirely lost what little of original form might have been their portion in days long departed. A huge bucket with water stood at one extremity of the room, and a clock of stupendous dimensions at the other.

Encompassed by the massy walls of this venerable academy, I passed, yet not in tedium or disgust, the years of the third lustrum of my life. The teeming brain of childhood requires no external world of incident to occupy or amuse it; and the apparently dismal monotony of a school was replete with more intense excitement than my riper youth has derived from luxury, or my full manhood from crime. Yet I must believe that my first mental development had in it much of the uncommon—even much of the *outré*. Upon mankind at large the events of very early existence rarely leave in mature age any definite impression. All is gray shadow—a weak and irregular remembrance—an indistinct regathering of feeble pleasures and phantasmagoric pains. With me this is not so. In childhood I must have felt with the energy of a man what I now find stamped upon memory in lines as vivid, as deep, and as durable as the *exergues* of the Carthaginian medals.

Yet in fact—in the fact of the world's view—how little was there to remember! The morning's awakening, the nightly summons to bed; the connings, the recitations; the periodical half-holidays, and perambulations; the play-ground, with its broils, its pastimes, its intrigues;—these, by a mental sorcery long forgotten, were made to involve a wilderness of sensation, a world of rich incident, an universe of varied emotion, of excitement the most passionate and spirit-stirring. "*Oh, le bon temps, que ce siècle de fer!*"

In truth, the ardor, the enthusiasm, and the imperiousness of my disposition, soon rendered me a marked character among my schoolmates, and by slow, but natural gradations, gave me an ascendancy over all not greatly older than myself;—over all with a single exception. This exception was found in the person of a scholar, who, although no relation, bore the same Christian and surname as myself;—a circumstance, in fact, little remarkable; for, notwithstanding a noble descent, mine was one of those everyday appellations which seem, by prescriptive right, to have been, time out of mind, the common property of the mob. In this narrative I have therefore designated myself as William Wilson,—a fictitious title not very dissimilar to the real. My namesake alone, of those who in school phraseology constituted "our set," presumed to compete with me in the studies of the class—in the sports and broils of the play-ground—to refuse implicit belief in my assertions, and submission to my will—indeed, to interfere with my arbitrary dictation in any respect whatsoever. If there is on earth a supreme and unqualified despotism, it is the despotism of a master mind in boyhood over the less energetic spirits of its companions.

Wilson's rebellion was a source of the greatest embarrassment to me—the more so as, in spite of the bravado with which in public I made a point of treating him and his pretensions, I secretly felt that I feared him, and could not help thinking the equality which he maintained so easily with myself, a proof of his true superiority; since not to be overcome cost me a perpetual struggle. Yet this superiority—even this equality—was in truth acknowledged by no one but myself; our associates, by some unaccountable blindness, seemed not even to suspect it. Indeed, his competition, his resistance, and especially his impertinent and dogged interference with my purposes, were not more pointed than private. He appeared to be destitute alike of the ambition which urged, and of the passionate energy of mind which enabled me to excel. In his rivalry he might have been supposed actuated solely by a whimsical desire to thwart, astonish, or mortify myself; although there were times when I could not help observing, with a feeling made up of wonder, abasement, and pique, that he mingled with his injuries, his insults, or his contradictions, a certain most inappropriate, and assuredly most unwelcome *affectionateness* of manner. I could only conceive this singular behavior to arise from a consummate self-conceit assuming the vulgar airs of patronage and protection.

Perhaps it was this latter trait in Wilson's conduct, conjoined with our identity of name, and the mere accident of our having entered the school upon the same day, which set afloat the notion that we were brothers, among the senior classes in the academy. These do not usually inquire with much strictness into the affairs of their juniors. I have before said, or should have said, that Wilson was not, in the most remote degree, connected with my family. But assuredly if we *had* been brothers we must have been twins; for, after leaving Dr. Bransby's, I casually learned that my namesake was born on the nineteenth of January, 1813—and this is a somewhat remarkable coincidence; for the day is precisely that of my own nativity.

It may seem strange that in spite of the continual anxiety occasioned me by the rivalry of Wilson, and his intolerable spirit of contradiction, I could not bring myself to hate him altogether. We had, to be sure, nearly every day a quarrel in which, yielding me publicly the palm of victory, he, in some manner, contrived to make me feel that it was he who had deserved it; yet a sense of pride on my part, and a veritable dignity on his own, kept us always upon what are called "speaking terms," while there were many points of strong congeniality in our tempers, operating to awake me in a sentiment which our position alone, perhaps, prevented from ripening into friendship. It is difficult, indeed, to define, or even to describe, my real feelings towards him. They formed a motley and heterogeneous admixture;—some petulant animosity, which was not yet hatred, some esteem, more respect, much fear, with a world of uneasy curiosity. To the moralist it will be unnecessary to say, in addition, that Wilson and myself were the most inseparable of companions.

It was no doubt the anomalous state of affairs existing between us, which turned all my attacks upon him (and they were many, either open or covert) into the channel of banter or practical joke (giving pain while assuming the aspect of mere fun) rather than into a more serious and determined hostility. But my endeavours on this head were by no means uniformly successful, even when my plans were the most wittily concocted; for my namesake had much about him, in character, of that unassuming and quiet austerity which, while enjoying the poignancy of its own jokes, has no heel of Achilles in itself, and absolutely refuses to be laughed at. I could find, indeed, but one vulnerable point, and that, lying in a personal peculiarity, arising, perhaps, from constitutional disease, would have been spared by any antagonist less at his wit's end than myself;—my rival had a weakness in the faucal or guttural organs, which precluded him from raising his voice at any time *above a very low whisper*. Of this defect I did not fall to take what poor advantage lay in my power.

Wilson's retaliations in kind were many; and there was one form of his practical wit that disturbed me beyond measure. How his sagacity first discovered at all that so petty a thing would vex me, is a question I never could solve; but, having discovered, he habitually practised the annoyance. I had always felt aversion to my uncourtly patronymic, and its very common, if not plebeian praenomen. The words were venom in my ears; and when, upon the day of my arrival, a second William Wilson came also to the academy, I felt angry with him for bearing the name, and doubly disgusted with the name because a stranger bore it, who would be the cause of its twofold repetition, who would be constantly in my presence, and whose concerns, in the ordinary routine of the school business, must inevitably, on account of the detestable coincidence, be often confounded with my own.

The feeling of vexation thus engendered grew stronger with every circumstance tending to show resemblance, moral or physical, between my rival and myself. I had not then discovered the remarkable fact that we were of the same age; but I saw that we were of the same height, and I perceived that we were even singularly alike in general contour of person and outline of feature. I was galled, too, by the rumor touching a relationship, which had grown current in the upper forms. In a word, nothing could more seriously disturb me (although I scrupulously concealed such disturbance), than any allusion to a similarity of mind, person, or condition existing between us. But, in truth, I had no reason to believe that (with the exception of the matter of relationship, and in the case of Wilson himself), this similarity had ever been made a subject of comment, or even observed at all by our schoolfellows. That *he* observed it in all its bearings, and as fixedly as I, was apparent; but that he could discover in such circumstances so fruitful a field of annoyance, can only be attributed, as I said before, to his more than ordinary penetration.

His cue, which was to perfect an imitation of myself, lay both in words and in actions; and most admirably did he play his part. My dress it was an easy matter to copy; my gait and general manner were, without difficulty, appropriated; in spite of his constitutional defect, even my voice did not escape him. My louder tones were, of course, unattempted, but then the key, it was identical; *and his singular whisper, it grew the very echo of my own.*

How greatly this most exquisite portraiture harassed me (for it could not justly be termed a caricature), I will not now venture to describe. I had but one consolation—in the fact that the imitation, apparently, was noticed by myself alone, and that I had to endure only the knowing and strangely sarcastic smiles of my namesake himself. Satisfied with having produced in my bosom the intended effect, he seemed to chuckle in secret over the sting he had inflicted, and was characteristically disregardful of the public applause which the success of his witty endeavours might have so easily elicited. That the school, indeed, did not feel his design, perceive its accomplishment, and participate in his sneer, was, for many anxious months, a riddle I could not resolve. Perhaps the *gradation* of his copy rendered it not so readily perceptible; or, more possibly, I owed my security to the master air of the copyist, who, disdaining the letter (which in a painting is all the obtuse can see), gave but the full spirit of his original for my individual contemplation and chagrin.

I have already more than once spoken of the disgusting air of patronage which he assumed toward me, and of his frequent officious interference withy my will. This interference often took the ungracious character of advice; advice not openly given, but hinted or insinuated. I received it with a repugnance which gained strength as I grew in years. Yet, at this distant day, let me do him the simple justice to acknowledge that I can recall no occasion when the suggestions of my rival were on the side of those errors or follies so usual to his immature age and seeming inexperience; that his moral sense, at least, if not his general talents and worldly wisdom, was far keener than my own; and that I might, to-day, have been a better, and thus a happier man, had I less frequently rejected the counsels embodied in those meaning whispers which I then but too cordially hated and too bitterly despised.

As it was, I at length grew restive in the extreme under his distasteful supervision, and daily resented more and more openly what I considered his intolerable arrogance. I have said that, in the first years of our connexion as schoolmates, my feelings in regard to him might have been easily ripened into friendship: but, in the latter months of my residence at the academy, although the intrusion of his ordinary manner had, beyond doubt, in some measure, abated, my sentiments, in nearly similar proportion, partook very much of positive hatred. Upon one occasion he saw this, I think, and afterwards avoided, or made a show of avoiding me.

It was about the same period, if I remember aright, that, in an altercation of violence with him, in which he was more than usually thrown off his guard, and spoke and acted with an openness of demeanor rather foreign to his nature, I discovered, or fancied I discovered, in his accent, his air, and general appearance, a something which first startled, and then deeply interested me, by bringing to mind dim visions of my earliest infancy—wild, confused and thronging memories of a time when memory herself was yet unborn. I cannot better describe the sensation which oppressed me than by saying that I could with difficulty shake off the belief of my having been acquainted with the being who stood before me, at some epoch very long ago—some point of the past even infinitely remote. The delusion, however, faded rapidly as it came; and I mention it at all but to define the day of the last conversation I there held with my singular namesake.

The huge old house, with its countless subdivisions, had several large chambers communicating with each other, where slept the greater number of the students. There were, however (as must necessarily happen in a building so awkwardly planned), many little nooks or recesses, the odds and ends of the structure; and these the economic ingenuity of Dr. Bransby had also fitted up as dormitories; although, being the merest closets, they were capable of accommodating but a single individual. One of these small apartments was occupied by Wilson.

One night, about the close of my fifth year at the school, and immediately after the altercation just mentioned, finding every one wrapped in sleep, I arose from bed, and, lamp in hand, stole through a wilderness of narrow passages from my own bedroom to that of my rival. I had long been plotting one of those ill-natured pieces of practical wit at his expense in which I had hitherto been so uniformly unsuccessful. It was my intention, now, to put my scheme in operation, and I resolved to make him feel the whole extent of the malice with which I was imbued. Having reached his closet, I noiselessly entered, leaving the lamp, with a shade over it, on the outside. I advanced a step, and listened to the sound of his tranquil breathing. Assured of his being asleep, I returned, took the light, and with it again approached the bed. Close curtains were around it, which, in the prosecution of my plan, I slowly and quietly withdrew, when the bright rays fell vividly upon the sleeper, and my eyes, at the same moment, upon his countenance. I looked;—and a numbness, an iciness of feeling instantly pervaded my frame. My breast heaved, my knees tottered, my whole spirit became possessed with an objectless yet intolerable horror. Gasping for breath, I lowered the lamp in still nearer proximity to the face. Were *these*—these the lineaments of William Wilson? I saw, indeed, that they were his, but I shook as if with a fit of the ague in fancying they were not. What *was* there about them to confound me in this manner? I gazed;—while my brain reeled with a multitude of incoherent thoughts. Not thus he appeared—assuredly not *thus*—in the vivacity of his waking hours. The same name! the same contour of person! the same day of arrival at the academy! And then his dogged and meaningless imitation of my gait, my voice, my habits, and my manner! Was it, in truth, within the bounds of human possibility, that *what I now saw* was the result, merely, of the habitual practice of this sarcastic imitation? Awe-stricken, and with a creeping shudder, I extinguished the lamp, passed silently from the chamber, and left, at once, the halls of that old academy, never to enter them again.

After a lapse of some months, spent at home in mere idleness, I found myself a student at Eton. The brief interval had been sufficient to enfeeble my remembrance of the events at Dr. Bransby's, or at least to effect a material change in the nature of the feelings with which I remembered them. The truth—the tragedy—of the drama was no more. I could now find room to doubt the evidence of my senses; and seldom called up the subject at all but with wonder at extent of human credulity, and a smile at the vivid force of the imagination which I hereditarily possessed. Neither was this species of scepticism likely to be diminished by the character of the life I led at Eton. The vortex of thoughtless folly into which I there so immediately and so recklessly plunged, washed away all but the froth of my past hours, engulfed at once every solid or serious impression, and left to memory only the veriest levities of a former existence.

I do not wish, however, to trace the course of my miserable profligacy here—a profligacy which set at defiance the laws, while it eluded the vigilance of the institution. Three years of folly, passed without profit, had but given me rooted habits of vice, and added, in a somewhat unusual degree, to my bodily stature, when, after a week of soulless dissipation, I invited a small party of the most dissolute students to a secret carousal in my chambers. We met at a late hour of the night; for our debaucheries were to be faithfully protracted until morning. The wine flowed freely, and there were not wanting other and perhaps more dangerous seductions; so that the gray dawn had already faintly appeared in the east, while our delirious extravagance was at its height. Madly flushed with cards and intoxication, I was in the act of insisting upon a toast of more than wonted profanity, when my attention was suddenly diverted by the violent, although partial unclosing of the door of the apartment, and by the eager voice of a servant from without. He said that some person, apparently in great haste, demanded to speak with me in the hall.

Wildly excited with wine, the unexpected interruption rather delighted than surprised me. I staggered forward at once, and a few steps brought me to the vestibule of the building. In this low and small room there hung no lamp; and now no light at all was admitted, save that of the exceedingly feeble dawn which made its way through the semicircular window. As I put my foot over the threshold, I became aware of the figure of a youth about my own height, and habited in a white kerseymere morning frock, cut in the novel fashion of the one I myself wore at the moment. This the faint light enabled me to perceive; but the features of his face I could not distinguish. Upon my entering he strode hurriedly up to me, and, seizing me by. the arm with a gesture of petulant impatience, whispered the words "William Wilson!" in my ear.

I grew perfectly sober in an instant.

There was that in the manner of the stranger, and in the tremulous shake of his uplifted finger, as he held it between my eyes and the light, which filled me with unqualified amazement; but it was not this which had so violently moved me. It was the pregnancy of solemn admonition in the singular, low, hissing utterance; and, above all, it was the character, the tone, *the key*, of those few, simple, and familiar, yet *whispered* syllables, which came with a thousand thronging memories of bygone days, and struck upon my soul with the shock of a galvanic battery. Ere I could recover the use of my senses he was gone.

Although this event failed not of a vivid effect upon my disordered imagination, yet was it evanescent as vivid. For some weeks, indeed, I busied myself in earnest inquiry, or was wrapped in a cloud of morbid speculation. I did not pretend to disguise from my perception the identity of the singular individual who thus perseveringly interfered with my affairs, and harassed me with his insinuated counsel. But who and what was this Wilson?—and whence came he?—and what were his purposes? Upon neither of these points could I be satisfied; merely ascertaining, in regard to him, that a sudden accident in his family had caused his removal from Dr. Bransby's academy on the afternoon of the day in which I myself had eloped. But in a brief period I ceased to think upon the subject; my attention being all absorbed in a contemplated departure for Oxford. Thither I soon went; the uncalculating vanity of my parents furnishing me with an outfit and annual establishment, which would enable me to indulge at will in the luxury already so dear to my heart,—to vie in profuseness of expenditure with the haughtiest heirs of the wealthiest earldoms in Great Britain.

Excited by such appliances to vice, my constitutional temperament broke forth with redoubled ardor, and I spurned even the common restraints of decency in the mad infatuation of my revels. But it were absurd to pause in the detail of my extravagance. Let it suffice, that among spendthrifts I out-Heroded Herod, and that, giving name to a multitude of novel follies, I added no brief appendix to the long catalogue of vices then usual in the most dissolute university of Europe.

It could hardly be credited, however, that I had, even here, so utterly fallen from the gentlemanly estate, as to seek acquaintance with the vilest arts of the gambler by profession, and, having become an adept in his despicable science, to practise it habitually as a means of increasing my already enormous income at the expense of the weak-minded among my fellow-collegians. Such, nevertheless, was the fact. And the very enormity of this offence against all manly and honourable sentiment proved, beyond doubt, the main if not the sole reason of the impunity with which it was committed. Who, indeed, among my most abandoned associates, would not rather have disputed the clearest evidence of his senses, than have suspected of such courses, the gay, the frank, the generous William Wilson—the noblest and most commoner at Oxford—him whose follies (said his parasites) were but the follies of youth and unbridled fancy—whose errors but inimitable whim—whose darkest vice but a careless and dashing extravagance?

I had been now two years successfully busied in this way, when there came to the university a young *parvenu* nobleman,

Glendinning—rich, said report, as Herodes Atticus—his riches, too, as easily acquired. I soon found him of weak intellect, and, of course, marked him as a fitting subject for my skill. I frequently engaged him in play, and contrived, with the gambler's usual art, to let him win considerable sums, the more effectually to entangle him in my snares. At length, my schemes being ripe, I met him (with the full intention that this meeting should be final and decisive) at the chambers of a fellow-commoner (Mr. Preston), equally intimate with both, but who, to do him Justice, entertained not even a remote suspicion of my design. To give to this a better colouring, I had contrived to have assembled a party of some eight or ten, and was solicitously careful that the introduction of cards should appear accidental, and originate in the proposal of my contemplated dupe himself. To be brief upon a vile topic, none of the low finesse was omitted, so customary upon similar occasions that it is a just matter for wonder how any are still found so besotted as to fall its victim.

We had protracted our sitting far into the night, and I had at length effected the manoeuvre of getting Glendinning as my sole antagonist. The game, too, was my favorite *écarté*! The rest of the company, interested in the extent of our play, had abandoned their own cards, and were standing around us as spectators. The *parvenu*, who had been induced by my artifices in the early part of the evening, to drink deeply, now shuffled, dealt, or played, with a wild nervousness of manner for which his intoxication, I thought, might partially, but could not altogether account. In a very short period he had become my debtor to a large amount, when, having taken a long draught of port, he did precisely what I had been coolly anticipating—he proposed to double our already extravagant stakes. With a well-feigned show of reluctance, and not until after my repeated refusal had seduced him into some angry words which gave a color of *pique* to my compliance, did I finally comply. The result, of course, did but prove how entirely the prey was in my toils; in less than an hour he had quadrupled his debt. For some time his countenance had been losing the florid tinge lent it by the wine; but now, to my astonishment, I perceived that it had grown to a pallor truly fearful. I say to my astonishment. Glendinning had been represented to my eager inquiries as immeasurably wealthy; and the sums which he had as yet lost, although in themselves vast, could not, I supposed, very seriously annoy, much less so violently affect him. That he was overcome by the wine just swallowed, was the idea which most readily presented itself; and, rather with a view to the preservation of my own character in the eyes of my associates, than from any less interested motive, I was about to insist, peremptorily, upon a discontinuance of the play, when some expressions at my elbow from among the company, and an ejaculation evincing utter despair on the part of Glendinning, gave me to understand that I had effected his total ruin under circumstances which, rendering him an object for the pity of all, should have protected him from the ill offices even of a fiend.

What now might have been my conduct it is difficult to say. The pitiable condition of my dupe had thrown an air of embarrassed gloom over all; and, for some moments, a profound silence was maintained, during which I could not help feeling my cheeks tingle with the many burning glances of scorn or reproach cast upon me by the less abandoned of the party. I will even own that an intolerable weight of anxiety was for a brief instant lifted from my bosom by the sudden and extraordinary interruption which ensued. The wide, heavy folding doors of the apartment were all at once thrown open, to their full extent, with a vigorous and rushing impetuosity that extinguished, as if by magic, every candle in the room. Their light, in dying, enabled us just to perceive that a stranger had entered, about my own height, and closely muffled in a cloak. The darkness, however, was now total; and we could only *feel* that he was standing in our midst. Before any one of us could recover from the extreme astonishment into which this rudeness had thrown all, we heard the voice of the intruder.

"Gentlemen," he said, in a low, distinct, and never-to-be-forgotten *whisper* which thrilled to the very marrow of my bones, "Gentlemen, I make no apology for this behaviour, because in thus behaving, I am but fulfilling a duty. You are, beyond doubt, uninformed of the true character of the person who has to-night won at *écarté* a large sum of money from Lord Glendinning. I will therefore put you upon an expeditious and decisive plan of obtaining this very necessary information. Please to examine, at your leisure, the inner linings of the cuff of his left sleeve, and the several little packages which may be found in the somewhat capacious pockets of his embroidered morning wrapper."

While he spoke, so profound was the stillness that one might have heard a pin drop upon the floor. In ceasing, he departed at once, and as abruptly as he had entered. Can I—shall I describe my sensations?—must I say that I felt all the horrors of the damned? Most assuredly I had little time given for reflection. Many hands roughly seized me upon the spot, and lights were immediately reprocured. A search ensued. In the lining of my sleeve were found all the court cards essential in *écarté*, and, in the pockets of my wrapper, a number of packs, facsimiles of those used at our sittings, with the single exception that mine were of the species called, technically, *arrondées*; the honours being slightly convex at the ends, the lower cards slightly convex at the sides. In this disposition, the dupe who cuts, as customary, at the length of the pack, will invariably find that he cuts his antagonist an honor; while the gambler, cutting at the breadth, will, as certainly, cut nothing for his victim which may count in the records of the game.

Any burst of indignation upon this discovery would have affected me less than the silent contempt, or the sarcastic composure, with which it was received.

"Mr. Wilson," said our host, stooping to remove from beneath his feet an exceedingly luxurious cloak of rare furs, "Mr. Wilson, this is your property." (The weather was cold; and, upon quitting my own room, I had thrown a cloak over my dressing wrapper, putting it off upon reaching the scene of play.) "I presume it is supererogatory to seek here (eyeing the folds of the garment with a bitter smile) for any farther evidence of your skill. Indeed, we have had enough. You will see the necessity, I hope, of quitting Oxford—at all events, of quitting instantly my chambers."

Abased, humbled to the dust as I then was, it is probable that I should have resented this galling language by immediate personal violence, had not my whole attention been at the moment arrested by a fact of the most startling character. The cloak which I had worn was of a rare description of fur; how rare, how extravagantly costly, I shall not venture to say. Its fashion, too, was of my own fantastic invention; for I was fastidious to an absurd degree of coxcombry, in matters of this frivolous nature. When, therefore, Mr. Preston reached me that which he had picked up upon the floor, and near the folding doors of the apartment, it was with an astonishment nearly bordering upon terror, that I perceived my own already hanging on my arm (where I had no doubt unwittingly placed it), and that the one presented me was but its exact counterpart in every, in even the minutest possible particular. The singular being who had so disastrously exposed me, had been muffled, I remembered, in a cloak; and none had been worn at all by any of the members of our party with the exception of myself. Retaining some presence of mind, I took the one offered me by Preston; placed it, unnoticed, over my own; left the apartment with a resolute scowl of defiance; and, next morning ere dawn of day, commenced a hurried journey from Oxford to the continent, in a perfect agony of horror and of shame.

I fled in vain. My evil destiny pursued me as if in exultation, and proved, indeed, that the exercise of its mysterious dominion had as yet only begun. Scarcely had I set foot in Paris ere I had fresh evidence of the detestable interest taken by this Wilson in my concerns. Years flew, while I experienced no relief. Villain!—at Rome, with how untimely, yet with how spectral an officiousness, stepped he in between me and my ambition! At Vienna, too—at Berlin—and at Moscow! Where, in truth, had I not bitter cause to curse him within my heart? From his inscrutable tyranny did I at length flee, panic-stricken, as from a pestilence; and to the very ends of the earth *I fled in vain.*

And again, and again, in secret communion with my own spirit, would I demand the questions "Who is he?—whence came he?—and what are his objects?" But no answer was there found. And then I scrutinized, with a minute scrutiny, the forms, and the methods, and the leading traits of his impertinent supervision. But even here there was very little upon which to base a conjecture. It was noticeable, indeed, that, in no one of the multiplied instances in which he had of late crossed my path, had he so crossed it except to frustrate those schemes, or to disturb those actions, which, if fully carried out, might have resulted in bitter mischief. Poor justification this, in truth, for an authority so imperiously assumed! Poor indemnity for natural rights of self-agency so pertinaciously, so insultingly denied!

I had also been forced to notice that my tormentor, for a very long period of time (while scrupulously and with miraculous dexterity maintaining his whim of an identity of apparel with myself), had so contrived it, in the execution of his varied interference with my will, that I saw not, at any moment, the features of his face. Be Wilson what he might, *this*, at least, was but the veriest of affectation, or of folly. Could he, for an instant, have supposed that, in my admonisher at Eton—in the destroyer of my honor at Oxford,—in him who thwarted my ambition at Rome, my revenge at Paris, my passionate love at Naples, or what he falsely termed my avarice in Egypt,—that in this, my arch-enemy and evil genius, could fall to recognise the William Wilson of my school boy days,—the namesake, the companion, the rival—the hated and dreaded rival at Dr. Bransby's? Impossible!—But let me hasten to the last eventful scene of the drama.

Thus far I had succumbed supinely to this imperious domination. The sentiment of deep awe with which I habitually regarded the elevated character, the majestic wisdom, the apparent omnipresence and omnipotence of Wilson, added to a feeling of even terror, with which certain other traits in his nature and assumptions inspired me, had operated, hitherto, to impress me with an idea of my own utter weakness and helplessness, and to suggest an implicit, although bitterly reluctant submission to his arbitrary will. But, of late days, I had given myself up entirely to wine; and its maddening influence upon my hereditary temper rendered me more and more impatient of control. I began to murmur,—to hesitate,—to resist. And was it only fancy which induced me to believe that, with the increase of my own firmness, that of my tormentor underwent a proportional diminution? Be this as it may, I now began to feel the inspiration of a burning hope, and at length nurtured in my secret thoughts a stern and desperate resolution that I would submit no longer to be enslaved.

It was at Rome, during the Carnival of 18—, that I attended a masquerade in the palazzo of the Neapolitan Duke Di Broglio. I had indulged more freely than usual in the excesses of the wine-table; and now the suffocating atmosphere of the crowded rooms irritated me beyond endurance. The difficulty, too, of forcing my way through the mazes of the company contributed not a little to the ruffling of my temper; for I was anxiously seeking (let me not say with what unworthy motive) the young, the gay, the beautiful wife of the aged and doting Di Broglio. With a too unscrupulous confidence she had previously communicated to me the secret of the costume in which she would be habited, and now, having caught a glimpse of her person, I was hurrying to make my way into her presence.—At this moment I felt a light hand placed upon my shoulder, and that ever-remembered, low, damnable *whisper* within my ear.

In an absolute phrenzy of wrath, I turned at once upon him who had thus interrupted me, and seized him violently by the collar. He was attired, as I had expected, in a costume altogether similar to my own; wearing a Spanish cloak of blue velvet, begirt about the waist with a crimson belt sustaining a rapier. A mask of black silk entirely covered his face.

"Scoundrel!" I said, in a voice husky with rage, while every syllable I uttered seemed as new fuel to my fury, "scoundrel! impostor! accursed villain! you shall not—you *shall not* dog me unto death! Follow me, or I stab you where you stand!"—and I broke my way from the ballroom into a small ante-chamber adjoining—dragging him unresistingly with me as I went.

Upon entering, I thrust him furiously from me. He staggered against the wall, while I closed the door with an oath, and commanded him to draw. He hesitated but for an instant; then, with a slight sigh, drew in silence, and put himself upon his defence.

The contest was brief indeed. I was frantic with every species of wild excitement, and felt within my single arm the energy and power of a multitude. In a few seconds I forced him by sheer strength against the wainscoting, and thus, getting him at mercy, plunged my sword, with brute ferocity, repeatedly through and through his bosom.

At that instant some person tried the latch of the door. I hastened to prevent an intrusion, and then immediately returned to my dying antagonist. But what human language can adequately portray *that* astonishment, *that* horror which possessed me at the spectacle then presented to view? The brief moment in which I averted my eyes had been sufficient to produce, apparently, a material change in the arrangements at the upper or farther end of the room. A large mirror,—so at first it seemed to me in my confusion—now stood where none had been perceptible before; and, as I stepped up to it in extremity of terror, mine own image, but with features all pale and dabbled in blood, advanced to meet me with a feeble and tottering gait.

Thus it appeared, I say, but was not. It was my antagonist—it was Wilson, who then stood before me in the agonies of his dissolution. His mask and cloak lay, where he had thrown them, upon the floor. Not a thread in all his raiment—not a line in all the marked and singular lineaments of his face which was not, even in the most absolute identity, *mine own*!

It was Wilson; but he spoke no longer in a whisper, and I could have fancied that I myself was speaking while he said:

> *"You have conquered, and I yield. Yet, henceforward art thou also dead—dead to the World, to Heaven and to Hope! In me didst thou exist—and, in my death, see by this image, which is thine own, how utterly thou hast murdered thyself."*

The Fall of the House of Usher

Son coeur est un luth suspendu;
Sitôt qu'on le touche il résonne.
De Béranger

During the whole of a dull, dark, and soundless day in the autumn of the year, when the clouds hung oppressively low in the heavens, I had been passing alone, on horseback, through a singularly dreary tract of country; and at length found myself, as the shades of the evening drew on, within view of the melancholy House of Usher. I know not how it was—but, with the first glimpse of the building, a sense of insufferable gloom pervaded my spirit. I say insufferable; for the feeling was unrelieved by any of that half-pleasurable, because poetic, sentiment, with which the mind usually receives even the sternest natural images of the desolate or terrible. I looked upon the scene before me—upon the mere house, and the simple landscape features of the domain—upon the bleak walls—upon the vacant eye-like windows—upon a few rank sedges—and upon a few white trunks of decayed trees—with an utter depression of soul which I can compare to no earthly sensation more properly than to the after-dream of the reveller upon opium—the bitter lapse into everyday life—the hideous dropping off of the veil. There was an iciness, a sinking, a sickening of the heart—an unredeemed dreariness of thought which no goading of the imagination could torture into aught of the sublime. What was it—I paused to think—what was it that so unnerved me in the contemplation of the House of Usher? It was a mystery all insoluble; nor could I grapple with the shadowy fancies that crowded upon me as I pondered. I was forced to fall back upon the unsatisfactory conclusion, that while, beyond doubt, there *are* combinations of very simple natural objects which have the power of thus affecting us, still the analysis of this power lies among considerations beyond our depth. It was possible, I reflected, that a mere different arrangement of the particulars of the scene, of the details of the picture, would be sufficient to modify, or perhaps to annihilate its capacity for sorrowful impression; and, acting upon this idea, I reined my horse to the precipitous brink of a black and lurid tarn that lay in unruffled lustre by the dwelling, and gazed down—but with a shudder even more thrilling than before—upon the remodelled and inverted images of the gray sedge, and the ghastly tree-stems, and the vacant and eye-like windows.

Nevertheless, in this mansion of gloom I now proposed to myself a sojourn of some weeks. Its proprietor, Roderick Usher, had been one of my boon companions in boyhood; but many years had elapsed since our last meeting. A letter, however, had lately reached me in a distant part of the country—a letter from him—which, in its wildly importunate nature, had admitted of no other than a personal reply. The MS. gave evidence of nervous agitation. The writer spoke of acute bodily illness—of a mental disorder which oppressed him—and of an earnest desire to see me, as his best, and indeed his only personal friend, with a view of attempting, by the cheerfulness of my society, some alleviation of his malady. It was the manner in which all this, and much more, was said—it was the apparent *heart* that went with his request—which allowed me no room for hesitation; and I accordingly obeyed forthwith what I still considered a very singular summons.

Although, as boys, we had been even intimate associates, yet I really knew little of my friend. His reserve had been always excessive and habitual. I was aware, however, that his very ancient family had been noted, time out of mind, for a peculiar sensibility of temperament, displaying itself, through long ages, in many works of exalted art, and manifested, of late, in repeated deeds of munificent yet unobtrusive charity, as well as in a passionate devotion to the intricacies, perhaps even more than to the orthodox and easily recognisable beauties, of musical science. I had learned, too, the very remarkable fact, that the stem of the Usher race, all time-honored as it was, had put forth, at no period, any enduring branch; in other words, that the entire family lay in the direct line of descent, and had always, with very trifling and very temporary variation, so lain. It was this deficiency, I considered, while running over in thought the perfect keeping of the character of the premises with the accredited character of the people, and while speculating upon the possible influence which the one, in the long lapse of centuries, might have exercised upon the other—it was this deficiency, perhaps, of collateral issue, and the consequent undeviating transmission, from sire to son, of the patrimony with the name, which had, at length, so identified the two as to merge the original title of the estate in the quaint and equivocal appellation of the "House of Usher"—an appellation which seemed to include, in the minds of the peasantry who used it, both the family and the family mansion.

I have said that the sole effect of my somewhat childish experiment—that of looking down within the tarn—had been to deepen the first singular impression. There can be no doubt that the consciousness of the rapid increase of my superstition—for why should I not so term it?—served mainly to accelerate the increase itself. Such, I have long known, is the paradoxical law of all sentiments having terror as a basis. And it might have been for this reason only, that, when I again uplifted my eyes to the house itself, from its image in the pool, there grew in my mind a strange fancy—a fancy so ridiculous, indeed, that I but mention it to show the vivid force of the sensations which oppressed me. I had so worked upon my imagination as really to believe that about the whole mansion and domain there hung an atmosphere peculiar to themselves and their immediate vicinity—an atmosphere which had no affinity with the air of heaven, but which had reeked up from the decayed trees, and the gray wall, and the silent tarn—a pestilent and mystic vapor, dull, sluggish, faintly discernible, and leaden-hued.

Shaking off from my spirit what *must* have been a dream, I scanned more narrowly the real aspect of the building. Its principal feature seemed to be that of an excessive antiquity. The discoloration of ages had been great. Minute fungi overspread the whole exterior, hanging in a fine tangled web-work from the eaves. Yet all this was apart from any extraordinary dilapidation. No portion of the masonry had fallen; and there appeared to be a wild inconsistency between its still perfect adaptation of parts, and the crumbling condition of the individual stones. In this there was much that reminded me of the specious totality of old wood-work which has rotted for long years in some neglected vault, with no disturbance from the breath of the external air. Beyond this indication of extensive decay, however, the fabric gave little token of instability. Perhaps the eye of a scrutinizing observer might have discovered a barely perceptible fissure, which, extending from the roof of the building in front, made its way down the wall in a zigzag direction, until it became lost in the sullen waters of the tarn.

Noticing these things, I rode over a short causeway to the house. A servant in waiting took my horse, and I entered the Gothic archway of the hall. A valet, of stealthy step, thence conducted me, in silence, through many dark and intricate passages in my progress to the *studio* of his master. Much that I encountered on the way contributed, I know not how, to heighten the vague sentiments of which I have already spoken. While the objects around me—while the carvings of the ceilings, the sombre tapestries of the walls, the ebon blackness of the floors, and the phantasmagoric armorial trophies which rattled as I strode, were but matters to which, or to such as which, I had been accustomed from my infancy—while I hesitated not to acknowledge how familiar was all this—I still wondered to find how unfamiliar were the fancies which ordinary images were stirring up. On one of the staircases, I met the physician of the family. His countenance, I thought, wore a mingled expression of low cunning and perplexity. He accosted me with trepidation and passed on. The valet now threw open a door and ushered me into the presence of his master.

The room in which I found myself was very large and lofty. The windows were long, narrow, and pointed, and at so vast a distance from the black oaken floor as to be altogether inaccessible from within. Feeble gleams of encrimsoned light made their way through the trellissed panes, and served to render sufficiently distinct the more prominent objects around; the eye, however, struggled in vain to reach the remoter angles of the chamber, or the recesses of the vaulted and fretted ceiling. Dark draperies hung upon the walls. The general furniture was profuse, comfortless, antique, and tattered. Many books and musical instruments lay scattered about, but failed to give any vitality to the scene. I felt that I breathed an atmosphere of sorrow. An air of stern, deep, and irredeemable gloom hung over and pervaded all.

Upon my entrance, Usher arose from a sofa on which he had been lying at full length, and greeted me with a vivacious warmth which had much in it, I at first thought, of an overdone cordiality—of the constrained effort of the *ennuyé*; man of the world. A glance, however, at his countenance, convinced me of his perfect sincerity. We sat down; and for some moments, while he spoke not, I gazed upon him with a feeling half of pity, half of awe. Surely, man had never before so terribly altered, in so brief a period, as had Roderick Usher! It was with difficulty that I could bring myself to admit the identity of the wan being before me with the companion of my early boyhood. Yet the character of his face had been at all times remarkable. A cadaverousness of complexion; an eye large, liquid, and luminous beyond comparison; lips somewhat thin and very pallid, but of a surpassingly beautiful curve; a nose of a delicate Hebrew model, but with a breadth of nostril unusual in similar formations; a finely moulded chin, speaking, in its want of prominence, of a want of moral energy; hair of a more than web-like softness and tenuity; these features, with an inordinate expansion above the regions of the temple, made up altogether a countenance not easily to be forgotten. And now in the mere exaggeration of the prevailing character of these features, and of the expression they were wont to convey, lay so much of change that I doubted to whom I spoke. The now ghastly pallor of the skin, and the now miraculous lustre of the eye, above all things startled and even awed me. The silken hair, too, had been suffered to grow all unheeded, and as, in its wild gossamer texture, it floated rather than fell about the face, I could not, even with effort, connect its Arabesque expression with any idea of simple humanity.

In the manner of my friend I was at once struck with an incoherence—an inconsistency; and I soon found this to arise from a series of feeble and futile struggles to overcome an habitual trepidancy—an excessive nervous agitation. For something of this nature I had indeed been prepared, no less by his letter, than by reminiscences of certain boyish traits, and by conclusions deduced from his peculiar physical conformation and temperament. His action was alternately vivacious and sullen. His voice varied rapidly from a tremulous indecision (when the animal spirits seemed utterly in abeyance) to that species of energetic concision—that abrupt, weighty, unhurried, and hollow-sounding enunciation—that leaden, self-balanced and perfectly modulated guttural utterance, which may be observed in the lost drunkard, or the irreclaimable eater of opium, during the periods of his most intense excitement.

It was thus that he spoke of the object of my visit, of his earnest desire to see me, and of the solace he expected me to afford him. He entered, at some length, into what he conceived to be the nature of his malady. It was, he said, a constitutional and a family evil, and one for which he despaired to find a remedy—a mere nervous affection, he immediately added, which would undoubtedly soon pass off. It displayed itself in a host of unnatural sensations. Some of these, as he detailed them, interested and bewildered me; although, perhaps, the terms, and the general manner of the narration had their weight. He suffered much from a morbid acuteness of the senses; the most insipid food was alone endurable; he could wear only garments of certain texture; the odors of all flowers were oppressive; his eyes were tortured by even a faint light; and there were but peculiar sounds, and these from stringed instruments, which did not inspire him with horror.

To an anomalous species of terror I found him a bounden slave. "I shall perish," said he, "I *must* perish in this deplorable folly. Thus, thus, and not otherwise, shall I be lost. I dread the events of the future, not in themselves, but in their results. I shudder at the thought of any, even the most trivial, incident, which may operate upon this intolerable agitation of soul. I have, indeed, no abhorrence of danger, except in its absolute effect—in terror. In this unnerved—in this pitiable condition—I feel that the period will sooner or later arrive when I must abandon life and reason together, in some struggle with the grim phantasm, *fear*."

I learned, moreover, at intervals, and through broken and equivocal hints, another singular feature of his mental condition. He was enchained by certain superstitious impressions in regard to the dwelling which he tenanted, and whence, for many years, he had never ventured forth—in regard to an influence whose supposititious force was conveyed in terms too shadowy here to be re-stated—an influence which some peculiarities in the mere form and substance of his family mansion, had, by dint of long sufferance, he said, obtained over his spirit—an effect which the *physique* of the gray walls and turrets, and of the dim tarn into which they all looked down, had, at length, brought about upon the *morale* of his existence.

He admitted, however, although with hesitation, that much of the peculiar gloom which thus afflicted him could be traced to a more natural and far more palpable origin—to the severe and long-continued illness—indeed to the evidently approaching dissolution—of a tenderly beloved sister—his sole companion for long years—his last and only relative on earth. "Her decease," he said, with a bitterness which I can never forget, "would leave him (him the hopeless and the frail) the last of the ancient race of the Ushers." While he spoke, the Lady Madeline (for so was she called) passed slowly through a remote portion of the apartment, and, without having noticed my presence, disappeared. I regarded her with an utter astonishment not unmingled with dread—and yet I found it impossible to account for such feelings. A sensation of stupor oppressed me, as my eyes followed her retreating steps. When a door, at length, closed upon her, my glance sought instinctively and eagerly the countenance of the brother—but he had buried his face in his hands, and I could only perceive that a far more than ordinary wanness had overspread the emaciated fingers through which trickled many passionate tears.

The disease of the Lady Madeline had long baffled the skill of her physicians. A settled apathy, a gradual wasting away of the person, and frequent although transient affections of a partially cataleptical character, were the unusual diagnosis. Hitherto she had steadily borne up against the pressure of her malady, and had not betaken herself finally to bed; but, on the closing in of the evening of my arrival at the house, she succumbed (as her brother told me at night with inexpressible agitation) to the prostrating power of the destroyer; and I learned that the glimpse I had obtained of her person would thus probably be the last I should obtain—that the lady, at least while living, would be seen by me no more.

For several days ensuing, her name was unmentioned by either Usher or myself: and during this period I was busied in earnest endeavors to alleviate the melancholy of my friend. We painted and read together; or I listened, as if in a dream, to the wild improvisations of his speaking guitar. And thus, as a closer and still closer intimacy admitted me more unreservedly into the recesses of his spirit, the more bitterly did I perceive the futility of all attempt at cheering a mind from which darkness, as if an inherent positive quality, poured forth upon all objects of the moral and physical universe, in one unceasing radiation of gloom.

I shall ever bear about me a memory of the many solemn hours I thus spent alone with the master of the House of Usher. Yet I should fail in any attempt to convey an idea of the exact character of the studies, or of the occupations, in which he involved me, or led me the way. An excited and highly distempered ideality threw a sulphureous lustre over all. His long improvised dirges will ring forever in my ears. Among other things, I hold painfully in mind a certain singular perversion and amplification of the wild air of the last waltz of Von Weber. From the paintings over which his elaborate fancy brooded, and which grew, touch by touch, into vaguenesses at which I shuddered the more thrillingly, because I shuddered knowing not why—from these paintings (vivid as their images now are before me) I would in vain endeavor to educe more than a small portion which should lie within the compass of merely written words. By the utter simplicity, by the nakedness of his designs, he arrested and overawed attention. If ever mortal painted an idea, that mortal was Roderick Usher. For me at least—in the circumstances then surrounding me—there arose out of the pure abstractions which the hypochondriac contrived to throw upon his canvass, an intensity of intolerable awe, no shadow of which felt I ever yet in the contemplation of the certainly glowing yet too concrete reveries of Fuseli.

One of the phantasmagoric conceptions of my friend, partaking not so rigidly of the spirit of abstraction, may be shadowed forth, although feebly, in words. A small picture presented the interior of an immensely long and rectangular vault or tunnel, with low walls, smooth, white, and without interruption or device. Certain accessory points of the design served well to convey the idea that this excavation lay at an exceeding depth below the surface of the earth. No outlet was observed in any portion of its vast extent, and no torch, or other artificial source of light was discernible; yet a flood of intense rays rolled throughout, and bathed the whole in a ghastly and inappropriate splendor.

I have just spoken of that morbid condition of the auditory nerve which rendered all music intolerable to the sufferer, with the exception of certain effects of stringed instruments. It was, perhaps, the narrow limits to which he thus confined himself upon the guitar, which gave birth, in great measure, to the fantastic character of his performances. But the fervid *facility* of his *impromptus* could not be so accounted for. They must have been, and were, in the notes, as well as in the words of his wild fantasias (for he not unfrequently accompanied himself with rhymed verbal improvisations), the result of that intense mental collectedness and concentration to which I have previously alluded as observable only in particular moments of the highest artificial excitement. The words of one of these rhapsodies I have easily remembered. I was, perhaps, the more forcibly impressed with it, as he gave it, because, in the under or mystic current of its meaning, I fancied that I perceived, and for the first time, a full consciousness on the part of Usher, of the tottering of his lofty reason upon her throne. The verses, which were entitled "The Haunted Palace," ran very nearly, if not accurately, thus:

I.

In the greenest of our valleys,
By good angels tenanted,
Once a fair and stately palace—
Radiant palace—reared its head.
In the monarch Thought's dominion—
It stood there!
Never seraph spread a pinion
Over fabric half so fair.

II.

Banners yellow, glorious, golden,
On its roof did float and flow;
(This—all this—was in the olden
Time long ago)
And every gentle air that dallied,
In that sweet day,

Along the ramparts plumed and pallid,
A winged odor went away.

III.

Wanderers in that happy valley
Through two luminous windows saw
Spirits moving musically
To a lute's well-tuned law,
Round about a throne, where sitting
(Porphyrogene!)
In state his glory well befitting,
The ruler of the realm was seen.

IV.

And all with pearl and ruby glowing
Was the fair palace door,
Through which came flowing, flowing, flowing,
And sparkling evermore,
A troop of Echoes whose sweet duty
Was but to sing,
In voices of surpassing beauty,
The wit and wisdom of their king.

V.

But evil things, in robes of sorrow,
Assailed the monarch's high estate;
(Ah, let us mourn, for never morrow
Shall dawn upon him, desolate!)
And, round about his home, the glory
That blushed and bloomed
Is but a dim-remembered story
Of the old time entombed.

VI.

And travellers now within that valley,
Through the red-litten windows, see
Vast forms that move fantastically
To a discordant melody;

While, like a rapid ghastly river,
Through the pale door,
A hideous throng rush out forever,
And laugh—but smile no more.

I well remember that suggestions arising from this ballad, led us into a train of thought wherein there became manifest an opinion of Usher's which I mention not so much on account of its novelty (for other men[1] have thought thus), as on account of the pertinacity with which he maintained it. This opinion, in its general form, was that of the sentience of all vegetable things. But, in his disordered fancy, the idea had assumed a more daring character, and trespassed, under certain conditions, upon the kingdom of inorganization. I lack words to express the full extent, or the earnest *abandon* of his persuasion. The belief, however, was connected (as I have previously hinted) with the gray stones of the home of his forefathers. The conditions of the sentience had been here, he imagined, fulfilled in the method of collocation of these stones—in the order of their arrangement, as well as in that of the many *fungi* which overspread them, and of the decayed trees which stood around—above all, in the long undisturbed endurance of this arrangement, and in its reduplication in the still waters of the tarn. Its evidence—the evidence of the sentience—was to be seen, he said (and I here started as he spoke), in the gradual yet certain condensation of an atmosphere of their own about the waters and the walls. The result was discoverable, he added, in that silent, yet importunate and terrible influence which for centuries had moulded the destinies of his family, and which made *him* what I now saw him—what he was. Such opinions need no comment, and I will make none.

Our books—the books which, for years, had formed no small portion of the mental existence of the invalid—were, as might be supposed, in strict keeping with this character of phantasm. We pored together over such works as the Ververt et Chartreuse of Gresset; the Belphegor of Machiavelli; the Heaven and Hell of Swedenborg; the Subterranean Voyage of Nicholas Klimm by Holberg; the Chiromancy of Robert Flud, of Jean D'Indagine, and of De la Chambre; the Journey into the Blue Distance of Tieck; and the City of the Sun of Campanella. One favorite volume was a small octavo edition of the *Directorium Inquisitorium*, by the Dominican

Eymeric de Gironne; and there were passages in Pomponius Mela, about the old African Satyrs and OEgipans, over which Usher would sit dreaming for hours. His chief delight, however, was found in the perusal of an exceedingly rare and curious book in quarto Gothic—the manual of a forgotten church—the *Vigiliae Mortuorum secundum Chorum Ecclesiae Maguntinae*.

I could not help thinking of the wild ritual of this work, and of its probable influence upon the hypochondriac, when, one evening, having informed me abruptly that the Lady Madeline was no more, he stated his intention of preserving her corpse for a fortnight (previously to its final interment), in one of the numerous vaults within the main walls of the building. The worldly reason, however, assigned for this singular proceeding, was one which I did not feel at liberty to dispute. The brother had been led to his resolution (so he told me) by consideration of the unusual character of the malady of the deceased, of certain obtrusive and eager inquiries on the part of her medical men, and of the remote and exposed situation of the burial-ground of the family. I will not deny that when I called to mind the sinister countenance of the person whom I met upon the staircase, on the day of my arrival at the house, I had no desire to oppose what I regarded as at best but a harmless, and by no means an unnatural, precaution.

At the request of Usher, I personally aided him in the arrangements for the temporary entombment. The body having been encoffined, we two alone bore it to its rest. The vault in which we placed it (and which had been so long unopened that our torches, half smothered in its oppressive atmosphere, gave us little opportunity for investigation) was small, damp, and entirely without means of admission for light; lying, at great depth, immediately beneath that portion of the building in which was my own sleeping apartment. It had been used, apparently, in remote feudal times, for the worst purposes of a donjon-keep, and, in later days, as a place of deposit for powder, or some other highly combustible substance, as a portion of its floor, and the whole interior of a long archway through which we reached it, were carefully sheathed with copper. The door, of massive iron, had been, also, similarly protected. Its immense weight caused an unusually sharp grating sound, as it moved upon its hinges.

Having deposited our mournful burden upon tressels within this region of horror, we partially turned aside the yet unscrewed lid of the coffin, and looked upon the face of the tenant. A striking similitude between the brother and sister now first arrested my attention; and Usher, divining, perhaps, my thoughts, murmured out some few words from which I learned that the deceased and himself had been twins, and that sympathies of a scarcely intelligible nature had always existed between them. Our glances, however, rested not long upon the dead—for we could not regard her unawed. The disease which had thus entombed the lady in the maturity of youth, had left, as usual in all maladies of a strictly cataleptical character, the mockery of a faint blush upon the bosom and the face, and that suspiciously lingering smile upon the lip which is so terrible in death. We replaced and screwed down the lid, and, having secured the door of iron, made our way, with toil, into the scarcely less gloomy apartments of the upper portion of the house.

And now, some days of bitter grief having elapsed, an observable change came over the features of the mental disorder of my friend. His ordinary manner had vanished. His ordinary occupations were neglected or forgotten. He roamed from chamber to chamber with hurried, unequal, and objectless step. The pallor of his countenance had assumed, if possible, a more ghastly hue—but the luminousness of his eye had utterly gone out. The once occasional huskiness of his tone was heard no more; and a tremulous quaver, as if of extreme terror, habitually characterized his utterance. There were times, indeed, when I thought his unceasingly agitated mind was laboring with some oppressive secret, to divulge which he struggled for the necessary courage. At times, again, I was obliged to resolve all into the mere inexplicable vagaries of madness, for I beheld him gazing upon vacancy for long hours, in an attitude of the profoundest attention, as if listening to some imaginary sound. It was no wonder that his condition terrified—that it infected me. I felt creeping upon me, by slow yet certain degrees, the wild influences of his own fantastic yet impressive superstitions.

It was, especially, upon retiring to bed late in the night of the seventh or eighth day after the placing of the Lady Madeline within the donjon, that I experienced the full power of such feelings. Sleep came not near my couch—while the hours waned and waned away. I struggled to reason off the nervousness which had dominion over me. I endeavored to believe that much, if not all of what I felt, was due to the bewildering influence of the gloomy furniture of the room—of the dark and tattered draperies, which, tortured into motion by the breath of a rising tempest, swayed fitfully to and fro upon the walls, and rustled uneasily about the decorations of the bed. But my efforts were fruitless. An irrepressible tremor gradually pervaded my frame; and, at length, there sat upon my very heart an incubus of utterly causeless alarm. Shaking this off with a gasp and a struggle, I uplifted myself upon the pillows, and, peering earnestly within the intense darkness of the chamber, harkened—I know not why, except that an instinctive spirit prompted me—to certain low and indefinite sounds which came, through the pauses of the storm, at long intervals, I knew not whence. Overpowered by an intense sentiment of horror, unaccountable yet unendurable, I threw on my clothes with haste (for I felt that I should sleep no more during the night), and endeavored to arouse myself from the pitiable condition into which I had fallen, by pacing rapidly to and fro through the apartment.

I had taken but few turns in this manner, when a light step on an adjoining staircase arrested my attention. I presently recognised it as that of Usher. In an instant afterward he rapped, with a gentle touch, at my door, and entered, bearing a lamp. His countenance was, as usual, cadaverously wan—but, moreover, there was a species of mad hilarity in his eyes—an evidently restrained *hysteria* in his whole demeanor. His air appalled me—but anything was preferable to the solitude which I had so long endured, and I even welcomed his presence as a relief.

"And you have not seen it?" he said abruptly, after having stared about him for some moments in silence—"you have not then seen it?—but, stay! you shall." Thus speaking, and having carefully shaded his lamp, he hurried to one of the casements, and threw it freely open to the storm.

The impetuous fury of the entering gust nearly lifted us from our feet. It was, indeed, a tempestuous yet sternly beautiful night, and one wildly singular in its terror and its beauty. A whirlwind had apparently collected its force in our vicinity; for there were frequent and violent alterations in the direction of the wind; and the exceeding density of the clouds (which hung so low as to press upon the turrets of the house) did not prevent our perceiving the life-like velocity with which they flew careering from all points against each other, without passing away into the distance. I say that even their exceeding density did not prevent our perceiving this—yet we had no glimpse of the moon or stars—nor was there any flashing forth of the lightning. But the under surfaces of the huge masses of agitated vapor, as well as all terrestrial objects immediately around us, were glowing in the unnatural light of a faintly luminous and distinctly visible gaseous exhalation which hung about and enshrouded the mansion.

"You must not—you shall not behold this!" said I, shudderingly, to Usher, as I led him, with a gentle violence, from the window to a seat. "These appearances, which bewilder you, are merely electrical phenomena not uncommon—or it may be that they have their ghastly origin in the rank miasma of the tarn. Let us close this casement—the air is chilling and dangerous to your frame. Here is one of your favorite romances. I will read, and you shall listen—and so we will pass away this terrible night together."

The antique volume which I had taken up was the *Mad Trist* of Sir Launcelot Canning; but I had called it a favorite of Usher's more in sad jest than in earnest; for, in truth, there is little in its uncouth and unimaginative prolixity which could have had interest for the lofty and spiritual ideality of my friend. It was, however, the only book immediately at hand; and I indulged a vague hope that the excitement which now agitated the hypochondriac, might find relief (for the history of mental disorder is full of similar anomalies) even in the extremeness of the folly which I should read. Could I have judged, indeed, by the wild overstrained air of vivacity with which he harkened, or apparently harkened, to the words of the tale, I might well have congratulated myself upon the success of my design.

I had arrived at that well-known portion of the story where Ethelred, the hero of the Trist, having sought in vain for peaceable admission into the dwelling of the hermit, proceeds to make good an entrance by force. Here, it will be remembered, the words of the narrative run thus:

"And Ethelred, who was by nature of a doughty heart, and who was now mighty withal, on account of the powerfulness of the wine which he had drunken, waited no longer to hold parley with the hermit, who, in sooth, was of an obstinate and maliceful turn, but, feeling the rain upon his shoulders, and fearing the rising of the tempest, uplifted his mace outright, and, with blows, made quickly room in the plankings of the door for his gauntleted hand; and now pulling therewith sturdily, he so cracked, and ripped, and tore all asunder, that the noise of the dry and hollow-sounding wood alarummed and reverberated throughout the forest."

At the termination of this sentence I started, and for a moment, paused; for it appeared to me (although I at once concluded that my excited fancy had deceived me)—it appeared to me that, from some very remote portion of the mansion, there came, indistinctly, to my ears, what might have been, in its exact similarity of character, the echo (but a stifled and dull one certainly) of the very cracking and ripping sound which Sir Launcelot had so particularly described. It was, beyond doubt, the coincidence alone which had arrested my attention; for, amid the rattling of the sashes of the casements, and the ordinary commingled noises of the still increasing storm, the sound, in itself, had nothing, surely, which should have interested or disturbed me. I continued the story:

"But the good champion Ethelred, now entering within the door, was sore enraged and amazed to perceive no signal of the maliceful hermit; but, in the stead thereof, a dragon of a scaly and prodigious demeanor, and of a fiery tongue, which sate in guard before a palace of gold, with a floor of silver; and upon the wall there hung a shield of shining brass with this legend enwritten:

Who entereth herein, a conqueror hath bin;
Who slayeth the dragon, the shield he shall win;

And Ethelred uplifted his mace, and struck upon the head of the dragon, which fell before him, and gave up his pesty breath, with a shriek so horrid and harsh, and withal so piercing, that Ethelred had fain to close his ears with his hands against the dreadful noise of it, the like whereof was never before heard."

Here again I paused abruptly, and now with a feeling of wild amazement—for there could be no doubt whatever that, in this instance, I did actually hear (although from what direction it proceeded I found it impossible to say) a low and apparently distant, but harsh, protracted, and most unusual screaming or grating sound—the exact counterpart of what my fancy had already conjured up for the dragon's unnatural shriek as described by the romancer.

Oppressed, as I certainly was, upon the occurrence of this second and most extraordinary coincidence, by a thousand conflicting sensations, in which wonder and extreme terror were predominant, I still retained sufficient presence of mind to avoid exciting, by any observation, the sensitive nervousness of my companion. I was by no means certain that he had noticed the sounds in question; although, assuredly, a strange alteration had, during the last few minutes, taken place in his demeanor. From a position fronting my own, he had gradually brought round his chair, so as to sit with his face to the door of the chamber; and thus I could but partially perceive his features, although I saw that his lips trembled as if he were murmuring inaudibly. His head had dropped upon his breast—yet I knew that he was not asleep, from the wide and rigid opening of the eye as I caught a glance of it in profile. The motion of his body, too, was at variance with this idea—for he rocked from side to side with a gentle yet constant and uniform sway. Having rapidly taken notice of all this, I resumed the narrative of Sir Launcelot, which thus proceeded:

"And now, the champion, having escaped from the terrible fury of the dragon, bethinking himself of the brazen shield, and of the breaking up of the enchantment which was upon it, removed the carcass from out of the way before him, and approached valorously over the silver pavement of the castle to where the shield was upon the wall; which in sooth the feet upon the silver floor, with a mighty great and terrible ringing sound."

No sooner had these syllables passed my lips, than—as if a shield of brass had indeed, at the moment, fallen heavily upon a floor of silver—I became aware of a distinct, hollow, metallic, and clangorous, yet apparently muffled reverberation. Completely unnerved, I leaped to my feet; but the measured rocking movement of Usher was undisturbed. I rushed to the chair in which he sat. His eyes were bent fixedly before him, and throughout his whole countenance there reigned a stony rigidity. But, as I placed my hand upon his shoulder, there came a strong shudder over his whole person; a sickly smile quivered about his lips; and I saw that he spoke in a low, hurried, and gibbering murmur, as if unconscious of my presence. Bending closely over him, I at length drank in the hideous import of his words.

"Not hear it?—yes, I hear it, and *have* heard it. Long—long—long—many minutes, many hours, many days, have I heard it—yet I dared not—oh, pity me, miserable wretch that I am!—I dared not—I *dared* not speak! *We have put her living in the tomb!* Said I not that my senses were acute? I *now* tell you that I heard her first feeble movements in the hollow coffin. I heard them—many, many days ago—yet I dared not—*I dared not speak!* And now—to-night—Ethelred—ha! ha!—the breaking of the hermit's door, and the death-cry of the dragon, and the clangor of the shield!—say, rather, the rending of her coffin, and the grating of the iron hinges of her prison, and her struggles within the coppered archway of the vault! Oh whither shall I fly? Will she not be here anon? Is she not hurrying to upbraid me for my haste? Have I not heard her footstep on the stair? Do I not distinguish that heavy and horrible beating of her heart? Madman!"—here he sprang furiously to his feet, and shrieked out his syllables, as if in the effort he were giving up his soul—"*Madman! I tell you that she now stands without the door!*"

As if in the superhuman energy of his utterance there had been found the potency of a spell—the huge antique panels to which the speaker pointed, threw slowly back, upon the instant, their ponderous and ebony jaws. It was the work of the rushing gust—but then without those doors there *did* stand the lofty and enshrouded figure of the Lady Madeline of Usher. There was blood upon her white robes, and the evidence of some bitter struggle upon every portion of her emaciated frame. For a moment she remained trembling and reeling to and fro upon the threshold—then, with a low moaning cry, fell heavily inward upon the person of her brother, and in her violent and now final death-agonies, bore him to the floor a corpse, and a victim to the terrors he had anticipated.

From that chamber, and from that mansion, I fled aghast. The storm was still abroad in all its wrath as I found myself crossing the old causeway. Suddenly there shot along the path a wild light, and I turned to see whence a gleam so unusual could have issued;

for the vast house and its shadows were alone behind me. The radiance was that of the full, setting, and blood-red moon, which now shone vividly through that once barely-discernible fissure, of which I have before spoken as extending from the roof of the building, in a zigzag direction, to the base. While I gazed, this fissure rapidly widened—there came a fierce breath of the whirlwind—the entire orb of the satellite burst at once upon my sight—my brain reeled as I saw the mighty walls rushing asunder—there was a long tumultuous shouting sound like the voice of a thousand waters—and the deep and dank tarn at my feet closed sullenly and silently over the fragments of the "House of Usher."

Note

1 Watson, Dr. Percival, Spallanzani, and especially the Bishop of Landaff.—See "Chemical Essays," vol v.

A Descent into the Maelström

> The ways of God in Nature, as in Providence, are not as our ways; nor are the models that we frame any way commensurate to the vastness, profundity, and unsearchableness of His works, which have a depth in them greater than the well of Democritus.
>
> *Joseph Glanville*

We had now reached the summit of the loftiest crag. For some minutes the old man seemed too much exhausted to speak.

"Not long ago," said he at length, "and I could have guided you on this route as well as the youngest of my sons; but, about three years past, there happened to me an event such as never happened to mortal man—or at least such as no man ever survived to tell of—and the six hours of deadly terror which I then endured have broken me up body and soul. You suppose me a *very* old man—but I am not. It took less than a single day to change these hairs from a jetty black to white, to weaken my limbs, and to unstring my nerves, so that I tremble at the least exertion, and am frightened at a shadow. Do you know I can scarcely look over this little cliff without getting giddy?"

The "little cliff," upon whose edge he had so carelessly thrown himself down to rest that the weightier portion of his body hung over it, while he was only kept from falling by the tenure of his elbow on its extreme and slippery edge—this "little cliff" arose, a sheer unobstructed precipice of black shining rock, some fifteen or sixteen hundred feet from the world of crags beneath us. Nothing would have tempted me to within half a dozen yards of its brink. In truth so deeply was I excited by the perilous position of my companion, that I fell at full length upon the ground, clung to the shrubs around me, and dared not even glance upward at the sky—while I struggled in vain to divest myself of the idea that the very foundations of the mountain were in danger from the fury of the winds. It was long before I could reason myself into sufficient courage to sit up and look out into the distance.

"You must get over these fancies," said the guide, "for I have brought you here that you might have the best possible view of the scene of that event I mentioned—and to tell you the whole story with the spot just under your eye."

"We are now," he continued, in that particularizing manner which distinguished him—"we are now close upon the Norwegian coast—in the sixty-eighth degree of latitude—in the great province of Nordland—and in the dreary district of Lofoden. The mountain upon whose top we sit is Helseggen, the Cloudy. Now raise yourself up a little higher—hold on to the grass if you feel giddy—so—and look out, beyond the belt of vapor beneath us, into the sea."

I looked dizzily, and beheld a wide expanse of ocean, whose waters wore so inky a hue as to bring at once to my mind the Nubian geographer's account of the *Mare Tenebrarum*. A panorama more deplorably desolate no human imagination can conceive. To the right and left, as far as the eye could reach, there lay outstretched, like ramparts of the world, lines of horridly black and beetling cliff, whose character of gloom was but the more forcibly illustrated by the surf which reared high up against its white and ghastly crest, howling and shrieking forever. Just opposite the promontory upon whose apex we were placed, and at a distance of some five or six miles out at sea, there was visible a small, bleak-looking island; or, more properly, its position was discernible through the wilderness of surge in which it was enveloped. About two miles nearer the land, arose another of smaller size, hideously craggy and barren, and encompassed at various intervals by a cluster of dark rocks.

The appearance of the ocean, in the space between the more distant island and the shore, had something very unusual about it. Although, at the time, so strong a gale was blowing landward that a brig in the remote offing lay to under a double-reefed trysail, and constantly plunged her whole hull out of sight, still there was here nothing like a regular swell, but only a short, quick, angry cross dashing of water in every direction—as well in the teeth of the wind as otherwise. Of foam there was little except in the immediate vicinity of the rocks.

"The island in the distance," resumed the old man, "is called by the Norwegians Vurrgh. The one midway is Moskoe. That a mile to the northward is Ambaaren. Yonder are Islesen, Hotholm, Keildhelm, Suarven, and Buckholm. Farther off—between Moskoe and Vurrgh—are Otterholm, Flimen, Sandflesen, and Stockholm. These are the true names of the places—but why it has been thought necessary to name them at all, is more than either you or I can understand. Do you hear anything? Do you see any change in the water?"

We had now been about ten minutes upon the top of Helseggen, to which we had ascended from the interior of Lofoden, so that we had caught no glimpse of the sea until it had burst upon us from the summit. As the old man spoke, I became aware of a loud and gradually increasing sound, like the moaning of a vast herd of buffaloes upon an American prairie; and at the same moment I perceived that what seamen term the *chopping* character of the ocean beneath us, was rapidly changing into a current which set to the eastward. Even while I gazed, this current acquired a monstrous velocity. Each moment added to its speed—to its headlong impetuosity. In five minutes the whole sea, as far as Vurrgh, was lashed into ungovernable fury; but it was between Moskoe and the coast that the main uproar held its sway. Here the vast bed of the waters, seamed and scarred into a thousand conflicting channels, burst suddenly into phrensied convulsion—heaving, boiling, hissing—gyrating in gigantic and innumerable vortices, and all whirling and plunging on to the eastward with a rapidity which water never elsewhere assumes except in precipitous descents.

In a few minutes more, there came over the scene another radical alteration. The general surface grew somewhat more smooth, and the whirlpools, one by one, disappeared, while prodigious streaks of foam became apparent where none had been seen before. These streaks, at length, spreading out to a great distance, and entering into combination, took unto themselves the gyratory motion of the subsided vortices, and seemed to form the germ of another more vast. Suddenly—very suddenly—this assumed a distinct and definite existence, in a circle of more than a mile in diameter. The edge of the whirl was represented by a broad belt of gleaming spray; but no particle of this slipped into the mouth of the terrific funnel, whose interior, as far as the eye could fathom it, was a smooth, shining, and jet-black wall of water, inclined to the horizon at an angle of some forty-five degrees, speeding dizzily round and round with a swaying and sweltering motion, and sending forth to the winds an appalling voice, half shriek, half roar, such as not even the mighty cataract of Niagara ever lifts up in its agony to Heaven.

The mountain trembled to its very base, and the rock rocked. I threw myself upon my face, and clung to the scant herbage in an excess of nervous agitation.

"This," said I at length, to the old man—"this *can* be nothing else than the great whirlpool of the Maelström."

"So it is sometimes termed," said he. "We Norwegians call it the Moskoe-ström, from the island of Moskoe in the midway."

The ordinary accounts of this vortex had by no means prepared me for what I saw. That of Jonas Ramus, which is perhaps the most circumstantial of any, cannot impart the faintest conception either of the magnificence, or of the horror of the scene—or of the wild bewildering sense of *the novel* which confounds the beholder. I am not sure from what point of view the writer in question surveyed it, nor at what time; but it could neither have been from the summit of Helseggen, nor during a storm. There are some passages of his description, nevertheless, which may be quoted for their details, although their effect is exceedingly feeble in conveying an impression of the spectacle.

"Between Lofoden and Moskoe," he says, "the depth of the water is between thirty-six and forty fathoms; but on the other side, toward Ver (Vurrgh) this depth decreases so as not to afford a convenient passage for a vessel, without the risk of splitting on the rocks, which happens even in the calmest weather. When it is flood, the stream runs up the country between Lofoden and Moskoe with a boisterous rapidity; but the roar of its impetuous ebb to the sea is scarce equalled by the loudest and most dreadful cataracts; the noise being heard several leagues off, and the vortices or pits are of such an extent and depth, that if a ship comes within its attraction, it is inevitably absorbed and carried down to the bottom, and there beat to pieces against the rocks; and when the water relaxes, the fragments thereof are thrown up again. But these intervals of tranquillity are only at the turn of the ebb and flood, and in calm weather, and last but a quarter of an hour, its violence gradually returning. When the stream is most boisterous, and its fury heightened by a storm, it is dangerous to come within a Norway mile of it. Boats, yachts, and ships have been carried away by not guarding against it before they were within its reach. It likewise happens frequently, that whales come too near the stream, and are overpowered by its violence; and then it is impossible to describe their howlings and bellowings in their fruitless struggles to disengage themselves. A bear once, attempting to swim from Lofoden to Moskoe, was caught by the stream and borne down, while he roared terribly, so as to be heard on shore. Large stocks of firs and pine trees, after being absorbed by the current, rise again broken and torn to such a degree as if bristles grew upon them. This plainly shows the bottom to consist of craggy rocks, among which they are whirled to and fro. This stream is regulated by the flux and reflux of the sea—it being constantly high and low water every six hours. In the year 1645, early in the morning of Sexagesima Sunday, it raged with such noise and impetuosity that the very stones of the houses on the coast fell to the ground."

In regard to the depth of the water, I could not see how this could have been ascertained at all in the immediate vicinity of the vortex. The "forty fathoms" must have reference only to portions of the channel close upon the shore either of Moskoe or Lofoden. The depth in the centre of the Moskoe-ström must be immeasurably greater; and no better proof of this fact is necessary than can be obtained from even the sidelong glance into the abyss of the whirl which may be had from the highest crag of Helseggen. Looking down from this pinnacle upon the howling Phlegethon below, I could not help smiling at the simplicity with which the honest Jonas Ramus records, as a matter difficult of belief, the anecdotes of the whales and the bears; for it appeared to me, in fact, a self-evident thing, that the largest ship of the line in existence, coming within the influence of that deadly attraction, could resist it as little as a feather the hurricane, and must disappear bodily and at once.

The attempts to account for the phenomenon—some of which, I remember, seemed to me sufficiently plausible in perusal—now wore a very different and unsatisfactory aspect. The idea generally received is that this, as well as three smaller vortices among the Ferroe islands, "have no other cause than the collision of waves rising and falling, at flux and reflux, against a ridge of rocks and shelves, which confines the water so that it precipitates itself like a cataract; and thus the higher the flood rises, the deeper must the fall be, and the natural result of all is a whirlpool or vortex, the prodigious suction of which is sufficiently known by lesser experiments."—These are the words of the Encyclopaedia Britannica. Kircher and others imagine that in the centre of the channel of the Maelström is an abyss penetrating the globe, and issuing in some very remote part—the Gulf of Bothnia being somewhat decidedly named in one instance. This opinion, idle in itself, was the one to which, as I gazed, my imagination most readily assented; and, mentioning it to the guide, I was rather surprised to hear him say that, although it was the view almost universally entertained of the subject by the Norwegians, it nevertheless was not his own. As to the former notion he confessed his inability to comprehend it; and here I agreed with him—for, however conclusive on paper, it becomes altogether unintelligible, and even absurd, amid the thunder of the abyss.

"You have had a good look at the whirl now," said the old man, "and if you will creep round this crag, so as to get in its lee, and deaden the roar of the water, I will tell you a story that will convince you I ought to know something of the Moskoe-ström."

I placed myself as desired, and he proceeded.

"Myself and my two brothers once owned a schooner-rigged smack of about seventy tons burthen, with which we were in the habit of fishing among the islands beyond Moskoe, nearly to Vurrgh. In all violent eddies at sea there is good fishing, at proper opportunities, if one has only the courage to attempt it; but among the whole of the Lofoden coastmen, we three were the only ones who made a regular business of going out to the islands, as I tell you. The usual grounds are a great way lower down to the southward. There fish can be got at all hours, without much risk, and therefore these places are preferred. The choice spots over here among the rocks, however, not only yield the finest variety, but in far greater abundance; so that we often got in a single day, what the more timid of the craft could not scrape together in a week. In fact, we made it a matter of desperate speculation—the risk of life standing instead of labor, and courage answering for capital.

"We kept the smack in a cove about five miles higher up the coast than this; and it was our practice, in fine weather, to take advantage of the fifteen minutes' slack to push across the main channel of the Moskoe-ström, far above the pool, and then drop down upon anchorage somewhere near Otterholm, or Sandflesen, where the eddies are not so violent as elsewhere. Here we used to remain until nearly time for slack-water again, when we weighed and made for home. We never set out upon this expedition without a steady side wind for going and coming—one that we felt sure would not fail us before our return—and we seldom made a mis-calculation upon this point. Twice, during six years, we were forced to stay all night at anchor on account of a dead calm, which is a rare thing indeed just about here; and once we had to remain on the grounds nearly a week, starving to death, owing to a gale which blew up shortly after our arrival, and made the channel too boisterous to be thought of. Upon this occasion we should have been driven out to sea in spite of everything (for the whirlpools threw us round and round so violently, that, at length, we fouled our anchor and dragged it) if it had not been that we drifted into one of the innumerable cross currents—here to-day and gone to-morrow—which drove us under the lee of Flimen, where, by good luck, we brought up.

"I could not tell you the twentieth part of the difficulties we encountered 'on the grounds'—it is a bad spot to be in, even in good weather—but we made shift always to run the gauntlet of the Moskoe-ström itself without accident; although at times my heart has been in my mouth when we happened to be a minute or so behind or before the slack. The wind sometimes was not as strong as we thought it at starting, and then we made rather less way than we could wish, while the current rendered the smack unmanageable. My eldest brother had a son eighteen years old, and I had two stout boys of my own. These would have been of great assistance at such times, in using the sweeps, as well as afterward in fishing—but, somehow, although we ran the risk ourselves, we had not the heart to let the young ones get into the danger—for, after all is said and done, it *was* a horrible danger, and that is the truth.

"It is now within a few days of three years since what I am going to tell you occurred. It was on the tenth day of July, 18—, a day which the people of this part of the world will never forget—for it was one in which blew the most terrible hurricane that ever came out of the heavens. And yet all the morning, and indeed until late in the afternoon, there was a gentle and steady breeze from the south-west, while the sun shone brightly, so that the oldest seaman among us could not have foreseen what was to follow.

"The three of us—my two brothers and myself—had crossed over to the islands about two o'clock P.M., and had soon nearly loaded the smack with fine fish, which, we all remarked, were more plenty that day than we had ever known them. It was just seven, *by my watch*, when we weighed and started for home, so as to make the worst of the Ström at slack water, which we knew would be at eight.

"We set out with a fresh wind on our starboard quarter, and for some time spanked along at a great rate, never dreaming of danger, for indeed we saw not the slightest reason to apprehend it. All at once we were taken aback by a breeze from over Helseggen. This was most unusual—something that had never happened to us before—and I began to feel a little uneasy, without exactly knowing why. We put the boat on the wind, but could make no headway at all for the eddies, and I was upon the point of proposing to return to the anchorage, when, looking astern, we saw the whole horizon covered with a singular copper-colored cloud that rose with the most amazing velocity.

"In the meantime the breeze that had headed us off fell away, and we were dead becalmed, drifting about in every direction. This state of things, however, did not last long enough to give us time to think about it. In less than a minute the storm was upon us—in less than two the sky was entirely overcast—and what with this and the driving spray, it became suddenly so dark that we could not see each other in the smack.

"Such a hurricane as then blew it is folly to attempt describing. The oldest seaman in Norway never experienced any thing like it. We had let our sails go by the run before it cleverly took us; but, at the first puff, both our masts went by the board as if they had been sawed off—the mainmast taking with it my youngest brother, who had lashed himself to it for safety.

"Our boat was the lightest feather of a thing that ever sat upon water. It had a complete flush deck, with only a small hatch near the bow, and this hatch it had always been our custom to batten down when about to cross the Ström, by way of precaution against the chopping seas. But for this circumstance we should have foundered at once—for we lay entirely buried for some moments. How my elder brother escaped destruction I cannot say, for I never had an opportunity of ascertaining. For my part, as soon as I had let the foresail run, I threw myself flat on deck, with my feet against the narrow gunwale of the bow, and with my hands grasping a ring-bolt near the foot of the fore-mast. It was mere instinct that prompted me to do this—which was undoubtedly the very best thing I could have done—for I was too much flurried to think.

"For some moments we were completely deluged, as I say, and all this time I held my breath, and clung to the bolt. When I could stand it no longer I raised myself upon my knees, still keeping hold with my hands, and thus got my head clear. Presently our little boat gave herself a shake, just as a dog does in coming out of the water, and thus rid herself, in some measure, of the seas. I was now trying to get the better of the stupor that had come over me, and to collect my senses so as to see what was to be done, when I felt somebody grasp my arm. It was my elder brother, and my heart leaped for joy, for I had made sure that he was overboard—but the next moment all this joy was turned into horror—for he put his mouth close to my ear, and screamed out the word '*Moskoe-ström!*'

"No one ever will know what my feelings were at that moment. I shook from head to foot as if I had had the most violent fit of the ague. I knew what he meant by that one word well enough—I knew what he wished to make me understand. With the wind that now drove us on, we were bound for the whirl of the Ström, and nothing could save us!

"You perceive that in crossing the Ström *channel*, we always went a long way up above the whirl, even in the calmest weather, and then had to wait and watch carefully for the slack—but now we were driving right upon the pool itself, and in such a hurricane as this! 'To be sure,' I thought, 'we shall get there just about the slack—there is some little hope in that'—but in the next moment I cursed myself for being so great a fool as to dream of hope at all. I knew very well that we were doomed, had we been ten times a ninety-gun ship.

"By this time the first fury of the tempest had spent itself, or perhaps we did not feel it so much, as we scudded before it, but at all events the seas, which at first had been kept down by the wind, and lay flat and frothing, now got up into absolute mountains. A singular change, too, had come over the heavens. Around in every direction it was still as black as pitch, but nearly overhead there burst out, all at once, a circular rift of clear sky—as clear as I ever saw—and of a deep bright blue—and through it there blazed forth the full moon with a lustre that I never before knew her to wear. She lit up every thing about us with the greatest distinctness—but, oh God, what a scene it was to light up!

"I now made one or two attempts to speak to my brother—but, in some manner which I could not understand, the din had so increased that I could not make him hear a single word, although I screamed at the top of my voice in his ear. Presently he shook his head, looking as pale as death, and held up one of his finger, as if to say *'listen!'*

"At first I could not make out what he meant—but soon a hideous thought flashed upon me. I dragged my watch from its fob. It was not going. I glanced at its face by the moonlight, and then burst into tears as I flung it far away into the ocean. *It had run down at seven o'clock! We were behind the time of the slack, and the whirl of the Ström was in full fury!*

"When a boat is well built, properly trimmed, and not deep laden, the waves in a strong gale, when she is going large, seem always to slip from beneath her—which appears very strange to a landsman—and this is what is called *riding*, in sea phrase. Well, so far we had ridden the swells very cleverly; but presently a gigantic sea happened to take us right under the counter, and bore us with it as it rose—up—up—as if into the sky. I would not have believed that any wave could rise so high. And then down we came with a sweep, a slide, and a plunge, that made me feel sick and dizzy, as if I was falling from some lofty mountain-top in a dream. But while we were up I had thrown a quick glance around—and that one glance was all sufficient. I saw our exact position in an instant. The Moskoe-ström whirlpool was about a quarter of a mile dead ahead—but no more like the every-day Moskoe-ström, than the whirl as you now see it is like a mill-race. If I had not known where we were, and what we had to expect, I should not have recognised the place at all. As it was, I involuntarily closed my eyes in horror. The lids clenched themselves together as if in a spasm.

"It could not have been more than two minutes afterward until we suddenly felt the waves subside, and were enveloped in foam. The boat made a sharp half turn to larboard, and then shot off in its new direction like a thunderbolt. At the same moment the roaring noise of the water was completely drowned in a kind of shrill shriek—such a sound as you might imagine given out by the waste-pipes of many thousand steam-vessels, letting off their steam all together. We were now in the belt of surf that always surrounds the whirl; and I thought, of course, that another moment would plunge us into the abyss—down which we could only see indistinctly on account of the amazing velocity with which we wore borne along. The boat did not seem to sink into the water at all, but to skim like an air-bubble upon the surface of the surge. Her starboard side was next the whirl, and on the larboard arose the world of ocean we had left. It stood like a huge writhing wall between us and the horizon.

"It may appear strange, but now, when we were in the very jaws of the gulf, I felt more composed than when we were only approaching it. Having made up my mind to hope no more, I got rid of a great deal of that terror which unmanned me at first. I suppose it was despair that strung my nerves.

"It may look like boasting—but what I tell you is truth—I began to reflect how magnificent a thing it was to die in such a manner, and how foolish it was in me to think of so paltry a consideration as my own individual life, in view of so wonderful a manifestation of God's power. I do believe that I blushed with shame when this idea crossed my mind. After a little while I became possessed with the keenest curiosity about the whirl itself. I positively felt a *wish* to explore its depths, even at the sacrifice I was going to make; and my principal grief was that I should never be able to tell my old companions on shore about the mysteries I should see. These, no doubt, were singular fancies to occupy a man's mind in such extremity—and I have often thought since, that the revolutions of the boat around the pool might have rendered me a little light-headed.

"There was another circumstance which tended to restore my self-possession; and this was the cessation of the wind, which could not reach us in our present situation—for, as you saw yourself, the belt of surf is considerably lower than the general bed of the ocean, and this latter now towered above us, a high, black, mountainous ridge. If you have never been at sea in a heavy gale, you can form no idea of the confusion of mind occasioned by the wind and spray together. They blind, deafen, and strangle you, and take away all power of action or reflection. But we were now, in a great measure, rid of these annoyances—just us death-condemned felons in prison are allowed petty indulgences, forbidden them while their doom is yet uncertain.

"How often we made the circuit of the belt it is impossible to say. We careered round and round for perhaps an hour, flying rather than floating, getting gradually more and more into the middle of the surge, and then nearer and nearer to its horrible inner edge. All this time I had never let go of the ring-bolt. My brother was at the stern, holding on to a small empty water-cask which had been securely lashed under the coop of the counter, and was the only thing on deck that had not been swept overboard when the gale first took us. As we approached the brink of the pit he let go his hold upon this, and made for the ring, from which, in the agony of his terror, he endeavored to force my hands, as it was not large enough to afford us both a secure grasp. I never felt deeper grief than when I saw him attempt this act—although I knew he was a madman when he did it—a raving maniac through sheer fright. I did not care, however, to contest the point with him. I knew it could make no difference whether either of us held on at all; so I let him have the bolt, and went astern to the cask. This there was no great difficulty in doing; for the smack flew round steadily enough, and upon an even keel—only swaying to and fro, with the immense sweeps and swelters of the whirl. Scarcely had I secured myself in my new position, when we gave a wild lurch to starboard, and rushed headlong into the abyss. I muttered a hurried prayer to God, and thought all was over.

"As I felt the sickening sweep of the descent, I had instinctively tightened my hold upon the barrel, and closed my eyes. For some seconds I dared not open them—while I expected instant destruction, and wondered that I was not already in my death-struggles with the water. But moment after moment elapsed. I still lived. The sense of falling had ceased; and the motion of the vessel seemed much as it had been before, while in the belt of foam, with the exception that she now lay more along. I took courage, and looked once again upon the scene.

"Never shall I forget the sensations of awe, horror, and admiration with which I gazed about me. The boat appeared to be hanging, as if by magic, midway down, upon the interior surface of a funnel vast in circumference, prodigious in depth, and whose perfectly smooth sides might have been mistaken for ebony, but for the bewildering rapidity with which they spun around, and for the gleaming and ghastly radiance they shot forth, as the rays of the full moon, from that circular rift amid the clouds which I have already described, streamed in a flood of golden glory along the black walls, and far away down into the inmost recesses of the abyss.

"At first I was too much confused to observe anything accurately. The general burst of terrific grandeur was all that I beheld. When I recovered myself a little, however, my gaze fell instinctively downward. In this direction I was able to obtain an unobstructed view, from the manner in which the smack hung on the inclined surface of the pool. She was quite upon an even keel—that is to say, her deck lay in a plane parallel with that of the water—but this latter sloped at an angle of more than forty-five degrees, so that we seemed to be lying upon our beam-ends. I could not help observing, nevertheless, that I had scarcely more difficulty in maintaining my hold and footing in this situation, than if we had been upon a dead level; and this, I suppose, was owing to the speed at which we revolved.

"The rays of the moon seemed to search the very bottom of the profound gulf; but still I could make out nothing distinctly, on account of a thick mist in which everything there was enveloped, and over which there hung a magnificent rainbow, like that narrow and tottering bridge which Mussulmen say is the only pathway between Time and Eternity. This mist, or spray, was no doubt occasioned by the clashing of the great walls of the funnel, as they all met together at the bottom—but the yell that went up to the Heavens from out of that mist, I dare not attempt to describe.

"Our first slide into the abyss itself, from the belt of foam above, had carried us a great distance down the slope; but our farther descent was by no means proportionate. Round and round we swept—not with any uniform movement—but in dizzying swings and jerks, that sent us sometimes only a few hundred yards—sometimes nearly the complete circuit of the whirl. Our progress downward, at each revolution, was slow, but very perceptible.

"Looking about me upon the wide waste of liquid ebony on which we were thus borne, I perceived that our boat was not the only object in the embrace of the whirl. Both above and below us were visible fragments of vessels, large masses of building timber and trunks of trees, with many smaller articles, such as pieces of house furniture, broken boxes, barrels and staves. I have already described the unnatural curiosity which had taken the place of my original terrors. It appeared to grow upon me as I drew nearer and nearer to my dreadful doom. I now began to watch, with a strange interest, the numerous things that floated in our company. I *must* have been delirious—for I even sought *amusement* in speculating upon the relative velocities of their several descents toward the foam below. 'This fir tree,' I found myself at one time saying, 'will certainly be the next thing that takes the awful plunge and disappears,'—and then I was disappointed to find that the wreck of a Dutch merchant ship overtook it and went down before. At length, after making several guesses of this nature, and being deceived in all—this fact—the fact of my invariable miscalculation—set me upon a train of reflection that made my limbs again tremble, and my heart beat heavily once more.

"It was not a new terror that thus affected me, but the dawn of a more exciting *hope*. This hope arose partly from memory, and partly from present observation. I called to mind the great variety of buoyant matter that strewed the coast of Lofoden, having been absorbed and then thrown forth by the Moskoe-ström. By far the greater number of the articles were shattered in the most extraordinary way—so chafed and roughened as to have the appearance of being stuck full of splinters—but then I distinctly recollected that there were *some* of them which were not disfigured at all. Now I could not account for this difference except by supposing that the roughened fragments were the only ones which had been *completely absorbed*—that the others had entered the whirl at so late a period of the tide, or, for some reason, had descended so slowly after entering, that they did not reach the bottom before the turn of the flood came, or of the ebb, as the case might be. I conceived it possible, in either instance, that they might thus be whirled up again to the level of the ocean, without undergoing the fate of those which had been drawn in more early, or absorbed more rapidly. I made, also, three important observations. The first was, that, as a general rule, the larger the bodies were, the more rapid their descent—the second, that, between two masses of equal extent, the one spherical, and the other *of any other shape*, the superiority in speed of descent was with the sphere—the third, that, between two masses of equal size, the one cylindrical, and the other of any other shape, the cylinder was absorbed the more slowly. Since my escape, I have had several conversations on this subject with an old school-master of the district; and it was from him that I learned the use of the words 'cylinder' and 'sphere.' He explained to me—although I have forgotten the explanation—how what I observed was, in fact, the natural consequence of the forms of the floating fragments—and showed me how it happened that a cylinder, swimming in a vortex, offered more resistance to its suction, and was drawn in with greater difficulty than an equally bulky body, of any form whatever.[1]

"There was one startling circumstance which went a great way in enforcing these observations, and rendering me anxious to turn them to account, and this was that, at every revolution, we passed something like a barrel, or else the yard or the mast of a vessel, while many of these things, which had been on our level when I first opened my eyes upon the wonders of the whirlpool, were now high up above us, and seemed to have moved but little from their original station.

"I no longer hesitated what to do. I resolved to lash myself securely to the water cask upon which I now held, to cut it loose from the counter, and to throw myself with it into the water. I attracted my brother's attention by signs, pointed to the floating barrels that came near us, and did everything in my power to make him understand what I was about to do. I thought at length that he comprehended my design—but, whether this was the case or not, he shook his head despairingly, and refused to move from his station by the ring-bolt. It was impossible to reach him; the emergency admitted of no delay; and so, with a bitter struggle, I resigned him to his fate, fastened myself to the cask by means of the lashings which secured it to the counter, and precipitated myself with it into the sea, without another moment's hesitation.

"The result was precisely what I had hoped it might be. As it is myself who now tell you this tale—as you see that I *did* escape—and as you are already in possession of the mode in which this escape was effected, and must therefore anticipate all that I have farther to say—I will bring my story quickly to conclusion. It might have been an hour, or thereabout, after my quitting the smack, when, having descended to a vast distance beneath me, it made three or four wild gyrations in rapid succession, and, bearing my loved brother with it, plunged headlong, at once and forever, into the chaos of foam below. The barrel to which I was attached sunk very little farther than half the distance between the bottom of the gulf and the spot at which I leaped overboard, before a great change took place in the character of the whirlpool. The slope of the sides of the vast funnel became momently less and less steep. The gyrations of the whirl grew, gradually, less and less violent. By degrees, the froth and the rainbow disappeared, and the bottom of the gulf seemed slowly to uprise. The sky was clear, the winds had gone down, and the full moon was setting radiantly in the west, when I found myself on the surface of the ocean, in full view of the shores of Lofoden, and above the spot where the pool of the Moskoe-ström *had been.* It was the hour of the slack—but the sea still heaved in mountainous waves from the effects of the hurricane. I was borne violently into the channel of the Ström, and in a few minutes was hurried down the coast into the 'grounds' of the fishermen. A boat picked me up—exhausted from fatigue—and (now that the danger was removed) speechless from the memory of its horror. Those who drew me on board were my old mates and daily companions—but they knew me no more than they would have known a traveller from the spirit-land. My hair which had been raven-black the day before, was as white as you see it now. They say too that the whole expression of my countenance had changed. I told them my story—they did not believe it. I now tell it to *you*—and I can scarcely expect you to put more faith in it than did the merry fishermen of Lofoden."

Note

[1] See Archimedes, "*De Incidentibus in Fluido.*"—lib. 2.

The Murders in the Rue Morgue

What song the Syrens sang, or what name Achilles assumed when he hid himself among women, although puzzling questions, are not beyond *all* conjecture.

—*Sir Thomas Browne*

The mental features discoursed of as the analytical, are, in themselves, but little susceptible of analysis. We appreciate them only in their effects. We know of them, among other things, that they are always to their possessor, when inordinately possessed, a source of the liveliest enjoyment. As the strong man exults in his physical ability, delighting in such exercises as call his muscles into action, so glories the analyst in that moral activity which *disentangles.* He derives pleasure from even the most trivial occupations bringing his talent into play. He is fond of enigmas, of conundrums, of hieroglyphics; exhibiting in his solutions of each a degree of *acumen* which appears to the ordinary apprehension preternatural. His results, brought about by the very soul and essence of method, have, in truth, the whole air of intuition.

The faculty of resolution is possibly much invigorated by mathematical study, and especially by that highest branch of it which, unjustly, and merely on account of its retrograde operations, has been called, as if *par excellence*, analysis. Yet to calculate is not in itself to analyze. A chess-player, for example, does the one without effort at the other. It follows that the game of chess, in its effects upon mental character, is greatly misunderstood. I am not now writing a treatise, but simply prefacing a somewhat peculiar narrative by observations very much at random; I will, therefore, take occasion to assert that the higher powers of the reflective intellect are more decidedly and more usefully tasked by the unostentatious game of draughts than by a the elaborate frivolity of chess. In this latter, where the pieces have different and *bizarre* motions, with various and variable values, what is only complex is mistaken (a not unusual error) for what is profound. The *attention* is here called powerfully into play. If it flag for an instant, an oversight is committed resulting in injury or defeat. The possible moves being not only manifold but involute, the chances of such oversights are multiplied; and in nine cases out of ten it is the more concentrative rather than the more acute player who conquers. In draughts, on the contrary, where the moves are *unique* and have but little variation, the probabilities of inadvertence are diminished, and the mere attention being left comparatively unemployed, what advantages are obtained by either party are obtained by superior *acumen*. To be less abstract, let us suppose a game of draughts where the pieces are reduced to four kings, and where, of course, no oversight is to be expected. It is obvious that here the victory can be decided (the players being at all equal) only by some *recherché* movement, the result of some strong exertion of the intellect. Deprived of ordinary resources, the analyst throws himself into the spirit of his opponent, identifies himself therewith, and not unfrequently sees thus, at a glance, the sole methods (sometime indeed absurdly simple ones) by which he may seduce into error or hurry into miscalculation.

Whist has long been noted for its influence upon what is termed the calculating power; and men of the highest order of intellect have been known to take an apparently unaccountable delight in it, while eschewing chess as frivolous. Beyond doubt there is nothing of a similar nature so greatly tasking the faculty of analysis. The best chess-player in Christendom *may* be little more than the best player of chess; but proficiency in whist implies capacity for success in all those more important undertakings where mind struggles with mind. When I say proficiency, I mean that perfection in the game which includes a comprehension of *all* the sources whence legitimate advantage may be derived. These are not only manifold but multiform, and lie frequently among recesses of thought altogether inaccessible to the ordinary understanding. To observe attentively is to remember distinctly; and, so far, the concentrative chess-player will do very well at whist; while the rules of Hoyle (themselves based upon the mere mechanism of the game) are sufficiently and generally comprehensible. Thus to have a retentive memory, and to proceed by "the book," are points commonly regarded as the sum total of good playing. But it is in matters beyond the limits of mere rule that the skill of the analyst is evinced. He makes, in silence, a host of observations and inferences. So, perhaps, do his companions; and the difference in the extent of the information obtained, lies not so much in the validity of the inference as in the quality of the observation. The necessary knowledge is that of *what* to observe. Our player confines himself not at all; nor, because the game is the object, does he reject deductions from things external to the game. He examines the countenance of his partner, comparing it carefully with that of each of his opponents. He considers the mode of assorting the cards in each hand; often counting trump by trump, and honor by honor, through the glances bestowed by their holders upon each. He notes every variation of face as the play progresses, gathering a fund of thought from the differences in the expression of certainty, of surprise, of triumph, or of chagrin. From the manner of gathering up a trick he judges whether the person taking it can make another in the suit. He recognises what is played through feint, by the air with which it is thrown upon the table. A casual or inadvertent word; the accidental dropping or turning of a card, with the accompanying anxiety or carelessness in regard to its concealment; the counting of the tricks, with the order of their arrangement; embarrassment, hesitation, eagerness or trepidation—all afford, to his apparently intuitive perception, indications of the true state of affairs. The first two or three rounds having been played, he is in full possession of the contents of each hand, and thenceforward puts down his cards with as absolute a precision of purpose as if the rest of the party had turned outward the faces of their own.

The analytical power should not be confounded with ample ingenuity; for while the analyst is necessarily ingenious, the ingenious man is often remarkably incapable of analysis. The constructive or combining power, by which ingenuity is usually manifested, and to which the phrenologists (I believe erroneously) have assigned a separate organ, supposing it a primitive faculty, has been so frequently seen in those whose intellect bordered otherwise upon idiocy, as to have attracted general observation among writers on morals. Between ingenuity and the analytic ability there exists a difference far greater, indeed, than that between the fancy and the imagination, but of a character very strictly analogous. It will be found, in fact, that the ingenious are always fanciful, and the *truly* imaginative never otherwise than analytic.

The narrative which follows will appear to the reader somewhat in the light of a commentary upon the propositions just advanced.

Residing in Paris during the spring and part of the summer of 18—, I there became acquainted with a Monsieur C. Auguste Dupin. This young gentleman was of an excellent—indeed of an illustrious family, but, by a variety of untoward events, had been reduced to such poverty that the energy of his character succumbed beneath it, and he ceased to bestir himself in the world, or to care for the retrieval of his fortunes. By courtesy of his creditors, there still remained in his possession a small remnant of his patrimony; and, upon the income arising from this, he managed, by means of a rigorous economy, to procure the necessaries of life, without troubling himself about its superfluities. Books, indeed, were his sole luxuries, and in Paris these are easily obtained.

Our first meeting was at an obscure library in the Rue Montmartre, where the accident of our both being in search of the same very rare and very remarkable volume, brought us into closer communion. We saw each other again and again. I was deeply interested in the little family history which he detailed to me with all that candor which a Frenchman indulges whenever mere self is his theme. I was astonished, too, at the vast extent of his reading; and, above all, I felt my soul enkindled within me by the wild fervor, and the vivid freshness of his imagination. Seeking in Paris the objects I then sought, I felt that the society of such a man would be to me a treasure beyond price; and this feeling I frankly confided to him. It was at length arranged that we should live together during my stay in the city; and as my worldly circumstances were somewhat less embarrassed than his own, I was permitted to be at the expense of renting, and furnishing in a style which suited the rather fantastic gloom of our common temper, a time-eaten and grotesque mansion, long deserted through superstitions into which we did not inquire, and tottering to its fall in a retired and desolate portion of the Faubourg St. Germain.

Had the routine of our life at this place been known to the world, we should have been regarded as madmen—although, perhaps, as madmen of a harmless nature. Our seclusion was perfect. We admitted no visitors. Indeed the locality of our retirement had been carefully kept a secret from my own former associates; and it had been many years since Dupin had ceased to know or be known in Paris. We existed within ourselves alone.

It was a freak of fancy in my friend (for what else shall I call it?) to be enamored of the night for her own sake; and into this *bizarrerie*, as into all his others, I quietly fell; giving myself up to his wild whims with a perfect *abandon*. The sable divinity would not herself dwell with us always; but we could counterfeit her presence. At the first dawn of the morning we closed all the messy shutters of our old building; lighting a couple of tapers which, strongly perfumed, threw out only the ghastliest and feeblest of rays. By the aid of these we then busied our souls in dreams—reading, writing, or conversing, until warned by the clock of the advent of the true Darkness. Then we sallied forth into the streets arm in arm, continuing the topics of the day, or roaming far and wide until a late hour, seeking, amid the wild lights and shadows of the populous city, that infinity of mental excitement which quiet observation can afford.

At such times I could not help remarking and admiring (although from his rich ideality I had been prepared to expect it) a peculiar analytic ability in Dupin. He seemed, too, to take an eager delight in its exercise—if not exactly in its display—and did not hesitate to confess the pleasure thus derived. He boasted to me, with a low chuckling laugh, that most men, in respect to himself, wore windows in their bosoms, and was wont to follow up such assertions by direct and very startling proofs of his intimate knowledge of my own. His manner at these moments was frigid and abstract; his eyes were vacant in expression; while his voice, usually a rich tenor, rose into a treble which would have sounded petulantly but for the deliberateness and entire distinctness of the enunciation. Observing him in these moods, I often dwelt meditatively upon the old philosophy of the Bi-Part Soul, and amused myself with the fancy of a double Dupin—the creative and the resolvent.

Let it not be supposed, from what I have just said, that I am detailing any mystery, or penning any romance. What I have described in the Frenchman, was merely the result of an excited, or perhaps of a diseased intelligence. But of the character of his remarks at the periods in question an example will best convey the idea.

We were strolling one night down a long dirty street in the vicinity of the Palais Royal. Being both, apparently, occupied with thought, neither of us had spoken a syllable for fifteen minutes at least. All at once Dupin broke forth with these words:

"He is a very little fellow, that's true, and would do better for the *Théâtre des Variétés*."

"There can be no doubt of that," I replied unwittingly, and not at first observing (so much had I been absorbed in reflection) the extraordinary manner in which the speaker had chimed in with my meditations. In an instant afterward I recollected myself, and my astonishment was profound.

"Dupin," said I, gravely, "this is beyond my comprehension. I do not hesitate to say that I am amazed, and can scarcely credit my senses. How was it possible you should know I was thinking of ——?" Here I paused, to ascertain beyond a doubt whether he really knew of whom I thought.

"Of Chantilly," said he, "why do you pause? You were remarking to yourself that his diminutive figure unfitted him for tragedy."

This was precisely what had formed the subject of my reflections. Chantilly was a *quondam* cobbler of the Rue St. Denis, who, becoming stage-mad, had attempted the *rôle* of Xerxes, in Crébillon's tragedy so called, and been notoriously Pasquinaded for his pains.

"Tell me, for Heaven's sake," I exclaimed, "the method—if method there is—by which you have been enabled to fathom my soul in this matter." In fact I was even more startled than I would have been willing to express.

"It was the fruiterer," replied my friend, "who brought you to the conclusion that the mender of soles was not of sufficient height for Xerxes *et id genus omne*."

"The fruiterer!—you astonish me—I know no fruiterer whomsoever."

"The man who ran up against you as we entered the street—it may have been fifteen minutes ago."

I now remembered that, in fact, a fruiterer, carrying upon his head a large basket of apples, had nearly thrown me down, by accident, as we passed from the Rue C —— into the thoroughfare where we stood; but what this had to do with Chantilly I could not possibly understand.

There was not a particle of *charlâtanerie* about Dupin. "I will explain," he said, "and that you may comprehend all clearly, we will first retrace the course of your meditations, from the moment in which I spoke to you until that of the *rencontre* with the fruiterer in question. The larger links of the chain run thus—Chantilly, Orion, Dr. Nichols, Epicurus, Stereotomy, the street stones, the fruiterer."

There are few persons who have not, at some period of their lives, amused themselves in retracing the steps by which particular conclusions of their own minds have been attained. The occupation is often full of interest and he who attempts it for the first time is astonished by the apparently illimitable distance and incoherence between the starting-point and the goal. What, then, must have been my amazement when I heard the Frenchman speak what he had just spoken, and when I could not help acknowledging that he had spoken the truth. He continued:

"We had been talking of horses, if I remember aright, just before leaving the Rue C ——. This was the last subject we discussed. As we crossed into this street, a fruiterer, with a large basket upon his head, brushing quickly past us, thrust you upon a pile of paving stones collected at a spot where the causeway is undergoing repair. You stepped upon one of the loose fragments, slipped, slightly strained your ankle, appeared vexed or sulky, muttered a few words, turned to look at the pile, and then proceeded in silence. I was not particularly attentive to what you did; but observation has become with me, of late, a species of necessity.

"You kept your eyes upon the ground—glancing, with a petulant expression, at the holes and ruts in the pavement (so that I saw you were still thinking of the stones), until we reached the little alley called Lamartine, which has been paved, by way of experiment, with the overlapping and riveted blocks. Here your countenance brightened up, and, perceiving your lips move, I could not doubt that you murmured the word 'stereotomy,' a term very affectedly applied to this species of pavement. I knew that you could not say to yourself 'stereotomy' without being brought to think of atomies, and thus of the theories of Epicurus; and since, when we discussed this subject not very long ago, I mentioned to you how singularly, yet with how little notice, the vague guesses of that noble Greek had met with confirmation in the late nebular cosmogony, I felt that you could not avoid casting your eyes upward to the great *nebula* in Orion, and I certainly expected that you would do so. You did look up; and I was now assured that I had correctly followed your steps. But in that bitter *tirade* upon Chantilly, which appeared in yesterday's *Musée*, the satirist, making some disgraceful allusions to the cobbler's change of name upon assuming the buskin, quoted a Latin line about which we have often conversed. I mean the line

Perdidit antiquum litera sonum.

"I had told you that this was in reference to Orion, formerly written Urion; and, from certain pungencies connected with this explanation, I was aware that you could not have forgotten it. It was clear, therefore, that you would not fail to combine the two ideas of Orion and Chantilly. That you did combine them I saw by the character of the smile which passed over your lips. You thought of the poor cobbler's immolation. So far, you had been stooping in your gait; but now I saw you draw yourself up to your full height. I was then sure that you reflected upon the diminutive figure of Chantilly. At this point I interrupted your meditations to remark that as, in fact, he was a very little fellow—that Chantilly—he would do better at the *Théâtre des Variétés*."

Not long after this, we were looking over an evening edition of the *Gazette des Tribunaux*, when the following paragraphs arrested our attention.

"Extraordinary Murders—This morning, about three o'clock, the inhabitants of the Quartier St. Roch were aroused from sleep by a succession of terrific shrieks, issuing, apparently, from the fourth story of a house in the Rue Morgue, known to be in the sole occupancy of one Madame L'Espanaye, and her daughter Mademoiselle Camille L'Espanaye. After some delay, occasioned by a fruitless attempt to procure admission in the usual manner, the gateway was broken in with a crowbar, and eight or ten of the neighbors entered accompanied by two *gendarmes*. By this time the cries had ceased; but, as the party rushed up the first flight of stairs, two or more rough voices in angry contention were distinguished and seemed to proceed from the upper part of the house. As the second landing was reached, these sounds, also, had ceased and everything remained perfectly quiet. The party spread themselves and hurried from room to room. Upon arriving at a large back chamber in the fourth story (the door of which, being found locked, with the key inside, was forced open), a spectacle presented itself which struck every one present not less with horror than with astonishment.

"The apartment was in the wildest disorder—the furniture broken and thrown about in all directions. There was only one bedstead; and from this the bed had been removed, and thrown into the middle of the floor. On a chair lay a razor, besmeared with blood. On the hearth were two or three long and thick tresses of grey human hair, also dabbled in blood, and seeming to have been pulled out by the roots. Upon the floor were found four Napoleons, an earring of topaz, three large silver spoons, three smaller of *métal d'Alger*, and two bags, containing nearly four thousand francs in gold. The drawers of a bureau, which stood in one corner were open, and had been, apparently, rifled, although many articles still remained in them. A small iron safe was discovered under the *bed* (not under the bedstead). It was open, with the key still in the door. It had no contents beyond a few old letters, and other papers of little consequence.

"Of Madame L'Espanaye no traces were here seen; but an unusual quantity of soot being observed in the fire-place, a search was made in the chimney, and (horrible to relate!) the corpse of the daughter, head downward, was dragged therefrom; it having been thus forced up the narrow aperture for a considerable distance. The body was quite warm. Upon examining it, many excoriations were perceived, no doubt occasioned by the violence with which it had been thrust up and disengaged. Upon the face were many severe scratches, and, upon the throat, dark bruises, and deep indentations of finger nails, as if the deceased had been throttled to death.

"After a thorough investigation of every portion of the house, without farther discovery, the party made its way into a small paved yard in the rear of the building, where lay the corpse of the old lady, with her throat so entirely cut that, upon an attempt to raise her, the head fell off. The body, as well as the head, was fearfully mutilated—the former so much so as scarcely to retain any semblance of humanity.

"To this horrible mystery there is not as yet, we believe, the slightest clue."

The next day's paper had these additional particulars.

"*The Tragedy in the Rue Morgue.* Many individuals have been examined in relation to this most extraordinary and frightful affair," [the word '*affaire*' has not yet, in France, that levity of import which it conveys with us], "but nothing whatever has transpired to throw light upon it. We give below all the material testimony elicited.

"*Pauline Dubourg*, laundress, deposes that she has known both the deceased for three years, having washed for them during that period. The old lady and her daughter seemed on good terms—very affectionate towards each other. They were excellent pay. Could not speak in regard to their mode or means of living. Believed that Madame L. told fortunes for a living. Was reputed to have money put by. Never met any persons in the house when she called for the clothes or took them home. Was sure that they had no servant in employ. There appeared to be no furniture in any part of the building except in the fourth story.

"*Pierre Moreau*, tobacconist, deposes that he has been in the habit of selling small quantities of tobacco and snuff to Madame L'Espanaye for nearly four years. Was born in the neighborhood, and has always resided there. The deceased and her daughter had occupied the house in which the corpses were found, for more than six years. It was formerly occupied by a jeweller, who under-let the upper rooms to various persons. The house was the property of Madame L. She became dissatisfied with the abuse of the premises by her tenant, and moved into them herself, refusing to let any portion. The old lady was childish. Witness had seen the daughter some five or six times during the six years. The two lived an exceedingly retired life—were reputed to have money. Had heard it said among the neighbors that Madame L. told fortunes—did not believe it. Had never seen any person enter the door except the old lady and her daughter, a porter once or twice, and a physician some eight or ten times.

"Many other persons, neighbors, gave evidence to the same

effect. No one was spoken of as frequenting the house. It was not known whether there were any living connexions of Madame L. and her daughter. The shutters of the front windows were seldom opened. Those in the rear were always closed, with the exception of the large back room, fourth story. The house was a good house—not very old.

"*Isidore Muset, gendarme*, deposes that he was called to the house about three o'clock in the morning, and found some twenty or thirty persons at the gateway, endeavoring to gain admittance. Forced it open, at length, with a bayonet—not with a crowbar. Had but little difficulty in getting it open, on account of its being a double or folding gate, and bolted neither at bottom not top. The shrieks were continued until the gate was forced—and then suddenly ceased. They seemed to be screams of some person (or persons) in great agony—were loud and drawn out, not short and quick. Witness led the way up stairs. Upon reaching the first landing, heard two voices in loud and angry contention—the one a gruff voice, the other much shriller—a very strange voice. Could distinguish some words of the former, which was that of a Frenchman. Was positive that it was not a woman's voice. Could distinguish the words '*sacré*' and '*diable*.' The shrill voice was that of a foreigner. Could not be sure whether it was the voice of a man or of a woman. Could not make out what was said, but believed the language to be Spanish. The state of the room and of the bodies was described by this witness as we described them yesterday.

"*Henri Duval*, a neighbor, and by trade a silversmith, deposes that he was one of the party who first entered the house. Corroborates the testimony of Musèt in general. As soon as they forced an entrance, they reclosed the door, to keep out the crowd, which collected very fast, notwithstanding the lateness of the hour. The shrill voice, this witness thinks, was that of an Italian. Was certain it was not French. Could not be sure that it was a man's voice. It might have been a woman's. Was not acquainted with the Italian language. Could not distinguish the words, but was convinced by the intonation that the speaker was an Italian. Knew Madame L. and her daughter. Had conversed with both frequently. Was sure that the shrill voice was not that of either of the deceased.

"——*Odenheimer, restaurateur*. This witness volunteered his

testimony. Not speaking French, was examined through an interpreter. Is a native of Amsterdam. Was passing the house at the time of the shrieks. They lasted for several minutes—probably ten. They were long and loud—very awful and distressing. Was one of those who entered the building. Corroborated the previous evidence in every respect but one. Was sure that the shrill voice was that of a man—of a Frenchman. Could not distinguish the words uttered. They were loud and quick—unequal—spoken apparently in fear as well as in anger. The voice was harsh—not so much shrill as harsh. Could not call it a shrill voice. The gruff voice said repeatedly '*sacré*,' '*diable*,' and once '*mon Dieu*.'

"*Jules Mignaud*, banker, of the firm of Mignaud et Fils, Rue Deloraine. Is the elder Mignaud. Madame L'Espanaye had some property. Had opened an account with his banking house in the spring of the year—(eight years previously). Made frequent deposits in small sums. Had checked for nothing until the third day before her death, when she took out in person the sum of 4,000 francs. This sum was paid in gold, and a clerk went home with the money.

"*Adolphe Le Bon*, clerk to Mignaud et Fils, deposes that on the day in question, about noon, he accompanied Madame L'Espanaye to her residence with the 4,000 francs, put up in two bags. Upon the door being opened, Mademoiselle L. appeared and took from his hands one of the bags, while the old lady relieved him of the other. He then bowed and departed. Did not see any person in the street at the time. It is a bye-street—very lonely.

"*William Bird*, tailor deposes that he was one of the party who entered the house. Is an Englishman. Has lived in Paris two years. Was one of the first to ascend the stairs. Heard the voices in contention. The gruff voice was that of a Frenchman. Could make out several words, but cannot now remember all. Heard distinctly '*sacré*' and '*mon Dieu*.' There was a sound at the moment as if of several persons struggling—a scraping and scuffling sound. The shrill voice was very loud—louder than the gruff one. Is sure that it was not the voice of an Englishman. Appeared to be that of a German. Might have been a woman's voice. Does not understand German.

"Four of the above-named witnesses, being recalled, deposed

that the door of the chamber in which was found the body of Mademoiselle L. was locked on the inside when the party reached it. Every thing was perfectly silent—no groans or noises of any kind. Upon forcing the door no person was seen. The windows, both of the back and front room, were down and firmly fastened from within. A door between the two rooms was closed, but not locked. The door leading from the front room into the passage was locked, with the key on the inside. A small room in the front of the house, on the fourth story, at the head of the passage was open, the door being ajar. This room was crowded with old beds, boxes, and so forth. These were carefully removed and searched. There was not an inch of any portion of the house which was not carefully searched. Sweeps were sent up and down the chimneys. The house was a four story one, with garrets (*mansardes*). A trap-door on the roof was nailed down very securely—did not appear to have been opened for years. The time elapsing between the hearing of the voices in contention and the breaking open of the room door, was variously stated by the witnesses. Some made it as short as three minutes—some as long as five. The door was opened with difficulty.

"*Alfonzo Garcio*, undertaker, deposes that he resides in the Rue Morgue. Is a native of Spain. Was one of the party who entered the house. Did not proceed up stairs. Is nervous, and was apprehensive of the consequences of agitation. Heard the voices in contention. The gruff voice was that of a Frenchman. Could not distinguish what was said. The shrill voice was that of an Englishman—is sure of this. Does not understand the English language, but judges by the intonation.

"*Alberto Montani*, confectioner, deposes that he was among the first to ascend the stairs. Heard the voices in question. The gruff voice was that of a Frenchman. Distinguished several words. The speaker appeared to be expostulating. Could not make out the words of the shrill voice. Spoke quick and unevenly. Thinks it the voice of a Russian. Corroborates the general testimony. Is an Italian. Never conversed with a native of Russia.

"Several witnesses, recalled, here testified that the chimneys of all the rooms on the fourth story were too narrow to admit the passage of a human being. By 'sweeps' were meant cylindrical sweeping brushes, such as are employed by those who clean chimneys. These brushes were passed up and down every flue in the house. There is no back passage by which any one could have descended while the party proceeded up stairs. The body of Mademoiselle L'Espanaye was so firmly wedged in the chimney that it could not be got down until four or five of the party united their strength.

"*Paul Dumas*, physician, deposes that he was called to view the bodies about day-break. They were both then lying on the sacking of the bedstead in the chamber where Mademoiselle L. was found. The corpse of the young lady was much bruised and excoriated. The fact that it had been thrust up the chimney would sufficiently account for these appearances. The throat was greatly chafed. There were several deep scratches just below the chin, together with a series of livid spots which were evidently the impression of fingers. The face was fearfully discolored, and the eye-balls protruded. The tongue had been partially bitten through. A large bruise was discovered upon the pit of the stomach, produced, apparently, by the pressure of a knee. In the opinion of M. Dumas, Mademoiselle L'Espanaye had been throttled to death by some person or persons unknown. The corpse of the mother was horribly mutilated. All the bones of the right leg and arm were more or less shattered. The left tibia much splintered, as well as all the ribs of the left side. Whole body dreadfully bruised and discolored. It was not possible to say how the injuries had been inflicted. A heavy club of wood, or a broad bar of iron—a chair—any large, heavy, and obtuse weapon would have produced such results, if wielded by the hands of a very powerful man. No woman could have inflicted the blows with any weapon. The head of the deceased, when seen by witness, was entirely separated from the body, and was also greatly shattered. The throat had evidently been cut with some very sharp instrument—probably with a razor.

"*Alexandre Etienne*, surgeon, was called with M.Dumas to view the bodies. Corroborated the testimony, and the opinions of M. Dumas.

"Nothing farther of importance was elicited, although several other persons were examined. A murder so mysterious, and so perplexing in all its particulars, was never before committed in Paris—if indeed a murder has been committed at all. The police are entirely at fault—an unusual occurrence in affairs of this nature. There is not, however, the shadow of a clue apparent."

The evening edition of the paper stated that the greatest excitement still continued in the Quartier St. Roch—that the premises in question had been carefully re-searched, and fresh examinations of witnesses instituted, but all to no purpose. A postscript, however, mentioned that Adolphe Le Bon had been arrested and imprisoned—although nothing appeared to criminate him, beyond the facts already detailed.

Dupin seemed singularly interested in the progress of this affair—at least so I judged from his manner, for he made no comments. It was only after the announcement that Le Bon had been imprisoned, that he asked me my opinion respecting the murders.

I could merely agree with all Paris in considering them an insoluble mystery. I saw no means by which it would be possible to trace the murderer.

"We must not judge of the means," said Dupin, "by this shell of an examination. The Parisian police, so much extolled for *acumen*, are cunning, but no more. There is no method in their proceedings, beyond the method of the moment. They make a vast parade of measures; but, not unfrequently, these are so ill adapted to the objects proposed, as to put us in mind of Monsieur Jourdain's calling for his *robe-de-chambre—pour mieux entendre la musique*. The results attained by them are not unfrequently surprising, but, for the most part, are brought about by simple diligence and activity. When these qualities are unavailing, their schemes fail. Vidocq, for example, was a good guesser and a persevering man. But, without educated thought, he erred continually by the very intensity of his investigations. He impaired his vision by holding the object too close. He might see, perhaps, one or two points with unusual clearness, but in so doing he, necessarily, lost sight of the matter as a whole. Thus there is such a thing as being too profound. Truth is not always in a well. In fact, as regards the more important knowledge, I do believe that she is invariably superficial. The depth lies in the valleys where we seek her, and not upon the mountain-tops where she is found. The modes and sources of this kind of error are well typified in the contemplation of the heavenly bodies. To look at a star by glances—to view it in a side-long way, by turning toward it the exterior portions of the *retina* (more susceptible of feeble impressions of light than the interior), is to behold the star distinctly—is to have the best appreciation of its lustre—a lustre which grows dim just in proportion as we turn our vision *fully* upon it. A greater number of rays actually fall upon the eye in the latter case, but, in the former, there is the more refined capacity for comprehension. By undue profundity we perplex and enfeeble thought; and it is possible to make even Venus herself vanish from the firmanent by a scrutiny too sustained, too concentrated, or too direct.

"As for these murders, let us enter into some examinations for ourselves, before we make up an opinion respecting them. An inquiry will afford us amusement" [I thought this an odd term, so applied, but said nothing], "and, besides, Le Bon once rendered me a service for which I am not ungrateful. We will go and see the premises with our own eyes. I know G——, the Prefect of Police, and shall have no difficulty in obtaining the necessary permission."

The permission was obtained, and we proceeded at once to the Rue Morgue. This is one of those miserable thoroughfares which intervene between the Rue Richelieu and the Rue St. Roch. It was late in the afternoon when we reached it; as this quarter is at a great distance from that in which we resided. The house was readily found; for there were still many persons gazing up at the closed shutters, with an objectless curiosity, from the opposite side of the way. It was an ordinary Parisian house, with a gateway, on one side of which was a glazed watch-box, with a sliding panel in the window, indicating a *loge de concierge*. Before going in we walked up the street, turned down an alley, and then, again turning, passed in the rear of the building—Dupin, meanwhile examining the whole neighborhood, as well as the house, with a minuteness of attention for which I could see no possible object.

Retracing our steps, we came again to the front of the dwelling, rang, and, having shown our credentials, were admitted by the agents in charge. We went up stairs—into the chamber where the body of Mademoiselle L'Espanaye had been found, and where both the deceased still lay. The disorders of the room had, as usual, been suffered to exist. I saw nothing beyond what had been stated in the *Gazette des Tribunaux*. Dupin scrutinized every thing—not excepting the bodies of the victims. We then went into the other rooms, and into the yard; a *gendarme* accompanying us throughout. The examination occupied us until dark, when we took our departure. On our way home my companion stepped in for a moment at the office of one of the daily papers.

I have said that the whims of my friend were manifold, and that *Je les ménagais*:—for this phrase there is no English equivalent. It was his humor, now, to decline all conversation on the subject of the murder, until about noon the next day. He then asked me, suddenly, if I had observed any thing *peculiar* at the scene of the atrocity.

There was something in his manner of emphasizing the word "peculiar," which caused me to shudder, without knowing why.

"No, nothing *peculiar*," I said; "nothing more, at least, than we both saw stated in the paper."

"The *Gazette*," he replied, "has not entered, I fear, into the unusual horror of the thing. But dismiss the idle opinions of this print. It appears to me that this mystery is considered insoluble, for the very reason which should cause it to be regarded as easy of solution—I mean for the *outré* character of its features. The police are confounded by the seeming absence of motive—not for the murder itself—but for the atrocity of the murder. They are puzzled, too, by the seeming impossibility of reconciling the voices heard in contention, with the facts that no one was discovered up stairs but the assassinated Mademoiselle L'Espanaye, and that there were no means of egress without the notice of the party ascending. The wild disorder of the room; the corpse thrust, with the head downward, up the chimney; the frightful mutilation of the body of the old lady; these considerations, with those just mentioned, and others which I need not mention, have sufficed to paralyze the powers, by putting completely at fault the boasted *acumen*, of the government agents. They have fallen into the gross but common error of confounding the unusual with the abstruse. But it is by these deviations from the plane of the ordinary, that reason feels its way, if at all, in its search for the true. In investigations such as we are now pursuing, it should not be so much asked 'what has occurred,' as 'what has occurred that has never occurred before.' In fact, the facility with which I shall arrive, or have arrived, at the solution of this mystery, is in the direct ratio of its apparent insolubility in the eyes of the police."

I stared at the speaker in mute astonishment.

"I am now awaiting," continued he, looking toward the door of our apartment—"I am now awaiting a person who, although perhaps not the perpetrator of these butcheries, must have been in some measure implicated in their perpetration. Of the worst portion of the crimes committed, it is probable that he is innocent. I hope that I am right in this supposition; for upon it I build my expectation of reading the entire riddle. I look for the man here—in this room—every moment. It is true that he may not arrive; but the probability is that he will. Should he come, it will be necessary to detain him. Here are pistols; and we both know how to use them when occasion demands their use."

I took the pistols, scarcely knowing what I did, or believing what I heard, while Dupin went on, very much as if in a soliloquy. I have already spoken of his abstract manner at such times. His discourse was addressed to myself; but his voice, although by no means loud, had that intonation which is commonly employed in speaking to some one at a great distance. His eyes, vacant in expression, regarded only the wall.

"That the voices heard in contention," he said, "by the party upon the stairs, were not the voices of the women themselves, was fully proved by the evidence. This relieves us of all doubt upon the question whether the old lady could have first destroyed the daughter and afterward have committed suicide. I speak of this point chiefly for the sake of method; for the strength of Madame L'Espanaye would have been utterly unequal to the task of thrusting her daughter's corpse up the chimney as it was found; and the nature of the wounds upon her own person entirely preclude the idea of self-destruction. Murder, then, has been committed by some third party; and the voices of this third party were those heard in contention. Let me now advert—not to the whole testimony respecting these voices—but to what was *peculiar* in that testimony. Did you observe any thing peculiar about it?"

I remarked that, while all the witnesses agreed in supposing the gruff voice to be that of a Frenchman, there was much disagreement in regard to the shrill, or, as one individual termed it, the harsh voice.

"That was the evidence itself," said Dupin, "but it was not the peculiarity of the evidence. You have observed nothing distinctive. Yet there *was* something to be observed. The witnesses, as you remark, agreed about the gruff voice; they were here unanimous. But in regard to the shrill voice, the peculiarity is—not that they disagreed—but that, while an Italian, an Englishman, a Spaniard, a Hollander, and a Frenchman attempted to describe it, each one spoke of it as that *of a foreigner*. Each is sure that it was not the voice of one of his own countrymen. Each likens it—not to the voice of an individual of any nation with whose language he is conversant—but the converse. The Frenchman supposes it the voice of a Spaniard, and 'might have distinguished some words *had he been acquainted with the Spanish*.' The Dutchman maintains it to have been that of a Frenchman; but we find it stated that '*not understanding French this witness was examined through an interpreter*.' The Englishman thinks it the voice of a German, and '*does not understand German*.' The Spaniard 'is sure' that it was that of an Englishman, but 'judges by the intonation' altogether, '*as he has no knowledge of the English*.' The Italian believes it the voice of a Russian, but '*has never conversed with a native of Russia*.' A second Frenchman differs, moreover, with the first, and is positive that the voice was that of an Italian; but, *not being cognizant of that tongue*, is, like the Spaniard, 'convinced by the intonation.' Now, how strangely unusual must that voice have really been, about which such testimony as this *could* have been elicited!—in whose *tones*, even, denizens of the five great divisions of Europe could recognise nothing familiar! You will say that it might have been the voice of an Asiatic—of an African. Neither Asiatics nor Africans abound in Paris; but, without denying the inference, I will now merely call your attention to three points. The voice is termed by one witness 'harsh rather than shrill.' It is represented by two others to have been 'quick and *unequal*.' No words—no sounds resembling words—were by any witness mentioned as distinguishable.

"I know not," continued Dupin, "what impression I may have made, so far, upon your own understanding; but I do not hesitate to say that legitimate deductions even from this portion of the testimony—the portion respecting the gruff and shrill voices—are in themselves sufficient to engender a suspicion which should give direction to all farther progress in the investigation of the mystery. I said 'legitimate deductions;' but my meaning is not thus fully expressed. I designed to imply that the deductions are the *sole* proper ones, and that the suspicion arises *inevitably* from them as the single result. What the suspicion is, however, I will not say just yet. I merely wish you to bear in mind that, with myself, it was sufficiently forcible to give a definite form—a certain tendency—to my inquiries in the chamber.

"Let us now transport ourselves, in fancy, to this chamber. What shall we first seek here? The means of egress employed by the murderers. It is not too much to say that neither of us believe in preternatural events. Madame and Mademoiselle L'Espanaye were not destroyed by spirits. The doers of the deed were material, and escaped materially. Then how? Fortunately, there is but one mode of reasoning upon the point, and that mode *must* lead us to a definite decision. Let us examine, each by each, the possible means of egress. It is clear that the assassins were in the room where Mademoiselle L'Espanaye was found, or at least in the room adjoining, when the party ascended the stairs. It is then only from these two apartments that we have to seek issues. The police have laid bare the floors, the ceilings, and the masonry of the walls, in every direction. No *secret* issues could have escaped their vigilance. But, not trusting to *their* eyes, I examined with my own. There were, then, *no* secret issues. Both doors leading from the rooms into the passage were securely locked, with the keys inside. Let us turn to the chimneys. These, although of ordinary width for some eight or ten feet above the hearths, will not admit, throughout their extent, the body of a large cat. The impossibility of egress, by means already stated, being thus absolute, we are reduced to the windows. Through those of the front room no one could have escaped without notice from the crowd in the street. The murderers *must* have passed, then, through those of the back room. Now, brought to this conclusion in so unequivocal a manner as we are, it is not our part, as reasoners, to reject it on account of apparent impossibilities. It is only left for us to prove that these apparent 'impossibilities' are, in reality, not such.

"There are two windows in the chamber. One of them is unobstructed by furniture, and is wholly visible. The lower portion of the other is hidden from view by the head of the unwieldy bedstead which is thrust close up against it. The former was found securely fastened from within. It resisted the utmost force of those who endeavored to raise it. A large gimlet-hole had been pierced in its frame to the left, and a very stout nail was found fitted therein, nearly to the head. Upon examining the other window, a similar nail was seen similarly fitted in it; and a vigorous attempt to raise this sash, failed also. The police were now entirely satisfied that egress had not been in these directions. And, *therefore*, it was thought a matter of supererogation to withdraw the nails and open the windows.

"My own examination was somewhat more particular, and was so for the reason I have just given—because here it was, I knew, that all apparent impossibilities *must* be proved to be not such in reality.

"I proceeded to think thus—*à posteriori*. The murderers did escape from one of these windows. This being so, they could not have refastened the sashes from the inside, as they were found fastened—the consideration which put a stop, through its obviousness, to the scrutiny of the police in this quarter. Yet the sashes *were* fastened. They *must*, then, have the power of fastening themselves. There was no escape from this conclusion. I stepped to the unobstructed casement, withdrew the nail with some difficulty and attempted to raise the sash. It resisted all my efforts, as I had anticipated. A concealed spring must, I now know, exist; and this corroboration of my idea convinced me that my premises at least, were correct, however mysterious still appeared the circumstances attending the nails. A careful search soon brought to light the hidden spring. I pressed it, and, satisfied with the discovery, forbore to upraise the sash.

"I now replaced the nail and regarded it attentively. A person passing out through this window might have reclosed it, and the spring would have caught—but the nail could not have been replaced. The conclusion was plain, and again narrowed in the field of my investigations. The assassins *must* have escaped through the other window. Supposing, then, the springs upon each sash to be the same, as was probable, there *must* be found a difference between the nails, or at least between the modes of their fixture. Getting upon the sacking of the bedstead, I looked over the head-board minutely at the second casement. Passing my hand down behind the board, I readily discovered and pressed the spring, which was, as I had supposed, identical in character with its neighbor. I now looked at the nail. It was as stout as the other, and apparently fitted in the same manner—driven in nearly up to the head.

"You will say that I was puzzled; but, if you think so, you must have misunderstood the nature of the inductions. To use a sporting phrase, I had not been once 'at fault.' The scent had never for an instant been lost. There was no flaw in any link of the chain. I had traced the secret to its ultimate result—and that result was *the nail.* It had, I say, in every respect, the appearance of its fellow in the other window; but this fact was an absolute nullity (conclusive us it might seem to be) when compared with the consideration that here, at this point, terminated the clue. 'There *must* be something wrong,' I said, 'about the nail.' I touched it; and the head, with about a quarter of an inch of the shank, came off in my fingers. The rest of the shank was in the gimlet-hole where it had been broken off. The fracture was an old one (for its edges were incrusted with rust), and had apparently been accomplished by the blow of a hammer, which had partially imbedded, in the top of the bottom sash, the head portion of the nail. I now carefully replaced this head portion in the indentation whence I had taken it, and the resemblance to a perfect nail was complete—the fissure was invisible. Pressing the spring, I gently raised the sash for a few inches; the head went up with it, remaining firm in its bed. I closed the window, and the semblance of the whole nail was again perfect.

"The riddle, so far, was now unriddled. The assassin had escaped through the window which looked upon the bed. Dropping of its own accord upon his exit (or perhaps purposely closed), it had become fastened by the spring; and it was the retention of this spring which had been mistaken by the police for that of the nail,—farther inquiry being thus considered unnecessary.

"The next question is that of the mode of descent. Upon this point I had been satisfied in my walk with you around the building. About five feet and a half from the casement in question there runs a lightning-rod. From this rod it would have been impossible for any one to reach the window itself, to say nothing of entering it. I observed, however, that the shutters of the fourth story were of the peculiar kind called by Parisian carpenters *ferrades*—a kind rarely employed at the present day, but frequently seen upon very old mansions at Lyons and Bourdeaux. They are in the form of an ordinary door (a single, not a folding door) except that the lower half is latticed or worked in open trellis—thus affording an excellent hold for the hands. In the present instance these shutters are fully three feet and a half broad. When we saw them from the rear of the house, they were both about half open—that is to say, they stood off at right angles from the wall. It is probable that the police, as well as myself, examined the back of the tenement; but, if so, in looking at these *ferrades* in the line of their breadth (as they must have done), they did not perceive this great breadth itself, or, at all events, failed to take it into due consideration. In fact, having once satisfied themselves that no egress could have been made in this quarter, they would *naturally* bestow here a very cursory examination. It was clear to me, however, that the shutter belonging to the window at the head of the bed, would, if swung fully back to the wall, reach to within two feet of the lightning-rod. It was also evident that, by exertion of a very unusual degree of activity and courage, an entrance into the window, from the rod, might have been thus effected.—By reaching to the distance of two feet and a half (we now suppose the shutter open to its whole extent) a robber might have taken a firm grasp upon the trellis-work. Letting go, then, his hold upon the rod, placing his feet securely against the wall, and springing boldly from it, he might have swung the shutter so as to close it, and, if we imagine the window open at the time, might even have swung himself into the room.

"I wish you to bear especially in mind that I have spoken of a *very* unusual degree of activity as requisite to success in so hazardous and so difficult a feat. It is my design to show you, first, that the thing might possibly have been accomplished—but, secondly and *chiefly*, I wish to impress upon your understanding the *very extraordinary*—the almost preternatural character of that agility which could have accomplished it.

"You will say, no doubt, using the language of the law, that 'to make out my case,' I should rather undervalue, than insist upon a full estimation of the activity required in this matter. This may be the practice in law, but it is not the usage of reason. My ultimate object is only the truth. My immediate purpose is to lead you to place in juxtaposition, that *very unusual* activity of which I have just spoken with that *very peculiar* shrill (or harsh) and *unequal* voice, about whose nationality no two persons could be found to agree, and in whose utterance no syllabification could be detected."

At these words a vague and half-formed conception of the meaning of Dupin flitted over my mind. I seemed to be upon the verge of comprehension without power to comprehend—men, at times, find themselves upon the brink of remembrance without being able, in the end, to remember. My friend went on with his discourse.

"You will see," he said, "that I have shifted the question from the mode of egress to that of ingress. It was my design to convey the idea that both were effected in the same manner, at the same point. Let us now revert to the interior of the room. Let us survey the appearances here. The drawers of the bureau, it is said, had been rifled, although many articles of apparel still remained within them. The conclusion here is absurd. It is a mere guess—a very silly one—and no more. How are we to know that the articles found in the drawers were not all these drawers had originally contained? Madame L'Espanaye and her daughter lived an exceedingly retired life—saw no company—seldom went out—had little use for numerous changes of habiliment. Those found were at least of as good quality as any likely to be possessed by these ladies. If a thief had taken any, why did he not take the best—why did he not take all? In a word, why did he abandon four thousand francs in gold to encumber himself with a bundle of linen? The gold *was* abandoned. Nearly the whole sum mentioned by Monsieur Mignaud, the banker, was discovered, in bags, upon the floor. I wish you, therefore, to discard from your thoughts the blundering idea of *motive*, engendered in the brains of the police by that portion of the evidence which speaks of money delivered at the door of the house. Coincidences ten times as remarkable as this (the delivery of the money, and murder committed within three days upon the party receiving it), happen to all of us every hour of our lives, without attracting even momentary notice. Coincidences, in general, are great stumbling blocks in the way of that class of thinkers who have been educated to know nothing of the theory of probabilities—that theory to which the most glorious objects of human research are indebted for the most glorious of illustration. In the present instance, had the gold been gone, the fact of its delivery three days before would have formed something more than a coincidence. It would have been corroborative of this idea of motive. But, under the real circumstances of the case, if we are to suppose gold the motive of this outrage, we must also imagine the perpetrator so vacillating an idiot as to have abandoned his gold and his motive together.

"Keeping now steadily in mind the points to which I have drawn your attention—that peculiar voice, that unusual agility, and that startling absence of motive in a murder so singularly atrocious as this—let us glance at the butchery itself. Here is a woman strangled to death by manual strength, and thrust up a chimney, head downward. Ordinary assassins employ no such modes of murder as this. Least of all, do they thus dispose of the murdered. In the manner of thrusting the corpse up the chimney, you will admit that there was something *excessively outré*—something altogether irreconcilable with our common notions of human action, even when we suppose the actors the most depraved of men. Think, too, how great must have been that strength which could have thrust the body *up* such an aperture so forcibly that the united vigor of several persons was found barely sufficient to drag it *down!*

"Turn, now, to other indications of the employment of a vigor most marvellous. On the hearth were thick tresses—very thick tresses—of grey human hair. These had been torn out by the roots. You are aware of the great force necessary in tearing thus from the head even twenty or thirty hairs together. You saw the locks in question as well as myself. Their roots (a hideous sight!) were clotted with fragments of the flesh of the scalp—sure token of the prodigious power which had been exerted in uprooting perhaps half a million of hairs at a time. The throat of the old lady was not merely cut, but the head absolutely severed from the body: the instrument was a mere razor. I wish you also to look at the *brutal* ferocity of these deeds. Of the bruises upon the body of Madame L'Espanaye I do not speak. Monsieur Dumas, and his worthy coadjutor Monsieur Etienne, have pronounced that they were inflicted by some obtuse instrument; and so far these gentlemen are very correct. The obtuse instrument was clearly the stone pavement in the yard, upon which the victim had fallen from the window which looked in upon the bed. This idea, however simple it may now seem, escaped the police for the same reason that the breadth of the shutters escaped them—because, by the affair of the nails, their perceptions had been hermetically sealed against the possibility of the windows having ever been opened at all.

"If now, in addition to all these things, you have properly reflected upon the odd disorder of the chamber, we have gone so far as to combine the ideas of an agility astounding, a strength superhuman, a ferocity brutal, a butchery without motive, a *grotesquerie* in horror absolutely alien from humanity, and a voice foreign in tone to the ears of men of many nations, and devoid of all distinct or intelligible syllabification. What result, then, has ensued? What impression have I made upon your fancy?"

I felt a creeping of the flesh as Dupin asked me the question. "A madman," I said, "has done this deed—some raving maniac, escaped from a neighboring *Maison de Santé*."

"In some respects," he replied, "your idea is not irrelevant. But the voices of madmen, even in their wildest paroxysms, are never found to tally with that peculiar voice heard upon the stairs. Madmen are of some nation, and their language, however incoherent in its words, has always the coherence of syllabification. Besides, the hair of a madman is not such as I now hold in my hand. I disentangled this little tuft from the rigidly clutched fingers of Madame L'Espanaye. Tell me what you can make of it."

"Dupin!" I said, completely unnerved; "this hair is most unusual—this is no *human* hair."

"I have not asserted that it is," said he; "but, before we decide this point, I wish you to glance at the little sketch I have here traced upon this paper. It is a *facsimile* drawing of what has been described in one portion of the testimony as 'dark bruises, and deep indentations of finger nails,' upon the throat of Mademoiselle L'Espanaye, and in another (by Messrs. Dumas and Etienne), as a 'series of livid spots, evidently the impression of fingers.'

"You will perceive," continued my friend, spreading out the paper upon the table before us, "that this drawing gives the idea of a firm and fixed hold. There is no *slipping* apparent. Each finger has retained—possibly until the death of the victim—the fearful grasp by which it originally imbedded itself. Attempt, now, to place all your fingers, at the same time, in the respective impressions as you see them."

I made the attempt in vain.

"We are possibly not giving this matter a fair trial," he said. "The paper is spread out upon a plane surface; but the human throat is cylindrical. Here is a billet of wood, the circumference of which is about that of the throat. Wrap the drawing around it, and try the experiment again."

I did so; but the difficulty was even more obvious than before. "This," I said, "is the mark of no human hand."

"Read now," replied Dupin, "this passage from Cuvier."

It was a minute anatomical and generally descriptive account of the large fulvous Ourang-Outang of the East Indian Islands. The gigantic stature, the prodigious strength and activity, the wild ferocity, and the imitative propensities of these mammalia are sufficiently well known to all. I understood the full horrors of the murder at once.

"The description of the digits," said I, as I made an end of reading, "is in exact accordance with this drawing. I see that no animal but an Ourang-Outang, of the species here mentioned, could have impressed the indentations as you have traced them. This tuft of tawny hair, too, is identical in character with that of the beast of Cuvier. But I cannot possibly comprehend the particulars of this frightful mystery. Besides, there were *two* voices heard in contention, and one of them was unquestionably the voice of a Frenchman."

"True; and you will remember an expression attributed almost unanimously, by the evidence, to this voice,—the expression, '*mon Dieu!*' This, under the circumstances, has been justly characterized by one of the witnesses (Montani, the confectioner), as an expression of remonstrance or expostulation. Upon these two words, therefore, I have mainly built my hopes of a full solution of the riddle. A Frenchman was cognizant of the murder. It is possible—indeed it is far more than probable—that he was innocent of all participation in the bloody transactions which took place. The Ourang-Outang may have escaped from him. He may have traced it to the chamber; but, under the agitating circumstances which ensued, he could never have recaptured it. It is still at large. I will not pursue these guesses—for I have no right to call them more—since the shades of reflection upon which they are based are scarcely of sufficient depth to be appreciable by my own intellect, and since I could not pretend to make them intelligible to the understanding of another. We will call them guesses then, and speak of them as such. If the Frenchman in question is indeed, as I suppose, innocent of this atrocity, this advertisement which I left last night, upon our return home, at the office of *Le Monde* (a paper devoted to the shipping interest, and much sought by sailors), will bring him to our residence."

He handed me a paper, and I read thus:

> CAUGHT—*In the Bois de Boulogne, early in the morning of the—inst.* (the morning of the murder), *a very large, tawny Ourang-Outang of the Bornese species. The owner (who is ascertained to be a sailor, belonging to a Maltese vessel), may have the animal again, upon identifying it satisfactorily, and paying a few charges arising from its capture and keeping. Call at No. ——, Rue ——, Faubourg St. Germain—au troisième.*

"How was it possible," I asked, "that you should know the man to be a sailor, and belonging to a Maltese vessel?"

"I do *not* know it," said Dupin. "I am not *sure* of it. Here, however, is a small piece of ribbon, which from its form, and from its greasy appearance, has evidently been used in tying the hair in one of those long *queues* of which sailors are so fond. Moreover, this knot is one which few besides sailors can tie, and is peculiar to the Maltese. I picked the ribbon up at the foot of the lightning-rod. It could not have belonged to either of the deceased. Now if, after all, I am wrong in my induction from this ribbon, that the Frenchman was a sailor belonging to a Maltese vessel, still I can have done no harm in saying what I did in the advertisement. If I am in error, he will merely suppose that I have been misled by some circumstance into which he will not take the trouble to inquire. But if I am right, a great point is gained. Cognizant although innocent of the murder, the Frenchman will *naturally* hesitate about replying to the advertisement—about demanding the Ourang-Outang. He will reason thus:—'I am innocent; I am poor; my Ourang-Outang is of great value—to one in my circumstances a fortune of itself—why should I lose it through idle apprehensions of danger? Here it is, within my grasp. It was found in the Bois de Boulogne—at a vast distance from the scene of that butchery. How can it ever be suspected that a brute beast should have done the deed? The police are at fault—they have failed to procure the slightest clew. Should they even trace the animal, it would be impossible to prove me cognizant of the murder, or to implicate me in guilt on account of that cognizance. Above all, *I am known.* The advertiser designates me as the possessor of the beast. I am not sure to what limit his knowledge may extend. Should I avoid claiming a property of so great value, which it is known that I possess, I will render the animal at least, liable to suspicion. It is not my policy to attract attention either to myself or to the beast. I will answer the advertisement, get the Ourang-Outang, and keep it close until this matter has blown over.'"

At this moment we heard a step upon the stairs.

"Be ready," said Dupin, "with your pistols, but neither use them nor show them until at a signal from myself."

The front door of the house had been left open, and the visiter had entered, without ringing, and advanced several steps upon the staircase. Now, however, he seemed to hesitate. Presently we heard him descending. Dupin was moving quickly to the door, when we again heard him coming up. He did not turn back a second time, but stepped up with decision, and rapped at the door of our chamber.

"Come in," said Dupin, in a cheerful and hearty tone.

A man entered. He was a sailor, evidently,—a tall, stout, and muscular-looking person, with a certain dare-devil expression of countenance, not altogether unprepossessing. His face, greatly sunburnt, was more than half hidden by whisker and mustachio. He had with him a huge oaken cudgel, but appeared to be otherwise unarmed. He bowed awkwardly, and bade us "good evening," in French accents, which, although somewhat Neufchatelish, were still sufficiently indicative of a Parisian origin.

"Sit down, my friend," said Dupin. "I suppose you have called about the Ourang-Outang. Upon my word, I almost envy you the possession of him; a remarkably fine, and no doubt a very valuable animal. How old do you suppose him to be?"

The sailor drew a long breath, with the air of a man relieved of some intolerable burden, and then replied, in an assured tone:

"I have no way of telling—but he can't be more than four or five years old. Have you got him here?"

"Oh no, we had no conveniences for keeping him here. He is at a livery stable in the Rue Dubourg, just by. You can get him in the morning. Of course you are prepared to identify the property?"

"To be sure I am, sir."

"I shall be sorry to part with him," said Dupin.

"I don't mean that you should be at all this trouble for nothing, sir," said the man. "Couldn't expect it. Am very willing to pay a reward for the finding of the animal—that is to say, any thing in reason."

"Well," replied my friend, "that is all very fair, to be sure. Let me think!—what should I have? Oh! I will tell you. My reward shall be this. You shall give me all the information in your power about these murders in the Rue Morgue."

Dupin said the last words in a very low tone, and very quietly. Just as quietly, too, he walked toward the door, locked it and put the key in his pocket. He then drew a pistol from his bosom and placed it, without the least flurry, upon the table.

The sailor's face flushed up as if he were struggling with suffocation. He started to his feet and grasped his cudgel, but the next moment he fell back into his seat, trembling violently, and with the countenance of death itself. He spoke not a word. I pitied him from the bottom of my heart.

"My friend," said Dupin, in a kind tone, "you are alarming yourself unnecessarily—you are indeed. We mean you no harm whatever. I pledge you the honor of a gentleman, and of a Frenchman, that we intend you no injury. I perfectly well know that you are innocent of the atrocities in the Rue Morgue. It will not do, however, to deny that you are in some measure implicated in them. From what I have already said, you must know that I have had means of information about this matter—means of which you could never have dreamed. Now the thing stands thus. You have done nothing which you could have avoided—nothing, certainly, which renders you culpable. You were not even guilty of robbery, when you might have robbed with impunity. You have nothing to conceal. You have no reason for concealment. On the other hand, you are bound by every principle of honor to confess all you know. An innocent man is now imprisoned, charged with that crime of which you can point out the perpetrator."

The sailor had recovered his presence of mind, in a great measure, while Dupin uttered these words; but his original boldness of bearing was all gone.

"So help me God," said he, after a brief pause, "I *will* tell you all I know about this affair;—but I do not expect you to believe one half I say—I would be a fool indeed if I did. Still, I *am* innocent, and I will make a clean breast if I die for it."

What he stated was, in substance, this. He had lately made a voyage to the Indian Archipelago. A party, of which he formed one, landed at Borneo, and passed into the interior on an excursion of pleasure. Himself and a companion had captured the Ourang-Outang. This companion dying, the animal fell into his own exclusive possession. After great trouble, occasioned by the intractable ferocity of his captive during the home voyage, he at length succeeded in lodging it safely at his own residence in Paris, where, not to attract toward himself the unpleasant curiosity of his neighbors, he kept it carefully secluded, until such time as it should recover from a wound in the foot, received from a splinter on board ship. His ultimate design was to sell it.

Returning home from some sailors' frolic the night, or rather in the morning of the murder, he found the beast occupying his own bed-room, into which it had broken from a closet adjoining, where it had been, as was thought, securely confined. Razor in hand, and fully lathered, it was sitting before a looking-glass, attempting the operation of shaving, in which it had no doubt previously watched its master through the key-hole of the closet. Terrified at the sight of so dangerous a weapon in the possession of an animal so ferocious, and so well able to use it, the man, for some moments, was at a loss what to do. He had been accustomed, however, to quiet the creature, even in its fiercest moods, by the use of a whip, and to this he now resorted. Upon sight of it, the Ourang-Outang sprang at once through the door of the chamber, down the stairs, and thence, through a window, unfortunately open, into the street.

The Frenchman followed in despair; the ape, razor still in hand, occasionally stopping to look back and gesticulate at its pursuer, until the latter had nearly come up with it. It then again made off. In this manner the chase continued for a long time. The streets were profoundly quiet, as it was nearly three o'clock in the morning. In passing down an alley in the rear of the Rue Morgue, the fugitive's attention was arrested by a light gleaming from the open window of Madame L'Espanaye's chamber, in the fourth story of her house.

Rushing to the building, it perceived the lightning rod, clambered up with inconceivable agility, grasped the shutter, which was thrown fully back against the wall, and, by its means, swung itself directly upon the headboard of the bed. The whole feat did not occupy a minute. The shutter was kicked open again by the Ourang-Outang as it entered the room.

The sailor, in the meantime, was both rejoiced and perplexed. He had strong hopes of now recapturing the brute, as it could scarcely escape from the trap into which it had ventured, except by the rod, where it might be intercepted as it came down. On the other hand, there was much cause for anxiety as to what it might do in the house. This latter reflection urged the man still to follow the fugitive. A lightning rod is ascended without difficulty, especially by a sailor; but, when he had arrived as high as the window, which lay far to his left, his career was stopped; the most that he could accomplish was to reach over so as to obtain a glimpse of the interior of the room. At this glimpse he nearly fell from his hold through excess of horror. Now it was that those hideous shrieks arose upon the night, which had startled from slumber the inmates of the Rue Morgue. Madame L'Espanaye and her daughter, habited in their night clothes, had apparently been occupied in arranging some papers in the iron chest already mentioned, which had been wheeled into the middle of the room. It was open, and its contents lay beside it on the floor. The victims must have been sitting with their backs toward the window; and, from the time elapsing between the ingress of the beast and the screams, it seems probable that it was not immediately perceived. The flapping-to of the shutter would *naturally* have been attributed to the wind.

As the sailor looked in, the gigantic animal had seized Madame L'Espanaye by the hair (which was loose, as she had been combing it), and was flourishing the razor about her face, in imitation of the motions of a barber. The daughter lay prostrate and motionless; she had swooned. The screams and struggles of the old lady (during which the hair was torn from her head) had the effect of changing the probably pacific purposes of the Ourang-Outang into those of wrath. With one determined sweep of its muscular arm it nearly severed her head from her body. The sight of blood inflamed its anger into phrenzy. Gnashing its teeth, and flashing fire from its eyes, it flew upon the body of the girl, and imbedded its fearful talons in her throat, retaining its grasp until she expired. Its wandering and wild glances fell at this moment upon the head of the bed, over which the face of its master, rigid with horror, was just discernible. The fury of the beast, who no doubt bore still in mind the dreaded whip, was instantly converted into fear. Conscious of having deserved punishment, it seemed desirous of concealing its bloody deeds, and skipped about the chamber in an agony of nervous agitation; throwing down and breaking the furniture as it moved, and dragging the bed from the bedstead. In conclusion, it seized first the corpse of the daughter, and thrust it up the chimney, as it was found; then that of the old lady, which it immediately hurled through the window headlong.

As the ape approached the casement with its mutilated burden, the sailor shrank aghast to the rod, and, rather gliding than clambering down it, hurried at once home—dreading the consequences of the butchery, and gladly abandoning, in his terror, all solicitude about the fate of the Ourang-Outang. The words heard by the party upon the staircase were the Frenchman's exclamations of horror and affright, commingled with the fiendish jabberings of the brute.

I have scarcely anything to add. The Ourang-Outang must have escaped from the chamber, by the rod, just before the break of the door. It must have closed the window as it passed through it. It was subsequently caught by the owner himself, who obtained for it a very large sum at the *Jardin des Plantes.* Le Don was instantly released, upon our narration of the circumstances (with some comments from Dupin) at the bureau of the Prefect of Police. This functionary, however well disposed to my friend, could not altogether conceal his chagrin at the turn which affairs had taken, and was fain to indulge in a sarcasm or two, about the propriety of every person minding his own business.

"Let him talk," said Dupin, who had not thought it necessary to reply. "Let him discourse; it will ease his conscience, I am satisfied with having defeated him in his own castle. Nevertheless, that he failed in the solution of this mystery, is by no means that matter for wonder which he supposes it; for, in truth, our friend the Prefect is somewhat too cunning to be profound. In his wisdom is no *stamen.* It is all head and no body, like the pictures of the Goddess

Laverna,—or, at best, all head and shoulders, like a codfish. But he is a good creature after all. I like him especially for one master stroke of cant, by which he has attained his reputation for ingenuity. I mean the way he has '*de nier ce qui est, et d'expliquer ce qui n'est pas.*'"[1]

Note

[1] Rousseau—*Nouvelle Héloïse.*

The Mystery of Marie Rogêt[1]

A Sequel to "The Murders in the Rue Morgue"

Es giebt eine Reihe idealischer Begebenheiten, die der Wirklichkeit parallel lauft. Selten fallen sie zusammen. Menschen und zufalle modifieiren gewohulich die idealische Begebenheit, so dass sie unvollkommen erscheint, und ihre Folgen gleichfalls unvollkommen sind. So bei der Reformation; statt des Protestantismus kam das Lutherthum hervor.

There are ideal series of events which run parallel with the realones. They rarely coincide. Men and circumstances generally modify the ideal train of events, so that it seems imperfect, and its consequences are equally imperfect. Thus with the Reformation; instead of Protestantism came Lutheranism.

—Novalis.[2] *Moral Ansichten*

There are few persons, even among the calmest thinkers, who have not occasionally been startled into a vague yet thrilling half-credence in the supernatural, by *coincidences* of so seemingly marvellous a character that, as mere coincidences, the intellect has been unable to receive them. Such sentiments—for the half-credences of which I speak have never the full force of *thought*—such sentiments are seldom thoroughly stifled unless by reference to the doctrine of chance, or, as it is technically termed, the Calculus of Probabilities. Now this Calculus is, in its essence, purely mathematical; and thus we have the anomaly of the most rigidly exact in science applied to the shadow and spirituality of the most intangible in speculation.

The extraordinary details which I am now called upon to make public, will be found to form, as regards sequence of time, the primary branch of a series of scarcely intelligible coincidences, whose secondary or concluding branch will be recognized by all readers in the late murder of MARY CECILA ROGERS, at New York.

When, in an article entitled "The Murders in the Rue Morgue," I endeavored, about a year ago, to depict some very remarkable features in the mental character of my friend, the Chevalier C. Auguste Dupin, it did not occur to me that I should ever resume the subject. This depicting of character constituted my design; and this design was thoroughly fulfilled in the wild train of circumstances brought to instance Dupin's idiosyncrasy. I might have adduced other examples, but I should have proven no more. Late events, however, in their surprising development, have startled me into some farther details, which will carry with them the air of extorted confession. Hearing what I have lately heard, it would be indeed strange should I remain silent in regard to what I both heard and saw so long ago.

Upon the winding up of the tragedy involved in the deaths of Madame L'Espanaye and her daughter, the Chevalier dismissed the affair at once from his attention, and relapsed into his old habits of moody reverie. Prone, at all times, to abstraction, I readily fell in with his humor; and, continuing to occupy our chambers in the Faubourg Saint Germain, we gave the Future to the winds, and slumbered tranquilly in the Present, weaving the dull world around us into dreams.

But these dreams were not altogether uninterrupted. It may readily be supposed that the part played by my friend, in the drama at the Rue Morgue, had not failed of its impression upon the fancies of the Parisian police. With its emissaries, the name of Dupin had grown into a household word. The simple character of those inductions by which he had disentangled the mystery never having been explained even to the Prefect, or to any other individual than myself, of course it is not surprising that the affair was regarded as little less than miraculous, or that the Chevalier's analytical abilities acquired for him the credit of intuition. His frankness would have led him to disabuse every inquirer of such prejudice; but his indolent humor forbade all farther agitation of a topic whose interest to himself had long ceased. It thus happened that he found himself the cynosure of the political eyes; and the cases were not few in which attempt was made to engage his services at the Prefecture. One of the most remarkable instances was that of the murder of a young girl named Marie Rogêt.

This event occurred about two years after the atrocity in the Rue Morgue. Marie, whose Christian and family name will at once arrest attention from their resemblance to those of the unfortunate "cigargirl," was the only daughter of the widow Estelle Rogêt. The father had died during the child's infancy, and from the period of his death, until within eighteen months before the assassination which forms the subject of our narrative, the mother and daughter had dwelt together in the Rue Pavée Saint Andrée;[3] Madame there keeping a *pension*, assisted by Marie. Affairs went on thus until the latter had attained her twenty-second year, when her great beauty attracted the notice of a perfumer, who occupied one of the shops in the basement of the Palais Royal, and whose custom lay chiefly among the desperate adventurers infesting that neighborhood. Monsieur Le Blanc[4] was not unaware of the advantages to be derived from the attendance of the fair Marie in his perfumery; and his liberal proposals were accepted eagerly by the girl, although with somewhat more of hesitation by Madame.

The anticipations of the shopkeeper were realized, and his rooms soon became notorious through the charms of the sprightly *grisette*. She had been in his employ about a year, when her admirers were thrown info confusion by her sudden disappearance from the shop. Monsieur Le Blanc was unable to account for her absence, and Madame Rogêt was distracted with anxiety and terror. The public papers immediately took up the theme, and the police were upon the point of making serious investigations, when, one fine morning, after the lapse of a week, Marie, in good health, but with a somewhat saddened air, made her re-appearance at her usual counter in the perfumery. All inquiry, except that of a private character, was of course immediately hushed. Monsieur Le Blanc professed total ignorance, as before. Marie, with Madame, replied to all questions, that the last week had been spent at the house of a relation in the country. Thus the affair died away, and was generally forgotten; for the girl, ostensibly to relieve herself from the impertinence of curiosity, soon bade a final adieu to the perfumer, and sought the shelter of her mother's residence in the Rue Pavée Saint Andrée.

It was about five months after this return home, that her friends were alarmed by her sudden disappearance for the second time. Three days elapsed, and nothing was heard of her. On the fourth her corpse was found floating in the Seine,[5] near the shore which is opposite the Quartier of the Rue Saint Andree, and at a point not very far distant from the secluded neighborhood of the Barrière du Roule.[6]

The atrocity of this murder (for it was at once evident that murder had been committed), the youth and beauty of the victim, and, above all, her previous notoriety, conspired to produce intense excitement in the minds of the sensitive Parisians. I can call to mind no similar occurrence producing so general and so intense an effect. For several weeks, in the discussion of this one absorbing theme, even the momentous political topics of the day were forgotten. The Prefect made unusual exertions; and the powers of the whole Parisian police were, of course, tasked to the utmost extent.

Upon the first discovery of the corpse, it was not supposed that the murderer would be able to elude, for more than a very brief period, the inquisition which was immediately set on foot. It was not until the expiration of a week that it was deemed necessary to offer a reward; and even then this reward was limited to a thousand francs. In the meantime the investigation proceeded with vigor, if not always with judgment, and numerous individuals were examined to no purpose; while, owing to the continual absence of all clue to the mystery, the popular excitement greatly increased. At the end of the tenth day it was thought advisable to double the sum originally proposed; and, at length, the second week having elapsed without leading to any discoveries, and the prejudice which always exists in Paris against the Police having given vent to itself in several serious *émeutes*, the Prefect took it upon himself to offer the sum of twenty thousand francs "for the conviction of the assassin," or, if more than one should prove to have been implicated, "for the conviction of any one of the assassins." In the proclamation setting forth this reward, a full pardon was promised to any accomplice who should come forward in evidence against his fellow; and to the whole was appended, wherever it appeared, the private placard of a committee of citizens, offering ten thousand francs, in addition to the amount proposed by the Prefecture. The entire reward thus stood at no less than thirty thousand francs, which will be regarded as an extraordinary sum when we consider the humble condition of the girl, and the great frequency, in large cities, of such atrocities as the one described.

No one doubted now that the mystery of this murder would be immediately brought to light. But although, in one or two instances, arrests were made which promised elucidation, yet nothing was elicited which could implicate the parties suspected; and they were discharged forthwith. Strange as it may appear, the third week from the discovery of the body had passed, and passed without any light being thrown upon the subject, before even a rumor of the events which had so agitated the public mind, reached the ears of Dupin and myself. Engaged in researches which absorbed our whole attention, it had been nearly a month since either of us had gone abroad, or received a visiter, or more than glanced at the leading political articles in one of the daily papers. The first intelligence of the murder was brought us by G ——, in person. He called upon us early in the afternoon of the thirteenth of July, 18—, and remained with us until late in the night. He had been piqued by the failure of all his endeavors to ferret out the assassins. His reputation—so he said with a peculiarly Parisian air—was at stake. Even his honor was concerned. The eyes of the public were upon him; and there was really no sacrifice which he would not be willing to make for the development of the mystery. He concluded a somewhat droll speech with a compliment upon what he was pleased to term the *tact* of Dupin, and made him a direct, and certainly a liberal proposition, the precise nature of which I do not feel myself at liberty to disclose, but which has no bearing upon the proper subject of my narrative.

The compliment my friend rebutted as best he could, but the proposition he accepted at once, although its advantages were altogether provisional. This point being settled, the Prefect broke forth at once into explanations of his own views, interspersing them with long comments upon the evidence; of which latter we were not yet in possession. He discoursed much, and beyond doubt, learnedly; while I hazarded an occasional suggestion as the night wore drowsily away. Dupin, sitting steadily in his accustomed arm-chair, was the embodiment of respectful attention. He wore spectacles, during the whole interview; and an occasional signal glance beneath their green glasses, sufficed to convince me that he slept not the less soundly, because silently, throughout the seven or eight leaden-footed hours which immediately preceded the departure of the Prefect.

In the morning, I procured, at the Prefecture, a full report of all the evidence elicited, and, at the various newspaper offices, a copy of every paper in which, from first to last, had been published any decisive information in regard to this sad affair. Freed from all that was positively disproved, this mass of information stood thus:

Marie Rogêt left the residence of her mother, in the Rue Pavée St. Andrée, about nine o'clock in the morning of Sunday June the twenty-second, 18—. In going out, she gave notice to a Monsieur Jacques St. Eustache,[7] and to him only, of her intention to spend the day with an aunt who resided in the Rue des Drômes. The Rue des Drômes is a short and narrow but populous thoroughfare, not far from the banks of the river, and at a distance of some two miles, in the most direct course possible, from the *pension* of Madame Rogêt. St. Eustache was the accepted suitor of Marie, and lodged, as well as took his meals, at the *pension*. He was to have gone for his betrothed at dusk, and to have escorted her home. In the afternoon, however, it came on to rain heavily; and, supposing that she would remain all night at her aunt's (as she had done under similar circumstances before), he did not think it necessary to keep his promise. As night drew on, Madame Rogêt (who was an infirm old lady, seventy years of age), was heard to express a fear "that she should never see Marie again"; but this observation attracted little attention at the time.

On Monday, it was ascertained that the girl had not been to the Rue des Drômes; and when the day elapsed without tidings of her, a tardy search was instituted at several points in the city, and its environs. It was not, however until the fourth day from the period of disappearance that any thing satisfactory was ascertained respecting her. On this day (Wednesday, the twenty-fifth of June), a Monsieur Beauvais,[8] who, with a friend, had been making inquiries for Marie near the Barrière du Roule, on the shore of the Seine which is opposite the Rue Pavée St. Andrée, was informed that a corpse had just been towed ashore by some fishermen, who had found it floating in the river. Upon seeing the body, Beauvais, after some hesitation, identified it as that of the perfumery-girl. His friend recognized it more promptly.

The face was suffused with dark blood, some of which issued from the mouth. No foam was seen, as in the case of the merely drowned. There was no discoloration in the cellular tissue. About the throat were bruises and impressions of fingers. The arms were bent over on the chest and were rigid. The right hand was clenched; the left partially open. On the left wrist were two circular excoriations, apparently the effect of ropes, or of a rope in more than one volution. A part of the right wrist, also, was much chafed, as well as the back throughout its extent, but more especially at the shoulder-blades. In bringing the body to the shore the fishermen had attached to it a rope; but none of the excoriations had been effected by this. The flesh of the neck was much swollen. There were no cuts apparent, or bruises which appeared the effect of blows. A piece of lace was found tied so tightly around the neck as to be hidden from sight; it was completely buried in the flesh, and was fasted by a knot which lay just under the left ear. This alone would have sufficed to produce death. The medical testimony spoke confidently of the virtuous character of the deceased. She had been subjected, it said, to brutal violence. The corpse was in such condition when found, that there could have been no difficulty in its recognition by friends.

The dress was much torn and otherwise disordered. In the outer garment, a slip, about a foot wide, had been torn upward from the bottom hem to the waist, but not torn off. It was wound three times around the waist, and secured by a sort of hitch in the back. The dress immediately beneath the frock was of fine muslin; and from this a slip eighteen inches wide had been torn entirely out—torn very evenly and with great care. It was found around her neck, fitting loosely, and secured with a hard knot. Over this muslin slip and the slip of lace, the strings of a bonnet were attached; the bonnet being appended. The knot by which the strings of the bonnet were fastened, was not a lady's, but a slip or sailor's knot.

After the recognition of the corpse, it was not, as usual, taken to the Morgue (this formality being superfluous), but hastily interred not far front the spot at which it was brought ashore. Through the exertions of Beauvais, the matter was industriously hushed up, as far as possible; and several days had elapsed before any public emotion resulted. A weekly paper,[9] however, at length took up the theme; the corpse was disinterred, and a re-examination instituted; but nothing was elicited beyond what has been already noted. The clothes, however, were now submitted to the mother and friends of the deceased, and fully identified as those worn by the girl upon leaving home.

Meantime, the excitement increased hourly. Several individuals were arrested and discharged. St. Eustache fell especially under suspicion; and he failed, at first, to give an intelligible account of his whereabouts during the Sunday on which Marie left home. Subsequently, however, he submitted to Monsieur G——, affidavits, accounting satisfactorily for every hour of the day in question. As time passed and no discovery ensued, a thousand contradictory rumors were circulated, and journalists busied themselves in suggestions. Among these, the one which attracted the most notice, was the idea that Marie Rogêt still lived—that the corpse found in the Seine was that of some other unfortunate. It will be proper that I submit to the reader some passages which embody the suggestion alluded to. These passages are *literal* translations from *L'Etoile*,[10] a paper conducted, in general, with much ability:

"Mademoiselle Rogêt left her mother's house on Sunday morning, June the twenty-second, 18—, with the ostensible purpose of going to see her aunt, or some other connexion, in the Rue des Drômes. From that hour, nobody is proved to have seen her. There is no trace or tidings of her at all.... There has no person, whatever, come forward, so far, who saw her at all, on that day, after she left her mother's door.... Now, though we have no evidence that Marie

Rogêt was in the land of the living after nine o'clock on Sunday, June the twenty-second, we have proof that, up to that hour, she was alive. On Wednesday noon, at twelve, a female body was discovered afloat on the shore of the Barrière de Roule. This was, even if we presume that Marie Rogêt was thrown into the river within three hours after she left her mother's house, only three days from the time she left her home—three days to an hour. But it is folly to suppose that the murder, if murder was committed on her body, could have been consummated soon enough to have enabled her murderers to throw the body into the river before midnight. Those who are guilty of such horrid crimes, choose darkness rather the light.... Thus we see that if the body found in the river was that of Marie Rogêt, it could only have been in the water two and a half days, or three at the outside. All experience has shown that drowned bodies, or bodies thrown into the water immediately after death by violence, require from six to ten days for decomposition to take place to bring them to the top of the water. Even where a cannon is fired over a corpse, and it rises before at least five or six days' immersion, it sinks again, if let alone. Now, we ask, what was there in this cave to cause a departure from the ordinary course of nature?... If the body had been kept in its mangled state on shore until Tuesday night, some trace would be found on shore of the murderers. It is a doubtful point, also, whether the body would be so soon afloat, even were it thrown in after having been dead two days. And, furthermore, it is exceedingly improbable that any villains who had committed such a murder as is here supposed, would have throw the body in without weight to sink it, when such a precaution could have so easily been taken."

The editor here proceeds to argue that the body must have been in the water "not three days merely, but, at least, five times three days," because it was so far decomposed that Beauvais had great difficulty in recognizing it. This latter point, however, was fully disproved. I continue the translation:

"What, then, are the facts on which M. Beauvais says that he has no doubt the body was that of Marie Rogêt? He ripped up the gown sleeve, and says he found marks which satisfied him of the identity. The public generally supposed those marks to have consisted of some description of scars. He rubbed the arm and found hair upon it—something as indefinite, we think, as can readily be imagined—as little conclusive as finding an arm in the sleeve. M. Beauvais did not return that night, but sent word to Madame Rogêt, at seven o'clock, on Wednesday evening, that an investigation was still in progress respecting her daughter. If we allow that Madame Rogêt, from her age and grief, could not go over (which is allowing a great deal), there certainly must have been some one who would have thought it worth while to go over and attend the investigation, if they thought the body was that of Marie. Nobody went over. There was nothing said or heard about the matter in the Rue Pavée St. Andrée, that reached even the occupants of the same building. M. St. Eustache, the lover and intended husband of Marie, who boarded in her mother's house, deposes that he did not hear of the discovery of the body of his intended until the next morning, when M. Beauvais came into his chamber and told him of it. For an item of news like this, it strikes us it was very coolly received."

In this way the journal endeavored to create the impression of an apathy on the part of the relatives of Marie, inconsistent with the supposition that these relatives believed the corpse to be hers. Its insinuations amount to this—that Marie, with the connivance of her friends, had absented herself from the city for reasons involving a charge against her chastity; and that these friends, upon the discovery of a corpse in the Seine, somewhat resembling that of the girl, had availed themselves of the opportunity to impress press the public with the belief of her death. But *L'Etoile* was again over-hasty. It was distinctly proved that no apathy, such as was imagined, existed; that the old lady was exceedingly feeble, and so agitated as to be unable to attend to any duty, that St. Eustache, so far from receiving the news coolly, was distracted with grief, and bore himself so frantically, that M. Beauvais prevailed upon a friend and relative to take charge of him, and prevent his attending the examination at the disinterment. Moreover, although it was stated by *L'Etoile*, that the corpse was re-interred at the public expense—that an advantageous offer of private sculpture was absolutely declined by the family—and that no member of the family attended the ceremonial:—although, I say, all this was asserted by *L'Etoile* in furtherance of the impression it designed to convey—yet all this was satisfactorily disproved. In a subsequent number of the paper, an attempt was made to throw suspicion upon Beauvais himself. The editor says:

"Now, then, a change comes over the matter. We are told that on one occasion, while a Madame B—— was at Madame Rogêt's house, M. Beauvais, who was going out, told her that a *gendarme* was expected there, and she, Madame B., must not say anything to the *gendarme* until he returned, but let the matter be for him.... In the present posture of affairs, M. Beauvais appears to have the whole matter looked up in his head. A single step cannot be taken without M. Beauvais; for, go which way you will, you run against him.... For some reason, he determined that nobody shall have any thing to do with the proceedings but himself, and he has elbowed the male relatives out of the way, according to their representations, in a very singular manner. He seems to have been very much averse to permitting the relatives to see the body."

By the following fact, some color was given to the suspicion thus thrown upon Beauvais. A visiter at his office, a few days prior to the girl's disappearance, and during the absence of its occupant, had observed a *rose* in the key-hole of the door, and the name "*Marie*" inscribed upon a slate which hung near at hand.

The general impression, so far as we were enabled to glean it from the newspapers, seemed to be, that Marie had been the victim of a *gang* of desperadoes—that by these she had been borne across the river, maltreated and murdered. *Le Commerciel*,[11] however, a print of extensive influence, was earnest in combating this popular idea. I quote a passage or two from its columns:

"We are persuaded that pursuit has hitherto been on a false scent, so far as it has been directed to the Barrière du Roule. It is impossible that a person so well known to thousands as this young woman was, should have passed three blocks without some one having seen her; and any one who saw her would have remembered it, for she interested all who knew her. It was when the streets were full of people, when she went out.... It is impossible that she could have gone to the Barrière du Roule, or to the Rue des Drômes, without being recognized by a dozen persons; yet no one has come forward who saw her outside of her mother's door, and there is no evidence, except the testimony concerning her *expressed intentions*, that she did go out at all. Her gown was torn, bound round her, and tied;

and by that the body was carried as a bundle. If the murder had been committed at the Barrière du Roule, there would have been no necessity for any such arrangement. The fact that the body was found floating near the Barrière, is no proof as to where it was thrown into the water... A piece of one of the unfortunate girl's petticoats, two feet long and one foot wide, was torn out and tied under her chin around the back of her head, probably to prevent screams. This was done by fellows who had no pocket-handkerchief."

A day or two before the Prefect called upon us, however, some important information reached the police, which seemed to overthrow, at least, the chief portion of *Le Commerciel's* argument. Two small boys, sons of a Madame Deluc, while roaming among the woods near the Barrière du Roule, chanced to penetrate a close thicket, within which were three or four large stones, forming a kind of seat, with a back and footstool. On the upper stone lay a white petticoat; on the second a silk scarf. A parasol, gloves, and a pocket-handkerchief were also here found. The handkerchief bore the name "Marie Rogêt." Fragments of dress were discovered on the brambles around. The earth was trampled, the bushes were broken, and there was every evidence of a struggle. Between the thicket and the river, the fences were found taken down, and the ground bore evidence of some heavy burthen having been dragged along it.

A weekly paper, *Le Soleil*,[12] had the following comments upon this discovery—comments which merely echoed the sentiment of the whole Parisian press:

"The things had all evidently been there at least three or four weeks; they were all mildewed down hard with the action of the rain and stuck together from mildew. The grass had grown around and over some of them. The silk on the parasol was strong, but the threads of it were run together within. The upper part, where it had been doubled and folded, was all mildewed and rotten, and tore on its being opened... The pieces of her frock torn out by the bushes were about three inches wide and six inches long. One part was the hem of the frock, and it had been mended; the other piece was part of the skirt, not the hem. They looked like strips torn off, and were on the thorn bush, about a foot from the ground... There can be no doubt, therefore, that the spot of this appalling outrage has been discovered."

Consequent upon this discovery, new evidence appeared. Madame Deluc testified that she keeps a roadside inn not far from the bank of the river, opposite the Barrière du Roule. The neighborhood is secluded—particularly so. It is the usual Sunday resort of blackguards from the city, who cross the river in boats. About three o'clock, in the afternoon of the Sunday in question, a young girl arrived at the inn, accompanied by a young man of dark complexion. The two remained here for some time. On their departure, they took the road to some thick woods in the vicinity. Madame Deluc's attention was called to the dress worn by the girl, on account of its resemblance to one worn by a deceased relative. A scarf was particularly noticed. Soon after the departure of the couple, a *gang* of miscreants made their appearance, behaved boisterously, ate and drank without making payment, followed in the route of the young man and girl, returned to the inn about dusk, and recrossed the river as if in great haste.

It was soon after dark, upon this same evening, that Madame Deluc, as well as her eldest son, heard the screams of a female in the vicinity of the inn. The screams were violent but brief. Madame D. recognized not only the scarf which was found in the thicket, but the dress which was discovered upon the corpse. An omnibus driver, Valence,[13] now also testified that he saw Marie Rogêt cross a ferry on the Seine, on the Sunday in question, in company with a young man of dark complexion. He, Valence, knew Marie, and could not be mistaken in her identity. The articles found in the thicket were fully identified by the relatives of Marie.

The items of evidence and information thus collected by myself, from the newspapers, at the suggestion of Dupin, embraced only one more point—but this was a point of seemingly vast consequence. It appears that, immediately after the discovery of the clothes as above described, the lifeless, or nearly lifeless body of St. Eustache, Marie's betrothed, was found in the vicinity of what all now supposed the scene of the outrage. A phial labelled "laudanum," and emptied, was found near him. His breath gave evidence of the poison. He died without speaking. Upon his person was found a letter, briefly stating his love for Marie, with his design of self-destruction.

"I need scarcely tell you," said Dupin, as he finished the perusal of my notes, "that this is a far more intricate case than that of the

Rue Morgue; from which it differs in one important respect. This is an *ordinary*, although an atrocious instance of crime. There is nothing peculiarly *outré* about it. You will observe that, for this reason, the mystery has been considered easy, when, for this reason, it should have been considered difficult, of solution. Thus; at first, it was thought unnecessary to offer a reward. The myrmidons of G—— were able at once to comprehend how and why such an atrocity *might have been* committed. They *could* picture to their imaginations a mode—many modes—and a motive—many motives; and because it was not impossible that either of these numerous modes and motives *could* have been the actual one, they have taken it for granted that one of them *must*. But the case with which these variable fancies were entertained, and the very plausibility which each assumed, should have been understood as indicative rather of the difficulties than of the facilities which must attend elucidation. I have before observed that it is by prominences above the plane of the ordinary, that reason feels her way, if at all, in her search for the true, and that the proper question in cases such as this, is not so much 'what has occurred?' as 'what has occurred that has never occurred before?' In the investigations at the house of Madame L'Espanaye,[14] the agents of G—— were discouraged and confounded by that very *unusualness* which, to a properly regulated intellect, would have afforded the surest omen of success; while this same intellect might have been plunged in despair at the ordinary character of all that met the eye in the case of the perfumery-girl, and yet told of nothing but easy triumph to the functionaries of the Prefecture.

"In the case of Madame L'Espanaye and her daughter there was, even at the beginning of our investigation, no doubt that murder had been committed. The idea of suicide was excluded at once. Here, too, we are freed, at the commencement, from all supposition of self-murder. The body found at the Barrière du Roule, was found under such circumstances as to leave us no room for embarrassment upon this important point. But it has been suggested that the corpse discovered, is not that of the Marie Rogêt for the conviction of whose assassin, or assassins, the reward is offered, and respecting whom, solely, our agreement has been arranged with the Prefect. We both know this gentleman well. It will not do to trust him too far. If, dating our inquiries from the body found, and thence tracing a murderer, we yet discover this body to be that of some other individual than Marie; or, if starting from the living Marie, we find her, yet find her unassassinated—in either case we lose our labor; since it is Monsieur G—— with whom we have to deal. For our own purpose, therefore, if not for the purpose of justice, it is indispensable that our first step should be the determination of the identity of the corpse with the Marie Rogêt who is missing.

"With the public the arguments of *L'Etoile* have had weight; and that the journal itself is convinced of their importance would appear from the manner in which it commences one of its essays upon the subject—'Several of the morning papers of the day,' it says, 'speak of the *conclusive* article in Monday's *Etoile*.' To me, this article appears conclusive of little beyond the zeal of its inditer. We should bear in mind that, in general, it is the object of our newspapers rather to create a sensation—to make a point—than to further the cause of truth. The latter end is only pursued when it seems coincident with the former. The print which merely falls in with ordinary opinion (however well founded this opinion may be) earns for itself no credit with the mob. The mass of the people regard as profound only him who suggests *pungent contradictions* of the general idea. In ratiocination, not less than in literature, it is the *epigram* which is the most immediately and the most universally appreciated. In both, it is of the lowest order of merit.

"What I mean to say is, that it is the mingled epigram and melodrame of the idea, that Marie Rogêt still lives, rather than any true plausibility in this idea, which have suggested it to *L'Etoile*, and secured it a favorable reception with the public. Let us examine the heads of this journal's argument; endeavoring to avoid the incoherence with which it is originally set forth.

"The first aim of the writer is to show, from the brevity of the interval between Marie's disappearance and the finding of the floating corpse, that this corpse cannot be that of Marie. The reduction of this interval to its smallest possible dimension, becomes thus, at once, an object with the reasoner. In the rash pursuit of this object, he rushes into mere assumption at the outset. 'It is folly to suppose,' he says, 'that the murder, if murder was committed on her body, could have been consummated soon enough to have enabled her murderers to throw the body into the river before midnight.' We demand at once, and very naturally, *why*? Why is it folly to suppose that the murder was committed *within five minutes* after the girl's quitting her mother's house? Why is it folly to suppose that the murder was committed at any given period of the day? There have been assassinations at all hours. But, had the murder taken place at any moment between nine o'clock in the morning of Sunday, and a quarter before midnight, there would still have been time enough 'to throw the body into the river before midnight.' This assumption, then, amounts precisely to this—that the murder was not committed on Sunday at all—and, if we allow *L'Etoile* to assume this, we may permit it any liberties whatever. The paragraph beginning 'It is folly to suppose that the murder, etc.,' however it appears as printed in *L'Etoile*, may be imagined to have existed actually *thus* in the brain of its inditer—'It is folly to suppose that the murder, if murder was committed on the body, could have been committed soon enough to have enabled her murderers to throw the body into the river before midnight; it is folly, we say, to suppose all this, and to suppose at the same time (as we are resolved to suppose), that the body was not thrown in until *after* midnight'—a sentence sufficiently inconsequential in itself, but not so utterly preposterous as the one printed.

"Were it my purpose," continued Dupin, "merely to *make out a case* against this passage of *L'Etoile's* argument, I might safely leave it where it is. It is not, however, with *L'Etoile* that we have to do, but with the truth. The sentence in question has but one meaning, as it stands; and this meaning I have fairly stated: but it is material that we go behind the mere words, for an idea which these words have obviously intended, and failed to convey. It was the design of the journalist to say that, at whatever period of the day or night of Sunday this murder was committed, it was improbable that the assassins would have ventured to bear the corpse to the river before midnight. And herein lies, really, the assumption of which I complain. It is assumed that the murder was committed at such a position, and under such circumstances, that *the bearing it* to the river became necessary. Now, the assassination might have taken place upon the river's brink, or on the river itself; and, thus, the throwing the corpse in the water might have been resorted to, at any period of the day or night, as the most obvious and most immediate mode of disposal. You will understand that I suggest nothing here as probable, or as cöincident with my own opinion. My design, so far, has no reference to the facts of the case. I wish merely to caution you against the whole tone of *L'Etoile's suggestion*, by calling your attention to its *ex parte* character at the outset.

"Having prescribed thus a limit to suit its own preconceived notions; having assumed that, if this were the body of Marie, it could have been in the water but a very brief time; the journal goes on to say:

"'All experience has shown that drowned bodies, or bodies thrown into the water immediately after death by violence, require from six to ten days for sufficient decomposition to take place to bring them to the top of the water. Even when a cannon is fired over a corpse, and it rises before at least five or six days' immersion, it sinks again if let alone.'"

"These assertions have been tacitly received by every paper in Paris, with the exception of *Le Moniteur*.[15] This latter print endeavors to combat that portion of the paragraph which has reference to 'drowned bodies' only, by citing some five or six instances in which the bodies of individuals known to be drowned were found floating after the lapse of less time than is insisted upon by *L'Etoile*. But there is something excessively unphilosophical in the attempt on the part of *Le Moniteur*, to rebut the general assertion of *L'Etoile*, by a citation of particular instances militating against that assertion. Had it been possible to adduce fifty instead of five examples of bodies found floating at the end of two or three days, these fifty examples could still have been properly regarded only as exceptions to *L'Etoile's* rule, until such time as the rule itself should be confuted. Admitting the rule (and this *Le Moniteur* does not deny, insisting merely upon its exceptions), the argument of *L'Etoile* is suffered to remain in full force; for this argument does not pretend to involve more than a question of the probability of the body having risen to the surface in less than three days; and this probability will be in favor of *L'Etoile's* position until the instances so childishly adduced shall be sufficient in number to establish an antagonistical rule.

"You will see at once that all argument upon this head should be urged, if at all, against the rule itself; and for this end we must examine the *rationale* of the rule. Now the human body, in general, is neither much lighter nor much heavier than the water of the Seine; that is to say, the specific gravity of the human body, in its natural condition, is about equal to the bulk of fresh water which it displaces. The bodies of fat and fleshy persons, with small bones, and of women generally, are lighter than those of the lean and large-boned, and of men; and the specific gravity of the water of a river is somewhat influenced by the presence of the tide from sea. But, leaving this tide out of question, it may be said that very few human bodies will sink at all, even in fresh water, *of their own accord*. Almost any one, falling into a river, will be enabled to float, if he suffer the specific gravity of the water fairly to be adduced in comparison with his own—that is to say, if he suffer his whole person to be immersed, with as little exception as possible. The proper position for one who cannot swim, is the upright position of the walker on land, with the head thrown fully back, and immersed; the mouth and nostrils alone remaining above the surface. Thus circumstanced, we shall find that we float without difficulty and without exertion. It is evident, however, that the gravities of the body, and of the bulk of water displaced, are very nicely balanced, and that a trifle will cause either to preponderate. An arm, for instance, uplifted from the water, and thus deprived of its support, is an additional weight sufficient to immerse the whole head, while the accidental aid of the smallest piece of timber will enable us to elevate the head so as to look about. Now, in the struggles of one unused to swimming, the arms are invariably thrown upwards, while an attempt is made to keep the head in its usual perpendicular position. The result is the immersion of the mouth and nostrils, and the inception, during efforts to breathe while beneath the surface, of water into the lungs. Much is also received into the stomach, and the whole body becomes heavier by the difference between the weight of the air originally distending these cavities, and that of the fluid which now fills them. This difference is sufficient to cause the body to sink, as a general rule; but is insufficient in the cases of individuals with small bones and an abnormal quantity of flaccid or fatty matter. Such individuals float even after drowning.

"The corpse, being supposed at the bottom of the river, will there remain until, by some means, its specific gravity again becomes less than that of the bulk of water which it displaces. This effect is brought about by decomposition, or otherwise. The result of decomposition is the generation of gas, distending the cellular tissues and all the cavities, and giving the *puffed* appearance which is so horrible. When this distension has so far progressed that the bulk of the corpse is materially increased without a corresponding increase of *mass* or weight, its specific gravity becomes less than that of the water displaced, and it forthwith makes its appearance at the surface. But decomposition is modified by innumerable circumstances—is hastened or retarded by innumerable agencies; for example, by the heat or cold of the season, by the mineral impregnation or purity of the water, by its depth or shallowness, by its currency or stagnation, by the temperament of the body, by its infection or freedom from disease before death. Thus it is evident that we can assign no period, with any thing like accuracy, at which the corpse shall rise through decomposition. Under certain conditions this result would be brought about within an hour; under others, it might not take place at all. There are chemical infusions by which the animal frame can be preserved *forever* from corruption; the Bi-chloride of Mercury is one. But, apart from decomposition, there may be, and very usually is, a generation of gas within the stomach, from the acetous fermentation of vegetable matter (or within other cavities from other causes) sufficient to induce a distension which will bring the body to the surface. The effect produced by the firing of a cannon is that of simple vibration. This may either loosen the corpse from the soft mud or ooze in which it is imbedded, thus permitting it to rise when other agencies have already prepared it for so doing; or it may overcome the tenacity of some putrescent portions of the cellular tissue; allowing the cavities to distend under the influence of the gas.

"Having thus before us the whole philosophy of this subject, we can easily test by it the assertions of *L'Etoile*. 'All experience shows,' says this paper, 'that drowned bodies, or bodies thrown into the water immediately after death by violence, require from six to ten days for sufficient decomposition to take place to bring them to the top of the water. Even when a cannon is fired over a corpse, and it rises before at least five or six days' immersion, it sinks again if let alone.'

"The whole of this paragraph must now appear a tissue of inconsequence and incoherence. All experience does not show that 'drowned bodies' *require* from six to ten days for sufficient decomposition to take place to bring them to the surface. Both science and experience show that the period of their rising is, and necessarily must be, indeterminate. If, moreover, a body has risen to the surface through firing of cannon, it will *not* 'sink again if let alone,' until decomposition has so far progressed as to permit the escape of the generated gas. But I wish to call your attention to the distinction which is made between 'drowned bodies,' and 'bodies thrown into the water immediately after death by violence.' Although the writer admits the distinction, he yet includes them all in the same category. I have shown how it is that the body of a drowning man becomes specifically heavier than its bulk of water, and that he would not sink at all, except for the struggles by which he elevates his arms above the surface, and his gasps for breath while beneath the surface—gasps which supply by water the place of the original air in the lungs. But these struggles and these gasps would not occur in the body 'thrown into the water immediately after death by violence.' Thus, in the latter instance, *the body, as a general rule, would not sink at all*—a fact of which *L'Etoile* is evidently ignorant. When decomposition had proceeded to a very great extent—when the flesh had in a great measure left the bones—then, indeed, but not till then, should we lose sight of the corpse.

"And now what are we to make of the argument, that the body found could not be that of Marie Rogêt, because, three days only having elapsed, this body was found floating? If drowned, being a woman, she might never have sunk; or having sunk, might have reappeared in twenty-four hours, or less. But no one supposes her to have been drowned; and, dying before being thrown into the river, she might have been found floating at any period afterwards whatever.

"'But,' says *L'Etoile*, 'if the body had been kept in its mangled state on shore until Tuesday night, some trace would be found on shore of the murderers.' Here it is at first difficult to perceive the intention of the reasoner. He means to anticipate what he imagines would be an objection to his theory—viz: that the body was kept on shore two days, suffering rapid decomposition—*more* rapid than if immersed in water. He supposes that, had this been the case, it *might* have appeared at the surface on the Wednesday, and thinks that *only* under such circumstances it could so have appeared. He is accordingly in haste to show that it was not kept on shore; for, if so, 'some trace would be found on shore of the murderers.' I presume you smile at the *sequitur*. You cannot be made to see how the mere duration of the corpse on the shore could operate to *multiply traces* of the assassins. Nor can I.

"'And furthermore it is exceedingly improbable,' continues our journal, 'that any villains who had committed such a murder as is here supposed, would have thrown the body in without weight to sink it, when such a precaution could have so easily been taken.' Observe, here, the laughable confusion of thought! No one—not even *L'Etoile*—disputes the murder committed *on the body found*. The marks of violence are too obvious. It is our reasoner's object merely to show that this body is not Marie's. He wishes to prove that *Marie* is not assassinated—not that the corpse was not. Yet his observation proves only the latter point. Here is a corpse without weight attached. Murderers, casting it in, would not have failed to attach a weight. Therefore it was not thrown in by murderers. This is all which is proved, if any thing is. The question of identity is not even approached, and *L'Etoile* has been at great pains merely to gainsay now what it has admitted only a moment before. 'We are perfectly convinced,' it says, 'that the body found was that of a murdered female.'

"Nor is this the sole instance, even in this division of his subject, where our reasoner unwittingly reasons against himself. His evident object, I have already said, is to reduce, us much as possible, the interval between Marie's disappearance and the finding of the corpse. Yet we find him *urging* the point that no person saw the girl from the moment of her leaving her mother's house. 'We have no evidence,' he says, 'that Marie Rogêt was in the land of the living after nine o'clock on Sunday, June the twenty-second.' As his argument is obviously an *ex parte* one, he should, at least, have left this matter out of sight; for had any one been known to see Marie, say on Monday, or on Tuesday, the interval in question would have been much reduced, and, by his own ratiocination, the probability much diminished of the corpse being that of the *grisette*. It is, nevertheless, amusing to observe that *L'Etoile* insists upon its point in the full belief of its furthering its general argument.

"Reperuse now that portion of this argument which has reference to the identification of the corpse by Beauvais. In regard to the *hair* upon the arm, *L'Etoile* has been obviously disingenuous. M. Beauvais, not being an idiot, could never have urged, in identification of the corpse, simply *hair upon its arm*. No arm is *without hair*. The *generality* of the expression of *L'Etoile* is a mere perversion of the witness' phraseology. He must have spoken of some *peculiarity* in this hair. It must have been a peculiarity of color, of quantity, of length, or of situation.

"'Her foot,' says the journal, 'was small—so are thousands of feet. Her garter is no proof whatever—nor is her shoe—for shoes and garters are sold in packages. The same may be said of the flowers in her hat. One thing upon which M. Beauvais strongly insists is, that the clasp on the garter found, had been set back to take it in. This amounts to nothing; for most women find it proper to take a pair of garters home and fit them to the size of the limbs they are to encircle, rather than to try them in the store where they purchase.' Here it is difficult to suppose the reasoner in earnest. Had M. Beauvais, in his search for the body of Marie, discovered a corpse corresponding in general size and appearance to the missing girl, he would have been warranted (without reference to the question of habiliment at all) in forming an opinion that his search had been successful. If, in addition to the point of general size and contour, he had found upon the arm a peculiar hairy appearance which he had observed upon the living Marie, his opinion might have been justly strengthened; and the increase of positiveness might well have been in the ratio of the peculiarity, or unusualness, of the hairy mark. If, the feet of Marie being small, those of the corpse were also small, the increase of probability that the body was that of Marie would not be an increase in a ratio merely arithmetical, but in one highly geometrical, or accumulative. Add to all this shoes such as she had been known to wear upon the day of her disappearance, and, although these shoes may be 'sold in packages,' you so far augment the probability as to verge upon the certain. What, of itself, would be no evidence of identity, becomes through its corroborative position, proof most sure. Give us, then, flowers in the hat corresponding to those worn by the missing girl, and we seek for nothing farther. If only *one* flower, we seek for nothing farther—what then if two or three, or more? Each successive one is multiple evidence—proof not *added* to proof, but *multiplied* by hundreds or thousands. Let us now discover, upon the deceased, garters such as the living used, and it is almost folly to proceed. But these garters are found to be tightened, by the setting back of a clasp, in just such a manner as her own had been tightened by Marie, shortly previous to her leaving home. It is now madness or hypocrisy to doubt. What *L'Etoile* says in respect to this abbreviation of the garter's being an usual occurrence, shows nothing beyond its own pertinacity in error. The elastic nature of the clasp-garter is self-demonstration of the *unusualness* of the abbreviation. What is made to adjust itself, must of necessity require foreign adjustment but rarely. It must have been by an accident, in its strictest sense, that these garters of Marie needed the tightening described. They alone would have amply established her identity. But it is not that the corpse was found to have the garters of the missing girl, or found to have her shoes, or her bonnet, or the flowers of her bonnet, or her feet, or a peculiar mark upon the arm, or her general size and appearance—it is that the corpse had each, and *all collectively*. Could it be proved that the editor of *L'Etoile* *really* entertained a doubt, under the circumstances, there would be no need, in his case, of a commission *de lunatico inquirendo*. He has thought it sagacious to echo the small talk of the lawyers, who, for the most part, content themselves with echoing the rectangular precepts of the courts. I would here observe that very much of what is rejected as evidence by a court, is the best of evidence to the intellect. For the court, guiding itself by the general principles of evidence—the recognized and *booked* principles—is averse from swerving at particular instances. And this steadfast adherence to principle, with rigorous disregard of the conflicting exception, is a sure mode of attaining the *maximum* of attainable truth, in any long sequence of time. The practice, *en mass*, is therefore philosophical; but it is not the less certain that it engenders vast individual error.[16]

"In respect to the insinuations levelled at Beauvais, you will be willing to dismiss them in a breath. You have already fathomed the true character of this good gentleman. He is a *busy-body*, with much of romance and little of wit. Any one so constituted will readily so conduct himself, upon occasion of real excitement, as to render himself liable to suspicion on the part of the over acute, or the ill-disposed. M. Beauvais (as it appears from your notes) had some personal interviews with the editor of *L'Etoile*, and offended him by venturing an opinion that the corpse, notwithstanding the theory of the editor, was, in sober fact, that of Marie. 'He persists,' says the paper, 'in asserting the corpse to be that of Marie, but cannot give a circumstance, in addition to those which we have commented upon, to make others believe.' Now, without re-adverting to the fact that stronger evidence 'to make others believe,' could *never* have been adduced, it may be remarked that a man may very well be understood to believe, in a case of this kind, without the ability to advance a single reason for the belief of a second party. Nothing is more vague than impressions of individual identity. Each man recognizes his neighbor, yet there are few instances in which any one is prepared to *give a reason* for his recognition. The editor of *L'Etoile* had no right to be offended at M. Beauvais' unreasoning belief.

"The suspicious circumstances which invest him, will be found to tally much better with my hypothesis of *romantic busy-bodyism*, than with the reasoner's suggestion of guilt. Once adopting the more charitable interpretation, we shall find no difficulty in comprehending the rose in the key-hole; the 'Marie' upon the slate; the 'elbowing the male relatives out of the way;' the 'aversion to permitting them to see the body;' the caution given to Madame B——, that she must hold no conversation with the *gendarme* until his return (Beauvais'); and, lastly, his apparent determination 'that nobody should have anything to do with the proceedings except himself.' It seems to me unquestionable that Beauvais was a suitor of Marie's; that she coquetted with him; and that he was ambitious of being thought to enjoy her fullest intimacy and confidence. I shall say nothing more upon this point; and, as the evidence fully rebuts the assertion of *L'Etoile*, touching the matter of *apathy* on the part of the mother and other relatives—an apathy inconsistent with the supposition of their believing the corpse to be that of the perfumery-girl—we shall now proceed as if the question of *identity* were settled to our perfect satisfaction."

"And what," I here demanded, "do you think of the opinions of *Le Commerciel*?"

"That, in spirit, they are far more worthy of attention than any which have been promulgated upon the subject. The deductions from the premises are philosophical and acute; but the premises, in two instances, at least, are founded in imperfect observation. *Le Commerciel* wishes to intimate that Marie was seized by some *gang* of low ruffians not far from her mother's door. 'It is impossible,' it urges, 'that a person so well known to thousands as this young woman was, should have passed three blocks without some one having seen her.' This is the idea of a man long resident in Paris—a public man—and one whose walks to and fro in the city, have been mostly limited to the vicinity of the public offices. He is aware that he seldom passes so far as a dozen blocks from his own bureau, without being recognized and accosted. And, knowing the extent of his personal acquaintance with others, and of others with him, he compares his notoriety with that of the perfumery-girl, finds no great difference between them, and reaches at once the conclusion that she, in her walks, would be equally liable to recognition with himself in his. This could only be the case were her walks of the same unvarying, methodical character, and within the same *species* of limited region as are his own. He passes to and fro, at regular intervals, within a confined periphery, abounding in individuals who are led to observation of his person through interest in the kindred nature of his occupation with their own. But the walks of Marie may, in general, be supposed discursive. In this particular instance, it will be understood as most probable, that she proceeded upon a route of more than average diversity from her accustomed ones. The parallel which we imagine to have existed in the mind of *Le Commerciel* would only be sustained in the event of the two individuals' traversing the whole city. In this case, granting the personal acquaintances to be equal, the chances would be also equal that an equal number of personal encounters would be made. For my own part, I should hold it not only as possible, but as very far more than probable, that Marie might have proceeded, at any given period, by any one of the many routes between her own residence and that of her aunt, without meeting a single individual whom she knew, or by whom she was known. In viewing this question in its full and proper light, we must hold steadily in mind the great disproportion between the personal acquaintances of even the most noted individual in Paris, and the entire population of Paris itself.

"But whatever force there may still appear to be in the suggestion of *Le Commerciel*, will be much diminished when we take into consideration the *hour* at which the girl went abroad. 'It was when the streets were full of people,' says *Le Commerciel*, 'that she went out.' But not so. It was at nine o'clock in the morning. Now at nine o'clock of every morning in the week, *with the exception of Sunday*, the streets of the city are, it is true, thronged with people. At nine on Sunday, the populace are chiefly within doors *preparing for church*. No observing person can have failed to notice the peculiarly deserted air of the town, from about eight until ten on the morning of every Sabbath. Between ten and eleven the streets are thronged, but not at so early a period as that designated.

"There is another point at which there seems a deficiency of *observation* on the part of *Le Commerciel*. 'A piece,' it says, 'of one of the unfortunate girl's petticoats, two feet long, and one foot wide, was torn out and tied under her chin, and around the back of her head, probably to prevent screams. This was done, by fellows who had no pocket-handkerchiefs.' Whether this idea is, or is not well founded, we will endeavor to see hereafter; but by 'fellows who have no pocket-handkerchiefs' the editor intends the lowest class of ruffians. These, however, are the very description of people who will always be found to have handkerchiefs even when destitute of shirts. You must have had occasion to observe how absolutely indispensable, of late years, to the thorough blackguard, has become the pocket-handkerchief."

"And what are we to think," I asked, "of the article in *Le Soleil*?"

"That it is a vast pity its inditer was not born a parrot—in which case he would have been the most illustrious parrot of his race. He has merely repeated the individual items of the already published opinion; collecting them, with a laudable industry, from this paper and from that. 'The things had all *evidently* been there,' he says, 'at least, three or four weeks, and there can be *no doubt* that the spot of this appalling outrage has been discovered.' The facts here re-stated by *Le Soleil*, are very far indeed from removing my own doubts upon this subject, and we will examine them more particularly hereafter in connexion with another division of the theme.

"At present we must occupy ourselves with other investigations You cannot fail to have remarked the extreme laxity of the examination of the corpse. To be sure, the question of identity was readily determined, or should have been; but there were other points to be ascertained. Had the body been in any respect *despoiled*? Had the deceased any articles of jewelry about her person upon leaving home? if so, had she any when found? These are important questions utterly untouched by the evidence; and there are others of equal moment, which have met with no attention. We must endeavor to satisfy ourselves by personal inquiry. The case of St. Eustache must be re-examined. I have no suspicion of this person; but let us proceed methodically. We will ascertain beyond a doubt the validity of the *affidavits* in regard to his whereabouts on the Sunday. Affidavits of this character are readily made matter of mystification. Should there be nothing wrong here, however, we will dismiss St. Eustache from our investigations. His suicide, however corroborative of suspicion, were there found to be deceit in the affidavits, is, without such deceit, in no respect an unaccountable circumstance, or one which need cause us to deflect from the line of ordinary analysis.

"In that which I now propose, we will discard the interior points of this tragedy, and concentrate our attention upon its outskirts. Not the least usual error, in investigations such as this, is the limiting of inquiry to the immediate, with total disregard of the collateral or circumstantial events. It is the mal-practice of the courts to confine evidence and discussion to the bounds of apparent relevancy. Yet experience has shown, and a true philosophy will always show, that a vast, perhaps the larger portion of truth, arises from the seemingly irrelevant. It is through the spirit of this principle, if not precisely through its letter, that modern science has resolved to *calculate upon the unforeseen*. But perhaps you do not comprehend me. The history of human knowledge has so uninterruptedly shown that to collateral, or incidental, or accidental events we are indebted for the most numerous and most valuable discoveries, that it has at length become necessary, in any prospective view of improvement, to make not only large, but the largest allowances for inventions that shall arise by chance, and quite out of the range of ordinary expectation. It is no longer philosophical to base, upon what has been, a vision of what is to be. *Accident* is admitted as a portion of the substructure. We make chance a matter of absolute calculation. We subject the unlooked for and unimagined, to the mathematical *formulae* of the schools.

"I repeat that it is no more than fact, that the *larger* portion of all truth has sprung from the collateral; and it is but in accordance with the spirit of the principle involved in this fact, that I would divert inquiry, in the present case, from the trodden and hitherto unfruitful ground of the event itself, to the contemporary circumstances which surround it. While you ascertain the validity of the affidavits, I will examine the newspapers more generally than you have as yet done. So far, we have only reconnoitred the field of investigation; but it will be strange indeed if a comprehensive survey, such as I propose, of the public prints, will not afford us some minute points which shall establish a *direction* for inquiry."

In pursuance of Dupin's suggestion, I made scrupulous examination of the affair of the affidavits. The result was a firm conviction of their validity, and of the consequent innocence of St. Eustache. In the meantime my friend occupied himself, with what seemed to me a minuteness altogether objectless, in a scrutiny of the various newspaper files. At the end of a week he placed before me the following extracts:

"About three years and a half ago, a disturbance very similar to the present, was caused by the disappearance of this same Marie Rogêt, from the *parfumerie* of Monsieur Le Blanc, in the Palais Royal. At the end of a week, however, she re-appeared at her customary *comptoir*, as well as ever, with the exception of a slight paleness not altogether usual. It was given out by Monsieur Le Blanc and her mother, that she had merely been on a visit to some friend in the country; and the affair was speedily hushed up. We presume that the present absence is a freak of the same nature, and that, at the expiration of a week, or perhaps of a month, we shall have her among us again."—*Evening Paper*, Monday June 23.[17]

"An evening journal of yesterday, refers to a former mysterious disappearance of Mademoiselle Rogêt. It is well known that, during the week of her absence from Le Blanc's *parfumerie*, she was in the company of a young naval officer, much noted for his debaucheries. A quarrel, it is supposed, providentially led to her return home.

We have the name of the Lothario in question, who is, at present, stationed in Paris, but, for obvious reasons, forbear to make it public."—*Le Mercurie*, Tuesday Morning, June 24.[18]

"An outrage of the most atrocious character was perpetrated near this city the day before yesterday. A gentleman, with his wife and daughter, engaged, about dusk, the services of six young men, who were idly rowing a boat to and fro near the banks of the Seine, to convey him across the river. Upon reaching the opposite shore, the three passengers stepped out, and had proceeded so far as to be beyond the view of the boat, when the daughter discovered that she had left in it her parasol. She returned for it, was seized by the *gang*, carried out into the stream, gagged, brutally treated, and finally taken to the shore at a point not far from that at which she had originally entered the boat with her parents. The villains have escaped for the time, but the police are upon their trail, and some of them will soon be taken."—*Morning Paper*, June 25.[19]

"We have received one or two communications, the object of which is to fasten the crime of the late atrocity upon Mennais;[20] but as this gentleman has been fully exonerated by a loyal inquiry, and as the arguments of our several correspondents appear to be more zealous than profound, we do not think it advisable to make them public."—*Morning Paper*, June 28.[21]

"We have received several forcibly written communications, apparently from various sources, and which go far to render it a matter of certainty that the unfortunate Marie Rogêt has become a victim of one of the numerous bands of blackguards which infest the vicinity of the city upon Sunday. Our own opinion is decidedly in favor of this supposition. We shall endeavor to make room for some of these arguments hereafter."—*Evening Paper*, Tuesday, June 31.[22]

"On Monday, one of the bargemen connected with the revenue service, saw a empty boat floating down the Seine. Sails were lying in the bottom of the boat. The bargeman towed it under the barge office. The next morning it was taken from thence, without the knowledge of any of the officers. The rudder is now at the barge office."—*Le Diligence*, Thursday, June 26.

Upon reading these various extracts, they not only seemed to me irrelevant, but I could perceive no mode in which any one of them could be brought to bear upon the matter in hand. I waited for some explanation from Dupin.

"It is not my present design," he said, "to *dwell* upon the first and second of those extracts. I have copied them chiefly to show you the extreme remissness of the police, who, as far as I can understand from the Prefect, have not troubled themselves, in any respect, with an examination of the naval officer alluded to. Yet it is mere folly to say that between the first and second disappearance of Marie, there is no *supposable* connection. Let us admit the first elopement to have resulted in a quarrel between the lovers, and the return home of the betrayed. We are now prepared to view a second *elopement* (if we *know* that an elopement has again taken place) as indicating a renewal of the betrayer's advances, rather than as the result of new proposals by a second individual—we are prepared to regard it as a 'making up' of the old *amour*, rather than as the commencement of a new one. The chances are ten to one, that he who had once eloped with Marie, would again propose an elopement, rather than that she to whom proposals of elopement had been made by one individual, should have them made to her by another. And here let me call your attention to the fact, that the time elapsing between the first ascertained, and the second supposed elopement, is a few months more than the general period of the cruises of our men-of-war. Had the lover been interrupted in his first villany by the necessity of departure to sea, and had he seized the first moment of his return to renew the base designs not yet altogether accomplished—or not yet altogether accomplished by *him?* Of all these things we know nothing.

"You will say, however, that, in the second instance, there was *no* elopement as imagined. Certainly not—but are we prepared to say that there was not the frustrated design? Beyond St. Eustache, and perhaps Beauvais, we find no recognized, no open, no honorable suitors of Marie. Of none other is there any thing said. Who, then, is the secret lover, of whom the relatives (*at least most of them*) know nothing, but whom Marie meets upon the morning of Sunday, and who is so deeply in her confidence, that she hesitates not to remain with him until the shades of the evening descend, amid the solitary groves of the Barrière du Roule? Who is that secret lover, I ask, of whom, at least, most of the relatives know nothing? And what means the singular prophecy of Madame Rogêt on the morning of Marie's departure?—'I fear that I shall never see Marie again.'

"But if we cannot imagine Madame Rogêt privy to the design of elopement, may we not at least suppose this design entertained by the girl? Upon quitting home, she gave it to be understood that she was about to visit her aunt in the Rue des Drômes and St. Eustache was requested to call for her at dark. Now, at first glance, this fact strongly militates against my suggestion;—but let us reflect. That she *did* meet some companion, and proceed with him across the river, reaching the Barrière du Roule at so late an hour as three o'clock in the afternoon, is known. But in consenting so to accompany this individual (*for whatever purpose—to her mother known or unknown*), she must have thought of her expressed intention when leaving home, and of the surprise and suspicion aroused in the bosom of her affianced suitor, St. Eustache, when, calling for her, at the hour appointed, in the Rue des Drômes, he should find that she had not been there, and when, moreover, upon returning to the *pension* with this alarming intelligence, he should become aware of her continued absence from home. She must have thought of these things, I say. She must have foreseen the chagrin of St. Eustache, the suspicion of all. She could not have thought of returning to brave this suspicion; but the suspicion becomes a point of trivial importance to her, if we suppose her *not* intending to return.

"We may imagine her thinking thus—'I am to meet a certain person for the purpose of elopement, or for certain other purposes known only to myself. It is necessary that there be no chance of interruption—there must be sufficient time given us to elude pursuit—I will give it to be understood that I shall visit and spend the day with my aunt at the Rue des Drômes—I well tell St. Eustache not to call for me until dark—in this way, my absence from home for the longest possible period, without causing suspicion or anxiety, will be accounted for, and I shall gain more time than in any other manner. If I bid St. Eustache call for me at dark, he will be sure not to call before; but, if I wholly neglect to bid him call, my time for escape will be diminished, since it will be expected that I return the earlier, and my absence will the sooner excite anxiety. Now, if it were my design to return *at all*—if I had in contemplation merely a stroll with the individual in question—it would not be my policy to bid St. Eustache call; for, calling, he will be *sure* to ascertain that I have played him false—a fact of which I might keep him for ever in ignorance, by leaving home without notifying him of my intention, by returning before dark, and by then stating that I had been to visit my aunt in the Rue des Drômes. But, as it is my design never to return—or not for some weeks—or not until certain concealments are effected—the gaining of time is the only point about which I need give myself any concern.'

"You have observed, in your notes, that the most general opinion in relation to this sad affair is, and was from the first, that the girl had been the victim of a *gang* of blackguards. Now, the popular opinion, under certain conditions, is not to be disregarded. When arising of itself—when manifesting itself in a strictly spontaneous manner—we should look upon it as analogous with that *intuition* which is the idiosyncrasy of the individual man of genius. In ninety-nine cases from the hundred I would abide by its decision. But it is important that we find no palpable traces of *suggestion*. The opinion must be rigorously *the public's own*; and the distinction is often exceedingly difficult to perceive and to maintain. In the present instance, it appears to me that this 'public opinion' in respect to a *gang*, has been superinduced by the collateral event which is detailed in the third of my extracts. All Paris is excited by the discovered corpse of Marie, a girl young, beautiful and notorious. This corpse is found, bearing marks of violence, and floating in the river. But it is now made known that, at the very period, or about the very period, in which it is supposed that the girl was assassinated, an outrage similar in nature to that endured by the deceased, although less in extent, was perpetuated, by a *gang* of young ruffians, upon the person of a second young female. Is it wonderful that the one known atrocity should influence the popular judgment in regard to the other unknown? This judgment awaited direction, and the known outrage seemed so opportunely to afford it! Marie, too, was found in the river; and upon this very river was this known outrage committed. The connexion of the two events had about it so much of the palpable, that the true wonder would have been a *failure* of the populace to appreciate and to seize it. But, in fact, the one atrocity, known to be so committed, is, if any thing, evidence that the other, committed at a time nearly coincident, was not so committed. It would have been a miracle indeed, if, while a *gang* of ruffians were perpetrating, at a given locality, a most unheard-of wrong, there should have been another similar *gang*, in a similar locality, in the same city, under the same circumstances, with the same means and appliances, engaged in a wrong of precisely the same aspect, at precisely the same period of time! Yet in what, if not in this marvellous train of coincidence, does the accidentally *suggested* opinion of the populace call upon us to believe?

"Before proceeding farther, let us consider the supposed scene of the assassination, in the thicket at the Barrière du Roule. This thicket, although dense, was in the close vicinity of a public road. Within were three or four large stones, forming a kind of seat with a back and footstool. On the upper stone was discovered a white petticoat; on the second, a silk scarf. A parasol, gloves, and a pocket-handkerchief, were also here found. The handkerchief bore the name, 'Marie Rogêt.' Fragments of dress were seen on the branches around. The earth was trampled, the bushes were broken, and there was every evidence of a violent struggle.

"Notwithstanding the acclamation with which the discovery of this thicket was received by the press, and the unanimity with which it was supposed to indicate the precise scene of the outrage, it must be admitted that there was some very good reason for doubt. That it *was* the scene, I may or I may not believe—but there was excellent reason for doubt. Had the *true* scene been, as *Le Commerciel* suggested, in the neighborhood of the Rue Pavée St. Andrée, the perpetrators of the crime, supposing them still resident in Paris, would *naturally* have been stricken with terror at the public attention thus acutely directed into the proper channel; and, in certain classes of minds, there would have arisen, at once, a sense of the necessity of some exertion to redivert this attention. And thus, the thicket of the Barrière du Roule having been already suspected, the idea of placing the articles where they were found, might have been *naturally* entertained. There is no real evidence, although *Le Soleil* so supposes, that the articles discovered had been more than a very few days in the thicket; while there is much circumstantial proof that they could not have remained there, without attracting attention, during the twenty days elapsing between the fatal Sunday and the afternoon upon which they were found by the boys. 'They were all *mildewed* down hard,' says *Le Soleil*, adopting the opinions of its predecessors, 'with the action of the rain, and stuck together from *mildew*. The grass had grown around and over some of them. The silk of the parasol was strong, but the threads of it were run together within. The upper part, where it bad been doubled and folded, was all *mildewed* and rotten, and tore on being opened.' In respect to the grass having 'grown around and over some of them,' it is obvious that the fact could only have been ascertained from the words, and thus from the recollections, of two small boys; for these boys removed the articles and took them home before they had been seen by a third party. But grass will grow, especially in warm and damp weather (such as was that of the period of the murder), as much as two or three inches in a single day. A parasol lying upon a newly turfed ground, might, in a single week, be entirely concealed from sight by the upspringing grass. And touching that *mildew* upon which the editor of *Le Soleil* so pertinaciously insists, that he employs the word no less than three times in the brief paragraph just quoted, is he really unaware of the nature of this *mildew*? Is he to be told that it is one of the many classes of fungus, of which the most ordinary feature is its upspringing and decadence within twenty-four hours?

"Thus we see, at a glance, that what has been most triumphantly adduced in support of the idea that the articles bad been 'for at least three or four weeks' in the thicket, is most absurdly null as regards any evidence of that fact. On the other hand, it is exceedingly difficult to believe that these articles could have remained in the thicket specified, for a longer period than a single week—for a longer period than from one Sunday to the next. Those who know any thing of the vicinity of Paris, know the extreme difficulty of finding *seclusion* unless at a great distance from its suburbs. Such a thing as an unexplored, or even an unfrequently visited recess, amid its woods or groves, is not for a moment to be imagined. Let any one who, being at heart a lover of nature, is yet chained by duty to the dust and heat of this great metropolis—let any such one attempt, even during the weekdays, to slake his thirst for solitude amid the scenes of natural loveliness which immediately surround us. At every second step, he will find the growing charm dispelled by the voice and personal intrusion of some ruffian or party of carousing blackguards. He will seek privacy amid the densest foliage, all in vain. Here are the very nooks where the unwashed most abound—here are the temples most desecrate. With sickness of the heart the wanderer will flee back to the polluted Paris as to a less odious because less incongruous sink of pollution. But if the vicinity of the city is so beset during the working days of the week, how much more so on the Sabbath! It is now especially that, released from the claims of labor, or deprived of the customary opportunities of crime, the town blackguard seeks the precincts of the town, not through love of the rural, which in his heart he despises, but by way of escape from the restraints and conventionalities of society. He desires less the fresh air and the green trees, than the utter *licence* of the country. Here, at the road-side inn, or beneath the foliage of the woods, he indulges, unchecked by any eye except those of his boon companions, in all the mad excess of a counterfeit hilarity—the joint offspring of liberty and of rum. I say nothing more than what must be obvious to every dispassionate observer, when I repeat that the circumstance of the articles in question having remained undiscovered, for a longer period—than from one Sunday to another, in *any* thicket in the immediate neighborhood of Paris, is to be looked upon as little less than miraculous.

"But there are not wanting other grounds for the suspicion that the articles were placed in the thicket with the view of diverting attention from the real scene of the outrage. And, first, let me direct your notice to the *date* of the discovery of the articles. Collate this with the date of the fifth extract made by myself from the newspapers. You will find that the discovery followed, almost immediately, the urgent communications sent to the evening paper. These communications, although various and apparently from various sources, tended all to the same point—viz., the directing of attention to a *gang* as the perpetrators of the outrage, and to the neighborhood of thc Barrière du Roule as its scene. Now here, of course, the suspicion is not that, in consequence of these communications, or of the public attention by them directed, the articles were found by the boys; but the suspicion might and may well have been, that the articles were not *before* found by the boys, for the reason that the articles had not before been in the thicket; having been deposited there only at so late a period as at the date, or shortly prior to the date of the communications by the guilty authors of these communications themselves.

"This thicket was a singular—an exceedingly singular one. It was unusually dense. Within its *naturally* walled enclosure were three extraordinary stones, *forming a seat with a back and footstool.* And this thicket, so full of a natural art, was in the immediate vicinity, *within a few rods*, of the dwelling of Madame Deluc, whose boys were in the habit of closely examining the shrubberies about them in search of the bark of the sassafras. Would it be a rash wager—a wager of one thousand to one—that *a day* never passed over the heads of these boys without finding at least one of them ensconced in the umbrageous hall, and enthroned upon its natural throne? Those who would hesitate at such a wager, have either never been boys themselves, or have forgotten the boyish nature. I repeat—it is exceedingly hard to comprehend how the articles could have remained in this thicket undiscovered, for a longer period than one or two days; and that thus there is good ground for suspicion, in spite of the dogmatic ignorance of *Le Soleil*, that they were, at a comparatively late date, deposited where found.

"But there are still other and stronger reasons for believing them so deposited, than any which I have as yet urged. And, now, let me beg your notice to the highly artificial arrangement of the articles. On the *upper* stone lay a white petticoat; on the *second* a silk scarf; scattered around, were a parasol, gloves, and a pocket-handkerchief bearing the name, 'Marie Rogêt.' Here is just such an arrangement as would *naturally* be made by a not over-acute person wishing to dispose the articles *naturally*. But it is by no means a *really* natural arrangement. I should rather have looked to see the things *all* lying on the ground and trampled under foot. In the narrow limits of that bower, it would have been scarcely possible that the petticoat and scarf should have retained a position upon the stones, when subjected to the brushing to and fro of many struggling persons. 'There was evidence,' it is said, 'of a struggle; and the earth was trampled, the bushes were broken,' but the petticoat and the scarf are found deposited as if upon shelves. 'The pieces of the frock torn out by the bushes were about three inches wide and six inches long. One part was the hem of the frock and it had been mended. They *looked like strips torn off*.' Here, inadvertently, *Le Soleil* has employed an exceedingly suspicious phrase. The pieces, as described, do indeed 'look like strips torn off'; but purposely and by hand. It is one of the rarest of accidents that a piece is 'torn off,' from any garment such as is now in question, by the agency of a *thorn*. From the very nature of such fabrics, a thorn or nail becoming entangled in them, tears them rectangularly—divides them into two longitudinal rents, at right angles with each other, and meeting at an apex where the thorn enters—but it is scarcely possible to conceive the piece 'torn off.' I never so knew it, nor did you. To tear a piece *off* from such fabric, two distinct forces, in different directions, will be, in almost every case, required. If there be two edges to the fabric—if, for example, it be a pocket-handkerchief, and it is desired to tear from it a slip, then, and then only, will the one force serve the purpose. But in the present case the question is of a dress, presenting but one edge. To tear a piece from the interior, where no edge is presented, could only be effected by a miracle through the agency of thorns, and no one thorn could accomplish it. But, even where an edge is presented, two thorns will be necessary, operating, the one in two distinct directions, and the other in one. And this in the supposition that the edge is unhemmed. If hemmed, the matter is nearly out of the question. We thus see the numerous and great obstacles in the way of pieces being 'torn off' through the simple agency of 'thorns'; yet we are required to believe not only that one piece but that many have been so torn. 'And one part,' too, '*was the hem of the frock!*' Another piece was '*part of the skirt, not the hem*,' that is to say, was torn completely out through the agency of thorns, from the uncaged interior of the dress! These, I say, are things which one may well be pardoned for disbelieving; yet, taken collectedly, they form, perhaps, less of reasonable ground for suspicion, than the one startling circumstance of the articles' having been left in this thicket at all, by any *murderers* who had enough precaution to think of removing the corpse. You will not have apprehended me rightly, however, if you suppose it my design to *deny* this thicket as the scene of the outrage. There might have been a wrong *here*, or, more possibly, an accident at Madame Deluc's. But, in fact, this is a point of minor importance. We are not engaged in an attempt to discover the scene, but to produce the perpetrators of the murder. What I have adduced, notwithstanding the minuteness with which

I have adduced it, has been with the view, first, to show the folly of the positive and headlong assertions of *Le Soleil*, but secondly and chiefly, to bring you, by the most natural route, to a further contemplation of the doubt whether this assassination has, or has not been, the work of a *gang*.

"We will resume this question by mere allusion to the revolting details of the surgeon examined at the inquest. It is only necessary to say that is published *inferences*, in regard to the number of ruffians, have been properly ridiculed as unjust and totally baseless, by all the reputable anatomists of Paris. Not that the matter might not have been as inferred, but that there was no ground for the inference:—was there not much for another?

"Let us reflect now upon 'the traces of a struggle'; and let me ask what these traces have been supposed to demonstrate. A *gang*. But do they not rather demonstrate the absence of a *gang*? What *struggle* could have taken place—what struggle so violent and so enduring as to have left its 'traces' in all directions—between a weak and defenceless girl and the *gang* of ruffians imagined? The silent grasp of a few rough arms and all would have been over. The victim must have been absolutely passive at their will. You will here bear in mind that the arguments urged against the thicket as the scene, are applicable in chief part, only against it as the scene of an outrage committed by *more than a single individual*. If we imagine but one violator, we can conceive, and thus only conceive, the struggle of so violent and so obstinate a nature as to have left the 'traces' apparent.

"And again. I have already mentioned the suspicion to be excited by the fact that the articles in question were suffered to remain *at all* in the thicket where discovered. It seems almost impossible that these evidences of guilt should have been accidentally left where found. There was sufficient presence of mind (it is supposed) to remove the corpse; and yet a more positive evidence than the corpse itself (whose features might have been quickly obliterated by decay), is allowed to lie conspicuously in the scene of the outrage—I allude to the handkerchief with the *name* of the deceased. If this was accident, it was not the accident of a *gang*. We can imagine it only the accident of an individual. Let us see. An individual has committed the murder. He is alone with the ghost of the departed. He is appalled by what lies motionless before him. The fury of his passion is over, and there is abundant room in his heart for the natural awe of the deed. His is none of that confidence which the presence of numbers inevitably inspires. He is *alone* with the dead. He trembles and is bewildered. Yet there is a necessity for disposing of the corpse. He bears it to the river, but leaves behind him the other evidences of guilt; for it is difficult, if not impossible to carry all the burthen at once, and it will be easy to return for what is left. But in his toilsome journey to the water his fears redouble within him. The sounds of life encompass his path. A dozen times he hears or fancies the step of an observer. Even the very lights from the city bewilder him. Yet, in time and by long and frequent pauses of deep agony, he reaches the river's brink, and disposes of his ghastly charge—perhaps through the medium of a boat. But now what treasure does the world hold—what threat of vengeance could it hold out—which would have power to urge the return of that lonely murderer over that toilsome and perilous path, to the thicket and its blood chilling recollections? He returns *not*, let the consequences be what they may. He *could* not return if he would. His sole thought is immediate escape. He turns his back *forever* upon those dreadful shrubberies and flees as from the wrath to come.

"But how with a gang? Their number would have inspired them with confidence; if, indeed confidence is ever wanting in the breast of the arrant blackguard; and of arrant blackguards alone are the supposed *gang*s ever constituted. Their number, I say, would have prevented the bewildering and unreasoning terror which I have imagined to paralyze the single man. Could we suppose an oversight in one, or two, or three, this oversight would have been remedied by a fourth. They would have left nothing behind them; for their number would have enabled them to carry *all* at once. There would have been no need of *return.*

"Consider now the circumstance that in the outer garment of the corpse when found, 'a slip, about a foot wide had been torn upward from the bottom hem to the waist wound three times round the waist, and secured by a sort of hitch in the back.' This was done with the obvious design of affording a *handle* by which to carry the body. But would any *number* of men have dreamed of resorting to such an expedient? To three or four, the limbs of the corpse would have afforded not only a sufficient, but the best possible hold. The device is that of a single individual; and this brings us to the fact that 'between the thicket and the river, the rails of the fences were found taken down, and the ground bore evident traces of some heavy burden having been dragged along it!' But would a *number* of men have put themselves to the superfluous trouble of taking down a fence, for the purpose of dragging through it a corpse which they might have lifted over any fence in an instant? Would a *number* of men have so *dragged* a corpse at all as to have left evident *traces* of the dragging?

"And here we must refer to an observation of *Le Commerciel*; an observation upon which I have already, in some measure, commented. 'A piece,' says this journal, 'of one of the unfortunate girl's petticoats was torn out and tied under her chin, and around the back of her head, probably to prevent screams. This was done by fellows who had no pocket-handkerchiefs.'

"I have before suggested that a genuine blackguard is never *without* a pocket-handkerchief. But it is not to this fact that I now especially advert. That it was not through want of a handkerchief for the purpose imagined by *Le Commerciel*, that this bandage was employed, is rendered apparent by the handkerchief left in the thicket; and that the object was not 'to prevent screams' appears, also, from the bandage having been employed in preference to what would so much better have answered the purpose. But the language of the evidence speaks of the strip in question as 'found around the neck, fitting loosely, and secured with a hard knot.' These words are sufficiently vague, but differ materially from those of *Le Commerciel*. The slip was eighteen inches wide, and therefore, although of muslin, would form a strong band when folded or rumpled longitudinally. And thus rumpled it was discovered. My inference is this. The solitary murderer, having borne the corpse, for some distance (whether from the thicket or elsewhere) by means of the bandage *hitched* around its middle, found the weight, in this mode of procedure, too much for his strength. He resolved to drag the burthen—the evidence goes to show that it was dragged. With this object in view, it became necessary to attach something like a rope to one of the extremities. It could be best attached about the neck, where the head would prevent its slipping off. And, now, the murderer bethought him, unquestionably, of the bandage about the loins. He would have used this, but for its volution about the corpse, the *hitch* which embarrassed it, and the reflection that it had not been 'torn off' from the garment. It was easier to tear a new slip from the petticoat. He tore it, made it fast about the neck, and so *dragged* his victim to the brink of the river. That this 'bandage,' only attainable with trouble and delay, and but imperfectly answering its purpose—that this bandage was employed *at all*, demonstrates that the necessity for its employment sprang from circumstances arising at a period when the handkerchief was no longer attainable—that is to say, arising, as we have imagined, after quitting the thicket (if the thicket it was), and on the road between the thicket and the river.

"But the evidence, you will say, of Madame Deluc (!) points especially to the presence of a *gang*, in the vicinity of the thicket, at or about the epoch of the murder. This I grant. I doubt if there were not a *dozen* gangs, such as described by Madame Deluc, in and about the vicinity of the Barrière du Roule at or *about* the period of this tragedy. But the *gang* which has drawn upon itself the pointed animadversion, although the somewhat tardy and very suspicious evidence of Madame Deluc, is the *only* gang which is represented by that honest and scrupulous old lady as having eaten her cakes and swallowed her brandy, without putting themselves to the trouble of making her payment. *Et hinc illae irae*?

"But what *is* the precise evidence of Madame Deluc? 'A gang of miscreants made their appearance, behaved boisterously, ate and drank without making payment, followed in the route of the young man and girl, returned to the inn *about dusk*, and recrossed the river as if in great haste.'

"Now this 'great haste' very possibly seemed *greater* haste in the eyes of Madame Deluc, since she dwelt lingeringly and lamentingly upon her violated cakes and ale—cakes and ale for which she might still have entertained a faint hope of compensation. Why, otherwise, since it was *about dusk*, should she make a point of the *haste*? It is no cause for wonder, surely, that even a gang of blackguards should make *haste* to get home, when a wide river is to be crossed in small boats, when storm impends, and when night *approaches*.

"I say *approaches*; for the night had *not yet arrived*. It was only *about dusk* that the indecent haste of these 'miscreants' offended the sober eyes of Madame Deluc. But we are told that it was upon this very evening that Madame Deluc, as well as her eldest son, 'heard the screams of a female in the vicinity of the inn.' And in what words does Madame Deluc designate the period of the evening at which these screams were heard? 'It was *soon after dark*,' she says. But 'soon *after* dark,' is, at least, *dark*; and '*about dusk*' is as certainly daylight. Thus it is abundantly clear that the *gang* quitted the Barrière du Roule *prior* to the screams overheard (?) by Madame Deluc. And although, in all the many reports of the evidence, the relative expressions in question are distinctly and invariably employed just as I have employed them in this conversation with yourself, no notice whatever of the gross discrepancy has, as yet, been taken by any of the public journals, or by any of the Myrmidons of police.

"I shall add but one to the arguments against a *gang*; but this *one* has, to my own understanding at least, a weight altogether irresistible. Under the circumstances of large reward offered, and full pardon to any King's evidence, it is not to be imagined, for a moment, that some member of a *gang* of low ruffians, or of any body of men, would not long ago have betrayed his accomplices. Each one of a *gang* so placed, is not so much greedy of reward, or anxious for escape, as *fearful of betrayal*. He betrays eagerly and early that *he may not himself be betrayed*. That the secret has not been divulged, is the very best of proof that it is, in fact, a secret. The horrors of this dark deed are known only to one, or two, living human beings, and to God.

"Let us sum up now the meagre yet certain fruits of our long analysis. We have attained the idea either of a fatal accident under the roof of Madame Deluc, or of a murder perpetrated, in the thicket at the Barrière du Roule, by a lover, or at least by an intimate and secret associate of the deceased. This associate is of swarthy complexion. This complexion, the 'hitch' in the bandage, and the 'sailor's knot,' with which the bonnet-ribbon is tied, point to a seaman. His companionship with the deceased, a gay, but not an abject young girl, designates him as above the grade of the common sailor. Here the well written and urgent communications to the journals are much in the way of corroboration. The circumstance of the first elopement, as mentioned by *Le Mercurie*, tends to blend the idea of this seaman with that of the 'naval officer' who is first known to have led the unfortunate into crime.

"And here, most fitly, comes the consideration of the continued absence of him of the dark complexion. Let me pause to observe that the complexion of this man is dark and swarthy; it was no common swarthiness which constituted the *sole* point of remembrance, both as regards Valence and Madame Deluc. But why is this man absent? Was he murdered by the gang? If so, why are there only *traces* of the assassinated *girl*? The scene of the two outrages will naturally be supposed identical. And where is his corpse? The assassins would most probably have disposed of both in the same way. But it may be said that this man lives, and is deterred from making himself known, through dread of being charged with the murder. This consideration might be supposed to operate upon him now—at this late period—since it has been given in evidence that he was seen with Marie—but it would have had no force at the period of the deed. The first impulse of an innocent man would have been to announce the outrage, and to aid in identifying the ruffians. This *policy* would have suggested. He had been seen with the girl. He had crossed the river with her in an open ferry-boat. The denouncing of the assassins would have appeared, even to an idiot, the surest and sole means of relieving himself from suspicion. We cannot suppose him, on the night of the fatal Sunday, both innocent himself and incognizant of an outrage committed. Yet only under such circumstances is it possible to imagine that he would have failed, if alive, in the denouncement of the assassins.

"And what means are ours, of attaining the truth? We shall find these means multiplying and gathering distinctness as we proceed. Let us sift to the bottom this affair of the first elopement. Let us know the full history of 'the officer,' with his present circumstances, and his whereabouts at the precise period of the murder. Let us carefully compare with each other the various communications sent to the evening paper, in which the object was to inculpate a *gang*. This done, let us compare these communications, both as regards style and MS., with those sent to the morning paper, at a previous period, and insisting so vehemently upon the guilt of Mennais. And, all this done, let us again compare these various communications with the known MSS. of the officer. Let us endeavor to ascertain, by repeated questionings of Madame Deluc and her boys, as well as of the omnibus driver, Valence, something more of the personal appearance and bearing of the 'man of dark complexion.' Queries, skilfully directed, will not fail to elicit, from some of these parties, information on this particular point (or upon others)—information which the parties themselves may not even be aware of possessing. And let us now trace *the boat* picked up by the bargeman on the morning of Monday the twenty-third of June, and which was removed from the barge-office, without the cognizance of the officer in attendance, and *without the rudder*, at some period prior to the discovery of the corpse. With a proper caution and perseverance we shall infallibly trace this boat; for not only can the bargeman who picked it up identify it, but the *rudder is at hand*. The rudder *of a sail-boat* would not have been abandoned, without inquiry, by one altogether at ease in heart. And here let me pause to insinuate a question. There was no *advertisement* of the picking up of this boat. It was silently taken to the barge-office, and as silently removed. But its owner or employer—how *happened* he, at so early a period as Tuesday morning, to be informed, without the agency of advertisement, of the locality of the boat taken up on Monday, unless we imagine some connexion with the *navy*—some personal permanent connexion leading to cognizance of its minute in interests—its petty local news?

"In speaking of the lonely assassin dragging his burden to the shore, I have already suggested the probability of his availing himself *of a boat*. Now we are to understand that Marie Rogêt *was* precipitated from *a boat*. This would naturally have been the case. The corpse could not have been trusted to the shallow waters of the shore. The peculiar marks on the back and shoulders of the victim tell of the bottom ribs of a boat. That the body was found without weight is also corroborative of the idea. If thrown from the shore a weight would have been attached. We can only account for its absence by supposing the murderer to have neglected the precaution of supplying himself with it before pushing off. In the act of consigning the corpse to the water, he would unquestionably have noticed his oversight; but then no remedy would have been at hand. Any risk would have been preferred to a return to that accursed shore. Having rid himself of his ghastly charge, the murderer would have hastened to the city. There, at some obscure wharf, he would have leaped on land. But the boat—would he have secured it?

He would have been in too great haste for such things as securing a boat. Moreover, in fastening it to the wharf, he would have felt as if securing evidence against himself. His natural thought would have been to cast from him, as far as possible, all that had held connection with his crime. He would not only have fled from the wharf, but he would not have permitted *the boat* to remain. Assuredly he would have cast it adrift. Let us pursue our fancies.—In the morning, the wretch is stricken with unutterable horror at finding that the boat has been picked up and detained at a locality which he is in the daily habit of frequenting—at a locality, perhaps, which his duty compels him to frequent. The next night, *without daring to ask for the rudder*, he removes it. Now *where* is that rudderless boat? Let it be one of our first purposes to discover. With the first glimpse we obtain of it, the dawn of our success shall begin. This boat shall guide us, with a rapidity which will surprise even ourselves, to him who employed it in the midnight of the fatal Sabbath. Corroboration will rise upon corroboration, and the murderer will be traced."

[For reasons which we shall not specify, but which to many readers will appear obvious, we have taken the liberty of here omitting, from the MSS. placed in our hands, such portion as details the following up of the apparently slight clew obtained by Dupin. We feel it advisable only to state, in brief, that the result desired was brought to pass; and that the Prefect fulfilled punctually, although with reluctance, the terms of his compact with the Chevalier. Mr. Poe's article concludes with the following words.—Eds.[23]]

It will be understood that I speak of coincidences *and no more*. What I have said above upon this topic must suffice. In my own heart there dwells no faith in preternature. That Nature and its God are two, no man who thinks, will deny. That the latter, creating the former, can, at will, control or modify it, is also unquestionable. I say "at will"; for the question is of will, and not, as the insanity of logic has assumed, of power. It is not that the Deity *cannot* modify his laws, but that we insult him in imagining a possible necessity for modification. In their origin these laws were fashioned to embrace all contingencies which *could* lie in the Future. With God all is *Now*.

I repeat, then, that I speak of these things only as of coincidences. And farther: in what I relate it will be seen that between the fate of the unhappy Mary Cecilia Rogers, so far as that fate is known, and the fate of one Marie Rogêt up to a certain epoch in her history, there has existed a parallel in the contemplation of whose wonderful exactitude the reason becomes embarrassed. I say all this will be seen. But let it not for a moment be supposed that, in proceeding with the sad narrative of Marie from the epoch just mentioned, and in tracing to its *dénouement* the mystery which enshrouded her, it is my covert design to hint at an extension of the parallel, or even to suggest that the measures adopted in Paris for the discovery of the assassin of a *grisette*, or measures founded in any similar ratiocination, would produce any similar result.

For, in respect to the latter branch of the supposition, it should be considered that the most trifling variation in the facts of the two cases might give rise to the most important miscalculations, by diverting thoroughly the two courses of events; very much as, in arithmetic, an error which, in its own individuality, may be inappreciable, produces, at length, by dint of multiplication at all points of the process, a result enormously at variance with truth. And, in regard to the former branch, we must not fail to hold in view that the very Calculus of Probabilities to which I have referred, forbids all idea of the extension of the parallel—forbids it with a positiveness strong and decided just in proportion as this parallel has already been long-drawn and exact. This is one of those anomalous propositions which, seemingly appealing to thought altogether apart from the mathematical, is yet one which only the mathematician can fully entertain. Nothing, for example, is more difficult than to convince the merely general reader that the fact of sixes having been thrown twice in succession by a player at dice, is sufficient cause for betting the largest odds that sixes will not be thrown in the third attempt. A suggestion to this effect is usually rejected by the intellect at once. It does not appear that the two throws which have been completed, and which lie now absolutely in the Past, can have influence upon the throw which exists only in the Future. The chance for throwing sixes seems to be precisely as it was at any ordinary time—that is to say, subject only to the influence of the various other throws which may be made by the dice. And this is a reflection which appears so exceedingly obvious that attempts to controvert it are received more frequently with a derisive smile than with anything like respectful attention. The error here involved—a gross error redolent of mischief—I cannot pretend to expose within the limits assigned me at present; and with the philosophical it needs no exposure. It may be sufficient here to say that it forms one of an infinite series of mistakes which arise in the path or Reason through her propensity for seeking truth *in detail*.

Notes

[1] Upon the original publication of "Marie Rogêt," the foot-notes now appended were considered unnecessary; but the lapse of several years since the tragedy upon which the tale is based, renders it expedient to give them, and also to say a few words in explanation of the general design. A young girl, Mary Cecilia Rogers, was murdered in the vicinity of New York; and, although her death occasioned an intense and long-enduring excitement, the mystery attending it had remained unsolved at the period when the present paper was written and published (November, 1842). Herein, under pretence of relating the fate of a Parisian *grisette*, the author has followed, in minute detail, the essential, while merely paralleling the inessential facts of the real murder of Mary Rogers. Thus all argument founded upon the fiction is applicable to the truth; and the investigation of the truth was the object.

The "Mystery of Marie Rogêt" was composed at a distance from the scene of the atrocity, and with no other means of investigation than the newspapers afforded. Thus much escaped the writer of which he could have availed himself had he been upon the spot, and visited the localities. It may not be improper to record, nevertheless, that the confessions of *two* persons (one of them the Madame Deluc of the narrative) made, at different periods, long subsequent to the publication, confirmed, in full, not only the general conclusion, but absolutely *all* the chief hypothetical details by which that conclusion was attained.

[2] The *nom de plume* of Von Hardenberg.

[3] Nassau Street.

[4] Anderson.

[5] The Hudson.

[6] Weehawken.

[7] Payne.

[8] Crommelin.

[9] The New York *Mercury*.

[10] The New York *Brother Jonathan*, edited by H. Hastings Weld, Esq.

[11] New York *Journal of Commerce*.

[12] Philadelphia *Saturday Evening Post*, edited by C. I. Peterson, Esq.

[13] Adam.

[14] See "Murders in the Rue Morgue."

[15] The New York *Commercial Advertiser*, edited by Col. Stone.

[16] "A theory based on the qualities of an object, will prevent its being unfolded according to its objects; and he who arranges topics in reference to their causes, will cease to value them according to their results. Thus the jurisprudence of every nation will show that, when law becomes a science and a system, it ceases to be justice. The errors into which a blind devotion to *principles* of classification has led the common law, will be seen by observing how often the legislature has been obliged to come forward to restore the equity its scheme had lost."—Landor.

[17] New York *Express*.

[18] New York *Herald*.

[19] New York *Courier* and *Inquirer*.

[20] Mennais was one of the parties originally suspected and arrested, but discharged through total lack of evidence.

[21] New York *Courier* and *Inquirer*.

[22] New York *Evening Post*.

[23] Of the Magazine in which the article was originally published.

The Masque of the Red Death

The "Red Death" had long devastated the country. No pestilence had ever been so fatal, or so hideous. Blood was its Avatar and its seal—the redness and the horror of blood. There were sharp pains, and sudden dizziness, and then profuse bleeding at the pores, with dissolution. The scarlet stains upon the body and especially upon the face of the victim, were the pest ban which shut him out from the aid and from the sympathy of his fellow-men. And the whole seizure, progress and termination of the disease, were the incidents of half an hour.

But the Prince Prospero was happy and dauntless and sagacious. When his dominions were half depopulated, he summoned to his presence a thousand hale and light-hearted friends from among the knights and dames of his court, and with these retired to the deep seclusion of one of his castellated abbeys. This was an extensive and magnificent structure, the creation of the prince's own eccentric yet august taste. A strong and lofty wall girdled it in. This wall had gates of iron. The courtiers, having entered, brought furnaces and massy hammers and welded the bolts. They resolved to leave means neither of ingress or egress to the sudden impulses of despair or of frenzy from within. The abbey was amply provisioned. With such precautions the courtiers might bid defiance to contagion. The external world could take care of itself. In the meantime it was folly to grieve, or to think. The prince had provided all the appliances of pleasure. There were buffoons, there were improvisatori, there were ballet-dancers, there were musicians, there was Beauty, there was wine. All these and security were within. Without was the "Red Death."

It was toward the close of the fifth or sixth month of his seclusion, and while the pestilence raged most furiously abroad, that the Prince Prospero entertained his thousand friends at a masked ball of the most unusual magnificence.

It was a voluptuous scene, that masquerade. But first let me tell of the rooms in which it was held. There were seven—an imperial suite. In many palaces, however, such suites form a long and straight vista, while the folding doors slide back nearly to the walls on either hand, so that the view of the whole extent is scarcely impeded. Here the case was very different; as might have been expected from the duke's love of the bizarre. The apartments were so irregularly disposed that the vision embraced but little more than one at a time. There was a sharp turn at every twenty or thirty yards, and at each turn a novel effect. To the right and left, in the middle of each wall, a tall and narrow Gothic window looked out upon a closed corridor which pursued the windings of the suite. These windows were of stained glass whose color varied in accordance with the prevailing hue of the decorations of the chamber into which it opened. That at the eastern extremity was hung, for example, in blue—and vividly blue were its windows. The second chamber was purple in its ornaments and tapestries, and here the panes were purple. The third was green throughout, and so were the casements. The fourth was furnished and lighted with orange—the fifth with white—the sixth with violet. The seventh apartment was closely shrouded in black velvet tapestries that hung all over the ceiling and down the walls, falling in heavy folds upon a carpet of the same material and hue. But in this chamber only, the color of the windows failed to correspond with the decorations. The panes here were scarlet—a deep blood color. Now in no one of the seven apartments was there any lamp or candelabrum, amid the profusion of golden ornaments that lay scattered to and fro or depended from the roof. There was no light of any kind emanating from lamp or candle within the suite of chambers. But in the corridors that followed the suite, there stood, opposite to each window, a heavy tripod, bearing a brazier of fire that protected its rays through the tinted glass and so glaringly illumined the room. And thus were produced a multitude of gaudy and fantastic appearances. But in the western or black chamber the effect of the fire-light that streamed upon the dark hangings through the blood-tinted panes, was ghastly in the extreme, and produced so wild a look upon the countenances of those who entered, that there were few of the company bold enough to set foot within its precincts at all.

It was in this apartment, also, that there stood against the western wall, a gigantic clock of ebony. Its pendulum swung to and fro with a dull, heavy, monotonous clang; and when the minute-hand made the circuit of the face, and the hour was to be stricken, there came from the brazen lungs of the clock a sound which was clear and loud and deep and exceedingly musical, but of so peculiar a note and emphasis that, at each lapse of an hour, the musicians of the orchestra were constrained to pause, momentarily, in their performance, to hearken to the sound; and thus the waltzers perforce ceased their evolutions; and there was a brief disconcert of the whole gay company; and, while the chimes of the clock yet rang, it was observed that the giddiest grew pale, and the more aged and sedate passed their hands over their brows as if in confused reverie or meditation. But when the echoes had fully ceased, a light laughter at once pervaded the assembly; the musicians looked at each other and smiled as if at their own nervousness and folly, and made whispering vows, each to the other, that the next chiming of the clock should produce in them no similar emotion; and then, after the lapse of sixty minutes (which embrace three thousand and six hundred seconds of the Time that flies), there came yet another chiming of the clock, and then were the same disconcert and tremulousness and meditation as before.

But, in spite of these things, it was a gay and magnificent revel. The tastes of the duke were peculiar. He had a fine eye for colors and effects. He disregarded the *decora* of mere fashion. His plans were bold and fiery, and his conceptions glowed with barbaric lustre. There are some who would have thought him mad. His followers felt that he was not. It was necessary to hear and see and touch him to be sure that he was not.

He had directed, in great part, the moveable embellishments of the seven chambers, upon occasion of this great *fête*; and it was his own guiding taste which had given character to the masqueraders. Be sure they were grotesque. There were much glare and glitter and piquancy and phantasm—much of what has been since seen in *Hernani*. There were arabesque figures with unsuited limbs and appointments. There were delirious fancies such as the madman fashions. There was much of the beautiful, much of the wanton, much of the bizarre, something of the terrible, and not a little of that which might have excited disgust. To and fro in the seven chambers there stalked, in fact, a multitude of dreams. And these—the dreams—writhed in and about, taking hue from the rooms, and causing the wild music of the orchestra to seem as the echo of their steps. And, anon, there strikes the ebony clock which stands in the hall of the velvet. And then, for a moment, all is still, and all is silent save the voice of the clock. The dreams are stiff-frozen as they stand. But the echoes of the chime die away—they have endured but an instant—and a light, half-subdued laughter floats after them as they depart. And now again the music swells, and the dreams live, and writhe to and fro more merrily than ever, taking hue from the many-tinted windows through which stream the rays from the tripods. But to the chamber which lies most westwardly of the seven, there are now none of the maskers who venture; for the night is waning away; and there flows a ruddier light through the blood-colored panes; and the blackness of the sable drapery appals; and to him whose foot falls upon the sable carpet, there comes from the near clock of ebony a muffled peal more solemnly emphatic than any which reaches their ears who indulge in the more remote gaieties of the other apartments.

But these other apartments were densely crowded, and in them beat feverishly the heart of life. And the revel went whirlingly on, until at length there commenced the sounding of midnight upon the clock. And then the music ceased, as I have told; and the evolutions of the waltzers were quieted; and there was an uneasy cessation of all things as before. But now there were twelve strokes to be sounded by the bell of the clock; and thus it happened, perhaps, that more of thought crept, with more of time, into the meditations of the thoughtful among those who revelled. And thus, too, it happened, perhaps, that before the last echoes of the last chime had utterly sunk into silence, there were many individuals in the crowd who had found leisure to become aware of the presence of a masked figure which had arrested the attention of no single individual before. And the rumor of this new presence having spread itself whisperingly around, there arose at length from the whole company a buzz, or murmur, expressive of disapprobation and surprise—then, finally, of terror, of horror, and of disgust.

In an assembly of phantasms such as I have painted, it may well be supposed that no ordinary appearance could have excited such sensation. In truth the masquerade licence of the night was nearly unlimited; but the figure in question had out-Heroded Herod, and gone beyond the bounds of even the prince's indefinite decorum. There are chords in the hearts of the most reckless which cannot be touched without emotion. Even with the utterly lost, to whom life and death are equally jests, there are matters of which no jest can be made. The whole company, indeed, seemed now deeply to feel that in the costume and bearing of the stranger neither wit nor propriety existed. The figure was tall and gaunt, and shrouded from head to foot in the habiliments of the grave. The mask which concealed the visage was made so nearly to resemble the countenance of a stiffened corpse that the closest scrutiny must have had difficulty in detecting the cheat. And yet all this might have been endured, if not approved, by the mad revellers around. But the mummer had gone so far as to assume the type of the Red Death. His vesture was dabbled in *blood*—and his broad brow, with all the features of the face, was besprinkled with the scarlet horror.

When the eyes of Prince Prospero fell upon this spectral image (which with a slow and solemn movement, as if more fully to sustain its role, stalked to and fro among the waltzers) he was seen to be convulsed, in the first moment with a strong shudder either of terror or distaste; but, in the next, his brow reddened with rage.

"Who dares?" he demanded hoarsely of the courtiers who stood near him—"who dares insult us with this blasphemous mockery? Seize him and unmask him—that we may know whom we have to hang at sunrise, from the battlements!"

It was in the eastern or blue chamber in which stood the Prince Prospero as he uttered these words. They rang throughout the seven rooms loudly and clearly—for the prince was a bold and robust man, and the music had become hushed at the waving of his hand.

It was in the blue room where stood the prince, with a group of pale courtiers by his side. At first, as he spoke, there was a slight rushing movement of this group in the direction of the intruder, who at the moment was also near at hand, and now, with deliberate and stately step, made closer approach to the speaker. But from a certain nameless awe with which the mad assumptions of the mummer had inspired the whole party, there were found none who put forth hand to seize him; so that, unimpeded, he passed within a yard of the prince's person; and, while the vast assembly, as if with one impulse, shrank from the centres of the rooms to the walls, he made his way uninterruptedly, but with the same solemn and measured step which had distinguished him from the first, through the blue chamber to the purple—through the purple to the green—through the green to the orange—through this again to the white—and even thence to the violet, ere a decided movement had been made to arrest him. It was then, however, that the Prince Prospero, maddening with rage and the shame of his own momentary cowardice, rushed hurriedly through the six chambers, while none followed him on account of a deadly terror that had seized upon all. He bore aloft a drawn dagger, and had approached, in rapid impetuosity, to within three or four feet of the retreating figure, when the latter, having attained the extremity of the velvet apartment, turned suddenly and confronted his pursuer. There was a sharp cry—and the dagger dropped gleaming upon the sable carpet, upon which, instantly afterwards, fell prostrate in death the Prince Prospero. Then, summoning the wild courage of despair, a throng of the revellers at once threw themselves into the black apartment, and, seizing the mummer, whose tall figure stood erect and motionless within the shadow of the ebony clock, gasped in unutterable horror at finding the grave-cerements and corpse-like mask which they handled with so violent a rudeness, untenanted by any tangible form.

And now was acknowledged the presence of the Red Death. He had come like a thief in the night. And one by one dropped the revellers in the blood-bedewed halls of their revel, and died each in the despairing posture of his fall. And the life of the ebony clock went out with that of the last of the gay. And the flames of the tripods expired. And Darkness and Decay and the Red Death held illimitable dominion over all.

The Pit and the Pendulum

Impia tortorum longos hic turba
furores
Sanguinis innocui, non satiata,
aluit.
Sospite nunc patria, fracto nunc
funeris antro,
Mors ubi dira fuit vita salusque
patent.

[Quatrain composed for the gates of a market to be erected upon the site of the Jacobin Club House at Paris.]

I was sick—sick unto death with that long agony; and when they at length unbound me, and I was permitted to sit, I felt that my senses were leaving me. The sentence—the dread sentence of death—was the last of distinct accentuation which reached my ears. After that, the sound of the inquisitorial voices seemed merged in one dreamy indeterminate hum. It conveyed to my soul the idea of *revolution*—perhaps from its association in fancy with the burr of a mill wheel. This only for a brief period; for presently I heard no more. Yet, for a while, I saw; but with how terrible an exaggeration! I saw the lips of the black-robed judges. They appeared to me white—whiter than the sheet upon which I trace these words—and thin even to grotesqueness; thin with the intensity of their expression of firmness—of immoveable resolution—of stern contempt of human torture. I saw that the decrees of what to me was Fate, were still issuing from those lips. I saw them writhe with a deadly locution. I saw them fashion the syllables of my name; and I shuddered because no sound succeeded. I saw, too, for a few moments of delirious horror, the soft and nearly imperceptible waving of the sable draperies which enwrapped the walls of the apartment. And then my vision fell upon the seven tall candles upon the table. At first they wore the aspect of charity, and seemed white and slender angels who would save me; but then, all at once, there came a most deadly nausea over my spirit, and I felt every fibre in my frame thrill as if I had touched the wire of a galvanic battery, while the angel forms became meaningless spectres, with heads of flame, and I saw that from them there would be no help. And then there stole into my fancy, like a rich musical note, the thought of what sweet rest there must be in the grave. The thought came gently and stealthily, and it seemed long before it attained full appreciation; but just as my spirit came at length properly to feel and entertain it, the figures of the judges vanished, as if magically, from before me; the tall candles sank into nothingness; their flames went out utterly; the blackness of darkness supervened; all sensations appeared swallowed up in a mad rushing descent as of the soul into Hades. Then silence, and stillness, night were the universe.

I had swooned; but still will not say that all of consciousness was lost. What of it there remained I will not attempt to define, or even to describe; yet all was not lost. In the deepest slumber—no! In delirium—no! In a swoon—no! In death—no! Even in the grave all *is not* lost. Else there is no immortality for man. Arousing from the most profound of slumbers, we break the gossamer web of *some* dream. Yet in a second afterward (so frail may that web have been), we remember not that we have dreamed. In the return to life from the swoon there are two stages; first, that of the sense of mental or spiritual; secondly, that of the sense of physical, existence. It seems probable that if, upon reaching the second stage, we could recall the impressions of the first, we should find these impressions eloquent in memories of the gulf beyond. And that gulf is—what? How at least shall we distinguish its shadows from those of the tomb? But if the impressions of what I have termed the first stage, are not, at will, recalled, yet, after long interval, do they not come unbidden, while we marvel whence they come? He who has never swooned, is not he who finds strange palaces and wildly familiar faces in coals that glow; is not he who beholds floating in mid-air the sad visions that the many may not view; is not he who ponders over the perfume of some novel flower—is not he whose brain grows bewildered with the meaning of some musical cadence which has never before arrested his attention.

Amid frequent and thoughtful endeavors to remember; amid earnest struggles to regather some token of the state of seeming nothingness into which my soul had lapsed, there have been moments when I have dreamed of success; there have been brief, very brief periods when I have conjured up remembrances which the lucid reason of a later epoch assures me could have had reference only to that condition of seeming unconsciousness. These shadows of memory tell, indistinctly, of tall figures that lifted and bore me in silence down—down—still down—till a hideous dizziness oppressed me at the mere idea of the interminableness of the descent. They tell also of a vague horror at my heart, on account of that heart's unnatural stillness. Then comes a sense of sudden motionlessness throughout all things; as if those who bore me (a ghastly train!) had outrun, in their descent, the limits of the limitless, and paused from the wearisomeness of their toil. After this I call to mind flatness and dampness; and then all is *madness*—the madness of a memory which busies itself among forbidden things.

Very suddenly there came back to my soul motion and sound—the tumultuous motion of the heart, and, in my ears, the sound of its beating. Then a pause in which all is blank. Then again sound, and motion, and touch—a tingling sensation pervading my frame. Then the mere consciousness of existence, without thought—a condition which lasted long. Then, very suddenly, *thought*, and shuddering terror, and earnest endeavor to comprehend my true state. Then a strong desire to lapse into insensibility. Then a rushing revival of soul and a successful effort to move. And now a full memory of the trial, of the judges, of the sable draperies, of the sentence, of the sickness, of the swoon. Then entire forgetfulness of all that followed; of all that a later day and much earnestness of endeavor have enabled me vaguely to recall.

So far, I had not opened my eyes. I felt that I lay upon my back, unbound. I reached out my hand, and it fell heavily upon something damp and hard. There I suffered it to remain for many minutes, while I strove to imagine where and *what* I could be. I longed, yet dared not to employ my vision. I dreaded the first glance at objects around me. It was not that I feared to look upon things horrible, but that I grew aghast lest there should be *nothing* to see. At length, with a wild desperation at heart, I quickly unclosed my eyes. My worst thoughts, then, were confirmed. The blackness of eternal night encompassed me. I struggled for breath. The intensity of the darkness seemed to oppress and stifle me. The atmosphere was intolerably close. I still lay quietly, and made effort to exercise my reason. I brought to mind the inquisitorial proceedings, and attempted from that point to deduce my real condition. The sentence had passed; and it appeared to me that a very long interval of time had since elapsed. Yet not for a moment did I suppose myself actually dead. Such a supposition, notwithstanding what we read in fiction, is altogether inconsistent with real existence;—but where and in what state was I? The condemned to death, I knew, perished usually at the *autos-da-fé*, and one of these had been held on the very night of the day of my trial. Had I been remanded to my dungeon, to await the next sacrifice, which would not take place for many months? This I at once saw could not be. Victims had been in immediate demand. Moreover, my dungeon, as well as all the condemned cells at Toledo, had stone floors, and light was not altogether excluded.

A fearful idea now suddenly drove the blood in torrents upon my heart, and for a brief period, I once more relapsed into insensibility. Upon recovering, I at once started to my feet, trembling convulsively in every fibre. I thrust my arms wildly above and around me in all directions. I felt nothing; yet dreaded to move a step, lest I should be impeded by the walls of a *tomb*. Perspiration burst from every pore, and stood in cold big beads upon my forehead. The agony of suspense grew at length intolerable, and I cautiously moved forward, with my arms extended, and my eyes straining from their sockets, in the hope of catching some faint ray of light. I proceeded for many paces; but still all was blackness and vacancy. I breathed more freely. It seemed evident that mine was not, at least, the most hideous of fates.

And now, as I still continued to step cautiously onward, there came thronging upon my recollection a thousand vague rumors of the horrors of Toledo. Of the dungeons there had been strange things narrated—fables I had always deemed them—but yet strange, and too ghastly to repeat, save in a whisper. Was I left to perish of starvation in this subterranean world of darkness; or what fate, perhaps even more fearful, awaited me? That the result would be death, and a death of more than customary bitterness, I knew too well the character of my judges to doubt. The mode and the hour were all that occupied or distracted me.

My outstretched hands at length encountered some solid obstruction. It was a wall, seemingly of stone masonry—very smooth, slimy, and cold. I followed it up; stepping with all the careful distrust with which certain antique narratives had inspired me. This process, however, afforded me no means of ascertaining the dimensions of my dungeon; as I might make its circuit, and return to the point whence I set out, without being aware of the fact; so perfectly uniform seemed the wall. I therefore sought the knife which had been in my pocket, when led into the inquisitorial chamber; but it was gone; my clothes had been exchanged for a wrapper of coarse serge. I had thought of forcing the blade in some minute crevice of the masonry, so as to identify my point of departure. The difficulty, nevertheless, was but trivial; although, in the disorder of my fancy, it seemed at first insuperable. I tore a part of the hem from the robe and placed the fragment at full length, and at right angles to the wall. In groping my way around the prison, I could not fail to encounter this rag upon completing the circuit. So, at least I thought: but I had not counted upon the extent of the dungeon, or upon my own weakness. The ground was moist and slippery. I staggered onward for some time, when I stumbled and fell. My excessive fatigue induced me to remain prostrate; and sleep soon overtook me as I lay.

Upon awaking, and stretching forth an arm, I found beside me a loaf and a pitcher with water. I was too much exhausted to reflect upon this circumstance, but ate and drank with avidity. Shortly afterward, I resumed my tour around the prison, and with much toil came at last upon the fragment of the serge. Up to the period when I fell I had counted fifty-two paces, and upon resuming my walk, I had counted forty-eight more;—when I arrived at the rag. There were in all, then, a hundred paces; and, admitting two paces to the yard, I presumed the dungeon to be fifty yards in circuit. I had met, however, with many angles in the wall, and thus I could form no guess at the shape of the vault; for vault I could not help supposing it to be.

I had little object—certainly no hope these researches; but a vague curiosity prompted me to continue them. Quitting the wall, I resolved to cross the area of the enclosure. At first I proceeded with extreme caution, for the floor, although seemingly of solid material, was treacherous with slime. At length, however, I took courage, and did not hesitate to step firmly; endeavoring to cross in as direct a line as possible. I had advanced some ten or twelve paces in this manner, when the remnant of the torn hem of my robe became entangled between my legs. I stepped on it, and fell violently on my face.

In the confusion attending my fall, I did not immediately apprehend a somewhat startling circumstance, which yet, in a few seconds afterward, and while I still lay prostrate, arrested my attention. It was this—my chin rested upon the floor of the prison, but my lips and the upper portion of my head, although seemingly at a less elevation than the chin, touched nothing. At the same time my forehead seemed bathed in a clammy vapor, and the peculiar smell of decayed fungus arose to my nostrils. I put forward my arm, and shuddered to find that I had fallen at the very brink of a circular pit, whose extent, of course, I had no means of ascertaining at the moment. Groping about the masonry just below the margin, I succeeded in dislodging a small fragment, and let it fall into the abyss. For many seconds I hearkened to its reverberations as it dashed against the sides of the chasm in its descent; at length there was a sullen plunge into water, succeeded by loud echoes. At the same moment there came a sound resembling the quick opening, and as rapid closing of a door overhead, while a faint gleam of light flashed suddenly through the gloom, and as suddenly faded away.

I saw clearly the doom which had been prepared for me, and congratulated myself upon the timely accident by which I had escaped. Another step before my fall, and the world had seen me no more. And the death just avoided, was of that very character which I had regarded as fabulous and frivolous in the tales respecting the Inquisition. To the victims of its tyranny, there was the choice of death with its direst physical agonies, or death with its most hideous moral horrors. I had been reserved for the latter. By long suffering my nerves had been unstrung, until I trembled at the sound of my own voice, and had become in every respect a fitting subject for the species of torture which awaited me.

Shaking in every limb, I groped my way back to the wall; resolving there to perish rather than risk the terrors of the wells, of which my imagination now pictured many in various positions about the dungeon. In other conditions of mind I might have had courage to end my misery at once by a plunge into one of these abysses; but now I was the veriest of cowards. Neither could I forget what I had read of these pits—that the *sudden* extinction of life formed no part of their most horrible plan.

Agitation of spirit kept me awake for many long hours; but at length I again slumbered. Upon arousing, I found by my side, as before, a loaf and a pitcher of water. A burning thirst consumed me, and I emptied the vessel at a draught. It must have been drugged; for scarcely had I drunk, before I became irresistibly drowsy. A deep sleep fell upon me—a sleep like that of death. How long it lasted of course, I know not; but when, once again, I unclosed my eyes, the objects around me were visible. By a wild sulphurous lustre, the origin of which I could not at first determine, I was enabled to see the extent and aspect of the prison.

In its size I had been greatly mistaken. The whole circuit of its walls did not exceed twenty-five yards. For some minutes this fact occasioned me a world of vain trouble; vain indeed! for what could be of less importance, under the terrible circumstances which environed me, then the mere dimensions of my dungeon? But my soul took a wild interest in trifles, and I busied myself in endeavors to account for the error I had committed in my measurement. The truth at length flashed upon me. In my first attempt at exploration I had counted fifty-two paces, up to the period when I fell; I must then have been within a pace or two of the fragment of serge; in fact, I had nearly performed the circuit of the vault. I then slept, and upon awaking, I must have returned upon my steps—thus supposing the circuit nearly double what it actually was. My confusion of mind prevented me from observing that I began my tour with the wall to the left, and ended it with the wall to the right.

I had been deceived, too, in respect to the shape of the enclosure. In feeling my way I had found many angles, and thus deduced an idea of great irregularity; so potent is the effect of total darkness upon one arousing from lethargy or sleep! The angles were simply those of a few slight depressions, or niches, at odd intervals. The general shape of the prison was square. What I had taken for masonry seemed now to be iron, or some other metal, in huge plates, whose sutures or joints occasioned the depression. The entire surface of this metallic enclosure was rudely daubed in all the hideous and repulsive devices to which the charnel superstition of the monks has given rise. The figures of fiends in aspects of menace, with skeleton forms, and other more really fearful images, overspread and disfigured the walls. I observed that the outlines of these monstrosities were sufficiently distinct, but that the colors seemed faded and blurred, as if from the effects of a damp atmosphere. I now noticed the floor, too, which was of stone. In the centre yawned the circular pit from whose jaws I had escaped; but it was the only one in the dungeon.

All this I saw indistinctly and by much effort: for my personal condition had been greatly changed during slumber. I now lay upon my back, and at full length, on a species of low framework of wood. To this I was securely bound by a long strap resembling a surcingle. It passed in many convolutions about my limbs and body, leaving at liberty only my head, and my left arm to such extent that I could, by dint of much exertion, supply myself with food from an earthen dish which lay by my side on the floor. I saw, to my horror, that the pitcher had been removed. I say to my horror; for I was consumed with intolerable thirst. This thirst it appeared to be the design of my persecutors to stimulate: for the food in the dish was meat pungently seasoned.

Looking upward, I surveyed the ceiling of my prison. It was some thirty or forty feet overhead, and constructed much as the side walls. In one of its panels a very singular figure riveted my whole attention. It was the painted figure of Time as he is commonly represented, save that, in lieu of a scythe, he held what, at a casual glance, I supposed to be the pictured image of a huge pendulum such as we see on antique clocks. There was something, however, in the appearance of this machine which caused me to regard it more attentively. While I gazed directly upward at it (for its position was immediately over my own) I fancied that I saw it in motion. In an instant afterward the fancy was confirmed. Its sweep was brief, and of course slow. I watched it for some minutes, somewhat in fear, but more in wonder. Wearied at length with observing its dull movement, I turned my eyes upon the other objects in the cell.

A slight noise attracted my notice, and, looking to the floor, I saw several enormous rats traversing it. They had issued from the well, which lay just within view to my right. Even then, while I gazed, they came up in troops, hurriedly, with ravenous eyes, allured by the scent of the meat. From this it required much effort and attention to scare them away.

It might have been half an hour, perhaps even an hour (for I could take but imperfect note of time), before I again cast my eyes upward. What I then saw confounded and amazed me. The sweep of the pendulum had increased in extent by nearly a yard. As a natural consequence, its velocity was also much greater. But what mainly disturbed me was the idea that had perceptibly *descended.* I now observed—with what horror it is needless to say—that its nether extremity was formed of a crescent of glittering steel, about a foot in length from horn to horn; the horns upward, and the under edge evidently as keen as that of a razor. Like a razor also, it seemed massy and heavy, tapering from the edge into a solid and broad structure above. It was appended to a weighty rod of brass, and the whole *hissed* as it swung through the air.

I could no longer doubt the doom prepared for me by monkish ingenuity in torture. My cognizance of the pit had become known to the inquisitorial agents—*the pit* whose horrors had been destined for so bold a recusant as myself—*the pit*, typical of hell, and regarded by rumor as the Ultima Thule of all their punishments. The plunge into this pit I had avoided by the merest of accidents, I knew that surprise, or entrapment into torment, formed an important portion of all the grotesquerie of these dungeon deaths. Having failed to fall, it was no part of the demon plan to hurl me into the abyss; and thus (there being no alternative) a different and a milder destruction awaited me. Milder! I half smiled in my agony as I thought of such application of such a term.

What boots it to tell of the long, long hours of horror more than mortal, during which I counted the rushing vibrations of the steel! Inch by inch—line by line—with a descent only appreciable at intervals that seemed ages—down and still down it came! Days passed—it might have been that many days passed—ere it swept so closely over me as to fan me with its acrid breath. The odor of the sharp steel forced itself into my nostrils. I prayed—I wearied heaven with my prayer for its more speedy descent. I grew frantically mad, and struggled to force myself upward against the sweep of the fearful scimitar. And then I fell suddenly calm, and lay smiling at the glittering death, as a child at some rare bauble.

There was another interval of utter insensibility; it was brief; for, upon again lapsing into life there had been no perceptible descent in the pendulum. But it might have been long; for I knew there were demons who took note of my swoon, and who could have arrested the vibration at pleasure. Upon my recovery, too, I felt very—oh, inexpressibly sick and weak, as if through long inanition. Even amid the agonies of that period, the human nature craved food. With painful effort I outstretched my left arm as far as my bonds permitted, and took possession of the small remnant which had been spared me by the rats. As I put a portion of it within my lips, there rushed to my mind a half formed thought of joy—of hope. Yet what business had *I* with hope? It was, as I say, a half formed thought—man has many such which are never completed. I felt that it was of joy—of hope; but felt also that it had perished in its formation. In vain I struggled to perfect—to regain it. Long suffering had nearly annihilated all my ordinary powers of mind. I was an imbecile—an idiot.

The vibration of the pendulum was at right angles to my length. I saw that the crescent was designed to cross the region of the heart. It would fray the serge of my robe—it would return and repeat its operations—again—and again. Notwithstanding terrifically wide sweep (some thirty feet or more) and the hissing vigor of its descent, sufficient to sunder these very walls of iron, still the fraying of my robe would be all that, for several minutes, it would accomplish. And at this thought I paused. I dared not go farther than this reflection. I dwelt upon it with a pertinacity of attention—as if, in so dwelling, I could arrest here the descent of the steel. I forced myself to ponder upon the sound of the crescent as it should pass across the garment—upon the peculiar thrilling sensation which the friction of cloth produces on the nerves. I pondered upon all this frivolity until my teeth were on edge.

Down—steadily down it crept. I took a frenzied pleasure in contrasting its downward with its lateral velocity. To the right—to the left—far and wide—with the shriek of a damned spirit; to my heart with the stealthy pace of the tiger! I alternately laughed and howled as the one or the other idea grew predominant.

Down—certainly, relentlessly down! It vibrated within three inches of my bosom! I struggled violently, furiously, to free my left arm. This was free only from the elbow to the hand. I could reach the latter, from the platter beside me, to my mouth, with great effort, but no farther. Could I have broken the fastenings above the elbow, I would have seized and attempted to arrest the pendulum. I might as well have attempted to arrest an avalanche!

Down—still unceasingly—still inevitably down! I gasped and struggled at each vibration. I shrunk convulsively at its every sweep. My eyes followed its outward or upward whirls with the eagerness of the most unmeaning despair; they closed themselves spasmodically at the descent, although death would have been a relief, oh! how unspeakable! Still I quivered in every nerve to think how slight a sinking of the machinery would precipitate that keen, glistening axe upon my bosom. It was *hope* that prompted the nerve to quiver—the frame to shrink. It was hope—the hope that triumphs on the rack—that whispers to the death-condemned even in the dungeons of the Inquisition.

I saw that some ten or twelve vibrations would bring the steel in actual contact with my robe, and with this observation there suddenly came over my spirit all the keen, collected calmness of despair. For the first time during many hours—or perhaps days—I *thought*. It now occurred to me that the bandage, or surcingle, which enveloped me, was *unique*. I was tied by no separate cord. The first stroke of the razorlike crescent athwart any portion of the band, would so detach it that it might be unwound from my person by means of my left hand. But how fearful, in that case, the proximity of the steel! The result of the slightest struggle how deadly! Was it likely, moreover, that the minions of the torturer had not foreseen and provided for this possibility! Was it probable that the bandage crossed my bosom in the track of the pendulum? Dreading to find my faint, and, as it seemed, in last hope frustrated, I so far elevated my head as to obtain a distinct view of my breast. The surcingle enveloped my limbs and body close in all directions—*save in the path of the destroying crescent.*

Scarcely had I dropped my head back into its original position, when there flashed upon my mind what I cannot better describe than as the unformed half of that idea of deliverance to which I have previously alluded, and of which a moiety only floated indeterminately through my brain when I raised food to my burning lips. The whole thought was now present—feeble, scarcely sane, scarcely definite—but still entire. I proceeded at once, with the nervous energy of despair, to attempt its execution.

For many hours the immediate vicinity of the low framework upon which I lay, had been literally swarming with rats. They were wild, bold, ravenous; their red eyes glaring upon me as if they waited but for motionlessness on my part to make me their prey. "To what food," I thought, "have they been accustomed in the well?"

They had devoured, in spite of all my efforts to prevent them, all but a small remnant of the contents of the dish. I had fallen into an habitual see-saw, or wave of the hand about the platter: and, at length, the unconscious uniformity of the movement deprived it of effect. In their voracity the vermin frequently fastened their sharp fangs in my fingers. With the particles of the oily and spicy viand which now remained, I thoroughly rubbed the bandage wherever I could reach it; then, raising my hand from the floor, I lay breathlessly still.

At first the ravenous animals were startled and terrified at the change—at the cessation of movement. They shrank alarmedly back; many sought the well. But this was only for a moment. I had not counted in vain upon their voracity. Observing that I remained without motion, one or two of the boldest leaped upon the framework, and smelt at the surcingle. This seemed the signal for a general rush. Forth from the well they hurried in fresh troops. They clung to the wood—they overran it, and leaped in hundreds upon my person. The measured movement of the pendulum disturbed them not at all. Avoiding its strokes they busied themselves with the anointed bandage. They pressed—they swarmed upon me in ever accumulating heaps. They writhed upon my throat; their cold lips sought my own; I was half stifled by their thronging pressure; disgust, for which the world has no name, swelled my bosom, and chilled, with a heavy clamminess, my heart. Yet one minute, and I felt that the struggle would be over. Plainly I perceived the loosening of the bandage. I knew that in more than one place it must be already severed. With a more than human resolution I lay still.

Nor had I erred in my calculations—nor had I endured in vain. I at length felt that I was *free*. The surcingle hung in ribands from my body. But the stroke of the pendulum already pressed upon my bosom. It had divided the serge of the robe. It had cut through the linen beneath. Twice again it swung, and a sharp sense of pain shot through every nerve. But the moment of escape had arrived. At a wave of my hand my deliverers hurried tumultuously away. With a steady movement—cautious, sidelong, shrinking, and slow—I slid from the embrace of the bandage and beyond the reach of the scimitar. For the moment, at least, *I was free*.

Free!—and in the grasp of the Inquisition! I had scarcely stepped from my wooden bed of horror upon the stone floor of the prison, when the motion of the hellish machine ceased and I beheld it drawn up, by some invisible force, through the ceiling. This was a lesson which I took desperately to heart. My every motion was undoubtedly watched. Free!—I had but escaped death in one form of agony, to be delivered unto worse than death in some other. With that thought I rolled my eves nervously around on the barriers of iron that hemmed me in. Something unusual—some change which, at first, I could not appreciate distinctly—it was obvious, had taken place in the apartment. For many minutes of a dreamy and trembling abstraction, I busied myself in vain, unconnected conjecture. During this period, I became aware, for the first time, of the origin of the sulphurous light which illumined the cell. It proceeded from a fissure, about half an inch in width, extending entirely around the prison at the base of the walls, which thus appeared, and were, completely separated from the floor. I endeavored, but of course in vain, to look through the aperture.

As I arose from the attempt, the mystery of the alteration in the chamber broke at once upon my understanding. I have observed that, although the outlines of the figures upon the walls were sufficiently distinct, yet the colors seemed blurred and indefinite. These colors had now assumed, and were momentarily assuming, a startling and most intense brilliancy, that gave to the spectral and fiendish portraitures an aspect that might have thrilled even firmer nerves than my own. Demon eyes, of a wild and ghastly vivacity, glared upon me in a thousand directions, where none had been visible before, and gleamed with the lurid lustre of a fire that I could not force my imagination to regard as unreal.

Unreal!—Even while I breathed there came to my nostrils the breath of the vapour of heated iron! A suffocating odour pervaded the prison! A deeper glow settled each moment in the eyes that glared at my agonies! A richer tint of crimson diffused itself over the pictured horrors of blood. I panted! I gasped for breath! There could be no doubt of the design of my tormentors—oh! most unrelenting! oh! most demoniac of men! I shrank from the glowing metal to the centre of the cell. Amid the thought of the fiery destruction that impended, the idea of the coolness of the well came over my soul like balm. I rushed to its deadly brink. I threw my straining vision below. The glare from the enkindled roof illumined its inmost recesses. Yet, for a wild moment, did my spirit refuse to comprehend the meaning of what I saw. At length it forced—it wrestled its way into my soul—it burned itself in upon my shuddering reason.—Oh! for a voice to speak!—oh! horror!—oh! any horror but this! With a shriek, I rushed from the margin, and buried my face in my hands—weeping bitterly.

The heat rapidly increased, and once again I looked up, shuddering as with a fit of the ague. There had been a second change in the cell—and now the change was obviously in the *form*. As before, it was in vain that I, at first, endeavoured to appreciate or understand what was taking place. But not long was I left in doubt. The Inquisitorial vengeance had been hurried by my two-fold escape, and there was to be no more dallying with the King of Terrors. The room had been square. I saw that two of its iron angles were now acute—two, consequently, obtuse. The fearful difference quickly increased with a low rumbling or moaning sound. In an instant the apartment had shifted its form into that of a lozenge. But the alteration stopped not here—I neither hoped nor desired it to stop. I could have clasped the red walls to my bosom as a garment of eternal peace. "Death," I said, "any death but that of the pit!" Fool! might I have not known that *into the pit* it was the object of the burning iron to urge me? Could I resist its glow? or, if even that, could I withstand its pressure And now, flatter and flatter grew the lozenge, with a rapidity that left me no time for contemplation. Its centre, and of course, its greatest width, came just over the yawning gulf. I shrank back—but the closing walls pressed me resistlessly onward. At length for my seared and writhing body there was no longer an inch of foothold on the firm floor of the prison. I struggled no more, but the agony of my soul found vent in one loud, long, and final scream of despair. I felt that I tottered upon the brink—I averted my eyes—

There was a discordant hum of human voices! There was a loud blast as of many trumpets! There was a harsh grating as of a thousand thunders! The fiery walls rushed back! An outstretched arm caught my own as I fell, fainting, into the abyss. It was that of General Lasalle. The French army had entered Toledo. The Inquisition was in the hands of its enemies.

The Black Cat

For the most wild, yet most homely narrative which I am about to pen, I neither expect nor solicit belief. Mad indeed would I be to expect it, in a case where my very senses reject their own evidence. Yet, mad am I not—and very surely do I not dream. But tomorrow I die, and to-day I would unburthen my soul. My immediate purpose is to place before the world, plainly, succinctly, and without comment, a series of mere household events. In their consequences, these events have terrified—have tortured—have destroyed me. Yet I will not attempt to expound them. To me, they have presented little but Horror—to many they will seem less terrible than *baroques*. Hereafter, perhaps, some intellect may be found which will reduce my phantasm to the common-place—some intellect more calm, more logical, and far less excitable than my own, which will perceive, in the circumstances I detail with awe, nothing more than an ordinary succession of very natural causes and effects.

From my infancy I was noted for the docility and humanity of my disposition. My tenderness of heart was even so conspicuous as to make me the jest of my companions. I was especially fond of animals, and was indulged by my parents with a great variety of pets. With these I spent most of my time, and never was so happy as when feeding and caressing them. This peculiarity of character grew with my growth, and in my manhood, I derived from it one of my principal sources of pleasure. To those who have cherished an affection for a faithful and sagacious dog, I need hardly be at the trouble of explaining the nature or the intensity of the gratification thus derivable. There is something in the unselfish and self-sacrificing love of a brute, which goes directly to the heart of him who has had frequent occasion to test the paltry friendship and gossamer fidelity of mere *Man*.

I married early, and was happy to find in my wife a disposition not uncongenial with my own. Observing my partiality for domestic pets, she lost no opportunity of procuring those of the most agreeable kind. We had birds, gold-fish, a fine dog, rabbits, a small monkey, and *a cat*.

This latter was a remarkably large and beautiful animal, entirely black, and sagacious to an astonishing degree. In speaking of his intelligence, my wife, who at heart was not a little tinctured with superstition, made frequent allusion to the ancient popular notion, which regarded all black cats as witches in disguise. Not that she was ever *serious* upon this point—and I mention the matter at all for no better reason than that it happens, just now, to be remembered.

Pluto—this was the cat's name—was my favorite pet and playmate. I alone fed him, and he attended me wherever I went about the house. It was even with difficulty that I could prevent him from following me through the streets.

Our friendship lasted, in this manner, for several years, during which my general temperament and character—through the instrumentality of the Fiend Intemperance—had (I blush to confess it) experienced a radical alteration for the worse. I grew, day by day, more moody, more irritable, more regardless of the feelings of others. I suffered myself to use intemperate language to my wife. At length, I even offered her personal violence. My pets, of course, were made to feel the change in my disposition. I not only neglected, but ill-used them. For Pluto, however, I still retained sufficient regard to restrain me from maltreating him, as I made no scruple of maltreating the rabbits, the monkey, or even the dog, when by accident, or through affection, they came in my way. But my disease grew upon me—for what disease is like Alcohol!—and at length even Pluto, who was now becoming old, and consequently somewhat peevish—even Pluto began to experience the effects of my ill temper.

One night, returning home, much intoxicated, from one of my haunts about town, I fancied that the cat avoided my presence. I seized him; when, in his fright at my violence, he inflicted a slight wound upon my hand with his teeth. The fury of a demon instantly possessed me. I knew myself no longer. My original soul seemed, at once, to take its flight from my body and a more than fiendish malevolence, gin-nurtured, thrilled every fibre of my frame. I took from my waistcoat-pocket a pen-knife, opened it, grasped the poor beast by the throat, and deliberately cut one of its eyes from the socket! I blush, I burn, I shudder, while I pen the damnable atrocity.

When reason returned with the morning—when I had slept off the fumes of the night's debauch—I experienced a sentiment half of horror, half of remorse, for the crime of which I had been guilty; but it was, at best, a feeble and equivocal feeling, and the soul remained untouched. I again plunged into excess, and soon drowned in wine all memory of the deed.

In the meantime the cat slowly recovered. The socket of the lost eye presented, it is true, a frightful appearance, but he no longer appeared to suffer any pain. He went about the house as usual, but, as might be expected, fled in extreme terror at my approach. I had so much of my old heart left, as to be at first grieved by this evident dislike on the part of a creature which had once so loved me. But this feeling soon gave place to irritation. And then came, as if to my final and irrevocable overthrow, the spirit of *perverseness*. Of this spirit philosophy takes no account. Yet I am not more sure that my soul lives, than I am that perverseness is one of the primitive impulses of the human heart—one of the indivisible primary faculties, or sentiments, which give direction to the character of Man. Who has not, a hundred times, found himself committing a vile or a silly action, for no other reason than because he knows he should *not*? Have we not a perpetual inclination, in the teeth of our best judgment, to violate that which is *Law*, merely because we understand it to be such? This spirit of perverseness, I say, came to my final overthrow. It was this unfathomable longing of the soul *to vex itself*—to offer violence to its own nature—to do wrong for the wrong's sake only—that urged me to continue and finally to consummate the injury I had inflicted upon the unoffending brute. One morning, in cool blood, I slipped a noose about its neck and hung it to the limb of a tree;—hung it with the tears streaming from my eyes, and with the bitterest remorse at my heart;—hung it *because* I knew that it had loved me, and *because* I felt it had given me no reason of offence;—hung it *because* I knew that in so doing I was committing a sin—a deadly sin that would so jeopardize my immortal soul as to place it—if such a thing wore possible—even beyond the reach of the infinite mercy of the most merciful and most terrible God.

On the night of the day on which this cruel deed was done, I was aroused from sleep by the cry of fire. The curtains of my bed were in flames. The whole house was blazing. It was with great difficulty that my wife, a servant, and myself, made our escape from the conflagration. The destruction was complete. My entire worldly wealth was swallowed up, and I resigned myself thenceforward to despair.

I am above the weakness of seeking to establish a sequence of cause and effect, between the disaster and the atrocity. But I am detailing a chain of facts—and wish not to leave even a possible link imperfect. On the day succeeding the fire, I visited the ruins. The walls, with one exception, had fallen in. This exception was found in a compartment wall, not very thick, which stood about the middle of the house, and against which had rested the head of my bed. The plastering had here, in great measure, resisted the action of the fire—a fact which I attributed to its having been recently spread. About this wall a dense crowd were collected, and many persons seemed to be examining a particular portion of it with very minute and eager attention. The words "strange!" "singular!" and other similar expressions, excited my curiosity. I approached and saw, as if graven in *bas relief* upon the white surface, the figure of a gigantic *cat*. The impression was given with an accuracy truly marvellous. There was a rope about the animal's neck.

When I first beheld this apparition—for I could scarcely regard it as less—my wonder and my terror were extreme. But at length reflection came to my aid. The cat, I remembered, had been hung in a garden adjacent to the house. Upon the alarm of fire, this garden had been immediately filled by the crowd—by some one of whom the animal must have been cut from the tree and thrown, through an open window, into my chamber. This had probably been done with the view of arousing me from sleep. The falling of other walls had compressed the victim of my cruelty into the substance of the freshly-spread plaster; the lime of which, with the flames, and the *ammonia* from the carcass, had then accomplished the portraiture as I saw it.

Although I thus readily accounted to my reason, if not altogether to my conscience, for the startling fact just detailed, it did not the less fail to make a deep impression upon my fancy. For months I could not rid myself of the phantasm of the cat; and, during this period, there came back into my spirit a half-sentiment that seemed, but was not, remorse. I went so far as to regret the loss of the animal, and to look about me, among the vile haunts which I now habitually frequented, for another pet of the same species, and of somewhat similar appearance, with which to supply its place.

One night as I sat, half stupefied, in a den of more than infamy, my attention was suddenly drawn to some black object, reposing upon the head of one of the immense hogsheads of Gin, or of Rum, which constituted the chief furniture of the apartment. I had been looking steadily at the top of this hogshead for some minutes, and what now caused me surprise was the fact that I had not sooner perceived the object thereupon. I approached it, and touched it with my hand. It was a black cat—a very large one—fully as large as Pluto, and closely resembling him in every respect but one. Pluto had not a white hair upon any portion of his body; but this cat had a large, although indefinite splotch of white, covering nearly the whole region of the breast.

Upon my touching him, he immediately arose, purred loudly, rubbed against my hand, and appeared delighted with my notice. This, then, was the very creature of which I was in search. I at once offered to purchase it of the landlord; but this person made no claim to it—knew nothing of it—had never seen it before.

I continued my caresses, and, when I prepared to go home, the animal evinced a disposition to accompany me. I permitted it to do so; occasionally stooping and patting it as I proceeded. When it reached the house it domesticated itself at once, and became immediately a great favorite with my wife.

For my own part, I soon found a dislike to it arising within me. This was just the reverse of what I had anticipated; but—I know not how or why it was—its evident fondness for myself rather disgusted and annoyed. By slow degrees, these feelings of disgust and annoyance rose into the bitterness of hatred. I avoided the creature; a certain sense of shame, and the remembrance of my former deed of cruelty, preventing me from physically abusing it. I did not, for some weeks, strike, or otherwise violently ill use it; but gradually—very gradually—I came to look upon it with unutterable loathing, and to flee silently from its odious presence, as from the breath of a pestilence.

What added, no doubt, to my hatred of the beast, was the discovery, on the morning after I brought it home, that, like Pluto, it also had been deprived of one of its eyes. This circumstance, however, only endeared it to my wife, who, as I have already said, possessed, in a high degree, that humanity of feeling which had once been my distinguishing trait, and the source of many of my simplest and purest pleasures.

With my aversion to this cat, however, its partiality for myself seemed to increase. It followed my footsteps with a pertinacity which it would be difficult to make the reader comprehend. Whenever I sat, it would crouch beneath my chair, or spring upon my knees, covering me with its loathsome caresses. If I arose to walk it would get between my feet and thus nearly throw me down, or, fastening its long and sharp claws in my dress, clamber, in this manner, to my breast. At such times, although I longed to destroy it with a blow, I was yet withheld from so doing, partly by a memory of my former crime, but chiefly—let me confess it at once—by absolute *dread* of the beast.

This dread was not exactly a dread of physical evil—and yet I should be at a loss how otherwise to define it. I am almost ashamed to own—yes, even in this felon's cell, I am almost ashamed to own—that the terror and horror with which the animal inspired me, had been heightened by one of the merest chimæras it would be possible to conceive. My wife had called my attention, more than once, to the character of the mark of white hair, of which I have spoken, and which constituted the sole visible difference between the strange beast and the one I had destroyed. The reader will remember that this mark, although large, had been originally very indefinite; but, by slow degrees—degrees nearly imperceptible, and which for a long time my Reason struggled to reject as fanciful—it had, at length, assumed a rigorous distinctness of outline. It was now the representation of an object that I shudder to name—and for this, above all, I loathed, and dreaded, and would have rid myself of the monster *had I dared*—it was now, I say, the image of a hideous—of a ghastly thing—of the *gallows*!—oh, mournful and terrible engine of Horror and of Crime—of Agony and of Death!

And now was I indeed wretched beyond the wretchedness of mere Humanity. And *a brute beast*—whose fellow I had contemptuously destroyed—*a brute beast* to work out for *me*—for me a man, fashioned in the image of the High God—so much of insufferable wo! Alas! neither by day nor by night knew I the blessing of Rest any more! During the former the creature left me no moment alone; and, in the latter, I started, hourly, from dreams of unutterable fear, to find the hot breath of *the thing* upon my face, and its vast weight—an incarnate Night-Mare that I had no power to shake off—incumbent eternally upon my *heart!*

Beneath the pressure of torments such as these, the feeble remnant of the good within me succumbed. Evil thoughts became my sole intimates—the darkest and most evil of thoughts. The moodiness of my usual temper increased to hatred of all things and of all mankind; while, from the sudden, frequent, and ungovernable outbursts of a fury to which I now blindly abandoned myself, my uncomplaining wife, alas! was the most usual and the most patient of sufferers.

One day she accompanied me, upon some household errand, into the cellar of the old building which our poverty compelled us to inhabit. The cat followed me down the steep stairs, and, nearly throwing me headlong, exasperated me to madness. Uplifting an axe, and forgetting, in my wrath, the childish dread which had hitherto stayed my hand, I aimed a blow at the animal which, of course, would have proved instantly fatal had it descended as I wished. But this blow was arrested by the hand of my wife. Goaded, by the interference, into a rage more than demoniacal, I withdrew my arm from her grasp and buried the axe in her brain. She fell dead upon the spot, without a groan.

This hideous murder accomplished, I set myself forthwith, and with entire deliberation, to the task of concealing the body. I knew that I could not remove it from the house, either by day or by night, without the risk of being observed by the neighbors. Many projects entered my mind. At one period I thought of cutting the corpse into minute fragments, and destroying them by fire. At another, I resolved to dig a grave for it in the floor of the cellar. Again, I deliberated about casting it in the well in the yard—about packing it in a box, as if merchandize, with the usual arrangements, and so getting a porter to take it from the house. Finally I hit upon what I considered a far better expedient than either of these. I determined to wall it up in the cellar—as the monks of the middle ages are recorded to have walled up their victims.

For a purpose such as this the cellar was well adapted. Its walls were loosely constructed, and had lately been plastered throughout with a rough plaster, which the dampness of the atmosphere had prevented from hardening. Moreover, in one of the walls was a projection, caused by a false chimney, or fireplace, that had been filled up, and made to resemble the red of the cellar. I made no doubt that I could readily displace the bricks at this point, insert the corpse, and wall the whole up as before, so that no eye could detect any thing suspicious.

And in this calculation I was not deceived. By means of a crow-bar I easily dislodged the bricks, and, having carefully deposited the body against the inner wall, I propped it in that position, while, with little trouble, I re-laid the whole structure as it originally stood. Having procured mortar, sand, and hair, with every possible precaution, I prepared a plaster which could not be distinguished from the old, and with this I very carefully went over the new brickwork. When I had finished, I felt satisfied that all was right. The wall did not present the slightest appearance of having been disturbed. The rubbish on the floor was picked up with the minutest care. I looked around triumphantly, and said to myself—"Here at least, then, my labor has not been in vain."

My next step was to look for the beast which had been the cause of so much wretchedness; for I had, at length, firmly resolved to put it to death. Had I been able to meet with it, at the moment, there could have been no doubt of its fate; but it appeared that the crafty animal had been alarmed at the violence of my previous anger, and forebore to present itself in my present mood. It is impossible to describe, or to imagine, the deep, the blissful sense of relief which the absence of the detested creature occasioned in my bosom. It did not make its appearance during the night—and thus for one night at least, since its introduction into the house, I soundly and tranquilly slept; aye, *slept* even with the burden of murder upon my soul!

The second and the third day passed, and still my tormentor came not. Once again I breathed as a freeman. The monster, in terror, had fled the premises forever! I should behold it no more! My happiness was supreme! The guilt of my dark deed disturbed me but little. Some few inquiries had been made, but these had been readily answered. Even a search had been instituted—but of course nothing was to be discovered. I looked upon my future felicity as secured.

Upon the fourth day of the assassination, a party of the police came, very unexpectedly, into the house, and proceeded again to make rigorous investigation of the premises. Secure, however, in the inscrutability of my place of concealment, I felt no embarrassment whatever. The officers bade me accompany them in their search. They left no nook or corner unexplored. At length, for the third or fourth time, they descended into the cellar. I quivered not in a muscle. My heart beat calmly as that of one who slumbers in innocence. I walked the cellar from end to end. I folded my arms upon my bosom, and roamed easily to and fro. The police were thoroughly satisfied and prepared to depart. The glee at my heart was too strong to be restrained. I burned to say if but one word, by way of triumph, and to render doubly sure their assurance of my guiltlessness.

"Gentlemen," I said at last, as the party ascended the steps, "I delight to have allayed your suspicions. I wish you all health, and a little more courtesy. By the bye, gentlemen, this—this is a very well constructed house." [In the rabid desire to say something easily, I scarcely knew what I uttered at all.]—"I may say an *excellently* well constructed house. These walls are you going, gentlemen?—these walls are solidly put together;" and here, through the mere phrenzy of bravado, I rapped heavily, with a cane which I held in my hand, upon that very portion of the brick-work behind which stood the corpse of the wife of my bosom.

But may God shield and deliver me from the fangs of the Arch-Fiend! No sooner had the reverberation of my blows sunk into silence, than I was answered by a voice from within the tomb!—by a cry, at first muffled and broken, like the sobbing of a child, and then quickly swelling into one long, loud, and continuous scream, utterly anomalous and inhuman—a howl—a wailing shriek, half of horror and half of triumph, such as might have arisen only out of hell, conjointly from the throats of the dammed in their agony and of the demons that exult in the damnation.

Of my own thoughts it is folly to speak. Swooning, I staggered to the opposite wall. For one instant the party upon the stairs remained motionless, through extremity of terror and of awe. In the next, a dozen stout arms were toiling at the wall. It fell bodily. The corpse, already greatly decayed and clotted with gore, stood erect before the eyes of the spectators. Upon its head, with red extended mouth and solitary eye of fire, sat the hideous beast whose craft had seduced me into murder, and whose informing voice had consigned me to the hangman. I had walled the monster up within the tomb!

The Tell-Tale Heart

True!—nervous—very, very dreadfully nervous I had been and am; but why *will* you say that I am mad? The disease had sharpened my senses—not destroyed—not dulled them. Above all was the sense of hearing acute. I heard all things in the heaven and in the earth. I heard many things in hell. How, then, am I mad? Hearken! and observe how healthily—how calmly I can tell you the whole story.

It is impossible to say how first the idea entered my brain; but once conceived, it haunted me day and night. Object there was none. Passion there was none. I loved the old man. He had never wronged me. He had never given me insult. For his gold I had no desire. I think it was his eye! yes, it was this! He had the eye of a vulture—a pale blue eye, with a film over it. Whenever it fell upon me, my blood ran cold; and so by degrees—very gradually—I made up my mind to take the life of the old man, and thus rid myself of the eye forever.

Now this is the point. You fancy me mad. Madmen know nothing. But you should have seen *me*. You should have seen how wisely I proceeded—with what caution—with what foresight—with what dissimulation I went to work! I was never kinder to the old man than during the whole week before I killed him. And every night, about midnight, I turned the latch of his door and opened it—oh so gently! And then, when I had made an opening sufficient for my head, I put in a dark lantern, all closed, closed, that no light shone out, and then I thrust in my head. Oh, you would have laughed to see how cunningly I thrust it in! I moved it slowly—very, very slowly, so that I might not disturb the old man's sleep. It took me an hour to place my whole head within the opening so far that I could see him as he lay upon his bed. Ha! would a madman have been so wise as this? And then, when my head was well in the room, I undid the lantern cautiously—oh, so cautiously—cautiously (for the hinges creaked)—I undid it just so much that a single thin ray fell upon the vulture eye. And this I did for seven long nights—every night just at midnight—but I found the eye always closed; and so it was impossible to do the work; for it was not the old man who vexed me, but his Evil Eye. And every morning, when the day broke, I went boldly into the chamber, and spoke courageously to him, calling him by name in a hearty tone, and inquiring how he has passed the night. So you see he would have been a very profound old man, indeed, to suspect that every night, just at twelve, I looked in upon him while he slept.

Upon the eighth night I was more than usually cautious in opening the door. A watch's minute hand moves more quickly than did mine. Never before that night had I *felt* the extent of my own powers—of my sagacity. I could scarcely contain my feelings of triumph. To think that there I was, opening the door, little by little, and he not even to dream of my secret deeds or thoughts. I fairly chuckled at the idea; and perhaps he heard me; for he moved on the bed suddenly, as if startled. Now you may think that I drew back—but no. His room was as black as pitch with the thick darkness (for the shutters were close fastened, through fear of robbers), and so I knew that he could not see the opening of the door, and I kept pushing it on steadily, steadily.

I had my head in, and was about to open the lantern, when my thumb slipped upon the tin fastening, and the old man sprang up in bed, crying out—"Who's there?"

I kept quite still and said nothing. For a whole hour I did not move a muscle, and in the meantime I did not hear him lie down. He was still sitting up in the bed listening;—just as I have done, night after night, hearkening to the death watches in the wall.

Presently I heard a slight groan, and I knew it was the groan of mortal terror. It was not a groan of pain or of grief—oh, no!—it was the low stifled sound that arises from the bottom of the soul when overcharged with awe. I knew the sound well. Many a night, just at midnight, when all the world slept, it has welled up from my own bosom, deepening, with its dreadful echo, the terrors that distracted me. I say I knew it well. I knew what the old man felt, and pitied him, although I chuckled at heart. I knew that he had been lying awake ever since the first slight noise, when he had turned in the bed. His fears had been ever since growing upon him. He had been trying to fancy them causeless, but could not. He had been saying to himself—"It is nothing but the wind in the chimney—it is only a mouse crossing the floor," or "It is merely a cricket which has made a single chirp." Yes, he had been trying to comfort himself with these suppositions: but he had found all in vain. *All in vain*; because Death, in approaching him had stalked with his black shadow before him, and enveloped the victim. And it was the mournful influence of the unperceived shadow that caused him to feel—although he neither saw nor heard—to *feel* the presence of my head within the room.

When I had waited a long time, very patiently, without hearing him lie down, I resolved to open a little—a very, very little crevice in the lantern. So I opened it—you cannot imagine how stealthily, stealthily—until, at length a simple dim ray, like the thread of the spider, shot from out the crevice and fell full upon the vulture eye.

It was open—wide, wide open—and I grew furious as I gazed upon it. I saw it with perfect distinctness—all a dull blue, with a hideous veil over it that chilled the very marrow in my bones; but I could see nothing else of the old man's face or person: for I had directed the ray as if by instinct, precisely upon the damned spot.

And have I not told you that what you mistake for madness is but over-acuteness of the senses?—now, I say, there came to my ears a low, dull, quick sound, such as a watch makes when enveloped in cotton. I knew *that* sound well, too. It was the beating of the old man's heart. It increased my fury, as the beating of a drum stimulates the soldier into courage.

But even yet I refrained and kept still. I scarcely breathed. I held the lantern motionless. I tried how steadily I could maintain the ray upon the eve. Meantime the hellish tattoo of the heart increased. It grew quicker and quicker, and louder and louder every instant. The old man's terror *must* have been extreme! It grew louder, I say, louder every moment!—do you mark me well I have told you that I am nervous: so I am. And now at the dead hour of the night, amid the dreadful silence of that old house, so strange a noise as this excited me to uncontrollable terror. Yet, for some minutes longer I refrained and stood still. But the beating grew louder, louder! I thought the heart must burst. And now a new anxiety seized me—the sound would be heard by a neighbour! The old man's hour had come! With a loud yell, I threw open the lantern and leaped into the room. He shrieked once—once only. In an instant I dragged him to the floor, and pulled the heavy bed over him. I then smiled gaily, to find the deed so far done. But, for many minutes, the heart beat on with a muffled sound. This, however, did not vex me; it would not be heard through the wall. At length it ceased. The old man was dead. I removed the bed and examined the corpse. Yes, he was stone, stone dead. I placed my hand upon the heart and held it there many minutes. There was no pulsation. He was stone dead. His eye would trouble me no more.

If still you think me mad, you will think so no longer when I describe the wise precautions I took for the concealment of the body. The night waned, and I worked hastily, but in silence. First of all I dismembered the corpse. I cut off the head and the arms and the legs.

I then took up three planks from the flooring of the chamber, and deposited all between the scantlings. I then replaced the boards so cleverly, so cunningly, that no human eye—not even *his*—could have detected any thing wrong. There was nothing to wash out—no stain of any kind—no blood-spot whatever. I had been too wary for that. A tub had caught all—ha! ha!

When I had made an end of these labors, it was four o'clock—still dark as midnight. As the bell sounded the hour, there came a knocking at the street door. I went down to open it with a light heart,—for what had I *now* to fear? There entered three men, who introduced themselves, with perfect suavity, as officers of the police. A shriek had been heard by a neighbour during the night; suspicion of foul play had been aroused; information had been lodged at the police office, and they (the officers) had been deputed to search the premises.

I smiled—for *what* had I to fear? I bade the gentlemen welcome. The shriek, I said, was my own in a dream. The old man, I mentioned, was absent in the country. I took my visitors all over the house. I bade them search—search *well*. I led them, at length, to *his* chamber. I showed them his treasures, secure, undisturbed. In the enthusiasm of my confidence, I brought chairs into the room, and desired them *here* to rest from their fatigues, while I myself, in the wild audacity of my perfect triumph, placed my own seat upon the very spot beneath which reposed the corpse of the victim.

The officers were satisfied. My manner had convinced them. I was singularly at ease. They sat, and while I answered cheerily, they chatted of familiar things. But, ere long, I felt myself getting pale and wished them gone. My head ached, and I fancied a ringing in my ears: but still they sat and still chatted. The ringing became more distinct:—It continued and became more distinct: I talked more freely to get rid of the feeling: but it continued and gained definiteness—until, at length, I found that the noise was *not* within my ears.

No doubt I now grew *very* pale;—but I talked more fluently, and with a heightened voice. Yet the sound increased—and what could I do? It was a low, *dull, quick sound—much such a sound as a watch makes when enveloped in cotton.* I gasped for breath—and yet the officers heard it not. I talked more quickly—more vehemently; but the noise steadily increased. I arose and argued about trifles, in a high key and with violent gesticulations; but the noise steadily increased. Why *would* they not be gone? I paced the floor to and fro with heavy strides, as if excited to fury by the observations of the men—but the noise steadily increased. Oh God! What *could* I do? I foamed—I raved—I swore! I swung the chair upon which I had been sitting, and grated it upon the boards, but the noise arose over all and continually increased. It grew louder—louder—*louder*! And still the men chatted pleasantly, and smiled. Was it possible they heard not? Almighty God!—no, no! They heard!—they suspected!—they *knew*!—they were making a mockery of my horror!—this I thought, and this I think. But anything was better than this agony! Anything was more tolerable than this derision! I could bear those hypocritical smiles no longer! I felt that I must scream or die! and now—again!—hark! louder! louder! louder! *louder*!

"Villains!" I shrieked, "dissemble no more! I admit the deed!—tear up the planks! here, here!—It is the beating of his hideous heart!"

The Gold Bug

> What ho! what ho! this fellow is dancing mad!
> He hath been bitten by the Tarantula.
>
> —*All in the Wrong*

Many years ago, I contracted an intimacy with a Mr. William Legrand. He was of an ancient Huguenot family, and had once been wealthy; but a series of misfortunes had reduced him to want. To avoid the mortification consequent upon his disasters, he left New Orleans, the city of his forefathers, and took up his residence at Sullivan's Island, near Charleston, South Carolina.

This island is a very singular one. It consists of little else than the sea sand, and is about three miles long. Its breadth at no point exceeds a quarter of a mile. It is separated from the main land by a scarcely perceptible creek, oozing its way through a wilderness of reeds and slime, a favorite resort of the marsh hen. The vegetation, as might be supposed, is scant, or at least dwarfish. No trees of any magnitude are to be seen. Near the western extremity, where Fort Moultrie stands, and where are some miserable frame buildings, tenanted, during summer, by the fugitives from Charleston dust and fever, may be found, indeed, the bristly palmetto; but the whole island, with the exception of this western point, and a line of hard, white beach on the seacoast, is covered with a dense undergrowth of the sweet myrtle, so much prized by the horticulturists of England. The shrub here often attains the height of fifteen or twenty feet, and forms an almost impenetrable coppice, burthening the air with its fragrance.

In the inmost recesses of this coppice, not far from the eastern or more remote end of the island, Legrand had built himself a small hut, which he occupied when I first, by mere accident, made his acquaintance. This soon ripened into friendship—for there was much in the recluse to excite interest and esteem. I found him well educated, with unusual powers of mind, but infected with misanthropy, and subject to perverse moods of alternate enthusiasm and melancholy. He had with him many books, but rarely employed them. His chief amusements were gunning and fishing, or sauntering along the beach and through the myrtles, in quest of shells or entomological specimens—his collection of the latter might have been envied by a Swammerdamm. In these excursions he was usually accompanied by an old negro, called Jupiter, who had been manumitted before the reverses of the family, but who could be induced, neither by threats nor by promises, to abandon what he considered his right of attendance upon the footsteps of his young "Massa Will." It is not improbable that the relatives of Legrand, conceiving him to be somewhat unsettled in intellect, had contrived to instill this obstinacy into Jupiter, with a view to the supervision and guardianship of the wanderer.

The winters in the latitude of Sullivan's Island are seldom very severe, and in the fall of the year it is a rare event indeed when a fire is considered necessary. About the middle of October, 18—, there occurred, however, a day of remarkable chilliness. Just before sunset I scrambled my way through the evergreens to the hut of my friend, whom I had not visited for several weeks—my residence being, at that time, in Charleston, a distance of nine miles from the Island, while the facilities of passage and re-passage were very far behind those of the present day. Upon reaching the hut I rapped, as was my custom, and getting no reply, sought for the key where I knew it was secreted, unlocked the door and went in. A fine fire was blazing upon the hearth. It was a novelty, and by no means an ungrateful one. I threw off an overcoat, took an arm-chair by the crackling logs, and awaited patiently the arrival of my hosts.

Soon after dark they arrived, and gave me a most cordial welcome. Jupiter, grinning from ear to ear, bustled about to prepare some marsh-hens for supper. Legrand was in one of his fits—how else shall I term them?—of enthusiasm. He had found an unknown bivalve, forming a new genus, and, more than this, he had hunted down and secured, with Jupiter's assistance, a *scarabaeus* which he believed to be totally new, but in respect to which he wished to have my opinion on the morrow.

"And why not tonight?" I asked, rubbing my hands over the blaze, and wishing the whole tribe of *scarabaei* at the devil.

"Ah, if I had only known you were here!" said Legrand, "but it's so long since I saw you; and how could I foresee that you would pay me a visit this very night of all others? As I was coming home I met Lieutenant G—, from the fort, and, very foolishly, I lent him the bug; so it will be impossible for you to see it until the morning. Stay here to-night, and I will send Jup down for it at sunrise. It is the loveliest thing in creation!"

"What?—sunrise?"

"Nonsense! no!—the bug. It is of a brilliant gold color—about the size of a large hickory-nut—with two jet black spots near one extremity of the back, and another, somewhat longer, at the other. The *antennae* are—"

"Dey aint *no* tin in him, Massa Will, I keep a tellin on you," here interrupted Jupiter; "de bug is a goole bug, solid, ebery bit of him, inside and all, sep him wing—neber feel half so hebby a bug in my life."

"Well, suppose it is, Jup," replied Legrand, somewhat more earnestly, it seemed to me, than the case demanded, "is that any reason for your letting the birds burn? The color"—here he turned to me—"is really almost enough to warrant Jupiter's idea. You never saw a more brilliant metallic lustre than the scales emit—but of this you cannot judge till tomorrow. In the meantime I can give you some idea of the shape." Saying this, he seated himself at a small table, on which were a pen and ink, but no paper. He looked for some in a drawer, but found none.

"Never mind," said he at length, "this will answer;" and he drew from his waistcoat pocket a scrap of what I took to be very dirty foolscap, and made upon it a rough drawing with the pen. While he did this, I retained my seat by the fire, for I was still chilly. When the design was complete, he handed it to me without rising. As I received it, a loud growl was heard, succeeded by a scratching at the door. Jupiter opened it, and a large Newfoundland, belonging to Legrand, rushed in, leaped upon my shoulders, and loaded me with caresses; for I had shown him much attention during previous visits. When his gambols were over, I looked at the paper, and, to speak the truth, found myself not a little puzzled at what my friend had depicted.

"Well!" I said, after contemplating it for some minutes, "this is a strange *scarabaeus*, I must confess: new to me: never saw anything like it before—unless it was a skull, or a death's-head—which it more nearly resembles than anything else that has come under *my* observation."

"A death's-head!" echoed Legrand—"Oh—yes—well, it has something of that appearance upon paper, no doubt. The two upper black spots look like eyes, eh? and the longer one at the bottom like a mouth—and then the shape of the whole is oval."

"Perhaps so," said I; "but, Legrand, I fear you are no artist. I must wait until I see the beetle itself, if I am to form any idea of its personal appearance."

"Well, I don't know," said he, a little nettled, "I draw tolerably—*should* do it at least—have had good masters, and flatter myself that I am not quite a blockhead."

"But, my dear fellow, you are joking then," said I, "this is a very passable *skull*—indeed, I may say that it is a very *excellent* skull, according to the vulgar notions about such specimens of physiology—and your *scarabaeus* must be the queerest *scarabaeus* in the world if it resembles it. Why, we may get up a very thrilling bit of superstition upon this hint. I presume you will call the bug *scarabaeus caput hominis*, or something of that kind—there are many similar titles in the Natural Histories. But where are the *antennae* you spoke of?"

"The *antennae*!" said Legrand, who seemed to be getting unaccountably warm upon the subject; "I am sure you must see the *antennae*. I made them as distinct as they are in the original insect, and I presume that is sufficient."

"Well, well," I said, "perhaps you have—still I don't see them;" and I handed him the paper without additional remark, not wishing to ruffle his temper; but I was much surprised at the turn affairs had taken; his ill humor puzzled me—and, as for the drawing of the beetle, there were positively *no antennae* visible, and the whole *did* bear a very close resemblance to the ordinary cuts of a death's-head.

He received the paper very peevishly, and was about to crumple it, apparently to throw it in the fire, when a casual glance at the design seemed suddenly to rivet his attention. In an instant his face grew violently red—in another as excessively pale. For some minutes he continued to scrutinize the drawing minutely where he sat. At length he arose, took a candle from the table, and proceeded to seat himself upon a sea-chest in the farthest corner of the room. Here again he made an anxious examination of the paper; turning it in all directions. He said nothing, however, and his conduct greatly astonished me; yet I thought it prudent not to exacerbate the growing moodiness of his temper by any comment. Presently he took from his coat pocket a wallet, placed the paper carefully in it, and deposited both in a writing-desk, which he locked. He now grew more composed in his demeanor; but his original air of enthusiasm had quite disappeared. Yet he seemed not so much sulky as abstracted. As the evening wore away he became more and more absorbed in reverie, from which no sallies of mine could arouse him. It had been my intention to pass the night at the hut, as I had frequently done before, but, seeing my host in this mood, I deemed it proper to take leave. He did not press me to remain, but, as I departed, he shook my hand with even more than his usual cordiality.

It was about a month after this (and during the interval I had seen nothing of Legrand) when I received a visit, at Charleston, from his man, Jupiter. I had never seen the good old negro look so dispirited, and I feared that some serious disaster had befallen my friend.

"Well, Jup," said I, "what is the matter now?—how is your master?"

"Why, to speak de troof, massa, him not so berry well as mought be."

"Not well! I am truly sorry to hear it. What does he complain of?"

"Dar! dat's it!—him neber plain of notin—but him berry sick for all dat."

"*Very* sick, Jupiter!—why didn't you say so at once? Is he confined to bed?"

"No, dat he aint!—he aint find nowhar—dat's just whar de shoe pinch—my mind is got to be berry hebby bout poor Massa Will."

"Jupiter, I should like to understand what it is you are talking about. You say your master is sick. Hasn't he told you what ails him?"

"Why, massa, taint worf while for to git mad about de matter—Massa Will say noffin at all aint de matter wid him—but den what make him go about looking dis here way, wid he head down and he soldiers up, and as white as a gose? And den he keep a syphon all de time—"

"Keeps a what, Jupiter?"

"Keeps a syphon wid de figgurs on de slate—de queerest figgurs I ebber did see. Ise gittin to be skeered, I tell you. Hab for to keep mighty tight eye pon him noovers. Todder day he gib me slip fore de sun up and was gone de whole ob de blessed day. I had a big stick ready cut for to gib him deuced good beating when he did come—but Ise sich a fool dat I hadn't de heart arter all—he look so berry poorly."

"Eh?—what?—ah yes!—upon the whole I think you had better not be too severe with the poor fellow—don't flog him, Jupiter—he can't very well stand it—but can you form no idea of what has occasioned this illness, or rather this change of conduct? Has anything unpleasant happened since I saw you?"

"No, massa, dey aint bin noffin unpleasant *since* den—'twas *fore* den I'm feared—'twas de berry day you was dare."

"How? what do you mean?"

"Why, massa, I mean de bug—dare now."

"The what?"

"De bug,—I'm berry sartain dat Massa Will bin bit somewhere bout de head by dat goole-bug."

"And what cause have you, Jupiter, for such a supposition?"

"Claws enuff, massa, and mouth too. I nebber did see sick a deuced bug—he kick and he bite ebery ting what cum near him. Massa Will cotch him fuss, but had for to let him go gin mighty quick, I tell you—den was de time he must ha got de bite. I didn't like de look oh de bug mouff, myself, no how, so I wouldn't take hold ob him wid my finger, but I cotch him wid a piece ob paper dat I found. I rap him up in de paper and stuff piece ob it in he mouff—dat was de way."

"And you think, then, that your master was really bitten by the beetle, and that the bite made him sick?"

"I don't tink noffin about it—I nose it. What make him dream bout de goole so much, if taint cause he bit by de goole-bug? Ise heerd bout dem goole-bugs fore dis."

"But how do you know he dreams about gold?"

"How I know? why cause he talk about it in he sleep—dat's how I nose."

"Well, Jup, perhaps you are right; but to what fortunate circumstance am I to attribute the honor of a visit from you today?"

"What de matter, massa?"

"Did you bring any message from Mr. Legrand?"

"No, massa, I bring dis here pissel;" and here Jupiter handed me a note which ran thus:

> MY DEAR ——
>
> Why have I not seen you for so long a time? I hope you have not been so foolish as to take offence at any little *brusquerie* of mine; but no, that is improbable.
>
> Since I saw you I have had great cause for anxiety. I have something to tell you, yet scarcely know how to tell it, or whether I should tell it at all.
>
> I have not been quite well for some days past, and poor old Jup annoys me, almost beyond endurance, by his well-meant attentions. Would you believe it?—he had prepared a huge stick, the other day, with which to chastise me for giving him the slip, and spending the day, *solus*, among the hills on the main land. I verily believe that my ill looks alone saved me a flogging.
>
> I have made no addition to my cabinet since we met.
>
> If you can, in any way, make it convenient, come over with Jupiter. *Do* come. I wish to see you *tonight*, upon business of importance. I assure you that it is of the *highest* importance.
>
> Ever yours,
> WILLIAM LEGRAND

There was something in the tone of this note which gave me great uneasiness. Its whole style differed materially from that of Legrand.

What could he be dreaming of? What new crotchet possessed his excitable brain? What "business of the highest importance" could *he* possibly have to transact? Jupiter's account of him boded no good. I dreaded lest the continued pressure of misfortune had, at length, fairly unsettled the reason of my friend. Without a moment's hesitation, therefore, I prepared to accompany the negro.

Upon reaching the wharf, I noticed a scythe and three spades, all apparently new, lying in the bottom of the boat in which we were to embark.

"What is the meaning of all this, Jup?" I inquired.

"Him syfe, massa, and spade."

"Very true; but what are they doing here?"

"Him de syfe and de spade what Massa Will sis pon my buying for him in de town, and de debbils own lot of money I had to gib for em."

"But what, in the name of all that is mysterious, is your 'Massa Will' going to do with scythes and spades?"

"Dat's more dan *I* know, and debbil take me if I don't blieve 'tis more dan he know, too. But it's all cum ob do bug."

Finding that no satisfaction was to be obtained of Jupiter, whose whole intellect seemed to be absorbed by "de bug," I now stepped into the boat and made sail. With a fair and strong breeze we soon ran into the little cove to the northward of Fort Moultrie, and a walk of some two miles brought us to the hut. It was about three in the afternoon when we arrived. Legrand had been awaiting us in eager expectation. He grasped my hand with a nervous *empressement* which alarmed me and strengthened the suspicions already entertained. His countenance was pale even to ghastliness, and his deep-set eyes glared with unnatural lustre. After some inquiries respecting his health, I asked him, not knowing what better to say, if he had yet obtained the *scarabaeus* from Lieutenant G ——.

"Oh, yes," he replied, coloring violently, "I got it from him the next morning. Nothing should tempt me to part with that *scarabaeus*. Do you know that Jupiter is quite right about it?"

"In what way?" I asked, with a sad foreboding at heart.

"In supposing it to be a bug of *real gold*." He said this with an air of profound seriousness, and I felt inexpressibly shocked.

"This bug is to make my fortune," he continued, with a

triumphant smile, "to reinstate me in my family possessions. Is it any wonder, then, that I prize it? Since Fortune has thought fit to bestow it upon me, I have only to use it properly and I shall arrive at the gold of which it is the index. Jupiter; bring me that *scarabaeus*!"

"What! de bug, massa? I'd rudder not go fer trubble dat bug—you mus git him for your own self." Hereupon Legrand arose, with a grave and stately air, and brought me the beetle from a glass case in which it was enclosed. It was a beautiful *scarabaeus*, and, at that time, unknown to naturalists—of course a great prize in a scientific point of view. There were two round, black spots near one extremity of the back, and a long one near the other. The scales were exceedingly hard and glossy, with all the appearance of burnished gold. The weight of the insect was very remarkable, and, taking all things into consideration, I could hardly blame Jupiter for his opinion respecting it; but what to make of Legrand's concordance with that opinion, I could not, for the life of me, tell.

"I sent for you," said he, in a grandiloquent tone, when I had completed my examination of the beetle, "I sent for you, that I might have your counsel and assistance in furthering the views of Fate and of the bug"—

"My dear Legrand," I cried, interrupting him, "you are certainly unwell, and had better use some little precautions. You shall go to bed, and I will remain with you a few days, until you get over this. You are feverish and"—

"Feel my pulse," said he.

I felt it, and, to say the truth, found not the slightest indication of fever.

"But you may be ill and yet have no fever. Allow me this once to prescribe for you. In the first place, go to bed. In the next"—

"You are mistaken," he interposed, "I am as well as I can expect to be under the excitement which I suffer. If you really wish me well, you will relieve this excitement."

"And how is this to be done?"

"Very easily. Jupiter and myself are going upon an expedition into the hills, upon the main land, and, in this expedition we shall need the aid of some person in whom we can confide. You are the only one we can trust. Whether we succeed or fail, the excitement which you now perceive in me will be equally allayed."

"I am anxious to oblige you in any way," I replied; "but do you mean to say that this infernal beetle has any connection with your expedition into the hills?"

"It has."

"Then, Legrand, I can become a party to no such absurd proceeding."

"I am sorry—very sorry—for we shall have to try it by ourselves."

"Try it by yourselves! The man is surely mad!—but stay!—how long do you propose to be absent?"

"Probably all night. We shall start immediately, and be back, at all events, by sunrise."

"And will you promise me, upon your honor, that when this freak of yours is over, and the bug business (good God!) settled to your satisfaction, you will then return home and follow my advice implicitly, as that of your physician?"

"Yes; I promise; and now let us be off, for we have no time to lose."

With a heavy heart I accompanied my friend. We started about four o'clock—Legrand, Jupiter, the dog, and myself. Jupiter had with him the scythe and spades—the whole of which he insisted upon carrying—more through fear, it seemed to me, of trusting either of the implements within reach of his master, than from any excess of industry or complaisance. His demeanor was dogged in the extreme, and "dat deuced bug" were the sole words which escaped his lips during the journey. For my own part, I had charge of a couple of dark lanterns, while Legrand contented himself with the *scarabaeus*, which he carried attached to the end of a bit of whip-cord; twirling it to and fro, with the air of a conjuror, as he went. When I observed this last, plain evidence of my friend's aberration of mind, I could scarcely refrain from tears. I thought it best, however, to humor his fancy, at least for the present, or until I could adopt some more energetic measures with a chance of success. In the meantime I endeavored, but all in vain, to sound him in regard to the object of the expedition. Having succeeded in inducing me to accompany him, he seemed unwilling to hold conversation upon any topic of minor importance, and to all my questions vouchsafed no other reply than "we shall see!"

We crossed the creek at the head of the island by means of a skiff; and, ascending the high grounds on the shore of the main land, proceeded in a northwesterly direction, through a tract of country excessively wild and desolate, where no trace of a human footstep was to be seen. Legrand led the way with decision; pausing only for an instant, here and there, to consult what appeared to be certain landmarks of his own contrivance upon a former occasion.

In this manner we journeyed for about two hours, and the sun was just setting when we entered a region infinitely more dreary than any yet seen. It was a species of table land, near the summit of an almost inaccessible hill, densely wooded from base to pinnacle, and interspersed with huge crags that appeared to lie loosely upon the soil, and in many cases were prevented from precipitating themselves into the valleys below, merely by the support of the trees against which they reclined. Deep ravines, in various directions, gave an air of still sterner solemnity to the scene.

The natural platform to which we had clambered was thickly overgrown with brambles, through which we soon discovered that it would have been impossible to force our way but for the scythe; and Jupiter, by direction of his master, proceeded to clear for us a path to the foot of an enormously tall tulip-tree, which stood, with some eight or ten oaks, upon the level, and far surpassed them all, and all other trees which I had then ever seen, in the beauty of its foliage and form, in the wide spread of its branches, and in the general majesty of its appearance. When we reached this tree, Legrand turned to Jupiter, and asked him if he thought he could climb it. The old man seemed a little staggered by the question, and for some moments made no reply. At length he approached the huge trunk, walked slowly around it, and examined it with minute attention. When he had completed his scrutiny, he merely said, "Yes, massa, Jup climb any tree he ebber see in he life."

"Then up with you as soon as possible, for it will soon be too dark to see what we are about."

"How far mus go up, massa?" inquired Jupiter.

"Get up the main trunk first, and then I will tell you which way to go—and here—stop! take this beetle with you."

"De bug, Massa Will!—de goole bug!" cried the negro, drawing back in dismay—"what for mus tote de bug way up de tree?—d—n if I do!"

"If you are afraid, Jup, a great big negro like you, to take hold of a harmless little dead beetle, why you can carry it up by this string—but, if you do not take it up with you in some way, I shall be under the necessity of breaking your head with this shovel."

"What de matter now, massa?" said Jup, evidently shamed into compliance; "always want for to raise fuss wid old nigger. Was only funnin any how. *Me* feered de bug! what I keer for de bug?" Here he took cautiously hold of the extreme end of the string, and, maintaining the insect as far from his person as circumstances would permit, prepared to ascend the tree.

In youth, the tulip tree, or *Liriodendron Tulipferum*, the most magnificent of American foresters, has a trunk peculiarly smooth, and often rises to a great height without lateral branches; but, in its riper age, the bark becomes gnarled and uneven, while many short limbs make their appearance on the stem. Thus the difficulty of ascension, in the present case, lay more in semblance than in reality. Embracing the huge cylinder, as closely as possible, with his arms and knees, seizing with his hands some projections, and resting his naked toes upon others, Jupiter, after one or two narrow escapes from falling, at length wriggled himself into the first great fork, and seemed to consider the whole business as virtually accomplished. The risk of the achievement was, in fact, now over, although the climber was some sixty or seventy feet from the ground.

"Which way mus go now, Massa Will?" he asked.

"Keep up the largest branch—the one on this side," said Legrand. The negro obeyed him promptly, and apparently with but little trouble; ascending higher and higher, until no glimpse of his squat figure could be obtained through the dense foliage which enveloped it. Presently his voice was heard in a sort of halloo.

"How much fudder is got for go?"

"How high up are you?" asked Legrand.

"Ebber so fur," replied the negro; "can see de sky fru de top ob de tree."

"Never mind the sky, but attend to what I say. Look down the trunk and count the limbs below you on this side. How many limbs have you passed?"

"One, two, tree, four, fibe—I done pass fibe big limb, massa, pon dis side."

"Then go one limb higher."

In a few minutes the voice was heard again, announcing that the seventh limb was attained.

"Now, Jup," cried Legrand, evidently much excited, "I want you to work your way out upon that limb as far as you can. If you see anything strange, let me know."

By this time what little doubt I might have entertained of my poor friend's insanity, was put finally at rest. I had no alternative but to conclude him stricken with lunacy, and I became seriously anxious about getting him home. While I was pondering upon what was best to be done, Jupiter's voice was again heard.

"Mos feerd for to ventur pon dis limb berry far—tis dead limb putty much all de way."

"Did you say it was a *dead* limb, Jupiter?" cried Legrand in a quavering voice.

"Yes, massa, him dead as de door-nail—done up for sartain—done departed dis here life."

"What in the name of heaven shall I do?" asked Legrand, seemingly in the greatest distress.

"Do!" said I, glad of an opportunity to interpose a word, "why come home and go to bed. Come now!—that's a fine fellow. It's getting late, and, besides, you remember your promise."

"Jupiter," cried he, without heeding me in the least, "do you hear me?"

"Yes, Massa Will, hear you ebber so plain."

"Try the wood well, then, with your knife, and see if you think it *very* rotten."

"Him rotten, massa, sure nuff," replied the negro in a few moments, "but not so berry rotten as mought be. Mought ventur out leetle way pon de limb by myself, dat's true."

"By yourself!—what do you mean?"

"Why I mean de bug. 'Tis *berry* hebby bug. Spose I drop him down fuss, and den de limb won't break wid just de weight ob one nigger."

"You infernal scoundrel!" cried Legrand, apparently much relieved, "what do you mean by telling me such nonsense as that? As sure as you drop that beetle I'll break your neck. Look here, Jupiter, do you hear me?"

"Yes, massa, needn't hollo at poor nigger dat style."

"Well! now listen!—if you will venture out on the limb as far as you think safe, and not let go the beetle, I'll make you a present of a silver dollar as soon as you get down."

"I'm gwine, Massa Will—deed I is," replied the negro very promptly—"mos out to the end now."

"*Out to the end!*" here fairly screamed Legrand, "do you say you are out to the end of that limb?"

"Soon be to de end, massa,—o-o-o-o-oh! Lor-gol-a-marcy! what *is* dis here pon de tree?"

"Well!" cried Legrand, highly delighted, "what is it?"

"Why taint noffin but a skull—somebody bin lef him head up de tree, and de crows done gobble ebery bit ob de meat off."

"A skull, you say!—very well!—how is it fastened to the limb?—what holds it on?"

"Sure nuff, massa; mus look. Why dis berry curous sarcumstance, pon my word—dare's a great big nail in de skull, what fastens ob it on to de tree."

"Well now, Jupiter, do exactly as I tell you—do you hear?"

"Yes, massa."

"Pay attention, then!—find the left eye of the skull."

"Hum! hoo! dat's good! why dare aint no eye lef at all."

"Curse your stupidity! do you know your right hand from your left?"

"Yes, I nose dat—nose all bout dat—tis my lef hand what I chops de wood wid."

"To be sure! you are left-handed; and your left eye is on the same side as your left hand. Now, I suppose, you can find the left eye of the skull, or the place where the left eye has been. Have you found it?"

Here was a long pause. At length the negro asked,

"Is de lef eye of de skull pon de same side as de lef hand of de skull, too?—cause de skull aint got not a bit ob a hand at all—nebber mind! I got de lef eye now—here de lef eye! what mus do wid it?"

"Let the beetle drop through it, as far as the string will reach—but be careful and not let go your hold of the string."

"All dat done, Massa Will; mighty easy ting for to put de bug fru de hole—look out for him dare below!"

During this colloquy no portion of Jupiter's person could be seen;

but the beetle, which he had suffered to descend, was now visible at the end of the string, and glistened, like a globe of burnished gold, in the last rays of the setting sun, some of which still faintly illumined the eminence upon which we stood. The *scarabaeus* hung quite clear of any branches, and, if allowed to fall, would have fallen at our feet. Legrand immediately took the scythe, and cleared with it a circular space, three or four yards in diameter, just beneath the insect, and, having accomplished this, ordered Jupiter to let go the string and come down from the tree.

Driving a peg, with great nicety, into the ground, at the precise spot where the beetle fell, my friend now produced from his pocket a tape measure. Fastening one end of this at that point of the trunk, of the tree which was nearest the peg, he unrolled it till it reached the peg, and thence farther unrolled it, in the direction already established by the two points of the tree and the peg, for the distance of fifty feet—Jupiter clearing away the brambles with the scythe. At the spot thus attained a second peg was driven, and about this, as a centre, a rude circle, about four feet in diameter, described. Taking now a spade himself, and giving one to Jupiter and one to me, Legrand begged us to set about digging as quickly as possible.

To speak the truth, I had no especial relish for such amusement at any time, and, at that particular moment, would most willingly have declined it; for the night was coming on, and I felt much fatigued with the exercise already taken; but I saw no mode of escape, and was fearful of disturbing my poor friend's equanimity by a refusal. Could I have depended, indeed, upon Jupiter's aid, I would have had no hesitation in attempting to get the lunatic home by force; but I was too well assured of the old negro's disposition, to hope that he would assist me, under any circumstances, in a personal contest with his master. I made no doubt that the latter had been infected with some of the innumerable Southern superstitions about money buried, and that his phantasy had received confirmation by the finding of the *scarabaeus*, or, perhaps, by Jupiter's obstinacy in maintaining it to be "a bug of real gold." A mind disposed to lunacy would readily be led away by such suggestions—especially if chiming in with favorite preconceived ideas—and then I called to mind the poor fellow's speech about the beetle's being "the index of his fortune." Upon the whole, I was sadly vexed and puzzled, but, at length, I concluded to make a virtue of necessity—to dig with a good will, and thus the sooner to convince the visionary, by ocular demonstration, of the fallacy of the opinions he entertained.

The lanterns having been lit, we all fell to work with a zeal worthy a more rational cause; and, as the glare fell upon our persons and implements, I could not help thinking how picturesque a group we composed, and how strange and suspicious our labors must have appeared to any interloper who, by chance, might have stumbled upon our whereabouts.

We dug very steadily for two hours. Little was said; and our chief embarrassment lay in the yelpings of the dog, who took exceeding interest in our proceedings. He, at length, became so obstreperous that we grew fearful of his giving the alarm to some stragglers in the vicinity;—or, rather, this was the apprehension of Legrand;—for myself, I should have rejoiced at any interruption which might have enabled me to get the wanderer home. The noise was, at length, very effectually silenced by Jupiter, who, getting out of the hole with a dogged air of deliberation, tied the brute's mouth up with one of his suspenders, and then returned, with a grave chuckle, to his task.

When the time mentioned had expired, we had reached a depth of five feet, and yet no signs of any treasure became manifest. A general pause ensued, and I began to hope that the farce was at an end. Legrand, however, although evidently much disconcerted, wiped his brow thoughtfully and recommenced. We had excavated the entire circle of four feet diameter, and now we slightly enlarged the limit, and went to the farther depth of two feet. Still nothing appeared. The gold-seeker, whom I sincerely pitied, at length clambered from the pit, with the bitterest disappointment imprinted upon every feature, and proceeded, slowly and reluctantly, to put on his coat, which he had thrown off at the beginning of his labor. In the meantime I made no remark. Jupiter, at a signal from his master, began to gather up his tools. This done, and the dog having been unmuzzled, we turned in profound silence towards home.

We had taken, perhaps, a dozen steps in this direction, when, with a loud oath, Legrand strode up to Jupiter, and seized him by the collar. The astonished negro opened his eyes and mouth to the fullest extent, let fall the spades, and fell upon his knees.

"You scoundrel," said Legrand, hissing out the syllables from between his clenched teeth—"you infernal black villain!—speak, I tell you!—answer me this instant, without prevarication!—which—which is your left eye?"

"Oh, my golly, Massa Will! aint dis here my lef eye for sartain?" roared the terrified Jupiter, placing his hand upon his *right* organ of vision, and holding it there with a desperate pertinacity, as if in immediate dread of his master's attempt at a gouge.

"I thought so!—I knew it! hurrah!" vociferated Legrand, letting the negro go, and executing a series of curvets and caracols, much to the astonishment of his valet, who, arising from his knees, looked, mutely, from his master to myself, and then from myself to his master.

"Come! we must go back," said the latter, "the game's not up yet;" and he again led the way to the tulip tree.

"Jupiter," said he, when we reached its foot, "come here! was the skull nailed to the limb with the face outwards, or with the face to the limb?"

"De face was out, massa, so dat de crows could get at de eyes good, widout any trouble."

"Well, then, was it this eye or that through which you dropped the beetle?"—here Legrand touched each of Jupiter's eyes.

"Twas dis eye, massa—de lef eye—jis as you tell me," and here it was his right eye that the negro indicated.

"That will do—must try it again."

Here my friend, about whose madness I now saw, or fancied that I saw, certain indications of method, removed the peg which marked the spot where the beetle fell, to a spot about three inches to the westward of its former position. Taking, now, the tape measure from the nearest point of the trunk to the peg, as before, and continuing the extension in a straight line to the distance of fifty feet, a spot was indicated, removed, by several yards, from the point at which we had been digging.

Around the new position a circle, somewhat larger than in the former instance, was now described, and we again set to work with the spades. I was dreadfully weary, but, scarcely understanding what had occasioned the change in my thoughts, I felt no longer any great aversion from the labor imposed. I had become most unaccountably interested—nay, even excited. Perhaps there was something, amid all the extravagant demeanor of Legrand—some air of forethought, or of deliberation, which impressed me. I dug eagerly, and now and then caught myself actually looking, with something that very much resembled expectation, for the fancied treasure, the vision of which had demented my unfortunate companion. At a period when such vagaries of thought most fully possessed me, and when we had been at work perhaps an hour and a half, we were again interrupted by the violent howlings of the dog. His uneasiness, in the first instance, had been, evidently, but the result of playfulness or caprice, but he now assumed a bitter and serious tone. Upon Jupiter's again attempting to muzzle him, he made furious resistance, and, leaping into the hole, tore up the mould frantically with his claws. In a few seconds he had uncovered a mass of human bones, forming two complete skeletons, intermingled with several buttons of metal, and what appeared to be the dust of decayed woollen. One or two strokes of a spade upturned the blade of a large Spanish knife, and, as we dug farther, three or four loose pieces of gold and silver coin came to light.

At sight of these the joy of Jupiter could scarcely be restrained, but the countenance of his master wore an air of extreme disappointment He urged us, however, to continue our exertions, and the words were hardly uttered when I stumbled and fell forward, having caught the toe of my boot in a large ring of iron that lay half buried in the loose earth.

We now worked in earnest, and never did I pass ten minutes of more intense excitement. During this interval we had fairly unearthed an oblong chest of wood, which, from its perfect preservation and wonderful hardness, had plainly been subjected to some mineralizing process—perhaps that of the Bi-chloride of Mercury. This box was three feet and a half long, three feet broad, and two and a half feet deep. It was firmly secured by bands of wrought iron, riveted, and forming a kind of open trelliswork over the whole. On each side of the chest, near the top, were three rings of iron—six in all—by means of which a firm hold could be obtained by six persons. Our utmost united endeavors served only to disturb the coffer very slightly in its bed. We at once saw the impossibility of removing so great a weight. Luckily, the sole fastenings of the lid consisted of two sliding bolts. These we drew back—trembling and panting with anxiety. In an instant, a treasure of incalculable value lay gleaming before us. As the rays of the lanterns fell within the pit, there flashed upwards a glow and a glare, from a confused heap of gold and of jewels, that absolutely dazzled our eyes.

I shall not pretend to describe the feelings with which I gazed. Amazement was, of course, predominant. Legrand appeared exhausted with excitement, and spoke very few words. Jupiter's countenance wore, for some minutes, as deadly a pallor as it is possible, in nature of things, for any negro's visage to assume. He seemed stupefied—thunderstricken. Presently he fell upon his knees in the pit, and, burying his naked arms up to the elbows in gold, let them there remain, as if enjoying the luxury of a bath. At length, with a deep sigh, he exclaimed, as if in a soliloquy, "And dis all cum ob de goole-bug! de putty goole bug! de poor little goole-bug, what I boosed in dat sabage kind ob style! Aint you shamed ob yourself, nigger?—answer me dat!"

It became necessary, at last, that I should arouse both master and valet to the expediency of removing the treasure. It was growing late, and it behooved us to make exertion, that we might get every thing housed before daylight. It was difficult to say what should be done, and much time was spent in deliberation—so confused were the ideas of all. We, finally, lightened the box by removing two thirds of its contents, when we were enabled, with some trouble, to raise it from the hole. The articles taken out were deposited among the brambles, and the dog left to guard them, with strict orders from Jupiter neither, upon any pretence, to stir from the spot, nor to open his mouth until our return. We then hurriedly made for home with the chest; reaching the hut in safety, but after excessive toil, at one o'clock in the morning. Worn out as we were, it was not in human nature to do more immediately. We rested until two, and had supper; starting for the hills immediately afterwards, armed with three stout sacks, which, by good luck, were upon the premises. A little before four we arrived at the pit, divided the remainder of the booty, as equally as might be, among us, and, leaving the holes unfilled, again set out for the hut, at which, for the second time, we deposited our golden burthens, just as the first faint streaks of the dawn gleamed from over the tree-tops in the East.

We were now thoroughly broken down; but the intense excitement of the time denied us repose. After an unquiet slumber of some three or four hours' duration, we arose, as if by preconcert, to make examination of our treasure.

The chest had been full to the brim, and we spent the whole day, and the greater part of the next night, in a scrutiny of its contents. There had been nothing like order or arrangement. Every thing had been heaped in promiscuously. Having assorted all with care, we found ourselves possessed of even vaster wealth than we had at first supposed. In coin there was rather more than four hundred and fifty thousand dollars—estimating the value of the pieces, as accurately as we could, by the tables of the period. There was not a particle of silver. All was gold of antique date and of great variety—French, Spanish, and German money, with a few English guineas, and some counters, of which we had never seen specimens before. There were several very large and heavy coins, so worn that we could make nothing of their inscriptions. There was no American money. The value of the jewels we found more difficulty in estimating. There were diamonds—some of them exceedingly large and fine—a hundred and ten in all, and not one of them small; eighteen rubies of remarkable brilliancy—three hundred and ten emeralds, all very beautiful; and twenty-one sapphires, with an opal. These stones had all been broken from their settings and thrown loose in the chest. The settings themselves, which we picked out from among the other gold, appeared to have been beaten up with hammers, as if to prevent identification. Besides all this, there was a vast quantity of solid gold ornaments;—nearly two hundred massive finger and earrings;—rich chains—thirty of these, if I remember—eighty-three very large and heavy crucifixes—five gold censers of great value;—a prodigious golden punch bowl, ornamented with richly chased vine-leaves and Bacchanalian figures; with two sword-handles exquisitely embossed, and many other smaller articles which I cannot recollect. The weight of these valuables exceeded three hundred and fifty pounds avoirdupois; and in this estimate I have not included one hundred and ninety-seven superb gold watches; three of the number being worth each five hundred dollars, if one. Many of them were very old, and as time keepers valueless; the works having suffered, more or less, from corrosion—but all were richly jewelled and in cases of great worth. We estimated the entire contents of the chest, that night, at a million and a half of dollars;

and upon the subsequent disposal of the trinkets and jewels (a few being retained for our own use), it was found that we had greatly undervalued the treasure.

When, at length, we had concluded our examination, and the intense excitement of the time had, in some measure, subsided, Legrand, who saw that I was dying with impatience for a solution of this most extraordinary riddle, entered into a full detail of all the circumstances connected with it.

"You remember;" said he, "the night when I handed you the rough sketch I had made of the *scarabaeus*. You recollect also, that I became quite vexed at you for insisting that my drawing resembled a death's-head. When you first made this assertion I thought you were jesting; but afterwards I called to mind the peculiar spots on the back of the insect, and admitted to myself that your remark had some little foundation in fact. Still, the sneer at my graphic powers irritated me—for I am considered a good artist—and, therefore, when you handed me the scrap of parchment, I was about to crumple it up and throw it angrily into the fire."

"The scrap of paper, you mean," said I.

"No; it had much of the appearance of paper, and at first I supposed it to be such, but when I came to draw upon it, I discovered it, at once, to be a piece of very thin parchment. It was quite dirty, you remember. Well, as I was in the very act of crumpling it up, my glance fell upon the sketch at which you had been looking, and you may imagine my astonishment when I perceived, in fact, the figure of a death's-head just where, it seemed to me, I had made the drawing of the beetle. For a moment I was too much amazed to think with accuracy. I knew that my design was very different in detail from this—although there was a certain similarity in general outline. Presently I took a candle, and seating myself at the other end of the room, proceeded to scrutinize the parchment more closely. Upon turning it over, I saw my own sketch upon the reverse, just as I had made it. My first idea, now, was mere surprise at the really remarkable similarity of outline—at the singular coincidence involved in the fact, that unknown to me, there should have been a skull upon the other side of the parchment, immediately beneath my figure of the *scarabaeus*, and that this skull, not only in outline, but in size, should so closely resemble my drawing. I say the singularity of this coincidence absolutely stupefied me for a time. This is the usual effect of such coincidences. The mind struggles to establish a connexion—a sequence of cause and effect—and, being unable to do so, suffers a species of temporary paralysis. But, when I recovered from this stupor, there dawned upon me gradually a conviction which startled me even far more than the coincidence. I began distinctly, positively, to remember that there had been *no* drawing upon the parchment when I made my sketch of the *scarabaeus*. I became perfectly certain of this; for I recollected turning up first one side and then the other, in search of the cleanest spot. Had the skull been then there, of course I could not have failed to notice it. Here was indeed a mystery which I felt it impossible to explain; but, even at that early moment, there seemed to glimmer, faintly, within the most remote and secret chambers of my intellect, a glow-worm-like conception of that truth which last night's adventure brought to so magnificent a demonstration. I arose at once, and putting the parchment securely away, dismissed all farther reflection until I should be alone.

"When you had gone, and when Jupiter was fast asleep, I betook myself to a more methodical investigation of the affair. In the first place I considered the manner in which the parchment had come into my possession. The spot where we discovered the *scarabaeus* was on the coast of the main land, about a mile eastward of the island, and but a short distance above high water mark. Upon my taking hold of it, it gave me a sharp bite, which caused me to let it drop. Jupiter, with his accustomed caution, before seizing the insect, which had flown towards him, looked about him for a leaf, or something of that nature, by which to take hold of it. It was at this moment that his eyes, and mine also, fell upon the scrap of parchment, which I then supposed to be paper. It was lying half buried in the sand, a corner sticking up. Near the spot where we found it, I observed the remnants of the hull of what appeared to have been a ship's long boat. The wreck seemed to have been there for a very great while; for the resemblance to boat timbers could scarcely be traced.

"Well, Jupiter picked up the parchment, wrapped the beetle in it, and gave it to me. Soon afterwards we turned to go home, and on the way met Lieutenant G—. I showed him the insect, and he begged me to let him take it to the fort. Upon my consenting, he thrust it forthwith into his waistcoat pocket, without the parchment in which it had been wrapped, and which I had continued to hold in my hand during his inspection. Perhaps he dreaded my changing my mind, and thought it best to make sure of the prize at once—you know how enthusiastic he is on all subjects connected with Natural History. At the same time, without being conscious of it, I must have deposited the parchment in my own pocket.

"You remember that when I went to the table, for the purpose of making a sketch of the beetle, I found no paper where it was usually kept. I looked in the drawer, and found none there. I searched my pockets, hoping to find an old letter, when my hand fell upon the parchment. I thus detail the precise mode in which it came into my possession; for the circumstances impressed me with peculiar force.

"No doubt you will think me fanciful—but I had already established a kind of *connection*. I had put together two links of a great chain. There was a boat lying upon a sea-coast, and not far from the boat was a parchment—*not a paper*—with a skull depicted upon it. You will, of course, ask 'where is the connexion?' I reply that the skull, or death's-head, is the well-known emblem of the pirate. The flag of the death's head is hoisted in all engagements.

"I have said that the scrap was parchment, and not paper. Parchment is durable—almost imperishable. Matters of little moment are rarely consigned to parchment; since, for the mere ordinary purposes of drawing or writing, it is not nearly so well adapted as paper. This reflection suggested some meaning—some relevancy—in the death's-head. I did not fail to observe, also, the form of the parchment. Although one of its corners had been, by some accident, destroyed, it could be seen that the original form was oblong. It was just such a slip, indeed, as might have been chosen for a memorandum—for a record of something to be long remembered and carefully preserved."

"But," I interposed, "you say that the skull was *not* upon the parchment when you made the drawing of the beetle. How then do you trace any connexion between the boat and the skull—since this latter, according to your own admission, must have been designed (God only knows how or by whom) at some period subsequent to your sketching the *scarabaeus*?"

"Ah, hereupon turns the whole mystery; although the secret, at this point, I had comparatively little difficulty in solving. My steps were sure, and could afford but a single result. I reasoned, for example, thus: When I drew the *scarabaeus*, there was no skull apparent upon the parchment. When I had completed the drawing I gave it to you, and observed you narrowly until you returned it. *You*, therefore, did not design the skull, and no one else was present to do it. Then it was not done by human agency. And nevertheless it was done.

"At this stage of my reflections I endeavored to remember, and *did* remember, with entire distinctness, every incident which occurred about the period in question. The weather was chilly (oh rare and happy accident!), and a fire was blazing upon the hearth. I was heated with exercise and sat near the table. You, however, had drawn a chair close to the chimney. Just as I placed the parchment in your hand, and as you were in the act of inspecting it, Wolf, the Newfoundland, entered, and leaped upon your shoulders. With your left hand you caressed him and kept him off, while your right, holding the parchment, was permitted to fall listlessly between your knees, and in close proximity to the fire. At one moment I thought the blaze had caught it, and was about to caution you, but, before I could speak, you had withdrawn it, and were engaged in its examination. When I considered all these particulars, I doubted not for a moment that *heat* had been the agent in bringing to light, upon the parchment, the skull which I saw designed upon it. You are well aware that chemical preparations exist, and have existed time out of mind, by means of which it is possible to write upon either paper or vellum, so that the characters shall become visible only when subjected to the action of fire. Zaffre, digested in *aqua regia*, and diluted with four times its weight of water, is sometimes employed; a green tint results. The regulus of cobalt, dissolved in spirit of nitre, gives a red. These colors disappear at longer or shorter intervals after the material written upon cools, but again become apparent upon the re-application of heat.

"I now scrutinized the death's-head with care. Its outer edges—the edges of the drawing nearest the edge of the vellum—were far more *distinct* than the others. It was clear that the action of the caloric had been imperfect or unequal. I immediately kindled a fire, and subjected every portion of the parchment to a glowing heat. At first, the only effect was the strengthening of the faint lines in the skull; but, upon persevering in the experiment, there became visible, at the corner of the slip, diagonally opposite to the spot in which the death's-head was delineated, the figure of what I at first supposed to be a goat. A closer scrutiny, however, satisfied me that it was intended for a kid."

"Ha! ha!" said I, "to be sure I have no right to laugh at you—a million and a half of money is too serious a matter for mirth—but you are not about to establish a third link in your chain—you will not find any especial connexion between your pirates and a goat—pirates, you know, have nothing to do with goats; they appertain to the farming interest."

"But I have just said that the figure was *not* that of a goat."

"Well, a kid then—pretty much the same thing."

"Pretty much, but not altogether," said Legrand. "You may have heard of one *Captain* Kidd. I at once looked upon the figure of the animal as a kind of punning or hieroglyphical signature. I say signature; because its position upon the vellum suggested this idea. The death's-head at the corner diagonally opposite, had, in the same manner, the air of a stamp, or seal. But I was sorely put out by the absence of all else—of the body to my imagined instrument—of the text for my context."

"I presume you expected to find a letter between the stamp and the signature."

"Something of that kind. The fact is, I felt irresistibly impressed with a presentiment of some vast good fortune impending. I can scarcely say why. Perhaps, after all, it was rather a desire than an actual belief;—but do you know that Jupiter's silly words, about the bug being of solid gold, had a remarkable effect upon my fancy? And then the series of accidents and coincidences—these were so *very* extraordinary. Do you observe how mere an accident it was that these events should have occurred upon the *sole* day of all the year in which it has been, or may be, sufficiently cool for fire, and that without the fire, or without the intervention of the dog at the precise moment in which he appeared, I should never have become aware of the death's-head, and so never the possessor of the treasure?"

"But proceed—I am all impatience."

"Well; you have heard, of course, the many stories current—the thousand vague rumors afloat about money buried, somewhere upon the Atlantic coast, by Kidd and his associates. These rumors must have had some foundation in fact. And that the rumors have existed so long and so continuous, could have resulted, it appeared to me, only from the circumstance of the buried treasure still *remaining* entombed. Had Kidd concealed his plunder for a time, and afterwards reclaimed it, the rumors would scarcely have reached us in their present unvarying form. You will observe that the stories told are all about money-seekers, not about money-finders. Had the pirate recovered his money, there the affair would have dropped. It seemed to me that some accident—say the loss of a memorandum indicating its locality—had deprived him of the means of recovering it, and that this accident had become known to his followers, who otherwise might never have heard that treasure had been concealed at all, and who, busying themselves in vain, because unguided attempts, to regain it, had given first birth, and then universal currency, to the reports which are now so common. Have you ever heard of any important treasure being unearthed along the coast?"

"Never."

"But that Kidd's accumulations were immense, is well known. I took it for granted, therefore, that the earth still held them; and you will scarcely be surprised when I tell you that I felt a hope, nearly amounting to certainty, that the parchment so strangely found, involved a lost record of the place of deposit."

"But how did you proceed?"

"I held the vellum again to the fire, after increasing the heat; but nothing appeared. I now thought it possible that the coating of dirt might have something to do with the failure; so I carefully rinsed the parchment by pouring warm water over it, and, having done this, I placed it in a tin pan, with the skull downwards, and put the pan upon a furnace of lighted charcoal. In a few minutes, the pan having become thoroughly heated, I removed the slip, and, to my inexpressible joy, found it spotted, in several places, with what appeared to be figures arranged in lines. Again I placed it in the pan, and suffered it to remain another minute. Upon taking it off, the whole was just as you see it now."

Here Legrand, having reheated the parchment, submitted it to my inspection. The following characters were rudely traced, in a red tint, between the death's-head and the goat:

53‡‡†305))6*;4826)4‡.)4‡);806*;48†8¶60))
85;1‡(;:‡*8†83(88)5*†;46(;88*96*?;8)*‡(;48
5);5*†2:*‡9;4956*2(5*—4)8¶8*;4069285);)6†
8)4‡‡;1(‡9;48081;8:8‡1;48†85;4)485†528806*
81(‡9;48;(88;4(‡?34;48)4‡;161;:188;‡?;

"But," said I, returning him the slip, "I am as much in the dark as ever. Were all the jewels of Golconda awaiting me upon my solution of this enigma, I am quite sure that I should be unable to earn them."

"And yet," said Legrand, "the solution is by no means so difficult as you might be lead to imagine from the first hasty inspection of the characters. These characters, as any one might readily guess, form a cipher—that is to say, they convey a meaning; but then, from what is known of Kidd, I could not suppose him capable of constructing any of the more abstruse cryptographs. I made up my mind, at once, that this was of a simple species—such, however, as would appear, to the crude intellect of the sailor, absolutely insoluble without the key."

"And you really solved it?"

"Readily; I have solved others of an abstruseness ten thousand times greater. Circumstances, and a certain bias of mind, have led me to take interest in such riddles, and it may well be doubted whether human ingenuity can construct an enigma of the kind which human ingenuity may not, by proper application, resolve. In fact, having once established connected and legible characters, I scarcely gave a thought to the mere difficulty of developing their import.

"In the present case—indeed in all cases of secret writing—the first question regards the *language* of the cipher; for the principles of solution, so far, especially, as the more simple ciphers are concerned, depend upon, and are varied by, the genius of the particular idiom. In general, there is no alternative but experiment (directed by probabilities) of every tongue known to him who attempts the solution, until the true one be attained. But, with the cipher now before us, all difficulty was removed by the signature. The pun upon the word 'Kidd' is appreciable in no other language than the

English. But for this consideration I should have begun my attempts with the Spanish and French, as the tongues in which a secret of this kind would most *naturally* have been written by a pirate of the Spanish main. As it was, I assumed the cryptograph to be English.

"You observe there are no divisions between the words. Had there been divisions, the task would have been comparatively easy. In such case I should have commenced with a collation and analysis of the shorter words, and, had a word of a single letter occurred, as is most likely (*a* or *I*, for example), I should have considered the solution as assured. But, there being no division, my first step was to ascertain the predominant letters, as well as the least frequent. Counting all, I constructed a table, thus:

Of the character 8	there are	33.
;	"	26.
4	"	19.
‡)	"	16.
*	"	13.
5	"	12.
6	"	11.
† 1	"	8.
0	"	6.
9 2	"	5.
: 3	"	4.
?	"	3.
¶	"	2.
— .	"	

"Now, in English, the letter which most frequently occurs is *e*. Afterwards, succession runs thus: *a o i d h n r s t u y c f g l m w b k p q x z*. *E* predominates so remarkably that an individual sentence of any length is rarely seen, in which it is not the prevailing character.

"Here, then, we leave, in the very beginning, the groundwork for something more than a mere guess. The general use which may be made of the table is obvious—but, in this particular cipher, we shall only very partially require its aid. As our predominant character is 8, we will commence by assuming it as the *e* of the natural alphabet.

To verify the supposition, let us observe if the 8 be seen often in couples—for *e* is doubled with great frequency in English—in such words, for example, as 'meet,' 'fleet,' 'speed,' 'seen,' been,' 'agree,' &c. In the present instance we see it doubled no less than five times, although the cryptograph is brief.

"Let us assume 8, then, as *e*. Now, of all *words* in the language, 'the' is most usual; let us see, therefore, whether there are not repetitions of any three characters, in the same order of collocation, the last of them being 8. If we discover repetitions of such letters, so arranged, they will most probably represent the word 'the.' Upon inspection, we find no less than seven such arrangements, the characters being ;48. We may, therefore, assume that ; represents *t*, 4 represents *h*, and 8 represents *e*—the last being now well confirmed. Thus a great step has been taken.

"But, having established a single word, we are enabled to establish a vastly important point; that is to say, several commencements and terminations of other words. Let us refer, for example, to the last instance but one, in which the combination ;48 occurs—not far from the end of the cipher. We know that the ; immediately ensuing is the commencement of a word, and, of the six characters succeeding this 'the,' we are cognizant of no less than five. Let us set these characters down, thus, by the letters we know them to represent, leaving a space for the unknown—

t eeth.

"Here we are enabled, at once, to discard the '*th*,' as forming no portion of the word commencing with the first *t*; since, by experiment of the entire alphabet for a letter adapted to the vacancy, we perceive that no word can be formed of which this *th* can be a part. We are thus narrowed into

t ee,

and, going through the alphabet, if necessary, as before, we arrive at the word 'tree,' as the sole possible reading. We thus gain another letter, *r*, represented by (, with the words 'the tree' in juxtaposition.

"Looking beyond these words, for a short distance, we again see the combination ;48, and employ it by way of *termination* to what immediately precedes. We have thus this arrangement:

the tree ;4(‡?34 the,

or, substituting the natural letters, where known, it reads thus:

the tree thr‡?3h the.

"Now, if, in place of the unknown characters, we leave blank spaces, or substitute dots, we read thus:

the tree thr . . . h the,

when the word '*through*' makes itself evident at once. But this discovery gives us three new letters, *o*, *u* and *g*, represented by ‡ ? and 3.

"Looking now, narrowly, through the cipher for combinations of known characters, we find, not very far from the beginning, this arrangement,

83(88, or egree,

which, plainly, is the conclusion of the word 'degree,' and gives us another letter, *d*, represented by †.

"Four letters beyond the word 'degree,' we perceive the combination

;46(;88*.

"Translating the known characters, and representing the unknown by dots, as before, we read thus:

th rtee.

an arrangement immediately suggestive of the word 'thirteen,' and again furnishing us with two new characters, *i* and *n*, represented by 6 and *.

"Referring, now, to the beginning of the cryptograph, we find the combination,

53‡‡†.

"Translating, as before, we obtain

.good,

which assures us that the first letter is *A*, and that the first two words are 'A good.'

"It is now time that we arrange our key, as far as discovered, in a tabular form, to avoid confusion. It will stand thus:

5	represents	a
†	"	d
8	"	e
3	"	g
4	"	h
6	"	i
*	"	n
‡	"	o
(	"	r
;	"	t

"We have, therefore, no less than ten of the most important letters represented, and it will be unnecessary to proceed with the details of the solution. I have said enough to convince you that ciphers of this nature are readily soluble, and to give you some insight into the *rationale* of their development. But be assured that the specimen before us appertains to the very simplest species of cryptograph. It now only remains to give you the full translation of the characters upon the parchment, as unriddled. Here it is:

> *'A good glass in the bishop's hostel in the devil's seat forty-one degrees and thirteen minutes northeast and by north main branch seventh limb east side shoot from the left eye of the death's-head a bee line from the tree through the shot fifty feet out.'"*

"But," said I, "the enigma seems still in as bad a condition as ever. How is it possible to extort a meaning from all this jargon about 'devil's seats,' 'death's heads,' and 'bishop's hotels?'"

"I confess," replied Legrand, "that the matter still wears a serious aspect, when regarded with a casual glance. My first endeavor was to divide the sentence into the natural division intended by the cryptographist."

"You mean, to punctuate it?"

"Something of that kind."

"But how was it possible to effect this?"

"I reflected that it had been a *point* with the writer to run his words together without division, so as to increase the difficulty of solution. Now, a not over-acute man, in pursuing such an object would be nearly certain to overdo the matter. When, in the course of his composition, he arrived at a break in his subject which would *naturally* require a pause, or a point, he would be exceedingly apt to run his characters, at this place, more than usually close together. If you will observe the MS., in the present instance, you will easily detect five such cases of unusual crowding. Acting upon this hint, I made the division thus:

> *'A good glass in the Bishop's hostel in the Devil's seat—forty-one degrees and thirteen minutes—northeast and by north—main branch seventh limb east side—shoot from the left eye of the death's-head—a bee-line from the tree through the shot fifty feet out.'* "

"Even this division," said I, "leaves me still in the dark."

"It left me also in the dark," replied Legrand, "for a few days; during which I made diligent inquiry, in the neighborhood of Sullivan's Island, for any building which went by the name of the 'Bishop's Hotel;' for, of course, I dropped the obsolete word 'hostel.' Gaining no information on the subject, I was on the point of extending my sphere of search, and proceeding in a more systematic manner, when, one morning, it entered into my head, quite suddenly, that this 'Bishop's Hostel' might have some reference to an old family, of the name of Bessop, which, time out of mind, had held possession of an ancient manor-house, about four miles to the northward of the Island. I accordingly went over to the plantation, and reinstituted my inquiries among the older negroes of the place. At length one of the most aged of the women said that she had heard of such a place as Bessop's Castle, and thought that she could guide me to it, but that it was not a castle nor a tavern, but a high rock.

"I offered to pay her well for her trouble, and, after some demur, she consented to accompany me to the spot. We found it without much difficulty, when, dismissing her, I proceeded to examine the place. The 'castle' consisted of an irregular assemblage of cliffs and rocks—one of the latter being quite remarkable for its height as well as for its insulated and artificial appearance I clambered to its apex, and then felt much at a loss as to what should be next done.

"While I was busied in reflection, my eyes fell upon a narrow ledge in the eastern face of the rock, perhaps a yard below the summit upon which I stood. This ledge projected about eighteen inches, and was not more than a foot wide, while a niche in the cliff just above it, gave it a rude resemblance to one of the hollow-backed chairs used by our ancestors. I made no doubt that here was the 'devil's seat' alluded to in the MS., and now I seemed to grasp the full secret of the riddle.

"The 'good glass,' I knew, could have reference to nothing but a telescope; for the word 'glass' is rarely employed in any other sense by seamen. Now here, I at once saw, was a telescope to be used, and a definite point of view, admitting no variation, from which to use it. Nor did I hesitate to believe that the phrases, 'forty-one degrees and thirteen minutes,' and 'northeast and by north,' were intended as directions for the levelling of the glass. Greatly excited by these discoveries, I hurried home, procured a telescope, and returned to the rock.

"I let myself down to the ledge, and found that it was impossible to retain a seat upon it except in one particular position. This fact confirmed my preconceived idea. I proceeded to use the glass. Of course, the 'forty-one degrees and thirteen minutes' could allude to nothing but elevation above the visible horizon, since the horizontal direction was clearly indicated by the words, 'northeast and by north.' This latter direction I at once established by means of a pocket-compass; then, pointing the glass as nearly at an angle of forty-one degrees of elevation as I could do it by guess, I moved it cautiously up or down, until my attention was arrested by a circular rift or opening in the foliage of a large tree that overtopped its fellows in the distance. In the centre of this rift I perceived a white spot, but could not, at first, distinguish what it was. Adjusting the focus of the telescope, I again looked, and now made it out to be a human skull.

"Upon this discovery I was so sanguine as to consider the enigma solved; for the phrase 'main branch, seventh limb, east side,' could refer only to the position of the skull upon the tree, while 'shoot from the left eye of the death's head' admitted, also, of but one interpretation, in regard to a search for buried treasure. I perceived that the design was to drop a bullet from the left eye of the skull, and that a bee-line, or, in other words, a straight line, drawn from the nearest point of the trunk through 'the shot,' (or the spot where the bullet fell), and thence extended to a distance of fifty feet, would indicate a definite point—and beneath this point I thought it at least *possible* that a deposit of value lay concealed."

"All this," I said, "is exceedingly clear, and, although ingenious, still simple and explicit. When you left the Bishop's Hotel, what then?"

"Why, having carefully taken the bearings of the tree, I turned homewards. The instant that I left 'the devil's seat,' however, the circular rift vanished; nor could I get a glimpse of it afterwards, turn as I would. What seems to me the chief ingenuity in this whole business, is the fact (for repeated experiment has convinced me it is a fact) that the circular opening in question is visible from no other attainable point of view than that afforded by the narrow ledge upon the face of the rock.

"In this expedition to the 'Bishop's Hotel' I had been attended by Jupiter, who had, no doubt, observed, for some weeks past, the abstraction of my demeanor, and took especial care not to leave me alone. But, on the next day, getting up very early, I contrived to give him the slip, and went into the hills in search of the tree. After much toil I found it. When I came home at night my valet proposed to give me a flogging. With the rest of the adventure I believe you are as well acquainted as myself."

"I suppose," said I, "you missed the spot, in the first attempt at digging, through Jupiter's stupidity in letting the bug fall through the right instead of through the left eye of the skull."

"Precisely. This mistake made a difference of about two inches and a half in the 'shot'—that is to say, in the position of the peg nearest the tree; and had the treasure been *beneath* the 'shot,' the error would have been of little moment; but 'the shot,' together with the nearest point of the tree, were merely two points for the establishment of a line of direction; of course the error, however trivial in the beginning, increased as we proceeded with the line, and by the time we had gone fifty feet, threw us quite off the scent. But for my deep-seated impressions that treasure was here somewhere actually buried, we might have had all our labor in vain."

"But your grandiloquence, and your conduct in swinging the beetle—how excessively odd! I was sure you were mad. And why did you insist upon letting fall the bug, instead of a bullet, from the skull?"

"Why, to be frank, I felt somewhat annoyed by your evident suspicions touching my sanity, and so resolved to punish you quietly, in my own way, by a little bit of sober mystification. For this reason I swung the beetle, and for this reason I let it fall it from the tree. An observation of yours about its great weight suggested the latter idea."

"Yes, I perceive; and now there is only one point which puzzles me. What are we to make of the skeletons found in the hole?"

"That is a question I am no more able to answer than yourself. There seems, however, only one plausible way of accounting for them—and yet it is dreadful to believe in such atrocity as my suggestion would imply. It is clear that Kidd—if Kidd indeed secreted this treasure, which I doubt not—it is clear that he must have had assistance in the labor. But this labor concluded, he may have thought it expedient to remove all participants in his secret. Perhaps a couple of blows with a mattock were sufficient, while his coadjutors were busy in the pit; perhaps it required a dozen—who shall tell?"

Diddling
Considered as One of the Exact Sciences

Hey, diddle diddle
The cat and the fiddle

Since the world began there have been two Jeremys. The one wrote a Jeremiad about usury, and was called Jeremy Bentham. He has been much admired by Mr. John Neal, and was a great man in a small way. The other gave name to the most important of the Exact Sciences, and was a great man in a *great* way—I may say, indeed, in the very greatest of ways.

Diddling—or the abstract idea conveyed by the verb to diddle—is sufficiently well understood. Yet the fact, the deed, the thing, *diddling*, is somewhat difficult to define. We may get, however, at a tolerably distinct conception of the matter in hand, by defining—not the thing, diddling, in itself—but man, as an animal that diddles. Had Plato but hit upon this, he would have been spared the affront of the picked chicken.

Very pertinently it was demanded of Plato, why a picked chicken, which was clearly "a biped without feathers," was not, according to his own definition, a man? But I am not to be bothered by any similar query. Man is an animal that diddles, and there is *no* animal that diddles *but* man. It will take an entire hen-coop of picked chickens to get over that.

What constitutes the essence, the nare, the principle of diddling is, in fact, peculiar to the class of creatures that wear coats and pantaloons. A crow thieves; a fox cheats; a weasel outwits; a man diddles. To diddle is his destiny. "Man was made to mourn," says the poet. But not so:—he was made to diddle. This is his aim—his object—his *end*. And for this reason when a man's diddled we say he's "*done*."

Diddling, rightly considered, is a compound, of which the ingredients are minuteness, interest, perseverance, ingenuity, audacity, *nonchalance*, originality, impertinence, and *grin*.

Minuteness:—Your diddler is minute. His operations are upon a small scale. His business is retail, for cash, or approved paper at sight. Should he ever be tempted into magnificent speculation, he then, at once, loses his distinctive features, and becomes what we term "financier." This latter word conveys the diddling idea in every respect except that of magnitude. A diddler may thus be regarded as a banker *in petto*—a "financial operation," as a diddle at Brobdignag. The one is to the other, as Homer to "Flaccus"—as a Mastodon to a mouse—as the tail of a comet to that of a pig.

Interest:—Your diddler is guided by self-interest. He scorns to diddle for the mere sake of the diddle. He has an object in view—his pocket—and yours. He regards always the main chance. He looks to Number One. You are Number Two, and must look to yourself.

Perseverance:—Your diddler perseveres. He is not readily discouraged. Should even the banks break, he cares nothing about it. He steadily pursues his end, and

Ut canis a corio nunquam absterrebitur uncto,

so he never lets go of his game.

Ingenuity:—Your diddler is ingenious. He has constructiveness large. He understands plot. He invents and circumvents. Were he not Alexander he would be Diogenes. Were he not a diddler, he would be a maker of patent rat-traps or an angler for trout.

Audacity:—Your diddler is audacious.—He is a bold man. He carries the war into Africa. He conquers all by assault. He would not fear the daggers of Frey Herren. With a little more prudence Dick Turpin would have made a good diddler; with a trifle less blarney, Daniel O'Connell; with a pound or two more brains Charles the Twelfth.

Nonchalance:—Your diddler is *nonchalant*. He is not at all nervous. He never *had* any nerves. He is never seduced into a flurry. He is never put out—unless put out of doors. He is cool—cool as a cucumber. He is calm—"calm as a smile from Lady Bury." He is easy—easy as an old glove, or the damsels of ancient Baiae.

Originality:—Your diddler is original—conscientiously so. His thoughts are his own. He would scorn to employ those of another. A stale trick is his aversion. He would return a purse, I am sure, upon discovering that he had obtained it by an unoriginal diddle.

Impertinence:—Your diddler is impertinent. He swaggers. He sets his arms a-kimbo. He thrusts his hands in his trowsers' pockets. He sneers in your face. He treads on your corns. He eats your dinner, he drinks your wine, he borrows your money, he pulls your nose, he kicks your poodle, and he kisses your wife.

Grin:—Your *true* diddler winds up all with a grin. But this nobody sees but himself. He grins when his daily work is done—when his allotted labors are accomplished—at night in his own closet, and altogether for his own private entertainment. He goes home. He locks his door. He divests himself of his clothes. He puts out his candle. He gets into bed. He places his head upon the pillow. All this done, and your diddler *grins*. This is no hypothesis. It is a matter of course. I reason *à priori*, and a diddle would be *no* diddle without a grin.

The origin of the diddle is referrable to the infancy of the Human Race. Perhaps the first diddler was Adam. At all events, we can trace the science back to a very remote period of antiquity. The moderns, however, have brought it to a perfection never dreamed of by our thick-headed progenitors. Without pausing to speak of the "old saws," therefore, I shall content myself with a compendious account of some of the more "modern instances."

A very good diddle is this. A housekeeper in want of a sofa, for instance, is seen to go in and out of several cabinet warehouses. At length she arrives at one offering an excellent variety. She is accosted, and invited to enter, by a polite and voluble individual at the door. She finds a sofa well adapted to her views, and upon inquiring the price, is surprised and delighted to hear a sum named at least twenty per cent. lower than her expectations. She hastens to make the purchase, gets a bill and receipt, leaves her address, with a request that the article be sent home as speedily as possible, and retires amid a profusion of bows from the shopkeeper. The night arrives and no sofa. A servant is sent to make inquiry about the delay. The whole transaction is denied. No sofa has been sold—no money received—except by the diddler, who played shop-keeper for the nonce.

Our cabinet warehouses are left entirely unattended, and thus afford every facility for a trick of this kind. Visiters enter, look at furniture, and depart unheeded and unseen. Should any one wish to purchase, or to inquire the price of an article, a bell is at hand, and this is considered amply sufficient.

Again, quite a respectable diddle is this. A well-dressed individual enters a shop, makes a purchase to the value of a dollar; finds, much to his vexation, that he has left his pocket-book in another coat pocket; and so says to the shopkeeper—

"My dear sir, never mind; just oblige me, will you, by sending the bundle home? But stay! I really believe that I have nothing less than a five dollar bill, even *there*. However, you can send four dollars in change *with* the bundle, you know."

"Very good, sir," replies the shop-keeper, who entertains, at once, a lofty opinion of the high-mindedness of his customer. "I know fellows," he says to himself, "who would just have put the goods under their arm, and walked off with a promise to call and pay the dollar as they came by in the afternoon."

A boy is sent with the parcel and change. On the route, quite accidentally, he is met by the purchaser, who exclaims:

"Ah! This is my bundle, I see—I thought you had been home with it, long ago. Well, go on! My wife, Mrs. Trotter, will give you the five dollars—I left instructions with her to that effect. The change you might as well give to *me*—I shall want some silver for the Post Office. Very good! One, two, is this a good quarter?—three, four—quite right! Say to Mrs. Trotter that you met me, and be sure now and *do* not loiter on the way."

The boy doesn't loiter at all—but he is a very long time in getting back from his errand—for no lady of the precise name of Mrs. Trotter is to be discovered. He consoles himself, however, that he has not been such a fool as to leave the goods without the money, and re-entering his shop with a self-satisfied air, feels sensibly hurt and indignant when his master asks him what has become of the change.

A very simple diddle, indeed, is this. The captain of a ship, which is about to sail, is presented by an official looking person with an unusually moderate bill of city charges. Glad to get off so easily, and confused by a hundred duties pressing upon him all at once, he discharges the claim forthwith. In about fifteen minutes, another and less reasonable bill is handed him by one who soon makes it evident that the first collector was a diddler, and the original collection a diddle.

And here, too, is a somewhat similar thing. A steamboat is casting loose from the wharf. A traveller, portmanteau in hand, is discovered running toward the wharf, at full speed. Suddenly, he makes a dead halt, stoops, and picks up something from the ground in a very agitated manner. It is a pocket-book, and—"Has any gentleman lost a pocket-book?" he cries. No one can say that he has exactly lost a pocket-book; but a great excitement ensues, when the treasure trove is found to be of value. The boat, however, must not be detained.

"Time and tide wait for no man," says the captain.

"For God's sake, stay only a few minutes," says the finder of the book—"the true claimant will presently appear."

"Can't wait!" replies the man in authority; "cast off there, d'ye hear?"

"What *am* I to do?" asks the finder, in great tribulation. "I am about to leave the country for some years, and I cannot conscientiously retain this large amount in my possession. I beg your pardon, sir," [here he addresses a gentleman on shore] "but you have the air of an honest man. *Will* you confer upon me the favor of taking charge of this pocket-book—I know I can trust you—and of advertising it? The notes, you see, amount to a very considerable sum. The owner will, no doubt, insist upon rewarding you for your trouble—"

"Me!—no, *you*!—it was *you* who found the book."

"Well, if you *must* have it so—I will take a small reward—just to satisfy your scruples. Let me see—why these notes are all hundreds—bless my soul! a hundred is too much to take—fifty would be quite enough, I am sure—"

"Cast off there!" says the captain.

"But then I have no change for a hundred, and upon the whole, you had better—

"Cast off there!" says the captain.

"Never mind!" cries the gentleman on shore, who has been examining his own pocket-book for the last minute or so—"never mind! *I* can fix it—here is a fifty on the Bank of North America—throw the book."

And the over-conscientious finder takes the fifty with marked reluctance, and throws the gentleman the book, as desired, while the steamboat fumes and fizzes on her way. In about half an hour after her departure, the "large amount" is seen to be a "counterfeit presentment," and the whole thing a capital diddle.

A bold diddle is this. A camp-meeting, or something similar, is to be held at a certain spot which is accessible only by means of a free bridge. A diddler stations himself upon this bridge, respectfully informs all passers by of the new county law, which establishes a toll of one cent for foot passengers, two for horses and donkeys, and so forth, and so forth. Some grumble but all submit, and the diddler goes home a wealthier man by some fifty or sixty dollars well earned. This taking a toll from a great crowd of people is an excessively troublesome thing.

A neat diddle is this. A friend holds one of the diddler's promises to pay, filled up and signed in due form, upon the ordinary blanks printed in red ink. The diddler purchases one or two dozen of these blanks, and every day dips one of them in his soup, makes his dog jump for it, and finally gives it to him as a *bonne bouche*. The note arriving at maturity, the diddler, with the diddler's dog, calls upon the friend, and the promise to pay is made the topic of discussion. The friend produces it from his *escritoire*, and is in the act of reaching it to the diddler, when up jumps the diddler's dog and devours it forthwith. The diddler is not only surprised but vexed and incensed at the absurd behavior of his dog, and expresses his entire readiness to cancel the obligation at any moment when the evidence of the obligation shall be forthcoming.

A very minute diddle is this. A lady is insulted in the street by a diddler's accomplice. The diddler himself flies to her assistance, and, giving his friend a comfortable thrashing, insists upon attending the lady to her own door. He bows, with his hand upon his heart, and most respectfully bids her adieu. She entreats him, as her deliverer, to walk in and be introduced to her big brother and her papa. With a sigh, he declines to do so. "Is there no way, then, sir," she murmurs, "in which I may be permitted to testify my gratitude?"

"Why, yes, madam, there is. Will you be kind enough to lend me a couple of shillings?"

In the first excitement of the moment the lady decides upon

fainting outright. Upon second thought, however, she opens her purse-strings and delivers the specie. Now this, I say, is a diddle minute—for one entire moiety of the sum borrowed has to be paid to the gentleman who had the trouble of performing the insult, and who had then to stand still and be thrashed for performing it.

Rather a small but still a scientific diddle is this. The diddler approaches the bar of a tavern, and demands a couple of twists of tobacco. These are handed to him, when, having slightly examined them, he says:

"I don't much like this tobacco. Here, take it back, and give me a glass of brandy and water in its place." The brandy and water is furnished and imbibed, and the diddler makes his way to the door. But the voice of the tavern-keeper arrests him.

"I believe, sir, you have forgotten to pay for your brandy and water."

"Pay for my brandy and water!—didn't I give you the tobacco for the brandy and water? What more would you have?"

"But, sir, if you please, I don't remember that you paid me for the tobacco."

"What do you mean by that, you scoundrel?—Didn't I give you back your tobacco? Isn't *that* your tobacco lying *there*? Do you expect me to pay for what I did not take?"

"But, sir," says the publican, now rather at a loss what to say, "but sir—"

"But me no buts, sir," interrupts the diddler, apparently in very high dudgeon, and slamming the door after him, as he makes his escape.—"But me no buts, sir, and none of your tricks upon travellers."

Here again is a very clever diddle, of which the simplicity is not its least recommendation. A purse, or pocket-book, being really lost, the loser inserts in *one* of the daily papers of a large city a fully descriptive advertisement.

Whereupon our diddler copies the *facts* of this advertisement, with a change of heading, of general phraseology and *address*. The original, for instance, is long, and verbose, is headed "A Pocket-Book Lost!" and requires the treasure, when found, to be left at No. 1 Tom Street. The copy is brief, and being headed with "Lost" only, indicates No. 2 Dick, or No. 3 Harry Street, as the locality at which the owner may be seen. Moreover, it is inserted in at least five or six of the daily papers of the day, while in point of time, it makes its appearance only a few hours after the original. Should it be read by the loser of the purse, he would hardly suspect it to have any reference to his own misfortune. But, of course, the chances are five or six to one, that the finder will repair to the address given by the diddler, rather than to that pointed out by the rightful proprietor. The former pays the reward, pockets the treasure and decamps.

Quite an analogous diddle is this. A lady of *ton* has dropped, some where in the street, a diamond ring of very unusual value. For its recovery, she offers some forty or fifty dollars reward—giving, in her advertisement, a very minute description of the gem, and of its settings, and declaring that, on its restoration at No. so and so, in such and such Avenue, the reward would be paid *instanter*, without a single question being asked. During the lady's absence from home, a day or two afterwards, a ring is heard at the door of No. so and so, in such and such Avenue; a servant appears; the lady of the house is asked for and is declared to be out, at which astounding information, the visitor expresses the most poignant regret. His business is of importance and concerns the lady herself. In fact, he had the good fortune to find her diamond ring. But perhaps it would be as well that he should call again. "By no means!" says the servant; and "By no means!" says the lady's sister and the lady's sister-in-law, who are summoned forthwith. The ring is clamorously identified, the reward is paid, and the finder nearly thrust out of doors. The lady returns and expresses some little dissatisfaction with her sister and sister-in-law, because they happen to have paid forty or fifty dollars for a fac-simile of her diamond ring—a *fac-simile* made out of real pinch-beck and unquestionable paste.

But as there is really no end to diddling, so there would be none to this essay, were I even to hint at half the variations, or inflections, of which this science is susceptible. I must bring this paper, perforce, to a conclusion, and this I cannot do better than by a summary notice of a very decent, but rather elaborate diddle, of which our own city was made the theatre, not very long ago, and which was subsequently repeated with success, in other still more verdant localities of the Union. A middle-aged gentleman arrives in town from parts unknown. He is remarkably precise, cautious, staid, and deliberate in his demeanor. His dress is scrupulously neat, but plain, unostentatious. He wears a white cravat, an ample waistcoat, made with an eye to comfort alone; thick-soled cosy-looking shoes, and pantaloons without straps. He has the whole air, in fact, of your well-to-do, sober-sided, exact, and respectable "man of business," *par excellence*—one of the stern and outwardly hard, internally soft, sort of people that we see in the crack high comedies—fellows whose words are so many bonds, and who are noted for giving away guineas, in charity, with the one hand, while, in the way of mere bargain, they exact the uttermost fraction of a farthing with the other.

He makes much ado before he can get suited with a boarding house. He dislikes children. He has been accustomed to quiet. His habits are methodical—and then he would prefer getting into a private and respectable small family, piously inclined. Terms, however, are no object—only he *must* insist upon settling his bill on the first of every month (it is now the second) and begs his landlady, when he finally obtains one to his mind, *not* on any account to forget his instructions upon this point—but to send in a bill, *and* receipt, precisely at ten o'clock, on the *first* day of every month, and under no circumstances to put it off to the second.

These arrangements made, our man of business rents an office in a reputable rather than a fashionable quarter of the town. There is nothing he more despises than pretense. "Where there is much show," he says, "there is seldom any thing very solid behind"—an observation which so profoundly impresses his landlady's fancy, that she makes a pencil memorandum of it forthwith, in her great family Bible, on the broad margin of the Proverbs of Solomon.

The next step is to advertise, after some such fashion as this, in the principal business six-pennies of the city—the pennies are eschewed as not "respectable"—and as demanding payment for all advertisements in advance. Our man of business holds it as a point of his faith that work should never be paid for until done.

> WANTED—The advertisers, being about to commence
> extensive business operations in this city, will
> require the services of three or four intelligent and
> competent clerks, to whom a liberal salary will
> be paid. The very best recommendations, not so

> much for capacity, as for integrity, will be expected. Indeed, as the duties to be performed involve high responsibilities, and large amounts of money must necessarily pass through the hands of those engaged, it is deemed advisable to demand a deposit of fifty dollars from each clerk employed. No person need apply, therefore, who is not prepared to leave this sum in the possession of the advertisers, and who cannot furnish the most satisfactory testimonials of morality. Young gentlemen piously inclined will be preferred. Application should be made between the hours of ten and eleven A.M., and four and five P.M., of Messrs.
>
> Bogs, Hogs Logs, Frogs & Co.
> No. 110 Dog Street

By the thirty-first day of the month, this advertisement has brought to the office of Messrs. Bogs, Hogs, Logs, Frogs, and Company, some fifteen or twenty young gentlemen piously inclined. But our man of business is in no hurry to conclude a contract with any—no man of business is *ever* precipitate—and it is not until the most rigid catechism in respect to the piety of each young gentleman's inclination, that his services are engaged and his fifty dollars receipted for, *just* by way of proper precaution, on the part of the respectable firm of Bogs, Hogs, Logs, Frogs, and Company. On the morning of the first day of the next month, the landlady does not present her bill, according to promise—a piece of neglect for which the comfortable head of the house ending in *ogs* would no doubt have chided her severely, could he have been prevailed upon to remain in town a day or two for that purpose.

As it is, the constables have had a sad time of it, running hither and thither, and all they can do is to declare the man of business most emphatically, a "hen knee high"—by which some persons imagine them to imply that, in fact, he is n. e. i.—by which again the very classical phrase *non est inventus*, is supposed to be understood. In the meantime the young gentlemen, one and all, are somewhat less piously inclined than before, while the landlady purchases a shilling's worth of the Indian rubber, and very carefully obliterates the pencil memorandum that some fool has made in her great family Bible, on the broad margin of the Proverbs of Solomon.

The Premature Burial

There are certain themes of which the interest is all-absorbing, but which are too entirely horrible for the purposes of legitimate fiction. These the mere romanticist must eschew, if he do not wish to offend or to disgust. They are with propriety handled only when the severity and majesty of Truth sanctify and sustain them. We thrill, for example, with the most intense of "pleasurable pain" over the accounts of the Passage of the Beresina, of the Earthquake at Lisbon, of the Plague at London, of the Massacre of St. Bartholomew, or of the stifling of the hundred and twenty-three prisoners in the Black Hole at Calcutta. But in these accounts it is the fact—it is the reality—it is the history which excites. As inventions, we should regard them with simple abhorrence.

I have mentioned some few of the more prominent and august calamities on record; but in these it is the extent, not less than the character of the calamity, which so vividly impresses the fancy. I need not remind the reader that, from the long and weird catalogue of human miseries, I might have selected many individual instances more replete with essential suffering than any of these vast generalities of disaster. The true wretchedness, indeed—the ultimate woe—is particular, not diffuse. That the ghastly extremes of agony are endured by man the unit, and never by man the mass—for this let us thank a merciful God!

To be buried while alive is, beyond question, the most terrific of these extremes which has ever fallen to the lot of mere mortality. That it has frequently, very frequently, so fallen will scarcely be denied by those who think. The boundaries which divide Life from Death are at best shadowy and vague. Who shall say where the one ends, and where the other begins? We know that there are diseases in which occur total cessations of all the apparent functions of vitality, and yet in which these cessations are merely suspensions, properly so called. They are only temporary pauses in the incomprehensible mechanism. A certain period elapses, and some unseen mysterious principle again sets in motion the magic pinions and the wizard wheels. The silver cord was not for ever loosed, nor the golden bowl irreparably broken. But where, meantime, was the soul?

Apart, however, from the inevitable conclusion, *à priori* that such causes must produce such effects—that the well-known occurrence of such cases of suspended animation must naturally give rise, now and then, to premature interments—apart from this consideration, we have the direct testimony of medical and ordinary experience to prove that a vast number of such interments have actually taken place. I might refer at once, if necessary to a hundred well authenticated instances. One of very remarkable character, and of which the circumstances may be fresh in the memory of some of my readers, occurred, not very long ago, in the neighboring city of Baltimore, where it occasioned a painful, intense, and widely—extended excitement. The wife of one of the most respectable citizens—a lawyer of eminence and a member of Congress—was seized with a sudden and unaccountable illness, which completely baffled the skill of her physicians. After much suffering she died, or was supposed to die. No one suspected, indeed, or had reason to suspect, that she was not actually dead. She presented all the ordinary appearances of death. The face assumed the usual pinched and sunken outline. The lips were of the usual marble pallor. The eyes were lustreless. There was no warmth. Pulsation had ceased. For three days the body was preserved unburied, during which it had acquired a stony rigidity. The funeral, in short, was hastened, on account of the rapid advance of what was supposed to be decomposition.

The lady was deposited in her family vault, which, for three subsequent years, was undisturbed. At the expiration of this term it was opened for the reception of a sarcophagus—but, alas! how fearful a shock awaited the husband, who, personally, threw open the door! As its portals swung outwardly back, some white-apparelled object fell rattling within his arms. It was the skeleton of his wife in her yet unmoulded shroud.

A careful investigation rendered it evident that she had revived within two days after her entombment; that her struggles within the coffin had caused it to fall from a ledge, or shelf to the floor, where it was so broken as to permit her escape. A lamp which had been accidentally left, full of oil, within the tomb, was found empty; it might have been exhausted, however, by evaporation. On the uttermost of the steps which led down into the dread chamber was a large fragment of the coffin, with which, it seemed, that she had endeavored to arrest attention by striking the iron door. While thus occupied, she probably swooned, or possibly died, through sheer terror; and, in failing, her shroud became entangled in some iron—work which projected interiorly. Thus she remained, and thus she rotted, erect.

In the year 1810, a case of living inhumation happened in France, attended with circumstances which go far to warrant the assertion that truth is, indeed, stranger than fiction. The heroine of the story was a Mademoiselle Victorine Lafourcade, a young girl of illustrious family, of wealth, and of great personal beauty. Among her numerous suitors was Julien Bossuet, a poor *litterateur*, or journalist of Paris. His talents and general amiability had recommended him to the notice of the heiress, by whom he seems to have been truly beloved; but her pride of birth decided her, finally, to reject him, and to wed a Monsieur Renelle, a banker and a diplomatist of some eminence. After marriage, however, this gentleman neglected, and, perhaps, even more positively ill-treated her. Having passed with him some wretched years, she died,—at least her condition so closely resembled death as to deceive every one who saw her. She was buried—not in a vault, but in an ordinary grave in the village of her nativity. Filled with despair, and still inflamed by the memory of a profound attachment, the lover journeys from the capital to the remote province in which the village lies, with the romantic purpose of disinterring the corpse, and possessing himself of its luxuriant tresses. He reaches the grave. At midnight he unearths the coffin, opens it, and is in the act of detaching the hair, when he is arrested by the unclosing of the beloved eyes. In fact, the lady had been buried alive. Vitality had not altogether departed, and she was aroused by the caresses of her lover from the lethargy which had been mistaken for death. He bore her frantically to his lodgings in the village. He employed certain powerful restoratives suggested by no little medical learning. In fine, she revived. She recognized her preserver. She remained with him until, by slow degrees, she fully recovered her original health. Her woman's heart was not adamant, and this last lesson of love sufficed to soften it. She bestowed it upon Bossuet. She returned no more to her husband, but, concealing from him her resurrection, fled with her lover to America. Twenty years afterward, the two returned to France, in the persuasion that time had so greatly altered the lady's appearance that her friends would be unable to recognize her. They were mistaken, however, for, at the first meeting, Monsieur Renelle did actually recognize and make claim to his wife. This claim she resisted, and a judicial tribunal sustained her in her resistance, deciding that the peculiar circumstances, with the long lapse of years, had extinguished, not only equitably, but legally, the authority of the husband.

The *Chirurgical Journal* of Leipsic—a periodical of high authority and merit, which some American bookseller would do well to translate and republish, records in a late number a very distressing event of the character in question.

An officer of artillery, a man of gigantic stature and of robust health, being thrown from an unmanageable horse, received a very severe contusion upon the head, which rendered him insensible at once; the skull was slightly fractured, but no immediate danger was apprehended. Trepanning was accomplished successfully. He was bled, and many other of the ordinary means of relief were adopted. Gradually, however, he fell into a more and more hopeless state of stupor, and, finally, it was thought that he died.

The weather was warm, and he was buried with indecent haste in one of the public cemeteries. His funeral took place on Thursday. On the Sunday following, the grounds of the cemetery were, as usual, much thronged with visiters, and about noon an intense excitement was created by the declaration of a peasant that, while sitting upon the grave of the officer, he had distinctly felt a commotion of the earth, as if occasioned by some one struggling beneath. At first little attention was paid to the man's asseveration; but his evident terror, and the dogged obstinacy with which he persisted in his story, had at length their natural effect upon the crowd. Spades were hurriedly procured, and the grave, which was shamefully shallow, was in a few minutes so far thrown open that the head of its occupant appeared. He was then seemingly dead; but he sat nearly erect within his coffin, the lid of which, in his furious struggles, he had partially uplifted.

He was forthwith conveyed to the nearest hospital, and there pronounced to be still living, although in an asphytic condition. After some hours he revived, recognized individuals of his acquaintance, and, in broken sentences spoke of his agonies in the grave.

From what he related, it was clear that he must have been conscious of life for more than an hour, while inhumed, before lapsing into insensibility. The grave was carelessly and loosely filled with an exceedingly porous soil; and thus some air was necessarily admitted. He heard the footsteps of the crowd overhead, and endeavored to make himself heard in turn. It was the tumult within the grounds of the cemetery, he said, which appeared to awaken him from a deep sleep, but no sooner was he awake than he became fully aware of the awful horrors of his position.

This patient, it is recorded, was doing well and seemed to be in a fair way of ultimate recovery, but fell a victim to the quackeries of medical experiment. The galvanic battery was applied, and he suddenly expired in one of those ecstatic paroxysms which, occasionally, it superinduces.

The mention of the galvanic battery, nevertheless, recalls to my memory a well known and very extraordinary case in point, where its action proved the means of restoring to animation a young attorney of London, who had been interred for two days. This occurred in 1831, and created, at the time, a very profound sensation wherever it was made the subject of converse.

The patient, Mr. Edward Stapleton, had died, apparently of typhus fever, accompanied with some anomalous symptoms which had excited the curiosity of his medical attendants. Upon his seeming decease, his friends were requested to sanction a *post-mortem* examination, but declined to permit it. As often happens, when such refusals are made, the practitioners resolved to disinter the body and dissect it at leisure, in private. Arrangements were easily effected with some of the numerous corps of body-snatchers, with which London abounds; and, upon the third night after the funeral, the supposed corpse was unearthed from a grave eight feet deep, and deposited in the opening chamber of one of the private hospitals.

An incision of some extent had been actually made in the abdomen, when the fresh and undecayed appearance of the subject suggested an application of the battery. One experiment succeeded another, and the customary effects supervened, with nothing to characterize them in any respect, except, upon one or two occasions, a more than ordinary degree of life-likeness in the convulsive action.

It grew late. The day was about to dawn; and it was thought expedient, at length, to proceed at once to the dissection. A student, however, was especially desirous of testing a theory of his own, and insisted upon applying the battery to one of the pectoral muscles. A rough gash was made, and a wire hastily brought in contact, when the patient, with a hurried but quite unconvulsive movement, arose from the table, stepped into the middle of the floor, gazed about him uneasily for a few seconds, and then—spoke. What he said was unintelligible, but words were uttered; the syllabification was distinct. Having spoken, he fell heavily to the floor.

For some moments all were paralyzed with awe—but the urgency of the case soon restored them their presence of mind. It was seen that Mr. Stapleton was alive, although in a swoon. Upon exhibition of ether he revived and was rapidly restored to health, and to the society of his friends—from whom, however, all knowledge of his resuscitation was withheld, until a relapse was no longer to be apprehended. Their wonder—their rapturous astonishment—may be conceived.

The most thrilling peculiarity of this incident, nevertheless, is involved in what Mr. S. himself asserts. He declares that at no period was he altogether insensible—that, dully and confusedly, he was aware of everything which happened to him, from the moment in which he was pronounced *dead* by his physicians, to that in which he fell swooning to the floor of the hospital. "I am alive," were the uncomprehended words which, upon recognizing the locality of the dissecting-room, he had endeavored, in his extremity, to utter.

It were an easy matter to multiply such histories as these—but I forbear—for, indeed, we have no need of such to establish the fact that premature interments occur. When we reflect how very rarely, from the nature of the case, we have it in our power to detect them, we must admit that they may *frequently* occur without our cognizance. Scarcely, in truth, is a graveyard ever encroached upon, for any purpose, to any great extent, that skeletons are not found in postures which suggest the most fearful of suspicions.

Fearful indeed the suspicion—but more fearful the doom! It

may be asserted, without hesitation, that *no* event is so terribly well adapted to inspire the supremeness of bodily and of mental distress, as is burial before death. The unendurable oppression of the lungs—the stifling fumes from the damp earth—the clinging to the death garments—the rigid embrace of the narrow house—the blackness of the absolute Night—the silence like a sea that overwhelms—the unseen but palpable presence of the Conqueror Worm—these things, with the thoughts of the air and grass above, with memory of dear friends who would fly to save us if but informed of our fate, and with consciousness that of this fate they can *never* be informed—that our hopeless portion is that of the really dead—these considerations, I say, carry into the heart, which still palpitates, a degree of appalling and intolerable horror from which the most daring imagination must recoil. We know of nothing so agonizing upon Earth—we can dream of nothing half so hideous in the realms of the nethermost Hell. And thus all narratives upon this topic have an interest profound; an interest, nevertheless, which, through the sacred awe of the topic itself, very properly and very peculiarly depends upon our conviction of the *truth* of the matter narrated. What I have now to tell is of my own actual knowledge—of my own positive and personal experience.

For several years I had been subject to attacks of the singular disorder which physicians have agreed to term catalepsy, in default of a more definitive title. Although both the immediate and the predisposing causes, and even the actual diagnosis, of this disease are still mysterious, its obvious and apparent character is sufficiently well understood. Its variations seem to be chiefly of degree. Sometimes the patient lies, for a day only, or even for a shorter period, in a species of exaggerated lethargy. He is senseless and externally motionless; but the pulsation of the heart is still faintly perceptible; some traces of warmth remain; a slight color lingers within the centre of the cheek; and, upon application of a mirror to the lips, we can detect a torpid, unequal, and vacillating action of the lungs. Then again the duration of the trance is for weeks—even for months; while the closest scrutiny, and the most rigorous medical tests, fail to establish any material distinction between the state of the sufferer and what we conceive of absolute death. Very usually he is saved from premature interment solely by the knowledge of his friends that he has been previously subject to catalepsy, by the consequent suspicion excited, and, above all, by the non-appearance of decay. The advances of the malady are, luckily, gradual. The first manifestations, although marked, are unequivocal. The fits grow successively more and more distinctive, and endure each for a longer term than the preceding. In this lies the principal security from inhumation. The unfortunate whose *first* attack should be of the extreme character which is occasionally seen, would almost inevitably be consigned alive to the tomb.

My own case differed in no important particular from those mentioned in medical books. Sometimes, without any apparent cause, I sank, little by little, into a condition of hemi-syncope, or half swoon; and, in this condition, without pain, without ability to stir, or, strictly speaking, to think, but with a dull lethargic consciousness of life and of the presence of those who surrounded my bed, I remained, until the crisis of the disease restored me, suddenly, to perfect sensation. At other times I was quickly and impetuously smitten. I grew sick, and numb, and chilly, and dizzy, and so fell prostrate at once. Then, for weeks, all was void, and black, and silent, and Nothing became the universe. Total annihilation could be no more. From these latter attacks I awoke, however, with a gradation slow in proportion to the suddenness of the seizure. Just as the day dawns to the friendless and houseless beggar who roams the streets throughout the long desolate winter night—just so tardily—just so wearily—just so cheerily came back the light of the Soul to me.

Apart from the tendency to trance, however, my general health appeared to be good; nor could I perceive that it was at all affected by the one prevalent malady—unless, indeed, an idiosyncrasy in my ordinary *sleep* may be looked upon as superinduced. Upon awaking from slumber, I could never gain, at once, thorough possession of my senses, and always remained, for many minutes, in much bewilderment and perplexity;—the mental faculties in general, but the memory in especial, being in a condition of absolute abeyance.

In all that I endured there was no physical suffering but of moral distress an infinitude. My fancy grew charnel, I talked "of worms, of tombs, and epitaphs." I was lost in reveries of death, and the idea of premature burial held continual possession of my brain. The ghastly Danger to which I was subjected haunted me day and night.

In the former, the torture of meditation was excessive—in the latter, supreme. When the grim Darkness overspread the Earth, then, with every horror of thought, I shook—shook as the quivering plumes upon the hearse. When Nature could endure wakefulness no longer, it was with a struggle that I consented to sleep—for I shuddered to reflect that, upon awaking, I might find myself the tenant of a grave. And when, finally, I sank into slumber, it was only to rush at once into a world of phantasms, above which, with vast, sable, overshadowing wing, hovered, predominant, the one sepulchral Idea.

From the innumerable images of gloom which thus oppressed me in dreams, I select for record but a solitary vision. Methought I was immersed in a cataleptic trance of more than usual duration and profundity. Suddenly there came an icy hand upon my forehead, and an impatient, gibbering voice whispered the word "Arise!" within my ear.

I sat erect. The darkness was total. I could not see the figure of him who had aroused me. I could call to mind neither the period at which I had fallen into the trance, nor the locality in which I then lay. While I remained motionless, and busied in endeavors to collect my thought, the cold hand grasped me fiercely by the wrist, shaking it petulantly, while the gibbering voice said again:

"Arise! did I not bid thee arise?"

"And who," I demanded, "art thou?"

"I have no name in the regions which I inhabit," replied the voice, mournfully; "I was mortal, but am fiend. I was merciless, but am pitiful. Thou dost feel that I shudder.—My teeth chatter as I speak, yet it is not with the chilliness of the night—of the night without end. But this hideousness is insufferable. How canst *thou* tranquilly sleep? I cannot rest for the cry of these great agonies. These sights are more than I can bear. Get thee up! Come with me into the outer Night, and let me unfold to thee the graves. Is not this a spectacle of woe?—Behold!"

I looked; and the unseen figure, which still grasped me by the wrist, had caused to be thrown open the graves of all mankind, and from each issued the faint phosphoric radiance of decay, so that I could see into the innermost recesses, and there view the shrouded bodies in their sad and solemn slumbers with the worm. But alas!

the real sleepers were fewer, by many millions, than those who slumbered not at all; and there was a feeble struggling; and there was a general sad unrest; and from out the depths of the countless pits there came a melancholy rustling from the garments of the buried. And of those who seemed tranquilly to repose, I saw that a vast number had changed, in a greater or less degree, the rigid and uneasy position in which they had originally been entombed. And the voice again said to me as I gazed:

"Is it not—oh! is it not a pitiful sight?"—but, before I could find words to reply, the figure had ceased to grasp my wrist, the phosphoric lights expired, and the graves were closed with a sudden violence, while from out them arose a tumult of despairing cries, saying again: "Is it not—O, God, is it *not* a very pitiful sight?"

Phantasies such as these, presenting themselves at night, extended their terrific influence far into my waking hours. My nerves became thoroughly unstrung, and I fell prey to perpetual horror. I hesitated to ride, or to walk, or to indulge in any exercise that would carry me from home. In fact, I no longer dared trust myself out of the immediate presence of those who were aware of my proneness to catalepsy, lest, falling into one of my usual fits, I should be buried before my real condition could be ascertained. I doubted the care, the fidelity of my dearest friends. I dreaded that, in some trance of more than customary duration, they might be prevailed upon to regard me as irrecoverable. I even went so far as to fear that, as I occasioned much trouble, they might be glad to consider any very protracted attack as sufficient excuse for getting rid of me altogether. It was in vain they endeavored to reassure me by the most solemn promises. I exacted the most sacred oaths, that under no circumstances they would bury me until decomposition had so materially advanced as to render farther preservation impossible. And, even then, my mortal terrors would listen to no reason—would accept no consolation. I entered into a series of elaborate precautions. Among other things, I had the family vault so remodelled as to admit of being readily opened from within. The slightest pressure upon a long lever that extended far into the tomb would cause the iron portal to fly back. There were arrangements also for the free admission of air and light, and convenient receptacles for food and water, within immediate reach of the coffin intended for my reception. This coffin was warmly and softly padded, and was provided with a lid, fashioned upon the principle of the vault-door, with the addition of springs so contrived that the feeblest movement of the body would be sufficient to set it at liberty. Besides all this, there was suspended from the roof of the tomb, a large bell, the rope of which, it was designed, should extend through a hole in the coffin, and so be fastened to one of the hands of the corpse. But, alas? what avails the vigilance against the Destiny of man? Not even these well-contrived securities sufficed to save from the uttermost agonies of living inhumation, a wretch to these agonies foredoomed!

There arrived an epoch—as often before there had arrived—in which I found myself emerging from total unconsciousness into the first feeble and indefinite sense of existence. Slowly—with a tortoise gradation—approached the faint gray dawn of the psychal day. A torpid uneasiness. An apathetic endurance of dull pain. No care—no hope—no effort. Then, after a long interval, a ringing in the ears; then, after a lapse still longer, a prickling or tingling sensation in the extremities; then a seemingly eternal period of pleasurable quiescence, during which the awakening feelings are struggling into thought; then a brief re-sinking into non-entity; then a sudden recovery. At length the slight quivering of an eyelid, and immediately thereupon, an electric shock of a terror, deadly and indefinite, which sends the blood in torrents from the temples to the heart. And now the first positive effort to think. And now the first endeavor to remember. And now a partial and evanescent success. And now the memory has so far regained its dominion, that, in some measure, I am cognizant of my state. I feel that I am not awaking from ordinary sleep. I recollect that I have been subject to catalepsy. And now, at last, as if by the rush of an ocean, my shuddering spirit is overwhelmed by the one grim Danger—by the one spectral and ever-prevalent idea.

For some minutes after this fancy possessed me, I remained without motion. And why? I could not summon courage to move. I dared not make the effort which was to satisfy me of my fate—and yet there was something at my heart which whispered me *it was sure*. Despair—such as no other species of wretchedness ever calls into being—despair alone urged me, after long irresolution, to uplift the heavy lids of my eyes. I uplifted them. It was dark—all dark. I knew that the fit was over. I knew that the crisis of my disorder had long passed. I knew that I had now fully recovered the use of my visual faculties—and yet it was dark—all dark—the intense and utter raylessness of the Night that endureth for evermore.

I endeavored to shriek; and my lips and my parched tongue moved convulsively together in the attempt—but no voice issued from the cavernous lungs, which oppressed as if by the weight of some incumbent mountain, gasped and palpitated, with the heart, at every elaborate and struggling inspiration.

The movement of the jaws, in this effort to cry aloud, showed me that they were bound up, as is usual with the dead. I felt, too, that I lay upon some hard substance, and by something similar my sides were, also, closely compressed. So far, I had not ventured to stir any of my limbs—but now I violently threw up my arms, which had been lying at length, with the wrists crossed. They struck a solid wooden substance, which extended above my person at an elevation of not more than six inches from my face. I could no longer doubt that I reposed within a coffin at last.

And now, amid all my infinite miseries, came sweetly the cherub Hope—for I thought of my precautions. I writhed, and made spasmodic exertions to force open the lid: it would not move. I felt my wrists for the bell-rope: it was not to be found. And now the Comforter fled for ever, and a still sterner Despair reigned triumphant; for I could not help perceiving the absence of the paddings which I had so carefully prepared—and then, too, there came suddenly to my nostrils the strong peculiar odor of moist earth. The conclusion was irresistible. I was not within the vault. I had fallen into a trance while absent from home—while among strangers—when, or how, I could not remember—and it was they who had buried me as a dog—nailed up in some common coffin—and thrust deep, deep, and for ever, into some ordinary and nameless *grave*.

As this awful conviction forced itself, thus, into the innermost chambers of my soul, I once again struggled to cry aloud. And in this second endeavor I succeeded. A long, wild, and continuous shriek, or yell of agony, resounded through the realms of the subterranean Night.

"Hillo! hillo, there!" said a gruff voice, in reply.

"What the devil's the matter now!" said a second.

"Get out o' that!" said a third.

"What do you mean by yowling in that ere kind of style, like a cattymount?" said a fourth; and hereupon I was seized and shaken without ceremony, for several minutes, by a junto of very rough-looking individuals. They did not arouse me from my slumber—for I was wide awake when I screamed—but they restored me to the full possession of my memory.

This adventure occurred near Richmond, in Virginia. Accompanied by a friend, I had proceeded, upon a gunning expedition, some miles down the banks of the James River. Night approached, and we were overtaken by a storm. The cabin of a small sloop lying at anchor in the stream, and laden with garden mould, afforded us the only available shelter. We made the best of it, and passed the night on board. I slept in one of the only two berths in the vessel—and the berths of a sloop of sixty or twenty tons need scarcely be described. That which I occupied had no bedding of any kind. Its extreme width was eighteen inches. The distance of its bottom from the deck overhead was precisely the same. I found it a matter of exceeding difficulty to squeeze myself in. Nevertheless, I slept soundly, and the whole of my vision—for it was no dream, and no nightmare—arose naturally from the circumstances of my position—from my ordinary bias of thought—and from the difficulty, to which I have alluded, of collecting my senses, and especially of regaining my memory, for a long time after awaking from slumber. The men who shook me were the crew of the sloop, and some laborers engaged to unload it. From the load itself came the earthly smell. The bandage about the jaws was a silk handkerchief in which I had bound up my head, in default of my customary nightcap.

The tortures endured, however, were indubitably quite equal for the time, to those of actual sepulture. They were fearfully—they were inconceivably hideous; but out of Evil proceeded Good; for their very excess wrought in my spirit an inevitable revulsion. My soul acquired tone—acquired temper. I went abroad. I took vigorous exercise. I breathed the free air of Heaven. I thought upon other subjects than Death. I discarded my medical books. Buchan I burned. I read no *Night Thoughts*—no fustian about churchyards—no bugaboo tales—*such as this*. In short, I became a new man, and lived a man's life. From that memorable night, I dismissed forever my charnel apprehensions, and with them vanished the cataleptic disorder, of which, perhaps, they had been less the consequence than the cause.

There are moments when, even to the sober eye of Reason, the world of our sad Humanity may assume the semblance of a Hell—but the imagination of man is no Carathis, to explore with impunity its every cavern. Alas! the grim legion of sepulchral terrors cannot be regarded as altogether fanciful—but, like the Demons in whose company Afrasiab made his voyage down the Oxus, they must sleep, or they will devour us—they must be suffered to slumber, or we perish.

The Purloined Letter

> Nil sapientiae odiosius acumine nimio.
>
> —*Seneca*

At Paris, just after dark one gusty evening in the autumn of 18—, I was enjoying the twofold luxury of meditation and a meerschaum, in company with my friend C. Auguste Dupin, in his little back library, or book-closet, *au troisieme,* No. 33, Rue Dunot, Faubourg St. Germain. For one hour at least we had maintained a profound silence; while each, to any casual observer, might have seemed intently and exclusively occupied with the curling eddies of smoke that oppressed the atmosphere of the chamber. For myself, however, I was mentally discussing certain topics which had formed matter for conversation between us at an earlier period of the evening; I mean the affair of the Rue Morgue, and the mystery attending the murder of Marie Rogêt. I looked upon it, therefore, as something of a coincidence, when the door of our apartment was thrown open and admitted our old acquaintance, Monsieur G—, the Prefect of the Parisian police.

We gave him a hearty welcome; for there was nearly half as much of the entertaining as of the contemptible about the man, and we had not seen him for several years. We had been sitting in the dark, and Dupin now arose for the purpose of lighting a lamp, but sat down again, without doing so, upon G.'s saying that he had called to consult us, or rather to ask the opinion of my friend, about some official business which had occasioned a great deal of trouble.

"If it is any point requiring reflection," observed Dupin, as he forebore to enkindle the wick, "we shall examine it to better purpose in the dark."

"That is another of your odd notions," said the Prefect, who had a fashion of calling every thing "odd" that was beyond his comprehension, and thus lived amid an absolute legion of "oddities."

"Very true," said Dupin, as he supplied his visiter with a pipe, and rolled towards him a comfortable chair.

"And what is the difficulty now?" I asked. "Nothing more in the assassination way, I hope?"

"Oh, no; nothing of that nature. The fact is, the business is *very* simple indeed, and I make no doubt that we can manage it sufficiently well ourselves; but then I thought Dupin would like to hear the details of it, because it is so excessively *odd*."

"Simple and odd," said Dupin.

"Why, yes; and not exactly that, either. The fact is, we have all been a good deal puzzled because the affair *is* so simple, and yet baffles us altogether."

"Perhaps it is the very simplicity of the thing which puts you at fault," said my friend.

"What nonsense you *do* talk!" replied the Prefect, laughing heartily.

"Perhaps the mystery is a little *too* plain," said Dupin.

"Oh, good heavens! who ever heard of such an idea?"

"A little *too* self-evident."

"Ha! ha! ha—ha! ha! ha!—ho! ho! ho!" roared our visiter, profoundly amused, "oh, Dupin, you will be the death of me yet!"

"And what, after all, *is* the matter on hand?" I asked.

"Why, I will tell you," replied the Prefect, as he gave a long, steady and contemplative puff, and settled himself in his chair. "I will tell you in a few words; but, before I begin, let me caution you that this is an affair demanding the greatest secrecy, and that I should most probably lose the position I now hold, were it known that I confided it to any one."

"Proceed," said I.

"Or not," said Dupin.

"Well, then; I have received personal information, from a very high quarter, that a certain document of the last importance, has been purloined from the royal apartments. The individual who purloined it is known; this beyond a doubt; he was seen to take it. It is known, also, that it still remains in his possession."

"How is this known?" asked Dupin.

"It is clearly inferred," replied the Prefect, "from the nature of the document, and from the non-appearance of certain results which would at once arise from its passing *out* of the robber's possession; that is to say, from his employing it as he must design in the end to employ it."

"Be a little more explicit," I said.

"Well, I may venture so far as to say that the paper gives its holder a certain power in a certain quarter where such power is immensely valuable." The Prefect was fond of the cant of diplomacy.

"Still I do not quite understand," said Dupin.

"No? Well; the disclosure of the document to a third person, who shall be nameless, would bring in question the honor of a personage of most exalted station; and this fact gives the holder of the document an ascendancy over the illustrious personage whose honor and peace are so jeopardized."

"But this ascendancy," I interposed, "would depend upon the robber's knowledge of the loser's knowledge of the robber. Who would dare—"

"The thief," said G., "is the Minister D—, who dares all things, those unbecoming as well as those becoming a man. The method of the theft was not less ingenious than bold. The document in question—a letter, to be frank—had been received by the personage robbed while alone in the royal *boudoir*. During its perusal she was suddenly interrupted by the entrance of the other exalted personage from whom especially it was her wish to conceal it. After a hurried and vain endeavor to thrust it in a drawer, she was forced to place it, open as it was, upon a table. The address, however, was uppermost, and, the contents thus unexposed, the letter escaped notice. At this juncture enters the Minister D—. His lynx eye immediately perceives the paper, recognises the handwriting of the address, observes the confusion of the personage addressed, and fathoms her secret. After some business transactions, hurried through in his ordinary manner, he produces a letter somewhat similar to the one in question, opens it, pretends to read it, and then places it in close juxtaposition to the other. Again he converses, for some fifteen minutes, upon the public affairs. At length, in taking leave, he takes also from the table the letter to which he had no claim. Its rightful owner saw, but, of course, dared not call attention to the act, in the presence of the third personage who stood at her elbow. The minister decamped; leaving his own letter—one of no importance—upon the table."

"Here, then," said Dupin to me, "you have precisely what you demand to make the ascendancy complete—the robber's knowledge of the loser's knowledge of the robber."

"Yes," replied the Prefect; "and the power thus attained has, for some months past, been wielded, for political purposes, to a very dangerous extent. The personage robbed is more thoroughly convinced, every day, of the necessity of reclaiming her letter. But this, of course, cannot be done openly. In fine, driven to despair, she has committed the matter to me."

"Than whom," said Dupin, amid a perfect whirlwind of smoke, "no more sagacious agent could, I suppose, be desired, or even imagined."

"You flatter me," replied the Prefect; "but it is possible that some such opinion may have been entertained."

"It is clear," said I, "as you observe, that the letter is still in possession of the minister; since it is this possession, and not any employment of the letter, which bestows the power. With the employment the power departs."

"True," said G.; "and upon this conviction I proceeded. My first care was to make thorough search of the minister's hotel; and here my chief embarrassment lay in the necessity of searching without his knowledge. Beyond all things, I have been warned of the danger which would result from giving him reason to suspect our design."

"But," said I, "you are quite *au fait* in these investigations. The Parisian police have done this thing often before."

"O yes; and for this reason I did not despair. The habits of the minister gave me, too, a great advantage. He is frequently absent from home all night. His servants are by no means numerous. They sleep at a distance from their master's apartment, and, being chiefly Neapolitans, are readily made drunk. I have keys, as you know, with which I can open any chamber or cabinet in Paris. For three months a night has not passed, during the greater part of which I have not been engaged, personally, in ransacking the D— Hotel. My honor is interested, and, to mention a great secret, the reward is enormous. So I did not abandon the search until I had become fully satisfied that the thief is a more astute man than myself. I fancy that I have investigated every nook and corner of the premises in which it is possible that the paper can be concealed."

"But is it not possible," I suggested, "that although the letter may be in possession of the minister, as it unquestionably is, he may have concealed it elsewhere than upon his own premises?"

"This is barely possible," said Dupin. "The present peculiar condition of affairs at court, and especially of those intrigues in which D— is known to be involved, would render the instant availability of the document—its susceptibility of being produced at a moment's notice—a point of nearly equal importance with its possession."

"Its susceptibility of being produced?" said I.

"That is to say, of being *destroyed*," said Dupin.

"True," I observed; "the paper is clearly then upon the premises. As for its being upon the person of the minister, we may consider that as out of the question."

"Entirely," said the Prefect. "He has been twice waylaid, as if by footpads, and his person rigorously searched under my own inspection."

"You might have spared yourself this trouble," said Dupin. "D—, I presume, is not altogether a fool, and, if not, must have anticipated these waylayings, as a matter of course."

"Not *altogether* a fool," said G., "but then he's a poet, which I take to be only one remove from a fool."

"True," said Dupin, after a long and thoughtful whiff from his meerschaum, "although I have been guilty of certain doggrel myself."

"Suppose you detail," said I, "the particulars of your search."

"Why the fact is, we took our time, and we searched *everywhere*. I have had long experience in these affairs. I took the entire building, room by room; devoting the nights of a whole week to each. We examined, first, the furniture of each apartment. We opened every possible drawer; and I presume you know that, to a properly trained police agent, such a thing as a 'secret' drawer is impossible. Any man is a dolt who permits a 'secret' drawer to escape him in a search of this kind. The thing is *so* plain. There is a certain amount of bulk—of space—to be accounted for in every cabinet. Then we have accurate rules. The fiftieth part of a line could not escape us.

After the cabinets we took the chairs. The cushions we probed with the fine long needles you have seen me employ. From the tables we removed the tops."

"Why so?"

"Sometimes the top of a table, or other similarly arranged piece of furniture, is removed by the person wishing to conceal an article; then the leg is excavated, the article deposited within the cavity, and the top replaced. The bottoms and tops of bedposts are employed in the same way."

"But could not the cavity be detected by sounding?" I asked.

"By no means, if, when the article is deposited, a sufficient wadding of cotton be placed around it. Besides, in our case, we were obliged to proceed without noise."

"But you could not have removed—you could not have taken to pieces *all* articles of furniture in which it would have been possible to make a deposit in the manner you mention. A letter may be compressed into a thin spiral roll, not differing much in shape or bulk from a large knitting-needle, and in this form it might be inserted into the rung of a chair, for example. You did not take to pieces all the chairs?"

"Certainly not; but we did better—we examined the rungs of every chair in the hotel, and, indeed the jointings of every description of furniture, by the aid of a most powerful microscope. Had there been any traces of recent disturbance we should not have failed to detect it instantly. A single grain of gimlet-dust, for example, would have been as obvious as an apple. Any disorder in the glueing—any unusual gaping in the joints—would have sufficed to insure detection."

"I presume you looked to the mirrors, between the boards and the plates, and you probed the beds and the bed-clothes, as well as the curtains and carpets."

"That of course; and when we had absolutely completed every particle of the furniture in this way, then we examined the house itself. We divided its entire surface into compartments, which we numbered, so that none might be missed; then we scrutinized each individual square inch throughout the premises, including the two houses immediately adjoining, with the microscope, as before."

"The two houses adjoining!" I exclaimed; "you must have had a great deal of trouble."

"We had; but the reward offered is prodigious!"

"You include the *grounds* about the houses?"

"All the grounds are paved with brick. They gave us comparatively little trouble. We examined the moss between the bricks, and found it undisturbed."

"You looked among D—'s papers, of course, and into the books of the library?"

"Certainly; we opened every package and parcel; we not only opened every book, but we turned over every leaf in each volume, not contenting ourselves with a mere shake, according to the fashion of some of our police officers. We also measured the thickness of every book-*cover*, with the most accurate admeasurement, and applied to each the most jealous scrutiny of the microscope. Had any of the bindings been recently meddled with, it would have been utterly impossible that the fact should have escaped observation. Some five or six volumes, just from the hands of the binder, we carefully probed, longitudinally, with the needles."

"You explored the floors beneath the carpets?"

"Beyond doubt. We removed every carpet, and examined the boards with the microscope."

"And the paper on the walls?"

"Yes."

"You looked into the cellars?"

"We did."

"Then," I said, "you have been making a miscalculation, and the letter is *not* upon the premises, as you suppose."

"I fear you are right there," said the Prefect. "And now, Dupin, what would you advise me to do?"

"To make a thorough re-search of the premises."

"That is absolutely needless," replied G—. "I am not more sure that I breathe than I am that the letter is not at the Hotel."

"I have no better advice to give you," said Dupin. "You have, of course, an accurate description of the letter?"

"Oh yes!"—And here the Prefect, producing a memorandum-book proceeded to read aloud a minute account of the internal, and especially of the external appearance of the missing document. Soon after finishing the perusal of this description, he took his departure, more entirely depressed in spirits than I had ever known the good gentleman before.

In about a month afterwards he paid us another visit, and found us occupied very nearly as before. He took a pipe and a chair and entered into some ordinary conversation.

At length I said,—"Well, but G—, what of the purloined letter? I presume you have at last made up your mind that there is no such thing as overreaching the Minister?"

"Confound him, say I—yes; I made the re-examination, however, as Dupin suggested—but it was all labor lost, as I knew it would be."

"How much was the reward offered, did you say?" asked Dupin.

"Why, a very great deal—a *very* liberal reward—I don't like to say how much, precisely; but one thing I *will* say, that I wouldn't mind giving my individual check for fifty thousand francs to any one who could obtain me that letter. The fact is, it is becoming of more and more importance every day; and the reward has been lately doubled. If it were trebled, however, I could do no more than I have done."

"Why, yes," said Dupin, drawlingly, between the whiffs of his meerschaum, "I really—think, G—, you have not exerted yourself—to the utmost in this matter. You might—do a little more, I think, eh?"

"How?—in what way?"

"Why—puff, puff—you might—puff, puff—employ counsel in the matter, eh?—puff, puff, puff. Do you remember the story they tell of Abernethy?"

"No; hang Abernethy!"

"To be sure! hang him and welcome. But, once upon a time, a certain rich miser conceived the design of spunging upon this Abernethy for a medical opinion. Getting up, for this purpose, an ordinary conversation in a private company, he insinuated his case to the physician, as that of an imaginary individual.

"'We will suppose,' said the miser, 'that his symptoms are such and such; now, doctor, what would *you* have directed him to take?'

"'Take!' said Abernethy, 'why, take *advice*, to be sure.'"

"But," said the Prefect, a little discomposed, "*I* am *perfectly* willing to take advice, and to pay for it. I would *really* give fifty thousand francs to any one who would aid me in the matter."

"In that case," replied Dupin, opening a drawer, and producing a check-book, "you may as well fill me up a check for the amount mentioned. When you have signed it, I will hand you the letter."

I was astounded. The Prefect appeared absolutely thunder-stricken. For some minutes he remained speechless and motionless, looking incredulously at my friend with open mouth, and eyes that seemed starting from their sockets; then, apparently recovering himself in some measure, he seized a pen, and after several pauses and vacant stares, finally filled up and signed a check for fifty thousand francs, and handed it across the table to Dupin. The latter examined it carefully and deposited it in his pocket-book; then, unlocking an *escritoire*, took thence a letter and gave it to the Prefect. This functionary grasped it in a perfect agony of joy, opened it with a trembling hand, cast a rapid glance at its contents, and then, scrambling and struggling to the door, rushed at length unceremoniously from the room and from the house, without having uttered a syllable since Dupin had requested him to fill up the check.

When he had gone, my friend entered into some explanations.

"The Parisian police," he said, "are exceedingly able in their way. They are persevering, ingenious, cunning, and thoroughly versed in the knowledge which their duties seem chiefly to demand. Thus, when G— detailed to us his made of searching the premises at the Hotel D—, I felt entire confidence in his having made a satisfactory investigation—so far as his labors extended."

"So far as his labors extended?" said I.

"Yes," said Dupin. "The measures adopted were not only the best of their kind, but carried out to absolute perfection. Had the letter been deposited within the range of their search, these fellows would, beyond a question, have found it."

I merely laughed—but he seemed quite serious in all that he said.

"The measures, then," he continued, "were good in their kind, and well executed; their defect lay in their being inapplicable to the case, and to the man. A certain set of highly ingenious resources are, with the Prefect, a sort of Procrustean bed, to which he forcibly adapts his designs. But he perpetually errs by being too deep or too shallow, for the matter in hand; and many a schoolboy is a better reasoner than he. I knew one about eight years of age, whose success at guessing in the game of 'even and odd' attracted universal admiration. This game is simple, and is played with marbles. One player holds in his hand a number of these toys, and demands of another whether that number is even or odd. If the guess is right, the guesser wins one; if wrong, he loses one. The boy to whom I allude won all the marbles of the school. Of course he had some principle of guessing; and this lay in mere observation and admeasurement of the astuteness of his opponents. For example, an arrant simpleton is his opponent, and, holding up his closed hand, asks, 'are they even or odd?' Our schoolboy replies, 'odd,' and loses; but upon the second trial he wins, for he then says to himself, 'the simpleton had them even upon the first trial, and his amount of cunning is just sufficient to make him have them odd upon the second; I will therefore guess odd'—he guesses odd, and wins. Now, with a simpleton a degree above the first, he would have reasoned thus: 'This fellow finds that in the first instance I guessed odd, and, in the second, he will propose to himself, upon the first impulse, a simple variation from even to odd, as did the first simpleton; but then a second thought will suggest that this is too simple a variation, and finally he will decide upon putting it even as before. I will therefore guess even;'—he guesses even, and wins. Now this mode of reasoning in the schoolboy, whom his fellows termed 'lucky'—what, in its last analysis, is it?"

"It is merely," I said, "an identification of the reasoner's intellect with that of his opponent."

"It is," said Dupin; "and, upon inquiring, of the boy by what means he effected the *thorough* identification in which his success consisted, I received answer as follows: 'When I wish to find out how wise, or how stupid, or how good, or how wicked is any one, or what are his thoughts at the moment, I fashion the expression of my face, as accurately as possible, in accordance with the expression of his, and then wait to see what thoughts or sentiments arise in my mind or heart, as if to match or correspond with the expression.' This response of the schoolboy lies at the bottom of all the spurious profundity which has been attributed to Rochefoucault, to La Bougive, to Machiavelli, and to Campanella."

"And the identification," I said, "of the reasoner's intellect with that of his opponent, depends, if I understand you aright, upon the accuracy with which the opponent's intellect is admeasured."

"For its practical value it depends upon this," replied Dupin; "and the Prefect and his cohort fail so frequently, first, by default of this identification, and, secondly, by ill-admeasurement, or rather through non-admeasurement, of the intellect with which they are engaged. They consider only their *own* ideas of ingenuity; and, in searching for anything hidden, advert only to the modes in which *they* would have hidden it. They are right in this much—that their own ingenuity is a faithful representative of that of *the mass*; but when the cunning of the individual felon is diverse in character from their own, the felon foils them, of course. This always happens when it is above their own, and very usually when it is below. They have no variation of principle in their investigations; at best, when urged by some unusual emergency—by some extraordinary reward—they extend or exaggerate their old modes of *practice*, without touching their principles. What, for example, in this case of D—, has been done to vary the principle of action? What is all this boring, and probing, and sounding, and scrutinizing with the microscope and dividing the surface of the building into registered square inches—what is it all but an exaggeration *of the application* of the one principle or set of principles of search, which are based upon the one set of notions regarding human ingenuity, to which the Prefect, in the long routine of his duty, has been accustomed? Do you not see he has taken it for granted that *all* men proceed to conceal a letter—not exactly in a gimlet hole bored in a chair-leg—but, at least, in *some* out-of-the-way hole or corner suggested by the same tenor of thought which would urge a man to secrete a letter in a gimlet-hole bored in a chair-leg? And do you not see also, that such *recherchés* nooks for concealment are adapted only for ordinary occasions, and would be adopted only by ordinary intellects; for, in all cases of concealment, a disposal of the article concealed—a disposal of it in this *recherché* manner—is, in the very first instance, presumable and presumed; and thus its discovery depends, not at all upon the acumen, but altogether upon the mere care, patience, and determination of the seekers; and where the case is of importance—or, what amounts to the same thing in the policial eyes, when the reward is of magnitude,—the qualities in question have *never* been known to fail. You will now understand what I meant in suggesting that, had the purloined letter been hidden any where within the limits of the Prefect's examination—in other words, had the principle of its concealment been comprehended within the principles of the Prefect—its discovery would have been a matter altogether beyond question. This functionary, however, has been thoroughly mystified; and the remote source of his defeat lies in the supposition that the Minister is a fool, because he has acquired renown as a poet. All fools are poets; this the Prefect feels; and he is merely guilty of a *non distributio medii* in thence inferring that all poets are fools."

"But is this really the poet?" I asked. "There are two brothers, I know; and both have attained reputation in letters. The Minister I believe has written learnedly on the Differential Calculus. He is a mathematician, and no poet."

"You are mistaken; I know him well; he is both. As poet *and* mathematician, he would reason well; as mere mathematician, he could not have reasoned at all, and thus would have been at the mercy of the Prefect."

"You surprise me," I said, "by these opinions, which have been contradicted by the voice of the world. You do not mean to set at naught the well-digested idea of centuries. The mathematical reason has long been regarded as the reason *par excellence*."

"'*Il ya à parier*,'" replied Dupin, quoting from Chamfort, "'*que toute idée publique, toute convention reçue est une sottise, car elle a convenue au plus grand nombre*.' The mathematicians, I grant you, have done their best to promulgate the popular error to which you allude, and which is none the less an error for its promulgation as truth. With an art worthy a better cause, for example, they have insinuated the term 'analysis' into application to algebra. The French are the originators of this particular deception; but if a term is of any importance—if words derive any value from applicability—then 'analysis' conveys 'algebra' about as much as, in Latin, '*ambitus*' implies 'ambition,' '*religio*' 'religion,' or '*homines* honesti,' a set of *honorable* men."

"You have a quarrel on hand, I see," said I, "with some of the algebraists of Paris; but proceed."

"I dispute the availability, and thus the value, of that reason which is cultivated in any especial form other than the abstractly logical. I dispute, in particular, the reason educed by mathematical study. The mathematics are the science of form and quantity; mathematical reasoning is merely logic applied to observation upon form and quantity. The great error lies in supposing that even the truths of what is called pure algebra, are abstract or general truths. And this error is so egregious that I am confounded at the universality with which it has been received. Mathematical axioms are not axioms of general truth. What is true of *relation*—of form and quantity—is often grossly false in regard to morals, for example. In this latter science it is very usually *untrue* that the aggregated parts are equal to the whole. In chemistry also the axiom fails. In the consideration of motive it fails; for two motives, each of a given value, have not, necessarily, a value when united, equal to the sum of their values apart. There are numerous other mathematical truths which are only truths within the limits of *relation*. But the mathematician argues, from his *finite truths*, through habit, as if they were of an absolutely general applicability—as the world indeed imagines them to be. Bryant, in his very learned *Mythology*, mentions an analogous source of error, when he says that 'although the Pagan fables are not believed, yet we forget ourselves continually, and make inferences from them as existing realities.' With the algebraists, however, who are Pagans themselves, the 'Pagan fables' *are* believed, and the inferences are made, not so much through lapse of memory, as through an unaccountable addling of the brains. In short, I never yet encountered the mere mathematician who could be trusted out of equal roots, or one who did not clandestinely hold it as a point of his faith that $x2 + px$ was absolutely and unconditionally equal to q. Say to one of these gentlemen, by way of experiment, if you please, that you believe occasions may occur where $x2 + px$ is not altogether equal to q, and, having made him understand what you mean, get out of his reach as speedily as convenient, for, beyond doubt, he will endeavor to knock you down.

"I mean to say," continued Dupin, while I merely laughed at his last observations, "that if the Minister had been no more than a mathematician, the Prefect would have been under no necessity of giving me this check. I know him, however, as both mathematician and poet, and my measures were adapted to his capacity, with reference to the circumstances by which he was surrounded. I knew him as a courtier, too, and as a bold *intriguant*. Such a man, I considered, could not fail to be aware of the ordinary policial modes of action. He could not have failed to anticipate—and events have proved that he did not fail to anticipate—the waylayings to which he was subjected. He must have foreseen, I reflected, the secret investigations of his premises. His frequent absences from home at night, which were hailed by the Prefect as certain aids to his success, I regarded only as *ruses*, to afford opportunity for thorough search to the police, and thus the sooner to impress them with the conviction to which G—, in fact, did finally arrive—the conviction that the letter was not upon the premises. I felt, also, that the whole train of thought, which I was at some pains in detailing to you just now, concerning the invariable principle of policial action in searches for articles concealed—I felt that this whole train of thought would necessarily pass through the mind of the Minister. It would imperatively lead him to despise all the ordinary *nooks* of concealment. *He* could not, I reflected, be so weak as not to see that the most intricate and remote recess of his hotel would be as open as his commonest closets to the eyes, to the probes, to the gimlets, and to the microscopes of the Prefect. I saw, in fine, that he would be driven, as a matter of course, to *simplicity*, if not deliberately induced to it as a matter of choice. You will remember, perhaps, how desperately the Prefect laughed when I suggested, upon our first interview, that it was just possible this mystery troubled him so much on account of its being so *very* self-evident."

"Yes," said I, "I remember his merriment well. I really thought he would have fallen into convulsions."

"The material world," continued Dupin, "abounds with very strict analogies to the immaterial; and thus some color of truth has been given to the rhetorical dogma, that metaphor, or simile, may be made to strengthen an argument, as well as to embellish a description. The principle of the *vis inertiae*, for example, seems to be identical in physics and metaphysics. It is not more true in the former, that a large body is with more difficulty set in motion than a smaller one, and that its subsequent *momentum* is commensurate with this difficulty, than it is, in the latter, that intellects of the vaster capacity, while more forcible, more constant, and more eventful in their movements than those of inferior grade, are yet the less readily moved, and more embarrassed and full of hesitation in the first few steps of their progress. Again: have you ever noticed which of the street signs, over the shop-doors, are the most attractive of attention?"

"I have never given the matter a thought," I said.

"There is a game of puzzles," he resumed, "which is played upon a map. One party playing requires another to find a given word—the name of town, river, state or empire—any word, in short, upon the motley and perplexed surface of the chart. A novice in the game generally seeks to embarrass his opponents by giving them the most minutely lettered names; but the adept selects such words as stretch, in large characters, from one end of the chart to the other. These, like the over-largely lettered signs and placards of the street, escape observation by dint of being excessively obvious; and here the physical oversight is precisely analogous with the moral inapprehension by which the intellect suffers to pass unnoticed those considerations which are too obtrusively and too palpably self-evident. But this is a point, it appears, somewhat above or beneath the understanding of the Prefect. He never once thought it probable, or possible, that the Minister had deposited the letter immediately beneath the nose of the whole world, by way of best preventing any portion of that world from perceiving it.

"But the more I reflected upon the daring, dashing, and discriminating ingenuity of D—; upon the fact that the document must always have been at *hand*, if he intended to use it to good purpose; and upon the decisive evidence, obtained by the Prefect, that it was not hidden within the limits of that dignitary's ordinary search—the more satisfied I became that, to conceal this letter, the Minister had resorted to the comprehensive and sagacious expedient of not attempting to conceal it at all.

"Full of these ideas, I prepared myself with a pair of green spectacles, and called one fine morning, quite by accident, at the Ministerial hotel. I found D— at home, yawning, lounging, and dawdling, as usual, and pretending to be in the last extremity of *ennui*. He is, perhaps, the most really energetic human being now alive—but that is only when nobody sees him.

"To be even with him, I complained of my weak eyes, and lamented the necessity of the spectacles, under cover of which I cautiously and thoroughly surveyed the whole apartment, while seemingly intent only upon the conversation of my host.

"I paid especial attention to a large writing-table near which he sat, and upon which lay confusedly, some miscellaneous letters and other papers, with one or two musical instruments and a few books. Here, however, after a long and very deliberate scrutiny, I saw nothing to excite particular suspicion.

"At length my eyes, in going the circuit of the room, fell upon a trumpery fillagree card-rack of pasteboard, that hung dangling by a dirty blue ribbon, from a little brass knob just beneath the middle of the mantel-piece. In this rack, which had three or four compartments, were five or six visiting cards and a solitary letter. This last was much soiled and crumpled. It was torn nearly in two, across the middle—as if a design, in the first instance, to tear it entirely up as worthless, had been altered, or stayed, in the second. It had a large black seal, bearing the D— cipher *very* conspicuously, and was addressed, in a diminutive female hand, to D—, the minister, himself. It was thrust carelessly, and even, as it seemed, contemptuously, into one of the uppermost divisions of the rack.

"No sooner had I glanced at this letter, than I concluded it to be that of which I was in search. To be sure, it was, to all appearance, radically different from the one of which the Prefect had read us so minute a description. Here the seal was large and black, with the D— cipher; there it was small and red, with the ducal arms of the S— family. Here, the address, to the Minister, diminutive and feminine; there the superscription, to a certain royal personage, was markedly bold and decided; the size alone formed a point of correspondence. But, then, the *radicalness* of these differences, which was excessive; the dirt; the soiled and torn condition of the paper, so inconsistent with the *true* methodical habits of D—, and so suggestive of a design to delude the beholder into an idea of the worthlessness of the document; these things, together with the hyper-obtrusive situation of this document, full in the view of every visiter, and thus exactly in accordance with the conclusions to which I had previously arrived; these things, I say, were strongly corroborative of suspicion, in one who came with the intention to suspect.

"I protracted my visit as long as possible, and, while I maintained a most animated discussion with the Minister upon a topic which I knew well had never failed to interest and excite him, I kept my attention really riveted upon the letter. In this examination, I committed to memory its external appearance and arrangement in the rack; and also fell, at length, upon a discovery which set at rest whatever trivial doubt I might have entertained. In scrutinizing the edges of the paper, I observed them to be more *chafed* than seemed necessary. They presented the *broken* appearance which is manifested when a stiff paper, having been once folded and pressed with a folder, is refolded in a reversed direction, in the same creases or edges which had formed the original fold. This discovery was sufficient. It was clear to me that the letter had been turned, as a glove, inside out, re-directed, and re-sealed. I bade the Minister good morning, and took my departure at once, leaving a gold snuff-box upon the table.

"The next morning I called for the snuff-box, when we resumed, quite eagerly, the conversation of the preceding day. While thus engaged, however, a loud report, as if of a pistol, was heard immediately beneath the windows of the hotel, and was succeeded by a series of fearful screams, and the shoutings of a terrified mob. D— rushed to a casement, threw it open, and looked out. In the meantime, I stepped to the card-rack took the letter, put it in my pocket, and replaced it by a *fac-simile* (so far as regards externals), which I had carefully prepared at my lodgings—imitating the D— cipher, very readily, by means of a seal formed of bread.

"The disturbance in the street had been occasioned by the frantic behavior of a man with a musket. He had fired it among a crowd of women and children. It proved, however, to have been without ball, and the fellow was suffered to go his way as a lunatic or a drunkard. When he had gone, D— came from the window, whither I had followed him immediately upon securing the object in view. Soon afterwards I bade him farewell. The pretended lunatic was a man in my own pay."

"But what purpose had you," I asked, "in replacing the letter by a *fac-simile*? Would it not have been better, at the first visit, to have seized it openly, and departed?"

"D—," replied Dupin, "is a desperate man, and a man of nerve. His hotel, too, is not without attendants devoted to his interests. Had I made the wild attempt you suggest, I might never have left the Ministerial presence alive. The good people of Paris might have heard of me no more. But I had an object apart from these considerations. You know my political prepossessions. In this matter, I act as a partisan of the lady concerned. For eighteen months the Minister has had her in his power. She has now him in hers—since, being unaware that the letter is not in his possession, he will proceed with his exactions as if it was. Thus will he inevitably commit himself, at once, to his political destruction. His downfall, too, will not be more precipitate than awkward. It is all very well to talk about the *facilis descensus Averni*; but in all kinds of climbing, as Catalani said of singing, it is far more easy to get up than to come down. In the present instance I have no sympathy—at least no pity—for him who descends. He is that *monstrum horrendum*, an unprincipled man of genius. I confess, however, that I should like very well to know the precise character of his thoughts, when, being defied by her whom the Prefect terms 'a certain personage' he is reduced to opening the letter which I left for him in the card-rack."

"How? did you put any thing particular in it?"

"Why—it did not seem altogether right to leave the interior blank—that would have been insulting. D—, at Vienna once, did me an evil turn, which I told him, quite good-humoredly, that I should remember. So, as I knew he would feel some curiosity in regard to the identity of the person who had outwitted him, I thought it a pity not to give him a clue. He is well acquainted with my MS., and I just copied into the middle of the blank sheet the words:

> '—*Un dessein si funeste,*
> *S'il n'est digne d'Atrée, est digne de Thyeste.*'

They are to be found in Crebillon's *Atrée*."

The Facts in the Case of M. Valdemar

Of course I shall not pretend to consider it any matter for wonder, that the extraordinary case of M. Valdemar has excited discussion. It would have been a miracle had it not—especially under the circumstances. Through the desire of all parties concerned, to keep the affair from the public, at least for the present, or until we had farther opportunities for investigation—through our endeavors to effect this—a garbled or exaggerated account made its way into society, and became the source of many unpleasant misrepresentations, and, very naturally, of a great deal of disbelief.

It is now rendered necessary that I give the *facts*—as far as I comprehend them myself. They are, succinctly, these:

My attention, for the last three years, had been repeatedly drawn to the subject of Mesmerism; and, about nine months ago it occurred to me, quite suddenly, that in the series of experiments made hitherto, there had been a very remarkable and most unaccountable omission:—no person had as yet been mesmerized *in articulo mortis*. It remained to be seen, first, whether, in such condition, there existed in the patient any susceptibility to the magnetic influence; secondly, whether, if any existed, it was impaired or increased by the condition; thirdly, to what extent, or for how long a period, the encroachments of Death might be arrested by the process. There were other points to be ascertained, but these most excited my curiosity—the last in especial, from the immensely important character of its consequences.

In looking around me for some subject by whose means I might test these particulars, I was brought to think of my friend, M. Ernest Valdemar, the well-known compiler of the *Bibliotheca Forensica*, and author (under the *nom de plume* of Issachar Marx) of the Polish versions of *Wallenstein* and *Gargantua*. M. Valdemar, who has resided principally at Harlaem, N.Y., since the year 1839, is (or was) particularly noticeable for the extreme spareness of his person—his lower limbs much resembling those of John Randolph; and, also, for the whiteness of his whiskers, in violent contrast to the blackness of his hair—the latter, in consequence, being very generally mistaken for a wig. His temperament was markedly nervous, and rendered him a good subject for mesmeric experiment. On two or three occasions I had put him to sleep with little difficulty, but was disappointed in other results which his peculiar constitution had naturally led me to anticipate. His will was at no period positively, or thoroughly, under my control, and in regard to *clairvoyance*, I could accomplish with him nothing to be relied upon. I always attributed my failure at these points to the disordered state of his health. For some months previous to my becoming acquainted with him, his physicians had declared him in a confirmed phthisis. It was his custom, indeed, to speak calmly of his approaching dissolution, as of a matter neither to be avoided nor regretted.

When the ideas to which I have alluded first occurred to me, it was of course very natural that I should think of M. Valdemar. I knew the steady philosophy of the man too well to apprehend any scruples from *him*; and he had no relatives in America who would be likely to interfere. I spoke to him frankly upon the subject; and, to my surprise, his interest seemed vividly excited. I say to my surprise, for, although he had always yielded his person freely to my experiments, he had never before given me any tokens of sympathy with what I did. His disease was if that character which would admit of exact calculation in respect to the epoch of its termination in death; and it was finally arranged between us that he would send for me about twenty-four hours before the period announced by his physicians as that of his decease.

It is now rather more than seven months since I received, from M. Valdemar himself, the subjoined note:

> My Dear P——,
>
> You may as well come now. D— and F— are agreed that I cannot hold out beyond tomorrow midnight; and I think they have hit the time very nearly.
>
> Valdemar

I received this note within half an hour after it was written, and in fifteen minutes more I was in the dying man's chamber. I had not seen him for ten days, and was appalled by the fearful alteration which the brief interval had wrought in him. His face wore a leaden hue; the eyes were utterly lustreless; and the emaciation was so extreme that the skin had been broken through by the cheek-bones. His expectoration was excessive. The pulse was barely perceptible. He retained, nevertheless, in a very remarkable manner, both his mental power and a certain degree of physical strength. He spoke with distinctness—took some palliative medicines without aid—and, when I entered the room, was occupied in penciling memoranda in a pocket-book. He was propped up in the bed by pillows. Doctors D—— and F—— were in attendance.

After pressing Valdemar's hand, I took these gentlemen aside, and obtained from them a minute account of the patient's condition. The left lung had been for eighteen months in a semi-osseous or cartilaginous state, and was, of course, entirely useless for all purposes of vitality. The right, in its upper portion, was also partially, if not thoroughly, ossified, while the lower region was merely a mass of purulent tubercles, running one into another. Several extensive perforations existed; and, at one point, permanent adhesion to the ribs had taken place. These appearances in the right lobe were of comparatively recent date. The ossification had proceeded with very unusual rapidity; no sign of it had discovered a month before, and the adhesion had only been observed during the three previous days. Independently of the phthisis, the patient was suspected of aneurism of the aorta; but on this point the osseous symptoms rendered an exact diagnosis impossible. It was the opinion of both physicians that M. Valdemar would die about midnight on the morrow (Sunday). It was then seven o'clock on Saturday evening.

On quitting the invalid's bed-side to hold conversation with myself, Doctors D— and F— had bidden him a final farewell. It had not been their intention to return; but, at my request, they agreed to look in upon the patient about ten the next night.

When they had gone, I spoke freely with M. Valdemar on the subject of his approaching dissolution, as well as, more particularly, of the experiment proposed. He still professed himself quite willing and even anxious to have it made, and urged me to commence it at once. A male and a female nurse were in attendance; but I did not feel myself altogether at liberty to engage in a task of this character with no more reliable witnesses than these people, in case of sudden accident, might prove. I therefore postponed operations until about eight the next night, when the arrival of a medical student with whom I had some acquaintance (Mr. Theodore L—l), relieved me from farther embarrassment. It had been my design, originally, to wait for the physicians; but I was induced to proceed, first, by the urgent entreaties of M. Valdemar, and secondly, by my conviction that I had not a moment to lose, as he was evidently sinking fast.

Mr. L—l was so kind as to accede to my desire that he would take notes of all that occurred, and it is from his memoranda that what I now have to relate is, for the most part, either condensed or copied *verbatim*.

It wanted about five minutes of eight when, taking the patient's hand, I begged him to state, as distinctly as he could, to Mr. L—l, whether he (M. Valdemar) was entirely willing that I should make the experiment of mesmerizing him in his then condition.

He replied feebly, yet quite audibly, "Yes, I wish to be. I fear you have mesmerized"—adding immediately afterwards, "deferred it too long."

While he spoke thus, I commenced the passes which I had already found most effectual in subduing him. He was evidently influenced with the first lateral stroke of my hand across his forehead; but although I exerted all my powers, no farther perceptible effect was induced until some minutes after ten o'clock, when Doctors D— and F— called, according to appointment. I explained to them, in a few words, what I designed, and as they opposed no objection, saying that the patient was already in the death agony, I proceeded without hesitation—exchanging, however, the lateral passes for downward ones, and directing my gaze entirely into the right eye of the sufferer.

By this time his pulse was imperceptible and his breathing was stertorous, and at intervals of half a minute.

This condition was nearly unaltered for a quarter of an hour. At the expiration of this period, however, a natural although a very deep sigh escaped the bosom of the dying man, and the stertorous breathing ceased—that is to say, its stertorousness was no longer apparent; the intervals were undiminished. The patient's extremities were of an icy coldness.

At five minutes before eleven I perceived unequivocal signs of the mesmeric influence. The glassy roll of the eye was changed for that expression of uneasy *inward* examination which is never seen except in cases of sleep-waking, and which it is quite impossible to mistake. With a few rapid lateral passes I made the lids quiver, as in incipient sleep, and with a few more I closed them altogether. I was not satisfied, however, with this, but continued the manipulations vigorously, and with the fullest exertion of the will, until I had completely stiffened the limbs of the slumberer, after placing them in a seemingly easy position. The legs were at full length; the arms were nearly so, and reposed on the bed at a moderate distance from the loin. The head was very slightly elevated.

When I had accomplished this, it was fully midnight, and I requested the gentlemen present to examine M. Valdemar's condition. After a few experiments, they admitted him to be an unusually perfect state of mesmeric trance. The curiosity of both the physicians was greatly excited. Dr. D—— resolved at once to remain with the patient all night, while Dr. F—— took leave with a promise to return at daybreak. Mr. L—l and the nurses remained.

We left M. Valdemar entirely undisturbed until about three o'clock in the morning, when I approached him and found him in precisely the same condition as when Dr. F— went away—that is to say, he lay in the same position; the pulse was imperceptible; the breathing was gentle (scarcely noticeable, unless through the application of a mirror to the lips); the eyes were closed naturally; and the limbs were as rigid and as cold as marble. Still, the general appearance was certainly not that of death.

As I approached M. Valdemar I made a kind of half effort to influence his right arm into pursuit of my own, as I passed the latter gently to and fro above his person. In such experiments with this patient had never perfectly succeeded before, and assuredly I had little thought of succeeding now; but to my astonishment, his arm very readily, although feebly, followed every direction I assigned it with mine. I determined to hazard a few words of conversation.

"M. Valdemar," I said, "are you asleep?" He made no answer, but I perceived a tremor about the lips, and was thus induced to repeat the question, again and again. At its third repetition, his whole frame was agitated by a very slight shivering; the eyelids unclosed themselves so far as to display a white line of the ball; the lips moved sluggishly, and from between them, in a barely audible whisper, issued the words:

"Yes;—asleep now. Do not wake me!—let me die so!"

I here felt the limbs and found them as rigid as ever. The right arm, as before, obeyed the direction of my hand. I questioned the sleep-waker again:

"Do you still feel pain in the breast, M. Valdemar?"

The answer now was immediate, but even less audible than before: "No pain—I am dying."

I did not think it advisable to disturb him farther just then, and nothing more was said or done until the arrival of Dr. F—, who came a little before sunrise, and expressed unbounded astonishment at finding the patient still alive. After feeling the pulse and applying a mirror to the lips, he requested me to speak to the sleep-waker again. I did so, saying: "M. Valdemar, do you still sleep?"

As before, some minutes elapsed ere a reply was made; and during the interval the dying man seemed to be collecting his energies to speak. At my fourth repetition of the question, he said very faintly, almost inaudibly: "Yes; still asleep—dying."

It was now the opinion, or rather the wish, of the physicians, that M. Valdemar should be suffered to remain undisturbed in his present apparently tranquil condition, until death should supervene—and this, it was generally agreed, must now take place within a few minutes. I concluded, however, to speak to him once more, and merely repeated my previous question.

While I spoke, there came a marked change over the countenance of the sleep-waker. The eyes rolled themselves slowly open, the pupils disappearing upwardly; the skin generally assumed a cadaverous hue, resembling not so much parchment as white paper; and the circular hectic spots which, hitherto, had been strongly defined in the centre of each cheek, *went out* at once. I use this expression, because the suddenness of their departure put me in mind of nothing so much as the extinguishment of a candle by a puff of the breath. The upper lip, at the same time, writhed itself away from the teeth, which it had previously covered completely; while the lower jaw fell with an audible jerk, leaving the mouth widely extended, and disclosing in full view the swollen and blackened tongue. I presume that no member of the party then present had been unaccustomed to death-bed horrors; but so hideous beyond conception was the appearance of M. Valdemar at this moment, that there was a general shrinking back from the region of the bed.

I now feel that I have reached a point of this narrative at which every reader will be startled into positive disbelief. It is my business, however, simply to proceed.

There was no longer the faintest sign of vitality in M. Valdemar; and concluding him to be dead, we were consigning him to the charge of the nurses, when a strong vibratory motion was observable in the tongue. This continued for perhaps a minute. At the expiration of this period, there issued from the distended and motionless jaws a voice—such as it would be madness in me to attempt describing. There are, indeed, two or three epithets which might be considered as applicable to it in part; I might say, for example, that the sound was harsh, and broken and hollow; but the hideous whole is indescribable, for the simple reason that no similar sounds have ever jarred upon the ear of humanity. There were two particulars, nevertheless, which I thought then, and still think, might fairly be stated as characteristic of the intonation—as well adapted to convey some idea of its unearthly peculiarity. In the first place, the voice seemed to reach our ears—at least mine—from a vast distance, or from some deep cavern within the earth. In the second place, it impressed me (I fear, indeed, that it will be impossible to make myself comprehended) as gelatinous or glutinous matters impress the sense of touch.

I have spoken both of "sound" and of "voice." I mean to say that the sound was one of distinct—of even wonderfully, thrillingly distinct—syllabification. M. Valdemar *spoke*—obviously in reply to the question I had propounded to him a few minutes before. I had asked him, it will be remembered, if he still slept. He now said:

"Yes!—no;—I *have been* sleeping—and now—now—*I am dead.*"

No person present even affected to deny, or attempted to repress, the unutterable, shuddering horror which these few words, thus uttered, were so well calculated to convey. Mr. L—l (the student) swooned. The nurses immediately left the chamber, and could not be induced to return. My own impressions I would not pretend to render intelligible to the reader. For nearly an hour, we busied ourselves, silently—without the utterance of a word—in endeavors to revive Mr. L—l. When he came to himself, we addressed ourselves again to an investigation of M. Valdemar's condition.

It remained in all respects as I have last described it, with the exception that the mirror no longer afforded evidence of respiration. An attempt to draw blood from the arm failed. I should mention, too, that this limb was no farther subject to my will. I endeavored in vain to make it follow the direction of my hand. The only real indication, indeed, of the mesmeric influence, was now found in the vibratory movement of the tongue, whenever I addressed M. Valdemar a question. He seemed to be making an effort to reply, but had no longer sufficient volition. To queries put to him by any other person than myself he seemed utterly insensible—although I endeavored to place each member of the company in mesmeric *rapport* with him. I believe that I have now related all that is necessary to an understanding of the sleep-waker's state at this epoch. Other nurses were procured; and at ten o'clock I left the house in company with the two physicians and Mr. L—l.

In the afternoon we all called again to see the patient. His condition remained precisely the same. We had now some discussion as to the propriety and feasibility of awakening him; but we had little difficulty in agreeing that no good purpose would be served by so doing. It was evident that, so far, death (or what is usually termed death) had been arrested by the mesmeric process. It seemed clear to us all that to awaken M. Valdemar would be merely to insure his instant, or at least his speedy dissolution.

From this period until the close of last week—*an interval of nearly seven months*—we continued to make daily calls at M. Valdemar's house, accompanied, now and then, by medical and other friends. All this time the sleeper-waker remained *exactly* as I have last described him. The nurses' attentions were continual.

It was on Friday last that we finally resolved to make the experiment of awakening or attempting to awaken him; and it is the (perhaps) unfortunate result of this latter experiment which has given rise to so much discussion in private circles—to so much of what I cannot help thinking unwarranted popular feeling.

For the purpose of relieving M. Valdemar from the mesmeric trance, I made use of the customary passes. These, for a time, were unsuccessful. The first indication of revival was afforded by a partial descent of the iris. It was observed, as especially remarkable, that this lowering of the pupil was accompanied by the profuse outflowing of a yellowish ichor (from beneath the lids) of a pungent and highly offensive odor.

It was now suggested that I should attempt to influence the patient's arm, as heretofore. I made the attempt and failed. Dr. F— then intimated a desire to have me put a question. I did so, as follows:

"M. Valdemar, can you explain to us what are your feelings or wishes now?"

There was an instant return of the hectic circles on the cheeks; the tongue quivered, or rather rolled violently in the mouth (although the jaws and lips remained rigid as before); and at length the same hideous voice which I have already described, broke forth:

"For God's sake!—quick!—quick!—put me to sleep—or, quick!—waken me!—quick!—*I say to you that I am dead!*"

I was thoroughly unnerved, and for an instant remained undecided what to do. At first I made an endeavor to re-compose the patient; but, failing in this through total abeyance of the will, I retraced my steps and as earnestly struggled to awaken him. In this attempt I soon saw that I should be successful—or at least I soon fancied that my success would be complete—and I am sure that all in the room were prepared to see the patient awaken.

For what really occurred, however, it is quite impossible that any human being could have been prepared.

As I rapidly made the mesmeric passes, amid ejaculations of "dead! dead!" absolutely *bursting* from the tongue and not from the lips of the sufferer, his whole frame at once—within the space of a single minute, or even less, shrunk—crumbled—absolutely *rotted* away beneath my hands. Upon the bed, before that whole company, there lay a nearly liquid mass of loathsome—of detestable putridity.

The Imp of the Perverse

In the consideration of the faculties and impulses—of the *prima mobilia* of the human soul, the phrenologists have failed to make room for a propensity which, although obviously existing as a radical, primitive, irreducible sentiment, has been equally overlooked by all the moralists who have preceded them. In the pure arrogance of the reason, we have all overlooked it. We have suffered its existence to escape our senses, solely through want of belief—of faith—whether it be faith in Revelation, or faith in the Kabbala. The idea of it has never occurred to us, simply because of its supererogation. We saw no *need* of the impulse—for the propensity. We could not perceive its necessity. We could not understand, that is to say, we could not have understood, had the notion of this *primum mobile* ever obtruded itself;—we could not have understood in what manner it might be made to further the objects of humanity, either temporal or eternal. It cannot be denied that phrenology and, in great measure, all metaphysicianism have been concocted *à priori*. The intellectual or logical man, rather than the understanding or observant man, set himself to imagine designs—to dictate purposes to God. Having thus fathomed, to his satisfaction, the intentions of Jehovah, out of these intentions he built his innumerable systems of mind. In the matter of phrenology, for example, we first determined, naturally enough, that it was the design of the Deity that man should eat. We then assigned to man an organ of alimentiveness, and this organ is the scourge with which the Deity compels man, will-I nill-I, into eating. Secondly, having settled it to be God's will that man should continue his species, we discovered an organ of amativeness, forthwith. And so with combativeness, with ideality, with causality, with constructiveness,—so, in short, with every organ, whether representing a propensity, a moral sentiment, or a faculty of the pure intellect. And in these arrangements of the *principia* of human action, the Spurzheimites, whether right or wrong, in part, or upon the whole, have but followed, in principle, the footsteps of their predecessors: deducing and establishing every thing from the preconceived destiny of man, and upon the ground of the objects of his Creator.

It would have been wiser, it would have been safer, to classify (if classify we must) upon the basis of what man usually or occasionally did, and was always occasionally doing, rather than upon the basis of what we took it for granted the Deity intended him to do. If we cannot comprehend God in his visible works, how then in his inconceivable thoughts, that call the works into being? If we cannot understand him in his objective creatures, how then in his substantive moods and phases of creation?

Induction, *à posteriori*, would have brought phrenology to admit, as an innate and primitive principle of human action, a paradoxical something, which we may call *perverseness*, for want of a more characteristic term. In the sense I intend, it is, in fact, a *mobile* without motive, a motive not *motivirt*. Through its promptings we act without comprehensible object; or, if this shall be understood as a contradiction in terms, we may so far modify the proposition as to say, that through its promptings we act, for the reason that we should *not*. In theory, no reason can be more unreasonable, but, in fact, there is none more strong. With certain minds, under certain conditions, it becomes absolutely irresistible. I am not more certain that I breathe, than that the assurance of the wrong or error of any action is often the one unconquerable *force* which impels us, and alone impels us to its prosecution. Nor will this overwhelming tendency to do wrong for the wrong's sake, admit of analysis, or resolution into ulterior elements. It is a radical, a primitive impulse-elementary. It will be said, I am aware, that when we persist in acts because we feel we should *not* persist in them, our conduct is but a modification of that which ordinarily springs from the *combativeness* of phrenology. But a glance will show the fallacy of this idea. The phrenological combativeness has for its essence, the necessity of self-defence. It is our safeguard against injury. Its principle regards our well-being; and thus the desire to be well is excited simultaneously with its development. It follows, that the desire to be well must be excited simultaneously with any principle which shall be merely a modification of combativeness, but in the case of that something which I term *perverseness*, the desire to be well is not only not aroused, but a strongly antagonistical sentiment exists.

An appeal to one's own heart is, after all, the best reply to the sophistry just noticed. No one who trustingly consults and thoroughly questions his own soul, will be disposed to deny the entire radicalness of the propensity in question. It is not more incomprehensible than distinctive. There lives no man who at some period has not been tormented, for example, by an earnest desire to tantalize a listener by circumlocution. The speaker is aware that he displeases; he has every intention to please, he is usually curt, precise, and clear, the most laconic and luminous language is struggling for utterance upon his tongue, it is only with difficulty that he restrains himself from giving it flow; he dreads and deprecates the anger of him whom he addresses; yet, the thought strikes him, that by certain involutions and parentheses this anger may be engendered. That single thought is enough. The impulse increases to a wish, the wish to a desire, the desire to an uncontrollable longing, and the longing (to the deep regret and mortification of the speaker, and in defiance of all consequences) is indulged.

We have a task before us which must be speedily performed. We know that it will be ruinous to make delay. The most important crisis of our life calls, trumpet-tongued, for immediate energy and action. We glow, we are consumed with eagerness to commence the work, with the anticipation of whose glorious result our whole souls are on fire. It must, it shall be undertaken today, and yet we put it off until to-morrow, and why? There is no answer, except that we feel *perverse*, using the word with no comprehension of the principle. Tomorrow arrives, and with it a more impatient anxiety to do our duty, but with this very increase of anxiety arrives, also, a nameless, a positively fearful, because unfathomable, craving for delay. This craving gathers strength as the moments fly. The last hour for action is at hand. We tremble with the violence of the conflict within us—of the definite with the indefinite—of the substance with the shadow. But, if the contest have proceeded thus far, it is the shadow which prevails—we struggle in vain. The clock strikes, and is the knell of our welfare. At the same time, it is the chanticleer—note to the ghost that has so long overawed us. It flies—it disappears—we are free. The old energy returns. We will labor now. Alas, it is *too late*!

We stand upon the brink of a precipice. We peer into the abyss—we grow sick and dizzy. Our first impulse is to shrink from the danger. Unaccountably we remain. By slow degrees our sickness and dizziness and horror become merged in a cloud of unnamable feeling. By gradations, still more imperceptible, this cloud assumes shape, as did the vapor from the bottle out of which arose the genius in the Arabian Nights. But out of this *our* cloud upon the precipice's edge, there grows into palpability, a shape, far more terrible than any genius or any demon of a tale, and yet it is but a thought, although a fearful one, and one which chills the very marrow of our bones with the fierceness of the delight of its horror. It is merely the idea of what would be our sensations during the sweeping precipitancy of a fall from such a height. And this fall—this rushing annihilation—for the very reason that it involves that one most ghastly and loathsome of all the most ghastly and loathsome images of death and suffering which have ever presented themselves to our imagination—for this very cause do we now the most vividly desire it. And because our reason violently deters us from the brink, *therefore* do we the most impetuously approach it. There is no passion in nature so demoniacally impatient, as that of him who, shuddering upon the edge of a precipice, thus meditates a Plunge. To indulge, for a moment, in any attempt at *thought*, is to be inevitably lost; for reflection but urges us to forbear, and *therefore* it is, I say, that we *cannot*. If there be no friendly arm to check us, or if we fail in a sudden effort to prostrate ourselves backward from the abyss, we plunge, and are destroyed.

Examine these similar actions as we will, we shall find them resulting solely from the spirit of the *Perverse*. We perpetrate them because we feel that we should *not*. Beyond or behind this there is no intelligible principle; and we might, indeed, deem this perverseness a direct instigation of the Arch-Fiend, were it not occasionally known to operate in furtherance of good.

I have said thus much, that in some measure I may answer your question, that I may explain to you why I am here, that I may assign to you something that shall have at least the faint aspect of a cause for my wearing these fetters, and for my tenanting this cell of the condemned. Had I not been thus prolix, you might either have misunderstood me altogether, or, with the rabble, have fancied me mad. As it is, you will easily perceive that I am one of the many uncounted victims of the Imp of the Perverse.

It is impossible that any deed could have been wrought with a more thorough deliberation. For weeks, for months, I pondered upon the means of the murder. I rejected a thousand schemes, because their accomplishment involved a chance of detection. At length, in reading some French Memoirs, I found an account of a nearly fatal illness that occurred to Madame Pilau, through the agency of a candle accidentally poisoned. The idea struck my fancy at once. I knew my victim's habit of reading in bed. I knew, too, that his apartment was narrow and ill-ventilated. But I need not vex you with impertinent details. I need not describe the easy artifices by which I substituted, in his bed-room candle-stand, a wax-light of my own making for the one which I there found. The next morning he was discovered dead in his bed, and the Coroner's verdict was—"Death by the visitation of God."

Having inherited his estate, all went well with me for years. The idea of detection never once entered my brain. Of the remains of the fatal taper I had myself carefully disposed. I had left no shadow of a clew by which it would be possible to convict, or even to suspect me of the crime. It is inconceivable how rich a sentiment of satisfaction arose in my bosom as I reflected upon my absolute security. For a very long period of time I was accustomed to revel in this sentiment. It afforded me more real delight than all the mere worldly advantages accruing from my sin. But there arrived at length an epoch, from which the pleasurable feeling grew, by scarcely perceptible gradations, into a haunting and harassing thought. It harassed because it haunted. I could scarcely get rid of it for an instant. It is quite a common thing to be thus annoyed with the ringing in our ears, or rather in our memories, of the burthen of some ordinary song, or some unimpressive snatches from an opera. Nor will we be the less tormented if the song in itself be good, or the opera air meritorious. In this manner, at last, I would perpetually catch myself pondering upon my security, and repeating, in a low undertone, the phrase, "I am safe."

One day, whilst sauntering along the streets, I arrested myself in the act of murmuring, half aloud, these customary syllables. In a fit of petulance, I remodelled them thus; "I am safe—I am safe—yes—if I be not fool enough to make open confession!"

No sooner had I spoken these words, than I felt an icy chill creep to my heart. I had had some experience in these fits of perversity (whose nature I have been at some trouble to explain), and I remembered well that in no instance I had successfully resisted their attacks. And now my own casual self-suggestion that I might possibly be fool enough to confess the murder of which I had been guilty, confronted me, as if the very ghost of him whom I had murdered—and beckoned me on to death.

At first, I made an effort to shake off this nightmare of the soul. I walked vigorously—faster—still faster—at length I ran. I felt a maddening desire to shriek aloud. Every succeeding wave of thought overwhelmed me with new terror, for, alas! I well, too well understood that to *think*, in my situation, was to be lost. I still quickened my pace. I bounded like a madman through the crowded thoroughfares. At length, the populace took the alarm, and pursued me. I felt *then* the consummation of my fate. Could I have torn out my tongue, I would have done it, but a rough voice resounded in my ears—a rougher grasp seized me by the shoulder. I turned—I gasped for breath. For a moment I experienced all the pangs of suffocation; I became blind, and deaf, and giddy; and then some invisible fiend, I thought, struck me with his broad palm upon the back. The long imprisoned secret burst forth from my soul.

They say that I spoke with a distinct enunciation, but with marked emphasis and passionate hurry, as if in dread of interruption before concluding the brief, but pregnant sentences that consigned me to the hangman and to hell.

Having related all that was necessary for the fullest judicial conviction, I fell prostrate in a swoon.

But why shall I say more? Today I wear these chains, and am here! To-morrow I shall be fetterless!—*but where?*

The Cask of Amontillado

The thousand injuries of Fortunato I had borne as I best could; but when he ventured upon insult, I vowed revenge. You, who so well know the nature of my soul, will not suppose, however, that I gave utterance to a threat. *At length* I would be avenged; this was a point definitively settled—but the very definitiveness with which it was resolved, precluded the idea of risk. I must not only punish, but punish with impunity. A wrong is unredressed when retribution overtakes its redresser. It is equally unredressed when the avenger fails to make himself felt as such to him who has done the wrong.

It must be understood, that neither by word nor deed had I given Fortunato cause to doubt my good will. I continued, as was my wont, to smile in his face, and he did not perceive that my smile *now* was at the thought of his immolation.

He had a weak point—this Fortunato—although in other regards he was a man to be respected and even feared. He prided himself on his connoisseurship in wine. Few Italians have the true virtuoso spirit. For the most part their enthusiasm is adopted to suit the time and opportunity—to practise imposture upon the British and Austrian *millionaires*. In painting and gemmary, Fortunato, like his countrymen, was a quack—but in the matter of old wines he was sincere. In this respect I did not differ from him materially: I was skilful in the Italian vintages myself, and bought largely whenever I could.

It was about dusk, one evening during the supreme madness of the carnival season, that I encountered my friend. He accosted me with excessive warmth, for he had been drinking much. The man wore motley. He had on a tight-fitting parti-striped dress, and his head was surmounted by the conical cap and bells. I was so pleased to see him, that I thought I should never have done wringing his hand.

I said to him—"My dear Fortunato, you are luckily met. How remarkably well you are looking today! But I have received a pipe of what passes for Amontillado, and I have my doubts."

"How?" said he. "Amontillado? A pipe? Impossible! And in the middle of the carnival!"

"I have my doubts," I replied; "and I was silly enough to pay the full Amontillado price without consulting you in the matter. You were not to be found, and I was fearful of losing a bargain."

"Amontillado!"

"I have my doubts."

"Amontillado!"

"And I must satisfy them."

"Amontillado!"

"As you are engaged, I am on my way to Luchesi. If any one has a critical turn, it is he. He will tell me—"

"Luchesi cannot tell Amontillado from Sherry."

"And yet some fools will have it that his taste is a match for your own."

"Come, let us go."

"Whither?"

"To your vaults."

"My friend, no; I will not impose upon your good nature. I perceive you have an engagement. Luchesi—"

"I have no engagement—come."

"My friend, no. It is not the engagement, but the severe cold with which I perceive you are afflicted. The vaults are insufferably damp. They are encrusted with nitre."

"Let us go, nevertheless. The cold is merely nothing. Amontillado! You have been imposed upon. And as for Luchesi, he cannot distinguish Sherry from Amontillado."

Thus speaking, Fortunato possessed himself of my arm. Putting on a mask of black silk, and drawing a *roquelaire* closely about my person, I suffered him to hurry me to my palazzo.

There were no attendants at home; they had absconded to make merry in honor of the time. I had told them that I should not return until the morning, and had given them explicit orders not to stir from the house. These orders were sufficient, I well knew, to insure their immediate disappearance, one and all, as soon as my back was turned.

I took from their sconces two flambeaux, and giving one to Fortunato, bowed him through several suites of rooms to the archway that led into the vaults. I passed down a long and winding staircase, requesting him to be cautious as he followed. We came at length to the foot of the descent, and stood together on the damp ground of the catacombs of the Montresors.

The gait of my friend was unsteady, and the bells upon his cap jingled as he strode.

"The pipe," said he.

"It is farther on," said I; "but observe the white web-work which gleams from these cavern walls."

He turned towards me, and looked into my eyes with two filmy orbs that distilled the rheum of intoxication.

"Nitre?" he asked, at length.

"Nitre," I replied. "How long have you had that cough?"

"Ugh! ugh! ugh!—ugh! ugh! ugh!—ugh! ugh! ugh!—ugh! ugh! ugh!—ugh! ugh! ugh!"

My poor friend found it impossible to reply for many minutes.

"It is nothing," he said, at last.

"Come," I said, with decision, "we will go back; your health is precious. You are rich, respected, admired, beloved; you are happy, as once I was. You are a man to be missed. For me it is no matter. We will go back; you will be ill, and I cannot be responsible. Besides, there is Luchesi—"

"Enough," he said; "the cough is a mere nothing; it will not kill me. I shall not die of a cough."

"True—true," I replied; "and, indeed, I had no intention of alarming you unnecessarily—but you should use all proper caution. A draught of this Medoc will defend us from the damps."

Here I knocked off the neck of a bottle which I drew from a long row of its fellows that lay upon the mould.

"Drink," I said, presenting him the wine.

He raised it to his lips with a leer. He paused and nodded to me familiarly, while his bells jingled.

"I drink," he said, "to the buried that repose around us."

"And I to your long life."

He again took my arm, and we proceeded.

"These vaults," he said, "are extensive."

"The Montresors," I replied, "were a great and numerous family."

"I forget your arms."

"A huge human foot d'or, in a field azure; the foot crushes a serpent rampant whose fangs are imbedded in the heel."

"And the motto?"

"*Nemo me impune lacessit.*"

"Good!" he said.

The wine sparkled in his eyes and the bells jingled. My own fancy grew warm with the Medoc. We had passed through walls of piled bones, with casks and puncheons intermingling, into the inmost recesses of the catacombs. I paused again, and this time I made bold to seize Fortunato by an arm above the elbow.

"The nitre!" I said: "see, it increases. It hangs like moss upon the vaults. We are below the river's bed. The drops of moisture trickle among the bones. Come, we will go back ere it is too late. Your cough—"

"It is nothing," he said; "let us go on. But first, another draught of the Medoc."

I broke and reached him a flaçon of De Grave. He emptied it at a breath. His eyes flashed with a fierce light. He laughed and threw the bottle upwards with a gesticulation I did not understand.

I looked at him in surprise. He repeated the movement—a grotesque one.

"You do not comprehend?" he said.

"Not I," I replied.

"Then you are not of the brotherhood."

"How?"

"You are not of the masons."

"Yes, yes," I said, "yes, yes."

"You? Impossible! A mason?"

"A mason," I replied.

"A sign," he said.

"It is this," I answered, producing a trowel from beneath the folds of my *roquelaire*.

"You jest," he exclaimed, recoiling a few paces. "But let us proceed to the Amontillado."

"Be it so," I said, replacing the tool beneath the cloak, and again offering him my arm. He leaned upon it heavily. We continued our route in search of the Amontillado. We passed through a range of low arches, descended, passed on, and descending again, arrived at a deep crypt, in which the foulness of the air caused our flambeaux rather to glow than flame.

At the most remote end of the crypt there appeared another less spacious. Its walls had been lined with human remains, piled to the vault overhead, in the fashion of the great catacombs of Paris. Three sides of this interior crypt were still ornamented in this manner. From the fourth the bones had been thrown down, and lay promiscuously upon the earth, forming at one point a mound of some size. Within the wall thus exposed by the displacing of the bones, we perceived a still interior recess, in depth about four feet, in width three, in height six or seven. It seemed to have been constructed for no especial use in itself, but formed merely the interval between two of the colossal supports of the roof of the catacombs, and was backed by one of their circumscribing walls of solid granite.

It was in vain that Fortunato, uplifting his dull torch, endeavored to pry into the depths of the recess. Its termination the feeble light did not enable us to see.

"Proceed," I said; "herein is the Amontillado. As for Luchesi—"

"He is an ignoramus," interrupted my friend, as he stepped unsteadily forward, while I followed immediately at his heels. In an instant he had reached the extremity of the niche, and finding his progress arrested by the rock, stood stupidly bewildered. A moment more and I had fettered him to the granite. In its surface were two iron staples, distant from each other about two feet, horizontally. From one of these depended a short chain, from the other a padlock. Throwing the links about his waist, it was but the work of a few seconds to secure it. He was too much astounded to resist. Withdrawing the key I stepped back from the recess.

"Pass your hand," I said, "over the wall; you cannot help feeling the nitre. Indeed it is *very* damp. Once more let me *implore* you to return. No? Then I must positively leave you. But I must first render you all the little attentions in my power."

"The Amontillado!" ejaculated my friend, not yet recovered from his astonishment.

"True," I replied; "the Amontillado."

As I said these words I busied myself among the pile of bones of which I have before spoken. Throwing them aside, I soon uncovered a quantity of building stone and mortar. With these materials and with the aid of my trowel, I began vigorously to wall up the entrance of the niche.

I had scarcely laid the first tier of my masonry when I discovered that the intoxication of Fortunato had in a great measure worn off. The earliest indication I had of this was a low moaning cry from the depth of the recess. It was *not* the cry of a drunken man. There was then a long and obstinate silence. I laid the second tier, and the third, and the fourth; and then I heard the furious vibrations of the chain. The noise lasted for several minutes, during which, that I might hearken to it with the more satisfaction, I ceased my labors and sat down upon the bones. When at last the clanking subsided, I resumed the trowel, and finished without interruption the fifth, the sixth, and the seventh tier. The wall was now nearly upon a level with my breast. I again paused, and holding the flambeaux over the mason-work, threw a few feeble rays upon the figure within.

A succession of loud and shrill screams, bursting suddenly from the throat of the chained form, seemed to thrust me violently back. For a brief moment I hesitated—I trembled. Unsheathing my rapier, I began to grope with it about the recess: but the thought of an instant reassured me. I placed my hand upon the solid fabric of the catacombs, and felt satisfied. I reapproached the wall. I replied to the yells of him who clamored. I re-echoed—I aided—I surpassed them in volume and in strength. I did this, and the clamorer grew still.

It was now midnight, and my task was drawing to a close. I had completed the eighth, the ninth, and the tenth tier. I had finished a portion of the last and the eleventh; there remained but a single stone to be fitted and plastered in. I struggled with its weight; I placed it partially in its destined position. But now there came from out the niche a low laugh that erected the hairs upon my head. It was succeeded by a sad voice, which I had difficulty in recognising as that of the noble Fortunato. The voice said—

"Ha! ha! ha!—he! he!—a very good joke indeed—an excellent jest. We will have many a rich laugh about it at the palazzo—he! he! he!—over our wine—he! he! he!"

"The Amontillado!" I said.

"He! he! he!—he! he! he!—yes, the Amontillado. But is it not getting late? Will not they be awaiting us at the palazzo, the Lady Fortunato and the rest? Let us be gone."

"Yes," I said, "let us be gone."

"*For the love of God, Montressor!*"

"Yes," I said, "for the love of God!"

But to these words I hearkened in vain for a reply. I grew impatient. I called aloud—

"Fortunato!"

No answer. I called again—

"Fortunato!"

No answer still. I thrust a torch through the remaining aperture and let it fall within. There came forth in return only a jingling of the bells. My heart grew sick—on account of the dampness of the catacombs. I hastened to make an end of my labor. I forced the last stone into its position; I plastered it up. Against the new masonry I re-erected the old rampart of bones. For the half of a century no mortal has disturbed them. *In pace requiescat!*

Hop-Frog

I never knew anyone so keenly alive to a joke as the king was. He seemed to live only for joking. To tell a good story of the joke kind, and to tell it well, was the surest road to his favor. Thus it happened that his seven ministers were all noted for their accomplishments as jokers. They all took after the king, too, in being large, corpulent, oily men, as well as inimitable jokers. Whether people grow fat by joking, or whether there is something in fat itself which predisposes to a joke, I have never been quite able to determine; but certain it is that a lean joker is a *rara avis in terris*.

About the refinements, or, as he called them, the "ghosts" of wit, the king troubled himself very little. He had an especial admiration for *breadth* in a jest, and would often put up with *length*, for the sake of it. Over-niceties wearied him. He would have preferred Rabelais' *Gargantua* to the *Zadig* of Voltaire: and, upon the whole, practical jokes suited his taste far better than verbal ones.

At the date of my narrative, professing jesters had not altogether gone out of fashion at court. Several of the great continental "powers" still retain their "fools," who wore motley, with caps and bells, and who were expected to be always ready with sharp witticisms, at a moment's notice, in consideration of the crumbs that fell from the royal table.

Our king, as a matter of course, retained his "fool." The fact is, he *required* something in the way of folly—if only to counterbalance the heavy wisdom of the seven wise men who were his ministers—not to mention himself.

His fool, or professional jester, was not *only* a fool, however. His value was trebled in the eyes of the king, by the fact of his being also a dwarf and a cripple. Dwarfs were as common at court, in those days, as fools; and many monarchs would have found it difficult to get through their days (days are rather longer at court than elsewhere) without both a jester to laugh *with*, and a dwarf to laugh *at*. But, as I have already observed, your jesters, in ninety-nine cases out of a hundred, are fat, round, and unwieldy—so that it was no small source of self-gratulation with our king that, in Hop-Frog (this was the fool's name), he possessed a triplicate treasure in one person.

I believe the name "Hop-Frog" was *not* that given to the dwarf by his sponsors at baptism, but it was conferred upon him, by general consent of the several ministers, on account of his inability to walk as other men do. In fact, Hop-Frog could only get along by a sort of interjectional gait—something between a leap and a wriggle—a movement that afforded illimitable amusement, and of course consolation, to the king, for (notwithstanding the protuberance of his stomach and a constitutional swelling of the head) the king, by his whole court, was accounted a capital figure.

But although Hop-Frog, through the distortion of his legs, could move only with great pain and difficulty along a road or floor, the prodigious muscular power which nature seemed to have bestowed upon his arms, by way of compensation for deficiency in the lower limbs, enabled him to perform many feats of wonderful dexterity, where trees or ropes were in question, or any thing else to climb. At such exercises he certainly much more resembled a squirrel, or a small monkey, than a frog.

I am not able to say, with precision, from what country Hop-Frog originally came. It was from some barbarous region, however, that no person ever heard of—a vast distance from the court of our king. Hop-Frog, and a young girl very little less dwarfish than himself (although of exquisite proportions, and a marvellous dancer), had been forcibly carried off from their respective homes in adjoining provinces, and sent as presents to the king, by one of his ever-victorious generals.

Under these circumstances, it is not to be wondered at that a close intimacy arose between the two little captives. Indeed, they soon became sworn friends. Hop-Frog, who, although he made a great deal of sport, was by no means popular, had it not in his power to render Trippetta many services; but *she*, on account of her grace and exquisite beauty (although a dwarf), was universally admired and petted; so she possessed much influence; and never failed to use it, whenever she could, for the benefit of Hop-Frog.

On some grand state occasion—I forgot what—the king determined to have a masquerade, and whenever a masquerade or any thing of that kind, occurred at our court, then the talents, both of Hop-Frog and Trippetta were sure to be called into play. Hop-Frog, in especial, was so inventive in the way of getting up pageants, suggesting novel characters, and arranging costumes, for masked balls, that nothing could be done, it seems, without his assistance.

The night appointed for the *fête* had arrived. A gorgeous hall had been fitted up, under Trippetta's eye, with every kind of device which could possibly give *éclât* to a masquerade. The whole court was in a fever of expectation. As for costumes and characters, it might well be supposed that everybody had come to a decision on such points. Many had made up their minds (as to what roles they should assume) a week, or even a month, in advance; and, in fact, there was not a particle of indecision anywhere—except in the case of the king and his seven minsters. Why *they* hesitated I never could tell, unless they did it by way of a joke. More probably, they found it difficult, on account of being so fat, to make up their minds. At all events, time flew; and, as a last resort they sent for Trippetta and Hop-Frog.

When the two little friends obeyed the summons of the king they found him sitting at his wine with the seven members of his cabinet council; but the monarch appeared to be in a very ill humor. He knew that Hop-Frog was not fond of wine, for it excited the poor cripple almost to madness; and madness is no comfortable feeling. But the king loved his practical jokes, and took pleasure in forcing Hop-Frog to drink and (as the king called it) "to be merry."

"Come here, Hop-Frog," said he, as the jester and his friend entered the room; "swallow this bumper to the health of your absent friends [here Hop-Frog sighed], and then let us have the benefit of your invention. We want characters—*characters*, man—something novel—out of the way. We are wearied with this everlasting sameness. Come, drink! the wine will brighten your wits."

Hop-Frog endeavored, as usual, to get up a jest in reply to these advances from the king; but the effort was too much. It happened to be the poor dwarf's birthday, and the command to drink to his "absent friends" forced the tears to his eyes. Many large, bitter drops fell into the goblet as he took it, humbly, from the hand of the tyrant.

"Ah! ha! ha!" roared the latter, as the dwarf reluctantly drained the beaker.—"See what a glass of good wine can do! Why, your eyes are shining already!"

Poor fellow! his large eyes *gleamed*, rather than shone; for the effect of wine on his excitable brain was not more powerful than instantaneous. He placed the goblet nervously on the table, and looked round upon the company with a half—insane stare. They all seemed highly amused at the success of the king's "*joke*."

"And now to business," said the prime minister, a *very* fat man.

"Yes," said the king; "come lend us your assistance. Characters, my fine fellow; we stand in need of characters—all of us—ha! ha! ha!" and as this was seriously meant for a joke, his laugh was chorused by the seven.

Hop-Frog also laughed, although feebly and somewhat vacantly.

"Come, come," said the king, impatiently, "have you nothing to suggest?"

"I am endeavoring to think of something *novel*," replied the dwarf, abstractedly, for he was quite bewildered by the wine.

"Endeavoring!" cried the tyrant, fiercely; "what do you mean by *that*? Ah, I perceive. You are sulky, and want more wine. Here, drink this!" and he poured out another goblet full and offered it to the cripple, who merely gazed at it, gasping for breath.

"Drink, I say!" shouted the monster, "or by the fiends—"

The dwarf hesitated. The king grew purple with rage. The courtiers smirked. Trippetta, pale as a corpse, advanced to the monarch's seat, and, falling on her knees before him, implored him to spare her friend.

The tyrant regarded her, for some moments, in evident wonder at her audacity. He seemed quite at a loss what to do or say—how most becomingly to express his indignation. At last, without uttering a syllable, he pushed her violently from him, and threw the contents of the brimming goblet in her face.

The poor girl got up the best she could, and, not daring even to sigh, resumed her position at the foot of the table.

There was a dead silence for about half a minute, during which the falling of a leaf, or of a feather, might have been heard. It was interrupted by a low, but harsh and protracted *grating* sound which seemed to come at once from every corner of the room.

"What—what—*what* are you making that noise for?" demanded the king, turning furiously to the dwarf.

The latter seemed to have recovered, in great measure, from his intoxication, and looking fixedly but quietly into the tyrant's face, merely ejaculated:

"I—I? How could it have been me?"

"The sound appeared to come from without," observed one of the courtiers. "I fancy it was the parrot at the window, whetting his bill upon his cage-wires."

"True," replied the monarch, as if much relieved by the suggestion; "but, on the honor of a knight, I could have sworn that it was the gritting of this vagabond's teeth."

Hereupon the dwarf laughed (the king was too confirmed a joker to object to any one's laughing), and displayed a set of large, powerful, and very repulsive teeth. Moreover, he avowed his perfect willingness to swallow as much wine as desired. The monarch was pacified; and having drained another bumper with no very perceptible ill effect, Hop-Frog entered at once, and with spirit, into the plans for the masquerade.

"I cannot tell what was the association of idea," observed he, very tranquilly, and as if he had never tasted wine in his life, "but *just after* your majesty, had struck the girl and thrown the wine in her face—*just after* your majesty had done this, and while the parrot was making that odd noise outside the window, there came into my mind a capital diversion—one of my own country frolics—often enacted among us, at our masquerades: but here it will be new altogether. Unfortunately, however, it requires a company of eight persons and—"

"Here we *are*!" cried the king, laughing at his acute discovery of the coincidence; "eight to a fraction—I and my seven ministers. Come! what is the diversion?"

"We call it," replied the cripple, "the Eight Chained Ourang-Outangs, and it really is excellent sport if well enacted."

"*We* will enact it," remarked the king, drawing himself up, and lowering his eyelids.

"The beauty of the game," continued Hop-Frog, "lies in the fright it occasions among the women."

"Capital!" roared in chorus the monarch and his ministry.

"*I* will equip you as ourang-outangs," proceeded the dwarf; "leave all that to me. The resemblance shall be so striking, that the company of masqueraders will take you for real beasts—and of course, they will be as much terrified as astonished."

"Oh, this is exquisite!" exclaimed the king. "Hop-Frog! I will make a man of you."

"The chains are for the purpose of increasing the confusion by their jangling. You are supposed to have escaped, *en masse*, from your keepers. Your majesty cannot conceive the *effect* produced, at a masquerade, by eight chained ourang-outangs, imagined to be real ones by most of the company; and rushing in with savage cries, among the crowd of delicately and gorgeously habited men and women. The *contrast* is inimitable!"

"It *must* be," said the king: and the council arose hurriedly (as it was growing late), to put in execution the scheme of Hop-Frog.

His mode of equipping the party as ourang-outangs was very simple, but effective enough for his purposes. The animals in question had, at the epoch of my story, very rarely been seen in any part of the civilized world; and as the imitations made by the dwarf were sufficiently beast-like and more than sufficiently hideous, their truthfulness to nature was thus thought to be secured.

The king and his ministers were first encased in tight-fitting stockinet shirts and drawers. They were then saturated with tar. At this stage of the process, some one of the party suggested feathers; but the suggestion was at once overruled by the dwarf, who soon convinced the eight, by ocular demonstration, that the hair of such a brute as the ourang-outang was much more efficiently represented by *flax*. A thick coating of the latter was accordingly plastered upon the coating of tar. A long chain was now procured. First, it was passed about the waist of the king, *and tied*, then about another of the party, and also tied; then about all successively, in the same manner. When this chaining arrangement was complete, and the party stood as far apart from each other as possible, they formed a circle; and to make all things appear natural, Hop-Frog passed the residue of the chain in two diameters, at right angles, across the circle, after the fashion adopted, at the present day, by those who capture Chimpanzees, or other large apes, in Borneo.

The grand saloon in which the masquerade was to take place, was a circular room, very lofty, and receiving the light of the sun only through a single window at top. At night (the season for which the apartment was especially designed) it was illuminated principally by a large chandelier, depending by a chain from the centre of the sky-light, and lowered, or elevated, by means of a counter-balance as usual; but (in order not to look unsightly) this latter passed outside the cupola and over the roof.

The arrangements of the room had been left to Trippetta's superintendence; but, in some particulars, it seems, she had been guided by the calmer judgment of her friend the dwarf. At his suggestion it was that, on this occasion, the chandelier was removed. Its waxen drippings (which, in weather so warm, it was quite impossible to prevent) would have been seriously detrimental to the rich dresses of the guests, who, on account of the crowded state of the saloon, could not *all* be expected to keep from out its centre; that is to say, from under the chandelier. Additional sconces were set in various parts of the hall, out of the war, and a flambeau, emitting sweet odor, was placed in the right hand of each of the Caryaides [Caryatides] that stood against the wall—some fifty or sixty altogether.

The eight ourang-outangs, taking Hop-Frog's advice, waited patiently until midnight (when the room was thoroughly filled with masqueraders) before making their appearance. No sooner had the clock ceased striking, however, than they rushed, or rather rolled in, all together—for the impediments of their chains caused most of the party to fall, and all to stumble as they entered.

The excitement among the masqueraders was prodigious, and filled the heart of the king with glee. As had been anticipated, there were not a few of the guests who supposed the ferocious-looking creatures to be beasts of *some* kind in reality, if not precisely ourang-outangs. Many of the women swooned with affright; and had not the king taken the precaution to exclude all weapons from the saloon, his party might soon have expiated their frolic in their blood. As it was, a general rush was made for the doors; but the king had ordered them to be locked immediately upon his entrance; and, at the dwarf's suggestion, the keys had been deposited with *him*.

While the tumult was at its height, and each masquerader attentive only to his own safety (for, in fact, there was much *real* danger from the pressure of the excited crowd), the chain by which the chandelier ordinarily hung, and which had been drawn up on its removal, might have been seen very gradually to descend, until its hooked extremity came within three feet of the floor.

Soon after this, the king and his seven friends having reeled about the hall in all directions, found themselves, at length, in its centre, and, of course, in immediate contact with the chain. While they were thus situated, the dwarf, who had followed noiselessly at their heels, inciting them to keep up the commotion, took hold of their own chain at the intersection of the two portions which crossed the circle diametrically and at right angles. Here, with the rapidity of thought, he inserted the hook from which the chandelier had been wont to depend; and, in an instant, by some unseen agency, the chandelier-chain was drawn so far upward as to take the hook out of reach, and, as an inevitable consequence, to drag the ourang-outangs together in close connection, and face to face.

The masqueraders, by this time, had recovered, in some measure, from their alarm; and, beginning to regard the whole matter as a well-contrived pleasantry, set up a loud shout of laughter at the predicament of the apes.

"Leave them to *me*!" now screamed Hop-Frog, his shrill voice making itself easily heard through all the din. "Leave them to *me*. I fancy *I* know them. If I can only get a good look at them, *I* can soon tell who they are."

Here, scrambling over the heads of the crowd, he managed to get to the wall; when, seizing a flambeau from one of the Caryatides, he returned, as he went, to the centre of the room-leaping, with the agility of a monkey, upon the kings head, and thence clambered a few feet up the chain; holding down the torch to examine the group of ourang-outangs, and still screaming: "*I* shall soon find out who they are!"

And now, while the whole assembly (the apes included) were convulsed with laughter, the jester suddenly uttered a shrill whistle; when the chain flew violently up for about thirty feet—dragging with it the dismayed and struggling ourang-outangs, and leaving them suspended in mid-air between the sky-light and the floor. Hop-Frog, clinging to the chain as it rose, still maintained his relative position in respect to the eight maskers, and still (as if nothing were the matter) continued to thrust his torch down toward them, as though endeavoring to discover who they were.

So thoroughly astonished was the whole company at this ascent, that a dead silence, of about a minute's duration, ensued. It was broken by just such a low, harsh, *grating* sound, as had before attracted the attention of the king and his councillors when the former threw the wine in the face of Trippetta. But, on the present occasion, there could be no question as to *whence* the sound issued. It came from the fang—like teeth of the dwarf, who ground them and gnashed them as he foamed at the mouth, and glared, with an expression of maniacal rage, into the upturned countenances of the king and his seven companions.

"Ah, ha!" said at length the infuriated jester. "Ah, ha! I begin to see who these people *are* now!" Here, pretending to scrutinize the king more closely, he held the flambeau to the flaxen coat which enveloped him, and which instantly burst into a sheet of vivid flame. In less than half a minute the whole eight ourang-outangs were blazing fiercely, amid the shrieks of the multitude who gazed at them from below, horror-stricken, and without the power to render them the slightest assistance.

At length the flames, suddenly increasing in virulence, forced the jester to climb higher up the chain, to be out of their reach; and, as he made this movement, the crowd again sank, for a brief instant, into silence. The dwarf seized his opportunity, and once more spoke:

"I now see *distinctly*," he said, "what manner of people these maskers are. They are a great king and his seven privy-councillors—a king who does not scruple to strike a defenceless girl and his seven councillors who abet him in the outrage. As for myself, I am simply Hop-Frog, the jester—and *this is my last jest*."

Owing to the high combustibility of both the flax and the tar to which it adhered, the dwarf had scarcely made an end of his brief speech before the work of vengeance was complete. The eight corpses swung in their chains, a fetid, blackened, hideous, and indistinguishable mass. The cripple hurled his torch at them, clambered leisurely to the ceiling, and disappeared through the sky-light.

It is supposed that Trippetta, stationed on the roof of the saloon, had been the accomplice of her friend in his fiery revenge, and that, together, they effected their escape to their own country: for neither was seen again.

Poems

Al Aaraaf[1]

Part I.

O! Nothing earthly save the ray
(Thrown back from flowers) of Beauty's eye,
As in those gardens where the day
Springs from the gems of Circassy—
O! nothing earthly save the thrill
Of melody in woodland rill—
Or (music of the passion-hearted)
Joy's voice so peacefully departed
That like the murmur in the shell,
Its echo dwelleth and will dwell—
Oh, nothing of the dross of ours—
Yet all the beauty—all the flowers
That list our Love, and deck our bowers—
Adorn yon world afar, afar—
The wandering star.

'Twas a sweet time for Nesace—for there
Her world lay lolling on the golden air,
Near four bright suns—a temporary rest—
An oasis in desert of the blest.
Away—away—'mid seas of rays that roll
Empyrean splendor o'er th' unchained soul—
The soul that scarce (the billows are so dense)
Can struggle to its destin'd eminence—
To distant spheres, from time to time, she rode,
And late to ours, the favour'd one of God—
But, now, the ruler of an anchor'd realm,
She throws aside the sceptre—leaves the helm,
And, amid incense and high spiritual hymns,
Laves in quadruple light her angel limbs.

Now happiest, loveliest in yon lovely Earth,
Whence sprang the "Idea of Beauty" into birth,
(Falling in wreaths thro' many a startled star,
Like woman's hair 'mid pearls, until, afar,
It lit on hills Achaian, and there dwelt)
She look'd into Infinity—and knelt.
Rich clouds, for canopies, about her curled—
Fit emblems of the model of her world—
Seen but in beauty—not impeding sight
Of other beauty glittering thro' the light—
A wreath that twined each starry form around,
And all the opal'd air in color bound.

All hurriedly she knelt upon a bed
Of flowers: of lilies such as rear'd the head
On the fair Capo Deucato, and sprang[2]
So eagerly around about to hang
Upon the flying footsteps of—deep pride—
Of her who lov'd a mortal—and so died.
The Sephalica, budding with young bees,
Uprear'd its purple stem around her knees:
And gemmy flower, of Trebizond misnam'd—[3]
Inmate of highest stars, where erst it sham'd
All other loveliness: its honied dew
(The fabled nectar that the heathen knew)
Deliriously sweet, was dropp'd from Heaven,
And fell on gardens of the unforgiven
In Trebizond—and on a sunny flower
So like its own above that, to this hour,
It still remaineth, torturing the bee
With madness, and unwonted reverie:
In Heaven, and all its environs, the leaf
And blossom of the fairy plant, in grief
Disconsolate linger—grief that hangs her head,
Repenting follies that full long have fled,
Heaving her white breast to the balmy air,
Like guilty beauty, chasten'd, and more fair:
Nyctanthes too, as sacred as the light

She fears to perfume, perfuming the night:
And Clytia pondering between many a sun,[4]
While pettish tears adown her petals run:
And that aspiring flower that sprang on Earth—[5]
And died, ere scarce exalted into birth,
Bursting its odorous heart in spirit to wing
Its way to Heaven, from garden of a king:
And Valisnerian lotus thither flown[6]
From struggling with the waters of the Rhone:
And thy most lovely purple perfume, Zante![7]
Isola d'oro!—Fior di Levante!
And the Nelumbo bud that floats for ever[8]
With Indian Cupid down the holy river—
Fair flowers, and fairy! to whose care is given
To bear the Goddess' song, in odors, up to Heaven:[9]

"Spirit! that dwellest where,
    In the deep sky,
The terrible and fair,
    In beauty vie!
Beyond the line of blue—
    The boundary of the star
Which turneth at the view
    Of thy barrier and thy bar—
Of the barrier overgone
    By the comets who were cast
From their pride, and from their throne
    To be drudges till the last—
To be carriers of fire
    (The red fire of their heart)
With speed that may not tire
    And with pain that shall not part—
Who livest—that we know—
    In Eternity—we feel—
But the shadow of whose brow
    What spirit shall reveal?
Tho' the beings whom thy Nesace,
    Thy messenger hath known

Have dream'd for thy Infinity
    A model of their own—[10]
Thy will is done, Oh, God!
    The star hath ridden high
Thro' many a tempest, but she rode
    Beneath thy burning eye;
And here, in thought, to thee—
    In thought that can alone
Ascend thy empire and so be
    A partner of thy throne—
By winged Fantasy,[11]
    My embassy is given,
Till secrecy shall knowledge be
    In the environs of Heaven."

She ceas'd—and buried then her burning cheek
Abash'd, amid the lilies there, to seek
A shelter from the fervour of His eye;
For the stars trembled at the Deity.
She stirr'd not—breath'd not—for a voice was there
How solemnly pervading the calm air!
A sound of silence on the startled ear
Which dreamy poets name "the music of the sphere."
Ours is a world of words: Quiet we call
"Silence"—which is the merest word of all.
All Nature speaks, and ev'n ideal things
Flap shadowy sounds from visionary wings—
But ah! not so when, thus, in realms on high
The eternal voice of God is passing by,
And the red winds are withering in the sky!

    "What tho' in worlds which sightless cycles run,[12]
Link'd to a little system, and one sun—
Where all my love is folly and the crowd
Still think my terrors but the thunder cloud,
The storm, the earthquake, and the ocean-wrath—
(Ah! will they cross me in my angrier path?)
What tho' in worlds which own a single sun

The sands of Time grow dimmer as they run,
Yet thine is my resplendency, so given
To bear my secrets thro' the upper Heaven.
Leave tenantless thy crystal home, and fly,
With all thy train, athwart the moony sky—
Apart—like fire-flies in Sicilian night,[13]
And wing to other worlds another light!
Divulge the secrets of thy embassy
To the proud orbs that twinkle—and so be
To ev'ry heart a barrier and a ban
Lest the stars totter in the guilt of man!"

Up rose the maiden in the yellow night,
The single-mooned eve!—on Earth we plight
Our faith to one love—and one moon adore—
The birth-place of young Beauty had no more.
As sprang that yellow star from downy hours
Up rose the maiden from her shrine of flowers,
And bent o'er sheeny mountain and dim plain
Her way—but left not yet her Therasaean reign.[14]

Part II.

High on a mountain of enamell'd head—
Such as the drowsy shepherd on his bed
Of giant pasturage lying at his ease,
Raising his heavy eyelid, starts and sees
With many a mutter'd "hope to be forgiven"
What time the moon is quadrated in Heaven—
Of rosy head, that towering far away
Into the sunlit ether, caught the ray
Of sunken suns at eve—at noon of night,
While the moon danc'd with the fair stranger light—
Uprear'd upon such height arose a pile
Of gorgeous columns on th' unburthen'd air,
Flashing from Parian marble that twin smile
Far down upon the wave that sparkled there,
And nursled the young mountain in its lair.

Of molten stars their pavement, such as fall[15]
Thro' the ebon air, besilvering the pall
Of their own dissolution, while they die—
Adorning then the dwellings of the sky.
A dome, by linked light from Heaven let down,
Sat gently on these columns as a crown—
A window of one circular diamond, there,
Look'd out above into the purple air,
And rays from God shot down that meteor chain
And hallow'd all the beauty twice again,
Save when, between th' Empyrean and that ring,
Some eager spirit flapp'd his dusky wing.
But on the pillars Seraph eyes have seen
The dimness of this world: that greyish green
That Nature loves the best for Beauty's grave
Lurk'd in each cornice, round each architrave—
And every sculptur'd cherub thereabout
That from his marble dwelling peered out
Seem'd earthly in the shadow of his niche—
Achaian statues in a world so rich?
Friezes from Tadmor and Persepolis—[16]
From Balbec, and the stilly, clear abyss
Of beautiful Gomorrah! O, the wave[17]
Is now upon thee—but too late to save!

Sound loves to revel in a summer night:
Witness the murmur of the grey twilight
That stole upon the ear, in Eyraco,[18]
Of many a wild star-gazer long ago—
That stealeth ever on the ear of him
Who, musing, gazeth on the distance dim.
And sees the darkness coming as a cloud—
Is not its form—its voice—most palpable and loud?[19]

But what is this?—it cometh—and it brings
A music with it—'tis the rush of wings—
A pause—and then a sweeping, falling strain
And Nesace is in her halls again.

From the wild energy of wanton haste
    Her cheeks were flushing, and her lips apart;
And zone that clung around her gentle waist
    Had burst beneath the heaving of her heart.
Within the centre of that hall to breathe
She paus'd and panted, Zanthe! all beneath,
The fairy light that kiss'd her golden hair
And long'd to rest, yet could but sparkle there!

    Young flowers were whispering in melody[20]
To happy flowers that night—and tree to tree;
Fountains were gushing music as they fell
In many a star-lit grove, or moon-lit dell;
Yet silence came upon material things—
Fair flowers, bright waterfalls and angel wings—
And sound alone that from the spirit sprang
Bore burthen to the charm the maiden sang:

"'Neath blue-bell or streamer—
    Or tufted wild spray
That keeps, from the dreamer,
    The moonbeam away—[21]
Bright beings! that ponder,
    With half closing eyes,
On the stars which your wonder
    Hath drawn from the skies,
Till they glance thro' the shade, and
    Come down to your brow
Like—eyes of the maiden
    Who calls on you now—
Arise! from your dreaming
    In violet bowers,
To duty beseeming
    These star-litten hours—
And shake from your tresses
    Encumber'd with dew
The breath of those kisses
    That cumber them too—

(O! how, without you, Love!
    Could angels be blest?)
Those kisses of true love
    That lull'd ye to rest!
Up!—shake from your wing
    Each hindering thing:
The dew of the night—
    It would weigh down your flight;
And true love caresses—
    O! leave them apart!
They are light on the tresses,
    But lead on the heart.

Ligeia! Ligeia!
    My beautiful one!
Whose harshest idea
    Will to melody run,
O! is it thy will
    On the breezes to toss?
Or, capriciously still,
    Like the lone Albatross,[22]
Incumbent on night
    (As she on the air)
To keep watch with delight
    On the harmony there?

Ligeia! whatever
    Thy image may be,
No magic shall sever
    Thy music from thee.
Thou hast bound many eyes
    In a dreamy sleep—
But the strains still arise
    Which *thy* vigilance keep—
The sound of the rain
    Which leaps down to the flower,
And dances again
    In the rhythm of the shower—

The murmur that springs[23]
    From the growing of grass
Are the music of things—
    But are modell'd, alas!—
Away, then my dearest,
    O! hie thee away
To springs that lie clearest
    Beneath the moon-ray—
To lone lake that smiles,
    In its dream of deep rest,
At the many star-isles
    That enjewel its breast—
Where wild flowers, creeping,
    Have mingled their shade,
On its margin is sleeping
    Full many a maid—
Some have left the cool glade, and
    Have slept with the bee—[24]
Arouse them my maiden,
    On moorland and lea—
Go! breathe on their slumber,
    All softly in ear,
The musical number
    They slumber'd to hear—
For what can awaken
    An angel so soon
Whose sleep hath been taken
    Beneath the cold moon,
As the spell which no slumber
    Of witchery may test,
The rythmical number
    Which lull'd him to rest?"

Spirits in wing, and angels to the view,
A thousand seraphs burst th' Empyrean thro',
Young dreams still hovering on their drowsy flight—
Seraphs in all but "Knowledge," the keen light
That fell, refracted, thro' thy bounds, afar

O Death! from eye of God upon that star:
Sweet was that error—sweeter still that death—
Sweet was that error—ev'n with *us* the breath
Of science dims the mirror of our joy—
To them 'twere the Simoom, and would destroy—
For what (to them) availeth it to know
That Truth is Falsehood—or that Bliss is Woe?
Sweet was their death—with them to die was rife
With the last ecstacy of satiate life—
Beyond that death no immortality—
But sleep that pondereth and is not "to be"—
And there—oh! may my weary spirit dwell—
Apart from Heaven's Eternity—and yet how far from Hell![25]

What guilty spirit, in what shrubbery dim,
Heard not the stirring summons of that hymn?
But two: they fell: for Heaven no grace imparts
To those who hear not for their beating hearts.
A maiden-angel and her seraph-lover—
O! where (and ye may seek the wide skies over)
Was Love, the blind, near sober Duty known?
Unguided Love hath fallen—'mid "tears of perfect moan."[26]

He was a goodly spirit—he who fell:
A wanderer by moss-y-mantled well—
A gazer on the lights that shine above—
A dreamer in the moonbeam by his love:
What wonder? For each star is eye-like there,
And looks so sweetly down on Beauty's hair—
And they, and ev'ry mossy spring were holy
To his love-haunted heart and melancholy.
The night had found (to him a night of wo)
Upon a mountain crag, young Angelo—
Beetling it bends athwart the solemn sky,
And scowls on starry worlds that down beneath it lie.
Here sate he with his love—his dark eye bent

With eagle gaze along the firmament:
Now turn'd it upon her—but ever then
It trembled to the orb of Earth again.

"Iante, dearest, see! how dim that ray!
How lovely 'tis to look so far away!
She seem'd not thus upon that autumn eve
I left her gorgeous halls—nor mourn'd to leave.
That eve—that eve—I should remember well—
The sun-ray dropp'd, in Lemnos, with a spell
On th'Arabesque carving of a gilded hall
Wherein I sate, and on the draperied wall—
And on my eye-lids—O the heavy light!
How drowsily it weigh'd them into night!
On flowers, before, and mist, and love they ran
With Persian Saadi in his Gulistan:
But O that light!—I slumber'd—Death, the while,
Stole o'er my senses in that lovely isle
So softly that no single silken hair
Awoke that slept—or knew that it was there.
The last spot of Earth's orb I trod upon
Was a proud temple call'd the Parthenon—[27]
More beauty clung around her column'd wall
Than ev'n thy glowing bosom beats withal,[28]
And when old Time my wing did disenthral
Thence sprang I—as the eagle from his tower,
And years I left behind me in an hour.
What time upon her airy bounds I hung
One half the garden of her globe was flung
Unrolling as a chart unto my view—
Tenantless cities of the desert too!
Ianthe, beauty crowded on me then,
And half I wish'd to be again of men."

"My Angelo! and why of them to be?
A brighter dwelling-place is here for thee—
And greener fields than in yon world above,
And women's loveliness—and passionate love."

"But, list, Ianthe! when the air so soft
Fail'd, as my pennon'd spirit leapt aloft,[29]
Perhaps my brain grew dizzy—but the world
I left so late was into chaos hurl'd—
Sprang from her station, on the winds apart,
And roll'd, a flame, the fiery Heaven athwart.
Methought, my sweet one, then I ceased to soar
And fell—not swiftly as I rose before,
But with a downward, tremulous motion thro'
Light, brazen rays, this golden star unto!
Nor long the measure of my falling hours,
For nearest of all stars was thine to ours—
Dread star! that came, amid a night of mirth,
A red Daedalion on the timid Earth.

"We came—and to thy Earth—but not to us
Be given our lady's bidding to discuss:
We came, my love; around, above, below,
Gay fire-fly of the night we come and go,
Nor ask a reason save the angel-nod
She grants to us, as granted by her God—
But, Angelo, than thine grey Time unfurl'd
Never his fairy wing o'er fairier world!
Dim was its little disk, and angel eyes
Alone could see the phantom in the skies,
When first Al Aaraaf knew her course to be
Headlong thitherward o'er the starry sea—
But when its glory swell'd upon the sky,
As glowing Beauty's bust beneath man's eye,
We paus'd before the heritage of men,
And thy star trembled—as doth Beauty then!"

Thus, in discourse, the lovers whiled away
The night that waned and waned and brought no day.
They fell: for Heaven to them no hope imparts
Who hear not for the beating of their hearts.

Notes

[1] A star was discovered by Tycho Brahe which appeared suddenly in the heavens—attained, in a few days, a brilliancy surpassing that of Jupiter—then as suddenly disappeared, and has never been seen since.

[2] On Santa Maura—*olim Deucadia.*

[3] This flower is much noticed by Lewenhoeck and Tournefort. The bee, feeding upon its blossom, becomes intoxicated.

[4] Clytia—The Chrysanthemum Peruvianum, or, to employ a better-known term, the turnsol—which continually turns towards the sun, covers itself, like Peru, the country from which it comes, with dewy clouds which cool and refresh its flowers during the most violent heat of the day.—*B. de St. Pierre*

[5] There is cultivated in the king's garden at Paris, a species of serpentine aloes without prickles, whose large and beautiful flower exhales a strong odour of the vanilla, during the time of its expansion, which is very short. It does not blow till towards the month of July—you then perceive it gradually open its petals—expand them—fade and die.—*St. Pierre.*

[6] There is found, in the Rhone, a beautiful lily of the Valisnerian kind. Its stem will stretch to the length of three or four feet—thus preserving its head above water in the swellings of the river.

[7] The Hyacinth.

[8] It is a fiction of the Indians, that Cupid was first seen floating in one of these down the river Ganges—and that he still loves the cradle of his childhood.

[9] And golden vials full of odors which are the prayers of the saints.—*Rev. St. John.*

[10] The Humanitarians held that God was to be understood as having a really human form.—*Vide Clarke's Sermons*, vol. 1, page 26, fol. edit.

The drift of Milton's argument, leads him to employ language which would appear, at first sight, to verge upon their doctrine; but it will be seen immediately, that he guards himself against the charge of having adopted one of the most ignorant errors of the dark ages of the church.—*Dr. Sumner's Notes on Milton's Christian Doctrine.*

This opinion, in spite of many testimonies to the contrary, could never have been very general. Andeus, a Syrian of Mesopotamia, was condemned for the opinion, as heretical. He lived in the beginning of the fourth century. His disciples were called Anthropmorphites.—*Vide Du Pin.*

[11] Seltsamen Tochter Jovis Seinem Schosskinde Der Phantasie.—*Göethe.*

[12] Sightless—too small to be seen—*Legge.*

13 I have often noticed a peculiar movement of the fire-flies—they will collect in a body and fly off, from a common centre, into innumerable radii.

14 Thersæa, or Therasea, the island mentioned by Seneca, which, in a moment, arose from the sea to the eyes of astonished mariners.

15 Some star which, from the ruin'd roof Of shak'd Olympus, by mischance, did fall.—*Milton.*

16 Voltaire, in speaking of Persepolis, says, "*Je connois bien l'admiration qu'inspirent ces ruines—mais un palais erige au pied d'une chaine des rochers sterils—peut il etre un chef d'oevure des arts!*" [*Voila les arguments de M. Voltaire.*]

17 "Oh! the wave"—Ula Degusi is the Turkish appellation; but, on its own shores, it is called Bahar Loth, or Almotanah. There were undoubtedly more than two cities engluphed in the "dead sea." In the valley of Siddim were five—Adrah, Zeboin, Zoar, Sodom and Gomorrah. Stephen of Byzantium mentions eight, and Strabo thirteeen (engulphed)—but the last is out of all reason.

18 Eyraco—Chaldea.

19 I have often thought I could distinctly hear the sound of the darkness as it stole over the horizon.

20 Fairies use flowers for their charactery.—*Merry Wives of Windsor.* [William Shakespeare]

21 In Scripture is this passage—"The sun shall not harm thee by day, nor the moon by night." It is perhaps not generally known that the moon, in Egypt, has the effect of producing blindness to those who sleep with the face exposed to its rays, to which circumstance the passage evidently alludes.

22 The Albatross is said to sleep on the wing.

23 I met with this idea in an old English tale, which I am now unable to obtain and quote from memory—"The verie essence and, as it were, springe-heade, and origine of all musiche is the verie pleasaunte sounde which the trees of the forest do make when they growe."

24 The wild bee will not sleep in the shade if there be moonlight. The rhyme in this verse, as in one about sixty lines before, has an appearance of affectation. It is, however, imitated from Sir W. Scott, or rather from Claud Halcro—in whose mouth I admired its effect.

25 With the Arabians there is a medium between Heaven and Hell, where men suffer no punishment, but yet do not attain that tranquil and even happiness which they suppose to be characteristic of heavenly enjoyment.

26 There be tears of perfect moan
Wept for thee in Helicon.—*Milton.*

27 It was entire in 1687—the most elevated spot in Athens.

28 Shadowing more beauty in their airy brows
Than have the white breasts of the Queen of Love.—*Marlowe.*

29 Pennon—for pinion.—*Milton.*

Sonnet—To Science

SCIENCE! true daughter of Old Time thou art!
  Who alterest all things with thy peering eyes.
Why preyest thou thus upon the poet's heart,
  Vulture, whose wings are dull realities?
How should he love thee? or how deem thee wise,
  Who wouldst not leave him in his wandering
To seek for treasure in the jewelled skies
  Albeit he soared with an undaunted wing?
Hast thou not dragged Diana from her car?
  And driven the Hamadryad from the wood
To seek a shelter in some happier star?
  Hast thous not torn the Naiad from her flood,
The Elfin from the green grass, and from me
The summer dream beneath the tamarind tree?

To Helen

Helen, thy beauty is to me
Like those Nicean barks of yore,
That gently, o'er a perfumed sea,
The weary way-worn wanderer bore
To his own native shore.
On desperate seas long wont to roam,
Thy hyacinth hair, thy classic face,
Thy Naiad airs have brought me home
To the glory that was Greece,
And the grandeur that was Rome.

Lo! in yon brilliant window-niche
How statue-like I me thee stand,
The agate lamp within thy hand!
Ah, Psyche, from the regions which
Are Holy-land!

The Coliseum

Type of the antique Rome! Rich reliquary
Of lofty contemplation left to Time
By buried centuries of pomp and power!
At length—at length—after so many days
Of weary pilgrimage and burning thirst,
(Thirst for the springs of lore that in thee lie),
I kneel, an altered and an humble man,
Amid thy shadows, and so drink within
My very soul thy grandeur, gloom, and glory!

Vastness! and Age! and Memories of Eld!
Silence! and Desolation! and dim Night!
I feel ye now—I feel ye in your strength—
O spells more sure than e'er Judaean king
Taught in the gardens of Gethsemane!
O charms more potent than the rapt Chaldee
Ever drew down from out the quiet stars!

Here, where a hero fell, a column falls!
Here, where the mimic eagle glared in gold,
A midnight vigil holds the swarthy bat!
Here, where the dames of Rome their gilded hair
Waved to the wind, now wave the reed and thistle!
Here, where on golden throne the monarch lolled,
Glides, spectre-like, unto his marble home,
Lit by the wanlight—wan light of the horned moon,
The swift and silent lizard of the stones!

But stay! these walls—these ivy-clad arcades—
These mouldering plinths—these sad and blackened shafts—
These vague entablatures—this crumbling frieze—

These shattered cornices—this wreck—this ruin—
These stones—alas! these gray stones—are they all—
All of the famed, and the colossal left
By the corrosive Hours to Fate and me?

"Not all"—the Echoes answer me—"not all!
Prophetic sounds and loud, arise forever
From us, and from all Ruin, unto the wise,
As melody from Memnon to the Sun.
We rule the hearts of mightiest men—we rule
With a despotic sway all giant minds.
We are not impotent—we pallid stones.
Not all our power is gone—not all our fame—
Not all the magic of our high renown—
Not all the wonder that encircles us—
Not all the mysteries that in us lie—
Not all the memories that hang upon
And cling around about us as a garment,
Clothing us in a robe of more than glory."

Hymn

At morn—at noon—at twilight dim—
Maria! thou hast heard my hymn!
In joy and wo—in good and ill—
Mother of God, be with me still!
When the Hours flew brightly by
And not a cloud obscured the sky,
My soul, lest it should truant be,
Thy grace did guide to thine and thee;
Now, when storms of Fate o'ercast
Darkly my Present and my Past,
Let my Future radiant shine
With sweet hopes of thee and thine!

Bridal Ballad

The ring is on my hand,
　　And the wreath is on my brow;
Satins and jewels grand
Are all at my command,
　　And I am happy now.

And my lord he loves me well;
　　But, when first he breathed his vow,
I felt my bosom swell—
For the words rang as a knell,
And the voice seemed *his* who fell
In the battle down the dell,
　　And who is happy now.

But he spoke to re-asure me,
　　And he kissed my pallid brow,
While a reverie came o're me,
And to the church-yard bore me,
And I sighed to him before me,
Thinking him dead D'Elormie,
　　"Oh, I am happy now!"

And thus the words were spoken,
　　And this the plighted vow,
And, though my faith be broken,
And, though my heart be broken,
Behold the golden token
　　That *proves* me happy now!

Would God I could awaken!
    For I dream I know not how,
And my soul is sorely shaken
Lest an evil step be taken,—
Lest the dead who is forsaken
    May not be happy now.

The Haunted Palace

In the greenest of our valleys
By good angels tenanted,
Once a fair and stately palace—
Radiant palace—reared its head.
In the monarch Thought's dominion—
It stood there!
Never seraph spread a pinion
Over fabric half so fair.

Banners yellow, glorious, golden,
On its roof did float and flow,
(This—all this—was in the olden
Time long ago),
And every gentle air that dallied,
In that sweet day,
Along the ramparts plumed and pallid,
A winged odour went away.

Wanderers in that happy valley,
Through two luminous windows, saw
Spirits moving musically,
To a lute's well-tuned law,
Round about a throne where, sitting
(Porphyrogene)
In state his glory well befitting,
The ruler of the realm was seen.

And all with pearl and ruby glowing
Was the fair palace door,
Through which came flowing, flowing, flowing,
And sparkling evermore,
A troop of Echoes, whose sweet duty

Was but to sing,
In voices of surpassing beauty,
The wit and wisdom of their king.

But evil things, in robes of sorrow,
Assailed the monarch's high estate.
(Ah, let us mourn!—for never sorrow
Shall dawn upon him desolate!)
And round about his home the glory
That blushed and bloomed,
Is but a dim-remembered story
Of the old time entombed.

And travellers, now, within that valley,
Through the red-litten windows see
Vast forms, that move fantastically
To a discordant melody,
While, lie a ghastly rapid river,
Through the pale door
A hideous throng rush out forever
And laugh—but smile no more.

Silence

There are some qualities—some incorporate things,
    That have a double life, which thus is made
A type of that twin entity which springs
    From matter and light, evinced in solid and shade.
There is a two-fold *Silence*—sea and shore—
    Body and soul. One dwells in lonely places,
    Newly with grass o'ergrown; some solemn graces,
Some human memories and tearful lore,
Render him terrorless: his name's "No More."
He is the corporate Silence: dread him not!
    No power hath he of evil in himself;
But should some urgent fate (untimely lot!)
    Bring thee to meet his shadow (nameless elf,
That haunteth the lone regions where hath trod
No foot of man), commend thyself to God!

A Pæan

I.

How shall the burial rite be read?
The solemn song be sung?
The requiem for the loveliest dead,
That ever died so young?

II.

Her friends are gazing on her,
And on her gaudy bier,
And weep!—oh! to dishonor
Dead beauty with a tear!

III.

They loved her for her wealth—
And they hated her for her pride—
But she grew in feeble health,
And they *love* her—that she died.

IV.

They tell me (while they speak
Of her "costly broider'd pall")
That my voice is growing weak—
That I should not sing at all—

V.

Or that my tone should be
Tun'd to such solemn song
So mournfully—so mournfully,
That the dead may feel no wrong.

VI.

But she is gone above,
With young Hope at her side,
And I am drunk with love
Of the dead, who is my bride.—

VII.

Of the dead—dead who lies
All perfum'd there,
With the death upon her eyes,
And the life upon her hair.

VIII.

Thus on the coffin loud and long
I strike—the murmur sent
Through the grey chambers to my song,
Shall be the accompaniment.

IX.

Thou died'st in thy life's June—
But thou did'st not die too fair:
Thou did'st not die too soon,
Nor with too calm an air.

X.

From more than fiends on earth,
Thy life and love are riven,
To join the untainted mirth
Of more than thrones in heaven—

XII.

Therefore, to thee this night
I will no requiem raise,
But waft thee on thy flight,
With a Paean of old days.

Lenore

Ah broken is the golden bowl! the spirit flown forever!
Let the bell toll!—a saintly soul floats on the Stygian river;
And, Guy De Vere, hast *thou* no tear?—weep now or never more!
See! on yon drear and rigid bier low lies thy love, Lenore!
Come! let the burial rite be read—the funeral song be sung!—
An anthem for the queenliest dead that ever died so young—
A dirge for her the doubly dead in that she died so young.

"Wretches! ye loved her for her wealth and hated her for her pride,
And when she fell in feeble health, ye blessed her—that she died!
How *shall* the ritual, then, be read?—the requiem how be sung
By you—by yours, the evil eye,—by yours, the slanderous tongue
That did to death the innocent that died, and died so young?"

Peccavimus; but rave not thus! and let a Sabbath song
Go up to God so solemnly the dead may feel so wrong!
The sweet Lenore hath "gone before," with Hope, that flew beside
Leaving thee wild for the dear child that should have been thy bride—
For her, the fair and debonair, that now so lowly lies,
The life upon her yellow hair but not within her eyes—
The life still there, upon her hair—the death upon her eyes.

"Avaunt! to-night my heart is light. No dirge will I upraise,
But waft the angel on her flight with a Paean of old days!
Let *no* bell toll!—lest her sweet soul, amid its hallowed mirth,
Should catch the note, as it doth float—up from the damned Earth.

To friends above, from fiends below, the indignant ghost is riven—
From Hell unto a high estate far up within the Heaven—
From grief and groan, to a golden throne, beside the King of Heaven."

Dream-Land

By a route obscure and lonely,
Haunted by ill angels only,
Where an Eidolon, named Night,
On a black throne reigns upright,
I have reached these lands but newly
From an ultimate dim Thule—
From a wild weird clime that lieth, sublime,
    Out of Space—out of Time.

Bottomless vales and boundless floods,
And chasms, and caves, and Titian woods,
With forms that no man can discover
For the dews that drip all over;
Mountains toppling evermore
Into seas without a shore;
Seas that restlessly aspire,
Surging, unto skies of fire;
Lakes that endlessly outspread
Their lone waters—lone and dead,—
Their still waters—still and chilly
With the snows of the lolling lily.

By the lakes that thus outspread
Their lone waters, lone and dead,—
Their sad waters, sad and chilly
With the snows of the lolling lily,—
By the mountains—near the river
Murmuring lowly, murmuring ever—
By the grey woods—by the swamp
Where the toad and the newt encamp—
By the dismal tarns and pools
    Where dwell the Ghouls—

By each spot the most unholy—
In each nook most melancholy—
There the traveller meets aghast
Sheeted Memories of the Past—
Shrouded forms that start and sigh
As they pass the wanderer by—
White-robed forms of friends long given,
In agony, to the Earth—and Heaven.

For the heart whose woes are legion
'Tis a peaceful, soothing region—
For the spirit that walks in shadow
'Tis—oh 'tis an Eldorado!
But the traveller, travelling through it,
May not—dare not openly view it;
Never its mysteries are exposed
To the weak human eye unclosed;
So wills its King, who hath forbid
The uplifting of the fringed lid;
And thus the sad Soul that here passes
Beholds it but through darkened glasses.

By a route obscure and lonely,
Haunted by ill angels only,
Where an Eidolon, named Night,
On a black throne reigns upright,
I have wandered home but newly
From this ultimate dim Thule.

The Raven[1]

Once upon a midnight dreary, while I pondered, weak and weary,
Over many a quaint and curious volume of forgotten lore,
While I nodded, nearly napping, suddenly there came a tapping,
As of some one gently rapping, rapping at my chamber door.
" 'Tis some visiter," I muttered, "tapping at my chamber door—
Only this, and nothing more."

Ah, distinctly I remember it was in the bleak December,
And each separate dying ember wrought its ghost upon the floor.
Eagerly I wished the morrow;—vainly I had sought to borrow
From my books surcease of sorrow—sorrow for the lost Lenore—
For the rare and radiant maiden whom the angels name Lenore—
Nameless *here* for evermore.

And the silken sad uncertain rustling of each purple curtain
Thrilled me—filled me with fantastic terrors never felt before;
So that now, to still the beating of my heart, I stood repeating
" 'Tis some visiter entreating entrance at my chamber door—
Some late visiter entreating entrance at my chamber door;—
This it is, and nothing more."

Presently my soul grew stronger; hesitating then no longer,
"Sir," said I, "or Madam, truly your forgiveness I implore;
But the fact is I was napping, and so gently you came rapping,
And so faintly you came tapping, tapping at my chamber door,
That I scarce was sure I heard you"—here I opened wide the door;—
Darkness there and nothing more.

Deep into that darkness peering, long I stood there wondering,
fearing,
Doubting, dreaming dreams no mortal ever dared to dream before;
But the silence was unbroken, and the darkness gave no token,

And the only word there spoken was the whispered word, "Lenore!"
This I whispered, and an echo murmured back the word, "Lenore!"—
Merely this, and nothing more.

Back into the chamber turning, all my soul within me burning,
Soon I heard again a tapping somewhat louder than before.
"Surely," said I, "surely that is something at my window lattice;
Let me see, then, what thereat is, and this mystery explore—
Let my heart be still a moment and this mystery explore;—
'Tis the wind and nothing more!"

Open here I flung the shutter, when, with many a flirt and flutter,
In there stepped a stately Raven of the saintly days of yore;
Not the least obeisance made he; not an instant stopped or stayed he;
But, with mien of lord or lady, perched above my chamber door—
Perched upon a bust of Pallas just above my chamber door—
Perched, and sat, and nothing more.

Then this ebony bird beguiling my sad fancy into smiling,
By the grave and stern decorum of the countenance it wore,
"Though thy crest be shorn and shaven, thou," I said, "art sure no craven,
Ghastly grim and ancient Raven wandering from the Nightly shore—
Tell me what thy lordly name is on the Night's Plutonian shore!"
Quoth the Raven, "Nevermore."

Much I marvelled this ungainly fowl to hear discourse so plainly,
Though its answer little meaning—little relevancy bore;
For we cannot help agreeing that no living human being
Ever yet was blessed with seeing bird above his chamber door—
Bird or beast upon the sculptured bust above his chamber door,
With such name as "Nevermore."

But the Raven, sitting lonely on the placid bust, spoke only
That one word, as if his soul in that one word he did outpour.
Nothing farther then he uttered—not a feather then he fluttered—
Till I scarcely more than muttered "Other friends have flown before—

On the morrow *he* will leave me, as my Hopes have flown before."
Then the bird said "Nevermore."

Startled at the stillness broken by reply so aptly spoken,
"Doubtless," said I, "what it utters is its only stock and store
Caught from some unhappy master whom unmerciful Disaster
Followed fast and followed faster till his songs one burden bore—
Till the dirges of his Hope that melancholy burden bore
Of "Never—nevermore."

But the Raven still beguiling all my sad soul into smiling,
Straight I wheeled a cushioned seat in front of bird, and bust and door;
Then, upon the velvet sinking, I betook myself to linking
Fancy unto fancy, thinking what this ominous bird of yore—
What this grim, ungainly, ghastly, gaunt and ominous bird of yore
Meant in croaking "Nevermore."

This I sat engaged in guessing, but no syllable expressing
To the fowl whose fiery eyes now burned into my bosom's core;
This and more I sat divining, with my head at ease reclining
On the cushion's velvet lining that the lamplght gloated o'er,
But whose velvet violet lining with the lamplight gloating o'er,
She shall press, ah, nevermore!

Then, methought, the air grew denser, perfumed from an unseen censer
Swung by Angels whose faint foot-falls tinkled on the tufted floor.
"Wretch," I cried, "thy God hath lent thee—by these angels he hath sent thee Respite—respite and nepenthe from thy memories of Lenore;
Quaff, oh quaff this kind nepenthe and forget this lost Lenore!"
Quoth the Raven, "Nevermore."

"Prophet!" said I, "thing of evil!—prophet still, if bird or devil!—
Whether Tempter sent, or whether tempest tossed thee here ashore,
Desolate yet all undaunted, on this desert land enchanted—
On this home by Horror haunted—tell me truly, I implore—

Is there—*is* there balm in Gilead?—tell me—tell me, I implore!"
            Quoth the raven, "Nevermore."

"Prophet!" said I, "thing of evil—prophet still, if bird or devil!
By that Heaven that bends above us—by that God we both adore—
Tell this soul with sorrow laden if, within the distant Aidenn,
It shall clasp a sainted maiden whom the angels name Lenore—
Clasp a rare and radiant maiden whom the angels name Lenore."
            Quoth the Raven, "Nevermore."

"Be that word our sign of parting, bird or fiend!" I shrieked, upstarting—
"Get thee back into the tempest and the Night's Plutonian shore!
Leave no black plume as a token of that lie thy soul hath spoken!
Leave my loneliness unbroken!—quit the bust above my door!
Take thy beak from out my heart, and take thy form from off my door!"
            Quoth the Raven, "Nevermore."

And the Raven, never flitting, still is sitting, *still* is sitting
On the pallid bust of Pallas just above my chamber door;
And his eyes have all the seeming of a demon's that is dreaming,
And the lamp-light o'er him streaming throws his shadow on the floor;
And my soul from out that shadow that lies floating on the floor
            Shall be lifted—nevermore!

Notes

1. "The Raven" was first published on the 29th January, 1845, in the New York *Evening Mirror*—a paper its author was then assistant editor of. It was prefaced by the following words, understood to have been written by N. P. Willis: "We are permitted to copy (in advance of publication) from the second number of the *American Review*, the following remarkable poem by Edgar Poe. In our opinion, it is the most effective single example of 'fugitive poetry' ever published in this country, and unsurpassed in English poetry for subtle conception, masterly ingenuity of versification, and consistent sustaining of imaginative lift and 'pokerishness.' It is one of those 'dainties bred in a book' which we feed on. It will stick to the memory of everybody who reads it." In the February number of the *American Review* the

poem was published as by "Quarles," and it was introduced by the following note, evidently suggested if not written by Poe himself.

["The following lines from a correspondent-besides the deep, quaint strain of the sentiment, and the curious introduction of some ludicrous touches amidst the serious and impressive, as was doubtless intended by the author—appears to us one of the most felicitous specimens of unique rhyming which has for some time met our eye. The resources of English rhythm for varieties of melody, measure, and sound, producing corresponding diversities of effect, having been thoroughly studied, much more perceived, by very few poets in the language. While the classic tongues, especially the Greek, possess, by power of accent, several advantages for versification over our own, chiefly through greater abundance of spondaic: feet, we have other and very great advantages of sound by the modern usage of rhyme. Alliteration is nearly the only effect of that kind which the ancients had in common with us. It will be seen that much of the melody of 'The Raven' arises from alliteration, and the studious use of similar sounds in unusual places. In regard to its measure, it may be noted that if all the verses were like the second, they might properly be placed merely in short lines, producing a not uncommon form; but the presence in all the others of one line-mostly the second in the verse" (stanza?)—"which flows continuously, with only an aspirate pause in the middle, like that before the short line in the Sapphic Adonic, while the fifth has at the middle pause no similarity of sound with any part besides, gives the versification an entirely different effect. We could wish the capacities of our noble language in prosody were better understood."—*ED. Am. Rev.*]

To Helen[1]

I saw thee once—once only—years ago:
I must not say *how* many—but *not* many.
It was a July midnight; and from out
A full-orbed moon, that, like thine own soul, soaring,
Sought a precipitate pathway up through heaven,
There fell a silvery-silken veil of light,
With quietude, and sultriness, and slumber,
Upon the upturned faces of a thousand
Roses that grew in an enchanted garden,
Where no wind dared to stir, unless on tiptoe—
Fell on the upturn'd faces of these roses
That gave out, in return for the love-light,
Their odorous souls in an ecstatic death—
Fell on the upturn'd faces of these roses
That smiled and died in this parterre, enchanted
By thee, and by the poetry of thy presence.

Clad all in white, upon a violet bank
I saw thee half reclining; while the moon
Fell on the upturn'd faces of the roses,
And on thine own, upturn'd—alas, in sorrow!

Was it not Fate, that, on this July midnight—
Was it not Fate (whose name is also Sorrow),
That bade me pause before that garden-gate,
To breathe the incense of those slumbering roses?
No footstep stirred: the hated world an slept,
Save only thee and me. (Oh, Heaven!—oh, God!
How my heart beats in coupling those two words!)
Save only thee and me. I paused—I looked—
And in an instant all things disappeared.
(Ah, bear in mind this garden was enchanted!)

The pearly lustre of the moon went out:
The mossy banks and the meandering paths,
The happy flowers and the repining trees,
Were seen no more: the very roses' odors
Died in the arms of the adoring airs.
All—all expired save thee—save less than thou:
Save only the divine light in thine eyes—
Save but the soul in thine uplifted eyes.
I saw but them—they were the world to me!
I saw but them—saw only them for hours,
Saw only them until the moon went down.
What wild heart-histories seemed to he enwritten
Upon those crystalline, celestial spheres!
How dark a woe, yet how sublime a hope!
How silently serene a sea of pride!
How daring an ambition; yet how deep—
How fathomless a capacity for love!

But now, at length, dear Dian sank from sight,
Into a western couch of thunder-cloud;
And thou, a ghost, amid the entombing trees
Didst glide away. *Only thine eyes remained*;
They *would not go*—they never yet have gone;
Lighting my lonely pathway home that night,
They have not left me (as my hopes have) since;
They follow me—they lead me through the years.
They are my ministers—yet I their slave.
Their office is to illumine and enkindle—
My duty, *to be saved* by their bright light,
And purified in their electric fire,
And sanctified in their elysian fire.
They fill my soul with Beauty (which is Hope),
And are far up in Heaven—the stars I kneel to
In the sad, silent watches of my night;
While even in the meridian glare of day
I see them still—two sweetly scintillant
Venuses, unextinguished by the sun!

Notes

1 "To Helen!" (Mrs. S. Helen Whitman) was not published until November, 1848, although written several months earlier. It first appeared in the *Union Magazine*, and with the omission, contrary to the knowledge or desire of Poe, of the line, "Oh, God! oh, Heaven—how my heart beats in coupling those two words."

The City in the Sea

Lo! Death has reared himself a throne
In a strange city lying alone
Far down within the dim West,
Where the good and the bad and the worst and the best
Have gone to their eternal rest.
There shrines and palaces and towers
(Time-eaten towers that tremble not!)
Resemble nothing that is ours.
Around, by lifting winds forgot,
Resignedly beneath the sky
The melancholy waters lie.

No rays from the holy heaven come down
On the long night-time of that town;
But light from out the lurid sea
Streams up the turrets silently—
Gleams up the pinnacles far and free—
Up domes—up spires—up kingly halls—
Up fanes—up Babylon-like walls—
Up shadowy long-forgotten bowers
Of scultured ivy and stone flowers—
Up many and many a marvellous shrine
Whose wreathed friezes intertwine
The viol, the violet, and the vine.

Resignedly beneath the sky
The melancholy waters lie.
So blend the turrets and shadows there
That all seem pendulous in air,
While from a proud tower in the town
Death looks gigantically down.

There open fanes and gaping graves
Yawn level with the luminous waves;
But not the riches there that lie
In each idol's diamond eye—
Not the gaily-jewelled dead
Tempt the waters from their bed;
For no ripples curl, alas!
Along that wilderness of glass—
No swellings tell that winds may be
Upon some far-off happier sea—
No heavings hint that winds have been
On seas less hideously serene.

But lo, a stir is in the air!
The wave—there is a movement there!
As if the towers had thrown aside,
In slightly sinking, the dull tide—
As if their tops had feebly given
A void within the filmy Heaven.
The waves have now a redder glow—
The hours are breathing faint and low—
And when, amid no earthly moans,
Down, down that town shall settle hence,
Hell, rising from a thousand thrones,
Shall do it reverence.

Ulalume[1]

The skies they were ashen and sober;
    The leaves they were crisped and sere—
    The leaves they were withering and sere;
It was night in the lonesome October
    Of my most immemorial year:
It was hard by the dim lake of Auber,
    In the misty mid region of Weir:—
It was down by the dank tarn of Auber,
    In the ghoul-haunted woodland of Weir.

Here once, through an alley Titanic,
    Of cypress, I roamed with my Soul—
    Of cypress, with Psyche, my Soul.
There were days when my heart was volcanic
    As the scoriac rivers that roll—
    As the lavas that restlessly roll
Their sulphurous currents down Yaanek,
    In the ultimate climes of the Pole—
That groan as they roll down Mount Yaanek
    In the realms of the Boreal Pole.

Our talk had been serious and sober,
    But our thoughts they were palsied and sere—
    Our memories were treacherous and sere;
For we knew not the month was October,
    And we marked not the night of the year—
    (Ah, night of all nights in the year!)
We noted not the dim lake of Auber,
    (Though once we had journeyed down here)
We remembered not the dank tarn of Auber,
    Nor the ghoul-haunted woodland of Weir.

And now, as the night was senescent,
And star-dials pointed to morn—
As the star-dials hinted of morn—
At the end of our path a liquescent
And nebulous lustre was born,
Out of which a miraculous crescent
Arose with a duplicate horn—
Astarte's bediamonded crescent,
Distinct with its duplicate horn.

And I said—"She is warmer than Dian:
She rolls through an ether of sighs—
She revels in a region of sighs.
She has seen that the tears are not dry on
These cheeks, where the worm never dies,
And has come past the stars of the Lion,
To point us the path to the skies—
To the Lethean peace of the skies—
Come up, in despite of the Lion,
To shine on us with her bright eyes—
Come up, through the lair of the Lion,
With love in her luminous eyes."

But Psyche, uplifting her finger,
Said—"Sadly this star I mistrust—
Her pallor I strangely mistrust—
Ah, hasten!—ah, let us not linger!
Ah, fly!—let us fly!—for we must."
In terror she spoke; letting sink her
Wings till they trailed in the dust—
In agony sobbed, letting sink her
Plumes till they trailed in the dust—
Till they sorrowfully trailed in the dust.

I replied—"This is nothing but dreaming.
Let us on, by this tremulous light!
Let us bathe in this crystalline light!
Its Sybillic splendor is beaming

With Hope and in Beauty to-night—
See!—it flickers up the sky through the night!
Ah, we safely may trust to its gleaming,
And be sure it will lead us aright—
We safely may trust to a gleaming
That cannot but guide us aright,
Since it flickers up to Heaven through the night."

Thus I pacified Psyche and kissed her,
And tempted her out of her gloom—
And conquered her scruples and gloom;
And we passed to the end of the vista—
But were stopped by the door of a tomb—
By the door of a legended tomb:—
And I said—"What is written, sweet sister,
On the door of this legended tomb?"
She replied—"Ulalume—Ulalume—
'Tis the vault of thy lost Ulalume!"

Then my heart it grew ashen and sober
As the leaves that were crisped and sere—
As the leaves that were withering and sere—
And I cried—"It was surely October
On *this* very night of last year,
That I journeyed—I journeyed down here!—
That I brought a dread burden down here—
On this night, of all nights in the year,
Ah, what demon has tempted me here?
Well I know, now, this dim lake of Auber—
This misty mid region of Weir:—
Well I know, now, this dank tarn of Auber—
This ghoul-haunted woodland of Weir."

Notes

1. This poem was first published in Colton's *American Review* for December, 1847, as "To—Ulalume: a Ballad." Being reprinted immediately in the *Home Journal*, it was copied into various publications with the name of the editor, N. P. Willis, appended, and was ascribed to him. When first published, it contained

the following additional stanza which Poe subsequently, at the suggestion of Mrs. Whitman, wisely suppressed:

> Said we then—we two, then—"Ah, can it
> Have been that the woodlandish ghouls—
> The pitiful, the merciful ghouls—
> To bar up our path and to ban it
> From the secret that lies in these wolds—
> Had drawn up the spectre of a planet
> From the limbo of lunary souls—
> This sinfully scintillant planet
> From the Hell of the planetary souls?"

The Bells[1]

I.

Hear the sledges with the bells—
Silver bells!
What a world of merriment their melody foretells!
How they tinkle, tinkle, tinkle,
In the icy air of night!
While the stars that oversprinkle
All the heavens, seem to twinkle
With a crystalline delight;
Keeping time, time, time,
In a sort of Runic rhyme,
To the tintinnabulation that so musically wells
From the bells, bells, bells, bells,
Bells, bells, bells—
From the jingling and the tinkling of the bells.

II.

Hear the mellow wedding-bells
Golden bells!
What a world of happiness their harmony foretells!
Through the balmy air of night
How they ring out their delight!—
From the molten-golden notes,
And all in tune,
What a liquid ditty floats
To the turtle-dove that listens, while she gloats
On the moon!
Oh, from out the sounding cells,
What a gush of euphony voluminously wells!
How it swells!
How it dwells

On the Future!—how it tells
Of the rapture that impels
To the swinging and the ringing
Of the bells, bells, bells—
Of the bells, bells, bells, bells,
Bells, bells, bells—
To the rhyming and the chiming of the bells!

III.

Hear the loud alarum bells—
Brazen bells!
What tale of terror, now, their turbulency tells!
In the startled ear of night
How they scream out their affright!
Too much horrified to speak,
They can only shriek, shriek,
Out of tune,
In a clamorous appealing to the mercy of the fire,
In a mad expostulation with the deaf and frantic fire,
Leaping higher, higher, higher,
With a desperate desire,
And a resolute endeavor
Now—now to sit, or never,
By the side of the pale-faced moon.
Oh, the bells, bells, bells!
What a tale their terror tells
Of despair!
How they clang, and clash, and roar!
What a horror they outpour
On the bosom of the palpitating air!
Yet the ear, it fully knows,
By the twanging
And the clanging,
How the danger ebbs and flows;
Yet, the ear distinctly tells,
In the jangling
And the wrangling,
How the danger sinks and swells,

By the sinking or the swelling in the anger of the bells—
Of the bells—
Of the bells, bells, bells, bells,
Bells, bells, bells—
In the clamour and the clangour of the bells!

IV.

Hear the tolling of the bells—
Iron bells!
What a world of solemn thought their monody compels!
In the silence of the night,
How we shiver with affright
At the melancholy meaning of their tone!
For every sound that floats
From the rust within their throats
Is a groan.
And the people—ah, the people—
They that dwell up in the steeple,
All alone,
And who, tolling, tolling, tolling,
In that muffled monotone,
Feel a glory in so rolling
On the human heart a stone—
They are neither man nor woman—
They are neither brute nor human—
They are Ghouls:—
And their king it is who tolls:—
And he rolls, rolls, rolls, rolls,
rolls
A Pæan from the bells!
And his merry bosom swells
With the Pæan of the bells!
And he dances, and he yells;
Keeping time, time, time,
In a sort of Runic rhyme,
To the paean of the bells—
Of the bells:—
Keeping time, time, time,

In a sort of Runic rhyme,
To the throbbing of the bells—
Of the bells, bells, bells—
To the sobbing of the bells:—
Keeping time, time, time,
As he knells, knells, knells,
In a happy Runic rhyme,
To the rolling of the bells—
Of the bells, bells, bells:—
To the tolling of the bells—
Of the bells, bells, bells, bells,
Bells, bells, bells—
To the moaning and the groaning of the bells.

Notes

1. The bibliographical history of "The Bells" is curious. The subject, and some lines of the original version, having been suggested by the poet's friend, Mrs. Shew, Poe, when he wrote out the first draft of the poem, headed it, "The Bells, By Mrs. M. A. Shew." This draft, now the editor's property, consists of only seventeen lines, and read thus:

I.

The bells!-ah, the bells!
The little silver bells!
How fairy-like a melody there floats
From their throats—
From their merry little throats—
From the silver, tinkling throats
Of the bells, bells, bells—
Of the bells!

II.

The bells!-ah, the bells!
The heavy iron bells!
How horrible a monody there floats
From their throats—
From their deep-toned throats—
From their melancholy throats!
How I shudder at the notes
Of the bells, bells, bells—
Of the bells!

In the autumn of 1848 Poe added another line to this poem, and sent it to the editor of the *Union Magazine*. It was not published. So, in the following February, the poet forwarded to the same periodical a much enlarged and altered transcript. Three months having elapsed without publication, another revision of the poem, similar to the current version, was sent, and in the following October was published in the *Union Magazine*.

Annabel Lee[1]

It was many and many a year ago,
    In a kingdom by the sea,
That a maiden lived whom you may know
    By the name of Annabel Lee;—
And this maiden she lived with no other thought
    Than to love and be loved by me.

I was a child and *she* was a child,
    In this kingdom by the sea,
But we loved with a love that was more than love—
    I and my Annabel Lee—
With a love that the winged seraphs of Heaven
    Coveted her and me.

And this was the reason that, long ago,
    In this kingdom by the sea,
A wind blew out of a cloud by night
    Chilling my Annabel Lee;
So that her high-born kinsmen came
    And bore her away from me,
To shut her up, in a sepulchre
    In this kingdom by the sea.

The angels, not half so happy in Heaven,
    Went envying her and me;
Yes! that was the reason (as all men know,
    In this kingdom by the sea)
That the wind came out of the cloud, chilling
    And killing my Annabel Lee.

But our love it was stronger by far than the love
    Of those who were older than we—

Of many far wiser than we—
    And neither the angels in Heaven above
Nor the demons down under the sea
    Can ever dissever my soul from the soul
Of the beautiful Annabel Lee,

For the moon never beams without bringing me dreams
    Of the beautiful Annabel Lee;
And the stars never rise but I see the bright eyes
    Of the beautiful Annabel Lee;
And so, all the night-tide, I lie down by the side
    Of my darling, my darling, my life and my bride
In her sepulchre there by the sea—
    In her tomb by the sounding sea.

Notes

1. "Annabel Lee" was written early in 1849, and is evidently an expression of the poet's undying love for his deceased bride, although at least one of his lady admirers deemed it a response to her admiration. Poe sent a copy of the ballad to the *Union Magazine*, in which publication it appeared in January, 1850, three months after the author's death. While suffering from "hope deferred" as to its fate, Poe presented a copy of "Annabel Lee" to the editor of the *Southern Literary Messenger*, who published it in the November number of his periodical, a month after Poe's death. In the meantime the poet's own copy, left among his papers, passed into the hands of the person engaged to edit his works, and he quoted the poem in an obituary of Poe, in the New York *Tribune*, before any one else had an opportunity of publishing it.

Eldorado[1]

Gaily bedight,
A gallant knight,
In sunshine and in shadow,
Had journeyed long,
Singing a song,
In search of Eldorado.

But he grew old—
This knight so bold—
And o'er his heart a shadow
Fell, as he found
No spot of ground
That looked like Eldorado.

And, as his strength
Failed him at length,
He met a pilgrim shadow—
"Shadow," said he,
"Where can it be—
This land of Eldorado?"

"Over the Mountains
Of the Moon,
Down the Valley of the Shadow,
Ride, boldly ride,"
The shade replied,—
"If you seek for Eldorado!"

Notes

1. Although "Eldorado" was published during Poe's lifetime, in 1849, in the *Flag of our Union*, it does not appear to have ever received the author's finishing touches.

A Dream within a Dream

Take this kiss upon the brow!
And, in parting from you now,
Thus much let me avow—
You are not wrong, who deem
That my days have been a dream;
Yet if hope has flown away
In a night, or in a day,
In a vision, or in none,
Is it therefore the less *gone*?
All that we see or seem
Is but a dream within a dream.

I stand amid the roar
Of a surf-tormented shore,
And I hold within my hand
Grains of the golden sand—
How few! yet how they creep
Through my fingers to the deep,
While I weep—while I weep!
O God! can I not grasp
Them with a tighter clasp?
O God! can I not save
One from the pitiless wave?
Is *all* that we see or seem
But a dream within a dream?

Word Cloud Classics

Adventures of Huckleberry Finn

The Adventures of Sherlock Holmes

The Adventures of Tom Sawyer

Aesop's Fables

The Age of Innocence

Alice's Adventures in Wonderland and Through the Looking-Glass

Anna Karenina

Anne of Green Gables

The Art of War

The Autobiography of Benjamin Franklin and Other Writings

The Awakening and Other Stories

The Beautiful and Damned and Other Stories

Black Beauty

The Brothers Grimm 101 Fairy Tales

The Brothers Grimm Volume II: 110 Grimmer Fairy Tales

Bulfinch's Mythology: Stories of Gods and Heroes

The Call of the Wild and Other Stories

A Christmas Carol and Other Holiday Treasures

Classic Horror Tales

Classic Science Fiction

Classic Stories of World War I

Classic Stories of World War II

Classic Tales of Mystery

Classic Westerns: Zane Grey

Common Sense and Selected Works of Thomas Paine

The Count of Monte Cristo

Crime and Punishment

Don Quixote

Dracula

Dubliners & A Portrait of the Artist as a Young Man and Other Works

Emma

Frankenstein

Great Expectations

Hans Christian Andersen Tales

H. P. Lovecraft Cthulhu Mythos Tales

The Hunchback of Notre Dame

The Inventions, Researches, and Writings of Nikola Tesla

Jane Eyre

The Jungle Book

Lady Chatterley's Lover

Leaves of Grass

Word Cloud Classics

The Legend of Sleepy Hollow and Other Tales

Les Misérables

Little Women

Love Poems

Madame Bovary

Mansfield Park

The Merry Adventures of Robin Hood

Moby-Dick

My Ántonia

Northanger Abbey

Odyssey

Persuasion

Peter Pan

The Phantom of the Opera

The Picture of Dorian Gray

The Poetry of Emily Dickinson

Presidential Inaugural Addresses

Pride and Prejudice

The Prince and Other Writings

The Prophet and Other Tales

The Romantic Poets

The Scarlet Letter

The Secret Garden

Selected Works of Alexander Hamilton

Selected Works of Edgar Allan Poe

Sense and Sensibility

Shakespeare's Sonnets and Other Poems

Strange Case of Dr. Jekyll and Mr. Hyde & Other Stories

A Tale of Two Cities

Tarzan of the Apes & The Return of Tarzan

The Three Musketeers

Treasure Island

Twenty Thousand Leagues Under the Sea

Uncle Tom's Cabin, or Life Among the Lowly

The U.S. Constitution and Other Key American Writings

Walden and Civil Disobedience

William Shakespeare Comedies

William Shakespeare Tragedies

The Wind in the Willows and Other Stories

The Wizard of Oz

Wuthering Heights

Frankenstein

Word Cloud Classics

Adventures of Huckleberry Finn

The Adventures of Sherlock Holmes

Aesop's Fables

The Age of Innocence

Alice's Adventures in Wonderland and Through the Looking-Glass

Anna Karenina

Anne of Green Gables

The Art of War

The Autobiography of Benjamin Franklin and Other Writings

The Awakening and Other Stories

The Beautiful and Damned and Other Stories

Black Beauty

The Brothers Grimm 101 Fairy Tales

The Brothers Grimm Volume II: 110 Grimmer Fairy Tales

Bulfinch's Mythology: Stories of Gods and Heroes

The Call of the Wild and Other Stories

A Christmas Carol and Other Holiday Treasures

Classic Horror Tales

Classic Westerns: Zane Grey

Common Sense and Selected Works of Thomas Paine

The Count of Monte Cristo

Crime and Punishment

Don Quixote

Dracula

Dubliners & A Portrait of the Artist as a Young Man and Other Works

Emma

Frankenstein

Great Expectations

Hans Christian Andersen Tales

H. P. Lovecraft Cthulhu Mythos Tales

Inferno

The Inventions, Researches, and Writings of Nikola Tesla

Jane Eyre

The Jungle Book

Lady Chatterley's Lover

Leaves of Grass

The Legend of Sleepy Hollow and Other Tales

Word Cloud Classics

Les Misérables

Little Women

Madame Bovary

Mansfield Park

The Merry Adventures of Robin Hood

Moby-Dick

My Ántonia

Narrative of the Life of Frederick Douglass and Other Works

Northanger Abbey

Odyssey

Persuasion

Peter Pan

The Phantom of the Opera

The Picture of Dorian Gray

The Poetry of Emily Dickinson

Presidential Inaugural Addresses

Pride and Prejudice

The Prince and Other Writings

The Red Badge of Courage and Other Stories

The Romantic Poets

The Scarlet Letter

The Secret Garden

Selected Works of Alexander Hamilton

Sense and Sensibility

Shakespeare's Sonnets and Other Poems

Strange Case of Dr. Jekyll and Mr. Hyde & Other Stories

Tarzan of the Apes & The Return of Tarzan

The Three Musketeers

Treasure Island

12 Years a Slave

Twenty Thousand Leagues Under the Sea

Uncle Tom's Cabin, or Life Among the Lowly

The U.S. Constitution and Other Key American Writings

Walden and Civil Disobedience

The Wind in the Willows and Other Stories

The Wizard of Oz

Wuthering Heights

Frankenstein

or

The Modern Prometheus

Mary Shelley

Word Cloud Classics
San Diego

Canterbury Classics
An imprint of Printers Row Publishing Group
9717 Pacific Heights Blvd, San Diego, CA 92121
www.canterburyclassicsbooks.com • mail@canterburyclassicsbooks.com

Correspondence concerning the content of this book should be sent to Canterbury Classics, Editorial Department, at the above address.

Publisher: Peter Norton • Associate Publisher: Ana Parker
Art Director: Charles McStravick
Senior Developmental Editor: April Graham
Publishing/Editorial Team: Kathryn C. Dalby, JoAnn Padgett, Melinda Allman, Dan Mansfield, Traci Douglas
Production/Design Team: Jonathan Lopes, Rusty von Dyl, Beno Chan, Julie Greene, Rosemary Rae

Spine art: gio_banfi/DigitalVision Vectors via Getty Images
Endpapers: Pobytov/DigitalVision Vectors via Getty Images

ISBN: 978-1-6672-0319-5

Printed in China
27 26 25 24 23   2 3 4 5 6

MIX
Paper | Supporting responsible forestry
FSC
www.fsc.org
FSC® C144853

Editor's Note: This work has been published in its original form to preserve the author's intent and style.

CONTENTS

VOLUME ONE

LETTER I

To Mrs. Saville, England.
St. Petersburgh, December 11th, 17—.

You will rejoice to hear that no disaster has accompanied the commencement of an enterprise which you have regarded with such evil forebodings. I arrived here yesterday, and my first task is to assure my dear sister of my welfare and increasing confidence in the success of my undertaking.

I am already far north of London, and as I walk in the streets of Petersburgh, I feel a cold northern breeze play upon my cheeks, which braces my nerves and fills me with delight. Do you understand this feeling? This breeze, which has travelled from the regions towards which I am advancing, gives me a foretaste of those icy climes. Inspirited by this wind of promise, my daydreams become more fervent and vivid. I try in vain to be persuaded that the pole is the seat of frost and desolation; it ever presents itself to my imagination as the region of beauty and delight. There, Margaret, the sun is forever visible, its broad disk just skirting the horizon and diffusing a perpetual splendour. There—for with your leave, my sister, I will put some trust in preceding navigators—there snow and frost are banished; and, sailing over a calm sea, we may be wafted to a land surpassing in wonders and in beauty every region hitherto discovered on the habitable globe. Its productions and features may be without example, as the phenomena of the heavenly bodies undoubtedly are in those undiscovered solitudes. What may not be expected in a country of eternal light? I may there discover the wondrous power which attracts the needle and may regulate a thousand celestial observations that require only this voyage to render their seeming eccentricities consistent forever. I shall satiate my ardent curiosity with the sight of a part of the world never before visited, and may tread a land never before imprinted by the foot of man. These are my enticements, and they are sufficient to conquer all fear of danger or death and to induce me to commence this laborious voyage with the joy a child feels when he embarks in a little boat, with his holiday mates, on an expedition of discovery up his native river. But supposing all these conjectures to be false, you cannot contest the inestimable benefit which I shall confer on all mankind, to the last generation, by discovering a passage near the pole to those countries, to reach which at present so many months are requisite; or by ascertaining the secret of the magnet, which, if at all possible, can only be effected by an undertaking such as mine.

These reflections have dispelled the agitation with which I began my letter, and I feel my heart glow with an enthusiasm which elevates me to heaven, for nothing contributes so much to tranquillize the mind as a steady purpose—a point on which the soul may fix its intellectual eye. This expedition has been the favourite dream of my early years. I have read with ardour the accounts of the various voyages which have been made in the prospect of arriving at the North Pacific Ocean through the seas which surround the pole. You may remember that a history of all the voyages made for purposes of discovery composed the whole of our good Uncle Thomas's library. My education was neglected, yet I was passionately fond of reading. These volumes were my study day and night, and my familiarity with them increased that regret which I had felt, as a child, on learning that my father's dying injunction had forbidden my uncle to allow me to embark in a seafaring life.

These visions faded when I perused, for the first time, those poets whose effusions entranced my soul and lifted it to heaven. I also became a poet and for one year lived in a paradise of my own creation; I imagined that I also might obtain a niche in the temple where the names of Homer and Shakespeare are consecrated. You are well acquainted with my failure and how heavily I bore the disappointment. But just at that time I inherited the fortune of my cousin, and my thoughts were turned into the channel of their earlier bent.

Six years have passed since I resolved on my present undertaking. I can, even now, remember the hour from which I dedicated myself to this great enterprise. I commenced by inuring my body to hardship. I accompanied the whale-fishers on several expeditions to the North Sea; I voluntarily endured cold, famine, thirst, and want of sleep; I often worked harder than the common sailors during the day and devoted my nights to the study of mathematics, the theory of medicine, and those branches of physical science from which a naval adventurer might derive the greatest practical advantage. Twice I actually hired myself as an under-mate in a Greenland whaler, and acquitted myself to admiration. I must own I felt a little proud when my captain offered me the second dignity in the vessel and entreated me to remain with the greatest earnestness, so valuable did he consider my services.

And now, dear Margaret, do I not deserve to accomplish some great purpose? My life might have been passed in ease and luxury, but I preferred glory to every enticement that wealth placed in my path. Oh, that some encouraging voice would answer in the affirmative! My courage and my resolution is firm; but my hopes fluctuate, and my spirits are often depressed. I am about to proceed on a long and difficult voyage, the emergencies of which will demand all my fortitude: I am required not only to raise the spirits of others, but sometimes to sustain my own, when theirs are failing.

This is the most favourable period for travelling in Russia. They fly quickly over the snow in their sledges; the motion is pleasant, and, in my opinion, far more agreeable than that of an English stagecoach. The cold is not excessive, if you are wrapped in furs—a dress which I have already adopted, for there is a great difference between walking the deck and remaining seated motionless for hours, when no exercise prevents the blood from actually freezing in your veins. I have no ambition to lose my life on the post-road between St. Petersburgh and Archangel.

I shall depart for the latter town in a fortnight or three weeks; and my intention is to hire a ship there, which can easily be done by paying the insurance for the owner, and to engage as many sailors as I think necessary among those who are accustomed to the whale-fishing. I do not intend to sail until the month of June; and when shall I return? Ah, dear sister, how can I answer this question? If I succeed, many, many months, perhaps years, will pass before you and I may meet. If I fail, you will see me again soon, or never.

Farewell, my dear, excellent Margaret. Heaven shower down blessings on you, and save me, that I may again and again testify my gratitude for all your love and kindness.

Your affectionate brother,
R. Walton

LETTER II

TO MRS. SAVILLE, ENGLAND.
Archangel, March 28th, 17—.

How slowly the time passes here, encompassed as I am by frost and snow! Yet a second step is taken towards my enterprise. I have hired a vessel and am occupied in collecting my sailors; those whom I have already engaged appear to be men on whom I can depend and are certainly possessed of dauntless courage.

But I have one want which I have never yet been able to satisfy, and the absence of the object of which I now feel as a most severe evil. I have no friend, Margaret: when I am glowing with the enthusiasm of success, there will be none to participate my joy; if I am assailed by disappointment, no one will endeavour to sustain me in dejection. I shall commit my thoughts to paper, it is true; but that is a poor medium for the communication of feeling. I desire the company of a man who could sympathise with me, whose eyes would reply to mine. You may deem me romantic, my dear sister, but I bitterly feel the want of a friend. I have no one near me, gentle yet courageous, possessed of a cultivated as well as of a capacious mind, whose tastes are like my own, to approve or amend my plans. How would such a friend repair the faults of your poor brother! I am too ardent in execution and too impatient of difficulties. But it is a still greater evil to me that I am self-educated: for the first fourteen years of my life I ran wild on a common and read nothing but our Uncle Thomas's books of voyages. At that age I became acquainted with the celebrated poets of our own country; but it was only when it had ceased to be in my power to derive its most important benefits from such a conviction that I perceived the necessity of becoming acquainted with more languages than that of my native country. Now I am twenty-eight and am in reality more illiterate than many schoolboys of fifteen. It is true that I have thought more and that my daydreams are more extended and magnificent, but they want (as the painters call it) *keeping*; and I greatly need a friend who would have sense enough not to despise me as romantic, and affection enough for me to endeavour to regulate my mind.

Well, these are useless complaints; I shall certainly find no friend on the wide ocean, nor even here in Archangel, among merchants and seamen. Yet some feelings, unallied to the dross of human nature, beat even in these rugged bosoms. My lieutenant, for instance, is a man of wonderful courage and enterprise; he is madly desirous of glory, or rather, to word my phrase more characteristically, of advancement in his profession. He is an Englishman, and in the midst of national and professional prejudices, unsoftened by cultivation, retains some of the noblest endowments of humanity. I first became acquainted with him on board a whale vessel; finding that he was unemployed in this city, I easily engaged him to assist in my enterprise.

The master is a person of an excellent disposition and is remarkable in the ship for his gentleness and the mildness of his discipline. This circumstance, added to his well-known integrity and dauntless courage, made me very desirous to engage him. A youth passed in solitude, my best years spent under your gentle and feminine fosterage, has so refined the groundwork of my character that I cannot overcome an intense distaste to the usual brutality exercised on board ship: I have never believed it to be necessary, and when I heard of a mariner equally noted for his kindliness of heart and the respect and obedience paid to him by his crew, I felt myself peculiarly fortunate in being able to secure his services. I heard of him first in rather a romantic manner, from a lady who owes to him the happiness of her life. This, briefly, is his story. Some years ago he loved a young Russian lady of moderate fortune, and having amassed a considerable sum in prize-money, the father of the girl consented to the match. He saw his mistress once before the destined ceremony; but she was bathed in tears, and throwing herself at his feet, entreated him to spare her, confessing at the same time that she loved another, but that he was poor, and that her father would never consent to the union. My generous friend reassured the suppliant, and on being informed of the name of her lover, instantly abandoned his pursuit. He had already bought a farm with his money, on which he had designed to pass the remainder of his life; but he bestowed the whole on his rival, together with the remains of his prize-money to purchase stock, and then himself solicited the young woman's father to consent to her marriage with her lover. But the old man decidedly refused, thinking himself bound in honour to my friend, who, when he found the father inexorable, quitted his country, nor returned until he heard that his former mistress was married according to her inclinations. "What a noble fellow!" you will exclaim. He is so; but then he is wholly uneducated: he is as silent as a Turk, and a kind of ignorant carelessness attends him, which, while it renders his conduct the more astonishing, detracts from the interest and sympathy which otherwise he would command.

Yet do not suppose, because I complain a little or because I can conceive a consolation for my toils which I may never know, that I am wavering in my resolutions. Those are as fixed as fate, and my voyage is only now delayed until the weather shall permit my embarkation. The winter has been dreadfully severe, but the spring promises well, and it is considered as a remarkably early season, so that perhaps I may sail sooner than I expected. I shall do nothing rashly: you know me sufficiently to confide in my prudence and considerateness whenever the safety of others is committed to my care.

I cannot describe to you my sensations on the near prospect of my undertaking. It is impossible to communicate to you a conception of the trembling sensation, half pleasurable and half fearful, with which I am preparing to depart. I am going to unexplored regions, to "the land of mist and snow," but I shall kill no albatross; therefore do not be alarmed for my safety or if I should come back to you as worn and woeful as the "Ancient Mariner." You will smile at my allusion, but I will disclose a secret. I have often attributed my attachment to, my passionate enthusiasm for, the dangerous mysteries of ocean to that production of the most imaginative of modern poets. There is something at work in my soul which I do not understand. I am practically industrious—painstaking, a workman to execute with perseverance and labour—but besides this there is a love for the marvellous, a belief in the marvellous, intertwined in all my projects, which hurries me out of the common pathways of men, even to the wild sea and unvisited regions I am about to explore.

But to return to dearer considerations. Shall I meet you again, after having traversed immense seas, and returned by the most southern cape of Africa or America? I dare not expect such success, yet I cannot bear to look on the reverse of the picture. Continue for the present to write to me by every opportunity: I may receive your letters on some occasions when I need them most to support my spirits. I love you very tenderly. Remember me with affection, should you never hear from me again.

Your affectionate brother,
ROBERT WALTON

LETTER III

TO MRS. SAVILLE, ENGLAND.
July 7th, 17—.

MY DEAR SISTER,

I write a few lines in haste to say that I am safe—and well advanced on my voyage. This letter will reach England by a merchantman now on its homeward voyage from Archangel; more fortunate than I, who may not see my native land, perhaps, for many years. I am, however, in good spirits: my men are bold and apparently firm of purpose, nor do the floating sheets of ice that continually pass us, indicating the dangers of the region towards which we are advancing, appear to dismay them. We have already reached a very high latitude; but it is the height of summer, and although not so warm as in England, the southern gales, which blow us speedily towards those shores which I so ardently desire to attain, breathe a degree of renovating warmth which I had not expected.

No incidents have hitherto befallen us that would make a figure in a letter. One or two stiff gales and the springing of a leak are accidents which experienced navigators scarcely remember to record, and I shall be well content if nothing worse happen to us during our voyage.

Adieu, my dear Margaret. Be assured that for my own sake, as well as yours, I will not rashly encounter danger. I will be cool, persevering, and prudent.

But success shall crown my endeavours. Wherefore not? Thus far I have gone, tracing a secure way over the pathless seas, the very stars themselves being witnesses and testimonies of my triumph. Why not still proceed over the untamed yet obedient element? What can stop the determined heart and resolved will of man?

My swelling heart involuntarily pours itself out thus. But I must finish. Heaven bless my beloved sister!

R.W.

LETTER IV

TO MRS. SAVILLE, ENGLAND.
August 5th, 17—.

So strange an accident has happened to us that I cannot forbear recording it, although it is very probable that you will see me before these papers can come into your possession.

Last Monday (July 31st) we were nearly surrounded by ice, which closed in the ship on all sides, scarcely leaving her the searoom in which she floated. Our situation was somewhat dangerous, especially as we were compassed round by a very thick fog. We accordingly lay to, hoping that some change would take place in the atmosphere and weather.

About two o'clock the mist cleared away, and we beheld, stretched out in every direction, vast and irregular plains of ice, which seemed to have no end. Some of my comrades groaned, and my own mind began to grow watchful with anxious thoughts, when a strange sight suddenly attracted our attention and diverted our solicitude from our own situation. We perceived a low carriage, fixed on a sledge and drawn by dogs, pass on towards the north, at the distance of half a mile; a being which had the shape of a man, but apparently of gigantic stature, sat in the sledge and guided the dogs. We watched the rapid progress of the traveller with our telescopes until he was lost among the distant inequalities of the ice.

This appearance excited our unqualified wonder. We were, as we believed, many hundred miles from any land; but this apparition seemed to denote that it was not, in reality, so distant as we had supposed. Shut in, however, by ice, it was impossible to follow his track, which we had observed with the greatest attention.

About two hours after this occurrence we heard the ground sea, and before night the ice broke and freed our ship. We, however, lay to until the morning, fearing to encounter in the dark those large loose masses which float about after the breaking up of the ice. I profited of this time to rest for a few hours.

In the morning, however, as soon as it was light, I went upon deck and found all the sailors busy on one side of the vessel, apparently talking to someone in the sea. It was, in fact, a sledge, like that we had seen before, which had drifted towards us in the night on a large fragment of ice. Only one dog remained alive; but there was a human being within it whom the sailors were persuading to enter the vessel. He was not, as the other traveller seemed to be, a savage inhabitant of some undiscovered island, but a European. When I appeared on deck the master said, "Here is our captain, and he will not allow you to perish on the open sea."

On perceiving me, the stranger addressed me in English, although with a foreign accent. "Before I come on board your vessel," said he, "will you have the kindness to inform me whither you are bound?"

You may conceive my astonishment on hearing such a question addressed to me from a man on the brink of destruction and to whom I should have supposed that my vessel would have been a resource which he would not have exchanged for the most precious wealth the earth can afford. I replied, however, that we were on a voyage of discovery towards the northern pole.

Upon hearing this he appeared satisfied and consented to come on board. Good God! Margaret, if you had seen the man who thus capitulated for his safety, your surprise would have been boundless. His limbs were nearly frozen, and his body dreadfully emaciated by fatigue and suffering. I never saw a man in so wretched a condition. We attempted to carry him into the cabin, but as soon as he had quitted the fresh air he fainted. We accordingly brought him back to the deck and restored him to animation by rubbing him with brandy and forcing him to swallow a small quantity. As soon as he showed signs of life we wrapped him up in blankets and placed him near the chimney of the kitchen stove. By slow degrees he recovered and ate a little soup, which restored him wonderfully.

Two days passed in this manner before he was able to speak, and I often feared that his sufferings had deprived him of understanding. When he had in some measure recovered, I removed him to my own cabin and attended on him as much as my duty would permit. I never saw a more interesting creature: his eyes have generally an expression of wildness, and even madness, but there are moments when, if anyone performs an act of kindness towards him or does him any the most trifling service, his whole countenance is lighted up, as it were, with a beam of benevolence and sweetness that I never saw equalled. But he is generally melancholy and despairing, and sometimes he gnashes his teeth, as if impatient of the weight of woes that oppresses him.

When my guest was a little recovered I had great trouble to keep off the men, who wished to ask him a thousand questions; but I would not allow him to be tormented by their idle curiosity, in a state of body and mind whose restoration evidently depended upon entire repose. Once, however, the lieutenant asked why he had come so far upon the ice in so strange a vehicle.

His countenance instantly assumed an aspect of the deepest gloom, and he replied, "To seek one who fled from me."

"And did the man whom you pursued travel in the same fashion?"

"Yes."

"Then I fancy we have seen him, for the day before we picked you up we saw some dogs drawing a sledge, with a man in it, across the ice."

This aroused the stranger's attention, and he asked a multitude of questions concerning the route which the daemon, as he called him, had pursued. Soon after, when he was alone with me, he said, "I have, doubtless, excited your curiosity, as well as that of these good people; but you are too considerate to make enquiries."

"Certainly; it would indeed be very impertinent and inhuman in me to trouble you with any inquisitiveness of mine."

"And yet you rescued me from a strange and perilous situation; you have benevolently restored me to life."

Soon after this he enquired if I thought that the breaking up of the ice had destroyed the other sledge. I replied that I could not answer with any degree of certainty, for the ice had not broken until near midnight, and the traveller might have arrived at a place of safety before that time; but of this I could not judge.

From this time a new spirit of life animated the decaying frame of the stranger. He manifested the greatest eagerness to be upon deck to watch for the sledge which had before appeared; but I have persuaded him to remain in the cabin, for he is far too weak to sustain the rawness of the atmosphere. I have promised that someone should watch for him and give him instant notice if any new object should appear in sight.

Such is my journal of what relates to this strange occurrence up to the present day. The stranger has gradually improved in health but is very silent and appears uneasy when anyone except myself enters his cabin. Yet his manners are so conciliating and gentle that the sailors are all interested in him, although they have had very little communication with him. For my own part, I begin to love him as a brother, and his constant and deep grief fills me with sympathy and compassion. He must have been a noble creature in his better days, being even now in wreck so attractive and amiable.

I said in one of my letters, my dear Margaret, that I should find no friend on the wide ocean; yet I have found a man who, before his spirit had been broken by misery, I should have been happy to have possessed as the brother of my heart.

I shall continue my journal concerning the stranger at intervals, should I have any fresh incidents to record.

August 13th, 17—.

My affection for my guest increases every day. He excites at once my admiration and my pity to an astonishing degree. How can I see so noble a creature destroyed by misery without feeling the most poignant grief? He is so gentle, yet so wise; his mind is so cultivated, and when he speaks, although his words are culled with the choicest art, yet they flow with rapidity and unparalleled eloquence.

He is now much recovered from his illness and is continually on the deck, apparently watching for the sledge that preceded his own. Yet, although unhappy, he is not so utterly occupied by his own misery but that he interests himself deeply in the projects of others. He has frequently conversed with me on mine, which I have communicated to him without disguise. He entered attentively into all my arguments in favour of my eventual success and into every minute detail of the measures I had taken to secure it. I was easily led by the sympathy which he evinced to use the language of my heart, to give utterance to the burning ardour of my soul and to say, with all the fervour that warmed me, how gladly I would sacrifice my fortune, my existence, my every hope, to the furtherance of my enterprise. One man's life or death were but a small price to pay for the acquirement of the knowledge which I sought, for the dominion I should acquire and transmit over the elemental foes of our race. As I spoke, a dark gloom spread over my listener's countenance. At first I perceived that he tried to suppress his emotion; he placed his hands before his eyes, and my voice quivered and failed me as I beheld tears trickle fast from between his fingers; a groan burst from his heaving breast. I paused; at length he spoke, in broken accents: "Unhappy man! Do you share my madness? Have you drunk also of the intoxicating draught? Hear me; let me reveal my tale, and you will dash the cup from your lips!"

Such words, you may imagine, strongly excited my curiosity; but the paroxysm of grief that had seized the stranger overcame his weakened powers, and many hours of repose and tranquil conversation were necessary to restore his composure.

Having conquered the violence of his feelings, he appeared to despise himself for being the slave of passion; and quelling the dark tyranny of despair, he led me again to converse concerning myself personally. He asked me the history of my earlier years. The tale was quickly told, but it awakened various trains of reflection. I spoke of my desire of finding a friend, of my thirst for a more intimate sympathy with a fellow mind than had ever fallen to my lot, and expressed my conviction that a man could boast of little happiness who did not enjoy this blessing.

"I agree with you," replied the stranger; "we are unfashioned creatures, but half made up, if one wiser, better, dearer than ourselves—such a friend ought to be—do not lend his aid to perfectionate our weak and faulty natures. I once had a friend, the most noble of human creatures, and am entitled, therefore, to judge respecting friendship. You have hope, and the world before you, and have no cause for despair. But I—I have lost everything and cannot begin life anew."

As he said this his countenance became expressive of a calm, settled grief that touched me to the heart. But he was silent and presently retired to his cabin.

Even broken in spirit as he is, no one can feel more deeply than he does the beauties of nature. The starry sky, the sea, and every sight afforded by these wonderful regions seem still to have the power of elevating his soul from earth. Such a man has a double existence: he may suffer misery and be overwhelmed by disappointments, yet when he has retired into himself, he will be like a celestial spirit that has a halo around him, within whose circle no grief or folly ventures.

Will you smile at the enthusiasm I express concerning this divine wanderer? You would not if you saw him. You have been tutored and refined by books and retirement from the world, and you are therefore somewhat fastidious; but this only renders you the more fit to appreciate the extraordinary merits of this wonderful man. Sometimes I have endeavoured to discover what quality it is which he possesses that elevates him so immeasurably above any other person I ever knew. I believe it to be an intuitive discernment, a quick but never-failing power of judgement, a penetration into the causes of things, unequalled for clearness and precision; add to this a facility of expression and a voice whose varied intonations are soul-subduing music.

August 19th, 17—.

Yesterday the stranger said to me, "You may easily perceive, Captain Walton, that I have suffered great and unparalleled misfortunes. I had determined at one time that the memory of these evils should die with me, but you have won me to alter my determination. You seek for knowledge and wisdom, as I once did; and I ardently hope that the gratification of your wishes may not be a serpent to sting you, as mine has been. I do not know that the relation of my disasters will be useful to you; yet, when I reflect that you are pursuing the same course, exposing yourself to the same dangers which have rendered me what I am, I imagine that you may deduce an apt moral from my tale, one that may direct you if you succeed in your undertaking and console you in case of failure. Prepare to hear of occurrences which are usually deemed marvellous. Were we among the tamer scenes of nature I might fear to encounter your unbelief, perhaps your ridicule; but many things will appear possible in these wild and mysterious regions which would provoke the laughter of those unacquainted with the ever-varied powers of nature; nor can I doubt but that my tale conveys in its series internal evidence of the truth of the events of which it is composed."

You may easily imagine that I was much gratified by the offered communication, yet I could not endure that he should renew his grief by a recital of his misfortunes. I felt the greatest eagerness to hear the promised narrative, partly from curiosity and partly from a strong desire to ameliorate his fate if it were in my power. I expressed these feelings in my answer.

"I thank you," he replied, "for your sympathy, but it is useless; my fate is nearly fulfilled. I wait but for one event, and then I shall repose in peace. I understand your feeling," continued he, perceiving that I wished to interrupt him; "but you are mistaken, my friend, if thus you will allow me to name you; nothing can alter my destiny; listen to my history, and you will perceive how irrevocably it is determined."

He then told me that he would commence his narrative the next day when I should be at leisure. This promise drew from me the warmest thanks. I have resolved every night, when I am not imperatively occupied by my duties, to record, as nearly as possible in his own words, what he has related during the day. If I should be engaged, I will at least make notes. This manuscript will doubtless afford you the greatest pleasure; but to me, who know him, and who hear it from his own lips—with what interest and sympathy shall I read it in some future day! Even now, as I commence my task, his full-toned voice swells in my ears; his lustrous eyes dwell on me with all their melancholy sweetness; I see his thin hand raised in animation, while the lineaments of his face are irradiated by the soul within. Strange and harrowing must be his story, frightful the storm which embraced the gallant vessel on its course and wrecked it—thus!

CHAPTER I

I am by birth a Genevese, and my family is one of the most distinguished of that republic. My ancestors had been for many years counsellors and syndics, and my father had filled several public situations with honour and reputation. He was respected by all who knew him for his integrity and indefatigable attention to public business. He passed his younger days perpetually occupied by the affairs of his country; a variety of circumstances had prevented his marrying early, nor was it until the decline of life that he became a husband and the father of a family.

As the circumstances of his marriage illustrate his character, I cannot refrain from relating them. One of his most intimate friends was a merchant who, from a flourishing state, fell, through numerous mischances, into poverty. This man, whose name was Beaufort, was of a proud and unbending disposition and could not bear to live in poverty and oblivion in the same country where he had formerly been distinguished for his rank and magnificence. Having paid his debts, therefore, in the most honourable manner, he retreated with his daughter to the town of Lucerne, where he lived unknown and in wretchedness. My father loved Beaufort with the truest friendship and was deeply grieved by his retreat in these unfortunate circumstances. He bitterly deplored the false pride which led his friend to a conduct so little worthy of the affection that united them. He lost no time in endeavouring to seek him out, with the hope of persuading him to begin the world again through his credit and assistance.

Beaufort had taken effectual measures to conceal himself, and it was ten months before my father discovered his abode. Overjoyed at this discovery, he hastened to the house, which was situated in a mean street near the Reuss. But when he entered, misery and despair alone welcomed him. Beaufort had saved but a very small sum of money from the wreck of his fortunes, but it was sufficient to provide him with sustenance for some months, and in the meantime he hoped to procure some respectable employment in a merchant's house. The interval was, consequently, spent in inaction; his grief only became more deep and rankling when he had leisure for reflection, and at length it took so fast hold of his mind that at the end of three months he lay on a bed of sickness, incapable of any exertion.

His daughter attended him with the greatest tenderness, but she saw with despair that their little fund was rapidly decreasing and that there was no other prospect of support. But Caroline Beaufort possessed a mind of an uncommon mould, and her courage rose to support her in her adversity. She procured plain work; she plaited straw and by various means contrived to earn a pittance scarcely sufficient to support life.

Several months passed in this manner. Her father grew worse; her time was more entirely occupied in attending him; her means of subsistence decreased; and in the tenth month her father died in her arms, leaving her an orphan and a beggar. This last blow overcame her, and she knelt by Beaufort's coffin weeping bitterly, when my father entered the chamber. He came like a protecting spirit to the poor girl, who committed herself to his care; and after the interment of his friend he conducted her to Geneva and placed her under the protection of a relation. Two years after this event Caroline became his wife.

There was a considerable difference between the ages of my parents, but this circumstance seemed to unite them only closer in bonds of devoted affection. There was a sense of justice in my father's upright mind which rendered it necessary that he should approve highly to love strongly. Perhaps during former years he had suffered from the late-discovered unworthiness of one beloved and so was disposed to set a greater value on tried worth. There was a show of gratitude and worship in his attachment to my mother, differing wholly from the doting fondness of age, for it was inspired by reverence for her virtues and a desire to be the means of, in some degree, recompensing her for the sorrows she had endured, but which gave inexpressible grace to his behaviour to her. Everything was made to yield to her wishes and her convenience. He strove to shelter her, as a fair exotic is sheltered by the gardener, from every rougher wind and to surround her with all that could tend to excite pleasurable emotion in her soft and benevolent mind. Her health, and even the tranquillity of her hitherto constant spirit, had been shaken by what she had gone through. During the two years that had elapsed previous to their marriage my father had gradually relinquished all his public functions; and immediately after their union they sought the pleasant climate of Italy, and the change of scene and interest attendant on a tour through that land of wonders, as a restorative for her weakened frame.

From Italy they visited Germany and France. I, their eldest child, was born at Naples, and as an infant accompanied them in their rambles. I remained for several years their only child. Much as they were attached to each other, they seemed to draw inexhaustible stores of affection from a very mine of love to bestow them upon me. My mother's tender caresses and my father's smile of benevolent pleasure while regarding me are my first recollections. I was their plaything and their idol, and something better—their child, the innocent and helpless creature bestowed on them by heaven, whom to bring up to good, and whose future lot it was in their hands to direct to happiness or misery, according as they fulfilled their duties towards me. With this deep consciousness of what they owed towards the being to which they had given life, added to the active spirit of tenderness that animated both, it may be imagined that while during every hour of my infant life I received a lesson of patience, of charity, and of self-control, I was so guided by a silken cord that all seemed but one train of enjoyment to me.

For a long time I was their only care. My mother had much desired to have a daughter, but I continued their single offspring. When I was about five years old, while making an excursion beyond the frontiers of Italy, they passed a week on the shores of the Lake of Como. Their benevolent disposition often made them enter the cottages of the poor. This, to my mother, was more than a duty; it was a necessity, a passion—remembering what she had suffered, and how she had been relieved—for her to act in her turn the guardian angel to the afflicted. During one of their walks a poor cot in the foldings of a vale attracted their notice as being singularly disconsolate, while the number of half-clothed children gathered about it spoke of penury in its worst shape. One day, when my father had gone by himself to Milan, my mother, accompanied by me, visited this abode. She found a peasant and his wife, hard working, bent down by care and labour, distributing a scanty meal to five hungry babes. Among these there was one which attracted my mother far above all the rest. She appeared of a different stock. The four others were dark-eyed, hardy little vagrants; this child was thin and very fair. Her hair was the brightest living gold, and despite the poverty of her clothing, seemed to set a crown of distinction on her head. Her brow was clear and ample, her blue eyes cloudless, and her lips and the moulding of her face so expressive of sensibility and sweetness that none could behold her without looking on her as of a distinct species, a being heaven-sent, and bearing a celestial stamp in all her features.

The peasant woman, perceiving that my mother fixed eyes of wonder and admiration on this lovely girl, eagerly communicated her history. She was not her child, but the daughter of a Milanese nobleman. Her mother was a German and had died on giving her birth. The infant had been placed with these good people to nurse: they were better off then. They had not been long married, and their eldest child was but just born. The father of their charge was one of those Italians nursed in the memory of the antique glory of Italy—one among the *schiavi ognor frementi*, who exerted himself to obtain the liberty of his country. He became the victim of its weakness. Whether he had died or still lingered in the dungeons of Austria was not known. His property was confiscated; his child became an orphan and a beggar. She continued with her foster parents and bloomed in their rude abode, fairer than a garden rose among dark-leaved brambles.

When my father returned from Milan, he found playing with me in the hall of our villa a child fairer than a pictured cherub—a creature who seemed to shed radiance from her looks and whose form and motions were lighter than the chamois of the hills. The apparition was soon explained. With his permission my mother prevailed on her rustic guardians to yield their charge to her. They were fond of the sweet orphan. Her presence had seemed a blessing to them, but it would be unfair to her to keep her in poverty and want when Providence afforded her such powerful protection. They consulted their village priest, and the result was that Elizabeth Lavenza became the inmate of my parents' house—my more than sister—the beautiful and adored companion of all my occupations and my pleasures.

Everyone loved Elizabeth. The passionate and almost reverential attachment with which all regarded her became, while I shared it, my pride and my delight. On the evening previous to her being brought to my home, my mother had said playfully, "I have a pretty present for my Victor—tomorrow he shall have it." And when, on the morrow, she presented Elizabeth to me as her promised gift, I, with childish seriousness, interpreted her words literally and looked upon Elizabeth as mine—mine to protect, love, and cherish. All praises bestowed on her I received as made to a possession of my own. We called each other familiarly by the name of cousin. No word, no expression could body forth the kind of relation in which she stood to me—my more than sister, since till death she was to be mine only.

CHAPTER II

We were brought up together; there was not quite a year difference in our ages. I need not say that we were strangers to any species of disunion or dispute. Harmony was the soul of our companionship, and the diversity and contrast that subsisted in our characters drew us nearer together. Elizabeth was of a calmer and more concentrated disposition; but, with all my ardour, I was capable of a more intense application and was more deeply smitten with the thirst for knowledge. She busied herself with following the aerial creations of the poets; and in the majestic and wondrous scenes which surrounded our Swiss home—the sublime shapes of the mountains, the changes of the seasons, tempest and calm, the silence of winter, and the life and turbulence of our Alpine summers—she found ample scope for admiration and delight. While my companion contemplated with a serious and satisfied spirit the magnificent appearances of things, I delighted in investigating their causes. The world was to me a secret which I desired to divine. Curiosity, earnest research to learn the hidden laws of nature, gladness akin to rapture, as they were unfolded to me, are among the earliest sensations I can remember.

On the birth of a second son, my junior by seven years, my parents gave up entirely their wandering life and fixed themselves in their native country. We possessed a house in Geneva, and a *campagne* on Belrive, the eastern shore of the lake, at the distance of rather more than a league from the city. We resided principally in the latter, and the lives of my parents were passed in considerable seclusion. It was my temper to avoid a crowd and to attach myself fervently to a few. I was indifferent, therefore, to my school-fellows in general; but I united myself in the bonds of the closest friendship to one among them. Henry Clerval was the son of a merchant of Geneva. He was a boy of singular talent and fancy. He loved enterprise, hardship, and even danger for its own sake. He was deeply read in books of chivalry and romance. He composed heroic songs and began to write many a tale of enchantment and knightly adventure. He tried to make us act plays and to enter into masquerades, in which the characters were drawn from the heroes of Roncesvalles, of the Round Table of King Arthur, and the chivalrous train who shed their blood to redeem the holy sepulchre from the hands of the infidels.

No human being could have passed a happier childhood than myself. My parents were possessed by the very spirit of kindness and indulgence. We felt that they were not the tyrants to rule our lot according to their caprice, but the agents and creators of all the many delights which we enjoyed. When I mingled with other families I distinctly discerned how peculiarly fortunate my lot was, and gratitude assisted the development of filial love.

My temper was sometimes violent, and my passions vehement; but by some law in my temperature they were turned not towards childish pursuits but to an eager desire to learn, and not to learn all things indiscriminately. I confess that neither the structure of languages, nor the code of governments, nor the politics of various states possessed attractions for me. It was the secrets of heaven and earth that I desired to learn; and whether it was the outward substance of things or the inner spirit of nature and the mysterious soul of man that occupied me, still my enquiries were directed to the metaphysical, or in its highest sense, the physical secrets of the world.

Meanwhile Clerval occupied himself, so to speak, with the moral relations of things. The busy stage of life, the virtues of heroes, and the actions of men were his theme; and his hope and his dream was to become one among those whose names are recorded in story as the gallant and adventurous benefactors of our species. The saintly soul of Elizabeth shone like a shrine-dedicated lamp in our peaceful home. Her sympathy was ours; her smile, her soft voice, the sweet glance of her celestial eyes, were ever there to bless and animate us. She was the living spirit of love to soften and attract; I might have become sullen in my study, rough through the ardour of my nature, but that she was there to subdue me to a semblance of her own gentleness. And Clerval—could aught ill entrench on the noble spirit of Clerval? Yet he might not have been so perfectly humane, so thoughtful in his generosity, so full of kindness and tenderness amidst his passion for adventurous exploit, had she not unfolded to him the real loveliness of beneficence and made the doing good the end and aim of his soaring ambition.

I feel exquisite pleasure in dwelling on the recollections of childhood, before misfortune had tainted my mind and changed its bright visions of extensive usefulness into gloomy and narrow reflections upon self.

Besides, in drawing the picture of my early days, I also record those events which led, by insensible steps, to my after tale of misery, for when I would account to myself for the birth of that passion which afterwards ruled my destiny I find it arise, like a mountain river, from ignoble and almost forgotten sources; but, swelling as it proceeded, it became the torrent which, in its course, has swept away all my hopes and joys.

Natural philosophy is the genius that has regulated my fate; I desire, therefore, in this narration, to state those facts which led to my predilection for that science. When I was thirteen years of age we all went on a party of pleasure to the baths near Thonon; the inclemency of the weather obliged us to remain a day confined to the inn. In this house I chanced to find a volume of the works of Cornelius Agrippa. I opened it with apathy; the theory which he attempts to demonstrate and the wonderful facts which he relates soon changed this feeling into enthusiasm. A new light seemed to dawn upon my mind, and bounding with joy, I communicated my discovery to my father. My father looked carelessly at the title page of my book and said, "Ah! Cornelius Agrippa! My dear Victor, do not waste your time upon this; it is sad trash."

If, instead of this remark, my father had taken the pains to explain to me that the principles of Agrippa had been entirely exploded and that a modern system of science had been introduced which possessed much greater powers than the ancient, because the powers of the latter were chimerical, while those of the former were real and practical, under such circumstances I should certainly have thrown Agrippa aside and have contented my imagination, warmed as it was, by returning with greater ardour to my former studies. It is even possible that the train of my ideas would never have received the fatal impulse that led to my ruin. But the cursory glance my father had taken of my volume by no means assured me that he was acquainted with its contents, and I continued to read with the greatest avidity.

When I returned home my first care was to procure the whole works of this author, and afterwards of Paracelsus and Albertus Magnus. I read and studied the wild fancies of these writers with delight; they appeared to me treasures known to few besides myself. I have described myself as always having been imbued with a fervent longing to penetrate the secrets of nature. In spite of the intense labour and wonderful discoveries of modern philosophers, I always came from my studies discontented and unsatisfied. Sir Isaac Newton is said to have avowed that he felt like a child picking up shells beside the great and unexplored ocean of truth. Those of his successors in each branch of natural philosophy with whom I was acquainted appeared even to my boy's apprehensions as tyros engaged in the same pursuit.

The untaught peasant beheld the elements around him and was acquainted with their practical uses. The most learned philosopher knew little more. He had partially unveiled the face of Nature, but her immortal lineaments were still a wonder and a mystery. He might dissect, anatomize, and give names; but, not to speak of a final cause, causes in their secondary and tertiary grades were utterly unknown to him. I had gazed upon the fortifications and impediments that seemed to keep human beings from entering the citadel of nature, and rashly and ignorantly I had repined.

But here were books, and here were men who had penetrated deeper and knew more. I took their word for all that they averred, and I became their disciple. It may appear strange that such should arise in the eighteenth century; but while I followed the routine of education in the schools of Geneva, I was, to a great degree, self-taught with regard to my favourite studies. My father was not scientific, and I was left to struggle with a child's blindness, added to a student's thirst for knowledge. Under the guidance of my new preceptors I entered with the greatest diligence into the search of the philosopher's stone and the elixir of life; but the latter soon obtained my undivided attention. Wealth was an inferior object, but what glory would attend the discovery if I could banish disease from the human frame and render man invulnerable to any but a violent death!

Nor were these my only visions. The raising of ghosts or devils was a promise liberally accorded by my favourite authors, the fulfilment of which I most eagerly sought; and if my incantations were always unsuccessful, I attributed the failure rather to my own inexperience and mistake than to a want of skill or fidelity in my instructors. And thus for a time I was occupied by exploded systems, mingling, like an unadept, a thousand contradictory theories, and floundering desperately in a very slough of multifarious knowledge, guided by an ardent imagination and childish reasoning, till an accident again changed the current of my ideas.

When I was about fifteen years old we had retired to our house near Belrive, when we witnessed a most violent and terrible thunderstorm. It advanced from behind the mountains of Jura, and the thunder burst at once with frightful loudness from various quarters of the heavens. I remained, while the storm lasted, watching its progress with curiosity and delight. As I stood at the door, on a sudden I beheld a stream of fire issue from an old and beautiful oak which stood about twenty yards from our house; and so soon as the dazzling light vanished, the oak had disappeared, and nothing remained but a blasted stump. When we visited it the next morning, we found the tree shattered in a singular manner. It was not splintered by the shock, but entirely reduced to thin ribbons of wood. I never beheld anything so utterly destroyed.

Before this I was not unacquainted with the more obvious laws of electricity. On this occasion a man of great research in natural philosophy was with us, and excited by this catastrophe, he entered on the explanation of a theory which he had formed on the subject of electricity and galvanism, which was at once new and astonishing to me. All that he said threw greatly into the shade Cornelius Agrippa, Albertus Magnus, and Paracelsus, the lords of my imagination; but by some fatality the overthrow of these men disinclined me to pursue my accustomed studies. It seemed to me as if nothing would or could ever be known. All that had so long engaged my attention suddenly grew despicable. By one of those caprices of the mind which we are perhaps most subject to in early youth, I at once gave up my former occupations, set down natural history and all its progeny as a deformed and abortive creation, and entertained the greatest disdain for a would-be science which could never even step within the threshold of real knowledge. In this mood of mind I betook myself to the mathematics and the branches of study appertaining to that science as being built upon secure foundations, and so worthy of my consideration.

Thus strangely are our souls constructed, and by such slight ligaments are we bound to prosperity or ruin. When I look back, it seems to me as if this almost miraculous change of inclination and will was the immediate suggestion of the guardian angel of my life—the last effort made by the spirit of preservation to avert the storm that was even then hanging in the stars and ready to envelop me. Her victory was announced by an unusual tranquillity and gladness of soul which followed the relinquishing of my ancient and latterly tormenting studies. It was thus that I was to be taught to associate evil with their prosecution, happiness with their disregard.

It was a strong effort of the spirit of good, but it was ineffectual. Destiny was too potent, and her immutable laws had decreed my utter and terrible destruction.

CHAPTER III

When I had attained the age of seventeen, my parents resolved that I should become a student at the university of Ingolstadt. I had hitherto attended the schools of Geneva, but my father thought it necessary for the completion of my education that I should be made acquainted with other customs than those of my native country. My departure was therefore fixed at an early date, but before the day resolved upon could arrive, the first misfortune of my life occurred—an omen, as it were, of my future misery.

Elizabeth had caught the scarlet fever; her illness was severe, and she was in the greatest danger. During her illness many arguments had been urged to persuade my mother to refrain from attending upon her. She had at first yielded to our entreaties, but when she heard that the life of her favourite was menaced, she could no longer control her anxiety. She attended her sickbed; her watchful attentions triumphed over the malignity of the distemper—Elizabeth was saved, but the consequences of this imprudence were fatal to her preserver. On the third day my mother sickened; her fever was accompanied by the most alarming symptoms, and the looks of her medical attendants prognosticated the worst event. On her deathbed the fortitude and benignity of this best of women did not desert her. She joined the hands of Elizabeth and myself. "My children," she said, "my firmest hopes of future happiness were placed on the prospect of your union. This expectation will now be the consolation of your father. Elizabeth, my love, you must supply my place to my younger children. Alas! I regret that I am taken from you; and, happy and beloved as I have been, is it not hard to quit you all? But these are not thoughts befitting me; I will endeavour to resign myself cheerfully to death and will indulge a hope of meeting you in another world."

She died calmly, and her countenance expressed affection even in death. I need not describe the feelings of those whose dearest ties are rent by that most irreparable evil, the void that presents itself to the soul, and the despair that is exhibited on the countenance. It is so long before the mind can persuade itself that she whom we saw every day and whose very existence appeared a part of our own can have departed forever—that the brightness of a beloved eye can have been extinguished and the sound of a voice so familiar and dear to the ear can be hushed, never more to be heard. These are the reflections of the first days; but when the lapse of time proves the reality of the evil, then the actual bitterness of grief commences. Yet from whom has not that rude hand rent away some dear connection? And why should I describe a sorrow which all have felt, and must feel? The time at length arrives when grief is rather an indulgence than a necessity; and the smile that plays upon the lips, although it may be deemed a sacrilege, is not banished. My mother was dead, but we had still duties which we ought to perform; we must continue our course with the rest and learn to think ourselves fortunate whilst one remains whom the spoiler has not seized.

My departure for Ingolstadt, which had been deferred by these events, was now again determined upon. I obtained from my father a respite of some weeks. It appeared to me sacrilege so soon to leave the repose, akin to death, of the house of mourning and to rush into the thick of life. I was new to sorrow, but it did not the less alarm me. I was unwilling to quit the sight of those that remained to me, and above all, I desired to see my sweet Elizabeth in some degree consoled.

She indeed veiled her grief and strove to act the comforter to us all. She looked steadily on life and assumed its duties with courage and zeal. She devoted herself to those whom she had been taught to call her uncle and cousins. Never was she so enchanting as at this time, when she recalled the sunshine of her smiles and spent them upon us. She forgot even her own regret in her endeavours to make us forget.

The day of my departure at length arrived. Clerval spent the last evening with us. He had endeavoured to persuade his father to permit him to accompany me and to become my fellow student, but in vain. His father was a narrow-minded trader and saw idleness and ruin in the aspirations and ambition of his son. Henry deeply felt the misfortune of being debarred from a liberal education. He said little, but when he spoke I read in his kindling eye and in his animated glance a restrained but firm resolve not to be chained to the miserable details of commerce.

We sat late. We could not tear ourselves away from each other nor persuade ourselves to say the word "Farewell!" It was said, and we retired under the pretence of seeking repose, each fancying that the other was deceived; but when at morning's dawn I descended to the carriage which was to convey me away, they were all there—my father again to bless me, Clerval to press my hand once more, my Elizabeth to renew her entreaties that I would write often and to bestow the last feminine attentions on her playmate and friend.

I threw myself into the chaise that was to convey me away and indulged in the most melancholy reflections. I, who had ever been surrounded by amiable companions, continually engaged in endeavouring to bestow mutual pleasure—I was now alone. In the university whither I was going I must form my own friends and be my own protector. My life had hitherto been remarkably secluded and domestic, and this had given me invincible repugnance to new countenances. I loved my brothers, Elizabeth, and Clerval; these were "old familiar faces," but I believed myself totally unfitted for the company of strangers. Such were my reflections as I commenced my journey; but as I proceeded, my spirits and hopes rose. I ardently desired the acquisition of knowledge. I had often, when at home, thought it hard to remain during my youth cooped up in one place and had longed to enter the world and take my station among other human beings. Now my desires were complied with, and it would, indeed, have been folly to repent.

I had sufficient leisure for these and many other reflections during my journey to Ingolstadt, which was long and fatiguing. At length the high white steeple of the town met my eyes. I alighted and was conducted to my solitary apartment to spend the evening as I pleased.

The next morning I delivered my letters of introduction and paid a visit to some of the principal professors. Chance—or rather the evil influence, the Angel of Destruction, which asserted omnipotent sway over me from the moment I turned my reluctant steps from my father's door—led me first to M. Krempe, professor of natural philosophy. He was an uncouth man, but deeply imbued in the secrets of his science. He asked me several questions concerning my progress in the different branches of science appertaining to natural philosophy. I replied carelessly, and partly in contempt, mentioned the names of my alchemists as the principal authors I had studied. The professor stared. "Have you," he said, "really spent your time in studying such nonsense?"

I replied in the affirmative. "Every minute," continued M. Krempe with warmth, "every instant that you have wasted on those books is utterly and entirely lost. You have burdened your memory with exploded systems and useless names. Good God! In what desert land have you lived, where no one was kind enough to inform you that these fancies which you have so greedily imbibed are a thousand years old and as musty as they are ancient? I little expected, in this enlightened and scientific age, to find a disciple of Albertus Magnus and Paracelsus. My dear sir, you must begin your studies entirely anew."

So saying, he stepped aside and wrote down a list of several books treating of natural philosophy which he desired me to procure, and dismissed me after mentioning that in the beginning of the following week he intended to commence a course of lectures upon natural philosophy in its general relations, and that M. Waldman, a fellow professor, would lecture upon chemistry the alternate days that he omitted.

I returned home, not disappointed, for I have said that I had long considered those authors useless whom the professor reprobated; but I returned not at all the more inclined to recur to these studies in any shape. M. Krempe was a little squat man with a gruff voice and a repulsive countenance; the teacher, therefore, did not prepossess me in favour of his pursuits. In rather a too philosophical and connected a strain, perhaps, I have given an account of the conclusions I had come to concerning them in my early years. As a child I had not been content with the results promised by the modern professors of natural science. With a confusion of ideas only to be accounted for by my extreme youth and my want of a guide on such matters, I had retrod the steps of knowledge along the paths of time and exchanged the discoveries of recent enquirers for the dreams of forgotten alchemists. Besides, I had a contempt for the uses of modern natural philosophy. It was very different when the masters of the science sought immortality and power; such views, although futile, were grand; but now the scene was changed. The ambition of the enquirer seemed to limit itself to the annihilation of those visions on which my interest in science was chiefly founded. I was required to exchange chimeras of boundless grandeur for realities of little worth.

Such were my reflections during the first two or three days of my residence at Ingolstadt, which were chiefly spent in becoming acquainted with the localities and the principal residents in my new abode. But as the ensuing week commenced, I thought of the information which

M. Krempe had given me concerning the lectures. And although I could not consent to go and hear that little conceited fellow deliver sentences out of a pulpit, I recollected what he had said of M. Waldman, whom I had never seen, as he had hitherto been out of town.

Partly from curiosity and partly from idleness, I went into the lecturing room, which M. Waldman entered shortly after. This professor was very unlike his colleague. He appeared about fifty years of age, but with an aspect expressive of the greatest benevolence; a few grey hairs covered his temples, but those at the back of his head were nearly black. His person was short but remarkably erect and his voice the sweetest I had ever heard. He began his lecture by a recapitulation of the history of chemistry and the various improvements made by different men of learning, pronouncing with fervour the names of the most distinguished discoverers. He then took a cursory view of the present state of the science and explained many of its elementary terms. After having made a few preparatory experiments, he concluded with a panegyric upon modern chemistry, the terms of which I shall never forget:

"The ancient teachers of this science," said he, "promised impossibilities and performed nothing. The modern masters promise very little; they know that metals cannot be transmuted and that the elixir of life is a chimera. But these philosophers, whose hands seem only made to dabble in dirt, and their eyes to pore over the microscope or crucible, have indeed performed miracles. They penetrate into the recesses of nature and show how she works in her hiding-places. They ascend into the heavens; they have discovered how the blood circulates, and the nature of the air we breathe. They have acquired new and almost unlimited powers; they can command the thunders of heaven, mimic the earthquake, and even mock the invisible world with its own shadows."

Such were the professor's words—rather let me say such the words of the fate—enounced to destroy me. As he went on I felt as if my soul were grappling with a palpable enemy; one by one the various keys were touched which formed the mechanism of my being; chord after chord was sounded, and soon my mind was filled with one thought, one conception, one purpose. So much has been done, exclaimed the soul of Frankenstein—more, far more, will I achieve; treading in the steps already marked, I will pioneer a new way, explore unknown powers, and unfold to the world the deepest mysteries of creation.

I closed not my eyes that night. My internal being was in a state of insurrection and turmoil; I felt that order would thence arise, but I had no power to produce it. By degrees, after the morning's dawn, sleep came. I awoke, and my yesternight's thoughts were as a dream. There only remained a resolution to return to my ancient studies and to devote myself to a science for which I believed myself to possess a natural talent. On the same day, I paid M. Waldman a visit. His manners in private were even more mild and attractive than in public, for there was a certain dignity in his mien during his lecture which in his own house was replaced by the greatest affability and kindness. I gave him pretty nearly the same account of my former pursuits as I had given to his fellow professor. He heard with attention the little narration concerning my studies and smiled at the names of Cornelius Agrippa and Paracelsus, but without the contempt that M. Krempe had exhibited. He said that "these were men to whose indefatigable zeal modern philosophers were indebted for most of the foundations of their knowledge. They had left to us, as an easier task, to give new names and arrange in connected classifications the facts which they in a great degree had been the instruments of bringing to light. The labours of men of genius, however erroneously directed, scarcely ever fail in ultimately turning to the solid advantage of mankind." I listened to his statement, which was delivered without any presumption or affectation, and then added that his lecture had removed my prejudices against modern chemists; I expressed myself in measured terms, with the modesty and deference due from a youth to his instructor, without letting escape (inexperience in life would have made me ashamed) any of the enthusiasm which stimulated my intended labours. I requested his advice concerning the books I ought to procure.

"I am happy," said M. Waldman, "to have gained a disciple; and if your application equals your ability, I have no doubt of your success. Chemistry is that branch of natural philosophy in which the greatest improvements have been and may be made; it is on that account that I have made it my peculiar study; but at the same time, I have not neglected the other branches of science. A man would make but a very sorry chemist if he attended to that department of human knowledge alone. If your wish is to become really a man of science and not merely a petty experimentalist, I should advise you to apply to every branch of natural philosophy, including mathematics."

He then took me into his laboratory and explained to me the uses of his various machines, instructing me as to what I ought to procure and promising me the use of his own when I should have advanced far enough in the science not to derange their mechanism. He also gave me the list of books which I had requested, and I took my leave.

Thus ended a day memorable to me: it decided my future destiny.

CHAPTER IV

From this day natural philosophy, and particularly chemistry, in the most comprehensive sense of the term, became nearly my sole occupation. I read with ardour those works, so full of genius and discrimination, which modern enquirers have written on these subjects. I attended the lectures and cultivated the acquaintance of the men of science of the university, and I found even in M. Krempe a great deal of sound sense and real information, combined, it is true, with a repulsive physiognomy and manners, but not on that account the less valuable. In M. Waldman I found a true friend. His gentleness was never tinged by dogmatism, and his instructions were given with an air of frankness and good nature that banished every idea of pedantry. In a thousand ways he smoothed for me the path of knowledge and made the most abstruse enquiries clear and facile to my apprehension. My application was at first fluctuating and uncertain; it gained strength as I proceeded and soon became so ardent and eager that the stars often disappeared in the light of morning whilst I was yet engaged in my laboratory.

As I applied so closely, it may be easily conceived that my progress was rapid. My ardour was indeed the astonishment of the students, and my proficiency that of the masters. Professor Krempe often asked me, with a sly smile, how Cornelius Agrippa went on, whilst M. Waldman expressed the most heartfelt exultation in my progress. Two years passed in this manner, during which I paid no visit to Geneva, but was engaged, heart and soul, in the pursuit of some discoveries which I hoped to make. None but those who have experienced them can conceive of the enticements of science. In other studies you go as far as others have gone before you, and there is nothing more to know; but in a scientific pursuit there is continual food for discovery and wonder. A mind of moderate capacity which closely pursues one study must infallibly arrive at great proficiency in that study; and I, who continually sought the attainment of one object of pursuit and was solely wrapped up in this, improved so rapidly that at the end of two years I made some discoveries in the improvement of some chemical instruments, which procured me great esteem and admiration at the university. When I had arrived at this point and had become as well acquainted with the theory and practice of natural philosophy as depended on the lessons of any of the professors at Ingolstadt, my residence there being no longer conducive to my improvements, I thought of returning to my friends and my native town, when an incident happened that protracted my stay.

One of the phenomena which had peculiarly attracted my attention was the structure of the human frame, and, indeed, any animal endued with life. Whence, I often asked myself, did the principle of life proceed? It was a bold question, and one which has ever been considered as a mystery; yet with how many things are we upon the brink of becoming acquainted, if cowardice or carelessness did not restrain our enquiries. I revolved these circumstances in my mind and determined thenceforth to apply myself more particularly to those branches of natural philosophy which relate to physiology. Unless I had been animated by an almost supernatural enthusiasm, my application to this study would have been irksome and almost intolerable. To examine the causes of life, we must first have recourse to death. I became acquainted with the science of anatomy, but this was not sufficient; I must also observe the natural decay and corruption of the human body. In my education my father had taken the greatest precautions that my mind should be impressed with no supernatural horrors. I do not ever remember to have trembled at a tale of superstition or to have feared the apparition of a spirit. Darkness had no effect upon my fancy, and a churchyard was to me merely the receptacle of bodies deprived of life, which, from being the seat of beauty and strength, had become food for the worm. Now I was led to examine the cause and progress of this decay and forced to spend days and nights in vaults and charnel-houses. My attention was fixed upon every object the most insupportable to the delicacy of the human feelings. I saw how the fine form of man was degraded and wasted; I beheld the corruption of death succeed to the blooming cheek of life; I saw how the worm inherited the wonders of the eye and brain. I paused, examining and analysing all the minutiae of causation, as exemplified in the change from life to death, and death to life, until from the midst of this darkness a sudden light broke in upon me—a light so brilliant and wondrous, yet so simple, that while I became dizzy with the immensity of the prospect which it illustrated, I was surprised that among so many men of genius who had directed their enquiries towards the same science, that I alone should be reserved to discover so astonishing a secret.

Remember, I am not recording the vision of a madman. The sun does not more certainly shine in the heavens than that which I now affirm is true. Some miracle might have produced it, yet the stages of the discovery were distinct and probable. After days and nights of incredible labour and fatigue, I succeeded in discovering the cause of generation and life; nay, more, I became myself capable of bestowing animation upon lifeless matter.

The astonishment which I had at first experienced on this discovery soon gave place to delight and rapture. After so much time spent in painful labour, to arrive at once at the summit of my desires was the most gratifying consummation of my toils. But this discovery was so great and overwhelming that all the steps by which I had been progressively led to it were obliterated, and I beheld only the result. What had been the study and desire of the wisest men since the creation of the world was now within my grasp. Not that, like a magic scene, it all opened upon me at once: the information I had obtained was of a nature rather to direct my endeavours so soon as I should point them towards the object of my search than to exhibit that object already accomplished. I was like the Arabian who had been buried with the dead and found a passage to life, aided only by one glimmering and seemingly ineffectual light.

I see by your eagerness and the wonder and hope which your eyes express, my friend, that you expect to be informed of the secret with which I am acquainted; that cannot be; listen patiently until the end of my story, and you will easily perceive why I am reserved upon that subject. I will not lead you on, unguarded and ardent as I then was, to your destruction and infallible misery. Learn from me, if not by my precepts, at least by my example, how dangerous is the acquirement of knowledge and how much happier that man is who believes his native town to be the world, than he who aspires to become greater than his nature will allow.

When I found so astonishing a power placed within my hands, I hesitated a long time concerning the manner in which I should employ it. Although I possessed the capacity of bestowing animation, yet to prepare a frame for the reception of it, with all its intricacies of fibres, muscles, and veins, still remained a work of inconceivable difficulty and labour. I doubted at first whether I should attempt the creation of a being like myself, or one of simpler organization; but my imagination was too much exalted by my first success to permit me to doubt of my ability to give life to an animal as complex and wonderful as man. The materials at present within my command hardly appeared adequate to so arduous an undertaking, but I doubted not that I should ultimately succeed. I prepared myself for a multitude of reverses; my operations might be incessantly baffled, and at last my work be imperfect, yet when I considered the improvement which every day takes place in science and mechanics, I was encouraged to hope my present attempts would at least lay the foundations of future success. Nor could I consider the magnitude and complexity of my plan as any argument of its impracticability. It was with these feelings that I began the creation of a human being. As the minuteness of the parts formed a great hindrance to my speed, I resolved, contrary to my first intention, to make the being of a gigantic stature, that is to say, about eight feet in height, and proportionably large. After having formed this determination and having spent some months in successfully collecting and arranging my materials, I began.

No one can conceive the variety of feelings which bore me onwards, like a hurricane, in the first enthusiasm of success. Life and death appeared to me ideal bounds, which I should first break through, and pour a torrent of light into our dark world. A new species would bless me as its creator and source; many happy and excellent natures would owe their being to me. No father could claim the gratitude of his child so completely as I should deserve theirs. Pursuing these reflections, I thought that if I could bestow animation upon lifeless matter, I might in process of time (although I now found it impossible) renew life where death had apparently devoted the body to corruption.

These thoughts supported my spirits, while I pursued my undertaking with unremitting ardour. My cheek had grown pale with study, and my person had become emaciated with confinement. Sometimes, on the very brink of certainty, I failed; yet still I clung to the hope which the next day or the next hour might realize. One secret which I alone possessed was the hope to which I had dedicated myself; and the moon gazed on my midnight labours, while, with unrelaxed and breathless eagerness, I pursued nature to her hiding-places. Who shall conceive the horrors of my secret toil as I dabbled among the unhallowed damps of the grave or tortured the living animal to animate the lifeless clay? My limbs now tremble, and my eyes swim with the remembrance;

but then a resistless and almost frantic impulse urged me forward; I seemed to have lost all soul or sensation but for this one pursuit. It was indeed but a passing trance, that only made me feel with renewed acuteness so soon as, the unnatural stimulus ceasing to operate, I had returned to my old habits. I collected bones from charnel-houses and disturbed, with profane fingers, the tremendous secrets of the human frame. In a solitary chamber, or rather cell, at the top of the house, and separated from all the other apartments by a gallery and staircase, I kept my workshop of filthy creation; my eyeballs were starting from their sockets in attending to the details of my employment. The dissecting room and the slaughter-house furnished many of my materials; and often did my human nature turn with loathing from my occupation, whilst, still urged on by an eagerness which perpetually increased, I brought my work near to a conclusion.

The summer months passed while I was thus engaged, heart and soul, in one pursuit. It was a most beautiful season; never did the fields bestow a more plentiful harvest or the vines yield a more luxuriant vintage, but my eyes were insensible to the charms of nature. And the same feelings which made me neglect the scenes around me caused me also to forget those friends who were so many miles absent, and whom I had not seen for so long a time. I knew my silence disquieted them, and I well remembered the words of my father: "I know that while you are pleased with yourself you will think of us with affection, and we shall hear regularly from you. You must pardon me if I regard any interruption in your correspondence as a proof that your other duties are equally neglected."

I knew well therefore what would be my father's feelings, but I could not tear my thoughts from my employment, loathsome in itself, but which had taken an irresistible hold of my imagination. I wished, as it were, to procrastinate all that related to my feelings of affection until the great object, which swallowed up every habit of my nature, should be completed.

I then thought that my father would be unjust if he ascribed my neglect to vice or faultiness on my part, but I am now convinced that he was justified in conceiving that I should not be altogether free from blame. A human being in perfection ought always to preserve a calm and peaceful mind and never to allow passion or a transitory desire to disturb his tranquillity. I do not think that the pursuit of knowledge is an exception to this rule. If the study to which you apply yourself has a tendency to weaken your affections and to destroy your taste for those simple pleasures in which no alloy can possibly mix, then that study is certainly unlawful, that is to say, not befitting the human mind. If this rule were always observed; if no man allowed any pursuit whatsoever to interfere with the tranquillity of his domestic affections, Greece had not been enslaved, Caesar would have spared his country, America would have been discovered more gradually, and the empires of Mexico and Peru had not been destroyed.

But I forget that I am moralizing in the most interesting part of my tale, and your looks remind me to proceed.

My father made no reproach in his letters and only took notice of my silence by enquiring into my occupations more particularly than before. Winter, spring, and summer passed away during my labours; but I did not watch the blossom or the expanding leaves—sights which before always yielded me supreme delight—so deeply was I engrossed in my occupation. The leaves of that year had withered before my work drew near to a close, and now every day showed me more plainly how well I had succeeded. But my enthusiasm was checked by my anxiety, and I appeared rather like one doomed by slavery to toil in the mines, or any other unwholesome trade than an artist occupied by his favourite employment. Every night I was oppressed by a slow fever, and I became nervous to a most painful degree; the fall of a leaf startled me, and I shunned my fellow creatures as if I had been guilty of a crime. Sometimes I grew alarmed at the wreck I perceived that I had become; the energy of my purpose alone sustained me: my labours would soon end, and I believed that exercise and amusement would then drive away incipient disease; and I promised myself both of these when my creation should be complete.

CHAPTER V

It was on a dreary night of November that I beheld the accomplishment of my toils. With an anxiety that almost amounted to agony, I collected the instruments of life around me, that I might infuse a spark of being into the lifeless thing that lay at my feet. It was already one in the morning; the rain pattered dismally against the panes, and my candle was nearly burnt out, when, by the glimmer of the half-extinguished light, I saw the dull yellow eye of the creature open; it breathed hard, and a convulsive motion agitated its limbs.

How can I describe my emotions at this catastrophe, or how delineate the wretch whom with such infinite pains and care I had endeavoured to form? His limbs were in proportion, and I had selected his features as beautiful. Beautiful! Great God! His yellow skin scarcely covered the work of muscles and arteries beneath; his hair was of a lustrous black, and flowing; his teeth of a pearly whiteness; but these luxuriances only formed a more horrid contrast with his watery eyes, that seemed almost of the same colour as the dun-white sockets in which they were set, his shrivelled complexion and straight black lips.

The different accidents of life are not so changeable as the feelings of human nature. I had worked hard for nearly two years, for the sole purpose of infusing life into an inanimate body. For this I had deprived myself of rest and health. I had desired it with an ardour that far exceeded moderation; but now that I had finished, the beauty of the dream vanished, and breathless horror and disgust filled my heart. Unable to endure the aspect of the being I had created, I rushed out of the room and continued a long time traversing my bedchamber, unable to compose my mind to sleep. At length lassitude succeeded to the tumult I had before endured, and I threw myself on the bed in my clothes, endeavouring to seek a few moments of forgetfulness. But it was in vain; I slept, indeed, but I was disturbed by the wildest dreams. I thought I saw Elizabeth, in the bloom of health, walking in the streets of Ingolstadt. Delighted and surprised, I embraced her, but as I imprinted the first kiss on her lips, they became livid with the hue of death; her features appeared to change, and I thought that I held the corpse of my dead mother in my arms; a shroud enveloped her form, and I saw the grave-worms crawling in the folds of the flannel. I started from my sleep with horror; a cold dew covered my forehead, my teeth chattered, and every limb became convulsed; when, by the dim and yellow light of the moon, as it forced its way through the window shutters, I beheld the wretch—the miserable monster whom I had created. He held up the curtain of the bed; and his eyes, if eyes they may be called, were fixed on me. His jaws opened, and he muttered some inarticulate sounds, while a grin wrinkled his cheeks. He might have spoken, but I did not hear; one hand was stretched out, seemingly to detain me, but I escaped and rushed downstairs. I took refuge in the courtyard belonging to the house which I inhabited, where I remained during the rest of the night, walking up and down in the greatest agitation, listening attentively, catching and fearing each sound as if it were to announce the approach of the demoniacal corpse to which I had so miserably given life.

Oh! No mortal could support the horror of that countenance. A mummy again endued with animation could not be so hideous as that wretch. I had gazed on him while unfinished; he was ugly then, but when those muscles and joints were rendered capable of motion, it became a thing such as even Dante could not have conceived.

I passed the night wretchedly. Sometimes my pulse beat so quickly and hardly that I felt the palpitation of every artery; at others, I nearly sank to the ground through languor and extreme weakness. Mingled with this horror, I felt the bitterness of disappointment; dreams that had been my food and pleasant rest for so long a space were now become a hell to me; and the change was so rapid, the overthrow so complete!

Morning, dismal and wet, at length dawned and discovered to my sleepless and aching eyes the church of Ingolstadt, its white steeple and clock, which indicated the sixth hour. The porter opened the gates of the court, which had that night been my asylum, and I issued into the streets, pacing them with quick steps, as if I sought to avoid the wretch whom I feared every turning of the street would present to my view. I did not dare return to the apartment which I inhabited, but felt impelled to hurry on, although drenched by the rain which poured from a black and comfortless sky.

I continued walking in this manner for some time, endeavouring by bodily exercise to ease the load that weighed upon my mind. I traversed the streets without any clear conception of where I was or what I was doing. My heart palpitated in the sickness of fear, and I hurried on with irregular steps, not daring to look about me:

> Like one who, on a lonely road,
> Doth walk in fear and dread,
> And, having once turned round, walks on,
> And turns no more his head;
> Because he knows a frightful fiend
> Doth close behind him tread.*

Continuing thus, I came at length opposite to the inn at which the various diligences and carriages usually stopped. Here I paused, I knew not why; but I remained some minutes with my eyes fixed on a coach that was coming towards me from the other end of the street. As it drew nearer I observed that it was the Swiss diligence; it stopped just where I was standing, and on the door being opened, I perceived Henry Clerval, who, on seeing me, instantly sprung out. "My dear Frankenstein," exclaimed he, "how glad I am to see you! How fortunate that you should be here at the very moment of my alighting!"

Nothing could equal my delight on seeing Clerval; his presence brought back to my thoughts my father, Elizabeth, and all those scenes of home so dear to my recollection. I grasped his hand, and in a moment forgot my horror and misfortune; I felt suddenly, and for the first time during many months, calm and serene joy. I welcomed my friend, therefore, in the most cordial manner, and we walked towards my college. Clerval continued talking for some time about our mutual friends and his own good fortune in being permitted to come to Ingolstadt. "You may easily believe," said he, "how great was the difficulty to persuade my father that all necessary knowledge was not comprised in the noble art of book-keeping; and, indeed, I believe I left him incredulous to the last, for his constant answer to my unwearied entreaties was the same as that of the Dutch schoolmaster in *The Vicar of Wakefield*: 'I have ten thousand florins a year without Greek, I eat heartily without Greek.' But his affection for me at length overcame his dislike of learning, and he has permitted me to undertake a voyage of discovery to the land of knowledge."

* Coleridge's *Ancient Mariner*

"It gives me the greatest delight to see you; but tell me how you left my father, brothers, and Elizabeth."

"Very well, and very happy, only a little uneasy that they hear from you so seldom. By the by, I mean to lecture you a little upon their account myself. But, my dear Frankenstein," continued he, stopping short and gazing full in my face, "I did not before remark how very ill you appear; so thin and pale; you look as if you had been watching for several nights."

"You have guessed right; I have lately been so deeply engaged in one occupation that I have not allowed myself sufficient rest, as you see; but I hope, I sincerely hope, that all these employments are now at an end and that I am at length free."

I trembled excessively; I could not endure to think of, and far less to allude to, the occurrences of the preceding night. I walked with a quick pace, and we soon arrived at my college. I then reflected, and the thought made me shiver, that the creature whom I had left in my apartment might still be there, alive and walking about. I dreaded to behold this monster, but I feared still more that Henry should see him. Entreating him, therefore, to remain a few minutes at the bottom of the stairs, I darted up towards my own room. My hand was already on the lock of the door before I recollected myself. I then paused, and a cold shivering came over me. I threw the door forcibly open, as children are accustomed to do when they expect a spectre to stand in waiting for them on the other side; but nothing appeared. I stepped fearfully in: the apartment was empty, and my bedroom was also freed from its hideous guest. I could hardly believe that so great a good fortune could have befallen me, but when I became assured that my enemy had indeed fled, I clapped my hands for joy and ran down to Clerval.

We ascended into my room, and the servant presently brought breakfast; but I was unable to contain myself. It was not joy only that possessed me; I felt my flesh tingle with excess of sensitiveness, and my pulse beat rapidly. I was unable to remain for a single instant in the same place; I jumped over the chairs, clapped my hands, and laughed aloud. Clerval at first attributed my unusual spirits to joy on his arrival, but when he observed me more attentively, he saw a wildness in my eyes for which he could not account, and my loud, unrestrained, heartless laughter frightened and astonished him.

"My dear Victor," cried he, "what, for God's sake, is the matter?

Do not laugh in that manner. How ill you are! What is the cause of all this?"

"Do not ask me," cried I, putting my hands before my eyes, for I thought I saw the dreaded spectre glide into the room; "*he* can tell. Oh, save me! Save me!" I imagined that the monster seized me; I struggled furiously and fell down in a fit.

Poor Clerval! What must have been his feelings? A meeting, which he anticipated with such joy, so strangely turned to bitterness. But I was not the witness of his grief, for I was lifeless and did not recover my senses for a long, long time.

This was the commencement of a nervous fever, which confined me for several months. During all that time Henry was my only nurse. I afterwards learned that, knowing my father's advanced age and unfitness for so long a journey, and how wretched my sickness would make Elizabeth, he spared them this grief by concealing the extent of my disorder. He knew that I could not have a more kind and attentive nurse than himself; and, firm in the hope he felt of my recovery, he did not doubt that, instead of doing harm, he performed the kindest action that he could towards them.

But I was in reality very ill, and surely nothing but the unbounded and unremitting attentions of my friend could have restored me to life. The form of the monster on whom I had bestowed existence was forever before my eyes, and I raved incessantly concerning him. Doubtless my words surprised Henry; he at first believed them to be the wanderings of my disturbed imagination, but the pertinacity with which I continually recurred to the same subject persuaded him that my disorder indeed owed its origin to some uncommon and terrible event.

By very slow degrees, and with frequent relapses that alarmed and grieved my friend, I recovered. I remember the first time I became capable of observing outward objects with any kind of pleasure, I perceived that the fallen leaves had disappeared and that the young buds were shooting forth from the trees that shaded my window. It was a divine spring, and the season contributed greatly to my convalescence. I felt also sentiments of joy and affection revive in my bosom; my gloom disappeared, and in a short time I became as cheerful as before I was attacked by the fatal passion.

"Dearest Clerval," exclaimed I, "how kind, how very good you are to me. This whole winter, instead of being spent in study, as you promised yourself, has been consumed in my sick room. How shall I ever repay you? I feel the greatest remorse for the disappointment of which I have been the occasion, but you will forgive me."

"You will repay me entirely if you do not discompose yourself, but get well as fast as you can; and since you appear in such good spirits, I may speak to you on one subject, may I not?"

I trembled. One subject! What could it be? Could he allude to an object on whom I dared not even think?

"Compose yourself," said Clerval, who observed my change of colour, "I will not mention it if it agitates you; but your father and cousin would be very happy if they received a letter from you in your own handwriting. They hardly know how ill you have been and are uneasy at your long silence."

"Is that all, my dear Henry? How could you suppose that my first thought would not fly towards those dear, dear friends whom I love and who are so deserving of my love?"

"If this is your present temper, my friend, you will perhaps be glad to see a letter that has been lying here some days for you; it is from your cousin, I believe."

CHAPTER VI

Clerval then put the following letter into my hands. It was from my own Elizabeth:

MY DEAREST COUSIN,

You have been ill, very ill, and even the constant letters of dear kind Henry are not sufficient to reassure me on your account. You are forbidden to write—to hold a pen; yet one word from you, dear Victor, is necessary to calm our apprehensions. For a long time I have thought that each post would bring this line, and my persuasions have restrained my uncle from undertaking a journey to Ingolstadt. I have prevented his encountering the inconveniences and perhaps dangers of so long a journey, yet how often have I regretted not being able to perform it myself! I figure to myself that the task of attending on your sickbed has devolved on some mercenary old nurse, who could never guess your wishes nor minister to them with the care and affection of your poor cousin. Yet that is over now: Clerval writes that indeed you are getting better. I eagerly hope that you will confirm this intelligence soon in your own handwriting.

Get well—and return to us. You will find a happy, cheerful home and friends who love you dearly. Your father's health is vigorous, and he asks but to see you, but to be assured that you are well; and not a care will ever cloud his benevolent countenance. How pleased you would be to remark the improvement of our Ernest! He is now sixteen and full of activity and spirit. He is desirous to be a true Swiss and to enter into foreign service, but we cannot part with him, at least until his elder brother returns to us. My uncle is not pleased with the idea of a military career in a distant country, but Ernest never had your powers of application. He looks upon study as an odious fetter; his time is spent in the open air, climbing the hills or rowing on the lake. I fear that he will become an idler unless we yield the point and permit him to enter on the profession which he has selected.

Little alteration, except the growth of our dear children, has taken place since you left us. The blue lake and snow-clad mountains—they never change; and I think our placid home and our contented hearts are regulated by the same immutable laws. My trifling occupations take up my time and amuse me, and I am rewarded for any exertions by seeing none but happy, kind faces around me. Since you left us, but one change has taken place in our little household. Do you remember on what occasion Justine Moritz entered our family? Probably you do not; I will relate her history, therefore in a few words. Madame Moritz, her mother, was a widow with four children, of whom Justine was the third. This girl had always been the favourite of her father, but through a strange perversity, her mother could not endure her, and after the death of M. Moritz, treated her very ill. My aunt observed this, and when Justine was twelve years of age, prevailed on her mother to allow her to live at our house. The republican institutions of our country have produced simpler and happier manners than those which prevail in the great monarchies that surround it. Hence there is less distinction between the several classes of its inhabitants; and the lower orders, being neither so poor nor so despised, their manners are more refined and moral. A servant in Geneva does not mean the same thing as a servant in France and England. Justine, thus received in our family, learned the duties of a servant, a condition which, in our fortunate country, does not include the idea of ignorance and a sacrifice of the dignity of a human being.

Justine, you may remember, was a great favourite of yours; and I recollect you once remarked that if you were in an ill humour, one glance from Justine could dissipate it, for the same reason that Ariosto gives concerning the beauty of Angelica—she looked so frank-hearted and happy. My aunt conceived a great attachment for her, by which she was induced to give her an education superior to that which she had at first intended. This benefit was fully repaid; Justine was the most grateful little creature in the world: I do not mean that she made any professions; I never heard one pass her lips, but you could see by her eyes that she almost adored her protectress. Although her disposition was gay and in many respects inconsiderate, yet she paid the greatest attention to every gesture of my aunt. She thought her the model of all excellence and endeavoured to imitate her phraseology and manners, so that even now she often reminds me of her.

When my dearest aunt died, everyone was too much occupied in their own grief to notice poor Justine, who had attended her during her illness with the most anxious affection. Poor Justine was very ill; but other trials were reserved for her.

One by one, her brothers and sister died; and her mother, with the exception of her neglected daughter, was left childless. The conscience of the woman was troubled; she began to think that the deaths of her favourites was a judgement from heaven to chastise her partiality. She was a Roman Catholic; and I believe her confessor confirmed the idea which she had conceived. Accordingly, a few months after your departure for Ingolstadt, Justine was called home by her repentant mother. Poor girl! She wept when she quitted our house; she was much altered since the death of my aunt; grief had given softness and a winning mildness to her manners, which had before been remarkable for vivacity. Nor was her residence at her mother's house of a nature to restore her gaiety. The poor woman was very vacillating in her repentance. She sometimes begged Justine to forgive her unkindness, but much oftener accused her of having caused the deaths of her brothers and sister. Perpetual fretting at length threw Madame Moritz into a decline, which at first increased her irritability, but she is now at peace forever. She died on the first approach of cold weather, at the beginning of this last winter. Justine has just returned to us; and I assure you I love her tenderly. She is very clever and gentle, and extremely pretty; as I mentioned before, her mien and her expression continually remind me of my dear aunt.

I must say also a few words to you, my dear cousin, of little darling William. I wish you could see him; he is very tall of his age, with sweet laughing blue eyes, dark eyelashes, and curling hair. When he smiles, two little dimples appear on each cheek, which are rosy with health. He has already had one or two little *wives*, but Louisa Biron is his favourite, a pretty little girl of five years of age.

Now, dear Victor, I dare say you wish to be indulged in a little gossip concerning the good people of Geneva. The pretty Miss Mansfield has already received the congratulatory visits on her approaching marriage with a young Englishman, John Melbourne, Esq. Her ugly sister, Manon, married M. Duvillard, the rich banker, last autumn. Your favourite school-fellow, Louis Manoir, has suffered several misfortunes since the departure of Clerval from Geneva. But he has already recovered his spirits, and is reported to be on the point of marrying a lively pretty Frenchwoman, Madame Tavernier. She is a widow, and much older than Manoir; but she is very much admired, and a favourite with everybody.

I have written myself into better spirits, dear cousin; but my anxiety returns upon me as I conclude. Write, dearest Victor—one line—one word will be a blessing to us. Ten thousand thanks to Henry for his kindness, his affection, and his many letters; we are sincerely grateful. Adieu, my cousin! Take care of yourself; and, I entreat you, write!

Elizabeth Lavenza.
Geneva, March 18th, 17—.

"Dear, dear Elizabeth!" I exclaimed, when I had read her letter: "I will write instantly and relieve them from the anxiety they must feel." I wrote, and this exertion greatly fatigued me; but my convalescence had commenced, and proceeded regularly. In another fortnight I was able to leave my chamber.

One of my first duties on my recovery was to introduce Clerval to the several professors of the university. In doing this, I underwent a kind of rough usage, ill befitting the wounds that my mind had sustained. Ever since the fatal night, the end of my labours, and the beginning of my misfortunes, I had conceived a violent antipathy even to the name of natural philosophy. When I was otherwise quite restored to health, the sight of a chemical instrument would renew all the agony of my nervous symptoms. Henry saw this, and had removed all my apparatus from my view. He had also changed my apartment; for he perceived that I had acquired a dislike for the room which had previously been my laboratory. But these cares of Clerval were made of no avail when I visited the professors. M. Waldman inflicted torture when he praised, with kindness and warmth, the astonishing progress I had made in the sciences. He soon perceived that I disliked the subject; but not guessing the real cause, he attributed my feelings to modesty, and changed the subject from my improvement to the science itself, with a desire, as I evidently saw, of drawing me out. What could I do? He meant to please, and he tormented me. I felt as if he had placed carefully, one by one, in my view those instruments which were to be afterwards used in putting me to a slow and cruel death. I writhed under his words, yet dared not exhibit the pain I felt. Clerval, whose eyes and feelings were always quick in discerning the sensations of others, declined the subject, alleging, in excuse, his total ignorance; and the conversation took a more general turn. I thanked my friend from my heart, but I did not speak. I saw plainly that he was surprised, but he never attempted to draw my secret from me; and although I loved him with a mixture of affection and reverence that knew no bounds, yet I could never persuade myself to confide in him that event which was so often present to my recollection, but which I feared the detail to another would only impress more deeply.

M. Krempe was not equally docile; and in my condition at that time, of almost insupportable sensitiveness, his harsh blunt encomiums gave me even more pain than the benevolent approbation of M. Waldman. "D—n the fellow!" cried he. "Why, M. Clerval, I assure you he has outstript us all. Ay, stare if you please; but it is nevertheless true. A youngster who, but a few years ago, believed in Cornelius Agrippa as firmly as in the gospel, has now set himself at the head of the university; and if he is not soon pulled down, we shall all be out of countenance. Ay, ay," continued he, observing my face expressive of suffering, "M. Frankenstein is modest; an excellent quality in a young man. Young men should be diffident of themselves, you know, M. Clerval: I was myself when young, but that wears out in a very short time."

M. Krempe had now commenced an eulogy on himself, which happily turned the conversation from a subject that was so annoying to me.

Clerval had never sympathised in my tastes for natural science; and his literary pursuits differed wholly from those which had occupied me. He came to the university with the design of making himself complete master of the Oriental languages, and thus he should open a field for the plan of life he had marked out for himself. Resolved to pursue no inglorious career, he turned his eyes toward the East, as affording scope for his spirit of enterprise. The Persian, Arabic, and Sanskrit languages engaged his attention, and I was easily induced to enter on the same studies. Idleness had ever been irksome to me, and now that I wished to fly from reflection, and hated my former studies, I felt great relief in being the fellow-pupil with my friend, and found not only instruction but consolation in the works of the Orientalists. I did not, like him, attempt a critical knowledge of their dialects, for I did not contemplate making any other use of them than temporary amusement. I read merely to understand their meaning, and they well repaid my labours. Their melancholy is soothing, and their joy elevating, to a degree I never experienced in studying the authors of any other country. When you read their writings, life appears to consist in a warm sun and a garden of roses, in the smiles and frowns of a fair enemy, and the fire that consumes your own heart. How different from the manly and heroical poetry of Greece and Rome!

Summer passed away in these occupations, and my return to Geneva was fixed for the latter end of autumn; but being delayed by several accidents, winter and snow arrived, the roads were deemed impassable, and my journey was retarded until the ensuing spring. I felt this delay very bitterly; for I longed to see my native town and my beloved friends. My return had only been delayed so long from an unwillingness to leave Clerval in a strange place, before he had become acquainted with any of its inhabitants. The winter, however, was spent cheerfully; and although the spring was uncommonly late, when it came its beauty compensated for its dilatoriness.

The month of May had already commenced, and I expected the letter daily which was to fix the date of my departure, when Henry proposed a pedestrian tour in the environs of Ingolstadt, that I might bid a personal farewell to the country I had so long inhabited. I acceded with pleasure to this proposition: I was fond of exercise, and Clerval had always been my favourite companion in the ramble of this nature that I had taken among the scenes of my native country.

We passed a fortnight in these perambulations: my health and spirits had long been restored, and they gained additional strength from the salubrious air I breathed, the natural incidents of our progress, and the conversation of my friend. Study had before secluded me from the intercourse of my fellow-creatures, and rendered me unsocial; but Clerval called forth the better feelings of my heart; he again taught me to love the aspect of nature, and the cheerful faces of children. Excellent friend! How sincerely you did love me, and endeavour to elevate my mind until it was on a level with your own. A selfish pursuit had cramped and narrowed me, until your gentleness and affection warmed and opened my senses; I became the same happy creature who, a few years ago, loved and beloved by all, had no sorrow or care. When happy, inanimate nature had the power of bestowing on me the most delightful sensations. A serene sky and verdant fields filled me with ecstasy. The present season was indeed divine; the flowers of spring bloomed in the hedges, while those of summer were already in bud. I was undisturbed by thoughts which during the preceding year had pressed upon me, notwithstanding my endeavours to throw them off, with an invincible burden.

Henry rejoiced in my gaiety, and sincerely sympathised in my feelings: he exerted himself to amuse me, while he expressed the sensations that filled his soul. The resources of his mind on this occasion were truly astonishing: his conversation was full of imagination; and very often, in imitation of the Persian and Arabic writers, he invented tales of wonderful fancy and passion. At other times he repeated my favourite poems, or drew me out into arguments, which he supported with great ingenuity.

We returned to our college on a Sunday afternoon: the peasants were dancing, and everyone we met appeared gay and happy. My own spirits were high, and I bounded along with feelings of unbridled joy and hilarity.

CHAPTER VII

On my return, I found the following letter from my father:

MY DEAR VICTOR,

You have probably waited impatiently for a letter to fix the date of your return to us; and I was at first tempted to write only a few lines, merely mentioning the day on which I should expect you. But that would be a cruel kindness, and I dare not do it. What would be your surprise, my son, when you expected a happy and glad welcome, to behold, on the contrary, tears and wretchedness? And how, Victor, can I relate our misfortune? Absence cannot have rendered you callous to our joys and griefs; and how shall I inflict pain on my long-absent son? I wish to prepare you for the woeful news, but I know it is impossible; even now your eye skims over the page to seek the words which are to convey to you the horrible tidings.

William is dead! That sweet child, whose smiles delighted and warmed my heart, who was so gentle, yet so gay! Victor, he is murdered!

I will not attempt to console you; but will simply relate the circumstances of the transaction.

Last Thursday (May 7th), I, my niece, and your two brothers went to walk in Plainpalais. The evening was warm and serene, and we prolonged our walk farther than usual. It was already dusk before we thought of returning; and then we discovered that William and Ernest, who had gone on before, were not to be found. We accordingly rested on a seat until they should return. Presently Ernest came, and enquired if we had seen his brother; he said that he had been playing with him, that William had run away to hide himself, and that he vainly sought for him, and afterwards waited for a long time, but that he did not return.

This account rather alarmed us, and we continued to search for him until night fell, when Elizabeth conjectured that he might have returned to the house. He was not there. We returned again, with torches; for I could not rest when I thought that my sweet boy had lost himself, and was exposed to all the damps and dews of night; Elizabeth also suffered extreme anguish. About five in the morning I discovered my lovely boy, whom the night before I had seen blooming and active in health, stretched on the grass livid and motionless; the print of the murderer's finger was on his neck.

He was conveyed home, and the anguish that was visible in my countenance betrayed the secret to Elizabeth. She was very earnest to see the corpse. At first I attempted to prevent her but she persisted, and entering the room where it lay, hastily examined the neck of the victim, and clasping her hands exclaimed, "O God! I have murdered my darling child!"

She fainted, and was restored with extreme difficulty. When she again lived, it was only to weep and sigh. She told me that that same evening William had teased her to let him wear a very valuable miniature that she possessed of your mother. This picture is gone, and was doubtless the temptation which urged the murderer to the deed. We have no trace of him at present, although our exertions to discover him are unremitted; but they will not restore my beloved William!

Come, dearest Victor; you alone can console Elizabeth. She weeps continually, and accuses herself unjustly as the cause of his death; her words pierce my heart. We are all unhappy; but will not that be an additional motive for you, my son, to return and be our comforter? Your dear mother! Alas, Victor! I now say, Thank God she did not live to witness the cruel, miserable death of her youngest darling!

Come, Victor; not brooding thoughts of vengeance against the assassin, but with feelings of peace and gentleness that will heal, instead of festering, the wounds of our minds. Enter the house of mourning, my friend, but with kindness and affection for those who love you, and not with hatred for your enemies.

Your affectionate and afflicted father,
ALPHONSE FRANKENSTEIN.
Geneva, May 12th, 17—.

Clerval, who had watched my countenance as I read this letter, was surprised to observe the despair that succeeded the joy I at first expressed on receiving news from my friends. I threw the letter on the table, and covered my face with my hands.

"My dear Frankenstein," exclaimed Henry, when he perceived me weep with bitterness, "are you always to be unhappy? My dear friend, what has happened?"

I motioned him to take up the letter, while I walked up and down the room in the extremest agitation. Tears also gushed from the eyes of Clerval, as he read the account of my misfortune.

"I can offer you no consolation, my friend," said he; "your disaster is irreparable. What do you intend to do?"

"To go instantly to Geneva: come with me, Henry, to order the horses."

During our walk, Clerval endeavoured to say a few words of consolation; he could only express his heartfelt sympathy. "Poor William!" said he. "Dear lovely child, he now sleeps with his angel mother! Who that had seen him bright and joyous in his young beauty, but must weep over his untimely loss! To die so miserably; to feel the murderer's grasp! How much more a murderer that could destroy radiant innocence! Poor little fellow! One only consolation have we; his friends mourn and weep, but he is at rest. The pang is over, his sufferings are at an end forever. A sod covers his gentle form, and he knows no pain. He can no longer be a subject for pity; we must reserve that for his miserable survivors."

Clerval spoke thus as we hurried through the streets; the words impressed themselves on my mind and I remembered them afterwards in solitude. But now, as soon as the horses arrived, I hurried into a cabriolet, and bade farewell to my friend.

My journey was very melancholy. At first I wished to hurry on, for I longed to console and sympathise with my loved and sorrowing friends; but when I drew near my native town, I slackened my progress. I could hardly sustain the multitude of feelings that crowded into my mind. I passed through scenes familiar to my youth, but which I had not seen for nearly six years. How altered everything might be during that time! One sudden and desolating change had taken place; but a thousand little circumstances might have by degrees worked other alterations, which, although they were done more tranquilly, might not be the less decisive.

Fear overcame me; I dared no advance, dreading a thousand nameless evils that made me tremble, although I was unable to define them.

I remained two days at Lausanne, in this painful state of mind. I contemplated the lake: the waters were placid; all around was calm; and the snowy mountains, "the palaces of nature," were not changed. By degrees the calm and heavenly scene restored me, and I continued my journey towards Geneva.

The road ran by the side of the lake, which became narrower as I approached my native town. I discovered more distinctly the black sides of Jura, and the bright summit of Mont Blanc. I wept like a child. "Dear mountains! My own beautiful lake! How do you welcome your wanderer? Your summits are clear; the sky and lake are blue and placid. Is this to prognosticate peace, or to mock at my unhappiness?"

I fear, my friend, that I shall render myself tedious by dwelling on these preliminary circumstances; but they were days of comparative happiness, and I think of them with pleasure. My country, my beloved country! Who but a native can tell the delight I took in again beholding thy streams, thy mountains, and, more than all, thy lovely lake!

Yet, as I drew nearer home, grief and fear again overcame me. Night also closed around; and when I could hardly see the dark mountains, I felt still more gloomily. The picture appeared a vast and dim scene of evil, and I foresaw obscurely that I was destined to become the most wretched of human beings. Alas! I prophesied truly, and failed only in one single circumstance, that in all the misery I imagined and dreaded, I did not conceive the hundredth part of the anguish I was destined to endure.

It was completely dark when I arrived in the environs of Geneva; the gates of the town were already shut; and I was obliged to pass the night at Secheron, a village at the distance of half a league from the city. The sky was serene; and, as I was unable to rest, I resolved to visit the spot where my poor William had been murdered. As I could not pass through the town, I was obliged to cross the lake in a boat to arrive at Plainpalais. During this short voyage I saw the lightning playing on the summit of Mont Blanc in the most beautiful figures. The storm appeared to approach rapidly, and, on landing, I ascended a low hill, that I might observe its progress. It advanced; the heavens were clouded, and I soon felt the rain coming slowly in large drops, but its violence quickly increased.

I quitted my seat and walked on, although the darkness and storm increased every minute, and the thunder burst with a terrific crash over my head. It was echoed from Salêve, the Juras, and the Alps of Savoy; vivid flashes of lightning dazzled my eyes, illuminating the lake, making it appear like a vast sheet of fire; then for an instant everything seemed of a pitchy darkness, until the eye recovered itself from the preceding flash. The storm, as is often the case in Switzerland, appeared at once in various parts of the heavens. The most violent storm hung exactly north of the town, over the part of the lake which lies between the promontory of Belrive and the village of Copêt. Another storm enlightened Jura with faint flashes; and another darkened and sometimes disclosed the Môle, a peaked mountain to the east of the lake.

While I watched the tempest, so beautiful yet terrific, I wandered on with a hasty step. This noble war in the sky elevated my spirits; I clasped my hands and exclaimed aloud, "William, dear angel! This is thy funeral, this thy dirge!" As I said these words, I perceived in the gloom a figure which stole from behind a clump of trees near me; I stood fixed, gazing intently: I could not be mistaken. A flash of lightning illuminated the object, and discovered its shape plainly to me; its gigantic stature, and the deformity of its aspect more hideous than belongs to humanity, instantly informed me that it was the wretch, the filthy daemon, to whom I had given life. What did he there? Could he be (I shuddered at the conception) the murderer of my brother? No sooner did that idea cross my imagination, than I became convinced of its truth; my teeth chattered, and I was forced to lean against a tree for support. The figure passed me quickly, and I lost it in the gloom. Nothing in human shape could have destroyed the fair child. *He* was the murderer! I could not doubt it. The mere presence of the idea was an irresistible proof of the fact. I thought of pursuing the devil; but it would have been in vain, for another flash discovered him to me hanging among the rocks of the nearly perpendicular ascent of Mont Salêve, a hill that bounds Plainpalais on the south. He soon reached the summit, and disappeared.

I remained motionless. The thunder ceased, but the rain still continued, and the scene was enveloped in an impenetrable darkness. I revolved in my mind the events which I had until now sought to forget: the whole train of my progress toward the creation; the appearance of the work of my own hands at my bedside; its departure. Two years had now nearly elapsed since the night on which he first received life; and was this his first crime? Alas! I had turned loose into the world a depraved wretch, whose delight was in carnage and misery; had he not murdered my brother?

No one can conceive the anguish I suffered during the remainder of the night, which I spent, cold and wet, in the open air. But I did not feel the inconvenience of the weather; my imagination was busy in scenes of evil and despair. I considered the being whom I had cast among mankind, and endowed with the will and power to effect purposes of horror, such as the deed which he had now done, nearly in the light of my own vampire, my own spirit let loose from the grave, and forced to destroy all that was dear to me.

Day dawned; and I directed my steps towards the town. The gates were open, and I hastened to my father's house. My first thought was to discover what I knew of the murderer, and cause instant pursuit to be made. But I paused when I reflected on the story that I had to tell. A being whom I myself had formed, and endued with life, had met me at midnight among the precipices of an inaccessible mountain. I remembered also the nervous fever with which I had been seized just at the time that I dated my creation, and which would give an air of delirium to a tale otherwise so utterly improbable. I well knew that if any other had communicated such a relation to me, I should have looked upon it as the ravings of insanity. Besides, the strange nature of the animal would elude all pursuit, even if I were so far credited as to persuade my relatives to commence it. And then of what use would be pursuit? Who could arrest a creature capable of scaling the overhanging sides of Mont Salêve? These reflections determined me, and I resolved to remain silent.

It was about five in the morning when I entered my father's house. I told the servants not to disturb the family, and went into the library to attend their usual hour of rising.

Six years had elapsed, passed in a dream but for one indelible trace, and I stood in the same place where I had last embraced my father before my departure for Ingolstadt. Beloved and venerable parent! He still remained to me. I gazed on the picture of my mother, which stood over the mantel-piece. It was an historical subject, painted at my father's desire, and represented Caroline Beaufort in an agony of despair, kneeling by the coffin of her dead father. Her garb was rustic, and her cheek pale; but there was an air of dignity and beauty, that hardly permitted the sentiment of pity. Below this picture was a miniature of William; and my tears flowed when I looked upon it. While I was thus engaged, Ernest entered: he had heard me arrive, and hastened to welcome me. "Welcome, my dearest Victor," said he. "Ah! I wish you had come three months ago, and then you would have found us all joyous and delighted. You come to us now to share a misery which nothing can alleviate; yet your presence will, I hope, revive our father, who seems sinking under his misfortune; and your persuasions will induce poor Elizabeth to cease her vain and tormenting self-accusations. Poor William! He was our darling and our pride!"

Tears, unrestrained, fell from my brother's eyes; a sense of mortal agony crept over my frame. Before, I had only imagined the wretchedness of my desolated home; the reality came on me as a new, and a not less terrible, disaster. I tried to calm Ernest; I enquired more minutely concerning my father, and her I named my cousin.

"She most of all," said Ernest, "requires consolation; she accused herself of having caused the death of my brother, and that made her very wretched. But since the murderer has been discovered—"

"The murderer discovered! Good God! How can that be? Who could attempt to pursue him? It is impossible; one might as well try to overtake the winds, or confine a mountain-stream with a straw. I saw him too; he was free last night!"

"I do not know what you mean," replied my brother, in accents of wonder, "but to us the discovery we have made completes our misery. No one would believe it at first; and even now Elizabeth will not be convinced, notwithstanding all the evidence. Indeed, who would credit that Justine Moritz, who was so amiable, and fond of all the family, could suddenly become so capable of so frightful, so appalling a crime?"

"Justine Moritz! Poor, poor girl, is she the accused? But it is wrongfully; everyone knows that; no one believes it, surely, Ernest?"

"No one did at first; but several circumstances came out that have almost forced conviction upon us; and her own behaviour has been so confused as to add to the evidence of facts a weight that, I fear, leaves no hope for doubt. But she will be tried today, and you will then hear all."

He then related that, the morning on which the murder of poor William had been discovered, Justine had been taken ill, and confined to her bed for several days. During this interval, one of the servants, happening to examine the apparel she had worn on the night of the murder, had discovered in her pocket the picture of my mother, which had been judged to be the temptation of the murderer. The servant instantly showed it to one of the others, who, without saying a word to any of the family, went to a magistrate; and, upon their deposition, Justine was apprehended. On being charged with the fact, the poor girl confirmed the suspicion in a great measure by her extreme confusion of manner.

This was a strange tale, but it did not shake my faith; and I replied earnestly, "You are all mistaken; I know the murderer. Justine, poor, good Justine, is innocent."

At that instant my father entered. I saw unhappiness deeply impressed on his countenance, but he endeavoured to welcome me cheerfully; and, after we had exchanged our mournful greeting, would have introduced some other topic than that of our disaster, had not Ernest exclaimed, "Good God, Papa! Victor says that he knows who was the murderer of poor William."

"We do also, unfortunately," replied my father, "for indeed I had rather have been forever ignorant than have discovered so much depravity and ingratitude in one I valued so highly."

"My dear father, you are mistaken; Justine is innocent."

"If she is, God forbid that she should suffer as guilty. She is to be tried today, and I hope, I sincerely hope, that she will be acquitted."

This speech calmed me. I was firmly convinced in my own mind that Justine, and indeed every human being, was guiltless of this murder. I had no fear, therefore, that any circumstantial evidence could be brought forward strong enough to convict her. My tale was not one to announce publicly; its astounding horror would be looked upon as madness by the vulgar. Did anyone indeed exist, except I, the creator, who would believe, unless his senses convinced him, in the existence of the living monument of presumption and rash ignorance which I had let loose upon the world?

We were soon joined by Elizabeth. Time had altered her since I last beheld her; it had endowed her with loveliness surpassing the beauty of her childish years. There was the same candour, the same vivacity, but it was allied to an expression more full of sensibility and intellect. She welcomed me with the greatest affection. "Your arrival, my dear cousin," said she, "fills me with hope. You perhaps will find some means to justify my poor guiltless Justine. Alas! Who is safe, if she be convicted of crime? I rely on her innocence as certainly as I do upon my own. Our misfortune is doubly hard to us; we have not only lost that lovely darling boy, but this poor girl, whom I sincerely love, is to be torn away by even a worse fate. If she is condemned, I never shall know joy more. But she will not, I am sure she will not; and then I shall be happy again, even after the sad death of my little William."

"She is innocent, my Elizabeth," said I, "and that shall be proved; fear nothing, but let your spirits be cheered by the assurance of her acquittal."

"How kind and generous you are! Everyone else believes in her guilt, and that made me wretched, for I knew that it was impossible: and to see everyone else prejudiced in so deadly a manner rendered me hopeless and despairing." She wept.

"Dearest niece," said my father, "dry your tears. If she is, as you believe, innocent, rely on the justice of our laws, and the activity with which I shall prevent the slightest shadow of partiality."

CHAPTER VIII

We passed a few sad hours until eleven o'clock, when the trial was to commence. My father and the rest of the family being obliged to attend as witnesses, I accompanied them to the court. During the whole of this wretched mockery of justice I suffered living torture. It was to be decided whether the result of my curiosity and lawless devices would cause the death of two of my fellow beings: one a smiling babe full of innocence and joy, the other far more dreadfully murdered, with every aggravation of infamy that could make the murder memorable in horror. Justine also was a girl of merit and possessed qualities which promised to render her life happy; now all was to be obliterated in an ignominious grave, and I the cause! A thousand times rather would I have confessed myself guilty of the crime ascribed to Justine, but I was absent when it was committed, and such a declaration would have been considered as the ravings of a madman and would not have exculpated her who suffered through me.

The appearance of Justine was calm. She was dressed in mourning, and her countenance, always engaging, was rendered, by the solemnity of her feelings, exquisitely beautiful. Yet she appeared confident in innocence and did not tremble, although gazed on and execrated by thousands, for all the kindness which her beauty might otherwise have excited was obliterated in the minds of the spectators by the imagination of the enormity she was supposed to have committed. She was tranquil, yet her tranquillity was evidently constrained; and as her confusion had before been adduced as a proof of her guilt, she worked up her mind to an appearance of courage. When she entered the court she threw her eyes round it and quickly discovered where we were seated. A tear seemed to dim her eye when she saw us, but she quickly recovered herself, and a look of sorrowful affection seemed to attest her utter guiltlessness.

The trial began, and after the advocate against her had stated the charge, several witnesses were called. Several strange facts combined against her, which might have staggered anyone who had not such proof of her innocence as I had. She had been out the whole of the night on which the murder had been committed and towards morning had been perceived by a market-woman not far from the spot where the body of the murdered child had been afterwards found. The woman asked her what she did there, but she looked very strangely and only returned a confused and unintelligible answer. She returned to the house about eight o'clock, and when one enquired where she had passed the night, she replied that she had been looking for the child and demanded earnestly if anything had been heard concerning him. When shown the body, she fell into violent hysterics and kept her bed for several days. The picture was then produced which the servant had found in her pocket; and when Elizabeth, in a faltering voice, proved that it was the same which, an hour before the child had been missed, she had placed round his neck, a murmur of horror and indignation filled the court.

Justine was called on for her defence. As the trial had proceeded, her countenance had altered. Surprise, horror, and misery were strongly expressed. Sometimes she struggled with her tears, but when she was desired to plead, she collected her powers and spoke in an audible although variable voice.

"God knows," she said, "how entirely I am innocent. But I do not pretend that my protestations should acquit me; I rest my innocence on a plain and simple explanation of the facts which have been adduced against me, and I hope the character I have always borne will incline my judges to a favourable interpretation where any circumstance appears doubtful or suspicious."

She then related that, by the permission of Elizabeth, she had passed the evening of the night on which the murder had been committed at the house of an aunt at Chêne, a village situated at about a league from Geneva. On her return, at about nine o'clock, she met a man who asked her if she had seen anything of the child who was lost. She was alarmed by this account and passed several hours in looking for him, when the gates of Geneva were shut, and she was forced to remain several hours of the night in a barn belonging to a cottage, being unwilling to call up the inhabitants, to whom she was well known. Most of the night she spent here watching; towards morning she believed that she slept for a few minutes; some steps disturbed her, and she awoke. It was dawn, and she quitted her asylum, that she might again endeavour to find my brother. If she had gone near the spot where his body lay, it was without her knowledge. That she had been bewildered when questioned by the market-woman was not surprising, since she had passed a sleepless night and the fate of poor William was yet uncertain. Concerning the picture she could give no account.

"I know," continued the unhappy victim, "how heavily and fatally this one circumstance weighs against me, but I have no power of explaining it; and when I have expressed my utter ignorance, I am only left to conjecture concerning the probabilities by which it might have been placed in my pocket. But here also I am checked. I believe that I have no enemy on earth, and none surely would have been so wicked as to destroy me wantonly. Did the murderer place it there? I know of no opportunity afforded him for so doing; or, if I had, why should he have stolen the jewel, to part with it again so soon?

"I commit my cause to the justice of my judges, yet I see no room for hope. I beg permission to have a few witnesses examined concerning my character, and if their testimony shall not overweigh my supposed guilt, I must be condemned, although I would pledge my salvation on my innocence."

Several witnesses were called who had known her for many years, and they spoke well of her; but fear and hatred of the crime of which they supposed her guilty rendered them timorous and unwilling to come forward. Elizabeth saw even this last resource, her excellent dispositions and irreproachable conduct, about to fail the accused, when, although violently agitated, she desired permission to address the court.

"I am," said she, "the cousin of the unhappy child who was murdered, or rather his sister, for I was educated by and have lived with his parents ever since and even long before his birth. It may therefore be judged indecent in me to come forward on this occasion, but when I see a fellow creature about to perish through the cowardice of her pretended friends, I wish to be allowed to speak, that I may say what I know of her character. I am well acquainted with the accused. I have lived in the same house with her, at one time for five and at another for nearly two years. During all that period she appeared to me the most amiable and benevolent of human creatures. She nursed Madame Frankenstein, my aunt, in her last illness, with the greatest affection and care and afterwards attended her own mother during a tedious illness, in a manner that excited the admiration of all who knew her, after which she again lived in my uncle's house, where she was beloved by all the family. She was warmly attached to the child who is now dead and acted towards him like a most affectionate mother. For my own part, I do not hesitate to say that, notwithstanding all the evidence produced against her, I believe and rely on her perfect innocence. She had no temptation for such an action; as to the bauble on which the chief proof rests, if she had earnestly desired it, I should have willingly given it to her, so much do I esteem and value her."

A murmur of approbation followed Elizabeth's simple and powerful appeal, but it was excited by her generous interference, and not in favour of poor Justine, on whom the public indignation was turned with renewed violence, charging her with the blackest ingratitude. She herself wept as Elizabeth spoke, but she did not answer. My own agitation and anguish was extreme during the whole trial. I believed in her innocence; I knew it. Could the daemon who had (I did not for a minute doubt) murdered my brother also in his hellish sport have betrayed the innocent to death and ignominy? I could not sustain the horror of my situation, and when I perceived that the popular voice and the countenances of the judges had already condemned my unhappy victim, I rushed out of the court in agony. The tortures of the accused did not equal mine; she was sustained by innocence, but the fangs of remorse tore my bosom and would not forego their hold.

I passed a night of unmingled wretchedness. In the morning I went to the court; my lips and throat were parched. I dared not ask the fatal question, but I was known, and the officer guessed the cause of my visit. The ballots had been thrown; they were all black, and Justine was condemned.

I cannot pretend to describe what I then felt. I had before experienced sensations of horror, and I have endeavoured to bestow upon them adequate expressions, but words cannot convey an idea of the heart-sickening despair that I then endured. The person to whom I addressed myself added that Justine had already confessed her guilt. "That evidence," he observed, "was hardly required in so glaring a case, but I am glad of it, and, indeed, none of our judges like to condemn a criminal upon circumstantial evidence, be it ever so decisive."

This was strange and unexpected intelligence; what could it mean? Had my eyes deceived me? And was I really as mad as the whole world would believe me to be if I disclosed the object of my suspicions? I hastened to return home, and Elizabeth eagerly demanded the result.

"My cousin," replied I, "it is decided as you may have expected; all judges had rather that ten innocent should suffer than that one guilty should escape. But she has confessed."

This was a dire blow to poor Elizabeth, who had relied with firmness upon Justine's innocence. "Alas!" said she. "How shall I ever again believe in human goodness? Justine, whom I loved and esteemed as my sister, how could she put on those smiles of innocence only to betray? Her mild eyes seemed incapable of any severity or guile, and yet she has committed a murder."

Soon after we heard that the poor victim had expressed a desire to see my cousin. My father wished her not to go but said that he left it to her own judgement and feelings to decide. "Yes," said Elizabeth, "I will go, although she is guilty; and you, Victor, shall accompany me; I cannot go alone." The idea of this visit was torture to me, yet I could not refuse.

We entered the gloomy prison chamber and beheld Justine sitting on some straw at the farther end; her hands were manacled, and her head rested on her knees. She rose on seeing us enter, and when we were left alone with her, she threw herself at the feet of Elizabeth, weeping bitterly. My cousin wept also.

"Oh, Justine!" said she. "Why did you rob me of my last consolation? I relied on your innocence, and although I was then very wretched, I was not so miserable as I am now."

"And do you also believe that I am so very, very wicked? Do you also join with my enemies to crush me, to condemn me as a murderer?" Her voice was suffocated with sobs.

"Rise, my poor girl," said Elizabeth; "why do you kneel, if you are innocent? I am not one of your enemies; I believed you guiltless, notwithstanding every evidence, until I heard that you had yourself declared your guilt. That report, you say, is false; and be assured, dear Justine, that nothing can shake my confidence in you for a moment, but your own confession."

"I did confess, but I confessed a lie. I confessed, that I might obtain absolution; but now that falsehood lies heavier at my heart than all my other sins. The God of heaven forgive me! Ever since I was condemned, my confessor has besieged me; he threatened and menaced, until I almost began to think that I was the monster that he said I was. He threatened excommunication and hell fire in my last moments if I continued obdurate. Dear lady, I had none to support me; all looked on me as a wretch doomed to ignominy and perdition. What could I do? In an evil hour I subscribed to a lie; and now only am I truly miserable."

She paused, weeping, and then continued: "I thought with horror, my sweet lady, that you should believe your Justine, whom your blessed aunt had so highly honoured, and whom you loved, was a creature capable of a crime which none but the devil himself could have perpetrated. Dear William! Dearest blessed child! I soon shall see you again in heaven, where we shall all be happy; and that consoles me, going as I am to suffer ignominy and death."

"Oh, Justine! Forgive me for having for one moment distrusted you. Why did you confess? But do not mourn, dear girl. Do not fear. I will proclaim, I will prove your innocence. I will melt the stony hearts of your enemies by my tears and prayers. You shall not die! You, my playfellow, my companion, my sister, perish on the scaffold! No! No! I never could survive so horrible a misfortune."

Justine shook her head mournfully. "I do not fear to die," she said; "that pang is past. God raises my weakness and gives me courage to endure the worst. I leave a sad and bitter world; and if you remember me and think of me as of one unjustly condemned, I am resigned to the fate awaiting me. Learn from me, dear lady, to submit in patience to the will of heaven!"

During this conversation I had retired to a corner of the prison room, where I could conceal the horrid anguish that possessed me. Despair! Who dared talk of that? The poor victim, who on the morrow was to pass the awful boundary between life and death, felt not, as I did, such deep and bitter agony. I gnashed my teeth and ground them together, uttering a groan that came from my inmost soul. Justine started. When she saw who it was, she approached me and said, "Dear sir, you are very kind to visit me; you, I hope, do not believe that I am guilty?"

I could not answer. "No, Justine," said Elizabeth; "he is more convinced of your innocence than I was, for even when he heard that you had confessed, he did not credit it."

"I truly thank him. In these last moments I feel the sincerest gratitude towards those who think of me with kindness. How sweet is the affection of others to such a wretch as I am! It removes more than half my misfortune, and I feel as if I could die in peace now that my innocence is acknowledged by you, dear lady, and your cousin."

Thus the poor sufferer tried to comfort others and herself. She indeed gained the resignation she desired. But I, the true murderer, felt the never-dying worm alive in my bosom, which allowed of no hope or consolation. Elizabeth also wept and was unhappy, but hers also was the misery of innocence, which, like a cloud that passes over the fair moon, for a while hides but cannot tarnish its brightness. Anguish and despair had penetrated into the core of my heart; I bore a hell within me which nothing could extinguish. We stayed several hours with Justine, and it was with great difficulty that Elizabeth could tear herself away. "I wish," cried she, "that I were to die with you; I cannot live in this world of misery."

Justine assumed an air of cheerfulness, while she with difficulty repressed her bitter tears. She embraced Elizabeth and said in a voice of half-suppressed emotion, "Farewell, sweet lady, dearest Elizabeth, my beloved and only friend; may heaven, in its bounty, bless and preserve you; may this be the last misfortune that you will ever suffer! Live, and be happy, and make others so."

And on the morrow Justine died. Elizabeth's heart-rending eloquence failed to move the judges from their settled conviction in the criminality of the saintly sufferer. My passionate and indignant appeals were lost upon them. And when I received their cold answers and heard the harsh, unfeeling reasoning of these men, my purposed avowal died away on my lips. Thus I might proclaim myself a madman, but not revoke the sentence passed upon my wretched victim. She perished on the scaffold as a murderess!

From the tortures of my own heart, I turned to contemplate the deep and voiceless grief of my Elizabeth. This also was my doing! And my father's woe, and the desolation of that late so smiling home—all was the work of my thrice-accursed hands! Ye weep, unhappy ones, but these are not your last tears! Again shall you raise the funeral wail, and the sound of your lamentations shall again and again be heard! Frankenstein, your son, your kinsman, your early, much-loved friend; he who would spend each vital drop of blood for your sakes, who has no thought nor sense of joy except as it is mirrored also in your dear countenances, who would fill the air with blessings and spend his life in serving you—he bids you weep, to shed countless tears; happy beyond his hopes, if thus inexorable fate be satisfied, and if the destruction pause before the peace of the grave have succeeded to your sad torments!

Thus spoke my prophetic soul, as, torn by remorse, horror, and despair, I beheld those I loved spend vain sorrow upon the graves of William and Justine, the first hapless victims to my unhallowed arts.

VOLUME TWO

CHAPTER I

Nothing is more painful to the human mind than, after the feelings have been worked up by a quick succession of events, the dead calmness of inaction and certainty which follows and deprives the soul both of hope and fear. Justine died, she rested, and I was alive. The blood flowed freely in my veins, but a weight of despair and remorse pressed on my heart which nothing could remove. Sleep fled from my eyes; I wandered like an evil spirit, for I had committed deeds of mischief beyond description horrible, and more, much more (I persuaded myself) was yet behind. Yet my heart overflowed with kindness and the love of virtue. I had begun life with benevolent intentions and thirsted for the moment when I should put them in practice and make myself useful to my fellow beings. Now all was blasted; instead of that serenity of conscience which allowed me to look back upon the past with self-satisfaction, and from thence to gather promise of new hopes, I was seized by remorse and the sense of guilt, which hurried me away to a hell of intense tortures such as no language can describe.

This state of mind preyed upon my health, which had perhaps never entirely recovered from the first shock it had sustained. I shunned the face of man; all sound of joy or complacency was torture to me; solitude was my only consolation—deep, dark, deathlike solitude.

My father observed with pain the alteration perceptible in my disposition and habits and endeavoured by arguments deduced from the feelings of his serene conscience and guiltless life to inspire me with fortitude and awaken in me the courage to dispel the dark cloud which brooded over me. "Do you think, Victor," said he, "that I do not suffer also? No one could love a child more than I loved your brother"—tears came into his eyes as he spoke—"but is it not a duty to the survivors that we should refrain from augmenting their unhappiness by an appearance of immoderate grief? It is also a duty owed to yourself, for excessive sorrow prevents improvement or enjoyment, or even the discharge of daily usefulness, without which no man is fit for society."

This advice, although good, was totally inapplicable to my case; I should have been the first to hide my grief and console my friends if remorse had not mingled its bitterness, and terror its alarm, with my other sensations. Now I could only answer my father with a look of despair and endeavour to hide myself from his view.

About this time we retired to our house at Belrive. This change was particularly agreeable to me. The shutting of the gates regularly at ten o'clock and the impossibility of remaining on the lake after that hour had rendered our residence within the walls of Geneva very irksome to me. I was now free. Often, after the rest of the family had retired for the night, I took the boat and passed many hours upon the water. Sometimes, with my sails set, I was carried by the wind; and sometimes, after rowing into the middle of the lake, I left the boat to pursue its own course and gave way to my own miserable reflections. I was often tempted, when all was at peace around me, and I the only unquiet thing that wandered restless in a scene so beautiful and heavenly—if I except some bat, or the frogs, whose harsh and interrupted croaking was heard only when I approached the shore—often, I say, I was tempted to plunge into the silent lake, that the waters might close over me and my calamities forever. But I was restrained, when I thought of the heroic and suffering Elizabeth, whom I tenderly loved, and whose existence was bound up in mine. I thought also of my father and surviving brother; should I by my base desertion leave them exposed and unprotected to the malice of the fiend whom I had let loose among them?

At these moments I wept bitterly and wished that peace would revisit my mind only that I might afford them consolation and happiness. But that could not be. Remorse extinguished every hope. I had been the author of unalterable evils, and I lived in daily fear lest the monster whom I had created should perpetrate some new wickedness. I had an obscure feeling that all was not over and that he would still commit some signal crime, which by its enormity should almost efface the recollection of the past. There was always scope for fear so long as anything I loved remained behind. My abhorrence of this fiend cannot be conceived. When I thought of him I gnashed my teeth, my eyes became inflamed, and I ardently wished to extinguish that life which I had so thoughtlessly bestowed. When I reflected on his crimes and malice, my hatred and revenge burst all bounds of moderation. I would have made a pilgrimage to the highest peak of the Andes, could I, when there, have precipitated him to their base. I wished to see him again, that I might wreak the utmost extent of abhorrence on his head and avenge the deaths of William and Justine.

Our house was the house of mourning. My father's health was deeply shaken by the horror of the recent events. Elizabeth was sad and desponding; she no longer took delight in her ordinary occupations; all pleasure seemed to her sacrilege toward the dead; eternal woe and tears she then thought was the just tribute she should pay to innocence so blasted and destroyed. She was no longer that happy creature who in earlier youth wandered with me on the banks of the lake and talked with ecstasy of our future prospects. The first of those sorrows which are sent to wean us from the earth had visited her, and its dimming influence quenched her dearest smiles.

"When I reflect, my dear cousin," said she, "on the miserable death of Justine Moritz, I no longer see the world and its works as they before appeared to me. Before, I looked upon the accounts of vice and injustice that I read in books or heard from others as tales of ancient days or imaginary evils; at least they were remote and more familiar to reason than to the imagination; but now misery has come home, and men appear to me as monsters thirsting for each other's blood. Yet I am certainly unjust. Everybody believed that poor girl to be guilty; and if she could have committed the crime for which she suffered, assuredly she would have been the most depraved of human creatures. For the sake of a few jewels, to have murdered the son of her benefactor and friend, a child whom she had nursed from its birth, and appeared to love as if it had been her own! I could not consent to the death of any human being, but certainly I should have thought such a creature unfit to remain in the society of men. But she was innocent. I know, I feel she was innocent; you are of the same opinion, and that confirms me. Alas! Victor, when falsehood can look so like the truth, who can assure themselves of certain happiness? I feel as if I were walking on the edge of a precipice, towards which thousands are crowding and endeavouring to plunge me into the abyss. William and Justine were assassinated, and the murderer escapes; he walks about the world free, and perhaps respected. But even if I were condemned to suffer on the scaffold for the same crimes, I would not change places with such a wretch."

I listened to this discourse with the extremest agony. I, not in deed, but in effect, was the true murderer. Elizabeth read my anguish in my countenance, and kindly taking my hand, said, "My dearest friend, you must calm yourself. These events have affected me, God knows how deeply; but I am not so wretched as you are. There is an expression of despair, and sometimes of revenge, in your countenance that makes me tremble. Dear Victor, banish these dark passions. Remember the friends around you, who centre all their hopes in you. Have we lost the power of rendering you happy? Ah! While we love, while we are true to each other, here in this land of peace and beauty, your native country, we may reap every tranquil blessing—what can disturb our peace?"

And could not such words from her whom I fondly prized before every other gift of fortune suffice to chase away the fiend that lurked in my heart? Even as she spoke I drew near to her, as if in terror, lest at that very moment the destroyer had been near to rob me of her.

Thus not the tenderness of friendship, nor the beauty of earth, nor of heaven, could redeem my soul from woe; the very accents of love were ineffectual. I was encompassed by a cloud which no beneficial influence could penetrate. The wounded deer dragging its fainting limbs to some untrodden brake, there to gaze upon the arrow which had pierced it, and to die, was but a type of me.

Sometimes I could cope with the sullen despair that overwhelmed me, but sometimes the whirlwind passions of my soul drove me to seek, by bodily exercise and by change of place, some relief from my intolerable sensations. It was during an access of this kind that I suddenly left my home, and bending my steps towards the near Alpine valleys, sought in the magnificence, the eternity of such scenes, to forget myself and my ephemeral, because human, sorrows. My wanderings were directed towards the valley of Chamounix. I had visited it frequently during my boyhood. Six years had passed since then: *I* was a wreck, but nought had changed in those savage and enduring scenes.

I performed the first part of my journey on horseback. I afterwards hired a mule, as the more sure-footed and least liable to receive injury on these rugged roads. The weather was fine; it was about the middle of the month of August, nearly two months after the death of Justine, that miserable epoch from which I dated all my woe. The weight upon my spirit was sensibly lightened as I plunged yet deeper in the ravine of Arve. The immense mountains and precipices that overhung me on every side—the sound of the river raging among the rocks, and the dashing of the waterfalls around spoke of a power mighty as Omnipotence—and I ceased to fear or to bend before any being less almighty than that which had created and ruled the elements, here displayed in their most terrific guise. Still, as I ascended higher, the valley assumed a more magnificent and astonishing character. Ruined castles hanging on the precipices of piny mountains, the impetuous Arve, and cottages every here and there peeping forth from among the trees formed a scene of singular beauty. But it was augmented and rendered sublime by the mighty Alps, whose white and shining pyramids and domes towered above all, as belonging to another earth, the habitations of another race of beings.

I passed the bridge of Pélissier, where the ravine, which the river forms, opened before me, and I began to ascend the mountain that overhangs it. Soon after, I entered the valley of Chamounix. This valley is more wonderful and sublime, but not so beautiful and picturesque as that of Servox, through which I had just passed. The high and snowy mountains were its immediate boundaries, but I saw no more ruined castles and fertile fields. Immense glaciers approached the road; I heard the rumbling thunder of the falling avalanche and marked the smoke of its passage. Mont Blanc, the supreme and magnificent Mont Blanc, raised itself from the surrounding *aiguilles*, and its tremendous *dôme* overlooked the valley.

A tingling long-lost sense of pleasure often came across me during this journey. Some turn in the road, some new object suddenly perceived and recognised, reminded me of days gone by, and were associated with the light-hearted gaiety of boyhood. The very winds whispered in soothing accents, and maternal nature bade me weep no more. Then again the kindly influence ceased to act—I found myself fettered again to grief and indulging in all the misery of reflection. Then I spurred on my animal, striving so to forget the world, my fears, and more than all, myself—or, in a more desperate fashion, I alighted and threw myself on the grass, weighed down by horror and despair.

At length I arrived at the village of Chamounix. Exhaustion succeeded to the extreme fatigue both of body and of mind which I had endured. For a short space of time I remained at the window watching the pallid lightnings that played above Mont Blanc and listening to the rushing of the Arve, which pursued its noisy way beneath. The same lulling sounds acted as a lullaby to my too keen sensations; when I placed my head upon my pillow, sleep crept over me; I felt it as it came and blessed the giver of oblivion.

CHAPTER II

I spent the following day roaming through the valley. I stood beside the sources of the Arveiron, which take their rise in a glacier that with slow pace is advancing down from the summit of the hills to barricade the valley. The abrupt sides of vast mountains were before me; the icy wall of the glacier overhung me; a few shattered pines were scattered around; and the solemn silence of this glorious presence-chamber of imperial nature was broken only by the brawling waves or the fall of some vast fragment, the thunder sound of the avalanche or the cracking, reverberated along the mountains, of the accumulated ice, which, through the silent working of immutable laws, was ever and anon rent and torn, as if it had been but a plaything in their hands. These sublime and magnificent scenes afforded me the greatest consolation that I was capable of receiving. They elevated me from all littleness of feeling, and although they did not remove my grief, they subdued and tranquillized it. In some degree, also, they diverted my mind from the thoughts over which it had brooded for the last month. I retired to rest at night; my slumbers, as it were, waited on and ministered to by the assemblance of grand shapes which I had contemplated during the day. They congregated round me; the unstained snowy mountain-top, the glittering pinnacle, the pine woods, and ragged bare ravine, the eagle, soaring amidst the clouds—they all gathered round me and bade me be at peace.

Where had they fled when the next morning I awoke? All of soul-inspiriting fled with sleep, and dark melancholy clouded every thought. The rain was pouring in torrents, and thick mists hid the summits of the mountains, so that I even saw not the faces of those mighty friends. Still I would penetrate their misty veil and seek them in their cloudy retreats. What were rain and storm to me? My mule was brought to the door, and I resolved to ascend to the summit of Montanvert. I remembered the effect that the view of the tremendous and ever-moving glacier had produced upon my mind when I first saw it. It had then filled me with a sublime ecstasy that gave wings to the soul and allowed it to soar from the obscure world to light and joy. The sight of the awful and majestic in nature had indeed always the effect of solemnizing my mind and causing me to forget the passing cares of life. I determined to go without a guide, for I was well acquainted with the path, and the presence of another would destroy the solitary grandeur of the scene.

The ascent is precipitous, but the path is cut into continual and short windings, which enable you to surmount the perpendicularity of the mountain. It is a scene terrifically desolate. In a thousand spots the traces of the winter avalanche may be perceived, where trees lie broken and strewed on the ground, some entirely destroyed, others bent, leaning upon the jutting rocks of the mountain or transversely upon other trees. The path, as you ascend higher, is intersected by ravines of snow, down which stones continually roll from above; one of them is particularly dangerous, as the slightest sound, such as even speaking in a loud voice, produces a concussion of air sufficient to draw destruction upon the head of the speaker. The pines are not tall or luxuriant, but they are sombre and add an air of severity to the scene. I looked on the valley beneath; vast mists were rising from the rivers which ran through it and curling in thick wreaths around the opposite mountains, whose summits were hid in the uniform clouds, while rain poured from the dark sky and added to the melancholy impression I received from the objects around me. Alas! Why does man boast of sensibilities superior to those apparent in the brute; it only renders them more necessary beings. If our impulses were confined to hunger, thirst, and desire, we might be nearly free; but now we are moved by every wind that blows and a chance word or scene that that word may convey to us.

> We rest; a dream has power to poison sleep.
> We rise; one wand'ring thought pollutes the day.
> We feel, conceive, or reason; laugh or weep,
> Embrace fond woe, or cast our cares away;
> It is the same: for, be it joy or sorrow,
> The path of its departure still is free.
> Man's yesterday may ne'er be like his morrow;
> Nought may endure but mutability!

It was nearly noon when I arrived at the top of the ascent. For some time I sat upon the rock that overlooks the sea of ice. A mist covered both that and the surrounding mountains. Presently a breeze dissipated the cloud, and I descended upon the glacier. The surface is very uneven, rising like the waves of a troubled sea, descending low, and interspersed by rifts that sink deep. The field of ice is almost a league in width, but I spent nearly two hours in crossing it. The opposite mountain is a bare perpendicular rock. From the side where I now stood Montanvert was exactly opposite, at the distance of a league; and above it rose Mont Blanc, in awful majesty. I remained in a recess of the rock, gazing on this wonderful and stupendous scene. The sea, or rather the vast river of ice, wound among its dependent mountains, whose aerial summits hung over its recesses. Their icy and glittering peaks shone in the sunlight over the clouds. My heart, which was before sorrowful, now swelled with something like joy; I exclaimed, "Wandering spirits, if indeed ye wander, and do not rest in your narrow beds, allow me this faint happiness, or take me, as your companion, away from the joys of life."

As I said this I suddenly beheld the figure of a man, at some distance, advancing towards me with superhuman speed. He bounded over the crevices in the ice, among which I had walked with caution; his stature, also, as he approached, seemed to exceed that of man. I was troubled; a mist came over my eyes, and I felt a faintness seize me, but I was quickly restored by the cold gale of the mountains. I perceived, as the shape came nearer (sight tremendous and abhorred!) that it was the wretch whom I had created. I trembled with rage and horror, resolving to wait his approach and then close with him in mortal combat. He approached; his countenance bespoke bitter anguish, combined with disdain and malignity, while its unearthly ugliness rendered it almost too horrible for human eyes. But I scarcely observed this; rage and hatred had at first deprived me of utterance, and I recovered only to overwhelm him with words expressive of furious detestation and contempt.

"Devil," I exclaimed, "do you dare approach me? And do not you fear the fierce vengeance of my arm wreaked on your miserable head? Begone, vile insect! Or rather, stay, that I may trample you to dust! And, oh, that I could, with the extinction of your miserable existence, restore those victims whom you have so diabolically murdered!"

"I expected this reception," said the daemon. "All men hate the wretched; how, then, must I be hated, who am miserable beyond all living things! Yet you, my creator, detest and spurn me, thy creature, to whom thou art bound by ties only dissoluble by the annihilation of one of us. You purpose to kill me. How dare you sport thus with life? Do your duty towards me, and I will do mine towards you and the rest of mankind. If you will comply with my conditions, I will leave them and you at peace; but if you refuse, I will glut the maw of death, until it be satiated with the blood of your remaining friends."

"Abhorred monster! Fiend that thou art! The tortures of hell are too mild a vengeance for thy crimes. Wretched devil! You reproach me with your creation; come on, then, that I may extinguish the spark which I so negligently bestowed."

My rage was without bounds; I sprang on him, impelled by all the feelings which can arm one being against the existence of another.

He easily eluded me, and said:

"Be calm! I entreat you to hear me before you give vent to your hatred on my devoted head. Have I not suffered enough, that you seek to increase my misery? Life, although it may only be an accumulation of anguish, is dear to me, and I will defend it. Remember, thou hast made me more powerful than thyself; my height is superior to thine, my joints more supple. But I will not be tempted to set myself in opposition to thee. I am thy creature, and I will be even mild and docile to my natural lord and king if thou wilt also perform thy part, the which thou owest me. Oh, Frankenstein, be not equitable to every other and trample upon me alone, to whom thy justice, and even thy clemency and affection, is most due. Remember that I am thy creature; I ought to be thy Adam, but I am rather the fallen angel, whom thou drivest from joy for no misdeed. Everywhere I see bliss, from which I alone am irrevocably excluded. I was benevolent and good; misery made me a fiend. Make me happy, and I shall again be virtuous."

"Begone! I will not hear you. There can be no community between you and me; we are enemies. Begone, or let us try our strength in a fight, in which one must fall."

"How can I move thee? Will no entreaties cause thee to turn a favourable eye upon thy creature, who implores thy goodness and compassion? Believe me, Frankenstein, I was benevolent; my soul glowed with love and humanity; but am I not alone, miserably alone? You, my creator, abhor me; what hope can I gather from your fellow creatures, who owe me nothing? They spurn and hate me. The desert mountains and dreary glaciers are my refuge. I have wandered here many days; the caves of ice, which I only do not fear, are a dwelling to me, and the only one which man does not grudge. These bleak skies I hail, for they are kinder to me than your fellow beings. If the multitude of mankind knew of my existence, they would do as you do, and arm themselves for my destruction. Shall I not then hate them who abhor me? I will keep no terms with my enemies. I am miserable, and they shall share my wretchedness. Yet it is in your power to recompense me, and deliver them from an evil which it only remains for you to make so great, that not only you and your family, but thousands of others, shall be swallowed up in the whirlwinds of its rage. Let your compassion be moved, and do not disdain me. Listen to my tale; when you have heard that, abandon or commiserate me, as you shall judge that I deserve. But hear me. The guilty are allowed, by human laws, bloody as they are, to speak in their own defence before they are condemned. Listen to me, Frankenstein. You accuse me of murder, and yet you would, with a satisfied conscience, destroy your own creature. Oh, praise the eternal justice of man! Yet I ask you not to spare me; listen to me, and then, if you can, and if you will, destroy the work of your hands."

"Why do you call to my remembrance," I rejoined, "circumstances of which I shudder to reflect, that I have been the miserable origin and author? Cursed be the day, abhorred devil, in which you first saw light! Cursed (although I curse myself) be the hands that formed you! You have made me wretched beyond expression. You have left me no power to consider whether I am just to you or not. Begone! Relieve me from the sight of your detested form."

"Thus I relieve thee, my creator," he said, and placed his hated hands before my eyes, which I flung from me with violence; "thus I take from thee a sight which you abhor. Still thou canst listen to me and grant me thy compassion. By the virtues that I once possessed, I demand this from you. Hear my tale; it is long and strange, and the temperature of this place is not fitting to your fine sensations; come to the hut upon the mountain. The sun is yet high in the heavens; before it descends to hide itself behind your snowy precipices and illuminate another world, you will have heard my story and can decide. On you it rests, whether I quit forever the neighbourhood of man and lead a harmless life, or become the scourge of your fellow creatures and the author of your own speedy ruin."

As he said this, he led the way across the ice; I followed. My heart was full, and I did not answer him, but as I proceeded, I weighed the various arguments that he had used and determined at least to listen to his tale. I was partly urged by curiosity, and compassion confirmed my resolution. I had hitherto supposed him to be the murderer of my brother, and I eagerly sought a confirmation or denial of this opinion. For the first time, also, I felt what the duties of a creator towards his creature were, and that I ought to render him happy before I complained of his wickedness. These motives urged me to comply with his demand. We crossed the ice, therefore, and ascended the opposite rock. The air was cold, and the rain again began to descend; we entered the hut, the fiend with an air of exultation, I with a heavy heart and depressed spirits. But I consented to listen, and seating myself by the fire which my odious companion had lighted, he thus began his tale.

CHAPTER III

It is with considerable difficulty that I remember the original era of my being; all the events of that period appear confused and indistinct. A strange multiplicity of sensations seized me, and I saw, felt, heard, and smelt at the same time; and it was, indeed, a long time before I learned to distinguish between the operations of my various senses. By degrees, I remember, a stronger light pressed upon my nerves, so that I was obliged to shut my eyes. Darkness then came over me and troubled me, but hardly had I felt this when, by opening my eyes, as I now suppose, the light poured in upon me again. I walked and, I believe, descended, but I presently found a great alteration in my sensations. Before, dark and opaque bodies had surrounded me, impervious to my touch or sight; but I now found that I could wander on at liberty, with no obstacles which I could not either surmount or avoid. The light became more and more oppressive to me, and the heat wearying me as I walked, I sought a place where I could receive shade. This was the forest near Ingolstadt; and here I lay by the side of a brook resting from my fatigue, until I felt tormented by hunger and thirst. This roused me from my nearly dormant state, and I ate some berries which I found hanging on the trees or lying on the ground. I slaked my thirst at the brook, and then lying down, was overcome by sleep.

"It was dark when I awoke; I felt cold also, and half frightened, as it were, instinctively, finding myself so desolate. Before I had quitted your apartment, on a sensation of cold, I had covered myself with some clothes, but these were insufficient to secure me from the dews of night. I was a poor, helpless, miserable wretch; I knew, and could distinguish, nothing; but feeling pain invade me on all sides, I sat down and wept.

"Soon a gentle light stole over the heavens and gave me a sensation of pleasure. I started up and beheld a radiant form rise from among the trees.* I gazed with a kind of wonder. It moved slowly, but it enlightened my path, and I again went out in search of berries. I was still cold when under one of the trees I found a huge cloak, with which I covered myself, and sat down upon the ground. No distinct ideas

* The moon (author's footnote)

occupied my mind; all was confused. I felt light, and hunger, and thirst, and darkness; innumerable sounds rang in my ears, and on all sides various scents saluted me; the only object that I could distinguish was the bright moon, and I fixed my eyes on that with pleasure.

"Several changes of day and night passed, and the orb of night had greatly lessened, when I began to distinguish my sensations from each other. I gradually saw plainly the clear stream that supplied me with drink and the trees that shaded me with their foliage. I was delighted when I first discovered that a pleasant sound, which often saluted my ears, proceeded from the throats of the little winged animals who had often intercepted the light from my eyes. I began also to observe, with greater accuracy, the forms that surrounded me and to perceive the boundaries of the radiant roof of light which canopied me. Sometimes I tried to imitate the pleasant songs of the birds but was unable. Sometimes I wished to express my sensations in my own mode, but the uncouth and inarticulate sounds which broke from me frightened me into silence again.

"The moon had disappeared from the night, and again, with a lessened form, showed itself, while I still remained in the forest. My sensations had by this time become distinct, and my mind received every day additional ideas. My eyes became accustomed to the light and to perceive objects in their right forms; I distinguished the insect from the herb, and by degrees, one herb from another. I found that the sparrow uttered none but harsh notes, whilst those of the blackbird and thrush were sweet and enticing.

"One day, when I was oppressed by cold, I found a fire which had been left by some wandering beggars, and was overcome with delight at the warmth I experienced from it. In my joy I thrust my hand into the live embers, but quickly drew it out again with a cry of pain. How strange, I thought, that the same cause should produce such opposite effects! I examined the materials of the fire, and to my joy found it to be composed of wood. I quickly collected some branches, but they were wet and would not burn. I was pained at this and sat still watching the operation of the fire. The wet wood which I had placed near the heat dried and itself became inflamed. I reflected on this, and by touching the various branches, I discovered the cause and busied myself in collecting a great quantity of wood, that I might dry it and have a plentiful supply of fire. When night came on and brought sleep with it, I was in the greatest fear lest my fire should be extinguished. I covered it carefully with dry wood and leaves and placed wet branches upon it; and then, spreading my cloak, I lay on the ground and sank into sleep.

"It was morning when I awoke, and my first care was to visit the fire. I uncovered it, and a gentle breeze quickly fanned it into a flame. I observed this also and contrived a fan of branches, which roused the embers when they were nearly extinguished. When night came again I found, with pleasure, that the fire gave light as well as heat and that the discovery of this element was useful to me in my food, for I found some of the offals that the travellers had left had been roasted, and tasted much more savoury than the berries I gathered from the trees. I tried, therefore, to dress my food in the same manner, placing it on the live embers. I found that the berries were spoiled by this operation, and the nuts and roots much improved.

"Food, however, became scarce, and I often spent the whole day searching in vain for a few acorns to assuage the pangs of hunger. When I found this, I resolved to quit the place that I had hitherto inhabited, to seek for one where the few wants I experienced would be more easily satisfied. In this emigration I exceedingly lamented the loss of the fire which I had obtained through accident and knew not how to reproduce it. I gave several hours to the serious consideration of this difficulty, but I was obliged to relinquish all attempt to supply it, and wrapping myself up in my cloak, I struck across the wood towards the setting sun. I passed three days in these rambles and at length discovered the open country. A great fall of snow had taken place the night before, and the fields were of one uniform white; the appearance was disconsolate, and I found my feet chilled by the cold damp substance that covered the ground.

"It was about seven in the morning, and I longed to obtain food and shelter; at length I perceived a small hut, on a rising ground, which had doubtless been built for the convenience of some shepherd. This was a new sight to me, and I examined the structure with great curiosity. Finding the door open, I entered. An old man sat in it, near a fire, over which he was preparing his breakfast. He turned on hearing a noise, and perceiving me, shrieked loudly, and quitting the hut, ran across the fields with a speed of which his debilitated form hardly appeared capable. His appearance, different from any I had ever before seen, and his flight somewhat surprised me. But I was enchanted by the appearance of the hut; here the snow and rain could not penetrate; the ground was dry; and it presented to me then as exquisite and divine a retreat as Pandemonium appeared to the daemons of hell after their sufferings in the lake of fire. I greedily devoured the remnants of the shepherd's breakfast, which consisted of bread, cheese, milk, and wine; the latter, however, I did not like. Then, overcome by fatigue, I lay down among some straw and fell asleep.

"It was noon when I awoke, and allured by the warmth of the sun, which shone brightly on the white ground, I determined to recommence my travels; and, depositing the remains of the peasant's breakfast in a wallet I found, I proceeded across the fields for several hours, until at sunset I arrived at a village. How miraculous did this appear! The huts, the neater cottages, and stately houses engaged my admiration by turns. The vegetables in the gardens, the milk and cheese that I saw placed at the windows of some of the cottages, allured my appetite. One of the best of these I entered, but I had hardly placed my foot within the door before the children shrieked, and one of the women fainted. The whole village was roused; some fled, some attacked me, until, grievously bruised by stones and many other kinds of missile weapons, I escaped to the open country and fearfully took refuge in a low hovel, quite bare, and making a wretched appearance after the palaces I had beheld in the village. This hovel, however, joined a cottage of a neat and pleasant appearance; but after my late dearly bought experience, I dared not enter it. My place of refuge was constructed of wood, but so low that I could with difficulty sit upright in it. No wood, however, was placed on the earth, which formed the floor, but it was dry; and although the wind entered it by innumerable chinks, I found it an agreeable asylum from the snow and rain.

"Here, then, I retreated and lay down happy to have found a shelter, however miserable, from the inclemency of the season, and still more from the barbarity of man.

"As soon as morning dawned I crept from my kennel, that I might view the adjacent cottage and discover if I could remain in the habitation I had found. It was situated against the back of the cottage and surrounded on the sides which were exposed by a pig sty and a clear pool of water. One part was open, and by that I had crept in; but now I covered every crevice by which I might be perceived with stones and wood, yet in such a manner that I might move them on occasion to pass out; all the light I enjoyed came through the sty, and that was sufficient for me.

"Having thus arranged my dwelling and carpeted it with clean straw, I retired, for I saw the figure of a man at a distance, and I remembered too well my treatment the night before to trust myself in his power. I had first, however, provided for my sustenance for that day by a loaf of coarse bread, which I purloined, and a cup with which I could drink more conveniently than from my hand of the pure water which flowed by my retreat. The floor was a little raised, so that it was kept perfectly dry, and by its vicinity to the chimney of the cottage it was tolerably warm.

"Being thus provided, I resolved to reside in this hovel until something should occur which might alter my determination. It was indeed a paradise compared to the bleak forest, my former residence, the rain-dropping branches, and dank earth. I ate my breakfast with pleasure and was about to remove a plank to procure myself a little water when I heard a step, and looking through a small chink, I beheld a young creature, with a pail on her head, passing before my hovel. The girl was young and of gentle demeanour, unlike what I have since found cottagers and farmhouse servants to be. Yet she was meanly dressed, a coarse blue petticoat and a linen jacket being her only garb; her fair hair was plaited but not adorned: she looked patient yet sad. I lost sight of her, and in about a quarter of an hour she returned bearing the pail, which was now partly filled with milk. As she walked along, seemingly incommoded by the burden, a young man met her, whose countenance expressed a deeper despondence. Uttering a few sounds with an air of melancholy, he took the pail from her head and bore it to the cottage himself. She followed, and they disappeared. Presently I saw the young man again, with some tools in his hand, cross the field behind the cottage; and the girl was also busied, sometimes in the house and sometimes in the yard.

"On examining my dwelling, I found that one of the windows of the cottage had formerly occupied a part of it, but the panes had been filled up with wood. In one of these was a small and almost imperceptible chink through which the eye could just penetrate. Through this crevice a small room was visible, whitewashed and clean but very bare of furniture. In one corner, near a small fire, sat an old man, leaning his head on his hands in a disconsolate attitude. The young girl was occupied in arranging the cottage; but presently she took something out of a drawer, which employed her hands, and she sat down beside the old man, who, taking up an instrument, began to play and to produce sounds sweeter than the voice of the thrush or the nightingale. It was a lovely sight, even to me, poor wretch who had never beheld aught beautiful before. The silver hair and benevolent countenance of the aged cottager won my reverence, while the gentle manners of the girl enticed my love. He played a sweet mournful air which I perceived drew tears from the eyes of his amiable companion, of which the old man took no notice, until she sobbed audibly; he then pronounced a few sounds, and the fair creature, leaving her work, knelt at his feet. He raised her and smiled with such kindness and affection that I felt sensations of a peculiar and overpowering nature; they were a mixture of pain and pleasure, such as I had never before experienced, either from hunger or cold, warmth or food; and I withdrew from the window, unable to bear these emotions.

"Soon after this the young man returned, bearing on his shoulders a load of wood. The girl met him at the door, helped to relieve him of his burden, and taking some of the fuel into the cottage, placed it on the fire; then she and the youth went apart into a nook of the cottage, and he showed her a large loaf and a piece of cheese. She seemed pleased and went into the garden for some roots and plants, which she placed in water, and then upon the fire. She afterwards continued her work, whilst the young man went into the garden and appeared busily employed in digging and pulling up roots. After he had been employed thus about an hour, the young woman joined him and they entered the cottage together.

"The old man had, in the meantime, been pensive, but on the appearance of his companions he assumed a more cheerful air, and they sat down to eat. The meal was quickly dispatched. The young woman was again occupied in arranging the cottage, the old man walked before the cottage in the sun for a few minutes, leaning on the arm of the youth. Nothing could exceed in beauty the contrast between these two excellent creatures. One was old, with silver hairs and a countenance beaming with benevolence and love; the younger was slight and graceful in his figure, and his features were moulded with the finest symmetry, yet his eyes and attitude expressed the utmost sadness and despondency. The old man returned to the cottage, and the youth, with tools different from those he had used in the morning, directed his steps across the fields.

"Night quickly shut in, but to my extreme wonder, I found that the cottagers had a means of prolonging light by the use of tapers, and was delighted to find that the setting of the sun did not put an end to the pleasure I experienced in watching my human neighbours. In the evening the young girl and her companion were employed in various occupations which I did not understand; and the old man again took up the instrument which produced the divine sounds that had enchanted me in the morning. So soon as he had finished, the youth began, not to play, but to utter sounds that were monotonous, and neither resembling the harmony of the old man's instrument nor the songs of the birds; I since found that he read aloud, but at that time I knew nothing of the science of words or letters.

"The family, after having been thus occupied for a short time, extinguished their lights and retired, as I conjectured, to rest."

CHAPTER IV

I lay on my straw, but I could not sleep. I thought of the occurrences of the day. What chiefly struck me was the gentle manners of these people, and I longed to join them, but dared not. I remembered too well the treatment I had suffered the night before from the barbarous villagers, and resolved, whatever course of conduct I might hereafter think it right to pursue, that for the present I would remain quietly in my hovel, watching and endeavouring to discover the motives which influenced their actions.

"The cottagers arose the next morning before the sun. The young woman arranged the cottage and prepared the food, and the youth departed after the first meal.

"This day was passed in the same routine as that which preceded it. The young man was constantly employed out of doors, and the girl in various laborious occupations within. The old man, whom I soon perceived to be blind, employed his leisure hours on his instrument or in contemplation. Nothing could exceed the love and respect which the younger cottagers exhibited towards their venerable companion. They performed towards him every little office of affection and duty with gentleness, and he rewarded them by his benevolent smiles.

"They were not entirely happy. The young man and his companion often went apart and appeared to weep. I saw no cause for their unhappiness, but I was deeply affected by it. If such lovely creatures were miserable, it was less strange that I, an imperfect and solitary being, should be wretched. Yet why were these gentle beings unhappy? They possessed a delightful house (for such it was in my eyes) and every luxury; they had a fire to warm them when chill and delicious viands when hungry; they were dressed in excellent clothes; and, still more, they enjoyed one another's company and speech, interchanging each day looks of affection and kindness. What did their tears imply? Did they really express pain? I was at first unable to solve these questions, but perpetual attention and time explained to me many appearances which were at first enigmatic.

"A considerable period elapsed before I discovered one of the causes of the uneasiness of this amiable family: it was poverty, and they suffered that evil in a very distressing degree. Their nourishment consisted entirely of the vegetables of their garden and the milk of one cow, which gave very little during the winter, when its masters could scarcely procure food to support it. They often, I believe, suffered the pangs of hunger very poignantly, especially the two younger cottagers, for several times they placed food before the old man when they reserved none for themselves.

"This trait of kindness moved me sensibly. I had been accustomed, during the night, to steal a part of their store for my own consumption, but when I found that in doing this I inflicted pain on the cottagers, I abstained and satisfied myself with berries, nuts, and roots which I gathered from a neighbouring wood.

"I discovered also another means through which I was enabled to assist their labours. I found that the youth spent a great part of each day in collecting wood for the family fire, and during the night I often took his tools, the use of which I quickly discovered, and brought home firing sufficient for the consumption of several days.

"I remember, the first time that I did this, the young woman, when she opened the door in the morning, appeared greatly astonished on seeing a great pile of wood on the outside. She uttered some words in a loud voice, and the youth joined her, who also expressed surprise. I observed, with pleasure, that he did not go to the forest that day, but spent it in repairing the cottage and cultivating the garden.

"By degrees I made a discovery of still greater moment. I found that these people possessed a method of communicating their experience and feelings to one another by articulate sounds. I perceived that the words they spoke sometimes produced pleasure or pain, smiles or sadness, in the minds and countenances of the hearers. This was indeed a godlike science, and I ardently desired to become acquainted with it. But I was baffled in every attempt I made for this purpose. Their pronunciation was quick, and the words they uttered, not having any apparent connection with visible objects, I was unable to discover any clue by which I could unravel the mystery of their reference. By great application, however, and after having remained during the space of several revolutions of the moon in my hovel, I discovered the names that were given to some of the most familiar objects of discourse; I learned and applied the words, 'fire,' 'milk,' 'bread,' and 'wood.' I learned also the names of the cottagers themselves. The youth and his companion had each of them several names, but the old man had only one, which was 'father.' The girl was called 'sister' or 'Agatha,' and the youth 'Felix,' 'brother,' or 'son.' I cannot describe the delight I felt when I learned the ideas appropriated to each of these sounds and was able to pronounce them. I distinguished several other words without being able as yet to understand or apply them, such as 'good,' 'dearest,' 'unhappy.'

"I spent the winter in this manner. The gentle manners and beauty of the cottagers greatly endeared them to me; when they were unhappy, I felt depressed; when they rejoiced, I sympathised in their joys. I saw few human beings besides them, and if any other happened to enter the cottage, their harsh manners and rude gait only enhanced to me the superior accomplishments of my friends. The old man, I could perceive, often endeavoured to encourage his children, as sometimes I found that he called them, to cast off their melancholy. He would talk in a cheerful accent, with an expression of goodness that bestowed pleasure even upon me. Agatha listened with respect, her eyes sometimes filled with tears, which she endeavoured to wipe away unperceived; but I generally found that her countenance and tone were more cheerful after having listened to the exhortations of her father. It was not thus with Felix. He was always the saddest of the group, and even to my unpractised senses, he appeared to have suffered more deeply than his friends. But if his countenance was more sorrowful, his voice was more cheerful than that of his sister, especially when he addressed the old man.

"I could mention innumerable instances which, although slight, marked the dispositions of these amiable cottagers. In the midst of poverty and want, Felix carried with pleasure to his sister the first little white flower that peeped out from beneath the snowy ground. Early in the morning, before she had risen, he cleared away the snow that obstructed her path to the milk-house, drew water from the well, and brought the wood from the outhouse, where, to his perpetual astonishment, he found his store always replenished by an invisible hand. In the day, I believe, he worked sometimes for a neighbouring farmer, because he often went forth and did not return until dinner, yet brought no wood with him. At other times he worked in the garden, but as there was little to do in the frosty season, he read to the old man and Agatha.

"This reading had puzzled me extremely at first, but by degrees I discovered that he uttered many of the same sounds when he read as when he talked. I conjectured, therefore, that he found on the paper signs for speech which he understood, and I ardently longed to comprehend these also; but how was that possible when I did not even understand the sounds for which they stood as signs? I improved, however, sensibly in this science, but not sufficiently to follow up any kind of conversation, although I applied my whole mind to the endeavour: for I easily perceived that, although I eagerly longed to discover myself to the cottagers, I ought not to make the attempt until I had first become master of their language, which knowledge might enable me to make them overlook the deformity of my figure, for with this also the contrast perpetually presented to my eyes had made me acquainted.

"I had admired the perfect forms of my cottagers—their grace, beauty, and delicate complexions; but how was I terrified when I viewed myself in a transparent pool! At first I started back, unable to believe that it was indeed I who was reflected in the mirror; and when I became fully convinced that I was in reality the monster that I am, I was filled with the bitterest sensations of despondence and mortification. Alas! I did not yet entirely know the fatal effects of this miserable deformity.

"As the sun became warmer and the light of day longer, the snow vanished, and I beheld the bare trees and the black earth. From this time Felix was more employed, and the heart-moving indications of impending famine disappeared. Their food, as I afterwards found, was coarse, but it was wholesome; and they procured a sufficiency of it. Several new kinds of plants sprang up in the garden, which they dressed; and these signs of comfort increased daily as the season advanced.

"The old man, leaning on his son, walked each day at noon, when it did not rain, as I found it was called when the heavens poured forth its waters. This frequently took place, but a high wind quickly dried the earth, and the season became far more pleasant than it had been.

"My mode of life in my hovel was uniform. During the morning I attended the motions of the cottagers, and when they were dispersed in various occupations, I slept; the remainder of the day was spent in observing my friends. When they had retired to rest, if there was any moon or the night was star-light, I went into the woods and collected my own food and fuel for the cottage. When I returned, as often as it was necessary, I cleared their path from the snow and performed those offices that I had seen done by Felix. I afterwards found that these labours, performed by an invisible hand, greatly astonished them; and once or twice I heard them, on these occasions, utter the words 'good spirit,' 'wonderful'; but I did not then understand the signification of these terms.

"My thoughts now became more active, and I longed to discover the motives and feelings of these lovely creatures; I was inquisitive to know why Felix appeared so miserable and Agatha so sad. I thought (foolish wretch!) that it might be in my power to restore happiness to these deserving people. When I slept or was absent, the forms of the venerable blind father, the gentle Agatha, and the excellent Felix flitted before me. I looked upon them as superior beings who would be the arbiters of my future destiny. I formed in my imagination a thousand pictures of presenting myself to them, and their reception of me. I imagined that they would be disgusted, until, by my gentle demeanour and conciliating words, I should first win their favour and afterwards their love.

"These thoughts exhilarated me and led me to apply with fresh ardour to the acquiring the art of language. My organs were indeed harsh, but supple; and although my voice was very unlike the soft music of their tones, yet I pronounced such words as I understood with tolerable ease. It was as the ass and the lap-dog; yet surely the gentle ass whose intentions were affectionate, although his manners were rude, deserved better treatment than blows and execration.

"The pleasant showers and genial warmth of spring greatly altered the aspect of the earth. Men who before this change seemed to have been hid in caves dispersed themselves and were employed in various arts of cultivation. The birds sang in more cheerful notes, and the leaves began to bud forth on the trees. Happy, happy earth! Fit habitation for gods, which, so short a time before, was bleak, damp, and unwholesome. My spirits were elevated by the enchanting appearance of nature; the past was blotted from my memory, the present was tranquil, and the future gilded by bright rays of hope and anticipations of joy."

CHAPTER V

I now hasten to the more moving part of my story. I shall relate events that impressed me with feelings which, from what I had been, have made me what I am.

"Spring advanced rapidly; the weather became fine and the skies cloudless. It surprised me that what before was desert and gloomy should now bloom with the most beautiful flowers and verdure. My senses were gratified and refreshed by a thousand scents of delight and a thousand sights of beauty.

"It was on one of these days, when my cottagers periodically rested from labour—the old man played on his guitar, and the children listened to him—that I observed the countenance of Felix was melancholy beyond expression; he sighed frequently, and once his father paused in his music, and I conjectured by his manner that he enquired the cause of his son's sorrow. Felix replied in a cheerful accent, and the old man was recommencing his music when someone tapped at the door.

"It was a lady on horseback, accompanied by a countryman as a guide. The lady was dressed in a dark suit and covered with a thick black veil. Agatha asked a question, to which the stranger only replied by pronouncing, in a sweet accent, the name of Felix. Her voice was musical but unlike that of either of my friends. On hearing this word, Felix came up hastily to the lady, who, when she saw him, threw up her veil, and I beheld a countenance of angelic beauty and expression. Her hair of a shining raven black, and curiously braided; her eyes were dark, but gentle, although animated; her features of a regular proportion, and her complexion wondrously fair, each cheek tinged with a lovely pink.

"Felix seemed ravished with delight when he saw her, every trait of sorrow vanished from his face, and it instantly expressed a degree of ecstatic joy, of which I could hardly have believed it capable; his eyes sparkled, as his cheek flushed with pleasure; and at that moment I thought him as beautiful as the stranger. She appeared affected by different feelings; wiping a few tears from her lovely eyes, she held out her hand to Felix, who kissed it rapturously and called her, as well as I could distinguish, his sweet Arabian. She did not appear to understand him, but smiled. He assisted her to dismount, and dismissing her guide, conducted her into the cottage. Some conversation took place between him and his father, and the young stranger knelt at the old man's feet and would have kissed his hand, but he raised her and embraced her affectionately.

"I soon perceived that although the stranger uttered articulate sounds and appeared to have a language of her own, she was neither understood by nor herself understood the cottagers. They made many signs which I did not comprehend, but I saw that her presence diffused gladness through the cottage, dispelling their sorrow as the sun dissipates the morning mists. Felix seemed peculiarly happy and with smiles of delight welcomed his Arabian. Agatha, the ever-gentle Agatha, kissed the hands of the lovely stranger, and pointing to her brother, made signs which appeared to me to mean that he had been sorrowful until she came. Some hours passed thus, while they, by their countenances, expressed joy, the cause of which I did not comprehend. Presently I found, by the frequent recurrence of some sound which the stranger repeated after them, that she was endeavouring to learn their language; and the idea instantly occurred to me that I should make use of the same instructions to the same end. The stranger learned about twenty words at the first lesson; most of them, indeed, were those which I had before understood, but I profited by the others.

"As night came on, Agatha and the Arabian retired early. When they separated, Felix kissed the hand of the stranger and said, 'Good night, sweet Safie.' He sat up much longer, conversing with his father, and by the frequent repetition of her name I conjectured that their lovely guest was the subject of their conversation. I ardently desired to understand them, and bent every faculty towards that purpose, but found it utterly impossible.

"The next morning Felix went out to his work, and after the usual occupations of Agatha were finished, the Arabian sat at the feet of the old man, and taking his guitar, played some airs so entrancingly beautiful that they at once drew tears of sorrow and delight from my eyes. She sang, and her voice flowed in a rich cadence, swelling or dying away like a nightingale of the woods.

"When she had finished, she gave the guitar to Agatha, who at first declined it. She played a simple air, and her voice accompanied it in sweet accents, but unlike the wondrous strain of the stranger. The old man appeared enraptured and said some words which Agatha endeavoured to explain to Safie, and by which he appeared to wish to express that she bestowed on him the greatest delight by her music.

"The days now passed as peaceably as before, with the sole alteration that joy had taken place of sadness in the countenances of my friends. Safie was always gay and happy; she and I improved rapidly in the knowledge of language, so that in two months I began to comprehend most of the words uttered by my protectors.

"In the meanwhile also the black ground was covered with herbage, and the green banks interspersed with innumerable flowers, sweet to the scent and the eyes, stars of pale radiance among the moonlight woods; the sun became warmer, the nights clear and balmy; and my nocturnal rambles were an extreme pleasure to me, although they were considerably shortened by the late setting and early rising of the sun, for I never ventured abroad during daylight, fearful of meeting with the same treatment I had formerly endured in the first village which I entered.

"My days were spent in close attention, that I might more speedily master the language; and I may boast that I improved more rapidly than the Arabian, who understood very little and conversed in broken accents, whilst I comprehended and could imitate almost every word that was spoken.

"While I improved in speech, I also learned the science of letters as it was taught to the stranger, and this opened before me a wide field for wonder and delight.

"The book from which Felix instructed Safie was Volney's *Ruins of Empires*. I should not have understood the purport of this book had not Felix, in reading it, given very minute explanations. He had chosen this work, he said, because the declamatory style was framed in imitation of the Eastern authors. Through this work I obtained a cursory knowledge of history and a view of the several empires at present existing in the world; it gave me an insight into the manners, governments, and religions of the different nations of the earth. I heard of the slothful Asiatics, of the stupendous genius and mental activity of the Grecians, of the wars and wonderful virtue of the early Romans—of their subsequent degenerating—of the decline of that mighty empire, of chivalry, Christianity, and kings. I heard of the discovery of the American hemisphere and wept with Safie over the hapless fate of its original inhabitants.

"These wonderful narrations inspired me with strange feelings. Was man, indeed, at once so powerful, so virtuous and magnificent, yet so vicious and base? He appeared at one time a mere scion of the evil principle and at another as all that can be conceived of noble and godlike. To be a great and virtuous man appeared the highest honour that can befall a sensitive being; to be base and vicious, as many on record have been, appeared the lowest degradation, a condition more abject than that of the blind mole or harmless worm. For a long time I could not conceive how one man could go forth to murder his fellow, or even why there were laws and governments; but when I heard details of vice and bloodshed, my wonder ceased and I turned away with disgust and loathing.

"Every conversation of the cottagers now opened new wonders to me. While I listened to the instructions which Felix bestowed upon the Arabian, the strange system of human society was explained to me. I heard of the division of property, of immense wealth and squalid poverty, of rank, descent, and noble blood.

"The words induced me to turn towards myself. I learned that the possessions most esteemed by your fellow creatures were high and unsullied descent united with riches. A man might be respected with only one of these advantages, but without either he was considered, except in very rare instances, as a vagabond and a slave, doomed to waste his powers for the profits of the chosen few! And what was I? Of my creation and creator I was absolutely ignorant, but I knew that I possessed no money, no friends, no kind of property. I was, besides, endued with a figure hideously deformed and loathsome; I was not even of the same nature as man. I was more agile than they and could subsist upon coarser diet; I bore the extremes of heat and cold with less injury to my frame; my stature far exceeded theirs. When I looked around I saw and heard of none like me. Was I, then, a monster, a blot upon the earth, from which all men fled and whom all men disowned?

"I cannot describe to you the agony that these reflections inflicted upon me; I tried to dispel them, but sorrow only increased with knowledge. Oh, that I had forever remained in my native wood, nor known nor felt beyond the sensations of hunger, thirst, and heat!

"Of what a strange nature is knowledge! It clings to the mind when it has once seized on it like a lichen on the rock. I wished sometimes to shake off all thought and feeling, but I learned that there was but one means to overcome the sensation of pain, and that was death—a state which I feared yet did not understand. I admired virtue and good feelings and loved the gentle manners and amiable qualities of my cottagers, but I was shut out from intercourse with them, except through means which I obtained by stealth, when I was unseen and unknown, and which rather increased than satisfied the desire I had of becoming one among my fellows. The gentle words of Agatha and the animated smiles of the charming Arabian were not for me. The mild exhortations of the old man and the lively conversation of the loved Felix were not for me. Miserable, unhappy wretch!

"Other lessons were impressed upon me even more deeply. I heard of the difference of sexes, and the birth and growth of children, how the father doted on the smiles of the infant, and the lively sallies of the older child, how all the life and cares of the mother were wrapped up in the precious charge, how the mind of youth expanded and gained knowledge, of brother, sister, and all the various relationships which bind one human being to another in mutual bonds.

"But where were my friends and relations? No father had watched my infant days, no mother had blessed me with smiles and caresses; or if they had, all my past life was now a blot, a blind vacancy in which I distinguished nothing. From my earliest remembrance I had been as I then was in height and proportion. I had never yet seen a being resembling me or who claimed any intercourse with me. What was I? The question again recurred, to be answered only with groans.

"I will soon explain to what these feelings tended, but allow me now to return to the cottagers, whose story excited in me such various feelings of indignation, delight, and wonder, but which all terminated in additional love and reverence for my protectors (for so I loved, in an innocent, half-painful self-deceit, to call them)."

CHAPTER VI

Some time elapsed before I learned the history of my friends. It was one which could not fail to impress itself deeply on my mind, unfolding as it did a number of circumstances, each interesting and wonderful to one so utterly inexperienced as I was.

"The name of the old man was De Lacey. He was descended from a good family in France, where he had lived for many years in affluence, respected by his superiors and beloved by his equals. His son was bred in the service of his country, and Agatha had ranked with ladies of the highest distinction. A few months before my arrival they had lived in a large and luxurious city called Paris, surrounded by friends and possessed of every enjoyment which virtue, refinement of intellect, or taste, accompanied by a moderate fortune, could afford.

"The father of Safie had been the cause of their ruin. He was a Turkish merchant and had inhabited Paris for many years, when, for some reason which I could not learn, he became obnoxious to the government. He was seized and cast into prison the very day that Safie arrived from Constantinople to join him. He was tried and condemned to death. The injustice of his sentence was very flagrant; all Paris was indignant; and it was judged that his religion and wealth rather than the crime alleged against him had been the cause of his condemnation.

"Felix had accidentally been present at the trial; his horror and indignation were uncontrollable when he heard the decision of the court. He made, at that moment, a solemn vow to deliver him and then looked around for the means. After many fruitless attempts to gain admittance to the prison, he found a strongly grated window in an unguarded part of the building, which lighted the dungeon of the unfortunate Muhammadan, who, loaded with chains, waited in despair the execution of the barbarous sentence. Felix visited the grate at night and made known to the prisoner his intentions in his favour. The Turk, amazed and delighted, endeavoured to kindle the zeal of his deliverer by promises of reward and wealth. Felix rejected his offers with contempt, yet when he saw the lovely Safie, who was allowed to visit her father and who by her gestures expressed her lively gratitude, the youth could not help owning to his own mind that the captive possessed a treasure which would fully reward his toil and hazard.

"The Turk quickly perceived the impression that his daughter had made on the heart of Felix and endeavoured to secure him more entirely in his interests by the promise of her hand in marriage so soon as he should be conveyed to a place of safety. Felix was too delicate to accept this offer, yet he looked forward to the probability of the event as to the consummation of his happiness.

"During the ensuing days, while the preparations were going forward for the escape of the merchant, the zeal of Felix was warmed by several letters that he received from this lovely girl, who found means to express her thoughts in the language of her lover by the aid of an old man, a servant of her father who understood French. She thanked him in the most ardent terms for his intended services towards her parent, and at the same time she gently deplored her own fate.

"I have copies of these letters, for I found means, during my residence in the hovel, to procure the implements of writing; and the letters were often in the hands of Felix or Agatha. Before I depart I will give them to you; they will prove the truth of my tale; but at present, as the sun is already far declined, I shall only have time to repeat the substance of them to you.

"Safie related that her mother was a Christian Arab, seized and made a slave by the Turks; recommended by her beauty, she had won the heart of the father of Safie, who married her. The young girl spoke in high and enthusiastic terms of her mother, who, born in freedom, spurned the bondage to which she was now reduced. She instructed her daughter in the tenets of her religion and taught her to aspire to higher powers of intellect and an independence of spirit forbidden to the female followers of Muhammad. This lady died, but her lessons were indelibly impressed on the mind of Safie, who sickened at the prospect of again returning to Asia and being immured within the walls of a harem, allowed only to occupy herself with infantile amusements, ill-suited to the temper of her soul, now accustomed to grand ideas and a noble emulation for virtue. The prospect of marrying a Christian and remaining in a country where women were allowed to take a rank in society was enchanting to her.

"The day for the execution of the Turk was fixed, but on the night previous to it he quitted his prison and before morning was distant many leagues from Paris. Felix had procured passports in the name of his father, sister, and himself. He had previously communicated his plan to the former, who aided the deceit by quitting his house, under the pretence of a journey and concealed himself, with his daughter, in an obscure part of Paris.

"Felix conducted the fugitives through France to Lyons and across Mont Cenis to Leghorn, where the merchant had decided to wait a favourable opportunity of passing into some part of the Turkish dominions.

"Safie resolved to remain with her father until the moment of his departure, before which time the Turk renewed his promise that she should be united to his deliverer; and Felix remained with them in expectation of that event; and in the meantime he enjoyed the society of the Arabian, who exhibited towards him the simplest and tenderest affection. They conversed with one another through the means of an interpreter, and sometimes with the interpretation of looks; and Safie sang to him the divine airs of her native country.

"The Turk allowed this intimacy to take place and encouraged the hopes of the youthful lovers, while in his heart he had formed far other plans. He loathed the idea that his daughter should be united to a Christian, but he feared the resentment of Felix if he should appear lukewarm, for he knew that he was still in the power of his deliverer if he should choose to betray him to the Italian state which they inhabited. He revolved a thousand plans by which he should be enabled to prolong the deceit until it might be no longer necessary, and secretly to take his daughter with him when he departed. His plans were facilitated by the news which arrived from Paris.

"The government of France were greatly enraged at the escape of their victim and spared no pains to detect and punish his deliverer. The plot of Felix was quickly discovered, and De Lacey and Agatha were thrown into prison. The news reached Felix and roused him from his dream of pleasure. His blind and aged father and his gentle sister lay in a noisome dungeon while he enjoyed the free air and the society of her whom he loved. This idea was torture to him. He quickly arranged with the Turk that if the latter should find a favourable opportunity for escape before Felix could return to Italy, Safie should remain as a boarder at a convent at Leghorn; and then, quitting the lovely Arabian, he hastened to Paris and delivered himself up to the vengeance of the law, hoping to free De Lacey and Agatha by this proceeding.

"He did not succeed. They remained confined for five months before the trial took place, the result of which deprived them of their fortune and condemned them to a perpetual exile from their native country.

"They found a miserable asylum in the cottage in Germany, where I discovered them. Felix soon learned that the treacherous Turk, for whom he and his family endured such unheard-of oppression, on discovering that his deliverer was thus reduced to poverty and ruin, became a traitor to good feeling and honour and had quitted Italy with his daughter, insultingly sending Felix a pittance of money to aid him, as he said, in some plan of future maintenance.

"Such were the events that preyed on the heart of Felix and rendered him, when I first saw him, the most miserable of his family. He could have endured poverty, and while this distress had been the meed of his virtue, he gloried in it; but the ingratitude of the Turk and the loss of his beloved Safie were misfortunes more bitter and irreparable. The arrival of the Arabian now infused new life into his soul.

"When the news reached Leghorn that Felix was deprived of his wealth and rank, the merchant commanded his daughter to think no more of her lover, but to prepare to return to her native country. The generous nature of Safie was outraged by this command; she attempted to expostulate with her father, but he left her angrily, reiterating his tyrannical mandate.

"A few days after, the Turk entered his daughter's apartment and told her hastily that he had reason to believe that his residence at Leghorn had been divulged and that he should speedily be delivered up to the French government; he had consequently hired a vessel to convey him to Constantinople, for which city he should sail in a few hours. He intended to leave his daughter under the care of a confidential servant, to follow at her leisure with the greater part of his property, which had not yet arrived at Leghorn.

"When alone, Safie resolved in her own mind the plan of conduct that it would become her to pursue in this emergency. A residence in Turkey was abhorrent to her; her religion and her feelings were alike averse to it. By some papers of her father which fell into her hands she heard of the exile of her lover and learnt the name of the spot where he then resided. She hesitated some time, but at length she formed her determination. Taking with her some jewels that belonged to her and a sum of money, she quitted Italy with an attendant, a native of Leghorn, but who understood the common language of Turkey, and departed for Germany.

"She arrived in safety at a town about twenty leagues from the cottage of De Lacey, when her attendant fell dangerously ill. Safie nursed her with the most devoted affection, but the poor girl died, and the Arabian was left alone, unacquainted with the language of the country and utterly ignorant of the customs of the world. She fell, however, into good hands. The Italian had mentioned the name of the spot for which they were bound, and after her death the woman of the house in which they had lived took care that Safie should arrive in safety at the cottage of her lover."

CHAPTER VII

Such was the history of my beloved cottagers. It impressed me deeply. I learned, from the views of social life which it developed, to admire their virtues and to deprecate the vices of mankind.

"As yet I looked upon crime as a distant evil, benevolence and generosity were ever present before me, inciting within me a desire to become an actor in the busy scene where so many admirable qualities were called forth and displayed. But in giving an account of the progress of my intellect, I must not omit a circumstance which occurred in the beginning of the month of August of the same year.

"One night during my accustomed visit to the neighbouring wood where I collected my own food and brought home firing for my protectors, I found on the ground a leathern portmanteau containing several articles of dress and some books. I eagerly seized the prize and returned with it to my hovel. Fortunately the books were written in the language, the elements of which I had acquired at the cottage; they consisted of *Paradise Lost*, a volume of Plutarch's *Lives*, and the *Sorrows of Werter*. The possession of these treasures gave me extreme delight; I now continually studied and exercised my mind upon these histories, whilst my friends were employed in their ordinary occupations.

"I can hardly describe to you the effect of these books. They produced in me an infinity of new images and feelings, that sometimes raised me to ecstasy, but more frequently sunk me into the lowest dejection. In the *Sorrows of Werter*, besides the interest of its simple and affecting story, so many opinions are canvassed and so many lights thrown upon what had hitherto been to me obscure subjects that I found in it a never-ending source of speculation and astonishment. The gentle and domestic manners it described, combined with lofty sentiments and feelings, which had for their object something out of self, accorded well with my experience among my protectors and with the wants which were forever alive in my own bosom. But I thought Werter himself a more divine being than I had ever beheld or imagined; his character contained no pretension, but it sank deep. The disquisitions upon death and suicide were calculated to fill me with wonder. I did not pretend to enter into the merits of the case, yet I inclined towards the opinions of the hero, whose extinction I wept, without precisely understanding it.

"As I read, however, I applied much personally to my own feelings and condition. I found myself similar yet at the same time strangely unlike to the beings concerning whom I read and to whose conversation I was a listener. I sympathised with and partly understood them, but I was unformed in mind; I was dependent on none and related to none. 'The path of my departure was free,' and there was none to lament my annihilation. My person was hideous and my stature gigantic. What did this mean? Who was I? What was I? Whence did I come? What was my destination? These questions continually recurred, but I was unable to solve them.

"The volume of Plutarch's *Lives* which I possessed contained the histories of the first founders of the ancient republics. This book had a far different effect upon me from the *Sorrows of Werter*. I learned from Werter's imaginations despondency and gloom, but Plutarch taught me high thoughts; he elevated me above the wretched sphere of my own reflections, to admire and love the heroes of past ages. Many things I read surpassed my understanding and experience. I had a very confused knowledge of kingdoms, wide extents of country, mighty rivers, and boundless seas. But I was perfectly unacquainted with towns and large assemblages of men. The cottage of my protectors had been the only school in which I had studied human nature, but this book developed new and mightier scenes of action. I read of men concerned in public affairs, governing or massacring their species. I felt the greatest ardour for virtue rise within me, and abhorrence for vice, as far as I understood the signification of those terms, relative as they were, as I applied them, to pleasure and pain alone. Induced by these feelings, I was of course led to admire peaceable lawgivers, Numa, Solon, and Lycurgus, in preference to Romulus and Theseus. The patriarchal lives of my protectors caused these impressions to take a firm hold on my mind; perhaps, if my first introduction to humanity had been made by a young soldier, burning for glory and slaughter, I should have been imbued with different sensations.

"But *Paradise Lost* excited different and far deeper emotions. I read it, as I had read the other volumes which had fallen into my hands, as a true history. It moved every feeling of wonder and awe that the picture of an omnipotent God warring with his creatures was capable of exciting. I often referred the several situations, as their similarity struck me, to my own. Like Adam, I was apparently united by no link to any other being in existence; but his state was far different from mine in every other respect. He had come forth from the hands of God a perfect creature, happy and prosperous, guarded by the especial care of his Creator; he was allowed to converse with and acquire knowledge from beings of a superior nature, but I was wretched, helpless, and alone. Many times I considered Satan as the fitter emblem of my condition, for often, like him, when I viewed the bliss of my protectors, the bitter gall of envy rose within me.

"Another circumstance strengthened and confirmed these feelings. Soon after my arrival in the hovel I discovered some papers in the pocket of the dress which I had taken from your laboratory. At first I had neglected them, but now that I was able to decipher the characters in which they were written, I began to study them with diligence. It was your journal of the four months that preceded my creation. You minutely described in these papers every step you took in the progress of your work; this history was mingled with accounts of domestic occurrences. You doubtless recollect these papers. Here they are. Everything is related in them which bears reference to my accursed origin; the whole detail of that series of disgusting circumstances which produced it is set in view; the minutest description of my odious and loathsome person is given, in language which painted your own horrors and rendered mine indelible. I sickened as I read. 'Hateful day when I received life!' I exclaimed in agony. 'Accursed creator! Why did you form a monster so hideous that even *you* turned from me in disgust? God, in pity, made man beautiful and alluring, after his own image; but my form is a filthy type of yours, more horrid even from the very resemblance. Satan had his companions, fellow devils, to admire and encourage him, but I am solitary and abhorred.'

"These were the reflections of my hours of despondency and solitude; but when I contemplated the virtues of the cottagers, their amiable and benevolent dispositions, I persuaded myself that when they should become acquainted with my admiration of their virtues they would compassionate me and overlook my personal deformity. Could they turn from their door one, however monstrous, who solicited their compassion and friendship? I resolved, at least, not to despair, but in every way to fit myself for an interview with them which would decide my fate. I postponed this attempt for some months longer, for the importance attached to its success inspired me with a dread lest I should fail. Besides, I found that my understanding improved so much with every day's experience that I was unwilling to commence this undertaking until a few more months should have added to my sagacity.

"Several changes, in the meantime, took place in the cottage. The presence of Safie diffused happiness among its inhabitants, and I also found that a greater degree of plenty reigned there. Felix and Agatha spent more time in amusement and conversation, and were assisted in their labours by servants. They did not appear rich, but they were contented and happy; their feelings were serene and peaceful, while mine became every day more tumultuous. Increase of knowledge only discovered to me more clearly what a wretched outcast I was. I cherished hope, it is true, but it vanished when I beheld my person reflected in water or my shadow in the moonshine, even as that frail image and that inconstant shade.

"I endeavoured to crush these fears and to fortify myself for the trial which in a few months I resolved to undergo; and sometimes I allowed my thoughts, unchecked by reason, to ramble in the fields of Paradise, and dared to fancy amiable and lovely creatures sympathising with my feelings and cheering my gloom; their angelic countenances breathed smiles of consolation. But it was all a dream; no Eve soothed my sorrows nor shared my thoughts; I was alone. I remembered Adam's supplication to his Creator. But where was mine? He had abandoned me, and in the bitterness of my heart I cursed him.

"Autumn passed thus. I saw, with surprise and grief, the leaves decay and fall, and nature again assume the barren and bleak appearance it had worn when I first beheld the woods and the lovely moon. Yet I did not heed the bleakness of the weather; I was better fitted by my conformation for the endurance of cold than heat. But my chief delights were the sight of the flowers, the birds, and all the gay apparel of summer; when those deserted me, I turned with more attention towards the cottagers. Their happiness was not decreased by the absence of summer. They loved and sympathised with one another; and their joys, depending on each other, were not interrupted by the casualties that took place around them. The more I saw of them, the greater became my desire to claim their protection and kindness; my heart yearned to be known and loved by these amiable creatures; to see their sweet looks directed towards me with affection was the utmost limit of my ambition. I dared not think that they would turn them from me with disdain and horror. The poor that stopped at their door were never driven away. I asked, it is true, for greater treasures than a little food or rest: I required kindness and sympathy; but I did not believe myself utterly unworthy of it.

"The winter advanced, and an entire revolution of the seasons had taken place since I awoke into life. My attention at this time was solely directed towards my plan of introducing myself into the cottage of my protectors. I revolved many projects, but that on which I finally fixed was to enter the dwelling when the blind old man should be alone. I had sagacity enough to discover that the unnatural hideousness of my person was the chief object of horror with those who had formerly beheld me. My voice, although harsh, had nothing terrible in it; I thought, therefore, that if in the absence of his children I could gain the good will and mediation of the old De Lacey, I might by his means be tolerated by my younger protectors.

"One day, when the sun shone on the red leaves that strewed the ground and diffused cheerfulness, although it denied warmth, Safie, Agatha, and Felix departed on a long country walk, and the old man, at his own desire, was left alone in the cottage. When his children had departed, he took up his guitar and played several mournful but sweet airs, more sweet and mournful than I had ever heard him play before. At first his countenance was illuminated with pleasure, but as he continued, thoughtfulness and sadness succeeded; at length, laying aside the instrument, he sat absorbed in reflection.

"My heart beat quick; this was the hour and moment of trial, which would decide my hopes or realize my fears. The servants were gone to a neighbouring fair. All was silent in and around the cottage; it was an excellent opportunity; yet, when I proceeded to execute my plan, my limbs failed me and I sank to the ground. Again I rose, and exerting all the firmness of which I was master, removed the planks which I had placed before my hovel to conceal my retreat. The fresh air revived me, and with renewed determination I approached the door of their cottage.

"I knocked. 'Who is there?' said the old man. 'Come in.'

"I entered. 'Pardon this intrusion,' said I; 'I am a traveller in want of a little rest; you would greatly oblige me if you would allow me to remain a few minutes before the fire.'

"'Enter,' said De Lacey, 'and I will try in what manner I can to relieve your wants; but, unfortunately, my children are from home, and as I am blind, I am afraid I shall find it difficult to procure food for you.'

"'Do not trouble yourself, my kind host; I have food; it is warmth and rest only that I need.'

"I sat down, and a silence ensued. I knew that every minute was precious to me, yet I remained irresolute in what manner to commence the interview, when the old man addressed me. 'By your language, stranger, I suppose you are my countryman; are you French?'

"'No; but I was educated by a French family and understand that language only. I am now going to claim the protection of some friends, whom I sincerely love, and of whose favour I have some hopes.'

"'Are they Germans?'

"'No, they are French. But let us change the subject. I am an unfortunate and deserted creature; I look around and I have no relation or friend upon earth. These amiable people to whom I go have never seen me and know little of me. I am full of fears, for if I fail there, I am an outcast in the world forever.'

"'Do not despair. To be friendless is indeed to be unfortunate, but the hearts of men, when unprejudiced by any obvious self-interest, are full of brotherly love and charity. Rely, therefore, on your hopes; and if these friends are good and amiable, do not despair.'

"'They are kind—they are the most excellent creatures in the world; but, unfortunately, they are prejudiced against me. I have good dispositions; my life has been hitherto harmless and in some degree beneficial; but a fatal prejudice clouds their eyes, and where they ought to see a feeling and kind friend, they behold only a detestable monster.'

"'That is indeed unfortunate; but if you are really blameless, cannot you undeceive them?'

"'I am about to undertake that task; and it is on that account that I feel so many overwhelming terrors. I tenderly love these friends; I have, unknown to them, been for many months in the habits of daily kindness towards them; but they believe that I wish to injure them, and it is that prejudice which I wish to overcome.'

"'Where do these friends reside?'

"'Near this spot.'

"The old man paused and then continued, 'If you will unreservedly confide to me the particulars of your tale, I perhaps may be of use in undeceiving them. I am blind and cannot judge of your countenance, but there is something in your words which persuades me that you are sincere. I am poor and an exile, but it will afford me true pleasure to be in any way serviceable to a human creature.'

"'Excellent man! I thank you and accept your generous offer. You raise me from the dust by this kindness; and I trust that, by your aid, I shall not be driven from the society and sympathy of your fellow creatures.'

"'Heaven forbid! Even if you were really criminal, for that can only drive you to desperation, and not instigate you to virtue. I also am unfortunate; I and my family have been condemned, although innocent; judge, therefore, if I do not feel for your misfortunes.'

"'How can I thank you, my best and only benefactor? From your lips first have I heard the voice of kindness directed towards me; I shall be forever grateful; and your present humanity assures me of success with those friends whom I am on the point of meeting.'

"'May I know the names and residence of those friends?'

"I paused. This, I thought, was the moment of decision, which was to rob me of or bestow happiness on me forever. I struggled vainly for firmness sufficient to answer him, but the effort destroyed all my remaining strength; I sank on the chair and sobbed aloud. At that moment I heard the steps of my younger protectors. I had not a moment to lose, but seizing the hand of the old man, I cried, 'Now is the time! Save and protect me! You and your family are the friends whom I seek. Do not you desert me in the hour of trial!'

"'Great God!' exclaimed the old man. 'Who are you?'

"At that instant the cottage door was opened, and Felix, Safie, and Agatha entered. Who can describe their horror and consternation on beholding me? Agatha fainted, and Safie, unable to attend to her friend, rushed out of the cottage. Felix darted forward, and with supernatural force tore me from his father, to whose knees I clung: in a transport of fury, he dashed me to the ground and struck me violently with a stick. I could have torn him limb from limb, as the lion rends the antelope. But my heart sank within me as with bitter sickness, and I refrained. I saw him on the point of repeating his blow, when, overcome by pain and anguish, I quitted the cottage, and in the general tumult escaped unperceived to my hovel."

CHAPTER VIII

Cursed, cursed creator! Why did I live? Why, in that instant, did I not extinguish the spark of existence which you had so wantonly bestowed? I know not; despair had not yet taken possession of me; my feelings were those of rage and revenge. I could with pleasure have destroyed the cottage and its inhabitants and have glutted myself with their shrieks and misery.

"When night came I quitted my retreat and wandered in the wood; and now, no longer restrained by the fear of discovery, I gave vent to my anguish in fearful howlings. I was like a wild beast that had broken the toils, destroying the objects that obstructed me and ranging through the wood with a staglike swiftness. Oh! What a miserable night I passed! The cold stars shone in mockery, and the bare trees waved their branches above me; now and then the sweet voice of a bird burst forth amidst the universal stillness. All, save I, were at rest or in enjoyment; I, like the archfiend, bore a hell within me, and finding myself unsympathised with, wished to tear up the trees, spread havoc and destruction around me, and then to have sat down and enjoyed the ruin.

"But this was a luxury of sensation that could not endure; I became fatigued with excess of bodily exertion and sank on the damp grass in the sick impotence of despair. There was none among the myriads of men that existed who would pity or assist me; and should I feel kindness towards my enemies? No; from that moment I declared everlasting war against the species, and more than all, against him who had formed me and sent me forth to this insupportable misery.

"The sun rose; I heard the voices of men and knew that it was impossible to return to my retreat during that day. Accordingly I hid myself in some thick underwood, determining to devote the ensuing hours to reflection on my situation.

"The pleasant sunshine and the pure air of day restored me to some degree of tranquillity; and when I considered what had passed at the cottage, I could not help believing that I had been too hasty in my conclusions. I had certainly acted imprudently. It was apparent that my conversation had interested the father in my behalf, and I was a fool in having exposed my person to the horror of his children. I ought to have familiarized the old De Lacey to me, and by degrees to have discovered myself to the rest of his family, when they should have been prepared for my approach. But I did not believe my errors to be irretrievable, and after much consideration I resolved to return to the cottage, seek the old man, and by my representations win him to my party.

"These thoughts calmed me, and in the afternoon I sank into a profound sleep; but the fever of my blood did not allow me to be visited by peaceful dreams. The horrible scene of the preceding day was forever acting before my eyes; the females were flying and the enraged Felix tearing me from his father's feet. I awoke exhausted, and finding that it was already night, I crept forth from my hiding-place, and went in search of food.

"When my hunger was appeased, I directed my steps towards the well-known path that conducted to the cottage. All there was at peace. I crept into my hovel and remained in silent expectation of the accustomed hour when the family arose. That hour passed, the sun mounted high in the heavens, but the cottagers did not appear. I trembled violently, apprehending some dreadful misfortune. The inside of the cottage was dark, and I heard no motion; I cannot describe the agony of this suspense.

"Presently two countrymen passed by, but pausing near the cottage, they entered into conversation, using violent gesticulations; but I did not understand what they said, as they spoke the language of the country, which differed from that of my protectors. Soon after, however, Felix approached with another man; I was surprised, as I knew that he had not quitted the cottage that morning, and waited anxiously to discover from his discourse the meaning of these unusual appearances.

" 'Do you consider,' said his companion to him, 'that you will be obliged to pay three months' rent and to lose the produce of your garden? I do not wish to take any unfair advantage, and I beg therefore that you will take some days to consider of your determination.'

" 'It is utterly useless,' replied Felix; 'we can never again inhabit your cottage. The life of my father is in the greatest danger, owing to the dreadful circumstance that I have related. My wife and my sister will never recover from their horror. I entreat you not to reason with me any more. Take possession of your tenement and let me fly from this place.'

"Felix trembled violently as he said this. He and his companion entered the cottage, in which they remained for a few minutes, and then departed. I never saw any of the family of De Lacey more.

"I continued for the remainder of the day in my hovel in a state of utter and stupid despair. My protectors had departed and had broken the only link that held me to the world. For the first time the feelings of revenge and hatred filled my bosom, and I did not strive to control them, but allowing myself to be borne away by the stream, I bent my mind towards injury and death. When I thought of my friends, of the mild voice of De Lacey, the gentle eyes of Agatha, and the exquisite beauty of the Arabian, these thoughts vanished and a gush of tears somewhat soothed me. But again when I reflected that they had spurned and deserted me, anger returned, a rage of anger, and unable to injure anything human, I turned my fury towards inanimate objects. As night advanced I placed a variety of combustibles around the cottage, and after having destroyed every vestige of cultivation in the garden, I waited with forced impatience until the moon had sunk to commence my operations.

"As the night advanced, a fierce wind arose from the woods and quickly dispersed the clouds that had loitered in the heavens; the blast tore along like a mighty avalanche and produced a kind of insanity in my spirits that burst all bounds of reason and reflection. I lighted the dry branch of a tree and danced with fury around the devoted cottage, my eyes still fixed on the western horizon, the edge of which the moon nearly touched. A part of its orb was at length hid, and I waved my brand; it sank, and with a loud scream I fired the straw, and heath, and bushes, which I had collected. The wind fanned the fire, and the cottage was quickly enveloped by the flames, which clung to it and licked it with their forked and destroying tongues.

"As soon as I was convinced that no assistance could save any part of the habitation, I quitted the scene and sought for refuge in the woods.

"And now, with the world before me, whither should I bend my steps? I resolved to fly far from the scene of my misfortunes; but to me, hated and despised, every country must be equally horrible. At length the thought of you crossed my mind. I learned from your papers that you were my father, my creator; and to whom could I apply with more fitness than to him who had given me life? Among the lessons that Felix had bestowed upon Safie, geography had not been omitted; I had learned from these the relative situations of the different countries of the earth. You had mentioned Geneva as the name of your native town, and towards this place I resolved to proceed.

"But how was I to direct myself? I knew that I must travel in a southwesterly direction to reach my destination, but the sun was my only guide. I did not know the names of the towns that I was to pass through, nor could I ask information from a single human being; but I did not despair. From you only could I hope for succour, although towards you I felt no sentiment but that of hatred. Unfeeling, heartless creator! You had endowed me with perceptions and passions and then cast me abroad an object for the scorn and horror of mankind. But on you only had I any claim for pity and redress, and from you I determined to seek that justice which I vainly attempted to gain from any other being that wore the human form.

"My travels were long and the sufferings I endured intense. It was late in autumn when I quitted the district where I had so long resided. I travelled only at night, fearful of encountering the visage of a human being. Nature decayed around me, and the sun became heatless; rain and snow poured around me; mighty rivers were frozen; the surface of the earth was hard and chill, and bare, and I found no shelter. Oh, earth! How often did I imprecate curses on the cause of my being! The mildness of my nature had fled, and all within me was turned to gall and bitterness. The nearer I approached to your habitation, the more deeply did I feel the spirit of revenge enkindled in my heart. Snow fell, and the waters were hardened, but I rested not. A few incidents now and then directed me, and I possessed a map of the country; but I often wandered wide from my path. The agony of my feelings allowed me no respite; no incident occurred from which my rage and misery could not extract its food; but a circumstance that happened when I arrived on the confines of Switzerland, when the sun had recovered its warmth and the earth again began to look green, confirmed in an especial manner the bitterness and horror of my feelings.

"I generally rested during the day and travelled only when I was secured by night from the view of man. One morning, however, finding that my path lay through a deep wood, I ventured to continue my journey after the sun had risen; the day, which was one of the first of spring, cheered even me by the loveliness of its sunshine and the balminess of the air. I felt emotions of gentleness and pleasure, that had long appeared dead, revive within me. Half surprised by the novelty of these sensations, I allowed myself to be borne away by them, and forgetting my solitude and deformity, dared to be happy. Soft tears again bedewed my cheeks, and I even raised my humid eyes with thankfulness towards the blessed sun, which bestowed such joy upon me.

"I continued to wind among the paths of the wood, until I came to its boundary, which was skirted by a deep and rapid river, into which many of the trees bent their branches, now budding with the fresh spring. Here I paused, not exactly knowing what path to pursue, when I heard the sound of voices, that induced me to conceal myself under the shade of a cypress. I was scarcely hid when a young girl came running towards the spot where I was concealed, laughing, as if she ran from someone in sport. She continued her course along the precipitous sides of the river, when suddenly her foot slipped, and she fell into the rapid stream. I rushed from my hiding-place and with extreme labour, from the force of the current, saved her and dragged her to shore. She was senseless, and I endeavoured by every means in my power to restore animation, when I was suddenly interrupted by the approach of a rustic, who was probably the person from whom she had playfully fled. On seeing me, he darted towards me, and tearing the girl from my arms, hastened towards the deeper parts of the wood. I followed speedily, I hardly knew why; but when the man saw me draw near, he aimed a gun, which he carried, at my body and fired. I sank to the ground, and my injurer, with increased swiftness, escaped into the wood.

"This was then the reward of my benevolence! I had saved a human being from destruction, and as a recompense I now writhed under the miserable pain of a wound which shattered the flesh and bone. The feelings of kindness and gentleness which I had entertained but a few moments before gave place to hellish rage and gnashing of teeth. Inflamed by pain, I vowed eternal hatred and vengeance to all mankind. But the agony of my wound overcame me; my pulses paused, and I fainted.

"For some weeks I led a miserable life in the woods, endeavouring to cure the wound which I had received. The ball had entered my shoulder, and I knew not whether it had remained there or passed through; at any rate I had no means of extracting it. My sufferings were augmented also by the oppressive sense of the injustice and ingratitude of their infliction. My daily vows rose for revenge—a deep and deadly revenge, such as would alone compensate for the outrages and anguish I had endured.

"After some weeks my wound healed, and I continued my journey. The labours I endured were no longer to be alleviated by the bright sun or gentle breezes of spring; all joy was but a mockery which insulted my desolate state and made me feel more painfully that I was not made for the enjoyment of pleasure.

"But my toils now drew near a close, and in two months from this time I reached the environs of Geneva.

"It was evening when I arrived, and I retired to a hiding-place among the fields that surround it to meditate in what manner I should apply to you. I was oppressed by fatigue and hunger and far too unhappy to enjoy the gentle breezes of evening or the prospect of the sun setting behind the stupendous mountains of Jura.

"At this time a slight sleep relieved me from the pain of reflection, which was disturbed by the approach of a beautiful child, who came running into the recess I had chosen, with all the sportiveness of infancy. Suddenly, as I gazed on him, an idea seized me that this little creature was unprejudiced and had lived too short a time to have imbibed a horror of deformity. If, therefore, I could seize him and educate him as my companion and friend, I should not be so desolate in this peopled earth.

"Urged by this impulse, I seized on the boy as he passed and drew him towards me. As soon as he beheld my form, he placed his hands before his eyes and uttered a shrill scream; I drew his hand forcibly from his face and said, 'Child, what is the meaning of this? I do not intend to hurt you; listen to me.'

"He struggled violently. 'Let me go,' he cried. 'Monster! Ugly wretch! You wish to eat me and tear me to pieces. You are an ogre. Let me go, or I will tell my papa.'

" 'Boy, you will never see your father again; you must come with me.'

" 'Hideous monster! Let me go. My papa is a syndic—he is M. Frankenstein—he will punish you. You dare not keep me.'

" 'Frankenstein! You belong then to my enemy—to him towards whom I have sworn eternal revenge; you shall be my first victim.'

"The child still struggled, and loaded me with epithets which carried despair to my heart; I grasped his throat to silence him, and in a moment he lay dead at my feet.

"I gazed on my victim, and my heart swelled with exultation and hellish triumph; clapping my hands, I exclaimed, 'I too can create desolation; my enemy is not invulnerable; this death will carry despair to him, and a thousand other miseries shall torment and destroy him.'

"As I fixed my eyes on the child, I saw something glittering on his breast. I took it; it was a portrait of a most lovely woman. In spite of my malignity, it softened and attracted me. For a few moments I gazed with delight on her dark eyes, fringed by deep lashes, and her lovely lips; but presently my rage returned; I remembered that I was forever deprived of the delights that such beautiful creatures could bestow and that she whose resemblance I contemplated would, in regarding me, have changed that air of divine benignity to one expressive of disgust and affright.

"Can you wonder that such thoughts transported me with rage? I only wonder that at that moment, instead of venting my sensations in exclamations and agony, I did not rush among mankind and perish in the attempt to destroy them.

"While I was overcome by these feelings, I left the spot where I had committed the murder, and seeking a more secluded hiding-place, I entered a barn which had appeared to me to be empty. A woman was sleeping on some straw; she was young, not indeed so beautiful as her whose portrait I held, but of an agreeable aspect and blooming in the loveliness of youth and health. Here, I thought, is one of those whose joy-imparting smiles are bestowed on all but me. And then I bent over her and whispered, 'Awake, fairest, thy lover is near—he who would give his life but to obtain one look of affection from thine eyes; my beloved, awake!'

"The sleeper stirred; a thrill of terror ran through me. Should she indeed awake, and see me, and curse me, and denounce the murderer? Thus would she assuredly act if her darkened eyes opened and she beheld me. The thought was madness; it stirred the fiend within me—not I, but she, shall suffer; the murder I have committed because I am forever robbed of all that she could give me, she shall atone. The crime had its source in her; be hers the punishment! Thanks to the lessons of Felix and the sanguinary laws of man, I had learned now to work mischief. I bent over her and placed the portrait securely in one of the folds of her dress. She moved again, and I fled.

"For some days I haunted the spot where these scenes had taken place, sometimes wishing to see you, sometimes resolved to quit the world and its miseries forever. At length I wandered towards these mountains, and have ranged through their immense recesses, consumed by a burning passion which you alone can gratify. We may not part until you have promised to comply with my requisition. I am alone and miserable; man will not associate with me; but one as deformed and horrible as myself would not deny herself to me. My companion must be of the same species and have the same defects. This being you must create."

CHAPTER IX

The being finished speaking, and fixed his looks upon me in the expectation of a reply. But I was bewildered, perplexed, and unable to arrange my ideas sufficiently to understand the full extent of his proposition. He continued.

"You must create a female for me, with whom I can live in the interchange of those sympathies necessary for my being. This you alone can do, and I demand it of you as a right which you must not refuse to concede."

The latter part of his tale had kindled anew in me the anger that had died away while he narrated his peaceful life among the cottagers, and as he said this I could no longer suppress the rage that burned within me.

"I do refuse it," I replied; "and no torture shall ever extort a consent from me. You may render me the most miserable of men, but you shall never make me base in my own eyes. Shall I create another like yourself, whose joint wickedness might desolate the world? Begone! I have answered you; you may torture me, but I will never consent."

"You are in the wrong," replied the fiend; "and instead of threatening, I am content to reason with you. I am malicious because I am miserable. Am I not shunned and hated by all mankind? You, my creator, would tear me to pieces and triumph; remember that, and tell me why I should pity man more than he pities me? You would not call it murder if you could precipitate me into one of those ice-rifts and destroy my frame, the work of your own hands. Shall I respect man when he condemns me? Let him live with me in the interchange of kindness, and instead of injury I would bestow every benefit upon him with tears of gratitude at his acceptance. But that cannot be; the human senses are insurmountable barriers to our union. Yet mine shall not be the submission of abject slavery. I will revenge my injuries; if I cannot inspire love, I will cause fear, and chiefly towards you my archenemy, because my creator, do I swear inextinguishable hatred. Have a care; I will work at your destruction, nor finish until I desolate your heart, so that you shall curse the hour of your birth."

A fiendish rage animated him as he said this; his face was wrinkled into contortions too horrible for human eyes to behold; but presently he calmed himself and proceeded.

"I intended to reason. This passion is detrimental to me, for you do not reflect that *you* are the cause of its excess. If any being felt emotions of benevolence towards me, I should return them a hundred and a hundredfold; for that one creature's sake I would make peace with the whole kind! But I now indulge in dreams of bliss that cannot be realized. What I ask of you is reasonable and moderate; I demand a creature of another sex, but as hideous as myself; the gratification is small, but it is all that I can receive, and it shall content me. It is true, we shall be monsters, cut off from all the world; but on that account we shall be more attached to one another. Our lives will not be happy, but they will be harmless and free from the misery I now feel. Oh! My creator, make me happy; let me feel gratitude towards you for one benefit! Let me see that I excite the sympathy of some existing thing; do not deny me my request!"

I was moved. I shuddered when I thought of the possible consequences of my consent, but I felt that there was some justice in his argument. His tale and the feelings he now expressed proved him to be a creature of fine sensations, and did I not as his maker owe him all the portion of happiness that it was in my power to bestow? He saw my change of feeling and continued.

"If you consent, neither you nor any other human being shall ever see us again; I will go to the vast wilds of South America. My food is not that of man; I do not destroy the lamb and the kid to glut my appetite; acorns and berries afford me sufficient nourishment. My companion will be of the same nature as myself and will be content with the same fare. We shall make our bed of dried leaves; the sun will shine on us as on man and will ripen our food. The picture I present to you is peaceful and human, and you must feel that you could deny it only in the wantonness of power and cruelty. Pitiless as you have been towards me, I now see compassion in your eyes; let me seize the favourable moment and persuade you to promise what I so ardently desire."

"You propose," replied I, "to fly from the habitations of man, to dwell in those wilds where the beasts of the field will be your only companions. How can you, who long for the love and sympathy of man, persevere in this exile? You will return and again seek their kindness, and you will meet with their detestation; your evil passions will be renewed, and you will then have a companion to aid you in the task of destruction. This may not be; cease to argue the point, for I cannot consent."

"How inconstant are your feelings! But a moment ago you were moved by my representations, and why do you again harden yourself to my complaints? I swear to you, by the earth which I inhabit, and by you that made me, that with the companion you bestow I will quit the neighbourhood of man and dwell, as it may chance, in the most savage of places. My evil passions will have fled, for I shall meet with sympathy! My life will flow quietly away, and in my dying moments I shall not curse my maker."

His words had a strange effect upon me. I compassionated him and sometimes felt a wish to console him, but when I looked upon him, when I saw the filthy mass that moved and talked, my heart sickened and my feelings were altered to those of horror and hatred. I tried to stifle these sensations; I thought that as I could not sympathise with him, I had no right to withhold from him the small portion of happiness which was yet in my power to bestow.

"You swear," I said, "to be harmless; but have you not already shown a degree of malice that should reasonably make me distrust you? May not even this be a feint that will increase your triumph by affording a wider scope for your revenge?"

"How is this? I must not be trifled with, and I demand an answer. If I have no ties and no affections, hatred and vice must be my portion; the love of another will destroy the cause of my crimes, and I shall become a thing of whose existence everyone will be ignorant. My vices are the children of a forced solitude that I abhor, and my virtues will necessarily arise when I live in communion with an equal. I shall feel the affections of a sensitive being and become linked to the chain of existence and events from which I am now excluded."

I paused some time to reflect on all he had related and the various arguments which he had employed. I thought of the promise of virtues which he had displayed on the opening of his existence and the subsequent blight of all kindly feeling by the loathing and scorn which his protectors had manifested towards him. His power and threats were not omitted in my calculations; a creature who could exist in the ice caves of the glaciers and hide himself from pursuit among the ridges of inaccessible precipices was a being possessing faculties it would be vain to cope with. After a long pause of reflection I concluded that the justice due both to him and my fellow creatures demanded of me that I should comply with his request. Turning to him, therefore, I said:

"I consent to your demand, on your solemn oath to quit Europe forever, and every other place in the neighbourhood of man, as soon as I shall deliver into your hands a female who will accompany you in your exile."

"I swear," he cried, "by the sun, and by the blue sky of heaven, and by the fire of love that burns my heart, that if you grant my prayer, while they exist you shall never behold me again. Depart to your home and commence your labours; I shall watch their progress with unutterable anxiety; and fear not but that when you are ready I shall appear."

Saying this, he suddenly quitted me, fearful, perhaps, of any change in my sentiments. I saw him descend the mountain with greater speed than the flight of an eagle, and quickly lost among the undulations of the sea of ice.

His tale had occupied the whole day, and the sun was upon the verge of the horizon when he departed. I knew that I ought to hasten my descent towards the valley, as I should soon be encompassed in darkness; but my heart was heavy, and my steps slow. The labour of winding among the little paths of the mountain and fixing my feet firmly as I advanced perplexed me, occupied as I was by the emotions which the occurrences of the day had produced. Night was far advanced when I came to the halfway resting-place and seated myself beside the fountain. The stars shone at intervals as the clouds passed from over them; the dark pines rose before me, and every here and there a broken tree lay on the ground; it was a scene of wonderful solemnity and stirred strange thoughts within me. I wept bitterly, and clasping my hands in agony, I exclaimed, "Oh! Stars and clouds and winds, ye are all about to mock me; if ye really pity me, crush sensation and memory; let me become as nought; but if not, depart, depart, and leave me in darkness."

These were wild and miserable thoughts, but I cannot describe to you how the eternal twinkling of the stars weighed upon me and how I listened to every blast of wind as if it were a dull ugly siroc on its way to consume me.

Morning dawned before I arrived at the village of Chamounix; I took no rest, but returned immediately to Geneva. Even in my own heart I could give no expression to my sensations—they weighed on me with a mountain's weight and their excess destroyed my agony beneath them. Thus I returned home, and entering the house, presented myself to the family. My haggard and wild appearance awoke intense alarm, but I answered no question, scarcely did I speak. I felt as if I were placed under a ban—as if I had no right to claim their sympathies—as if never more might I enjoy companionship with them. Yet even thus I loved them to adoration; and to save them, I resolved to dedicate myself to my most abhorred task. The prospect of such an occupation made every other circumstance of existence pass before me like a dream, and that thought only had to me the reality of life.

VOLUME THREE

CHAPTER I

Day after day, week after week, passed away on my return to Geneva; and I could not collect the courage to recommence my work. I feared the vengeance of the disappointed fiend, yet I was unable to overcome my repugnance to the task which was enjoined me. I found that I could not compose a female without again devoting several months to profound study and laborious disquisition. I had heard of some discoveries having been made by an English philosopher, the knowledge of which was material to my success, and I sometimes thought of obtaining my father's consent to visit England for this purpose; but I clung to every pretence of delay and shrank from taking the first step in an undertaking whose immediate necessity began to appear less absolute to me. A change indeed had taken place in me; my health, which had hitherto declined, was now much restored; and my spirits, when unchecked by the memory of my unhappy promise, rose proportionably. My father saw this change with pleasure, and he turned his thoughts towards the best method of eradicating the remains of my melancholy, which every now and then would return by fits, and with a devouring blackness overcast the approaching sunshine. At these moments I took refuge in the most perfect solitude. I passed whole days on the lake alone in a little boat, watching the clouds and listening to the rippling of the waves, silent and listless. But the fresh air and bright sun seldom failed to restore me to some degree of composure, and on my return I met the salutations of my friends with a readier smile and a more cheerful heart.

It was after my return from one of these rambles that my father, calling me aside, thus addressed me:

"I am happy to remark, my dear son, that you have resumed your former pleasures and seem to be returning to yourself. And yet you are still unhappy and still avoid our society. For some time I was lost in conjecture as to the cause of this, but yesterday an idea struck me, and if it is well founded, I conjure you to avow it. Reserve on such a point would be not only useless, but draw down treble misery on us all."

I trembled violently at his exordium, and my father continued:

"I confess, my son, that I have always looked forward to your marriage with our dear Elizabeth as the tie of our domestic comfort and the stay of my declining years. You were attached to each other from your earliest infancy; you studied together, and appeared, in dispositions and tastes, entirely suited to one another. But so blind is the experience of man that what I conceived to be the best assistants to my plan may have entirely destroyed it. You, perhaps, regard her as your sister, without any wish that she might become your wife. Nay, you may have met with another whom you may love; and considering yourself as bound in honour to Elizabeth, this struggle may occasion the poignant misery which you appear to feel."

"My dear father, reassure yourself. I love my cousin tenderly and sincerely. I never saw any woman who excited, as Elizabeth does, my warmest admiration and affection. My future hopes and prospects are entirely bound up in the expectation of our union."

"The expression of your sentiments of this subject, my dear Victor, gives me more pleasure than I have for some time experienced. If you feel thus, we shall assuredly be happy, however present events may cast a gloom over us. But it is this gloom which appears to have taken so strong a hold of your mind that I wish to dissipate. Tell me, therefore, whether you object to an immediate solemnization of the marriage. We have been unfortunate, and recent events have drawn us from that everyday tranquillity befitting my years and infirmities. You are younger; yet I do not suppose, possessed as you are of a competent fortune, that an early marriage would at all interfere with any future plans of honour and utility that you may have formed. Do not suppose, however, that I wish to dictate happiness to you or that a delay on your part would cause me any serious uneasiness. Interpret my words with candour and answer me, I conjure you, with confidence and sincerity."

I listened to my father in silence and remained for some time incapable of offering any reply. I revolved rapidly in my mind a multitude of thoughts and endeavoured to arrive at some conclusion. Alas! To me the idea of an immediate union with my Elizabeth was one of horror and dismay. I was bound by a solemn promise which I had not yet fulfilled and dared not break, or if I did, what manifold miseries might not impend over me and my devoted family! Could I enter into a festival with this deadly weight yet hanging round my neck and bowing me to the ground? I must perform my engagement and let the monster depart with his mate before I allowed myself to enjoy the delight of a union from which I expected peace.

I remembered also the necessity imposed upon me of either journeying to England or entering into a long correspondence with those philosophers of that country whose knowledge and discoveries were of indispensable use to me in my present undertaking. The latter method of obtaining the desired intelligence was dilatory and unsatisfactory; besides, I had an insurmountable aversion to the idea of engaging myself in my loathsome task in my father's house while in habits of familiar intercourse with those I loved. I knew that a thousand fearful accidents might occur, the slightest of which would disclose a tale to thrill all connected with me with horror. I was aware also that I should often lose all self-command, all capacity of hiding the harrowing sensations that would possess me during the progress of my unearthly occupation. I must absent myself from all I loved while thus employed. Once commenced, it would quickly be achieved, and I might be restored to my family in peace and happiness. My promise fulfilled, the monster would depart forever. Or (so my fond fancy imaged) some accident might meanwhile occur to destroy him and put an end to my slavery forever.

These feelings dictated my answer to my father. I expressed a wish to visit England, but concealing the true reasons of this request, I clothed my desires under a guise which excited no suspicion, while I urged my desire with an earnestness that easily induced my father to comply. After so long a period of an absorbing melancholy that resembled madness in its intensity and effects, he was glad to find that I was capable of taking pleasure in the idea of such a journey, and he hoped that change of scene and varied amusement would, before my return, have restored me entirely to myself.

The duration of my absence was left to my own choice; a few months, or at most a year, was the period contemplated. One paternal kind precaution he had taken to ensure my having a companion. Without previously communicating with me, he had, in concert with Elizabeth, arranged that Clerval should join me at Strasbourg. This interfered with the solitude I coveted for the prosecution of my task; yet at the commencement of my journey the presence of my friend could in no way be an impediment, and truly I rejoiced that thus I should be saved many hours of lonely, maddening reflection. Nay, Henry might stand between me and the intrusion of my foe. If I were alone, would he not at times force his abhorred presence on me to remind me of my task or to contemplate its progress?

To England, therefore, I was bound, and it was understood that my union with Elizabeth should take place immediately on my return. My father's age rendered him extremely averse to delay. For myself, there was one reward I promised myself from my detested toils—one consolation for my unparalleled sufferings; it was the prospect of that day when, enfranchised from my miserable slavery, I might claim Elizabeth and forget the past in my union with her.

I now made arrangements for my journey, but one feeling haunted me which filled me with fear and agitation. During my absence I should leave my friends unconscious of the existence of their enemy and unprotected from his attacks, exasperated as he might be by my departure. But he had promised to follow me wherever I might go, and would he not accompany me to England? This imagination was dreadful in itself, but soothing inasmuch as it supposed the safety of my friends. I was agonised with the idea of the possibility that the reverse of this might happen. But through the whole period during which I was the slave of my creature I allowed myself to be governed by the impulses of the moment; and my present sensations strongly intimated that the fiend would follow me and exempt my family from the danger of his machinations.

It was in the latter end of August that I again quitted my native country. My journey had been my own suggestion, and Elizabeth therefore acquiesced, but she was filled with disquiet at the idea of my suffering, away from her, the inroads of misery and grief. It had been her care which provided me a companion in Clerval—and yet a man is blind to a thousand minute circumstances which call forth a woman's sedulous attention. She longed to bid me hasten my return; a thousand conflicting emotions rendered her mute as she bade me a tearful, silent farewell.

I threw myself into the carriage that was to convey me away, hardly knowing whither I was going, and careless of what was passing around. I remembered only, and it was with a bitter anguish that I reflected on it, to order that my chemical instruments should be packed to go with me. Filled with dreary imaginations, I passed through many beautiful and majestic scenes, but my eyes were fixed and unobserving. I could only think of the bourne of my travels and the work which was to occupy me whilst they endured.

After some days spent in listless indolence, during which I traversed many leagues, I arrived at Strasbourg, where I waited two days for Clerval. He came. Alas, how great was the contrast between us! He was alive to every new scene, joyful when he saw the beauties of the setting sun, and more happy when he beheld it rise and recommence a new day. He pointed out to me the shifting colours of the landscape and the appearances of the sky. "This is what it is to live," he cried; "how I enjoy existence! But you, my dear Frankenstein, wherefore are you desponding and sorrowful?" In truth, I was occupied by gloomy thoughts and neither saw the descent of the evening star nor the golden sunrise reflected in the Rhine. And you, my friend, would be far more amused with the journal of Clerval, who observed the scenery with an eye of feeling and delight, than in listening to my reflections. I, a miserable wretch, haunted by a curse that shut up every avenue to enjoyment.

We had agreed to descend the Rhine in a boat from Strasbourg to Rotterdam, whence we might take shipping for London. During this voyage we passed many willowy islands and saw several beautiful towns. We stayed a day at Mannheim, and on the fifth from our departure from Strasbourg, arrived at Mainz. The course of the Rhine below Mainz becomes much more picturesque. The river descends rapidly and winds between hills, not high, but steep, and of beautiful forms. We saw many ruined castles standing on the edges of precipices, surrounded by black woods, high and inaccessible. This part of the Rhine, indeed, presents a singularly variegated landscape. In one spot you view rugged hills, ruined castles overlooking tremendous precipices, with the dark Rhine rushing beneath; and on the sudden turn of a promontory, flourishing vineyards with green sloping banks and a meandering river and populous towns occupy the scene.

We travelled at the time of the vintage and heard the song of the labourers as we glided down the stream. Even I, depressed in mind, and my spirits continually agitated by gloomy feelings, even I was pleased. I lay at the bottom of the boat, and as I gazed on the cloudless blue sky, I seemed to drink in a tranquillity to which I had long been a stranger. And if these were my sensations, who can describe those of Henry? He felt as if he had been transported to Fairy-land and enjoyed a happiness seldom tasted by man. "I have seen," he said, "the most beautiful scenes of my own country; I have visited the lakes of Lucerne and Uri, where the snowy mountains descend almost perpendicularly to the water, casting black and impenetrable shades, which would cause a gloomy and mournful appearance were it not for the most verdant islands that relieve the eye by their gay appearance; I have seen this lake agitated by a tempest, when the wind tore up whirlwinds of water and gave you an idea of what the waterspout must be on the great ocean; and the waves dash with fury the base of the mountain, where the priest and his mistress were overwhelmed by an avalanche and where their dying voices are still said to be heard amid the pauses of the nightly wind; I have seen the mountains of La Valais, and the Pays de Vaud; but this country, Victor, pleases me more than all those wonders. The mountains of Switzerland are more majestic and strange, but there is a charm in the banks of this divine river that I never before saw equalled. Look at that castle which overhangs yon precipice; and that also on the island, almost concealed amongst the foliage of those lovely trees; and now that group of labourers coming from among their vines; and that village half hid in the recess of the mountain. Oh, surely the spirit that inhabits and guards this place has a soul more in harmony with man than those who pile the glacier or retire to the inaccessible peaks of the mountains of our own country."

Clerval! Beloved friend! Even now it delights me to record your words and to dwell on the praise of which you are so eminently deserving. He was a being formed in the "very poetry of nature." His wild and enthusiastic imagination was chastened by the sensibility of his heart. His soul overflowed with ardent affections, and his friendship was of that devoted and wondrous nature that the worldly-minded teach us to look for only in the imagination. But even human sympathies were not sufficient to satisfy his eager mind. The scenery of external nature, which others regard only with admiration, he loved with ardour:

> The sounding cataract
> Haunted him like a passion: the tall rock,
> The mountain, and the deep and gloomy wood,
> Their colours and their forms, were then to him
> An appetite; a feeling, and a love,
> That had no need of a remoter charm,
> By thought supplied, or any interest
> Unborrow'd from the eye.*

* Wordsworth's "Tintern Abbey"

And where does he now exist? Is this gentle and lovely being lost forever? Has this mind, so replete with ideas, imaginations fanciful and magnificent, which formed a world, whose existence depended on the life of its creator—has this mind perished? Does it now only exist in my memory? No, it is not thus; your form so divinely wrought, and beaming with beauty, has decayed, but your spirit still visits and consoles your unhappy friend.

Pardon this gush of sorrow; these ineffectual words are but a slight tribute to the unexampled worth of Henry, but they soothe my heart, overflowing with the anguish which his remembrance creates. I will proceed with my tale.

Beyond Cologne we descended to the plains of Holland; and we resolved to post the remainder of our way, for the wind was contrary and the stream of the river was too gentle to aid us.

Our journey here lost the interest arising from beautiful scenery, but we arrived in a few days at Rotterdam, whence we proceeded by sea to England. It was on a clear morning, in the latter days of September, that I first saw the white cliffs of Britain. The banks of the Thames presented a new scene; they were flat but fertile, and almost every town was marked by the remembrance of some story. We saw Tilbury Fort and remembered the Spanish Armada; Gravesend, Woolwich, and Greenwich—places which I had heard of even in my country.

At length we saw the numerous steeples of London, St. Paul's towering above all, and the Tower, famed in English history.

CHAPTER II

London was our present point of rest; we determined to remain several months in this wonderful and celebrated city. Clerval desired the intercourse of the men of genius and talent who flourished at this time, but this was with me a secondary object; I was principally occupied with the means of obtaining the information necessary for the completion of my promise and quickly availed myself of the letters of introduction that I had brought with me, addressed to the most distinguished natural philosophers.

If this journey had taken place during my days of study and happiness, it would have afforded me inexpressible pleasure. But a blight had come over my existence, and I only visited these people for the sake of the information they might give me on the subject in which my interest was so terribly profound. Company was irksome to me; when alone, I could fill my mind with the sights of heaven and earth; the voice of Henry soothed me, and I could thus cheat myself into a transitory peace. But busy, uninteresting, joyous faces brought back despair to my heart. I saw an insurmountable barrier placed between me and my fellow men; this barrier was sealed with the blood of William and Justine, and to reflect on the events connected with those names filled my soul with anguish.

But in Clerval I saw the image of my former self; he was inquisitive and anxious to gain experience and instruction. The difference of manners which he observed was to him an inexhaustible source of instruction and amusement. He was also pursuing an object he had long had in view. His design was to visit India, in the belief that he had in his knowledge of its various languages, and in the views he had taken of its society, the means of materially assisting the progress of European colonization and trade. In Britain only could he further the execution of his plan. He was forever busy, and the only check to his enjoyments was my sorrowful and dejected mind. I tried to conceal this as much as possible, that I might not debar him from the pleasures natural to one who was entering on a new scene of life, undisturbed by any care or bitter recollection. I often refused to accompany him, alleging another engagement, that I might remain alone. I now also began to collect the materials necessary for my new creation, and this was to me like the torture of single drops of water continually falling on the head. Every thought that was devoted to it was an extreme anguish, and every word that I spoke in allusion to it caused my lips to quiver, and my heart to palpitate.

After passing some months in London, we received a letter from a person in Scotland who had formerly been our visitor at Geneva. He mentioned the beauties of his native country and asked us if those were not sufficient allurements to induce us to prolong our journey as far north as Perth, where he resided. Clerval eagerly desired to accept this invitation, and I, although I abhorred society, wished to view again mountains and streams and all the wondrous works with which Nature adorns her chosen dwelling-places.

We had arrived in England at the beginning of October, and it was now February. We accordingly determined to commence our journey towards the north at the expiration of another month. In this expedition we did not intend to follow the great road to Edinburgh, but to visit Windsor, Oxford, Matlock, and the Cumberland lakes, resolving to arrive at the completion of this tour about the end of July. I packed up my chemical instruments and the materials I had collected, resolving to finish my labours in some obscure nook in the northern highlands of Scotland.

We quitted London on the 27th of March and remained a few days at Windsor, rambling in its beautiful forest. This was a new scene to us mountaineers; the majestic oaks, the quantity of game, and the herds of stately deer were all novelties to us.

From thence we proceeded to Oxford. As we entered this city our minds were filled with the remembrance of the events that had been transacted there more than a century and a half before. It was here that Charles I had collected his forces. This city had remained faithful to him, after the whole nation had forsaken his cause to join the standard of Parliament and liberty. The memory of that unfortunate king and his companions, the amiable Falkland, the insolent Goring, his queen, and son, gave a peculiar interest to every part of the city which they might be supposed to have inhabited. The spirit of elder days found a dwelling here, and we delighted to trace its footsteps. If these feelings had not found an imaginary gratification, the appearance of the city had yet in itself sufficient beauty to obtain our admiration. The colleges are ancient and picturesque; the streets are almost magnificent; and the lovely Isis, which flows beside it through meadows of exquisite verdure, is spread forth into a placid expanse of waters, which reflects its majestic assemblage of towers, and spires, and domes, embosomed among aged trees.

I enjoyed this scene, and yet my enjoyment was embittered both by the memory of the past and the anticipation of the future. I was formed for peaceful happiness. During my youthful days discontent never visited my mind, and if I was ever overcome by ennui, the sight of what is beautiful in nature or the study of what is excellent and sublime in the productions of man could always interest my heart and communicate elasticity to my spirits. But I am a blasted tree; the bolt has entered my soul; and I felt then that I should survive to exhibit what I shall soon cease to be—a miserable spectacle of wrecked humanity, pitiable to others and intolerable to myself.

We passed a considerable period at Oxford, rambling among its environs and endeavouring to identify every spot which might relate to the most animating epoch of English history. Our little voyages of discovery were often prolonged by the successive objects that presented themselves. We visited the tomb of the illustrious Hampden and the field on which that patriot fell. For a moment my soul was elevated from its debasing and miserable fears to contemplate the divine ideas of liberty and self-sacrifice of which these sights were the monuments and the remembrancers. For an instant I dared to shake off my chains and look around me with a free and lofty spirit, but the iron had eaten into my flesh, and I sank again, trembling and hopeless, into my miserable self.

We left Oxford with regret and proceeded to Matlock, which was our next place of rest. The country in the neighbourhood of this village resembled, to a greater degree, the scenery of Switzerland; but everything is on a lower scale, and the green hills want the crown of distant white Alps which always attend on the piny mountains of my native country. We visited the wondrous cave and the little cabinets of natural history, where the curiosities are disposed in the same manner as in the collections at Servox and Chamounix. The latter name made me tremble when pronounced by Henry, and I hastened to quit Matlock, with which that terrible scene was thus associated.

From Derby, still journeying northwards, we passed two months in Cumberland and Westmorland. I could now almost fancy myself among the Swiss mountains. The little patches of snow which yet lingered on the northern sides of the mountains, the lakes, and the dashing of the rocky streams were all familiar and dear sights to me. Here also we made some acquaintances, who almost contrived to cheat me into happiness. The delight of Clerval was proportionably greater than mine; his mind expanded in the company of men of talent, and he found in his own nature greater capacities and resources than he could have imagined himself to have possessed while he associated with his inferiors. "I could pass my life here," said he to me; "and among these mountains I should scarcely regret Switzerland and the Rhine."

But he found that a traveller's life is one that includes much pain amidst its enjoyments. His feelings are forever on the stretch; and when he begins to sink into repose, he finds himself obliged to quit that on which he rests in pleasure for something new, which again engages his attention, and which also he forsakes for other novelties.

We had scarcely visited the various lakes of Cumberland and Westmorland and conceived an affection for some of the inhabitants when the period of our appointment with our Scotch friend approached, and we left them to travel on. For my own part I was not sorry. I had now neglected my promise for some time, and I feared the effects of the daemon's disappointment. He might remain in Switzerland and wreak his vengeance on my relatives. This idea pursued me and tormented me at every moment from which I might otherwise have snatched repose and peace. I waited for my letters with feverish impatience; if they were delayed I was miserable and overcome by a thousand fears; and when they arrived and I saw the superscription of Elizabeth or my father, I hardly dared to read and ascertain my fate. Sometimes I thought that the fiend followed me and might expedite my remissness by murdering my companion. When these thoughts possessed me, I would not quit Henry for a moment, but followed him as his shadow, to protect him from the fancied rage of his destroyer. I felt as if I had committed some great crime, the consciousness of which haunted me. I was guiltless, but I had indeed drawn down a horrible curse upon my head, as mortal as that of crime.

I visited Edinburgh with languid eyes and mind; and yet that city might have interested the most unfortunate being. Clerval did not like it so well as Oxford, for the antiquity of the latter city was more pleasing to him. But the beauty and regularity of the new town of Edinburgh, its romantic castle and its environs, the most delightful in the world, Arthur's Seat, St. Bernard's Well, and the Pentland Hills compensated him for the change and filled him with cheerfulness and admiration. But I was impatient to arrive at the termination of my journey.

We left Edinburgh in a week, passing through Coupar, St. Andrew's, and along the banks of the Tay, to Perth, where our friend expected us. But I was in no mood to laugh and talk with strangers or enter into their feelings or plans with the good humour expected from a guest; and accordingly I told Clerval that I wished to make the tour of Scotland alone. "Do you," said I, "enjoy yourself, and let this be our rendezvous. I may be absent a month or two; but do not interfere with my motions, I entreat you; leave me to peace and solitude for a short time; and when I return, I hope it will be with a lighter heart, more congenial to your own temper."

Henry wished to dissuade me, but seeing me bent on this plan, ceased to remonstrate. He entreated me to write often. "I had rather be with you," he said, "in your solitary rambles, than with these Scotch people, whom I do not know; hasten, then, my dear friend, to return, that I may again feel myself somewhat at home, which I cannot do in your absence."

Having parted from my friend, I determined to visit some remote spot of Scotland and finish my work in solitude. I did not doubt but that the monster followed me and would discover himself to me when I should have finished, that he might receive his companion.

With this resolution I traversed the northern highlands and fixed on one of the remotest of the Orkneys as the scene of my labours. It was a place fitted for such a work, being hardly more than a rock whose high sides were continually beaten upon by the waves. The soil was barren, scarcely affording pasture for a few miserable cows, and oatmeal for its inhabitants, which consisted of five persons, whose gaunt and scraggy limbs gave tokens of their miserable fare. Vegetables and bread, when they indulged in such luxuries, and even fresh water, was to be procured from the mainland, which was about five miles distant.

On the whole island there were but three miserable huts, and one of these was vacant when I arrived. This I hired. It contained but two rooms, and these exhibited all the squalidness of the most miserable penury. The thatch had fallen in, the walls were unplastered, and the door was off its hinges. I ordered it to be repaired, bought some furniture, and took possession, an incident which would doubtless have occasioned some surprise had not all the senses of the cottagers been benumbed by want and squalid poverty. As it was, I lived ungazed at and unmolested, hardly thanked for the pittance of food and clothes which I gave, so much does suffering blunt even the coarsest sensations of men.

In this retreat I devoted the morning to labour; but in the evening, when the weather permitted, I walked on the stony beach of the sea to listen to the waves as they roared and dashed at my feet. It was a monotonous yet ever-changing scene. I thought of Switzerland; it was far different from this desolate and appalling landscape. Its hills are covered with vines, and its cottages are scattered thickly in the plains. Its fair lakes reflect a blue and gentle sky, and when troubled by the winds, their tumult is but as the play of a lively infant when compared to the roarings of the giant ocean.

In this manner I distributed my occupations when I first arrived, but as I proceeded in my labour, it became every day more horrible and irksome to me. Sometimes I could not prevail on myself to enter my laboratory for several days, and at other times I toiled day and night in order to complete my work. It was, indeed, a filthy process in which I was engaged. During my first experiment, a kind of enthusiastic frenzy had blinded me to the horror of my employment; my mind was intently fixed on the consummation of my labour, and my eyes were shut to the horror of my proceedings. But now I went to it in cold blood, and my heart often sickened at the work of my hands.

Thus situated, employed in the most detestable occupation, immersed in a solitude where nothing could for an instant call my attention from the actual scene in which I was engaged, my spirits became unequal; I grew restless and nervous. Every moment I feared to meet my persecutor. Sometimes I sat with my eyes fixed on the ground, fearing to raise them lest they should encounter the object which I so much dreaded to behold. I feared to wander from the sight of my fellow creatures lest when alone he should come to claim his companion.

In the meantime I worked on, and my labour was already considerably advanced. I looked towards its completion with a tremulous and eager hope, which I dared not trust myself to question but which was intermixed with obscure forebodings of evil that made my heart sicken in my bosom.

CHAPTER III

I sat one evening in my laboratory; the sun had set, and the moon was just rising from the sea; I had not sufficient light for my employment, and I remained idle, in a pause of consideration of whether I should leave my labour for the night or hasten its conclusion by an unremitting attention to it. As I sat, a train of reflection occurred to me which led me to consider the effects of what I was now doing. Three years before, I was engaged in the same manner and had created a fiend whose unparalleled barbarity had desolated my heart and filled it forever with the bitterest remorse. I was now about to form another being of whose dispositions I was alike ignorant; she might become ten thousand times more malignant than her mate and delight, for its own sake, in murder and wretchedness. He had sworn to quit the neighbourhood of man and hide himself in deserts, but she had not; and she, who in all probability was to become a thinking and reasoning animal, might refuse to comply with a compact made before her creation. They might even hate each other; the creature who already lived loathed his own deformity, and might he not conceive a greater abhorrence for it when it came before his eyes in the female form? She also might turn with disgust from him to the superior beauty of man; she might quit him, and he be again alone, exasperated by the fresh provocation of being deserted by one of his own species.

Even if they were to leave Europe and inhabit the deserts of the new world, yet one of the first results of those sympathies for which the daemon thirsted would be children, and a race of devils would be propagated upon the earth who might make the very existence of the species of man a condition precarious and full of terror. Had I right, for my own benefit, to inflict this curse upon everlasting generations? I had before been moved by the sophisms of the being I had created; I had been struck senseless by his fiendish threats; but now, for the first time, the wickedness of my promise burst upon me; I shuddered to think that future ages might curse me as their pest, whose selfishness had not hesitated to buy its own peace at the price, perhaps, of the existence of the whole human race.

I trembled, and my heart failed within me, when, on looking up, I saw by the light of the moon the daemon at the casement. A ghastly grin wrinkled his lips as he gazed on me, where I sat fulfilling the task which he had allotted to me. Yes, he had followed me in my travels; he had loitered in forests, hid himself in caves, or taken refuge in wide and desert heaths; and he now came to mark my progress and claim the fulfilment of my promise.

As I looked on him, his countenance expressed the utmost extent of malice and treachery. I thought with a sensation of madness on my promise of creating another like to him, and trembling with passion, tore to pieces the thing on which I was engaged. The wretch saw me destroy the creature on whose future existence he depended for happiness, and with a howl of devilish despair and revenge, withdrew.

I left the room, and locking the door, made a solemn vow in my own heart never to resume my labours; and then, with trembling steps, I sought my own apartment. I was alone; none were near me to dissipate the gloom and relieve me from the sickening oppression of the most terrible reveries.

Several hours passed, and I remained near my window gazing on the sea; it was almost motionless, for the winds were hushed, and all nature reposed under the eye of the quiet moon. A few fishing vessels alone specked the water, and now and then the gentle breeze wafted the sound of voices as the fishermen called to one another. I felt the silence, although I was hardly conscious of its extreme profundity, until my ear was suddenly arrested by the paddling of oars near the shore, and a person landed close to my house.

In a few minutes after, I heard the creaking of my door, as if someone endeavoured to open it softly. I trembled from head to foot; I felt a presentiment of who it was and wished to rouse one of the peasants who dwelt in a cottage not far from mine; but I was overcome by the sensation of helplessness, so often felt in frightful dreams, when you in vain endeavour to fly from an impending danger, and was rooted to the spot.

Presently I heard the sound of footsteps along the passage; the door opened, and the wretch whom I dreaded appeared. Shutting the door, he approached me and said in a smothered voice:

"You have destroyed the work which you began; what is it that you intend? Do you dare to break your promise? I have endured toil and misery; I left Switzerland with you; I crept along the shores of the

Rhine, among its willow islands and over the summits of its hills. I have dwelt many months in the heaths of England and among the deserts of Scotland. I have endured incalculable fatigue, and cold, and hunger; do you dare destroy my hopes?"

"Begone! I do break my promise; never will I create another like yourself, equal in deformity and wickedness."

"Slave, I before reasoned with you, but you have proved yourself unworthy of my condescension. Remember that I have power; you believe yourself miserable, but I can make you so wretched that the light of day will be hateful to you. You are my creator, but I am your master—obey!"

"The hour of my irresolution is past, and the period of your power is arrived. Your threats cannot move me to do an act of wickedness; but they confirm me in a determination of not creating you a companion in vice. Shall I, in cool blood, set loose upon the earth a daemon whose delight is in death and wretchedness? Begone! I am firm, and your words will only exasperate my rage."

The monster saw my determination in my face and gnashed his teeth in the impotence of anger. "Shall each man," cried he, "find a wife for his bosom, and each beast have his mate, and I be alone? I had feelings of affection, and they were requited by detestation and scorn. Man! You may hate, but beware! Your hours will pass in dread and misery, and soon the bolt will fall which must ravish from you your happiness forever. Are you to be happy while I grovel in the intensity of my wretchedness? You can blast my other passions, but revenge remains—revenge, henceforth dearer than light or food! I may die, but first you, my tyrant and tormentor, shall curse the sun that gazes on your misery. Beware, for I am fearless and therefore powerful. I will watch with the wiliness of a snake, that I may sting with its venom. Man, you shall repent of the injuries you inflict."

"Devil, cease; and do not poison the air with these sounds of malice. I have declared my resolution to you, and I am no coward to bend beneath words. Leave me; I am inexorable."

"It is well. I go; but remember, I shall be with you on your wedding-night."

I started forward and exclaimed, "Villain! Before you sign my death-warrant, be sure that you are yourself safe."

I would have seized him, but he eluded me and quitted the house with precipitation. In a few moments I saw him in his boat, which shot across the waters with an arrowy swiftness and was soon lost amidst the waves.

All was again silent, but his words rang in my ears. I burned with rage to pursue the murderer of my peace and precipitate him into the ocean. I walked up and down my room hastily and perturbed, while my imagination conjured up a thousand images to torment and sting me. Why had I not followed him and closed with him in mortal strife? But I had suffered him to depart, and he had directed his course towards the mainland. I shuddered to think who might be the next victim sacrificed to his insatiate revenge. And then I thought again of his words—*"I will be with you on your wedding-night."* That, then, was the period fixed for the fulfilment of my destiny. In that hour I should die and at once satisfy and extinguish his malice. The prospect did not move me to fear; yet when I thought of my beloved Elizabeth, of her tears and endless sorrow, when she should find her lover so barbarously snatched from her, tears, the first I had shed for many months, streamed from my eyes, and I resolved not to fall before my enemy without a bitter struggle.

The night passed away, and the sun rose from the ocean; my feelings became calmer, if it may be called calmness when the violence of rage sinks into the depths of despair. I left the house, the horrid scene of the last night's contention, and walked on the beach of the sea, which I almost regarded as an insuperable barrier between me and my fellow creatures; nay, a wish that such should prove the fact stole across me. I desired that I might pass my life on that barren rock, wearily, it is true, but uninterrupted by any sudden shock of misery. If I returned, it was to be sacrificed or to see those whom I most loved die under the grasp of a daemon whom I had myself created.

I walked about the isle like a restless spectre, separated from all it loved and miserable in the separation. When it became noon, and the sun rose higher, I lay down on the grass and was overpowered by a deep sleep. I had been awake the whole of the preceding night, my nerves were agitated, and my eyes inflamed by watching and misery. The sleep into which I now sank refreshed me; and when I awoke, I again felt as if I belonged to a race of human beings like myself, and I began to reflect upon what had passed with greater composure; yet still the words of the fiend rang in my ears like a death-knell; they appeared like a dream, yet distinct and oppressive as a reality.

The sun had far descended, and I still sat on the shore, satisfying my appetite, which had become ravenous, with an oaten cake, when I saw a fishing-boat land close to me, and one of the men brought me a packet; it contained letters from Geneva, and one from Clerval entreating me to join him. He said that he was wearing away his time fruitlessly where he was, that letters from the friends he had formed in London desired his return to complete the negotiation they had entered into for his Indian enterprise. He could not any longer delay his departure; but as his journey to London might be followed, even sooner than he now conjectured, by his longer voyage, he entreated me to bestow as much of my society on him as I could spare. He besought me, therefore, to leave my solitary isle and to meet him at Perth, that we might proceed southwards together. This letter in a degree recalled me to life, and I determined to quit my island at the expiration of two days.

Yet, before I departed, there was a task to perform, on which I shuddered to reflect: I must pack up my chemical instruments, and for that purpose I must enter the room which had been the scene of my odious work, and I must handle those utensils the sight of which was sickening to me. The next morning, at daybreak, I summoned sufficient courage and unlocked the door of my laboratory. The remains of the half-finished creature, whom I had destroyed, lay scattered on the floor, and I almost felt as if I had mangled the living flesh of a human being. I paused to collect myself and then entered the chamber. With trembling hand I conveyed the instruments out of the room, but I reflected that I ought not to leave the relics of my work to excite the horror and suspicion of the peasants; and I accordingly put them into a basket, with a great quantity of stones, and laying them up, determined to throw them into the sea that very night; and in the meantime I sat upon the beach, employed in cleaning and arranging my chemical apparatus.

Nothing could be more complete than the alteration that had taken place in my feelings since the night of the appearance of the daemon. I had before regarded my promise with a gloomy despair as a thing that, with whatever consequences, must be fulfilled; but I now felt as if a film had been taken from before my eyes and that I for the first time saw clearly. The idea of renewing my labours did not for one instant occur to me; the threat I had heard weighed on my thoughts, but I did not reflect that a voluntary act of mine could avert it. I had resolved in my own mind that to create another like the fiend I had first made would be an act of the basest and most atrocious selfishness, and I banished from my mind every thought that could lead to a different conclusion.

Between two and three in the morning the moon rose; and I then, putting my basket aboard a little skiff, sailed out about four miles from the shore. The scene was perfectly solitary; a few boats were returning towards land, but I sailed away from them. I felt as if I was about the commission of a dreadful crime and avoided with shuddering anxiety any encounter with my fellow-creatures. At one time the moon, which had before been clear, was suddenly overspread by a thick cloud, and I took advantage of the moment of darkness and cast my basket into the sea; I listened to the gurgling sound as it sank and then sailed away from the spot. The sky became clouded, but the air was pure, although chilled by the northeast breeze that was then rising. But it refreshed me and filled me with such agreeable sensations that I resolved to prolong my stay on the water, and fixing the rudder in a direct position, stretched myself at the bottom of the boat. Clouds hid the moon, everything was obscure, and I heard only the sound of the boat as its keel cut through the waves; the murmur lulled me, and in a short time I slept soundly.

I do not know how long I remained in this situation, but when I awoke I found that the sun had already mounted considerably. The wind was high, and the waves continually threatened the safety of my little skiff. I found that the wind was northeast and must have driven me far from the coast from which I had embarked. I endeavoured to change my course but quickly found that if I again made the attempt the boat would be instantly filled with water.

Thus situated, my only resource was to drive before the wind. I confess that I felt a few sensations of terror. I had no compass with me and was so slenderly acquainted with the geography of this part of the world that the sun was of little benefit to me. I might be driven into the wide Atlantic and feel all the tortures of starvation or be swallowed up in the immeasurable waters that roared and buffeted around me. I had already been out many hours and felt the torment of a burning thirst, a prelude to my other sufferings. I looked on the heavens, which were covered by clouds that flew before the wind, only to be replaced by others; I looked upon the sea; it was to be my grave. “Fiend,” I exclaimed, “your task is already fulfilled!” I thought of Elizabeth, of my father, and of Clerval—all left behind, on whom the monster might satisfy his sanguinary and merciless passions. This idea plunged me into a reverie so despairing and frightful that even now, when the scene is on the point of closing before me forever, I shudder to reflect on it.

Some hours passed thus; but by degrees, as the sun declined towards the horizon, the wind died away into a gentle breeze and the sea became free from breakers. But these gave place to a heavy swell; I felt sick and hardly able to hold the rudder, when suddenly I saw a line of high land towards the south.

Almost spent, as I was, by fatigue and the dreadful suspense I endured for several hours, this sudden certainty of life rushed like a flood of warm joy to my heart, and tears gushed from my eyes.

How mutable are our feelings, and how strange is that clinging love we have of life even in the excess of misery! I constructed another sail with a part of my dress and eagerly steered my course towards the land. It had a wild and rocky appearance, but as I approached nearer I easily perceived the traces of cultivation. I saw vessels near the shore and found myself suddenly transported back to the neighbourhood of civilised man. I carefully traced the windings of the land and hailed a steeple which I at length saw issuing from behind a small promontory. As I was in a state of extreme debility, I resolved to sail directly towards the town, as a place where I could most easily procure nourishment. Fortunately I had money with me. As I turned the promontory I perceived a small neat town and a good harbour, which I entered, my heart bounding with joy at my unexpected escape.

As I was occupied in fixing the boat and arranging the sails, several people crowded towards the spot. They seemed much surprised at my appearance, but instead of offering me any assistance, whispered together with gestures that at any other time might have produced in me a slight sensation of alarm. As it was, I merely remarked that they spoke English, and I therefore addressed them in that language. "My good friends," said I, "will you be so kind as to tell me the name of this town and inform me where I am?"

"You will know that soon enough," replied a man with a hoarse voice. "Maybe you are come to a place that will not prove much to your taste, but you will not be consulted as to your quarters, I promise you."

I was exceedingly surprised on receiving so rude an answer from a stranger, and I was also disconcerted on perceiving the frowning and angry countenances of his companions. "Why do you answer me so roughly?" I replied. "Surely it is not the custom of Englishmen to receive strangers so inhospitably."

"I do not know," said the man, "what the custom of the English may be, but it is the custom of the Irish to hate villains."

While this strange dialogue continued, I perceived the crowd rapidly increase. Their faces expressed a mixture of curiosity and anger, which annoyed and in some degree alarmed me. I enquired the way to the inn, but no one replied. I then moved forward, and a murmuring sound arose from the crowd as they followed and surrounded me, when an ill-looking man approaching tapped me on the shoulder and said, "Come, sir, you must follow me to Mr. Kirwin's, to give an account of yourself."

"Who is Mr. Kirwin? Why am I to give an account of myself? Is not this a free country?"

"Ay, sir, free enough for honest folks. Mr. Kirwin is a magistrate, and you are to give an account of the death of a gentleman who was found murdered here last night."

This answer startled me, but I presently recovered myself. I was innocent; that could easily be proved; accordingly I followed my conductor in silence and was led to one of the best houses in the town. I was ready to sink from fatigue and hunger, but being surrounded by a crowd, I thought it politic to rouse all my strength, that no physical debility might be construed into apprehension or conscious guilt. Little did I then expect the calamity that was in a few moments to overwhelm me and extinguish in horror and despair all fear of ignominy or death.

I must pause here, for it requires all my fortitude to recall the memory of the frightful events which I am about to relate, in proper detail, to my recollection.

CHAPTER IV

I was soon introduced into the presence of the magistrate, an old benevolent man with calm and mild manners. He looked upon me, however, with some degree of severity, and then, turning towards my conductors, he asked who appeared as witnesses on this occasion.

About half a dozen men came forward; and, one being selected by the magistrate, he deposed that he had been out fishing the night before with his son and brother-in-law, Daniel Nugent, when, about ten o'clock, they observed a strong northerly blast rising, and they accordingly put in for port. It was a very dark night, as the moon had not yet risen; they did not land at the harbour, but, as they had been accustomed, at a creek about two miles below. He walked on first, carrying a part of the fishing tackle, and his companions followed him at some distance. As he was proceeding along the sands, he struck his foot against something and fell at his length on the ground. His companions came up to assist him, and by the light of their lantern they found that he had fallen on the body of a man, who was to all appearance dead. Their first supposition was that it was the corpse of some person who had been drowned and was thrown on shore by the waves, but on examination they found that the clothes were not wet and even that the body was not then cold. They instantly carried it to the cottage of an old woman near the spot and endeavoured, but in vain, to restore it to life. It appeared to be a handsome young man, about five and twenty years of age. He had apparently been strangled, for there was no sign of any violence except the black mark of fingers on his neck.

The first part of this deposition did not in the least interest me, but when the mark of the fingers was mentioned I remembered the murder of my brother and felt myself extremely agitated; my limbs trembled, and a mist came over my eyes, which obliged me to lean on a chair for support. The magistrate observed me with a keen eye and of course drew an unfavourable augury from my manner.

The son confirmed his father's account, but when Daniel Nugent was called he swore positively that just before the fall of his companion, he saw a boat, with a single man in it, at a short distance from the shore;

and as far as he could judge by the light of a few stars, it was the same boat in which I had just landed.

A woman deposed that she lived near the beach and was standing at the door of her cottage, waiting for the return of the fishermen, about an hour before she heard of the discovery of the body, when she saw a boat with only one man in it push off from that part of the shore where the corpse was afterwards found.

Another woman confirmed the account of the fishermen having brought the body into her house; it was not cold. They put it into a bed and rubbed it, and Daniel went to the town for an apothecary, but life was quite gone.

Several other men were examined concerning my landing, and they agreed that, with the strong north wind that had arisen during the night, it was very probable that I had beaten about for many hours and had been obliged to return nearly to the same spot from which I had departed. Besides, they observed that it appeared that I had brought the body from another place, and it was likely that as I did not appear to know the shore, I might have put into the harbour ignorant of the distance of the town of —— from the place where I had deposited the corpse.

Mr. Kirwin, on hearing this evidence, desired that I should be taken into the room where the body lay for interment, that it might be observed what effect the sight of it would produce upon me. This idea was probably suggested by the extreme agitation I had exhibited when the mode of the murder had been described. I was accordingly conducted, by the magistrate and several other persons, to the inn. I could not help being struck by the strange coincidences that had taken place during this eventful night; but, knowing that I had been conversing with several persons in the island I had inhabited about the time that the body had been found, I was perfectly tranquil as to the consequences of the affair.

I entered the room where the corpse lay, and was led up to the coffin. How can I describe my sensations on beholding it? I feel yet parched with horror, nor can I reflect on that terrible moment without shuddering and agony. The examination, the presence of the magistrate and witnesses, passed like a dream from my memory when I saw the lifeless form of Henry Clerval stretched before me. I gasped for breath, and throwing myself on the body, I exclaimed, "Have my murderous machinations deprived you also, my dearest Henry, of life? Two I have already destroyed; other victims await their destiny; but you, Clerval, my friend, my benefactor—"

The human frame could no longer support the agonies that I endured, and I was carried out of the room in strong convulsions.

A fever succeeded to this. I lay for two months on the point of death; my ravings, as I afterwards heard, were frightful; I called myself the murderer of William, of Justine, and of Clerval. Sometimes I entreated my attendants to assist me in the destruction of the fiend by whom I was tormented; and at others I felt the fingers of the monster already grasping my neck, and screamed aloud with agony and terror. Fortunately, as I spoke my native language, Mr. Kirwin alone understood me; but my gestures and bitter cries were sufficient to affright the other witnesses.

Why did I not die? More miserable than man ever was before, why did I not sink into forgetfulness and rest? Death snatches away many blooming children, the only hopes of their doting parents; how many brides and youthful lovers have been one day in the bloom of health and hope, and the next a prey for worms and the decay of the tomb! Of what materials was I made that I could thus resist so many shocks, which, like the turning of the wheel, continually renewed the torture?

But I was doomed to live, and in two months found myself as awaking from a dream, in a prison, stretched on a wretched bed, surrounded by jailers, turnkeys, bolts, and all the miserable apparatus of a dungeon. It was morning, I remember, when I thus awoke to understanding; I had forgotten the particulars of what had happened and only felt as if some great misfortune had suddenly overwhelmed me; but when I looked around and saw the barred windows and the squalidness of the room in which I was, all flashed across my memory and I groaned bitterly.

This sound disturbed an old woman who was sleeping in a chair beside me. She was a hired nurse, the wife of one of the turnkeys, and her countenance expressed all those bad qualities which often characterize that class. The lines of her face were hard and rude, like that of persons accustomed to see without sympathising in sights of misery. Her tone expressed her entire indifference; she addressed me in English, and the voice struck me as one that I had heard during my sufferings:

"Are you better now, sir?" said she.

I replied in the same language, with a feeble voice, "I believe I am; but if it be all true, if indeed I did not dream, I am sorry that I am still alive to feel this misery and horror."

"For that matter," replied the old woman, "if you mean about the gentleman you murdered, I believe that it were better for you if you were dead, for I fancy it will go hard with you! However, that's none of my business; I am sent to nurse you and get you well; I do my duty with a safe conscience; it were well if everybody did the same."

I turned with loathing from the woman who could utter so unfeeling a speech to a person just saved, on the very edge of death; but I felt languid and unable to reflect on all that had passed. The whole series of my life appeared to me as a dream; I sometimes doubted if indeed it were all true, for it never presented itself to my mind with the force of reality.

As the images that floated before me became more distinct, I grew feverish; a darkness pressed around me; no one was near me who soothed me with the gentle voice of love; no dear hand supported me. The physician came and prescribed medicines, and the old woman prepared them for me; but utter carelessness was visible in the first, and the expression of brutality was strongly marked in the visage of the second. Who could be interested in the fate of a murderer but the hangman who would gain his fee?

These were my first reflections, but I soon learned that Mr. Kirwin had shown me extreme kindness. He had caused the best room in the prison to be prepared for me (wretched indeed was the best); and it was he who had provided a physician and a nurse. It is true, he seldom came to see me, for although he ardently desired to relieve the sufferings of every human creature, he did not wish to be present at the agonies and miserable ravings of a murderer. He came, therefore, sometimes to see that I was not neglected, but his visits were short and with long intervals.

One day, while I was gradually recovering, I was seated in a chair, my eyes half open and my cheeks livid like those in death. I was overcome by gloom and misery and often reflected I had better seek death than desire to remain in a world which to me was replete with wretchedness. At one time I considered whether I should not declare myself guilty and suffer the penalty of the law, less innocent than poor Justine had been. Such were my thoughts when the door of my apartment was opened and Mr. Kirwin entered. His countenance expressed sympathy and compassion; he drew a chair close to mine and addressed me in French:

"I fear that this place is very shocking to you; can I do anything to make you more comfortable?"

"I thank you, but all that you mention is nothing to me; on the whole earth there is no comfort which I am capable of receiving."

"I know that the sympathy of a stranger can be but of little relief to one borne down as you are by so strange a misfortune. But you will, I hope, soon quit this melancholy abode, for doubtless evidence can easily be brought to free you from the criminal charge."

"That is my least concern; I am, by a course of strange events, become the most miserable of mortals. Persecuted and tortured as I am and have been, can death be any evil to me?"

"Nothing indeed could be more unfortunate and agonising than the strange chances that have lately occurred. You were thrown, by some surprising accident, on this shore, renowned for its hospitality, seized immediately, and charged with murder. The first sight that was presented to your eyes was the body of your friend, murdered in so unaccountable a manner and placed, as it were, by some fiend across your path."

As Mr. Kirwin said this, notwithstanding the agitation I endured on this retrospect of my sufferings, I also felt considerable surprise at the knowledge he seemed to possess concerning me. I suppose some astonishment was exhibited in my countenance, for Mr. Kirwin hastened to say:

"Immediately upon your being taken ill, all the papers that were on your person were brought me, and I examined them that I might discover some trace by which I could send to your relations an account of your misfortune and illness. I found several letters, and, among others, one which I discovered from its commencement to be from your father. I instantly wrote to Geneva; nearly two months have elapsed since the departure of my letter. But you are ill; even now you tremble; you are unfit for agitation of any kind."

"This suspense is a thousand times worse than the most horrible event; tell me what new scene of death has been acted, and whose murder I am now to lament?"

"Your family is perfectly well," said Mr. Kirwin with gentleness; "and someone, a friend, is come to visit you."

I know not by what chain of thought the idea presented itself, but it instantly darted into my mind that the murderer had come to mock at my misery and taunt me with the death of Clerval, as a new incitement for me to comply with his hellish desires. I put my hand before my eyes, and cried out in agony, "Oh! Take him away! I cannot see him; for God's sake, do not let him enter!"

Mr. Kirwin regarded me with a troubled countenance. He could not help regarding my exclamation as a presumption of my guilt and said in rather a severe tone:

"I should have thought, young man, that the presence of your father would have been welcome instead of inspiring such violent repugnance."

"My father!" cried I, while every feature and every muscle was relaxed from anguish to pleasure. "Is my father indeed come? How kind, how very kind! But where is he, why does he not hasten to me?"

My change of manner surprised and pleased the magistrate; perhaps he thought that my former exclamation was a momentary return of delirium, and now he instantly resumed his former benevolence. He rose and quitted the room with my nurse, and in a moment my father entered it.

Nothing, at this moment, could have given me greater pleasure than the arrival of my father. I stretched out my hand to him and cried:

"Are you, then, safe—and Elizabeth—and Ernest?"

My father calmed me with assurances of their welfare and endeavoured, by dwelling on these subjects so interesting to my heart, to raise my desponding spirits; but he soon felt that a prison cannot be the abode of cheerfulness. "What a place is this that you inhabit, my son!" said he, looking mournfully at the barred windows and wretched appearance of the room. "You travelled to seek happiness, but a fatality seems to pursue you. And poor Clerval—"

The name of my unfortunate and murdered friend was an agitation too great to be endured in my weak state; I shed tears.

"Alas! Yes, my father," replied I; "some destiny of the most horrible kind hangs over me, and I must live to fulfil it, or surely I should have died on the coffin of Henry."

We were not allowed to converse for any length of time, for the precarious state of my health rendered every precaution necessary that could ensure tranquillity. Mr. Kirwin came in and insisted that my strength should not be exhausted by too much exertion. But the appearance of my father was to me like that of my good angel, and I gradually recovered my health.

As my sickness quitted me, I was absorbed by a gloomy and black melancholy that nothing could dissipate. The image of Clerval was forever before me, ghastly and murdered. More than once the agitation into which these reflections threw me made my friends dread a dangerous relapse. Alas! Why did they preserve so miserable and detested a life? It was surely that I might fulfil my destiny, which is now drawing to a close. Soon, oh, very soon, will death extinguish these throbbings and relieve me from the mighty weight of anguish that bears me to the dust; and, in executing the award of justice, I shall also sink to rest. Then the appearance of death was distant, although the wish was ever present to my thoughts; and I often sat for hours motionless and speechless, wishing for some mighty revolution that might bury me and my destroyer in its ruins.

The season of the assizes approached. I had already been three months in prison, and although I was still weak and in continual danger of a relapse, I was obliged to travel nearly a hundred miles to the country town where the court was held. Mr. Kirwin charged himself with every care of collecting witnesses and arranging my defence. I was spared the disgrace of appearing publicly as a criminal, as the case was not brought before the court that decides on life and death. The grand jury rejected the bill, on its being proved that I was on the Orkney Islands at the hour the body of my friend was found; and a fortnight after my removal I was liberated from prison.

My father was enraptured on finding me freed from the vexations of a criminal charge, that I was again allowed to breathe the fresh atmosphere and permitted to return to my native country. I did not participate in these feelings, for to me the walls of a dungeon or a palace were alike hateful. The cup of life was poisoned forever, and although the sun shone upon me, as upon the happy and gay of heart, I saw around me nothing but a dense and frightful darkness, penetrated by no light but the glimmer of two eyes that glared upon me. Sometimes they were the expressive eyes of Henry, languishing in death, the dark orbs nearly covered by the lids and the long black lashes that fringed them; sometimes it was the watery, clouded eyes of the monster, as I first saw them in my chamber at Ingolstadt.

My father tried to awaken in me the feelings of affection. He talked of Geneva, which I should soon visit, of Elizabeth and Ernest; but these words only drew deep groans from me. Sometimes, indeed, I felt a wish for happiness and thought with melancholy delight of my beloved cousin or longed, with a devouring *maladie du pays*, to see once more the blue lake and rapid Rhône, that had been so dear to me in early childhood; but my general state of feeling was a torpor in which a prison was as welcome a residence as the divinest scene in nature; and these fits were seldom interrupted but by paroxysms of anguish and despair. At these moments I often endeavoured to put an end to the existence I loathed, and it required unceasing attendance and vigilance to restrain me from committing some dreadful act of violence.

Yet one duty remained to me, the recollection of which finally triumphed over my selfish despair. It was necessary that I should return without delay to Geneva, there to watch over the lives of those I so fondly loved and to lie in wait for the murderer, that if any chance led me to the place of his concealment, or if he dared again to blast me by his presence, I might, with unfailing aim, put an end to the existence of the monstrous image which I had endued with the mockery of a soul still more monstrous. My father still desired to delay our departure, fearful that I could not sustain the fatigues of a journey, for I was a shattered wreck—the shadow of a human being. My strength was gone. I was a mere skeleton, and fever night and day preyed upon my wasted frame.

Still, as I urged our leaving Ireland with such inquietude and impatience, my father thought it best to yield. We took our passage on board a vessel bound for Havre-de-Grâce and sailed with a fair wind from the Irish shores. It was midnight. I lay on the deck looking at the stars and listening to the dashing of the waves. I hailed the darkness that shut Ireland from my sight, and my pulse beat with a feverish joy when I reflected that I should soon see Geneva. The past appeared to me in the light of a frightful dream; yet the vessel in which I was, the wind that blew me from the detested shore of Ireland, and the sea which surrounded me told me too forcibly that I was deceived by no vision and that Clerval, my friend and dearest companion, had fallen a victim to me and the monster of my creation. I repassed, in my memory, my whole life—my quiet happiness while residing with my family in Geneva, the death of my mother, and my departure for Ingolstadt. I remembered, shuddering, the mad enthusiasm that hurried me on to the creation of my hideous enemy, and I called to mind the night in which he first lived. I was unable to pursue the train of thought; a thousand feelings pressed upon me, and I wept bitterly.

Ever since my recovery from the fever I had been in the custom of taking every night a small quantity of laudanum, for it was by means of this drug only that I was enabled to gain the rest necessary for the preservation of life. Oppressed by the recollection of my various misfortunes, I now swallowed double my usual quantity and soon slept profoundly. But sleep did not afford me respite from thought and misery; my dreams presented a thousand objects that scared me. Towards morning I was possessed by a kind of nightmare; I felt the fiend's grasp in my neck and could not free myself from it; groans and cries rang in my ears. My father, who was watching over me, perceiving my restlessness, awoke me; the dashing waves were around, the cloudy sky above; the fiend was not here: a sense of security, a feeling that a truce was established between the present hour and the irresistible, disastrous future imparted to me a kind of calm forgetfulness, of which the human mind is by its structure peculiarly susceptible.

CHAPTER V

The voyage came to an end. We landed, and proceeded to Paris. I soon found that I had overtaxed my strength and that I must repose before I could continue my journey. My father's care and attentions were indefatigable, but he did not know the origin of my sufferings and sought erroneous methods to remedy the incurable ill. He wished me to seek amusement in society. I abhorred the face of man. Oh, not abhorred! They were my brethren, my fellow beings, and I felt attracted even to the most repulsive among them, as to creatures of an angelic nature and celestial mechanism. But I felt that I had no right to share their intercourse. I had unchained an enemy among them whose joy it was to shed their blood and to revel in their groans. How they would, each and all, abhor me and hunt me from the world did they know my unhallowed acts and the crimes which had their source in me!

My father yielded at length to my desire to avoid society and strove by various arguments to banish my despair. Sometimes he thought that I felt deeply the degradation of being obliged to answer a charge of murder, and he endeavoured to prove to me the futility of pride.

"Alas! My father," said I, "how little do you know me. Human beings, their feelings and passions, would indeed be degraded if such a wretch as I felt pride. Justine, poor unhappy Justine, was as innocent as I, and she suffered the same charge; she died for it; and I am the cause of this—I murdered her. William, Justine, and Henry—they all died by my hands."

My father had often, during my imprisonment, heard me make the same assertion; when I thus accused myself, he sometimes seemed to desire an explanation, and at others he appeared to consider it as the offspring of delirium, and that, during my illness, some idea of this kind had presented itself to my imagination, the remembrance of which I preserved in my convalescence. I avoided explanation and maintained a continual silence concerning the wretch I had created. I had a persuasion that I should be supposed mad, and this in itself would forever have chained my tongue. But, besides, I could not bring myself to disclose a secret which would fill my hearer with consternation and make fear and unnatural horror the inmates of his breast. I checked, therefore, my impatient thirst for sympathy and was silent when I would have given the world to have confided the fatal secret. Yet, still, words like those I have recorded would burst uncontrollably from me. I could offer no explanation of them, but their truth in part relieved the burden of my mysterious woe.

Upon this occasion my father said, with an expression of unbounded wonder, "My dearest Victor, what infatuation is this? My dear son, I entreat you never to make such an assertion again."

"I am not mad," I cried energetically; "the sun and the heavens, who have viewed my operations, can bear witness of my truth. I am the assassin of those most innocent victims; they died by my machinations. A thousand times would I have shed my own blood, drop by drop, to have saved their lives; but I could not, my father, indeed I could not sacrifice the whole human race."

The conclusion of this speech convinced my father that my ideas were deranged, and he instantly changed the subject of our conversation and endeavoured to alter the course of my thoughts. He wished as much as possible to obliterate the memory of the scenes that had taken place in Ireland and never alluded to them or suffered me to speak of my misfortunes.

As time passed away I became more calm; misery had her dwelling in my heart, but I no longer talked in the same incoherent manner of my own crimes; sufficient for me was the consciousness of them. By the utmost self-violence I curbed the imperious voice of wretchedness, which sometimes desired to declare itself to the whole world, and my manners were calmer and more composed than they had ever been since my journey to the sea of ice. A few days before we left Paris on our way to Switzerland, I received the following letter from Elizabeth:

> My dear Friend,
>
> It gave me the greatest pleasure to receive a letter from my uncle dated at Paris; you are no longer at a formidable distance, and I may hope to see you in less than a fortnight. My poor cousin, how much you must have suffered! I expect to see you looking even more ill than when you quitted Geneva. This winter has been passed most miserably, tortured as I have been by anxious suspense; yet I hope to see peace in your countenance

and to find that your heart is not totally void of comfort and tranquillity.

Yet I fear that the same feelings now exist that made you so miserable a year ago, even perhaps augmented by time. I would not disturb you at this period, when so many misfortunes weigh upon you, but a conversation that I had with my uncle previous to his departure renders some explanation necessary before we meet.

Explanation! You may possibly say, What can Elizabeth have to explain? If you really say this, my questions are answered and all my doubts satisfied. But you are distant from me, and it is possible that you may dread and yet be pleased with this explanation; and in a probability of this being the case, I dare not any longer postpone writing what, during your absence, I have often wished to express to you but have never had the courage to begin.

You well know, Victor, that our union had been the favourite plan of your parents ever since our infancy. We were told this when young, and taught to look forward to it as an event that would certainly take place. We were affectionate playfellows during childhood, and, I believe, dear and valued friends to one another as we grew older. But as brother and sister often entertain a lively affection towards each other without desiring a more intimate union, may not such also be our case? Tell me, dearest Victor. Answer me, I conjure you by our mutual happiness, with simple truth—Do you not love another?

You have travelled; you have spent several years of your life at Ingolstadt; and I confess to you, my friend, that when I saw you last autumn so unhappy, flying to solitude from the society of every creature, I could not help supposing that you might regret our connection and believe yourself bound in honour to fulfil the wishes of your parents, although they opposed themselves to your inclinations. But this is false reasoning. I confess to you, my friend, that I love you and that in my airy dreams of futurity you have been my constant friend and companion. But it is your happiness I desire as well as my own when I declare to you that our marriage would render me eternally miserable unless it were the dictate of your own free choice. Even now

I weep to think that, borne down as you are by the cruellest misfortunes, you may stifle, by the word 'honour,' all hope of that love and happiness which would alone restore you to yourself. I, who have so disinterested an affection for you, may increase your miseries tenfold by being an obstacle to your wishes. Ah! Victor, be assured that your cousin and playmate has too sincere a love for you not to be made miserable by this supposition. Be happy, my friend; and if you obey me in this one request, remain satisfied that nothing on earth will have the power to interrupt my tranquillity.

Do not let this letter disturb you; do not answer tomorrow, or the next day, or even until you come, if it will give you pain. My uncle will send me news of your health, and if I see but one smile on your lips when we meet, occasioned by this or any other exertion of mine, I shall need no other happiness.

Elizabeth Lavenza
Geneva, May 18th, 17—.

This letter revived in my memory what I had before forgotten, the threat of the fiend—*"I will be with you on your wedding-night!"* Such was my sentence, and on that night would the daemon employ every art to destroy me and tear me from the glimpse of happiness which promised partly to console my sufferings. On that night he had determined to consummate his crimes by my death. Well, be it so; a deadly struggle would then assuredly take place, in which if he were victorious I should be at peace and his power over me be at an end. If he were vanquished, I should be a free man. Alas! What freedom? Such as the peasant enjoys when his family have been massacred before his eyes, his cottage burnt, his lands laid waste, and he is turned adrift, homeless, penniless, and alone, but free. Such would be my liberty except that in my Elizabeth I possessed a treasure, alas, balanced by those horrors of remorse and guilt which would pursue me until death.

Sweet and beloved Elizabeth! I read and reread her letter, and some softened feelings stole into my heart and dared to whisper paradisiacal dreams of love and joy; but the apple was already eaten, and the angel's arm bared to drive me from all hope. Yet I would die to make her happy. If the monster executed his threat, death was inevitable; yet, again, I considered whether my marriage would hasten my fate. My destruction might indeed arrive a few months sooner, but if my torturer should suspect that I postponed it, influenced by his menaces, he would surely find other and perhaps more dreadful means of revenge.

He had vowed *to be with me on my wedding-night*, yet he did not consider that threat as binding him to peace in the meantime, for as if to show me that he was not yet satiated with blood, he had murdered Clerval immediately after the enunciation of his threats. I resolved, therefore, that if my immediate union with my cousin would conduce either to hers or my father's happiness, my adversary's designs against my life should not retard it a single hour.

In this state of mind I wrote to Elizabeth. My letter was calm and affectionate. "I fear, my beloved girl," I said, "little happiness remains for us on earth; yet all that I may one day enjoy is centred in you. Chase away your idle fears; to you alone do I consecrate my life and my endeavours for contentment. I have one secret, Elizabeth, a dreadful one; when revealed to you, it will chill your frame with horror, and then, far from being surprised at my misery, you will only wonder that I survive what I have endured. I will confide this tale of misery and terror to you the day after our marriage shall take place, for, my sweet cousin, there must be perfect confidence between us. But until then, I conjure you, do not mention or allude to it. This I most earnestly entreat, and I know you will comply."

In about a week after the arrival of Elizabeth's letter, we returned to Geneva. The sweet girl welcomed me with warm affection, yet tears were in her eyes as she beheld my emaciated frame and feverish cheeks. I saw a change in her also. She was thinner and had lost much of that heavenly vivacity that had before charmed me; but her gentleness and soft looks of compassion made her a more fit companion for one blasted and miserable as I was.

The tranquillity which I now enjoyed did not endure. Memory brought madness with it, and when I thought of what had passed, a real insanity possessed me; sometimes I was furious and burnt with rage, sometimes low and despondent. I neither spoke nor looked at anyone, but sat motionless, bewildered by the multitude of miseries that overcame me.

Elizabeth alone had the power to draw me from these fits; her gentle voice would soothe me when transported by passion and inspire me with human feelings when sunk in torpor. She wept with me and for me. When reason returned, she would remonstrate and endeavour to inspire me with resignation. Ah! It is well for the unfortunate to be resigned, but for the guilty there is no peace. The agonies of remorse poison the luxury there is otherwise sometimes found in indulging the excess of grief.

Soon after my arrival my father spoke of my immediate marriage with Elizabeth. I remained silent.

"Have you, then, some other attachment?"

"None on earth. I love Elizabeth and look forward to our union with delight. Let the day therefore be fixed; and on it I will consecrate myself, in life or death, to the happiness of my cousin."

"My dear Victor, do not speak thus. Heavy misfortunes have befallen us, but let us only cling closer to what remains and transfer our love for those whom we have lost to those who yet live. Our circle will be small but bound close by the ties of affection and mutual misfortune. And when time shall have softened your despair, new and dear objects of care will be born to replace those of whom we have been so cruelly deprived."

Such were the lessons of my father. But to me the remembrance of the threat returned; nor can you wonder that, omnipotent as the fiend had yet been in his deeds of blood, I should almost regard him as invincible, and that when he had pronounced the words "*I shall be with you on your wedding-night*," I should regard the threatened fate as unavoidable. But death was no evil to me if the loss of Elizabeth were balanced with it, and I therefore, with a contented and even cheerful countenance, agreed with my father that if my cousin would consent, the ceremony should take place in ten days, and thus put, as I imagined, the seal to my fate.

Great God! If for one instant I had thought what might be the hellish intention of my fiendish adversary, I would rather have banished myself forever from my native country and wandered a friendless outcast over the earth than have consented to this miserable marriage. But, as if possessed of magic powers, the monster had blinded me to his real intentions; and when I thought that I had prepared only my own death, I hastened that of a far dearer victim.

As the period fixed for our marriage drew nearer, whether from cowardice or a prophetic feeling, I felt my heart sink within me. But

I concealed my feelings by an appearance of hilarity that brought smiles and joy to the countenance of my father, but hardly deceived the ever-watchful and nicer eye of Elizabeth. She looked forward to our union with placid contentment, not unmingled with a little fear, which past misfortunes had impressed, that what now appeared certain and tangible happiness might soon dissipate into an airy dream and leave no trace but deep and everlasting regret.

Preparations were made for the event, congratulatory visits were received, and all wore a smiling appearance. I shut up, as well as I could, in my own heart the anxiety that preyed there and entered with seeming earnestness into the plans of my father, although they might only serve as the decorations of my tragedy. Through my father's exertions a part of the inheritance of Elizabeth had been restored to her by the Austrian government. A small possession on the shores of Como belonged to her. It was agreed that, immediately after our union, we should proceed to Villa Lavenza and spend our first days of happiness beside the beautiful lake near which it stood.

In the meantime I took every precaution to defend my person in case the fiend should openly attack me. I carried pistols and a dagger constantly about me and was ever on the watch to prevent artifice, and by these means gained a greater degree of tranquillity. Indeed, as the period approached, the threat appeared more as a delusion, not to be regarded as worthy to disturb my peace, while the happiness I hoped for in my marriage wore a greater appearance of certainty as the day fixed for its solemnization drew nearer and I heard it continually spoken of as an occurrence which no accident could possibly prevent.

Elizabeth seemed happy; my tranquil demeanour contributed greatly to calm her mind. But on the day that was to fulfil my wishes and my destiny, she was melancholy, and a presentiment of evil pervaded her; and perhaps also she thought of the dreadful secret which I had promised to reveal to her on the following day. My father was in the meantime overjoyed and in the bustle of preparation only recognized in the melancholy of his niece the diffidence of a bride.

After the ceremony was performed a large party assembled at my father's, but it was agreed that Elizabeth and I should commence our journey by water, sleeping that night at Evian and continuing our voyage on the following day. The day was fair, the wind favourable; all smiled on our nuptial embarkation.

Those were the last moments of my life during which I enjoyed the feeling of happiness. We passed rapidly along; the sun was hot, but we were sheltered from its rays by a kind of canopy while we enjoyed the beauty of the scene, sometimes on one side of the lake, where we saw Mont Salêve, the pleasant banks of Montalègre, and at a distance, surmounting all, the beautiful Mont Blanc and the assemblage of snowy mountains that in vain endeavour to emulate her; sometimes coasting the opposite banks, we saw the mighty Jura opposing its dark side to the ambition that would quit its native country, and an almost insurmountable barrier to the invader who should wish to enslave it.

I took the hand of Elizabeth. "You are sorrowful, my love. Ah! If you knew what I have suffered and what I may yet endure, you would endeavour to let me taste the quiet and freedom from despair that this one day at least permits me to enjoy."

"Be happy, my dear Victor," replied Elizabeth; "there is, I hope, nothing to distress you; and be assured that if a lively joy is not painted in my face, my heart is contented. Something whispers to me not to depend too much on the prospect that is opened before us, but I will not listen to such a sinister voice. Observe how fast we move along and how the clouds, which sometimes obscure and sometimes rise above the dome of Mont Blanc, render this scene of beauty still more interesting. Look also at the innumerable fish that are swimming in the clear waters, where we can distinguish every pebble that lies at the bottom. What a divine day! How happy and serene all nature appears!"

Thus Elizabeth endeavoured to divert her thoughts and mine from all reflection upon melancholy subjects. But her temper was fluctuating; joy for a few instants shone in her eyes, but it continually gave place to distraction and reverie.

The sun sank lower in the heavens; we passed the river Drance and observed its path through the chasms of the higher and the glens of the lower hills. The Alps here come closer to the lake, and we approached the amphitheatre of mountains which forms its eastern boundary. The spire of Evian shone under the woods that surrounded it and the range of mountain above mountain by which it was overhung.

The wind, which had hitherto carried us along with amazing rapidity, sank at sunset to a light breeze; the soft air just ruffled the water and caused a pleasant motion among the trees as we approached the shore, from which it wafted the most delightful scent of flowers and hay. The sun sank beneath the horizon as we landed, and as I touched the shore I felt those cares and fears revive which soon were to clasp me and cling to me forever.

CHAPTER VI

It was eight o'clock when we landed; we walked for a short time on the shore, enjoying the transitory light, and then retired to the inn and contemplated the lovely scene of waters, woods, and mountains, obscured in darkness, yet still displaying their black outlines.

The wind, which had fallen in the south, now rose with great violence in the west. The moon had reached her summit in the heavens and was beginning to descend; the clouds swept across it swifter than the flight of the vulture and dimmed her rays, while the lake reflected the scene of the busy heavens, rendered still busier by the restless waves that were beginning to rise. Suddenly a heavy storm of rain descended.

I had been calm during the day, but so soon as night obscured the shapes of objects, a thousand fears arose in my mind. I was anxious and watchful, while my right hand grasped a pistol which was hidden in my bosom; every sound terrified me, but I resolved that I would sell my life dearly and not shrink from the conflict until my own life or that of my adversary was extinguished.

Elizabeth observed my agitation for some time in timid and fearful silence, but there was something in my glance which communicated terror to her, and trembling, she asked, "What is it that agitates you, my dear Victor? What is it you fear?"

"Oh! Peace, peace, my love," replied I; "this night, and all will be safe; but this night is dreadful, very dreadful."

I passed an hour in this state of mind, when suddenly I reflected how fearful the combat which I momentarily expected would be to my wife, and I earnestly entreated her to retire, resolving not to join her until I had obtained some knowledge as to the situation of my enemy.

She left me, and I continued some time walking up and down the passages of the house and inspecting every corner that might afford a retreat to my adversary. But I discovered no trace of him and was beginning to conjecture that some fortunate chance had intervened to prevent the execution of his menaces when suddenly I heard a shrill and dreadful scream. It came from the room into which Elizabeth had retired. As I heard it, the whole truth rushed into my mind, my arms dropped, the motion of every muscle and fibre was suspended; I could feel the blood trickling in my veins and tingling in the extremities of my limbs. This state lasted but for an instant; the scream was repeated, and I rushed into the room.

Great God! Why did I not then expire! Why am I here to relate the destruction of the best hope and the purest creature on earth? She was there, lifeless and inanimate, thrown across the bed, her head hanging down and her pale and distorted features half covered by her hair. Everywhere I turn I see the same figure—her bloodless arms and relaxed form flung by the murderer on its bridal bier. Could I behold this and live? Alas! Life is obstinate and clings closest where it is most hated. For a moment only did I lose recollection; I fell senseless on the ground.

When I recovered, I found myself surrounded by the people of the inn; their countenances expressed a breathless terror, but the horror of others appeared only as a mockery, a shadow of the feelings that oppressed me. I escaped from them to the room where lay the body of Elizabeth, my love, my wife, so lately living, so dear, so worthy. She had been moved from the posture in which I had first beheld her, and now, as she lay, her head upon her arm and a handkerchief thrown across her face and neck, I might have supposed her asleep. I rushed towards her and embraced her with ardour, but the deadly languor and coldness of the limbs told me that what I now held in my arms had ceased to be the Elizabeth whom I had loved and cherished. The murderous mark of the fiend's grasp was on her neck, and the breath had ceased to issue from her lips.

While I still hung over her in the agony of despair, I happened to look up. The windows of the room had before been darkened, and I felt a kind of panic on seeing the pale yellow light of the moon illuminate the chamber. The shutters had been thrown back, and with a sensation of horror not to be described, I saw at the open window a figure the most hideous and abhorred. A grin was on the face of the monster; he seemed to jeer, as with his fiendish finger he pointed towards the corpse of my wife. I rushed towards the window, and drawing a pistol from my bosom, fired; but he eluded me, leaped from his station, and running with the swiftness of lightning, plunged into the lake.

The report of the pistol brought a crowd into the room. I pointed to the spot where he had disappeared, and we followed the track with boats; nets were cast, but in vain. After passing several hours, we returned hopeless, most of my companions believing it to have been a form conjured up by my fancy. After having landed, they proceeded to search the country, parties going in different directions among the woods and vines.

I attempted to accompany them, and proceeded a short distance from the house, but my head whirled round, my steps were like those of a drunken man, I fell at last in a state of utter exhaustion; a film covered my eyes, and my skin was parched with the heat of fever. In this state I was carried back and placed on a bed, hardly conscious of what had happened; my eyes wandered round the room as if to seek something that I had lost.

After an interval I arose, and as if by instinct, crawled into the room where the corpse of my beloved lay. There were women weeping around; I hung over it and joined my sad tears to theirs; all this time no distinct idea presented itself to my mind, but my thoughts rambled to various subjects, reflecting confusedly on my misfortunes and their cause. I was bewildered, in a cloud of wonder and horror. The death of William, the execution of Justine, the murder of Clerval, and lastly of my wife; even at that moment I knew not that my only remaining friends were safe from the malignity of the fiend; my father even now might be writhing under his grasp, and Ernest might be dead at his feet. This idea made me shudder and recalled me to action. I started up and resolved to return to Geneva with all possible speed.

There were no horses to be procured, and I must return by the lake; but the wind was unfavourable, and the rain fell in torrents. However, it was hardly morning, and I might reasonably hope to arrive by night. I hired men to row and took an oar myself, for I had always experienced relief from mental torment in bodily exercise. But the overflowing misery I now felt, and the excess of agitation that I endured rendered me incapable of any exertion. I threw down the oar, and leaning my head upon my hands, gave way to every gloomy idea that arose. If I looked up, I saw scenes which were familiar to me in my happier time and which I had contemplated but the day before in the company of her who was now but a shadow and a recollection. Tears streamed from my eyes. The rain had ceased for a moment, and I saw the fish play in the waters as they had done a few hours before; they had then been observed by Elizabeth. Nothing is so painful to the human mind as a great and sudden change. The sun might shine or the clouds might lower, but nothing could appear to me as it had done the day before.

A fiend had snatched from me every hope of future happiness; no creature had ever been so miserable as I was; so frightful an event is single in the history of man.

But why should I dwell upon the incidents that followed this last overwhelming event? Mine has been a tale of horrors; I have reached their acme, and what I must now relate can but be tedious to you. Know that, one by one, my friends were snatched away; I was left desolate. My own strength is exhausted, and I must tell, in a few words, what remains of my hideous narration.

I arrived at Geneva. My father and Ernest yet lived, but the former sunk under the tidings that I bore. I see him now, excellent and venerable old man! His eyes wandered in vacancy, for they had lost their charm and their delight—his Elizabeth, his more than daughter, whom he doted on with all that affection which a man feels, who in the decline of life, having few affections, clings more earnestly to those that remain. Cursed, cursed be the fiend that brought misery on his grey hairs and doomed him to waste in wretchedness! He could not live under the horrors that were accumulated around him; the springs of existence suddenly gave way; he was unable to rise from his bed, and in a few days he died in my arms.

What then became of me? I know not; I lost sensation, and chains and darkness were the only objects that pressed upon me. Sometimes, indeed, I dreamt that I wandered in flowery meadows and pleasant vales with the friends of my youth, but I awoke and found myself in a dungeon. Melancholy followed, but by degrees I gained a clear conception of my miseries and situation and was then released from my prison. For they had called me mad, and during many months, as I understood, a solitary cell had been my habitation.

Liberty, however, had been a useless gift to me, had I not, as I awakened to reason, at the same time awakened to revenge. As the memory of past misfortunes pressed upon me, I began to reflect on their cause—the monster whom I had created, the miserable daemon whom I had sent abroad into the world for my destruction. I was possessed by a maddening rage when I thought of him, and desired and ardently prayed that I might have him within my grasp to wreak a great and signal revenge on his cursed head.

Nor did my hate long confine itself to useless wishes; I began to reflect on the best means of securing him; and for this purpose, about a month after my release, I repaired to a criminal judge in the town and told him that I had an accusation to make, that I knew the destroyer of my family, and that I required him to exert his whole authority for the apprehension of the murderer.

The magistrate listened to me with attention and kindness. "Be assured, sir," said he, "no pains or exertions on my part shall be spared to discover the villain."

"I thank you," replied I; "listen, therefore, to the deposition that I have to make. It is indeed a tale so strange that I should fear you would not credit it were there not something in truth which, however wonderful, forces conviction. The story is too connected to be mistaken for a dream, and I have no motive for falsehood." My manner as I thus addressed him was impressive but calm; I had formed in my own heart a resolution to pursue my destroyer to death, and this purpose quieted my agony and for an interval reconciled me to life. I now related my history briefly but with firmness and precision, marking the dates with accuracy and never deviating into invective or exclamation.

The magistrate appeared at first perfectly incredulous, but as I continued he became more attentive and interested; I saw him sometimes shudder with horror; at others a lively surprise, unmingled with disbelief, was painted on his countenance.

When I had concluded my narration I said, "This is the being whom I accuse and for whose seizure and punishment I call upon you to exert your whole power. It is your duty as a magistrate, and I believe and hope that your feelings as a man will not revolt from the execution of those functions on this occasion."

This address caused a considerable change in the physiognomy of my own auditor. He had heard my story with that half kind of belief that is given to a tale of spirits and supernatural events; but when he was called upon to act officially in consequence, the whole tide of his incredulity returned. He, however, answered mildly, "I would willingly afford you every aid in your pursuit, but the creature of whom you speak appears to have powers which would put all my exertions to defiance. Who can follow an animal which can traverse the sea of ice and inhabit caves and dens where no man would venture to intrude? Besides, some months have elapsed since the commission of his crimes, and no one can conjecture to what place he has wandered or what region he may now inhabit."

"I do not doubt that he hovers near the spot which I inhabit, and if he has indeed taken refuge in the Alps, he may be hunted like the chamois and destroyed as a beast of prey. But I perceive your thoughts; you do not credit my narrative and do not intend to pursue my enemy with the punishment which is his desert."

As I spoke, rage sparkled in my eyes; the magistrate was intimidated. "You are mistaken," said he. "I will exert myself, and if it is in my power to seize the monster, be assured that he shall suffer punishment proportionate to his crimes. But I fear, from what you have yourself described to be his properties, that this will prove impracticable; and thus, while every proper measure is pursued, you should make up your mind to disappointment."

"That cannot be; but all that I can say will be of little avail. My revenge is of no moment to you; yet, while I allow it to be a vice, I confess that it is the devouring and only passion of my soul. My rage is unspeakable when I reflect that the murderer, whom I have turned loose upon society, still exists. You refuse my just demand; I have but one resource, and I devote myself, either in my life or death, to his destruction."

I trembled with excess of agitation as I said this; there was a frenzy in my manner, and something, I doubt not, of that haughty fierceness which the martyrs of old are said to have possessed. But to a Genevan magistrate, whose mind was occupied by far other ideas than those of devotion and heroism, this elevation of mind had much the appearance of madness. He endeavoured to soothe me as a nurse does a child and reverted to my tale as the effects of delirium.

"Man," I cried, "how ignorant art thou in thy pride of wisdom! Cease; you know not what it is you say."

I broke from the house angry and disturbed and retired to meditate on some other mode of action.

CHAPTER VII

My present situation was one in which all voluntary thought was swallowed up and lost. I was hurried away by fury; revenge alone endowed me with strength and composure; it moulded my feelings and allowed me to be calculating and calm at periods when otherwise delirium or death would have been my portion.

My first resolution was to quit Geneva forever; my country, which, when I was happy and beloved, was dear to me, now, in my adversity, became hateful. I provided myself with a sum of money, together with a few jewels which had belonged to my mother, and departed.

And now my wanderings began which are to cease but with life. I have traversed a vast portion of the earth and have endured all the hardships which travellers in deserts and barbarous countries are wont to meet. How I have lived I hardly know; many times have I stretched my failing limbs upon the sandy plain and prayed for death. But revenge kept me alive; I dared not die and leave my adversary in being.

When I quitted Geneva my first labour was to gain some clue by which I might trace the steps of my fiendish enemy. But my plan was unsettled, and I wandered many hours round the confines of the town, uncertain what path I should pursue. As night approached I found myself at the entrance of the cemetery where William, Elizabeth, and my father reposed. I entered it and approached the tomb which marked their graves. Everything was silent except the leaves of the trees, which were gently agitated by the wind; the night was nearly dark, and the scene would have been solemn and affecting even to an uninterested observer. The spirits of the departed seemed to flit around and to cast a shadow, which was felt but not seen, around the head of the mourner.

The deep grief which this scene had at first excited quickly gave way to rage and despair. They were dead, and I lived; their murderer also lived, and to destroy him I must drag out my weary existence. I knelt on the grass and kissed the earth and with quivering lips exclaimed, "By the sacred earth on which I kneel, by the shades that wander near me, by the deep and eternal grief that I feel, I swear; and by thee, O Night, and the spirits that preside over thee, to pursue the daemon who caused this misery, until he or I shall perish in mortal conflict. For this purpose

I will preserve my life; to execute this dear revenge will I again behold the sun and tread the green herbage of earth, which otherwise should vanish from my eyes forever. And I call on you, spirits of the dead, and on you, wandering ministers of vengeance, to aid and conduct me in my work. Let the cursed and hellish monster drink deep of agony; let him feel the despair that now torments me."

I had begun my adjuration with solemnity and an awe which almost assured me that the shades of my murdered friends heard and approved my devotion, but the furies possessed me as I concluded, and rage choked my utterance.

I was answered through the stillness of night by a loud and fiendish laugh. It rang on my ears long and heavily; the mountains re-echoed it, and I felt as if all hell surrounded me with mockery and laughter. Surely in that moment I should have been possessed by frenzy and have destroyed my miserable existence but that my vow was heard and that I was reserved for vengeance. The laughter died away, when a well-known and abhorred voice, apparently close to my ear, addressed me in an audible whisper, "I am satisfied, miserable wretch! You have determined to live, and I am satisfied."

I darted towards the spot from which the sound proceeded, but the devil eluded my grasp. Suddenly the broad disk of the moon arose and shone full upon his ghastly and distorted shape as he fled with more than mortal speed.

I pursued him, and for many months this has been my task. Guided by a slight clue, I followed the windings of the Rhône, but vainly. The blue Mediterranean appeared, and by a strange chance, I saw the fiend enter by night and hide himself in a vessel bound for the Black Sea. I took my passage in the same ship, but he escaped, I know not how.

Amidst the wilds of Tartary and Russia, although he still evaded me, I have ever followed in his track. Sometimes the peasants, scared by this horrid apparition, informed me of his path; sometimes he himself, who feared that if I lost all trace of him I should despair and die, left some mark to guide me. The snows descended on my head, and I saw the print of his huge step on the white plain. To you first entering on life, to whom care is new and agony unknown, how can you understand what I have felt and still feel? Cold, want, and fatigue were the least pains which I was destined to endure; I was cursed by some devil and carried about with me my eternal hell; yet still a spirit of good followed and directed my steps and when I most murmured would suddenly extricate me from seemingly insurmountable difficulties. Sometimes, when nature, overcome by hunger, sank under the exhaustion, a repast was prepared for me in the desert that restored and inspirited me. The fare was, indeed, coarse, such as the peasants of the country ate, but I will not doubt that it was set there by the spirits that I had invoked to aid me. Often, when all was dry, the heavens cloudless, and I was parched by thirst, a slight cloud would bedim the sky, shed the few drops that revived me, and vanish.

I followed, when I could, the courses of the rivers; but the daemon generally avoided these, as it was here that the population of the country chiefly collected. In other places human beings were seldom seen, and I generally subsisted on the wild animals that crossed my path. I had money with me and gained the friendship of the villagers by distributing it; or I brought with me some food that I had killed, which, after taking a small part, I always presented to those who had provided me with fire and utensils for cooking.

My life, as it passed thus, was indeed hateful to me, and it was during sleep alone that I could taste joy. O blessed sleep! Often, when most miserable, I sank to repose, and my dreams lulled me even to rapture. The spirits that guarded me had provided these moments, or rather hours, of happiness that I might retain strength to fulfil my pilgrimage. Deprived of this respite, I should have sunk under my hardships. During the day I was sustained and inspirited by the hope of night, for in sleep I saw my friends, my wife, and my beloved country; again I saw the benevolent countenance of my father, heard the silver tones of my Elizabeth's voice, and beheld Clerval enjoying health and youth. Often, when wearied by a toilsome march, I persuaded myself that I was dreaming until night should come and that I should then enjoy reality in the arms of my dearest friends. What agonising fondness did I feel for them! How did I cling to their dear forms, as sometimes they haunted even my waking hours, and persuade myself that they still lived! At such moments vengeance, that burned within me, died in my heart, and I pursued my path towards the destruction of the daemon more as a task enjoined by heaven, as the mechanical impulse of some power of which I was unconscious, than as the ardent desire of my soul.

What his feelings were whom I pursued I cannot know. Sometimes, indeed, he left marks in writing on the barks of the trees or cut in stone that guided me and instigated my fury. "My reign is not yet over"—these words were legible in one of these inscriptions—"you live, and my power is complete. Follow me; I seek the everlasting ices of the north, where you will feel the misery of cold and frost, to which I am impassive. You will find near this place, if you follow not too tardily, a dead hare; eat and be refreshed. Come on, my enemy; we have yet to wrestle for our lives, but many hard and miserable hours must you endure until that period shall arrive."

Scoffing devil! Again do I vow vengeance; again do I devote thee, miserable fiend, to torture and death. Never will I give up my search until he or I perish; and then with what ecstasy shall I join my Elizabeth and my departed friends, who even now prepare for me the reward of my tedious toil and horrible pilgrimage!

As I still pursued my journey to the northward, the snows thickened and the cold increased in a degree almost too severe to support. The peasants were shut up in their hovels, and only a few of the most hardy ventured forth to seize the animals whom starvation had forced from their hiding-places to seek for prey. The rivers were covered with ice, and no fish could be procured; and thus I was cut off from my chief article of maintenance.

The triumph of my enemy increased with the difficulty of my labours. One inscription that he left was in these words: "Prepare! Your toils only begin; wrap yourself in furs and provide food, for we shall soon enter upon a journey where your sufferings will satisfy my everlasting hatred."

My courage and perseverance were invigorated by these scoffing words; I resolved not to fail in my purpose, and calling on heaven to support me, I continued with unabated fervour to traverse immense deserts, until the ocean appeared at a distance and formed the utmost boundary of the horizon. Oh! How unlike it was to the blue seasons of the south! Covered with ice, it was only to be distinguished from land by its superior wildness and ruggedness. The Greeks wept for joy when they beheld the Mediterranean from the hills of Asia, and hailed with rapture the boundary of their toils. I did not weep, but I knelt down and with a full heart thanked my guiding spirit for conducting me in safety to the place where I hoped, notwithstanding my adversary's gibe, to meet and grapple with him.

Some weeks before this period I had procured a sledge and dogs and thus traversed the snows with inconceivable speed. I know not whether the fiend possessed the same advantages, but I found that, as before I had daily lost ground in the pursuit, I now gained on him, so much so that when I first saw the ocean he was but one day's journey in advance, and I hoped to intercept him before he should reach the beach. With new courage, therefore, I pressed on, and in two days arrived at a wretched hamlet on the seashore. I enquired of the inhabitants concerning the fiend and gained accurate information. A gigantic monster, they said, had arrived the night before, armed with a gun and many pistols, putting to flight the inhabitants of a solitary cottage through fear of his terrific appearance. He had carried off their store of winter food, and placing it in a sledge, to draw which he had seized on a numerous drove of trained dogs, he had harnessed them, and the same night, to the joy of the horror-struck villagers, had pursued his journey across the sea in a direction that led to no land; and they conjectured that he must speedily be destroyed by the breaking of the ice or frozen by the eternal frosts.

On hearing this information, I suffered a temporary access of despair. He had escaped me, and I must commence a destructive and almost endless journey across the mountainous ices of the ocean, amidst cold that few of the inhabitants could long endure and which I, the native of a genial and sunny climate, could not hope to survive. Yet at the idea that the fiend should live and be triumphant, my rage and vengeance returned, and like a mighty tide, overwhelmed every other feeling. After a slight repose, during which the spirits of the dead hovered round and instigated me to toil and revenge, I prepared for my journey.

I exchanged my land-sledge for one fashioned for the inequalities of the frozen ocean, and purchasing a plentiful stock of provisions, I departed from land.

I cannot guess how many days have passed since then, but I have endured misery which nothing but the eternal sentiment of a just retribution burning within my heart could have enabled me to support. Immense and rugged mountains of ice often barred up my passage, and I often heard the thunder of the ground sea, which threatened my destruction. But again the frost came and made the paths of the sea secure.

By the quantity of provision which I had consumed, I should

guess that I had passed three weeks in this journey; and the continual protraction of hope, returning back upon the heart, often wrung bitter drops of despondency and grief from my eyes. Despair had indeed almost secured her prey, and I should soon have sunk beneath this misery. Once, after the poor animals that conveyed me had with incredible toil gained the summit of a sloping ice mountain, and one, sinking under his fatigue, died, I viewed the expanse before me with anguish, when suddenly my eye caught a dark speck upon the dusky plain. I strained my sight to discover what it could be and uttered a wild cry of ecstasy when I distinguished a sledge and the distorted proportions of a well-known form within. Oh! With what a burning gush did hope revisit my heart! Warm tears filled my eyes, which I hastily wiped away, that they might not intercept the view I had of the daemon; but still my sight was dimmed by the burning drops, until, giving way to the emotions that oppressed me, I wept aloud.

But this was not the time for delay: I disencumbered the dogs of their dead companion, gave them a plentiful portion of food, and after an hour's rest, which was absolutely necessary, and yet which was bitterly irksome to me, I continued my route. The sledge was still visible, nor did I again lose sight of it except at the moments when for a short time some ice-rock concealed it with its intervening crags. I indeed perceptibly gained on it, and when, after nearly two days' journey, I beheld my enemy at no more than a mile distant, my heart bounded within me.

But now, when I appeared almost within grasp of my foe, my hopes were suddenly extinguished, and I lost all trace of him more utterly than I had ever done before. A ground sea was heard; the thunder of its progress, as the waters rolled and swelled beneath me, became every moment more ominous and terrific. I pressed on, but in vain. The wind arose; the sea roared; and, as with the mighty shock of an earthquake, it split and cracked with a tremendous and overwhelming sound. The work was soon finished; in a few minutes a tumultuous sea rolled between me and my enemy, and I was left drifting on a scattered piece of ice that was continually lessening and thus preparing for me a hideous death. In this manner many appalling hours passed; several of my dogs died, and I myself was about to sink under the accumulation of distress when I saw your vessel riding at anchor and holding forth to me hopes of succour and life. I had no conception that vessels ever came so far north and was astounded at the sight. I quickly destroyed part of my sledge to construct oars, and by these means was enabled, with infinite fatigue, to move my ice raft in the direction of your ship. I had determined, if you were going southwards, still to trust myself to the mercy of the seas rather than abandon my purpose. I hoped to induce you to grant me a boat with which I could pursue my enemy. But your direction was northwards. You took me on board when my vigour was exhausted, and I should soon have sunk under my multiplied hardships into a death which I still dread—for my task is unfulfilled.

Oh! When will my guiding spirit, in conducting me to the daemon, allow me the rest I so much desire; or must I die, and he yet live? If I do, swear to me, Walton, that he shall not escape, that you will seek him and satisfy my vengeance in his death. And do I dare to ask of you to undertake my pilgrimage, to endure the hardships that I have undergone? No; I am not so selfish. Yet, when I am dead, if he should appear, if the ministers of vengeance should conduct him to you, swear that he shall not live—swear that he shall not triumph over my accumulated woes and survive to add to the list of his dark crimes. He is eloquent and persuasive, and once his words had even power over my heart; but trust him not. His soul is as hellish as his form, full of treachery and fiend-like malice. Hear him not; call on the names of William, Justine, Clerval, Elizabeth, my father, and of the wretched Victor, and thrust your sword into his heart. I will hover near and direct the steel aright.

WALTON, IN CONTINUATION.
August 26th, 17—.

You have read this strange and terrific story, Margaret; and do you not feel your blood congeal with horror, like that which even now curdles mine? Sometimes, seized with sudden agony, he could not continue his tale; at others, his voice broken, yet piercing, uttered with difficulty the words so replete with anguish. His fine and lovely eyes were now lighted up with indignation, now subdued to downcast sorrow and quenched in infinite wretchedness. Sometimes he commanded his countenance and tones and related the most horrible incidents with a tranquil voice, suppressing every mark of agitation; then, like a volcano bursting forth, his face would suddenly change to an expression of the wildest rage as he shrieked out imprecations on his persecutor.

His tale is connected and told with an appearance of the simplest truth, yet I own to you that the letters of Felix and Safie, which he showed me, and the apparition of the monster seen from our ship, brought to me a greater conviction of the truth of his narrative than his asseverations, however earnest and connected. Such a monster has, then, really existence! I cannot doubt it, yet I am lost in surprise and admiration. Sometimes I endeavoured to gain from Frankenstein the particulars of his creature's formation, but on this point he was impenetrable.

"Are you mad, my friend?" said he. "Or whither does your senseless curiosity lead you? Would you also create for yourself and the world a demoniacal enemy? Peace, peace! Learn my miseries and do not seek to increase your own."

Frankenstein discovered that I made notes concerning his history; he asked to see them and then himself corrected and augmented them in many places, but principally in giving the life and spirit to the conversations he held with his enemy. "Since you have preserved my narration," said he, "I would not that a mutilated one should go down to posterity."

Thus has a week passed away, while I have listened to the strangest tale that ever imagination formed. My thoughts and every feeling of my soul have been drunk up by the interest for my guest which this tale and his own elevated and gentle manners have created. I wish to soothe him, yet can I counsel one so infinitely miserable, so destitute of every hope of consolation, to live? Oh, no! The only joy that he can now know will be when he composes his shattered spirit to peace and death. Yet he enjoys one comfort, the offspring of solitude and delirium; he believes that when in dreams he holds converse with his friends and derives from that communion consolation for his miseries or excitements to his vengeance, that they are not the creations of his fancy, but the beings themselves who visit him from the regions of a remote world. This faith gives a solemnity to his reveries that render them to me almost as imposing and interesting as truth.

Our conversations are not always confined to his own history and misfortunes. On every point of general literature he displays unbounded knowledge and a quick and piercing apprehension. His eloquence is forcible and touching; nor can I hear him, when he relates a pathetic incident or endeavours to move the passions of pity or love, without tears. What a glorious creature must he have been in the days of his prosperity, when he is thus noble and godlike in ruin! He seems to feel his own worth and the greatness of his fall.

"When younger," said he, "I believed myself destined for some great enterprise. My feelings are profound, but I possessed a coolness of judgement that fitted me for illustrious achievements. This sentiment of the worth of my nature supported me when others would have been oppressed, for I deemed it criminal to throw away in useless grief those talents that might be useful to my fellow creatures. When I reflected on the work I had completed, no less a one than the creation of a sensitive and rational animal, I could not rank myself with the herd of common projectors. But this thought, which supported me in the commencement of my career, now serves only to plunge me lower in the dust. All my speculations and hopes are as nothing, and like the archangel who aspired to omnipotence, I am chained in an eternal hell. My imagination was vivid, yet my powers of analysis and application were intense; by the union of these qualities I conceived the idea and executed the creation of a man. Even now I cannot recollect without passion my reveries while the work was incomplete. I trod heaven in my thoughts, now exulting in my powers, now burning with the idea of their effects. From my infancy I was imbued with high hopes and a lofty ambition; but how am I sunk! Oh! My friend, if you had known me as I once was, you would not recognize me in this state of degradation. Despondency rarely visited my heart; a high destiny seemed to bear me on, until I fell, never, never again to rise."

Must I then lose this admirable being? I have longed for a friend; I have sought one who would sympathise with and love me. Behold, on these desert seas I have found such a one, but I fear I have gained him only to know his value and lose him. I would reconcile him to life, but he repulses the idea.

"I thank you, Walton," he said, "for your kind intentions towards so miserable a wretch; but when you speak of new ties and fresh affections, think you that any can replace those who are gone? Can any man be to me as Clerval was, or any woman another Elizabeth? Even where the affections are not strongly moved by any superior excellence, the companions of our childhood always possess a certain power over our minds which hardly any later friend can obtain. They know our infantine dispositions, which, however they may be afterwards modified, are never eradicated; and they can judge of our actions with more certain conclusions as to the integrity of our motives. A sister or a brother can never, unless indeed such symptoms have been shown early, suspect the other of fraud or false dealing, when another friend, however strongly he may be attached, may, in spite of himself, be contemplated with suspicion. But I enjoyed friends, dear not only through habit and association, but from their own merits; and wherever I am, the soothing voice of my Elizabeth and the conversation of Clerval will be ever whispered in my ear. They are dead, and but one feeling in such a solitude can persuade me to preserve my life. If I were engaged in any high undertaking or design, fraught with extensive utility to my fellow creatures, then could I live to fulfil it. But such is not my destiny; I must pursue and destroy the being to whom I gave existence; then my lot on earth will be fulfilled, and I may die."

September 2nd.

My beloved Sister,

I write to you, encompassed by peril and ignorant whether I am ever doomed to see again dear England and the dearer friends that inhabit it. I am surrounded by mountains of ice which admit of no escape and threaten every moment to crush my vessel. The brave fellows whom I have persuaded to be my companions look towards me for aid, but I have none to bestow. There is something terribly appalling in our situation, yet my courage and hopes do not desert me. Yet it is terrible to reflect that the lives of all these men are endangered through me. If we are lost, my mad schemes are the cause.

And what, Margaret, will be the state of your mind? You will not hear of my destruction, and you will anxiously await my return. Years will pass, and you will have visitings of despair and yet be tortured by hope. Oh! My beloved sister, the sickening failing of your heartfelt expectations is, in prospect, more terrible to me than my own death. But you have a husband and lovely children; you may be happy. Heaven bless you and make you so!

My unfortunate guest regards me with the tenderest compassion. He endeavours to fill me with hope and talks as if life were a possession which he valued. He reminds me how often the same accidents have happened to other navigators who have attempted this sea, and in spite of myself, he fills me with cheerful auguries. Even the sailors feel the power of his eloquence; when he speaks, they no longer despair; he rouses their energies, and while they hear his voice they believe these vast mountains of ice are molehills which will vanish before the resolutions of man. These feelings are transitory; each day of expectation delayed fills them with fear, and I almost dread a mutiny caused by this despair.

September 5th.

A scene has just passed of such uncommon interest that, although it is highly probable that these papers may never reach you, yet I cannot forbear recording it.

We are still surrounded by mountains of ice, still in imminent danger of being crushed in their conflict. The cold is excessive, and many of my unfortunate comrades have already found a grave amidst this scene of desolation. Frankenstein has daily declined in health; a feverish fire still glimmers in his eyes, but he is exhausted, and when suddenly roused to any exertion, he speedily sinks again into apparent lifelessness.

I mentioned in my last letter the fears I entertained of a mutiny. This morning, as I sat watching the wan countenance of my friend—his eyes half closed and his limbs hanging listlessly—I was roused by half a dozen of the sailors, who demanded admission into the cabin. They entered, and their leader addressed me. He told me that he and his companions had been chosen by the other sailors to come in deputation to me to make me a requisition which, in justice, I could not refuse.

We were immured in ice and should probably never escape, but they feared that if, as was possible, the ice should dissipate and a free passage be opened, I should be rash enough to continue my voyage and lead them into fresh dangers, after they might happily have surmounted this. They insisted, therefore, that I should engage with a solemn promise that if the vessel should be freed I would instantly direct my course southwards.

This speech troubled me. I had not despaired, nor had I yet conceived the idea of returning if set free. Yet could I, in justice, or even in possibility, refuse this demand? I hesitated before I answered, when Frankenstein, who had at first been silent, and indeed appeared hardly to have force enough to attend, now roused himself; his eyes sparkled, and his cheeks flushed with momentary vigour. Turning towards the men, he said:

"What do you mean? What do you demand of your captain? Are you, then, so easily turned from your design? Did you not call this a glorious expedition? And wherefore was it glorious? Not because the way was smooth and placid as a southern sea, but because it was full of dangers and terror, because at every new incident your fortitude was to be called forth and your courage exhibited, because danger and death surrounded it, and these you were to brave and overcome. For this was it a glorious, for this was it an honourable undertaking. You were hereafter to be hailed as the benefactors of your species, your names adored as belonging to brave men who encountered death for honour and the benefit of mankind. And now, behold, with the first imagination of danger, or, if you will, the first mighty and terrific trial of your courage, you shrink away and are content to be handed down as men who had not strength enough to endure cold and peril; and so, poor souls, they were chilly and returned to their warm firesides. Why, that requires not this preparation; ye need not have come thus far and dragged your captain to the shame of a defeat merely to prove yourselves cowards. Oh! Be men, or be more than men. Be steady to your purposes and firm as a rock. This ice is not made of such stuff as your hearts may be; it is mutable and cannot withstand you if you say that it shall not. Do not return to your families with the stigma of disgrace marked on your brows. Return as heroes who have fought and conquered and who know not what it is to turn their backs on the foe."

He spoke this with a voice so modulated to the different feelings expressed in his speech, with an eye so full of lofty design and heroism, that can you wonder that these men were moved? They looked at one another and were unable to reply. I spoke; I told them to retire and consider of what had been said, that I would not lead them farther north if they strenuously desired the contrary, but that I hoped that, with reflection, their courage would return.

They retired, and I turned towards my friend, but he was sunk in languor and almost deprived of life.

How all this will terminate, I know not, but I had rather die than return shamefully, my purpose unfulfilled. Yet I fear such will be my fate; the men, unsupported by ideas of glory and honour, can never willingly continue to endure their present hardships.

September 7th.

The die is cast; I have consented to return if we are not destroyed. Thus are my hopes blasted by cowardice and indecision; I come back ignorant and disappointed. It requires more philosophy than I possess to bear this injustice with patience.

September 12th.

It is past; I am returning to England. I have lost my hopes of utility and glory; I have lost my friend. But I will endeavour to detail these bitter circumstances to you, my dear sister; and while I am wafted towards England and towards you, I will not despond.

September 9th, the ice began to move, and roarings like thunder were heard at a distance as the islands split and cracked in every direction. We were in the most imminent peril, but as we could only remain passive, my chief attention was occupied by my unfortunate guest whose illness increased in such a degree that he was entirely confined to his bed. The ice cracked behind us and was driven with force towards the north; a breeze sprang from the west, and on the 11th the passage towards the south became perfectly free. When the sailors saw this and that their return to their native country was apparently assured, a shout of tumultuous joy broke from them, loud and long-continued. Frankenstein, who was dozing, awoke and asked the cause of the tumult. "They shout," I said, "because they will soon return to England."

"Do you, then, really return?"

"Alas! Yes; I cannot withstand their demands. I cannot lead them unwillingly to danger, and I must return."

"Do so, if you will; but I will not. You may give up your purpose, but mine is assigned to me by heaven, and I dare not. I am weak, but surely the spirits who assist my vengeance will endow me with sufficient strength." Saying this, he endeavoured to spring from the bed, but the exertion was too great for him; he fell back and fainted.

It was long before he was restored, and I often thought that life was entirely extinct. At length he opened his eyes; he breathed with difficulty and was unable to speak. The surgeon gave him a composing draught and ordered us to leave him undisturbed. In the meantime he told me that my friend had certainly not many hours to live.

His sentence was pronounced, and I could only grieve and be patient. I sat by his bed, watching him; his eyes were closed, and I thought he slept; but presently he called to me in a feeble voice, and bidding me come near, said:

"Alas! The strength I relied on is gone; I feel that I shall soon die, and he, my enemy and persecutor, may still be in being. Think not, Walton, that in the last moments of my existence I feel that burning hatred and ardent desire of revenge I once expressed; but I feel myself justified in desiring the death of my adversary. During these last days I have been occupied in examining my past conduct; nor do I find it blamable. In a fit of enthusiastic madness I created a rational creature and was bound towards him to assure, as far as was in my power, his happiness and well-being. This was my duty, but there was another still paramount to that. My duties towards the beings of my own species had greater claims to my attention because they included a greater proportion of happiness or misery. Urged by this view, I refused, and I did right in refusing, to create a companion for the first creature. He showed unparalleled malignity and selfishness in evil; he destroyed my friends; he devoted to destruction beings who possessed exquisite sensations, happiness, and wisdom; nor do I know where this thirst for vengeance may end. Miserable himself that he may render no other wretched, he ought to die. The task of his destruction was mine, but I have failed. When actuated by selfish and vicious motives, I asked you to undertake my unfinished work, and I renew this request now, when I am only induced by reason and virtue.

"Yet I cannot ask you to renounce your country and friends to fulfil this task; and now that you are returning to England, you will have little chance of meeting with him. But the consideration of these points, and the well balancing of what you may esteem your duties, I leave to you; my judgement and ideas are already disturbed by the near approach of death. I dare not ask you to do what I think right, for I may still be misled by passion.

"That he should live to be an instrument of mischief disturbs me; in other respects, this hour, when I momentarily expect my release, is the only happy one which I have enjoyed for several years. The forms of the beloved dead flit before me, and I hasten to their arms. Farewell, Walton! Seek happiness in tranquillity and avoid ambition, even if it be only the apparently innocent one of distinguishing yourself in science and discoveries. Yet why do I say this? I have myself been blasted in these hopes, yet another may succeed."

His voice became faint as he spoke, and at length, exhausted by his effort, he sank into silence. About half an hour afterwards he attempted again to speak but was unable; he pressed my hand feebly, and his eyes closed forever, while the irradiation of a gentle smile passed away from his lips.

Margaret, what comment can I make on the untimely extinction of this glorious spirit? What can I say that will enable you to understand the depth of my sorrow? All that I should express would be inadequate and feeble. My tears flow; my mind is overshadowed by a cloud of disappointment. But I journey towards England, and I may there find consolation.

I am interrupted. What do these sounds portend? It is

midnight; the breeze blows fairly, and the watch on deck scarcely stir. Again there is a sound as of a human voice, but hoarser; it comes from the cabin where the remains of Frankenstein still lie. I must arise and examine. Good night, my sister.

Great God! What a scene has just taken place! I am yet dizzy with the remembrance of it. I hardly know whether I shall have the power to detail it; yet the tale which I have recorded would be incomplete without this final and wonderful catastrophe.

I entered the cabin where lay the remains of my ill-fated and admirable friend. Over him hung a form which I cannot find words to describe—gigantic in stature, yet uncouth and distorted in its proportions. As he hung over the coffin, his face was concealed by long locks of ragged hair; but one vast hand was extended, in colour and apparent texture like that of a mummy. When he heard the sound of my approach, he ceased to utter exclamations of grief and horror and sprung towards the window. Never did I behold a vision so horrible as his face, of such loathsome yet appalling hideousness. I shut my eyes involuntarily and endeavoured to recollect what were my duties with regard to this destroyer. I called on him to stay.

He paused, looking on me with wonder, and again turning towards the lifeless form of his creator, he seemed to forget my presence, and every feature and gesture seemed instigated by the wildest rage of some uncontrollable passion.

"That is also my victim!" he exclaimed. "In his murder my crimes are consummated; the miserable series of my being is wound to its close! Oh, Frankenstein! Generous and self-devoted being! What does it avail that I now ask thee to pardon me? I, who irretrievably destroyed thee by destroying all thou lovedst. Alas! He is cold, he cannot answer me."

His voice seemed suffocated, and my first impulses, which had suggested to me the duty of obeying the dying request of my friend in destroying his enemy, were now suspended by a mixture of curiosity and compassion. I approached this tremendous being; I dared not again raise my eyes to his face, there was something so scaring and unearthly in his ugliness. I attempted to speak, but the words died away on my lips. The monster continued to utter wild and incoherent self-reproaches. At length

I gathered resolution to address him in a pause of the tempest of his passion. "Your repentance," I said, "is now superfluous. If you had listened to the voice of conscience and heeded the stings of remorse before you had urged your diabolical vengeance to this extremity, Frankenstein would yet have lived."

"And do you dream?" said the daemon. "Do you think that I was then dead to agony and remorse? He," he continued, pointing to the corpse, "he suffered not in the consummation of the deed. Oh! Not the ten-thousandth portion of the anguish that was mine during the lingering detail of its execution. A frightful selfishness hurried me on, while my heart was poisoned with remorse. Think you that the groans of Clerval were music to my ears? My heart was fashioned to be susceptible of love and sympathy, and when wrenched by misery to vice and hatred, it did not endure the violence of the change without torture such as you cannot even imagine.

"After the murder of Clerval, I returned to Switzerland, heartbroken and overcome. I pitied Frankenstein; my pity amounted to horror; I abhorred myself. But when I discovered that he, the author at once of my existence and of its unspeakable torments, dared to hope for happiness, that while he accumulated wretchedness and despair upon me he sought his own enjoyment in feelings and passions from the indulgence of which I was forever barred, then impotent envy and bitter indignation filled me with an insatiable thirst for vengeance. I recollected my threat and resolved that it should be accomplished. I knew that I was preparing for myself a deadly torture, but I was the slave, not the master, of an impulse which I detested yet could not disobey. Yet when she died! Nay, then I was not miserable. I had cast off all feeling, subdued all anguish, to riot in the excess of my despair. Evil thenceforth became my good. Urged thus far, I had no choice but to adapt my nature to an element which I had willingly chosen. The completion of my demoniacal design became an insatiable passion. And now it is ended; there is my last victim!"

I was at first touched by the expressions of his misery; yet, when I called to mind what Frankenstein had said of his powers of eloquence and persuasion, and when I again cast my eyes on the lifeless form of my friend, indignation was rekindled within me. "Wretch!" I said. "It is well that you come here to whine over the desolation that you have made. You throw a torch into a pile of buildings, and when they are consumed, you sit among the ruins and lament the fall. Hypocritical fiend! If he whom you mourn still lived, still would he be the object, again would he become the prey, of your accursed vengeance. It is not pity that you feel; you lament only because the victim of your malignity is withdrawn from your power."

"Oh, it is not thus—not thus," interrupted the being. "Yet such must be the impression conveyed to you by what appears to be the purport of my actions. Yet I seek not a fellow feeling in my misery. No sympathy may I ever find. When I first sought it, it was the love of virtue, the feelings of happiness and affection with which my whole being overflowed, that I wished to be participated. But now that virtue has become to me a shadow, and that happiness and affection are turned into bitter and loathing despair, in what should I seek for sympathy? I am content to suffer alone while my sufferings shall endure; when I die, I am well satisfied that abhorrence and opprobrium should load my memory. Once my fancy was soothed with dreams of virtue, of fame, and of enjoyment. Once I falsely hoped to meet with beings who, pardoning my outward form, would love me for the excellent qualities which I was capable of unfolding. I was nourished with high thoughts of honour and devotion. But now crime has degraded me beneath the meanest animal. No guilt, no mischief, no malignity, no misery, can be found comparable to mine. When I run over the frightful catalogue of my sins, I cannot believe that I am the same creature whose thoughts were once filled with sublime and transcendent visions of the beauty and the majesty of goodness. But it is even so; the fallen angel becomes a malignant devil. Yet even that enemy of God and man had friends and associates in his desolation; I am alone.

"You, who call Frankenstein your friend, seem to have a knowledge of my crimes and his misfortunes. But in the detail which he gave you of them he could not sum up the hours and months of misery which I endured wasting in impotent passions. For while I destroyed his hopes, I did not satisfy my own desires. They were forever ardent and craving; still I desired love and fellowship, and I was still spurned. Was there no injustice in this? Am I to be thought the only criminal, when all humankind sinned against me? Why do you not hate Felix, who drove his friend from his door with contumely? Why do you not execrate the rustic who sought to destroy the saviour of his child? Nay, these are virtuous and immaculate beings! I, the miserable and the abandoned, am an abortion, to be spurned at, and kicked, and trampled on. Even now my blood boils at the recollection of this injustice.

"But it is true that I am a wretch. I have murdered the lovely and the helpless; I have strangled the innocent as they slept and grasped to death his throat who never injured me or any other living thing. I have devoted my creator, the select specimen of all that is worthy of love and admiration among men, to misery; I have pursued him even to that irremediable ruin. There he lies, white and cold in death. You hate me, but your abhorrence cannot equal that with which I regard myself. I look on the hands which executed the deed; I think on the heart in which the imagination of it was conceived and long for the moment when these hands will meet my eyes, when that imagination will haunt my thoughts no more.

"Fear not that I shall be the instrument of future mischief. My work is nearly complete. Neither yours nor any man's death is needed to consummate the series of my being and accomplish that which must be done, but it requires my own. Do not think that I shall be slow to perform this sacrifice. I shall quit your vessel on the ice raft which brought me thither and shall seek the most northern extremity of the globe; I shall collect my funeral pile and consume to ashes this miserable frame, that its remains may afford no light to any curious and unhallowed wretch who would create such another as I have been. I shall die. I shall no longer feel the agonies which now consume me or be the prey of feelings unsatisfied, yet unquenched. He is dead who called me into being; and when I shall be no more, the very remembrance of us both will speedily vanish. I shall no longer see the sun or stars or feel the winds play on my cheeks. Light, feeling, and sense will pass away; and in this condition must I find my happiness. Some years ago, when the images which this world affords first opened upon me, when I felt the cheering warmth of summer and heard the rustling of the leaves and the warbling of the birds, and these were all to me, I should have wept to die; now it is my only consolation. Polluted by crimes and torn by the bitterest remorse, where can I find rest but in death?

"Farewell! I leave you, and in you the last of humankind whom these eyes will ever behold. Farewell, Frankenstein! If thou wert yet alive and yet cherished a desire of revenge against me, it would be better satiated in my life than in my destruction. But it was not so; thou didst seek my extinction, that I might not cause greater wretchedness; and if yet, in some mode unknown to me, thou hadst not ceased to think and feel, thou wouldst not desire against me a vengeance greater than that which I feel. Blasted as thou wert, my agony was still superior to thine, for the bitter sting of remorse will not cease to rankle in my wounds until death shall close them forever.

"But soon," he cried with sad and solemn enthusiasm, "I shall die, and what I now feel be no longer felt. Soon these burning miseries will be extinct. I shall ascend my funeral pile triumphantly and exult in the agony of the torturing flames. The light of that conflagration will fade away; my ashes will be swept into the sea by the winds. My spirit will sleep in peace, or if it thinks, it will not surely think thus. Farewell."

He sprang from the cabin window as he said this, upon the ice raft which lay close to the vessel. He was soon borne away by the waves and lost in darkness and distance.

The Legend of Sleepy Hollow and Other Tales

The Legend of Sleepy Hollow and Other Tales

WASHINGTON IRVING

Word Cloud Classics
Word Cloud Classics
San Diego

Canterbury Classics
An imprint of Printers Row Publishing Group
9717 Pacific Heights Blvd, San Diego, CA 92121
www.canterburyclassicsbooks.com • mail@canterburyclassicsbooks.com

Printers Row Publishing Group is a division of Readerlink Distribution Services, LLC. Canterbury Classics and Word Cloud Classics are registered trademarks of Readerlink Distribution Services, LLC.

Correspondence concerning the content of this book should be sent to Canterbury Classics, Editorial Department, at the above address.

Publisher: Peter Norton • Associate Publisher: Ana Parker
Art Director: Charles McStravick
Senior Developmental Editor: April Graham
Editorial Team: Lori Asbury, Laura Vignale, JoAnn Padgett, Melinda Allman, Traci Douglas
Production/Design Team: Blake Mitchum, Rusty von Dyl, Lidija Tomas, Beno Chan, Julie Greene, Rosemary Rae

Spine art: gio_banfi/DigitalVision Vectors via Getty Images
Endpapers: Pobytov/DigitalVision Vectors via Getty Images

ISBN: 978-1-6672-0320-1

Printed in China
27 26 25 24 23 2 3 4 5 6

FSC www.fsc.org MIX Paper | Supporting responsible forestry FSC® C144853

Editor's Note: These works have been published in their original form to preserve the author's intent and style.

CONTENTS

PUBLISHER'S NOTE

This collection of stories by Washington Irving was first published as a serial in 1819 and 1820 under the title *The Sketch Book of Geoffrey Crayon, Gent*. Included here is the complete text of the revised edition, first published in 1848.

PREFACE TO THE REVISED EDITION

The following papers, with two exceptions, were written in England, and formed but part of an intended series for which I had made notes and memorandums. Before I could mature a plan, however, circumstances compelled me to send them piecemeal to the United States, where they were published from time to time in portions or numbers. It was not my intention to publish them in England, being conscious that much of their contents could be interesting only to American readers, and, in truth, being deterred by the severity with which American productions had been treated by the British press.

By the time the contents of the first volume had appeared in this occasional manner, they began to find their way across the Atlantic, and to be inserted, with many kind encomiums, in the London Literary Gazette. It was said, also, that a London bookseller intended to publish them in a collective form. I determined, therefore, to bring them forward myself, that they might at least have the benefit of my superintendence and revision. I accordingly took the printed numbers which I had received from the United States, to Mr. John Murray, the eminent publisher, from whom I had already received friendly attentions, and left them with him for examination, informing him that should he be inclined to bring them before the public, I had materials enough on hand for a second volume. Several days having elapsed without any communication from Mr. Murray, I addressed a note to him, in which I construed his silence into a tacit rejection of my work, and begged that the numbers I had left with him might be returned to me. The following was his reply:

> My Dear Sir:
>
> I entreat you to believe that I feel truly obliged by your kind intentions towards me, and that I entertain the most unfeigned respect for your most tasteful talents. My house is completely filled with workpeople at this time, and I have only an office to transact business in; and yesterday I was

wholly occupied, or I should have done myself the pleasure of seeing you.

If it would not suit me to engage in the publication of your present work, it is only because I do not see that scope in the nature of it which would enable me to make those satisfactory accounts between us, without which I really feel no satisfaction in engaging—but I will do all I can to promote their circulation, and shall be most ready to attend to any future plan of yours.

With much regard, I remain, dear sir,
Your faithful servant,
John Murray

This was disheartening, and might have deterred me from any further prosecution of the matter, had the question of republication in Great Britain rested entirely with me; but I apprehended the appearance of a spurious edition. I now thought of Mr. Archibald Constable as publisher, having been treated by him with much hospitality during a visit to Edinburgh; but first I determined to submit my work to Sir Walter (then Mr.) Scott, being encouraged to do so by the cordial reception I had experienced from him at Abbotsford a few years previously, and by the favorable opinion he had expressed to others of my earlier writings. I accordingly sent him the printed numbers of the Sketch-Book in a parcel by coach, and at the same time wrote to him, hinting that since I had had the pleasure of partaking of his hospitality, a reverse had taken place in my affairs which made the successful exercise of my pen all important to me; I begged him, therefore, to look over the literary articles I had forwarded to him, and, if he thought they would bear European republication, to ascertain whether Mr. Constable would be inclined to be the publisher.

The parcel containing my work went by coach to Scott's address in Edinburgh; the letter went by mail to his residence in the country. By the very first post I received a reply, before he had seen my work.

"I was down at Kelso," said he, "when your letter reached Abbotsford. I am now on my way to town, and will converse with Constable, and do all in my power to forward your views—I assure you nothing will give me more pleasure."

The hint, however, about a reverse of fortune had struck the quick apprehension of Scott, and, with that practical and efficient goodwill which belonged to his nature, he had already devised a way of aiding me. A weekly periodical, he went on to inform me, was about to be set up in Edinburgh, supported by the most respectable talents, and amply furnished with all the necessary information. The appointment of the editor, for which ample funds were provided, would be five hundred pounds sterling a year, with the reasonable prospect of further advantages. This situation, being apparently at his disposal, he frankly offered to me. The work, however, he intimated, was to have somewhat of a political bearing, and he expressed an apprehension that the tone it was desired to adopt might not suit me. "Yet I risk the question," added he, "because I know no man so well qualified for this important task, and perhaps because it will necessarily bring you to Edinburgh. If my proposal does not suit, you need only keep the matter secret and there is no harm done. 'And for my love I pray you wrong me not.' If on the contrary you think it could be made to suit you, let me know as soon as possible, addressing Castle Street, Edinburgh."

In a postscript, written from Edinburgh, he adds, "I am just come here, and have glanced over the Sketch Book. It is positively beautiful, and increases my desire to crimp you, if it be possible. Some difficulties there always are in managing such a matter, especially at the outset; but we will obviate them as much as we possibly can."

The following is from an imperfect draught of my reply, which underwent some modifications in the copy sent:

"I cannot express how much I am gratified by your letter. I had begun to feel as if I had taken an unwarrantable liberty; but, somehow or other, there is a genial sunshine about you that warms every creeping thing into heart and confidence. Your literary proposal both surprises and flatters me, as it evinces a much higher opinion of my talents than I have myself."

I then went on to explain that I found myself peculiarly unfitted for the situation offered to me, not merely by my political opinions, but by the very constitution and habits of my mind. "My whole course of life," I observed, "has been desultory, and I am unfitted for any periodically recurring task, or any stipulated labor of body or mind. I have no command of my talents, such as they are, and have to watch the varyings of my mind as I would those of a weather cock. Practice and training may bring me more into rule; but at present I am as useless for regular service as one of my own country Indians or a Don Cossack.

"I must, therefore, keep on pretty much as I have begun; writing when I can, not when I would. I shall occasionally shift my residence and write whatever is suggested by objects before me, or whatever rises in my imagination; and hope to write better and more copiously by and by.

"I am playing the egotist, but I know no better way of answering your proposal than by showing what a very good-for-nothing kind of being I am. Should Mr. Constable feel inclined to make a bargain for the wares I have on hand, he will encourage me to further enterprise; and it will be something like trading with a gypsy for the fruits of his prowlings, who may at one time have nothing but a wooden bowl to offer, and at another time a silver tankard."

In reply, Scott expressed regret, but not surprise, at my declining what might have proved a troublesome duty. He then recurred to the original subject of our correspondence; entered into a detail of the various terms upon which arrangements were made between authors and booksellers, that I might take my choice; expressing the most encouraging confidence of the success of my work, and of previous works which I had produced in America. "I did no more," added he, "than open the trenches with Constable; but I am sure if you will take the trouble to write to him, you will find him disposed to treat your overtures with every degree of attention. Or, if you think it of consequence in the first place to see me, I shall be in London in the course of a month, and whatever my experience can command is most heartily at your command. But I can add little to what I have said above, except my earnest recommendation to Constable to enter into the negotiation."*

* I cannot avoid subjoining in a note a succeeding paragraph of Scott's letter, which, though it does not relate to the main subject of our correspondence, was too characteristic to be emitted. Some time previously I had sent Miss Sophia Scott small duodecimo American editions of her father's poems published in Edinburgh in quarto volumes; showing the "nigromancy" of the American press, by which a quart of wine is conjured into a pint bottle. Scott observes: "In my hurry, I have not thanked you in Sophia's name for the kind attention which furnished her with the American volumes. I am not quite sure I can add my own, since you have made her acquainted with much more of papa's folly than she would ever otherwise have learned; for I had taken special care they should never see any of those things during their earlier years. I think I have told you that Walter is sweeping the firmament with a feather like a maypole and indenting the pavement with a sword like a scythe—in other words, he has become a whiskered hussar in the 18th Dragoons."

Before the receipt of this most obliging letter, however, I had determined to look to no leading bookseller for a launch, but to throw my work before the public at my own risk, and let it sink or swim according to its merits. I wrote to that effect to Scott, and soon received a reply:

"I observe with pleasure that you are going to come forth in Britain. It is certainly not the very best way to publish on one's own accompt; for the booksellers set their face against the circulation of such works as do not pay an amazing toll to themselves. But they have lost the art of altogether damming up the road in such cases between the author and the public, which they were once able to do as effectually as Diabolus in John Bunyan's Holy War closed up the windows of my Lord Understanding's mansion. I am sure of one thing, that you have only to be known to the British public to be admired by them, and I would not say so unless I really was of that opinion.

"If you ever see a witty but rather local publication called Blackwood's Edinburgh Magazine, you will find some notice of your works in the last number: the author is a friend of mine, to whom I have introduced you in your literary capacity. His name is Lockhart, a young man of very considerable talent, and who will soon be intimately connected with my family. My faithful friend Knickerbocker is to be next examined and illustrated. Constable was extremely willing to enter into consideration of a treaty for your works, but I foresee will be still more so when

> Your name is up, and may go From Toledo to Madrid.

——And that will soon be the case. I trust to be in London about the middle of the month, and promise myself great pleasure in once again shaking you by the hand."

The first volume of the Sketch Book was put to press in London, as I had resolved, at my own risk, by a bookseller unknown to fame, and without any of the usual arts by which a work is trumpeted into notice. Still some attention had been called to it by the extracts which had previously appeared in the Literary Gazette, and by the kind word spoken by the editor of that periodical, and it was getting into fair circulation, when my worthy bookseller failed before the first month was over, and the sale was interrupted.

At this juncture Scott arrived in London. I called to him for help, as

I was sticking in the mire, and, more propitious than Hercules, he put his own shoulder to the wheel. Through his favorable representations, Murray was quickly induced to undertake the future publication of the work which he had previously declined. A further edition of the first volume was struck off and the second volume was put to press, and from that time Murray became my publisher, conducting himself in all his dealings with that fair, open, and liberal spirit which had obtained for him the well-merited appellation of the Prince of Booksellers.

Thus, under the kind and cordial auspices of Sir Walter Scott, I began my literary career in Europe; and I feel that I am but discharging, in a trifling degree, my debt of gratitude to the memory of that golden-hearted man in acknowledging my obligations to him. But who of his literary contemporaries ever applied to him for aid or counsel that did not experience the most prompt, generous, and effectual assistance?

W. I.
Sunnyside, 1848.

THE SKETCH
BOOK

THE AUTHOR'S ACCOUNT OF HIMSELF

> I am of this mind with Homer, that as the snaile that crept out of her shel was turned eftsoones into a toad, and thereby was forced to make a stoole to sit on; so the traveller that stragleth from his owne country is in a short time transformed into so monstrous a shape, that he is faine to alter his mansion with his manners, and to live where he can, not where he would.
>
> —Lyly's Euphes

I was always fond of visiting new scenes, and observing strange characters and manners. Even when a mere child I began my travels, and made many tours of discovery into foreign parts and unknown regions of my native city, to the frequent alarm of my parents, and the emolument of the town cryer. As I grew into boyhood, I extended the range of my observations. My holy day afternoons were spent in rambles about the surrounding country. I made myself familiar with all its places famous in history or fable. I knew every spot where a murder or robbery had been committed, or a ghost seen. I visited the neighboring villages, and added greatly to my stock of knowledge, by noting their habits and customs, and conversing with their sages and great men. I even journeyed one long summer's day to the summit of the most distant hill, whence I stretched my eye over many a mile of terra incognita, and was astonished to find how vast a globe I inhabited.

This rambling propensity strengthened with my years. Books of voyages and travels became my passion, and in devouring their contents, I neglected the regular exercises of the school. How wistfully would I wander about the pier heads in fine weather, and watch the parting ships, bound to distant climes; with what longing eyes would I gaze after their lessening sails, and waft myself in imagination to the ends of the earth!

Further reading and thinking, though they brought this vague inclination into more reasonable bounds, only served to make it more decided. I visited various parts of my own country; and had I been merely a lover of fine scenery, I should have felt little desire to seek elsewhere its gratification, for on no country had the charms of nature been more prodigally lavished. Her mighty lakes, her oceans of liquid silver; her mountains, with their bright aerial tints; her valleys, teeming with wild fertility; her tremendous cataracts, thundering in their solitudes; her boundless plains, waving with spontaneous verdure; her broad, deep rivers, rolling in solemn silence to the ocean; her trackless forests, where vegetation puts forth all its magnificence; her skies, kindling with the magic of summer clouds and glorious sunshine;—no, never need an American look beyond his own country for the sublime and beautiful of natural scenery.

But Europe held forth all the charms of storied and poetical association. There were to be seen the masterpieces of art, the refinements of highly cultivated society, the quaint peculiarities of ancient and local custom. My native country was full of youthful promise; Europe was rich in the accumulated treasures of age. Her very ruins told the history of the times gone by, and every mouldering stone was a chronicle. I longed to wander over the scenes of renowned achievement—to tread, as it were, in the footsteps of antiquity—to loiter about the ruined castle—to meditate on the falling tower—to escape, in short, from the commonplace realities of the present, and lose myself among the shadowy grandeurs of the past.

I had, besides all this, an earnest desire to see the great men of the earth. We have, it is true, our great men in America: not a city but has an ample share of them. I have mingled among them in my time, and been almost withered by the shade into which they cast me; for there is nothing so baleful to a small man as the shade of a great one, particularly the great man of a city. But I was anxious to see the great men of Europe; for I had read in the works of various philosophers, that all animals degenerated in America, and man among the number. A great man of Europe, thought I, must therefore be as superior to a great man of America, as a peak of the Alps to a highland of the Hudson; and in this idea I was confirmed by observing the comparative importance and swelling magnitude of many English travellers among us, who, I was assured, were very little people in their own country. I will visit this land of wonders, thought I, and see the gigantic race from which I am degenerated.

It has been either my good or evil lot to have my roving passion gratified. I have wandered through different countries and witnessed many of the shifting scenes of life. I cannot say that I have studied them with the eye of a philosopher, but rather with the sauntering gaze with which humble lovers of the picturesque stroll from the window of one print-shop to another; caught sometimes by the delineations of beauty, sometimes by the distortions of caricature, and sometimes by the loveliness of landscape. As it is the fashion for modern tourists to travel pencil in hand, and bring home their portfolios filled with sketches, I am disposed to get up a few for the entertainment of my friends. When, however, I look over the hints and memorandums I have taken down for the purpose, my heart almost fails me, at finding how my idle humor has led me astray from the great object studied by every regular traveller who would make a book. I fear I shall give equal disappointment with an unlucky landscape-painter, who had travelled on the Continent, but following the bent of his vagrant inclination, had sketched in nooks, and corners, and by-places. His sketch-book was accordingly crowded with cottages, and landscapes, and obscure ruins; but he had neglected to paint St. Peter's, or the Coliseum, the cascade of Terni, or the bay of Naples, and had not a single glacier or volcano in his whole collection.

THE VOYAGE

Ships, ships, I will descrie you
Amidst the main,
I will come and try you,
What you are protecting,
And projecting,
What's your end and aim.
One goes abroad for merchandise and trading,
Another stays to keep his country from invading,
A third is coming home with rich and wealthy lading.
Hallo! my fancie, whither wilt thou go?
—Old Poem

To an American visiting Europe, the long voyage he has to make is an excellent preparative. The temporary absence of worldly scenes and employments produces a state of mind peculiarly fitted to receive new and vivid impressions. The vast space of waters that separate the hemispheres is like a blank page in existence. There is no gradual transition by which, as in Europe, the features and population of one country blend almost imperceptibly with those of another. From the moment you lose sight of the land you have left, all is vacancy, until you step on the opposite shore, and are launched at once into the bustle and novelties of another world.

In travelling by land there is a continuity of scene, and a connected succession of persons and incidents, that carry on the story of life, and lessen the effect of absence and separation. We drag, it is true, "a lengthening chain" at each remove of our pilgrimage; but the chain is unbroken; we can trace it back link by link; and we feel that the last still grapples us to home. But a wide sea voyage severs us at once. It makes us conscious of being cast loose from the secure anchorage of settled life, and sent adrift upon a doubtful world. It interposes a gulf, not merely imaginary, but real, between us and our homes—a gulf, subject to tempest, and fear, and uncertainty, rendering distance palpable, and return precarious.

Such, at least, was the case with myself. As I saw the last blue lines of my native land fade away like a cloud in the horizon, it seemed as if I had closed one volume of the world and its concerns, and had time for meditation, before I opened another. That land, too, now vanishing from my view, which contained all most dear to me in life; what vicissitudes might occur in it—what changes might take place in me, before I should visit it again. Who can tell, when he sets forth to wander, whither he may be driven by the uncertain currents of existence; or when he may return; or whether it may be ever his lot to revisit the scenes of his childhood?

I said, that at sea all is vacancy; I should correct the impression. To one given to day-dreaming, and fond of losing himself in reveries, a sea voyage is full of subjects for meditation; but then they are the wonders of the deep and of the air, and rather tend to abstract the mind from worldly themes. I delighted to loll over the quarter-railing or climb to the main-top, of a calm day, and muse for hours together on the tranquil bosom of a summer's sea; to gaze upon the piles of golden clouds just peering above the horizon, fancy them some fairy realms, and people them with a creation of my own;—to watch the gently undulating billows rolling their silver volumes, as if to die away on those happy shores.

There was a delicious sensation of mingled security and awe with which I looked down, from my giddy height, on the monsters of the deep at their uncouth gambols: shoals of porpoises tumbling about the bow of the ship; the grampus, slowly heaving his huge form above the surface; or the ravenous shark, darting, like a spectre, through the blue waters. My imagination would conjure up all that I had heard or read of the watery world beneath me; of the finny herds that roam its fathomless valleys; of the shapeless monsters that lurk among the very foundations of the earth; and of those wild phantasms that swell the tales of fishermen and sailors.

Sometimes a distant sail, gliding along the edge of the ocean, would be another theme of idle speculation. How interesting this fragment of a world, hastening to rejoin the great mass of existence! What a glorious monument of human invention; which has in a manner triumphed over wind and wave; has brought the ends of the world into communion;

has established an interchange of blessings, pouring into the sterile regions of the north all the luxuries of the south; has diffused the light of knowledge, and the charities of cultivated life; and has thus bound together those scattered portions of the human race, between which nature seemed to have thrown an insurmountable barrier.

We one day described some shapeless object drifting at a distance. At sea, every thing that breaks the monotony of the surrounding expanse attracts attention. It proved to be the mast of a ship that must have been completely wrecked; for there were the remains of handkerchiefs, by which some of the crew had fastened themselves to this spar, to prevent their being washed off by the waves. There was no trace by which the name of the ship could be ascertained. The wreck had evidently drifted about for many months; clusters of shell-fish had fastened about it, and long sea weeds flaunted at its sides.

But where, thought I, is the crew? Their struggle has long been over—they have gone down amidst the roar of the tempest—their bones lie whitening among the caverns of the deep. Silence, oblivion, like the waves, have closed over them, and no one can tell the story of their end. What sighs have been wafted after that ship! what prayers offered up at the deserted fireside of home! How often has the mistress, the wife, the mother, pored over the daily news, to catch some casual intelligence of this rover of the deep! How has expectation darkened into anxiety—anxiety into dread—and dread into despair! Alas! not one memento may ever return for love to cherish. All that may ever be known, is that she sailed from her port, "and was never heard of more!"

The sight of this wreck, as usual, gave rise to many dismal anecdotes. This was particularly the case in the evening, when the weather, which had hitherto been fair, began to look wild and threatening, and gave indications of one of those sudden storms that will sometimes break in upon the serenity of a summer voyage. As we sat round the dull light of a lamp, in the cabin, that made the gloom more ghastly, everyone had his tale of shipwreck and disaster. I was particularly struck with a short one related by the captain:

"As I was once sailing," said he, "in a fine, stout ship, across the banks of Newfoundland, one of those heavy fogs that prevail in those parts rendered it impossible for us to see far ahead, even in the daytime; but at night the weather was so thick that we could not distinguish any object at twice the length of the ship. I kept lights at the mast-head, and a constant watch forward to look out for fishing smacks, which are accustomed to anchor of the banks. The wind was blowing a smacking breeze, and we were going at a great rate through the water. Suddenly the watch gave the alarm of 'a sail ahead!'—it was scarcely uttered before we were upon her. She was a small schooner, at anchor, with her broadside toward us. The crew were all asleep, and had neglected to hoist a light. We struck her just amidships. The force, the size, and weight of our vessel, bore her down below the waves; we passed over her and were hurried on our course. As the crashing wreck was sinking beneath us, I had a glimpse of two or three half-naked wretches, rushing from her cabin; they just started from their beds to be swallowed shrieking by the waves. I heard their drowning cry mingling with the wind. The blast that bore it to our ears, swept us out of all further hearing. I shall never forget that cry! It was some time before we could put the ship about, she was under such headway. We returned, as nearly as we could guess, to the place where the smack had anchored. We cruised about for several hours in the dense fog. We fired signal-guns, and listened if we might hear the halloo of any survivors: but all was silent—we never saw or heard any thing of them more!"

I confess these stories, for a time, put an end to all my fine fancies. The storm increased with the night. The sea was lashed into tremendous confusion. There was a fearful, sullen sound of rushing waves and broken surges. Deep called unto deep. At times the black volume of clouds overhead seemed rent asunder by flashes of lightning which quivered along the foaming billows, and made the succeeding darkness doubly terrible. The thunders bellowed over the wild waste of waters, and were echoed and prolonged by the mountain waves. As I saw the ship staggering and plunging among these roaring caverns, it seemed miraculous that she regained her balance, or preserved her buoyancy. Her yards would dip into the water; her bow was almost buried beneath the waves. Sometimes an impending surge appeared ready to overwhelm her, and nothing but a dexterous movement of the helm preserved her from the shock.

When I retired to my cabin, the awful scene still followed me.

The whistling of the wind through the rigging sounded like funereal wailings. The creaking of the masts; the straining and groaning of bulkheads, as the ship labored in the weltering sea, were frightful. As I heard the waves rushing along the side of the ship, and roaring in my very ear, it seemed as if Death were raging around this floating prison, seeking for his prey: the mere starting of a nail, the yawning of a seam, might give him entrance.

A fine day, however, with a tranquil sea and favoring breeze, soon put all these dismal reflections to flight. It is impossible to resist the gladdening influence of fine weather and fair wind at sea. When the ship is decked out in all her canvas, every sail swelled, and careering gayly over the curling waves, how lofty, how gallant, she appears—how she seems to lord it over the deep!

I might fill a volume with the reveries of a sea voyage; for with me it is almost a continual reverie—but it is time to get to shore.

It was a fine sunny morning when the thrilling cry of "land!" was given from the mast-head. None but those who have experienced it can form an idea of the delicious throng of sensations which rush into an American's bosom, when he first comes in sight of Europe. There is a volume of associations with the very name. It is the land of promise, teeming with everything of which his childhood has heard, or on which his studious years have pondered.

From that time, until the moment of arrival, it was all feverish excitement. The ships of war, that prowled like guardian giants along the coast; the headlands of Ireland, stretching out into the channel; the Welsh mountains towering into the clouds;—all were objects of intense interest. As we sailed up the Mersey, I reconnoitred the shores with a telescope. My eye dwelt with delight on neat cottages, with their trim shrubberies and green grass plots. I saw the mouldering ruin of an abbey overrun with ivy, and the taper spire of a village church rising from the brow of a neighboring hill;—all were characteristic of England.

The tide and wind were so favorable, that the ship was enabled to come at once to her pier. It was thronged with people; some idle lookers-on; others, eager expectants of friends or relations. I could distinguish the merchant to whom the ship was consigned. I knew him by his calculating brow and restless air. His hands were thrust into his pockets; he was whistling thoughtfully, and walking to and fro, a small space having been accorded him by the crowd, in deference to his temporary importance. There were repeated cheerings and salutations interchanged between the shore and the ship, as friends happened to recognize each other. I particularly noticed one young woman of humble dress, but interesting demeanor. She was leaning forward from among the crowd; her eye hurried over the ship as it neared the shore, to catch some wished-for countenance. She seemed disappointed and sad; when I heard a faint voice call her name. It was from a poor sailor who had been ill all the voyage, and had excited the sympathy of every one on board. When the weather was fine, his messmates had spread a mattress for him on deck in the shade, but of late his illness had so increased that he had taken to his hammock, and only breathed a wish that he might see his wife before he died. He had been helped on deck as we came up the river, and was now leaning against the shrouds, with a countenance so wasted, so pale, so ghastly, that it was no wonder even the eye of affection did not recognize him. But at the sound of his voice, her eye darted on his features: it read, at once, a whole volume of sorrow—she clasped her hands, uttered a faint shriek, and stood wringing them in silent agony.

All now was hurry and bustle. The meetings of acquaintances—the greetings of friends—the consultations of men of business. I alone was solitary and idle. I had no friend to meet, no cheering to receive. I stepped upon the land of my forefathers—but felt that I was a stranger in the land.

ROSCOE

In the service of mankind to be
A guardian god below; still to employ
The mind's brave ardor in heroic aims,
Such as may raise us o'er the grovelling herd,
And make us shine for ever—that is life.
—THOMSON

One of the first places to which a stranger is taken in Liverpool is the Athenæum. It is established on a liberal and judicious plan; it contains a good library, and spacious reading room, and is the great literary resort of the place. Go there at what hour you may, you are sure to find it filled with grave-looking personages, deeply absorbed in the study of newspapers.

As I was once visiting this haunt of the learned, my attention was attracted to a person just entering the room. He was advanced in life, tall, and of a form that might once have been commanding, but it was a little bowed by time—perhaps by care. He had a noble Roman style of countenance; a a head that would have pleased a painter; and though some slight furrows on his brow showed that wasting thought had been busy there, yet his eye beamed with the fire of a poetic soul. There was something in his whole appearance that indicated a being of a different order from the bustling race round him.

I inquired his name, and was informed that it was Roscoe. I drew back with an involuntary feeling of veneration. This, then, was an author of celebrity; this was one of those men whose voices have gone forth to the ends of the earth; with whose minds I have communed even in the solitudes of America. Accustomed, as we are in our country, to know European writers only by their works, we cannot conceive of them, as of other men, engrossed by trivial or sordid pursuits, and jostling with the crowd of common minds in the dusty paths of life. They pass before our imaginations like superior beings, radiant with the emanations of their genius, and surrounded by a halo of literary glory.

To find, therefore, the elegant historian of the Medici mingling among the busy sons of traffic, at first shocked my poetical ideas; but it is from the very circumstances and situation in which he has been placed, that Mr. Roscoe derives his highest claims to admiration. It is interesting to notice how some minds seem almost to create themselves, springing up under every disadvantage, and working their solitary but irresistible way through a thousand obstacles. Nature seems to delight in disappointing the assiduities of art, with which it would rear legitimate dullness to maturity; and to glory in the vigor and luxuriance of her chance productions. She scatters the seeds of genius to the winds, and though some may perish among the stony places of the world, and some be choked, by the thorns and brambles of early adversity, yet others will now and then strike root even in the clefts of the rock, struggle bravely up into sunshine, and spread over their sterile birthplace all the beauties of vegetation.

Such has been the case with Mr. Roscoe. Born in a place apparently ungenial to the growth of literary talent—in the very market-place of trade; without fortune, family connections, or patronage; self-prompted, self-sustained, and almost self-taught, he has conquered every obstacle, achieved his way to eminence, and, having become one of the ornaments of the nation, has turned the whole force of his talents and influence to advance and embellish his native town.

Indeed, it is this last trait in his character which has given him the greatest interest in my eyes, and induced me particularly to point him out to my countrymen. Eminent as are his literary merits, he is but one among the many distinguished authors of this intellectual nation. They, however, in general, live but for their own fame, or their own pleasures. Their private history presents no lesson to the world, or, perhaps, a humiliating one of human frailty or inconsistency. At best, they are prone to steal away from the bustle and commonplace of busy existence; to indulge in the selfishness of lettered ease; and to revel in scenes of mental, but exclusive enjoyment.

Mr. Roscoe, on the contrary, has claimed none of the accorded privileges of talent. He has shut himself up in no garden of thought, nor elysium of fancy; but has gone forth into the highways and thoroughfares of life, he has planted bowers by the wayside, for the refreshment of the pilgrim and the sojourner, and has opened pure fountains where the laboring man may turn aside from the dust and heat of the day, and drink of the living streams of knowledge. There is a "daily beauty in his life," on which mankind may meditate, and grow better. It exhibits no lofty and almost useless, because inimitable, example of excellence; but presents a picture of active, yet simple and imitable virtues, which are within every man's reach, but which, unfortunately, are not exercised by many, or this world would be a paradise.

But his private life is peculiarly worthy the attention of the citizens of our young and busy country, where literature and the elegant arts must grow up side by side with the coarser plants of daily necessity; and must depend for their culture, not on the exclusive devotion of time and wealth; nor the quickening rays of titled patronage; but on hours and seasons snatched from the purest of worldly interests, by intelligent and public-spirited individuals.

He has shown how much may be done for a place in hours of leisure by one master spirit, and how completely it can give its own impress to surrounding objects. Like his own Lorenzo de' Medici, on whom he seems to have fixed his eye, as on a pure model of antiquity, he has interwoven the history of his life with the history of his native town, and has made the foundations of his fame the monuments of his virtues. Wherever you go, in Liverpool, you perceive traces of his footsteps in all that is elegant and liberal. He found the tide of wealth flowing merely in the channels of traffic; he has diverted from it invigorating rills to refresh the garden of literature. By his own example and constant exertions, he has effected that union of commerce and the intellectual pursuits, so eloquently recommended in one of his latest writings;* and has practically proved how beautifully they may be brought to harmonize, and to benefit each other. The noble institutions for literary and scientific purposes, which reflect such credit on Liverpool, and are giving such an impulse to the public mind, have mostly been originated, and have all been effectively promoted, by Mr. Roscoe; and when we consider the rapidly increasing opulence and magnitude of that town, which promises to vie in commercial importance with the metropolis, it will be perceived that in awakening an ambition of mental improvement among its inhabitants, he has effected a great benefit to the cause of British literature.

* Address on the opening of the Liverpool Institution.

In America, we know Mr. Roscoe only as the author; in Liverpool he is spoken of as the banker; and I was told of his having been unfortunate in business. I could not pity him, as I heard some rich men do. I considered him far above the reach of pity. Those who live only for the world, and in the world, may be cast down by the frowns of adversity; but a man like Roscoe is not to be overcome by the reverses of fortune. They do but drive him in upon the resources of his own mind, to the superior society of his own thoughts; which the best of men are apt sometimes to neglect, and to roam abroad in search of less worthy associates. He is independent of the world around him. He lives with antiquity, and with posterity: with antiquity, in the sweet communion of studious retirement; and with posterity, in the generous aspirings after future renown. The solitude of such a mind is its state of highest enjoyment. It is then visited by those elevated meditations which are the proper aliment of noble souls, and are, like manna, sent from heaven, in the wilderness of this world.

While my feelings were yet alive on the subject, it was my fortune to light on further traces of Mr. Roscoe. I was riding out with a gentleman, to view the environs of Liverpool, when he turned off, through a gate, into some ornamented grounds. After riding a short distance, we came to a spacious mansion of freestone, built in the Grecian style. It was not in the purest style, yet it had an air of elegance, and the situation was delightful. A fine lawn sloped away from it, studded with clumps of trees, so disposed as to break a soft fertile country into a variety of landscapes. The Mersey was seen winding a broad quiet sheet of water through an expanse of green meadow land, while the Welsh mountains, blended with clouds, and melting into distance, bordered the horizon.

This was Roscoe's favorite residence during the days of his prosperity. It had been the seat of elegant hospitality and literary retirement. The house was now silent and deserted. I saw the windows of the study, which looked out upon the soft scenery I have mentioned. The windows were closed—the library was gone. Two or three ill-favored beings were loitering about the place, whom my fancy pictured into retainers of the law. It was like visiting some classic fountain, that had once welled its pure waters in a sacred shade, but finding it dry and dusty, with the lizard and the toad brooding over the shattered marbles.

I inquired after the fate of Mr. Roscoe's library, which had consisted of scarce and foreign books, from many of which he had drawn the materials for his Italian histories. It had passed under the hammer of the auctioneer, and was dispersed about the country. The good people of the vicinity thronged liked wreckers to get some part of the noble vessel that had been driven on shore. Did such a scene admit of ludicrous associations, we might imagine something whimsical in this strange irruption in the regions of learning. Pigmies rummaging the armory of a giant, and contending for the possession of weapons which they could not wield. We might picture to ourselves some knot of speculators, debating with calculating brow over the quaint binding and illuminated margin of an obsolete author; of the air of intense but baffled sagacity with which some successful purchaser attempted to dive into the black-letter bargain he had secured.

It is a beautiful incident in the story of Mr. Roscoe's misfortunes, and one which cannot fail to interest the studious mind, that the parting with his books seems to have touched upon his tenderest feelings, and to have been the only circumstance that could provoke the notice of his muse. The scholar only knows how dear these silent, yet eloquent, companions of pure thoughts and innocent hours become in the season of adversity. When all that is worldly turns to dross around us, these only retain their steady value. When friends grow cold, and the converse of intimates languishes into vapid civility and commonplace, these only continue the unaltered countenance of happier days, and cheer us with that true friendship which never deceived hope, nor deserted sorrow.

I do not wish to censure; but, surely, if the people of Liverpool had been properly sensible of what was due to Mr. Roscoe and themselves, his library would never have been sold. Good worldly reasons may, doubtless, be given for the circumstance, which it would be difficult to combat with others that might seem merely fanciful; but it certainly appears to me such an opportunity as seldom occurs, of cheering a noble mind struggling under misfortunes by one of the most delicate, but most expressive tokens of public sympathy. It is difficult, however, to estimate a man of genius properly who is daily before our eyes. He becomes mingled and confounded with other men. His great qualities lose their novelty; we become too familiar with the common materials which form the basis even of the loftiest character. Some of Mr. Roscoe's townsmen may regard him merely as a man of business; others, as a politician; all find him engaged like themselves in ordinary occupations, and surpassed, perhaps, by themselves on some points of worldly wisdom. Even that amiable and unostentatious simplicity of character, which gives the nameless grace to real excellence, may cause him to be undervalued by some coarse minds, who do not know that true worth is always void of glare and pretension. But the man of letters, who speaks of Liverpool, speaks of it as the residence of Roscoe. The intelligent traveller who visits it inquires where Roscoe is to be seen. He is the literary landmark of the place, indicating its existence to the distant scholar. He is like Pompey's column at Alexandria, towering alone in classic dignity.

The following sonnet, addressed by Mr. Roscoe to his books, on parting with them, has already been alluded to. If anything can add effect to the pure feeling and elevated thought here displayed, it is the conviction, that the whole is no effusion of fancy, but a faithful transcript from the writer's heart.

To My Books

As one who, destined from his friends to part,
Regrets his loss, but hopes again erewhile
To share their converse and enjoy their smile,
And tempers as he may, affliction's dart;

Thus, loved associates, chiefs of elder art,
Teachers of wisdom, who could once beguile
My tedious hours and lighten every toil
I now resign you; nor with fainting heart;

For pass a few short years, or days, or hours,
And happier seasons may their dawn unfold,
And all your sacred fellowship restore;
When, freed from earth, unlimited its powers.
Mind shall with mind direct communion hold,
And kindred spirits meet to part no more.

THE WIFE

> The treasures of the deep are not so precious
> As are the concealed comforts of a man
> Lock'd up in woman's love. I scent the air
> Of blessings, when I came but near the house,
> What a delicious breath marriage sends forth,
> The violet bed's no sweeter!
>
> —MIDDLETON

I have often had occasion to remark the fortitude with which women sustain the most overwhelming reverses of fortune. Those disasters which break down the spirit of a man, and prostrate him in the dust, seem to call forth all the energies of the softer sex, and give such intrepidity and elevation to their character, that at times it approaches to sublimity. Nothing can be more touching, than to behold a soft and tender female, who had been all weakness and dependence, and alive to every trivial roughness, while threading the prosperous paths of life, suddenly rising in mental force to be the comforter and support of her husband under misfortune, and abiding with unshrinking firmness the bitterest blasts of adversity.

As the vine which has long twined its graceful foliage about the oak, and been lifted by it into sunshine, will, when the hardy plant is rifted by the thunderbolt, cling round it with its caressing tendrils, and bind up its shattered boughs, so is it beautifully ordered by Providence, that woman, who is the mere dependent and ornament of man in his happier hours, should be his stay and solace when smitten with sudden calamity; winding herself into the rugged recesses of his nature, tenderly supporting the drooping head, and binding up the broken heart.

I was once congratulating a friend, who had around him a blooming family, knit together in the strongest affection. "I can wish you no better lot," said he, with enthusiasm, "than to have a wife and children. If you are prosperous, there they are to share your prosperity; if otherwise, there they are to comfort you." And, indeed, I have observed that a married man falling into misfortune, is more apt to retrieve his situation in the world than a single one; partly, because he is more stimulated to exertion by the necessities of the helpless and beloved beings who depend upon him for subsistence, but chiefly because his spirits are soothed and relieved by domestic endearments, and his self-respect kept alive by finding, that, though all abroad is darkness and humiliation, yet there is still a little world of love at home, of which he is the monarch. Whereas, a single man is apt to run to waste and self-neglect; to fancy himself lonely and abandoned, and his heart to fall to ruin, like some deserted mansion, for want of an inhabitant.

These observations call to mind a little domestic story, of which I was once a witness. My intimate friend, Leslie, had married a beautiful and accomplished girl, who had been brought up in the midst of fashionable life. She had, it is true, no fortune, but that of my friend was ample; and he delighted in the anticipation of indulging her in every elegant pursuit, and administering to those delicate tastes and fancies that spread a kind of witchery about the sex. "Her life," said he, "shall be like a fairy tale."

The very difference in their characters produced a harmonious combination; he was of a romantic, and somewhat serious cast; she was all life and gladness. I have often noticed the mute rapture with which he would gaze upon her in company, of which her sprightly powers made her the delight: and how, in the midst of applause, her eye would still turn to him, as if there alone she sought favor and acceptance. When leaning on his arm, her slender form contrasted finely with his tall, manly person. The fond, confiding air with which she looked up to him seemed to call forth a flush of triumphant pride and cherishing tenderness, as if he doted on his lovely burden from its very helplessness. Never did a couple set forward on the flowery path of early and well-suited marriage with a fairer prospect of felicity.

It was the misfortune of my friend, however, to have embarked his property in large speculations; and he had not been married many months, when, by a succession of sudden disasters, it was swept from him, and he found himself reduced to almost penury. For a time he kept his situation to himself, and went about with a haggard countenance, and a breaking heart. His life was but a protracted agony; and what rendered it more insupportable was the necessity of keeping up a smile in the presence of his wife; for he could not bring himself to overwhelm her with the news. She saw, however, with the quick eyes of affection, that all was not well with him. She marked his altered looks and stifled sighs, and was not to be deceived by his sickly and vapid attempts at cheerfulness. She tasked all her sprightly powers and tender blandishments to win him back to happiness; but she only drove the arrow deeper into his soul. The more he saw cause to love her, the more torturing was the thought that he was soon to make her wretched. A little while, thought he, and the smile will vanish from that cheek—the song will die away from those lips—the lustre of those eyes will be quenched with sorrow and the happy heart which now beats lightly in that bosom, will be weighed down, like mine, by the cares and miseries of the world.

At length he came to me one day, and related his whole situation in a tone of the deepest despair. When I had heard him through, I inquired: "Does your wife know all this?"—At the question he burst into an agony of tears. "For God's sake!" cried he, "if you have any pity on me don't mention my wife; it is the thought of her that drives me almost to madness!"

"And why not?" said I. "She must know it sooner or later: you cannot keep it long from her, and the intelligence may break upon her in a more startling manner than if imparted by yourself; for the accents of those we love soften the harshest tidings. Besides, you are depriving yourself of the comforts of her sympathy; and not merely that, but also endangering the only bond that can keep hearts together—an unreserved community of thought and feeling. She will soon perceive that something is secretly preying upon your mind; and true love will not brook reserve; it feels undervalued and outraged, when even the sorrows of those it loves are concealed from it."

"Oh, but my friend! to think what a blow I am to give to all her future prospects—how I am to strike her very soul to the earth, by telling her that her husband is a beggar! that she is to forego all the elegancies of life—all the pleasures of society—to shrink with me into indigence and obscurity! To tell her that I have dragged her down from the sphere in which she might have continued to move in constant brightness—the light of every eye—the admiration of every heart!—How can she bear poverty? She has been brought up in all the refinements of opulence. How can she bear neglect? She has been the idol of society. Oh, it will break her heart—it will break her heart!"

I saw his grief was eloquent, and I let it have its flow; for sorrow relieves itself by words. When his paroxysm had subsided, and he had relapsed into moody silence, I resumed the subject gently, and urged him to break his situation at once to his wife. He shook his head mournfully, but positively.

"But how are you to keep it from her? It is necessary she should know it, that you may take the steps proper to the alteration of your circumstances. You must change your style of living—nay," observing a pang to pass across his countenance, "don't let that afflict you. I am sure you have never placed your happiness in outward show—you have yet friends, warm friends, who will not think the worse of you for being less splendidly lodged: and surely it does not require a palace to be happy with Mary—"

"I could be happy with her," cried he, convulsively, "in a hovel!—I could go down with her into poverty and the dust!—I could—I could—God bless her!—God bless her!" cried he, bursting into a transport of grief and tenderness.

"And believe me, my friend," said I, stepping up, and grasping him warmly by the hand, "believe me, she can be the same with you. Ay, more; it will be a source of pride and triumph to her—it will call forth all the latent energies and fervent sympathies of her nature; for she will rejoice to prove that she loves you for yourself. There is in every true woman's heart a spark of heavenly fire, which lies dormant in the broad daylight of prosperity; but which kindles up, and beams, and blazes in the dark hour of adversity. No man knows what the wife of his bosom is—no man knows what a ministering angel she is—until he has gone with her through the fiery trials of this world."

There was something in the earnestness of my manner, and the figurative style of my language, that caught the excited imagination of Leslie. I knew the auditor I had to deal with; and following up the impression I had made, I finished by persuading him to go home and unburden his sad heart to his wife.

I must confess, notwithstanding all I had said, I felt some little solicitude for the result. Who can calculate on the fortitude of one whose life has been a round of pleasures? Her gay spirits might revolt at the dark, downward path of low humility suddenly pointed out before her, and might cling to the sunny regions in which they had hitherto revelled. Besides, ruin in fashionable life is accompanied by so many galling mortifications, to which, in other ranks, it is a stranger. In short, I could not meet Leslie, the next morning, without trepidation. He had made the disclosure.

"And how did she bear it?"

"Like an angel! It seemed rather to be a relief to her mind, for she threw her arms around my neck, and asked if this was all that had lately made me unhappy.—But, poor girl," added he, "she cannot realize the change we must undergo. She has no idea of poverty but in the abstract; she has only read of it in poetry, where it is allied to love. She feels as yet no privation; she suffers no loss of accustomed conveniences nor elegancies. When we come practically to experience its sordid cares, its paltry wants, its petty humiliations—then will be the real trial."

"But," said I, "now that you have got over the severest task, that of breaking it to her, the sooner you let the world into the secret the better. The disclosure may be mortifying; but then it is a single misery, and soon over: whereas you otherwise suffer it, in anticipation, every hour in the day. It is not poverty, so much as pretence, that harasses a ruined man—the struggle between a proud mind and an empty purse—the keeping up a hollow show that must soon come to an end. Have the courage to appear poor, and you disarm poverty of its sharpest sting." On this point I found Leslie perfectly prepared. He had no false pride himself, and as to his wife, she was only anxious to conform to their altered fortunes.

Some days afterwards, he called upon me in the evening. He had disposed of his dwelling-house, and taken a small cottage in the country, a few miles from town. He had been busied all day in sending out furniture. The new establishment required few articles, and those of the simplest kind. All the splendid furniture of his late residence had been sold, excepting his wife's harp. That, he said, was too closely associated with the idea of herself—it belonged to the little story of their loves—for some of the sweetest moments of their courtship were those when he had leaned over that instrument, and listened to the melting tones of her voice.—I could not but smile at this instance of romantic gallantry in a doating husband.

He was now going out to the cottage, where his wife had been all day superintending its arrangement. My feelings had become strongly interested in the progress of his family story, and, as it was a fine evening, I offered to accompany him.

He was wearied with the fatigues of the day, and, as we walked out, fell into a fit of gloomy musing.

"Poor Mary!" at length broke, with a heavy sigh, from his lips.

"And what of her," asked I, "has anything happened to her?"

"What," said he, darting an impatient glance, "is it nothing to be reduced to this paltry situation—to be caged in a miserable cottage—to be obliged to toil almost in the menial concerns of her wretched habitation?"

Has she then repined at the change?

"Repined! she has been nothing but sweetness and good-humor. Indeed, she seems in better spirits than I have ever known her; she has been to me all love, and tenderness, and comfort!"

"Admirable girl!" exclaimed I. "You call yourself poor, my friend; you never were so rich,—you never knew the boundless treasures of excellence you possessed in that woman."

"Oh! but, my friend, if this first meeting at the cottage were over, I think I could then be comfortable. But this is her first day of real experience; she has been introduced into our humble dwelling,—she has been employed all day in arranging its miserable equipments,—she has, for the first time, known the fatigues of domestic employment,—she has, for the first time, looked around her on a home destitute of every thing elegant—almost of every thing convenient; and may now be sitting down, exhausted and spiritless, brooding over a prospect of future poverty."

There was a degree of probability in this picture that I could not gainsay, so we walked on in silence.

After turning from the main road up a narrow lane, so thickly shaded with forest-trees as to give it a complete air of seclusion, we came in sight of the cottage. It was humble enough in its appearance for the most pastoral poet; and yet it had a pleasing rural look. A wild vine had overrun one end with a profusion of foliage; a few trees threw their branches gracefully over it; and I observed several pots of flowers tastefully disposed about the door, and on the grass plot in front. A small wicket gate opened upon a footpath that wound through some shrubbery to the door. Just as we approached, we heard the sound of music—Leslie grasped my arm; we paused and listened. It was Mary's voice singing, in a style of the most touching simplicity, a little air of which her husband was peculiarly fond.

I felt Leslie's hand tremble on my arm. He stepped forward, to hear more distinctly. His step made a noise on the gravel-walk. A bright beautiful face glanced out at the window, and vanished—a light footstep was heard—and Mary came tripping forth to meet us. She was in a pretty rural dress of white; a few wild flowers were twisted in her fine hair; a fresh bloom was on her cheek; her whole countenance beamed with smiles—I had never seen her look so lovely.

"My dear George," cried she, "I am so glad you are come; I have been watching and watching for you; and running down the lane, and looking out for you. I've set out a table under a beautiful tree behind the cottage; and I've been gathering some of the most delicious strawberries, for I know you are fond of them—and we have such excellent cream—and everything is so sweet and still here—Oh!"—said she, putting her arm within his, and looking up brightly in his face, "Oh, we shall be so happy!"

Poor Leslie was overcome.—He caught her to his bosom—he folded his arms round her—he kissed her again and again—he could not speak, but the tears gushed into his eyes; and he has often assured me, that though the world has since gone prosperously with him, and his life has, indeed, been a happy one, yet never has he experienced a moment of more exquisite felicity.

RIP VAN WINKLE

A Posthumous Writing of Diedrich Knickerbocker

By Woden, God of Saxons,
From whence comes Wensday, that is Wodensday,
Truth is a thing that ever I will keep
Unto thylke day in which I creep into
My sepulchre—

—Cartwright

The following Tale was found among the papers of the late Diedrich Knickerbocker, an old gentleman of New York, who was very curious in the Dutch History of the province and the manners of the descendants from its primitive settlers. His historical researches, however, did not lie so much among books as among men; for the former are lamentably scanty on his favorite topics; whereas he found the old burghers, and still more, their wives, rich in that legendary lore, so invaluable to true history. Whenever, therefore, he happened upon a genuine Dutch family, snugly shut up in its low-roofed farm house, under a spreading sycamore, he looked upon it as a little clasped volume of black letter, and studied it with the zeal of a bookworm.

The result of all these researches was a history of the province, during the reign of the Dutch governors, which he published some years since. There have been various opinions as to the literary character of his work, and, to tell the truth, it is not a whit better than it should be. Its chief merit is its scrupulous accuracy, which indeed was a little questioned on its first appearance, but has since been completely established; and it is now admitted into all historical collections, as a book of unquestionable authority.

The old gentleman died shortly after the publication of his work; and now that he is dead and gone, it cannot do much harm to his memory to say that his time might have been much better employed in weightier labors. He, however, was apt to ride his hobby his own way; and though it did now and then kick up the dust a little in the eyes of his neighbors, and grieve the spirit of some friends, for whom he felt the truest deference and affection, yet his errors and follies are remembered "more in sorrow than in anger," and it begins to be suspected that he never intended to injure or offend. But however his memory may be appreciated by critics, it is still held dear among many folk whose good opinion is well worth having; particularly by certain biscuit-bakers, who have gone so far as to imprint his likeness on their new-year cakes, and have thus given him a chance for immortality, almost equal to the being stamped on a Waterloo medal, or a Queen Anne's farthing.

* * *

Whoever has made a voyage up the Hudson must remember the Kaatskill mountains. They are a dismembered branch of the great Appalachian family, and are seen away to the west of the river, swelling up to a noble height, and lording it over the surrounding country. Every change of season, every change of weather, indeed, every hour of the day produces some change in the magical hues and shapes of these mountains; and they are regarded by all the good wives, far and near, as perfect barometers. When the weather is fair and settled, they are clothed in blue and purple, and print their bold outlines on the clear evening sky; but sometimes, when the rest of the landscape is cloudless, they will gather a hood of gray vapors about their summits, which, in the last rays of the setting sun, will glow and light up like a crown of glory.

At the foot of these fairy mountains, the voyager may have descried the light smoke curling up from a village, whose shingle roofs gleam among the trees, just where the blue tints of the upland melt away into the fresh green of the nearer landscape. It is a little village of great antiquity, having been founded by some of the Dutch colonists, in the early times of the province, just about the beginning of the government of the good Peter Stuyvesant (may he rest in peace!), and there were some of the houses of the original settlers standing within a few years, built of small yellow bricks, brought from Holland, having latticed windows and gable fronts, surmounted with weathercocks.

In that same village, and in one of these very houses (which, to tell the precise truth, was sadly time-worn and weather-beaten), there lived, many years since, while the country was yet a province of Great Britain, a simple, good-natured fellow, of the name of Rip Van Winkle. He was a descendant of the Van Winkles who figured so gallantly in the chivalrous days of Peter Stuyvesant, and accompanied him to the siege of Fort Christina. He inherited, however, but little of the martial character of his ancestors. I have observed that he was a simple, good-natured man; he was, moreover, a kind neighbor, and an obedient, henpecked husband. Indeed, to the latter circumstance might be owing that meekness of spirit which gained him such universal popularity; for those men are apt to be obsequious and conciliating abroad, who are under the discipline of shrews at home. Their tempers, doubtless, are rendered pliant and malleable in the fiery furnace of domestic tribulation, and a curtain lecture is worth all the sermons in the world for teaching the virtues of patience and long suffering. A termagant wife may, therefore, in some respects, be considered a tolerable blessing, and if so, Rip Van Winkle was thrice blessed.

Certain it is that he was a great favorite among all the good wives of the village, who, as usual with the amiable sex, took his part in all family squabbles, and never failed, whenever they talked those matters over in their evening gossipings, to lay all the blame on Dame Van Winkle. The children of the village, too, would shout with joy whenever he approached. He assisted at their sports, made their playthings, taught them to fly kites and shoot marbles, and told them long stories of ghosts, witches, and Indians. Whenever he went dodging about the village, he was surrounded by a troop of them hanging on his skirts, clambering on his back, and playing a thousand tricks on him with impunity; and not a dog would bark at him throughout the neighborhood.

The great error in Rip's composition was an insuperable aversion to all kinds of profitable labor. It could not be for want of assiduity or perseverance; for he would sit on a wet rock, with a rod as long and heavy as a Tartar's lance, and fish all day without a murmur, even though he should not be encouraged by a single nibble. He would carry a fowling piece on his shoulder, for hours together, trudging through woods and swamps, and up hill and down dale, to shoot a few squirrels or wild pigeons. He would never refuse to assist a neighbor even in the roughest toil, and was a foremost man in all country frolics for husking

Indian corn, or building stone fences; the women of the village, too, used to employ him to run their errands, and to do such little odd jobs as their less obliging husbands would not do for them. In a word, Rip was ready to attend to anybody's business but his own; but as to doing family duty, and keeping his farm in order, he found it impossible.

In fact, he declared it was of no use to work on his farm; it was the most pestilent little piece of ground in the whole country; everything about it went wrong, and would go wrong, in spite of him. His fences were continually falling to pieces; his cow would either go astray, or get among the cabbages; weeds were sure to grow quicker in his fields than anywhere else; the rain always made a point of setting in just as he had some outdoor work to do; so that though his patrimonial estate had dwindled away under his management, acre by acre, until there was little more left than a mere patch of Indian corn and potatoes, yet it was the worst-conditioned farm in the neighborhood.

His children, too, were as ragged and wild as if they belonged to nobody. His son Rip, an urchin begotten in his own likeness, promised to inherit the habits, with the old clothes, of his father. He was generally seen trooping like a colt at his mother's heels, equipped in a pair of his father's cast-off galligaskins, which he had much ado to hold up with one hand, as a fine lady does her train in bad weather.

Rip Van Winkle, however, was one of those happy mortals of foolish, well-oiled dispositions, who take the world easy, eat white bread or brown, whichever can be got with least thought or trouble, and would rather starve on a penny than work for a pound. If left to himself, he would have whistled life away, in perfect contentment; but his wife kept continually dinning in his ears about his idleness, his carelessness, and the ruin he was bringing on his family. Morning, noon, and night, her tongue was incessantly going, and every thing he said or did was sure to produce a torrent of household eloquence. Rip had but one way of replying to all lectures of the kind, and that, by frequent use, had grown into a habit. He shrugged his shoulders, shook his head, cast up his eyes, but said nothing. This, however, always provoked a fresh volley from his wife, so that he was fain to draw off his forces, and take to the outside of the house—the only side which, in truth, belongs to a henpecked husband.

Rip's sole domestic adherent was his dog Wolf, who was as much henpecked as his master; for Dame Van Winkle regarded them as companions in idleness, and even looked upon Wolf with an evil eye, as the cause of his master's going so often astray. True it is, in all points of spirit befitting in honorable dog, he was as courageous an animal as ever scoured the woods—but what courage can withstand the evil-doing and all-besetting terrors of a woman's tongue? The moment Wolf entered the house, his crest fell, his tail drooped to the ground, or curled between his legs, he sneaked about with a gallows air, casting many a sidelong glance at Dame Van Winkle, and at the least flourish of a broomstick or ladle, he would fly to the door with yelping precipitation.

Times grew worse and worse with Rip Van Winkle as years of matrimony rolled on; a tart temper never mellows with age, and a sharp tongue is the only edged tool that grows keener with constant use. For a long while he used to console himself, when driven from home, by frequenting a kind of perpetual club of the sages, philosophers, and other idle personages of the village, which held its sessions on a bench before a small inn, designated by a rubicund portrait of his Majesty George the Third. Here they used to sit in the shade through a long, lazy summer's day, talking listlessly over village gossip, or telling endless, sleepy stories about nothing. But it would have been worth any statesman's money to have heard the profound discussions which sometimes took place, when by chance an old newspaper fell into their hands from some passing traveller. How solemnly they would listen to the contents, as drawled out by Derrick Van Bummel, the schoolmaster, a dapper learned little man, who was not to be daunted by the most gigantic word in the dictionary; and how sagely they would deliberate upon public events some months after they had taken place.

The opinions of this junto were completely controlled by Nicholas Vedder, a patriarch of the village, and landlord of the inn, at the door of which he took his seat from morning till night, just moving sufficiently to avoid the sun and keep in the shade of a large tree; so that the neighbors could tell the hour by his movements as accurately as by a sun-dial. It is true, he was rarely heard to speak, but smoked his pipe incessantly. His adherents, however (for every great man has his adherents), perfectly understood him, and knew how to gather his opinions. When anything that was read or related displeased him, he was observed to smoke his pipe vehemently, and to send forth, frequent, and angry puffs; but when pleased, he would inhale the smoke slowly and tranquilly and emit it in light and placid clouds, and sometimes taking the pipe from his mouth, and letting the fragrant vapor curl about his nose, would gravely nod his head in token of perfect approbation.

From even this stronghold the unlucky Rip was at length routed by his termagant wife, who would suddenly break in upon the tranquillity of the assemblage, and call the members all to naught; nor was that august personage Nicholas Vedder himself, sacred from the daring tongue of this terrible virago, who charged him outright with encouraging her husband in habits of idleness.

Poor Rip was at last reduced almost to despair; and his only alternative, to escape from the labor of the farm and the clamor of his wife, was to take gun in hand, and stroll away into the woods. Here he would sometimes seat himself at the foot of a tree, and share the contents of his wallet with Wolf, with whom he sympathized as a fellow-sufferer in persecution. "Poor Wolf," he would say, "thy mistress leads thee a dog's life of it; but never mind, my lad, whilst I live thou shalt never want a friend to stand by thee!" Wolf would wag his tail, look wistfully in his master's face, and if dogs can feel pity, I verily believe he reciprocated the sentiment with all his heart.

In a long ramble of the kind on a fine autumnal day, Rip had unconsciously scrambled to one of the highest parts of the Kaatskill mountains. He was after his favorite sport of squirrel shooting, and the still solitudes had echoed and re-echoed with the reports of his gun. Panting and fatigued, he threw himself, late in the afternoon, on a green knoll, covered with mountain herbage, that crowned the brow of a precipice. From an opening between the trees, he could overlook all the lower country for many a mile of rich woodland. He saw at a distance the lordly Hudson, far, far below him, moving on its silent but majestic course, with the reflection of a purple cloud, or the sail of a lagging bark here and there sleeping on its glassy bosom and at last losing itself in the blue highlands.

On the other side he looked down into a deep mountain glen,

wild, lonely, and shagged, the bottom filled with fragments from the impending cliffs, and scarcely lighted by the reflected rays of the setting sun. For some time Rip lay musing on this scene; evening was gradually advancing; the mountains began to throw their long blue shadows over the valleys; he saw that it would be dark long before he could reach the village; and he heaved a heavy sigh when he thought of encountering the terrors of Dame Van Winkle.

As he was about to descend, he heard a voice from a distance hallooing: "Rip Van Winkle! Rip Van Winkle!" He looked around, but could see nothing but a crow winging its solitary flight across the mountain. He thought his fancy must have deceived him, and turned again to descend, when he heard the same cry ring through the still evening air, "Rip Van Winkle! Rip Van Winkle!"—at the same time Wolf bristled up his back, and giving a low growl, skulked to his master's side, looking fearfully down into the glen. Rip now felt a vague apprehension stealing over him; he looked anxiously in the same direction, and perceived a strange figure slowly toiling up the rocks, and bending under the weight of something he carried on his back. He was surprised to see any human being in this lonely and unfrequented place, but supposing it to be some one of the neighborhood in need of his assistance, he hastened down to yield it.

On nearer approach, he was still more surprised at the singularity of the stranger's appearance. He was a short, square-built old fellow, with thick bushy hair and a grizzled beard. His dress was of the antique Dutch fashion, a cloth jerkin strapped round the waist, several pairs of breeches, the outer one of ample volume, decorated with rows of buttons down the sides, and bunches at the knees. He bore on his shoulders a stout keg, that seemed full of liquor, and made signs for Rip to approach and assist him with the load. Though rather shy and distrustful of this new acquaintance, Rip complied with his usual alacrity; and mutually relieving each other, they clambered up a narrow gully, apparently the dry bed of a mountain torrent. As they ascended, Rip every now and then heard long rolling peals, like distant thunder, that seemed to issue out of a deep ravine or rather cleft between lofty rocks, toward which their rugged path conducted. He paused for an instant, but supposing it to be the muttering of one of those transient thunder showers which often take place in the mountain heights, he proceeded. Passing through the ravine, they came to a hollow, like a small amphitheatre, surrounded by perpendicular precipices, over the brinks of which impending trees shot their branches, so that you only caught glimpses of the azure sky, and the bright evening cloud. During the whole time Rip and his companion had labored on in silence; for though the former marvelled greatly what could be the object of carrying a keg of liquor up this wild mountain, yet there was something strange and incomprehensible about the unknown, that inspired awe, and checked familiarity.

On entering the amphitheatre, new objects of wonder presented themselves. On a level spot in the centre was a company of odd-looking personages playing at ninepins. They were dressed in quaint outlandish fashion; some wore short doublets, others jerkins, with long knives in their belts, and most of them had enormous breeches, of similar style with that of the guide's. Their visages, too, were peculiar; one had a large head, broad face, and small piggish eyes; the face of another seemed to consist entirely of nose, and was surmounted by a white sugar-loaf hat, set off with a little red cock's tail. They all had beards, of various shapes and colors. There was one who seemed to be the commander. He was a stout old gentleman, with a weather-beaten countenance; he wore a laced doublet, broad belt and hanger, high-crowned hat and feather, red stockings, and high-heeled shoes, with roses in them. The whole group reminded Rip of the figures in an old Flemish painting, in the parlor of Dominie Van Schaick, the village parson, and which had been brought over from Holland at the time of the settlement.

What seemed particularly odd to Rip was, that though these folks were evidently amusing themselves, yet they maintained the gravest faces, the most mysterious silence, and were, withal, the most melancholy party of pleasure he had ever witnessed. Nothing interrupted the stillness of the scene but the noise of the balls, which, whenever they were rolled, echoed along the mountains like rumbling peals of thunder.

As Rip and his companion approached them, they suddenly desisted from their play, and stared at him with such a fixed statue-like gaze, and such strange uncouth, lack-lustre countenances, that his heart turned within him, and his knees smote together. His companion now emptied the contents of the keg into large flagons, and made signs to him to wait upon the company. He obeyed with fear and trembling; they quaffed the liquor in profound silence, and then returned to their game.

By degrees, Rip's awe and apprehension subsided. He even ventured, when no eye was fixed upon him, to taste the beverage which he found had much of the flavor of excellent Hollands. He was naturally a thirsty soul, and was soon tempted to repeat the draught. One taste provoked another; and he reiterated his visits to the flagon so often, that at length his senses were overpowered, his eyes swam in his head, his head gradually declined, and he fell into a deep sleep.

On waking, he found himself on the green knoll whence he had first seen the old man of the glen. He rubbed his eyes—it was a bright sunny morning. The birds were hopping and twittering among the bushes, and the eagle was wheeling aloft, and breasting the pure mountain breeze. "Surely," thought Rip, "I have not slept here all night." He recalled the occurrences before he fell asleep. The strange man with the keg of liquor—the mountain ravine—the wild retreat among the rocks—the woe-begone party at ninepins—the flagon—"Oh! that flagon! that wicked flagon!" thought Rip—"what excuse shall I make to Dame Van Winkle?"

He looked round for his gun, but in place of the clean well-oiled fowling-piece, he found an old firelock lying by him, the barrel encrusted with rust, the lock falling off, and the stock worm-eaten. He now suspected that the grave roysterers of the mountains had put a trick upon him, and, having dosed him with liquor, had robbed him of his gun. Wolf, too, had disappeared, but he might have strayed away after a squirrel or partridge. He whistled after him and shouted his name, but all in vain; the echoes repeated his whistle and shout, but no dog was to be seen.

He determined to revisit the scene of the last evening's gambol, and if he met with any of the party, to demand his dog and gun. As he rose to walk, he found himself stiff in the joints, and wanting in his usual activity. "These mountain beds do not agree with me," thought Rip, "and if this frolic should lay me up with a fit of the rheumatism, I shall have a blessed time with Dame Van Winkle." With some difficulty he got down into the glen: he found the gully up which he and his companion had ascended the preceding evening; but to his astonishment a mountain stream was now foaming down it, leaping from rock to rock, and filling the glen with babbling murmurs. He, however, made shift to scramble up its sides, working his toilsome way through thickets of birch, sassafras, and witch-hazel; and sometimes tripped up or entangled by the wild grape vines that twisted their coils and tendrils from tree to tree, and spread a kind of network in his path.

At length he reached to where the ravine had opened through the cliffs to the amphitheatre; but no traces of such opening remained. The rocks presented a high impenetrable wall over which the torrent came tumbling in a sheet of feathery foam, and fell into a broad deep basin, black from the shadows of the surrounding forest. Here, then, poor Rip was brought to a stand. He again called and whistled after his dog; he was only answered by the cawing of a flock of idle crows, sporting high in the air about a dry tree that overhung a sunny precipice; and who, secure in their elevation, seemed to look down and scoff at the poor man's perplexities.

What was to be done? The morning was passing away, and Rip felt famished for want of his breakfast. He grieved to give up his dog and gun; he dreaded to meet his wife; but it would not do to starve among the mountains. He shook his head, shouldered the rusty firelock, and, with a heart full of trouble and anxiety, turned his steps homeward.

As he approached the village, he met a number of people, but none whom he new, which somewhat surprised him, for he had thought himself acquainted with every one in the country round. Their dress, too, was of a different fashion from that to which he was accustomed. They all stared at him with equal marks of surprise, and whenever they cast eyes upon him, invariably stroked their chins. The constant recurrence of this gesture, induced Rip involuntarily to do the same, when to his astonishment he found his beard had grown a foot long!

He had now entered the skirts of the village. A troop of strange children ran at his heels, hooting after him, and pointing at his gray beard. The dogs, too, not one of which he recognized for an old acquaintance, barked at him as he passed. The very village was altered: it was larger and more populous. There were rows of houses which he had never seen before, and those which had been his familiar haunts had disappeared. Strange names were over the doors—strange faces at the windows—everything was strange. His mind now misgave him; he began to doubt whether both he and the world around him were not bewitched. Surely this was his native village, which he had left but a day before. There stood the Kaatskill mountains—there ran the silver Hudson at a distance—there was every hill and dale precisely as it had always been—Rip was sorely perplexed—"That flagon last night," thought he, "has addled my poor head sadly!"

It was with some difficulty that he found the way to his own house, which he approached with silent awe, expecting every moment to hear the shrill voice of Dame Van Winkle. He found the house gone to decay—the roof had fallen in, the windows shattered, and the doors off the hinges. A half-starved dog, that looked like Wolf, was skulking about it. Rip called him by name, but the cur snarled, showed his teeth, and passed on. This was an unkind cut indeed.—"My very dog," sighed poor Rip, "has forgotten me!"

He entered the house, which, to tell the truth, Dame Van Winkle had always kept in neat order. It was empty, forlorn, and apparently abandoned. This desolateness overcame all his connubial fears—he called loudly for his wife and children—the lonely chambers rang for a moment with his voice, and then all again was silence.

He now hurried forth, and hastened to his old resort, the village inn—but it too was gone. A large rickety wooden building stood in its place, with great gaping windows, some of them broken, and mended with old hats and petticoats, and over the door was painted, "The Union Hotel, by Jonathan Doolittle." Instead of the great tree that used to shelter the quiet little Dutch inn of yore, there now was reared a tall naked pole with something on the top that looked like a red nightcap, and from it was fluttering a flag, on which was a singular assemblage of stars and stripes—all this was strange and incomprehensible. He recognized on the sign, however, the ruby face of King George, under which he had smoked so many a peaceful pipe, but even this was singularly metamorphosed. The red coat was changed for one of blue and buff, a sword was held in the hand instead of a sceptre, the head was decorated with a cocked hat, and underneath was painted in large characters, *General Washington.*

There was, as usual, a crowd of folk about the door, but none that Rip recollected. The very character of the people seemed changed. There was a busy, bustling, disputatious tone about it, instead of the accustomed phlegm and drowsy tranquillity. He looked in vain for the sage Nicholas Vedder, with his broad face, double chin, and fair long pipe, uttering clouds of tobacco-smoke, instead of idle speeches; or Van Bummel, the schoolmaster, doling forth the contents of an ancient newspaper. In place of these, a lean, bilious-looking fellow, with his pockets full of handbills, was haranguing, vehemently about rights of citizens-elections—members of Congress—liberty—Bunker's hill—heroes of seventy-six-and other words, which were a perfect Babylonish jargon to the bewildered Van Winkle.

The appearance of Rip, with his long, grizzled beard, his rusty fowling piece, his uncouth dress, and the army of women and children at his heels, soon attracted the attention of the tavern politicians. They crowded round him, eying him from head to foot, with great curiosity. The orator bustled up to him, and, drawing him partly aside, inquired, "on which side he voted?" Rip stared in vacant stupidity. Another short but busy little fellow pulled him by the arm, and rising on tiptoe, inquired in his ear, "whether he was Federal or Democrat." Rip was equally at a loss to comprehend the question; when a knowing, self-important old gentleman, in a sharp cocked hat, made his way through the crowd, putting them to the right and left with his elbows as he passed, and planting himself before Van Winkle, with one arm akimbo, the other resting on his cane, his keen eyes and sharp hat penetrating, as it were, into his very soul, demanded in an austere tone, "What brought him to the election with a gun on his shoulder, and a mob at his heels; and whether he meant to breed a riot in the village?"

"Alas! gentlemen," cried Rip, somewhat dismayed, "I am a poor, quiet man, a native of the place, and a loyal subject of the King, God bless him!"

Here a general shout burst from the bystanders—"a tory! a tory! a spy! a refugee! hustle him! away with him!" It was with great difficulty that the self-important man in the cocked hat restored order; and having assumed a tenfold austerity of brow, demanded again of the unknown culprit, what he came there for, and whom he was seeking. The poor man humbly assured him that he meant no harm, but merely came there in search of some of his neighbors, who used to keep about the tavern.

"Well—who are they?—name them."

Rip bethought himself a moment, and inquired, "Where's Nicholas Vedder?"

There was a silence for a little while, when an old man replied, in a thin, piping voice, "Nicholas Vedder? why, he is dead and gone these eighteen years! There was a wooden tombstone in the churchyard that used to tell all about him, but that's rotten and gone too."

"Where's Brom Dutcher?"

"Oh, he went off to the army in the beginning of the war; some say he was killed at the storming of Stony-Point—others say he was drowned in a squall at the foot of Antony's Nose. I don't know—he never came back again."

"Where's Van Bummel, the schoolmaster?"

"He went off to the wars, too; was a great militia general, and is now in Congress."

Rip's heart died away, at hearing of these sad changes in his home and friends, and finding himself thus alone in the world. Every answer puzzled him too, by treating of such enormous lapses of time, and of matters which he could not understand: war—Congress-Stony-Point;—he had no courage to ask after any more friends, but cried out in despair, "Does nobody here know Rip Van Winkle?"

"Oh, Rip Van Winkle!" exclaimed two or three. "Oh, to be sure! that's Rip Van Winkle yonder, leaning against the tree."

Rip looked, and beheld a precise counterpart of himself as he went up the mountain; apparently as lazy, and certainly as ragged. The poor fellow was now completely confounded. He doubted his own identity, and whether he was himself or another man. In the midst of his bewilderment, the man in the cocked hat demanded who he was, and what was his name?

"God knows!" exclaimed he at his wit's end; "I'm not myself—I'm somebody else—that's me yonder-no—that's somebody else, got into my shoes—I was myself last night, but I fell asleep on the mountain, and they've changed my gun, and everything's changed, and I'm changed, and I can't tell what's my name, or who I am!"

The bystanders began now to look at each other, nod, wink significantly, and tap their fingers against their foreheads. There was a whisper also about securing the gun, and keeping the old fellow from doing mischief; at the very suggestion of which, the self-important man with the cocked hat retired with some precipitation. At this critical moment a fresh, likely-looking woman pressed through the throng to get a peep at the gray-bearded man. She had a chubby child in her arms, which, frightened at his looks, began to cry. "Hush, Rip," cried she, "hush, you little fool; the old man won't hurt you." The name of the child, the air of the mother, the tone of her voice, all awakened a train of recollections in his mind.

"What is your name, my good woman?" asked he.

"Judith Cardenier."

"And your father's name?"

"Ah, poor man, Rip Van Winkle was his name, but it's twenty years since he went away from home with his gun, and never has been heard of since,—his dog came home without him; but whether he shot himself, or was carried away by the Indians, nobody can tell. I was then but a little girl."

Rip had but one more question to ask; but he put it with a faltering voice:

"Where's your mother?"

"Oh, she too had died but a short time since; she broke a blood-vessel in a fit of passion at a New-England pedler."

There was a drop of comfort at least in this intelligence. The honest man could contain himself no longer. He caught his daughter and her child in his arms. "I am your father!" cried he—"Young Rip Van Winkle once—old Rip Van Winkle now—Does nobody know poor Rip Van Winkle!"

All stood amazed, until an old woman, tottering out from among the crowd, put her hand to her brow, and peering under it in his face for a moment exclaimed, "sure enough! it is Rip Van Winkle—it is himself. Welcome home again, old neighbor. Why, where have you been these twenty long years?"

Rip's story was soon told, for the whole twenty years had been to him but as one night. The neighbors stared when they heard it; some were seen to wink at each other, and put their tongues in their cheeks; and the self-important man in the cocked hat, who, when the alarm was over, had returned to the field, screwed down the corners of his mouth, and shook his head—upon which there was a general shaking of the head throughout the assemblage.

It was determined, however, to take the opinion of old Peter Vanderdonk, who was seen slowly advancing up the road. He was a descendant of the historian of that name, who wrote one of the earliest accounts of the province. Peter was the most ancient inhabitant of the village, and well versed in all the wonderful events and traditions of the neighborhood. He recollected Rip at once, and corroborated his story in the most satisfactory manner. He assured the company that it was a fact, handed down from his ancestor, the historian, that the Kaatskill mountains had always been haunted by strange beings. That it was affirmed that the great Hendrick Hudson, the first discoverer of the river and country, kept a kind of vigil there every twenty years, with his crew of the Half Moon; being permitted in this way to revisit the scenes of his enterprise and keep a guardian eye upon the river and the great city called by his name. That his father had once seen them in their old Dutch dresses playing at ninepins in the hollow of the mountain; and that he himself had heard, one summer afternoon, the sound of their balls, like distant peals of thunder.

To make a long story short, the company broke up, and returned to the more important concerns of the election. Rip's daughter took him home to live with her; she had a snug, well-furnished house, and a stout cheery farmer for a husband, whom Rip recollected for one of the urchins that used to climb upon his back. As to Rip's son and heir, who was the ditto of himself, seen leaning against the tree, he was employed to work on the farm; but evinced an hereditary disposition to attend to any thing else but his business.

Rip now resumed his old walks and habits; he soon found many of his former cronies, though all rather the worse for the wear and tear of time; and preferred making friends among the rising generation, with whom he soon grew into great favor.

Having nothing to do at home, and being arrived at that happy age when a man can be idle with impunity, he took his place once more on the bench, at the inn door, and was reverenced as one of the patriarchs of the village, and a chronicle of the old times "before the war." It was some time before he could get into the regular track of gossip, or could be made to comprehend the strange events that had taken place during his torpor. How that there had been a revolutionary war—that the country had thrown off the yoke of old England—and that, instead of being a subject to his Majesty George the Third, he was now a free citizen of the United States. Rip, in fact, was no politician; the changes of states and empires made but little impression on him; but there was one species of despotism under which he had long groaned, and that was petticoat government. Happily, that was at an end; he had got his neck out of the yoke of matrimony, and could go in and out whenever he pleased, without dreading the tyranny of Dame Van Winkle. Whenever her name was mentioned, however, he shook his head, shrugged his shoulders, and cast up his eyes; which might pass either for an expression of resignation to his fate, or joy at his deliverance.

He used to tell his story to every stranger that arrived at Mr. Doolittle's hotel. He was observed, at first, to vary on some points every time he told it, which was, doubtless, owing to his having so recently awaked. It at last settled down precisely to the tale I have related, and not a man, woman, or child in the neighborhood, but knew it by heart. Some always pretended to doubt the reality of it, and insisted that Rip had been out of his head, and that this was one point on which he always remained flighty. The old Dutch inhabitants, however, almost universally gave it full credit. Even to this day, they never hear a thunder-storm of a summer afternoon about the Kaatskill, but they say Hendrick Hudson and his crew are at their game of ninepins; and it is a common wish of all henpecked husbands in the neighborhood, when life hangs heavy on their hands, that they might have a quieting draught out of Rip Van Winkle's flagon.

Note

The foregoing tale, one would suspect, had been suggested to Mr. Knickerbocker by a little German superstition about the Emperor Frederick der Rothbart and the Kypphauser mountain; the subjoined note, however, which had appended to the tale, shows that it is an absolute fact, narrated with his usual fidelity.

"The story of Rip Van Winkle may seem incredible to many, but nevertheless I give it my full belief, for I know the vicinity of our old Dutch settlements to have been very subject to marvellous events and appearances. Indeed, I have heard many stranger stories than this, in the villages along the Hudson; all of which were too well authenticated to admit of a doubt. I have even talked with Rip Van Winkle myself, who, when last I saw him, was a very venerable old man, and so perfectly rational and consistent on every other point, that I think no conscientious person could refuse to take this into the bargain; nay, I have seen a certificate on the subject taken before a country justice, and signed with cross, in the justice's own handwriting. The story, therefore, is beyond the possibility of doubt.

D. K."

Postscript

The following are travelling notes from a memorandum-book of Mr. Knickerbocker:

The Kaatsberg or Catskill mountains have always been a region full of fable. The Indians considered them the abode of spirits, who influenced the weather, spreading sunshine or clouds over the landscape, and sending good or bad hunting seasons. They were ruled by an old squaw spirit, said to be their mother. She dwelt on the highest peak of the Catskills, and had charge of the doors of day and night to open and shut them at the proper hour. She hung up the new moons in the skies, and cut up the old ones into stars. In times of drought, if properly propitiated, she would spin light summer clouds out of cobwebs and morning dew, and send them off from the crest of the mountain, flake after flake, like flakes of carded cotton, to float in the air; until, dissolved by the heat of the sun, they would fall in gentle showers, causing the grass to spring, the fruits to ripen, and the corn to grow an inch an hour. If displeased, however, she would brew up clouds black as ink, sitting in the midst of them like a bottle-bellied spider in the midst of its web; and when these clouds broke, woe betide the valleys!

In old times, say the Indian traditions, there was a kind of Manitou or Spirit, who kept about the wildest recesses of the Catskill mountains, and took a mischievous pleasure in wreaking all kind of evils and vexations upon the red men. Sometimes he would assume the form of a bear, a panther, or a deer, lead the bewildered hunter a weary chase through tangled forests and among ragged rocks, and then spring off with a loud ho! ho! leaving him aghast on the brink of a beetling precipice or raging torrent.

The favorite abode of this Manitou is still shown. It is a rock or cliff on the loneliest port of the mountains, and, from the flowering vines which clamber about it, and the wild flowers which abound in its neighborhood, is known by the name of the Garden Rock. Near the foot of it is a small lake, the haunt of the solitary bittern, with water snakes basking in the sun on the leaves of the pond-lilies which lie on the surface. This place was held in great awe by the Indians, insomuch that the boldest hunter would not pursue his game within its precincts. Once upon a time, however, a hunter who had lost his way penetrated to the Garden Rock, where he beheld a number of gourds placed in the crotches of trees. One of these he seized and made off with it, but in the hurry of his retreat he let it fall among the rocks, when a great stream gushed forth, which washed him away and swept him down precipices, where he was dished to pieces, and the stream made its way to the Hudson, and continues to flow to the present day, being the identical stream known by the name of the Kaaterskill.

ENGLISH WRITERS ON AMERICA

> Methinks I see in my mind a noble and puissant nation rousting herself like a strong man after sleep, and shaking her invincible locks; methinks I see her as an eagle mewing her mighty youth, and kindling her endazzled eyes at the full mid-day beam.
>
> —Milton on the Liberty of the Press

It is with feelings of deep regret that I observe the literary animosity daily growing up between England and America. Great curiosity has been awakened of late with respect to the United States, and the London press has teemed with volumes of travels through the republic; but they seem intended to diffuse error rather than knowledge; and so successful have they been, that, notwithstanding the constant intercourse between the nations, there is no people concerning whom the great mass of the British public have less pure information, or entertain more numerous prejudices.

English travellers are the best and the worst in the world. Where no motives of pride or interest intervene, none can equal them for profound and philosophical views of society, or faithful and graphical description of external objects; but when either the interest or reputation of their own country comes in collision with that of another, they go to the opposite extreme, and forget their usual probity and candor, in the indulgence of splenetic remark, and an illiberal spirit of ridicule.

Hence, their travels are more honest and accurate, the more remote the country described. I would place implicit confidence in an Englishman's description of the regions beyond the cataracts of the Nile; of unknown islands in the Yellow Sea; of the interior of India; or of any other tract which other travellers might be apt to picture out with the illusions of their fancies. But I would cautiously receive his account of his immediate neighbors, and of those nations with which he is in habits of most frequent intercourse. However I might be disposed to trust his probity, I dare not trust his prejudices.

It has also been the peculiar lot of our country to be visited by the worst kind of English travellers. While men of philosophical spirit and cultivated minds have been sent from England to ransack the poles, to penetrate the deserts, and to study the manners and customs of barbarous nations, with which she can have no permanent intercourse of profit or pleasure; it has been left to the broken-down tradesman, the scheming adventurer, the wandering mechanic, the Manchester and Birmingham agent, to be her oracles respecting America. From such sources she is content to receive her information respecting a country in a singular state of moral and physical development; a country in which one of the greatest political experiments in the history of the world is now performing; and which presents the most profound and momentous studies to the statesman and the philosopher.

That such men should give prejudicial accounts of America, is not a matter of surprise. The themes it offers for contemplation are too vast and elevated for their capacities. The national character is yet in a state of fermentation: it may have its frothiness and sediment, but its ingredients are sound and wholesome; it has already given proofs of powerful and generous qualities; and the whole promises to settle down into something substantially excellent. But the causes which are operating to strengthen and ennoble it, and its daily indications of admirable properties, are all lost upon these purblind observers; who are only affected by the little asperities incident to its present situation. They are capable of judging only of the surface of things; of those matters which come in contact with their private interests and personal gratifications. They miss some of the snug conveniences and petty comforts which belong to an old, highly finished, and over-populous state of society, where the ranks of useful labor are crowded, and many earn a painful and servile subsistence, by studying the very caprices of appetite and self-indulgence. These minor comforts, however, are all-important in the estimation of narrow minds; which either do not perceive, or will not acknowledge, that they are more than counterbalanced among us, by great and generally diffused blessings.

They may, perhaps, have been disappointed in some unreasonable expectation of sudden gain. They may have pictured America to themselves an El Dorado, where gold and silver abounded, and the natives were lacking in sagacity, and where they were to become strangely and suddenly rich, in some unforeseen but easy manner. The same weakness of mind that indulges absurd expectations, produces petulance in disappointment. Such persons become embittered against the country on finding that there, as everywhere else, a man must sow before he can reap; must win wealth by industry and talent; and must contend with the common difficulties of nature, and the shrewdness of an intelligent and enterprising people.

Perhaps, through mistaken or ill-directed hospitality, or from the prompt disposition to cheer and countenance the stranger, prevalent among my countrymen, they may have been treated with unwonted respect in America; and, having been accustomed all their lives to consider themselves below the surface of good society, and brought up in a servile feeling of inferiority, they become arrogant, on the common boon of civility; they attribute to the lowliness of others their own elevation; and underrate a society where there are no artificial distinctions, and where, by any chance, such individuals as themselves can rise to consequence.

One would suppose, however, that information coming from such sources, on a subject where the truth is so desirable, would be received with caution by the censors of the press; that the motives of these men, their veracity, their opportunities of inquiry and observation, and their capacities for judging correctly, would be rigorously scrutinized, before their evidence was admitted in such sweeping extent, against a kindred nation. The very reverse, however, is the case, and it furnishes a striking instance of human inconsistency. Nothing can surpass the vigilance with which English critics will examine the credibility of the traveller who publishes an account of some distant and comparatively unimportant country. How warily will they compare the measurements of a pyramid, or the description of a ruin; and how sternly will they censure any inaccuracy in these contributions of merely curious knowledge, while they will receive, with eagerness and unhesitating faith, the gross misrepresentations of coarse and obscure writers, concerning a country with which their own is placed in the most important and delicate relations. Nay, they will even make these apocryphal volumes text-books, on which to enlarge, with a zeal and an ability worthy of a more generous cause.

I shall not, however, dwell on this irksome and hackneyed topic; nor should I have adverted to it, but for the undue interest apparently taken in it by my countrymen, and certain injurious effects which I apprehend it might produce upon the national feeling. We attach too much consequence to these attacks. They cannot do us any essential injury. The tissue of misrepresentations attempted to be woven round us, are like cobwebs woven round the limbs of an infant giant. Our country continually outgrows them. One falsehood after another falls off of itself. We have but to live on, and every day we live a whole volume of refutation.

All the writers of England united, if we could for a moment suppose their great minds stooping to so unworthy a combination, could not conceal our rapidly growing importance and matchless prosperity. They could not conceal that these are owing, not merely to physical and local, but also to moral causes—to the political liberty, the general diffusion of knowledge, the prevalence of sound, moral, and religious principles, which give force and sustained energy to the character of a people, and which in fact, have been the acknowledged and wonderful supporters of their own national power and glory.

But why are we so exquisitely alive to the aspersions of England? Why do we suffer ourselves to be so affected by the contumely she has endeavored to cast upon us? It is not in the opinion of England alone that honor lives, and reputation has its being. The world at large is the arbiter of a nation's fame: with its thousand eyes it witnesses a nation's deeds, and from their collective testimony is national glory or national disgrace established.

For ourselves, therefore, it is comparatively of but little importance whether England does us justice or not; it is, perhaps, of far more importance to herself. She is instilling anger and resentment into the bosom of a youthful nation, to grow with its growth, and strengthen with its strength. If in America, as some of her writers are laboring to convince her, she is hereafter to find an invidious rival and a gigantic foe, she may thank those very writers for having provoked rivalship, and irritated hostility. Every one knows the all-pervading influence of literature at the present day, and how much the opinions and passions of mankind are under its control. The mere contests of the sword are temporary; their wounds are but in the flesh, and it is the pride of the generous to forgive and forget them; but the slanders of the pen pierce to the heart; they rankle longest in the noblest spirits; they dwell ever present in the mind, and render it morbidly sensitive to the most trifling collision. It is but seldom that any one overt act produces hostilities between two nations; there exists, most commonly, a previous jealousy and ill will, a predisposition to take offence. Trace these to their cause, and how often will they be found to originate in the mischievous effusions of mercenary writers, who, secure in their closets, and for ignominious bread, concoct and circulate the venom that is to inflame the generous and the brave.

I am not laying too much stress upon this point; for it applies most emphatically to our particular case. Over no nation does the press hold a more absolute control than over the people of America; for the universal education of the poorest classes makes every individual a reader. There is nothing published in England on the subject of our country, that does not circulate through every part of it. There is not a calumny dropt from an English pen, nor an unworthy sarcasm uttered by an English statesman, that does not go to blight good will, and add to the mass of latent resentment. Possessing, then, as England does, the fountain-head whence the literature of the language flows, how completely is it in her power, and how truly is it her duty, to make it the medium of amiable and magnanimous feeling—a stream where the two nations might meet together and drink in peace and kindness. Should she, however, persist in turning it to waters of bitterness, the time may come when she may repent her folly. The present friendship of America may be of but little moment to her; but the future destinies of that country do not admit of a doubt; over those of England, there lower some shadows of uncertainty. Should, then, a day of gloom arrive—should those reverses overtake her, from which the proudest empires have not been exempt—she may look back with regret at her infatuation, in repulsing from her side a nation she might have grappled to her bosom, and thus destroying her only chance for real friendship beyond the boundaries of her own dominions.

There is a general impression in England that the people of the United States are inimical to the parent country. It is one of the errors which have been diligently propagated by designing writers. There is, doubtless, considerable political hostility, and a general soreness at the illiberality of the English press; but, collectively speaking, the prepossessions of the people are strongly in favor of England. Indeed, at one time they amounted, in many parts of the Union, to an absurd degree of bigotry. The bare name of Englishman was a passport to the confidence and hospitality of every family, and too often gave a transient currency to the worthless and the ungrateful. Throughout the country there was something of enthusiasm connected with the idea of England. We looked to it with a hallowed feeling of tenderness and veneration, as the land of our forefathers—the august repository of the monuments and antiquities of our race—the birthplace and mausoleum of the sages and heroes of our paternal history. After our own country, there was none in whose glory we more delighted—none whose good opinion we were more anxious to possess—none toward which our hearts yearned with such throbbings of warm consanguinity. Even during the late war, whenever there was the least opportunity for kind feelings to spring forth, it was the delight of the generous spirits of our country to show that in the midst of hostilities they still kept alive the sparks of future friendship.

Is all this to be at an end? Is this golden band of kindred sympathies, so rare between nations, to be broken forever?—Perhaps it is for the best—it may dispel an illusion which might have kept us in mental vassalage; which might have interfered occasionally with our true interests, and prevented the growth of proper national pride. But it is hard to give up the kindred tie! and there are feelings dearer than interest—closer to the heart than pride—that will still make us cast back a look of regret as we wander farther and farther from the paternal roof, and lament the waywardness of the parent that would repel the affections of the child.

Short-sighted and injudicious, however, as the conduct or England may be in this system of aspersion, recrimination on our part would be equally ill judged. I speak not of a prompt and spirited vindication of our country, or the keenest castigation of her slanderers—but I allude to a disposition to retaliate in kind, to retort sarcasm and inspire prejudice, which seems to be spreading widely among our writers.

Let us guard particularly against such a temper; for it would double the evil, instead of redressing the wrong. Nothing is so easy and inviting as the retort of abuse and sarcasm; but it is a paltry and an unprofitable contest. It is the alternative of a morbid mind fretted into petulance rather than warmed into indignation. If England is willing to permit the mean jealousies of trade or the rancorous animosities of politics to deprave the integrity of her press, and poison the fountain of public opinion, let us beware of her example. She may deem it her interest to diffuse error, and engender antipathy, for the purpose of checking emigration: we have no purpose of the kind to serve. Neither have we any spirit of national jealousy to gratify; for as yet, in all our rivalships with England, we are the rising and the gaining party. There can be no end to answer, therefore, but the gratification of resentment—a mere spirit of retaliation—and even that is impotent. Our retorts are never republished in England; they fall short, therefore, of their aim; but they foster a querulous and peevish temper among our writers; they sour the sweet flow of our early literature, and sow thorns and brambles among its blossoms. What is still worse, they circulate through our own country, and, as far as they have effect, excite virulent national prejudices. This last is the evil most especially to be deprecated. Governed, as we are, entirely by public opinion, the utmost care should be taken to preserve the purity of the public mind. Knowledge is power, and truth is knowledge; whoever, therefore, knowingly propagates a prejudice, wilfully saps the foundation of his country's strength.

The members of a republic, above all other men, should be candid and dispassionate. They are, individually, portions of the sovereign mind and sovereign will, and should be enabled to come to all questions of national concern with calm and unbiassed judgments. From the peculiar nature of our relations with England, we must have more frequent questions of a difficult and delicate character with her, than with any other nation—questions that affect the most acute and excitable feelings: and as in the adjustment of these, our national measures must ultimately be determined by popular sentiment, we cannot be too anxiously attentive to purify it from all latent passion or prepossession.

Opening, too, as we do, an asylum for strangers every portion of the earth, we should receive all with impartiality. It should be our pride to exhibit an example of one nation, at least, destitute of national antipathies, and exercising, not merely the overt acts of hospitality, but those more rare and noble courtesies which spring from liberality of opinion.

What have we to do with national prejudices? They are the inveterate diseases of old countries, contracted in rude and ignorant ages, when nations knew but little of each other, and looked beyond their own boundaries with distrust and hostility. We, on the contrary, have sprung into national existence in an enlightened and philosophic age, when the different parts of the habitable world, and the various branches of the human family, have been indefatigably studied and made known to each other; and we forego the advantages of our birth, if we do not shake off the national prejudices, as we would the local superstitions, of the old world.

But above all, let us not be influenced by any angry feelings so far as to shut our eyes to the perception of what is really excellent and amiable in the English character. We are a young people, necessarily an imitative one, and must take our examples and models, in a great degree, from the existing nations of Europe. There is no country more worthy of our study than England. The spirit of her constitution is most analogous to ours. The manners of her people—their intellectual activity—their freedom of opinion—their habits of thinking on those subjects which concern the dearest interests and most sacred charities of private life, are all congenial to the American character; and, in fact, are all intrinsically excellent: for it is in the moral feeling of the people that the deep foundations of British prosperity are laid; and however the superstructure may be time worn, or overrun by abuses, there must be something solid in the basis, admirable in the materials, and stable in the structure of an edifice that so long has towered unshaken amidst the tempests of the world.

Let it be the pride of our writers, therefore, discarding all feelings of irritation and disdaining to retaliate the illiberality of British authors, to speak of the English nation without prejudice, and with determined candor. While they rebuke the indiscriminating bigotry with which some of our countrymen admire and imitate every thing English, merely because it is English, let them frankly point out what is really worthy of approbation. We may thus place England before us as a perpetual volume of reference, wherein are recorded sound deductions from ages of experience; and while we avoid the errors and absurdities which may have crept into the page, we may draw thence golden maxims of practical wisdom, wherewith to strengthen and to embellish our national character.

RURAL LIFE IN ENGLAND

> Oh! friendly to the best pursuits of man,
> Friendly to thought, to virtue and to peace,
> Domestic life in rural pleasures pass'd!
>
> —Cowper

The stranger who would form a correct opinion of the English character must not confine his observations to the metropolis. He must go forth into the country; he must sojourn in villages and hamlets; he must visit castles, villas, farm-houses, cottages; he must wander through parks and gardens; along hedges and green lanes; he must loiter about country churches; attend wakes and fairs, and other rural festivals; and cope with the people in all their conditions, and all their habits and humors.

In some countries, the large cities absorb the wealth and fashion of the nation; they are the only fixed abodes of elegant and intelligent society, and the country is inhabited almost entirely by boorish peasantry. In England, on the contrary, the metropolis is a mere gathering-place, or general rendezvous, of the polite circles, where they devote a small portion of the year to a hurry of gaiety and dissipation, and, having indulged this kind of carnival, return again to the apparently more congenial habits of rural life. The various orders of society are therefore diffused over the whole surface of the kingdom, and the most retired neighborhoods afford specimens of the different ranks.

The English, in fact, are strongly gifted with the rural feeling. They possess a quick sensibility to the beauties of nature, and a keen relish for the pleasures and employments of the country. This passion seems inherent in them. Even the inhabitants of cities, born and brought up among brick walls and bustling streets, enter with facility into rural habits and evince a tact for rural occupation. The merchant has his snug retreat in the vicinity of the metropolis, where he often displays as much pride and zeal in the cultivation of his flower garden and the maturing of his fruits as he does in the conduct of his business and the success of a commercial enterprise. Even those less fortunate individuals, who are doomed to pass their lives in the midst of din and traffic, contrive to have something that shall remind them of the green aspect of nature. In the most dark and dingy quarters of the city, the drawing-room window resembles frequently a bank of flowers; every spot capable of vegetation has its grass plot and flower bed; and every square its mimic park, laid out with picturesque taste, and gleaming with refreshing verdure.

Those who see the Englishman only in town are apt to form an unfavorable opinion of his social character. He is either absorbed in business, or distracted by the thousand engagements that dissipate time, thought, and feeling, in this huge metropolis. He has, therefore, too commonly a look of hurry and abstraction. Wherever he happens to be, he is on the point of going somewhere else; at the moment he is talking on one subject, his mind is wandering to another; and while paying a friendly visit, he is calculating how he shall economize time so as to pay the other visits allotted to the morning. An immense metropolis like London is calculated to make men selfish and uninteresting. In their casual and transient meetings, they can but deal briefly in commonplaces. They present but the cold superfices of character—its rich and genial qualities have no time to be warmed into a flow.

It is in the country that the Englishman gives scope to his natural feelings. He breaks loose gladly from the cold formalities and negative civilities of town; throws off his habits of shy reserve, and becomes joyous and free-hearted. He manages to collect round him all the conveniences and elegancies of polite life, and to banish its restraints. His country seat abounds with every requisite, either for studious retirement, tasteful gratification, or rural exercise. Books, paintings, music, horses, dogs, and sporting implements of all kinds are at hand. He puts no constraint either upon his guests or himself, but in the true spirit of hospitality, provides the means of enjoyment, and leaves every one to partake according to his inclination.

The taste of the English in the cultivation of land and in what is called landscape gardening is unrivalled. They have studied nature intently and discovered an exquisite sense of her beautiful forms and harmonious combinations. Those charms which in other countries she lavishes in wild solitudes are here assembled round the haunts of domestic life. They seem to have caught her coy and furtive graces, and spread them, like witchery, about their rural abodes.

Nothing can be more imposing than the magnificence of English park scenery. Vast lawns that extend like sheets of vivid green, with here and there clumps of gigantic trees heaping up rich piles of foliage. The solemn pomp of groves and woodland glades with the deer trooping in silent herds across them; the hare bounding away to the covert; or the pheasant suddenly bursting upon the wing. The brook, taught to wind in natural meanderings or expand into a glassy lake—the sequestered pool reflecting the quivering trees, with the yellow leaf sleeping on its bosom, and the trout roaming fearlessly about its limpid waters; while some rustic temple or sylvan statue, grown green and dank with age, gives an air of classic sanctity to the seclusion.

These are but a few of the features of park scenery; but what most delights me is the creative talent with which the English decorate the unostentatious abodes of middle life. The rudest habitation, the most unpromising and scanty portion of land, in the hands of an Englishman of taste, becomes a little paradise. With a nicely discriminating eye, he seizes at once upon its capabilities, and pictures in his mind the future landscape. The sterile spot grows into loveliness under his hand; and yet the operations of art which produce the effect are scarcely to be perceived. The cherishing and training of some trees; the cautious pruning of others; the nice distribution of flowers and plants of tender and graceful foliage; the introduction of a green slope of velvet turf; the partial opening to a peep of blue distance, or silver gleam of water—all these are managed with a delicate tact, a pervading yet quiet assiduity, like the magic touchings with which a painter finishes up a favorite picture.

The residence of people of fortune and refinement in the country has diffused a degree of taste and elegance in rural economy that descends to the lowest class. The very laborer, with his thatched cottage and narrow slip of ground, attends to their embellishment. The trim hedge, the grass plot before the door, the little flower bed bordered with snug box, the woodbine trained up against the wall and hanging its blossoms about the lattice; the pot of flowers in the window;

the holly, providently planted about the house, to cheat winter of its dreariness, and to throw in a semblance of green summer to cheer the fireside—all these bespeak the influence of taste, flowing down from high sources, and pervading the lowest levels of the public mind. If ever love, as poets sing, delights to visit a cottage, it must be the cottage of an English peasant.

The fondness for rural life among the higher classes of the English has had a great and salutary effect upon the national character. I do not know a finer race of men than the English gentlemen. Instead of the softness and effeminacy which characterize the men of rank in most countries, they exhibit a union of elegance and strength, a robustness of frame and freshness of complexion, which I am inclined to attribute to their living so much in the open air, and pursuing so eagerly the invigorating recreations of the country. The hardy exercises produce also a healthful tone of mind and spirits, a manliness and simplicity of manners, which even the follies and dissipations of the town cannot easily pervert, and can never entirely destroy. In the country, too, the different orders of society seem to approach more freely, to be more disposed to blend and operate favorably upon each other. The distinctions between them do not appear to be so marked and impassable as in the cities. The manner in which property has been distributed into small estates and farms has established a regular gradation from the noblemen, through the classes of gentry, small landed proprietors, and substantial farmers, down to the laboring peasantry; and while it has thus banded the extremes of society together, has infused into each intermediate rank a spirit of independence. This, it must be confessed, is not so universally the case at present as it was formerly; the larger estates having, in late years of distress, absorbed the smaller, and, in some parts of the country, almost annihilated the sturdy race of small farmers. These, however, I believe are but casual breaks in the general system I have mentioned.

In rural occupation, there is nothing mean and debasing. It leads a man forth among scenes of natural grandeur and beauty; it leaves him to the workings of his own mind operated upon by the purest and most elevating of external influences. Such a man may be simple and rough, but he cannot be vulgar. The man of refinement, therefore, finds nothing revolting in an intercourse with the lower orders in rural life, as he does when he casually mingles with the lower orders of cities. He lays aside his distance and reserve, and is glad to waive the distinctions of rank, and to enter into the honest, heartfelt enjoyments of common life. Indeed, the very amusements of the country bring men more and more together; and the sound of hound and horn blend all feelings into harmony. I believe this is one great reason why the nobility and gentry are more popular among the inferior orders in England than they are in any other country; and why the latter have endured so many excessive pressures and extremities, without repining more generally at the unequal distribution of fortune and privilege.

To this mingling of cultivated and rustic society may also be attributed the rural feeling that runs through British literature—the frequent use of illustrations from rural life; those incomparable descriptions of nature, that abound in the British poets, that have continued down from "The Flower and the Leaf," of Chaucer, and have brought into our closets all the freshness and fragrance of the dewy landscape. The pastoral writers of other countries appear as if they had paid nature an occasional visit, and become acquainted with her general charms; but the British poets have lived and revelled with her—they have wooed her in her most secret haunts; they have watched her minutest caprices. A spray could not tremble in the breeze; a leaf could not rustle to the ground; a diamond drop could not patter in the stream; a fragrance could not exhale from the humble violet, nor a daisy unfold its crimson tints to the morning, but it has been noticed by these impassioned and delicate observers, and wrought up into some beautiful morality.

The effect of this devotion of elegant minds to rural occupations has been wonderful on the face of the country. A great part of the island is rather level, and would be monotonous were it not for the charms of culture, but it is studded and gemmed, as it were, with castles and palaces, and embroidered with parks and gardens. It does not abound in grand and sublime prospects, but rather in little home scenes of rural repose and sheltered quiet. Every antique farm-house and moss-grown cottage is a picture; and as the roads are continually winding, and the view is shut in by groves and hedges, the eye is delighted by a continual succession of small landscapes of captivating loveliness.

The great charm, however, of English scenery, is the moral feeling that seems to pervade it. It is associated in the mind with ideas of order, of quiet, of sober well-established principles, of hoary usage and reverend custom. Every thing seems to be the growth of ages of regular and peaceful existence. The old church of remote architecture, with its low, massive portal; its gothic tower; its windows rich with tracery and painted glass in scrupulous preservation; its stately monuments of warriors and worthies of the olden time, ancestors of the present lords of the soil; its tombstones recording successive generations of sturdy yeomanry, whose progeny still plough the same fields, and kneel at the same altar. The parsonage, a quaint irregular pile, partly antiquated, but repaired and altered in the tastes of various ages and occupants. The stile and foot-path leading from the churchyard, across pleasant fields, and along shady hedgerows, according to an immemorial right of way. The neighboring village, with its venerable cottages, its public green sheltered by trees under which the forefathers of the present race have sported. The antique family mansion, standing apart in some little rural domain, but looking down with a protecting air on the surrounding scene—all these common features of English landscape evince a calm and settled security, a hereditary transmission of home-bred virtues and local attachments, that speak deeply and touchingly for the moral character of the nation.

It is a pleasing sight of a Sunday morning, when the bell is sending its sober melody across the quiet fields, to behold the peasantry in their best finery, with ruddy faces, and modest cheerfulness, thronging tranquilly along the green lanes to church; but it is still more pleasing to see them in the evenings, gathering about their cottage doors, and appearing to exult in the humble comforts and embellishments which their own hands have spread around them.

It is this sweet home feeling, this settled repose of affection in the domestic scene that is, after all, the parent of the steadiest virtues and purest enjoyments; and I cannot close these desultory remarks better, than by quoting the words of a modern English poet, who has depicted it with remarkable felicity:

> Through each gradation, from the castled hall,
> The city dome, the villa crown'd with shade,

But chief from modest mansions numberless,
In town or hamlet, shelt'ring middle life,
Down to the cottag'd vale, and straw-roof'd shed,
This western isle has long been famed for scenes
Where bliss domestic finds a dwelling-place:
Domestic bliss, that, like a harmless dove,
(Honor and sweet endearment keeping guard,)
Can centre in a little quiet nest
All that desire would fly for through the earth;
That can, the world eluding, be itself
A world enjoy'd; that wants no witnesses
But its own sharers, and approving heaven;
That, like a flower deep hid in rock cleft,
Smiles, though 'tis looking only at the sky.*

* From a poem on the death of the Princess Charlotte, by the Reverend Rann Kennedy, A.M.

THE BROKEN HEART

I never heard
Of any true affection, but 'twas nipt
With care, that, like the caterpillar, eats
The leaves of the spring's sweetest book, the rose.
—MIDDLETON

'Tis a common practice with those who have outlived the susceptibility of early feeling, or have been brought up in the gay heartlessness of dissipated life, to laugh at all love stories, and to treat the tales of romantic passion as mere fictions of novelists and poets. My observations on human nature have induced me to think otherwise. They have convinced me that, however the surface of the character may be chilled and frozen by the cares of the world, or cultivated into mere smiles by the arts of society, still there are dormant fires lurking in the depths of the coldest bosom, which, when once enkindled, become impetuous, and are sometimes desolating in their effects. Indeed, I am a true believer in the blind deity, and go to the full extent of his doctrines. Shall I confess it?—I believe in broken hearts, and the possibility of dying of disappointed love! I do not, however, consider it a malady often fatal to my own sex; but I firmly believe that it withers down many a lovely woman into an early grave.

Man is the creature of interest and ambition. His nature leads him forth into the struggle and bustle of the world. Love is but the embellishment of his early life, or a song piped in the intervals of the acts. He seeks for fame, for fortune, for space in the world's thought, and dominion over his fellow men. But a woman's whole life is a history of the affections. The heart is her world; it is there her ambition strives for empire—it is there her avarice seeks for hidden treasures. She sends forth her sympathies on adventure; she embarks her whole soul in the traffic of affection; and if shipwrecked, her case is hopeless—for it is a bankruptcy of the heart.

To a man, the disappointment of love may occasion some bitter pangs; it wounds some feelings of tenderness—it blasts some prospects of felicity; but he is an active being—he may dissipate his thoughts in the whirl of varied occupation, or may plunge into the tide of pleasure; or, if the scene of disappointment be too full of painful associations, he can shift his abode at will, and taking, as it were, the wings of the morning, can "fly to the uttermost parts of the earth, and be at rest."

But woman's is comparatively a fixed, a secluded, and meditative life. She is more the companion of her own thoughts and feelings; and if they are turned to ministers of sorrow, where shall she look for consolation? Her lot is to be wooed and won; and if unhappy in her love, her heart is like some fortress that has been captured, and sacked, and abandoned, and left desolate.

How many bright eyes grow dim—how many soft cheeks grow pale—how many lovely forms fade away into the tomb, and none can tell the cause that blighted their loveliness. As the dove will clasp its wings to its side, and cover and conceal the arrow that is preying on its vitals—so is it the nature of woman, to hide from the world the pangs of wounded affection. The love of a delicate female is always shy and silent. Even when fortunate, she scarcely breathes it to herself; but when otherwise, she buries it in the recesses of her bosom, and there lets it cower and brood among the ruins of her peace. With her, the desire of her heart has failed—the great charm of existence is at an end. She neglects all the cheerful exercises which gladden the spirits, quicken the pulses, and send the tide of life in healthful currents through the veins. Her rest is broken—the sweet refreshment of sleep is poisoned by melancholy dreams—"dry sorrow drinks her blood," until her enfeebled frame sinks under the slightest external injury. Look for her, after a little while, and you find friendship weeping over her untimely grave, and wondering that one, who but lately glowed with all the radiance of health and beauty, should so speedily be brought down to "darkness and the worm." You will be told of some wintry chill, some casual indisposition, that laid her low—but no one knows of the mental malady which previously sapped her strength, and made her so easy a prey to the spoiler.

She is like some tender tree, the pride and beauty of the grove; graceful in its form, bright in its foliage, but with the worm preying at its heart. We find it suddenly withering, when it should be most fresh and luxuriant. We see it drooping its branches to the earth, and shedding leaf by leaf, until, wasted and perished away, it falls even in the stillness of the forest; and as we muse over the beautiful ruin, we strive in vain to recollect the blast or thunderbolt that could have smitten it with decay.

I have seen many instances of women running to waste and self-neglect, and disappearing gradually from the earth, almost as if they had been exhaled to heaven; and have repeatedly fancied that I could trace their deaths through the various declensions of consumption, cold, debility, languor, melancholy, until I reached the first symptom of disappointed love. But an instance of the kind was lately told to me; the circumstances are well known in the country where they happened, and I shall but give them in the manner in which they were related.

Every one must recollect the tragical story of young E—, the Irish patriot; it was too touching to be soon forgotten. During the troubles in Ireland, he was tried, condemned, and executed, on a charge of treason. His fate made a deep impression on public sympathy. He was so young—so intelligent—so generous—so brave—so every thing that we are apt to like in a young man. His conduct under trial, too, was so lofty and intrepid. The noble indignation with which he repelled the charge of treason against his country—the eloquent vindication of his name—and his pathetic appeal to posterity, in the hopeless hour of condemnation—all these entered deeply into every generous bosom, and even his enemies lamented the stern policy that dictated his execution.

But there was one heart whose anguish it would be impossible to describe. In happier days and fairer fortunes, he had won the affections of a beautiful and interesting girl, the daughter of a late celebrated Irish barrister. She loved him with the disinterested fervor of a woman's first and early love. When every worldly maxim arrayed itself against him; when blasted in fortune, and disgrace and danger darkened around his name, she loved him the more ardently for his very sufferings. If, then, his fate could awaken the sympathy even of his foes, what must have been the agony of her, whose whole soul was occupied by his image? Let those tell who have had the portals of the tomb suddenly closed between them and the being they most loved on earth—who have sat at its threshold, as one shut out in a cold and lonely world, whence all that was most lovely and loving had departed.

But then the horrors of such a grave!—so frightful, so dishonored! There was nothing for memory to dwell on that could soothe the pang of separation—none of those tender though melancholy circumstances which endear the parting scene—nothing to melt sorrow into those blessed tears, sent like the dews of heaven, to revive the heart in the parting hour of anguish.

To render her widowed situation more desolate, she had incurred her father's displeasure by her unfortunate attachment, and was an exile from the parental roof. But could the sympathy and kind offices of friends have reached a spirit so shocked and driven in by horror, she would have experienced no want of consolation, for the Irish are a people of quick and generous sensibilities. The most delicate and cherishing attentions were paid her by families of wealth and distinction. She was led into society, and they tried by all kinds of occupation and amusement to dissipate her grief, and wean her from the tragical story of her loves. But it was all in vain. There are some strokes of calamity that scathe and scorch the soul—which penetrate to the vital seat of happiness—and blast it, never again to put forth bud or blossom. She never objected to frequent the haunts of pleasure, but was as much alone there as in the depths of solitude; walking about in a sad reverie, apparently unconscious of the world around her. She carried with her an inward woe that mocked at all the blandishments of friendship, and "heeded not the song of the charmer, charm he never so wisely."

The person who told me her story had seen her at a masquerade. There can be no exhibition of far-gone wretchedness more striking and painful than to meet it in such a scene. To find it wandering like a spectre, lonely and joyless, where all around is gay—to see it dressed out in the trappings of mirth, and looking so wan and woe-begone, as if it had tried in vain to cheat the poor heart into momentary forgetfulness of sorrow. After strolling through the splendid rooms and giddy crowd with an air of utter abstraction, she sat herself down on the steps of an orchestra, and, looking about for some time with a vacant air, that showed her insensibility to the garish scene, she began, with the capriciousness of a sickly heart, to warble a little plaintive air. She had an exquisite voice; but on this occasion it was so simple, so touching, it breathed forth such a soul of wretchedness—that she drew a crowd, mute and silent, around her and melted every one into tears.

The story of one so true and tender could not but excite great interest in a country remarkable for enthusiasm. It completely won the heart of a brave officer, who paid his addresses to her, and thought that one so true to the dead, could not but prove affectionate to the living. She declined his attentions, for her thoughts were irrevocably engrossed by the memory of her former lover. He, however, persisted in his suit. He solicited not her tenderness, but her esteem. He was assisted by her conviction of his worth, and her sense of her own destitute and dependent situation, for she was existing on the kindness of friends. In a word, he at length succeeded in gaining her hand, though with the solemn assurance that her heart was unalterably another's.

He took her with him to Sicily, hoping that a change of scene might wear out the remembrance of early woes. She was an amiable and exemplary wife, and made an effort to be a happy one; but nothing could cure the silent and devouring melancholy that had entered into her very soul. She wasted away in a slow but hopeless decline, and at length sunk into the grave, the victim of a broken heart.

It was on her that Moore, the distinguished Irish poet, composed the following lines:

She is far from the land where her young hero sleeps,
   And lovers around her are sighing:
But coldly she turns from their gaze, and weeps,
   For her heart in his grave is lying.

She sings the wild song of her dear native plains,
   Every note which he lov'd awaking—
Ah! little they think, who delight in her strains,
   How the heart of the minstrel is breaking!

He had liv'd for his love—for his country he died,
   They were all that to life had entwin'd him—
Nor soon shall the tears of his country be dried,
   Nor long will his love stay behind him!

Oh! make her a grave where the sunbeams rest,
    When they promise a glorious morrow;
They'll shine o'er her sleep, like a smile from the west,
    From her own lov'd island of sorrow!

THE ART OF BOOK-MAKING

> If that severe doom of Synesius be true, "It is a greater offence to steal dead men's labor, than their clothes," what shall become of most writers?
>
> —Burton's Anatomy of Melancholy

I have often wondered at the extreme fecundity of the press, and how it comes to pass that so many heads, on which nature seems to have inflicted the curse of barrenness, should teem with voluminous productions. As a man travels on, however, in the journey of life, his objects of wonder daily diminish, and he is continually finding out some very simple cause for some great matter of marvel. Thus have I chanced, in my peregrinations about this great metropolis, to blunder upon a scene which unfolded to me some of the mysteries of the book-making craft, and at once put an end to my astonishment.

I was one summer's day loitering through the great saloons of the British Museum, with that listlessness with which one is apt to saunter about a museum in warm weather; sometimes lolling over the glass cases of minerals, sometimes studying the hieroglyphics on an Egyptian mummy, and some times trying, with nearly equal success, to comprehend the allegorical paintings on the lofty ceilings. Whilst I was gazing about in this idle way, my attention was attracted to a distant door, at the end of a suite of apartments. It was closed, but every now and then it would open, and some strange favored being, generally clothed in black, would steal forth and glide through the rooms without noticing any of the surrounding objects. There was an air of mystery about this that piqued my languid curiosity, and I determined to attempt the passage of that strait, and to explore the unknown regions beyond. The door yielded to my hand, with all that facility with which the portals of enchanted castles yield to the adventurous knight-errant. I found myself in a spacious chamber, surrounded with great cases of venerable books. Above the cases, and just under the cornice, were arranged a great number of black-looking portraits of ancient authors.

About the room were placed long tables, with stands for reading and writing, at which sat many pale, studious personages, poring intently over dusty volumes, rummaging among mouldy manuscripts, and taking copious notes of their contents. A hushed stillness reigned through this mysterious apartment, excepting that you might hear the racing of pens over sheets of paper, or occasionally the deep sigh of one of these sages as he shifted his position to turn over the page of an old folio; doubtless arising from that hollowness and flatulency incident to learned research.

Now and then one of these personages would write something on a small slip of paper and ring a bell, whereupon a familiar would appear, take the paper in profound silence, glide out of the room, and return shortly loaded with ponderous tomes, upon which the other would fall, tooth and nail, with famished voracity. I had no longer a doubt that I had happened upon a body of Magi, deeply engaged in the study of occult sciences. The scene reminded me of an old Arabian tale, of a philosopher shut up in an enchanted library, in the bosom of a mountain, which opened only once a year; where he made the spirits of the place bring him books of all kinds of dark knowledge, so that at the end of the year, when the magic portal once more swung open on its hinges, he issued forth so versed in forbidden lore, as to be able to soar above the heads of the multitude, and to control the powers of nature.

My curiosity being now fully aroused, I whispered to one of the familiars, as he was about to leave the room, and begged an interpretation of the strange scene before me. A few words were sufficient for the purpose. I found that these mysterious personages, whom I had mistaken for Magi, were principally authors, and were in the very act of manufacturing books. I was, in fact, in the reading-room of the great British Library, an immense collection of volumes of all ages and languages, many of which are now forgotten, and most of which are seldom read: one of these sequestered pools of obsolete literature to which modern authors repair, and draw buckets full of classic lore, or "pure English, undefiled," wherewith to swell their own scanty rills of thought.

Being now in possession of the secret, I sat down in a corner, and watched the process of this book manufactory. I noticed one lean, bilious-looking wight, who sought none but the most worm-eaten volumes, printed in black letter. He was evidently constructing some work of profound erudition, that would be purchased by every man who wished to be thought learned, placed upon a conspicuous shelf of his library, or laid open upon his table—but never read. I observed him, now and then, draw a large fragment of biscuit out of his pocket, and gnaw; whether it was his dinner, or whether he was endeavoring to keep off that exhaustion of the stomach, produced by much pondering over dry works, I leave to harder students than myself to determine.

There was one dapper little gentleman in bright-colored clothes, with a chirping, gossiping expression of countenance, who had all the appearance of an author on good terms with his bookseller. After considering him attentively, I recognized in him a diligent getter-up of miscellaneous works, which bustled off well with the trade. I was curious to see how he manufactured his wares. He made more stir and show of business than any of the others; dipping into various books, fluttering over the leaves of manuscripts, taking a morsel out of one, a morsel out of another, line upon line, precept upon precept, here a little and there a little. The contents of his book seemed to be as heterogeneous as those of the witches' cauldron in Macbeth. It was here a finger and there a thumb, toe of frog and blind worm's sting, with his own gossip poured in like "baboon's blood," to make the medley "slab and good."

After all, thought I, may not this pilfering disposition be implanted in authors for wise purposes? may it not be the way in which Providence has taken care that the seeds of knowledge and wisdom shall be preserved from age to age, in spite of the inevitable decay of the works in which they were first produced? We see that Nature has wisely, though whimsically, provided for the conveyance of seeds from clime to clime, in the maws of certain birds; so that animals, which, in themselves, are little better than carrion, and apparently the lawless plunderers of the orchard and the corn field, are, in fact, nature's carriers to disperse and perpetuate her blessings. In like manner, the beauties and fine thoughts of ancient and obsolete authors are caught up by these flights of predatory writers, and cast forth, again to flourish and bear fruit in a remote and distant tract of time. Many of their works, also, undergo a kind of metempsychosis and spring up under new forms. What was formerly a ponderous history, revives in the shape of a romance—an old legend changes into a modern play—and a sober philosophical treatise furnishes the body for a whole series of bouncing and sparkling essays. Thus it is in the clearing of our American woodlands; where we burn down a forest of stately pines, a progeny of dwarf oaks start up in their place; and we never see the prostrate trunk of a tree mouldering into soil, but it gives birth to a whole tribe of fungi.

Let us not then, lament over the decay and oblivion into which ancient writers descend; they do but submit to the great law of Nature, which declares that all sublunary shapes of matter shall be limited in their duration, but which decrees also that their element shall never perish. Generation after generation, both in animal and vegetable life, passes away, but the vital principle is transmitted to posterity, and the species continue to flourish. Thus also do authors beget authors, and having produced a numerous progeny, in a good old age they sleep with their fathers; that is to say, with the authors who preceded them—and from whom they had stolen.

Whilst I was indulging in these rambling fancies I had leaned my head against a pile of reverend folios. Whether it was owing to the soporific emanations for these works, or to the profound quiet of the room; or to the lassitude arising from much wandering, or to an unlucky habit of napping at improper times and places, with which I am grievously afflicted, so it was that I fell into a doze. Still, however, my imagination continued busy, and indeed the same scene continued before my mind's eye, only a little changed in some of the details. I dreamt that the chamber was still decorated with the portraits of ancient authors, but that the number was increased. The long tables had disappeared, and, in place of the sage Magi, I beheld a ragged, threadbare throng, such as may be seen plying about the great repository of cast-off clothes, Monmouth Street. Whenever they seized upon a book, by one of those incongruities common to dreams, methought it turned into a garment of foreign or antique fashion, with which they proceeded to equip themselves. I noticed, however, that no one pretended to clothe himself from any particular suit, but took a sleeve from one, a cape from another, a skirt from a third, thus decking himself out piecemeal, while some of his original rags would peep out from among his borrowed finery.

There was a portly, rosy, well-fed parson whom I observed ogling several mouldy polemical writers through an eyeglass. He soon contrived to slip on the voluminous mantle of one of the old fathers, and having purloined the gray beard of another, endeavored to look exceedingly wise; but the smirking commonplace of his countenance set at naught all the trappings of wisdom. One sickly-looking gentleman was busied embroidering a very flimsy garment with gold thread drawn out of several old court-dresses of the reign of Queen Elizabeth. Another had trimmed himself magnificently from an illuminated manuscript, had stuck a nosegay in his bosom, culled from "The Paradise of Dainty Devices," and having put Sir Philip Sidney's hat on one side of his head, strutted off with an exquisite air of vulgar elegance. A third, who was but of puny dimensions, had bolstered himself out bravely with the spoils from several obscure tracts of philosophy, so that he had a very imposing front, but he was lamentably tattered in rear, and I perceived that he had patched his small clothes with scraps of parchment from a Latin author.

There were some well-dressed gentlemen, it is true, who only helped themselves to a gem or so, which sparkled among their own ornaments, without eclipsing them. Some, too, seemed to contemplate the costumes of the old writers, merely to imbibe their principles of taste, and to catch their air and spirit; but I grieve to say, that too many were apt to array themselves, from top to toe, in the patchwork manner I have mentioned. I shall not omit to speak of one genius in drab breeches and gaiters, and an Arcadian hat, who had a violent propensity to the pastoral, but whose rural wanderings had been confined to the classic haunts of Primrose Hill, and the solitudes of the Regent's Park. He had decked himself in wreaths and ribbons from all the old pastoral poets, and, hanging his head on one side, went about with a fantastical, lackadaisical air, "babbling about green fields." But the personage that most struck my attention was a pragmatical old gentleman in clerical robes, with a remarkably large and square but bald head. He entered the room wheezing and puffing, elbowed his way through the throng with a look of sturdy self-confidence, and having laid hands upon a thick

Greek quarto, clapped it upon his head, and swept majestically away in a formidable frizzled wig.

In the height of this literary masquerade, a cry suddenly resounded from every side, of "Thieves! thieves!" I looked, and lo! the portraits about the walls became animated! The old authors thrust out, first a head, then a shoulder, from the canvas, looked down curiously for an instant upon the motley throng, and then descended, with fury in their eyes, to claim their rifled property. The scene of scampering and hubbub that ensued baffles all description. The unhappy culprits endeavored in vain to escape with their plunder. On one side might be seen half a dozen old monks, stripping a modern professor; on another, there was sad devastation carried into the ranks of modern dramatic writers. Beaumont and Fletcher, side by side, raged round the field like Castor and Pollux, and sturdy Ben Jonson enacted more wonders than when a volunteer with the army in Flanders. As to the dapper little compiler of farragoes mentioned some time since, he had arrayed himself in as many patches and colors as harlequin, and there was as fierce a contention of claimants about him, as about the dead body of Patroclus. I was grieved to see many men, to whom I had been accustomed to look up with awe and reverence, fain to steal off with scarce a rag to cover their nakedness. Just then my eye was caught by the pragmatical old gentleman in the Greek grizzled wig, who was scrambling away in sore affright with half a score of authors in full cry after him. They were close upon his haunches; in a twinkling off went his wig; at every turn some strip of raiment was peeled away, until in a few moments, from his domineering pomp, he shrunk into a little, pursy, "chopp'd bald shot," and made his exit with only a few tags and rags fluttering at his back.

There was something so ludicrous in the catastrophe of this learned Theban that I burst into an immoderate fit of laughter, which broke the whole illusion. The tumult and the scuffle were at an end. The chamber resumed its usual appearance. The old authors shrunk back into their picture frames and hung in shadowy solemnity along the walls. In short, I found myself wide awake in my corner, with the whole assemblage of hookworms gazing at me with astonishment. Nothing of the dream had been real but my burst of laughter, a sound never before heard in that grave sanctuary, and so abhorrent to the ears of wisdom, as to electrify the fraternity.

The librarian now stepped up to me, and demanded whether I had a card of admission. At first I did not comprehend him, but I soon found that the library was a kind of literary "preserve," subject to game laws, and that no one must presume to hunt there without special license and permission. In a word, I stood convicted of being an arrant poacher, and was glad to make a precipitate retreat, lest I should have a whole pack of authors let loose upon me.

A ROYAL POET

Though your body be confin'd
  And soft love a prisoner bound,
Yet the beauty of your mind
  Neither check nor chain hath found.
Look out nobly, then, and dare
Even the fetters that you wear.
—FLETCHER

On a soft sunny morning in the genial month of May, I made an excursion to Windsor Castle. It is a place full of storied and poetical associations. The very external aspect of the proud old pile is enough to inspire high thought. It rears its irregular walls and massive towers, like a mural crown around the brow of a lofty ridge, waves its royal banner in the clouds, and looks down with a lordly air upon the surrounding world.

On this morning, the weather was of that voluptuous vernal kind which calls forth all the latent romance of a man's temperament, filling his mind with music, and disposing him to quote poetry and dream of beauty. In wandering through the magnificent saloons and long echoing galleries of the castle, I passed with indifference by whole rows of portraits of warriors and statesmen, but lingered in the chamber where hang the likenesses of the beauties which graced the gay court of Charles the Second; and as I gazed upon them, depicted with amorous, half-dishevelled tresses, and the sleepy eye of love, I blessed the pencil of Sir Peter Lely, which had thus enabled me to bask in the reflected rays of beauty. In traversing also the "large green courts," with sunshine beaming on the gray walls and glancing along the velvet turf, my mind was engrossed with the image of the tender, the gallant, but hapless Surrey, and his account of his loiterings about them in his stripling days, when enamoured of the Lady Geraldine—

With eyes cast up unto the maiden's tower,
With easie sighs, such as men draw in love.

In this mood of mere poetical susceptibility, I visited the ancient keep of the castle, where James the First of Scotland, the pride and theme of Scottish poets and historians, was for many years of his youth detained a prisoner of state. It is a large gray tower that has stood the brunt of ages, and is still in good preservation. It stands on a mound which elevates it above the other parts of the castle, and a great flight of steps leads to the interior. In the armory, a gothic hall furnished with weapons of various kinds and ages, I was shown a coat of armor hanging against the wall, which had once belonged to James. Hence I was conducted up a staircase to a suite of apartments of faded magnificence, hung with storied tapestry, which formed his prison, and the scene of that passionate and fanciful amour, which has woven into the web of his story the magical hues of poetry and fiction.

The whole history of this amiable but unfortunate prince is highly romantic. At the tender age of eleven, he was sent from home by his father, Robert III, and destined for the French court, to be reared under the eye of the French monarch, secure from the treachery and danger that surrounded the royal house of Scotland. It was his mishap in the course of his voyage to fall into the hands of the English, and he was detained prisoner by Henry IV, notwithstanding that a truce existed between the two countries.

The intelligence of his capture, coming in the train of many sorrows and disasters, proved fatal to his unhappy father. "The news," we are told, "was brought to him while at supper, and did so overwhelm him with grief that he was almost ready to give up the ghost into the hands of the servants that attended him. But being carried to his bedchamber, he abstained from all food, and in three days died of hunger and grief at Rothesay."*

James was detained in captivity above eighteen years; but, though deprived of personal liberty, he was treated with the respect due to his rank. Care was taken to instruct him in all the branches of useful knowledge cultivated at that period, and to give him those mental and personal accomplishments deemed proper for a prince. Perhaps in this respect his imprisonment was an advantage, as it enabled him to apply himself the more exclusively to his improvement, and quietly to imbibe

* Buchanan

that rich fund of knowledge and to cherish those elegant tastes which have given such a lustre to his memory. The picture drawn of him in early life by the Scottish historians is highly captivating, and seems rather the description of a hero of romance than of a character in real history. He was well learnt, we are told, "to fight with the sword, to joust, to tourney, to wrestle, to sing and dance; he was an expert mediciner, right crafty in playing both of lute and harp, and sundry other instruments of music, and was expert in grammar, oratory, and poetry."*

With this combination of manly and delicate accomplishments, fitting him to shine both in active and elegant life, and calculated to give him an intense relish for joyous existence, it must have been a severe trial, in an age of bustle and chivalry, to pass the spring-time of his years in monotonous captivity. It was the good fortune of James, however, to be gifted with a powerful poetic fancy, and to be visited in his prison by the choicest inspirations of the muse. Some minds corrode and grow inactive, under the loss of personal liberty; others grow morbid and irritable; but it is the nature of the poet to become tender and imaginative in the loneliness of confinement. He banquets upon the honey of his own thoughts, and, like the captive bird, pours forth his soul in melody.

Have you not seen the nightingale,
A pilgrim coop'd into a cage,
How doth she chant her wonted tale,
In that her lonely hermitage!
Even there her charming melody doth prove
That all her boughs are trees, her cage a grove.†

Indeed, it is the divine attribute of the imagination, that it is irrepressible, unconfinable—that when the real world is shut out, it can create a world for itself, and with a necromantic power, can conjure up glorious shapes and forms and brilliant visions, to make solitude populous, and irradiate the gloom of the dungeon. Such was the world of pomp and pageant that lived round Tasso in his dismal cell at Ferrara, when he conceived the splendid scenes of his Jerusalem; and we may

* Ballenden's translation of Hector Boyce

† Roger L'Estrange

consider "The King's Quair"* composed by James during his captivity at Windsor, as another of those beautiful breakings forth of the soul from the restraint and gloom of the prison-house.

The subject of the poem is his love for the lady Jane Beaufort, daughter of the Earl of Somerset, and a princess of the blood royal of England, of whom he became enamoured in the course of his captivity. What gives it a peculiar value is that it may be considered a transcript of the royal bard's true feelings, and the story of his real loves and fortunes. It is not often that sovereigns write poetry or that poets deal in fact. It is gratifying to the pride of a common man, to find a monarch thus suing, as it were, for admission into his closet, and seeking to win his favor by administering to his pleasures. It is a proof of the honest equality of intellectual competition, which strips off all the trappings of factitious dignity, brings the candidate down to a level with his fellow men, and obliges him to depend on his own native powers for distinction. It is curious, too, to get at the history of a monarch's heart, and to find the simple affections of human nature throbbing under the ermine. But James had learnt to be a poet before he was a king; he was schooled in adversity, and reared in the company of his own thoughts. Monarchs have seldom time to parley with their hearts or to meditate their minds into poetry; and had James been brought up amidst the adulation and gaiety of a court, we should never, in all probability, have had such a poem as the Quair.

I have been particularly interested by those parts of the poem which breathe his immediate thoughts concerning his situation, or which are connected with the apartment in the tower. They have thus a personal and local charm, and are given with such circumstantial truth as to make the reader present with the captive in his prison and the companion of his meditations.

Such is the account which he gives of his weariness of spirit, and of the incident which first suggested the idea of writing the poem. It was the still mid-watch of a clear moonlight night; the stars, he says, were twinkling as fire in the high vault of heaven, and "Cynthia rinsing her golden locks in Aquarius." He lay in bed wakeful and restless, and took a book to beguile the tedious hours. The book he chose was Boetius'

* Quair, an old term for book

Consolations of Philosophy, a work popular among the writers of that day, and which had been translated by his great prototype, Chaucer. From the high eulogium in which he indulges, it is evident this was one of his favorite volumes while in prison; and indeed it is an admirable text-book for meditation under adversity. It is the legacy of a noble and enduring spirit, purified by sorrow and suffering, bequeathing to its successors in calamity the maxims of sweet morality, and the trains of eloquent but simple reasoning, by which it was enabled to bear up against the various ills of life. It is a talisman, which the unfortunate may treasure up in his bosom, or, like the good King James, lay upon his nightly pillow.

After closing the volume he turns its contents over in his mind, and gradually falls into a fit of musing on the fickleness of fortune, the vicissitudes of his own life, and the evils that had overtaken him even in his tender youth. Suddenly he hears the bell ringing to matins, but its sound, chiming in with his melancholy fancies, seems to him like a voice exhorting him to write his story. In the spirit of poetic errantry he determines to comply with this intimation; he therefore takes pen in hand, makes with it a sign of the cross to implore a benediction, and sallies forth into the fairy-land of poetry. There is something extremely fanciful in all this, and it is interesting as furnishing a striking and beautiful instance of the simple manner in which whole trains of poetical thought are sometimes awakened and literary enterprises suggested to the mind.

In the course of his poem, he more than once bewails the peculiar hardness of his fate, thus doomed to lonely and inactive life, and shut up from the freedom and pleasure of the world in which the meanest animal indulges unrestrained. There is a sweetness, however, in his very complaints; they are the lamentations of an amiable and social spirit at being denied the indulgence of its kind and generous propensities; there is nothing in them harsh nor exaggerated; they flow with a natural and touching pathos, and are perhaps rendered more touching by their simple brevity. They contrast finely with those elaborate and iterated repinings which we sometimes meet with in poetry the effusions of morbid minds sickening under miseries of their own creating, and venting their bitterness upon an unoffending world. James speaks of his privations with acute sensibility, but having mentioned them passes on, as if his manly mind disdained to brood over unavoidable calamities.

When such a spirit breaks forth into complaint, however brief, we are aware how great must be the suffering that extorts the murmur. We sympathize with James, a romantic, active, and accomplished prince, cut off in the lustihood of youth from all the enterprise, the noble uses, and vigorous delights of life, as we do with Milton, alive to all the beauties of nature and glories of art, when he breathes forth brief but deep-toned lamentations over his perpetual blindness.

Had not James evinced a deficiency of poetic artifice, we might almost have suspected that these lowerings of gloomy reflection were meant as preparative to the brightest scene of his story, and to contrast with that refulgence of light and loveliness, that exhilarating accompaniment of bird and song, and foliage and flower, and all the revel of, the year with which he ushers in the lady of his heart. It is this scene, in particular, which throws all the magic of romance about the old castle keep. He had risen, he says, at daybreak, according to custom, to escape from the dreary meditations of a sleepless pillow. "Bewailing in his chamber thus alone," despairing of all joy and remedy, "fortired of thought, and woebegone," he had wandered to the window to indulge the captive's miserable solace, of gazing wistfully upon the world from which he is excluded. The window looked forth upon a small garden which lay at the foot of the tower. It was a quiet, sheltered spot, adorned with arbors and green alleys, and protected from the passing gaze by trees and hawthorn hedges.

Now was there made fast by the tower's wall,
 A garden faire, and in the corners set
An arbour green with wandis long and small
 Railed about, and so with leaves beset
Was all the place and hawthorn hedges knet,
 That lyf* was none, walkyng there forbye,
 That might within scarce any wight espye.

So thick the branches and the leves grene,
 Beshaded all the alleys that there were,
And midst of every arbour might be seen
 The sharpe, grene, swete juniper,

* Lyf, person

Growing so fair, with branches here and there,
That as it seemed to a lyf without,
The boughs did spread the arbour all about.

And on the small grene twistis* set
The lytel swete nightingales, and sung
So loud and clear, the hymnis consecrate
Of lovis use, now soft, now loud among,
That all the garden and the wallis rung
Right of their song— †

It was the month of May, when every thing was in bloom, and he interprets the song of the nightingale into the language of his enamoured feeling:

Worship, all ye that lovers be, this May,
For of your bliss the kalends are begun,
And sing with us, away, winter, away.
Come, summer, come, the sweet season and sun.

As he gazes on the scene, and listens to the notes of the birds, he gradually relapses into one of those tender and undefinable reveries, which fill the youthful bosom in this delicious season. He wonders what this love may be of which he has so often read, and which thus seems breathed forth in the quickening breath of May, and melting all nature into ecstasy and song. If it really be so great a felicity, and if it be a boon thus generally dispensed to the most insignificant beings, why is he alone cut off from its enjoyments?

Oft would I think, O Lord, what may this be,
That love is of such noble myght and kynde?
Loving his folke, and such prosperitee,
Is it of him, as we in books do find;
May he oure hertes setten‡ and unbynd:

* Twistis, small boughs or twigs
† Note—The language of the quotations is generally modernized.
‡ Setten, incline

Hath he upon oure hertes such maistrye?
Or is all this but feynit fantasye?
For giff he be of so grete excellence
    That he of every wight hath care and charge,
What have I gilt* to him, or done offense,
    That I am thral'd, and birdis go at large?

In the midst of his musing, as he casts his eye downward, he beholds "the fairest and the freshest young floure" that ever he had seen. It is the lovely Lady Jane, walking in the garden to enjoy the beauty of that "fresh May morrowe." Breaking thus suddenly upon his sight in a moment of loneliness and excited susceptibility, she at once captivates the fancy of the romantic prince, and becomes the object of his wandering wishes, the sovereign of his ideal world.

There is, in this charming scene, an evident resemblance to the early part of Chaucer's Knight's Tale, where Palamon and Arcite fall in love with Emilia, whom they see walking in the garden of their prison. Perhaps the similarity of the actual fact to the incident which he had read in Chaucer may have induced James to dwell on it in his poem. His description of the Lady Jane is given in the picturesque and minute manner of his master, and, being doubtless taken from the life, is a perfect portrait of a beauty of that day. He dwells, with the fondness of a lover, on every article of her apparel, from the net of pearl, splendent with emeralds and sapphires, that confined her golden hair, even to the "goodly chaine of small orfeverye"† about her neck, whereby there hung a ruby in shape of a heart, that seemed, he says, like a spark of fire burning upon her white bosom. Her dress of white tissue was looped up to enable her to walk with more freedom. She was accompanied by two female attendants, and about her sported a little hound decorated with bells, probably the small Italian hound of exquisite symmetry which was a parlor favorite and pet among the fashionable dames of ancient times. James closes his description by a burst of general eulogium:

In her was youth, beauty, with humble port,
    Bounty, richesse, and womanly feature;

* Gilt, what injury have I done, etc.

† Wrought gold

God better knows than my pen can report,
   Wisdom, largesse,* estate,† and cunning‡ sure.
In every point so guided her measure,
   In word, in deed, in shape, in countenance,
   That nature might no more her child advance.

The departure of the Lady Jane from the garden puts an end to this transient riot of the heart. With her departs the amorous illusion that had shed a temporary charm over the scene of his captivity, and he relapses into loneliness, now rendered tenfold more intolerable by this passing beam of unattainable beauty. Through the long and weary day he repines at his unhappy lot, and when evening approaches, and Phoebus, as he beautifully expresses it, had "bade farewell to every leaf and flower," he still lingers at the window, and, laying his head upon the cold stone, gives vent to a mingled flow of love and sorrow, until, gradually lulled by the mute melancholy of the twilight hour, he lapses, "half-sleeping, half swoon," into a vision which occupies the remainder of the poem, and in which is allegorically shadowed out the history of his passion.

When he wakes from his trance, he rises from his stony pillow, and, pacing his apartment, full of dreary reflections, questions his spirit, whither it has been wandering; whether, indeed, all that has passed before his dreaming fancy has been conjured up by preceding circumstances, or whether it is a vision intended to comfort and assure him in his despondency. If the latter, he prays that some token may be sent to confirm the promise of happier days, given him in his slumbers. Suddenly, a turtle dove of the purest whiteness comes flying in at the window, and alights upon his hand, bearing in her bill a branch of red gilliflower, on the leaves of which is written, in letters of gold, the following sentence:

Awake! Awake! I bring, lover, I bring
   The newis glad, that blissful is and sure
Of thy comfort; now laugh, and play, and sing,
   For in the heaven decretit is thy cure.

* Largesse, bounty
† Estate, dignity
‡ Cunning, discretion

He receives the branch with mingled hope and dread; reads it with rapture; and this he says was the first token of his succeeding happiness. Whether this is a mere poetic fiction, or whether the Lady Jane did actually send him a token of her favor in this romantic way, remains to be determined according to the fate or fancy of the reader. He concludes his poem by intimating that the promise conveyed in the vision and by the flower, is fulfilled by his being restored to liberty, and made happy in the possession of the sovereign of his heart.

Such is the poetical account given by James of his love adventures in Windsor Castle. How much of it is absolute fact, and how much the embellishment of fancy, it is fruitless to conjecture; let us not, however, reject every romantic incident as incompatible with real life, but let us sometimes take a poet at his word. I have noticed merely those parts of the poem immediately connected with the tower, and have passed over a large part which was in the allegorical vein, so much cultivated at that day. The language, of course, is quaint and antiquated, so that the beauty of many of its golden phrases will scarcely be perceived at the present day, but it is impossible not to be charmed with the genuine sentiment, the delightful artlessness and urbanity, which prevail throughout it. The descriptions of nature too, with which it is embellished, are given with a truth, a discrimination, and a freshness, worthy of the most cultivated periods of the art.

As an amatory poem, it is edifying, in these days of coarser thinking, to notice the nature, refinement, and exquisite delicacy which pervade it; banishing every gross thought, or immodest expression, and presenting female loveliness, clothed in all its chivalrous attributes of almost supernatural purity and grace.

James flourished nearly about the time of Chaucer and Gower, and was evidently an admirer and studier of their writings. Indeed, in one of his stanzas he acknowledges them as his masters; and in some parts of his poem we find traces of similarity to their productions, more especially to those of Chaucer. There are always, however, general features of resemblance in the works of contemporary authors, which are not so much borrowed from each other as from the times. Writers, like bees, toll their sweets in the wide world; they incorporate with their own conceptions, the anecdotes and thoughts current in society; and thus each generation has some features in common, characteristic of the age in which it lives.

James belongs to one of the most brilliant eras of our literary history, and establishes the claims of his country to a participation in its primitive honors. Whilst a small cluster of English writers are constantly cited as the fathers of our verse, the name of their great Scottish compeer is apt to be passed over in silence; but he is evidently worthy of being enrolled in that little constellation of remote but never-failing luminaries who shine in the highest firmament of literature, and who, like morning stars, sang together at the bright dawning of British poesy.

Such of my readers as may not be familiar with Scottish history (though the manner in which it has of late been woven with captivating fiction has made it a universal study) may be curious to learn something of the subsequent history of James and the fortunes of his love. His passion for the Lady Jane, as it was the solace of his captivity, so it facilitated his release, it being imagined by the Court that a connection with the blood royal of England would attach him to its own interests. He was ultimately restored to his liberty and crown, having previously espoused the Lady Jane, who accompanied him to Scotland, and made him a most tender and devoted wife.

He found his kingdom in great confusion, the feudal chieftains having taken advantage of the troubles and irregularities of a long interregnum, to strengthen themselves in their possessions, and place themselves above the power of the laws. James sought to found the basis of his power in the affections of his people. He attached the lower orders to him by the reformation of abuses, the temperate and equable administration of justice, the encouragement of the arts of peace, and the promotion of every thing that could diffuse comfort, competency, and innocent enjoyment through the humblest ranks of society. He mingled occasionally among the common people in disguise; visited their firesides; entered into their cares, their pursuits, and their amusements; informed himself of the mechanical arts, and how they could best be patronized and improved; and was thus an all-pervading spirit, watching with a benevolent eye over the meanest of his subjects. Having in this generous manner made himself strong in the hearts of the common people, he turned himself to curb the power of the factious nobility; to strip them of those dangerous immunities which they had usurped; to punish such as had been guilty of flagrant offences; and to bring the whole into proper obedience to the Crown. For some time they bore this with outward submission, but with secret impatience and brooding resentment. A conspiracy was at length formed against his life, at the head of which was his own uncle, Robert Stewart, Earl of Athol, who, being too old himself for the perpetration of the deed of blood, instigated his grandson, Sir Robert Stewart, together with Sir Robert Graham, and others of less note, to commit the deed. They broke into his bedchamber at the Dominican convent near Perth, where he was residing, and barbarously murdered him by oft-repeated wounds. His faithful queen, rushing to throw her tender body between him and the sword, was twice wounded in the ineffectual attempt to shield him from the assassin; and it was not until she had been forcibly torn from his person, that the murder was accomplished.

It was the recollection of this romantic tale of former times, and of the golden little poem, which had its birthplace in this tower, that made me visit the old pile with more than common interest. The suit of armor hanging up in the hall, richly gilt and embellished, as if to figure in the tourney, brought the image of the gallant and romantic prince vividly before my imagination. I paced the deserted chambers where he had composed his poem; I leaned upon the window, and endeavored to persuade myself it was the very one where he had been visited by his vision; I looked out upon the spot where he had first seen the Lady Jane. It was the same genial and joyous month; the birds were again vying with each other in strains of liquid melody; every thing was bursting into vegetation, and budding forth the tender promise of the year. Time, which delights to obliterate the sterner memorials of human pride, seems to have passed lightly over this little scene of poetry and love, and to have withheld his desolating hand. Several centuries have gone by, yet the garden still flourishes at the foot of the tower. It occupies what was once the moat of the keep; and, though some parts have been separated by dividing walls, yet others have still their arbors and shaded walks, as in the days of James, and the whole is sheltered, blooming, and retired. There is a charm about the spot that has been printed by the footsteps of departed beauty, and consecrated by the inspirations of the poet, which is heightened, rather than impaired, by the lapse of ages. It is, indeed, the gift of poetry, to hallow every place in which it moves; to breathe around nature an odor more exquisite than the perfume of the rose, and to shed over it a tint more magical than the blush of morning.

Others may dwell on the illustrious deeds of James as a warrior and a legislator; but I have delighted to view him merely as the companion of his fellow-men, the benefactor of the human heart, stooping from his high estate to sow the sweet flowers of poetry and song in the paths of common life. He was the first to cultivate the vigorous and hardy plant of Scottish genius, which has since become so prolific of the most wholesome and highly flavored fruit. He carried with him into the sterner regions of the north, all the fertilizing arts of southern refinement. He did every thing in his power to win his countrymen to the gay, the elegant, and gentle arts, which soften and refine the character of a people, and wreathe a grace round the loftiness of a proud and warlike spirit. He wrote many poems, which, unfortunately for the fulness of his fame, are now lost to the world; one, which is still preserved, called "Christ's Kirk of the Green," shows how diligently he had made himself acquainted with the rustic sports and pastimes, which constitute such a source of kind and social feeling among the Scottish peasantry; and with what simple and happy humor he could enter into their enjoyments. He contributed greatly to improve the national music; and traces of his tender sentiment and elegant taste are said to exist in those witching airs, still piped among the wild mountains and lonely glens of Scotland. He has thus connected his image with whatever is most gracious and endearing in the national character; he has embalmed his memory in song, and floated his name to after-ages in the rich streams of Scottish melody. The recollection of these things was kindling at my heart, as I paced the silent scene of his imprisonment. I have visited Vaucluse with as much enthusiasm as a pilgrim would visit the shrine at Loretto; but I have never felt more poetical devotion than when contemplating the old tower and the little garden at Windsor, and musing over the romantic loves of the Lady Jane, and the Royal Poet of Scotland.

THE COUNTRY CHURCH

A gentleman!
What o' the woolpack? or the sugar-chest?
Or lists of velvet? which is't, pound, or yard,
You vend your gentry by?
—BEGGAR'S BUSH

Here are few places more favorable to the study of character than an English country church. I was once passing a few weeks at the seat of a friend who resided in the vicinity of one the appearance of which particularly struck my fancy. It was one of those rich morsels of quaint antiquity which gives such a peculiar charm to English landscape. It stood in the midst of a country filled with ancient families, and contained within its cold and silent aisles the congregated dust of many noble generations. The interior walls were encrusted with monuments of every age and style. The light streamed through windows dimmed with armorial bearings, richly emblazoned in stained glass. In various parts of the church were tombs of knights and high-born dames, of gorgeous workmanship, with their effigies in colored marble. On every side, the eye was struck with some instance of aspiring mortality, some haughty memorial which human pride had erected over its kindred dust in this temple of the most humble of all religions.

The congregation was composed of the neighboring people of rank, who sat in pews sumptuously lined and cushioned, furnished with richly gilded prayer books, and decorated with their arms upon the pew doors—of the villagers and peasantry, who filled the back seats, and a small gallery beside the organ; and of the poor of the parish, who were ranged on benches in the aisles.

The service was performed by a snuffling, well-fed vicar, who had a snug dwelling near the church. He was a privileged guest at all the tables of the neighborhood, and had been the keenest fox-hunter in the country, until age and good living had disabled him from doing anything more than ride to see the hounds throw off, and make one at the hunting dinner.

Under the ministry of such a pastor, I found it impossible to get into the train of thought suitable to the time and place; so, having, like many other feeble Christians, compromised with my conscience, by laying the sin of my own delinquency at another person's threshold, I occupied myself by making observations on my neighbors.

I was as yet a stranger in England, and curious to notice the manners of its fashionable classes. I found, as usual, that there was the least pretension where there was the most acknowledged title to respect. I was particularly struck, for instance, with the family of a nobleman of high rank, consisting of several sons and daughters. Nothing could be more simple and unassuming than their appearance. They generally came to church in the plainest equipage, and often on foot. The young ladies would stop and converse in the kindest manner with the peasantry, caress the children, and listen to the stories of the humble cottagers. Their countenances were open and beautifully fair, with an expression of high refinement, but at the same time a frank cheerfulness and engaging affability. Their brothers were tall and elegantly formed. They were dressed fashionably, but simply—with strict neatness and propriety, but without any mannerism or foppishness. Their whole demeanor was easy and natural, with that lofty grace and noble frankness which bespeak free-born souls that have never been checked in their growth by feelings of inferiority. There is a healthful hardiness about real dignity, that never dreads contact and communion with others, however humble. It is only spurious pride that is morbid and sensitive, and shrinks from every touch. I was pleased to see the manner in which they would converse with the peasantry about those rural concerns and fieldsports in which the gentlemen of the country so much delight. In these conversations there was neither haughtiness on the one part, nor servility on the other, and you were only reminded of the difference of rank by the habitual respect of the peasant.

In contrast to these was the family of a wealthy citizen, who had amassed a vast fortune, and having purchased the estate and mansion of a ruined nobleman in the neighborhood, was endeavoring to assume all the style and dignity of an hereditary lord of the soil. The family always came to church *en prince*. They were rolled majestically along in a carriage emblazoned with arms. The crest glittered in silver radiance from every part of the harness where a crest could possibly be placed. A fat coachman, in a three-cornered hat, richly laced, and a flaxen wig, curling close round his rosy face, was seated on the box, with a sleek Danish dog beside him. Two footmen in gorgeous liveries, with huge bouquets, and gold-headed canes, lolled behind. The carriage rose and sunk on its long springs with a peculiar stateliness of motion. The very horses champed their bits, arched their necks, and glanced their eyes more proudly than common horses; either because they had caught a little of the family feeling, or were reined up more tightly than ordinary.

I could not but admire the style with which this splendid pageant was brought up to the gate of the churchyard. There was a vast effect produced at the turning of an angle of the wall—a great smacking of the whip, straining and scrambling of the horses, glistening of harness, and flashing of wheels through gravel. This was the moment of triumph and vainglory to the coachman. The horses were urged and checked, until they were fretted into a foam. They threw out their feet in a prancing trot, dashing about pebbles at every step. The crowd of villagers sauntering quietly to church opened precipitately to the right and left, gaping in vacant admiration. On reaching the gate, the horses were pulled up with a suddenness that produced an immediate stop, and almost threw them on their haunches.

There was an extraordinary hurry of the footmen to alight, pull down the steps, and prepare everything for the descent on earth of this august family. The old citizen first emerged his round red face from out the door, looking about him with the pompous air of a man accustomed to rule on change, and shake the stock market with a nod. His consort, a fine, fleshy, comfortable dame, followed him. There seemed, I must confess, but little pride in her composition. She was the picture of broad, honest, vulgar enjoyment. The world went well with her; and she liked the world. She had fine clothes, a fine house, a fine carriage, fine children—everything was fine about her: it was nothing but driving about and visiting and feasting. Life was to her a perpetual revel; it was one long Lord Mayor's Day.

Two daughters succeeded to this goodly couple. They certainly were handsome, but had a supercilious air that chilled admiration and disposed the spectator to be critical. They were ultra-fashionables in dress, and, though no one could deny the richness of their decorations, yet their appropriateness might be questioned amidst the simplicity of a country church. They descended loftily from the carriage, and moved up the line of peasantry with a step that seemed dainty of the soil it trod on. They cast an excursive glance around, that passed coldly over the burly faces of the peasantry, until they met the eyes of the nobleman's family, when their countenances immediately brightened into smiles, and they made the most profound and elegant courtesies, which were returned in a manner that showed they were but slight acquaintances.

I must not forget the two sons of this inspiring citizen, who came to church in a dashing curricle with outriders. They were arrayed in the extremity of the mode, with all that pedantry of dress which marks the man of questionable pretensions to style. They kept entirely by themselves, eying every one askance that came near them, as if measuring his claims to respectability; yet they were without conversation, except the exchange of an occasional cant phrase. They even moved artificially, for their bodies, in compliance with the caprice of the day, had been disciplined into the absence of all ease and freedom. Art had done everything to accomplish them as men of fashion, but nature had denied them the nameless grace. They were vulgarly shaped, like men formed for the common purposes of life, and had that air of supercilious assumption which is never seen in the true gentleman.

I have been rather minute in drawing the pictures of these two families, because I considered them specimens of what is often to be met with in this country—the unpretending great, and the arrogant little. I have no respect for titled rank, unless it be accompanied with true nobility of soul; but I have remarked, in all countries where artificial distinctions exist, that the very highest classes are always the most courteous and unassuming. Those who are well assured of their own standing are least apt to trespass on that of others; whereas, nothing is so offensive as the aspirings of vulgarity, which thinks to elevate itself by humiliating its neighbor.

As I have brought these families into contrast, I must notice their behavior in church. That of the nobleman's family was quiet, serious, and attentive. Not that they appeared to have any fervor of devotion, but rather a respect for sacred things, and sacred places, inseparable from good-breeding. The others, on the contrary, were in a perpetual flutter and whisper; they betrayed a continual consciousness of finery, and the sorry ambition of being the wonders of a rural congregation.

The old gentleman was the only one really attentive to the service. He took the whole burden of family devotion upon himself; standing bolt upright, and uttering the responses with a loud voice that might be heard all over the church. It was evident that he was one of these thorough Church-and-King men, who connect the idea of devotion and loyalty; who consider the deity, somehow or other, of the government party, and religion "a very excellent sort of thing, that ought to be countenanced and kept up."

When he joined so loudly in the service, it seemed more by way of example to the lower orders, to show them that, though so great and wealthy, he was not above being religious; as I have seen a turtle-fed alderman swallow publicly a basin of charity soup, smacking his lips at every mouthful and pronouncing it "excellent food for the poor."

When the service was at an end, I was curious to witness the several exits of my groups. The young noblemen and their sisters, as the day was fine, preferred strolling home across the fields, chatting with the country people as they went. The others departed as they came, in grand parade. Again were the equipages wheeled up to the gate. There was again the smacking of whips, the clattering of hoofs, and the glittering of harness. The horses started off almost at a bound; the villagers again hurried to right and left; the wheels threw up a cloud of dust, and the aspiring family was rapt out of sight in a whirlwind.

THE WIDOW AND HER SON

> Pittie olde age, within whose silver haires
> Honour and reverence evermore have raign'd.
> —Marlowe's Tamburlaine

Those who are in the habit of remarking such matters must have noticed the passive quiet of an English landscape on Sunday. The clacking of the mill, the regularly recurring stroke of the flail, the din of the blacksmith's hammer, the whistling of the ploughman, the rattling of the cart, and all other sounds of rural labor are suspended. The very farm-dogs bark less frequently, being less disturbed by passing travellers. At such times I have almost fancied the wind sunk into quiet, and that the sunny landscape, with its fresh green tints melting into blue haze, enjoyed the hallowed calm.

> Sweet day, so pure, so calm, so bright
> The bridal of the earth and sky.

Well was it ordained that the day of devotion should be a day of rest. The holy repose which reigns over the face of nature has its moral influence; every restless passion is charmed down, and we feel the natural religion of the soul gently springing up within us. For my part, there are feelings that visit me, in a country church, amid the beautiful serenity of nature, which I experience nowhere else; and if not a more religious, I think I am a better man on Sunday than on any other day of the seven.

During my recent residence in the country, I used frequently to attend at the old village church. Its shadowy aisles, its mouldering monuments, its dark oaken panelling, all reverend with the gloom of departed years, seemed to fit it for the haunt of solemn meditation; but, being in a wealthy, aristocratic neighborhood, the glitter of fashion penetrated even into the sanctuary; and I felt myself continually thrown back upon the world, by the frigidity and pomp of the poor worms around me. The only being in the whole congregation who appeared thoroughly to feel the humble and prostrate piety of a true Christian was a poor decrepit old woman, bending under the weight of years and infirmities. She bore the traces of something better than abject poverty. The lingerings of decent pride were visible in her appearance. Her dress, though humble in the extreme, was scrupulously clean. Some trivial respect, too, had been awarded her, for she did not take her seat among the village poor, but sat alone on the steps of the altar. She seemed to have survived all love, all friendship, all society, and to have nothing left her but the hopes of heaven. When I saw her feebly rising and bending her aged form in prayer; habitually conning her prayer-book, which her palsied hand and failing eyes could not permit her to read, but which she evidently knew by heart, I felt persuaded that the faltering voice of that poor woman arose to heaven far before the responses of the clerk, the swell of the organ, or the chanting of the choir.

I am fond of loitering about country churches, and this was so delightfully situated, that it frequently attracted me. It stood on a knoll, round which a small stream made a beautiful bend and then wound its way through a long reach of soft meadow scenery. The church was surrounded by yew trees, which seemed almost coeval with itself. Its tall gothic spire shot up lightly from among them, with rooks and crows generally wheeling about it. I was seated there one still sunny morning watching two laborers who were digging a grave. They had chosen one of the most remote and neglected corners of the churchyard, where, from the number of nameless graves around, it would appear that the indigent and friendless were huddled into the earth. I was told that the new-made grave was for the only son of a poor widow. While I was meditating on the distinctions of worldly rank, which extend thus down into the very dust, the toll of the bell announced the approach of the funeral. They were the obsequies of poverty, with which pride had nothing to do. A coffin of the plainest materials, without pall or other covering, was borne by some of the villagers. The sexton walked before with an air of cold indifference. There were no mock mourners in the trappings of affected woe, but there was one real mourner who feebly tottered after the corpse. It was the aged mother of the deceased, the poor old woman whom I had seen seated on the steps of the altar. She was supported by a humble friend, who was endeavoring to comfort her. A few of the neighboring poor had joined the train, and some children of the village were running hand in hand, now shouting with unthinking mirth, and now pausing to gaze, with childish curiosity on the grief of the mourner.

As the funeral train approached the grave, the parson issued from the church-porch, arrayed in the surplice, with prayer-book in hand, and attended by the clerk. The service, however, was a mere act of charity. The deceased had been destitute, and the survivor was penniless. It was shuffled through, therefore, in form, but coldly and unfeeling. The well-fed priest moved but a few steps from the church door; his voice could scarcely be heard at the grave; and never did I hear the funeral service, that sublime and touching ceremony, turned into such a frigid mummery of words.

I approached the grave. The coffin was placed on the ground. On it were inscribed the name and age of the deceased—"George Somers, aged 26 years." The poor mother had been assisted to kneel down at the head of it. Her withered hands were clasped, as if in prayer; but I could perceive, by a feeble rocking of the body, and a convulsive motion of the lips, that she was gazing on the last relics of her son with the yearnings of a mother's heart.

Preparations were made to deposit the coffin in the earth. There was that bustling stir, which breaks so harshly on the feelings of grief and affection; directions given in the cold tones of business; the striking of spades into sand and gravel; which, at the grave of those we love, is, of all sounds, the most withering. The bustle around seemed to waken the mother from a wretched reverie. She raised her glazed eyes, and looked about with a faint wildness. As the men approached with cords to lower the coffin into the grave, she wrung her hands, and broke into an agony of grief. The poor woman who attended her took her by the arm, endeavoring to raise her from the earth, and to whisper something like consolation: "Nay, now—nay, now—don't take it so sorely to heart." She could only shake her head, and wring her hands, as one not to be comforted.

As they lowered the body into the earth, the creaking of the cords seemed to agonize her; but when, on some accidental obstruction, there was a jostling of the coffin, all the tenderness of the mother burst forth, as if any harm could come to him who was far beyond the reach of worldly suffering.

I could see no more—my heart swelled into my throat—my eyes filled with tears; I felt as if I were acting a barbarous part in standing by and gazing idly on this scene of maternal anguish. I wandered to another part of the churchyard, where I remained until the funeral train had dispersed.

When I saw the mother slowly and painfully quitting the grave, leaving behind her the remains of all that was dear to her on earth, and returning to silence and destitution, my heart ached for her. What, thought I, are the distresses of the rich? They have friends to soothe—pleasures to beguile—a world to divert and dissipate their griefs. What are the sorrows of the young? Their growing minds soon close above the wound—their elastic spirits soon rise beneath the pressure—their green and ductile affections soon twine round new objects. But the sorrows of the poor, who have no outward appliances to soothe—the sorrows of the aged, with whom life at best is but a wintry day, and who can look for no after-growth of joy—the sorrows of a widow, aged, solitary, destitute, mourning over an only son, the last solace of her years—these are indeed sorrows which make us feel the impotency of consolation.

It was some time before I left the churchyard. On my way homeward, I met with the woman who had acted as comforter: she was just returning from accompanying the mother to her lonely habitation, and I drew from her some particulars connected with the affecting scene I had witnessed.

The parents of the deceased had resided in the village from childhood. They had inhabited one of the neatest cottages, and by various rural occupations, and the assistance of a small garden, had supported themselves creditably and comfortably, and led a happy and a blameless life. They had one son, who had grown up to be the staff and pride of their age. "Oh, sir!" said the good woman, "he was such a comely lad, so sweet-tempered, so kind to every one around him, so dutiful to his parents! It did one's heart good to see him of a Sunday, drest out in his best, so tall, so straight, so cheery, supporting his old mother to church; for she was always fonder of leaning on George's arm than on her good man's; and, poor soul, she might well be proud of him, for a finer lad there was not in the country round."

Unfortunately, the son was tempted, during a year of scarcity and agricultural hardship, to enter into the service of one of the small craft that plied on a neighboring river. He had not been long in this employ, when he was entrapped by a press-gang, and carried off to sea. His parents received tidings of his seizure, but beyond that they could learn nothing. It was the loss of their main prop. The father, who was already infirm, grew heartless and melancholy and sunk into his grave. The widow, left lonely in her age and feebleness, could no longer support herself, and came upon the parish. Still there was a kind feeling towards her throughout the village, and a certain respect as being one of the oldest inhabitants. As no one applied for the cottage in which she had passed so many happy days, she was permitted to remain in it, where she lived solitary and almost helpless. The few wants of nature were chiefly supplied from the scanty productions of her little garden, which the neighbors would now and then cultivate for her. It was but a few days before the time at which these circumstances were told me, that she was gathering some vegetables for her repast, when she heard the cottage-door which faced the garden, suddenly opened. A stranger came out, and seemed to be looking eagerly and wildly around. He was dressed in seamen's clothes, was emaciated and ghastly pale, and bore the air of one broken by sickness and hardships. He saw her and hastened towards her, but his steps were faint and faltering; he sank on his knees before her and sobbed like a child. The poor woman gazed upon him with a vacant and wandering eye. "Oh, my dear, dear mother! don't you know your son? your poor boy, George?" It was, indeed, the wreck of her once noble lad; who shattered by wounds, by sickness and foreign imprisonment, had, at length, dragged his wasted limbs homeward, to repose among the scenes of his childhood.

I will not attempt to detail the particulars of such a meeting, where sorrow and joy were so completely blended: still, he was alive! he was come home! he might yet live to comfort and cherish her old age! Nature, however, was exhausted in him; and if any thing had been wanting to finish the work of fate, the desolation of his native cottage would have been sufficient. He stretched himself on the pallet on which his widowed mother had passed many a sleepless night, and he never rose from it again.

The villagers, when they heard that George Somers had returned, crowded to see him, offering every comfort and assistance that their humble means afforded. He was too weak, however, to talk—he could only look his thanks. His mother was his constant attendant; and he seemed unwilling to be helped by any other hand.

There is something in sickness that breaks down the pride of manhood, that softens the heart, and brings it back to the feelings of infancy. Who that has languished, even in advanced life, in sickness and despondency, who that has pined on a weary bed in the neglect and loneliness of a foreign land, but has thought on the mother "that looked on his childhood," that smoothed his pillow, and administered to his helplessness? Oh, there is an enduring tenderness in the love of a mother to a son, that transcends all other affections of the heart. It is neither to be chilled by selfishness, nor daunted by danger, nor weakened by worthlessness, nor stifled by ingratitude. She will sacrifice every comfort to his convenience; she will surrender every pleasure to his enjoyment; she will glory in his fame and exult in his prosperity; and, if misfortune overtake him, he will be the dearer to her from misfortune; and if disgrace settle upon his name, she will still love and cherish him in spite of his disgrace; and if all the world beside cast him off, she will be all the world to him.

Poor George Somers had known what it was to be in sickness, and none to soothe—lonely and in prison, and none to visit him. He could not endure his mother from his sight; if she moved away, his eye would follow her. She would sit for hours by his bed watching him as he slept. Sometimes he would start from a feverish dream, and look anxiously up until he saw her bending over him; when he would take her hand, lay it on his bosom, and fall asleep with the tranquillity of a child. In this way he died.

My first impulse on hearing this humble tale of affliction was to visit the cottage of the mourner, and administer pecuniary assistance, and, if possible, comfort. I found, however, on inquiry, that the good feelings of the villagers had prompted them to do everything that the case admitted; and as the poor know best how to console each other's sorrows, I did not venture to intrude.

The next Sunday I was at the village church, when, to my surprise, I saw the poor old woman tottering down the aisle to her accustomed seat on the steps of the altar.

She had made an effort to put on something like mourning for her son; and nothing could be more touching than this struggle between pious affection and utter poverty—a black ribbon or so, a faded black handkerchief, and one or two more such humble attempts to express by outward signs that grief which passes show. When I looked round upon the storied monuments, the stately hatchments, the cold marble pomp with which grandeur mourned magnificently over departed pride, and turned to this poor widow, bowed down by age and sorrow at the altar of her God, and offering up the prayers and praises of a pious though a broken heart, I felt that this living monument of real grief was worth them all.

I related her story to some of the wealthy members of the congregation, and they were moved by it. They exerted themselves to render her situation more comfortable, and to lighten her afflictions. It was, however, but smoothing a few steps to the grave. In the course of a Sunday or two after, she was missed from her usual seat at church, and before I left the neighborhood I heard, with a feeling of satisfaction, that she had quietly breathed her last, and had gone to rejoin those she loved, in that world where sorrow is never known and friends are never parted.

A SUNDAY IN LONDON[*]

In a preceding paper I have spoken of an English Sunday in the country and its tranquillizing effect upon the landscape; but where is its sacred influence more strikingly apparent than in the very heart of that great Babel, London? On this sacred day the gigantic monster is charmed into repose. The intolerable din and struggle of the week are at an end. The shops are shut. The fires of forges and manufactories are extinguished, and the sun, no longer obscured by murky clouds of smoke, pours down a sober yellow radiance into the quiet streets. The few pedestrians we meet, instead of hurrying forward with anxious countenances, move leisurely along; their brows are smoothed from the wrinkles of business and care; they have put on their Sunday looks and Sunday manners with their Sunday clothes, and are cleansed in mind as well as in person.

And now the melodious clangor of bells from church towers summons their several flocks to the fold. Forth issues from his mansion the family of the decent tradesman, the small children in the advance; then the citizen and his comely spouse, followed by the grown-up daughters, with small morocco-bound prayer-books laid in the folds of their pocket-handkerchiefs. The housemaid looks after them from the window, admiring the finery of the family, and receiving, perhaps, a nod and smile from her young mistresses, at whose toilet she has assisted.

Now rumbles along the carriage of some magnate of the city, peradventure an alderman or a sheriff, and now the patter of many feet announces a procession of charity scholars in uniforms of antique cut, and each with a prayer-book under his arm.

The ringing of bells is at an end; the rumbling of the carriage has ceased; the pattering of feet is heard no more; the flocks are folded in ancient churches, cramped up in by-lanes and corners of the crowded city, where the vigilant beadle keeps watch, like the shepherd's dog,

* Part of a sketch omitted in the preceding editions.

round the threshold of the sanctuary. For a time everything is hushed, but soon is heard the deep, pervading sound of the organ, rolling and vibrating through the empty lanes and courts, and the sweet chanting of the choir making them resound with melody and praise. Never have I been more sensible of the sanctifying effect of church music than when I have heard it thus poured forth, like a river of joy, through the inmost recesses of this great metropolis, elevating it, as it were, from all the sordid pollutions of the week, and bearing the poor world-worn soul on a tide of triumphant harmony to heaven.

The morning service is at an end. The streets are again alive with the congregations returning to their homes, but soon again relapse into silence. Now comes on the Sunday dinner, which, to the city tradesman, is a meal of some importance. There is more leisure for social enjoyment at the board. Members of the family can now gather together, who are separated by the laborious occupations of the week. A school-boy may be permitted on that day to come to the paternal home; an old friend of the family takes his accustomed Sunday seat at the board, tells over his well-known stories, and rejoices young and old with his well-known jokes.

On Sunday afternoon the city pours forth its lesions to breathe the fresh air and enjoy the sunshine of the parks and rural environs. Satirists may say what they please about the rural enjoyments of a London citizen on Sunday, but to me there is something delightful in beholding the poor prisoner of the crowded and dusty city enabled thus to come forth once a week and throw himself upon the green bosom of nature. He is like a child restored to the mother's breast; and they who first spread out these noble parks and magnificent pleasure-grounds which surround this huge metropolis have done at least as much for its health and morality as if they had expended the amount of cost in hospitals, prisons, and penitentiaries.

THE BOAR'S HEAD TAVERN, EAST CHEAP

A Shakespearean Research

> A tavern is the rendezvous, the exchange, the staple of good fellows. I have heard my great-grandfather tell, how his great-great-grandfather should say, that it was an old proverb when his great-grandfather was a child, that "it was a good wind that blew a man to the wine."
>
> —Mother Bombie

It is a pious custom in some Catholic countries to honor the memory of saints by votive lights burnt before their pictures. The popularity of a saint, therefore, may be known by the number of these offerings. One, perhaps, is left to moulder in the darkness of his little chapel; another may have a solitary lamp to throw its blinking rays athwart his effigy; while the whole blaze of adoration is lavished at the shrine of some beatified father of renown. The wealthy devotee brings his huge luminary of wax, the eager zealot his seven-branched candlestick; and even the mendicant pilgrim is by no means satisfied that sufficient light is thrown upon the deceased unless he hangs up his little lamp of smoking oil. The consequence is, that in the eagerness to enlighten, they are often apt to obscure; and I have occasionally seen an unlucky saint almost smoked out of countenance by the officiousness of his followers.

In like manner has it fared with the immortal Shakespeare. Every writer considers it his bounden duty to light up some portion of his character or works, and to rescue some merit from oblivion. The commentator, opulent in words, produces vast tomes of dissertations; the common herd of editors send up mists of obscurity from their notes at the bottom of each page; and every casual scribbler brings his farthing rush light of eulogy or research to swell the cloud of incense and of smoke.

As I honor all established usages of my brethren of the quill, I thought it but proper to contribute my mite of homage to the memory of the illustrious bard. I was for some time, however, sorely puzzled in what way I should discharge this duty. I found myself anticipated in every attempt at a new reading; every doubtful line had been explained a dozen different ways, and perplexed beyond the reach of elucidation; and as to fine passages, they had all been amply praised by previous admirers; nay, so completely had the bard of late been overlarded with panegyric by a great German critic that it was difficult now to find even a fault that had not been argued into a beauty.

In this perplexity I was one morning turning over his pages when I casually opened upon the comic scenes of Henry IV, and was, in a moment, completely lost in the madcap revelry of the Boar's Head Tavern. So vividly and naturally are these scenes of humor depicted, and with such force and consistency are the characters sustained, that they become mingled up in the mind with the facts and personages of real life. To few readers does it occur that these are all ideal creations of a poet's brain, and that, in sober truth, no such knot of merry roisterers ever enlivened the dull neighborhood of Eastcheap.

For my part, I love to give myself up to the illusions of poetry. A hero of fiction that never existed is just as valuable to me as a hero of history that existed a thousand years since; and, if I may be excused such an insensibility to the common ties of human nature, I would not give up fat Jack for half the great men of ancient chronicle. What have the heroes of yore done for me or men like me? They have conquered countries of which I do not enjoy an acre, or they have gained laurels of which I do not inherit a leaf, or they have furnished examples of hair-brained prowess, which I have neither the opportunity nor the inclination to follow. But old Jack Falstaff! kind Jack Falstaff! sweet Jack Falstaff! has enlarged the boundaries of human enjoyment; he has added vast regions of wit and good humor, in which the poorest man may revel, and has bequeathed a never-failing inheritance of jolly laughter, to make mankind merrier and better to the latest posterity.

A thought suddenly struck me. "I will make a pilgrimage to Eastcheap," said I, closing the book, "and see if the old Boar's Head Tavern still exists. Who knows but I may light upon some legendary traces of Dame Quickly and her guests? At any rate, there will be a kindred pleasure in treading the halls once vocal with their mirth, to that the toper enjoys in smelling to the empty cask, once filled with generous wine."

The resolution was no sooner formed than put in execution. I forbear to treat of the various adventures and wonders I encountered in my travels; of the haunted regions of Cock Lane; of the faded glories of Little Britain and the parts adjacent; what perils I ran in Cateaton Street and Old Jewry; of the renowned Guildhall and its two stunted giants, the pride and wonder of the city and the terror of all unlucky urchins; and how I visited London Stone, and struck my staff upon it in imitation of that arch-rebel Jack Cade.

Let it suffice to say, that I at length arrived in merry Eastcheap, that ancient region of wit and wassail, where the very names of the streets relished of good cheer, as Pudding Lane bears testimony even at the present day. For Eastcheap, says old Stow, "was always famous for its convivial doings. The cookes cried hot ribbes of beef roasted, pies well baked, and other victuals: there was clattering of pewter pots, harpe, pipe, and sawtrie." Alas! how sadly is the scene changed since the roaring days of Falstaff and old Stow! The madcap roisterer has given place to the plodding tradesman; the clattering of pots and the sound of "harpe and sawtrie," to the din of carts and the accurst dinging of the dustman's bell; and no song is heard, save, haply, the strain of some syren from Billingsgate, chanting the eulogy of deceased mackerel.

I sought, in vain, for the ancient abode of Dame Quickly. The only relict of it is a boar's head, carved in relief in stone, which formerly served as the sign, but at present is built into the parting line of two houses which stand on the site of the renowned old tavern.

For the history of this little abode of good fellowship I was referred to a tallow-chandler's widow opposite, who had been born and brought up on the spot, and was looked up to as the indisputable chronicler of the neighborhood. I found her seated in a little back parlor, the window of which looked out upon a yard about eight feet square laid out as a flower garden, while a glass door opposite afforded a distant view of the street, through a vista of soap and tallow candles—the two views which comprised, in all probability, her prospects in life and the little world in which she had lived and moved and had her being for the better part of a century.

To be versed in the history of Eastcheap, great and little, from London Stone even unto the Monument, was doubtless, in her opinion, to be acquainted with the history of the universe. Yet, with all this, she possessed the simplicity of true wisdom, and that liberal communicative disposition which I have generally remarked in intelligent old ladies knowing in the concerns of their neighborhood.

Her information, however, did not extend far back into antiquity. She could throw no light upon the history of the Boar's Head from the time that Dame Quickly espoused the valiant Pistol until the great fire of London when it was unfortunately burnt down. It was soon rebuilt, and continued to flourish under the old name and sign, until a dying landlord, struck with remorse for double scores, bad measures, and other iniquities which are incident to the sinful race of publicans, endeavored to make his peace with Heaven by bequeathing the tavern to St. Michael's Church, Crooked Lane, toward the supporting of a chaplain. For some time the vestry meetings were regularly held there, but it was observed that the old Boar never held up his head under church government. He gradually declined, and finally gave his last gasp about thirty years since. The tavern was then turned into shops; but she informed me that a picture of it was still preserved in St. Michael's Church, which stood just in the rear. To get a sight of this picture was now my determination; so, having informed myself of the abode of the sexton, I took my leave of the venerable chronicler of Eastcheap, my visit having doubtless raised greatly her opinion of her legendary lore and furnished an important incident in the history of her life.

It cost me some difficulty and much curious inquiry to ferret out the humble hanger-on to the church. I had to explore Crooked Lane and divers little alleys and elbows and dark passages with which this old city is perforated like an ancient cheese, or a worm-eaten chest of drawers. At length I traced him to a corner of a small court surrounded by lofty houses, where the inhabitants enjoy about as much of the face of heaven as a community of frogs at the bottom of a well.

The sexton was a meek, acquiescing little man, of a bowing, lowly habit, yet he had a pleasant twinkling in his eye, and if encouraged, would now and then hazard a small pleasantry, such as a man of his low estate might venture to make in the company of high churchwardens and other mighty men of the earth. I found him in company with the deputy organist, seated apart, like Milton's angels, discoursing, no doubt, on high doctrinal points, and settling the affairs of the church over a friendly pot of ale; for the lower classes of English seldom deliberate on any weighty matter without the assistance of a cool tankard to clear their understandings. I arrived at the moment when they had finished their ale and their argument, and were about to repair to the church to put it in order; so, having made known my wishes, I received their gracious permission to accompany them.

The church of St. Michael's, Crooked Lane, standing a short distance from Billingsgate, is enriched with the tombs of many fishmongers of renown; and as every profession has its galaxy of glory and its constellation of great men, I presume the monument of a mighty fishmonger of the olden time is regarded with as much reverence by succeeding generations of the craft, as poets feel on contemplating the tomb of Virgil or soldiers the monument of a Marlborough or Turenne.

I cannot but turn aside, while thus speaking of illustrious men, to observe that St. Michael's, Crooked Lane, contains also the ashes of that doughty champion, William Walworth, Knight, who so manfully clove down the sturdy wight, Wat Tyler, in Smithfield—a hero worthy of honorable blazon, as almost the only Lord Mayor on record famous for deeds of arms, the sovereigns of Cockney being generally renowned as the most pacific of all potentates.*

* The following was the ancient inscription on the monument of this worthy, which, unhappily, was destroyed in the great conflagration.

Hereunder lyth a man of Fame,
William Walworth callyd by name:
Fishmonger he was in lyfftime here,
And twise Lord Maior, as in books appere;
Who, with courage stout and manly myght,
Slew Jack Straw in Kyng Richard's sight.
For which act done, and trew entent,
The Kyng made him knyght incontinent
And gave him armes, as here you see,
To declare his fact and chivaldrie.
He left this lyff the yere of our God
Thirteen hundred fourscore and three odd.

An error in the foregoing inscription has been corrected by the venerable Stow. "Whereas," saith he, "it hath been far spread abroad by vulgar opinion, that the rebel smitten down so manfully by Sir William Walworth, the then worthy Lord Maior, was named Jack Straw, and not Wat Tyler, I thought good to reconcile this rash-conceived doubt by such testimony

Adjoining the church, in a small cemetery, immediately under the back window of what was once the Boar's Head, stands the tombstone of Robert Preston, whilom drawer at the tavern. It is now nearly a century since this trusty drawer of good liquor closed his bustling career and was thus quietly deposited within call of his customers. As I was clearing away the weeds from his epitaph the little sexton drew me on one side with a mysterious air, and informed me in a low voice that once upon a time, on a dark wintry night, when the wind was unruly, howling, and whistling, banging about doors and windows, and twirling weathercocks, so that the living were frightened out of their beds, and even the dead could not sleep quietly in their graves, the ghost of honest Preston, which happened to be airing itself in the churchyard, was attracted by the well-known call of "Waiter!" from the Boar's Head, and made its sudden appearance in the midst of a roaring club, just as the parish clerk was singing a stave from the "mirre garland of Captain Death;" to the discomfiture of sundry train-band captains and the conversion of an infidel attorney, who became a zealous Christian on the spot, and was never known to twist the truth afterwards, except in the way of business.

I beg it may be remembered, that I do not pledge myself for the authenticity of this anecdote, though it is well known that the churchyards and by-corners of this old metropolis are very much infested with perturbed spirits; and every one must have heard of the Cock Lane ghost, and the apparition that guards the regalia in the Tower which has frightened so many bold sentinels almost out of their wits.

Be all this as it may, this Robert Preston seems to have been a worthy successor to the nimbletongued Francis, who attended upon the revels of Prince Hal; to have been equally prompt with his "Anon, anon, sir;" and to have transcended his predecessor in honesty; for Falstaff, the veracity of whose taste no man will venture to impeach, flatly accuses Francis of putting lime in his sack, whereas honest Preston's epitaph lauds him for the sobriety of his conduct, the soundness of his wine, and the fairness of his measure.* The worthy dignitaries of the church,

as I find in ancient and good records. The principal leaders, or captains, of the commons, were Wat Tyler, as the first man; the second was John, or Jack, Straw, etc., etc."
—Stow's London.

* As this inscription is rife with excellent morality, I transcribe it for the admonition of

however, did not appear much captivated by the sober virtues of the tapster; the deputy organist, who had a moist look out of the eye, made some shrewd remark on the abstemiousness of a man brought up among full hogsheads, and the little sexton corroborated his opinion by a significant wink and a dubious shake of the head.

Thus far my researches, though they threw much light on the history of tapsters, fishmongers, and Lord Mayors, yet disappointed me in the great object of my quest, the picture of the Boar's Head Tavern. No such painting was to be found in the church of St. Michael's. "Marry and amen," said I, "here endeth my research!" So I was giving the matter up, with the air of a baffled antiquary, when my friend the sexton, perceiving me to be curious in everything relative to the old tavern, offered to show me the choice vessels of the vestry, which had been handed down from remote times when the parish meetings were held at the Boar's Head. These were deposited in the parish club-room, which had been transferred, on the decline of the ancient establishment, to a tavern in the neighborhood.

A few steps brought us to the house, which stands No. 12 Miles Lane, bearing the title of The Mason's Arms, and is kept by Master Edward Honeyball, the "bully-rock" of the establishment. It is one of those little taverns which abound in the heart of the city and form the centre of gossip and intelligence of the neighborhood.

We entered the barroom, which was narrow and darkling, for in these close lanes but few rays of reflected light are enabled to struggle down to the inhabitants, whose broad day is at best but a tolerable twilight. The room was partitioned into boxes, each containing a table spread with a clean white cloth, ready for dinner. This showed that the guests were

---

delinquent tapsters. It is no doubt, the production of some choice spirit who once frequented the Boar's Head.

Bacchus, to give the toping world surprise,
Produced one sober son, and here he lies.
Though rear'd among full hogsheads, he defy'd
The charms of wine, and every one beside.
O reader, if to justice thou'rt inclined,
Keep honest Preston daily in thy mind.
He drew good wine, took care to fill his pots,
Had sundry virtues that excused his faults.
You that on Bacchus have the like dependence,
Pray copy Bob in measure and attendance.

of the good old stamp, and divided their day equally, for it was but just one o'clock. At the lower end of the room was a clear coal fire, before which a breast of lamb was roasting. A row of bright brass candlesticks and pewter mugs glistened along the mantelpiece, and an old-fashioned clock ticked in one corner. There was something primitive in this medley of kitchen, parlor, and hall that carried me back to earlier times, and pleased me. The place, indeed, was humble, but everything had that look of order and neatness which bespeaks the superintendence of a notable English housewife. A group of amphibious-looking beings, who might be either fishermen or sailors, were regaling themselves in one of the boxes. As I was a visitor of rather higher pretensions, I was ushered into a little misshapen back room, having at least nine corners. It was lighted by a sky-light, furnished with antiquated leathern chairs, and ornamented with the portrait of a fat pig. It was evidently appropriated to particular customers, and I found a shabby gentleman in a red nose and oil-cloth hat seated in one corner meditating on a half empty pot of porter.

The old sexton had taken the landlady aside, and with an air of profound importance imparted to her my errand. Dame Honeyball was a likely, plump, bustling little woman, and no bad substitute for that paragon of hostesses, Dame Quickly. She seemed delighted with an opportunity to oblige, and, hurrying upstairs to the archives of her house, where the precious vessels of the parish club were deposited, she returned, smiling and courtesying, with them in her hands.

The first she presented me was a japanned iron tobacco-box of gigantic size, out of which, I was told, the vestry had smoked at their stated meetings since time immemorial, and which was never suffered to be profaned by vulgar hands, or used on common occasions, I received it with becoming reverence, but what was my delight at beholding on its cover the identical painting of which I was in quest! There was displayed the outside of the Boar's Head Tavern, and before the door was to be seen the whole convivial group at table, in full revel, pictured with that wonderful fidelity and force with which the portraits of renowned generals and commodores are illustrated on tobacco-boxes, for the benefit of posterity. Lest, however, there should be any mistake, the cunning limner had warily inscribed the names of Prince Hal and Falstaff on the bottoms of their chairs.

On the inside of the cover was an inscription, nearly obliterated, recording that this box was the gift of Sir Richard Gore, for the use of the vestry meetings at the Boar's Head Tavern, and that it was "repaired and beautified by his successor, Mr. John Packard, 1767." Such is a faithful description of this august and venerable relic, and I question whether the learned Scriblerius contemplated his Roman shield, or the Knights of the Round Table the long-sought Sangreal, with more exultation.

While I was meditating on it with enraptured gaze, Dame Honeyball, who was highly gratified by the interest it excited, put in my hands a drinking-cup or goblet which also belonged to the vestry, and was descended from the old Boar's Head. It bore the inscription of having been the gift of Francis Wythers, Knight, and was held, she told me, in exceeding great value, being considered very "antyke." This last opinion was strengthened by the shabby gentleman with the red nose and oilcloth hat, and whom I strongly suspected of being a lineal descendant from the variant Bardolph. He suddenly aroused from his meditation on the pot of porter, and casting a knowing look at the goblet, exclaimed, "Ay, ay! the head don't ache now that made that there article."

The great importance attached to this memento of ancient revelry by modern churchwardens, at first puzzled me; but there is nothing sharpens the apprehension so much as antiquarian research; for I immediately perceived that this could be no other than the identical "parcel-gilt goblet," on which Falstaff made his loving but faithless vow to Dame Quickly, and which would, of course, be treasured up with care among the regalia of her domains, as a testimony of that solemn contract.*

Mine hostess, indeed, gave me a long history how the goblet had been handed down from generation to generation. She also entertained me with many particulars concerning the worthy vestrymen who have seated themselves thus quietly on the stools of the ancient roisterers of Eastcheap, and, like so many commentators, utter clouds of smoke in honor of Shakespeare. These I forbear to relate, lest my readers

* "Thou didst swear to me upon a parcel-gilt goblet, sitting in my Dolphin chamber, at the round table, by a sea coal fire, on Wednesday, in Whitsun-week, when the prince broke thy head for likening his father to a singing man at Windsor; thou didst swear to me then, as I was washing thy wound, to marry me, and make me my lady, thy wife. Canst thou deny it?"—Henry IV, Part 2

should not be as curious in these matters as myself. Suffice it to say, the neighbors, one and all about Eastcheap, believe that Falstaff and his merry crew actually lived and revelled there. Nay, there are several legendary anecdotes concerning him still extant among the oldest frequenters of the Mason's Arms, which they give as transmitted down from their forefathers; and Mr. McKash, an Irish hair-dresser, whose shop stands on the site of the old Boar's Head, has several dry jokes of Fat Jack's, not laid down in the books, with which he makes his customers ready to die of laughter.

I now turned to my friend the sexton to make some further inquiries, but I found him sunk in pensive meditation. His head had declined a little on one side; a deep sigh heaved from the very bottom of his stomach, and, though I could not see a tear trembling in his eye, yet a moisture was evidently stealing from a corner of his mouth. I followed the direction of his eye through the door which stood open, and found it fixed wistfully on the savory breast of lamb, roasting in dripping richness before the fire.

I now called to mind that in the eagerness of my recondite investigation, I was keeping the poor man from his dinner. My bowels yearned with sympathy, and putting in his hand a small token of my gratitude and goodness, I departed with a hearty benediction on him, Dame Honeyball, and the parish club of Crooked Lane—not forgetting my shabby but sententious friend in the oil-cloth hat and copper nose.

Thus have I given a "tedious brief" account of this interesting research, for which, if it prove too short and unsatisfactory, I can only plead my inexperience in this branch of literature, so deservedly popular at the present day. I am aware that a more skilful illustrator of the immortal bard would have swelled the materials I have touched upon to a good merchantable bulk, comprising the biographies of William Walworth, Jack Straw, and Robert Preston; some notice of the eminent fishmongers of St. Michael's; the history of Eastcheap, great and little; private anecdotes of Dame Honeyball and her pretty daughter, whom I have not even mentioned; to say nothing of a damsel tending the breast of lamb (and whom, by the way, I remarked to be a comely lass with a neat foot and ankle);—the whole enlivened by the riots of Wat Tyler, and illuminated by the great fire of London.

All this I leave, as a rich mine, to be worked by future commentators, nor do I despair of seeing the tobacco-box, and the "parcel-gilt goblet" which I have thus brought to light, the subject of future engravings, and almost as fruitful of voluminous dissertations and disputes as the shield of Achilles or the far-famed Portland Vase.

THE MUTABILITY OF LITERATURE

A Colloqy in Westminster Abbey

I know that all beneath the moon decays,
And what by mortals in this world is brought,
In time's great periods shall return to nought.
I know that all the muses' heavenly layes,
With toil of sprite which are so dearly bought,
As idle sounds of few or none are sought,
That there is nothing lighter than mere praise.
—Drummond of Hawthornden

There are certain half-dreaming moods of mind in which we naturally steal away from noise and glare, and seek some quiet haunt where we may indulge our reveries and build our air castles undisturbed. In such a mood I was loitering about the old gray cloisters of Westminster Abbey, enjoying that luxury of wandering thought which one is apt to dignify with the name of reflection, when suddenly an irruption of madcap boys from Westminster school, playing at football, broke in upon the monastic stillness of the place, making the vaulted passages and mouldering tombs echo with their merriment. I sought to take refuge from their noise by penetrating still deeper into the solitudes of the pile, and applied to one of the vergers for admission to the library. He conducted me through a portal rich with the crumbling sculpture of former ages, which opened upon a gloomy passage leading to the chapter-house and the chamber in which Doomsday Book is deposited. Just within the passage is a small door on the left. To this the verger applied a key; it was double locked, and opened with some difficulty, as if seldom used. We now ascended a dark narrow staircase, and passing through a second door, entered the library.

I found myself in a lofty antique hall, the roof supported by massive joists of old English oak. It was soberly lighted by a row of gothic windows at a considerable height from the floor, and which apparently opened upon the roofs of the cloisters. An ancient picture of some reverend dignitary of the Church in his robes hung over the fireplace. Around the hall and in a small gallery were the books, arranged in carved oaken cases. They consisted principally of old polemical writers, and were much more worn by time than use. In the center of the library was a solitary table with two or three books on it, an inkstand without ink, and a few pens parched by long disuse. The place seemed fitted for quiet study and profound meditation. It was buried deep among the massive walls of the abbey and shut up from the tumult of the world. I could only hear now and then the shouts of the school-boys faintly swelling from the cloisters, and the sound of a bell tolling for prayers echoing soberly along the roofs of the abbey. By degrees the shouts of merriment grew fainter and fainter, and at length died away; the bell ceased to toll, and a profound silence reigned through the dusky hall.

I had taken down a little thick quarto, curiously bound in parchment, with brass clasps, and seated myself at the table in a venerable elbow-chair. Instead of reading, however, I was beguiled by the solemn monastic air and lifeless quiet of the place, into a train of musing. As I looked around upon the old volumes in their mouldering covers, thus ranged on the shelves and apparently never disturbed in their repose, I could not but consider the library a kind of literary catacomb, where authors, like mummies, are piously entombed and left to blacken and moulder in dusty oblivion.

How much, thought I, has each of these volumes, now thrust aside with such indifference, cost some aching head! how many weary days! how many sleepless nights! How have their authors buried themselves in the solitude of cells and cloisters, shut themselves up from the face of man, and the still more blessed face of nature; and devoted themselves to painful research and intense reflection! And all for what? To occupy an inch of dusty shelf—to have the titles of their works read now and then in a future age by some drowsy churchman or casual straggler like myself, and in another age to be lost even to remembrance. Such is the amount of this boasted immortality. A mere temporary rumor, a local sound; like the tone of that bell which has tolled among these towers, filling the ear for a moment, lingering transiently in echo, and then passing away, like a thing that was not!

While I sat half-murmuring, half-meditating, these unprofitable speculations with my head resting on my hand, I was thrumming with the other hand upon the quarto, until I accidentally loosened the clasps; when, to my utter astonishment, the little book gave two or three yawns, like one awaking from a deep sleep, then a husky hem, and at length began to talk. At first its voice was very hoarse and broken, being much troubled by a cobweb which some studious spider had woven across it, and having probably contracted a cold from long exposure to the chills and damps of the abbey. In a short time, however, it became more distinct, and I soon found it an exceedingly fluent, conversable little tome. Its language, to be sure, was rather quaint and obsolete, and its pronunciation what, in the present day, would be deemed barbarous; but I shall endeavor, as far as I am able, to render it in modern parlance.

It began with railings about the neglect of the world, about merit being suffered to languish in obscurity, and other such commonplace topics of literary repining, and complained bitterly that it had not been opened for more than two centuries—that the dean only looked now and then into the library, sometimes took down a volume or two, trifled with them for a few moments, and then returned them to their shelves. "What a plague do they mean?" said the little quarto, which I began to perceive was somewhat choleric—"what a plague do they mean by keeping several thousand volumes of us shut up here, and watched by a set of old vergers, like so many beauties in a harem, merely to be looked at now and then by the dean? Books were written to give pleasure and to be enjoyed; and I would have a rule passed that the dean should pay each of us a visit at least once a year; or, if he is not equal to the task, let them once in a while turn loose the whole school of Westminster among us, that at any rate we may now and then have an airing."

"Softly, my worthy friend," replied I; "you are not aware how much better you are off than most books of your generation. By being stored away in this ancient library you are like the treasured remains of those saints and monarchs which lie enshrined in the adjoining chapels, while the remains of their contemporary mortals, left to the ordinary course of nature, have long since returned to dust."

"Sir," said the little tome, ruffling his leaves and looking big, "I was written for all the world, not for the bookworms of an abbey. I was intended to circulate from hand to hand, like other great contemporary works; but here have I been clasped up for more than two centuries, and might have silently fallen a prey to these worms that are playing the very vengeance with my intestines if you had not by chance given me an opportunity of uttering a few last words before I go to pieces."

"My good friend," rejoined I, "had you been left to the circulation of which you speak, you would long ere this have been no more. To judge from your physiognomy, you are now well stricken in years: very few of your contemporaries can be at present in existence, and those few owe their longevity to being immured like yourself in old libraries; which, suffer me to add, instead of likening to harems, you might more properly and gratefully have compared to those infirmaries attached to religious establishments for the benefit of the old and decrepit, and where, by quiet fostering and no employment, they often endure to an amazingly good-for-nothing old age. You talk of your contemporaries as if in circulation. Where do we meet with their works? What do we hear of Robert Grosteste of Lincoln? No one could have toiled harder than he for immortality. He is said to have written nearly two hundred volumes. He built, as it were, a pyramid of books to perpetuate his name: but, alas! the pyramid has long since fallen, and only a few fragments are scattered in various libraries, where they are scarcely disturbed even by the antiquarian. What do we hear of Giraldus Cambrensis, the historian, antiquary, philosopher, theologian, and poet? He declined two bishoprics that he might shut himself up and write for posterity; but posterity never inquires after his labors. What of Henry of Huntingdon, who, besides a learned history of England, wrote a treatise on the contempt of the world, which the world has revenged by forgetting him? What is quoted of Joseph of Exeter, styled the miracle of his age in classical composition? Of his three great heroic poems, one is lost forever, excepting a mere fragment; the others are known only to a few of the curious in literature; and as to his love verses and epigrams, they have entirely disappeared. What is in current use of John Wallis the Franciscan, who acquired the name of the tree of life? Of William of Malmsbury—of Simeon of Durham—of Benedict of Peterborough—of John Hanvill of St. Albans—of—"

"Prithee, friend," cried the quarto in a testy tone, "how old do you think me? You are talking of authors that lived long before my time, and wrote either in Latin or French, so that they in a manner expatriated themselves, and deserved to be forgotten;* but I, sir, was ushered into the world from the press of the renowned Wynkyn de Worde. I was written in my own native tongue, at a time when the language had become fixed; and indeed I was considered a model of pure and elegant English."

(I should observe that these remarks were couched in such intolerably antiquated terms, that I have had infinite difficulty in rendering them into modern phraseology.)

"I cry you mercy," said I, "for mistaking your age; but it matters little. Almost all the writers of your time have likewise passed into forgetfulness, and De Worde's publications are mere literary rarities among book-collectors. The purity and stability of language, too, on which you found your claims to perpetuity, have been the fallacious dependence of authors of every age, even back to the times of the worthy Robert of Gloucester, who wrote his history in rhymes of mongrel Saxon.† Even now many talk of Spenser's 'well of pure English undefiled,' as if the language ever sprang from a well or fountain-head, and was not rather a mere confluence of various tongues perpetually subject to changes and intermixtures. It is this which has made English literature so extremely mutable, and the reputation built upon it so fleeting. Unless thought can be committed to something more permanent and unchangeable than such a medium, even thought must share the fate of everything else, and fall into decay. This should serve as a check upon the vanity and exultation of the most popular writer. He finds the language in which he has embarked his fame gradually altering and subject to the dilapidations of time and the caprice of fashion. He looks back and beholds the early authors of his country, once the favorites of

* "In Latin and French hath many soueraine wittes had great delyte to endite, and have many noble thinges fulfilde, but certes there ben some that speaken their poisye in French, of which speche the Frenchmen have as good a fantasye as we have in herying of Frenchmen's Englishe."—Chaucer's Testament of Love

† Holinshed in his Chronicle, observes, "afterward, also, by diligent travell Geffray Chaucer and John Gowre, in the time of Richard the Second, and after them of John Scogan and John Lydgate, monke of Berrie, our said toong was brought to an excellent passe, notwithstanding that it never came unto the type of perfection until the time of Queen Elizabeth, wherein John Jewell, Bishop of Sarum, John Fox, and sundrie learned and excellent writers, have fully accomplished the ornature of the same, to their great praise and immortal commendation."

their day, supplanted by modern writers. A few short ages have covered them with obscurity, and their merits can only be relished by the quaint taste of the bookworm. And such, he anticipates, will be the fate of his own work, which, however it may be admired in its day and held up as a model of purity, will in the course of years grow antiquated and obsolete, until it shall become almost as unintelligible in its native land as an Egyptian obelisk or one of those Runic inscriptions said to exist in the deserts of Tartary. I declare," added I, with some emotion, "when I contemplate a modern library, filled with new works in all the bravery of rich gilding and binding, I feel disposed to sit down and weep, like the good Xerxes, when he surveyed his army, pranked out in all the splendor of military array, and reflected that in one hundred years not one of them would be in existence!"

"Ah," said the little quarto, with a heavy sigh, "I see how it is: these in modern scribblers have superseded all the good old authors. I suppose nothing is read nowadays but Sir Philip Sidney's Arcadia, Sackville's stately plays and Mirror for Magistrates, or the fine-spun euphuisms of the 'unparalleled John Lyly.'"

"There you are again mistaken," said I; "the writers whom you suppose in vogue, because they happened to be so when you were last in circulation, have long since had their day. Sir Philip Sidney's Arcadia, the immortality of which was so fondly predicted by his admirers,* and which, in truth, was full of noble thoughts, delicate images, and graceful turns of language, is now scarcely ever mentioned. Sackville has strutted into obscurity; and even Lyly, though his writings were once the delight of a court, and apparently perpetuated by a proverb, is now scarcely known even by name. A whole crowd of authors who wrote and wrangled at the time, have likewise gone down with all their writings and their controversies. Wave after wave of succeeding literature has rolled over them, until they are buried so deep, that it is only now and then that some industrious diver after fragments of antiquity brings up a specimen for the gratification of the curious.

* "Live ever sweete booke; the simple image of his gentle witt, and the golden pillar of his noble courage; and ever notify unto the world that thy writer was the secretary of eloquence, the breath of the muses, the honey bee of the dayntiest flowers of witt and arte, the pith of morale and intellectual virtues, the arme of Bellona in the field, the tongue of Suada in the chamber, the spirite of Practise in esse, and the paragon of excellence in print."—Harvey Pierce's Supererogation

"For my part," I continued, "I consider this mutability of language a wise precaution of Providence for the benefit of the world at large, and of authors in particular. To reason from analogy, we daily behold the varied and beautiful tribes of vegetables springing up, flourishing, adorning the fields for a short time, and then fading into dust, to make way for their successors. Were not this the case, the fecundity of nature would be a grievance instead of a blessing. The earth would groan with rank and excessive vegetation, and its surface become a tangled wilderness. In like manner, the works of genius and learning decline and make way for subsequent productions. Language gradually varies, and with it fade away the writings of authors who have flourished their allotted time; otherwise the creative powers of genius would overstock the world, and the mind would be completely bewildered in the endless mazes of literature. Formerly there were some restraints on this excessive multiplication. Works had to be transcribed by hand, which was a slow and laborious operation; they were written either on parchment, which was expensive, so that one work was often erased to make way for another; or on papyrus, which was fragile and extremely perishable. Authorship was a limited and unprofitable craft, pursued chiefly by monks in the leisure and solitude of their cloisters. The accumulation of manuscripts was slow and costly, and confined almost entirely to monasteries. To these circumstances it may, in some measure, be owing that we have not been inundated by the intellect of antiquity—that the fountains of thought have not been broken up, and modern genius drowned in the deluge. But the inventions of paper and the press have put an end to all these restraints. They have made every one a writer, and enabled every mind to pour itself into print, and diffuse itself over the whole intellectual world. The consequences are alarming. The stream of literature has swollen into a torrent—augmented into a river—expanded into a sea. A few centuries since five or six hundred manuscripts constituted a great library; but what would you say to libraries, such as actually exist, containing three or four hundred thousand volumes; legions of authors at the same time busy; and the press going on with fearfully increasing activity, to double and quadruple the number? Unless some unforeseen mortality should break out among the progeny of the Muse, now that she has become so prolific, I tremble for posterity. I fear the mere fluctuation of language will not be sufficient. Criticism may do much; it increases with the increase of literature, and resembles one of those salutary checks on population spoken of by economists. All possible encouragement, therefore, should be given to the growth of critics, good or bad. But I fear all will be in vain; let criticism do what it may, writers will write, printers will print, and the world will inevitably be overstocked with good books. It will soon be the employment of a lifetime merely to learn their names. Many a man of passable information at the present day reads scarcely anything but reviews, and before long a man of erudition will be little better than a mere walking catalogue."

"My very good sir," said the little quarto, yawning most drearily in my face, "excuse my interrupting you, but I perceive you are rather given to prose. I would ask the fate of an author who was making some noise just as I left the world. His reputation, however, was considered quite temporary. The learned shook their heads at him, for he was a poor, half-educated varlet, that knew little of Latin, and nothing of Greek, and had been obliged to run the country for deer-stealing. I think his name was Shakespeare. I presume he soon sunk into oblivion."

"On the contrary," said I, "it is owing to that very man that the literature of his period has experienced a duration beyond the ordinary term of English literature. There rise authors now and then who seem proof against the mutability of language because they have rooted themselves in the unchanging principles of human nature. They are like gigantic trees that we sometimes see on the banks of a stream, which, by their vast and deep roots, penetrating through the mere surface and laying hold on the very foundations of the earth, preserve the soil around them from being swept away by the ever-flowing current, and hold up many a neighboring plant, and perhaps worthless weed, to perpetuity. Such is the case with Shakespeare, whom we behold defying the encroachments of time, retaining in modern use the language and literature of his day, and giving duration to many an indifferent author, merely from having flourished in his vicinity. But even he, I grieve to say, is gradually assuming the tint of age, and his whole form is overrun by a profusion of commentators, who, like clambering vines and creepers, almost bury the noble plant that upholds them."

Here the little quarto began to heave his sides and chuckle, until at length he broke out into a plethoric fit of laughter that had well nigh choked him by reason of his excessive corpulency. "Mighty well!" cried he, as soon as he could recover breath, "mighty well! and so you would persuade me that the literature of an age is to be perpetuated by a vagabond deer-stealer! by a man without learning! by a poet! forsooth—a poet!" And here he wheezed forth another fit of laughter.

I confess that I felt somewhat nettled at this rudeness, which, however, I pardoned on account of his having flourished in a less polished age. I determined, nevertheless, not to give up my point.

"Yes," resumed I positively, "a poet; for of all writers he has the best chance for immortality. Others may write from the head, but he writes from the heart, and the heart will always understand him. He is the faithful portrayer of nature, whose features are always the same and always interesting. Prose writers are voluminous and unwieldy; their pages crowded with commonplaces, and their thoughts expanded into tediousness. But with the true poet every thing is terse, touching, or brilliant. He gives the choicest thoughts in the choicest language. He illustrates them by everything that he sees most striking in nature and art. He enriches them by pictures of human life, such as it is passing before him. His writings, therefore, contain the spirit, the aroma, if I may use the phrase, of the age in which he lives. They are caskets which inclose within a small compass the wealth of the language—its family jewels, which are thus transmitted in a portable form to posterity. The setting may occasionally be antiquated, and require now and then to be renewed, as in the case of Chaucer; but the brilliancy and intrinsic value of the gems continue unaltered. Cast a look back over the long reach of literary history. What vast valleys of dulness, filled with monkish legends and academical controversies! What bogs of theological speculations! What dreary wastes of metaphysics! Here and there only do we behold the heaven-illumined bards, elevated like beacons on their widely separated heights, to transmit the pure light of poetical intelligence from age to age."*

* Thorow earth and waters deepe,
The pen by skill doth passe:

I was just about to launch forth into eulogiums upon the poets of the day when the sudden opening of the door caused me to turn my head. It was the verger, who came to inform me that it was time to close the library. I sought to have a parting word with the quarto, but the worthy little tome was silent; the clasps were closed: and it looked perfectly unconscious of all that had passed. I have been to the library two or three times since, and have endeavored to draw it into further conversation, but in vain; and whether all this rambling colloquy actually took place, or whether it was another of those odd day-dreams to which I am subject, I have never, to this moment, been able to discover.

And featly nyps the worldes abuse,
And shoes us in a glasse,
The vertu and the vice
Of every wight alyve;
The honey combe that bee doth make
Is not so sweet in hyve,
As are the golden leves
That drop from poet's head!
Which doth surmount our common talke
As farre as dros doth lead. —Churchyard

RURAL FUNERALS

> Here's a few flowers; but about midnight more:
> The herbs that have on them cold dew o' the night
> Are strewings fitt'st for graves—
> You were as flowers now wither'd; even so
> These herblets shall, which we upon you strow.
>
> —CYMBELINE

Among the beautiful and simple-hearted customs of rural life which still linger in some parts of England are those of strewing flowers before the funerals and planting them at the graves of departed friends. These, it is said, are the remains of some of the rites of the primitive church; but they are of still higher antiquity, having been observed among the Greeks and Romans, and frequently mentioned by their writers, and were no doubt the spontaneous tributes of unlettered affection, originating long before art had tasked itself to modulate sorrow into song or story it on the monument. They are now only to be met with in the most distant and retired places of the kingdom, where fashion and innovation have not been able to throng in and trample out all the curious and interesting traces of the olden time.

In Glamorganshire, we are told, the bed whereon the corpse lies is covered with flowers, a custom alluded to in one of the wild and plaintive ditties of Ophelia:

> White his shroud as the mountain snow,
> Larded all with sweet flowers;
> Which be-wept to the grave did go,
> With true-love showers.

There is also a most delicate and beautiful rite observed in some of the remote villages of the south at the funeral of a female who has died young and unmarried. A chaplet of white flowers is borne before the corpse by a young girl nearest in age, size, and resemblance, and is afterwards hung up in the church over the accustomed seat of the deceased. These chaplets are sometimes made of white paper, in imitation of flowers, and inside of them is generally a pair of white gloves. They are intended as emblems of the purity of the deceased, and the crown of glory which she has received in heaven.

In some parts of the country, also, the dead are carried to the grave with the singing of psalms and hymns—a kind of triumph, "to show," says Bourne, "that they have finished their course with joy, and are become conquerors." This, I am informed, is observed in some of the northern counties, particularly in Northumberland, and it has a pleasing, though melancholy effect to hear of a still evening in some lonely country scene the mournful melody of a funeral dirge swelling from a distance, and to see the train slowly moving along the landscape.

> Thus, thus, and thus, we compass round
> Thy harmless and unhaunted ground,
> And as we sing thy dirge, we will,
> The daffodill
> And other flowers lay upon
> The altar of our love, thy stone.
> —Herrick

There is also a solemn respect paid by the traveller to the passing funeral in these sequestered places; for such spectacles, occurring among the quiet abodes of nature, sink deep into the soul. As the mourning train approaches he pauses, uncovered, to let it go by; he then follows silently in the rear; sometimes quite to the grave, at other times for a few hundred yards, and, having paid this tribute of respect to the deceased, turns and resumes his journey.

The rich vein of melancholy which runs through the English character, and gives it some of its most touching and ennobling graces, is finely evidenced in these pathetic customs, and in the solicitude shown by the common people for an honored and a peaceful grave. The humblest peasant, whatever may be his lowly lot while living, is anxious that some little respect may be paid to his remains. Sir Thomas Overbury, describing the "faire and happy milkmaid," observes, "thus lives she, and all her care is, that she may die in the spring-time, to have store of flowers stucke upon her winding-sheet." The poets, too, who always breathe the feeling of a nation, continually advert to this fond solicitude about the grave. In "The Maid's Tragedy," by Beaumont and Fletcher, there is a beautiful instance of the kind describing the capricious melancholy of a broken-hearted girl:

> When she sees a bank
> Stuck full of flowers, she, with a sigh, will tell
> Her servants, what a pretty place it were
> To bury lovers in; and made her maids
> Pluck 'em, and strew her over like a corse.

The custom of decorating graves was once universally prevalent: osiers were carefully bent over them to keep the turf uninjured, and about them were planted evergreens and flowers. "We adorn their graves," says Evelyn, in his Sylva, "with flowers and redolent plants, just emblems of the life of man, which has been compared in Holy Scriptures to those fading beauties whose roots, being buried in dishonor, rise, again in glory." This usage has now become extremely rare in England; but it may still be met with in the churchyards of retired villages, among the Welsh mountains; and I recollect an instance of it at the small town of Ruthven, which lies at the head of the beautiful vale of Clewyd. I have been told also by a friend, who was present at the funeral of a young girl in Glamorganshire, that the female attendants had their aprons full of flowers, which, as soon as the body was interred, they stuck about the grave. He noticed several graves which had been decorated in the same manner. As the flowers had been merely stuck in the ground, and not planted, they had soon withered, and might be seen in various states of decay; some drooping, others quite perished. They were afterwards to be supplanted by holly, rosemary, and other evergreens, which on some graves had grown to great luxuriance, and overshadowed the tombstones.

There was formerly a melancholy fancifulness in the arrangement of these rustic offerings that had something in it truly poetical. The rose was sometimes blended with the lily, to form a general emblem of frail mortality. "This sweet flower," said Evelyn, "borne on a branch set with thorns and accompanied with the lily, are natural hieroglyphics of our fugitive, umbratile, anxious, and transitory life, which, making so fair a show for a time, is not yet without its thorns and crosses." The nature and color of the flowers, and of the ribbons with which they were tied, had often a particular reference to the qualities or story of the deceased, or were expressive of the feelings of the mourner. In an old poem, entitled "Corydon's Doleful Knell," a lover specifies the decorations he intends to use:

> A garland shall be framed
>   By art and nature's skill,
> Of sundry-colored flowers,
>   In token of good-will.
>
> And sundry-colored ribbons
>   On it I will bestow;
> But chiefly blacke and yellowe
>   With her to grave shall go.
>
> I'll deck her tomb with flowers
>   The rarest ever seen;
> And with my tears as showers
>   I'll keep them fresh and green.

The white rose, we are told, was planted at the grave of a virgin; her chaplet was tied with white ribbons, in token of her spotless innocence, though sometimes black ribbons were intermingled, to bespeak the grief of the survivors. The red rose was occasionally used, in remembrance of such as had been remarkable for benevolence; but roses in general were appropriated to the graves of lovers. Evelyn tells us that the custom was not altogether extinct in his time, near his dwelling in the county of Surrey, "where the maidens yearly planted and decked the graves of their defunct sweethearts with rose-bushes." And Camden likewise remarks, in his Britannia: "Here is also a certain custom, observed time out of mind, of planting rose-trees upon the graves, especially by the young men and maids who have lost their loves; so that this churchyard is now full of them."

When the deceased had been unhappy in their loves, emblems of a more gloomy character were used, such as the yew and cypress, and if flowers were strewn, they were of the most melancholy colors. Thus, in poems by Thomas Stanley, Esq. (published in 1651), is the following stanza:

> Yet strew
> Upon my dismall grave
> Such offerings as you have,
> Forsaken cypresse and yewe;
> For kinder flowers can take no birth
> Or growth from such unhappy earth.

In *The Maid's Tragedy*, a pathetic little air, is introduced, illustrative of this mode of decorating the funerals of females who had been disappointed in love:

> Lay a garland on my hearse
> Of the dismall yew,
> Maidens willow branches wear,
> Say I died true.
>
> My love was false, but I was firm,
> From my hour of birth;
> Upon my buried body lie
> Lightly, gentle earth.

The natural effect of sorrow over the dead is to refine and elevate the mind; and we have a proof of it in the purity of sentiment and the unaffected elegance of thought which pervaded the whole of these funeral observances. Thus it was an especial precaution that none but sweet-scented evergreens and flowers should be employed. The intention seems to have been to soften the horrors of the tomb, to beguile the mind from brooding over the disgraces of perishing mortality, and to associate the memory of the deceased with the most delicate and beautiful objects in nature. There is a dismal process going on in the grave, ere dust can return to its kindred dust, which the imagination shrinks from contemplating; and we seek still to think of the form we have loved, with those refined associations which it awakened when blooming before us in youth and beauty. "Lay her i' the earth," says Laertes, of his virgin sister,

And from her fair and unpolluted flesh
May violets spring.

Herrick, also, in his "Dirge of Jephtha," pours forth a fragrant flow of poetical thought and image, which in a manner embalms the dead in the recollections of the living.

Sleep in thy peace, thy bed of spice,
And make this place all Paradise:
May sweets grow here! and smoke from hence
Fat frankincense.
Let balme and cassia send their scent
From out thy maiden monument.

* * *

May all shie maids at wonted hours
Come forth to strew thy tombe with flowers!
May virgins, when they come to mourn
Male incense burn
Upon thine altar! then return
And leave thee sleeping in thy urn.

I might crowd my pages with extracts from the older British poets, who wrote when these rites were more prevalent, and delighted frequently to allude to them; but I have already quoted more than is necessary. I cannot, however, refrain from giving a passage from Shakespeare, even though it should appear trite, which illustrates the emblematical meaning often conveyed in these floral tributes, and at the same time possesses that magic of language and appositeness of imagery for which he stands pre-eminent.

With fairest flowers,
Whilst summer lasts, and I live here, Fidele,
I'll sweeten thy sad grave; thou shalt not lack
The flower that's like thy face, pale primrose; nor
The azured harebell like thy veins; no, nor

The leaf of eglantine; whom not to slander,
Outsweetened not thy breath.

There is certainly something more affecting in these prompt and spontaneous offerings of nature than in the most costly monuments of art; the hand strews the flower while the heart is warm, and the tear falls on the grave as affection is binding the osier round the sod; but pathos expires under the slow labor of the chisel, and is chilled among the cold conceits of sculptured marble.

It is greatly to be regretted that a custom so truly elegant and touching has disappeared from general use, and exists only in the most remote and insignificant villages. But it seems as if poetical custom always shuns the walks of cultivated society. In proportion as people grow polite they cease to be poetical. They talk of poetry, but they have learnt to check its free impulses, to distrust its sallying emotions, and to supply its most affecting and picturesque usages by studied form and pompous ceremonial. Few pageants can be more stately and frigid than an English funeral in town. It is made up of show and gloomy parade: mourning carriages, mourning horses, mourning plumes, and hireling mourners, who make a mockery of grief. "There is a grave digged," says Jeremy Taylor, "and a solemn mourning, and a great talk in the neighborhood, and when the daies are finished, they shall be, and they shall be remembered no more." The associate in the gay and crowded city is soon forgotten; the hurrying succession of new intimates and new pleasures effaces him from our minds, and the very scenes and circles in which he moved are incessantly fluctuating. But funerals in the country are solemnly impressive. The stroke of death makes a wider space in the village circle, and is an awful event in the tranquil uniformity of rural life. The passing bell tolls its knell in every ear; it steals with its pervading melancholy over hill and vale, and saddens all the landscape.

The fixed and unchanging features of the country also perpetuate the memory of the friend with whom we once enjoyed them, who was the companion of our most retired walks, and gave animation to every lonely scene. His idea is associated with every charm of nature; we hear his voice in the echo which he once delighted to awaken; his spirit haunts the grove which he once frequented; we think of him in the wild upland solitude or amidst the pensive beauty of the valley. In the freshness of joyous morning we remember his beaming smiles and bounding gayety; and when sober evening returns with its gathering shadows and subduing quiet, we call to mind many a twilight hour of gentle talk and sweet-souled melancholy.

> Each lonely place shall him restore,
> For him the tear be duly shed;
> Beloved till life can charm no more,
> And mourn'd, till pity's self be dead.

Another cause that perpetuates the memory of the deceased in the country is that the grave is more immediately in sight of the survivors. They pass it on their way to prayer; it meets their eyes when their hearts are softened by the exercises of devotion; they linger about it on the Sabbath, when the mind is disengaged from worldly cares and most disposed to turn aside from present pleasures and present loves and to sit down among the solemn mementos of the past. In North Wales the peasantry kneel and pray over the graves of their deceased friends for several Sundays after the interment; and where the tender rite of strewing and planting flowers is still practised, it is always renewed on Easter, Whitsuntide, and other festivals, when the season brings the companion of former festivity more vividly to mind. It is also invariably performed by the nearest relatives and friends; no menials nor hirelings are employed, and if a neighbor yields assistance, it would be deemed an insult to offer compensation.

I have dwelt upon this beautiful rural custom because, as it is one of the last, so is it one of the holiest offices of love. The grave is the ordeal of true affection. It is there that the divine passion of the soul manifests its superiority to the instinctive impulse of mere animal attachment. The latter must be continually refreshed and kept alive by the presence of its object, but the love that is seated in the soul can live on long remembrance. The mere inclinations of sense languish and decline with the charms which excited them, and turn with shuddering disgust from the dismal precincts of the tomb; but it is thence that truly spiritual affection rises, purified from every sensual desire, and returns, like a holy flame, to illumine and sanctify the heart of the survivor.

The sorrow for the dead is the only sorrow from which we refuse to be divorced. Every other wound we seek to heal, every other affliction to forget; but this wound we consider it a duty to keep open, this affliction we cherish and brood over in solitude. Where is the mother who would willingly forget the infant that perished like a blossom from her arms though every recollection is a pang? Where is the child that would willingly forget the most tender of parents, though to remember be but to lament? Who, even in the hour of agony, would forget the friend over whom he mourns? Who, even when the tomb is closing upon the remains of her he most loved, when he feels his heart, as it were, crushed in the closing of its portal, would accept of consolation that must be bought by forgetfulness? No, the love which survives the tomb is one of the noblest attributes of the soul. If it has its woes, it has likewise its delights; and when the overwhelming burst of grief is calmed into the gentle tear of recollection, when the sudden anguish and the convulsive agony over the present ruins of all that we most loved is softened away into pensive meditation on all that it was in the days of its loveliness, who would root out such a sorrow from the heart? Though it may sometimes throw a passing cloud over the bright hour of gayety, or spread a deeper sadness over the hour of gloom, yet who would exchange it even for the song of pleasure or the burst of revelry? No, there is a voice from the tomb sweeter than song. There is a remembrance of the dead to which we turn even from the charms of the living. Oh, the grave! the grave! It buries every error, covers every defect, extinguishes every resentment! From its peaceful bosom spring none but fond regrets and tender recollections. Who can look down upon the grave even of an enemy, and not feel a compunctious throb that he should ever have warred with the poor handful of earth that lies mouldering before him?

But the grave of those we loved—what a place for meditation! There it is that we call up in long review the whole history of virtue and gentleness, and the thousand endearments lavished upon us almost unheeded in the daily intercourse of intimacy; there it is that we dwell upon the tenderness, the solemn, awful tenderness, of the parting scene. The bed of death, with all its stifled griefs—its noiseless attendance—its mute, watchful assiduities. The last testimonies of expiring love! The feeble, fluttering, thrilling—oh, how thrilling!—pressure of the hand! The faint, faltering accents, struggling in death to give one more assurance of affection! The last fond look of the glazing eye, turning upon us even from the threshold of existence!

Ay, go to the grave of buried love and meditate! There settle the account with thy conscience for every past benefit unrequited—every past endearment unregarded, of that departed being who can never—never—never return to be soothed by thy contrition!

If thou art a child, and hast ever added a sorrow to the soul or a furrow to the silvered brow of an affectionate parent; if thou art a husband, and hast ever caused the fond bosom that ventured its whole happiness in thy arms to doubt one moment of thy kindness or thy truth; if thou art a friend, and hast ever wronged, in thought or word or deed, the spirit that generously confided in thee; if thou art a lover, and hast ever given one unmerited pang to that true heart which now lies cold and still beneath thy feet;—then be sure that every unkind look, every ungracious word, every ungentle action will come thronging back upon thy memory and knocking dolefully at thy soul—then be sure that thou wilt lie down sorrowing and repentant on the grave, and utter the unheard groan and pour the unavailing tear, more deep, more bitter because unheard and unavailing.

Then weave thy chaplet of flowers and strew the beauties of Nature about the grave; console thy broken spirit, if thou canst, with these tender yet futile tributes of regret; but take warning by the bitterness of this thy contrite affliction over the dead, and henceforth be more faithful and affectionate in the discharge of thy duties to the living.

In writing the preceding article it was not intended to give a full detail of the funeral customs of the English peasantry, but merely to furnish a few hints and quotations illustrative of particular rites, to be appended, by way of note, to another paper, which has been withheld. The article swelled insensibly into its present form, and this is mentioned as an apology for so brief and casual a notice of these usages after they have been amply and learnedly investigated in other works.

I must observe, also, that I am well aware that this custom of adorning graves with flowers prevails in other countries besides England. Indeed, in some it is much more general, and is observed even by the rich and fashionable; but it is then apt to lose its simplicity and to degenerate into affectation. Bright, in his travels in Lower Hungary, tells of monuments of marble and recesses formed for retirement, with seats placed among bowers of greenhouse plants, and that the graves generally are covered with the gayest flowers of the season. He gives a casual picture of filial piety which I cannot but transcribe; for I trust it is as useful as it is delightful to illustrate the amiable virtues of the sex. "When I was at Berlin," says he, "I followed the celebrated Iffland to the grave. Mingled with some pomp you might trace much real feeling. In the midst of the ceremony my attention was attracted by a young woman who stood on a mound of earth newly covered with turf, which she anxiously protected from the feet of the passing crowd. It was the tomb of her parent; and the figure of this affectionate daughter presented a monument more striking than the most costly work of art."

I will barely add an instance of sepulchral decoration that I once met with among the mountains of Switzerland. It was at the village of Gersau, which stands on the borders of the Lake of Lucerne, at the foot of Mount Rigi. It was once the capital of a miniature republic shut up between the Alps and the lake, and accessible on the land side only by footpaths. The whole force of the republic did not exceed six hundred fighting men, and a few miles of circumference, scooped out as it were from the bosom of the mountains, comprised its territory. The village of Gersau seemed separated from the rest of the world, and retained the golden simplicity of a purer age. It had a small church, with a burying-ground adjoining. At the heads of the graves were placed crosses of wood or iron. On some were affixed miniatures, rudely executed, but evidently attempts at likenesses of the deceased. On the crosses were hung chaplets of flowers, some withering, others fresh, as if occasionally renewed. I paused with interest at this scene: I felt that I was at the source of poetical description, for these were the beautiful but unaffected offerings of the heart which poets are fain to record. In a gayer and more populous place I should have suspected them to have been suggested by factitious sentiment derived from books; but the good people of Gersau knew little of books; there was not a novel nor a love-poem in the village, and I question whether any peasant of the place dreamt, while he was twining a fresh chaplet for the grave of his mistress, that he was fulfilling one of the most fanciful rites of poetical devotion, and that he was practically a poet.

THE INN KITCHEN

Shall I not take mine ease in mine inn?
—FALSTAFF

During a journey that I once made through the Netherlands, I had arrived one evening at the Pomme d'Or, the principal inn of a small Flemish village. It was after the hour of the *table d'hote*, so that I was obliged to make a solitary supper from the relics of its ampler board. The weather was chilly; I was seated alone in one end of a great gloomy dining-room, and, my repast being over, I had the prospect before me of a long dull evening, without any visible means of enlivening it. I summoned mine host and requested something to read; he brought me the whole literary stock of his household, a Dutch family Bible, an almanac in the same language, and a number of old Paris newspapers. As I sat dozing over one of the latter, reading old news and stale criticisms, my ear was now and then struck with bursts of laughter which seemed to proceed from the kitchen. Every one that has travelled on the Continent must know how favorite a resort the kitchen of a country inn is to the middle and inferior order of travellers, particularly in that equivocal kind of weather when a fire becomes agreeable toward evening. I threw aside the newspaper and explored my way to the kitchen, to take a peep at the group that appeared to be so merry. It was composed partly of travellers who had arrived some hours before in a diligence, and partly of the usual attendants and hangers-on of inns. They were seated round a great burnished stove, that might have been mistaken for an altar at which they were worshipping. It was covered with various kitchen vessels of resplendent brightness, among which steamed and hissed a huge copper tea-kettle. A large lamp threw a strong mass of light upon the group, bringing out many odd features in strong relief. Its yellow rays partially illumined the spacious kitchen, dying duskily away into remote corners, except where they settled in mellow radiance on the broad side of a flitch of bacon or were reflected back from well-scoured utensils that gleamed from the midst of obscurity. A strapping Flemish lass, with long golden pendants in her ears and a necklace with a golden heart suspended to it, was the presiding priestess of the temple.

Many of the company were furnished with pipes, and most of them with some kind of evening potation. I found their mirth was occasioned by anecdotes which a little swarthy Frenchman, with a dry weazen face and large whiskers, was giving of his love-adventures; at the end of each of which there was one of those bursts of honest unceremonious laughter in which a man indulges in that temple of true liberty, an inn.

As I had no better mode of getting through a tedious blustering evening, I took my seat near the stove, and listened to a variety of travellers' tales, some very extravagant and most very dull. All of them, however, have faded from my treacherous memory except one, which I will endeavor to relate. I fear, however, it derived its chief zest from the manner in which it was told, and the peculiar air and appearance of the narrator. He was a corpulent old Swiss, who had the look of a veteran traveller. He was dressed in a tarnished green travelling-jacket, with a broad belt round his waist, and a pair of overalls with buttons from the hips to the ankles. He was of a full rubicund countenance, with a double chin, aquiline nose, and a pleasant twinkling eye. His hair was light, and curled from under an old green velvet travelling-cap stuck on one side of his head. He was interrupted more than once by the arrival of guests or the remarks of his auditors, and paused now and then to replenish his pipe; at which times he had generally a roguish leer and a sly joke for the buxom kitchen-maid.

I wish my readers could imagine the old fellow lolling in a huge arm-chair, one arm a-kimbo, the other holding a curiously twisted tobacco-pipe formed of genuine *écume de mer*, decorated with silver chain and silken tassel, his head cocked on one side, and a whimsical cut of the eye occasionally as he related the following story.

THE SPECTRE BRIDEGROOM

A TRAVELLER'S TALE*

He that supper for is dight,
He lyes full cold, I trow, this night!
Yestreen to chamber I him led,
This night Gray-steel has made his bed!
—SIR EGER, SIR GRAHAME, AND SIR GRAY-STEEL

On the summit of one of the heights of the Odenwald, a wild and romantic tract of Upper Germany that lies not far from the confluence of the Main and the Rhine, there stood many, many years since the castle of the Baron Von Landshort. It is now quite fallen to decay, and almost buried among beech trees and dark firs; above which, however, its old watch-tower may still be seen struggling, like the former possessor I have mentioned, to carry a high head and look down upon the neighboring country.

The baron was a dry branch of the great family of Katzenellenbogen,† and inherited the relics of the property, and all the pride, of his ancestors. Though the warlike disposition of his predecessors had much impaired the family possessions, yet the baron still endeavored to keep up some show of former state. The times were peaceable, and the German nobles in general had abandoned their inconvenient old castles, perched like eagles' nests among the mountains, and had built more convenient residences in the valleys; still, the baron remained proudly drawn up in his little fortress, cherishing with hereditary inveteracy all the old family feuds, so that he was on ill terms with some of his nearest neighbors, on account of disputes that had happened between their great-great-grandfathers.

The baron had but one child, a daughter, but nature, when she grants

* The erudite reader, well versed in good-for-nothing lore, will perceive that the above tale must have been suggested to the old Swiss by a little French anecdote, a circumstance said to have taken place in Paris.

† i.e., Catselbow—the name of a family of those parts, and very powerful in former times. The appellation, we are told, was given in compliment to a peerless dame of the family, celebrated for a fine arm.

but one child, always compensates by making it a prodigy; and so it was with the daughter of the baron. All the nurses, gossips, and country cousins assured her father that she had not her equal for beauty in all Germany; and who should know better than they? She had, moreover, been brought up with great care under the superintendence of two maiden aunts, who had spent some years of their early life at one of the little German courts, and were skilled in all branches of knowledge necessary to the education of a fine lady. Under their instructions, she became a miracle of accomplishments. By the time she was eighteen she could embroider to admiration, and had worked whole histories of the saints in tapestry with such strength of expression in their countenances that they looked like so many souls in purgatory. She could read without great difficulty, and had spelled her way through several Church legends and almost all the chivalric wonders of the Heldenbuch. She had even made considerable proficiency in writing; could sign her own name without missing a letter, and so legibly that her aunts could read it without spectacles. She excelled in making little elegant good-for-nothing, lady-like knicknacks of all kinds, was versed in the most abstruse dancing of the day, played a number of airs on the harp and guitar, and knew all the tender ballads of the Minne-lieders by heart.

Her aunts, too, having been great flirts and coquettes in their younger days, were admirably calculated to be vigilant guardians and strict censors of the conduct of their niece; for there is no duenna so rigidly prudent and inexorably decorous as a superannuated coquette. She was rarely suffered out of their sight; never went beyond the domains of the castle unless well attended, or rather well watched; had continual lectures read to her about strict decorum and implicit obedience; and, as to the men—pah!—she was taught to hold them at such a distance and in such absolute distrust that, unless properly authorized, she would not have cast a glance upon the handsomest cavalier in the world—no, not if he were even dying at her feet.

The good effects of this system were wonderfully apparent. The young lady was a pattern of docility and correctness. While others were wasting their sweetness in the glare of the world, and liable to be plucked and thrown aside by every hand, she was coyly blooming into fresh and lovely womanhood under the protection of those immaculate spinsters, like a rosebud blushing forth among guardian thorns. Her aunts looked upon her with pride and exultation, and vaunted that, though all the other young ladies in the world might go astray, yet thank Heaven, nothing of the kind could happen to the heiress of Katzenellenbogen.

But, however scantily the Baron Von Landshort might be provided with children, his household was by no means a small one; for Providence had enriched him with abundance of poor relations. They, one and all, possessed the affectionate disposition common to humble relatives—were wonderfully attached to the baron, and took every possible occasion to come in swarms and enliven the castle. All family festivals were commemorated by these good people at the baron's expense; and when they were filled with good cheer they would declare that there was nothing on earth so delightful as these family meetings, these jubilees of the heart.

The baron, though a small man, had a large soul, and it swelled with satisfaction at the consciousness of being the greatest man in the little world about him. He loved to tell long stories about the stark old warriors whose portraits looked grimly down from the walls around, and he found no listeners equal to those who fed at his expense. He was much given to the marvellous, and a firm believer in all those supernatural tales with which every mountain and valley in Germany abounds. The faith of his guests exceeded even his own: they listened to every tale of wonder with open eyes and mouth, and never failed to be astonished, even though repeated for the hundredth time. Thus lived the Baron Von Landshort, the oracle of his table, the absolute monarch of his little territory, and happy, above all things, in the persuasion that he was the wisest man of the age.

At the time of which my story treats, there was a great family gathering at the castle on an affair of the utmost importance: it was to receive the destined bridegroom of the baron's daughter. A negotiation had been carried on between the father and an old nobleman of Bavaria to unite the dignity of their houses by the marriage of their children. The preliminaries had been conducted with proper punctilio. The young people were betrothed without seeing each other, and the time was appointed for the marriage ceremony. The young Count Von Altenburg had been recalled from the army for the purpose, and was actually on his way to the baron's to receive his bride. Missives had even been received from him from Wurtzburg, where he was accidentally detained, mentioning the day and hour when he might be expected to arrive.

The castle was in a tumult of preparation to give him a suitable welcome. The fair bride had been decked out with uncommon care. The two aunts had superintended her toilet, and quarrelled the whole morning about every article of her dress. The young lady had taken advantage of their contest to follow the bent of her own taste; and fortunately it was a good one. She looked as lovely as youthful bridegroom could desire, and the flutter of expectation heightened the lustre of her charms.

The suffusions that mantled her face and neck, the gentle heaving of the bosom, the eye now and then lost in reverie, all betrayed the soft tumult that was going on in her little heart. The aunts were continually hovering around her, for maiden aunts are apt to take great interest in affairs of this nature. They were giving her a world of staid counsel how to deport herself, what to say, and in what manner to receive the expected lover.

The baron was no less busied in preparations. He had, in truth, nothing exactly to do; but he was naturally a fuming, bustling little man, and could not remain passive when all the world was in a hurry. He worried from top to bottom of the castle with an air of infinite anxiety; he continually called the servants from their work to exhort them to be diligent; and buzzed about every hall and chamber, as idly restless and importunate as a blue-bottle fly on a warm summer's day.

In the meantime, the fatted calf had been killed; the forests had rung with the clamor of the huntsmen; the kitchen was crowded with good cheer; the cellars had yielded up whole oceans of *Rhein-wein* and *Ferne-wein*; and even the great Heidelberg tun had been laid under contribution. Everything was ready to receive the distinguished guest with *Saus und Braus* in the true spirit of German hospitality; but the guest delayed to make his appearance. Hour rolled after hour. The sun, that had poured his downward rays upon the rich forest of the

Odenwald, now just gleamed along the summits of the mountains. The baron mounted the highest tower and strained his eyes in hopes of catching a distant sight of the count and his attendants. Once he thought he beheld them; the sound of horns came floating from the valley, prolonged by the mountain-echoes. A number of horsemen were seen far below slowly advancing along the road; but when they had nearly reached the foot of the mountain they suddenly struck off in a different direction. The last ray of sunshine departed, the bats began to flit by in the twilight, the road grew dimmer and dimmer to the view, and nothing appeared stirring in it but now and then a peasant lagging homeward from his labor.

While the old castle of Landshort was in this state of perplexity, a very interesting scene was transacting in a different part of the Odenwald.

The young Count Von Altenburg was tranquilly pursuing his route in that sober jog-trot way in which a man travels toward matrimony when his friends have taken all the trouble and uncertainty of courtship off his hands, and a bride is waiting for him as certainly as a dinner at the end of his journey. He had encountered at Wurtzburg a youthful companion-in-arms with whom he had seen some service on the frontiers—Herman Von Starkenfaust, one of the stoutest hands and worthiest hearts of German chivalry—who was now returning from the army. His father's castle was not far distant from the old fortress of Landshort, although an hereditary feud rendered the families hostile and strangers to each other.

In the warm-hearted moment of recognition, the young friends related all their past adventures and fortunes, and the count gave the whole history of his intended nuptials with a young lady whom he had never seen, but of whose charms he had received the most enrapturing descriptions.

As the route of the friends lay in the same direction, they agreed to perform the rest of their journey together, and that they might do it the more leisurely, set off from Wurtzburg at an early hour, the count having given directions for his retinue to follow and overtake him.

They beguiled their wayfaring with recollections of their military scenes and adventures; but the count was apt to be a little tedious now and then about the reputed charms of his bride and the felicity that awaited him.

In this way they had entered among the mountains of the Odenwald, and were traversing one of its most lonely and thickly wooded passes. It is well known that the forests of Germany have always been as much infested by robbers as its castles by spectres; and at this time the former were particularly numerous, from the hordes of disbanded soldiers wandering about the country. It will not appear extraordinary, therefore, that the cavaliers were attacked by a gang of these stragglers, in the midst of the forest. They defended themselves with bravery, but were nearly overpowered when the count's retinue arrived to their assistance. At sight of them the robbers fled, but not until the count had received a mortal wound. He was slowly and carefully conveyed back to the city of Wurtzburg, and a friar summoned from a neighboring convent who was famous for his skill in administering to both soul and body; but half of his skill was superfluous; the moments of the unfortunate count were numbered.

With his dying breath he entreated his friend to repair instantly to the castle of Landshort and explain the fatal cause of his not keeping his appointment with his bride. Though not the most ardent of lovers, he was one of the most punctilious of men, and appeared earnestly solicitous that his mission should be speedily and courteously executed. "Unless this is done," said he, "I shall not sleep quietly in my grave." He repeated these last words with peculiar solemnity. A request at a moment so impressive admitted no hesitation. Starkenfaust endeavored to soothe him to calmness, promised faithfully to execute his wish, and gave him his hand in solemn pledge. The dying man pressed it in acknowledgment, but soon lapsed into delirium—raved about his bride, his engagements, his plighted word—ordered his horse, that he might ride to the castle of Landshort, and expired in the fancied act of vaulting into the saddle.

Starkenfaust bestowed a sigh and a soldier's tear on the untimely fate of his comrade and then pondered on the awkward mission he had undertaken. His heart was heavy and his head perplexed; for he was to present himself an unbidden guest among hostile people, and to damp their festivity with tidings fatal to their hopes. Still, there were certain whisperings of curiosity in his bosom to see this far-famed beauty of

Katzenellenbogen, so cautiously shut up from the world; for he was a passionate admirer of the sex, and there was a dash of eccentricity and enterprise in his character that made him fond of all singular adventure.

Previous to his departure he made all due arrangements with the holy fraternity of the convent for the funeral solemnities of his friend, who was to be buried in the cathedral of Wurtzburg near some of his illustrious relatives, and the mourning retinue of the count took charge of his remains.

It is now high time that we should return to the ancient family of Katzenellenbogen, who were impatient for their guest, and still more for their dinner, and to the worthy little baron, whom we left airing himself on the watch-tower.

Night closed in, but still no guest arrived. The baron descended from the tower in despair. The banquet, which had been delayed from hour to hour, could no longer be postponed. The meats were already overdone, the cook in an agony, and the whole household had the look of a garrison, that had been reduced by famine. The baron was obliged reluctantly to give orders for the feast without the presence of the guest. All were seated at table, and just on the point of commencing, when the sound of a horn from without the gate gave notice of the approach of a stranger. Another long blast filled the old courts of the castle with its echoes, and was answered by the warder from the walls. The baron hastened to receive his future son-in-law.

The drawbridge had been let down, and the stranger was before the gate. He was a tall gallant cavalier, mounted on a black steed. His countenance was pale, but he had a beaming, romantic eye and an air of stately melancholy. The baron was a little mortified that he should have come in this simple, solitary style. His dignity for a moment was ruffled, and he felt disposed to consider it a want of proper respect for the important occasion and the important family with which he was to be connected. He pacified himself, however, with the conclusion that it must have been youthful impatience which had induced him thus to spur on sooner than his attendants.

"I am sorry," said the stranger, "to break in upon you thus unseasonably—"

Here the baron interrupted him with a world of compliments and greetings, for, to tell the truth, he prided himself upon his courtesy and eloquence. The stranger attempted once or twice to stem the torrent of words, but in vain, so he bowed his head and suffered it to flow on. By the time the baron had come to a pause they had reached the inner court of the castle, and the stranger was again about to speak, when he was once more interrupted by the appearance of the female part of the family, leading forth the shrinking and blushing bride. He gazed on her for a moment as one entranced; it seemed as if his whole soul beamed forth in the gaze and rested upon that lovely form. One of the maiden aunts whispered something in her ear; she made an effort to speak; her moist blue eye was timidly raised, gave a shy glance of inquiry on the stranger, and was cast again to the ground. The words died away, but there was a sweet smile playing about her lips, and a soft dimpling of the cheek that showed her glance had not been unsatisfactory. It was impossible for a girl of the fond age of eighteen, highly predisposed for love and matrimony, not to be pleased with so gallant a cavalier.

The late hour at which the guest had arrived left no time for parley. The baron was peremptory, and deferred all particular conversation until the morning, and led the way to the untasted banquet.

It was served up in the great hall of the castle. Around the walls hung the hard-favored portraits of the heroes of the house of Katzenellenbogen, and the trophies which they had gained in the field, and in the chase. Hacked corselets, splintered jousting-spears, and tattered banners were mingled with the spoils of sylvan warfare: the jaws of the wolf and the tusks of the boar grinned horribly among crossbows and battle-axes, and a huge pair of antlers branched immediately over the head of the youthful bridegroom.

The cavalier took but little notice of the company or the entertainment. He scarcely tasted the banquet, but seemed absorbed in admiration of his bride. He conversed in a low tone that could not be overheard, for the language of love is never loud; but where is the female ear so dull that it cannot catch the softest whisper of the lover? There was a mingled tenderness and gravity in his manner that appeared to have a powerful effect upon the young lady. Her color came and went as she listened with deep attention. Now and then she made some blushing reply, and when his eye was turned away she would steal a sidelong glance at his romantic countenance, and heave a gentle sigh of tender happiness. It was evident that the young couple were completely enamored. The aunts, who were deeply versed in the mysteries of the heart, declared that they had fallen in love with each other at first sight.

The feast went on merrily, or at least noisily, for the guests were all blessed with those keen appetites that attend upon light purses and mountain air. The baron told his best and longest stories, and never had he told them so well or with such great effect. If there was anything marvellous, his auditors were lost in astonishment; and if anything facetious, they were sure to laugh exactly in the right place. The baron, it is true, like most great men, was too dignified to utter any joke but a dull one; it was always enforced, however, by a bumper of excellent Hockheimer, and even a dull joke at one's own table, served up with jolly old wine, is irresistible. Many good things were said by poorer and keener wits that would not bear repeating, except on similar occasions; many sly speeches whispered in ladies' ears that almost convulsed them with suppressed laughter; and a song or two roared out by a poor but merry and broad-faced cousin of the baron that absolutely made the maiden aunts hold up their fans.

Amidst all this revelry the stranger guest maintained a most singular and unseasonable gravity. His countenance assumed a deeper cast of dejection as the evening advanced, and, strange as it may appear, even the baron's jokes seemed only to render him the more melancholy. At times he was lost in thought, and at times there was a perturbed and restless wandering of the eye that bespoke a mind but ill at ease. His conversations with the bride became more and more earnest and mysterious. Lowering clouds began to steal over the fair serenity of her brow, and tremors to run through her tender frame.

All this could not escape the notice of the company. Their gayety was chilled by the unaccountable gloom of the bridegroom; their spirits were infected; whispers and glances were interchanged, accompanied by shrugs and dubious shakes of the head. The song and the laugh grew less and less frequent: there were dreary pauses in the conversation, which were at length succeeded by wild tales and supernatural legends. One dismal story produced another still more dismal, and the baron nearly frightened some of the ladies into hysterics with the history of the goblin horseman that carried away the fair Leonora—a dreadful story which has since been put into excellent verse, and is read and believed by all the world.

The bridegroom listened to this tale with profound attention. He kept his eyes steadily fixed on the baron, and, as the story drew to a close, began gradually to rise from his seat, growing taller and taller, until in the baron's entranced eye he seemed almost to tower into a giant. The moment the tale was finished he heaved a deep sigh and took a solemn farewell of the company. They were all amazement. The baron was perfectly thunderstruck.

"What! going to leave the castle at midnight? Why, everything was prepared for his reception; a chamber was ready for him if he wished to retire."

The stranger shook his head mournfully and mysteriously: "I must lay my head in a different chamber to-night."

There was something in this reply and the tone in which it was uttered that made the baron's heart misgive him; but he rallied his forces and repeated his hospitable entreaties.

The stranger shook his head silently, but positively, at every offer, and, waving his farewell to the company, stalked slowly out of the hall. The maiden aunts were absolutely petrified; the bride hung her head and a tear stole to her eye.

The baron followed the stranger to the great court of the castle, where the black charger stood pawing the earth and snorting with impatience. When they had reached the portal, whose deep archway was dimly lighted by a cresset, the stranger paused, and addressed the baron in a hollow tone of voice, which the vaulted roof rendered still more sepulchral.

"Now that we are alone," said he, "I will impart to you the reason of my going. I have a solemn, an indispensable engagement—"

"Why," said the baron, "cannot you send some one in your place?"

"It admits of no substitute—I must attend it in person; I must away to Wurtzburg cathedral—"

"Ay," said the baron, plucking up spirit, "but not until to-morrow—to-morrow you shall take your bride there."

"No! no!" replied the stranger, with tenfold solemnity, "my engagement is with no bride—the worms! the worms expect me! I am a dead man—I have been slain by robbers—my body lies at Wurtzburg—at midnight I am to be buried—the grave is waiting for me—I must keep my appointment!"

He sprang on his black charger, dashed over the drawbridge, and the clattering of his horse's hoofs was lost in the whistling of the night blast.

The baron returned to the hall in the utmost consternation, and related what had passed. Two ladies fainted outright, others sickened at the idea of having banqueted with a spectre. It was the opinion of some that this might be the wild huntsman, famous in German legend. Some talked of mountain-sprites, of wood-demons, and of other supernatural beings with which the good people of Germany have been so grievously harassed since time immemorial. One of the poor relations ventured to suggest that it might be some sportive evasion of the young cavalier, and that the very gloominess of the caprice seemed to accord with so melancholy a personage. This, however, drew on him, the indignation of the whole company, and especially of the baron, who looked upon him as little better than an infidel; so that he was fain to abjure his heresy as speedily as possible and come into the faith of the true believers.

But, whatever may have been the doubts entertained, they were completely put to an end by the arrival next day of regular missives confirming the intelligence of the young count's murder and his interment in Wurtzburg cathedral.

The dismay at the castle may well be imagined. The baron shut himself up in his chamber. The guests, who had come to rejoice with him, could not think of abandoning him in his distress. They wandered about the courts or collected in groups in the hall, shaking their heads and shrugging their shoulders at the troubles of so good a man, and sat longer than ever at table, and ate and drank more stoutly than ever, by way of keeping up their spirits. But the situation of the widowed bride was the most pitiable. To have lost a husband before she had even embraced him—and such a husband! If the very spectre could be so gracious and noble, what must have been the living man? She filled the house with lamentations.

On the night of the second day of her widowhood she had retired to her chamber, accompanied by one of her aunts, who insisted on sleeping with her. The aunt, who was one of the best tellers of ghost-stories in all Germany, had just been recounting one of her longest, and had fallen asleep in the very midst of it. The chamber was remote and overlooked a small garden. The niece lay pensively gazing at the beams of the rising moon as they trembled on the leaves of an aspen tree before the lattice. The castle clock had just tolled midnight when a soft strain of music stole up from the garden. She rose hastily from her bed and stepped lightly to the window. A tall figure stood among the shadows of the trees. As it raised its head a beam of moonlight fell upon the countenance. Heaven and earth! she beheld the Spectre Bridegroom! A loud shriek at that moment burst upon her ear, and her aunt, who had been awakened by the music and had followed her silently to the window, fell into her arms. When she looked again the spectre had disappeared.

Of the two females, the aunt now required the most soothing, for she was perfectly beside herself with terror. As to the young lady, there was something even in the spectre of her lover that seemed endearing. There was still the semblance of manly beauty, and, though the shadow of a man is but little calculated to satisfy the affections of a lovesick girl, yet where the substance is not to be had even that is consoling. The aunt declared she would never sleep in that chamber again; the niece, for once, was refractory, and declared as strongly that she would sleep in no other in the castle: the consequence was, that she had to sleep in it alone; but she drew a promise from her aunt not to relate the story of the spectre, lest she should be denied the only melancholy pleasure left her on earth—that of inhabiting the chamber over which the guardian shade of her lover kept its nightly vigils.

How long the good old lady would have observed this promise is uncertain, for she dearly loved to talk of the marvellous, and there is a triumph in being the first to tell a frightful story; it is, however, still quoted in the neighborhood as a memorable instance of female secrecy that she kept it to herself for a whole week, when she was suddenly absolved from all further restraint by intelligence brought to the breakfast-table one morning that the young lady was not to be found. Her room was empty—the bed had not been slept in—the window was open and the bird had flown!

The astonishment and concern with which the intelligence was received can only be imagined by those who have witnessed the agitation which the mishaps of a great man cause among his friends. Even the poor relations paused for a moment from the indefatigable labors of the trencher, when the aunt, who had at first been struck speechless, wrung her hands and shrieked out, "The goblin! the goblin! she's carried away by the goblin!"

In a few words she related the fearful scene of the garden, and concluded that the spectre must have carried off his bride. Two of the domestics corroborated the opinion, for they had heard the clattering of a horse's hoofs down the mountain about midnight, and had no doubt that it was the spectre on his black charger bearing her away to the tomb. All present were struck with the direful probability for events of the kind are extremely common in Germany, as many well-authenticated histories bear witness.

What a lamentable situation was that of the poor baron! What a heartrending dilemma for a fond father and a member of the great family of Katzenellenbogen! His only daughter had either been rapt away to the grave, or he was to have some wood-demon for a son-in-law, and perchance a troop of goblin grandchildren. As usual, he was completely bewildered, and all the castle in an uproar. The men were ordered to take horse and scour every road and path and glen of the Odenwald. The baron himself had just drawn on his jack-boots, girded on his sword, and was about to mount his steed to sally forth on the doubtful quest, when he was brought to a pause by a new apparition. A lady was seen approaching the castle mounted on a palfrey, attended by a cavalier on horseback. She galloped up to the gate, sprang from her horse, and, falling at the baron's feet, embraced his knees. It was his lost daughter, and her companion—the Spectre Bridegroom! The baron was astounded. He looked at his daughter, then at the spectre, and almost doubted the evidence of his senses. The latter, too, was wonderfully improved in his appearance since his visit to the world of spirits. His dress was splendid, and set off a noble figure of manly symmetry. He was no longer pale and melancholy. His fine countenance was flushed with the glow of youth, and joy rioted in his large dark eye.

The mystery was soon cleared up. The cavalier (for, in truth, as you must have known all the while, he was no goblin) announced himself as Sir Herman Von Starkenfaust. He related his adventure with the young count. He told how he had hastened to the castle to deliver the unwelcome tidings, but that the eloquence of the baron had interrupted him in every attempt to tell his tale. How the sight of the bride had completely captivated him and that to pass a few hours near her he had tacitly suffered the mistake to continue. How he had been sorely perplexed in what way to make a decent retreat, until the baron's goblin stories had suggested his eccentric exit. How, fearing the feudal hostility of the family, he had repeated his visits by stealth—had haunted the garden beneath the young lady's window—had wooed—had won—had borne away in triumph—and, in a word, had wedded the fair.

Under any other circumstances the baron would have been inflexible, for he was tenacious of paternal authority and devoutly obstinate in all family feuds; but he loved his daughter; he had lamented her as lost; he rejoiced to find her still alive; and, though her husband was of a hostile house, yet, thank Heaven! he was not a goblin. There was something, it must be acknowledged, that did not exactly accord with his notions of strict veracity in the joke the knight had passed upon him of his being a dead man; but several old friends present, who had served in the wars, assured him that every stratagem was excusable in love, and that the cavalier was entitled to especial privilege, having lately served as a trooper.

Matters, therefore, were happily arranged. The baron pardoned the young couple on the spot. The revels at the castle were resumed. The poor relations overwhelmed this new member of the family with loving kindness; he was so gallant, so generous—and so rich. The aunts, it is true, were somewhat scandalized that their system of strict seclusion and passive obedience should be so badly exemplified, but attributed it all to their negligence in not having the windows grated. One of them was particularly mortified at having her marvellous story marred, and that the only spectre she had ever seen should turn out a counterfeit; but the niece seemed perfectly happy at having found him substantial flesh and blood. And so the story ends.

WESTMINSTER ABBEY

When I behold, with deepe astonishment,
To famous Westminster how there resorte,
Living in brasse or stoney monyment,
The princes and the worthies of all sorte:
Doe not I see reformde nobilitie,
Without contempt, or pride, or ostentation,
And looke upon offenselesse majesty,
Naked of pomp or earthly domination?
And how a play-game of a painted stone
Contents the quiet now and silent sprites,
Whome all the world which late they stood upon,
Could not content nor quench their appetites.
    Life is a froste of cold felicitie,
    And death the thaw of all our vanitie.
— Christolero's Epigrams, by T. B. 1598

On one of those sober and rather melancholy days in the latter part of autumn, when the shadows of morning and evening almost mingle together, and throw a gloom over the decline of the year, I passed several hours in rambling about Westminster Abbey. There was something congenial to the season in the mournful magnificence of the old pile; and as I passed its threshold it seemed like stepping back into the regions of antiquity and losing myself among the shades of former ages.

I entered from the inner court of Westminster School, through a long, low, vaulted passage that had an almost subterranean look, being dimly lighted in one part by circular perforations in the massive walls. Through this dark avenue I had a distant view of the cloisters, with the figure of an old verger in his black gown moving along their shadowy vaults, and seeming like a spectre from one of the neighboring tombs. The approach to the abbey through these gloomy monastic remains prepares the mind for its solemn contemplation. The cloisters still retain something of the quiet and seclusion of former days. The gray walls are discolored by damps and crumbling with age; a coat of hoary moss has gathered over the inscriptions of the mural monuments, and obscured the death's heads and other funereal emblems. The sharp touches of the chisel are gone from the rich tracery of the arches; the roses which adorned the keystones have lost their leafy beauty; everything bears marks of the gradual dilapidations of time, which yet has something touching and pleasing in its very decay.

The sun was pouring down a yellow autumnal ray into the square of the cloisters, beaming upon a scanty plot of grass in the centre, and lighting up an angle of the vaulted passage with a kind of dusky splendor. From between the arcades the eye glanced up to a bit of blue sky or a passing cloud, and beheld the sun-gilt pinnacles of the abbey towering into the azure heaven.

As I paced the cloisters, sometimes contemplating this mingled picture of glory and decay, and sometimes endeavoring to decipher the inscriptions on the tombstones which formed the pavement beneath my feet, my eye was attracted to three figures rudely carved in relief, but nearly worn away by the footsteps of many generations. They were the effigies of three of the early abbots; the epitaphs were entirely effaced; the names alone remained, having no doubt been renewed in later times (Vitalis. Abbas. 1082, and Gislebertus Crispinus. Abbas. 1114, and Laurentius. Abbas. 1176). I remained some little while, musing over these casual relics of antiquity thus left like wrecks upon this distant shore of time, telling no tale but that such beings had been and had perished, teaching no moral but the futility of that pride which hopes still to exact homage in its ashes and to live in an inscription. A little longer, and even these faint records will be obliterated and the monument will cease to be a memorial. Whilst I was yet looking down upon the gravestones, I was roused by the sound of the abbey clock, reverberating from buttress to buttress and echoing among the cloisters. It is almost startling to hear this warning of departed time sounding among the tombs and telling the lapse of the hour, which, like a billow, has rolled us onward towards the grave. I pursued my walk to an arched door opening to the interior of the abbey. On entering here, the magnitude of the building breaks fully upon the mind, contrasted with the vaults of the cloisters. The eye gazes with wonder at clustered columns of gigantic dimensions, with arches springing from them to such an amazing height; and man wandering about their bases, shrunk into insignificance in comparison with his own handiwork. The spaciousness and gloom of this vast edifice produce a profound and mysterious awe. We step cautiously and softly about, as if fearful of disturbing the hallowed silence of the tomb, while every footfall whispers along the walls and chatters among the sepulchres, making us more sensible of the quiet we have interrupted.

It seems as if the awful nature of the place presses down upon the soul and hushes the beholder into noiseless reverence. We feel that we are surrounded by the congregated bones of the great men of past times, who have filled history with their deeds and the earth with their renown. And yet it almost provokes a smile at the vanity of human ambition to see how they are crowded together and jostled in the dust; what parsimony is observed in doling out a scanty nook, a gloomy corner, a little portion of earth, to those whom, when alive, kingdoms could not satisfy: and how many shapes and forms and artifices are devised to catch the casual notice of the passenger, and save from forgetfulness for a few short years a name which once aspired to occupy ages of the world's thought and admiration.

I passed some time in Poet's Corner, which occupies an end of one of the transepts or cross aisles of the abbey. The monuments are generally simple, for the lives of literary men afford no striking themes for the sculptor. Shakespeare and Addison have statues erected to their memories, but the greater part have busts, medallions, and sometimes mere inscriptions. Notwithstanding the simplicity of these memorials, I have always observed that the visitors to the abbey remained longest about them. A kinder and fonder feeling takes place of that cold curiosity or vague admiration with which they gaze on the splendid monuments of the great and the heroic. They linger about these as about the tombs of friends and companions, for indeed there is something of companionship between the author and the reader. Other men are known to posterity only through the medium of history, which is continually growing faint and obscure; but the intercourse between the author and his fellowmen is ever new, active and immediate. He has lived for them more than for himself; he has sacrificed surrounding enjoyments, and shut himself up from the delights of social life, that he might the more intimately commune with distant minds and distant ages. Well may the world cherish his renown, for it has been purchased not by deeds of violence and blood, but by the diligent dispensation of pleasure. Well may posterity be grateful to his memory, for he has left it an inheritance not of empty names and sounding actions, but whole treasures of wisdom, bright gems of thought, and golden veins of language.

From Poet's Corner I continued my stroll towards that part of the abbey which contains the sepulchres of the kings. I wandered among what once were chapels, but which are now occupied by the tombs and monuments of the great. At every turn I met with some illustrious name; or the cognizance of some powerful house renowned in history. As the eye darts into these dusky chambers of death, it catches glimpses of quaint effigies—some kneeling in niches, as if in devotion; others stretched upon the tombs, with hands piously pressed together; warriors in armor, as if reposing after battle; prelates, with crosiers and mitres; and nobles in robes and coronets, lying as it were in state. In glancing over this scene, so strangely populous, yet where every form is so still and silent, it seems almost as if we were treading a mansion of that fabled city where every being had been suddenly transmuted into stone.

I paused to contemplate a tomb on which lay the effigy of a knight in complete armor. A large buckler was on one arm; the hands were pressed together in supplication upon the breast; the face was almost covered by the morion; the legs were crossed, in token of the warrior's having been engaged in the holy war. It was the tomb of a crusader, of one of those military enthusiasts who so strangely mingled religion and romance, and whose exploits form the connecting link between fact and fiction, between the history and the fairy tale. There is something extremely picturesque in the tombs of these adventurers, decorated as they are with rude armorial bearings and gothic sculpture. They comport with the antiquated chapels in which they are generally found; and in considering them, the imagination is apt to kindle with the legendary associations, the romantic fiction, the chivalrous pomp and pageantry which poetry has spread over the wars for the sepulchre of Christ. They are the relics of times utterly gone by; of beings passed from recollection; of customs and manners with which ours have no affinity. They are like objects from some strange and distant land of which we have no certain knowledge, and about which all our conceptions are vague and visionary. There is something extremely solemn and awful in those effigies on gothic tombs, extended as if in the sleep of death or in the supplication of the dying hour. They have an effect infinitely more impressive on my feelings than the fanciful attitudes, the over-wrought conceits, the allegorical groups which abound on modern monuments. I have been struck, also, with the superiority of many of the old sepulchral inscriptions. There was a noble way in former times of saying things simply, and yet saying them proudly; and I do not know an epitaph that breathes a loftier consciousness of family worth and honorable lineage than one which affirms of a noble house that "all the brothers were brave and all the sisters virtuous."

In the opposite transept to Poet's Corner stands a monument which is among the most renowned achievements of modern art, but which to me appears horrible rather than sublime. It is the tomb of Mrs. Nightingale, by Roubillac. The bottom of the monument is represented as throwing open its marble doors, and a sheeted skeleton is starting forth. The shroud is falling from his fleshless frame as he launches his dart at his victim. She is sinking into her affrighted husband's arms, who strives with vain and frantic effort to avert the blow. The whole is executed with terrible truth and spirit; we almost fancy we hear the gibbering yell of triumph bursting from the distended jaws of the spectre. But why should we thus seek to clothe death with unnecessary terrors, and to spread horrors round the tomb of those we love? The grave should be surrounded by everything that might inspire tenderness and veneration for the dead, or that might win the living to virtue. It is the place not of disgust and dismay, but of sorrow and meditation.

While wandering about these gloomy vaults and silent aisles, studying the records of the dead, the sound of busy existence from without occasionally reaches the ear—the rumbling of the passing equipage, the murmur of the multitude, or perhaps the light laugh of pleasure. The contrast is striking with the deathlike repose around: and it has a strange effect upon the feelings thus to hear the surges of active life hurrying along and beating against the very walls of the sepulchre.

I continued in this way to move from tomb to tomb and from chapel to chapel. The day was gradually wearing away; the distant tread of loiterers about the abbey grew less and less frequent; the sweet-tongued bell was summoning to evening prayers; and I saw at a distance the choristers in their white surplices crossing the aisle and entering the choir. I stood before the entrance to Henry the Seventh's chapel. A flight of steps leads up to it through a deep and gloomy but magnificent arch. Great gates of brass, richly and delicately wrought, turn heavily upon their hinges, as if proudly reluctant to admit the feet of common mortals into this most gorgeous of sepulchres.

On entering, the eye is astonished by the pomp of architecture and the elaborate beauty of sculptured detail. The very walls are wrought into universal ornament encrusted with tracery, and scooped into niches crowded with the statues of saints and martyrs. Stone seems, by the cunning labor of the chisel, to have been robbed of its weight and density, suspended aloft as if by magic, and the fretted roof achieved with the wonderful minuteness and airy security of a cobweb.

Along the sides of the chapel are the lofty stalls of the Knights of the Bath, richly carved of oak, though with the grotesque decorations of gothic architecture. On the pinnacles of the stalls are affixed the helmets and crests of the knights, with their scarfs and swords, and above them are suspended their banners, emblazoned with armorial bearings, and contrasting the splendor of gold and purple and crimson with the cold gray fretwork of the roof. In the midst of this grand mausoleum stands the sepulchre of its founder—his effigy, with that of his queen, extended on a sumptuous tomb—and the whole surrounded by a superbly wrought brazen railing.

There is a sad dreariness in this magnificence: this strange mixture of tombs and trophies, these emblems of living and aspiring ambition, close beside mementos which show the dust and oblivion in which all must sooner or later terminate. Nothing impresses the mind with a deeper feeling of loneliness than to tread the silent and deserted scene of former throng and pageant. On looking round on the vacant stalls of the knights and their esquires, and on the rows of dusty but gorgeous banners that were once borne before them, my imagination conjured up the scene when this hall was bright with the valor and beauty of the land, glittering with the splendor of jewelled rank and military array, alive with the tread of many feet and the hum of an admiring multitude.

All had passed away; the silence of death had settled again upon the place, interrupted only by the casual chirping of birds, which had found their way into the chapel and built their nests among its friezes and pendants—sure signs of solitariness and desertion.

When I read the names inscribed on the banners, they were those of men scattered far and wide about the world; some tossing upon distant seas; some under arms in distant lands; some mingling in the busy intrigues of courts and cabinets; all seeking to deserve one more distinction in this mansion of shadowy honors—the melancholy reward of a monument.

Two small aisles on each side of this chapel present a touching instance of the equality of the grave, which brings down the oppressor to a level with the oppressed and mingles the dust of the bitterest enemies together. In one is the sepulchre of the haughty Elizabeth; in the other is that of her victim, the lovely and unfortunate Mary. Not an hour in the day but some ejaculation of pity is uttered over the fate of the latter, mingled with indignation at her oppressor. The walls of Elizabeth's sepulchre continually echo with the sighs of sympathy heaved at the grave of her rival.

A peculiar melancholy reigns over the aisle where Mary lies buried. The light struggles dimly through windows darkened by dust. The greater part of the place is in deep shadow, and the walls are stained and tinted by time and weather. A marble figure of Mary is stretched upon the tomb, round which is an iron railing, much corroded, bearing her national emblem—the thistle. I was weary with wandering, and sat down to rest myself by the monument, revolving in my mind the chequered and disastrous story of poor Mary.

The sound of casual footsteps had ceased from the abbey. I could only hear, now and then, the distant voice of the priest repeating the evening service and the faint responses of the choir; these paused for a time, and all was hushed. The stillness, the desertion, and obscurity that were gradually prevailing around gave a deeper and more solemn interest to the place:

> For in the silent grave no conversation,
> No joyful tread of friends, no voice of lovers,
> No careful father's counsel—nothing's heard,

For nothing is, but all oblivion,
Dust, and an endless darkness.

Suddenly the notes of the deep-laboring organ burst upon the ear, falling with doubled and redoubled intensity, and rolling, as it were, huge billows of sound. How well do their volume and grandeur accord with this mighty building! With what pomp do they swell through its vast vaults, and breathe their awful harmony through these caves of death, and make the silent sepulchre vocal! And now they rise in triumphant acclamation, heaving higher and higher their accordant notes and piling sound on sound. And now they pause, and the soft voices of the choir break out into sweet gushes of melody; they soar aloft and warble along the roof, and seem to play about these lofty vaults like the pure airs of heaven. Again the pealing organ heaves its thrilling thunders, compressing air into music, and rolling it forth upon the soul. What long-drawn cadences! What solemn sweeping concords! It grows more and more dense and powerful; it fills the vast pile and seems to jar the very walls—the ear is stunned—the senses are overwhelmed. And now it is winding up in full jubilee—it is rising from the earth to heaven—the very soul seems rapt away and floated upwards on this swelling tide of harmony!

I sat for some time lost in that kind of reverie which a strain of music is apt sometimes to inspire: the shadows of evening were gradually thickening round me; the monuments began to cast deeper and deeper gloom; and the distant clock again gave token of the slowly waning day.

I rose and prepared to leave the abbey. As I descended the flight of steps which lead into the body of the building, my eye was caught by the shrine of Edward the Confessor, and I ascended the small staircase that conducts to it, to take from thence a general survey of this wilderness of tombs. The shrine is elevated upon a kind of platform, and close around it are the sepulchres of various kings and queens. From this eminence the eye looks down between pillars and funeral trophies to the chapels and chambers below, crowded with tombs, where warriors, prelates, courtiers, and statesmen lie mouldering in their "beds of darkness." Close by me stood the great chair of coronation, rudely carved of oak in the barbarous taste of a remote and gothic age. The scene seemed almost as if contrived with theatrical artifice to produce an effect upon the beholder. Here was a type of the beginning and the end of human pomp and power; here it was literally but a step from the throne to the sepulchre. Would not one think that these incongruous mementos had been gathered together as a lesson to living greatness?—to show it, even in the moment of its proudest exaltation, the neglect and dishonor to which it must soon arrive—how soon that crown which encircles its brow must pass away, and it must lie down in the dust and disgraces of the tomb, and be trampled upon by the feet of the meanest of the multitude. For, strange to tell, even the grave is here no longer a sanctuary. There is a shocking levity in some natures which leads them to sport with awful and hallowed things, and there are base minds which delight to revenge on the illustrious dead the abject homage and grovelling servility which they pay to the living. The coffin of Edward the Confessor has been broken open, and his remains despoiled of their funereal ornaments; the sceptre has been stolen from the hand of the imperious Elizabeth; and the effigy of Henry the Fifth lies headless. Not a royal monument but bears some proof how false and fugitive is the homage of mankind. Some are plundered, some mutilated, some covered with ribaldry and insult—all more or less outraged and dishonored.

The last beams of day were now faintly streaming through the painted windows in the high vaults above me; the lower parts of the abbey were already wrapped in the obscurity of twilight. The chapels and aisles grew darker and darker. The effigies of the kings faded into shadows; the marble figures of the monuments assumed strange shapes in the uncertain light; the evening breeze crept through the aisles like the cold breath of the grave; and even the distant footfall of a verger, traversing the Poet's Corner, had something strange and dreary in its sound. I slowly retraced my morning's walk, and as I passed out at the portal of the cloisters, the door, closing with a jarring noise behind me, filled the whole building with echoes.

I endeavored to form some arrangement in my mind of the objects I had been contemplating, but found they were already falling into indistinctness and confusion. Names, inscriptions, trophies, had all become confounded in my recollection, though I had scarcely taken my foot from off the threshold. What, thought I, is this vast assemblage of sepulchres but a treasury of humiliation—a huge pile of reiterated homilies on the emptiness of renown and the certainty of oblivion? It is, indeed, the empire of death; his great shadowy palace, where he sits in state mocking at the relics of human glory and spreading dust and forgetfulness on the monuments of princes. How idle a boast, after all, is the immortality of a name! Time is ever silently turning over his pages; we are too much engrossed by the story of the present to think of the characters and anecdotes that gave interest to the past; and each age is a volume thrown aside to be speedily forgotten. The idol of to-day pushes the hero of yesterday out of our recollection, and will in turn be supplanted by his successor of tomorrow. "Our fathers," says Sir Thomas Browne, "find their graves in our short memories, and sadly tell us how we may be buried in our survivors." History fades into fable; fact becomes clouded with doubt and controversy; the inscription moulders from the tablet; the statue falls from the pedestal. Columns, arches, pyramids, what are they but heaps of sand, and their epitaphs but characters written in the dust? What is the security of a tomb or the perpetuity of an embalmment? The remains of Alexander the Great have been scattered to the wind, and his empty sarcophagus is now the mere curiosity of a museum. "The Egyptian mummies, which Cambyses or time hath spared, avarice now consumeth; Mizraim cures wounds, and Pharaoh is sold for balsams."*

What then is to ensure this pile which now towers above me from sharing the fate of mightier mausoleums? The time must come when its gilded vaults which now spring so loftily, shall lie in rubbish beneath the feet; when instead of the sound of melody and praise the wind shall whistle through the broken arches and the owl hoot from the shattered tower; when the garish sunbeam shall break into these gloomy mansions of death, and the ivy twine round the fallen column; and the fox-glove hang its blossoms about the nameless urn, as if in mockery of the dead. Thus man passes away; his name passes from record and recollection; his history is as a tale that is told, and his very monument becomes a ruin.

* Sir T. Browne.

CHRISTMAS

But is old, old, good old Christmas gone? Nothing but the hair of his good, gray old head and beard left? Well, I will have that, seeing I cannot have more of him.

—Hue and Cry After Christmas

A man might then behold
  At Christmas, in each hall
Good fires to curb the cold,
  And meat for great and small.
The neighbors were friendly bidden,
  And all had welcome true,
The poor from the gates were not chidden
  When this old cap was new.

—Old Song

Nothing in England exercises a more delightful spell over my imagination than the lingerings of the holiday customs and rural games of former times. They recall the pictures my fancy used to draw in the May morning of life, when as yet I only knew the world through books, and believed it to be all that poets had painted it; and they bring with them the flavor of those honest days of yore, in which, perhaps with equal fallacy, I am apt to think the world was more homebred, social, and joyous than at present. I regret to say that they are daily growing more and more faint, being gradually worn away by time, but still more obliterated by modern fashion. They resemble those picturesque morsels of gothic architecture which we see crumbling in various parts of the country, partly dilapidated by the waste of ages and partly lost in the additions and alterations of latter days. Poetry, however, clings with cherishing fondness about the rural game and holiday revel from which it has derived so many of its themes, as the ivy winds its rich foliage about the gothic arch and mouldering tower, gratefully repaying their support by clasping together their tottering remains, and, as it were, embalming them in verdure.

Of all the old festivals, however, that of Christmas awakens the strongest and most heartfelt associations. There is a tone of solemn and sacred feeling that blends with our conviviality and lifts the spirit to a state of hallowed and elevated enjoyment. The services of the Church about this season are extremely tender and inspiring. They dwell on the beautiful story of the origin of our faith and the pastoral scenes that accompanied its announcement. They gradually increase in fervor and pathos during the season of Advent, until they break forth in full jubilee on the morning that brought peace and good-will to men. I do not know a grander effect of music on the moral feelings than to hear the full choir and the pealing organ performing a Christmas anthem in a cathedral, and filling every part of the vast pile with triumphant harmony.

It is a beautiful arrangement, also, derived from days of yore, that this festival, which commemorates the announcement of the religion of peace and love, has been made the season for gathering together of family connections, and drawing closer again those bands of kindred hearts which the cares and pleasures and sorrows of the world are continually operating to cast loose; of calling back the children of a family who have launched forth in life and wandered widely asunder, once more to assemble about the paternal hearth, that rallying-place of the affections, there to grow young and loving again among the endearing mementos of childhood.

There is something in the very season of the year that gives a charm to the festivity of Christmas. At other times we derive a great portion of our pleasures from the mere beauties of nature. Our feelings sally forth and dissipate themselves over the sunny landscape, and we "live abroad and everywhere." The song of the bird, the murmur of the stream, the breathing fragrance of spring, the soft voluptuousness of summer, the golden pomp of autumn, earth with its mantle of refreshing green, and heaven with it deep delicious blue and its cloudy magnificence—all fill us with mute but exquisite delight, and we revel in the luxury of mere sensation. But in the depth of winter, when nature lies despoiled of every charm and wrapped in her shroud of sheeted snow, we turn for our gratifications to moral sources. The dreariness and desolation of the landscape, the short gloomy days and darksome nights, while they circumscribe our wanderings, shut in our feelings also from rambling abroad, and make us more keenly disposed for the pleasure of the social circle. Our thoughts are more concentrated; our friendly sympathies more aroused. We feel more sensibly the charm of each other's society, and are brought more closely together by dependence on each other for enjoyment. Heart calleth unto heart, and we draw our pleasures from the deep wells of loving kindness which lie in the quiet recesses of our bosoms, and which, when resorted to, furnish forth the pure element of domestic felicity.

The pitchy gloom without makes the heart dilate on entering the room filled with the glow and warmth of the evening fire. The ruddy blaze diffuses an artificial summer and sunshine through the room, and lights up each countenance in a kindlier welcome. Where does the honest face of hospitality expand into a broader and more cordial smile, where is the shy glance of love more sweetly eloquent, than by the winter fireside? and as the hollow blast of wintry wind rushes through the hall, claps the distant door, whistles about the casement, and rumbles down the chimney, what can be more grateful than that feeling of sober and sheltered security with which we look round upon the comfortable chamber and the scene of domestic hilarity?

The English, from the great prevalence of rural habit throughout every class of society, have always been found of those festivals and holidays which agreeably interrupt the stillness of country life; and they were, in former days, particularly observant of the religious and social rites of Christmas. It is inspiring to read even the dry details which some antiquaries have given of the quaint humors, the burlesque pageants, the complete abandonment to mirth and good fellowship with which this festival was celebrated. It seemed to throw open every door and unlock every heart. It brought the peasant and the peer together, and blended all ranks in one warm, generous flow of joy and kindness. The old halls of castles and manor houses resounded with the harp and the Christmas carol, and their ample boards groaned under the weight of hospitality. Even the poorest cottage welcomed the festive season with green decorations of bay and holly—the cheerful fire glanced its rays through the lattice, inviting the passengers to raise the latch and join the gossip knot huddled round the hearth beguiling the long evening with legendary jokes and oft-told Christmas tales.

One of the least pleasing effects of modern refinement is the havoc it has made among the hearty old holiday customs. It has completely taken off the sharp touchings and spirited reliefs of these embellishments of life, and has worn down society into a more smooth and polished, but certainly a less characteristic, surface. Many of the games and ceremonials of Christmas have entirely disappeared, and, like the sherris sack of old Falstaff, are become matters of speculation and dispute among commentators. They flourished in times full of spirit and lustihood, when men enjoyed life roughly, but heartily and vigorously—times wild and picturesque, which have furnished poetry with its richest materials and the drama with its most attractive variety of characters and manners. The world has become more worldly. There is more of dissipation, and less of enjoyment. Pleasure has expanded into a broader, but a shallower stream, and has forsaken many of those deep and quiet channels where it flowed sweetly through the calm bosom of domestic life. Society has acquired a more enlightened and elegant tone, but it has lost many of its strong local peculiarities, its homebred feelings, its honest fireside delights. The traditionary customs of golden-hearted antiquity, its feudal hospitalities, and lordly wassailings, have passed away with the baronial castles and stately manor houses in which they were celebrated. They comported with the shadowy hall, the great oaken gallery, and the tapestried parlor, but are unfitted to the light showy saloons and gay drawing rooms of the modern villa.

Shorn, however, as it is, of its ancient and festive honors, Christmas is still a period of delightful excitement in England. It is gratifying to see that home feeling completely aroused which holds so powerful a place in every English bosom. The preparations making on every side for the social board that is again to unite friends and kindred; the presents of good cheer passing and repassing, those tokens of regard and quickeners of kind feelings; the evergreens distributed about houses and churches, emblems of peace and gladness—all these have the most pleasing effect in producing fond associations and kindling benevolent sympathies. Even the sound of the Waits, rude as may be their minstrelsy, breaks upon the mid-watches of a winter night with the effect of perfect harmony. As I have been awakened by them in that still and solemn hour "when deep sleep falleth upon man," I have listened with a hushed delight, and connecting them with the sacred and joyous occasion, have almost fancied them into another celestial choir announcing peace and good-will to mankind.

How delightfully the imagination, when wrought upon by these moral influences, turns everything to melody and beauty. The very crowing of the cock, heard sometimes in the profound repose of the country, "telling the night-watches to his feathery dames," was thought by the common people to announce the approach of this sacred festival.

> Some say that ever 'gainst that season comes
> Wherein our Saviour's birth is celebrated,
> This bird of dawning singeth all night long;
> And then, they say, no spirit dares stir abroad,
> The nights are wholesome—then no planets strike,
> No fairy takes, no witch hath power to charm,
> So hallow'd and so gracious is the time.

Amidst the general call to happiness, the bustle of the spirits, and stir of the affections which prevail at this period, what bosom can remain insensible? It is, indeed, the season of regenerated feeling—the season for kindling not merely the fire of hospitality in the hall, but the genial flame of charity in the heart.

The scene of early love again rises green to memory beyond the sterile waste of years; and the idea of home, fraught with the fragrance of home-dwelling joys, reanimates the drooping spirit, as the Arabian breeze will sometimes waft the freshness of the distant fields to the weary pilgrim of the desert.

Stranger and sojourner as I am in the land, though for me no social hearth may blaze, no hospitable roof throw open its doors, nor the warm grasp of friendship welcome me at the threshold, yet I feel the influence of the season beaming into my soul from the happy looks of those around me. Surely happiness is reflective, like the light of heaven, and every countenance, bright with smiles and glowing with innocent enjoyment, is a mirror transmitting to others the rays of a supreme and ever-shining benevolence. He who can turn churlishly away from contemplating the felicity of his fellow-beings, and can sit down darkling and repining in his loneliness when all around is joyful, may have his moments of strong excitement and selfish gratification, but he wants the genial and social sympathies which constitute the charm of a merry Christmas.

THE STAGE-COACH

Omne benè
Sine poenâ
Tempua est ludendi.
Venit hora
Absque morâ
Libros deponendi.
—Old Holiday School Song

In the preceding paper I have made some general observations on the Christmas festivities of England, and am tempted to illustrate them by some anecdotes of a Christmas passed in the country: in perusing which I would most courteously invite my reader to lay aside the austerity of wisdom, and to put on that genuine holiday spirit which is tolerant of folly and anxious only for amusement.

In the course of a December tour in Yorkshire, I rode for a long distance in one of the public coaches on the day preceding Christmas. The coach was crowded, both inside and out, with passengers who, by their talk, seemed principally bound to the mansions of relations or friends to eat the Christmas dinner. It was loaded also with hampers of game, and baskets and boxes of delicacies, and hares hung dangling their long ears about the coachman's box, presents from distant friends for the impending feast. I had three fine rosy-cheeked school boys for my fellow-passengers inside, full of the buxom health and manly spirit which I have observed in the children of this country. They were returning home for the holidays in high glee, and promising themselves a world of enjoyment. It was delightful to hear the gigantic plans of the little rogues, and the impracticable feats they were to perform during their six weeks' emancipation from the abhorred thraldom of book, birch, and pedagogue. They were full of anticipations of the meeting with the family and household, down to the very cat and dog, and of the joy they were to give their little sisters by the presents with which their pockets were crammed; but the meeting to which they seemed to look forward with the greatest impatience was with Bantam, which I found to be a pony, and, according to their talk, possessed of more virtues than any steed since the days of Bucephalus. How he could trot! how he could run! and then such leaps as he would take!—there was not a hedge in the whole country that he could not clear.

They were under the particular guardianship of the coachman, to whom, whenever an opportunity presented, they addressed a host of questions, and pronounced him one of the best fellows in the world. Indeed, I could not but notice the more than ordinary air of bustle and importance of the coachman, who wore his hat a little on one side and had a large bunch of Christmas greens stuck in the buttonhole of his coat. He is always a personage full of mighty care and business, but he is particularly so during this season, having so many commissions to execute in consequence of the great interchange of presents. And here, perhaps, it may not be unacceptable to my untravelled readers to have a sketch that may serve as a general representation of this very numerous and important class of functionaries, who have a dress, a manner, a language, an air peculiar to themselves and prevalent throughout the fraternity; so that wherever an English stage-coachman may be seen he cannot be mistaken for one of any other craft or mystery.

He has commonly a broad, full face, curiously mottled with red, as if the blood had been forced by hard feeding into every vessel of the skin; he is swelled into jolly dimensions by frequent potations of malt liquors, and his bulk is still further increased by a multiplicity of coats, in which he is buried like a cauliflower, the upper one reaching to his heels. He wears a broad-brimmed, low-crowned hat; a huge roll of colored handkerchief about his neck, knowingly knotted and tucked in at the bosom; and has in summer-time a large bouquet of flowers in his buttonhole, the present, most probably, of some enamored country lass. His waistcoat is commonly of some bright color, striped, and his small-clothes extend far below the knees, to meet a pair of jockey boots which reach about halfway up his legs.

All this costume is maintained with much precision; he has a pride in having his clothes of excellent materials, and, notwithstanding the seeming grossness of his appearance, there is still discernible that neatness and propriety of person which is almost inherent in an

Englishman. He enjoys great consequence and consideration along the road; has frequent conferences with the village housewives, who look upon him as a man of great trust and dependence; and he seems to have a good understanding with every bright-eyed country lass. The moment he arrives where the horses are to be changed, he throws down the reins with something of an air and abandons the cattle to the care of the hostler, his duty being merely to drive from one stage to another. When off the box his hands are thrust into the pockets of his great coat, and he rolls about the inn yard with an air of the most absolute lordliness. Here he is generally surrounded by an admiring throng of hostlers, stableboys, shoeblacks, and those nameless hangers-on that infest inns and taverns, and run errands and do all kind of odd jobs for the privilege of battening on the drippings of the kitchen and the leakage of the tap-room. These all look up to him as to an oracle, treasure up his cant phrases, echo his opinions about horses and other topics of jockey lore, and, above all, endeavor to imitate his air and carriage. Every ragamuffin that has a coat to his back thrusts his hands in the pockets, rolls in his gait, talks slang, and is an embryo Coachey.

Perhaps it might be owing to the pleasing serenity that reigned in my own mind that I fancied I saw cheerfulness in every countenance throughout the journey. A stage-coach, however, carries animation always with it, and puts the world in motion as it whirls along. The horn, sounded at the entrance of the village, produces a general bustle. Some hasten forth to meet friends; some with bundles and bandboxes to secure places, and in the hurry of the moment can hardly take leave of the group that accompanies them. In the meantime the coachman has a world of small commissions to execute. Sometimes he delivers a hare or pheasant; sometimes jerks a small parcel or newspaper to the door of a public house; and sometimes, with knowing leer and words of sly import, hands to some half-blushing, half-laughing house-maid an odd-shaped billet-doux from some rustic admirer. As the coach rattles through the village every one runs to the window, and you have glances on every side of fresh country faces and blooming giggling girls. At the corners are assembled juntos of village idlers and wise men, who take their stations there for the important purpose of seeing company pass; but the sagest knot is generally at the blacksmith's, to whom the passing of the coach is an event fruitful of much speculation. The smith, with the horse's heel in his lap, pauses as the vehicle whirls by; the cyclops round the anvil suspend their ringing hammers and suffer the iron to grow cool; and the sooty spectre in brown paper cap laboring at the bellows leans on the handle for a moment, and permits the asthmatic engine to heave a long-drawn sigh, while he glares through the murky smoke and sulphurous gleams of the smithy.

Perhaps the impending holiday might have given a more than usual animation to the country, for it seemed to me as if everybody was in good looks and good spirits. Game, poultry, and other luxuries of the table were in brisk circulation in the villages; the grocers', butchers', and fruiterers' shops were thronged with customers. The housewives were stirring briskly about, putting their dwellings in order, and the glossy branches of holly with their bright-red berries began to appear at the windows. The scene brought to mind an old writer's account of Christmas preparation: "Now capons and hens, besides turkeys, geese, and ducks, with beef and mutton, must all die, for in twelve days a multitude of people will not be fed with a little. Now plums and spice, sugar and honey, square it among pies and broth. Now or never must music be in tune, for the youth must dance and sing to get them a heat, while the aged sit by the fire. The country maid leaves half her market, and must be sent again if she forgets a pack of cards on Christmas Eve. Great is the contention of holly and ivy whether master or dame wears the breeches. Dice and cards benefit the butler; and if the cook do not lack wit, he will sweetly lick his fingers."

I was roused from this fit of luxurious meditation by a shout from my little travelling companions. They had been looking out of the coach-windows for the last few miles, recognizing every tree and cottage as they approached home, and now there was a general burst of joy. "There's John! and there's old Carlo! and there's Bantam!" cried the happy little rogues, clapping their hands.

At the end of a lane there was an old sober-looking servant in livery waiting for them; he was accompanied by a superannuated pointer and by the redoubtable Bantam, a little old rat of a pony with a shaggy mane and long rusty tail, who stood dozing quietly by the roadside, little dreaming of the bustling times that awaited him.

I was pleased to see the fondness with which the little fellows leaped about the steady old footman and hugged the pointer, who wriggled his whole body for joy. But Bantam was the great object of interest; all wanted to mount at once, and it was with some difficulty that John arranged that they should ride by turns and the eldest should ride first.

Off they set at last, one on the pony, with the dog bounding and barking before him, and the others holding John's hands, both talking at once and overpowering him with questions about home and with school anecdotes. I looked after them with a feeling in which I do not know whether pleasure or melancholy predominated; for I was reminded of those days when, like them, I had known neither care nor sorrow and a holiday was the summit of earthly felicity. We stopped a few moments afterwards to water the horses, and on resuming our route a turn of the road brought us in sight of a neat country-seat. I could just distinguish the forms of a lady and two young girls in the portico, and I saw my little comrades, with Bantam, Carlo, and old John, trooping along the carriage-road. I leaned out of the coach-window, in hopes of witnessing the happy meeting, but a grove of trees shut it from my sight.

In the evening we reached a village where I had determined to pass the night. As we drove into the great gateway of the inn, I saw on one side the light of a rousing kitchen-fire beaming through a window. I entered, and admired, for the hundredth time, that picture of convenience, neatness, and broad honest enjoyment, the kitchen of an English inn. It was of spacious dimensions, hung round with copper and tin vessels highly polished, and decorated here and there with a Christmas green. Hams, tongues, and flitches of bacon were suspended from the ceiling; a smoke-jack made its ceaseless clanking beside the fireplace, and a clock ticked in one corner. A well-scoured deal table extended along one side of the kitchen, with a cold round of beef and other hearty viands upon it, over which two foaming tankards of ale seemed mounting guard. Travellers of inferior order were preparing to attack this stout repast, while others sat smoking and gossiping over their ale on two high-backed oaken settles beside the fire. Trim housemaids were hurrying backwards and forwards under the directions of a fresh bustling landlady, but still seizing an occasional moment to exchange a flippant word and have a rallying laugh with the group round the fire. The scene completely realized Poor Robin's humble idea of the comforts of midwinter:

> Now trees their leafy hats do bare
> To reverence Winter's silver hair;
> A handsome hostess, merry host,
> A pot of ale now and a toast,
> Tobacco and a good coal fire,
> Are things this season doth require.*

I had not been long at the inn when a post-chaise drove up to the door. A young gentleman stept out, and by the light of the lamps I caught a glimpse of a countenance which I thought I knew. I moved forward to get a nearer view, when his eye caught mine. I was not mistaken; it was Frank Bracebridge, a sprightly, good-humored young fellow with whom I had once travelled on the Continent. Our meeting was extremely cordial, for the countenance of an old fellow-traveller always brings up the recollection of a thousand pleasant scenes, odd adventures, and excellent jokes. To discuss all these in a transient interview at an inn was impossible; and, finding that I was not pressed for time and was merely making a tour of observation, he insisted that I should give him a day or two at his father's country-seat, to which he was going to pass the holidays and which lay at a few miles' distance. "It is better than eating a solitary Christmas dinner at an inn," said he, "and I can assure you of a hearty welcome in something of the old-fashioned style." His reasoning was cogent, and I must confess the preparation I had seen for universal festivity and social enjoyment had made me feel a little impatient of my loneliness. I closed, therefore, at once with his invitation; the chaise drove up to the door, and in a few moments I was on my way to the family mansion of the Bracebridges.

* Poor Robin's Almanack, 1684.

CHRISTMAS EVE

Saint Francis and Saint Benedight
Blesse this house from wicked wight;
From the night-mare and the goblin,
That is hight good fellow Robin;
Keep it from all evil spirits,
Fairies, weezels, rats, and ferrets:
From curfew-time
To the next prime.

—Cartwright

It was a brilliant moonlight night, but extremely cold; our chaise whirled rapidly over the frozen ground; the postboy smacked his whip incessantly, and a part of the time his horses were on a gallop. "He knows where he is going," said my companion, laughing, "and is eager to arrive in time for some of the merriment and good cheer of the servants' hall. My father, you must know, is a bigoted devotee of the old school, and prides himself upon keeping up something of old English hospitality. He is a tolerable specimen of what you will rarely meet with nowadays in its purity, the old English country gentleman; for our men of fortune spend so much of their time in town, and fashion is carried so much into the country, that the strong rich peculiarities of ancient rural life are almost polished away. My father, however, from early years, took honest Peacham* for his textbook, instead of Chesterfield; he determined in his own mind that there was no condition more truly honorable and enviable than that of a country gentleman on his paternal lands, and therefore passes the whole of his time on his estate. He is a strenuous advocate for the revival of the old rural games and holiday observances, and is deeply read in the writers, ancient and modern, who have treated on the subject. Indeed, his favorite range of reading is among the authors who flourished at least two centuries since, who, he insists, wrote and thought more like true Englishmen

* Peacham's Complete Gentleman, 1622

than any of their successors. He even regrets sometimes that he had not been born a few centuries earlier, when England was itself and had its peculiar manners and customs. As he lives at some distance from the main road, in rather a lonely part of the country, without any rival gentry near him, he has that most enviable of all blessings to an Englishman—an opportunity of indulging the bent of his own humor without molestation. Being representative of the oldest family in the neighborhood, and a great part of the peasantry being his tenants, he is much looked up to, and in general is known simply by the appellation of 'The Squire'—a title which has been accorded to the head of the family since time immemorial. I think it best to give you these hints about my worthy old father, to prepare you for any eccentricities that might otherwise appear absurd."

We had passed for some time along the wall of a park, and at length the chaise stopped at the gate. It was in a heavy, magnificent old style, of iron bars fancifully wrought at top into flourishes and flowers. The huge square columns that supported the gate were surmounted by the family crest. Close adjoining was the porter's lodge, sheltered under dark fir trees and almost buried in shrubbery.

The postboy rang a large porter's bell, which resounded though the still frosty air, and was answered by the distant barking of dogs, with which the mansion-house seemed garrisoned. An old woman immediately appeared at the gate. As the moonlight fell strongly upon her, I had a full view of a little primitive dame, dressed very much in the antique taste, with a neat kerchief and stomacher, and her silver hair peeping from under a cap of snowy whiteness. She came curtseying forth, with many expressions of simple joy at seeing her young master. Her husband, it seemed, was up at the house keeping Christmas Eve in the servants' hall; they could not do without him, as he was the best hand at a song and story in the household.

My friend proposed that we should alight and walk through the park to the hall, which was at no great distance, while the chaise should follow on. Our road wound through a noble avenue of trees, among the naked branches of which the moon glittered as she rolled through the deep vault of a cloudless sky. The lawn beyond was sheeted with a slight covering of snow, which here and there sparkled as the moonbeams caught a frosty crystal, and at a distance might be seen a thin transparent vapor stealing up from the low grounds and threatening gradually to shroud the landscape.

My companion looked around him with transport. "How often," said he, "have I scampered up this avenue on returning home on school vacations! How often have I played under these trees when a boy! I feel a degree of filial reverence for them, as we look up to those who have cherished us in childhood. My father was always scrupulous in exacting our holidays and having us around him on family festivals. He used to direct and superintend our games with the strictness that some parents do the studies of their children. He was very particular that we should play the old English games according to their original form, and consulted old books for precedent and authority for every 'merrie disport;' yet I assure you there never was pedantry so delightful. It was the policy of the good old gentleman to make his children feel that home was the happiest place in the world; and I value this delicious home feeling as one of the choicest gifts a parent could bestow."

We were interrupted by the clamor of a troop of dogs of all sorts and sizes, "mongrel, puppy, whelp, and hound, and curs of lower degree," that disturbed by the ring of the porter's bell and the rattling of the chaise, came bounding, open-mouthed, across the lawn.

"'—The little dogs and all,
Tray, Blanch, and Sweetheart, see, they bark at me!'"

cried Bracebridge, laughing. At the sound of his voice the bark was changed into a yelp of delight, and in a moment he was surrounded and almost overpowered by the caresses of the faithful animals.

We had now come in full view of the old family mansion, partly thrown in deep shadow and partly lit up by the cold moonshine. It was an irregular building of some magnitude, and seemed to be of the architecture of different periods. One wing was evidently very ancient, with heavy stone-shafted bow windows jutting out and overrun with ivy, from among the foliage of which the small diamond-shaped panes of glass glittered with the moonbeams. The rest of the house was in the French taste of Charles the Second's time, having been repaired and altered, as my friend told me, by one of his ancestors who returned with that monarch at the Restoration. The grounds about the house were laid out in the old formal manner of artificial flower-beds, clipped shrubberies, raised terraces, and heavy stone balustrades, ornamented with urns, a leaden statue or two, and a jet of water. The old gentleman, I was told, was extremely careful to preserve this obsolete finery in all its original state. He admired this fashion in gardening; it had an air of magnificence, was courtly and noble, and befitting good old family style. The boasted imitation of nature in modern gardening had sprung up with modern republican notions, but did not suit a monarchical government; it smacked of the leveling system. I could not help smiling at this introduction of politics into gardening, though I expressed some apprehension that I should find the old gentleman rather intolerant in his creed. Frank assured me, however, that it was almost the only instance in which he had ever heard his father meddle with politics; and he believed that he had got this notion from a member of Parliament who once passed a few weeks with him. The squire was glad of any argument to defend his clipped yew trees and formal terraces, which had been occasionally attacked by modern landscape gardeners.

As we approached the house we heard the sound of music, and now and then a burst of laughter from one end of the building. This, Bracebridge said, must proceed from the servants' hall, where a great deal of revelry was permitted, and even encouraged, by the squire throughout the twelve days of Christmas, provided everything was done conformably to ancient usage. Here were kept up the old games of hoodman blind, shoe the wild mare, hot cockles, steal the white loaf, bob apple, and snap dragon; the Yule-clog and Christmas candle were regularly burnt, and the mistletoe with its white berries hung up, to the imminent peril of all the pretty housemaids.*

So intent were the servants upon their sports that we had to ring repeatedly before we could make ourselves heard. On our arrival being announced the squire came out to receive us, accompanied by his two other sons—one a young officer in the army, home on a leave of absence; the other an Oxonian, just from the university. The squire was a fine healthy-looking old gentleman, with silver hair curling lightly

* The mistletoe is still hung up in farm-houses and kitchens at Christmas, and the young men have the privilege of kissing the girls under it, plucking each time a berry from the bush. When the berries are all plucked the privilege ceases.

round an open florid countenance, in which the physiognomist, with the advantage, like myself, of a previous hint or two, might discover a singular mixture of whim and benevolence.

The family meeting was warm and affectionate; as the evening was far advanced, the squire would not permit us to change our travelling dresses, but ushered us at once to the company, which was assembled in a large old-fashioned hall. It was composed of different branches of a numerous family connection, where there were the usual proportion of old uncles and aunts, comfortable married dames, superannuated spinsters, blooming country cousins, half-fledged striplings, and bright-eyed boarding-school hoydens. They were variously occupied—some at a round game of cards; others conversing around the fireplace; at one end of the hall was a group of the young folks, some nearly grown up, others of a more tender and budding age, fully engrossed by a merry game; and a profusion of wooden horses, penny trumpets, and tattered dolls about the floor showed traces of a troop of little fairy beings who, having frolicked through a happy day, had been carried off to slumber through a peaceful night.

While the mutual greetings were going on between young Bracebridge and his relatives I had time to scan the apartment. I have called it a hall, for so it had certainly been in old times, and the squire had evidently endeavored to restore it to something of its primitive state. Over the heavy projecting fireplace was suspended a picture of a warrior in armor, standing by a white horse, and on the opposite wall hung a helmet, buckler, and lance. At one end an enormous pair of antlers were inserted in the wall, the branches serving as hooks on which to suspend hats, whips, and spurs, and in the corners of the apartment were fowling-pieces, fishing-rods, and other sporting implements. The furniture was of the cumbrous workmanship of former days, though some articles of modern convenience had been added and the oaken floor had been carpeted, so that the whole presented an odd mixture of parlor and hall.

The grate had been removed from the wide overwhelming fireplace to make way for a fire of wood, in the midst of which was an enormous log glowing and blazing, and sending forth a vast volume of light and heat: this, I understood, was the Yule-clog, which the squire was particular in having brought in and illumined on a Christmas Eve, according to ancient custom.*

It was really delightful to see the old squire seated in his hereditary elbow-chair by the hospitable fireside of his ancestors, and looking around him like the sun of a system, beaming warmth and gladness to every heart. Even the very dog that lay stretched at his feet, as he lazily shifted his position and yawned, would look fondly up in his master's face, wag his tail against the floor, and stretch himself again to sleep, confident of kindness and protection. There is an emanation from the heart in genuine hospitality which cannot be described, but is immediately felt and puts the stranger at once at his ease. I had not been seated many minutes by the comfortable hearth of the worthy old cavalier before I found myself as much at home as if I had been one of the family.

Supper was announced shortly after our arrival. It was served up in a spacious oaken chamber, the panels of which shone with wax, and around which were several family portraits decorated with holly and ivy. Besides the accustomed lights, two great wax tapers, called Christmas candles, wreathed with greens, were placed on a highly polished beaufet among the family plate. The table was abundantly spread with substantial fare; but the squire made his supper of frumenty, a dish made of wheat cakes boiled in milk with rich spices, being a standing dish in old times for Christmas Eve. I was happy to find my old friend, minced pie, in the retinue of the feast and, finding him to be

* The Yule-clog is a great log of wood, sometimes the root of a tree, brought into the house with great ceremony on Christmas Eve, laid in the fireplace, and lighted with the brand of last year's clog. While it lasted there was great drinking, singing, and telling of tales. Sometimes it was accompanied by Christmas candles; but in the cottages the only light was from the ruddy blaze of the great wood fire. The Yule-clog was to burn all night; if it went out, it was considered a sign of ill luck.
Herrick mentions it in one of his songs:

> Come, bring with a noise,
> My metric, merrie boyes,
> The Christmas Log to the firing;
> While my good dame, she
> Bids ye all be free,
> And drink to your hearts' desiring.

The Yule-clog is still burnt in many farm-houses and kitchens in England, particularly in the north, and there are several superstitions connected with it among the peasantry. If a squinting person come to the house while it is burning, or a person barefooted, it is considered an ill omen. The brand remaining from the Yule-clog is carefully put away to light the next year's Christmas fire.

perfectly orthodox, and that I need not be ashamed of my predilection, I greeted him with all the warmth wherewith we usually greet an old and very genteel acquaintance.

The mirth of the company was greatly promoted by the humors of an eccentric personage whom Mr. Bracebridge always addressed with the quaint appellation of Master Simon. He was a tight brisk little man, with the air of an arrant old bachelor. His nose was shaped like the bill of a parrot; his face slightly pitted with the small-pox, with a dry perpetual bloom on it, like a frostbitten leaf in autumn. He had an eye of great quickness and vivacity, with a drollery and lurking waggery of expression that was irresistible. He was evidently the wit of the family, dealing very much in sly jokes and innuendoes with the ladies, and making infinite merriment by harping upon old themes, which, unfortunately, my ignorance of the family chronicles did not permit me to enjoy. It seemed to be his great delight during supper to keep a young girl next to him in a continual agony of stifled laughter, in spite of her awe of the reproving looks of her mother, who sat opposite. Indeed, he was the idol of the younger part of the company, who laughed at everything he said or did and at every turn of his countenance. I could not wonder at it; for he must have been a miracle of accomplishments in their eyes. He could imitate Punch and Judy; make an old woman of his hand, with the assistance of a burnt cork and pocket-handkerchief; and cut an orange into such a ludicrous caricature that the young folks were ready to die with laughing.

I was let briefly into his history by Frank Bracebridge. He was an old bachelor, of a small independent income, which by careful management was sufficient for all his wants. He revolved through the family system like a vagrant comet in its orbit, sometimes visiting one branch, and sometimes another quite remote, as is often the case with gentlemen of extensive connections and small fortunes in England. He had a chirping, buoyant disposition, always enjoying the present moment; and his frequent change of scene and company prevented his acquiring those rusty, unaccommodating habits with which old bachelors are so uncharitably charged. He was a complete family chronicle, being versed in the genealogy, history, and intermarriages of the whole house of Bracebridge, which made him a great favorite with the old folks; he was a beau of all the elder ladies and superannuated spinsters, among whom he was habitually considered rather a young fellow; and he was master of the revels among the children, so that there was not a more popular being in the sphere in which he moved than Mr. Simon Bracebridge. Of late years he had resided almost entirely with the squire, to whom he had become a factotum, and whom he particularly delighted by jumping with his humor in respect to old times and by having a scrap of an old song to suit every occasion. We had presently a specimen of his last-mentioned talent, for no sooner was supper removed and spiced wines and other beverages peculiar to the season introduced, than Master Simon was called on for a good old Christmas song. He bethought himself for a moment, and then, with a sparkle of the eye and a voice that was by no means bad, excepting that it ran occasionally into a falsetto like the notes of a split reed, he quavered forth a quaint old ditty:

> Now Christmas is come,
> Let us beat up the drum,
> And call all our neighbors together;
> And when they appear,
> Let us make them such cheer,
> As will keep out the wind and the weather, &c.

The supper had disposed every one to gayety, and an old harper was summoned from the servants' hall, where he had been strumming all the evening, and to all appearance comforting himself with some of the squire's home-brewed. He was a kind of hanger-on, I was told, of the establishment, and, though ostensibly a resident of the village, was oftener to be found in the squire's kitchen than his own home, the old gentleman being fond of the sound of "harp in hall."

The dance, like most dances after supper, was a merry one: some of the older folks joined in it, and the squire himself figured down several couple with a partner with whom he affirmed he had danced at every Christmas for nearly half a century. Master Simon, who seemed to be a kind of connecting link between the old times and the new, and to be withal a little antiquated in the taste of his accomplishments, evidently piqued himself on his dancing, and was endeavoring to gain credit by the heel and toe, rigadoon, and other graces of the ancient school; but he had unluckily assorted himself with a little romping girl from boarding-school, who by her wild vivacity kept him continually on the stretch and defeated all his sober attempts at elegance: such are the ill-sorted matches to which antique gentlemen are unfortunately prone.

The young Oxonian, on the contrary, had led out one of his maiden aunts, on whom the rogue played a thousand little knaveries with impunity: he was full of practical jokes, and his delight was to tease his aunts and cousins, yet, like all madcap youngsters, he was a universal favorite among the women. The most interesting couple in the dance was the young officer and a ward of the squire's, a beautiful blushing girl of seventeen. From several shy glances which I had noticed in the course of the evening I suspected there was a little kindness growing up between them; and indeed the young soldier was just the hero to captivate a romantic girl. He was tall, slender, and handsome, and, like most young British officers of late years, had picked up various small accomplishments on the Continent: he could talk French and Italian, draw landscapes, sing very tolerably, dance divinely, but, above all, he had been wounded at Waterloo. What girl of seventeen, well read in poetry and romance, could resist such a mirror of chivalry and perfection?

The moment the dance was over he caught up a guitar, and, lolling against the old marble fireplace in an attitude which I am half inclined to suspect was studied, began the little French air of the Troubadour. The squire, however, exclaimed against having anything on Christmas Eve but good old English; upon which the young minstrel, casting up his eye for a moment as if in an effort of memory, struck into another strain, and with a charming air of gallantry gave Herrick's "night-piece to Julia."

Her eyes the glow-worm lend thee,
The shooting stars attend thee,
　　And the elves also,
　　Whose little eyes glow
Like the sparks of fire, befriend thee.

No Will-o'-the-Wisp mislight thee;
Nor snake nor slow-worm bite thee;
    But on thy way,
    Not making a stay,
Since ghost there is none to affright thee,

Then let not the dark thee cumber;
What though the moon does slumber,
    The stars of the night
    Will lend thee their light,
Like tapers clear without number.

Then, Julia, let me woo thee,
Thus, thus to come unto me,
    And when I shall meet
    Thy silvery feet,
My soul I'll pour into thee.

The song might or might not have been intended in compliment to the fair Julia, for so I found his partner was called; she, however, was certainly unconscious of any such application, for she never looked at the singer, but kept her eyes cast upon the floor. Her face was suffused, it is true, with a beautiful blush, and there was a gentle heaving of the bosom, but all that was doubtless caused by the exercise of the dance; indeed, so great was her indifference that she amused herself with plucking to pieces a choice bouquet of hot-house flowers, and by the time the song was concluded the nosegay lay in ruins on the floor.

The party now broke up for the night with the kind-hearted old custom of shaking hands. As I passed through the hall on my way to my chamber, the dying embers of the Yule-clog still sent forth a dusky glow, and had it not been the season when "no spirit dares stir abroad," I should have been half tempted to steal from my room at midnight and peep whether the fairies might not be at their revels about the hearth.

My chamber was in the old part of the mansion, the ponderous furniture of which might have been fabricated in the days of the giants. The room was panelled, with cornices of heavy carved work, in which flowers and grotesque faces were strangely intermingled, and a row of black-looking portraits stared mournfully at me from the walls. The bed was of rich though faded damask, with a lofty tester, and stood in a niche opposite a bow window. I had scarcely got into bed when a strain of music seemed to break forth in the air just below the window. I listened, and found it proceeded from a band which I concluded to be the Waits from some neighboring village. They went round the house, playing under the windows. I drew aside the curtains to hear them more distinctly. The moonbeams fell through the upper part of the casement; partially lighting up the antiquated apartment. The sounds, as they receded, became more soft and aerial, and seemed to accord with the quiet and moonlight. I listened and listened—they became more and more tender and remote, and, as they gradually died away, my head sunk upon the pillow and I fell asleep.

CHRISTMAS DAY

Dark and dull night, flie hence away,
And give the honor to this day
That sees December turn'd to May.

Why does the chilling winter's morne
Smile like a field beset with corn?
Or smell like to a meade new-shorne,
Thus on the sudden?—come and see
The cause why things thus fragrant be.

—HERRICK

When I woke the next morning it seemed as if all the events of the preceding evening had been a dream, and nothing but the identity of the ancient chamber convinced me of their reality. While I lay musing on my pillow I heard the sound of little feet pattering outside of the door, and a whispering consultation. Presently a choir of small voices chanted forth an old Christmas carol, the burden of which was—

Rejoice, our Saviour he was born
On Christmas Day in the morning.

I rose softly, slipt on my clothes, opened the door suddenly, and beheld one of the most beautiful little fairy groups that a painter could imagine. It consisted of a boy and two girls, the eldest not more than six, and lovely as seraphs. They were going the rounds of the house and singing at every chamber door, but my sudden appearance frightened them into mute bashfulness. They remained for a moment playing on their lips with their fingers, and now and then stealing a shy glance from under their eyebrows, until, as if by one impulse, they scampered away, and as they turned an angle of the gallery I heard them laughing in triumph at their escape.

Everything conspired to produce kind and happy feelings in this stronghold of old-fashioned hospitality. The window of my chamber looked out upon what in summer would have been a beautiful landscape. There was a sloping lawn, a fine stream winding at the foot of it, and a tract of park beyond, with noble clumps of trees and herds of deer. At a distance was a neat hamlet, with the smoke from the cottage chimneys hanging over it, and a church with its dark spire in strong relief against the clear cold sky. The house was surrounded with evergreens, according to the English custom, which would have given almost an appearance of summer; but the morning was extremely frosty; the light vapor of the preceding evening had been precipitated by the cold, and covered all the trees and every blade of grass with its fine crystalizations. The rays of a bright morning sun had a dazzling effect among the glittering foliage. A robin, perched upon the top of a mountain-ash that hung its clusters of red berries just before my window, was basking himself in the sunshine and piping a few querulous notes, and a peacock was displaying all the glories of his train and strutting with the pride and gravity of a Spanish grandee on the terrace walk below.

I had scarcely dressed myself when a servant appeared to invite me to family prayers. He showed me the way to a small chapel in the old wing of the house, where I found the principal part of the family already assembled in a kind of gallery furnished with cushions, hassocks, and large prayer-books; the servants were seated on benches below. The old gentleman read prayers from a desk in front of the gallery, and Master Simon acted as clerk and made the responses; and I must do him the justice to say that he acquitted himself with great gravity and decorum.

The service was followed by a Christmas carol, which Mr. Bracebridge himself had constructed from a poem of his favorite author, Herrick, and it had been adapted to an old church melody by Master Simon. As there were several good voices among the household, the effect was extremely pleasing, but I was particularly gratified by the exaltation of heart and sudden sally of grateful feeling with which the worthy squire delivered one stanza, his eye glistening and his voice rambling out of all the bounds of time and tune:

> Tis Thou that crown'st my glittering hearth
>   With guiltlesse mirth,

And giv'st me Wassaile bowles to drink
  Spic'd to the brink;
Lord, 'tis Thy plenty-dropping hand
  That soiles my land;
And giv'st me for my bushell sowne,
  Twice ten for one.

I afterwards understood that early morning service was read on every Sunday and saint's day throughout the year, either by Mr. Bracebridge or by some member of the family. It was once almost universally the case at the seats of the nobility and gentry of England, and it is much to be regretted that the custom is falling into neglect; for the dullest observer must be sensible of the order and serenity prevalent in those households where the occasional exercise of a beautiful form of worship in the morning gives, as it were, the keynote to every temper for the day and attunes every spirit to harmony.

Our breakfast consisted of what the squire denominated true old English fare. He indulged in some bitter lamentations over modern breakfasts of tea and toast, which he censured as among the causes of modern effeminacy and weak nerves and the decline of old English heartiness; and, though he admitted them to his table to suit the palates of his guests, yet there was a brave display of cold meats, wine, and ale on the sideboard.

After breakfast I walked about the grounds with Frank Bracebridge and Master Simon, or Mr. Simon, as he was called by everybody but the squire. We were escorted by a number of gentlemanlike dogs, that seemed loungers about the establishment, from the frisking spaniel to the steady old stag-hound, the last of which was of a race that had been in the family time out of mind; they were all obedient to a dog-whistle which hung to Master Simon's buttonhole, and in the midst of their gambols would glance an eye occasionally upon a small switch he carried in his hand.

The old mansion had a still more venerable look in the yellow sunshine than by pale moonlight; and I could not but feel the force of the squire's idea that the formal terraces, heavily moulded balustrades, and clipped yew trees carried with them an air of proud aristocracy. There appeared to be an unusual number of peacocks about the place, and I was making some remarks upon what I termed a flock of them that were basking under a sunny wall, when I was gently corrected in my phraseology by Master Simon, who told me that according to the most ancient and approved treatise on hunting I must say a *muster* of peacocks. "In the same way," added he, with a slight air of pedantry, "we say a flight of doves or swallows, a bevy of quails, a herd of deer, of wrens, or cranes, a skulk of foxes, or a building of rooks." He went on to inform me that, according to Sir Anthony Fitzherbert, we ought to ascribe to this bird "both understanding and glory; for, being praised, he will presently set up his tail, chiefly against the sun, to the intent you may the better behold the beauty thereof. But at the fall of the leaf, when his tail falleth, he will mourn and hide himself in corners till his tail come again as it was."

I could not help smiling at this display of small erudition on so whimsical a subject; but I found that the peacocks were birds of some consequence at the hall, for Frank Bracebridge informed me that they were great favorites with his father, who was extremely careful to keep up the breed; partly because they belonged to chivalry, and were in great request at the stately banquets of the olden time, and partly because they had a pomp and magnificence about them highly becoming an old family mansion. Nothing, he was accustomed to say, had an air of greater state and dignity than a peacock perched upon an antique stone balustrade.

Master Simon had now to hurry off, having an appointment at the parish church with the village choristers, who were to perform some music of his selection. There was something extremely agreeable in the cheerful flow of animal spirits of the little man; and I confess I had been somewhat surprised at his apt quotations from authors who certainly were not in the range of every-day reading. I mentioned this last circumstance to Frank Bracebridge, who told me with a smile that Master Simon's whole stock of erudition was confined to some half a dozen old authors, which the squire had put into his hands, and which he read over and over whenever he had a studious fit, as he sometimes had on a rainy day or a long winter evening. Sir Anthony Fitzherbert's Book of Husbandry; Markham's Country Contentments; the Tretyse of Hunting, by Sir Thomas Cockayne; Knight, Isaac Walton's Angler, and two or three more such ancient worthies of the pen were his standard authorities; and, like all men who know but a few books, he looked up to them with a kind of idolatry and quoted them on all occasions. As to his songs, they were chiefly picked out of old books in the squire's library, and adapted to tunes that were popular among the choice spirits of the last century. His practical application of scraps of literature, however, had caused him to be looked upon as a prodigy of book-knowledge by all the grooms, huntsmen, and small sportsmen of the neighborhood.

While we were talking we heard the distant toll of the village bell, and I was told that the squire was a little particular in having his household at church on a Christmas morning, considering it a day of pouring out of thanks and rejoicing; for, as old Tusser observed,—

> At Christmas be merry, *and thankful withal*,
> And feast thy poor neighbors, the great with the small.

"If you are disposed to go to church," said Frank Bracebridge, "I can promise you a specimen of my cousin Simon's musical achievements. As the church is destitute of an organ, he has formed a band from the village amateurs, and established a musical club for their improvement; he has also sorted a choir, as he sorted my father's pack of hounds, according to the directions of Jervaise Markham in his Country Contentments: for the bass he has sought out all the 'deep, solemn mouths,' and for the tenor the 'loud-ringing mouths,' among the country bumpkins, and for 'sweet-mouths,' he has culled with curious taste among the prettiest lasses in the neighborhood; though these last, he affirms, are the most difficult to keep in tune, your pretty female singer being exceedingly wayward and capricious, and very liable to accident."

As the morning, though frosty, was remarkably fine and clear, the most of the family walked to the church, which was a very old building of gray stone, and stood near a village about half a mile from the park gate. Adjoining it was a low snug parsonage which seemed coeval with the church. The front of it was perfectly matted with a yew tree that had been trained against its walls, through the dense foliage of which, apertures had been formed to admit light into the small antique lattices. As we passed this sheltered nest the parson issued forth and preceded us.

I had expected to see a sleek well-conditioned pastor, such as is often found in a snug living in the vicinity of a rich patron's table, but I was disappointed. The parson was a little, meagre, black-looking man, with a grizzled wig that was too wide and stood off from each ear; so that his head seemed to have shrunk away within it, like a dried filbert in its shell. He wore a rusty coat, with great skirts and pockets that would have held the church Bible and prayer-book: and his small legs seemed still smaller from being planted in large shoes decorated with enormous buckles.

I was informed by Frank Bracebridge that the parson had been a chum of his father's at Oxford, and had received this living shortly after the latter had come to his estate. He was a complete black-letter hunter, and would scarcely read a work printed in the Roman character. The editions of Caxton and Wynkyn de Worde were his delight, and he was indefatigable in his researches after such old English writers as have fallen into oblivion from their worthlessness. In deference, perhaps, to the notions of Mr. Bracebridge he had made diligent investigations into the festive rites and holiday customs of former times, and had been as zealous in the inquiry as if he had been a boon companion; but it was merely with that plodding spirit with which men of adust temperament follow up any track of study, merely because it is denominated learning; indifferent to its intrinsic nature, whether it be the illustration of the wisdom or of the ribaldry and obscenity of antiquity. He had pored over these old volumes so intensely that they seemed to have been reflected into his countenance; which, if the face be indeed an index of the mind, might be compared to a title-page of black-letter.

On reaching the church-porch we found the parson rebuking the gray-headed sexton for having used mistletoe among the greens with which the church was decorated. It was, he observed, an unholy plant, profaned by having been used by the Druids in their mystic ceremonies; and, though it might be innocently employed in the festive ornamenting of halls and kitchens, yet it had been deemed by the Fathers of the Church as unhallowed and totally unfit for sacred purposes. So tenacious was he on this point that the poor sexton was obliged to strip down a great part of the humble trophies of his taste before the parson would consent to enter upon the service of the day.

The interior of the church was venerable, but simple; on the walls were several mural monuments of the Bracebridges, and just beside the altar was a tomb of ancient workmanship, on which lay the effigy of a warrior in armor with his legs crossed, a sign of his having been a crusader. I was told it was one of the family who had signalized himself in the Holy Land, and the same whose picture hung over the fireplace in the hall.

During service Master Simon stood up in the pew and repeated the responses very audibly, evincing that kind of ceremonious devotion punctually observed by a gentleman of the old school and a man of old family connections. I observed too that he turned over the leaves of a folio prayer-book with something of a flourish; possibly to show off an enormous seal-ring which enriched one of his fingers and which had the look of a family relic. But he was evidently most solicitous about the musical part of the service, keeping his eye fixed intently on the choir, and beating time with much gesticulation and emphasis.

The orchestra was in a small gallery, and presented a most whimsical grouping of heads piled one above the other, among which I particularly noticed that of the village tailor, a pale fellow with a retreating forehead and chin, who played on the clarinet, and seemed to have blown his face to a point; and there was another, a short pursy man, stooping and laboring at a bass-viol, so as to show nothing but the top of a round bald head, like the egg of an ostrich. There were two or three pretty faces among the female singers, to which the keen air of a frosty morning had given a bright rosy tint; but the gentlemen choristers had evidently been chosen, like old Cremona fiddles, more for tone than looks; and as several had to sing from the same book, there were clusterings of odd physiognomies not unlike those groups of cherubs we sometimes see on country tombstones.

The usual services of the choir were managed tolerably well, the vocal parts generally lagging a little behind the instrumental, and some loitering fiddler now and then making up for lost time by travelling over a passage with prodigious celerity and clearing more bars than the keenest fox-hunter to be in at the death. But the great trial was an anthem that had been prepared and arranged by Master Simon, and on which he had founded great expectations. Unluckily, there was a blunder at the very outset: the musicians became flurried; Master Simon was in a fever; everything went on lamely and irregularly until they came to a chorus beginning, "Now let us sing with one accord," which seemed to be a signal for parting company: all became discord and confusion: each shifted for himself, and got to the end as well—or, rather, as soon—as he could, excepting one old chorister in a pair of horn spectacles bestriding and pinching a long sonorous nose, who happened to stand a little apart, and, being wrapped up in his own melody, kept on a quavering course, wriggling his head, ogling his book, and winding all up by a nasal solo of at least three bars' duration.

The parson gave us a most erudite sermon on the rites and ceremonies of Christmas, and the propriety of observing it not merely as a day of thanksgiving but of rejoicing, supporting the correctness of his opinions by the earliest usages of the Church, and enforcing them by the authorities of Theophilus of Caesarea, St. Cyprian, St. Chrysostom, St. Augustine, and a cloud more of saints and fathers, from whom he made copious quotations. I was a little at a loss to perceive the necessity of such a mighty array of forces to maintain a point which no one present seemed inclined to dispute; but I soon found that the good man had a legion of ideal adversaries to contend with, having in the course of his researches on the subject of Christmas got completely embroiled in the sectarian controversies of the Revolution, when the Puritans made such a fierce assault upon the ceremonies of the Church, and poor old Christmas was driven out of the land by proclamation of Parliament.* The worthy parson lived but with times past, and knew but little of the present.

Shut up among worm-eaten tomes in the retirement of his antiquated little study, the pages of old times were to him as the gazettes of the day, while the era of the Revolution was mere modern history. He forgot that nearly two centuries had elapsed since the fiery persecution of poor

* From the "Flying Eagle," a small gazette, published December 24, 1652: "The House spent much time this day about the business of the Navy, for settling the affairs at sea, and before they rose, were presented with a terrible remonstrance against Christmas day, grounded upon divine Scriptures, 2 Cor. v. 16; I Cor. xv. 14, 17; and in honor of the Lord's Day, grounded upon these Scriptures, John xx. I; Rev. i. 10; Psalms cxviii. 24; Lev. xxiii. 7, 11; Mark xv. 8; Psalms lxxxiv. 10, in which Christmas is called Anti- christ's masse, and those Masse-mongers and Papists who observe it, etc. In consequence of which parliament spent some time in consultation about the abolition of Christmas day, passed orders to that effect, and resolved to sit on the following day, which was commonly called Christmas day."

mince-pie throughout the land; when plum porridge was denounced as "mere popery," and roast beef as anti-christian, and that Christmas had been brought in again triumphantly with the merry court of King Charles at the Restoration. He kindled into warmth with the ardor of his contest and the host of imaginary foes with whom he had to combat; he had a stubborn conflict with old Prynne and two or three other forgotten champions of the Roundheads on the subject of Christmas festivity; and concluded by urging his hearers, in the most solemn and affecting manner, to stand to the traditional customs of their fathers and feast and make merry on this joyful anniversary of the Church.

I have seldom known a sermon attended apparently with more immediate effects, for on leaving the church the congregation seemed one and all possessed with the gayety of spirit so earnestly enjoined by their pastor. The elder folks gathered in knots in the churchyard, greeting and shaking hands, and the children ran about crying Ule! Ule! and repeating some uncouth rhymes,* which the parson, who had joined us, informed me had been handed down from days of yore. The villagers doffed their hats to the squire as he passed, giving him the good wishes of the season with every appearance of heartfelt sincerity, and were invited by him to the hall to take something to keep out the cold of the weather; and I heard blessings uttered by several of the poor, which convinced me that, in the midst of his enjoyments, the worthy old cavalier had not forgotten the true Christmas virtue of charity.

On our way homeward his heart seemed overflowed with generous and happy feelings. As we passed over a rising ground which commanded something of a prospect, the sounds of rustic merriment now and then reached our ears: the squire paused for a few moments and looked around with an air of inexpressible benignity. The beauty of the day was of itself sufficient to inspire philanthropy. Notwithstanding the frostiness of the morning, the sun in his cloudless journey had acquired sufficient power to melt away the thin covering of snow from every southern declivity, and to bring out the living green which adorns an English landscape even in mid-winter. Large tracts of smiling verdure contrasted with the dazzling whiteness of the shaded slopes and hollows.

* "Ule! Ule!
Three puddings in a pule;
Crack nuts and cry ule!"

Every sheltered bank on which the broad rays rested yielded its silver rill of cold and limpid water, glittering through the dripping grass, and sent up slight exhalations to contribute to the thin haze that hung just above the surface of the earth. There was something truly cheering in this triumph of warmth and verdure over the frosty thraldom of winter; it was, as the squire observed, an emblem of Christmas hospitality breaking through the chills of ceremony and selfishness and thawing every heart into a flow. He pointed with pleasure to the indications of good cheer reeking from the chimneys of the comfortable farm-houses and low thatched cottages. "I love," said he, "to see this day well kept by rich and poor; it is a great thing to have one day in the year, at least, when you are sure of being welcome wherever you go, and of having, as it were, the world all thrown open to you; and I am almost disposed to join with Poor Robin in his malediction on every churlish enemy to this honest festival:

Those who at Christmas do repine,
And would fain hence dispatch him,
May they with old Duke Humphry dine,
Or else may Squire Ketch catch'em.

The squire went on to lament the deplorable decay of the games and amusements which were once prevalent at this season among the lower orders and countenanced by the higher, when the old halls of castles and manor-houses were thrown open at daylight; when the tables were covered with brawn and beef and humming ale; when the harp and the carol resounded all day long; and when rich and poor were alike welcome to enter and make merry.* "Our old games and local customs," said he, "had a great effect in making the peasant fond of his home, and the promotion of them by the gentry made him fond of his lord. They made the times merrier and kinder and better, and I can truly say, with one of our old poets,

* "An English gentleman, at the opening of the great day— i.e. on Christmas Day in the morning—had all his tenants and neighbors enter his hall by daybreak. The strong beer was broached, and the black-jacks went plentifully about, with toast, sugar and nutmeg, and good Cheshire cheese. The Hackin (the great sausage) must be boiled by daybreak, or else two young men must take the maiden (i.e. the cook) by the arms and run her round the market-place till she is shamed of her laziness."—Round about Our Sea-Coal Fire

I like them well—the curious preciseness
And all-pretended gravity of those
That seek to banish hence these harmless sports,
Have thrust away much ancient honesty.

"The nation," continued he, "is altered; we have almost lost our simple true-hearted peasantry. They have broken asunder from the higher classes, and seem to think their interests are separate. They have become too knowing, and begin to read newspapers, listen to ale-house politicians, and talk of reform. I think one mode to keep them in good-humor in these hard times would be for the nobility and gentry to pass more time on their estates, mingle more among the country-people, and set the merry old English games going again."

Such was the good squire's project for mitigating public discontent: and, indeed, he had once attempted to put his doctrine in practice, and a few years before had kept open house during the holidays in the old style. The country-people, however, did not understand how to play their parts in the scene of hospitality; many uncouth circumstances occurred; the manor was overrun by all the vagrants of the country, and more beggars drawn into the neighborhood in one week than the parish officers could get rid of in a year. Since then he had contented himself with inviting the decent part of the neighboring peasantry to call at the hall on Christmas Day, and with distributing beef, and bread, and ale among the poor, that they might make merry in their own dwellings.

We had not been long home when the sound of music was heard from a distance. A band of country lads, without coats, their shirt-sleeves fancifully tied with ribbons, their hats decorated with greens, and clubs in their hands, was seen advancing up the avenue, followed by a large number of villagers and peasantry. They stopped before the hall door, where the music struck up a peculiar air, and the lads performed a curious and intricate dance, advancing, retreating, and striking their clubs together, keeping exact time to the music; while one, whimsically crowned with a fox's skin, the tail of which flaunted down his back, kept capering round the skirts of the dance and rattling a Christmas box with many antic gesticulations.

The squire eyed this fanciful exhibition with great interest and delight, and gave me a full account of its origin, which he traced to the times when the Romans held possession of the island, plainly proving that this was a lineal descendant of the sword dance of the ancients. "It was now," he said, "nearly extinct, but he had accidentally met with traces of it in the neighborhood, and had encouraged its revival; though, to tell the truth, it was too apt to be followed up by the rough cudgel play and broken heads in the evening."

After the dance was concluded the whole party was entertained with brawn and beef and stout home-brewed. The squire himself mingled among the rustics, and was received with awkward demonstrations of deference and regard. It is true I perceived two or three of the younger peasants, as they were raising their tankards to their mouths, when the squire's back was turned making something of a grimace, and giving each other the wink; but the moment they caught my eye they pulled grave faces and were exceedingly demure. With Master Simon, however, they all seemed more at their ease. His varied occupations and amusements had made him well known throughout the neighborhood. He was a visitor at every farm-house and cottage, gossiped with the farmers and their wives, romped with their daughters, and, like that type of a vagrant bachelor, the humble bee, tolled the sweets from all the rosy lips of the country round.

The bashfulness of the guests soon gave way before good cheer and affability. There is something genuine and affectionate in the gayety of the lower orders when it is excited by the bounty and familiarity of those above them; the warm glow of gratitude enters into their mirth, and a kind word or a small pleasantry frankly uttered by a patron gladdens the heart of the dependant more than oil and wine. When the squire had retired, the merriment increased, and there was much joking and laughter, particularly between Master Simon and a hale, ruddy-faced, white-headed farmer who appeared to be the wit of the village; for I observed all his companions to wait with open months for his retorts, and burst into a gratuitous laugh before they could well understand them.

The whole house indeed seemed abandoned to merriment: as I passed to my room to dress for dinner, I heard the sound of music in a small court, and, looking through a window that commanded it, I perceived a band of wandering musicians with pandean pipes and tambourine; a pretty coquettish housemaid was dancing a jig with a smart country lad, while several of the other servants were looking on. In the midst of her sport the girl caught a glimpse of my face at the window, and, coloring up, ran off with an air of roguish affected confusion.

THE CHRISTMAS DINNER

Lo, now is come our joyful'st feast!
  Let every man be jolly.
Eache roome with yvie leaves is drest,
  And every post with holly.
Now all our neighbours' chimneys smoke,
  And Christmas blocks are burning;
Their ovens they with bak't meats choke
  And all their spits are turning.
    Without the door let sorrow lie,
      And if, for cold, it hap to die,
    Wee'le bury 't in a Christmas pye,
      And evermore be merry.

—WITHERS' JUVENILIA

I had finished my toilet, and was loitering with Frank Bracebridge in the library, when we heard a distant thwacking sound, which he informed me was a signal for the serving up of the dinner. The squire kept up old customs in kitchen as well as hall, and the rolling-pin, struck upon the dresser by the cook, summoned the servants to carry in the meats.

Just in this nick the cook knock'd thrice,
And all the waiters in a trice
  His summons did obey;
Each serving-man, with dish in hand,
March'd boldly up, like our train-band,
  Presented, and away.*

The dinner was served up in the great hall, where the squire always held his Christmas banquet. A blazing, crackling fire of logs had been heaped on to warm the spacious apartment, and the flame went sparkling and wreathing up the wide-mouthed chimney. The great picture of the

* Sir John Suckling

crusader and his white horse had been profusely decorated with greens for the occasion, and holly and ivy had likewise been wreathed round the helmet and weapons on the opposite wall, which I understood were the arms of the same warrior. I must own, by the by, I had strong doubts about the authenticity of the painting and armor as having belonged to the crusader, they certainly having the stamp of more recent days; but I was told that the painting had been so considered time out of mind; and that as to the armor, it had been found in a lumber-room and elevated to its present situation by the squire, who at once determined it to be the armor of the family hero; and as he was absolute authority on all such subjects in his own household, the matter had passed into current acceptation. A sideboard was set out just under this chivalric trophy, on which was a display of plate that might have vied (at least in variety) with Belshazzar's parade of the vessels of the temple: "flagons, cans, cups, beakers, goblets, basins, and ewers," the gorgeous utensils of good companionship that had gradually accumulated through many generations of jovial housekeepers. Before these stood the two Yule candles, beaming like two stars of the first magnitude; other lights were distributed in branches, and the whole array glittered like a firmament of silver.

We were ushered into this banqueting scene with the sound of minstrelsy, the old harper being seated on a stool beside the fireplace and twanging, his instrument with a vast deal more power than melody. Never did Christmas board display a more goodly and gracious assemblage of countenances; those who were not handsome were at least happy, and happiness is a rare improver of your hard-favored visage. I always consider an old English family as well worth studying as a collection of Holbein's portraits or Albert Durer's prints. There is much antiquarian lore to be acquired, much knowledge of the physiognomies of former times. Perhaps it may be from having continually before their eyes those rows of old family portraits, with which the mansions of this country are stocked; certain it is that the quaint features of antiquity are often most faithfully perpetuated in these ancient lines, and I have traced an old family nose through a whole picture-gallery, legitimately handed down from generation to generation almost from the time of the Conquest. Something of the kind was to be observed in the worthy company around me. Many of their faces had evidently originated in a gothic age, and been merely copied by succeeding generations; and there was one little girl in particular, of staid demeanor, with a high Roman nose and an antique vinegar aspect, who was a great favorite of the squire's, being, as he said, a Bracebridge all over, and the very counterpart of one of his ancestors who figured in the court of Henry VIII.

The parson said grace, which was not a short familiar one, such as is commonly addressed to the Deity in these unceremonious days, but a long, courtly, well-worded one of the ancient school. There was now a pause, as if something was expected, when suddenly the butler entered the hall with some degree of bustle: he was attended by a servant on each side with a large wax-light, and bore a silver dish on which was an enormous pig's head decorated with rosemary, with a lemon in its mouth, which was placed with great formality at the head of the table. The moment this pageant made its appearance the harper struck up a flourish; at the conclusion of which the young Oxonian, on receiving a hint from the squire, gave, with an air of the most comic gravity, an old carol, the first verse of which was as follows

Caput apri defero
Reddens laudes Domino.
The boar's head in hand bring I,
With garlands gay and rosemary.
I pray you all synge merily
Qui estis in convivio.

Though prepared to witness many of these little eccentricities, from being apprised of the peculiar hobby of mine host, yet I confess the parade with which so odd a dish was introduced somewhat perplexed me, until I gathered from the conversation of the squire and the parson that it was meant to represent the bringing in of the boar's head, a dish formerly served up with much ceremony and the sound of minstrelsy and song at great tables on Christmas Day. "I like the old custom," said the squire, "not merely because it is stately and pleasing in itself, but because it was observed at the college at Oxford at which I was educated. When I hear the old song chanted it brings to mind the time when I was young and gamesome, and the noble old college hall, and my fellow-students loitering about in their black gowns; many of whom, poor lads! are now in their graves."

The parson, however, whose mind was not haunted by such associations, and who was always more taken up with the text than the sentiment, objected to the Oxonian's version of the carol, which he affirmed was different from that sung at college. He went on, with the dry perseverance of a commentator, to give the college reading, accompanied by sundry annotations, addressing himself at first to the company at large; but, finding their attention gradually diverted to other talk and other objects, he lowered his tone as his number of auditors diminished, until he concluded his remarks in an under voice to a fat-headed old gentleman next him who was silently engaged in the discussion of a huge plateful of turkey.*

The table was literally loaded with good cheer, and presented an epitome of country abundance in this season of overflowing larders. A distinguished post was allotted to "ancient sirloin," as mine host termed it, being, as he added, "the standard of old English hospitality, and a joint of goodly presence, and full of expectation." There were several dishes quaintly decorated, and which had evidently something

* The old ceremony of serving up the boar's head on Christmas Day is still observed in the hall of Queen's College, Oxford. I was favored by the parson with a copy of the carol as now sung, and as it may be acceptable to such of my readers as are curious in these grave and learned matters, I give it entire:

The boar's head in hand bear I,
Bedeck'd with bays and rosemary
And I pray you, my masters, be merry
  Quot estis in convivio
    Caput apri defero,
    Reddens laudes domino.

The boar's head, as I understand,
Is the rarest dish in all this land,
Which thus bedeck'd with a gay garland
  Let us servire cantico.
    Caput apri defero, etc.

Our steward hath provided this
In honor of the King of Bliss,
Which on this day to be served is
  In Reginensi Atrio.
    Caput apri defero,
      etc., etc., etc.

traditional in their embellishments, but about which, as I did not like to appear overcurious, I asked no questions.

I could not, however, but notice a pie magnificently decorated with peacock's feathers, in imitation of the tail of that bird, which overshadowed a considerable tract of the table. This, the squire confessed with some little hesitation, was a pheasant pie, though a peacock pie was certainly the most authentical; but there had been such a mortality among the peacocks this season that he could not prevail upon himself to have one killed.*

It would be tedious, perhaps, to my wiser readers, who may not have that foolish fondness for odd and obsolete things to which I am a little given, were I to mention the other makeshifts or this worthy old humorist, by which he was endeavoring to follow up, though at humble distance, the quaint customs of antiquity. I was pleased, however, to see the respect shown to his whims by his children and relatives; who, indeed, entered readily into the full spirit of them, and seemed all well versed in their parts, having doubtless been present at many a rehearsal. I was amused, too, at the air of profound gravity with which the butler and other servants executed the duties assigned them, however eccentric. They had an old-fashioned look, having, for the most part, been brought up in the household and grown into keeping with the antiquated mansion and the humors of its lord, and most probably looked upon all his whimsical regulations as the established laws of honorable housekeeping.

When the cloth was removed the butler brought in a huge silver vessel of rare and curious workmanship, which he placed before the

---

* The peacock was anciently in great demand for stately entertainments. Sometimes it was made into a pie, at one end of which the head appeared above the crust in all its plumage, with the beak richly gilt; at the other end the tail was displayed. Such pies were served up at the solemn banquets of chivalry, when knights-errant pledged themselves to undertake any perilous enterprise, whence came the ancient oath, used by Justice Shallow, "by cock and pie."

The peacock was also an important dish for the Christmas feast; and Massinger, in his "City Madam," gives some idea of the extravagance with which this, as well as other dishes, was prepared for the gorgeous revels of the olden times:

> Men may talk of Country Christmasses,
> Their thirty pound butter'd eggs, their pies of carps' tongues;
> Their pheasants drench'd with ambergris: the carcases of three fat
> wethers bruised for gravy to make sauce for a single peacock!

squire. Its appearance was hailed with acclamation, being the Wassail Bowl, so renowned in Christmas festivity. The contents had been prepared by the squire himself; for it was a beverage in the skilful mixture of which he particularly prided himself, alleging that it was too abstruse and complex for the comprehension of an ordinary servant. It was a potation, indeed, that might well make the heart of a toper leap within him, being composed of the richest and raciest wines, highly spiced and sweetened, with roasted apples bobbing about the surface.*

The old gentleman's whole countenance beamed with a serene look of indwelling delight as he stirred this mighty bowl. Having raised it to his lips, with a hearty wish of a merry Christmas to all present, he sent it brimming round the board, for every one to follow his example, according to the primitive style, pronouncing it "the ancient fountain of good feeling, where all hearts met together."†

There was much laughing and rallying as the honest emblem of Christmas joviality circulated and was kissed rather coyly by the ladies. When it reached Master Simon, he raised it in both hands, and with the air of a boon companion struck up an old Wassail Chanson:

The brown bowle,
The merry brown bowle,
As it goes round-about-a,
Fill
Still,
Let the world say what it will,
And drink your fill all out-a.

---

* The Wassail Bowl was sometimes composed of ale instead of wine, with nutmeg, sugar, toast, ginger, and roasted crabs; in this way the nut-brown beverage is still prepared in some old families and round the hearths of substantial farmers at Christmas. It is also called Lamb's Wool, and is celebrated by Herrick in his "Twelfth Night":

Next crowne the bowle full
With gentle Lamb's Wooll;
Add sugar, nutmeg, and ginger,
With store of ale too;
And thus ye must doe
To make the Wassaile a swinger.

† "The custom of drinking out of the same cup gave place to each having his cup. When the steward came to the doore with the Wassel, he was to cry three times,
Wassel, Wassel, Wassel, and then the chappell (chaplain) was to answer with a song."
—Archaeologia

The deep canne,
The merry deep canne,
As thou dost freely quaff-a,
Sing
Fling,
Be as merry as a king,
And sound a lusty laugh-a.*

Much of the conversation during dinner turned upon family topics, to which I was a stranger. There was, however, a great deal of rallying of Master Simon about some gay widow with whom he was accused of having a flirtation. This attack was commenced by the ladies, but it was continued throughout the dinner by the fat-headed old gentleman next the parson with the persevering assiduity of a slow hound, being one of those long-winded jokers who, though rather dull at starting game, are unrivalled for their talents in hunting it down. At every pause in the general conversation he renewed his bantering in pretty much the same terms, winking hard at me with both eyes whenever he gave Master Simon what he considered a home thrust. The latter, indeed, seemed fond of being teased on the subject, as old bachelors are apt to be, and he took occasion to inform me, in an undertone, that the lady in question was a prodigiously fine woman and drove her own curricle.

The dinner-time passed away in this flow of innocent hilarity, and, though the old hall may have resounded in its time with many a scene of broader rout and revel, yet I doubt whether it ever witnessed more honest and genuine enjoyment. How easy it is for one benevolent being to diffuse pleasure around him! and how truly is a kind heart a fountain of gladness, making everything in its vicinity to freshen into smiles! The joyous disposition of the worthy squire was perfectly contagious; he was happy himself, and disposed to make all the world happy, and the little eccentricities of his humor did but season, in a manner, the sweetness of his philanthropy.

When the ladies had retired, the conversation, as usual, became still more animated; many good things were broached which had been thought of during dinner, but which would not exactly do for a lady's ear; and, though I cannot positively affirm that there was much wit

* From Poor Robin's Almanack

uttered, yet I have certainly heard many contests of rare wit produce much less laughter. Wit, after all, is a mighty tart, pungent ingredient, and much too acid for some stomachs; but honest good-humor is the oil and wine of a merry meeting, and there is no jovial companionship equal to that where the jokes are rather small and the laughter abundant.

The squire told several long stories of early college pranks and adventures, in some of which the parson had been a sharer, though in looking at the latter it required some effort of imagination to figure such a little dark anatomy of a man into the perpetrator of a madcap gambol. Indeed, the two college chums presented pictures of what men may be made by their different lots in life. The squire had left the university to live lustily on his paternal domains in the vigorous enjoyment of prosperity and sunshine, and had flourished on to a hearty and florid old age; whilst the poor parson, on the contrary, had dried and withered away among dusty tomes in the silence and shadows of his study. Still, there seemed to be a spark of almost extinguished fire feebly glimmering in the bottom of his soul; and as the squire hinted at a sly story of the parson and a pretty milkmaid whom they once met on the banks of the Isis, the old gentleman made an "alphabet of faces," which, as far as I could decipher his physiognomy, I verily believe was indicative of laughter; indeed, I have rarely met with an old gentleman that took absolute offence at the imputed gallantries of his youth.

I found the tide of wine and wassail fast gaining on the dry land of sober judgment. The company grew merrier and louder as their jokes grew duller. Master Simon was in as chirping a humor as a grasshopper filled with dew; his old songs grew of a warmer complexion, and he began to talk maudlin about the widow. He even gave a long song about the wooing of a widow which he informed me he had gathered from an excellent black-letter work entitled Cupid's Solicitor for Love, containing store of good advice for bachelors, and which he promised to lend me; the first verse was to this effect:

> He that will woo a widow must not dally
>   He must make hay while the sun doth shine;
> He must not stand with her, shall I, shall I,
>   But boldly say, Widow, thou must be mine.

This song inspired the fat-headed old gentleman, who made several attempts to tell a rather broad story out of Joe Miller that was pat to the purpose; but he always stuck in the middle, everybody recollecting the latter part excepting himself. The parson, too, began to show the effects of good cheer, having gradually settled down into a doze and his wig sitting most suspiciously on one side. Just at this juncture we were summoned to the drawing room, and I suspect, at the private instigation of mine host, whose joviality seemed always tempered with a proper love of decorum.

After the dinner-table was removed the hall was given up to the younger members of the family, who, prompted to all kind of noisy mirth by the Oxonian and Master Simon, made its old walls ring with their merriment as they played at romping games. I delight in witnessing the gambols of children, and particularly at this happy holiday season, and could not help stealing out of the drawing-room on hearing one of their peals of laughter. I found them at the game of blindman's-buff. Master Simon, who was the leader of their revels, and seemed on all occasions to fulfill the office of that ancient potentate, the Lord of Misrule,* was blinded in the midst of the hall. The little beings were as busy about him as the mock fairies about Falstaff, pinching him, plucking at the skirts of his coat, and tickling him with straws. One fine blue-eyed girl of about thirteen, with her flaxen hair all in beautiful confusion, her frolic face in a glow, her frock half torn off her shoulders, a complete picture of a romp, was the chief tormentor; and, from the slyness with which Master Simon avoided the smaller game and hemmed this wild little nymph in corners, and obliged her to jump shrieking over chairs, I suspected the rogue of being not a whit more blinded than was convenient.

When I returned to the drawing-room, I found the company seated round the fire listening to the parson, who was deeply ensconced in a high-backed oaken chair, the work of some cunning artificer of yore, which had been brought from the library for his particular accommodation. From this venerable piece of furniture, with which his shadowy figure and dark weazen face so admirably accorded, he was

* At Christmasse there was in the Kinges house, wheresoever hee was lodged, a lorde of misrule or mayster of merie disportes, and the like had ye in the house of every nobleman of honor, or good worshipper were he spirituall or temporall.—Stow

dealing out strange accounts of the popular superstitions and legends of the surrounding country, with which he had become acquainted in the course of his antiquarian researches. I am half inclined to think that the old gentleman was himself somewhat tinctured with superstition, as men are very apt to be who live a recluse and studious life in a sequestered part of the country and pore over black-letter tracts, so often filled with the marvelous and supernatural. He gave us several anecdotes of the fancies of the neighboring peasantry concerning the effigy of the crusader which lay on the tomb by the church altar. As it was the only monument of the kind in that part of the country, it had always been regarded with feelings of superstition by the good wives of the village. It was said to get up from the tomb and walk the rounds of the churchyard in stormy nights, particularly when it thundered; and one old woman, whose cottage bordered on the churchyard, had seen it through the windows of the church, when the moon shone, slowly pacing up and down the aisles. It was the belief that some wrong had been left unredressed by the deceased, or some treasure hidden, which kept the spirit in a state of trouble and restlessness. Some talked of gold and jewels buried in the tomb, over which the spectre kept watch; and there was a story current of a sexton in old times who endeavored to break his way to the coffin at night, but just as he reached it received a violent blow from the marble hand of the effigy, which stretched him senseless on the pavement. These tales were often laughed at by some of the sturdier among the rustics, yet when night came on, there were many of the stoutest unbelievers that were shy of venturing alone in the footpath that led across the churchyard.

From these and other anecdotes that followed, the crusader appeared to be the favorite hero of ghost-stories throughout the vicinity. His picture, which hung up in the hall, was thought by the servants to have something supernatural about it; for they remarked that in whatever part of the hall you went, the eyes of the warrior were still fixed on you. The old porter's wife, too, at the lodge, who had been born and brought up in the family, and was a great gossip among the maid-servants, affirmed that in her young days she had often heard say that on Midsummer Eve, when it was well known all kinds of ghosts, goblins, and fairies become visible and walk abroad, the crusader used to mount his horse, come down from his picture, ride about the house, down the avenue, and so to the church to visit the tomb; on which occasion the church-door most civilly swung open of itself; not that he needed it, for he rode through closed gates, and even stone walls, and had been seen by one of the dairymaids to pass between two bars of the great park gate, making himself as thin as a sheet of paper.

All these superstitions I found had been very much countenanced by the squire, who, though not superstitious himself, was very fond of seeing others so. He listened to every goblin tale of the neighboring gossips with infinite gravity, and held the porter's wife in high favor on account of her talent for the marvellous. He was himself a great reader of old legends and romances, and often lamented that he could not believe in them; for a superstitious person, he thought, must live in a kind of fairy-land.

Whilst we were all attention to the parson's stories, our ears were suddenly assailed by a burst of heterogeneous sounds from the hall, in which were mingled something like the clang of rude minstrelsy with the uproar of many small voices and girlish laughter. The door suddenly flew open, and a train came trooping into the room that might almost have been mistaken for the breaking up of the court of Fairy. That indefatigable spirit, Master Simon, in the faithful discharge of his duties as lord of misrule, had conceived the idea of a Christmas mummery or masking; and having called in to his assistance the Oxonian and the young officer, who were equally ripe for anything that should occasion romping and merriment, they had carried it into instant effect. The old housekeeper had been consulted; the antique clothes presses and wardrobes rummaged and made to yield up the relics of finery that had not seen the light for several generations; the younger part of the company had been privately convened from the parlor and hall, and the whole had been bedizened out into a burlesque imitation of an antique masque.*

Master Simon led the van, as "Ancient Christmas," quaintly apparelled in a ruff, a short cloak, which had very much the aspect

* Masquings or mummeries were favorite sports at Christmas in old times, and the wardrobes at halls and manor-houses were often laid under contribution to furnish dresses and fantastic disguisings. I strongly suspect Master Simon to have taken the idea of his from Ben Jonson's "Masque of Christmas."

of one of the old housekeeper's petticoats, and a hat that might have served for a village steeple, and must indubitably have figured in the days of the Covenanters. From under this his nose curved boldly forth, flushed with a frost-bitten bloom that seemed the very trophy of a December blast. He was accompanied by the blue-eyed romp, dished up, as "Dame Mince Pie," in the venerable magnificence of a faded brocade, long stomacher, peaked hat, and high-heeled shoes. The young officer appeared as Robin Hood, in a sporting dress of Kendal green and a foraging cap with a gold tassel.

The costume, to be sure, did not bear testimony to deep research, and there was an evident eye to the picturesque, natural to a young gallant in the presence of his mistress. The fair Julia hung on his arm in a pretty rustic dress as "Maid Marian." The rest of the train had been metamorphosed in various ways; the girls trussed up in the finery of the ancient belles of the Bracebridge line, and the striplings bewhiskered with burnt cork, and gravely clad in broad skirts, hanging sleeves, and full-bottomed wigs, to represent the character of Roast Beef, Plum Pudding, and other worthies celebrated in ancient masquings. The whole was under the control of the Oxonian in the appropriate character of Misrule; and I observed that he exercised rather a mischievous sway with his wand over the smaller personages of the pageant.

The irruption of this motley crew, with beat of drum, according to ancient custom, was the consummation of uproar and merriment. Master Simon covered himself with glory by the stateliness with which, as Ancient Christmas, he walked a minuet with the peerless, though giggling, Dame Mince Pie. It was followed by a dance of all the characters, which from its medley of costumes seemed as though the old family portraits had skipped down from their frames to join in the sport. Different centuries were figuring at cross hands and right and left; the Dark Ages were cutting pirouettes and rigadoons; and the days of Queen Bess jigging merrily down the middle, through a line of succeeding generations.

The worthy squire contemplated these fantastic sports and this resurrection of his old wardrobe with the simple relish of childish delight. He stood chuckling and rubbing his hands, and scarcely hearing a word the parson said, notwithstanding that the latter was discoursing most authentically on the ancient and stately dance of the Pavon, or peacock, from which he conceived the minuet to be derived.* For my part, I was in a continual excitement from the varied scenes of whim and innocent gayety passing before me. It was inspiring to see wild-eyed frolic and warm-hearted hospitality breaking out from among the chills and glooms of winter, and old age throwing off his apathy and catching once more the freshness of youthful enjoyment. I felt also an interest in the scene from the consideration that these fleeting customs were posting fast into oblivion, and that this was perhaps the only family in England in which the whole of them was still punctiliously observed. There was a quaintness, too, mingled with all this revelry that gave it a peculiar zest: it was suited to the time and place; and as the old manor-house almost reeled with mirth and wassail, it seemed echoing back the joviality of long departed years.†

But enough of Christmas and its gambols; it is time for me to pause in this garrulity. Methinks I hear the questions asked by my graver readers, "To what purpose is all this? how is the world to be made wiser by this talk?" Alas! is there not wisdom enough extant for the instruction of the world? And if not, are there not thousands of abler pens laboring for its improvement? It is so much pleasanter to please than to instruct—to play the companion rather than the preceptor. What, after all, is the mite of wisdom that I could throw into the mass of knowledge! or how am I sure that my sagest deductions may be safe guides for the opinions of others? But in writing to amuse, if I fail, the only evil is in my own disappointment. If, however, I can by any lucky chance, in these days of evil, rub out one wrinkle from the brow of care or beguile the heavy heart of one moment of sorrow; if I can now and then penetrate through the gathering film of misanthropy, prompt a

---

* Sir John Hawkins, speaking of the dance called the Pavon, from pavo, a peacock, says, "It is a grave and majestic dance; the method of dancing it anciently was by gentlemen dressed with caps and swords, by those of the long robe in their gowns, by the peers in their mantles, and by the ladies in gowns with long trains, the motion whereof, in dancing, resembled that of a peacock."—History of Music

† At the time of the first publication of this paper, the picture of an old-fashioned Christmas in the country was pronounced by some as out of date. The author had afterwards an opportunity of witnessing almost all the customs above described, existing in unexpected vigor in the skirts of Derbyshire and Yorkshire, where he passed the Christmas holidays. The reader will find some notice of them in the author's account of his sojourn at Newstead Abbey.

benevolent view of human nature, and make my reader more in good-humor with his fellow-beings and himself—surely, surely, I shall not then have written entirely in vain.

LONDON ANTIQUES

—I do walk
Methinks like Guido Vaux, with my dark lanthorn,
Stealing to set the town o' fire; i' th' country
I should be taken for William o' the Wisp,
Or Robin Goodfellow.

—FLETCHER

I am somewhat of an antiquity-hunter, and am fond of exploring London in quest of the relics of old times. These are principally to be found in the depths of the city, swallowed up and almost lost in a wilderness of brick and mortar, but deriving poetical and romantic interest from the commonplace, prosaic world around them. I was struck with an instance of the kind in the course of a recent summer ramble into the city; for the city is only to be explored to advantage in summer-time, when free from the smoke and fog and rain and mud of winter. I had been buffeting for some time against the current of population setting through Fleet Street. The warm weather had unstrung my nerves and made me sensitive to every jar and jostle and discordant sound. The flesh was weary, the spirit faint, and I was getting out of humor with the bustling busy throng through which I had to struggle, when in a fit of desperation I tore my way through the crowd, plunged into a by-lane, and, after passing through several obscure nooks and angles, emerged into a quaint and quiet court with a grass plot in the centre overhung by elms, and kept perpetually fresh and green by a fountain with its sparkling jet of water. A student with book in hand was seated on a stone bench, partly reading, partly meditating on the movements of two or three trim nursery-maids with their infant charges.

I was like an Arab who had suddenly come upon an oasis amid the panting sterility of the desert. By degrees, the quiet and coolness of the place soothed my nerves and refreshed my spirit. I pursued my walk and came, hard by, to a very ancient chapel with a low-browed

Saxon portal of massive and rich architecture. The interior was circular and lofty and lighted from above. Around were monumental tombs of ancient date on which were extended the marble effigies of warriors in armor. Some had the hands devoutly crossed upon the breast; others grasped the pommel of the sword, menacing hostility even in the tomb, while the crossed legs of several indicated soldiers of the Faith who had been on crusades to the Holy Land.

I was, in fact, in the chapel of the Knights Templars, strangely situated in the very centre of sordid traffic; and I do not know a more impressive lesson for the many of the world than thus suddenly to turn aside from the highway of busy money-seeking life, and sit down among these shadowy sepulchres, where all is twilight, dust, and forgetfulness.

In a subsequent tour of observation I encountered another of these relics of a "foregone world" locked up in the heart of the city. I had been wandering for some time through dull monotonous streets, destitute of anything to strike the eye or excite the imagination, when I beheld before me a gothic gateway of mouldering antiquity. It opened into a spacious quadrangle forming the courtyard of a stately gothic pile, the portal of which stood invitingly open.

It was apparently a public edifice, and, as I was antiquity-hunting, I ventured in, though with dubious steps. Meeting no one either to oppose or rebuke my intrusion, I continued on until I found myself in a great hall with a lofty arched roof and oaken gallery, all of gothic architecture. At one end of the hall was an enormous fireplace, with wooden settles on each side; at the other end was a raised platform or dais, the seat of state, above which was the portrait of a man in antique garb with a long robe, a ruff, and a venerable gray beard.

The whole establishment had an air of monastic quiet and seclusion, and what gave it a mysterious charm was, that I had not met with a human being since I had passed the threshold.

Encouraged by this loneliness, I seated myself in a recess of a large bow window which admitted a broad flood of yellow sunshine, checkered here and there by tints from panes of colored glass, while an open casement let in the soft summer air. Here, leaning my head on my hand and my arm on an old oaken table, I indulged in a sort of reverie about what might have been the ancient uses of this edifice. It had evidently been of monastic origin; perhaps one of those collegiate establishments built of yore for the promotion of learning, where the patient monk, in the ample solitude of the cloister, added page to page and volume to volume, emulating in the productions of his brain the magnitude of the pile he inhabited.

As I was seated in this musing mood, a small panelled door in an arch at the upper end of the hall was opened and a number of gray-headed old men, clad in long black cloaks, came forth one by one, proceeding in that manner through the hall, without uttering a word, each turning a pale face on me as he passed, and disappearing through a door at the lower end.

I was singularly struck with their appearance; their black cloaks and antiquated air comported with the style of this most venerable and mysterious pile. It was as if the ghosts of the departed years, about which I had been musing, were passing in review before me. Pleasing myself with such fancies, I set out, in the spirit of romance, to explore what I pictured to myself a realm of shadows existing in the very centre of substantial realities.

My ramble led me through a labyrinth of interior courts and corridors and dilapidated cloisters, for the main edifice had many additions and dependencies, built at various times and in various styles. In one open space a number of boys, who evidently belonged to the establishment, were at their sports, but everywhere I observed those mysterious old gray men in black mantles, sometimes sauntering alone, sometimes conversing in groups; they appeared to be the pervading genii of the place. I now called to mind what I had read of certain colleges in old times, where judicial astrology, geomancy, necromancy, and other forbidden and magical sciences were taught. Was this an establishment of the kind, and were these black-cloaked old men really professors of the black art?

These surmises were passing through my mind as my eye glanced into a chamber hung round with all kinds of strange and uncouth objects—implements of savage warfare; strange idols and stuffed alligators; bottled serpents and monsters decorated the mantelpiece; while on the high tester of an old-fashioned bedstead grinned a human skull, flanked on each side by a dried cat.

I approached to regard more narrowly this mystic chamber, which seemed a fitting laboratory for a necromancer, when I was startled at beholding a human countenance staring at me from a dusky corner. It was that of a small, shrivelled old man with thin cheeks, bright eyes, and gray, wiry, projecting eyebrows. I at first doubted whether it were not a mummy curiously preserved, but it moved, and I saw that it was alive. It was another of these black-cloaked old men, and, as I regarded his quaint physiognomy, his obsolete garb, and the hideous and sinister objects by which he was surrounded, I began to persuade myself that I had come upon the arch-mage who ruled over this magical fraternity.

Seeing me pausing before the door, he rose and invited me to enter. I obeyed with singular hardihood, for how did I know whether a wave of his wand might not metamorphose me into some strange monster or conjure me into one of the bottles on his mantelpiece? He proved, however, to be anything but a conjurer, and his simple garrulity soon dispelled all the magic and mystery with which I had enveloped this antiquated pile and its no less antiquated inhabitants.

It appeared that I had made my way into the centre of an ancient asylum for superannuated tradesmen and decayed householders, with which was connected a school for a limited number of boys. It was founded upwards of two centuries since on an old monastic establishment, and retained somewhat of the conventual air and character. The shadowy line of old men in black mantles who had passed before me in the hall, and whom I had elevated into magi, turned out to be the pensioners returning from morning service in the chapel.

John Hallum, the little collector of curiosities whom I had made the arch magician, had been for six years a resident of the place, and had decorated this final nestling-place of his old age with relics and rarities picked up in the course of his life. According to his own account, he had been somewhat of a traveller, having been once in France, and very near making a visit to Holland. He regretted not having visited the latter country, "as then he might have said he had been there." He was evidently a traveller of the simple kind.

He was aristocratical too in his notions, keeping aloof, as I found, from the ordinary run of pensioners. His chief associates were a blind man who spoke Latin and Greek, of both which languages Hallum was profoundly ignorant, and a broken-down gentleman who had run through a fortune of forty thousand pounds left him by his father, and ten thousand pounds, the marriage portion of his wife. Little Hallum seemed to consider it an indubitable sign of gentle blood as well as of lofty spirit to be able to squander such enormous sums.

* * *

P.S. The picturesque remnant of old times into which I have thus beguiled the reader is what is called the Charter House, originally the Chartreuse. It was founded in 1611, on the remains of an ancient convent, by Sir Thomas Sutton, being one of those noble charities set on foot by individual munificence, and kept up with the quaintness and sanctity of ancient times amidst the modern changes and innovations of London. Here eighty broken-down men, who have seen better days, are provided in their old age with food, clothing, fuel, and a yearly allowance for private expenses. They dine together, as did the monks of old, in the hall which had been the refectory of the original convent. Attached to the establishment is a school for forty-four boys.

Stow, whose work I have consulted on the subject, speaking of the obligations of the gray-headed pensioners, says, "They are not to intermeddle with any business touching the affairs of the hospital, but to attend only to the service of God, and take thankfully what is provided for them, without muttering, murmuring, or grudging. None to wear weapon, long hair, colored boots, spurs, or colored shoes, feathers in their hats, or any ruffian-like or unseemly apparel, but such as becomes hospital-men to wear." "And in truth," adds Stow, "happy are they that are so taken from the cares and sorrows of the world, and fixed in so good a place as these old men are; having nothing to care for but the good of their souls, to serve God, and to live in brotherly love."

* * *

For the amusement of such as have been interested by the preceding sketch, taken down from my own observation, and who may wish to know a little more about the mysteries of London, I subjoin a modicum of local history put into my hands by an odd-looking old gentleman, in a small brown wig and a snuff-colored coat, with whom I became acquainted shortly after my visit to the Charter House. I confess I was a little dubious at first whether it was not one of those apocryphal tales often passed off upon inquiring travellers like myself, and which have brought our general character for veracity into such unmerited reproach. On making proper inquiries, however, I have received the most satisfactory assurances of the author's probity, and indeed have been told that he is actually engaged in a full and particular account of the very interesting region in which he resides, of which the following may be considered merely as a foretaste.

LITTLE BRITAIN

> What I write is most true. I have a whole booke of cases lying by me, which if I should sette foorth, some grave auntients (within the hearing of Bow bell) would bee out of charity with me.
>
> —Nashe

In the centre of the great City of London lies a small neighborhood, consisting of a cluster of narrow streets and courts, of very venerable and debilitated houses, which goes by the name of Little Britain. Christ Church School and St. Bartholomew's Hospital bound it on the west; Smithfield and Long Lane on the north; Aldersgate Street, like an arm of the sea, divides it from the eastern part of the city; whilst the yawning gulf of Bull-and-Mouth Street separates it from Butcher Lane and the regions of Newgate. Over this little territory, thus bounded and designated, the great dome of St. Paul's, swelling above the intervening houses of Paternoster Row, Amen Corner, and Ave-Maria Lane, looks down with an air of motherly protection.

This quarter derives its appellation from having been, in ancient times, the residence of the Dukes of Brittany. As London increased, however, rank and fashion rolled off to the west, and trade, creeping on at their heels, took possession of their deserted abodes. For some time Little Britain became the great mart of learning, and was peopled by the busy and prolific race of booksellers: these also gradually deserted it, and, emigrating beyond the great strait of Newgate Street, settled down in Paternoster Row and St. Paul's Churchyard, where they continue to increase and multiply even at the present day.

But, though thus fallen into decline, Little Britain still bears traces of its former splendor. There are several houses ready to tumble down, the fronts of which are magnificently enriched with old oaken carvings of hideous faces, unknown birds, beasts, and fishes, and fruits and flowers which it would perplex a naturalist to classify. There are also, in Aldersgate Street, certain remains of what were once spacious and lordly family mansions, but which have in latter days been subdivided into several tenements. Here may often be found the family of a petty tradesman, with its trumpery furniture, burrowing among the relics of antiquated finery in great rambling time-stained apartments with fretted ceilings, gilded cornices, and enormous marble fireplaces. The lanes and courts also contain many smaller houses, not on so grand a scale, but, like your small ancient gentry, sturdily maintaining their claims to equal antiquity. These have their gable ends to the street, great bow windows with diamond panes set in lead, grotesque carvings, and low arched doorways.*

In this most venerable and sheltered little nest have I passed several quiet years of existence, comfortably lodged in the second floor of one of the smallest but oldest edifices. My sitting-room is an old wainscoted chamber, with small panels and set off with a miscellaneous array of furniture. I have a particular respect for three or four high-backed, claw-footed chairs, covered with tarnished brocade, which bear the marks of having seen better days, and have doubtless figured in some of the old palaces of Little Britain. They seem to me to keep together and to look down with sovereign contempt upon their leathern-bottomed neighbors, as I have seen decayed gentry carry a high head among the plebeian society with which they were reduced to associate. The whole front of my sitting-room is taken up with a bow window, on the panes of which are recorded the names of previous occupants for many generations, mingled with scraps of very indifferent gentleman-like poetry, written in characters which I can scarcely decipher, and which extol the charms of many a beauty of Little Britain who has long, long since bloomed, faded, and passed away. As I am an idle personage, with no apparent occupation, and pay my bill regularly every week, I am looked upon as the only independent gentleman of the neighborhood, and, being curious to learn the internal state of a community so apparently shut up within itself, I have managed to work my way into all the concerns and secrets of the place.

Little Britain may truly be called the heart's core of the city, the stronghold of true John Bullism. It is a fragment of London as it was in its better days, with its antiquated folks and fashions. Here flourish

* It is evident that the author of this interesting communication has included, in his general title of Little Britain, man of those little lanes and courts that belong immediately to Cloth Fair.

in great preservation many of the holiday games and customs of yore. The inhabitants most religiously eat pancakes on Shrove Tuesday, hot cross-buns on Good Friday, and roast goose at Michaelmas; they send love-letters on Valentine's Day, burn the Pope on the Fifth of November, and kiss all the girls under the mistletoe at Christmas. Roast beef and plum-pudding are also held in superstitious veneration, and port and sherry maintain their grounds as the only true English wines, all others being considered vile outlandish beverages.

Little Britain has its long catalogue of city wonders, which its inhabitants consider the wonders of the world, such as the great bell of St. Paul's, which sours all the beer when it tolls; the figures that strike the hours at St. Dunstan's clock; the Monument; the lions in the Tower; and the wooden giants in Guildhall. They still believe in dreams and fortune-telling, and an old woman that lives in Bull-and-Mouth Street makes a tolerable subsistence by detecting stolen goods and promising the girls good husbands. They are apt to be rendered uncomfortable by comets and eclipses, and if a dog howls dolefully at night it is looked upon as a sure sign of death in the place. There are even many ghost-stories current, particularly concerning the old mansion-houses, in several of which it is said strange sights are sometimes seen. Lords and ladies, the former in full-bottomed wigs, hanging sleeves, and swords, the latter in lappets, stays, hoops, and brocade, have been seen walking up and down the great waste chambers on moonlight nights, and are supposed to be the shades of the ancient proprietors in their court dresses.

Little Britain has likewise its sages and great men. One of the most important of the former is a tall, dry old gentleman of the name of Skryme, who keeps a small apothecary's shop. He has a cadaverous countenance, full of cavities and projections, with a brown circle round each eye, like a pair of horn spectacles. He is much thought of by the old women, who consider him as a kind of conjurer because he has two or three stuffed alligators hanging up in his shop and several snakes in bottles. He is a great reader of almanacs and newspapers, and is much given to pore over alarming accounts of plots, conspiracies, fires, earthquakes, and volcanic eruptions; which last phenomena he considers as signs of the times. He has always some dismal tale of the kind to deal out to his customers with their doses, and thus at the same time puts both soul and body into an uproar. He is a great believer in omens and predictions; and has the prophecies of Robert Nixon and Mother Shipton by heart. No man can make so much out of an eclipse, or even an unusually dark day; and he shook the tail of the last comet over the heads of his customers and disciples until they were nearly frightened out of their wits. He has lately got hold of a popular legend or prophecy, on which he has been unusually eloquent. There has been a saying current among the ancient sibyls, who treasure up these things, that when the grasshopper on the top of the Exchange shook hands with the dragon on the top of Bow Church steeple, fearful events would take place. This strange conjunction, it seems, has as strangely come to pass. The same architect has been engaged lately on the repairs of the cupola of the Exchange and the steeple of Bow Church; and, fearful to relate, the dragon and the grasshopper actually lie, cheek by jole, in the yard of his workshop.

"Others," as Mr. Skryme is accustomed to say, "may go star-gazing, and look for conjunctions in the heavens, but here is a conjunction on the earth, near at home and under our own eyes, which surpasses all the signs and calculations of astrologers." Since these portentous weathercocks have thus laid their heads together, wonderful events had already occurred. The good old king, notwithstanding that he had lived eighty-two years, had all at once given up the ghost; another king had mounted the throne; a royal duke had died suddenly; another, in France, had been murdered; there had been radical meetings in all parts of the kingdom; the bloody scenes at Manchester; the great plot in Cato Street;—and, above all, the queen had returned to England! All these sinister events are recounted by Mr. Skyrme with a mysterious look and a dismal shake of the head; and being taken with his drugs, and associated in the minds of his auditors with stuffed sea-monsters, bottled serpents, and his own visage, which is a title-page of tribulation, they have spread great gloom through the minds of the people of Little Britain. They shake their heads whenever they go by Bow Church, and observe that they never expected any good to come of taking down that steeple, which in old times told nothing but glad tidings, as the history of Whittington and his Cat bears witness.

The rival oracle of Little Britain is a substantial cheesemonger, who lives in a fragment of one of the old family mansions, and is as magnificently lodged as a round-bellied mite in the midst of one of his own Cheshires. Indeed, he is a man of no little standing and importance, and his renown extends through Huggin Lane and Lad Lane, and even unto Aldermanbury. His opinion is very much taken in affairs of state, having read the Sunday papers for the last half century, together with the Gentleman's Magazine, Rapin's History of England, and the Naval Chronicle. His head is stored with invaluable maxims which have borne the test of time and use for centuries. It is his firm opinion that "it is a moral impossible," so long as England is true to herself, that anything can shake her: and he has much to say on the subject of the national debt, which, somehow or other, he proves to be a great national bulwark and blessing. He passed the greater part of his life in the purlieus of Little Britain until of late years, when, having become rich and grown into the dignity of a Sunday cane, he begins to take his pleasure and see the world. He has therefore made several excursions to Hampstead, Highgate, and other neighboring towns, where he has passed whole afternoons in looking back upon the metropolis through a telescope and endeavoring to descry the steeple of St. Bartholomew's. Not a stage-coachman of Bull-and-Mouth Street but touches his hat as he passes, and he is considered quite a patron at the coach-office of the Goose and Gridiron, St. Paul's Churchyard. His family have been very urgent for him to make an expedition to Margate, but he has great doubts of those new gimcracks, the steamboats, and indeed thinks himself too advanced in life to undertake sea-voyages.

Little Britain has occasionally its factions and divisions, and party spirit ran very high at one time, in consequence of two rival "Burial Societies" being set up in the place. One held its meeting at the Swan and Horse-Shoe, and was patronized by the cheesemonger; the other at the Cock and Crown, under the auspices of the apothecary: it is needless to say that the latter was the most flourishing. I have passed an evening or two at each, and have acquired much valuable information as to the best mode of being buried, the comparative merits of churchyards, together with divers hints on the subject of patent iron coffins. I have heard the question discussed in all its bearings as to the legality of prohibiting the latter on account of their durability. The feuds occasioned by these societies have happily died of late; but they were for a long time prevailing themes of controversy, the people of Little Britain being extremely solicitous of funeral honors and of lying comfortably in their graves.

Besides these two funeral societies there is a third of quite a different cast, which tends to throw the sunshine of good-humor over the whole neighborhood. It meets once a week at a little old-fashioned house kept by a jolly publican of the name of Wagstaff, and bearing for insignia a resplendent half-moon, with a most seductive bunch of grapes. The whole edifice is covered with inscriptions to catch the eye of the thirsty wayfarer; such as "Truman, Hanbury, and Co's Entire," "Wine, Rum, and Brandy Vaults," "Old Tom, Rum, and Compounds," etc. This indeed has been a temple of Bacchus and Momus from time immemorial. It has always been in the family of the Wagstaffs, so that its history is tolerably preserved by the present landlord. It was much frequented by the gallants and cavalieros of the reign of Elizabeth, and was looked into now and then by the wits of Charles the Second's day. But what Wagstaff principally prides himself upon is that Henry the Eighth, in one of his nocturnal rambles, broke the head of one of his ancestors with his famous walking staff. This, however, is considered as rather a dubious and vain-glorious boast of the landlord.

The club which now holds its weekly sessions here goes by the name of "the Roaring Lads of Little Britain." They abound in old catches, glees, and choice stories that are traditional in the place and not to be met with in any other part of the metropolis. There is a madcap undertaker who is inimitable at a merry song; but the life of the club, and indeed the prime wit of Little Britain, is bully Wagstaff himself. His ancestors were all wags before him, and he has inherited with the inn a large stock of songs and jokes, which go with it from generation to generation as heirlooms. He is a dapper little fellow, with bandy legs and pot belly, a red face with a moist merry eye, and a little shock of gray hair behind. At the opening of every club night he is called in to sing his "Confession of Faith," which is the famous old drinking trowl from Gammer Gurton's Needle. He sings it, to be sure, with many variations, as he received it from his father's lips; for it has been a standing favorite at the Half-Moon and Bunch of Grapes ever since it was written; nay, he affirms that his predecessors have often had the honor of singing it before the nobility and gentry at Christmas mummeries, when Little Britain was in all its glory.*

It would do one's heart good to hear, on a club night, the shouts of

* As mine host of the Half-Moon's Confession of Faith may not be familiar to the majority of readers, and as it is a specimen of the current songs of Little Britain, I subjoin it in its original orthography. I would observe that the whole club always join in the chorus with a fearful thumping on the table and clattering of pewter pots.

I cannot eate but lytle meate,
My stomacke is not good,
But sure I thinke that I can drinke
With him that weares a hood.
Though I go bare, take ye no care,
I nothing am a colde,
I stuff my skyn so full within,
Of joly good ale and olde.

Chorus. Backe and syde go bare, go bare,
Booth foote and hand go colde,
But, belly, God send thee good ale ynoughe,
Whether it be new or olde.

I love no rost, but a nut browne toste
And a crab laid in the fyre;
A little breade shall do me steade,
Much breade I not desyre.
No frost nor snow, nor winde, I trowe,
Can hurte mee, if I wolde,
I am so wrapt and throwly lapt
Of joly good ale and olde.

Chorus. Backe and syde go bare, go bare, etc.

And Tyb my wife, that, as her lyfe,
Loveth well good ale to seeke,
Full oft drynkes shee, tyll ye may see,
The teares run downe her cheeke.
Then doth shee trowle to me the bowle,
Even as a mault-worme sholde,
And sayth, sweete harte, I took my parte
Of this joly good ale and olde.

Chorus. Backe and syde go bare, go bare, etc.

Now let them drynke, tyll they nod and winke,
Even as goode fellowes sholde doe,
They shall not mysse to have the blisse,
Good ale doth bring men to;
And all poore soules that have scowred bowles,
Or have them lustily trolde,
God save the lyves of them and their wives,
Whether they be yonge or olde.

Chorus. Backe and syde go bare, go bare, etc.

merriment, the snatches of song, and now and then the choral bursts of half a dozen discordant voices, which issue from this jovial mansion. At such times the street is lined with listeners, who enjoy a delight equal to that of gazing into a confectioner's window or snuffing up the steams of a cook-shop.

There are two annual events which produce great stir and sensation in Little Britain: these are St. Bartholomew's Fair and the Lord Mayor's Day. During the time of the Fair, which is held in the adjoining regions of Smithfield, there is nothing going on but gossiping and gadding about. The late quiet streets of Little Britain are overrun with an irruption of strange figures and faces; every tavern is a scene of rout and revel. The fiddle and the song are heard from the taproom morning, noon, and night; and at each window may be seen some group of boon companions, with half-shut eyes, hats on one side, pipe in mouth and tankard in hand, fondling and prosing, and singing maudlin songs over their liquor. Even the sober decorum of private families, which I must say is rigidly kept up at other times among my neighbors, is no proof against this saturnalia. There is no such thing as keeping maid-servants within doors. Their brains are absolutely set madding with Punch and the Puppet-Show, the Flying Horses, Signior Polito, the Fire-Eater, the celebrated Mr. Paap, and the Irish Giant. The children too lavish all their holiday money in toys and gilt gingerbread, and fill the house with the Lilliputian din of drums, trumpets, and penny whistles.

But the Lord Mayor's Day is the great anniversary. The Lord Mayor is looked up to by the inhabitants of Little Britain as the greatest potentate upon earth, his gilt coach with six horses as the summit of human splendor, and his procession, with all the sheriffs and aldermen in his train, as the grandest of earthly pageants. How they exult in the idea that the king himself dare not enter the city without first knocking at the gate of Temple Bar and asking permission of the Lord Mayor; for if he did, heaven and earth! there is no knowing what might be the consequence. The man in armor who rides before the Lord Mayor, and is the city champion, has orders to cut down everybody that offends against the dignity of the city; and then there is the little man with a velvet porringer on his head, who sits at the window of the state coach and holds the city sword, as long as a pikestaff. Odd's blood! if he once draws that sword, Majesty itself is not safe.

Under the protection of this mighty potentate, therefore, the good people of Little Britain sleep in peace. Temple Bar is an effectual barrier against all interior foes; and as to foreign invasion, the Lord Mayor has but to throw himself into the Tower, call in the train-bands, and put the standing army of Beef-eaters under arms, and he may bid defiance to the world!

Thus wrapped up in its own concerns, its own habits, and its own opinions, Little Britain has long flourished as a sound heart to this great fungous metropolis. I have pleased myself with considering it as a chosen spot, where the principles of sturdy John Bullism were garnered up, like seed corn, to renew the national character when it had run to waste and degeneracy. I have rejoiced also in the general spirit of harmony that prevailed throughout it; for though there might now and then be a few clashes of opinion between the adherents of the cheesemonger and the apothecary, and an occasional feud between the burial societies, yet these were but transient clouds and soon passed away. The neighbors met with good-will, parted with a shake of the hand, and never abused each other except behind their backs.

I could give rare descriptions of snug junketing parties at which I have been present, where we played at All-Fours, Pope-Joan, Tom-come-tickle-me, and other choice old games, and where we sometimes had a good old English country dance to the tune of Sir Roger de Coverley. Once a year also the neighbors would gather together and go on a gypsy party to Epping Forest. It would have done any man's heart good to see the merriment that took place here as we banqueted on the grass under the trees. How we made the woods ring with bursts of laughter at the songs of little Wagstaff and the merry undertaker! After dinner, too, the young folks would play at blind-man's-buff and hide-and-seek, and it was amusing to see them tangled among the briars, and to hear a fine romping girl now and then squeak from among the bushes. The elder folks would gather round the cheesemonger and the apothecary to hear them talk politics, for they generally brought out a newspaper in their pockets to pass away time in the country. They would now and then, to be sure, get a little warm in argument; but their disputes were always adjusted by reference to a worthy old umbrella-maker in a double chin, who, never exactly comprehending the subject, managed somehow or other to decide in favor of both parties.

All empires, however, says some philosopher or historian, are doomed to changes and revolutions. Luxury and innovation creep in, factions arise, and families now and then spring up whose ambition and intrigues throw the whole system into confusion. Thus in letter days has the tranquillity of Little Britain been grievously disturbed and its golden simplicity of manners threatened with total subversion by the aspiring family of a retired butcher.

The family of the Lambs had long been among the most thriving and popular in the neighborhood: the Miss Lambs were the belles of Little Britain, and everybody was pleased when Old Lamb had made money enough to shut up shop and put his name on a brass plate on his door. In an evil hour, however, one of the Miss Lambs had the honor of being a lady in attendance on the Lady Mayoress at her grand annual ball, on which occasion she wore three towering ostrich feathers on her head. The family never got over it; they were immediately smitten with a passion for high life; set up a one-horse carriage, put a bit of gold lace round the errand-boy's hat, and have been the talk and detestation of the whole neighborhood ever since. They could no longer be induced to play at Pope-Joan or blind-man's-buff; they could endure no dances but quadrilles, which nobody had ever heard of in Little Britain; and they took to reading novels, talking bad French, and playing upon the piano. Their brother, too, who had been articled to an attorney, set up for a dandy and a critic, characters hitherto unknown in these parts, and he confounded the worthy folks exceedingly by talking about Kean, the Opera, and the "Edinburgh Review."

What was still worse, the Lambs gave a grand ball, to which they neglected to invite any of their old neighbors; but they had a great deal of genteel company from Theobald's Road, Red Lion Square, and other parts towards the west. There were several beaux of their brother's acquaintance from Gray's Inn Lane and Hatton Garden, and not less than three aldermen's ladies with their daughters. This was not to be forgotten or forgiven. All Little Britain was in an uproar with the smacking of whips, the lashing of in miserable horses, and the rattling and jingling of hackney-coaches. The gossips of the neighborhood might be seen popping their night-caps out at every window, watching the crazy vehicles rumble by; and there was a knot of virulent old cronies that kept a lookout from a house just opposite the retired butcher's and scanned and criticised every one that knocked at the door.

This dance was a cause of almost open war, and the whole neighborhood declared they would have nothing more to say to the Lambs. It is true that Mrs. Lamb, when she had no engagements with her quality acquaintance, would give little humdrum tea-junketings to some of her old cronies, "quite," as she would say, "in a friendly way;" and it is equally true that her invitations were always accepted, in spite of all previous vows to the contrary. Nay, the good ladies would sit and be delighted with the music of the Miss Lambs, who would condescend to strum an Irish melody for them on the piano; and they would listen with wonderful interest to Mrs. Lamb's anecdotes of Alderman Plunket's family of Portsoken Ward, and the Miss Timberlakes, the rich heiresses of Crutched Friars; but then they relieved their consciences and averted the reproaches of their confederates by canvassing at the next gossiping convocation everything that had passed, and pulling the Lambs and their rout all to pieces.

The only one of the family that could not be made fashionable was the retired butcher himself. Honest Lamb, in spite of the meekness of his name, was a rough, hearty old fellow, with the voice of a lion, a head of black hair like a shoe-brush, and a broad face mottled like his own beef. It was in vain that the daughters always spoke of him as "the old gentleman," addressed him as "papa" in tones of infinite softness, and endeavored to coax him into a dressing-gown and slippers and other gentlemanly habits. Do what they might, there was no keeping down the butcher. His sturdy nature would break through all their glozings. He had a hearty vulgar good humor that was irrepressible. His very jokes made his sensitive daughters shudder, and he persisted in wearing his blue cotton coat of a morning, dining at two o'clock, and having a "bit of sausage with his tea."

He was doomed, however, to share the unpopularity of his family.

He found his old comrades gradually growing cold and civil to him, no longer laughing at his jokes, and now and then throwing out a fling at "some people" and a hint about "quality binding." This both nettled and perplexed the honest butcher; and his wife and daughters, with the consummate policy of the shrewder sex, taking advantage of the circumstance, at length prevailed upon him to give up his afternoon's pipe and tankard at Wagstaff's, to sit after dinner by himself and take his pint of port—a liquor he detested—and to nod in his chair in solitary and dismal gentility.

The Miss Lambs might now be seen flaunting along the streets in French bonnets with unknown beaux, and talking and laughing so loud that it distressed the nerves of every good lady within hearing. They even went so far as to attempt patronage, and actually induced a French dancing master to set up in the neighborhood; but the worthy folks of Little Britain took fire at it, and did so persecute the poor Gaul that he was fain to pack up fiddle and dancing-pumps and decamp with such precipitation that he absolutely forgot to pay for his lodgings.

I had flattered myself, at first, with the idea that all this fiery indignation on the part of the community was merely the overflowing of their zeal for good old English manners and their horror of innovation, and I applauded the silent contempt they were so vociferous in expressing for upstart pride, French fashions and the Miss Lambs. But I grieve to say that I soon perceived the infection had taken hold, and that my neighbors, after condemning, were beginning to follow their example. I overheard my landlady importuning her husband to let their daughters have one quarter at French and music, and that they might take a few lessons in quadrille. I even saw, in the course of a few Sundays, no less than five French bonnets, precisely like those of the Miss Lambs, parading about Little Britain.

I still had my hopes that all this folly would gradually die away, that the Lambs might move out of the neighborhood, might die, or might run away with attorneys' apprentices, and that quiet and simplicity might be again restored to the community. But unluckily a rival power arose. An opulent oilman died, and left a widow with a large jointure and a family of buxom daughters. The young ladies had long been repining in secret at the parsimony of a prudent father, which kept down all their elegant aspirings. Their ambition, being now no longer restrained, broke out into a blaze, and they openly took the field against the family of the butcher. It is true that the Lambs, having had the first start, had naturally an advantage of them in the fashionable career. They could speak a little bad French, play the piano, dance quadrilles, and had formed high acquaintances; but the Trotters were not to be distanced. When the Lambs appeared with two feathers in their hats, the Miss Trotters mounted four and of twice as fine colors. If the Lambs gave a dance, the Trotters were sure not to be behind hand; and, though they might not boast of as good company, yet they had double the number and were twice as merry.

The whole community has at length divided itself into fashionable factions under the banners of these two families. The old games of Pope-Joan and Tom-come-tickle-me are entirely discarded; there is no such thing as getting up an honest country dance; and on my attempting to kiss a young lady under the mistletoe last Christmas, I was indignantly repulsed, the Miss Lambs having pronounced it "shocking vulgar." Bitter rivalry has also broken out as to the most fashionable part of Little Britain, the Lambs standing up for the dignity of Cross-Keys Square, and the Trotters for the vicinity of St. Bartholomew's.

Thus is this little territory torn by factions and internal dissensions, like the great empire whose name it bears; and what will be the result would puzzle the apothecary himself, with all his talent at prognostics, to determine, though I apprehend that it will terminate in the total downfall of genuine John Bullism.

The immediate effects are extremely unpleasant to me. Being a single man, and, as I observed before, rather an idle good-for-nothing personage, I have been considered the only gentleman by profession in the place. I stand therefore in high favor with both parties, and have to hear all their cabinet counsels and mutual backbitings. As I am too civil not to agree with the ladies on all occasions, I have committed myself most horribly with both parties by abusing their opponents. I might manage to reconcile this to my conscience, which is a truly accommodating one, but I cannot to my apprehension: if the Lambs and Trotters ever come to a reconciliation and compare notes, I am ruined!

I have determined, therefore, to beat a retreat in time, and am actually looking out for some other nest in this great city where old English manners are still kept up; where French is neither eaten, drunk, danced, nor spoken; and where there are no fashionable families of retired tradesmen. This found, I will, like a veteran rat, hasten away before I have an old house about my ears, bid a long, though a sorrowful adieu to my present abode, and leave the rival factions of the Lambs and the Trotters to divide the distracted empire of Little Britain.

STRATFORD-ON-AVON

Thou soft-flowing Avon, by thy silver stream
Of things more than mortal sweet Shakespeare would dream;
The fairies by moonlight dance round his green bed,
For hallow'd the turf is which pillow'd his head.

—Garrick

To a homeless man, who has no spot on this wide world which he can truly call his own, there is a momentary feeling of something like independence and territorial consequence when, after a weary day's travel, he kicks off his boots, thrusts his feet into slippers, and stretches himself before an inn fire. Let the world without go as it may, let kingdoms rise or fall, so long as he has the wherewithal to pay his bill he is, for the time being, the very monarch of all he surveys. The armchair is his throne, the poker his sceptre, and the little parlor, some twelve feet square, his undisputed empire. It is a morsel of certainly snatched from the midst of the uncertainties of life; it is a sunny moment gleaming out kindly on a cloudy day: and he who has advanced some way on the pilgrimage of existence knows the importance of husbanding even morsels and moments of enjoyment. "Shall I not take mine ease in mine inn?" thought I, as I gave the fire a stir, lolled back in my elbow-chair, and cast a complacent look about the little parlor of the Red Horse, at Stratford-on-Avon.

The words of sweet Shakespeare were just passing through my mind as the clock struck midnight from the tower of the church in which he lies buried. There was a gentle tap at the door, and a pretty chambermaid, putting in her smiling face, inquired, with a hesitating air, whether I had rung. I understood it as a modest hint that it was time to retire. My dream of absolute dominion was at an end; so abdicating my throne, like a prudent potentate, to avoid being deposed, and putting the Stratford Guide-Book under my arm as a pillow companion, I went to bed, and dreamt all night of Shakespeare, the jubilee, and David Garrick.

The next morning was one of those quickening mornings which we sometimes have in early spring, for it was about the middle of March. The chills of a long winter had suddenly given way; the north wind had spent its last gasp; and a mild air came stealing from the west, breathing the breath of life into Nature, and wooing every bud and flower to burst forth into fragrance and beauty.

I had come to Stratford on a poetical pilgrimage. My first visit was to the house where Shakespeare was born, and where, according to tradition, he was brought up to his father's craft of wool-combing. It is a small mean-looking edifice of wood and plaster, a true nestling-place of genius, which seems to delight in hatching its offspring in by-corners. The walls of its squalid chambers are covered with names and inscriptions in every language by pilgrims of all nations, ranks, and conditions, from the prince to the peasant, and present a simple but striking instance of the spontaneous and universal homage of mankind to the great poet of nature.

The house is shown by a garrulous old lady in a frosty red face, lighted up by a cold blue anxious eye, and garnished with artificial locks of flaxen hair curling from under an exceedingly dirty cap. She was peculiarly assiduous in exhibiting the relics with which this, like all other celebrated shrines, abounds. There was the shattered stock of the very matchlock with which Shakespeare shot the deer on his poaching exploits. There, too, was his tobacco-box, which proves that he was a rival smoker of Sir Walter Raleigh: the sword also with which he played Hamlet; and the identical lantern with which Friar Laurence discovered Romeo and Juliet at the tomb! There was an ample supply also of Shakespeare's mulberry tree, which seems to have as extraordinary powers of self-multiplication as the wood of the true cross, of which there is enough extant to build a ship of the line.

The most favorite object of curiosity, however, is Shakespeare's chair. It stands in a chimney-nook of a small gloomy chamber just behind what was his father's shop. Here he may many a time have sat when a boy, watching the slowly revolving spit with all the longing of an urchin, or of an evening listening to the cronies and gossips of Stratford dealing forth church-yard tales and legendary anecdotes of the troublesome times of England. In this chair it is the custom of every one that visits the house to sit: whether this be done with the hope of imbibing any of the inspiration of the bard I am at a loss to say; I merely mention the fact, and mine hostess privately assured me that, though built of solid oak, such was the fervent zeal of devotees the chair had to be new bottomed at least once in three years. It is worthy of notice also, in the history of this extraordinary chair, that it partakes something of the volatile nature of the Santa Casa of Loretto, or the flying chair of the Arabian enchanter; for, though sold some few years since to a northern princess, yet, strange to tell, it has found its way back again to the old chimney-corner.

I am always of easy faith in such matters, and am ever willing to be deceived where the deceit is pleasant and costs nothing. I am therefore a ready believer in relics, legends, and local anecdotes of goblins and great men, and would advise all travellers who travel for their gratification to be the same. What is it to us whether these stories be true or false, so long as we can persuade ourselves into the belief of them and enjoy all the charm of the reality? There is nothing like resolute good-humored credulity in these matters; and on this occasion I went even so far as willingly to believe the claims of mine hostess to a lineal descent from the poet, when, unluckily for my faith, she put into my hands a play of her own composition, which set all belief in her own consanguinity at defiance.

From the birthplace of Shakespeare a few paces brought me to his grave. He lies buried in the chancel of the parish church, a large and venerable pile, mouldering with age, but richly ornamented. It stands on the banks of the Avon on an embowered point, and separated by adjoining gardens from the suburbs of the town. Its situation is quiet and retired; the river runs murmuring at the foot of the church-yard, and the elms which grow upon its banks droop their branches into its clear bosom. An avenue of limes, the boughs of which are curiously interlaced, so as to form in summer an arched way of foliage, leads up from the gate of the yard to the church porch. The graves are overgrown with grass; the gray tombstones, some of them nearly sunk into the earth, are half covered with moss, which has likewise tinted the reverend old building. Small birds have built their nests among the cornices and fissures of the walls, and keep up a continual flutter and chirping; and rooks are sailing and cawing about its lofty gray spire.

In the course of my rambles I met with the gray-headed sexton, Edmonds, and accompanied him home to get the key of the church. He had lived in Stratford, man and boy, for eighty years, and seemed still to consider himself a vigorous man, with the trivial exception that he had nearly lost the use of his legs for a few years past. His dwelling was a cottage looking out upon the Avon and its bordering meadows, and was a picture of that neatness, order, and comfort which pervade the humblest dwellings in this country. A low whitewashed room, with a stone floor carefully scrubbed, served for parlor, kitchen, and hall. Rows of pewter and earthen dishes glittered along the dresser. On an old oaken table, well rubbed and polished, lay the family Bible and prayer-book, and the drawer contained the family library, composed of about half a score of well-thumbed volumes. An ancient clock, that important article of cottage furniture, ticked on the opposite side of the room, with a bright warming-pan hanging on one side of it, and the old man's horn-handled Sunday cane on the other. The fireplace, as usual, was wide and deep enough to admit a gossip knot within its jambs. In one corner sat the old man's granddaughter sewing, a pretty blue-eyed girl, and in the opposite corner was a superannuated crony whom he addressed by the name of John Ange, and who, I found, had been his companion from childhood. They had played together in infancy; they had worked together in manhood; they were now tottering about and gossiping away the evening of life; and in a short time they will probably be buried together in the neighboring church-yard. It is not often that we see two streams of existence running thus evenly and tranquilly side by side; it is only in such quiet "bosom scenes" of life that they are to be met with.

I had hoped to gather some traditionary anecdotes of the bard from these ancient chroniclers, but they had nothing new to impart. The long interval during which Shakespeare's writings lay in comparative neglect has spread its shadow over his history, and it is his good or evil lot that scarcely anything remains to his biographers but a scanty handful of conjectures.

The sexton and his companion had been employed as carpenters on the preparations for the celebrated Stratford Jubilee, and they remembered Garrick, the prime mover of the fête, who superintended the arrangements, and who, according to the sexton, was "a short punch man, very lively and bustling." John Ange had assisted also in cutting down Shakespeare's mulberry tree, of which he had a morsel in his pocket for sale; no doubt a sovereign quickener of literary conception.

I was grieved to hear these two worthy wights speak very dubiously of the eloquent dame who shows the Shakespeare house. John Ange shook his head when I mentioned her valuable and inexhaustible collection of relics, particularly her remains of the mulberry tree; and the old sexton even expressed a doubt as to Shakespeare having been born in her house. I soon discovered that he looked upon her mansion with an evil eye, as a rival to the poet's tomb, the latter having comparatively but few visitors. Thus it is that historians differ at the very outset, and mere pebbles make the stream of truth diverge into different channels even at the fountain head.

We approached the church through the avenue of limes, and entered by a gothic porch, highly ornamented, with carved doors of massive oak. The interior is spacious, and the architecture and embellishments superior to those of most country churches. There are several ancient monuments of nobility and gentry, over some of which hang funeral escutcheons and banners dropping piecemeal from the walls. The tomb of Shakespeare is in the chancel. The place is solemn and sepulchral. Tall elms wave before the pointed windows, and the Avon, which runs at a short distance from the walls, keeps up a low perpetual murmur. A flat stone marks the spot where the bard is buried. There are four lines inscribed on it, said to have been written by himself, and which have in them something extremely awful. If they are indeed his own, they show that solicitude about the quiet of the grave which seems natural to fine sensibilities and thoughtful minds:

> Good friend, for Jesus' sake, forbeare
> To dig the dust inclosed here.
> Blessed be he that spares these stones,
> And curst be he that moves my bones.

Just over the grave, in a niche of the wall, is a bust of Shakespeare, put up shortly after his death and considered as a resemblance. The aspect is pleasant and serene, with a finely arched forehead; and I thought I could read in it clear indications of that cheerful, social disposition by which he was as much characterized among his contemporaries as by the vastness of his genius. The inscription mentions his age at the time of his decease, fifty-three years—an untimely death for the world, for what fruit might not have been expected from the golden autumn of such a mind, sheltered as it was from the stormy vicissitudes of life, and flourishing in the sunshine of popular and royal favor?

The inscription on the tombstone has not been without its effect. It has prevented the removal of his remains from the bosom of his native place to Westminster Abbey, which was at one time contemplated. A few years since also, as some laborers were digging to make an adjoining vault, the earth caved in, so as to leave a vacant space almost like an arch, through which one might have reached into his grave. No one, however, presumed to meddle with his remains so awfully guarded by a malediction; and lest any of the idle or the curious or any collector of relics should be tempted to commit depredations, the old sexton kept watch over the place for two days, until the vault was finished and the aperture closed again. He told me that he had made bold to look in at the hole, but could see neither coffin nor bones—nothing but dust. It was something, I thought, to have seen the dust of Shakespeare.

Next to this grave are those of his wife, his favorite daughter, Mrs. Hall, and others of his family. On a tomb close by, also, is a full-length effigy of his old friend John Combe, of usurious memory, on whom he is said to have written a ludicrous epitaph. There are other monuments around, but the mind refuses to dwell on anything that is not connected with Shakespeare. His idea pervades the place; the whole pile seems but as his mausoleum. The feelings, no longer checked and thwarted by doubt, here indulge in perfect confidence: other traces of him may be false or dubious, but here is palpable evidence and absolute certainty. As I trod the sounding pavement there was something intense and thrilling in the idea that in very truth the remains of Shakespeare were mouldering beneath my feet. It was a long time before I could prevail upon myself to leave the place; and as I passed through the church-yard I plucked a branch from one of the yew trees, the only relic that I have brought from Stratford.

I had now visited the usual objects of a pilgrim's devotion, but I had a desire to see the old family seat of the Lucys at Charlecot, and to ramble through the park where Shakespeare, in company with some of the roisterers of Stratford, committed his youthful offence of deer-stealing. In this harebrained exploit we are told that he was taken prisoner and carried to the keeper's lodge, where he remained all night in doleful captivity. When brought into the presence of Sir Thomas Lucy, his treatment must have been galling and humiliating; for it so wrought upon his spirit as to produce a rough pasquinade which was affixed to the park gate at Charlecot.*

This flagitious attack upon the dignity of the knight so incensed him that he applied to a lawyer at Warwick to put the severity of the laws in force against the rhyming deer-stalker. Shakespeare did not wait to brave the united puissance of a knight of the shire and a country attorney. He forthwith abandoned the pleasant banks of the Avon and his paternal trade; wandered away to London; became a hanger-on to the theatres; then an actor; and finally wrote for the stage; and thus, through the persecution of Sir Thomas Lucy, Stratford lost an indifferent wool-comber and the world gained an immortal poet. He retained, however, for a long time, a sense of the harsh treatment of the Lord of Charlecot, and revenged himself in his writings, but in the sportive way of a good-natured mind. Sir Thomas is said to be the original of Justice Shallow, and the satire is slyly fixed upon him by the justice's armorial bearings, which, like those of the knight, had white luces† in the quarterings.

Various attempts have been made by his biographers to soften and explain away this early transgression of the poet; but I look upon it as one of those thoughtless exploits natural to his situation and turn

* The following is the only stanza extant of this lampoon:

A parliament member, a justice of peace,
At home a poor scarecrow, at London an asse,
If lowsie is Lucy, as some volke miscalle it,
Then Lucy is lowsie, whatever befall it.
  He thinks himself great;
Yet an asse in his state,
We allow by his ears but with asses to mate,
If Lucy is lowsie, as some volke miscalle it,
Then sing lowsie Lucy whatever befall it.

† The luce is a pike or jack, and abounds in the Avon about Charlecot.

of mind. Shakespeare, when young, had doubtless all the wildness and irregularity of an ardent, undisciplined, and undirected genius. The poetic temperament has naturally something in it of the vagabond. When left to itself it runs loosely and wildly, and delights in everything eccentric and licentious. It is often a turn-up of a die, in the gambling freaks of fate, whether a natural genius shall turn out a great rogue or a great poet; and had not Shakespeare's mind fortunately taken a literary bias, he might have as daringly transcended all civil as he has all dramatic laws.

I have little doubt that, in early life, when running like an unbroken colt about the neighborbood of Stratford, he was to be found in the company of all kinds of odd anomalous characters; that he associated with all the madcaps of the place, and was one of those unlucky urchins at mention of whom old men shake their heads and predict that they will one day come to the gallows. To him the poaching in Sir Thomas Lucy's park was doubtless like a foray to a Scottish knight, and struck his eager, and as yet untamed, imagination as something delightfully adventurous.*

The old mansion of Charlecot and its surrounding park still remain in the possession of the Lucy family, and are peculiarly interesting

* A proof of Shakespeare's random habits and associates in his youthful days may be found in a traditionary anecdote, picked up at Stratford by the elder Ireland, and mentioned in his "Picturesque Views on the Avon."

About seven miles from Stratford lies the thirsty little market-town of Bedford, famous for its ale. Two societies of the village yeomanry used to meet, under the appellation of the Bedford topers, and to challenge the lovers of good ale of the neighboring villages to a contest of drinking. Among others, the people of Stratford were called out to prove the strength of their heads; and in the number of the champions was Shakespeare, who, in spite of the proverb that "they who drink beer will think beer," was as true to his ale as Falstaff to his sack. The chivalry of Stratford was staggered at the first onset, and sounded a retreat while they had yet the legs to carry them off the field. They had scarcely marched a mile when, their legs failing them, they were forced to lie down under a crab tree, where they passed the night. It was still standing, and goes by the name of Shakespeare's tree.

In the morning his companions awaked the bard, and proposed returning to Bedford, but he declined, saying he had enough, having drank with

Piping Pebworth, Dancing Marston,
Haunted Hilbro', Hungry Grafton,
Dudging Exhall, Papist Wicksford,
Beggarly Broom, and Drunken Bedford.

"The villages here alluded to," says Ireland, "still bear the epithets thus given them: the people of Pebworth are still famed for their skill on the pipe and tabor; Hilborough is now called Haunted Hilborough; and Grafton is famous for the poverty of its soil."

frombeing connected with this whimsical but eventful circumstance in the scanty history of the bard. As the house stood at little more than three miles' distance from Stratford, I resolved to pay it a pedestrian visit, that I might stroll leisurely through some of those scenes from which Shakespeare must have derived his earliest ideas of rural imagery.

The country was yet naked and leafless, but English scenery is always verdant, and the sudden change in the temperature of the weather was surprising in its quickening effects upon the landscape. It was inspiring and animating to witness this first awakening of spring; to feel its warm breath stealing over the senses; to see the moist mellow earth beginning to put forth the green sprout and the tender blade, and the trees and shrubs, in their reviving tints and bursting buds, giving the promise of returning foliage and flower. The cold snow-drop, that little borderer on the skirts of winter, was to be seen with its chaste white blossoms in the small gardens before the cottages. The bleating of the new-dropt lambs was faintly heard from the fields. The sparrow twittered about the thatched eaves and budding hedges; the robin threw a livelier note into his late querulous wintry strain; and the lark, springing up from the reeking bosom of the meadow, towered away into the bright fleecy cloud, pouring forth torrents of melody. As I watched the little songster mounting up higher and higher, until his body was a mere speck on the white bosom of the cloud, while the ear was still filled with his music, it called to mind Shakespeare's exquisite little song in *Cymbeline*:

> Hark! hark! the lark at heav'n's gate sings,
> And Phœbus 'gins arise,
> His steeds to water at those springs,
> On chaliced flowers that lies.
>
> And winking mary-buds begin
> To ope their golden eyes;
> With every thing that pretty bin,
> My lady sweet arise!

Indeed, the whole country about here is poetic ground: everything is associated with the idea of Shakespeare. Every old cottage that I saw I fancied into some resort of his boyhood, where he had acquired his intimate knowledge of rustic life and manners, and heard those legendary tales and wild superstitions which he has woven like witchcraft into his dramas. For in his time, we are told, it was a popular amusement in winter evenings "to sit round the fire, and tell merry tales of errant knights, queens, lovers, lords, ladies, giants, dwarfs, thieves, cheaters, witches, fairies, goblins, and friars."*

My route for a part of the way lay in sight of the Avon, which made a variety of the most fancy doublings and windings through a wide and fertile valley; sometimes glittering from among willows which fringed its borders; sometimes disappearing among groves or beneath green banks; and sometimes rambling out into full view and making an azure sweep round a slope of meadow-land. This beautiful bosom of country is called the Vale of the Red Horse. A distant line of undulating blue hills seems to be its boundary, whilst all the soft intervening landscape lies in a manner enchained in the silver links of the Avon.

After pursuing the road for about three miles, I turned off into a footpath, which led along the borders of fields and under hedgerows to a private gate of the park; there was a stile, however, for the benefit of the pedestrian, there being a public right of way through the grounds. I delight in these hospitable estates, in which every one has a kind of property—at least as far as the footpath is concerned. It in some measure reconciles a poor man to his lot, and, what is more, to the better lot of his neighbor, thus to have parks and pleasure-grounds thrown open for his recreation. He breathes the pure air as freely and lolls as luxuriously under the shade as the lord of the soil; and if he has not the privilege of calling all that he sees his own, he has not, at the same time, the trouble of paying for it and keeping it in order.

I now found myself among noble avenues of oaks and elms, whose vast size bespoke the growth of centuries. The wind sounded solemnly among their branches, and the rooks cawed from their hereditary nests in the tree tops. The eye ranged through a long lessening vista, with

* Scot, in his "Discoverie of Witchcraft," enumerates a host of these fireside fancies: "And they have so fraid us with bull-beggars, spirits, witches, urchins, elves, hags, fairies, satyrs, pans, faunes, syrens, kit with the can ,sticke, tritons, centaurs, dwarfes, giantes, imps, calcars, conjurors, nymphes, changelings, incubus, Robin-good-fellow, the spoorne, the mare, the man in the oke, the hell-waine, the fier drake, the puckle, Tom Thombe, hobgoblins, Tom Tumbler, boneless, and such other bugs, that we were afraid of our own shadowes."

nothing to interrupt the view but a distant statue and a vagrant deer stalking like a shadow across the opening.

There is something about these stately old avenues that has the effect of gothic architecture, not merely from the pretended similarity of form, but from their bearing the evidence of long duration, and of having had their origin in a period of time with which we associate ideas of romantic grandeur. They betoken also the long-settled dignity and proudly concentrated independence of an ancient family; and I have heard a worthy but aristocratic old friend observe, when speaking of the sumptuous palaces of modern gentry, that "money could do much with stone and mortar, but thank Heaven! there was no such thing as suddenly building up an avenue of oaks."

It was from wandering in early life among this rich scenery, and about the romantic solitudes of the adjoining park of Fullbroke, which then formed a part of the Lucy estate, that some of Shakepeare's commentators have supposed he derived his noble forest meditations of Jaques and the enchanting woodland pictures in "As You Like It." It is in lonely wanderings through such scenes that the mind drinks deep but quiet draughts of inspiration, and becomes intensely sensible of the beauty and majesty of nature. The imagination kindles into reverie and rapture, vague but exquisite images and ideas keep breaking upon it, and we revel in a mute and almost incommunicable luxury of thought. It was in some such mood, and perhaps under one of those very trees before me, which threw their broad shades over the grassy banks and quivering waters of the Avon, that the poet's fancy may have sallied forth into that little song which breathes the very soul of a rural voluptuary:

Unto the green wood tree,
Who loves to lie with me,
And tune his merry throat
Unto the sweet bird's note,
Come hither, come hither, come hither.
Here shall he see
No enemy,
But winter and rough weather.

I had now come in sight of the house. It is a large building of brick with stone quoins, and is in the gothic style of Queen Elizabeth's day, having been built in the first year of her reign. The exterior remains very nearly in its original state, and may be considered a fair specimen of the residence of a wealthy country gentleman of those days. A great gateway opens from the park into a kind of courtyard in front of the house, ornamented with a grass-plot, shrubs, and flower-beds. The gateway is in imitation of the ancient barbacan, being a kind of outpost and flanked by towers, though evidently for mere ornament, instead of defence. The front of the house is completely in the old style with stone-shafted casements, a great bow-window of heavy stone-work, and a portal with armorial bearings over it carved in stone. At each corner of the building is an octagon tower surmounted by a gilt ball and weathercock.

The Avon, which winds through the park, makes a bend just at the foot of a gently sloping bank which sweeps down from the rear of the house. Large herds of deer were feeding or reposing upon its borders, and swans were sailing majestically upon its bosom. As I contemplated the venerable old mansion, I called to mind Falstaff's encomium on Justice Shallow's abode, and the affected indifference and real vanity of the latter:

> FALSTAFF. You have a goodly dwelling and a rich.
> SHALLOW. Barren, barren, barren; beggars all, beggars all,
> Sir John:—marry, good air.

Whatever may have been the joviality of the old mansion in the days of Shakespeare, it had now an air of stillness and solitude. The great iron gateway that opened into the courtyard was locked; there was no show of servants bustling about the place; the deer gazed quietly at me as I passed, being no longer harried by the moss-troopers of Stratford. The only sign of domestic life that I met with was a white cat stealing with wary look and stealthy pace towards the stables, as if on some nefarious expedition. I must not omit to mention the carcass of a scoundrel crow which I saw suspended against the barn wall, as it shows that the Lucys still inherit that lordly abhorrence of poachers and maintain that rigorous exercise of territorial power which was so strenuously manifested in the case of the bard.

After prowling about for some time, I at length found my way to a lateral portal, which was the every-day entrance to the mansion. I was courteously received by a worthy old housekeeper, who, with the civility and communicativeness of her order, showed me the interior of the house. The greater part has undergone alterations and been adapted to modern tastes and modes of living: there is a fine old oaken staircase, and the great hall, that noble feature in an ancient manor-house, still retains much of the appearance it must have had in the days of Shakespeare. The ceiling is arched and lofty, and at one end is a gallery in which stands an organ. The weapons and trophies of the chase, which formerly adorned the hall of a country gentleman, have made way for family portraits. There is a wide, hospitable fireplace, calculated for an ample old-fashioned wood fire, formerly the rallying place of winter festivity. On the opposite side of the hall is the huge Gothic bow-window, with stone shafts, which looks out upon the courtyard. Here are emblazoned in stained glass the armorial bearings of the Lucy family for many generations, some being dated in 1558. I was delighted to observe in the quarterings the three white luces by which the character of Sir Thomas was first identified with that of Justice Shallow. They are mentioned in the first scene of the "Merry Wives of Windsor," where the justice is in a rage with Falstaff for having "beaten his men, killed his deer, and broken into his lodge." The poet had no doubt the offences of himself and his comrades in mind at the time, and we may suppose the family pride and vindictive threats of the puissant Shallow to be a caricature of the pompous indignation of Sir Thomas.

> SHALLOW. Sir Hugh, persuade me not: I will make a Star-Chamber matter of it; if he were twenty John Falstaffs, he shall not abuse Sir Robert Shallow, Esq.
> SLENDER. In the county of Gloster, justice of peace and coram.
> SHALLOW. Ay, cousin Slender, and custalorum.
> SLENDER. Ay, and ratolorum too, and a gentleman born, master parson; who writes himself Armigero in any bill, warrant, quittance, or obligation, Armigero.
> SHALLOW. Ay, that I do; and have done any time these three hundred years.

SLENDER. All his successors gone before him have done 't, and all his ancestors that come after him may; they may give the dozen white luces in their coat . . . .
SHALLOW. The council shall hear it; it is a riot.
EVANS. It is not meet the council hear of a riot; there is no fear of Got in a riot; the council, hear you, shall desire to hear the fear of Got, and not to hear a riot; take your vizaments in that.
SHALLOW. Ha! o' my life, if I were young again, the sword should end it!

Near the window thus emblazoned hung a portrait, by Sir Peter Lely, of one of the Lucy family, a great beauty of the time of Charles the Second: the old housekeeper shook her head as she pointed to the picture, and informed me that this lady had been sadly addicted to cards, and had gambled away a great portion of the family estate, among which was that part of the park where Shakespeare and his comrades had killed the deer. The lands thus lost had not been entirely regained by the family even at the present day. It is but justice to this recreant dame to confess that she had a surpassingly fine hand and arm.

The picture which most attracted my attention was a great painting over the fireplace, containing likenesses of Sir Thomas Lucy and his family who inhabited the hall in the latter part of Shakespeare's lifetime. I at first thought that it was the vindictive knight himself, but the housekeeper assured me that it was his son; the only likeness extant of the former being an effigy upon his tomb in the church of the neighboring hamlet of Charlecot.*

* This effigy is in white marble, and represents the knight in complete armor. Near him lies the effigy of his wife, and on her tomb is the following inscription; which, if really composed by her husband, places him quite above the intellectual level of Master Shallow:

Here lyeth the Lady Joyce Lucy wife of Sir Thomas Lucy of Charlecot in ye county of Warwick, Knight, Daughter and heir of Thomas Acton of Sutton in ye county of Worcester Esquire who departed out of this wretched world to her heavenly kingdom ye 10 day of February in ye yeare of our Lord God 1595 and of her age 60 and three. All the time of her lyfe a true and faythful servant of her good God, never detected of any cryme or vice. In religion most sounde, in love to her husband most faythful and true. In friendship most constant; to what in trust was committed unto her most secret. In wisdom excelling. In governing of her house, bringing up of youth in ye fear of God that did converse with her moste rare and singular. A great maintayner of hospitality. Greatly esteemed of her betters;

The picture gives a lively idea of the costume and manners of the time. Sir Thomas is dressed in ruff and doublet, white shoes with roses in them, and has a peaked yellow, or, as Master Slender would say, "a cane-colored beard." His lady is seated on the opposite side of the picture in wide ruff and long stomacher, and the children have a most venerable stiffness and formality of dress. Hounds and spaniels are mingled in the family group; a hawk is seated on his perch in the foreground, and one of the children holds a bow, all intimating the knight's skill in hunting, hawking, and archery, so indispensable to an accomplished gentleman in those days.*

I regretted to find that the ancient furniture of the hall had disappeared; for I had hoped to meet with the stately elbow-chair of carved oak in which the country squire of former days was wont to sway the sceptre of empire over his rural domains, and in which it might be presumed the redoubled Sir Thomas sat enthroned in awful state when the recreant Shakespeare was brought before him. As I like to deck out pictures for my own entertainment, I pleased myself with the idea that this very hall had been the scene of the unlucky bard's examination on the morning after his captivity in the lodge. I fancied to myself the rural potentate surrounded by his body-guard of butler, pages, and blue-coated serving-men with their badges, while the luckless culprit was brought in, forlorn and chap-fallen, in the custody of gamekeepers, huntsmen, and whippers-in, and followed by a rabble rout of country clowns. I fancied bright faces of curious housemaids peeping from the half-opened doors, while from the gallery the fair daughters of the knight leaned gracefully forward, eyeing the youthful prisoner with that pity "that dwells in womanhood." Who would have

misliked of none unless of the envyous. When all is spoken that can be saide a woman so garnished with virtue as not to be bettered and hardly to be equalled by any. As shee lived most virtuotisly so shee died most Godly. Set downe by him yt best did knowe what hath byn written to be true. Thomas Lucye.

* Bishop Earle, speaking of the country gentleman of his time, observes, "His housekeeping is seen much in the different families of dogs and serving-men attendant on their kennels; and the deepness of their throats is the depth of his discourse. A hawk he esteems the true burden of nobility, and is exceedingly ambitious to seem delighted with the sport, and have his fist gloved with his jesses." And Gilpin, in his description of a Mr. Hastings, remarks, "He kept all sorts of hounds that run buck, fox, hare, otter, and badger; and had hawks of all kinds both long and short winged. His great hall was commonly strewed with marrow-bones, and full of hawk perches, hounds, spaniels, and terriers. On a broad hearth, paved with brick, lay some of the choicest terriers, hounds, and spaniels."

thought that this poor varlet, thus trembling before the brief authority of a country squire, and the sport of rustic boors, was soon to become the delight of princes, the theme of all tongues and ages, the dictator to the human mind, and was to confer immortality on his oppressor by a caricature and a lampoon?

I was now invited by the butler to walk into the garden, and I felt inclined to visit the orchard and arbor where the justice treated Sir John Falstaff and Cousin Silence "to a last year's pippin of his own grafting, with a dish of caraways;" but I had already spent so much of the day in my ramblings that I was obliged to give up any further investigations. When about to take my leave I was gratified by the civil entreaties of the housekeeper and butler that I would take some refreshment: an instance of good old hospitality which, I grieve to say, we castle-hunters seldom meet with in modern days. I make no doubt it is a virtue which the present representative of the Lucys inherits from his ancestor; for Shakespeare, even in his caricature, makes Justice Shallow importunate in this respect, as witness his pressing instances to Falstaff:

> By cock and pye, Sir, you shall not away to-night . . . I will not excuse you; you shall not be excused; excuses shall not be admitted; there is no excuse shall serve; you shall not be excused . . . Some pigeons, Davy, a couple of short-legged hens; a joint of mutton; and any pretty little tiny kickshaws, tell William Cook.

I now bade a reluctant farewell to the old hall. My mind had become so completely possessed by the imaginary scenes and characters connected with it that I seemed to be actually living among them. Everything brought them as it were before my eyes, and as the door of the dining-room opened I almost expected to hear the feeble voice of Master Silence quavering forth his favorite ditty:

> 'Tis merry in hall, when beards wag all,
> And welcome merry Shrove-tide!

On returning to my inn, I could not but reflect on the singular gift of the poet; to be able thus to spread the magic of his mind over the very face of nature; to give to things and places a charm and character not their own, and to turn this "working-day world" into a perfect fairy-land. He is indeed the true enchanter, whose spell operates, not upon the senses, but upon the imagination and the heart. Under the wizard influence of Shakespeare I had been walking all day in a complete delusion. I had surveyed the landscape through the prism of poetry, which tinged every object with the hues of the rainbow. I had been surrounded with fancied beings, with mere airy nothings conjured up by poetic power, yet which, to me, had all the charm of reality. I had heard Jaques soliloquize beneath his oak; had beheld the fair Rosalind and her companion adventuring through the woodlands; and, above all, had been once more present in spirit with fat Jack Falstaff and his contemporaries, from the august Justice Shallow down to the gentle Master Slender and the sweet Anne Page. Ten thousand honors and blessings on the bard who has thus gilded the dull realities of life with innocent illusions, who has spread exquisite and unbought pleasures in my chequered path, and beguiled my spirit in many a lonely hour with all the cordial and cheerful sympathies of social life!

As I crossed the bridge over the Avon on my return, I paused to contemplate the distant church in which the poet lies buried, and could not but exult in the malediction which has kept his ashes undisturbed in its quiet and hallowed vaults. What honor could his name have derived from being mingled in dusty companionship with the epitaphs and escutcheons and venal eulogiums of a titled multitude? What would a crowded corner in Westminster Abbey have been, compared with this reverend pile, which seems to stand in beautiful loneliness as his sole mausoleum! The solitude about the grave may be but the offspring of an overwrought sensibility; but human nature is made up of foibles and prejudices, and its best and tenderest affections are mingled with these factitious feelings. He who has sought renown about the world, and has reaped a full harvest of worldly favor, will find, after all, that there is no love, no admiration, no applause, so sweet to the soul as that which springs up in his native place. It is there that he seeks to be gathered in peace and honor among his kindred and his early friends. And when the weary heart and failing head begin to warn him that the evening of life is drawing on, he turns as fondly as does the infant to the mother's arms to sink to sleep in the bosom of the scene of his childhood.

How would it have cheered the spirit of the youthful bard when, wandering forth in disgrace upon a doubtful world, he cast back a heavy look upon his paternal home, could he have foreseen that before many years he should return to it covered with renown; that his name should become the boast and glory of his native place; that his ashes should be religiously guarded as its most precious treasure; and that its lessening spire, on which his eyes were fixed in tearful contemplation, should one day become the beacon towering amidst the gentle landscape to guide the literary pilgrim of every nation to his tomb!

TRAITS OF INDIAN CHARACTER

"I appeal to any white man if ever he entered Logan's cabin hungry, and he gave him not to eat; if ever he came cold and naked, and he clothed him not."

—Speech of au Indian Chief

There is something in the character and habits of the North American savage, taken in connection with the scenery over which he is accustomed to range, its vast lakes, boundless forests, majestic rivers, and trackless plains, that is, to my mind, wonderfully striking and sublime. He is formed for the wilderness, as the Arab is for the desert. His nature is stern, simple, and enduring, fitted to grapple with difficulties and to support privations. There seems but little soil in his heart for the support of the kindly virtues; and yet, if we would but take the trouble to penetrate through that proud stoicism and habitual taciturnity which lock up his character from casual observation, we should find him linked to his fellow-man of civilized life by more of those sympathies and affections than are usually ascribed to him.

It has been the lot of the unfortunate aborigines of America, in the early periods of colonization, to be doubly wronged by the white men. They have been dispossessed of their hereditary possessions by mercenary and frequently wanton warfare, and their characters have been traduced by bigoted and interested writers. The colonists often treated them like beasts of the forest, and the author has endeavored to justify him in his outrages. The former found it easier to exterminate than to civilize; the latter to vilify than to discriminate. The appellations of savage and pagan were deemed sufficient to sanction the hostilities of both; and thus the poor wanderers of the forest were persecuted and defamed, not because they were guilty, but because they were ignorant.

The rights of the savage have seldom been properly appreciated or respected by the white man. In peace he has too often been the dupe of artful traffic; in war he has been regarded as a ferocious animal whose life or death was a question of mere precaution and convenience. Man is cruelly wasteful of life when his own safety is endangered and he is sheltered by impunity, and little mercy is to be expected from him when he feels the sting of the reptile and is conscious of the power to destroy.

The same prejudices, which were indulged thus early, exist in common circulation at the present day. Certain learned societies have, it is true, with laudable diligence, endeavored to investigate and record the real characters and manners of the Indian tribes; the American government, too, has wisely and humanely exerted itself to inculcate a friendly and forbearing spirit towards them and to protect them from fraud and injustice.* The current opinion of the Indian character, however, is too apt to be formed from the miserable hordes which infest the frontiers and hang on the skirts of the settlements. These are too commonly composed of degenerate beings, corrupted and enfeebled by the vices of society, without being benefited by its civilization. That proud independence which formed the main pillar of savage virtue has been shaken down, and the whole moral fabric lies in ruins. Their spirits are humiliated and debased by a sense of inferiority, and their native courage cowed and daunted by the superior knowledge and power of their enlightened neighbors. Society has advanced upon them like one of those withering airs that will sometimes breed desolation over a whole region of fertility. It has enervated their strength, multiplied their diseases, and superinduced upon their original barbarity the low vices of artificial life. It has given them a thousand superfluous wants, whilst it has diminished their means of mere existence. It has driven before it the animals of the chase, who fly from the sound of the axe and the smoke of the settlement and seek refuge in the depths of remoter forests and yet untrodden wilds. Thus do we too often find the Indians on our frontiers to be the mere wrecks and remnants of once powerful tribes, who have lingered in the vicinity of the settlements and sunk into precarious and vagabond existence. Poverty, repining and hopeless poverty, a canker of the mind unknown in savage life, corrodes their spirits and blights every free and noble quality of their natures. They

* The American Government has been indefatigable in its exertions to ameliorate the situation of the Indians, and to introduce among them the arts of civilization, and civil and religious knowledge. To protect them from the frauds of the white traders, no purchase of land from them by individuals is permitted; nor is any person allowed to receive lands from them as a present without the express sanction of government. These precautions are strictly enforced.

become drunken, indolent, feeble, thievish, and pusillanimous. They loiter like vagrants about the settlements, among spacious dwellings replete with elaborate comforts, which only render them sensible of the comparative wretchedness of their own condition. Luxury spreads its ample board before their eyes, but they are excluded from the banquet. Plenty revels over the fields, but they are starving in the midst of its abundance; the whole wilderness has blossomed into a garden, but they feel as reptiles that infest it.

How different was their state while yet the undisputed lords of the soil! Their wants were few and the means of gratification within their reach. They saw every one round them sharing the same lot, enduring the same hardships, feeding on the same aliments, arrayed in the same rude garments. No roof then rose but was open to the homeless stranger; no smoke curled among the trees but he was welcome to sit down by its fire and join the hunter in his repast. "For," says an old historian of New England, "their life is so void of care, and they are so loving also, that they make use of those things they enjoy as common goods, and are therein so compassionate that rather than one should starve through want, they would starve all; thus they pass their time merrily, not regarding our pomp, but are better content with their own, which some men esteem so meanly of." Such were the Indians whilst in the pride and energy of their primitive natures: they resembled those wild plants which thrive best in the shades of the forest, but shrink from the hand of cultivation and perish beneath the influence of the sun.

In discussing the savage character, writers have been too prone to indulge in vulgar prejudice and passionate exaggeration, instead of the candid temper of true philosophy. They have not sufficiently considered the peculiar circumstances in which the Indians have been placed, and the peculiar principles under which they have been educated. No being acts more rigidly from rule than the Indian. His whole conduct is regulated according to some general maxims early implanted in his mind. The moral laws that govern him are, to be sure, but few; but then he conforms to them all; the white man abounds in laws of religion, morals, and manners, but how many does he violate!

A frequent ground of accusation against the Indians is their disregard of treaties, and the treachery and wantonness with which, in time of apparent peace, they will suddenly fly to hostilities. The intercourse of the white men with the Indians, however, is too apt to be cold, distrustful, oppressive, and insulting. They seldom treat them with that confidence and frankness which are indispensable to real friendship, nor is sufficient caution observed not to offend against those feelings of pride or superstition which often prompt the Indian to hostility quicker than mere considerations of interest. The solitary savage feels silently, but acutely. His sensibilities are not diffused over so wide a surface as those of the white man, but they run in steadier and deeper channels. His pride, his affections, his superstitions, are all directed towards fewer objects, but the wounds inflicted on them are proportionably severe, and furnish motives of hostility which we cannot sufficiently appreciate. Where a community is also limited in number, and forms one great patriarchal family, as in an Indian tribe, the injury of an individual is the injury of the whole, and the sentiment of vengeance is almost instantaneously diffused. One council fire is sufficient for the discussion and arrangement of a plan of hostilities. Here all the fighting men and sages assemble. Eloquence and superstition combine to inflame the minds of the warriors. The orator awakens their martial ardor, and they are wrought up to a kind of religious desperation by the visions of the prophet and the dreamer.

An instance of one of those sudden exasperations, arising from a motive peculiar to the Indian character, is extant in an old record of the early settlement of Massachusetts. The planters of Plymouth had defaced the monuments of the dead at Passonagessit, and had plundered the grave of the Sachem's mother of some skins with which it had been decorated. The Indians are remarkable for the reverence which they entertain for the sepulchres of their kindred. Tribes that have passed generations exiled from the abodes of their ancestors, when by chance they have been travelling in the vicinity, have been known to turn aside from the highway, and, guided by wonderfully accurate tradition, have crossed the country for miles to some tumulus, buried perhaps in woods, where the bones of their tribe were anciently deposited, and there have passed hours in silent meditation. Influenced by this sublime and holy feeling, the Sachem whose mother's tomb had been violated gathered his men together, and addressed them in the following beautifully simple and pathetic harangue—a curious specimen of Indian eloquence and an affecting instance of filial piety in a savage:

> When last the glorious light of all the sky was underneath this globe and birds grew silent, I began to settle, as my custom is, to take repose. Before mine eyes were fast closed methought I saw a vision, at which my spirit was much troubled; and trembling at that doleful sight, a spirit cried aloud, 'Behold, my son, whom I have cherished, see the breasts that gave thee suck, the hands that lapped thee warm and fed thee oft. Canst thou forget to take revenge of those wild people who have defaced my monument in a despiteful manner, disdaining our antiquities and honorable customs? See, now, the Sachem's grave lies like the common people, defaced by an ignoble race. Thy mother doth complain and implores thy aid against this thievish people who have newly intruded on our land. If this be suffered, I shall not rest quiet in my everlasting habitation.' This said, the spirit vanished, and I, all in a sweat, not able scarce to speak, began to get some strength and recollect my spirits that were fled, and determined to demand your counsel and assistance.

I have adduced this anecdote at some length, as it tends to show how these sudden acts of hostility, which have been attributed to caprice and perfidy, may often arise from deep and generous motives, which our inattention to Indian character and customs prevents our properly appreciating.

Another ground of violent outcry against the Indians is their barbarity to the vanquished. This had its origin partly in policy and partly in superstition. The tribes, though sometimes called nations, were never so formidable in their numbers but that the loss of several warriors was sensibly felt; this was particularly the case when they had been frequently engaged in warfare; and many an instance occurs in Indian history where a tribe that had long been formidable to its neighbors has been broken up and driven away by the capture and massacre of its principal fighting men. There was a strong temptation, therefore, to the victor to be merciless, not so much to gratify any cruel revenge, as to provide for future security. The Indians had also the superstitious belief, frequent among barbarous nations and prevalent also among the ancients, that the manes of their friends who had fallen in battle were soothed by the blood of the captives. The prisoners, however, who are not thus sacrificed are adopted into their families in the place of the slain, and are treated with the confidence and affection of relatives and friends; nay, so hospitable and tender is their entertainment that when the alternative is offered them they will often prefer to remain with their adopted brethren rather than return to the home and the friends of their youth.

The cruelty of the Indians towards their prisoners has been heightened since the colonization of the whites. What was formerly a compliance with policy and superstition has been exasperated into a gratification of vengeance. They cannot but be sensible that the white men are the usurpers of their ancient dominion, the cause of their degradation, and the gradual destroyers of their race. They go forth to battle smarting with injuries and indignities which they have individually suffered, and they are driven to madness and despair by the wide-spreading desolation and the overwhelming ruin of European warfare. The whites have too frequently set them an example of violence by burning their villages and laying waste their slender means of subsistence, and yet they wonder that savages do not show moderation and magnanimity towards those who have left them nothing but mere existence and wretchedness.

We stigmatize the Indians, also, as cowardly and treacherous, because they use stratagem in warfare in preference to open force; but in this they are fully justified by their rude code of honor. They are early taught that stratagem is praiseworthy; the bravest warrior thinks it no disgrace to lurk in silence, and take every advantage of his foe: he triumphs in the superior craft and sagacity by which he has been enabled to surprise and destroy an enemy. Indeed, man is naturally more prone to subtilty than open valor, owing to his physical weakness in comparison with other animals. They are endowed with natural weapons of defence, with horns, with tusks, with hoofs, and talons; but man has to depend on his superior sagacity. In all his encounters with these, his proper enemies, he resorts to stratagem; and when he perversely turns his hostility against his fellow man, he at first continues the same subtle mode of warfare.

The natural principle of war is to do the most harm to our enemy with the least harm to ourselves; and this of course is to be effected by stratagem. That chivalrous courage which induces us to despise the suggestions of prudence and to rush in the face of certain danger is the offspring of society and produced by education. It is honorable, because it is in fact the triumph of lofty sentiment over an instinctive repugnance to pain, and over those yearnings after personal ease and security which society has condemned as ignoble. It is kept alive by pride and the fear of shame; and thus the dread of real evil is overcome by the superior dread of an evil which exists but in the imagination. It has been cherished and stimulated also by various means. It has been the theme of spirit-stirring song and chivalrous story. The poet and minstrel have delighted to shed round it the splendors of fiction, and even the historian has forgotten the sober gravity of narration and broken forth into enthusiasm and rhapsody in its praise. Triumphs and gorgeous pageants have been its reward: monuments, on which art has exhausted its skill and opulence its treasures, have been erected to perpetuate a nation's gratitude and admiration. Thus artificially excited, courage has risen to an extraordinary and factitious degree of heroism, and, arrayed in all the glorious "pomp and circumstance of war," this turbulent quality has even been able to eclipse many of those quiet but invaluable virtues which silently ennoble the human character and swell the tide of human happiness.

But if courage intrinsically consists in the defiance of danger and pain, the life of the Indian is a continual exhibition of it. He lives in a state of perpetual hostility and risk. Peril and adventure are congenial to his nature, or rather seem necessary to arouse his faculties and to give an interest to his existence. Surrounded by hostile tribes, whose mode of warfare is by ambush and surprisal, he is always prepared for fight and lives with his weapons in his hands. As the ship careers in fearful singleness through the solitudes of ocean; as the bird mingles among clouds and storms, and wings its way, a mere speck, across the pathless fields of air, so the Indian holds his course, silent, solitary, but undaunted, through the boundless bosom of the wilderness. His expeditions may vie in distance and danger with the pilgrimage of the devotee or the crusade of the knight-errant. He traverses vast forests exposed to the hazards of lonely sickness, of lurking enemies, and pining famine. Stormy lakes, those great inland seas, are no obstacles to his wanderings: in his light canoe of bark he sports like a feather on their waves, and darts with the swiftness of an arrow down the roaring rapids of the rivers. His very subsistence is snatched from the midst of toil and peril. He gains his food by the hardships and dangers of the chase: he wraps himself in the spoils of the bear, the panther, and the buffalo, and sleeps among the thunders of the cataract.

No hero of ancient or modern days can surpass the Indian in his lofty contempt of death and the fortitude with which he sustains his cruelest affliction. Indeed, we here behold him rising superior to the white man in consequence of his peculiar education. The latter rushes to glorious death at the cannon's mouth; the former calmly contemplates its approach, and triumphantly endures it amidst the varied torments of surrounding foes and the protracted agonies of fire. He even takes a pride in taunting his persecutors and provoking their ingenuity of torture; and as the devouring flames prey on his very vitals and the flesh shrinks from the sinews, he raises his last song of triumph, breathing the defiance of an unconquered heart and invoking the spirits of his fathers to witness that he dies without a groan.

Notwithstanding the obloquy with which the early historians have overshadowed the characters of the unfortunate natives, some bright gleams occasionally break through which throw a degree of melancholy lustre on their memories. Facts are occasionally to be met with in the rude annals of the eastern provinces which, though recorded with the coloring of prejudice and bigotry, yet speak for themselves, and will be dwelt on with applause and sympathy when prejudice shall have passed away.

In one of the homely narratives of the Indian wars in New England there is a touching account of the desolation carried into the tribe of the Pequod Indians. Humanity shrinks from the cold-blooded detail of indiscriminate butchery. In one place we read of the surprisal of an Indian fort in the night, when the wigwams were wrapped in flames and the miserable inhabitants shot down and slain in attempting to escape, "all being despatched and ended in the course of an hour." After a series of similar transactions, "our soldiers," as the historian piously observes, "being resolved by God's assistance to make a final destruction of them," the unhappy savages being hunted from their homes and fortresses and pursued with fire and sword, a scanty but gallant band, the sad remnant of the Pequod warriors, with their wives and children took refuge in a swamp.

Burning with indignation and rendered sullen by despair, with hearts bursting with grief at the destruction of their tribe, and spirits galled and sore at the fancied ignominy of their defeat, they refused to ask their lives at the hands of an insulting foe, and preferred death to submission.

As the night drew on they were surrounded in their dismal retreat, so as to render escape impracticable. Thus situated, their enemy "plied them with shot all the time, by which means many were killed and buried in the mire." In the darkness and fog that preceded the dawn of day some few broke through the besiegers and escaped into the woods; "the rest were left to the conquerors, of which many were killed in the swamp, like sullen dogs who would rather, in their self-willedness and madness, sit still and be shot through or cut to pieces" than implore for mercy. When the day broke upon this handful of forlorn but dauntless spirits, the soldiers, we are told, entering the swamp, "saw several heaps of them sitting close together, upon whom they discharged their pieces, laden with ten or twelve pistol bullets at a time, putting the muzzles of the pieces under the boughs, within a few yards of them; so as, besides those that were found dead, many more were killed and sunk into the mire, and never were minded more by friend or foe."

Can any one read this plain unvarnished tale without admiring the stern resolution, the unbending pride, the loftiness of spirit that seemed to nerve the hearts of these self-taught heroes and to raise them above the instinctive feelings of human nature? When the Gauls laid waste the city of Rome, they found the senators clothed in their robes and seated with stern tranquillity in their curule chairs; in this manner they suffered death without resistance or even supplication. Such conduct was in them applauded as noble and magnanimous; in the hapless Indian it was reviled as obstinate and sullen. How truly are we the dupes of show and circumstance! How different is virtue clothed in purple and enthroned in state, from virtue naked and destitute and perishing obscurely in a wilderness!

But I forbear to dwell on these gloomy pictures. The eastern tribes have long since disappeared; the forests that sheltered them have been laid low, and scarce any traces remain of them in the thickly settled States of New England, excepting here and there the Indian name of a village or a stream. And such must, sooner or later, be the fate of those other tribes which skirt the frontiers, and have occasionally been inveigled from their forests to mingle in the wars of white men. In a little while, and they will go the way that their brethren have gone before. The few hordes which still linger about the shores of Huron and Superior and the tributary streams of the Mississippi will share the fate of those tribes that once spread over Massachusetts and Connecticut and lorded it along the proud banks of the Hudson, of that gigantic race said to have existed on the borders of the Susquehanna, and of those various nations that flourished about the Potomac and the Rappahannock and that peopled the forests of the vast valley of Shenandoah. They will vanish like a vapor from the face of the earth; their very history will be lost in forgetfulness; and "the places that now know them will know them no more forever." Or if, perchance, some dubious memorial of them should survive, it may be in the romantic dreams of the poet, to people in imagination his glades and groves, like the fauns and satyrs and sylvan deities of antiquity. But should he venture upon the dark story of their wrongs and wretchedness, should he tell how they were invaded, corrupted, despoiled, driven from their native abodes and the sepulchres of their fathers, hunted like wild beasts about the earth, and sent down with violence and butchery to the grave, posterity will either turn with horror and incredulity from the tale or blush with indignation at the inhumanity of their forefathers. "We are driven back," said an old warrior, "until we can retreat no farther—our hatchets are broken, our bows are snapped, our fires are nearly extinguished; a little longer and the white man will cease to persecute us, for we shall cease to exist!"

PHILIP OF POKANOKET

An Indian Memoir

As monumental bronze unchanged his look:
A soul that pity touch'd, but never shook;
Train'd from his tree-rock'd cradle to his bier,
The fierce extremes of good and ill to brook
Impassive—fearing but the shame of fear—
A stoic of the woods—a man without a tear.
—Campbell

It is to be regretted that those early writers who treated of the discovery and settlement of America have not given us more particular and candid accounts of the remarkable characters that flourished in savage life. The scanty anecdotes which have reached us are full of peculiarity and interest; they furnish us with nearer glimpses of human nature, and show what man is in a comparatively primitive state and what he owes to civilization. There is something of the charm of discovery in lighting upon these wild and unexplored tracts of human nature—in witnessing, as it were, the native growth of moral sentiment, and perceiving those generous and romantic qualities which have been artificially cultivated by society vegetating in spontaneous hardihood and rude magnificence.

In civilized life, where the happiness, and indeed almost the existence, of man depends so much upon the opinion of his fellow men, he is constantly acting a studied part. The bold and peculiar traits of native character are refined away or softened down by the levelling influence of what is termed good breeding, and he practises so many petty deceptions, and affects so many generous sentiments for the purposes of popularity, that it is difficult to distinguish his real from his artificial character. The Indian, on the contrary, free from the restraints and refinements of polished life, and in a great degree a solitary and independent being, obeys the impulses of his inclination or the dictates of his judgment; and thus the attributes of his nature, being freely indulged, grow singly great and striking. Society is like a lawn, where every roughness is smoothed, every bramble eradicated, and where the eye is delighted by the smiling verdure of a velvet surface; he, however, who would study nature in its wildness and variety must plunge into the forest, must explore the glen, must stem the torrent, and dare the precipice.

These reflections arose on casually looking through a volume of early colonial history wherein are recorded, with great bitterness, the outrages of the Indians and their wars with the settlers, New England. It is painful to perceive, even from these partial narratives, how the footsteps of civilization may be traced in the blood of the aborigines; how easily the colonists were moved to hostility by the lust of conquest; how merciless and exterminating was their warfare. The imagination shrinks at the idea of how many intellectual beings were hunted from the earth, how many brave and noble hearts, of nature's sterling coinage, were broken down and trampled in the dust.

Such was the fate of Philip of Pokanoket, an Indian warrior whose name was once a terror throughout Massachusetts and Connecticut. He was the most distinguished of a number of contemporary sachems who reigned over the Pequods, the Narragansetts, the Wampanoags, and the other eastern tribes at the time of the first settlement of New England—a band of native untaught heroes who made the most generous struggle of which human nature is capable, fighting to the last gasp in the cause of their country, without a hope of victory or a thought of renown. Worthy of an age of poetry and fit subjects for local story and romantic fiction, they have left scarcely any authentic traces on the page of history, but stalk like gigantic shadows in the dim twilight of tradition.*

When the Pilgrims, as the Plymouth settlers are called by their descendants, first took refuge on the shores of the New World from the religious persecutions of the Old, their situation was to the last degree gloomy and disheartening. Few in number, and that number rapidly perishing away through sickness and hardships, surrounded by a howling wilderness and savage tribes, exposed to the rigors of an almost arctic winter and the vicissitudes of an ever-shifting climate,

* While correcting the proof-sheets of this article the author is informed that a celebrated English poet has nearly finished an heroic poem on the story of Philip of Pokanoket.

their minds were filled with doleful forebodings, and nothing preserved them from sinking into despondency but the strong excitement of religious enthusiasm. In this forlorn situation they were visited by Massasoit, chief sagamore of the Wampanoags, a powerful chief who reigned over a great extent of country. Instead of taking advantage of the scanty number of the strangers and expelling them from his territories, into which they had intruded, he seemed at once to conceive for them a generous friendship, and extended towards them the rites of primitive hospitality. He came early in the spring to their settlement of New Plymouth, attended by a mere handful of followers, entered into a solemn league of peace and amity, sold them a portion of the soil, and promised to secure for them the good-will of his savage allies. Whatever may be said of Indian perfidy, it is certain that the integrity and good faith of Massasoit have never been impeached. He continued a firm and magnanimous friend of the white men, suffering them to extend their possessions and to strengthen themselves in the land, and betraying no jealousy of their increasing power and prosperity. Shortly before his death, he came once more to New Plymouth with his son Alexander, for the purpose of renewing the covenant of peace and of securing it to his posterity.

At this conference he endeavored to protect the religion of his forefathers from the encroaching zeal of the missionaries, and stipulated that no further attempt should be made to draw off his people from their ancient faith; but, finding the English obstinately opposed to any such condition, he mildly relinquished the demand. Almost the last act of his life was to bring his two sons, Alexander and Philip (as they had been named by the English), to the residence of a principal settler, recommending mutual kindness and confidence, and entreating that the same love and amity which had existed between the white men and himself might be continued afterwards with his children. The good old sachem died in peace, and was happily gathered to his fathers before sorrow came upon his tribe; his children remained behind to experience the ingratitude of white men.

His eldest son, Alexander, succeeded him. He was of a quick and impetuous temper, and proudly tenacious of his hereditary rights and dignity. The intrusive policy and dictatorial conduct of the strangers excited his indignation, and he beheld with uneasiness their exterminating wars with the neighboring tribes. He was doomed soon to incur their hostility, being accused of plotting with the Narragansetts to rise against the English and drive them from the land. It is impossible to say whether this accusation was warranted by facts or was grounded on mere suspicions. It is evident, however, by the violent and overbearing measures of the settlers, that they had by this time begun to feel conscious of the rapid increase of their power, and to grow harsh and inconsiderate in their treatment of the natives. They despatched an armed force to seize upon Alexander and to bring him before their courts. He was traced to his woodland haunts, and surprised at a hunting house where he was reposing with a band of his followers, unarmed, after the toils of the chase. The suddenness of his arrest and the outrage offered to his sovereign dignity so preyed upon the irascible feelings of this proud savage as to throw him into a raging fever. He was permitted to return home on condition of sending his son as a pledge for his reappearance; but the blow he had received was fatal, and before he reached his home he fell a victim to the agonies of a wounded spirit.

The successor of Alexander was Metamocet, or King Philip, as he was called by the settlers on account of his lofty spirit and ambitious temper. These, together with his well-known energy and enterprise, had rendered him an object of great jealousy and apprehension, and he was accused of having always cherished a secret and implacable hostility towards the whites. Such may very probably and very naturally have been the case. He considered them as originally but mere intruders into the country, who had presumed upon indulgence and were extending an influence baneful to savage life. He saw the whole race of his countrymen melting before them from the face of the earth, their territories slipping from their hands, and their tribes becoming feeble, scattered, and dependent. It may be said that the soil was originally purchased by the settlers; but who does not know the nature of Indian purchases in the early periods of colonization? The Europeans always made thrifty bargains through their superior adroitness in traffic, and they gained vast accessions of territory by easily provoked hostilities. An uncultivated savage is never a nice inquirer into the refinements of law by which an injury may be gradually and legally inflicted. Leading facts are all by which he judges; and it was enough for Philip to know that before the intrusion of the Europeans, his countrymen were lords of the soil, and that now they were becoming vagabonds in the land of their fathers.

But whatever may have been his feelings of general hostility and his particular indignation at the treatment of his brother, he suppressed them for the present, renewed the contract with the settlers, and resided peaceably for many years at Pokanoket, or as, it was called by the English, Mount Hope,* the ancient seat of dominion of his tribe. Suspicions, however, which were at first but vague and indefinite, began to acquire form and substance, and he was at length charged with attempting to instigate the various eastern tribes to rise at once, and by a simultaneous effort to throw off the yoke of their oppressors. It is difficult at this distant period to assign the proper credit due to these early accusations against the Indians. There was a proneness to suspicion and an aptness to acts of violence on the part of the whites that gave weight and importance to every idle tale. Informers abounded where tale-bearing met with countenance and reward, and the sword was readily unsheathed when its success was certain and it carved out empire.

The only positive evidence on record against Philip is the accusation of one Sausaman, a renegado Indian, whose natural cunning had been quickened by a partial education which he had received among the settlers. He changed his faith and his allegiance two or three times with a facility that evinced the looseness of his principles. He had acted for some time as Philip's confidential secretary and counsellor, and had enjoyed his bounty and protection. Finding, however, that the clouds of adversity were gathering round his patron, he abandoned his service and went over to the whites, and in order to gain their favor charged his former benefactor with plotting against their safety. A rigorous investigation took place. Philip and several of his subjects submitted to be examined, but nothing was proved against them. The settlers, however, had now gone too far to retract; they had previously determined that Philip was a dangerous neighbor; they had publicly evinced their distrust, and had done enough to insure his hostility;

* Now Bristol, Rhode Island

according, therefore, to the usual mode of reasoning in these cases, his destruction had become necessary to their security. Sausaman, the treacherous informer, was shortly afterwards found dead in a pond, having fallen a victim to the vengeance of his tribe. Three Indians, one of whom was a friend and counsellor of Philip, were apprehended and tried, and on the testimony of one very questionable witness were condemned and executed as murderers.

This treatment of his subjects and ignominious punishment of his friend outraged the pride and exasperated the passions of Philip. The bolt which had fallen thus at his very feet awakened him to the gathering storm, and he determined to trust himself no longer in the power of the white men. The fate of his insulted and broken-hearted brother still rankled in his mind; and he had a further warning in the tragical story of Miantonimo, a great Sachem of the Narragansetts, who, after manfully facing his accusers before a tribunal of the colonists, exculpating himself from a charge of conspiracy and receiving assurances of amity, had been perfidiously despatched at their instigation. Philip therefore gathered his fighting men about him, persuaded all strangers that he could to join his cause, sent the women and children to the Narragansetts for safety, and wherever he appeared was continually surrounded by armed warriors.

When the two parties were thus in a state of distrust and irritation, the least spark was sufficient to set them in a flame. The Indians, having weapons in their hands, grew mischievous and committed various petty depredations. In one of their maraudings, a warrior was fired on and killed by a settler. This was the signal for open hostilities; the Indians pressed to revenge the death of their comrade, and the alarm of war resounded through the Plymouth colony.

In the early chronicles of these dark and melancholy times, we meet with many indications of the diseased state of the public mind. The gloom of religious abstraction and the wildness of their situation among trackless forests and savage tribes had disposed the colonists to superstitious fancies, and had filled their imaginations with the frightful chimeras of witchcraft and spectrology. They were much given also to a belief in omens. The troubles with Philip and his Indians were preceded, we are told, by a variety of those awful warnings which forerun great and public calamities. The perfect form of an Indian bow appeared in the air at New Plymouth, which was looked upon by the inhabitants as a "prodigious apparition." At Hadley, Northampton, and other towns in their neighborhood "was heard the report of a great piece of ordnance, with a shaking of the earth and a considerable echo."* Others were alarmed on a still sunshiny morning by the discharge of guns and muskets; bullets seemed to whistle past them, and the noise of drums resounded in the air, seeming to pass away to the westward; others fancied that they heard the galloping of horses over their heads; and certain monstrous births which took place about the time filled the superstitious in some towns with doleful forebodings. Many of these portentous sights and sounds may be ascribed to natural phenomena—to the northern lights which occur vividly in those latitudes, the meteors which explode in the air, the casual rushing of a blast through the top branches of the forest, the crash of fallen trees or disrupted rocks, and to those other uncouth sounds and echoes which will sometimes strike the ear so strangely amidst the profound stillness of woodland solitudes. These may have startled some melancholy imaginations, may have been exaggerated by the love for the marvellous, and listened to with that avidity with which we devour whatever is fearful and mysterious. The universal currency of these superstitious fancies and the grave record made of them by one of the learned men of the day are strongly characteristic of the times.

The nature of the contest that ensued was such as too often distinguishes the warfare between civilized men and savages. On the part of the whites it was conducted with superior skill and success, but with a wastefulness of the blood and a disregard of the natural rights of their antagonists: on the part of the Indians it was waged with the desperation of men fearless of death, and who had nothing to expect from peace but humiliation, dependence, and decay.

The events of the war are transmitted to us by a worthy clergyman of the time, who dwells with horror and indignation on every hostile act of the Indians, however justifiable, whilst he mentions with applause the most sanguinary atrocities of the whites. Philip is reviled as a murderer and a traitor, without considering that he was a true-

* The Rev. Increase Mather's History

born prince gallantly fighting at the head of his subjects to avenge the wrongs of his family, to retrieve the tottering power of his line, and to deliver his native land from the oppression of usurping strangers.

The project of a wide and simultaneous revolt, if such had really been formed, was worthy of a capacious mind, and had it not been prematurely discovered might have been overwhelming in its consequences. The war that actually broke out was but a war of detail, a mere succession of casual exploits and unconnected enterprises. Still, it sets forth the military genius and daring prowess of Philip, and wherever, in the prejudiced and passionate narrations that have been given of it, we can arrive at simple facts, we find him displaying a vigorous mind, a fertility of expedients, a contempt of suffering and hardship, and an unconquerable resolution that command our sympathy and applause.

Driven from his paternal domains at Mount Hope, he threw himself into the depths of those vast and trackless forests that skirted the settlements and were almost impervious to anything but a wild beast or an Indian. Here he gathered together his forces, like the storm accumulating its stores of mischief in the bosom of the thundercloud, and would suddenly emerge at a time and place least expected, carrying havoc and dismay into the villages. There were now and then indications of these impending ravages that filled the minds of the colonists with awe and apprehension. The report of a distant gun would perhaps be heard from the solitary woodland, where there was known to be no white man; the cattle which had been wandering in the woods would sometimes return home wounded; or an Indian or two would be seen lurking about the skirts of the forests and suddenly disappearing, as the lightning will sometimes be seen playing silently about the edge of the cloud that is brewing up the tempest.

Though sometimes pursued and even surrounded by the settlers, yet Philip as often escaped almost miraculously from their toils, and, plunging into the wilderness, would be lost to all search or inquiry until he again emerged at some far distant quarter, laying the country desolate. Among his strongholds were the great swamps or morasses which extend in some parts of New England, composed of loose bogs of deep black mud, perplexed with thickets, brambles, rank weeds, the shattered and mouldering trunks of fallen trees, overshadowed by lugubrious hemlocks. The uncertain footing and the tangled mazes of these shaggy wilds rendered them almost impracticable to the white man, though the Indian could thread their labyrinths with the agility of a deer. Into one of these, the great swamp of Pocasset Neck, was Philip once driven with a band of his followers. The English did not dare to pursue him, fearing to venture into these dark and frightful recesses, where they might perish in fens and miry pits or be shot down by lurking foes. They therefore invested the entrance to the Neck, and began to build a fort with the thought of starving out the foe; but Philip and his warriors wafted themselves on a raft over an arm of the sea in the dead of night, leaving the women and children behind, and escaped away to the westward, kindling the flames of war among the tribes of Massachusetts and the Nipmuck country and threatening the colony of Connecticut.

In this way Philip became a theme of universal apprehension. The mystery in which he was enveloped exaggerated his real terrors. He was an evil that walked in darkness, whose coming none could foresee and against which none knew when to be on the alert. The whole country abounded with rumors and alarms. Philip seemed almost possessed of ubiquity, for in whatever part of the widely extended frontier an irruption from the forest took place, Philip was said to be its leader. Many superstitious notions also were circulated concerning him. He was said to deal in necromancy, and to be attended by an old Indian witch or prophetess, whom he consulted and who assisted him by her charms and incantations. This, indeed, was frequently the case with Indian chiefs, either through their own credulity or to act upon that of their followers; and the influence of the prophet and the dreamer over Indian superstition has been fully evidenced in recent instances of savage warfare.

At the time that Philip effected his escape from Pocasset, his fortunes were in a desperate condition. His forces had been thinned by repeated fights and he had lost almost the whole of his resources. In this time of adversity he found a faithful friend in Canonchet, chief Sachem of all the Narragansetts. He was the son and heir of Miantonimo, the great sachem who, as already mentioned, after an honorable acquittal of the charge of conspiracy, had been privately put to death at the perfidious instigations of the settlers. "He was the heir," says the old chronicler, "of all his father's pride and insolence, as well as of his malice towards the English;" he certainly was the heir of his insults and injuries and the legitimate avenger of his murder. Though he had forborne to take an active part in this hopeless war, yet he received Philip and his broken forces with open arms and gave them the most generous countenance and support. This at once drew upon him the hostility of the English, and it was determined to strike a signal blow that should involve both the Sachems in one common ruin. A great force was therefore gathered together from Massachusetts, Plymouth, and Connecticut, and was sent into the Narragansett country in the depth of winter, when the swamps, being frozen and leafless, could be traversed with comparative facility and would no longer afford dark and impenetrable fastnesses to the Indians.

Apprehensive of attack, Canonchet had conveyed the greater part of his stores, together with the old, the infirm, the women and children of his tribe, to a strong fortress, where he and Philip had likewise drawn up the flower of their forces. This fortress, deemed by the Indians impregnable, was situated upon a rising mound or kind of island of five or six acres in the midst of a swamp; it was constructed with a degree of judgment and skill vastly superior to what is usually displayed in Indian fortification, and indicative of the martial genius of these two chieftains.

Guided by a renegado Indian, the English penetrated, through December snows, to this stronghold and came upon the garrison by surprise. The fight was fierce and tumultuous. The assailants were repulsed in their first attack, and several of their bravest officers were shot down in the act of storming the fortress, sword in hand. The assault was renewed with greater success. A lodgment was effected. The Indians were driven from one post to another. They disputed their ground inch by inch, fighting with the fury of despair. Most of their veterans were cut to pieces, and after a long and bloody battle, Philip and Canonchet, with a handful of surviving warriors, retreated from the fort and took refuge in the thickets of the surrounding forest.

The victors set fire to the wigwams and the fort; the whole was soon in a blaze; many of the old men, the women, and the children perished in the flames. This last outrage overcame even the stoicism of the savage. The neighboring woods resounded with the yells of rage and despair uttered by the fugitive warriors, as they beheld the destruction of their dwellings and heard the agonizing cries of their wives and offspring. "The burning of the wigwams," says a contemporary writer, "the shrieks and cries of the women and children, and the yelling of the warriors, exhibited a most horrible and affecting scene, so that it greatly moved some of the soldiers." The same writer cautiously adds, "They were in *much doubt* then, and afterwards seriously inquired, whether burning their enemies alive could be consistent with humanity, and the benevolent principles of the gospel."*

The fate of the brave and generous Canonchet is worthy of particular mention: the last scene of his life is one of the noblest instances on record of Indian magnanimity.

Broken down in his power and resources by this signal defeat, yet faithful to his ally and to the hapless cause which he had espoused, he rejected all overtures of peace offered on condition of betraying Philip and his followers, and declared that "he would fight it out to the last man, rather than become a servant to the English." His home being destroyed, his country harassed and laid waste by the incursions of the conquerors, he was obliged to wander away to the banks of the Connecticut, where he formed a rallying point to the whole body of western Indians and laid waste several of the English settlements.

Early in the spring he departed on a hazardous expedition, with only thirty chosen men, to penetrate to Seaconck, in the vicinity of Mount Hope, and to procure seed corn to plant for the sustenance of his troops. This little hand of adventurers had passed safely through the Pequod country, and were in the centre of the Narragansett, resting at some wigwams near Pautucket River, when an alarm was given of an approaching enemy. Having but seven men by him at the time, Canonchet despatched two of them to the top of a neighboring hill to bring intelligence of the foe.

Panic-struck by the appearance of a troop of English and Indians rapidly advancing, they fled in breathless terror past their chieftain, without stopping to inform him of the danger. Canonchet sent another

* MS. of the Rev. W. Ruggles

scout, who did the same. He then sent two more, one of whom, hurrying back in confusion and affright, told him that the whole British army was at hand. Canonchet saw there was no choice but immediate flight. He attempted to escape round the hill, but was perceived and hotly pursued by the hostile Indians and a few of the fleetest of the English. Finding the swiftest pursuer close upon his heels, he threw off, first his blanket, then his silver-laced coat and belt of peag, by which his enemies knew him to be Canonchet and redoubled the eagerness of pursuit.

At length, in dashing through the river, his foot slipped upon a stone, and he fell so deep as to wet his gun. This accident so struck him with despair that, as he afterwards confessed, "his heart and his bowels turned within him, and he became like a rotten stick, void of strength."

To such a degree was he unnerved that, being seized by a Pequod Indian within a short distance of the river, he made no resistance, though a man of great vigor of body and boldness of heart. But on being made prisoner the whole pride of his spirit arose within him, and from that moment we find, in the anecdotes given by his enemies, nothing but repeated flashes of elevated and prince-like heroism. Being questioned by one of the English who first came up with him, and who had not attained his twenty-second year, the proud-hearted warrior, looking with lofty contempt upon his youthful countenance, replied, "You are a child—you cannot understand matters of war; let your brother or your chief come: him will I answer."

Though repeated offers were made to him of his life on condition of submitting with his nation to the English, yet he rejected them with disdain, and refused to send any proposals of the kind to the great body of his subjects, saying that he knew none of them would comply. Being reproached with his breach of faith towards the whites, his boast that he would not deliver up a Wampanoag nor the paring of a Wampanoag's nail; and his threat that he would burn the English alive in their houses, he disdained to justify himself, haughtily answering that others were as forward for the war as himself, and "he desired to hear no more thereof."

So noble and unshaken a spirit, so true a fidelity to his cause and his friend, might have touched the feelings of the generous and the brave; but Canonchet was an Indian, a being towards whom war had no courtesy, humanity no law, religion no compassion: he was condemned to die. The last words of his that are recorded are worthy the greatness of his soul. When sentence of death was passed upon him, he observed "that he liked it well, for he should die before his heart was soft or he had spoken anything unworthy of himself." His enemies gave him the death of a soldier, for he was shot at Stonington by three young sachems of his own rank.

The defeat at the Narraganset fortress and the death of Canonchet, were fatal blows to the fortunes of King Philip. He made an ineffectual attempt to raise a head of war by stirring up the Mohawks to take arms; but, though possessed of the native talents of a statesman, his arts were counteracted by the superior arts of his enlightened enemies, and the terror of their warlike skill began to subdue the resolution of the neighboring tribes. The unfortunate chieftain saw himself daily stripped of power, and his ranks rapidly thinning around him. Some were suborned by the whites; others fell victims to hunger and fatigue and to the frequent attacks by which they were harassed. His stores were all captured; his chosen friends were swept away from before his eyes; his uncle was shot down by his side; his sister was carried into captivity; and in one of his narrow escapes, he was compelled to leave his beloved wife and only son to the mercy of the enemy. "His ruin," says the historian, "being thus gradually carried on, his misery was not prevented, but augmented thereby; being himself made acquainted with the sense and experimental feeling of the captivity of his children, loss of friends, slaughter of his subjects, bereavement of all family relations, and being stripped of all outward comforts before his own life should be taken away."

To fill up the measure of his misfortunes, his own followers began to plot against his life, that by sacrificing him they might purchase dishonorable safety. Through treachery a number of his faithful adherents, the subjects of Wetamoe, an Indian princess of Pocasset, a near kinswoman and confederate of Philip, were betrayed into the hands of the enemy. Wetamoe was among them at the time, and attempted to make her escape by crossing a neighboring river: either exhausted by swimming or starved with cold and hunger, she was found dead and naked near the water side. But persecution ceased not at the grave. Even death, the refuge of the wretched, where the wicked commonly cease from troubling, was no protection to this outcast female, whose great crime was affectionate fidelity to her kinsman and her friend. Her corpse was the object of unmanly and dastardly vengeance: the head was severed from the body and set upon a pole, and was thus exposed at Taunton to the view of her captive subjects. They immediately recognized the features of their unfortunate queen, and were so affected at this barbarous spectacle that we are told they broke forth into the "most horrid and diabolical lamentations."

However Philip had borne up against the complicated miseries and misfortunes that surrounded him, the treachery of his followers seemed to wring his heart and reduce him to despondency. It is said that "he never rejoiced afterwards, nor had success in any of his designs." The spring of hope was broken—the ardor of enterprise was extinguished—he looked around, and all was danger and darkness; "there was no eye to pity nor any arm that could bring deliverance." With a scanty band of followers, who still remained true to his desperate fortunes, the unhappy Philip wandered back to the vicinity of Mount Hope, the ancient dwelling of his fathers. Here he lurked about like a spectre among the scenes of former power and prosperity, now bereft of home, of family, and of friend. There needs no better picture of his destitute and piteous situation than that furnished by the homely pen of the chronicler, who is unwarily enlisting the feelings of the reader in favor of the hapless warrior whom he reviles. "Philip," he says, "like a savage wild beast, having been hunted by the English forces through the woods above a hundred miles backward and forward, at last was driven to his own den upon Mount Hope, where he retired, with a few of his best friends, into a swamp, which proved but a prison to keep him fast till the messengers of death came by divine permission to execute vengeance upon him."

Even in this last refuge of desperation and despair, a sullen grandeur gathers round his memory. We picture him to ourselves seated among his care worn followers, brooding in silence over his blasted fortunes, and acquiring a savage sublimity from the wildness and dreariness of his lurking place. Defeated, but not dismayed—crushed to the earth, but not humiliated—he seemed to grow more haughty beneath disaster, and to experience a fierce satisfaction in draining the last dregs of bitterness. Little minds are tamed and subdued by misfortune, but great minds rise above it. The very idea of submission awakened the fury of Philip, and he smote to death one of his followers who proposed an expedient of peace. The brother of the victim made his escape, and in revenge betrayed the retreat of his chieftain. A body of white men and Indians were immediately despatched to the swamp where Philip lay crouched, glaring with fury and despair. Before he was aware of their approach they had begun to surround him. In a little while he saw five of his trustiest followers laid dead at his feet; all resistance was vain; he rushed forth from his covert, and made a headlong attempt at escape, but was shot through the heart by a renegado Indian of his own nation.

Such is the scanty story of the brave but unfortunate King Philip, persecuted while living, slandered and dishonored when dead. If, however, we consider even the prejudiced anecdotes furnished us by his enemies, we may perceive in them traces of amiable and lofty character sufficient to awaken sympathy for his fate and respect for his memory. We find that amidst all the harassing cares and ferocious passions of constant warfare, he was alive to the softer feelings of connubial love and paternal tenderness and to the generous sentiment of friendship. The captivity of his "beloved wife and only son" are mentioned with exultation as causing him poignant misery: the death of any near friend is triumphantly recorded as a new blow on his sensibilities; but the treachery and desertion of many of his followers, in whose affections he had confided, is said to have desolated his heart and to have bereaved him of all further comfort. He was a patriot attached to his native soil—a prince true to his subjects and indignant of their wrongs—a soldier daring in battle, firm in adversity, patient of fatigue, of hunger, of every variety of bodily suffering, and ready to perish in the cause he had espoused. Proud of heart and with an untamable love of natural liberty, he preferred to enjoy it among the beasts of the forests or in the dismal and famished recesses of swamps and morasses, rather than bow his haughty spirit to submission and live dependent and despised in the ease and luxury of the settlements.

With heroic qualities and bold achievements that would have graced a civilized warrior, and have rendered him the theme of the poet and the historian, he lived a wanderer and a fugitive in his native land, and went down, like a lonely bark foundering amid darkness and tempest, without a pitying eye to weep his fall or a friendly hand to record his struggle.

JOHN BULL

An old song, made by an aged old pate,
Of an old worshipful gentleman who had a great estate,
That kept a brave old house at a bountiful rate,
And an old porter to relieve the poor at his gate.

With an old study fill'd full of learned old books,
With an old reverend chaplain, you might know him by his looks,
With an old buttery-hatch worn quite off the hooks,
And an old kitchen that maintained half-a-dozen old cooks.
Like an old courtier, etc.

—Old Song

There is no species of humor in which the English more excel than that which consists in caricaturing and giving ludicrous appellations or nicknames. In this way they have whimsically designated, not merely individuals, but nations, and in their fondness for pushing a joke, they have not spared even themselves. One would think that in personifying itself, a nation would be apt to picture something grand, heroic, and imposing; but it is characteristic of the peculiar humor of the English, and of their love for what is blunt, comic, and familiar, that they have embodied their national oddities in the figure of a sturdy, corpulent old fellow with a three-cornered hat, red waistcoat, leather breeches, and stout oaken cudgel. Thus they have taken a singular delight in exhibiting their most private foibles in a laughable point of view, and have been so successful in their delineations that there is scarcely a being in actual existence more absolutely present to the public mind than that eccentric personage, John Bull.

Perhaps the continual contemplation of the character thus drawn of them has contributed to fix it upon the nation, and thus to give reality to what at first may have been painted in a great measure from the imagination. Men are apt to acquire peculiarities that are continually ascribed to them. The common orders of English seem wonderfully captivated with the *beau ideal* which they have formed of John Bull, and endeavor to act up to the broad caricature that is perpetually before their eyes. Unluckily, they sometimes make their boasted Bullism an apology for their prejudice or grossness; and this I have especially noticed among those truly homebred and genuine sons of the soil who have never migrated beyond the sound of Bow bells. If one of these should be a little uncouth in speech and apt to utter impertinent truths, he confesses that he is a real John Bull and always speaks his mind. If he now and then flies into an unreasonable burst of passion about trifles, he observes that John Bull is a choleric old blade, but then his passion is over in a moment and he bears no malice. If he betrays a coarseness of taste and an insensibility to foreign refinements, he thanks Heaven for his ignorance—he is a plain John Bull and has no relish for frippery and knick-knacks. His very proneness to be gulled by strangers and to pay extravagantly for absurdities is excused under the plea of munificence, for John is always more generous than wise.

Thus, under the name of John Bull he will contrive to argue every fault into a merit, and will frankly convict himself of being the honestest fellow in existence.

However little, therefore, the character may have suited in the first instance, it has gradually adapted itself to the nation, or rather they have adapted themselves to each other; and a stranger who wishes to study English peculiarities may gather much valuable information from the innumerable portraits of John Bull as exhibited in the windows of the caricature-shops. Still, however, he is one of those fertile humorists that are continually throwing out new portraits and presenting different aspects from different points of view; and, often as he has been described, I cannot resist the temptation to give a slight sketch of him such as he has met my eye.

John Bull, to all appearance, is a plain, downright, matter-of-fact fellow, with much less of poetry about him than rich prose. There is little of romance in his nature, but a vast deal of strong natural feeling. He excels in humor more than in wit; is jolly rather than gay; melancholy rather than morose; can easily be moved to a sudden tear or surprised into a broad laugh; but he loathes sentiment and has no turn for light pleasantry. He is a boon companion, if you allow him in to have his humor and to talk about himself; and he will stand by a friend in a quarrel with life and purse, however soundly he may be cudgelled.

In this last respect, to tell the truth, he has a propensity to be somewhat too ready. He is a busy-minded personage, who thinks not merely for himself and family, but for all the country round, and is most generously disposed to be everybody's champion. He is continually volunteering his services to settle his neighbor's affairs, and takes it in great dudgeon if they engage in any matter of consequence without asking his advice, though he seldom engages in any friendly office of the kind without finishing by getting into a squabble with all parties, and then railing bitterly at their ingratitude. He unluckily took lessons in his youth in the noble science of defence, and having accomplished himself in the use of his limbs and his weapons and become a perfect master at boxing and cudgel-play, he has had a troublesome life of it ever since. He cannot hear of a quarrel between the most distant of his neighbors but he begins incontinently to fumble with the head of his cudgel, and consider whether his interest or honor does not require that he should meddle in the broil. Indeed, he has extended his relations of pride and policy so completely over the whole country that no event can take place without infringing some of his finely spun rights and dignities. Couched in his little domain, with these filaments stretching forth in every direction, he is like some choleric, bottle-bellied old spider who has woven his web over a whole chamber, so that a fly cannot buzz nor a breeze blow without startling his repose and causing him to sally forth wrathfully from his den.

Though really a good-hearted, good-tempered old fellow at bottom, yet he is singularly fond of being in the midst of contention. It is one of his peculiarities, however, that he only relishes the beginning of an affray; he always goes into a fight with alacrity, but comes out of it grumbling even when victorious; and though no one fights with more obstinacy to carry a contested point, yet when the battle is over and he comes to the reconciliation he is so much taken up with the mere shaking of hands that he is apt to let his antagonist pocket all that they have been quarrelling about. It is not, therefore, fighting that he ought so much to be on his guard against as making friends. It is difficult to cudgel him out of a farthing, but put him in a good humor and you may bargain him out of all the money in his pocket. He is like a stout ship which will weather the roughest storm uninjured, but roll its masts overboard in the succeeding calm.

He is a little fond of playing the magnifico abroad, of pulling out a long purse, flinging his money bravely about at boxing matches, horse races, cock fights, and carrying a high head among "gentlemen of the fancy:" but immediately after one of these fits of extravagance he will be taken with violent qualms of economy; stop short at the most trivial expenditure; talk desperately of being ruined and brought upon the parish; and in such moods will not pay the smallest tradesman's bill without violent altercation. He is, in fact, the most punctual and discontented paymaster in the world, drawing his coin out of his breeches pocket with infinite reluctance, paying to the uttermost farthing, but accompanying every guinea with a growl.

With all his talk of economy, however, he is a bountiful provider and a hospitable housekeeper. His economy is of a whimsical kind, its chief object being to devise how he may afford to be extravagant; for he will begrudge himself a beefsteak and pint of port one day that he may roast an ox whole, broach a hogshead of ale, and treat all his neighbors on the next.

His domestic establishment is enormously expensive, not so much from any great outward parade as from the great consumption of solid beef and pudding, the vast number of followers he feeds and clothes, and his singular disposition to pay hugely for small services. He is a most kind and indulgent master, and, provided his servants humor his peculiarities, flatter his vanity a little now and then, and do not peculate grossly on him before his face, they may manage him to perfection. Everything that lives on him seems to thrive and grow fat. His house-servants are well paid and pampered and have little to do. His horses are sleek and lazy and prance slowly before his state carriage; and his house dogs sleep quietly about the door and will hardly bark at a house-breaker.

His family mansion is an old castellated manor-house, gray with age, and of a most venerable though weather-beaten appearance. It has been built upon no regular plan, but is a vast accumulation of parts erected in various tastes and ages. The centre bears evident traces of

Saxon architecture, and is as solid as ponderous stone and old English oak can make it. Like all the relics of that style, it is full of obscure passages, intricate mazes, and dusky chambers; and, though these have been partially lighted up in modern days, yet there are many places where you must still grope in the dark. Additions have been made to the original edifice from time to time, and great alterations have taken place: towers and battlements have been erected during wars and tumults; wings built in time of peace; and outhouses, lodges, and offices run up according to the whim or convenience of different generations, until it has become one of the most spacious, rambling tenements imaginable. An entire wing is taken up with the family chapel, a reverend pile that must have been exceedingly sumptuous, and, indeed, in spite of having been altered and simplified at various periods, has still a look of solemn religious pomp. Its walls within are storied with the monuments of John's ancestors, and it is snugly fitted up with soft cushions and well-lined chairs, where such of his family as are inclined to church services may doze comfortably in the discharge of their duties.

To keep up this chapel has cost John much money; but he is staunch in his religion and piqued in his zeal, from the circumstance that many dissenting chapels have been erected in his vicinity, and several of his neighbors, with whom he has had quarrels, are strong papists.

To do the duties of the chapel, he maintains, at a large expense, a pious and portly family chaplain. He is a most learned and decorous personage and a truly well-bred Christian, who always backs the old gentleman in his opinions, winks discreetly at his little peccadilloes, rebukes the children when refractory, and is of great use in exhorting the tenants to read their Bibles, say their prayers, and, above all, to pay their rents punctually and without grumbling.

The family apartments are in a very antiquated taste, somewhat heavy and often inconvenient, but full of the solemn magnificence of former times, fitted up with rich though faded tapestry, unwieldy furniture, and loads of massy, gorgeous old plate. The vast fireplaces, ample kitchens, extensive cellars, and sumptuous banqueting-halls all speak of the roaring hospitality of days of yore, of which the modern festivity at the manor-house is but a shadow. There are, however, complete suites of rooms apparently deserted and time-worn, and towers and turrets that are tottering to decay, so that in high winds there is danger of their tumbling about the ears of the household.

John has frequently been advised to have the old edifice thoroughly overhauled, and to have some of the useless parts pulled down, and the others strengthened with their materials; but the old gentleman always grows testy on this subject. He swears the house is an excellent house: that it is tight and weather-proof, and not to be shaken by tempests; that it has stood for several hundred years, and therefore is not likely to tumble down now; that as to its being inconvenient, his family is accustomed to the inconveniences and would not be comfortable without them; that as to its unwieldy size and irregular construction, these result from its being the growth of centuries and being improved by the wisdom of every generation; that an old family, like his, requires a large house to dwell in; new, upstart families may live in modern cottages and snug boxes; but an old English family should inhabit an old English manor-house. If you point out any part of the building as superfluous, he insists that it is material to the strength or decoration of the rest and the harmony of the whole, and swears that the parts are so built into each other that if you pull down one, you run the risk of having the whole about your ears.

The secret of the matter is, that John has a great disposition to protect and patronize. He thinks it indispensable to the dignity of an ancient and honorable family to be bounteous in its appointments and to be eaten up by dependents; and so, partly from pride and partly from kind-heartedness, he makes it a rule always to give shelter and maintenance to his superannuated servants.

The consequence is, that like many other venerable family establishments, his manor is incumbered by old retainers whom he cannot turn off, and an old style which he cannot lay down. His mansion is like a great hospital of invalids, and, with all its magnitude, is not a whit too large for its inhabitants. Not a nook or corner but is of use in housing some useless personage. Groups of veteran beef-eaters, gouty pensioners, and retired heroes of the buttery and the larder are seen lolling about its ways, crawling over its lawns, dozing under its tree, or sunning themselves upon the benches at its doors. Every office and outhouse is garrisoned by these supernumeraries and their families; for they are amazingly prolific, and when they die off are sure to leave John a legacy of hungry mouths to be provided for. A mattock cannot be struck against the most mouldering, tumble-down tower but out pops, from some cranny or loophole, the gray pate of some superannuated hanger-on, who has lived at John's expense all his life, and makes the most grievous outcry at their pulling down the roof from over the head of a worn-out servant of the family. This is an appeal that John's honest heart never can withstand; so that a man who has faithfully eaten his beef and pudding all his life is sure to be rewarded with a pipe and tankard in his old days.

A great part of his park also is turned into paddocks, where his broken-down chargers are turned loose to graze undisturbed for the remainder of their existence—a worthy example of grateful recollection which, if some of his neighbors were to imitate, would not be to their discredit. Indeed, it is one of his great pleasures to point out these old steeds to his visitors, to dwell on their good qualities, extol their past services, and boast, with some little vain-glory, of the perilous adventures and hardy exploits through which they have carried him.

He is given, however, to indulge his veneration for family usages and family encumbrances to a whimsical extent. His manor is infested by gangs of gypsies; yet he will not suffer them to be driven off, because they have infested the place time out of mind and been regular poachers upon every generation of the family. He will scarcely permit a dry branch to be lopped from the great trees that surround the house, lest it should molest the rooks that have bred there for centuries. Owls have taken possession of the dovecote, but they are hereditary owls and must not be disturbed. Swallows have nearly choked up every chimney with their nests; martins build in every frieze and cornice; crows flutter about the towers and perch on every weather-cock; and old gray-headed rats may be seen in every quarter of the house, running in and out of their holes undauntedly in broad daylight. In short, John has such a reverence for everything that has been long in the family that he will not hear even of abuses being reformed, because they are good old family abuses.

All these whims and habits have concurred woefully to drain the old gentleman's purse; and as he prides himself on punctuality in money matters, and wishes to maintain his credit in the neighborhood, they have caused him great perplexity in meeting his engagements. This, too, has been increased by the altercations and heart-burnings which are continually taking place in his family. His children have been brought up to different callings and are of different ways of thinking; and as they have always been allowed to speak their minds freely, they do not fail to exercise the privilege most clamorously in the present posture of his affairs. Some stand up for the honor of the race, and are clear that the old establishment should be kept up in all its state, whatever may be the cost; others, who are more prudent and considerate, entreat the old gentleman to retrench his expenses and to put his whole system of housekeeping on a more moderate footing. He has, indeed, at times, seemed inclined to listen to their opinions, but their wholesome advice has been completely defeated by the obstreperous conduct of one of his sons. This is a noisy, rattle-pated fellow of rather low habits, who neglects his business to frequent ale-houses—is the orator of village clubs and a complete oracle among the poorest of his father's tenants. No sooner does he hear any of his brothers mention reform or retrenchment than up he jumps, takes the words out of their mouths, and roars out for an overturn. When his tongue is once going, nothing can stop it. He rants about the room; hectors the old man about his spendthrift practices; ridicules his tastes and pursuits; insists that he shall turn the old servants out of doors, give the broken-down horses to the hounds, send the fat chaplain packing, and take a field-preacher in his place; nay, that the whole family mansion shall be levelled with the ground, and a plain one of brick and mortar built in its place. He rails at every social entertainment and family festivity, and skulks away growling to the ale-house whenever an equipage drives up to the door. Though constantly complaining of the emptiness of his purse, yet he scruples not to spend all his pocket-money in these tavern convocations, and even runs up scores for the liquor over which he preaches about his father's extravagance.

It may readily be imagined how little such thwarting agrees with the old cavalier's fiery temperament. He has become so irritable from repeated crossings that the mere mention of retrenchment or reform is a signal for a brawl between him and the tavern oracle. As the latter is too sturdy and refractory for paternal discipline, having grown out of all fear of the cudgel, they have frequent scenes of wordy warfare, which at times run so high that John is fain to call in the aid of his son Tom, an officer who has served abroad, but is at present living at home on half-pay. This last is sure to stand by the old gentleman, right or wrong; likes nothing so much as a rocketing, roistering life, and is ready at a wink or nod to out sabre and flourish it over the orator's head if he dares to array himself against parental authority.

These family dissensions, as usual, have got abroad, and are rare food for scandal in John's neighborhood. People begin to look wise and shake their heads whenever his affairs are mentioned. They all "hope that matters are not so bad with him as represented; but when a man's own children begin to rail at his extravagance, things must be badly managed. They understand he is mortgaged over head and ears and is continually dabbling with money-lenders. He is certainly an open-handed old gentleman, but they fear he has lived too fast; indeed, they never knew any good come of this fondness for hunting, racing revelling, and prize-fighting. In short, Mr. Bull's estate is a very fine one and has been in the family a long while, but, for all that, they have known many finer estates come to the hammer."

What is worst of all, is the effect which these pecuniary embarrassments and domestic feuds have had on the poor man himself. Instead of that jolly round corporation and smug rosy face which he used to present, he has of late become as shrivelled and shrunk as a frost-bitten apple. His scarlet gold-laced waistcoat, which bellied out so bravely in those prosperous days when he sailed before the wind, now hangs loosely about him like a mainsail in a calm. His leather breeches are all in folds and wrinkles, and apparently have much ado to hold up the boots that yawn on both sides of his once sturdy legs.

Instead of strutting about as formerly with his three-cornered hat on one side, flourishing his cudgel, and bringing it down every moment with a hearty thump upon the ground, looking every one sturdily in the face, and trolling out a stave of a catch or a drinking-song, he now goes about whistling thoughtfully to himself, with his head drooping down, his cudgel tucked under his arm, and his hands thrust to the bottom of his breeches pockets, which are evidently empty.

Such is the plight of honest John Bull at present, yet for all this the old fellow's spirit is as tall and as gallant as ever. If you drop the least expression of sympathy or concern, he takes fire in an instant; swears that he is the richest and stoutest fellow in the country; talks of laying out large sums to adorn his house or buy another estate; and with a valiant swagger and grasping of his cudgel, longs exceedingly to have another bout at quarter-staff.

Though there may be something rather whimsical in all this, yet I confess I cannot look upon John's situation without strong feelings of interest. With all his odd humors and obstinate prejudices, he is a sterling-hearted old blade. He may not be so wonderfully fine a fellow as he thinks himself, but he is at least twice as good as his neighbors represent him. His virtues are all his own—all plain, homebred, and unaffected. His very faults smack of the raciness of his good qualities. His extravagance savors of his generosity, his quarrelsomeness of his courage, his credulity of his open faith, his vanity of his pride, and his bluntness of his sincerity. They are all the redundancies of a rich and liberal character. He is like his own oak, rough without, but sound and solid within; whose bark abounds with excrescences in proportion to the growth and grandeur of the timber; and whose branches make a fearful groaning and murmuring in the least storm from their very magnitude and luxuriance. There is something, too, in the appearance of his old family mansion that is extremely poetical and picturesque; and as long as it can be rendered comfortably habitable, I should almost tremble to see it meddled with during the present conflict of tastes and opinions. Some of his advisers are no doubt good architects that might be of service; but many, I fear, are mere levellers, who, when they had once got to work with their mattocks on this venerable edifice, would never stop until they had brought it to the ground, and perhaps buried themselves among the ruins. All that I wish is that John's present troubles may teach him more prudence in future—that he may cease to distress his mind about other people's affairs; that he may give up the fruitless attempt to promote the good of his neighbors and the peace and happiness of the world, by dint of the cudgel; that he may remain quietly at home; gradually get his house into repair; cultivate his rich estate according to his fancy; husband his income, if he thinks proper; bring his unruly children into order, if he can; renew the jovial scenes of ancient prosperity; and long enjoy on his paternal lands a green, an honorable, and a merry old age.

THE PRIDE OF THE VILLAGE

May no wolfe howle; no screech owle stir
A wing about thy sepulchre!
No boysterous winds or stormes come hither,
    To starve or wither
Thy soft sweet earth! but, like a spring,
Love kept it ever flourishing.

—HERRICK

In the course of an excursion through one of the remote counties of England, I had struck into one of those crossroads that lead through the more secluded parts of the country, and stopped one afternoon at a village, the situation of which was beautifully rural and retired. There was an air of primitive simplicity about its inhabitants, not to be found in the villages which lie on the great coach-roads. I determined to pass the night there, and having taken an early dinner, strolled out to enjoy the neighboring scenery.

My ramble, as is usually the case with travellers, soon led me to the church, which stood at a little distance from the village. Indeed, it was an object of some curiosity, its old tower being completely overrun with ivy, so that only here and there a jutting buttress, an angle of gray wall, or a fantastically carved ornament peered through the verdant covering. It was a lovely evening. The early part of the day had been dark and showery, but in the afternoon it had cleared up, and though sullen clouds still hung overhead, yet there was a broad tract of golden sky in the west, from which the setting sun gleamed through the dripping leaves and lit up all nature into a melancholy smile. It seemed like the parting hour of a good Christian smiling on the sins and sorrows of the world, and giving, in the serenity of his decline, an assurance that he will rise again in glory.

I had seated myself on a half-sunken tombstone, and was musing, as one is apt to do at this sober-thoughted hour, on past scenes and early friends—on those who were distant and those who were dead—and indulging in that kind of melancholy fancying which has in it something sweeter even than pleasure. Every now and then the stroke of a bell from the neighboring tower fell on my ear; its tones were in unison with the scene, and, instead of jarring, chimed in with my feelings; and it was some time before I recollected that it must be tolling the knell of some new tenant of the tomb.

Presently I saw a funeral train moving across the village green; it wound slowly along a lane, was lost, and reappeared through the breaks of the hedges, until it passed the place where I was sitting. The pall was supported by young girls dressed in white, and another, about the age of seventeen, walked before, bearing a chaplet of white flowers—a token that the deceased was a young and unmarried female. The corpse was followed by the parents. They were a venerable couple of the better order of peasantry. The father seemed to repress his feelings, but his fixed eye, contracted brow, and deeply furrowed face showed the struggle that was passing within. His wife hung on his arm, and wept aloud with the convulsive bursts of a mother's sorrow.

I followed the funeral into the church. The bier was placed in the centre aisle, and the chaplet of white flowers, with a pair of white gloves, was hung over the seat which the deceased had occupied.

Every one knows the soul-subduing pathos of the funeral service, for who is so fortunate as never to have followed someone he has loved to the tomb? But when performed over the remains of innocence and beauty, thus laid low in the bloom of existence, what can be more affecting? At that simple but most solemn consignment of the body to the grave"—Earth to earth, ashes to ashes, dust to dust!"—the tears of the youthful companions of the deceased flowed unrestrained. The father still seemed to struggle with his feelings, and to comfort himself with the assurance that the dead are blessed which die in the Lord; but the mother only thought of her child as a flower of the field cut down and withered in the midst of its sweetness; she was like Rachel, "mourning over her children, and would not be comforted."

On returning to the inn I learnt the whole story of the deceased. It was a simple one, and such as has often been told. She had been the beauty and pride of the village. Her father had once been an opulent farmer, but was reduced in circumstances. This was an only child, and brought up entirely at home in the simplicity of rural life. She had been the pupil of the village pastor, the favorite lamb of his little flock. The good man watched over her education with paternal care; it was limited and suitable to the sphere in which she was to move, for he only sought to make her an ornament to her station in life, not to raise her above it. The tenderness and indulgence of her parents and the exemption from all ordinary occupations had fostered a natural grace and delicacy of character that accorded with the fragile loveliness of her form. She appeared like some tender plant of the garden blooming accidentally amid the hardier natives of the fields.

The superiority of her charms was felt and acknowledged by her companions, but without envy, for it was surpassed by the unassuming gentleness and winning kindness of her manners. It might be truly said of her:

> This is the prettiest low-born lass, that ever
> Ran on the green-sward: nothing she does or seems
> But smacks of something greater than herself;
> Too noble for this place.

The village was one of those sequestered spots which still retain some vestiges of old English customs. It had its rural festivals and holiday pastimes, and still kept up some faint observance of the once popular rites of May. These, indeed, had been promoted by its present pastor, who was a lover of old customs and one of those simple Christians that think their mission fulfilled by promoting joy on earth and good-will among mankind. Under his auspices the May-pole stood from year to year in the centre of the village green; on Mayday it was decorated with garlands and streamers, and a queen or lady of the May was appointed, as in former times, to preside at the sports and distribute the prizes and rewards. The picturesque situation of the village and the fancifulness of its rustic fetes would often attract the notice of casual visitors. Among these, on one May-day, was a young officer whose regiment had been recently quartered in the neighborhood. He was charmed with the native taste that pervaded this village pageant, but, above all, with the dawning loveliness of the queen of May. It was the village favorite who was crowned with flowers, and blushing and smiling in all the beautiful confusion of girlish diffidence and delight. The artlessness of rural habits enabled him readily to make her acquaintance; he gradually won his way into her intimacy, and paid his court to her in that unthinking way in which young officers are too apt to trifle with rustic simplicity.

There was nothing in his advances to startle or alarm. He never even talked of love, but there are modes of making it more eloquent than language, and which convey it subtilely and irresistibly to the heart. The beam of the eye, the tone of voice, the thousand tendernesses which emanate from every word and look and action,—these form the true eloquence of love, and can always be felt and understood, but never described. Can we wonder that they should readily win a heart young, guileless, and susceptible? As to her, she loved almost unconsciously; she scarcely inquired what was the growing passion that was absorbing every thought and feeling, or what were to be its consequences. She, indeed, looked not to the future. When present, his looks and words occupied her whole attention; when absent, she thought but of what had passed at their recent interview. She would wander with him through the green lanes and rural scenes of the vicinity. He taught her to see new beauties in nature; he talked in the language of polite and cultivated life, and breathed into her ear the witcheries of romance and poetry.

Perhaps there could not have been a passion between the sexes more pure than this innocent girl's. The gallant figure of her youthful admirer and the splendor of his military attire might at first have charmed her eye, but it was not these that had captivated her heart. Her attachment had something in it of idolatry. She looked up to him as to a being of a superior order. She felt in his society the enthusiasm of a mind naturally delicate and poetical, and now first awakened to a keen perception of the beautiful and grand. Of the sordid distinctions of rank and fortune she thought nothing; it was the difference of intellect, of demeanor, of manners, from those of the rustic society to which she had been accustomed, that elevated him in her opinion. She would listen to him with charmed ear and downcast look of mute delight, and her cheek would mantle with enthusiasm; or if ever she ventured a shy glance of timid admiration, it was as quickly withdrawn, and she would sigh and blush at the idea of her comparative unworthiness.

Her lover was equally impassioned, but his passion was mingled with feelings of a coarser nature. He had begun the connection in levity, for he had often heard his brother-officers boast of their village conquests, and thought some triumph of the kind necessary to his reputation as a man of spirit. But he was too full of youthful fervor. His heart had not yet been rendered sufficiently cold and selfish by a wandering and a dissipated life: it caught fire from the very flame it sought to kindle, and before he was aware of the nature of his situation he became really in love.

What was he to do? There were the old obstacles which so incessantly occur in these heedless attachments. His rank in life, the prejudices of titled connections, his dependence upon a proud and unyielding father, all forbade him to think of matrimony; but when he looked down upon this innocent being, so tender and confiding, there was a purity in her manners, a blamelessness in her life, and a beseeching modesty in her looks that awed down every licentious feeling. In vain did he try to fortify himself by a thousand heartless examples of men of fashion, and to chill the glow of generous sentiment with that cold derisive levity with which he had heard them talk of female virtue: whenever he came into her presence she was still surrounded by that mysterious but impassive charm of virgin purity in whose hallowed sphere no guilty thought can live.

The sudden arrival of orders for the regiment to repair to the Continent completed the confusion of his mind. He remained for a short time in a state of the most painful irresolution; he hesitated to communicate the tidings until the day for marching was at hand, when he gave her the intelligence in the course of an evening ramble.

The idea of parting had never before occurred to her. It broke in at once upon her dream of felicity; she looked upon it as a sudden and insurmountable evil, and wept with the guileless simplicity of a child. He drew her to his bosom and kissed the tears from her soft cheek; nor did he meet with a repulse, for there are moments of mingled sorrow and tenderness which hallow the caresses of affection. He was naturally impetuous, and the sight of beauty apparently yielding in his arms, the confidence of his power over her, and the dread of losing her forever all conspired to overwhelm his better feelings: he ventured to propose that she should leave her home and be the companion of his fortunes.

He was quite a novice in seduction, and blushed and faltered at his own baseness; but so innocent of mind was his intended victim that she was at first at a loss to comprehend his meaning, and why she should leave her native village and the humble roof of her parents. When at last the nature of his proposal flashed upon her pure mind, the effect was withering. She did not weep; she did not break forth into reproach; she said not a word, but she shrunk back aghast as from a viper, gave him a look of anguish that pierced to his very soul, and, clasping her hands in agony, fled, as if for refuge, to her father's cottage.

The officer retired confounded, humiliated, and repentant. It is uncertain what might have been the result of the conflict of his feelings, had not his thoughts been diverted by the bustle of departure. New scenes, new pleasures, and new companions soon dissipated his self-reproach and stifled his tenderness; yet, amidst the stir of camps, the revelries of garrisons, the array of armies, and even the din of battles, his thoughts would sometimes steal back to the scenes of rural quiet and village simplicity—the white cottage, the footpath along the silver brook and up the hawthorn hedge, and the little village maid loitering along it, leaning on his arm and listening to him with eyes beaming with unconscious affection.

The shock which the poor girl had received in the destruction of all her ideal world had indeed been cruel. Faintings and hysterics had at first shaken her tender frame, and were succeeded by a settled and pining melancholy. She had beheld from her window the march of the departing troops. She had seen her faithless lover borne off, as if in triumph, amidst the sound of drum and trumpet and the pomp of arms. She strained a last aching gaze after him as the morning sun glittered about his figure and his plume waved in the breeze; he passed away like a bright vision from her sight, and left her all in darkness.

It would be trite to dwell on the particulars of her after story. It was, like other tales of love, melancholy. She avoided society and wandered out alone in the walks she had most frequented with her lover. She sought, like the stricken deer, to weep in silence and loneliness and brood over the barbed sorrow that rankled in her soul. Sometimes she would be seen late of an evening sitting in the porch of the village church, and the milkmaids, returning from the fields, would now and then overhear her singing some plaintive ditty in the hawthorn walk. She became fervent in her devotions at church, and as the old people saw her approach, so wasted away, yet with a hectic gloom and that hallowed air which melancholy diffuses round the form, they would make way for her as for something spiritual, and looking after her, would shake their heads in gloomy foreboding.

She felt a conviction that she was hastening to the tomb, but looked forward to it as a place of rest. The silver cord that had bound her to existence was loosed, and there seemed to be no more pleasure under the sun. If ever her gentle bosom had entertained resentment against her lover, it was extinguished. She was incapable of angry passions, and in a moment of saddened tenderness she penned him a farewell letter. It was couched in the simplest language, but touching from its very simplicity. She told him that she was dying, and did not conceal from him that his conduct was the cause. She even depicted the sufferings which she had experienced, but concluded with saying that she could not die in peace until she had sent him her forgiveness and her blessing.

By degrees her strength declined that she could no longer leave the cottage. She could only totter to the window, where, propped up in her chair, it was her enjoyment to sit all day and look out upon the landscape. Still she uttered no complaint nor imparted to any one the malady that was preying on her heart. She never even mentioned her lover's name, but would lay her head on her mother's bosom and weep in silence. Her poor parents hung in mute anxiety over this fading blossom of their hopes, still flattering themselves that it might again revive to freshness and that the bright unearthly bloom which sometimes flushed her cheek might be the promise of returning health.

In this way she was seated between them one Sunday afternoon; her hands were clasped in theirs, the lattice was thrown open, and the soft air that stole in brought with it the fragrance of the clustering honeysuckle which her own hands had trained round the window.

Her father had just been reading a chapter in the Bible: it spoke of the vanity of worldly things and of the joys of heaven: it seemed to have diffused comfort and serenity through her bosom. Her eye was fixed on the distant village church: the bell had tolled for the evening service; the last villager was lagging into the porch, and everything had sunk into that hallowed stillness peculiar to the day of rest. Her parents were gazing on her with yearning hearts. Sickness and sorrow, which pass so roughly over some faces, had given to hers the expression of a seraph's. A tear trembled in her soft blue eye. Was she thinking of her faithless lover? or were her thoughts wandering to that distant churchyard, into whose bosom she might soon be gathered?

Suddenly the clang of hoofs was heard: a horseman galloped to the cottage; he dismounted before the window; the poor girl gave a faint exclamation and sunk back in her chair: it was her repentant lover. He rushed into the house and flew to clasp her to his bosom; but her wasted form, her deathlike countenance—so wan, yet so lovely in its desolation—smote him to the soul, and he threw himself in agony at her feet. She was too faint to rise—she attempted to extend her trembling hand—her lips moved as if she spoke, but no word was articulated; she looked down upon him with a smile of unutterable tenderness, and closed her eyes forever.

Such are the particulars which I gathered of this village story. They are but scanty, and I am conscious have little novelty to recommend them. In the present rage also for strange incident and high-seasoned narrative, they may appear trite and insignificant, but they interested me strongly at the time; and, taken in connection with the affecting ceremony which I had just witnessed, left a deeper impression on my mind than many circumstances of a more striking nature. I have passed through the place since, and visited the church again from a better motive than mere curiosity. It was a wintry evening: the trees were stripped of their foliage, the churchyard looked naked and mournful, and the wind rustled coldly through the dry grass. Evergreens, however, had been planted about the grave of the village favorite, and osiers were bent over it to keep the turf uninjured.

The church door was open and I stepped in. There hung the chaplet of flowers and the gloves, as on the day of the funeral: the flowers were withered, it is true, but care seemed to have been taken that no dust should soil their whiteness. I have seen many monuments where art has exhausted its powers to awaken the sympathy of the spectator, but I have met with none that spoke more touchingly to my heart than this simple but delicate memento of departed innocence.

THE ANGLER

This day Dame Nature seem'd in love,
The lusty sap began to move,
Fresh juice did stir th' embracing vines,
And birds had drawn their valentines.
The jealous trout that low did lie,
Rose at a well-dissembled flie.
There stood my friend, with patient skill,
Attending of his trembling quill.
—Sir H. Wotton

It is said that many an unlucky urchin is induced to run away from his family and betake himself to a seafaring life from reading the history of Robinson Crusoe; and I suspect that, in like manner, many of those worthy gentlemen who are given to haunt the sides of pastoral streams with angle-rods in hand may trace the origin of their passion to the seductive pages of honest Izaak Walton. I recollect studying his Complete Angler several years since in company with a knot of friends in America, and moreover that we were all completely bitten with the angling mania. It was early in the year, but as soon as the weather was auspicious, and that the spring began to melt into the verge of summer, we took rod in hand and sallied into the country, as stark mad as was ever Don Quixote from reading books of chivalry.

One of our party had equalled the Don in the fulness of his equipments, being attired cap-a-pie for the enterprise. He wore a broad-skirted fustian coat, perplexed with half a hundred pockets; a pair of stout shoes and leathern gaiters; a basket slung on one side for fish; a patent rod, a landing net, and a score of other inconveniences only to be found in the true angler's armory. Thus harnessed for the field, he was as great a matter of stare and wonderment among the country folk, who had never seen a regular angler, as was the steel-clad hero of La Mancha among the goatherds of the Sierra Morena.

Our first essay was along a mountain brook among the highlands of the Hudson—a most unfortunate place for the execution of those piscatory tactics which had been invented along the velvet margins of quiet English rivulets. It was one of those wild streams that lavish, among our romantic solitudes, unheeded beauties enough to fill the sketch-book of a hunter of the picturesque. Sometimes it would leap down rocky shelves, making small cascades, over which the trees threw their broad balancing sprays and long nameless weeds hung in fringes from the impending banks, dripping with diamond drops. Sometimes it would brawl and fret along a ravine in the matted shade of a forest, filling it with murmurs, and after this termagant career would steal forth into open day with the most placid, demure face imaginable, as I have seen some pestilent shrew of a housewife, after filling her home with uproar and ill-humor, come dimpling out of doors, swimming and curtseying and smiling upon all the world.

How smoothly would this vagrant brook glide at such times through some bosom of green meadow land among the mountains, where the quiet was only interrupted by the occasional tinkling of a bell from the lazy cattle among the clover or the sound of a woodcutter's axe from the neighboring forest.

For my part, I was always a bungler at all kinds of sport that required either patience or adroitness, and had not angled above half an hour before I had completely "satisfied the sentiment," and convinced myself of the truth of Izaak Walton's opinion, that angling is something like poetry—a man must be born to it. I hooked myself instead of the fish, tangled my line in every tree, lost my bait, broke my rod, until I gave up the attempt in despair, and passed the day under the trees reading old Izaak, satisfied that it was his fascinating vein of honest simplicity and rural feeling that had bewitched me, and not the passion for angling. My companions, however, were more persevering in their delusion. I have them at this moment before eyes, stealing along the border of the brook where it lay open to the day or was merely fringed by shrubs and bushes. I see the bittern rising with hollow scream as they break in upon his rarely invaded haunt; the kingfisher watching them suspiciously from his dry tree that overhangs the deep black millpond in the gorge of the hills; the tortoise letting himself slip sideways from off the stone or log on which he is sunning himself; and the panic-struck frog plumping in headlong as they approach, and spreading an alarm throughout the watery world around.

I recollect also that, after toiling and watching and creeping about for the greater part of a day, with scarcely any success in spite of all our admirable apparatus, a lubberly country urchin came down from the hills with a rod made from a branch of a tree, a few yards of twine, and, as Heaven shall help me! I believe a crooked pin for a hook, baited with a vile earthworm—and in half an hour caught more fish than we had nibbles throughout the day!

But, above all, I recollect the "good, honest, wholesome, hungry" repast which we made under a beech tree just by a spring of pure sweet water that stole out of the side of a hill, and how, when it was over, one of the party read old Izaak Walton's scene with the milkmaid, while I lay on the grass and built castles in a bright pile of clouds until I fell asleep. All this may appear like mere egotism, yet I cannot refrain from uttering these recollections, which are passing like a strain of music over my mind and have been called up by an agreeable scene which I witnessed not long since.

In the morning's stroll along the banks of the Alun, a beautiful little stream which flows down from the Welsh hills and throws itself into the Dee, my attention was attracted to a group seated on the margin. On approaching I found it to consist of a veteran angler and two rustic disciples. The former was an old fellow with a wooden leg, with clothes very much but very carefully patched, betokening poverty honestly come by and decently maintained. His face bore the marks of former storms, but present fair weather; its furrows had been worn into an habitual smile, his iron-gray locks hung about his ears, and he had altogether the good-humored air of a constitutional philosopher who was disposed to take the world as it went. One of his companions was a ragged wight with the skulking look of an arrant poacher, and I'll warrant could find his way to any gentleman's fish-pond in the neighborhood in the darkest night. The other was a tall, awkward country lad, with a lounging gait, and apparently somewhat of a rustic beau. The old man was busy in examining the maw of a trout which he had just killed, to discover by its contents what insects were seasonable for bait, and was lecturing on the subject to his companions, who appeared to listen with infinite deference.

I have a kind feeling towards all "brothers of the angle" ever since I read Izaak Walton. They are men, he affirms, of a "mild, sweet, and peaceable spirit;" and my esteem for them has been increased since I met with an old "Tretyse of fishing with the Angle," in which are set forth many of the maxims of their inoffensive fraternity. "Take good hede," sayeth this honest little tretyse, "that in going about your disportes ye open no man's gates but that ye shet them again. Also ye shall not use this forsayd crafti disport for no covetousness to the encreasing and sparing of your money only, but principally for your solace, and to cause the helth of your body and specyally of your soule."*

I thought that I could perceive in the veteran angler before me an exemplification of what I had read; and there was a cheerful contentedness in his looks that quite drew me towards him. I could not but remark the gallant manner in which he stumped from one part of the brook to another, waving his rod in the air to keep the line from dragging on the ground or catching among the bushes, and the adroitness with which he would throw his fly to any particular place, sometimes skimming it lightly along a little rapid, sometimes casting it into one of those dark holes made by a twisted root or overhanging bank in which the large trout are apt to lurk. In the meanwhile he was giving instructions to his two disciples, showing them the manner in which they should handle their rods, fix their flies, and play them along the surface of the stream. The scene brought to my mind the instructions of the sage Piscator to his scholar. The country around was of that pastoral kind which Walton is fond of describing. It was a part of the great plain of Cheshire, close by the beautiful vale of Gessford, and just where the inferior Welsh hills begin to swell up from among fresh, sweet-smelling meadows. The day too, like that recorded in his work, was mild and sunshiny, with now and then a soft-dropping shower that sowed the whole earth with diamonds.

I soon fell into conversation with the old angler, and was so much entertained that, under pretext of receiving instructions in his art, I kept

* From this same treatise it would appear that angling is a more industrious and devout employment than it is generally considered: "For when ye purpose to go on your disportes in fishynge ye will not desyre greatlye many persons with you, which might let you of your game. And that ye may serve God devoutly in saying effectually your customable prayers. And thus doying, ye shall eschew and also avoyde many vices, as ydelness, which is princi-pall cause to induce man to many other vices, as it is right well known."

company with him almost the whole day, wandering along the banks of the stream and listening to his talk. He was very communicative, having all the easy garrulity of cheerful old age, and I fancy was a little flattered by having an opportunity of displaying his piscatory lore, for who does not like now and then to play the sage?

He had been much of a rambler in his day, and had passed some years of his youth in America, particularly in Savannah, where he had entered into trade and had been ruined by the indiscretion of a partner. He had afterwards experienced many ups and downs in life until he got into the navy, where his leg was carried away by a cannon-ball at the battle of Camperdown. This was the only stroke of real good-fortune he had ever experienced, for it got him a pension, which, together with some small paternal property, brought him in a revenue of nearly forty pounds. On this he retired to his native village, where he lived quietly and independently, and devoted the remainder of his life to the "noble art of angling."

I found that he had read Izaak Walton attentively, and he seemed to have imbibed all his simple frankness and prevalent good humor. Though he had been sorely buffeted about the world, he was satisfied that the world, in itself, was good and beautiful. Though he had been as roughly used in different countries as a poor sheep that is fleeced by every hedge and thicket, yet he spoke of every nation with candor and kindness, appearing to look only on the good side of things; and, above all, he was almost the only man I had ever met with who had been an unfortunate adventurer in America and had honesty and magnanimity enough to take the fault to his own door, and not to curse the country. The lad that was receiving his instructions, I learnt, was the son and heir-apparent of a fat old widow who kept the village inn, and of course a youth of some expectation, and much courted by the idle gentleman-like personages of the place. In taking him under his care, therefore, the old man had probably an eye to a privileged corner in the tap-room and an occasional cup of cheerful ale free of expense.

There is certainly something in angling—if we could forget, which anglers are apt to do, the cruelties and tortures inflicted on worms and insects—that tends to produce a gentleness of spirit and a pure serenity of mind. As the English are methodical even in their recreations, and are the most scientific of sportsmen, it has been reduced among them to perfect rule and system. Indeed, it is an amusement peculiarly adapted to the mild and highly cultivated scenery of England, where every roughness has been softened away from the landscape. It is delightful to saunter along those limpid streams which wander, like veins of silver, through the bosom of this beautiful country, leading one through a diversity of small home scenery: sometimes winding through ornamented grounds; sometimes brimming along through rich pasturage, where the fresh green is mingled with sweet-smelling flowers; sometimes venturing in sight of villages and hamlets, and then running capriciously away into shady retirements. The sweetness and serenity of nature and the quiet watchfulness of the sport gradually bring on pleasant fits of musing, which are now and then agreeably interrupted by the song of a bird, the distant whistle of the peasant, or perhaps the vagary of some fish leaping out of the still water and skimming transiently about its glassy surface. "When I would beget content," says Izaak Walton, "and increase confidence in the power and wisdom and providence of Almighty God, I will walk the meadows by some gliding stream, and there contemplate the lilies that take no care, and those very many other little living creatures that are not only created, but fed (man knows not how) by the goodness of the God of Nature, and therefore trust in Him."

I cannot forbear to give another quotation from one of those ancient champions of angling which breathes the same innocent and happy spirit:

> Let me live harmlessly, and near the brink
>   Of Trent or Avon have a dwelling-place:
> Where I may see my quill, or cork, down sink
>   With eager bite of Pike, or Bleak, or Dace;
> And on the world and my Creator think:
>   Whilst some men strive ill-gotten goods t' embrace:
> And others spend their time in base excess
>   Of wine, or worse, in war or wantonness.
>
> Let them that will, these pastimes still pursue,
>   And on such pleasing fancies feed their fill;

So I the fields and meadows green may view,
And daily by fresh rivers walk at will,
Among the daisies and the violets blue,
Red hyacinth and yellow daffodil.*

On parting with the old angler I inquired after his place of abode, and, happening to be in the neighborhood of the village a few evenings afterwards, I had the curiosity to seek him out. I found him living in a small cottage containing only one room, but a perfect curiosity in its method and arrangement. It was on the skirts of the village, on a green bank a little back from the road, with a small garden in front stocked with kitchen herbs and adorned with a few flowers. The whole front of the cottage was overrun with a honeysuckle. On the top was a ship for a weathercock. The interior was fitted up in a truly nautical style, his ideas of comfort and convenience having been acquired on the berth-deck of a man-of-war. A hammock was slung from the ceiling which in the daytime was lashed up so as to take but little room. From the centre of the chamber hung a model of a ship, of his own workmanship. Two or three chairs, a table, and a large sea-chest formed the principal movables. About the wall were stuck up naval ballads, such as "Admiral Hosier's Ghost," "All in the Downs," and "Tom Bowling," intermingled with pictures of sea fights, among which the battle of Camperdown held a distinguished place. The mantelpiece was decorated with seashells, over which hung a quadrant, flanked by two woodcuts of most bitter-looking naval commanders. His implements for angling were carefully disposed on nails and hooks about the room. On a shelf was arranged his library, containing a work on angling, much worn, a Bible covered with canvas, an odd volume or two of voyages, a nautical almanac, and a book of songs.

His family consisted of a large black cat with one eye, and a parrot which he had caught and tamed and educated himself in the course of one of his voyages, and which uttered a variety of sea-phrases with the hoarse brattling tone of a veteran boatswain. The establishment reminded me of that of the renowned Robinson Crusoe; it was kept in neat order, everything being "stowed away" with the regularity of

* J. Davors.

a ship of war; and he informed me that he "scoured the deck every morning and swept it between meals."

I found him seated on a bench before the door, smoking his pipe in the soft evening sunshine. His cat was purring soberly on the threshold, and his parrot describing some strange evolutions in an iron ring that swung in the centre of his cage. He had been angling all day, and gave me a history of his sport with as much minuteness as a general would talk over a campaign; being particularly animated in relating the manner in which he had taken a large trout, which had completely tasked all his skill and wariness, and which he had sent as a trophy to mine hostess of the inn.

How comforting it is to see a cheerful and contented old age, and to behold a poor fellow like this, after being tempest-tost through life, safely moored in a snug and quiet harbor in the evening of his days! His happiness, however, sprung from within himself and was independent of external circumstances, for he had that inexhaustible good nature which is the most precious gift of heaven, spreading itself like oil over the troubled sea of thought, and keeping the mind smooth and equable in the roughest weather.

On inquiring further about him, I learnt that he was a universal favorite in the village and the oracle of the tap-room, where he delighted the rustics with his songs, and, like Sindbad, astonished them with his stories of strange lands and shipwrecks and sea fights. He was much noticed too by gentlemen sportsmen of the neighborhood; had taught several of them the art of angling, and was a privileged visitor to their kitchens. The whole tenor of his life was quiet and inoffensive, being principally passed about the neighboring streams when the weather and season were favorable; and at other times he employed himself at home, preparing his fishing-tackle for the next campaign or manufacturing rods, nets, and flies for his patrons and pupils among the gentry.

He was a regular attendant at church on Sundays, though he generally fell asleep during the sermon. He had made it his particular request that when he died he should be buried in a green spot which he could see from his seat in church, and which he had marked out ever since he was a boy, and had thought of when far from home on the raging sea in danger of being food for the fishes: it was the spot where his father and mother had been buried.

I have done, for I fear that my reader is growing weary; but I could not refrain from drawing the picture of this worthy "brother of the angle," who has made me more than ever in love with the theory, though I fear I shall never be adroit in the practice, of his art; and I will conclude this rambling sketch in the words of honest Izaak Walton, by craving the blessing of St. Peter's Master upon my reader, "and upon all that are true lovers of virtue, and dare trust in His providence, and be quiet, and go a-angling."

THE LEGEND OF SLEEPY HOLLOW

(Found among the papers of the late Diedrich Knickerbocker)

> A pleasing land of drowsy head it was,
> Of dreams that wave before the half-shut eye,
> And of gay castles in the clouds that pass,
> Forever flushing round a summer sky.
>
> —Castle of Indolence

In the bosom of one of those spacious coves which indent the eastern shore of the Hudson, at that broad expansion of the river denominated by the ancient Dutch navigators the Tappan Zee, and where they always prudently shortened sail, and implored the protection of St. Nicholas when they crossed, there lies a small market town or rural port which by some is called Greensburg, but which is more generally and properly known by the name of Tarry Town. This name was given, we are told, in former days by the good housewives of the adjacent country from the inveterate propensity of their husbands to linger about the village tavern on market days. Be that as it may, I do not vouch for the fact, but merely advert to it, for the sake of being precise and authentic. Not far from this village, perhaps about two miles, there is a little valley, or rather lap of land, among high hills, which is one of the quietest places in the whole world. A small brook glides through it, with just murmur enough to lull one to repose, and the occasional whistle of a quail or tapping of a woodpecker is almost the only sound that ever breaks in upon the uniform tranquillity.

I recollect that when a stripling, my first exploit in squirrel-shooting was in a grove of tall walnut trees that shades one side of the valley. I had wandered into it at noontime, when all nature is peculiarly quiet, and was startled by the roar of my own gun as it broke the sabbath stillness around and was prolonged and reverberated by the angry echoes. If ever I should wish for a retreat, whither I might steal from the world and its distractions and dream quietly away the remnant of a troubled life, I know of none more promising than this little valley.

From the listless repose of the place and the peculiar character of its inhabitants, who are descendants from the original Dutch settlers, this sequestered glen has long been known by the name of Sleepy Hollow, and its rustic lads are called the Sleepy Hollow Boys throughout all the neighboring country. A drowsy, dreamy influence seems to hang over the land and to pervade the very atmosphere. Some say that the place was bewitched by a High German doctor during the early days of the settlement; others, that an old Indian chief, the prophet or wizard of his tribe, held his powwows there before the country was discovered by Master Hendrick Hudson. Certain it is, the place still continues under the sway of some witching power that holds a spell over the minds of the good people, causing them to walk in a continual reverie. They are given to all kinds of marvellous beliefs, are subject to trances and visions, and frequently see strange sights and hear music and voices in the air. The whole neighborhood abounds with local tales, haunted spots, and twilight superstitions; stars shoot and meteors glare oftener across the valley than in any other part of the country, and the nightmare, with her whole ninefold, seems to make it the favorite scene of her gambols.

The dominant spirit, however, that haunts this enchanted region, and seems to be commander-in-chief of all the powers of the air, is the apparition of a figure on horseback without a head. It is said by some to be the ghost of a Hessian trooper whose head had been carried away by a cannonball in some nameless battle during the Revolutionary War, and who is ever and anon seen by the country-folk hurrying along in the gloom of night as if on the wings of the wind. His haunts are not confined to the valley, but extend at times to the adjacent roads, and especially to the vicinity of a church at no great distance. Indeed, certain of the most authentic historians of those parts, who have been careful in collecting and collating the floating facts concerning this spectre, allege that the body of the trooper, having been buried in the churchyard, the ghost rides forth to the scene of battle in nightly quest of his head, and that the rushing speed with which he sometimes passes along the Hollow, like a midnight blast, is owing to his being belated and in a hurry to get back to the church-yard before daybreak.

Such is the general purport of this legendary superstition, which has furnished materials for many a wild story in that region of shadows; and the spectre is known at all the country firesides by the name of the Headless Horseman of Sleepy Hollow.

It is remarkable that the visionary propensity I have mentioned is not confined to the native inhabitants of the valley, but is unconsciously imbibed by every one who resides there for a time. However wide awake they may have been before they entered that sleepy region, they are sure in a little time to inhale the witching influence of the air and begin to grow imaginative—to dream dreams and see apparitions.

I mention this peaceful spot with all possible laud; for it is in such little retired Dutch valleys, found here and there embosomed in the great State of New York, that population, manners, and customs remain fixed, while the great torrent of migration and improvement, which is making such incessant changes in other parts of this restless country, sweeps by them unobserved. They are like those little nooks of still water which border a rapid stream, where we may see the straw and bubble riding quietly at anchor or slowly revolving in their mimic harbor, undisturbed by the rush of the passing current. Though many years have elapsed since I trod the drowsy shades of Sleepy Hollow, yet I question whether I should not still find the same trees and the same families vegetating in its sheltered bosom.

In this by-place of nature there abode, in a remote period of American history—that is to say, some thirty years since—a worthy wight of the name of Ichabod Crane, who sojourned, or, as he expressed it, "tarried," in Sleepy Hollow for the purpose of instructing the children of the vicinity. He was a native of Connecticut, a state which supplies the Union with pioneers for the mind as well as for the forest, and sends forth yearly its legions of frontier woodmen and country schoolmasters. The cognomen of Crane was not inapplicable to his person. He was tall, but exceedingly lank, with narrow shoulders, long arms and legs, hands that dangled a mile out of his sleeves, feet that might have served for shovels, and his whole frame most loosely hung together. His head was small, and flat at top, with huge ears, large green glassy eyes, and a long snipe nose, so that it looked like a weathercock perched upon his spindle neck, to tell which way the wind blew. To see him striding along the profile of a hill on a windy day, with his clothes bagging and fluttering about him, one might have mistaken him for the genius of famine descending upon the earth or some scarecrow eloped from a cornfield.

His school-house was a low building of one large room, rudely constructed of logs, the windows partly glazed and partly patched with leaves of old copybooks. It was most ingeniously secured at vacant hours by a withe twisted in the handle of the door and stakes set against the window shutters; so that, though a thief might get in with perfect ease, he would find some embarrassment in getting out—-an idea most probably borrowed by the architect, Yost Van Houten, from the mystery of an eel-pot. The school-house stood in a rather lonely but pleasant situation, just at the foot of a woody hill, with a brook running close by and a formidable birch tree growing at one end of it. From hence the low murmur of his pupils' voices, conning over their lessons, might be heard in a drowsy summer's day like the hum of a bee-hive, interrupted now and then by the authoritative voice of the master in the tone of menace or command, or, peradventure, by the appalling sound of the birch as he urged some tardy loiterer along the flowery path of knowledge. Truth to say, he was a conscientious man, and ever bore in mind the golden maxim, "Spare the rod and spoil the child." Ichabod Crane's scholars certainly were not spoiled.

I would not have it imagined, however, that he was one of those cruel potentates of the school who joy in the smart of their subjects; on the contrary, he administered justice with discrimination rather than severity, taking the burden off the backs of the weak and laying it on those of the strong. Your mere puny stripling, that winced at the least flourish of the rod, was passed by with indulgence; but the claims of justice were satisfied by inflicting a double portion on some little tough, wrong-headed, broad-skirted Dutch urchin, who sulked and swelled and grew dogged and sullen beneath the birch. All this he called "doing his duty by their parents;" and he never inflicted a chastisement without following it by the assurance, so consolatory to the smarting urchin, that "he would remember it and thank him for it the longest day he had to live."

When school hours were over, he was even the companion and playmate of the larger boys, and on holiday afternoons would convoy some of the smaller ones home who happened to have pretty sisters or good housewives for mothers, noted for the comforts of the cupboard. Indeed, it behooved him to keep on good terms with his pupils. The revenue arising from his school was small, and would have been scarcely sufficient to furnish him with daily bread, for he was a huge feeder, and, though lank, had the dilating powers of an anaconda; but to help out his maintenance he was, according to country custom in those parts, boarded and lodged at the houses of the farmers whose children he instructed. With these he lived successively a week at a time, thus going the rounds of the neighborhood with all his worldly effects tied up in a cotton handkerchief.

That all this might not be too onerous on the purses of his rustic patrons, who are apt to consider the costs of schooling a grievous burden and schoolmasters as mere drones, he had various ways of rendering himself both useful and agreeable. He assisted the farmers occasionally in the lighter labors of their farms, helped to make hay, mended the fences, took the horses to water, drove the cows from pasture, and cut wood for the winter fire. He laid aside, too, all the dominant dignity and absolute sway with which he lorded it in his little empire, the school, and became wonderfully gentle and ingratiating. He found favor in the eyes of the mothers by petting the children, particularly the youngest; and like the lion bold, which whilom so magnanimously the lamb did hold, he would sit with a child on one knee and rock a cradle with his foot for whole hours together.

In addition to his other vocations, he was the singing master of the neighborhood and picked up many bright shillings by instructing the young folks in psalmody. It was a matter of no little vanity to him on Sundays to take his station in front of the church gallery with a band of chosen singers, where, in his own mind, he completely carried away the palm from the parson. Certain it is, his voice resounded far above all the rest of the congregation, and there are peculiar quavers still to be heard in that church, and which may even be heard half a mile off, quite to the opposite side of the mill pond on a still Sunday morning, which are said to be legitimately descended from the nose of Ichabod Crane. Thus, by divers little makeshifts in that ingenious way which is commonly denominated "by hook and by crook," the worthy pedagogue got on tolerably enough, and was thought, by all who understood nothing of the labor of headwork, to have a wonderfully easy life of it.

The schoolmaster is generally a man of some importance in the female circle of a rural neighborhood, being considered a kind of idle, gentleman-like personage of vastly superior taste and accomplishments to the rough country swains, and, indeed, inferior in learning only to the parson. His appearance, therefore, is apt to occasion some little stir at the tea-table of a farmhouse and the addition of a supernumerary dish of cakes or sweetmeats, or, peradventure, the parade of a silver teapot. Our man of letters, therefore, was peculiarly happy in the smiles of all the country damsels. How he would figure among them in the church-yard between services on Sundays, gathering grapes for them from the wild vines that overrun the surrounding trees; reciting for their amusement all the epitaphs on the tombstones; or sauntering, with a whole bevy of them, along the banks of the adjacent mill pond, while the more bashful country bumpkins hung sheepishly back, envying his superior elegance and address.

From his half-itinerant life, also, he was a kind of travelling gazette, carrying the whole budget of local gossip from house to house, so that his appearance was always greeted with satisfaction. He was, moreover, esteemed by the women as a man of great erudition, for he had read several books quite through, and was a perfect master of Cotton Mather's History of New England Witchcraft, in which, by the way, he most firmly and potently believed.

He was, in fact, an odd mixture of small shrewdness and simple credulity. His appetite for the marvellous and his powers of digesting it, were equally extraordinary, and both had been increased by his residence in this spellbound region. No tale was too gross or monstrous for his capacious swallow. It was often his delight, after his school was dismissed in the afternoon, to stretch himself on the rich bed of clover bordering the little brook that whimpered by his school-house, and there con over old Mather's direful tales until the gathering dusk of the evening made the printed page a mere mist before his eyes. Then, as he wended his way by swamp and stream and awful woodland to the farmhouse where he happened to be quartered, every sound of nature at that witching hour fluttered his excited imagination—the moan of the whip-poor-will* from the hillside; the boding cry of the tree-toad, that harbinger of storm; the dreary hooting of the screech-owl; or the sudden rustling in the thicket of birds frightened from their roost. The fire-flies, too, which sparkled most vividly in the darkest places, now and then startled him as one of uncommon brightness would stream across his path; and if, by chance, a huge blockhead of a beetle came winging his blundering flight against him, the poor varlet was ready to give up the ghost, with the idea that he was struck with a witch's token. His only resource on such occasions, either to drown thought or drive away evil spirits, was to sing psalm tunes; and the good people of Sleepy Hollow, as they sat by their doors of an evening, were often filled with awe at hearing his nasal melody, "in linked sweetness long drawn out," floating from the distant hill or along the dusky road.

Another of his sources of fearful pleasure was to pass long winter evenings with the old Dutch wives as they sat spinning by the fire, with a row of apples roasting and spluttering along the hearth, and listen to their marvellous tales of ghosts and goblins, and haunted fields, and haunted brooks, and haunted bridges, and haunted houses, and particularly of the headless horseman, or Galloping Hessian of the Hollow, as they sometimes called him. He would delight them equally by his anecdotes of witchcraft and of the direful omens and portentous sights and sounds in the air which prevailed in the earlier times of Connecticut; and would frighten them woefully with speculations upon comets and shooting stars, and with the alarming fact that the world did absolutely turn round and that they were half the time topsy-turvy.

But if there was a pleasure in all this, while snugly cuddling in the chimney-corner of a chamber that was all of a ruddy glow from the crackling wood fire, and where, of course, no spectre dared to show its face, it was dearly purchased by the terrors of his subsequent walk homewards. What fearful shapes and shadows beset his path amidst the dim and ghastly glare of a snowy night! With what wistful look did he eye every trembling ray of light streaming across the waste fields from some distant window! How often was he appalled by some shrub covered with snow, which, like a sheeted spectre, beset his very path! How often did he shrink with curdling awe at the sound of his own

* The whip-poor-will is a bird which is only heard at night. It receives its name from its note, which is thought to resemble those words.

steps on the frosty crust beneath his feet, and dread to look over his shoulder, lest he should behold some uncouth being tramping close behind him! And how often was he thrown into complete dismay by some rushing blast howling among the trees, in the idea that it was the Galloping Hessian on one of his nightly scourings!

All these, however, were mere terrors of the night, phantoms of the mind, that walk in darkness; and though he had seen many spectres in his time, and been more than once beset by Satan in divers shapes in his lonely perambulations, yet daylight put an end to all these evils; and he would have passed a pleasant life of it, in despite of the devil and all his works, if his path had not been crossed by a being that causes more perplexity to mortal man than ghosts, goblins, and the whole race of witches put together, and that was—a woman.

Among the musical disciples who assembled one evening in each week to receive his instructions in psalmody was Katrina Van Tassel, the daughter and only child of a substantial Dutch farmer. She was a blooming lass of fresh eighteen; plump as a partridge, ripe and melting and rosy-cheeked as one of her father's peaches, and universally famed, not merely for her beauty, but her vast expectations. She was withal a little of a coquette, as might be perceived even in her dress, which was a mixture of ancient and modern fashions, as most suited to set off her charms. She wore the ornaments of pure yellow gold which her great-great-grandmother had brought over from Saardam; the tempting stomacher of the olden time, and withal a provokingly short petticoat, to display the prettiest foot and ankle in the country round.

Ichabod Crane had a soft and foolish heart towards the sex, and it is not to be wondered at that so tempting a morsel soon found favor in his eyes, more especially after he had visited her in her paternal mansion. Old Baltus Van Tassel was a perfect picture of a thriving, contented, liberal-hearted farmer. He seldom, it is true, sent either his eyes or his thoughts beyond the boundaries of his own farm, but within those everything was snug, happy, and well conditioned. He was satisfied with his wealth but not proud of it, and piqued himself upon the hearty abundance, rather than the style, in which he lived. His stronghold was situated on the banks of the Hudson, in one of those green, sheltered, fertile nooks in which the Dutch farmers are so fond of nestling. A great elm tree spread its broad branches over it, at the foot of which bubbled up a spring of the softest and sweetest water in a little well formed of a barrel, and then stole sparkling away through the grass to a neighboring brook that bubbled along among alders and dwarf willows. Hard by the farmhouse was a vast barn, that might have served for a church; every window and crevice of which seemed bursting forth with the treasures of the farm; the flail was busily resounding within it from morning to night; swallows and martins skimmed twittering about the eaves; and rows of pigeons, some with one eye turned up, as if watching the weather, some with their heads under their wings or buried in their bosoms, and others, swelling, and cooing, and bowing about their dames, were enjoying the sunshine on the roof. Sleek, unwieldy porkers were grunting in the repose and abundance of their pens, whence sallied forth, now and then, troops of sucking pigs as if to snuff the air. A stately squadron of snowy geese were riding in an adjoining pond, convoying whole fleets of ducks; regiments of turkeys were gobbling through the farmyard, and guinea fowls fretting about it, like ill-tempered housewives, with their peevish, discontented cry. Before the barn door strutted the gallant cock, that pattern of a husband, a warrior, and a fine gentleman, clapping his burnished wings and crowing in the pride and gladness of his heart—sometimes tearing up the earth with his feet, and then generously calling his ever-hungry family of wives and children to enjoy the rich morsel which he had discovered.

The pedagogue's mouth watered as he looked upon this sumptuous promise of luxurious winter fare. In his devouring mind's eye he pictured to himself every roasting-pig running about with a pudding in his belly and an apple in his mouth; the pigeons were snugly put to bed in a comfortable pie and tucked in with a coverlet of crust; the geese were swimming in their own gravy; and the ducks pairing cosily in dishes, like snug married couples, with a decent competency of onion sauce. In the porkers he saw carved out the future sleek side of bacon and juicy relishing ham; not a turkey but he beheld daintily trussed up, with its gizzard under its wing, and, peradventure, a necklace of savory sausages; and even bright Chanticleer himself lay sprawling on his back in a side-dish, with uplifted claws, as if craving that quarter which his chivalrous spirit disdained to ask while living.

As the enraptured Ichabod fancied all this, and as he rolled his great green eyes over the fat meadow lands, the rich fields of wheat, of rye, of buckwheat, and Indian corn, and the orchards burdened with ruddy fruit, which surrounded the warm tenement of Van Tassel, his heart yearned after the damsel who was to inherit these domains, and his imagination expanded with the idea how they might be readily turned into cash and the money invested in immense tracts of wild land and shingle palaces in the wilderness. Nay, his busy fancy already realized his hopes, and presented to him the blooming Katrina, with a whole family of children, mounted on the top of a wagon loaded with household trumpery, with pots and kettles dangling beneath, and he beheld himself bestriding a pacing mare, with a colt at her heels, setting out for Kentucky, Tennessee, or the Lord knows where!

When he entered the house, the conquest of his heart was complete. It was one of those spacious farmhouses with high-ridged but lowly sloping roofs, built in the style handed down from the first Dutch settlers, the low projecting eaves forming a piazza along the front capable of being closed up in bad weather. Under this were hung flails, harness, various utensils of husbandry, and nets for fishing in the neighboring river. Benches were built along the sides for summer use, and a great spinning wheel at one end and a churn at the other showed the various uses to which this important porch might be devoted. From this piazza, the wondering Ichabod entered the hall, which formed the centre of the mansion and the place of usual residence. Here rows of resplendent pewter, ranged on a long dresser, dazzled his eyes. In one corner stood a huge bag of wool ready to be spun; in another a quantity of linsey-woolsey just from the loom; ears of Indian corn and strings of dried apples and peaches hung in gay festoons along the walls, mingled with the gaud of red peppers; and a door left ajar gave him a peep into the best parlor, where the claw-footed chairs and dark mahogany tables shone like mirrors; andirons, with their accompanying shovel and tongs, glistened from their covert of asparagus tops; mock-oranges and conch shells decorated the mantelpiece; strings of various-colored birds' eggs were suspended above it; a great ostrich egg was hung from the centre of the room, and a corner cupboard, knowingly left open, displayed immense treasures of old silver and well-mended china.

From the moment Ichabod laid his eyes upon these regions of delight, the peace of his mind was at an end, and his only study was how to gain the affections of the peerless daughter of Van Tassel. In this enterprise, however, he had more real difficulties than generally fell to the lot of a knight-errant of yore, who seldom had anything but giants, enchanters, fiery dragons, and such-like easily conquered adversaries to contend with; and had to make his way merely through gates of iron and brass and walls of adamant to the castle keep, where the lady of his heart was confined; all which he achieved as easily as a man would carve his way to the centre of a Christmas pie, and then the lady gave him her hand as a matter of course. Ichabod, on the contrary, had to win his way to the heart of a country coquette, beset with a labyrinth of whims and caprices, which were forever presenting new difficulties and impediments, and he had to encounter a host of fearful adversaries of real flesh and blood, the numerous rustic admirers who beset every portal to her heart, keeping a watchful and angry eye upon each other, but ready to fly out in the common cause against any new competitor.

Among these, the most formidable was a burly, roaring, roistering blade of the name of Abraham—or, according to the Dutch abbreviation, Brom—Van Brunt, the hero of the country round, which rang with his feats of strength and hardihood. He was broad-shouldered and double-jointed, with short curly black hair and a bluff but not unpleasant countenance, having a mingled air of fun and arrogance. From his Herculean frame and great powers of limb, he had received the nickname of Brom Bones, by which he was universally known. He was famed for great knowledge and skill in horsemanship, being as dexterous on horseback as a Tartar. He was foremost at all races and cock-fights, and, with the ascendancy which bodily strength acquires in rustic life, was the umpire in all disputes, setting his hat on one side and giving his decisions with an air and tone admitting of no gainsay or appeal. He was always ready for either a fight or a frolic, but had more mischief than ill will in his composition; and with all his overbearing roughness, there was a strong dash of waggish good humor at bottom. He had three or four boon companions who regarded him as their model, and at the head of whom he scoured the country, attending every scene of feud or merriment for miles around. In cold weather he was distinguished by a fur cap surmounted with a flaunting fox's tail; and when the folks at a country gathering descried this well-known crest at a distance, whisking about among a squad of hard riders, they always stood by for a squall. Sometimes his crew would be heard dashing along past the farm houses at midnight with whoop and halloo, like a troop of Don Cossacks, and the old dames, startled out of their sleep, would listen for a moment till the hurry-scurry had clattered by, and then exclaim, "Ay, there goes Brom Bones and his gang!" The neighbors looked upon him with a mixture of awe, admiration, and good will; and when any madcap prank or rustic brawl occurred in the vicinity, always shook their heads and warranted Brom Bones was at the bottom of it.

This rantipole hero had for some time singled out the blooming Katrina for the object of his uncouth gallantries, and, though his amorous toyings were something like the gentle caresses and endearments of a bear, yet it was whispered that she did not altogether discourage his hopes. Certain it is, his advances were signals for rival candidates to retire who felt no inclination to cross a line in his amours; insomuch, that when his horse was seen tied to Van Tassel's paling on a Sunday night, a sure sign that his master was courting—or, as it is termed, "sparking"—within, all other suitors passed by in despair and carried the war into other quarters.

Such was the formidable rival with whom Ichabod Crane had to contend, and, considering all things, a stouter man than he would have shrunk from the competition and a wiser man would have despaired. He had, however, a happy mixture of pliability and perseverance in his nature; he was in form and spirit like a supple jack—yielding, but although; though he bent, he never broke and though he bowed beneath the slightest pressure, yet the moment it was away, jerk! he was as erect and carried his head as high as ever.

To have taken the field openly against his rival would have been madness; for he was not man to be thwarted in his amours, any more than that stormy lover, Achilles. Ichabod, therefore, made his advances in a quiet and gently insinuating manner. Under cover of his character of singing master, he made frequent visits at the farmhouse; not that he had anything to apprehend from the meddlesome interference of parents, which is so often a stumbling block in the path of lovers. Balt Van Tassel was an easy, indulgent soul; he loved his daughter better even than his pipe, and like a reasonable man and an excellent father, let her have her way in everything. His notable little wife, too, had enough to do to attend to her housekeeping and manage her poultry, for as she sagely observed, ducks and geese are foolish things and must be looked after, but girls can take care of themselves. Thus while the busy dame bustled about the house or plied her spinning wheel at one end of the piazza, honest Balt would sit smoking his evening pipe at the other, watching the achievements of a little wooden warrior who, armed with a sword in each hand, was most valiantly fighting the wind on the pinnacle of the barn. In the meantime, Ichabod would carry on his suit with the daughter by the side of the spring under the great elm, or sauntering along in the twilight, that hour so favorable to the lover's eloquence.

I profess not to know how women's hearts are wooed and won. To me they have always been matters of riddle and admiration. Some seem to have but one vulnerable point, or door of access, while others have a thousand avenues and may be captured in a thousand different ways. It is a great triumph of skill to gain the former, but still greater proof of generalship to maintain possession of the latter, for the man must battle for his fortress at every door and window. He who wins a thousand common hearts is therefore entitled to some renown, but he who keeps undisputed sway over the heart of a coquette is indeed a hero. Certain it is, this was not the case with the redoubtable Brom Bones; and from the moment Ichabod Crane made his advances, the interests of the former evidently declined; his horse was no longer seen tied at the palings on Sunday nights, and a deadly feud gradually arose between him and the preceptor of Sleepy Hollow.

Brom, who had a degree of rough chivalry in his nature, would fain have carried matters to open warfare, and have settled their pretensions to the lady according to the mode of those most concise and simple reasoners, the knights-errant of yore—by single combat; but Ichabod was too conscious of the superior might of his adversary to enter the lists against him: he had overheard a boast of Bones, that he would "double the schoolmaster up and lay him on a shelf of his own school-house;" and he was too wary to give him an opportunity. There was something extremely provoking in this obstinately pacific system; it left Brom no alternative but to draw upon the funds of rustic waggery in his disposition and to play off boorish practical jokes upon his rival. Ichabod became the object of whimsical persecution to Bones and his gang of rough riders. They harried his hitherto peaceful domains; smoked out his singing school by stopping up the chimney; broke into the school-house at night in spite of its formidable fastenings of withe and window stakes, and turned everything topsy-turvy; so that the poor schoolmaster began to think all the witches in the country held their meetings there. But, what was still more annoying, Brom took all opportunities of turning him into ridicule in presence of his mistress, and had a scoundrel dog whom he taught to whine in the most ludicrous manner, and introduced as a rival of Ichabod's, to instruct her in psalmody.

In this way, matters went on for some time without producing any material effect on the relative situation of the contending powers. On a fine autumnal afternoon Ichabod, in pensive mood, sat enthroned on the lofty stool whence he usually watched all the concerns of his little literary realm. In his hand he swayed a ferule, that sceptre of despotic power; the birch of justice reposed on three nails behind the throne, a constant terror to evil-doers; while on the desk before him might be seen sundry contraband articles and prohibited weapons detected upon the persons of idle urchins, such as half-munched apples, popguns, whirligigs, fly-cages, and whole legions of rampant little paper game-cocks. Apparently there had been some appalling act of justice recently inflicted, for his scholars were all busily intent upon their books or slyly whispering behind them with one eye kept upon the master, and a kind of buzzing stillness reigned throughout the school-room. It was suddenly interrupted by the appearance of a negro in tow-cloth jacket and trowsers, a round-crowned fragment of a hat like the cap of Mercury, and mounted on the back of a ragged, wild, half-broken colt, which he managed with a rope by way of halter. He came clattering up to the school door with an invitation to Ichabod to attend a merry-making or "quilting frolic" to be held that evening at Mynheer Van Tassel's; and, having delivered his message with that air of importance and effort at fine language which a negro is apt to display on petty embassies of the kind, he dashed over the brook, and was seen scampering away up the hollow, full of the importance and hurry of his mission.

All was now bustle and hubbub in the late quiet school-room. The scholars were hurried through their lessons without stopping at trifles; those who were nimble skipped over half with impunity, and those who were tardy had a smart application now and then in the rear to quicken their speed or help them over a tall word. Books were flung aside without being put away on the shelves; inkstands were overturned, benches thrown down, and the whole school was turned loose an hour before the usual time, bursting forth like a legion of young imps, yelping and racketing about the green in joy at their early emancipation.

The gallant Ichabod now spent at least an extra half hour at his toilet, brushing and furbishing up his best, and indeed only, suit of rusty black, and arranging his looks by a bit of broken looking-glass that hung up in the school-house. That he might make his appearance before his mistress in the true style of a cavalier, he borrowed a horse from the farmer with whom he was domiciliated, a choleric old Dutchman of the name of Hans Van Ripper, and, thus gallantly mounted, issued forth like a knight-errant in quest of adventures. But it is meet I should, in the true spirit of romantic story, give some account of the looks and equipments of my hero and his steed. The animal he bestrode was a broken-down plough-horse that had outlived almost everything but his viciousness. He was gaunt and shagged, with a ewe neck and a head like a hammer; his rusty mane and tail were tangled and knotted with burrs; one eye had lost its pupil and was glaring and spectral, but the other had the gleam of a genuine devil in it. Still, he must have had fire and mettle in his day, if we may judge from the name he bore of Gunpowder. He had, in fact, been a favorite steed of his master's, the choleric Van Ripper, who was a furious rider, and had infused, very probably, some of his own spirit into the animal; for, old and broken down as he looked, there was more of the lurking devil in him than in any young filly in the country.

Ichabod was a suitable figure for such a steed. He rode with short stirrups, which brought his knees nearly up to the pommel of the saddle;

his sharp elbows stuck out like grasshoppers'; he carried his whip perpendicularly in his hand like a sceptre; and as his horse jogged on, the motion of his arms was not unlike the flapping of a pair of wings. A small wool hat rested on the top of his nose, for so his scanty strip of forehead might be called, and the skirts of his black coat fluttered out almost to his horse's tail. Such was the appearance of Ichabod and his steed as they shambled out of the gate of Hans Van Ripper, and it was altogether such an apparition as is seldom to be met with in broad daylight.

It was, as I have said, a fine autumnal day, the sky was clear and serene, and nature wore that rich and golden livery which we always associate with the idea of abundance. The forests had put on their sober brown and yellow, while some trees of the tenderer kind had been nipped by the frosts into brilliant dyes of orange, purple, and scarlet. Streaming files of wild-ducks began to make their appearance high in the air; the bark of the squirrel might be heard from the groves of beech and hickory nuts, and the pensive whistle of the quail at intervals from the neighboring stubble field.

The small birds were taking their farewell banquets. In the fulness of their revelry they fluttered, chirping and frolicking, from bush to bush and tree to tree, capricious from the very profusion and variety around them. There was the honest cock robin, the favorite game of stripling sportsmen, with its loud querulous note; and the twittering blackbirds, flying in sable clouds; and the golden-winged woodpecker, with his crimson crest, his broad black gorget, and splendid plumage; and the cedar bird, with its red-tipt wings and yellow-tipt tail, and its little monteiro cap of feathers; and the blue jay, that noisy coxcomb, in his gay light-blue coat and white under-clothes, screaming and chattering, bobbing and nodding and bowing, and pretending to be on good terms with every songster of the grove.

As Ichabod jogged slowly on his way, his eye, ever open to every symptom of culinary abundance, ranged with delight over the treasures of jolly autumn. On all sides he beheld vast store of apples—some hanging in oppressive opulence on the trees, some gathered into baskets and barrels for the market, others heaped up in rich piles for the cider press. Farther on he beheld great fields of Indian corn, with its golden ears peeping from their leafy coverts and holding out the promise of cakes and hasty pudding; and the yellow pumpkins lying beneath them, turning up their fair round bellies to the sun, and giving ample prospects of the most luxurious of pies; and anon he passed the fragrant buckwheat fields, breathing the odor of the beehive, and as he beheld them, soft anticipations stole over his mind of dainty slapjacks, well buttered and garnished with honey or treacle by the delicate little dimpled hand of Katrina Van Tassel.

Thus feeding his mind with many sweet thoughts and "sugared suppositions," he journeyed along the sides of a range of hills which look out upon some of the goodliest scenes of the mighty Hudson. The sun gradually wheeled his broad disk down into the west. The wide bosom of the Tappan Zee lay motionless and glassy, excepting that here and there a gentle undulation waved and prolonged the blue shadow of the distant mountain. A few amber clouds floated in the sky, without a breath of air to move them. The horizon was of a fine golden tint, changing gradually into a pure apple green, and from that into the deep blue of the mid-heaven. A slanting ray lingered on the woody crests of the precipices that overhung some parts of the river, giving greater depth to the dark-gray and purple of their rocky sides. A sloop was loitering in the distance, dropping slowly down with the tide, her sail hanging uselessly against the mast, and as the reflection of the sky gleamed along the still water it seemed as if the vessel was suspended in the air.

It was toward evening that Ichabod arrived at the castle of the Heer Van Tassel, which he found thronged with the pride and flower of the adjacent country—old farmers, a spare leathern-faced race, in homespun coats and breeches, blue stockings, huge shoes, and magnificent pewter buckles; their brisk withered little dames, in close crimped caps, long-waisted shortgowns, homespun petticoats, with scissors and pincushions and gay calico pockets hanging on the outside; buxom lasses, almost as antiquated as their mothers, excepting where a straw hat, a fine ribbon, or perhaps a white frock, gave symptoms of city innovation. The sons, in short square-skirted coats with rows of stupendous brass buttons, and their hair generally queued in the fashion of the times, especially if they could procure an eel-skin for the purpose, it being esteemed throughout the country as a potent nourisher and strengthener of the hair.

Brom Bones, however, was the hero of the scene, having come to the gathering on his favorite steed Daredevil—a creature, like himself full of metal and mischief, and which no one but himself could manage. He was, in fact, noted for preferring vicious animals, given to all kinds of tricks, which kept the rider in constant risk of his neck, for he held a tractable, well-broken horse as unworthy of a lad of spirit.

Fain would I pause to dwell upon the world of charms that burst upon the enraptured gaze of my hero as he entered the state parlor of Van Tassel's mansion. Not those of the bevy of buxom lasses with their luxurious display of red and white, but the ample charms of a genuine Dutch country tea-table in the sumptuous time of autumn. Such heaped-up platters of cakes of various and almost indescribable kinds, known only to experienced Dutch housewives! There was the doughty doughnut, the tenderer oly koek, and the crisp and crumbling cruller; sweet cakes and short cakes, ginger cakes and honey cakes, and the whole family of cakes. And then there were apple pies and peach pies and pumpkin pies; besides slices of ham and smoked beef; and moreover delectable dishes of preserved plums, and peaches, and pears, and quinces; not to mention broiled shad and roasted chickens; together with bowls of milk and cream, all mingled higgledy-piggledy, pretty much as I have enumerated them, with the motherly teapot sending up its clouds of vapor from the midst. Heaven bless the mark! I want breath and time to discuss this banquet as it deserves, and am too eager to get on with my story. Happily, Ichabod Crane was not in so great a hurry as his historian, but did ample justice to every dainty.

He was a kind and thankful creature, whose heart dilated in proportion as his skin was filled with good cheer, and whose spirits rose with eating as some men's do with drink. He could not help, too, rolling his large eyes round him as he ate, and chuckling with the possibility that he might one day be lord of all this scene of almost unimaginable luxury and splendor. Then, he thought, how soon he'd turn his back upon the old school-house; snap his fingers in the face of Hans Van Ripper and every other niggardly patron, and kick any itinerant pedagogue out of doors that should dare to call him comrade!

Old Baltus Van Tassel moved about among his guests with a face dilated with content and good humor, round and jolly as the harvest moon. His hospitable attentions were brief, but expressive, being confined to a shake of the hand, a slap on the shoulder, a loud laugh, and a pressing invitation to "fall to and help themselves."

And now the sound of the music from the common room, or hall, summoned to the dance. The musician was an old gray-headed negro who had been the itinerant orchestra of the neighborhood for more than half a century. His instrument was as old and battered as himself. The greater part of the time he scraped on two or three strings, accompanying every movement of the bow with a motion of the head, bowing almost to the ground and stamping with his foot whenever a fresh couple were to start.

Ichabod prided himself upon his dancing as much as upon his vocal powers. Not a limb, not a fibre about him was idle; and to have seen his loosely hung frame in full motion and clattering about the room you would have thought Saint Vitus himself, that blessed patron of the dance, was figuring before you in person. He was the admiration of all the negroes, who, having gathered, of all ages and sizes, from the farm and the neighborhood, stood forming a pyramid of shining black faces at every door and window, gazing with delight at the scene, rolling their white eyeballs, and showing grinning rows of ivory from ear to ear. How could the flogger of urchins be otherwise than animated and joyous? The lady of his heart was his partner in the dance, and smiling graciously in reply to all his amorous oglings, while Brom Bones, sorely smitten with love and jealousy, sat brooding by himself in one corner.

When the dance was at an end, Ichabod was attracted to a knot of the sager folks, who, with old Van Tassel, sat smoking at one end of the piazza gossiping over former times and drawing out long stories about the war.

This neighborhood, at the time of which I am speaking, was one of those highly favored places which abound with chronicle and great men. The British and American line had run near it during the war; it had, therefore, been the scene of marauding, and infested with refugees, cow-boys, and all kinds of border chivalry. Just sufficient time had elapsed to enable each storyteller to dress up his tale with a little becoming fiction, and in the indistinctness of his recollection to make himself the hero of every exploit.

There was the story of Doffue Martling, a large blue-bearded Dutchman, who had nearly taken a British frigate with an old iron nine-pounder from a mud breastwork, only that his gun burst at the sixth discharge. And there was an old gentleman who shall be nameless, being too rich a mynheer to be lightly mentioned, who, in the battle of Whiteplains, being an excellent master of defence, parried a musket-ball with a small sword, insomuch that he absolutely felt it whiz round the blade and glance off at the hilt: in proof of which he was ready at any time to show the sword, with the hilt a little bent. There were several more that had been equally great in the field, not one of whom but was persuaded that he had a considerable hand in bringing the war to a happy termination.

But all these were nothing to the tales of ghosts and apparitions that succeeded. The neighborhood is rich in legendary treasures of the kind. Local tales and superstitions thrive best in these sheltered, long-settled retreats; but are trampled under foot by the shifting throng that forms the population of most of our country places. Besides, there is no encouragement for ghosts in most of our villages, for they have scarcely had time to finish their first nap and turn themselves in their graves before their surviving friends have travelled away from the neighborhood; so that when they turn out at night to walk their rounds, they have no acquaintance left to call upon. This is perhaps the reason why we so seldom hear of ghosts except in our long-established Dutch communities.

The immediate causes however, of the prevalence of supernatural stories in these parts, was doubtless owing to the vicinity of Sleepy Hollow. There was a contagion in the very air that blew from that haunted region; it breathed forth an atmosphere of dreams and fancies infecting all the land. Several of the Sleepy Hollow people were present at Van Tassel's, and, as usual, were doling out their wild and wonderful legends. Many dismal tales were told about funeral trains, and mourning cries and wailings heard and seen about the great tree where the unfortunate Major André was taken, and which stood in the neighborhood. Some mention was made also of the woman in white that haunted the dark glen at Raven Rock, and was often heard to shriek on winter nights before a storm, having perished there in the snow. The chief part of the stories, however, turned upon the favorite spectre of Sleepy Hollow, the headless horseman, who had been heard several times of late patrolling the country, and, it was said, tethered his horse nightly among the graves in the churchyard.

The sequestered situation of this church seems always to have made it a favorite haunt of troubled spirits. It stands on a knoll surrounded by locust trees and lofty elms, from among which its decent whitewashed walls shine modestly forth, like Christian purity beaming through the shades of retirement. A gentle slope descends from it to a silver sheet of water bordered by high trees, between which peeps may be caught at the blue hills of the Hudson. To look upon its grass-grown yard, where the sunbeams seem to sleep so quietly, one would think that there at least the dead might rest in peace. On one side of the church extends a wide woody dell, along which raves a large brook among broken rocks and trunks of fallen trees. Over a deep black part of the stream, not far from the church, was formerly thrown a wooden bridge; the road that led to it and the bridge itself were thickly shaded by overhanging trees, which cast a gloom about it even in the daytime; but occasioned a fearful darkness at night. Such was one of the favorite haunts of the headless horseman, and the place where he was most frequently encountered. The tale was told of old Brouwer, a most heretical disbeliever in ghosts, how he met the horseman returning from his foray into Sleepy Hollow, and was obliged to get up behind him; how they galloped over bush and brake, over hill and swamp, until they reached the bridge, when the horseman suddenly turned into a skeleton, threw old Brouwer into the brook, and sprang away over the tree-tops with a clap of thunder.

This story was immediately matched by a thrice-marvellous adventure of Brom Bones, who made light of the galloping Hessian as an arrant jockey. He affirmed that on returning one night from the neighboring village of Sing-Sing, he had been overtaken by this midnight trooper; that he had offered to race with him for a bowl of punch, and should have won it too, for Daredevil beat the goblin horse all hollow, but just as they came to the church bridge the Hessian bolted, and vanished in a flash of fire.

All these tales, told in that drowsy undertone with which men talk in the dark, the countenances of the listeners only now and then receiving a casual gleam from the glare of a pipe, sank deep in the mind of Ichabod. He repaid them in kind with large extracts from his invaluable author, Cotton Mather, and added many marvellous events that had taken place in his native state of Connecticut and fearful sights which he had seen in his nightly walks about Sleepy Hollow.

The revel now gradually broke up. The old farmers gathered together their families in their wagons, and were heard for some time rattling along the hollow roads and over the distant hills. Some of the damsels mounted on pillions behind their favorite swains, and their light-hearted laughter, mingling with the clatter of hoofs, echoed along the silent woodlands, sounding fainter and fainter until they gradually died away, and the late scene of noise and frolic was all silent and deserted. Ichabod only lingered behind, according to the custom of country lovers, to have a tête-à-tête with the heiress, fully convinced that he was now on the high road to success. What passed at this interview I will not pretend to say, for in fact I do not know. Something, however, I fear me, must have gone wrong, for he certainly sallied forth, after no very great interval, with an air quite desolate and chop-fallen. Oh these women! these women! Could that girl have been playing off any of her coquettish tricks? Was her encouragement of the poor pedagogue all a mere sham to secure her conquest of his rival? Heaven only knows, not I! Let it suffice to say, Ichabod stole forth with the air of one who had been sacking a hen-roost, rather than a fair lady's heart. Without looking to the right or left to notice the scene of rural wealth on which he had so often gloated, he went straight to the stable, and with several hearty cuffs and kicks, roused his steed most uncourteously from the comfortable quarters in which he was soundly sleeping, dreaming of mountains of corn and oats and whole valleys of timothy and clover.

It was the very witching time of night that Ichabod, heavy-hearted and crestfallen, pursued his travel homewards along the sides of the lofty hills which rise above Tarry Town, and which he had traversed so cheerily in the afternoon. The hour was as dismal as himself. Far below him the Tappan Zee spread its dusky and indistinct waste of waters, with here and there the tall mast of a sloop riding quietly at anchor under the land. In the dead hush of midnight he could even hear the barking of the watch-dog from the opposite shore of the Hudson; but it was so vague and faint as only to give an idea of his distance from this faithful companion of man. Now and then, too, the long-drawn crowing of a cock, accidentally awakened, would sound far, far off, from some farmhouse away among the hills; but it was like a dreaming sound in his ear. No signs of life occurred near him, but occasionally the melancholy chirp of a cricket, or perhaps the guttural twang of a bull-frog from a neighboring marsh, as if sleeping uncomfortably and turning suddenly in his bed.

All the stories of ghosts and goblins that he had heard in the afternoon now came crowding upon his recollection. The night grew darker and darker; the stars seemed to sink deeper in the sky, and driving clouds occasionally had them from his sight. He had never felt so lonely and dismal. He was, moreover, approaching the very place where many of the scenes of the ghost stories had been laid. In the centre of the road stood an enormous tulip tree, which towered like a giant above all the other trees of the neighborhood and formed a kind of landmark. Its limbs were gnarled and fantastic, large enough to form trunks for ordinary trees, twisting down almost to the earth and rising again into the air. It was connected with the tragical story of the unfortunate André, who had been taken prisoner hard by, and was universally known by the name of Major André's tree. The common people regarded it with a mixture of respect and superstition, partly out of sympathy for the fate of its ill-starred namesake, and partly from the tales of strange sights and doleful lamentations told concerning it.

As Ichabod approached this fearful tree, he began to whistle: he thought his whistle was answered—it was but a blast sweeping sharply through the dry branches. As he approached a little nearer, he thought he saw something white hanging in the midst of the tree: he paused and ceased whistling, but on looking more narrowly, perceived that it was a place where the tree had been scathed by lightning and the white wood laid bare. Suddenly he heard a groan—his teeth chattered and his knees smote against the saddle; it was but the rubbing of one huge bough upon another as they were swayed about by the breeze. He passed the tree in safety, but new perils lay before him.

About two hundred yards from the tree, a small brook crossed the road, and ran into a marshy and thickly-wooded glen known by the name of Wiley's Swamp. A few rough logs, laid side by side, served for a bridge over this stream. On that side of the road where the brook entered the wood, a group of oaks and chestnuts, matted thick with wild grapevines, threw a cavernous gloom over it. To pass this bridge was the severest trial. It was at this identical spot that the unfortunate André was captured, and under the covert of those chestnuts and vines were the sturdy yeomen concealed who surprised him. This has ever since been considered a haunted stream, and fearful are the feelings of the schoolboy who has to pass it alone after dark.

As he approached the stream his heart began to thump; he summoned up, however, all his resolution, gave his horse half a score of kicks in the ribs, and attempted to dash briskly across the bridge; but instead of starting forward, the perverse old animal made a lateral movement and ran broadside against the fence. Ichabod, whose fears increased with the delay, jerked the reins on the other side and kicked lustily with the contrary foot: it was all in vain; his steed started, it is true, but it was only to plunge to the opposite side of the road into a thicket of brambles and alder bushes. The schoolmaster now bestowed both whip and heel upon the starveling ribs of old Gunpowder, who dashed forward, snuffing and snorting, but came to a stand just by the bridge with a suddenness that had nearly sent his rider sprawling over his head. Just at this moment, a plashy tramp by the side of the bridge caught the sensitive ear of Ichabod. In the dark shadow of the grove, on the margin of the brook, he beheld something huge, misshapen, black, and towering. It stirred not, but seemed gathered up in the gloom, like some gigantic monster ready to spring upon the traveller.

The hair of the affrighted pedagogue rose upon his head with terror. What was to be done? To turn and fly was now too late; and besides, what chance was there of escaping ghost or goblin, if such it was, which could ride upon the wings of the wind? Summoning up, therefore, a show of courage, he demanded in stammering accents, "Who are you?" He received no reply. He repeated his demand in a still more agitated voice. Still there was no answer. Once more he cudgelled the sides of the inflexible Gunpowder, and, shutting his eyes, broke forth with involuntary fervor into a psalm tune. Just then the shadowy object of alarm put itself in motion, and with a scramble and a bound stood at once in the middle of the road. Though the night was dark and dismal, yet the form of the unknown might now in some degree be ascertained. He appeared to be a horseman of large dimensions and mounted on a black horse of powerful frame. He made no offer of molestation or sociability, but kept aloof on one side of the road, jogging along on the blind side of old Gunpowder, who had now got over his fright and waywardness.

Ichabod, who had no relish for this strange midnight companion, and bethought himself of the adventure of Brom Bones with the Galloping Hessian, now quickened his steed in hopes of leaving him behind. The stranger, however, quickened his horse to an equal pace. Ichabod pulled up, and fell into a walk, thinking to lag behind; the other did the same. His heart began to sink within him; he endeavored to resume his psalm tune, but his parched tongue clove to the roof of his mouth and he could not utter a stave. There was something in the moody and dogged silence of this pertinacious companion that was mysterious and appalling. It was soon fearfully accounted for. On mounting a rising ground, which brought the figure of his fellow-traveller in relief against the sky, gigantic in height and muffled in a cloak, Ichabod was horror-struck on perceiving that he was headless! but his horror was still more increased on observing that the head, which should have rested on his shoulders, was carried before him on the pommel of the saddle. His terror rose to desperation, he rained a shower of kicks and blows upon Gunpowder, hoping by a sudden movement to give his companion the slip; but the spectre started full jump with him. Away then they dashed, through thick and thin, stones flying and sparks flashing at every bound. Ichabod's flimsy garments fluttered in the air as he stretched his long lank body away over his horse's head in the eagerness of his flight.

They had now reached the road which turns off to Sleepy Hollow; but Gunpowder, who seemed possessed with a demon, instead of keeping up it, made an opposite turn and plunged headlong down hill to the left. This road leads through a sandy hollow shaded by trees for about a quarter of a mile, where it crosses the bridge famous in goblin story, and just beyond swells the green knoll on which stands the whitewashed church.

As yet the panic of the steed had given his unskillful rider an apparent advantage in the chase; but just as he had got halfway through the hollow, the girths of the saddle gave away and he felt it slipping from under him. He seized it by the pommel and endeavored to hold it firm, but in vain, and had just time to save himself by clasping old Gunpowder round the neck, when the saddle fell to the earth, and he heard it trampled under foot by his pursuer. For a moment the terror of Hans Van Ripper's wrath passed across his mind, for it was his Sunday saddle; but this was no time for petty fears; the goblin was hard on his haunches, and (unskilled rider that he was) he had much ado to maintain his seat, sometimes slipping on one side, sometimes on another, and sometimes jolted on the high ridge of his horse's back-bone with a violence that he verily feared would cleave him asunder.

An opening in the trees now cheered him with the hopes that the church bridge was at hand. The wavering reflection of a silver star in the bosom of the brook told him that he was not mistaken. He saw the walls of the church dimly glaring under the trees beyond. He recollected the place where Brom Bones' ghostly competitor had disappeared. "If I can but reach that bridge," thought Ichabod, "I am safe." Just then he heard the black steed panting and blowing close behind him; he even fancied that he felt his hot breath. Another convulsive kick in the ribs, and old Gunpowder sprang upon the bridge; he thundered over the resounding planks; he gained the opposite side; and now Ichabod cast a look behind to see if his pursuer should vanish, according to rule, in a flash of fire and brimstone. Just then he saw the goblin rising in his stirrups, and in the very act of hurling his head at him. Ichabod endeavored to dodge the horrible missile, but too late. It encountered his cranium with a tremendous crash; he was tumbled headlong into the dust, and Gunpowder, the black steed, and the goblin rider passed by like a whirlwind.

The next morning the old horse was found, without his saddle and with the bridle under his feet, soberly cropping the grass at his master's gate. Ichabod did not make his appearance at breakfast; dinner-hour came, but no Ichabod. The boys assembled at the school-house and strolled idly about the banks of the brook but no schoolmaster. Hans Van Ripper now began to feel some uneasiness about the fate of poor Ichabod and his saddle. An inquiry was set on foot, and after diligent investigation they came upon his traces. In one part of the road leading to the church was found the saddle trampled in the dirt; the tracks of horses' hoofs, deeply dented in the road and evidently at furious speed, were traced to the bridge, beyond which, on the bank of a broad part of the brook, where the water ran deep and black, was found the hat of the unfortunate Ichabod, and close beside it a shattered pumpkin.

The brook was searched, but the body of the schoolmaster was not to be discovered. Hans Van Ripper, as executor of his estate, examined the bundle which contained all his worldly effects. They consisted of two shirts and a half, two stocks for the neck, a pair or two of worsted stockings, an old pair of corduroy small-clothes, a rusty razor, a book of psalm tunes full of dog's ears, and a broken pitch-pipe. As to the books and furniture of the school-house, they belonged to the community, excepting Cotton Mather's History of Witchcraft, a New England Almanac, and a book of dreams and fortune-telling; in which last was a sheet of foolscap much scribbled and blotted in several fruitless attempts to make a copy of verses in honor of the heiress of Van Tassel. These magic books and the poetic scrawl were forthwith consigned to the flames by Hans Van Ripper, who from that time forward determined to send his children no more to school, observing that he never knew any good come of this same reading and writing. Whatever money the schoolmaster possessed—and he had received his quarter's pay but a day or two before—he must have had about his person at the time of his disappearance.

The mysterious event caused much speculation at the church on the following Sunday. Knots of gazers and gossips were collected in the churchyard, at the bridge, and at the spot where the hat and pumpkin had been found. The stories of Brouwer, of Bones, and a whole budget of others were called to mind; and when they had diligently considered them all, and compared them with the symptoms of the present case, they shook their heads and came to the conclusion that Ichabod had been carried off by the galloping Hessian. As he was a bachelor and in nobody's debt, nobody troubled his head any more about him, the school was removed to a different quarter of the hollow and another pedagogue reigned in his stead.

It is true an old farmer, who had been down to New York on a visit several years after, and from whom this account of the ghostly adventure was received, brought home the intelligence that Ichabod Crane was still alive; that he had left the neighborhood, partly through fear of the goblin and Hans Van Ripper, and partly in mortification at having been suddenly dismissed by the heiress; that he had changed his quarters to a distant part of the country, had kept school and studied law at the same time, had been admitted to the bar, turned politician, electioneered, written for the newspapers, and finally had been made a justice of the Ten Pound Court. Brom Bones too, who shortly after his rival's disappearance conducted the blooming Katrina in triumph to the altar, was observed to look exceedingly knowing whenever the story of Ichabod was related, and always burst into a hearty laugh at the mention of the pumpkin; which led some to suspect that he knew more about the matter than he chose to tell.

The old country wives, however, who are the best judges of these matters, maintain to this day that Ichabod was spirited away by supernatural means; and it is a favorite story often told about the neighborhood round the winter evening fire. The bridge became more than ever an object of superstitious awe, and that may be the reason why the road has been altered of late years, so as to approach the church by the border of the mill-pond. The schoolhouse, being deserted, soon fell to decay, and was reported to be haunted by the ghost of the unfortunate pedagogue; and the plough-boy, loitering homeward of a still summer evening, has often fancied his voice at a distance, chanting a melancholy psalm tune among the tranquil solitudes of Sleepy Hollow.

Postscript Found in the Handwriting of Mr. Knickerbocker.

The preceding tale is given almost in the precise words in which I heard it related at a Corporation meeting of the ancient city of Manhattoes, at which were present many of its sagest and most illustrious burghers. The narrator was a pleasant, shabby, gentlemanly old fellow in pepper-and-salt clothes, with a sadly humorous face, and one whom I strongly suspected of being poor, he made such efforts to be entertaining. When his story was concluded, there was much laughter and approbation, particularly from two or three deputy aldermen who had been asleep the greater part of the time. There was, however, one tall, dry-looking old gentleman, with beetling eyebrows, who maintained a grave and rather severe face throughout, now and then folding his arms, inclining his head, and looking down upon the floor, as if turning a doubt over in his mind. He was one of your wary men, who never laugh but upon good grounds—when they have reason and the law on their side. When the mirth of the rest of the company had subsided and silence was restored, he leaned one arm on the elbow of his chair, and sticking the other akimbo, demanded, with a slight but exceedingly sage motion of the head and contraction of the brow, what was the moral of the story and what it went to prove.

The story-teller, who was just putting a glass of wine to his lips as a refreshment after his toils, paused for a moment, looked at his inquirer with an air of infinite deference, and, lowering the glass slowly to the table, observed that the story was intended most logically to prove—

"That there is no situation in life but has its advantages and pleasures, provided we will but take a joke as we find it;

"That, therefore, he that runs races with goblin troopers is likely to have rough riding of it;

"Ergo, for a country schoolmaster to be refused the hand of a Dutch heiress is a certain step to high preferment in the state."

The cautious old gentleman knit his brows tenfold closer after this explanation, being sorely puzzled by the ratiocination of the syllogism, while methought the one in pepper-and-salt eyed him with something of a triumphant leer. At length he observed that all this was very well, but still he thought the story a little on the extravagant—there were one or two points on which he had his doubts.

"Faith, sir," replied the story-teller, "as to that matter, I don't believe one-half of it myself."

D. K.

*L'ENVOY**

Go, little booke, God send thee good passage,
And specially let this be thy prayere,
Unto them all that thee will read or hear,
Where thou art wrong, after their help to call,
Thee to correct in any part or all.
—Chaucer's Belle Dame sans Mercie

In concluding a second volume of the Sketch Book, the Author cannot but express his deep sense of the indulgence with which his first has been received, and of the liberal disposition that has been evinced to treat him with kindness as a stranger. Even the critics, whatever may be said of them by others, he has found to be a singularly gentle and good-natured race; it is true that each has in turn objected to some one or two articles, and that these individual exceptions, taken in the aggregate, would amount almost to a total condemnation of his work; but then he has been consoled by observing that what one has particularly censured another has as particularly praised; and thus, the encomiums being set off against the objections, he finds his work, upon the whole, commended far beyond its deserts.

He is aware that he runs a risk of forfeiting much of this kind favor by not following the counsel that has been liberally bestowed upon him; for where abundance of valuable advice is given gratis, it may seem a man's own fault if he should go astray. He only can say in his vindication that he faithfully determined for a time to govern himself in his second volume by the opinions passed upon his first; but he was soon brought to a stand by the contrariety of excellent counsel. One kindly advised him to avoid the ludicrous; another to shun the pathetic; a third assured him that he was tolerable at description, but cautioned him to leave narrative alone; while a fourth declared that he had a very pretty knack at turning a story, and was really entertaining when in a pensive mood, but was grievously mistaken if he imagined himself to possess a spirit of humor.

* Closing the second volume of the London edition.

Thus perplexed by the advice of his friends, who each in turn closed some particular path, but left him all the world beside to range in, he found that to follow all their counsels would, in fact, be to stand still. He remained for a time sadly embarrassed, when all at once the thought struck him to ramble on as he had begun; that his work being miscellaneous and written for different humors, it could not be expected that any one would be pleased with the whole; but that if it should contain something to suit each reader, his end would be completely answered. Few guests sit down to a varied table with an equal appetite for every dish. One has an elegant horror of a roasted pig; another holds a curry or a devil in utter abomination; a third cannot tolerate the ancient flavor of venison and wild fowl; and a fourth, of truly masculine stomach, looks with sovereign contempt on those knick-knacks here and there dished up for the ladies. Thus each article is in condemned in its turn; and yet amidst this variety of appetites, seldom does a dish go away from the table without being tasted and relished by some one or other of the guests.

With these considerations he ventures to serve up this second volume in the same heterogeneous way with his first; simply requesting the reader, if he should find here and there something to please him, to rest assured that it was written expressly for intelligent readers like himself; but entreating him, should he find anything to dislike, to tolerate it, as one of those articles which the author has been obliged to write for readers of a less refined taste.

To be serious: The author is conscious of the numerous faults and imperfections of his work, and well aware how little he is disciplined and accomplished in the arts of authorship. His deficiencies are also increased by a diffidence arising from his peculiar situation. He finds himself writing in a strange land, and appearing before a public which he has been accustomed from childhood to regard with the highest feelings of awe and reverence. He is full of solicitude to deserve their approbation, yet finds that very solicitude continually embarrassing his powers and depriving him of that case and confidence which are necessary to successful exertion. Still, the kindness with which he is treated encourages him to go on, hoping that in time he may acquire a steadier footing; and thus he proceeds, half venturing, half shrinking, surprised at his own goodfortune and wondering at his own temerity.

Word Cloud Classics

12 Years a Slave

A Christmas Carol and Other Holiday Treasures

Adventures of Huckleberry Finn

The Adventures of Sherlock Holmes

Aesop's Fables

The Age of Innocence

Alice's Adventures in Wonderland and Through the Looking-Glass

Anna Karenina

Anne of Green Gables

The Art of War

The Autobiography of Benjamin Franklin and Other Writings

The Awakening and Other Stories

Black Beauty

The Brothers Grimm 101 Fairy Tales

The Brothers Grimm Volume II: 110 Grimmer Fairy Tales

Bulfinch's Mythology: Stories of Gods and Heroes

The Call of the Wild and Other Stories

Classic Horror Tales

Classic Westerns: Zane Grey

Common Sense and Selected Works of Thomas Paine

The Count of Monte Cristo

Crime and Punishment

Don Quixote

Dracula

Emma

Frankenstein

Great Expectations

Hans Christian Andersen Tales

H. P. Lovecraft Cthulhu Mythos Tales

Inferno

Jane Eyre

The Jungle Book

Lady Chatterley's Lover

Leaves of Grass

The Legend of Sleepy Hollow and Other Tales

Les Misérables

Little Women

Word Cloud Classics

Madame Bovary

Mansfield Park

The Merry Adventures of Robin Hood

Moby-Dick

My Ántonia

Narrative of the Life of Frederick Douglass and Other Works

Northanger Abbey

Odyssey

Persuasion

Peter Pan

The Phantom of the Opera

The Picture of Dorian Gray

The Poetry of Emily Dickinson

Pride and Prejudice

The Prince and Other Writings

The Red Badge of Courage and Other Stories

The Romantic Poets

The Scarlet Letter

The Secret Garden

Selected Works of Alexander Hamilton

Sense and Sensibility

Shakespeare's Sonnets and Other Poems

Strange Case of Dr. Jekyll and Mr. Hyde & Other Stories

Tarzan of the Apes & The Return of Tarzan

The Three Musketeers

Treasure Island

Twenty Thousand Leagues Under the Sea

Uncle Tom's Cabin, or Life Among the Lowly

The U.S. Constitution and Other Key American Writings

Walden and Civil Disobedience

The Wizard of Oz

Wuthering Heights

Dracula

Bram Stoker

Word Cloud Classics
San Diego

Canterbury Classics
An imprint of Printers Row Publishing Group
9717 Pacific Heights Blvd, San Diego, CA 92121
www.canterburyclassicsbooks.com • mail@canterburyclassicsbooks.com

Correspondence concerning the content of this book should be sent to Canterbury Classics, Editorial Department, at the above address.

Publisher: Peter Norton • Associate Publisher: Ana Parker
Art Director: Charles McStravick
Senior Developmental Editor: April Graham
Publishing/Editorial Team: Kathryn C. Dalby, JoAnn Padgett, Melinda Allman, Dan Mansfield, Traci Douglas
Production/Design Team: Jonathan Lopes, Rusty von Dyl, Beno Chan, Julie Greene, Rosemary Rae

Spine art: gio_banfi/DigitalVision Vectors via Getty Images
Endpapers: Pobytov/DigitalVision Vectors via Getty Images

ISBN: 978-1-6672-0316-4

MIX
Paper | Supporting responsible forestry
FSC
www.fsc.org
FSC® C144853

Printed in China
27 26 25 24 23 2 3 4 5 6

Editor's Note: This work has been published in its original form to preserve the author's intent and style.

How these papers have been placed in sequence will be made manifest in the reading of them. All needless matters have been eliminated, so that a history almost at variance with the possibilities of latter-day belief may stand forth as simple fact. There is throughout no statement of past things wherein memory may err, for all the records chosen are exactly contemporary, given from the standpoints and within the range of knowledge of those who made them.

CHAPTER I

Jonathan Harker's Journal
(*Kept in Shorthand*)

3 May. Bistritz.

Left Munich at 8:35 p.m., on 1st May, arriving at Vienna early next morning; should have arrived at 6:46, but train was an hour late. Buda-Pesth seems a wonderful place, from the glimpse which I got of it from the train and the little I could walk through the streets. I feared to go very far from the station, as we had arrived late and would start as near the correct time as possible. The impression I had was that we were leaving the West and entering the East; the most western of splendid bridges over the Danube, which is here of noble width and depth, took us among the traditions of Turkish rule.

We left in pretty good time, and came after nightfall to Klausenburgh. Here I stopped for the night at the Hotel Royale. I had for dinner, or rather supper, a chicken done up some way with red pepper, which was very good but thirsty. (*Mem.*, get recipe for Mina.) I asked the waiter, and he said it was called "paprika hendl," and that, as it was a national dish, I should be able to get it anywhere along the Carpathians. I found my smattering of German very useful here; indeed, I don't know how I should be able to get on without it.

Having had some time at my disposal when in London, I had visited the British Museum, and made search among the books and maps in the library regarding Transylvania; it had struck me that some foreknowledge of the country could hardly fail to have some importance in dealing with a nobleman of that country. I find that the district he named is in the extreme east of the country, just on the borders of three states, Transylvania, Moldavia, and Bukovina, in the midst of the Carpathian mountains; one of the wildest and least known portions of Europe.

I was not able to light on any map or work giving the exact locality of the Castle Dracula, as there are no maps of this country as yet to compare with our own Ordnance Survey Maps; but I found that Bistritz, the post town named by Count Dracula, is a fairly well-known place.

I shall enter here some of my notes, as they may refresh my memory when I talk over my travels with Mina.

In the population of Transylvania there are four distinct nationalities: Saxons in the South, and mixed with them the Wallachs, who are the descendants of the Dacians; Magyars in the West, and Szekelys in the East and North. I am going among the latter, who claim to be descended from Attila and the Huns. This may be so, for when the Magyars conquered the country in the eleventh century they found the Huns settled in it. I read that every known superstition in the world is gathered into the horseshoe of the Carpathians, as if it were the centre of some sort of imaginative whirlpool; if so my stay may be very interesting. (*Mem.*, I must ask the Count all about them.)

I did not sleep well, though my bed was comfortable enough, for I had all sorts of queer dreams. There was a dog howling all night under my window, which may have had something to do with it; or it may have been the paprika, for I had to drink up all the water in my carafe, and was still thirsty. Towards morning I slept and was wakened by the continuous knocking at my door, so I guess I must have been sleeping soundly then. I had for breakfast more paprika, and a sort of porridge of maize flour which they said was "mamaliga," and eggplant stuffed with forcemeat, a very excellent dish, which they call "impletata." (*Mem.*, get recipe for this also.) I had to hurry breakfast, for the train started a little before eight, or rather it ought to have done so, for after rushing to the station at 7:30 I had to sit in the carriage for more than an hour before we began to move. It seems to me that the further east you go the more unpunctual are the trains. What ought they to be in China?

All day long we seemed to dawdle through a country which was full of beauty of every kind. Sometimes we saw little towns or castles on the top of steep hills such as we see in old missals; sometimes we ran by rivers and streams which seemed from the wide stony margin on each side of them to be subject to great floods. It takes a lot of water, and running strong, to sweep the outside edge of a river clear. At every station there were groups of people, sometimes crowds, and in all sorts of attire. Some of them were just like the peasants at home or those I saw coming through France and Germany, with short jackets, and round hats, and home-made trousers; but others were very picturesque. The women looked pretty, except when you got near them, but they were very clumsy about the waist. They had all full white sleeves of some kind or other, and most of them had big belts with a lot of strips of something fluttering from them like the dresses in a ballet, but of course there were petticoats under them. The strangest figures we saw were the Slovaks, who were more barbarian than the rest, with their big cowboy hats, great baggy dirty-white trousers, white linen shirts, and enormous heavy leather belts, nearly a foot wide, all studded over with brass nails. They wore high boots, with their trousers tucked into them, and had long black hair and heavy black moustaches. They are very picturesque, but do not look prepossessing. On the stage they would be set down at once as some old Oriental band of brigands. They are, however, I am told, very harmless and rather wanting in natural self-assertion.

It was on the dark side of twilight when we got to Bistritz, which is a very interesting old place. Being practically on the frontier—for the Borgo Pass leads from it into Bukovina—it has had a very stormy existence, and it certainly shows marks of it. Fifty years ago a series of great fires took place, which made terrible havoc on five separate occasions. At the very beginning of the seventeenth century it underwent a siege of three weeks and lost 13,000 people, the casualties of war proper being assisted by famine and disease.

Count Dracula had directed me to go to the Golden Krone Hotel, which I found, to my great delight, to be thoroughly old-fashioned, for of course I wanted to see all I could of the ways of the country. I was evidently expected, for when I got near the door I faced a cheery-looking elderly woman in the usual peasant dress—white undergarment with a long double apron, front, and back, of coloured stuff fitting almost too tight for modesty. When I came close she bowed and said, "The Herr Englishman?"

"Yes," I said, "Jonathan Harker."

She smiled, and gave some message to an elderly man in white shirtsleeves, who had followed her to the door. He went, but immediately returned with a letter:

> My friend,
>
> Welcome to the Carpathians. I am anxiously expecting you. Sleep well tonight. At three tomorrow the diligence will start for Bukovina; a place on it is kept for you. At the Borgo Pass my carriage will await you and will bring you to me. I

trust that your journey from London has been a happy one, and that you will enjoy your stay in my beautiful land.

Your friend,

DRACULA.

4 May.

I found that my landlord had got a letter from the Count, directing him to secure the best place on the coach for me; but on making inquiries as to details he seemed somewhat reticent, and pretended that he could not understand my German. This could not be true, because up to then he had understood it perfectly; at least, he answered my questions exactly as if he did. He and his wife, the old lady who had received me, looked at each other in a frightened sort of way. He mumbled out that the money had been sent in a letter, and that was all he knew. When I asked him if he knew Count Dracula, and could tell me anything of his castle, both he and his wife crossed themselves, and, saying that they knew nothing at all, simply refused to speak further. It was so near the time of starting that I had no time to ask anyone else, for it was all very mysterious and not by any means comforting.

Just before I was leaving, the old lady came up to my room and said in a hysterical way, "Must you go? Oh! Young Herr, must you go?" She was in such an excited state that she seemed to have lost her grip of what German she knew, and mixed it all up with some other language which I did not know at all. I was just able to follow her by asking many questions. When I told her that I must go at once, and that I was engaged on important business, she asked again:

"Do you know what day it is?" I answered that it was the fourth of May. She shook her head as she said again:

"Oh, yes! I know that! I know that, but do you know what day it is?"

On my saying that I did not understand, she went on:

"It is the eve of St. George's Day. Do you not know that tonight, when the clock strikes midnight, all the evil things in the world will have full sway? Do you know where you are going, and what you are going to?" She was in such evident distress that I tried to comfort her, but without effect. Finally, she went down on her knees and implored me not to go; at least to wait a day or two before starting. It was all very ridiculous but I did not feel comfortable. However, there was business to be done, and I could allow nothing to interfere with it. I tried to raise her up, and said, as gravely as I could, that I thanked her, but my duty was imperative, and that I must go. She then rose and dried her eyes, and taking a crucifix from her neck offered it to me. I did not know what to do, for, as an English Churchman, I have been taught to regard such things as in some measure idolatrous, and yet it seemed so ungracious to refuse an old lady meaning so well and in such a state of mind. She saw, I suppose, the doubt in my face, for she put the rosary round my neck and said, "For your mother's sake," and went out of the room. I am writing up this part of the diary whilst I am waiting for the coach, which is, of course, late; and the crucifix is still round my neck. Whether it is the old lady's fear, or the many ghostly traditions of this place, or the crucifix itself, I do not know, but I am not feeling nearly as easy in my mind as usual. If this book should ever reach Mina before I do, let it bring my goodbye. Here comes the coach!

5 May. The Castle.

The gray of the morning has passed, and the sun is high over the distant horizon, which seems jagged, whether with trees or hills I know not, for it is so far off that big things and little are mixed. I am not sleepy, and, as I am not to be called till I awake, naturally I write till sleep comes. There are many odd things to put down, and, lest who reads them may fancy that I dined too well before I left Bistritz, let me put down my dinner exactly. I dined on what they called "robber steak"—bits of bacon, onion, and beef, seasoned with red pepper, and strung on sticks, and roasted over the fire, in simple style of the London cat's meat! The wine was Golden Mediasch, which produces a queer sting on the tongue, which is, however, not disagreeable. I had only a couple of glasses of this, and nothing else.

When I got on the coach, the driver had not taken his seat, and I saw him talking to the landlady. They were evidently talking of me, for every now and then they looked at me, and some of the people who were sitting on the bench outside the door—which they call by a name meaning "wood bearer"—came and listened, and then looked at me, most of them pityingly. I could hear a lot of words often repeated, queer words, for there were many nationalities in the crowd, so I quietly got my polyglot dictionary from my bag and looked them out. I must say they were not cheering to me, for amongst them were "Ordog"—Satan, "Pokol"—hell, "stregoica"—witch, "vrolok" and "vlkoslak"—

both mean the same thing, one being Slovak and the other Servian for something that is either werewolf or vampire. (*Mem.*, I must ask the Count about these superstitions.)

When we started, the crowd round the inn door, which had by this time swelled to a considerable size, all made the sign of the cross and pointed two fingers towards me. With some difficulty, I got a fellow passenger to tell me what they meant. He would not answer at first, but on learning that I was English, he explained that it was a charm or guard against the evil eye. This was not very pleasant for me, just starting for an unknown place to meet an unknown man. But everyone seemed so kind-hearted, and so sorrowful, and so sympathetic that I could not but be touched. I shall never forget the last glimpse which I had of the inn yard and its crowd of picturesque figures, all crossing themselves, as they stood round the wide archway, with its background of rich foliage of oleander and orange trees in green tubs clustered in the centre of the yard. Then our driver, whose wide linen drawers covered the whole front of the boxseat—"gotza" they call them—cracked his big whip over his four small horses, which ran abreast, and we set off on our journey.

I soon lost sight and recollection of ghostly fears in the beauty of the scene as we drove along, although had I known the language, or rather languages, which my fellow-passengers were speaking, I might not have been able to throw them off so easily. Before us lay a green sloping land full of forests and woods, with here and there steep hills, crowned with clumps of trees or with farmhouses, the blank gable end to the road. There was everywhere a bewildering mass of fruit blossom—apple, plum, pear, cherry. And as we drove by I could see the green grass under the trees spangled with the fallen petals. In and out amongst these green hills of what they call here the "Mittel Land" ran the road, losing itself as it swept round the grassy curve, or was shut out by the straggling ends of pine woods, which here and there ran down the hillsides like tongues of flame. The road was rugged, but still we seemed to fly over it with a feverish haste. I could not understand then what the haste meant, but the driver was evidently bent on losing no time in reaching Borgo Prund. I was told that this road is in summertime excellent, but that it had not yet been put in order after the winter snows. In this respect it is different from the general run of roads in the Carpathians, for it is an old tradition that they are not to be kept in too good order. Of old the Hospadars would not repair them, lest the Turk should think that they were preparing to bring in foreign troops, and so hasten the war which was always really at loading point.

Beyond the green swelling hills of the Mittel Land rose mighty slopes of forest up to the lofty steeps of the Carpathians themselves. Right and left of us they towered, with the afternoon sun falling full upon them and bringing out all the glorious colours of this beautiful range, deep blue and purple in the shadows of the peaks, green and brown where grass and rock mingled, and an endless perspective of jagged rock and pointed crags, till these were themselves lost in the distance, where the snowy peaks rose grandly. Here and there seemed mighty rifts in the mountains, through which, as the sun began to sink, we saw now and again the white gleam of falling water. One of my companions touched my arm as we swept round the base of a hill and opened up the lofty, snow-covered peak of a mountain, which seemed, as we wound on our serpentine way, to be right before us.

"Look! Isten szek!"—"God's seat!"—and he crossed himself reverently. As we wound on our endless way, and the sun sank lower and lower behind us, the shadows of the evening began to creep round us. This was emphasized by the fact that the snowy mountain-top still held the sunset, and seemed to glow out with a delicate cool pink. Here and there we passed Cszeks and Slovaks, all in picturesque attire, but I noticed that goitre was painfully prevalent. By the roadside were many crosses, and as we swept by, my companions all crossed themselves. Here and there was a peasant man or woman kneeling before a shrine, who did not even turn round as we approached, but seemed in the self-surrender of devotion to have neither eyes nor ears for the outer world. There were many things new to me. For instance, hay-ricks in the trees, and here and there very beautiful masses of weeping birch, their white stems shining like silver through the delicate green of the leaves. Now and again we passed a leiter-wagon—the ordinary peasants's cart, with its long, snakelike vertebra, calculated to suit the inequalities of the road. On this were sure to be seated quite a group of homecoming peasants, the Cszeks with their white, and the Slovaks with their coloured sheepskins, the latter carrying lance-fashion their long staves, with axe at end. As the evening fell it began to get very cold, and the growing twilight seemed to merge into one dark mistiness the gloom of the trees, oak, beech, and pine, though in the valleys which ran deep between the spurs of the hills, as we ascended through the Pass, the dark firs stood out here and there against the background of late-lying snow. Sometimes, as the road was cut through the pine woods that seemed in the darkness to be closing down upon us, great masses of grayness which here and there bestrewed the trees, produced a peculiarly weird and solemn effect, which carried on the thoughts and grim fancies engendered earlier in the evening, when the falling sunset threw into strange relief the ghost-like clouds which amongst the Carpathians seem to wind ceaselessly through the valleys. Sometimes the hills were so steep that, despite our driver's haste, the horses could only go slowly. I wished to get down and walk up them, as we do at home, but the driver would not hear of it. "No, no," he said. "You must not walk here. The dogs are too fierce." And then he added, with what he evidently meant for grim pleasantry—for he looked round to catch the approving smile of the rest—"And you may have enough of such matters before you go to sleep." The only stop he would make was a moment's pause to light his lamps.

When it grew dark there seemed to be some excitement amongst the passengers, and they kept speaking to him, one after the other, as though urging him to further speed. He lashed the horses unmercifully with his long whip, and with wild cries of encouragement urged them on to further exertions. Then through the darkness I could see a sort of patch of gray light ahead of us, as though there were a cleft in the hills. The excitement of the passengers grew greater. The crazy coach rocked on its great leather springs, and swayed like a boat tossed on a stormy sea. I had to hold on. The road grew more level, and we appeared to fly along. Then the mountains seemed to come nearer to us on each side and to frown down upon us. We were entering on the Borgo Pass. One by one several of the passengers offered me gifts, which they pressed upon me with an earnestness which would take no denial. These were certainly of an odd and varied kind, but each was given in simple good faith, with a kindly word, and a blessing, and that same strange mixture of fear-meaning movements which I had seen outside the hotel at Bistritz—the sign of the cross and the guard against the evil eye. Then, as we flew along, the driver leaned forward, and on each side the passengers, craning over the edge of the coach, peered eagerly into the darkness. It was evident that something very exciting was either happening or expected, but though I asked each passenger, no one would give me the slightest explanation. This state of excitement kept on for some little time. And at last we saw before us the Pass opening out on the eastern side. There were dark, rolling clouds overhead, and in the air the heavy, oppressive sense of thunder. It seemed as though the mountain range had separated two atmospheres, and that now we had got into the thunderous one. I was now myself looking out for the conveyance which was to take me to the Count. Each moment I expected to see the glare of lamps through the blackness, but all was dark. The only light was the flickering rays of our own lamps, in which the steam from our hard-driven horses rose in a white cloud. We could see now the sandy road lying white before us, but there was on it no sign of a vehicle. The passengers drew back with a sigh of gladness, which seemed to mock my own disappointment. I was already thinking what I had best do, when the driver, looking at his watch, said to the others something which I could hardly hear, it was spoken so quietly and in so low a tone, I thought it was "An hour less than the time."

Then turning to me, he spoke in German worse than my own. "There is no carriage here. The Herr is not expected after all. He will now come on to Bukovina, and return tomorrow or the next day, better the next day." Whilst he was speaking the horses began to neigh and snort and plunge wildly, so that the driver had to hold them up. Then, amongst a chorus of screams from the peasants and a universal crossing of themselves, a calèche, with four horses, drove up behind us, overtook us, and drew up beside the coach. I could see from the flash of our lamps as the rays fell on them, that the horses were coal-black and splendid animals. They were driven by a tall man, with a long brown beard and a great black hat, which seemed to hide his face from us. I could only see the gleam of a pair of very bright eyes, which seemed red in the lamplight, as he turned to us.

He said to the driver, "You are early tonight, my friend."

The man stammered in reply, "The English Herr was in a hurry."

To which the stranger replied, "That is why, I suppose, you wished him to go on to Bukovina. You cannot deceive me, my friend. I know too much, and my horses are swift." As he spoke he smiled, and the lamplight fell on a hard-looking mouth, with very red lips and sharp-looking teeth, as white as ivory. One of my companions whispered to another the line from Burger's "Lenore":

"Denn die Todten reiten Schnell."
("For the dead travel fast.")

The strange driver evidently heard the words, for he looked up with a gleaming smile. The passenger turned his face away, at the same time putting out his two fingers and crossing himself. "Give me the Herr's luggage," said the driver, and with exceeding alacrity my bags were handed out and put in the calèche. Then I descended from the side of the coach, as the calèche was close alongside, the driver helping me with a hand which caught my arm in a grip of steel. His strength must have been prodigious. Without a word he shook his reins, the horses turned, and we swept into the darkness of the pass. As I looked back I saw the steam from the horses of the coach by the light of the lamps, and projected against it the figures of my late companions crossing themselves. Then the driver cracked his whip and called to his horses, and off they swept on their way to Bukovina.

As they sank into the darkness I felt a strange chill, and a lonely feeling come over me. But a cloak was thrown over my shoulders, and a rug across my knees, and the driver said in excellent German, "The night is chill, mein Herr, and my master the Count bade me take all care of you. There is a flask of slivovitz (the plum brandy of the country) underneath the seat, if you should require it."

I did not take any, but it was a comfort to know it was there all the same. I felt a little strangely, and not a little frightened. I think had there been any alternative I should have taken it, instead of prosecuting that unknown night journey. The carriage went at a hard pace straight along, then we made a complete turn and went along another straight road. It seemed to me that we were simply going over and over the same ground again, and so I took note of some salient point, and found that this was so. I would have liked to have asked the driver what this all meant, but I really feared to do so, for I thought that, placed as I was, any protest would have had no effect in case there had been an intention to delay. By-and-by, however, as I was curious to know how time was passing, I struck a match, and by its flame looked at my watch. It was within a few minutes of midnight. This gave me a sort of shock, for I suppose the general superstition about midnight was increased by my recent experiences. I waited with a sick feeling of suspense.

Then a dog began to howl somewhere in a farmhouse far down the road, a long, agonized wailing, as if from fear. The sound was taken up by another dog, and then another and another, till, borne on the wind which now sighed softly through the Pass, a wild howling began, which seemed to come from all over the country, as far as the imagination could grasp it through the gloom of the night. At the first howl the horses began to strain and rear, but the driver spoke to them soothingly, and they quieted down, but shivered and sweated as though after a runaway from sudden fright. Then, far off in the distance, from the mountains on each side of us began a louder and a sharper howling, that of wolves, which affected both the horses and myself in the same way. For I was minded to jump from the calèche and run, whilst they reared again and plunged madly, so that the driver had to use all his great strength to keep them from bolting. In a few minutes, however, my own ears got accustomed to the sound, and the horses so far became quiet that the driver was able to descend and to stand before them. He petted and soothed them, and whispered something in their ears, as I have heard of horse-tamers doing, and with extraordinary effect, for under his caresses they became quite manageable again, though they still trembled. The driver again took his seat, and shaking his reins, started off at a great pace. This time, after going to the far side of the Pass, he suddenly turned down a narrow roadway which ran sharply to the right.

Soon we were hemmed in with trees, which in places arched right over the roadway till we passed as through a tunnel. And again great frowning rocks guarded us boldly on either side. Though we were in shelter, we could hear the rising wind, for it moaned and whistled through the rocks, and the branches of the trees crashed together as we swept along. It grew colder and colder still, and fine, powdery snow began to fall, so that soon we and all around us were covered with a white blanket. The keen wind still carried the howling of the dogs, though this grew fainter as we went on our way. The baying of the wolves sounded nearer and nearer, as though they were closing round on us from every side. I grew dreadfully afraid, and the horses shared my fear. The driver, however, was not in the least disturbed. He kept turning his head to left and right, but I could not see anything through the darkness.

Suddenly, away on our left, I saw a faint flickering blue flame. The driver saw it at the same moment. He at once checked the horses, and, jumping to the ground, disappeared into the darkness. I did not know what to do, the less as the howling of the wolves grew closer. But while I wondered, the driver suddenly appeared again, and without a word took his seat, and we resumed our journey. I think I must have fallen asleep and kept dreaming of the incident, for it seemed to be repeated endlessly, and now looking back, it is like a sort of awful nightmare. Once the flame appeared so near the road, that even in the darkness around us I could watch the driver's motions. He went rapidly to where the blue flame arose—it must have been very faint, for it did not seem to illumine the place around it at all—and gathering a few stones, formed them into some device. Once there appeared a strange optical effect. When he stood between me and the flame he did not obstruct it, for I could see its ghostly flicker all the same. This startled me, but as the effect was only momentary, I took it that my eyes deceived me straining through the darkness. Then for a time there were no blue flames, and we sped onwards through the gloom, with the howling of the wolves around us, as though they were following in a moving circle.

At last there came a time when the driver went further afield than he had yet gone, and during his absence, the horses began to tremble worse than ever and to snort and scream with fright. I could not see any cause for it, for the howling of the wolves had ceased altogether. But just then the moon, sailing through the black clouds, appeared behind the jagged crest of a beetling, pine-clad rock, and by its light I saw around us a ring of wolves, with white teeth and lolling red tongues, with long, sinewy limbs and shaggy hair. They were a hundred times more terrible in the grim silence which held them than even when they howled. For myself, I felt a sort of paralysis of fear. It is only when a man feels himself face to face with such horrors that he can understand their true import.

All at once the wolves began to howl as though the moonlight had had some peculiar effect on them. The horses jumped about and reared, and looked helplessly round with eyes that rolled in a way painful to see. But the living ring of terror encompassed them on every side, and they had perforce to remain within it. I called to the coachman to come, for it seemed to me that our only chance was to try to break out through the ring and to aid his approach. I shouted and beat the side of the calèche, hoping by the noise to scare the wolves from the side, so as to give him a chance of reaching the trap. How he came there, I know not, but I heard his voice raised in a tone of imperious command, and looking towards the sound, saw him stand in the roadway. As he swept his long arms, as though brushing aside some impalpable obstacle, the wolves fell back and back further still. Just then a heavy cloud passed across the face of the moon, so that we were again in darkness.

When I could see again the driver was climbing into the calèche, and the wolves disappeared. This was all so strange and uncanny that a dreadful fear came upon me, and I was afraid to speak or move. The time seemed interminable as we swept on our way, now in almost complete darkness, for the rolling clouds obscured the moon. We kept on ascending, with occasional periods of quick descent, but in the main always ascending. Suddenly, I became conscious of the fact that the driver was in the act of pulling up the horses in the courtyard of a vast ruined castle, from whose tall black windows came no ray of light, and whose broken battlements showed a jagged line against the sky.

CHAPTER II

Jonathan Harker's Journal, Continued

5 May.

I must have been asleep, for certainly if I had been fully awake I must have noticed the approach of such a remarkable place. In the gloom the courtyard looked of considerable size, and as several dark ways led from it under great round arches, it perhaps seemed bigger than it really is. I have not yet been able to see it by daylight.

When the calèche stopped, the driver jumped down and held out his hand to assist me to alight. Again I could not but notice his prodigious strength. His hand actually seemed like a steel vice that could have crushed mine if he had chosen. Then he took my traps, and placed them on the ground beside me as I stood close to a great door, old and studded with large iron nails, and set in a projecting doorway of massive stone. I could see even in the dim light that the stone was massively carved, but that the carving had been much worn by time and weather. As I stood, the driver jumped again into his seat and shook the reins. The horses started forward, and trap and all disappeared down one of the dark openings.

I stood in silence where I was, for I did not know what to do. Of bell or knocker there was no sign. Through these frowning walls and dark window openings it was not likely that my voice could penetrate. The time I waited seemed endless, and I felt doubts and fears crowding upon me. What sort of place had I come to, and among what kind of people? What sort of grim adventure was it on which I had embarked? Was this a customary incident in the life of a solicitor's clerk sent out to explain the purchase of a London estate to a foreigner? Solicitor's clerk! Mina would not like that. Solicitor, for just before leaving London I got word that my examination was successful, and I am now a full-blown solicitor! I began to rub my eyes and pinch myself to see if I were awake. It all seemed like a horrible nightmare to me, and I expected that I should suddenly awake, and find myself at home, with the dawn struggling in through the windows, as I had now and again felt in the morning after a day of overwork. But my flesh answered the pinching test, and my eyes were not to be deceived. I was indeed awake and among the Carpathians. All I could do now was to be patient, and to wait the coming of morning.

Just as I had come to this conclusion I heard a heavy step approaching behind the great door, and saw through the chinks the gleam of a coming light. Then there was the sound of rattling chains and the clanking of massive bolts drawn back. A key was turned with the loud grating noise of long disuse, and the great door swung back.

Within, stood a tall old man, clean shaven save for a long white moustache, and clad in black from head to foot, without a single speck of colour about him anywhere. He held in his hand an antique silver lamp, in which the flame burned without a chimney or globe of any kind, throwing long quivering shadows as it flickered in the draught of the open door. The old man motioned me in with his right hand with a courtly gesture, saying in excellent English, but with a strange intonation.

"Welcome to my house! Enter freely and of your own free will!" He made no motion of stepping to meet me, but stood like a statue, as though his gesture of welcome had fixed him into stone. The instant, however, that I had stepped over the threshold, he moved impulsively forward, and holding out his hand grasped mine with a strength which made me wince, an effect which was not lessened by the fact that it seemed cold as ice, more like the hand of a dead than a living man.

Again he said, "Welcome to my house! Enter freely. Go safely, and leave something of the happiness you bring!" The strength of the handshake was so much akin to that which I had noticed in the driver, whose face I had not seen, that for a moment I doubted if it were not the same person to whom I was speaking. So to make sure, I said interrogatively, "Count Dracula?"

He bowed in a courtly way as he replied, "I am Dracula, and I bid you welcome, Mr. Harker, to my house. Come in, the night air is chill, and you must need to eat and rest." As he was speaking, he put the lamp on a bracket on the wall, and stepping out, took my luggage. He had carried it in before I could forestall him. I protested, but he insisted.

"Nay, sir, you are my guest. It is late, and my people are not available. Let me see to your comfort myself." He insisted on carrying my traps along the passage, and then up a great winding stair, and along another great passage, on whose stone floor our steps rang heavily. At the end of this he threw open a heavy door, and I rejoiced to see within a well-lit room in which a table was spread for supper, and on whose mighty hearth a great fire of logs, freshly replenished, flamed and flared.

The Count halted, putting down my bags, closed the door, and crossing the room, opened another door, which led into a small octagonal room lit by a single lamp, and seemingly without a window of any sort. Passing through this, he opened another door, and motioned me to enter. It was a welcome sight. For here was a great bedroom well lighted and warmed with another log fire, also added to but lately, for the top logs were fresh, which sent a hollow roar up the wide chimney.

The Count himself left my luggage inside and withdrew, saying, before he closed the door, "You will need, after your journey, to refresh yourself by making your toilet. I trust you will find all you wish. When you are ready, come into the other room, where you will find your supper prepared."

The light and warmth and the Count's courteous welcome seemed to have dissipated all my doubts and fears. Having then reached my normal state, I discovered that I was half famished with hunger. So making a hasty toilet, I went into the other room.

I found supper already laid out. My host, who stood on one side of the great fireplace, leaning against the stonework, made a graceful wave of his hand to the table, and said, "I pray you, be seated and sup how you please. You will I trust, excuse me that I do not join you, but I have dined already, and I do not sup."

I handed to him the sealed letter which Mr. Hawkins had entrusted to me. He opened it and read it gravely. Then, with a charming smile, he handed it to me to read. One passage of it, at least, gave me a thrill of pleasure:

> "I must regret that an attack of gout, from which malady I am a constant sufferer, forbids absolutely any travelling on my part for some time to come. But I am happy to say I can send a sufficient substitute, one in whom I have every possible confidence. He is a young man, full of energy and talent in his own way, and of a very faithful disposition. He is discreet and silent, and has grown into manhood in my service. He shall be ready to attend on you when you will during his stay, and shall take your instructions in all matters."

The count himself came forward and took off the cover of a dish, and I fell to at once on an excellent roast chicken. This, with some cheese and a salad and a bottle of old Tokay, of which I had two glasses, was my supper. During the time I was eating it the Count asked me many questions as to my journey, and I told him by degrees all I had experienced.

By this time I had finished my supper, and by my host's desire had drawn up a chair by the fire and begun to smoke a cigar which he offered me, at the same time excusing himself that he did not smoke. I had now an opportunity of observing him, and found him of a very marked physiognomy.

His face was a strong—a very strong— aquiline, with high bridge of the thin nose and peculiarly arched nostrils, with lofty domed forehead, and hair growing scantily round the temples but profusely elsewhere. His eyebrows were very massive, almost meeting over the nose, and with bushy hair that seemed to curl in its own profusion. The mouth, so far as I could see it under the heavy moustache, was fixed and rather cruel-looking, with peculiarly sharp white teeth. These protruded over the lips, whose remarkable ruddiness showed astonishing vitality in a man of his years. For the rest, his ears were pale, and at the tops extremely pointed. The chin was broad and strong, and the cheeks firm though thin. The general effect was one of extraordinary pallor.

Hitherto I had noticed the backs of his hands as they lay on his knees in the firelight, and they had seemed rather white and fine. But seeing them now close to me, I could not but notice that they were rather coarse, broad, with squat fingers. Strange to say, there were hairs in the centre of the palm. The nails were long and fine, and cut to a sharp point. As the Count leaned over me and his hands touched me, I could not repress a shudder. It may have been that his breath was rank, but a horrible feeling of nausea came over me, which, do what I would, I could not conceal. The Count, evidently noticing it, drew back. And with a grim sort of smile, which showed more than he had yet done his protruberant teeth, sat himself down again on his own side of the fireplace. We were both silent for a while, and as I looked towards the window I saw the first dim streak of the coming dawn. There seemed a strange stillness over everything. But as I listened, I heard as if from down below in the valley the howling of many wolves.

The Count's eyes gleamed, and he said, "Listen to them, the

children of the night. What music they make!" Seeing, I suppose, some expression in my face strange to him, he added, "Ah, sir, you dwellers in the city cannot enter into the feelings of the hunter." Then he rose and said, "But you must be tired. Your bedroom is all ready, and tomorrow you shall sleep as late as you will. I have to be away till the afternoon, so sleep well and dream well!" With a courteous bow, he opened for me himself the door to the octagonal room, and I entered my bedroom.

I am all in a sea of wonders. I doubt. I fear. I think strange things, which I dare not confess to my own soul. God keep me, if only for the sake of those dear to me!

7 May.

It is again early morning, but I have rested and enjoyed the last twenty-four hours. I slept till late in the day, and awoke of my own accord. When I had dressed myself I went into the room where we had supped, and found a cold breakfast laid out, with coffee kept hot by the pot being placed on the hearth. There was a card on the table, on which was written:

I have to be absent for a while. Do not wait for me. —D.

So I set to and enjoyed a hearty meal. When I had done, I looked for a bell, so that I might let the servants know I had finished, but I could not find one. There are certainly odd deficiencies in the house, considering the extraordinary evidences of wealth which are round me. The table service is of gold, and so beautifully wrought that it must be of immense value. The curtains and upholstery of the chairs and sofas and the hangings of my bed are of the costliest and most beautiful fabrics, and must have been of fabulous value when they were made, for they are centuries old, though in excellent order. I saw something like them in Hampton Court, but they were worn and frayed and moth-eaten. But still in none of the rooms is there a mirror. There is not even a toilet glass on my table, and I had to get the little shaving glass from my bag before I could either shave or brush my hair. I have not yet seen a servant anywhere, or heard a sound near the castle except the howling of wolves. Some time after I had finished my meal—I do not know whether to call it breakfast or dinner, for it was between five and six o'clock when I had it—I looked about for something to read, for I did not like to go about the castle until I had asked the Count's permission. There was absolutely nothing in the room, book, newspaper, or even writing materials, so I opened another door in the room and found a sort of library. The door opposite mine I tried, but found locked.

In the library I found, to my great delight, a vast number of English books, whole shelves full of them, and bound volumes of magazines and newspapers. A table in the centre was littered with English magazines and newspapers, though none of them were of very recent date. The books were of the most varied kind, history, geography, politics, political economy, botany, geology, law, all relating to England and English life and customs and manners. There were even such books of reference as the London Directory, the "Red" and "Blue" books, Whitaker's Almanack, the Army and Navy Lists, and—it somehow gladdened my heart to see it—the Law List.

Whilst I was looking at the books, the door opened, and the Count entered. He saluted me in a hearty way, and hoped that I had had a good night's rest. Then he went on, "I am glad you found your way in here, for I am sure there is much that will interest you. These companions," and he laid his hand on some of the books, "have been good friends to me, and for some years past, ever since I had the idea of going to London, have given me many, many hours of pleasure. Through them I have come to know your great England, and to know her is to love her. I long to go through the crowded streets of your mighty London, to be in the midst of the whirl and rush of humanity, to share its life, its change, its death, and all that makes it what it is. But alas! As yet I only know your tongue through books. To you, my friend, I look that I know it to speak."

"But, Count," I said, "you know and speak English thoroughly!"

He bowed gravely. "I thank you, my friend, for your all too-flattering estimate, but yet I fear that I am but a little way on the road I would travel. True, I know the grammar and the words, but yet I know not how to speak them."

"Indeed," I said, "you speak excellently."

"Not so," he answered. "Well, I know that, did I move and speak in your London, none there are who would not know me for a stranger. That is not enough for me. Here I am noble. I am a *boyar*. The common people know me, and I am master. But a stranger in a strange land, he is no one. Men know him not, and to know not is to care not for. I am content if I am like the rest, so that no man stops if he sees me, or pauses in his speaking if he hears my words, 'Ha, ha! A stranger!' I have been so long master that I would be master still, or at least that none other should be master of me. You come to me not alone as agent of my friend Peter Hawkins, of Exeter, to tell me all about my new estate in London. You shall, I trust, rest here with me a while, so that by our talking I may learn the English intonation. And I would that you tell me when I make error, even of the smallest, in my speaking. I am sorry that I had to be away so long today, but you will, I know, forgive one who has so many important affairs in hand."

Of course I said all I could about being willing, and asked if I might come into that room when I chose. He answered, "Yes, certainly," and added, "You may go anywhere you wish in the castle, except where the doors are locked, where of course you will not wish to go. There is reason that all things are as they are, and did you see with my eyes and know with my knowledge, you would perhaps better understand." I said I was sure of this, and then he went on. "We are in Transylvania, and Transylvania is not England. Our ways are not your ways, and there shall be to you many strange things. Nay, from what you have told me of your experiences already, you know something of what strange things there may be."

This led to much conversation, and as it was evident that he wanted to talk, if only for talking's sake, I asked him many questions regarding things that had already happened to me or come within my notice. Sometimes he sheered off the subject, or turned the conversation by pretending not to understand, but generally he answered all I asked most frankly. Then as time went on, and I had got somewhat bolder, I asked him of some of the strange things of the preceding night, as for instance, why the coachman went to the places where he had seen the blue flames. He then explained to me that it was commonly believed that on a certain night of the year—last night, in fact, when all evil spirits are supposed to have unchecked sway—a blue flame is seen over any place where treasure has been concealed. "That treasure has been hidden," he went on, "in the region through which you came last night, there can be but little doubt. For it was the ground fought over for centuries by the Wallachian, the Saxon, and the Turk. Why, there is hardly a foot of soil in all this region that has not been enriched by the blood of men, patriots or invaders. In the old days there were stirring times, when the Austrian and the Hungarian came up in hordes, and the patriots went out to meet them—men and women, the aged and the children too—and waited their coming on the rocks above the passes, that they might sweep destruction on them with their artificial avalanches. When the invader was triumphant he found but little, for whatever there was had been sheltered in the friendly soil."

"But how," said I, "can it have remained so long undiscovered, when there is a sure index to it if men will but take the trouble to look?" The Count smiled, and as his lips ran back over his gums, the long, sharp, canine teeth showed out strangely.

He answered, "Because your peasant is at heart a coward and a fool! Those flames only appear on one night, and on that night no man of this land will, if he can help it, stir without his doors. And, dear sir, even if he did he would not know what to do. Why, even the peasant that you tell me of who marked the place of the flame would not know where to look in daylight even for his own work. Even you would not, I dare be sworn, be able to find these places again?"

"There you are right," I said. "I know no more than the dead where even to look for them." Then we drifted into other matters.

"Come," he said at last, "tell me of London and of the house which you have procured for me." With an apology for my remissness, I went into my own room to get the papers from my bag. Whilst I was placing them in order I heard a rattling of china and silver in the next room, and as I passed through, noticed that the table had been cleared and the lamp lit, for it was by this time deep into the dark. The lamps were also lit in the study or library, and I found the Count lying on the sofa, reading, of all things in the world, an English Bradshaw's Guide. When I came in he cleared the books and papers from the table, and with him I went into plans and deeds and figures of all sorts. He was interested in everything, and asked me a myriad questions about the place and its surroundings. He clearly had studied beforehand all he could get on the subject of the neighbourhood, for he evidently at the end knew very much more than I did.

When I remarked this, he answered, "Well, but, my friend, is it not needful that I should? When I go there I shall be all alone, and my friend Harker Jonathan—nay, pardon me; I fall into my country's habit of putting your patronymic first—my friend Jonathan Harker will not be by my side to correct and aid me. He will be in Exeter, miles away, probably working at papers of the law with my other friend, Peter Hawkins. So!"

We went thoroughly into the business of the purchase of the estate at Purfleet. When I had told him the facts and got his signature to the necessary papers, and had written a letter with them ready to post to Mr. Hawkins, he began to ask me how I had come across so suitable a place. I read to him the notes which I had made at the time, and which I inscribe here:

> "At Purfleet, on a byroad, I came across just such a place as seemed to be required, and where was displayed a dilapidated notice that the place was for sale. It was surrounded by a high wall, of ancient structure, built of heavy stones, and has not been repaired for a large number of years. The closed gates are of heavy old oak and iron, all eaten with rust.
>
> "The estate is called Carfax, no doubt a corruption of the old *Quatre Face*, as the house is four sided, agreeing with the cardinal points of the compass. It contains in all some twenty acres, quite surrounded by the solid stone wall above mentioned. There are many trees on it, which make it in places gloomy, and there is a deep, dark-looking pond or small lake, evidently fed by some springs, as the water is clear and flows away in a fair-sized stream. The house is very large and of all periods back, I should say, to mediaeval times, for one part is of stone immensely thick, with only a few windows high up and heavily barred with iron. It looks like part of a keep, and is close to an old chapel or church. I could not enter it, as I had not the key of the door leading to it from the house, but I have taken with my Kodak views of it from various points. The house had been added to, but in a very straggling way, and I can only guess at the amount of ground it covers, which must be very great. There are but few houses close at hand, one being a very large house only recently added to and formed into a private lunatic asylum. It is not, however, visible from the grounds."

When I had finished, he said, "I am glad that it is old and big. I myself am of an old family, and to live in a new house would kill me. A house cannot be made habitable in a day, and after all, how few days go to make up a century. I rejoice also that there is a chapel of old times. We Transylvanian nobles love not to think that our bones may lie amongst the common dead. I seek not gaiety nor mirth, not the bright voluptuousness of much sunshine and sparkling waters which please the young and gay. I am no longer young, and my heart, through weary years of mourning over the dead, is not attuned to mirth. Moreover, the walls of my castle are broken. The shadows are many, and the wind breathes cold through the broken battlements and casements. I love the shade and the shadow, and would be alone with my thoughts when I may."

Somehow his words and his look did not seem to accord, or else it was that his cast of face made his smile look malignant and saturnine.

Presently, with an excuse, he left me, asking me to pull my papers together. He was some little time away, and I began to look at some of the books around me. One was an atlas, which I found opened naturally to England, as if that map had been much used. On looking at it I found in certain places little rings marked, and on examining these I noticed that one was near London on the east side, manifestly where his new estate was situated. The other two were Exeter, and Whitby on the Yorkshire coast.

It was the better part of an hour when the Count returned. "Aha!" he said. "Still at your books? Good! But you must not work always. Come! I am informed that your supper is ready." He took my arm, and we went into the next room, where I found an excellent supper ready on the table. The Count again excused himself, as he had dined out on his being away from home. But he sat as on the previous night, and chatted whilst I ate. After supper I smoked, as on the last evening, and the Count stayed with me, chatting and asking questions on every conceivable subject, hour after hour. I felt that it was getting very late indeed, but I did not say anything, for I felt under obligation to meet my host's wishes in every way. I was not sleepy, as the long sleep yesterday had fortified me, but I could not help experiencing that chill which comes over one at the coming of the dawn, which is like, in its way, the turn of the tide. They say that people who are near death die generally at the change to dawn or at the turn of the tide. Anyone who has when tired, and tied as it were to his post, experienced this change in the atmosphere can well believe it. All at once we heard the crow of the cock coming up with preternatural shrillness through the clear morning air.

Count Dracula, jumping to his feet, said, "Why, there is the morning again! How remiss I am to let you stay up so long. You must make your conversation regarding my dear new country of England less interesting, so that I may not forget how time flies by us," and with a courtly bow, he quickly left me.

I went into my room and drew the curtains, but there was little to notice. My window opened into the courtyard, all I could see was the warm gray of quickening sky. So I pulled the curtains again, and have written of this day.

8 May.

I began to fear as I wrote in this book that I was getting too diffuse. But now I am glad that I went into detail from the first, for there is something so strange about this place and all in it that I cannot but feel uneasy. I wish I were safe out of it, or that I had never come. It may be that this strange night existence is telling on me, but would that that were all! If there were anyone to talk to I could bear it, but there is no one. I have only the Count to speak with, and he—I fear I am myself the only living soul within the place. Let me be prosaic so far as facts can be. It will help me to bear up, and imagination must not run riot with me. If it does I am lost. Let me say at once how I stand—or seem to.

I only slept a few hours when I went to bed, and feeling that I could not sleep any more, got up. I had hung my shaving glass by the window, and was just beginning to shave. Suddenly I felt a hand on my shoulder, and heard the Count's voice saying to me, "Good morning." I started, for it amazed me that I had not seen him, since the reflection of the glass covered the whole room behind me. In starting I had cut myself slightly, but did not notice it at the moment. Having answered the Count's salutation, I turned to the glass again to see how I had been mistaken. This time there could be no error, for the man was close to me, and I could see him over my shoulder. But there was no reflection of him in the mirror! The whole room behind me was displayed, but there was no sign of a man in it, except myself.

This was startling, and coming on the top of so many strange things, was beginning to increase that vague feeling of uneasiness which I always have when the Count is near. But at the instant I saw that the cut had bled a little, and the blood was trickling over my chin. I laid down the razor, turning as I did so half round to look for some sticking plaster. When the Count saw my face, his eyes blazed with a sort of demoniac fury, and he suddenly made a grab at my throat. I drew away and his hand touched the string of beads which held the crucifix. It made an instant change in him, for the fury passed so quickly that I could hardly believe that it was ever there.

"Take care," he said, "take care how you cut yourself. It is more dangerous than you think in this country." Then seizing the shaving glass, he went on, "And this is the wretched thing that has done the mischief. It is a foul bauble of man's vanity. Away with it!" And opening the window with one wrench of his terrible hand, he flung out the glass, which was shattered into a thousand pieces on the stones of the courtyard far below. Then he withdrew without a word. It is very annoying, for I do not see how I am to shave, unless in my watch-case or the bottom of the shaving pot, which is fortunately of metal.

When I went into the dining room, breakfast was prepared, but I could not find the Count anywhere. So I breakfasted alone. It is strange that as yet I have not seen the Count eat or drink. He must be a very peculiar man! After breakfast I did a little exploring in the castle. I went out on the stairs, and found a room looking towards the south. The view was magnificent, and from where I stood there was every opportunity of seeing it. The castle is on the very edge of a terrific precipice. A stone falling from the window would fall a thousand feet without touching anything! As far as the eye can reach is a sea of green tree tops, with occasionally a deep rift where there is a chasm. Here and there are silver threads where the rivers wind in deep gorges through the forests.

But I am not in heart to describe beauty, for when I had seen the view I explored further. Doors, doors, doors everywhere, and all locked and bolted. In no place save from the windows in the castle walls is there an available exit.

The castle is a veritable prison, and I am a prisoner!

CHAPTER III

Jonathan Harker's Journal, Continued

When I found that I was a prisoner a sort of wild feeling came over me. I rushed up and down the stairs, trying every door and peering out of every window I could find, but after a little the conviction of my helplessness overpowered all other feelings. When I look back after a few hours I think I must have been mad for the time, for I behaved much as a rat does in a trap. When, however, the conviction had come to me that I was helpless I sat down quietly—as quietly as I have ever done anything in my life—and began to think over what was best to be done. I am thinking still, and as yet have come to no definite conclusion. Of one thing only am I certain. That it is no use making my ideas known to the Count. He knows well that I am imprisoned, and as he has done it himself, and has doubtless his own motives for it, he would only deceive me if I trusted him fully with the facts. So far as I can see, my only plan will be to keep my knowledge and my fears to myself, and my eyes open. I am, I know, either being deceived, like a baby, by my own fears, or else I am in desperate straits, and if the latter be so, I need, and shall need, all my brains to get through. I had hardly come to this conclusion when I heard the great door below shut, and knew that the Count had returned. He did not come at once into the library, so I went cautiously to my own room and found him making the bed. This was odd, but only confirmed what I had all along thought—that there are no servants in the house. When later I saw him through the chink of the hinges of the door laying the table in the dining room, I was assured of it. For if he does himself all these menial offices, surely it is proof that there is no one else in the castle, it must have been the Count himself who was the driver of the coach that brought me here. This is a terrible thought, for if so, what does it mean that he could control the wolves, as he did, by only holding up his hand for silence? How was it that all the people at Bistritz and on the coach had some terrible fear for me? What meant the giving of the crucifix, of the garlic, of the wild rose, of the mountain ash? Bless that good, good woman who hung the crucifix round my neck! For it is a comfort and a strength to me whenever I touch it. It is odd that a thing which I have been taught to regard with disfavour and as idolatrous should in a time of loneliness and trouble be of help. Is it that there is something in the essence of the thing itself, or that it is a medium, a tangible help, in conveying memories of sympathy and comfort? Some time, if it may be, I must examine this matter and try to make up my mind about it. In the meantime I must find out all I can about Count Dracula, as it may help me to understand. Tonight he may talk of himself, if I turn the conversation that way. I must be very careful, however, not to awake his suspicion.

Midnight.

I have had a long talk with the Count. I asked him a few questions on Transylvanian history, and he warmed up to the subject wonderfully. In his speaking of things and people, and especially of battles, he spoke as if he had been present at them all. This he afterwards explained by saying that to a *boyar* the pride of his house and name is his own pride, that their glory is his glory, that their fate is his fate. Whenever he spoke of his house he always said "we," and spoke almost in the plural, like a king speaking. I wish I could put down all he said exactly as he said it, for to me it was most fascinating. It seemed to have in it a whole history of the country. He grew excited as he spoke, and walked about the room pulling his great white moustache and grasping anything on which he laid his hands as though he would crush it by main strength. One thing he said which I shall put down as nearly as I can, for it tells in its way the story of his race:

"We Szekelys have a right to be proud, for in our veins flows the blood of many brave races who fought as the lion fights, for lordship. Here, in the whirlpool of European races, the Ugric tribe bore down from Iceland the fighting spirit which Thor and Wodin gave them, which their Berserkers displayed to such fell intent on the seaboards of Europe, aye, and of Asia and Africa too, till the peoples thought that the werewolves themselves had come. Here, too, when they came, they found the Huns, whose warlike fury had swept the earth like a living flame, till the dying peoples held that in their veins ran the blood of those old witches, who, expelled from Scythia had mated with the devils in the desert. Fools, fools! What devil or what witch was ever so great as Attila, whose blood is in these veins?" He held up his arms. "Is it a wonder that we were a conquering race, that we were proud, that when the Magyar, the Lombard, the Avar, the Bulgar, or the Turk poured his thousands on our frontiers, we drove them back? Is it strange that when Arpad and his legions swept through the Hungarian fatherland he found us here when he reached the frontier, that the Honfoglalas was completed there? And when the Hungarian flood swept eastward, the Szekelys were claimed as kindred by the victorious Magyars, and to us for centuries was trusted the guarding of the frontier of Turkeyland. Aye, and more than that, endless duty of the frontier guard, for as the Turks say, 'water sleeps, and the enemy is sleepless.' Who more gladly than we throughout the Four Nations received the 'bloody sword,' or at its warlike call flocked quicker to the standard of the King? When was redeemed that great shame of my nation, the shame of Cassova, when the flags of the Wallach and the Magyar went down beneath the Crescent? Who was it but one of my own race who as Voivode crossed the Danube and beat the Turk on his own ground? This was a Dracula indeed! Woe was it that his own unworthy brother, when he had fallen, sold his people to the Turk and brought the shame of slavery on them! Was it not this Dracula, indeed, who inspired that other of his race who in a later age again and again brought his forces over the great river into Turkeyland, who, when he was beaten back, came again, and again, though he had to come alone from the bloody field where his troops were being slaughtered, since he knew that he alone could ultimately triumph! They said that he thought only of himself. Bah! What good are peasants without a leader? Where ends the war without a brain and heart to conduct it? Again, when, after the battle of Mohacs, we threw off the Hungarian yoke, we of the Dracula blood were amongst their leaders, for our spirit would not brook that we were not free. Ah, young sir, the Szekelys—and the Dracula as their heart's blood, their brains, and their swords—can boast a record that mushroom growths like the Hapsburgs and the Romanoffs can never reach. The warlike days are over. Blood is too precious a thing in these days of dishonourable peace, and the glories of the great races are as a tale that is told."

It was by this time close on morning, and we went to bed. (*Mem.*, this diary seems horribly like the beginning of the "Arabian Nights," for everything has to break off at cock-crow, or like the ghost of Hamlet's father.)

12 May.

Let me begin with facts—bare, meager facts, verified by books and figures, and of which there can be no doubt. I must not confuse them with experiences which will have to rest on my own observation, or my memory of them. Last evening when the Count came from his room he began by asking me questions on legal matters and on the doing of certain kinds of business. I had spent the day wearily over books, and, simply to keep my mind occupied, went over some of the matters I had been examined in at Lincoln's Inn. There was a certain method in the Count's inquiries, so I shall try to put them down in sequence. The knowledge may somehow or some time be useful to me.

First, he asked if a man in England might have two solicitors or more. I told him he might have a dozen if he wished, but that it would not be wise to have more than one solicitor engaged in one transaction, as only one could act at a time, and that to change would be certain to militate against his interest. He seemed thoroughly to understand, and went on to ask if there would be any practical difficulty in having one man to attend, say, to banking, and another to look after shipping, in case local help were needed in a place far from the home of the banking solicitor.

I asked to explain more fully, so that I might not by any chance mislead him, so he said, "I shall illustrate. Your friend and mine, Mr. Peter Hawkins, from under the shadow of your beautiful cathedral at Exeter, which is far from London, buys for me through your good self my place at London. Good! Now here let me say frankly, lest you should think it strange that I have sought the services of one so far off from London instead of someone resident there, that my motive was that no local interest might be served save my wish only, and as one of London residence might, perhaps, have some purpose of himself or friend to serve, I went thus afield to seek my agent, whose labours should be only to my interest. Now, suppose I, who have much of affairs, wish to ship goods, say, to Newcastle, or Durham, or Harwich, or Dover, might it not be that it could with more ease be done by consigning to one in these ports?" I answered that certainly it would be most easy, but that we solicitors had a system of agency one for the other, so that local work could be done locally on instruction from any solicitor, so that the client, simply placing himself in the hands of one man, could have his wishes carried out by him without further trouble.

"But," said he, "I could be at liberty to direct myself. Is it not so?"

"Of course," I replied, and "Such is often done by men of business, who do not like the whole of their affairs to be known by any one person."

"Good!" he said, and then went on to ask about the means of making consignments and the forms to be gone through, and of all sorts of difficulties which might arise, but by forethought could be guarded against. I explained all these things to him to the best of my ability, and he certainly left me under the impression that he would have made a wonderful solicitor, for there was nothing that he did not think of or foresee. For a man who was never in the country, and who did not evidently do much in the way of business, his knowledge and acumen were wonderful. When he had satisfied himself on these points of which he had spoken, and I had verified all as well as I could by the books available, he suddenly stood up and said, "Have you written since your first letter to our friend Mr. Peter Hawkins, or to any other?" It was with some bitterness in my heart that I answered that I had not, that as yet I had not seen any opportunity of sending letters to anybody.

"Then write now, my young friend," he said, laying a heavy hand on my shoulder, "write to our friend and to any other, and say, if it will please you, that you shall stay with me until a month from now."

"Do you wish me to stay so long?" I asked, for my heart grew cold at the thought.

"I desire it much, nay I will take no refusal. When your master, employer, what you will, engaged that someone should come on his behalf, it was understood that my needs only were to be consulted. I have not stinted. Is it not so?"

What could I do but bow acceptance? It was Mr. Hawkins' interest, not mine, and I had to think of him, not myself, and besides, while Count Dracula was speaking, there was that in his eyes and in his bearing which made me remember that I was a prisoner, and that if I wished it I could have no choice. The Count saw his victory in my bow, and his mastery in the trouble of my face, for he began at once to use them, but in his own smooth, resistless way.

"I pray you, my good young friend, that you will not discourse of things other than business in your letters. It will doubtless please your friends to know that you are well, and that you look forward to getting home to them. Is it not so?" As he spoke he handed me three sheets of note paper and three envelopes. They were all of the thinnest foreign post, and looking at them, then at him, and noticing his quiet smile, with the sharp, canine teeth lying over the red underlip, I understood as well as if he had spoken that I should be more careful what I wrote, for he would be able to read it. So I determined to write only formal notes now, but to write fully to Mr. Hawkins in secret, and also to Mina, for to her I could write shorthand, which would puzzle the Count, if he did see it. When I had written my two letters I sat quiet, reading a book whilst the Count wrote several notes, referring as he wrote them to some books on his table. Then he took up my two and placed them with his own, and put by his writing materials, after which, the instant the door had closed behind him, I leaned over and looked at the letters, which were face down on the table. I felt no compunction in doing so for under the circumstances I felt that I should protect myself in every way I could.

One of the letters was directed to Samuel F. Billington, No. 7, The Crescent, Whitby, another to Herr Leutner, Varna. The third was to Coutts & Co., London, and the fourth to Herren Klopstock & Billreuth, bankers, Buda-Pesth. The second and fourth were unsealed. I was just about to look at them when I saw the door handle move. I sank back in my seat, having just had time to resume my book before the Count, holding still another letter in his hand, entered the room.

He took up the letters on the table and stamped them carefully, and then turning to me, said, "I trust you will forgive me, but I have much work to do in private this evening. You will, I hope, find all things as you wish." At the door he turned, and after a moment's pause said, "Let me advise you, my dear young friend. Nay, let me warn you with all seriousness, that should you leave these rooms you will not by any chance go to sleep in any other part of the castle. It is old, and has many memories, and there are bad dreams for those who sleep unwisely. Be warned! Should sleep now or ever overcome you, or be like to do, then haste to your own chamber or to these rooms, for your rest will then be safe. But if you be not careful in this respect, then," He finished his speech in a gruesome way, for he motioned with his hands as if he were washing them. I quite understood. My only doubt was as to whether any dream could be more terrible than the unnatural, horrible net of gloom and mystery which seemed closing around me.

Later.

I endorse the last words written, but this time there is no doubt in question. I shall not fear to sleep in any place where he is not. I have placed the crucifix over the head of my bed, I imagine that my rest is thus freer from dreams, and there it shall remain.

When he left me I went to my room. After a little while, not hearing any sound, I came out and went up the stone stair to where I could look out towards the South. There was some sense of freedom in the vast expanse, inaccessible though it was to me, as compared with the narrow darkness of the courtyard. Looking out on this, I felt that I was indeed in prison, and I seemed to want a breath of fresh air, though it were of the night. I am beginning to feel this nocturnal existence tell on me. It is destroying my nerve. I start at my own shadow, and am full of all sorts of horrible imaginings. God knows that there is ground for my terrible fear in this accursed place! I looked out over the beautiful expanse, bathed in soft yellow moonlight till it was almost as light as day. In the soft light the distant hills became melted, and the shadows in the valleys and gorges of velvety blackness. The mere beauty seemed to cheer me. There was peace and comfort in every breath I drew. As I leaned from the window my eye was caught by something moving a storey below me, and somewhat to my left, where I imagined, from the order of the rooms, that the windows of the Count's own room would look out. The window at which I stood was tall and deep, stone-mullioned, and though weatherworn, was still complete. But it was evidently many a day since the case had been there. I drew back behind the stonework, and looked carefully out.

What I saw was the Count's head coming out from the window. I did not see the face, but I knew the man by the neck and the movement of his back and arms. In any case I could not mistake the hands which I had had some many opportunities of studying. I was at first interested and somewhat amused, for it is wonderful how small a matter will interest and amuse a man when he is a prisoner. But my very feelings changed to repulsion and terror when I saw the whole man slowly emerge from the window and begin to crawl down the castle wall over the dreadful abyss, *face down* with his cloak spreading out around him like great wings. At first I could not believe my eyes. I thought it was some trick of the moonlight, some weird effect of shadow, but I kept looking, and it could be no delusion. I saw the fingers and toes grasp the corners of the stones, worn clear of the mortar by the stress of years, and by thus using every projection and inequality move downwards with considerable speed, just as a lizard moves along a wall.

What manner of man is this, or what manner of creature, is it in the semblance of man? I feel the dread of this horrible place overpowering me. I am in fear—in awful fear—and there is no escape for me. I am encompassed about with terrors that I dare not think of . . .

15 May.

Once more have I seen the count go out in his lizard fashion. He moved downwards in a sidelong way, some hundred feet down, and a good deal to the left. He vanished into some hole or window. When his head had disappeared, I leaned out to try and see more, but without avail. The distance was too great to allow a proper angle of sight. I knew he had left the castle now, and thought to use the opportunity to explore more than I had dared to do as yet. I went back to the room, and taking a lamp, tried all the doors. They were all locked, as I had expected, and the locks were comparatively new. But I went down the stone stairs to the hall where I had entered originally. I found I could pull back the bolts easily enough and unhook the great chains. But the door was locked, and the key was gone! That key must be in the Count's room. I must watch should his door be unlocked, so that I may get it and escape. I went on to make a thorough examination of the various stairs and passages, and to try the doors that opened from them. One or two small rooms near the hall were open, but there was nothing to see in them except old furniture, dusty with age and moth-eaten. At last, however, I found one door at the top of the stairway which, though it seemed locked, gave a little under pressure. I tried it harder, and found that it was not really locked, but that the resistance came from the fact that the hinges had fallen somewhat, and the heavy door rested on the floor. Here was an opportunity which I might not have again, so I exerted myself, and with many efforts forced it back so that I could enter. I was now in a wing of the castle further to the right than the rooms I knew and a storey lower down. From the windows I could see that the suite of rooms lay along to the south of the castle, the windows of the end room looking out both west and south. On the latter side, as well as to the former, there was a great precipice.

The castle was built on the corner of a great rock, so that on three sides it was quite impregnable, and great windows were placed here where sling, or bow, or culverin could not reach, and consequently light and comfort, impossible to a position which had to be guarded, were secured. To the west was a great valley, and then, rising far away, great jagged mountain fastnesses, rising peak on peak, the sheer rock studded with mountain ash and thorn, whose roots clung in cracks and crevices and crannies of the stone. This was evidently the portion of the castle occupied by the ladies in bygone days, for the furniture had more an air of comfort than any I had seen. The windows were curtainless, and the yellow moonlight, flooding in through the diamond panes, enabled one to see even colours, whilst it softened the wealth of dust which lay over all and disguised in some measure the ravages of time and moth. My lamp seemed to be of little effect in the brilliant moonlight, but I was glad to have it with me, for there was a dread loneliness in the place which chilled my heart and made my nerves tremble. Still, it was better than living alone in the rooms which I had come to hate from the presence of the Count, and after trying a little to school my nerves, I found a soft quietude come over me. Here I am, sitting at a little oak table where in old times possibly some fair lady sat to pen, with much thought and many blushes, her ill-spelt love letter, and writing in my diary in shorthand all that has happened since I closed it last. It is the nineteenth century up-to-date with a vengeance. And yet, unless my senses deceive me, the old centuries had, and have, powers of their own which mere "modernity" cannot kill.

Later: the morning of 16 May.

God preserve my sanity, for to this I am reduced. Safety and the assurance of safety are things of the past. Whilst I live on here there is but one thing to hope for, that I may not go mad, if, indeed, I be not mad already. If I be sane, then surely it is maddening to think that of all the foul things that lurk in this hateful place the Count is the least dreadful to me, that to him alone I can look for safety, even though this be only whilst I can serve his purpose. Great God! Merciful God, let me be calm, for out of that way lies madness indeed. I begin to get new lights on certain things which have puzzled me. Up to now I never quite knew what Shakespeare meant when he made Hamlet say:

> "My tablets! Quick, my tablets!
> 'Tis meet that I put it down," etc.

For now, feeling as though my own brain were unhinged or as if the shock had come which must end in its undoing, I turn to my diary for repose. The habit of entering accurately must help to soothe me.

The Count's mysterious warning frightened me at the time. It frightens me more not when I think of it, for in the future he has a fearful hold upon me. I shall fear to doubt what he may say!

When I had written in my diary and had fortunately replaced the book and pen in my pocket I felt sleepy. The Count's warning came into my mind, but I took pleasure in disobeying it. The sense of sleep was upon me, and with it the obstinacy which sleep brings as outrider. The soft moonlight soothed, and the wide expanse without gave a sense of freedom which refreshed me. I determined not to return tonight to the gloom-haunted rooms, but to sleep here, where, of old, ladies had sat and sung and lived sweet lives whilst their gentle breasts were sad for their menfolk away in the midst of remorseless wars. I drew a great couch out of its place near the corner, so that as I lay, I could look at the lovely view to east and south, and unthinking of and uncaring for the dust, composed myself for sleep.

I suppose I must have fallen asleep. I hope so, but I fear, for all that followed was startlingly real, so real that now sitting here in the broad, full sunlight of the morning, I cannot in the least believe that it was all sleep.

I was not alone. The room was the same, unchanged in any way since I came into it. I could see along the floor, in the brilliant moonlight, my own footsteps marked where I had disturbed the long accumulation of dust. In the moonlight opposite me were three young women, ladies by their dress and manner. I thought at the time that I must be dreaming when I saw them, they threw no shadow on the floor. They came close to me, and looked at me for some time, and then whispered together. Two were dark, and had high aquiline noses, like the Count, and great dark, piercing eyes, that seemed to be almost red when contrasted with the pale yellow moon. The other was fair, as fair as can be, with great masses of golden hair and eyes like pale sapphires. I seemed somehow to know her face, and to know it in connection with some dreamy fear, but I could not recollect at the moment how or where. All three had brilliant white teeth that shone like pearls against the ruby of their voluptuous lips. There was something about them that made me uneasy, some longing and at the same time some deadly fear. I felt in my heart a wicked, burning desire that they would kiss me with those red lips. It is not good to note this down, lest someday it should meet Mina's eyes and cause her pain, but it is the truth. They whispered together, and then they all three laughed, such a silvery, musical laugh, but as hard as though the sound never could have come through the softness of human lips. It was like the intolerable, tingling sweetness of waterglasses when played on by a cunning hand. The fair girl shook her head coquettishly, and the other two urged her on.

One said, "Go on! You are first, and we shall follow. Yours is the right to begin."

The other added, "He is young and strong. There are kisses for us all."

I lay quiet, looking out from under my eyelashes in an agony of delightful anticipation. The fair girl advanced and bent over me till I could feel the movement of her breath upon me. Sweet it was in one sense, honey-sweet, and sent the same tingling through the nerves as her voice, but with a bitter underlying the sweet, a bitter offensiveness, as one smells in blood.

I was afraid to raise my eyelids, but looked out and saw perfectly under the lashes. The girl went on her knees, and bent over me, simply gloating. There was a deliberate voluptuousness which was both thrilling and repulsive, and as she arched her neck she actually licked her lips like an animal, till I could see in the moonlight the moisture shining on the scarlet lips and on the red tongue as it lapped the white sharp teeth. Lower and lower went her head as the lips went below the range of my mouth and chin and seemed to fasten on my throat. Then she paused, and I could hear the churning sound of her tongue as it licked her teeth and lips, and I could feel the hot breath on my neck. Then the skin of my throat began to tingle as one's flesh does when the hand that is to tickle it approaches nearer, nearer. I could feel the soft, shivering touch of the lips on the super sensitive skin of my throat, and the hard dents of two sharp teeth, just touching and pausing there. I closed my eyes in languorous ecstasy and waited, waited with beating heart.

But at that instant, another sensation swept through me as quick as lightning. I was conscious of the presence of the Count, and of his being as if lapped in a storm of fury. As my eyes opened involuntarily I saw his strong hand grasp the slender neck of the fair woman and with giant's power draw it back, the blue eyes transformed with fury, the white teeth champing with rage, and the fair cheeks blazing red with passion. But the Count! Never did I imagine such wrath and fury, even to the demons of the pit. His eyes were positively blazing. The red light in them was lurid, as if the flames of hell-fire blazed behind them. His face was deathly pale, and the lines of it were hard like drawn wires. The thick eyebrows that met over the nose now seemed like a heaving bar of white-hot metal. With a fierce sweep of his arm, he hurled the woman from him, and then motioned to the others, as though he were beating them back. It was the same imperious gesture that I had seen used to the wolves.

In a voice which, though low and almost in a whisper seemed to cut through the air and then ring in the room he said, "How dare you touch him, any of you? How dare you cast eyes on him when I had forbidden it? Back, I tell you all! This man belongs to me! Beware how you meddle with him, or you'll have to deal with me."

The fair girl, with a laugh of ribald coquetry, turned to answer him. "You yourself never loved. You never love!" On this the other women joined, and such a mirthless, hard, soulless laughter rang through the room that it almost made me faint to hear. It seemed like the pleasure of fiends.

Then the Count turned, after looking at my face attentively, and said in a soft whisper, "Yes, I too can love. You yourselves can tell it from the past. Is it not so? Well, now I promise you that when I am done with him you shall kiss him at your will. Now go! Go! I must awaken him, for there is work to be done."

"Are we to have nothing tonight?" said one of them, with a low laugh, as she pointed to the bag which he had thrown upon the floor, and which moved as though there were some living thing within it. For answer he nodded his head. One of the women jumped forward and opened it. If my ears did not deceive me there was a gasp and a low wail, as of a half smothered child. The women closed round, whilst I was aghast with horror. But as I looked, they disappeared, and with them the dreadful bag. There was no door near them, and they could not have passed me without my noticing. They simply seemed to fade into the rays of the moonlight and pass out through the window, for I could see outside the dim, shadowy forms for a moment before they entirely faded away.

Then the horror overcame me, and I sank down unconscious.

CHAPTER IV

Jonathan Harker's Journal, Continued

I awoke in my own bed. If it be that I had not dreamt, the Count must have carried me here. I tried to satisfy myself on the subject, but could not arrive at any unquestionable result. To be sure, there were certain small evidences, such as that my clothes were folded and laid by in a manner which was not my habit. My watch was still unwound, and I am rigorously accustomed to wind it the last thing before going to bed, and many such details. But these things are no proof, for they may have been evidences that my mind was not as usual, and, for some cause or another, I had certainly been much upset. I must watch for proof. Of one thing I am glad. If it was that the Count carried me here and undressed me, he must have been hurried in his task, for my pockets are intact. I am sure this diary would have been a mystery to him which he would not have brooked. He would have taken or destroyed it. As I look round this room, although it has been to me so full of fear, it is now a sort of sanctuary, for nothing can be more dreadful than those awful women, who were—who are—waiting to suck my blood.

18 May.

I have been down to look at that room again in daylight, for I *must* know the truth. When I got to the doorway at the top of the stairs I found it closed. It had been so forcibly driven against the jamb that part of the woodwork was splintered. I could see that the bolt of the lock had not been shot, but the door is fastened from the inside. I fear it was no dream, and must act on this surmise.

19 May.

I am surely in the toils. Last night the Count asked me in the suavest tones to write three letters, one saying that my work here was nearly done, and that I should start for home within a few days, another that I was starting on the next morning from the time of the letter, and the third that I had left the castle and arrived at Bistritz. I would fain have rebelled, but felt that in the present state of things it would be madness to quarrel openly with the Count whilst I am so absolutely in his power. And to refuse would be to excite his suspicion and to arouse his anger. He knows that I know too much, and that I must not live, lest I be dangerous to him. My only chance is to prolong my opportunities. Something may occur which will give me a chance to escape. I saw in his eyes something of that gathering wrath which was manifest when he hurled that fair woman from him. He explained to me that posts were few and uncertain, and that my writing now would ensure ease of mind to my friends. And he assured me with so much impressiveness that he would countermand the later letters, which would be held over at Bistritz until due time in case chance would admit of my prolonging my stay, that to oppose him would have been to create new suspicion. I therefore pretended to fall in with his views, and asked him what dates I should put on the letters.

He calculated a minute, and then said, "The first should be June 12, the second June 19, and the third June 29."

I know now the span of my life. God help me!

28 May.

There is a chance of escape, or at any rate of being able to send word home. A band of Szgany have come to the castle, and are encamped in the courtyard. These Szgany are gypsies; I have notes of them in my book. They are peculiar to this part of the world, though allied to the ordinary gipsies all the world over. There are thousands of them in Hungary and Transylvania, who are almost outside all law. They attach themselves as a rule to some great noble or *boyar*, and call themselves by his name. They are fearless and without religion, save superstition, and they talk only their own varieties of the Romany tongue.

I shall write some letters home, and shall try to get them to have them posted. I have already spoken to them through my window to begin acquaintanceship. They took their hats off and made obeisance and many signs, which however, I could not understand any more than I could their spoken language . . .

I have written the letters. Mina's is in shorthand, and I simply ask Mr. Hawkins to communicate with her. To her I have explained my situation, but without the horrors which I may only surmise. It would shock and frighten her to death were I to expose my heart to her. Should the letters not carry, then the Count shall not yet know my secret or the extent of my knowledge . . .

I have given the letters. I threw them through the bars of my window with a gold piece, and made what signs I could to have them posted. The man who took them pressed them to his heart and bowed, and then put them in his cap. I could do no more. I stole back to the study, and began to read. As the Count did not come in, I have written here . . .

The Count has come. He sat down beside me, and said in his smoothest voice as he opened two letters, "The Szgany has given me these, of which, though I know not whence they come, I shall, of course, take care. See!"—he must have looked at it—"one is from you, and to my friend Peter Hawkins. The other"—here he caught sight of the strange symbols as he opened the envelope, and the dark look came into his face, and his eyes blazed wickedly—"the other is a vile thing, an outrage upon friendship and hospitality! It is not signed. Well! So it cannot matter to us." And he calmly held letter and envelope in the flame of the lamp till they were consumed.

Then he went on, "The letter to Hawkins, that I shall, of course send on, since it is yours. Your letters are sacred to me. Your pardon, my friend, that unknowingly I did break the seal. Will you not cover it again?" He held out the letter to me, and with a courteous bow handed me a clean envelope. I could only redirect it and hand it to him in silence. When he went out of the room I could hear the key turn softly. A minute later I went over and tried it, and the door was locked.

When, an hour or two after, the Count came quietly into the room, his coming awakened me, for I had gone to sleep on the sofa. He was very courteous and very cheery in his manner, and seeing that I had been sleeping, he said, "So, my friend, you are tired? Get to bed. There is the surest rest. I may not have the pleasure of talk tonight, since there are many labours to me, but you will sleep, I pray." I passed to my room and went to bed, and, strange to say, slept without dreaming. Despair has its own calms.

31 May.

This morning when I woke I thought I would provide myself with some papers and envelopes from my bag and keep them in my pocket, so that I might write in case I should get an opportunity, but again a surprise, again a shock!

Every scrap of paper was gone, and with it all my notes, my memoranda, relating to railways and travel, my letter of credit, in fact all that might be useful to me were I once outside the castle. I sat and pondered a while, and then some thought occurred to me, and I made search of my portmanteau and in the wardrobe where I had placed my clothes.

The suit in which I had travelled was gone, and also my overcoat and rug. I could find no trace of them anywhere. This looked like some new scheme of villainy . . .

17 June.

This morning, as I was sitting on the edge of my bed cudgelling my brains, I heard without a crackling of whips and pounding and scraping of horses' feet up the rocky path beyond the courtyard. With joy I hurried to the window, and saw drive into the yard two great leiter-wagons, each drawn by eight sturdy horses, and at the head of each pair a Slovak, with his wide hat, great nail-studded belt, dirty sheepskin, and high boots. They had also their long staves in hand. I ran to the door, intending to descend and try and join them through the main hall, as I thought that way might be opened for them. Again a shock, my door was fastened on the outside.

Then I ran to the window and cried to them. They looked up at me stupidly and pointed, but just then the "hetman" of the Szgany came out, and seeing them pointing to my window, said something, at which they laughed. Henceforth no effort of mine, no piteous cry or agonized entreaty, would make them even look at me. They resolutely turned away. The leiter-wagons contained great, square boxes, with handles of thick rope. These were evidently empty by the ease with which the Slovaks handled them, and by their resonance as they were roughly moved. When they were all unloaded and packed in a great heap in one corner of the yard, the Slovaks were given some money by the Szgany, and spitting on it for luck, lazily went each to his horse's head. Shortly afterwards, I heard the crackling of their whips die away in the distance.

24 June, before morning.

Last night the Count left me early, and locked himself into his own room. As soon as I dared I ran up the winding stair, and looked out of the window, which opened South. I thought I would watch for the Count, for there is something going on. The Szgany are quartered somewhere in the castle and are doing work of some kind. I know it, for now and then, I hear a far-away muffled sound as of mattock and spade, and, whatever it is, it must be the end of some ruthless villainy.

I had been at the window somewhat less than half an hour, when I saw something coming out of the Count's window. I drew back and watched carefully, and saw the whole man emerge. It was a new shock to me to find that he had on the suit of clothes which I had worn whilst travelling here, and slung over his shoulder the terrible bag which I had seen the women take away. There could be no doubt as to his quest, and in my garb, too! This, then, is his new scheme of evil, that he will allow others to see me, as they think, so that he may both leave evidence that I have been seen in the towns or villages posting my own letters, and that any wickedness which he may do shall by the local people be attributed to me.

It makes me rage to think that this can go on, and whilst I am shut up here, a veritable prisoner, but without that protection of the law which is even a criminal's right and consolation.

I thought I would watch for the Count's return, and for a long time sat doggedly at the window. Then I began to notice that there were some quaint little specks floating in the rays of the moonlight. They were like the tiniest grains of dust, and they whirled round and gathered in clusters in a nebulous sort of way. I watched them with a sense of soothing, and a sort of calm stole over me. I leaned back in the embrasure in a more comfortable position, so that I could enjoy more fully the aerial gambolling.

Something made me start up, a low, piteous howling of dogs somewhere far below in the valley, which was hidden from my sight. Louder it seemed to ring in my ears, and the floating moats of dust to take new shapes to the sound as they danced in the moonlight. I felt myself struggling to awake to some call of my instincts. Nay, my very soul was struggling, and my half-remembered sensibilities were striving to answer the call. I was becoming hypnotized! Quicker and quicker danced the dust. The moonbeams seemed to quiver as they went by me into the mass of gloom beyond. More and more they gathered till they seemed to take dim phantom shapes. And then I started, broad awake and in full possession of my senses, and ran screaming from the place. The phantom shapes, which were becoming gradually materialised from the moonbeams, were those three ghostly women to whom I was doomed. I fled, and felt somewhat safer in my own room, where there was no moonlight, and where the lamp was burning brightly.

When a couple of hours had passed I heard something stirring in the Count's room, something like a sharp wail quickly suppressed. And then there was silence, deep, awful silence, which chilled me. With a beating heart, I tried the door, but I was locked in my prison, and could do nothing. I sat down and simply cried.

As I sat I heard a sound in the courtyard without—the agonized cry of a woman. I rushed to the window, and throwing it up, peered between the bars. There, indeed, was a woman with dishevelled hair, holding her hands over her heart as one distressed with running. She was leaning against the corner of the gateway. When she saw my face at the window she threw herself forward, and shouted in a voice laden with menace, "Monster, give me my child!"

She threw herself on her knees, and raising up her hands, cried the same words in tones which wrung my heart. Then she tore her hair and beat her breast, and abandoned herself to all the violences of extravagant emotion. Finally, she threw herself forward, and though I could not see her, I could hear the beating of her naked hands against the door.

Somewhere high overhead, probably on the tower, I heard the voice of the Count calling in his harsh, metallic whisper. His call seemed to be answered from far and wide by the howling of wolves. Before many minutes had passed a pack of them poured, like a pent-up dam when liberated, through the wide entrance into the courtyard.

There was no cry from the woman, and the howling of the wolves was but short. Before long they streamed away singly, licking their lips.

I could not pity her, for I knew now what had become of her child, and she was better dead.

What shall I do? What can I do? How can I escape from this dreadful thing of night, gloom, and fear?

25 June, morning.

No man knows till he has suffered from the night how sweet and dear to his heart and eye the morning can be. When the sun grew so high this morning that it struck the top of the great gateway opposite my window, the high spot which it touched seemed to me as if the dove from the ark had lighted there. My fear fell from me as if it had been a vaporous garment which dissolved in the warmth. I must take action of some sort whilst the courage of the day is upon me. Last night one of my post-dated letters went to post, the first of that fatal series which is to blot out the very traces of my existence from the earth.

Let me not think of it. Action!

It has always been at night-time that I have been molested or threatened, or in some way in danger or in fear. I have not yet seen the Count in the daylight. Can it be that he sleeps when others wake, that he may be awake whilst they sleep? If I could only get into his room! But there is no possible way. The door is always locked, no way for me.

Yes, there is a way, if one dares to take it. Where his body has gone why may not another body go? I have seen him myself crawl from his window. Why should not I imitate him, and go in by his window? The chances are desperate, but my need is more desperate still. I shall risk it. At the worst it can only be death, and a man's death is not a calf's, and the dreaded Hereafter may still be open to me. God help me in my task! Goodbye, Mina, if I fail. Goodbye, my faithful friend and second father. Goodbye, all, and last of all Mina!

Same day, later.

I have made the effort, and God helping me, have come safely back to this room. I must put down every detail in order. I went whilst my courage was fresh straight to the window on the south side, and at once got outside on this side. The stones are big and roughly cut, and the mortar has by process of time been washed away between them. I took off my boots, and ventured out on the desperate way. I looked down once, so as to make sure that a sudden glimpse of the awful depth would not overcome me, but after that kept my eyes away from it. I know pretty well the direction and distance of the Count's window, and made for it as well as I could, having regard to the opportunities available. I did not feel dizzy, I suppose I was too excited, and the time seemed ridiculously short till I found myself standing on the window sill and trying to raise up the sash. I was filled with agitation, however, when I bent down and slid feet foremost in through the window. Then I looked around for the Count, but with surprise and gladness, made a discovery. The room was empty! It was barely furnished with odd things, which seemed to have never been used. The furniture was something the same style as that in the south rooms, and was covered with dust. I looked for the key, but it was not in the lock, and I could not find it anywhere. The only thing I found was a great heap of gold in one corner—gold of all kinds, Roman, and British, and Austrian, and Hungarian, and Greek and Turkish money, covered with a film of dust, as though it had lain long in the ground. None of it that I noticed was less than three hundred years old. There were also chains and ornaments, some jewelled, but all of them old and stained.

At one corner of the room was a heavy door. I tried it, for, since I could not find the key of the room or the key of the outer door, which was the main object of my search, I must make further examination, or all my efforts would be in vain. It was open, and led through a stone passage to a circular stairway, which went steeply down. I descended, minding carefully where I went, for the stairs were dark, being only lit by loopholes in the heavy masonry. At the bottom there was a dark, tunnel-like passage, through which came a deathly, sickly odour, the odour of old earth newly turned. As I went through the passage the smell grew closer and heavier. At last I pulled open a heavy door which stood ajar, and found myself in an old ruined chapel, which had evidently been used as a graveyard. The roof was broken, and in two places were steps leading to vaults, but the ground had recently been dug over, and the earth placed in great wooden boxes, manifestly those which had been brought by the Slovaks. There was nobody about, and I made a search over every inch of the ground, so as not to lose a chance. I went down even into the vaults, where the dim light struggled, although to do so was a dread to my very soul. Into two of these I went, but saw nothing except fragments of old coffins and piles of dust. In the third, however, I made a discovery.

There, in one of the great boxes, of which there were fifty in all, on a pile of newly dug earth, lay the Count! He was either dead or asleep. I could not say which, for eyes were open and stony, but without the glassiness of death, and the cheeks had the warmth of life through all their pallor. The lips were as red as ever. But there was no sign of movement, no pulse, no breath, no beating of the heart. I bent over him, and tried to find any sign of life, but in vain. He could not have lain there long, for the earthy smell would have passed away in a few hours. By the side of the box was its cover, pierced with holes here and there. I thought he might have the keys on him, but when I went to search I saw the dead eyes, and in them dead though they were, such a look of hate, though unconscious of me or my presence, that I fled from the place, and leaving the Count's room by the window, crawled again up the castle wall. Regaining my room, I threw myself panting upon the bed and tried to think . . .

29 June.

Today is the date of my last letter, and the Count has taken steps to prove that it was genuine, for again I saw him leave the castle by the same window, and in my clothes. As he went down the wall, lizard fashion, I wished I had a gun or some lethal weapon, that I might destroy him. But I fear that no weapon wrought along by man's hand would have any effect on him. I dared not wait to see him return, for I feared to see those weird sisters. I came back to the library, and read there till I fell asleep.

I was awakened by the Count, who looked at me as grimly as a man could look as he said, "Tomorrow, my friend, we must part. You return to your beautiful England, I to some work which may have such an end that we may never meet. Your letter home has been despatched. Tomorrow I shall not be here, but all shall be ready for your journey. In the morning come the Szgany, who have some labours of their own here, and also come some Slovaks. When they have gone, my carriage shall come for you, and shall bear you to the Borgo Pass to meet the diligence from Bukovina to Bistritz. But I am in hopes that I shall see more of you at Castle Dracula."

I suspected him, and determined to test his sincerity. Sincerity! It seems like a profanation of the word to write it in connection with such a monster, so I asked him point-blank, "Why may I not go tonight?"

"Because, dear sir, my coachman and horses are away on a mission."

"But I would walk with pleasure. I want to get away at once."

He smiled, such a soft, smooth, diabolical smile that I knew there was some trick behind his smoothness. He said, "And your baggage?"

"I do not care about it. I can send for it some other time."

The Count stood up, and said, with a sweet courtesy which made me rub my eyes, it seemed so real, "You English have a saying which is close to my heart, for its spirit is that which rules our *boyars*, 'Welcome the coming, speed the parting guest.' Come with me, my dear young friend. Not an hour shall you wait in my house against your will, though sad am I at your going, and that you so suddenly desire it. Come!" With a stately gravity, he, with the lamp, preceded me down the stairs and along the hall. Suddenly he stopped. "Hark!"

Close at hand came the howling of many wolves. It was almost as if the sound sprang up at the rising of his hand, just as the music of a great orchestra seems to leap under the baton of the conductor. After a pause of a moment, he proceeded, in his stately way, to the door, drew back the ponderous bolts, unhooked the heavy chains, and began to draw it open.

To my intense astonishment I saw that it was unlocked. Suspiciously, I looked all round, but could see no key of any kind.

As the door began to open, the howling of the wolves without grew louder and angrier. Their red jaws, with champing teeth, and their blunt-clawed feet as they leaped, came in through the opening door. I knew than that to struggle at the moment against the Count was useless. With such allies as these at his command, I could do nothing. But still the door continued slowly to open, and only the Count's body stood in the gap. Suddenly it struck me that this might be the moment and means of my doom. I was to be given to the wolves, and at my own instigation. There was a diabolical wickedness in the idea great enough for the Count, and as the last chance I cried out, "Shut the door! I shall wait till morning." And I covered my face with my hands to hide my tears of bitter disappointment. With one sweep of his powerful arm, the Count threw the door shut, and the great bolts clanged and echoed through the hall as they shot back into their places.

In silence we returned to the library, and after a minute or two I went to my own room. The last I saw of Count Dracula was his kissing his hand to me, with a red light of triumph in his eyes, and with a smile that Judas in hell might be proud of.

When I was in my room and about to lie down, I thought I heard a whispering at my door. I went to it softly and listened. Unless my ears deceived me, I heard the voice of the Count.

"Back! Back to your own place! Your time is not yet come. Wait! Have patience! Tonight is mine. Tomorrow night is yours!" There was a low, sweet ripple of laughter, and in a rage I threw open the door, and saw without the three terrible women licking their lips. As I appeared, they all joined in a horrible laugh, and ran away.

I came back to my room and threw myself on my knees. It is then so near the end? Tomorrow! Tomorrow! Lord, help me, and those to whom I am dear!

30 June, morning.

These may be the last words I ever write in this diary. I slept till just before the dawn, and when I woke threw myself on my knees, for I determined that if Death came he should find me ready.

At last I felt that subtle change in the air, and knew that the morning had come. Then came the welcome cock-crow, and I felt that I was safe. With a glad heart, I opened the door and ran down the hall. I had seen that the door was unlocked, and now escape was before me. With hands that trembled with eagerness, I unhooked the chains and threw back the massive bolts.

But the door would not move. Despair seized me. I pulled and pulled at the door, and shook it till, massive as it was, it rattled in its casement. I could see the bolt shot. It had been locked after I left the Count.

Then a wild desire took me to obtain the key at any risk, and I determined then and there to scale the wall again, and gain the Count's room. He might kill me, but death now seemed the happier choice of evils. Without a pause I rushed up to the east window, and scrambled down the wall, as before, into the Count's room. It was empty, but that was as I expected. I could not see a key anywhere, but the heap of gold remained. I went through the door in the corner and down the winding stair and along the dark passage to the old chapel. I knew now well enough where to find the monster I sought.

The great box was in the same place, close against the wall, but the lid was laid on it, not fastened down, but with the nails ready in their places to be hammered home. I knew I must reach the body for the key, so I raised the lid, and laid it back against the wall. And then I saw something which filled my very soul with horror. There lay the Count, but looking as if his youth had been half restored. For the white hair and moustache were changed to dark iron-gray. The cheeks were fuller, and the white skin seemed ruby-red underneath. The mouth was redder than ever, for on the lips were gouts of fresh blood, which trickled from the corners of the mouth and ran down over the chin and neck. Even the deep, burning eyes seemed set amongst swollen flesh, for the lids and pouches underneath were bloated. It seemed as if the whole awful creature were simply gorged with blood. He lay like a filthy leech, exhausted with his repletion. I shuddered as I bent over to touch him, and every sense in me revolted at the contact, but I had to search, or I was lost. The coming night might see my own body a banquet in a similar war to those horrid three. I felt all over the body, but no sign could I find of the key. Then I stopped and looked at the Count. There was a mocking smile on the bloated face which seemed to drive me mad. This was the being I was helping to transfer to London, where, perhaps, for centuries to come he might, amongst its teeming millions, satiate his lust for blood, and create a new and ever-widening circle of semi-demons to batten on the helpless. The very thought drove me mad. A terrible desire came upon me to rid the world of such a monster. There was no lethal weapon at hand, but I seized a shovel which the workmen had been using to fill the cases, and lifting it high, struck, with the edge downward, at the hateful face. But as I did so the head turned, and the eyes fell upon me, with all their blaze of basilisk horror. The sight seemed to paralyze me, and the shovel turned in my hand and glanced from the face, merely making a deep gash above the forehead. The shovel fell from my hand across the box, and as I pulled it away the flange of the blade caught the edge of the lid which fell over again, and hid the horrid thing from my sight. The last glimpse I had was of the bloated face, blood-stained and fixed with a grin of malice which would have held its own in the nethermost hell.

I thought and thought what should be my next move, but my brain seemed on fire, and I waited with a despairing feeling growing over me. As I waited I heard in the distance a gypsy song sung by merry voices coming closer, and through their song the rolling of heavy wheels and the cracking of whips. The Szgany and the Slovaks of whom the Count had spoken were coming. With a last look around and at the box which contained the vile body, I ran from the place and gained the Count's room, determined to rush out at the moment the door should be opened. With strained ears, I listened, and heard downstairs the grinding of the key in the great lock and the falling back of the heavy door. There must have been some other means of entry, or someone had a key for one of the locked doors. Then there came the sound of many feet tramping and dying away in some passage which sent up a clanging echo. I turned to run down again towards the vault, where I might find the new entrance, but at the moment there seemed to come a violent puff of wind, and the door to the winding stair blew to with a shock that set the dust from the lintels flying. When I ran to push it open, I found that it was hopelessly fast. I was again a prisoner, and the net of doom was closing round me more closely.

As I write there is in the passage below a sound of many tramping feet and the crash of weights being set down heavily, doubtless the boxes, with their freight of earth. There was a sound of hammering. It is the box being nailed down. Now I can hear the heavy feet tramping again along the hall, with many other idle feet coming behind them.

The door is shut, the chains rattle. There is a grinding of the key in the lock. I can hear the key withdrawn, then another door opens and shuts. I hear the creaking of lock and bolt.

Hark! In the courtyard and down the rocky way the roll of heavy wheels, the crack of whips, and the chorus of the Szgany as they pass into the distance.

I am alone in the castle with those horrible women. Faugh! Mina is a woman, and there is nought in common. They are devils of the Pit!

I shall not remain alone with them. I shall try to scale the castle wall farther than I have yet attempted. I shall take some of the gold with me, lest I want it later. I may find a way from this dreadful place.

And then away for home! Away to the quickest and nearest train! Away from the cursed spot, from this cursed land, where the devil and his children still walk with earthly feet!

At least God's mercy is better than that of those monsters, and the precipice is steep and high. At its foot a man may sleep, as a man. Goodbye, all. Mina!

CHAPTER V

LETTER FROM MISS MINA MURRAY TO MISS LUCY WESTENRA

9 May.

My dearest Lucy,

Forgive my long delay in writing, but I have been simply overwhelmed with work. The life of an assistant schoolmistress is sometimes trying. I am longing to be with you, and by the sea, where we can talk together freely and build our castles in the air. I have been working very hard lately, because I want to keep up with Jonathan's studies, and I have been practicing shorthand very assiduously. When we are married I shall be able to be useful to Jonathan, and if I can stenograph well enough I can take down what he wants to say in this way and write it out for him on the typewriter, at which also I am practicing very hard. He and I sometimes write letters in shorthand, and he is keeping a stenographic journal of his travels abroad. When I am with you I shall keep a diary in the same way. I don't mean one of those two-pages-to-the-week-with-Sunday-squeezed-in-a-corner diaries, but a sort of journal which I can write in whenever I feel inclined. I do not suppose there will be much of interest to other people, but it is not intended for them. I may show it to Jonathan someday if there is in it anything worth sharing, but it is really an exercise book. I shall try to do what I see lady journalists do, interviewing and writing descriptions and trying to remember conversations. I am told that, with a little practice, one can remember all that goes on or that one hears said during a day. However, we shall see. I will tell you of my little plans when we meet. I have just had a few hurried lines from Jonathan from Transylvania. He is well, and will be returning in about a week. I am longing to hear all his news. It must be nice to see strange countries. I wonder if we—I mean Jonathan and I—shall ever see them together. There is the ten o'clock bell ringing. Goodbye.

Your loving

MINA.

Tell me all the news when you write. You have not told me anything for a long time. I hear rumours, and especially of a tall, handsome, curly-haired man???

LETTER, LUCY WESTENRA TO MINA MURRAY

17, Chatham Street,
Wednesday

My dearest Mina,

I must say you tax me *very* unfairly with being a bad correspondent. I wrote you *twice* since we parted, and your last letter was only your *second*. Besides, I have nothing to tell you. There is really nothing to interest you. Town is very pleasant just now, and we go a great deal to picture-galleries and for walks and rides in the park. As to the tall, curly-haired man, I suppose it was the one who was with me at the last Pop. Someone has evidently been telling tales. That was Mr. Holmwood. He often comes to see us, and he and Mamma get on very well together, they have so many things to talk about in common. We met some time ago a man that would just *do for you*, if you were not already engaged to Jonathan. He is an excellent *parti*, being handsome, well off, and of good birth. He is a doctor and really clever. Just fancy! He is only nine-and-twenty, and he has an immense lunatic asylum all under his own care. Mr. Holmwood introduced him to me, and he called here to see us, and often comes now. I think he is one of the most resolute men I ever saw, and yet the most calm. He seems absolutely imperturbable. I can fancy what a wonderful power he must have over his patients. He has a curious habit of looking one straight in the face, as if trying to read one's thoughts. He tries this on very much with me, but I flatter myself he has got a tough nut to crack. I know that from my glass. Do you ever try to read your own face? I do, and I can tell you it is not a bad study, and gives you more trouble than you can well fancy if you have never tried it. He says that I afford him a curious psychological study, and I humbly think I do. I do not, as you know, take sufficient interest in dress to be able to describe the new fashions. Dress is a bore. That is slang again, but never mind. Arthur says that every day. There, it is all out. Mina, we have told all our secrets to each other since we were *children*. We have slept together and eaten together, and laughed and cried together, and now, though I have spoken, I would like to speak more. Oh, Mina, couldn't you guess? I love him. I am blushing as I write, for although I *think* he loves me, he has not told me so in words. But, oh, Mina, I love him. I love him! There, that does me good. I wish I were with you, dear, sitting by the fire undressing, as we used to sit, and I would try to tell you what I feel. I do not know how I am writing this even to you. I am afraid to stop, or I should tear up the letter, and I don't want to stop, for I *do so* want to tell you all. Let me hear from you *at once*, and tell me all that you think about it. Mina, I must stop. Good night. Bless me in your prayers; and, Mina, pray for my happiness.

LUCY.

P.S. I need not tell you this is a secret. Good night again. L.

LETTER, LUCY WESTENRA TO MINA MURRAY

24 May.

My dearest Mina,

Thanks, and thanks, and thanks again for your sweet letter. It was so nice to be able to tell you and to have your sympathy.

My dear, it never rains but it pours. How true the old proverbs are. Here am I, who shall be twenty in September, and yet I never had a proposal till today, not a real proposal, and today I had three. Just fancy! Three proposals in one day! Isn't it awful! I feel sorry, really and truly sorry, for two of the poor fellows. Oh, Mina, I am so happy that I don't know what to do with myself. And three proposals! But, for goodness' sake, don't tell any of the girls, or they would be getting all sorts of extravagant ideas, and imagining themselves injured and slighted if in their very first day at home they did not get six at least. Some girls are so vain! You and I, Mina dear, who are engaged and are going to settle down soon soberly into old married women, can despise vanity. Well, I must tell you about the three, but you must keep it a secret, dear, from every one except, of course, Jonathan. You will tell him, because I would, if I were in your place, certainly tell Arthur. A woman ought to tell her husband everything. Don't you think so, dear? And I must be fair. Men like women, certainly their wives, to be quite as fair as they are. And women, I am afraid, are not always quite as fair as they should be. Well, my dear, number one came just before lunch. I told you of him, Dr. John Seward, the lunatic asylum man, with the strong jaw and the good forehead. He was very cool outwardly, but was nervous all the same. He had evidently been schooling himself as to all sorts of little things, and remembered them, but he almost managed to sit down on his silk hat, which men don't generally do when they are cool, and then when he wanted to appear at ease he kept playing with a lancet in a way that made me nearly scream. He spoke to me, Mina, very straightforwardly. He told me how dear I was to him, though he had known me so little, and what his life would be with me to help and cheer him. He was going to tell me how unhappy he would be if I did not care for him, but when he saw me cry he said he was a brute and would not add to my present trouble. Then he broke off and asked if I could love him in time, and when I shook my head his hands trembled, and then with some hesitation he asked me if I cared already for anyone else. He put it very nicely, saying that he did not want to wring my confidence from me, but only to know, because if a woman's heart was free a man might have hope. And then, Mina, I felt a sort of duty to tell him that there was someone. I only told him that much, and then he stood up, and he looked very strong and very grave as he took both my hands in his and said he hoped I would be happy, and that If I ever wanted a friend I must count him one of my best. Oh, Mina dear, I can't help crying, and you must excuse this letter being all blotted. Being proposed to is all very nice and all that sort of thing, but it isn't at all a happy thing when you have to see a poor fellow, whom you know loves you honestly, going away and looking all broken hearted, and to know that, no matter what he may say at the moment, you are passing out of his life. My dear, I must stop here at present, I feel so miserable, though I am so happy.

Evening.

Arthur has just gone, and I feel in better spirits than when I left off, so I can go on telling you about the day. Well, my dear, number two came after lunch. He is such a nice fellow, an American from Texas, and he looks so young and so fresh that it seems almost impossible that he has been to so many places and has such adventures. I sympathize with poor Desdemona when she had such a stream poured in her ear, even by a black man. I suppose that we women are such cowards that we think a man will save us from fears, and we marry him. I know now what I would do if I were a man and wanted to make a girl love me. No, I don't, for there was Mr. Morris telling us his stories, and

Arthur never told any, and yet—my dear, I am somewhat previous. Mr. Quincy P. Morris found me alone. It seems that a man always does find a girl alone. No, he doesn't, for Arthur tried twice to *make* a chance, and I helping him all I could, I am not ashamed to say it now. I must tell you beforehand that Mr. Morris doesn't always speak slang, that is to say, he never does so to strangers or before them, for he is really well educated and has exquisite manners, but he found out that it amused me to hear him talk American slang, and whenever I was present, and there was no one to be shocked, he said such funny things. I am afraid, my dear, he has to invent it all, for it fits exactly into whatever else he has to say. But this is a way slang has. I do not know myself if I shall ever speak slang. I do not know if Arthur likes it, as I have never heard him use any as yet. Well, Mr. Morris sat down beside me and looked as happy and jolly as he could, but I could see all the same that he was very nervous. He took my hand in his, and said ever so sweetly—

"Miss Lucy, I know I ain't good enough to regulate the fixin's of your little shoes, but I guess if you wait till you find a man that is you will go join them seven young women with the lamps when you quit. Won't you just hitch up alongside of me and let us go down the long road together, driving in double harness?"

Well, he did look so good humoured and so jolly that it didn't seem half so hard to refuse him as it did poor Dr. Seward. So I said, as lightly as I could, that I did not know anything of hitching, and that I wasn't broken to harness at all yet. Then he said that he had spoken in a light manner, and he hoped that if he had made a mistake in doing so on so grave, so momentous, and occasion for him, I would forgive him. He really did look serious when he was saying it, and I couldn't help feeling a sort of exultation that he was number two in one day. And then, my dear, before I could say a word he began pouring out a perfect torrent of love-making, laying his very heart and soul at my feet. He looked so earnest over it that I shall never again think that a man must be playful always, and never earnest, because he is merry at times. I suppose he saw something in my face which checked him, for he suddenly stopped, and said with a sort of manly fervour that I could have loved him for if I had been free—

"Lucy, you are an honest-hearted girl, I know. I should not be here speaking to you as I am now if I did not believe you clean grit, right through to the very depths of your soul. Tell me, like one good fellow to another, is there anyone else that you care for? And if there is I'll never trouble you a hair's breadth again, but will be, if you will let me, a very faithful friend."

My dear Mina, why are men so noble when we women are so little worthy of them? Here was I almost making fun of this great-hearted, true gentleman. I burst into tears, I am afraid, my dear, you will think this a very sloppy letter in more ways than one, and I really felt very badly.

Why can't they let a girl marry three men, or as many as want her, and save all this trouble? But this is heresy, and I must not say it. I am glad to say that, though I was crying, I was able to look into Mr. Morris' brave eyes, and I told him out straight—

"Yes, there is someone I love, though he has not told me yet that he even loves me." I was right to speak to him so frankly, for quite a light came into his face, and he put out both his hands and took mine—I think I put them into his—and said in a hearty way, "That's my brave girl. It's better worth being late for a chance of winning you than being in time for any other girl in the world. Don't cry, my dear. If it's for me, I'm a hard nut to crack, and I take it standing up. If that other fellow doesn't know his happiness, well, he'd better look for it soon, or he'll have to deal with me. Little girl, your honesty and pluck have made me a friend, and that's rarer than a lover, it's more selfish anyhow. My dear, I'm going to have a pretty lonely walk between this and Kingdom Come. Won't you give me one kiss? It'll be something to keep off the darkness now and then. You can, you know, if you like, for that other good fellow—he must be a good fellow, my dear, and a fine fellow, or you could not love him—hasn't spoken yet." That quite won me, Mina, for it was brave and sweet of him, and noble too, to a rival, wasn't it? And he so sad, so I leant over and kissed him. He stood up with my two hands in his, and as he looked down into my face, I am afraid I was blushing very much, he said, "Little girl, I hold your hand, and you've kissed me, and if these things don't make us friends nothing ever will. Thank you for your sweet honesty to me, and goodbye." He wrung my hand, and taking up his hat, went straight out of the room without looking back, without a tear or a quiver or a pause, and I am crying like a baby. Oh, why must a man like that be made unhappy when there are lots of girls about who would worship the very ground he trod on? I know I would if I were free, only I don't want to be free. My dear, this quite upset me, and I feel I cannot write of happiness just at once, after telling you of it, and I don't wish to tell of the number three until it can be all happy.

Ever your loving
LUCY

P.S. Oh, about number three—I needn't tell you of number three, need I? Besides, it was all so confused. It seemed only a moment from his coming into the room till both his arms were round me, and he was kissing me. I am very, very happy, and I don't know what I have done to deserve it. I must only try in the future to show that I am not ungrateful to God for all His goodness to me in sending to me such a lover, such a husband, and such a friend.

Goodbye.

DR. SEWARD'S DIARY (KEPT IN PHONOGRAPH)

25 May.

Ebb tide in appetite today. Cannot eat, cannot rest, so diary instead. Since my rebuff of yesterday I have a sort of empty feeling. Nothing in the world seems of sufficient importance to be worth the doing. As I knew that the only cure for this sort of thing was work, I went amongst the patients. I picked out one who has afforded me a study of much interest. He is so quaint that I am determined to understand him as well as I can. Today I seemed to get nearer than ever before to the heart of his mystery.

I questioned him more fully than I had ever done, with a view to making myself master of the facts of his hallucination. In my manner of doing it there was, I now see, something of cruelty. I seemed to wish to keep him to the point of his madness—a thing which I avoid with the patients as I would the mouth of hell. (*Mem.*, Under what circumstances would I not avoid the pit of hell?) *Omnia Romae venalia sunt.* Hell has its price! If there be anything behind this instinct it will be valuable to trace it afterwards accurately, so I had better commence to do so, therefore—

R. M. Renfield, age 59. Sanguine temperament, great physical strength, morbidly excitable, periods of gloom ending in some fixed idea which I cannot make out. I presume that the sanguine temperament itself and the disturbing influence end in a mentally-accomplished finish, a possibly dangerous man, probably dangerous if unselfish. In selfish men caution is as secure an armour for their foes as for themselves. What I think of on this point is, when self is the fixed point the centripetal force is balanced with the centrifugal. When duty, a cause, etc., is the fixed point, the latter force is paramount, and only accident or a series of accidents can balance it.

LETTER, QUINCEY P. MORRIS TO HON. ARTHUR HOLMWOOD

25 May.

My dear Art,

We've told yarns by the campfire in the prairies, and dressed one another's wounds after trying a landing at the Marquesas, and drunk healths on the shore of Titicaca. There are more yarns to be told, and other wounds to be healed, and another health to be drunk. Won't you let this be at my campfire tomorrow night? I have no hesitation in asking you, as I know a certain lady is engaged to a certain dinner party, and that you are free. There will only be one other, our old pal at the Korea, Jack Seward. He's coming, too, and we both want to mingle our weeps over the wine cup, and to drink a health with all our hearts to the happiest man in all the wide world, who has won the noblest heart that God has made and best worth winning. We promise you a hearty welcome, and a loving greeting, and a health as true as your own right hand. We shall both swear to leave you at home if you drink too deep to a certain pair of eyes. Come!

Yours, as ever and always,
QUINCEY P. MORRIS

TELEGRAM FROM ARTHUR HOLMWOOD
TO QUINCEY P. MORRIS

26 May.

Count me in every time. I bear messages which will make both your ears tingle.

ART.

CHAPTER VI

Mina Murray's Journal

24 July. Whitby.

Lucy met me at the station, looking sweeter and lovelier than ever, and we drove up to the house at the Crescent in which they have rooms. This is a lovely place. The little river, the Esk, runs through a deep valley, which broadens out as it comes near the harbour. A great viaduct runs across, with high piers, through which the view seems somehow further away than it really is. The valley is beautifully green, and it is so steep that when you are on the high land on either side you look right across it, unless you are near enough to see down. The houses of the old town—the side away from us–are all red-roofed, and seem piled up one over the other anyhow, like the pictures we see of Nuremberg. Right over the town is the ruin of Whitby Abbey, which was sacked by the Danes, and which is the scene of part of "Marmion," where the girl was built up in the wall. It is a most noble ruin, of immense size, and full of beautiful and romantic bits. There is a legend that a white lady is seen in one of the windows. Between it and the town there is another church, the parish one, round which is a big graveyard, all full of tombstones. This is to my mind the nicest spot in Whitby, for it lies right over the town, and has a full view of the harbour and all up the bay to where the headland called Kettleness stretches out into the sea. It descends so steeply over the harbour that part of the bank has fallen away, and some of the graves have been destroyed. In one place part of the stonework of the graves stretches out over the sandy pathway far below. There are walks, with seats beside them, through the churchyard, and people go and sit there all day long looking at the beautiful view and enjoying the breeze. I shall come and sit here often myself and work. Indeed, I am writing now, with my book on my knee, and listening to the talk of three old men who are sitting beside me. They seem to do nothing all day but sit here and talk.

The harbour lies below me, with, on the far side, one long granite wall stretching out into the sea, with a curve outwards at the end of it, in the middle of which is a lighthouse. A heavy seawall runs along outside of it. On the near side, the seawall makes an elbow crooked inversely, and its end too has a lighthouse. Between the two piers there is a narrow opening into the harbour, which then suddenly widens.

It is nice at high water, but when the tide is out it shoals away to nothing, and there is merely the stream of the Esk, running between banks of sand, with rocks here and there. Outside the harbour on this side there rises for about half a mile a great reef, the sharp of which runs straight out from behind the south lighthouse. At the end of it is a buoy with a bell, which swings in bad weather, and sends in a mournful sound on the wind. They have a legend here that when a ship is lost bells are heard out at sea. I must ask the old man about this. He is coming this way . . .

He is a funny old man. He must be awfully old, for his face is gnarled and twisted like the bark of a tree. He tells me that he is nearly a hundred, and that he was a sailor in the Greenland fishing fleet when Waterloo was fought. He is, I am afraid, a very sceptical person, for when I asked him about the bells at sea and the White Lady at the abbey he said very brusquely, "I wouldn't fash masel' about them, miss. Them things be all wore out. Mind, I don't say that they never was, but I do say that they wasn't in my time. They be all very well for comers and trippers, an' the like, but not for a nice young lady like you. Them feet-folks from York and Leeds that be always eatin' cured herrin's and drinkin' tea an' lookin' out to buy cheap jet would creed aught. I wonder masel' who'd be bothered tellin' lies to them, even the newspapers, which is full of fool-talk."

I thought he would be a good person to learn interesting things from, so I asked him if he would mind telling me something about the whale fishing in the old days. He was just settling himself to begin when the clock struck six, whereupon he laboured to get up, and said, "I must gang ageeanwards home now, miss. My grand-daughter doesn't like to be kept waitin' when the tea is ready, for it takes me time to crammle aboon the grees, for there be a many of 'em, and miss, I lack belly-timber sairly by the clock."

He hobbled away, and I could see him hurrying, as well as he could, down the steps. The steps are a great feature on the place. They lead from the town to the church, there are hundreds of them—I do not know how many—and they wind up in a delicate curve. The slope is so gentle that a horse could easily walk up and down them.

I think they must originally have had something to do with the abbey. I shall go home too. Lucy went out, visiting with her mother, and as they were only duty calls, I did not go.

1 August.

I came up here an hour ago with Lucy, and we had a most interesting talk with my old friend and the two others who always come and join him. He is evidently the Sir Oracle of them, and I should think must have been in his time a most dictatorial person. He will not admit anything, and downfaces everybody. If he can't out-argue them he bullies them, and then takes their silence for agreement with his views. Lucy was looking sweetly pretty in her white lawn frock. She has got a beautiful colour since she has been here. I noticed that the old men did not lose any time in coming and sitting near her when we sat down. She is so sweet with old people, I think they all fell in love with her on the spot. Even my old man succumbed and did not contradict her, but gave me double share instead. I got him on the subject of the legends, and he went off at once into a sort of sermon. I must try to remember it and put it down.

"It be all fool-talk, lock, stock, and barrel, that's what it be and nowt else. These bans an' wafts an' boh-ghosts an' bar-guests an' bogles an' all anent them is only fit to set bairns an' dizzy women a'belderin'. They be nowt but air-blebs. They, an' all grims an' signs an' warnin's, be all invented by parsons an' illsome berk-bodies an' railway touters to skeer an' scunner hafflin's, an' to get folks to do somethin' that they don't other incline to. It makes me ireful to think o' them. Why, it's them that, not content with printin' lies on paper an' preachin' them out of pulpits, does want to be cuttin' them on the tombstones. Look here all around you in what airt ye will. All them steans, holdin' up their heads as well as they can out of their pride, is acant, simply tumblin' down with the weight o' the lies wrote on them, 'Here lies the body' or 'Sacred to the memory' wrote on all of them, an' yet in nigh half of them there bean't no bodies at all, an' the memories of them bean't cared a pinch of snuff about, much less sacred. Lies all of them, nothin' but lies of one kind or another! My gog, but it'll be a quare scowderment at the Day of Judgment when they come tumblin' up in their death-sarks, all jouped together an' tryin' to drag their tombsteans with them to prove how good they was, some of them trimmlin' an' dithering, with their hands that dozzened an' slippery from lyin' in the sea that they can't even keep their gurp o' them."

I could see from the old fellow's self-satisfied air and the way in which he looked round for the approval of his cronies that he was "showing off," so I put in a word to keep him going.

"Oh, Mr. Swales, you can't be serious. Surely these tombstones are not all wrong?"

"Yabblins! There may be a poorish few not wrong, savin' where they make out the people too good, for there be folk that do think a balm-bowl be like the sea, if only it be their own. The whole thing be only lies. Now look you here. You come here a stranger, an' you see this kirkgarth."

I nodded, for I thought it better to assent, though I did not quite understand his dialect. I knew it had something to do with the church.

He went on, "And you consate that all these steans be aboon folk that be haped here, snod an' snog?" I assented again. "Then that be just where the lie comes in. Why, there be scores of these laybeds that be toom as old Dun's 'baccabox on Friday night."

He nudged one of his companions, and they all laughed. "And, my gog! How could they be otherwise? Look at that one, the aftest abaft the bier-bank, read it!"

I went over and read:

> "Edward Spencelagh, master mariner, murdered by pirates off the coast of Andres, April, 1854, age 30."

When I came back Mr. Swales went on, "Who brought him home, I wonder, to hap him here? Murdered off the coast of Andres! An' you consated his body lay under! Why, I could name ye a dozen whose bones lie in the Greenland seas above,"—he pointed northwards—"or where the currants may have drifted them. There be the steans around ye. Ye can, with your young eyes, read the small print of the lies from here. This Braithwaite Lowery— I knew his father, lost in the *Lively* off Greenland in '20; or Andrew Woodhouse, drowned in the same seas in 1777; or John Paxton, drowned off Cape Farewell a year later; or old John Rawlings, whose grandfather sailed with me, drowned in the Gulf of Finland in '50. Do ye think that all these men will have to make a rush to Whitby when the trumpet sounds? I have me antherums aboot it! I tell ye that when they got here they'd be jommlin' and jostlin' one another that way that it 'ud be like a fight up on the ice in the old days, when we'd be at one another from daylight to dark, an' tryin' to tie up our cuts by the aurora borealis." This was evidently local pleasantry, for the old man cackled over it, and his cronies joined in with gusto.

"But," I said, "surely you are not quite correct, for you start on the assumption that all the poor people, or their spirits, will have to take their tombstones with them on the Day of Judgment. Do you think that will be really necessary?"

"Well, what else be they tombsteans for? Answer me that, miss!"

"To please their relatives, I suppose."

"To please their relatives, you suppose!" This he said with intense scorn. "How will it pleasure their relatives to know that lies is wrote over them, and that everybody in the place knows that they be lies?" He pointed to a stone at our feet which had been laid down as a slab, on which the seat was rested, close to the edge of the cliff. "Read the lies on that thruff-stean," he said. The letters were upside down to me from where I sat, but Lucy was more opposite to them, so she leant over and read, "Sacred to the memory of George Canon, who died, in the hope of a glorious resurrection, on July 29, 1873, falling from the rocks at Kettleness. This tomb was erected by his sorrowing mother to her dearly beloved son. 'He was the only son of his mother, and she was a widow.' Really, Mr. Swales, I don't see anything very funny in that!" She spoke her comment very gravely and somewhat severely.

"Ye don't see aught funny! Ha-ha! But that's because ye don't gawm the sorrowin' mother was a hell-cat that hated him because he was acrewk'd, a regular lamiter he was, an' he hated her so that he committed suicide in order that she mightn't get an insurance she put on his life. He blew nigh the top of his head off with an old musket that they had for scarin' crows with. 'Twarn't for crows then, for it brought the clegs and the dowps to him. That's the way he fell off the rocks. And, as to hopes of a glorious resurrection, I've often heard him say masel' that he hoped he'd go to hell, for his mother was so pious that she'd be sure to go to heaven, an' he didn't want to addle where she was. Now isn't that stean at any rate," he hammered it with his stick as he spoke, "a pack of lies? And won't it make Gabriel keckle when Geordie comes pantin' ut the grees with the tombstean balanced on his hump, and asks to be took as evidence!"

I did not know what to say, but Lucy turned the conversation as she said, rising up, "Oh, why did you tell us of this? It is my favourite seat, and I cannot leave it, and now I find I must go on sitting over the grave of a suicide."

"That won't harm ye, my pretty, an' it may make poor Geordie gladsome to have so trim a lass sittin' on his lap. That won't hurt ye. Why, I've sat here off an' on for nigh twenty years past, an' it hasn't done me no harm. Don't ye fash about them as lies under ye, or that doesn' lie there either! It'll be time for ye to be getting scart when ye see the tombsteans all run away with, and the place as bare as a stubble-field. There's the clock, and I must gang. My service to ye, ladies!" And off he hobbled.

Lucy and I sat awhile, and it was all so beautiful before us that we took hands as we sat, and she told me all over again about Arthur and their coming marriage. That made me just a little heart-sick, for I haven't heard from Jonathan for a whole month.

The same day.

I came up here alone, for I am very sad. There was no letter for me. I hope there cannot be anything the matter with Jonathan. The clock has just struck nine. I see the lights scattered all over the town, sometimes in rows where the streets are, and sometimes singly. They run right up the Esk and die away in the curve of the valley. To my left the view is cut off by a black line of roof of the old house next to the abbey. The sheep and lambs are bleating in the fields away behind me, and there is a clatter of donkeys' hoofs up the paved road below. The band on the pier is playing a harsh waltz in good time, and further along the quay there is a Salvation Army meeting in a back street. Neither of the bands hears the other, but up here I hear and see them both. I wonder where Jonathan is and if he is thinking of me! I wish he were here.

Dr. Seward's Diary

5 June.

The case of Renfield grows more interesting the more I get to understand the man. He has certain qualities very largely developed, selfishness, secrecy, and purpose. I wish I could get at what is the object of the latter. He seems to have some settled scheme of his own, but what it is I do not know. His redeeming quality is a love of animals, though, indeed, he has such curious turns in it that I sometimes imagine he is only abnormally cruel. His pets are of odd sorts. Just now his hobby is catching flies. He has at present such a quantity that I have had myself to expostulate. To my astonishment, he did not break out into a fury, as I expected, but took the matter in simple seriousness. He thought for a moment, and then said, "May I have three days? I shall clear them away." Of course, I said that would do. I must watch him.

18 June.

He has turned his mind now to spiders, and has got several very big fellows in a box. He keeps feeding them his flies, and the number of the latter is becoming sensibly diminished, although he has used half his food in attracting more flies from outside to his room.

1 July.

His spiders are now becoming as great a nuisance as his flies, and today I told him that he must get rid of them. He looked very sad at this, so I said that he must clear out some of them, at all events. He cheerfully acquiesced in this, and I gave him the same time as before for reduction. He disgusted me much while with him, for when a horrid blowfly, bloated with some carrion food, buzzed into the room, he caught it, held it exultantly for a few moments between his finger and thumb, and before I knew what he was going to do, put it in his mouth and ate it. I scolded him for it, but he argued quietly that it was very good and very wholesome, that it was life, strong life, and gave life to him. This gave me an idea, or the rudiment of one. I must watch how he gets rid of his spiders.

He has evidently some deep problem in his mind, for he keeps a little notebook in which he is always jotting down something. Whole pages of it are filled with masses of figures, generally single numbers added up in batches, and then the totals added in batches again, as though he were "focussing" some account, as the auditors put it.

8 July.

There is a method in his madness, and the rudimentary idea in my mind is growing. It will be a whole idea soon, and then, oh, unconscious cerebration, you will have to give the wall to your conscious brother. I kept away from my friend for a few days, so that

I might notice if there were any change. Things remain as they were except that he has parted with some of his pets and got a new one. He has managed to get a sparrow, and has already partially tamed it. His means of taming is simple, for already the spiders have diminished. Those that do remain, however, are well fed, for he still brings in the flies by tempting them with his food.

19 July.

We are progressing. My friend has now a whole colony of sparrows, and his flies and spiders are almost obliterated. When I came in he ran to me and said he wanted to ask me a great favour, a very, very great favour. And as he spoke, he fawned on me like a dog.

I asked him what it was, and he said, with a sort of rapture in his voice and bearing, "A kitten, a nice, little, sleek playful kitten, that I can play with, and teach, and feed—and feed—and feed!" I was not unprepared for this request, for I had noticed how his pets went on increasing in size and vivacity, but I did not care that his pretty family of tame sparrows should be wiped out in the same manner as the flies and spiders. So I said I would see about it, and asked him if he would not rather have a cat than a kitten.

His eagerness betrayed him as he answered, "Oh, yes, I would like a cat! I only asked for a kitten lest you should refuse me a cat. No one would refuse me a kitten, would they?"

I shook my head, and said that at present I feared it would not be possible, but that I would see about it. His face fell, and I could see a warning of danger in it, for there was a sudden fierce, sidelong look which meant killing. The man is an undeveloped homicidal maniac. I shall test him with his present craving and see how it will work out, then I shall know more.

10 p.m.

I have visited him again and found him sitting in a corner brooding. When I came in he threw himself on his knees before me and implored me to let him have a cat, that his salvation depended upon it. I was firm, however, and told him that he could not have it, whereupon he went without a word, and sat down, gnawing his fingers, in the corner where I had found him. I shall see him in the morning early.

20 July.

Visited Renfield very early, before attendant went his rounds. Found him up and humming a tune. He was spreading out his sugar, which he had saved, in the window, and was manifestly beginning his fly-catching again, and beginning it cheerfully and with a good grace. I looked around for his birds, and not seeing them, asked him where they were. He replied, without turning round, that they had all flown away. There were a few feathers about the room and on his pillow a drop of blood. I said nothing, but went and told the keeper to report to me if there were anything odd about him during the day.

11 a.m.

The attendant has just been to see me to say that Renfield has been very sick and has disgorged a whole lot of feathers. "My belief is, doctor," he said, "that he has eaten his birds, and that he just took and ate them raw!"

11:00 p.m.

I gave Renfield a strong opiate tonight, enough to make even him sleep, and took away his pocketbook to look at it. The thought that has been buzzing about my brain lately is complete, and the theory proved. My homicidal maniac is of a peculiar kind. I shall have to invent a new classification for him, and call him a zoophagous (life-eating) maniac. What he desires is to absorb as many lives as he can, and he has laid himself out to achieve it in a cumulative way. He gave many flies to one spider and many spiders to one bird, and then wanted a cat to eat the many birds. What would have been his later steps? It would almost be worth while to complete the experiment. It might be done if there were only a sufficient cause. Men sneered at vivisection, and yet look at its results today! Why not advance science in its most difficult and vital aspect—the knowledge of the brain? Had I even the secret of one such mind—did I hold the key to the fancy of even one lunatic—I might advance my own branch of science to a pitch compared with which Burdon-Sanderson's physiology or Ferrier's brain knowledge would be as nothing. If only there were a sufficient cause! I must not think too much of this, or I may be tempted. A good cause might turn the scale with me, for may not I too be of an exceptional brain, congenitally?

How well the man reasoned. Lunatics always do within their own scope. I wonder at how many lives he values a man, or if at only one. He has closed the account most accurately, and today begun a new record. How many of us begin a new record with each day of our lives?

To me it seems only yesterday that my whole life ended with my new hope, and that truly I began a new record. So it shall be until the Great Recorder sums me up and closes my ledger account with a balance to profit or loss. Oh, Lucy, Lucy, I cannot be angry with you, nor can I be angry with my friend whose happiness is yours, but I must only wait on hopeless and work. Work! Work!

If I could have as strong a cause as my poor mad friend there, a good, unselfish cause to make me work, that would be indeed happiness.

Mina Murray's Journal

26 July.

I am anxious, and it soothes me to express myself here. It is like whispering to one's self and listening at the same time. And there is also something about the shorthand symbols that makes it different from writing. I am unhappy about Lucy and about Jonathan. I had not heard from Jonathan for some time, and was very concerned, but yesterday dear Mr. Hawkins, who is always so kind, sent me a letter from him. I had written asking him if he had heard, and he said the enclosed had just been received. It is only a line dated from Castle Dracula, and says that he is just starting for home. That is not like Jonathan. I do not understand it, and it makes me uneasy. Then, too, Lucy, although she is so well, has lately taken to her old habit of walking in her sleep. Her mother has spoken to me about it, and we have decided that I am to lock the door of our room every night. Mrs. Westenra has got an idea that sleep-walkers always go out on roofs of houses and along the edges of cliffs and then get suddenly wakened and fall over with a despairing cry that echoes all over the place. Poor dear, she is naturally anxious about Lucy, and she tells me that her husband, Lucy's father, had the same habit, that he would get up in the night and dress himself and go out, if he were not stopped. Lucy is to be married in the autumn, and she is already planning out her dresses and how her house is to be arranged. I sympathise with her, for I do the same, only Jonathan and I will start in life in a very simple way, and shall have to try to make both ends meet. Mr. Holmwood—he is the Hon. Arthur Holmwood, only son of Lord Godalming, is coming up here very shortly, as soon as he can leave town, for his father is not very well, and I think dear Lucy is counting the moments till he comes. She wants to take him up in the seat on the churchyard cliff and show him the beauty of Whitby. I daresay it is the waiting which disturbs her. She will be all right when he arrives.

27 July.

No news from Jonathan. I am getting quite uneasy about him, though why I should I do not know, but I *do* wish that he would write, if it were only a single line. Lucy walks more than ever, and each night I am awakened by her moving about the room. Fortunately, the weather is so hot that she cannot get cold. But still, the anxiety and the perpetually being awakened is beginning to tell on me, and I am getting nervous and wakeful myself. Thank God, Lucy's health keeps up. Mr. Holmwood has been suddenly called to Ring to see his father, who has been taken seriously ill. Lucy frets at the postponement of seeing him, but it does not touch her looks. She is a trifle stouter, and her cheeks are a lovely rose-pink. She has lost the anemic look which she had. I pray it will all last.

3 August.

Another week gone by, and no news from Jonathan, not even to Mr. Hawkins, from whom I have heard. Oh, I do hope he is not ill. He surely would have written. I look at that last letter of his, but somehow it does not satisfy me. It does not read like him, and yet it is his writing. There is no mistake of that. Lucy has not walked much in her sleep the last week, but there is an odd concentration about her which I do not understand, even in her sleep she seems to be watching me. She tries the door, and finding it locked, goes about the room searching for the key.

6 August.

Another three days, and no news. This suspense is getting dreadful. If I only knew where to write to or where to go to, I should feel easier. But no one has heard a word of Jonathan since that last letter. I must only pray to God for patience. Lucy is more excitable than ever, but is otherwise well. Last night was very threatening, and the fishermen say that we are in for a storm. I must try to watch it and learn the weather signs. Today is a gray day, and the sun as I write is hidden in thick clouds, high over Kettleness. Everything is gray—except the green grass, which seems like emerald amongst it, gray earthy rock, gray clouds, tinged with the sunburst at the far edge, hang over the gray sea, into which the sandpoints stretch like gray figures. The sea is tumbling in over the shallows and the sandy flats with a roar, muffled in the sea-mists drifting inland. The horizon is lost in a gray mist. All vastness, the clouds are piled up like giant rocks, and there is a "brool" over the sea that sounds like some passage of doom. Dark figures are on the beach here and there, sometimes half shrouded in the mist, and seem "men like trees walking." The fishing boats are racing for home, and rise and dip in the ground swell as they sweep into the harbour, bending to the scuppers. Here comes old Mr. Swales. He is making straight for me, and I can see, by the way he lifts his hat, that he wants to talk.

I have been quite touched by the change in the poor old man. When he sat down beside me, he said in a very gentle way, "I want to say something to you, miss." I could see he was not at ease, so I took his poor old wrinkled hand in mine and asked him to speak fully.

So he said, leaving his hand in mine, "I'm afraid, my deary, that I must have shocked you by all the wicked things I've been sayin' about the dead, and such like, for weeks past, but I didn't mean them, and I want ye to remember that when I'm gone. We aud folks that be daffled, and with one foot abaft the krok-hooal, don't altogether like to think of it, and we don't want to feel scart of it, and that's why I've took to makin' light of it, so that I'd cheer up my own heart a bit. But, Lord love ye, miss, I ain't afraid of dyin,' not a bit, only I don't want to die if I can help it. My time must be nigh at hand now, for I be aud, and a hundred years is too much for any man to expect. And I'm so nigh it that the Aud Man is already whettin' his scythe. Ye see, I can't get out o' the habit of caffin' about it all at once. The chafts will wag as they be used to. Someday soon the Angel of Death will sound his trumpet for me. But don't ye dooal an' greet, my deary!"—for he saw that I was crying—"If he should come this very night I'd not refuse to answer his call. For life be, after all, only a waitin' for somethin' else than what we're doin,' and death be all that we can rightly depend on. But I'm content, for it's comin' to me, my deary, and comin' quick. It may be comin' while we be lookin' and wonderin'. Maybe it's in that wind out over the sea that's bringin' with it loss and wreck, and sore distress, and sad hearts. Look! Look!" he cried suddenly. "There's something in that wind and in the hoast beyont that sounds, and looks, and tastes, and smells like death. It's in the air. I feel it comin'. Lord, make me answer cheerful, when my call comes!" He held up his arms devoutly, and raised his hat. His mouth moved as though he were praying. After a few minutes' silence, he got up, shook hands with me, and blessed me, and said goodbye, and hobbled off. It all touched me, and upset me very much.

I was glad when the coastguard came along, with his spyglass under his arm. He stopped to talk with me, as he always does, but all the time kept looking at a strange ship.

"I can't make her out," he said. "She's a Russian, by the look of her. But she's knocking about in the queerest way. She doesn't know her mind a bit. She seems to see the storm coming, but can't decide whether to run up north in the open, or to put in here. Look there again! She is steered mighty strangely, for she doesn't mind the hand on the wheel, changes about with every puff of wind. We'll hear more of her before this time tomorrow."

CHAPTER VII

Cutting from the *Dailygraph*, 8 August (Pasted in Mina Murray's Journal)

From a correspondent

Whitby.

One of the greatest and suddenest storms on record has just been experienced here, with results both strange and unique. The weather had been somewhat sultry, but not to any degree uncommon in the month of August. Saturday evening was as fine as was ever known, and the great body of holiday-makers laid out yesterday for visits to Mulgrave Woods, Robin Hood's Bay, Rig Mill, Runswick, Staithes, and the various trips in the neighborhood of Whitby. The steamers *Emma* and *Scarborough* made trips up and down the coast, and there was an unusual amount of "tripping" both to and from Whitby. The day was unusually fine till the afternoon, when some of the gossips who frequent the East Cliff churchyard, and from the commanding eminence watch the wide sweep of sea visible to the north and east, called attention to a sudden show of "mares tails" high in the sky to the northwest. The wind was then blowing from the south-west in the mild degree which in barometrical language is ranked "No. 2: light breeze."

The coastguard on duty at once made report, and one old fisherman, who for more than half a century has kept watch on weather signs from the East Cliff, foretold in an emphatic manner the coming of a sudden storm. The approach of sunset was so very beautiful, so grand in its masses of splendidly coloured clouds, that there was quite an assemblage on the walk along the cliff in the old churchyard to enjoy the beauty. Before the sun dipped below the black mass of Kettleness, standing boldly athwart the western sky, its downward way was marked by myriad clouds of every sunset colour—flame, purple, pink, green, violet, and all the tints of gold, with here and there masses not large, but of seemingly absolute blackness, in all sorts of shapes, as well outlined as colossal silhouettes. The experience was not lost on the painters, and doubtless some of the sketches of the "Prelude to the Great Storm" will grace the R. A and R. I. walls in May next.

More than one captain made up his mind then and there that his "cobble" or his "mule," as they term the different classes of boats, would remain in the harbour till the storm had passed. The wind fell away entirely during the evening, and at midnight there was a dead calm, a sultry heat, and that prevailing intensity which, on the approach of thunder, affects persons of a sensitive nature.

There were but few lights in sight at sea, for even the coasting steamers, which usually hug the shore so closely, kept well to seaward, and but few fishing boats were in sight. The only sail noticeable was a foreign schooner with all sails set, which was seemingly going westwards. The foolhardiness or ignorance of her officers was a prolific theme for comment whilst she remained in sight, and efforts were made to signal her to reduce sail in the face of her danger. Before the night shut down she was seen with sails idly flapping as she gently rolled on the undulating swell of the sea.

As idle as a painted ship upon a painted ocean.

Shortly before ten o'clock the stillness of the air grew quite oppressive, and the silence was so marked that the bleating of a sheep inland or the barking of a dog in the town was distinctly heard, and the band on the pier, with its lively French air, was like a dischord in the great harmony of nature's silence. A little after midnight came a strange sound from over the sea, and high overhead the air began to carry a strange, faint, hollow booming.

Then without warning the tempest broke. With a rapidity which, at the time, seemed incredible, and even afterwards is impossible to realize, the whole aspect of nature at once became convulsed. The waves rose in growing fury, each over-topping its fellow, till in a very few minutes the lately glassy sea was like a roaring and devouring monster. White-crested waves beat madly on the level sands and rushed up the shelving cliffs. Others broke over the piers, and with their spume swept the lanthorns of the lighthouses which rise from the end of either pier of Whitby Harbour.

The wind roared like thunder, and blew with such force that it was with difficulty that even strong men kept their feet, or clung with grim clasp to the iron stanchions. It was found necessary to clear the entire pier from the mass of onlookers, or else the fatalities of the night would have increased manifold. To add to the difficulties and dangers of the time, masses of sea-fog came drifting inland. White, wet clouds, which swept by in ghostly fashion, so dank and damp and cold that it needed but little effort of imagination to think that the spirits of those lost at sea were touching their living brethren with the clammy hands of death, and many a one shuddered as the wreaths of sea-mist swept by.

At times the mist cleared, and the sea for some distance could be seen in the glare of the lightning, which came thick and fast, followed by such peals of thunder that the whole sky overhead seemed trembling under the shock of the footsteps of the storm.

Some of the scenes thus revealed were of immeasurable grandeur and of absorbing interest. The sea, running mountains high, threw skywards with each wave mighty masses of white foam, which the tempest seemed to snatch at and whirl away into space. Here and there a fishing boat, with a rag of sail, running madly for shelter before the blast, now and again the white wings of a storm-tossed seabird. On the summit of the East Cliff the new searchlight was ready for experiment, but had not yet been tried. The officers in charge of it got it into working order, and in the pauses of onrushing mist swept with it the surface of the sea. Once or twice its service was most effective, as when a fishing boat, with gunwale under water, rushed into the harbour, able, by the guidance of the sheltering light, to avoid the danger of dashing against the piers. As each boat achieved the safety of the port there was a shout of joy from the mass of people on the shore, a shout which for a moment seemed to cleave the gale and was then swept away in its rush.

Before long the searchlight discovered some distance away a schooner with all sails set, apparently the same vessel which had been noticed earlier in the evening. The wind had by this time backed to the east, and there was a shudder amongst the watchers on the cliff as they realized the terrible danger in which she now was. Between her and the port lay the great flat reef on which so many good ships have from time to time suffered, and, with the wind blowing from its present quarter, it would be quite impossible that she should fetch the entrance of the harbour. It was now nearly the hour of high tide, but the waves were so great that in their troughs the shallows of the shore were almost visible, and the schooner, with all sails set, was rushing with such speed that, in the words of one old salt, "she must fetch up somewhere, if it was only in hell." Then came another rush of sea-fog, greater than any hitherto, a mass of dank mist, which seemed to close on all things like a gray pall, and left available to men only the organ of hearing, for the roar of the tempest, and the crash of the thunder, and the booming of the mighty billows came through the damp oblivion even louder than before. The rays of the searchlight were kept fixed on the harbour mouth across the East Pier, where the shock was expected, and men waited breathless.

The wind suddenly shifted to the northeast, and the remnant of the sea fog melted in the blast. And then, *mirabile dictu*, between the piers, leaping from wave to wave as it rushed at headlong speed, swept the strange schooner before the blast, with all sail set, and gained the safety of the harbour. The searchlight followed her, and a shudder ran through all who saw her, for lashed to the helm was a corpse, with drooping head, which swung horribly to and fro at each motion of the ship. No other form could be seen on the deck at all.

A great awe came on all as they realised that the ship, as if by a miracle, had found the harbour, unsteered save by the hand of a dead man! However, all took place more quickly than it takes to write these words. The schooner paused not, but rushing across the harbour, pitched herself on that accumulation of sand and gravel washed by many tides and many storms into the southeast corner of the pier jutting under the East Cliff, known locally as Tate Hill Pier.

There was of course a considerable concussion as the vessel drove up on the sand heap. Every spar, rope, and stay was strained, and some of the "top-hammer" came crashing down. But, strangest of all, the very instant the shore was touched, an immense dog sprang up on deck from below, as if shot up by the concussion, and running forward, jumped from the bow on the sand.

Making straight for the steep cliff, where the churchyard hangs over the laneway to the East Pier so steeply that some of the flat tombstones, thruffsteans or through-stones, as they call them in Whitby vernacular, actually project over where the sustaining cliff has fallen away, it disappeared in the darkness, which seemed intensified just beyond the focus of the searchlight.

It so happened that there was no one at the moment on Tate Hill Pier, as all those whose houses are in close proximity were either in bed or were out on the heights above. Thus the coastguard on duty on the eastern side of the harbour, who at once ran down to the little pier, was the first to climb aboard. The men working the searchlight, after scouring the entrance of the harbour without seeing anything, then turned the light on the derelict and kept it there. The coastguard ran aft, and when he came beside the wheel, bent over to examine it, and recoiled at once as though under some sudden emotion. This seemed to pique general curiosity, and quite a number of people began to run.

It is a good way round from the West Cliff by the Draw-bridge to Tate Hill Pier, but your correspondent is a fairly good runner, and came well ahead of the crowd. When I arrived, however, I found already assembled on the pier a crowd, whom the coastguard and police refused to allow to come on board. By the courtesy of the chief boatman, I was, as your correspondent, permitted to climb on deck, and was one of a small group who saw the dead seaman whilst actually lashed to the wheel.

It was no wonder that the coastguard was surprised, or even awed, for not often can such a sight have been seen. The man was simply fastened by his hands, tied one over the other, to a spoke of the wheel. Between the inner hand and the wood was a crucifix, the set of beads on which it was fastened being around both wrists and wheel, and all kept fast by the binding cords. The poor fellow may have been seated at one time, but the flapping and buffeting of the sails had worked through the rudder of the wheel and had dragged him to and fro, so that the cords with which he was tied had cut the flesh to the bone.

Accurate note was made of the state of things, and a doctor—Surgeon J. M. Caffyn, of 33, East Elliot Place—who came immediately after me, declared, after making examination, that the man must have been dead for quite two days.In his pocket was a bottle, carefully corked, empty save for a little roll of paper, which proved to be the addendum to the log.

The coastguard said the man must have tied up his own hands, fastening the knots with his teeth. The fact that a coastguard was the first on board may save some complications later on, in the Admiralty Court, for coastguards cannot claim the salvage which is the right of the first civilian entering on a derelict. Already, however, the legal tongues are wagging, and one young law student is loudly asserting that the rights of the owner are already completely sacrificed, his property being held in contravention of the statues of mortmain, since the tiller, as emblemship, if not proof, of delegated possession, is held in a *dead hand*.

It is needless to say that the dead steersman has been reverently removed from the place where he held his honourable watch and ward till death, a steadfastness as noble as that of the young Casabianca, and placed in the mortuary to await inquest.

Already the sudden storm is passing, and its fierceness is abating. Crowds are scattering backward, and the sky is beginning to redden over the Yorkshire wolds.

I shall send, in time for your next issue, further details of the derelict ship which found her way so miraculously into harbour in the storm.

Whitby. 9 August.

The sequel to the strange arrival of the derelict in the storm last night is almost more startling than the thing itself. It turns out that the schooner is Russian from Varna, and is called the *Demeter*. She is almost entirely in ballast of silver sand, with only a small amount of cargo, a number of great wooden boxes filled with mould. This cargo was consigned to a Whitby solicitor, Mr. S.F. Billington, of 7, The Crescent, who this morning went aboard and took formal possession of the goods consigned to him. The Russian consul, too, acting for the charter-party, took formal possession of the ship, and paid all harbour dues, etc. Nothing is talked about here today except the strange coincidence. The officials of the Board of Trade have been most exacting in seeing that every compliance has been made with existing regulations. As the matter is to be a "nine days wonder," they are evidently determined that there shall be no cause of other complaint. A good deal of interest was abroad concerning the dog which landed when the ship struck, and more than a few of the members of the S.P.C.A., which is very strong in Whitby, have tried to befriend the animal. To the general disappointment, however, it was not to be found. It seems to have disappeared entirely from the town. It may be that it was frightened and made its way on to the moors, where it is still hiding in terror. There are some who look with dread on such a possibility, lest later on it should in itself become a danger, for it is evidently a fierce brute. Early this morning a large dog, a half-bred mastiff belonging to a coal merchant close to Tate Hill Pier, was found dead in the roadway opposite its master's yard. It had been fighting, and manifestly had had a savage opponent, for its throat was torn away, and its belly was slit open as if with a savage claw.

Later.

By the kindness of the Board of Trade inspector, I have been permitted to look over the log book of the *Demeter*, which was in order up to within three days, but contained nothing of special interest except as to facts of missing men. The greatest interest, however, is with regard to the paper found in the bottle, which was today produced at the inquest. And a more strange narrative than the two between them unfold it has not been my lot to come across. As there is no motive for concealment, I am permitted to use them, and accordingly send you a transcript, simply omitting technical details of seamanship and supercargo. It almost seems as though the captain had been seized with some kind of mania before he had got well into blue water, and that this had developed persistently throughout the voyage. Of course my statement must be taken *cum grano*, since I am writing from the dictation of a clerk of the Russian consul, who kindly translated for me, time being short.

LOG OF THE *DEMETER*

VARNA TO WHITBY

WRITTEN 18 JULY, THINGS SO STRANGE HAPPENING, THAT I SHALL KEEP ACCURATE NOTE HENCEFORTH TILL WE LAND.

On 6 July we finished taking in cargo, silver sand and boxes of earth. At noon set sail. East wind, fresh. Crew, five hands . . . two mates, cook, and myself, (captain).

On 11 July at dawn entered Bosphorus. Boarded by Turkish Customs officers. Backsheesh. All correct. Under way at 4 p.m.

On 12 July through Dardanelles. More Customs officers and flagboat of guarding squadron. Backsheesh again. Work of officers thorough, but quick. Want us off soon. At dark passed into Archipelago.

On 13 July passed Cape Matapan. Crew dissatisfied about something. Seemed scared, but would not speak out.

On 14 July was somewhat anxious about crew. Men all steady fellows, who sailed with me before. Mate could not make out what was wrong. They only told him there was *something*, and crossed themselves. Mate lost temper with one of them that day and struck him. Expected fierce quarrel, but all was quiet.

On 16 July mate reported in the morning that one of the crew, Petrofsky, was missing. Could not account for it. Took larboard watch eight bells last night, was relieved by Amramoff, but did not go to bunk. Men more downcast than ever. All said they expected something of the kind, but would not say more than there was *something* aboard. Mate getting very impatient with them. Feared some trouble ahead.

On 17 July, yesterday, one of the men, Olgaren, came to my cabin, and in an awestruck way confided to me that he thought there was a strange man aboard the ship. He said that in his watch he had been sheltering behind the deckhouse, as there was a rain storm, when he saw a tall, thin man, who was not like any of the crew, come up the companionway, and go along the deck forward and disappear. He followed cautiously, but when he got to bows found no one, and the hatchways were all closed. He was in a panic of superstitious fear, and I am afraid the panic may spread. To allay it, I shall today search the entire ship carefully from stem to stern.

Later in the day I got together the whole crew, and told them, as they evidently thought there was someone in the ship, we would search from stem to stern. First mate angry, said it was folly, and to yield to such foolish ideas would demoralise the men, said he would engage to keep them out of trouble with the handspike. I let him take the helm, while the rest began a thorough search, all keeping abreast, with lanterns. We left no corner unsearched. As there were only the big wooden boxes, there were no odd corners where a man could hide. Men much relieved when search over, and went back to work cheerfully. First mate scowled, but said nothing.

22 July.

Rough weather last three days, and all hands busy with sails, no time to be frightened. Men seem to have forgotten their dread. Mate cheerful again, and all on good terms. Praised men for work in bad weather. Passed Gibraltar and out through Straits. All well.

24 July.

There seems some doom over this ship. Already a hand short, and entering the Bay of Biscay with wild weather ahead, and yet last night another man lost, disappeared. Like the first, he came off his watch and was not seen again. Men all in a panic of fear, sent a round robin, asking to have double watch, as they fear to be alone. Mate angry.

Fear there will be some trouble, as either he or the men will do some violence.

28 July.

Four days in hell, knocking about in a sort of maelstrom, and the wind a tempest. No sleep for anyone. Men all worn out. Hardly know how to set a watch, since no one fit to go on. Second mate volunteered to steer and watch, and let men snatch a few hours sleep. Wind abating, seas still terrific, but feel them less, as ship is steadier.

29 July.

Another tragedy. Had single watch tonight, as crew too tired to double. When morning watch came on deck could find no one except steersman. Raised outcry, and all came on deck. Thorough search, but no one found. Are now without second mate, and crew in a panic. Mate and I agreed to go armed henceforth and wait for any sign of cause.

30 July.

Last night. Rejoiced we are nearing England. Weather fine, all sails set. Retired worn out, slept soundly, awakened by mate telling me that both man of watch and steersman missing. Only self and mate and two hands left to work ship.

1 August.

Two days of fog, and not a sail sighted. Had hoped when in the English Channel to be able to signal for help or get in somewhere. Not having power to work sails, have to run before wind. Dare not lower, as could not raise them again. We seem to be drifting to some terrible doom. Mate now more demoralised than either of men. His stronger nature seems to have worked inwardly against himself. Men are beyond fear, working stolidly and patiently, with minds made up to worst. They are Russian, he Roumanian.

2 August, midnight.

Woke up from few minutes sleep by hearing a cry, seemingly outside my port. Could see nothing in fog. Rushed on deck, and ran against mate. Tells me he heard cry and ran, but no sign of man on watch. One more gone. Lord, help us! Mate says we must be past Straits of Dover, as in a moment of fog lifting he saw North Foreland, just as he heard the man cry out. If so we are now off in the North Sea, and only God can guide us in the fog, which seems to move with us, and God seems to have deserted us.

3 August.

At midnight I went to relieve the man at the wheel and when I got to it found no one there. The wind was steady, and as we ran before it there was no yawing. I dared not leave it, so shouted for the mate. After a few seconds, he rushed up on deck in his flannels. He looked wild-eyed and haggard, and I greatly fear his reason has given way. He came close to me and whispered hoarsely, with his mouth to my ear, as though fearing the very air might hear. "It is here. I know it now. On the watch last night I saw It, like a man, tall and thin, and ghastly pale. It was in the bows, and looking out. I crept behind It, and gave It my knife, but the knife went through It, empty as the air." And as he spoke he took the knife and drove it savagely into space. Then he went on, "But It is here, and I'll find It. It is in the hold, perhaps in one of those boxes. I'll unscrew them one by one and see. You work the helm." And with a warning look and his finger on his lip, he went below. There was springing up a choppy wind, and I could not leave the helm. I saw him come out on deck again with a tool chest and lantern, and go down the forward hatchway. He is mad, stark, raving mad, and it's no use my trying to stop him. He can't hurt those big boxes, they are invoiced as clay, and to pull them about is as harmless a thing as he can do. So here I stay and mind the helm, and write these notes. I can only trust in God and wait till the fog clears. Then, if I can't steer to any harbour with the wind that is, I shall cut down sails, and lie by, and signal for help . . .

It is nearly all over now. Just as I was beginning to hope that the mate would come out calmer, for I heard him knocking away at something in the hold, and work is good for him—there came up the hatchway a sudden, startled scream, which made my blood run cold, and up on the deck he came as if shot from a gun—a raging madman, with his eyes rolling and his face convulsed with fear. "Save me! Save me!" he cried, and then looked round on the blanket of fog. His horror turned to despair, and in a steady voice he said, "You had better come too, captain, before it is too late. He is there! I know the secret now. The sea will save me from Him, and it is all that is left!" Before I could say a word, or move forward to seize him, he sprang on the bulwark and deliberately threw himself into the sea. I suppose I know the secret too, now. It was this madman who had got rid of the men one by one, and now he has followed them himself. God help me! How am I to account for all these horrors when I get to port? When I get to port! Will that ever be?

4 August.

Still fog, which the sunrise cannot pierce, I know there is sunrise because I am a sailor, why else I know not. I dared not go below, I dared not leave the helm, so here all night I stayed, and in the dimness of the night I saw It—Him! God, forgive me, but the mate was right to jump overboard. It was better to die like a man. To die like a sailor in blue water, no man can object. But I am captain, and I must not leave my ship. But I shall baffle this fiend or monster, for I shall tie my hands to the wheel when my strength begins to fail, and along with them I shall tie that which He—It—dare not touch. And then, come good wind or foul, I shall save my soul, and my honour as a captain. I am growing weaker, and the night is coming on. If He can look me in the face again, I may not have time to act . . . If we are wrecked, mayhap this bottle may be found, and those who find it may understand. If not . . . well, then all men shall know that I have been true to my trust. God and the Blessed Virgin and the Saints help a poor ignorant soul trying to do his duty . . .

Of course the verdict was an open one. There is no evidence to adduce, and whether or not the man himself committed the murders there is now none to say. The folk here hold almost universally that the captain is simply a hero, and he is to be given a public funeral. Already it is arranged that his body is to be taken with a train of boats up the Esk for a piece and then brought back to Tate Hill Pier and up the abbey steps, for he is to be buried in the churchyard on the cliff. The owners of more than a hundred boats have already given in their names as wishing to follow him to the grave.

No trace has ever been found of the great dog, at which there is much mourning, for, with public opinion in its present state, he would, I believe, be adopted by the town. Tomorrow will see the funeral, and so will end this one more "mystery of the sea."

Mina Murray's Journal

8 August.

Lucy was very restless all night, and I too, could not sleep. The storm was fearful, and as it boomed loudly among the chimney pots, it made me shudder. When a sharp puff came it seemed to be like a distant gun. Strangely enough, Lucy did not wake, but she got up twice and dressed herself. Fortunately, each time I awoke in time and managed to undress her without waking her, and got her back to bed. It is a very strange thing, this sleep-walking, for as soon as her will is thwarted in any physical way, her intention, if there be any, disappears, and she yields herself almost exactly to the routine of her life.

Early in the morning we both got up and went down to the harbour to see if anything had happened in the night. There were very few people about, and though the sun was bright, and the air clear and fresh, the big, grim-looking waves, that seemed dark themselves because the foam that topped them was like snow, forced themselves in through the mouth of the harbour, like a bullying man going through a crowd. Somehow I felt glad that Jonathan was not on the sea last night, but on land. But, oh, is he on land or sea? Where is he, and how? I am getting fearfully anxious about him. If I only knew what to do, and could do anything!

10 August.

The funeral of the poor sea captain today was most touching. Every boat in the harbour seemed to be there, and the coffin was carried by captains all the way from Tate Hill Pier up to the churchyard. Lucy came with me, and we went early to our old seat, whilst the cortege of boats went up the river to the Viaduct and came down again. We had a lovely view, and saw the procession nearly all the way. The poor fellow was laid to rest near our seat so that we stood on it, when the time came and saw everything. Poor Lucy seemed much upset. She was restless and uneasy all the time, and I cannot but think that her dreaming at night is telling on her. She is quite odd in one thing. She will not admit to me that there is any cause for restlessness, or if there be, she does not understand it herself. There is an additional cause in that poor Mr. Swales was found dead this morning on our seat, his neck being broken.

He had evidently, as the doctor said, fallen back in the seat in some sort of fright, for there was a look of fear and horror on his face that the men said made them shudder. Poor dear old man! Lucy is so sweet and sensitive that she feels influences more acutely than other people do. Just now she was quite upset by a little thing which I did not much heed, though I am myself very fond of animals. One of the men who came up here often to look for the boats was followed by his dog. The dog is always with him. They are both quiet persons, and I never saw the man angry, nor heard the dog bark. During the service the dog would not come to its master, who was on the seat with us, but kept a few yards off, barking and howling. Its master spoke to it gently, and then harshly, and then angrily. But it would neither come nor cease to make a noise. It was in a fury, with its eyes savage, and all its hair bristling out like a cat's tail when puss is on the war path. Finally the man too got angry, and jumped down and kicked the dog, and then took it by the scruff of the neck and half dragged and half threw it on the tombstone on which the seat is fixed. The moment it touched the stone the poor thing began to tremble. It did not try to get away, but crouched down, quivering and cowering, and was in such a pitiable state of terror that I tried, though without effect, to comfort it. Lucy was full of pity, too, but she did not attempt to touch the dog, but looked at it in an agonised sort of way. I greatly fear that she is of too super sensitive a nature to go through the world without trouble. She will be dreaming of this tonight, I am sure. The whole agglomeration of things, the ship steered into port by a dead man, his attitude, tied to the wheel with a crucifix and beads, the touching funeral, the dog, now furious and now in terror, will all afford material for her dreams.

I think it will be best for her to go to bed tired out physically, so I shall take her for a long walk by the cliffs to Robin Hood's Bay and back. She ought not to have much inclination for sleep-walking then.

CHAPTER VIII

Mina Murray's Journal

Same day, 11 p.m.

Oh, but I am tired! If it were not that I had made my diary a duty I should not open it tonight. We had a lovely walk. Lucy, after a while, was in gay spirits, owing, I think, to some dear cows who came nosing towards us in a field close to the lighthouse, and frightened the wits out of us. I believe we forgot everything, except of course, personal fear, and it seemed to wipe the slate clean and give us a fresh start. We had a capital "severe tea" at Robin Hood's Bay in a sweet little old-fashioned inn, with a bow window right over the seaweed-covered rocks of the strand. I believe we should have shocked the "New Woman" with our appetites. Men are more tolerant, bless them! Then we walked home with some, or rather many, stoppages to rest, and with our hearts full of a constant dread of wild bulls. Lucy was really tired, and we intended to creep off to bed as soon as we could. The young curate came in, however, and Mrs. Westenra asked him to stay for supper. Lucy and I had both a fight for it with the dusty miller. I know it was a hard fight on my part, and I am quite heroic. I think that someday the bishops must get together and see about breeding up a new class of curates, who don't take supper, no matter how hard they may be pressed to, and who will know when girls are tired. Lucy is asleep and breathing softly. She has more colour in her cheeks than usual, and looks, oh so sweet. If Mr. Holmwood fell in love with her seeing her only in the drawing room, I wonder what he would say if he saw her now. Some of the "New Women" writers will someday start an idea that men and women should be allowed to see each other asleep before proposing or accepting. But I suppose the "New Woman" won't condescend in future to accept. She will do the proposing herself. And a nice job she will make of it too! There's some consolation in that. I am so happy tonight, because dear Lucy seems better. I really believe she has turned the corner, and that we are over her troubles with dreaming. I should be quite happy if I only knew if Jonathan . . . God bless and keep him.

11 August, 3 a.m.

Diary again. No sleep now, so I may as well write. I am too agitated to sleep. We have had such an adventure, such an agonizing experience. I fell asleep as soon as I had closed my diary. . . . Suddenly I became broad awake, and sat up, with a horrible sense of fear upon me, and of some feeling of emptiness around me. The room was dark, so I could not see Lucy's bed. I stole across and felt for her. The bed was empty. I lit a match and found that she was not in the room. The door was shut, but not locked, as I had left it. I feared to wake her mother, who has been more than usually ill lately, so threw on some clothes and got ready to look for her. As I was leaving the room it struck me that the clothes she wore might give me some clue to her dreaming intention. Dressing-gown would mean house, dress outside. Dressing-gown and dress were both in their places. "Thank God," I said to myself, "she cannot be far, as she is only in her nightdress." I ran downstairs and looked in the sitting room. Not there! Then I looked in all the other rooms of the house, with an ever-growing fear chilling my heart. Finally, I came to the hall door and found it open. It was not wide open, but the catch of the lock had not caught. The people of the house are careful to lock the door every night, so I feared that Lucy must have gone out as she was. There was no time to think of what might happen. A vague overmastering fear obscured all details. I took a big, heavy shawl and ran out. The clock was striking one as I was in the Crescent, and there was not a soul in sight. I ran along the North Terrace, but could see no sign of the white figure which I expected. At the edge of the West Cliff above the pier I looked across the harbour to the East Cliff, in the hope or fear—I don't know which—of seeing Lucy in our favourite seat. There was a bright full moon, with heavy black, driving clouds, which threw the whole scene into a fleeting diorama of light and shade as they sailed across. For a moment or two I could see nothing, as the shadow of a cloud obscured St. Mary's Church and all around it. Then as the cloud passed I could see the ruins of the abbey coming into view, and as the edge of a narrow band of light as sharp as a sword-cut moved along, the church and churchyard became gradually visible. Whatever my expectation was, it was not disappointed, for there, on our favourite seat, the silver light of the moon struck a half-reclining figure, snowy white. The coming of the cloud was too quick for me to see much, for shadow shut down on light almost immediately, but it seemed to me as though something dark stood behind the seat where the white figure shone, and bent over it. What it was, whether man or beast, I could not tell. I did not wait to catch another glance, but flew down the steep steps to the pier and along by the fish-market to the bridge, which was the only way to reach the East Cliff. The town seemed as dead, for not a soul did I see. I rejoiced that it was so, for I wanted no witness of poor Lucy's condition. The time and distance seemed endless, and my knees trembled and my breath came laboured as I toiled up the endless steps to the abbey. I must have gone fast, and yet it seemed to me as if my feet were weighted with lead, and as though every joint in my body were rusty. When I got almost to the top I could see the seat and the white figure, for I was now close enough to distinguish it even through the spells of shadow. There was undoubtedly something, long and black, bending over the half-reclining white figure. I called in fright, "Lucy! Lucy!" and something raised a head, and from where I was I could see a white face and red, gleaming eyes. Lucy did not answer, and I ran on to the entrance of the churchyard. As I entered, the church was between me and the seat, and for a minute or so I lost sight of her. When I came in view again the cloud had passed, and the moonlight struck so brilliantly that I could see Lucy half reclining with her head lying over the back of the seat. She was quite alone, and there was not a sign of any living thing about.

When I bent over her I could see that she was still asleep. Her lips were parted, and she was breathing, not softly as usual with her, but in long, heavy gasps, as though striving to get her lungs full at every breath. As I came close, she put up her hand in her sleep and pulled the collar of her nightdress close around her, as though she felt the cold. I flung the warm shawl over her, and drew the edges tight around her neck, for I dreaded lest she should get some deadly chill from the night air, unclad as she was. I feared to wake her all at once, so, in order to have my hands free to help her, I fastened the shawl at her throat with a big safety pin. But I must have been clumsy in my anxiety and pinched or pricked her with it, for by-and-by, when her breathing became quieter, she put her hand to her throat again and moaned. When I had her carefully wrapped up I put my shoes on her feet, and then began very gently to wake her. At first she did not respond, but gradually she became more and more uneasy in her sleep, moaning and sighing occasionally. At last, as time was passing fast, and for many other reasons, I wished to get her home at once, I shook her forcibly, till finally she opened her eyes and awoke. She did not seem surprised to see me, as, of course, she did not realize all at once where she was. Lucy always wakes prettily, and even at such a time, when her body must have been chilled with cold, and her mind somewhat appalled at waking unclad in a churchyard at night, she did not lose her grace. She trembled a little, and clung to me. When I told her to come at once with me home, she rose without a word, with the obedience of a child. As we passed along, the gravel hurt my feet, and Lucy noticed me wince. She stopped and wanted to insist upon my taking my shoes, but I would not. However, when we got to the pathway outside the churchyard, where there was a puddle of water, remaining from the storm, I daubed my feet with mud, using each foot in turn on the other, so that as we went home, no one, in case we should meet anyone, should notice my bare feet.

Fortune favoured us, and we got home without meeting a soul. Once we saw a man, who seemed not quite sober, passing along a street in front of us. But we hid in a door till he had disappeared up an opening such as there are here, steep little closes, or "wynds," as they call them in Scotland. My heart beat so loud all the time sometimes I thought I should faint. I was filled with anxiety about Lucy, not only for her health, lest she should suffer from the exposure, but for her reputation in case the story should get wind. When we got in, and had washed our feet, and had said a prayer of thankfulness together, I tucked her into bed. Before falling asleep she asked—even implored—me not to say a word to anyone, even her mother, about her sleep-walking adventure. I hesitated at first, to promise, but on thinking of the state of her mother's health, and how the knowledge of such a thing would fret her, and think too, of how such a story might become distorted—nay, infallibly would—in case it should leak out, I thought it wiser to do so. I hope I did right. I have locked the door, and the key is tied to my wrist, so perhaps I shall not be again disturbed. Lucy is sleeping soundly. The reflex of the dawn is high and far over the sea . . .

Same day, noon.

All goes well. Lucy slept till I woke her and seemed not to have even changed her side. The adventure of the night does not seem to have harmed her, on the contrary, it has benefited her, for she looks better this morning than she has done for weeks. I was sorry to notice that my clumsiness with the safety-pin hurt her. Indeed, it might have been serious, for the skin of her throat was pierced. I must have pinched up a piece of loose skin and have transfixed it, for there are two little red points like pin-pricks, and on the band of her nightdress was a drop of blood. When I apologised and was concerned about it, she laughed and petted me, and said she did not even feel it. Fortunately it cannot leave a scar, as it is so tiny.

Same day, night.

We passed a happy day. The air was clear, and the sun bright, and there was a cool breeze. We took our lunch to Mulgrave Woods, Mrs. Westenra driving by the road and Lucy and I walking by the cliff-path and joining her at the gate. I felt a little sad myself, for I could not but feel how absolutely happy it would have been had Jonathan been with me. But there! I must only be patient. In the evening we strolled in the Casino Terrace, and heard some good music by Spohr and Mackenzie, and went to bed early. Lucy seems more restful than she has been for some time, and fell asleep at once. I shall lock the door and secure the key the same as before, though I do not expect any trouble tonight.

12 August.

My expectations were wrong, for twice during the night I was wakened by Lucy trying to get out. She seemed, even in her sleep, to be a little impatient at finding the door shut, and went back to bed under a sort of protest. I woke with the dawn, and heard the birds chirping outside of the window. Lucy woke, too, and I was glad to see, was even better than on the previous morning. All her old gaiety of manner seemed to have come back, and she came and snuggled in beside me and told me all about Arthur. I told her how anxious I was about Jonathan, and then she tried to comfort me. Well, she succeeded somewhat, for, though sympathy can't alter facts, it can make them more bearable.

13 August.

Another quiet day, and to bed with the key on my wrist as before. Again I awoke in the night, and found Lucy sitting up in bed, still asleep, pointing to the window. I got up quietly, and pulling aside the blind, looked out. It was brilliant moonlight, and the soft effect of the light over the sea and sky, merged together in one great silent mystery, was beautiful beyond words. Between me and the moonlight flitted a great bat, coming and going in great whirling circles. Once or twice it came quite close, but was, I suppose, frightened at seeing me, and flitted away across the harbour towards the abbey. When I came back from the window Lucy had lain down again, and was sleeping peacefully. She did not stir again all night.

14 August.

On the East Cliff, reading and writing all day. Lucy seems to have become as much in love with the spot as I am, and it is hard to get her away from it when it is time to come home for lunch or tea or dinner. This afternoon she made a funny remark. We were coming home for dinner, and had come to the top of the steps up from the West Pier and stopped to look at the view, as we generally do. The setting sun, low down in the sky, was just dropping behind Kettleness. The red light was thrown over on the East Cliff and the old abbey, and seemed to bathe everything in a beautiful rosy glow.

We were silent for a while, and suddenly Lucy murmured as if to herself, "His red eyes again! They are just the same." It was such an odd expression, coming apropos of nothing, that it quite startled me. I slewed round a little, so as to see Lucy well without seeming to stare at her, and saw that she was in a half dreamy state, with an odd look on her face that I could not quite make out, so I said nothing, but followed her eyes. She appeared to be looking over at our own seat, whereon was a dark figure seated alone. I was quite a little startled myself, for it seemed for an instant as if the stranger had great eyes like burning flames, but a second look dispelled the illusion. The red sunlight was shining on the windows of St. Mary's Church behind our seat, and as the sun dipped there was just sufficient change in the refraction and reflection to make it appear as if the light moved. I called Lucy's attention to the peculiar effect, and she became herself with a start, but she looked sad all the same. It may have been that she was thinking of that terrible night up there. We never refer to it, so I said nothing, and we went home to dinner. Lucy had a headache and went early to bed. I saw her asleep, and went out for a little stroll myself. I walked along the cliffs to the westward, and was full of sweet sadness, for I was thinking of Jonathan. When coming home, it was then bright moonlight, so bright that, though the front of our part of the Crescent was in shadow, everything could be well seen, I threw a glance up at our window, and saw Lucy's head leaning out. I opened my handkerchief and waved it. She did not notice or make any movement whatever. Just then, the moonlight crept round an angle of the building, and the light fell on the window. There distinctly was Lucy with her head lying up against the side of the window sill and her eyes shut. She was fast asleep, and by her, seated on the window sill, was something that looked like a good-sized bird. I was afraid she might get a chill, so I ran upstairs, but as I came into the room she was moving back to her bed, fast asleep, and breathing heavily. She was holding her hand to her throat, as though to protect if from the cold.

I did not wake her, but tucked her up warmly. I have taken care that the door is locked and the window securely fastened.

She looks so sweet as she sleeps, but she is paler than is her wont, and there is a drawn, haggard look under her eyes which I do not like. I fear she is fretting about something. I wish I could find out what it is.

15 August.

Rose later than usual. Lucy was languid and tired, and slept on after we had been called. We had a happy surprise at breakfast. Arthur's father is better, and wants the marriage to come off soon. Lucy is full of quiet joy, and her mother is glad and sorry at once. Later on in the day she told me the cause. She is grieved to lose Lucy as her very own, but she is rejoiced that she is soon to have someone to protect her. Poor dear, sweet lady! She confided to me that she has got her death warrant. She has not told Lucy, and made me promise secrecy. Her doctor told her that within a few months, at most, she must die, for her heart is weakening. At any time, even now, a sudden shock would be almost sure to kill her. Ah, we were wise to keep from her the affair of the dreadful night of Lucy's sleep-walking.

17 August.

No diary for two whole days. I have not had the heart to write. Some sort of shadowy pall seems to be coming over our happiness. No news from Jonathan, and Lucy seems to be growing weaker, whilst her mother's hours are numbering to a close. I do not understand Lucy's fading away as she is doing. She eats well and sleeps well, and enjoys the fresh air, but all the time the roses in her cheeks are fading, and she gets weaker and more languid day by day. At night I hear her gasping as if for air. I keep the key of our door always fastened to my wrist at night, but she gets up and walks about the room, and sits at the open window. Last night I found her leaning out when I woke up, and when I tried to wake her I could not. She was in a faint. When I managed to restore her, she was weak as water, and cried silently between long, painful struggles for breath. When I asked her how she came to be at the window she shook her head and turned away. I trust her feeling ill may not be from that unlucky prick of the safety-pin. I looked at her throat just now as she lay asleep, and the tiny wounds seem not to have healed. They are still open, and, if anything, larger than before, and the edges of them are faintly white. They are like little white dots with red centres. Unless they heal within a day or two, I shall insist on the doctor seeing about them.

Letter, Samuel F. Billington & Son, Solicitors Whitby, to Messrs. Carter, Paterson & Co., London

17 August.

Dear Sirs,

Herewith please receive invoice of goods sent by Great Northern Railway. Same are to be delivered at Carfax, near Purfleet, immediately on receipt at goods station King's Cross. The house is at present empty, but enclosed please find keys, all of which are labelled.

You will please deposit the boxes, fifty in number, which form the consignment, in the partially ruined building forming part of the house and marked "A" on rough diagrams enclosed. Your agent will easily recognize the locality, as it is the ancient chapel of the mansion. The goods leave by the train at 9:30 tonight, and will be due at King's Cross at 4:30 tomorrow afternoon. As our client wishes the delivery made as soon as possible, we shall be obliged by your having teams ready at King's Cross at the time named and forthwith conveying the goods to destination. In order to obviate any delays possible through any routine requirements as to payment in your departments, we enclose cheque herewith for ten pounds, receipt of which please acknowledge. Should the charge be less than this amount, you can return balance, if greater, we shall at once send cheque for difference on hearing from you. You are to leave the keys on coming away in the main hall of the house, where the proprietor may get them on his entering the house by means of his duplicate key.

Pray do not take us as exceeding the bounds of business courtesy in pressing you in all ways to use the utmost expedition.

We are, dear Sirs,
Faithfully yours,
SAMUEL F. BILLINGTON & SON

LETTER, MESSRS. CARTER, PATERSON & CO., LONDON, TO MESSRS. BILLINGTON & SON, WHITBY

21 August.

Dear Sirs,

We beg to acknowledge 10 pounds received and to return cheque of 1 pound, 17s, 9d, amount of overplus, as shown in receipted account herewith. Goods are delivered in exact accordance with instructions, and keys left in parcel in main hall, as directed.

We are, dear Sirs,
Yours respectfully,
PRO CARTER, PATERSON & CO.

MINA MURRAY'S JOURNAL

18 August.

I am happy today, and write sitting on the seat in the churchyard. Lucy is ever so much better. Last night she slept well all night, and did not disturb me once.

The roses seem coming back already to her cheeks, though she is still sadly pale and wan-looking. If she were in any way anemic I could understand it, but she is not. She is in gay spirits and full of life and cheerfulness. All the morbid reticence seems to have passed from her, and she has just reminded me, as if I needed any reminding, of *that* night, and that it was here, on this very seat, I found her asleep.

As she told me she tapped playfully with the heel of her boot on the stone slab and said, "My poor little feet didn't make much noise then! I daresay poor old Mr. Swales would have told me that it was because I didn't want to wake up Geordie."

As she was in such a communicative humour, I asked her if she had dreamed at all that night. Before she answered, that sweet, puckered look came into her forehead, which Arthur—I call him Arthur from her habit—says he loves, and indeed, I don't wonder that he does. Then she went on in a half-dreaming kind of way, as if trying to recall it to herself.

"I didn't quite dream, but it all seemed to be real. I only wanted to be here in this spot. I don't know why, for I was afraid of something, I don't know what. I remember, though I suppose I was asleep, passing through the streets and over the bridge. A fish leaped as I went by, and I leaned over to look at it, and I heard a lot of dogs howling. The whole town seemed as if it must be full of dogs all howling at once, as I went up the steps. Then I had a vague memory of something long and dark with red eyes, just as we saw in the sunset, and something very sweet and very bitter all around me at once. And then I seemed sinking into deep green water, and there was a singing in my ears, as I have heard there is to drowning men, and then everything seemed passing away from me. My soul seemed to go out from my body and float about the air. I seem to remember that once the West Lighthouse was right under me, and then there was a sort of agonizing feeling, as if I were in an earthquake, and I came back and found you shaking my body. I saw you do it before I felt you."

Then she began to laugh. It seemed a little uncanny to me, and I listened to her breathlessly. I did not quite like it, and thought it better not to keep her mind on the subject, so we drifted on to another subject, and Lucy was like her old self again. When we got home the fresh breeze had braced her up, and her pale cheeks were really more rosy. Her mother rejoiced when she saw her, and we all spent a very happy evening together.

19 August.

Joy, joy, joy! Although not all joy. At last, news of Jonathan. The dear fellow has been ill, that is why he did not write. I am not afraid to think it or to say it, now that I know. Mr. Hawkins sent me on the letter, and wrote himself, oh so kindly. I am to leave in the morning and go over to Jonathan, and to help to nurse him if necessary, and to bring him home. Mr. Hawkins says it would not be a bad thing if we were to be married out there. I have cried over the good Sister's letter till I can feel it wet against my bosom, where it lies. It is of Jonathan, and must be near my heart, for he is in my heart. My journey is all mapped out, and my luggage ready. I am only taking one change of dress. Lucy will bring my trunk to London and keep it till I send for it, for it may be that . . . I must write no more. I must keep it to say to Jonathan, my husband. The letter that he has seen and touched must comfort me till we meet.

Letter, Sister Agatha, Hospital of St. Joseph and Ste. Mart Buda-Pesth, to Miss Willhelmina Murray

12 August.

Dear Madam,

I write by desire of Mr. Jonathan Harker, who is himself not strong enough to write, though progressing well, thanks to God and St. Joseph and Ste. Mary. He has been under our care for nearly six weeks, suffering from a violent brain fever. He wishes me to convey his love, and to say that by this post I write for him to Mr. Peter Hawkins, Exeter, to say, with his dutiful respects, that he is sorry for his delay, and that all of his work is completed. He will require some few weeks' rest in our sanatorium in the hills, but will then return. He wishes me to say that he has not sufficient money with him, and that he would like to pay for his staying here, so that others who need shall not be wanting for help.

Believe me,
Yours, with sympathy and all blessings.
Sister Agatha

P.S. My patient being asleep, I open this to let you know something more. He has told me all about you, and that you are shortly to be his wife. All blessings to you both! He has had some fearful shock—so says our doctor—and in his delirium his ravings have been dreadful, of wolves and poison and blood, of ghosts and demons, and I fear to say of what. Be careful of him always that there may be nothing to excite him of this kind for a long time to come. The traces of such an illness as his do not lightly die away. We should have written long ago, but we knew nothing of his friends, and there was nothing on him, nothing that anyone could understand. He came in the train from Klausenburg, and the guard was told by the station master there that he rushed into the station shouting for a ticket for home. Seeing from his violent demeanour that he was English, they gave him a ticket for the furthest station on the way thither that the train reached.

Be assured that he is well cared for. He has won all hearts by his sweetness and gentleness. He is truly getting on well, and I have no doubt will in a few weeks be all himself. But be careful of him for safety's sake. There are, I pray God and St. Joseph and Ste. Mary, many, many, happy years for you both.

Dr. Seward's Diary

19 August.

Strange and sudden change in Renfield last night. About eight o'clock he began to get excited and sniff about as a dog does when setting. The attendant was struck by his manner, and knowing my interest in him, encouraged him to talk. He is usually respectful to the attendant and at times servile, but tonight, the man tells me, he was quite haughty. Would not condescend to talk with him at all.

All he would say was, "I don't want to talk to you. You don't count now. The master is at hand."

The attendant thinks it is some sudden form of religious mania which has seized him. If so, we must look out for squalls, for a strong man with homicidal and religious mania at once might be dangerous. The combination is a dreadful one. At nine o'clock I visited him myself. His attitude to me was the same as that to the attendant. In his sublime self-feeling the difference between myself and the attendant seemed to him as nothing. It looks like religious mania, and he will soon think that he himself is God. These infinitesimal distinctions between man and man are too paltry for an Omnipotent Being. How these madmen give themselves away! The real God taketh heed lest a sparrow fall. But the God created from human vanity sees no difference between an eagle and a sparrow. Oh, if men only knew!

For half an hour or more Renfield kept getting excited in greater and greater degree. I did not pretend to be watching him, but I kept strict observation all the same. All at once that shifty look came into his eyes which we always see when a madman has seized an idea, and with it the shifty movement of the head and back which asylum attendants come to know so well. He became quite quiet, and went and sat on the edge of his bed resignedly, and looked into space with lack-luster eyes. I thought I would find out if his apathy were real or only assumed, and tried to lead him to talk of his pets, a theme which had never failed to excite his attention.

At first he made no reply, but at length said testily, "Bother them all! I don't care a pin about them."

"What?" I said. "You don't mean to tell me you don't care about spiders?" (Spiders at present are his hobby and the notebook is filling up with columns of small figures.)

To this he answered enigmatically, "The Bride maidens rejoice the eyes that wait the coming of the bride. But when the bride draweth nigh, then the maidens shine not to the eyes that are filled." He would not explain himself, but remained obstinately seated on his bed all the time I remained with him.

I am weary tonight and low in spirits. I cannot but think of Lucy, and how different things might have been. If I don't sleep at once, chloral, the modern Morpheus—$C_2HCl_3OH_2O$! I must be careful not to let it grow into a habit. No, I shall take none tonight! I have thought of Lucy, and I shall not dishonour her by mixing the two. If need be, tonight shall be sleepless.

Later.

Glad I made the resolution, gladder that I kept to it. I had lain tossing about, and had heard the clock strike only twice, when the night watchman came to me, sent up from the ward, to say that Renfield had escaped. I threw on my clothes and ran down at once. My patient is too dangerous a person to be roaming about. Those ideas of his might work out dangerously with strangers. The attendant was waiting for me. He said he had seen him not ten minutes before, seemingly asleep in his bed, when he had looked through the observation trap in the door. His attention was called by the sound of the window being wrenched out. He ran back and saw his feet disappear through the window, and had at once sent up for me. He was only in his night gear, and cannot be far off. The attendant thought it would be more useful to watch where he should go than to follow him, as he might lose sight of him whilst getting out of the building by the door. He is a bulky man, and couldn't get through the window. I am thin, so, with his aid, I got out, but feet foremost, and as we were only a few feet above ground landed unhurt.

The attendant told me the patient had gone to the left, and had taken a straight line, so I ran as quickly as I could. As I got through the belt of trees I saw a white figure scale the high wall which separates our grounds from those of the deserted house.

I ran back at once, told the watchman to get three or four men immediately and follow me into the grounds of Carfax, in case our friend might be dangerous. I got a ladder myself, and crossing the wall, dropped down on the other side. I could see Renfield's figure just disappearing behind the angle of the house, so I ran after him. On the far side of the house I found him pressed close against the old iron-bound oak door of the chapel. He was talking, apparently to someone, but I was afraid to go near enough to hear what he was saying, lest I might frighten him, and he should run off. Chasing an errant swarm of bees is nothing to following a naked lunatic, when the fit of escaping is upon him! After a few minutes, however, I could see that he did not take note of anything around him, and so ventured to draw nearer to him, the more so as my men had now crossed the wall and were closing him in.

I heard him say, "I am here to do your bidding, Master. I am your slave, and you will reward me, for I shall be faithful. I have worshipped you long and afar off. Now that you are near, I await your commands, and you will not pass me by, will you, dear Master, in your distribution of good things?"

He *is* a selfish old beggar anyhow. He thinks of the loaves and fishes even when he believes he is in a Real Presence. His manias make a startling combination. When we closed in on him he fought like a tiger. He is immensely strong, for he was more like a wild beast than a man. I never saw a lunatic in such a paroxysm of rage before, and I hope I shall not again. It is a mercy that we have found out his strength and his danger in good time. With strength and determination like his, he might have done wild work before he was caged. He is safe now, at any rate. Jack Sheppard himself couldn't get free from the strait waistcoat that keeps him restrained, and he's chained to the wall in the padded room. His cries are at times awful, but the silences that follow are more deadly still, for he means murder in every turn and movement.

Just now he spoke coherent words for the first time. "I shall be patient, Master. It is coming—coming—coming!"

So I took the hint, and came too. I was too excited to sleep, but this diary has quieted me, and I feel I shall get some sleep tonight.

CHAPTER IX

Letter, Mina Harker to Lucy Westenra

Buda-Pesth, 24 August.

My dearest Lucy,

I know you will be anxious to hear all that has happened since we parted at the railway station at Whitby.

Well, my dear, I got to Hull all right, and caught the boat to Hamburg, and then the train on here. I feel that I can hardly recall anything of the journey, except that I knew I was coming to Jonathan, and that as I should have to do some nursing, I had better get all the sleep I could. I found my dear one, oh, so thin and pale and weak-looking. All the resolution has gone out of his dear eyes, and that quiet dignity which I told you was in his face has vanished. He is only a wreck of himself, and he does not remember anything that has happened to him for a long time past. At least, he wants me to believe so, and I shall never ask. He has had some terrible shock, and I fear it might tax his poor brain if he were to try to recall it. Sister Agatha, who is a good creature and a born nurse, tells me that he wanted her to tell me what they were, but she would only cross herself, and say she would never tell. That the ravings of the sick were the secrets of God, and that if a nurse through her vocation should hear them, she should respect her trust.

She is a sweet, good soul, and the next day, when she saw I was troubled, she opened up the subject my poor dear raved about, added, "I can tell you this much, my dear. That it was not about anything which he has done wrong himself, and you, as his wife to be, have no cause to be concerned. He has not forgotten you or what he owes to you. His fear was of great and terrible things, which no mortal can treat of."

I do believe the dear soul thought I might be jealous lest my poor dear should have fallen in love with any other girl. The idea of my being jealous about Jonathan! And yet, my dear, let me whisper, I felt a thrill of joy through me when I knew that no other woman was a cause for trouble. I am now sitting by his bedside, where I can see his face while he sleeps. He is waking!

When he woke he asked me for his coat, as he wanted to get something from the pocket. I asked Sister Agatha, and she brought all his things. I saw amongst them was his notebook, and was going to ask him to let me look at it, for I knew that I might find some clue to his trouble, but I suppose he must have seen my wish in my eyes, for he sent me over to the window, saying he wanted to be quite alone for a moment.

Then he called me back, and he said to me very solemnly, "Wilhelmina." I knew then that he was in deadly earnest, for he has never called me by that name since he asked me to marry him. "You know, dear, my ideas of the trust between husband and wife. There should be no secret, no concealment. I have had a great shock, and when I try to think of what it is I feel my head spin round, and I do not know if it was real or the dreaming of a madman. You know I had brain fever, and that is to be mad. The secret is here, and I do not want to know it. I want to take up my life here, with our marriage." For, my dear, we had decided to be married as soon as the formalities are complete. "Are you willing, Wilhelmina, to share my ignorance? Here is the book. Take it and keep it, read it if you will, but never let me know unless, indeed, some solemn duty should come upon me to go back to the bitter hours, asleep or awake, sane or mad, recorded here." He fell back exhausted, and I put the book under his pillow, and kissed him. I have asked Sister Agatha to beg the Superior to let our wedding be this afternoon, and am waiting her reply . . .

She has come and told me that the Chaplain of the English mission church has been sent for. We are to be married in an hour, or as soon after as Jonathan awakes.

Lucy, the time has come and gone. I feel very solemn, but very, very happy. Jonathan woke a little after the hour, and all was ready, and he sat up in bed, propped up with pillows. He answered his "I will" firmly and strong. I could hardly speak. My heart was so full that even those words seemed to choke me. The dear sisters were so kind. Please, God, I shall never, never forget them, nor the grave and sweet responsibilities I have taken upon me. I must tell you of my wedding present. When the chaplain and the sisters had left me alone with my husband—oh, Lucy, it is the first time I have written the words "my husband"—left me alone with my husband, I took the book from under his pillow, and wrapped it up in white paper, and tied it with a little bit of pale blue ribbon which was round my neck, and sealed it over the knot with sealing wax, and for my seal I used my wedding ring. Then I kissed it and showed it to my husband, and told him that I would keep it so, and then it would be an outward and visible sign for us all our lives that we trusted each other, that I would never open it unless it were for his own dear sake or for the sake of some stern duty. Then he took my hand in his, and oh, Lucy, it was the first time he took his wife's hand, and said that it was the dearest thing in all the wide world, and that he would go through all the past again to win it, if need be. The poor dear meant to have said a part of the past, but he cannot think of time yet, and I shall not wonder if at first he mixes up not only the month, but the year.

Well, my dear, what could I say? I could only tell him that I was the happiest woman in all the wide world, and that I had nothing to give him except myself, my life, and my trust, and that with these went my love and duty for all the days of my life. And, my dear, when he kissed me, and drew me to him with his poor weak hands, it was like a solemn pledge between us.

Lucy dear, do you know why I tell you all this? It is not only because it is all sweet to me, but because you have been, and are, very dear to me. It was my privilege to be your friend and guide when you came from the schoolroom to prepare for the world of life. I want you to see now, and with the eyes of a very happy wife, whither duty has led me, so that in your own married life you too may be all happy, as I am. My dear, please Almighty God, your life may be all it promises, a long day of sunshine, with no harsh wind, no forgetting duty, no distrust. I must not wish you no pain, for that can never be, but I do hope you will be always as happy as I am now. Goodbye, my dear. I shall post this at once, and perhaps, write you very soon again. I must stop, for Jonathan is waking. I must attend my husband!

Your ever-loving

Mina Harker.

Letter, Lucy Westenra to Mina Harker

Whitby, 30 August.

My dearest Mina,

Oceans of love and millions of kisses, and may you soon be in your own home with your husband. I wish you were coming home soon enough to stay with us here. The strong air would soon restore Jonathan. It has quite restored me. I have an appetite like a cormorant, am full of life, and sleep well. You will be glad to know that I have quite given up walking in my sleep. I think I have not stirred out of my bed for a week, that is when I once got into it at night. Arthur says I am getting fat. By the way, I forgot to tell you that Arthur is here. We have such walks and drives, and rides, and rowing, and tennis, and fishing together, and I love him more than ever. He tells me that he loves me more, but I doubt that, for at first he told me that he couldn't love me more than he did then. But this is nonsense. There he is, calling to me. So no more just at present from your loving,

LUCY

P.S. Mother sends her love. She seems better, poor dear.

P.P.S. We are to be married on 28 September.

Dr. Seward's Diary

20 August.

The case of Renfield grows even more interesting. He has now so far quieted that there are spells of cessation from his passion. For the first week after his attack he was perpetually violent. Then one night, just as the moon rose, he grew quiet, and kept murmuring to himself. "Now I can wait. Now I can wait." The attendant came to tell me, so I ran down at once to have a look at him. He was still in the strait waistcoat and in the padded room, but the suffused look had gone from his face, and his eyes had something of their old pleading. I might almost say, cringing, softness. I was satisfied with his present condition, and directed him to be relieved. The attendants hesitated, but finally carried out my wishes without protest.

It was a strange thing that the patient had humour enough to see their distrust, for, coming close to me, he said in a whisper, all the while looking furtively at them, "They think I could hurt you! Fancy me hurting you! The fools!"

It was soothing, somehow, to the feelings to find myself disassociated even in the mind of this poor madman from the others, but all the same I do not follow his thought. Am I to take it that I have anything in common with him, so that we are, as it were, to stand together. Or has he to gain from me some good so stupendous that my well being is needful to Him? I must find out later on. Tonight he will not speak. Even the offer of a kitten or even a full-grown cat will not tempt him.

He will only say, "I don't take any stock in cats. I have more to think of now, and I can wait. I can wait."

After a while I left him. The attendant tells me that he was quiet until just before dawn, and that then he began to get uneasy, and at length violent, until at last he fell into a paroxysm which exhausted him so that he swooned into a sort of coma.

. . . Three nights has the same thing happened, violent all day then quiet from moonrise to sunrise. I wish I could get some clue to the cause. It would almost seem as if there was some influence which came and went. Happy thought! We shall tonight play sane wits against mad ones. He escaped before without our help. Tonight he shall escape with it. We shall give him a chance, and have the men ready to follow in case they are required.

23 August.

"The expected always happens." How well Disraeli knew life. Our bird when he found the cage open would not fly, so all our subtle arrangements were for nought. At any rate, we have proved one thing, that the spells of quietness last a reasonable time. We shall in future be able to ease his bonds for a few hours each day. I have given orders to the night attendant merely to shut him in the padded room, when once he is quiet, until the hour before sunrise. The poor soul's body will enjoy the relief even if his mind cannot appreciate it. Hark! The unexpected again! I am called. The patient has once more escaped.

Later.

Another night adventure. Renfield artfully waited until the attendant was entering the room to inspect. Then he dashed out past him and flew down the passage. I sent word for the attendants to follow. Again he went into the grounds of the deserted house, and we found him in the same place, pressed against the old chapel door. When he saw me he became furious, and had not the attendants seized him in time, he would have tried to kill me. As we were holding him a strange thing happened. He suddenly redoubled his efforts, and then as suddenly grew calm. I looked round instinctively, but could see nothing. Then I caught the patient's eye and followed it, but could trace nothing as it looked into the moonlight sky, except a big bat, which was flapping its silent and ghostly way to the west. Bats usually wheel about, but this one seemed to go straight on, as if it knew where it was bound for or had some intention of its own.

The patient grew calmer every instant, and presently said, "You needn't tie me. I shall go quietly!" Without trouble, we came back to the house. I feel there is something ominous in his calm, and shall not forget this night.

Lucy Westenra's Diary

Hillingham, 24 August.

I must imitate Mina, and keep writing things down. Then we can have long talks when we do meet. I wonder when it will be. I wish she were with me again, for I feel so unhappy. Last night I seemed to be dreaming again just as I was at Whitby. Perhaps it is the change of air, or getting home again. It is all dark and horrid to me, for I can remember nothing. But I am full of vague fear, and I feel so weak and worn out. When Arthur came to lunch he looked quite grieved when he saw me, and I hadn't the spirit to try to be cheerful. I wonder if I could sleep in mother's room tonight. I shall make an excuse to try.

25 August.

Another bad night. Mother did not seem to take to my proposal. She seems not too well herself, and doubtless she fears to worry me. I tried to keep awake, and succeeded for a while, but when the clock struck twelve it waked me from a doze, so I must have been falling asleep. There was a sort of scratching or flapping at the window, but I did not mind it, and as I remember no more, I suppose I must have fallen asleep. More bad dreams. I wish I could remember them. This morning I am horribly weak. My face is ghastly pale, and my throat pains me. It must be something wrong with my lungs, for I don't seem to be getting air enough. I shall try to cheer up when Arthur comes, or else I know he will be miserable to see me so.

Letter, Arthur to Dr. Seward

Albemarle Hotel, 31 August.

My dear Jack,

I want you to do me a favour. Lucy is ill; that is she has no special disease, but she looks awful, and is getting worse every day. I have asked her if there is any cause, I not dare to ask her mother, for to disturb the poor lady's mind about her daughter in her present state of health would be fatal. Mrs. Westenra has confided to me that her doom is spoken—disease of the heart—though poor Lucy does not know it yet. I am sure that there is something preying on my dear girl's mind. I am almost distracted when I think of her. To look at her gives me a pang. I told her I should ask you to see her, and though she demurred at first—I know why, old fellow—she finally consented. It will be a painful task for you, I know, old friend, but it is for her sake, and I must not hesitate to ask, or you to act. You are to come to lunch at Hillingham tomorrow, two o'clock, so as not to arouse any suspicion in Mrs. Westenra, and after lunch Lucy will take an opportunity of being alone with you. I am filled with anxiety, and want to consult with you alone as soon as I can after you have seen her. Do not fail!

Arthur.

Telegram, Arthur Holmwood to Seward

1 September.

Am summoned to see my father, who is worse. Am writing. Write me fully by tonight's post to Ring. Wire me if necessary.

Letter from Dr. Seward to Arthur Holmwood

2 September.

My dear old fellow,

With regard to Miss Westenra's health I hasten to let you know at once that in my opinion there is not any functional disturbance or any malady that I know of. At the same time, I am not by any means satisfied with her appearance. She is woefully different from what she was when I saw her last. Of course you must bear in mind that I did not have full opportunity of examination such as I should wish. Our very friendship makes a little difficulty which not even medical science or custom can bridge over. I had better tell you exactly what happened, leaving you to draw, in a measure, your own conclusions. I shall then say what I have done and propose doing.

I found Miss Westenra in seemingly gay spirits. Her mother was present, and in a few seconds I made up my mind that she was trying all she knew to mislead her mother and prevent her from being anxious. I have no doubt she guesses, if she does not know, what need of caution there is. We lunched alone, and as we all exerted ourselves to be cheerful, we got, as some kind of reward for our labours, some real cheerfulness amongst us. Then Mrs. Westenra went to lie down, and Lucy was left with me. We went into her boudoir, and till we got there her gaiety remained, for the servants were coming and going. As soon as the door was closed, however, the mask fell from her face, and she sank down into a chair with a great sigh, and hid her eyes with her hand. When I saw that her high spirits had failed, I at once took advantage of her reaction to make a diagnosis.

She said to me very sweetly, "I cannot tell you how I loathe talking about myself." I reminded her that a doctor's confidence was sacred, but that you were grievously anxious about her. She caught on to my meaning at once, and settled that matter in a word. "Tell Arthur everything you choose. I do not care for myself, but for him!" So I am quite free.

I could easily see that she was somewhat bloodless, but I could not see the usual anemic signs, and by the chance, I was able to test the actual quality of her blood, for in opening a window which was stiff a cord gave way, and she cut her hand slightly with broken glass. It was a slight matter in itself, but it gave me an evident chance, and I secured a few drops of the blood and have analysed them. The qualitative analysis give a quite normal condition, and shows, I should infer, in itself a vigorous state of health. In other physical matters I was quite satisfied that there is no need for anxiety, but as there must be a cause somewhere, I have come to the conclusion that it must be something mental. She complains of difficulty breathing satisfactorily at times, and of heavy, lethargic sleep, with dreams that frighten her, but regarding which she can remember nothing. She says that as a child, she used to walk in her sleep, and that when in Whitby the habit came back, and that once she walked out in the night and went to East Cliff, where

Miss Murray found her. But she assures me that of late the habit has not returned. I am in doubt, and so have done the best thing I know of. I have written to my old friend and master, Professor Van Helsing, of Amsterdam, who knows as much about obscure diseases as anyone in the world. I have asked him to come over, and as you told me that all things were to be at your charge, I have mentioned to him who you are and your relations to Miss Westenra. This, my dear fellow, is in obedience to your wishes, for I am only too proud and happy to do anything I can for her. Van Helsing would, I know, do anything for me for a personal reason, so no matter on what ground he comes, we must accept his wishes. He is a seemingly arbitrary man, this is because he knows what he is talking about better than anyone else. He is a philosopher and a metaphysician, and one of the most advanced scientists of his day, and he has, I believe, an absolutely open mind. This, with an iron nerve, a temper of the ice-brook, and indomitable resolution, self-command, and toleration exalted from virtues to blessings, and the kindliest and truest heart that beats, these form his equipment for the noble work that he is doing for mankind, work—both in theory and practice, for his views are as wide as his all-embracing sympathy. I tell you these facts that you may know why I have such confidence in him. I have asked him to come at once. I shall see Miss Westenra tomorrow again. She is to meet me at the Stores, so that I may not alarm her mother by too early a repetition of my call.

Yours always,

John Seward.

Letter, Abraham Van Helsing, MD, DPh, D. Lit, etc., etc., to Dr. Seward

2 September.

My good Friend,

When I received your letter I am already coming to you. By good fortune I can leave just at once, without wrong to any of those who have trusted me. Were fortune other, then it were bad for those who have trusted, for I come to my friend when he call me to aid those he holds dear. Tell your friend that when that time you suck from my wound so swiftly the poison of the gangrene from that knife that our other friend, too nervous, let slip, you did more for him when he wants my aids and you call for them than all his great fortune could do. But it is pleasure added to do for him, your friend, it is to you that I come. Have near at hand, and please it so arrange that we may see the young lady not too late on tomorrow, for it is likely that I may have to return here that night. But if need be I shall come again in three days, and stay longer if it must. Till then goodbye, my friend John.

VAN HELSING.

LETTER, DR. SEWARD TO HON. ARTHUR HOLMWOOD

3 September.

My dear Art,

Van Helsing has come and gone. He came on with me to Hillingham, and found that, by Lucy's discretion, her mother was lunching out, so that we were alone with her.

Van Helsing made a very careful examination of the patient. He is to report to me, and I shall advise you, for of course I was not present all the time. He is, I fear, much concerned, but says he must think. When I told him of our friendship and how you trust to me in the matter, he said, "You must tell him all you think. Tell him what I think, if you can guess it, if you will. Nay, I am not jesting. This is no jest, but life and death, perhaps more." I asked what he meant by that, for he was very serious. This was when we had come back to town, and he was having a cup of tea before starting on his return to Amsterdam. He would not give me any further clue. You must not be angry with me, Art, because his very reticence means that all his brains are working for her good. He will speak plainly enough when the time comes, be sure. So I told him I would simply write an account of our visit, just as if I were doing a descriptive special article for the *Daily Telegraph*. He seemed not to notice, but remarked that the smuts of London were not quite so bad as they used to be when he was a student here. I am to get his report tomorrow if he can possibly make it. In any case I am to have a letter.

Well, as to the visit, Lucy was more cheerful than on the day I first saw her, and certainly looked better. She had lost something of the ghastly look that so upset you, and her breathing was normal. She was very sweet to the Professor (as she always is), and tried to make him feel at ease, though I could see the poor girl was making a hard struggle for it. I believe Van Helsing saw it, too, for I saw the quick look under his bushy brows that I knew of old. Then he began to chat of all things except ourselves and diseases and with such an infinite geniality that I could see poor Lucy's pretense of animation merge into reality.

Then, without any seeming change, he brought the conversation gently round to his visit, and suavely said, "My dear young miss, I have the so great pleasure because you are so much beloved. That is much, my dear, even were there that which I do not see. They told me you were down in the spirit, and that you were of a ghastly pale. To them I say 'Pouf!'" And he snapped his fingers at me and went on. "But you and I shall show them how wrong they are. How can he,"—and he pointed at me with the same look and gesture as that with which he pointed me out in his class, on, or rather after, a particular occasion which he never fails to remind me of—"know anything of a young ladies? He has his madmen to play with, and to bring them back to happiness, and to those that love them. It is much to do, and, oh, but there are rewards in that we can bestow such happiness. But the young ladies! He has no wife nor daughter, and the young do not tell themselves to the young, but to the old, like me, who have known so many sorrows and the causes of them. So, my dear, we will send him away to smoke the cigarette in the garden, whiles you and I have little talk all to ourselves." I took the hint, and strolled about, and presently the professor came to the window and called me in. He looked grave, but said, "I have made careful examination, but there is no functional cause. With you I agree that there has been much blood lost, it has been but is not. But the conditions of her are in no way anemic. I have asked her to send me her maid, that I may ask just one or two questions, that so I may not chance to miss nothing. I know well what she will say. And yet there is cause. There is always cause for everything. I must go back home and think. You must send me the telegram every day, and if there be cause I shall come again. The disease—for not to be well is a disease—interest me, and the sweet, young dear, she interest me too. She charm me, and for her, if not for you or disease, I come."

As I tell you, he would not say a word more, even when we were alone. And so now, Art, you know all I know. I shall keep stern watch. I trust your poor father is rallying. It must be a terrible thing to you, my dear old fellow, to be placed in such a position between two people who are both so dear to you. I know your idea of duty to your father, and you are right to stick to it. But if need be, I shall send you word to come at once to Lucy, so do not be over-anxious unless you hear from me.

Dr. Seward's Diary

4 September.

Zoophagous patient still keeps up our interest in him. He had only one outburst and that was yesterday at an unusual time. Just before the stroke of noon he began to grow restless. The attendant knew the symptoms, and at once summoned aid. Fortunately the men came at a run, and were just in time, for at the stroke of noon he became so violent that it took all their strength to hold him. In about five minutes, however, he began to get more quiet, and finally sank into a sort of melancholy, in which state he has remained up to now. The attendant tells me that his screams whilst in the paroxysm were really appalling. I found my hands full when I got in, attending to some of the other patients who were frightened by him. Indeed, I can quite understand the effect, for the sounds disturbed even me, though I was some distance away. It is now after the dinner hour of the asylum, and as yet my patient sits in a corner brooding, with a dull, sullen, woe-begone look in his face, which seems rather to indicate than to show something directly. I cannot quite understand it.

Later.

Another change in my patient. At five o'clock I looked in on him, and found him seemingly as happy and contented as he used to be. He was catching flies and eating them, and was keeping note of his capture by making nailmarks on the edge of the door between the ridges of padding. When he saw me, he came over and apologized for his bad conduct, and asked me in a very humble, cringing way to be led back to his own room, and to have his notebook again. I thought it well to humour him, so he is back in his room with the window open. He has the sugar of his tea spread out on the window sill, and is reaping quite a harvest of flies. He is not now eating them, but putting them into a box, as of old, and is already examining the corners of his room to find a spider. I tried to get him to talk about the past few days, for any clue to his thoughts would be of immense help to me, but he would not rise. For a moment or two he looked very sad, and said in a sort of far away voice, as though saying it rather to himself than to me.

"All over! All over! He has deserted me. No hope for me now unless I do it myself!" Then suddenly turning to me in a resolute way, he said,

"Doctor, won't you be very good to me and let me have a little more sugar? I think it would be very good for me."

"And the flies?" I said.

"Yes! The flies like it, too, and I like the flies, therefore I like it." And there are people who know so little as to think that madmen do not argue. I procured him a double supply, and left him as happy a man as, I suppose, any in the world. I wish I could fathom his mind.

Midnight.

Another change in him. I had been to see Miss Westenra, whom I found much better, and had just returned, and was standing at our own gate looking at the sunset, when once more I heard him yelling. As his room is on this side of the house, I could hear it better than in the morning. It was a shock to me to turn from the wonderful smoky beauty of a sunset over London, with its lurid lights and inky shadows and all the marvellous tints that come on foul clouds even as on foul water, and to realize all the grim sternness of my own cold stone building, with its wealth of breathing misery, and my own desolate heart to endure it all. I reached him just as the sun was going down, and from his window saw the red disc sink. As it sank he became less and less frenzied, and just as it dipped he slid from the hands that held him, an inert mass, on the floor. It is wonderful, however, what intellectual recuperative power lunatics have, for within a few minutes he stood up quite calmly and looked around him. I signalled to the attendants not to hold him, for I was anxious to see what he would do. He went straight over to the window and brushed out the crumbs of sugar. Then he took his fly box, and emptied it outside, and threw away the box. Then he shut the window, and crossing over, sat down on his bed. All this surprised me, so I asked him, "Are you going to keep flies any more?"

"No," said he. "I am sick of all that rubbish!" He certainly is a wonderfully interesting study. I wish I could get some glimpse of his mind or of the cause of his sudden passion. Stop. There may be a clue after all, if we can find why today his paroxysms came on at high noon and at sunset. Can it be that there is a malign influence of the sun at periods which affects certain natures, as at times the moon does others? We shall see.

TELEGRAM, SEWARD, LONDON, TO VAN HELSING, AMSTERDAM

4 September.

Patient still better today.

TELEGRAM, SEWARD, LONDON, TO VAN HELSING, AMSTERDAM

5 September.

Patient greatly improved. Good appetite, sleeps naturally, good spirits, colour coming back.

TELEGRAM, SEWARD, LONDON, TO VAN HELSING, AMSTERDAM

6 September.

Terrible change for the worse. Come at once. Do not lose an hour. I hold over telegram to Holmwood till have seen you.

CHAPTER X

Letter, Dr. Seward to Hon. Arthur Holmwood

6 September.

My dear Art,

My news today is not so good. Lucy this morning had gone back a bit. There is, however, one good thing which has arisen from it. Mrs. Westenra was naturally anxious concerning Lucy, and has consulted me professionally about her. I took advantage of the opportunity, and told her that my old master, Van Helsing, the great specialist, was coming to stay with me, and that I would put her in his charge conjointly with myself. So now we can come and go without alarming her unduly, for a shock to her would mean sudden death, and this, in Lucy's weak condition, might be disastrous to her. We are hedged in with difficulties, all of us, my poor fellow, but, please God, we shall come through them all right. If any need I shall write, so that, if you do not hear from me, take it for granted that I am simply waiting for news, In haste,

Yours ever,

John Seward.

Dr. Seward's Diary

7 September.

The first thing Van Helsing said to me when we met at Liverpool Street was, "Have you said anything to our young friend, the lover of her?"

"No," I said. "I waited till I had seen you, as I said in my telegram. I wrote him a letter simply telling him that you were coming, as Miss Westenra was not so well, and that I should let him know if need be."

"Right, my friend," he said. "Quite right! Better he not know as yet. Perhaps he will never know. I pray so, but if it be needed, then he shall know all. And, my good friend John, let me caution you. You deal with the madmen. All men are mad in some way or the other, and inasmuch as you deal discreetly with your madmen, so deal with God's madmen too, the rest of the world. You tell not your madmen what you do nor why you do it. You tell them not what you think. So you shall keep knowledge in its place, where it may rest, where it may gather its kind around it and breed. You and I shall keep as yet what we know here, and here." He touched me on the heart and on the forehead, and then touched himself the same way. "I have for myself thoughts at the present. Later I shall unfold to you."

"Why not now?" I asked. "It may do some good. We may arrive at some decision."

He looked at me and said, "My friend John, when the corn is grown, even before it has ripened, while the milk of its mother earth is in him, and the sunshine has not yet begun to paint him with his gold, the husbandman he pull the ear and rub him between his rough hands, and blow away the green chaff, and say to you, 'Look! He's good corn, he will make a good crop when the time comes.'" I did not see the application and told him so. For reply he reached over and took my ear in his hand and pulled it playfully, as he used long ago to do at lectures, and said, "The good husbandman tell you so then because he knows, but not till then. But you do not find the good husbandman dig up his planted corn to see if he grow. That is for the children who play at husbandry, and not for those who take it as of the work of their life. See you now, friend John? I have sown my corn, and Nature has her work to do in making it sprout, if he sprout at all, there's some promise; and I wait till the ear begins to swell." He broke off, for he evidently saw that I understood.

Then he went on gravely, "You were always a careful student, and your case book was ever more full than the rest. And I trust that good habit have not fail. Remember, my friend, that knowledge is stronger than memory, and we should not trust the weaker. Even if you have not kept the good practice, let me tell you that this case of our dear miss is one that may be, mind, I say *may be*, of such interest to us and others that all the rest may not make him kick the beam, as your people say. Take then good note of it. Nothing is too small. I counsel you, put down in record even your doubts and surmises. Hereafter it may be of interest to you to see how true you guess. We learn from failure, not from success!"

When I described Lucy's symptoms—the same as before, but infinitely more marked—he looked very grave, but said nothing. He took with him a bag in which were many instruments and drugs, "the ghastly paraphernalia of our beneficial trade," as he once called, in one of his lectures, the equipment of a professor of the healing craft.

When we were shown in, Mrs. Westenra met us. She was alarmed, but not nearly so much as I expected to find her. Nature in one of her beneficient moods has ordained that even death has some antidote to its own terrors. Here, in a case where any shock may prove fatal, matters are so ordered that, from some cause or other, the things not personal, even the terrible change in her daughter to whom she is so attached, do not seem to reach her. It is something like the way dame Nature gathers round a foreign body an envelope of some insensitive tissue which can protect from evil that which it would otherwise harm by contact. If this be an ordered selfishness, then we should pause before we condemn anyone for the vice of egoism, for there may be deeper root for its causes than we have knowledge of.

I used my knowledge of this phase of spiritual pathology, and set down a rule that she should not be present with Lucy, or think of her illness more than was absolutely required. She assented readily, so readily that I saw again the hand of Nature fighting for life. Van Helsing and I were shown up to Lucy's room. If I was shocked when I saw her yesterday, I was horrified when I saw her today.

She was ghastly, chalkily pale. The red seemed to have gone even from her lips and gums, and the bones of her face stood out prominently. Her breathing was painful to see or hear. Van Helsing's face grew set as marble, and his eyebrows converged till they almost touched over his nose. Lucy lay motionless, and did not seem to have strength to speak, so for a while we were all silent. Then Van Helsing beckoned to me, and we went gently out of the room. The instant we had closed the door he stepped quickly along the passage to the next door, which was open. Then he pulled me quickly in with him and closed the door. "My God!" he said. "This is dreadful. There is not time to be lost. She will die for sheer want of blood to keep the heart's action as it should be. There must be a transfusion of blood at once. Is it you or me?"

"I am younger and stronger, Professor. It must be me."

"Then get ready at once. I will bring up my bag. I am prepared."

I went downstairs with him, and as we were going there was a knock at the hall door. When we reached the hall, the maid had just opened the door, and Arthur was stepping quickly in.

He rushed up to me, saying in an eager whisper, "Jack, I was so anxious. I read between the lines of your letter, and have been in an agony. The dad was better, so I ran down here to see for myself. Is not that gentleman Dr. Van Helsing? I am so thankful to you, sir, for coming." When first the Professor's eye had lit upon him, he had been angry at his interruption at such a time, but now, as he took in his stalwart proportions and recognized the strong young manhood which seemed to emanate from him, his eyes gleamed.

Without a pause he said to him as he held out his hand, "Sir, you have come in time. You are the lover of our dear miss. She is bad, very, very bad. Nay, my child, do not go like that." For he suddenly grew pale and sat down in a chair almost fainting. "You are to help her. You can do more than any that live, and your courage is your best help."

"What can I do?" asked Arthur hoarsely. "Tell me, and I shall do it. My life is hers, and I would give the last drop of blood in my body for her."

The Professor has a strongly humorous side, and I could from old knowledge detect a trace of its origin in his answer.

"My young sir, I do not ask so much as that, not the last!"

"What shall I do?" There was fire in his eyes, and his open nostrils quivered with intent. Van Helsing slapped him on the shoulder.

"Come!" he said. "You are a man, and it is a man we want. You are better than me, better than my friend John." Arthur looked bewildered, and the Professor went on by explaining in a kindly way.

"Young miss is bad, very bad. She wants blood, and blood she must have or die. My friend John and I have consulted, and we are about to perform what we call transfusion of blood, to transfer from full veins of one to the empty veins which pine for him. John was to give his blood, as he is the more young and strong than me." Here Arthur took my hand and wrung it hard in silence. "But now you are here, you are more good than us, old or young, who toil much in the world of thought. Our nerves are not so calm and our blood so bright than yours!"

Arthur turned to him and said, "If you only knew how gladly I would die for her you would understand . . ." He stopped with a sort of choke in his voice.

"Good boy!" said Van Helsing. "In the not-so-far-off you will be happy that you have done all for her you love. Come now and be silent. You shall kiss her once before it is done, but then you must go, and you must leave at my sign. Say no word to Madame. You know how it is with her. There must be no shock, any knowledge of this would be one. Come!"

We all went up to Lucy's room. Arthur by direction remained outside. Lucy turned her head and looked at us, but said nothing. She was not asleep, but she was simply too weak to make the effort. Her eyes spoke to us, that was all.

Van Helsing took some things from his bag and laid them on a little table out of sight. Then he mixed a narcotic, and coming over to the bed, said cheerily, "Now, little miss, here is your medicine. Drink it off, like a good child. See, I lift you so that to swallow is easy. Yes." She had made the effort with success.

It astonished me how long the drug took to act. This, in fact, marked the extent of her weakness. The time seemed endless until sleep began to flicker in her eyelids. At last, however, the narcotic began to manifest its potency, and she fell into a deep sleep. When the Professor was satisfied, he called Arthur into the room, and bade him strip off his coat. Then he added, "You may take that one little kiss whiles I bring over the table. Friend John, help to me!" So neither of us looked whilst he bent over her.

Van Helsing, turning to me, said, "He is so young and strong, and of blood so pure that we need not defibrinate it."

Then with swiftness, but with absolute method, Van Helsing performed the operation. As the transfusion went on, something like life seemed to come back to poor Lucy's cheeks, and through Arthur's growing pallor the joy of his face seemed absolutely to shine. After a bit I began to grow anxious, for the loss of blood was telling on Arthur, strong man as he was. It gave me an idea of what a terrible strain Lucy's system must have undergone that what weakened Arthur only partially restored her.

But the Professor's face was set, and he stood watch in hand, and with his eyes fixed now on the patient and now on Arthur. I could hear my own heart beat. Presently, he said in a soft voice, "Do not stir an instant. It is enough. You attend him. I will look to her."

When all was over, I could see how much Arthur was weakened. I dressed the wound and took his arm to bring him away, when Van Helsing spoke without turning round, the man seems to have eyes in the back of his head, "The brave lover, I think, deserve another kiss, which he shall have presently." And as he had now finished his operation, he adjusted the pillow to the patient's head. As he did so the narrow black velvet band which she seems always to wear round her throat, buckled with an old diamond buckle which her lover had given her, was dragged a little up, and showed a red mark on her throat.

Arthur did not notice it, but I could hear the deep hiss of indrawn breath which is one of Van Helsing's ways of betraying emotion. He said nothing at the moment, but turned to me, saying, "Now take down our brave young lover, give him of the port wine, and let him lie down a while. He must then go home and rest, sleep much and eat much, that he may be recruited of what he has so given to his love. He must not stay here. Hold a moment! I may take it, sir, that you are anxious of result. Then bring it with you, that in all ways the operation is successful. You have saved her life this time, and you can go home and rest easy in mind that all that can be is. I shall tell her all when she is well. She shall love you none the less for what you have done. Goodbye."

When Arthur had gone I went back to the room. Lucy was sleeping gently, but her breathing was stronger. I could see the counterpane move as her breast heaved. By the bedside sat Van Helsing, looking at her intently. The velvet band again covered the red mark. I asked the Professor in a whisper, "What do you make of that mark on her throat?"

"What do you make of it?"

"I have not examined it yet," I answered, and then and there proceeded to loose the band. Just over the external jugular vein there were two punctures, not large, but not wholesome looking. There was no sign of disease, but the edges were white and worn looking, as if by some trituration. It at once occurred to me that that this wound, or whatever it was, might be the means of that manifest loss of blood. But I abandoned the idea as soon as it formed, for such a thing could not be. The whole bed would have been drenched to a scarlet with the blood which the girl must have lost to leave such a pallor as she had before the transfusion.

"Well?" said Van Helsing.

"Well," said I. "I can make nothing of it."

The Professor stood up. "I must go back to Amsterdam tonight," he said. "There are books and things there which I want. You must remain here all night, and you must not let your sight pass from her."

"Shall I have a nurse?" I asked.

"We are the best nurses, you and I. You keep watch all night. See that she is well fed, and that nothing disturbs her. You must not sleep all the night. Later on we can sleep, you and I. I shall be back as soon as possible. And then we may begin."

"May begin?" I said. "What on earth do you mean?"

"We shall see!" he answered, as he hurried out. He came back a moment later and put his head inside the door and said with a warning finger held up, "Remember, she is your charge. If you leave her, and harm befall, you shall not sleep easy hereafter!"

Dr. Seward's Diary, Continued

8 September.

I sat up all night with Lucy. The opiate worked itself off towards dusk, and she waked naturally. She looked a different being from what she had been before the operation. Her spirits even were good, and she was full of a happy vivacity, but I could see evidences of the absolute prostration which she had undergone. When I told Mrs. Westenra that Dr. Van Helsing had directed that I should sit up with her, she almost pooh-poohed the idea, pointing out her daughter's renewed strength and excellent spirits. I was firm, however, and made preparations for my long vigil. When her maid had prepared her for the night I came in, having in the meantime had supper, and took a seat by the bedside.

She did not in any way make objection, but looked at me gratefully whenever I caught her eye. After a long spell she seemed sinking off to sleep, but with an effort seemed to pull herself together and shook it off. It was apparent that she did not want to sleep, so I tackled the subject at once.

"You do not want to sleep?"

"No. I am afraid."

"Afraid to go to sleep! Why so? It is the boon we all crave for."

"Ah, not if you were like me, if sleep was to you a presage of horror!"

"A presage of horror! What on earth do you mean?"

"I don't know. Oh, I don't know. And that is what is so terrible. All this weakness comes to me in sleep, until I dread the very thought."

"But, my dear girl, you may sleep tonight. I am here watching you, and I can promise that nothing will happen."

"Ah, I can trust you!" she said.

I seized the opportunity, and said, "I promise that if I see any evidence of bad dreams I will wake you at once."

"You will? Oh, will you really? How good you are to me. Then I will sleep!" And almost at the word she gave a deep sigh of relief, and sank back, asleep.

All night long I watched by her. She never stirred, but slept on and on in a deep, tranquil, life-giving, health-giving sleep. Her lips were slightly parted, and her breast rose and fell with the regularity of a pendulum. There was a smile on her face, and it was evident that no bad dreams had come to disturb her peace of mind.

In the early morning her maid came, and I left her in her care and took myself back home, for I was anxious about many things. I sent a short wire to Van Helsing and to Arthur, telling them of the excellent result of the operation. My own work, with its manifold arrears, took me all day to clear off. It was dark when I was able to inquire about my zoophagous patient. The report was good. He had been quite quiet for the past day and night. A telegram came from Van Helsing at Amsterdam whilst I was at dinner, suggesting that I should be at Hillingham tonight, as it might be well to be at hand, and stating that he was leaving by the night mail and would join me early in the morning.

9 September.

I was pretty tired and worn out when I got to Hillingham. For two nights I had hardly had a wink of sleep, and my brain was beginning to feel that numbness which marks cerebral exhaustion. Lucy was up and in cheerful spirits.

When she shook hands with me she looked sharply in my face and said, "No sitting up tonight for you. You are worn out. I am quite well again. Indeed, I am, and if there is to be any sitting up, it is I who will sit up with you."

I would not argue the point, but went and had my supper. Lucy came with me, and, enlivened by her charming presence, I made an excellent meal, and had a couple of glasses of the more than excellent port. Then Lucy took me upstairs, and showed me a room next her own, where a cozy fire was burning. "Now," she said. "You must stay here. I shall leave this door open and my door too. You can lie on the sofa for I know that nothing would induce any of you doctors to go to bed whilst there is a patient above the horizon. If I want anything I shall call out, and you can come to me at once." I could not but acquiesce, for I was dog tired, and could not have sat up had I tried. So, on her renewing her promise to call me if she should want anything, I lay on the sofa, and forgot all about everything.

Lucy Westenra's Diary

9 September.

I feel so happy tonight. I have been so miserably weak, that to be able to think and move about is like feeling sunshine after a long spell of east wind out of a steel sky. Somehow Arthur feels very, very close to me. I seem to feel his presence warm about me. I suppose it is that sickness and weakness are selfish things and turn our inner eyes and sympathy on ourselves, whilst health and strength give love rein, and in thought and feeling he can wander where he wills. I know where my thoughts are. If only Arthur knew! My dear, my dear, your ears must tingle as you sleep, as mine do waking. Oh, the blissful rest of last night! How I slept, with that dear, good Dr. Seward watching me. And tonight I shall not fear to sleep, since he is close at hand and within call. Thank everybody for being so good to me. Thank God! Good night, Arthur.

Dr. Seward's Diary

10 September.

I was conscious of the Professor's hand on my head, and started awake all in a second. That is one of the things that we learn in an asylum, at any rate.

"And how is our patient?"

"Well, when I left her, or rather when she left me," I answered.

"Come, let us see," he said. And together we went into the room.

The blind was down, and I went over to raise it gently, whilst Van Helsing stepped, with his soft, cat-like tread, over to the bed.

As I raised the blind, and the morning sunlight flooded the room, I heard the Professor's low hiss of inspiration, and knowing its rarity, a deadly fear shot through my heart. As I passed over he moved back, and his exclamation of horror, "Gott in Himmel!" needed no enforcement from his agonized face. He raised his hand and pointed to the bed, and his iron face was drawn and ashen white. I felt my knees begin to tremble.

There on the bed, seemingly in a swoon, lay poor Lucy, more horribly white and wan-looking than ever. Even the lips were white, and the gums seemed to have shrunken back from the teeth, as we sometimes see in a corpse after a prolonged illness. Van Helsing raised his foot to stamp in anger, but the instinct of his life and all the long years of habit stood to him, and he put it down again softly. "Quick!" he said. "Bring the brandy." I flew to the dining room, and returned with the decanter. He wetted the poor white lips with it, and together we rubbed palm and wrist and heart.

He felt her heart, and after a few moments of agonizing suspense said, "It is not too late. It beats, though but feebly. All our work is undone. We must begin again. There is no young Arthur here now. I have to call on you yourself this time, friend John." As he spoke, he was dipping into his bag, and producing the instruments of transfusion. I had taken off my coat and rolled up my shirt sleeve. There was no possibility of an opiate just at present, and no need of one; and so, without a moment's delay, we began the operation. After a time—it did not seem a short time either, for the draining away of one's blood, no matter how willingly it be given, is a terrible feeling—Van Helsing held up a warning finger. "Do not stir," he said. "But I fear that with growing strength she may wake, and that would make danger, oh, so much danger. But I shall precaution take. I shall give hypodermic injection of morphia." He proceeded then, swiftly and deftly, to carry out his intent. The effect on Lucy was not bad, for the faint seemed to merge subtly into the narcotic sleep. It was with a feeling of personal pride that I could see a faint tinge of colour steal back into the pallid cheeks and lips. No man knows, till he experiences it, what it is to feel his own lifeblood drawn away into the veins of the woman he loves.

The Professor watched me critically. "That will do," he said. "Already?" I remonstrated. "You took a great deal more from Art."

To which he smiled a sad sort of smile as he replied, "He is her lover, her *fiancé*. You have work, much work to do for her and for others, and the present will suffice."

When we stopped the operation, he attended to Lucy, whilst I applied digital pressure to my own incision. I laid down, while I waited his leisure to attend to me, for I felt faint and a little sick. By and by he bound up my wound, and sent me downstairs to get a glass of wine for myself.

As I was leaving the room, he came after me, and half whispered,

"Mind, nothing must be said of this. If our young lover should turn up unexpected, as before, no word to him. It would at once frighten him and enjealous him, too. There must be none. So!"

When I came back he looked at me carefully, and then said, "You are not much the worse. Go into the room, and lie on your sofa, and rest awhile, then have much breakfast and come here to me."

I followed out his orders, for I knew how right and wise they were. I had done my part, and now my next duty was to keep up my strength. I felt very weak, and in the weakness lost something of the amazement at what had occurred. I fell asleep on the sofa, however, wondering over and over again how Lucy had made such a retrograde movement, and how she could have been drained of so much blood with no sign any where to show for it. I think I must have continued my wonder in my dreams, for, sleeping and waking my thoughts always came back to the little punctures in her throat and the ragged, exhausted appearance of their edges, tiny though they were.

Lucy slept well into the day, and when she woke she was fairly well and strong, though not nearly so much so as the day before. When Van Helsing had seen her, he went out for a walk, leaving me in charge, with strict injunctions that I was not to leave her for a moment. I could hear his voice in the hall, asking the way to the nearest telegraph office.

Lucy chatted with me freely, and seemed quite unconscious that anything had happened. I tried to keep her amused and interested.

When her mother came up to see her, she did not seem to notice any change whatever, but said to me gratefully, "We owe you so much, Dr. Seward, for all you have done, but you really must now take care not to overwork yourself. You are looking pale yourself. You want a wife to nurse and look after you a bit, that you do!" As she spoke, Lucy turned crimson, though it was only momentarily, for her poor wasted veins could not stand for long an unwonted drain to the head. The reaction came in excessive pallor as she turned imploring eyes on me. I smiled and nodded, and laid my finger on my lips. With a sigh, she sank back amid her pillows.

Van Helsing returned in a couple of hours, and presently said to me: "Now you go home, and eat much and drink enough. Make yourself strong. I stay here tonight, and I shall sit up with little miss myself. You and I must watch the case, and we must have none other to know. I have grave reasons. No, do not ask me. Think what you will. Do not fear to think even the most not-improbable. Good night."

In the hall two of the maids came to me, and asked if they or either of them might not sit up with Miss Lucy. They implored me to let them, and when I said it was Dr. Van Helsing's wish that either he or I should sit up, they asked me quite piteously to intercede with the "foreign gentleman." I was much touched by their kindness. Perhaps it is because I am weak at present, and perhaps because it was on Lucy's account, that their devotion was manifested. For over and over again have I seen similar instances of woman's kindness. I got back here in time for a late dinner, went my rounds—all well; and set this down whilst waiting for sleep. It is coming.

11 September.

This afternoon I went over to Hillingham. Found Van Helsing in excellent spirits, and Lucy much better. Shortly after I had arrived, a big parcel from abroad came for the Professor. He opened it with much impressment, assumed, of course, and showed a great bundle of white flowers.

"These are for you, Miss Lucy," he said.

"For me? Oh, Dr. Van Helsing!"

"Yes, my dear, but not for you to play with. These are medicines." Here Lucy made a wry face. "Nay, but they are not to take in a decoction or in nauseous form, so you need not snub that so charming nose, or I shall point out to my friend Arthur what woes he may have to endure in seeing so much beauty that he so loves so much distort. Aha, my pretty miss, that bring the so nice nose all straight again. This is medicinal, but you do not know how. I put him in your window, I make pretty wreath, and hang him round your neck, so you sleep well. Oh, yes! They, like the lotus flower, make your trouble forgotten. It smell so like the waters of Lethe, and of that fountain of youth that the Conquistadores sought for in the Floridas, and find him all too late."

Whilst he was speaking, Lucy had been examining the flowers and smelling them. Now she threw them down saying, with half laughter, and half disgust, "Oh, Professor, I believe you are only putting up a joke on me. Why, these flowers are only common garlic."

To my surprise, Van Helsing rose up and said with all his sternness, his iron jaw set and his bushy eyebrows meeting, "No trifling with me! I never jest! There is grim purpose in what I do, and I warn you that you do not thwart me. Take care, for the sake of others if not for your own." Then seeing poor Lucy scared, as she might well be, he went on more gently, "Oh, little miss, my dear, do not fear me. I only do for your good, but there is much virtue to you in those so common flowers. See, I place them myself in your room. I make myself the wreath that you are to wear. But hush! No telling to others that make so inquisitive questions. We must obey, and silence is a part of obedience, and obedience is to bring you strong and well into loving arms that wait for you. Now sit still a while. Come with me, friend John, and you shall help me deck the room with my garlic, which is all the way from Haarlem, where my friend Vanderpool raise herb in his glass houses all the year. I had to telegraph yesterday, or they would not have been here."

We went into the room, taking the flowers with us. The Professor's actions were certainly odd and not to be found in any pharmacopeia that I ever heard of. First he fastened up the windows and latched them securely. Next, taking a handful of the flowers, he rubbed them all over the sashes, as though to ensure that every whiff of air that might get in would be laden with the garlic smell. Then with the wisp he rubbed all over the jamb of the door, above, below, and at each side, and round the fireplace in the same way. It all seemed grotesque to me, and presently I said, "Well, Professor, I know you always have a reason for what you do, but this certainly puzzles me. It is well we have no sceptic here, or he would say that you were working some spell to keep out an evil spirit."

"Perhaps I am!" he answered quietly as he began to make the wreath which Lucy was to wear round her neck.

We then waited whilst Lucy made her toilet for the night, and when she was in bed he came and himself fixed the wreath of garlic round her neck.

The last words he said to her were, "Take care you do not disturb it, and even if the room feel close, do not tonight open the window or the door."

"I promise," said Lucy. "And thank you both a thousand times for all your kindness to me! Oh, what have I done to be blessed with such friends?"

As we left the house in my fly, which was waiting, Van Helsing said, "Tonight I can sleep in peace, and sleep I want—two nights of travel, much reading in the day between, and much anxiety on the day to follow, and a night to sit up, without to wink. Tomorrow in the morning early you call for me, and we come together to see our pretty miss, so much more strong for my 'spell' which I have work. Ho, ho!"

He seemed so confident that I, remembering my own confidence two nights before and with the baneful result, felt awe and vague terror. It must have been my weakness that made me hesitate to tell it to my friend, but I felt it all the more, like unshed tears.

CHAPTER XI

Lucy Westenra's Diary

12 September.

How good they all are to me. I quite love that dear Dr. Van Helsing. I wonder why he was so anxious about these flowers. He positively frightened me, he was so fierce. And yet he must have been right, for I feel comfort from them already. Somehow, I do not dread being alone tonight, and I can go to sleep without fear. I shall not mind any flapping outside the window. Oh, the terrible struggle that I have had against sleep so often of late, the pain of sleeplessness, or the pain of the fear of sleep, and with such unknown horrors as it has for me! How blessed are some people, whose lives have no fears, no dreads, to whom sleep is a blessing that comes nightly, and brings nothing but sweet dreams. Well, here I am tonight, hoping for sleep, and lying like Ophelia in the play, with "virgin crants and maiden strewments." I never liked garlic before, but tonight it is delightful! There is peace in its smell. I feel sleep coming already. Good night, everybody.

Dr. Seward's Diary

13 September.

Called at the Berkeley and found Van Helsing, as usual, up to time. The carriage ordered from the hotel was waiting. The Professor took his bag, which he always brings with him now.

Let all be put down exactly. Van Helsing and I arrived at Hillingham at eight o'clock. It was a lovely morning. The bright sunshine and all the fresh feeling of early autumn seemed like the completion of nature's annual work. The leaves were turning to all kinds of beautiful colours, but had not yet begun to drop from the trees. When we entered we met Mrs. Westenra coming out of the morning room. She is always an early riser. She greeted us warmly and said, "You will be glad to know that Lucy is better. The dear child is still asleep. I looked into her room and saw her, but did not go in, lest I should disturb her."

The Professor smiled, and looked quite jubilant. He rubbed his hands together, and said, "Aha! I thought I had diagnosed the case. My treatment is working."

To which she replied, "You must not take all the credit to yourself, doctor. Lucy's state this morning is due in part to me."

"How do you mean, ma'am?" asked the Professor.

"Well, I was anxious about the dear child in the night, and went into her room. She was sleeping soundly, so soundly that even my coming did not wake her. But the room was awfully stuffy. There were a lot of those horrible, strong-smelling flowers about everywhere, and she had actually a bunch of them round her neck. I feared that the heavy odour would be too much for the dear child in her weak state, so I took them all away and opened a bit of the window to let in a little fresh air. You will be pleased with her, I am sure."

She moved off into her boudoir, where she usually breakfasted early. As she had spoken, I watched the Professor's face, and saw it turn ashen gray. He had been able to retain his self-command whilst the poor lady was present, for he knew her state and how mischievous a shock would be. He actually smiled on her as he held open the door for her to pass into her room. But the instant she had disappeared he pulled me, suddenly and forcibly, into the dining room and closed the door.

Then, for the first time in my life, I saw Van Helsing break down. He raised his hands over his head in a sort of mute despair, and then beat his palms together in a helpless way. Finally he sat down on a chair, and putting his hands before his face, began to sob, with loud, dry sobs that seemed to come from the very racking of his heart. Then he raised his arms again, as though appealing to the whole universe. "God! God! God!" he said. "What have we done, what has this poor thing done, that we are so sore beset? Is there fate amongst us still, send down from the pagan world of old, that such things must be, and in such way? This poor mother, all unknowing, and all for the best as she think, does such thing as lose her daughter body and soul, and we must not tell her, we must not even warn her, or she die, then both die. Oh, how we are beset! How are all the powers of the devils against us!" Suddenly he jumped to his feet. "Come," he said, "come, we must see and act. Devils or no devils, or all the devils at once, it matters not. We must fight him all the same." He went to the hall door for his bag, and together we went up to Lucy's room.

Once again I drew up the blind, whilst Van Helsing went towards the bed. This time he did not start as he looked on the poor face with the same awful, waxen pallor as before. He wore a look of stern sadness and infinite pity.

"As I expected," he murmured, with that hissing inspiration of his which meant so much. Without a word he went and locked the door, and then began to set out on the little table the instruments for yet another operation of transfusion of blood. I had long ago recognized the necessity, and begun to take off my coat, but he stopped me with a warning hand. "No!" he said. "Today you must operate. I shall provide. You are weakened already." As he spoke he took off his coat and rolled up his shirtsleeve.

Again the operation. Again the narcotic. Again some return of colour to the ashy cheeks, and the regular breathing of healthy sleep. This time I watched whilst Van Helsing recruited himself and rested.

Presently he took an opportunity of telling Mrs. Westenra that she must not remove anything from Lucy's room without consulting him. That the flowers were of medicinal value, and that the breathing of their odour was a part of the system of cure. Then he took over the care of the case himself, saying that he would watch this night and the next, and would send me word when to come.

After another hour Lucy waked from her sleep, fresh and bright and seemingly not much the worse for her terrible ordeal.

What does it all mean? I am beginning to wonder if my long habit of life amongst the insane is beginning to tell upon my own brain.

Lucy Westenra's Diary

17 September.

Four days and nights of peace. I am getting so strong again that I hardly know myself. It is as if I had passed through some long nightmare, and had just awakened to see the beautiful sunshine and feel the fresh air of the morning around me. I have a dim half remembrance of long, anxious times of waiting and fearing, darkness in which there was not even the pain of hope to make present distress more poignant. And then long spells of oblivion, and the rising back to life as a diver coming up through a great press of water. Since, however, Dr. Van Helsing has been with me, all this bad dreaming seems to have passed away. The noises that used to frighten me out of my wits—the flapping against the windows, the distant voices which seemed so close to me, the harsh sounds that came from I know not where and commanded me to do I know not what—have all ceased. I go to bed now without any fear of sleep. I do not even try to keep awake. I have grown quite fond of the garlic, and a boxful arrives for me every day from Haarlem. Tonight Dr. Van Helsing is going away, as he has to be for a day in Amsterdam. But I need not be watched. I am well enough to be left alone. Thank God for Mother's sake, and dear Arthur's, and for all our friends who have been so kind! I shall not even feel the change, for last night Dr. Van Helsing slept in his chair a lot of the time. I found him asleep twice when I awoke. But I did not fear to go to sleep again, although the boughs or bats or something flapped almost angrily against the window panes.

THE *PALL MALL GAZETTE* , 18 SEPTEMBER

THE ESCAPED WOLF

PERILOUS ADVENTURE OF OUR INTERVIEWER

INTERVIEW WITH THE KEEPER IN THE ZOOLOGICAL GARDENS

After many inquiries and almost as many refusals, and perpetually using the words "*Pall Mall Gazette*" as a sort of talisman, I managed to find the keeper of the section of the Zoological Gardens in which the wolf department is included. Thomas Bilder lives in one of the cottages in the enclosure behind the elephant house, and was just sitting down to his tea when I found him. Thomas and his wife are hospitable folk, elderly, and without children, and if the specimen I enjoyed of their hospitality be of the average kind, their lives must be pretty comfortable. The keeper would not enter on what he called business until the supper was over, and we were all satisfied.

Then when the table was cleared, and he had lit his pipe, he said, "Now, Sir, you can go on and arsk me what you want. You'll excoose me refoosin' to talk of perfeshunal subjucts afore meals. I gives the wolves and the jackals and the hyenas in all our section their tea afore I begins to arsk them questions."

"How do you mean, ask them questions?" I queried, wishful to get him into a talkative humor.

"'Ittin' of them over the 'ead with a pole is one way. Scratchin' of their ears in another, when gents as is flush wants a bit of a show-orf to their gals. I don't so much mind the fust, the 'ittin of the pole part afore I chucks in their dinner, but I waits till they've 'ad their sherry and kawffee, so to speak, afore I tries on with the ear scratchin'. Mind you," he added philosophically, "there's a deal of the same nature in us as in them theer animiles. Here's you a-comin' and arskin' of me questions about my business, and I that grump-like that only for your bloomin' 'arf-quid I'd 'a' seen you blowed fust 'fore I'd answer. Not even when you arsked me sarcastic like if I'd like you to arsk the Superintendent if you might arsk me questions. Without offence did I tell yer to go to 'ell?"

"You did."

"An' when you said you'd report me for usin' obscene language that was 'ittin' me over the 'ead. But the 'arf-quid made that all right. I weren't a-goin' to fight, so I waited for the food, and did with my 'owl as the wolves and lions and tigers does. But, lor' love yer 'art, now that the old 'ooman has stuck a chunk of her tea-cake in me, an' rinsed me out with her bloomin' old teapot, and I've lit hup, you may scratch my ears for all you're worth, and won't even get a growl out of me. Drive along with your questions. I know what yer a-comin' at, that 'ere escaped wolf."

"Exactly. I want you to give me your view of it. Just tell me how it happened, and when I know the facts I'll get you to say what you consider was the cause of it, and how you think the whole affair will end."

"All right, guv'nor. This 'ere is about the 'ole story. That 'ere wolf what we called Bersicker was one of three gray ones that came from Norway to Jamrach's, which we bought off him four years ago. He was a nice well-behaved wolf, that never gave no trouble to talk of. I'm more surprised at 'im for wantin' to get out nor any other animile in the place. But, there, you can't trust wolves no more nor women."

"Don't you mind him, Sir!" broke in Mrs. Tom, with a cheery laugh. "'E's got mindin' the animiles so long that blest if he ain't like a old wolf 'isself! But there ain't no 'arm in 'im."

"Well, Sir, it was about two hours after feedin' yesterday when I first hear my disturbance. I was makin' up a litter in the monkey house for a young puma which is ill. But when I heard the yelpin' and 'owlin' I kem away straight. There was Bersicker a-tearin' like a mad thing at the bars as if he wanted to get out. There wasn't much people about that day, and close at hand was only one man, a tall, thin chap, with a 'ook nose and a pointed beard, with a few white hairs runnin' through it. He had a 'ard, cold look and red eyes, and I took a sort of mislike to him, for it seemed as if it was 'im as they was hirritated at. He 'ad white kid gloves on 'is 'ands, and he pointed out the animiles to me and says, 'Keeper, these wolves seem upset at something.'

"'Maybe it's you,' says I, for I did not like the airs as he give 'isself. He didn't get angry, as I 'oped he would, but he smiled a kind of insolent smile, with a mouth full of white, sharp teeth. 'Oh no, they wouldn't like me,' 'e says.

"'Ow yes, they would,' says I, a-imitatin' of him. 'They always like a bone or two to clean their teeth on about tea time, which you 'as a bagful.'

"Well, it was a odd thing, but when the animiles see us a-talkin' they lay down, and when I went over to Bersicker he let me stroke his ears same as ever. That there man kem over, and blessed but if he didn't put in his hand and stroke the old wolf's ears too!

"'Tyke care,' says I. 'Bersicker is quick.'

"'Never mind,' he says. I'm used to 'em!'

"'Are you in the business yourself?' I says, tyking off my 'at, for a man what trades in wolves, anceterer, is a good friend to keepers.

"'No,' says he, 'not exactly in the business, but I 'ave made pets of several.' And with that he lifts his 'at as perlite as a lord, and walks away. Old Bersicker kep' a-lookin' arter 'im till 'e was out of sight, and then went and lay down in a corner and wouldn't come hout the 'ole hevening. Well, larst night, so soon as the moon was hup, the wolves here all began a-'owling. There warn't nothing for them to 'owl at. There warn't no one near, except someone that was evidently a-callin' a dog somewheres out back of the gardings in the Park road. Once or twice I went out to see that all was right, and it was, and then the 'owling stopped. Just before twelve o'clock I just took a look round afore turnin' in, an,'bust me, but when I kem opposite to old Bersicker's cage I see the rails broken and twisted about and the cage empty. And that's all I know for certing."

"Did anyone else see anything?"

"One of our gard'ners was a-comin' 'ome about that time from a 'armony, when he sees a big gray dog comin' out through the garding 'edges. At least, so he says, but I don't give much for it myself, for if he did 'e never said a word about it to his missis when 'e got 'ome, and it was only after the escape of the wolf was made known, and we had been up all night a-huntin' of the Park for Bersicker, that he remembered seein' anything. My own belief was that the 'armony 'ad got into his 'ead."

"Now, Mr. Bilder, can you account in any way for the escape of the wolf?"

"Well, Sir," he said, with a suspicious sort of modesty, "I think I can, but I don't know as 'ow you'd be satisfied with the theory."

"Certainly I shall. If a man like you, who knows the animals from experience, can't hazard a good guess at any rate, who is even to try?"

"Well then, Sir, I accounts for it this way. It seems to me that 'ere wolf escaped—simply because he wanted to get out."

From the hearty way that both Thomas and his wife laughed at the joke I could see that it had done service before, and that the whole explanation was simply an elaborate sell. I couldn't cope in badinage with the worthy Thomas, but I thought I knew a surer way to his heart, so I said, "Now, Mr. Bilder, we'll consider that first half-sovereign worked off, and this brother of his is waiting to be claimed when you've told me what you think will happen."

"Right y'are, Sir," he said briskly. "Ye'll excoose me, I know, for a-chaffin' of ye, but the old woman here winked at me, which was as much as telling me to go on."

"Well, I never!" said the old lady.

"My opinion is this: that 'ere wolf is a-'idin' of, somewheres. The gard'ner wot didn't remember said he was a-gallopin' northward faster than a horse could go, but I don't believe him, for, yer see, Sir, wolves don't gallop no more nor dogs does, they not bein' built that way. Wolves is fine things in a storybook, and I dessay when they gets in packs and does be chivyin' somethin' that's more afeared than they is they can make a devil of a noise and chop it up, whatever it is. But, Lor' bless you, in real life a wolf is only a low creature, not half so clever or bold as a good dog, and not half a quarter so much fight in 'im. This one ain't been used to fightin' or even to providin' for hisself, and more like he's somewhere round the Park a'hidin' an' a'shiverin' of, and if he thinks at all, wonderin' where he is to get his breakfast from. Or maybe he's got down some area and is in a coal cellar. My eye, won't some cook get a rum start when she sees his green eyes a-shinin' at her out of the dark! If he can't get food he's bound to look for it, and mayhap he may chance to light on a butcher's shop in time. If he doesn't, and some nursemaid goes out walkin' or orf with a soldier, leavin' of the hinfant in the perambulator—well, then I shouldn't be surprised if the census is one babby the less. That's all."

I was handing him the half-sovereign, when something came bobbing up against the window, and Mr. Bilder's face doubled its natural length with surprise.

"God bless me!" he said. "If there ain't old Bersicker come back by 'isself!"

He went to the door and opened it, a most unnecessary proceeding it seemed to me. I have always thought that a wild animal never looks so well as when some obstacle of pronounced durability is between us. A personal experience has intensified rather than diminished that idea.

After all, however, there is nothing like custom, for neither Bilder nor his wife thought any more of the wolf than I should of a dog. The animal itself was a peaceful and well-behaved as that father of all picture-wolves—Red Riding Hood's quondam friend, whilst moving her confidence in masquerade.

The whole scene was an unutterable mixture of comedy and pathos. The wicked wolf that for a half a day had paralyzed London and set all the children in town shivering in their shoes, was there in a sort of penitent mood, and was received and petted like a sort of vulpine prodigal son.

Old Bilder examined him all over with most tender solicitude, and when he had finished with his penitent said, "There, I knew the poor old chap would get into some kind of trouble. Didn't I say it all along? Here's his head all cut and full of broken glass. 'E's been a-gettin' over some bloomin' wall or other. It's a shyme that people are allowed to top their walls with broken bottles. This 'ere's what comes of it. Come along, Bersicker."

He took the wolf and locked him up in a cage, with a piece of meat that satisfied, in quantity at any rate, the elementary conditions of the fatted calf, and went off to report.

I came off too, to report the only exclusive information that is given today regarding the strange escapade at the Zoo.

Dr. Seward's Diary

17 September.

I was engaged after dinner in my study posting up my books, which, through press of other work and the many visits to Lucy, had fallen sadly into arrear. Suddenly the door was burst open, and in rushed my patient, with his face distorted with passion. I was thunderstruck, for such a thing as a patient getting of his own accord into the Superintendent's study is almost unknown. Without an instant's notice he made straight at me. He had a dinner knife in his hand, and as I saw he was dangerous, I tried to keep the table between us. He was too quick and too strong for me, however, for before I could get my balance he had struck at me and cut my left wrist rather severely. Before he could strike again, however, I got in my right hand and he was sprawling on his back on the floor. My wrist bled freely, and quite a little pool trickled on to the carpet. I saw that my friend was not intent on further effort, and occupied myself binding up my wrist, keeping a wary eye on the prostrate figure all the time. When the attendants rushed in, and we turned our attention to him, his employment positively sickened me. He was lying on his belly on the floor licking up, like a dog, the blood which had fallen from my wounded wrist. He was easily secured, and to my surprise, went with the attendants quite placidly, simply repeating over and over again, "The blood is the life! The blood is the life!"

I cannot afford to lose blood just at present. I have lost too much of late for my physical good, and then the prolonged strain of Lucy's illness and its horrible phases is telling on me. I am over excited and weary, and I need rest, rest, rest. Happily Van Helsing has not summoned me, so I need not forego my sleep. Tonight I could not well do without it.

Telegram, Van Helsing, Antwerp, to Seward, Carfax (Sent to Carfax, Sussex, as no county given; delivered late by twenty-two hours.)

17 September.

Do not fail to be at Hilllingham tonight. If not watching all the time, frequently visit and see that flowers are as placed, very important, do not fail. Shall be with you as soon as possible after arrival.

Dr. Seward's Diary

18 September.

Just off train to London. The arrival of Van Helsing's telegram filled me with dismay. A whole night lost, and I know by bitter experience what may happen in a night. Of course it is possible that all may be well, but what may have happened? Surely there is some horrible doom hanging over us that every possible accident should thwart us in all we try to do. I shall take this cylinder with me, and then I can complete my entry on Lucy's phonograph.

Memorandum Left by Lucy Westenra

17 September. Night.

I write this and leave it to be seen, so that no one may by any chance get into trouble through me. This is an exact record of what took place tonight. I feel I am dying of weakness, and have barely strength to write, but it must be done if I die in the doing.

I went to bed as usual, taking care that the flowers were placed as Dr. Van Helsing directed, and soon fell asleep.

I was waked by the flapping at the window, which had begun after that sleep-walking on the cliff at Whitby when Mina saved me, and which now I know so well. I was not afraid, but I did wish that Dr. Seward was in the next room—as Dr. Van Helsing said he would be—so that I might have called him. I tried to sleep, but I could not. Then there came to me the old fear of sleep, and I determined to keep awake. Perversely sleep would try to come then when I did not want it. So, as I feared to be alone, I opened my door and called out, "Is there anybody there?" There was no answer. I was afraid to wake mother, and so closed my door again. Then outside in the shrubbery I heard a sort of howl like a dog's, but more fierce and deeper. I went to the window and looked out, but could see nothing, except a big bat, which had evidently been buffeting its wings against the window. So I went back to bed again, but determined not to go to sleep. Presently the door opened, and mother looked in. Seeing by my moving that I was not asleep, she came in and sat by me.

She said to me even more sweetly and softly than her wont, "I was uneasy about you, darling, and came in to see that you were all right."

I feared she might catch cold sitting there, and asked her to come in and sleep with me, so she came into bed, and lay down beside me. She did not take off her dressing gown, for she said she would only stay a while and then go back to her own bed. As she lay there in my arms, and I in hers the flapping and buffeting came to the window again. She was startled and a little frightened, and cried out, "What is that?" I tried to pacify her, and at last succeeded, and she lay quiet. But I could hear her poor dear heart still beating terribly. After a while there was the howl again out in the shrubbery, and shortly after there was a crash at the window, and a lot of broken glass was hurled on the floor. The window blind blew back with the wind that rushed in, and in the aperture of the broken panes there was the head of a great, gaunt gray wolf. Mother cried out in a fright, and struggled up into a sitting posture, and clutched wildly at anything that would help her. Amongst other things, she clutched the wreath of flowers that Dr. Van Helsing insisted on my wearing round my neck, and tore it away from me. For a second or two she sat up, pointing at the wolf, and there was a strange and horrible gurgling in her throat. Then she fell over, as if struck with lightning, and her head hit my forehead and made me dizzy for a moment or two. The room and all round seemed to spin round. I kept my eyes fixed on the window, but the wolf drew his head back, and a whole myriad of little specks seems to come blowing in through the broken window, and wheeling and circling round like the pillar of dust that travellers describe when there is a simoom in the desert. I tried to stir, but there was some spell upon me, and dear Mother's poor body, which seemed to grow cold already—for her dear heart had ceased to beat—weighed me down, and I remembered no more for a while.

The time did not seem long, but very, very awful, till I recovered consciousness again. Somewhere near, a passing bell was tolling. The dogs all round the neighbourhood were howling, and in our shrubbery, seemingly just outside, a nightingale was singing. I was dazed and stupid with pain and terror and weakness, but the sound of the nightingale seemed like the voice of my dead mother come back to comfort me. The sounds seemed to have awakened the maids, too, for I could hear their bare feet pattering outside my door. I called to them, and they came in, and when they saw what had happened, and what it was that lay over me on the bed, they screamed out. The wind rushed in through the broken window, and the door slammed to. They lifted off the body of my dear mother, and laid her, covered up with a sheet, on the bed after I had got up. They were all so frightened and nervous that I directed them to go to the dining room and each have a glass of wine. The door flew open for an instant and closed again. The maids shrieked, and then went in a body to the dining room, and I laid what flowers I had on my dear mother's breast. When they were there I remembered what Dr. Van Helsing had told me, but I didn't like to remove them, and besides, I would have some of the servants to sit up with me now. I was surprised that the maids did not come back. I called them, but got no answer, so I went to the dining room to look for them.

My heart sank when I saw what had happened. They all four lay helpless on the floor, breathing heavily. The decanter of sherry was on the table half full, but there was a queer, acrid smell about. I was suspicious, and examined the decanter. It smelt of laudanum, and looking on the sideboard, I found that the bottle which Mother's doctor uses for her—oh! did use—was empty. What am I to do? What am I to do? I am back in the room with Mother. I cannot leave her, and I am alone, save for the sleeping servants, whom someone has drugged. Alone with the dead! I dare not go out, for I can hear the low howl of the wolf through the broken window.

The air seems full of specks, floating and circling in the draught from the window, and the lights burn blue and dim. What am I to do? God shield me from harm this night! I shall hide this paper in my breast, where they shall find it when they come to lay me out. My dear mother gone! It is time that I go too. Goodbye, dear Arthur, if I should not survive this night. God keep you, dear, and God help me!

CHAPTER XII

Dr. Seward's Diary

18 September.

I drove at once to Hillingham and arrived early. Keeping my cab at the gate, I went up the avenue alone. I knocked gently and rang as quietly as possible, for I feared to disturb Lucy or her mother, and hoped to only bring a servant to the door. After a while, finding no response, I knocked and rang again, still no answer. I cursed the laziness of the servants that they should lie abed at such an hour, for it was now ten o'clock, and so rang and knocked again, but more impatiently, but still without response. Hitherto I had blamed only the servants, but now a terrible fear began to assail me. Was this desolation but another link in the chain of doom which seemed drawing tight round us? Was it indeed a house of death to which I had come, too late? I know that minutes, even seconds of delay, might mean hours of danger to Lucy, if she had had again one of those frightful relapses, and I went round the house to try if I could find by chance an entry anywhere.

I could find no means of ingress. Every window and door was fastened and locked, and I returned baffled to the porch. As I did so, I heard the rapid pit-pat of a swiftly driven horse's feet. They stopped at the gate, and a few seconds later I met Van Helsing running up the avenue. When he saw me, he gasped out, "Then it was you, and just arrived. How is she? Are we too late? Did you not get my telegram?"

I answered as quickly and coherently as I could that I had only got his telegram early in the morning, and had not a minute in coming here, and that I could not make anyone in the house hear me. He paused and raised his hat as he said solemnly, "Then I fear we are too late. God's will be done!"

With his usual recuperative energy, he went on, "Come. If there be no way open to get in, we must make one. Time is all in all to us now."

We went round to the back of the house, where there was a kitchen window. The Professor took a small surgical saw from his case, and handing it to me, pointed to the iron bars which guarded the window.

I attacked them at once and had very soon cut through three of them. Then with a long, thin knife we pushed back the fastening of the sashes and opened the window. I helped the Professor in, and followed him. There was no one in the kitchen or in the servants' rooms, which were close at hand. We tried all the rooms as we went along, and in the dining room, dimly lit by rays of light through the shutters, found four servant women lying on the floor. There was no need to think them dead, for their stertorous breathing and the acrid smell of laudanum in the room left no doubt as to their condition. Van Helsing and I looked at each other, and as we moved away he said, "We can attend to them later." Then we ascended to Lucy's room. For an instant or two we paused at the door to listen, but there was no sound that we could hear. With white faces and trembling hands, we opened the door gently, and entered the room.

How shall I describe what we saw? On the bed lay two women, Lucy and her mother. The latter lay farthest in, and she was covered with a white sheet, the edge of which had been blown back by the draught through the broken window, showing the drawn, white, face, with a look of terror fixed upon it. By her side lay Lucy, with face white and still more drawn. The flowers which had been round her neck we found upon her mother's bosom, and her throat was bare, showing the two little wounds which we had noticed before, but looking horribly white and mangled. Without a word the Professor bent over the bed, his head almost touching poor Lucy's breast. Then he gave a quick turn of his head, as of one who listens, and leaping to his feet, he cried out to me, "It is not yet too late! Quick! Quick! Bring the brandy!"

I flew downstairs and returned with it, taking care to smell and taste it, lest it, too, were drugged like the decanter of sherry which I found on the table. The maids were still breathing, but more restlessly, and I fancied that the narcotic was wearing off. I did not stay to make sure, but returned to Van Helsing. He rubbed the brandy, as on another occasion, on her lips and gums and on her wrists and the palms of her hands. He said to me, "I can do this, all that can be at the present. You go wake those maids. Flick them in the face with a wet towel, and flick them hard. Make them get heat and fire and a warm bath. This poor soul is nearly as cold as that beside her. She will need be heated before we can do anything more."

I went at once, and found little difficulty in waking three of the women. The fourth was only a young girl, and the drug had evidently affected her more strongly so I lifted her on the sofa and let her sleep. The others were dazed at first, but as remembrance came back to them they cried and sobbed in a hysterical manner. I was stern with them, however, and would not let them talk. I told them that one life was bad enough to lose, and if they delayed they would sacrifice Miss Lucy. So, sobbing and crying they went about their way, half clad as they were, and prepared fire and water. Fortunately, the kitchen and boiler fires were still alive, and there was no lack of hot water. We got a bath and carried Lucy out as she was and placed her in it. Whilst we were busy chafing her limbs there was a knock at the hall door. One of the maids ran off, hurried on some more clothes, and opened it. Then she returned and whispered to us that there was a gentleman who had come with a message from Mr. Holmwood. I bade her simply tell him that he must wait, for we could see no one now. She went away with the message, and, engrossed with our work, I clean forgot all about him.

I never saw in all my experience the Professor work in such deadly earnest. I knew, as he knew, that it was a stand-up fight with death, and in a pause told him so. He answered me in a way that I did not understand, but with the sternest look that his face could wear. "If that were all, I would stop here where we are now, and let her fade away into peace, for I see no light in life over her horizon." He went on with his work with, if possible, renewed and more frenzied vigour.

Presently we both began to be conscious that the heat was beginning to be of some effect. Lucy's heart beat a trifle more audibly to the stethoscope, and her lungs had a perceptible movement. Van Helsing's face almost beamed, and as we lifted her from the bath and rolled her in a hot sheet to dry her he said to me, "The first gain is ours! Check to the King!"

We took Lucy into another room, which had by now been prepared, and laid her in bed and forced a few drops of brandy down her throat. I noticed that Van Helsing tied a soft silk handkerchief round her throat. She was still unconscious, and was quite as bad as, if not worse than, we had ever seen her.

Van Helsing called in one of the women, and told her to stay with her and not to take her eyes off her till we returned, and then beckoned me out of the room.

"We must consult as to what is to be done," he said as we descended the stairs. In the hall he opened the dining room door, and we passed in, he closing the door carefully behind him. The shutters had been opened, but the blinds were already down, with that obedience to the etiquette of death which the British woman of the lower classes always rigidly observes. The room was, therefore, dimly dark. It was, however, light enough for our purposes. Van Helsing's sternness was somewhat relieved by a look of perplexity. He was evidently torturing his mind about something, so I waited for an instant, and he spoke.

"What are we to do now? Where are we to turn for help? We must have another transfusion of blood, and that soon, or that poor girl's life won't be worth an hour's purchase. You are exhausted already. I am exhausted too. I fear to trust those women, even if they would have courage to submit. What are we to do for someone who will open his veins for her?"

"What's the matter with me, anyhow?"

The voice came from the sofa across the room, and its tones brought relief and joy to my heart, for they were those of Quincey Morris. Van Helsing started angrily at the first sound, but his face softened and a glad look came into his eyes as I cried out, "Quincey Morris!" and rushed towards him with outstretched hands.

"What brought you here?" I cried as our hands met.

"I guess Art is the cause."

He handed me a telegram.

> "Have not heard from Seward for three days, and am terribly anxious. Cannot leave. Father still in same condition. Send me word how Lucy is. Do not delay.
>
> HOLMWOOD."

"I think I came just in the nick of time. You know you have only to tell me what to do."

Van Helsing strode forward, and took his hand, looking him straight in the eyes as he said, "A brave man's blood is the best thing on this earth when a woman is in trouble. You're a man and no mistake. Well, the devil may work against us for all he's worth, but God sends us men when we want them."

Once again we went through that ghastly operation. I have not the heart to go through with the details. Lucy had got a terrible shock and it told on her more than before, for though plenty of blood went into her veins, her body did not respond to the treatment as well as on the other occasions. Her struggle back into life was something frightful to see and hear. However, the action of both heart and lungs improved, and Van Helsing made a subcutaneous injection of morphia, as before, and with good effect. Her faint became a profound slumber. The Professor watched whilst I went downstairs with Quincey Morris, and sent one of the maids to pay off one of the cabmen who were waiting. I left Quincey lying down after having a glass of wine, and told the cook to get ready a good breakfast. Then a thought struck me, and I went back to the room where Lucy now was. When I came softly in, I found Van Helsing with a sheet or two of note paper in his hand. He had evidently read it, and was thinking it over as he sat with his hand to his brow. There was a look of grim satisfaction in his face, as of one who has had a doubt solved. He handed me the paper saying only, "It dropped from Lucy's breast when we carried her to the bath."

When I had read it, I stood looking at the Professor, and after a pause asked him, "In God's name, what does it all mean? Was she, or is she, mad;or what sort of horrible danger is it?" I was so bewildered that I did not know what to say more.

Van Helsing put out his hand and took the paper, saying, "Do not trouble about it now. Forget it for the present. You shall know and understand it all in good time, but it will be later. And now what is it that you came to me to say?" This brought me back to fact, and I was all myself again.

"I came to speak about the certificate of death. If we do not act properly and wisely, there may be an inquest, and that paper would have to be produced. I am in hopes that we need have no inquest, for if we had it would surely kill poor Lucy, if nothing else did. I know, and you know, and the other doctor who attended her knows, that Mrs. Westenra had disease of the heart, and we can certify that she died of it. Let us fill up the certificate at once, and I shall take it myself to the registrar and go on to the undertaker."

"Good, oh my friend John! Well thought of! Truly Miss Lucy, if she be sad in the foes that beset her, is at least happy in the friends that love her. One, two, three, all open their veins for her, besides one old man. Ah, yes, I know, friend John. I am not blind! I love you all the more for it! Now go."

In the hall I met Quincey Morris, with a telegram for Arthur telling him that Mrs. Westenra was dead, that Lucy also had been ill, but was now going on better, and that Van Helsing and I were with her. I told him where I was going, and he hurried me out, but as I was going said, "When you come back, Jack, may I have two words with you all to ourselves?" I nodded in reply and went out. I found no difficulty about the registration, and arranged with the local undertaker to come up in the evening to measure for the coffin and to make arrangements.

When I got back Quincey was waiting for me. I told him I would see him as soon as I knew about Lucy, and went up to her room. She was still sleeping, and the Professor seemingly had not moved from his seat at her side. From his putting his finger to his lips, I gathered that he expected her to wake before long and was afraid of fore-stalling nature. So I went down to Quincey and took him into the breakfast room, where the blinds were not drawn down, and which was a little more cheerful, or rather less cheerless, than the other rooms.

When we were alone, he said to me, "Jack Seward, I don't want to shove myself in anywhere where I've no right to be, but this is no ordinary case. You know I loved that girl and wanted to marry her, but although that's all past and gone, I can't help feeling anxious about her all the same. What is it that's wrong with her? The Dutchman, and a fine old fellow he is, I can see that, said that time you two came into the room, that you must have another transfusion of blood, and that both you and he were exhausted. Now I know well that you medical men speak in camera, and that a man must not expect to know what they consult about in private. But this is no common matter, and whatever it is, I have done my part. Is not that so?"

"That's so," I said, and he went on.

"I take it that both you and Van Helsing had done already what I did today. Is not that so?"

"That's so."

"And I guess Art was in it too. When I saw him four days ago down at his own place he looked queer. I have not seen anything pulled down so quick since I was on the Pampas and had a mare that I was fond of go to grass all in a night. One of those big bats that they call vampires had got at her in the night, and what with his gorge and the vein left open, there wasn't enough blood in her to let her stand up, and I had to put a bullet through her as she lay. Jack, if you may tell me without betraying confidence, Arthur was the first, is not that so?" As he spoke the poor fellow looked terribly anxious. He was in a torture of suspense regarding the woman he loved, and his utter ignorance of the terrible mystery which seemed to surround her intensified his pain. His very heart was bleeding, and it took all the manhood of him—and there was a royal lot of it, too—to keep him from breaking down. I paused before answering, for I felt that I must not betray anything which the Professor wished kept secret, but already he knew so much, and guessed so much, that there could be no reason for not answering, so I answered in the same phrase.

"That's so."

"And how long has this been going on?"

"About ten days."

"Ten days! Then I guess, Jack Seward, that that poor pretty creature that we all love has had put into her veins within that time the blood of four strong men. Man alive, her whole body wouldn't hold it." Then coming close to me, he spoke in a fierce half-whisper. "What took it out?"

I shook my head. "That," I said, "is the crux. Van Helsing is simply frantic about it, and I am at my wits' end. I can't even hazard a guess. There has been a series of little circumstances which have thrown out all our calculations as to Lucy being properly watched. But these shall not occur again. Here we stay until all be well, or ill."

Quincey held out his hand. "Count me in," he said. "You and the Dutchman will tell me what to do, and I'll do it."

When she woke late in the afternoon, Lucy's first movement was to feel in her breast, and to my surprise, produced the paper which Van Helsing had given me to read. The careful Professor had replaced it where it had come from, lest on waking she should be alarmed. Her eyes then lit on Van Helsing and on me too, and gladdened. Then she looked round the room, and seeing where she was, shuddered. She gave a loud cry, and put her poor thin hands before her pale face. We both understood what was meant, that she had realized to the full her mother's death. So we tried what we could to comfort her. Doubtless sympathy eased her somewhat, but she was very low in thought and spirit, and wept silently and weakly for a long time. We told her that either or both of us would now remain with her all the time, and that seemed to comfort her. Towards dusk she fell into a doze. Here a very odd thing occurred. Whilst still asleep she took the paper from her breast and tore it in two.

Van Helsing stepped over and took the pieces from her. All the same, however, she went on with the action of tearing, as though the material were still in her hands. Finally she lifted her hands and opened them as though scattering the fragments. Van Helsing seemed surprised, and his brows gathered as if in thought, but he said nothing.

19 September.

All last night she slept fitfully, being always afraid to sleep, and something weaker when she woke from it. The Professor and I took in turns to watch, and we never left her for a moment unattended. Quincey Morris said nothing about his intention, but I knew that all night long he patrolled round and round the house.

When the day came, its searching light showed the ravages in poor Lucy's strength. She was hardly able to turn her head, and the little nourishment which she could take seemed to do her no good. At times she slept, and both Van Helsing and I noticed the difference in her, between sleeping and waking. Whilst asleep she looked stronger, although more haggard, and her breathing was softer. Her open mouth showed the pale gums drawn back from the teeth, which looked positively longer and sharper than usual. When she woke the softness of her eyes evidently changed the expression, for she looked her own self, although a dying one. In the afternoon she asked for Arthur, and we telegraphed for him. Quincey went off to meet him at the station.

When he arrived it was nearly six o'clock, and the sun was setting full and warm, and the red light streamed in through the window and gave more colour to the pale cheeks. When he saw her, Arthur was simply choking with emotion, and none of us could speak. In the hours that had passed, the fits of sleep, or the comatose condition that passed for it, had grown more frequent, so that the pauses when conversation was possible were shortened. Arthur's presence, however, seemed to act as a stimulant. She rallied a little, and spoke to him more brightly than she had done since we arrived. He too pulled himself together, and spoke as cheerily as he could, so that the best was made of everything.

It is now nearly one o'clock, and he and Van Helsing are sitting with her. I am to relieve them in a quarter of an hour, and I am entering this on Lucy's phonograph. Until six o'clock they are to try to rest. I fear that tomorrow will end our watching, for the shock has been too great. The poor child cannot rally. God help us all.

Letter, Mina Harker to Lucy Westenra (*Unopened by Her*)

17 September.

My dearest Lucy,

It seems an age since I heard from you, or indeed since I wrote. You will pardon me, I know, for all my faults when you have read all my budget of news. Well, I got my husband back all right. When we arrived at Exeter there was a carriage waiting for us, and in it, though he had an attack of gout, Mr. Hawkins. He took us to his house, where there were rooms for us all nice and comfortable, and we dined together. After dinner Mr. Hawkins said, "My dears, I want to drink your health and prosperity, and may every blessing attend you both. I know you both from children, and have, with love and pride, seen you grow up. Now I want you to make your home here with me. I have left to me neither chick nor child. All are gone, and in my will I have left you everything." I cried, Lucy dear, as Jonathan and the old man clasped hands. Our evening was a very, very happy one.

So here we are, installed in this beautiful old house, and from both my bedroom and the drawing room I can see the great elms of the cathedral close, with their great black stems standing out against the old yellow stone of the cathedral, and I can hear the rooks overhead cawing and cawing and chattering and chattering and gossiping all day, after the manner of rooks—and humans. I am busy, I need not tell you, arranging things and housekeeping. Jonathan and Mr. Hawkins are busy all day, for now that Jonathan is a partner, Mr. Hawkins wants to tell him all about the clients.

How is your dear mother getting on? I wish I could run up to town for a day or two to see you, dear, but I dare not go yet, with so much on my shoulders, and Jonathan wants looking after still. He is beginning to put some flesh on his bones again, but he was terribly weakened by the long illness. Even now he sometimes starts out of his sleep in a sudden way and awakes all trembling until I can coax him back to his usual placidity. However, thank God, these occasions grow less frequent as the days go on, and they will in time pass away altogether, I trust. And now I have told you my news, let me ask yours. When are you to be married, and where, and who is to perform the ceremony, and what are you to wear, and is it to be a public or private wedding? Tell me all about it, dear, tell me all about everything, for there is nothing which interests you which will not be dear to me. Jonathan asks me to send his "respectful duty," but I do not think that is good enough from the junior partner of the important firm Hawkins & Harker. And so, as you love me, and he loves me, and I love you with all the moods and tenses of the verb, I send you simply his "love" instead. Goodbye, my dearest Lucy, and blessings on you.

Yours,

MINA HARKER.

REPORT FROM PATRICK HENNESSEY, MD, MRCS, LK, QCPI, ETC., ETC., TO JOHN SEWARD, MD

20 September.

My dear Sir,

In accordance with your wishes, I enclose report of the conditions of everything left in my charge. With regard to patient, Renfield, there is more to say. He has had another outbreak, which might have had a dreadful ending, but which, as it fortunately happened, was unattended with any unhappy results. This afternoon a carrier's cart with two men made a call at the empty house whose grounds abut on ours, the house to which, you will remember, the patient twice ran away. The men stopped at our gate to ask the porter their way, as they were strangers I was myself looking out of the study window, having a smoke after dinner, and saw one of them come up to the house. As he passed the window of Renfield's room, the patient began to rate him from within, and called him all the foul names he could lay his tongue to. The man, who seemed a decent fellow enough, contented himself by telling him to "shut up for a foul-mouthed beggar," whereon our man accused him of robbing him and wanting to murder him and said that he would hinder him if he were to swing for it. I opened the window and signed to the man not to notice, so he contented himself after looking the place over and making up his mind as to what kind of place he had got to by saying, "Lor' bless yer, sir, I wouldn't mind what was said to me in a bloomin' madhouse. I pity ye and the guv'nor for havin' to live in the house with a wild beast like that." Then he asked his way civilly enough, and I told him where the gate of the empty house was. He went away followed by threats and curses and revilings from our man. I went down to see if I could make out any cause for his anger, since he is usually such a well-behaved man, and except his violent fits nothing of the kind had ever occurred. I found him, to my astonishment, quite composed and most genial in his manner. I tried to get him to talk of the incident, but he blandly asked me questions as to what I meant, and led me to believe that he was completely oblivious of the affair. It was, I am sorry to say, however, only another instance of his cunning, for within half an hour I heard of him again. This time he had broken out through the window of his room, and was running down the avenue. I called to the attendants to follow me, and ran after him, for I feared he was intent on some mischief. My fear was justified when I saw the same cart which had passed before coming down the road, having on it some great wooden boxes. The men were wiping their foreheads, and were flushed in the face, as if with violent exercise. Before I could get up to him, the patient rushed at them, and pulling one of them off the cart, began to knock his head against the ground. If I had not seized him just at the moment, I believe he would have killed the man there and then. The other fellow jumped down and struck him over the head with the butt end of his heavy whip. It was a horrible blow, but he did not seem to mind it, but seized him also, and struggled with the three of us, pulling us to and fro as if we were kittens. You know I am no lightweight, and the others were both burly men. At first he was silent in his fighting, but as we began to master him, and the attendants were putting a strait waistcoat on him, he began to shout, "I'll frustrate them! They shan't rob me! They shan't murder me by inches! I'll fight for my Lord and Master!" and all sorts of similar incoherent ravings. It was with very considerable difficulty that they got him back to the house and put him in the padded room. One of the attendants, Hardy, had a finger broken. However, I set it all right, and he is going on well.

The two carriers were at first loud in their threats of actions for damages, and promised to rain all the penalties of the law on us. Their threats were, however, mingled with some sort of indirect apology for the defeat of the two of them by a feeble madman. They said that if it had not been for the way their strength had been spent in carrying and raising the heavy boxes to the cart they would have made short work of him. They gave as another reason for their defeat the extraordinary state of drouth to which they had been reduced by the dusty nature of their occupation and the reprehensible distance from the scene of their labors of any place of public entertainment. I quite understood their drift, and after a stiff glass of strong grog, or rather more of the same, and with each a sovereign in hand, they made light of the attack, and swore that they would encounter a worse madman any day for the pleasure of meeting so "bloomin' good a bloke" as your correspondent. I took their names and addresses, in case they might be needed. They are as follows: Jack Smollet, of Dudding's Rents, King George's Road, Great Walworth, and Thomas Snelling, Peter Farley's Row, Guide Court, Bethnal Green. They are both in the employment of Harris & Sons, Moving and Shipment Company, Orange Master's Yard, Soho.

I shall report to you any matter of interest occurring here, and shall wire you at once if there is anything of importance.

Believe me, dear Sir,
Yours faithfully,
PATRICK HENNESSEY.

LETTER, MINA HARKER TO LUCY WESTENRA (UNOPENED BY HER)

18 September.

My dearest Lucy,

Such a sad blow has befallen us. Mr. Hawkins has died very suddenly. Some may not think it so sad for us, but we had both come to so love him that it really seems as though we had lost a father. I never knew either father or mother, so that the dear old man's death is a real blow to me. Jonathan is greatly distressed. It is not only that he feels sorrow, deep sorrow, for the dear, good man who has befriended him all his life, and now at the end has treated him like his own son and left him a fortune which to people of our modest bringing up is wealth beyond the dream of avarice, but Jonathan feels it on another account. He says the amount of responsibility which it puts upon him makes him nervous. He begins to doubt himself. I try to cheer him up, and *my* belief in *him* helps him to have a belief in himself. But it is here that the grave shock that he experienced tells upon him the most. Oh, it is too hard that a sweet, simple, noble, strong nature such as his—a nature which enabled him by our dear, good friend's aid to rise from clerk to master in a few years—should be so injured that the very essence of its strength is gone. Forgive me, dear, if I worry you with my troubles in the midst of your own happiness, but Lucy dear, I must tell someone, for the strain of keeping up a brave and cheerful appearance to Jonathan tries me, and I have no one here that I can confide in. I dread coming up to London, as we must do that day after tomorrow, for poor Mr. Hawkins left in his will that he was to be buried in the grave with his father. As there are no relations at all, Jonathan will have to be chief mourner. I shall try to run over to see you, dearest, if only for a few minutes. Forgive me for troubling you. With all blessings,

Your loving

MINA HARKER.

DR. SEWARD'S DIARY

20 September.

Only resolution and habit can let me make an entry tonight. I am too miserable, too low spirited, too sick of the world and all in it, including life itself, that I would not care if I heard this moment the flapping of the wings of the angel of death. And he has been flapping those grim wings to some purpose of late, Lucy's mother and Arthur's father, and now . . . Let me get on with my work.

I duly relieved Van Helsing in his watch over Lucy. We wanted Arthur to go to rest also, but he refused at first. It was only when I told him that we should want him to help us during the day, and that we must not all break down for want of rest, lest Lucy should suffer, that he agreed to go. Van Helsing was very kind to him. "Come, my child," he said. "Come with me. You are sick and weak, and have had much sorrow and much mental pain, as well as that tax on your strength that we know of. You must not be alone, for to be alone is to be full of fears and alarms. Come to the drawing room, where there is a big fire, and there are two sofas. You shall lie on one, and I on the other, and our sympathy will be comfort to each other, even though we do not speak, and even if we sleep." Arthur went off with him, casting back a longing look on Lucy's face, which lay in her pillow, almost whiter than the lawn. She lay quite still, and I looked around the room to see that all was as it should be. I could see that the Professor had carried out in this room, as in the other, his purpose of using the garlic. The whole of the window sashes reeked with it, and round Lucy's neck, over the silk handkerchief which Van Helsing made her keep on, was a rough chaplet of the same odorous flowers. Lucy was breathing somewhat stertorously, and her face was at its worst, for the open mouth showed the pale gums. Her teeth, in the dim, uncertain light, seemed longer and sharper than they had been in the morning. In particular, by some trick of the light, the canine teeth looked longer and sharper than the rest. I sat down beside her, and presently she moved uneasily. At the same moment there came a sort of dull flapping or buffeting at the window. I went over to it softly, and peeped out by the corner of the blind. There was a full moonlight, and I could see that the noise was made by a great bat, which wheeled around—doubtless attracted by the light—although so dim, and every now and again struck the window with its wings. When I came back to my seat, I found that Lucy had moved slightly, and had torn away the garlic flowers from her throat. I replaced them as well as I could, and sat watching her.

Presently she woke, and I gave her food, as Van Helsing had prescribed. She took but a little, and that languidly. There did not seem to be with her now the unconscious struggle for life and strength that had hitherto so marked her illness. It struck me as curious that the moment she became conscious she pressed the garlic flowers close to her. It was certainly odd that whenever she got into that lethargic state, with the stertorous breathing, she put the flowers from her, but that when she waked she clutched them close. There was no possibility of making any mistake about this, for in the long hours that followed, she had many spells of sleeping and waking and repeated both actions many times.

At six o'clock Van Helsing came to relieve me. Arthur had then fallen into a doze, and he mercifully let him sleep on. When he saw Lucy's face I could hear the hissing indraw of breath, and he said to me in a sharp whisper. "Draw up the blind. I want light!" Then he bent down, and, with his face almost touching Lucy's, examined her carefully. He removed the flowers and lifted the silk handkerchief from her throat. As he did so he started back and I could hear his ejaculation, "Mein Gott!" as it was smothered in his throat. I bent over and looked, too, and as I noticed some queer chill came over me.

The wounds on the throat had absolutely disappeared.

For fully five minutes Van Helsing stood looking at her, with his face at its sternest. Then he turned to me and said calmly, "She is dying. It will not be long now. It will be much difference, mark me, whether she dies conscious or in her sleep. Wake that poor boy, and let him come and see the last. He trusts us, and we have promised him."

I went to the dining room and waked him. He was dazed for a moment, but when he saw the sunlight streaming in through the edges of the shutters he thought he was late, and expressed his fear. I assured him that Lucy was still asleep, but told him as gently as I could that both Van Helsing and I feared that the end was near. He covered his face with his hands, and slid down on his knees by the sofa, where he remained, perhaps a minute, with his head buried, praying, whilst his shoulders shook with grief. I took him by the hand and raised him up. "Come," I said, "my dear old fellow, summon all your fortitude. It will be best and easiest for *her*."

When we came into Lucy's room I could see that Van Helsing had, with his usual forethought, been putting matters straight and making everything look as pleasing as possible. He had even brushed Lucy's hair, so that it lay on the pillow in its usual sunny ripples. When we came into the room she opened her eyes, and seeing him, whispered softly, "Arthur! Oh, my love, I am so glad you have come!"

He was stooping to kiss her, when Van Helsing motioned him back. "No," he whispered, "not yet! Hold her hand, it will comfort her more."

So Arthur took her hand and knelt beside her, and she looked her best, with all the soft lines matching the angelic beauty of her eyes. Then gradually her eyes closed, and she sank to sleep. For a little bit her breast heaved softly, and her breath came and went like a tired child's.

And then insensibly there came the strange change which I had noticed in the night. Her breathing grew stertorous, the mouth opened, and the pale gums, drawn back, made the teeth look longer and sharper than ever. In a sort of sleep-waking, vague, unconscious way she opened her eyes, which were now dull and hard at once, and said in a soft, voluptuous voice, such as I had never heard from her lips, "Arthur! Oh, my love, I am so glad you have come! Kiss me!"

Arthur bent eagerly over to kiss her, but at that instant Van Helsing, who, like me, had been startled by her voice, swooped upon him, and catching him by the neck with both hands, dragged him back with a fury of strength which I never thought he could have possessed, and actually hurled him almost across the room.

"Not on your life!" he said. "Not for your living soul and hers!" And he stood between them like a lion at bay.

Arthur was so taken aback that he did not for a moment know what to do or say, and before any impulse of violence could seize him he realized the place and the occasion, and stood silent, waiting.

I kept my eyes fixed on Lucy, as did Van Helsing, and we saw a spasm as of rage flit like a shadow over her face. The sharp teeth clamped together. Then her eyes closed, and she breathed heavily.

Very shortly after she opened her eyes in all their softness, and putting out her poor, pale, thin hand, took Van Helsing's great brown one, drawing it close to her, she kissed it. "My true friend," she said, in a faint voice, but with untellable pathos, "my true friend, and his! Oh, guard him, and give me peace!"

"I swear it!" he said solemnly, kneeling beside her and holding up his hand, as one who registers an oath. Then he turned to Arthur, and said to him, "Come, my child, take her hand in yours, and kiss her on the forehead, and only once."

Their eyes met instead of their lips, and so they parted.

Lucy's eyes closed, and Van Helsing, who had been watching closely, took Arthur's arm, and drew him away.

And then Lucy's breathing became stertorous again, and all at once it ceased.

"It is all over," said Van Helsing. "She is dead!"

I took Arthur by the arm, and led him away to the drawing room, where he sat down, and covered his face with his hands, sobbing in a way that nearly broke me down to see.

I went back to the room, and found Van Helsing looking at poor Lucy, and his face was sterner than ever. Some change had come over her body. Death had given back part of her beauty, for her brow and cheeks had recovered some of their flowing lines. Even the lips had lost their deadly pallor. It was as if the blood, no longer needed for the working of the heart, had gone to make the harshness of death as little rude as might be.

> We thought her dying whilst she slept,
> And sleeping when she died.

I stood beside Van Helsing, and said, "Ah well, poor girl, there is peace for her at last. It is the end!"

He turned to me, and said with grave solemnity, "Not so, alas! Not so. It is only the beginning!"

When I asked him what he meant, he only shook his head and answered, "We can do nothing as yet. Wait and see."

CHAPTER XIII

Dr. Seward's Diary, Continued

The funeral was arranged for the next succeeding day, so that Lucy and her mother might be buried together. I attended to all the ghastly formalities, and the urbane undertaker proved that his staff was afflicted—or blessed—with something of his own obsequious suavity. Even the woman who performed the last offices for the dead remarked to me, in a confidential, brother-professional way, when she had come out from the death chamber, "She makes a very beautiful corpse, sir. It's quite a privilege to attend on her. It's not too much to say that she will do credit to our establishment!"

I noticed that Van Helsing never kept far away. This was possible from the disordered state of things in the household. There were no relatives at hand, and as Arthur had to be back the next day to attend at his father's funeral, we were unable to notify anyone who should have been bidden. Under the circumstances, Van Helsing and I took it upon ourselves to examine papers, etc. He insisted upon looking over Lucy's papers himself. I asked him why, for I feared that he, being a foreigner, might not be quite aware of English legal requirements, and so might in ignorance make some unnecessary trouble.

He answered me, "I know, I know. You forget that I am a lawyer as well as a doctor. But this is not altogether for the law. You knew that, when you avoided the coroner. I have more than him to avoid. There may be papers more—such as this."

As he spoke he took from his pocket book the memorandum which had been in Lucy's breast, and which she had torn in her sleep.

"When you find anything of the solicitor who is for the late Mrs. Westenra, seal all her papers, and write him tonight. For me, I watch here in the room and in Miss Lucy's old room all night, and I myself search for what may be. It is not well that her very thoughts go into the hands of strangers."

I went on with my part of the work, and in another half hour had found the name and address of Mrs. Westenra's solicitor and had written to him. All the poor lady's papers were in order. Explicit directions regarding the place of burial were given. I had hardly sealed the letter, when, to my surprise, Van Helsing walked into the room, saying, "Can I help you, friend John? I am free, and if I may, my service is to you."

"Have you got what you looked for?" I asked.

To which he replied, "I did not look for any specific thing. I only hoped to find, and find I have, all that there was, only some letters and a few memoranda, and a diary new begun. But I have them here, and we shall for the present say nothing of them. I shall see that poor lad tomorrow evening, and, with his sanction, I shall use some."

When we had finished the work in hand, he said to me, "And now, friend John, I think we may to bed. We want sleep, both you and I, and rest to recuperate. Tomorrow we shall have much to do, but for the tonight there is no need of us. Alas!"

Before turning in we went to look at poor Lucy. The undertaker had certainly done his work well, for the room was turned into a small chapelle ardente. There was a wilderness of beautiful white flowers, and death was made as little repulsive as might be. The end of the winding sheet was laid over the face. When the Professor bent over and turned it gently back, we both started at the beauty before us. The tall wax candles showing a sufficient light to note it well. All Lucy's loveliness had come back to her in death, and the hours that had passed, instead of leaving traces of "decay's effacing fingers," had but restored the beauty of life, till positively I could not believe my eyes that I was looking at a corpse.

The Professor looked sternly grave. He had not loved her as I had, and there was no need for tears in his eyes. He said to me, "Remain till I return," and left the room. He came back with a handful of wild garlic from the box waiting in the hall, but which had not been opened, and placed the flowers amongst the others on and around the bed. Then he took from his neck, inside his collar, a little gold crucifix, and placed it over the mouth. He restored the sheet to its place, and we came away.

I was undressing in my own room, when, with a premonitory tap at the door, he entered, and at once began to speak.

"Tomorrow I want you to bring me, before night, a set of post-mortem knives."

"Must we make an autopsy?" I asked.

"Yes and no. I want to operate, but not what you think. Let me tell you now, but not a word to another. I want to cut off her head and take out her heart. Ah! You a surgeon, and so shocked! You, whom I have seen with no tremble of hand or heart, do operations of life and death that make the rest shudder. Oh, but I must not forget, my dear friend John, that you loved her, and I have not forgotten it for is I that shall operate, and you must not help. I would like to do it tonight, but for Arthur I must not. He will be free after his father's funeral tomorrow, and he will want to see her, to see it. Then, when she is coffined ready for the next day, you and I shall come when all sleep. We shall unscrew the coffin lid, and shall do our operation, and then replace all, so that none know, save we alone."

"But why do it at all? The girl is dead. Why mutilate her poor body without need? And if there is no necessity for a post-mortem and nothing to gain by it, no good to her, to us, to science, to human knowledge, why do it? Without such it is monstrous."

For answer he put his hand on my shoulder, and said, with infinite tenderness, "Friend John, I pity your poor bleeding heart, and I love you the more because it does so bleed. If I could, I would take on myself the burden that you do bear. But there are things that you know not, but that you shall know, and bless me for knowing, though they are not pleasant things. John, my child, you have been my friend now many years, and yet did you ever know me to do any without good cause? I may err, I am but man, but I believe in all I do. Was it not for these causes that you send for me when the great trouble came? Yes! Were you not amazed, nay horrified, when I would not let Arthur kiss his love, though she was dying, and snatched him away by all my strength? Yes! And yet you saw how she thanked me, with her so beautiful dying eyes, her voice, too, so weak, and she kiss my rough old hand and bless me? Yes! And did you not hear me swear promise to her, that so she closed her eyes grateful? Yes!

"Well, I have good reason now for all I want to do. You have for many years trust me. You have believe me weeks past, when there be things so strange that you might have well doubt. Believe me yet a little, friend John. If you trust me not, then I must tell what I think, and that is not perhaps well. And if I work, as work I shall, no matter trust or no trust, without my friend trust in me, I work with heavy heart and feel oh so lonely when I want all help and courage that may be!" He paused a moment and went on solemnly, "Friend John, there are strange and terrible days before us. Let us not be two, but one, that so we work to a good end. Will you not have faith in me?"

I took his hand, and promised him. I held my door open as he went away, and watched him go to his room and close the door. As I stood without moving, I saw one of the maids pass silently along the passage—she had her back to me, so did not see me—and go into the room where Lucy lay. The sight touched me. Devotion is so rare, and we are so grateful to those who show it unasked to those we love. Here was a poor girl putting aside the terrors which she naturally had of death to go watch alone by the bier of the mistress whom she loved, so that the poor clay might not be lonely till laid to eternal rest.

I must have slept long and soundly, for it was broad daylight when Van Helsing waked me by coming into my room. He came over to my bedside and said, "You need not trouble about the knives. We shall not do it."

"Why not?" I asked. For his solemnity of the night before had greatly impressed me.

"Because," he said sternly, "it is too late, or too early. See!" Here he held up the little golden crucifix.

"This was stolen in the night."

"How stolen," I asked in wonder, "since you have it now?"

"Because I get it back from the worthless wretch who stole it, from the woman who robbed the dead and the living. Her punishment will surely come, but not through me. She knew not altogether what she did, and thus unknowing, she only stole. Now we must wait." He went away on the word, leaving me with a new mystery to think of, a new puzzle to grapple with.

The forenoon was a dreary time, but at noon the solicitor came, Mr. Marquand, of Wholeman, Sons, Marquand & Lidderdale. He was very genial and very appreciative of what we had done, and took off our hands all cares as to details. During lunch he told us that Mrs. Westenra had for some time expected sudden death from her heart, and had put her affairs in absolute order. He informed us that, with the exception of a certain entailed property of Lucy's father which now, in default of direct issue, went back to a distant branch of the family, the whole estate, real and personal, was left absolutely to Arthur Holmwood. When he had told us so much he went on, "Frankly we did our best to prevent such a testamentary disposition, and pointed out certain contingencies that might leave her daughter either penniless or not so free as she should be to act regarding a matrimonial alliance. Indeed, we pressed the matter so far that we almost came into collision, for she asked us if we were or were not prepared to carry out her wishes. Of course, we had then no alternative but to accept. We were right in principle, and ninety-nine times out of a hundred we should have proved, by the logic of events, the accuracy of our judgment. "Frankly, however, I must admit that in this case any other form of disposition would have rendered impossible the carrying out of her wishes. For by her predeceasing her daughter the latter would have come into possession of the property, and, even had she only survived her mother by five minutes, her property would, in case there were no will, and a will was a practical impossibility in such a case, have been treated at her decease as under intestacy. In which case Lord Godalming, though so dear a friend, would have had no claim in the world. And the inheritors, being remote, would not be likely to abandon their just rights, for sentimental reasons regarding an entire stranger. I assure you, my dear sirs, I am rejoiced at the result, perfectly rejoiced."

He was a good fellow, but his rejoicing at the one little part—in which he was officially interested—of so great a tragedy, was an object-lesson in the limitations of sympathetic understanding.

He did not remain long, but said he would look in later in the day and see Lord Godalming. His coming, however, had been a certain comfort to us, since it assured us that we should not have to dread hostile criticism as to any of our acts. Arthur was expected at five o'clock, so a little before that time we visited the death chamber. It was so in very truth, for now both mother and daughter lay in it. The undertaker, true to his craft, had made the best display he could of his goods, and there was a mortuary air about the place that lowered our spirits at once. Van Helsing ordered the former arrangement to be adhered to, explaining that, as Lord Godalming was coming very soon, it would be less harrowing to his feelings to see all that was left of his *fiancée* quite alone. The undertaker seemed shocked at his own stupidity and exerted himself to restore things to the condition in which we left them the night before, so that when Arthur came such shocks to his feelings as we could avoid were saved.

Poor fellow! He looked desperately sad and broken. Even his stalwart manhood seemed to have shrunk somewhat under the strain of his much-tried emotions. He had, I knew, been very genuinely and devotedly attached to his father, and to lose him, and at such a time, was a bitter blow to him. With me he was warm as ever, and to Van Helsing he was sweetly courteous. But I could not help seeing that there was some constraint with him. The professor noticed it too, and motioned me to bring him upstairs.

I did so, and left him at the door of the room, as I felt he would like to be quite alone with her, but he took my arm and led me in, saying huskily, "You loved her too, old fellow. She told me all about it, and there was no friend had a closer place in her heart than you. I don't know how to thank you for all you have done for her. I can't think yet . . ."

Here he suddenly broke down, and threw his arms round my shoulders and laid his head on my breast, crying, "Oh, Jack! Jack! What shall I do? The whole of life seems gone from me all at once, and there is nothing in the wide world for me to live for."

I comforted him as well as I could. In such cases men do not need much expression. A grip of the hand, the tightening of an arm over the shoulder, a sob in unison, are expressions of sympathy dear to a man's heart. I stood still and silent till his sobs died away, and then I said softly to him, "Come and look at her."

Together we moved over to the bed, and I lifted the lawn from her face. God! How beautiful she was. Every hour seemed to be enhancing her loveliness. It frightened and amazed me somewhat. And as for Arthur, he fell to trembling, and finally was shaken with doubt as with an ague. At last, after a long pause, he said to me in a faint whisper, "Jack, is she really dead?"

I assured him sadly that it was so, and went on to suggest—for I felt that such a horrible doubt should not have life for a moment longer than I could help—that it often happened that after death faces become softened and even resolved into their youthful beauty, that this was especially so when death had been preceded by any acute or prolonged suffering. I seemed to quite do away with any doubt, and after kneeling beside the couch for a while and looking at her lovingly and long, he turned aside. I told him that that must be goodbye, as the coffin had to be prepared, so he went back and took her dead hand in his and kissed it, and bent over and kissed her forehead. He came away, fondly looking back over his shoulder at her as he came.

I left him in the drawing room, and told Van Helsing that he had said goodbye, so the latter went to the kitchen to tell the undertaker's men to proceed with the preparations and to screw up the coffin. When he came out of the room again I told him of Arthur's question, and he replied, "I am not surprised. Just now I doubted for a moment myself!"

We all dined together, and I could see that poor Art was trying to make the best of things. Van Helsing had been silent all dinner time, but when we had lit our cigars he said, "Lord—" but Arthur interrupted him.

"No, no, not that, for God's sake! Not yet at any rate. Forgive me, sir. I did not mean to speak offensively. It is only because my loss is so recent."

The Professor answered very sweetly, "I only used that name because I was in doubt. I must not call you 'Mr.' and I have grown to love you—yes, my dear boy, to love you—as Arthur."

Arthur held out his hand, and took the old man's warmly. "Call me what you will," he said. "I hope I may always have the title of a friend. And let me say that I am at a loss for words to thank you for your goodness to my poor dear." He paused a moment, and went on, "I know that she understood your goodness even better than I do. And if I was rude or in any way wanting at that time you acted so, you remember"—the Professor nodded—"you must forgive me."

He answered with a grave kindness, "I know it was hard for you to quite trust me then, for to trust such violence needs to understand, and I take it that you do not—that you cannot—trust me now, for you do not yet understand. And there may be more times when I shall want you to trust when you cannot—and may not—and must not yet understand. But the time will come when your trust shall be whole and complete in me, and when you shall understand as though the sunlight himself shone through. Then you shall bless me from first to last for your own sake, and for the sake of others, and for her dear sake to whom I swore to protect."

"And indeed, indeed, sir," said Arthur warmly, "I shall in all ways trust you. I know and believe you have a very noble heart, and you are Jack's friend, and you were hers. You shall do what you like."

The Professor cleared his throat a couple of times, as though about to speak, and finally said, "May I ask you something now?"

"Certainly."

"You know that Mrs. Westenra left you all her property?"

"No, poor dear. I never thought of it."

"And as it is all yours, you have a right to deal with it as you will.

I want you to give me permission to read all Miss Lucy's papers and letters. Believe me, it is no idle curiosity. I have a motive of which, be sure, she would have approved. I have them all here. I took them before we knew that all was yours, so that no strange hand might touch them—no strange eye look through words into her soul. I shall keep them, if I may. Even you may not see them yet, but I shall keep them safe. No word shall be lost, and in the good time I shall give them back to you. It is a hard thing that I ask, but you will do it, will you not, for Lucy's sake?"

Arthur spoke out heartily, like his old self, "Dr. Van Helsing, you may do what you will. I feel that in saying this I am doing what my dear one would have approved. I shall not trouble you with questions till the time comes."

The old Professor stood up as he said solemnly, "And you are right. There will be pain for us all, but it will not be all pain, nor will this pain be the last. We and you too—you most of all, dear boy—will have to pass through the bitter water before we reach the sweet. But we must be brave of heart and unselfish, and do our duty, and all will be well!"

I slept on a sofa in Arthur's room that night. Van Helsing did not go to bed at all. He went to and fro, as if patroling the house, and was never out of sight of the room where Lucy lay in her coffin, strewn with the wild garlic flowers, which sent through the odour of lily and rose, a heavy, overpowering smell into the night.

Mina Harker's Journal

22 September.

In the train to Exeter. Jonathan sleeping. It seems only yesterday that the last entry was made, and yet how much between then, in Whitby and all the world before me, Jonathan away and no news of him, and now, married to Jonathan, Jonathan a solicitor, a partner, rich, master of his business, Mr. Hawkins dead and buried, and Jonathan with another attack that may harm him. Someday he may ask me about it. Down it all goes. I am rusty in my shorthand—see what unexpected prosperity does for us, so it may be as well to freshen it up again with an exercise anyhow.

The service was very simple and very solemn. There were only ourselves and the servants there, one or two old friends of his from Exeter, his London agent, and a gentleman representing Sir John

Paxton, the President of the Incorporated Law Society. Jonathan and I stood hand in hand, and we felt that our best and dearest friend was gone from us.

We came back to town quietly, taking a bus to Hyde Park Corner. Jonathan thought it would interest me to go into the Row for a while, so we sat down. But there were very few people there, and it was sad-looking and desolate to see so many empty chairs. It made us think of the empty chair at home. So we got up and walked down Piccadilly. Jonathan was holding me by the arm, the way he used to in the old days before I went to school. I felt it very improper, for you can't go on for some years teaching etiquette and decorum to other girls without the pedantry of it biting into yourself a bit. But it was Jonathan, and he was my husband, and we didn't know anybody who saw us—and we didn't care if they did—so on we walked. I was looking at a very beautiful girl, in a big cart-wheel hat, sitting in a victoria outside Guiliano's, when I felt Jonathan clutch my arm so tight that he hurt me, and he said under his breath, "My God!" I am always anxious about Jonathan, for I fear that some nervous fit may upset him again. So I turned to him quickly, and asked him what it was that disturbed him.

He was very pale, and his eyes seemed bulging out as, half in terror and half in amazement, he gazed at a tall, thin man, with a beaky nose and black moustache and pointed beard, who was also observing the pretty girl. He was looking at her so hard that he did not see either of us, and so I had a good view of him. His face was not a good face. It was hard, and cruel, and sensual, and big white teeth, that looked all the whiter because his lips were so red, were pointed like an animal's. Jonathan kept staring at him, till I was afraid he would notice. I feared he might take it ill, he looked so fierce and nasty. I asked Jonathan why he was disturbed, and he answered, evidently thinking that I knew as much about it as he did, "Do you see who it is?"

"No, dear," I said. "I don't know him; who is it?" His answer seemed to shock and thrill me, for it was said as if he did not know that it was me, Mina, to whom he was speaking.

"It is the man himself!"

The poor dear was evidently terrified at something, very greatly terrified. I do believe that if he had not had me to lean on and to support him he would have sunk down. He kept staring. A man came out of the shop with a small parcel, and gave it to the lady, who then drove off.

The dark man kept his eyes fixed on her, and when the carriage moved up Piccadilly he followed in the same direction, and hailed a hansom.

Jonathan kept looking after him, and said, as if to himself, "I believe it is the Count, but he has grown young. My God, if this be so! Oh, my God! My God! If only I knew! If only I knew!" He was distressing himself so much that I feared to keep his mind on the subject by asking him any questions, so I remained silent. I drew away quietly, and he, holding my arm, came easily. We walked a little further, and then went in and sat for a while in the Green Park. It was a hot day for autumn, and there was a comfortable seat in a shady place. After a few minutes' staring at nothing, Jonathan's eyes closed, and he went quickly into a sleep, with his head on my shoulder. I thought it was the best thing for him, so did not disturb him.

In about twenty minutes he woke up, and said to me quite cheerfully, "Why, Mina, have I been asleep! Oh, do forgive me for being so rude. Come, and we'll have a cup of tea somewhere." He had evidently forgotten all about the dark stranger, as in his illness he had forgotten all that this episode had reminded him of. I don't like this lapsing into forgetfulness. It may make or continue some injury to the brain. I must not ask him, for fear I shall do more harm than good, but I must somehow learn the facts of his journey abroad. The time is come, I fear, when I must open the parcel, and know what is written. Oh, Jonathan, you will, I know, forgive me if I do wrong, but it is for your own dear sake.

Later.

A sad homecoming in every way, the house empty of the dear soul who was so good to us. Jonathan still pale and dizzy under a slight relapse of his malady, and now a telegram from Van Helsing, whoever he may be.

"You will be grieved to hear that Mrs. Westenra died five days ago, and that Lucy died the day before yesterday. They were both buried today."

Oh, what a wealth of sorrow in a few words! Poor Mrs. Westenra! Poor Lucy! Gone, gone, never to return to us! And poor, poor Arthur, to have lost such a sweetness out of his life! God help us all to bear our troubles.

Dr. Seward's Diary, Continued

22 September.

It is all over. Arthur has gone back to Ring, and has taken Quincey Morris with him. What a fine fellow is Quincey! I believe in my heart of hearts that he suffered as much about Lucy's death as any of us, but he bore himself through it like a moral Viking. If America can go on breeding men like that, she will be a power in the world indeed. Van Helsing is lying down, having a rest preparatory to his journey. He goes to Amsterdam tonight, but says he returns tomorrow night, that he only wants to make some arrangements which can only be made personally. He is to stop with me then, if he can. He says he has work to do in London which may take him some time. Poor old fellow! I fear that the strain of the past week has broken down even his iron strength. All the time of the burial he was, I could see, putting some terrible restraint on himself. When it was all over, we were standing beside Arthur, who, poor fellow, was speaking of his part in the operation where his blood had been transfused to his Lucy's veins. I could see Van Helsing's face grow white and purple by turns. Arthur was saying that he felt since then as if they two had been really married, and that she was his wife in the sight of God. None of us said a word of the other operations, and none of us ever shall. Arthur and Quincey went away together to the station, and Van Helsing and I came on here. The moment we were alone in the carriage he gave way to a regular fit of hysterics. He has denied to me since that it was hysterics, and insisted that it was only his sense of humor asserting itself under very terrible conditions. He laughed till he cried, and I had to draw down the blinds lest anyone should see us and misjudge. And then he cried, till he laughed again, and laughed and cried together, just as a woman does. I tried to be stern with him, as one is to a woman under the circumstances, but it had no effect. Men and women are so different in manifestations of nervous strength or weakness! Then when his face grew grave and stern again I asked him why his mirth, and why at such a time. His reply was in a way characteristic of him, for it was logical and forceful and mysterious.

He said, "Ah, you don't comprehend, friend John. Do not think that I am not sad, though I laugh. See, I have cried even when the laugh did choke me. But no more think that I am all sorry when I cry, for the laugh he come just the same. Keep it always with you that laughter who knock at your door and say, 'May I come in?' is not true laughter. No! He is a king, and he come when and how he like. He ask no person, he choose no time of suitability. He say, 'I am here.' Behold, in example I grieve my heart out for that so sweet young girl. I give my blood for her, though I am old and worn. I give my time, my skill, my sleep. I let my other sufferers want that she may have all. And yet I can laugh at her very grave, laugh when the clay from the spade of the sexton drop upon her coffin and say 'Thud, thud!' to my heart, till it send back the blood from my cheek. My heart bleed for that poor boy, that dear boy, so of the age of mine own boy had I been so blessed that he live, and with his hair and eyes the same. "There, you know now why I love him so. And yet when he say things that touch my husband-heart to the quick, and make my father-heart yearn to him as to no other man—not even you, friend John, for we are more level in experiences than father and son—yet even at such a moment King Laugh he come to me and shout and bellow in my ear, 'Here I am! Here I am!' till the blood come dance back and bring some of the sunshine that he carry with him to my cheek. Oh, friend John, it is a strange world, a sad world, a world full of miseries, and woes, and troubles. And yet when King Laugh come, he make them all dance to the tune he play. Bleeding hearts, and dry bones of the churchyard, and tears that burn as they fall, all dance together to the music that he make with that smileless mouth of him. And believe me, friend John, that he is good to come, and kind. Ah, we men and women are like ropes drawn tight with strain that pull us different ways. Then tears come, and like the rain on the ropes, they brace us up, until perhaps the strain become too great, and we break. But King Laugh he come like the sunshine, and he ease off the strain again, and we bear to go on with our labor, what it may be."

I did not like to wound him by pretending not to see his idea, but as I did not yet understand the cause of his laughter, I asked him.

As he answered me his face grew stern, and he said in quite a different tone, "Oh, it was the grim irony of it all, this so lovely lady garlanded with flowers, that looked so fair as life, till one by one we wondered if she were truly dead, she laid in that so fine marble house in that lonely churchyard, where rest so many of her kin, laid there with the mother who loved her, and whom she loved, and that sacred bell going 'Toll! Toll! Toll!' so sad and slow, and those holy men, with the white garments of the angel, pretending to read books, and yet all the time their eyes never on the page, and all of us with the bowed head. And all for what? She is dead, so! Is it not?"

"Well, for the life of me, Professor," I said, "I can't see anything to laugh at in all that. Why, your expression makes it a harder puzzle than before. But even if the burial service was comic, what about poor Art and his trouble? Why his heart was simply breaking."

"Just so. Said he not that the transfusion of his blood to her veins had made her truly his bride?"

"Yes, and it was a sweet and comforting idea for him."

"Quite so. But there was a difficulty, friend John. If so that, then what about the others? Ho, ho! Then this so sweet maid is a polyandrist, and me, with my poor wife dead to me, but alive by Church's law, though no wits, all gone—even I, who am faithful husband to this now-no-wife, am bigamist."

"I don't see where the joke comes in there either!" I said, and I did not feel particularly pleased with him for saying such things.

He laid his hand on my arm, and said, "Friend John, forgive me if I pain. I showed not my feeling to others when it would wound, but only to you, my old friend, whom I can trust. If you could have looked into my heart then when I want to laugh, if you could have done so when the laugh arrived, if you could do so now, when King Laugh have pack up his crown, and all that is to him—for he go far, far away from me, and for a long, long time—maybe you would perhaps pity me the most of all."

I was touched by the tenderness of his tone, and asked why.

"Because I know!"

And now we are all scattered, and for many a long day loneliness will sit over our roofs with brooding wings. Lucy lies in the tomb of her kin, a lordly death house in a lonely churchyard, away from teeming London, where the air is fresh, and the sun rises over Hampstead Hill, and where wild flowers grow of their own accord.

So I can finish this diary, and God only knows if I shall ever begin another. If I do, or if I even open this again, it will be to deal with different people and different themes, for here at the end, where the romance of my life is told, ere I go back to take up the thread of my life-work, I say sadly and without hope,

"*Finis.*"

The *Westminster Gazette*, 25 September

A Hampstead Mystery

The neighborhood of Hampstead is just at present exercised with a series of events which seem to run on lines parallel to those of what was known to the writers of headlines as "The Kensington Horror," or "The Stabbing Woman," or "The Woman in Black." During the past two or three days several cases have occurred of young children straying from home or neglecting to return from their playing on the Heath. In all these cases the children were too young to give any properly intelligible account of themselves, but the consensus of their excuses is that they had been with a "bloofer lady." It has always been late in the evening when they have been missed, and on two occasions the children have not been found until early in the following morning. It is generally supposed in the neighborhood that, as the first child missed gave as his reason for being away that a "bloofer lady" had asked him to come for a walk, the others had picked up the phrase and used it as occasion served. This is the more natural as the favourite game of the little ones at present is luring each other away by wiles. A correspondent writes us that to see some of the tiny tots pretending to be the "bloofer lady" is supremely funny. Some of our caricaturists might, he says, take a lesson in the irony of grotesque by comparing the reality and the picture. It is only in accordance with general principles of human nature that the "bloofer lady" should be the popular role at these *al fresco* performances. Our correspondent naively says that even Ellen Terry could not be so winningly attractive as some of these grubby-faced little children pretend—and even imagine themselves—to be.

There is, however, possibly a serious side to the question, for some of the children, indeed all who have been missed at night, have been slightly torn or wounded in the throat. The wounds seem such as might be made by a rat or a small dog, and although of not much importance individually, would tend to show that whatever animal inflicts them has a system or method of its own. The police of the division have been instructed to keep a sharp lookout for straying children, especially when very young, in and around Hampstead Heath, and for any stray dog which may be about.

Westminster Gazette, 25 September, *Extra Special*

THE HAMPSTEAD HORROR
Another Child Injured
"The Bloofer Lady"

We have just received intelligence that another child, missed last night, was only discovered late in the morning under a furze bush at the Shooter's Hill side of Hampstead Heath, which is, perhaps, less frequented than the other parts. It has the same tiny wound in the throat as has been noticed in other cases. It was terribly weak, and looked quite emaciated. It too, when partially restored, had the common story to tell of being lured away by the "bloofer lady."

CHAPTER XIV

Mina Harker's Journal

23 September.

Jonathan is better after a bad night. I am so glad that he has plenty of work to do, for that keeps his mind off the terrible things, and oh, I am rejoiced that he is not now weighed down with the responsibility of his new position. I knew he would be true to himself, and now how proud I am to see my Jonathan rising to the height of his advancement and keeping pace in all ways with the duties that come upon him. He will be away all day till late, for he said he could not lunch at home. My household work is done, so I shall take his foreign journal, and lock myself up in my room and read it.

24 September.

I hadn't the heart to write last night, that terrible record of Jonathan's upset me so. Poor dear! How he must have suffered, whether it be true or only imagination. I wonder if there is any truth in it at all. Did he get his brain fever, and then write all those terrible things, or had he some cause for it all? I suppose I shall never know, for I dare not open the subject to him. And yet that man we saw yesterday! He seemed quite certain of him, poor fellow! I suppose it was the funeral upset him and sent his mind back on some train of thought.

He believes it all himself. I remember how on our wedding day he said "Unless some solemn duty come upon me to go back to the bitter hours, asleep or awake, mad or sane . . ." There seems to be through it all some thread of continuity. That fearful Count was coming to London. If it should be, and he came to London, with its teeming millions . . . There may be a solemn duty, and if it come we must not shrink from it. I shall be prepared. I shall get my typewriter this very hour and begin transcribing. Then we shall be ready for other eyes if required. And if it be wanted, then, perhaps, if I am ready, poor Jonathan may not be upset, for I can speak for him and never let him be troubled or worried with it at all. If ever Jonathan quite gets over the nervousness he may want to tell me of it all, and I can ask him questions and find out things, and see how I may comfort him.

Letter, Van Helsing to Mrs. Harker

24 September.
(Confidence)

Dear Madam,

I pray you to pardon my writing, in that I am so far friend as that I sent to you sad news of Miss Lucy Westenra's death. By the kindness of Lord Godalming, I am empowered to read her letters and papers, for I am deeply concerned about certain matters vitally important. In them I find some letters from you, which show how great friends you were and how you love her. Oh, Madam Mina, by that love, I implore you, help me. It is for others' good that I ask, to redress great wrong, and to lift much and terrible troubles, that may be more great than you can know. May it be that I see you? You can trust me. I am friend of Dr. John Seward and of Lord Godalming (that was Arthur of Miss Lucy). I must keep it private for the present from all. I should come to Exeter to see you at once if you tell me I am privilege to come, and where and when. I implore your pardon, Madam. I have read your letters to poor Lucy, and know how good you are and how your husband suffer. So I pray you, if it may be, enlighten him not, least it may harm. Again your pardon, and forgive me.

Van Helsing.

Telegram, Mrs. Harker to Van Helsing

25 September.

Come today by quarter past ten train if you can catch it. Can see you any time you call.

Wilhelmina Harker.

Mina Harker's Journal

25 September.

I cannot help feeling terribly excited as the time draws near for the visit of Dr. Van Helsing, for somehow I expect that it will throw some light upon Jonathan's sad experience, and as he attended poor dear Lucy in her last illness, he can tell me all about her. That is the reason of his coming. It is concerning Lucy and her sleep-walking, and not about Jonathan. Then I shall never know the real truth now! How silly I am. That awful journal gets hold of my imagination and tinges everything with something of its own colour. Of course it is about Lucy. That habit came back to the poor dear, and that awful night on the cliff must have made her ill. I had almost forgotten in my own affairs how ill she was afterwards. She must have told him of her sleep-walking adventure on the cliff, and that I knew all about it, and now he wants me to tell him what I know, so that he may understand. I hope I did right in not saying anything of it to Mrs. Westenra. I should never forgive myself if any act of mine, were it even a negative one, brought harm on poor dear Lucy. I hope too, Dr. Van Helsing will not blame me. I have had so much trouble and anxiety of late that I feel I cannot bear more just at present.

I suppose a cry does us all good at times—clears the air as other rain does. Perhaps it was reading the journal yesterday that upset me, and then Jonathan went away this morning to stay away from me a whole day and night, the first time we have been parted since our marriage. I do hope the dear fellow will take care of himself, and that nothing will occur to upset him. It is two o'clock, and the doctor will be here soon now. I shall say nothing of Jonathan's journal unless he asks me. I am so glad I have typewritten out my own journal, so that, in case he asks about Lucy, I can hand it to him. It will save much questioning.

Later.

He has come and gone. Oh, what a strange meeting, and how it all makes my head whirl round. I feel like one in a dream. Can it be all possible, or even a part of it? If I had not read Jonathan's journal first, I should never have accepted even a possibility. Poor, poor, dear Jonathan! How he must have suffered. Please the good God, all this may not upset him again. I shall try to save him from it. But it may be even a consolation and a help to him—terrible though it be and awful in its consequences—to know for certain that his eyes and ears and brain did not deceive him, and that it is all true. It may be that it is the doubt which haunts him, that when the doubt is removed, no matter which—waking or dreaming—may prove the truth, he will be more satisfied and better able to bear the shock. Dr. Van Helsing must be a good man as well as a clever one if he is Arthur's friend and Dr. Seward's, and if they brought him all the way from Holland to look after Lucy. I feel from having seen him that he is good and kind and of a noble nature. When he comes tomorrow I shall ask him about Jonathan. And then, please God, all this sorrow and anxiety may lead to a good end. I used to think I would like to practice interviewing. Jonathan's friend on the *Exeter News* told him that memory is everything in such work, that you must be able to put down exactly almost every word spoken, even if you had to refine some of it afterwards. Here was a rare interview. I shall try to record it *verbatim*.

It was half-past two o'clock when the knock came. I took my courage *a deux mains* and waited. In a few minutes Mary opened the door and announced, "Dr. Van Helsing."

I rose and bowed, and he came towards me, a man of medium weight, strongly built, with his shoulders set back over a broad, deep chest and a neck well balanced on the trunk as the head is on the neck. The poise of the head strikes me at once as indicative of thought and power. The head is noble, well-sized, broad, and large behind the ears. The face, clean-shaven, shows a hard, square chin, a large resolute, mobile mouth, a good-sized nose, rather straight, but with quick, sensitive nostrils, that seem to broaden as the big bushy brows come down and the mouth tightens. The forehead is broad and fine, rising at first almost straight and then sloping back above two bumps or ridges wide apart, such a forehead that the reddish hair cannot possibly tumble over it, but falls naturally back and to the sides. Big, dark blue eyes are set widely apart, and are quick and tender or stern with the man's moods.

He said to me, "Mrs. Harker, is it not?" I bowed assent.

"That was Miss Mina Murray?" Again I assented.

"It is Mina Murray that I came to see that was friend of that poor dear child Lucy Westenra. Madam Mina, it is on account of the dead that I come."

"Sir," I said, "you could have no better claim on me than that you were a friend and helper of Lucy Westenra." And I held out my hand. He took it and said tenderly,

"Oh, Madam Mina, I know that the friend of that poor little girl must be good, but I had yet to learn—" He finished his speech with a courtly bow. I asked him what it was that he wanted to see me about, so he at once began.

"I have read your letters to Miss Lucy. Forgive me, but I had to begin to inquire somewhere, and there was none to ask. I know that you were with her at Whitby. She sometimes kept a diary—you need not look surprised, Madam Mina. It was begun after you had left, and was an imitation of you—and in that diary she traces by inference certain things to a sleep-walking in which she puts down that you saved her. In great perplexity then I come to you, and ask you out of your so much kindness to tell me all of it that you can remember."

"I can tell you, I think, Dr. Van Helsing, all about it."

"Ah, then you have good memory for facts, for details? It is not always so with young ladies."

"No, doctor, but I wrote it all down at the time. I can show it to you if you like."

"Oh, Madam Mina, I well be grateful. You will do me much favour."

I could not resist the temptation of mystifying him a bit, I suppose it is some taste of the original apple that remains still in our mouths, so I handed him the shorthand diary. He took it with a grateful bow, and said, "May I read it?"

"If you wish," I answered as demurely as I could. He opened it, and for an instant his face fell. Then he stood up and bowed.

"Oh, you so clever woman!" he said. "I knew long that Mr. Jonathan was a man of much thankfulness, but see, his wife have all the good things. And will you not so much honour me and so help me as to read it for me? Alas! I know not the shorthand."

By this time my little joke was over, and I was almost ashamed. So I took the typewritten copy from my work basket and handed it to him.

"Forgive me," I said. "I could not help it, but I had been thinking that it was of dear Lucy that you wished to ask, and so that you might not have time to wait—not on my account, but because I know your time must be precious—I have written it out on the typewriter for you."

He took it and his eyes glistened. "You are so good," he said. "And may I read it now? I may want to ask you some things when I have read."

"By all means," I said, "read it over whilst I order lunch, and then you can ask me questions whilst we eat."

He bowed and settled himself in a chair with his back to the light, and became so absorbed in the papers, whilst I went to see after lunch chiefly in order that he might not be disturbed. When I came back, I found him walking hurriedly up and down the room, his face all ablaze with excitement. He rushed up to me and took me by both hands.

"Oh, Madam Mina," he said, "how can I say what I owe to you? This paper is as sunshine. It opens the gate to me. I am dazed, I am dazzled, with so much light, and yet clouds roll in behind the light every time. But that you do not, cannot comprehend. Oh, but I am grateful to you, you so clever woman. Madame," he said this very solemnly, "if ever Abraham Van Helsing can do anything for you or yours, I trust you will let me know. It will be pleasure and delight if I may serve you as a friend, as a friend, but all I have ever learned, all I can ever do, shall be for you and those you love. There are darknesses in life, and there are lights. You are one of the lights. You will have a happy life and a good life, and your husband will be blessed in you."

"But, doctor, you praise me too much—and you do not know me."

"Not know you—I, who am old, and who have studied all my life men and women, I who have made my specialty the brain and all that belongs to him and all that follow from him! And I have read your diary that you have so goodly written for me, and which breathes out truth in every line. I, who have read your so sweet letter to poor Lucy of your marriage and your trust, not know you! Oh, Madam Mina, good women tell all their lives, and by day and by hour and by minute, such things that angels can read. And we men who wish to know have in us something of angels' eyes. Your husband is noble nature, and you are noble too, for you trust, and trust cannot be where there is mean nature. And your husband, tell me of him. Is he quite well? Is all that fever gone, and is he strong and hearty?"

I saw here an opening to ask him about Jonathan, so I said, "He was almost recovered, but he has been greatly upset by Mr. Hawkins's death."

He interrupted, "Oh, yes. I know. I know. I have read your last two letters."

I went on, "I suppose this upset him, for when we were in town on Thursday last he had a sort of shock."

"A shock, and after brain fever so soon! That is not good. What kind of shock was it?"

"He thought he saw someone who recalled something terrible, something which led to his brain fever." And here the whole thing seemed to overwhelm me in a rush. The pity for Jonathan, the horror which he experienced, the whole fearful mystery of his diary, and the fear that has been brooding over me ever since, all came in a tumult. I suppose I was hysterical, for I threw myself on my knees and held up my hands to him, and implored him to make my husband well again. He took my hands and raised me up, and made me sit on the sofa, and sat by me.

He held my hand in his, and said to me with, oh, such infinite sweetness, "My life is a barren and lonely one, and so full of work that I have not had much time for friendships, but since I have been summoned to here by my friend John Seward I have known so many good people and seen such nobility that I feel more than ever, and it has grown with my advancing years, the loneliness of my life. Believe me, then, that I come here full of respect for you, and you have given me hope—hope, not in what I am seeking of, but that there are good women still left to make life happy, good women, whose lives and whose truths may make good lesson for the children that are to be. I am glad, glad, that I may here be of some use to you. For if your husband suffer, he suffer within the range of my study and experience. I promise you that I will gladly do all for him that I can, all to make his life strong and manly, and your life a happy one. Now you must eat. You are overwrought and perhaps over-anxious. Husband Jonathan would not like to see you so pale, and what he like not where he love, is not to his good. Therefore for his sake you must eat and smile. You have told me about Lucy, and so now we shall not speak of it, lest it distress. I shall stay in Exeter tonight, for I want to think much over what you have told me, and when I have thought I will ask you questions, if I may. And then too, you will tell me of husband Jonathan's trouble so far as you can, but not yet. You must eat now, afterwards you shall tell me all."

After lunch, when we went back to the drawing room, he said to me, "And now tell me all about him."

When it came to speaking to this great learned man, I began to fear that he would think me a weak fool, and Jonathan a madman, that journal is all so strange, and I hesitated to go on. But he was so sweet and kind, and he had promised to help, and I trusted him, so I said, "Dr. Van Helsing, what I have to tell you is so queer that you must not laugh at me or at my husband. I have been since yesterday in a sort of fever of doubt. You must be kind to me, and not think me foolish that I have even half believed some very strange things."

He reassured me by his manner as well as his words when he said, "Oh, my dear, if you only know how strange is the matter regarding which I am here, it is you who would laugh. I have learned not to think little of anyone's belief, no matter how strange it may be. I have tried to keep an open mind, and it is not the ordinary things of life that could close it, but the strange things, the extraordinary things, the things that make one doubt if they be mad or sane."

"Thank you, thank you, a thousand times! You have taken a weight off my mind. If you will let me, I shall give you a paper to read. It is long, but I have typewritten it out. It will tell you my trouble and Jonathan's. It is the copy of his journal when abroad, and all that happened. I dare not say anything of it. You will read for yourself and judge. And then when I see you, perhaps, you will be very kind and tell me what you think."

"I promise," he said as I gave him the papers. "I shall in the morning, as soon as I can, come to see you and your husband, if I may."

"Jonathan will be here at half-past eleven, and you must come to lunch with us and see him then. You could catch the quick 3:34 train, which will leave you at Paddington before eight." He was surprised at my knowledge of the trains offhand, but he does not know that I have made up all the trains to and from Exeter, so that I may help Jonathan in case he is in a hurry.

So he took the papers with him and went away, and I sit here thinking—thinking I don't know what.

Letter (by Hand), Van Helsing to Mrs. Harker

25 September, 6 p.m.

Dear Madam Mina,

I have read your husband's so wonderful diary. You may sleep without doubt. Strange and terrible as it is, it is true! I will pledge my life on it. It may be worse for others, but for him and you there is no dread. He is a noble fellow, and let me tell you from experience of men, that one who would do as he did in going down that wall and to that room—aye, and going a second time—is not one to be injured in permanence by a shock. His brain and his heart are all right, this I swear, before I have even seen him, so be at rest. I shall have much to ask him of other things. I am blessed that today I come to see you, for

I have learn all at once so much that again I am dazzled—dazzled more than ever, and I must think.

Yours the most faithful,
ABRAHAM VAN HELSING.

LETTER, MRS. HARKER TO VAN HELSING

25 September, 6:30 p.m.

My dear Dr. Van Helsing,

A thousand thanks for your kind letter, which has taken a great weight off my mind. And yet, if it be true, what terrible things there are in the world, and what an awful thing if that man, that monster, be really in London! I fear to think. I have this moment, whilst writing, had a wire from Jonathan, saying that he leaves by the 6:25 tonight from Launceston and will be here at 10:18, so that I shall have no fear tonight. Will you, therefore, instead of lunching with us, please come to breakfast at eight o'clock, if this be not too early for you? You can get away, if you are in a hurry, by the 10:30 train, which will bring you to Paddington by 2:35. Do not answer this, as I shall take it that, if I do not hear, you will come to breakfast.

Believe me,
Your faithful and grateful friend,
MINA HARKER.

JONATHAN HARKER'S JOURNAL

26 September.

I thought never to write in this diary again, but the time has come. When I got home last night Mina had supper ready, and when we had supped she told me of Van Helsing's visit, and of her having given him the two diaries copied out, and of how anxious she has been about me. She showed me in the doctor's letter that all I wrote down was true. It seems to have made a new man of me. It was the doubt as to the reality of the whole thing that knocked me over. I felt impotent, and in the dark, and distrustful. But, now that I *know*, I am not afraid, even of the Count. He has succeeded after all, then, in his design in getting to London, and it was he I saw. He has got younger, and how? Van Helsing is the man to unmask him and hunt him out, if he is anything like what Mina says. We sat late, and talked it over. Mina is dressing, and I shall call at the hotel in a few minutes and bring him over.

He was, I think, surprised to see me. When I came into the room where he was, and introduced myself, he took me by the shoulder, and turned my face round to the light, and said, after a sharp scrutiny, "But Madam Mina told me you were ill, that you had had a shock."

It was so funny to hear my wife called "Madam Mina" by this kindly, strong-faced old man. I smiled, and said, "I was ill, I have had a shock, but you have cured me already."

"And how?"

"By your letter to Mina last night. I was in doubt, and then everything took a hue of unreality, and I did not know what to trust, even the evidence of my own senses. Not knowing what to trust, I did not know what to do, and so had only to keep on working in what had hitherto been the groove of my life. The groove ceased to avail me, and I mistrusted myself. Doctor, you don't know what it is to doubt everything, even yourself. No, you don't, you couldn't with eyebrows like yours."

He seemed pleased, and laughed as he said, "So! You are a physiognomist. I learn more here with each hour. I am with so much pleasure coming to you to breakfast, and, oh, sir, you will pardon praise from an old man, but you are blessed in your wife." I would listen to him go on praising Mina for a day, so I simply nodded and stood silent.

"She is one of God's women, fashioned by His own hand to show us men and other women that there is a heaven where we can enter, and that its light can be here on earth. So true, so sweet, so noble, so little an egoist—and that, let me tell you, is much in this age, so sceptical and selfish. And you, sir—I have read all the letters to poor Miss Lucy, and some of them speak of you, so I know you since some days from the knowing of others, but I have seen your true self since last night. You will give me your hand, will you not? And let us be friends for all our lives."

We shook hands, and he was so earnest and so kind that it made me quite choky.

"And now," he said, "may I ask you for some more help? I have a great task to do, and at the beginning it is to know. You can help me here. Can you tell me what went before your going to Transylvania? Later on I may ask more help, and of a different kind, but at first this will do."

"Look here, Sir," I said, "does what you have to do concern the Count?"

"It does," he said solemnly.

"Then I am with you heart and soul. As you go by the 10:30 train, you will not have time to read them, but I shall get the bundle of papers. You can take them with you and read them in the train."

After breakfast I saw him to the station. When we were parting he said, "Perhaps you will come to town if I send for you, and take Madam Mina too."

"We shall both come when you will," I said.

I had got him the morning papers and the London papers of the previous night, and while we were talking at the carriage window, waiting for the train to start, he was turning them over. His eyes suddenly seemed to catch something in one of them, the *Westminster Gazette*—I knew it by the colour—and he grew quite white. He read something intently, groaning to himself, "Mein Gott! Mein Gott! So soon! So soon!" I do not think he remembered me at the moment. Just then the whistle blew, and the train moved off. This recalled him to himself, and he leaned out of the window and waved his hand, calling out, "Love to Madam Mina. I shall write so soon as ever I can."

Dr. Seward's Diary

26 September.

Truly there is no such thing as finality. Not a week since I said "Finis," and yet here I am starting fresh again, or rather going on with the record. Until this afternoon I had no cause to think of what is done. Renfield had become, to all intents, as sane as he ever was. He was already well ahead with his fly business, and he had just started in the spider line also, so he had not been of any trouble to me. I had a letter from Arthur, written on Sunday, and from it I gather that he is bearing up wonderfully well. Quincey Morris is with him, and that is much of a help, for he himself is a bubbling well of good spirits. Quincey wrote me a line too, and from him I hear that Arthur is beginning to recover something of his old buoyancy, so as to them all my mind is at rest. As for myself, I was settling down to my work with the enthusiasm which I used to have for it, so that I might fairly have said that the wound which poor Lucy left on me was becoming cicatrised.

Everything is, however, now reopened, and what is to be the end God only knows. I have an idea that Van Helsing thinks he knows, too, but he will only let out enough at a time to whet curiosity. He went to Exeter yesterday, and stayed there all night. Today he came back, and almost bounded into the room at about half-past five o'clock, and thrust last night's *Westminster Gazette* into my hand.

"What do you think of that?" he asked as he stood back and folded his arms.

I looked over the paper, for I really did not know what he meant, but he took it from me and pointed out a paragraph about children being decoyed away at Hampstead. It did not convey much to me, until I reached a passage where it described small puncture wounds on their throats. An idea struck me, and I looked up.

"Well?" he said.

"It is like poor Lucy's."

"And what do you make of it?"

"Simply that there is some cause in common. Whatever it was that injured her has injured them." I did not quite understand his answer.

"That is true indirectly, but not directly."

"How do you mean, Professor?" I asked. I was a little inclined to take his seriousness lightly—for, after all, four days of rest and freedom from burning, harrowing, anxiety does help to restore one's spirits, but when I saw his face, it sobered me. Never, even in the midst of our despair about poor Lucy, had he looked more stern.

"Tell me!" I said. "I can hazard no opinion. I do not know what to think, and I have no data on which to found a conjecture."

"Do you mean to tell me, friend John, that you have no suspicion as to what poor Lucy died of, not after all the hints given, not only by events, but by me?"

"Of nervous prostration following a great loss or waste of blood."

"And how was the blood lost or wasted?" I shook my head.

He stepped over and sat down beside me, and went on, "You are a clever man, friend John. You reason well, and your wit is bold, but you are too prejudiced. You do not let your eyes see nor your ears hear, and that which is outside your daily life is not of account to you. Do you not think that there are things which you cannot understand, and yet which are, that some people see things that others cannot? But there are things old and new which must not be contemplated by men's eyes, because they know—or think they know—some things which other men have told them. Ah, it is the fault of our science that it wants to explain all, and if it explain not, then it says there is nothing to explain. But yet we see around us every day the growth of new beliefs, which think themselves new, and which are yet but the old, which pretend to be young—like the fine ladies at the opera. I suppose now you do not believe in corporeal transference. No? Nor in materialization. No? Nor in astral bodies. No? Nor in the reading of thought. No? Nor in hypnotism—"

"Yes," I said. "Charcot has proved that pretty well."

He smiled as he went on, "Then you are satisfied as to it. Yes? And of course then you understand how it act, and can follow the mind of the great Charcot—alas that he is no more!—into the very soul of the patient that he influence. No? Then, friend John, am I to take it that you simply accept fact, and are satisfied to let from premise to conclusion be a blank? No? Then tell me—for I am a student of the brain—how you accept hypnotism and reject the thought reading. Let me tell you, my friend, that there are things done today in electrical science which would have been deemed unholy by the very man who discovered electricity, who would themselves not so long before been burned as wizards. There are always mysteries in life. Why was it that Methuselah lived nine hundred years, and 'Old Parr' one hundred and sixty-nine, and yet that poor Lucy, with four men's blood in her poor veins, could not live even one day? For, had she lived one more day, we could save her. Do you know all the mystery of life and death? Do you know the altogether of comparative anatomy and can say wherefore the qualities of brutes are in some men, and not in others? Can you tell me why, when other spiders die small and soon, that one great spider lived for centuries in the tower of the old Spanish church and grew and grew, till, on descending, he could drink the oil of all the church lamps? Can you tell me why in the Pampas, ay and elsewhere, there are bats that come out at night and open the veins of cattle and horses and suck dry their veins, how in some islands of the Western seas there are bats which hang on the trees all day, and those who have seen describe as like giant nuts or pods, and that when the sailors sleep on the deck, because that it is hot, flit down on them and then—and then in the morning are found dead men, white as even Miss Lucy was?"

"Good God, Professor!" I said, starting up. "Do you mean to tell me that Lucy was bitten by such a bat, and that such a thing is here in London in the nineteenth century?"

He waved his hand for silence, and went on, "Can you tell me why the tortoise lives more long than generations of men, why the elephant goes on and on till he have sees dynasties, and why the parrot never die only of bite of cat of dog or other complaint? Can you tell me why men believe in all ages and places that there are men and women who cannot die? We all know, because science has vouched for the fact, that there have been toads shut up in rocks for thousands of years, shut in one so small hole that only hold him since the youth of the world. Can you tell me how the Indian fakir can make himself to die and have been buried, and his grave sealed and corn sowed on it, and the corn reaped and be cut and sown and reaped and cut again, and then men come and take away the unbroken seal and that there lie the Indian fakir, not dead, but that rise up and walk amongst them as before?"

Here I interrupted him. I was getting bewildered. He so crowded on my mind his list of nature's eccentricities and possible impossibilities that my imagination was getting fired. I had a dim idea that he was teaching me some lesson, as long ago he used to do in his study at Amsterdam. But he used them to tell me the thing, so that I could have the object of thought in mind all the time. But now I was without his help, yet I wanted to follow him, so I said, "Professor, let me be your pet student again. Tell me the thesis, so that I may apply your knowledge as you go on. At present I am going in my mind from point to point as a madman, and not a sane one, follows an idea. I feel like a novice lumbering through a bog in a midst, jumping from one tussock to another in the mere blind effort to move on without knowing where I am going."

"That is a good image," he said. "Well, I shall tell you. My thesis is this, I want you to believe."

"To believe what?"

"To believe in things that you cannot. Let me illustrate. I heard once of an American who so defined faith, 'that faculty which enables us to believe things which we know to be untrue.' For one, I follow that man. He meant that we shall have an open mind, and not let a little bit of truth check the rush of the big truth, like a small rock does a railway truck. We get the small truth first. Good! We keep him, and we value him, but all the same we must not let him think himself all the truth in the universe."

"Then you want me not to let some previous conviction inure the receptivity of my mind with regard to some strange matter. Do I read your lesson aright?"

"Ah, you are my favourite pupil still. It is worth to teach you. Now that you are willing to understand, you have taken the first step to understand. You think then that those so small holes in the children's throats were made by the same that made the holes in Miss Lucy?"

"I suppose so."

He stood up and said solemnly, "Then you are wrong. Oh, would it were so! But alas! No. It is worse, far, far worse."

"In God's name, Professor Van Helsing, what do you mean?" I cried.

He threw himself with a despairing gesture into a chair, and placed his elbows on the table, covering his face with his hands as he spoke.

"They were made by Miss Lucy!"

CHAPTER XV

Dr. Seward's Diary, Continued

For a while sheer anger mastered me. It was as if he had during her life struck Lucy on the face. I smote the table hard and rose up as I said to him, "Dr. Van Helsing, are you mad?"

He raised his head and looked at me, and somehow the tenderness of his face calmed me at once. "Would I were!" he said. "Madness were easy to bear compared with truth like this. Oh, my friend, why, think you, did I go so far round, why take so long to tell so simple a thing? Was it because I hate you and have hated you all my life? Was it because I wished to give you pain? Was it that I wanted, now so late, revenge for that time when you saved my life, and from a fearful death? Ah no!"

"Forgive me," said I.

He went on, "My friend, it was because I wished to be gentle in the breaking to you, for I know you have loved that so sweet lady. But even yet I do not expect you to believe. It is so hard to accept at once any abstract truth, that we may doubt such to be possible when we have always believed the 'no' of it. It is more hard still to accept so sad a concrete truth, and of such a one as Miss Lucy. Tonight I go to prove it. Dare you come with me?"

This staggered me. A man does not like to prove such a truth, Byron excepted from the category, jealousy.

"And prove the very truth he most abhorred."

He saw my hesitation, and spoke: "The logic is simple, no madman's logic this time, jumping from tussock to tussock in a misty bog. If it not be true, then proof will be relief. At worst it will not harm. If it be true! Ah, there is the dread. Yet every dread should help my cause, for in it is some need of belief. Come, I tell you what I propose. First, that we go off now and see that child in the hospital. Dr. Vincent, of the North Hospital, where the papers say the child is, is a friend of mine, and I think of yours since you were in class at Amsterdam. He will let two scientists see his case, if he will not let two friends. We shall tell him nothing, but only that we wish to learn. And then—"

"And then?"

He took a key from his pocket and held it up. "And then we spend the night, you and I, in the churchyard where Lucy lies. This is the key that lock the tomb. I had it from the coffin man to give to Arthur." My heart sank within me, for I felt that there was some fearful ordeal before us. I could do nothing, however, so I plucked up what heart I could and said that we had better hasten, as the afternoon was passing.

We found the child awake. It had had a sleep and taken some food, and altogether was going on well. Dr. Vincent took the bandage from its throat, and showed us the punctures. There was no mistaking the similarity to those which had been on Lucy's throat. They were smaller, and the edges looked fresher, that was all. We asked Vincent to what he attributed them, and he replied that it must have been a bite of some animal, perhaps a rat, but for his own part, he was inclined to think it was one of the bats which are so numerous on the northern heights of London. "Out of so many harmless ones," he said, "there may be some wild specimen from the South of a more malignant species. Some sailor may have brought one home, and it managed to escape, or even from the Zoological Gardens a young one may have got loose, or one be bred there from a vampire. These things do occur, you, know. Only ten days ago a wolf got out, and was, I believe, traced up in this direction. For a week after, the children were playing nothing but Red Riding Hood on the Heath and in every alley in the place until this 'bloofer lady' scare came along, since then it has been quite a gala time with them. Even this poor little mite, when he woke up today, asked the nurse if he might go away. When she asked him why he wanted to go, he said he wanted to play with the 'bloofer lady.'"

"I hope," said Van Helsing, "that when you are sending the child home you will caution its parents to keep strict watch over it. These fancies to stray are most dangerous, and if the child were to remain out another night, it would probably be fatal. But in any case I suppose you will not let it away for some days?"

"Certainly not, not for a week at least, longer if the wound is not healed."

Our visit to the hospital took more time than we had reckoned on, and the sun had dipped before we came out. When Van Helsing saw how dark it was, he said, "There is not hurry. It is more late than I thought. Come, let us seek somewhere that we may eat, and then we shall go on our way."

We dined at Jack Straw's Castle along with a little crowd of bicyclists and others who were genially noisy. About ten o'clock we started from the inn. It was then very dark, and the scattered lamps made the darkness greater when we were once outside their individual radius. The Professor had evidently noted the road we were to go, for he went on unhesitatingly, but, as for me, I was in quite a mixup as to locality. As we went further, we met fewer and fewer people, till at last we were somewhat surprised when we met even the patrol of horse police going their usual suburban round. At last we reached the wall of the churchyard, which we climbed over. With some little difficulty—for it was very dark—and the whole place seemed so strange to us—we found the Westenra tomb. The Professor took the key, opened the creaky door, and standing back, politely, but quite unconsciously, motioned me to precede him. There was a delicious irony in the offer, in the courtliness of giving preference on such a ghastly occasion. My companion followed me quickly, and cautiously drew the door to, after carefully ascertaining that the lock was a falling, and not a spring one. In the latter case we should have been in a bad plight. Then he fumbled in his bag, and taking out a matchbox and a piece of candle, proceeded to make a light. The tomb in the daytime, and when wreathed with fresh flowers, had looked grim and gruesome enough, but now, some days afterwards, when the flowers hung lank and dead, their whites turning to rust and their greens to browns, when the spider and the beetle had resumed their accustomed dominance, when the time-discoloured stone, and dust-encrusted mortar, and rusty, dank iron, and tarnished brass, and clouded silver-plating gave back the feeble glimmer of a candle, the effect was more miserable and sordid than could have been imagined. It conveyed irresistibly the idea that life, animal life, was not the only thing which could pass away.

Van Helsing went about his work systematically. Holding his candle so that he could read the coffin plates, and so holding it that the sperm dropped in white patches which congealed as they touched the metal, he made assurance of Lucy's coffin. Another search in his bag, and he took out a turnscrew.

"What are you going to do?" I asked.

"To open the coffin. You shall yet be convinced." Straightway he began taking out the screws, and finally lifted off the lid, showing the casing of lead beneath. The sight was almost too much for me. It seemed to be as much an affront to the dead as it would have been to have stripped off her clothing in her sleep whilst living. I actually took hold of his hand to stop him.

He only said, "You shall see," and again fumbling in his bag took out a tiny fret saw. Striking the turnscrew through the lead with a swift downward stab, which made me wince, he made a small hole, which was, however, big enough to admit the point of the saw. I had expected a rush of gas from the week-old corpse. We doctors, who have had to study our dangers, have to become accustomed to such things, and I drew back towards the door. But the Professor never stopped for a moment. He sawed down a couple of feet along one side of the lead coffin, and then across, and down the other side. Taking the edge of the loose flange, he bent it back towards the foot of the coffin, and holding up the candle into the aperture, motioned to me to look.

I drew near and looked. The coffin was empty. It was certainly a surprise to me, and gave me a considerable shock, but Van Helsing was unmoved. He was now more sure than ever of his ground, and so emboldened to proceed in his task. "Are you satisfied now, friend John?" he asked.

I felt all the dogged argumentativeness of my nature awake within me as I answered him, "I am satisfied that Lucy's body is not in that coffin, but that only proves one thing."

"And what is that, friend John?"

"That it is not there."

"That is good logic," he said, "so far as it goes. But how do you—how can you—account for it not being there?"

"Perhaps a body-snatcher," I suggested. "Some of the undertaker's people may have stolen it." I felt that I was speaking folly, and yet it was the only real cause which I could suggest.

The Professor sighed. "Ah, well!" he said. "We must have more proof. Come with me."

He put on the coffin lid again, gathered up all his things and placed them in the bag, blew out the light, and placed the candle also in the bag. We opened the door, and went out. Behind us he closed the door and locked it. He handed me the key, saying, "Will you keep it? You had better be assured."

I laughed, it was not a very cheerful laugh, I am bound to say, as I motioned him to keep it. "A key is nothing," I said, "there are many duplicates, and anyhow it is not difficult to pick a lock of this kind." He said nothing, but put the key in his pocket. Then he told me to watch at one side of the churchyard whilst he would watch at the other. I took up my place behind a yew tree, and I saw his dark figure move until the intervening headstones and trees hid it from my sight.

It was a lonely vigil. Just after I had taken my place I heard a distant clock strike twelve, and in time came one and two. I was chilled and unnerved, and angry with the Professor for taking me on such an errand and with myself for coming. I was too cold and too sleepy to be keenly observant, and not sleepy enough to betray my trust, so altogether I had a dreary, miserable time.

Suddenly, as I turned round, I thought I saw something like a white streak, moving between two dark yew trees at the side of the churchyard farthest from the tomb. At the same time a dark mass moved from the Professor's side of the ground, and hurriedly went towards it. Then I too moved, but I had to go round headstones and railed-off tombs, and I stumbled over graves. The sky was overcast, and somewhere far off an early cock crew. A little ways off, beyond a line of scattered juniper trees, which marked the pathway to the church, a white dim figure flitted in the direction of the tomb. The tomb itself was hidden by trees, and I could not see where the figure had disappeared. I heard the rustle of actual movement where I had first seen the white figure, and coming over, found the Professor holding in his arms a tiny child. When he saw me he held it out to me, and said, "Are you satisfied now?"

"No," I said, in a way that I felt was aggressive.

"Do you not see the child?"

"Yes, it is a child, but who brought it here? And is it wounded?"

"We shall see," said the Professor, and with one impulse we took our way out of the churchyard, he carrying the sleeping child.

When we had got some little distance away, we went into a clump of trees, and struck a match, and looked at the child's throat. It was without a scratch or scar of any kind.

"Was I right?" I asked triumphantly.

"We were just in time," said the Professor thankfully.

We had now to decide what we were to do with the child, and so consulted about it. If we were to take it to a police station we should have to give some account of our movements during the night. At least, we should have had to make some statement as to how we had come to find the child. So finally we decided that we would take it to the Heath, and when we heard a policeman coming, would leave it where he could not fail to find it. We would then seek our way home as quickly as we could. All fell out well. At the edge of Hampstead Heath we heard a policeman's heavy tramp, and laying the child on the pathway, we waited and watched until he saw it as he flashed his lantern to and fro. We heard his exclamation of astonishment, and then we went away silently. By good chance we got a cab near the "Spainiards," and drove to town.

I cannot sleep, so I make this entry. But I must try to get a few hours' sleep, as Van Helsing is to call for me at noon. He insists that I go with him on another expedition.

27 September.

It was two o'clock before we found a suitable opportunity for our attempt. The funeral held at noon was all completed, and the last stragglers of the mourners had taken themselves lazily away, when, looking carefully from behind a clump of alder trees, we saw the sexton lock the gate after him. We knew that we were safe till morning did we desire it, but the Professor told me that we should not want more than an hour at most. Again I felt that horrid sense of the reality of things, in which any effort of imagination seemed out of place, and I realized distinctly the perils of the law which we were incurring in our unhallowed work. Besides, I felt it was all so useless. Outrageous as it was to open a leaden coffin, to see if a woman dead nearly a week were really dead, it now seemed the height of folly to open the tomb again, when we knew, from the evidence of our own eyesight, that the coffin was empty. I shrugged my shoulders, however, and rested silent, for Van Helsing had a way of going on his own road, no matter who remonstrated. He took the key, opened the vault, and again courteously motioned me to precede. The place was not so gruesome as last night, but oh, how unutterably mean looking when the sunshine streamed in. Van Helsing walked over to Lucy's coffin, and I followed. He bent over and again forced back the leaden flange, and a shock of surprise and dismay shot through me.

There lay Lucy, seemingly just as we had seen her the night before her funeral. She was, if possible, more radiantly beautiful than ever, and I could not believe that she was dead. The lips were red, nay redder than before, and on the cheeks was a delicate bloom.

"Is this a juggle?" I said to him.

"Are you convinced now?" said the Professor, in response, and as he spoke he put over his hand, and in a way that made me shudder, pulled back the dead lips and showed the white teeth. "See," he went on, "they are even sharper than before. With this and this," and he touched one of the canine teeth and that below it, "the little children can be bitten. Are you of belief now, friend John?"

Once more argumentative hostility woke within me. I *could* not accept such an overwhelming idea as he suggested. So, with an attempt to argue of which I was even at the moment ashamed, I said, "She may have been placed here since last night."

"Indeed? That is so, and by whom?"

"I do not know. Someone has done it."

"And yet she has been dead one week. Most peoples in that time would not look so."

I had no answer for this, so was silent. Van Helsing did not seem to notice my silence. At any rate, he showed neither chagrin nor triumph. He was looking intently at the face of the dead woman, raising the eyelids and looking at the eyes, and once more opening the lips and examining the teeth.

Then he turned to me and said, "Here, there is one thing which is different from all recorded. Here is some dual life that is not as the common. She was bitten by the vampire when she was in a trance, sleep-walking—oh, you start; you do not know that, friend John, but you shall know it later—and in trance could he best come to take more blood. In trance she dies, and in trance she is Undead, too. So it is that she differ from all other. Usually when the Undead sleep at home,"—as he spoke he made a comprehensive sweep of his arm to designate what to a vampire was "home"—"Their face show what they are, but this so sweet that was when she not Undead she go back to the nothings of the common dead. There is no malign there, see, and so it make hard that I must kill her in her sleep."

This turned my blood cold, and it began to dawn upon me that I was accepting Van Helsing's theories. But if she were really dead, what was there of terror in the idea of killing her?

He looked up at me, and evidently saw the change in my face, for he said almost joyously, "Ah, you believe now?"

I answered, "Do not press me too hard all at once. I am willing to accept. How will you do this bloody work?"

"I shall cut off her head and fill her mouth with garlic, and I shall drive a stake through her body."

It made me shudder to think of so mutilating the body of the woman whom I had loved. And yet the feeling was not so strong as I had expected. I was, in fact, beginning to shudder at the presence of this being, this Undead, as Van Helsing called it, and to loathe it. Is it possible that love is all subjective, or all objective?

I waited a considerable time for Van Helsing to begin, but he stood as if wrapped in thought. Presently he closed the catch of his bag with a snap, and said, "I have been thinking, and have made up my mind as to what is best. If I did simply follow my inclining I would do now, at this moment, what is to be done. But there are other things to follow, and things that are thousand times more difficult in that them we do not know. This is simple. She have yet no life taken, though that is of time, and to act now would be to take danger from her forever. But then we may have to want Arthur, and how shall we tell him of this? If you, who saw the wounds on Lucy's throat, and saw the wounds so similar on the child's at the hospital, if you, who saw the coffin empty last night and full today with a woman who have not change only to be more rose and more beautiful in a whole week, after she die—if you know of this and know of the white figure last night that brought the child to the churchyard, and yet of your own senses you did not believe, how then, can I expect Arthur, who know none of those things, to believe?" He doubted me when I took him from her kiss when she was dying. I know he has forgiven me because in some mistaken idea I have done things that prevent him say goodbye as he ought, and he may think that in some more mistaken idea this woman was buried alive, and that in most mistake of all we have killed her. He will then argue back that it is we, mistaken ones, that have killed her by our ideas, and so he will be much unhappy always. Yet he never can be sure, and that is the worst of all. And he will sometimes think that she he loved was buried alive, and that will paint his dreams with horrors of what she must have suffered, and again, he will think that we may be right, and that his so beloved was, after all, an Undead. No! I told him once, and since then I learn much. Now, since I know it is all true, a hundred thousand times more do I know that he must pass through the bitter waters to reach the sweet. He, poor fellow, must have one hour that will make the very face of heaven grow black to him, then we can act for good all round and send him peace. My mind is made up. Let us go. You return home for tonight to your asylum, and see that all be well. As for me, I shall spend the night here in this churchyard in my own way. Tomorrow night you will come to me to the Berkeley Hotel at ten of the clock. I shall send for Arthur to come too, and also that so fine young man of America that gave his blood. Later we shall all have work to do. I come with you so far as Piccadilly and there dine, for I must be back here before the sun set."

So we locked the tomb and came away, and got over the wall of the churchyard, which was not much of a task, and drove back to Piccadilly.

Note Left by Van Helsing in His Portmanteau, Berkeley Hotel, Directed to John Seward, MD (Not Delivered)

27 September.

Friend John,

I write this in case anything should happen. I go alone to watch in that churchyard. It pleases me that the Undead, Miss Lucy, shall not leave tonight, that so on the morrow night she may be more eager. Therefore I shall fix some things she like not—garlic and a crucifix—and so seal up the door of the tomb. She is young as Undead, and will heed. Moreover, these are only to prevent her coming out. They may not prevail on her wanting to get in, for then the Undead is desperate, and must find the line of least resistance, whatsoever it may be. I shall be at hand all the night from sunset till after sunrise, and if there be aught that may be learned I shall learn it. For Miss Lucy or from her, I have no fear, but that other to whom is there that she is Undead, he have not the power to seek her tomb and find shelter. He is cunning, as I know from Mr. Jonathan and from the way that all along he have fooled us when he played with us for Miss Lucy's life, and we lost, and in many ways the Undead are strong. He have always the strength in his hand of twenty men, even we four who gave our strength to Miss Lucy it also is all to him. Besides, he can summon his wolf and I know not what. So if it be that he came thither on this night he shall find me. But none other shall—until it be too late. But it may be that he will not attempt the place. There is no reason why he should. His hunting ground is more full of game than the churchyard where the Undead woman sleeps, and the one old man watch.

Therefore I write this in case . . . Take the papers that are with this, the diaries of Harker and the rest, and read them, and then find this great Undead, and cut off his head and burn his heart or drive a stake through it, so that the world may rest from him.

If it be so, farewell.

VAN HELSING.

DR. SEWARD'S DIARY

28 September.

It is wonderful what a good night's sleep will do for one. Yesterday I was almost willing to accept Van Helsing's monstrous ideas, but now they seem to start out lurid before me as outrages on common sense. I have no doubt that he believes it all. I wonder if his mind can have become in any way unhinged. Surely there must be some rational explanation of all these mysterious things. Is it possible that the Professor can have done it himself? He is so abnormally clever that if he went off his head he would carry out his intent with regard to some fixed idea in a wonderful way. I am loathe to think it, and indeed it would be almost as great a marvel as the other to find that Van Helsing was mad, but anyhow I shall watch him carefully. I may get some light on the mystery.

29 September, morning.

Last night, at a little before ten o'clock, Arthur and Quincey came into Van Helsing's room. He told us all what he wanted us to do, but especially addressing himself to Arthur, as if all our wills were centred in his. He began by saying that he hoped we would all come with him too, "for," he said, "there is a grave duty to be done there. You were doubtless surprised at my letter?" This query was directly addressed to Lord Godalming.

"I was. It rather upset me for a bit. There has been so much trouble around my house of late that I could do without any more. I have been curious, too, as to what you mean.

"Quincey and I talked it over, but the more we talked, the more puzzled we got, till now I can say for myself that I'm about up a tree as to any meaning about anything."

"Me too," said Quincey Morris laconically.

"Oh," said the Professor, "then you are nearer the beginning, both of you, than friend John here, who has to go a long way back before he can even get so far as to begin."

It was evident that he recognized my return to my old doubting frame of mind without my saying a word. Then, turning to the other two, he said with intense gravity, "I want your permission to do what I think good this night. It is, I know, much to ask, and when you know what it is I propose to do you will know, and only then how much. Therefore may I ask that you promise me in the dark, so that afterwards, though you may be angry with me for a time—I must not disguise from myself the possibility that such may be—you shall not blame yourselves for anything."

"That's frank anyhow," broke in Quincey. "I'll answer for the Professor. I don't quite see his drift, but I swear he's honest, and that's good enough for me."

"I thank you, Sir," said Van Helsing proudly. "I have done myself the honour of counting you one trusting friend, and such endorsement is dear to me." He held out a hand, which Quincey took.

Then Arthur spoke out, "Dr. Van Helsing, I don't quite like to 'buy a pig in a poke,' as they say in Scotland, and if it be anything in which my honour as a gentleman or my faith as a Christian is concerned, I cannot make such a promise. If you can assure me that what you intend does not violate either of these two, then I give my consent at once, though for the life of me, I cannot understand what you are driving at."

"I accept your limitation," said Van Helsing, "and all I ask of you is that if you feel it necessary to condemn any act of mine, you will first consider it well and be satisfied that it does not violate your reservations."

"Agreed!" said Arthur. "That is only fair. And now that the *pourparlers* are over, may I ask what it is we are to do?"

"I want you to come with me, and to come in secret, to the churchyard at Kingstead."

Arthur's face fell as he said in an amazed sort of way, "Where poor Lucy is buried?"

The Professor bowed.

Arthur went on, "And when there?"

"To enter the tomb!"

Arthur stood up. "Professor, are you in earnest, or is it some monstrous joke? Pardon me, I see that you are in earnest." He sat down again, but I could see that he sat firmly and proudly, as one who is on his dignity. There was silence until he asked again, "And when in the tomb?"

"To open the coffin."

"This is too much!" he said, angrily rising again. "I am willing to be patient in all things that are reasonable, but in this, this desecration of the grave—of one who—" He fairly choked with indignation.

The Professor looked pityingly at him. "If I could spare you one pang, my poor friend," he said, "God knows I would. But this night our feet must tread in thorny paths, or later, and for ever, the feet you love must walk in paths of flame!"

Arthur looked up with set white face and said, "Take care, sir, take care!"

"Would it not be well to hear what I have to say?" said Van Helsing. "And then you will at least know the limit of my purpose. Shall I go on?"

"That's fair enough," broke in Morris.

After a pause Van Helsing went on, evidently with an effort, "Miss Lucy is dead, is it not so? Yes! Then there can be no wrong to her. But if she be not dead—"

Arthur jumped to his feet, "Good God!" he cried. "What do you mean? Has there been any mistake, has she been buried alive?" He groaned in anguish that not even hope could soften.

"I did not say she was alive, my child. I did not think it. I go no further than to say that she might be Undead."

"Undead! Not alive! What do you mean? Is this all a nightmare, or what is it?"

"There are mysteries which men can only guess at, which age by age they may solve only in part. Believe me, we are now on the verge of one. But I have not done. May I cut off the head of dead Miss Lucy?"

"Heavens and earth, no!" cried Arthur in a storm of passion. "Not for the wide world will I consent to any mutilation of her dead body. Dr. Van Helsing, you try me too far. What have I done to you that you should torture me so? What did that poor, sweet girl do that you should want to cast such dishonour on her grave? Are you mad, that you speak of such things, or am I mad to listen to them? Don't dare think more of such a desecration. I shall not give my consent to anything you do. I have a duty to do in protecting her grave from outrage, and by God, I shall do it!"

Van Helsing rose up from where he had all the time been seated, and said, gravely and sternly, "My Lord Godalming, I too, have a duty to do, a duty to others, a duty to you, a duty to the dead, and by God, I shall do it! All I ask you now is that you come with me, that you look and listen, and if when later I make the same request you do not be more eager for its fulfillment even than I am, then, I shall do my duty, whatever it may seem to me. And then, to follow your Lordship's wishes I shall hold myself at your disposal to render an account to you, when and where you will." His voice broke a little, and he went on with a voice full of pity. "But I beseech you, do not go forth in anger with me. In a long life of acts which were often not pleasant to do, and which sometimes did wring my heart, I have never had so heavy a task as now. Believe me that if the time comes for you to change your mind towards me, one look from you will wipe away all this so sad hour, for I would do what a man can to save you from sorrow. Just think. For why should I give myself so much labor and so much of sorrow? I have come here from my own land to do what I can of good, at the first to please my friend John, and then to help a sweet young lady, whom too, I come to love. For her—I am ashamed to say so much, but I say it in kindness—I gave what you gave, the blood of my veins. I gave it, I who was not, like you, her lover, but only her physician and her friend. I gave her my nights and days, before death, after death, and if my death can do her good even now, when she is the dead Undead, she shall have it freely." He said this with a very grave, sweet pride, and Arthur was much affected by it.

He took the old man's hand and said in a broken voice, "Oh, it is hard to think of it, and I cannot understand, but at least I shall go with you and wait."

CHAPTER XVI

Dr. Seward's Diary, Continued

It was just a quarter before twelve o'clock when we got into the churchyard over the low wall. The night was dark with occasional gleams of moonlight between the dents of the heavy clouds that scudded across the sky. We all kept somehow close together, with Van Helsing slightly in front as he led the way. When we had come close to the tomb I looked well at Arthur, for I feared the proximity to a place laden with so sorrowful a memory would upset him, but he bore himself well. I took it that the very mystery of the proceeding was in some way a counteractant to his grief. The Professor unlocked the door, and seeing a natural hesitation amongst us for various reasons, solved the difficulty by entering first himself. The rest of us followed, and he closed the door. He then lit a dark lantern and pointed to a coffin. Arthur stepped forward hesitatingly. Van Helsing said to me, "You were with me here yesterday. Was the body of Miss Lucy in that coffin?"

"It was."

The Professor turned to the rest saying, "You hear, and yet there is no one who does not believe with me."

He took his screwdriver and again took off the lid of the coffin. Arthur looked on, very pale but silent. When the lid was removed he stepped forward. He evidently did not know that there was a leaden coffin, or at any rate, had not thought of it. When he saw the rent in the lead, the blood rushed to his face for an instant, but as quickly fell away again, so that he remained of a ghastly whiteness. He was still silent. Van Helsing forced back the leaden flange, and we all looked in and recoiled.

The coffin was empty!

For several minutes no one spoke a word. The silence was broken by Quincey Morris, "Professor, I answered for you. Your word is all I want. I wouldn't ask such a thing ordinarily, I wouldn't so dishonour you as to imply a doubt, but this is a mystery that goes beyond any honour or dishonour. Is this your doing?"

"I swear to you by all that I hold sacred that I have not removed or touched her. What happened was this. Two nights ago my friend Seward and I came here—with good purpose, believe me. I opened that coffin, which was then sealed up, and we found it as now, empty. We then waited, and saw something white come through the trees. The next day we came here in daytime and she lay there. Did she not, friend John?"

"Yes."

"That night we were just in time. One more so small child was missing, and we find it, thank God, unharmed amongst the graves. Yesterday I came here before sundown, for at sundown the Undead can move. I waited here all night till the sun rose, but I saw nothing. It was most probable that it was because I had laid over the clamps of those doors garlic, which the Undead cannot bear, and other things which they shun. Last night there was no exodus, so tonight before the sundown I took away my garlic and other things. And so it is we find this coffin empty. But bear with me. So far there is much that is strange. Wait you with me outside, unseen and unheard, and things much stranger are yet to be. So,"—here he shut the dark slide of his lantern—"now to the outside." He opened the door, and we filed out, he coming last and locking the door behind him.

Oh! But it seemed fresh and pure in the night air after the terror of that vault. How sweet it was to see the clouds race by, and the passing gleams of the moonlight between the scudding clouds crossing and passing—like the gladness and sorrow of a man's life. How sweet it was to breathe the fresh air, that had no taint of death and decay. How humanizing to see the red lighting of the sky beyond the hill, and to hear far away the muffled roar that marks the life of a great city. Each in his own way was solemn and overcome. Arthur was silent, and was, I could see, striving to grasp the purpose and the inner meaning of the mystery. I was myself tolerably patient, and half inclined again to throw aside doubt and to accept Van Helsing's conclusions. Quincey Morris was phlegmatic in the way of a man who accepts all things, and accepts them in the spirit of cool bravery, with hazard of all he has at stake. Not being able to smoke, he cut himself a good-sized plug of tobacco and began to chew. As to Van Helsing, he was employed in a definite way. First he took from his bag a mass of what looked like thin, wafer-like biscuit, which was carefully rolled up in a white napkin. Next he took out a double handful of some whitish stuff, like dough or putty. He crumbled the wafer up fine and worked it into the mass between his hands. This he then took, and rolling it into thin strips, began to lay them into the crevices between the door and its setting in the tomb. I was somewhat puzzled at this, and being close, asked him what it was that he was doing. Arthur and Quincey drew near also, as they too were curious.

He answered, "I am closing the tomb so that the Undead may not enter."

"And is that stuff you have there going to do it?"

"It is."

"What is that which you are using?" This time the question was by Arthur.

Van Helsing reverently lifted his hat as he answered. "The Host. I brought it from Amsterdam. I have an Indulgence."

It was an answer that appalled the most sceptical of us, and we felt individually that in the presence of such earnest purpose as the Professor's, a purpose which could thus use the to him most sacred of things, it was impossible to distrust. In respectful silence we took the places assigned to us close round the tomb, but hidden from the sight of anyone approaching. I pitied the others, especially Arthur. I had myself been apprenticed by my former visits to this watching horror, and yet I, who had up to an hour ago repudiated the proofs, felt my heart sink within me. Never did tombs look so ghastly white. Never did cypress, or yew, or juniper so seem the embodiment of funeral gloom. Never did tree or grass wave or rustle so ominously. Never did bough creak so mysteriously, and never did the far-away howling of dogs send such a woeful presage through the night.

There was a long spell of silence, a big, aching, void, and then from the Professor a keen "S-s-s-s!" He pointed, and far down the avenue of yews we saw a white figure advance—a dim white figure, which held something dark at its breast. The figure stopped, and at the moment a ray of moonlight fell upon the masses of driving clouds, and showed in startling prominence a dark-haired woman, dressed in the cerements of the grave. We could not see the face, for it was bent down over what we saw to be a fair-haired child. There was a pause and a sharp little cry, such as a child gives in sleep, or a dog as it lies before the fire and dreams. We were starting forward, but the Professor's warning hand, seen by us as he stood behind a yew tree, kept us back. And then as we looked the white figure moved forwards again. It was now near enough for us to see clearly, and the moonlight still held. My own heart grew cold as ice, and I could hear the gasp of Arthur, as we recognized the features of Lucy Westenra. Lucy Westenra, but yet how changed. The sweetness was turned to adamantine, heartless cruelty, and the purity to voluptuous wantonness.

Van Helsing stepped out, and obedient to his gesture, we all advanced too. The four of us ranged in a line before the door of the tomb. Van Helsing raised his lantern and drew the slide. By the concentrated light that fell on Lucy's face we could see that the lips were crimson with fresh blood, and that the stream had trickled over her chin and stained the purity of her lawn death-robe.

We shuddered with horror. I could see by the tremulous light that even Van Helsing's iron nerve had failed. Arthur was next to me, and if I had not seized his arm and held him up, he would have fallen.

When Lucy, I call the thing that was before us Lucy because it bore her shape, saw us she drew back with an angry snarl, such as a cat gives when taken unawares, then her eyes ranged over us. Lucy's eyes in form and colour, but Lucy's eyes unclean and full of hell fire, instead of the pure, gentle orbs we knew. At that moment the remnant of my love passed into hate and loathing. Had she then to be killed, I could have done it with savage delight. As she looked, her eyes blazed with unholy light, and the face became wreathed with a voluptuous smile. Oh, God, how it made me shudder to see it! With a careless motion, she flung to the ground, callous as a devil, the child that up to now she had clutched strenuously to her breast, growling over it as a dog growls over a bone. The child gave a sharp cry, and lay there moaning. There was a cold-bloodedness in the act which wrung a groan from Arthur. When she advanced to him with outstretched arms and a wanton smile he fell back and hid his face in his hands.

She still advanced, however, and with a languorous, voluptuous grace, said, "Come to me, Arthur. Leave these others and come to me. My arms are hungry for you. Come, and we can rest together. Come, my husband, come!"

There was something diabolically sweet in her tones, something of the tinkling of glass when struck, which rang through the brains even of us who heard the words addressed to another. As for Arthur, he seemed under a spell, moving his hands from his face, he opened wide his arms. She was leaping for them, when Van Helsing sprang forward and held between them his little golden crucifix. She recoiled from it, and, with a suddenly distorted face, full of rage, dashed past him as if to enter the tomb.

When within a foot or two of the door, however, she stopped, as if arrested by some irresistible force. Then she turned, and her face was shown in the clear burst of moonlight and by the lamp, which had now no quiver from Van Helsing's nerves. Never did I see such baffled malice on a face, and never, I trust, shall such ever be seen again by mortal eyes. The beautiful colour became livid, the eyes seemed to throw out sparks of hell fire, the brows were wrinkled as though the folds of flesh were the coils of Medusa's snakes, and the lovely, blood-stained mouth grew to an open square, as in the passion masks of the Greeks and Japanese. If ever a face meant death—if looks could kill—we saw it at that moment.

And so for full half a minute, which seemed an eternity, she remained between the lifted crucifix and the sacred closing of her means of entry.

Van Helsing broke the silence by asking Arthur, "Answer me, oh my friend! Am I to proceed in my work?"

Arthur threw himself on his knees, and hid his face in his hands, as he answered, "Do as you will, friend. Do as you will. There can be no horror like this ever any more." And he groaned in spirit.

Quincey and I simultaneously moved towards him, and took his arms. We could hear the click of the closing lantern as Van Helsing held it down. Coming close to the tomb, he began to remove from the chinks some of the sacred emblem which he had placed there. We all looked on with horrified amazement as we saw, when he stood back, the woman, with a corporeal body as real at that moment as our own, pass through the interstice where scarce a knife blade could have gone. We all felt a glad sense of relief when we saw the Professor calmly restoring the strings of putty to the edges of the door.

When this was done, he lifted the child and said, "Come now, my friends. We can do no more till tomorrow. There is a funeral at noon, so here we shall all come before long after that. The friends of the dead will all be gone by two, and when the sexton locks the gate we shall remain. Then there is more to do, but not like this of tonight. As for this little one, he is not much harmed, and by tomorrow night he shall be well. We shall leave him where the police will find him, as on the other night, and then to home."

Coming close to Arthur, he said, "My friend Arthur, you have had a sore trial, but after, when you look back, you will see how it was necessary. You are now in the bitter waters, my child. By this time tomorrow you will, please God, have passed them, and have drunk of the sweet waters. So do not mourn over-much. Till then I shall not ask you to forgive me."

Arthur and Quincey came home with me, and we tried to cheer each other on the way. We had left behind the child in safety, and were tired. So we all slept with more or less reality of sleep.

29 September, night.

A little before twelve o'clock we three—Arthur, Quincey Morris, and myself—called for the Professor. It was odd to notice that by common consent we had all put on black clothes. Of course, Arthur wore black, for he was in deep mourning, but the rest of us wore it by instinct. We got to the graveyard by half-past one, and strolled about, keeping out of official observation, so that when the gravediggers had completed their task and the sexton, under the belief that every one had gone, had locked the gate, we had the place all to ourselves. Van Helsing, instead of his little black bag, had with him a long leather one, something like a cricketing bag. It was manifestly of fair weight.

When we were alone and had heard the last of the footsteps die out up the road, we silently, and as if by ordered intention, followed the Professor to the tomb. He unlocked the door, and we entered, closing it behind us. Then he took from his bag the lantern, which he lit, and also two wax candles, which, when lighted, he stuck by melting their own ends, on other coffins, so that they might give light sufficient to work by. When he again lifted the lid off Lucy's coffin we all looked—Arthur trembling like an aspen—and saw that the corpse lay there in all its death beauty. But there was no love in my own heart, nothing but loathing for the foul Thing which had taken Lucy's shape without her soul. I could see even Arthur's face grow hard as he looked. Presently he said to Van Helsing, "Is this really Lucy's body, or only a demon in her shape?"

"It is her body, and yet not it. But wait a while, and you shall see her as she was, and is."

She seemed like a nightmare of Lucy as she lay there, the pointed teeth, the blood stained, voluptuous mouth—which made one shudder to see—the whole carnal and unspirited appearance, seeming like a devilish mockery of Lucy's sweet purity. Van Helsing, with his usual methodicalness, began taking the various contents from his bag and placing them ready for use. First he took out a soldering iron and some plumbing solder, and then small oil lamp, which gave out, when lit in a corner of the tomb, gas which burned at a fierce heat with a blue flame, then his operating knives, which he placed to hand, and last a round wooden stake, some two and a half or three inches thick and about three feet long. One end of it was hardened by charring in the fire, and was sharpened to a fine point. With this stake came a heavy hammer, such as in households is used in the coal cellar for breaking the lumps. To me, a doctor's preparations for work of any kind are stimulating and bracing, but the effect of these things on both Arthur and Quincey was to cause them a sort of consternation. They both, however, kept their courage, and remained silent and quiet.

When all was ready, Van Helsing said, "Before we do anything, let me tell you this. It is out of the lore and experience of the ancients and of all those who have studied the powers of the Undead. When they become such, there comes with the change the curse of immortality. They cannot die, but must go on age after age adding new victims and multiplying the evils of the world. For all that die from the preying of the Undead become themselves Undead, and prey on their kind. And so the circle goes on ever widening, like as the ripples from a stone thrown in the water. Friend Arthur, if you had met that kiss which you know of before poor Lucy die, or again, last night when you open your arms to her, you would in time, when you had died, have become *nosferatu*, as they call it in Eastern Europe, and would for all time make more of those Undeads that so have filled us with horror. The career of this so unhappy dear lady is but just begun. Those children whose blood she sucked are not as yet so much the worse, but if she lives on, Undead, more and more they lose their blood and by her power over them they come to her, and so she draw their blood with that so wicked mouth. But if she die in truth, then all cease. The tiny wounds of the throats disappear, and they go back to their play unknowing ever of what has been. But of the most blessed of all, when this now Undead be made to rest as true dead, then the soul of the poor lady whom we love shall again be free. Instead of working wickedness by night and growing more debased in the assimilating of it by day, she shall take her place with the other Angels. So that, my friend, it will be a blessed hand for her that shall strike the blow that sets her free. To this I am willing, but is there none amongst us who has a better right? Will it be no joy to think of hereafter in the silence of the night when sleep is not, 'It was my hand that sent her to the stars. It was the hand of him that loved her best, the hand that of all she would herself have chosen, had it been to her to choose?' Tell me if there be such a one amongst us?"

We all looked at Arthur. He saw too, what we all did, the infinite kindness which suggested that his should be the hand which would restore Lucy to us as a holy, and not an unholy, memory. He stepped forward and said bravely, though his hand trembled, and his face was as pale as snow, "My true friend, from the bottom of my broken heart I thank you. Tell me what I am to do, and I shall not falter!"

Van Helsing laid a hand on his shoulder, and said, "Brave lad! A moment's courage, and it is done. This stake must be driven through her. It well be a fearful ordeal—be not deceived in that—but it will be only a short time, and you will then rejoice more than your pain was great. From this grim tomb you will emerge as though you tread on air. But you must not falter when once you have begun. Only think that we, your true friends, are round you, and that we pray for you all the time."

"Go on," said Arthur hoarsely. "Tell me what I am to do."

"Take this stake in your left hand, ready to place to the point over the heart, and the hammer in your right. Then when we begin our prayer for the dead—I shall read him, I have here the book, and the others shall follow—strike in God's name, that so all may be well with the dead that we love and that the Undead pass away."

Arthur took the stake and the hammer, and when once his mind was set on action his hands never trembled nor even quivered. Van Helsing opened his missal and began to read, and Quincey and I followed as well as we could. Arthur placed the point over the heart, and as I looked I could see its dint in the white flesh. Then he struck with all his might.

The Thing in the coffin writhed, and a hideous, blood-curdling screech came from the opened red lips. The body shook and quivered and twisted in wild contortions. The sharp white teeth champed together till the lips were cut, and the mouth was smeared with a crimson foam. But Arthur never faltered. He looked like a figure of Thor as his untrembling arm rose and fell, driving deeper and deeper the mercy-bearing stake, whilst the blood from the pierced heart welled and spurted up around it. His face was set, and high duty seemed to shine through it. The sight of it gave us courage so that our voices seemed to ring through the little vault.

And then the writhing and quivering of the body became less, and the teeth seemed to champ, and the face to quiver. Finally it lay still. The terrible task was over.

The hammer fell from Arthur's hand. He reeled and would have fallen had we not caught him. The great drops of sweat sprang from his forehead, and his breath came in broken gasps. It had indeed been an awful strain on him, and had he not been forced to his task by more than human considerations he could never have gone through with it. For a few minutes we were so taken up with him that we did not look towards the coffin. When we did, however, a murmur of startled surprise ran from one to the other of us. We gazed so eagerly that Arthur rose, for he had been seated on the ground, and came and looked too, and then a glad strange light broke over his face and dispelled altogether the gloom of horror that lay upon it.

There, in the coffin lay no longer the foul Thing that we had so dreaded and grown to hate that the work of her destruction was yielded as a privilege to the one best entitled to it, but Lucy as we had seen her in life, with her face of unequalled sweetness and purity. True that there were there, as we had seen them in life, the traces of care and pain and waste. But these were all dear to us, for they marked her truth to what we knew. One and all we felt that the holy calm that lay like sunshine over the wasted face and form was only an earthly token and symbol of the calm that was to reign for ever.

Van Helsing came and laid his hand on Arthur's shoulder, and said to him, "And now, Arthur my friend, dear lad, am I not forgiven?"

The reaction of the terrible strain came as he took the old man's hand in his, and raising it to his lips, pressed it, and said, "Forgiven! God bless you that you have given my dear one her soul again, and me peace." He put his hands on the Professor's shoulder, and laying his head on his breast, cried for a while silently, whilst we stood unmoving.

When he raised his head Van Helsing said to him, "And now, my child, you may kiss her. Kiss her dead lips if you will, as she would have you to, if for her to choose. For she is not a grinning devil now, not any more a foul Thing for all eternity. No longer she is the devil's Undead.

She is God's true dead, whose soul is with Him!"

Arthur bent and kissed her, and then we sent him and Quincey out of the tomb. The Professor and I sawed the top off the stake, leaving the point of it in the body. Then we cut off the head and filled the mouth with garlic. We soldered up the leaden coffin, screwed on the coffin lid, and gathering up our belongings, came away. When the Professor locked the door he gave the key to Arthur.

Outside the air was sweet, the sun shone, and the birds sang, and it seemed as if all nature were tuned to a different pitch. There was gladness and mirth and peace everywhere, for we were at rest ourselves on one account, and we were glad, though it was with a tempered joy.

Before we moved away Van Helsing said, "Now, my friends, one step of our work is done, one the most harrowing to ourselves. But there remains a greater task: to find out the author of all this our sorrow and to stamp him out. I have clues which we can follow, but it is a long task, and a difficult one, and there is danger in it, and pain. Shall you not all help me? We have learned to believe, all of us—is it not so? And since so, do we not see our duty? Yes! And do we not promise to go on to the bitter end?"

Each in turn, we took his hand, and the promise was made. Then said the Professor as we moved off, "Two nights hence you shall meet with me and dine together at seven of the clock with friend John. I shall entreat two others, two that you know not as yet, and I shall be ready to all our work show and our plans unfold. Friend John, you come with me home, for I have much to consult you about, and you can help me. Tonight I leave for Amsterdam, but shall return tomorrow night. And then begins our great quest. But first I shall have much to say, so that you may know what to do and to dread. Then our promise shall be made to each other anew. For there is a terrible task before us, and once our feet are on the ploughshare we must not draw back."

CHAPTER XVII

Dr. Seward's Diary, Continued

When we arrived at the Berkeley Hotel, Van Helsing found a telegram waiting for him.

> "Am coming up by train. Jonathan at Whitby. Important news. Mina Harker."

The Professor was delighted. "Ah, that wonderful Madam Mina," he said, "pearl among women! She arrive, but I cannot stay. She must go to your house, friend John. You must meet her at the station. Telegraph her *en route* so that she may be prepared."

When the wire was dispatched he had a cup of tea. Over it he told me of a diary kept by Jonathan Harker when abroad, and gave me a typewritten copy of it, as also of Mrs. Harker's diary at Whitby. "Take these," he said, "and study them well. When I have returned you will be master of all the facts, and we can then better enter on our inquisition. Keep them safe, for there is in them much of treasure. You will need all your faith, even you who have had such an experience as that of today. What is here told," he laid his hand heavily and gravely on the packet of papers as he spoke, "may be the beginning of the end to you and me and many another, or it may sound the knell of the Undead who walk the earth. Read all, I pray you, with the open mind, and if you can add in any way to the story here told do so, for it is all important. You have kept a diary of all these so strange things, is it not so? Yes! Then we shall go through all these together when we meet." He then made ready for his departure and shortly drove off to Liverpool Street. I took my way to Paddington, where I arrived about fifteen minutes before the train came in.

The crowd melted away, after the bustling fashion common to arrival platforms, and I was beginning to feel uneasy, lest I might miss my guest, when a sweet-faced, dainty looking girl stepped up to me, and after a quick glance said, "Dr. Seward, is it not?"

"And you are Mrs. Harker!" I answered at once, whereupon she held out her hand.

"I knew you from the description of poor dear Lucy, but—" She stopped suddenly, and a quick blush overspread her face.

The blush that rose to my own cheeks somehow set us both at ease, for it was a tacit answer to her own. I got her luggage, which included a typewriter, and we took the Underground to Fenchurch Street, after I had sent a wire to my housekeeper to have a sitting room and a bedroom prepared at once for Mrs. Harker.

In due time we arrived. She knew, of course, that the place was a lunatic asylum, but I could see that she was unable to repress a shudder when we entered.

She told me that, if she might, she would come presently to my study, as she had much to say. So here I am finishing my entry in my phonograph diary whilst I await her. As yet I have not had the chance of looking at the papers which Van Helsing left with me, though they lie open before me. I must get her interested in something, so that I may have an opportunity of reading them. She does not know how precious time is, or what a task we have in hand. I must be careful not to frighten her. Here she is!

Mina Harker's Journal

29 September.

After I had tidied myself, I went down to Dr. Seward's study. At the door I paused a moment, for I thought I heard him talking with someone. As, however, he had pressed me to be quick, I knocked at the door, and on his calling out, "Come in," I entered.

To my intense surprise, there was no one with him. He was quite alone, and on the table opposite him was what I knew at once from the description to be a phonograph. I had never seen one, and was much interested.

"I hope I did not keep you waiting," I said, "but I stayed at the door as I heard you talking, and thought there was someone with you."

"Oh," he replied with a smile, "I was only entering my diary."

"Your diary?" I asked him in surprise.

"Yes," he answered. "I keep it in this." As he spoke he laid his hand on the phonograph. I felt quite excited over it, and blurted out, "Why, this beats even shorthand! May I hear it say something?"

"Certainly," he replied with alacrity, and stood up to put it in train for speaking. Then he paused, and a troubled look overspread his face.

"The fact is," he began awkwardly, "I only keep my diary in it, and as it is entirely—almost entirely—about my cases it may be awkward—that is, I mean—" He stopped, and I tried to help him out of his embarrassment.

"You helped to attend dear Lucy at the end. Let me hear how she died, for all that I know of her, I shall be very grateful. She was very, very dear to me."

To my surprise, he answered, with a horrorstruck look in his face, "Tell you of her death? Not for the wide world!"

"Why not?" I asked, for some grave, terrible feeling was coming over me.

Again he paused, and I could see that he was trying to invent an excuse. At length, he stammered out, "You see, I do not know how to pick out any particular part of the diary." Even while he was speaking an idea dawned upon him, and he said with unconscious simplicity, in a different voice, and with the naivete of a child, "That's quite true, upon my honour. Honest Indian!"

I could not but smile, at which he grimaced. "I gave myself away that time!" he said. "But do you know that, although I have kept the diary for months past, it never once struck me how I was going to find any particular part of it in case I wanted to look it up?" By this time my mind was made up that the diary of a doctor who attended Lucy might have something to add to the sum of our knowledge of that terrible Being, and I said boldly, "Then, Dr. Seward, you had better let me copy it out for you on my typewriter."

He grew to a positively deathly pallor as he said, "No! No! No! For all the world. I wouldn't let you know that terrible story!"

Then it was terrible. My intuition was right! For a moment, I thought, and as my eyes ranged the room, unconsciously looking for something or some opportunity to aid me, they lit on a great batch of typewriting on the table. His eyes caught the look in mine, and without his thinking, followed their direction. As they saw the parcel he realized my meaning.

"You do not know me," I said. "When you have read those papers—my own diary and my husband's also, which I have typed—you will know me better. I have not faltered in giving every thought of my own heart in this cause. But, of course, you do not know me, yet, and I must not expect you to trust me so far."

He is certainly a man of noble nature. Poor dear Lucy was right about him. He stood up and opened a large drawer, in which were arranged in order a number of hollow cylinders of metal covered with dark wax, and said, "You are quite right. I did not trust you because I did not know you. But I know you now, and let me say that I should have known you long ago. I know that Lucy told you of me. She told me of you too. May I make the only atonement in my power? Take the cylinders and hear them. The first half-dozen of them are personal to me, and they will not horrify you. Then you will know me better. Dinner will by then be ready. In the meantime I shall read over some of these documents, and shall be better able to understand certain things." He carried the phonograph himself up to my sitting room and adjusted it for me. Now I shall learn something pleasant, I am sure. For it will tell me the other side of a true love episode of which I know one side already.

Dr. Seward's Diary

29 September.

I was so absorbed in that wonderful diary of Jonathan Harker and that other of his wife that I let the time run on without thinking. Mrs. Harker was not down when the maid came to announce dinner, so I said, "She is possibly tired. Let dinner wait an hour," and I went on with my work. I had just finished Mrs. Harker's diary, when she came in. She looked sweetly pretty, but very sad, and her eyes were flushed with crying. This somehow moved me much. Of late I have had cause for tears, God knows! But the relief of them was denied me, and now the sight of those sweet eyes, brightened by recent tears, went straight to my heart. So I said as gently as I could, "I greatly fear I have distressed you."

"Oh, no, not distressed me," she replied. "But I have been more touched than I can say by your grief. That is a wonderful machine, but it is cruelly true. It told me, in its very tones, the anguish of your heart. It was like a soul crying out to Almighty God. No one must hear them spoken ever again! See, I have tried to be useful. I have copied out the words on my typewriter, and none other need now hear your heart beat, as I did."

"No one need ever know, shall ever know," I said in a low voice. She laid her hand on mine and said very gravely, "Ah, but they must!"

"Must! But why?" I asked.

"Because it is a part of the terrible story, a part of poor Lucy's death and all that led to it. Because in the struggle which we have before us to rid the earth of this terrible monster we must have all the knowledge and all the help which we can get. I think that the cylinders which you gave me contained more than you intended me to know. But I can see that there are in your record many lights to this dark mystery. You will let me help, will you not? I know all up to a certain point, and I see already, though your diary only took me to 7 September, how poor Lucy was beset, and how her terrible doom was being wrought out. Jonathan and I have been working day and night since Professor Van Helsing saw us. He is gone to Whitby to get more information, and he will be here tomorrow to help us. We need have no secrets amongst us. Working together and with absolute trust, we can surely be stronger than if some of us were in the dark." She looked at me so appealingly, and at the same time manifested such courage and resolution in her bearing, that I gave in at once to her wishes. "You shall," I said, "do as you like in the matter. God forgive me if I do wrong! There are terrible things yet to learn of, but if you have so far traveled on the road to poor Lucy's death, you will not be content, I know, to remain in the dark. Nay, the end—the very end—may give you a gleam of peace. Come, there is dinner. We must keep one another strong for what is before us. We have a cruel and dreadful task. When you have eaten you shall learn the rest, and I shall answer any questions you ask—if there be anything which you do not understand, though it was apparent to us who were present."

Mina Harker's Journal

29 September.

After dinner I came with Dr. Seward to his study. He brought back the phonograph from my room, and I took a chair, and arranged the phonograph so that I could touch it without getting up, and showed me how to stop it in case I should want to pause. Then he very thoughtfully took a chair, with his back to me, so that I might be as free as possible, and began to read. I put the forked metal to my ears and listened.

When the terrible story of Lucy's death, and all that followed, was done, I lay back in my chair powerless. Fortunately I am not of a fainting disposition. When Dr. Seward saw me he jumped up with a horrified exclamation, and hurriedly taking a case bottle from the cupboard, gave me some brandy, which in a few minutes somewhat restored me. My brain was all in a whirl, and only that there came through all the multitude of horrors, the holy ray of light that my dear Lucy was at last at peace, I do not think I could have borne it without making a scene. It is all so wild and mysterious, and strange that if I had not known Jonathan's experience in Transylvania I could not have believed. As it was, I didn't know what to believe, and so got out of my difficulty by attending to something else.

I took the cover off my typewriter, and said to Dr. Seward,"Let me write this all out now. We must be ready for Dr. Van Helsing when he comes. I have sent a telegram to Jonathan to come on here when he arrives in London from Whitby. In this matter dates are everything, and I think that if we get all of our material ready, and have every item put in chronological order, we shall have done much. "You tell me that Lord Godalming and Mr. Morris are coming too. Let us be able to tell them when they come."

He accordingly set the phonograph at a slow pace, and I began to typewrite from the beginning of the seventeenth cylinder. I used manifold, and so took three copies of the diary, just as I had done with the rest. It was late when I got through, but Dr. Seward went about his work of going his round of the patients. When he had finished he came back and sat near me, reading, so that I did not feel too lonely whilst I worked. How good and thoughtful he is. The world seems full of good men—even if there *are* monsters in it.

Before I left him I remembered what Jonathan put in his diary of the Professor's perturbation at reading something in an evening paper at the station at Exeter, so, seeing that Dr. Seward keeps his newspapers, I borrowed the files of the *Westminster Gazette* and the *Pall Mall Gazette* and took them to my room. I remember how much the *Dailygraph* and the *Whitby Gazette*, of which I had made cuttings, had helped us to understand the terrible events at Whitby when Count Dracula landed, so I shall look through the evening papers since then, and perhaps I shall get some new light. I am not sleepy, and the work will help to keep me quiet.

Dr. Seward's Diary

30 September.

Mr. Harker arrived at nine o'clock. He got his wife's wire just before starting. He is uncommonly clever, if one can judge from his face, and full of energy. If this journal be true—and judging by one's own wonderful experiences, it must be—he is also a man of great nerve. That going down to the vault a second time was a remarkable piece of daring. After reading his account of it I was prepared to meet a good specimen of manhood, but hardly the quiet, businesslike gentleman who came here today.

Later.

After lunch Harker and his wife went back to their own room, and as I passed a while ago I heard the click of the typewriter. They are hard at it. Mrs. Harker says that they are knitting together in chronological order every scrap of evidence they have. Harker has got the letters between the consignee of the boxes at Whitby and the carriers in London who took charge of them. He is now reading his wife's transcript of my diary. I wonder what they make out of it. Here it is . . .

Strange that it never struck me that the very next house might be the Count's hiding place! Goodness knows that we had enough clues from the conduct of the patient Renfield! The bundle of letters relating to the purchase of the house were with the transcript. Oh, if we had only had them earlier we might have saved poor Lucy! Stop! That way madness lies! Harker has gone back, and is again collecting material. He says that by dinner time they will be able to show a whole connected narrative. He thinks that in the meantime I should see Renfield, as hitherto he has been a sort of index to the coming and going of the Count. I hardly see this yet, but when I get at the dates I suppose I shall. What a good thing that Mrs. Harker put my cylinders into type! We never could have found the dates otherwise.

I found Renfield sitting placidly in his room with his hands folded, smiling benignly. At the moment he seemed as sane as anyone I ever saw. I sat down and talked with him on a lot of subjects, all of which he treated naturally. He then, of his own accord, spoke of going home, a subject he has never mentioned to my knowledge during his sojourn here. In fact, he spoke quite confidently of getting his discharge at once.

I believe that, had I not had the chat with Harker and read the letters and the dates of his outbursts, I should have been prepared to sign for him after a brief time of observation. As it is, I am darkly suspicious. All those outbreaks were in some way linked with the proximity of the Count. What then does this absolute content mean? Can it be that his instinct is satisfied as to the vampire's ultimate triumph? Stay. He is himself zoophagous, and in his wild ravings outside the chapel door of the deserted house he always spoke of "master." This all seems confirmation of our idea. However, after a while I came away. My friend is just a little too sane at present to make it safe to probe him too deep with questions. He might begin to think, and then—! So I came away. I mistrust these quiet moods of his, so I have given the attendant a hint to look closely after him, and to have a strait waistcoat ready in case of need.

Jonathan Harker's Journal

29 September, in train to London.

When I received Mr. Billington's courteous message that he would give me any information in his power I thought it best to go down to Whitby and make, on the spot, such inquiries as I wanted. It was now my object to trace that horrid cargo of the Count's to its place in London. Later, we may be able to deal with it. Billington junior, a nice lad, met me at the station, and brought me to his father's house, where they had decided that I must spend the night. They are hospitable, with true Yorkshire hospitality, give a guest everything and leave him to do as he likes. They all knew that I was busy, and that my stay was short, and Mr. Billington had ready in his office all the papers concerning the consignment of boxes. It gave me almost a turn to see again one of the letters which I had seen on the Count's table before I knew of his diabolical plans. Everything had been carefully thought out, and done systematically and with precision. He seemed to have been prepared for every obstacle which might be placed by accident in the way of his intentions being carried out. To use an Americanism, he had "taken no chances," and the absolute accuracy with which his instructions were fulfilled was simply the logical result of his care. I saw the invoice, and took note of it. "Fifty cases of common earth, to be used for experimental purposes." Also the copy of the letter to Carter Paterson, and their reply. Of both these I got copies. This was all the information Mr. Billington could give me, so I went down to the port and saw the coastguards, the Customs Officers and the harbour master, who kindly put me in communication with the men who had actually received the boxes. Their tally was exact with the list, and they had nothing to add to the simple description "fifty cases of common earth," except that the boxes were "main and mortal heavy," and that shifting them was dry work. One of them added that it was hard lines that there wasn't any gentleman "such like as like yourself, squire," to show some sort of appreciation of their efforts in a liquid form. Another put in a rider that the thirst then generated was such that even the time which had elapsed had not completely allayed it. Needless to add, I took care before leaving to lift, forever and adequately, this source of reproach.

30 September.

The station master was good enough to give me a line to his old companion the station master at King's Cross, so that when I arrived there in the morning I was able to ask him about the arrival of the boxes. He, too, put me at once in communication with the proper officials, and I saw that their tally was correct with the original invoice. The opportunities of acquiring an abnormal thirst had been here limited. A noble use of them had, however, been made, and again I was compelled to deal with the result in *ex post facto* manner.

From thence I went to Carter Paterson's central office, where I met with the utmost courtesy. They looked up the transaction in their day book and letter book, and at once telephoned to their King's Cross office for more details. By good fortune, the men who did the teaming were waiting for work, and the official at once sent them over, sending also by one of them the way-bill and all the papers connected with the delivery of the boxes at Carfax. Here again I found the tally agreeing exactly. The carriers' men were able to supplement the paucity of the written words with a few more details. These were, I shortly found, connected almost solely with the dusty nature of the job, and the consequent thirst engendered in the operators. On my affording an opportunity, through the medium of the currency of the realm, of the allaying, at a later period, this beneficial evil, one of the men remarked,

"That 'ere 'ouse, guv'nor, is the rummiest I ever was in. Blyme! But it ain't been touched sence a hundred years. There was dust that thick in the place that you might have slep' on it without 'urtin' of yer bones. An' the place was that neglected that yer might 'ave smelled ole Jerusalem in it. But the old chapel, that took the cike, that did! Me and my mate, we thort we wouldn't never git out quick enough. Lor', I wouldn't take less nor a quid a moment to stay there arter dark."

Having been in the house, I could well believe him, but if he knew what I know, he would, I think, have raised his terms.

Of one thing I am now satisfied. That all those boxes which arrived at Whitby from Varna in the Demeter were safely deposited in the old chapel at Carfax. There should be fifty of them there, unless any have since been removed, as from Dr. Seward's diary I fear.

I shall try to see the carter who took away the boxes from Carfax when Renfield attacked them. By following up this clue we may learn a good deal.

Later.

Mina and I have worked all day, and we have put all the papers into order.

Mina Harker's Journal

30 September.

I am so glad that I hardly know how to contain myself. It is, I suppose, the reaction from the haunting fear which I have had, that this terrible affair and the reopening of his old wound might act detrimentally on Jonathan. I saw him leave for Whitby with as brave a face as could, but I was sick with apprehension. The effort has, however, done him good. He was never so resolute, never so strong, never so full of volcanic energy, as at present. It is just as that dear, good Professor Van Helsing said, he is true grit, and he improves under strain that would kill a weaker nature. He came back full of life and hope and determination. We have got everything in order for tonight. I feel myself quite wild with excitement. I suppose one ought to pity anything so hunted as the Count. That is just it. This thing is not human—not even a beast. To read Dr. Seward's account of poor Lucy's death, and what followed, is enough to dry up the springs of pity in one's heart.

Later.

Lord Godalming and Mr. Morris arrived earlier than we expected.

Dr. Seward was out on business, and had taken Jonathan with him, so I had to see them. It was to me a painful meeting, for it brought back all poor dear Lucy's hopes of only a few months ago. Of course they had heard Lucy speak of me, and it seemed that Dr. Van Helsing, too, had been quite "blowing my trumpet," as Mr. Morris expressed it. Poor fellows, neither of them is aware that I know all about the proposals they made to Lucy. They did not quite know what to say or do, as they were ignorant of the amount of my knowledge. So they had to keep on neutral subjects. However, I thought the matter over, and came to the conclusion that the best thing I could do would be to post them on affairs right up to date. I knew from Dr. Seward's diary that they had been at Lucy's death—her real death—and that I need not fear to betray any secret before the time. So I told them, as well as I could, that I had read all the papers and diaries, and that my husband and I, having typewritten them, had just finished putting them in order. I gave them each a copy to read in the library. When Lord Godalming got his and turned it over—it does make a pretty good pile—he said, "Did you write all this, Mrs. Harker?"

I nodded, and he went on.

"I don't quite see the drift of it, but you people are all so good and kind, and have been working so earnestly and so energetically, that all I can do is to accept your ideas blindfold and try to help you. I have had one lesson already in accepting facts that should make a man humble to the last hour of his life. Besides, I know you loved my Lucy—" Here he turned away and covered his face with his hands. I could hear the tears in his voice. Mr. Morris, with instinctive delicacy, just laid a hand for a moment on his shoulder, and then walked quietly out of the room. I suppose there is something in a woman's nature that makes a man free to break down before her and express his feelings on the tender or emotional side without feeling it derogatory to his manhood. For when Lord Godalming found himself alone with me he sat down on the sofa and gave way utterly and openly. I sat down beside him and took his hand. I hope he didn't think it forward of me, and that if he ever thinks of it afterwards he never will have such a thought. There I wrong him. I *know* he never will. He is too true a gentleman. I said to him, for I could see that his heart was breaking, "I loved dear Lucy, and I know what she was to you, and what you were to her. She and I were like sisters, and now she is gone, will you not let me be like a sister to you in your trouble? I know what sorrows you have had, though I cannot measure the depth of them. If sympathy and pity can help in your affliction, won't you let me be of some little service—for Lucy's sake?"

In an instant the poor dear fellow was overwhelmed with grief. It seemed to me that all that he had of late been suffering in silence found a vent at once. He grew quite hysterical, and raising his open hands, beat his palms together in a perfect agony of grief. He stood up and then sat down again, and the tears rained down his cheeks. I felt an infinite pity for him, and opened my arms unthinkingly. With a sob he laid his head on my shoulder and cried like a wearied child, whilst he shook with emotion.

We women have something of the mother in us that makes us rise above smaller matters when the mother spirit is invoked. I felt this big sorrowing man's head resting on me, as though it were that of a baby that someday may lie on my bosom, and I stroked his hair as though he were my own child. I never thought at the time how strange it all was.

After a little bit his sobs ceased, and he raised himself with an apology, though he made no disguise of his emotion. He told me that for days and nights past—weary days and sleepless nights—he had been unable to speak with anyone, as a man must speak in his time of sorrow. There was no woman whose sympathy could be given to him, or with whom, owing to the terrible circumstance with which his sorrow was surrounded, he could speak freely. "I know now how I suffered," he said, as he dried his eyes, "but I do not know even yet, and none other can ever know, how much your sweet sympathy has been to me today. I shall know better in time, and believe me that, though I am not ungrateful now, my gratitude will grow with my understanding. You will let me be like a brother, will you not, for all our lives—for dear Lucy's sake?"

"For dear Lucy's sake," I said as we clasped hands. "Ay, and for your own sake," he added, "for if a man's esteem and gratitude are ever worth the winning, you have won mine today. If ever the future should bring to you a time when you need a man's help, believe me, you will not call in vain. God grant that no such time may ever come to you to break the sunshine of your life, but if it should ever come, promise me that you will let me know." He was so earnest, and his sorrow was so fresh, that I felt it would comfort him, so I said, "I promise."

As I came along the corridor I saw Mr. Morris looking out of a window. He turned as he heard my footsteps. "How is Art?" he said. Then noticing my red eyes, he went on, "Ah, I see you have been comforting him. Poor old fellow! He needs it. No one but a woman can help a man when he is in trouble of the heart, and he had no one to comfort him."

He bore his own trouble so bravely that my heart bled for him. I saw the manuscript in his hand, and I knew that when he read it he would realize how much I knew, so I said to him, "I wish I could comfort all who suffer from the heart. Will you let me be your friend, and will you come to me for comfort if you need it? You will know later why I speak." He saw that I was in earnest, and stooping, took my hand, and raising it to his lips, kissed it. It seemed but poor comfort to so brave and unselfish a soul, and impulsively I bent over and kissed him. The tears rose in his eyes, and there was a momentary choking in his throat. He said quite calmly, "Little girl, you will never forget that true hearted kindness, so long as ever you live!" Then he went into the study to his friend.

"Little girl!" The very words he had used to Lucy, and, oh, but he proved himself a friend.

CHAPTER XVIII

Dr. Seward's Diary

30 September.

I got home at five o'clock, and found that Godalming and Morris had not only arrived, but had already studied the transcript of the various diaries and letters which Harker had not yet returned from his visit to the carriers' men, of whom Dr. Hennessey had written to me. Mrs. Harker gave us a cup of tea, and I can honestly say that, for the first time since I have lived in it, this old house seemed like *home*.

When we had finished, Mrs. Harker said, "Dr. Seward, may I ask a favour? I want to see your patient, Mr. Renfield. Do let me see him. What you have said of him in your diary interests me so much!" She looked so appealing and so pretty that I could not refuse her, and there was no possible reason why I should, so I took her with me.

When I went into the room, I told the man that a lady would like to see him, to which he simply answered, "Why?"

"She is going through the house, and wants to see every one in it," I answered.

"Oh, very well," he said, "let her come in, by all means, but just wait a minute till I tidy up the place."

His method of tidying was peculiar, he simply swallowed all the flies and spiders in the boxes before I could stop him. It was quite evident that he feared, or was jealous of, some interference. When he had got through his disgusting task, he said cheerfully, "Let the lady come in," and sat down on the edge of his bed with his head down, but with his eyelids raised so that he could see her as she entered. For a moment I thought that he might have some homicidal intent. I remembered how quiet he had been just before he attacked me in my own study, and I took care to stand where I could seize him at once if he attempted to make a spring at her. She came into the room with an easy gracefulness which would at once command the respect of any lunatic, for easiness is one of the qualities mad people most respect. She walked over to him, smiling pleasantly, and held out her hand.

"Good evening, Mr. Renfield," said she. "You see, I know you, for

Dr. Seward has told me of you." He made no immediate reply, but eyed her all over intently with a set frown on his face. This look gave way to one of wonder, which merged in doubt, then to my intense astonishment he said, "You're not the girl the doctor wanted to marry, are you? You can't be, you know, for she's dead."

Mrs. Harker smiled sweetly as she replied, "Oh no! I have a husband of my own, to whom I was married before I ever saw Dr. Seward, or he me. I am Mrs. Harker."

"Then what are you doing here?"

"My husband and I are staying on a visit with Dr. Seward."

"Then don't stay."

"But why not?"

I thought that this style of conversation might not be pleasant to Mrs. Harker, any more than it was to me, so I joined in, "How did you know I wanted to marry anyone?"

His reply was simply contemptuous, given in a pause in which he turned his eyes from Mrs. Harker to me, instantly turning them back again, "What an asinine question!"

"I don't see that at all, Mr. Renfield," said Mrs. Harker, at once championing me.

He replied to her with as much courtesy and respect as he had shown contempt to me, "You will, of course, understand, Mrs. Harker, that when a man is so loved and honoured as our host is, everything regarding him is of interest in our little community. Dr. Seward is loved not only by his household and his friends, but even by his patients, who, being some of them hardly in mental equilibrium, are apt to distort causes and effects. Since I myself have been an inmate of a lunatic asylum, I cannot but notice that the sophistic tendencies of some of its inmates lean towards the errors of *non causa* and *ignoratio elenche*." I positively opened my eyes at this new development. Here was my own pet lunatic—the most pronounced of his type that I had ever met with—talking elemental philosophy, and with the manner of a polished gentleman. I wonder if it was Mrs. Harker's presence which had touched some chord in his memory. If this new phase was spontaneous, or in any way due to her unconscious influence, she must have some rare gift or power.

We continued to talk for some time, and seeing that he was seemingly quite reasonable, she ventured, looking at me questioningly as she began, to lead him to his favourite topic. I was again astonished, for he addressed himself to the question with the impartiality of the completest sanity. He even took himself as an example when he mentioned certain things.

"Why, I myself am an instance of a man who had a strange belief. Indeed, it was no wonder that my friends were alarmed, and insisted on my being put under control. I used to fancy that life was a positive and perpetual entity, and that by consuming a multitude of live things, no matter how low in the scale of creation, one might indefinitely prolong life. At times I held the belief so strongly that I actually tried to take human life. The doctor here will bear me out that on one occasion I tried to kill him for the purpose of strengthening my vital powers by the assimilation with my own body of his life through the medium of his blood—relying of course, upon the Scriptural phrase, 'For the blood is the life.' Though, indeed, the vendor of a certain nostrum has vulgarized the truism to the very point of contempt. Isn't that true, doctor?" I nodded assent, for I was so amazed that I hardly knew what to either think or say, it was hard to imagine that I had seen him eat up his spiders and flies not five minutes before. Looking at my watch, I saw that I should go to the station to meet Van Helsing, so I told Mrs. Harker that it was time to leave.

She came at once, after saying pleasantly to Mr. Renfield, "Goodbye, and I hope I may see you often, under auspices pleasanter to yourself."

To which, to my astonishment, he replied, "Goodbye, my dear. I pray God I may never see your sweet face again. May He bless and keep you!"

When I went to the station to meet Van Helsing I left the boys behind me. Poor Art seemed more cheerful than he has been since Lucy first took ill, and Quincey is more like his own bright self than he has been for many a long day.

Van Helsing stepped from the carriage with the eager nimbleness of a boy. He saw me at once, and rushed up to me, saying, "Ah, friend John, how goes all? Well? So! I have been busy, for I come here to stay if need be. All affairs are settled with me, and I have much to tell. Madam Mina is with you? Yes. And her so fine husband? And Arthur and my friend Quincey, they are with you, too? Good!"

As I drove to the house I told him of what had passed, and of how my own diary had come to be of some use through Mrs. Harker's suggestion, at which the Professor interrupted me.

"Ah, that wonderful Madam Mina! She has man's brain—a brain

that a man should have were he much gifted—and a woman's heart. The good God fashioned her for a purpose, believe me, when He made that so good combination. Friend John, up to now fortune has made that woman of help to us, after tonight she must not have to do with this so terrible affair. It is not good that she run a risk so great. We men are determined—nay, are we not pledged—to destroy this monster? But it is no part for a woman. Even if she be not harmed, her heart may fail her in so much and so many horrors and hereafter she may suffer—both in waking, from her nerves, and in sleep, from her dreams. And, besides, she is young woman and not so long married, there may be other things to think of some time, if not now. You tell me she has wrote all, then she must consult with us, but tomorrow she say goodbye to this work, and we go alone." I agreed heartily with him, and then I told him what we had found in his absence, that the house which Dracula had bought was the very next one to my own. He was amazed, and a great concern seemed to come on him. "Oh that we had known it before!" he said. "For then we might have reached him in time to save poor Lucy. However, 'the milk that is spilt cries not out afterwards,' as you say. We shall not think of that, but go on our way to the end." Then he fell into a silence that lasted till we entered my own gateway.

Before we went to prepare for dinner he said to Mrs. Harker, "I am told, Madam Mina, by my friend John that you and your husband have put up in exact order all things that have been, up to this moment."

"Not up to this moment, Professor," she said impulsively, "but up to this morning."

"But why not up to now? We have seen hitherto how good light all the little things have made. We have told our secrets, and yet no one who has told is the worse for it."

Mrs. Harker began to blush, and taking a paper from her pockets, she said, "Dr. Van Helsing, will you read this, and tell me if it must go in. It is my record of today. I too have seen the need of putting down at present everything, however trivial, but there is little in this except what is personal. Must it go in?"

The Professor read it over gravely, and handed it back, saying, "It need not go in if you do not wish it, but I pray that it may. It can but make your husband love you the more, and all us, your friends, more honour you—as well as more esteem and love." She took it back with another blush and a bright smile.

And so now, up to this very hour, all the records we have are complete and in order. The Professor took away one copy to study after dinner, and before our meeting, which is fixed for nine o'clock. The rest of us have already read everything, so when we meet in the study we shall all be informed as to facts, and can arrange our plan of battle with this terrible and mysterious enemy.

Mina Harker's Journal

30 September.

When we met in Dr. Seward's study two hours after dinner, which had been at six o'clock, we unconsciously formed a sort of board or committee. Professor Van Helsing took the head of the table, to which Dr. Seward motioned him as he came into the room. He made me sit next to him on his right, and asked me to act as secretary. Jonathan sat next to me. Opposite us were Lord Godalming, Dr. Seward, and Mr. Morris, Lord Godalming being next the Professor, and Dr. Seward in the centre.

The Professor said, "I may, I suppose, take it that we are all acquainted with the facts that are in these papers." We all expressed assent, and he went on, "Then it were, I think, good that I tell you something of the kind of enemy with which we have to deal. I shall then make known to you something of the history of this man, which has been ascertained for me. So we then can discuss how we shall act, and can take our measure according.

"There are such beings as vampires, some of us have evidence that they exist. Even had we not the proof of our own unhappy experience, the teachings and the records of the past give proof enough for sane peoples. I admit that at the first I was sceptic. Were it not that through long years I have trained myself to keep an open mind, I could not have believed until such time as that fact thunder on my ear. 'See! See! I prove, I prove.' Alas! Had I known at first what now I know—nay, had I even guess at him—one so precious life had been spared to many of us who did love her. But that is gone, and we must so work, that other poor souls perish not, whilst we can save. The *nosferatu* do not die like the bee when he sting once. He is only stronger, and being stronger, have yet more power to work evil. This vampire which is amongst us is of himself so strong in person as twenty men, he is of cunning more than mortal, for his cunning be the growth of ages, he have still the aids of necromancy, which is, as his etymology imply, the divination by the dead, and all the dead that he can come nigh to are for him at command; he is brute, and more than brute; he is devil in callous, and the heart of him is not; he can, within his range, direct the elements, the storm, the fog, the thunder; he can command all the meaner things, the rat, and the owl, and the bat—the moth, and the fox, and the wolf, he can grow and become small; and he can at times vanish and come unknown. How then are we to begin our strike to destroy him? How shall we find his where, and having found it, how can we destroy? My friends, this is much, it is a terrible task that we undertake, and there may be consequence to make the brave shudder. For if we fail in this our fight he must surely win, and then where end we? Life is nothings, I heed him not. But to fail here, is not mere life or death. It is that we become as him, that we henceforward become foul things of the night like him—without heart or conscience, preying on the bodies and the souls of those we love best. To us forever are the gates of heaven shut, for who shall open them to us again? We go on for all time abhorred by all, a blot on the face of God's sunshine, an arrow in the side of Him who died for man. But we are face to face with duty, and in such case must we shrink? For me, I say no, but then I am old, and life, with his sunshine, his fair places, his song of birds, his music and his love, lie far behind. You others are young. Some have seen sorrow, but there are fair days yet in store. What say you?"

Whilst he was speaking, Jonathan had taken my hand. I feared, oh so much, that the appalling nature of our danger was overcoming him when I saw his hand stretch out, but it was life to me to feel its touch—so strong, so self reliant, so resolute. A brave man's hand can speak for itself, it does not even need a woman's love to hear its music.

When the Professor had done speaking my husband looked in my eyes, and I in his, there was no need for speaking between us.

"I answer for Mina and myself," he said.

"Count me in, Professor," said Mr. Quincey Morris, laconically as usual.

"I am with you," said Lord Godalming, "for Lucy's sake, if for no other reason."

Dr. Seward simply nodded.

The Professor stood up and, after laying his golden crucifix on the table, held out his hand on either side. I took his right hand, and Lord

Godalming his left, Jonathan held my right with his left and stretched across to Mr. Morris. So as we all took hands our solemn compact was made. I felt my heart icy cold, but it did not even occur to me to draw back. We resumed our places, and Dr. Van Helsing went on with a sort of cheerfulness which showed that the serious work had begun. It was to be taken as gravely, and in as businesslike a way, as any other transaction of life.

"Well, you know what we have to contend against, but we too, are not without strength. We have on our side power of combination—a power denied to the vampire kind, we have sources of science, we are free to act and think, and the hours of the day and the night are ours equally. In fact, so far as our powers extend, they are unfettered, and we are free to use them. We have self-devotion in a cause and an end to achieve which is not a selfish one. These things are much.

"Now let us see how far the general powers arrayed against us are restrict, and how the individual cannot. In fine, let us consider the limitations of the vampire in general, and of this one in particular.

"All we have to go upon are traditions and superstitions. These do not at the first appear much, when the matter is one of life and death—nay of more than either life or death. Yet must we be satisfied, in the first place because we have to be—no other means is at our control—and secondly, because, after all these things—tradition and superstition—are everything. Does not the belief in vampires rest for others—though not, alas! for us—on them? A year ago which of us would have received such a possibility, in the midst of our scientific, sceptical, matter-of-fact nineteenth century? We even scouted a belief that we saw justified under our very eyes. Take it, then, that the vampire, and the belief in his limitations and his cure, rest for the moment on the same base. For, let me tell you, he is known everywhere that men have been. In old Greece, in old Rome, he flourish in Germany all over, in France, in India, even in the Chermosese, and in China, so far from us in all ways, there even is he, and the peoples for him at this day. He have follow the wake of the berserker Icelander, the devil-begotten Hun, the Slav, the Saxon, the Magyar. "So far, then, we have all we may act upon, and let me tell you that very much of the beliefs are justified by what we have seen in our own so unhappy experience. The vampire live on, and cannot die by mere passing of the time, he can flourish when that he can fatten on the blood of the living. Even more, we have seen amongst us that he can even grow younger, that his vital faculties grow strenuous, and seem as though they refresh themselves when his special pabulum is plenty. "But he cannot flourish without this diet, he eat not as others. Even friend Jonathan, who lived with him for weeks, did never see him eat, never! He throws no shadow, he make in the mirror no reflect, as again Jonathan observe. He has the strength of many of his hand—witness again Jonathan when he shut the door against the wolves, and when he help him from the diligence too. He can transform himself to wolf, as we gather from the ship arrival in Whitby, when he tear open the dog, he can be as bat, as Madam Mina saw him on the window at Whitby, and as friend John saw him fly from this so near house, and as my friend Quincey saw him at the window of Miss Lucy. "He can come in mist which he create—that noble ship's captain proved him of this, but, from what we know, the distance he can make this mist is limited, and it can only be round himself. "He come on moonlight rays as elemental dust—as again Jonathan saw those sisters in the castle of Dracula. He become so small—we ourselves saw Miss Lucy, ere she was at peace, slip through a hairbreadth space at the tomb door. He can, when once he find his way, come out from anything or into anything, no matter how close it be bound or even fused up with fire—solder you call it. He can see in the dark—no small power this, in a world which is one half shut from the light. Ah, but hear me through. "He can do all these things, yet he is not free. Nay, he is even more prisoner than the slave of the galley, than the madman in his cell. He cannot go where he lists, he who is not of nature has yet to obey some of nature's laws, why we know not. He may not enter anywhere at the first, unless there be someone of the household who bid him to come, though afterwards he can come as he please. His power ceases, as does that of all evil things, at the coming of the day. "Only at certain times can he have limited freedom. If he be not at the place whither he is bound, he can only change himself at noon or at exact sunrise or sunset. These things we are told, and in this record of ours we have proof by inference. Thus, whereas he can do as he will within his limit, when he have his earth-home, his coffin-home, his hell-home, the place unhallowed, as we saw when he went to the grave of the suicide at Whitby, still at other time he can only change when the time come. It is said, too, that he can only pass running water at the slack or the flood of the tide. Then there are things which so afflict him that he has no power, as the garlic that we know of, and as for things sacred, as this symbol, my crucifix, that was amongst us even now when we resolve, to them he is nothing, but in their presence he take his place far off and silent with respect. There are others, too, which I shall tell you of, lest in our seeking we may need them. "The branch of wild rose on his coffin keep him that he move not from it, a sacred bullet fired into the coffin kill him so that he be true dead, and as for the stake through him, we know already of its peace, or the cut off head that giveth rest. We have seen it with our eyes.

"Thus when we find the habitation of this man-that-was, we can confine him to his coffin and destroy him, if we obey what we know. But he is clever. I have asked my friend Arminius, of Buda-Pesth University, to make his record, and from all the means that are, he tell me of what he has been. He must, indeed, have been that Voivode Dracula who won his name against the Turk, over the great river on the very frontier of Turkeyland. If it be so, then was he no common man, for in that time, and for centuries after, he was spoken of as the cleverest and the most cunning, as well as the bravest of the sons of the 'land beyond the forest.' That mighty brain and that iron resolution went with him to his grave, and are even now arrayed against us. The Draculas were, says Arminius, a great and noble race, though now and again were scions who were held by their coevals to have had dealings with the Evil One. They learned his secrets in the Scholomance, amongst the mountains over Lake Hermanstadt, where the devil claims the tenth scholar as his due. In the records are such words as 'stregoica'—witch, 'ordog' and 'pokol'—Satan and hell, and in one manuscript this very Dracula is spoken of as 'wampyr,' which we all understand too well. There have been from the loins of this very one great men and good women, and their graves make sacred the earth where alone this foulness can dwell. For it is not the least of its terrors that this evil thing is rooted deep in all good, in soil barren of holy memories it cannot rest."

Whilst they were talking Mr. Morris was looking steadily at the window, and he now got up quietly, and went out of the room. There was a little pause, and then the Professor went on.

"And now we must settle what we do. We have here much data, and we must proceed to lay out our campaign. We know from the inquiry of Jonathan that from the castle to Whitby came fifty boxes of earth, all of which were delivered at Carfax, we also know that at least some of these boxes have been removed. It seems to me, that our first step should be to ascertain whether all the rest remain in the house beyond that wall where we look today, or whether any more have been removed. If the latter, we must trace—"

Here we were interrupted in a very startling way. Outside the house came the sound of a pistol shot, the glass of the window was shattered with a bullet, which ricochetting from the top of the embrasure, struck the far wall of the room. I am afraid I am at heart a coward, for I shrieked out. The men all jumped to their feet, Lord Godalming flew over to the window and threw up the sash. As he did so we heard Mr. Morris' voice without, "Sorry! I fear I have alarmed you. I shall come in and tell you about it."

A minute later he came in and said, "It was an idiotic thing of me to do, and I ask your pardon, Mrs. Harker, most sincerely, I fear I must have frightened you terribly. But the fact is that whilst the Professor was talking there came a big bat and sat on the window sill. I have got such a horror of the damned brutes from recent events that I cannot stand them, and I went out to have a shot, as I have been doing of late of evenings, whenever I have seen one. You used to laugh at me for it then, Art."

"Did you hit it?" asked Dr. Van Helsing.

"I don't know, I fancy not, for it flew away into the wood." Without saying any more he took his seat, and the Professor began to resume his statement.

"We must trace each of these boxes, and when we are ready, we must either capture or kill this monster in his lair, or we must, so to speak, sterilize the earth, so that no more he can seek safety in it. Thus in the end we may find him in his form of man between the hours of noon and sunset, and so engage with him when he is at his most weak.

"And now for you, Madam Mina, this night is the end until all be well. You are too precious to us to have such risk. When we part tonight, you no more must question. We shall tell you all in good time. We are men and are able to bear, but you must be our star and our hope, and we shall act all the more free that you are not in the danger, such as we are."

All the men, even Jonathan, seemed relieved, but it did not seem to me good that they should brave danger and, perhaps lessen their safety—strength being the best safety—through care of me, but their minds were made up, and though it was a bitter pill for me to swallow, I could say nothing, save to accept their chivalrous care of me.

Mr. Morris resumed the discussion, "As there is no time to lose, I vote we have a look at his house right now. Time is everything with him, and swift action on our part may save another victim."

I own that my heart began to fail me when the time for action came so close, but I did not say anything, for I had a greater fear that if I appeared as a drag or a hindrance to their work, they might even leave me out of their counsels altogether. They have now gone off to Carfax, with means to get into the house.

Manlike, they had told me to go to bed and sleep, as if a woman can sleep when those she loves are in danger! I shall lie down, and pretend to sleep, lest Jonathan have added anxiety about me when he returns.

Dr. Seward's Diary

1 October, 4 a.m.

Just as we were about to leave the house, an urgent message was brought to me from Renfield to know if I would see him at once, as he had something of the utmost importance to say to me. I told the messenger to say that I would attend to his wishes in the morning, I was busy just at the moment.

The attendant added, "He seems very importunate, sir. I have never seen him so eager. I don't know but what, if you don't see him soon, he will have one of his violent fits." I knew the man would not have said this without some cause, so I said, "All right, I'll go now," and I asked the others to wait a few minutes for me, as I had to go and see my "patient."

"Take me with you, friend John," said the Professor. "His case in your diary interest me much, and it had bearing, too, now and again on *our* case. I should much like to see him, and especial when his mind is disturbed."

"May I come also?" asked Lord Godalming.

"Me too?" said Quincey Morris. "May I come?" said Harker. I nodded, and we all went down the passage together.

We found him in a state of considerable excitement, but far more rational in his speech and manner than I had ever seen him. There was an unusual understanding of himself, which was unlike anything I had ever met with in a lunatic, and he took it for granted that his reasons would prevail with others entirely sane. We all five went into the room, but none of the others at first said anything. His request was that I would at once release him from the asylum and send him home. This he backed up with arguments regarding his complete recovery, and adduced his own existing sanity. "I appeal to your friends," he said. "They will, perhaps, not mind sitting in judgement on my case. By the way, you have not introduced me."

I was so much astonished, that the oddness of introducing a madman in an asylum did not strike me at the moment, and besides, there was a certain dignity in the man's manner, so much of the habit of equality, that I at once made the introduction, "Lord Godalming, Professor Van Helsing, Mr. Quincey Morris, of Texas, Mr. Jonathan Harker, Mr. Renfield."

He shook hands with each of them, saying in turn, "Lord Godalming, I had the honour of seconding your father at the Windham; I grieve to know, by your holding the title, that he is no more. He was a man loved and honoured by all who knew him, and in his youth was, I have heard, the inventor of a burnt rum punch, much patronized on Derby night. Mr. Morris, you should be proud of your great state. Its reception into the Union was a precedent which may have far-reaching effects hereafter, when the Pole and the Tropics may hold alliance to the Stars and Stripes. The power of Treaty may yet prove a vast engine of enlargement, when the Monroe doctrine takes its true place as a political fable. What shall any man say of his pleasure at meeting Van Helsing? Sir, I make no apology for dropping all forms of conventional prefix. When an individual has revolutionized therapeutics by his discovery of the continuous evolution of brain matter, conventional forms are unfitting, since they would seem to limit him to one of a class. You, gentlemen, who by nationality, by heredity, or by the possession of natural gifts, are fitted to hold your respective places in the moving world, I take to witness that I am as sane as at least the majority of men who are in full possession of their liberties. And I am sure that you, Dr. Seward, humanitarian and medico-jurist as well as scientist, will deem it a moral duty to deal with me as one to be considered as under exceptional circumstances." He made this last appeal with a courtly air of conviction which was not without its own charm.

I think we were all staggered. For my own part, I was under the conviction, despite my knowledge of the man's character and history, that his reason had been restored, and I felt under a strong impulse to tell him that I was satisfied as to his sanity, and would see about the necessary formalities for his release in the morning. I thought it better to wait, however, before making so grave a statement, for of old I knew the sudden changes to which this particular patient was liable. So I contented myself with making a general statement that he appeared to be improving very rapidly, that I would have a longer chat with him in the morning, and would then see what I could do in the direction of meeting his wishes.

This did not at all satisfy him, for he said quickly, "But I fear, Dr. Seward, that you hardly apprehend my wish. I desire to go at once—here—now—this very hour—this very moment, if I may. Time presses, and in our implied agreement with the old scytheman it is of the essence of the contract. I am sure it is only necessary to put before so admirable a practitioner as Dr. Seward so simple, yet so momentous a wish, to ensure its fulfilment."

He looked at me keenly, and seeing the negative in my face, turned to the others, and scrutinized them closely. Not meeting any sufficient response, he went on, "Is it possible that I have erred in my supposition?"

"You have," I said frankly, but at the same time, as I felt, brutally.

There was a considerable pause, and then he said slowly, "Then I suppose I must only shift my ground of request. Let me ask for this concession—boon, privilege, what you will. I am content to implore in such a case, not on personal grounds, but for the sake of others. I am not at liberty to give you the whole of my reasons, but you may, I assure you, take it from me that they are good ones, sound and unselfish, and spring from the highest sense of duty.

"Could you look, sir, into my heart, you would approve to the full the sentiments which animate me. Nay, more, you would count me amongst the best and truest of your friends."

Again he looked at us all keenly. I had a growing conviction that this sudden change of his entire intellectual method was but yet another phase of his madness, and so determined to let him go on a little longer, knowing from experience that he would, like all lunatics, give himself away in the end. Van Helsing was gazing at him with a look of utmost intensity, his bushy eyebrows almost meeting with the fixed concentration of his look. He said to Renfield in a tone which did not surprise me at the time, but only when I thought of it afterwards—for it was as of one addressing an equal, "Can you not tell frankly your real reason for wishing to be free tonight? I will undertake that if you will satisfy even me, a stranger, without prejudice, and with the habit of keeping an open mind, Dr. Seward will give you, at his own risk and on his own responsibility, the privilege you seek."

He shook his head sadly, and with a look of poignant regret on his face. The Professor went on, "Come, sir, bethink yourself. You claim the privilege of reason in the highest degree, since you seek to impress us with your complete reasonableness. You do this, whose sanity we have reason to doubt, since you are not yet released from medical treatment for this very defect. If you will not help us in our effort to choose the wisest course, how can we perform the duty which you yourself put upon us? Be wise, and help us, and if we can we shall aid you to achieve your wish."

He still shook his head as he said, "Dr. Van Helsing, I have nothing to say. Your argument is complete, and if I were free to speak I should not hesitate a moment, but I am not my own master in the matter. I can only ask you to trust me. If I am refused, the responsibility does not rest with me."

I thought it was now time to end the scene, which was becoming too comically grave, so I went towards the door, simply saying, "Come, my friends, we have work to do. Goodnight."

As, however, I got near the door, a new change came over the patient. He moved towards me so quickly that for the moment I feared that he was about to make another homicidal attack. My fears, however, were groundless, for he held up his two hands imploringly, and made his petition in a moving manner. As he saw that the very excess of his emotion was militating against him, by restoring us more to our old relations, he became still more demonstrative. I glanced at Van Helsing, and saw my conviction reflected in his eyes, so I became a little more fixed in my manner, if not more stern, and motioned to him that his efforts were unavailing. I had previously seen something of the same constantly growing excitement in him when he had to make some request of which at the time he had thought much, such for instance, as when he wanted a cat, and I was prepared to see the collapse into the same sullen acquiescence on this occasion. My expectation was not realized, for when he found that his appeal would not be successful, he got into quite a frantic condition. He threw himself on his knees, and held up his hands, wringing them in plaintive supplication, and poured forth a torrent of entreaty, with the tears rolling down his cheeks, and his whole face and form expressive of the deepest emotion.

"Let me entreat you, Dr. Seward, oh, let me implore you, to let me out of this house at once. Send me away how you will and where you will, send keepers with me with whips and chains, let them take me in a strait waistcoat, manacled and leg-ironed, even to gaol, but let me go out of this. You don't know what you do by keeping me here. I am speaking from the depths of my heart—of my very soul. You don't know whom you wrong, or how, and I may not tell. Woe is me! I may not tell. By all you hold sacred—by all you hold dear—by your love that is lost—by your hope that lives—for the sake of the Almighty, take me out of this and save my soul from guilt! Can't you hear me, man? Can't you understand? Will you never learn? Don't you know that I am sane and earnest now, that I am no lunatic in a mad fit, but a sane man fighting for his soul? Oh, hear me! Hear me! Let me go, let me go, let me go!"

I thought that the longer this went on the wilder he would get, and so would bring on a fit, so I took him by the hand and raised him up.

"Come," I said sternly, "no more of this, we have had quite enough already. Get to your bed and try to behave more discreetly."

He suddenly stopped and looked at me intently for several moments. Then, without a word, he rose and moving over, sat down on the side of the bed. The collapse had come, as on former occasions, just as I had expected.

When I was leaving the room, last of our party, he said to me in a quiet, well-bred voice, "You will, I trust, Dr. Seward, do me the justice to bear in mind, later on, that I did what I could to convince you tonight."

CHAPTER XIX

JONATHAN HARKER'S JOURNAL

1 October, 5 a.m.

I went with the party to the search with an easy mind, for I think I never saw Mina so absolutely strong and well. I am so glad that she consented to hold back and let us men do the work. Somehow, it was a dread to me that she was in this fearful business at all, but now that her work is done, and that it is due to her energy and brains and foresight that the whole story is put together in such a way that every point tells, she may well feel that her part is finished, and that she can henceforth leave the rest to us. We were, I think, all a little upset by the scene with Mr. Renfield. When we came away from his room we were silent till we got back to the study.

Then Mr. Morris said to Dr. Seward, "Say, Jack, if that man wasn't attempting a bluff, he is about the sanest lunatic I ever saw. I'm not sure, but I believe that he had some serious purpose, and if he had, it was pretty rough on him not to get a chance."

Lord Godalming and I were silent, but Dr. Van Helsing added, "Friend John, you know more lunatics than I do, and I'm glad of it, for I fear that if it had been to me to decide I would before that last hysterical outburst have given him free. But we live and learn, and in our present task we must take no chance, as my friend Quincey would say. All is best as they are."

Dr. Seward seemed to answer them both in a dreamy kind of way, "I don't know but that I agree with you. If that man had been an ordinary lunatic I would have taken my chance of trusting him, but he seems so mixed up with the Count in an indexy kind of way that I am afraid of doing anything wrong by helping his fads. I can't forget how he prayed with almost equal fervor for a cat, and then tried to tear my throat out with his teeth. Besides, he called the Count 'lord and master,' and he may want to get out to help him in some diabolical way. That horrid thing has the wolves and the rats and his own kind to help him, so I suppose he isn't above trying to use a respectable lunatic. He certainly did seem earnest, though. I only hope we have done what is best. These things, in conjunction with the wild work we have in hand, help to unnerve a man."

The Professor stepped over, and laying his hand on his shoulder, said in his grave, kindly way, "Friend John, have no fear. We are trying to do our duty in a very sad and terrible case, we can only do as we deem best. What else have we to hope for, except the pity of the good God?" Lord Godalming had slipped away for a few minutes, but now he returned.

He held up a little silver whistle as he remarked, "That old place may be full of rats, and if so, I've got an antidote on call." Having passed the wall, we took our way to the house, taking care to keep in the shadows of the trees on the lawn when the moonlight shone out. When we got to the porch the Professor opened his bag and took out a lot of things, which he laid on the step, sorting them into four little groups, evidently one for each. Then he spoke.

"My friends, we are going into a terrible danger, and we need arms of many kinds. Our enemy is not merely spiritual. Remember that he has the strength of twenty men, and that, though our necks or our windpipes are of the common kind—and therefore breakable or crushable—his are not amenable to mere strength. A stronger man, or a body of men more strong in all than him, can at certain times hold him, but they cannot hurt him as we can be hurt by him. We must, therefore, guard ourselves from his touch. Keep this near your heart." As he spoke he lifted a little silver crucifix and held it out to me, I being nearest to him. "Put these flowers round your neck." Here he handed to me a wreath of withered garlic blossoms. "For other enemies more mundane, this revolver and this knife, and for aid in all, these so small electric lamps, which you can fasten to your breast, and for all, and above all at the last, this, which we must not desecrate needless." This was a portion of Sacred Wafer, which he put in an envelope and handed to me. Each of the others was similarly equipped. "Now," he said, "friend John, where are the skeleton keys? If so that we can open the door, we need not break house by the window, as before at Miss Lucy's."

Dr. Seward tried one or two skeleton keys, his mechanical dexterity as a surgeon standing him in good stead. Presently he got one to suit, after a little play back and forward the bolt yielded, and with a rusty clang, shot back. We pressed on the door, the rusty hinges creaked, and it slowly opened. It was startlingly like the image conveyed to me in Dr. Seward's diary of the opening of Miss Westenra's tomb, I fancy that the same idea seemed to strike the others, for with one accord they shrank back. The Professor was the first to move forward, and stepped into the open door.

"*In manus tuas, Domine*!" he said, crossing himself as he passed over the threshold. We closed the door behind us, lest when we should have lit our lamps we should possibly attract attention from the road. The Professor carefully tried the lock, lest we might not be able to open it from within should we be in a hurry making our exit. Then we all lit our lamps and proceeded on our search.

The light from the tiny lamps fell in all sorts of odd forms, as the rays crossed each other, or the opacity of our bodies threw great shadows. I could not for my life get away from the feeling that there was someone else amongst us. I suppose it was the recollection, so powerfully brought home to me by the grim surroundings, of that terrible experience in Transylvania. I think the feeling was common to us all, for I noticed that the others kept looking over their shoulders at every sound and every new shadow, just as I felt myself doing.

The whole place was thick with dust. The floor was seemingly inches deep, except where there were recent footsteps, in which on holding down my lamp I could see marks of hobnails where the dust was cracked. The walls were fluffy and heavy with dust, and in the corners were masses of spider's webs, whereon the dust had gathered till they looked like old tattered rags as the weight had torn them partly down. On a table in the hall was a great bunch of keys, with a time-yellowed label on each. They had been used several times, for on the table were several similar rents in the blanket of dust, similar to that exposed when the Professor lifted them.

He turned to me and said, "You know this place, Jonathan. You have copied maps of it, and you know it at least more than we do. Which is the way to the chapel?"I had an idea of its direction, though on my former visit I had not been able to get admission to it, so I led the way, and after a few wrong turnings found myself opposite a low, arched oaken door, ribbed with iron bands.

"This is the spot," said the Professor as he turned his lamp on a small map of the house, copied from the file of my original correspondence regarding the purchase. With a little trouble we found the key on the bunch and opened the door. We were prepared for some unpleasantness, for as we were opening the door a faint, malodorous air seemed to exhale through the gaps, but none of us ever expected such an odour as we encountered. None of the others had met the Count at all at close quarters, and when I had seen him he was either in the fasting stage of his existence in his rooms or, when he was bloated with fresh blood, in a ruined building open to the air, but here the place was small and close, and the long disuse had made the air stagnant and foul. There was an earthy smell, as of some dry miasma, which came through the fouler air. But as to the odour itself, how shall I describe it? It was not alone that it was composed of all the ills of mortality and with the pungent, acrid smell of blood, but it seemed as though corruption had become itself corrupt. Faugh! It sickens me to think of it. Every breath exhaled by that monster seemed to have clung to the place and intensified its loathsomeness.

Under ordinary circumstances such a stench would have brought our enterprise to an end, but this was no ordinary case, and the high and terrible purpose in which we were involved gave us a strength which rose above merely physical considerations. After the involuntary shrinking consequent on the first nauseous whiff, we one and all set about our work as though that loathsome place were a garden of roses.

We made an accurate examination of the place, the Professor saying as we began, "The first thing is to see how many of the boxes are left, we must then examine every hole and corner and cranny and see if we cannot get some clue as to what has become of the rest." A glance was sufficient to show how many remained, for the great earth chests were bulky, and there was no mistaking them.

There were only twenty-nine left out of the fifty! Once I got a fright, for, seeing Lord Godalming suddenly turn and look out of the vaulted door into the dark passage beyond, I looked too, and for an instant my heart stood still. Somewhere, looking out from the shadow, I seemed to see the high lights of the Count's evil face, the ridge of the nose, the red eyes, the red lips, the awful pallor. It was only for a moment, for, as Lord Godalming said, "I thought I saw a face, but it was only the shadows," and resumed his inquiry, I turned my lamp in the direction, and stepped into the passage. There was no sign of anyone, and as there were no corners, no doors, no aperture of any kind, but only the solid walls of the passage, there could be no hiding place even for *him*. I took it that fear had helped imagination, and said nothing.

A few minutes later I saw Morris step suddenly back from a corner, which he was examining. We all followed his movements with our eyes, for undoubtedly some nervousness was growing on us, and we saw a whole mass of phosphorescence, which twinkled like stars. We all instinctively drew back. The whole place was becoming alive with rats.

For a moment or two we stood appalled, all save Lord Godalming, who was seemingly prepared for such an emergency. Rushing over to the great iron-bound oaken door, which Dr. Seward had described from the outside, and which I had seen myself, he turned the key in the lock, drew the huge bolts, and swung the door open. Then, taking his little silver whistle from his pocket, he blew a low, shrill call. It was answered from behind Dr. Seward's house by the yelping of dogs, and after about a minute three terriers came dashing round the corner of the house. Unconsciously we had all moved towards the door, and as we moved I noticed that the dust had been much disturbed. The boxes which had been taken out had been brought this way. But even in the minute that had elapsed the number of the rats had vastly increased. They seemed to swarm over the place all at once, till the lamplight, shining on their moving dark bodies and glittering, baleful eyes, made the place look like a bank of earth set with fireflies. The dogs dashed on, but at the threshold suddenly stopped and snarled, and then, simultaneously lifting their noses, began to howl in most lugubrious fashion. The rats were multiplying in thousands, and we moved out.

Lord Godalming lifted one of the dogs, and carrying him in, placed him on the floor. The instant his feet touched the ground he seemed to recover his courage, and rushed at his natural enemies. They fled before him so fast that before he had shaken the life out of a score, the other dogs, who had by now been lifted in the same manner, had but small prey ere the whole mass had vanished.

With their going it seemed as if some evil presence had departed, for the dogs frisked about and barked merrily as they made sudden darts at their prostrate foes, and turned them over and over and tossed them in the air with vicious shakes. We all seemed to find our spirits rise. Whether it was the purifying of the deadly atmosphere by the opening of the chapel door, or the relief which we experienced by finding ourselves in the open I know not, but most certainly the shadow of dread seemed to slip from us like a robe, and the occasion of our coming lost something of its grim significance, though we did not slacken a whit in our resolution. We closed the outer door and barred and locked it, and bringing the dogs with us, began our search of the house. We found nothing throughout except dust in extraordinary proportions, and all untouched save for my own footsteps when I had made my first visit. Never once did the dogs exhibit any symptom of uneasiness, and even when we returned to the chapel they frisked about as though they had been rabbit hunting in a summer wood.

The morning was quickening in the east when we emerged from the front. Dr. Van Helsing had taken the key of the hall door from the bunch, and locked the door in orthodox fashion, putting the key into his pocket when he had done.

"So far," he said, "our night has been eminently successful. No harm has come to us such as I feared might be and yet we have ascertained how many boxes are missing. More than all do I rejoice that this, our first—and perhaps our most difficult and dangerous—step has been accomplished without the bringing thereinto our most sweet Madam Mina or troubling her waking or sleeping thoughts with sights and sounds and smells of horror which she might never forget. One lesson, too, we have learned, if it be allowable to argue a *particulari*, that the brute beasts which are to the Count's command are yet themselves not amenable to his spiritual power, for look, these rats that would come to his call, just as from his castle top he summon the wolves to your going and to that poor mother's cry, though they come to him, they run pell-mell from the so little dogs of my friend Arthur. We have other matters before us, other dangers, other fears, and that monster—he has not used his power over the brute world for the only or the last time tonight. So be it that he has gone elsewhere. Good! It has given us opportunity to cry 'check' in some ways in this chess game, which we play for the stake of human souls. And now let us go home. The dawn is close at hand, and we have reason to be content with our first night's work. It may be ordained that we have many nights and days to follow, if full of peril, but we must go on, and from no danger shall we shrink."

The house was silent when we got back, save for some poor creature who was screaming away in one of the distant wards, and a low, moaning sound from Renfield's room. The poor wretch was doubtless torturing himself, after the manner of the insane, with needless thoughts of pain.

I came tiptoe into our own room, and found Mina asleep, breathing so softly that I had to put my ear down to hear it. She looks paler than usual. I hope the meeting tonight has not upset her. I am truly thankful that she is to be left out of our future work, and even of our deliberations. It is too great a strain for a woman to bear. I did not think so at first, but I know better now. Therefore I am glad that it is settled. There may be things which would frighten her to hear, and yet to conceal them from her might be worse than to tell her if once she suspected that there was any concealment. Henceforth our work is to be a sealed book to her, till at least such time as we can tell her that all is finished, and the earth free from a monster of the nether world. I daresay it will be difficult to begin to keep silence after such confidence as ours, but I must be resolute, and tomorrow I shall keep dark over tonight's doings, and shall refuse to speak of anything that has happened. I rest on the sofa, so as not to disturb her.

1 October, later.

I suppose it was natural that we should have all overslept ourselves, for the day was a busy one, and the night had no rest at all. Even Mina must have felt its exhaustion, for though I slept till the sun was high, I was awake before her, and had to call two or three times before she awoke. Indeed, she was so sound asleep that for a few seconds she did not recognize me, but looked at me with a sort of blank terror, as one looks who has been waked out of a bad dream. She complained a little of being tired, and I let her rest till later in the day. We now know of twenty-one boxes having been removed, and if it be that several were taken in any of these removals we may be able to trace them all. Such will, of course, immensely simplify our labor, and the sooner the matter is attended to the better. I shall look up Thomas Snelling today.

Dr. Seward's Diary

1 October.

It was towards noon when I was awakened by the Professor walking into my room. He was more jolly and cheerful than usual, and it is quite evident that last night's work has helped to take some of the brooding weight off his mind.

After going over the adventure of the night he suddenly said, "Your patient interests me much. May it be that with you I visit him this morning? Or if that you are too occupy, I can go alone if it may be.

It is a new experience to me to find a lunatic who talk philosophy, and reason so sound." I had some work to do which pressed, so I told him that if he would go alone I would be glad, as then I should not have to keep him waiting, so I called an attendant and gave him the necessary instructions. Before the Professor left the room I cautioned him against getting any false impression from my patient. "But," he answered, "I want him to talk of himself and of his delusion as to consuming live things. He said to Madam Mina, as I see in your diary of yesterday, that he had once had such a belief. Why do you smile, friend John?"

"Excuse me," I said, "but the answer is here." I laid my hand on the typewritten matter. "When our sane and learned lunatic made that very statement of how he used to consume life, his mouth was actually nauseous with the flies and spiders which he had eaten just before Mrs. Harker entered the room."

Van Helsing smiled in turn. "Good!" he said. "Your memory is true, friend John. I should have remembered. And yet it is this very obliquity of thought and memory which makes mental disease such a fascinating study. Perhaps I may gain more knowledge out of the folly of this madman than I shall from the teaching of the most wise. Who knows?" I went on with my work, and before long was through that in hand. It seemed that the time had been very short indeed, but there was Van Helsing back in the study.

"Do I interrupt?" he asked politely as he stood at the door.

"Not at all," I answered. "Come in. My work is finished, and I am free. I can go with you now, if you like."

"It is needless, I have seen him!"

"Well?"

"I fear that he does not appraise me at much. Our interview was short. When I entered his room he was sitting on a stool in the centre, with his elbows on his knees, and his face was the picture of sullen discontent. I spoke to him as cheerfully as I could, and with such a measure of respect as I could assume. He made no reply whatever. 'Don't you know me?' I asked. His answer was not reassuring: 'I know you well enough; you are the old fool Van Helsing. I wish you would take yourself and your idiotic brain theories somewhere else. Damn all thick-headed Dutchmen!' Not a word more would he say, but sat in his implacable sullenness as indifferent to me as though I had not been in the room at all. Thus departed for this time my chance of much learning from this so clever lunatic, so I shall go, if I may, and cheer myself with a few happy words with that sweet soul Madam Mina. Friend John, it does rejoice me unspeakable that she is no more to be pained, no more to be worried with our terrible things. Though we shall much miss her help, it is better so."

"I agree with you with all my heart," I answered earnestly, for I did not want him to weaken in this matter. "Mrs. Harker is better out of it. Things are quite bad enough for us, all men of the world, and who have been in many tight places in our time, but it is no place for a woman, and if she had remained in touch with the affair, it would in time infallibly have wrecked her."

So Van Helsing has gone to confer with Mrs. Harker and Harker, Quincey and Art are all out following up the clues as to the earth boxes. I shall finish my round of work and we shall meet tonight.

Mina Harker's Journal

1 October.

It is strange to me to be kept in the dark as I am today, after Jonathan's full confidence for so many years, to see him manifestly avoid certain matters, and those the most vital of all. This morning I slept late after the fatigues of yesterday, and though Jonathan was late too, he was the earlier. He spoke to me before he went out, never more sweetly or tenderly, but he never mentioned a word of what had happened in the visit to the Count's house. And yet he must have known how terribly anxious I was. Poor dear fellow! I suppose it must have distressed him even more than it did me. They all agreed that it was best that I should not be drawn further into this awful work, and I acquiesced. But to think that he keeps anything from me! And now I am crying like a silly fool, when I know it comes from my husband's great love and from the good, good wishes of those other strong men.

That has done me good. Well, someday Jonathan will tell me all. And lest it should ever be that he should think for a moment that I kept anything from him, I still keep my journal as usual. Then if he has feared of my trust I shall show it to him, with every thought of my heart put down for his dear eyes to read. I feel strangely sad and low-spirited today. I suppose it is the reaction from the terrible excitement.

Last night I went to bed when the men had gone, simply because they told me to. I didn't feel sleepy, and I did feel full of devouring anxiety.

I kept thinking over everything that has been ever since Jonathan came to see me in London, and it all seems like a horrible tragedy, with fate pressing on relentlessly to some destined end. Everything that one does seems, no matter how right it may be, to bring on the very thing which is most to be deplored. If I hadn't gone to Whitby, perhaps poor dear Lucy would be with us now. She hadn't taken to visiting the churchyard till I came, and if she hadn't come there in the day time with me she wouldn't have walked in her sleep. And if she hadn't gone there at night and asleep, that monster couldn't have destroyed her as he did. Oh, why did I ever go to Whitby? There now, crying again! I wonder what has come over me today. I must hide it from Jonathan, for if he knew that I had been crying twice in one morning—I, who never cried on my own account, and whom he has never caused to shed a tear—the dear fellow would fret his heart out. I shall put a bold face on, and if I do feel weepy, he shall never see it. I suppose it is just one of the lessons that we poor women have to learn . . .

I can't quite remember how I fell asleep last night. I remember hearing the sudden barking of the dogs and a lot of queer sounds, like praying on a very tumultuous scale, from Mr. Renfield's room, which is somewhere under this. And then there was silence over everything, silence so profound that it startled me, and I got up and looked out of the window. All was dark and silent, the black shadows thrown by the moonlight seeming full of a silent mystery of their own. Not a thing seemed to be stirring, but all to be grim and fixed as death or fate, so that a thin streak of white mist, that crept with almost imperceptible slowness across the grass towards the house, seemed to have a sentience and a vitality of its own. I think that the digression of my thoughts must have done me good, for when I got back to bed I found a lethargy creeping over me. I lay a while, but could not quite sleep, so I got out and looked out of the window again. The mist was spreading, and was now close up to the house, so that I could see it lying thick against the wall, as though it were stealing up to the windows. The poor man was more loud than ever, and though I could not distinguish a word he said, I could in some way recognize in his tones some passionate entreaty on his part. Then there was the sound of a struggle, and I knew that the attendants were dealing with him. I was so frightened that I crept into bed, and pulled the clothes over my head, putting my fingers in my ears. I was not then a bit sleepy, at least so I thought, but I must have fallen asleep, for except dreams, I do not remember anything until the morning, when Jonathan woke me. I think that it took me an effort and a little time to realize where I was, and that it was Jonathan who was bending over me. My dream was very peculiar, and was almost typical of the way that waking thoughts become merged in, or continued in, dreams.

I thought that I was asleep, and waiting for Jonathan to come back. I was very anxious about him, and I was powerless to act, my feet, and my hands, and my brain were weighted, so that nothing could proceed at the usual pace. And so I slept uneasily and thought. Then it began to dawn upon me that the air was heavy, and dank, and cold. I put back the clothes from my face, and found, to my surprise, that all was dim around. The gaslight which I had left lit for Jonathan, but turned down, came only like a tiny red spark through the fog, which had evidently grown thicker and poured into the room. Then it occurred to me that I had shut the window before I had come to bed. I would have got out to make certain on the point, but some leaden lethargy seemed to chain my limbs and even my will. I lay still and endured, that was all. I closed my eyes, but could still see through my eyelids. (It is wonderful what tricks our dreams play us, and how conveniently we can imagine.) The mist grew thicker and thicker and I could see now how it came in, for I could see it like smoke—or with the white energy of boiling water—pouring in, not through the window, but through the joinings of the door. It got thicker and thicker, till it seemed as if it became concentrated into a sort of pillar of cloud in the room, through the top of which I could see the light of the gas shining like a red eye. Things began to whirl through my brain just as the cloudy column was now whirling in the room, and through it all came the scriptural words "a pillar of cloud by day and of fire by night." Was it indeed such spiritual guidance that was coming to me in my sleep? But the pillar was composed of both the day and the night guiding, for the fire was in the red eye, which at the thought got a new fascination for me, till, as I looked, the fire divided, and seemed to shine on me through the fog like two red eyes, such as Lucy told me of in her momentary mental wandering when, on the cliff, the dying sunlight struck the windows of St. Mary's Church. Suddenly the horror burst upon me that it was thus that Jonathan had seen those awful women growing into reality through the whirling mist in the moonlight, and in my dream I must have fainted, for all became black darkness. The last conscious effort which imagination made was to show me a livid white face bending over me out of the mist. I must be careful of such dreams, for they would unseat one's reason if there were too much of them. I would get Dr. Van Helsing or Dr. Seward to prescribe something for me which would make me sleep, only that I fear to alarm them. Such a dream at the present time would become woven into their fears for me. Tonight I shall strive hard to sleep naturally. If I do not, I shall tomorrow night get them to give me a dose of chloral, that cannot hurt me for once, and it will give me a good night's sleep. Last night tired me more than if I had not slept at all.

2 October, 10 p.m.

Last night I slept, but did not dream. I must have slept soundly, for I was not waked by Jonathan coming to bed, but the sleep has not refreshed me, for today I feel terribly weak and spiritless. I spent all yesterday trying to read, or lying down dozing. In the afternoon, Mr. Renfield asked if he might see me. Poor man, he was very gentle, and when I came away he kissed my hand and bade God bless me. Some way it affected me much. I am crying when I think of him. This is a new weakness, of which I must be careful. Jonathan would be miserable if he knew I had been crying. He and the others were out till dinner time, and they all came in tired. I did what I could to brighten them up, and I suppose that the effort did me good, for I forgot how tired I was. After dinner they sent me to bed, and all went off to smoke together, as they said, but I knew that they wanted to tell each other of what had occurred to each during the day. I could see from Jonathan's manner that he had something important to communicate. I was not so sleepy as I should have been, so before they went I asked Dr. Seward to give me a little opiate of some kind, as I had not slept well the night before. He very kindly made me up a sleeping draught, which he gave to me, telling me that it would do me no harm, as it was very mild . . . I have taken it, and am waiting for sleep, which still keeps aloof. I hope I have not done wrong, for as sleep begins to flirt with me, a new fear comes: that I may have been foolish in thus depriving myself of the power of waking. I might want it. Here comes sleep. Good night.

CHAPTER XX

Jonathan Harker's Journal

1 October, evening.

I found Thomas Snelling in his house at Bethnal Green, but unhappily he was not in a condition to remember anything. The very prospect of beer which my expected coming had opened to him had proved too much, and he had begun too early on his expected debauch. I learned, however, from his wife, who seemed a decent, poor soul, that he was only the assistant of Smollet, who of the two mates was the responsible person. So off I drove to Walworth, and found Mr. Joseph Smollet at home and in his shirtsleeves, taking a late tea out of a saucer. He is a decent, intelligent fellow, distinctly a good, reliable type of workman, and with a headpiece of his own. He remembered all about the incident of the boxes, and from a wonderful dog-eared notebook, which he produced from some mysterious receptacle about the seat of his trousers, and which had hieroglyphical entries in thick, half-obliterated pencil, he gave me the destinations of the boxes. There were, he said, six in the cartload which he took from Carfax and left at 197 Chicksand Street, Mile End New Town, and another six which he deposited at Jamaica Lane, Bermondsey. If then the Count meant to scatter these ghastly refuges of his over London, these places were chosen as the first of delivery, so that later he might distribute more fully. The systematic manner in which this was done made me think that he could not mean to confine himself to two sides of London. He was now fixed on the far east on the northern shore, on the east of the southern shore, and on the south. The north and west were surely never meant to be left out of his diabolical scheme, let alone the City itself and the very heart of fashionable London in the south-west and west. I went back to Smollet, and asked him if he could tell us if any other boxes had been taken from Carfax.

He replied, "Well guv'nor, you've treated me very 'an'some," I had given him half a sovereign, "an I'll tell yer all I know. I heard a man by the name of Bloxam say four nights ago in the 'Are an' 'Ounds, in Pincher's Alley, as 'ow he an' his mate 'ad 'ad a rare dusty job in a old 'ouse at Purfleet. There ain't a many such jobs as this 'ere, an' I'm thinkin' that maybe Sam Bloxam could tell ye summut."

I asked if he could tell me where to find him. I told him that if he could get me the address it would be worth another half sovereign to him. So he gulped down the rest of his tea and stood up, saying that he was going to begin the search then and there.

At the door he stopped, and said, "Look 'ere, guv'nor, there ain't no sense in me a keepin' you 'ere. I may find Sam soon, or I mayn't, but anyhow he ain't like to be in a way to tell ye much tonight. Sam is a rare one when he starts on the booze. If you can give me a envelope with a stamp on it, and put yer address on it, I'll find out where Sam is to be found and post it ye tonight. But ye'd better be up arter 'im soon in the mornin,' never mind the booze the night afore."

This was all practical, so one of the children went off with a penny to buy an envelope and a sheet of paper, and to keep the change. When she came back, I addressed the envelope and stamped it, and when Smollet had again faithfully promised to post the address when found, I took my way to home. We're on the track anyhow. I am tired tonight, and I want to sleep. Mina is fast asleep, and looks a little too pale. Her eyes look as though she had been crying. Poor dear, I've no doubt it frets her to be kept in the dark, and it may make her doubly anxious about me and the others. But it is best as it is. It is better to be disappointed and worried in such a way now than to have her nerve broken. The doctors were quite right to insist on her being kept out of this dreadful business. I must be firm, for on me this particular burden of silence must rest. I shall not ever enter on the subject with her under any circumstances. Indeed, It may not be a hard task, after all, for she herself has become reticent on the subject, and has not spoken of the Count or his doings ever since we told her of our decision.

2 October, evening.

A long and trying and exciting day. By the first post I got my directed envelope with a dirty scrap of paper enclosed, on which was written with a carpenter's pencil in a sprawling hand, "Sam Bloxam, Korkrans, 4 Poters Cort, Bartel Street, Walworth. Arsk for the depite."

I got the letter in bed, and rose without waking Mina. She looked heavy and sleepy and pale, and far from well. I determined not to wake her, but that when I should return from this new search, I would arrange for her going back to Exeter. I think she would be happier in our own home, with her daily tasks to interest her, than in being here amongst us and in ignorance. I only saw Dr. Seward for a moment, and told him where I was off to, promising to come back and tell the rest so soon as I should have found out anything. I drove to Walworth and found, with some difficulty, Potter's Court. Mr. Smollet's spelling misled me, as I asked for Poter's Court instead of Potter's Court. However, when I had found the court, I had no difficulty in discovering Corcoran's lodging house.

When I asked the man who came to the door for the "depite," he shook his head, and said, "I dunno 'im. There ain't no such a person 'ere. I never 'eard of 'im in all my bloomin' days. Don't believe there ain't nobody of that kind livin' 'ere or anywheres."

I took out Smollet's letter, and as I read it it seemed to me that the lesson of the spelling of the name of the court might guide me. "What are you?" I asked.

"I'm the depity," he answered.

I saw at once that I was on the right track. Phonetic spelling had again misled me. A half crown tip put the deputy's knowledge at my disposal, and I learned that Mr. Bloxam, who had slept off the remains of his beer on the previous night at Corcoran's, had left for his work at Poplar at five o'clock that morning. He could not tell me where the place of work was situated, but he had a vague idea that it was some kind of a "new-fangled ware'us," and with this slender clue I had to start for Poplar. It was twelve o'clock before I got any satisfactory hint of such a building, and this I got at a coffee shop, where some workmen were having their dinner. One of them suggested that there was being erected at Cross Angel Street a new "cold storage" building, and as this suited the condition of a "new-fangled ware'us," I at once drove to it. An interview with a surly gatekeeper and a surlier foreman, both of whom were appeased with the coin of the realm, put me on the track of Bloxam. He was sent for on my suggestion that I was willing to pay his days wages to his foreman for the privilege of asking him a few questions on a private matter. He was a smart enough fellow, though rough of speech and bearing. When I had promised to pay for his information and given him an earnest, he told me that he had made two journeys between Carfax and a house in Piccadilly, and had taken from this house to the latter nine great boxes, "main heavy ones," with a horse and cart hired by him for this purpose.

I asked him if he could tell me the number of the house in Piccadilly, to which he replied, "Well, guv'nor, I forgits the number, but it was only a few door from a big white church, or somethink of the kind, not long built. It was a dusty old 'ouse, too, though nothin' to the dustiness of the 'ouse we tooked the bloomin' boxes from."

"How did you get in if both houses were empty?"

"There was the old party what engaged me a waitin' in the 'ouse at Purfleet. He 'elped me to lift the boxes and put them in the dray. Curse me, but he was the strongest chap I ever struck, an' him a old feller, with a white moustache, one that thin you would think he couldn't throw a shadder."

How this phrase thrilled through me!

"Why, 'e took up 'is end o' the boxes like they was pounds of tea, and me a puffin' an' a blowin' afore I could upend mine anyhow—an' I'm no chicken, neither."

"How did you get into the house in Piccadilly?" I asked.

"He was there too. He must 'a started off and got there afore me, for when I rung of the bell he kem an' opened the door 'isself an' 'elped me carry the boxes into the 'all."

"The whole nine?" I asked.

"Yus, there was five in the first load an' four in the second. It was main dry work, an' I don't so well remember 'ow I got 'ome."

I interrupted him, "Were the boxes left in the hall?"

"Yus, it was a big 'all, an' there was nothin' else in it."

I made one more attempt to further matters. "You didn't have any key?"

"Never used no key nor nothink. The old gent, he opened the door 'isself an' shut it again when I druv off. I don't remember the last time, but that was the beer."

"And you can't remember the number of the house?"

"No, sir. But ye needn't have no difficulty about that. It's a 'igh 'un with a stone front with a bow on it, an' 'igh steps up to the door. I know them steps, 'avin' 'ad to carry the boxes up with three loafers what come round to earn a copper. The old gent give them shillin's, an' they seein' they got so much, they wanted more. But 'e took one of them by the shoulder and was like to throw 'im down the steps, till the lot of them went away cussin'."

I thought that with this description I could find the house, so having paid my friend for his information, I started off for Piccadilly. I had gained a new painful experience. The Count could, it was evident, handle the earth boxes himself. If so, time was precious, for now that he had achieved a certain amount of distribution, he could, by choosing his own time, complete the task unobserved. At Piccadilly Circus I discharged my cab, and walked westward. Beyond the Junior Constitutional I came across the house described and was satisfied that this was the next of the lairs arranged by Dracula. The house looked as though it had been long untenanted. The windows were encrusted with dust, and the shutters were up. All the framework was black with time, and from the iron the paint had mostly scaled away. It was evident that up to lately there had been a large notice board in front of the balcony. It had, however, been roughly torn away, the uprights which had supported it still remaining. Behind the rails of the balcony I saw there were some loose boards, whose raw edges looked white. I would have given a good deal to have been able to see the notice board intact, as it would, perhaps, have given some clue to the ownership of the house. I remembered my experience of the investigation and purchase of Carfax, and I could not but feel that if I could find the former owner there might be some means discovered of gaining access to the house.

There was at present nothing to be learned from the Piccadilly side, and nothing could be done, so I went around to the back to see if anything could be gathered from this quarter. The mews were active, the Piccadilly houses being mostly in occupation. I asked one or two of the grooms and helpers whom I saw around if they could tell me anything about the empty house. One of them said that he heard it had lately been taken, but he couldn't say from whom. He told me, however, that up to very lately there had been a notice board of "For Sale" up, and that perhaps Mitchell, Sons & Candy the house agents could tell me something, as he thought he remembered seeing the name of that firm on the board. I did not wish to seem too eager, or to let my informant know or guess too much, so thanking him in the usual manner, I strolled away. It was now growing dusk, and the autumn night was closing in, so I did not lose any time. Having learned the address of Mitchell, Sons & Candy from a directory at the Berkeley, I was soon at their office in Sackville Street.

The gentleman who saw me was particularly suave in manner, but uncommunicative in equal proportion. Having once told me that the Piccadilly house, which throughout our interview he called a "mansion," was sold, he considered my business as concluded. When I asked who had purchased it, he opened his eyes a thought wider, and paused a few seconds before replying, "It is sold, sir."

"Pardon me," I said, with equal politeness, "but I have a special reason for wishing to know who purchased it."

Again he paused longer, and raised his eyebrows still more. "It is sold, sir," was again his laconic reply.

"Surely," I said, "you do not mind letting me know so much."

"But I do mind," he answered. "The affairs of their clients are absolutely safe in the hands of Mitchell, Sons & Candy."

This was manifestly a prig of the first water, and there was no use arguing with him. I thought I had best meet him on his own ground, so I said, "Your clients, sir, are happy in having so resolute a guardian of their confidence. I am myself a professional man."

Here I handed him my card. "In this instance I am not prompted by curiosity, I act on the part of Lord Godalming, who wishes to know something of the property which was, he understood, lately for sale."

These words put a different complexion on affairs. He said, "I would like to oblige you if I could, Mr. Harker, and especially would I like to oblige his lordship. We once carried out a small matter of renting some chambers for him when he was the honourable Arthur Holmwood. If you will let me have his lordship's address I will consult the House on the subject, and will, in any case, communicate with his lordship by tonight's post. It will be a pleasure if we can so far deviate from our rules as to give the required information to his lordship."

I wanted to secure a friend, and not to make an enemy, so I thanked him, gave the address at Dr. Seward's and came away. It was now dark, and I was tired and hungry. I got a cup of tea at the Aerated Bread Company and came down to Purfleet by the next train.

I found all the others at home. Mina was looking tired and pale, but she made a gallant effort to be bright and cheerful. It wrung my heart to think that I had had to keep anything from her and so caused her inquietude. Thank God, this will be the last night of her looking on at our conferences, and feeling the sting of our not showing our confidence. It took all my courage to hold to the wise resolution of keeping her out of our grim task. She seems somehow more reconciled, or else the very subject seems to have become repugnant to her, for when any accidental allusion is made she actually shudders. I am glad we made our resolution in time, as with such a feeling as this, our growing knowledge would be torture to her.

I could not tell the others of the day's discovery till we were alone, so after dinner—followed by a little music to save appearances even amongst ourselves—I took Mina to her room and left her to go to bed. The dear girl was more affectionate with me than ever, and clung to me as though she would detain me, but there was much to be talked of and I came away. Thank God, the ceasing of telling things has made no difference between us.

When I came down again I found the others all gathered round the fire in the study. In the train I had written my diary so far, and simply read it off to them as the best means of letting them get abreast of my own information.

When I had finished, Van Helsing said, "This has been a great day's work, friend Jonathan. Doubtless we are on the track of the missing boxes. If we find them all in that house, then our work is near the end. But if there be some missing, we must search until we find them. Then shall we make our final *coup*, and hunt the wretch to his real death."

We all sat silent awhile and all at once Mr. Morris spoke, "Say! How are we going to get into that house?"

"We got into the other," answered Lord Godalming quickly.

"But, Art, this is different. We broke house at Carfax, but we had night and a walled park to protect us. It will be a mighty different thing to commit burglary in Piccadilly, either by day or night. I confess I don't see how we are going to get in unless that agency duck can find us a key of some sort."

Lord Godalming's brows contracted, and he stood up and walked about the room. By-and-by he stopped and said, turning from one to another of us, "Quincey's head is level. This burglary business is getting serious. We got off once all right, but we have now a rare job on hand. Unless we can find the Count's key basket."

As nothing could well be done before morning, and as it would be at least advisable to wait till Lord Godalming should hear from Mitchell's, we decided not to take any active step before breakfast time. For a good while we sat and smoked, discussing the matter in its various lights and bearings. I took the opportunity of bringing this diary right up to the moment. I am very sleepy and shall go to bed . . .

Just a line. Mina sleeps soundly and her breathing is regular. Her forehead is puckered up into little wrinkles, as though she thinks even in her sleep. She is still too pale, but does not look so haggard as she did this morning. Tomorrow will, I hope, mend all this. She will be herself at home in Exeter. Oh, but I am sleepy!

Dr. Seward's Diary

1 October.

I am puzzled afresh about Renfield. His moods change so rapidly that I find it difficult to keep touch of them, and as they always mean something more than his own well-being, they form a more than interesting study. This morning, when I went to see him after his repulse of Van Helsing, his manner was that of a man commanding destiny. He was, in fact, commanding destiny—subjectively. He did not really care for any of the things of mere earth, he was in the clouds and looked down on all the weaknesses and wants of us poor mortals.

I thought I would improve the occasion and learn something, so I asked him, "What about the flies these times?"

He smiled on me in quite a superior sort of way, such a smile as would have become the face of Malvolio, as he answered me, "The fly, my dear sir, has one striking feature. Its wings are typical of the aerial powers of the psychic faculties. The ancients did well when they typified the soul as a butterfly!"

I thought I would push his analogy to its utmost logically, so I said quickly, "Oh, it is a soul you are after now, is it?"

His madness foiled his reason, and a puzzled look spread over his face as, shaking his head with a decision which I had but seldom seen in him.

He said, "Oh, no, oh no! I want no souls. Life is all I want." Here he brightened up. "I am pretty indifferent about it at present. Life is all right. I have all I want. You must get a new patient, doctor, if you wish to study zoophagy!"

This puzzled me a little, so I drew him on. "Then you command life. You are a god, I suppose?"

He smiled with an ineffably benign superiority. "Oh no! Far be it from me to arrogate to myself the attributes of the Deity. I am not even concerned in His especially spiritual doings. If I may state my intellectual position I am, so far as concerns things purely terrestrial, somewhat in the position which Enoch occupied spiritually!"

This was a poser to me. I could not at the moment recall Enoch's appositeness, so I had to ask a simple question, though I felt that by so doing I was lowering myself in the eyes of the lunatic. "And why with Enoch?"

"Because he walked with God."

I could not see the analogy, but did not like to admit it, so I harked back to what he had denied. "So you don't care about life and you don't want souls. Why not?" I put my question quickly and somewhat sternly, on purpose to disconcert him.

The effort succeeded, for an instant he unconsciously relapsed into his old servile manner, bent low before me, and actually fawned upon me as he replied. "I don't want any souls, indeed, indeed! I don't. I couldn't use them if I had them. They would be no manner of use to me. I couldn't eat them or—" He suddenly stopped and the old cunning look spread over his face, like a wind sweep on the surface of the water. "And doctor, as to life, what is it after all? When you've got all you require, and you know that you will never want, that is all. I have friends—good friends—like you, Dr. Seward." This was said with a leer of inexpressible cunning. "I know that I shall never lack the means of life!"

I think that through the cloudiness of his insanity he saw some antagonism in me, for he at once fell back on the last refuge of such as he, a dogged silence. After a short time I saw that for the present it was useless to speak to him. He was sulky, and so I came away.

Later in the day he sent for me. Ordinarily I would not have come without special reason, but just at present I am so interested in him that I would gladly make an effort. Besides, I am glad to have anything to help pass the time. Harker is out, following up clues, and so are Lord Godalming and Quincey. Van Helsing sits in my study poring over the record prepared by the Harkers. He seems to think that by accurate knowledge of all details he will light up on some clue. He does not wish to be disturbed in the work, without cause. I would have taken him with me to see the patient, only I thought that after his last repulse he might not care to go again. There was also another reason. Renfield might not speak so freely before a third person as when he and I were alone.

I found him sitting in the middle of the floor on his stool, a pose which is generally indicative of some mental energy on his part. When I came in, he said at once, as though the question had been waiting on his lips. "What about souls?"

It was evident then that my surmise had been correct. Unconscious cerebration was doing its work, even with the lunatic. I determined to have the matter out.

"What about them yourself?" I asked.

He did not reply for a moment but looked all around him, and up and down, as though he expected to find some inspiration for an answer.

"I don't want any souls!" he said in a feeble, apologetic way. The matter seemed preying on his mind, and so I determined to use it, to "be cruel only to be kind." So I said, "You like life, and you want life?"

"Oh yes! But that is all right. You needn't worry about that!"

"But," I asked, "how are we to get the life without getting the soul also?"

This seemed to puzzle him, so I followed it up, "A nice time you'll have some time when you're flying out here, with the souls of thousands of flies and spiders and birds and cats buzzing and twittering and moaning all around you. You've got their lives, you know, and you must put up with their souls!" Something seemed to affect his imagination, for he put his fingers to his ears and shut his eyes, screwing them up tightly just as a small boy does when his face is being soaped. There was something pathetic in it that touched me. It also gave me a lesson, for it seemed that before me was a child, only a child, though the features were worn, and the stubble on the jaws was white. It was evident that he was undergoing some process of mental disturbance, and knowing how his past moods had interpreted things seemingly foreign to himself, I thought I would enter into his mind as well as I could and go with him.

The first step was to restore confidence, so I asked him, speaking pretty loud so that he would hear me through his closed ears, "Would you like some sugar to get your flies around again?"

He seemed to wake up all at once, and shook his head. With a laugh he replied, "Not much! Flies are poor things, after all!" After a pause he added, "But I don't want their souls buzzing round me, all the same."

"Or spiders?" I went on.

"Blow spiders! What's the use of spiders? There isn't anything in them to eat or—" He stopped suddenly as though reminded of a forbidden topic.

"So, so!" I thought to myself, "this is the second time he has suddenly stopped at the word 'drink.' What does it mean?"

Renfield seemed himself aware of having made a lapse, for he hurried on, as though to distract my attention from it, "I don't take any stock at all in such matters. 'Rats and mice and such small deer,' as Shakespeare has it, 'chicken feed of the larder' they might be called. I'm past all that sort of nonsense. You might as well ask a man to eat molecules with a pair of chopsticks, as to try to interest me about the less carnivora, when I know of what is before me."

"I see," I said. "You want big things that you can make your teeth meet in? How would you like to breakfast on an elephant?"

"What ridiculous nonsense you are talking?" He was getting too wide awake, so I thought I would press him hard.

"I wonder," I said reflectively, "what an elephant's soul is like!"

The effect I desired was obtained, for he at once fell from his high-horse and became a child again.

"I don't want an elephant's soul, or any soul at all!" he said. For a few moments he sat despondently. Suddenly he jumped to his feet, with his eyes blazing and all the signs of intense cerebral excitement. "To hell with you and your souls!" he shouted. "Why do you plague me about souls? Haven't I got enough to worry, and pain, to distract me already, without thinking of souls?"

He looked so hostile that I thought he was in for another homicidal fit, so I blew my whistle.

The instant, however, that I did so he became calm, and said apologetically, "Forgive me, Doctor. I forgot myself. You do not need any help. I am so worried in my mind that I am apt to be irritable. If you only knew the problem I have to face, and that I am working out, you would pity, and tolerate, and pardon me. Pray do not put me in a strait waistcoat. I want to think and I cannot think freely when my body is confined. I am sure you will understand!" He had evidently self-control, so when the attendants came I told them not to mind, and they withdrew. Renfield watched them go. When the door was closed he said with considerable dignity and sweetness, "Dr. Seward, you have been very considerate towards me. Believe me that I am very, very grateful to you!" I thought it well to leave him in this mood, and so I came away. There is certainly something to ponder over in this man's state. Several points seem to make what the American interviewer calls "a story," if one could only get them in proper order. Here they are:

Will not mention "drinking."

Fears the thought of being burdened with the "soul" of anything.

Has no dread of wanting "life" in the future.

Despises the meaner forms of life altogether, though he dreads being haunted by their souls.

Logically all these things point one way! He has assurance of some kind that he will acquire some higher life.

He dreads the consequence—the burden of a soul. Then it is a human life he looks to!

And the assurance—?

Merciful God! The Count has been to him, and there is some new scheme of terror afoot!

Later.

I went after my round to Van Helsing and told him my suspicion. He grew very grave, and after thinking the matter over for a while asked me to take him to Renfield. I did so. As we came to the door we heard the lunatic within singing gaily, as he used to do in the time which now seems so long ago. When we entered we saw with amazement that he had spread out his sugar as of old. The flies, lethargic with the autumn, were beginning to buzz into the room. We tried to make him talk of the subject of our previous conversation, but he would not attend. He went on with his singing, just as though we had not been present. He had got a scrap of paper and was folding it into a notebook. We had to come away as ignorant as we went in.

His is a curious case indeed. We must watch him tonight.

LETTER, MITCHELL, SONS & CANDY TO LORD GODALMING

1 October.

My Lord,

We are at all times only too happy to meet your wishes. We beg, with regard to the desire of your Lordship, expressed by Mr. Harker on your behalf, to supply the following information concerning the sale and purchase of No. 347, Piccadilly. The original vendors are the executors of the late Mr. Archibald Winter-Suffield. The purchaser is a foreign nobleman, Count de Ville, who effected the purchase himself paying the purchase money in notes "over the counter," if your Lordship will pardon us using so vulgar an expression. Beyond this we know nothing whatever of him.

We are, my Lord,
Your Lordship's humble servants,
MITCHELL, SONS & CANDY.

DR. SEWARD'S DIARY

2 October.

I placed a man in the corridor last night, and told him to make an accurate note of any sound he might hear from Renfield's room, and gave him instructions that if there should be anything strange he was to call me. After dinner, when we had all gathered round the fire in the study—Mrs. Harker having gone to bed—we discussed the attempts and discoveries of the day. Harker was the only one who had any result, and we are in great hopes that his clue may be an important one.

Before going to bed I went round to the patient's room and looked in through the observation trap. He was sleeping soundly, his heart rose and fell with regular respiration.

This morning the man on duty reported to me that a little after midnight he was restless and kept saying his prayers somewhat loudly. I asked him if that was all. He replied that it was all he heard. There was something about his manner, so suspicious that I asked him point blank if he had been asleep. He denied sleep, but admitted to having "dozed" for a while. It is too bad that men cannot be trusted unless they are watched.

Today Harker is out following up his clue, and Art and Quincey are looking after horses. Godalming thinks that it will be well to have horses always in readiness, for when we get the information which we seek there will be no time to lose. We must sterilize all the imported earth between sunrise and sunset. We shall thus catch the Count at his weakest, and without a refuge to fly to. Van Helsing is off to the British Museum looking up some authorities on ancient medicine. The old physicians took account of things which their followers do not accept, and the Professor is searching for witch and demon cures which may be useful to us later.

I sometimes think we must be all mad and that we shall wake to sanity in strait waistcoats.

Later.

We have met again. We seem at last to be on the track, and our work of tomorrow may be the beginning of the end. I wonder if Renfield's quiet has anything to do with this. His moods have so followed the doings of the Count, that the coming destruction of the monster may be carried to him some subtle way. If we could only get some hint as to what passed in his mind, between the time of my argument with him today and his resumption of fly-catching, it might afford us a valuable clue. He is now seemingly quiet for a spell . . . Is he? That wild yell seemed to come from his room . . .

The attendant came bursting into my room and told me that Renfield had somehow met with some accident. He had heard him yell, and when he went to him found him lying on his face on the floor, all covered with blood. I must go at once . . .

CHAPTER XXI

Dr. Seward's Diary

3 October.

Let me put down with exactness all that happened, as well as I can remember, since last I made an entry. Not a detail that I can recall must be forgotten. In all calmness I must proceed.

When I came to Renfield's room I found him lying on the floor on his left side in a glittering pool of blood. When I went to move him, it became at once apparent that he had received some terrible injuries. There seemed none of the unity of purpose between the parts of the body which marks even lethargic sanity. As the face was exposed I could see that it was horribly bruised, as though it had been beaten against the floor. Indeed it was from the face wounds that the pool of blood originated.

The attendant who was kneeling beside the body said to me as we turned him over, "I think, sir, his back is broken. See, both his right arm and leg and the whole side of his face are paralysed." How such a thing could have happened puzzled the attendant beyond measure.

He seemed quite bewildered, and his brows were gathered in as he said, "I can't understand the two things. He could mark his face like that by beating his own head on the floor. I saw a young woman do it once at the Eversfield Asylum before anyone could lay hands on her. And I suppose he might have broken his neck by falling out of bed, if he got in an awkward kink. But for the life of me I can't imagine how the two things occurred. If his back was broke, he couldn't beat his head, and if his face was like that before the fall out of bed, there would be marks of it."

I said to him, "Go to Dr. Van Helsing, and ask him to kindly come here at once. I want him without an instant's delay." The man ran off, and within a few minutes the Professor, in his dressing gown and slippers, appeared. When he saw Renfield on the ground, he looked keenly at him a moment, and then turned to me. I think he recognized my thought in my eyes, for he said very quietly, manifestly for the ears of the attendant, "Ah, a sad accident! He will need very careful watching, and much attention. I shall stay with you myself, but I shall first dress myself. If you will remain I shall in a few minutes join you."

The patient was now breathing stertorously and it was easy to see that he had suffered some terrible injury.

Van Helsing returned with extraordinary celerity, bearing with him a surgical case. He had evidently been thinking and had his mind made up, for almost before he looked at the patient, he whispered to me, "Send the attendant away. We must be alone with him when he becomes conscious, after the operation."

I said, "I think that will do now, Simmons. We have done all that we can at present. You had better go your round, and Dr. Van Helsing will operate. Let me know instantly if there be anything unusual anywhere."

The man withdrew, and we went into a strict examination of the patient. The wounds of the face were superficial. The real injury was a depressed fracture of the skull, extending right up through the motor area.

The Professor thought a moment and said, "We must reduce the pressure and get back to normal conditions, as far as can be. The rapidity of the suffusion shows the terrible nature of his injury. The whole motor area seems affected. The suffusion of the brain will increase quickly, so we must trephine at once or it may be too late." As he was speaking there was a soft tapping at the door. I went over and opened it and found in the corridor without, Arthur and Quincey in pajamas and slippers; the former spoke, "I heard your man call up Dr. Van Helsing and tell him of an accident. So I woke Quincey or rather called for him as he was not asleep. Things are moving too quickly and too strangely for sound sleep for any of us these times. I've been thinking that tomorrow night will not see things as they have been. We'll have to look back, and forward a little more than we have done. May we come in?" I nodded, and held the door open till they had entered, then I closed it again.

When Quincey saw the attitude and state of the patient, and noted the horrible pool on the floor, he said softly, "My God! What has happened to him? Poor, poor devil!"

I told him briefly, and added that we expected he would recover consciousness after the operation, for a short time, at all events. He went at once and sat down on the edge of the bed, with Godalming beside him. We all watched in patience.

"We shall wait," said Van Helsing, "just long enough to fix the best spot for trephining, so that we may most quickly and perfectly remove the blood clot, for it is evident that the haemorrhage is increasing."

The minutes during which we waited passed with fearful slowness. I had a horrible sinking in my heart, and from Van Helsing's face I gathered that he felt some fear or apprehension as to what was to come. I dreaded the words Renfield might speak. I was positively afraid to think. But the conviction of what was coming was on me, as I have read of men who have heard the death watch. The poor man's breathing came in uncertain gasps. Each instant he seemed as though he would open his eyes and speak, but then would follow a prolonged stertorous breath, and he would relapse into a more fixed insensibility. Inured as I was to sick beds and death, this suspense grew and grew upon me. I could almost hear the beating of my own heart, and the blood surging through my temples sounded like blows from a hammer. The silence finally became agonizing. I looked at my companions, one after another, and saw from their flushed faces and damp brows that they were enduring equal torture. There was a nervous suspense over us all, as though overhead some dread bell would peal out powerfully when we should least expect it.

At last there came a time when it was evident that the patient was sinking fast. He might die at any moment. I looked up at the Professor and caught his eyes fixed on mine. His face was sternly set as he spoke, "There is no time to lose. His words may be worth many lives. I have been thinking so, as I stood here. It may be there is a soul at stake! We shall operate just above the ear."

Without another word he made the operation. For a few moments the breathing continued to be stertorous. Then there came a breath so prolonged that it seemed as though it would tear open his chest. Suddenly his eyes opened, and became fixed in a wild, helpless stare. This was continued for a few moments, then it was softened into a glad surprise, and from his lips came a sigh of relief. He moved convulsively, and as he did so, said, "I'll be quiet, Doctor. Tell them to take off the strait waistcoat. I have had a terrible dream, and it has left me so weak that I cannot move. What's wrong with my face? It feels all swollen, and it smarts dreadfully."

He tried to turn his head, but even with the effort his eyes seemed to grow glassy again so I gently put it back. Then Van Helsing said in a quiet grave tone, "Tell us your dream, Mr. Renfield."

As he heard the voice his face brightened, through its mutilation, and he said, "That is Dr. Van Helsing. How good it is of you to be here. Give me some water, my lips are dry, and I shall try to tell you. I dreamed—" He stopped and seemed fainting.

I called quietly to Quincey, "The brandy—it is in my study—quick!" He flew and returned with a glass, the decanter of brandy and a carafe of water. We moistened the parched lips, and the patient quickly revived.

It seemed, however, that his poor injured brain had been working in the interval, for when he was quite conscious, he looked at me piercingly with an agonized confusion which I shall never forget, and said, "I must not deceive myself. It was no dream, but all a grim reality." Then his eyes roved round the room. As they caught sight of the two figures sitting patiently on the edge of the bed he went on, "If I were not sure already, I would know from them."

For an instant his eyes closed—not with pain or sleep but voluntarily, as though he were bringing all his faculties to bear. When he opened them he said, hurriedly, and with more energy than he had yet displayed, "Quick, Doctor, quick, I am dying! I feel that I have but a few minutes, and then I must go back to death—or worse! Wet my lips with brandy again. I have something that I must say before I die. Or before my poor crushed brain dies anyhow. Thank you! It was that night after you left me, when I implored you to let me go away. I couldn't speak then, for I felt my tongue was tied. But I was as sane then, except in that way, as I am now. I was in an agony of despair for a long time after you left me, it seemed hours. Then there came a sudden peace to me. My brain seemed to become cool again, and I realized where I was. I heard the dogs bark behind our house, but not where He was!"

As he spoke, Van Helsing's eyes never blinked, but his hand came out and met mine and gripped it hard. He did not, however, betray himself. He nodded slightly and said, "Go on," in a low voice.

Renfield proceeded. "He came up to the window in the mist, as I had seen him often before, but he was solid then, not a ghost, and his eyes were fierce like a man's when angry. He was laughing with his red mouth, the sharp white teeth glinted in the moonlight when he turned to look back over the belt of trees, to where the dogs were barking. I wouldn't ask him to come in at first, though I knew he wanted to, just as he had wanted all along. Then he began promising me things—not in words but by doing them."

He was interrupted by a word from the Professor: "How?"

"By making them happen. Just as he used to send in the flies when the sun was shining. Great big fat ones with steel and sapphire on their wings. And big moths, in the night, with skull and cross-bones on their backs."

Van Helsing nodded to him as he whispered to me unconsciously, "The *Acherontia atropos* of the Sphinges—what you call the 'death's-head moth'?"

The patient went on without stopping, "Then he began to whisper. 'Rats, rats, rats! Hundreds, thousands, millions of them, and every one a life. And dogs to eat them, and cats too. All lives! All red blood, with years of life in it, and not merely buzzing flies!' I laughed at him, for I wanted to see what he could do. Then the dogs howled, away beyond the dark trees in His house. He beckoned me to the window. I got up and looked out, and He raised his hands, and seemed to call out without using any words. A dark mass spread over the grass, coming on like the shape of a flame of fire. And then He moved the mist to the right and left, and I could see that there were thousands of rats with their eyes blazing red, like His only smaller. He held up his hand, and they all stopped, and I thought he seemed to be saying, 'All these lives will I give you, ay, and many more and greater, through countless ages, if you will fall down and worship me!' And then a red cloud, like the colour of blood, seemed to close over my eyes, and before I knew what I was doing, I found myself opening the sash and saying to Him, 'Come in, Lord and Master!' The rats were all gone, but He slid into the room through the sash, though it was only open an inch wide—just as the Moon herself has often come in through the tiniest crack and has stood before me in all her size and splendour."

His voice was weaker, so I moistened his lips with the brandy again, and he continued, but it seemed as though his memory had gone on working in the interval for his story was further advanced. I was about to call him back to the point, but Van Helsing whispered to me, "Let him go on. Do not interrupt him. He cannot go back, and maybe could not proceed at all if once he lost the thread of his thought."

He proceeded, "All day I waited to hear from him, but he did not send me anything, not even a blowfly, and when the moon got up I was pretty angry with him. When he did slide in through the window, though it was shut, and did not even knock, I got mad with him. He sneered at me, and his white face looked out of the mist with his red eyes gleaming, and he went on as though he owned the whole place, and I was no one. He didn't even smell the same as he went by me. I couldn't hold him. I thought that, somehow, Mrs. Harker had come into the room."

The two men sitting on the bed stood up and came over, standing behind him so that he could not see them, but where they could hear better. They were both silent, but the Professor started and quivered. His face, however, grew grimmer and sterner still. Renfield went on without noticing, "When Mrs. Harker came in to see me this afternoon she wasn't the same. It was like tea after the teapot has been watered." Here we all moved, but no one said a word.

He went on, "I didn't know that she was here till she spoke, and she didn't look the same. I don't care for the pale people. I like them with lots of blood in them, and hers all seemed to have run out. I didn't think of it at the time, but when she went away I began to think, and it made me mad to know that He had been taking the life out of her." I could feel that the rest quivered, as I did; but we remained otherwise still. "So when He came tonight I was ready for Him. I saw the mist stealing in, and I grabbed it tight. I had heard that madmen have unnatural strength. And as I knew I was a madman, at times anyhow, I resolved to use my power. Ay, and He felt it too, for He had to come out of the mist to struggle with me. I held tight, and I thought I was going to win, for I didn't mean Him to take any more of her life, till I saw His eyes. They burned into me, and my strength became like water. He slipped through it, and when I tried to cling to Him, He raised me up and flung me down. There was a red cloud before me, and a noise like thunder, and the mist seemed to steal away under the door." His voice was becoming fainter and his breath more stertorous. Van Helsing stood up instinctively.

"We know the worst now," he said. "He is here, and we know his purpose. It may not be too late. Let us be armed, the same as we were the other night, but lose no time, there is not an instant to spare."

There was no need to put our fear, nay our conviction, into words, we shared them in common. We all hurried and took from our rooms the same things that we had when we entered the Count's house. The Professor had his ready, and as we met in the corridor he pointed to them significantly as he said, "They never leave me, and they shall not till this unhappy business is over. Be wise also, my friends. It is no common enemy that we deal with Alas! Alas! That dear Madam Mina should suffer!" He stopped, his voice was breaking, and I do not know if rage or terror predominated in my own heart.

Outside the Harkers' door we paused. Art and Quincey held back, and the latter said, "Should we disturb her?"

"We must," said Van Helsing grimly. "If the door be locked, I shall break it in."

"May it not frighten her terribly? It is unusual to break into a lady's room!"

Van Helsing said solemnly, "You are always right. But this is life and death. All chambers are alike to the doctor. And even were they not they are all as one to me tonight. Friend John, when I turn the handle, if the door does not open, do you put your shoulder down and shove; and you too, my friends. Now!"

He turned the handle as he spoke, but the door did not yield. We threw ourselves against it. With a crash it burst open, and we almost fell headlong into the room. The Professor did actually fall, and I saw across him as he gathered himself up from hands and knees. What I saw appalled me. I felt my hair rise like bristles on the back of my neck, and my heart seemed to stand still.

The moonlight was so bright that through the thick yellow blind the room was light enough to see. On the bed beside the window lay Jonathan Harker, his face flushed and breathing heavily as though in a stupor. Kneeling on the near edge of the bed facing outwards was the white-clad figure of his wife. By her side stood a tall, thin man, clad in black. His face was turned from us, but the instant we saw we all recognized the Count—in every way, even to the scar on his forehead. With his left hand he held both Mrs. Harker's hands, keeping them away with her arms at full tension. His right hand gripped her by the back of the neck, forcing her face down on his bosom. Her white nightdress was smeared with blood, and a thin stream trickled down the man's bare chest which was shown by his torn-open dress. The attitude of the two had a terrible resemblance to a child forcing a kitten's nose into a saucer of milk to compel it to drink. As we burst into the room, the Count turned his face, and the hellish look that I had heard described seemed to leap into it. His eyes flamed red with devilish passion. The great nostrils of the white aquiline nose opened wide and quivered at the edge, and the white sharp teeth, behind the full lips of the blood dripping mouth, clamped together like those of a wild beast. With a wrench, which threw his victim back upon the bed as though hurled from a height, he turned and sprang at us. But by this time the Professor had gained his feet, and was holding towards him the envelope which contained the Sacred Wafer. The Count suddenly stopped, just as poor Lucy had done outside the tomb, and cowered back. Further and further back he cowered, as we, lifting our crucifixes, advanced. The moonlight suddenly failed, as a great black cloud sailed across the sky. And when the gaslight sprang up under Quincey's match, we saw nothing but a faint vapour. This, as we looked, trailed under the door, which with the recoil from its bursting open, had swung back to its old position. Van Helsing, Art, and I moved forward to Mrs. Harker, who by this time had drawn her breath and with it had given a scream so wild, so ear-piercing, so despairing that it seems to me now that it will ring in my ears till my dying day. For a few seconds she lay in her helpless attitude and disarray. Her face was ghastly, with a pallor which was accentuated by the blood which smeared her lips and cheeks and chin. From her throat trickled a thin stream of blood. Her eyes were mad with terror. Then she put before her face her poor crushed hands, which bore on their whiteness the red mark of the Count's terrible grip, and from behind them came a low desolate wail which made the terrible scream seem only the quick expression of an endless grief. Van Helsing stepped forward and drew the coverlet gently over her body, whilst Art, after looking at her face for an instant despairingly, ran out of the room.

Van Helsing whispered to me, "Jonathan is in a stupor such as we know the Vampire can produce. We can do nothing with poor Madam Mina for a few moments till she recovers herself. I must wake him!" He dipped the end of a towel in cold water and with it began to flick him on the face, his wife all the while holding her face between her hands and sobbing in a way that was heart breaking to hear. I raised the blind, and looked out of the window. There was much moonshine, and as I looked I could see Quincey Morris run across the lawn and hide himself in the shadow of a great yew tree. It puzzled me to think why he was doing this. But at the instant I heard Harker's quick exclamation as he woke to partial consciousness, and turned to the bed. On his face, as there might well be, was a look of wild amazement. He seemed dazed for a few seconds, and then full consciousness seemed to burst upon him all at once, and he started up. His wife was aroused by the quick movement, and turned to him with her arms stretched out, as though to embrace him. Instantly, however, she drew them in again, and putting her elbows together, held her hands before her face, and shuddered till the bed beneath her shook.

"In God's name what does this mean?" Harker cried out. "Dr. Seward, Dr. Van Helsing, what is it? What has happened? What is wrong? Mina, dear what is it? What does that blood mean? My God, my God! Has it come to this!" And, raising himself to his knees, he beat his hands wildly together. "Good God, help us! Help her! Oh, help her!"

With a quick movement he jumped from bed, and began to pull on his clothes, all the man in him awake at the need for instant exertion. "What has happened? Tell me all about it!" he cried without pausing. "Dr. Van Helsing, you love Mina, I know. Oh, do something to save her. It cannot have gone too far yet. Guard her while I look for him!"

His wife, through her terror and horror and distress, saw some sure danger to him. Instantly forgetting her own grief, she seized hold of him and cried out. "No! No! Jonathan, you must not leave me. I have suffered enough tonight, God knows, without the dread of his harming you. You must stay with me. Stay with these friends who will watch over you!" Her expression became frantic as she spoke. And, he yielding to her, she pulled him down sitting on the bedside, and clung to him fiercely.

Van Helsing and I tried to calm them both. The Professor held up his golden crucifix, and said with wonderful calmness, "Do not fear, my dear. We are here, and whilst this is close to you no foul thing can approach. You are safe for tonight, and we must be calm and take counsel together."

She shuddered and was silent, holding down her head on her husband's breast. When she raised it, his white nightrobe was stained with blood where her lips had touched, and where the thin open wound in the neck had sent forth drops. The instant she saw it she drew back, with a low wail, and whispered, amidst choking sobs. "Unclean, unclean! I must touch him or kiss him no more. Oh, that it should be that it is I who am now his worst enemy, and whom he may have most cause to fear."

To this he spoke out resolutely, "Nonsense, Mina. It is a shame to me to hear such a word. I would not hear it of you. And I shall not hear it from you. May God judge me by my deserts, and punish me with more bitter suffering than even this hour, if by any act or will of mine anything ever come between us!"

He put out his arms and folded her to his breast. And for a while she lay there sobbing. He looked at us over her bowed head, with eyes that blinked damply above his quivering nostrils. His mouth was set as steel. After a while her sobs became less frequent and more faint, and then he said to me, speaking with a studied calmness which I felt tried his nervous power to the utmost.

"And now, Dr. Seward, tell me all about it. Too well I know the broad fact. Tell me all that has been."

I told him exactly what had happened and he listened with seeming impassiveness, but his nostrils twitched and his eyes blazed as I told how the ruthless hands of the Count had held his wife in that terrible and horrid position, with her mouth to the open wound in his breast. It interested me, even at that moment, to see that whilst the face of white set passion worked convulsively over the bowed head, the hands tenderly and lovingly stroked the ruffled hair. Just as I had finished, Quincey and Godalming knocked at the door. They entered in obedience to our summons. Van Helsing looked at me questioningly. I understood him to mean if we were to take advantage of their coming to divert if possible the thoughts of the unhappy husband and wife from each other and from themselves. So on nodding acquiescence to him he asked them what they had seen or done. To which Lord Godalming answered.

"I could not see him anywhere in the passage, or in any of our rooms. I looked in the study but, though he had been there, he had gone. He had, however . . ." He stopped suddenly, looking at the poor drooping figure on the bed.

Van Helsing said gravely, "Go on, friend Arthur. We want here no more concealments. Our hope now is in knowing all. Tell freely!"

So Art went on, "He had been there, and though it could only have been for a few seconds, he made rare hay of the place. All the manuscript had been burned, and the blue flames were flickering amongst the white ashes. The cylinders of your phonograph too were thrown on the fire, and the wax had helped the flames."

Here I interrupted. "Thank God there is the other copy in the safe!"

His face lit for a moment, but fell again as he went on. "I ran downstairs then, but could see no sign of him. I looked into Renfield's room, but there was no trace there except—" Again he paused.

"Go on," said Harker hoarsely. So he bowed his head and moistening his lips with his tongue, added, "except that the poor fellow is dead."

Mrs. Harker raised her head, looking from one to the other of us she said solemnly, "God's will be done!"

I could not but feel that Art was keeping back something. But, as I took it that it was with a purpose, I said nothing.

Van Helsing turned to Morris and asked, "And you, friend Quincey, have you any to tell?"

"A little," he answered. "It may be much eventually, but at present I can't say. I thought it well to know if possible where the Count would go when he left the house. I did not see him, but I saw a bat rise from Renfield's window, and flap westward. I expected to see him in some shape go back to Carfax, but he evidently sought some other lair. He will not be back tonight, for the sky is reddening in the east, and the dawn is close. We must work tomorrow!"

He said the latter words through his shut teeth. For a space of perhaps a couple of minutes there was silence, and I could fancy that I could hear the sound of our hearts beating.

Then Van Helsing said, placing his hand tenderly on Mrs. Harker's head, "And now, Madam Mina, poor dear, dear, Madam Mina, tell us exactly what happened. God knows that I do not want that you be pained, but it is need that we know all. For now more than ever has all work to be done quick and sharp, and in deadly earnest. The day is close to us that must end all, if it may be so, and now is the chance that we may live and learn."

The poor dear lady shivered, and I could see the tension of her nerves as she clasped her husband closer to her and bent her head lower and lower still on his breast. Then she raised her head proudly, and held out one hand to Van Helsing who took it in his, and after stooping and kissing it reverently, held it fast. The other hand was locked in that of her husband, who held his other arm thrown round her protectingly. After a pause in which she was evidently ordering her thoughts, she began.

"I took the sleeping draught which you had so kindly given me, but for a long time it did not act. I seemed to become more wakeful, and myriads of horrible fancies began to crowd in upon my mind. All of them connected with death, and vampires, with blood, and pain, and trouble." Her husband involuntarily groaned as she turned to him and said lovingly, "Do not fret, dear. You must be brave and strong, and help me through the horrible task. If you only knew what an effort it is to me to tell of this fearful thing at all, you would understand how much I need your help. Well, I saw I must try to help the medicine to its work with my will, if it was to do me any good, so I resolutely set myself to sleep. Sure enough sleep must soon have come to me, for I remember no more. Jonathan coming in had not waked me, for he lay by my side when next I remember. There was in the room the same thin white mist that I had before noticed. But I forget now if you know of this. You will find it in my diary which I shall show you later. I felt the same vague terror which had come to me before and the same sense of some presence. I turned to wake Jonathan, but found that he slept so soundly that it seemed as if it was he who had taken the sleeping draught, and not I. I tried, but I could not wake him. This caused me a great fear, and I looked around terrified. Then indeed, my heart sank within me. Beside the bed, as if he had stepped out of the mist—or rather as if the mist had turned into his figure, for it had entirely disappeared—stood a tall, thin man, all in black. I knew him at once from the description of the others. The waxen face, the high aquiline nose, on which the light fell in a thin white line, the parted red lips, with the sharp white teeth showing between, and the red eyes that I had seemed to see in the sunset on the windows of St. Mary's Church at Whitby. I knew, too, the red scar on his forehead where Jonathan had struck him. For an instant my heart stood still, and I would have screamed out, only that I was paralyzed. In the pause he spoke in a sort of keen, cutting whisper, pointing as he spoke to Jonathan.

"'Silence! If you make a sound I shall take him and dash his brains out before your very eyes.' I was appalled and was too bewildered to do or say anything. With a mocking smile, he placed one hand upon my shoulder and, holding me tight, bared my throat with the other, saying as he did so, 'First, a little refreshment to reward my exertions. You may as well be quiet. It is not the first time, or the second, that your veins have appeased my thirst!' I was bewildered, and strangely enough, I did not want to hinder him. I suppose it is a part of the horrible curse that such is, when his touch is on his victim. And oh, my God, my God, pity me! He placed his reeking lips upon my throat!" Her husband groaned again. She clasped his hand harder, and looked at him pityingly, as if he were the injured one, and went on.

"I felt my strength fading away, and I was in a half swoon. How long this horrible thing lasted I know not, but it seemed that a long time must have passed before he took his foul, awful, sneering mouth away. I saw it drip with the fresh blood!" The remembrance seemed for a while to overpower her, and she drooped and would have sunk down but for her husband's sustaining arm. With a great effort she recovered herself and went on.

"Then he spoke to me mockingly, 'And so you, like the others, would play your brains against mine. You would help these men to hunt me and frustrate me in my design! You know now, and they know in part already, and will know in full before long, what it is to cross my path. They should have kept their energies for use closer to home. Whilst they played wits against me, against me who commanded nations, and intrigued for them, and fought for them, hundreds of years before they were born, I was countermining them. And you, their best beloved one, are now to me, flesh of my flesh, blood of my blood, kin of my kin, my bountiful wine-press for a while, and shall be later on my companion and my helper. You shall be avenged in turn, for not one of them but shall minister to your needs. But as yet you are to be punished for what you have done. You have aided in thwarting me. Now you shall come to my call. When my brain says "Come!" to you, you shall cross land or sea to do my bidding. And to that end this!'"

With that he pulled open his shirt, and with his long sharp nails opened a vein in his breast. When the blood began to spurt out, he took my hands in one of his, holding them tight, and with the other seized my neck and pressed my mouth to the wound, so that I must either suffocate or swallow some to the—oh, my God! My God! What have I done? What have I done to deserve such a fate, I who have tried to walk in meekness and righteousness all my days. God pity me! Look down on a poor soul in worse than mortal peril. And in mercy pity those to whom she is dear!" Then she began to rub her lips as though to cleanse them from pollution.

As she was telling her terrible story, the eastern sky began to quicken, and everything became more and more clear. Harker was still and quiet; but over his face, as the awful narrative went on, came a gray look which deepened and deepened in the morning light, till when the first red streak of the coming dawn shot up, the flesh stood darkly out against the whitening hair.

We have arranged that one of us is to stay within call of the unhappy pair till we can meet together and arrange about taking action.

Of this I am sure. The sun rises today on no more miserable house in all the great round of its daily course.

CHAPTER XXII

Jonathan Harker's Journal

3 October.

As I must do something or go mad, I write this diary. It is now six o'clock, and we are to meet in the study in half an hour and take something to eat, for Dr. Van Helsing and Dr. Seward are agreed that if we do not eat we cannot work our best. Our best will be, God knows, required today. I must keep writing at every chance, for I dare not stop to think. All, big and little, must go down. Perhaps at the end the little things may teach us most. The teaching, big or little, could not have landed Mina or me anywhere worse than we are today. However, we must trust and hope. Poor Mina told me just now, with the tears running down her dear cheeks, that it is in trouble and trial that our faith is tested. That we must keep on trusting, and that God will aid us up to the end. The end! Oh my God! What end? . . . To work! To work!

When Dr. Van Helsing and Dr. Seward had come back from seeing poor Renfield, we went gravely into what was to be done. First, Dr. Seward told us that when he and Dr. Van Helsing had gone down to the room below they had found Renfield lying on the floor, all in a heap. His face was all bruised and crushed in, and the bones of the neck were broken.

Dr. Seward asked the attendant who was on duty in the passage if he had heard anything. He said that he had been sitting down—he confessed to half dozing—when he heard loud voices in the room, and then Renfield had called out loudly several times, "God! God! God!" After that there was a sound of falling, and when he entered the room he found him lying on the floor, face down, just as the doctors had seen him. Van Helsing asked if he had heard "voices" or "a voice," and he said he could not say. That at first it had seemed to him as if there were two, but as there was no one in the room it could have been only one. He could swear to it, if required, that the word "God" was spoken by the patient.

Dr. Seward said to us, when we were alone, that he did not wish to go into the matter. The question of an inquest had to be considered, and it would never do to put forward the truth, as no one would believe it. As it was, he thought that on the attendant's evidence he could give a certificate of death by misadventure in falling from bed. In case the coroner should demand it, there would be a formal inquest, necessarily to the same result.

When the question began to be discussed as to what should be our next step, the very first thing we decided was that Mina should be in full confidence. That nothing of any sort—no matter how painful—should be kept from her. She herself agreed as to its wisdom, and it was pitiful to see her so brave and yet so sorrowful, and in such a depth of despair.

"There must be no concealment," she said. "Alas! We have had too much already. And besides there is nothing in all the world that can give me more pain than I have already endured, than I suffer now! Whatever may happen, it must be of new hope or of new courage to me!"

Van Helsing was looking at her fixedly as she spoke, and said, suddenly but quietly, "But dear Madam Mina, are you not afraid. Not for yourself, but for others from yourself, after what has happened?"

Her face grew set in its lines, but her eyes shone with the devotion of a martyr as she answered, "Ah no! For my mind is made up!"

"To what?" he asked gently, whilst we were all very still, for each in our own way we had a sort of vague idea of what she meant.

Her answer came with direct simplicity, as though she was simply stating a fact, "Because if I find in myself—and I shall watch keenly for it—a sign of harm to any that I love, I shall die!"

"You would not kill yourself?" he asked, hoarsely.

"I would. If there were no friend who loved me, who would save me such a pain, and so desperate an effort!" She looked at him meaningly as she spoke.

He was sitting down, but now he rose and came close to her and put his hand on her head as he said solemnly. "My child, there is such an one if it were for your good. For myself I could hold it in my account with God to find such an euthanasia for you, even at this moment if it were best. Nay, were it safe! But my child—" For a moment he seemed choked, and a great sob rose in his throat. He gulped it down and went on, "There are here some who would stand between you and death. You must not die. You must not die by any hand, but least of all your own. Until the other, who has fouled your sweet life, is true dead you must not die. For if he is still with the quick Undead, your death would make you even as he is. No, you must live! You must struggle and strive to live, though death would seem a boon unspeakable. You must fight Death himself, though he come to you in pain or in joy. By the day, or the night, in safety or in peril! On your living soul I charge you that you do not die. Nay, nor think of death, till this great evil be past." The poor dear grew white as death, and shook and shivered, as I have seen a quicksand shake and shiver at the incoming of the tide. We were all silent. We could do nothing.

At length she grew more calm and turning to him said sweetly, but oh so sorrowfully, as she held out her hand, "I promise you, my dear friend, that if God will let me live, I shall strive to do so. Till, if it may be in His good time, this horror may have passed away from me." She was so good and brave that we all felt that our hearts were strengthened to work and endure for her, and we began to discuss what we were to do. I told her that she was to have all the papers in the safe, and all the papers or diaries and phonographs we might hereafter use, and was to keep the record as she had done before. She was pleased with the prospect of anything to do—if "pleased" could be used in connection with so grim an interest.

As usual Van Helsing had thought ahead of everyone else, and was prepared with an exact ordering of our work.

"It is perhaps well," he said, "that at our meeting after our visit to Carfax we decided not to do anything with the earth boxes that lay there. Had we done so, the Count must have guessed our purpose, and would doubtless have taken measures in advance to frustrate such an effort with regard to the others. But now he does not know our intentions. Nay, more, in all probability, he does not know that such a power exists to us as can sterilize his lairs, so that he cannot use them as of old.

"We are now so much further advanced in our knowledge as to their disposition that, when we have examined the house in Piccadilly, we may track the very last of them. Today then, is ours, and in it rests our hope. The sun that rose on our sorrow this morning guards us in its course. Until it sets tonight, that monster must retain whatever form he now has. He is confined within the limitations of his earthly envelope. He cannot melt into thin air nor disappear through cracks or chinks or crannies. If he go through a doorway, he must open the door like a mortal. And so we have this day to hunt out all his lairs and sterilize them. So we shall, if we have not yet catch him and destroy him, drive him to bay in some place where the catching and the destroying shall be, in time, sure." Here I started up for I could not contain myself at the thought that the minutes and seconds so preciously laden with Mina's life and happiness were flying from us, since whilst we talked action was impossible. But Van Helsing held up his hand warningly. "Nay, friend Jonathan," he said, "in this, the quickest way home is the longest way, so your proverb say. We shall all act and act with desperate quick, when the time has come. But think, in all probable the key of the situation is in that house in Piccadilly. The Count may have many houses which he has bought. Of them he will have deeds of purchase, keys and other things. He will have paper that he write on. He will have his book of cheques. There are many belongings that he must have somewhere. Why not in this place so central, so quiet, where he come and go by the front or the back at all hours, when in the very vast of the traffic there is none to notice. We shall go there and search that house. And when we learn what it holds, then we do what our friend Arthur call, in his phrases of hunt 'stop the earths' and so we run down our old fox—so? Is it not?"

"Then let us come at once," I cried, "we are wasting the precious, precious time!"

The Professor did not move, but simply said, "And how are we to get into that house in Piccadilly?"

"Any way!" I cried. "We shall break in if need be."

"And your police? Where will they be, and what will they say?"

I was staggered, but I knew that if he wished to delay he had a good reason for it. So I said, as quietly as I could, "Don't wait more than need be. You know, I am sure, what torture I am in."

"Ah, my child, that I do. And indeed there is no wish of me to add to your anguish. But just think, what can we do, until all the world be at movement. Then will come our time. I have thought and thought, and it seems to me that the simplest way is the best of all. Now we wish to get into the house, but we have no key. Is it not so?" I nodded.

"Now suppose that you were, in truth, the owner of that house, and could not still get in. And think there was to you no conscience of the housebreaker, what would you do?"

"I should get a respectable locksmith, and set him to work to pick the lock for me."

"And your police, they would interfere, would they not?"

"Oh no! Not if they knew the man was properly employed."

"Then," he looked at me as keenly as he spoke, "all that is in doubt is the conscience of the employer, and the belief of your policemen as to whether or not that employer has a good conscience or a bad one. Your police must indeed be zealous men and clever—oh so clever—in reading the heart, that they trouble themselves in such matter. No, no, my friend Jonathan, you go take the lock off a hundred empty houses in this your London, or of any city in the world, and if you do it as such things are rightly done, and at the time such things are rightly done, no one will interfere. I have read of a gentleman who owned a so fine house in London, and when he went for months of summer to Switzerland and lock up his house, some burglar come and broke window at back and got in. Then he went and made open the shutters in front and walk out and in through the door, before the very eyes of the police. Then he have an auction in that house, and advertise it, and put up big notice. And when the day come he sell off by a great auctioneer all the goods of that other man who own them. Then he go to a builder, and he sell him that house, making an agreement that he pull it down and take all away within a certain time. And your police and other authority help him all they can. And when that owner come back from his holiday in Switzerland he find only an empty hole where his house had been. This was all done *en règle*, and in our work we shall be *en règle* too. We shall not go so early that the policemen who have then little to think of, shall deem it strange. But we shall go after ten o'clock, when there are many about, and such things would be done were we indeed owners of the house."

I could not but see how right he was and the terrible despair of Mina's face became relaxed in thought. There was hope in such good counsel.

Van Helsing went on, "When once within that house we may find more clues. At any rate some of us can remain there whilst the rest find the other places where there be more earth boxes, at Bermondsey and Mile End."

Lord Godalming stood up. "I can be of some use here," he said. "I shall wire to my people to have horses and carriages where they will be most convenient."

"Look here, old fellow," said Morris, "it is a capital idea to have all ready in case we want to go horse backing, but don't you think that one of your snappy carriages with its heraldic adornments in a byway of Walworth or Mile End would attract too much attention for our purpose? It seems to me that we ought to take cabs when we go south or east. And even leave them somewhere near the neighbourhood we are going to."

"Friend Quincey is right!" said the Professor. "His head is what you call in plane with the horizon. It is a difficult thing that we go to do, and we do not want no peoples to watch us if so it may."

Mina took a growing interest in everything and I was rejoiced to see that the exigency of affairs was helping her to forget for a time the terrible experience of the night. She was very, very pale—almost ghastly, and so thin that her lips were drawn away, showing her teeth in somewhat of prominence. I did not mention this last, lest it should give her needless pain, but it made my blood run cold in my veins to think of what had occurred with poor Lucy when the Count had sucked her blood. As yet there was no sign of the teeth growing sharper, but the time as yet was short, and there was time for fear.

When we came to the discussion of the sequence of our efforts and of the disposition of our forces, there were new sources of doubt. It was finally agreed that before starting for Piccadilly we should destroy the Count's lair close at hand. In case he should find it out too soon, we should thus be still ahead of him in our work of destruction. And his presence in his purely material shape, and at his weakest, might give us some new clue.

As to the disposal of forces, it was suggested by the Professor that, after our visit to Carfax, we should all enter the house in Piccadilly. That the two doctors and I should remain there, whilst Lord Godalming and Quincey found the lairs at Walworth and Mile End and destroyed them. It was possible, if not likely, the Professor urged, that the Count might appear in Piccadilly during the day, and that if so we might be able to cope with him then and there. At any rate, we might be able to follow him in force. To this plan I strenuously objected, and so far as my going was concerned, for I said that I intended to stay and protect Mina. I thought that my mind was made up on the subject, but Mina would not listen to my objection. She said that there might be some law matter in which I could be useful. That amongst the Count's papers might be some clue which I could understand out of my experience in Transylvania. And that, as it was, all the strength we could muster was required to cope with the Count's extraordinary power. I had to give in, for Mina's resolution was fixed. She said that it was the last hope for her that we should all work together.

"As for me," she said, "I have no fear. Things have been as bad as they can be. And whatever may happen must have in it some element of hope or comfort. Go, my husband! God can, if He wishes it, guard me as well alone as with anyone present."

So I started up crying out, "Then in God's name let us come at once, for we are losing time. The Count may come to Piccadilly earlier than we think."

"Not so!" said Van Helsing, holding up his hand.

"But why?" I asked.

"Do you forget," he said, with actually a smile, "that last night he banqueted heavily, and will sleep late?"

Did I forget! Shall I ever—can I ever! Can any of us ever forget that terrible scene! Mina struggled hard to keep her brave countenance, but the pain overmastered her and she put her hands before her face, and shuddered whilst she moaned. Van Helsing had not intended to recall her frightful experience. He had simply lost sight of her and her part in the affair in his intellectual effort.

When it struck him what he said, he was horrified at his thoughtlessness and tried to comfort her.

"Oh, Madam Mina," he said, "dear, dear, Madam Mina, alas! That I of all who so reverence you should have said anything so forgetful. These stupid old lips of mine and this stupid old head do not deserve so, but you will forget it, will you not?" He bent low beside her as he spoke.

She took his hand, and looking at him through her tears, said hoarsely, "No, I shall not forget, for it is well that I remember. And with it I have so much in memory of you that is sweet, that I take it all together. Now, you must all be going soon. Breakfast is ready, and we must all eat that we may be strong."

Breakfast was a strange meal to us all. We tried to be cheerful and encourage each other, and Mina was the brightest and most cheerful of us. When it was over, Van Helsing stood up and said, "Now, my dear friends, we go forth to our terrible enterprise. Are we all armed, as we were on that night when first we visited our enemy's lair. Armed against ghostly as well as carnal attack?"

We all assured him.

"Then it is well. Now, Madam Mina, you are in any case *quite* safe here until the sunset. And before then we shall return—if—We shall return! But before we go let me see you armed against personal attack. I have myself, since you came down, prepared your chamber by the placing of things of which we know, so that He may not enter. Now let me guard yourself. On your forehead I touch this piece of Sacred Wafer in the name of the Father, the Son, and . . ."

There was a fearful scream which almost froze our hearts to hear. As he had placed the Wafer on Mina's forehead, it had seared it—had burned into the flesh as though it had been a piece of white-hot metal. My poor darling's brain had told her the significance of the fact as quickly as her nerves received the pain of it, and the two so overwhelmed her that her overwrought nature had its voice in that dreadful scream. But the words to her thought came quickly. The echo of the scream had not ceased to ring on the air when there came the reaction, and she sank on her knees on the floor in an agony of abasement. Pulling her beautiful hair over her face, as the leper of old his mantle, she wailed out.

"Unclean! Unclean! Even the Almighty shuns my polluted flesh! I must bear this mark of shame upon my forehead until the Judgement Day." They all paused. I had thrown myself beside her in an agony of helpless grief, and putting my arms around held her tight. For a few minutes our sorrowful hearts beat together, whilst the friends around us turned away their eyes that ran tears silently. Then Van Helsing turned and said gravely. So gravely that I could not help feeling that he was in some way inspired, and was stating things outside himself.

"It may be that you may have to bear that mark till God himself see fit, as He most surely shall, on the Judgement Day, to redress all wrongs of the earth and of His children that He has placed thereon. And oh, Madam Mina, my dear, my dear, may we who love you be there to see, when that red scar, the sign of God's knowledge of what has been, shall pass away, and leave your forehead as pure as the heart we know. For so surely as we live, that scar shall pass away when God sees right to lift the burden that is hard upon us. Till then we bear our Cross, as His Son did in obedience to His Will. It may be that we are chosen instruments of His good pleasure, and that we ascend to His bidding as that other through stripes and shame. Through tears and blood. Through doubts and fear, and all that makes the difference between God and man."

There was hope in his words, and comfort. And they made for resignation. Mina and I both felt so, and simultaneously we each took one of the old man's hands and bent over and kissed it. Then without a word we all knelt down together, and all holding hands, swore to be true to each other. We men pledged ourselves to raise the veil of sorrow from the head of her whom, each in his own way, we loved. And we prayed for help and guidance in the terrible task which lay before us.

It was then time to start. So I said farewell to Mina, a parting which neither of us shall forget to our dying day, and we set out.

To one thing I have made up my mind. If we find out that Mina must be a vampire in the end, then she shall not go into that unknown and terrible land alone. I suppose it is thus that in old times one vampire meant many. Just as their hideous bodies could only rest in sacred earth, so the holiest love was the recruiting sergeant for their ghastly ranks.

We entered Carfax without trouble and found all things the same as on the first occasion. It was hard to believe that amongst so prosaic surroundings of neglect and dust and decay there was any ground for such fear as already we knew. Had not our minds been made up, and had there not been terrible memories to spur us on, we could hardly have proceeded with our task. We found no papers, or any sign of use in the house. And in the old chapel the great boxes looked just as we had seen them last.

Dr. Van Helsing said to us solemnly as we stood before him, "And now, my friends, we have a duty here to do. We must sterilize this earth, so sacred of holy memories, that he has brought from a far distant land for such fell use. He has chosen this earth because it has been holy. Thus we defeat him with his own weapon, for we make it more holy still. It was sanctified to such use of man, now we sanctify it to God." As he spoke he took from his bag a screwdriver and a wrench, and very soon the top of one of the cases was thrown open. The earth smelled musty and close, but we did not somehow seem to mind, for our attention was concentrated on the Professor. Taking from his box a piece of the Sacred Wafer he laid it reverently on the earth, and then shutting down the lid began to screw it home, we aiding him as he worked.

One by one we treated in the same way each of the great boxes, and left them as we had found them to all appearance. But in each was a portion of the Host.

When we closed the door behind us, the Professor said solemnly, "So much is already done. It may be that with all the others we can be so successful, then the sunset of this evening may shine of Madam Mina's forehead all white as ivory and with no stain!"

As we passed across the lawn on our way to the station to catch our train we could see the front of the asylum. I looked eagerly, and in the window of my own room saw Mina. I waved my hand to her, and nodded to tell that our work there was successfully accomplished. She nodded in reply to show that she understood. The last I saw, she was waving her hand in farewell. It was with a heavy heart that we sought the station and just caught the train, which was steaming in as we reached the platform.

I have written this in the train.

Piccadilly, 12:30 p.m.

Just before we reached Fenchurch Street Lord Godalming said to me, "Quincey and I will find a locksmith. You had better not come with us in case there should be any difficulty. For under the circumstances it wouldn't seem so bad for us to break into an empty house. But you are a solicitor and the Incorporated Law Society might tell you that you should have known better." I demurred as to my not sharing any danger even of odium, but he went on, "Besides, it will attract less attention if there are not too many of us. My title will make it all right with the locksmith, and with any policeman that may come along. You had better go with Jack and the Professor and stay in the Green Park. Somewhere in sight of the house, and when you see the door opened and the smith has gone away, do you all come across. We shall be on the lookout for you, and shall let you in."

"The advice is good!" said Van Helsing, so we said no more. Godalming and Morris hurried off in a cab, we following in another. At the corner of Arlington Street our contingent got out and strolled into the Green Park. My heart beat as I saw the house on which so much of our hope was centred, looming up grim and silent in its deserted condition amongst its more lively and spruce-looking neighbours. We sat down on a bench within good view, and began to smoke cigars so as to attract as little attention as possible. The minutes seemed to pass with leaden feet as we waited for the coming of the others.

At length we saw a four-wheeler drive up. Out of it, in leisurely fashion, got Lord Godalming and Morris. And down from the box descended a thick-set working man with his rush-woven basket of tools. Morris paid the cabman, who touched his hat and drove away. Together the two ascended the steps, and Lord Godalming pointed out what he wanted done. The workman took off his coat leisurely and hung it on one of the spikes of the rail, saying something to a policeman who just then sauntered along. The policeman nodded acquiescence, and the man kneeling down placed his bag beside him. After searching through it, he took out a selection of tools which he proceeded to lay beside him in orderly fashion. Then he stood up, looked in the keyhole, blew into it, and turning to his employers, made some remark. Lord Godalming smiled, and the man lifted a good sized bunch of keys. Selecting one of them, he began to probe the lock, as if feeling his way with it. After fumbling about for a bit he tried a second, and then a third. All at once the door opened under a slight push from him, and he and the two others entered the hall. We sat still. My own cigar burnt furiously, but Van Helsing's went cold altogether. We waited patiently as we saw the workman come out and bring his bag. Then he held the door partly open, steadying it with his knees, whilst he fitted a key to the lock. This he finally handed to Lord Godalming, who took out his purse and gave him something. The man touched his hat, took his bag, put on his coat and departed. Not a soul took the slightest notice of the whole transaction.

When the man had fairly gone, we three crossed the street and knocked at the door. It was immediately opened by Quincey Morris, beside whom stood Lord Godalming lighting a cigar.

"The place smells so vilely," said the latter as we came in. It did indeed smell vilely—like the old chapel at Carfax—and with our previous experience it was plain to us that the Count had been using the place pretty freely. We moved to explore the house, all keeping together in case of attack, for we knew we had a strong and wily enemy to deal with, and as yet we did not know whether the Count might not be in the house. In the dining room, which lay at the back of the hall, we found eight boxes of earth. Eight boxes only out of the nine which we sought! Our work was not over, and would never be until we should have found the missing box. First we opened the shutters of the window which looked out across a narrow stone flagged yard at the blank face of a stable, pointed to look like the front of a miniature house. There were no windows in it, so we were not afraid of being overlooked. We did not lose any time in examining the chests. With the tools which we had brought with us we opened them, one by one, and treated them as we had treated those others in the old chapel. It was evident to us that the Count was not at present in the house, and we proceeded to search for any of his effects.

After a cursory glance at the rest of the rooms, from basement to attic, we came to the conclusion that the dining room contained any effects which might belong to the Count. And so we proceeded to minutely examine them. They lay in a sort of orderly disorder on the great dining room table. There were title deeds of the Piccadilly house in a great bundle, deeds of the purchase of the houses at Mile End and Bermondsey, notepaper, envelopes, and pens and ink. All were covered up in thin wrapping paper to keep them from the dust. There were also a clothes brush, a brush and comb, and a jug and basin—the latter containing dirty water which was reddened as if with blood. Last of all was a little heap of keys of all sorts and sizes, probably those belonging to the other houses. When we had examined this last find, Lord Godalming and Quincey Morris taking accurate notes of the various addresses of the houses in the East and the South, took with them the keys in a great bunch, and set out to destroy the boxes in these places. The rest of us are, with what patience we can, waiting their return, or the coming of the Count.

CHAPTER XXIII

Dr. Seward's Diary

3 October.

The time seemed terribly long whilst we were waiting for the coming of Godalming and Quincey Morris. The Professor tried to keep our minds active by using them all the time. I could see his beneficent purpose, by the side glances which he threw from time to time at Harker. The poor fellow is overwhelmed in a misery that is appalling to see. Last night he was a frank, happy-looking man, with strong, youthful face, full of energy, and with dark brown hair. Today he is a drawn, haggard old man, whose white hair matches well with the hollow burning eyes and grief-written lines of his face. His energy is still intact. In fact, he is like a living flame. This may yet be his salvation, for if all go well, it will tide him over the despairing period. He will then, in a kind of way, wake again to the realities of life. Poor fellow, I thought my own trouble was bad enough, but his—! The Professor knows this well enough, and is doing his best to keep his mind active. What he has been saying was, under the circumstances, of absorbing interest. So well as I can remember, here it is:

"I have studied, over and over again since they came into my hands, all the papers relating to this monster, and the more I have studied, the greater seems the necessity to utterly stamp him out. All through there are signs of his advance. Not only of his power, but of his knowledge of it. As I learned from the researches of my friend Arminius of Buda-Pesth, he was in life a most wonderful man. Soldier, statesman, and alchemist—which latter was the highest development of the science knowledge of his time. He had a mighty brain, a learning beyond compare, and a heart that knew no fear and no remorse. He dared even to attend the Scholomance, and there was no branch of knowledge of his time that he did not essay. Well, in him the brain powers survived the physical death. Though it would seem that memory was not all complete. In some faculties of mind he has been, and is, only a child. But he is growing, and some things that were childish at the first are now of man's stature. He is experimenting, and doing it well. And if it had not been that we have crossed his path he would be yet—he may be yet if we fail—the father or furtherer of a new order of beings, whose road must lead through Death, not Life."

Harker groaned and said, "And this is all arrayed against my darling! But how is he experimenting? The knowledge may help us to defeat him!"

"He has all along, since his coming, been trying his power, slowly but surely. That big child-brain of his is working. Well for us, it is as yet a child-brain. For had he dared, at the first, to attempt certain things he would long ago have been beyond our power. However, he means to succeed, and a man who has centuries before him can afford to wait and to go slow. *Festina lente* may well be his motto."

"I fail to understand," said Harker wearily. "Oh, do be more plain to me! Perhaps grief and trouble are dulling my brain."

The Professor laid his hand tenderly on his shoulder as he spoke, "Ah, my child, I will be plain. Do you not see how, of late, this monster has been creeping into knowledge experimentally. How he has been making use of the zoophagous patient to effect his entry into friend John's home. For your Vampire, though in all afterwards he can come when and how he will, must at the first make entry only when asked thereto by an inmate. But these are not his most important experiments. Do we not see how at the first all these so great boxes were moved by others. He knew not then but that must be so. But all the time that so great child-brain of his was growing, and he began to consider whether he might not himself move the box. So he began to help. And then, when he found that this be all right, he try to move them all alone. And so he progress, and he scatter these graves of him. And none but he know where they are hidden. "He may have intend to bury them deep in the ground. So that only he use them in the night, or at such time as he can change his form, they do him equal well, and none may know these are his hiding place! But, my child, do not despair, this knowledge came to him just too late! Already all of his lairs but one be sterilize as for him. And before the sunset this shall be so. Then he have no place where he can move and hide. I delayed this morning that so we might be sure. Is there not more at stake for us than for him? Then why not be more careful than him? By my clock it is one hour and already, if all be well, friend Arthur and Quincey are on their way to us. Today is our day, and we must go sure, if slow, and lose no chance. See! There are five of us when those absent ones return."

Whilst we were speaking we were startled by a knock at the hall door, the double postman's knock of the telegraph boy. We all moved out to the hall with one impulse, and Van Helsing, holding up his hand to us to keep silence, stepped to the door and opened it. The boy handed in a dispatch. The Professor closed the door again, and after looking at the direction, opened it and read aloud.

> "Look out for D. He has just now, 12:45, come from Carfax hurriedly and hastened towards the South. He seems to be going the round and may want to see you: MINA."

There was a pause, broken by Jonathan Harker's voice, "Now, God be thanked, we shall soon meet!"

Van Helsing turned to him quickly and said, "God will act in His own way and time. Do not fear, and do not rejoice as yet. For what we wish for at the moment may be our own undoings."

"I care for nothing now," he answered hotly, "except to wipe out this brute from the face of creation. I would sell my soul to do it!"

"Oh, hush, hush, my child!" said Van Helsing. "God does not purchase souls in this wise, and the Devil, though he may purchase, does not keep faith. But God is merciful and just, and knows your pain and your devotion to that dear Madam Mina. Think you, how her pain would be doubled, did she but hear your wild words. Do not fear any of us, we are all devoted to this cause, and today shall see the end. The time is coming for action. Today this Vampire is limit to the powers of man, and till sunset he may not change. It will take him time to arrive here, see it is twenty minutes past one, and there are yet some times before he can hither come, be he never so quick. What we must hope for is that my Lord Arthur and Quincey arrive first."

About half an hour after we had received Mrs. Harker's telegram, there came a quiet, resolute knock at the hall door. It was just an ordinary knock, such as is given hourly by thousands of gentlemen, but it made the Professor's heart and mine beat loudly. We looked at each other, and together moved out into the hall. We each held ready to use our various armaments, the spiritual in the left hand, the mortal in the right. Van Helsing pulled back the latch, and holding the door half open, stood back, having both hands ready for action. The gladness of our hearts must have shown upon our faces when on the step, close to the door, we saw Lord Godalming and Quincey Morris. They came quickly in and closed the door behind them, the former saying, as they moved along the hall:

"It is all right. We found both places. Six boxes in each and we destroyed them all."

"Destroyed?" asked the Professor.

"For him!" We were silent for a minute, and then Quincey said, "There's nothing to do but to wait here. If, however, he doesn't turn up by five o'clock, we must start off. For it won't do to leave Mrs. Harker alone after sunset."

"He will be here before long now," said Van Helsing, who had been consulting his pocketbook. "*Nota bene*, in Madam's telegram he went south from Carfax. That means he went to cross the river, and he could only do so at slack of tide, which should be something before one o'clock. That he went south has a meaning for us. He is as yet only suspicious, and he went from Carfax first to the place where he would suspect interference least. You must have been at Bermondsey only a short time before him. That he is not here already shows that he went to Mile End next. This took him some time, for he would then have to be carried over the river in some way. Believe me, my friends, we shall not have long to wait now. We should have ready some plan of attack, so that we may throw away no chance. Hush, there is no time now. Have all your arms! Be ready!" He held up a warning hand as he spoke, for we all could hear a key softly inserted in the lock of the hall door.

I could not but admire, even at such a moment, the way in which a dominant spirit asserted itself. In all our hunting parties and adventures in different parts of the world, Quincey Morris had always been the one to arrange the plan of action, and Arthur and I had been accustomed to obey him implicitly. Now, the old habit seemed to be renewed instinctively. With a swift glance around the room, he at once laid out our plan of attack, and without speaking a word, with a gesture, placed us each in position. Van Helsing, Harker, and I were just behind the door, so that when it was opened the Professor could guard it whilst we two stepped between the incomer and the door. Godalming behind and Quincey in front stood just out of sight ready to move in front of the window. We waited in a suspense that made the seconds pass with nightmare slowness. The slow, careful steps came along the hall. The Count was evidently prepared for some surprise—at least he feared it.

Suddenly with a single bound he leaped into the room. Winning a way past us before any of us could raise a hand to stay him. There was something so pantherlike in the movement—something so unhuman, that it seemed to sober us all from the shock of his coming. The first to act was Harker, who with a quick movement, threw himself before the door leading into the room in the front of the house. As the Count saw us, a horrible sort of snarl passed over his face, showing the eyeteeth long and pointed. But the evil smile as quickly passed into a cold stare of lion-like disdain. His expression again changed as, with a single impulse, we all advanced upon him. It was a pity that we had not some better organized plan of attack, for even at the moment I wondered what we were to do. I did not myself know whether our lethal weapons would avail us anything. Harker evidently meant to try the matter, for he had ready his great Kukri knife and made a fierce and sudden cut at him. The blow was a powerful one; only the diabolical quickness of the Count's leap back saved him. A second less and the trenchant blade had shorn through his heart. As it was, the point just cut the cloth of his coat, making a wide gap whence a bundle of bank notes and a stream of gold fell out. The expression of the Count's face was so hellish, that for a moment I feared for Harker, though I saw him throw the terrible knife aloft again for another stroke. Instinctively I moved forward with a protective impulse, holding the Crucifix and Wafer in my left hand. I felt a mighty power fly along my arm, and it was without surprise that I saw the monster cower back before a similar movement made spontaneously by each one of us. It would be impossible to describe the expression of hate and baffled malignity—of anger and hellish rage—which came over the Count's face. His waxen hue became greenish-yellow by the contrast of his burning eyes, and the red scar on the forehead showed on the pallid skin like a palpitating wound. The next instant, with a sinuous dive he swept under Harker's arm, ere his blow could fall, and grasping a handful of the money from the floor, dashed across the room, threw himself at the window. Amid the crash and glitter of the falling glass, he tumbled into the flagged area below. Through the sound of the shivering glass I could hear the "ting" of the gold, as some of the sovereigns fell on the flagging.

We ran over and saw him spring unhurt from the ground. He,

rushing up the steps, crossed the flagged yard, and pushed open the stable door. There he turned and spoke to us.

"You think to baffle me, you—with your pale faces all in a row, like sheep in a butcher's. You shall be sorry yet, each one of you! You think you have left me without a place to rest, but I have more. My revenge is just begun! I spread it over centuries, and time is on my side. Your girls that you all love are mine already. And through them you and others shall yet be mine—my creatures, to do my bidding and to be my jackals when I want to feed. Bah!" With a contemptuous sneer, he passed quickly through the door, and we heard the rusty bolt creak as he fastened it behind him. A door beyond opened and shut. The first of us to speak was the Professor. Realizing the difficulty of following him through the stable, we moved toward the hall.

"We have learnt something—much! Notwithstanding his brave words, he fears us. He fears time, he fears want! For if not, why he hurry so? His very tone betray him, or my ears deceive. Why take that money? You follow quick. You are hunters of the wild beast, and understand it so. For me, I make sure that nothing here may be of use to him, if so that he returns." As he spoke he put the money remaining in his pocket, took the title deeds in the bundle as Harker had left them, and swept the remaining things into the open fireplace, where he set fire to them with a match.

Godalming and Morris had rushed out into the yard, and Harker had lowered himself from the window to follow the Count. He had, however, bolted the stable door, and by the time they had forced it open there was no sign of him. Van Helsing and I tried to make inquiry at the back of the house. But the mews was deserted and no one had seen him depart.

It was now late in the afternoon, and sunset was not far off. We had to recognize that our game was up. With heavy hearts we agreed with the Professor when he said, "Let us go back to Madam Mina. Poor, poor dear Madam Mina. All we can do just now is done, and we can there, at least, protect her. But we need not despair. There is but one more earth box, and we must try to find it. When that is done all may yet be well." I could see that he spoke as bravely as he could to comfort Harker. The poor fellow was quite broken down, now and again he gave a low groan which he could not suppress. He was thinking of his wife.

With sad hearts we came back to my house, where we found Mrs. Harker waiting us, with an appearance of cheerfulness which did honour to her bravery and unselfishness. When she saw our faces, her own became as pale as death. For a second or two her eyes were closed as if she were in secret prayer.

And then she said cheerfully, "I can never thank you all enough. Oh, my poor darling!" As she spoke, she took her husband's gray head in her hands and kissed it. "Lay your poor head here and rest it. All will yet be well, dear! God will protect us if He so will it in His good intent." The poor fellow groaned. There was no place for words in his sublime misery.

We had a sort of perfunctory supper together, and I think it cheered us all up somewhat. It was, perhaps, the mere animal heat of food to hungry people—for none of us had eaten anything since breakfast, or the sense of companionship may have helped us, but anyhow we were all less miserable, and saw the morrow as not altogether without hope. True to our promise, we told Mrs. Harker everything which had passed. And although she grew snowy white at times when danger had seemed to threaten her husband, and red at others when his devotion to her was manifested, she listened bravely and with calmness. When we came to the part where Harker had rushed at the Count so recklessly, she clung to her husband's arm, and held it tight as though her clinging could protect him from any harm that might come. She said nothing, however, till the narration was all done, and matters had been brought up to the present time. Then without letting go her husband's hand she stood up amongst us and spoke. Oh, that I could give any idea of the scene. Of that sweet, sweet, good, good woman in all the radiant beauty of her youth and animation, with the red scar on her forehead, of which she was conscious, and which we saw with grinding of our teeth, remembering whence and how it came. Her loving kindness against our grim hate. Her tender faith against all our fears and doubting. And we, knowing that so far as symbols went, she with all her goodness and purity and faith, was outcast from God.

"Jonathan," she said, and the word sounded like music on her lips it was so full of love and tenderness, "Jonathan dear, and you all my true, true friends, I want you to bear something in mind through all this dreadful time. I know that you must fight—that you must destroy even as you destroyed the false Lucy so that the true Lucy might live hereafter. But it is not a work of hate. That poor soul who has wrought all this misery is the saddest case of all. Just think what will be his joy when he, too, is destroyed in his worser part that his better part may have spiritual immortality. You must be pitiful to him, too, though it may not hold your hands from his destruction."

As she spoke I could see her husband's face darken and draw together, as though the passion in him were shriveling his being to its core. Instinctively the clasp on his wife's hand grew closer, till his knuckles looked white. She did not flinch from the pain which I knew she must have suffered, but looked at him with eyes that were more appealing than ever.

As she stopped speaking he leaped to his feet, almost tearing his hand from hers as he spoke. "May God give him into my hand just for long enough to destroy that earthly life of him which we are aiming at. If beyond it I could send his soul forever and ever to burning hell I would do it!"

"Oh, hush! Oh, hush in the name of the good God. Don't say such things, Jonathan, my husband, or you will crush me with fear and horror. Just think, my dear . . . I have been thinking all this long, long day of it—that . . . perhaps . . . someday . . . I, too, may need such pity, and that some other like you, and with equal cause for anger—may deny it to me! Oh, my husband! My husband, indeed I would have spared you such a thought had there been another way. But I pray that God may not have treasured your wild words, except as the heart-broken wail of a very loving and sorely stricken man. Oh, God, let these poor white hairs go in evidence of what he has suffered, who all his life has done no wrong, and on whom so many sorrows have come."

We men were all in tears now. There was no resisting them, and we wept openly. She wept, too, to see that her sweeter counsels had prevailed. Her husband flung himself on his knees beside her, and putting his arms round her, hid his face in the folds of her dress. Van Helsing beckoned to us and we stole out of the room, leaving the two loving hearts alone with their God.

Before they retired the Professor fixed up the room against any coming of the Vampire, and assured Mrs. Harker that she might rest in peace. She tried to school herself to the belief, and manifestly for her husband's sake, tried to seem content. It was a brave struggle, and was, I think and believe, not without its reward. Van Helsing had placed at hand a bell which either of them was to sound in case of any emergency. When they had retired, Quincey, Godalming, and I arranged that we should sit up, dividing the night between us, and watch over the safety of the poor stricken lady. The first watch falls to Quincey, so the rest of us shall be off to bed as soon as we can. Godalming has already turned in, for his is the second watch. Now that my work is done I, too, shall go to bed.

Jonathan Harker's Journal

3–4 October, close to midnight.

I thought yesterday would never end. There was over me a yearning for sleep, in some sort of blind belief that to wake would be to find things changed, and that any change must now be for the better. Before we parted, we discussed what our next step was to be, but we could arrive at no result. All we knew was that one earth box remained, and that the Count alone knew where it was. If he chooses to lie hidden, he may baffle us for years. And in the meantime—the thought is too horrible, I dare not think of it even now. This I know, that if ever there was a woman who was all perfection, that one is my poor wronged darling. I loved her a thousand times more for her sweet pity of last night, a pity that made my own hate of the monster seem despicable. Surely God will not permit the world to be the poorer by the loss of such a creature. This is hope to me. We are all drifting reefwards now, and faith is our only anchor. Thank God! Mina is sleeping, and sleeping without dreams. I fear what her dreams might be like, with such terrible memories to ground them in. She has not been so calm, within my seeing, since the sunset. Then, for a while, there came over her face a repose which was like spring after the blasts of March. I thought at the time that it was the softness of the red sunset on her face, but somehow now I think it has a deeper meaning. I am not sleepy myself, though I am weary—weary to death. However, I must try to sleep. For there is tomorrow to think of, and there is no rest for me until . . .

Later.

I must have fallen asleep, for I was awakened by Mina, who was sitting up in bed, with a startled look on her face. I could see easily, for we did not leave the room in darkness. She had placed a warning hand over my mouth, and now she whispered in my ear, "Hush! There is someone in the corridor!" I got up softly, and crossing the room, gently opened the door.

Just outside, stretched on a mattress, lay Mr. Morris, wide awake. He raised a warning hand for silence as he whispered to me, "Hush! Go back to bed. It is all right. One of us will be here all night. We don't mean to take any chances!"

His look and gesture forbade discussion, so I came back and told Mina. She sighed and positively a shadow of a smile stole over her poor, pale face as she put her arms round me and said softly, "Oh, thank God for good brave men!" With a sigh she sank back again to sleep. I write this now as I am not sleepy, though I must try again.

4 October, morning.

Once again during the night I was wakened by Mina. This time we had all had a good sleep, for the gray of the coming dawn was making the windows into sharp oblongs, and the gas flame was like a speck rather than a disc of light.

She said to me hurriedly, "Go, call the Professor. I want to see him at once."

"Why?" I asked.

"I have an idea. I suppose it must have come in the night, and matured without my knowing it. He must hypnotize me before the dawn, and then I shall be able to speak. Go quick, dearest, the time is getting close."

I went to the door. Dr. Seward was resting on the mattress, and seeing me, he sprang to his feet.

"Is anything wrong?" he asked, in alarm.

"No," I replied. "But Mina wants to see Dr. Van Helsing at once."

"I will go," he said, and hurried into the Professor's room.

Two or three minutes later Van Helsing was in the room in his dressing gown, and Mr. Morris and Lord Godalming were with Dr. Seward at the door asking questions. When the Professor saw Mina a smile, a positive smile ousted the anxiety of his face.

He rubbed his hands as he said, "Oh, my dear Madam Mina, this is indeed a change. See! Friend Jonathan, we have got our dear Madam Mina, as of old, back to us today!" Then turning to her, he said cheerfully, "And what am I to do for you? For at this hour you do not want me for nothing."

"I want you to hypnotize me!" she said. "Do it before the dawn, for I feel that then I can speak, and speak freely. Be quick, for the time is short!" Without a word he motioned her to sit up in bed.

Looking fixedly at her, he commenced to make passes in front of her, from over the top of her head downward, with each hand in turn. Mina gazed at him fixedly for a few minutes, during which my own heart beat like a trip hammer, for I felt that some crisis was at hand. Gradually her eyes closed, and she sat, stock still. Only by the gentle heaving of her bosom could one know that she was alive. The Professor made a few more passes and then stopped, and I could see that his forehead was covered with great beads of perspiration. Mina opened her eyes, but she did not seem the same woman. There was a far-away look in her eyes, and her voice had a sad dreaminess which was new to me. Raising his hand to impose silence, the Professor motioned to me to bring the others in. They came on tiptoe, closing the door behind them, and stood at the foot of the bed, looking on. Mina appeared not to see them. The stillness was broken by Van Helsing's voice speaking in a low level tone which would not break the current of her thoughts.

"Where are you?" The answer came in a neutral way.

"I do not know. Sleep has no place it can call its own." For several minutes there was silence. Mina sat rigid, and the Professor stood staring at her fixedly.

The rest of us hardly dared to breathe. The room was growing lighter. Without taking his eyes from Mina's face, Dr. Van Helsing motioned me to pull up the blind. I did so, and the day seemed just upon us. A red streak shot up, and a rosy light seemed to diffuse itself through the room. On the instant the Professor spoke again.

"Where are you now?"

The answer came dreamily, but with intention. It were as though she were interpreting something. I have heard her use the same tone when reading her shorthand notes.

"I do not know. It is all strange to me!"

"What do you see?"

"I can see nothing. It is all dark."

"What do you hear?" I could detect the strain in the Professor's patient voice.

"The lapping of water. It is gurgling by, and little waves leap. I can hear them on the outside."

"Then you are on a ship?"

We all looked at each other, trying to glean something each from the other. We were afraid to think.

The answer came quick. "Oh, yes!"

"What else do you hear?"

"The sound of men stamping overhead as they run about. There is the creaking of a chain, and the loud tinkle as the check of the capstan falls into the ratchet."

"What are you doing?"

"I am still, oh so still. It is like death!" The voice faded away into a deep breath as of one sleeping, and the open eyes closed again.

By this time the sun had risen, and we were all in the full light of day. Dr. Van Helsing placed his hands on Mina's shoulders, and laid her head down softly on her pillow. She lay like a sleeping child for a few moments, and then, with a long sigh, awoke and stared in wonder to see us all around her.

"Have I been talking in my sleep?" was all she said. She seemed, however, to know the situation without telling, though she was eager to know what she had told. The Professor repeated the conversation, and she said, "Then there is not a moment to lose. It may not be yet too late!"

Mr. Morris and Lord Godalming started for the door but the Professor's calm voice called them back.

"Stay, my friends. That ship, wherever it was, was weighing anchor at the moment in your so great Port of London. Which of them is it that you seek? God be thanked that we have once again a clue, though whither it may lead us we know not. We have been blind somewhat. Blind after the manner of men, since we can look back we see what we might have seen looking forward if we had been able to see what we might have seen! Alas, but that sentence is a puddle, is it not? We can know now what was in the Count's mind, when he seize that money, though Jonathan's so fierce knife put him in the danger that even he dread. He meant escape. Hear me, *escape*! He saw that with but one earth box left, and a pack of men following like dogs after a fox, this London was no place for him. He have take his last earth box on board a ship, and he leave the land. He think to escape, but no! We follow him. Tallyho! As friend Arthur would say when he put on his red frock! Our old fox is wily. Oh! So wily, and we must follow with wile. I, too, am wily and I think his mind in a little while. In meantime we may rest and in peace, for there are between us which he do not want to pass, and which he could not if he would—unless the ship were to touch the land, and then only at full or slack tide. See, and the sun is just rose, and all day to sunset is us. Let us take bath, and dress, and have breakfast which we all need, and which we can eat comfortably since he be not in the same land with us."

Mina looked at him appealingly as she asked, "But why need we seek him further, when he is gone away from us?"

He took her hand and patted it as he replied, "Ask me nothing as yet. When we have breakfast, then I answer all questions." He would say no more, and we separated to dress.

After breakfast Mina repeated her question. He looked at her gravely for a minute and then said sorrowfully, "Because my dear, dear Madam Mina, now more than ever must we find him even if we have to follow him to the jaws of Hell!"

She grew paler as she asked faintly, "Why?"

"Because," he answered solemnly, "he can live for centuries, and you are but mortal woman. Time is now to be dreaded, since once he put that mark upon your throat."

I was just in time to catch her as she fell forward in a faint.

CHAPTER XXIV

Dr. Seward's Phonograph Diary
Spoken by Van Hesling

This to Jonathan Harker.

You are to stay with your dear Madam Mina. We shall go to make our search—if I can call it so, for it is not search but knowing, and we seek confirmation only. But do you stay and take care of her today. This is your best and most holiest office. This day nothing can find him here.

Let me tell you that so you will know what we four know already, for I have tell them. He, our enemy, have gone away. He have gone back to his Castle in Transylvania. I know it so well, as if a great hand of fire wrote it on the wall. He have prepare for this in some way, and that last earth box was ready to ship somewheres. For this he took the money. For this he hurry at the last, lest we catch him before the sun go down. It was his last hope, save that he might hide in the tomb that he think poor Miss Lucy, being as he thought like him, keep open to him. But there was not of time. When that fail he make straight for his last resource—his last earth-work I might say did I wish *double entente*. He is clever, oh so clever! He know that his game here was finish. And so he decide he go back home. He find ship going by the route he came, and he go in it. We go off now to find what ship, and whither bound. When we have discover that, we come back and tell you all. Then we will comfort you and poor Madam Mina with new hope. For it will be hope when you think it over, that all is not lost. This very creature that we pursue, he take hundreds of years to get so far as London. And yet in one day, when we know of the disposal of him we drive him out. He is finite, though he is powerful to do much harm and suffers not as we do. But we are strong, each in our purpose, and we are all more strong together. Take heart afresh, dear husband of Madam Mina. This battle is but begun and in the end we shall win—so sure as that God sits on high to watch over His children. Therefore be of much comfort till we return.

Van Helsing.

Jonathan Harker's Journal

4 October.

When I read to Mina, Van Helsing's message in the phonograph, the poor girl brightened up considerably. Already the certainty that the Count is out of the country has given her comfort. And comfort is strength to her. For my own part, now that his horrible danger is not face to face with us, it seems almost impossible to believe in it. Even my own terrible experiences in Castle Dracula seem like a long forgotten dream. Here in the crisp autumn air in the bright sunlight—

Alas! How can I disbelieve! In the midst of my thought my eye fell on the red scar on my poor darling's white forehead. Whilst that lasts, there can be no disbelief. Mina and I fear to be idle, so we have been over all the diaries again and again. Somehow, although the reality seem greater each time, the pain and the fear seem less. There is something of a guiding purpose manifest throughout, which is comforting. Mina says that perhaps we are the instruments of ultimate good. It may be! I shall try to think as she does. We have never spoken to each other yet of the future. It is better to wait till we see the Professor and the others after their investigations.

The day is running by more quickly than I ever thought a day could run for me again. It is now three o'clock.

Mina Harker's Journal

5 October, 5 p.m.

Our meeting for report. Present: Professor Van Helsing, Lord Godalming, Dr. Seward, Mr. Quincey Morris, Jonathan Harker, Mina Harker.

Dr. Van Helsing described what steps were taken during the day to discover on what boat and whither bound Count Dracula made his escape.

"As I knew that he wanted to get back to Transylvania, I felt sure that he must go by the Danube mouth, or by somewhere in the Black Sea, since by that way he come. It was a dreary blank that was before us. *Omne ignotum pro magnifico*; and so with heavy hearts we start to find what ships leave for the Black Sea last night. He was in sailing ship, since Madam Mina tell of sails being set. These not so important as to go in your list of the shipping in the *Times*, and so we go, by suggestion of Lord Godalming, to your Lloyd's, where are note of all ships that sail, however so small. There we find that only one Black Sea bound ship go out with the tide. She is the *Czarina Catherine*, and she sail from Doolittle's Wharf for Varna, and thence to other ports and up the Danube. 'So!' said I. 'This is the ship whereon is the Count.' So off we go to Doolittle's Wharf, and there we find a man in an office. From him we inquire of the goings of the *Czarina Catherine*. He swear much, and he red face and loud of voice, but he good fellow all the same. And when Quincey give him something from his pocket which crackle as he roll it up, and put it in a so small bag which he have hid deep in his clothing, he still better fellow and humble servant to us. He come with us, and ask many men who are rough and hot. These be better fellows too when they have been no more thirsty. They say much of blood and bloom, and of others which I comprehend not, though I guess what they mean. But nevertheless they tell us all things which we want to know.

"They make known to us among them, how last afternoon at about five o'clock comes a man so hurry. A tall man, thin and pale, with high nose and teeth so white, and eyes that seem to be burning. That he be all in black, except that he have a hat of straw which suit not him or the time. That he scatter his money in making quick inquiry as to what ship sails for the Black Sea and for where. Some took him to the office and then to the ship, where he will not go aboard but halt at shore end of gangplank, and ask that the captain come to him. The captain come, when told that he will be pay well, and though he swear much at the first he agree to term. Then the thin man go and someone tell him where horse and cart can be hired. He go there and soon he come again, himself driving cart on which a great box. This he himself lift down, though it take several to put it on truck for the ship. He give much talk to captain as to how and where his box is to be place. But the captain like it not and swear at him in many tongues, and tell him that if he like he can come and see where it shall be. But he say 'no,' that he come not yet, for that he have much to do. Whereupon the captain tell him that he had better be quick—with blood—for that his ship will leave the place—of blood—before the turn of the tide—with blood. Then the thin man smile and say that of course he must go when he think fit, but he will be surprise if he go quite so soon. The captain swear again, polyglot, and the thin man make him bow, and thank him, and say that he will so far intrude on his kindness as to come aboard before the sailing. Final the captain, more red than ever, and in more tongues, tell him that he doesn't want no Frenchmen, with bloom upon them and also with blood—in his ship—with blood on her also. And so, after asking where he might purchase ship forms, he departed.

"No one knew where he went 'or bloomin' well cared' as they said, for they had something else to think of—well with blood again. For it soon became apparent to all that the *Czarina Catherine* would not sail as was expected. A thin mist began to creep up from the river, and it grew, and grew. Till soon a dense fog enveloped the ship and all around her. The captain swore polyglot—very polyglot—polyglot with bloom and blood, but he could do nothing. The water rose and rose, and he began to fear that he would lose the tide altogether. He was in no friendly mood, when just at full tide, the thin man came up the gangplank again and asked to see where his box had been stowed. Then the captain replied that he wished that he and his box—old and with much bloom and blood—were in hell. But the thin man did not be offend, and went down with the mate and saw where it was place, and came up and stood awhile on deck in fog. He must have come off by himself, for none notice him. Indeed they thought not of him, for soon the fog begin to melt away, and all was clear again. My friends of the thirst and the language that was of bloom and blood laughed, as they told how the captain's swears exceeded even his usual polyglot, and was more than ever full of picturesque, when on questioning other mariners who were on movement up and down the river that hour, he found that few of them had seen any of fog at all, except where it lay round the wharf. However, the ship went out on the ebb tide, and was doubtless by morning far down the river mouth. She was then, when they told us, well out to sea.

"And so, my dear Madam Mina, it is that we have to rest for a time, for our enemy is on the sea, with the fog at his command, on his way to the Danube mouth. To sail a ship takes time, go she never so quick. And when we start to go on land more quick, and we meet him there. Our best hope is to come on him when in the box between sunrise and sunset. For then he can make no struggle, and we may deal with him as we should. There are days for us, in which we can make ready our plan. We know all about where he go. For we have seen the owner of the ship, who have shown us invoices and all papers that can be. The box we seek is to be landed in Varna, and to be given to an agent, one Ristics who will there present his credentials. And so our merchant friend will have done his part. When he ask if there be any wrong, for that so, he can telegraph and have inquiry made at Varna, we say 'no,' for what is to be done is not for police or of the customs. It must be done by us alone and in our own way."

When Dr. Van Helsing had done speaking, I asked him if he were certain that the Count had remained on board the ship. He replied, "We have the best proof of that, your own evidence, when in the hypnotic trance this morning." I asked him again if it were really necessary that they should pursue the Count, for oh! I dread Jonathan leaving me, and I know that he would surely go if the others went. He answered in growing passion, at first quietly. As he went on, however, he grew more angry and more forceful, till in the end we could not but see wherein was at least some of that personal dominance which made him so long a master amongst men.

"Yes, it is necessary—necessary—necessary! For your sake in the first, and then for the sake of humanity. This monster has done much harm already, in the narrow scope where he find himself, and in the short time when as yet he was only as a body groping his so small measure in darkness and not knowing. All this have I told these others. You, my dear Madam Mina, will learn it in the phonograph of my friend John, or in that of your husband. I have told them how the measure of leaving his own barren land, barren of peoples, and coming to a new land where life of man teems till they are like the multitude of standing corn, was the work of centuries. Were another of the Undead, like him, to try to do what he has done, perhaps not all the centuries of the world that have been, or that will be, could aid him. With this one, all the forces of nature that are occult and deep and strong must have worked together in some wonderous way. The very place, where he have been alive, Undead for all these centuries, is full of strangeness of the geologic and chemical world. There are deep caverns and fissures that reach none know whither. There have been volcanoes, some of whose openings still send out waters of strange properties, and gases that kill or make to vivify. Doubtless, there is something magnetic or electric in some of these combinations of occult forces which work for physical life in strange way, and in himself were from the first some great qualities. In a hard and warlike time he was celebrate that he have more iron nerve, more subtle brain, more braver heart, than any man. In him some vital principle have in strange way found their utmost. And as his body keep strong and grow and thrive, so his brain grow too. All this without that diabolic aid which is surely to him. For it have to yield to the powers that come from, and are, symbolic of good. And now this is what he is to us. He have infect you, oh forgive me, my dear, that I must say such, but it is for good of you that I speak. He infect you in such wise, that even if he do no more, you have only to live, to live in your own old, sweet way, and so in time, death, which is of man's common lot and with God's sanction, shall make you like to him. This must not be! We have sworn together that it must not. Thus are we ministers of God's own wish. That the world, and men for whom His Son die, will not be given over to monsters, whose very existence would defame Him. He have allowed us to redeem one soul already, and we go out as the old knights of the Cross to redeem more. Like them we shall travel towards the sunrise. And like them, if we fall, we fall in good cause."

He paused and I said, "But will not the Count take his rebuff wisely? Since he has been driven from England, will he not avoid it, as a tiger does the village from which he has been hunted?"

"Aha!" he said. "Your simile of the tiger good, for me, and I shall adopt him. Your maneater, as they of India call the tiger who has once tasted blood of the human, care no more for the other prey, but prowl unceasing till he get him. This that we hunt from our village is a tiger, too, a maneater, and he never cease to prowl. Nay, in himself he is not one to retire and stay afar. In his life, his living life, he go over the Turkey frontier and attack his enemy on his own ground. He be beaten back, but did he stay? No! He come again, and again, and again. Look at his persistence and endurance. With the child-brain that was to him he have long since conceive the idea of coming to a great city. What does he do? He find out the place of all the world most of promise for him. Then he deliberately set himself down to prepare for the task. He find in patience just how is his strength, and what are his powers. He study new tongues. He learn new social life, new environment of old ways, the politics, the law, the finance, the science, the habit of a new land and a new people who have come to be since he was. His glimpse that he have had, whet his appetite only and enkeen his desire. Nay, it help him to grow as to his brain. For it all prove to him how right he was at the first in his surmises. He have done this alone, all alone! From a ruin tomb in a forgotten land. What more may he not do when the greater world of thought is open to him. He that can smile at death, as we know him. Who can flourish in the midst of diseases that kill off whole peoples. Oh! If such an one was to come from God, and not the Devil, what a force for good might he not be in this old world of ours. But we are pledged to set the world free. Our toil must be in silence, and our efforts all in secret. For in this enlightened age, when men believe not even what they see, the doubting of wise men would be his greatest strength. It would be at once his sheath and his armor, and his weapons to destroy us, his enemies, who are willing to peril even our own souls for the safety of one we love—for the good of mankind, and for the honour and glory of God."

After a general discussion it was determined that for tonight nothing be definitely settled. That we should all sleep on the facts, and try to think out the proper conclusions. Tomorrow, at breakfast, we are to meet again, and after making our conclusions known to one another, we shall decide on some definite cause of action . . .

I feel a wonderful peace and rest tonight. It is as if some haunting presence were removed from me. Perhaps . . .

My surmise was not finished, could not be, for I caught sight in the mirror of the red mark upon my forehead, and I knew that I was still unclean.

Dr. Seward's Diary

5 October.

We all arose early, and I think that sleep did much for each and all of us. When we met at early breakfast there was more general cheerfulness than any of us had ever expected to experience again.

It is really wonderful how much resilience there is in human nature. Let any obstructing cause, no matter what, be removed in any way—even by death—and we fly back to first principles of hope and enjoyment. More than once as we sat around the table, my eyes opened in wonder whether the whole of the past days had not been a dream. It was only when I caught sight of the red blotch on Mrs. Harker's forehead that I was brought back to reality. Even now, when I am gravely revolving the matter, it is almost impossible to realize that the cause of all our trouble is still existent. Even Mrs. Harker seems to lose sight of her trouble for whole spells. It is only now and again, when something recalls it to her mind, that she thinks of her terrible scar. We are to meet here in my study in half an hour and decide on our course of action. I see only one immediate difficulty, I know it by instinct rather than reason. We shall all have to speak frankly. And yet I fear that in some mysterious way poor Mrs. Harker's tongue is tied. I know that she forms conclusions of her own, and from all that has been I can guess how brilliant and how true they must be. But she will not, or cannot, give them utterance. I have mentioned this to Van Helsing, and he and I are to talk it over when we are alone. I suppose it is some of that horrid poison which has got into her veins beginning to work. The Count had his own purposes when he gave her what Van Helsing called "the Vampire's baptism of blood." Well, there may be a poison that distills itself out of good things. In an age when the existence of ptomaines is a mystery we should not wonder at anything! One thing I know, that if my instinct be true regarding poor Mrs. Harker's silences, then there is a terrible difficulty—an unknown danger—in the work before us. The same power that compels her silence may compel her speech. I dare not think further, for so I should in my thoughts dishonour a noble woman!

Van Helsing is coming to my study a little before the others. I shall try to open the subject with him.

Later.

When the Professor came in, we talked over the state of things. I could see that he had something on his mind, which he wanted to say, but felt some hesitancy about broaching the subject. After beating about the bush a little, he said, "Friend John, there is something that you and I must talk of alone, just at the first at any rate. Later, we may have to take the others into our confidence."

Then he stopped, so I waited. He went on, "Madam Mina, our poor, dear Madam Mina is changing."

A cold shiver ran through me to find my worst fears thus endorsed. Van Helsing continued.

"With the sad experience of Miss Lucy, we must this time be warned before things go too far. Our task is now in reality more difficult than ever, and this new trouble makes every hour of the direst importance.

I can see the characteristics of the vampire coming in her face. It is now but very, very slight. But it is to be seen if we have eyes to notice without prejudge. Her teeth are sharper, and at times her eyes are more hard. But these are not all, there is to her the silence now often, as so it was with Miss Lucy. She did not speak, even when she wrote that which she wished to be known later. Now my fear is this. If it be that she can, by our hypnotic trance, tell what the Count see and hear, is it not more true that he who have hypnotize her first, and who have drink of her very blood and make her drink of his, should if he will, compel her mind to disclose to him that which she know?"

I nodded acquiescence. He went on, "Then, what we must do is to prevent this. We must keep her ignorant of our intent, and so she cannot tell what she know not. This is a painful task! Oh, so painful that it heartbreak me to think of it, but it must be. When today we meet, I must tell her that for reason which we will not to speak she must not more be of our council, but be simply guarded by us." He wiped his forehead, which had broken out in profuse perspiration at the thought of the pain which he might have to inflict upon the poor soul already so tortured. I knew that it would be some sort of comfort to him if I told him that I also had come to the same conclusion. For at any rate it would take away the pain of doubt. I told him, and the effect was as I expected.

It is now close to the time of our general gathering. Van Helsing has gone away to prepare for the meeting, and his painful part of it. I really believe his purpose is to be able to pray alone.

Later.

At the very outset of our meeting a great personal relief was experienced by both Van Helsing and myself. Mrs. Harker had sent a message by her husband to say that she would not join us at present, as she thought it better that we should be free to discuss our movements without her presence to embarrass us. The Professor and I looked at each other for an instant, and somehow we both seemed relieved. For my own part, I thought that if Mrs. Harker realized the danger herself, it was much pain as well as much danger averted. Under the circumstances we agreed, by a questioning look and answer, with finger on lip, to preserve silence in our suspicions, until we should have been able to confer alone again. We went at once into our Plan of Campaign.

Van Helsing roughly put the facts before us first, "The *Czarina Catherine* left the Thames yesterday morning. It will take her at the quickest speed she has ever made at least three weeks to reach Varna. But we can travel overland to the same place in three days. Now, if we allow for two days less for the ship's voyage, owing to such weather influences as we know that the Count can bring to bear, and if we allow a whole day and night for any delays which may occur to us, then we have a margin of nearly two weeks. Thus, in order to be quite safe, we must leave here on 17th at latest. Then we shall at any rate be in Varna a day before the ship arrives, and able to make such preparations as may be necessary. Of course we shall all go armed—armed against evil things—spiritual as well as physical."

Here Quincey Morris added, "I understand that the Count comes from a wolf country, and it may be that he shall get there before us. I propose that we add Winchesters to our armament. I have a kind of belief in a Winchester when there is any trouble of that sort around. Do you remember, Art, when we had the pack after us at Tobolsk? What wouldn't we have given then for a repeater apiece!"

"Good!" said Van Helsing, "Winchesters it shall be. Quincey's head is level at times, but most so when there is to hunt, metaphor be more dishonour to science than wolves be of danger to man. In the meantime we can do nothing here. And as I think that Varna is not familiar to any of us, why not go there more soon? It is as long to wait here as there. Tonight and tomorrow we can get ready, and then if all be well, we four can set out on our journey."

"We four?" said Harker interrogatively, looking from one to another of us.

"Of course!" answered the Professor quickly. "You must remain to take care of your so sweet wife!"

Harker was silent for awhile and then said in a hollow voice, "Let us talk of that part of it in the morning. I want to consult with Mina."

I thought that now was the time for Van Helsing to warn him not to disclose our plan to her, but he took no notice. I looked at him significantly and coughed. For answer he put his finger to his lips and turned away.

Jonathan Harker's Journal

5 October, afternoon.

For some time after our meeting this morning I could not think. The new phases of things leave my mind in a state of wonder which allows no room for active thought. Mina's determination not to take any part in the discussion set me thinking. And as I could not argue the matter with her, I could only guess. I am as far as ever from a solution now. The way the others received it, too puzzled me. The last time we talked of the subject we agreed that there was to be no more concealment of anything amongst us. Mina is sleeping now, calmly and sweetly like a little child. Her lips are curved and her face beams with happiness. Thank God, there are such moments still for her.

Later.

How strange it all is. I sat watching Mina's happy sleep, and I came as near to being happy myself as I suppose I shall ever be. As the evening drew on, and the earth took its shadows from the sun sinking lower, the silence of the room grew more and more solemn to me.

All at once Mina opened her eyes, and looking at me tenderly said, "Jonathan, I want you to promise me something on your word of honour. A promise made to me, but made holily in God's hearing, and not to be broken though I should go down on my knees and implore you with bitter tears. Quick, you must make it to me at once."

"Mina," I said, "a promise like that, I cannot make at once. I may have no right to make it."

"But, dear one," she said, with such spiritual intensity that her eyes were like pole stars, "it is I who wish it. And it is not for myself. You can ask Dr. Van Helsing if I am not right. If he disagrees you may do as you will. Nay, more if you all agree, later you are absolved from the promise."

"I promise!" I said, and for a moment she looked supremely happy. Though to me all happiness for her was denied by the red scar on her forehead.

She said, "Promise me that you will not tell me anything of the plans formed for the campaign against the Count. Not by word, or inference, or implication, not at any time whilst this remains to me!" And she solemnly pointed to the scar. I saw that she was in earnest, and said solemnly, "I promise!" and as I said it I felt that from that instant a door had been shut between us.

Later, midnight.

Mina has been bright and cheerful all the evening. So much so that all the rest seemed to take courage, as if infected somewhat with her gaiety. As a result even I myself felt as if the pall of gloom which weighs us down were somewhat lifted. We all retired early. Mina is now sleeping like a little child. It is wonderful thing that her faculty of sleep remains to her in the midst of her terrible trouble. Thank God for it, for then at least she can forget her care. Perhaps her example may affect me as her gaiety did tonight. I shall try it. Oh! For a dreamless sleep.

6 October, morning.

Another surprise. Mina woke me early, about the same time as yesterday, and asked me to bring Dr. Van Helsing. I thought that it was another occasion for hypnotism, and without question went for the Professor. He had evidently expected some such call, for I found him dressed in his room. His door was ajar, so that he could hear the opening of the door of our room. He came at once. As he passed into the room, he asked Mina if the others might come, too.

"No," she said quite simply, "it will not be necessary. You can tell them just as well. I must go with you on your journey."

Dr. Van Helsing was as startled as I was. After a moment's pause he asked, "But why?"

"You must take me with you. I am safer with you, and you shall be safer, too."

"But why, dear Madam Mina? You know that your safety is our solemnest duty. We go into danger, to which you are, or may be, more liable than any of us from—from circumstances—things that have been." He paused embarrassed.

As she replied, she raised her finger and pointed to her forehead. "I know. That is why I must go. I can tell you now, whilst the sun is coming up. I may not be able again. I know that when the Count wills me I must go. I know that if he tells me to come in secret, I must by wile. By any device to hoodwink, even Jonathan." God saw the look that she turned on me as she spoke, and if there be indeed a Recording Angel that look is noted to her ever-lasting honour. I could only clasp her hand. I could not speak. My emotion was too great for even the relief of tears.

She went on. "You men are brave and strong. You are strong in your numbers, for you can defy that which would break down the human endurance of one who had to guard alone. Besides, I may be of service, since you can hypnotize me and so learn that which even I myself do not know."

Dr. Van Helsing said gravely, "Madam Mina, you are, as always, most wise. You shall with us come. And together we shall do that which we go forth to achieve."

When he had spoken, Mina's long spell of silence made me look at her. She had fallen back on her pillow asleep. She did not even wake when I had pulled up the blind and let in the sunlight which flooded the room. Van Helsing motioned to me to come with him quietly. We went to his room, and within a minute Lord Godalming, Dr. Seward, and Mr. Morris were with us also.

He told them what Mina had said, and went on. "In the morning we shall leave for Varna. We have now to deal with a new factor, Madam Mina. Oh, but her soul is true. It is to her an agony to tell us so much as she has done. But it is most right, and we are warned in time. There must be no chance lost, and in Varna we must be ready to act the instant when that ship arrives."

"What shall we do exactly?" asked Mr. Morris laconically.

The Professor paused before replying, "We shall at the first board that ship. Then, when we have identified the box, we shall place a branch of the wild rose on it. This we shall fasten, for when it is there none can emerge, so that at least says the superstition. And to superstition must we trust at the first. It was man's faith in the early, and it have its root in faith still. Then, when we get the opportunity that we seek, when none are near to see, we shall open the box, and—and all will be well."

"I shall not wait for any opportunity," said Morris. "When I see the box I shall open it and destroy the monster, though there were a thousand men looking on, and if I am to be wiped out for it the next moment!" I grasped his hand instinctively and found it as firm as a piece of steel. I think he understood my look. I hope he did.

"Good boy," said Dr. Van Helsing. "Brave boy. Quincey is all man. God bless him for it. My child, believe me none of us shall lag behind or pause from any fear. I do but say what we may do . . . what we must do. But, indeed, indeed we cannot say what we may do. There are so many things which may happen, and their ways and their ends are so various that until the moment we may not say. We shall all be armed, in all ways. And when the time for the end has come, our effort shall not be lack. Now let us today put all our affairs in order. Let all things which touch on others dear to us, and who on us depend, be complete. For none of us can tell what, or when, or how, the end may be. As for me, my own affairs are regulate, and as I have nothing else to do, I shall go make arrangements for the travel. I shall have all tickets and so forth for our journey."

There was nothing further to be said, and we parted. I shall now settle up all my affairs of earth, and be ready for whatever may come.

Later.

It is done. My will is made, and all complete. Mina if she survive is my sole heir. If it should not be so, then the others who have been so good to us shall have remainder.

It is now drawing towards the sunset. Mina's uneasiness calls my attention to it. I am sure that there is something on her mind which the time of exact sunset will reveal. These occasions are becoming harrowing times for us all. For each sunrise and sunset opens up some new danger—some new pain, which however, may in God's will be means to a good end. I write all these things in the diary since my darling must not hear them now. But if it may be that she can see them again, they shall be ready.

She is calling to me.

CHAPTER XXV

Dr. Seward's Diary

11 October, evening.

Jonathan Harker has asked me to note this, as he says he is hardly equal to the task, and he wants an exact record kept.

I think that none of us were surprised when we were asked to see Mrs. Harker a little before the time of sunset. We have of late come to understand that sunrise and sunset are to her times of peculiar freedom. When her old self can be manifest without any controlling force subduing or restraining her, or inciting her to action. This mood or condition begins some half hour or more before actual sunrise or sunset, and lasts till either the sun is high, or whilst the clouds are still aglow with the rays streaming above the horizon. At first there is a sort of negative condition, as if some tie were loosened, and then the absolute freedom quickly follows. When, however, the freedom ceases the change back or relapse comes quickly, preceded only by a spell of warning silence.

Tonight, when we met, she was somewhat constrained, and bore all the signs of an internal struggle. I put it down myself to her making a violent effort at the earliest instant she could do so. A very few minutes, however, gave her complete control of herself. Then, motioning her husband to sit beside her on the sofa where she was half reclining, she made the rest of us bring chairs up close.

Taking her husband's hand in hers, she began, "We are all here together in freedom, for perhaps the last time! I know that you will always be with me to the end." This was to her husband whose hand had, as we could see, tightened upon her. "In the morning we go out upon our task, and God alone knows what may be in store for any of us. You are going to be so good to me to take me with you. I know that all that brave earnest men can do for a poor weak woman, whose soul perhaps is lost—no, no, not yet, but is at any rate at stake—you will do. But you must remember that I am not as you are. There is a poison in my blood, in my soul, which may destroy me, which must destroy me, unless some relief comes to us. Oh, my friends, you know as well as I do, that my soul is at stake. And though I know there is one way out for me, you must not and I must not take it!" She looked appealingly to us all in turn, beginning and ending with her husband.

"What is that way?" asked Van Helsing in a hoarse voice. "What is that way, which we must not—may not—take?"

"That I may die now, either by my own hand or that of another, before the greater evil is entirely wrought. I know, and you know, that were I once dead you could and would set free my immortal spirit, even as you did my poor Lucy's. Were death, or the fear of death, the only thing that stood in the way I would not shrink to die here now, amidst the friends who love me. But death is not all. I cannot believe that to die in such a case, when there is hope before us and a bitter task to be done, is God's will. Therefore, I on my part, give up here the certainty of eternal rest, and go out into the dark where may be the blackest things that the world or the nether world holds!" We were all silent, for we knew instinctively that this was only a prelude. The faces of the others were set, and Harker's grew ashen gray. Perhaps, he guessed better than any of us what was coming.

She continued, "This is what I can give into the hotch-pot." I could not but note the quaint legal phrase which she used in such a place, and with all seriousness. "What will each of you give? Your lives I know," she went on quickly, "that is easy for brave men. Your lives are God's, and you can give them back to Him, but what will you give to me?" She looked again questioningly, but this time avoided her husband's face. Quincey seemed to understand, he nodded, and her face lit up. "Then I shall tell you plainly what I want, for there must be no doubtful matter in this connection between us now. You must promise me, one and all—even you, my beloved husband—that should the time come, you will kill me."

"What is that time?" The voice was Quincey's, but it was low and strained.

"When you shall be convinced that I am so changed that it is better that I die that I may live. When I am thus dead in the flesh, then you will, without a moment's delay, drive a stake through me and cut off my head, or do whatever else may be wanting to give me rest!"

Quincey was the first to rise after the pause. He knelt down before her and taking her hand in his said solemnly, "I'm only a rough fellow, who hasn't, perhaps, lived as a man should to win such a distinction, but I swear to you by all that I hold sacred and dear that, should the time ever come, I shall not flinch from the duty that you have set us. And I promise you, too, that I shall make all certain, for if I am only doubtful I shall take it that the time has come!"

"My true friend!" was all she could say amid her fast-falling tears, as bending over, she kissed his hand.

"I swear the same, my dear Madam Mina!" said Van Helsing.

"And I!" said Lord Godalming, each of them in turn kneeling to her to take the oath. I followed, myself.

Then her husband turned to her wan-eyed and with a greenish pallor which subdued the snowy whiteness of his hair, and asked, "And must I, too, make such a promise, oh, my wife?"

"You too, my dearest," she said, with infinite yearning of pity in her voice and eyes. "You must not shrink. You are nearest and dearest and all the world to me. Our souls are knit into one, for all life and all time. Think, dear, that there have been times when brave men have killed their wives and their womenkind, to keep them from falling into the hands of the enemy. Their hands did not falter any the more because those that they loved implored them to slay them. It is men's duty towards those whom they love, in such times of sore trial! And oh, my dear, if it is to be that I must meet death at any hand, let it be at the hand of him that loves me best. Dr. Van Helsing, I have not forgotten your mercy in poor Lucy's case to him who loved." She stopped with a flying blush, and changed her phrase, "to him who had best right to give her peace. If that time shall come again, I look to you to make it a happy memory of my husband's life that it was his loving hand which set me free from the awful thrall upon me."

"Again I swear!" came the Professor's resonant voice.

Mrs. Harker smiled, positively smiled, as with a sigh of relief she leaned back and said, "And now one word of warning, a warning which you must never forget. This time, if it ever come, may come quickly and unexpectedly, and in such case you must lose no time in using your opportunity. At such a time I myself might be—nay! If the time ever come, *shall* be—leagued with your enemy against you.

"One more request," she became very solemn as she said this, "it is not vital and necessary like the other, but I want you to do one thing for me, if you will."

We all acquiesced, but no one spoke. There was no need to speak.

"I want you to read the Burial Service." She was interrupted by a deep groan from her husband. Taking his hand in hers, she held it over her heart, and continued. "You must read it over me someday. Whatever may be the issue of all this fearful state of things, it will be a sweet thought to all or some of us. You, my dearest, will I hope read it, for then it will be in your voice in my memory forever—come what may!"

"But oh, my dear one," he pleaded, "death is afar off from you."

"Nay," she said, holding up a warning hand. "I am deeper in death at this moment than if the weight of an earthly grave lay heavy upon me!"

"Oh, my wife, must I read it?" he said, before he began.

"It would comfort me, my husband!" was all she said, and he began to read when she had got the book ready.

How can I—how could anyone—tell of that strange scene, its solemnity, its gloom, its sadness, its horror, and withal, its sweetness. Even a sceptic, who can see nothing but a travesty of bitter truth in anything holy or emotional, would have been melted to the heart had he seen that little group of loving and devoted friends kneeling round that stricken and sorrowing lady; or heard the tender passion of her husband's voice, as in tones so broken and emotional that often he had to pause, he read the simple and beautiful service from the Burial of the Dead. I cannot go on—words—and v-voices—f-fail m-me!

She was right in her instinct. Strange as it was, bizarre as it may hereafter seem even to us who felt its potent influence at the time, it comforted us much. And the silence, which showed Mrs. Harker's coming relapse from her freedom of soul, did not seem so full of despair to any of us as we had dreaded.

Jonathan Harker's Journal

15 October, Varna.

We left Charing Cross on the morning of the 12th, got to Paris the same night, and took the places secured for us in the Orient Express. We traveled night and day, arriving here at about five o'clock. Lord Godalming went to the Consulate to see if any telegram had arrived for him, whilst the rest of us came on to this hotel, the Odessus. The journey may have had incidents. I was, however, too eager to get on, to care for them. Until the *Czarina Catherine* comes into port there will be no interest for me in anything in the wide world. Thank God! Mina is well, and looks to be getting stronger. Her colour is coming back. She sleeps a great deal. Throughout the journey she slept nearly all the time. Before sunrise and sunset, however, she is very wakeful and alert. And it has become a habit for Van Helsing to hypnotize her at such times. At first, some effort was needed, and he had to make many passes. But now, she seems to yield at once, as if by habit, and scarcely any action is needed. He seems to have power at these particular moments to simply will, and her thoughts obey him. He always asks her what she can see and hear.

She answers to the first, "Nothing, all is dark."

And to the second, "I can hear the waves lapping against the ship, and the water rushing by. Canvas and cordage strain and masts and yards creak. The wind is high—I can hear it in the shrouds, and the bow throws back the foam."

It is evident that the *Czarina Catherine* is still at sea, hastening on her way to Varna. Lord Godalming has just returned. He had four telegrams, one each day since we started, and all to the same effect. That the *Czarina Catherine* had not been reported to Lloyd's from anywhere. He had arranged before leaving London that his agent should send him every day a telegram saying if the ship had been reported. He was to have a message even if she were not reported, so that he might be sure that there was a watch being kept at the other end of the wire.

We had dinner and went to bed early. Tomorrow we are to see the Vice Consul, and to arrange, if we can, about getting on board the ship as soon as she arrives. Van Helsing says that our chance will be to get on the boat between sunrise and sunset. The Count, even if he takes the form of a bat, cannot cross the running water of his own volition, and so cannot leave the ship. As he dare not change to man's form without suspicion—which he evidently wishes to avoid—he must remain in the box. If, then, we can come on board after sunrise, he is at our mercy, for we can open the box and make sure of him, as we did of poor Lucy, before he wakes. What mercy he shall get from us all will not count for much. We think that we shall not have much trouble with officials or the seamen. Thank God! This is the country where bribery can do anything, and we are well supplied with money. We have only to make sure that the ship cannot come into port between sunset and sunrise without our being warned, and we shall be safe. Judge Moneybag will settle this case, I think!

16 October.

Mina's report still the same. Lapping waves and rushing water, darkness and favouring winds. We are evidently in good time, and when we hear of the *Czarina Catherine* we shall be ready. As she must pass the Dardanelles we are sure to have some report.

17 October.

Everything is pretty well fixed now, I think, to welcome the Count on his return from his tour. Godalming told the shippers that he fancied that the box sent aboard might contain something stolen from a friend of his, and got a half consent that he might open it at his own risk. The owner gave him a paper telling the Captain to give him every facility in doing whatever he chose on board the ship, and also a similar authorization to his agent at Varna. We have seen the agent, who was much impressed with Godalming's kindly manner to him, and we are all satisfied that whatever he can do to aid our wishes will be done. We have already arranged what to do in case we get the box open. If the Count is there, Van Helsing and Seward will cut off his head at once and drive a stake through his heart. Morris and Godalming and I shall prevent interference, even if we have to use the arms which we shall have ready. The Professor says that if we can so treat the Count's body, it will soon after fall into dust. In such case there would be no evidence against us, in case any suspicion of murder were aroused. But even if it were not, we should stand or fall by our act, and perhaps someday this very script may be evidence to come between some of us and a rope. For myself, I should take the chance only too thankfully if it were to come. We mean to leave no stone unturned to carry out our intent. We have arranged with certain officials that the instant the *Czarina Catherine* is seen, we are to be informed by a special messenger.

24 October.

A whole week of waiting. Daily telegrams to Godalming, but only the same story. "Not yet reported." Mina's morning and evening hypnotic answer is unvaried. Lapping waves, rushing water, and creaking masts.

Telegram, October 24th, Rufus Smith, Lloyd's, London, to Lord Godalming, Care of H. B. M. Vice Consul, Varna

"*Czarina Catherine* reported this morning from Dardanelles."

Dr. Seward's Diary

25 October.

How I miss my phonograph! To write a diary with a pen is irksome to me! But Van Helsing says I must. We were all wild with excitement yesterday when Godalming got his telegram from Lloyd's. I know now what men feel in battle when the call to action is heard. Mrs. Harker, alone of our party, did not show any signs of emotion. After all, it is not strange that she did not, for we took special care not to let her know anything about it, and we all tried not to show any excitement when we were in her presence. In old days she would, I am sure, have noticed, no matter how we might have tried to conceal it. But in this way she is greatly changed during the past three weeks. The lethargy grows upon her, and though she seems strong and well, and is getting back some of her colour, Van Helsing and I are not satisfied. We talk of her often. We have not, however, said a word to the others. It would break poor Harker's heart, certainly his nerve, if he knew that we had even a suspicion on the subject. Van Helsing examines, he tells me, her teeth very carefully, whilst she is in the hypnotic condition, for he says that so long as they do not begin to sharpen there is no active danger of a change in her. If this change should come, it would be necessary to take steps! We both know what those steps would have to be, though we do not mention our thoughts to each other. We should neither of us shrink from the task, awful though it be to contemplate. "Euthanasia" is an excellent and a comforting word! I am grateful to whoever invented it.

It is only about 24 hours' sail from the Dardanelles to here, at the rate the *Czarina Catherine* has come from London. She should therefore arrive some time in the morning, but as she cannot possibly get in before noon, we are all about to retire early. We shall get up at one o'clock, so as to be ready.

25 October, noon.

No news yet of the ship's arrival. Mrs. Harker's hypnotic report this morning was the same as usual, so it is possible that we may get news at any moment. We men are all in a fever of excitement, except Harker, who is calm. His hands are cold as ice, and an hour ago I found him whetting the edge of the great Ghoorka knife which he now always carries with him. It will be a bad lookout for the Count if the edge of that "Kukri" ever touches his throat, driven by that stern, ice-cold hand!

Van Helsing and I were a little alarmed about Mrs. Harker today. About noon she got into a sort of lethargy which we did not like. Although we kept silence to the others, we were neither of us happy about it. She had been restless all the morning, so that we were at first glad to know that she was sleeping. When, however, her husband mentioned casually that she was sleeping so soundly that he could not wake her, we went to her room to see for ourselves. She was breathing naturally and looked so well and peaceful that we agreed that the sleep was better for her than anything else. Poor girl, she has so much to forget that it is no wonder that sleep, if it brings oblivion to her, does her good.

Later.

Our opinion was justified, for when after a refreshing sleep of some hours she woke up, she seemed brighter and better than she had been for days. At sunset she made the usual hypnotic report. Wherever he may be in the Black Sea, the Count is hurrying to his destination. To his doom, I trust!

26 October.

Another day and no tidings of the *Czarina Catherine*. She ought to be here by now. That she is still journeying *somewhere* is apparent, for Mrs. Harker's hypnotic report at sunrise was still the same. It is possible that the vessel may be lying by, at times, for fog. Some of the steamers which came in last evening reported patches of fog both to north and south of the port. We must continue our watching, as the ship may now be signalled any moment.

27 October, noon.

Most strange. No news yet of the ship we wait for. Mrs. Harker reported last night and this morning as usual. "Lapping waves and rushing water," though she added that "the waves were very faint." The telegrams from London have been the same, "no further report." Van Helsing is terribly anxious, and told me just now that he fears the Count is escaping us.

He added significantly, "I did not like that lethargy of Madam Mina's. Souls and memories can do strange things during trance." I was about to ask him more, but Harker just then came in, and he held up a warning hand. We must try tonight at sunset to make her speak more fully when in her hypnotic state.

28 October.

Telegram. Rufus Smith, London, to Lord Godalming, care H. B. M. Vice Consul, Varna:

Czarina Catherine reported entering Galatz at one o'clock today.

Dr. Seward's Diary

28 October.

When the telegram came announcing the arrival in Galatz I do not think it was such a shock to any of us as might have been expected. True, we did not know whence, or how, or when, the bolt would come. But I think we all expected that something strange would happen. The day of arrival at Varna made us individually satisfied that things would not be just as we had expected. We only waited to learn where the change would occur. None the less, however, it was a surprise. I suppose that nature works on such a hopeful basis that we believe against ourselves that things will be as they ought to be, not as we should know that they will be. Transcendentalism is a beacon to the angels, even if it be a will-o'-the-wisp to man. Van Helsing raised his hand over his head for a moment, as though in remonstrance with the Almighty. But he said not a word, and in a few seconds stood up with his face sternly set. Lord Godalming grew very pale, and sat breathing heavily. I was myself half stunned and looked in wonder at one after another. Quincey Morris tightened his belt with that quick movement which I knew so well. In our old wandering days it meant "action." Mrs. Harker grew ghastly white, so that the scar on her forehead seemed to burn, but she folded her hands meekly and looked up in prayer. Harker smiled—actually smiled—the dark, bitter smile of one who is without hope, but at the same time his action belied his words, for his hands instinctively sought the hilt of the great Kukri knife and rested there.

"When does the next train start for Galatz?" said Van Helsing to us generally.

"At 6:30 tomorrow morning!" We all started, for the answer came from Mrs. Harker.

"How on earth do you know?" said Art.

"You forget, or perhaps you do not know, though Jonathan does and so does Dr. Van Helsing, that I am the train fiend. At home in Exeter I always used to make up the time tables, so as to be helpful to my husband. I found it so useful sometimes, that I always make a study of the time tables now. I knew that if anything were to take us to Castle Dracula we should go by Galatz, or at any rate through Bucharest, so I learned the times very carefully. Unhappily there are not many to learn, as the only train tomorrow leaves as I say."

"Wonderful woman!" murmured the Professor.

"Can't we get a special?" asked Lord Godalming.

Van Helsing shook his head, "I fear not. This land is very different from yours or mine. Even if we did have a special, it would probably not arrive as soon as our regular train. Moreover, we have something to prepare. We must think. Now let us organize. You, friend Arthur, go to the train and get the tickets and arrange that all be ready for us to go in the morning. Do you, friend Jonathan, go to the agent of the ship and get from him letters to the agent in Galatz, with authority to make a search of the ship just as it was here. Quincey Morris, you see the Vice Consul, and get his aid with his fellow in Galatz and all he can do to make our way smooth, so that no times be lost when over the Danube. John will stay with Madam Mina and me, and we shall consult. For so if time be long you may be delayed. And it will not matter when the sun set, since I am here with Madam to make report."

"And I," said Mrs. Harker brightly, and more like her old self than she had been for many a long day, "shall try to be of use in all ways, and shall think and write for you as I used to do. Something is shifting from me in some strange way, and I feel freer than I have been of late!"

The three younger men looked happier at the moment as they seemed to realize the significance of her words. But Van Helsing and

I, turning to each other, met each a grave and troubled glance. We said nothing at the time, however.

When the three men had gone out to their tasks Van Helsing asked Mrs. Harker to look up the copy of the diaries and find him the part of Harker's journal at the Castle. She went away to get it.

When the door was shut upon her he said to me, "We mean the same! Speak out!"

"Here is some change. It is a hope that makes me sick, for it may deceive us."

"Quite so. Do you know why I asked her to get the manuscript?"

"No!" said I, "unless it was to get an opportunity of seeing me alone."

"You are in part right, friend John, but only in part. I want to tell you something. And oh, my friend, I am taking a great—a terrible—risk. But I believe it is right. In the moment when Madam Mina said those words that arrest both our understanding, an inspiration came to me. In the trance of three days ago the Count sent her his spirit to read her mind. Or more like he took her to see him in his earth box in the ship with water rushing, just as it go free at rise and set of sun. He learn then that we are here, for she have more to tell in her open life with eyes to see ears to hear than he, shut as he is, in his coffin box. Now he make his most effort to escape us. At present he want her not.

"He is sure with his so great knowledge that she will come at his call. But he cut her off, take her, as he can do, out of his own power, that so she come not to him. Ah! There I have hope that our man brains that have been of man so long and that have not lost the grace of God, will come higher than his child-brain that lie in his tomb for centuries, that grow not yet to our stature, and that do only work selfish and therefore small. Here comes Madam Mina. Not a word to her of her trance! She knows it not, and it would overwhelm her and make despair just when we want all her hope, all her courage, when most we want all her great brain which is trained like man's brain, but is of sweet woman and have a special power which the Count give her, and which he may not take away altogether—though he think not so. Hush! Let me speak, and you shall learn. Oh, John, my friend, we are in awful straits. I fear, as I never feared before. We can only trust the good God. Silence! Here she comes!"

I thought that the Professor was going to break down and have hysterics, just as he had when Lucy died, but with a great effort he controlled himself and was at perfect nervous poise when Mrs. Harker tripped into the room, bright and happy looking and, in the doing of work, seemingly forgetful of her misery. As she came in, she handed a number of sheets of typewriting to Van Helsing. He looked over them gravely, his face brightening up as he read.

Then holding the pages between his finger and thumb he said, "Friend John, to you with so much experience already, and you too, dear Madam Mina, that are young, here is a lesson. Do not fear ever to think. A half thought has been buzzing often in my brain, but I fear to let him loose his wings. Here now, with more knowledge, I go back to where that half thought come from and I find that he be no half thought at all. That be a whole thought, though so young that he is not yet strong to use his little wings. Nay, like the 'Ugly Duck' of my friend Hans Andersen, he be no duck thought at all, but a big swan thought that sail nobly on big wings, when the time come for him to try them. See, I read here what Jonathan have written.

"That other of his race who, in a later age, again and again, brought his forces over the Great River into Turkey Land, who when he was beaten back, came again, and again, and again, though he had to come alone from the bloody field where his troops were being slaughtered, since he knew that he alone could ultimately triumph.

"What does this tell us? Not much? No! The Count's child thought see nothing, therefore he speak so free. Your man thought see nothing. My man thought see nothing, till just now. No! But there comes another word from someone who speak without thought because she, too, know not what it mean, what it might mean. Just as there are elements which rest, yet when in nature's course they move on their way and they touch, the pouf! And there comes a flash of light, heaven wide, that blind and kill and destroy some. But that show up all earth below for leagues and leagues. Is it not so? Well, I shall explain. To begin, have you ever study the philosophy of crime? 'Yes' and 'No.' You, John, yes, for it is a study of insanity. You, no, Madam Mina, for crime touch you not, not but once. Still, your mind works true, and argues not *a particulari ad universale*. There is this peculiarity in criminals. It is so constant, in all countries and at all times, that even police, who know not much from philosophy, come to know it empirically, that it is. That is to be empiric. The criminal always work at one crime, that is the true criminal who seems predestinate to crime, and who will of none other. This criminal has not full man brain. He is clever and cunning and resourceful, but he be not of man stature as to brain. He be of child brain in much. Now this criminal of ours is predestinate to crime also. He, too, have child brain, and it is of the child to do what he have done. The little bird, the little fish, the little animal learn not by principle, but empirically. And when he learn to do, then there is to him the ground to start from to do more. '*Dos pou sto*,' said Archimedes. 'Give me a fulcrum, and I shall move the world!' To do once, is the fulcrum whereby child brain become man brain. And until he have the purpose to do more, he continue to do the same again every time, just as he have done before! Oh, my dear, I see that your eyes are opened, and that to you the lightning flash show all the leagues," for Mrs. Harker began to clap her hands and her eyes sparkled.

He went on, "Now you shall speak. Tell us two dry men of science what you see with those so bright eyes." He took her hand and held it whilst he spoke. His finger and thumb closed on her pulse, as I thought instinctively and unconsciously, as she spoke.

"The Count is a criminal and of criminal type. Nordau and Lombroso would so classify him, and qua criminal he is of an imperfectly formed mind. Thus, in a difficulty he has to seek resource in habit. His past is a clue, and the one page of it that we know—and that from his own lips—tells that once before, when in what Mr. Morris would call a 'tight place,' he went back to his own country from the land he had tried to invade, and thence, without losing purpose, prepared himself for a new effort. He came again better equipped for his work, and won. So he came to London to invade a new land. He was beaten, and when all hope of success was lost, and his existence in danger, he fled back over the sea to his home. Just as formerly he had fled back over the Danube from Turkey Land."

"Good, good! Oh, you so clever lady!" said Van Helsing, enthusiastically, as he stooped and kissed her hand. A moment later he said to me, as calmly as though we had been having a sick room consultation, "Seventy-two only, and in all this excitement. I have hope."

Turning to her again, he said with keen expectation, "But go on. Go on! There is more to tell if you will. Be not afraid. John and I know. I do in any case, and shall tell you if you are right. Speak, without fear!"

"I will try to. But you will forgive me if I seem too egotistical."

"Nay! Fear not, you must be egotist, for it is of you that we think."

"Then, as he is criminal he is selfish. And as his intellect is small and his action is based on selfishness, he confines himself to one purpose. That purpose is remorseless. As he fled back over the Danube, leaving his forces to be cut to pieces, so now he is intent on being safe, careless of all. So his own selfishness frees my soul somewhat from the terrible power which he acquired over me on that dreadful night. I felt it! Oh, I felt it! Thank God, for His great mercy! My soul is freer than it has been since that awful hour. And all that haunts me is a fear lest in some trance or dream he may have used my knowledge for his ends."

The Professor stood up. "He has so used your mind, and by it he has left us here in Varna, whilst the ship that carried him rushed through enveloping fog up to Galatz, where, doubtless, he had made preparation for escaping from us. But his child mind only saw so far. And it may be that as ever is in God's Providence, the very thing that the evil doer most reckoned on for his selfish good, turns out to be his chiefest harm. The hunter is taken in his own snare, as the great Psalmist says. For now that he think he is free from every trace of us all, and that he has escaped us with so many hours to him, then his selfish child brain will whisper him to sleep. He think, too, that as he cut himself off from knowing your mind, there can be no knowledge of him to you. There is where he fail! That terrible baptism of blood which he give you makes you free to go to him in spirit, as you have as yet done in your times of freedom, when the sun rise and set. At such times you go by my volition and not by his. And this power to good of you and others, you have won from your suffering at his hands. This is now all more precious that he know it not, and to guard himself have even cut himself off from his knowledge of our where. We, however, are not selfish, and we believe that God is with us through all this blackness, and these many dark hours. We shall follow him, and we shall not flinch, even if we peril ourselves that we become like him. Friend John, this has been a great hour, and it have done much to advance us on our way. You must be scribe and write him all down, so that when the others return from their work you can give it to them, then they shall know as we do."

And so I have written it whilst we wait their return, and Mrs. Harker has written with the typewriter all since she brought the MS to us.

CHAPTER XXVI

Dr. Seward's Diary

29 October.

This is written in the train from Varna to Galatz. Last night we all assembled a little before the time of sunset. Each of us had done his work as well as he could, so far as thought, and endeavour, and opportunity go, we are prepared for the whole of our journey, and for our work when we get to Galatz. When the usual time came round Mrs. Harker prepared herself for her hypnotic effort, and after a longer and more serious effort on the part of Van Helsing than has been usually necessary, she sank into the trance. Usually she speaks on a hint, but this time the Professor had to ask her questions, and to ask them pretty resolutely, before we could learn anything. At last her answer came.

"I can see nothing. We are still. There are no waves lapping, but only a steady swirl of water softly running against the hawser. I can hear men's voices calling, near and far, and the roll and creak of oars in the rowlocks. A gun is fired somewhere, the echo of it seems far away. There is tramping of feet overhead, and ropes and chains are dragged along. What is this? There is a gleam of light. I can feel the air blowing upon me."

Here she stopped. She had risen, as if impulsively, from where she lay on the sofa, and raised both her hands, palms upwards, as if lifting a weight. Van Helsing and I looked at each other with understanding. Quincey raised his eyebrows slightly and looked at her intently, whilst Harker's hand instinctively closed round the hilt of his Kukri. There was a long pause. We all knew that the time when she could speak was passing, but we felt that it was useless to say anything.

Suddenly she sat up, and as she opened her eyes said sweetly, "Would none of you like a cup of tea? You must all be so tired!"

We could only make her happy, and so acqueisced. She bustled off to get tea. When she had gone Van Helsing said, "You see, my friends. *He* is close to land. He has left his earth chest. But he has yet to get on shore. In the night he may lie hidden somewhere, but if he be not carried on shore, or if the ship do not touch it, he cannot achieve the land. In such case he can, if it be in the night, change his form and jump or fly on shore, then, unless he be carried he cannot escape. And if he be carried, then the customs men may discover what the box contain. Thus, in fine, if he escape not on shore tonight, or before dawn, there will be the whole day lost to him. We may then arrive in time. For if he escape not at night we shall come on him in daytime, boxed up and at our mercy. For he dare not be his true self, awake and visible, lest he be discovered."

There was no more to be said, so we waited in patience until the dawn, at which time we might learn more from Mrs. Harker.

Early this morning we listened, with breathless anxiety, for her response in her trance. The hypnotic stage was even longer in coming than before, and when it came the time remaining until full sunrise was so short that we began to despair. Van Helsing seemed to throw his whole soul into the effort. At last, in obedience to his will she made reply.

"All is dark. I hear lapping water, level with me, and some creaking as of wood on wood." She paused, and the red sun shot up. We must wait till tonight.

And so it is that we are travelling towards Galatz in an agony of expectation. We are due to arrive between two and three in the morning. But already, at Bucharest, we are three hours late, so we cannot possibly get in till well after sunup. Thus we shall have two more hypnotic messages from Mrs. Harker! Either or both may possibly throw more light on what is happening.

Later.

Sunset has come and gone. Fortunately it came at a time when there was no distraction. For had it occurred whilst we were at a station, we might not have secured the necessary calm and isolation. Mrs. Harker yielded to the hypnotic influence even less readily than this morning. I am in fear that her power of reading the Count's sensations may die away, just when we want it most. It seems to me that her imagination is beginning to work. Whilst she has been in the trance hitherto she has confined herself to the simplest of facts. If this goes on it may ultimately mislead us. If I thought that the Count's power over her would die away equally with her power of knowledge it would be a happy thought. But I am afraid that it may not be so.

When she did speak, her words were enigmatical, "Something is going out. I can feel it pass me like a cold wind. I can hear, far off, confused sounds, as of men talking in strange tongues, fierce falling water, and the howling of wolves." She stopped and a shudder ran through her, increasing in intensity for a few seconds, till at the end, she shook as though in a palsy. She said no more, even in answer to the Professor's imperative questioning. When she woke from the trance, she was cold, and exhausted, and languid, but her mind was all alert. She could not remember anything, but asked what she had said. When she was told, she pondered over it deeply for a long time and in silence.

30 October, 7 a.m.

We are near Galatz now, and I may not have time to write later. Sunrise this morning was anxiously looked for by us all. Knowing of the increasing difficulty of procuring the hypnotic trance, Van Helsing began his passes earlier than usual. They produced no effect, however, until the regular time, when she yielded with a still greater difficulty, only a minute before the sun rose. The Professor lost no time in his questioning.

Her answer came with equal quickness, "All is dark. I hear water swirling by, level with my ears, and the creaking of wood on wood. Cattle low far off. There is another sound, a queer one like—" She stopped and grew white, and whiter still.

"Go on, go on! Speak, I command you!" said Van Helsing in an agonized voice. At the same time there was despair in his eyes, for the risen sun was reddening even Mrs. Harker's pale face. She opened her eyes, and we all started as she said, sweetly and seemingly with the utmost unconcern.

"Oh, Professor, why ask me to do what you know I can't? I don't remember anything." Then, seeing the look of amazement on our faces, she said, turning from one to the other with a troubled look, "What have I said? What have I done? I know nothing, only that I was lying here, half asleep, and heard you say 'go on! speak, I command you!' It seemed so funny to hear you order me about, as if I were a bad child!"

"Oh, Madam Mina," he said, sadly, "it is proof, if proof be needed, of how I love and honour you, when a word for your good, spoken more earnest than ever, can seem so strange because it is to order her whom I am proud to obey!"

The whistles are sounding. We are nearing Galatz. We are on fire with anxiety and eagerness.

Mina Harker's Journal

30 October.

Mr. Morris took me to the hotel where our rooms had been ordered by telegraph, he being the one who could best be spared, since he does not speak any foreign language. The forces were distributed much as they had been at Varna, except that Lord Godalming went to the Vice Consul, as his rank might serve as an immediate guarantee of some sort to the official, we being in extreme hurry. Jonathan and the two doctors went to the shipping agent to learn particulars of the arrival of the *Czarina Catherine*.

Later.

Lord Godalming has returned. The Consul is away, and the Vice Consul sick. So the routine work has been attended to by a clerk. He was very obliging, and offered to do anything in his power.

Jonathan Harker's Journal

30 October.

At nine o'clock Dr. Van Helsing, Dr. Seward, and I called on Messrs. Mackenzie & Steinkoff, the agents of the London firm of Hapgood. They had received a wire from London, in answer to Lord Godalming's telegraphed request, asking them to show us any civility in their power. They were more than kind and courteous, and took us at once on board the *Czarina Catherine*, which lay at anchor out in the river harbor. There we saw the Captain, Donelson by name, who told us of his voyage. He said that in all his life he had never had so favourable a run.

"Man!" he said, "but it made us afeard, for we expect it that we should have to pay for it wi' some rare piece o' ill luck, so as to keep up the average. It's no canny to run frae London to the Black Sea wi' a wind ahint ye, as though the Deil himself were blawin' on yer sail for his ain purpose. An' a' the time we could no speer a thing. Gin we were nigh a ship, or a port, or a headland, a fog fell on us and travelled wi' us, till when after it had lifted and we looked out, the deil a thing could we see. We ran by Gibraltar wi' oot bein' able to signal. An' til we came to the Dardanelles and had to wait to get our permit to pass, we never were within hail o' aught. At first I inclined to slack off sail and beat about till the fog was lifted. But whiles, I thocht that if the Deil was minded to get us into the Black Sea quick, he was like to do it whether we would or no. If we had a quick voyage it would be no to our miscredit wi' the owners, or no hurt to our traffic, an' the Old Mon who had served his ain purpose wad be decently grateful to us for no hinderin' him."

This mixture of simplicity and cunning, of superstition and commercial reasoning, aroused Van Helsing, who said, "Mine friend, that Devil is more clever than he is thought by some, and he know when he meet his match!"

The skipper was not displeased with the compliment, and went on, "When we got past the Bosphorus the men began to grumble. Some o' them, the Roumanians, came and asked me to heave overboard a big box which had been put on board by a queer lookin' old man just before we had started frae London. I had seen them speer at the fellow, and put out their twa fingers when they saw him, to guard them against the evil eye. Man! but the supersteetion of foreigners is pairfectly rideeculous! I sent them aboot their business pretty quick, but as just after a fog closed in on us I felt a wee bit as they did anent something, though I wouldn't say it was again the big box. Well, on we went, and as the fog didn't let up for five days I joost let the wind carry us, for if the Deil wanted to get somewheres—well, he would fetch it up a'reet. An' if he didn't, well, we'd keep a sharp lookout anyhow. Sure eneuch, we had a fair way and deep water all the time. And two days ago, when the mornin' sun came through the fog, we found ourselves just in the river opposite Galatz. The Roumanians were wild, and wanted me right or wrong to take out the box and fling it in the river. I had to argy wi' them aboot it wi' a handspike. An' when the last o' them rose off the deck wi' his head in his hand, I had convinced them that, evil eye or no evil eye, the property and the trust of my owners were better in my hands than in the river Danube. They had, mind ye, taken the box on the deck ready to fling in, and as it was marked Galatz *via* Varna, I thocht I'd let it lie till we discharged in the port an' get rid o't althegither. We didn't do much clearin' that day, an' had to remain the nicht at anchor. But in the mornin,' braw an' airly, an hour before sunup, a man came aboard wi' an order, written to him from England, to receive a box marked for one Count Dracula. Sure eneuch the matter was one ready to his hand. He had his papers a' reet, an' glad I was to be rid o' the dam' thing, for I was beginnin' masel' to feel uneasy at it. If the Deil did have any luggage aboord the ship, I'm thinkin' it was nane ither than that same!"

"What was the name of the man who took it?" asked Dr. Van Helsing with restrained eagerness.

"I'll be tellin' ye quick!" he answered, and stepping down to his cabin, produced a receipt signed "Immanuel Hildesheim." Burgen-strasse 16 was the address. We found out that this was all the Captain knew, so with thanks we came away.

We found Hildesheim in his office, a Hebrew of rather the Adelphi Theatre type, with a nose like a sheep, and a fez. His arguments were pointed with specie—we doing the punctuation—and with a little bargaining he told us what he knew. This turned out to be simple but important. He had received a letter from Mr. de Ville of London, telling him to receive, if possible before sunrise so as to avoid customs, a box which would arrive at Galatz in the *Czarina Catherine*. This he was to give in charge to a certain Petrof Skinsky, who dealt with the Slovaks who traded down the river to the port. He had been paid for his work by an English bank note, which had been duly cashed for gold at the Danube International Bank. When Skinsky had come to him, he had taken him to the ship and handed over the box, so as to save porterage. That was all he knew.

We then sought for Skinsky, but were unable to find him. One of his neighbors, who did not seem to bear him any affection, said that he had gone away two days before, no one knew whither. This was corroborated by his landlord, who had received by messenger the key of the house together with the rent due, in English money. This had been between ten and eleven o'clock last night. We were at a standstill again.

Whilst we were talking one came running and breathlessly gasped out that the body of Skinsky had been found inside the wall of the churchyard of St. Peter, and that the throat had been torn open as if by some wild animal. Those we had been speaking with ran off to see the horror, the women crying out. "This is the work of a Slovak!" We hurried away lest we should have been in some way drawn into the affair, and so detained.

As we came home we could arrive at no definite conclusion. We were all convinced that the box was on its way, by water, to somewhere, but where that might be we would have to discover. With heavy hearts we came home to the hotel to Mina.

When we met together, the first thing was to consult as to taking Mina again into our confidence. Things are getting desperate, and it is at least a chance, though a hazardous one. As a preliminary step, I was released from my promise to her.

Mina Harker's Journal

30 October, evening.

They were so tired and worn out and dispirited that there was nothing to be done till they had some rest, so I asked them all to lie down for half an hour whilst I should enter everything up to the moment. I feel so grateful to the man who invented the "Traveller's" typewriter, and to Mr. Morris for getting this one for me. I should have felt quite astray doing the work if I had to write with a pen . . .

It is all done. Poor dear, dear Jonathan, what he must have suffered, what he must be suffering now. He lies on the sofa hardly seeming to breathe, and his whole body appears in collapse. His brows are knit. His face is drawn with pain. Poor fellow, maybe he is thinking, and I can see his face all wrinkled up with the concentration of his thoughts. Oh! if I could only help at all. I shall do what I can.

I have asked Dr. Van Helsing, and he has got me all the papers that I have not yet seen. Whilst they are resting, I shall go over all carefully, and perhaps I may arrive at some conclusion. I shall try to follow the Professor's example, and think without prejudice on the facts before me . . .

I do believe that under God's providence I have made a discovery. I shall get the maps and look over them.

I am more than ever sure that I am right. My new conclusion is ready, so I shall get our party together and read it. They can judge it. It is well to be accurate, and every minute is precious.

Mina Harker's Memorandum
(Entered in her journal)

Ground of inquiry.

Count Dracula's problem is to get back to his own place.

(a) He must be *brought back* by someone. This is evident; for had he power to move himself as he wished he could go either as man, or wolf, or bat, or in some other way. He evidently fears discovery or interference, in the state of helplessness in which he must be—confined as he is between dawn and sunset in his wooden box.

(b) *How is he to be taken?* Here a process of exclusions may help us. By road, by rail, by water?

1. By Road. There are endless difficulties, especially in leaving the city.

(x) There are people. And people are curious, and investigate. A hint, a surmise, a doubt as to what might be in the box, would destroy him.

(y) There are, or there may be, customs and octroi officers to pass.

(z) His pursuers might follow. This is his highest fear. And in order to prevent his being betrayed he has repelled, so far as he can, even his victim—me!

2. By Rail. There is no one in charge of the box. It would have to take its chance of being delayed, and delay would be fatal, with enemies on the track. True, he might escape at night. But what would he be, if left in a strange place with no refuge that he could fly to? This is not what he intends, and he does not mean to risk it.

3. By Water. Here is the safest way, in one respect, but with most danger in another. On the water he is powerless except at night. Even then he can only summon fog and storm and snow and his wolves. But were he wrecked, the living water would engulf him, helpless, and he would indeed be lost. He could have the vessel drive to land, but if it were unfriendly land, wherein he was not free to move, his position would still be desperate.

We know from the record that he was on the water, so what we have to do is to ascertain *what* water.

The first thing is to realize exactly what he has done as yet. We may, then, get a light on what his task is to be.

Firstly. We must differentiate between what he did in London as part of his general plan of action, when he was pressed for moments and had to arrange as best he could.

Secondly. We must see, as well as we can surmise it from the facts we know of, what he has done here.

As to the first, he evidently intended to arrive at Galatz, and sent invoice to Varna to deceive us lest we should ascertain his means of exit from England. His immediate and sole purpose then was to escape. The proof of this, is the letter of instructions sent to Immanuel Hildesheim to clear and take away the box *before sunrise*. There is also the instruction to Petrof Skinsky. These we must only guess at, but there must have been some letter or message, since Skinsky came to Hildesheim.

That, so far, his plans were successful we know. The *Czarina Catherine* made a phenomenally quick journey—so much so that Captain Donelson's suspicions were aroused. But his superstition united with his canniness played the Count's game for him, and he ran with his favouring wind through fogs and all till he brought up blindfold at Galatz. That the Count's arrangements were well made, has been proved. Hildesheim cleared the box, took it off, and gave it to Skinsky. Skinsky took it—and here we lose the trail. We only know that the box is somewhere on the water, moving along. The customs and the octroi, if there be any, have been avoided.

Now we come to what the Count must have done after his arrival—*on land*, at Galatz.

The box was given to Skinsky before sunrise. At sunrise the Count could appear in his own form. Here, we ask why Skinsky was chosen at all to aid in the work? In my husband's diary, Skinsky is mentioned as dealing with the Slovaks who trade down the river to the port. And the man's remark, that the murder was the work of a Slovak, showed the general feeling against his class. The Count wanted isolation.

My surmise is this: that in London the Count decided to get back to his castle by water, as the most safe and secret way. He was brought from the castle by Szgany, and probably they delivered their cargo to Slovaks who took the boxes to Varna, for there they were shipped to London. Thus the Count had knowledge of the persons who could arrange this service. When the box was on land, before sunrise or after sunset, he came out from his box, met Skinsky and instructed him what to do as to arranging the carriage of the box up some river. When this was done, and he knew that all was in train, he blotted out his traces, as he thought, by murdering his agent.

I have examined the map and find that the river most suitable for the Slovaks to have ascended is either the Pruth or the Sereth. I read in the typescript that in my trance I heard cows low and water swirling level with my ears and the creaking of wood. The Count in his box, then, was on a river in an open boat—propelled probably either by oars or poles, for the banks are near and it is working against stream. There would be no such if floating downstream.

Of course it may not be either the Sereth or the Pruth, but we may possibly investigate further. Now of these two, the Pruth is the more easily navigated, but the Sereth is, at Fundu, joined by the Bistritza which runs up round the Borgo Pass. The loop it makes is manifestly as close to Dracula's castle as can be got by water.

Mina Harker's Journal, Continued

When I had done reading, Jonathan took me in his arms and kissed me. The others kept shaking me by both hands, and Dr. Van Helsing said, "Our dear Madam Mina is once more our teacher. Her eyes have been where we were blinded. Now we are on the track once again, and this time we may succeed. Our enemy is at his most helpless. And if we can come on him by day, on the water, our task will be over. He has a start, but he is powerless to hasten, as he may not leave this box lest those who carry him may suspect. For them to suspect would be to prompt them to throw him in the stream where he perish. This he knows, and will not. Now men, to our Council of War, for here and now, we must plan what each and all shall do."

"I shall get a steam launch and follow him," said Lord Godalming.

"And I, horses to follow on the bank lest by chance he land," said Mr. Morris.

"Good!" said the Professor, "both good. But neither must go alone. There must be force to overcome force if need be. The Slovak is strong and rough, and he carries rude arms." All the men smiled, for amongst them they carried a small arsenal.

Said Mr. Morris, "I have brought some Winchesters. They are pretty handy in a crowd, and there may be wolves. The Count, if you remember, took some other precautions. He made some requisitions on others that Mrs. Harker could not quite hear or understand. We must be ready at all points."

Dr. Seward said, "I think I had better go with Quincey. We have been accustomed to hunt together, and we two, well armed, will be a match for whatever may come along. You must not be alone, Art. It may be necessary to fight the Slovaks, and a chance thrust—for I don't suppose these fellows carry guns—would undo all our plans. There must be no chances, this time. We shall not rest until the Count's head and body have been separated, and we are sure that he cannot reincarnate."

He looked at Jonathan as he spoke, and Jonathan looked at me. I could see that the poor dear was torn about in his mind. Of course he wanted to be with me. But then the boat service would, most likely, be the one which would destroy the . . . the . . . Vampire. (Why did I hesitate to write the word?)

He was silent awhile, and during his silence Dr. Van Helsing spoke, "Friend Jonathan, this is to you for twice reasons. First, because you are young and brave and can fight, and all energies may be needed at the last. And again that it is your right to destroy him—that—which has wrought such woe to you and yours. Be not afraid for Madam Mina. She will be my care, if I may. I am old. My legs are not so quick to run as once. And I am not used to ride so long or to pursue as need be, or to fight with lethal weapons. But I can be of other service. I can fight in other way. And I can die, if need be, as well as younger men. Now let me say that what I would is this. While you, my Lord Godalming and friend Jonathan go in your so swift little steamboat up the river, and whilst John and Quincey guard the bank where perchance he might be landed, I will take Madam Mina right into the heart of the enemy's country. Whilst the old fox is tied in his box, floating on the running stream whence he cannot escape to land—where he dares not raise the lid of his coffin box lest his Slovak carriers should in fear leave him to perish—we shall go in the track where Jonathan went—from Bistritz over the Borgo, and find our way to the Castle of Dracula. Here, Madam Mina's hypnotic power will surely help, and we shall find our way—all dark and unknown otherwise—after the first sunrise when we are near that fateful place. There is much to be done, and other places to be made sanctify, so that that nest of vipers be obliterated."

Here Jonathan interrupted him hotly, "Do you mean to say, Professor Van Helsing, that you would bring Mina, in her sad case and tainted as she is with that devil's illness, right into the jaws of his deathtrap? Not for the world! Not for Heaven or Hell!"

He became almost speechless for a minute, and then went on, "Do you know what the place is? Have you seen that awful den of hellish infamy—with the very moonlight alive with grisly shapes, and every speck of dust that whirls in the wind a devouring monster in embryo? Have you felt the Vampire's lips upon your throat?"

Here he turned to me, and as his eyes lit on my forehead he threw up his arms with a cry, "Oh, my God, what have we done to have this terror upon us?" and he sank down on the sofa in a collapse of misery.

The Professor's voice, as he spoke in clear, sweet tones, which seemed to vibrate in the air, calmed us all.

"Oh, my friend, it is because I would save Madam Mina from that awful place that I would go. God forbid that I should take her into that place. There is work—wild work—to be done before that place can be purify. Remember that we are in terrible straits. If the Count escape us this time—and he is strong and subtle and cunning—he may choose to sleep him for a century, and then in time our dear one," he took my hand, "would come to him to keep him company, and would be as those others that you, Jonathan, saw. You have told us of their gloating lips. You heard their ribald laugh as they clutched the moving bag that the Count threw to them. You shudder, and well may it be. Forgive me that I make you so much pain, but it is necessary. My friend, is it not a dire need for that which I am giving, possibly my life? If it were that anyone went into that place to stay, it is I who would have to go to keep them company."

"Do as you will," said Jonathan, with a sob that shook him all over, "we are in the hands of God!"

Later.

Oh, it did me good to see the way that these brave men worked. How can women help loving men when they are so earnest, and so true, and so brave! And, too, it made me think of the wonderful power of money! What can it not do when basely used. I felt so thankful that Lord Godalming is rich, and both he and Mr. Morris, who also has plenty of money, are willing to spend it so freely. For if they did not, our little expedition could not start, either so promptly or so well equipped, as it will within another hour. It is not three hours since it was arranged what part each of us was to do. And now Lord Godalming and Jonathan have a lovely steam launch, with steam up ready to start at a moment's notice. Dr. Seward and Mr. Morris have half a dozen good horses, well appointed. We have all the maps and appliances of various kinds that can be had. Professor Van Helsing and I are to leave by the 11:40 train tonight for Veresti, where we are to get a carriage to drive to the Borgo Pass. We are bringing a good deal of ready money, as we are to buy a carriage and horses. We shall drive ourselves, for we have no one whom we can trust in the matter. The Professor knows something of a great many languages, so we shall get on all right. We have all got arms, even for me a large bore revolver. Jonathan would not be happy unless I was armed like the rest. Alas! I cannot carry one arm that the rest do, the scar on my forehead forbids that. Dear Dr. Van Helsing comforts me by telling me that I am fully armed as there may be wolves. The weather is getting colder every hour, and there are snow flurries which come and go as warnings.

Later.

It took all my courage to say goodbye to my darling. We may never meet again. Courage, Mina! The Professor is looking at you keenly. His look is a warning. There must be no tears now—unless it may be that God will let them fall in gladness.

Jonathan Harker's Journal

30 October, night.

I am writing this in the light from the furnace door of the steam launch. Lord Godalming is firing up. He is an experienced hand at the work, as he has had for years a launch of his own on the Thames, and another on the Norfolk Broads. Regarding our plans, we finally decided that Mina's guess was correct, and that if any waterway was chosen for the Count's escape back to his Castle, the Sereth and then the Bistritza at its junction, would be the one. We took it, that somewhere about the 47th degree, north latitude, would be the place chosen for crossing the country between the river and the Carpathians. We have no fear in running at good speed up the river at night. There is plenty of water, and the banks are wide enough apart to make steaming, even in the dark, easy enough. Lord Godalming tells me to sleep for a while, as it is enough for the present for one to be on watch. But I cannot sleep—how can I with the terrible danger hanging over my darling, and her going out into that awful place . . . My only comfort is that we are in the hands of God. Only for that faith it would be easier to die than to live, and so be quit of all the trouble. Mr. Morris and Dr. Seward were off on their long ride before we started. They are to keep up the right bank, far enough off to get on higher lands where they can see a good stretch of river and avoid the following of its curves. They have, for the first stages, two men to ride and lead their spare horses—four in all—so as not to excite curiosity. When they dismiss the men, which shall be shortly, they shall themselves look after the horses. It may be necessary for us to join forces. If so they can mount our whole party. One of the saddles has a moveable horn, and can be easily adapted for Mina, if required.

It is a wild adventure we are on. Here, as we are rushing along through the darkness, with the cold from the river seeming to rise up and strike us, with all the mysterious voices of the night around us, it all comes home. We seem to be drifting into unknown places and unknown ways. Into a whole world of dark and dreadful things. Godalming is shutting the furnace door . . .

31 October.

Still hurrying along. The day has come, and Godalming is sleeping. I am on watch. The morning is bitterly cold, the furnace heat is grateful, though we have heavy fur coats. As yet we have passed only a few open boats, but none of them had on board any box or package of anything like the size of the one we seek. The men were scared every time we turned our electric lamp on them, and fell on their knees and prayed.

1 November, evening.

No news all day. We have found nothing of the kind we seek. We have now passed into the Bistritza, and if we are wrong in our surmise our chance is gone. We have overhauled every boat, big and little. Early this morning, one crew took us for a Government boat, and treated us accordingly. We saw in this a way of smoothing matters, so at Fundu, where the Bistritza runs into the Sereth, we got a Roumanian flag which we now fly conspicuously. With every boat which we have overhauled since then this trick has succeeded. We have had every deference shown to us, and not once any objection to whatever we chose to ask or do. Some of the Slovaks tell us that a big boat passed them, going at more than usual speed as she had a double crew on board. This was before they came to Fundu, so they could not tell us whether the boat turned into the Bistritza or continued on up the Sereth. At Fundu we could not hear of any such boat, so she must have passed there in the night. I am feeling very sleepy. The cold is perhaps beginning to tell upon me, and nature must have rest some time. Godalming insists that he shall keep the first watch. God bless him for all his goodness to poor dear Mina and me.

2 November, morning.

It is broad daylight. That good fellow would not wake me. He says it would have been a sin to, for I slept peacefully and was forgetting my trouble. It seems brutally selfish to me to have slept so long, and let him watch all night, but he was quite right. I am a new man this morning. And, as I sit here and watch him sleeping, I can do all that is necessary both as to minding the engine, steering, and keeping watch. I can feel that my strength and energy are coming back to me. I wonder where Mina is now, and Van Helsing. They should have got to Veresti about noon on Wednesday. It would take them some time to get the carriage and horses. So if they had started and travelled hard, they would be about now at the Borgo Pass. God guide and help them! I am afraid to think what may happen. If we could only go faster. But we cannot. The engines are throbbing and doing their utmost. I wonder how Dr. Seward and Mr. Morris are getting on. There seem to be endless streams running down the mountains into this river, but as none of them are very large, at present, at all events, though they are doubtless terrible in winter and when the snow melts, the horsemen may not have met much obstruction. I hope that before we get to Strasba we may see them. For if by that time we have not overtaken the Count, it may be necessary to take counsel together what to do next.

Dr. Seward's Diary

2 November.

Three days on the road. No news, and no time to write it if there had been, for every moment is precious. We have had only the rest needful for the horses. But we are both bearing it wonderfully. Those adventurous days of ours are turning up useful. We must push on. We shall never feel happy till we get the launch in sight again.

3 November.

We heard at Fundu that the launch had gone up the Bistritza. I wish it wasn't so cold. There are signs of snow coming. And if it falls heavy it will stop us. In such case we must get a sledge and go on, Russian fashion.

4 November.

Today we heard of the launch having been detained by an accident when trying to force a way up the rapids. The Slovak boats get up all right, by aid of a rope and steering with knowledge. Some went up only a few hours before. Godalming is an amateur fitter himself, and evidently it was he who put the launch in trim again. Finally, they got up the rapids all right, with local help, and are off on the chase afresh. I fear that the boat is not any better for the accident, the peasantry tell us that after she got upon smooth water again, she kept stopping every now and again so long as she was in sight. We must push on harder than ever. Our help may be wanted soon.

Mina Harker's Journal

31 October.

Arrived at Veresti at noon. The Professor tells me that this morning at dawn he could hardly hypnotize me at all, and that all I could say was, "dark and quiet." He is off now buying a carriage and horses. He says that he will later on try to buy additional horses, so that we may be able to change them on the way. We have something more than 70 miles before us. The country is lovely, and most interesting. If only we were under different conditions, how delightful it would be to see it all. If Jonathan and I were driving through it alone what a pleasure it would be. To stop and see people, and learn something of their life, and to fill our minds and memories with all the colour and picturesqueness of the whole wild, beautiful country and the quaint people! But, alas!

Later.

Dr. Van Helsing has returned. He has got the carriage and horses. We are to have some dinner, and to start in an hour. The landlady is putting us up a huge basket of provisions. It seems enough for a company of soldiers. The Professor encourages her, and whispers to me that it may be a week before we can get any food again. He has been shopping too, and has sent home such a wonderful lot of fur coats and wraps, and all sorts of warm things. There will not be any chance of our being cold.

We shall soon be off. I am afraid to think what may happen to us. We are truly in the hands of God. He alone knows what may be, and I pray Him, with all the strength of my sad and humble soul, that He will watch over my beloved husband. That whatever may happen, Jonathan may know that I loved him and honoured him more than I can say, and that my latest and truest thought will be always for him.

CHAPTER XXVII

Mina Harker's Journal

1 November.

All day long we have travelled, and at a good speed. The horses seem to know that they are being kindly treated, for they go willingly their full stage at best speed. We have now had so many changes and find the same thing so constantly that we are encouraged to think that the journey will be an easy one. Dr. Van Helsing is laconic, he tells the farmers that he is hurrying to Bistritz, and pays them well to make the exchange of horses. We get hot soup, or coffee, or tea, and off we go. It is a lovely country. Full of beauties of all imaginable kinds, and the people are brave, and strong, and simple, and seem full of nice qualities. They are *very, very* superstitious. In the first house where we stopped, when the woman who served us saw the scar on my forehead, she crossed herself and put out two fingers towards me, to keep off the evil eye. I believe they went to the trouble of putting an extra amount of garlic into our food, and I can't abide garlic. Ever since then I have taken care not to take off my hat or veil, and so have escaped their suspicions. We are travelling fast, and as we have no driver with us to carry tales, we go ahead of scandal. But I daresay that fear of the evil eye will follow hard behind us all the way. The Professor seems tireless. All day he would not take any rest, though he made me sleep for a long spell. At sunset time he hypnotized me, and he says I answered as usual, "darkness, lapping water and creaking wood." So our enemy is still on the river. I am afraid to think of Jonathan, but somehow I have now no fear for him, or for myself. I write this whilst we wait in a farmhouse for the horses to be ready. Dr. Van Helsing is sleeping. Poor dear, he looks very tired and old and gray, but his mouth is set as firmly as a conqueror's. Even in his sleep he is intense with resolution. When we have well started I must make him rest whilst I drive. I shall tell him that we have days before us, and he must not break down when most of all his strength will be needed . . . All is ready. We are off shortly.

2 November, morning.

I was successful, and we took turns driving all night. Now the day is on us, bright though cold. There is a strange heaviness in the air—I say heaviness for want of a better word. I mean that it oppresses us both. It is very cold, and only our warm furs keep us comfortable. At dawn Van Helsing hypnotized me. He says I answered "darkness, creaking wood and roaring water," so the river is changing as they ascend. I do hope that my darling will not run any chance of danger—more than need be, but we are in God's hands.

2 November, night.

All day long driving. The country gets wilder as we go, and the great spurs of the Carpathians, which at Veresti seemed so far from us and so low on the horizon, now seem to gather round us and tower in front. We both seem in good spirits. I think we make an effort each to cheer the other, in the doing so we cheer ourselves. Dr. Van Helsing says that by morning we shall reach the Borgo Pass. The houses are very few here now, and the Professor says that the last horse we got will have to go on with us, as we may not be able to change. He got two in addition to the two we changed, so that now we have a rude four-in-hand. The dear horses are patient and good, and they give us no trouble. We are not worried with other travellers, and so even I can drive. We shall get to the Pass in daylight. We do not want to arrive before. So we take it easy, and have each a long rest in turn. Oh, what will tomorrow bring to us? We go to seek the place where my poor darling suffered so much. God grant that we may be guided aright, and that He will deign to watch over my husband and those dear to us both, and who are in such deadly peril. As for me, I am not worthy in His sight. Alas! I am unclean to His eyes, and shall be until He may deign to let me stand forth in His sight as one of those who have not incurred His wrath.

Memorandum by Abraham Van Helsing

4 November.

This to my old and true friend John Seward, MD, of Purfleet, London, in case I may not see him. It may explain. It is morning, and I write by a fire which all the night I have kept alive, Madam Mina aiding me. It is cold, cold. So cold that the gray heavy sky is full of snow, which when it falls will settle for all winter as the ground is hardening to receive it. It seems to have affected Madam Mina. She has been so heavy of head all day that she was not like herself. She sleeps, and sleeps, and sleeps! She who is usual so alert, have done literally nothing all the day. She even have lost her appetite. She make no entry into her little diary, she who write so faithful at every pause. Something whisper to me that all is not well. However, tonight she is more *vif*. Her long sleep all day have refresh and restore her, for now she is all sweet and bright as ever. At sunset I try to hypnotize her, but alas! with no effect. The power has grown less and less with each day, and tonight it fail me altogether. Well, God's will be done—whatever it may be, and whithersoever it may lead!

Now to the historical, for as Madam Mina write not in her stenography, I must, in my cumbrous old fashion, that so each day of us may not go unrecorded.

We got to the Borgo Pass just after sunrise yesterday morning. When I saw the signs of the dawn I got ready for the hypnotism. We stopped our carriage, and got down so that there might be no disturbance. I made a couch with furs, and Madam Mina, lying down, yield herself as usual, but more slow and more short time than ever, to the hypnotic sleep. As before, came the answer, "darkness and the swirling of water." Then she woke, bright and radiant and we go on our way and soon reach the Pass. At this time and place, she become all on fire with zeal. Some new guiding power be in her manifested, for she point to a road and say, "This is the way."

"How know you it?" I ask.

"Of course I know it," she answer, and with a pause, add, "Have not my Jonathan travelled it and wrote of his travel?"

At first I think somewhat strange, but soon I see that there be only one such byroad. It is used but little, and very different from the coach road from the Bukovina to Bistritz, which is more wide and hard, and more of use.

So we came down this road. When we meet other ways, not always were we sure that they were roads at all, for they be neglect and light snow have fallen—the horses know and they only. I give rein to them, and they go on so patient. By and by we find all the things which Jonathan have note in that wonderful diary of him. Then we go on for long, long hours and hours. At the first, I tell Madam Mina to sleep.

She try, and she succeed. She sleep all the time, till at the last, I feel myself to suspicious grow, and attempt to wake her. But she sleep on, and I may not wake her though I try. I do not wish to try too hard lest I harm her. For I know that she have suffer much, and sleep at times be all-in-all to her. I think I drowse myself, for all of sudden I feel guilt, as though I have done something. I find myself bolt up, with the reins in my hand, and the good horses go along jog, jog, just as ever. I look down and find Madam Mina still asleep. It is now not far off sunset time, and over the snow the light of the sun flow in big yellow flood, so that we throw great long shadow on where the mountain rise so steep. For we are going up, and up, and all is oh so wild and rocky, as though it were the end of the world.

Then I arouse Madam Mina. This time she wake with not much trouble, and then I try to put her to hypnotic sleep. But she sleep not, being as though I were not. Still I try and try, till all at once I find her and myself in dark, so I look round, and find that the sun have gone down. Madam Mina laugh, and I turn and look at her. She is now quite awake, and look so well as I never saw her since that night at Carfax when we first enter the Count's house. I am amaze, and not at ease then. But she is so bright and tender and thoughtful for me that I forget all fear. I light a fire, for we have brought supply of wood with us, and she prepare food while I undo the horses and set them, tethered in shelter, to feed. Then when I return to the fire she have my supper ready. I go to help her, but she smile, and tell me that she have eat already. That she was so hungry that she would not wait. I like it not, and I have grave doubts. But I fear to affright her, and so I am silent of it. She help me and I eat alone, and then we wrap in fur and lie beside the fire, and I tell her to sleep while I watch. But presently I forget all of watching. And when I sudden remember that I watch, I find her lying quiet, but awake, and looking at me with so bright eyes. Once, twice more the same occur, and I get much sleep till before morning. When I wake I try to hypnotize her, but alas! though she shut her eyes obedient, she may not sleep. The sun rise up, and up, and up, and then sleep come to her too late, but so heavy that she will not wake. I have to lift her up, and place her sleeping in the carriage when I have harnessed the horses and made all ready. Madam still sleep, and she look in her sleep more healthy and more redder than before. And I like it not. And I am afraid, afraid, afraid!—I am afraid of all things— even to think but I must go on my way. The stake we play for is life and death, or more than these, and we must not flinch.

5 November, morning.

Let me be accurate in everything, for though you and I have seen some strange things together, you may at the first think that I, Van Helsing, am mad. That the many horrors and the so long strain on nerves has at the last turn my brain.

All yesterday we travel, always getting closer to the mountains, and moving into a more and more wild and desert land. There are great, frowning precipices and much falling water, and Nature seem to have held sometime her carnival. Madam Mina still sleep and sleep. And though I did have hunger and appeased it, I could not waken her, even for food. I began to fear that the fatal spell of the place was upon her, tainted as she is with that Vampire baptism. "Well," said I to myself, "if it be that she sleep all the day, it shall also be that I do not sleep at night." As we travel on the rough road, for a road of an ancient and imperfect kind there was, I held down my head and slept. Again I waked with a sense of guilt and of time passed, and found Madam Mina still sleeping, and the sun low down. But all was indeed changed. The frowning mountains seemed further away, and we were near the top of a steep rising hill, on summit of which was such a castle as Jonathan tell of in his diary. At once I exulted and feared. For now, for good or ill, the end was near.

I woke Madam Mina, and again tried to hypnotize her, but alas! unavailing till too late. Then, ere the great dark came upon us—for even after down sun the heavens reflected the gone sun on the snow, and all was for a time in a great twilight—I took out the horses and fed them in what shelter I could. Then I make a fire, and near it I make Madam Mina, now awake and more charming than ever, sit comfortable amid her rugs. I got ready food, but she would not eat, simply saying that she had not hunger. I did not press her, knowing her unavailingness. But I myself eat, for I must needs now be strong for all. Then, with the fear on me of what might be, I drew a ring so big for her comfort, round where Madam Mina sat. And over the ring I passed some of the wafer, and I broke it fine so that all was well guarded. She sat still all the time—so still as one dead. And she grew whiter and even whiter till the snow was not more pale, and no word she said. But when I drew near, she clung to me, and I could know that the poor soul shook her from head to feet with a tremor that was pain to feel.

I said to her presently, when she had grown more quiet, "Will you not come over to the fire?" for I wished to make a test of what she could. She rose obedient, but when she have made a step she stopped, and stood as one stricken.

"Why not go on?" I asked. She shook her head, and coming back, sat down in her place. Then, looking at me with open eyes, as of one waked from sleep, she said simply, "I cannot!" and remained silent. I rejoiced, for I knew that what she could not, none of those that we dreaded could. Though there might be danger to her body, yet her soul was safe!

Presently the horses began to scream, and tore at their tethers till I came to them and quieted them. When they did feel my hands on them, they whinnied low as in joy, and licked at my hands and were quiet for a time. Many times through the night did I come to them, till it arrive to the cold hour when all nature is at lowest, and every time my coming was with quiet of them. In the cold hour the fire began to die, and I was about stepping forth to replenish it, for now the snow came in flying sweeps and with it a chill mist. Even in the dark there was a light of some kind, as there ever is over snow, and it seemed as though the snow flurries and the wreaths of mist took shape as of women with trailing garments. All was in dead, grim silence only that the horses whinnied and cowered, as if in terror of the worst. I began to fear—horrible fears. But then came to me the sense of safety in that ring wherein I stood. I began too, to think that my imaginings were of the night, and the gloom, and the unrest that I have gone through, and all the terrible anxiety. It was as though my memories of all Jonathan's horrid experience were befooling me. For the snow flakes and the mist began to wheel and circle round, till I could get as though a shadowy glimpse of those women that would have kissed him. And then the horses cowered lower and lower, and moaned in terror as men do in pain. Even the madness of fright was not to them, so that they could break away. I feared for my dear Madam Mina when these weird figures drew near and circled round. I looked at her, but she sat calm, and smiled at me. When I would have stepped to the fire to replenish it, she caught me and held me back, and whispered, like a voice that one hears in a dream, so low it was.

"No! No! Do not go without. Here you are safe!"

I turned to her, and looking in her eyes said, "But you? It is for you that I fear!"

Whereat she laughed, a laugh low and unreal, and said, "Fear for *me*! Why fear for me? None safer in all the world from them than I am," and as I wondered at the meaning of her words, a puff of wind made the flame leap up, and I see the red scar on her forehead. Then, alas! I knew. Did I not, I would soon have learned, for the wheeling figures of mist and snow came closer, but keeping ever without the Holy circle. Then they began to materialize till—if God have not taken away my reason, for I saw it through my eyes—there were before me in actual flesh the same three women that Jonathan saw in the room, when they would have kissed his throat. I knew the swaying round forms, the bright hard eyes, the white teeth, the ruddy colour, the voluptuous lips. They smiled ever at poor dear Madam Mina. And as their laugh came through the silence of the night, they twined their arms and pointed to her, and said in those so sweet tingling tones that Jonathan said were of the intolerable sweetness of the water glasses, "Come, sister. Come to us. Come!"

In fear I turned to my poor Madam Mina, and my heart with gladness leapt like flame. For oh! the terror in her sweet eyes, the repulsion, the horror, told a story to my heart that was all of hope. God be thanked she was not, yet, of them. I seized some of the firewood which was by me, and holding out some of the Wafer, advanced on them towards the fire. They drew back before me, and laughed their low horrid laugh. I fed the fire, and feared them not. For I knew that we were safe within the ring, which she could not leave no more than they could enter. The horses had ceased to moan, and lay still on the ground. The snow fell on them softly, and they grew whiter. I knew that there was for the poor beasts no more of terror.

And so we remained till the red of the dawn began to fall through the snow gloom. I was desolate and afraid, and full of woe and terror. But when that beautiful sun began to climb the horizon life was to me again. At the first coming of the dawn the horrid figures melted in the whirling mist and snow. The wreaths of transparent gloom moved away towards the castle, and were lost.

Instinctively, with the dawn coming, I turned to Madam Mina, intending to hypnotize her. But she lay in a deep and sudden sleep, from which I could not wake her. I tried to hypnotize through her sleep, but she made no response, none at all, and the day broke. I fear yet to stir.

I have made my fire and have seen the horses, they are all dead. Today I have much to do here, and I keep waiting till the sun is up high. For there may be places where I must go, where that sunlight, though snow and mist obscure it, will be to me a safety.

I will strengthen me with breakfast, and then I will do my terrible work. Madam Mina still sleeps, and God be thanked! She is calm in her sleep . . .

Jonathan Harker's Journal

4 November, evening.

The accident to the launch has been a terrible thing for us. Only for it we should have overtaken the boat long ago, and by now my dear Mina would have been free. I fear to think of her, off on the wolds near that horrid place. We have got horses, and we follow on the track. I note this whilst Godalming is getting ready. We have our arms. The Szgany must look out if they mean to fight. Oh, if only Morris and Seward were with us. We must only hope! If I write no more Goodbye Mina! God bless and keep you.

Dr. Seward's Diary

5 November.

With the dawn we saw the body of Szgany before us dashing away from the river with their leiter wagon. They surrounded it in a cluster, and hurried along as though beset. The snow is falling lightly and there is a strange excitement in the air. It may be our own feelings, but the depression is strange. Far off I hear the howling of wolves. The snow brings them down from the mountains, and there are dangers to all of us, and from all sides. The horses are nearly ready, and we are soon off. We ride to death of someone. God alone knows who, or where, or what, or when, or how it may be . . .

Dr. Van Helsing's Memorandum

5 November, afternoon.

I am at least sane. Thank God for that mercy at all events, though the proving it has been dreadful. When I left Madam Mina sleeping within the Holy circle, I took my way to the castle. The blacksmith hammer which I took in the carriage from Veresti was useful, though the doors were all open I broke them off the rusty hinges, lest some ill intent or ill chance should close them, so that being entered I might not get out. Jonathan's bitter experience served me here. By memory of his diary I found my way to the old chapel, for I knew that here my work lay. The air was oppressive. It seemed as if there was some sulphurous fume, which at times made me dizzy. Either there was a roaring in my ears or I heard afar off the howl of wolves. Then I bethought me of my dear Madam Mina, and I was in terrible plight. The dilemma had me between his horns.

Her, I had not dare to take into this place, but left safe from the Vampire in that Holy circle. And yet even there would be the wolf! I resolve me that my work lay here, and that as to the wolves we must submit, if it were God's will. At any rate it was only death and freedom beyond. So did I choose for her. Had it but been for myself the choice had been easy, the maw of the wolf were better to rest in than the grave of the Vampire! So I make my choice to go on with my work.

I knew that there were at least three graves to find—graves that are inhabit. So I search, and search, and I find one of them. She lay in her Vampire sleep, so full of life and voluptuous beauty that I shudder as though I have come to do murder. Ah, I doubt not that in the old time, when such things were, many a man who set forth to do such a task as mine, found at the last his heart fail him, and then his nerve. So he delay, and delay, and delay, till the mere beauty and the fascination of the wanton Undead have hypnotize him. And he remain on and on, till sunset come, and the Vampire sleep be over. Then the beautiful eyes of the fair woman open and look love, and the voluptuous mouth present to a kiss, and the man is weak. And there remain one more victim in the Vampire fold. One more to swell the grim and grisly ranks of the Undead! . . .

There is some fascination, surely, when I am moved by the mere presence of such an one, even lying as she lay in a tomb fretted with age and heavy with the dust of centuries, though there be that horrid odour such as the lairs of the Count have had. Yes, I was moved—I, Van Helsing, with all my purpose and with my motive for hate—I was moved to a yearning for delay which seemed to paralyze my faculties and to clog my very soul. It may have been that the need of natural sleep, and the strange oppression of the air were beginning to overcome me. Certain it was that I was lapsing into sleep, the open eyed sleep of one who yields to a sweet fascination, when there came through the snow-stilled air a long, low wail, so full of woe and pity that it woke me like the sound of a clarion. For it was the voice of my dear Madam Mina that I heard.

Then I braced myself again to my horrid task, and found by wrenching away tomb tops one other of the sisters, the other dark one. I dared not pause to look on her as I had on her sister, lest once more I should begin to be enthrall. But I go on searching until, presently, I find in a high great tomb as if made to one much beloved that other fair sister which, like Jonathan I had seen to gather herself out of the atoms of the mist. She was so fair to look on, so radiantly beautiful, so exquisitely voluptuous, that the very instinct of man in me, which calls some of my sex to love and to protect one of hers, made my head whirl with new emotion. But God be thanked, that soul wail of my dear Madam Mina had not died out of my ears. And, before the spell could be wrought further upon me, I had nerved myself to my wild work. By this time I had searched all the tombs in the chapel, so far as I could tell. And as there had been only three of these Undead phantoms around us in the night, I took it that there were no more of active Undead existent. There was one great tomb more lordly than all the rest. Huge it was, and nobly proportioned. On it was but one word.

DRACULA

This then was the Undead home of the King Vampire, to whom so many more were due. Its emptiness spoke eloquent to make certain what I knew. Before I began to restore these women to their dead selves through my awful work, I laid in Dracula's tomb some of the Wafer, and so banished him from it, Undead, for ever.

Then began my terrible task, and I dreaded it. Had it been but one, it had been easy, comparative. But three! To begin twice more after I had been through a deed of horror. For it was terrible with the sweet Miss Lucy, what would it not be with these strange ones who had survived through centuries, and who had been strengthened by the passing of the years. Who would, if they could, have fought for their foul lives . . .

Oh, my friend John, but it was butcher work. Had I not been nerved by thoughts of other dead, and of the living over whom hung such a pall of fear, I could not have gone on. I tremble and tremble even yet, though till all was over, God be thanked, my nerve did stand. Had I not seen the repose in the first place, and the gladness that stole over it just ere the final dissolution came, as realization that the soul had been won, I could not have gone further with my butchery. I could not have endured the horrid screeching as the stake drove home, the plunging of writhing form, and lips of bloody foam. I should have fled in terror and left my work undone. But it is over! And the poor souls, I can pity them now and weep, as I think of them placid each in her full sleep of death for a short moment ere fading. For, friend John, hardly had my knife severed the head of each, before the whole body began to melt away and crumble into its native dust, as though the death that should have come centuries ago had at last assert himself and say at once and loud, "I am here!"

Before I left the castle I so fixed its entrances that never more can the Count enter there Undead.

When I stepped into the circle where Madam Mina slept, she woke from her sleep and, seeing me, cried out in pain that I had endured too much.

"Come!" she said, "come away from this awful place! Let us go to meet my husband who is, I know, coming towards us." She was looking thin and pale and weak. But her eyes were pure and glowed with fervour. I was glad to see her paleness and her illness, for my mind was full of the fresh horror of that ruddy vampire sleep.

And so with trust and hope, and yet full of fear, we go eastward to meet our friends—and *him*—whom Madam Mina tell me that she know are coming to meet us.

Mina Harker's Journal

6 November.

It was late in the afternoon when the Professor and I took our way towards the east whence I knew Jonathan was coming. We did not go fast, though the way was steeply downhill, for we had to take heavy rugs and wraps with us. We dared not face the possibility of being left without warmth in the cold and the snow. We had to take some of our provisions too, for we were in a perfect desolation, and so far as we could see through the snowfall, there was not even the sign of habitation. When we had gone about a mile, I was tired with the heavy walking and sat down to rest. Then we looked back and saw where the clear line of Dracula's castle cut the sky. For we were so deep under the hill whereon it was set that the angle of perspective of the Carpathian mountains was far below it. We saw it in all its grandeur, perched a thousand feet on the summit of a sheer precipice, and with seemingly a great gap between it and the steep of the adjacent mountain on any side. There was something wild and uncanny about the place. We could hear the distant howling of wolves. They were far off, but the sound, even though coming muffled through the deadening snowfall, was full of terror. I knew from the way Dr. Van Helsing was searching about that he was trying to seek some strategic point, where we would be less exposed in case of attack. The rough roadway still led downwards. We could trace it through the drifted snow.

In a little while the Professor signalled to me, so I got up and joined him. He had found a wonderful spot, a sort of natural hollow in a rock, with an entrance like a doorway between two boulders. He took me by the hand and drew me in. "See!" he said. "Here you will be in shelter. And if the wolves do come I can meet them one by one." He brought in our furs, and made a snug nest for me, and got out some provisions and forced them upon me. But I could not eat, to even try to do so was repulsive to me, and much as I would have liked to please him, I could not bring myself to the attempt. He looked very sad, but did not reproach me. Taking his field glasses from the case, he stood on the top of the rock, and began to search the horizon.

Suddenly he called out, "Look! Madam Mina, look! Look!" I sprang up and stood beside him on the rock. He handed me his glasses and pointed. The snow was now falling more heavily, and swirled about fiercely, for a high wind was beginning to blow. However, there were times when there were pauses between the snow flurries and I could see a long way round. From the height where we were it was possible to see a great distance. And far off, beyond the white waste of snow, I could see the river lying like a black ribbon in kinks and curls as it wound its way. Straight in front of us and not far off—in fact so near that I wondered we had not noticed before—came a group of mounted men hurrying along. In the midst of them was a cart, a long leiter wagon which swept from side to side, like a dog's tail wagging, with each stern inequality of the road. Outlined against the snow as they were, I could see from the men's clothes that they were peasants or gypsies of some kind.

On the cart was a great square chest. My heart leaped as I saw it, for

I felt that the end was coming. The evening was now drawing close, and well I knew that at sunset the Thing, which was till then imprisoned there, would take new freedom and could in any of many forms elude pursuit. In fear I turned to the Professor. To my consternation, however, he was not there. An instant later, I saw him below me. Round the rock he had drawn a circle, such as we had found shelter in last night.

When he had completed it he stood beside me again saying, "At least you shall be safe here from *him*!" He took the glasses from me, and at the next lull of the snow swept the whole space below us. "See," he said, "they come quickly. They are flogging the horses, and galloping as hard as they can."

He paused and went on in a hollow voice, "They are racing for the sunset. We may be too late. God's will be done!" Down came another blinding rush of driving snow, and the whole landscape was blotted out. It soon passed, however, and once more his glasses were fixed on the plain.

Then came a sudden cry, "Look! Look! Look! See, two horsemen follow fast, coming up from the south. It must be Quincey and John. Take the glass. Look before the snow blots it all out!" I took it and looked. The two men might be Dr. Seward and Mr. Morris. I knew at all events that neither of them was Jonathan. At the same time I knew that Jonathan was not far off. Looking around I saw on the north side of the coming party two other men, riding at breakneck speed. One of them I knew was Jonathan, and the other I took, of course, to be Lord Godalming. They too, were pursuing the party with the cart. When I told the Professor he shouted in glee like a schoolboy, and after looking intently till a snow fall made sight impossible, he laid his Winchester rifle ready for use against the boulder at the opening of our shelter.

"They are all converging," he said. "When the time comes we shall have gypsies on all sides." I got out my revolver ready to hand, for whilst we were speaking the howling of wolves came louder and closer. When the snow storm abated a moment we looked again. It was strange to see the snow falling in such heavy flakes close to us, and beyond, the sun shining more and more brightly as it sank down towards the far mountain tops. Sweeping the glass all around us I could see here and there dots moving singly and in twos and threes and larger numbers. The wolves were gathering for their prey.

Every instant seemed an age whilst we waited. The wind came now in fierce bursts, and the snow was driven with fury as it swept upon us in circling eddies. At times we could not see an arm's length before us. But at others, as the hollow sounding wind swept by us, it seemed to clear the air space around us so that we could see afar off. We had of late been so accustomed to watch for sunrise and sunset, that we knew with fair accuracy when it would be. And we knew that before long the sun would set.

It was hard to believe that by our watches it was less than an hour that we waited in that rocky shelter before the various bodies began to converge close upon us. The wind came now with fiercer and more bitter sweeps, and more steadily from the north. It seemingly had driven the snow clouds from us, for with only occasional bursts, the snow fell. We could distinguish clearly the individuals of each party, the pursued and the pursuers. Strangely enough those pursued did not seem to realize, or at least to care, that they were pursued. They seemed, however, to hasten with redoubled speed as the sun dropped lower and lower on the mountain tops.

Closer and closer they drew. The Professor and I crouched down behind our rock, and held our weapons ready. I could see that he was determined that they should not pass. One and all were quite unaware of our presence.

All at once two voices shouted out to "Halt!" One was my Jonathan's, raised in a high key of passion. The other Mr. Morris' strong resolute tone of quiet command. The gypsies may not have known the language, but there was no mistaking the tone, in whatever tongue the words were spoken. Instinctively they reined in, and at the instant Lord Godalming and Jonathan dashed up at one side and Dr. Seward and Mr. Morris on the other. The leader of the gypsies, a splendid looking fellow who sat his horse like a centaur, waved them back, and in a fierce voice gave to his companions some word to proceed. They lashed the horses which sprang forward. But the four men raised their Winchester rifles, and in an unmistakable way commanded them to stop. At the same moment Dr. Van Helsing and I rose behind the rock and pointed our weapons at them. Seeing that they were surrounded the men tightened their reins and drew up. The leader turned to them and gave a word at which every man of the gypsy party drew what weapon he carried, knife or pistol, and held himself in readiness to attack. Issue was joined in an instant.

The leader, with a quick movement of his rein, threw his horse out in front, and pointed first to the sun, now close down on the hill tops, and then to the castle, said something which I did not understand. For answer, all four men of our party threw themselves from their horses and dashed towards the cart. I should have felt terrible fear at seeing Jonathan in such danger, but that the ardor of battle must have been upon me as well as the rest of them. I felt no fear, but only a wild, surging desire to do something. Seeing the quick movement of our parties, the leader of the gypsies gave a command. His men instantly formed round the cart in a sort of undisciplined endeavour, each one shouldering and pushing the other in his eagerness to carry out the order.

In the midst of this I could see that Jonathan on one side of the ring of men, and Quincey on the other, were forcing a way to the cart. It was evident that they were bent on finishing their task before the sun should set. Nothing seemed to stop or even to hinder them. Neither the levelled weapons nor the flashing knives of the gypsies in front, nor the howling of the wolves behind, appeared to even attract their attention. Jonathan's impetuosity, and the manifest singleness of his purpose, seemed to overawe those in front of him. Instinctively they cowered aside and let him pass. In an instant he had jumped upon the cart, and with a strength which seemed incredible, raised the great box, and flung it over the wheel to the ground. In the meantime, Mr. Morris had had to use force to pass through his side of the ring of Szgany. All the time I had been breathlessly watching Jonathan I had, with the tail of my eye, seen him pressing desperately forward, and had seen the knives of the gypsies flash as he won a way through them, and they cut at him. He had parried with his great bowie knife, and at first I thought that he too had come through in safety. But as he sprang beside Jonathan, who had by now jumped from the cart, I could see that with his left hand he was clutching at his side, and that the blood was spurting through his fingers. He did not delay notwithstanding this, for as Jonathan, with desperate energy, attacked one end of the chest, attempting to prize off the lid with his great Kukri knife, he attacked the other frantically with his bowie. Under the efforts of both men the lid began to yield. The nails drew with a screeching sound, and the top of the box was thrown back.

By this time the gypsies, seeing themselves covered by the Winchesters, and at the mercy of Lord Godalming and Dr. Seward, had given in and made no further resistance. The sun was almost down on the mountain tops, and the shadows of the whole group fell upon the snow. I saw the Count lying within the box upon the earth, some of which the rude falling from the cart had scattered over him. He was deathly pale, just like a waxen image, and the red eyes glared with the horrible vindictive look which I knew so well.

As I looked, the eyes saw the sinking sun, and the look of hate in them turned to triumph.

But, on the instant, came the sweep and flash of Jonathan's great knife. I shrieked as I saw it shear through the throat. Whilst at the same moment Mr. Morris's bowie knife plunged into the heart.

It was like a miracle, but before our very eyes, and almost in the drawing of a breath, the whole body crumbled into dust and passed from our sight.

I shall be glad as long as I live that even in that moment of final dissolution, there was in the face a look of peace, such as I never could have imagined might have rested there.

The Castle of Dracula now stood out against the red sky, and every stone of its broken battlements was articulated against the light of the setting sun.

The gypsies, taking us as in some way the cause of the extraordinary disappearance of the dead man, turned, without a word, and rode away as if for their lives. Those who were unmounted jumped upon the leiter wagon and shouted to the horsemen not to desert them. The wolves, which had withdrawn to a safe distance, followed in their wake, leaving us alone.

Mr. Morris, who had sunk to the ground, leaned on his elbow, holding his hand pressed to his side. The blood still gushed through his fingers. I flew to him, for the Holy circle did not now keep me back; so did the two doctors. Jonathan knelt behind him and the wounded man laid back his head on his shoulder. With a sigh he took, with a feeble effort, my hand in that of his own which was unstained.

He must have seen the anguish of my heart in my face, for he smiled at me and said, "I am only too happy to have been of service! Oh, God!" he cried suddenly, struggling to a sitting posture and pointing to me. "It was worth for this to die! Look! Look!"

The sun was now right down upon the mountain top, and the red gleams fell upon my face, so that it was bathed in rosy light. With one impulse the men sank on their knees and a deep and earnest "Amen" broke from all as their eyes followed the pointing of his finger.

The dying man spoke, "Now God be thanked that all has not been in vain! See! The snow is not more stainless than her forehead! The curse has passed away!"

And, to our bitter grief, with a smile and in silence, he died, a gallant gentleman.

Note

Seven years ago we all went through the flames. And the happiness of some of us since then is, we think, well worth the pain we endured. It is an added joy to Mina and to me that our boy's birthday is the same day as that on which Quincey Morris died. His mother holds, I know, the secret belief that some of our brave friend's spirit has passed into him. His bundle of names links all our little band of men together. But we call him Quincey.

In the summer of this year we made a journey to Transylvania, and went over the old ground which was, and is, to us so full of vivid and terrible memories. It was almost impossible to believe that the things which we had seen with our own eyes and heard with our own ears were living truths. Every trace of all that had been was blotted out. The castle stood as before, reared high above a waste of desolation.

When we got home we were talking of the old time, which we could all look back on without despair, for Godalming and Seward are both happily married. I took the papers from the safe where they had been ever since our return so long ago. We were struck with the fact, that in all the mass of material of which the record is composed, there is hardly one authentic document. Nothing but a mass of typewriting, except the later notebooks of Mina and Seward and myself, and Van Helsing's memorandum. We could hardly ask anyone, even did we wish to, to accept these as proofs of so wild a story. Van Helsing summed it all up as he said, with our boy on his knee.

"We want no proofs. We ask none to believe us! This boy will someday know what a brave and gallant woman his mother is. Already he knows her sweetness and loving care. Later on he will understand how some men so loved her, that they did dare much for her sake."

Jonathan Harker

Word Cloud Classics

Adventures of Huckleberry Finn

The Adventures of Sherlock Holmes

Aesop's Fables

Alice's Adventures in Wonderland and Through the Looking-Glass

Anna Karenina

Anne of Green Gables

The Art of War

The Autobiography of Benjamin Franklin and Other Writings

The Awakening and Other Stories

The Brothers Grimm 101 Fairy Tales

The Brothers Grimm Volume II: 110 Grimmer Fairy Tales

Classic Horror Tales

Classic Westerns: Zane Grey

The Count of Monte Cristo

Crime and Punishment

Don Quixote

Frankenstein

Hans Christian Andersen Tales

H. P. Lovecraft Cthulhu Mythos Tales

The Jungle Book

Leaves of Grass

Les Misérables

My Ántonia

Narrative of the Life of Frederick Douglass and Other Works

Odyssey

Peter Pan

The Phantom of the Opera

The Picture of Dorian Gray

Pride and Prejudice

The Romantic Poets

Selected Works of Alexander Hamilton

Sense and Sensibility

Shakespeare's Sonnets and Other Poems

Treasure Island

Twenty Thousand Leagues Under the Sea

Uncle Tom's Cabin, or Life Among the Lowly

The Wizard of Oz

Wuthering Heights

Classic Horror Tales

Classic Horror Tales

Word Cloud Classics
San Diego

Canterbury Classics
An imprint of Printers Row Publishing Group
9717 Pacific Heights Blvd, San Diego, CA 92121
www.canterburyclassicsbooks.com • mail@canterburyclassicsbooks.com

Correspondence concerning the content of this book should be sent to Canterbury Classics, Editorial Department, at the above address.

Publisher: Peter Norton • Associate Publisher: Ana Parker
Art Director: Charles McStravick
Senior Developmental Editor: April Graham
Publishing/Editorial Team: Kathryn C. Dalby, JoAnn Padgett, Melinda Allman, Dan Mansfield, Traci Douglas
Production/Design Team: Jonathan Lopes, Rusty von Dyl, Beno Chan, Julie Greene, Rosemary Rae

Spine art: gio_banfi/DigitalVision Vectors via Getty Images
Endpapers: Pobytov/DigitalVision Vectors via Getty Images

ISBN: 978-1-6672-0321-8

MIX
Paper | Supporting responsible forestry
FSC® C144853
www.fsc.org

Printed in China
27 26 25 24 23   2 3 4 5 6

Editor's Note: These works have been published in their original form to preserve the authors' intent and style.

CONTENTS

The Tell-Tale Heart

Edgar Allan Poe

True!—nervous—very, very dreadfully nervous I had been and am; but why will you say that I am mad? The disease had sharpened my senses—not destroyed—not dulled them. Above all was the sense of hearing acute. I heard all things in the heaven and in the earth. I heard many things in hell. How, then, am I mad? Hearken! and observe how healthily—how calmly I can tell you the whole story.

It is impossible to say how first the idea entered my brain; but once conceived, it haunted me day and night. Object there was none. Passion there was none. I loved the old man. He had never wronged me. He had never given me insult. For his gold I had no desire. I think it was his eye! yes, it was this! He had the eye of a vulture—a pale blue eye, with a film over it. Whenever it fell upon me, my blood ran cold; and so by degrees—very gradually—I made up my mind to take the life of the old man, and thus rid myself of the eye forever.

Now this is the point. You fancy me mad. Madmen know nothing. But you should have seen me. You should have seen how wisely I proceeded—with what caution—with what foresight—with what dissimulation I went to work! I was never kinder to the old man than during the whole week before I killed him. And every night, about midnight, I turned the latch of his door and opened it—oh so gently! And then, when I had made an opening sufficient for my head, I put in a dark lantern, all closed, closed, that no light shone out, and then I thrust in my head. Oh, you would have laughed to see how cunningly I thrust it in! I moved it slowly—very, very slowly, so that I might not disturb the old man's sleep. It took me an hour to place my whole head within the opening so far that I could see him as he lay upon his bed. Ha! would a madman have been so wise as this? And then, when my head was well in the room, I undid the lantern cautiously—oh, so cautiously—cautiously (for the hinges creaked)—I undid it just so much that a single thin ray fell upon the vulture eye. And this I did for seven long nights—every night just at midnight—but I found the eye always closed; and so it was impossible to do the work; for it was not the old man who vexed me, but his Evil Eye. And every morning, when the day broke, I went boldly into the chamber, and spoke courageously to him, calling him by name in a hearty tone, and inquiring how he has passed the night. So you see he would have been a very profound old man, indeed, to suspect that every night, just at twelve, I looked in upon him while he slept.

Upon the eighth night I was more than usually cautious in opening the door. A watch's minute hand moves more quickly than did mine. Never before that night had I felt the extent of my own powers—of my sagacity. I could scarcely contain my feelings of triumph. To think that there I was, opening the door, little by little, and he not even to dream of my secret deeds or thoughts. I fairly chuckled at the idea; and perhaps he heard me; for he moved on the bed suddenly, as if startled. Now you may think that I drew back—but no. His room was as black as pitch with the thick darkness, (for the shutters were close fastened, through fear of robbers,) and so I knew that he could not see the opening of the door, and I kept pushing it on steadily, steadily.

I had my head in, and was about to open the lantern, when my thumb slipped upon the tin fastening, and the old man sprang up in bed, crying out—"Who's there?"

I kept quite still and said nothing. For a whole hour I did not move a muscle, and in the meantime I did not hear him lie down. He was still sitting up in the bed listening;—just as I have done, night after night, hearkening to the death watches in the wall.

Presently I heard a slight groan, and I knew it was the groan of mortal terror. It was not a groan of pain or of grief—oh, no!—it was the low stifled sound that arises from the bottom of the soul when overcharged with awe. I knew the sound well. Many a night, just at midnight, when all the world slept, it has welled up from my own bosom, deepening, with its dreadful echo, the terrors that distracted me. I say I knew it well. I knew what the old man felt, and pitied him, although I chuckled at heart. I knew that he had been lying awake ever since the first slight noise, when he had turned in the bed. His fears had been ever since growing upon him. He had been trying to fancy them causeless, but could not. He had been saying to himself—"It is nothing but the wind in the chimney—it is only a mouse crossing the floor," or "It is merely a cricket which has made a single chirp." Yes, he had been trying to comfort himself with these suppositions: but he had found all in vain. *All in vain;* because Death, in approaching him had stalked with his black shadow before him, and enveloped the victim. And it was the mournful influence of the unperceived shadow that caused him to feel—although he neither saw nor heard—to feel the presence of my head within the room.

When I had waited a long time, very patiently, without hearing him lie down, I resolved to open a little—a very, very little crevice in the lantern. So

I opened it—you cannot imagine how stealthily, stealthily—until, at length a simple dim ray, like the thread of the spider, shot from out the crevice and fell full upon the vulture eye.

It was open—wide, wide open—and I grew furious as I gazed upon it. I saw it with perfect distinctness—all a dull blue, with a hideous veil over it that chilled the very marrow in my bones; but I could see nothing else of the old man's face or person: for I had directed the ray as if by instinct, precisely upon the damned spot.

And have I not told you that what you mistake for madness is but over-acuteness of the sense?—now, I say, there came to my ears a low, dull, quick sound, such as a watch makes when enveloped in cotton. I knew *that* sound well, too. It was the beating of the old man's heart. It increased my fury, as the beating of a drum stimulates the soldier into courage.

But even yet I refrained and kept still. I scarcely breathed. I held the lantern motionless. I tried how steadily I could maintain the ray upon the eye. Meantime the hellish tattoo of the heart increased. It grew quicker and quicker, and louder and louder every instant. The old man's terror *must* have been extreme! It grew louder, I say, louder every moment!—do you mark me well I have told you that I am nervous: so I am. And now at the dead hour of the night, amid the dreadful silence of that old house, so strange a noise as this excited me to uncontrollable terror. Yet, for some minutes longer I refrained and stood still. But the beating grew louder, louder! I thought the heart must burst. And now a new anxiety seized me—the sound would be heard by a neighbour! The old man's hour had come! With a loud yell, I threw open the lantern and leaped into the room. He shrieked once—once only. In an instant I dragged him to the floor, and pulled the heavy bed over him. I then smiled gaily, to find the deed so far done. But, for many minutes, the heart beat on with a muffled sound. This, however, did not vex me; it would not be heard through the wall. At length it ceased. The old man was dead. I removed the bed and examined the corpse. Yes, he was stone, stone dead. I placed my hand upon the heart and held it there many minutes. There was no pulsation. He was stone dead. His eye would trouble me no more.

If still you think me mad, you will think so no longer when I describe the wise precautions I took for the concealment of the body. The night waned, and I worked hastily, but in silence. First of all I dismembered the corpse. I cut off the head and the arms and the legs.

I then took up three planks from the flooring of the chamber, and deposited all between the scantlings. I then replaced the boards so cleverly, so cunningly, that no human eye—not even *his*—could have detected any thing wrong. There was nothing to wash out—no stain of any kind—no blood-spot whatever. I had been too wary for that. A tub had caught all—ha! ha!

When I had made an end of these labors, it was four o'clock—still dark as midnight. As the bell sounded the hour, there came a knocking at the street door. I went down to open it with a light heart,—for what had I now to fear? There entered three men, who introduced themselves, with perfect suavity, as officers of the police. A shriek had been heard by a neighbour during the night; suspicion of foul play had been aroused; information had been lodged at the police office, and they (the officers) had been deputed to search the premises.

I smiled—for *what* had I to fear? I bade the gentlemen welcome. The shriek, I said, was my own in a dream. The old man, I mentioned, was absent in the country. I took my visitors all over the house. I bade them search—search well. I led them, at length, to *his* chamber. I showed them his treasures, secure, undisturbed. In the enthusiasm of my confidence, I brought chairs into the room, and desired them here to rest from their fatigues, while I myself, in the wild audacity of my perfect triumph, placed my own seat upon the very spot beneath which reposed the corpse of the victim.

The officers were satisfied. My manner had convinced them. I was singularly at ease. They sat, and while I answered cheerily, they chatted of familiar things. But, ere long, I felt myself getting pale and wished them gone. My head ached, and I fancied a ringing in my ears: but still they sat and still chatted. The ringing became more distinct:—It continued and became more distinct: I talked more freely to get rid of the feeling: but it continued and gained definiteness—until, at length, I found that the noise was not within my ears.

No doubt I now grew *very* pale;—but I talked more fluently, and with a heightened voice. Yet the sound increased—and what could I do? It was a low, *dull, quick sound—much such a sound as a watch makes when enveloped in cotton*. I gasped for breath—and yet the officers heard it not. I talked more quickly—more vehemently; but the noise steadily increased. I arose and argued about trifles, in a high key and with violent gesticulations; but the noise steadily increased. Why *would* they not be gone? I paced the floor to and fro with heavy strides, as if excited to fury by the observations of the men—but the noise steadily increased. Oh God! What *could* I do? I foamed—I raved—I swore! I swung the chair upon which I had been sitting, and grated it upon the boards, but the noise arose over all and continually increased. It grew louder—louder—*louder!* And still the men chatted pleasantly, and smiled.

Was it possible they heard not? Almighty God!—no, no! They heard!—they suspected!—they *knew!*—they were making a mockery of my horror!—this I thought, and this I think. But anything was better than this agony! Anything was more tolerable than this derision! I could bear those hypocritical smiles no longer! I felt that I must scream or die! and now—again!—hark! louder! louder! louder! *louder!*

"Villains!" I shrieked, "dissemble no more! I admit the deed!—tear up the planks! here, here!—It is the beating of his hideous heart!"

Dracula's Guest

Bram Stoker

When we started for our drive the sun was shining brightly on Munich, and the air was full of the joyousness of early summer. Just as we were about to depart, Herr Delbrück (the maître d'hôtel of the Quatre Saisons, where I was staying) came down, bareheaded, to the carriage and, after wishing me a pleasant drive, said to the coachman, still holding his hand on the handle of the carriage door:

"Remember you are back by nightfall. The sky looks bright but there is a shiver in the north wind that says there may be a sudden storm. But I am sure you will not be late." Here he smiled, and added, "for you know what night it is."

Johann answered with an emphatic, "Ja, mein Herr," and, touching his hat, drove off quickly. When we had cleared the town, I said, after signalling to him to stop:

"Tell me, Johann, what is tonight?"

He crossed himself, as he answered laconically: "Walpurgis nacht." Then he took out his watch, a great, old-fashioned German silver thing as big as a turnip, and looked at it, with his eyebrows gathered together and a little impatient shrug of his shoulders. I realised that this was his way of respectfully protesting against the unnecessary delay, and sank back in the carriage, merely motioning him to proceed. He started off rapidly, as if to make up for lost time. Every now and then the horses seemed to throw up their heads and sniffed the air suspiciously. On such occasions I often looked round in alarm. The road was pretty bleak, for we were traversing a sort of high, wind-swept plateau. As we drove, I saw a road that looked but little used, and which seemed to dip through a little, winding valley. It looked so inviting that, even at the risk of offending him, I called Johann to stop—and when he had pulled up, I told him I would like to drive down that road. He made all sorts of excuses, and frequently crossed himself as he spoke. This somewhat piqued my curiosity, so I asked him various questions. He answered fencingly, and repeatedly looked at his watch in protest. Finally I said:

"Well, Johann, I want to go down this road. I shall not ask you to come unless you like; but tell me why you do not like to go, that is all I ask." For answer he seemed to throw himself off the box, so quickly did he reach the ground. Then he stretched out his hands appealingly to me, and implored me not to go. There was just enough of English mixed with the German for me to understand the drift of his talk. He seemed always just about to tell me something—the very idea of which evidently frightened him; but each time he pulled himself up, saying, as he crossed himself: "Walpurgis-Nacht!"

I tried to argue with him, but it was difficult to argue with a man when I did not know his language. The advantage certainly rested with him, for although he began to speak in English, of a very crude and broken kind, he always got excited and broke into his native tongue—and every time he did so, he looked at his watch. Then the horses became restless and sniffed the air. At this he grew very pale, and, looking around in a frightened way, he suddenly jumped forward, took them by the bridles and led them on some twenty feet. I followed, and asked why he had done this. For answer he crossed himself, pointed to the spot we had left and drew his carriage in the direction of the other road, indicating a cross, and said, first in German, then in English: "Buried him—him what killed themselves."

I remembered the old custom of burying suicides at cross-roads: "Ah! I see, a suicide. How interesting!" But for the life of me I could not make out why the horses were frightened.

Whilst we were talking, we heard a sort of sound between a yelp and a bark. It was far away; but the horses got very restless, and it took Johann all his time to quiet them. He was pale, and said, "It sounds like a wolf—but yet there are no wolves here now."

"No?" I said, questioning him; "isn't it long since the wolves were so near the city?"

"Long, long," he answered, "in the spring and summer; but with the snow the wolves have been here not so long."

Whilst he was petting the horses and trying to quiet them, dark clouds drifted rapidly across the sky. The sunshine passed away, and a breath of cold wind seemed to drift past us. It was only a breath, however, and more in the nature of a warning than a fact, for the sun came out brightly again. Johann looked under his lifted hand at the horizon and said:

"The storm of snow, he comes before long time." Then he looked at his watch again, and, straightway holding his reins firmly—for the horses were still pawing the ground restlessly and shaking their heads—he climbed to his box as though the time had come for proceeding on our journey.

I felt a little obstinate and did not at once get into the carriage.

"Tell me," I said, "about this place where the road leads," and I pointed down.

Again he crossed himself and mumbled a prayer, before he answered, "It is unholy."

"What is unholy?" I enquired.

"The village."

"Then there is a village?"

"No, no. No one lives there hundreds of years."

My curiosity was piqued, "But you said there was a village."

"There was."

"Where is it now?"

Whereupon he burst out into a long story in German and English, so mixed up that I could not quite understand exactly what he said, but roughly I gathered that long ago, hundreds of years, men had died there and been buried in their graves; and sounds were heard under the clay, and when the graves were opened, men and women were found rosy with life, and their mouths red with blood. And so, in haste to save their lives (aye, and their souls!—and here he crossed himself) those who were left fled away to other places, where the living lived, and the dead were dead and not—not something. He was evidently afraid to speak the last words. As he proceeded with his narration, he grew more and more excited. It seemed as if his imagination had got hold of him, and he ended in a perfect paroxysm of fear—white-faced, perspiring, trembling and looking round him, as if expecting that some dreadful presence would manifest itself there in the bright sunshine on the open plain. Finally, in an agony of desperation, he cried:

"Walpurgis nacht!" and pointed to the carriage for me to get in. All my English blood rose at this, and, standing back, I said:

"You are afraid, Johann—you are afraid. Go home; I shall return alone; the walk will do me good." The carriage door was open. I took from the seat my oak walking-stick—which I always carry on my holiday excursions—and closed the door, pointing back to Munich, and said, "Go home, Johann—Walpurgis-nacht doesn't concern Englishmen."

The horses were now more restive than ever, and Johann was trying to hold them in, while excitedly imploring me not to do anything so foolish. I pitied the poor fellow, he was deeply in earnest; but all the same I could not help laughing. His English was quite gone now. In his anxiety he had forgotten that his only means of making me understand was to talk my language, so he jabbered away in his native German. It began to be a little tedious. After giving the direction, "Home!" I turned to go down the cross-road into the valley.

With a despairing gesture, Johann turned his horses towards Munich. I leaned on my stick and looked after him. He went slowly along the road for a while: then there came over the crest of the hill a man tall and thin. I could see so much in the distance. When he drew near the horses, they began to jump and kick about, then to scream with terror. Johann could not hold them in; they bolted down the road, running away madly. I watched them out of sight, then looked for the stranger, but I found that he, too, was gone.

With a light heart I turned down the side road through the deepening valley to which Johann had objected. There was not the slightest reason, that I could see, for his objection; and I daresay I tramped for a couple of hours without thinking of time or distance, and certainly without seeing a person or a house. So far as the place was concerned, it was desolation itself. But I did not notice this particularly till, on turning a bend in the road, I came upon a scattered fringe of wood; then I recognised that I had been impressed unconsciously by the desolation of the region through which I had passed.

I sat down to rest myself, and began to look around. It struck me that it was considerably colder than it had been at the commencement of my walk—a sort of sighing sound seemed to be around me, with, now and then, high overhead, a sort of muffled roar. Looking upwards I noticed that great thick clouds were drifting rapidly across the sky from North to South at a great height. There were signs of coming storm in some lofty stratum of the air. I was a little chilly, and, thinking that it was the sitting still after the exercise of walking, I resumed my journey.

The ground I passed over was now much more picturesque. There were no striking objects that the eye might single out; but in all there was a charm of beauty. I took little heed of time and it was only when the deepening twilight forced itself upon me that I began to think of how I should find my way home. The brightness of the day had gone. The air was cold, and the drifting of clouds high overhead was more marked. They were accompanied by a sort of far-away rushing sound, through which seemed to come at intervals that mysterious cry which the driver had said came from a wolf. For a while I hesitated. I had said I would see the deserted village, so on I went, and presently came on a wide stretch of open country, shut in by hills all around. Their sides were covered with trees which spread down to the plain, dotting, in clumps, the gentler slopes and hollows which showed here and there. I followed with my eye the winding of the road, and saw that it curved close to one of the densest of these clumps and was lost behind it.

As I looked there came a cold shiver in the air, and the snow began to fall. I thought of the miles and miles of bleak country I had passed, and then hurried on to seek the shelter of the wood in front. Darker and darker grew the sky, and faster and heavier fell the snow, till the earth before and around me was a glistening white carpet the further edge of which was lost in misty vagueness. The road was here but crude, and when on the level its boundaries were not so marked, as when it passed through the cuttings; and in a little while I found that I must have strayed from it, for I missed underfoot the hard surface, and my feet sank deeper in the grass and moss. Then the wind grew stronger and blew with ever increasing force, till I was fain to run before it. The air became icy-cold, and in spite of my exercise I began to suffer. The snow was now falling so thickly and whirling around me in such rapid eddies that I could hardly keep my eyes open. Every now and then the heavens were torn asunder by vivid lightning, and in the flashes I could see ahead of me a great mass of trees, chiefly yew and cypress all heavily coated with snow.

I was soon amongst the shelter of the trees, and there, in comparative silence, I could hear the rush of the wind high overhead. Presently the blackness of the storm had become merged in the darkness of the night. By-and-by the storm seemed to be passing away: it now only came in fierce puffs or blasts. At such moments the weird sound of the wolf appeared to be echoed by many similar sounds around me.

Now and again, through the black mass of drifting cloud, came a straggling ray of moonlight, which lit up the expanse, and showed me that I was at the edge of a dense mass of cypress and yew trees. As the snow had ceased to fall, I walked out from the shelter and began to investigate more closely. It appeared to me that, amongst so many old foundations as I had passed, there might be still standing a house in which, though in ruins, I could find some sort of shelter for a while. As I skirted the edge of the copse, I found that a low wall encircled it, and following this I presently found an opening. Here the cypresses formed an alley leading up to a square mass of some kind of building. Just as I caught sight of this, however, the drifting clouds obscured the moon, and I passed up the path in darkness. The wind must have grown colder, for I felt myself shiver as I walked; but there was hope of shelter, and I groped my way blindly on.

I stopped, for there was a sudden stillness. The storm had passed; and, perhaps in sympathy with nature's silence, my heart seemed to cease to beat. But this was only momentarily; for suddenly the moonlight broke through the clouds, showing me that I was in a graveyard, and that the square object before me was a great massive tomb of marble, as white as the snow that lay on and all around it. With the moonlight there came a fierce sigh of the storm, which appeared to resume its course with a long, low howl, as of many dogs or wolves. I was awed and shocked, and felt the cold perceptibly grow upon me till it seemed to grip me by the heart. Then while the flood of moonlight still fell on the marble tomb, the storm gave further evidence of renewing, as though it was returning on its track. Impelled by some sort of fascination, I approached the sepulchre to see what it was, and why such a thing stood alone in such a place. I walked around it, and read, over the Doric door, in German:

COUNTESS DOLINGEN OF GRATZ
IN STYRIA
SOUGHT AND FOUND DEATH
1801

On the top of the tomb, seemingly driven through the solid marble—for the structure was composed of a few vast blocks of stone—was a great iron spike or stake. On going to the back I saw, graven in great Russian letters:

"The dead travel fast."

There was something so weird and uncanny about the whole thing that it gave me a turn and made me feel quite faint. I began to wish, for the first time, that I had taken Johann's advice. Here a thought struck me, which came under almost mysterious circumstances and with a terrible shock. This was Walpurgis Night!

Walpurgis Night, when, according to the belief of millions of people, the devil was abroad—when the graves were opened and the dead came forth and walked. When all evil things of earth and air and water held revel. This very place the driver had specially shunned. This was the depopulated village of centuries ago. This was where the suicide lay; and this was the place where I was alone—unmanned, shivering with cold in a shroud of snow with a wild storm gathering again upon me! It took all my philosophy, all the religion I had been taught, all my courage, not to collapse in a paroxysm of fright.

And now a perfect tornado burst upon me. The ground shook as though thousands of horses thundered across it; and this time the storm bore on its icy wings, not snow, but great hailstones which drove with such violence that they might have come from the thongs of Balearic slingers—hailstones that beat down leaf and branch and made the shelter of the cypresses of no more avail than though their stems were standing-corn. At the first I had rushed to the nearest tree; but I was soon fain to leave it and seek the only spot that seemed to afford refuge, the deep Doric doorway of the marble tomb. There, crouching against the massive bronze door, I gained a certain amount of protection from the beating of the hailstones, for now they only drove against me as they ricocheted from the ground and the side of the marble.

As I leaned against the door, it moved slightly and opened inwards. The shelter of even a tomb was welcome in that pitiless tempest, and I was about to enter it when there came a flash of forked-lightning that lit up the whole expanse of the heavens. In the instant, as I am a living man, I saw, as my eyes were turned into the darkness of the tomb, a beautiful woman, with rounded cheeks and red lips, seemingly sleeping on a bier. As the thunder broke overhead, I was grasped as by the hand of a giant and hurled out into the storm. The whole thing was so sudden that, before I could realise the shock, moral as well as physical, I found the hailstones beating me down. At the same time I had a strange, dominating feeling that I was not alone. I looked towards the tomb. Just then there came another blinding flash, which seemed to strike the iron stake that surmounted the tomb and to pour through to the earth, blasting and crumbling the marble, as in a burst of flame. The dead woman rose for a moment of agony, while she was lapped in the flame, and her bitter scream of pain was drowned in the thundercrash. The last thing I heard was this mingling of dreadful sound, as again I was seized in the giant-grasp and dragged away, while the hailstones beat on me, and the air around seemed reverberant with the howling of wolves. The last sight that I remembered was a vague, white, moving mass, as if all the graves around me had sent out the phantoms of their sheeted-dead, and that they were closing in on me through the white cloudiness of the driving hail.

* * * * *

Gradually there came a sort of vague beginning of consciousness; then a sense of weariness that was dreadful. For a time I remembered nothing; but slowly my senses returned. My feet seemed positively racked with pain, yet I could not move them. They seemed to be numbed. There was an icy feeling at the back of my neck and all down my spine, and my ears, like my feet, were dead, yet in torment; but there was in my breast a sense of warmth which was, by comparison, delicious. It was as a nightmare—a physical nightmare, if one may use such an expression; for some heavy weight on my chest made it difficult for me to breathe.

This period of semi-lethargy seemed to remain a long time, and as it faded away I must have slept or swooned. Then came a sort of loathing, like the first stage of sea-sickness, and a wild desire to be free from something—I knew not what. A vast stillness enveloped me, as though all the world were asleep or dead—only broken by the low panting as of some animal close to me. I felt a warm rasping at my throat, then came a consciousness of the awful truth, which chilled me to the heart and sent the blood surging up through my brain. Some great animal was lying on me and now licking my throat. I feared to stir, for some instinct of prudence bade me lie still; but the brute seemed to realise that there was now some change in me, for it raised its head. Through my eyelashes I saw above me the two great flaming eyes of a gigantic wolf. Its sharp white teeth gleamed in the gaping red mouth, and I could feel its hot breath fierce and acrid upon me.

For another spell of time I remembered no more. Then I became conscious of a low growl, followed by a yelp, renewed again and again. Then, seemingly very far away, I heard a "Holloa! holloa!" as of many voices calling in unison. Cautiously I raised my head and looked in the direction whence the sound came; but the cemetery blocked my view. The wolf still continued to yelp in a strange way, and a red glare began to move round the grove of cypresses, as though following the sound. As the voices drew closer, the wolf yelped faster and louder. I feared to make either sound or motion. Nearer came the red glow, over the white pall which stretched into the darkness around me. Then all at once from beyond the trees there came at a trot a troop of horsemen bearing torches. The wolf rose from my breast and made for the cemetery. I saw one of the horsemen (soldiers by their caps and their long military cloaks) raise his carbine and take aim. A companion knocked up his arm, and I heard the ball whizz over my head. He had evidently taken my body for that of the wolf. Another sighted the animal as it slunk away, and a shot followed. Then, at a gallop, the troop rode forward—some towards me, others following the wolf as it disappeared amongst the snow-clad cypresses.

As they drew nearer I tried to move, but was powerless, although I could see and hear all that went on around me. Two or three of the soldiers jumped from their horses and knelt beside me. One of them raised my head, and placed his hand over my heart.

"Good news, comrades!" he cried. "His heart still beats!"

Then some brandy was poured down my throat; it put vigour into me, and I was able to open my eyes fully and look around. Lights and shadows were moving among the trees, and I heard men call to one another. They drew together, uttering frightened exclamations; and the lights flashed as the others came pouring out of the cemetery pell-mell, like men possessed. When the further ones came close to us, those who were around me asked them eagerly:

"Well, have you found him?"

The reply rang out hurriedly:

"No! no! Come away quick—quick! This is no place to stay, and on this of all nights!"

"What was it?" was the question, asked in all manner of keys. The answer came variously and all indefinitely as though the men were moved by some common impulse to speak, yet were restrained by some common fear from giving their thoughts.

"It—it—indeed!" gibbered one, whose wits had plainly given out for the moment.

"A wolf—and yet not a wolf!" another put in shudderingly.

"No use trying for him without the sacred bullet," a third remarked in a more ordinary manner.

"Serve us right for coming out on this night! Truly we have earned our thousand marks!" were the ejaculations of a fourth.

"There was blood on the broken marble," another said after a pause—"the lightning never brought that there. And for him—is he safe? Look at his throat! See, comrades, the wolf has been lying on him and keeping his blood warm."

The officer looked at my throat and replied:

"He is all right; the skin is not pierced. What does it all mean? We should never have found him but for the yelping of the wolf."

"What became of it?" asked the man who was holding up my head, and who seemed the least panic-stricken of the party, for his hands were steady and without tremor. On his sleeve was the chevron of a petty officer.

"It went to its home," answered the man, whose long face was pallid, and who actually shook with terror as he glanced around him fearfully. "There are graves enough there in which it may lie. Come, comrades—come quickly! Let us leave this cursed spot."

The officer raised me to a sitting posture, as he uttered a word of command; then several men placed me upon a horse. He sprang to the saddle behind me, took me in his arms, gave the word to advance; and, turning our faces away from the cypresses, we rode away in swift, military order.

As yet my tongue refused its office, and I was perforce silent. I must have fallen asleep; for the next thing I remembered was finding myself standing up, supported by a soldier on each side of me. It was almost broad daylight, and to the north a red streak of sunlight was reflected, like a path of blood, over the waste of snow. The officer was telling the men to say nothing of what they had seen, except that they found an English stranger, guarded by a large dog.

"Dog! that was no dog," cut in the man who had exhibited such fear. "I think I know a wolf when I see one."

The young officer answered calmly: "I said a dog."

"Dog!" reiterated the other ironically. It was evident that his courage was rising with the sun; and, pointing to me, he said, "Look at his throat. Is that the work of a dog, master?"

Instinctively I raised my hand to my throat, and as I touched it I cried out in pain. The men crowded round to look, some stooping down from their saddles; and again there came the calm voice of the young officer:

"A dog, as I said. If aught else were said we should only be laughed at."

I was then mounted behind a trooper, and we rode on into the suburbs of Munich. Here we came across a stray carriage, into which I was lifted, and it was driven off to the Quatre Saisons—the young officer accompanying me, whilst a trooper followed with his horse, and the others rode off to their barracks.

When we arrived, Herr Delbrück rushed so quickly down the steps to meet me, that it was apparent he had been watching within. Taking me by both hands he solicitously led me in. The officer saluted me and was turning to withdraw, when I recognised his purpose, and insisted that he should come to my rooms. Over a glass of wine I warmly thanked him and his brave comrades for saving me. He replied simply that he was more than glad, and that Herr Delbrück had at the first taken steps to make all the searching party pleased; at which ambiguous utterance the maître d'hôtel smiled, while the officer pleaded duty and withdrew.

"But Herr Delbrück," I enquired, "how and why was it that the soldiers searched for me?"

He shrugged his shoulders, as if in depreciation of his own deed, as he replied:

"I was so fortunate as to obtain leave from the commander of the regiment in which I served, to ask for volunteers."

"But how did you know I was lost?" I asked.

"The driver came hither with the remains of his carriage, which had been upset when the horses ran away."

"But surely you would not send a search-party of soldiers merely on this account?"

"Oh, no!" he answered; "but even before the coachman arrived, I had this telegram from the Boyar whose guest you are," and he took from his pocket a telegram which he handed to me, and I read:

Bistritz.

Be careful of my guest—his safety is most precious to me. Should aught happen to him, or if he be missed, spare nothing to find him and ensure his safety. He is English and therefore adventurous. There are often dangers from snow and wolves and night. Lose not a moment if you suspect harm to him. I answer your zeal with my fortune.

—Dracula.

As I held the telegram in my hand, the room seemed to whirl around me; and, if the attentive maître d'hôtel had not caught me, I think I should have fallen. There was something so strange in all this, something so weird and impossible to imagine, that there grew on me a sense of my being in some way the sport of opposite forces—the mere vague idea of which seemed in a way to paralyse me. I was certainly under some form of mysterious protection. From a distant country had come, in the very nick of time, a message that took me out of the danger of the snow-sleep and the jaws of the wolf.

Kerfol

Edith Wharton

I

"You ought to buy it," said my host; "its just the place for a solitary-minded devil like you. And it would be rather worth while to own the most romantic house in Brittany. The present people are dead broke, and it's going for a song—you ought to buy it."

It was not with the least idea of living up to the character my friend Lanrivain ascribed to me (as a matter of fact, under my unsociable exterior I have always had secret yearnings for domesticity) that I took his hint one autumn afternoon and went to Kerfol. My friend was motoring over to Quimper on business: he dropped me on the way, at a cross-road on a heath, and said: "First turn to the right and second to the left. Then straight ahead till you see an avenue. If you meet any peasants, don't ask your way. They don't understand French, and they would pretend they did and mix you up. I'll be back for you here by sunset—and don't forget the tombs in the chapel."

I followed Lanrivain's directions with the hesitation occasioned by the usual difficulty of remembering whether he had said the first turn to the right and second to the left, or the contrary. If I had met a peasant I should certainly have asked, and probably been sent astray; but I had the desert landscape to myself, and so stumbled on the right turn and walked across the heath till I came to an avenue. It was so unlike any other avenue I have ever seen that I instantly knew it must be *the* avenue. The grey-trunked trees sprang up straight to a great height and then interwove their pale-grey branches in a long tunnel through which the autumn light fell faintly. I know most trees by name, but I haven't to this day been able to decide what those trees were. They had the tall curve of elms, the tenuity of poplars, the ashen colour of olives under a rainy sky; and they stretched ahead of me for half a mile or more without a break in their arch. If ever I saw an avenue that unmistakably led to something, it was the avenue at Kerfol. My heart beat a little as I began to walk down it.

Presently the trees ended and I came to a fortified gate in a long wall. Between me and the wall was an open space of grass, with other grey avenues radiating from it. Behind the wall were tall slate roofs mossed with silver, a chapel belfry, the top of a keep. A moat filled with wild shrubs and brambles surrounded the place; the drawbridge had been replaced by a stone arch, and the portcullis by an iron gate. I stood for a long time on the hither side of the moat, gazing about me, and letting the influence of the place sink in. I said to myself: "If I wait long enough, the guardian will turn up and show me the tombs—" and I rather hoped he wouldn't turn up too soon.

I sat down on a stone and lit a cigarette. As soon as I had done it, it struck me as a puerile and portentous thing to do, with that great blind house looking down at me, and all the empty avenues converging on me. It may have been the depth of the silence that made me so conscious of my gesture. The squeak of my match sounded as loud as the scraping of a brake, and I almost fancied I heard it fall when I tossed it onto the grass. But there was more than that: a sense of irrelevance, of littleness, of futile bravado, in sitting there puffing my cigarette-smoke into the face of such a past.

I knew nothing of the history of Kerfol—I was new to Brittany, and Lanrivain had never mentioned the name to me till the day before—but one couldn't as much as glance at that pile without feeling in it a long accumulation of history. What kind of history I was not prepared to guess: perhaps only that sheer weight of many associated lives and deaths which gives a majesty to all old houses. But the aspect of Kerfol suggested something more—a perspective of stern and cruel memories stretching away, like its own grey avenues, into a blur of darkness.

Certainly no house had ever more completely and finally broken with the present. As it stood there, lifting its proud roofs and gables to the sky, it might have been its own funeral monument. "Tombs in the chapel? The whole place is a tomb!" I reflected. I hoped more and more that the guardian would not come. The details of the place, however striking, would seem trivial compared with its collective impressiveness; and I wanted only to sit there and be penetrated by the weight of its silence.

"It's the very place for you!" Lanrivain had said; and I was overcome by the almost blasphemous frivolity of suggesting to any living being that Kerfol was the place for him. "Is it possible that any one could *not* see—?" I wondered. I did not finish the thought: what I meant was undefinable. I stood up and wandered toward the gate. I was beginning to want to know more; not to *see* more—I was by now so sure it was not a question of seeing—but to feel more: feel all the place had to communicate. "But to get in one will have to rout out the keeper," I thought reluctantly, and hesitated. Finally I crossed the bridge and tried the iron gate. It yielded, and I walked through the tunnel formed by the thickness of the *chemin de ronde*. At the farther end, a wooden barricade had been laid across the entrance, and beyond it was a court enclosed in noble architecture. The main building faced me; and I now saw that one half was a mere ruined front, with gaping windows through which the wild growths of the moat and the trees of the park were visible. The rest of the house was still in its robust beauty. One end abutted on the round tower, the other on the small traceried chapel, and in an angle of the building stood a graceful well-head crowned with mossy urns. A few roses grew against the walls, and on an upper window-sill I remember noticing a pot of fuchsias.

My sense of the pressure of the invisible began to yield to my architectural interest. The building was so fine that I felt a desire to explore it for its own sake. I looked about the court, wondering in which corner the guardian lodged. Then I pushed open the barrier and went in. As I did so, a dog barred my way. He was such a remarkably beautiful little dog that for a moment he made me forget the splendid place he was defending. I was not sure of his breed at the time, but have since learned that it was Chinese, and that he was of a rare variety called the "Sleeve-dog." He was very small and golden brown, with large brown eyes and a ruffled throat: he looked like a large tawny chrysanthemum. I said to myself: "These little beasts always snap and scream, and somebody will be out in a minute."

The little animal stood before me, forbidding, almost menacing: there was anger in his large brown eyes. But he made no sound, he came no nearer. Instead, as I advanced, he gradually fell back, and I noticed that another dog, a vague rough brindled thing, had limped up on a lame leg. "There'll be a hubbub now," I thought; for at the same moment a third dog, a long-haired white mongrel, slipped out of a doorway and joined the others. All three stood looking at me with grave eyes; but not a sound came from them. As I advanced they continued to fall back on muffled paws, still watching me. "At a given point, they'll all charge at my ankles: it's one of the jokes that dogs who live together put up on one," I thought. I was not alarmed, for they were neither large nor formidable. But they let me wander about the court as I pleased, following me at a little distance—always the same distance—and always keeping their eyes on me. Presently I looked across at the ruined facade, and saw that in one of its empty window-frames another dog stood: a white pointer with one brown ear. He was an old grave dog, much more experienced than the others; and he seemed to be observing me with a deeper intentness. "I'll hear from him," I said to myself; but he stood in the window-frame, against the trees of the park, and continued to watch me without moving. I stared back at him for a time, to see if the sense that he was being watched would not rouse him. Half the width of the court lay between us, and we gazed at each other silently across it. But he did not stir, and at last I turned away. Behind me I found the rest of the pack, with a newcomer added: a small black greyhound with pale agate-coloured eyes. He was shivering a little, and his expression was more timid than that of the others. I noticed that he kept a little behind them. And still there was not a sound.

I stood there for fully five minutes, the circle about me—waiting, as they seemed to be waiting. At last I went up to the little golden-brown dog and stooped to pat him. As I did so, I heard myself give a nervous laugh. The little dog did not start, or growl, or take his eyes from me—he simply slipped back about a yard, and then paused and continued to look at me. "Oh, hang it!" I exclaimed, and walked across the court toward the well.

As I advanced, the dogs separated and slid away into different corners of the court. I examined the urns on the well, tried a locked door or two, and looked up and down the dumb facade; then I faced about toward the chapel. When I turned I perceived that all the dogs had disappeared except the old pointer, who still watched me from the window. It was rather a relief to be rid of that cloud of witnesses; and I began to look about me for a way to the back of the house. "Perhaps there'll be somebody in the garden," I thought. I found a way across the moat, scrambled over a wall smothered in brambles, and got into the garden. A few lean hydrangeas and geraniums pined in the flower-beds, and the ancient house looked down on them indifferently. Its garden side was plainer and severer than the other: the long granite front, with its few windows and steep roof, looked like a fortress-prison. I walked around the farther wing, went up some disjointed steps, and entered the deep twilight of a narrow and incredibly old box-walk. The walk was just wide enough for one person to slip through, and its branches met overhead. It was like the ghost of a box-walk, its lustrous green all turning to the shadowy greyness of the avenues. I walked on and on, the branches hitting me in the face and springing back with a dry rattle; and at length I came out on the grassy top of the *chemin de ronde*. I walked along it to the gate-tower, looking down into the court, which was just below me. Not a human being was in sight; and neither were the dogs. I found a flight of steps in the thickness of the wall and went down them; and when I emerged again into the court, there stood the circle of dogs, the golden-brown one a little ahead of the others, the black greyhound shivering in the rear.

"Oh, hang it—you uncomfortable beasts, you!" I exclaimed, my voice startling me with a sudden echo. The dogs stood motionless, watching me. I knew by this time that they would not try to prevent my approaching the house, and the knowledge left me free to examine them. I had a feeling that they must be horribly cowed to be so silent and inert. Yet they did not look hungry or ill-treated. Their coats were smooth and they were not thin, except the shivering greyhound. It was more as if they had lived a long time with people who never spoke to them or looked at them: as though the silence of the place had gradually benumbed their busy inquisitive natures. And this strange passivity, this almost human lassitude, seemed to me sadder than the misery of starved and beaten animals. I should have liked to rouse them for a minute, to coax them into a game or a scamper; but the longer I looked into their fixed and weary eyes the more preposterous the idea became. With the windows of that house looking down on us, how could I have imagined such a thing? The dogs knew better: they knew what the house would tolerate and what it would not. I even fancied that they knew what was passing through my mind, and pitied me for my frivolity. But even that feeling probably reached them through a thick fog of listlessness. I had an idea that their distance from me was as nothing to my remoteness from them. The impression they produced was that of having in common one memory so deep and dark that nothing that had happened since was worth either a growl or a wag.

"I say," I broke out abruptly, addressing myself to the dumb circle, "do you know what you look like, the whole lot of you? You look as if you'd seen a ghost—that's how you look! I wonder if there is a ghost here, and nobody but you left for it to appear to?" The dogs continued to gaze at me without moving . . .

* * * * *

It was dark when I saw Lanrivain's motor lamps at the cross-roads—and I wasn't exactly sorry to see them. I had the sense of having escaped from the loneliest place in the whole world, and of not liking loneliness—to that degree—as much as I had imagined I should. My friend had brought his solicitor back from Quimper for the night, and seated beside a fat and affable stranger I felt no inclination to talk of Kerfol . . .

But that evening, when Lanrivain and the solicitor were closeted in the study, Madame de Lanrivain began to question me in the drawing-room.

"Well—are you going to buy Kerfol?" she asked, tilting up her gay chin from her embroidery.

"I haven't decided yet. The fact is, I couldn't get into the house," I said, as if I had simply postponed my decision, and meant to go back for another look.

"You couldn't get in? Why, what happened? The family are mad to sell the place, and the old guardian has orders—"

"Very likely. But the old guardian wasn't there."

"What a pity! He must have gone to market. But his daughter—?"

"There was nobody about. At least I saw no one."

"How extraordinary! Literally nobody?"

"Nobody but a lot of dogs—a whole pack of them—who seemed to have the place to themselves."

Madame de Lanrivain let the embroidery slip to her knee and folded her hands on it. For several minutes she looked at me thoughtfully.

"A pack of dogs—you saw them?"

"Saw them? I saw nothing else!"

"How many?" She dropped her voice a little. "I've always wondered—"

I looked at her with surprise: I had supposed the place to be familiar to her. "Have you never been to Kerfol?" I asked.

"Oh, yes: often. But never on that day."

"What day?"

"I'd quite forgotten—and so had Hervé, I'm sure. If we'd remembered, we never should have sent you today—but then, after all, one doesn't half believe that sort of thing, does one?"

"What sort of thing?" I asked, involuntarily sinking my voice to the level of hers. Inwardly I was thinking: "I knew there was something . . ."

Madame de Lanrivain cleared her throat and produced a reassuring smile. "Didn't Hervé tell you the story of Kerfol? An ancestor of his was mixed up in it. You know every Breton house has its ghost-story; and some of them are rather unpleasant."

"Yes—but those dogs?"

"Well, those dogs are the ghosts of Kerfol. At least, the peasants say there's one day in the year when a lot of dogs appear there; and that day the keeper and his daughter go off to Morlaix and get drunk. The women in Brittany drink dreadfully." She stooped to match a silk; then she lifted her charming inquisitive Parisian face. "Did you really see a lot of dogs? There isn't one at Kerfol," she said.

II

Lanrivain, the next day, hunted out a shabby calf volume from the back of an upper shelf of his library.

"Yes—here it is. What does it call itself? *A History of the Assizes of the Duchy of Brittany. Quimper*, 1702. The book was written about a hundred years later than the Kerfol affair; but I believe the account is transcribed pretty literally from the judicial records. Anyhow, it's queer reading. And there's a

Hervé de Lanrivain mixed up in it—not exactly *my* style, as you'll see. But then he's only a collateral. Here, take the book up to bed with you. I don't exactly remember the details; but after you've read it I'll bet anything you'll leave your light burning all night!"

I left my light burning all night, as he had predicted; but it was chiefly because, till near dawn, I was absorbed in my reading. The account of the trial of Anne de Cornault, wife of the lord of Kerfol, was long and closely printed. It was, as my friend had said, probably an almost literal transcription of what took place in the court-room; and the trial lasted nearly a month. Besides, the type of the book was very bad . . .

At first I thought of translating the old record. But it is full of wearisome repetitions, and the main lines of the story are forever straying off into side issues. So I have tried to disentangle it, and give it here in a simpler form. At times, however, I have reverted to the text because no other words could have conveyed so exactly the sense of what I felt at Kerfol; and nowhere have I added anything of my own.

III

It was in the year 16— that Yves de Cornault, lord of the domain of Kerfol, went to the pardon of Locronan to perform his religious duties. He was a rich and powerful noble, then in his sixty-second year, but hale and sturdy, a great horseman and hunter and a pious man. So all his neighbours attested. In appearance he was short and broad, with a swarthy face, legs slightly bowed from the saddle, a hanging nose and broad hands with black hairs on them. He had married young and lost his wife and son soon after, and since then had lived alone at Kerfol. Twice a year he went to Morlaix, where he had a handsome house by the river, and spent a week or ten days there; and occasionally he rode to Rennes on business. Witnesses were found to declare that during these absences he led a life different from the one he was known to lead at Kerfol, where he busied himself with his estate, attended mass daily, and found his only amusement in hunting the wild boar and water-fowl. But these rumours are not particularly relevant, and it is certain that among people of his own class in the neighbourhood he passed for a stern and even austere man, observant of his religious obligations, and keeping strictly to himself. There was no talk of any familiarity with the women on his estate, though at that time the nobility were very free with their peasants. Some people said he had never looked at a woman since his wife's death; but such things are hard to prove, and the evidence on this point was not worth much.

Well, in his sixty-second year, Yves de Cornault went to the pardon at Locronan, and saw there a young lady of Douarnenez, who had ridden over pillion behind her father to do her duty to the saint. Her name was Anne de Barrigan, and she came of good old Breton stock, but much less great and powerful than that of Yves de Cornault; and her father had squandered his fortune at cards, and lived almost like a peasant in his little granite manor on the moors . . . I have said I would add nothing of my own to this bald statement of a strange case; but I must interrupt myself here to describe the young lady who rode up to the lych-gate of Locronan at the very moment when the Baron de Cornault was also dismounting there. I take my description from a faded drawing in red crayon, sober and truthful enough to be by a late pupil of the Clouets, which hangs in Lanrivain's study, and is said to be a portrait of Anne de Barrigan. It is unsigned and has no mark of identity but the initials A. B., and the date 16—, the year after her marriage. It represents a young woman with a small oval face, almost pointed, yet wide enough for a full mouth with a tender depression at the corners. The nose is small, and the eyebrows are set rather high, far apart, and as lightly pencilled as the eyebrows in a Chinese painting. The forehead is high and serious, and the hair, which one feels to be fine and thick and fair, is drawn off it and lies close like a cap. The eyes are neither large nor small, hazel probably, with a look at once shy and steady. A pair of beautiful long hands are crossed below the lady's breast . . .

The chaplain of Kerfol, and other witnesses, averred that when the Baron came back from Locronan he jumped from his horse, ordered another to be instantly saddled, called to a young page to come with him, and rode away that same evening to the south. His steward followed the next morning with coffers laden on a pair of pack mules. The following week Yves de Cornault rode back to Kerfol, sent for his vassals and tenants, and told them he was to be married at All Saints to Anne de Barrigan of Douarnenez. And on All Saints' Day the marriage took place.

As to the next few years, the evidence on both sides seems to show that they passed happily for the couple. No one was found to say that Yves de Cornault had been unkind to his wife, and it was plain to all that he was content with his bargain. Indeed, it was admitted by the chaplain and other witnesses for the prosecution that the young lady had a softening influence on her husband, and that he became less exacting with his tenants, less harsh to peasants and dependents, and less subject to the fits of gloomy silence which had darkened his widowhood. As to his wife, the only grievance her champions could call up in her behalf was that Kerfol was a lonely place, and that when her husband was away on business at Bennes or Morlaix—whither she was never taken—she was not allowed so much as to walk in the park unaccompanied. But no one asserted that she was unhappy, though one servant-woman said she had surprised her crying, and had heard her say that she was a woman accursed to have no child, and nothing in life to call her own. But that was a natural enough feeling in a wife attached to her husband; and certainly it must have been a great grief to Yves de Cornault that she bore no son. Yet he never made her feel her childlessness as a reproach—she admits this in her evidence—but seemed to try to make her forget it by showering gifts and favours on her. Rich though he was, he had never been openhanded; but nothing was too fine for his wife, in the way of silks or gems or linen, or whatever else she fancied. Every wandering merchant was welcome at Kerfol, and when the master was called away he never came back without bringing his wife a handsome present—something curious and particular—from Morlaix or Rennes or Quimper. One of the waiting-women gave, in cross-examination, an interesting list of one year's gifts, which I copy. From Morlaix, a carved ivory junk, with Chinamen at the oars, that a strange sailor had brought back as a votive offering for Notre Dame de la Clarté, above Ploumanac'h; from Quimper, an embroidered gown, worked by the nuns of the Assumption; from Rennes, a silver rose that opened and showed an amber Virgin with a crown of garnets; from Morlaix, again, a length of Damascus velvet shot with gold, bought of a Jew from Syria; and for Michaelmas that same year, from Rennes, a necklet or bracelet of round stones—emeralds and pearls and rubies—strung like beads on a fine gold chain. This was the present that pleased the lady best, the woman said. Later on, as it happened, it was produced at the trial, and appears to have struck the Judges and the public as a curious and valuable jewel.

The very same winter, the Baron absented himself again, this time as far as Bordeaux, and on his return he brought his wife something even odder and prettier than the bracelet. It was a winter evening when he rode up to Kerfol and, walking into the hall, found her sitting by the hearth, her chin on her hand, looking into the fire. He carried a velvet box in his hand and, setting it down, lifted the lid and let out a little golden-brown dog.

Anne de Cornault exclaimed with pleasure as the little creature bounded toward her. "Oh, it looks like a bird or a butterfly!" she cried as she picked it up; and the dog put its paws on her shoulders and looked at her with eyes "like a Christian's." After that she would never have it out of her sight, and petted and talked to it as if it had been a child—as indeed it was the nearest thing to a child she was to know. Yves de Cornault was much pleased with his purchase.

The dog had been brought to him by a sailor from an East India merchantman, and the sailor had bought it of a pilgrim in a bazaar at Jaffa, who had stolen it from a nobleman's wife in China: a perfectly permissible thing to do, since the pilgrim was a Christian and the nobleman a heathen doomed to hell-fire.

Yves de Cornault had paid a long price for the dog, for they were beginning to be in demand at the French court, and the sailor knew he had got hold of a good thing; but Anne's pleasure was so great that, to see her laugh and play with the little animal, her husband would doubtless have given twice the sum.

* * * * *

So far, all the evidence is at one, and the narrative plain sailing; but now the steering becomes difficult. I will try to keep as nearly as possible to Anne's own statements; though toward the end, poor thing . . .

Well, to go back. The very year after the little brown dog was brought to Kerfol, Yves de Cornault, one winter night, was found dead at the head of a narrow flight of stairs leading down from his wife's rooms to a door opening on the court. It was his wife who found him and gave the alarm, so distracted, poor wretch, with fear and horror—for his blood was all over her—that at first the roused household could not make out what she was saying, and thought she had suddenly gone mad. But there, sure enough, at the top of the stairs lay her husband, stone dead, and head foremost, the blood from his wounds dripping down to the steps below him. He had been dreadfully scratched and gashed about the face and throat, as if with curious pointed weapons; and one of his legs had a deep tear in it which had cut an artery, and probably caused his death. But how did he come there, and who had murdered him?

His wife declared that she had been asleep in her bed, and hearing his cry had rushed out to find him lying on the stairs; but this was immediately questioned. In the first place, it was proved that from her room she could not have heard the struggle on the stairs, owing to the thickness of the walls and the length of the intervening passage; then it was evident that she had not been in bed and asleep, since she was dressed when she roused the house, and her bed had not been slept in. Moreover, the door at the bottom of the stairs was ajar, and it was noticed by the chaplain (an observant man) that the dress she wore was stained with blood about the knees, and that there were traces of small blood-stained hands low down on the staircase walls, so that it was conjectured that she had really been at the postern-door when her husband fell and, feeling her way up to him in the darkness on her hands and knees, had been stained by his blood dripping down on her. Of course it was argued on the other side that the blood-marks on her dress might have been caused by her kneeling down by her husband when she rushed out of her room; but there was the open door below, and the fact that the finger-marks in the staircase all pointed upward.

The accused held to her statement for the first two days, in spite of its improbability; but on the third day word was brought to her that Hervé de Lanrivain, a young nobleman of the neighbourhood, had been arrested for complicity in the crime. Two or three witnesses thereupon came forward to say that it was known throughout the country that Lanrivain had formerly been on good terms with the lady of Cornault; but that he had been absent from Brittany for over a year, and people had ceased to associate their names. The witnesses who made this statement were not of a very reputable sort. One was an old herb-gatherer suspected of witchcraft, another a drunken clerk from a neighbouring parish, the third a half-witted shepherd who could be made to say anything; and it was clear that the prosecution was not satisfied with its case, and would have liked to find more definite proof of Lanrivain's complicity than the statement of the herb-gatherer, who swore to having seen him climbing the wall of the park on the night of the murder. One way of patching out incomplete proofs in those days was to put some sort of pressure, moral or physical, on the accused person. It is not clear what pressure was put on Anne de Cornault; but on the third day, when she was brought in court, she "appeared weak and wandering," and after being encouraged to collect herself and speak the truth, on her honour and the wounds of her Blessed Redeemer, she confessed that she had in fact gone down the stairs to speak with Hervé de Lanrivain (who denied everything), and had been surprised there by the sound of her husband's fall. That was better; and the prosecution rubbed its hands with satisfaction. The satisfaction increased when various dependents living at Kerfol were induced to say—with apparent sincerity—that during the year or two preceding his death their master had once more grown uncertain and irascible, and subject to the fits of brooding silence which his household had learned to dread before his second marriage. This seemed to show that things had not been going well at Kerfol; though no one could be found to say that there had been any signs of open disagreement between husband and wife.

Anne de Cornault, when questioned as to her reason for going down at night to open the door to Hervé de Lanrivain, made an answer which must have sent a smile around the court. She said it was because she was lonely and wanted to talk with the young man. Was this the only reason? she was asked; and replied: "Yes, by the Cross over your Lordships' heads." "But why at midnight?" the court asked. "Because I could see him in no other way." I can see the exchange of glances across the ermine collars under the Crucifix.

Anne de Cornault, further questioned, said that her married life had been extremely lonely: "desolate" was the word she used. It was true that her husband seldom spoke harshly to her; but there were days when he did not speak at all. It was true that he had never struck or threatened her; but he kept her like a prisoner at Kerfol, and when he rode away to Morlaix or Quimper or Rennes he set so close a watch on her that she could not pick a flower in the garden without having a waiting-woman at her heels. "I am no Queen, to need such honours," she once said to him; and he had answered that a man who has a treasure does not leave the key in the lock when he goes out. "Then take me with you," she urged; but to this he said that towns were pernicious places, and young wives better off at their own firesides.

"But what did you want to say to Hervé de Lanrivain?" the court asked; and she answered: "To ask him to take me away."

"Ah—you confess that you went down to him with adulterous thoughts?"

"No."

"Then why did you want him to take you away?"

"Because I was afraid for my life."

"Of whom were you afraid?"

"Of my husband."

"Why were you afraid of your husband?"

"Because he had strangled my little dog."

Another smile must have passed around the courtroom: in days when any nobleman had a right to hang his peasants—and most of them exercised it—pinching a pet animal's wind-pipe was nothing to make a fuss about.

At this point one of the Judges, who appears to have had a certain sympathy for the accused, suggested that she should be allowed to explain herself in her own way; and she thereupon made the following statement.

The first years of her marriage had been lonely; but her husband had not been unkind to her. If she had had a child she would not have been unhappy; but the days were long, and it rained too much.

It was true that her husband, whenever he went away and left her, brought her a handsome present on his return; but this did not make up for the loneliness. At least nothing had, till he brought her the little brown dog from the East: after that she was much less unhappy. Her husband seemed pleased that she was so fond of the dog; he gave her leave to put her jewelled bracelet around its neck, and to keep it always with her.

One day she had fallen asleep in her room, with the dog at her feet, as his habit was. Her feet were bare and resting on his back. Suddenly she was waked by her husband: he stood beside her, smiling not unkindly.

"You look like my great-grandmother, Juliane de Cornault, lying in the chapel with her feet on a little dog," he said.

The analogy sent a chill through her, but she laughed and answered: "Well, when I am dead you must put me beside her, carved in marble, with my dog at my feet."

"Oho—we'll wait and see," he said, laughing also, but with his black brows close together. "The dog is the emblem of fidelity."

"And do you doubt my right to lie with mine at my feet?"

"When I'm in doubt I find out," he answered. "I am an old man," he added, "and people say I make you lead a lonely life. But I swear you shall have your monument if you earn it."

"And I swear to be faithful," she returned, "if only for the sake of having my little dog at my feet."

Not long afterward he went on business to the Quimper Assizes; and while he was away his aunt, the widow of a great nobleman of the duchy, came to spend a night at Kerfol on her way to the *pardon* of Ste. Barbe. She was a woman of piety and consequence, and much respected by Yves de Cornault, and when she proposed to Anne to go with her to Ste. Barbe no one could object, and even the chaplain declared himself in favour of the pilgrimage. So Anne set out for Ste. Barbe, and there for the first time she talked with Hervé de Lanrivain. He had come once or twice to Kerfol with his father, but she had never before exchanged a dozen words with him. They did not talk for more than five minutes now: it was under the chestnuts, as the procession was coming out of the chapel. He said: "I pity you," and she was surprised, for she had not supposed that any one thought her an object of pity. He added: "Call for me when you need me," and she smiled a little, but was glad afterward, and thought often of the meeting.

She confessed to having seen him three times afterward: not more. How or where she would not say—one had the impression that she feared to implicate some one. Their meetings had been rare and brief; and at the last he had told her that he was starting the next day for a foreign country, on a mission which was not without peril and might keep him for many months absent. He asked her for a remembrance, and she had none to give him but the collar about the little dog's neck. She was sorry afterward that she had given it, but he was so unhappy at going that she had not had the courage to refuse.

Her husband was away at the time. When he returned a few days later he picked up the animal to pet it, and noticed that its collar was missing. His wife told him that the dog had lost it in the undergrowth of the park, and that she and her maids had hunted a whole day for it. It was true, she explained to the court, that she had made the maids search for the necklet—they all believed the dog had lost it in the park . . .

Her husband made no comment, and that evening at supper he was in his usual mood, between good and bad: you could never tell which. He talked a good deal, describing what he had seen and done at Rennes; but now and then he stopped and looked hard at her, and when she went to bed she found her little dog strangled on her pillow. The little thing was dead, but still warm; she stooped to lift it, and her distress turned to horror when she discovered that it had been strangled by twisting twice round its throat the necklet she had given to Lanrivain.

The next morning at dawn she buried the dog in the garden, and hid the necklet in her breast. She said nothing to her husband, then or later, and he said nothing to her; but that day he had a peasant hanged for stealing a faggot in the park, and the next day he nearly beat to death a young horse he was breaking.

Winter set in, and the short days passed, and the long nights, one by one; and she heard nothing of Hervé de Lanrivain. It might be that her husband had killed him; or merely that he had been robbed of the necklet. Day after day by the hearth among the spinning maids, night after night alone on her bed, she wondered and trembled. Sometimes at table her husband looked across at her and smiled; and then she felt sure that Lanrivain was dead. She dared not try to get news of him, for she was sure her husband would find out if she did: she had an idea that he could find out anything. Even when a witchwoman who was a noted seer, and could show you the whole world in her crystal, came to the castle for a night's shelter, and the maids flocked to her, Anne held back.

The winter was long and black and rainy. One day, in Yves de Cornault's absence, some gypsies came to Kerfol with a troop of performing dogs. Anne bought the smallest and cleverest, a white dog with a feathery coat and one blue and one brown eye. It seemed to have been ill-treated by the gypsies, and clung to her plaintively when she took it from them. That evening her husband came back, and when she went to bed she found the dog strangled on her pillow.

After that she said to herself that she would never have another dog; but one bitter cold evening a poor lean greyhound was found whining at the castle-gate, and she took him in and forbade the maids to speak of him to her husband.

She hid him in a room that no one went to, smuggled food to him from her own plate, made him a warm bed to lie on and petted him like a child.

Yves de Cornault came home, and the next day she found the greyhound strangled on her pillow. She wept in secret, but said nothing, and resolved that even if she met a dog dying of hunger she would never bring him into the castle; but one day she found a young sheepdog, a brindled puppy with good blue eyes, lying with a broken leg in the snow of the park. Yves de Cornault was at Bennes, and she brought the dog in, warmed and fed it, tied up its leg and hid it in the castle till her husband's return. The day before, she gave it to a peasant woman who lived a long way off, and paid her handsomely to care for it and say nothing; but that night she heard a whining and scratching at her door, and when she opened it the lame puppy, drenched and shivering, jumped up on her with little sobbing barks. She hid him in her bed, and the next morning was about to have him taken back to the peasant woman when she heard her husband ride into the court. She shut the dog in a chest, and went down to receive him. An hour or two later, when she returned to her room, the puppy lay strangled on her pillow . . .

After that she dared not make a pet of any other dog; and her loneliness became almost unendurable. Sometimes, when she crossed the court of the castle, and thought no one was looking, she stopped to pat the old pointer at the gate. But one day as she was caressing him her husband came out of the chapel; and the next day the old dog was gone . . .

This curious narrative was not told in one sitting of the court, or received without impatience and incredulous comment. It was plain that the Judges were surprised by its puerility, and that it did not help the accused in the eyes of the public. It was an odd tale, certainly; but what did it prove? That Yves de Cornault disliked dogs, and that his wife, to gratify her own fancy, persistently ignored this dislike. As for pleading this trivial disagreement as an excuse for her relations—whatever their nature—with her supposed accomplice, the argument was so absurd that her own lawyer manifestly regretted having let her make use of it, and tried several times to cut short her story. But she went on to the end, with a kind of hypnotized insistence, as though the scenes she evoked were so real to her that she had forgotten where she was and imagined herself to be re-living them.

At length the Judge who had previously shown a certain kindness to her said (leaning forward a little, one may suppose, from his row of dozing colleagues): "Then you would have us believe that you murdered your husband because he would not let you keep a pet dog?"

"I did not murder my husband."

"Who did, then? Hervé de Lanrivain?"

"No."

"Who then? Can you tell us?"

"Yes, I can tell you. The dogs—" At that point she was carried out of the court in a swoon.

* * * * *

It was evident that her lawyer tried to get her to abandon this line of defense. Possibly her explanation, whatever it was, had seemed convincing when she poured it out to him in the heat of their first private colloquy; but now that it was exposed to the cold daylight of judicial scrutiny, and the banter of the town, he was thoroughly ashamed of it, and would have sacrificed her without a scruple to save his professional reputation. But the obstinate Judge—who perhaps, after all, was more inquisitive than kindly—evidently wanted to hear the story out, and she was ordered, the next day, to continue her deposition.

She said that after the disappearance of the old watchdog nothing particular happened for a month or two. Her husband was much as usual: she did not remember any special incident. But one evening a pedlar woman came to the castle and was selling trinkets to the maids. She had no heart for trinkets, but she stood looking on while the women made their choice. And then, she did not know how, but the pedlar coaxed her into buying for herself a pear-shaped pomander with a strong scent in it—she had once seen something of the kind on a gypsy woman. She had no desire for the pomander, and did not know why she had bought it. The pedlar said that whoever wore it had the power to read the future; but she did not really believe that, or care much either. However, she bought the thing and took it up to her room, where she sat turning it about in her hand. Then the strange scent attracted her and she began to wonder what kind of spice was in the box. She opened it and found a grey bean rolled in a strip of paper; and on the paper she saw a sign she knew, and a message from Hervé de Lanrivain, saying that he was at home again and would be at the door in the court that night after the moon had set . . .

She burned the paper and sat down to think. It was nightfall, and her husband was at home . . . She had no way of warning Lanrivain, and there was nothing to do but to wait . . .

At this point I fancy the drowsy court-room beginning to wake up. Even to the oldest hand on the bench there must have been a certain relish in picturing the feelings of a woman on receiving such a message at nightfall from a man living twenty miles away, to whom she had no means of sending a warning . . .

She was not a clever woman, I imagine; and as the first result of her cogitation she appears to have made the mistake of being, that evening, too kind to her husband. She could not ply him with wine, according to the traditional expedient, for though he drank heavily at times he had a strong head; and when he drank beyond its strength it was because he chose to, and not because a woman coaxed him. Not his wife, at any rate—she was an old story by now. As I read the case, I fancy there was no feeling for her left in him but the hatred occasioned by his supposed dishonour.

At any rate, she tried to call up her old graces; but early in the evening he complained of pains and fever, and left the hall to go up to the closet where he sometimes slept. His servant carried him a cup of hot wine, and brought back word that he was sleeping and not to be disturbed; and an hour later, when Anne lifted the tapestry and listened at his door, she heard his loud regular breathing. She thought it might be a feint, and stayed a long time barefooted in the passage, her ear to the crack; but the breathing went on too steadily and naturally to be other than that of a man in a sound sleep. She crept back to her room reassured, and stood in the window watching the moon set through the trees of the park. The sky was misty and starless, and after the moon went down the night was black as pitch. She knew the time had come, and stole along the passage, past her husband's door—where she stopped again to listen to his breathing—to the top of the stairs. There she paused a moment, and assured herself that no one was following her; then she began to go down the stairs in the darkness. They were so steep and winding that she had to go very slowly, for fear of stumbling. Her one thought was to get the door unbolted, tell Lanrivain to make his escape, and hasten back to her room. She had tried the bolt earlier in the evening, and managed to put a little grease on it; but nevertheless, when she drew it, it gave a squeak . . . not loud, but it made her heart stop; and the next minute, overhead, she heard a noise . . .

"What noise?" the prosecution interposed.

"My husband's voice calling out my name and cursing me."

"What did you hear after that?"

"A terrible scream and a fall."

"Where was Hervé de Lanrivain at this time?"

"He was standing outside in the court. I just made him out in the darkness. I told him for God's sake to go, and then I pushed the door shut."

"What did you do next?"

"I stood at the foot of the stairs and listened."

"What did you hear?"

"I heard dogs snarling and panting." (Visible discouragement of the bench, boredom of the public, and exasperation of the lawyer for the defense. Dogs again—! But the inquisitive Judge insisted.)

"What dogs?"

She bent her head and spoke so low that she had to be told to repeat her answer: "I don't know."

"How do you mean—you don't know?"

"I don't know what dogs . . ."

The Judge again intervened: "Try to tell us exactly what happened. How long did you remain at the foot of the stairs?"

"Only a few minutes."

"And what was going on meanwhile overhead?"

"The dogs kept on snarling and panting. Once or twice he cried out. I think he moaned once. Then he was quiet."

"Then what happened?"

"Then I heard a sound like the noise of a pack when the wolf is thrown to them—gulping and lapping."

(There was a groan of disgust and repulsion through the court, and another attempted intervention by the distracted lawyer. But the inquisitive Judge was still inquisitive.)

"And all the while you did not go up?"

"Yes—I went up then—to drive them off."

"The dogs?"

"Yes."

"Well—?"

"When I got there it was quite dark. I found my husband's flint and steel and struck a spark. I saw him lying there. He was dead."

"And the dogs?"

"The dogs were gone."

"Gone—whereto?"

"I don't know. There was no way out—and there were no dogs at Kerfol."

She straightened herself to her full height, threw her arms above her head, and fell down on the stone floor with a long scream. There was a moment of confusion in the court-room. Some one on the bench was heard to say: "This is clearly a case for the ecclesiastical authorities"—and the prisoner's lawyer doubtless jumped at the suggestion.

After this, the trial loses itself in a maze of cross-questioning and squabbling. Every witness who was called corroborated Anne de Cornault's statement that there were no dogs at Kerfol: had been none for several months. The master of the house had taken a dislike to dogs, there was no denying it. But, on the other hand, at the inquest, there had been long and bitter discussions as to the nature of the dead man's wounds. One of the surgeons called in had spoken of marks that looked like bites. The suggestion of witchcraft was revived, and the opposing lawyers hurled tomes of necromancy at each other.

At last Anne de Cornault was brought back into court—at the instance of the same Judge—and asked if she knew where the dogs she spoke of could have come from. On the body of her Redeemer she swore that she did not. Then the Judge put his final question: "If the dogs you think you heard had been known to you, do you think you would have recognized them by their barking?"

"Yes."

"Did you recognize them?"

"Yes."

"What dogs do you take them to have been?"

"My dead dogs," she said in a whisper . . . She was taken out of court, not to reappear there again. There was some kind of ecclesiastical investigation, and the end of the business was that the Judges disagreed with each other, and with the ecclesiastical committee, and that Anne de Cornault was finally handed over to the keeping of her husband's family, who shut her up in the keep of Kerfol, where she is said to have died many years later, a harmless mad-woman.

So ends her story. As for that of Hervé de Lanrivain, I had only to apply to his collateral descendant for its subsequent details. The evidence against the young man being insufficient, and his family influence in the duchy considerable, he was set free, and left soon afterward for Paris. He was probably in no mood for a worldly life, and he appears to have come almost immediately under the influence of the famous M. Arnauld d'Andilly and the gentlemen of Port Royal. A year or two later he was received into their Order, and without achieving any particular distinction he followed its good and evil fortunes till his death some twenty years later. Lanrivain showed me a portrait of him by a pupil of Philippe de Champaigne: sad eyes, an impulsive mouth and a narrow brow. Poor Hervé de Lanrivain: it was a grey ending. Yet as I looked at his stiff and sallow effigy, in the dark dress of the Janséniste, I almost found myself envying his fate. After all, in the course of his life two great things had happened to him: he had loved romantically, and he must have talked with Pascal . . .

The Case of Lady Sannox

Arthur Conan Doyle

The relations between Douglas Stone and the notorious Lady Sannox were very well known both among the fashionable circles of which she was a brilliant member, and the scientific bodies which numbered him among their most illustrious confreres. There was naturally, therefore, a very widespread interest when it was announced one morning that the lady had absolutely and for ever taken the veil, and that the world would see her no more. When, at the very tail of this rumour, there came the assurance that the celebrated operating surgeon, the man of steel nerves, had been found in the morning by his valet, seated on one side of his bed, smiling pleasantly upon the universe, with both legs jammed into one side of his breeches and his great brain about as valuable as a cap full of porridge, the matter was strong enough to give quite a little thrill of interest to folk who had never hoped that their jaded nerves were capable of such a sensation.

Douglas Stone in his prime was one of the most remarkable men in England. Indeed, he could hardly be said to have ever reached his prime, for he was but nine-and-thirty at the time of this little incident. Those who knew him best were aware that famous as he was as a surgeon, he might have succeeded with even greater rapidity in any of a dozen lines of life. He could have cut his way to fame as a soldier, struggled to it as an explorer, bullied for it in the courts, or built it out of stone and iron as an engineer. He was born to be great, for he could plan what another man dare not do, and he could do what another man dare not plan. In surgery none could follow him. His nerve, his judgement, his intuition, were things apart. Again and again his knife cut away death, but grazed the very springs of life in doing it, until his assistants were as white as the patient. His energy, his audacity, his full-blooded self-confidence—does not the memory of them still linger to the south of Marylebone Road and the north of Oxford Street?

His vices were as magnificent as his virtues, and infinitely more picturesque. Large as was his income, and it was the third largest of all professional men in London, it was far beneath the luxury of his living. Deep in his complex nature lay a rich vein of sensualism, at the sport of which he placed all the prizes of his life. The eye, the ear, the touch, the palate, all were his masters. The bouquet of old vintages, the scent of rare exotics, the curves and tints of the daintiest potteries of Europe, it was to these that the quick-running stream of gold was transformed. And then there came his sudden mad passion for Lady Sannox, when a single interview with two challenging glances and a whispered word set him ablaze. She was the loveliest woman in London and the only one to him. He was one of the handsomest men in London, but not the only one to her. She had a liking for new experiences, and was gracious to most men who wooed her. It may have been cause or it may have been effect that Lord Sannox looked fifty, though he was but six-and-thirty.

He was a quiet, silent, neutral-tinted man, this lord, with thin lips and heavy eyelids, much given to gardening, and full of home-like habits. He had at one time been fond of acting, had even rented a theatre in London, and on its boards had first seen Miss Marion Dawson, to whom he had offered his hand, his title, and the third of a county. Since his marriage his early hobby had become distasteful to him. Even in private theatricals it was no longer possible to persuade him to exercise the talent which he had often showed that he possessed. He was happier with a spud and a watering-can among his orchids and chrysanthemums.

It was quite an interesting problem whether he was absolutely devoid of sense, or miserably wanting in spirit. Did he know his lady's ways and condone them, or was he a mere blind, doting fool? It was a point to be discussed over the teacups in snug little drawing-rooms, or with the aid of a cigar in the bow windows of clubs. Bitter and plain were the comments among men upon his conduct. There was but one who had a good word to say for him, and he was the most silent member in the smoking-room. He had seen him break in a horse at the University, and it seemed to have left an impression upon his mind.

But when Douglas Stone became the favourite all doubts as to Lord Sannox's knowledge or ignorance were set for ever at rest. There was no subterfuge about Stone. In his high-handed, impetuous fashion, he set all caution and discretion at defiance. The scandal became notorious. A learned body intimated that his name had been struck from the list of its vice-presidents. Two friends implored him to consider his professional credit. He cursed them all three, and spent forty guineas on a bangle to take with him to the lady. He was at her house every evening, and she drove in his carriage in the afternoons. There was not an attempt on either side to conceal their relations; but there came at last a little incident to interrupt them.

It was a dismal winter's night, very cold and gusty, with the wind whooping in the chimneys and blustering against the window-panes. A thin spatter of rain tinkled on the glass with each fresh sough of the gale, drowning for the instant the dull gurgle and drip from the eaves. Douglas Stone had finished his dinner, and sat by his fire in the study, a glass of rich port upon the malachite table at his elbow. As he raised it to his lips, he held it up against the lamplight, and watched with the eye of a connoisseur the tiny scales of beeswing which floated in its rich ruby depths. The fire, as it spurted up, threw fitful lights upon his bald, clear-cut face, with its widely-opened grey eyes, its thick and yet firm lips, and the deep, square jaw, which had something Roman in its strength and its animalism. He smiled from time to time as he nestled back in his luxurious chair. Indeed, he had a right to feel well pleased, for, against the advice of six colleagues, he had performed an operation that day of which only two cases were on record, and the result had been brilliant beyond all expectation. No other man in London would have had the daring to plan, or the skill to execute, such a heroic measure.

But he had promised Lady Sannox to see her that evening and it was already half-past eight. His hand was outstretched to the bell to order the carriage when he heard the dull thud of the knocker. An instant later there was the shuffling of feet in the hall, and the sharp closing of a door.

"A patient to see you, sir, in the consulting room," said the butler.

"About himself?"

"No, sir; I think he wants you to go out."

"It is too late," cried Douglas Stone peevishly. "I won't go."

"This is his card, sir."

The butler presented it upon the gold salver which had been given to his master by the wife of a Prime Minister.

"'Hamil Ali, Smyrna.' Hum! The fellow is a Turk, I suppose."

"Yes, sir. He seems as if he came from abroad, sir. And he's in a terrible way."

"Tut, tut! I have an engagement. I must go somewhere else. But I'll see him. Show him in here, Pim."

A few moments later the butler swung open the door and ushered in a small and decrepit man, who walked with a bent back and with the forward push of the face and blink of the eyes which goes with extreme short sight. His face was swarthy, and his hair and beard of the deepest black. In one hand he held a turban of white muslin striped with red, in the other a small chamois-leather bag.

"Good evening," said Douglas Stone, when the butler had closed the door. "You speak English, I presume?"

"Yes, sir. I am from Asia Minor, but I speak English when I speak slow."

"You wanted me to go out, I understand?"

"Yes, sir. I wanted very much that you should see my wife."

"I could come in the morning, but I have an engagement which prevents me from seeing your wife tonight."

The Turk's answer was a singular one. He pulled the string which closed the mouth of the chamois-leather bag, and poured a flood of gold on to the table.

"There are one hundred pounds there," said he, "and I promise you that it will not take you an hour. I have a cab ready at the door."

Douglas Stone glanced at his watch. An hour would not make it too late to visit Lady Sannox. He had been there later. And the fee was an extraordinarily high one. He had been pressed by his creditors lately, and he could not afford to let such a chance pass. He would go.

"What is the case?" he asked.

"Oh, it is so sad a one! So sad a one! You have not, perhaps heard of the daggers of the Almohades?"

"Never."

"Ah, they are Eastern daggers of a great age and of a singular shape, with the hilt like what you call a stirrup. I am a curiosity dealer, you understand, and that is why I have come to England from Smyrna, but next week I go back once more. Many things I brought with me, and I have a few things left, but among them, to my sorrow, is one of these daggers."

"You will remember that I have an appointment, sir," said the surgeon, with some irritation; "pray confine yourself to the necessary details."

"You will see that it is necessary. Today my wife fell down in a faint in the room in which I keep my wares, and she cut her lower lip upon this cursed dagger of Almohades."

"I see," said Douglas Stone, rising. "And you wish me to dress the wound?"

"No, no, it is worse than that."

"What then?"

"These daggers are poisoned."

"Poisoned!"

"Yes, and there is no man, East or West, who can tell now what is the poison or what the cure. But all that is known I know, for my father was in this trade before me, and we have had much to do with these poisoned weapons."

"What are the symptoms?"

"Deep sleep, and death in thirty hours."

"And you say there is no cure. Why then should you pay me this considerable fee?"

"No drug can cure, but the knife may."

"And how?"

"The poison is slow of absorption. It remains for hours in the wound."

"Washing, then, might cleanse it?"

"No more than in a snake bite. It is too subtle and too deadly."

"Excision of the wound, then?"

"That is it. If it be on the finger, take the finger off. So said my father always. But think of where this wound is, and that it is my wife. It is dreadful!"

But familiarity with such grim matters may take the finer edge from a man's sympathy. To Douglas Stone this was already an interesting case, and he brushed aside as irrelevant the feeble objections of the husband.

"It appears to be that or nothing," said he brusquely. "It is better to lose a lip than a life."

"Ah, yes, I know that you are right. Well, well, it is kismet, and it must be faced. I have the cab, and you will come with me and do this thing."

Douglas Stone took his case of bistouries from a drawer, and placed it with a roll of bandage and a compress of lint in his pocket. He must waste no more time if he were to see Lady Sannox.

"I am ready," said he, pulling on his overcoat. "Will you take a glass of wine before you go out into this cold air?"

His visitor shrank away, with a protesting hand upraised.

"You forget that I am a Mussulman, and a true follower of the Prophet," said he. "But tell me what is the bottle of green glass which you have placed in your pocket?"

"It is chloroform."

"Ah, that also is forbidden to us. It is a spirit, and we make no use of such things."

"What! You would allow your wife to go through an operation without an anaesthetic?"

"Ah! she will feel nothing, poor soul. The deep sleep has already come on, which is the first working of the poison. And then I have given her of our Smyrna opium. Come, sir, for already an hour has passed."

As they stepped out into the darkness, a sheet of rain was driven in upon their faces, and the hall lamp, which dangled from the arm of a marble Caryatid, went out with a fluff. Pim, the butler, pushed the heavy door to, straining hard with his shoulder against the wind, while the two men groped their way towards the yellow glare which showed where the cab was waiting. An instant later they were rattling upon their journey.

"Is it far?" asked Douglas Stone.

"Oh, no. We have a very little quiet place off the Euston Road."

The surgeon pressed the spring of his repeater and listened to the little tings which told him the hour. It was a quarter past nine. He calculated the distances, and the short time which it would take him to perform so trivial an operation. He ought to reach Lady Sannox by ten o'clock. Through the fogged windows he saw the blurred gas lamps dancing past, with occasionally the broader glare of a shop front. The rain was pelting and rattling upon the leathern top of the carriage, and the wheels swashed as they rolled through puddle and mud. Opposite to him the white headgear of his companion gleamed faintly through the obscurity. The surgeon felt in his pockets and arranged his needles, his ligatures and his safety-pins, that no time might be wasted when they arrived. He chafed with impatience and drummed his foot upon the floor.

But the cab slowed down at last and pulled up. In an instant Douglas Stone was out, and the Smyrna merchant's toe was at his very heel.

"You can wait," said he to the driver.

It was a mean-looking house in a narrow and sordid street. The surgeon, who knew his London well, cast a swift glance into the shadows, but there was nothing distinctive—no shop, no movement, nothing but a double line of dull, flat-faced houses, a double stretch of wet flagstones which gleamed in the lamplight, and a double rush of water in the gutters which swirled and gurgled towards the sewer gratings. The door which faced them was blotched and discoloured, and a faint light in the fan pane above, it served to show the dust and the grime which covered it. Above in one of the bedroom windows, there was a dull yellow glimmer. The merchant knocked loudly, and, as he turned his dark face towards the light, Douglas Stone could see that it was contracted with anxiety. A bolt was drawn, and an elderly woman with a taper stood in the doorway, shielding the thin flame with her gnarled hand.

"Is all well?" gasped the merchant.

"She is as you left her, sir."

"She has not spoken?"

"No, she is in a deep sleep."

The merchant closed the door, and Douglas Stone walked down the narrow passage, glancing about him in some surprise as he did so. There was no oil-cloth, no mat, no hat-rack. Deep grey dust and heavy festoons of cobwebs met his eyes everywhere. Following the old woman up the winding stair, his firm footfall echoed harshly through the silent house. There was no carpet.

The bedroom was on the second landing. Douglas Stone followed the old nurse into it, with the merchant at his heels. Here, at least, there was furniture and to spare. The floor was littered and the corners piled with Turkish cabinets, inlaid tables, coats of chain mail, strange pipes, and grotesque weapons. A single small lamp stood upon a bracket on the wall. Douglas Stone took it down, and picking his way among the lumber, walked over to a couch in the corner, on which lay a woman dressed in the Turkish fashion, with yashmak and veil. The lower part of the face was exposed, and the surgeon saw a jagged cut which zigzagged along the border of the under lip.

"You will forgive the yashmak," said the Turk. "You know our views about women in the East."

But the surgeon was not thinking about the yashmak. This was no longer a woman to him. It was a case. He stooped and examined the wound carefully.

"There are no signs of irritation," said he. "We might delay the operation until local symptoms develop."

The husband wrung his hands in uncontrollable agitation.

"Oh! sir, sir," he cried. "Do not trifle. You do not know. It is deadly. I know, and I give you my assurance that an operation is absolutely necessary. Only the knife can save her."

"And yet I am inclined to wait," said Douglas Stone.

"That is enough," the Turk cried, angrily. "Every minute is of importance, and I cannot stand here and see my wife allowed to sink. It only remains for me to give you my thanks for having come, and to call in some other surgeon before it is too late."

Douglas Stone hesitated. To refund that hundred pounds was no pleasant matter. But of course if he left the case he must return the money. And if the Turk were right and the woman died, his position before a coroner might be an embarrassing one.

"You have had personal experience of this poison?" he asked.

"I have."

"And you assure me that an operation is needful."

"I swear it by all that I hold sacred."

"The disfigurement will be frightful."

"I can understand that the mouth will not be a pretty one to kiss."

Douglas Stone turned fiercely upon the man. The speech was a brutal one. But the Turk has his own fashion of talk and of thought, and there was no time for wrangling. Douglas Stone drew a bistoury from his case, opened it and felt the keen straight edge with his forefinger. Then he held the lamp closer to the bed. Two dark eyes were gazing up at him through the slit in the yashmak. They were all iris, and the pupil was hardly to be seen.

"You have given her a very heavy dose of opium."

"Yes, she has had a good dose."

He glanced again at the dark eyes which looked straight at his own. They were dull and lustreless, but, even as he gazed, a little shifting sparkle came into them, and the lips quivered.

"She is not absolutely unconscious," said he.

"Would it not be well to use the knife while it will be painless?"

The same thought had crossed the surgeon's mind. He grasped the wounded lip with his forceps, and with two swift cuts he took out a broad V-shaped piece. The woman sprang up on the couch with a dreadful gurgling scream. Her covering was torn from her face. It was a face that he knew. In spite of that protruding upper lip and that slobber of blood, it was a face that he knew. She kept on putting her hand up to the gap and screaming. Douglas Stone sat down at the foot of the couch with his knife and his forceps. The room was whirling round, and he had felt something go like a ripping seam behind his ear. A bystander would have said that his face was the more ghastly of the two. As in a dream, or as if he had been looking at something at the play, he was conscious that the Turk's hair and beard lay upon the table, and that Lord Sannox was leaning against the wall with his hand to his side, laughing silently. The screams had died away now, and the dreadful head had dropped back again upon the pillow, but Douglas Stone still sat motionless, and Lord Sannox still chuckled quietly to himself.

"It was really very necessary for Marion, this operation," said he, "not physically, but morally, you know, morally."

Douglas Stone stooped for yards and began to play with the fringe of the coverlet. His knife tinkled down upon the ground, but he still held the forceps and something more.

"I had long intended to make a little example," said Lord Sannox, suavely. "Your note of Wednesday miscarried, and I have it here in my pocket-book. I took some pains in carrying out my idea. The wound, by the way, was from nothing more dangerous than my signet ring."

He glanced keenly at his silent companion, and cocked the small revolver which he held in his coat pocket. But Douglas Stone was still picking at the coverlet.

"You see you have kept your appointment after all," said Lord Sannox.

And at that Douglas Stone began to laugh. He laughed long and loudly. But Lord Sannox did not laugh now. Something like fear sharpened and hardened his features. He walked from the room, and he walked on tiptoe. The old woman was waiting outside.

"Attend to your mistress when she awakes," said Lord Sannox.

Then he went down to the street. The cab was at the door, and the driver raised his hand to his hat.

"John," said Lord Sannox, "you will take the doctor home first. He will want leading downstairs, I think. Tell his butler that he has been taken ill at a case."

"Very good, sir."

"Then you can take Lady Sannox home."

"And how about yourself, sir?"

"Oh, my address for the next few months will be Hotel di Roma, Venice. Just see that the letters are sent on. And tell Stevens to exhibit all the purple chrysanthemums next Monday, and to wire me the result."

Young Goodman Brown

Nathaniel Hawthorne

Young Goodman Brown came forth at sunset into the street at Salem village; but put his head back, after crossing the threshold, to exchange a parting kiss with his young wife. And Faith, as the wife was aptly named, thrust her own pretty head into the street, letting the wind play with the pink ribbons of her cap while she called to Goodman Brown.

"Dearest heart," whispered she, softly and rather sadly, when her lips were close to his ear, "prithee put off your journey until sunrise and sleep in your own bed tonight. A lone woman is troubled with such dreams and such thoughts that she's afeard of herself sometimes. Pray tarry with me this night, dear husband, of all nights in the year."

"My love and my Faith," replied young Goodman Brown, "of all nights in the year, this one night must I tarry away from thee. My journey, as thou callest it, forth and back again, must needs be done 'twixt now and sunrise. What, my sweet, pretty wife, dost thou doubt me already, and we but three months married?"

"Then God bless you!" said Faith, with the pink ribbons; "and may you find all well when you come back."

"Amen!" cried Goodman Brown. "Say thy prayers, dear Faith, and go to bed at dusk, and no harm will come to thee."

So they parted; and the young man pursued his way until, being about to turn the corner by the meeting-house, he looked back and saw the head of Faith still peeping after him with a melancholy air, in spite of her pink ribbons.

"Poor little Faith!" thought he, for his heart smote him. "What a wretch am I to leave her on such an errand! She talks of dreams, too. Methought as she spoke there was trouble in her face, as if a dream had warned her what work is to be done tonight. But no, no; 't would kill her to think it. Well, she's a blessed angel on earth; and after this one night I'll cling to her skirts and follow her to heaven."

With this excellent resolve for the future, Goodman Brown felt himself justified in making more haste on his present evil purpose. He had taken a dreary road, darkened by all the gloomiest trees of the forest, which barely stood aside to let the narrow path creep through, and closed immediately behind. It was all as lonely as could be; and there is this peculiarity in such a solitude, that the traveller knows not who may be concealed by the innumerable trunks and the thick boughs overhead; so that with lonely footsteps he may yet be passing through an unseen multitude.

"There may be a devilish Indian behind every tree," said Goodman Brown to himself; and he glanced fearfully behind him as he added, "What if the devil himself should be at my very elbow!"

His head being turned back, he passed a crook of the road, and, looking forward again, beheld the figure of a man, in grave and decent attire, seated at the foot of an old tree. He arose at Goodman Brown's approach and walked onward side by side with him.

"You are late, Goodman Brown," said he. "The clock of the Old South was striking as I came through Boston, and that is full fifteen minutes agone."

"Faith kept me back a while," replied the young man, with a tremor in his voice, caused by the sudden appearance of his companion, though not wholly unexpected.

It was now deep dusk in the forest, and deepest in that part of it where these two were journeying. As nearly as could be discerned, the second traveller was about fifty years old, apparently in the same rank of life as Goodman Brown, and bearing a considerable resemblance to him, though perhaps more in expression than features. Still they might have been taken for father and son. And yet, though the elder person was as simply clad as the younger, and as simple in manner too, he had an indescribable air of one who knew the world, and who would not have felt abashed at the governor's dinner table or in King William's court, were it possible that his affairs should call him thither. But the only thing about him that could be fixed upon as remarkable was his staff, which bore the likeness of a great black snake, so curiously wrought that it might almost be seen to twist and wriggle itself like a living serpent. This, of course, must have been an ocular deception, assisted by the uncertain light.

"Come, Goodman Brown," cried his fellow-traveller, "this is a dull pace for the beginning of a journey. Take my staff, if you are so soon weary."

"Friend," said the other, exchanging his slow pace for a full stop, "having kept covenant by meeting thee here, it is my purpose now to return whence I came. I have scruples touching the matter thou wot'st of."

"Sayest thou so?" replied he of the serpent, smiling apart. "Let us walk on, nevertheless, reasoning as we go; and if I convince thee not thou shalt turn back. We are but a little way in the forest yet."

"Too far! too far!" exclaimed the goodman, unconsciously resuming his walk. "My father never went into the woods on such an errand, nor his father before him. We have been a race of honest men and good Christians since the days of the martyrs; and shall I be the first of the name of Brown that ever took this path and kept—"

"Such company, thou wouldst say," observed the elder person, interpreting his pause. "Well said, Goodman Brown! I have been as well acquainted with your family as with ever a one among the Puritans; and that's no trifle to say. I helped your grandfather, the constable, when he lashed the Quaker woman so smartly through the streets of Salem; and it was I that brought your father a pitch-pine knot, kindled at my own hearth, to set fire to an Indian village, in King Philip's war. They were my good friends, both; and many a pleasant walk have we had along this path, and returned merrily after midnight. I would fain be friends with you for their sake."

"If it be as thou sayest," replied Goodman Brown, "I marvel they never spoke of these matters; or, verily, I marvel not, seeing that the least rumor of the sort would have driven them from New England. We are a people of prayer, and good works to boot, and abide no such wickedness."

"Wickedness or not," said the traveller with the twisted staff, "I have a very general acquaintance here in New England. The deacons of many a church have drunk the communion wine with me; the selectmen of divers towns make me their chairman; and a majority of the Great and General Court are firm supporters of my interest. The governor and I, too—But these are state secrets."

"Can this be so?" cried Goodman Brown, with a stare of amazement at his undisturbed companion. "Howbeit, I have nothing to do with the governor and council; they have their own ways, and are no rule for a simple husbandman like me. But, were I to go on with thee, how should I meet the eye of that good old man, our minister, at Salem village? Oh, his voice would make me tremble both Sabbath day and lecture day."

Thus far the elder traveller had listened with due gravity; but now burst into a fit of irrepressible mirth, shaking himself so violently that his snake-like staff actually seemed to wriggle in sympathy.

"Ha! ha! ha!" shouted he again and again; then composing himself, "Well, go on, Goodman Brown, go on; but, prithee, don't kill me with laughing."

"Well, then, to end the matter at once," said Goodman Brown, considerably nettled, "there is my wife, Faith. It would break her dear little heart; and I'd rather break my own."

"Nay, if that be the case," answered the other, "e'en go thy ways, Goodman Brown. I would not for twenty old women like the one hobbling before us that Faith should come to any harm."

As he spoke he pointed his staff at a female figure on the path, in whom Goodman Brown recognized a very pious and exemplary dame, who had taught him his catechism in youth, and was still his moral and spiritual adviser, jointly with the minister and Deacon Gookin.

"A marvel, truly, that Goody Cloyse should be so far in the wilderness at nightfall," said he. "But with your leave, friend, I shall take a cut through the woods until we have left this Christian woman behind. Being a stranger to you, she might ask whom I was consorting with and whither I was going."

"Be it so," said his fellow-traveller. "Betake you to the woods, and let me keep the path."

Accordingly the young man turned aside, but took care to watch his companion, who advanced softly along the road until he had come within a staff's length of the old dame. She, meanwhile, was making the best of her way, with singular speed for so aged a woman, and mumbling some indistinct words—a prayer, doubtless—as she went. The traveller put forth his staff and touched her withered neck with what seemed the serpent's tail.

"The devil!" screamed the pious old lady.

"Then Goody Cloyse knows her old friend?" observed the traveller, confronting her and leaning on his writhing stick.

"Ah, forsooth, and is it your worship indeed?" cried the good dame. "Yea, truly is it, and in the very image of my old gossip, Goodman Brown, the grandfather of the silly fellow that now is. But—would your worship believe it?—my broomstick hath strangely disappeared, stolen, as I suspect, by that unhanged witch, Goody Cory, and that, too, when I was all anointed with the juice of smallage, and cinquefoil, and wolf's bane."

"Mingled with fine wheat and the fat of a new-born babe," said the shape of old Goodman Brown.

"Ah, your worship knows the recipe," cried the old lady, cackling aloud. "So, as I was saying, being all ready for the meeting, and no horse to ride on, I made up my mind to foot it; for they tell me there is a nice young man to be taken into communion tonight. But now your good worship will lend me your arm, and we shall be there in a twinkling."

"That can hardly be," answered her friend. "I may not spare you my arm, Goody Cloyse; but here is my staff, if you will."

So saying, he threw it down at her feet, where, perhaps, it assumed life, being one of the rods which its owner had formerly lent to the Egyptian magi. Of this fact, however, Goodman Brown could not take cognizance. He had cast up his eyes in astonishment, and, looking down again, beheld neither Goody

Cloyse nor the serpentine staff, but his fellow-traveller alone, who waited for him as calmly as if nothing had happened.

"That old woman taught me my catechism," said the young man; and there was a world of meaning in this simple comment.

They continued to walk onward, while the elder traveller exhorted his companion to make good speed and persevere in the path, discoursing so aptly that his arguments seemed rather to spring up in the bosom of his auditor than to be suggested by himself. As they went, he plucked a branch of maple to serve for a walking stick, and began to strip it of the twigs and little boughs, which were wet with evening dew. The moment his fingers touched them they became strangely withered and dried up as with a week's sunshine. Thus the pair proceeded, at a good free pace, until suddenly, in a gloomy hollow of the road, Goodman Brown sat himself down on the stump of a tree and refused to go any farther.

"Friend," said he, stubbornly, "my mind is made up. Not another step will I budge on this errand. What if a wretched old woman do choose to go to the devil when I thought she was going to heaven: is that any reason why I should quit my dear Faith and go after her?"

"You will think better of this by and by," said his acquaintance, composedly. "Sit here and rest yourself a while; and when you feel like moving again, there is my staff to help you along."

Without more words, he threw his companion the maple stick, and was as speedily out of sight as if he had vanished into the deepening gloom. The young man sat a few moments by the roadside, applauding himself greatly, and thinking with how clear a conscience he should meet the minister in his morning walk, nor shrink from the eye of good old Deacon Gookin. And what calm sleep would be his that very night, which was to have been spent so wickedly, but so purely and sweetly now, in the arms of Faith! Amidst these pleasant and praiseworthy meditations, Goodman Brown heard the tramp of horses along the road, and deemed it advisable to conceal himself within the verge of the forest, conscious of the guilty purpose that had brought him thither, though now so happily turned from it.

On came the hoof tramps and the voices of the riders, two grave old voices, conversing soberly as they drew near. These mingled sounds appeared to pass along the road, within a few yards of the young man's hiding-place; but, owing doubtless to the depth of the gloom at that particular spot, neither the travellers nor their steeds were visible. Though their figures brushed the small boughs by the wayside, it could not be seen that they intercepted, even for a moment, the faint gleam from the strip of bright sky athwart which they must have passed. Goodman Brown alternately crouched and stood on tiptoe, pulling aside the branches and thrusting forth his head as far as he durst without discerning so much as a shadow. It vexed him the more, because he could have sworn, were such a thing possible, that he recognized the voices of the minister and Deacon Gookin, jogging along quietly, as they were wont to do, when bound to some ordination or ecclesiastical council. While yet within hearing, one of the riders stopped to pluck a switch.

"Of the two, reverend sir," said the voice like the deacon's, "I had rather miss an ordination dinner than tonight's meeting. They tell me that some of our community are to be here from Falmouth and beyond, and others from Connecticut and Rhode Island, besides several of the Indian powwows, who, after their fashion, know almost as much deviltry as the best of us. Moreover, there is a goodly young woman to be taken into communion."

"Mighty well, Deacon Gookin!" replied the solemn old tones of the minister. "Spur up, or we shall be late. Nothing can be done, you know, until I get on the ground."

The hoofs clattered again; and the voices, talking so strangely in the empty air, passed on through the forest, where no church had ever been gathered or solitary Christian prayed. Whither, then, could these holy men be journeying so deep into the heathen wilderness? Young Goodman Brown caught hold of a tree for support, being ready to sink down on the ground, faint and overburdened with the heavy sickness of his heart. He looked up to the sky, doubting whether there really was a heaven above him. Yet there was the blue arch, and the stars brightening in it.

"With heaven above and Faith below, I will yet stand firm against the devil!" cried Goodman Brown.

While he still gazed upward into the deep arch of the firmament and had lifted his hands to pray, a cloud, though no wind was stirring, hurried across the zenith and hid the brightening stars. The blue sky was still visible, except directly overhead, where this black mass of cloud was sweeping swiftly northward. Aloft in the air, as if from the depths of the cloud, came a confused and doubtful sound of voices. Once the listener fancied that he could distinguish the accents of towns-people of his own, men and women, both pious and ungodly, many of whom he had met at the communion table, and had seen others rioting at the tavern. The next moment, so indistinct were the sounds, he doubted whether he had heard aught but the murmur of the old forest, whispering without a wind. Then came a stronger swell of those familiar tones, heard daily in the sunshine at Salem village, but never until now from a cloud of night. There was one voice of a young woman, uttering lamentations, yet with an uncertain sorrow, and entreating for some favor, which, perhaps, it would grieve her to obtain; and all the unseen multitude, both saints and sinners, seemed to encourage her onward.

"Faith!" shouted Goodman Brown, in a voice of agony and desperation; and the echoes of the forest mocked him, crying, "Faith! Faith!" as if bewildered wretches were seeking her all through the wilderness.

The cry of grief, rage, and terror was yet piercing the night, when the unhappy husband held his breath for a response. There was a scream, drowned immediately in a louder murmur of voices, fading into far-off laughter, as the dark cloud swept away, leaving the clear and silent sky above Goodman Brown. But something fluttered lightly down through the air and caught on the branch of a tree. The young man seized it, and beheld a pink ribbon.

"My Faith is gone!" cried he, after one stupefied moment. "There is no good on earth; and sin is but a name. Come, devil; for to thee is this world given."

And, maddened with despair, so that he laughed loud and long, did Goodman Brown grasp his staff and set forth again, at such a rate that he seemed to fly along the forest path rather than to walk or run. The road grew wilder and drearier and more faintly traced, and vanished at length, leaving him in the heart of the dark wilderness, still rushing onward with the instinct that guides mortal man to evil. The whole forest was peopled with frightful sounds—the creaking of the trees, the howling of wild beasts, and the yell of Indians; while sometimes the wind tolled like a distant church bell, and sometimes gave a broad roar around the traveller, as if all Nature were laughing him to scorn. But he was himself the chief horror of the scene, and shrank not from its other horrors.

"Ha! ha! ha!" roared Goodman Brown when the wind laughed at him. "Let us hear which will laugh loudest. Think not to frighten me with your deviltry. Come witch, come wizard, come Indian powwow, come devil himself, and here comes Goodman Brown. You may as well fear him as he fear you."

In truth, all through the haunted forest there could be nothing more frightful than the figure of Goodman Brown. On he flew among the black pines, brandishing his staff with frenzied gestures, now giving vent to an inspiration of horrid blasphemy, and now shouting forth such laughter as set all the echoes of the forest laughing like demons around him. The fiend in his own shape is less hideous than when he rages in the breast of man. Thus sped the demoniac on his course, until, quivering among the trees, he saw a red light before him, as when the felled trunks and branches of a clearing have been set on fire, and throw up their lurid blaze against the sky, at the hour of midnight. He paused, in a lull of the tempest that had driven him onward, and heard the swell of what seemed a hymn, rolling solemnly from a distance with the weight of many voices. He knew the tune; it was a familiar one in the choir of the village meeting-house. The verse died heavily away, and was lengthened by a chorus, not of human voices, but of all the sounds of the benighted wilderness pealing in awful harmony together. Goodman Brown cried out, and his cry was lost to his own ear by its unison with the cry of the desert.

In the interval of silence he stole forward until the light glared full upon his eyes. At one extremity of an open space, hemmed in by the dark wall of the forest, arose a rock, bearing some rude, natural resemblance either to an altar or a pulpit, and surrounded by four blazing pines, their tops aflame, their stems untouched, like candles at an evening meeting. The mass of foliage that had overgrown the summit of the rock was all on fire, blazing high into the night and fitfully illuminating the whole field. Each pendent twig and leafy festoon was in a blaze. As the red light arose and fell, a numerous congregation alternately shone forth, then disappeared in shadow, and again grew, as it were, out of the darkness, peopling the heart of the solitary woods at once.

"A grave and dark-clad company," quoth Goodman Brown.

In truth they were such. Among them, quivering to and fro between gloom and splendor, appeared faces that would be seen next day at the council board of the province, and others which, Sabbath after Sabbath, looked devoutly heavenward, and benignantly over the crowded pews, from the holiest pulpits in the land. Some affirm that the lady of the governor was there. At least there were high dames well known to her, and wives of honored husbands, and widows, a great multitude, and ancient maidens, all of excellent repute, and fair young girls, who trembled lest their mothers should espy them. Either the sudden gleams of light flashing over the obscure field bedazzled Goodman Brown, or he recognized a score of the church members of Salem village famous for their especial sanctity. Good old Deacon Gookin had arrived, and waited at the skirts of that venerable saint, his revered pastor. But, irreverently consorting with these grave, reputable, and pious people, these elders of the church, these chaste dames and dewy virgins, there were men of dissolute lives and women of spotted fame, wretches given over to all mean and filthy vice, and suspected even of horrid crimes. It was strange to see that the good shrank not from the wicked, nor were the sinners abashed by the saints. Scattered also among their pale-faced enemies were the Indian priests, or powwows, who had often scared their native forest with more hideous incantations than any known to English witchcraft.

"But where is Faith?" thought Goodman Brown; and, as hope came into his heart, he trembled.

Another verse of the hymn arose, a slow and mournful strain, such as the pious love, but joined to words which expressed all that our nature can conceive of sin, and darkly hinted at far more. Unfathomable to mere mortals is the lore of fiends. Verse after verse was sung; and still the chorus of the desert swelled between like the deepest tone of a mighty organ; and with the final peal of that dreadful anthem there came a sound, as if the roaring wind, the rushing streams, the howling beasts, and every other voice of the unconcerted wilderness were mingling and according with the voice of guilty man in homage to the prince of all. The four blazing pines threw up a loftier flame, and obscurely discovered shapes and visages of horror on the smoke wreaths above the impious assembly. At the same moment the fire on the rock shot redly forth and formed a glowing arch above its base, where now appeared a figure. With reverence be it spoken, the figure bore no slight similitude, both in garb and manner, to some grave divine of the New England churches.

"Bring forth the converts!" cried a voice that echoed through the field and rolled into the forest.

At the word, Goodman Brown stepped forth from the shadow of the trees and approached the congregation, with whom he felt a loathful brotherhood by the sympathy of all that was wicked in his heart. He could have well-nigh sworn that the shape of his own dead father beckoned him to advance, looking downward from a smoke wreath, while a woman, with dim features of despair, threw out her hand to warn him back. Was it his mother? But he had no power to retreat one step, nor to resist, even in thought, when the minister and good old Deacon Gookin seized his arms and led him to the blazing rock. Thither came also the slender form of a veiled female, led between Goody Cloyse, that pious teacher of the catechism, and Martha Carrier, who had received the devil's promise to be queen of hell. A rampant hag was she. And there stood the proselytes beneath the canopy of fire.

"Welcome, my children," said the dark figure, "to the communion of your race. Ye have found thus young your nature and your destiny. My children, look behind you!"

They turned; and flashing forth, as it were, in a sheet of flame, the fiend worshippers were seen; the smile of welcome gleamed darkly on every visage.

"There," resumed the sable form, "are all whom ye have reverenced from youth. Ye deemed them holier than yourselves, and shrank from your own sin, contrasting it with their lives of righteousness and prayerful aspirations heavenward. Yet here are they all in my worshipping assembly. This night it shall be granted you to know their secret deeds: how hoary-bearded elders of the church have whispered wanton words to the young maids of their households; how many a woman, eager for widows' weeds, has given her husband a drink at bedtime and let him sleep his last sleep in her bosom; how beardless youths have made haste to inherit their fathers' wealth; and how fair damsels—blush not, sweet ones—have dug little graves in the garden, and bidden me, the sole guest to an infant's funeral. By the sympathy of your human hearts for sin ye shall scent out all the places—whether in church, bedchamber, street, field, or forest—where crime has been committed, and shall exult to behold the whole earth one stain of guilt, one mighty blood spot. Far more than this. It shall be yours to penetrate, in every bosom, the deep mystery of sin, the fountain of all wicked arts, and which inexhaustibly supplies more evil impulses than human power—than my power at its utmost—can make manifest in deeds. And now, my children, look upon each other."

They did so; and, by the blaze of the hell-kindled torches, the wretched man beheld his Faith, and the wife her husband, trembling before that unhallowed altar.

"Lo, there ye stand, my children," said the figure, in a deep and solemn tone, almost sad with its despairing awfulness, as if his once angelic nature could yet mourn for our miserable race. "Depending upon one another's hearts, ye had still hoped that virtue were not all a dream. Now are ye undeceived. Evil is the nature of mankind. Evil must be your only happiness. Welcome again, my children, to the communion of your race."

"Welcome," repeated the fiend worshippers, in one cry of despair and triumph.

And there they stood, the only pair, as it seemed, who were yet hesitating on the verge of wickedness in this dark world. A basin was hollowed, naturally, in the rock. Did it contain water, reddened by the lurid light? or was it blood? or, perchance, a liquid flame? Herein did the shape of evil dip his hand and prepare to lay the mark of baptism upon their foreheads, that they might be partakers of the mystery of sin, more conscious of the secret guilt of others, both in deed and thought, than they could now be of their own. The husband cast one look at his pale wife, and Faith at him. What polluted wretches would the next glance show them to each other, shuddering alike at what they disclosed and what they saw!

"Faith! Faith!" cried the husband, "look up to heaven, and resist the wicked one."

Whether Faith obeyed he knew not. Hardly had he spoken when he found himself amid calm night and solitude, listening to a roar of the wind which died heavily away through the forest. He staggered against the rock, and felt it chill and damp; while a hanging twig, that had been all on fire, besprinkled his cheek with the coldest dew.

The next morning young Goodman Brown came slowly into the street of Salem village, staring around him like a bewildered man. The good old minister was taking a walk along the graveyard to get an appetite for breakfast and meditate his sermon, and bestowed a blessing, as he passed, on Goodman Brown. He shrank from the venerable saint as if to avoid an anathema. Old Deacon Gookin was at domestic worship, and the holy words of his prayer were heard through the open window. "What God doth the wizard pray to?" quoth Goodman Brown. Goody Cloyse, that excellent old Christian, stood in the early sunshine at her own lattice, catechizing a little girl who had brought her a pint of morning's milk. Goodman Brown snatched away the child as from the grasp of the fiend himself. Turning the corner by the meeting-house, he spied the head of Faith, with the pink ribbons, gazing anxiously forth, and bursting into such joy at sight of him that she skipped along the street and almost kissed her husband before the whole village. But Goodman Brown looked sternly and sadly into her face, and passed on without a greeting.

Had Goodman Brown fallen asleep in the forest and only dreamed a wild dream of a witch-meeting?

Be it so if you will; but, alas! it was a dream of evil omen for young Goodman Brown. A stern, a sad, a darkly meditative, a distrustful, if not a desperate man did he become from the night of that fearful dream. On the Sabbath day, when the congregation were singing a holy psalm, he could not listen because an anthem of sin rushed loudly upon his ear and drowned all the blessed strain. When the minister spoke from the pulpit with power and fervid eloquence, and, with his hand on the open Bible, of the sacred truths of our religion, and of saint-like lives and triumphant deaths, and of future bliss or misery unutterable, then did Goodman Brown turn pale, dreading lest the roof should thunder down upon the gray blasphemer and his hearers. Often, waking suddenly at midnight, he shrank from the bosom of Faith; and at morning or eventide, when the family knelt down at prayer, he scowled and muttered to himself, and gazed sternly at his wife, and turned away. And when he had lived long, and was borne to his grave a hoary corpse, followed by Faith, an aged woman, and children and grandchildren, a goodly procession, besides neighbors not a few, they carved no hopeful verse upon his tombstone, for his dying hour was gloom.

The Turn of the Screw

Henry James

The story had held us, round the fire, sufficiently breathless, but except the obvious remark that it was gruesome, as, on Christmas Eve in an old house, a strange tale should essentially be, I remember no comment uttered till somebody happened to say that it was the only case he had met in which such a visitation had fallen on a child. The case, I may mention, was that of an apparition in just such an old house as had gathered us for the occasion—an appearance, of a dreadful kind, to a little boy sleeping in the room with his mother and waking her up in the terror of it; waking her not to dissipate his dread and soothe him to sleep again, but to encounter also, herself, before she had succeeded in doing so, the same sight that had shaken him. It was this observation that drew from Douglas—not immediately, but later in the evening—a reply that had the interesting consequence to which I call attention. Someone else told a story not particularly effective, which I saw he was not following. This I took for a sign that he had himself something to produce and that we should only have to wait. We waited in fact till two nights later; but that same evening, before we scattered, he brought out what was in his mind.

"I quite agree—in regard to Griffin's ghost, or whatever it was—that its appearing first to the little boy, at so tender an age, adds a particular touch. But it's not the first occurrence of its charming kind that I know to have involved a child. If the child gives the effect another turn of the screw, what do you say to *two* children—?"

"We say, of course," somebody exclaimed, "that they give two turns! Also that we want to hear about them."

I can see Douglas there before the fire, to which he had got up to present his back, looking down at his interlocutor with his hands in his pockets. "Nobody but me, till now, has ever heard. It's quite too horrible." This, naturally, was declared by several voices to give the thing the utmost price, and our friend, with quiet art, prepared his triumph by turning his eyes over the rest of us and going on: "It's beyond everything. Nothing at all that I know touches it."

"For sheer terror?" I remember asking.

He seemed to say it was not so simple as that; to be really at a loss how to qualify it. He passed his hand over his eyes, made a little wincing grimace. "For dreadful—dreadfulness!"

"Oh, how delicious!" cried one of the women.

He took no notice of her; he looked at me, but as if, instead of me, he saw what he spoke of. "For general uncanny ugliness and horror and pain."

"Well then," I said, "just sit right down and begin."

He turned round to the fire, gave a kick to a log, watched it an instant. Then as he faced us again: "I can't begin. I shall have to send to town." There was a unanimous groan at this, and much reproach; after which, in his preoccupied way, he explained. "The story's written. It's in a locked drawer—it has not been out for years. I could write to my man and enclose the key; he could send down the packet as he finds it." It was to me in particular that he appeared to propound this—appeared almost to appeal for aid not to hesitate. He had broken a thickness of ice, the formation of many a winter; had had his reasons for a long silence. The others resented postponement, but it was just his scruples that charmed me. I adjured him to write by the first post and to agree with us for an early hearing; then I asked him if the experience in question had been his own. To this his answer was prompt. "Oh, thank God, no!"

"And is the record yours? You took the thing down?"

"Nothing but the impression. I took that *here*"—he tapped his heart. "I've never lost it."

"Then your manuscript—?"

"Is in old, faded ink, and in the most beautiful hand." He hung fire again. "A woman's. She has been dead these twenty years. She sent me the pages in question before she died." They were all listening now, and of course there was somebody to be arch, or at any rate to draw the inference. But if he put the inference by without a smile it was also without irritation. "She was a most charming person, but she was ten years older than I. She was my sister's governess," he quietly said. "She was the most agreeable woman I've ever known in her position; she would have been worthy of any whatever. It was long ago, and this episode was long before. I was at Trinity, and I found her at home on my coming down the second summer. I was much there that year—it was a beautiful one; and we had, in her off-hours, some strolls and talks in the garden—talks in which she struck me as awfully clever and nice. Oh yes; don't grin: I liked her extremely and am glad to this day to think she liked me, too. If she hadn't she wouldn't have told me. She had never told anyone. It wasn't simply that she said so, but that I knew she hadn't. I was sure; I could see. You'll easily judge why when you hear."

"Because the thing had been such a scare?"

He continued to fix me. "You'll easily judge," he repeated: "You will."

I fixed him, too. "I see. She was in love."

He laughed for the first time. "You *are* acute. Yes, she was in love. That is, she had been. That came out—she couldn't tell her story without its coming out. I saw it, and she saw I saw it; but neither of us spoke of it. I remember the time and the place—the corner of the lawn, the shade of the great beeches and the long, hot summer afternoon. It wasn't a scene for a shudder; but oh—!" He quitted the fire and dropped back into his chair.

"You'll receive the packet Thursday morning?" I inquired.

"Probably not till the second post."

"Well then; after dinner—"

"You'll all meet me here?" He looked us round again. "Isn't anybody going?" It was almost the tone of hope.

"Everybody will stay!"

"*I* will"—and "I will!" cried the ladies whose departure had been fixed. Mrs. Griffin, however, expressed the need for a little more light. "Who was it she was in love with?"

"The story will tell," I took upon myself to reply.

"Oh, I can't wait for the story!"

"The story *won't* tell," said Douglas; "not in any literal, vulgar way."

"More's the pity, then. That's the only way I ever understand."

"Won't *you* tell, Douglas?" somebody else inquired.

He sprang to his feet again. "Yes—tomorrow. Now I must go to bed. Good night." And quickly catching up a candlestick, he left us slightly bewildered. From our end of the great brown hall we heard his step on the stair; whereupon Mrs. Griffin spoke. "Well, if I don't know who she was in love with, I know who *he* was."

"She was ten years older," said her husband.

"Raison de plus—at that age! But it's rather nice, his long reticence."

"Forty years!" Griffin put in.

"With this outbreak at last."

"The outbreak," I returned, "will make a tremendous occasion of Thursday night"; and everyone so agreed with me that, in the light of it, we lost all attention for everything else. The last story, however incomplete and like the mere opening of a serial, had been told; we handshook and "candlestuck," as somebody said, and went to bed.

I knew the next day that a letter containing the key had, by the first post, gone off to his London apartments; but in spite of—or perhaps just on account of—the eventual diffusion of this knowledge we quite let him alone till after dinner, till such an hour of the evening, in fact, as might best accord with the kind of emotion on which our hopes were fixed. Then he became as communicative as we could desire and indeed gave us his best reason for being so. We had it from him again before the fire in the hall, as we had had our mild wonders of the previous night. It appeared that the narrative he had promised to read us really required for a proper intelligence a few words of prologue. Let me say here distinctly, to have done with it, that this narrative, from an exact transcript of my own made much later, is what I shall presently give. Poor Douglas, before his death—when it was in sight—committed to me the manuscript that reached him on the third of these days and that, on the same spot, with immense effect, he began to read to our hushed little circle on the night of the fourth. The departing ladies who had said they would stay didn't, of course, thank heaven, stay: they departed, in consequence of arrangements made, in a rage of curiosity, as they professed, produced by the touches with which he had already worked us up. But that only made his little final auditory more compact and select, kept it, round the hearth, subject to a common thrill.

The first of these touches conveyed that the written statement took up the tale at a point after it had, in a manner, begun. The fact to be in possession of was therefore that his old friend, the youngest of several daughters of a poor country parson, had, at the age of twenty, on taking service for the first time in the schoolroom, come up to London, in trepidation, to answer in person an advertisement that had already placed her in brief correspondence with the advertiser. This person proved, on her presenting herself, for judgment, at a house in Harley Street, that impressed her as vast and imposing—this prospective patron proved a gentleman, a bachelor in the prime of life, such a figure as had never risen, save in a dream or an old novel, before a fluttered, anxious girl out of a Hampshire vicarage. One could easily fix his type; it never, happily, dies out. He was handsome and bold and pleasant, offhand and gay and kind. He struck her, inevitably, as gallant and splendid, but what took her most of all and gave her the courage she afterward showed was that he put the whole thing to her as a kind of favor, an obligation he should gratefully incur. She conceived him as rich, but as fearfully extravagant—saw him all in a glow of high fashion, of good looks, of expensive habits, of charming ways with women. He had for his own town residence a big house filled with the spoils of travel and the trophies of the chase; but it was to his country home, an old family place in Essex, that he wished her immediately to proceed.

He had been left, by the death of their parents in India, guardian to a small nephew and a small niece, children of a younger, a military brother, whom he had lost two years before. These children were, by the strangest of chances for a man in his position—a lone man without the right sort of experience or a grain of patience—very heavily on his hands. It had all been a great worry and, on his own part doubtless, a series of blunders, but he immensely pitied the poor chicks and had done all he could; had in particular sent them down to his other house, the proper place for them being of course the country, and kept them there, from the first, with the best people he could find to look after them, parting even with his own servants to wait on them and going down himself, whenever he might, to see how they were doing. The awkward thing was that they had practically no other relations and that his own affairs took up all his time. He had put them in possession of Bly, which was healthy and secure, and had placed at the head of their little establishment—but below stairs only—an excellent woman, Mrs. Grose, whom he was sure his visitor would like and who had formerly been maid to his mother. She was now housekeeper and was also acting for the time as superintendent to the little girl, of whom, without children of her own, she was, by good luck, extremely fond. There were plenty of people to help, but of course the young lady who should go down as governess would be in supreme authority. She would also have, in holidays, to look after the small boy, who had been for a term at school—young as he was to be sent, but what else could be done?—and who, as the holidays were about to begin, would be back from one day to the other. There had been for the two children at first a young lady whom they had had the misfortune to lose. She had done for them quite beautifully—she was a most respectable person—till her death, the great awkwardness of which had, precisely, left no alternative but the school for little Miles. Mrs. Grose, since then, in the way of manners and things, had done as she could for Flora; and there were, further, a cook, a housemaid, a dairywoman, an old pony, an old groom, and an old gardener, all likewise thoroughly respectable.

So far had Douglas presented his picture when someone put a question. "And what did the former governess die of?—of so much respectability?"

Our friend's answer was prompt. "That will come out. I don't anticipate."

"Excuse me—I thought that was just what you *are* doing."

"In her successor's place," I suggested, "I should have wished to learn if the office brought with it—"

"Necessary danger to life?" Douglas completed my thought. "She did wish to learn, and she did learn. You shall hear tomorrow what she learned. Meanwhile, of course, the prospect struck her as slightly grim. She was young, untried, nervous: it was a vision of serious duties and little company, of really great loneliness. She hesitated—took a couple of days to consult and consider.

But the salary offered much exceeded her modest measure, and on a second interview she faced the music, she engaged." And Douglas, with this, made a pause that, for the benefit of the company, moved me to throw in—

"The moral of which was of course the seduction exercised by the splendid young man. She succumbed to it."

He got up and, as he had done the night before, went to the fire, gave a stir to a log with his foot, then stood a moment with his back to us. "She saw him only twice."

"Yes, but that's just the beauty of her passion."

A little to my surprise, on this, Douglas turned round to me. "It was the beauty of it. There were others," he went on, "who hadn't succumbed. He told her frankly all his difficulty—that for several applicants the conditions had been prohibitive. They were, somehow, simply afraid. It sounded dull—it sounded strange; and all the more so because of his main condition."

"Which was—?"

"That she should never trouble him—but never, never: neither appeal nor complain nor write about anything; only meet all questions herself, receive all moneys from his solicitor, take the whole thing over and let him alone. She promised to do this, and she mentioned to me that when, for a moment, disburdened, delighted, he held her hand, thanking her for the sacrifice, she already felt rewarded."

"But was that all her reward?" one of the ladies asked.

"She never saw him again."

"Oh!" said the lady; which, as our friend immediately left us again, was the only other word of importance contributed to the subject till, the next night, by the corner of the hearth, in the best chair, he opened the faded red cover of a thin old-fashioned gilt-edged album. The whole thing took indeed more nights than one, but on the first occasion the same lady put another question. "What is your title?"

"I haven't one."

"Oh, *I* have!" I said. But Douglas, without heeding me, had begun to read with a fine clearness that was like a rendering to the ear of the beauty of his author's hand.

I

I remember the whole beginning as a succession of flights and drops, a little seesaw of the right throbs and the wrong. After rising, in town, to meet his appeal, I had at all events a couple of very bad days—found myself doubtful again, felt indeed sure I had made a mistake. In this state of mind I spent the long hours of bumping, swinging coach that carried me to the stopping place at which I was to be met by a vehicle from the house. This convenience, I was told, had been ordered, and I found, toward the close of the June afternoon, a commodious fly in waiting for me. Driving at that hour, on a lovely day, through a country to which the summer sweetness seemed to offer me a friendly welcome, my fortitude mounted afresh and, as we turned into the avenue, encountered a reprieve that was probably but a proof of the point to which it had sunk. I suppose I had expected, or had dreaded, something so melancholy that what greeted me was a good surprise. I remember as a most pleasant impression the broad, clear front, its open windows and fresh curtains and the pair of maids looking out; I remember the lawn and the bright flowers and the crunch of my wheels on the gravel and the clustered treetops over which the rooks circled and cawed in the golden sky. The scene had a greatness that made it a different affair from my own scant home, and there immediately appeared at the door, with a little girl in her hand, a civil person who dropped me as decent a curtsy as if I had been the mistress or a distinguished visitor. I had received in Harley Street a narrower notion of the place, and that, as I recalled it, made me think the proprietor still more of a gentleman, suggested that what I was to enjoy might be something beyond his promise.

I had no drop again till the next day, for I was carried triumphantly through the following hours by my introduction to the younger of my pupils. The little girl who accompanied Mrs. Grose appeared to me on the spot a creature so charming as to make it a great fortune to have to do with her. She was the most beautiful child I had ever seen, and I afterward wondered that my employer had not told me more of her. I slept little that night—I was too much excited; and this astonished me, too, I recollect, remained with me, adding to my sense of the liberality with which I was treated. The large, impressive room, one of the best in the house, the great state bed, as I almost felt it, the full, figured draperies, the long glasses in which, for the first time, I could see myself from head to foot, all struck me—like the extraordinary charm of my small charge—as so many things thrown in. It was thrown in as well, from the first moment, that I should get on with Mrs. Grose in a relation over which, on my way, in the coach, I fear I had rather brooded. The only thing indeed that in this early outlook might have made me shrink again was the clear circumstance of her being so glad to see me. I perceived within half an hour that she was so glad—stout, simple, plain, clean, wholesome woman—as to be positively on her guard against showing it too much. I wondered even then a little why she should wish not to show it, and that, with reflection, with suspicion, might of course have made me uneasy.

But it was a comfort that there could be no uneasiness in a connection with anything so beatific as the radiant image of my little girl, the vision of whose angelic beauty had probably more than anything else to do with the restlessness that, before morning, made me several times rise and wander about my room to take in the whole picture and prospect; to watch, from my open window, the faint summer dawn, to look at such portions of the rest of the house as I could catch, and to listen, while, in the fading dusk, the first birds began to twitter, for the possible recurrence of a sound or two, less natural and not without, but within, that I had fancied I heard. There had been a moment when I believed I recognized, faint and far, the cry of a child; there had been another when I found myself just consciously starting as at the passage, before my door, of a light footstep. But these fancies were not marked enough not to be thrown off, and it is only in the light, or the gloom, I should rather say, of other and subsequent matters that they now come back to me. To watch, teach, "form" little Flora would too evidently be the making of a happy and useful life. It had been agreed between us downstairs that after this first occasion I should have her as a matter of course at night, her small white bed being already arranged, to that end, in my room. What I had undertaken was the whole care of her, and she had remained, just this last time, with Mrs. Grose only as an effect of our consideration for my inevitable strangeness and her natural timidity. In spite of this timidity—which the child herself, in the oddest way in the world, had been perfectly frank and brave about, allowing it, without a sign of uncomfortable consciousness, with the deep, sweet serenity indeed of one of Raphael's holy infants, to be discussed, to be imputed to her, and to determine us—I feel quite sure she would presently like me. It was part of what I already liked Mrs. Grose herself for, the pleasure I could see her feel in my admiration and wonder as I sat at supper with four tall candles and with my pupil, in a high chair and a bib, brightly facing me, between them, over bread and milk. There were naturally things that in Flora's presence could pass between us only as prodigious and gratified looks, obscure and roundabout allusions.

"And the little boy—does he look like her? Is he too so very remarkable?"

One wouldn't flatter a child. "Oh, miss, *most* remarkable. If you think well of this one!"—and she stood there with a plate in her hand, beaming at our companion, who looked from one of us to the other with placid heavenly eyes that contained nothing to check us.

"Yes; if I do—?"

"You *will* be carried away by the little gentleman!"

"Well, that, I think, is what I came for—to be carried away. I'm afraid, however," I remember feeling the impulse to add, "I'm rather easily carried away. I was carried away in London!"

I can still see Mrs. Grose's broad face as she took this in. "In Harley Street?"

"In Harley Street."

"Well, miss, you're not the first—and you won't be the last."

"Oh, I've no pretension," I could laugh, "to being the only one. My other pupil, at any rate, as I understand, comes back tomorrow?"

"Not tomorrow—Friday, miss. He arrives, as you did, by the coach, under care of the guard, and is to be met by the same carriage."

I forthwith expressed that the proper as well as the pleasant and friendly thing would be therefore that on the arrival of the public conveyance I should be in waiting for him with his little sister; an idea in which Mrs. Grose concurred so heartily that I somehow took her manner as a kind of comforting pledge—never falsified, thank heaven!—that we should on every question be quite at one. Oh, she was glad I was there!

What I felt the next day was, I suppose, nothing that could be fairly called a reaction from the cheer of my arrival; it was probably at the most only a slight oppression produced by a fuller measure of the scale, as I walked round them, gazed up at them, took them in, of my new circumstances. They had, as it were, an extent and mass for which I had not been prepared and in the presence of which I found myself, freshly, a little scared as well as a little proud. Lessons, in this agitation, certainly suffered some delay; I reflected that my first duty was, by the gentlest arts I could contrive, to win the child into the sense of knowing me. I spent the day with her out-of-doors; I arranged with her, to her great satisfaction, that it should be she, she only, who might show me the place. She showed it step by step and room by room and secret by secret, with droll, delightful, childish talk about it and with the result, in half an hour, of our becoming immense friends. Young as she was, I was struck, throughout our little tour, with her confidence and courage with the way, in empty chambers and dull corridors, on crooked staircases that made me pause and even on the summit of an old machicolated square tower that made me dizzy, her morning music, her disposition to tell me so many more things than she asked, rang out and led me on. I have not seen Bly since the day I left it, and I daresay that to my older and more informed eyes it would now appear sufficiently contracted. But as my little conductress, with her hair of gold and her frock of blue, danced before me round corners and pattered down passages, I had the view of a castle of romance inhabited by a rosy sprite, such a place as would somehow, for diversion of the young idea, take all color out of storybooks and fairytales. Wasn't it just a storybook over which I had fallen adoze and adream? No; it was a big, ugly, antique, but convenient house, embodying a few features of a building still older, half-replaced and half-utilized, in which I had the fancy of our being almost as lost as a handful of passengers in a great drifting ship. Well, I was, strangely, at the helm!

II

This came home to me when, two days later, I drove over with Flora to meet, as Mrs. Grose said, the little gentleman; and all the more for an incident that, presenting itself the second evening, had deeply disconcerted me. The first day had been, on the whole, as I have expressed, reassuring; but I was to see it wind up in keen apprehension. The postbag, that evening—it came late—contained a letter for me, which, however, in the hand of my employer, I found to be composed but of a few words enclosing another, addressed to himself, with a seal still unbroken. "This, I recognize, is from the headmaster, and the headmaster's an awful bore. Read him, please; deal with him; but mind you don't report. Not a word. I'm off!" I broke the seal with a great effort—so great a one that I was a long time coming to it; took the unopened missive at last up to my room and only attacked it just before going to bed. I had better have let it wait till morning, for it gave me a second sleepless night. With no counsel to take, the next day, I was full of distress; and it finally got so the better of me that I determined to open myself at least to Mrs. Grose.

"What does it mean? The child's dismissed his school."

She gave me a look that I remarked at the moment; then, visibly, with a quick blankness, seemed to try to take it back. "But aren't they all—?"

"Sent home—yes. But only for the holidays. Miles may never go back at all."

Consciously, under my attention, she reddened. "They won't take him?"

"They absolutely decline."

At this she raised her eyes, which she had turned from me; I saw them fill with good tears. "What has he done?"

I hesitated; then I judged best simply to hand her my letter—which, however, had the effect of making her, without taking it, simply put her hands behind her. She shook her head sadly. "Such things are not for me, miss."

My counselor couldn't read! I winced at my mistake, which I attenuated as I could, and opened my letter again to repeat it to her; then, faltering in the act and folding it up once more, I put it back in my pocket. "Is he really *bad?*"

The tears were still in her eyes. "Do the gentlemen say so?"

"They go into no particulars. They simply express their regret that it should be impossible to keep him. That can have only one meaning." Mrs. Grose listened with dumb emotion; she forbore to ask me what this meaning might be; so that, presently, to put the thing with some coherence and with the mere aid of her presence to my own mind, I went on: "That he's an injury to the others."

At this, with one of the quick turns of simple folk, she suddenly flamed up. "Master Miles! *Him* an injury?"

There was such a flood of good faith in it that, though I had not yet seen the child, my very fears made me jump to the absurdity of the idea. I found myself, to meet my friend the better, offering it, on the spot, sarcastically. "To his poor little innocent mates!"

"It's too dreadful," cried Mrs. Grose, "to say such cruel things! Why, he's scarce ten years old."

"Yes, yes; it would be incredible."

She was evidently grateful for such a profession. "See him, miss, first. Then believe it!" I felt forthwith a new impatience to see him; it was the beginning of a curiosity that, for all the next hours, was to deepen almost to pain. Mrs. Grose was aware, I could judge, of what she had produced in me, and she followed it up with assurance. "You might as well believe it of the little lady. Bless her," she added the next moment—"*look* at her!"

I turned and saw that Flora, whom, ten minutes before, I had established in the schoolroom with a sheet of white paper, a pencil, and a copy of nice "round o's," now presented herself to view at the open door. She expressed in her little way an extraordinary detachment from disagreeable duties, looking to me, however, with a great childish light that seemed to offer it as a mere result of the affection she had conceived for my person, which had rendered necessary that she should follow me. I needed nothing more than this to feel the full force of Mrs. Grose's comparison, and, catching my pupil in my arms, covered her with kisses in which there was a sob of atonement.

Nonetheless, the rest of the day I watched for further occasion to approach my colleague, especially as, toward evening, I began to fancy she rather sought to avoid me. I overtook her, I remember, on the staircase; we went down together, and at the bottom I detained her, holding her there with a hand on her arm. "I take what you said to me at noon as a declaration that you've never known him to be bad."

She threw back her head; she had clearly, by this time, and very honestly, adopted an attitude. "Oh, never known him—I don't pretend *that!*"

I was upset again. "Then you *have* known him—?"

"Yes indeed, miss, thank God!"

On reflection I accepted this. "You mean that a boy who never is—?"

"Is no boy for *me!*"

I held her tighter. "You like them with the spirit to be naughty?" Then, keeping pace with her answer, "So do I!" I eagerly brought out. "But not to the degree to contaminate—"

"To contaminate?"—my big word left her at a loss. I explained it. "To corrupt."

She stared, taking my meaning in; but it produced in her an odd laugh. "Are you afraid he'll corrupt *you?*" She put the question with such a fine bold humor that, with a laugh, a little silly doubtless, to match her own, I gave way for the time to the apprehension of ridicule.

But the next day, as the hour for my drive approached, I cropped up in another place. "What was the lady who was here before?"

"The last governess? She was also young and pretty—almost as young and almost as pretty, miss, even as you."

"Ah, then, I hope her youth and her beauty helped her!" I recollect throwing off. "He seems to like us young and pretty!"

"Oh, he *did*," Mrs. Grose assented: "it was the way he liked everyone!" She had no sooner spoken indeed than she caught herself up. "I mean that's *his* way—the master's."

I was struck. "But of whom did you speak first?"

She looked blank, but she colored. "Why, of *him*."

"Of the master?"

"Of who else?"

There was so obviously no one else that the next moment I had lost my impression of her having accidentally said more than she meant; and I merely asked what I wanted to know. "Did *she* see anything in the boy—?"

"That wasn't right? She never told me."

I had a scruple, but I overcame it. "Was she careful—particular?"

Mrs. Grose appeared to try to be conscientious. "About some things—yes."

"But not about all?"

Again she considered. "Well, miss—she's gone. I won't tell tales."

"I quite understand your feeling," I hastened to reply; but I thought it, after an instant, not opposed to this concession to pursue: "Did she die here?"

"No—she went off."

I don't know what there was in this brevity of Mrs. Grose's that struck me as ambiguous. "Went off to die?" Mrs. Grose looked straight out of the window, but I felt that, hypothetically, I had a right to know what young persons engaged for Bly were expected to do. "She was taken ill, you mean, and went home?"

"She was not taken ill, so far as appeared, in this house. She left it, at the end of the year, to go home, as she said, for a short holiday, to which the time she had put in had certainly given her a right. We had then a young woman—a nursemaid who had stayed on and who was a good girl and clever; and *she* took the children altogether for the interval. But our young lady never came back, and at the very moment I was expecting her I heard from the master that she was dead."

I turned this over. "But of what?"

"He never told me! But please, miss," said Mrs. Grose, "I must get to my work."

III

Her thus turning her back on me was fortunately not, for my just preoccupations, a snub that could check the growth of our mutual esteem. We met, after I had brought home little Miles, more intimately than ever on the ground of my stupefaction, my general emotion: so monstrous was I then ready to pronounce it that such a child as had now been revealed to me should be under an interdict. I was a little late on the scene, and I felt, as he stood wistfully looking out for me before the door of the inn at which the coach had put him down, that I had seen him, on the instant, without and within, in the great glow of freshness, the same positive fragrance of purity, in which I had, from the first moment, seen his little sister. He was incredibly beautiful, and Mrs. Grose had put her finger on it: everything but a sort of passion of tenderness for him was swept away by his presence. What I then and there took him to my heart for was something divine that I have never found to the same degree in any child—his indescribable little air of knowing nothing in the world but love. It would have been impossible to carry a bad name with a greater sweetness of innocence, and by the time I had got back to Bly with him I remained merely bewildered—so far, that is, as I was not outraged—by the sense of the horrible letter locked up in my room, in a drawer. As soon as I could compass a private word with Mrs. Grose I declared to her that it was grotesque.

She promptly understood me. "You mean the cruel charge—?"

"It doesn't live an instant. My dear woman, *look* at him!"

She smiled at my pretention to have discovered his charm. "I assure you, miss, I do nothing else! What will you say, then?" she immediately added.

"In answer to the letter?" I had made up my mind. "Nothing."

"And to his uncle?"

I was incisive. "Nothing."

"And to the boy himself?"

I was wonderful. "Nothing."

She gave with her apron a great wipe to her mouth. "Then I'll stand by you. We'll see it out."

"We'll see it out!" I ardently echoed, giving her my hand to make it a vow.

She held me there a moment, then whisked up her apron again with her detached hand. "Would you mind, miss, if I used the freedom—"

"To kiss me? No!" I took the good creature in my arms and, after we had embraced like sisters, felt still more fortified and indignant.

This, at all events, was for the time: a time so full that, as I recall the way it went, it reminds me of all the art I now need to make it a little distinct. What I look back at with amazement is the situation I accepted. I had undertaken, with my companion, to see it out, and I was under a charm, apparently, that could smooth away the extent and the far and difficult connections of such an effort. I was lifted aloft on a great wave of infatuation and pity. I found it simple, in my ignorance, my confusion, and perhaps my conceit, to assume that I could deal with a boy whose education for the world was all on the point of beginning. I am unable even to remember at this day what proposal I framed for the end of his holidays and the resumption of his studies. Lessons with me, indeed, that charming summer, we all had a theory that he was to have; but I now feel that, for weeks, the lessons must have been rather my own. I learned something—at first, certainly—that had not been one of the teachings of my small, smothered life; learned to be amused, and even amusing, and not to think for the morrow. It was the first time, in a manner, that I had known space and air and freedom, all the music of summer and all the mystery of nature. And then there was consideration—and consideration was sweet. Oh, it was a trap—not designed, but deep—to my imagination, to my delicacy, perhaps to my vanity; to whatever, in me, was most excitable. The best way to picture it all is to say that I was off my guard. They gave me so little trouble—they were of a gentleness so extraordinary. I used to speculate—but even this with a dim disconnectedness—as to how the rough future (for all futures are rough!) would handle them and might bruise them. They had the bloom of health and happiness; and yet, as if I had been in charge of a pair of little grandees, of princes of the blood, for whom everything, to be right, would have to be enclosed and protected, the only form that, in my fancy, the afteryears could take for them was that of a romantic, a really royal extension of the garden and the park. It may be, of course, above all, that what suddenly broke into this gives the previous time a charm of stillness—that hush in which something gathers or crouches. The change was actually like the spring of a beast.

In the first weeks the days were long; they often, at their finest, gave me what I used to call my own hour, the hour when, for my pupils, teatime and bedtime having come and gone, I had, before my final retirement, a small interval alone. Much as I liked my companions, this hour was the thing in the day I liked most; and I liked it best of all when, as the light faded—or rather, I should say, the day lingered and the last calls of the last birds sounded, in a flushed sky, from the old trees—I could take a turn into the grounds and enjoy, almost with a sense of property that amused and flattered me, the beauty and dignity of the place. It was a pleasure at these moments to feel myself tranquil and justified; doubtless, perhaps, also to reflect that by my discretion, my quiet good sense and general high propriety, I was giving pleasure—if he ever thought of it!—to the person to whose pressure I had responded. What I was doing was what he had earnestly hoped and directly asked of me, and that I *could*, after all, do it proved even a greater joy than I had expected. I daresay I fancied myself, in short, a remarkable young woman and took comfort in the faith that this would more publicly appear. Well, I needed to be remarkable to offer a front to the remarkable things that presently gave their first sign.

It was plump, one afternoon, in the middle of my very hour: the children were tucked away, and I had come out for my stroll. One of the thoughts that, as I don't in the least shrink now from noting, used to be with me in these wanderings was that it would be as charming as a charming story suddenly to meet someone. Someone would appear there at the turn of a path and would stand before me and smile and approve. I didn't ask more than that—I only asked that he should *know;* and the only way to be sure he knew would be to see it, and the kind light of it, in his handsome face. That was exactly present to me—by which I mean the face was—when, on the first of these occasions, at the end of a long June day, I stopped short on emerging from one of the plantations and coming into view of the house. What arrested me on the spot—and with a shock much greater than any vision had allowed for—was the sense that my imagination had, in a flash, turned real. He did stand there!—but high up, beyond the lawn and at the very top of the tower to which, on that first morning, little Flora had conducted me. This tower was one of a pair—square, incongruous, crenelated structures—that were distinguished, for some reason, though I could see little difference, as the new and the old. They flanked opposite ends of the house and were probably architectural absurdities, redeemed in a measure indeed by not being wholly disengaged nor of a height too pretentious, dating, in their gingerbread antiquity, from a romantic revival that was already a respectable past. I admired them, had fancies about them, for we could all profit in a degree, especially when they loomed through the dusk, by the grandeur of their actual battlements; yet it was not at such an elevation that the figure I had so often invoked seemed most in place.

It produced in me, this figure, in the clear twilight, I remember, two distinct gasps of emotion, which were, sharply, the shock of my first and that of my second surprise. My second was a violent perception of the mistake of my first: the man who met my eyes was not the person I had precipitately supposed. There came to me thus a bewilderment of vision of which, after these years, there is no living view that I can hope to give. An unknown man in a lonely place is a permitted object of fear to a young woman privately bred; and the figure that faced me was—a few more seconds assured me—as little anyone else I knew as it was the image that had been in my mind. I had not seen it in Harley Street—I had not seen it anywhere. The place, moreover, in the strangest way in the world, had, on the instant, and by the very fact of its appearance, become a solitude. To me at least, making my statement here with a deliberation with which I have never made it, the whole feeling of the moment returns. It was as if, while I took in—what I did take in—all the rest of the scene had been stricken with death. I can hear again, as I write, the intense hush in which the sounds of evening dropped. The rooks stopped cawing in the golden sky, and the friendly hour lost, for the minute, all its voice. But there was no other change in nature, unless indeed it were a change that I saw with a stranger sharpness. The gold was still in the sky, the clearness in the air, and the man who looked at me over the battlements was as definite as a picture in a frame. That's how I thought, with extraordinary quickness, of each person that he might have been and that he was not. We were confronted across our distance quite long enough for me to ask myself with intensity who then he was and to feel, as an effect of my inability to say, a wonder that in a few instants more became intense.

The great question, or one of these, is, afterward, I know, with regard to certain matters, the question of how long they have lasted. Well, this matter of mine, think what you will of it, lasted while I caught at a dozen possibilities, none of which made a difference for the better, that I could see, in there having been in the house—and for how long, above all?—a person of whom I was in ignorance. It lasted while I just bridled a little with the sense that my office demanded that there should be no such ignorance and no such person. It lasted while this visitant, at all events—and there was a touch of the strange freedom, as I remember, in the sign of familiarity of his wearing no hat—seemed to fix me, from his position, with just the question, just the scrutiny through the fading light, that his own presence provoked. We were too far apart to call to each other, but there was a moment at which, at shorter range, some challenge between us, breaking the hush, would have been the right result of our straight mutual stare. He was in one of the angles, the one away from the house, very erect, as it struck me, and with both hands on the ledge. So I saw him as I see the letters I form on this page; then, exactly, after a minute, as if to add to the spectacle, he slowly changed his place—passed, looking at me hard all the while, to the opposite corner of the platform. Yes, I had the sharpest sense that during this transit he never took his eyes from me, and I can see at this moment the way his hand, as he went, passed from one of the crenelations to the next. He stopped at the other corner, but less long, and even as he turned away still markedly fixed me. He turned away; that was all I knew.

IV

It was not that I didn't wait, on this occasion, for more, for I was rooted as deeply as I was shaken. Was there a "secret" at Bly—a mystery of Udolpho or an insane, an unmentionable relative kept in unsuspected confinement? I can't say how long I turned it over, or how long, in a confusion of curiosity and dread, I remained where I had had my collision; I only recall that when I re-entered the house darkness had quite closed in. Agitation, in the interval, certainly had held me and driven me, for I must, in circling about the place, have walked three miles; but I was to be, later on, so much more overwhelmed that this mere dawn of alarm was a comparatively human chill. The most singular part of it, in fact—singular as the rest had been—was the part I became, in the hall, aware of in meeting Mrs. Grose. This picture comes back to me in the general train—the impression, as I received it on my return, of the wide white panelled space, bright in the lamplight and with its portraits and red carpet, and of the good surprised look of my friend, which immediately told me she had missed me. It came to me straightway, under her contact, that, with plain heartiness, mere relieved anxiety at my appearance, she knew nothing whatever that could bear upon the incident I had there ready for her. I had not suspected in advance that her comfortable face would pull me up, and

I somehow measured the importance of what I had seen by my thus finding myself hesitate to mention it. Scarce anything in the whole history seems to me so odd as this fact that my real beginning of fear was one, as I may say, with the instinct of sparing my companion. On the spot, accordingly, in the pleasant hall and with her eyes on me, I, for a reason that I couldn't then have phrased, achieved an inward resolution—offered a vague pretext for my lateness and, with the plea of the beauty of the night and of the heavy dew and wet feet, went as soon as possible to my room.

Here it was another affair; here, for many days after, it was a queer affair enough. There were hours, from day to day—or at least there were moments, snatched even from clear duties—when I had to shut myself up to think. It was not so much yet that I was more nervous than I could bear to be as that I was remarkably afraid of becoming so; for the truth I had now to turn over was, simply and clearly, the truth that I could arrive at no account whatever of the visitor with whom I had been so inexplicably and yet, as it seemed to me, so intimately concerned. It took little time to see that I could sound without forms of inquiry and without exciting remark any domestic complications. The shock I had suffered must have sharpened all my senses; I felt sure, at the end of three days and as the result of mere closer attention, that I had not been practiced upon by the servants nor made the object of any "game." Of whatever it was that I knew, nothing was known around me. There was but one sane inference: someone had taken a liberty rather gross. That was what, repeatedly, I dipped into my room and locked the door to say to myself. We had been, collectively, subject to an intrusion; some unscrupulous traveler, curious in old houses, had made his way in unobserved, enjoyed the prospect from the best point of view, and then stolen out as he came. If he had given me such a bold hard stare, that was but a part of his indiscretion. The good thing, after all, was that we should surely see no more of him.

This was not so good a thing, I admit, as not to leave me to judge that what, essentially, made nothing else much signify was simply my charming work. My charming work was just my life with Miles and Flora, and through nothing could I so like it as through feeling that I could throw myself into it in trouble. The attraction of my small charges was a constant joy, leading me to wonder afresh at the vanity of my original fears, the distaste I had begun by entertaining for the probable gray prose of my office. There was to be no gray prose, it appeared, and no long grind; so how could work not be charming that presented itself as daily beauty? It was all the romance of the nursery and the poetry of the schoolroom. I don't mean by this, of course, that we studied only fiction and verse; I mean I can express no otherwise the sort of interest my companions inspired. How can I describe that except by saying that instead of growing used to them—and it's a marvel for a governess: I call the sisterhood to witness!—I made constant fresh discoveries. There was one direction, assuredly, in which these discoveries stopped: deep obscurity continued to cover the region of the boy's conduct at school. It had been promptly given me, I have noted, to face that mystery without a pang. Perhaps even it would be nearer the truth to say that—without a word—he himself had cleared it up. He had made the whole charge absurd. My conclusion bloomed there with the real rose flush of his innocence: he was only too fine and fair for the little horrid, unclean school world, and he had paid a price for it. I reflected acutely that the sense of such differences, such superiorities of quality, always, on the part of the majority—which could include even stupid, sordid headmasters—turn infallibly to the vindictive.

Both the children had a gentleness (it was their only fault, and it never made Miles a muff) that kept them—how shall I express it?—almost impersonal and certainly quite unpunishable. They were like the cherubs of the anecdote, who had—morally, at any rate—nothing to whack! I remember feeling with Miles in especial as if he had had, as it were, no history. We expect of a small child a scant one, but there was in this beautiful little boy something extraordinarily sensitive, yet extraordinarily happy, that, more than in any creature of his age I have seen, struck me as beginning anew each day. He had never for a second suffered. I took this as a direct disproof of his having really been chastised. If he had been wicked he would have "caught" it, and I should have caught it by the rebound—I should have found the trace. I found nothing at all, and he was therefore an angel. He never spoke of his school, never mentioned a comrade or a master; and I, for my part, was quite too much disgusted to allude to them. Of course I was under the spell, and the wonderful part is that, even at the time, I perfectly knew I was. But I gave myself up to it; it was an antidote to any pain, and I had more pains than one. I was in receipt in these days of disturbing letters from home, where things were not going well. But with my children, what things in the world mattered? That was the question I used to put to my scrappy retirements. I was dazzled by their loveliness.

There was a Sunday—to get on—when it rained with such force and for so many hours that there could be no procession to church; in consequence of which, as the day declined, I had arranged with Mrs. Grose that, should the evening show improvement, we would attend together the late service. The rain happily stopped, and I prepared for our walk, which, through the park and by the good road to the village, would be a matter of twenty minutes. Coming downstairs to meet my colleague in the hall, I remembered a pair of gloves that had required three stitches and that had received them—with a publicity perhaps not edifying—while I sat with the children at their tea, served on Sundays, by exception, in that cold, clean temple of mahogany and brass, the "grown-up" dining room. The gloves had been dropped there, and I turned in to recover them. The day was gray enough, but the afternoon light still lingered, and it enabled me, on crossing the threshold, not only to recognize, on a chair near the wide window, then closed, the articles I wanted, but to become aware of a person on the other side of the window and looking straight in. One step into the room had sufficed; my vision was instantaneous; it was all there. The person looking straight in was the person who had already appeared to me. He appeared thus again with I won't say greater distinctness, for that was impossible, but with a nearness that represented a forward stride in our intercourse and made me, as I met him, catch my breath and turn cold. He was the same—he was the same, and seen, this time, as he had been seen before, from the waist up, the window, though the dining room was on the ground floor, not going down to the terrace on which he stood. His face was close to the glass, yet the effect of this better view was, strangely, only to show me how intense the former had been. He remained but a few seconds—long enough to convince me he also saw and recognized; but it was as if I had been looking at him for years and had known him always. Something, however, happened this time that had not happened before; his stare into my face, through the glass and across the room, was as deep and hard as then, but it quitted me for a moment during which I could still watch it, see it fix successively several other things. On the spot there came to me the added shock of a certitude that it was not for me he had come there. He had come for someone else.

The flash of this knowledge—for it was knowledge in the midst of dread—produced in me the most extraordinary effect, started as I stood there, a sudden vibration of duty and courage. I say courage because I was beyond all doubt already far gone. I bounded straight out of the door again, reached that of the house, got, in an instant, upon the drive, and, passing along the terrace as fast as I could rush, turned a corner and came full in sight. But it was in sight of nothing now—my visitor had vanished. I stopped, I almost dropped, with the real relief of this; but I took in the whole scene—I gave him time to reappear. I call it time, but how long was it? I can't speak to the purpose today of the duration of these things. That kind of measure must have left me: they couldn't have lasted as they actually appeared to me to last. The terrace and the whole place, the lawn and the garden beyond it, all I could see of the park, were empty with a great emptiness. There were shrubberies and big trees, but I remember the clear assurance I felt that none of them concealed him. He was there or was not there: not there if I didn't see him. I got hold of this; then, instinctively, instead of returning as I had come, went to the window. It was confusedly present to me that I ought to place myself where he had stood. I did so; I applied my face to the pane and looked, as he had looked, into the room. As if, at this moment, to show me exactly what his range had been, Mrs. Grose, as I had done for himself just before, came in from the hall. With this I had the full image of a repetition of what had already occurred. She saw me as I had seen my own visitant; she pulled up short as I had done; I gave her something of the shock that I had received. She turned white, and this made me ask myself if I had blanched as much. She stared, in short, and retreated on just my lines, and I knew she had then passed out and come round to me and that I should presently meet her. I remained where I was, and while I waited I thought of more things than one. But there's only one I take space to mention. I wondered why *she* should be scared.

V

Oh, she let me know as soon as, round the corner of the house, she loomed again into view. "What in the name of goodness is the matter—?" She was now flushed and out of breath.

I said nothing till she came quite near. "With me?" I must have made a wonderful face. "Do I show it?"

"You're as white as a sheet. You look awful."

I considered; I could meet on this, without scruple, any innocence. My need to respect the bloom of Mrs. Grose's had dropped, without a rustle, from my shoulders, and if I wavered for the instant it was not with what I kept back. I put out my hand to her and she took it; I held her hard a little, liking to feel her close to me. There was a kind of support in the shy heave of her surprise. "You came for me for church, of course, but I can't go."

"Has anything happened?"

"Yes. You must know now. Did I look very queer?"

"Through this window? Dreadful!"

"Well," I said, "I've been frightened." Mrs. Grose's eyes expressed plainly that *she* had no wish to be, yet also that she knew too well her place not to be ready to share with me any marked inconvenience. Oh, it was quite settled that she *must* share! "Just what you saw from the dining room a minute ago was the effect of that. What I saw—just before—was much worse."

Her hand tightened. "What was it?"

"An extraordinary man. Looking in."

"What extraordinary man?"

"I haven't the least idea."

Mrs. Grose gazed round us in vain. "Then where is he gone?"

"I know still less."

"Have you seen him before?"

"Yes—once. On the old tower."

She could only look at me harder. "Do you mean he's a stranger?"

"Oh, very much!"

"Yet you didn't tell me?"

"No—for reasons. But now that you've guessed—"

Mrs. Grose's round eyes encountered this charge. "Ah, I haven't guessed!" she said very simply. "How can I if *you* don't imagine?"

"I don't in the very least."

"You've seen him nowhere but on the tower?"

"And on this spot just now."

Mrs. Grose looked round again. "What was he doing on the tower?"

"Only standing there and looking down at me."

She thought a minute. "Was he a gentleman?"

I found I had no need to think. "No." She gazed in deeper wonder. "No."

"Then nobody about the place? Nobody from the village?"

"Nobody—nobody. I didn't tell you, but I made sure."

She breathed a vague relief: this was, oddly, so much to the good. It only went indeed a little way. "But if he isn't a gentleman—"

"What *is* he? He's a horror."

"A horror?"

"He's—God help me if I know what he is!"

Mrs. Grose looked round once more; she fixed her eyes on the duskier distance, then, pulling herself together, turned to me with abrupt inconsequence. "It's time we should be at church."

"Oh, I'm not fit for church!"

"Won't it do you good?"

"It won't do *them*—!" I nodded at the house.

"The children?"

"I can't leave them now."

"You're afraid—?"

I spoke boldly. "I'm afraid of *him*."

Mrs. Grose's large face showed me, at this, for the first time, the faraway faint glimmer of a consciousness more acute: I somehow made out in it the delayed dawn of an idea I myself had not given her and that was as yet quite obscure to me. It comes back to me that I thought instantly of this as something I could get from her; and I felt it to be connected with the desire she presently showed to know more. "When was it—on the tower?"

"About the middle of the month. At this same hour."

"Almost at dark," said Mrs. Grose.

"Oh, no, not nearly. I saw him as I see you."

"Then how did he get in?"

"And how did he get out?" I laughed. "I had no opportunity to ask him! This evening, you see," I pursued, "he has not been able to get in."

"He only peeps?"

"I hope it will be confined to that!" She had now let go my hand; she turned away a little. I waited an instant; then I brought out: "Go to church. Goodbye. I must watch."

Slowly she faced me again. "Do you fear for them?"

We met in another long look. "Don't *you?*" Instead of answering she came nearer to the window and, for a minute, applied her face to the glass. "You see how he could see," I meanwhile went on.

She didn't move. "How long was he here?"

"Till I came out. I came to meet him."

Mrs. Grose at last turned round, and there was still more in her face. "I couldn't have come out."

"Neither could I!" I laughed again. "But I did come. I have my duty."

"So have I mine," she replied; after which she added: "What is he like?"

"I've been dying to tell you. But he's like nobody."

"Nobody?" she echoed.

"He has no hat." Then seeing in her face that she already, in this, with a deeper dismay, found a touch of picture, I quickly added stroke to stroke. "He has red hair, very red, close-curling, and a pale face, long in shape, with straight, good features and little, rather queer whiskers that are as red as his hair. His eyebrows are, somehow, darker; they look particularly arched and as if they might move a good deal. His eyes are sharp, strange—awfully; but I only know clearly that they're rather small and very fixed. His mouth's wide, and his lips are thin, and except for his little whiskers he's quite clean-shaven. He gives me a sort of sense of looking like an actor."

"An actor!" It was impossible to resemble one less, at least, than Mrs. Grose at that moment.

"I've never seen one, but so I suppose them. He's tall, active, erect," I continued, "but never—no, never!—a gentleman."

My companion's face had blanched as I went on; her round eyes started and her mild mouth gaped. "A gentleman?" she gasped, confounded, stupefied: "a gentleman *he?*"

"You know him then?"

She visibly tried to hold herself. "But he is handsome?"

I saw the way to help her. "Remarkably!"

"And dressed—?"

"In somebody's clothes."

"They're smart, but they're not his own."

She broke into a breathless affirmative groan: "They're the master's!"

I caught it up. "You *do* know him?"

She faltered but a second. "Quint!" she cried.

"Quint?"

"Peter Quint—his own man, his valet, when he was here!"

"When the master was?"

Gaping still, but meeting me, she pieced it all together. "He never wore his hat, but he did wear—well, there were waistcoats missed. They were both here—last year. Then the master went, and Quint was alone."

I followed, but halting a little. "Alone?"

"Alone with *us*." Then, as from a deeper depth, "In charge," she added.

"And what became of him?"

She hung fire so long that I was still more mystified. "He went, too," she brought out at last.

"Went where?"

Her expression, at this, became extraordinary. "God knows where! He died."

"Died?" I almost shrieked.

She seemed fairly to square herself, plant herself more firmly to utter the wonder of it. "Yes. Mr. Quint is dead."

VI

It took of course more than that particular passage to place us together in presence of what we had now to live with as we could—my dreadful liability to impressions of the order so vividly exemplified, and my companion's knowledge, henceforth—a knowledge half consternation and half compassion—of that liability. There had been, this evening, after the revelation left me, for an hour, so prostrate—there had been, for either of us, no attendance on any service but a little service of tears and vows, of prayers and promises, a climax to the series of mutual challenges and pledges that had straightway ensued on our retreating together to the schoolroom and shutting ourselves up there to have everything out. The result of our having everything out was simply to reduce our situation to the last rigor of its elements. She herself had seen nothing, not the shadow of a shadow, and nobody in the house but the governess was in the governess's plight; yet she accepted without directly impugning my sanity the truth as I gave it to her, and ended by showing me, on this ground, an awestricken tenderness, an expression of the sense of my more than questionable privilege, of which the very breath has remained with me as that of the sweetest of human charities.

What was settled between us, accordingly, that night, was that we thought we might bear things together; and I was not even sure that, in spite of her exemption, it was she who had the best of the burden. I knew at this hour, I think, as well as I knew later, what I was capable of meeting to shelter my pupils; but it took me some time to be wholly sure of what my honest ally was prepared for to keep terms with so compromising a contract. I was queer company enough—quite as queer as the company I received; but as I trace over what we went through I see how much common ground we must have found in the one idea that, by good fortune, *could* steady us. It was the idea, the second movement, that led me straight out, as I may say, of the inner chamber of my dread. I could take the air in the court, at least, and there Mrs. Grose could join me. Perfectly can I recall now the particular way strength came to me before we separated for the night. We had gone over and over every feature of what I had seen.

"He was looking for someone else, you say—someone who was not you?"

"He was looking for little Miles." A portentous clearness now possessed me. "That's whom he was looking for."

"But how do you know?"

"I know, I know, I know!" My exaltation grew. "And you know, my dear!"

She didn't deny this, but I required, I felt, not even so much telling as that. She resumed in a moment, at any rate: "What if he should see him?"

"Little Miles? That's what he wants!"

She looked immensely scared again. "The child?"

"Heaven forbid! The man. He wants to appear to *them*." That he might was an awful conception, and yet, somehow, I could keep it at bay; which, moreover, as we lingered there, was what I succeeded in practically proving. I had an absolute certainty that I should see again what I had already seen, but something within me said that by offering myself bravely as the sole subject of such experience, by accepting, by inviting, by surmounting it all, I should serve as an expiatory victim and guard the tranquility of my companions. The children, in especial, I should thus fence about and absolutely save. I recall one of the last things I said that night to Mrs. Grose.

"It does strike me that my pupils have never mentioned—"

She looked at me hard as I musingly pulled up. "His having been here and the time they were with him?"

"The time they were with him, and his name, his presence, his history, in any way."

"Oh, the little lady doesn't remember. She never heard or knew."

"The circumstances of his death?" I thought with some intensity. "Perhaps not. But Miles would remember—Miles would know."

"Ah, don't try him!" broke from Mrs. Grose.

I returned her the look she had given me. "Don't be afraid." I continued to think. "It *is* rather odd."

"That he has never spoken of him?"

"Never by the least allusion. And you tell me they were 'great friends'?"

"Oh, it wasn't *him!*" Mrs. Grose with emphasis declared. "It was Quint's own fancy. To play with him, I mean—to spoil him." She paused a moment; then she added: "Quint was much too free."

This gave me, straight from my vision of his face—such a face!—a sudden sickness of disgust. "Too free with *my* boy?"

"Too free with everyone!"

I forbore, for the moment, to analyze this description further than by the reflection that a part of it applied to several of the members of the household, of the half-dozen maids and men who were still of our small colony. But there was everything, for our apprehension, in the lucky fact that no discomfortable legend, no perturbation of scullions, had ever, within anyone's memory attached to the kind old place. It had neither bad name nor ill fame, and Mrs. Grose, most apparently, only desired to cling to me and to quake in silence. I even put her, the very last thing of all, to the test. It was when, at midnight, she had her hand on the schoolroom door to take leave. "I have it from you then—for it's of great importance—that he was definitely and admittedly bad?"

"Oh, not admittedly. I knew it—but the master didn't."

"And you never told him?"

"Well, he didn't like tale-bearing—he hated complaints. He was terribly short with anything of that kind, and if people were all right to *him*—"

"He wouldn't be bothered with more?" This squared well enough with my impressions of him: he was not a trouble-loving gentleman, nor so very particular perhaps about some of the company *he* kept. All the same, I pressed my interlocutress. "I promise you I would have told!"

She felt my discrimination. "I daresay I was wrong. But, really, I was afraid."

"Afraid of what?"

"Of things that man could do. Quint was so clever—he was so deep."

I took this in still more than, probably, I showed. "You weren't afraid of anything else? Not of his effect—?"

"His effect?" she repeated with a face of anguish and waiting while I faltered.

"On innocent little precious lives. They were in your charge."

"No, they were not in mine!" she roundly and distressfully returned. "The master believed in him and placed him here because he was supposed not to be well and the country air so good for him. So he had everything to say. Yes"—she let me have it—"even about *them*."

"Them—that creature?" I had to smother a kind of howl. "And you could bear it!"

"No. I couldn't—and I can't now!" And the poor woman burst into tears.

A rigid control, from the next day, was, as I have said, to follow them; yet how often and how passionately, for a week, we came back together to the subject! Much as we had discussed it that Sunday night, I was, in the immediate later hours in especial—for it may be imagined whether I slept—still haunted with the shadow of something she had not told me. I myself had kept back nothing, but there was a word Mrs. Grose had kept back. I was sure, moreover, by morning, that this was not from a failure of frankness, but because on every side there were fears. It seems to me indeed, in retrospect, that by the time the morrow's sun was high I had restlessly read into the fact before us almost all the meaning they were to receive from subsequent and more cruel occurrences. What they gave me above all was just the sinister figure of the living man—the dead one would keep awhile!—and of the months he had continuously passed at Bly, which, added up, made a formidable stretch. The limit of this evil time had arrived only when, on the dawn of a winter's morning, Peter Quint was found, by a laborer going to early work, stone dead on the road from the village: a catastrophe explained—superficially at least—by a visible wound to his head; such a wound as might have been produced—and as, on the final evidence, *had* been—by a fatal slip, in the dark and after leaving the public house, on the steepish icy slope, a wrong path altogether, at the bottom of which he lay. The icy slope, the turn mistaken at night and in liquor, accounted for much—practically, in the end and after the inquest and boundless chatter, for everything; but there had been matters in his life—strange passages and perils, secret disorders, vices more than suspected—that would have accounted for a good deal more.

I scarce know how to put my story into words that shall be a credible picture of my state of mind; but I was in these days literally able to find a joy in the extraordinary flight of heroism the occasion demanded of me. I now saw that I had been asked for a service admirable and difficult; and there would be a greatness in letting it be seen—oh, in the right quarter!—that I could succeed where many another girl might have failed. It was an immense help to me—I confess I rather applaud myself as I look back!—that I saw my service so strongly and so simply. I was there to protect and defend the little creatures in the world the most bereaved and the most lovable, the appeal of whose helplessness had suddenly become only too explicit, a deep, constant ache of one's own committed heart. We were cut off, really, together; we were united in our danger. They had nothing but me, and I—well, I *had* them. It was in short a magnificent chance. This chance presented itself to me in an image richly material. I was a screen—I was to stand before them. The more I saw, the less they would. I began to watch them in a stifled suspense, a disguised excitement that might well, had it continued too long, have turned to something like madness. What saved me, as I now see, was that it turned to something else altogether. It didn't last as suspense—it was superseded by horrible proofs. Proofs, I say, yes—from the moment I really took hold.

This moment dated from an afternoon hour that I happened to spend in the grounds with the younger of my pupils alone. We had left Miles indoors, on the red cushion of a deep window seat; he had wished to finish a book, and I had been glad to encourage a purpose so laudable in a young man whose only defect was an occasional excess of the restless. His sister, on the contrary, had been alert to come out, and I strolled with her half an hour, seeking the shade, for the sun was still high and the day exceptionally warm. I was aware afresh, with her, as we went, of how, like her brother, she contrived—it was the charming thing in both children—to let me alone without appearing to drop me and to accompany me without appearing to surround. They were never importunate and yet never listless. My attention to them all really went to seeing them amuse themselves immensely without me: this was a spectacle they seemed actively to prepare and that engaged me as an active admirer. I walked in a world of their invention—they had no occasion whatever to draw upon mine; so that my time was taken only with being, for them, some remarkable person or thing that the game of the moment required and that was merely, thanks to my superior, my exalted stamp, a happy and highly distinguished sinecure. I forget what I was on the present occasion; I only remember that I was something very important and very quiet and that Flora was playing very hard. We were on the edge of the lake, and, as we had lately begun geography, the lake was the Sea of Azof.

Suddenly, in these circumstances, I became aware that, on the other side of the Sea of Azof, we had an interested spectator. The way this knowledge gathered in me was the strangest thing in the world—the strangest, that is, except the very much stranger in which it quickly merged itself. I had sat down with a piece of work—for I was something or other that could sit—on the old stone bench which overlooked the pond; and in this position I began to take in with certitude, and yet without direct vision, the presence, at a distance, of a third person. The old trees, the thick shrubbery, made a great and pleasant shade, but it was all suffused with the brightness of the hot, still hour. There was no ambiguity in anything; none whatever, at least, in the conviction I from one moment to another found myself forming as to what I should see straight before me and across the lake as a consequence of raising my eyes. They were attached at this juncture to the stitching in which I was engaged, and I can feel once more the spasm of my effort not to move them till I should so have steadied myself as to be able to make up my mind what to do. There was an alien object in view—a figure whose right of presence I instantly, passionately questioned. I recollect counting over perfectly the possibilities, reminding myself that nothing was more natural, for instance, then the appearance of one of the men about the place, or even of a messenger, a postman, or a tradesman's boy, from the village. That reminder had as little effect on my practical certitude as I was conscious—still even without looking—of its having upon the character and attitude of our visitor. Nothing was more natural than that these things should be the other things that they absolutely were not.

Of the positive identity of the apparition I would assure myself as soon as the small clock of my courage should have ticked out the right second; meanwhile, with an effort that was already sharp enough, I transferred my eyes straight to little Flora, who, at the moment, was about ten yards away. My heart had stood still for an instant with the wonder and terror of the question whether she too would see; and I held my breath while I waited for what a cry from her, what some sudden innocent sign either of interest or of alarm, would tell me. I waited, but nothing came; then, in the first place—and there is something more dire in this, I feel, than in anything I have to relate—I was determined by a sense that, within a minute, all sounds from her had previously dropped; and, in the second, by the circumstance that, also within the minute, she had, in her play, turned her back to the water. This was her attitude when I at last looked at her—looked with the confirmed conviction that we were still, together, under direct personal notice. She had picked up a small flat piece of wood, which happened to have in it a little hole that had evidently suggested to her the idea of sticking in another fragment that might figure as a mast and make the thing a boat. This second morsel, as I watched her, she was very markedly and intently attempting to tighten in its place. My apprehension of what she was doing sustained me so that after some seconds I felt I was ready for more. Then I again shifted my eyes—I faced what I had to face.

VII

I got hold of Mrs. Grose as soon after this as I could; and I can give no intelligible account of how I fought out the interval. Yet I still hear myself cry as I fairly threw myself into her arms: "They know—it's too monstrous: they know, they *know!*"

"And what on earth—?" I felt her incredulity as she held me.

"Why, all that we know—and heaven knows what else besides!" Then, as she released me, I made it out to her, made it out perhaps only now with full coherency even to myself. "Two hours ago, in the garden"—I could scarce articulate—"Flora *saw!*"

Mrs. Grose took it as she might have taken a blow in the stomach. "She has told you?" she panted.

"Not a word—that's the horror. She kept it to herself! The child of eight, *that* child!" Unutterable still, for me, was the stupefaction of it.

Mrs. Grose, of course, could only gape the wider. "Then how do you know?"

"I was there—I saw with my eyes: saw that she was perfectly aware."

"Do you mean aware of *him?*"

"No—of *her.*" I was conscious as I spoke that I looked prodigious things, for I got the slow reflection of them in my companion's face. "Another person—this time; but a figure of quite as unmistakable horror and evil: a woman in black, pale and dreadful—with such an air also, and such a face!—on the other side of the lake. I was there with the child—quiet for the hour; and in the midst of it she came."

"Came how—from where?"

"From where they come from! She just appeared and stood there—but not so near."

"And without coming nearer?"

"Oh, for the effect and the feeling, she might have been as close as you!"

My friend, with an odd impulse, fell back a step. "Was she someone you've never seen?"

"Yes. But someone the child has. Someone *you* have." Then, to show how I had thought it all out: "My predecessor—the one who died."

"Miss Jessel?"

"Miss Jessel. You don't believe me?" I pressed.

She turned right and left in her distress. "How can you be sure?"

This drew from me, in the state of my nerves, a flash of impatience. "Then ask Flora—*she's* sure!" But I had no sooner spoken than I caught myself up. "No, for God's sake, *don't!* She'll say she isn't—she'll lie!"

Mrs. Grose was not too bewildered instinctively to protest. "Ah, how *can* you?"

"Because I'm clear. Flora doesn't want me to know."

"It's only then to spare you."

"No, no—there are depths, depths! The more I go over it, the more I see in it, and the more I see in it, the more I fear. I don't know what I *don't* see—what I *don't* fear!"

Mrs. Grose tried to keep up with me. "You mean you're afraid of seeing her again?"

"Oh, no; that's nothing—now!" Then I explained. "It's of not *seeing* her."

But my companion only looked wan. "I don't understand you."

"Why, it's that the child may keep it up—and that the child assuredly *will*—without my knowing it."

At the image of this possibility Mrs. Grose for a moment collapsed, yet presently to pull herself together again, as if from the positive force of the sense of what, should we yield an inch, there would really be to give way to. "Dear, dear—we must keep our heads! And after all, if she doesn't mind it—!" She even tried a grim joke. "Perhaps she likes it!"

"Likes *such* things—a scrap of an infant!"

"Isn't it just a proof of her blessed innocence?" my friend bravely inquired.

She brought me, for the instant, almost round. "Oh, we must clutch at *that*—we must cling to it! If it isn't a proof of what you say, it's a proof of—God knows what! For the woman's a horror of horrors."

Mrs. Grose, at this, fixed her eyes a minute on the ground; then at last raising them, "Tell me how you know," she said.

"Then you admit it's what she was?" I cried.

"Tell me how you know," my friend simply repeated.

"Know? By seeing her! By the way she looked."

"At you, do you mean—so wickedly?"

"Dear me, no—I could have borne that. She gave me never a glance. She only fixed the child."

Mrs. Grose tried to see it. "Fixed her?"

"Ah, with such awful eyes!"

She stared at mine as if they might really have resembled them. "Do you mean of dislike?"

"God help us, no. Of something much worse."

"Worse than dislike?"—this left her indeed at a loss.

"With a determination—indescribable. With a kind of fury of intention."

I made her turn pale. "Intention?"

"To get hold of her." Mrs. Grose—her eyes just lingering on mine—gave a shudder and walked to the window; and while she stood there looking out I completed my statement. "*That's* what Flora knows."

After a little she turned round. "The person was in black, you say?"

"In mourning—rather poor, almost shabby. But—yes—with extraordinary beauty." I now recognized to what I had at last, stroke by stroke, brought the victim of my confidence, for she quite visibly weighed this. "Oh, handsome—very, very," I insisted; "wonderfully handsome. But infamous."

She slowly came back to me. "Miss Jessel—was infamous." She once more took my hand in both her own, holding it as tight as if to fortify me against the increase of alarm I might draw from this disclosure. "They were both infamous," she finally said.

So, for a little, we faced it once more together; and I found absolutely a degree of help in seeing it now so straight. "I appreciate," I said, "the great decency of your not having hitherto spoken; but the time has certainly come to give me the whole thing." She appeared to assent to this, but still only in silence; seeing which I went on: "I must have it now. Of what did she die? Come, there was something between them."

"There was everything."

"In spite of the difference—?"

"Oh, of their rank, their condition"—she brought it woefully out. "She was a lady."

I turned it over; I again saw. "Yes—she was a lady."

"And he so dreadfully below," said Mrs. Grose.

I felt that I doubtless needn't press too hard, in such company, on the place of a servant in the scale; but there was nothing to prevent an acceptance of my companion's own measure of my predecessor's abasement. There was a way to deal with that, and I dealt; the more readily for my full vision—on the evidence—of our employer's late clever, good-looking "own" man; impudent, assured, spoiled, depraved. "The fellow was a hound."

Mrs. Grose considered as if it were perhaps a little a case for a sense of shades. "I've never seen one like him. He did what he wished."

"With *her?*"

"With them all."

It was as if now in my friend's own eyes Miss Jessel had again appeared. I seemed at any rate, for an instant, to see their evocation of her as distinctly as I had seen her by the pond; and I brought out with decision: "It must have been also what she wished!"

Mrs. Grose's face signified that it had been indeed, but she said at the same time: "Poor woman—she paid for it!"

"Then you do know what she died of?" I asked.

"No—I know nothing. I wanted not to know; I was glad enough I didn't; and I thanked heaven she was well out of this!"

"Yet you had, then, your idea—"

"Of her real reason for leaving? Oh, yes—as to that. She couldn't have stayed. Fancy it here—for a governess! And afterward I imagined—and I still imagine. And what I imagine is dreadful."

"Not so dreadful as what *I* do," I replied; on which I must have shown her—as I was indeed but too conscious—a front of miserable defeat. It brought out again all her compassion for me, and at the renewed touch of her kindness my power to resist broke down. I burst, as I had, the other time, made her burst, into tears; she took me to her motherly breast, and my lamentation overflowed. "I don't do it!" I sobbed in despair; "I don't save or shield them! It's far worse than I dreamed—they're lost!"

VIII

What I had said to Mrs. Grose was true enough: there were in the matter I had put before her depths and possibilities that I lacked resolution to sound; so that when we met once more in the wonder of it we were of a common mind about the duty of resistance to extravagant fancies. We were to keep our heads if we should keep nothing else—difficult indeed as that might be in the face of what, in our prodigious experience, was least to be questioned. Late that night, while the house slept, we had another talk in my room, when she went all the way with me as to its being beyond doubt that I had seen exactly what I had seen. To hold her perfectly in the pinch of that, I found I had only to ask her how, if I had "made it up," I came to be able to give, of each of the persons appearing to me, a picture disclosing, to the last detail, their special marks—a portrait on the exhibition of which she had instantly recognized and named them. She wished of course—small blame to her!—to sink the whole subject; and I was quick to assure her that my own interest in it had now violently taken the form of a search for the way to escape from it. I encountered her on the ground of a probability that with recurrence—for recurrence we took for granted—I should get used to my danger, distinctly professing that my personal exposure had suddenly become the least of my discomforts. It was my new suspicion that was intolerable; and yet even to this complication the later hours of the day had brought a little ease.

On leaving her, after my first outbreak, I had of course returned to my pupils, associating the right remedy for my dismay with that sense of their charm which I had already found to be a thing I could positively cultivate and which had never failed me yet. I had simply, in other words, plunged afresh into Flora's special society and there become aware—it was almost a luxury!—that she could put her little conscious hand straight upon the spot that ached. She had looked at me in sweet speculation and then had accused me to my face of having "cried." I had supposed I had brushed away the ugly signs: but I could literally—for the time, at all events—rejoice, under this fathomless charity, that they had not entirely disappeared. To gaze into the depths of blue of the child's eyes and pronounce their loveliness a trick of premature cunning was to be guilty of a cynicism in preference to which I naturally preferred to abjure my judgment and, so far as might be, my agitation. I couldn't abjure for merely wanting to, but I could repeat to Mrs. Grose—as I did there, over and over, in the small hours—that with their voices in the air, their pressure on one's heart, and their fragrant faces against one's cheek, everything fell to the ground but their incapacity and their beauty. It was a pity that, somehow, to settle this once for all, I had equally to re-enumerate the signs of subtlety that, in the afternoon, by the lake had made a miracle of my show of self-possession. It was a pity to be obliged to reinvestigate the certitude of the moment itself and repeat how it had come to me as a revelation that the inconceivable communion I then surprised was a matter, for either party, of habit. It was a pity that I should have had to quaver out again the reasons for my not having, in my delusion, so much as questioned that the little girl saw our visitant even as I actually saw Mrs. Grose herself, and that she wanted, by just so much as she did thus see, to make me suppose she didn't, and at the same time, without showing anything, arrive at a guess as to whether I myself did! It was a pity that I needed once more to describe the portentous little activity by which she sought to divert my attention—the perceptible increase of movement, the greater intensity of play, the singing, the gabbling of nonsense, and the invitation to romp.

Yet if I had not indulged, to prove there was nothing in it, in this review, I should have missed the two or three dim elements of comfort that still remained to me. I should not for instance have been able to asseverate to my friend that I was certain—which was so much to the good—that I at least had not betrayed myself. I should not have been prompted, by stress of need, by desperation of mind—I scarce know what to call it—to invoke such further aid to intelligence as might spring from pushing my colleague fairly to the wall. She had told me, bit by bit, under pressure, a great deal; but a small shifty spot on the wrong side of it all still sometimes brushed my brow like the wing of a bat; and I remember how on this occasion—for the sleeping house and the concentration alike of our danger and our watch seemed to help—I felt the importance of giving the last jerk to the curtain. "I don't believe anything so horrible," I recollect saying; "no, let us put it definitely, my dear, that I don't. But if I did, you know, there's a thing I should require now, just without sparing you the least bit more—oh, not a scrap, come!—to get out of you. What was it you had in mind when, in our distress, before Miles came back, over the letter from his school, you said, under my insistence, that you didn't pretend for him that he had not literally ever been 'bad'? He has not literally 'ever,' in these weeks that I myself have lived with him and so closely watched him; he has been an imperturbable little prodigy of delightful, lovable goodness. Therefore you might perfectly have made the claim for him if you had not, as it happened, seen an exception to take. What was your exception, and to what passage in your personal observation of him did you refer?"

It was a dreadfully austere inquiry, but levity was not our note, and, at any rate, before the gray dawn admonished us to separate I had got my answer. What my friend had had in mind proved to be immensely to the purpose. It was neither more nor less than the circumstance that for a period of several months Quint and the boy had been perpetually together. It was in fact the very appropriate truth that she had ventured to criticize the propriety, to hint at the incongruity, of so close an alliance, and even to go so far on the subject as a frank overture to Miss Jessel. Miss Jessel had, with a most strange manner, requested her to mind her business, and the good woman had, on this, directly approached little Miles. What she had said to him, since I pressed, was that she liked to see young gentlemen not forget their station.

I pressed again, of course, at this. "You reminded him that Quint was only a base menial?"

"As you might say! And it was his answer, for one thing, that was bad."

"And for another thing?" I waited. "He repeated your words to Quint?"

"No, not that. It's just what he *wouldn't!*" she could still impress upon me. "I was sure, at any rate," she added, "that he didn't. But he denied certain occasions."

"What occasions?"

"When they had been about together quite as if Quint were his tutor—and a very grand one—and Miss Jessel only for the little lady. When he had gone off with the fellow, I mean, and spent hours with him."

"He then prevaricated about it—he said he hadn't?" Her assent was clear enough to cause me to add in a moment: "I see. He lied."

"Oh!" Mrs. Grose mumbled. This was a suggestion that it didn't matter; which indeed she backed up by a further remark. "You see, after all, Miss Jessel didn't mind. She didn't forbid him."

I considered. "Did he put that to you as a justification?"

At this she dropped again. "No, he never spoke of it."

"Never mentioned her in connection with Quint?"

She saw, visibly flushing, where I was coming out. "Well, he didn't show anything. He denied," she repeated; "he denied."

Lord, how I pressed her now! "So that you could see he knew what was between the two wretches?"

"I don't know—I don't know!" the poor woman groaned.

"You do know, you dear thing," I replied; "only you haven't my dreadful boldness of mind, and you keep back, out of timidity and modesty and delicacy, even the impression that, in the past, when you had, without my aid, to flounder about in silence, most of all made you miserable. But I shall get it out of you yet! There was something in the boy that suggested to you," I continued, "that he covered and concealed their relation."

"Oh, he couldn't prevent—"

"Your learning the truth? I daresay! But, heavens," I fell, with vehemence, athinking, "what it shows that they must, to that extent, have succeeded in making of him!"

"Ah, nothing that's not nice *now!*" Mrs. Grose lugubriously pleaded.

"I don't wonder you looked queer," I persisted, "when I mentioned to you the letter from his school!"

"I doubt if I looked as queer as you!" she retorted with homely force. "And if he was so bad then as that comes to, how is he such an angel now?"

"Yes, indeed—and if he was a fiend at school! How, how, how? Well," I said in my torment, "you must put it to me again, but I shall not be able to tell you for some days. Only, put it to me again!" I cried in a way that made my friend stare. "There are directions in which I must not for the present let myself go." Meanwhile I returned to her first example—the one to which she had just previously referred—of the boy's happy capacity for an occasional slip. "If Quint—on your remonstrance at the time you speak of—was a base menial, one of the things Miles said to you, I find myself guessing, was that you were another." Again her admission was so adequate that I continued: "And you forgave him that?"

"Wouldn't *you?*"

"Oh, yes!" And we exchanged there, in the stillness, a sound of the oddest amusement. Then I went on: "At all events, while he was with the man—"

"Miss Flora was with the woman. It suited them all!"

It suited me, too, I felt, only too well; by which I mean that it suited exactly the particularly deadly view I was in the very act of forbidding myself to entertain. But I so far succeeded in checking the expression of this view that I will throw, just here, no further light on it than may be offered by the mention of my final observation to Mrs. Grose. "His having lied and been impudent are, I confess, less engaging specimens than I had hoped to have from you of the outbreak in him of the little natural man. Still," I mused, "They must do, for they make me feel more than ever that I must watch."

It made me blush, the next minute, to see in my friend's face how much more unreservedly she had forgiven him than her anecdote struck me as presenting to my own tenderness an occasion for doing. This came out when, at the schoolroom door, she quitted me. "Surely you don't accuse *him*—"

"Of carrying on an intercourse that he conceals from me? Ah, remember that, until further evidence, I now accuse nobody." Then, before shutting her out to go, by another passage, to her own place, "I must just wait," I wound up.

IX

I waited and waited, and the days, as they elapsed, took something from my consternation. A very few of them, in fact, passing, in constant sight of my pupils, without a fresh incident, sufficed to give to grievous fancies and even to odious memories a kind of brush of the sponge. I have spoken of the surrender to their extraordinary childish grace as a thing I could actively cultivate, and it may be imagined if I neglected now to address myself to this source for whatever it would yield. Stranger than I can express, certainly, was the effort to struggle against my new lights; it would doubtless have been, however, a greater tension still had it not been so frequently successful. I used to wonder how my little charges could help guessing that I thought strange things about them; and the circumstances that these things only made them more interesting was not by itself a direct aid to keeping them in the dark. I trembled lest they should see that they were so immensely more interesting. Putting things at the worst, at all events, as in meditation I so often did, any clouding of their innocence could only be—blameless and foredoomed as they were—a reason the more for taking risks. There were moments when, by an irresistible impulse, I found myself catching them up and pressing them to my heart. As soon as I had done so I used to say to myself: "What will they think of that? Doesn't it betray too much?" It would have been easy to get into a sad, wild tangle about how much I might betray; but the real account, I feel, of the hours of peace that I could still enjoy was that the immediate charm of my companions was a beguilement still effective even under the shadow of the possibility that it was studied. For if it occurred to me that I might occasionally excite suspicion by the little outbreaks of my sharper passion for them, so too I remember wondering if I mightn't see a queerness in the traceable increase of their own demonstrations.

They were at this period extravagantly and preternaturally fond of me; which, after all, I could reflect, was no more than a graceful response in children perpetually bowed over and hugged. The homage of which they were so lavish succeeded, in truth, for my nerves, quite as well as if I never appeared to myself, as I may say, literally to catch them at a purpose in it. They had never, I think, wanted to do so many things for their poor protectress; I mean—though they got their lessons better and better, which was naturally what would please her most—in the way of diverting, entertaining, surprising her; reading her passages, telling her stories, acting her charades, pouncing out at her, in disguises, as animals and historical characters, and above all astonishing her by the "pieces" they had secretly got by heart and could interminably recite. I should never get to the bottom—were I to let myself go even now—of the prodigious private commentary, all under still more private correction, with which, in these days, I overscored their full hours. They had shown me from the first a facility for everything, a general faculty which, taking a fresh start, achieved remarkable flights. They got their little tasks as if they loved them, and indulged, from the mere exuberance of the gift, in the most unimposed little miracles of memory. They not only popped out at me as tigers and as Romans, but as Shakespeareans, astronomers, and navigators. This was so singularly the case that it had presumably much to do with the fact as to which, at the present day, I am at a loss for a different explanation: I allude to my unnatural composure on the subject of another school for Miles. What I remember is that I was content not, for the time, to open the question, and that contentment must have sprung from the sense of his perpetually striking show of cleverness. He was too clever for a bad governess, for a parson's daughter, to spoil; and the strangest if not the brightest thread in the pensive embroidery I just spoke of was the impression I might have got, if I had dared to work it out, that he was under some influence operating in his small intellectual life as a tremendous incitement.

If it was easy to reflect, however, that such a boy could postpone school, it was at least as marked that for such a boy to have been "kicked out" by a schoolmaster was a mystification without end. Let me add that in their company now—and I was careful almost never to be out of it—I could follow no scent very far. We lived in a cloud of music and love and success and private theatricals. The musical sense in each of the children was of the quickest, but the elder in especial had a marvelous knack of catching and repeating. The schoolroom piano broke into all gruesome fancies; and when that failed there were confabulations in corners, with a sequel of one of them going out in the highest spirits in order to "come in" as something new. I had had brothers myself, and it was no revelation to me that little girls could be slavish idolaters of little boys. What surpassed everything was that there was a little boy in the world who could have for the inferior age, sex, and intelligence so fine a consideration. They were extraordinarily at one, and to say that they never either quarreled or complained is to make the note of praise coarse for their quality of sweetness. Sometimes, indeed, when I dropped into coarseness, I perhaps came across traces of little understandings between them by which one of them should keep me occupied while the other slipped away. There is a naive side, I suppose, in all diplomacy; but if my pupils practiced upon me, it was surely with the minimum of grossness. It was all in the other quarter that, after a lull, the grossness broke out.

I find that I really hang back; but I must take my plunge. In going on with the record of what was hideous at Bly, I not only challenge the most liberal faith—for which I little care; but—and this is another matter—I renew what I myself suffered, I again push my way through it to the end. There came suddenly an hour after which, as I look back, the affair seems to me to have been all pure suffering; but I have at least reached the heart of it, and the straightest road out is doubtless to advance. One evening—with nothing to lead up or to prepare it—I felt the cold touch of the impression that had breathed on me the night of my arrival and which, much lighter then, as I have mentioned, I should probably have made little of in memory had my subsequent sojourn been less agitated. I had not gone to bed; I sat reading by a couple of candles. There was a roomful of old books at Bly—last-century fiction, some of it, which, to the extent of a distinctly deprecated renown, but never to so much as that of a stray specimen, had reached the sequestered home and appealed to the unavowed curiosity of my youth. I remember that the book I had in my hand was Fielding's *Amelia;* also that I was wholly awake. I recall further both a general conviction that it was horribly late and a particular objection to looking at my watch. I figure, finally, that the white curtain draping, in the fashion of those days, the head of Flora's little bed, shrouded, as I had assured myself long before, the perfection of childish rest. I recollect in short that, though I was deeply interested in my author, I found myself, at the turn of a page and with his spell all scattered, looking straight up from him and hard at the door of my room. There was a moment during which I listened, reminded of the faint sense I had had, the first night, of there being something undefinably astir in the house, and noted the soft breath of the open casement just move the half-drawn blind. Then, with all the marks of a deliberation that must have seemed magnificent had there been anyone to admire it, I laid down my book, rose to my feet, and, taking a candle, went straight out of the room and, from the passage, on which my light made little impression, noiselessly closed and locked the door.

I can say now neither what determined nor what guided me, but I went straight along the lobby, holding my candle high, till I came within sight of the tall window that presided over the great turn of the staircase. At this point I precipitately found myself aware of three things. They were practically simultaneous, yet they had flashes of succession. My candle, under a bold flourish, went out, and I perceived, by the uncovered window, that the yielding dusk of earliest morning rendered it unnecessary. Without it, the next instant, I saw that there was someone on the stair. I speak of sequences, but I required no lapse of seconds to stiffen myself for a third encounter with Quint. The apparition had reached the landing halfway up and was therefore on the spot nearest the window, where at sight of me, it stopped short and fixed me exactly as it had fixed me from the tower and from the garden. He knew me as well as I knew him; and so, in the cold, faint twilight, with a glimmer in the high glass and another on the polish of the oak stair below, we faced each other in our common intensity. He was absolutely, on this occasion, a living, detestable, dangerous presence. But that was not the wonder of wonders; I reserve this distinction for quite another circumstance: the circumstance that dread had unmistakably quitted me and that there was nothing in me there that didn't meet and measure him.

I had plenty of anguish after that extraordinary moment, but I had, thank God, no terror. And he knew I had not—I found myself at the end of an instant magnificently aware of this. I felt, in a fierce rigor of confidence, that if I stood my ground a minute I should cease—for the time, at least—to have him to reckon with; and during the minute, accordingly, the thing was as human and hideous as a real interview: hideous just because it was human, as human as to have met alone, in the small hours, in a sleeping house, some enemy, some adventurer, some criminal. It was the dead silence of our long gaze at such close quarters that gave the whole horror, huge as it was, its only note of the unnatural. If I had met a murderer in such a place and at such an hour, we still at least would have spoken. Something would have passed, in life, between us; if nothing had passed, one of us would have moved. The moment was so prolonged that it would have taken but little more to make me doubt if even I were in life. I can't express what followed it save by saying that the silence itself—which was indeed in a manner an attestation of my strength—became the element into which I saw the figure disappear; in which I definitely saw it turn as I might have seen the low wretch to which it had once belonged turn on receipt of an order, and pass, with my eyes on the villainous back that no hunch could have more disfigured, straight down the staircase and into the darkness in which the next bend was lost.

X

I remained awhile at the top of the stair, but with the effect presently of understanding that when my visitor had gone, he had gone: then I returned to my room. The foremost thing I saw there by the light of the candle I had left burning was that Flora's little bed was empty; and on this I caught my breath with all the terror that, five minutes before, I had been able to resist. I dashed at the place in which I had left her lying and over which (for the small silk counterpane and the sheets were disarranged) the white curtains had been deceivingly pulled forward; then my step, to my unutterable relief, produced an answering sound: I perceived an agitation of the window blind, and the child, ducking down, emerged rosily from the other side of it. She stood there in so much of her candor and so little of her nightgown, with her pink bare feet and the golden glow of her curls. She looked intensely grave, and I had never had such a sense of losing an advantage acquired (the thrill of which had just been so prodigious) as on my consciousness that she addressed me with a reproach. "You naughty: where have you been?"—instead of challenging her own irregularity I found myself arraigned and explaining. She herself explained, for that matter, with the loveliest, eagerest simplicity. She had known suddenly, as she lay there, that I was out of the room, and had jumped up to see what had become of me. I had dropped, with the joy of her reappearance, back into my chair—feeling then, and then only, a little faint; and she had pattered straight over to me, thrown herself upon my knee, given herself to be held with the flame of the candle full in the wonderful little face that was still flushed with sleep. I remember closing my eyes an instant, yieldingly, consciously, as before the excess of something beautiful that shone out of the blue of her own. "You were looking for me out of the window?" I said. "You thought I might be walking in the grounds?"

"Well, you know, I thought someone was"—she never blanched as she smiled out that at me.

Oh, how I looked at her now! "And did you see anyone?"

"Ah, *no!*" she returned, almost with the full privilege of childish inconsequence, resentfully, though with a long sweetness in her little drawl of the negative.

At that moment, in the state of my nerves, I absolutely believed she lied; and if I once more closed my eyes it was before the dazzle of the three or four possible ways in which I might take this up. One of these, for a moment, tempted me with such singular intensity that, to withstand it, I must have gripped my little girl with a spasm that, wonderfully, she submitted to without a cry or a sign of fright. Why not break out at her on the spot and have it all over?—give it to her straight in her lovely little lighted face? "You see, you see, you *know* that you do and that you already quite suspect I believe it; therefore, why not frankly confess it to me, so that we may at least live with it together and learn perhaps, in the strangeness of our fate, where we are and what it means?" This solicitation dropped, alas, as it came: if I could immediately have succumbed to it I might have spared myself—well, you'll see what. Instead of succumbing I sprang again to my feet, looked at her bed, and took a helpless middle way. "Why did you pull the curtain over the place to make me think you were still there?"

Flora luminously considered; after which, with her little divine smile: "Because I don't like to frighten you!"

"But if I had, by your idea, gone out—?"

She absolutely declined to be puzzled; she turned her eyes to the flame of the candle as if the question were as irrelevant, or at any rate as impersonal, as Mrs. Marcet or nine-times-nine. "Oh, but you know," she quite adequately answered, "that you might come back, you dear, and that you *have!*" And after a little, when she had got into bed, I had, for a long time, by almost sitting on her to hold her hand, to prove that I recognized the pertinence of my return.

You may imagine the general complexion, from that moment, of my nights. I repeatedly sat up till I didn't know when; I selected moments when my roommate unmistakably slept, and, stealing out, took noiseless turns in the passage and even pushed as far as to where I had last met Quint. But I never met him there again; and I may as well say at once that I on no other occasion saw him in the house. I just missed, on the staircase, on the other hand, a different adventure. Looking down it from the top I once recognized the presence of a woman seated on one of the lower steps with her back presented to me, her body half-bowed and her head, in an attitude of woe, in her hands. I had been there but an instant, however, when she vanished without looking round at me. I knew, nonetheless, exactly what dreadful face she had to show; and I wondered whether, if instead of being above I had been below, I should have had, for going up, the same nerve I had lately shown Quint. Well, there continued to be plenty of chance for nerve. On the eleventh night after my latest encounter with that gentleman—they were all numbered now—I had an alarm that perilously skirted it and that indeed, from the particular quality of its unexpectedness, proved quite my sharpest shock. It was precisely the first night during this series that, weary with watching, I had felt that I might again without laxity lay myself down at my old hour. I slept immediately and, as I afterward knew, till about one o'clock; but when I woke it was to sit straight up, as completely roused as if a hand had shook me. I had left a light burning, but it was now out, and I felt an instant certainty that Flora had extinguished it. This brought me to my feet and straight, in the darkness, to her bed, which I found she had left. A glance at the window enlightened me further, and the striking of a match completed the picture.

The child had again got up—this time blowing out the taper, and had again, for some purpose of observation or response, squeezed in behind the blind and was peering out into the night. That she now saw—as she had not, I had satisfied myself, the previous time—was proved to me by the fact that she was disturbed neither by my reillumination nor by the haste I made to get into slippers and into a wrap. Hidden, protected, absorbed, she evidently rested on the sill—the casement opened forward—and gave herself up. There was a great still moon to help her, and this fact had counted in my quick decision. She was face to face with the apparition we had met at the lake, and could now communicate with it as she had not then been able to do. What I, on my side, had to care for was, without disturbing her, to reach, from the corridor, some other window in the same quarter. I got to the door without her hearing me; I got out of it, closed it, and listened, from the other side, for some sound from her. While I stood in the passage I had my eyes on her brother's door, which was but ten steps off and which, indescribably, produced in me a renewal of the strange impulse that I lately spoke of as my temptation. What if I should go straight in and march to *his* window?—what if, by risking to his boyish bewilderment a revelation of my motive, I should throw across the rest of the mystery the long halter of my boldness?

This thought held me sufficiently to make me cross to his threshold and pause again. I preternaturally listened; I figured to myself what might portentously be; I wondered if his bed were also empty and he too were secretly at watch. It was a deep, soundless minute, at the end of which my impulse failed. He was quiet; he might be innocent; the risk was hideous; I turned away. There was a figure in the grounds—a figure prowling for a sight, the visitor with whom Flora was engaged; but it was not the visitor most concerned with my boy. I hesitated afresh, but on other grounds and only for a few seconds; then I had made my choice. There were empty rooms at Bly, and it was only a question of choosing the right one. The right one suddenly presented itself to me as the lower one—though high above the gardens—in the solid corner of the house that I have spoken of as the old tower. This was a large, square chamber, arranged with some state as a bedroom, the extravagant size of which made it so inconvenient that it had not for years, though kept by Mrs. Grose in exemplary order, been occupied. I had often admired it and I knew my way about in it; I had only, after just faltering at the first chill gloom of its disuse, to pass across it and unbolt as quietly as I could one of the shutters. Achieving this transit, I uncovered the glass without a sound and, applying my face to the pane, was able, the darkness without being much less than within, to see that I commanded the right direction. Then I saw something more. The moon made the night extraordinarily penetrable and showed me on the lawn a person, diminished by distance, who stood there motionless and as if fascinated, looking up to where I had appeared—looking, that is, not so much straight at me as at something that was apparently above me. There was clearly another person above me—there was a person on the tower; but the presence on the lawn was not in the least what I had conceived and had confidently hurried to meet. The presence on the lawn—I felt sick as I made it out—was poor little Miles himself.

XI

It was not till late next day that I spoke to Mrs. Grose; the rigor with which I kept my pupils in sight making it often difficult to meet her privately, and the more as we each felt the importance of not provoking—on the part of the servants quite as much as on that of the children—any suspicion of a secret flurry or that of a discussion of mysteries. I drew a great security in this particular from her mere smooth aspect. There was nothing in her fresh face to pass on to others my horrible confidences. She believed me, I was sure, absolutely: if she hadn't I don't know what would have become of me, for I couldn't have borne the business alone. But she was a magnificent monument to the blessing of a want of imagination, and if she could see in our little charges nothing but their beauty and amiability, their happiness and cleverness, she had no direct communication with the sources of my trouble. If they had been at all visibly blighted or battered, she would doubtless have grown, on tracing it back, haggard enough to match them; as matters stood, however, I could feel her, when she surveyed them, with her large white arms folded and the habit of serenity in all her look, thank the Lord's mercy that if they were ruined the pieces would still serve. Flights of fancy gave place, in her mind, to a steady fireside glow, and I had already begun to perceive how, with the development of the conviction that—as time went on without a public accident—our young things could, after all, look out for themselves, she addressed her greatest solicitude to the sad case presented by their instructress. That, for myself, was a sound simplification: I could engage that, to the world, my face should tell no tales, but it would have been, in the conditions, an immense added strain to find myself anxious about hers.

At the hour I now speak of she had joined me, under pressure, on the terrace, where, with the lapse of the season, the afternoon sun was now agreeable; and we sat there together while, before us, at a distance, but within call if we wished, the children strolled to and fro in one of their most manageable moods. They moved slowly, in unison, below us, over the lawn, the boy, as they went, reading aloud from a storybook and passing his arm round his sister to keep her quite in touch. Mrs. Grose watched them with positive placidity; then I caught the suppressed intellectual creak with which she conscientiously turned to take from me a view of the back of the tapestry. I had made her a receptacle of lurid things, but there was an odd recognition of my superiority—my accomplishments and my function—in her patience under my pain. She offered her mind to my disclosures as, had I wished to mix a witch's broth and proposed it with assurance, she would have held out a large clean saucepan. This had become thoroughly her attitude by the time that, in my recital of the events of the night, I reached the point of what Miles had said to me when, after seeing him, at such a monstrous hour, almost on the very spot where he happened now to be, I had gone down to bring him in; choosing then, at the window, with a concentrated need of not alarming the house, rather that method than a signal more resonant. I had left her meanwhile in little doubt of my small hope of representing with success even to her actual sympathy my sense of the real splendor of the little inspiration with which, after I had got him into the house, the boy met my final articulate challenge. As soon as I appeared in the moonlight on the terrace, he had come to me as straight as possible; on which I had taken his hand without a word and led him, through the dark spaces, up the staircase where Quint had so hungrily hovered for him, along the lobby where I had listened and trembled, and so to his forsaken room.

Not a sound, on the way, had passed between us, and I had wondered—oh, how I had wondered!—if he were groping about in his little mind for something plausible and not too grotesque. It would tax his invention, certainly, and I felt, this time, over his real embarrassment, a curious thrill of triumph. It was a sharp trap for the inscrutable! He couldn't play any longer at innocence; so how the deuce would he get out of it? There beat in me indeed, with the passionate throb of this question an equal dumb appeal as to how the deuce *I* should. I was confronted at last, as never yet, with all the risk attached even now to sounding my own horrid note. I remember in fact that as we pushed into his little chamber, where the bed had not been slept in at all and the window, uncovered to the moonlight, made the place so clear that there was no need of striking a match—I remember how I suddenly dropped, sank upon the edge of the bed from the force of the idea that he must know how he really, as they say, "had" me. He could do what he liked, with all his cleverness to help him, so long as I should continue to defer to the old tradition of the criminality of those caretakers of the young who minister to superstitions and fears. He "had" me indeed, and in a cleft stick; for who would ever absolve me, who would consent that I should go unhung, if, by the faintest tremor of an overture, I were the first to introduce into our perfect intercourse an element so dire? No, no: it was useless to attempt to convey to Mrs. Grose, just as it is scarcely less so to attempt to suggest here, how, in our short, stiff brush in the dark, he fairly shook me with admiration. I was of course thoroughly kind and merciful; never, never yet had I placed on his little shoulders hands of such tenderness as those with which, while I rested against the bed, I held him there well under fire. I had no alternative but, in form at least, to put it to him.

"You must tell me now—and all the truth. What did you go out for? What were you doing there?"

I can still see his wonderful smile, the whites of his beautiful eyes, and the uncovering of his little teeth shine to me in the dusk. "If I tell you why, will you understand?" My heart, at this, leaped into my mouth. *Would* he tell me why? I found no sound on my lips to press it, and I was aware of replying only with a vague, repeated, grimacing nod. He was gentleness itself, and while I wagged my head at him he stood there more than ever a little fairy prince. It was his brightness indeed that gave me a respite. Would it be so great if he were really going to tell me? "Well," he said at last, "just exactly in order that you should do this."

"Do what?"

"Think me—for a change—*bad!*" I shall never forget the sweetness and gaiety with which he brought out the word, nor how, on top of it, he bent forward and kissed me. It was practically the end of everything. I met his kiss and I had to make, while I folded him for a minute in my arms, the most stupendous effort not to cry. He had given exactly the account of himself that permitted least of my going behind it, and it was only with the effect of confirming my acceptance of it that, as I presently glanced about the room, I could say—

"Then you didn't undress at all?"

He fairly glittered in the gloom. "Not at all. I sat up and read."

"And when did you go down?"

"At midnight. When I'm bad I *am* bad!"

"I see, I see—it's charming. But how could you be sure I would know it?"

"Oh, I arranged that with Flora." His answers rang out with a readiness! "She was to get up and look out."

"Which is what she did do." It was I who fell into the trap!

"So she disturbed you, and, to see what she was looking at, you also looked—you saw."

"While you," I concurred, "caught your death in the night air!"

He literally bloomed so from this exploit that he could afford radiantly to assent. "How otherwise should I have been bad enough?" he asked. Then, after another embrace, the incident and our interview closed on my recognition of all the reserves of goodness that, for his joke, he had been able to draw upon.

XII

The particular impression I had received proved in the morning light, I repeat, not quite successfully presentable to Mrs. Grose, though I reinforced it with the mention of still another remark that he had made before we separated. "It all lies in half a dozen words," I said to her, "words that really settle the matter. 'Think, you know, what I might do!' He threw that off to show me how good he is. He knows down to the ground what he 'might' do. That's what he gave them a taste of at school."

"Lord, you do change!" cried my friend.

"I don't change—I simply make it out. The four, depend upon it, perpetually meet. If on either of these last nights you had been with either child, you would clearly have understood. The more I've watched and waited the more I've felt that if there were nothing else to make it sure it would be made so by the systematic silence of each. *Never*, by a slip of the tongue, have they so much as alluded to either of their old friends, any more than Miles has alluded to his expulsion. Oh, yes, we may sit here and look at them, and they may show off to us there to their fill; but even while they pretend to be lost in their fairytale they're steeped in their vision of the dead restored. He's not reading to her," I declared; "they're talking of *them*—they're talking horrors! I go on, I know, as if I were crazy; and it's a wonder I'm not. What I've seen would have made you so; but it has only made me more lucid, made me get hold of still other things."

My lucidity must have seemed awful, but the charming creatures who were victims of it, passing and repassing in their interlocked sweetness, gave my colleague something to hold on by; and I felt how tight she held as, without stirring in the breath of my passion, she covered them still with her eyes. "Of what other things have you got hold?"

"Why, of the very things that have delighted, fascinated, and yet, at bottom, as I now so strangely see, mystified and troubled me. Their more than earthly beauty, their absolutely unnatural goodness. It's a game," I went on; "it's a policy and a fraud!"

"On the part of little darlings—?"

"As yet mere lovely babies? Yes, mad as that seems!" The very act of bringing it out really helped me to trace it—follow it all up and piece it all together. "They haven't been good—they've only been absent. It has been easy to live with them, because they're simply leading a life of their own. They're not mine—they're not ours. They're his and they're hers!"

"Quint's and that woman's?"

"Quint's and that woman's. They want to get to them."

Oh, how, at this, poor Mrs. Grose appeared to study them! "But for what?"

"For the love of all the evil that, in those dreadful days, the pair put into them. And to ply them with that evil still, to keep up the work of demons, is what brings the others back."

"Laws!" said my friend under her breath. The exclamation was homely, but it revealed a real acceptance of my further proof of what, in the bad time—for there had been a worse even than this!—must have occurred. There could have been no such justification for me as the plain assent of her experience to whatever depth of depravity I found credible in our brace of scoundrels. It was in obvious submission of memory that she brought out after a moment: "They *were* rascals! But what can they now do?" she pursued.

"Do?" I echoed so loud that Miles and Flora, as they passed at their distance, paused an instant in their walk and looked at us. "Don't they do enough?" I demanded in a lower tone, while the children, having smiled and nodded and kissed hands to us, resumed their exhibition. We were held by it a minute; then I answered: "They can destroy them!" At this my companion did turn, but the inquiry she launched was a silent one, the effect of which was to make me more explicit. "They don't know, as yet, quite how—but they're trying hard. They're seen only across, as it were, and beyond—in strange places and on high places, the top of towers, the roof of houses, the outside of windows, the further edge of pools; but there's a deep design, on either side, to shorten the distance and overcome the obstacle; and the success of the tempters is only a question of time. They've only to keep to their suggestions of danger."

"For the children to come?"

"And perish in the attempt!" Mrs. Grose slowly got up, and I scrupulously added: "Unless, of course, we can prevent!"

Standing there before me while I kept my seat, she visibly turned things over. "Their uncle must do the preventing. He must take them away."

"And who's to make him?"

She had been scanning the distance, but she now dropped on me a foolish face. "You, miss."

"By writing to him that his house is poisoned and his little nephew and niece mad?"

"But if they *are*, miss?"

"And if I am myself, you mean? That's charming news to be sent him by a governess whose prime undertaking was to give him no worry."

Mrs. Grose considered, following the children again. "Yes, he do hate worry. That was the great reason—"

"Why those fiends took him in so long? No doubt, though his indifference must have been awful. As I'm not a fiend, at any rate, I shouldn't take him in."

My companion, after an instant and for all answer, sat down again and grasped my arm. "Make him at any rate come to you."

I stared. "To *me?*" I had a sudden fear of what she might do. "'Him'?"

"He ought to *be* here—he ought to help."

I quickly rose, and I think I must have shown her a queerer face than ever yet. "You see me asking him for a visit?" No, with her eyes on my face she evidently couldn't. Instead of it even—as a woman reads another—she could see what I myself saw: his derision, his amusement, his contempt for the breakdown of my resignation at being left alone and for the fine machinery I had set in motion to attract his attention to my slighted charms. She didn't know—no one knew—how proud I had been to serve him and to stick to our terms; yet she nonetheless took the measure, I think, of the warning I now gave her. "If you should so lose your head as to appeal to him for me—"

She was really frightened. "Yes, miss?"

"I would leave, on the spot, both him and you."

XIII

It was all very well to join them, but speaking to them proved quite as much as ever an effort beyond my strength—offered, in close quarters, difficulties as insurmountable as before. This situation continued a month, and with new aggravations and particular notes, the note above all, sharper and sharper, of the small ironic consciousness on the part of my pupils. It was not, I am as sure today as I was sure then, my mere infernal imagination: it was absolutely traceable that they were aware of my predicament and that this strange relation made, in a manner, for a long time, the air in which we moved. I don't mean that they had their tongues in their cheeks or did anything vulgar, for that was not one of their dangers: I do mean, on the other hand, that the element of the unnamed and untouched became, between us, greater than any other, and that so much avoidance could not have been so successfully effected without a great deal of tacit arrangement. It was as if, at moments, we were perpetually coming into sight of subjects before which we must stop short, turning suddenly out of alleys that we perceived to be blind, closing with a little bang that made us look at each other—for, like all bangs, it was something louder than we had intended—the doors we had indiscreetly opened. All roads lead to Rome, and there were times when it might have struck us that almost every branch of study or subject of conversation skirted forbidden ground. Forbidden ground was the question of the return of the dead in general and of whatever, in especial, might survive, in memory, of the friends little children had lost. There were days when I could have sworn that one of them had, with a small invisible nudge, said to the other: "She thinks she'll do it this time—but she *won't!*" To "do it" would have been to indulge for instance—and for once in a way—in some direct reference to the lady who had prepared them for my discipline. They had a delightful endless appetite for passages in my own history, to which I had again and again treated them; they were in possession of everything that had ever happened to me, had had, with every circumstance the story of my smallest adventures and of those of my brothers and sisters and of the cat and the dog at home, as well as many particulars of the eccentric nature of my father, of the furniture and arrangement of our house, and of the conversation of the old women of our village. There were things enough, taking one with another, to chatter about, if one went very fast and knew by instinct when to go round. They pulled with an art of their own the strings of my invention and my memory; and nothing else perhaps, when I thought of such occasions afterward, gave me so the suspicion of being watched from under cover. It was in any case over my life, my past, and my friends alone that we could take anything like our ease—a state of affairs that led them sometimes without the least pertinence to break out into sociable reminders. I was invited—with no visible connection—to repeat afresh Goody Gosling's celebrated mot or to confirm the details already supplied as to the cleverness of the vicarage pony.

It was partly at such junctures as these and partly at quite different ones that, with the turn my matters had now taken, my predicament, as I have called it, grew most sensible. The fact that the days passed for me without another encounter ought, it would have appeared, to have done something toward soothing my nerves. Since the light brush, that second night on the upper landing, of the presence of a woman at the foot of the stair, I had seen nothing, whether in or out of the house, that one had better not have seen. There was many a corner round which I expected to come upon Quint, and many a situation that, in a merely sinister way, would have favored the appearance of Miss Jessel. The summer had turned, the summer had gone; the autumn had dropped upon Bly and had blown out half our lights. The place, with its gray sky and withered garlands, its bared spaces and scattered dead leaves, was like a theater after the performance—all strewn with crumpled playbills. There were exactly states of the air, conditions of sound and of stillness, unspeakable impressions of the *kind* of ministering moment, that brought back to me, long enough to catch it, the feeling of the medium in which, that June evening out of doors, I had had my first sight of Quint, and in which, too, at those other instants, I had, after seeing him through the window, looked for him in vain in the circle of shrubbery. I recognized the signs, the portents—I recognized the moment, the spot. But they remained unaccompanied and empty, and I continued unmolested; if unmolested one could call a young woman whose sensibility had, in the most extraordinary fashion, not declined but deepened. I had said in my talk with Mrs. Grose on that horrid scene of Flora's by the lake—and had perplexed her by so saying—that it would from that moment distress me much more to lose my power than to keep it. I had then expressed what was vividly in my mind: the truth that, whether the children really saw or not—since, that is, it was not yet definitely proved—I greatly preferred, as a safeguard, the fullness of my own exposure. I was ready to know the very worst that was to be known. What I had then had an ugly glimpse of was that my eyes might be sealed just while theirs were most opened. Well, my eyes were sealed, it appeared, at present—a consummation for which it seemed blasphemous not to thank God. There was, alas, a difficulty about that: I would have thanked him with all my soul had I not had in a proportionate measure this conviction of the secret of my pupils.

How can I retrace today the strange steps of my obsession? There were times of our being together when I would have been ready to swear that, literally, in my presence, but with my direct sense of it closed, they had visitors who were known and were welcome. Then it was that, had I not been deterred by the very chance that such an injury might prove greater than the injury to be averted, my exultation would have broken out. "They're here, they're here, you little wretches," I would have cried, "and you can't deny it now!" The little wretches denied it with all the added volume of their sociability and their tenderness, in just the crystal depths of which—like the flash of a fish in a stream—the mockery of their advantage peeped up. The shock, in truth, had sunk into me still deeper than I knew on the night when, looking out to see either Quint or Miss Jessel under the stars, I had beheld the boy over whose rest I watched and who had immediately brought in with him—had straightway, there, turned it on me—the lovely upward look with which, from the battlements above me, the hideous apparition of Quint had played. If it was a question of a scare, my discovery on this occasion had scared me more than any other, and it was in the condition of nerves produced by it that I made my actual inductions. They harassed me so that sometimes, at odd moments, I shut myself up audibly to rehearse—it was at once a fantastic relief and a renewed despair—the manner in which I might come to the point. I approached it from one side and the other while, in my room, I flung myself about, but I always broke down in the monstrous utterance of names. As they died away on my lips, I said to myself that I should indeed help them to represent something infamous, if, by pronouncing them, I should violate as rare a little case of instinctive delicacy as any schoolroom, probably, had ever known. When I said to myself: "*They* have the manners to be silent, and you, trusted as you are, the baseness to speak!" I felt myself crimson and I covered my face with my hands. After these secret scenes I chattered more than ever, going on volubly enough till one of our prodigious, palpable hushes occurred—I can call them nothing else—the strange, dizzy lift or swim (I try for terms!) into a stillness, a pause of all life, that had nothing to do with the more or less noise that at the moment we might be engaged in making and that I could hear through any deepened exhilaration or quickened recitation or louder strum of the piano. Then it was that the others, the outsiders, were there. Though they were not angels, they "passed," as the French say, causing me, while they stayed, to tremble with the fear of their addressing to their younger victims some yet more infernal message or more vivid image than they had thought good enough for myself.

What it was most impossible to get rid of was the cruel idea that, whatever I had seen, Miles and Flora saw more—things terrible and unguessable and that sprang from dreadful passages of intercourse in the past. Such things naturally left on the surface, for the time, a chill which we vociferously denied that we felt; and we had, all three, with repetition, got into such splendid training that we went, each time, almost automatically, to mark the close of the incident, through the very same movements. It was striking of the children, at all events, to kiss me inveterately with a kind of wild irrelevance and never to fail—one or the other—of the precious question that had helped us through many a peril. "When do you think he *will* come? Don't you think we ought to write?"—there was nothing like that inquiry, we found by experience, for carrying off an awkwardness. "He" of course was their uncle in Harley Street; and we lived in much profusion of theory that he might at any moment arrive to mingle in our circle. It was impossible to have given less encouragement than he had done to such a doctrine, but if we had not had the doctrine to fall back upon we should have deprived each other of some of our finest exhibitions. He never wrote to them—that may have been selfish, but it was a part of the flattery of his trust of me; for the way in which a man pays his highest tribute to a woman is apt to be but by the more festal celebration of one of the sacred laws of his comfort; and I held that I carried out the spirit of the pledge given not to appeal to him when I let my charges understand that their own letters were but charming literary exercises. They were too beautiful to be posted; I kept them myself; I have them all to this hour. This was a rule indeed which only added to the satiric effect of my being plied with the supposition that he might at any moment be among us. It was exactly as if my charges knew how almost more awkward than anything else that might be for me. There appears to me, moreover, as I look back, no note in all this more extraordinary than the mere fact that, in spite of my tension and of their triumph, I never lost patience with them. Adorable they must in truth have been, I now reflect, that I didn't in these days hate them! Would exasperation, however, if relief had longer been postponed, finally have betrayed me? It little matters, for relief arrived. I call it relief, though it was only the relief that a snap brings to a strain or the burst of a thunderstorm to a day of suffocation. It was at least change, and it came with a rush.

XIV

Walking to church a certain Sunday morning, I had little Miles at my side and his sister, in advance of us and at Mrs. Grose's, well in sight. It was a crisp, clear day, the first of its order for some time; the night had brought a touch of frost, and the autumn air, bright and sharp, made the church bells almost gay. It was an odd accident of thought that I should have happened at such a moment to be particularly and very gratefully struck with the obedience of my little charges. Why did they never resent my inexorable, my perpetual society? Something or other had brought nearer home to me that I had all but pinned the boy to my shawl and that, in the way our companions were marshaled before me, I might have appeared to provide against some danger of rebellion. I was like a gaoler with an eye to possible surprises and escapes. But all this belonged—I mean their magnificent little surrender—just to the special array of the facts that were most abysmal. Turned out for Sunday by his uncle's tailor, who had had a free hand and a notion of pretty waistcoats and of his grand little air, Miles's whole title to independence, the rights of his sex and situation, were so stamped upon him that if he had suddenly struck for freedom

I should have had nothing to say. I was by the strangest of chances wondering how I should meet him when the revolution unmistakably occurred. I call it a revolution because I now see how, with the word he spoke, the curtain rose on the last act of my dreadful drama, and the catastrophe was precipitated. "Look here, my dear, you know," he charmingly said, "when in the world, please, am I going back to school?"

Transcribed here the speech sounds harmless enough, particularly as uttered in the sweet, high, casual pipe with which, at all interlocutors, but above all at his eternal governess, he threw off intonations as if he were tossing roses. There was something in them that always made one "catch," and I caught, at any rate, now so effectually that I stopped as short as if one of the trees of the park had fallen across the road. There was something new, on the spot, between us, and he was perfectly aware that I recognized it, though, to enable me to do so, he had no need to look a whit less candid and charming than usual. I could feel in him how he already, from my at first finding nothing to reply, perceived the advantage he had gained. I was so slow to find anything that he had plenty of time, after a minute, to continue with his suggestive but inconclusive smile: "You know, my dear, that for a fellow to be with a lady *always*—!" His "my dear" was constantly on his lips for me, and nothing could have expressed more the exact shade of the sentiment with which I desired to inspire my pupils than its fond familiarity. It was so respectfully easy.

But, oh, how I felt that at present I must pick my own phrases! I remember that, to gain time, I tried to laugh, and I seemed to see in the beautiful face with which he watched me how ugly and queer I looked. "And always with the same lady?" I returned.

He neither blanched nor winked. The whole thing was virtually out between us. "Ah, of course, she's a jolly, 'perfect' lady; but, after all, I'm a fellow, don't you see? that's—well, getting on."

I lingered there with him an instant ever so kindly. "Yes, you're getting on." Oh, but I felt helpless!

I have kept to this day the heartbreaking little idea of how he seemed to know that and to play with it. "And you can't say I've not been awfully good, can you?"

I laid my hand on his shoulder, for, though I felt how much better it would have been to walk on, I was not yet quite able. "No, I can't say that, Miles."

"Except just that one night, you know—!"

"That one night?" I couldn't look as straight as he.

"Why, when I went down—went out of the house."

"Oh, yes. But I forget what you did it for."

"You forget?"—he spoke with the sweet extravagance of childish reproach. "Why, it was to show you I could!"

"Oh, yes, you could."

"And I can again."

I felt that I might, perhaps, after all, succeed in keeping my wits about me. "Certainly. But you won't."

"No, not *that* again. It was nothing."

"It was nothing," I said. "But we must go on."

He resumed our walk with me, passing his hand into my arm. "Then when am I going back?"

I wore, in turning it over, my most responsible air. "Were you very happy at school?"

He just considered. "Oh, I'm happy enough anywhere!"

"Well, then," I quavered, "if you're just as happy here—!"

"Ah, but that isn't everything! Of course *you* know a lot—"

"But you hint that you know almost as much?" I risked as he paused.

"Not half I want to!" Miles honestly professed. "But it isn't so much that."

"What is it, then?"

"Well—I want to see more life."

"I see; I see." We had arrived within sight of the church and of various persons, including several of the household of Bly, on their way to it and clustered about the door to see us go in. I quickened our step; I wanted to get there before the question between us opened up much further; I reflected hungrily that, for more than an hour, he would have to be silent; and I thought with envy of the comparative dusk of the pew and of the almost spiritual help of the hassock on which I might bend my knees. I seemed literally to be running a race with some confusion to which he was about to reduce me, but I felt that he had got in first when, before we had even entered the churchyard, he threw out—

"I want my own sort!"

It literally made me bound forward. "There are not many of your own sort, Miles!" I laughed. "Unless perhaps dear little Flora!"

"You really compare me to a baby girl?"

This found me singularly weak. "Don't you, then, *love* our sweet Flora?"

"If I didn't—and you, too; if I didn't—!" he repeated as if retreating for a jump, yet leaving his thought so unfinished that, after we had come into the gate, another stop, which he imposed on me by the pressure of his arm, had become inevitable. Mrs. Grose and Flora had passed into the church, the other worshippers had followed, and we were, for the minute, alone among the old, thick graves. We had paused, on the path from the gate, by a low, oblong, tablelike tomb.

"Yes, if you didn't—?"

He looked, while I waited, at the graves. "Well, you know what!" But he didn't move, and he presently produced something that made me drop straight down on the stone slab, as if suddenly to rest. "Does my uncle think what you think?"

I markedly rested. "How do you know what I think?"

"Ah, well, of course I don't; for it strikes me you never tell me. But I mean does *he* know?"

"Know what, Miles?"

"Why, the way I'm going on."

I perceived quickly enough that I could make, to this inquiry, no answer that would not involve something of a sacrifice of my employer. Yet it appeared to me that we were all, at Bly, sufficiently sacrificed to make that venial. "I don't think your uncle much cares."

Miles, on this, stood looking at me. "Then don't you think he can be made to?"

"In what way?"

"Why, by his coming down."

"But who'll get him to come down?"

"*I* will!" the boy said with extraordinary brightness and emphasis. He gave me another look charged with that expression and then marched off alone into church.

XV

The business was practically settled from the moment I never followed him. It was a pitiful surrender to agitation, but my being aware of this had somehow no power to restore me. I only sat there on my tomb and read into what my little friend had said to me the fullness of its meaning; by the time I had grasped the whole of which I had also embraced, for absence, the pretext that I was ashamed to offer my pupils and the rest of the congregation such an example of delay. What I said to myself above all was that Miles had got something out of me and that the proof of it, for him, would be just this awkward collapse. He had got out of me that there was something I was much afraid of and that he should probably be able to make use of my fear to gain, for his own purpose, more freedom. My fear was of having to deal with the intolerable question of the grounds of his dismissal from school, for that was really but the question of the horrors gathered behind. That his uncle should arrive to treat with me of these things was a solution that, strictly speaking, I ought now to have desired to bring on; but I could so little face the ugliness and the pain of it that I simply procrastinated and lived from hand to mouth. The boy, to my deep discomposure, was immensely in the right, was in a position to say to me: "Either you clear up with my guardian the mystery of this interruption of my studies, or you cease to expect me to lead with you a life that's so unnatural for a boy." What was so unnatural for the particular boy I was concerned with was this sudden revelation of a consciousness and a plan.

That was what really overcame me, what prevented my going in. I walked round the church, hesitating, hovering; I reflected that I had already, with him, hurt myself beyond repair. Therefore I could patch up nothing, and it was too extreme an effort to squeeze beside him into the pew: he would be so much more sure than ever to pass his arm into mine and make me sit there for an hour in close, silent contact with his commentary on our talk. For the first minute since his arrival I wanted to get away from him. As I paused beneath the high east window and listened to the sounds of worship, I was taken with an impulse that might master me, I felt, completely should I give it the least encouragement. I might easily put an end to my predicament by getting away altogether. Here was my chance; there was no one to stop me; I could give the whole thing up—turn my back and retreat. It was only a question of hurrying again, for a few preparations, to the house which the attendance at church of so many of the servants would practically have left unoccupied. No one, in short, could blame me if I should just drive desperately off. What was it to get away if I got away only till dinner? That would be in a couple of hours, at the end of which—I had the acute prevision—my little pupils would play at innocent wonder about my nonappearance in their train.

"What *did* you do, you naughty, bad thing? Why in the world, to worry us so—and take our thoughts off, too, don't you know?—did you desert us at the very door?" I couldn't meet such questions nor, as they asked them, their false little lovely eyes; yet it was all so exactly what I should have to meet that, as the prospect grew sharp to me, I at last let myself go.

I got, so far as the immediate moment was concerned, away; I came straight out of the churchyard and, thinking hard, retraced my steps through the park. It seemed to me that by the time I reached the house I had made up my mind I would fly. The Sunday stillness both of the approaches and of the interior, in which I met no one, fairly excited me with a sense of opportunity. Were I to get off quickly, this way, I should get off without a scene, without a word. My quickness would have to be remarkable, however, and the question of a conveyance was the great one to settle. Tormented, in the hall, with difficulties and obstacles, I remember sinking down at the foot of the staircase—suddenly collapsing there on the lowest step and then, with a revulsion, recalling that it was exactly where more than a month before, in the darkness of night and just so bowed with evil things, I had seen the specter of the most horrible of women. At this I was able to straighten myself; I went the rest of the way up; I made, in my bewilderment, for the schoolroom, where there were objects belonging to me that I should have to take. But I opened the door to find again, in a flash, my eyes unsealed. In the presence of what I saw I reeled straight back upon my resistance.

Seated at my own table in clear noonday light I saw a person whom, without my previous experience, I should have taken at the first blush for some housemaid who might have stayed at home to look after the place and who, availing herself of rare relief from observation and of the schoolroom table and my pens, ink, and paper, had applied herself to the considerable effort of a letter to her sweetheart. There was an effort in the way that, while her arms rested on the table, her hands with evident weariness supported her head; but at the moment I took this in I had already become aware that, in spite of my entrance, her attitude strangely persisted. Then it was—with the very act of its announcing itself—that her identity flared up in a change of posture. She rose, not as if she had heard me, but with an indescribable grand melancholy of indifference and detachment, and, within a dozen feet of me, stood there as my vile predecessor. Dishonored and tragic, she was all before me; but even as I fixed and, for memory, secured it, the awful image passed away. Dark as midnight in her black dress, her haggard beauty and her unutterable woe, she had looked at me long enough to appear to say that her right to sit at my table was as good as mine to sit at hers. While these instants lasted, indeed, I had the extraordinary chill of feeling that it was I who was the intruder. It was as a wild protest against it that, actually addressing her—"You terrible, miserable woman!"—I heard myself break into a sound that, by the open door, rang through the long passage and the empty house. She looked at me as if she heard me, but I had recovered myself and cleared the air. There was nothing in the room the next minute but the sunshine and a sense that I must stay.

XVI

I had so perfectly expected that the return of my pupils would be marked by a demonstration that I was freshly upset at having to take into account that they were dumb about my absence. Instead of gaily denouncing and caressing me, they made no allusion to my having failed them, and I was left, for the time, on perceiving that she too said nothing, to study Mrs. Grose's odd face. I did this to such purpose that I made sure they had in some way bribed her to silence; a silence that, however, I would engage to break down on the first private opportunity. This opportunity came before tea: I secured five minutes with her in the housekeeper's room, where, in the twilight, amid a smell of lately baked bread, but with the place all swept and garnished, I found her sitting in pained placidity before the fire. So I see her still, so I see her best: facing the flame from her straight chair in the dusky, shining room, a large clean image of the "put away"—of drawers closed and locked and rest without a remedy.

"Oh, yes, they asked me to say nothing; and to please them—so long as they were there—of course I promised. But what had happened to you?"

"I only went with you for the walk," I said. "I had then to come back to meet a friend."

She showed her surprise. "A friend—*you?*"

"Oh, yes, I have a couple!" I laughed. "But did the children give you a reason?"

"For not alluding to your leaving us? Yes; they said you would like it better. Do you like it better?"

My face had made her rueful. "No, I like it worse!" But after an instant I added: "Did they say why I should like it better?"

"No; Master Miles only said, 'We must do nothing but what she likes!' "

"I wish indeed he would. And what did Flora say?"

"Miss Flora was too sweet. She said, 'Oh, of course, of course!'—and I said the same."

I thought a moment. "You were too sweet, too—I can hear you all. But nonetheless, between Miles and me, it's now all out."

"All out?" My companion stared. "But what, miss?"

"Everything. It doesn't matter. I've made up my mind. I came home, my dear," I went on, "for a talk with Miss Jessel."

I had by this time formed the habit of having Mrs. Grose literally well in hand in advance of my sounding that note; so that even now, as she bravely blinked under the signal of my word, I could keep her comparatively firm. "A talk! Do you mean she spoke?"

"It came to that. I found her, on my return, in the schoolroom."

"And what did she say?" I can hear the good woman still, and the candor of her stupefaction.

"That she suffers the torments—!"

It was this, of a truth, that made her, as she filled out my picture, gape. "Do you mean," she faltered, "—of the lost?"

"Of the lost. Of the damned. And that's why, to share them—" I faltered myself with the horror of it.

But my companion, with less imagination, kept me up. "To share them—?"

"She wants Flora." Mrs. Grose might, as I gave it to her, fairly have fallen away from me had I not been prepared. I still held her there, to show I was. "As I've told you, however, it doesn't matter."

"Because you've made up your mind? But to what?"

"To everything."

"And what do you call 'everything'?"

"Why, sending for their uncle."

"Oh, miss, in pity do," my friend broke out. "Ah, but I will, I *will!* I see it's the only way. What's 'out,' as I told you, with Miles is that if he thinks I'm afraid to—and has ideas of what he gains by that—he shall see he's mistaken. Yes, yes; his uncle shall have it here from me on the spot (and before the boy himself, if necessary) that if I'm to be reproached with having done nothing again about more school—"

"Yes, miss—" my companion pressed me.

"Well, there's that awful reason."

There were now clearly so many of these for my poor colleague that she was excusable for being vague. "But—a—which?"

"Why, the letter from his old place."

"You'll show it to the master?"

"I ought to have done so on the instant."

"Oh, no!" said Mrs. Grose with decision.

"I'll put it before him," I went on inexorably, "that I can't undertake to work the question on behalf of a child who has been expelled—"

"For we've never in the least known what!" Mrs. Grose declared.

"For wickedness. For what else—when he's so clever and beautiful and perfect? Is he stupid? Is he untidy? Is he infirm? Is he ill-natured? He's exquisite—so it can be only *that;* and that would open up the whole thing. After all," I said, "it's their uncle's fault. If he left here such people—!"

"He didn't really in the least know them. The fault's mine." She had turned quite pale.

"Well, you shan't suffer," I answered.

"The children shan't!" she emphatically returned.

I was silent awhile; we looked at each other. "Then what am I to tell him?"

"You needn't tell him anything. *I'll* tell him."

I measured this. "Do you mean you'll write—?" Remembering she couldn't, I caught myself up. "How do you communicate?"

"I tell the bailiff. *He* writes."

"And should you like him to write our story?"

My question had a sarcastic force that I had not fully intended, and it made her, after a moment, inconsequently break down. The tears were again in her eyes. "Ah, miss, you write!"

"Well—tonight," I at last answered; and on this we separated.

XVII

I went so far, in the evening, as to make a beginning. The weather had changed back, a great wind was abroad, and beneath the lamp, in my room, with Flora at peace beside me, I sat for a long time before a blank sheet of paper and listened to the lash of the rain and the batter of the gusts. Finally I went out, taking a candle; I crossed the passage and listened a minute at Miles's door. What, under my endless obsession, I had been impelled to listen for was some betrayal of his not being at rest, and I presently caught one, but not in the form I had expected. His voice tinkled out. "I say, you there—come in." It was a gaiety in the gloom!

I went in with my light and found him, in bed, very wide awake, but very much at his ease. "Well, what are *you* up to?" he asked with a grace of sociability in which it occurred to me that Mrs. Grose, had she been present, might have looked in vain for proof that anything was "out."

I stood over him with my candle. "How did you know I was there?"

"Why, of course I heard you. Did you fancy you made no noise? You're like a troop of cavalry!" he beautifully laughed.

"Then you weren't asleep?"

"Not much! I lie awake and think."

I had put my candle, designedly, a short way off, and then, as he held out his friendly old hand to me, had sat down on the edge of his bed. "What is it," I asked, "that you think of?"

"What in the world, my dear, but you?"

"Ah, the pride I take in your appreciation doesn't insist on that! I had so far rather you slept."

"Well, I think also, you know, of this queer business of ours."

I marked the coolness of his firm little hand. "Of what queer business, Miles?"

"Why, the way you bring me up. And all the rest!"

I fairly held my breath a minute, and even from my glimmering taper there was light enough to show how he smiled up at me from his pillow. "What do you mean by all the rest?"

"Oh, you know, you know!"

I could say nothing for a minute, though I felt, as I held his hand and our eyes continued to meet, that my silence had all the air of admitting his charge and that nothing in the whole world of reality was perhaps at that moment so fabulous as our actual relation. "Certainly you shall go back to school," I said, "if it be that that troubles you. But not to the old place—we must find another, a better. How could I know it did trouble you, this question, when you never told me so, never spoke of it at all?" His clear, listening face, framed in its smooth whiteness, made him for the minute as appealing as some wistful patient in a children's hospital; and I would have given, as the resemblance came to me, all I possessed on earth really to be the nurse or the sister of charity who might have helped to cure him. Well, even as it was, I perhaps might help! "Do you know you've never said a word to me about your school—I mean the old one; never mentioned it in any way?"

He seemed to wonder; he smiled with the same loveliness. But he clearly gained time; he waited, he called for guidance. "Haven't I?" It wasn't for *me* to help him—it was for the thing I had met!

Something in his tone and the expression of his face, as I got this from him, set my heart aching with such a pang as it had never yet known; so unutterably touching was it to see his little brain puzzled and his little resources taxed to play, under the spell laid on him, a part of innocence and consistency. "No, never—from the hour you came back. You've never mentioned to me one of your masters, one of your comrades, nor the least little thing that ever happened to you at school. Never, little Miles—no, never—have you given me an inkling of anything that *may* have happened there. Therefore you can fancy how much I'm in the dark. Until you came out, that way, this morning, you had, since the first hour I saw you, scarce even made a reference to anything in your previous life. You seemed so perfectly to accept the present." It was extraordinary how my absolute conviction of his secret precocity (or whatever I might call the poison of an influence that I dared but half to phrase) made him, in spite of the faint breath of his inward trouble, appear as accessible as an older person—imposed him almost as an intellectual equal. "I thought you wanted to go on as you are."

It struck me that at this he just faintly colored. He gave, at any rate, like a convalescent slightly fatigued, a languid shake of his head. "I don't—I don't. I want to get away."

"You're tired of Bly?"

"Oh, no, I like Bly."

"Well, then—?"

"Oh, *you* know what a boy wants!"

I felt that I didn't know so well as Miles, and I took temporary refuge. "You want to go to your uncle?"

Again, at this, with his sweet ironic face, he made a movement on the pillow. "Ah, you can't get off with that!"

I was silent a little, and it was I, now, I think, who changed color. "My dear, I don't want to get off!"

"You can't, even if you do. You can't, you can't!"—he lay beautifully staring. "My uncle must come down, and you must completely settle things."

"If we do," I returned with some spirit, "you may be sure it will be to take you quite away."

"Well, don't you understand that that's exactly what I'm working for? You'll have to tell him—about the way you've let it all drop: you'll have to tell him a tremendous lot!"

The exultation with which he uttered this helped me somehow, for the instant, to meet him rather more. "And how much will you, Miles, have to tell him? There are things he'll ask you!"

He turned it over. "Very likely. But what things?"

"The things you've never told me. To make up his mind what to do with you. He can't send you back—"

"Oh, I don't want to go back!" he broke in. "I want a new field."

He said it with admirable serenity, with positive unimpeachable gaiety; and doubtless it was that very note that most evoked for me the poignancy, the unnatural childish tragedy, of his probable reappearance at the end of three months with all this bravado and still more dishonor. It overwhelmed me now that I should never be able to bear that, and it made me let myself go. I threw myself upon him and in the tenderness of my pity I embraced him. "Dear little Miles, dear little Miles—!"

My face was close to his, and he let me kiss him, simply taking it with indulgent good humor. "Well, old lady?"

"Is there nothing—nothing at all that you want to tell me?"

He turned off a little, facing round toward the wall and holding up his hand to look at as one had seen sick children look. "I've told you—I told you this morning."

Oh, I was sorry for him! "That you just want me not to worry you?"

He looked round at me now, as if in recognition of my understanding him; then ever so gently, "To let me alone," he replied.

There was even a singular little dignity in it, something that made me release him, yet, when I had slowly risen, linger beside him. God knows I never wished to harass him, but I felt that merely, at this, to turn my back on him was to abandon or, to put it more truly, to lose him. "I've just begun a letter to your uncle," I said.

"Well, then, finish it!"

I waited a minute. "What happened before?"

He gazed up at me again. "Before what?"

"Before you came back. And before you went away."

For some time he was silent, but he continued to meet my eyes. "What happened?"

It made me, the sound of the words, in which it seemed to me that I caught for the very first time a small faint quaver of consenting consciousness—it made me drop on my knees beside the bed and seize once more the chance of possessing him. "Dear little Miles, dear little Miles, if you knew how I want to help you! It's only that, it's nothing but that, and I'd rather die than give you a pain or do you a wrong—I'd rather die than hurt a hair of you. Dear little Miles"—oh, I brought it out now even if I *should* go too far—"I just want you to help me to save you!" But I knew in a moment after this that I had gone too far. The answer to my appeal was instantaneous, but it came in the form of an extraordinary blast and chill, a gust of frozen air, and a shake of the room as great as if, in the wild wind, the casement had crashed in. The boy gave a loud, high shriek, which, lost in the rest of the shock of sound, might have seemed, indistinctly, though I was so close to him, a note either of jubilation or of terror. I jumped to my feet again and was conscious of darkness. So for a moment we remained, while I stared about me and saw that the drawn curtains were unstirred and the window tight. "Why, the candle's out!" I then cried.

"It was I who blew it, dear!" said Miles.

XVIII

The next day, after lessons, Mrs. Grose found a moment to say to me quietly: "Have you written, miss?"

"Yes—I've written." But I didn't add—for the hour—that my letter, sealed and directed, was still in my pocket. There would be time enough to send it before the messenger should go to the village. Meanwhile there had been, on the part of my pupils, no more brilliant, more exemplary morning. It was exactly as if they had both had at heart to gloss over any recent little friction. They performed the dizziest feats of arithmetic, soaring quite out of my feeble range, and perpetrated, in higher spirits than ever, geographical and historical jokes. It was conspicuous of course in Miles in particular that he appeared to wish to show how easily he could let me down. This child, to my memory, really lives in a setting of beauty and misery that no words can translate; there was a distinction all his own in every impulse he revealed; never was a small natural creature, to the uninitiated eye all frankness and freedom, a more ingenious, a more extraordinary little gentleman. I had perpetually to guard against the wonder of contemplation into which my initiated view betrayed me; to check the irrelevant gaze and discouraged sigh in which I constantly both attacked and renounced the enigma of what such a little gentleman could have done that deserved a penalty. Say that, by the dark prodigy I knew, the imagination of all evil *had* been opened up to him: all the justice within me ached for the proof that it could ever have flowered into an act.

He had never, at any rate, been such a little gentleman as when, after our early dinner on this dreadful day, he came round to me and asked if I shouldn't like him, for half an hour, to play to me. David playing to Saul could never have shown a finer sense of the occasion. It was literally a charming exhibition of tact, of magnanimity, and quite tantamount to his saying outright: "The true knights we love to read about never push an advantage too far. I know what you mean now: you mean that—to be let alone yourself and not followed up—you'll cease to worry and spy upon me, won't keep me so close to you, will let me go and come. Well, I 'come,' you see—but I don't go! There'll be plenty of time for that. I do really delight in your society, and I only want to show you that I contended for a principle." It may be imagined whether I resisted this appeal or failed to accompany him again, hand in hand, to the schoolroom. He sat down at the old piano and played as he had never played; and if there are those who think he had better have been kicking a football I can only say that I wholly agree with them. For at the end of a time that under his influence I had quite ceased to measure, I started up with a strange sense of having literally slept at my post. It was after luncheon, and by the schoolroom fire, and yet I hadn't really, in the least, slept: I had only done something much worse—I had forgotten. Where, all this time, was Flora? When I put the question to Miles, he played on a minute before answering and then could only say: "Why, my dear, how do *I* know?"—breaking moreover into a happy laugh which, immediately after, as if it were a vocal accompaniment, he prolonged into incoherent, extravagant song.

I went straight to my room, but his sister was not there; then, before going downstairs, I looked into several others. As she was nowhere about she would surely be with Mrs. Grose, whom, in the comfort of that theory, I accordingly proceeded in quest of. I found her where I had found her the evening before, but she met my quick challenge with blank, scared ignorance. She had only supposed that, after the repast, I had carried off both the children; as to which she was quite in her right, for it was the very first time I had allowed the little girl out of my sight without some special provision. Of course now indeed she might be with the maids, so that the immediate thing was to look for her without an air of alarm. This we promptly arranged between us; but when, ten minutes later and in pursuance of our arrangement, we met in the hall, it was only to report on either side that after guarded inquiries we had altogether failed to trace her. For a minute there, apart from observation, we exchanged mute alarms, and I could feel with what high interest my friend returned me all those I had from the first given her.

"She'll be above," she presently said—"in one of the rooms you haven't searched."

"No; she's at a distance." I had made up my mind. "She has gone out."

Mrs. Grose stared. "Without a hat?"

I naturally also looked volumes. "Isn't that woman always without one?"

"She's with *her?*"

"She's with *her!*" I declared. "We must find them."

My hand was on my friend's arm, but she failed for the moment, confronted with such an account of the matter, to respond to my pressure. She communed, on the contrary, on the spot, with her uneasiness. "And where's Master Miles?"

"Oh, *he's* with Quint. They're in the schoolroom."

"Lord, miss!" My view, I was myself aware—and therefore I suppose my tone—had never yet reached so calm an assurance.

"The trick's played," I went on; "they've successfully worked their plan. He found the most divine little way to keep me quiet while she went off."

"'Divine'?" Mrs. Grose bewilderedly echoed.

"Infernal, then!" I almost cheerfully rejoined. "He has provided for himself as well. But come!"

She had helplessly gloomed at the upper regions. "You leave him—?"

"So long with Quint? Yes—I don't mind that now."

She always ended, at these moments, by getting possession of my hand, and in this manner she could at present still stay me. But after gasping an instant at my sudden resignation, "Because of your letter?" she eagerly brought out.

I quickly, by way of answer, felt for my letter, drew it forth, held it up, and then, freeing myself, went and laid it on the great hall table. "Luke will take it," I said as I came back. I reached the house door and opened it; I was already on the steps.

My companion still demurred: the storm of the night and the early morning had dropped, but the afternoon was damp and gray. I came down to the drive while she stood in the doorway. "You go with nothing on?"

"What do I care when the child has nothing? I can't wait to dress," I cried, "and if you must do so, I leave you. Try meanwhile, yourself, upstairs."

"With them?" Oh, on this, the poor woman promptly joined me!

XIX

We went straight to the lake, as it was called at Bly, and I daresay rightly called, though I reflect that it may in fact have been a sheet of water less remarkable than it appeared to my untraveled eyes. My acquaintance with sheets of water was small, and the pool of Bly, at all events on the few occasions of my consenting, under the protection of my pupils, to affront its surface in the old flat-bottomed boat moored there for our use, had impressed me both with its extent and its agitation. The usual place of embarkation was half a mile from the house, but I had an intimate conviction that, wherever Flora might be, she was not near home. She had not given me the slip for any small adventure, and, since the day of the very great one that I had shared with her by the pond, I had been aware, in our walks, of the quarter to which she most inclined. This was why I had now given to Mrs. Grose's steps so marked a direction—a direction that made her, when she perceived it, oppose a resistance that showed me she was freshly mystified. "You're going to the water, Miss?—you think she's *in*—?"

"She may be, though the depth is, I believe, nowhere very great. But what I judge most likely is that she's on the spot from which, the other day, we saw together what I told you."

"When she pretended not to see—?"

"With that astounding self-possession? I've always been sure she wanted to go back alone. And now her brother has managed it for her."

Mrs. Grose still stood where she had stopped. "You suppose they really *talk* of them?"

"I could meet this with a confidence! They say things that, if we heard them, would simply appall us."

"And if she *is* there—"

"Yes?"

"Then Miss Jessel is?"

"Beyond a doubt. You shall see."

"Oh, thank you!" my friend cried, planted so firm that, taking it in, I went straight on without her. By the time I reached the pool, however, she was close behind me, and I knew that, whatever, to her apprehension, might befall me, the exposure of my society struck her as her least danger. She exhaled a moan of relief as we at last came in sight of the greater part of the water without a sight of the child. There was no trace of Flora on that nearer side of the bank where my observation of her had been most startling, and none on the opposite edge, where, save for a margin of some twenty yards, a thick copse came down to the water. The pond, oblong in shape, had a width so scant compared to its length that, with its ends out of view, it might have been taken for a scant river. We looked at the empty expanse, and then I felt the suggestion of my friend's eyes. I knew what she meant and I replied with a negative headshake.

"No, no; wait! She has taken the boat."

My companion stared at the vacant mooring place and then again across the lake. "Then where is it?"

"Our not seeing it is the strongest of proofs. She has used it to go over, and then has managed to hide it."

"All alone—that child?"

"She's not alone, and at such times she's not a child: she's an old, old woman." I scanned all the visible shore while Mrs. Grose took again, into the queer element I offered her, one of her plunges of submission; then I pointed out that the boat might perfectly be in a small refuge formed by one of the recesses of the pool, an indentation masked, for the hither side, by a projection of the bank and by a clump of trees growing close to the water.

"But if the boat's there, where on earth's *she?*" my colleague anxiously asked.

"That's exactly what we must learn." And I started to walk further.

"By going all the way round?"

"Certainly, far as it is. It will take us but ten minutes, but it's far enough to have made the child prefer not to walk. She went straight over."

"Laws!" cried my friend again; the chain of my logic was ever too much for her. It dragged her at my heels even now, and when we had got halfway round—a devious, tiresome process, on ground much broken and by a path choked with overgrowth—I paused to give her breath. I sustained her with a grateful arm, assuring her that she might hugely help me; and this started us afresh, so that in the course of but few minutes more we reached a point from which we found the boat to be where I had supposed it. It had been intentionally left as much as possible out of sight and was tied to one of the stakes of a fence that came, just there, down to the brink and that had been an assistance to disembarking. I recognized, as I looked at the pair of short, thick oars, quite safely drawn up, the prodigious character of the feat for a little girl; but I had lived, by this time, too long among wonders and had panted to too many livelier measures. There was a gate in the fence, through which we passed, and that brought us, after a trifling interval, more into the open. Then, "There she is!" we both exclaimed at once.

Flora, a short way off, stood before us on the grass and smiled as if her performance was now complete. The next thing she did, however, was to stoop straight down and pluck—quite as if it were all she was there for—a big, ugly spray of withered fern. I instantly became sure she had just come out of the copse. She waited for us, not herself taking a step, and I was conscious of the rare solemnity with which we presently approached her. She smiled and smiled, and we met; but it was all done in a silence by this time flagrantly ominous. Mrs. Grose was the first to break the spell: she threw herself on her knees and, drawing the child to her breast, clasped in a long embrace the little tender, yielding body. While this dumb convulsion lasted I could only watch it—which I did the more intently when I saw Flora's face peep at me over our companion's shoulder. It was serious now—the flicker had left it; but it strengthened the pang with which I at that moment envied Mrs. Grose the simplicity of *her* relation. Still, all this while, nothing more passed between us save that Flora had let her foolish fern again drop to the ground. What she and I had virtually said to each other was that pretexts were useless now. When Mrs. Grose finally got up she kept the child's hand, so that the two were still before me; and the singular reticence of our communion was even more marked in the frank look she launched me. "I'll be hanged," it said, "if *I'll* speak!"

It was Flora who, gazing all over me in candid wonder, was the first. She was struck with our bareheaded aspect. "Why, where are your things?"

"Where yours are, my dear!" I promptly returned.

She had already got back her gaiety, and appeared to take this as an answer quite sufficient. "And where's Miles?" she went on.

There was something in the small valor of it that quite finished me: these three words from her were, in a flash like the glitter of a drawn blade, the jostle of the cup that my hand, for weeks and weeks, had held high and full to the brim that now, even before speaking, I felt overflow in a deluge. "I'll tell you if you'll tell *me*—" I heard myself say, then heard the tremor in which it broke.

"Well, what?"

Mrs. Grose's suspense blazed at me, but it was too late now, and I brought the thing out handsomely. "Where, my pet, is Miss Jessel?"

XX

Just as in the churchyard with Miles, the whole thing was upon us. Much as I had made of the fact that this name had never once, between us, been sounded, the quick, smitten glare with which the child's face now received it fairly likened my breach of the silence to the smash of a pane of glass. It added to the interposing cry, as if to stay the blow, that Mrs. Grose, at the same instant, uttered over my violence—the shriek of a creature scared, or rather wounded, which, in turn, within a few seconds, was completed by a gasp of my own. I seized my colleague's arm. "She's there, she's there!"

Miss Jessel stood before us on the opposite bank exactly as she had stood the other time, and I remember, strangely, as the first feeling now produced in me, my thrill of joy at having brought on a proof. She was there, and I was justified; she was there, and I was neither cruel nor mad. She was there for poor scared Mrs. Grose, but she was there most for Flora; and no moment of my monstrous time was perhaps so extraordinary as that in which I consciously threw out to her—with the sense that, pale and ravenous demon as she was, she would catch and understand it—an inarticulate message of gratitude. She rose erect on the spot my friend and I had lately quitted, and there was not, in all the long reach of her desire, an inch of her evil that fell short. This first vividness of vision and emotion were things of a few seconds, during which Mrs. Grose's dazed blink across to where I pointed struck me as a sovereign sign that she too at last saw, just as it carried my own eyes precipitately to the child. The revelation then of the manner in which Flora was affected startled me, in truth, far more than it would have done to find her also merely agitated, for direct dismay was of course not what I had expected. Prepared and on her guard as our pursuit had actually made her, she would repress every betrayal; and I was therefore shaken, on the spot, by my first glimpse of the particular one for which I had not allowed. To see her, without a convulsion of her small pink face, not even feign to glance in the direction of the prodigy I announced, but only, instead of that, turn at me an expression of hard, still gravity, an expression absolutely new and unprecedented and that appeared to read and accuse and judge me—this was a stroke that somehow converted the little girl herself into the very presence that could make me quail. I quailed even though my certitude that she thoroughly saw was never greater than at that instant, and in the immediate need to defend myself I called it passionately to witness. "She's there, you little unhappy thing—there, there, *there*, and you see her as well as you see me!" I had said shortly before to Mrs. Grose that she was not at these times a child, but an old, old woman, and that description of her could not have been more strikingly confirmed than in the way in which, for all answer to this, she simply showed me, without a concession, an admission, of her eyes, a countenance of deeper and deeper, of indeed suddenly quite fixed, reprobation. I was by this time—if I can put the whole thing at all together—more appalled at what I may properly call her manner than at anything else, though it was simultaneously with this that I became aware of having Mrs. Grose also, and very formidably, to reckon with. My elder companion, the next moment, at any rate, blotted out everything but her own flushed face and her loud, shocked protest, a burst of high disapproval. "What a dreadful turn, to be sure, miss! Where on earth do you see anything?"

I could only grasp her more quickly yet, for even while she spoke the hideous plain presence stood undimmed and undaunted. It had already lasted a minute, and it lasted while I continued, seizing my colleague, quite thrusting her at it and presenting her to it, to insist with my pointing hand. "You don't see her exactly as *we* see?—you mean to say you don't now—*now?* She's as big as a blazing fire! Only look, dearest woman, *look*—!" She looked, even as I did, and gave me, with her deep groan of negation, repulsion, compassion—the mixture with her pity of her relief at her exemption—a sense, touching to me even then, that she would have backed me up if she could. I might well have needed that, for with this hard blow of the proof that her eyes were hopelessly sealed I felt my own situation horribly crumble, I felt—I saw—my livid predecessor press, from her position, on my defeat, and I was conscious, more than all, of what I should have from this instant to deal with in the astounding little attitude of Flora. Into this attitude Mrs. Grose immediately and violently entered, breaking, even while there pierced through my sense of ruin a prodigious private triumph, into breathless reassurance.

"She isn't there, little lady, and nobody's there—and you never see nothing, my sweet! How can poor Miss Jessel—when poor Miss Jessel's dead and buried? We know, don't we, love?"—and she appealed, blundering in, to the child. "It's all a mere mistake and a worry and a joke—and we'll go home as fast as we can!"

Our companion, on this, had responded with a strange, quick primness of propriety, and they were again, with Mrs. Grose on her feet, united, as it were, in pained opposition to me. Flora continued to fix me with her small mask of reprobation, and even at that minute I prayed God to forgive me for seeming to see that, as she stood there holding tight to our friend's dress, her incomparable childish beauty had suddenly failed, had quite vanished. I've said it already—she was literally, she was hideously, hard; she had turned common and almost ugly. "I don't know what you mean. I see nobody. I see nothing. I never have. I think you're cruel. I don't like you!" Then, after this deliverance, which might have been that of a vulgarly pert little girl in the street, she hugged Mrs. Grose more closely and buried in her skirts the dreadful little face. In this position she produced an almost furious wail. "Take me away, take me away—oh, take me away from *her!*"

"From *me?*" I panted.

"From you—from you!" she cried.

Even Mrs. Grose looked across at me dismayed, while I had nothing to do but communicate again with the figure that, on the opposite bank, without a movement, as rigidly still as if catching, beyond the interval, our voices, was as vividly there for my disaster as it was not there for my service. The wretched child had spoken exactly as if she had got from some outside source each of her stabbing little words, and I could therefore, in the full despair of all I had to accept, but sadly shake my head at her. "If I had ever doubted, all my doubt would at present have gone. I've been living with the miserable truth, and now it has only too much closed round me. Of course I've lost you: I've interfered, and you've seen—under *her* dictation"—with which I faced, over the pool again, our infernal witness—"the easy and perfect way to meet it. I've done my best, but I've lost you. Goodbye." For Mrs. Grose I had an imperative, an almost frantic "Go, go!" before which, in infinite distress, but mutely possessed of the little girl and clearly convinced, in spite of her blindness, that something awful had occurred and some collapse engulfed us, she retreated, by the way we had come, as fast as she could move.

Of what first happened when I was left alone I had no subsequent memory. I only knew that at the end of, I suppose, a quarter of an hour, an odorous dampness and roughness, chilling and piercing my trouble, had made me understand that I must have thrown myself, on my face, on the ground and given way to a wildness of grief. I must have lain there long and cried and sobbed, for when I raised my head the day was almost done. I got up and looked a moment, through the twilight, at the gray pool and its blank, haunted edge, and then I took, back to the house, my dreary and difficult course. When I reached the gate in the fence the boat, to my surprise, was gone, so that I had a fresh reflection to make on Flora's extraordinary command of the situation. She passed that night, by the most tacit, and I should add, were not the word so grotesque a false note, the happiest of arrangements, with Mrs. Grose. I saw neither of them on my return, but, on the other hand, as by an ambiguous compensation, I saw a great deal of Miles. I saw—I can use no other phrase—so much of him that it was as if it were more than it had ever been. No evening I had passed at Bly had the portentous quality of this one; in spite of which—and in spite also of the deeper depths of consternation that had opened beneath my feet—there was literally, in the ebbing actual, an extraordinarily sweet sadness. On reaching the house I had never so much as looked for the boy; I had simply gone straight to my room to change what I was wearing and to take in, at a glance, much material testimony to Flora's rupture. Her little belongings had all been removed. When later, by the schoolroom fire, I was served with tea by the usual maid, I indulged, on the article of my other pupil, in no inquiry whatever. He had his freedom now—he might have it to the end! Well, he did have it; and it consisted—in part at least—of his coming in at about eight o'clock and sitting down with me in silence. On the removal of the tea things I had blown out the candles and drawn my chair closer: I was conscious of a mortal coldness and felt as if I should never again be warm. So, when he appeared, I was sitting in the glow with my thoughts. He paused a moment by the door as if to look at me; then—as if to share them—came to the other side of the hearth and sank into a chair. We sat there in absolute stillness; yet he wanted, I felt, to be with me.

XXI

Before a new day, in my room, had fully broken, my eyes opened to Mrs. Grose, who had come to my bedside with worse news. Flora was so markedly feverish that an illness was perhaps at hand; she had passed a night of extreme unrest, a night agitated above all by fears that had for their subject not in the least her former, but wholly her present, governess. It was not against the possible re-entrance of Miss Jessel on the scene that she protested—it was conspicuously and passionately against mine. I was promptly on my feet of course, and with an immense deal to ask; the more that my friend had discernibly now girded her loins to meet me once more. This I felt as soon as I had put to her the question of her sense of the child's sincerity as against my own. "She persists in denying to you that she saw, or has ever seen, anything?"

My visitor's trouble, truly, was great. "Ah, miss, it isn't a matter on which I can push her! Yet it isn't either, I must say, as if I much needed to. It has made her, every inch of her, quite old."

"Oh, I see her perfectly from here. She resents, for all the world like some high little personage, the imputation on her truthfulness and, as it were, her respectability. 'Miss Jessel indeed—she!' Ah, she's 'respectable,' the chit! The impression she gave me there yesterday was, I assure you, the very strangest of all; it was quite beyond any of the others. I *did* put my foot in it! She'll never speak to me again."

Hideous and obscure as it all was, it held Mrs. Grose briefly silent; then she granted my point with a frankness which, I made sure, had more behind it. "I think indeed, miss, she never will. She do have a grand manner about it!"

"And that manner"—I summed it up—"is practically what's the matter with her now!"

Oh, that manner, I could see in my visitor's face, and not a little else besides! "She asks me every three minutes if I think you're coming in."

"I see—I see." I, too, on my side, had so much more than worked it out. "Has she said to you since yesterday—except to repudiate her familiarity with anything so dreadful—a single other word about Miss Jessel?"

"Not one, miss. And of course you know," my friend added, "I took it from her, by the lake, that, just then and there at least, there was nobody."

"Rather! and, naturally, you take it from her still."

"I don't contradict her. What else can I do?"

"Nothing in the world! You've the cleverest little person to deal with. They've made them—their two friends, I mean—still cleverer even than nature did; for it was wondrous material to play on! Flora has now her grievance, and she'll work it to the end."

"Yes, miss; but to *what* end?"

"Why, that of dealing with me to her uncle. She'll make me out to him the lowest creature—!"

I winced at the fair show of the scene in Mrs. Grose's face; she looked for a minute as if she sharply saw them together. "And him who thinks so well of you!"

"He has an odd way—it comes over me now," I laughed, "—of proving it! But that doesn't matter. What Flora wants, of course, is to get rid of me."

My companion bravely concurred. "Never again to so much as look at you."

"So that what you've come to me now for," I asked, "is to speed me on my way?" Before she had time to reply, however, I had her in check. "I've a better idea—the result of my reflections. My going *would* seem the right thing, and on Sunday I was terribly near it. Yet that won't do. It's *you* who must go. You must take Flora."

My visitor, at this, did speculate. "But where in the world—?"

"Away from here. Away from *them*. Away, even most of all, now, from me. Straight to her uncle."

"Only to tell on you—?"

"No, not 'only'! To leave me, in addition, with my remedy."

She was still vague. "And what *is* your remedy?"

"Your loyalty, to begin with. And then Miles's."

She looked at me hard. "Do you think he—?"

"Won't, if he has the chance, turn on me? Yes, I venture still to think it. At all events, I want to try. Get off with his sister as soon as possible and leave me with him alone." I was amazed, myself, at the spirit I had still in reserve, and therefore perhaps a trifle the more disconcerted at the way in which, in spite of this fine example of it, she hesitated. "There's one thing, of course," I went on: "they mustn't, before she goes, see each other for three seconds." Then it came over me that, in spite of Flora's presumable sequestration from the instant of her return from the pool, it might already be too late. "Do you mean," I anxiously asked, "that they *have* met?"

At this she quite flushed. "Ah, miss, I'm not such a fool as that! If I've been obliged to leave her three or four times, it has been each time with one of the maids, and at present, though she's alone, she's locked in safe. And yet—and yet!" There were too many things.

"And yet what?"

"Well, are you so sure of the little gentleman?"

"I'm not sure of anything but *you*. But I have, since last evening, a new hope. I think he wants to give me an opening. I do believe that—poor little exquisite wretch!—he wants to speak. Last evening, in the firelight and the silence, he sat with me for two hours as if it were just coming."

Mrs. Grose looked hard, through the window, at the gray, gathering day. "And did it come?"

"No, though I waited and waited, I confess it didn't, and it was without a breach of the silence or so much as a faint allusion to his sister's condition and absence that we at last kissed for good night. All the same," I continued, "I can't, if her uncle sees her, consent to his seeing her brother without my having given the boy—and most of all because things have got so bad—a little more time."

My friend appeared on this ground more reluctant than I could quite understand. "What do you mean by more time?"

"Well, a day or two—really to bring it out. He'll then be on my side—of which you see the importance. If nothing comes, I shall only fail, and you will, at the worst, have helped me by doing, on your arrival in town, whatever you may have found possible." So I put it before her, but she continued for a little so inscrutably embarrassed that I came again to her aid. "Unless, indeed," I wound up, "you really want *not* to go."

I could see it, in her face, at last clear itself; she put out her hand to me as a pledge. "I'll go—I'll go. I'll go this morning."

I wanted to be very just. "If you should wish still to wait, I would engage she shouldn't see me."

"No, no: it's the place itself. She must leave it." She held me a moment with heavy eyes, then brought out the rest. "Your idea's the right one. I myself, miss—"

"Well?"

"I can't stay."

The look she gave me with it made me jump at possibilities. "You mean that, since yesterday, you *have* seen—?"

She shook her head with dignity. "I've *heard*—!"

"Heard?"

"From that child—horrors! There!" she sighed with tragic relief. "On my honor, miss, she says things—!" But at this evocation she broke down; she dropped, with a sudden sob, upon my sofa and, as I had seen her do before, gave way to all the grief of it.

It was quite in another manner that I, for my part, let myself go. "Oh, thank God!"

She sprang up again at this, drying her eyes with a groan. "'Thank God'?"

"It so justifies me!"

"It does that, miss!"

I couldn't have desired more emphasis, but I just hesitated. "She's so horrible?"

I saw my colleague scarce knew how to put it. "Really shocking."

"And about me?"

"About you, miss—since you must have it. It's beyond everything, for a young lady; and I can't think wherever she must have picked up—"

"The appalling language she applied to me? I can, then!" I broke in with a laugh that was doubtless significant enough.

It only, in truth, left my friend still more grave. "Well, perhaps I ought to also—since I've heard some of it before! Yet I can't bear it," the poor woman went on while, with the same movement, she glanced, on my dressing table, at the face of my watch. "But I must go back."

I kept her, however. "Ah, if you can't bear it—!"

"How can I stop with her, you mean? Why, just for that: to get her away. Far from this," she pursued, "far from *them*—"

"She may be different? She may be free?" I seized her almost with joy. "Then, in spite of yesterday, you *believe*—"

"In such doings?" Her simple description of them required, in the light of her expression, to be carried no further, and she gave me the whole thing as she had never done. "I believe."

Yes, it was a joy, and we were still shoulder to shoulder: if I might continue sure of that I should care but little what else happened. My support in the presence of disaster would be the same as it had been in my early need of confidence, and if my friend would answer for my honesty, I would answer for all the rest. On the point of taking leave of her, nonetheless, I was to some extent embarrassed. "There's one thing, of course—it occurs to me—to remember. My letter, giving the alarm, will have reached town before you."

I now perceived still more how she had been beating about the bush and how weary at last it had made her. "Your letter won't have got there. Your letter never went."

"What then became of it?"

"Goodness knows! Master Miles—"

"Do you mean he took it?" I gasped.

She hung fire, but she overcame her reluctance. "I mean that I saw yesterday, when I came back with Miss Flora, that it wasn't where you had put it. Later in the evening I had the chance to question Luke, and he declared that he had neither noticed nor touched it." We could only exchange, on this, one of our deeper mutual soundings, and it was Mrs. Grose who first brought up the plumb with an almost elated "You see!"

"Yes, I see that if Miles took it instead he probably will have read it and destroyed it."

"And don't you see anything else?"

I faced her a moment with a sad smile. "It strikes me that by this time your eyes are open even wider than mine."

They proved to be so indeed, but she could still blush, almost, to show it. "I make out now what he must have done at school." And she gave, in her simple sharpness, an almost droll disillusioned nod. "He stole!"

I turned it over—I tried to be more judicial. "Well—perhaps."

She looked as if she found me unexpectedly calm. "He stole *letters!*"

She couldn't know my reasons for a calmness after all pretty shallow; so I showed them off as I might. "I hope then it was to more purpose than in this case! The note, at any rate, that I put on the table yesterday," I pursued, "will have given him so scant an advantage—for it contained only the bare demand for an interview—that he is already much ashamed of having gone so far for so little, and that what he had on his mind last evening was precisely the need of confession." I seemed to myself, for the instant, to have mastered it, to see it all. "Leave us, leave us"—I was already, at the door, hurrying her off. "I'll get it out of him. He'll meet me—he'll confess. If he confesses, he's saved. And if he's saved—"

"Then you are?" The dear woman kissed me on this, and I took her farewell. "I'll save you without him!" she cried as she went.

XXII

Yet it was when she had got off—and I missed her on the spot—that the great pinch really came. If I had counted on what it would give me to find myself alone with Miles, I speedily perceived, at least, that it would give me a measure. No hour of my stay in fact was so assailed with apprehensions as that of my coming down to learn that the carriage containing Mrs. Grose and my younger pupil had already rolled out of the gates. Now I was, I said to myself, face to face with the elements, and for much of the rest of the day, while I fought my weakness, I could consider that I had been supremely rash. It was a tighter place still than I had yet turned round in; all the more that, for the first time, I could see in the aspect of others a confused reflection of the crisis. What had happened naturally caused them all to stare; there was too little of the explained, throw out whatever we might, in the suddenness of my colleague's act. The maids and the men looked blank; the effect of which on my nerves was an aggravation until I saw the necessity of making it a positive aid. It was precisely, in short, by just clutching the helm that I avoided total wreck; and I dare say that, to bear up at all, I became, that morning, very grand and very dry. I welcomed the consciousness that I was charged with much to do, and I caused it to be known as well that, left thus to myself, I was quite remarkably firm. I wandered with that manner, for the next hour or two, all over the place and looked, I have no doubt, as if I were ready for any onset. So, for the benefit of whom it might concern, I paraded with a sick heart.

The person it appeared least to concern proved to be, till dinner, little Miles himself. My perambulations had given me, meanwhile, no glimpse of him, but they had tended to make more public the change taking place in our relation as a consequence of his having at the piano, the day before, kept me, in Flora's interest, so beguiled and befooled. The stamp of publicity had of course been fully given by her confinement and departure, and the change itself was now ushered in by our nonobservance of the regular custom of the schoolroom. He had already disappeared when, on my way down, I pushed open his door, and I learned below that he had breakfasted—in the presence of a couple of the maids—with Mrs. Grose and his sister. He had then gone out, as he said, for a stroll; than which nothing, I reflected, could better have expressed his frank view of the abrupt transformation of my office. What he would not permit this office to consist of was yet to be settled: there was a queer relief, at all events—I mean for myself in especial—in the renouncement of one pretension. If so much had sprung to the surface, I scarce put it too strongly in saying that what had perhaps sprung highest was the absurdity of our prolonging the fiction that I had anything more to teach him. It sufficiently stuck out that, by tacit little tricks in which even more than myself he carried out the care for my dignity, I had had to appeal to him to let me off straining to meet him on the ground of his true capacity. He had at any rate his freedom now; I was never to touch it again; as I had amply shown, moreover, when, on his joining me in the schoolroom the previous night, I had uttered, on the subject of the interval just concluded, neither challenge nor hint. I had too much, from this moment, my other ideas. Yet when he at last arrived, the difficulty of applying them, the accumulations of my problem, were brought straight home to me by the beautiful little presence on which what had occurred had as yet, for the eye, dropped neither stain nor shadow.

To mark, for the house, the high state I cultivated I decreed that my meals with the boy should be served, as we called it, downstairs; so that I had been awaiting him in the ponderous pomp of the room outside of the window of which I had had from Mrs. Grose, that first scared Sunday, my flash of something it would scarce have done to call light. Here at present I felt afresh—for I had felt it again and again—how my equilibrium depended on the success of my rigid will, the will to shut my eyes as tight as possible to the truth that what I had to deal with was, revoltingly, against nature. I could only get on at all by taking "nature" into my confidence and my account, by treating my monstrous ordeal as a push in a direction unusual, of course, and unpleasant, but demanding, after all, for a fair front, only another turn of the screw of ordinary human virtue. No attempt, nonetheless, could well require more tact than just this attempt to supply, one's self, all the nature. How could I put even a little of that article into a suppression of reference to what had occurred? How, on the other hand, could I make reference without a new plunge into the hideous obscure? Well, a sort of answer, after a time, had come to me, and it was so far confirmed as that I was met, incontestably, by the quickened vision of what was rare in my little companion. It was indeed as if he had found even now—as he had so often found at lessons—still some other delicate way to ease me off. Wasn't there light in the fact which, as we shared our solitude, broke out with a specious glitter it had never yet quite worn?—the fact that (opportunity aiding, precious opportunity which had now come) it would be preposterous, with a child so endowed, to forego the help one might wrest from absolute intelligence? What had his intelligence been given him for but to save him? Mightn't one, to reach his mind, risk the stretch of an angular arm over his character? It was as if, when we were face to face in the dining room, he had literally shown me the way. The roast mutton was on the table, and I had dispensed with attendance. Miles, before he sat down, stood a moment with his hands in his pockets and looked at the joint, on which he seemed on the point of passing some humorous judgment. But what he presently produced was: "I say, my dear, is she really very awfully ill?"

"Little Flora? Not so bad but that she'll presently be better. London will set her up. Bly had ceased to agree with her. Come here and take your mutton."

He alertly obeyed me, carried the plate carefully to his seat, and, when he was established, went on. "Did Bly disagree with her so terribly suddenly?"

"Not so suddenly as you might think. One had seen it coming on."

"Then why didn't you get her off before?"

"Before what?"

"Before she became too ill to travel."

I found myself prompt. "She's *not* too ill to travel: she only might have become so if she had stayed. This was just the moment to seize. The journey will dissipate the influence"—oh, I was grand!—"and carry it off."

"I see, I see"—Miles, for that matter, was grand, too. He settled to his repast with the charming little "table manner" that, from the day of his arrival, had relieved me of all grossness of admonition. Whatever he had been driven from school for, it was not for ugly feeding. He was irreproachable, as always, today; but he was unmistakably more conscious. He was discernibly trying to take for granted more things than he found, without assistance, quite easy; and he dropped into peaceful silence while he felt his situation. Our meal was of the briefest—mine a vain pretense, and I had the things immediately removed. While this was done Miles stood again with his hands in his little pockets and his back to me—stood and looked out of the wide window through which, that other day, I had seen what pulled me up. We continued silent while the maid was with us—as silent, it whimsically occurred to me, as some young couple who, on their wedding journey, at the inn, feel shy in the presence of the waiter. He turned round only when the waiter had left us. "Well—so we're alone!"

XXIII

"Oh, more or less." I fancy my smile was pale. "Not absolutely. We shouldn't like that!" I went on.

"No—I suppose we shouldn't. Of course we have the others."

"We have the others—we have indeed the others," I concurred.

"Yet even though we have them," he returned, still with his hands in his pockets and planted there in front of me, "they don't much count, do they?"

I made the best of it, but I felt wan. "It depends on what you call 'much'!"

"Yes"—with all accommodation—"everything depends!" On this, however, he faced to the window again and presently reached it with his vague, restless, cogitating step. He remained there awhile, with his forehead against the glass, in contemplation of the stupid shrubs I knew and the dull things of November. I had always my hypocrisy of "work," behind which, now, I gained the sofa. Steadying myself with it there as I had repeatedly done at those moments of torment that I have described as the moments of my knowing the children to be given to something from which I was barred, I sufficiently obeyed my habit of being prepared for the worst. But an extraordinary impression dropped on me as I extracted a meaning from the boy's embarrassed back—none other than the impression that I was not barred now. This inference grew in a few minutes to sharp intensity and seemed bound up with the direct perception that it was positively *he* who was. The frames and squares of the great window were a kind of image, for him, of a kind of failure. I felt that I saw him, at any rate, shut in or shut out. He was admirable, but not comfortable: I took it in with a throb of hope. Wasn't he looking, through the haunted pane, for something he couldn't see?—and wasn't it the first time in the whole business that he had known such a lapse? The first, the very first: I found it a splendid portent. It made him anxious, though he watched himself; he had been anxious all day and, even while in his usual sweet little manner he sat at table, had needed all his small strange genius to give it a gloss. When he at last turned round to meet me, it was almost as if this genius had succumbed. "Well, I think I'm glad Bly agrees with me!"

"You would certainly seem to have seen, these twenty-four hours, a good deal more of it than for some time before. I hope," I went on bravely, "that you've been enjoying yourself."

"Oh, yes, I've been ever so far; all round about—miles and miles away. I've never been so free."

He had really a manner of his own, and I could only try to keep up with him. "Well, do you like it?"

He stood there smiling; then at last he put into two words—"Do *you?*"—more discrimination than I had ever heard two words contain. Before I had time to deal with that, however, he continued as if with the sense that this was an impertinence to be softened. "Nothing could be more charming than the way you take it, for of course if we're alone together now it's you that are alone most. But I hope," he threw in, "you don't particularly mind!"

"Having to do with you?" I asked. "My dear child, how can I help minding? Though I've renounced all claim to your company—you're so beyond me—I at least greatly enjoy it. What else should I stay on for?"

He looked at me more directly, and the expression of his face, graver now, struck me as the most beautiful I had ever found in it. "You stay on just for *that?*"

"Certainly. I stay on as your friend and from the tremendous interest I take in you till something can be done for you that may be more worth your while. That needn't surprise you." My voice trembled so that I felt it impossible to suppress the shake. "Don't you remember how I told you, when I came and sat on your bed the night of the storm, that there was nothing in the world I wouldn't do for you?"

"Yes, yes!" He, on his side, more and more visibly nervous, had a tone to master; but he was so much more successful than I that, laughing out through his gravity, he could pretend we were pleasantly jesting. "Only that, I think, was to get me to do something for *you!*"

"It was partly to get you to do something," I conceded. "But, you know, you didn't do it."

"Oh, yes," he said with the brightest superficial eagerness, "you wanted me to tell you something."

"That's it. Out, straight out. What you have on your mind, you know."

"Ah, then, is *that* what you've stayed over for?"

He spoke with a gaiety through which I could still catch the finest little quiver of resentful passion; but I can't begin to express the effect upon me of an implication of surrender even so faint. It was as if what I had yearned for had come at last only to astonish me. "Well, yes—I may as well make a clean breast of it, it was precisely for that."

He waited so long that I supposed it for the purpose of repudiating the assumption on which my action had been founded; but what he finally said was: "Do you mean now—here?"

"There couldn't be a better place or time." He looked round him uneasily, and I had the rare—oh, the queer!—impression of the very first symptom I had seen in him of the approach of immediate fear. It was as if he were suddenly afraid of me—which struck me indeed as perhaps the best thing to make him. Yet in the very pang of the effort I felt it vain to try sternness, and I heard myself the next instant so gentle as to be almost grotesque. "You want so to go out again?"

"Awfully!" He smiled at me heroically, and the touching little bravery of it was enhanced by his actually flushing with pain. He had picked up his hat, which he had brought in, and stood twirling it in a way that gave me, even as I was just nearly reaching port, a perverse horror of what I was doing. To do it in *any* way was an act of violence, for what did it consist of but the obtrusion of the idea of grossness and guilt on a small helpless creature who had been for me a revelation of the possibilities of beautiful intercourse? Wasn't it base to create for a being so exquisite a mere alien awkwardness? I suppose I now read into our situation a clearness it couldn't have had at the time, for I seem to see our poor eyes already lighted with some spark of a prevision of the anguish that was to come. So we circled about, with terrors and scruples, like fighters not daring to close. But it was for each other we feared! That kept us a little longer suspended and unbruised. "I'll tell you everything," Miles said—"I mean I'll tell you anything you like. You'll stay on with me, and we shall both be all right, and I *will* tell you—I *will*. But not now."

"Why not now?"

My insistence turned him from me and kept him once more at his window in a silence during which, between us, you might have heard a pin drop. Then he was before me again with the air of a person for whom, outside, someone who had frankly to be reckoned with was waiting. "I have to see Luke."

I had not yet reduced him to quite so vulgar a lie, and I felt proportionately ashamed. But, horrible as it was, his lies made up my truth. I achieved thoughtfully a few loops of my knitting. "Well, then, go to Luke, and I'll wait for what you promise. Only, in return for that, satisfy, before you leave me, one very much smaller request."

He looked as if he felt he had succeeded enough to be able still a little to bargain. "Very much smaller—?"

"Yes, a mere fraction of the whole. Tell me"—oh, my work preoccupied me, and I was offhand!—"if, yesterday afternoon, from the table in the hall, you took, you know, my letter."

XXIV

My sense of how he received this suffered for a minute from something that I can describe only as a fierce split of my attention—a stroke that at first, as I sprang straight up, reduced me to the mere blind movement of getting hold of him, drawing him close, and, while I just fell for support against the nearest piece of furniture, instinctively keeping him with his back to the window. The appearance was full upon us that I had already had to deal with here: Peter Quint had come into view like a sentinel before a prison. The next thing I saw was that, from outside, he had reached the window, and then I knew that, close to the glass and glaring in through it, he offered once more to the room his white face of damnation. It represents but grossly what took place within me at the sight to say that on the second my decision was made; yet I believe that no woman so overwhelmed ever in so short a time recovered her grasp of the *act*. It came to me in the very horror of the immediate presence that the act would be, seeing and facing what I saw and faced, to keep the boy himself unaware. The inspiration—I can call it by no other name—was that I felt how voluntarily, how transcendently, I *might*. It was like fighting with a demon for a human soul, and when I had fairly so appraised it I saw how the human soul—held out, in the tremor of my hands, at arm's length—had a perfect dew of sweat on a lovely childish forehead. The face that was close to mine was as white as the face against the glass, and out of it presently came a sound, not low nor weak, but as if from much further away, that I drank like a waft of fragrance.

"Yes—I took it."

At this, with a moan of joy, I enfolded, I drew him close; and while I held him to my breast, where I could feel in the sudden fever of his little body the tremendous pulse of his little heart, I kept my eyes on the thing at the window and saw it move and shift its posture. I have likened it to a sentinel, but its slow wheel, for a moment, was rather the prowl of a baffled beast. My present quickened courage, however, was such that, not too much to let it through, I had to shade, as it were, my flame. Meanwhile the glare of the face was again at the window, the scoundrel fixed as if to watch and wait. It was the very confidence that I might now defy him, as well as the positive certitude, by this time, of the child's unconsciousness, that made me go on. "What did you take it for?"

"To see what you said about me."

"You opened the letter?"

"I opened it."

My eyes were now, as I held him off a little again, on Miles's own face, in which the collapse of mockery showed me how complete was the ravage of uneasiness. What was prodigious was that at last, by my success, his sense was sealed and his communication stopped: he knew that he was in presence, but knew not of what, and knew still less that I also was and that I did know. And what did this strain of trouble matter when my eyes went back to the window only to see that the air was clear again and—by my personal triumph—the influence quenched? There was nothing there. I felt that the cause was mine and that I should surely get *all*. "And you found nothing!"—I let my elation out.

He gave the most mournful, thoughtful little headshake. "Nothing."

"Nothing, nothing!" I almost shouted in my joy.

"Nothing, nothing," he sadly repeated.

I kissed his forehead; it was drenched. "So what have you done with it?"

"I've burned it."

"Burned it?" It was now or never. "Is that what you did at school?"

Oh, what this brought up! "At school?"

"Did you take letters?—or other things?"

"Other things?" He appeared now to be thinking of something far off and that reached him only through the pressure of his anxiety. Yet it did reach him. "Did I *steal?*"

I felt myself redden to the roots of my hair as well as wonder if it were more strange to put to a gentleman such a question or to see him take it with allowances that gave the very distance of his fall in the world. "Was it for that you mightn't go back?"

The only thing he felt was rather a dreary little surprise. "Did you know I mightn't go back?"

"I know everything."

He gave me at this the longest and strangest look. "Everything?"

"Everything. Therefore *did* you—?" But I couldn't say it again.

Miles could, very simply. "No. I didn't steal."

My face must have shown him I believed him utterly; yet my hands—but it was for pure tenderness—shook him as if to ask him why, if it was all for nothing, he had condemned me to months of torment. "What then did you do?"

He looked in vague pain all round the top of the room and drew his breath, two or three times over, as if with difficulty. He might have been standing at the bottom of the sea and raising his eyes to some faint green twilight. "Well—I said things."

"Only that?"

"They thought it was enough!"

"To turn you out for?"

Never, truly, had a person "turned out" shown so little to explain it as this little person! He appeared to weigh my question, but in a manner quite detached and almost helpless. "Well, I suppose I oughtn't."

"But to whom did you say them?"

He evidently tried to remember, but it dropped—he had lost it. "I don't know!"

He almost smiled at me in the desolation of his surrender, which was indeed practically, by this time, so complete that I ought to have left it there. But I was infatuated—I was blind with victory, though even then the very effect that was to have brought him so much nearer was already that of added separation. "Was it to everyone?" I asked.

"No; it was only to—" But he gave a sick little headshake. "I don't remember their names."

"Were they then so many?"

"No—only a few. Those I liked."

Those he liked? I seemed to float not into clearness, but into a darker obscure, and within a minute there had come to me out of my very pity the appalling alarm of his being perhaps innocent. It was for the instant confounding and bottomless, for if he *were* innocent, what then on earth was *I?* Paralyzed, while it lasted, by the mere brush of the question, I let him go a little, so that, with a deep-drawn sigh, he turned away from me again; which, as he faced toward the clear window, I suffered, feeling that I had nothing now there to keep him from. "And did they repeat what you said?" I went on after a moment.

He was soon at some distance from me, still breathing hard and again with the air, though now without anger for it, of being confined against his will. Once more, as he had done before, he looked up at the dim day as if, of what had hitherto sustained him, nothing was left but an unspeakable anxiety. "Oh, yes," he nevertheless replied—"they must have repeated them. To those *they* liked," he added.

There was, somehow, less of it than I had expected; but I turned it over. "And these things came round—?"

"To the masters? Oh, yes!" he answered very simply. "But I didn't know they'd tell."

"The masters? They didn't—they've never told. That's why I ask you."

He turned to me again his little beautiful fevered face. "Yes, it was too bad."

"Too bad?"

"What I suppose I sometimes said. To write home."

I can't name the exquisite pathos of the contradiction given to such a speech by such a speaker; I only know that the next instant I heard myself throw off with homely force: "Stuff and nonsense!" But the next after that I must have sounded stern enough. "What were these things?"

My sternness was all for his judge, his executioner; yet it made him avert himself again, and that movement made *me*, with a single bound and an irrepressible cry, spring straight upon him. For there again, against the glass, as if to blight his confession and stay his answer, was the hideous author of our woe—the white face of damnation. I felt a sick swim at the drop of my victory and all the return of my battle, so that the wildness of my veritable leap only served as a great betrayal. I saw him, from the midst of my act, meet it with a divination, and on the perception that even now he only guessed, and that the window was still to his own eyes free, I let the impulse flame up to convert the climax of his dismay into the very proof of his liberation. "No more, no more, no more!" I shrieked, as I tried to press him against me, to my visitant.

"Is she *here?*" Miles panted as he caught with his sealed eyes the direction of my words. Then as his strange "she" staggered me and, with a gasp, I echoed it, "Miss Jessel, Miss Jessel!" he with a sudden fury gave me back.

I seized, stupefied, his supposition—some sequel to what we had done to Flora, but this made me only want to show him that it was better still than that. "It's not Miss Jessel! But it's at the window—straight before us. It's *there*—the coward horror, there for the last time!"

At this, after a second in which his head made the movement of a baffled dog's on a scent and then gave a frantic little shake for air and light, he was at me in a white rage, bewildered, glaring vainly over the place and missing wholly, though it now, to my sense, filled the room like the taste of poison, the wide, overwhelming presence. "It's *he?*"

I was so determined to have all my proof that I flashed into ice to challenge him. "Whom do you mean by 'he'?"

"Peter Quint—you devil!" His face gave again, round the room, its convulsed supplication. "*Where?*"

They are in my ears still, his supreme surrender of the name and his tribute to my devotion. "What does he matter now, my own?—what will he *ever* matter? I have you," I launched at the beast, "but he has lost you forever!" Then, for the demonstration of my work, "There, *there!*" I said to Miles.

But he had already jerked straight round, stared, glared again, and seen but the quiet day. With the stroke of the loss I was so proud of he uttered the cry of a creature hurled over an abyss, and the grasp with which I recovered him might have been that of catching him in his fall. I caught him, yes, I held him—it may be imagined with what a passion; but at the end of a minute I began to feel what it truly was that I held. We were alone with the quiet day, and his little heart, dispossessed, had stopped.

The Man Who Found Out

Algernon Blackwood

I

Professor Mark Ebor, the scientist, led a double life, and the only persons who knew it were his assistant, Dr. Laidlaw, and his publishers. But a double life need not always be a bad one, and, as Dr. Laidlaw and the gratified publishers well knew, the parallel lives of this particular man were equally good, and indefinitely produced would certainly have ended in a heaven somewhere that can suitably contain such strangely opposite characteristics as his remarkable personality combined.

For Mark Ebor, F.R.S., etc., etc., was that unique combination hardly ever met with in actual life, a man of science and a mystic.

As the first, his name stood in the gallery of the great, and as the second—but there came the mystery! For under the pseudonym of "Pilgrim" (the author of that brilliant series of books that appealed to so many), his identity was as well concealed as that of the anonymous writer of the weather reports in a daily newspaper. Thousands read the sanguine, optimistic, stimulating little books that issued annually from the pen of "Pilgrim," and thousands bore their daily burdens better for having read; while the Press generally agreed that the author, besides being an incorrigible enthusiast and optimist, was also—a woman; but no one ever succeeded in penetrating the veil of anonymity and discovering that "Pilgrim" and the biologist were one and the same person.

Mark Ebor, as Dr. Laidlaw knew him in his laboratory, was one man; but Mark Ebor, as he sometimes saw him after work was over, with rapt eyes and ecstatic face, discussing the possibilities of "union with God" and the future of the human race, was quite another.

"I have always held, as you know," he was saying one evening as he sat in the little study beyond the laboratory with his assistant and intimate, "that Vision should play a large part in the life of the awakened man—not to be regarded as infallible, of course, but to be observed and made use of as a guide-post to possibilities—"

"I am aware of your peculiar views, sir," the young doctor put in deferentially, yet with a certain impatience.

"For Visions come from a region of the consciousness where observation and experiment are out of the question," pursued the other with enthusiasm, not noticing the interruption, "and, while they should be checked by reason afterwards, they should not be laughed at or ignored. All inspiration, I hold, is of the nature of interior Vision, and all our best knowledge has come—such is my confirmed belief—as a sudden revelation to the brain prepared to receive it—"

"Prepared by hard work first, by concentration, by the closest possible study of ordinary phenomena," Dr. Laidlaw allowed himself to observe.

"Perhaps," sighed the other; "but by a process, none the less, of spiritual illumination. The best match in the world will not light a candle unless the wick be first suitably prepared."

It was Laidlaw's turn to sigh. He knew so well the impossibility of arguing with his chief when he was in the regions of the mystic, but at the same time the respect he felt for his tremendous attainments was so sincere that he always listened with attention and deference, wondering how far the great man would go and to what end this curious combination of logic and "illumination" would eventually lead him.

"Only last night," continued the elder man, a sort of light coming into his rugged features, "the vision came to me again—the one that has haunted me at intervals ever since my youth, and that will not be denied."

Dr. Laidlaw fidgeted in his chair.

"About the Tablets of the Gods, you mean—and that they lie somewhere hidden in the sands," he said patiently. A sudden gleam of interest came into his face as he turned to catch the professor's reply.

"And that I am to be the one to find them, to decipher them, and to give the great knowledge to the world—"

"Who will not believe," laughed Laidlaw shortly, yet interested in spite of his thinly-veiled contempt.

"Because even the keenest minds, in the right sense of the word, are hopelessly—unscientific," replied the other gently, his face positively aglow with the memory of his vision. "Yet what is more likely," he continued after a moment's pause, peering into space with rapt eyes that saw things too wonderful for exact language to describe, "than that there should have been given to man in the first ages of the world some record of the purpose and problem that had been set him to solve? In a word," he cried, fixing his shining eyes upon the face of his perplexed assistant, "that God's messengers in the far-off ages should have given to His creatures some full statement of the secret of the world, of the secret of the soul, of the meaning of life and death—the explanation of our being here, and to what great end we are destined in the ultimate fullness of things?"

Dr. Laidlaw sat speechless. These outbursts of mystical enthusiasm he had witnessed before. With any other man he would not have listened to a single sentence, but to Professor Ebor, man of knowledge and profound investigator, he listened with respect, because he regarded this condition as temporary and pathological, and in some sense a reaction from the intense strain of the prolonged mental concentration of many days.

He smiled, with something between sympathy and resignation as he met the other's rapt gaze.

"But you have said, sir, at other times, that you consider the ultimate secrets to be screened from all possible—"

"The ultimate secrets, yes," came the unperturbed reply; "but that there lies buried somewhere an indestructible record of the secret meaning of life, originally known to men in the days of their pristine innocence, I am convinced. And, by this strange vision so often vouchsafed to me, I am equally sure that one day it shall be given to me to announce to a weary world this glorious and terrific message."

And he continued at great length and in glowing language to describe the species of vivid dream that had come to him at intervals since earliest childhood, showing in detail how he discovered these very Tablets of the Gods, and proclaimed their splendid contents—whose precise nature was always, however, withheld from him in the vision—to a patient and suffering humanity.

"The Scrutator, sir, well described 'Pilgrim' as the Apostle of Hope," said the young doctor gently, when he had finished; "and now, if that reviewer could hear you speak and realize from what strange depths comes your simple faith—"

The professor held up his hand, and the smile of a little child broke over his face like sunshine in the morning.

"Half the good my books do would be instantly destroyed," he said sadly; "they would say that I wrote with my tongue in my cheek. But wait," he added significantly; "wait till I find these Tablets of the Gods! Wait till I hold the solutions of the old world-problems in my hands! Wait till the light of this new revelation breaks upon confused humanity, and it wakes to find its bravest hopes justified! Ah, then, my dear Laidlaw—"

He broke off suddenly; but the doctor, cleverly guessing the thought in his mind, caught him up immediately.

"Perhaps this very summer," he said, trying hard to make the suggestion keep pace with honesty; "in your explorations in Assyria—your digging in the remote civilization of what was once Chaldea, you may find—what you dream of—"

The professor held up his hand, and the smile of a fine old face.

"Perhaps," he murmured softly, "perhaps!"

And the young doctor, thanking the gods of science that his leader's aberrations were of so harmless a character, went home strong in the certitude of his knowledge of externals, proud that he was able to refer his visions to self-suggestion, and wondering complaisantly whether in his old age he might not after all suffer himself from visitations of the very kind that afflicted his respected chief.

And as he got into bed and thought again of his master's rugged face, and finely shaped head, and the deep lines traced by years of work and self-discipline, he turned over on his pillow and fell asleep with a sigh that was half of wonder, half of regret.

II

It was in February, nine months later, when Dr. Laidlaw made his way to Charing Cross to meet his chief after his long absence of travel and exploration. The vision about the so-called Tablets of the Gods had meanwhile passed almost entirely from his memory.

There were few people in the train, for the stream of traffic was now running the other way, and he had no difficulty in finding the man he had come to meet. The shock of white hair beneath the low-crowned felt hat was alone enough to distinguish him by easily.

"Here I am at last!" exclaimed the professor, somewhat wearily, clasping his friend's hand as he listened to the young doctor's warm greetings and questions. "Here I am—a little older, and much dirtier than when you last saw me!" He glanced down laughingly at his travel-stained garments.

"And much wiser," said Laidlaw, with a smile, as he bustled about the platform for porters and gave his chief the latest scientific news.

At last they came down to practical considerations.

"And your luggage—where is that? You must have tons of it, I suppose?" said Laidlaw.

"Hardly anything," Professor Ebor answered. "Nothing, in fact, but what you see."

"Nothing but this hand-bag?" laughed the other, thinking he was joking.

"And a small portmanteau in the van," was the quiet reply. "I have no other luggage."

"You have no other luggage?" repeated Laidlaw, turning sharply to see if he were in earnest.

"Why should I need more?" the professor added simply.

Something in the man's face, or voice, or manner—the doctor hardly knew which—suddenly struck him as strange. There was a change in him, a change so profound—so little on the surface, that is—that at first he had not become aware of it. For a moment it was as though an utterly alien personality stood before him in that noisy, bustling throng. Here, in all the homely, friendly turmoil of a Charing Cross crowd, a curious feeling of cold passed over his heart, touching his life with icy finger, so that he actually trembled and felt afraid.

He looked up quickly at his friend, his mind working with startled and unwelcome thoughts.

"Only this?" he repeated, indicating the bag. "But where's all the stuff you went away with? And—have you brought nothing home—no treasures?"

"This is all I have," the other said briefly. The pale smile that went with the words caused the doctor a second indescribable sensation of uneasiness. Something was very wrong, something was very queer; he wondered now that he had not noticed it sooner.

"The rest follows, of course, by slow freight," he added tactfully, and as naturally as possible. "But come, sir, you must be tired and in want of food after your long journey. I'll get a taxi at once, and we can see about the other luggage afterwards."

It seemed to him he hardly knew quite what he was saying; the change in his friend had come upon him so suddenly and now grew upon him more and more distressingly. Yet he could not make out exactly in what it consisted. A terrible suspicion began to take shape in his mind, troubling him dreadfully.

"I am neither very tired, nor in need of food, thank you," the professor said quietly. "And this is all I have. There is no luggage to follow. I have brought home nothing—nothing but what you see."

His words conveyed finality. They got into a taxi, tipped the porter, who had been staring in amazement at the venerable figure of the scientist, and were conveyed slowly and noisily to the house in the north of London where the laboratory was, the scene of their labours of years.

And the whole way Professor Ebor uttered no word, nor did Dr. Laidlaw find the courage to ask a single question.

It was only late that night, before he took his departure, as the two men were standing before the fire in the study—that study where they had discussed so many problems of vital and absorbing interest—that Dr. Laidlaw at last found strength to come to the point with direct questions. The professor had been giving him a superficial and desultory account of his travels, of his journeys by camel, of his encampments among the mountains and in the desert, and of his explorations among the buried temples, and, deeper, into the waste of the pre-historic sands, when suddenly the doctor came to the desired point with a kind of nervous rush, almost like a frightened boy.

"And you found—" he began stammering, looking hard at the other's dreadfully altered face, from which every line of hope and cheerfulness seemed to have been obliterated as a sponge wipes markings from a slate—"you found—"

"I found," replied the other, in a solemn voice, and it was the voice of the mystic rather than the man of science—"I found what I went to seek. The vision never once failed me. It led me straight to the place like a star in the heavens. I found—the Tablets of the Gods."

Dr. Laidlaw caught his breath, and steadied himself on the back of a chair. The words fell like particles of ice upon his heart. For the first time the professor had uttered the well-known phrase without the glow of light and wonder in his face that always accompanied it.

"You have—brought them?" he faltered.

"I have brought them home," said the other, in a voice with a ring like iron; "and I have—deciphered them."

Profound despair, the bloom of outer darkness, the dead sound of a hopeless soul freezing in the utter cold of space seemed to fill in the pauses between the brief sentences. A silence followed, during which Dr. Laidlaw saw nothing but the white face before him alternately fade and return. And it was like the face of a dead man.

"They are, alas, indestructible," he heard the voice continue, with its even, metallic ring.

"Indestructible," Laidlaw repeated mechanically, hardly knowing what he was saying.

Again a silence of several minutes passed, during which, with a creeping cold about his heart, he stood and stared into the eyes of the man he had known and loved so long—aye, and worshipped, too; the man who had first opened his own eyes when they were blind, and had led him to the gates of knowledge, and no little distance along the difficult path beyond; the man who, in another direction, had passed on the strength of his faith into the hearts of thousands by his books.

"I may see them?" he asked at last, in a low voice he hardly recognized as his own. "You will let me know—their message?"

Professor Ebor kept his eyes fixedly upon his assistant's face as he answered, with a smile that was more like the grin of death than a living human smile.

"When I am gone," he whispered; "when I have passed away. Then you shall find them and read the translation I have made. And then, too, in your turn, you must try, with the latest resources of science at your disposal to aid you, to compass their utter destruction." He paused a moment, and his face grew pale as the face of a corpse. "Until that time," he added presently, without looking up, "I must ask you not to refer to the subject again—and to keep my confidence meanwhile—*ab—so—lute—ly*."

III

A year passed slowly by, and at the end of it Dr. Laidlaw had found it necessary to sever his working connexion with his friend and one-time leader. Professor Ebor was no longer the same man. The light had gone out of his life; the laboratory was closed; he no longer put pen to paper or applied his mind to a single problem. In the short space of a few months he had passed from a hale and hearty man of late middle life to the condition of old age—a man collapsed and on the edge of dissolution. Death, it was plain, lay waiting for him in the shadows of any day—and he knew it.

To describe faithfully the nature of this profound alteration in his character and temperament is not easy, but Dr. Laidlaw summed it up to himself in three words: *Loss of Hope*. The splendid mental powers remained indeed undimmed, but the incentive to use them—to use them for the help of others—had gone. The character still held to its fine and unselfish habits of years, but the far goal to which they had been the leading strings had faded away. The desire for knowledge—knowledge for its own sake—had died, and the passionate hope which hitherto had animated with tireless energy the heart and brain of this splendidly equipped intellect had suffered total eclipse. The central fires had gone out. Nothing was worth doing, thinking, working for. There was nothing to work for any longer!

The professor's first step was to recall as many of his books as possible; his second to close his laboratory and stop all research. He gave no explanation, he invited no questions. His whole personality crumbled away, so to speak, till his daily life became a mere mechanical process of clothing the body, feeding the body, keeping it in good health so as to avoid physical discomfort, and, above all, doing nothing that could interfere with sleep. The professor did everything he could to lengthen the hours of sleep, and therefore of forgetfulness.

It was all clear enough to Dr. Laidlaw. A weaker man, he knew, would have sought to lose himself in one form or another of sensual indulgence—sleeping-draughts, drink, the first pleasures that came to hand. Self-destruction would have been the method of a little bolder type; and deliberate evil-doing, poisoning with his awful knowledge all he could, the means of still another kind of man. Mark Ebor was none of these. He held himself under fine control, facing silently and without complaint the terrible facts he honestly believed himself to have been unfortunate enough to discover. Even to his intimate friend and assistant, Dr. Laidlaw, he vouchsafed no word of true explanation or lament. He went straight forward to the end, knowing well that the end was not very far away.

And death came very quietly one day to him, as he was sitting in the arm-chair of the study, directly facing the doors of the laboratory—the doors that no longer opened. Dr. Laidlaw, by happy chance, was with him at the time, and just able to reach his side in response to the sudden painful efforts for breath; just in time, too, to catch the murmured words that fell from the pallid lips like a message from the other side of the grave.

"Read them, if you must; and, if you can—destroy. But"—his voice sank so low that Dr. Laidlaw only just caught the dying syllables—"but—never, never—give them to the world."

And like a grey bundle of dust loosely gathered up in an old garment the professor sank back into his chair and expired.

But this was only the death of the body. His spirit had died two years before.

IV

The estate of the dead man was small and uncomplicated, and Dr. Laidlaw, as sole executor and residuary legatee, had no difficulty in settling it up. A month after the funeral he was sitting alone in his upstairs library, the last sad duties completed, and his mind full of poignant memories and regrets for the loss of a friend he had revered and loved, and to whom his debt was so incalculably great. The last two years, indeed, had been for him terrible. To watch the swift decay of the greatest combination of heart and brain he had ever known, and to realize he was powerless to help, was a source of profound grief to him that would remain to the end of his days.

At the same time an insatiable curiosity possessed him. The study of dementia was, of course, outside his special province as a specialist, but he knew enough of it to understand how small a matter might be the actual cause of how great an illusion, and he had been devoured from the very beginning by a ceaseless and increasing anxiety to know what the professor had found in the sands of "Chaldea," what these precious Tablets of the Gods might be, and particularly—for this was the real cause that had sapped the man's sanity and hope—what the inscription was that he had believed to have deciphered thereon.

The curious feature of it all to his own mind was, that whereas his friend had dreamed of finding a message of glorious hope and comfort, he had apparently found (so far as he had found anything intelligible at all, and not invented the whole thing in his dementia) that the secret of the world, and the meaning of life and death, was of so terrible a nature that it robbed the heart of courage and the soul of hope. What, then, could be the contents of the little brown parcel the professor had bequeathed to him with his pregnant dying sentences?

Actually his hand was trembling as he turned to the writing-table and began slowly to unfasten a small old-fashioned desk on which the small gilt initials "M.E." stood forth as a melancholy memento. He put the key into the lock and half turned it. Then, suddenly, he stopped and looked about him. Was that a sound at the back of the room? It was just as though someone had laughed and then tried to smother the laugh with a cough. A slight shiver ran over him as he stood listening.

"This is absurd," he said aloud; "too absurd for belief—that I should be so nervous! It's the effect of curiosity unduly prolonged." He smiled a little sadly and his eyes wandered to the blue summer sky and the plane trees swaying in the wind below his window. "It's the reaction," he continued. "The curiosity of two years to be quenched in a single moment! The nervous tension, of course, must be considerable."

He turned back to the brown desk and opened it without further delay. His hand was firm now, and he took out the paper parcel that lay inside without a tremor. It was heavy. A moment later there lay on the table before him a couple of weather-worn plaques of grey stone—they looked like stone, although they felt like metal—on which he saw markings of a curious character that might have been the mere tracings of natural forces through the ages, or, equally well, the half-obliterated hieroglyphics cut upon their surface in past centuries by the more or less untutored hand of a common scribe.

He lifted each stone in turn and examined it carefully. It seemed to him that a faint glow of heat passed from the substance into his skin, and he put them down again suddenly, as with a gesture of uneasiness.

"A very clever, or a very imaginative man," he said to himself, "who could squeeze the secrets of life and death from such broken lines as those!"

Then he turned to a yellow envelope lying beside them in the desk, with the single word on the outside in the writing of the professor—the word *Translation*.

"Now," he thought, taking it up with a sudden violence to conceal his nervousness, "now for the great solution. Now to learn the meaning of the worlds, and why mankind was made, and why discipline is worth while, and sacrifice and pain the true law of advancement."

There was the shadow of a sneer in his voice, and yet something in him shivered at the same time. He held the envelope as though weighing it in his hand, his mind pondering many things. Then curiosity won the day, and he suddenly tore it open with the gesture of an actor who tears open a letter on the stage, knowing there is no real writing inside at all.

A page of finely written script in the late scientist's handwriting lay before him. He read it through from beginning to end, missing no word, uttering each syllable distinctly under his breath as he read.

The pallor of his face grew ghastly as he neared the end. He began to shake all over as with ague. His breath came heavily in gasps. He still gripped the sheet of paper, however, and deliberately, as by an intense effort of will, read it through a second time from beginning to end. And this time, as the last syllable dropped from his lips, the whole face of the man flamed with a sudden and terrible anger. His skin became deep, deep red, and he clenched his teeth. With all the strength of his vigorous soul he was struggling to keep control of himself.

For perhaps five minutes he stood there beside the table without stirring a muscle. He might have been carved out of stone. His eyes were shut, and only the heaving of the chest betrayed the fact that he was a living being. Then, with a strange quietness, he lit a match and applied it to the sheet of paper he held in his hand. The ashes fell slowly about him, piece by piece, and he blew them from the window-sill into the air, his eyes following them as they floated away on the summer wind that breathed so warmly over the world.

He turned back slowly into the room. Although his actions and movements were absolutely steady and controlled, it was clear that he was on the edge of violent action. A hurricane might burst upon the still room any moment. His muscles were tense and rigid. Then, suddenly, he whitened, collapsed, and sank backwards into a chair, like a tumbled bundle of inert matter. He had fainted.

In less than half an hour he recovered consciousness and sat up. As before, he made no sound. Not a syllable passed his lips. He rose quietly and looked about the room.

Then he did a curious thing.

Taking a heavy stick from the rack in the corner he approached the mantlepiece, and with a heavy shattering blow he smashed the clock to pieces. The glass fell in shivering atoms.

"Cease your lying voice for ever," he said, in a curiously still, even tone. "There is no such thing as time!"

He took the watch from his pocket, swung it round several times by the long gold chain, smashed it into smithereens against the wall with a single blow, and then walked into his laboratory next door, and hung its broken body on the bones of the skeleton in the corner of the room.

"Let one damned mockery hang upon another," he said smiling oddly. "Delusions, both of you, and cruel as false!"

He slowly moved back to the front room. He stopped opposite the bookcase where stood in a row the "Scriptures of the World," choicely bound and exquisitely printed, the late professor's most treasured possession, and next to them several books signed "Pilgrim."

One by one he took them from the shelf and hurled them through the open window.

"A devil's dreams! A devil's foolish dreams!" he cried, with a vicious laugh.

Presently he stopped from sheer exhaustion. He turned his eyes slowly to the wall opposite, where hung a weird array of Eastern swords and daggers, scimitars and spears, the collections of many journeys. He crossed the room and ran his finger along the edge. His mind seemed to waver.

"No," he muttered presently; "not that way. There are easier and better ways than that."

He took his hat and passed downstairs into the street.

V

It was five o'clock, and the June sun lay hot upon the pavement. He felt the metal door-knob burn the palm of his hand.

"Ah, Laidlaw, this is well met," cried a voice at his elbow; "I was in the act of coming to see you. I've a case that will interest you, and besides, I remembered that you flavoured your tea with orange leaves!—and I admit—"

It was Alexis Stephen, the great hypnotic doctor.

"I've had no tea today," Laidlaw said, in a dazed manner, after staring for a moment as though the other had struck him in the face. A new idea had entered his mind.

"What's the matter?" asked Dr. Stephen quickly. "Something's wrong with you. It's this sudden heat, or overwork. Come, man, let's go inside."

A sudden light broke upon the face of the younger man, the light of a heaven-sent inspiration. He looked into his friend's face, and told a direct lie.

"Odd," he said, "I myself was just coming to see you. I have something of great importance to test your confidence with. But in your house, please," as Stephen urged him towards his own door—"in your house. It's only round the corner, and I—I cannot go back there—to my rooms—till I have told you.

"I'm your patient—for the moment," he added stammeringly as soon as they were seated in the privacy of the hypnotist's sanctum, "and I want—er—"

"My dear Laidlaw," interrupted the other, in that soothing voice of command which had suggested to many a suffering soul that the cure for its pain lay in the powers of its own reawakened will, "I am always at your service, as you know. You have only to tell me what I can do for you, and I will do it." He showed every desire to help him out. His manner was indescribably tactful and direct.

Dr. Laidlaw looked up into his face.

"I surrender my will to you," he said, already calmed by the other's healing presence, "and I want you to treat me hypnotically—and at once. I want you to suggest to me"—his voice became very tense—"that I shall forget—forget till I die—everything that has occurred to me during the last two hours; till I die, mind," he added, with solemn emphasis, "till I die."

He floundered and stammered like a frightened boy. Alexis Stephen looked at him fixedly without speaking.

"And further," Laidlaw continued, "I want you to ask me no questions. I wish to forget for ever something I have recently discovered—something so terrible and yet so obvious that I can hardly understand why it is not patent to every mind in the world—for I have had a moment of absolute clear vision—of merciless clairvoyance. But I want no one else in the whole world to know what it is—least of all, old friend, yourself."

He talked in utter confusion, and hardly knew what he was saying. But the pain on his face and the anguish in his voice were an instant passport to the other's heart.

"Nothing is easier," replied Dr. Stephen, after a hesitation so slight that the other probably did not even notice it. "Come into my other room where we shall not be disturbed. I can heal you. Your memory of the last two hours shall be wiped out as though it had never been. You can trust me absolutely."

"I know I can," Laidlaw said simply, as he followed him in.

VI

An hour later they passed back into the front room again. The sun was already behind the houses opposite, and the shadows began to gather.

"I went off easily?" Laidlaw asked.

"You were a little obstinate at first. But though you came in like a lion, you went out like a lamb. I let you sleep a bit afterwards."

Dr. Stephen kept his eyes rather steadily upon his friend's face.

"What were you doing by the fire before you came here?" he asked, pausing, in a casual tone, as he lit a cigarette and handed the case to his patient.

"I? Let me see. Oh, I know; I was worrying my way through poor old Ebor's papers and things. I'm his executor, you know. Then I got weary and came out for a whiff of air." He spoke lightly and with perfect naturalness. Obviously he was telling the truth. "I prefer specimens to papers," he laughed cheerily.

"I know, I know," said Dr. Stephen, holding a lighted match for the cigarette. His face wore an expression of content. The experiment had been a complete success. The memory of the last two hours was wiped out utterly. Laidlaw was already chatting gaily and easily about a dozen other things that interested him. Together they went out into the street, and at his door Dr. Stephen left him with a joke and a wry face that made his friend laugh heartily.

"Don't dine on the professor's old papers by mistake," he cried, as he vanished down the street.

Dr. Laidlaw went up to his study at the top of the house. Half way down he met his housekeeper, Mrs. Fewings. She was flustered and excited, and her face was very red and perspiring.

"There've been burglars here," she cried excitedly, "or something funny! All your things is just any'ow, sir. I found everything all about everywhere!" She was very confused. In this orderly and very precise establishment it was unusual to find a thing out of place.

"Oh, my specimens!" cried the doctor, dashing up the rest of the stairs at top speed. "Have they been touched or—"

He flew to the door of the laboratory. Mrs. Fewings panted up heavily behind him.

"The labatry ain't been touched," she explained, breathlessly, "but they smashed the libry clock and they've 'ung your gold watch, sir, on the skelinton's hands. And the books that weren't no value they flung out er the window just like so much rubbish. They must have been wild drunk, Dr. Laidlaw, sir!"

The young scientist made a hurried examination of the rooms. Nothing of value was missing. He began to wonder what kind of burglars they were. He looked up sharply at Mrs. Fewings standing in the doorway. For a moment he seemed to cast about in his mind for something.

"Odd," he said at length. "I only left here an hour ago and everything was all right then."

"Was it, sir? Yes, sir." She glanced sharply at him. Her room looked out upon the courtyard, and she must have seen the books come crashing down, and also have heard her master leave the house a few minutes later.

"And what's this rubbish the brutes have left?" he cried, taking up two slabs of worn gray stone, on the writing-table. "Bath brick, or something, I do declare."

He looked very sharply again at the confused and troubled housekeeper.

"Throw them on the dust heap, Mrs. Fewings, and—and let me know if anything is missing in the house, and I will notify the police this evening."

When she left the room he went into the laboratory and took his watch off the skeleton's fingers. His face wore a troubled expression, but after a moment's thought it cleared again. His memory was a complete blank.

"I suppose I left it on the writing-table when I went out to take the air," he said. And there was no one present to contradict him.

He crossed to the window and blew carelessly some ashes of burned paper from the sill, and stood watching them as they floated away lazily over the tops of the trees.

The Pit and the Pendulum

Edgar Allan Poe

Impia tortorum longos hic turba furores
Sanguinis innocui, non satiata, aluit.
Sospite nunc patria, fracto nunc funeris antro,
Mors ubi dira fuit vita salusque patent.
[Quatrain composed for the gates of a market to be erected upon the site of the Jacobin Club House at Paris.]

I was sick—sick unto death with that long agony; and when they at length unbound me, and I was permitted to sit, I felt that my senses were leaving me. The sentence—the dread sentence of death—was the last of distinct accentuation which reached my ears. After that, the sound of the inquisitorial voices seemed merged in one dreamy indeterminate hum. It conveyed to my soul the idea of *revolution*—perhaps from its association in fancy with the burr of a mill wheel. This only for a brief period; for presently I heard no more. Yet, for a while, I saw; but with how terrible an exaggeration! I saw the lips of the black-robed judges. They appeared to me white—whiter than the sheet upon which I trace these words—and thin even to grotesqueness; thin with the intensity of their expression of firmness—of immoveable resolution—of stern contempt of human torture. I saw that the decrees of what to me was Fate, were still issuing from those lips. I saw them writhe with a deadly locution. I saw them fashion the syllables of my name; and I shuddered because no sound succeeded. I saw, too, for a few moments of delirious horror, the soft and nearly imperceptible waving of the sable draperies which enwrapped the walls of the apartment. And then my vision fell upon the seven tall candles upon the table. At first they wore the aspect of charity, and seemed white and slender angels who would save me; but then, all at once, there came a most deadly nausea over my spirit, and I felt every fibre in my frame thrill as if I had touched the wire of a galvanic battery, while the angel forms became meaningless spectres, with heads of flame, and I saw that from them there would be no help. And then there stole into my fancy, like a rich musical note, the thought of what sweet rest there must be in the grave. The thought came gently and stealthily, and it seemed long before it attained full appreciation; but just as my spirit came at length properly to feel and entertain it, the figures of the judges vanished, as if magically, from before me; the tall candles sank into nothingness; their flames went out utterly; the blackness of darkness supervened; all sensations appeared swallowed up in a mad rushing descent as of the soul into Hades. Then silence, and stillness, night were the universe.

I had swooned; but still will not say that all of consciousness was lost. What of it there remained I will not attempt to define, or even to describe; yet all was not lost. In the deepest slumber—no! In delirium—no! In a swoon—no! In death—no! Even in the grave all *is not* lost. Else there is no immortality for man. Arousing from the most profound of slumbers, we break the gossamer web of some dream. Yet in a second afterward (so frail may that web have been), we remember not that we have dreamed. In the return to life from the swoon there are two stages; first, that of the sense of mental or spiritual; secondly, that of the sense of physical, existence. It seems probable that if, upon reaching the second stage, we could recall the impressions of the first, we should find these impressions eloquent in memories of the gulf beyond. And that gulf is—what? How at least shall we distinguish its shadows from those of the tomb? But if the impressions of what I have termed the first stage, are not, at will, recalled, yet, after long interval, do they not come unbidden, while we marvel whence they come? He who has never swooned, is not he who finds strange palaces and wildly familiar faces in coals that glow; is not he who beholds floating in mid-air the sad visions that the many may not view; is not he who ponders over the perfume of some novel flower—is not he whose brain grows bewildered with the meaning of some musical cadence which has never before arrested his attention.

Amid frequent and thoughtful endeavors to remember; amid earnest struggles to regather some token of the state of seeming nothingness into which my soul had lapsed, there have been moments when I have dreamed of success; there have been brief, very brief periods when I have conjured up remembrances which the lucid reason of a later epoch assures me could have had reference only to that condition of seeming unconsciousness. These shadows of memory tell, indistinctly, of tall figures that lifted and bore me in silence down—down—still down—till a hideous dizziness oppressed me at the mere idea of the interminableness of the descent. They tell also of a vague horror at my heart, on account of that heart's unnatural stillness. Then comes a sense of sudden motionlessness throughout all things; as if those who bore me (a ghastly train!) had outrun, in their descent, the limits of the limitless, and paused from the wearisomeness of their toil. After this I call to mind flatness and dampness; and then all is madness—the madness of a memory which busies itself among forbidden things.

Very suddenly there came back to my soul motion and sound—the tumultuous motion of the heart, and, in my ears, the sound of its beating. Then a pause in which all is blank. Then again sound, and motion, and touch—a tingling sensation pervading my frame. Then the mere consciousness of existence, without thought—a condition which lasted long. Then, very suddenly, thought, and shuddering terror, and earnest endeavor to comprehend my true state. Then a strong desire to lapse into insensibility. Then a rushing revival of soul and a successful effort to move. And now a full memory of the trial, of the judges, of the sable draperies, of the sentence, of the sickness, of the swoon. Then entire forgetfulness of all that followed; of all that a later day and much earnestness of endeavor have enabled me vaguely to recall.

So far, I had not opened my eyes. I felt that I lay upon my back, unbound. I reached out my hand, and it fell heavily upon something damp and hard. There I suffered it to remain for many minutes, while I strove to imagine where and what I could be. I longed, yet dared not to employ my vision. I dreaded the first glance at objects around me. It was not that I feared to look upon things horrible, but that I grew aghast lest there should be *nothing* to see. At length, with a wild desperation at heart, I quickly unclosed my eyes. My worst thoughts, then, were confirmed. The blackness of eternal night encompassed me. I struggled for breath. The intensity of the darkness seemed to oppress and stifle me. The atmosphere was intolerably close. I still lay quietly, and made effort to exercise my reason. I brought to mind the inquisitorial proceedings, and attempted from that point to deduce my real condition. The sentence had passed; and it appeared to me that a very long interval of time had since elapsed. Yet not for a moment did I suppose myself actually dead. Such a supposition, notwithstanding what we read in fiction, is altogether inconsistent with real existence;—but where and in what state was I? The condemned to death, I knew, perished usually at the *autos-da-fé*, and one of these had been held on the very night of the day of my trial. Had I been remanded to my dungeon, to await the next sacrifice, which would not take place for many months? This I at once saw could not be. Victims had been in immediate demand. Moreover, my dungeon, as well as all the condemned cells at Toledo, had stone floors, and light was not altogether excluded.

A fearful idea now suddenly drove the blood in torrents upon my heart, and for a brief period, I once more relapsed into insensibility. Upon recovering, I at once started to my feet, trembling convulsively in every fibre. I thrust my arms wildly above and around me in all directions. I felt nothing; yet dreaded to move a step, lest I should be impeded by the walls of a *tomb*. Perspiration burst from every pore, and stood in cold big beads upon my forehead. The agony of suspense grew at length intolerable, and I cautiously moved forward, with my arms extended, and my eyes straining from their sockets, in the hope of catching some faint ray of light. I proceeded for many paces; but still all was blackness and vacancy. I breathed more freely. It seemed evident that mine was not, at least, the most hideous of fates.

And now, as I still continued to step cautiously onward, there came thronging upon my recollection a thousand vague rumors of the horrors of Toledo. Of the dungeons there had been strange things narrated—fables I had always deemed them—but yet strange, and too ghastly to repeat, save in a whisper. Was I left to perish of starvation in this subterranean world of darkness; or what fate, perhaps even more fearful, awaited me? That the result would be death, and a death of more than customary bitterness, I knew too well the character of my judges to doubt. The mode and the hour were all that occupied or distracted me.

My outstretched hands at length encountered some solid obstruction. It was a wall, seemingly of stone masonry—very smooth, slimy, and cold. I followed it up; stepping with all the careful distrust with which certain antique narratives had inspired me. This process, however, afforded me no means of ascertaining the dimensions of my dungeon; as I might make its circuit, and return to the point whence I set out, without being aware of the fact; so perfectly uniform seemed the wall. I therefore sought the knife which had been in my pocket, when led into the inquisitorial chamber; but it was gone; my clothes had been exchanged for a wrapper of coarse serge. I had thought of forcing the blade in some minute crevice of the masonry, so as to identify my point of departure. The difficulty, nevertheless, was but trivial; although, in the disorder of my fancy, it seemed at first insuperable. I tore a part of the hem from the robe and placed the fragment at full length, and at right angles to the wall. In groping my way around the prison, I could not fail to encounter this rag upon completing the circuit. So, at least I thought: but I had not counted upon the extent of the dungeon, or upon my own weakness. The ground was moist and slippery. I staggered onward for some time, when I stumbled and fell. My excessive fatigue induced me to remain prostrate; and sleep soon overtook me as I lay.

Upon awaking, and stretching forth an arm, I found beside me a loaf and a pitcher with water. I was too much exhausted to reflect upon this circumstance, but ate and drank with avidity. Shortly afterward, I resumed my tour around the prison, and with much toil came at last upon the fragment of the serge. Up to the period when I fell I had counted fifty-two paces, and upon resuming my walk, I had counted forty-eight more;—when I arrived at the rag. There were in all, then, a hundred paces; and, admitting two paces to the yard, I presumed the dungeon to be fifty yards in circuit. I had met, however, with many angles in the wall, and thus I could form no guess at the shape of the vault; for vault I could not help supposing it to be.

I had little object—certainly no hope these researches; but a vague curiosity prompted me to continue them. Quitting the wall, I resolved to cross the area of the enclosure. At first I proceeded with extreme caution, for the floor, although seemingly of solid material, was treacherous with slime. At length, however, I took courage, and did not hesitate to step firmly; endeavoring to cross in as direct a line as possible. I had advanced some ten or twelve paces in this manner, when the remnant of the torn hem of my robe became entangled between my legs. I stepped on it, and fell violently on my face.

In the confusion attending my fall, I did not immediately apprehend a somewhat startling circumstance, which yet, in a few seconds afterward, and while I still lay prostrate, arrested my attention. It was this—my chin rested upon the floor of the prison, but my lips and the upper portion of my head, although seemingly at a less elevation than the chin, touched nothing. At the same time my forehead seemed bathed in a clammy vapor, and the peculiar smell of decayed fungus arose to my nostrils. I put forward my arm, and shuddered to find that I had fallen at the very brink of a circular pit, whose extent, of course, I had no means of ascertaining at the moment. Groping about the masonry just below the margin, I succeeded in dislodging a small fragment, and let it fall into the abyss. For many seconds I hearkened to its reverberations as it dashed against the sides of the chasm in its descent; at length there was a sullen plunge into water, succeeded by loud echoes. At the same moment there came a sound resembling the quick opening, and as rapid closing of a door overhead, while a faint gleam of light flashed suddenly through the gloom, and as suddenly faded away.

I saw clearly the doom which had been prepared for me, and congratulated myself upon the timely accident by which I had escaped. Another step before my fall, and the world had seen me no more. And the death just avoided, was of that very character which I had regarded as fabulous and frivolous in the tales respecting the Inquisition. To the victims of its tyranny, there was the choice of death with its direst physical agonies, or death with its most hideous moral horrors. I had been reserved for the latter. By long suffering my nerves had been unstrung, until I trembled at the sound of my own voice, and had become in every respect a fitting subject for the species of torture which awaited me.

Shaking in every limb, I groped my way back to the wall; resolving there to perish rather than risk the terrors of the wells, of which my imagination now pictured many in various positions about the dungeon. In other conditions of mind I might have had courage to end my misery at once by a plunge into one of these abysses; but now I was the veriest of cowards. Neither could I forget what I had read of these pits—that the sudden extinction of life formed no part of their most horrible plan.

Agitation of spirit kept me awake for many long hours; but at length I again slumbered. Upon arousing, I found by my side, as before, a loaf and a pitcher of water. A burning thirst consumed me, and I emptied the vessel at a draught. It must have been drugged; for scarcely had I drunk, before I became irresistibly drowsy. A deep sleep fell upon me—a sleep like that of death. How long it lasted of course, I know not; but when, once again, I unclosed my eyes, the objects around me were visible. By a wild sulphurous lustre, the origin of which I could not at first determine, I was enabled to see the extent and aspect of the prison.

In its size I had been greatly mistaken. The whole circuit of its walls did not exceed twenty-five yards. For some minutes this fact occasioned me a world of vain trouble; vain indeed! for what could be of less importance, under the terrible circumstances which environed me, then the mere dimensions of my dungeon? But my soul took a wild interest in trifles, and I busied myself in endeavors to account for the error I had committed in my measurement. The truth at length flashed upon me. In my first attempt at exploration I had counted fifty-two paces, up to the period when I fell; I must then have been within a pace or two of the fragment of serge; in fact, I had nearly performed the circuit of the vault. I then slept, and upon awaking, I must have returned upon my steps—thus supposing the circuit nearly double what it actually was. My confusion of mind prevented me from observing that I began my tour with the wall to the left, and ended it with the wall to the right.

I had been deceived, too, in respect to the shape of the enclosure. In feeling my way I had found many angles, and thus deduced an idea of great irregularity; so potent is the effect of total darkness upon one arousing from lethargy or sleep! The angles were simply those of a few slight depressions, or niches, at odd intervals. The general shape of the prison was square. What I had taken for masonry seemed now to be iron, or some other metal, in huge plates, whose sutures or joints occasioned the depression. The entire surface of this metallic enclosure was rudely daubed in all the hideous and repulsive devices to which the charnel superstition of the monks has given rise. The figures of fiends in aspects of menace, with skeleton forms, and other more really fearful images, overspread and disfigured the walls. I observed that the outlines of these monstrosities were sufficiently distinct, but that the colors seemed faded and blurred, as if from the effects of a damp atmosphere. I now noticed the floor, too, which was of stone. In the centre yawned the circular pit from whose jaws I had escaped; but it was the only one in the dungeon.

All this I saw indistinctly and by much effort: for my personal condition had been greatly changed during slumber. I now lay upon my back, and at full length, on a species of low framework of wood. To this I was securely bound by a long strap resembling a surcingle. It passed in many convolutions about my limbs and body, leaving at liberty only my head, and my left arm to such extent that I could, by dint of much exertion, supply myself with food from an earthen dish which lay by my side on the floor. I saw, to my horror, that the pitcher had been removed. I say to my horror; for I was consumed with intolerable thirst. This thirst it appeared to be the design of my persecutors to stimulate: for the food in the dish was meat pungently seasoned.

Looking upward, I surveyed the ceiling of my prison. It was some thirty or forty feet overhead, and constructed much as the side walls. In one of its panels a very singular figure riveted my whole attention. It was the painted figure of Time as he is commonly represented, save that, in lieu of a scythe, he held what, at a casual glance, I supposed to be the pictured image of a huge pendulum such as we see on antique clocks. There was something, however, in the appearance of this machine which caused me to regard it more attentively. While I gazed directly upward at it (for its position was immediately over my own) I fancied that I saw it in motion. In an instant afterward the fancy was confirmed. Its sweep was brief, and of course slow. I watched it for some minutes, somewhat in fear, but more in wonder. Wearied at length with observing its dull movement, I turned my eyes upon the other objects in the cell.

A slight noise attracted my notice, and, looking to the floor, I saw several enormous rats traversing it. They had issued from the well, which lay just within view to my right. Even then, while I gazed, they came up in troops, hurriedly, with ravenous eyes, allured by the scent of the meat. From this it required much effort and attention to scare them away.

It might have been half an hour, perhaps even an hour (for I could take but imperfect note of time), before I again cast my eyes upward. What I then saw confounded and amazed me. The sweep of the pendulum had increased in extent by nearly a yard. As a natural consequence, its velocity was also much greater. But what mainly disturbed me was the idea that had perceptibly descended. I now observed—with what horror it is needless to say—that its nether extremity was formed of a crescent of glittering steel, about a foot in length from horn to horn; the horns upward, and the under edge evidently as keen as that of a razor. Like a razor also, it seemed massy and heavy, tapering from the edge into a solid and broad structure above. It was appended to a weighty rod of brass, and the whole hissed as it swung through the air.

I could no longer doubt the doom prepared for me by monkish ingenuity in torture. My cognizance of the pit had become known to the inquisitorial agents—the pit whose horrors had been destined for so bold a recusant as myself—*the pit*, typical of hell, and regarded by rumor as the Ultima Thule of all their punishments. The plunge into this pit I had avoided by the merest of accidents, I knew that surprise, or entrapment into torment, formed an important portion of all the grotesquerie of these dungeon deaths. Having failed to fall, it was no part of the demon plan to hurl me into the abyss; and thus (there being no alternative) a different and a milder destruction awaited me. Milder! I half smiled in my agony as I thought of such application of such a term.

What boots it to tell of the long, long hours of horror more than mortal, during which I counted the rushing vibrations of the steel! Inch by inch—line by line—with a descent only appreciable at intervals that seemed ages—down and still down it came! Days passed—it might have been that many days passed—ere it swept so closely over me as to fan me with its acrid breath. The odor of the sharp steel forced itself into my nostrils. I prayed—I wearied heaven with my prayer for its more speedy descent. I grew frantically mad, and struggled to force myself upward against the sweep of the fearful scimitar. And then I fell suddenly calm, and lay smiling at the glittering death, as a child at some rare bauble.

There was another interval of utter insensibility; it was brief; for, upon again lapsing into life there had been no perceptible descent in the pendulum. But it might have been long; for I knew there were demons who took note of my swoon, and who could have arrested the vibration at pleasure. Upon my recovery, too, I felt very—oh, inexpressibly sick and weak, as if through long inanition. Even amid the agonies of that period, the human nature craved food. With painful effort I outstretched my left arm as far as my bonds permitted, and took possession of the small remnant which had been spared me by the rats. As I put a portion of it within my lips, there rushed to my mind a half formed thought of joy—of hope. Yet what business had I with hope? It was, as I say, a half formed thought—man has many such which are never completed. I felt that it was of joy—of hope; but felt also that it had perished in its formation. In vain I struggled to perfect—to regain it. Long suffering had nearly annihilated all my ordinary powers of mind. I was an imbecile—an idiot.

The vibration of the pendulum was at right angles to my length. I saw that the crescent was designed to cross the region of the heart. It would fray the serge of my robe—it would return and repeat its operations—again—and again. Notwithstanding terrifically wide sweep (some thirty feet or more) and the hissing vigor of its descent, sufficient to sunder these very walls of iron, still the fraying of my robe would be all that, for several minutes, it would accomplish. And at this thought I paused. I dared not go farther than this reflection. I dwelt upon it with a pertinacity of attention—as if, in so dwelling, I could arrest here the descent of the steel. I forced myself to ponder upon the sound of the crescent as it should pass across the garment—upon the peculiar thrilling sensation which the friction of cloth produces on the nerves. I pondered upon all this frivolity until my teeth were on edge.

Down—steadily down it crept. I took a frenzied pleasure in contrasting its downward with its lateral velocity. To the right—to the left—far and wide—with the shriek of a damned spirit; to my heart with the stealthy pace of the tiger! I alternately laughed and howled as the one or the other idea grew predominant.

Down—certainly, relentlessly down! It vibrated within three inches of my bosom! I struggled violently, furiously, to free my left arm. This was free only from the elbow to the hand. I could reach the latter, from the platter beside me, to my mouth, with great effort, but no farther. Could I have broken the fastenings above the elbow, I would have seized and attempted to arrest the pendulum. I might as well have attempted to arrest an avalanche!

Down—still unceasingly—still inevitably down! I gasped and struggled at each vibration. I shrunk convulsively at its every sweep. My eyes followed its outward or upward whirls with the eagerness of the most unmeaning despair; they closed themselves spasmodically at the descent, although death would have been a relief, oh! how unspeakable! Still I quivered in every nerve to think how slight a sinking of the machinery would precipitate that keen, glistening axe upon my bosom. It was hope that prompted the nerve to quiver—the frame to shrink. It was hope—the hope that triumphs on the rack—that whispers to the death-condemned even in the dungeons of the Inquisition.

I saw that some ten or twelve vibrations would bring the steel in actual contact with my robe, and with this observation there suddenly came over my spirit all the keen, collected calmness of despair. For the first time during many hours—or perhaps days—I *thought*. It now occurred to me that the bandage, or surcingle, which enveloped me, was *unique*. I was tied by no separate cord. The first stroke of the razorlike crescent athwart any portion of the band, would so detach it that it might be unwound from my person by means of my left hand. But how fearful, in that case, the proximity of the steel! The result of the slightest struggle how deadly! Was it likely, moreover, that the minions of the torturer had not foreseen and provided for this possibility! Was it probable that the bandage crossed my bosom in the track of the pendulum? Dreading to find my faint, and, as it seemed, in last hope frustrated, I so far elevated my head as to obtain a distinct view of my breast. The surcingle enveloped my limbs and body close in all directions—*save in the path of the destroying crescent.*

Scarcely had I dropped my head back into its original position, when there flashed upon my mind what I cannot better describe than as the unformed half of that idea of deliverance to which I have previously alluded, and of which a moiety only floated indeterminately through my brain when I raised food to my burning lips. The whole thought was now present—feeble, scarcely sane, scarcely definite—but still entire. I proceeded at once, with the nervous energy of despair, to attempt its execution.

For many hours the immediate vicinity of the low framework upon which I lay, had been literally swarming with rats. They were wild, bold, ravenous; their red eyes glaring upon me as if they waited but for motionlessness on my part to make me their prey. "To what food," I thought, "have they been accustomed in the well?"

They had devoured, in spite of all my efforts to prevent them, all but a small remnant of the contents of the dish. I had fallen into an habitual see-saw, or wave of the hand about the platter: and, at length, the unconscious uniformity of the movement deprived it of effect. In their voracity the vermin frequently fastened their sharp fangs in my fingers. With the particles of the oily and spicy viand which now remained, I thoroughly rubbed the bandage wherever I could reach it; then, raising my hand from the floor, I lay breathlessly still.

At first the ravenous animals were startled and terrified at the change—at the cessation of movement. They shrank alarmedly back; many sought the well. But this was only for a moment. I had not counted in vain upon their voracity. Observing that I remained without motion, one or two of the boldest leaped upon the frame-work, and smelt at the surcingle. This seemed the signal for a general rush. Forth from the well they hurried in fresh troops. They clung to the wood—they overran it, and leaped in hundreds upon my person. The measured movement of the pendulum disturbed them not at all. Avoiding its strokes they busied themselves with the anointed bandage. They pressed—they swarmed upon me in ever accumulating heaps. They writhed upon my throat; their cold lips sought my own; I was half stifled by their thronging pressure; disgust, for which the world has no name, swelled my bosom, and chilled, with a heavy clamminess, my heart. Yet one minute, and I felt that the struggle would be over. Plainly I perceived the loosening of the bandage. I knew that in more than one place it must be already severed. With a more than human resolution I lay still.

Nor had I erred in my calculations—nor had I endured in vain. I at length felt that I was free. The surcingle hung in ribands from my body. But the stroke of the pendulum already pressed upon my bosom. It had divided the serge of the robe. It had cut through the linen beneath. Twice again it swung, and a sharp sense of pain shot through every nerve. But the moment of escape had arrived. At a wave of my hand my deliverers hurried tumultuously away. With a steady movement—cautious, sidelong, shrinking, and slow—I slid from the embrace of the bandage and beyond the reach of the scimitar. For the moment, at least, *I was free*.

Free!—and in the grasp of the Inquisition! I had scarcely stepped from my wooden bed of horror upon the stone floor of the prison, when the motion of the hellish machine ceased and I beheld it drawn up, by some invisible force, through the ceiling. This was a lesson which I took desperately to heart. My every motion was undoubtedly watched. Free!—I had but escaped death in one form of agony, to be delivered unto worse than death in some other. With that thought I rolled my eves nervously around on the barriers of iron that hemmed me in. Something unusual—some change which, at first, I could not appreciate distinctly—it was obvious, had taken place in the apartment. For many minutes of a dreamy and trembling abstraction, I busied myself in vain, unconnected conjecture. During this period, I became aware, for the first time, of the origin of the sulphurous light which illumined the cell. It proceeded from a fissure, about half an inch in width, extending entirely around the prison at the base of the walls, which thus appeared, and were, completely separated from the floor. I endeavored, but of course in vain, to look through the aperture.

As I arose from the attempt, the mystery of the alteration in the chamber broke at once upon my understanding. I have observed that, although the outlines of the figures upon the walls were sufficiently distinct, yet the colors seemed blurred and indefinite. These colors had now assumed, and were momentarily assuming, a startling and most intense brilliancy, that gave to the spectral and fiendish portraitures an aspect that might have thrilled even firmer nerves than my own. Demon eyes, of a wild and ghastly vivacity, glared upon me in a thousand directions, where none had been visible before, and gleamed with the lurid lustre of a fire that I could not force my imagination to regard as unreal.

Unreal!—Even while I breathed there came to my nostrils the breath of the vapour of heated iron! A suffocating odour pervaded the prison! A deeper glow settled each moment in the eyes that glared at my agonies! A richer tint of crimson diffused itself over the pictured horrors of blood. I panted! I gasped for breath! There could be no doubt of the design of my tormentors—oh! most unrelenting! oh! most demoniac of men! I shrank from the glowing metal to the centre of the cell. Amid the thought of the fiery destruction that impended, the idea of the coolness of the well came over my soul like balm. I rushed to its deadly brink. I threw my straining vision below. The glare from the enkindled roof illumined its inmost recesses. Yet, for a wild moment, did my spirit refuse to comprehend the meaning of what I saw. At length it forced—it wrestled its way into my soul—it burned itself in upon my shuddering reason.—Oh! for a voice to speak!—oh! horror!—oh! any horror but this! With a shriek, I rushed from the margin, and buried my face in my hands—weeping bitterly.

The heat rapidly increased, and once again I looked up, shuddering as with a fit of the ague. There had been a second change in the cell—and now the change was obviously in the form. As before, it was in vain that I, at first, endeavoured to appreciate or understand what was taking place. But not long was I left in doubt. The Inquisitorial vengeance had been hurried by my two-fold escape, and there was to be no more dallying with the King of Terrors. The room had been square. I saw that two of its iron angles were now acute—two, consequently, obtuse. The fearful difference quickly increased with a low rumbling or moaning sound. In an instant the apartment had shifted its form into that of a lozenge. But the alteration stopped not here—I neither hoped nor desired it to stop. I could have clasped the red walls to my bosom as a garment of eternal peace. "Death," I said, "any death but that of the pit!" Fool! Might I have not known that *into the pit* it was the object of the burning iron to urge me? Could I resist its glow? Or, if even that, could I withstand its pressure? And now, flatter and flatter grew the lozenge, with a rapidity that left me no time for contemplation. Its centre, and of course, its greatest width, came just over the yawning gulf. I shrank back—but the closing walls pressed me resistlessly onward. At length for my seared and writhing body there was no longer an inch of foothold on the firm floor of the prison. I struggled no more, but the agony of my soul found vent in one loud, long, and final scream of despair. I felt that I tottered upon the brink—I averted my eyes—

There was a discordant hum of human voices! There was a loud blast as of many trumpets! There was a harsh grating as of a thousand thunders! The fiery walls rushed back! An outstretched arm caught my own as I fell, fainting, into the abyss. It was that of General Lasalle. The French army had entered Toledo. The Inquisition was in the hands of its enemies.

The Vampyre

John William Polidori

It happened that in the midst of the dissipations attendant upon a London winter, there appeared at the various parties of the leaders of the *ton* a nobleman, more remarkable for his singularities, than his rank. He gazed upon the mirth around him, as if he could not participate therein. Apparently, the light laughter of the fair only attracted his attention, that he might by a look quell it, and throw fear into those breasts where thoughtlessness reigned. Those who felt this sensation of awe, could not explain whence it arose: some attributed it to the dead grey eye, which, fixing upon the object's face, did not seem to penetrate, and at one glance to pierce through to the inward workings of the heart; but fell upon the cheek with a leaden ray that weighed upon the skin it could not pass. His peculiarities caused him to be invited to every house; all wished to see him, and those who had been accustomed to violent excitement, and now felt the weight of ennui, were pleased at having something in their presence capable of engaging their attention. In spite of the deadly hue of his face, which never gained a warmer tint, either from the blush of modesty, or from the strong emotion of passion, though its form and outline were beautiful, many of the female hunters after notoriety attempted to win his attentions, and gain, at least, some marks of what they might term affection: Lady Mercer, who had been the mockery of every monster shewn in drawing-rooms since her marriage, threw herself in his way, and did all but put on the dress of a mountebank, to attract his notice—though in vain—when she stood before him, though his eyes were apparently fixed upon hers, still it seemed as if they were unperceived—even her unappalled impudence was baffled, and she left the field. But though the common adultress could not influence even the guidance of his eyes, it was not that the female sex was indifferent to him: yet such was the apparent caution with which he spoke to the virtuous wife and innocent daughter, that few knew he ever addressed himself to females. He had, however, the reputation of a winning tongue; and whether it was that it even overcame the dread of his singular character, or that they were moved by his apparent hatred of vice, he was as often among those females who form the boast of their sex from their domestic virtues, as among those who sully it by their vices.

About the same time, there came to London a young gentleman of the name of Aubrey: he was an orphan left with an only sister in the possession of great wealth, by parents who died while he was yet in childhood. Left also to himself by guardians, who thought it their duty merely to take care of his fortune, while they relinquished the more important charge of his mind to the care of mercenary subalterns, he cultivated more his imagination than his judgment. He had, hence, that high romantic feeling of honour and candour, which daily ruins so many milliners' apprentices. He believed all to sympathise with virtue, and thought that vice was thrown in by Providence merely for the picturesque effect of the scene, as we see in romances: he thought that the misery of a cottage merely consisted in the vesting of clothes, which were as warm, but which were better adapted to the painter's eye by their irregular folds and various coloured patches. He thought, in fine, that the dreams of poets were the realities of life. He was handsome, frank, and rich: for these reasons, upon his entering into the gay circles, many mothers surrounded him, striving which should describe with least truth their languishing or romping favourites: the daughters at the same time, by their brightening countenances when he approached, and by their sparkling eyes, when he opened his lips, soon led him into false notions of his talents and his merit. Attached as he was to the romance of his solitary hours, he was startled at finding, that, except in the tallow and wax candles that flickered, not from the presence of a ghost, but from want of snuffing, there was no foundation in real life for any of that congeries of pleasing pictures and descriptions contained in those volumes, from which he had formed his study. Finding, however, some compensation in his gratified vanity, he was about to relinquish his dreams, when the extraordinary being we have above described, crossed him in his career.

He watched him; and the very impossibility of forming an idea of the character of a man entirely absorbed in himself, who gave few other signs of his observation of external objects, than the tacit assent to their existence, implied by the avoidance of their contact: allowing his imagination to picture every thing that flattered its propensity to extravagant ideas, he soon formed this object into the hero of a romance, and determined to observe the offspring of his fancy, rather than the person before him. He became acquainted with him, paid him attentions, and so far advanced upon his notice, that his presence was always recognised. He gradually learnt that Lord Ruthven's affairs were embarrassed, and soon found, from the notes of preparation in —— Street, that he was about to travel. Desirous of gaining some information respecting this singular character, who, till now, had only whetted his curiosity, he hinted to his guardians, that it was time for him to perform the tour, which for many generations has been thought necessary to enable the young to take some rapid steps in the career of vice towards putting themselves upon an equality with the aged, and not allowing them to appear as if fallen from the skies, whenever scandalous intrigues are mentioned as the subjects of pleasantry or of praise, according to the degree of skill shewn in carrying them on. They consented: and Aubrey immediately mentioning his intentions to Lord Ruthven, was surprised to receive from him a proposal to join him. Flattered by such a mark of esteem from him, who, apparently, had nothing in common with other men, he gladly accepted it, and in a few days they had passed the circling waters.

Hitherto, Aubrey had had no opportunity of studying Lord Ruthven's character, and now he found, that, though many more of his actions were exposed to his view, the results offered different conclusions from the apparent motives to his conduct. His companion was profuse in his liberality—the idle, the vagabond, and the beggar, received from his hand more than enough to relieve their immediate wants. But Aubrey could not avoid remarking, that it was not upon the virtuous, reduced to indigence by the misfortunes attendant even upon virtue, that he bestowed his alms;—these were sent from the door with hardly suppressed sneers; but when the profligate came to ask something, not to relieve his wants, but to allow him to wallow in his lust, or to sink him still deeper in his iniquity, he was sent away with rich charity. This was, however, attributed by him to the greater importunity of the vicious, which generally prevails over the retiring bashfulness of the virtuous indigent. There was one circumstance about the charity of his Lordship, which was still more impressed upon his mind: all those upon whom it was bestowed, inevitably found that there was a curse upon it, for they were all either led to the scaffold, or sunk to the lowest and the most abject misery. At Brussels and other towns through which they passed, Aubrey was surprized at the apparent eagerness with which his companion sought for the centres of all fashionable vice; there he entered into all the spirit of the faro table: he betted, and always gambled with success, except where the known sharper was his antagonist, and then he lost even more than he gained; but it was always with the same unchanging face, with which he generally watched the society around: it was not, however, so when he encountered the rash youthful novice, or the luckless father of a numerous family; then his very wish seemed fortune's law—this apparent abstractedness of mind was laid aside, and his eyes sparkled with more fire than that of the cat whilst dallying with the half-dead mouse. In every town, he left the formerly affluent youth, torn from the circle he adorned, cursing, in the solitude of a dungeon, the fate that had drawn him within the reach of this fiend; whilst many a father sat frantic, amidst the speaking looks of mute hungry children, without a single farthing of his late immense wealth, wherewith to buy even sufficient to satisfy their present craving. Yet he took no money from the gambling table; but immediately lost, to the ruiner of many, the last gilder he had just snatched from the convulsive grasp of the innocent: this might but be the result of a certain degree of knowledge, which was not, however, capable of combating the cunning of the more experienced. Aubrey often wished to represent this to his friend, and beg him to resign that charity and pleasure which proved the ruin of all, and did not tend to his own profit;—but he delayed it—for each day he hoped his friend would give him some opportunity of speaking frankly and openly to him; however, this never occurred. Lord Ruthven in his carriage, and amidst the various wild and rich scenes of nature, was always the same: his eye spoke less than his lip; and though Aubrey was near the object of his curiosity, he obtained no greater gratification from it than the constant excitement of vainly wishing to break that mystery, which to his exalted imagination began to assume the appearance of something supernatural.

They soon arrived at Rome, and Aubrey for a time lost sight of his companion; he left him in daily attendance upon the morning circle of an Italian countess, whilst he went in search of the memorials of another almost deserted city. Whilst he was thus engaged, letters arrived from England, which he opened with eager impatience; the first was from his sister, breathing nothing but affection; the others were from his guardians, the latter astonished him; if it had before entered into his imagination that there was an evil power resident in his companion, these seemed to give him sufficient reason for the belief. His guardians insisted upon his immediately leaving his friend, and urged, that his character was dreadfully vicious, for that the possession of irresistible powers of seduction, rendered his licentious habits more dangerous to society. It had been discovered, that his contempt for the adultress had not originated in hatred of her character; but that he had required, to enhance his gratification, that his victim, the partner of his guilt, should be hurled from the pinnacle of unsullied virtue, down to the lowest abyss of infamy and degradation: in fine, that all those females whom he had sought, apparently on account of their virtue, had, since his departure, thrown even the mask aside, and had not scrupled to expose the whole deformity of their vices to the public gaze.

Aubrey determined upon leaving one, whose character had not yet shown a single bright point on which to rest the eye. He resolved to invent some plausible pretext for abandoning him altogether, purposing, in the mean while, to watch him more closely, and to let no slight circumstances pass by unnoticed. He entered into the same circle, and soon perceived, that his Lordship was endeavouring to work upon the inexperience of the daughter of the lady whose house he chiefly frequented. In Italy, it is seldom that an unmarried female is met with in society; he was therefore obliged to carry on his plans in secret; but Aubrey's eye followed him in all his windings, and soon discovered that an assignation had been appointed, which would most likely end in the ruin of an innocent, though thoughtless girl. Losing no time, he entered the apartment of Lord Ruthven, and abruptly asked him his intentions with respect to the lady, informing him at the same time that he was aware of his being about to meet her that very night. Lord Ruthven answered, that his intentions were such as he supposed all would have upon such an occasion; and upon being pressed whether he intended to marry her, merely laughed. Aubrey retired; and, immediately writing a note, to say, that from that moment he must decline accompanying his Lordship in the remainder of their proposed tour, he ordered his servant to seek other apartments, and calling upon the mother of the lady, informed her of all he knew, not only with regard to her daughter, but also concerning the character of his Lordship. The assignation was prevented. Lord Ruthven next day merely sent his servant to notify his complete assent to a separation; but did not hint any suspicion of his plans having been foiled by Aubrey's interposition.

Having left Rome, Aubrey directed his steps towards Greece, and crossing the Peninsula, soon found himself at Athens. He then fixed his residence in the house of a Greek; and soon occupied himself in tracing the faded records of ancient glory upon monuments that apparently, ashamed of chronicling the deeds of freemen only before slaves, had hidden themselves beneath the sheltering soil or many coloured lichen. Under the same roof as himself, existed a being, so beautiful and delicate, that she might have formed the model for a painter, wishing; to pourtray on canvass the promised hope of the faithful in Mahomet's paradise, save that her eyes spoke too much mind for any one to think she could belong to those who had no souls. As she danced upon the plain, or tripped along the mountain's side, one would have thought the gazelle a poor type of her beauties; for who would have exchanged her eye, apparently the eye of animated nature, for that sleepy luxurious look of the animal suited but to the taste of an epicure. The light step of Ianthe often accompanied Aubrey in his search after antiquities, and often would the unconscious girl, engaged in the pursuit of a Kashmere butterfly, show the whole beauty of her form, floating as it were upon the wind, to the eager gaze of him, who forgot the letters he had just decyphered upon an almost effaced tablet, in the contemplation of her sylph-like figure. Often would her tresses falling, as she flitted around, exhibit in the sun's ray such delicately brilliant and swiftly fading hues, its might well excuse the forgetfulness of the antiquary, who let escape from his mind the very object he had before thought of vital importance to the proper interpretation of a passage in Pausanias. But why attempt to describe charms which all feel, but none can appreciate? It was innocence, youth, and beauty, unaffected by crowded drawing-rooms and stifling balls. Whilst he drew those remains of which he wished to preserve a memorial for his future hours, she would stand by, and watch the magic effects of his pencil, in tracing the scenes of her native place; she would then describe to him the circling dance upon the open plain, would paint, to him in all the glowing colours of youthful memory, the marriage pomp she remembered viewing in her infancy; and then, turning to subjects that had evidently made a greater impression upon her mind, would tell him all the supernatural tales of her nurse. Her earnestness and apparent belief of what she narrated, excited the interest even of Aubrey; and often as she told him the tale of the living vampyre, who had passed years amidst his friends, and dearest ties, forced every year, by feeding upon the life of a lovely female to prolong his existence for the ensuing months, his blood would run cold, whilst he attempted to laugh her out of such idle and horrible fantasies; but Ianthe cited to him the names of old men, who had at last detected one living among themselves, after several of their near relatives and children had been found marked with the stamp of the fiend's appetite; and when she found him so incredulous, she begged of him to believe her, for it had been remarked that those who had dared to question their existence, always had some proof given, which obliged them, with grief and heartbreaking, to confess it was true. She detailed to him the traditional appearance of these monsters, and his horror was increased, by hearing a pretty accurate description of Lord Ruthven; he, however, still persisted in persuading her, that there could be no truth in her fears, though at the same time he wondered at the many coincidences which had all tended to excite a belief in the supernatural power of Lord Ruthven.

Aubrey began to attach himself more and more to Ianthe; her innocence, so contrasted with all the affected virtues of the women among whom he had sought for his vision of romance, won his heart; and while he ridiculed the idea of a young man of English habits, marrying an uneducated Greek girl, still he found himself more and more attached to the almost fairy form before him. He would tear himself at times from her, and, forming a plan for some antiquarian research, he would depart, determined not to return until his object was attained; but he always found it impossible to fix his attention upon the ruins around him, whilst in his mind he retained an image that seemed alone the rightful possessor of his thoughts. Ianthe was unconscious of his love, and was ever the same frank infantile being he had first known. She always seemed to part from him with reluctance; but it was because she had no longer any one with whom she could visit her favourite haunts, whilst her guardian was occupied in sketching or uncovering some fragment which had yet escaped the destructive hand of time. She had appealed to her parents on the subject of Vampyres, and they both, with several present, affirmed their existence, pale with horror at the very name. Soon after, Aubrey determined to proceed upon one of his excursions, which was to detain him for a few hours; when they heard the name of the place, they all at once begged of him not to return at night, as he must necessarily pass through a wood, where no Greek would ever remain, after the day had closed, upon any consideration. They described it as the resort of the vampyres in their nocturnal orgies, and denounced the most heavy evils as impending upon him who dared to cross their path. Aubrey made light of their representations, and tried to laugh them out of the idea; but when he saw them shudder at his daring thus to mock a superior, infernal power, the very name of which apparently made their blood freeze, he was silent.

Next morning Aubrey set off upon his excursion unattended; he was surprised to observe the melancholy face of his host, and was concerned to find that his words, mocking the belief of those horrible fiends, had inspired them with such terror. When he was about to depart, Ianthe came to the side of his horse, and earnestly begged of him to return, ere night allowed the power of these beings to be put in action—he promised. He was, however, so occupied in his research, that he did not perceive that day-light would soon end, and that in the horizon there was one of those specks which, in the warmer climates, so rapidly gather into a tremendous mass, and pour all their rage upon the devoted country. He at last, however, mounted his horse, determined to make up by speed for his delay: but it was too late. Twilight, in these southern climates, is almost unknown; immediately the sun sets, night begins: and ere he had advanced far, the power of the storm was above—its echoing thunders had scarcely an interval of rest—its thick heavy rain forced its way through the canopying foliage, whilst the blue forked lightning seemed to fall and radiate at his very feet. Suddenly his horse took fright, and he was carried with dreadful rapidity through the entangled forest. The animal at last, through fatigue, stopped, and he found, by the glare of lightning, that he was in the neighbourhood of a hovel that hardly lifted itself up from the masses of dead leaves and brushwood which surrounded it. Dismounting, he approached, hoping to find some one to guide him to the town, or at least trusting to obtain shelter from the pelting of the storm. As he approached, the thunders, for a moment silent, allowed him to hear the dreadful shrieks of a woman mingling with the stifled, exultant mockery of a laugh, continued in one almost unbroken sound;—he was startled: but, roused by the thunder which again rolled over his head, he, with a sudden effort, forced open the door of the hut. He found himself in utter darkness: the sound, however, guided him. He was apparently unperceived; for, though he called, still the sounds continued, and no notice was taken of him. He found himself in contact with some one, whom he immediately seized; when a voice cried, "Again baffled!" to which a loud laugh succeeded; and he felt himself grappled by one whose strength seemed superhuman: determined to sell his life as dearly as he could, he struggled; but it was in vain: he was lifted from his feet and hurled with enormous force against the ground—his enemy threw himself upon him, and kneeling upon his breast, had placed his hands upon his throat—when the glare of many torches penetrating through the hole that gave light in the day, disturbed him—he instantly rose, and, leaving his prey, rushed through the door, and in a moment the crashing of the branches, as he broke through the wood, was no longer heard. The storm was now still; and Aubrey, incapable of moving, was soon heard by those without. They entered; the light of their torches fell upon the mud walls, and the thatch loaded on every individual straw with heavy flakes of soot. At the desire of Aubrey they searched for her who had attracted him by her cries; he was again left in darkness; but what was his horror, when the light of the torches once more burst upon him, to perceive the airy form of his fair conductress brought in a lifeless corse. He shut his eyes, hoping that it was but a vision arising from his disturbed imagination; but he again saw the same form, when he unclosed them, stretched by his side. There was no colour upon her cheek, not even upon her lip; yet there was a stillness about her face that seemed almost as attaching as the life that once dwelt there—upon her neck and breast was blood, and upon her throat were the marks of teeth having opened the vein—to this the men pointed, crying, simultaneously struck with horror, "A Vampyre! a Vampyre!" A litter was quickly formed, and Aubrey was laid by the side of her who had lately been to him the object of so many bright and fairy visions, now fallen with the flower of life that had died within her. He knew not what his thoughts were—his mind was benumbed and seemed to shun reflection, and take refuge in vacancy—he held almost unconsciously in his hand a naked dagger of a particular construction, which had been found in the hut. They were soon met by different parties who had been engaged in the search of her whom a mother had missed. Their lamentable cries, as they approached the city, forewarned the parents of some dreadful catastrophe. To describe their grief would be impossible; but when they ascertained the cause of their child's death, they looked at Aubrey, and pointed to the corse. They were inconsolable; both died broken-hearted.

Aubrey being put to bed was seized with a most violent fever, and was often delirious; in these intervals he would call upon Lord Ruthven and upon Ianthe—by some unaccountable combination he seemed to beg of his former companion to spare the being he loved. At other times he would imprecate maledictions upon his head, and curse him as her destroyer. Lord Ruthven, chanced at this time to arrive at Athens, and, from whatever motive, upon hearing of the state of Aubrey, immediately placed himself in the same house, and became his constant attendant. When the latter recovered from his delirium, he was horrified and startled at the sight of him whose image he had now combined with that of a Vampyre; but Lord Ruthven, by his kind words, implying almost repentance for the fault that had caused their separation, and still more by the attention, anxiety, and care which he showed, soon reconciled him to his presence. His lordship seemed quite changed; he no longer appeared that apathetic being who had so astonished Aubrey; but as soon as his convalescence began to be rapid, he again gradually retired into the same state of mind, and Aubrey perceived no difference from the former man, except that at times he was surprised to meet his gaze fixed intently upon him, with a smile of malicious exultation playing upon his lips: he knew not why, but this smile haunted him. During the last stage of the invalid's recovery, Lord Ruthven was apparently engaged in watching the tideless waves raised by the cooling breeze, or in marking the progress of those orbs, circling, like our world, the moveless sun—indeed, he appeared to wish to avoid the eyes of all.

Aubrey's mind, by this shock, was much weakened, and that elasticity of spirit which had once so distinguished him now seemed to have fled for ever. He was now as much a lover of solitude and silence as Lord Ruthven; but much as he wished for solitude, his mind could not find it in the neighbourhood of Athens; if he sought it amidst the ruins he had formerly frequented, Ianthe's form stood by his side—if he sought it in the woods, her light step would appear wandering amidst the underwood, in quest of the modest violet; then suddenly turning round, would show, to his wild imagination, her pale face and wounded throat, with a meek smile upon her lips. He determined to fly scenes, every feature of which created such bitter associations in his mind. He proposed to Lord Ruthven, to whom he held himself bound by the tender care he had taken of him during his illness, that they should visit those parts of Greece neither had yet seen. They travelled in every direction, and sought every spot to which a recollection could be attached: but though they thus hastened from place to place, yet they seemed not to heed what they gazed upon. They heard much of robbers, but they gradually began to slight these reports, which they imagined were only the invention of individuals, whose interest it was to excite the generosity of those whom they defended from pretended dangers. In consequence of thus neglecting the advice of the inhabitants, on one occasion they travelled with only a few guards, more to serve as guides than as a defence. Upon entering, however, a narrow defile, at the bottom of which was the bed of a torrent, with large masses of rock brought down from the neighbouring precipices, they had reason to repent their negligence; for scarcely were the whole of the party engaged in the narrow pass, when they were startled by the whistling of bullets close to their heads, and by the echoed report of several guns. In an instant their guards had left them, and, placing themselves behind rocks, had begun to fire in the direction whence the report came. Lord Ruthven and Aubrey, imitating their example, retired for a moment behind the sheltering turn of the defile: but ashamed of being thus detained by a foe, who with insulting shouts bade them advance, and being exposed to unresisting slaughter, if any of the robbers should climb above and take them in the rear, they determined at once to rush forward in search of the enemy. Hardly had they lost the shelter of the rock, when Lord Ruthven received a shot in the shoulder, which brought him to the ground. Aubrey hastened to his assistance; and, no longer heeding the contest or his own peril, was soon surprised by seeing the robbers' faces around him—his guards having, upon Lord Ruthven's being wounded, immediately thrown up their arms and surrendered.

By promises of great reward, Aubrey soon induced them to convey his wounded friend to a neighbouring cabin; and having agreed upon a ransom, he was no more disturbed by their presence—they being content merely to guard the entrance till their comrade should return with the promised sum, for which he had an order. Lord Ruthven's strength rapidly decreased; in two days mortification ensued, and death seemed advancing with hasty steps. His conduct and appearance had not changed; he seemed as unconscious of pain as he had been of the objects about him: but towards the close of the last evening, his mind became apparently uneasy, and his eye often fixed upon Aubrey, who was induced to offer his assistance with more than usual earnestness—"Assist me! you may save me—you may do more than that—I mean not my life, I heed the death of my existence as little as that of the passing day; but you may save my honour, your friend's honour."—"How? tell me how? I would do any thing," replied Aubrey. "I need but little—my life ebbs apace—I cannot explain the whole—but if you would conceal all you know of me, my honour were free from stain in the world's mouth—and if my death were unknown for some time in England—I—I—but life."—"It shall not be known."—"Swear!" cried the dying man, raising himself with exultant violence, "Swear by all your soul reveres, by all your nature fears, swear that, for a year and a day you will not impart your knowledge of my crimes or death to any living being in any way, whatever may happen, or whatever you may see." His eyes seemed bursting from their sockets: "I swear!" said Aubrey; he sunk laughing upon his pillow, and breathed no more.

Aubrey retired to rest, but did not sleep; the many circumstances attending his acquaintance with this man rose upon his mind, and he knew not why; when he remembered his oath a cold shivering came over him, as if from the presentiment of something horrible awaiting him. Rising early in the morning, he was about to enter the hovel in which he had left the corpse, when a robber met him, and informed him that it was no longer there, having been conveyed by himself and comrades, upon his retiring, to the pinnacle of a neighbouring mount, according to a promise they had given his lordship, that it should be exposed to the first cold ray of the moon that rose after his death. Aubrey astonished, and taking several of the men, determined to go and bury it upon the spot where it lay. But, when he had mounted to the summit he found no trace of either the corpse or the clothes, though the robbers swore they pointed out the identical rock on which they had laid the body. For a time his mind was bewildered in conjectures, but he at last returned, convinced that they had buried the corpse for the sake of the clothes.

Weary of a country in which he had met with such terrible misfortunes, and in which all apparently conspired to heighten that superstitious melancholy that had seized upon his mind, he resolved to leave it, and soon arrived at Smyrna. While waiting for a vessel to convey him to Otranto, or to Naples, he occupied himself in arranging those effects he had with him belonging to Lord Ruthven. Amongst other things there was a case containing several weapons of offence, more or less adapted to ensure the death of the victim. There were several daggers and ataghans. Whilst turning them over, and examining their curious forms, what was his surprise at finding a sheath apparently ornamented in the same style as the dagger discovered in the fatal hut—he shuddered—hastening to gain further proof, he found the weapon, and his horror may be imagined when he discovered that it fitted, though peculiarly shaped, the sheath he held in his hand. His eyes seemed to need no further certainty—they seemed gazing to be bound to the dagger; yet still he wished to disbelieve; but the particular form, the same varying tints upon the haft and sheath were alike in splendour on both, and left no room for doubt; there were also drops of blood on each.

He left Smyrna, and on his way home, at Rome, his first inquiries were concerning the lady he had attempted to snatch from Lord Ruthven's seductive arts. Her parents were in distress, their fortune ruined, and she had not been heard of since the departure of his lordship. Aubrey's mind became almost broken under so many repeated horrors; he was afraid that this lady had fallen a victim to the destroyer of Ianthe. He became morose and silent; and his only occupation consisted in urging the speed of the postilions, as if he were going to save the life of some one he held dear. He arrived at Calais; a breeze, which seemed obedient to his will, soon wafted him to the English shores; and he hastened to the mansion of his fathers, and there, for a moment, appeared to lose, in the embraces and caresses of his sister, all memory of the past. If she before, by her infantine caresses, had gained his affection, now that the woman began to appear, she was still more attaching as a companion.

Miss Aubrey had not that winning grace which gains the gaze and applause of the drawing-room assemblies. There was none of that light brilliancy which only exists in the heated atmosphere of a crowded apartment. Her blue eye was never lit up by the levity of the mind beneath. There was a melancholy charm about it which did not seem to arise from misfortune, but from some feeling within, that appeared to indicate a soul conscious of a brighter realm. Her step was not that light footing, which strays where'er a butterfly or a colour may attract—it was sedate and pensive. When alone, her face was never brightened by the smile of joy; but when her brother breathed to her his affection, and would in her presence forget those griefs she knew destroyed his rest, who would have exchanged her smile for that of the voluptuary? It seemed as if those eyes,—that face were then playing in the light of their own native sphere. She was yet only eighteen, and had not been presented to the world, it having been thought by her guardians more fit that her presentation should be delayed until her brother's return from the continent, when he might be her protector. It was now, therefore, resolved that the next drawing-room, which was fast approaching, should be the epoch of her entry into the "busy scene." Aubrey would rather have remained in the mansion of his fathers, and fed upon the melancholy which overpowered him. He could not feel interest about the frivolities of fashionable strangers, when his mind had been so torn by the events he had witnessed; but he determined to sacrifice his own comfort to the protection of his sister. They soon arrived in town, and prepared for the next day, which had been announced as a drawing-room.

The crowd was excessive—a drawing-room had not been held for a long time, and all who were anxious to bask in the smile of royalty, hastened thither. Aubrey was there with his sister. While he was standing in a corner by himself, heedless of all around him, engaged in the remembrance that the first time he had seen Lord Ruthven was in that very place—he felt himself suddenly seized by the arm, and a voice he recognized too well, sounded in his ear—"Remember your oath." He had hardly courage to turn, fearful of seeing a spectre that would blast him, when he perceived, at a little distance, the same figure which had attracted his notice on this spot upon his first entry into society. He gazed till his limbs almost refusing to bear their weight, he was obliged to take the arm of a friend, and forcing a passage through the crowd, he threw himself into his carriage, and was driven home. He paced the room with hurried steps, and fixed his hands upon his head, as if he were afraid his thoughts were bursting from his brain. Lord Ruthven again before him—circumstances started up in dreadful array—the dagger—his oath.—He roused himself, he could not believe it possible—the dead rise again!—He thought his imagination had conjured up the image, his mind was resting upon. It was impossible that it could be real—he determined, therefore, to go again into society; for though he attempted to ask concerning Lord Ruthven, the name hung upon his lips, and he could not succeed in gaining information. He went a few nights after with his sister to the assembly of a near relation. Leaving her under the protection of a matron, he retired into a recess, and there gave himself up to his own devouring thoughts. Perceiving, at last, that many were leaving, he roused himself, and entering another room, found his sister surrounded by several, apparently in earnest conversation; he attempted to pass and get near her, when one, whom he requested to move, turned round, and revealed to him those features he most abhorred. He sprang forward, seized his sister's arm, and, with hurried step, forced her towards the street: at the door he found himself impeded by the crowd of servants who were waiting for their lords; and while he was engaged in passing them, he again heard that voice whisper close to him—"Remember your oath!"—He did not dare to turn, but, hurrying his sister, soon reached home.

Aubrey became almost distracted. If before his mind had been absorbed by one subject, how much more completely was it engrossed, now that the certainty of the monster's living again pressed upon his thoughts. His sister's attentions were now unheeded, and it was in vain that she intreated him to explain to her what had caused his abrupt conduct. He only uttered a few words, and those terrified her. The more he thought, the more he was bewildered. His oath startled him;—was he then to allow this monster to roam, bearing ruin upon his breath, amidst all he held dear, and not avert its progress? His very sister might have been touched by him. But even if he were to break his oath, and disclose his suspicions, who would believe him? He thought of employing his own hand to free the world from such a wretch; but death, he remembered, had been already mocked. For days he remained in this state; shut up in his room, he saw no one, and eat only when his sister came, who, with eyes streaming with tears, besought him, for her sake, to support nature. At last, no longer capable of bearing stillness and solitude, he left his house, roamed from street to street, anxious to fly that image which haunted him. His dress became neglected, and he wandered, as often exposed to the noon-day sun as to the midnight damps. He was no longer to be recognized; at first he returned with the evening to the house; but at last he laid him down to rest wherever fatigue overtook him. His sister, anxious for his safety, employed people to follow him; but they were soon distanced by him who fled from a pursuer swifter than any—from thought. His conduct, however, suddenly changed. Struck with the idea that he left by his absence the whole of his friends, with a fiend amongst them, of whose presence they were unconscious, he determined to enter again into society, and watch him closely, anxious to forewarn, in spite of his oath, all whom Lord Ruthven approached with intimacy. But when he entered into a room, his haggard and suspicious looks were so striking, his inward shudderings so visible, that his sister was at last obliged to beg of him to abstain from seeking, for her sake, a society which affected him so strongly. When, however, remonstrance proved unavailing, the guardians thought proper to interpose, and, fearing that his mind was becoming alienated, they thought it high time to resume again that trust which had been before imposed upon them by Aubrey's parents.

Desirous of saving him from the injuries and sufferings he had daily encountered in his wanderings, and of preventing him from exposing to the general eye those marks of what they considered folly, they engaged a physician to reside in the house, and take constant care of him. He hardly appeared to notice it, so completely was his mind absorbed by one terrible subject. His incoherence became at last so great, that he was confined to his chamber. There he would often lie for days, incapable of being roused. He had become emaciated, his eyes had attained a glassy lustre—the only sign of affection and recollection remaining displayed itself upon the entry of his sister; then he would sometimes start, and, seizing her hands, with looks that severely afflicted her, he would desire her not to touch him. "Oh, do not touch him—if your love for me is aught, do not go near him!" When, however, she inquired to whom he referred, his only answer was, "True! true!" and again he sank into a state, whence not even she could rouse him. This lasted many months: gradually, however, as the year was passing, his incoherences became less frequent, and his mind threw off a portion of its gloom, whilst his guardians observed, that several times in the day he would count upon his fingers a definite number, and then smile.

The time had nearly elapsed, when, upon the last day of the year, one of his guardians entering his room, began to converse with his physician upon the melancholy circumstance of Aubrey's being in so awful a situation, when his sister was going next day to be married. Instantly Aubrey's attention was attracted; he asked anxiously to whom. Glad of this mark of returning intellect, of which they feared he had been deprived, they mentioned the name of the Earl of Marsden. Thinking this was a young Earl whom he had met with in society, Aubrey seemed pleased, and astonished them still more by his expressing his intention to be present at the nuptials, and desiring to see his sister. They answered not, but in a few minutes his sister was with him. He was apparently again capable of being affected by the influence of her lovely smile; for he pressed her to his breast, and kissed her cheek, wet with tears, flowing at the thought of her brother's being once more alive to the feelings of affection. He began to speak with all his wonted warmth, and to congratulate her upon her marriage with a person so distinguished for rank and every accomplishment; when he suddenly perceived a locket upon her breast; opening it, what was his surprise at beholding the features of the monster who had so long influenced his life. He seized the portrait in a paroxysm of rage, and trampled it under foot. Upon her asking him why he thus destroyed the resemblance of her future husband, he looked as if he did not understand her—then seizing her hands, and gazing on her with a frantic expression of countenance, he bade her swear that she would never wed this monster, for he—

But he could not advance—it seemed as if that voice again bade him remember his oath—he turned suddenly round, thinking Lord Ruthven was near him but saw no one. In the meantime the guardians and physician, who had heard the whole, and thought this was but a return of his disorder, entered, and forcing him from Miss Aubrey, desired her to leave him. He fell upon his knees to them, he implored, he begged of them to delay but for one day. They, attributing this to the insanity they imagined had taken possession of his mind, endeavoured to pacify him, and retired.

Lord Ruthven had called the morning after the drawing-room, and had been refused with every one else. When he heard of Aubrey's ill health, he readily understood himself to be the cause of it; but when he learned that he was deemed insane, his exultation and pleasure could hardly be concealed from those among whom he had gained this information. He hastened to the house of his former companion, and, by constant attendance, and the pretence of great affection for the brother and interest in his fate, he gradually won the ear of Miss Aubrey. Who could resist his power? His tongue had dangers and toils to recount—could speak of himself as of an individual having no sympathy with any being on the crowded earth, save with her to whom he addressed himself;—could tell how, since he knew her, his existence, had begun to seem worthy of preservation, if it were merely that he might listen to her soothing accents;—in fine, he knew so well how to use the serpent's art, or such was the will of fate, that he gained her affections. The title of the elder branch falling at length to him, he obtained an important embassy, which served as an excuse for hastening the marriage (in spite of her brother's deranged state), which was to take place the very day before his departure for the continent.

Aubrey, when he was left by the physician and his guardians, attempted to bribe the servants, but in vain. He asked for pen and paper; it was given him; he wrote a letter to his sister, conjuring her, as she valued her own happiness, her own honour, and the honour of those now in the grave, who once held her in their arms as their hope and the hope of their house, to delay but for a few hours that marriage, on which he denounced the most heavy curses. The servants promised they would deliver it; but giving it to the physician, he thought it better not to harass any more the mind of Miss Aubrey by, what he considered, the ravings of a maniac. Night passed on without rest to the busy inmates of the house; and Aubrey heard, with a horror that may more easily be conceived than described, the notes of busy preparation. Morning came, and the sound of carriages broke upon his ear. Aubrey grew almost frantic. The curiosity of the servants at last overcame their vigilance, they gradually stole away, leaving him in the custody of an helpless old woman. He seized the opportunity, with one bound was out of the room, and in a moment found himself in the apartment where all were nearly assembled. Lord Ruthven was the first to perceive him: he immediately approached, and, taking his arm by force, hurried him from the room, speechless with rage. When on the staircase,

Lord Ruthven whispered in his ear—"Remember your oath, and know, if not my bride to day, your sister is dishonoured. Women are frail!" So saying, he pushed him towards his attendants, who, roused by the old woman, had come in search of him. Aubrey could no longer support himself; his rage not finding vent, had broken a blood-vessel, and he was conveyed to bed. This was not mentioned to his sister, who was not present when he entered, as the physician was afraid of agitating her. The marriage was solemnized, and the bride and bridegroom left London.

Aubrey's weakness increased; the effusion of blood produced symptoms of the near approach of death. He desired his sister's guardians might be called, and when the midnight hour had struck, he related composedly what the reader has perused—he died immediately after.

The guardians hastened to protect Miss Aubrey; but when they arrived, it was too late. Lord Ruthven had disappeared, and Aubrey's sister had glutted the thirst of a *Vampyre!*

One Summer Night

Ambrose Bierce

The fact that Henry Armstrong was buried did not seem to him to prove that he was dead: he had always been a hard man to convince. That he really was buried, the testimony of his senses compelled him to admit. His posture—flat upon his back, with his hands crossed upon his stomach and tied with something that he easily broke without profitably altering the situation—the strict confinement of his entire person, the black darkness and profound silence, made a body of evidence impossible to controvert and he accepted it without cavil. But dead—no; he was only very, very ill. He had, withal, the invalid's apathy and did not greatly concern himself about the uncommon fate that had been allotted to him. No philosopher was he—just a plain, commonplace person gifted, for the time being, with a pathological indifference: the organ that he feared consequences with was torpid. So, with no particular apprehension for his immediate future, he fell asleep and all was peace with Henry Armstrong. But something was going on overhead. It was a dark summer night, shot through with infrequent shimmers of lightning silently firing a cloud lying low in the west and portending a storm. These brief, stammering illuminations brought out with ghastly distinctness the monuments and headstones of the cemetery and seemed to set them dancing. It was not a night in which any credible witness was likely to be straying about a cemetery, so the three men who were there, digging into the grave of Henry Armstrong, felt reasonably secure. Two of them were young students from a medical college a few miles away; the third was a gigantic negro known as Jess. For many years Jess had been employed about the cemetery as a man-of-all-work and it was his favourite pleasantry that he knew "every soul in the place." From the nature of what he was now doing it was inferable that the place was not so populous as its register may have shown it to be. Outside the wall, at the part of the grounds farthest from the public road, were a horse and a light wagon, waiting. The work of excavation was not difficult: the earth with which the grave had been loosely filled a few hours before offered little resistance and was soon thrown out. Removal of the casket from its box was less easy, but it was taken out, for it was a perquisite of Jess, who carefully unscrewed the cover and laid it aside, exposing the body in black trousers and white shirt. At that instant the air sprang to flame, a cracking shock of thunder shook the stunned world and Henry Armstrong tranquilly sat up. With inarticulate cries the men fled in terror, each in a different direction. For nothing on earth could two of them have been persuaded to return. But Jess was of another breed. In the grey of the morning the two students, pallid and haggard from anxiety and with the terror of their adventure still beating tumultuously in their blood, met at the medical college. "You saw it?" cried one. "God! yes—what are we to do?" They went around to the rear of the building, where they saw a horse, attached to a light wagon, hitched to a gatepost near the door of the dissecting-room. Mechanically they entered the room. On a bench in the obscurity sat the negro Jess. He rose, grinning, all eyes and teeth. "I'm waiting for my pay," he said. Stretched naked on a long table lay the body of Henry Armstrong, the head defiled with blood and clay from a blow with a spade.

For the Blood Is the Life

F. Marion Crawford

We had dined at sunset on the broad roof of the old tower, because it was cooler there during the great heat of summer. Besides, the little kitchen was built at one corner of the great square platform, which made it more convenient than if the dishes had to be carried down the steep stone steps, broken in places and everywhere worn with age. The tower was one of those built all down the west coast of Calabria by the Emperor Charles V early in the sixteenth century, to keep off the Barbary pirates, when the unbelievers were allied with Francis I against the Emperor and the Church. They have gone to ruin, a few still stand intact, and mine is one of the largest. How it came into my possession ten years ago, and why I spend a part of each year in it, are matters which do not concern this tale. The tower stands in one of the loneliest spots in Southern Italy, at the extremity of a curving rocky promontory, which forms a small but safe natural harbour at the southern extremity of the Gulf of Policastro, and just north of Cape Scalea, the birthplace of Judas Iscariot, according to the old local legend. The tower stands alone on this hooked spur of the rock, and there is not a house to be seen within three miles of it. When I go there I take a couple of sailors, one of whom is a fair cook, and when I am away it is in charge of a gnome-like little being who was once a miner and who attached himself to me long ago.

My friend, who sometimes visits me in my summer solitude, is an artist by profession, a Scandinavian by birth, and a cosmopolitan by force of circumstances. We had dined at sunset; the sunset glow had reddened and faded again, and the evening purple steeped the vast chain of the mountains that embrace the deep gulf to eastward and rear themselves higher and higher toward the south. It was hot, and we sat at the landward corner of the platform, waiting for the night breeze to come down from the lower hills. The colour sank out of the air, there was a little interval of deep-grey twilight, and a lamp sent a yellow streak from the open door of the kitchen, where the men were getting their supper.

Then the moon rose suddenly above the crest of the promontory, flooding the platform and lighting up every little spur of rock and knoll of grass below us, down to the edge of the motionless water. My friend lighted his pipe and sat looking at a spot on the hillside. I knew that he was looking at it, and for a long time past I had wondered whether he would ever see anything there that would fix his attention. I knew that spot well. It was clear that he was interested at last, though it was a long time before he spoke. Like most painters, he trusts to his own eyesight, as a lion trusts his strength and a stag his speed, and he is always disturbed when he cannot reconcile what he sees with what he believes that he ought to see.

"It's strange," he said. "Do you see that little mound just on this side of the boulder?"

"Yes," I said, and I guessed what was coming.

"It looks like a grave," observed Holger.

"Very true. It does look like a grave."

"Yes," continued my friend, his eyes still fixed on the spot. "But the strange thing is that I see the body lying on the top of it. Of course," continued Holger, turning his head on one side as artists do, "it must be an effect of light. In the first place, it is not a grave at all. Secondly, if it were, the body would be inside and not outside. Therefore, it's an effect of the moonlight. Don't you see it?"

"Perfectly; I always see it on moonlight nights."

"It doesn't seem to interest you much," said Holger.

"On the contrary, it does interest me, though I am used to it. You're not so far wrong, either. The mound is really a grave."

"Nonsense!" cried Holger, incredulously. "I suppose you'll tell me what I see lying on it is really a corpse!"

"No," I answered, "it's not. I know, because I have taken the trouble to go down and see."

"Then what is it?" asked Holger.

"It's nothing."

"You mean that it's an effect of light, I suppose?"

"Perhaps it is. But the inexplicable part of the matter is that it makes no difference whether the moon is rising or setting, or waxing or waning. If there's any moonlight at all, from east or west or overhead, so long as it shines on the grave you can see the outline of the body on top."

Holger stirred up his pipe with the point of his knife, and then used his finger for a stopper. When the tobacco burned well he rose from his chair.

"If you don't mind," he said, "I'll go down and take a look at it."

He left me, crossed the roof, and disappeared down the dark steps. I did not move, but sat looking down until he came out of the tower below. I heard him humming an old Danish song as he crossed the open space in the bright moonlight, going straight to the mysterious mound. When he was ten paces from it, Holger stopped short, made two steps forward, and then three or four backward, and then stopped again. I know what that meant. He had reached the spot where the Thing ceased to be visible—where, as he would have said, the effect of light changed.

Then he went on till he reached the mound and stood upon it. I could see the Thing still, but it was no longer lying down; it was on its knees now, winding its white arms round Holger's body and looking up into his face. A cool breeze stirred my hair at that moment, as the night wind began to come down from the hills, but it felt like a breath from another world.

The Thing seemed to be trying to climb to its feet, helping itself up by Holger's body while he stood upright, quite unconscious of it and apparently looking toward the tower, which is very picturesque when the moonlight falls upon it on that side.

"Come along!" I shouted. "Don't stay there all night!"

It seemed to me that he moved reluctantly as he stepped from the mound, or else with difficulty. That was it. The Thing's arms were still round his waist, but its feet could not leave the grave. As he came slowly forward it was drawn and lengthened like a wreath of mist, thin and white, till I saw distinctly that Holger shook himself, as a man does who feels a chill. At the same instant a little wail of pain came to me on the breeze—it might have been the cry of the small owl that lives among the rocks—and the misty presence floated swiftly back from Holger's advancing figure and lay once more at its length upon the mound.

Again I felt the cool breeze in my hair, and this time an icy thrill of dread ran down my spine. I remembered very well that I had once gone down there alone in the moonlight; that presently, being near, I had seen nothing; that, like Holger, I had gone and had stood upon the mound; and I remembered how, when I came back, sure that there was nothing there, I had felt the sudden conviction that there was something after all if I would only look behind me. I remembered the strong temptation to look back, a temptation I had resisted as unworthy of a man of sense, until, to get rid of it, I had shaken myself just as Holger did.

And now I knew that those white, misty arms had been round me too; I knew it in a flash, and I shuddered as I remembered that I had heard the night owl then too. But it had not been the night owl. It was the cry of the Thing.

I refilled my pipe and poured out a cup of strong southern wine; in less than a minute Holger was seated beside me again.

"Of course there's nothing there," he said, "but it's creepy, all the same.

Do you know, when I was coming back I was so sure that there was something behind me that I wanted to turn round and look? It was an effort not to."

He laughed a little, knocked the ashes out of his pipe, and poured himself out some wine. For a while neither of us spoke, and the moon rose higher, and we both looked at the Thing that lay on the mound.

"You might make a story about that," said Holger after a long time.

"There is one," I answered. "If you're not sleepy, I'll tell it to you."

"Go ahead," said Holger, who likes stories.

* * * * *

Old Alario was dying up there in the village behind the hill. You remember him, I have no doubt. They say that he made his money by selling sham jewellery in South America, and escaped with his gains when he was found out. Like all those fellows, if they bring anything back with them, he at once set to work to enlarge his house, and as there are no masons here, he sent all the way to Paola for two workmen. They were a rough-looking pair of scoundrels—a Neapolitan who had lost one eye and a Sicilian with an old scar half an inch deep across his left cheek. I often saw them, for on Sundays they used to come down here and fish off the rocks. When Alario caught the fever that killed him the masons were still at work. As he had agreed that part of their pay should be their board and lodging, he made them sleep in the house. His wife was dead, and he had an only son called Angelo, who was a much better sort than himself. Angelo was to marry the daughter of the richest man in the village, and, strange to say, though the marriage was arranged by their parents, the young people were said to be in love with each other.

For that matter, the whole village was in love with Angelo, and among the rest a wild, good-looking creature called Cristina, who was more like a gipsy than any girl I ever saw about here. She had very red lips and very black eyes, she was built like a greyhound, and had the tongue of the devil. But Angelo did not care a straw for her. He was rather a simple-minded fellow, quite different from his old scoundrel of a father, and under what I should call normal circumstances I really believe that he would never have looked at any girl except the nice plump little creature, with a fat dowry, whom his father meant him to marry. But things turned up which were neither normal nor natural.

On the other hand, a very handsome young shepherd from the hills above Maratea was in love with Cristina, who seems to have been quite indifferent to him. Cristina had no regular means of subsistence, but she was a good girl and willing to do any work or go on errands to any distance for the sake of a loaf of bread or a mess of beans, and permission to sleep under cover. She was especially glad when she could get something to do about the house of Angelo's father. There is no doctor in the village, and when the neighbours saw that old Alario was dying they sent Cristina to Scalea to fetch one. That was late in the afternoon, and if they had waited so long, it was because the dying miser refused to allow any such extravagance while he was able to speak. But while Cristina was gone matters grew rapidly worse, the priest was brought to the bedside, and when he had done what he could he gave it as his opinion to the bystanders that the old man was dead, and left the house.

You know these people. They have a physical horror of death. Until the priest spoke, the room had been full of people. The words were hardly out of his mouth before it was empty. It was night now. They hurried down the dark steps and out into the street.

Angelo, as I have said, was away, Cristina had not come back—the simple woman-servant who had nursed the sick man fled with the rest, and the body was left alone in the flickering light of the earthen oil lamp.

Five minutes later two men looked in cautiously and crept forward toward the bed. They were the one-eyed Neapolitan mason and his Sicilian companion. They knew what they wanted. In a moment they had dragged from under the bed a small but heavy iron-bound box, and long before any one thought of coming back to the dead man they had left the house and the village under cover of the darkness. It was easy enough, for Alario's house is the last toward the gorge which leads down here, and the thieves merely went out by the back door, got over the stone wall, and had nothing to risk after that except the possibility of meeting some belated countryman, which was very small indeed, since few of the people use that path. They had a mattock and shovel, and they made their way here without accident.

I am telling you this story as it must have happened, for, of course, there were no witnesses to this part of it. The men brought the box down by the gorge, intending to bury it until they should be able to come back and take it away in a boat. They must have been clever enough to guess that some of the money would be in paper notes, for they would otherwise have buried it on the beach in the wet sand, where it would have been much safer. But the paper would have rotted if they had been obliged to leave it there long, so they dug their hole down there, close to that boulder. Yes, just where the mound is now.

Cristina did not find the doctor in Scalea, for he had been sent for from a place up the valley, halfway to San Domenico. If she had found him, he would have come on his mule by the upper road, which is smoother but much longer. But Cristina took the short cut by the rocks, which passes about fifty feet above the mound, and goes round that corner. The men were digging when she passed, and she heard them at work. It would not have been like her to go by without finding out what the noise was, for she was never afraid of anything in her life, and, besides, the fishermen sometimes come ashore here at night to get a stone for an anchor or to gather sticks to make a little fire. The night was dark, and Cristina probably came close to the two men before she could see what they were doing. She knew them, of course, and they knew her, and understood instantly that they were in her power. There was only one thing to be done for their safety, and they did it. They knocked her on the head, they dug the hole deep, and they buried her quickly with the iron-bound chest. They must have understood that their only chance of escaping suspicion lay in getting back to the village before their absence was noticed, for they returned immediately, and were found half an hour later gossiping quietly with the man who was making Alario's coffin. He was a crony of theirs, and had been working at the repairs in the old man's house. So far as I have been able to make out, the only persons who were supposed to know where Alario kept his treasure were Angelo and the one woman-servant I have mentioned. Angelo was away; it was the woman who discovered the theft.

It is easy enough to understand why no one else knew where the money was. The old man kept his door locked and the key in his pocket when he was out, and did not let the woman enter to clean the place unless he was there himself. The whole village knew that he had money somewhere, however, and the masons had probably discovered the whereabouts of the chest by climbing in at the window in his absence. If the old man had not been delirious until he lost consciousness, he would have been in frightful agony of mind for his riches. The faithful woman-servant forgot their existence only for a few moments when she fled with the rest, overcome by the horror of death. Twenty minutes had not passed before she returned with the two hideous old hags who are always called in to prepare the dead for burial. Even then she had not at first the courage to go near the bed with them, but she made a pretence of dropping something, went down on her knees as if to find it, and looked under the bedstead. The walls of the room were newly whitewashed down to the floor, and she saw at a glance that the chest was gone. It had been there in the afternoon, it had therefore been stolen in the short interval since she had left the room.

There are no carabineers stationed in the village; there is not so much as a municipal watchman, for there is no municipality. There never was such a place, I believe. Scalea is supposed to look after it in some mysterious way, and it takes a couple of hours to get anybody from there. As the old woman had lived in the village all her life, it did not even occur to her to apply to any civil authority for help. She simply set up a howl and ran through the village in the dark, screaming out that her dead master's house had been robbed. Many of the people looked out, but at first no one seemed inclined to help her. Most of them, judging her by themselves, whispered to each other that she had probably stolen the money herself. The first man to move was the father of the girl whom Angelo was to marry; having collected his household, all of whom felt a personal interest in the wealth which was to have come into the family, he declared it to be his opinion that the chest had been stolen by the two journeyman masons who lodged in the house. He headed a search for them, which naturally began in Alario's house and ended in the carpenter's workshop, where the thieves were found discussing a measure of wine with the carpenter over the half-finished coffin, by the light of one earthen lamp filled with oil and tallow. The search party at once accused the delinquents of the crime, and threatened to lock them up in the cellar till the carabineers could be fetched from Scalea. The two men looked at each other for one moment, and then without the slightest hesitation they put out the single light, seized the unfinished coffin between them, and using it as a sort of battering ram, dashed upon their assailants in the dark. In a few moments they were beyond pursuit.

That is the end of the first part of the story. The treasure had disappeared, and as no trace of it could be found the people naturally supposed that the thieves had succeeded in carrying it off. The old man was buried, and when Angelo came back at last he had to borrow money to pay for the miserable funeral, and had some difficulty in doing so. He hardly needed to be told that in losing his inheritance he had lost his bride. In this part of the world marriages are made on strictly business principles, and if the promised cash is not forthcoming on the appointed day the bride or the bridegroom whose parents have failed to produce it may as well take themselves off, for there will be no wedding. Poor Angelo knew that well enough. His father had been possessed of hardly any land, and now that the hard cash which he had brought from South America was gone, there was nothing left but debts for the building materials that were to have been used for enlarging and improving the old house. Angelo was beggared, and the nice plump little creature who was to have been his turned up her nose at him in the most approved fashion. As for Cristina, it was several days before she was missed, for no one remembered that she had been sent to Scalea for the doctor, who had never come. She often disappeared in the same way for days together, when she could find a little work here and there at the distant farms among the hills. But when she did not come back at all, people began to wonder, and at last made up their minds that she had connived with the masons and had escaped with them.

* * * * *

I paused and emptied my glass.

"That sort of thing could not happen anywhere else," observed Holger, filling his everlasting pipe again. "It is wonderful what a natural charm there is about murder and sudden death in a romantic country like this. Deeds that would be simply brutal and disgusting anywhere else become dramatic and mysterious because this is Italy and we are living in a genuine tower of Charles V built against genuine Barbary pirates."

"There's something in that," I admitted. Holger is the most romantic man in the world inside of himself, but he always thinks it necessary to explain why he feels anything.

"I suppose they found the poor girl's body with the box," he said presently.

"As it seems to interest you," I answered, "I'll tell you the rest of the story."

The moon had risen high by this time; the outline of the Thing on the mound was clearer to our eyes than before.

* * * * *

The village very soon settled down to its small, dull life. No one missed old Alario, who had been away so much on his voyages to South America that he had never been a familiar figure in his native place. Angelo lived in the half-finished house, and because he had no money to pay the old woman-servant she would not stay with him, but once in a long time she would come and wash a shirt for him for old acquaintance' sake. Besides the house, he had inherited a small patch of ground at some distance from the village; he tried to cultivate it, but he had no heart in the work, for he knew he could never pay the taxes on it and on the house, which would certainly be confiscated by the Government, or seized for the debt of the building material, which the man who had supplied it refused to take back.

Angelo was very unhappy. So long as his father had been alive and rich, every girl in the village had been in love with him; but that was all changed now. It had been pleasant to be admired and courted, and invited to drink wine by fathers who had girls to marry. It was hard to be stared at coldly, and sometimes laughed at because he had been robbed of his inheritance. He cooked his miserable meals for himself, and from being sad became melancholy and morose.

At twilight, when the day's work was done, instead of hanging about in the open space before the church with young fellows of his own age, he took to wandering in lonely places on the outskirts of the village till it was quite dark. Then he slunk home and went to bed to save the expense of a light. But in those lonely twilight hours he began to have strange waking dreams. He was not always alone, for often when he sat on the stump of a tree, where the narrow path turns down the gorge, he was sure that a woman came up noiselessly over the rough stones, as if her feet were bare; and she stood under a clump of chestnut trees only half a dozen yards down the path, and beckoned to him without speaking. Though she was in the shadow he knew that her lips were red, and that when they parted a little and smiled at him she showed two small sharp teeth. He knew this at first rather than saw it, and he knew that it was Cristina, and that she was dead. Yet he was not afraid; he only wondered whether it was a dream, for he thought that if he had been awake he should have been frightened.

Besides, the dead woman had red lips, and that could only happen in a dream. Whenever he went near the gorge after sunset she was already there waiting for him, or else she very soon appeared, and he began to be sure that she came a little nearer to him every day. At first he had only been sure of her blood-red mouth, but now each feature grew distinct, and the pale face looked at him with deep and hungry eyes.

It was the eyes that grew dim. Little by little he came to know that some day the dream would not end when he turned away to go home, but would lead him down the gorge out of which the vision rose. She was nearer now when she beckoned to him. Her cheeks were not livid like those of the dead, but pale with starvation, with the furious and unappeased physical hunger of her eyes that devoured him. They feasted on his soul and cast a spell over him, and at last they were close to his own and held him. He could not tell whether her breath was as hot as fire or as cold as ice; he could not tell whether her red lips burned his or froze them, or whether her five fingers on his wrists seared scorching scars or bit his flesh like frost; he could not tell whether he was awake or asleep, whether she was alive or dead, but he knew that she loved him, she alone of all creatures, earthly or unearthly, and her spell had power over him.

When the moon rose high that night the shadow of that Thing was not alone down there upon the mound.

Angelo awoke in the cool dawn, drenched with dew and chilled through flesh, and blood, and bone. He opened his eyes to the faint grey light, and saw the stars still shining overhead. He was very weak, and his heart was beating so slowly that he was almost like a man fainting. Slowly he turned his head on the mound, as on a pillow, but the other face was not there. Fear seized him suddenly, a fear unspeakable and unknown; he sprang to his feet and fled up the gorge, and he never looked behind him until he reached the door of the house on the outskirts of the village. Drearily he went to his work that day, and wearily the hours dragged themselves after the sun, till at last he touched the sea and sank, and the great sharp hills above Maratea turned purple against the dove-coloured eastern sky.

Angelo shouldered his heavy hoe and left the field. He felt less tired now than in the morning when he had begun to work, but he promised himself that he would go home without lingering by the gorge, and eat the best supper he could get himself, and sleep all night in his bed like a Christian man. Not again would he be tempted down the narrow way by a shadow with red lips and icy breath; not again would he dream that dream of terror and delight. He was near the village now; it was half an hour since the sun had set, and the cracked church bell sent little discordant echoes across the rocks and ravines to tell all good people that the day was done. Angelo stood still a moment where the path forked, where it led toward the village on the left, and down to the gorge on the right, where a clump of chestnut trees overhung the narrow way. He stood still a minute, lifting his battered hat from his head and gazing at the fast-fading sea westward, and his lips moved as he silently repeated the familiar evening prayer. His lips moved, but the words that followed them in his brain lost their meaning and turned into others, and ended in a name that he spoke aloud—Cristina! With the name, the tension of his will relaxed suddenly, reality went out and the dream took him again, and bore him on swiftly and surely like a man walking in his sleep, down, down, by the steep path in the gathering darkness. And as she glided beside him, Cristina whispered strange, sweet things in his ear, which somehow, if he had been awake, he knew that he could not quite have understood; but now they were the most wonderful words he had ever heard in his life. And she kissed him also, but not upon his mouth. He felt her sharp kisses upon his white throat, and he knew that her lips were red. So the wild dream sped on through twilight and darkness and moonrise, and all the glory of the summer's night. But in the chilly dawn he lay as one half dead upon the mound down there, recalling and not recalling, drained of his blood, yet strangely longing to give those red lips more. Then came the fear, the awful nameless panic, the mortal horror that guards the confines of the world we see not, neither know of as we know of other things, but which we feel when its icy chill freezes our bones and stirs our hair with the touch of a ghostly hand. Once more Angelo sprang from the mound and fled up the gorge in the breaking day, but his step was less sure this time, and he panted for breath as he ran; and when he came to the bright spring of water that rises halfway up the hillside, he dropped upon his knees and hands and plunged his whole face in and drank as he had never drunk before—for it was the thirst of the wounded man who has lain bleeding all night long upon the battle-field.

She had him fast now, and he could not escape her, but would come to her every evening at dusk until she had drained him of his last drop of blood. It was in vain that when the day was done he tried to take another turning and to go home by a path that did not lead near the gorge. It was in vain that he made promises to himself each morning at dawn when he climbed the lonely way up from the shore to the village. It was all in vain, for when the sun sank burning into the sea, and the coolness of the evening stole out as from a hiding-place to delight the weary world, his feet turned toward the old way, and she was waiting for him in the shadow under the chestnut trees; and then all happened as before, and she fell to kissing his white throat even as she flitted lightly down the way, winding one arm about him. And as his blood failed, she grew more hungry and more thirsty every day, and every day when he awoke in the early dawn it was harder to rouse himself to the effort of climbing the steep path to the village; and when he went to his work his feet dragged painfully, and there was hardly strength in his arms to wield the heavy hoe. He scarcely spoke to any one now, but the people said he was "consuming himself" for love of the girl he was to have married when he lost his inheritance; and they laughed heartily at the thought, for this is not a very romantic country. At this time, Antonio, the man who stays here to look after the tower, returned from a visit to his people, who live near Salerno. He had been away all the time since before Alario's death and knew nothing of what had happened. He has told me that he came back late in the afternoon and shut himself up in the tower to eat and sleep, for he was very tired. It was past midnight when he awoke, and when he looked out the waning moon was rising over the shoulder of the hill. He looked out toward the mound, and he saw something, and he did not sleep again that night. When he went out again in the morning it was broad daylight, and there was nothing to be seen on the mound but loose stones and driven sand. Yet he did not go very near it; he went straight up the path to the village and directly to the house of the old priest.

"I have seen an evil thing this night," he said; "I have seen how the dead drink the blood of the living. And the blood is the life."

"Tell me what you have seen," said the priest in reply.

Antonio told him everything he had seen.

"You must bring your book and your holy water tonight," he added. "I will be here before sunset to go down with you, and if it pleases your reverence to sup with me while we wait, I will make ready."

"I will come," the priest answered, "for I have read in old books of these strange beings which are neither quick nor dead, and which lie ever fresh in their graves, stealing out in the dusk to taste life and blood."

Antonio cannot read, but he was glad to see that the priest understood the business; for, of course, the books must have instructed him as to the best means of quieting the half-living Thing for ever.

So Antonio went away to his work, which consists largely in sitting on the shady side of the tower, when he is not perched upon a rock with a fishing-line catching nothing. But on that day he went twice to look at the mound in the bright sunlight, and he searched round and round it for some hole through which the being might get in and out; but he found none. When the sun began to sink and the air was cooler in the shadows, he went up to fetch the old priest, carrying a little wicker basket with him; and in this they placed a bottle of holy water, and the basin, and sprinkler, and the stole which the priest would need; and they came down and waited in the door of the tower till it should be dark. But while the light still lingered very grey and faint, they saw something moving, just there, two figures, a man's that walked, and a woman's that flitted beside him, and while her head lay on his shoulder she kissed his throat. The priest has told me that, too, and that his teeth chattered and he grasped Antonio's arm. The vision passed and disappeared into the shadow. Then Antonio got the leathern flask of strong liquor, which he kept for great occasions, and poured such a draught as made the old man feel almost young again; and he got the lantern, and his pick and shovel, and gave the priest his stole to put on and the holy water to carry, and they went out together toward the spot where the work was to be done. Antonio says that in spite of the rum his own knees shook together, and the priest stumbled over his Latin. For when they were yet a few yards from the mound the flickering light of the lantern fell upon Angelo's white face, unconscious as if in sleep, and on his upturned throat, over which a very thin red line of blood trickled down into his collar; and the flickering light of the lantern played upon another face that looked up from the feast—upon two deep, dead eyes that saw in spite of death—upon parted lips redder than life itself—upon two gleaming teeth on which glistened a rosy drop. Then the priest, good old man, shut his eyes tight and showered holy water before him, and his cracked voice rose almost to a scream; and then Antonio, who is no coward after all, raised his pick in one hand and the lantern in the other, as he sprang forward, not knowing what the end should be; and then he swears that he heard a woman's cry, and the Thing was gone, and Angelo lay alone on the mound unconscious, with the red line on his throat and the beads of deathly sweat on his cold forehead. They lifted him, half-dead as he was, and laid him on the ground close by; then Antonio went to work, and the priest helped him, though he was old and could not do much; and they dug deep, and at last Antonio, standing in the grave, stooped down with his lantern to see what he might see.

His hair used to be dark brown, with grizzled streaks about the temples; in less than a month from that day he was as grey as a badger. He was a miner when he was young, and most of these fellows have seen ugly sights now and then, when accidents have happened, but he had never seen what he saw that night—that Thing which is neither alive nor dead, that Thing that will abide neither above ground nor in the grave. Antonio had brought something with him which the priest had not noticed. He had made it that afternoon—a sharp stake shaped from a piece of tough old driftwood. He had it with him now, and he had his heavy pick, and he had taken the lantern down into the grave. I don't think any power on earth could make him speak of what happened then, and the old priest was too frightened to look in. He says he heard Antonio breathing like a wild beast, and moving as if he were fighting with something almost as strong as himself; and he heard an evil sound also, with blows, as of something violently driven through flesh and bone; and then the most awful sound of all—a woman's shriek, the unearthly scream of a woman neither dead nor alive, but buried deep for many days. And he, the poor old priest, could only rock himself as he knelt there in the sand, crying aloud his prayers and exorcisms to drown these dreadful sounds. Then suddenly a small iron-bound chest was thrown up and rolled over against the old man's knee, and in a moment more Antonio was beside him, his face as white as tallow in the flickering light of the lantern, shovelling the sand and pebbles into the grave with furious haste, and looking over the edge till the pit was half full; and the priest said that there was much fresh blood on Antonio's hands and on his clothes.

* * * * *

I had come to the end of my story. Holger finished his wine and leaned back in his chair.

"So Angelo got his own again," he said. "Did he marry the prim and plump young person to whom he had been betrothed?"

"No; he had been badly frightened. He went to South America, and has not been heard of since."

"And that poor thing's body is there still, I suppose," said Holger. "Is it quite dead yet, I wonder?"

I wonder, too. But whether it be dead or alive, I should hardly care to see it, even in broad daylight. Antonio is as grey as a badger, and he has never been quite the same man since that night.

Count Magnus

M. R. James

By what means the papers out of which I have made a connected story came into my hands is the last point which the reader will learn from these pages. But it is necessary to prefix to my extracts from them a statement of the form in which I possess them.

They consist, then, partly of a series of collections for a book of travels, such a volume as was a common product of the forties and fifties. Horace Marryat's *Journal of a Residence in Jutland and the Danish Isles* is a fair specimen of the class to which I allude. These books usually treated of some unknown district on the Continent. They were illustrated with woodcuts or steel plates. They gave details of hotel accommodation and of means of communication, such as we now expect to find in any well-regulated guide-book, and they dealt largely in reported conversations with intelligent foreigners, racy innkeepers, and garrulous peasants. In a word, they were chatty.

Begun with the idea of furnishing material for such a book, my papers as they progressed assumed the character of a record of one single personal experience, and this record was continued up to the very eve, almost, of its termination.

The writer was a Mr. Wraxall. For my knowledge of him I have to depend entirely on the evidence his writings afford, and from these I deduce that he was a man past middle age, possessed of some private means, and very much alone in the world. He had, it seems, no settled abode in England, but was a denizen of hotels and boarding-houses. It is probable that he entertained the idea of settling down at some future time which never came; and I think it also likely that the Pantechnicon fire in the early seventies must have destroyed a great deal that would have thrown light on his antecedents, for he refers once or twice to property of his that was warehoused at that establishment.

It is further apparent that Mr. Wraxall had published a book, and that it treated of a holiday he had once taken in Brittany. More than this I cannot say about his work, because a diligent search in bibliographical works has convinced me that it must have appeared either anonymously or under a pseudonym.

As to his character, it is not difficult to form some superficial opinion. He must have been an intelligent and cultivated man. It seems that he was near being a Fellow of his college at Oxford—Brasenose, as I judge from the

Calendar. His besetting fault was pretty clearly that of over-inquisitiveness, possibly a good fault in a traveller, certainly a fault for which this traveller paid dearly enough in the end.

On what proved to be his last expedition, he was plotting another book. Scandinavia, a region not widely known to Englishmen forty years ago, had struck him as an interesting field. He must have alighted on some old books of Swedish history or memoirs, and the idea had struck him that there was room for a book descriptive of travel in Sweden, interspersed with episodes from the history of some of the great Swedish families. He procured letters of introduction, therefore, to some persons of quality in Sweden, and set out thither in the early summer of 1863.

Of his travels in the North there is no need to speak, nor of his residence of some weeks in Stockholm. I need only mention that some savant resident there put him on the track of an important collection of family papers belonging to the proprietors of an ancient manor-house in Vestergothland, and obtained for him permission to examine them.

The manor-house, or *herrgard*, in question is to be called Råbäck (pronounced something like Roebeck), though that is not its name. It is one of the best buildings of its kind in all the country, and the picture of it in Dahlenberg's *Suecia antiqua et moderna*, engraved in 1694, shows it very much as the tourist may see it today. It was built soon after 1600, and is, roughly speaking, very much like an English house of that period in respect of material—red-brick with stone facings—and style. The man who built it was a scion of the great house of De la Gardie, and his descendants possess it still. De la Gardie is the name by which I will designate them when mention of them becomes necessary.

They received Mr. Wraxall with great kindness and courtesy, and pressed him to stay in the house as long as his researches lasted. But, preferring to be independent, and mistrusting his powers of conversing in Swedish, he settled himself at the village inn, which turned out quite sufficiently comfortable, at any rate during the summer months. This arrangement would entail a short walk daily to and from the manor-house of something under a mile. The house itself stood in a park, and was protected—we should say grown up—with large old timber. Near it you found the walled garden, and then entered a close wood fringing one of the small lakes with which the whole country is pitted. Then came the wall of the demesne, and you climbed a steep knoll—a knob of rock lightly covered with soil—and on the top of this stood the church, fenced in with tall dark trees. It was a curious building to English eyes. The nave and aisles were low, and filled with pews and galleries. In the western gallery stood the handsome old organ, gaily painted, and with silver pipes. The ceiling was flat, and had been adorned by a seventeenth-century artist with a strange and hideous "Last Judgement," full of lurid flames, falling cities, burning ships, crying souls, and brown and smiling demons. Handsome brass coronae hung from the roof; the pulpit was like a doll's-house covered with little painted wooden cherubs and saints; a stand with three hour-glasses was hinged to the preacher's desk. Such sights as these may be seen in many a church in Sweden now, but what distinguished this one was an addition to the original building. At the eastern end of the north aisle the builder of the manor-house had erected a mausoleum for himself and his family. It was a largish eight-sided building, lighted by a series of oval windows, and it had a domed roof, topped by a kind of pumpkin-shaped object rising into a spire, a form in which Swedish architects greatly delighted. The roof was of copper externally, and was painted black, while the walls, in common with those of the church, were staringly white. To this mausoleum there was no access from the church. It had a portal and steps of its own on the northern side.

Past the churchyard the path to the village goes, and not more than three or four minutes bring you to the inn door.

On the first day of his stay at Råbäck Mr. Wraxall found the church door open, and made these notes of the interior which I have epitomized. Into the mausoleum, however, he could not make his way. He could by looking through the keyhole just descry that there were fine marble effigies and sarcophagi of copper, and a wealth of armorial ornament, which made him very anxious to spend some time in investigation.

The papers he had come to examine at the manor-house proved to be of just the kind he wanted for his book. There were family correspondence, journals, and account-books of the earliest owners of the estate, very carefully kept and clearly written, full of amusing and picturesque detail. The first De la Gardie appeared in them as a strong and capable man. Shortly after the building of the mansion there had been a period of distress in the district, and the peasants had risen and attacked several châteaux and done some damage. The owner of Råbäck took a leading part in supressing trouble, and there was reference to executions of ring-leaders and severe punishments inflicted with no sparing hand.

The portrait of this Magnus de la Gardie was one of the best in the house, and Mr. Wraxall studied it with no little interest after his day's work. He gives no detailed description of it, but I gather that the face impressed him rather by its power than by its beauty or goodness; in fact, he writes that Count Magnus was an almost phenomenally ugly man.

On this day Mr. Wraxall took his supper with the family, and walked back in the late but still bright evening.

"I must remember," he writes, "to ask the sexton if he can let me into the mausoleum at the church. He evidently has access to it himself, for I saw him tonight standing on the steps, and, as I thought, locking or unlocking the door."

I find that early on the following day Mr. Wraxall had some conversation with his landlord. His setting it down at such length as he does surprised me at first; but I soon realized that the papers I was reading were, at least in their beginning, the materials for the book he was meditating, and that it was to have been one of those quasi-journalistic productions which admit of the introduction of an admixture of conversational matter.

His object, he says, was to find out whether any traditions of Count Magnus de la Gardie lingered on in the scenes of that gentleman's activity, and whether the popular estimate of him were favourable or not. He found that the Count was decidedly not a favourite. If his tenants came late to their work on the days which they owed to him as Lord of the Manor, they were set on the wooden horse, or flogged and branded in the manor-house yard. One or two cases there were of men who had occupied lands which encroached on the lord's domain, and whose houses had been mysteriously burnt on a winter's night, with the whole family inside. But what seemed to dwell on the innkeeper's mind most—for he returned to the subject more than once—was that the Count had been on the Black Pilgrimage, and had brought something or someone back with him.

You will naturally inquire, as Mr. Wraxall did, what the Black Pilgrimage may have been. But your curiosity on the point must remain unsatisfied for the time being, just as his did. The landlord was evidently unwilling to give a full answer, or indeed any answer, on the point, and, being called out for a moment, trotted out with obvious alacrity, only putting his head in at the door a few minutes afterwards to say that he was called away to Skara, and should not be back till evening.

So Mr. Wraxall had to go unsatisfied to his day's work at the manor-house. The papers on which he was just then engaged soon put his thoughts into another channel, for he had to occupy himself with glancing over the correspondence between Sophia Albertina in Stockholm and her married cousin Ulrica Leonora at Råbäck in the years 1705–10. The letters were of exceptional interest from the light they threw upon the culture of that period in Sweden, as anyone can testify who has read the full edition of them in the publications of the Swedish Historical Manuscripts Commission.

In the afternoon he had done with these, and after returning the boxes in which they were kept to their places on the shelf, he proceeded, very naturally, to take down some of the volumes nearest to them, in order to determine which of them had best be his principal subject of investigation next day. The shelf he had hit upon was occupied mostly by a collection of account-books in the writing of the first Count Magnus. But one among them was not an account-book, but a book of alchemical and other tracts in another sixteenth-century hand. Not being very familiar with alchemical literature, Mr. Wraxall spends much space which he might have spared in setting out the names and beginnings of the various treatises: The book of the Phoenix, book of the Thirty Words, book of the Toad, book of Miriam, Turba philosophorum, and so forth; and then he announces with a good deal of circumstance his delight at finding, on a leaf originally left blank near the middle of the book, some writing of Count Magnus himself headed "Liber nigrae peregrinationis." It is true that only a few lines were written, but there was quite enough to show that the landlord had that morning been referring to a belief at least as old as the time of Count Magnus, and probably shared by him. This is the English of what was written:

"If any man desires to obtain a long life, if he would obtain a faithful messenger and see the blood of his enemies, it is necessary that he should first go into the city of Chorazin, and there salute the prince . . ." Here there was an erasure of one word, not very thoroughly done, so that Mr. Wraxall felt pretty sure that he was right in reading it as aeris ("of the air"). But there was no more of the text copied, only a line in Latin: *Quaere reliqua hujus materiei inter secretiora*. (See the rest of this matter among the more private things.)

It could not be denied that this threw a rather lurid light upon the tastes and beliefs of the Count; but to Mr. Wraxall, separated from him by nearly three centuries, the thought that he might have added to his general forcefulness alchemy, and to alchemy something like magic, only made him a more picturesque figure, and when, after a rather prolonged contemplation of his picture in the hall, Mr. Wraxall set out on his homeward way, his mind was full of the thought of Count Magnus. He had no eyes for his surroundings, no perception of the evening scents of the woods or the evening light on the lake; and when all of a sudden he pulled up short, he was astonished to find himself already at the gate of the churchyard, and within a few minutes of his dinner. His eyes fell on the mausoleum.

"Ah," he said, "Count Magnus, there you are. I should dearly like to see you."

"Like many solitary men," he writes, "I have a habit of talking to myself aloud; and, unlike some of the Greek and Latin particles, I do not expect an answer. Certainly, and perhaps fortunately in this case, there was neither voice nor any that regarded: only the woman who, I suppose, was cleaning up the church, dropped some metallic object on the floor, whose clang startled me. Count Magnus, I think, sleeps sound enough."

That same evening the landlord of the inn, who had heard Mr. Wraxall say that he wished to see the clerk or deacon (as he would be called in Sweden) of the parish, introduced him to that official in the inn parlour. A visit to the De la Gardie tomb-house was soon arranged for the next day, and a little general conversation ensued.

Mr. Wraxall, remembering that one function of Scandinavian deacons is to teach candidates for Confirmation, thought he would refresh his own memory on a Biblical point.

"Can you tell me," he said, "anything about Chorazin?"

The deacon seemed startled, but readily reminded him how that village had once been denounced.

"To be sure," said Mr. Wraxall; "it is, I suppose, quite a ruin now?"

"So I expect," replied the deacon. "I have heard some of our old priests say that Antichrist is to be born there; and there are tales—"

"Ah! what tales are those?" Mr. Wraxall put in.

"Tales, I was going to say, which I have forgotten," said the deacon; and soon after that he said good night.

The landlord was now alone, and at Mr. Wraxall's mercy; and that inquirer was not inclined to spare him.

"Herr Nielsen," he said, "I have found out something about the Black Pilgrimage. You may as well tell me what you know. What did the Count bring back with him?"

Swedes are habitually slow, perhaps, in answering, or perhaps the landlord was an exception. I am not sure; but Mr. Wraxall notes that the landlord spent at least one minute in looking at him before he said anything at all. Then he came close up to his guest, and with a good deal of effort he spoke:

"Mr. Wraxall, I can tell you this one little tale, and no more—not any more. You must not ask anything when I have done. In my grandfather's time—that is, ninety-two years ago—there were two men who said: 'The Count is dead; we do not care for him. We will go tonight and have a free hunt in his wood'—the long wood on the hill that you have seen behind Råbäck. Well, those that heard them say this, they said: 'No, do not go; we are sure you will meet with persons walking who should not be walking. They should be resting, not walking.' These men laughed. There were no forestmen to keep the wood, because no one wished to live there. The family were not here at the house. These men could do what they wished.

"Very well, they go to the wood that night. My grandfather was sitting here in this room. It was the summer, and a light night. With the window open, he could see out to the wood, and hear.

"So he sat there, and two or three men with him, and they listened. At first they hear nothing at all; then they hear someone—you know how far away it is—they hear someone scream, just as if the most inside part of his soul was twisted out of him. All of them in the room caught hold of each other, and they sat so for three-quarters of an hour. Then they hear someone else, only about three hundred ells off. They hear him laugh out loud: it was not one of those two men that laughed, and, indeed, they have all of them said that it was not any man at all. After that they hear a great door shut.

"Then, when it was just light with the sun, they all went to the priest. They said to him:

" 'Father, put on your gown and your ruff, and come to bury these men, Anders Bjornsen and Hans Thorbjorn.'

"You understand that they were sure these men were dead. So they went to the wood—my grandfather never forgot this. He said they were all like so many dead men themselves. The priest, too, he was in a white fear. He said when they came to him:

" 'I heard one cry in the night, and I heard one laugh afterwards. If I cannot forget that, I shall not be able to sleep again.'

"So they went to the wood, and they found these men on the edge of the wood. Hans Thorbjorn was standing with his back against a tree, and all the time he was pushing with his hands—pushing something away from him which was not there. So he was not dead. And they led him away, and took him to the house at Nykjoping, and he died before the winter; but he went on pushing with his hands. Also Anders Bjornsen was there; but he was dead. And I tell you this about Anders Bjornsen, that he was once a beautiful man, but now his face was not there, because the flesh of it was sucked away off the bones. You understand that? My grandfather did not forget that. And they laid him on the bier which they brought, and they put a cloth over his head, and the priest walked before; and they began to sing the psalm for the dead as well as they could. So, as they were singing the end of the first verse, one fell down, who was carrying the head of the bier, and the others looked back, and they saw that the cloth had fallen off, and the eyes of Anders Bjornsen were looking up, because there was nothing to close over them. And this they could not bear.

Therefore the priest laid the cloth upon him, and sent for a spade, and they buried him in that place."

The next day Mr. Wraxall records that the deacon called for him soon after his breakfast, and took him to the church and mausoleum. He noticed that the key of the latter was hung on a nail just by the pulpit, and it occurred to him that, as the church door seemed to be left unlocked as a rule, it would not be difficult for him to pay a second and more private visit to the monuments if there proved to be more of interest among them than could be digested at first. The building, when he entered it, he found not unimposing. The monuments, mostly large erections of the seventeenth and eighteenth centuries, were dignified if luxuriant, and the epitaphs and heraldry were copious. The central space of the domed room was occupied by three copper sarcophagi, covered with finely-engraved ornament. Two of them had, as is commonly the case in Denmark and Sweden, a large metal crucifix on the lid. The third, that of Count Magnus, as it appeared, had, instead of that, a full-length effigy engraved upon it, and round the edge were several bands of similar ornament representing various scenes. One was a battle, with cannon belching out smoke, and walled towns, and troops of pikemen. Another showed an execution. In a third, among trees, was a man running at full speed, with flying hair and outstretched hands. After him followed a strange form; it would be hard to say whether the artist had intended it for a man, and was unable to give the requisite similitude, or whether it was intentionally made as monstrous as it looked. In view of the skill with which the rest of the drawing was done, Mr. Wraxall felt inclined to adopt the latter idea. The figure was unduly short, and was for the most part muffled in a hooded garment which swept the ground. The only part of the form which projected from that shelter was not shaped like any hand or arm. Mr. Wraxall compares it to the tentacle of a devil-fish, and continues: "On seeing this, I said to myself, 'This, then, which is evidently an allegorical representation of some kind—a fiend pursuing a hunted soul—may be the origin of the story of Count Magnus and his mysterious companion. Let us see how the huntsman is pictured: doubtless it will be a demon blowing his horn.'" But, as it turned out, there was no such sensational figure, only the semblance of a cloaked man on a hillock, who stood leaning on a stick, and watching the hunt with an interest which the engraver had tried to express in his attitude.

Mr. Wraxall noted the finely-worked and massive steel padlocks—three in number—which secured the sarcophagus. One of them, he saw, was detached, and lay on the pavement. And then, unwilling to delay the deacon longer or to waste his own working-time, he made his way onward to the manor-house.

"It is curious," he notes, "how, on retracing a familiar path, one's thoughts engross one to the absolute exclusion of surrounding objects. Tonight, for the second time, I had entirely failed to notice where I was going (I had planned a private visit to the tomb-house to copy the epitaphs), when I suddenly, as it were, awoke to consciousness, and found myself (as before) turning in at the churchyard gate, and, I believe, singing or chanting some such words as, 'Are you awake, Count Magnus? Are you asleep, Count Magnus?' and then something more which I have failed to recollect. It seemed to me that I must have been behaving in this nonsensical way for some time."

He found the key of the mausoleum where he had expected to find it, and copied the greater part of what he wanted; in fact, he stayed until the light began to fail him.

"I must have been wrong," he writes, "in saying that one of the padlocks of my Count's sarcophagus was unfastened; I see tonight that two are loose. I picked both up, and laid them carefully on the window-ledge, after trying unsuccessfully to close them. The remaining one is still firm, and, though I take it to be a spring lock, I cannot guess how it is opened. Had I succeeded in undoing it, I am almost afraid I should have taken the liberty of opening the sarcophagus. It is strange, the interest I feel in the personality of this, I fear, somewhat ferocious and grim old noble."

The day following was, as it turned out, the last of Mr. Wraxall's stay at Råbäck. He received letters connected with certain investments which made it desirable that he should return to England; his work among the papers was practically done, and travelling was slow. He decided, therefore, to make his farewells, put some finishing touches to his notes, and be off.

These finishing touches and farewells, as it turned out, took more time than he had expected. The hospitable family insisted on his staying to dine with them—they dined at three—and it was verging on half past six before he was outside the iron gates of Råbäck. He dwelt on every step of his walk by the lake, determined to saturate himself, now that he trod it for the last time, in the sentiment of the place and hour. And when he reached the summit of the churchyard knoll, he lingered for many minutes, gazing at the limitless prospect of woods near and distant, all dark beneath a sky of liquid green. When at last he turned to go, the thought struck him that surely he must bid farewell to Count Magnus as well as the rest of the De la Gardies. The church was but twenty yards away, and he knew where the key of the mausoleum hung. It was not long before he was standing over the great copper coffin, and, as usual, talking to himself aloud: "You may have been a bit of a rascal in your time, Magnus," he was saying, "but for all that I should like to see you, or, rather—"

"Just at that instant," he says, "I felt a blow on my foot. Hastily enough I drew it back, and something fell on the pavement with a clash. It was the third, the last of the three padlocks which had fastened the sarcophagus. I stooped to pick it up, and—Heaven is my witness that I am writing only the bare truth—before I had raised myself there was a sound of metal hinges creaking, and I distinctly saw the lid shifting upwards. I may have behaved like a coward, but I could not for my life stay for one moment. I was outside that dreadful building in less time than I can write—almost as quickly as I could have said—the words; and what frightens me yet more, I could not turn the key in the lock. As I sit here in my room noting these facts, I ask myself (it was not twenty minutes ago) whether that noise of creaking metal continued, and I cannot tell whether it did or not. I only know that there was something more than I have written that alarmed me, but whether it was sound or sight I am not able to remember. What is this that I have done?"

* * * * *

Poor Mr. Wraxall! He set out on his journey to England on the next day, as he had planned, and he reached England in safety; and yet, as I gather from his changed hand and inconsequent jottings, a broken man. One of the several small note-books that have come to me with his papers gives, not a key to, but a kind of inkling of, his experiences. Much of his journey was made by canal-boat, and I find not less than six painful attempts to enumerate and describe his fellow-passengers. The entries are of this kind:

24. Pastor of village in Skane. Usual black coat and soft black hat.
25. Commercial traveller from Stockholm going to Trollhättan.
    Black cloak, brown hat.
26. Man in long black cloak, broad-leafed hat, very old-fashioned.

This entry is lined out, and a note added: "Perhaps identical with No. 13. Have not yet seen his face." On referring to No. 13, I find that he is a Roman priest in a cassock.

The net result of the reckoning is always the same. Twenty-eight people appear in the enumeration, one being always a man in a long black cloak and broad hat, and another a "short figure in dark cloak and hood." On the other hand, it is always noted that only twenty-six passengers appear at meals, and that the man in the cloak is perhaps absent, and the short figure is certainly absent.

On reaching England, it appears that Mr. Wraxall landed at Harwich, and that he resolved at once to put himself out of the reach of some person or persons whom he never specifies, but whom he had evidently come to regard as his pursuers. Accordingly he took a vehicle—it was a closed fly—not trusting the railway and drove across country to the village of Belchamp St. Paul. It was about nine o'clock on a moonlight August night when he neared the place. He was sitting forward, and looking out of the window at the fields and thickets—there was little else to be seen—racing past him. Suddenly he came to a cross-road. At the corner two figures were standing motionless; both were in dark cloaks; the taller one wore a hat, the shorter a hood. He had no time to see their faces, nor did they make any motion that he could discern. Yet the horse shied violently and broke into a gallop, and Mr. Wraxall sank back into his seat in something like desperation. He had seen them before.

Arrived at Belchamp St. Paul, he was fortunate enough to find a decent furnished lodging, and for the next twenty-four hours he lived, comparatively speaking, in peace. His last notes were written on this day. They are too disjointed and ejaculatory to be given here in full, but the substance of them is clear enough. He is expecting a visit from his pursuers—how or when he knows not—and his constant cry is "What has he done?" and "Is there no hope?" Doctors, he knows, would call him mad, policemen would laugh at him. The parson is away. What can he do but lock his door and cry to God?

People still remember last year at Belchamp St. Paul how a strange gentleman came one evening in August years back; and how the next morning but one he was found dead, and there was an inquest; and the jury that viewed the body fainted, seven of 'em did, and none of 'em wouldn't speak to what they see, and the verdict was visitation of God; and how the people as kep' the 'ouse moved out that same week, and went away from that part. But they do not, I think, know that any glimmer of light has ever been thrown, or could be thrown, on the mystery. It so happened that last year the little house came into my hands as part of a legacy. It had stood empty since 1863, and there seemed no prospect of letting it; so I had it pulled down, and the papers of which I have given you an abstract were found in a forgotten cupboard under the window in the best bedroom.

The Body-Snatcher

Robert Louis Stevenson

Every night in the year, four of us sat in the small parlour of the George at Debenham—the undertaker, and the landlord, and Fettes, and myself. Sometimes there would be more; but blow high, blow low, come rain or snow or frost, we four would be each planted in his own particular arm-chair. Fettes was an old drunken Scotchman, a man of education obviously, and a man of some property, since he lived in idleness. He had come to Debenham years ago, while still young, and by a mere continuance of living had grown to be an adopted townsman. His blue camlet cloak was a local antiquity, like the church-spire. His place in the parlour at the George, his absence from church, his old, crapulous, disreputable vices, were all things of course in Debenham. He had some vague Radical opinions and some fleeting infidelities, which he would now and again set forth and emphasise with tottering slaps upon the table. He drank rum—five glasses regularly every evening; and for the greater portion of his nightly visit to the George sat, with his glass in his right hand, in a state of melancholy alcoholic saturation. We called him the Doctor, for he was supposed to have some special knowledge of medicine, and had been known, upon a pinch, to set a fracture or reduce a dislocation; but beyond these slight particulars, we had no knowledge of his character and antecedents.

One dark winter night—it had struck nine some time before the landlord joined us—there was a sick man in the George, a great neighbouring proprietor suddenly struck down with apoplexy on his way to Parliament; and the great man's still greater London doctor had been telegraphed to his bedside. It was the first time that such a thing had happened in Debenham, for the railway was but newly open, and we were all proportionately moved by the occurrence.

"He's come," said the landlord, after he had filled and lighted his pipe.

"He?" said I. "Who?—not the doctor?"

"Himself," replied our host.

"What is his name?"

"Doctor Macfarlane," said the landlord.

Fettes was far through his third tumbler, stupidly fuddled, now nodding over, now staring mazily around him; but at the last word he seemed to awaken, and repeated the name "Macfarlane" twice, quietly enough the first time, but with sudden emotion at the second.

"Yes," said the landlord, "that's his name, Doctor Wolfe Macfarlane."

Fettes became instantly sober; his eyes awoke, his voice became clear, loud, and steady, his language forcible and earnest. We were all startled by the transformation, as if a man had risen from the dead.

"I beg your pardon," he said, "I am afraid I have not been paying much attention to your talk. Who is this Wolfe Macfarlane?" And then, when he had heard the landlord out, "It cannot be, it cannot be," he added; "and yet I would like well to see him face to face."

"Do you know him, Doctor?" asked the undertaker, with a gasp.

"God forbid!" was the reply. "And yet the name is a strange one; it were too much to fancy two. Tell me, landlord, is he old?"

"Well," said the host, "he's not a young man, to be sure, and his hair is white; but he looks younger than you."

"He is older, though; years older. But," with a slap upon the table, "it's the rum you see in my face—rum and sin. This man, perhaps, may have an easy conscience and a good digestion. Conscience! Hear me speak. You would think I was some good, old, decent Christian, would you not? But no, not I; I never canted. Voltaire might have canted if he'd stood in my shoes; but the brains"—with a rattling fillip on his bald head—"the brains were clear and active, and I saw and made no deductions."

"If you know this doctor," I ventured to remark, after a somewhat awful pause, "I should gather that you do not share the landlord's good opinion."

Fettes paid no regard to me.

"Yes," he said, with sudden decision, "I must see him face to face."

There was another pause, and then a door was closed rather sharply on the first floor, and a step was heard upon the stair.

"That's the doctor," cried the landlord. "Look sharp, and you can catch him."

It was but two steps from the small parlour to the door of the old George Inn; the wide oak staircase landed almost in the street; there was room for a Turkey rug and nothing more between the threshold and the last round of the descent; but this little space was every evening brilliantly lit up, not only by the light upon the stair and the great signal-lamp below the sign, but by the warm radiance of the bar-room window. The George thus brightly advertised itself to passers-by in the cold street. Fettes walked steadily to the spot, and we, who were hanging behind, beheld the two men meet, as one of them had phrased it, face to face. Dr. Macfarlane was alert and vigorous. His white hair set off his pale and placid, although energetic, countenance. He was richly dressed in the finest of broadcloth and the whitest of linen, with a great gold watch-chain, and studs and spectacles of the same precious material. He wore a broad-folded tie, white and speckled with lilac, and he carried on his arm a comfortable driving-coat of fur. There was no doubt but he became his years, breathing, as he did, of wealth and consideration; and it was a surprising contrast to see our parlour sot—bald, dirty, pimpled, and robed in his old camlet cloak—confront him at the bottom of the stairs.

"Macfarlane!" he said somewhat loudly, more like a herald than a friend.

The great doctor pulled up short on the fourth step, as though the familiarity of the address surprised and somewhat shocked his dignity.

"Toddy Macfarlane!" repeated Fettes.

The London man almost staggered. He stared for the swiftest of seconds at the man before him, glanced behind him with a sort of scare, and then in a startled whisper, "Fettes!" he said, "You!"

"Ay," said the other, "me! Did you think I was dead too? We are not so easy shut of our acquaintance."

"Hush, hush!" exclaimed the doctor. "Hush, hush! this meeting is so unexpected—I can see you are unmanned. I hardly knew you, I confess, at first; but I am overjoyed—overjoyed to have this opportunity. For the present it must be how-d'ye-do and good-bye in one, for my fly is waiting, and I must not fail the train; but you shall—let me see—yes—you shall give me your address, and you can count on early news of me. We must do something for you, Fettes. I fear you are out at elbows; but we must see to that for auld lang syne, as once we sang at suppers."

"Money!" cried Fettes; "money from you! The money that I had from you is lying where I cast it in the rain."

Dr. Macfarlane had talked himself into some measure of superiority and confidence, but the uncommon energy of this refusal cast him back into his first confusion.

A horrible, ugly look came and went across his almost venerable countenance. "My dear fellow," he said, "be it as you please; my last thought is to offend you. I would intrude on none. I will leave you my address, however—"

"I do not wish it—I do not wish to know the roof that shelters you," interrupted the other. "I heard your name; I feared it might be you; I wished to know if, after all, there were a God; I know now that there is none. Begone!"

He still stood in the middle of the rug, between the stair and doorway; and the great London physician, in order to escape, would be forced to step to one side. It was plain that he hesitated before the thought of this humiliation. White as he was, there was a dangerous glitter in his spectacles; but while he still paused uncertain, he became aware that the driver of his fly was peering in from the street at this unusual scene and caught a glimpse at the same time of our little body from the parlour, huddled by the corner of the bar. The presence of so many witnesses decided him at once to flee. He crouched together, brushing on the wainscot, and made a dart like a serpent, striking for the door. But his tribulation was not yet entirely at an end, for even as he was passing Fettes clutched him by the arm and these words came in a whisper, and yet painfully distinct, "Have you seen it again?"

The great rich London doctor cried out aloud with a sharp, throttling cry; he dashed his questioner across the open space, and, with his hands over his head, fled out of the door like a detected thief. Before it had occurred to one of us to make a movement the fly was already rattling toward the station. The scene was over like a dream, but the dream had left proofs and traces of its passage. Next day the servant found the fine gold spectacles broken on the threshold, and that very night we were all standing breathless by the bar-room window, and Fettes at our side, sober, pale, and resolute in look.

"God protect us, Mr. Fettes!" said the landlord, coming first into possession of his customary senses. "What in the universe is all this? These are strange things you have been saying."

Fettes turned toward us; he looked us each in succession in the face. "See if you can hold your tongues," said he. "That man Macfarlane is not safe to cross; those that have done so already have repented it too late."

And then, without so much as finishing his third glass, far less waiting for the other two, he bade us good-bye and went forth, under the lamp of the hotel, into the black night.

We three turned to our places in the parlour, with the big red fire and four clear candles; and as we recapitulated what had passed, the first chill of our surprise soon changed into a glow of curiosity. We sat late; it was the latest session I have known in the old George. Each man, before we parted, had his theory that he was bound to prove; and none of us had any nearer business in this world than to track out the past of our condemned companion, and surprise the secret that he shared with the great London doctor. It is no great boast, but I believe I was a better hand at worming out a story than either of my fellows at the George; and perhaps there is now no other man alive who could narrate to you the following foul and unnatural events.

In his young days Fettes studied medicine in the schools of Edinburgh. He had talent of a kind, the talent that picks up swiftly what it hears and readily retails it for its own. He worked little at home; but he was civil, attentive, and intelligent in the presence of his masters. They soon picked him out as a lad who listened closely and remembered well; nay, strange as it seemed to me when I first heard it, he was in those days well favoured, and pleased by his exterior. There was, at that period, a certain extramural teacher of anatomy, whom I shall here designate by the letter K. His name was subsequently too well known. The man who bore it skulked through the streets of Edinburgh in disguise, while the mob that applauded at the execution of Burke called loudly for the blood of his employer. But Mr. K— was then at the top of his vogue; he enjoyed a popularity due partly to his own talent and address, partly to the incapacity of his rival, the university professor. The students, at least, swore by his name, and Fettes believed himself, and was believed by others, to have laid the foundations of success when he had acquired the favour of this meteorically famous man. Mr. K— was a bon vivant as well as an accomplished teacher; he liked a sly illusion no less than a careful preparation. In both capacities Fettes enjoyed and deserved his notice, and by the second year of his attendance he held the half-regular position of second demonstrator or sub-assistant in his class.

In this capacity the charge of the theatre and lecture-room devolved in particular upon his shoulders. He had to answer for the cleanliness of the premises and the conduct of the other students, and it was a part of his duty to supply, receive, and divide the various subjects. It was with a view to this last—at that time very delicate—affair that he was lodged by Mr. K— in the same wynd, and at last in the same building, with the dissecting-rooms. Here, after a night of turbulent pleasures, his hand still tottering, his sight still misty and confused, he would be called out of bed in the black hours before the winter dawn by the unclean and desperate interlopers who supplied the table. He would open the door to these men, since infamous throughout the land. He would help them with their tragic burden, pay them their sordid price, and remain alone, when they were gone, with the unfriendly relics of humanity. From such a scene he would return to snatch another hour or two of slumber, to repair the abuses of the night, and refresh himself for the labours of the day.

Few lads could have been more insensible to the impressions of a life thus passed among the ensigns of mortality. His mind was closed against all general considerations. He was incapable of interest in the fate and fortunes of another, the slave of his own desires and low ambitions. Cold, light, and selfish in the last resort, he had that modicum of prudence, miscalled morality, which keeps a man from inconvenient drunkenness or punishable theft. He coveted, besides, a measure of consideration from his masters and his fellow-pupils, and he had no desire to fail conspicuously in the external parts of life. Thus he made it his pleasure to gain some distinction in his studies, and day after day rendered unimpeachable eye-service to his employer, Mr. K—. For his day of work he indemnified himself by nights of roaring, blackguardly enjoyment; and when that balance had been struck, the organ that he called his conscience declared itself content.

The supply of subjects was a continual trouble to him as well as to his master. In that large and busy class, the raw material of the anatomists kept perpetually running out; and the business thus rendered necessary was not only unpleasant in itself, but threatened dangerous consequences to all who were concerned. It was the policy of Mr. K— to ask no questions in his dealings with the trade. "They bring the body, and we pay the price," he used to say, dwelling on the alliteration—"*quid pro quo*." And, again, and somewhat profanely, "Ask no questions," he would tell his assistants, "for conscience' sake." There was no understanding that the subjects were provided by the crime of murder. Had that idea been broached to him in words, he would have recoiled in horror; but the lightness of his speech upon so grave a matter was, in itself, an offence against good manners, and a temptation to the men with whom he dealt. Fettes, for instance, had often remarked to himself upon the singular freshness of the bodies. He had been struck again and again by the hang-dog, abominable looks of the ruffians who came to him before the dawn; and putting things together clearly in his private thoughts, he perhaps attributed a meaning too immoral and too categorical to the unguarded counsels of his master. He understood his duty, in short, to have three branches: to take what was brought, to pay the price, and to avert the eye from any evidence of crime.

One November morning this policy of silence was put sharply to the test. He had been awake all night with a racking toothache—pacing his room like a caged beast or throwing himself in fury on his bed—and had fallen at last into that profound, uneasy slumber that so often follows on a night of pain, when he was awakened by the third or fourth angry repetition of the concerted signal. There was a thin, bright moonshine; it was bitter cold, windy, and frosty; the town had not yet awakened, but an indefinable stir already preluded the noise and business of the day. The ghouls had come later than usual, and they seemed more than usually eager to be gone. Fettes, sick with sleep, lighted them upstairs. He heard their grumbling Irish voices through a dream; and as they stripped the sack from their sad merchandise he leaned dozing, with his shoulder propped against the wall; he had to shake himself to find the men their money. As he did so his eyes lighted on the dead face. He started; he took two steps nearer, with the candle raised.

"God Almighty!" he cried. "That is Jane Galbraith!"

The men answered nothing, but they shuffled nearer the door.

"I know her, I tell you," he continued. "She was alive and hearty yesterday. It's impossible she can be dead; it's impossible you should have got this body fairly."

"Sure, sir, you're mistaken entirely," said one of the men.

But the other looked Fettes darkly in the eyes, and demanded the money on the spot.

It was impossible to misconceive the threat or to exaggerate the danger. The lad's heart failed him. He stammered some excuses, counted out the sum, and saw his hateful visitors depart. No sooner were they gone than he hastened to confirm his doubts. By a dozen unquestionable marks he identified the girl he had jested with the day before. He saw, with horror, marks upon her body that might well betoken violence. A panic seized him, and he took refuge in his room. There he reflected at length over the discovery that he had made; considered soberly the bearing of Mr. K—'s instructions and the danger to himself of interference in so serious a business, and at last, in sore perplexity, determined to wait for the advice of his immediate superior, the class assistant.

This was a young doctor, Wolfe Macfarlane, a high favourite among all the reckless students, clever, dissipated, and unscrupulous to the last degree. He had travelled and studied abroad. His manners were agreeable and a little forward. He was an authority on the stage, skilful on the ice or the links with skate or golf-club; he dressed with nice audacity, and, to put the finishing touch upon his glory, he kept a gig and a strong trotting-horse. With Fettes he was on terms of intimacy; indeed, their relative positions called for some community of life; and when subjects were scarce the pair would drive far into the country in Macfarlane's gig, visit and desecrate some lonely graveyard, and return before dawn with their booty to the door of the dissecting-room.

On that particular morning Macfarlane arrived somewhat earlier than his wont. Fettes heard him, and met him on the stairs, told him his story, and showed him the cause of his alarm. Macfarlane examined the marks on her body.

"Yes," he said with a nod, "it looks fishy."

"Well, what should I do?" asked Fettes.

"Do?" repeated the other. "Do you want to do anything? Least said soonest mended, I should say."

"Some one else might recognise her," objected Fettes. "She was as well known as the Castle Rock."

"We'll hope not," said Macfarlane, "and if anybody does—well, you didn't, don't you see, and there's an end. The fact is, this has been going on too long. Stir up the mud, and you'll get K— into the most unholy trouble; you'll be in a shocking box yourself. So will I, if you come to that. I should like to know how any one of us would look, or what the devil we should have to say for ourselves, in any Christian witness-box. For me, you know there's one thing certain—that, practically speaking, all our subjects have been murdered."

"Macfarlane!" cried Fettes.

"Come now!" sneered the other. "As if you hadn't suspected it yourself!"

"Suspecting is one thing—"

"And proof another. Yes, I know; and I'm as sorry as you are this should have come here," tapping the body with his cane. "The next best thing for me is not to recognise it; and," he added coolly, "I don't. You may, if you please. I don't dictate, but I think a man of the world would do as I do; and I may add, I fancy that is what K— would look for at our hands. The question is, Why did he choose us two for his assistants? And I answer, because he didn't want old wives."

This was the tone of all others to affect the mind of a lad like Fettes. He agreed to imitate Macfarlane. The body of the unfortunate girl was duly dissected, and no one remarked or appeared to recognise her.

One afternoon, when his day's work was over, Fettes dropped into a popular tavern and found Macfarlane sitting with a stranger. This was a small man, very pale and dark, with coal-black eyes. The cut of his features gave a promise of intellect and refinement which was but feebly realised in his manners, for he proved, upon a nearer acquaintance, coarse, vulgar, and stupid. He exercised, however, a very remarkable control over Macfarlane; issued orders like the Great Bashaw; became inflamed at the least discussion or delay, and commented rudely on the servility with which he was obeyed. This most offensive person took a fancy to Fettes on the spot, plied him with drinks, and honoured him with unusual confidences on his past career. If a tenth part of what he confessed were true, he was a very loathsome rogue; and the lad's vanity was tickled by the attention of so experienced a man.

"I'm a pretty bad fellow myself," the stranger remarked, "but Macfarlane is the boy—Toddy Macfarlane I call him. Toddy, order your friend another glass." Or it might be, "Toddy, you jump up and shut the door." "Toddy hates me," he said again. "Oh yes, Toddy, you do!"

"Don't you call me that confounded name," growled Macfarlane.

"Hear him! Did you ever see the lads play knife? He would like to do that all over my body," remarked the stranger.

"We medicals have a better way than that," said Fettes. "When we dislike a dead friend of ours, we dissect him."

Macfarlane looked up sharply, as though this jest were scarcely to his mind.

The afternoon passed. Gray, for that was the stranger's name, invited Fettes to join them at dinner, ordered a feast so sumptuous that the tavern was thrown into commotion, and when all was done commanded Macfarlane to settle the bill. It was late before they separated; the man Gray was incapably drunk. Macfarlane, sobered by his fury, chewed the cud of the money he had been forced to squander and the slights he had been obliged to swallow. Fettes, with various liquors singing in his head, returned home with devious footsteps and a mind entirely in abeyance. Next day Macfarlane was absent from the class, and Fettes smiled to himself as he imagined him still squiring the intolerable Gray from tavern to tavern. As soon as the hour of liberty had struck he posted from place to place in quest of his last night's companions. He could find them, however, nowhere; so returned early to his rooms, went early to bed, and slept the sleep of the just.

At four in the morning he was awakened by the well-known signal. Descending to the door, he was filled with astonishment to find Macfarlane with his gig, and in the gig one of those long and ghastly packages with which he was so well acquainted.

"What?" he cried. "Have you been out alone? How did you manage?"

But Macfarlane silenced him roughly, bidding him turn to business. When they had got the body upstairs and laid it on the table, Macfarlane made at first as if he were going away. Then he paused and seemed to hesitate; and then, "You had better look at the face," said he, in tones of some constraint. "You had better," he repeated, as Fettes only stared at him in wonder.

"But where, and how, and when did you come by it?" cried the other.

"Look at the face," was the only answer.

Fettes was staggered; strange doubts assailed him. He looked from the young doctor to the body, and then back again. At last, with a start, he did as he was bidden. He had almost expected the sight that met his eyes, and yet the shock was cruel. To see, fixed in the rigidity of death and naked on that coarse layer of sackcloth, the man whom he had left well clad and full of meat and sin upon the threshold of a tavern, awoke, even in the thoughtless Fettes, some of the terrors of the conscience. It was a *cras tibi* which re-echoed in his soul, that two whom he had known should have come to lie upon these icy tables. Yet these were only secondary thoughts. His first concern regarded Wolfe. Unprepared for a challenge so momentous, he knew not how to look his comrade in the face. He durst not meet his eye, and he had neither words nor voice at his command.

It was Macfarlane himself who made the first advance. He came up quietly behind and laid his hand gently but firmly on the other's shoulder.

"Richardson," said he, "may have the head."

Now Richardson was a student who had long been anxious for that portion of the human subject to dissect. There was no answer, and the murderer resumed: "Talking of business, you must pay me; your accounts, you see, must tally."

Fettes found a voice, the ghost of his own: "Pay you!" he cried. "Pay you for that?"

"Why, yes, of course you must. By all means and on every possible account, you must," returned the other. "I dare not give it for nothing, you dare not take it for nothing; it would compromise us both. This is another case like Jane Galbraith's. The more things are wrong the more we must act as if all were right. Where does old K— keep his money?"

"There," answered Fettes hoarsely, pointing to a cupboard in the corner.

"Give me the key, then," said the other, calmly, holding out his hand.

There was an instant's hesitation, and the die was cast. Macfarlane could not suppress a nervous twitch, the infinitesimal mark of an immense relief, as he felt the key between his fingers. He opened the cupboard, brought out pen and ink and a paper-book that stood in one compartment, and separated from the funds in a drawer a sum suitable to the occasion.

"Now, look here," he said, "there is the payment made—first proof of your good faith: first step to your security. You have now to clinch it by a second. Enter the payment in your book, and then you for your part may defy the devil."

The next few seconds were for Fettes an agony of thought; but in balancing his terrors it was the most immediate that triumphed. Any future difficulty seemed almost welcome if he could avoid a present quarrel with Macfarlane. He set down the candle which he had been carrying all this time, and with a steady hand entered the date, the nature, and the amount of the transaction.

"And now," said Macfarlane, "it's only fair that you should pocket the lucre. I've had my share already. By the bye, when a man of the world falls into a bit of luck, has a few shillings extra in his pocket—I'm ashamed to speak of it, but there's a rule of conduct in the case. No treating, no purchase of expensive class-books, no squaring of old debts; borrow, don't lend."

"Macfarlane," began Fettes, still somewhat hoarsely, "I have put my neck in a halter to oblige you."

"To oblige me?" cried Wolfe. "Oh, come! You did, as near as I can see the matter, what you downright had to do in self-defence. Suppose I got into trouble, where would you be? This second little matter flows clearly from the first. Mr. Gray is the continuation of Miss Galbraith. You can't begin and then stop. If you begin, you must keep on beginning; that's the truth. No rest for the wicked."

A horrible sense of blackness and the treachery of fate seized hold upon the soul of the unhappy student.

"My God!" he cried, "but what have I done? and when did I begin? To be made a class assistant—in the name of reason, where's the harm in that? Service wanted the position; Service might have got it. Would he have been where I am now?"

"My dear fellow," said Macfarlane, "what a boy you are! What harm has come to you? What harm can come to you if you hold your tongue? Why, man, do you know what this life is? There are two squads of us—the lions and the lambs. If you're a lamb, you'll come to lie upon these tables like Gray or Jane Galbraith; if you're a lion, you'll live and drive a horse like me, like K—, like all the world with any wit or courage. You're staggered at the first. But look at K—! My dear fellow, you're clever, you have pluck. I like you, and K— likes you. You were born to lead the hunt; and I tell you, on my honour and my experience of life, three days from now you'll laugh at all these scarecrows like a High School boy at a farce."

And with that Macfarlane took his departure and drove off up the wynd in his gig to get under cover before daylight. Fettes was thus left alone with his regrets. He saw the miserable peril in which he stood involved. He saw, with inexpressible dismay, that there was no limit to his weakness, and that, from concession to concession, he had fallen from the arbiter of Macfarlane's destiny to his paid and helpless accomplice. He would have given the world to have been a little braver at the time, but it did not occur to him that he might still be brave. The secret of Jane Galbraith and the cursed entry in the day-book closed his mouth.

Hours passed; the class began to arrive; the members of the unhappy Gray were dealt out to one and to another, and received without remark. Richardson was made happy with the head; and before the hour of freedom rang Fettes trembled with exultation to perceive how far they had already gone toward safety.

For two days he continued to watch, with increasing joy, the dreadful process of disguise.

On the third day Macfarlane made his appearance. He had been ill, he said; but he made up for lost time by the energy with which he directed the students. To Richardson in particular he extended the most valuable assistance and advice, and that student, encouraged by the praise of the demonstrator, burned high with ambitious hopes, and saw the medal already in his grasp.

Before the week was out Macfarlane's prophecy had been fulfilled. Fettes had outlived his terrors and had forgotten his baseness. He began to plume himself upon his courage, and had so arranged the story in his mind that he could look back on these events with an unhealthy pride. Of his accomplice he saw but little. They met, of course, in the business of the class; they received their orders together from Mr. K—. At times they had a word or two in private, and Macfarlane was from first to last particularly kind and jovial. But it was plain that he avoided any reference to their common secret; and even when Fettes whispered to him that he had cast in his lot with the lions and foresworn the lambs, he only signed to him smilingly to hold his peace.

At length an occasion arose which threw the pair once more into a closer union. Mr. K— was again short of subjects; pupils were eager, and it was a part of this teacher's pretensions to be always well supplied. At the same time there came the news of a burial in the rustic graveyard of Glencorse. Time has little changed the place in question. It stood then, as now, upon a cross road, out of call of human habitations, and buried fathom deep in the foliage of six cedar trees. The cries of the sheep upon the neighbouring hills, the streamlets upon either hand, one loudly singing among pebbles, the other dripping furtively from pond to pond, the stir of the wind in mountainous old flowering chestnuts, and once in seven days the voice of the bell and the old tunes of the precentor, were the only sounds that disturbed the silence around the rural church. The Resurrection Man—to use a byname of the period—was not to be deterred by any of the sanctities of customary piety. It was part of his trade to despise and desecrate the scrolls and trumpets of old tombs, the paths worn by the feet of worshippers and mourners, and the offerings and the inscriptions of bereaved affection. To rustic neighbourhoods, where love is more than commonly tenacious, and where some bonds of blood or fellowship unite the entire society of a parish, the body-snatcher, far from being repelled by natural respect, was attracted by the ease and safety of the task. To bodies that had been laid in earth, in joyful expectation of a far different awakening, there came that hasty, lamp-lit, terror-haunted resurrection of the spade and mattock. The coffin was forced, the cerements torn, and the melancholy relics, clad in sackcloth, after being rattled for hours on moonless byways, were at length exposed to uttermost indignities before a class of gaping boys.

Somewhat as two vultures may swoop upon a dying lamb, Fettes and Macfarlane were to be let loose upon a grave in that green and quiet resting-place. The wife of a farmer, a woman who had lived for sixty years, and been known for nothing but good butter and a godly conversation, was to be rooted from her grave at midnight and carried, dead and naked, to that far-away city that she had always honoured with her Sunday's best; the place beside her family was to be empty till the crack of doom; her innocent and almost venerable members to be exposed to that last curiosity of the anatomist.

Late one afternoon the pair set forth, well wrapped in cloaks and furnished with a formidable bottle. It rained without remission—a cold, dense, lashing rain. Now and again there blew a puff of wind, but these sheets of falling water kept it down. Bottle and all, it was a sad and silent drive as far as Penicuik, where they were to spend the evening. They stopped once, to hide their implements in a thick bush not far from the churchyard, and once again at the Fisher's Tryst, to have a toast before the kitchen fire and vary their nips of whisky with a glass of ale. When they reached their journey's end the gig was housed, the horse was fed and comforted, and the two young doctors in a private room sat down to the best dinner and the best wine the house afforded. The lights, the fire, the beating rain upon the window, the cold, incongruous work that lay before them, added zest to their enjoyment of the meal. With every glass their cordiality increased. Soon Macfarlane handed a little pile of gold to his companion.

"A compliment," he said. "Between friends these little d—d accommodations ought to fly like pipe-lights."

Fettes pocketed the money, and applauded the sentiment to the echo. "You are a philosopher," he cried. "I was an ass till I knew you. You and K— between you, by the Lord Harry! but you'll make a man of me."

"Of course we shall," applauded Macfarlane. "A man? I tell you, it required a man to back me up the other morning. There are some big, brawling, forty-year-old cowards who would have turned sick at the look of the d—d thing; but not you—you kept your head. I watched you."

"Well, and why not?" Fettes thus vaunted himself. "It was no affair of mine. There was nothing to gain on the one side but disturbance, and on the other I could count on your gratitude, don't you see?" And he slapped his pocket till the gold pieces rang.

Macfarlane somehow felt a certain touch of alarm at these unpleasant words. He may have regretted that he had taught his young companion so successfully, but he had no time to interfere, for the other noisily continued in this boastful strain:—

"The great thing is not to be afraid. Now, between you and me, I don't want to hang—that's practical; but for all cant, Macfarlane, I was born with a contempt. Hell, God, Devil, right, wrong, sin, crime, and all the old gallery of curiosities—they may frighten boys, but men of the world, like you and me, despise them. Here's to the memory of Gray!"

It was by this time growing somewhat late. The gig, according to order, was brought round to the door with both lamps brightly shining, and the young men had to pay their bill and take the road. They announced that they were bound for Peebles, and drove in that direction till they were clear of the last houses of the town; then, extinguishing the lamps, returned upon their course, and followed a by-road toward Glencorse. There was no sound but that of their own passage, and the incessant, strident pouring of the rain. It was pitch dark; here and there a white gate or a white stone in the wall guided them for a short space across the night; but for the most part it was at a foot pace, and almost groping, that they picked their way through that resonant blackness to their solemn and isolated destination. In the sunken woods that traverse the neighbourhood of the burying-ground the last glimmer failed them, and it became necessary to kindle a match and re-illumine one of the lanterns of the gig. Thus, under the dripping trees, and environed by huge and moving shadows, they reached the scene of their unhallowed labours.

They were both experienced in such affairs, and powerful with the spade; and they had scarce been twenty minutes at their task before they were rewarded by a dull rattle on the coffin lid. At the same moment Macfarlane, having hurt his hand upon a stone, flung it carelessly above his head. The grave, in which they now stood almost to the shoulders, was close to the edge of the plateau of the graveyard; and the gig lamp had been propped, the better to illuminate their labours, against a tree, and on the immediate verge of the steep bank descending to the stream. Chance had taken a sure aim with the stone. Then came a clang of broken glass; night fell upon them; sounds alternately dull and ringing announced the bounding of the lantern down the bank, and its occasional collision with the trees. A stone or two, which it had dislodged in its descent, rattled behind it into the profundities of the glen; and then silence, like night, resumed its sway; and they might bend their hearing to its utmost pitch, but naught was to be heard except the rain, now marching to the wind, now steadily falling over miles of open country.

They were so nearly at an end of their abhorred task that they judged it wisest to complete it in the dark. The coffin was exhumed and broken open; the body inserted in the dripping sack and carried between them to the gig; one mounted to keep it in its place, and the other, taking the horse by the mouth, groped along by wall and bush until they reached the wider road by the Fisher's Tryst. Here was a faint, diffused radiancy, which they hailed like daylight; by that they pushed the horse to a good pace and began to rattle along merrily in the direction of the town.

They had both been wetted to the skin during their operations, and now, as the gig jumped among the deep ruts, the thing that stood propped between them fell now upon one and now upon the other. At every repetition of the horrid contact each instinctively repelled it with the greater haste; and the process, natural although it was, began to tell upon the nerves of the companions. Macfarlane made some ill-favoured jest about the farmer's wife, but it came hollowly from his lips, and was allowed to drop in silence. Still their unnatural burden bumped from side to side; and now the head would be laid, as if in confidence, upon their shoulders, and now the drenching sack-cloth would flap icily about their faces. A creeping chill began to possess the soul of Fettes. He peered at the bundle, and it seemed somehow larger than at first. All over the country-side, and from every degree of distance, the farm dogs accompanied their passage with tragic ululations; and it grew and grew upon his mind that some unnatural miracle had been accomplished, that some nameless change had befallen the dead body, and that it was in fear of their unholy burden that the dogs were howling.

"For God's sake," said he, making a great effort to arrive at speech, "for God's sake, let's have a light!"

Seemingly Macfarlane was affected in the same direction; for, though he made no reply, he stopped the horse, passed the reins to his companion, got down, and proceeded to kindle the remaining lamp. They had by that time got no farther than the cross-road down to Auchenclinny. The rain still poured as though the deluge were returning, and it was no easy matter to make a light in such a world of wet and darkness. When at last the flickering blue flame had been transferred to the wick and began to expand and clarify, and shed a wide circle of misty brightness round the gig, it became possible for the two young men to see each other and the thing they had along with them. The rain had moulded the rough sacking to the outlines of the body underneath; the head was distinct from the trunk, the shoulders plainly modelled; something at once spectral and human riveted their eyes upon the ghastly comrade of their drive.

For some time Macfarlane stood motionless, holding up the lamp. A nameless dread was swathed, like a wet sheet, about the body, and tightened the white skin upon the face of Fettes; a fear that was meaningless, a horror of what could not be, kept mounting to his brain. Another beat of the watch, and he had spoken. But his comrade forestalled him.

"That is not a woman," said Macfarlane, in a hushed voice.

"It was a woman when we put her in," whispered Fettes.

"Hold that lamp," said the other. "I must see her face."

And as Fettes took the lamp his companion untied the fastenings of the sack and drew down the cover from the head. The light fell very clear upon the dark, well-moulded features and smooth-shaven cheeks of a too familiar countenance, often beheld in dreams of both of these young men. A wild yell rang up into the night; each leaped from his own side into the roadway: the lamp fell, broke, and was extinguished; and the horse, terrified by this unusual commotion, bounded and went off toward Edinburgh at a gallop, bearing along with it, sole occupant of the gig, the body of the dead and long-dissected Gray.

Sredni Vashtar

Saki

Conradin was ten years old, and the doctor had pronounced his professional opinion that the boy would not live another five years. The doctor was silky and effete, and counted for little, but his opinion was endorsed by Mrs. De Ropp, who counted for nearly everything. Mrs. De Ropp was Conradin's cousin and guardian, and in his eyes she represented those three-fifths of the world that are necessary and disagreeable and real; the other two-fifths, in perpetual antagonism to the foregoing, were summed up in himself and his imagination. One of these days Conradin supposed he would succumb to the mastering pressure of wearisome necessary things—such as illnesses and coddling restrictions and drawn-out dullness. Without his imagination, which was rampant under the spur of loneliness, he would have succumbed long ago.

Mrs. De Ropp would never, in her honestest moments, have confessed to herself that she disliked Conradin, though she might have been dimly aware that thwarting him "for his good" was a duty which she did not find particularly irksome. Conradin hated her with a desperate sincerity which he was perfectly able to mask. Such few pleasures as he could contrive for himself gained an added relish from the likelihood that they would be displeasing to his guardian, and from the realm of his imagination she was locked out—an unclean thing, which should find no entrance.

In the dull, cheerless garden, overlooked by so many windows that were ready to open with a message not to do this or that, or a reminder that medicines were due, he found little attraction. The few fruit-trees that it contained were set jealously apart from his plucking, as though they were rare specimens of their kind blooming in an arid waste; it would probably have been difficult to find a market-gardener who would have offered ten shillings for their entire yearly produce. In a forgotten corner, however, almost hidden behind a dismal shrubbery, was a disused tool-shed of respectable proportions, and within its walls Conradin found a haven, something that took on the varying aspects of a playroom and a cathedral. He had peopled it with a legion of familiar phantoms, evoked partly from fragments of history and partly from his own brain, but it also boasted two inmates of flesh and blood. In one corner lived a ragged-plumaged Houdan hen, on which the boy lavished an affection that had scarcely another outlet. Further back in the gloom stood a large hutch, divided into two compartments, one of which was fronted with close iron bars. This was the abode of a large polecat-ferret, which a friendly butcher-boy had once smuggled, cage and all, into its present quarters, in exchange for a long-secreted hoard of small silver. Conradin was dreadfully afraid of the lithe, sharp-fanged beast, but it was his most treasured possession. Its very presence in the tool-shed was a secret and fearful joy, to be kept scrupulously from the knowledge of the Woman, as he privately dubbed his cousin. And one day, out of Heaven knows what material, he spun the beast a wonderful name, and from that moment it grew into a god and a religion. The Woman indulged in religion once a week at a church near by, and took Conradin with her, but to him the church service was an alien rite in the House of Rimmon. Every Thursday, in the dim and musty silence of the tool-shed, he worshipped with mystic and elaborate ceremonial before the wooden hutch where dwelt Sredni Vashtar, the great ferret. Red flowers in their season and scarlet berries in the winter-time were offered at his shrine, for he was a god who laid some special stress on the fierce impatient side of things, as opposed to the Woman's religion, which, as far as Conradin could observe, went to great lengths in the contrary direction. And on great festivals powdered nutmeg was strewn in front of his hutch, an important feature of the offering being that the nutmeg had to be stolen. These festivals were of irregular occurrence, and were chiefly appointed to celebrate some passing event. On one occasion, when Mrs. De Ropp suffered from acute toothache for three days, Conradin kept up the festival during the entire three days, and almost succeeded in persuading himself that Sredni Vashtar was personally responsible for the toothache. If the malady had lasted for another day the supply of nutmeg would have given out.

The Houdan hen was never drawn into the cult of Sredni Vashtar. Conradin had long ago settled that she was an Anabaptist. He did not pretend to have the remotest knowledge as to what an Anabaptist was, but he privately hoped that it was dashing and not very respectable. Mrs. De Ropp was the ground plan on which he based and detested all respectability.

After a while Conradin's absorption in the tool-shed began to attract the notice of his guardian. "It is not good for him to be pottering down there in all weathers," she promptly decided, and at breakfast one morning she announced that the Houdan hen had been sold and taken away overnight. With her short-sighted eyes she peered at Conradin, waiting for an outbreak of rage and sorrow, which she was ready to rebuke with a flow of excellent precepts and reasoning. But Conradin said nothing: there was nothing to be said. Something perhaps in his white set face gave her a momentary qualm, for at tea that afternoon there was toast on the table, a delicacy which she usually banned on the ground that it was bad for him; also because the making of it "gave trouble," a deadly offence in the middle-class feminine eye.

"I thought you liked toast," she exclaimed, with an injured air, observing that he did not touch it.

"Sometimes," said Conradin.

In the shed that evening there was an innovation in the worship of the hutch-god. Conradin had been wont to chant his praises, tonight he asked a boon.

"Do one thing for me, Sredni Vashtar."

The thing was not specified. As Sredni Vashtar was a god he must be supposed to know. And choking back a sob as he looked at that other empty corner, Conradin went back to the world he so hated.

And every night, in the welcome darkness of his bedroom, and every evening in the dusk of the tool-shed, Conradin's bitter litany went up: "Do one thing for me, Sredni Vashtar."

Mrs. De Ropp noticed that the visits to the shed did not cease, and one day she made a further journey of inspection.

"What are you keeping in that locked hutch?" she asked. "I believe it's guinea-pigs. I'll have them all cleared away."

Conradin shut his lips tight, but the Woman ransacked his bedroom till she found the carefully hidden key, and forthwith marched down to the shed to complete her discovery. It was a cold afternoon, and Conradin had been bidden to keep to the house. From the furthest window of the dining-room the door of the shed could just be seen beyond the corner of the shrubbery, and there Conradin stationed himself. He saw the Woman enter, and then he imagined her opening the door of the sacred hutch and peering down with her short-sighted eyes into the thick straw bed where his god lay hidden. Perhaps she would prod at the straw in her clumsy impatience. And Conradin fervently breathed his prayer for the last time. But he knew as he prayed that he did not believe. He knew that the Woman would come out presently with that pursed smile he loathed so well on her face, and that in an hour or two the gardener would carry away his wonderful god, a god no longer, but a simple brown ferret in a hutch. And he knew that the Woman would triumph always as she triumphed now, and that he would grow ever more sickly under her pestering and domineering and superior wisdom, till one day nothing would matter much more with him, and the doctor would be proved right. And in the sting and misery of his defeat, he began to chant loudly and defiantly the hymn of his threatened idol:

Sredni Vashtar went forth,
His thoughts were red thoughts and his teeth were white.
His enemies called for peace, but he brought them death.
Sredni Vashtar the Beautiful.

And then of a sudden he stopped his chanting and drew closer to the window-pane. The door of the shed still stood ajar as it had been left, and the minutes were slipping by. They were long minutes, but they slipped by nevertheless. He watched the starlings running and flying in little parties across the lawn; he counted them over and over again, with one eye always on that swinging door. A sour-faced maid came in to lay the table for tea, and still Conradin stood and waited and watched. Hope had crept by inches into his heart, and now a look of triumph began to blaze in his eyes that had only known the wistful patience of defeat. Under his breath, with a furtive exultation, he began once again the paean of victory and devastation. And presently his eyes were rewarded: out through that doorway came a long, low, yellow-and-brown beast, with eyes a-blink at the waning daylight, and dark wet stains around the fur of jaws and throat. Conradin dropped on his knees. The great polecat-ferret made its way down to a small brook at the foot of the garden, drank for a moment, then crossed a little plank bridge and was lost to sight in the bushes. Such was the passing of Sredni Vashtar.

"Tea is ready," said the sour-faced maid; "where is the mistress?"

"She went down to the shed some time ago," said Conradin.

And while the maid went to summon her mistress to tea, Conradin fished a toasting-fork out of the sideboard drawer and proceeded to toast himself a piece of bread. And during the toasting of it and the buttering of it with much butter and the slow enjoyment of eating it, Conradin listened to the noises and silences which fell in quick spasms beyond the dining-room door. The loud foolish screaming of the maid, the answering chorus of wondering ejaculations from the kitchen region, the scuttering footsteps and hurried embassies for outside help, and then, after a lull, the scared sobbings and the shuffling tread of those who bore a heavy burden into the house.

"Whoever will break it to the poor child? I couldn't for the life of me!" exclaimed a shrill voice. And while they debated the matter among themselves, Conradin made himself another piece of toast.

The Horla

Guy de Maupassant

Translated by Jonathan Sturges

May 8th.
What a magnificent day! I spent the whole morning stretched on the grass, before my house, under the great plane-tree which entirely covers, shelters, and shades it. I love this country, and I love to live here, because here I have my roots, those deep, fine roots which attach a man to the soil where his forefathers were born and buried, which attach him to what is thought there and to what is eaten, to its customs as to its dishes, to its localisms of speech, to the peculiar intonation of its peasants, to the smell of its earth, of its villages, of its very air.

I love the house where I have grown up. From my windows I see the Seine, flowing by my garden; on the other side of the road, almost on my own property: the great, wide Seine that goes to Havre from Rouen, covered with the passing boats.

To the left, down there, Rouen the great city of blue roofs swarming far and wide below a crowd of pointed Gothic bell-towers. These, ponderous or slender, are innumerable, overtowered by the cathedral's cast-iron spire, and filled with bells which ring in the blue air on fine mornings. Their sweet and distant iron humming, their brazen chant, reaches out to me, brought by the breeze, and now louder, now lower, as the breeze now wakes, now drowses.

How fine it was this morning!

About eleven o'clock, I remember, a long tow of ships defiled past my garden railings. They were pulled by a tug the size of a fly; it groaned and vomited forth a thick, black smoke.

Just behind two English schooners, whose red flag waved against the sky, came a superb Brazilian three-master, quite white, admirably clean and shining. This ship gave me so much pleasure that I saluted her, I don't know why.

May 12th.
For some days I have had a little fever; I feel unwell, or rather, properly speaking, I feel depressed.

Whence come these mysterious influences which change our happiness into discouragement and our confidence into distress? One would almost say that the air, the invisible air, was full of unknowable Powers, to whose mysterious proximity we submit. I awake full of gayety, with desires to sing in my throat. Why? I go down to the waterside, and suddenly, after a short walk, return distressed, as though some misfortune awaited me at home. Why? Is it a shiver of cold which, brushing across my skin, has unsettled my nerves and darkened my soul? Is it the shapes of the clouds, or the colors of the day, or the changeable colors of things which have passed in through my eyes, and have troubled my thoughts? Do we know? Everything about us, everything which we see without observing, everything which we brush against without recognizing, everything which we touch without feeling, everything which we encounter without clearly distinguishing, may have upon us, upon our senses, and, through them, upon our minds and upon our hearts, instant effects which are wonderful and not to be explained.

Ah! but it is deep, this mystery of the Invisible! No, we may not sound it with our wretched senses, with our eyes which can perceive neither what is too small nor too great, nor too near nor too far, nor the inhabitants of a planet nor the inhabitants of a drop of water. And we may not sound it with our ears which deceive us, transmitting air-waves in the form of sonorous notes. They are the fairies who perform the miracle of changing movement into sound, and by this metamorphosis they give birth to music and to Nature's dumb agitation the power of singing. No, we may not sound it with our sense of smell feebler than that of the dog; nor with our taste which can hardly discern the age of wine!

Ah, if we had only other organs which would perform in our favor other miracles like that miracle of music, what new things we should discover all about our lives!

May 16th.
I am certainly ill. Last month I was so well! I have a fever, a dreadful fever, or rather a feeling of feverish enervation which causes my mind to suffer as much as my body. I experience that awful sense of some menacing danger, that apprehension of coming misfortune or approaching death, that curious presentiment which is no doubt really the stroke of a still unrecognized sickness germinating in body and in blood.

May 18th.
I have just been to consult my physician, for I was not able to sleep. He found my pulse rapid, my eye dilated, my nerves disturbed, but no alarming symptoms. I must take shower-baths and drink a little bromide of potassium.

May 25th.

No change. My condition is truly curious. With the approach of evening a strange anxiety invades me, as if the night concealed for me some dreadful menace. I dine quickly, then try to read, but I do not comprehend the words. I barely distinguish the letters. Then I pace my drawing-room backward and forward, under the oppression of a confused and resistless fear, the fear of sleep and the fear of my bed.

Towards ten o'clock I go up-stairs to my room. As soon as I get inside the door I double-lock it and I push the bolts; I am afraid . . . of what? . . .

Hitherto I feared nothing . . . I open my closets, I look under my bed; I listen . . .

I listen for what? . . . Is it not strange that a simple indisposition, a difficulty in the circulation perhaps, an irritated nerve, a slight congestion, a little disturbance of the works of my delicate, imperfect human machinery, can out of a merry man make a melancholy one out of a brave man make a coward? Then I go to bed, and I await sleep as one might await an executioner. I wait with terror for its coming. And my heart beats, and my limbs quiver, and my whole body trembles under the warmth of the bedclothes, until the moment when I fall suddenly into slumber, as a man might fall, to drown himself, into a gulf of stagnant water. I do not feel sleep coming in the way I used to feel it coming calmly. For this sleep, hidden somewhere near me, is perfidious, and it watches and will soon seize me by the head, and close my eyes, and destroy me.

I sleep long two or three hours then a dream—no, a nightmare grips me in its arms. I feel that I am in bed and that I am sleeping . . . I feel it and I know it . . . and I also feel that some one approaches me, looks at me, touches me, mounts upon my bed, kneels upon my breast, seizes my neck in his hands and presses . . . presses . . . with all his force, to strangle me.

I writhe, bound fast by that awful powerlessness which paralyzes us in dreams. I desire to shout, I cannot; to move, I cannot; I try, with fearful efforts, panting, to turn myself, to throw off this being who is crushing and suffocating me; I cannot.

And suddenly I awake, wild, covered with perspiration. I light a candle. I am alone.

After this crisis, which recurs every night, I sleep at last calmly until dawn.

June 2d.

My condition is still worse. What is the matter with me? The bromide has no effect; the shower-baths have no effect. Just now, in order to tire myself out (though Heaven knows I am languid enough already!) I went to walk in the forest of Roumare. I thought at first that the fresh, buoyant, balmy air, full of the perfume of herbs and leaves, was pouring new blood into my veins, new energy into my heart. I took a wide glade. Then I turned towards La Bouille, along a narrow *allée*, between two armies of great trees which built a thick, green, almost black roof between the sky and myself.

Suddenly a shiver seized me, not a shiver of cold, but a strange shiver of anguish.

I quickened my pace, uneasy at being alone in the wood, terrified without reason, stupidly, by the profound loneliness. All at once it seemed to me that I was being followed, that some one was treading on my heels, on the point—on the point—on the point of touching me.

I turned abruptly. I was alone. I saw behind me only the straight, wide glade empty, high, fearfully empty; and in front of me also it stretched out of sight just the same dreadful!

I closed my eyes. Why? And I began to turn round and round on my heel, quickly, like a top. I came near falling. I opened my eyes again; the trees danced; the earth swam; I was obliged to sit down. Then, of course, I no longer knew from which direction I had come! Fantastic thought! Strange! Fantastic thought! I set off to the right, and happened into the same avenue which had led me to the middle of the forest.

June 3d.
The night was horrible. I shall go away for a few weeks. A little journey will no doubt set me on my feet again.

July 2d.
At home again. I am cured; and, besides that, I have made a charming trip. I have visited Mont Saint Michel, where I had never been.

What a vision, when one arrives, as I did, at Avranches towards the end of the day! The city is on a little hill; a guide took me to the public garden at the end of the town. A great bay stretched away before me out of sight, between two lonely shores which lost themselves far off in the mists; and in the midst of this immense yellow bay, beneath a golden and glittering sky, rose, sombre and pointed, a strange mount in the midst of the sands. The sun had just disappeared, and against the still flaming horizon there was designed the profile of that fantastic rock which bears upon its summit a fantastic monument.

By daybreak I was on my way towards it. The tide was low, as yesterday at evening, and I watched that wonder-arousing abbey growing taller and taller before me as I approached. After several hours of walking I reached the enormous block of stones which bears the little town dominated by the great church. Having ascended the narrow and steep street, I entered the most admirable Gothic dwelling which has ever been constructed for God on earth, vast as a city, full of low passages borne down by heavy arches, of high galleries borne up by slender columns. I entered that gigantic granite jewel, light as a bit of lace, covered with towers and with slender belfries linked one to the other by fine-carved arches. They are climbed by twisting stair-ways, and they dart into the blue sky of day and into the black sky of night, their fantastic heads bristling with chimeras, with Devils, and with strange Beasts.

When I reached the top I said to the monk who accompanied me, "Father, you must be well off here."

He answered: "There's a great deal of wind, Monsieur"; and we fell into conversation while we watched the rising sea spread over the sand and cover it with a steely cuirass.

And the monk told me stories—all the old stories of the place—legends, always legends.

One of them impressed me very strongly. The country people, those of the mount, pretend that talking is heard on the sands by night, then the bleating of two goats, the one with a voice which is high, the other with a voice which is deep. Unbelievers maintain it is the sea-birds' crying, which resembles now a bleat, and now a human wail; but belated fishermen swear that they have met, wandering on the sands, between two tides, about the little city cast out so far from the rest of the world, an old shepherd whose head, shrouded in a cloak, is always invisible, and who leads behind him a he-goat with the face of a man, and a she-goat with the face of a woman. They have long white hair, and they talk incessantly, quarrelling together in an unknown tongue; then suddenly they cease crying and begin to bleat with all their might.

I said to the monk: "Do you believe it?"

He murmured: "I do not know."

I continued: "If there really existed on the earth any other beings beside ourselves, how is it possible that we should not have known them long ago? How should you have seen them, you? How should I not have seen them, I?"

He answered: "Do we see the hundred-thousandth part of what exists? For instance, take the wind, which is the greatest force in nature, which knocks down men, lays low buildings, tears up trees by the roots, heaps the sea into mountains of water, destroys coasts, and hurls great ships upon the breakers, the wind which kills, which whistles, which moans, which roars, have you ever seen it? Can you see it? It exists, nevertheless."

I was silent before this simple reasoning. This man was a wise man or perhaps a fool. I could not have decided which; but I was silent. What he had just said I had often thought.

July 3d.

I have slept badly; there is certainly something feverish in the air here, for my coachman suffers from the same complaint as myself. On my return yesterday I noticed that he was looking curiously pale. I asked him: "What is the matter, Jean?"

"It is that I cannot sleep, Monsieur; my nights eat up my days. Since Monsieur went away, it holds me like a charm."

The other servants, however, are well; but I myself am in great fear of a relapse.

July 4th.

Yes, I have had a relapse. My old nightmares have returned. Last night I felt some one squatting on my chest with his mouth to mine, drinking my life out through my lips. Yes, like a leech he drew it out of my throat. Then when he was satiated he arose, and I, I awoke, so nearly murdered, so exhausted, so broken, that I had no longer power to move. If this continues many days more I shall certainly go away again.

July 5th.

Have I lost my reason? That which has happened, that which I saw last night, is so strange that my head turns when I think of it!

I had, as I now do every evening, locked my door; then, being thirsty, I drank half a glass of water, and I noticed by mere chance that the water-bottle was full up to the glass stopper.

After that I went to bed and fell into one of my dreadful slumbers, from which, two hours later, I was drawn by a shock more awful yet.

Imagine a man who sleeps, who is being murdered, and who awakes with a knife in his breast, and who groans covered with blood, and who cannot breathe, and who is dying, and who does not understand. It was like that!

Having at last recovered my reason, I again felt thirsty; I lit a candle and I went to the table where the water-bottle stood. I raised it, tipping it over the glass; nothing came out. It was empty! It was completely empty! At first I did not understand; then, all at once, I experienced so terrible an emotion that I had to sit down, or rather that I simply fell, upon a chair! Then, with a start, I jumped to my feet, and looked about me! Then, again, I sat down, dazed with astonishment and with fear, before the transparent glass! I glared at it with staring eyes, trying to understand. My hands trembled! Had some one really drunk that water? Who—I? I, without a doubt. It could only be I. Then I was a somnambulist, I was living, without knowing it, that mysterious double life which makes us wonder whether we are in ourselves two beings, or whether some strange being, unknowable and invisible, may not animate, at moments when our will is weak, our bodies captive and more obedient to this stranger than to us.

Ah! who will understand my abominable anguish? Who will understand the emotion of a man, perfectly sane, well educated, full of reason, and yet contemplating in terror, through the glass of a water-bottle, the disappearance, while he slept, of a little water! And I remained there until morning, not daring to go back to bed.

July 6th.

I am going mad. The water was again drunk by some one last night; or, rather, I drank it!

But, is it—is it I? Who should it be? Who? Oh, my God! I am going mad. Who shall save me?

July 10th.

I have just established the most wonder-arousing proofs.

Yes, I am mad! And yet?

On the 6th of July, before going to bed, I placed some wine, some milk, some water, some bread, and some strawberries on my table.

Some one drank—I drank—all the water, and a little milk. The wine, the bread, and the strawberries were not touched.

On the 7th of July I made the same experiment, with the same result.

On the 8th of July I suppressed the water and the milk. Nothing was touched at all.

Finally, on the 9th of July, I put only the milk and the water on my table, being careful to wrap up the bottles in cloths of white muslin and to tie down the stoppers. Then I rubbed my lips, my beard, my hands, with black-lead, and I retired.

The invincible slumber seized me, soon followed by the dreadful awaking. I had not stirred; my very sheets bore no stains. I rushed to the table. The cloths covering the bottles were immaculate. I untied the cords, trembling with fear. Some one had drunk all the water! Some one had drunk all the milk! Oh, my God! . . .

I leave today for Paris.

July 12th.

Paris. I must have lost my head completely these last days. I have been undoubtedly the plaything of a nervous imagination, unless, that is, I am really a somnambulist, or that I have been subjected to one of those influences, admitted but not yet explained, which are called "suggestions." In any case my perturbation came near insanity, and twenty-four hours of Paris have sufficed to put me on my feet again.

Yesterday, after taking a drive and making some visits which caused a new, revivifying air to pass into my soul, I finished the evening at the Theatre Francais. They were playing a piece by Alexandre Dumas *fils;* and that strong, alert spirit completed my cure. Solitude is certainly dangerous for an active intelligence. We need around us men who think and talk. When we are long alone, we people the void with phantoms.

I returned to the hotel in great good spirits, along the boulevards. Reminded by the jostling of the crowd, I thought, not without irony, of my terrors and imaginings of last week, when I believed, yes, really believed, that an invisible being was dwelling under my roof. How easily we lose our heads, how weakly and quickly we become wild with fear the moment we encounter some little incident which cannot be explained!

Instead of concluding with the words: "The reason I do not understand is that the cause as yet escapes me," we immediately proceed to imagine some dreadful mystery, some supernatural power.

July 14th.

Fête de la République. I took a walk in the streets. The flags and the fireworks amused me like a child. Nevertheless, it is simply an absurdity—this being joyous on a fixed date, by Government decree. The people is an imbecile herd, now stupidly patient, now ferociously rebellious. Some one says to it: "Make merry." It makes merry. Some one says to it: "Go and fight with your neighbors." It goes and fights. Some one says to it: "Vote for the Emperor." It votes for the Emperor. Then some one says to it: "Vote for the Republic." And it votes for the Republic.

Those who give it these orders are fools, also, but instead of obeying men, they obey principles, things whose stupidity, whose barrenness, whose falsity appears in the very name Principles! Ideas supposed certain and immutable in this world where one is sure of nothing, where even light, even sound are illusions, merely states in the brain, merely states in the brain!

July 16th.

Yesterday I saw something which disturbed me very much.

I was dining with my cousin Mme. Sablé, whose husband commands the 76th Chasseurs at Limoges. At dinner there were two young ladies, and the husband of one of them, a Doctor Parent, a nerve-specialist, much interested in the extraordinary developments brought to light by the experiments now making in Hypnotism and Suggestion.

He gave us a long account of the prodigious results obtained by English scientists and by the physicians of the school at Nancy.

The facts which he advanced appeared to me so extremely fantastic that I declared myself entirely sceptical.

"We are," he maintained, "on the point of discovering one of Nature's most important secrets—I mean to say, one of her most important terrestrial secrets; since, of course, she hides forever others quite as important up there in the stars. Ever since Man has been able to think, ever since he has been able to speak and write his thoughts, he has from time to time felt brushing against him the touch of a mystery which is impenetrable to his gross, imperfect senses; and he has tried to supplement this weakness of his bodily organs by an effort of his mind. While his intelligence remained in the rudimentary state this notion of phenomena, all about him, yet invisible, took on shapes of the most vulgar terror. From it were born popular beliefs in the supernatural, legends of wandering spirits, of fairies, of gnomes, of ghosts—I might even add, the vulgar idea of God; for the ordinary conception of a workman-creator, in whatever religion it springs up, is, of all the inventions of the human brain, the most common, the most stupid, the most unacceptable. Nothing is truer than Voltaire's epigram: 'God made man in his own image, and man has returned the compliment.'

"But about a century ago people began to have dim forebodings of something new. Mesmer and several others started us on an unexpected track, and now, and especially in the last three or four years, we have arrived at wonderful results."

My cousin, as unbelieving as myself, smiled. Doctor Parent said to her: "May I try to hypnotize you, madame?"

"Certainly you may."

She seated herself in an arm-chair, and, trying to fascinate her gaze, he looked at her fixedly. As for me, I felt suddenly troubled—my heart beating, a choking in my throat. I saw the eyes of Mme. Sablé droop, her mouth work, her breast heave. At the end of ten minutes she slept.

"Put yourself behind her," said the physician.

And I seated myself behind her. In her hands he placed a visiting-card, saying: "This is a mirror; what do you see in it?"

She answered: "I see my cousin."

"What is he doing?"

"He is twisting his mustache."

"What now?"

"He is taking a photograph out of his pocket."

"A photograph of whom?"

"Of himself."

It was true! And the photograph had been sent home only that evening to my hotel.

"How does he look in the photograph?"

"He is standing up, with his hat in his hand."

So then she saw in this card, in this white card, as well as she would have seen in a glass!

The young ladies, very much frightened, cried: "Enough! Enough! Enough!"

But the doctor gave her an order: "You will rise at eight o'clock tomorrow morning; and you will go to find your cousin at his hotel; and you will beg him to lend you five thousand francs, which your husband has said he needs, and hopes to get from you when he comes up shortly to town."

Then he awoke her.

While returning to the hotel I meditated on this curious séance, and I was assailed by doubts, not of the absolute, the indubitable good faith of my cousin, whom I have known like a sister from childhood up, but of a possible trick on the part of the doctor. Might he not, at the same time with his visiting-card, have held before the sleeping lady a mirror hidden in his hand? Professional prestidigitators perform equally extraordinary feats.

So I went home and to bed.

But this morning, about half after eight, I was awaked by my man, who said: "It is Mme. Sablé. She asks to speak with you, sir, immediately."

I dressed in all haste, and I bid him show her in.

Very much embarrassed, she sat down, lowering her eyes, not lifting her veil; and she said: "My dear cousin, I have to ask you for a great favor."

"What is it, cousin?"

"I hate to ask you, and yet I must. I need—I need five thousand francs; I need it very much."

"Oh, come now! You?"

"Yes, I. Or, rather, my husband. He says I must get the money for him somehow."

I was so stupefied that I stammered. I asked myself if this were not a joke on me which she was playing with Doctor Parent; if this were not a simple farce rehearsed in advance, and very well acted.

But, when I looked at her carefully, all my doubts vanished. She trembled with anguish, the proceeding was so painful for her; and I saw that her throat was full of sobs.

I knew she was very rich, and I continued: "What! Your husband has not five thousand francs at his disposal? Come! Think a little. Are you sure he told you to ask me for it?"

For some seconds she hesitated as though making a great effort to remember, then she answered: "Yes . . . Yes . . . I am sure of it."

"Has he written?"

Again she hesitated, reflecting. I divined how she was tortured by the working of her thoughts. She did not know. She knew simply that she must borrow from me, for her husband, five thousand francs. But she gained the courage to lie.

"Yes, he wrote to me."

"When, then? You said nothing to me of it yesterday."

"I got the letter this morning."

"Can you show it me?"

"No . . . no . . . no . . . it had private matters in it . . . too personal . . . I . . . I burnt it."

"Oh I suppose then he's been getting into debt."

Again she hesitated; then murmured: "I do not know."

I announced, abruptly: "The fact is at the moment I haven't five thousand francs to my hand, cousin."

She uttered a kind of suffering cry.

"Oh, oh! I beg you, I beg you to get it somehow, somehow."

She grew excited, clasped her hands before me as though she were praying! I heard her voice change tone; she wept and stammered; she was tormented, overpowered, dominated by the irresistible order which had been laid upon her.

"Oh, oh! I beg you . . . if you knew how I suffer . . . I must have it today."

I took pity on her.

"You shall have it, and very soon, I promise."

"Oh, thank you! thank you! You are good."

I continued: "Do you remember what happened at your house last night?"

"Yes."

"Do you remember that Doctor Parent put you to sleep?"

"Yes."

"Well, he ordered you to come to me this morning, and borrow five thousand francs. And at this moment you are obeying his suggestion."

She reflected for a few seconds, and answered:

"But it's my husband who wants it."

For an hour I tried in vain to convince her.

As soon as she had gone, I hurried to the Doctor. He was on the point of going out; and he listened to me with a smile. Then he said: "Do you believe now?"

"Yes, I must."

"Let us go to your cousin."

She was already dozing in a long chair, exhausted with fatigue. The physician felt her pulse, looked at her for a time, his raised hand pointing towards her eyes. Little by little she closed them, submitting to the resistless strength of the magnetic power.

When she slumbered:

"Your husband has no longer any need of five thousand francs. You will therefore forget that you have asked your cousin to lend you them; and if he speaks to you of it, you will not understand him."

Then he awoke her. I drew out a pocket-book.

"Here, my dear cousin, here is what you asked me for this morning."

She was so surprised that I did not dare to insist. Nevertheless, I tried to arouse her memory; but she denied everything with vehemence, thought I was making fun of her, and at last came near being angry.

* * * * *

There it is! I have just returned; and I was so disturbed by this experience that at luncheon I could eat nothing.

July 19th.
Several people to whom I have related this adventure have made fun of me. I do not know what to think. The wise man says: "It may be."

July 21st.
I've been to dine at Bougival; afterwards I went to the Watermen's Ball.

Decidedly everything depends on circumstance and place. To believe in the supernatural on the island of La Grenouilliere would be the height of folly indeed . . . But on the top of Mont St. Michel? . . . But in the Far East? We are subject fearsomely to the influence of what surrounds us. Next week I shall go home.

July 30th.
I arrived yesterday. All well.

August 2d.
Nothing new. Beautiful weather. I pass my days watching the Seine flow.

August 4th.
Quarrels among the servants. They say that some one breaks the glass at night in the closets. My man accuses the cook, who accuses the laundress, who accuses the two maids. Which one is guilty? It would take a wise man to say.

August 6th.
This time I am not mad. I have seen . . . I have seen! . . . I have seen! . . . I can doubt no more . . . I have seen! . . . I am still chilled to my very finger-nails . . .

I am still afraid to the very marrow . . . I have seen! . . .

I was taking a walk about two o'clock, in broad daylight, in my rose-garden . . . along a row of autumn roses which are already beginning to bloom.

Pausing to look at a Géant des Batailles, which bore three magnificent buds, I saw, I distinctly saw, quite near me the stem of one of these roses bend as though twisted by an invisible hand, then break, as though that hand had plucked it! Then the flower lifted itself, following the curve which would have been described by an arm carrying it to a mouth; and it remained hanging in the empty air, alone, motionless, a terrifying red stain three paces from my eyes.

Maddened, I threw myself forward to seize it! I found nothing; it had disappeared. Then I was overcome with violent anger against myself, since a man who is serious and reasonable should not allow himself to have such hallucinations as this.

But was it really an hallucination? I turned to look for the stem, and I discovered it almost immediately, on the plant, freshly broken, between the two other roses which remained upon the tree.

So I went back to the house with a troubled soul; for now I am certain that near me there exists an invisible being who lives on milk and on water; who can touch objects; can take them up and change their places; whose nature, therefore, though imperceptible to our sense, is material, and who, like myself, dwells under my roof . . .

August 7th.

I slept quietly. He drank all the water in my bottle, but did not disturb my sleep.

I ask myself if I am mad. While walking just now along the river, doubts about my reason came to me; not vague doubts such as I have hitherto experienced, but doubts precise and absolute. I have seen lunatics, I have known some who remained intelligent, clear-headed, lucid on every subject save one. They talked clearly, easily, profoundly, then suddenly their intelligence, striking on the rock of their monomania, there ground itself to pieces, was broken up and foundered in that terrible, furious sea, full of heaving waves and mists and squalls, the sea which we call "Madness."

I should certainly believe that I was mad, quite mad, if I were not so entirely self-conscious, if I did not recognize my condition so perfectly, if I were not always sounding it by an analysis which is so completely clear. I am, then, only a man who suffers from an hallucination, but who is in full possession of his reason? Some trouble has occurred in my brain, one of those troubles which psychologists nowadays endeavor to note and particularize? And this trouble has induced a profound lapse in my intellect, in the order and logic of my thoughts? A similar phenomenon occurs in dreams, where we are led through the most improbable of phantasmagoria without feeling a shadow of surprise, simply for the reason that the verifying apparatus, our sense of control, is asleep, while our imaginative faculty wakes and is active. May it not be, therefore, that one of the invisible keys of my cerebral piano is paralyzed? People very often, in consequence of an accident, lose their memory of proper names, or of verbs, or of figures, or simply of dates. That the various little bundles of thought are specially localized is now considered proved. Hence what is there surprising if my power of controlling the unreality of certain hallucinations finds itself at the present moment torpid? I pondered on all this as I followed the bank of the river. The sun covered the stream with radiance, made the earth delicious, filled my eyes with love for life, for the swallows whose swift motions are a joy to look at, for the grasses by the water's edge whose rustling is a joy to me when I listen. Little by little, however, I was penetrated by a strange uneasiness. It seemed to me that a force, an occult force, benumbed me, checked me, prevented me from going farther, called me back. I experienced a mournful feeling that I must return, a feeling like that which oppresses us when, having left at home some sick person whom we love, we are suddenly seized by a presentiment that she is worse.

So I turned back, against my will, certain that I should find bad news at home, a letter, or a telegram. There was nothing, and I remained more surprised and uneasy than if I had again seen some fantastic vision.

August 8th.
I passed a dreadful evening yesterday. He no longer makes his presence evident, but I feel him near me, spying, watching, penetrating me, dominating me, more terrible while thus concealed than if he manifested by supernatural phenomena his invisible and constant presence.

I slept, however.

August 9th.
Nothing. But I am afraid.

August 10th.
Nothing. What will happen tomorrow?

August 11th.
Still nothing; I cannot stay at home any longer with this fear and these thoughts in my soul; I shall go away.

August 12th: 10 p.m.
All day I have wanted to be off; I could not go. I wished to perform an act of free-will, very easy and very simple: going out of my door getting into my carriage driving to Rouen. I was not able. Why?

August 13th.
When one is attacked by certain maladies all the powers of the physical being seem broken, all the energies destroyed, all the muscles relaxed, the bones

becoming soft as flesh and the flesh liquid as water. I experience this in my moral state after a strange and appalling fashion. I have no longer any strength, courage, self-control, no power to put in motion my own will. I can no longer will; but some one wills for me, and I obey.

August 14th.

I am lost! Some one is in possession of my soul and governs it. Some one orders all my acts, all my movements, all my thoughts. I am no longer anything in myself; I am nothing but an enslaved and terrified spectator of the things which I accomplish. I desire to go out; I cannot he does not wish it, and I remain, frightened, trembling, in the arm-chair where he holds me seated. I desire simply to rise, to get up, so as to prove that I am still my own master. I cannot! I am riveted to my seat, and my seat adheres to the ground with such force that no power could lift us up.

Then, on a sudden, I must, I must, I must go to the end of the garden and pick some strawberries and eat them. And I go. I pick the berries and I eat them. Oh, my God! my God! If there be a God, deliver me, save me, help me! Pardon! Pity! Grace! Save me! Oh, what suffering! what torture! what horror!

August 15th.

Yes, this is the way in which my poor cousin was possessed and dominated when she came to me to borrow five thousand francs. She submitted to a strange will which had entered into her like a new soul—like a new parasite and dominant soul. Is the world ending?

But this being who governs me—what is he, this invisible? Who is he, this unknowable, this prowler of a supernatural race?

And so the Invisibles exist! How is it, then, that since the beginning of the world they have never manifested themselves as they have to me? I never read of any such things as have happened here in my house. Oh, if I could leave it! If I could go away—flee and never return—I should be saved! But I cannot.

August 16th.

I was able to make my escape today for two hours, like a prisoner who finds the door of his dungeon, by chance, open. I suddenly felt that I was free, and that he was far away. I ordered the carriage instantly, and I got as far as Rouen. Oh, what joy to say to a man who obeys you—"Go to Rouen."

I had myself driven to the library, and I took out Hermann Herestauss's great treatise, *The Unrecognized Inhabitants of the Ancient and Modern World.*

Then, as I was getting back into my brougham I wanted to say: "To the station!" but cried—I did not say, I shouted—with a voice so loud that the people in the street turned round—"Home!" and I fell, mad with despair, on the cushions of the carriage. He had found and captured me again.

August 17th.

Ah! what a night! what a night! And yet it occurs to me that I ought to rejoice. I read till one o'clock in the morning. Hermann Herestauss is a doctor of philosophy and of theogony; he has written a complete history of the manifestations of those beings which wander mostly invisible about mankind, or are imagined by him as so doing; he treats exhaustively of their origin, of their domain, of the power which they exercise; and not one of them resembles the one who haunts me. One would say that ever since man could think he has had dim forebodings and fears of a new being, stronger than himself, his successor in the world; and that, feeling him near at hand, and being unable to foresee the real nature of this new master, he has in terror created all that fantastic crowd of occult beings vague phantoms born of fear.

But to continue. Having read till one o'clock, I went and seated myself at an open window to refresh brow and brain in the calm air of darkness.

The night was gentle and warm. How I should have loved this kind of a night long ago!

No moon. The stars at the back of the black sky glittered and trembled. Who dwell in those worlds up there? What forms? what living things? what animals? what plants? That which thinks in those distant universes, what knows it more than we? What power has it more than we? What sees it that we know not? And some day or another will not one of those beings, traversing space, appear upon the earth and conquer it, just as the Normans of old crossed the sea to subdue more feeble races?

We are so weak, so defenseless, so ignorant, so little, we here on this revolving speck of mud and water.

Thus dozing in the fresh evening breeze, I drowsed off.

But after I had slept about forty minutes, I opened my eyes, making no other movement, awoke by some confused fantastical emotion. At first I saw nothing; then, on a sudden, it seemed to me that a page of the open book lying on my table had just turned by itself. No breath of air came through the window. I was surprised, and I waited. At the end of about four minutes I saw, I saw, yes, I saw with my eyes another page lift itself and fold over down on the preceding one as though a finger had turned it. My arm-chair was empty, seemed empty; but

I understood that he was there, he, seated in my place, and that he was reading. With one furious leap, with the bound of a beast who has rebelled at last, and fallen on his master to tear him open, I crossed the room to seize, to grip him in my hands, to kill him! . . . But my chair, before I had reached it, was overturned, as though someone fled before me . . . my table tottered, my lamp fell and was extinguished, and my window shut itself as though a detected thief had leaped out into the night by catching both the sashes in his hands.

So, he fled! He was afraid, he was afraid of me!

Then . . . then . . . tomorrow . . . or the day after . . . or some day . . . I shall be able to get him down under my hands, and to crush him against the earth! Do not dogs sometimes bite and throttle their masters?

August 18th.
I have reflected all day. Oh yes, I shall obey him, follow his suggestions, accomplish all his desires, appear humble, submissive, cowardly! He is the strongest. But an hour will come . . .

August 19th.
I know . . . I know . . . I know all! I have read as follows in the *Revue du Monde Scientifique*: "Information of a curious nature comes to us from Rio de Janeiro. An epidemic of madness, comparable to those contagious crazes which attacked the European peoples during the Middle Ages, is, it seems, at present, raging in the Province of San Paulo. The inhabitants are leaving their houses in dismay, deserting their villages, and abandoning their crops, maintaining that they are being pursued, taken possession of, governed like a human herd of cattle, by certain invisible but tangible beings, resembling vampires, who suck upon their life-blood during their sleep, and who, besides that, take water and milk, but no other nourishment.

"Professor Don Pedro Henriquez, accompanied by several other scientists of the medical profession, is on his way to the province of San Paulo, to study on the spot the causes and the manifestations of this curious mania; he will then propose to the Emperor whatever measures he decides best for recalling these unhappy lunatics to their reason."

Ah! Ah! I remember, I remember the beautiful Brazilian three-master which passed up the Seine under my windows on the 8th of last May! I thought it so beautiful, so white, so gay! The Being was aboard it, coming from that distant country where his race was born! And he saw me! He saw that my dwelling was white, likewise; and he leaped from the ship to the river-banks. Oh, my God!

And now, I know, I divine. The kingdom of man is ended.

He has come. He whom primitive peoples dreaded with a naive terror, He who was exorcised by anxious priests, He whom sorcerers invoked in vain on sombre nights, He to whom the forebodings of man, the transitory master of the earth, have given the monstrous or gracious forms of gnomes and ghosts, of genii, of fairies, and of familiar spirits. After the vulgar conceptions of primitive fear came the clearer presentations of more highly developed minds. Mesmer first divined Him; and the doctors, as long as ten years ago, discovered the exact nature of His power before He himself had ever used it. They have played with this weapon of the new Lord, this domination of a mysterious will over a human soul made captive. They have called it magnetism, hypnotism, suggestion . . . what not? I have seen them, like careless children, amusing themselves with that dreadful power! Woe to us! Woe to Man! He is come, the . . . the . . . how calls he himself . . . the . . . it seems to me that he is crying out his name, and that I cannot hear it . . . the . . . yes . . . he is crying it . . . I am listening . . . I cannot . . . I repeat . . . the . . . Horla . . . I heard . . . the Horla . . . it is he . . . the Horla . . . he has come! . . .

Ah! the vulture has devoured the dove, and the wolf has devoured the sheep, the lion has devoured the buffalo with the pointed horns; and the man has slain the lion by arrows and by his knife and by powder. But the Horla will make of man what man has made of the horse, and of the ox: his thing, his servant, his food, by the sole power of his will. Woe unto us!

Nevertheless, the animal sometimes revolts and kills his master . . . and I, too, I wish . . . I shall be able . . . but I must first know what he is like, I must touch him, see him! Scientists say that the eyes of animals are different from ours, and do not distinguish things as ours do . . . Just so my eyes cannot distinguish this new-comer who oppresses me.

Why? Oh! now I remember the word; of the monk of Mont St. Michel: "Do we see the hundred-thousandth part of what exists? For instance, take the wind, which is the greatest force in nature, which knocks down men, lays low buildings, tears up trees by the roots, heaps the sea into mountains of water, destroys coasts, and hurls great ships upon the breakers, the wind which kills, which whistles, which moans, which roars, have you ever seen it? Can you see it? It exists, nevertheless."

And I continued to reflect: "My eye is so feeble, so imperfect, that it does not even distinguish solid bodies, if they are transparent such as glass! . . . And if a mirror without a quicksilver back bars the way, my eye allows me to throw myself up against it like a bird which, straying into a room, dashes its head to pieces against the window-panes. A thousand things beside deceive and confuse it. Then what wonder if it cannot see this new transparent body?"

A new being! Why not? Inevitably he must have arisen! Why should we be the last? We cannot see him as we do other beings created before ourselves? That is simply because his nature is more perfect, because his body is more subtilely and highly developed than ours, than ours so feeble, than ours conceived so roughly, encumbered with organs like over-complex springs, always fatigued, and always straining. For our body lives like a plant and like a beast, gaining a painful sustenance from air, from grasses, and from flesh. A living machine, the prey to sickness, to deformity, and to decay, it is of dust; a work at once coarse and delicate, irregular, pitifully simple, fantastic, and ill-made ingeniously; the first rough sketch of a being which might sometime be developed into something intelligent and perfect.

There are, after all, from the oyster up to the man, so few of us here on the earth. Why not one more, once the period which separates the appearances of different successive species has been accomplished?

Why not one more? Why not other trees with immense flowers dazzling and suffusing entire regions with their perfume? Why not other elements besides Fire, Air, Earth, and Water? They are four, only four, these nursing fathers of being! What a pity! Why are they not forty, four hundred, four thousand? How poor, how mean, how wretched is everything! Granted, but not freely; conceived, but without genius; executed, but with no lightness of touch! The elephant, forsooth, the hippopotamus, how graceful! The camel, how elegant!

But what say you of the butterfly, that flying flower? I dream of one large as a hundred worlds, with wings whose shape, whose beauty, whose color, and whose manner of motion I cannot even describe. But I see it . . . it is going from star to star refreshing and perfuming each with the light and harmonious breathing of its course! . . . And whole peoples, high up there, watch, in ecstasy and ravishment, its passing! . . .

* * * * *

What is the matter with me? It is he, he, the Horla, who haunts me and makes me dream such follies! He is within me. He has become my soul; I shall kill him!

August 20th.

I shall kill him. I have seen him. I sat down last night at my table, and I pretended to be absorbed in writing. I knew very well that he would come and prowl round me, very near, so near that perhaps I should be able to touch him, to seize him. And then! . . . then I should have the strength of desperation; I should have hands and knees, breast, and brow, and teeth, to strangle, to crush, to bite, to tear.

And, straining every sense, I watched for him.

I had lit my two lamps and the eight candles on my mantel, exactly as though the light would help me to discover him!

Before me was my bed, an old oak bedstead with columns. On my right the chimney-piece. On my left the door, which I had carefully shut, after leaving it open for a while in order to attract him. Behind me, a tall wardrobe, with a looking-glass which I used every day for shaving and for dressing, and in which, every time I passed it, I had a habit of looking myself over from head to foot.

So I pretended to write in order to deceive him; for he, too, was watching. And suddenly I felt, I was certain, that he was reading over my shoulder, that he was there almost brushing my ear.

I jumped up with out-stretched hands, and turned round so quickly that I almost fell. Well? In my chamber it was as light as day, but I did not see myself in the glass! . . . It was empty, clear, deep, full of light! My image was not in it . . . and I stood there right in front of it, I! The great glass was clear from top to bottom. And with wild eyes I stared at this thing; and I did not dare to advance, I did not dare to move, feeling indeed that he was there, but that he would escape me, he, whose invisible body had absorbed the reflection of mine.

What fear I suffered! Then, all of a sudden, I began to perceive myself in a mist at the back of the mirror, in a mist as though through a sheet of water; and it seemed to me that this water glided from left to right, slowly, making my figure clearer, from second to second. It was like the ending of an eclipse. That which concealed me did not appear to possess sharp outlines, but merely a kind of opaque transparence, rarefying itself little by little.

At last I could distinguish my whole figure, just as I do each day when I look.

I had seen him! The terror of it remains still on me, causing me still to shiver.

August 21st.

Kill him? How? Since I cannot reach him? Poison? But he would see me mixing it in the water; and, besides, would our poisons have any effect on his supersensual body? No . . . no . . . of course not . . . What then? . . . what then?

August 22d.
I have had up a locksmith from Rouen, and I have ordered for my room some iron shutters like those which certain private houses in Paris have on the ground-floor as a protection against robbers. He is also to make me an iron door. I am appearing like a great coward, but at that I laugh! . . .

Sept. 10th.
Rouen. Hôtel Continental. It is accomplished . . . it is accomplished . . . but is he dead? My soul is overwhelmed by what I have seen.

Yesterday the locksmith, having fitted my shutters and my iron door, I left everything open until midnight, although it began to be very cold.

All of a sudden I felt that he was there, and a joy, a mad joy seized me. I rose gently, and I walked up and down for a long time in order to put him off his guard. Then I carelessly took off my boots and put on my slippers. Then I closed my iron shutters, and, returning tranquilly to the door, I closed that also and double-locked it. Again returning to the window, I secured the shutter with a padlock, and put the key in my pocket.

All of a sudden I understood that he was stirring anxiously round me; that, in his turn now, he was afraid; that he was commanding me to open. I came near yielding; I did not yield, but, setting my back against the door, I opened it on a crack just wide enough for me to pass through backward; and as I am very tall, my head touched the lintel. I was sure that he could not have escaped, and I shut him in all alone—all alone! What happiness! I had him fast! Then I went downstairs, running. In the drawing-room under my bedchamber I took the two lamps, and I poured oil over the carpet, over the furniture, over everything; then I set fire to it and I escaped from the house after having double-locked on the outside the great hall door.

And I hid myself at the bottom of the garden in a thicket of laurels. How long it was! How long it was! All remained black, silent, immobile; not a breath of air, not a star in the great mountains of clouds which I could not see, but which rested on my soul so heavily, so heavily.

I watched my house and I waited. How long it was! I had begun to think that the fire had gone out of itself, or that he had extinguished it. Then one of the windows on the ground-floor cracked under the pressure of the inner conflagration, and a tongue of flame—a great tongue of red and yellow flame—long and soft and caressing, climbed up along the white wall and kissed the very roof. A glow ran over the trees, the branches, the leaves, and a shiver—a shiver of fear also! The birds awoke; a dog began to howl; it seemed to me that the day itself was getting up! Soon two other windows burst open, and I saw that the whole ground-floor of my house was nothing but a dreadful brazier. But a cry—an awful cry—sharp, heart-rending—a woman's shriek—came out into the night, and two windows in the garret opened! I had forgotten my servants! I saw their wild faces, their waving arms! . . .

Then, mad with horror, I set off running to the village, shouting "Help! help! Fire! fire!" I met people already hastening to the scene, and I returned with them to look!

The house was now simply a horrible and magnificent stake—a monstrous stake—illuminating all the country—a stake at which men were burning, and at which he burned also—He, He, my prisoner, the new Being, the new master, the Horla!

Suddenly the entire roof fell in between the walls, and a volcano of flame shot upward to the sky. Through the windows open upon the furnace I saw the fiery vat, and I thought: he is there in that burning oven—dead . . .

Dead? Perhaps . . . But his body? His body, which the light of day could pass through, is it not perhaps indestructible by such means as destroy our bodies?

What if he be not dead? . . . Time alone, perhaps, has power over the Being Invisible, the Being Terrible. Why a transparent body? why an imperceptible body? why the body of a Spirit, if he too must fear misfortunes, wounds, infirmities, premature destruction?

Premature destruction? All human terror springs from the idea of that. After Man, the Horla. After him who can die any day, any hour, any moment, by any accident, has come He who shall die only on his appointed day, at his appointed hour, at his appointed minute, having touched the appointed limit of existence!

No . . . no . . . there is no doubt, there is no doubt . . . I have not killed him . . . Then . . . then . . . I see . . . it is plain . . . yes, it is plain that I must . . . kill . . . myself!

The Willows

Algernon Blackwood

I

After leaving Vienna, and long before you come to Budapest, the Danube enters a region of singular loneliness and desolation, where its waters spread away on all sides regardless of a main channel, and the country becomes a swamp for miles upon miles, covered by a vast sea of low willow-bushes. On the big maps this deserted area is painted in a fluffy blue, growing fainter in color as it leaves the banks, and across it may be seen in large straggling letters the word *Sümpfe*, meaning marshes.

In high flood this great acreage of sand, shingle-beds, and willow-grown islands is almost topped by the water, but in normal seasons the bushes bend and rustle in the free winds, showing their silver leaves to the sunshine in an ever-moving plain of bewildering beauty. These willows never attain to the dignity of trees; they have no rigid trunks; they remain humble bushes, with rounded tops and soft outline, swaying on slender stems that answer to the least pressure of the wind; supple as grasses, and so continually shifting that they somehow give the impression that the entire plain is moving and alive. For the wind sends waves rising and falling over the whole surface, waves of leaves instead of waves of water, green swells like the sea, too, until the branches turn and lift, and then silvery white as their underside turns to the sun.

Happy to slip beyond the control of the stern banks, the Danube here wanders about at will among the intricate network of channels intersecting the islands everywhere with broad avenues down which the waters pour with a shouting sound; making whirlpools, eddies, and foaming rapids; tearing at the sandy banks; carrying away masses of shore and willow-clumps; and forming new islands innumerably which shift daily in size and shape and possess at best an impermanent life, since the flood-time obliterates their very existence.

Properly speaking, this fascinating part of the river's life begins soon after leaving Pressburg, and we, in our Canadian canoe, with gipsy tent and frying-pan on board, reached it on the crest of a rising flood about mid-July. That very same morning, when the sky was reddening before sunrise, we had slipped swiftly through still-sleeping Vienna, leaving it a couple of hours later a mere patch of smoke against the blue hills of the Wienerwald on the horizon; we had breakfasted below Fischeramend under a grove of birch trees roaring in the wind; and had then swept on the tearing current past Orth, Hainburg, Petronell (the old Roman Carnuntum of Marcus Aurelius), and so under the frowning heights of Thelsen on a spur of the Carpathians, where the March steals in quietly from the left and the frontier is crossed between Austria and Hungary.

Racing along at twelve kilometers an hour soon took us well into Hungary, and the muddy waters—sure sign of flood—sent us aground on many a shingle-bed, and twisted us like a cork in many a sudden belching whirlpool before the towers of Pressburg (Hungarian, Poszony) showed against the sky; and then the canoe, leaping like a spirited horse, flew at top speed under the grey walls, negotiated safely the sunken chain of the Fliegende Brucke ferry, turned the corner sharply to the left, and plunged on yellow foam into the wilderness of islands, sandbanks, and swamp-land beyond—the land of the willows.

The change came suddenly, as when a series of bioscope pictures snaps down on the streets of a town and shifts without warning into the scenery of lake and forest. We entered the land of desolation on wings, and in less than half an hour there was neither boat nor fishing-hut nor red roof, nor any single sign of human habitation and civilization within sight. The sense of remoteness from the world of humankind, the utter isolation, the fascination of this singular world of willows, winds, and waters, instantly laid its spell upon us both, so that we allowed laughingly to one another that we ought by rights to have held some special kind of passport to admit us, and that we had, somewhat audaciously, come without asking leave into a separate little kingdom of wonder and magic—a kingdom that was reserved for the use of others who had a right to it, with everywhere unwritten warnings to trespassers for those who had the imagination to discover them.

Though still early in the afternoon, the ceaseless buffetings of a most tempestuous wind made us feel weary, and we at once began casting about for a suitable camping-ground for the night. But the bewildering character of the islands made landing difficult; the swirling flood carried us in shore and then swept us out again; the willow branches tore our hands as we seized them to stop the canoe, and we pulled many a yard of sandy bank into the water before at length we shot with a great sideways blow from the wind into a backwater and managed to beach the bows in a cloud of spray. Then we lay panting and laughing after our exertions on the hot yellow sand, sheltered from the wind, and in the full blaze of a scorching sun, a cloudless blue sky above, and an immense army of dancing, shouting willow bushes, closing in from all sides, shining with spray and clapping their thousand little hands as though to applaud the success of our efforts.

"What a river!" I said to my companion, thinking of all the way we had traveled from the source in the Black Forest, and how he had often been obliged to wade and push in the upper shallows at the beginning of June.

"Won't stand much nonsense now, will it?" he said, pulling the canoe a little farther into safety up the sand, and then composing himself for a nap.

I lay by his side, happy and peaceful in the bath of the elements—water, wind, sand, and the great fire of the sun—thinking of the long journey that lay behind us, and of the great stretch before us to the Black Sea, and how lucky I was to have such a delightful and charming traveling companion as my friend, the Swede.

We had made many similar journeys together, but the Danube, more than any other river I knew, impressed us from the very beginning with its aliveness. From its tiny bubbling entry into the world among the pinewood gardens of Donaueschingen, until this moment when it began to play the great river-game of losing itself among the deserted swamps, unobserved, unrestrained, it had seemed to us like following the growth of some living creature. Sleepy at first, but later developing violent desires as it became conscious of its deep soul, it rolled, like some huge fluid being, through all the countries we had passed, holding our little craft on its mighty shoulders, playing roughly with us sometimes, yet always friendly and well-meaning, till at length we had come inevitably to regard it as a Great Personage.

How, indeed, could it be otherwise, since it told us so much of its secret life? At night we heard it singing to the moon as we lay in our tent, uttering that odd sibilant note peculiar to itself and said to be caused by the rapid tearing of the pebbles along its bed, so great is its hurrying speed. We knew, too, the voice of its gurgling whirlpools, suddenly bubbling up on a surface previously quite calm; the roar of its shallows and swift rapids; its constant steady thundering below all mere surface sounds; and that ceaseless tearing of its icy waters at the banks. How it stood up and shouted when the rains fell flat upon its face! And how its laughter roared out when the wind blew up-stream and tried to stop its growing speed! We knew all its sounds and voices, its tumblings and foamings, its unnecessary splashing against the bridges; that self-conscious chatter when there were hills to look on; the affected dignity of its speech when it passed through the little towns, far too important to laugh; and all these faint, sweet whisperings when the sun caught it fairly in some slow curve and poured down upon it till the steam rose.

It was full of tricks, too, in its early life before the great world knew it. There were places in the upper reaches among the Swabian forests, when yet the first whispers of its destiny had not reached it, where it elected to disappear through holes in the ground, to appear again on the other side of the porous limestone hills and start a new river with another name; leaving, too, so little water in its own bed that we had to climb out and wade and push the canoe through miles of shallows.

And a chief pleasure, in those early days of its irresponsible youth, was to lie low, like Brer Fox, just before the little turbulent tributaries came to join it from the Alps, and to refuse to acknowledge them when in, but to run for miles side by side, the dividing line well marked, the very levels different, the Danube utterly declining to recognize the newcomer. Below Passau, however, it gave up this particular trick, for there the Inn comes in with a thundering power impossible to ignore, and so pushes and incommodes the parent river that there is hardly room for them in the long twisting gorge that follows, and the Danube is shoved this way and that against the cliffs, and forced to hurry itself with great waves and much dashing to and fro in order to get through in time. And during the fight our canoe slipped down from its shoulder to its breast, and had the time of its life among the struggling waves. But the Inn taught the old river a lesson, and after Passau it no longer pretended to ignore new arrivals.

This was many days back, of course, and since then we had come to know other aspects of the great creature, and across the Bavarian wheat plain of Straubing she wandered so slowly under the blazing June sun that we could well imagine only the surface inches were water, while below there moved, concealed as by a silken mantle, a whole army of Undines, passing silently and unseen down to the sea, and very leisurely too, lest they be discovered.

Much, too, we forgave her because of her friendliness to the birds and animals that haunted the shores. Cormorants lined the banks in lonely places in rows like short black palings; grey crows crowded the shingle-beds; storks stood fishing in the vistas of shallower water that opened up between the islands, and hawks, swans, and marsh birds of all sorts filled the air with glinting wings and singing, petulant cries. It was impossible to feel annoyed with the river's vagaries after seeing a deer leap with a splash into the water at sunrise and swim past the bows of the canoe; and often we saw fawns peering at us from the underbrush, or looked straight into the brown eyes of a stag as we charged full tilt round a corner and entered another reach of the river. Foxes, too, everywhere haunted the banks, tripping daintily among the driftwood and disappearing so suddenly that it was impossible to see how they managed it.

But now, after leaving Pressburg, everything changed a little, and the Danube became more serious. It ceased trifling. It was half-way to the Black

Sea, within seeming distance almost of other, stranger countries where no tricks would be permitted or understood. It became suddenly grown-up, and claimed our respect and even our awe. It broke out into three arms, for one thing, that only met again a hundred kilometers farther down, and for a canoe there were no indications which one was intended to be followed.

"If you take a side channel," said the Hungarian officer we met in the Pressburg shop while buying provisions, "you may find yourselves, when the flood subsides, forty miles from anywhere, high and dry, and you may easily starve. There are no people, no farms, no fishermen. I warn you not to continue. The river, too, is still rising, and this wind will increase."

The rising river did not alarm us in the least, but the matter of being left high and dry by a sudden subsidence of the waters might be serious, and we had consequently laid in an extra stock of provisions. For the rest, the officer's prophecy held true, and the wind, blowing down a perfectly clear sky, increased steadily till it reached the dignity of a westerly gale.

It was earlier than usual when we camped, for the sun was a good hour or two from the horizon, and leaving my friend still asleep on the hot sand, I wandered about in desultory examination of our hotel. The island, I found, was less than an acre in extent, a mere sandy bank standing some two or three feet above the level of the river. The far end, pointing into the sunset, was covered with flying spray which the tremendous wind drove off the crests of the broken waves. It was triangular in shape, with the apex up stream.

I stood there for several minutes, watching the impetuous crimson flood bearing down with a shouting roar, dashing in waves against the bank as though to sweep it bodily away, and then swirling by in two foaming streams on either side. The ground seemed to shake with the shock and rush, while the furious movement of the willow bushes as the wind poured over them increased the curious illusion that the island itself actually moved. Above, for a mile or two, I could see the great river descending upon me; it was like looking up the slope of a sliding hill, white with foam, and leaping up everywhere to show itself to the sun.

The rest of the island was too thickly grown with willows to make walking pleasant, but I made the tour, nevertheless. From the lower end the light, of course, changed, and the river looked dark and angry. Only the backs of the flying waves were visible, streaked with foam, and pushed forcibly by the great puffs of wind that fell upon them from behind. For a short mile it was visible, pouring in and out among the islands, and then disappearing with a huge sweep into the willows, which closed about it like a herd of monstrous antediluvian creatures crowding down to drink. They made me think of gigantic sponge-like growths that sucked the river up into themselves. They caused it to vanish from sight. They herded there together in such overpowering numbers.

Altogether it was an impressive scene, with its utter loneliness, its bizarre suggestion; and as I gazed, long and curiously, a singular emotion began to stir somewhere in the depths of me. Midway in my delight of the wild beauty, there crept, unbidden and unexplained, a curious feeling of disquietude, almost of alarm.

A rising river, perhaps, always suggests something of the ominous; many of the little islands I saw before me would probably have been swept away by the morning; this resistless, thundering flood of water touched the sense of awe. Yet I was aware that my uneasiness lay deeper far than the emotions of awe and wonder. It was not that I felt. Nor had it directly to do with the power of the driving wind—this shouting hurricane that might almost carry up a few acres of willows into the air and scatter them like so much chaff over the landscape. The wind was simply enjoying itself, for nothing rose out of the flat landscape to stop it, and I was conscious of sharing its great game with a kind of pleasurable excitement. Yet this novel emotion had nothing to do with the wind. Indeed, so vague was the sense of distress I experienced, that it was impossible to trace it to its source and deal with it accordingly, though I was aware somehow that it had to do with my realization of our utter insignificance before this unrestrained power of the elements about me. The huge-grown river had something to do with it too—a vague, unpleasant idea that we had somehow trifled with these great elemental forces in whose power we lay helpless every hour of the day and night. For here, indeed, they were gigantically at play together, and the sight appealed to the imagination.

But my emotion, so far as I could understand it, seemed to attach itself more particularly to the willow bushes, to these acres and acres of willows, crowding, so thickly growing there, swarming everywhere the eye could reach, pressing upon the river as though to suffocate it, standing in dense array mile after mile beneath the sky, watching, waiting, listening. And, apart quite from the elements, the willows connected themselves subtly with my malaise, attacking the mind insidiously somehow by reason of their vast numbers, and contriving in some way or other to represent to the imagination a new and mighty power, a power, moreover, not altogether friendly to us.

Great revelations of nature, of course, never fail to impress in one way or another, and I was no stranger to moods of the kind. Mountains overawe and oceans terrify, while the mystery of great forests exercises a spell peculiarly its own. But all these, at one point or another, somewhere link on intimately with human life and human experience. They stir comprehensible, even if alarming, emotions. They tend on the whole to exalt.

With this multitude of willows, however, it was something far different, I felt. Some essence emanated from them that besieged the heart. A sense of awe awakened, true, but of awe touched somewhere by a vague terror. Their serried ranks, growing everywhere darker about me as the shadows deepened, moving furiously yet softly in the wind, woke in me the curious and unwelcome suggestion that we had trespassed here upon the borders of an alien world, a world where we were intruders, a world where we were not wanted or invited to remain—where we ran grave risks perhaps!

The feeling, however, though it refused to yield its meaning entirely to analysis, did not at the time trouble me by passing into menace. Yet it never left me quite, even during the very practical business of putting up the tent in a hurricane of wind and building a fire for the stew-pot. It remained, just enough to bother and perplex, and to rob a most delightful camping-ground of a good portion of its charm. To my companion, however, I said nothing, for he was a man I considered devoid of imagination. In the first place, I could never have explained to him what I meant, and in the second, he would have laughed stupidly at me if I had.

There was a slight depression in the center of the island, and here we pitched the tent. The surrounding willows broke the wind a bit.

"A poor camp," observed the imperturbable Swede when at last the tent stood upright, "no stones and precious little firewood. I'm for moving on early tomorrow—eh? This sand won't hold anything."

But the experience of a collapsing tent at midnight had taught us many devices, and we made the cozy gipsy house as safe as possible, and then set about collecting a store of wood to last till bed-time. Willow bushes drop no branches, and driftwood was our only source of supply. We hunted the shores pretty thoroughly. Everywhere the banks were crumbling as the rising flood tore at them and carried away great portions with a splash and a gurgle.

"The island's much smaller than when we landed," said the accurate Swede. "It won't last long at this rate. We'd better drag the canoe close to the tent, and be ready to start at a moment's notice. I shall sleep in my clothes."

He was a little distance off, climbing along the bank, and I heard his rather jolly laugh as he spoke.

"By Jove!" I heard him call, a moment later, and turned to see what had caused his exclamation. But for the moment he was hidden by the willows, and I could not find him.

"What in the world's this?" I heard him cry again, and this time his voice had become serious.

I ran up quickly and joined him on the bank. He was looking over the river, pointing at something in the water.

"Good heavens, it's a man's body!" he cried excitedly. "Look!"

A black thing, turning over and over in the foaming waves, swept rapidly past. It kept disappearing and coming up to the surface again. It was about twenty feet from the shore, and just as it was opposite to where we stood it lurched round and looked straight at us. We saw its eyes reflecting the sunset, and gleaming an odd yellow as the body turned over. Then it gave a swift, gulping plunge, and dived out of sight in a flash.

"An otter, by gad!" we exclaimed in the same breath, laughing.

It was an otter, alive, and out on the hunt; yet it had looked exactly like the body of a drowned man turning helplessly in the current. Far below it came to the surface once again, and we saw its black skin, wet and shining in the sunlight.

Then, too, just as we turned back, our arms full of driftwood, another thing happened to recall us to the river bank. This time it really was a man, and what was more, a man in a boat. Now a small boat on the Danube was an unusual sight at any time, but here in this deserted region, and at flood time, it was so unexpected as to constitute a real event. We stood and stared.

Whether it was due to the slanting sunlight, or the refraction from the wonderfully illumined water, I cannot say, but, whatever the cause, I found it difficult to focus my sight properly upon the flying apparition. It seemed, however, to be a man standing upright in a sort of flat-bottomed boat, steering with a long oar, and being carried down the opposite shore at a tremendous pace. He apparently was looking across in our direction, but the distance was too great and the light too uncertain for us to make out very plainly what he was about. It seemed to me that he was gesticulating and making signs at us. His voice came across the water to us shouting something furiously, but the wind drowned it so that no single word was audible. There was something curious about the whole appearance—man, boat, signs, voice—that made an impression on me out of all proportion to its cause.

"He's crossing himself!" I cried. "Look, he's making the sign of the Cross!"

"I believe you're right," the Swede said, shading his eyes with his hand and watching the man out of sight. He seemed to be gone in a moment, melting away down there into the sea of willows where the sun caught them in the bend of the river and turned them into a great crimson wall of beauty. Mist, too, had begun to ruse, so that the air was hazy.

"But what in the world is he doing at nightfall on this flooded river?" I said, half to myself. "Where is he going at such a time, and what did he mean by his signs and shouting? D'you think he wished to warn us about something?"

"He saw our smoke, and thought we were spirits probably," laughed my companion. "These Hungarians believe in all sorts of rubbish; you remember the shopwoman at Pressburg warning us that no one ever landed here because it belonged to some sort of beings outside man's world! I suppose they believe in fairies and elementals, possibly demons, too. That peasant in the boat saw people on the islands for the first time in his life," he added, after a slight pause, "and it scared him, that's all."

The Swede's tone of voice was not convincing, and his manner lacked something that was usually there. I noted the change instantly while he talked, though without being able to label it precisely.

"If they had enough imagination," I laughed loudly—I remember trying to make as much noise as I could—"they might well people a place like this with the old gods of antiquity. The Romans must have haunted all this region more or less with their shrines and sacred groves and elemental deities."

The subject dropped and we returned to our stew-pot, for my friend was not given to imaginative conversation as a rule. Moreover, just then I remember feeling distinctly glad that he was not imaginative; his stolid, practical nature suddenly seemed to me welcome and comforting. It was an admirable temperament, I felt; he could steer down rapids like a red Indian, shoot dangerous bridges and whirlpools better than any white man I ever saw in a canoe. He was a grand fellow for an adventurous trip, a tower of strength when untoward things happened. I looked at his strong face and light curly hair as he staggered along under his pile of driftwood (twice the size of mine!), and I experienced a feeling of relief. Yes, I was distinctly glad just then that the Swede was—what he was, and that he never made remarks that suggested more than they said.

"The river's still rising, though," he added, as if following out some thoughts of his own, and dropping his load with a gasp. "This island will be under water in two days if it goes on."

"I wish the wind would go down," I said. "I don't care a fig for the river."

The flood, indeed, had no terrors for us; we could get off at ten minutes' notice, and the more water the better we liked it. It meant an increasing current and the obliteration of the treacherous shingle-beds that so often threatened to tear the bottom out of our canoe.

Contrary to our expectations, the wind did not go down with the sun. It seemed to increase with the darkness, howling overhead and shaking the willows round us like straws. Curious sounds accompanied it sometimes, like the explosion of heavy guns, and it fell upon the water and the island in great flat blows of immense power. It made me think of the sounds a planet must make, could we only hear it, driving along through space.

But the sky kept wholly clear of clouds, and soon after supper the full moon rose up in the east and covered the river and the plain of shouting willows with a light like the day.

We lay on the sandy patch beside the fire, smoking, listening to the noises of the night round us, and talking happily of the journey we had already made, and of our plans ahead. The map lay spread in the door of the tent, but the high wind made it hard to study, and presently we lowered the curtain and extinguished the lantern. The firelight was enough to smoke and see each other's faces by, and the sparks flew about overhead like fireworks. A few yards beyond, the river gurgled and hissed, and from time to time a heavy splash announced the falling away of further portions of the bank.

Our talk, I noticed, had to do with the faraway scenes and incidents of our first camps in the Black Forest, or of other subjects altogether remote from the present setting, for neither of us spoke of the actual moment more than was necessary—almost as though we had agreed tacitly to avoid discussion of the camp and its incidents. Neither the otter nor the boatman, for instance, received the honor of a single mention, though ordinarily these would have furnished discussion for the greater part of the evening. They were, of course, distinct events in such a place.

The scarcity of wood made it a business to keep the fire going, for the wind, that drove the smoke in our faces wherever we sat, helped at the same time to make a forced draught. We took it in turn to make some foraging expeditions into the darkness, and the quantity the Swede brought back always made me feel that he took an absurdly long time finding it; for the fact was I did not care much about being left alone, and yet it always seemed to be my turn to grub about among the bushes or scramble along the slippery banks in the moonlight. The long day's battle with wind and water—such wind and such water!—had tired us both, and an early bed was the obvious program. Yet neither of us made the move for the tent. We lay there, tending the fire, talking in desultory fashion, peering about us into the dense willow bushes, and listening to the thunder of wind and river. The loneliness of the place had entered our very bones, and silence seemed natural, for after a bit the sound of our voices became a trifle unreal and forced; whispering would have been the fitting mode of communication, I felt, and the human voice, always rather absurd amid the roar of the elements, now carried with it something almost illegitimate. It was like talking out loud in church, or in some place where it was not lawful, perhaps not quite safe, to be overheard.

The eeriness of this lonely island, set among a million willows, swept by a hurricane, and surrounded by hurrying deep waters, touched us both, I fancy. Untrodden by man, almost unknown to man, it lay there beneath the moon, remote from human influence, on the frontier of another world, an alien world, a world tenanted by willows only and the souls of willows. And we, in our rashness, had dared to invade it, even to make use of it! Something more than the power of its mystery stirred in me as I lay on the sand, feet to fire, and peered up through the leaves at the stars. For the last time I rose to get firewood.

"When this has burnt up," I said firmly, "I shall turn in," and my companion watched me lazily as I moved off into the surrounding shadows.

For an unimaginative man I thought he seemed unusually receptive that night, unusually open to suggestion of things other than sensory. He too was touched by the beauty and loneliness of the place. I was not altogether pleased, I remember, to recognize this slight change in him, and instead of immediately collecting sticks, I made my way to the far point of the island where the moonlight on plain and river could be seen to better advantage. The desire to be alone had come suddenly upon me; my former dread returned in force; there was a vague feeling in me I wished to face and probe to the bottom.

When I reached the point of sand jutting out among the waves, the spell of the place descended upon me with a positive shock. No mere "scenery" could have produced such an effect. There was something more here, something to alarm.

I gazed across the waste of wild waters; I watched the whispering willows; I heard the ceaseless beating of the tireless wind; and, one and all, each in its own way, stirred in me this sensation of a strange distress. But the willows especially; for ever they went on chattering and talking among themselves, laughing a little, shrilly crying out, sometimes sighing—but what it was they made so much to-do about belonged to the secret life of the great plain they inhabited. And it was utterly alien to the world I knew, or to that of the wild yet kindly elements. They made me think of a host of beings from another plane of life, another evolution altogether, perhaps, all discussing a mystery known only to themselves. I watched them moving busily together, oddly shaking their big bushy heads, twirling their myriad leaves even when there was no wind. They moved of their own will as though alive, and they touched, by some incalculable method, my own keen sense of the horrible.

There they stood in the moonlight, like a vast army surrounding our camp, shaking their innumerable silver spears defiantly, formed all ready for an attack.

The psychology of places, for some imaginations at least, is very vivid; for the wanderer, especially, camps have their "note" either of welcome or rejection. At first it may not always be apparent, because the busy preparations of tent and cooking prevent, but with the first pause—after supper usually—it comes and announces itself. And the note of this willow-camp now became unmistakably plain to me; we were interlopers, trespassers; we were not welcomed. The sense of unfamiliarity grew upon me as I stood there watching. We touched the frontier of a region where our presence was resented. For a night's lodging we might perhaps be tolerated; but for a prolonged and inquisitive stay—No! by all the gods of the trees and wilderness, no! We were the first human influences upon this island, and we were not wanted. The willows were against us.

Strange thoughts like these, bizarre fancies, borne I know not whence, found lodgment in my mind as I stood listening. What, I thought, if, after all, these crouching willows proved to be alive; if suddenly they should rise up, like a swarm of living creatures, marshaled by the gods whose territory we had invaded, sweep towards us off the vast swamps, booming overhead in the night—and then settle down! As I looked it was so easy to imagine they actually moved, crept nearer, retreated a little, huddled together in masses, hostile, waiting for the great wind that should finally start them a-running. I could have sworn their aspect changed a little, and their ranks deepened and pressed more closely together.

The melancholy shrill cry of a night-bird sounded overhead, and suddenly I nearly lost my balance as the piece of bank I stood upon fell with a great splash into the river, undermined by the flood. I stepped back just in time, and went on hunting for firewood again, half laughing at the odd fancies that crowded so thickly into my mind and cast their spell upon me. I recalled the Swede's remark about moving on next day, and I was just thinking that I fully agreed with him, when I turned with a start and saw the subject of my thoughts standing immediately in front of me. He was quite close. The roar of the elements had covered his approach.

II

"You've been gone so long," he shouted above the wind, "I thought something must have happened to you."

But there was that in his tone, and a certain look in his face as well, that conveyed to me more than his usual words, and in a flash I understood the real reason for his coming. It was because the spell of the place had entered his soul too, and he did not like being alone.

"River still rising," he cried, pointing to the flood in the moonlight, "and the wind's simply awful."

He always said the same things, but it was the cry for companionship that gave the real importance to his words.

"Lucky," I cried back, "our tent's in the hollow. I think it'll hold all right." I added something about the difficulty of finding wood, in order to explain my absence, but the wind caught my words and flung them across the river, so that he did not hear, but just looked at me through the branches, nodding his head.

"Lucky if we get away without disaster!" he shouted, or words to that effect; and I remember feeling half angry with him for putting the thought into words, for it was exactly what I felt myself. There was disaster impending somewhere, and the sense of presentiment lay unpleasantly upon me.

We went back to the fire and made a final blaze, poking it up with our feet. We took a last look round. But for the wind the heat would have been unpleasant. I put this thought into words, and I remember my friend's reply struck me oddly: that he would rather have the heat, the ordinary July weather, than this "diabolical wind."

Everything was snug for the night; the canoe lying turned over beside the tent, with both yellow paddles beneath her; the provision sack hanging from a willow-stem, and the washed-up dishes removed to a safe distance from the fire, all ready for the morning meal.

We smothered the embers of the fire with sand, and then turned in. The flap of the tent door was up, and I saw the branches and the stars and the white moonlight. The shaking willows and the heavy buffetings of the wind against our taut little house were the last things I remembered as sleep came down and covered all with its soft and delicious forgetfulness.

Suddenly I found myself lying awake, peering from my sandy mattress through the door of the tent. I looked at my watch pinned against the canvas, and saw by the bright moonlight that it was past twelve o'clock—the threshold of a new day—and I had therefore slept a couple of hours. The Swede was asleep still beside me; the wind howled as before; something plucked at my heart and made me feel afraid. There was a sense of disturbance in my immediate neighborhood.

I sat up quickly and looked out. The trees were swaying violently to and fro as the gusts smote them, but our little bit of green canvas lay snugly safe in the hollow, for the wind passed over it without meeting enough resistance to make it vicious. The feeling of disquietude did not pass, however, and I crawled quietly out of the tent to see if our belongings were safe. I moved carefully so as not to waken my companion. A curious excitement was on me.

I was half-way out, kneeling on all fours, when my eye first took in that the tops of the bushes opposite, with their moving tracery of leaves, made shapes against the sky. I sat back on my haunches and stared. It was incredible, surely, but there, opposite and slightly above me, were shapes of some indeterminate sort among the willows, and as the branches swayed in the wind they seemed to group themselves about these shapes, forming a series of monstrous outlines that shifted rapidly beneath the moon. Close, about fifty feet in front of me, I saw these things.

My first instinct was to waken my companion, that he too might see them, but something made me hesitate—the sudden realization, probably, that I should not welcome corroboration; and meanwhile I crouched there staring in amazement with smarting eyes. I was wide awake. I remember saying to myself that I was not dreaming.

They first became properly visible, these huge figures, just within the tops of the bushes—immense, bronze-colored, moving, and wholly independent of the swaying of the branches. I saw them plainly and noted, now I came to examine them more calmly, that they were very much larger than human, and indeed that something in their appearance proclaimed them to be not human at all. Certainly they were not merely the moving tracery of the branches against the moonlight. They shifted independently. They rose upwards in a continuous stream from earth to sky, vanishing utterly as soon as they reached the dark of the sky. They were interlaced one with another, making a great column, and I saw their limbs and huge bodies melting in and out of each other, forming this serpentine line that bent and swayed and twisted spirally with the contortions of the wind-tossed trees. They were nude, fluid shapes, passing up the bushes, within the leaves almost—rising up in a living column into the heavens. Their faces I never could see. Unceasingly they poured upwards, swaying in great bending curves, with a hue of dull bronze upon their skins.

I stared, trying to force every atom of vision from my eyes. For a long time I thought they must every moment disappear and resolve themselves into the movements of the branches and prove to be an optical illusion. I searched everywhere for a proof of reality, when all the while I understood quite well that the standard of reality had changed. For the longer I looked the more certain I became that these figures were real and living, though perhaps not according to the standards that the camera and the biologist would insist upon.

Far from feeling fear, I was possessed with a sense of awe and wonder such as I have never known. I seemed to be gazing at the personified elemental forces of this haunted and primeval region. Our intrusion had stirred the powers of the place into activity. It was we who were the cause of the disturbance, and my brain filled to bursting with stories and legends of the spirits and deities of places that have been acknowledged and worshipped by men in all ages of the world's history. But, before I could arrive at any possible explanation, something impelled me to go farther out, and I crept forward on the sand and stood upright. I felt the ground still warm under my bare feet; the wind tore at my hair and face; and the sound of the river burst upon my ears with a sudden roar. These things, I knew, were real, and proved that my senses were acting normally. Yet the figures still rose from earth to heaven, silent, majestically, in a great spiral of grace and strength that overwhelmed me at length with a genuine deep emotion of worship. I felt that I must fall down and worship—absolutely worship.

Perhaps in another minute I might have done so, when a gust of wind swept against me with such force that it blew me sideways, and I nearly stumbled and fell. It seemed to shake the dream violently out of me. At least it gave me another point of view somehow. The figures still remained, still ascended into heaven from the heart of the night, but my reason at last began to assert itself. It must be a subjective experience, I argued—none the less real for that, but still subjective. The moonlight and the branches combined to work out these pictures upon the mirror of my imagination, and for some reason I projected them outwards and made them appear objective. I knew this must be the case, of course. I took courage, and began to move forward across the open patches of sand. By Jove, though, was it all hallucination? Was it merely subjective? Did not my reason argue in the old futile way from the little standard of the known?

I only know that great column of figures ascended darkly into the sky for what seemed a very long period of time, and with a very complete measure of reality as most men are accustomed to gauge reality. Then suddenly they were gone!

And, once they were gone and the immediate wonder of their great presence had passed, fear came down upon me with a cold rush. The esoteric meaning of this lonely and haunted region suddenly flamed up within me, and I began to tremble dreadfully. I took a quick look round—a look of horror that came near to panic—calculating vainly ways of escape; and then, realizing how helpless

I was to achieve anything really effective, I crept back silently into the tent and lay down again upon my sandy mattress, first lowering the door-curtain to shut out the sight of the willows in the moonlight, and then burying my head as deeply as possible beneath the blankets to deaden the sound of the terrifying wind.

As though further to convince me that I had not been dreaming, I remember that it was a long time before I fell again into a troubled and restless sleep; and even then only the upper crust of me slept, and underneath there was something that never quite lost consciousness, but lay alert and on the watch.

But this second time I jumped up with a genuine start of terror. It was neither the wind nor the river that woke me, but the slow approach of something that caused the sleeping portion of me to grow smaller and smaller till at last it vanished altogether, and I found myself sitting bolt upright—listening.

Outside there was a sound of multitudinous little patterings. They had been coming, I was aware, for a long time, and in my sleep they had first become audible. I sat there nervously wide awake as though I had not slept at all. It seemed to me that my breathing came with difficulty, and that there was a great weight upon the surface of my body. In spite of the hot night, I felt clammy with cold and shivered. Something surely was pressing steadily against the sides of the tent and weighing down upon it from above. Was it the body of the wind? Was this the pattering rain, the dripping of the leaves? The spray blown from the river by the wind and gathering in big drops? I thought quickly of a dozen things.

Then suddenly the explanation leaped into my mind: a bough from the poplar, the only large tree on the island, had fallen with the wind. Still half caught by the other branches, it would fall with the next gust and crush us, and meanwhile its leaves brushed and tapped upon the tight canvas surface of the tent. I raised a loose flap and rushed out, calling to the Swede to follow.

But when I got out and stood upright I saw that the tent was free. There was no hanging bough; there was no rain or spray; nothing approached.

A cold, grey light filtered down through the bushes and lay on the faintly gleaming sand. Stars still crowded the sky directly overhead, and the wind howled magnificently, but the fire no longer gave out any glow, and I saw the east reddening in streaks through the trees. Several hours must have passed since I stood there before watching the ascending figures, and the memory of it now came back to me horribly, like an evil dream. Oh, how tired it made me feel, that ceaseless raging wind! Yet, though the deep lassitude of a sleepless night was on me, my nerves were tingling with the activity of an equally tireless apprehension, and all idea of repose was out of the question. The river I saw had risen further. Its thunder filled the air, and a fine spray made itself felt through my thin sleeping shirt.

Yet nowhere did I discover the slightest evidence of anything to cause alarm. This deep, prolonged disturbance in my heart remained wholly unaccounted for.

My companion had not stirred when I called him, and there was no need to waken him now. I looked about me carefully, noting everything; the turned-over canoe; the yellow paddles—two of them, I'm certain; the provision sack and the extra lantern hanging together from the tree; and, crowding everywhere about me, enveloping all, the willows, those endless, shaking willows. A bird uttered its morning cry, and a string of duck passed with whirring flight overhead in the twilight. The sand whirled, dry and stinging, about my bare feet in the wind.

I walked round the tent and then went out a little way into the bush, so that I could see across the river to the farther landscape, and the same profound yet indefinable emotion of distress seized upon me again as I saw the interminable sea of bushes stretching to the horizon, looking ghostly and unreal in the wan light of dawn. I walked softly here and there, still puzzling over that odd sound of infinite pattering, and of that pressure upon the tent that had wakened me. It must have been the wind, I reflected—the wind bearing upon the loose, hot sand, driving the dry particles smartly against the taut canvas—the wind dropping heavily upon our fragile roof.

Yet all the time my nervousness and malaise increased appreciably.

I crossed over to the farther shore and noted how the coast-line had altered in the night, and what masses of sand the river had torn away. I dipped my hands and feet into the cool current, and bathed my forehead. Already there was a glow of sunrise in the sky and the exquisite freshness of coming day. On my way back I passed purposely beneath the very bushes where I had seen the column of figures rising into the air, and midway among the clumps I suddenly found myself overtaken by a sense of vast terror. From the shadows a large figure went swiftly by. Someone passed me, as sure as ever man did . . .

It was a great staggering blow from the wind that helped me forward again, and once out in the more open space, the sense of terror diminished strangely. The winds were about and walking, I remember saying to myself, for the winds often move like great presences under the trees. And altogether the fear that hovered about me was such an unknown and immense kind of fear, so unlike anything I had ever felt before, that it woke a sense of awe and wonder in me that did much to counteract its worst effects; and when I reached a high point in the middle of the island from which I could see the wide stretch of river, crimson in the sunrise, the whole magical beauty of it all was so overpowering that a sort of wild yearning woke in me and almost brought a cry up into the throat.

But this cry found no expression, for as my eyes wandered from the plain beyond to the island round me and noted our little tent half hidden among the willows, a dreadful discovery leaped out at me, compared to which my terror of the walking winds seemed as nothing at all.

For a change, I thought, had somehow come about in the arrangement of the landscape. It was not that my point of vantage gave me a different view, but that an alteration had apparently been effected in the relation of the tent to the willows, and of the willows to the tent. Surely the bushes now crowded much closer—unnecessarily, unpleasantly close. They had moved nearer.

Creeping with silent feet over the shifting sands, drawing imperceptibly nearer by soft, unhurried movements, the willows had come closer during the night. But had the wind moved them, or had they moved of themselves? I recalled the sound of infinite small patterings and the pressure upon the tent and upon my own heart that caused me to wake in terror. I swayed for a moment in the wind like a tree, finding it hard to keep my upright position on the sandy hillock. There was a suggestion here of personal agency, of deliberate intention, of aggressive hostility, and it terrified me into a sort of rigidity.

Then the reaction followed quickly. The idea was so bizarre, so absurd, that I felt inclined to laugh. But the laughter came no more readily than the cry, for the knowledge that my mind was so receptive to such dangerous imaginings brought the additional terror that it was through our minds and not through our physical bodies that the attack would come, and was coming.

The wind buffeted me about, and, very quickly it seemed, the sun came up over the horizon, for it was after four o'clock, and I must have stood on that little pinnacle of sand longer than I knew, afraid to come down to close quarters with the willows. I returned quietly, creepily, to the tent, first taking another exhaustive look round and—yes, I confess it—making a few measurements. I paced out on the warm sand the distances between the willows and the tent, making a note of the shortest distance particularly.

I crawled stealthily into my blankets. My companion, to all appearances, still slept soundly, and I was glad that this was so. Provided my experiences were not corroborated, I could find strength somehow to deny them, perhaps. With the daylight I could persuade myself that it was all a subjective hallucination, a fantasy of the night, a projection of the excited imagination.

Nothing further came in to disturb me, and I fell asleep almost at once, utterly exhausted, yet still in dread of hearing again that weird sound of multitudinous pattering, or of feeling the pressure upon my heart that had made it difficult to breathe.

The sun was high in the heavens when my companion woke me from a heavy sleep and announced that the porridge was cooked and there was just time to bathe. The grateful smell of frizzling bacon entered the tent door.

"River still rising," he said, "and several islands out in mid-stream have disappeared altogether. Our own island's much smaller."

"Any wood left?" I asked sleepily.

"The wood and the island will finish tomorrow in a dead heat," he laughed, "but there's enough to last us till then."

I plunged in from the point of the island, which had indeed altered a lot in size and shape during the night, and was swept down in a moment to the landing-place opposite the tent. The water was icy, and the banks flew by like the country from an express train. Bathing under such conditions was an exhilarating operation, and the terror of the night seemed cleansed out of me by a process of evaporation in the brain. The sun was blazing hot; not a cloud showed itself anywhere; the wind, however, had not abated one little jot.

Quite suddenly then the implied meaning of the Swede's words flashed across me, showing that he no longer wished to leave post-haste, and had changed his mind. "Enough to last till tomorrow"—he assumed we should stay on the island another night. It struck me as odd. The night before he was so positive the other way. How had the change come about?

Great crumblings of the banks occurred at breakfast, with heavy splashings and clouds of spray which the wind brought into our frying-pan, and my fellow-traveler talked incessantly about the difficulty the Vienna-Pesth steamers must have to find the channel in flood. But the state of his mind interested and impressed me far more than the state of the river or the difficulties of the steamers. He had changed somehow since the evening before. His manner was different—a trifle excited, a trifle shy, with a sort of suspicion about his voice and gestures. I hardly know how to describe it now in cold blood, but at the time I remember being quite certain of one thing—that he had become frightened!

He ate very little breakfast, and for once omitted to smoke his pipe. He had the map spread open beside him, and kept studying its markings.

"We'd better get off sharp in an hour," I said presently, feeling for an opening that must bring him indirectly to a partial confession at any rate. And his answer puzzled me uncomfortably: "Rather! If they'll let us."

"Who'll let us? The elements?" I asked quickly, with affected indifference.

"The powers of this awful place, whoever they are," he replied, keeping his eyes on the map. "The gods are here, if they are anywhere at all in the world."

"The elements are always the true immortals," I replied, laughing as naturally as I could manage, yet knowing quite well that my face reflected my true feelings when he looked up gravely at me and spoke across the smoke:

"We shall be fortunate if we get away without further disaster."

This was exactly what I had dreaded, and I screwed myself up to the point of the direct question. It was like agreeing to allow the dentist to extract the tooth; it had to come anyhow in the long run, and the rest was all pretence.

"Further disaster! Why, what's happened?"

"For one thing—the steering paddle's gone," he said quietly.

"The steering paddle gone!" I repeated, greatly excited, for this was our rudder, and the Danube in flood without a rudder was suicide. "But what—"

"And there's a tear in the bottom of the canoe," he added, with a genuine little tremor in his voice.

I continued staring at him, able only to repeat the words in his face somewhat foolishly. There, in the heat of the sun, and on this burning sand, I was aware of a freezing atmosphere descending round us. I got up to follow him, for he merely nodded his head gravely and led the way towards the tent a few yards on the other side of the fireplace. The canoe still lay there as I had last seen her in the night, ribs uppermost, the paddles, or rather, the paddle, on the sand beside her.

"There's only one," he said, stooping to pick it up. "And here's the rent in the base-board."

It was on the tip of my tongue to tell him that I had clearly noticed two paddles a few hours before, but a second impulse made me think better of it, and I said nothing. I approached to see.

There was a long, finely made tear in the bottom of the canoe where a little slither of wood had been neatly taken clean out; it looked as if the tooth of a sharp rock or snag had eaten down her length, and investigation showed that the hole went through. Had we launched out in her without observing it we must inevitably have foundered. At first the water would have made the wood swell so as to close the hole, but once out in mid-stream the water must have poured in, and the canoe, never more than two inches above the surface, would have filled and sunk very rapidly.

"There, you see an attempt to prepare a victim for the sacrifice," I heard him saying, more to himself than to me, "two victims rather," he added as he bent over and ran his fingers along the slit.

I began to whistle—a thing I always do unconsciously when utterly nonplussed—and purposely paid no attention to his words. I was determined to consider them foolish.

"It wasn't there last night," he said presently, straightening up from his examination and looking anywhere but at me.

"We must have scratched her in landing, of course," I stopped whistling to say. "The stones are very sharp."

I stopped abruptly, for at that moment he turned round and met my eye squarely. I knew just as well as he did how impossible my explanation was. There were no stones, to begin with.

"And then there's this to explain too," he added quietly, handing me the paddle and pointing to the blade.

A new and curious emotion spread freezingly over me as I took and examined it. The blade was scraped down all over, beautifully scraped, as though someone had sand-papered it with care, making it so thin that the first vigorous stroke must have snapped it off at the elbow.

"One of us walked in his sleep and did this thing," I said feebly, "or—or it has been filed by the constant stream of sand particles blown against it by the wind, perhaps."

"Ah," said the Swede, turning away, laughing a little, "you can explain everything."

"The same wind that caught the steering paddle and flung it so near the bank that it fell in with the next lump that crumbled," I called out after him, absolutely determined to find an explanation for everything he showed me.

"I see," he shouted back, turning his head to look at me before disappearing among the willow bushes.

Once alone with these perplexing evidences of personal agency, I think my first thoughts took the form of "One of us must have done this thing, and it certainly was not I." But my second thought decided how impossible it was to suppose, under all the circumstances, that either of us had done it. That my companion, the trusted friend of a dozen similar expeditions, could have knowingly had a hand in it, was a suggestion not to be entertained for a moment. Equally absurd seemed the explanation that this imperturbable and densely practical nature had suddenly become insane and was busied with insane purposes.

Yet the fact remained that what disturbed me most, and kept my fear actively alive even in this blaze of sunshine and wild beauty, was the clear certainty that some curious alteration had come about in his mind—that he was nervous, timid, suspicious, aware of goings on he did not speak about, watching a series of secret and hitherto unmentionable events—waiting, in a word, for a climax that he expected, and, I thought, expected very soon. This grew up in my mind intuitively—I hardly knew how.

I made a hurried examination of the tent and its surroundings, but the measurements of the night remained the same. There were deep hollows formed in the sand I now noticed for the first time, basin-shaped and of various depths and sizes, varying from that of a tea-cup to a large bowl. The wind, no doubt, was responsible for these miniature craters, just as it was for lifting the paddle and tossing it towards the water. The rent in the canoe was the only thing that seemed quite inexplicable; and, after all, it was conceivable that a sharp point had caught it when we landed. The examination I made of the shore did not assist this theory, but all the same I clung to it with that diminishing portion of my intelligence which I called my "reason." An explanation of some kind was an absolute necessity, just as some working explanation of the universe is necessary—however absurd—to the happiness of every individual who seeks to do his duty in the world and face the problems of life. The simile seemed to me at the time an exact parallel.

I at once set the pitch melting, and presently the Swede joined me at the work, though under the best conditions in the world the canoe could not be safe for traveling till the following day. I drew his attention casually to the hollows in the sand.

"Yes," he said, "I know. They're all over the island. But you can explain them, no doubt!"

"Wind, of course," I answered without hesitation. "Have you never watched those little whirlwinds in the street that twist and twirl everything into a circle? This sand's loose enough to yield, that's all."

He made no reply, and we worked on in silence for a bit. I watched him surreptitiously all the time, and I had an idea he was watching me. He seemed, too, to be always listening attentively to something I could not hear, or perhaps for something that he expected to hear, for he kept turning about and staring into the bushes, and up into the sky, and out across the water where it was visible through the openings among the willows. Sometimes he even put his hand to his ear and held it there for several minutes. He said nothing to me, however, about it, and I asked no questions. And meanwhile, as he mended that torn canoe with the skill and address of a red Indian, I was glad to notice his absorption in the work, for there was a vague dread in my heart that he would speak of the changed aspect of the willows. And, if he had noticed that, my imagination could no longer be held a sufficient explanation of it.

III

At length, after a long pause, he began to talk.

"Queer thing," he added in a hurried sort of voice, as though he wanted to say something and get it over. "Queer thing. I mean, about that otter last night."

I had expected something so totally different that he caught me with surprise, and I looked up sharply.

"Shows how lonely this place is. Otters are awfully shy things—"

"I don't mean that, of course," he interrupted. "I mean—do you think—did you think it really was an otter?"

"What else, in the name of Heaven, what else?"

"You know, I saw it before you did, and at first it seemed—so much bigger than an otter."

"The sunset as you looked up-stream magnified it, or something," I replied.

He looked at me absently a moment, as though his mind were busy with other thoughts.

"It had such extraordinary yellow eyes," he went on half to himself.

"That was the sun too," I laughed, a trifle boisterously. "I suppose you'll wonder next if that fellow in the boat—"

I suddenly decided not to finish the sentence. He was in the act again of listening, turning his head to the wind, and something in the expression of his face made me halt. The subject dropped, and we went on with our caulking. Apparently he had not noticed my unfinished sentence. Five minutes later, however, he looked at me across the canoe, the smoking pitch in his hand, his face exceedingly grave.

"I did rather wonder, if you want to know," he said slowly, "what that thing in the boat was. I remember thinking at the time it was not a man. The whole business seemed to rise quite suddenly out of the water."

I laughed again boisterously in his face, but this time there was impatience, and a strain of anger too, in my feeling.

"Look here now," I cried, "this place is quite queer enough without going out of our way to imagine things! That boat was an ordinary boat, and the man in it was an ordinary man, and they were both going down-stream as fast as they could lick. And that otter was an otter, so don't let's play the fool about it!"

He looked steadily at me with the same grave expression. He was not in the least annoyed. I took courage from his silence.

"And, for Heaven's sake," I went on, "don't keep pretending you hear things, because it only gives me the jumps, and there's nothing to hear but the river and this cursed old thundering wind."

"You fool!" he answered in a low, shocked voice, "you utter fool. That's just the way all victims talk. As if you didn't understand just as well as I do!" he sneered with scorn in his voice, and a sort of resignation. "The best thing you can do is to keep quiet and try to hold your mind as firm as possible. This feeble attempt at self-deception only makes the truth harder when you're forced to meet it."

My little effort was over, and I found nothing more to say, for I knew quite well his words were true, and that I was the fool, not he. Up to a certain stage in the adventure he kept ahead of me easily, and I think I felt annoyed to be out of it, to be thus proved less psychic, less sensitive than himself to these extraordinary happenings, and half ignorant all the time of what was going on under my very nose. He knew from the very beginning, apparently. But at the moment I wholly missed the point of his words about the necessity of there being a victim, and that we ourselves were destined to satisfy the want. I dropped all pretence thenceforward, but thenceforward likewise my fear increased steadily to the climax.

"But you're quite right about one thing," he added, before the subject passed, "and that is that we're wiser not to talk about it, or even to think about it, because what one thinks finds expression in words, and what one says, happens."

That afternoon, while the canoe dried and hardened, we spent trying to fish, testing the leak, collecting wood, and watching the enormous flood of rising water. Masses of driftwood swept near our shores sometimes, and we fished for them with long willow branches. The island grew perceptibly smaller as the banks were torn away with great gulps and splashes. The weather kept brilliantly fine till about four o'clock, and then for the first time for three days the wind showed signs of abating. Clouds began to gather in the south-west, spreading thence slowly over the sky.

This lessening of the wind came as a great relief, for the incessant roaring, banging, and thundering had irritated our nerves. Yet the silence that came about five o'clock with its sudden cessation was in a manner quite as oppressive. The booming of the river had everything in its own way then;

it filled the air with deep murmurs, more musical than the wind noises, but infinitely more monotonous. The wind held many notes, rising, falling always beating out some sort of great elemental tune; whereas the river's song lay between three notes at most—dull pedal notes, that held a lugubrious quality foreign to the wind, and somehow seemed to me, in my then nervous state, to sound wonderfully well the music of doom.

It was extraordinary, too, how the withdrawal suddenly of bright sunlight took everything out of the landscape that made for cheerfulness; and since this particular landscape had already managed to convey the suggestion of something sinister, the change of course was all the more unwelcome and noticeable. For me, I know, the darkening outlook became distinctly more alarming, and I found myself more than once calculating how soon after sunset the full moon would get up in the east, and whether the gathering clouds would greatly interfere with her lighting of the little island.

With this general hush of the wind—though it still indulged in occasional brief gusts—the river seemed to me to grow blacker, the willows to stand more densely together. The latter, too, kept up a sort of independent movement of their own, rustling among themselves when no wind stirred, and shaking oddly from the roots upwards. When common objects in this way become charged with the suggestion of horror, they stimulate the imagination far more than things of unusual appearance; and these bushes, crowding huddled about us, assumed for me in the darkness a bizarre grotesquerie of appearance that lent to them somehow the aspect of purposeful and living creatures. Their very ordinariness, I felt, masked what was malignant and hostile to us. The forces of the region drew nearer with the coming of night. They were focusing upon our island, and more particularly upon ourselves. For thus, somehow, in the terms of the imagination, did my really indescribable sensations in this extraordinary place present themselves.

I had slept a good deal in the early afternoon, and had thus recovered somewhat from the exhaustion of a disturbed night, but this only served apparently to render me more susceptible than before to the obsessing spell of the haunting. I fought against it, laughing at my feelings as absurd and childish, with very obvious physiological explanations, yet, in spite of every effort, they gained in strength upon me so that I dreaded the night as a child lost in a forest must dread the approach of darkness.

The canoe we had carefully covered with a waterproof sheet during the day, and the one remaining paddle had been securely tied by the Swede to the base of a tree, lest the wind should rob us of that too. From five o'clock onwards I busied myself with the stew-pot and preparations for dinner, it being my turn to cook that night. We had potatoes, onions, bits of bacon fat to add flavor, and a general thick residue from former stews at the bottom of the pot; with black bread broken up into it the result was most excellent, and it was followed by a stew of plums with sugar and a brew of strong tea with dried milk. A good pile of wood lay close at hand, and the absence of wind made my duties easy. My companion sat lazily watching me, dividing his attentions between cleaning his pipe and giving useless advice—an admitted privilege of the off-duty man. He had been very quiet all the afternoon, engaged in re-caulking the canoe, strengthening the tent ropes, and fishing for driftwood while I slept. No more talk about undesirable things had passed between us, and I think his only remarks had to do with the gradual destruction of the island, which he declared was not fully a third smaller than when we first landed.

The pot had just begun to bubble when I heard his voice calling to me from the bank, where he had wandered away without my noticing. I ran up.

"Come and listen," he said, "and see what you make of it." He held his hand cupwise to his ear, as so often before.

"Now do you hear anything?" he asked, watching me curiously.

We stood there, listening attentively together. At first I heard only the deep note of the water and the hissings rising from its turbulent surface. The willows, for once, were motionless and silent. Then a sound began to reach my ears faintly, a peculiar sound—something like the humming of a distant gong. It seemed to come across to us in the darkness from the waste of swamps and willows opposite. It was repeated at regular intervals, but it was certainly neither the sound of a bell nor the hooting of a distant steamer. I can liken it to nothing so much as to the sound of an immense gong, suspended far up in the sky, repeating incessantly its muffled metallic note, soft and musical, as it was repeatedly struck. My heart quickened as I listened.

"I've heard it all day," said my companion. "While you slept this afternoon it came all round the island. I hunted it down, but could never get near enough to see—to localize it correctly. Sometimes it was overhead, and sometimes it seemed under the water. Once or twice, too, I could have sworn it was not outside at all, but within myself—you know—the way a sound in the fourth dimension is supposed to come."

I was too much puzzled to pay much attention to his words. I listened carefully, striving to associate it with any known familiar sound I could think of, but without success. It changed in the direction, too, coming nearer, and then sinking utterly away into remote distance. I cannot say that it was ominous in quality, because to me it seemed distinctly musical, yet I must admit it set going a distressing feeling that made me wish I had never heard it.

"The wind blowing in those sand-funnels," I said determined to find an explanation, "or the bushes rubbing together after the storm perhaps."

"It comes off the whole swamp," my friend answered. "It comes from everywhere at once." He ignored my explanations. "It comes from the willow bushes somehow—"

"But now the wind has dropped," I objected. "The willows can hardly make a noise by themselves, can they?"

His answer frightened me, first because I had dreaded it, and secondly, because I knew intuitively it was true.

"It is because the wind has dropped we now hear it. It was drowned before. It is the cry, I believe, of the—"

I dashed back to my fire, warned by the sound of bubbling that the stew was in danger, but determined at the same time to escape further conversation. I was resolute, if possible, to avoid the exchanging of views. I dreaded, too, that he would begin about the gods, or the elemental forces, or something else disquieting, and I wanted to keep myself well in hand for what might happen later. There was another night to be faced before we escaped from this distressing place, and there was no knowing yet what it might bring forth.

"Come and cut up bread for the pot," I called to him, vigorously stirring the appetizing mixture. That stew-pot held sanity for us both, and the thought made me laugh.

He came over slowly and took the provision sack from the tree, fumbling in its mysterious depths, and then emptying the entire contents upon the ground-sheet at his feet.

"Hurry up!" I cried; "it's boiling."

The Swede burst out into a roar of laughter that startled me. It was forced laughter, not artificial exactly, but mirthless.

"There's nothing here!" he shouted, holding his sides.

"Bread, I mean."

"It's gone. There is no bread. They've taken it!"

I dropped the long spoon and ran up. Everything the sack had contained lay upon the ground-sheet, but there was no loaf.

The whole dead weight of my growing fear fell upon me and shook me. Then I burst out laughing too. It was the only thing to do: and the sound of my laughter also made me understand his. The stain of psychical pressure caused it—this explosion of unnatural laughter in both of us; it was an effort of repressed forces to seek relief; it was a temporary safety-valve. And with both of us it ceased quite suddenly.

"How criminally stupid of me!" I cried, still determined to be consistent and find an explanation. "I clean forgot to buy a loaf at Pressburg. That chattering woman put everything out of my head, and I must have left it lying on the counter or—"

"The oatmeal, too, is much less than it was this morning," the Swede interrupted.

Why in the world need he draw attention to it? I thought angrily.

"There's enough for tomorrow," I said, stirring vigorously, "and we can get lots more at Komorn or Gran. In twenty-four hours we shall be miles from here."

"I hope so—to God," he muttered, putting the things back into the sack, "unless we're claimed first as victims for the sacrifice," he added with a foolish laugh. He dragged the sack into the tent, for safety's sake, I suppose, and I heard him mumbling to himself, but so indistinctly that it seemed quite natural for me to ignore his words.

Our meal was beyond question a gloomy one, and we ate it almost in silence, avoiding one another's eyes, and keeping the fire bright. Then we washed up and prepared for the night, and, once smoking, our minds unoccupied with any definite duties, the apprehension I had felt all day long became more and more acute. It was not then active fear, I think, but the very vagueness of its origin distressed me far more than if I had been able to ticket and face it squarely. The curious sound I have likened to the note of a gong became now almost incessant, and filled the stillness of the night with a faint, continuous ringing rather than a series of distinct notes. At one time it was behind and at another time in front of us. Sometimes I fancied it came from the bushes on our left, and then again from the clumps on our right. More often it hovered directly overhead like the whirring of wings. It was really everywhere at once, behind, in front, at our sides and over our heads, completely surrounding us. The sound really defies description. But nothing within my knowledge is like that ceaseless muffled humming rising off the deserted world of swamps and willows.

We sat smoking in comparative silence, the strain growing every minute greater. The worst feature of the situation seemed to me that we did not know what to expect, and could therefore make no sort of preparation by way of defense. We could anticipate nothing. My explanations made in the sunshine, moreover, now came to haunt me with their foolish and wholly unsatisfactory nature, and it was more and more clear to us that some kind of plain talk with my companion was inevitable, whether I liked it or not. After all, we had to spend the night together, and to sleep in the same tent side by side. I saw that I could not get along much longer without the support of his mind, and for that, of course, plain talk was imperative. As long as possible, however, I postponed this little climax, and tried to ignore or laugh at the occasional sentences he flung into the emptiness.

Some of these sentences, moreover, were confoundedly disquieting to me, coming as they did to corroborate much that I felt myself; corroboration, too—which made it so much more convincing—from a totally different point of view. He composed such curious sentences, and hurled them at me in such an inconsequential sort of way, as though his main line of thought was secret to himself, and these fragments were mere bits he found it impossible to digest. He got rid of them by uttering them. Speech relieved him. It was like being sick.

"There are things about us, I'm sure, that make for disorder, disintegration, destruction, our destruction," he said once, while the fire blazed between us. "We've strayed out of a safe line somewhere."

And, another time, when the gong sounds had come nearer, ringing much louder than before, and directly over our heads, he said as though talking to himself:

"I don't think a gramophone would show any record of that. The sound doesn't come to me by the ears at all. The vibrations reach me in another manner altogether, and seem to be within me, which is precisely how a fourth dimensional sound might be supposed to make itself heard."

I purposely made no reply to this, but I sat up a little closer to the fire and peered about me into the darkness. The clouds were massed all over the sky, and no trace of moonlight came through. Very still, too, everything was, so that the river and the frogs had things all their own way.

"It has that about it," he went on, "which is utterly out of common experience. It is unknown. Only one thing describes it really; it is a non-human sound; I mean a sound outside humanity."

Having rid himself of this indigestible morsel, he lay quiet for a time, but he had so admirably expressed my own feeling that it was a relief to have the thought out, and to have confined it by the limitation of words from dangerous wandering to and fro in the mind.

The solitude of that Danube camping-place, can I ever forget it? The feeling of being utterly alone on an empty planet! My thoughts ran incessantly upon cities and the haunts of men. I would have given my soul, as the saying is, for the "feel" of those Bavarian villages we had passed through by the score; for the normal, human commonplaces; peasants drinking beer, tables beneath the trees, hot sunshine, and a ruined castle on the rocks behind the red-roofed church. Even the tourists would have been welcome.

Yet what I felt of dread was no ordinary ghostly fear. It was infinitely greater, stranger, and seemed to arise from some dim ancestral sense of terror more profoundly disturbing than anything I had known or dreamed of. We had "strayed," as the Swede put it, into some region or some set of conditions where the risks were great, yet unintelligible to us; where the frontiers of some unknown world lay close about us. It was a spot held by the dwellers in some outer space, a sort of peep-hole whence they could spy upon the earth, themselves unseen, a point where the veil between had worn a little thin. As the final result of too long a sojourn here, we should be carried over the border and deprived of what we called "our lives," yet by mental, not physical, processes. In that sense, as he said, we should be the victims of our adventure—a sacrifice.

It took us in different fashion, each according to the measure of his sensitiveness and powers of resistance. I translated it vaguely into a personification of the mightily disturbed elements, investing them with the horror of a deliberate and malefic purpose, resentful of our audacious intrusion into their breeding-place; whereas my friend threw it into the unoriginal form at first of a trespass on some ancient shrine, some place where the old gods still held sway, where the emotional forces of former worshippers still clung, and the ancestral portion of him yielded to the old pagan spell.

At any rate, here was a place unpolluted by men, kept clean by the winds from coarsening human influences, a place where spiritual agencies were within reach and aggressive. Never, before or since, have I been so attacked by indescribable suggestions of a "beyond region," of another scheme of life, another revolution not parallel to the human. And in the end our minds would succumb under the weight of the awful spell, and we should be drawn across the frontier into their world.

Small things testified to the amazing influence of the place, and now in the silence round the fire they allowed themselves to be noted by the mind. The very atmosphere had proved itself a magnifying medium to distort every indication: the otter rolling in the current, the hurrying boatman making signs, the shifting willows, one and all had been robbed of its natural character, and revealed in something of its other aspect—as it existed across the border to that other region. And this changed aspect I felt was now not merely to me, but to the race. The whole experience whose verge we touched was unknown to humanity at all. It was a new order of experience, and in the true sense of the word unearthly.

"It's the deliberate, calculating purpose that reduces one's courage to zero," the Swede said suddenly, as if he had been actually following my thoughts. "Otherwise imagination might count for much. But the paddle, the canoe, the lessening food—"

"Haven't I explained all that once?" I interrupted viciously.

"You have," he answered dryly; "you have indeed."

He made other remarks too, as usual, about what he called the "plain determination to provide a victim"; but, having now arranged my thoughts better, I recognized that this was simply the cry of his frightened soul against the knowledge that he was being attacked in a vital part, and that he would be somehow taken or destroyed. The situation called for a courage and calmness of reasoning that neither of us could compass, and I have never before been so clearly conscious of two persons in me—the one that explained everything, and the other that laughed at such foolish explanations, yet was horribly afraid.

Meanwhile, in the pitchy night the fire died down and the wood pile grew small. Neither of us moved to replenish the stock, and the darkness consequently came up very close to our faces. A few feet beyond the circle of firelight it was inky black. Occasionally a stray puff of wind set the willows shivering about us, but apart from this not very welcome sound a deep and depressing silence reigned, broken only by the gurgling of the river and the humming in the air overhead.

We both missed, I think, the shouting company of the winds.

At length, at a moment when a stray puff prolonged itself as though the wind were about to rise again, I reached the point for me of saturation, the point where it was absolutely necessary to find relief in plain speech, or else to betray myself by some hysterical extravagance that must have been far worse in its effect upon both of us. I kicked the fire into a blaze, and turned to my companion abruptly. He looked up with a start.

"I can't disguise it any longer," I said; "I don't like this place, and the darkness, and the noises, and the awful feelings I get. There's something here that beats me utterly. I'm in a blue funk, and that's the plain truth. If the other shore was—different, I swear I'd be inclined to swim for it!"

The Swede's face turned very white beneath the deep tan of sun and wind. He stared straight at me and answered quietly, but his voice betrayed his huge excitement by its unnatural calmness. For the moment, at any rate, he was the strong man of the two. He was more phlegmatic, for one thing.

"It's not a physical condition we can escape from by running away," he replied, in the tone of a doctor diagnosing some grave disease; "we must sit tight and wait. There are forces close here that could kill a herd of elephants in a second as easily as you or I could squash a fly. Our only chance is to keep perfectly still. Our insignificance perhaps may save us."

I put a dozen questions into my expression of face, but found no words. It was precisely like listening to an accurate description of a disease whose symptoms had puzzled me.

"I mean that so far, although aware of our disturbing presence, they have not found us—not 'located' us, as the Americans say," he went on. "They're blundering about like men hunting for a leak of gas. The paddle and canoe and provisions prove that. I think they feel us, but cannot actually see us. We must keep our minds quiet—it's our minds they feel. We must control our thoughts, or it's all up with us."

"Death, you mean?" I stammered, icy with the horror of his suggestion.

"Worse—by far," he said. "Death, according to one's belief, means either annihilation or release from the limitations of the senses, but it involves no change of character. You don't suddenly alter just because the body's gone. But this means a radical alteration, a complete change, a horrible loss of oneself by substitution—far worse than death, and not even annihilation. We happen to have camped in a spot where their region touches ours, where the veil between has worn thin"—horrors! he was using my very own phrase, my actual words—"so that they are aware of our being in their neighborhood."

"But who are aware?" I asked.

I forgot the shaking of the willows in the windless calm, the humming overhead, everything except that I was waiting for an answer that I dreaded more than I can possibly explain.

He lowered his voice at once to reply, leaning forward a little over the fire, an indefinable change in his face that made me avoid his eyes and look down upon the ground.

"All my life," he said, "I have been strangely, vividly conscious of another region—not far removed from our own world in one sense, yet wholly different in kind—where great things go on unceasingly, where immense and terrible personalities hurry by, intent on vast purposes compared to which earthly affairs, the rise and fall of nations, the destinies of empires, the fate of armies and continents, are all as dust in the balance; vast purposes, I mean, that deal directly with the soul, and not indirectly with more expressions of the soul—"

"I suggest just now—" I began, seeking to stop him, feeling as though I was face to face with a madman. But he instantly overbore me with his torrent that had to come.

"You think," he said, "it is the spirit of the elements, and I thought perhaps it was the old gods. But I tell you now it is—neither. These would be comprehensible entities, for they have relations with men, depending upon them for worship or sacrifice, whereas these beings who are now about us have absolutely nothing to do with mankind, and it is mere chance that their space happens just at this spot to touch our own."

The mere conception, which his words somehow made so convincing, as I listened to them there in the dark stillness of that lonely island, set me shaking a little all over. I found it impossible to control my movements.

"And what do you propose?" I began again.

"A sacrifice, a victim, might save us by distracting them until we could get away," he went on, "just as the wolves stop to devour the dogs and give the sleigh another start. But—I see no chance of any other victim now."

I stared blankly at him. The gleam in his eye was dreadful. Presently he continued.

IV

"It's the willows, of course. The willows mask the others, but the others are feeling about for us. If we let our minds betray our fear, we're lost, lost utterly." He looked at me with an expression so calm, so determined, so sincere, that I no longer had any doubts as to his sanity. He was as sane as any man ever was. "If we can hold out through the night," he added, "we may get off in the daylight unnoticed, or rather, undiscovered."

"But you really think a sacrifice would—"

That gong-like humming came down very close over our heads as I spoke, but it was my friend's scared face that really stopped my mouth.

"Hush!" he whispered, holding up his hand. "Do not mention them more than you can help. Do not refer to them by name. To name is to reveal; it is the inevitable clue, and our only hope lies in ignoring them, in order that they may ignore us."

"Even in thought?" He was extraordinarily agitated.

"Especially in thought. Our thoughts make spirals in their world. We must keep them out of our minds at all costs if possible."

I raked the fire together to prevent the darkness having everything its own way. I never longed for the sun as I longed for it then in the awful blackness of that summer night.

"Were you awake all last night?" he went on suddenly.

"I slept badly a little after dawn," I replied evasively, trying to follow his instructions, which I knew instinctively were true, "but the wind, of course—"

"I know. But the wind won't account for all the noises."

"Then you heard it too?"

"The multiplying countless little footsteps I heard," he said, adding, after a moment's hesitation, "and that other sound—"

"You mean above the tent, and the pressing down upon us of something tremendous, gigantic?"

He nodded significantly.

"It was like the beginning of a sort of inner suffocation?" I said.

"Partly, yes. It seemed to me that the weight of the atmosphere had been altered—had increased enormously, so that we should have been crushed."

"And that," I went on, determined to have it all out, pointing upwards where the gong-like note hummed ceaselessly, rising and falling like wind. "What do you make of that?"

"It's their sound," he whispered gravely. "It's the sound of their world, the humming in their region. The division here is so thin that it leaks through somehow. But, if you listen carefully, you'll find it's not above so much as around us. It's in the willows. It's the willows themselves humming, because here the willows have been made symbols of the forces that are against us."

I could not follow exactly what he meant by this, yet the thought and idea in my mind were beyond question the thought and idea in his. I realized what he realized, only with less power of analysis than his. It was on the tip of my tongue to tell him at last about my hallucination of the ascending figures and the moving bushes, when he suddenly thrust his face again close into mine across the firelight and began to speak in a very earnest whisper. He amazed me by his calmness and pluck, his apparent control of the situation. This man I had for years deemed unimaginative, stolid!

"Now listen," he said. "The only thing for us to do is to go on as though nothing had happened, follow our usual habits, go to bed, and so forth; pretend we feel nothing and notice nothing. It is a question wholly of the mind, and the less we think about them the better our chance of escape. Above all, don't think, for what you think happens!"

"All right," I managed to reply, simply breathless with his words and the strangeness of it all; "all right, I'll try, but tell me one more thing first. Tell me what you make of those hollows in the ground all about us, those sand-funnels?"

"No!" he cried, forgetting to whisper in his excitement. "I dare not, simply dare not, put the thought into words. If you have not guessed I am glad. Don't try to. They have put it into my mind; try your hardest to prevent their putting it into yours."

He sank his voice again to a whisper before he finished, and I did not press him to explain. There was already just about as much horror in me as I could hold. The conversation came to an end, and we smoked our pipes busily in silence.

Then something happened, something unimportant apparently, as the way is when the nerves are in a very great state of tension, and this small thing for a brief space gave me an entirely different point of view. I chanced to look down at my sand-shoe—the sort we used for the canoe—and something to do with the hole at the toe suddenly recalled to me the London shop where I had bought them, the difficulty the man had in fitting me, and other details of the uninteresting but practical operation. At once, in its train, followed a wholesome view of the modern skeptical world I was accustomed to move in at home. I thought of roast beef, and ale, motor-cars, policemen, brass bands, and a dozen other things that proclaimed the soul of ordinariness or utility. The effect was immediate and astonishing even to myself. Psychologically, I suppose, it was simply a sudden and violent reaction after the strain of living in an atmosphere of things that to the normal consciousness must seem impossible and incredible. But, whatever the cause, it momentarily lifted the spell from my heart, and left me for the short space of a minute feeling free and utterly unafraid. I looked up at my friend opposite.

"You damned old pagan!" I cried, laughing aloud in his face. "You imaginative idiot! You superstitious idolater! You—"

I stopped in the middle, seized anew by the old horror. I tried to smother the sound of my voice as something sacrilegious. The Swede, of course, heard it too—the strange cry overhead in the darkness—and that sudden drop in the air as though something had come nearer.

He had turned ashen white under the tan. He stood bolt upright in front of the fire, stiff as a rod, staring at me.

"After that," he said in a sort of helpless, frantic way, "we must go! We can't stay now; we must strike camp this very instant and go on—down the river."

He was talking, I saw, quite wildly, his words dictated by abject terror—the terror he had resisted so long, but which had caught him at last.

"In the dark?" I exclaimed, shaking with fear after my hysterical outburst, but still realizing our position better than he did. "Sheer madness! The river's in flood, and we've only got a single paddle. Besides, we only go deeper into their country! There's nothing ahead for fifty miles but willows, willows, willows!"

He sat down again in a state of semi-collapse. The positions, by one of those kaleidoscopic changes nature loves, were suddenly reversed, and the control of our forces passed over into my hands. His mind at last had reached the point where it was beginning to weaken.

"What on earth possessed you to do such a thing?" he whispered with the awe of genuine terror in his voice and face.

I crossed round to his side of the fire. I took both his hands in mine, kneeling down beside him and looking straight into his frightened eyes.

"We'll make one more blaze," I said firmly, "and then turn in for the night. At sunrise we'll be off full speed for Komorn. Now, pull yourself together a bit, and remember your own advice about not thinking fear!"

He said no more, and I saw that he would agree and obey. In some measure, too, it was a sort of relief to get up and make an excursion into the darkness for more wood. We kept close together, almost touching, groping among the bushes and along the bank. The humming overhead never ceased, but seemed to me to grow louder as we increased our distance from the fire. It was shivery work!

We were grubbing away in the middle of a thickish clump of willows where some driftwood from a former flood had caught high among the branches, when my body was seized in a grip that made me half drop upon the sand. It was the Swede. He had fallen against me, and was clutching me for support. I heard his breath coming and going in short gasps.

"Look! By my soul!" he whispered, and for the first time in my experience I knew what it was to hear tears of terror in a human voice. He was pointing to the fire, some fifty feet away. I followed the direction of his finger, and I swear my heart missed a beat.

There, in front of the dim glow, something was moving.

I saw it through a veil that hung before my eyes like the gauze drop-curtain used at the back of a theater—hazily a little. It was neither a human figure nor an animal. To me it gave the strange impression of being as large as several animals grouped together, like horses, two or three, moving slowly. The Swede, too, got a similar result, though expressing it differently, for he thought it was shaped and sized like a clump of willow bushes, rounded at the top, and moving all over upon its surface—"coiling upon itself like smoke," he said afterwards.

"I watched it settle downwards through the bushes," he sobbed at me. "Look, by God! It's coming this way! Oh, oh!"—he gave a kind of whistling cry. "They've found us."

I gave one terrified glance, which just enabled me to see that the shadowy form was swinging towards us through the bushes, and then I collapsed backwards with a crash into the branches. These failed, of course, to support my weight, so that with the Swede on top of me we fell in a struggling heap upon the sand. I really hardly knew what was happening. I was conscious only of a sort of enveloping sensation of icy fear that plucked the nerves out of their fleshly covering, twisted them this way and that, and replaced them quivering. My eyes were tightly shut; something in my throat choked me; a feeling that my consciousness was expanding, extending out into space, swiftly gave way to another feeling that I was losing it altogether, and about to die.

An acute spasm of pain passed through me, and I was aware that the Swede had hold of me in such a way that he hurt me abominably. It was the way he caught at me in falling.

But it was the pain, he declared afterwards, that saved me; it caused me to forget them and think of something else at the very instant when they were about to find me. It concealed my mind from them at the moment of discovery, yet just in time to evade their terrible seizing of me. He himself, he says, actually swooned at the same moment, and that was what saved him.

I only know that at a later date, how long or short is impossible to say, I found myself scrambling up out of the slippery network of willow branches, and saw my companion standing in front of me holding out a hand to assist me. I stared at him in a dazed way, rubbing the arm he had twisted for me. Nothing came to me to say, somehow.

"I lost consciousness for a moment or two," I heard him say. "That's what saved me. It made me stop thinking about them."

"You nearly broke my arm in two," I said, uttering my only connected thought at the moment. A numbness came over me.

"That's what saved you!" he replied. "Between us, we've managed to set them off on a false tack somewhere. The humming has ceased. It's gone—for the moment at any rate!"

A wave of hysterical laughter seized me again, and this time spread to my friend too—great healing gusts of shaking laughter that brought a tremendous sense of relief in their train. We made our way back to the fire and put the wood on so that it blazed at once. Then we saw that the tent had fallen over and lay in a tangled heap upon the ground.

We picked it up, and during the process tripped more than once and caught our feet in sand.

"It's those sand-funnels," exclaimed the Swede, when the tent was up again and the firelight lit up the ground for several yards about us. "And look at the size of them!"

All round the tent and about the fireplace where we had seen the moving shadows there were deep funnel-shaped hollows in the sand, exactly similar to the ones we had already found over the island, only far bigger and deeper, beautifully formed, and wide enough in some instances to admit the whole of my foot and leg.

Neither of us said a word. We both knew that sleep was the safest thing we could do, and to bed we went accordingly without further delay, having first thrown sand on the fire and taken the provision sack and the paddle inside the tent with us. The canoe, too, we propped in such a way at the end of the tent that our feet touched it, and the least motion would disturb and wake us.

In case of emergency, too, we again went to bed in our clothes, ready for a sudden start.

It was my firm intention to lie awake all night and watch, but the exhaustion of nerves and body decreed otherwise, and sleep after a while came over me with a welcome blanket of oblivion. The fact that my companion also slept quickened its approach. At first he fidgeted and constantly sat up, asking me if I "heard this" or "heard that." He tossed about on his cork mattress, and said the tent was moving and the river had risen over the point of the island, but each time I went out to look I returned with the report that all was well, and finally he grew calmer and lay still. Then at length his breathing became regular and I heard unmistakable sounds of snoring—the first and only time in my life when snoring has been a welcome and calming influence.

This, I remember, was the last thought in my mind before dozing off.

A difficulty in breathing woke me, and I found the blanket over my face. But something else besides the blanket was pressing upon me, and my first thought was that my companion had rolled off his mattress on to my own in his sleep. I called to him and sat up, and at the same moment it came to me that the tent was surrounded. That sound of multitudinous soft pattering was again audible outside, filling the night with horror.

I called again to him, louder than before. He did not answer, but I missed the sound of his snoring, and also noticed that the flap of the tent was down. This was the unpardonable sin. I crawled out in the darkness to hook it back securely, and it was then for the first time I realized positively that the Swede was not here. He had gone.

I dashed out in a mad run, seized by a dreadful agitation, and the moment I was out I plunged into a sort of torrent of humming that surrounded me completely and came out of every quarter of the heavens at once. It was that same familiar humming—gone mad! A swarm of great invisible bees might have been about me in the air. The sound seemed to thicken the very atmosphere, and I felt that my lungs worked with difficulty.

But my friend was in danger, and I could not hesitate.

The dawn was just about to break, and a faint whitish light spread upwards over the clouds from a thin strip of clear horizon. No wind stirred. I could just make out the bushes and river beyond, and the pale sandy patches. In my excitement I ran frantically to and fro about the island, calling him by name, shouting at the top of my voice the first words that came into my head. But the willows smothered my voice, and the humming muffled it, so that the sound only traveled a few feet round me. I plunged among the bushes, tripping headlong, tumbling over roots, and scraping my face as I tore this way and that among the preventing branches.

Then, quite unexpectedly, I came out upon the island's point and saw a dark figure outlined between the water and the sky. It was the Swede. And already he had one foot in the river! A moment more and he would have taken the plunge.

I threw myself upon him, flinging my arms about his waist and dragging him shorewards with all my strength. Of course he struggled furiously, making a noise all the time just like that cursed humming, and using the most outlandish phrases in his anger about "going inside to Them," and "taking the way of the water and the wind," and God only knows what more besides, that I tried in vain to recall afterwards, but which turned me sick with horror and amazement as I listened. But in the end I managed to get him into the comparative safety of the tent, and flung him breathless and cursing upon the mattress where I held him until the fit had passed.

I think the suddenness with which it all went and he grew calm, coinciding as it did with the equally abrupt cessation of the humming and pattering outside—I think this was almost the strangest part of the whole business perhaps. For he had just opened his eyes and turned his tired face up to me so that the dawn threw a pale light upon it through the doorway, and said, for all the world just like a frightened child:

"My life, old man—it's my life I owe you. But it's all over now anyhow. They've found a victim in our place!"

Then he dropped back upon his blankets and went to sleep literally under my eyes. He simply collapsed, and began to snore again as healthily as though nothing had happened and he had never tried to offer his own life as a sacrifice by drowning. And when the sunlight woke him three hours later—hours of ceaseless vigil for me—it became so clear to me that he remembered absolutely nothing of what he had attempted to do, that I deemed it wise to hold my peace and ask no dangerous questions.

He woke naturally and easily, as I have said, when the sun was already high in a windless hot sky, and he at once got up and set about the preparation of the fire for breakfast. I followed him anxiously at bathing, but he did not attempt to plunge in, merely dipping his head and making some remark about the extra coldness of the water.

"River's falling at last," he said, "and I'm glad of it."

"The humming has stopped too," I said.

He looked up at me quietly with his normal expression. Evidently he remembered everything except his own attempt at suicide.

"Everything has stopped," he said, "because—"

He hesitated. But I knew some reference to that remark he had made just before he fainted was in his mind, and I was determined to know it.

"Because 'They've found another victim'?" I said, forcing a little laugh.

"Exactly," he answered, "exactly! I feel as positive of it as though—as though—I feel quite safe again, I mean," he finished.

He began to look curiously about him. The sunlight lay in hot patches on the sand. There was no wind. The willows were motionless. He slowly rose to feet.

"Come," he said; "I think if we look, we shall find it."

He started off on a run, and I followed him. He kept to the banks, poking with a stick among the sandy bays and caves and little back-waters, myself always close on his heels.

"Ah!" he exclaimed presently, "ah!"

The tone of his voice somehow brought back to me a vivid sense of the horror of the last twenty-four hours, and I hurried up to join him. He was pointing with his stick at a large black object that lay half in the water and half on the sand. It appeared to be caught by some twisted willow roots so that the river could not sweep it away. A few hours before the spot must have been under water.

"See," he said quietly, "the victim that made our escape possible!"

And when I peered across his shoulder I saw that his stick rested on the body of a man. He turned it over. It was the corpse of a peasant, and the face was hidden in the sand. Clearly the man had been drowned, but a few hours before, and his body must have been swept down upon our island somewhere about the hour of the dawn—at the very time the fit had passed.

"We must give it a decent burial, you know."

"I suppose so," I replied. I shuddered a little in spite of myself, for there was something about the appearance of that poor drowned man that turned me cold.

The Swede glanced up sharply at me, an undecipherable expression on his face, and began clambering down the bank. I followed him more leisurely. The current, I noticed, had torn away much of the clothing from the body, so that the neck and part of the chest lay bare.

Halfway down the bank my companion suddenly stopped and held up his hand in warning; but either my foot slipped, or I had gained too much momentum to bring myself quickly to a halt, for I bumped into him and sent him forward with a sort of leap to save himself. We tumbled together on to the hard sand so that our feet splashed into the water. And, before anything could be done, we had collided a little heavily against the corpse.

The Swede uttered a sharp cry. And I sprang back as if I had been shot.

At the moment we touched the body there rose from its surface the loud sound of humming—the sound of several hummings—which passed with a vast commotion as of winged things in the air about us and disappeared upwards into the sky, growing fainter and fainter till they finally ceased in the distance. It was exactly as though we had disturbed some living yet invisible creatures at work.

My companion clutched me, and I think I clutched him, but before either of us had time properly to recover from the unexpected shock, we saw that a movement of the current was turning the corpse round so that it became released from the grip of the willow roots. A moment later it had turned completely over, the dead face uppermost, staring at the sky. It lay on the edge of the main stream. In another moment it would be swept away.

The Swede started to save it, shouting again something I did not catch about a "proper burial"—and then abruptly dropped upon his knees on the sand and covered his eyes with his hands. I was beside him in an instant.

I saw what he had seen.

For just as the body swung round to the current the face and the exposed chest turned full towards us, and showed plainly how the skin and flesh were indented with small hollows, beautifully formed, and exactly similar in shape and kind to the sand-funnels that we had found all over the island.

"Their mark!" I heard my companion mutter under his breath. "Their awful mark!"

And when I turned my eyes again from his ghastly face to the river, the current had done its work, and the body had been swept away into mid-stream and was already beyond our reach and almost out of sight, turning over and over on the waves like an otter.

The Yellow Wallpaper

Charlotte Perkins Gilman

It is very seldom that mere ordinary people like John and myself secure ancestral halls for the summer.

A colonial mansion, a hereditary estate, I would say a haunted house, and reach the height of romantic felicity—but that would be asking too much of fate!

Still I will proudly declare that there is something queer about it.

Else, why should it be let so cheaply? And why have stood so long untenanted?

John laughs at me, of course, but one expects that in marriage.

John is practical in the extreme. He has no patience with faith, an intense horror of superstition, and he scoffs openly at any talk of things not to be felt and seen and put down in figures.

John is a physician, and *perhaps*—(I would not say it to a living soul, of course, but this is dead paper and a great relief to my mind)—*perhaps* that is one reason I do not get well faster.

You see he does not believe I am sick!

And what can one do?

If a physician of high standing, and one's own husband, assures friends and relatives that there is really nothing the matter with one but temporary nervous depression—a slight hysterical tendency—what is one to do?

My brother is also a physician, and also of high standing, and he says the same thing.

So I take phosphates or phosphites—whichever it is, and tonics, and journeys, and air, and exercise, and am absolutely forbidden to "work" until I am well again.

Personally, I disagree with their ideas.

Personally, I believe that congenial work, with excitement and change, would do me good.

But what is one to do?

I did write for a while in spite of them; but it does exhaust me a good deal—having to be so sly about it, or else meet with heavy opposition.

I sometimes fancy that in my condition if I had less opposition and more society and stimulus—but John says the very worst thing I can do is to think about my condition, and I confess it always makes me feel bad.

So I will let it alone and talk about the house.

The most beautiful place! It is quite alone, standing well back from the road, quite three miles from the village. It makes me think of English places that you read about, for there are hedges and walls and gates that lock, and lots of separate little houses for the gardeners and people.

There is a delicious garden! I never saw such a garden—large and shady, full of box-bordered paths, and lined with long grape-covered arbors with seats under them.

There were greenhouses, too, but they are all broken now.

There was some legal trouble, I believe, something about the heirs and coheirs; anyhow, the place has been empty for years.

That spoils my ghostliness, I am afraid, but I don't care—there is something strange about the house—I can feel it.

I even said so to John one moonlight evening, but he said what I felt was a draught, and shut the window.

I get unreasonably angry with John sometimes. I'm sure I never used to be so sensitive. I think it is due to this nervous condition.

But John says if I feel so, I shall neglect proper self-control; so I take pains to control myself—before him, at least, and that makes me very tired.

I don't like our room a bit. I wanted one downstairs that opened on the piazza and had roses all over the window, and such pretty old-fashioned chintz hangings! but John would not hear of it.

He said there was only one window and not room for two beds, and no near room for him if he took another.

He is very careful and loving, and hardly lets me stir without special direction.

I have a schedule prescription for each hour in the day; he takes all care from me, and so I feel basely ungrateful not to value it more.

He said we came here solely on my account, that I was to have perfect rest and all the air I could get. "Your exercise depends on your strength, my dear," said he, "and your food somewhat on your appetite; but air you can absorb all the time." So we took the nursery at the top of the house.

It is a big, airy room, the whole floor nearly, with windows that look all ways, and air and sunshine galore. It was nursery first and then playroom and gymnasium, I should judge; for the windows are barred for little children, and there are rings and things in the walls.

The paint and paper look as if a boys' school had used it. It is stripped off—the paper—in great patches all around the head of my bed, about as far as I can reach, and in a great place on the other side of the room low down. I never saw a worse paper in my life.

One of those sprawling flamboyant patterns committing every artistic sin.

It is dull enough to confuse the eye in following, pronounced enough to constantly irritate and provoke study, and when you follow the lame uncertain curves for a little distance they suddenly commit suicide—plunge off at outrageous angles, destroy themselves in unheard of contradictions.

The color is repellent, almost revolting; a smouldering unclean yellow, strangely faded by the slow-turning sunlight.

It is a dull yet lurid orange in some places, a sickly sulphur tint in others.

No wonder the children hated it! I should hate it myself if I had to live in this room long.

There comes John, and I must put this away,—he hates to have me write a word.

We have been here two weeks, and I haven't felt like writing before, since that first day.

I am sitting by the window now, up in this atrocious nursery, and there is nothing to hinder my writing as much as I please, save lack of strength.

John is away all day, and even some nights when his cases are serious.

I am glad my case is not serious!

But these nervous troubles are dreadfully depressing.

John does not know how much I really suffer. He knows there is no reason to suffer, and that satisfies him.

Of course it is only nervousness. It does weigh on me so not to do my duty in any way!

I meant to be such a help to John, such a real rest and comfort, and here I am a comparative burden already!

Nobody would believe what an effort it is to do what little I am able,—to dress and entertain, and order things.

It is fortunate Mary is so good with the baby. Such a dear baby!

And yet I cannot be with him, it makes me so nervous.

I suppose John never was nervous in his life. He laughs at me so about this wallpaper!

At first he meant to repaper the room, but afterwards he said that I was letting it get the better of me, and that nothing was worse for a nervous patient than to give way to such fancies.

He said that after the wallpaper was changed it would be the heavy bedstead, and then the barred windows, and then that gate at the head of the stairs, and so on.

"You know the place is doing you good," he said, "and really, dear, I don't care to renovate the house just for a three months' rental."

"Then do let us go downstairs," I said, "there are such pretty rooms there."

Then he took me in his arms and called me a blessed little goose, and said he would go down to the cellar, if I wished, and have it whitewashed into the bargain.

But he is right enough about the beds and windows and things.

It is an airy and comfortable room as any one need wish, and, of course, I would not be so silly as to make him uncomfortable just for a whim.

I'm really getting quite fond of the big room, all but that horrid paper.

Out of one window I can see the garden, those mysterious deepshaded arbors, the riotous old-fashioned flowers, and bushes and gnarly trees.

Out of another I get a lovely view of the bay and a little private wharf belonging to the estate. There is a beautiful shaded lane that runs down there from the house. I always fancy I see people walking in these numerous paths and arbors, but John has cautioned me not to give way to fancy in the least. He says that with my imaginative power and habit of story-making, a nervous weakness like mine is sure to lead to all manner of excited fancies, and that I ought to use my will and good sense to check the tendency. So I try.

I think sometimes that if I were only well enough to write a little it would relieve the press of ideas and rest me.

But I find I get pretty tired when I try.

It is so discouraging not to have any advice and companionship about my work. When I get really well, John says we will ask Cousin Henry and Julia down for a long visit; but he says he would as soon put fireworks in my pillow-case as to let me have those stimulating people about now.

I wish I could get well faster.

But I must not think about that. This paper looks to me as if it knew what a vicious influence it had!

There is a recurrent spot where the pattern lolls like a broken neck and two bulbous eyes stare at you upside down.

I get positively angry with the impertinence of it and the everlastingness. Up and down and sideways they crawl, and those absurd, unblinking eyes are everywhere. There is one place where two breadths didn't match, and the eyes go all up and down the line, one a little higher than the other.

I never saw so much expression in an inanimate thing before, and we all know how much expression they have! I used to lie awake as a child and get more entertainment and terror out of blank walls and plain furniture than most children could find in a toy store.

I remember what a kindly wink the knobs of our big, old bureau used to have, and there was one chair that always seemed like a strong friend.

I used to feel that if any of the other things looked too fierce I could always hop into that chair and be safe.

The furniture in this room is no worse than inharmonious, however, for we had to bring it all from downstairs. I suppose when this was used as a playroom they had to take the nursery things out, and no wonder! I never saw such ravages as the children have made here.

The wallpaper, as I said before, is torn off in spots, and it sticketh closer than a brother—they must have had perseverance as well as hatred.

Then the floor is scratched and gouged and splintered, the plaster itself is dug out here and there, and this great heavy bed which is all we found in the room, looks as if it had been through the wars.

But I don't mind it a bit—only the paper.

There comes John's sister. Such a dear girl as she is, and so careful of me! I must not let her find me writing.

She is a perfect and enthusiastic housekeeper, and hopes for no better profession. I verily believe she thinks it is the writing which made me sick!

But I can write when she is out, and see her a long way off from these windows.

There is one that commands the road, a lovely shaded winding road, and one that just looks off over the country. A lovely country, too, full of great elms and velvet meadows.

This wallpaper has a kind of sub-pattern in a different shade, a particularly irritating one, for you can only see it in certain lights, and not clearly then.

But in the places where it isn't faded and where the sun is just so—I can see a strange, provoking, formless sort of figure, that seems to skulk about behind that silly and conspicuous front design.

There's sister on the stairs!

Well, the Fourth of July is over! The people are gone and I am tired out. John thought it might do me good to see a little company, so we just had mother and Nellie and the children down for a week.

Of course I didn't do a thing. Jennie sees to everything now.

But it tired me all the same.

John says if I don't pick up faster he shall send me to Weir Mitchell in the fall.

But I don't want to go there at all. I had a friend who was in his hands once, and she says he is just like John and my brother, only more so!

Besides, it is such an undertaking to go so far.

I don't feel as if it was worth while to turn my hand over for anything, and I'm getting dreadfully fretful and querulous.

I cry at nothing, and cry most of the time.

Of course I don't when John is here, or anybody else, but when I am alone.

And I am alone a good deal just now. John is kept in town very often by serious cases, and Jennie is good and lets me alone when I want her to.

So I walk a little in the garden or down that lovely lane, sit on the porch under the roses, and lie down up here a good deal.

I'm getting really fond of the room in spite of the wallpaper. Perhaps *because* of the wallpaper.

It dwells in my mind so!

I lie here on this great immovable bed—it is nailed down, I believe—and follow that pattern about by the hour. It is as good as gymnastics, I assure you. I start, we'll say, at the bottom, down in the corner over there where it has not been touched, and I determine for the thousandth time that I will follow that pointless pattern to some sort of a conclusion.

I know a little of the principle of design, and I know this thing was not arranged on any laws of radiation, or alternation, or repetition, or symmetry, or anything else that I ever heard of.

It is repeated, of course, by the breadths, but not otherwise.

Looked at in one way each breadth stands alone, the bloated curves and flourishes—a kind of "debased Romanesque" with delirium tremens—go waddling up and down in isolated columns of fatuity.

But, on the other hand, they connect diagonally, and the sprawling outlines run off in great slanting waves of optic horror, like a lot of wallowing seaweeds in full chase.

The whole thing goes horizontally, too, at least it seems so, and I exhaust myself in trying to distinguish the order of its going in that direction.

They have used a horizontal breadth for a frieze, and that adds wonderfully to the confusion.

There is one end of the room where it is almost intact, and there, when the crosslights fade and the low sun shines directly upon it, I can almost fancy radiation after all,—the interminable grotesques seem to form around a common centre and rush off in headlong plunges of equal distraction.

It makes me tired to follow it. I will take a nap I guess.

I don't know why I should write this.

I don't want to.

I don't feel able.

And I know John would think it absurd. But I must say what I feel and think in some way—it is such a relief!

But the effort is getting to be greater than the relief.

Half the time now I am awfully lazy, and lie down ever so much.

John says I mustn't lose my strength, and has me take cod liver oil and lots of tonics and things, to say nothing of ale and wine and rare meat.

Dear John! He loves me very dearly, and hates to have me sick. I tried to have a real earnest reasonable talk with him the other day, and tell him how I wish he would let me go and make a visit to Cousin Henry and Julia.

But he said I wasn't able to go, nor able to stand it after I got there; and I did not make out a very good case for myself, for I was crying before I had finished.

It is getting to be a great effort for me to think straight. Just this nervous weakness I suppose.

And dear John gathered me up in his arms, and just carried me upstairs and laid me on the bed, and sat by me and read to me till it tired my head.

He said I was his darling and his comfort and all he had, and that I must take care of myself for his sake, and keep well.

He says no one but myself can help me out of it, that I must use my will and self-control and not let any silly fancies run away with me.

There's one comfort, the baby is well and happy, and does not have to occupy this nursery with the horrid wallpaper.

If we had not used it, that blessed child would have! What a fortunate escape! Why, I wouldn't have a child of mine, an impressionable little thing, live in such a room for worlds.

I never thought of it before, but it is lucky that John kept me here after all, I can stand it so much easier than a baby, you see.

Of course I never mention it to them any more—I am too wise—but I keep watch of it all the same.

There are things in that paper that nobody knows but me, or ever will.

Behind that outside pattern the dim shapes get clearer every day.

It is always the same shape, only very numerous.

And it is like a woman stooping down and creeping about behind that pattern. I don't like it a bit. I wonder—I begin to think—I wish John would take me away from here!

It is so hard to talk with John about my case, because he is so wise, and because he loves me so.

But I tried it last night.

It was moonlight. The moon shines in all around just as the sun does.

I hate to see it sometimes, it creeps so slowly, and always comes in by one window or another.

John was asleep and I hated to waken him, so I kept still and watched the moonlight on that undulating wallpaper till I felt creepy.

The faint figure behind seemed to shake the pattern, just as if she wanted to get out.

I got up softly and went to feel and see if the paper *did* move, and when I came back John was awake.

"What is it, little girl?" he said. "Don't go walking about like that—you'll get cold."

I thought it was a good time to talk, so I told him that I really was not gaining here, and that I wished he would take me away.

"Why darling!" said he, "our lease will be up in three weeks, and I can't see how to leave before.

"The repairs are not done at home, and I cannot possibly leave town just now. Of course if you were in any danger, I could and would, but you really are better, dear, whether you can see it or not. I am a doctor, dear, and I know. You are gaining flesh and color, your appetite is better, I feel really much easier about you."

"I don't weigh a bit more," said I, "nor as much; and my appetite may be better in the evening when you are here, but it is worse in the morning when you are away!"

"Bless her little heart!" said he with a big hug, "she shall be as sick as she pleases! But now let's improve the shining hours by going to sleep, and talk about it in the morning!"

"And you won't go away?" I asked gloomily.

"Why, how can I, dear? It is only three weeks more and then we will take a nice little trip of a few days while Jennie is getting the house ready. Really dear you are better!"

"Better in body perhaps—" I began, and stopped short, for he sat up straight and looked at me with such a stern, reproachful look that I could not say another word.

"My darling," said he, "I beg of you, for my sake and for our child's sake, as well as for your own, that you will never for one instant let that idea enter your mind! There is nothing so dangerous, so fascinating, to a temperament like yours. It is a false and foolish fancy. Can you not trust me as a physician when I tell you so?"

So of course I said no more on that score, and we went to sleep before long. He thought I was asleep first, but I wasn't, and lay there for hours trying to decide whether that front pattern and the back pattern really did move together or separately.

On a pattern like this, by daylight, there is a lack of sequence, a defiance of law, that is a constant irritant to a normal mind.

The color is hideous enough, and unreliable enough, and infuriating enough, but the pattern is torturing.

You think you have mastered it, but just as you get well underway in following, it turns a back-somersault and there you are. It slaps you in the face, knocks you down, and tramples upon you. It is like a bad dream.

The outside pattern is a florid arabesque, reminding one of a fungus. If you can imagine a toadstool in joints, an interminable string of toadstools, budding and sprouting in endless convolutions—why, that is something like it.

That is, sometimes!

There is one marked peculiarity about this paper, a thing nobody seems to notice but myself, and that is that it changes as the light changes.

When the sun shoots in through the east window—I always watch for that first long, straight ray—it changes so quickly that I never can quite believe it.

That is why I watch it always.

By moonlight—the moon shines in all night when there is a moon—I wouldn't know it was the same paper.

At night in any kind of light, in twilight, candle light, lamplight, and worst of all by moonlight, it becomes bars! The outside pattern I mean, and the woman behind it is as plain as can be.

I didn't realize for a long time what the thing was that showed behind, that dim sub-pattern, but now I am quite sure it is a woman.

By daylight she is subdued, quiet. I fancy it is the pattern that keeps her so still. It is so puzzling. It keeps me quiet by the hour.

I lie down ever so much now. John says it is good for me, and to sleep all I can.

Indeed he started the habit by making me lie down for an hour after each meal.

It is a very bad habit I am convinced, for you see I don't sleep.

And that cultivates deceit, for I don't tell them I'm awake—O no!

The fact is I am getting a little afraid of John.

He seems very queer sometimes, and even Jennie has an inexplicable look.

It strikes me occasionally, just as a scientific hypothesis,—that perhaps it is the paper!

I have watched John when he did not know I was looking, and come into the room suddenly on the most innocent excuses, and I've caught him several times looking at the paper! And Jennie too. I caught Jennie with her hand on it once.

She didn't know I was in the room, and when I asked her in a quiet, a very quiet voice, with the most restrained manner possible, what she was doing with the paper—she turned around as if she had been caught stealing, and looked quite angry—asked me why I should frighten her so!

Then she said that the paper stained everything it touched, that she had found yellow smooches on all my clothes and John's, and she wished we would be more careful!

Did not that sound innocent? But I know she was studying that pattern, and I am determined that nobody shall find it out but myself!

Life is very much more exciting now than it used to be. You see I have something more to expect, to look forward to, to watch. I really do eat better, and am more quiet than I was.

John is so pleased to see me improve! He laughed a little the other day, and said I seemed to be flourishing in spite of my wallpaper.

I turned it off with a laugh. I had no intention of telling him it was *because* of the wallpaper—he would make fun of me. He might even want to take me away.

I don't want to leave now until I have found it out. There is a week more, and I think that will be enough.

I'm feeling ever so much better! I don't sleep much at night, for it is so interesting to watch developments; but I sleep a good deal in the daytime.

In the daytime it is tiresome and perplexing.

There are always new shoots on the fungus, and new shades of yellow all over it. I cannot keep count of them, though I have tried conscientiously.

It is the strangest yellow, that wallpaper! It makes me think of all the yellow things I ever saw—not beautiful ones like buttercups, but old foul, bad yellow things.

But there is something else about that paper—the smell! I noticed it the moment we came into the room, but with so much air and sun it was not bad. Now we have had a week of fog and rain, and whether the windows are open or not, the smell is here.

It creeps all over the house.

I find it hovering in the dining-room, skulking in the parlor, hiding in the hall, lying in wait for me on the stairs.

It gets into my hair.

Even when I go to ride, if I turn my head suddenly and surprise it—there is that smell!

Such a peculiar odor, too! I have spent hours in trying to analyze it, to find what it smelled like.

It is not bad—at first, and very gentle, but quite the subtlest, most enduring odor I ever met.

In this damp weather it is awful, I wake up in the night and find it hanging over me.

It used to disturb me at first. I thought seriously of burning the house—to reach the smell.

But now I am used to it. The only thing I can think of that it is like is the *color* of the paper! A yellow smell.

There is a very funny mark on this wall, low down, near the mopboard. A streak that runs round the room. It goes behind every piece of furniture, except the bed, a long, straight, even smooch, as if it had been rubbed over and over.

I wonder how it was done and who did it, and what they did it for. Round and round and round—round and round and round—it makes me dizzy!

I really have discovered something at last.

Through watching so much at night, when it changes so, I have finally found out.

The front pattern *does* move—and no wonder! The woman behind shakes it!

Sometimes I think there are a great many women behind, and sometimes only one, and she crawls around fast, and her crawling shakes it all over.

Then in the very bright spots she keeps still, and in the very shady spots she just takes hold of the bars and shakes them hard.

And she is all the time trying to climb through. But nobody could climb through that pattern—it strangles so; I think that is why it has so many heads.

They get through, and then the pattern strangles them off and turns them upside down, and makes their eyes white!

If those heads were covered or taken off it would not be half so bad.

I think that woman gets out in the daytime!

And I'll tell you why—privately—I've seen her!

I can see her out of every one of my windows!

It is the same woman, I know, for she is always creeping, and most women do not creep by daylight.

I see her on that long road under the trees, creeping along, and when a carriage comes she hides under the blackberry vines.

I don't blame her a bit. It must be very humiliating to be caught creeping by daylight!

I always lock the door when I creep by daylight. I can't do it at night, for I know John would suspect something at once.

And John is so queer now, that I don't want to irritate him. I wish he would take another room! Besides, I don't want anybody to get that woman out at night but myself.

I often wonder if I could see her out of all the windows at once.

But, turn as fast as I can, I can only see out of one at one time.

And though I always see her, she *may* be able to creep faster than I can turn!

I have watched her sometimes away off in the open country, creeping as fast as a cloud shadow in a high wind.

If only that top pattern could be gotten off from the under one! I mean to try it, little by little.

I have found out another funny thing, but I shan't tell it this time! It does not do to trust people too much.

There are only two more days to get this paper off, and I believe John is beginning to notice. I don't like the look in his eyes.

And I heard him ask Jennie a lot of professional questions about me. She had a very good report to give.

She said I slept a good deal in the daytime.

John knows I don't sleep very well at night, for all I'm so quiet!

He asked me all sorts of questions, too, and pretended to be very loving and kind.

As if I couldn't see through him!

Still, I don't wonder he acts so, sleeping under this paper for three months.

It only interests me, but I feel sure John and Jennie are secretly affected by it.

Hurrah! This is the last day, but it is enough. John is to stay in town over night, and won't be out until this evening.

Jennie wanted to sleep with me—the sly thing! but I told her I should undoubtedly rest better for a night all alone.

That was clever, for really I wasn't alone a bit! As soon as it was moonlight and that poor thing began to crawl and shake the pattern, I got up and ran to help her.

I pulled and she shook, I shook and she pulled, and before morning we had peeled off yards of that paper.

A strip about as high as my head and half around the room.

And then when the sun came and that awful pattern began to laugh at me, I declared I would finish it today!

We go away tomorrow, and they are moving all my furniture down again to leave things as they were before.

Jennie looked at the wall in amazement, but I told her merrily that I did it out of pure spite at the vicious thing.

She laughed and said she wouldn't mind doing it herself, but I must not get tired.

How she betrayed herself that time!

But I am here, and no person touches this paper but me—not *alive!*

She tried to get me out of the room—it was too patent! But I said it was so quiet and empty and clean now that I believed I would lie down again and sleep all I could; and not to wake me even for dinner—I would call when I woke.

So now she is gone, and the servants are gone, and the things are gone, and there is nothing left but that great bedstead nailed down, with the canvas mattress we found on it.

We shall sleep downstairs tonight, and take the boat home tomorrow.

I quite enjoy the room, now it is bare again.

How those children did tear about here!

This bedstead is fairly gnawed!

But I must get to work.

I have locked the door and thrown the key down into the front path.

I don't want to go out, and I don't want to have anybody come in, till John comes.

I want to astonish him.

I've got a rope up here that even Jennie did not find. If that woman does get out, and tries to get away, I can tie her!

But I forgot I could not reach far without anything to stand on!

This bed will not move!

I tried to lift and push it until I was lame, and then I got so angry I bit off a little piece at one corner—but it hurt my teeth.

Then I peeled off all the paper I could reach standing on the floor. It sticks horribly and the pattern just enjoys it! All those strangled heads and bulbous eyes and waddling fungus growths just shriek with derision!

I am getting angry enough to do something desperate. To jump out of the window would be admirable exercise, but the bars are too strong even to try.

Besides I wouldn't do it. Of course not. I know well enough that a step like that is improper and might be misconstrued.

I don't like to look out of the windows even—there are so many of those creeping women, and they creep so fast.

I wonder if they all come out of that wallpaper as I did?

But I am securely fastened now by my well-hidden rope—you don't get me out in the road there!

I suppose I shall have to get back behind the pattern when it comes night, and that is hard!

It is so pleasant to be out in this great room and creep around as I please!

I don't want to go outside. I won't, even if Jennie asks me to.

For outside you have to creep on the ground, and everything is green instead of yellow.

But here I can creep smoothly on the floor, and my shoulder just fits in that long smooch around the wall, so I cannot lose my way.

Why there's John at the door!

It is no use, young man, you can't open it!

How he does call and pound!

Now he's crying for an axe.

It would be a shame to break down that beautiful door!

"John dear!" said I in the gentlest voice, "the key is down by the front steps, under a plantain leaf!"

That silenced him for a few moments.

Then he said—very quietly indeed, "Open the door, my darling!"

"I can't," said I. "The key is down by the front door under a plantain leaf!"

And then I said it again, several times, very gently and slowly, and said it so often that he had to go and see, and he got it of course, and came in. He stopped short by the door.

"What is the matter?" he cried. "For God's sake, what are you doing!"

I kept on creeping just the same, but I looked at him over my shoulder.

"I've got out at last," said I, "in spite of you and Jane. And I've pulled off most of the paper, so you can't put me back!"

Now why should that man have fainted? But he did, and right across my path by the wall, so that I had to creep over him every time!

The Masque of the Red Death

Edgar Allan Poe

The "Red Death" had long devastated the country. No pestilence had ever been so fatal, or so hideous. Blood was its Avatar and its seal—the redness and the horror of blood. There were sharp pains, and sudden dizziness, and then profuse bleeding at the pores, with dissolution. The scarlet stains upon the body and especially upon the face of the victim, were the pest ban which shut him out from the aid and from the sympathy of his fellow-men. And the whole seizure, progress and termination of the disease, were the incidents of half an hour.

But the Prince Prospero was happy and dauntless and sagacious. When his dominions were half depopulated, he summoned to his presence a thousand hale and light-hearted friends from among the knights and dames of his court, and with these retired to the deep seclusion of one of his castellated abbeys. This was an extensive and magnificent structure, the creation of the prince's own eccentric yet august taste. A strong and lofty wall girdled it in. This wall had gates of iron. The courtiers, having entered, brought furnaces and massy hammers and welded the bolts. They resolved to leave means neither of ingress or egress to the sudden impulses of despair or of frenzy from within. The abbey was amply provisioned. With such precautions the courtiers might bid defiance to contagion. The external world could take care of itself. In the meantime it was folly to grieve, or to think. The prince had provided all the appliances of pleasure. There were buffoons, there were improvisatori, there were ballet-dancers, there were musicians, there was Beauty, there was wine. All these and security were within. Without was the "Red Death."

It was toward the close of the fifth or sixth month of his seclusion, and while the pestilence raged most furiously abroad, that the Prince Prospero entertained his thousand friends at a masked ball of the most unusual magnificence.

It was a voluptuous scene, that masquerade. But first let me tell of the rooms in which it was held. There were seven—an imperial suite. In many palaces, however, such suites form a long and straight vista, while the folding doors slide back nearly to the walls on either hand, so that the view of the whole extent is scarcely impeded. Here the case was very different; as might have been expected from the duke's love of the bizarre. The apartments were so irregularly disposed that the vision embraced but little more than one at a time. There was a sharp turn at every twenty or thirty yards, and at each turn a novel effect. To the right and left, in the middle of each wall, a tall and narrow Gothic window looked out upon a closed corridor which pursued the windings of the suite. These windows were of stained glass whose color varied in accordance with the prevailing hue of the decorations of the chamber into which it opened. That at the eastern extremity was hung, for example, in blue—and vividly blue were its windows. The second chamber was purple in its ornaments and tapestries, and here the panes were purple. The third was green throughout, and so were the casements. The fourth was furnished and lighted with orange—the fifth with white—the sixth with violet. The seventh apartment was closely shrouded in black velvet tapestries that hung all over the ceiling and down the walls, falling in heavy folds upon a carpet of the same material and hue. But in this chamber only, the color of the windows failed to correspond with the decorations. The panes here were scarlet—a deep blood color. Now in no one of the seven apartments was there any lamp or candelabrum, amid the profusion of golden ornaments that lay scattered to and fro or depended from the roof. There was no light of any kind emanating from lamp or candle within the suite of chambers. But in the corridors that followed the suite, there stood, opposite to each window, a heavy tripod, bearing a brazier of fire that protected its rays through the tinted glass and so glaringly illumined the room. And thus were produced a multitude of gaudy and fantastic appearances. But in the western or black chamber the effect of the fire-light that streamed upon the dark hangings through the blood-tinted panes, was ghastly in the extreme, and produced so wild a look upon the countenances of those who entered, that there were few of the company bold enough to set foot within its precincts at all.

It was in this apartment, also, that there stood against the western wall, a gigantic clock of ebony. Its pendulum swung to and fro with a dull, heavy, monotonous clang; and when the minute-hand made the circuit of the face, and the hour was to be stricken, there came from the brazen lungs of the clock a sound which was clear and loud and deep and exceedingly musical, but of so peculiar a note and emphasis that, at each lapse of an hour, the musicians of the orchestra were constrained to pause, momentarily, in their performance, to hearken to the sound; and thus the waltzers perforce ceased their evolutions; and there was a brief disconcert of the whole gay company; and, while the chimes of the clock yet rang, it was observed that the giddiest grew pale, and the more aged and sedate passed their hands over their brows as if in confused reverie or meditation. But when the echoes had fully ceased, a light laughter at once pervaded the assembly; the musicians looked at each other and smiled as if at their own nervousness and folly, and made whispering vows, each to the other, that the next chiming of the clock should produce in them no similar emotion; and then, after the lapse of sixty minutes (which embrace three thousand and six hundred seconds of the Time that flies), there came yet another chiming of the clock, and then were the same disconcert and tremulousness and meditation as before.

But, in spite of these things, it was a gay and magnificent revel. The tastes of the duke were peculiar. He had a fine eye for colors and effects. He disregarded the decora of mere fashion. His plans were bold and fiery, and his conceptions glowed with barbaric lustre. There are some who would have thought him mad. His followers felt that he was not. It was necessary to hear and see and touch him to be sure that he was not.

He had directed, in great part, the moveable embellishments of the seven chambers, upon occasion of this great fête; and it was his own guiding taste which had given character to the masqueraders. Be sure they were grotesque. There were much glare and glitter and piquancy and phantasm—much of what has been since seen in Hernani. There were arabesque figures with unsuited limbs and appointments. There were delirious fancies such as the madman fashions. There was much of the beautiful, much of the wanton, much of the bizarre, something of the terrible, and not a little of that which might have excited disgust. To and fro in the seven chambers there stalked, in fact, a multitude of dreams. And these—the dreams—writhed in and about, taking hue from the rooms, and causing the wild music of the orchestra to seem as the echo of their steps. And, anon, there strikes the ebony clock which stands in the hall of the velvet. And then, for a moment, all is still, and all is silent save the voice of the clock. The dreams are stiff-frozen as they stand. But the echoes of the chime die away—they have endured but an instant—and a light, half-subdued laughter floats after them as they depart. And now again the music swells, and the dreams live, and writhe to and fro more merrily than ever, taking hue from the many-tinted windows through which stream the rays from the tripods. But to the chamber which lies most westwardly of the seven, there are now none of the maskers who venture; for the night is waning away; and there flows a ruddier light through the blood-colored panes; and the blackness of the sable drapery appals; and to him whose foot falls upon the sable carpet, there comes from the near clock of ebony a muffled peal more solemnly emphatic than any which reaches their ears who indulge in the more remote gaieties of the other apartments.

But these other apartments were densely crowded, and in them beat feverishly the heart of life. And the revel went whirlingly on, until at length there commenced the sounding of midnight upon the clock. And then the music ceased, as I have told; and the evolutions of the waltzers were quieted; and there was an uneasy cessation of all things as before. But now there were twelve strokes to be sounded by the bell of the clock; and thus it happened, perhaps, that more of thought crept, with more of time, into the meditations of the thoughtful among those who revelled. And thus, too, it happened, perhaps, that before the last echoes of the last chime had utterly sunk into silence, there were many individuals in the crowd who had found leisure to become aware of the presence of a masked figure which had arrested the attention of no single individual before. And the rumor of this new presence having spread itself whisperingly around, there arose at length from the whole company a buzz, or murmur, expressive of disapprobation and surprise—then, finally, of terror, of horror, and of disgust.

In an assembly of phantasms such as I have painted, it may well be supposed that no ordinary appearance could have excited such sensation. In truth the masquerade license of the night was nearly unlimited; but the figure in question had out-Heroded Herod, and gone beyond the bounds of even the prince's indefinite decorum. There are chords in the hearts of the most reckless which cannot be touched without emotion. Even with the utterly lost, to whom life and death are equally jests, there are matters of which no jest can be made. The whole company, indeed, seemed now deeply to feel that in the costume and bearing of the stranger neither wit nor propriety existed. The figure was tall and gaunt, and shrouded from head to foot in the habiliments of the grave. The mask which concealed the visage was made so nearly to resemble the countenance of a stiffened corpse that the closest scrutiny must have had difficulty in detecting the cheat. And yet all this might have been endured, if not approved, by the mad revellers around. But the mummer had gone so far as to assume the type of the Red Death. His vesture was dabbled in *blood*—and his broad brow, with all the features of the face, was besprinkled with the scarlet horror.

When the eyes of Prince Prospero fell upon this spectral image (which with a slow and solemn movement, as if more fully to sustain its role, stalked to and fro among the waltzers) he was seen to be convulsed, in the first moment with a strong shudder either of terror or distaste; but, in the next, his brow reddened with rage.

"Who dares?" he demanded hoarsely of the courtiers who stood near him—"who dares insult us with this blasphemous mockery? Seize him and unmask him—that we may know whom we have to hang at sunrise, from the battlements!"

It was in the eastern or blue chamber in which stood the Prince Prospero as he uttered these words. They rang throughout the seven rooms loudly and clearly—for the prince was a bold and robust man, and the music had become hushed at the waving of his hand.

It was in the blue room where stood the prince, with a group of pale courtiers by his side. At first, as he spoke, there was a slight rushing movement of this group in the direction of the intruder, who at the moment was also near at hand, and now, with deliberate and stately step, made closer approach to the speaker. But from a certain nameless awe with which the mad assumptions of the mummer had inspired the whole party, there were found none who put forth hand to seize him; so that, unimpeded, he passed within a yard of the prince's person; and, while the vast assembly, as if with one impulse, shrank from the centres of the rooms to the walls, he made his way uninterruptedly, but with the same solemn and measured step which had distinguished him from the first, through the blue chamber to the purple—through the purple to the green—through the green to the orange—through this again to the white—and even thence to the violet, ere a decided movement had been made to arrest him. It was then, however, that the Prince Prospero, maddening with rage and the shame of his own momentary cowardice, rushed hurriedly through the six chambers, while none followed him on account of a deadly terror that had seized upon all. He bore aloft a drawn dagger, and had approached, in rapid impetuosity, to within three or four feet of the retreating figure, when the latter, having attained the extremity of the velvet apartment, turned suddenly and confronted his pursuer. There was a sharp cry—and the dagger dropped gleaming upon the sable carpet, upon which, instantly afterwards, fell prostrate in death the Prince Prospero. Then, summoning the wild courage of despair, a throng of the revellers at once threw themselves into the black apartment, and, seizing the mummer, whose tall figure stood erect and motionless within the shadow of the ebony clock, gasped in unutterable horror at finding the grave-cerements and corpse-like mask which they handled with so violent a rudeness, untenanted by any tangible form.

And now was acknowledged the presence of the Red Death. He had come like a thief in the night. And one by one dropped the revellers in the blood-bedewed halls of their revel, and died each in the despairing posture of his fall. And the life of the ebony clock went out with that of the last of the gay. And the flames of the tripods expired. And Darkness and Decay and the Red Death held illimitable dominion over all.

The Outsider

H. P. Lovecraft

That night the Baron dreamt of many a woe;
And all his warrior-guests, with shade and form
Of witch, and demon, and large coffin-worm,
Were long be-nightmared.

—KEATS

Unhappy is he to whom the memories of childhood bring only fear and sadness. Wretched is he who looks back upon lone hours in vast and dismal chambers with brown hangings and maddening rows of antique books, or upon awed watches in twilight groves of grotesque, gigantic, and vine-encumbered trees that silently wave twisted branches far aloft. Such a lot the gods gave to me—to me, the dazed, the disappointed; the barren, the broken. And yet I am strangely content, and cling desperately to those sere memories, when my mind momentarily threatens to reach beyond to the other.

I know not where I was born, save that the castle was infinitely old and infinitely horrible; full of dark passages and having high ceilings where the eye could find only cobwebs and shadows. The stones in the crumbling corridors seemed always hideously damp, and there was an accursed smell everywhere, as of the piled-up corpses of dead generations. It was never light, so that I used sometimes to light candles and gaze steadily at them for relief; nor was there any sun outdoors, since the terrible trees grew high above the topmost accessible tower. There was one black tower which reached above the trees into the unknown outer sky, but that was partly ruined and could not be ascended save by a well-nigh impossible climb up the sheer wall, stone by stone.

I must have lived years in this place, but I cannot measure the time. Beings must have cared for my needs, yet I cannot recall any person except myself; or anything alive but the noiseless rats and bats and spiders. I think that whoever nursed me must have been shockingly aged, since my first conception of a living person was that of something mockingly like myself, yet distorted, shrivelled, and decaying like the castle. To me there was nothing grotesque in the bones and skeletons that strowed some of the stone crypts deep down among the foundations. I fantastically associated these things with every-day events, and thought them more natural than the coloured pictures of living beings which I found in many of the mouldy books. From such books I learned all that I know. No teacher urged or guided me, and I do not recall hearing any human voice in all those years—not even my own; for although I had read of speech, I had never thought to try to speak aloud. My aspect was a matter equally unthought of, for there were no mirrors in the castle, and I merely regarded myself by instinct as akin to the youthful figures I saw drawn and painted in the books. I felt conscious of youth because I remembered so little.

Outside, across the putrid moat and under the dark mute trees, I would often lie and dream for hours about what I read in the books; and would longingly picture myself amidst gay crowds in the sunny world beyond the endless forest. Once I tried to escape from the forest, but as I went farther from the castle the shade grew denser and the air more filled with brooding fear; so that I ran frantically back lest I lose my way in a labyrinth of nighted silence.

So through endless twilights I dreamed and waited, though I knew not what I waited for. Then in the shadowy solitude my longing for light grew so frantic that I could rest no more, and I lifted entreating hands to the single black ruined tower that reached above the forest into the unknown outer sky. And at last I resolved to scale that tower, fall though I might; since it were better to glimpse the sky and perish, than to live without ever beholding day.

In the dank twilight I climbed the worn and aged stone stairs till I reached the level where they ceased, and thereafter clung perilously to small footholds leading upward. Ghastly and terrible was that dead, stairless cylinder of rock; black, ruined, and deserted, and sinister with startled bats whose wings made no noise. But more ghastly and terrible still was the slowness of my progress; for climb as I might, the darkness overhead grew no thinner, and a new chill as of haunted and venerable mould assailed me. I shivered as I wondered why I did not reach the light, and would have looked down had I dared. I fancied that night had come suddenly upon me, and vainly groped with one free hand for a window embrasure, that I might peer out and above, and try to judge the height I had attained.

All at once, after an infinity of awesome, sightless crawling up that concave and desperate precipice, I felt my head touch a solid thing, and I knew I must have gained the roof, or at least some kind of floor. In the darkness I raised my free hand and tested the barrier, finding it stone and immovable. Then came a deadly circuit of the tower, clinging to whatever holds the slimy wall could give; till finally my testing hand found the barrier yielding, and I turned upward again, pushing the slab or door with my head as I used both hands in my fearful ascent. There was no light revealed above, and as my hands went higher I knew that my climb was for the nonce ended; since the slab was the trap-door of an aperture leading to a level stone surface of greater circumference than the lower tower, no doubt the floor of some lofty and capacious observation chamber. I crawled through carefully, and tried to prevent the heavy slab from falling back into place; but failed in the latter attempt. As I lay exhausted on the stone floor I heard the eerie echoes of its fall, but hoped when necessary to pry it open again.

Believing I was now at a prodigious height, far above the accursed branches of the wood, I dragged myself up from the floor and fumbled about for windows, that I might look for the first time upon the sky, and the moon and stars of which I had read. But on every hand I was disappointed; since all that I found were vast shelves of marble, bearing odious oblong boxes of disturbing size. More and more I reflected, and wondered what hoary secrets might abide in this high apartment so many aeons cut off from the castle below. Then unexpectedly my hands came upon a doorway, where hung a portal of stone, rough with strange chiselling. Trying it, I found it locked; but with a supreme burst of strength I overcame all obstacles and dragged it open inward. As I did so there came to me the purest ecstasy I have ever known; for shining tranquilly through an ornate grating of iron, and down a short stone passageway of steps that ascended from the newly found doorway, was the radiant full moon, which I had never before seen save in dreams and in vague visions I dared not call memories.

Fancying now that I had attained the very pinnacle of the castle, I commenced to rush up the few steps beyond the door; but the sudden veiling of the moon by a cloud caused me to stumble, and I felt my way more slowly in the dark. It was still very dark when I reached the grating—which I tried carefully and found unlocked, but which I did not open for fear of falling from the amazing height to which I had climbed. Then the moon came out.

Most daemoniacal of all shocks is that of the abysmally unexpected and grotesquely unbelievable. Nothing I had before undergone could compare in terror with what I now saw; with the bizarre marvels that sight implied. The sight itself was as simple as it was stupefying, for it was merely this: instead of a dizzying prospect of treetops seen from a lofty eminence, there stretched around me on a level through the grating nothing less than the solid ground, decked and diversified by marble slabs and columns, and overshadowed by an ancient stone church, whose ruined spire gleamed spectrally in the moonlight.

Half unconscious, I opened the grating and staggered out upon the white gravel path that stretched away in two directions. My mind, stunned and chaotic as it was, still held the frantic craving for light; and not even the fantastic wonder which had happened could stay my course. I neither knew nor cared whether my experience was insanity, dreaming, or magic; but was determined to gaze on brilliance and gaiety at any cost. I knew not who I was or what I was, or what my surroundings might be; though as I continued to stumble along I became conscious of a kind of fearsome latent memory that made my progress not wholly fortuitous. I passed under an arch out of that region of slabs and columns, and wandered through the open country; sometimes following the visible road, but sometimes leaving it curiously to tread across meadows where only occasional ruins bespoke the ancient presence of a forgotten road. Once I swam across a swift river where crumbling, mossy masonry told of a bridge long vanished.

Over two hours must have passed before I reached what seemed to be my goal, a venerable ivied castle in a thickly wooded park; maddeningly familiar, yet full of perplexing strangeness to me. I saw that the moat was filled in, and that some of the well-known towers were demolished; whilst new wings existed to confuse the beholder. But what I observed with chief interest and delight were the open windows—gorgeously ablaze with light and sending forth sound of the gayest revelry. Advancing to one of these I looked in and saw an oddly dressed company, indeed; making merry, and speaking brightly to one another. I had never, seemingly, heard human speech before; and could guess only vaguely what was said. Some of the faces seemed to hold expressions that brought up incredibly remote recollections; others were utterly alien.

I now stepped through the low window into the brilliantly lighted room, stepping as I did so from my single bright moment of hope to my blackest convulsion of despair and realisation. The nightmare was quick to come; for as I entered, there occurred immediately one of the most terrifying demonstrations I had ever conceived. Scarcely had I crossed the sill when there descended upon the whole company a sudden and unheralded fear of hideous intensity, distorting every face and evoking the most horrible screams from nearly every throat. Flight was universal, and in the clamour and panic several fell in a swoon and were dragged away by their madly fleeing companions. Many covered their eyes with their hands, and plunged blindly and awkwardly in their race to escape; overturning furniture and stumbling against the walls before they managed to reach one of the many doors.

The cries were shocking; and as I stood in the brilliant apartment alone and dazed, listening to their vanishing echoes, I trembled at the thought of what might be lurking near me unseen. At a casual inspection the room seemed deserted, but when I moved toward one of the alcoves I thought I detected a presence there—a hint of motion beyond the golden-arched doorway leading to another and somewhat similar room. As I approached the arch I began to perceive the presence more clearly; and then, with the first and last sound I ever uttered—a ghastly ululation that revolted me almost as poignantly as its noxious cause—I beheld in full, frightful vividness the inconceivable, indescribable, and unmentionable monstrosity which had by its simple appearance changed a merry company to a herd of delirious fugitives.

I cannot even hint what it was like, for it was a compound of all that is unclean, uncanny, unwelcome, abnormal, and detestable. It was the ghoulish shade of decay, antiquity, and desolation; the putrid, dripping eidolon of unwholesome revelation; the awful baring of that which the merciful earth should always hide. God knows it was not of this world—or no longer of this world—yet to my horror I saw in its eaten-away and bone-revealing outlines a leering, abhorrent travesty on the human shape; and in its mouldy, disintegrating apparel an unspeakable quality that chilled me even more.

I was almost paralysed, but not too much so to make a feeble effort toward flight; a backward stumble which failed to break the spell in which the nameless, voiceless monster held me. My eyes, bewitched by the glassy orbs which stared loathsomely into them, refused to close; though they were mercifully blurred, and shewed the terrible object but indistinctly after the first shock. I tried to raise my hand to shut out the sight, yet so stunned were my nerves that my arm could not fully obey my will. The attempt, however, was enough to disturb my balance; so that I had to stagger forward several steps to avoid falling. As I did so I became suddenly and agonisingly aware of the nearness of the carrion thing, whose hideous hollow breathing I half fancied I could hear. Nearly mad, I found myself yet able to throw out a hand to ward off the foetid apparition which pressed so close; when in one cataclysmic second of cosmic nightmarishness and hellish accident *my fingers touched the rotting outstretched paw of the monster beneath the golden arch.*

I did not shriek, but all the fiendish ghouls that ride the night-wind shrieked for me as in that same second there crashed down upon my mind a single and fleeting avalanche of soul-annihilating memory. I knew in that second all that had been; I remembered beyond the frightful castle and the trees, and recognised the altered edifice in which I now stood; I recognised, most terrible of all, the unholy abomination that stood leering before me as I withdrew my sullied fingers from its own.

But in the cosmos there is balm as well as bitterness, and that balm is nepenthe. In the supreme horror of that second I forgot what had horrified me, and the burst of black memory vanished in a chaos of echoing images. In a dream I fled from that haunted and accursed pile, and ran swiftly and silently in the moonlight. When I returned to the churchyard place of marble and went down the steps I found the stone trap-door immovable; but I was not sorry, for I had hated the antique castle and the trees. Now I ride with the mocking and friendly ghouls on the night-wind, and play by day amongst the catacombs of Nephren-Ka in the sealed and unknown valley of Hadoth by the Nile. I know that light is not for me, save that of the moon over the rock tombs of Neb, nor any gaiety save the unnamed feasts of Nitokris beneath the Great Pyramid; yet in my new wildness and freedom I almost welcome the bitterness of alienage.

For although nepenthe has calmed me, I know always that I am an outsider; a stranger in this century and among those who are still men. This I have known ever since I stretched out my fingers to the abomination within that great gilded frame; stretched out my fingers and touched *a cold and unyielding surface of polished glass.*

Canon Alberic's Scrap-book

M. R. James

St. Bertrand de Comminges is a decayed town on the spurs of the Pyrenees, not very far from Toulouse, and still nearer to Bagnères-de-Luchon. It was the site of a bishopric until the Revolution, and has a cathedral which is visited by a certain number of tourists. In the spring of 1883 an Englishman arrived at this old-world place—I can hardly dignify it with the name of city, for there are not a thousand inhabitants. He was a Cambridge man, who had come specially from Toulouse to see St. Bertrand's Church, and had left two friends, who were less keen archaeologists than himself, in their hotel at Toulouse, under promise to join him on the following morning. Half an hour at the church would satisfy *them*, and all three could then pursue their journey in the direction of Auch. But our Englishman had come early on the day in question, and proposed to himself to fill a note-book and to use several dozens of plates in the process of describing and photographing every corner of the wonderful church that dominates the little hill of Comminges. In order to carry out this design satisfactorily, it was necessary to monopolize the verger of the church for the day. The verger or sacristan (I prefer the latter appellation, inaccurate as it may be) was accordingly sent for by the somewhat brusque lady who keeps the inn of the Chapeau Rouge; and when he came, the Englishman found him an unexpectedly interesting object of study. It was not in the personal appearance of the little, dry, wizened old man that the interest lay, for he was precisely like dozens of other church-guardians in France, but in a curious furtive or rather hunted and oppressed air which he had. He was perpetually half glancing behind him; the muscles of his back and shoulders seemed to be hunched in a continual nervous contraction, as if he were expecting every moment to find himself in the clutch of an enemy. The Englishman hardly knew whether to put him down as a man haunted by a fixed delusion, or as one oppressed by a guilty conscience, or as an unbearably henpecked husband. The probabilities, when reckoned up, certainly pointed to the last idea; but, still, the impression conveyed was that of a more formidable persecutor even than a termagant wife.

However, the Englishman (let us call him Dennistoun) was soon too deep in his note-book and too busy with his camera to give more than an occasional glance to the sacristan. Whenever he did look at him, he found him at no great distance, either huddling himself back against the wall or crouching in one of the gorgeous stalls. Dennistoun became rather fidgety after a time. Mingled suspicions that he was keeping the old man from his *déjeuner*, that he was regarded as likely to make away with St. Bertrand's ivory crozier, or with the dusty stuffed crocodile that hangs over the font, began to torment him.

"Won't you go home?" he said at last; "I'm quite well able to finish my notes alone; you can lock me in if you like. I shall want at least two hours more here, and it must be cold for you, isn't it?"

"Good heavens!" said the little man, whom the suggestion seemed to throw into a state of unaccountable terror, "such a thing cannot be thought of for a moment. Leave monsieur alone in the church? No, no; two hours, three hours, all will be the same to me. I have breakfasted, I am not at all cold, with many thanks to monsieur."

"Very well, my little man," quoth Dennistoun to himself: "you have been warned, and you must take the consequences."

Before the expiration of the two hours, the stalls, the enormous dilapidated organ, the choir-screen of Bishop John de Mauléon, the remnants of glass and tapestry, and the objects in the treasure-chamber had been well and truly examined; the sacristan still keeping at Dennistoun's heels, and every now and then whipping round as if he had been stung, when one or other of the strange noises that trouble a large empty building fell on his ear. Curious noises they were, sometimes.

"Once," Dennistoun said to me, "I could have sworn I heard a thin metallic voice laughing high up in the tower. I darted an inquiring glance at my sacristan. He was white to the lips. 'It is he—that is—it is no one; the door is locked,' was all he said, and we looked at each other for a full minute."

Another little incident puzzled Dennistoun a good deal. He was examining a large dark picture that hangs behind the altar, one of a series illustrating the miracles of St. Bertrand. The composition of the picture is well-nigh indecipherable, but there is a Latin legend below, which runs thus:

Qualiter S. Bertrandus liberavit hominem quem diabolus diu volebat strangulare. (How St. Bertrand delivered a man whom the Devil long sought to strangle.)

Dennistoun was turning to the sacristan with a smile and a jocular remark of some sort on his lips, but he was confounded to see the old man on his knees, gazing at the picture with the eye of a suppliant in agony, his hands tightly clasped, and a rain of tears on his cheeks. Dennistoun naturally pretended to have noticed nothing, but the question would not go away from him, "Why should a daub of this kind affect anyone so strongly?" He seemed to himself to be getting some sort of clue to the reason of the strange look that had been puzzling him all the day: the man must be a monomaniac; but what was his monomania?

It was nearly five o'clock; the short day was drawing in, and the church began to fill with shadows, while the curious noises—the muffled footfalls and distant talking voices that had been perceptible all day—seemed, no doubt because of the fading light and the consequently quickened sense of hearing, to become more frequent and insistent.

The sacristan began for the first time to show signs of hurry and impatience. He heaved a sigh of relief when camera and note-book were finally packed up and stowed away, and hurriedly beckoned Dennistoun to the western door of the church, under the tower. It was time to ring the Angelus. A few pulls at the reluctant rope, and the great bell Bertrande, high in the tower, began to speak, and swung her voice up among the pines and down to the valleys, loud with mountain-streams, calling the dwellers on those lonely hills to remember and repeat the salutation of the angel to her whom he called Blessed among women. With that a profound quiet seemed to fall for the first time that day upon the little town, and Dennistoun and the sacristan went out of the church.

On the doorstep they fell into conversation.

"Monsieur seemed to interest himself in the old choir-books in the sacristy."

"Undoubtedly. I was going to ask you if there were a library in the town."

"No, monsieur; perhaps there used to be one belonging to the Chapter, but it is now such a small place—" Here came a strange pause of irresolution, as it seemed; then, with a sort of plunge, he went on: "But if monsieur is *amateur des vieux livres*, I have at home something that might interest him. It is not a hundred yards."

At once all Dennistoun's cherished dreams of finding priceless manuscripts in untrodden corners of France flashed up, to die down again the next moment. It was probably a stupid missal of Plantin's printing, about 1580. Where was the likelihood that a place so near Toulouse would not have been ransacked long ago by collectors? However, it would be foolish not to go; he would reproach himself for ever after if he refused. So they set off. On the way the curious irresolution and sudden determination of the sacristan recurred to Dennistoun, and he wondered in a shamefaced way whether he was being decoyed into some purlieu to be made away with as a supposed rich Englishman. He contrived, therefore, to begin talking with his guide, and to drag in, in a rather clumsy fashion, the fact that he expected two friends to join him early the next morning. To his surprise, the announcement seemed to relieve the sacristan at once of some of the anxiety that oppressed him.

"That is well," he said quite brightly—"that is very well. Monsieur will travel in company with his friends: they will be always near him. It is a good thing to travel thus in company—sometimes."

The last word appeared to be added as an afterthought and to bring with it a relapse into gloom for the poor little man.

They were soon at the house, which was one rather larger than its neighbours, stone-built, with a shield carved over the door, the shield of Alberic de Mauléon, a collateral descendant, Dennistoun tells me, of Bishop John de Mauléon. This Alberic was a Canon of Comminges from 1680 to 1701. The upper windows of the mansion were boarded up, and the whole place bore, as does the rest of Comminges, the aspect of decaying age.

Arrived on his doorstep, the sacristan paused a moment.

"Perhaps," he said, "perhaps, after all, monsieur has not the time?"

"Not at all—lots of time—nothing to do till tomorrow. Let us see what it is you have got."

The door was opened at this point, and a face looked out, a face far younger than the sacristan's, but bearing something of the same distressing look: only here it seemed to be the mark, not so much of fear for personal safety as of acute anxiety on behalf of another. Plainly the owner of the face was the sacristan's daughter; and, but for the expression I have described, she was a handsome girl enough. She brightened up considerably on seeing her father accompanied by an able-bodied stranger. A few remarks passed between father and daughter of which Dennistoun only caught these words, said by the sacristan: "He was laughing in the church," words which were answered only by a look of terror from the girl.

But in another minute they were in the sitting-room of the house, a small, high chamber with a stone floor, full of moving shadows cast by a wood-fire that flickered on a great hearth. Something of the character of an oratory was imparted to it by a tall crucifix, which reached almost to the ceiling on one side; the figure was painted of the natural colours, the cross was black. Under this stood a chest of some age and solidity, and when a lamp had been brought, and chairs set, the sacristan went to this chest, and produced therefrom, with growing excitement and nervousness, as Dennistoun thought, a large book, wrapped in a white cloth, on which cloth a cross was rudely embroidered in red thread. Even before the wrapping had been removed, Dennistoun began to be interested by the size and shape of the volume. "Too large for a missal," he thought, "and not the shape of an antiphoner; perhaps it may be something good, after all." The next moment the book was open, and Dennistoun felt that he had at last lit upon something better than good. Before him lay a large folio, bound, perhaps, late in the seventeenth century, with the arms of Canon Alberic de Mauléon stamped in gold on the sides. There may have been a hundred and fifty leaves of paper in the book, and on almost every one of them was fastened a leaf from an illuminated manuscript. Such a collection Dennistoun had hardly dreamed of in his wildest moments. Here were ten leaves from a copy of Genesis, illustrated with pictures, which could not be later than A.D. 700. Further on was a complete set of pictures from a Psalter, of English execution, of the very finest kind that the thirteenth century could produce; and, perhaps best of all, there were twenty leaves of uncial writing in Latin, which, as a few words seen here and there told him at once, must belong to some very early unknown patristic treatise. Could it possibly be a fragment of the copy of Papias "On the Words of Our Lord," which was known to have existed as late as the twelfth century at Nimes?* In any case, his mind was made up; that book must return to Cambridge with him, even if he had to draw the whole of his balance from the bank and stay at St. Bertrand till the money came. He glanced up at the sacristan to see if his face yielded any hint that the book was for sale. The sacristan was pale, and his lips were working.

"If monsieur will turn on to the end," he said.

So monsieur turned on, meeting new treasures at every rise of a leaf; and at the end of the book he came upon two sheets of paper, of much more recent date than anything he had seen yet, which puzzled him considerably. They must be contemporary, he decided, with the unprincipled Canon Alberic, who had doubtless plundered the Chapter library of St. Bertrand to form this priceless scrap-book. On the first of the paper sheets was a plan, carefully drawn and instantly recognizable by a person who knew the ground, of the south aisle and cloisters of St. Bertrand's. There were curious signs looking like planetary symbols, and a few Hebrew words in the corners; and in the north-west angle of the cloister was a cross drawn in gold paint. Below the plan were some lines of writing in Latin, which ran thus:

Responsa 12(mi) Dec. 1694. Interrogatum est: Inveniamne? Responsum est: Invenies. Fiamne dives? Fies. Vivamne invidendus? Vives. Moriarne in lecto meo? Ita.

(Answers of the 12th of December, 1694. It was asked: Shall I find it? Answer: Thou shalt. Shall I become rich? Thou wilt. Shall I live an object of envy? Thou wilt. Shall I die in my bed? Thou wilt.)

* We now know that these leaves did contain an actual fragment of that work, if not of that actual copy of it.

"A good specimen of the treasure-hunter's record—quite reminds one of Mr. Minor-Canon Quatremain in *Old St. Paul's*," was Dennistoun's comment, and he turned the leaf.

What he then saw impressed him, as he has often told me, more than he could have conceived any drawing or picture capable of impressing him. And, though the drawing he saw is no longer in existence, there is a photograph of it (which I possess) which fully bears out that statement. The picture in question was a sepia drawing at the end of the seventeenth century, representing, one would say at first sight, a Biblical scene; for the architecture (the picture represented an interior) and the figures had that semi-classical flavour about them which the artists of two hundred years ago thought appropriate to illustrations of the Bible. On the right was a king on his throne, the throne elevated on twelve steps, a canopy overhead, soldiers on either side—evidently King Solomon. He was bending forward with outstretched sceptre, in attitude of command; his face expressed horror and disgust, yet there was in it also the mark of imperious command and confident power. The left half of the picture was the strangest, however. The interest plainly centred there.

On the pavement before the throne were grouped four soldiers, surrounding a crouching figure which must be described in a moment. A fifth soldier lay dead on the pavement, his neck distorted, and his eye-balls starting from his head. The four surrounding guards were looking at the King. In their faces, the sentiment of horror was intensified; they seemed, in fact, only restrained from flight by their implicit trust in their master. All this terror was plainly excited by the being that crouched in their midst.

I entirely despair of conveying by any words the impression which this figure makes upon anyone who looks at it. I recollect once showing the photograph of the drawing to a lecturer on morphology—a person of, I was going to say, abnormally sane and unimaginative habits of mind. He absolutely refused to be alone for the rest of that evening, and he told me afterwards that for many nights he had not dared to put out his light before going to sleep. However, the main traits of the figure I can at least indicate.

At first you saw only a mass of coarse, matted black hair; presently it was seen that this covered a body of fearful thinness, almost a skeleton, but with the muscles standing out like wires. The hands were of a dusky pallor, covered, like the body, with long, coarse hairs, and hideously taloned. The eyes, touched in with a burning yellow, had intensely black pupils, and were fixed upon the throned King with a look of beast-like hate. Imagine one of the awful bird-catching spiders of South America translated into human form, and endowed with intelligence just less than human, and you will have some faint conception of the terror inspired by the appalling effigy. One remark is universally made by those to whom I have shown the picture: "It was drawn from the life."

As soon as the first shock of his irresistible fright had subsided, Dennistoun stole a look at his hosts. The sacristan's hands were pressed upon his eyes; his daughter, looking up at the cross on the wall, was telling her beads feverishly.

At last the question was asked: "Is this book for sale?"

There was the same hesitation, the same plunge of determination that he had noticed before, and then came the welcome answer: "If monsieur pleases."

"How much do you ask for it?"

"I will take two hundred and fifty francs."

This was confounding. Even a collector's conscience is sometimes stirred, and Dennistoun's conscience was tenderer than a collector's.

"My good man!" he said again and again, "your book is worth far more than two hundred and fifty francs. I assure you—far more."

But the answer did not vary: "I will take two hundred and fifty francs—not more."

There was really no possibility of refusing such a chance. The money was paid, the receipt signed, a glass of wine drunk over the transaction, and then the sacristan seemed to become a new man. He stood upright, he ceased to throw those suspicious glances behind him, he actually laughed or tried to laugh. Dennistoun rose to go.

"I shall have the honour of accompanying monsieur to his hotel?" said the sacristan.

"Oh, no, thanks! it isn't a hundred yards. I know the way perfectly, and there is a moon."

The offer was pressed three or four times and refused as often.

"Then, monsieur will summon me if—if he finds occasion; he will keep the middle of the road, the sides are so rough."

"Certainly, certainly," said Dennistoun, who was impatient to examine his prize by himself; and he stepped out into the passage with his book under his arm.

Here he was met by the daughter; she, it appeared, was anxious to do a little business on her own account; perhaps, like Gehazi, to "take somewhat" from the foreigner whom her father had spared.

"A silver crucifix and chain for the neck; monsieur would perhaps be good enough to accept it?"

Well, really, Dennistoun hadn't much use for these things. What did mademoiselle want for it?

"Nothing—nothing in the world. Monsieur is more than welcome to it."

The tone in which this and much more was said was unmistakably genuine, so that Dennistoun was reduced to profuse thanks, and submitted to have the chain put round his neck. It really seemed as if he had rendered the father and daughter some service which they hardly knew how to repay. As he set off with his book they stood at the door looking after him, and they were still looking when he waved them a last good night from the steps of the Chapeau Rouge.

Dinner was over, and Dennistoun was in his bedroom, shut up alone with his acquisition. The landlady had manifested a particular interest in him since he had told her that he had paid a visit to the sacristan and bought an old book from him. He thought, too, that he had heard a hurried dialogue between her and the said sacristan in the passage outside the *salle à manger*; some words to the effect that "Pierre and Bertrand would be sleeping in the house" had closed the conversation.

All this time a growing feeling of discomfort had been creeping over him—nervous reaction, perhaps, after the delight of his discovery. Whatever it was, it resulted in a conviction that there was someone behind him, and that he was far more comfortable with his back to the wall. All this, of course, weighed light in the balance as against the obvious value of the collection he had acquired. And now, as I said, he was alone in his bedroom, taking stock of Canon Alberic's treasures, in which every moment revealed something more charming.

"Bless Canon Alberic!" said Dennistoun, who had an inveterate habit of talking to himself. "I wonder where he is now? Dear me! I wish that landlady would learn to laugh in a more cheering manner; it makes one feel as if there was someone dead in the house. Half a pipe more, did you say? I think perhaps you are right. I wonder what that crucifix is that the young woman insisted on giving me? Last century, I suppose. Yes, probably. It is rather a nuisance of a thing to have round one's neck—just too heavy. Most likely her father has been wearing it for years. I think I might give it a clean up before I put it away."

He had taken the crucifix off, and laid it on the table, when his attention was caught by an object lying on the red cloth just by his left elbow. Two or three ideas of what it might be flitted through his brain with their own incalculable quickness.

A penwiper? No, no such thing in the house. A rat? No, too black. A large spider? I trust to goodness not—no. Good God! a hand like the hand in that picture!

In another infinitesimal flash he had taken it in. Pale, dusky skin, covering nothing but bones and tendons of appalling strength; coarse black hairs, longer than ever grew on a human hand; nails rising from the ends of the fingers and curving sharply down and forward, grey, horny, and wrinkled.

He flew out of his chair with deadly, inconceivable terror clutching at his heart. The shape, whose left hand rested on the table, was rising to a standing posture behind his seat, its right hand crooked above his scalp. There was black and tattered drapery about it; the coarse hair covered it as in the drawing. The lower jaw was thin—what can I call it?—shallow, like a beast's; teeth showed behind the black lips; there was no nose; the eyes, of a fiery yellow, against which the pupils showed black and intense, and the exulting hate and thirst to destroy life which shone there, were the most horrifying features in the whole vision. There was intelligence of a kind in them—intelligence beyond that of a beast, below that of a man.

The feelings which this horror stirred in Dennistoun were the intensest physical fear and the most profound mental loathing. What did he do? What could he do? He has never been quite certain what words he said, but he knows that he spoke, that he grasped blindly at the silver crucifix, that he was conscious of a movement towards him on the part of the demon, and that he screamed with the voice of an animal in hideous pain.

Pierre and Bertrand, the two sturdy little serving-men, who rushed in, saw nothing, but felt themselves thrust aside by something that passed out between them, and found Dennistoun in a swoon. They sat up with him that night, and his two friends were at St. Bertrand by nine o'clock next morning. He himself, though still shaken and nervous, was almost himself by that time, and his story found credence with them, though not until they had seen the drawing and talked with the sacristan.

Almost at dawn the little man had come to the inn on some pretence, and had listened with the deepest interest to the story retailed by the landlady. He showed no surprise.

"It is he—it is he! I have seen him myself," was his only comment; and to all questionings but one reply was vouchsafed: "Deux fois je l'ai vu: mille fois je l'ai senti." He would tell them nothing of the provenance of the book, nor any details of his experiences. "I shall soon sleep, and my rest will be sweet. Why should you trouble me?" he said.*

We shall never know what he or Canon Alberic de Mauléon suffered. At the back of that fateful drawing were some lines of writing which may be supposed to throw light on the situation:

* He died that summer; his daughter married, and settled at St. Papoul. She never understood the circumstances of her father's "obsession."

*Contradictio Salomonis cum demonio nocturno. Albericus de Mauléone delineavit. V. Deus in adiutorium. Ps. Qui habitat. Sancte Bertrande, demoniorum effugator, intercede pro me miserrimo. Primum uidi nocte 12(mi) Dec. 1694: uidebo mox ultimum. Peccaui et passus sum, plura adhuc passurus. Dec. 29, 1701.**

The "Gallia Christiana" gives the date of the Canon's death as December 31, 1701, "in bed, of a sudden seizure." Details of this kind are not common in the great work of the Sammarthani.

I have never quite understood what was Dennistoun's view of the events I have narrated. He quoted to me once a text from Ecclesiasticus: "Some spirits there be that are created for vengeance, and in their fury lay on sore strokes." On another occasion he said: "Isaiah was a very sensible man; doesn't he say something about night monsters living in the ruins of Babylon? These things are rather beyond us at present."

Another confidence of his impressed me rather, and I sympathized with it. We had been, last year, to Comminges, to see Canon Alberic's tomb. It is a great marble erection with an effigy of the Canon in a large wig and soutane, and an elaborate eulogy of his learning below. I saw Dennistoun talking for some time with the Vicar of St. Bertrand's, and as we drove away he said to me: "I hope it isn't wrong: you know I am a Presbyterian—but I—I believe there will be 'saying of Mass and singing of dirges' for Alberic de Mauléon's rest. Then he added, with a touch of the Northern British in his tone, "I had no notion they came so dear."

* * * * *

The book is in the Wentworth Collection at Cambridge. The drawing was photographed and then burnt by Dennistoun on the day when he left Comminges on the occasion of his first visit.

* The Dispute of Solomon with a demon of the night. Drawn by Alberic de Mauléon. Versicle. O Lord, make haste to help me. Psalm. Whoso dwelleth xci. Saint Bernard, who puttest devils to flight, pray for me most unhappy. I saw it first on the night of Dec. 12, 1694: soon I shall see it for the last time. I have sinned and suffered, and have more to suffer yet. Dec. 29, 1701.

The Trial for Murder

Charles Dickens

I have always noticed a prevalent want of courage, even among persons of superior intelligence and culture, as to imparting their own psychological experiences when those have been of a strange sort. Almost all men are afraid that what they could relate in such wise would find no parallel or response in a listener's internal life, and might be suspected or laughed at. A truthful traveller, who should have seen some extraordinary creature in the likeness of a sea-serpent, would have no fear of mentioning it; but the same traveller, having had some singular presentiment, impulse, vagary of thought, vision (so-called), dream, or other remarkable mental impression, would hesitate considerably before he would own to it. To this reticence I attribute much of the obscurity in which such subjects are involved. We do not habitually communicate our experiences of these subjective things as we do our experiences of objective creation. The consequence is, that the general stock of experience in this regard appears exceptional, and really is so, in respect of being miserably imperfect.

In what I am going to relate, I have no intention of setting up, opposing, or supporting, any theory whatever. I know the history of the Bookseller of Berlin, I have studied the case of the wife of a late Astronomer Royal as related by Sir David Brewster, and I have followed the minutest details of a much more remarkable case of Spectral Illusion occurring within my private circle of friends. It may be necessary to state as to this last, that the sufferer (a lady) was in no degree, however distant, related to me. A mistaken assumption on that head might suggest an explanation of a part of my own case—but only a part—which would be wholly without foundation. It cannot be referred to my inheritance of any developed peculiarity, nor had I ever before any at all similar experience, nor have I ever had any at all similar experience since.

It does not signify how many years ago, or how few, a certain murder was committed in England, which attracted great attention. We hear more than enough of murderers as they rise in succession to their atrocious eminence, and I would bury the memory of this particular brute, if I could, as his body was buried, in Newgate Jail. I purposely abstain from giving any direct clue to the criminal's individuality.

When the murder was first discovered, no suspicion fell—or I ought rather to say, for I cannot be too precise in my facts, it was nowhere publicly hinted that any suspicion fell—on the man who was afterwards brought to trial. As no reference was at that time made to him in the newspapers, it is obviously impossible that any description of him can at that time have been given in the newspapers. It is essential that this fact be remembered.

Unfolding at breakfast my morning paper, containing the account of that first discovery, I found it to be deeply interesting, and I read it with close attention. I read it twice, if not three times. The discovery had been made in a bedroom, and, when I laid down the paper, I was aware of a flash—rush—flow—I do not know what to call it,—no word I can find is satisfactorily descriptive,—in which I seemed to see that bedroom passing through my room, like a picture impossibly painted on a running river. Though almost instantaneous in its passing, it was perfectly clear; so clear that I distinctly, and with a sense of relief, observed the absence of the dead body from the bed.

It was in no romantic place that I had this curious sensation, but in chambers in Piccadilly, very near to the corner of St. James's Street. It was entirely new to me. I was in my easy-chair at the moment, and the sensation was accompanied with a peculiar shiver which started the chair from its position. (But it is to be noted that the chair ran easily on castors.) I went to one of the windows (there are two in the room, and the room is on the second floor) to refresh my eyes with the moving objects down in Piccadilly. It was a bright autumn morning, and the street was sparkling and cheerful. The wind was high. As I looked out, it brought down from the Park a quantity of fallen leaves, which a gust took, and whirled into a spiral pillar. As the pillar fell and the leaves dispersed, I saw two men on the opposite side of the way, going from West to East. They were one behind the other. The foremost man often looked back over his shoulder. The second man followed him, at a distance of some thirty paces, with his right hand menacingly raised. First, the singularity and steadiness of this threatening gesture in so public a thoroughfare attracted my attention; and next, the more remarkable circumstance that nobody heeded it. Both men threaded their way among the other passengers with a smoothness hardly consistent even with the action of walking on a pavement; and no single creature, that I could see, gave them place, touched them, or looked after them. In passing before my windows, they both stared up at me. I saw their two faces very distinctly, and I knew that I could recognise them anywhere. Not that I had consciously noticed anything very remarkable in either face, except that the man who went first had an unusually lowering appearance, and that the face of the man who followed him was of the colour of impure wax.

I am a bachelor, and my valet and his wife constitute my whole establishment. My occupation is in a certain Branch Bank, and I wish that my duties as head of a Department were as light as they are popularly supposed to be. They kept me in town that autumn, when I stood in need of change. I was not ill, but I was not well. My reader is to make the most that can be reasonably made of my feeling jaded, having a depressing sense upon me of a monotonous life, and being "slightly dyspeptic." I am assured by my renowned doctor that my real state of health at that time justifies no stronger description, and I quote his own from his written answer to my request for it.

As the circumstances of the murder, gradually unravelling, took stronger and stronger possession of the public mind, I kept them away from mine by knowing as little about them as was possible in the midst of the universal excitement. But I knew that a verdict of Wilful Murder had been found against the suspected murderer, and that he had been committed to Newgate for trial. I also knew that his trial had been postponed over one Sessions of the Central Criminal Court, on the ground of general prejudice and want of time for the preparation of the defence. I may further have known, but I believe I did not, when, or about when, the Sessions to which his trial stood postponed would come on.

My sitting-room, bedroom, and dressing-room, are all on one floor. With the last there is no communication but through the bedroom. True, there is a door in it, once communicating with the staircase; but a part of the fitting of my bath has been—and had then been for some years—fixed across it. At the same period, and as a part of the same arrangement,—the door had been nailed up and canvased over.

I was standing in my bedroom late one night, giving some directions to my servant before he went to bed. My face was towards the only available door of communication with the dressing-room, and it was closed. My servant's back was towards that door. While I was speaking to him, I saw it open, and a man look in, who very earnestly and mysteriously beckoned to me. That man was the man who had gone second of the two along Piccadilly, and whose face was of the colour of impure wax.

The figure, having beckoned, drew back, and closed the door. With no longer pause than was made by my crossing the bedroom, I opened the dressing-room door, and looked in. I had a lighted candle already in my hand. I felt no inward expectation of seeing the figure in the dressing-room, and I did not see it there.

Conscious that my servant stood amazed, I turned round to him, and said:

"Derrick, could you believe that in my cool senses I fancied I saw a—" As I there laid my hand upon his breast, with a sudden start he trembled violently, and said, "O Lord, yes, sir! A dead man beckoning!"

Now I do not believe that this John Derrick, my trusty and attached servant for more than twenty years, had any impression whatever of having seen any such figure, until I touched him. The change in him was so startling, when I touched him, that I fully believe he derived his impression in some occult manner from me at that instant.

I bade John Derrick bring some brandy, and I gave him a dram, and was glad to take one myself. Of what had preceded that night's phenomenon, I told him not a single word. Reflecting on it, I was absolutely certain that I had never seen that face before, except on the one occasion in Piccadilly. Comparing its expression when beckoning at the door with its expression when it had stared up at me as I stood at my window, I came to the conclusion that on the first occasion it had sought to fasten itself upon my memory, and that on the second occasion it had made sure of being immediately remembered.

I was not very comfortable that night, though I felt a certainty, difficult to explain, that the figure would not return. At daylight I fell into a heavy sleep, from which I was awakened by John Derrick's coming to my bedside with a paper in his hand.

This paper, it appeared, had been the subject of an altercation at the door between its bearer and my servant. It was a summons to me to serve upon a Jury at the forthcoming Sessions of the Central Criminal Court at the Old Bailey. I had never before been summoned on such a Jury, as John Derrick well knew. He believed—I am not certain at this hour whether with reason or otherwise—that that class of Jurors were customarily chosen on a lower qualification than mine, and he had at first refused to accept the summons. The man who served it had taken the matter very coolly. He had said that my attendance or non-attendance was nothing to him; there the summons was; and I should deal with it at my own peril, and not at his.

For a day or two I was undecided whether to respond to this call, or take no notice of it. I was not conscious of the slightest mysterious bias, influence, or attraction, one way or other. Of that I am as strictly sure as of every other statement that I make here. Ultimately I decided, as a break in the monotony of my life, that I would go.

The appointed morning was a raw morning in the month of November. There was a dense brown fog in Piccadilly, and it became positively black and in the last degree oppressive East of Temple Bar. I found the passages and staircases of the Court-House flaringly lighted with gas, and the Court itself similarly illuminated. I think that, until I was conducted by officers into the Old Court and saw its crowded state, I did not know that the Murderer was to be tried that day. I think that, until I was so helped into the Old Court with considerable difficulty, I did not know into which of the two Courts sitting my summons would take me. But this must not be received as a positive assertion, for I am not completely satisfied in my mind on either point.

I took my seat in the place appropriated to Jurors in waiting, and I looked about the Court as well as I could through the cloud of fog and breath that was heavy in it. I noticed the black vapour hanging like a murky curtain outside the great windows, and I noticed the stifled sound of wheels on the straw or tan that was littered in the street; also, the hum of the people gathered there, which a shrill whistle, or a louder song or hail than the rest, occasionally pierced. Soon afterwards the Judges, two in number, entered, and took their seats. The buzz in the Court was awfully hushed. The direction was given to put the Murderer to the bar. He appeared there. And in that same instant I recognised in him the first of the two men who had gone down Piccadilly.

If my name had been called then, I doubt if I could have answered to it audibly. But it was called about sixth or eighth in the panel, and I was by that time able to say, "Here!" Now, observe. As I stepped into the box, the prisoner, who had been looking on attentively, but with no sign of concern, became violently agitated, and beckoned to his attorney. The prisoner's wish to challenge me was so manifest, that it occasioned a pause, during which the attorney, with his hand upon the dock, whispered with his client, and shook his head. I afterwards had it from that gentleman, that the prisoner's first affrighted words to him were, *"At all hazards, challenge that man!"* But that, as he would give no reason for it, and admitted that he had not even known my name until he heard it called and I appeared, it was not done.

Both on the ground already explained, that I wish to avoid reviving the unwholesome memory of that Murderer, and also because a detailed account of his long trial is by no means indispensable to my narrative, I shall confine myself closely to such incidents in the ten days and nights during which we, the Jury, were kept together, as directly bear on my own curious personal experience. It is in that, and not in the Murderer, that I seek to interest my reader. It is to that, and not to a page of the Newgate Calendar, that I beg attention.

I was chosen Foreman of the Jury. On the second morning of the trial, after evidence had been taken for two hours (I heard the church clocks strike), happening to cast my eyes over my brother jurymen, I found an inexplicable difficulty in counting them. I counted them several times, yet always with the same difficulty. In short, I made them one too many.

I touched the brother jurymen whose place was next me, and I whispered to him, "Oblige me by counting us." He looked surprised by the request, but turned his head and counted. "Why," says he, suddenly, "we are thirt—; but no, it's not possible. No. We are twelve."

According to my counting that day, we were always right in detail, but in the gross we were always one too many. There was no appearance—no figure—to account for it; but I had now an inward foreshadowing of the figure that was surely coming.

The Jury were housed at the London Tavern. We all slept in one large room on separate tables, and we were constantly in the charge and under the eye of the officer sworn to hold us in safe-keeping. I see no reason for suppressing the real name of that officer. He was intelligent, highly polite, and obliging, and (I was glad to hear) much respected in the City. He had an agreeable presence, good eyes, enviable black whiskers, and a fine sonorous voice. His name was Mr. Harker.

When we turned into our twelve beds at night, Mr. Harker's bed was drawn across the door. On the night of the second day, not being disposed to lie down, and seeing Mr. Harker sitting on his bed, I went and sat beside him, and offered him a pinch of snuff. As Mr. Harker's hand touched mine in taking it from my box, a peculiar shiver crossed him, and he said, "Who is this?"

Following Mr. Harker's eyes, and looking along the room, I saw again the figure I expected,—the second of the two men who had gone down Piccadilly. I rose, and advanced a few steps; then stopped, and looked round at Mr. Harker. He was quite unconcerned, laughed, and said in a pleasant way, "I thought for a moment we had a thirteenth juryman, without a bed. But I see it is the moonlight."

Making no revelation to Mr. Harker, but inviting him to take a walk with me to the end of the room, I watched what the figure did. It stood for a few moments by the bedside of each of my eleven brother jurymen, close to the pillow. It always went to the right-hand side of the bed, and always passed out crossing the foot of the next bed. It seemed, from the action of the head, merely to look down pensively at each recumbent figure. It took no notice of me, or of my bed, which was that nearest to Mr. Harker's. It seemed to go out where the moonlight came in, through a high window, as by an aërial flight of stairs.

Next morning at breakfast, it appeared that everybody present had dreamed of the murdered man last night, except myself and Mr. Harker.

I now felt as convinced that the second man who had gone down Piccadilly was the murdered man (so to speak), as if it had been borne into my comprehension by his immediate testimony. But even this took place, and in a manner for which I was not at all prepared.

On the fifth day of the trial, when the case for the prosecution was drawing to a close, a miniature of the murdered man, missing from his bedroom upon the discovery of the deed, and afterwards found in a hiding-place where the Murderer had been seen digging, was put in evidence. Having been identified by the witness under examination, it was handed up to the Bench, and thence handed down to be inspected by the Jury. As an officer in a black gown was making his way with it across to me, the figure of the second man who had gone down Piccadilly impetuously started from the crowd, caught the miniature from the officer, and gave it to me with his own hands, at the same time saying, in a low and hollow tone,—before I saw the miniature, which was in a locket,—*"I was younger then, and my face was not then drained of blood."* It also came between me and the brother juryman to whom I would have given the miniature, and between him and the brother juryman to whom he would have given it, and so passed it on through the whole of our number, and back into my possession. Not one of them, however, detected this.

At table, and generally when we were shut up together in Mr. Harker's custody, we had from the first naturally discussed the day's proceedings a good deal. On that fifth day, the case for the prosecution being closed, and we having that side of the question in a completed shape before us, our discussion was more animated and serious. Among our number was a vestryman,—the densest idiot I have ever seen at large,—who met the plainest evidence with the most preposterous objections, and who was sided with by two flabby parochial parasites; all the three impanelled from a district so delivered over to Fever that they ought to have been upon their own trial for five hundred Murders. When these mischievous blockheads were at their loudest, which was towards midnight, while some of us were already preparing for bed, I again saw the murdered man. He stood grimly behind them, beckoning to me. On my going towards them, and striking into the conversation, he immediately retired. This was the beginning of a separate series of appearances, confined to that long room in which we were confined. Whenever a knot of my brother jurymen laid their heads together, I saw the head of the murdered man among theirs. Whenever their comparison of notes was going against him, he would solemnly and irresistibly beckon to me.

It will be borne in mind that down to the production of the miniature, on the fifth day of the trial, I had never seen the Appearance in Court. Three changes occurred now that we entered on the case for the defence. Two of them I will mention together, first. The figure was now in Court continually, and it never there addressed itself to me, but always to the person who was speaking at the time. For instance: the throat of the murdered man had been cut straight across. In the opening speech for the defence, it was suggested that the deceased might have cut his own throat. At that very moment, the figure, with its throat in the dreadful condition referred to (this it had concealed before), stood at the speaker's elbow, motioning across and across its windpipe, now with the right hand, now with the left, vigorously suggesting to the speaker himself the impossibility of such a wound having been self-inflicted by either hand. For another instance: a witness to character, a woman, deposed to the prisoner's being the most amiable of mankind. The figure at that instant stood on the floor before her, looking her full in the face, and pointing out the prisoner's evil countenance with an extended arm and an outstretched finger.

The third change now to be added impressed me strongly as the most marked and striking of all. I do not theorise upon it; I accurately state it, and there leave it. Although the Appearance was not itself perceived by those whom it addressed, its coming close to such persons was invariably attended by some trepidation or disturbance on their part. It seemed to me as if it were prevented, by laws to which I was not amenable, from fully revealing itself to others, and yet as if it could invisibly, dumbly, and darkly overshadow their minds. When the leading counsel for the defence suggested that hypothesis of suicide, and the figure stood at the learned gentleman's elbow, frightfully sawing at its severed throat, it is undeniable that the counsel faltered in his speech, lost for a few seconds the thread of his ingenious discourse, wiped his forehead with his handkerchief, and turned extremely pale. When the witness to character was confronted by the Appearance, her eyes most certainly did follow the direction of its pointed finger, and rest in great hesitation and trouble upon the prisoner's face. Two additional illustrations will suffice. On the eighth day of the trial, after the pause which was every day made early in the afternoon for a few minutes' rest and refreshment, I came back into Court with the rest of the Jury some little time before the return of the Judges. Standing up in the box and looking about me, I thought the figure was not there, until, chancing to raise my eyes to the gallery, I saw it bending forward, and leaning over a very decent woman, as if to assure itself whether the Judges had resumed their seats or not. Immediately afterwards that woman screamed, fainted, and was carried out. So with the venerable, sagacious, and patient Judge who conducted the trial. When the case was over, and he settled himself and his papers to sum up, the murdered man, entering by the Judges' door, advanced to his Lordship's desk, and looked eagerly over his shoulder at the pages of his notes which he was turning. A change came over his Lordship's face; his hand stopped; the peculiar shiver, that I knew so well, passed over him; he faltered, "Excuse me, gentlemen, for a few moments. I am somewhat oppressed by the vitiated air"; and did not recover until he had drunk a glass of water.

Through all the monotony of six of those interminable ten days,—the same Judges and others on the bench, the same Murderer in the dock, the same lawyers at the table, the same tones of question and answer rising to the roof of the court, the same scratching of the Judge's pen, the same ushers going in and out, the same lights kindled at the same hour when there had been any natural light of day, the same foggy curtain outside the great windows when it was foggy, the same rain pattering and dripping when it was rainy, the same footmarks of turnkeys and prisoner day after day on the same sawdust, the same keys locking and unlocking the same heavy doors,—through all the wearisome monotony which made me feel as if I had been Foreman of the Jury for a vast period of time, and Piccadilly had flourished coevally with Babylon, the murdered man never lost one trace of his distinctness in my eyes, nor was he at any moment less distinct than anybody else. I must not omit, as a matter of fact, that I never once saw the Appearance which I call by the name of the murdered man look at the Murderer. Again and again I wondered, "Why does he not?" But he never did.

Nor did he look at me, after the production of the miniature, until the last closing minutes of the trial arrived. We retired to consider, at seven minutes before ten at night. The idiotic vestryman and his two parochial parasites gave us so much trouble that we twice returned into Court to beg to have certain extracts from the Judge's notes re-read. Nine of us had not the smallest doubt about those passages, neither, I believe, had any one in the Court; the dunder-headed triumvirate, having no idea but obstruction, disputed them for that very reason. At length we prevailed, and finally the Jury returned into Court at ten minutes past twelve.

The murdered man at that time stood directly opposite the Jury-box, on the other side of the Court. As I took my place, his eyes rested on me with great attention; he seemed satisfied, and slowly shook a great gray veil, which he carried on his arm for the first time, over his head and whole form. As I gave in our verdict, "Guilty," the veil collapsed, all was gone, and his place was empty. The Murderer, being asked by the Judge, according to usage, whether he had anything to say before sentence of Death should be passed upon him, indistinctly muttered something which was described in the leading newspapers of the following day as "a few rambling, incoherent, and half-audible words, in which he was understood to complain that he had not had a fair trial, because the Foreman of the Jury was prepossessed against him."

The remarkable declaration that he really made was this: *"My Lord, I knew I was a doomed man, when the Foreman of my Jury came into the box. My Lord, I knew he would never let me off, because, before I was taken, he somehow got to my bedside in the night, woke me, and put a rope round my neck."*

The Succubus

Honoré de Balzac

Translated by Jacques Le Clercq

Prologue

A number of persons of the noble country of Touraine, considerably edified by the warm search which the author is making into the antiquities, adventures, good jokes, and pretty tales of that blessed land, and believing for certain that he should know everything, have asked him (after drinking with him of course understood), if he had discovered the etymological reason, concerning which all the ladies of the town are so curious, and from which a certain street in Tours is called the Rue Chaude. By him it was replied, that he was much astonished to see that the ancient inhabitants had forgotten the great number of convents situated in this street, where the severe continence of the monks and nuns might have caused the walls to be made so hot that some woman of position should increase in size from walking too slowly along them to vespers. A troublesome fellow, wishing to appear learned, declared that formerly all the scandalmongers of the neighbourhood were wont to meet in this place. Another entangled himself in the minute suffrages of science, and poured forth golden words without being understood, qualifying words, harmonising the melodies of the ancient and modern, congregating customs, distilling verbs, alchemising all languages since the Deluge, of the Hebrew, Chaldeans, Egyptians, Greeks, Latins, and of Turnus, the ancient founder of Tours; and the good man finished by declaring that chaude or chaulde with the exception of the H and the L, came from Cauda, and that there was a tail in the affair, but the ladies only understood the end of it. An old man observed that in this same place was formerly a source of thermal water, of which his great great grandfather had drunk. In short, in less time than it takes a fly to embrace its sweetheart, there had been a pocketful of etymologies, in which the truth of the matter had been less easily found than a louse in the filthy beard of a Capuchin friar. But a man well learned and well informed, through having left his footprint in many monasteries, consumed much midnight oil, and manured his brain with many a volume—himself more encumbered with pieces, dyptic fragments, boxes, charters, and registers concerning the history of Touraine than is a gleaner with stalks of straw in the month of August—this man, old, infirm, and gouty, who had been drinking in his corner without saying a word, smiled the smile of a wise man and knitted his brows, the said smile finally resolving itself into a pish! well articulated, which the Author heard and understood it to be big with an adventure historically good, the delights of which he would be able to unfold in this sweet collection.

To be brief, on the morrow this gouty old fellow said to him, "By your poem, which is called 'The Venial Sin,' you have forever gained my esteem, because everything therein is true from head to foot—which I believe to be a precious superabundance in such matters. But doubtless you do not know what became of the Moor placed in religion by the said knight, Bruyn de la Roche-Corbon. I know very well. Now if this etymology of the street harass you, and also the Egyptian nun, I will lend you a curious and antique parchment, found by me in the Olim of the episcopal palace, of which the libraries were a little knocked about at a period when none of us knew if he would have the pleasure of his head's society on the morrow. Now will not this yield you a perfect contentment?"

"Good!" said the author.

Then this worthy collector of truths gave certain rare and dusty parchments to the author, the which he has, not without great labour, translated into French, and which were fragments of a most ancient ecclesiastical process. He has believed that nothing would be more amusing than the actual resurrection of this antique affair, wherein shines forth the illiterate simplicity of the good old times. Now, then, give ear. This is the order in which were the manuscripts, of which the author has made use in his own fashion, because the language was devilishly difficult.

I
What the Succubus Was

In nomine Patris, et Filii, et Spiritus Sancti. Amen.

In the year of our Lord, one thousand two hundred and seventy-one, before me, Hierome Cornille, grand inquisitor and ecclesiastical judge (thereto commissioned by the members of the chapter of Saint Maurice, the cathedral of Tours, having of this deliberated in the presence of our Lord Jean de Montsoreau, archbishop—namely, the grievances and complaints of the inhabitants of the said town, whose request is here subjoined), have appeared certain noblemen, citizens, and inhabitants of the diocese, who have stated the following facts concerning a demon suspected of having taken the features of a woman, who has much afflicted the minds of the diocese, and is at present a prisoner in the jail of the chapter; and in order to arrive at the truth of the said charge we have opened the present court, this Monday, the eleventh day of December, after mass, to communicate the evidence of each witness to the said demon, to interrogate her upon the said crimes to her imputed, and to judge her according to the laws enforced *contra demonios*.

In this inquiry has assisted me to write the evidence therein given, Guillaume Tournebouche, rubrican of the chapter, a learned man.

Firstly has come before us one Jehan, surnamed Tortebras, a citizen of Tours, keeping by licence the hostelry of La Cigoyne, situated on the Place du Pont, and who has sworn by the salvation of his soul, his hand upon the holy Evangelists, to state no other thing than that which by himself hath been seen and heard.

He hath stated as here followeth:—

"I declare that about two years before the feast of St. Jehan, upon which are the grand illuminations, a gentleman, at first unknown to me, but belonging without doubt to our lord the King, and at that time returned to our country from the Holy Land, came to me with the proposition that I should let to him at rental a certain country-house by me built, in the quit rent of the chapter over against the place called of St. Etienne, and the which I let to him for nine years, for the consideration of three besans of fine gold. In the said house was placed by the said knight a fair wench having the appearance of a woman, dressed in the strange fashion of the Saracens Mohammedans, whom he would allow by none to be seen or to be approached within a bow-shot, but whom I have seen with mine own eyes, weird feathers upon her head, and eyes so flaming that I cannot adequately describe them, and from which gleamed forth a fire of hell. The defunct knight having threatened with death whoever should appear to spy about the said house, I have by reason of great fear left the said house, and I have until this day secretly kept to my mind certain presumptions and doubts concerning the bad appearance of the said foreigner, who was more strange than any woman, her equal not having as yet by me been seen.

"Many persons of all conditions having at the time believed the said knight to be dead, but kept upon his feet by virtue of the said charms, philters, spells, and diabolical sorceries of this seeming woman, who wished to settle in our country, I declare that I have always seen the said knight so ghastly pale that I can only compare his face to the wax of a Paschal candle, and to the knowledge of all the people of the hostelry of La Cigoyne, this knight was interred nine days after his first coming. According to the statement of his groom, the defunct had been chalorously coupled with the said Moorish woman during seven whole days shut up in my house, without coming out from her, the which

I heard him horribly avow upon his deathbed. Certain persons at the present time have accused this she-devil of holding the said gentleman in her clutches by her long hair, the which was furnished with certain warm properties by means of which are communicated to Christians the flames of hell in the form of love, which work in them until their souls are by this means drawn from their bodies and possessed by Satan. But I declare that I have seen nothing of this excepting the said dead knight, bowelless, emaciated, wishing, in spite of his confessor, still to go to this wench; and then he has been recognized as the lord de Bueil, who was a crusader, and who was, according to certain persons of the town, under the spell of a demon whom he had met in the Asiatic country of Damascus or elsewhere.

"Afterwards I have let my house to the said unknown lady, according to the clauses of the deed of lease. The said lord of Bueil, being defunct, I had nevertheless been into my house in order to learn from the said foreign woman if she wished to remain in my dwelling, and after great trouble was led before her by a strange, half-naked black man, whose eyes were white.

"Then I have seen the said Moorish woman in a little room, shining with gold and jewels, lighted with strange lights, upon an Asiatic carpet, where she was seated, lightly attired, with another gentleman, who was there imperiling his soul; and I had not the heart bold enough to look upon her, seeing that her eyes would have incited me immediately to yield myself up to her, for already her voice thrilled into my very belly, filled my brain, and debauched my mind. Finding this, from the fear of God, and also of hell, I have departed with swift feet, leaving my house to her as long as she liked to retain it, so dangerous was it to behold that Moorish complexion from which radiated diabolical heats, besides a foot smaller than it was lawful in a real woman to possess; and to hear her voice, which pierced into one's heart! And from that day I have lacked the courage to enter my house from great fear of falling into hell. I have said my say."

To the said Tortebras we have then shown an Abyssinian, Nubian or Ethiopian, who, black from head to foot, had been found wanting in certain virile properties with which all good Christians are usually furnished, who, having persevered in his silence, after having been tormented and tortured many times, not without much moaning, has persisted in being unable to speak the language of our country. And the said Tortebras has recognized the said Abyss heretic as having been in his house in company with the said demoniacal spirit, and is suspected of having lent his aid to her sorcery.

And the said Tortebras has confessed his great faith in the Catholic religion, and declared no other things to be within his knowledge save certain rumours which were known to every one, of which he had been in no way a witness except in the hearing of them.

In obedience to the citations served upon him, has appeared then, Matthew, surname Cognefestu, a day-labourer of St. Etienne, whom, after having sworn by the holy Evangelists to speak the truth, has confessed to us always to have seen a bright light in the dwelling of the said foreign woman, and heard much wild and diabolical laughter on the days and nights of feasts and fasts, notably during the days of the holy and Christmas weeks, as if a great number of people were in the house. And he has sworn to have seen by the windows of the said dwellings, green buds of all kinds in the winter, growing as if by magic, especially roses in a time of frost, and other things for which there was a need of a great heat; but of this he was in no way astonished, seeing that the said foreigner threw out so much heat that when she walked in the evening by the side of his wall he found on the morrow his salad grown; and on certain occasions she had by the touching of her petticoats, caused the trees to put forth leaves and hasten the buds. Finally, the said, Cognefestu has declared to us to know no more, because he worked from early morning, and went to bed at the same hour as the fowls.

Afterwards the wife of the aforesaid Cognefestu has by us been required to state also upon oath the things come to her cognisance in this process, and has avowed naught save praises of the said foreigner, because since her coming her man had treated her better in consequence of the neighborhood of this good lady, who filled the air with love, as the sun did light, and other incongruous nonsense, which we have not committed to writing.

To the said Cognefestu and to his wife we have shown the said unknown African, who has been seen by them in the gardens of the house, and is stated by them for certain to belong to the said demon. In the third place, has advanced Harduin V, lord of Maille, who being by us reverentially begged to enlighten the religion of the church, has expressed his willingness so to do, and has, moreover, engaged his word, as a gallant knight, to say no other thing than that which he has seen. Then he has testified to have known in the army of the Crusades the demon in question, and in the town of Damascus to have seen the knight of Bueil, since defunct, fight at close quarters to be her sole possessor. The above-mentioned wench, or demon, belonged at that time to the knight Geoffroy IV, Lord of Roche-Pozay, by whom she was said to have been brought from Touraine, although she was a Saracen; concerning which the knights of France marvelled much, as well as at her beauty, which made a great noise and a thousand scandalous ravages in the camp. During the voyage this wench was the cause of many deaths, seeing that Roche-Pozay had already discomfited certain Crusaders, who wished to keep her to themselves, because she shed, according to certain knights petted by her in secret, joys around her comparable to none others. But in the end the knight of Bueil, having killed Geoffroy de la Roche-Pozay, became lord and master of this young murderess, and placed her in a convent, or harem, according to the Saracen custom. About this time one used to see her and hear her chattering as entertainment many foreign dialects, such as the Greek or the Latin empire, Moorish, and, above all, French better than any of those who knew the language of France best in the Christian host, from which sprang the belief that she was demoniacal.

The said knight Harduin has confessed to us not to have tilted for her in the Holy Land, not from fear, coldness or other cause, so much as that he believed the time had arrived for him to bear away a portion of the true cross, and also he had belonging to him a noble lady of the Greek country, who saved him from this danger in denuding him of love, morning and night, seeing that she took all of it substantially from him, leaving him none in his heart or elsewhere for others.

And the said knight has assured us that the woman living in the country house of Tortebras, was really the said Saracen woman, come into the country from Syria, because he had been invited to a midnight feast at her house by the young Lord of Croixmare, who expired the seventh day afterwards, according to the statement of the Dame de Croixmare, his mother, ruined all points by the said wench, whose commerce with him had consumed his vital spirit, and whose strange phantasies had squandered his fortune.

Afterwards questioned in his quality of a man full of prudence, wisdom and authority in this country, upon the ideas entertained concerning the said woman, and summoned by us to open his conscience, seeing that it was a question of a most abominable case of Christian faith and divine justice, answer has been made by the said knight:—

That by certain of the host of Crusaders it has been stated to him that always this she-devil was a maid to him who embraced her, and that Mammon was for certain occupied in her, making for her a new virtue for each of her lovers, and a thousand other foolish sayings of drunken men, which were not of a nature to form a fifth gospel. But for a fact, he, an old knight on that turn of life, and knowing nothing more of the aforesaid, felt himself again a young man in that last supper with which he had been regaled by the lord of Croixmare; then the voice of this demon went straight to his heart before flowing into his ears, and had awakened so great a love in his body that his life was ebbing from the place whence it should flow, and that eventually, but for the assistance of Cyprus wine, which he had drunk to blind his sight, and his getting under the table in order no longer to gaze upon the fiery eyes of his diabolical hostess, and not to rend his heart from her, without doubt he would have fought the young Croixmare, in order to enjoy for a single moment this supernatural woman. Since then he had had absolution from his confessor for the wicked thought. Then, by advice from on high, he had carried back to his house his portion of the true Cross, and had remained in his own manor, where, in spite of his Christian precautions, the said voice still at certain times tickled his brain, and in the morning often had he in remembrance this demon, warm as brimstone; and because the look of this wench was so warm that it made him burn like a young man, be half dead, and because it cost him then many transshipments of the vital spirit, the said knight has requested us not to confront him with the empress of love to whom, if it were not the devil, God the Father had granted strange liberties with the minds of men. Afterwards, he retired, after reading over his statement, not without having first recognized the above-mentioned African to be the servant and page of the lady.

In the fourth place, upon the faith pledged in us in the name of the Chapter and of our Lord Archbishop, that he should not be tormented, tortured, nor harassed in any manner, nor further cited after his statement, in consequence of his commercial journeys, and upon the assurance that he should retire in perfect freedom, has come before us a Jew, Salomon al Rastchid, who, in spite of the infamy of his person and his Judaism, has been heard by us to this one end, to know everything concerning the conduct of the aforesaid demon. Thus he has not been required to take any oath this Salomon, seeing that he is beyond the pale of the Church, separated from us by the blood of our saviour (*trucidatus Salvatore inter nos*). Interrogated by us as to why he appeared without the green cap upon his head, and the yellow wheel in the apparent locality of the heart in his garment, according to the ecclesiastical and royal ordinances, the said de Rastchid has exhibited to us letters patent of the seneschal of Touraine and Poitou. Then the said Jew has declared to us to have done a large business for the lady dwelling in the house of the innkeeper Tortebras, to have sold to her golden chandeliers, with many branches, minutely engraved, plates of red silver, cups enriched with stones, emeralds and rubies; to have brought for her from the Levant a number of rare stuffs, Persian carpets, silks, and fine linen; in fact, things so magnificent that no queen in Christendom could say she was so well furnished with jewels and household goods; and that he had for his part received from her three hundred thousand pounds for the rarity of the purchases in which he had been employed, such as Indian flowers, poppingjays, birds' feathers, spices, Greek wines, and diamonds. Requested by us, the judge, to say if he had furnished certain ingredients of magical conjuration, the blood of new-born children, conjuring books, and things generally and whatsoever made use of by sorcerers, giving him licence to state his case without that thereupon he should be the subject to any further inquest or inquiry, the said al Rastchid has sworn by his Hebrew faith never to have had any such commerce; and has stated that he was involved in too high interests to give himself to such miseries, seeing that he was the agent of certain most powerful lords, such as the Marquis de Montferrat, the King of England, the King of Cyprus and Jerusalem, the Court of Provence, lords of Venice, and many German gentleman; to have belonging to him merchant galleys of all kinds, going into Egypt with the permission of the Sultan, and he trafficking in precious articles of silver and of gold, which took him often into the exchange of Tours. Moreover, he has declared that he considered the said lady, the subject of inquiry, to be a right royal and natural woman, with the sweetest limbs, and the smallest he has ever seen. That in consequence of her renown for a diabolical spirit, pushed by a wild imagination, and also because that he was smitten with her, he had heard once that she was husbandless, proposed to her to be her gallant, to which proposition she willingly acceded. Now, although from that night he felt his bones disjointed and his bowels crushed, he had not yet experienced, as certain persons say, that who once yielded was free no more; he went to his fate as lead into the crucible of the alchemist. Then the said Salomon, to whom we have granted his liberty according to the safe conduct, in spite of the statement, which proves abundantly his commerce with the devil, because he had been saved there where all Christians have succumbed, has admitted to us an agreement concerning the said demon. To make known that he had made an offer to the chapter of the cathedral to give for the said semblance of a woman such a ransom, if she were condemned to be burned alive, that the highest of the towers of the Church of St. Maurice, at present in course of construction, could therewith be finished.

The which we have noted to be deliberated upon at an opportune time by the assembled chapter. And the said Salomon has taken his departure without being willing to indicate his residence, and has told us that he can be informed of the deliberation of the chapter by a Jew of the synagogue of Tours, a name Tobias Nathaneus. The said Jew has before his departure been shown the African, and has recognised him as the page of the demon, and has stated the Saracens to have the custom of mutilating their slaves thus, to commit to them the task of guarding their women by an ancient usage, as it appears in the profane histories of Narsez, general of Constantinople, and others.

On the morrow after mass has appeared before us the most noble and illustrious lady of Croixmare. The same has worn her faith in the holy Evangelists, and has related to us with tears how she had placed her eldest son beneath the earth, dead by reason of his extravagant amours with this female demon. The which noble gentleman was three-and-twenty years of age; of good complexion, very manly and well bearded like his defunct sire. Notwithstanding his great vigour, in ninety days he had little by little withered, ruined by his commerce with the succubus of the Rue Chaude, according to the statement of the common people; and her maternal authority over the son had been powerless. Finally in his latter days he appeared like a poor dried up worm, such as housekeepers meet with in a corner when they clean out the dwelling-rooms. And always, so long as he had the strength to go, he went to shorten his life with this cursed woman; where, also, he emptied his cash-box. When he was in his bed, and knew his last hour had come, he swore at, cursed, and threatened and heaped upon all—his sister, his brother, and upon her his mother—a thousand insults, rebelled in the face of the chaplain; denied God, and wished to die in damnation; at which were much afflicted the retainers of the family, who, to save his soul and pluck it from hell, have founded two annual masses in the cathedral. And in order to have him buried in consecrated ground, the house of Croixmare has undertaken to give to the chapter, during one hundred years, the wax candles for the chapels and the church, upon the day of the Paschal feast. And, in conclusion, saving the wicked words heard by the reverend person, Dom Loys Pot, a nun of Marmoustiers, who came to assist in his last hours the said Baron de Croixmaire affirms never to have heard any words offered by the defunct, touching the demon who had undone him.

And therewith has retired the noble and illustrious lady in deep mourning.

In the sixth place has appeared before us, after adjournment, Jacquette, called Vieux-Oing, a kitchen scullion, going to houses to wash dishes, residing at present in the Fishmarket, who, after having placed her word to say nothing she did not hold to be true, has declared as here follows:—Namely, that one day she, being come into the kitchen of the said demon, of whom she had no fear, because she was wont to regale herself only upon males, she had the opportunity of seeing in the garden this female demon, superbly attired, walking in company with a knight, with whom she was laughing, like a natural woman. Then she had recognised in this demon that true likeness of the Moorish woman placed as a nun in the convent of Notre Dame de l'Egrignolles by the defunct seneschal of Touraine and Poitou, Messire Bruyn, Count of Roche-Corbon, the which Moorish woman had been left in the situation and place of the image of our Lady the Virgin, the mother of our Blessed Saviour, stolen by the Egyptians about eighteen years since. Of this time, in consequence of the troubles come about in Touraine, no record has been kept. This girl, aged about twelve years, was saved from the stake at which she would have been burned by being baptised; and the said defunct and his wife had then been godfather and godmother to this child of hell. Being at that time laundress at the convent, she who bears witness has remembrance of the flight which the said Egyptian took twenty months after her entry into the convent, so subtilely that it has never been known how or by what means she escaped. At that time it was thought by all, that with the devil's aid she had flown away in the air, seeing that not withstanding much search, no trace of her flight was found in the convent, where everything remained in its accustomed order.

The African having been shown to the said scullion, she has declared not to have seen him before, although she was curious to do so, as he was commissioned to guard the place in which the Moorish woman combated with those whom she drained through the spigot.

In the seventh place has been brought before us Hugues de Fou, son of the Sieur de Bridore, who, aged twenty years, has been placed in the hands of his father, under caution of his estates, and by him is represented in this process, whom it concerns if should be duly attained and convicted of having, assisted by several unknown and bad young men, laid siege to the jail of the archbishop and of the chapter, and of having lent himself to disturb the force of ecclesiastical justice, by causing the escape of the demon now under consideration. In spite of the evil disposition we have commanded the said Hugues de Fou to testify truly, touching the things he should know concerning the said demon, with whom he is vehemently reputed to have had commerce, pointing out to him that it was a question of his salvation and of the life of the said demon. He, after having taken the oath, he said:—

"I swear by my eternal salvation, and by the holy Evangelists here present under my hand, to hold the woman suspected of being a demon to be an angel, a perfect woman, and even more so in mind than in body, living in all honesty, full of the migniard charms and delights of love, in no way wicked, but most generous, assisting greatly the poor and suffering. I declare that I have seen her weeping veritable tears for the death of my friend, the knight of Croixmare. And because on that day she had made a vow to our Lady the Virgin no more to receive the love of young noblemen too weak in her service; she has to me constantly and with great courage denied the enjoyment of her body, and has only granted to me love, and the possession of her heart, of which she has made sovereign. Since this gracious gift, in spite of my increasing flame I have remained alone in her dwelling, where I have spent the greater part of my days, happy in seeing and in hearing her. Oh! I would eat near her, partake of the air which entered into her lungs, of the light which shone in her sweet eyes, and found in this occupation more joy than have the lords of paradise. Elected by me to be forever my lady, chosen to be one day my dove, my wife, and only sweetheart, I, poor fool, have received from her no advances on the joys of the future, but, on the contrary, a thousand virtuous admonitions; such as that I should acquire renown as a good knight, become a strong man and a fine one, fear nothing except God; honour the ladies, serve but one and love them in memory of that one; that when I should be strengthened by the work of war, if her heart still pleased mine, at that time only would she be mine, because she would be able to wait for me, loving me so much."

So saying the young Sire Hugues wept, and weeping, added:—

"That thinking of this graceful and feeble woman, whose arms seemed scarcely large enough to sustain the light weight of her golden chains, he did not know how to contain himself while fancying the irons which would wound her, and the miseries with which she would traitorously be loaded, and from this cause came his rebellion. And that he had licence to express his sorrow before justice, because his life was so bound up with that of his delicious mistress and sweetheart that on the day when evil came to her he would surely die."

And the same young man has vociferated a thousand other praises of the said demon, which bear witness to the vehement sorcery practised upon him, and prove, moreover, the abominable, unalterable, and incurable life and the fraudulent witcheries to which he is at present subject, concerning which our lord the archbishop will judge, in order to save by exorcisms and penitences this young soul from the snares of hell, if the devil has not gained too strong a hold of it.

Then we have handed back the said young nobleman into the custody of the noble lord his father, after that by the said Hugues, the African has been recognised as the servant of the accused.

In the eighth place, before us, have the footguards of our lord the archbishop led in great state the *Most High and Reverend Lady Jacqueline de Champchevrier, Abbess of the Convent of Notre-Dame*, under the invocation of Mount Carmel, to whose control has been submitted by the late seneschal of Touraine, father of Monseigneur the Count of Roche-Corbon, present advocate of the said convent, the Egyptian, named at the baptismal font Blanche Bruyn.

To the said abbess we have shortly stated the present cause, in which is involved the holy church, the glory of God, and the eternal future of the people of the diocese afflicted with a demon, and also the life of a creature who it was possible might be quite innocent. Then the cause elaborated, we have requested the said noble abbess to testify that which was within her knowledge concerning the magical disappearance of her daughter in God, Blanche Bruyn, espoused by our Saviour under the name of Sister Clare.

Then has stated the very high, very noble, and very illustrious lady abbess as follows:—

"The Sister Clare, of origin to her unknown, but suspected to be of an heretic father and mother, people inimical to God, has truly been placed in religion in the convent of which the government had canonically come to her in spite of her unworthiness; that the said sister had properly concluded her noviciate, and made her vows according to the holy rule of the order. That the vows taken, she had fallen into great sadness, and had much drooped. Interrogated by her, the abbess, concerning her melancholy malady, the said sister had replied with tears that she herself did not know the cause. That one thousand and one tears engendered themselves in her at feeling no more her splendid hair upon her head; that besides this she thirsted for air, and could not resist her desire to jump up into the trees, to climb and tumble about according to her wont during her open air life; that she passed her nights in tears, dreaming of the forests under the leaves of which in other days she slept; and in remembrance of this she abhorred the quality of the air of the cloisters, which troubled her respiration; that in her inside she was troubled with evil vapours; that at times she was inwardly diverted in church by thoughts which made her lose countenance. Then I have repeated over and over again to the poor creature the holy directions of the church, have reminded her of the eternal happiness which women without seeing enjoy in paradise, and how transitory was life here below, and certain the goodness of God, who for first certain bitter pleasures lost, kept for us a love without end. In spite of this wise maternal advice the evil spirit has persisted in the said sister; and always would she gaze upon the leaves of the trees and grass of the meadows through the windows of the church during the offices and times of prayer; and persisted in becoming as white as linen in order that she might stay in her bed, and at certain times she would run about the cloisters like a goat broken loose from its fastening. Finally, she had grown thin, lost much of the great beauty, and shrunk away to nothing. While in this condition by us, the abbess her mother, was she placed in the sick-room, we daily expecting her to die. One winter's morning the said sister had fled, without leaving any trace of her steps, without breaking the door, forcing of locks, or opening of windows, nor any sign whatever of the manner of her passage; a frightful adventure which was believed to have taken place by the aid of the demon which has annoyed and tormented her. For the rest it was settled by the authorities of the metropolitan church that the mission of this daughter of hell was to divert the nuns from their holy ways, and blinded by their perfect lives, she had returned through the air on the wings of the sorcerer, who had left her for mockery of our holy religion in the place of our Virgin Mary."

The which having said, the lady abbess was, with great honour and according to the command of our lord the archbishop, accompanied as far as the convent of Carmel.

In the ninth place, before us has come, agreeably to the citation served upon him, Joseph, called Leschalopier, a money-changer, living on the bridge at the sign of the Besant d'Or, who, after having pledged his Catholic faith to say no other thing than the truth, and that known to him, touching the process before the ecclesiastical tribunal, has testified as follows:—

"I am a poor father, much afflicted by the sacred will of God. Before the coming of the Succubus of the Rue Chaude, I had, for all good, a son as handsome as a noble, learned as a clerk, and having made more than a dozen voyages into foreign lands; for the rest a good Catholic; keeping himself on guard against the needles of love, because he avoided marriage, knowing himself to be the support of my old days, the love for my eyes, and the constant delight of my heart. He was a son of whom the King of France might have been proud—a good and courageous man, the light on my commerce, the joy of my roof, and, above all, an inestimable blessing, seeing that I am alone in the world, having had the misfortune to lose my wife, and being too old to take another. Now, monseigneur, this treasure without equal has been taken from me, and cast into hell by the demon. Yes, my lord judge, directly he beheld this mischievous jade, this she-devil, in whom it is a whole workshop of perdition, a conjunction of pleasure and delectation, and whom nothing can satiate, my poor child stuck himself fast into the gluepot of love, and afterwards lived only between the columns of Venus, and there did not live long, because in that place like so great a heat that nothing can satisfy the thirst of this gulf, not even should you plunge therein the germs of the entire world. Alas! then, my poor boy—his fortune, his generative hopes, his eternal future, his entire self, more than himself, have been engulfed in this sewer, like a grain of corn in the jaws of a bull. By this means become an old orphan I, who speak, shall have no greater joy than to see burning, this demon, nourished with blood and gold. This Arachne who has drawn out and sucked more marriages, more families in the seed, more hearts, more Christians then there are lepers in all the lazar houses or Christendom.

Burn, torment this fiend—this vampire who feeds on souls, this tigerish nature that drinks blood, this amorous lamp in which burns the venom of all the vipers. Close this abyss, the bottom of which no man can find . . . I offer my deniers to the chapter for the stake, and my arm to light the fire. Watch well, my lord judge, to surely guard this devil, seeing that she has a fire more flaming than all other terrestrial fires; she has all the fire of hell in her, the strength of Samson in her hair, and the sound of celestial music in her voice. She charms to kill the body and the soul at one stroke; she smiles to bite, she kisses to devour; in short, she would wheedle an angel, and make him deny his God. My son! my son! where is he at this hour? The flower of my life—a flower cut by this feminine needlecase as with scissors. Ha, lord! why have I been called? Who will give me back my son, whose soul has been absorbed by a womb which gives death to all, and life to none? The devil alone copulates, and engenders not. This is my evidence, which I pray Master Tournebouche to write without omitting one iota, and to grant me a schedule, that I may tell it to God every evening in my prayer, to this end to make the blood of the innocent cry aloud into His ears, and to obtain from His infinite mercy the pardon for my son."

Here followed twenty and seven other statements, of which the transcription in their true objectivity, in all their quality of space would be over-fastidious, would draw to a great length, and divert the thread of this curious process—a narrative which, according to ancient precepts, should go straight to the fact, like a bull to his principal office. Therefore, here is, in a few words, the substance of these testimonies.

A great number of good Christians, townsmen and townswomen, inhabitants of the noble town of Tours, testified the demon to have held every day wedding feasts and royal festivities, never to have been seen in any church, to have cursed God, to have mocked the priests, never to have crossed herself in any place; to have spoken all the languages of the earth—a gift which has only been granted by God to the blessed Apostles; to have been many times met in the fields, mounted upon an unknown animal who went before the clouds; not to grow old, and to have always a youthful face; to have received the father and the son on the same day, saying that her door sinned not; to have visible malign influences which flowed from her, for that a pastrycook, seated on a bench at her door, having perceived her one evening, received such a gust of warm love that, going in and getting to bed, he had with great passion embraced his wife, and was found dead on the morrow, that the old men of the town went to spend the remainder of their days and of their money with her, to taste the joys of the sins of their youth, and that they died like fleas on their bellies, and that certain of them, while dying, became as black as Moors; that this demon never allowed herself to be seen neither at dinner, nor at breakfast, nor at supper, but ate alone, because she lived upon human brains; that several had seen her during the night go to the cemeteries, and there embrace the young dead men, because she was not able to assuage otherwise the devil who worked in her entrails, and there raged like a tempest, and from that came the astringent biting, nitrous shooting, precipitant, and diabolical movements, squeezings, and writhings of love and voluptuousness, from which several men had emerged bruised, torn, bitten, pinched and crushed; and that since the coming of our Saviour, who had imprisoned the master devil in the bellies of the swine, no malignant beast had ever been seen in any portion of the earth so mischievous, venomous and so clutching; so much so that if one threw the town of Tours into this field of Venus, she would there transmute it into the grain of cities, and this demon would swallow it like a strawberry.

And a thousand other statements, sayings, and depositions, from which was evident in perfect clearness the infernal generation of this woman, daughter, sister, niece, spouse, or brother of the devil, beside abundant proofs of her evil doing, and of the calamity spread by her in all families. And if it were possible to put them here conformably with the catalogue preserved by the good man to whom he accused the discovery, it would seem like a sample of the horrible cries which the Egyptians gave forth on the day of the seventh plague. Also this examination has covered with great honour Messire Guillaume Tournebouche, by whom are quoted all the memoranda. In the tenth vacation was thus closed this inquest, arriving at a maturity of proof, furnished with authentic testimony and sufficiently engrossed with the particulars, plaints, interdicts, contradictions, charges, assignments, withdrawals, confessions public and private, oaths, adjournments, appearances and controversies, to which the said demon must reply. And the townspeople say everywhere if there were really a she-devil, and furnished with internal horns planted in her nature, with which she drank the men, and broke them, this woman might swim a long time in this sea of writing before being landed safe and sound in hell.

II

The Proceedings Taken Relative to This Female Vampire

In nomine Patris, et Filii, et Spiritus Sancti. Amen.

In the year of our Lord one thousand two hundred and seventy-one, before us, Hierome Cornille, grand penitentiary and ecclesiastical judge to this, canonically appointed, have appeared—

The Sire Philippe d'Idre, bailiff of the town and city of Tours and province of Touraine, living in his hotel in the Rue de la Rotisserie, in Chateauneuf; Master Jehan Ribou, provost of the brotherhood and company of drapers, residing on the Quay de Bretaingne, at the image of St. Pierre-es-liens; Messire Antoine Jehan, alderman and chief of the Brotherhood of Changers, residing in the Place du Pont, at the image of St. Mark-counting-tournoise-pounds; Master Martin Beaupertuys, captain of the archers of the town residing at the castle; Jehan Rabelais, a ships' painter and boat maker residing at the port at the isle of St. Jacques, treasurer of the brotherhood of the mariners of the Loire; Mark Hierome, called Maschefer, hosier, at the sign of Saint-Sebastian, president of the trades council; and Jacques, called de Villedomer, master tavern-keeper and vine dresser, residing in the High Street, at the Pomme de Pin; to the said Sire d'Idre, and to the said citizens, we have read the following petition by them, written, signed, and deliberated upon, to be brought under the notice of the ecclesiastical tribunal:—

PETITION

We, the undersigned, all citizens of Tours, are come into the hotel of his worship the Sire d'Idre, bailiff of Touraine, in the absence of our mayor, and have requested him to hear our plaints and statements concerning the following facts, which we intend to bring before the tribunal of the archbishop, the judge of ecclesiastical crimes, to whom should be deferred the conduct of the cause which we here expose:—

A long time ago there came into this town a wicked demon in the form of a woman, who lives in the parish of Saint-Etienne, in the house of the innkeeper Tortebras, situated in the quit-rent of the chapter, and under the temporal jurisdiction of the archiepiscopal domain. The which foreigner carries on the business of a gay woman in a prodigal and abusive manner, and with such increase of infamy that she threatens to ruin the Catholic faith in this town, because those who go to her come back again with their souls lost in every way, and refuse the assistance of the Church with a thousand scandalous discourses.

Now considering that a great number of those who yielded to her are dead, and that arrived in our town with no other wealth than her beauty, she has, according to public clamour, infinite riches and right royal treasure, the acquisition of which is vehemently attributed to sorcery, or at least to robberies committed by the aid of magical attractions and her supernaturally amorous person.

Considering that it is a question of the honour and security of our families, and that never before has been seen in this country a woman wild of body or a daughter of pleasure, carrying on with such mischief of vocation of light o' love, and menacing so openly and bitterly the life, the savings, the morals, chastity, religion, and the everything of the inhabitants of this town;

Considering that there is need of a inquiry into her person, her wealth and her deportment, in order to verify if these effects of love are legitimate, and to not proceed, as would seem indicated by her manners, from a bewitchment of Satan, who often visits Christianity under the form of a female, as appears in the holy books, in which it is stated that our blessed Saviour was carried away into a mountain, from which Lucifer or Astaroth showed him the fertile plains of Judea and that in many places have been seen succubi or demons, having the faces of women, who, not wishing to return to hell, and having with them an insatiable fire, attempt to refresh and sustain themselves by sucking in souls;

Considering that in the case of the said woman a thousand proofs of diablerie are met with, of which certain inhabitants speak openly, and that it is necessary for the repose of the said woman that the matter be sifted, in order that she shall not be attacked by certain people, ruined by the result of her wickedness;

For these causes we pray that it will please you to submit to our spiritual lord, father of this diocese, the most noble and blessed archbishop Jehan de Monsoreau, the troubles of his afflicted flock, to the end that he may advise upon them.

By doing so you will fulfil the duties of your office, as we do those of preservers of the security of this town, each one according to the things of which he has charge in his locality.

And we have signed the present, in the year of our Lord one thousand two hundred and seventy-one, of All Saints' Day, after mass.

Master Tournebouche having finished the reading of this petition, by us, Hierome Cornille, has it been said to the petitioners—

"Gentlemen, do you, at the present time, persist in these statements? have you proofs other than those come within your own knowledge, and do you undertake to maintain the truth of this before God, before man, and before the accused?"

All, with the exception of Master Jehan Rabelais, have persisted in their belief, and the aforesaid Rabelais has withdrawn from the process, saying that he considered the said Moorish woman to be a natural woman and a good wench who had no other fault than that of keeping up a very high temperature of love.

Then we, the judge appointed, have, after mature deliberation, found matter upon which to proceed in the petition of the aforesaid citizens, and have commanded that the woman at present in the jail of the chapter shall be proceeded against by all legal methods, as written in the canons and ordinances, *contra demonios*. The said ordinance, embodied in a writ, shall be published by the town-crier in all parts, and with the sound of the trumpet, in order to make it known to all, and that each witness may, according to his knowledge, be confronted with the said demon, and finally the said accused to be provided with a defender, according to custom, and the interrogations, and the process to be congruously conducted.

(Signed) HIEROME CORNILLE.

And, lower down.

TOURNEBOUCHE.

In nomine Patris, et Filii, et Spiritus Sancti. Amen.

In the year of our Lord one thousand two hundred and seventy-one, the 10th day of February, after mass, by command of us, Hierome Cornille, ecclesiastical judge, has been brought from the jail of the chapter and led before us the woman taken in the house of the innkeeper Tortebras, situated in the domains of the chapter and the cathedral of St. Maurice, and are subject to the temporal and seigneurial justice of the Archbishop of Tours; besides which, in consequence of the nature of the crimes imputed to her, she is liable to the tribunal and council of ecclesiastical justice, the which we have made known to her, to the end that she should not ignore it.

And after a serious reading, entirely at will understood by her, in the first place of the petition of the town, then of the statements, plaints, accusations, and proceedings which written in twenty-four quires by Master Tournebouche, and are above related, we have, with the invocation and assistance of God and the Church, resolved to ascertain the truth, first by interrogatories made to the said accused.

In the first interrogation we have requested the aforesaid to inform us in what land or town she had been born. By her who speaks was it answered: "In Mauritania."

We have then inquired: "If she had a father or mother, or any relations?" By her who speaks has it been replied: "That she had never known them." By us requested to declare her name. By her who speaks has been replied: "Zulma," in Arabian tongue.

By us has it been demanded: "Why she spoke our language?" By her who speaks has it been said: "Because she had come into this country." By us has it been asked: "At what time?" By her who speaks has it been replied: "About twelve years."

By us has it been asked: "What age she then was?" By her who speaks has it been answered: "Fifteen years or thereabout."

By us has it been said: "Then you acknowledge yourself to be twenty-seven years of age?" By her who speaks has it been replied: "Yes."

By us has it been said to her: "That she was then the Moorish child found in the niche of Madame the Virgin, baptised by the Archbishop, held at the font by the late Lord of Roche-Corbon and the Lady of Azay, his wife, afterwards by them placed in religion at the convent of Mount Carmel, where by her had been made vows of chastity, poverty, silence, and the love of God, under the divine assistance of St. Clare?" By her who speaks has been said: "That is true."

By us has it been asked her: "If, then, she allowed to be true the declarations of the very noble and illustrious lady the abbess of Mount Carmel, also the statements of Jacquette, called Vieux-Oing, being kitchen scullion?" By the accused has been answered: "These words are true in great measure."

Then by us has it been said to her: "Then you are a Christian?" And by her who speaks has been answered: "Yes, my father."

Then by us has she been requested to make the sign of the cross, and to take holy water from the brush placed by Master Tournebouche in her hand; the which having been done, and by us having been witnessed, it has been admitted as an indisputable fact, that Zulma, the Moorish woman, called in our country Blanche Bruyn, a nun of the convent under the invocation of Mount Carmel, there named Sister Clare, and suspected to be the false appearance of a woman under which is concealed a demon, has in our presence made act of religion and thus recognised the justice of the ecclesiastical tribunal.

Then by us have these words been said to her: "My daughter, you are vehemently suspected to have had recourse to the devil from the manner in which you left the convent, which was supernatural in every way." By her who speaks has it been stated, that she at that time gained naturally the fields by the street door after vespers, enveloped in the robes of Jehan de Marsilis, visitor of the convent, who had hidden her, the person speaking, in a little hovel belonging to him, situated in the Cupidon Lane, near a tower in the town. That there this said priest had to her then speaking, at great length, and most thoroughly taught the depths of love, of which she then speaking was before in all points ignorant, for which delights she had a great taste, finding them of great use. That the Sire d'Amboise having perceived her then speaking at the window of this retreat, had been smitten with a great love for her. That she loved him more heartily than the monk, and fled from the hovel where she was detained for profit of his pleasure by Don Marsilis. And then she had gone in great haste to Amboise, the castle of the said lord, where she had had a thousand pastimes, hunting, and dancing, and beautiful dresses fit for a queen. One day the Sire de la Roche-Pozay having been invited by the Sire d'Amboise to come and feast and enjoy himself, the Baron d'Amboise had allowed him to see her then speaking, as she came out naked from her bath. That at this sight the said Sire de la Roche-Pozay having fallen violently in love with her, had on the morrow discomfited in single combat the Sire d'Amboise, and by great violence, had, is spite of her tears, taken her to the Holy Land, where she who was speaking had lived the life of a woman well beloved, and had been held in great respect on account of her great beauty. That after numerous adventures, she who was speaking had returned into this country in spite of the apprehensions of misfortune, because such was the will of her lord and master, the Baron de Bueil, who was dying of grief in Asiatic lands, and desired to return to his patrimonial manor. Now he had promised her who was speaking to preserve her from peril. Now she who was speaking had faith and belief in him, the more so as she loved him very much; but on his arrival in this country, the Sire de Bueil was seized with an illness, and died deplorably, without taking any remedies, this spite of the fervent requests which she who was speaking had addressed to him, but without success, because he hated physicians, master surgeons, and apothecaries; and that this was the whole truth.

Then by us has it been said to the accused that she then held to be true the statements of the good Sire Harduin and of the innkeeper Tortebras. By her who speaks has it been replied, that she recognized as evidence the greater part, and also as malicious, calumnious, and imbecile certain portions.

Then by us has the accused been required to declare if she had had pleasure and carnal commerce with all the men, nobles, citizens, and others as set forth in the plaints and declarations of the inhabitants. To which her who speaks has it been answered with great effrontery: "Pleasure, yes! Commerce, I do not know."

By us has it been said to her, that all had died by her acts. By her who speaks has it been said that their deaths could not be the result of her acts, because she had always refused herself to them, and the more she fled from them the more they came and embraced her with infinite passion, and that when she who was speaking was taken by them she gave herself up to them with all her strength, by the grace of God, because she had in that more joy than in anything, and has stated, she who speaks, that she avows her secret sentiments solely because she had been requested by us to state the whole truth, and that she the speaker stood in great fear of the torments of the torturers.

Then by us has she been requested to answer, under pain of torture, in what state of mind she was when a young nobleman died in consequence of his commerce with her. Then by her speaking has it been replied, that she remained quite melancholy and wished to destroy herself; and prayed God, the Virgin, and the saints to receive her into Paradise, because never had she met with any but lovely and good hearts in which was no guile, and beholding them die she fell into a great sadness, fancying herself to be an evil creature or subject to an evil fate, which she communicated like the plague.

Then by us has she been requested to state where she paid her orisons.

By her speaking has it been said that she played in her oratory on her knees before God, who according to the Evangelists, sees and hears all things and resides in all places.

Then by us has it been demanded why she never frequented the churches, the offices, nor the feasts. To this by her speaking has it been answered, that those who came to love her had elected the feast days for that purpose, and that she speaking did all things to their liking.

By us has it been remonstrated that, by so doing, she was submissive to man rather than to the commandments of God.

Then by her speaking has it been stated, that for those who loved her well she speaking would have thrown herself into a flaming pile, never having followed in her love any course but that of nature, and that for the weight of the world in gold she would not have lent her body or her love to a king who did not love her with his heart, feet, hair, forehead, and all over. In short and moreover the speaker had never made an act of harlotry in selling one single grain of love to a man whom she had not chosen to be hers, and that he who held her in his arms one hour or kissed her on the mouth a little, possessed her for the remainder of her days.

Then by us has she been requested to state whence preceded the jewels, gold plate, silver, precious stones, regal furniture, carpets, et cetera, worth 200,000 doubloons, according to the inventory found in her residence and placed in the custody of the treasurer of the chapter. By the speaker answer has been made, that in us she placed all her hopes, even as much as in God, but that she dare not reply to this, because it involved the sweetest things of love upon which she had always lived. And interpellated anew, the speaker has said that if the judge knew with what fervour she held him she loved, with what obedience she followed him in good or evil ways, with what study she submitted to him, with what happiness she listened to his desires, and inhaled the sacred words with which his mouth gratified her, in what adoration she held his person, even we, an old judge, would believe with her well-beloved, that no sum could pay for this great affection which all the men ran after. After the speaker has declared never from any man loved by her, to have solicited any present or gift, and that she rested perfectly contented to live in their hearts, that she would there curl herself up with indestructible and ineffable pleasure, finding herself richer with this heart than with anything, and thinking of no other thing than to give them more pleasure and happiness than she received from them. But in spite of the iterated refusals of the speaker her lovers persisted in graciously rewarding her. At times one came to her with a necklace of pearls, saying, "This is to show my darling that the satin of her skin did not falsely appear to me whiter than pearls" and would put it on the speaker's neck, kissing her lovingly. The speaker would be angry at these follies, but could not refuse to keep a jewel that gave them pleasure to see it there where they placed it. Each one had a different fancy. At times another liked to tear the precious garments which the speaker wore to gratify him; another to deck out the speaker with sapphires on her arms, on her legs, on her neck, and in her hair; another to seat her on the carpet, clad in silk or black velvet, and to remain for days together in ecstasy at the perfections of the speaker the whom the things desired by her lovers gave infinite pleasure, because these things rendered them quite happy. And the speaker has said, that as we love nothing so much as our pleasure, and wish that everything should shine in beauty and harmonize, outside as well as inside the heart, so they all wished to see the place inhabited by the speaker adorned with handsome objects, and from this idea all her lovers were pleased as much as she was in spreading thereabout gold, silks and flowers. Now seeing that these lovely things spoil nothing, the speaker had no force or commandment by which to prevent a knight, or even a rich citizen beloved by her, having his will, and thus found herself constrained to receive rare perfumes and other satisfaction with which the speaker was loaded, and that such was the source of the gold, plate, carpets, and jewels seized at her house by the officers of justice. This terminates the first interrogation made to the said Sister Clare, suspected to be a demon, because we the judge and Guillaume Tournebouche, are greatly fatigued with having the voice of the aforesaid, in our ears, and finding our understanding in every way muddled.

By us the judge has the second interrogatory been appointed, three days from today, in order that the proofs of the possession and presence of the demon in the body of the aforesaid may be sought, and the accused, according to the order of the judge, has been taken back to the jail under the conduct of Master Guillaume Tournebouche.

In nomine Patris, et Filii, et Spiritus Sancti. Amen.

On the thirteenth day following of the said month of the February before us, Hierome Cornille, et cetera, has been produced the Sister Clare abovementioned, in order to be interrogated upon the facts and deeds to her imputed, and of them to be convicted.

By us, the judge, has it been said to the accused that, looking at the divers responses by her given to the proceeding interrogatories, it was certain that it never had been in the power of a simple woman, even if she were authorised, if such licence were allowed to lead the life of a loose woman, to give pleasure to all, to cause so many deaths, and to accomplish sorceries so perfect, without the assistance of a special demon lodged in her body, and to whom her soul had been sold by an especial compact. That it had been clearly demonstrated that under her outward appearance lies and moves a demon, the author of these evils, and that she was now called upon to declare at what age she had received the demon, to vow the agreement existing between herself and him, and to tell the truth concerning their common evil doings. By the speaker was it replied that she would answer us, man, as to God, who would be judge of all of us. Then has the speaker pretended never to have seen the demon, neither to have spoken with him, nor in any way to desire to see him; never to have led the life of a courtesan, because she, the speaker, had never practised the various delights that love invents, other than those furnished by the pleasure which the Sovereign Creator has put in the thing, and to have always been incited more from the desire of being sweet and good to the dear lord loved by her, then by an incessantly raging desire. But if such had been her inclination, the speaker begged us to bear in mind that she was a poor African girl, in whom God had placed very hot blood, and in her brain so easy an understanding of the delights of love, that if a man only looked at her she felt greatly moved in her heart. That if from desire of acquaintance an amorous gentleman touched the speaker her on any portion of the body, there passing his hand, she was, in spite of everything, under his power, because her heart failed her instantly. By this touch, the apprehension and remembrance of all the sweet joys of love woke again in her breast, and there caused an intense heat, which mounted up, flamed in her veins, and made her love and joy from head to foot. And since the day when Don Marsilis had first awakened the understanding of the speaker concerning these things, she had never had any other thought, and thenceforth recognized love to be a thing so perfectly concordant with her nature, that it had since been proved to the speaker that in default of love and natural relief she would have died, withered at the said convent. As evidence of which, the speaker affirms as a certainty, that after her flight from the said convent she had not passed a single day or one particle of time in melancholy and sadness, but always was she joyous, and thus followed the sacred will of God, which she believed to have been diverted during the time lost by her in the convent.

To this was it objected by us, Hierome Cornille, to the said demon, that in this response she had openly blasphemed against God, because we had all been made to his greater glory, and placed in the world to honour and to serve Him, to have before our eyes His blessed commandments, and to live in sanctity, in order to gain eternal life, and not to be always in bed, doing that which even the beasts only do at a certain time. Then by the said sister, has answer been made, that she honoured God greatly, that in all countries she had taken care of the poor and suffering, giving them both money and raiment, and that at the last judgement-day she hoped to have around her a goodly company of holy works pleasant to God, which would intercede for her. That but for her humility, a fear of being reproached and of displeasing the gentlemen of the chapter, she would with joy have spent her wealth in finishing the cathedral of St. Maurice, and there have established foundations for the welfare of her soul—would have spared therein neither her pleasure nor her person, and that with this idea she would have taken double pleasure in her nights, because each one of her amours would have added a stone to the building of this basilic. Also the more this purpose, and for the eternal welfare of the speaker, would they have right heartily given their wealth.

Then by us has it been said to this demon that she could not justify the fact of her sterility, because in spite of so much commerce, no child had been born of her, the which proved the presence of a demon in her. Moreover, Astaroth alone, or an apostle, could speak all languages, and she spoke after the manner of all countries, the which proved the presence of the devil in her. Thereupon the speaker has asked: "In what consisted the said diversity of language?"—that of Greek she knew nothing but a Kyrie eleison, of which she made great use; of Latin, nothing, save Amen, which she said to God, wishing therewith to obtain her liberty. That for the rest the speaker had felt great sorrow, being without children, and if the good wives had them, she believed it was because they took so little pleasure in the business, and she, the speaker, a little too much. But that such was doubtless the will of God, who thought that from too great happiness, the world would be in danger of perishing. Taking this into consideration, and a thousand other reasons, which sufficiently establish the presence of the devil in the body of the sister, because the peculiar property of Lucifer is to always find arguments having the semblance of truth, we have ordered that in our presence the torture be applied to the said accused, and that she be well tormented in order to reduce the said demon by suffering to submit to the authority of the Church, and have requested to render us assistance one Francois de Hangest, master surgeon and doctor to the chapter, charging him by a codicil hereunder written to investigate the qualities of the feminine nature (*virtutes vulvae*) of the above-mentioned woman, to enlighten our religion on the methods employed by this demon to lay hold of souls in that way, and see if any article was there apparent.

Then the said Moorish women had wept bitterly, tortured in advance, and in spite of her irons, has knelt down imploring with cries and clamour the revocation of this order, objecting that her limbs were in such a feeble state, and her bones so tender, that they would break like glass; and finally, has offered to purchase her freedom from this by the gift all her goods to the chapter, and to quit incontinently the country.

Upon this, by us has she been required to voluntarily declare herself to be, and to have always been, demon of the nature of the Succubus, which is a female devil whose business it is to corrupt Christians by the blandishments and flagitious delights of love. To this the speaker has replied that the affirmation would be an abominable falsehood, seeing that she had always felt herself to be a most natural woman.

Then her irons being struck off by the torturer, the aforesaid has removed her dress, and has maliciously and with evil design bewildered and attacked our understandings with the sight of her body, the which, for a fact, exercises upon a man supernatural coercion.

Master Guillaume Tournebouche has, by reason of nature, quitted the pen at this period, and retired, objecting that he was unable, without incredible temptations, which worked in his brain, to be a witness of this torture, because he felt the devil violently gaining his person.

This finishes the second interrogatory; and as the apparitor and janitor of the chapter have stated Master Francois de Hangest to be in the country, the torture and interrogations are appointed for tomorrow at the hour of noon after mass.

This has been written verbally by me, Hierome, in the absence of Master Guillaume Tournebouche, on whose behalf it is signed.

HIEROME CORNILLE Grand Penitentiary.

PETITION

Today, the fourteenth day of the month of February, in the presence of me, Hierome Cornille, have appeared the said Masters Jehan Ribou, Antoine Jehan, Martin Beaupertuys, Hierome Maschefer, Jacques de Ville d'Omer, and the Sire d'Idre, in place of the mayor of the city of Tours, for the time absent.

All plaintiffs designated in the act of process made at the Town Hall, to whom we have, at the request of Blanche Bruyn (now confessing herself a nun of the convent of Mount Carmel, under the name of Sister Clare), declared the appeal made to the Judgment of God by the said person accused of demonical possession, and her offer to pass through the ordeal of fire and water, in presence of the Chapter and of the town of Tours, in order to prove her reality as a woman and her innocence.

To this request have agreed for their parts, the said accusers, who, on condition that the town is security for it, have engaged to prepare a suitable place and a pile, to be approved by the godparents of the accused.

Then by us, the judge, has the first day of the new year been appointed for the day of the ordeal—which will be next Paschal Day—and we have indicated the hour of noon, after mass, each of the parties having acknowledged this delay to be sufficient.

And the present proclamation shall be cited, at the suit of each of them, in all the towns, boroughs, and castles of Touraine and the land of France, at their request and at their cost and suit.

HIEROME CORNILLE.

III

What the Succubus Did to Suck Out the Soul of the Old Judge, and What Came of the Diabolical Delectation

This the act of extreme confession made the first day of the month of March, in the year one thousand two hundred and seventy-one, after the coming of our blessed Saviour, by Hierome Cornille, priest, canon of the chapter of the cathedral of St. Maurice, grand penitentiary, of all acknowledging himself unworthy, who, finding his last hour to be come, and contrite of his sins, evil doings, forfeits, bad deeds, and wickednesses, has desired his avowal to be published to serve the preconisation of the truth, the glory of God, the justice of the tribunal, and to be an alleviation to him of his punishment, in the other world. The said Hierome Cornille being on his deathbed, there had been convoked to hear his declarations, Jehan de la Haye (de Hago), vicar of the church of St. Maurice; Pietro Guyard, treasurer of the chapter, appointed by our Lord Jean de Monsoreau, Archbishop, to write his words; and Dom Louis Pot, a monk of maius *Monasterium* (Marmoustier), chosen by him for a spiritual father and confessor; all three assisted by the great and illustrious Dr Guillaume de Censoris, Roman Archdeacon, at present sent into the diocese (legatus), by our Holy Father the Pope; and, finally, in the presence of a great number of Christians come to be witnesses of the death of the said Hierome Cornille, upon his known wish to make act of public repentance, seeing that he was fast sinking, and that his words might open the eyes of Christians about to fall into hell.

And before him, Hierome, who, by reason of his great weakness could not speak, has Dom Louis Pot read the following confession to the great agitation of the said company:—

"My brethren, until the seventy-first year of my age, which is the one in which I now am, with the exception of the little sins through which, all holy though he be, a Christian renders himself culpable before God, but which it is allowed to us to repurchase by penitence, I believe I led a Christian life, and merited the praise and renown bestowed upon me in this diocese, where I was raised to the high office of grand penitentiary, of which I am unworthy. Now, struck with the knowledge of the infinite glory of God, horrified at the agonies which await the wicked and prevaricators in hell, I have thought to lessen the enormity of my sins by the greatest penitence I can show in the extreme hour at which I am. Thus I have prayed of the Church, whom I have deceived and betrayed, whose rights and judicial renown I have sold, to grant me the opportunity of accusing myself publicly in the manner of ancient Christians. I hoped, in order to show my great repentance, to have still enough life in me to be reviled at the door of the cathedral by all my brethren, to remain there an entire day on my knees, holding a candle, a cord around my neck, and my feet naked, seeing that I had followed the way of hell with regard to the sacred instincts of the Church. But in this great shipwreck of my fragile virtue, which will be to you as a warning to fly from vice and the snares of the demon, and to take refuge in the Church, where all help is, I have been so bewitched by Lucifer that our Saviour Jesus Christ will take, by the intercession of all you whose help and prayers I request, pity on me, a poor abused Christian, whose eyes now stream with tears. So would I have another life to spend in works of penitence. Now then listen and tremble with great fear! Elected by the assembled Chapter to carry it out, instruct, and complete the process commenced against a demon, who had appeared in a feminine shape, in the person of a relapse nun—an abominable person, denying God, and bearing the name of Zulma in the infidel country whence she comes; the which devil is known in the diocese under that of Clare, of the convent of Mount Carmel, and has much afflicted the town by putting herself under an infinite number of men to gain their souls to Mammon, Astaroth, and Satan—princes of hell, by making them leave this world in a state of mortal sin, and causing their death where life has its source, I have, I the judge, fallen in my latter days into this snare, and have lost my senses, while acquitting myself traitorously of the functions committed with great confidence by the Chapter to my cold senility. Hear how subtle the demon is, and stand firm against her artifices. While listening to the first response of the aforesaid Succubus, I saw with horror that the irons placed upon her feet and hands left no mark there, and was astonished at her hidden strength and at her apparent weakness. Then my mind was troubled suddenly at the sight of the natural perfections with which the devil was endowed. I listened to the music of her voice, which warmed me from head to foot, and made me desire to be young, to give myself up to this demon, thinking that for an hour passed in her company my eternal salvation was but poor payment for the pleasure of love tasted in those slender arms. Then I lost that firmness with which all judges should be furnished. This demon by me questioned, reasoned with me in such a manner that at the second interrogatory I was firmly persuaded I should be committing a crime in fining and torturing a poor little creature who cried like an innocent child. Then warned by a voice from on high to do my duty, and that these golden words, the music of celestial appearance, were diabolical mummeries, that this body, so pretty, so infatuating, would transmute itself into a bristly beast with sharp claws, those eyes so soft into flames of hell, her behind into a scaly tail, the pretty rosebud mouth and gentle lips into the jaws of a crocodile, I came back to my intention of having the said Succubus tortured until she avowed her permission, as this practice had already been followed in Christianity. Now when this demon showed herself stripped to me, to be put to the torture, I was suddenly placed in her power by magical conjurations. I felt my old bones crack, my brain received a warm light, my heart transhipped young and boiling blood. I was light in myself, and by virtue of the magic philter thrown into my eyes the snows on my forehead melted away. I lost all conscience of my Christian life and found myself a schoolboy, running about the country, escaped from class and stealing apples. I had not the power to make the sign of the cross, neither did I remember the Church, God the Father, nor the sweet Saviour of men. A prey to this design, I went about the streets thinking over the delights of that voice, the abominable, pretty body of this demon, and saying a thousand wicked things to myself. Then pierced and drawn by a blow of the devil's fork, who had planted himself already in my head as a serpent in an oak, I was conducted by this sharp prong towards the jail, in spite of my guardian angel, who from time to time pulled me by the arm and defended me against these temptations, but in spite of his holy advice and his assistance I was dragged by a million claws stuck into my heart, and soon found myself in the jail. As soon as the door was opened to me I saw no longer any appearance of a prison, because the Succubus had there, with the assistance of evil genii or fays, constructed a pavilion of purple and silk, full of perfumes and flowers, where she was seated, superbly attired with neither irons on her neck nor chains on her feet. I allowed myself to be stripped of my ecclesiastical vestments, and was put into a scent bath. Then the demon covered me with a Saracen robe, entertained me with a repast of rare viands contained in precious vases, gold cups, Asiatic wines, songs and marvellous music, and a thousand sweet sounds that tickled my soul by means of my ears. At my side kept always the said Succubus, and her sweet, delectable embrace distilled new ardour into my members. My guardian angel quitted me. Then I lived only by the terrible light of the Moorish woman's eyes, coveted the warm embraces of the delicate body, wished always to feel her red lips, that I believed natural, and had no fear of the bite of those teeth which drew me to the bottom of hell, I delighted to feel the unequalled softness of her hands without thinking that they were unnatural claws. In short, I acted like husband desiring to go to his affianced without thinking that that spouse was everlasting death. I had no thought for the things of this world nor the interests of God, dreaming only of love, of the sweet breasts of this woman, who made me burn, and of the gate of hell in which I wished to cast myself. Alas! my brethren, during three days and three nights was I thus constrained to toil without being able to stop the stream which flowed from my reins, in which were plunged, like two pikes, the hands of the Succubus, which communicated to my poor old age and to my dried up bones, I know not what sweat of love. At first this demon, to draw me to her, caused to flow in my inside the softness of milk, then came poignant joys which pricked like a hundred needles my bones, my marrow, my brain, and my nerves. Then all this gone, all things became inflamed, my head, my blood, my nerves, my flesh, my bones, and then I burned with the real fire of hell, which caused me torments in my joints, and an incredible, intolerable, tearing voluptuousness which loosened the bonds of my life. The tresses of this demon, which enveloped my poor body, poured upon me a stream of flame, and I felt each lock like a bar of red iron. During this mortal delectation I saw the ardent face of the said Succubus, who laughed and addressed to me a thousand exciting words; such as that I was her knight, her lord, her lance, her day, her joy, her hero, her life, her good, her rider, and that she would like to clasp me even closer, wishing to be in my skin or have me in hers. Hearing which, under the prick of this tongue which sucked out my soul, I plunged and precipitated myself finally into hell without finding the bottom. And then when I had no more a drop of blood in my veins, when my heart no longer beat in my body, and I was ruined at all points, the demon, still fresh, white, rubicund, glowing, and laughing, said to me—

"'Poor fool, to think me a demon! Had I asked thee to sell thy soul for a kiss, wouldst thou not give it to me with all thy heart?'

"'Yes,' said I.

"'And if always to act thus it were necessary for thee to nourish thyself with the blood of new-born children in order always to have new life to spend in my arms, would you not imbibe it willingly?'

"'Yes,' said I.

"'And to be always my gallant horseman, gay as a man in his prime, feeling life, drinking pleasure, plunging to the depths of joy as a swimmer into the Loire, wouldst thou not deny God, wouldst thou not spit in the face of Jesus?'

"'Yes,' said I.

"Then I felt a hundred sharp claws which tore my diaphragm as if the beaks of a thousand birds there took their bellyfuls, shrieking. Then I was lifted suddenly above the earth upon the said Succubus, who had spread her wings, and cried to me—

"'Ride, ride, my gallant rider! Hold yourself firmly on the back of thy mule, by her mane, by her neck; and ride, ride, my gallant rider—everything rides!' And then I saw, as a thick fog, the cities of the earth, where by a special gift I perceived each one coupled with a female demon, and tossing about, and engendering in great concupiscence, all shrieking a thousand words of love and exclamations of all kinds, and all toiling away with ecstasy. Then my horse with the Moorish head pointed out to me, still flying and galloping beyond the clouds, the earth coupled with the sun in a conjunction, from which proceeded a germ of stars, and there each female world was embracing a male world; but in place of the words used by creatures, the worlds were giving forth the howls of tempests, throwing up lightnings and crying thunders. Then still rising, I saw overhead the female nature of all things in love with the Prince of Movement. Now, by way of mockery, the Succubus placed me in the centre of this horrible and perpetual conflict, where I was lost as a grain of sand in the sea. Then still cried my white mare to me, 'Ride, ride my gallant rider—all things ride!' Now, thinking how little was a priest in this torment of the seed of worlds, nature always clasped together, and metals, stones, waters, airs, thunders, fish, plants, animals, men, spirits, worlds and planets, all embracing with rage, I denied the Catholic faith. Then the Succubus, pointing out to me the great patch of stars seen in heavens, said to me, 'That way is a drop of celestial seed escaped from great flow of the worlds in conjunction.' Thereupon I instantly clasped the Succubus with passion by the light of a thousand million of stars, and I wished in clasping her to feel the nature of those thousand million creatures. Then by this great effort of love I fell impotent in every way, and heard a great infernal laugh. Then I found myself in my bed, surrounded by my servitors, who had had the courage to struggle with the demon, throwing into the bed where I was stretched a basin full of holy water, and saying fervent prayers to God. Then had I to sustain, in spite of this assistance, a horrible combat with the said Succubus, whose claws still clutched my heart, causing me infinite pains; still, while reanimated by the voice of my servitors, relations, and friends, I tried to make the sacred sign of the cross; the Succubus perched on my bed, on the bolster, at the foot, everywhere, occupying herself in distracting my nerves, laughing, grimacing, putting before my eyes a thousand obscene images, and causing me a thousand wicked desires. Nevertheless, taking pity on me, my lord the Archbishop caused the relics of St. Gatien to be brought, and the moment the shrine had touched my bed the said Succubus was obliged to depart, leaving an odour of sulphur and of hell, which made the throats of my servants, friends, and others sore for a whole day. Then the celestial light of God having enlightened my soul, I knew I was, through my sins and my combat with the evil spirit, in great danger of dying. Then did I implore the especial mercy, to live just a little time to render glory to God and his Church, objecting the infinite merits of Jesus dead upon the cross for the salvation of the Christians. By this prayer I obtained the favour of recovering sufficient strength to accuse myself of my sins, and to beg of the members of the Church of St. Maurice their aid and assistance to deliver me from purgatory, where I am about to atone for my faults by infinite agonies. Finally, I declare that my proclamation, wherein the said demon appeals the judgment of God by the ordeals of holy water and a fire, is a subterfuge due to an evil design suggested by the said demon, who would thus have had the power to escape the justice of the tribunal of the Archbishop and of the Chapter, seeing that she secretly confessed to me, to be able to make another demon accustomed to the ordeal appear in her place. And, in conclusion, I give and bequeath to the Chapter of the Church of St. Maurice my property of all kinds, to found a chapter in the said church, to build it and adorn it and put it under the invocation of St. Hierome and St. Gatien, of whom one is my patron and the other the saviour of my soul."

This, heard by all the company, has been brought to the notice of the ecclesiastical tribunal by Jehan to la Haye (Johannes de Haga).

We, Jehan de la Haye (Johannes de Haga), elected grand penitentiary of St. Maurice by the general assembly of the Chapter, according to the usage and custom of that church, and appointed to pursue afresh the trial of the demon Succubus, at present in the jail of the Chapter, have ordered a new inquest, at which will be heard all those of this diocese having cognisance of the facts relative thereto. We declared void the other proceedings, interrogations, and decrees, and annul them in the name of the members of the Church in general, and sovereign Chapter assembled, and declare that the appeal to God, traitorously made by the demon, shall not take place, in consequence of the notorious treachery of the devil in this affair. And the said judgment shall be cried by sound of trumpet in all parts of the diocese in which have been published the false edicts of the preceding month, all notoriously due to the instigation of the demon, according to the confession of the late Hierome Cornille.

Let all good Christians be of assistance to our Holy Church, and to her commandments.

JEHAN DE LA HAYE.

IV

How the Moorish Woman of the Rue Chaude Twisted About So Briskly that with Great Difficulty Was She Burned and Cooked Alive, to the Great Loss of the Infernal Regions

This was written in the month of May, of the year 1360, after the manner of a testament.

"My very dear and well-beloved son, when it shall be lawful for thee to read this I shall be, I thy father, reposing in the tomb, imploring thy prayers, and supplicating thee to conduct thyself in life as it will be commanded thee in this rescript, bequeathed for the good government of thy family, thy future, and safety; for I have done this at a period when I had my senses and understanding, still recently affected by the sovereign injustice of men. In my virile age I had a great ambition to raise myself in the Church, and therein to obtain the highest dignities, because no life appeared to me more splendid. Now with this earnest idea, I learned to read and write, and with great trouble became in a fit condition to enter the clergy. But because I had no protection, or good advice to superintend my training I had an idea of becoming the writer, tabellion, and rubrican of the Chapter of St. Maurice, in which were the highest and richest personages of Christendom, since the King of France is only therein a simple canon. Now there I should be able better than anywhere else to find services to render to certain lords, and thus to find a master or gain patronage, and by this assistance enter into religion, and be mitred and esconced in an archiepiscopal chair, somewhere or other. But this first vision was over credulous, and a little too ambitious, the which God caused me clearly to perceive by the sequel. In fact, Messire Jepan de Villedomer, who afterwards became cardinal, was given this appointment, and I was rejected, discomfited. Now in this unhappy hour I received an alleviation of my troubles, by the advice of the good old Hierome Cornille, of whom I have often spoken to you. This dear man induced me, by his kindness, to become penman to the Chapter of St. Maurice and the Archbishop of Tours, the which offer I accepted with joy, since I was reputed a scrivener. At the time I was about to enter into the presbytery commenced the famous process against the devil of the Rue Chaude, of which the old folk still talk, and which in its time, has been recounted in every home in France. Now, believing that it would be of great advantage to my ambition, and that for this assistance the Chapter would raise me to some dignity, my good master had me appointed for the purpose of writing all of that should be in this grave cause, subject to writing. At the very outset Monseigneur Hierome Cornille, a man approaching eighty years, of great sense, justice, and sound understanding, suspected some spitefulness in this cause, although he was not partial to immodest girls, and had never been involved with a woman in his life, and was holy and venerable, with a sanctity which had caused him to be selected as a judge, all this not withstanding. As soon as the depositions were completed, and the poor wench heard, it remained clear that although this merry doxy had broken her religious vows, she was innocent of all devilry, and that her great wealth was coveted by her enemies, and other persons, whom I must not name to thee for reasons of prudence. At this time every one believed her to be so well furnished with silver and gold that she could have bought the whole county of Touraine, if so it had pleased her. A thousand falsehoods and calumnious words concerning the girl, envied by all the honest women, were circulated and believed in as gospel. At this period Master Hierome Cornille, having ascertained that no demon other than that of love was in the girl, made her consent to remain in a convent for the remainder of her days. And having ascertained certain noble knights brave in war and rich in domains, that they would do everything to save her, he invited her secretly to demand of her accusers the judgment of God, at the same time giving her goods to the chapter, in order to silence mischievous tongues. By this means would be saved from the stake the most delicate flower that ever heaven has allowed to fall upon our earth; the which flower yielded only from excessive tenderness and amiability to the malady of love, cast by her eyes into the hearts of all her pursuers. But the real devil, under the form of a monk, mixed himself up in this affair; in this wise: great enemy of the virtue, wisdom, and sanctity of Monsignor Hierome Cornille, named Jehan de la Haye, having learned that in the jail, the poor girl was treated like a queen, wickedly accused the grand penitentiary of connivance with her and of being her servitor, because, said this wicked priest, she makes him young, amorous, and happy, from which the poor old man died of grief in one day, knowing by this that Jehan de la Haye had worn his ruin and coveted his dignities. In fact, our lord the archbishop visited the jail, and found the Moorish woman in a pleasant place, reposing comfortably, and without irons, because, having placed a diamond in a place when none could have believed she could have held it, she had purchased the clemency of her jailer. At the time certain persons said that this jailer was smitten with her, and that from love, or perhaps in great fear of the young barons, lovers of this woman, he had planned her escape. The good man Cornille being at the point of death, through the treachery of Jehan de la Haye, the Chapter thinking it necessary to make null and void the proceedings taken by the penitentiary, and also his decrees, the said Jehan de la Haye, at that time a simple vicar of the cathedral, pointed out that to do this it would be sufficient to obtain a public confession from the good man on his death-bed. Then was the moribund tortured and tormented by the gentleman of the Chapter, those of Saint Martin, those of Marmoustiers, by the archbishop and also by the Pope's legate, in order that he might recant to the advantage of the Church, to which the good man would not consent. But after a thousand ills, the public confession was prepared, at which the most noteworthy people of the town assisted, and the which spread more horror and consternation than I can describe. The churches of the diocese held public prayers for this calamity, and every one expected to see the devil tumble into his house by the chimney. But the truth of it is that the good Master Hierome had a fever, and saw cows in his room, and then was this recantation obtained of him. The access passed, the poor saint wept copiously on learning this trick from me. In fact, he died in my arms, assisted by his physicians, heartbroken at this mummery, telling us that he was going to the feet of God to pray to prevent the consummation of this deplorable iniquity. The poor Moorish woman had touched him much by her tears and repentance, seing that before making her demand for the judgment of God he had minutely confessed her, and by that means had disentangled the soul divine which was in the body, and of which he spoke as of a diamond worthy of adorning the holy crown of

God, when she should have departed this life, after repenting her sins. Then, my dear son, knowing by the statements made in the town, and by the naive responses of this unhappy wretch, all the trickery of this affair, I determined by the advice of Master Francois de Hangest, physician of the chapter, to feign an illness and quit the service of the Church of St. Maurice and of the archbishopric, in order not to dip my hands in the innocent blood, which still cries and will continue to cry aloud unto God until the day of the last judgment. Then was the jailer dismissed, and in his place was put the second son of the torturer, who threw the Moorish woman into a dungeon, and inhumanly put upon her hands and feet chains weighing fifty pounds, besides a wooden waistband; and the jail were watched by the crossbowmen of the town and the people of the archbishop. The wench was tormented and tortured, and her bones were broken; conquered by sorrow, she made an avowal according to the wishes of Jehan de la Haye, and was instantly condemned to be burned in the enclosure of St. Etienne, having been previously placed in the portals of the church, attired in a chemise of sulphur, and her goods given over to the Chapter, et cetera. This order was the cause of great disturbances and fighting in the town, because three young knights of Touraine swore to die in the service of the poor girl, and to deliver her in all possible ways. Then they came into the town, accompanied by thousands of sufferers, labouring people, old soldiers, warriors, courtesans, and others, whom the said girls had succoured, saved from misfortune, from hunger and misery, and searched all the poor dwellings of the town where lay those to whom she had done good. Thus all were stirred up and called together to the plain of Mount-Louis under the protection of the soldiers of the said lords; they had for companions all the scape-graces of the said twenty leagues around, and came one morning to lay siege to the prison of the archbishop, demanding that the Moorish woman should be given up to them as though they would put her to death, but in fact to set her free, and to place her secretly upon a swift horse, that she might gain the open country, seeing that she rode like a groom. Then in this frightful tempest of men have we seen between the battlements of the archiepiscopal palace and the bridges, more than ten thousand men swarming, besides those who were perched upon the roofs of the houses and climbing on all the balconies to see the sedition; in short it was easy to hear the horrible cries of the Christians, who were terribly in earnest, and of those who surrounded the jail with the intention of setting the poor girl free, across the Loire, the other side of Saint Symphorien. The suffocation and squeezing of bodies was so great in this immense crowd, bloodthirsty for the poor creature at whose knees they would have fallen had they had the opportunity of seeing her, that seven children, eleven women, and eight citizens were crushed and smashed beyond all recognition, since they were like splodges of mud; in short, so wide open was the great mouth of this popular leviathan, this horrible monster, that the clamour was heard at Montils-les-Tours. All cried 'Death to the Succubus! Throw out the demon! Ha! I'd like a quarter! I'll have her skin! The foot for me, the mane for thee! The head for me! The something for me! Is it red? Shall we see? Will it be grilled? Death to her! death!' Each one had his say. But the cry, 'Largesse to God! Death to the Succubus!' was yelled at the same time by the crowd so hoarsely and so cruelly that one's ears and heart bled therefrom; and the other cries were scarcely heard in the houses. The archbishop decided, in order to calm this storm which threatened to overthrow everything, to come out with great pomp from the church, bearing the host, which would deliver the Chapter from ruin, since the wicked young men and the lords had sworn to destroy and burn the cloisters and all the canons. Now by this stratagem the crowd was obliged to break up, and from lack of provisions return to their houses. Then the monks of Touraine, the lords, and the citizens, in great apprehension of pillage on the morrow, held a nocturnal council, and accepted the advice of the Chapter. By their efforts the men-at-arms, archers, knights, and citizens, in a large number, kept watch, and killed a party of shepherds, road menders, and vagrants, who, knowing the disturbed state of Tours, came to swell the ranks of the malcontents. The Sire Harduin de Maille, an old nobleman, reasoned with the young knights, who were the champions of the Moorish woman, and argued sagely with them, asking them if for so small a woman they wished to put Touraine to fire and sword; that even if they were victorious they would be masters of the bad characters brought together by them; that these said freebooters, after having sacked the castles of their enemies, would turn to those of their chiefs. That the rebellion commenced had had no success in the first attack, because up to that time the place was untouched, could they have any over the church, which would invoke the aid of the king? And a thousand other arguments. To these reasons the young knights replied, that it was easy for the Chapter to aid the girl's escape in the night, and that thus the cause of the sedition would be removed. To this humane and wise requests replied Monseigneur de Censoris, the Pope's legate, that it was necessary that strength should remain with the religion of the Church. And thereupon the poor wench payed for all, since it was agreed that no inquiry should be made concerning this sedition.

"Then the Chapter had full licence to proceed to the penance of the girl, to which act and ecclesiastical ceremony the people came from twelve leagues around. So that on the day when, after divine satisfaction, the Succubus was to be delivered up to secular justice, in order to be publicly burnt at a stake, not for a gold pound would a lord or even an abbott have been found lodging in the town of Tours. The night before many camped outside the town in tents, or slept upon straw. Provisions were lacking, and many who came with their bellies full, returned with their bellies empty, having seen nothing but the reflection of the fire in the distance. And the bad characters did good strokes of business by the way.

"The poor courtesan was half dead; her hair had whitened. She was, to tell the truth, nothing but a skeleton, scarcely covered with flesh, and her chains weighed more than she did. If she had had joy in her life, she paid dearly for it at this moment. Those who saw her pass say that she wept and shrieked in a way that should have earned the pity of her hardest pursuers; and in the church there were compelled to put a piece of wood in her mouth, which she bit as a lizard bites a stick. Then the executioner tied her to a stake to sustain her, since she let herself roll at times and fell for want of strength. Then she suddenly recovered a vigorous handful, because, this notwithstanding, she was able, it is said to break her cords and escape into the church, where in remembrance of her old vocation, she climbed quickly into galleries above, flying like a bird along the little columns and small friezes. She was about to escape on to the roof when a soldier perceived her, and thrust his spear in the sole of her foot. In spite of her foot half cut through, the poor girl still ran along the church without noticing it, going along with her bones broken and her blood gushing out, so great fear had she of the flames of the stake. At last she was taken and bound, thrown into a tumbrel and led to the stake, without being afterwards heard to utter a cry. The account of her flight in the church assisted in making the common people believe that she was the devil, and some of them said that she had flown in the air. As soon as the executioner of the town threw her into the flames, she made two or three horrible leaps and fell down into the bottom of the pile, which burned day and night. On the following evening I went to see if anything remained of this gentle girl, so sweet, so loving, but I found nothing but a fragment of the 'os stomachal,' in which, is spite of this, there still remained some moisture, and which some say still trembled like a woman does in the same place. It is impossible to tell, my dear son, the sadnesses, without number and without equal, which for about ten years weighed upon me; always was I thinking of this angel burnt by wicked men, and always I beheld her with her eyes full of love. In short the supernatural gifts of this artless child were shining day and night before me, and I prayed for her in the church, where she had been martyred. At length I had neither the strength nor the courage to look without trembling upon the grand penitentiary Jehan de la Haye, who died eaten up by lice. Leprosy was his punishment. Fire burned his house and his wife; and all those who had a hand in the burning had their own hands singed.

"This, my well-beloved son, was the cause of a thousand ideas, which I have here put into writing to be forever the rule of conduct in our family.

"I quitted the service of the church, and espoused your mother, from whom I received infinite blessings, and with whom I shared my life, my goods, my soul, and all. And she agreed with me in following precepts—Firstly, that to live happily, it is necessary to keep far away from church people, to honour them much without giving them leave to enter your house, any more than to those who by right, just or unjust, are supposed to be superior to us. Secondly, to take a modest condition, and to keep oneself in it without wishing to appear in any way rich. To have a care to excite no envy, nor strike anyonesoever in any manner, because it is needful to be as strong as an oak, which kills the plants at its feet, to crush envious heads, and even then would one succumb, since human oaks are especially rare and that no Tournebouche should flatter himself that he is one, granting that he be a Tournebouche. Thirdly, never to spend more than one quarter of one's income, conceal one's wealth, hide one's goods and chattels, to undertake no office, to go to church like other people, and always keep one's thoughts to oneself, seeing that they belong to you and not to others, who twist them about, turn them after their own fashion, and make calumnies therefrom. Fourthly, always to remain in the condition of the Tournebouches, who are now and forever drapers. To marry your daughters to good drapers, send your sons to be drapers in other towns of France furnished with these wise precepts, and to bring them up to the honour of drapery, and without leaving any dream of ambition in their minds. A draper like a Tournebouche should be their glory, their arms, their name, their motto, their life. Thus by being always drapers, they will be always Tournebouches, and rub on like the good little insects, who, once lodged in the beam, made their dens, and go on with security to the end of their ball of thread. Fifthly never to speak any other language than that of drapery, and never to dispute concerning religion or government. And even though the government of the state, the province, religion, and God turn about, or have a fancy to go to the right or to the left, always in your quality of Tournebouche, stick to your cloth. Thus unnoticed by the others of the town, the Tournebouches will live in peace with their little Tournebouches—paying the tithes and taxes, and all that they are required by force to give, be it to God, or to the king, to the town or to the parish, with all of whom it is unwise to struggle. Also it is necessary to keep the patrimonial treasure, to have peace and to buy peace, never to owe anything, to have corn in the house, and enjoy yourselves with the doors and windows shut.

"By this means none will take from the Tournebouches, neither the state, nor the Church, nor the Lords, to whom should the case be that force is employed, you will lend a few crowns without cherishing the idea of ever seeing him again—I mean the crowns.

"Thus, in all seasons people will love the Tournebouches, will mock the Tournebouches as poor people—as the slow Tournebouches, as Tournebouches of no understanding. Let the know-nothings say on. The Tournebouches will neither be burned nor hanged, to the advantage of King or Church, or other people; and the wise Tournebouches will have secretly money in their pockets, and joy in their houses, hidden from all.

"Now, my dear son, follow this the counsel of a modest and middle-class life. Maintain this in thy family as a county charter; and when you die, let your successor maintain it as the sacred gospel of the Tournebouches, until God wills it that there be no longer Tournebouches in this world."

This letter has been found at the time of the inventory made in the house of Francois Tournebouche, lord of Veretz, chancellor to Monseigneur the Dauphin, and condemned at the time of the rebellion of the said lord against the King to lose his head, and have all his goods confiscated by order of the Parliament of Paris. The said letter has been handed to the Governor of Touraine as an historical curiosity, and joined to the pieces of the process in the archbishopric of Tours, by me, Pierre Gaultier, Sheriff, President of the Trades Council.

The author having finished the transcription and deciphering of these parchments, translating them from their strange language into French, the donor of them declared that the Rue Chaude at Tours was so called, according to certain people, because the sun remained there longer than in all other parts. But in spite of this version, people of lofty understanding will find, in the warm way of the said Succubus, the real origin of the said name. In which acquiesces the author. This teaches us not to abuse our body, but use it wisely in view of our salvation.

The Damned Thing

Ambrose Bierce

I
One Does Not Always Eat What Is on the Table

By the light of a tallow candle, which had been placed on one end of a rough table, a man was reading something written in a book. It was an old account book, greatly worn; and the writing was not, apparently, very legible, for the man sometimes held the page close to the flame of the candle to get a stronger light upon it. The shadow of the book would then throw into obscurity a half of the room, darkening a number of faces and figures; for besides the reader, eight other men were present. Seven of them sat against the rough log walls, silent and motionless, and, the room being small, not very far from the table. By extending an arm any one of them could have touched the eighth man, who lay on the table, face upward, partly covered by a sheet, his arms at his sides. He was dead.

The man with the book was not reading aloud, and no one spoke; all seemed to be waiting for something to occur; the dead man only was without expectation. From the blank darkness outside came in, through the aperture that served for a window, all the ever unfamiliar noises of night in the wilderness—the long, nameless note of a distant coyote; the stilly pulsing thrill of tireless insects in the trees; strange cries of night birds, so different from those of the birds of day; the drone of great blundering beetles and all that mysterious chorus of small sounds that seemed always to have been but half heard when they have suddenly ceased, as if conscious of an indiscretion. But nothing of all this was noted in that company; its members were not overmuch addicted to idle interest in matters of no practical importance; that was obvious in every line of their rugged faces—obvious even in the dim light of the single candle. They were evidently men of the vicinity—farmers and woodmen.

The person reading was a trifle different; one would have said of him that he was of the world, worldly, albeit there was that in his attire which attested a certain fellowship with the organisms of his environment. His coat would hardly have passed muster in San Francisco: his footgear was not of urban origin, and the hat that lay by him on the floor (he was the only one uncovered) was such that if one had considered it as an article of mere personal adornment he would have missed its meaning. In countenance the man was rather prepossessing, with just a hint of sternness; though that he may have assumed or cultivated, as appropriate to one in authority. For he was a coroner. It was by virtue of his office that he had possession of the book in which he was reading; it had been found among the dead man's effects—in his cabin, where the inquest was now taking place.

When the coroner had finished reading he put the book into his breast pocket. At that moment the door was pushed open and a young man entered. He, clearly, was not of mountain birth and breeding: he was clad as those who dwell in cities. His clothing was dusty, however, as from travel. He had, in fact, been riding hard to attend the inquest.

The coroner nodded; no one else greeted him.

"We have waited for you," said the coroner. "It is necessary to have done with this business tonight."

The young man smiled. "I am sorry to have kept you," he said, "I went away, not to evade your summons, but to post to my newspaper an account of what I suppose I am called back to relate."

The coroner smiled.

"The account that you posted to your newspaper," he said, "differs probably from that which you will give here under oath."

"That," replied the other, rather hotly and with a visible flush, "is as you choose. I used manifold paper and have a copy of what I sent. It was not written as news, for it is incredible, but as fiction. It may go as a part of my testimony under oath."

"But you say it is incredible."

"That is nothing to you, sir, if I also swear that it is true."

The coroner was apparently not greatly affected by the young man's manifest resentment. He was silent for some moments, his eyes upon the floor. The men about the sides of the cabin talked in whispers, but seldom withdrew their gaze from the face of the corpse. Presently the coroner lifted his eyes and said: "We will resume the inquest."

The men removed their hats. The witness was sworn.

"What is your name?" the coroner asked.

"William Harker."

"Age?"

"Twenty-seven."

"You knew the deceased, Hugh Morgan?"

"Yes."

"You were with him when he died?"

"Near him."

"How did that happen—your presence, I mean?"

"I was visiting him at his place to shoot and fish. A part of my purpose, however, was to study him, and his odd, solitary way of life. He seemed a good model for a character in fiction. I sometimes write stories."

"I sometimes read them."

"Thank you."

"Stories in general—not yours."

Some of the jurors laughed. Against a sombre background humour shows high lights. Soldiers in the intervals of battle laugh easily, and a jest in the death chamber conquers by surprise.

"Relate the circumstances of this man's death," said the coroner. "You may use any notes or memoranda that you please."

The witness understood. Pulling a manuscript from his breast pocket he held it near the candle, and turning the leaves until he found the passage that he wanted, began to read.

II
What May Happen in a Field of Wild Oats

". . . The sun had hardly risen when we left the house. We were looking for quail, each with a shot-gun, but we had only one dog. Morgan said that our best ground was beyond a certain ridge that he pointed out, and we crossed it by trail through the chaparral. On the other side was comparatively level ground, thickly covered with wild oats. As we emerged from the chaparral, Morgan was but a few yards in advance. Suddenly, we heard, at a little distance to our right, and partly in front, a noise as of some animal thrashing about in the bushes, which we could see were violently agitated.

" 'We've started a deer,' I said. 'I wish we had brought a rifle.'

"Morgan, who had stopped and was intently watching the agitated chaparral, said nothing, but had cocked both barrels of his gun, and was holding it in readiness to aim. I thought him a trifle excited, which surprised me, for he had a reputation for exceptional coolness, even in moments of sudden and imminent peril.

" 'O, come!' I said. 'You are not going to fill up a deer with quail-shot, are you?'

"Still he did not reply; but, catching a sight of his face as he turned it slightly toward me, I was struck by the pallor of it. Then I understood that we had serious business on hand, and my first conjecture was that we had 'jumped' a grizzly. I advanced to Morgan's side, cocking my piece as I moved.

"The bushes were now quiet, and the sounds had ceased, but Morgan was as attentive to the place as before.

" 'What is it? What the devil is it?' I asked.

" 'That Damned Thing!' he replied, without turning his head. His voice was husky and unnatural. He trembled visibly.

"I was about to speak further, when I observed the wild oats near the place of the disturbance moving in the most inexplicable way. I can hardly describe it. It seemed as if stirred by a streak of wind, which not only bent it, but pressed it down—crushed it so that it did not rise, and this movement was slowly prolonging itself directly toward us.

"Nothing that I had ever seen had affected me so strangely as this unfamiliar and unaccountable phenomenon, yet I am unable to recall any sense of fear. I remember—and tell it here because, singularly enough, I recollected it then—that once, in looking carelessly out of an open window, I momentarily mistook a small tree close at hand for one of a group of larger trees at a little distance away. It looked the same size as the others, but, being more distinctly and sharply defined in mass and details, seemed out of harmony with them. It was a mere falsification of the law of aerial perspective, but it startled, almost terrified me. We so rely upon the orderly operation of familar natural laws that any seeming suspension of them is noted as a menace to our safety, a warning of unthinkable calamity. So now the apparently causeless movement of the herbage, and the slow, undeviating approach of the line of disturbance were distinctly disquieting. My companion appeared actually frightened, and I could hardly credit my senses when I saw him suddenly throw his gun to his shoulders and fire both barrels at the agitated grass! Before the smoke of the discharge had cleared away I heard a loud savage cry—a scream like that of a wild animal—and, flinging his gun upon the ground, Morgan sprang away and ran swiftly from the spot. At the same instant I was thrown violently to the ground by the impact of something unseen in the smoke—some soft, heavy substance that seemed thrown against me with great force.

"Before I could get upon my feet and recover my gun, which seemed to have been struck from my hands, I heard Morgan crying out as if in mortal agony, and mingling with his cries were such hoarse, savage sounds as one hears from fighting dogs. Inexpressibly terrified, I struggled to my feet and looked in the direction of Morgan's retreat; and may heaven in mercy spare me from another sight like that! At a distance of less than thirty yards was my friend, down upon one knee, his head thrown back at a frightful angle, hatless, his long hair in disorder and his whole body in violent movement from side to side, backward and forward. His right arm was lifted and seemed to lack the hand—at least, I could see none. The other arm was invisible. At times, as my memory now reports this extraordinary scene, I could discern but a part of his body; it was as if he had been partly blotted out—I cannot otherwise express it—then a shifting of his position would bring it all into view again.

"All this must have occurred within a few seconds, yet in that time Morgan assumed all the postures of a determined wrestler vanquished by superior weight and strength. I saw nothing but him, and him not always distinctly. During the entire incident his shouts and curses were heard, as if through an enveloping uproar of such sounds of rage and fury as I had never heard from the throat of man or brute!

"For a moment only I stood irresolute, then throwing down my gun, I ran forward to my friend's assistance. I had a vague belief that he was suffering from a fit or some form of convulsion. Before I could reach his side he was down and quiet. All sounds had ceased, but, with a feeling of such terror as even these awful events had not inspired, I now saw the same mysterious movement of the wild oats prolonging itself from the trampled area about the prostrate man toward the edge of a wood. It was only when it had reached the wood that I was able to withdraw my eyes and look at my companion. He was dead."

III
A Man Though Naked May Be in Rags

The coroner rose from his seat and stood beside the dead man. Lifting an edge of the sheet he pulled it away, exposing the entire body, altogether naked and showing in the candle-light a clay-like yellow. It had, however, broad maculations of bluish-black, obviously caused by extravasated blood from contusions. The chest and sides looked as if they had been beaten with a bludgeon. There were dreadful lacerations; the skin was torn in strips and shreds.

The coroner moved round to the end of the table and undid a silk handkerchief, which had been passed under the chin and knotted on the top of the head. When the handkerchief was drawn away it exposed what had been the throat. Some of the jurors who had risen to get a better view repented their curiosity, and turned away their faces. Witness Harker went to the open window and leaned out across the sill, faint and sick. Dropping the handkerchief upon the dead man's neck, the coroner stepped to an angle of the room, and from a pile of clothing produced one garment after another, each of which he held up a moment for inspection. All were torn, and stiff with blood. The jurors did not make a closer inspection. They seemed rather uninterested. They had, in truth, seen all this before; the only thing that was new to them being Harker's testimony.

"Gentlemen," the coroner said, "we have no more evidence, I think. Your duty has been already explained to you; if there is nothing you wish to ask you may go outside and consider your verdict."

The foreman rose—a tall, bearded man of sixty, coarsely clad.

"I should like to ask one question, Mr. Coroner," he said. "What asylum did this yer last witness escape from?"

"Mr. Harker," said the coroner, gravely and tranquilly, "from what asylum did you last escape?"

Harker flushed crimson again, but said nothing, and the seven jurors rose and solemnly filed out of the cabin.

"If you have done insulting me, sir," said Harker, as soon as he and the officer were left alone with the dead man, "I suppose I am at liberty to go?"

"Yes."

Harker started to leave, but paused, with his hand on the door latch. The habit of his profession was strong in him—stronger than his sense of personal dignity. He turned about and said:

"The book that you have there—I recognise it as Morgan's diary. You seemed greatly interested in it; you read in it while I was testifying. May I see it? The public would like—"

"The book will cut no figure in this matter," replied the official, slipping it into his coat pocket; "all the entries in it were made before the writer's death."

As Harker passed out of the house the jury re-entered and stood about the table, on which the now covered corpse showed under the sheet with sharp definition. The foreman seated himself near the candle, produced from his breast pocket a pencil and scrap of paper, and wrote rather laboriously the following verdict, which with various degrees of effort all signed:

"We, the jury, do find that the remains come to their death at the hands of a mountain lion, but some of us thinks, all the same, they had fits."

IV
An Explanation from the Tomb

In the dairy of the late Hugh Morgan are certain interesting entries having, possibly, a scientific value as suggestions. At the inquest upon his body the book was not put in evidence; possibly the coroner thought it not worth while to confuse the jury. The date of the first of the entries mentioned cannot be ascertained; the upper part of the leaf is torn away; the part of the entry remaining is as follows:

". . . would run in a half circle, keeping his head turned always toward the centre and again he would stand still, barking furiously. At last he ran away into the brush as fast as he could go. I thought at first that he had gone mad, but on returning to the house found no other alteration in his manner than what was obviously due to fear of punishment.

"Can a dog see with his nose? Do odours impress some olfactory centre with images of the thing emitting them? . . .

"Sept. 2.—Looking at the stars last night as they rose above the crest of the ridge east of the house, I observed them successively disappear—from left to right. Each was eclipsed but an instant, and only a few at the same time, but along the entire length of the ridge all that were within a degree or two of the crest were blotted out. It was as if something had passed along between me and them; but I could not see it, and the stars were not thick enough to define its outline. Ugh! I don't like this . . ."

Several weeks' entries are missing, three leaves being torn from the book.

"Sept. 27.—It has been about here again—I find evidences of its presence every day. I watched again all of last night in the same cover, gun in hand, double-charged with buckshot. In the morning the fresh footprints were there, as before. Yet I would have sworn that I did not sleep—indeed, I hardly sleep at all. It is terrible, insupportable! If these amazing experiences are real I shall go mad; if they are fanciful I am mad already.

"Oct. 3.—I shall not go—it shall not drive me away. No, this is my house, my land. God hates a coward . . .

"Oct. 5.—I can stand it no longer; I have invited Harker to pass a few weeks with me—he has a level head. I can judge from his manner if he thinks me mad.

"Oct. 7.—I have the solution of the problem; it came to me last night—suddenly, as by revelation. How simple—how terribly simple!

"There are sounds that we cannot hear. At either end of the scale are notes that stir no chord of that imperfect instrument, the human ear. They are too high or too grave. I have observed a flock of blackbirds occupying an entire tree-top—the tops of several trees—and all in full song. Suddenly—in a moment—at absolutely the same instant—all spring into the air and fly away. How? They could not all see one another—whole tree-tops intervened. At no point could a leader have been visible to all. There must have been a signal of warning or command, high and shrill above the din, but by me unheard. I have observed, too, the same simultaneous flight when all were silent, among not only blackbirds, but other birds—quail, for example, widely separated by bushes—even on opposite sides of a hill.

"It is known to seamen that a school of whales basking or sporting on the surface of the ocean, miles apart, with the convexity of the earth between them, will sometimes dive at the same instant—all gone out of sight in a moment. The signal has been sounded—too grave for the ear of the sailor at the masthead and his comrades on the deck—who nevertheless feel its vibrations in the ship as the stones of a cathedral are stirred by the bass of the organ.

"As with sounds, so with colours. At each end of the solar spectrum the chemist can detect the presence of what are known as 'actinic' rays. They represent colours—integral colours in the composition of light—which we are unable to discern. The human eye is an imperfect instrument; its range is but a few octaves of the real 'chromatic scale.' I am not mad; there are colours that we cannot see.

"And, God help me! the Damned Thing is of such a colour!"

In the Penal Colony

Franz Kafka

Translated by Ian Johnston

"It's a peculiar apparatus," said the Officer to the Traveler, gazing with a certain admiration at the device, with which he was, of course, thoroughly familiar. It appeared that the Traveler had responded to the invitation of the Commandant only out of politeness, when he had been invited to attend the execution of a soldier condemned for disobeying and insulting his superior. Of course, interest in the execution was not very high, not even in the penal colony itself. At least, here in the small, deep, sandy valley, closed in on all sides by barren slopes, apart from the Officer and the Traveler there were present only the Condemned, a vacant-looking man with a broad mouth and dilapidated hair and face, and the Soldier, who held the heavy chain to which were connected the small chains which bound the Condemned Man by his feet and wrist bones, as well as by his neck, and which were also linked to each other by connecting chains. The Condemned Man had an expression of such dog-like resignation that it looked as if one could set him free to roam around the slopes and would only have to whistle at the start of the execution for him to return.

The Traveler had little interest in the apparatus and walked back and forth behind the Condemned Man, almost visibly indifferent, while the Officer took care of the final preparations. Sometimes he crawled under the apparatus, which was built deep into the earth, and sometimes he climbed up a ladder to inspect the upper parts. These were really jobs which could have been left to a mechanic, but the Officer carried them out with great enthusiasm, maybe because he was particularly fond of this apparatus or maybe because there was some other reason why one could not trust the work to anyone else. "It's all ready now!" he finally cried and climbed back down the ladder. He was unusually tired, breathing with his mouth wide open, and he had pushed two fine lady's handkerchiefs under the collar of his uniform.

"These uniforms are really too heavy for the tropics," the Traveler said, instead of asking some questions about the apparatus, as the Officer had expected. "That's true," said the Officer. He washed the oil and grease from his dirty hands in a bucket of water standing ready, "but they mean home, and we don't want to lose our homeland." "Now, have a look at this apparatus," he added immediately, drying his hands with a towel and pointing to the device. "Up to this point I had to do some work by hand, but from now on the apparatus should work entirely on its own." The Traveler nodded and followed the Officer. The latter tried to protect himself against all eventualities by saying, "Of course, breakdowns do happen. I really hope none will occur today, but we must be prepared for it. The apparatus is supposed to keep going for twelve hours without interruption. But if any breakdowns do occur, they'll only be very minor, and we'll deal with them right away."

"Don't you want to sit down?" he asked finally, as he pulled out a chair from a pile of cane chairs and offered it to the Traveler. The latter could not refuse. He sat on the edge of the pit, into which he cast a fleeting glance. It was not very deep. On one side of the hole the piled earth was heaped up into a wall; on the other side stood the apparatus. "I don't know," the officer said, "whether the Commandant has already explained the apparatus to you." The Traveler made a vague gesture with his hand. That was good enough for the Officer, for now he could explain the apparatus himself.

"This apparatus," he said, grasping a connecting rod and leaning against it, "is our previous Commandant's invention. I also worked with him on the very first tests and took part in all the work right up to its completion. However, the credit for the invention belongs to him alone. Have you heard of our previous Commandant? No? Well, I'm not claiming too much when I say that the organization of the entire penal colony is his work. We, his friends, already knew at the time of his death that the administration of the colony was so self-contained that even if his successor had a thousand new plans in mind, he would not be able to alter anything of the old plan, at least not for several years. And our prediction has held. The New Commandant has had to recognize that. It's a shame that you didn't know the previous Commandant!"

"However," the Officer said, interrupting himself, "I'm chattering, and his apparatus stands here in front of us. As you see, it consists of three parts. With the passage of time certain popular names have been developed for each of these parts. The one underneath is called the bed, the upper one is called the inscriber, and here in the middle, this moving part is called the harrow." "The harrow?" the Traveler asked. He had not been listening with full attention. The sun was excessively strong, trapped in the shadowless valley, and one could hardly collect one's thoughts. So the Officer appeared to him all the more admirable in his tight tunic weighed down with epaulettes and festooned with braid, ready to go on parade, as he explained the matter so eagerly and, while he was talking, adjusted screws here and there with a screwdriver.

The Soldier appeared to be in a state similar to the Traveler. He had wound the Condemned Man's chain around both his wrists and was supporting himself with his hand on his weapon, letting his head hang backward, not bothering about anything. The Traveler was not surprised at that, for the Officer spoke French, and clearly neither the Soldier nor the Condemned Man understood the language. So it was all the more striking that the Condemned Man, in spite of that, did what he could to follow the Officer's explanation. With a sort of sleepy persistence he kept directing his gaze to the place where the Officer had just pointed, and when the question from the Traveler interrupted the Officer, the Condemned Man looked at the Traveler, too, just as the Officer was doing.

"Yes, the harrow," said the Officer. "The name fits. The needles are arranged as in a harrow, and the whole thing is driven like a harrow, although it stays in one place and is, in principle, much more artistic. You'll understand in a moment. The condemned is laid out here on the bed. First, I'll describe the apparatus and only then let the procedure go to work. That way you'll be able to follow it better. Also a sprocket in the inscriber is excessively worn. It really squeaks. When it's in motion one can hardly make oneself understood. Unfortunately replacement parts are difficult to come by in this place. So, here is the bed, as I said. The whole thing is completely covered with a layer of cotton wool, the purpose of which you'll find out in a moment. The condemned man is laid out on his stomach on the cotton wool—naked, of course. There are straps for the hands here, for the feet here, and for the throat here, to tie him in securely. At the head of the bed here, where the man, as I have mentioned, first lies face down, is this small protruding lump of felt, which can easily be adjusted so that it presses right into the man's mouth. Its purpose is to prevent him screaming and biting his tongue to pieces. Of course, the man has to let the felt in his mouth—otherwise the straps around his throat would break his neck." "That's cotton wool?" asked the Traveler and bent down. "Yes, it is," said the Officer smiling, "feel it for yourself."

He took the Traveler's hand and led him over to the bed. "It's a specially prepared cotton wool. That's why it looks so unrecognizable. I'll get around to mentioning its purpose in a moment." The Traveler was already being won over a little to the apparatus. With his hand over his eyes to protect them from the sun, he looked at the apparatus in the hole. It was a massive construction. The bed and the inscriber were the same size and looked like two dark chests. The inscriber was set about two meters above the bed, and the two were joined together at the corners by four brass rods, which almost reflected the sun. The harrow hung between the chests on a band of steel.

The Officer had hardly noticed the earlier indifference of the Traveler, but he did have a sense now of how the latter's interest was being aroused for the first time. So he paused in his explanation in order to allow the Traveler time to observe the apparatus undisturbed. The Condemned Man imitated the Traveler, but since he could not put his hand over his eyes, he blinked upward with his eyes uncovered.

"So now the man is lying down," said the Traveler. He leaned back in his chair and crossed his legs.

"Yes," said the Officer, pushing his cap back a little and running his hand over his hot face. "Now, listen. Both the bed and the inscriber have their own electric batteries. The bed needs them for itself, and the inscriber for the harrow. As soon as the man is strapped in securely, the bed is set in motion. It quivers with tiny, very rapid oscillations from side to side and up and down simultaneously. You will have seen similar devices in mental hospitals. Only with our bed all movements are precisely calibrated, for they must be meticulously coordinated with the movements of the harrow. But it's the harrow which has the job of actually carrying out the sentence."

"What is the sentence?" the Traveler asked. "You don't even know that?" asked the Officer in astonishment and bit his lip. "Forgive me if my explanations are perhaps confused. I really do beg your pardon. Previously it was the Commandant's habit to provide such explanations. But the New Commandant has excused himself from this honorable duty. The fact that with such an eminent visitor"—the traveler tried to deflect the honor with both hands, but the officer insisted on the expression—"that with such an eminent visitor he didn't even once make him aware of the form of our sentencing is yet again something new, which . . ." He had a curse on his lips, but controlled himself and said merely: "I was not informed about it. It's not my fault. In any case, I am certainly the person best able to explain our style of sentencing, for here I am carrying"—he patted his breast pocket—"the relevant diagrams drawn by the previous Commandant."

"Diagrams made by the Commandant himself?" asked the Traveler. "Then was he in his own person a combination of everything? Was he soldier, judge, engineer, chemist, and draftsman?"

"He was indeed," said the Officer, nodding his head with a fixed and thoughtful expression. Then he looked at his hands, examining them. They didn't seem to him clean enough to handle the diagrams. So he went to the bucket and washed them again. Then he pulled out a small leather folder and said, "Our sentence does not sound severe. The law which a Condemned Man has violated is inscribed on his body with the harrow. This Condemned Man, for example," and the Officer pointed to the man, "will have inscribed on his body, 'Honor your superiors.' "

The Traveler had a quick look at the man. When the Officer was pointing at him, the man kept his head down and appeared to be directing all his energy into listening in order to learn something. But the movements of his thick pouting lips showed clearly that he was incapable of understanding anything. The Traveler wanted to raise various questions, but after looking at the Condemned Man he merely asked, "Does he know his sentence?" "No," said the Officer. He wished to get on with his explanation right away, but the Traveler interrupted him: "He doesn't know his own sentence?" "No," said the Officer once more. He then paused for a moment, as if he was asking the Traveler for a more detailed reason for his question, and said, "It would be useless to give him that information. He experiences it on his own body." The Traveler really wanted to keep quiet at this point, but he felt how the Condemned Man was gazing at him—he seemed to be asking whether he could approve of the process the Officer had described. So the Traveler, who had up to this point been leaning back, bent forward again and kept up his questions, "But does he nonetheless have some general idea that he's been condemned?" "Not that either," said the Officer, and he smiled at the Traveler, as if he was still waiting for some strange revelations from him. "No?" said the Traveler, wiping his forehead, "then does the man also not yet know how his defense was received?" "He has had no opportunity to defend himself," said the Officer and looked away, as if he was talking to himself and wished not to embarrass the Traveler with an explanation of matters so self-evident to him. "But he must have had a chance to defend himself," said the Traveler and stood up from his chair.

The Officer recognized that he was in danger of having his explanation of the apparatus held up for a long time. So he went to the Traveler, took him by the arm, pointed with his hand at the Condemned Man, who stood there stiffly now that the attention was so clearly directed at him—the Soldier was also pulling on his chain—and said, "The matter stands like this. Here in the penal colony I have been appointed judge. In spite of my youth. For I stood at the side of our Old Commandant in all matters of punishment, and I also know the most about the apparatus. The basic principle I use for my decisions is this: Guilt is always beyond a doubt. Other courts could not follow this principle, for they are made up of many heads and, in addition, have even higher courts above them. But that is not the case here, or at least it was not that way with the previous Commandant. It's true the New Commandant has already shown a desire to get mixed up in my court, but I've succeeded so far in fending him off. And I'll continue to be successful. You want this case explained. It's simple—just like all of them. This morning a captain laid a charge that this man, who is assigned to him as a servant and who sleeps before his door, had been sleeping on duty. For his task is to stand up every time the clock strikes the hour and salute in front of the captain's door. That's certainly not a difficult duty—and it's necessary, since he is supposed to remain fresh both for guarding and for service. Yesterday night the captain wanted to check whether his servant was fulfilling his duty. He opened the door on the stroke of two and found him curled up asleep. He got his horsewhip and hit him across the face. Now, instead of standing up and begging for forgiveness, the man grabbed his master by the legs, shook him, and cried out, 'Throw away that whip or I'll eat you up.' Those are the facts. The captain came to me an hour ago. I wrote up his statement and right after that the sentence. Then I had the man chained up. It was all very simple. If I had first summoned the man and interrogated him, the result would have been confusion. He would have lied, and if I had been successful in refuting his lies, he would have replaced them with new lies, and so forth. But now I have him, and I won't release him again. Now, does that clarify everything? But time is passing. We should be starting the execution, and I haven't finished explaining the apparatus yet."

He urged the Traveler to sit down in his chair, moved to the apparatus again, and started, "As you see, the shape of the harrow corresponds to the shape of a man. This is the harrow for the upper body, and here are the harrows for the legs. This small cutter is the only one designated for the head. Is that clear to you?" He leaned forward to the Traveler in a friendly way, ready to give the most comprehensive explanation.

The Traveler looked at the harrow with a wrinkled frown. The information about the judicial procedures had not satisfied him. However, he had to tell himself that here it was a matter of a penal colony, that in this place special regulations were necessary, and that one had to give precedence to military measures right down to the last detail. Beyond that, however, he had some hopes in the New Commandant, who obviously, although slowly, was intending to introduce a new procedure which the limited understanding of this Officer could not cope with.

Following this train of thought, the Traveler asked, "Will the Commandant be present at the execution?" "That is not certain," said the Officer, embarrassingly affected by the sudden question, and his friendly expression made a grimace. "That's why we need to hurry up. As much as I regret the fact, I'll have to make my explanation even shorter. But tomorrow, once the apparatus is clean again—the fact that it gets so very dirty is its only fault—I could add a detailed explanation. So now, only the most important things. When the man is lying on the bed and it starts quivering, the harrow sinks onto the body. It positions itself automatically in such a way that it touches the body only lightly with the needle tips. Once the machine is set in this position, this steel cable tightens up into a rod. And now the performance begins. Someone who is not an initiate sees no external difference among the punishments. The harrow seems to do its work uniformly. As it quivers, it sticks the tips of its needles into the body, which is also vibrating from the movement of the bed. Now, to enable someone to check on how the sentence is being carried out, the harrow is made of glass. That gave rise to certain technical difficulties with fastening the needles securely, but after several attempts we were successful. We didn't spare any efforts. And now, as the inscription is made on the body, everyone can see through the glass. Don't you want to come closer and see the needles for yourself."

The Traveler stood slowly, moved up, and bent over the harrow. "You see," the Officer said, "two sorts of needles in a multiple arrangement. Each long needle has a short one next to it. The long one inscribes, and the short one squirts water out to wash away the blood and keep the inscription always clear. The bloody water is then channeled here in small grooves and finally flows into these main gutters, and the outlet pipe takes it to the pit." The Officer pointed with his finger to the exact path which the bloody water had to take. As he began to demonstrate with both hands at the mouth of the outlet pipe, in order to make his account as clear as possible, the Traveler raised his head and, feeling behind him with his hand, wanted to return to his chair. Then he saw to his horror that the Condemned Man had also, like him, accepted the Officer's invitation to inspect the arrangement of the harrow up close. He had pulled the sleeping Soldier holding the chain a little forward and was also bending over the glass. One could see how with a confused gaze he also was looking for what the two gentlemen had just observed, but how he didn't succeed because he lacked the explanation. He leaned forward this way and that. He kept running his eyes over the glass again and again. The Traveler wanted to push him back, for what he was doing was probably punishable. But the Officer held the Traveler firmly with one hand, and with the other he took a lump of earth from the wall and threw it at the Soldier. The latter opened his eyes with a start, saw what the Condemned Man had dared to do, let his weapon fall, braced his heels in the earth, and pulled the Condemned Man back, so that he immediately collapsed. The Soldier looked down at him, as he writhed around, making his chain clink. "Stand him up," cried the Officer. Then he noticed that the Condemned Man was distracting the Traveler too much. The latter was even leaning out away from the harrow, without paying any attention to it, wanting to find out what was happening to the Condemned Man. "Handle him carefully," the Officer yelled again. He ran around the apparatus, personally grabbed the Condemned Man under the armpits and, with the help of the Soldier, stood the man, whose feet kept slipping, upright.

"Now I know all about it," said the Traveler, as the Officer turned back to him again. "Except the most important thing," said the latter, grabbing the Traveler by the arm and pointing up high. "There in the inscriber is the mechanism which determines the movement of the harrow, and this mechanism is arranged according to the diagram on which the sentence is set down. I still use the diagrams of the previous Commandant. Here they are." He pulled some pages out of the leather folder. "Unfortunately I can't hand them to you. They are the most cherished thing I possess. Sit down, and I'll show you them from this distance. Then you'll be able to see it all well." He showed the first sheet. The Traveler would have been happy to say something appreciative, but all he saw was a labyrinthine series of lines, criss-crossing each other in all sort of ways. These covered the paper so thickly that only with difficulty could one make out the white spaces in between. "Read it," said the Officer. "I can't," said the Traveler. "But it's clear," said the Officer. "It's very elaborate," said the Traveler evasively, "but I can't decipher it."

"Yes," said the Officer, smiling and putting the folder back again, "it's not calligraphy for school children. One has to read it a long time. You too will finally understand it clearly. Of course, it has to be a script that isn't simple. You see, it's not supposed to kill right away, but on average over a period of twelve hours. The turning point is set for the sixth hour. There must also be many, many embellishments surrounding the basic script. The essential script moves around the body only in a narrow belt. The rest of the body is reserved for decoration. Can you now appreciate the work of the harrow and the whole apparatus? Just look at it!" He jumped up the ladder, turned a wheel, and called down, "Watch out—move to the side!" Everything started moving. If the wheel had not squeaked, it would have been marvelous. The officer threatened the wheel with his fist, as if he was surprised by the disturbance it created. Then he spread his arms, apologizing to the traveler, and quickly clambered down, in order to observe the operation of the apparatus from below.

Something was still not working properly, something only he noticed. He clambered up again and reached with both hands into the inside of the inscriber. Then, in order to descend more quickly, instead of using the ladder, he slid down on one of the poles and, to make himself understandable through the noise, strained his voice to the limit as he yelled in the Traveler's ear, "Do you understand the process? The harrow is starting to write. When it's finished with the first part of the script on the man's back, the layer of cotton wool rolls and turns the body slowly onto its side to give the harrow a new area. Meanwhile those parts lacerated by the inscription are lying on the cotton wool which, because it has been specially treated, immediately stops the bleeding and prepares the script for a further deepening. Here, as the body continues to rotate, prongs on the edge of the harrow then pull the cotton wool from the wounds, throw it into the pit, and the harrow goes to work again. In this way it keeps making the inscription deeper for twelve hours. For the first six hours the Condemned Man goes on living almost as before. He suffers nothing but pain. After two hours, the felt is removed, for at that point the man has no more energy for screaming. Here at the head of the bed warm rice pudding is put in this electrically heated bowl. From this the man, if he feels like it, can help himself to what he can lap up with his tongue. No one passes up this opportunity. I don't know of a single one, and I have had a lot of experience. He first loses his pleasure in eating around the sixth hour. I usually kneel down at this point and observe the phenomenon. The man rarely swallows the last bit. He turns it around in his mouth and spits it into the pit. When he does that, I have to lean aside or else he'll get me in the face. But how quiet the man becomes around the sixth hour! The most stupid of them begin to understand. It starts around the eyes and spreads out from there. A look that could tempt one to lie down under the harrow. Nothing else happens. The man simply begins to decipher the inscription. He purses his lips, as if he is listening. You've seen that it's not easy to figure out the inscription with your eyes, but our man deciphers it with his wounds. True, it takes a lot of work. It requires six hours to complete. But then the harrow spits him right out and throws him into the pit, where he splashes down into the bloody water and cotton wool. Then the judgment is over, and we, the Soldier and I, quickly bury him."

The Traveler had leaned his ear towards the Officer and, with his hands in his coat pockets, was observing the machine at work. The Condemned Man was also watching, but without understanding. He bent forward a little and followed the moving needles, as the Soldier, after a signal from the Officer, cut through his shirt and trousers with a knife from the back, so that they fell off the Condemned Man. He wanted to grab the falling garments to cover his bare flesh, but the Soldier held him up and shook the last rags from him. The Officer turned the machine off, and in the silence which then ensued the Condemned Man was laid out under the harrow. The chains were taken off and the straps fastened in their place. For the Condemned Man it seemed at first glance to signify almost a relief. And now the harrow sunk down a stage lower, for the Condemned was a thin man. As the needle tips touched him, a shudder went over his skin. While the Soldier was busy with the right hand, the Condemned Man stretched out his left, with no sense of its direction. But it was pointing to where the Traveler was standing. The Officer kept looking at the Traveler from the side, without taking his eyes off him, as if he was trying to read from his face the impression he was getting of the execution, which he had now explained to him, at least superficially.

The strap meant to hold the wrist ripped off. The Soldier probably had pulled on it too hard. The Soldier showed the Officer the torn-off piece of strap, wanting him to help. So the Officer went over to him and said, with his face turned towards the Traveler, "The machine is very complicated. Now and then something has to tear or break. One shouldn't let that detract from one's overall opinion. Anyway, we have an immediate replacement for the strap. I'll use a chain—even though that will affect the sensitivity of the movements for the right arm." And while he put the chain in place, he kept talking, "Our resources for maintaining the machine are very limited at the moment. Under the previous Commandant, I had free access to a cash box specially set aside for this purpose. There was a store room here in which all possible replacement parts were kept. I admit I made almost extravagant use of it. I mean earlier, not now, as the New Commandant claims. For him everything serves only as a pretext to fight against the old arrangements. Now he keeps the cash box for machinery under his own control, and if I ask him for a new strap, he demands the torn one as a piece of evidence, the new one doesn't arrive for ten days, and it's an inferior brand, of not much use to me. But how I am supposed to get the machine to work in the meantime without a strap—no one's concerned about that."

The Traveler was thinking: it's always questionable to intervene decisively in strange circumstances. He was neither a citizen of the penal colony nor a citizen of the state to which it belonged. If he wanted to condemn the execution or even hinder it, people could say to him: You're a foreigner—keep quiet. He would have nothing in response to that, but could only add that he did not understand what he was doing on this occasion, for the purpose of his traveling was merely to observe and not to alter other people's judicial systems in any way. True, at this point the way things were turning out it was very tempting. The injustice of the process and the inhumanity of the execution were beyond doubt. No one could assume that the Traveler was acting out of any sense of his own self-interest, for the Condemned Man was a stranger to him, not a countryman and not someone who invited sympathy in any way. The Traveler himself had letters of reference from high officials and had been welcomed here with great courtesy. The fact that he had been invited to this execution even seemed to indicate that people were asking for his judgment of this trial. This was all the more likely since the Commandant, as he had now heard only too clearly, was no supporter of this process and maintained an almost hostile relationship with the Officer.

Then the Traveler heard a cry of rage from the Officer. He had just shoved the stub of felt in the Condemned Man's mouth, not without difficulty, when the Condemned Man, overcome by an irresistible nausea, shut his eyes and threw up. The Officer quickly yanked him up off the stump and wanted to turn his head aside toward the pit. But it was too late. The vomit was already flowing down onto the machine. "This is all the Commandant's fault!" cried the Officer and mindlessly rattled the brass rods at the front. "My machine's as filthy as a pigsty." With trembling hands he showed the Traveler what had happened. "Haven't I spent hours trying to make the Commandant understand that a day before the execution there should be no more food served. But the new lenient administration has a different opinion. Before the man is led away, the Commandant's women cram sugary things down his throat. His whole life he's fed himself on stinking fish, and now he has to eat sweets! But that would be all right—I'd have no objections—but why don't they get a new felt, the way I've been asking him for three months now? How can anyone take this felt into his mouth without feeling disgusted—something that a hundred men have sucked and bitten on it as they were dying?"

The Condemned Man had laid his head down and appeared peaceful. The Soldier was busy cleaning up the machine with the Condemned Man's shirt. The Officer went up to the Traveler, who, feeling some premonition, took a step backwards. But the Officer grasped him by the hand and pulled him aside. "I want to speak a few words to you in confidence," he said. "May I do that?" "Of course," said the Traveler and listened with his eyes lowered.

"This process and execution, which you now have an opportunity to admire, have no more open supporters in our colony. I am its only defender, just as I am the single advocate for the legacy of the Old Commandant. I can no longer think about a more extensive organization of the process—I'm using all my powers to maintain what there is at present. When the Old Commandant was alive, the colony was full of his supporters. I have something of the Old Commandant's power of persuasion, but I completely lack his power, and as a result the supporters have gone into hiding. There are still a lot of them, but no one admits to it. If you go into a tea house today—that is to say, on a day of execution—and keep your ears open, perhaps you'll hear nothing but ambiguous remarks. They are all supporters, but under the present Commandant, considering his present views, they are totally useless to me. And now I'm asking you: Should such a life's work," he pointed to the machine, "come to nothing because of this Commandant and the women influencing him? Should people let that happen? Even if one is a foreigner and only on our island for a couple of days? But there's no time to lose. People are already preparing something against my judicial proceedings. Discussions are already taking place in the Commandant's headquarters, to which I am not invited. Even your visit today seems to me typical of the whole situation. People are cowards and send you out—a foreigner. You should have seen the executions in earlier days! The entire valley was overflowing with people, even a day before the execution. They all came merely to watch. Early in the morning the Commandant appeared with his women. Fanfares woke up the entire campsite. I delivered the news that everything was ready. The whole society—and every high official had to attend—arranged itself around the machine. This pile of cane chairs is a sorry leftover from that time. The machine was freshly cleaned and glowed. For almost every execution I had new replacement parts. In front of hundreds of eyes—all the spectators stood on tip toe right up to the hills there—the Condemned Man was laid down under the harrow by the Commandant himself. What nowadays is done by a common soldier was then my work as the senior judge, and it was a honor for me. And then the execution began! No discordant note disturbed the work of the machine. Many people did not look any more at all, but lay down with closed eyes in the sand. They all knew: now justice was being carried out. In silence people listened to nothing but the groans of the Condemned Man, muffled by the felt. These days the machine no longer manages to squeeze a strong groan out of the Condemned Man—something the felt is not capable of smothering. But back then the needles which made the inscription dripped a caustic liquid which we are not permitted to use any more today. Well, then came the sixth hour. It was impossible to grant all the requests people made to be allowed to watch from up close. The Commandant, in his wisdom, arranged that the children should be taken care of before all the rest. Naturally, I was always allowed to stand close by, because of my official position. Often I crouched down there with two small children in my arms, on my right and left. How we all took in the expression of transfiguration on the martyred face! How we held our cheeks in the glow of this justice, finally attained and already passing away! What times we had, my friend!"

The Officer had obviously forgotten who was standing in front of him. He had put his arm around the Traveler and laid his head on his shoulder. The Traveler was extremely embarrassed. Impatiently he looked away over the Officer's head. The Soldier had ended his task of cleaning and had just shaken some rice pudding into the bowl from a tin. No sooner had the Condemned Man, who seemed to have fully recovered already, noticed this than his tongue began to lick at the pudding. The Soldier kept pushing him away, for the pudding was probably meant for a later time, but in any case it was not proper for the Soldier to reach in and grab some food with his dirty hands and eat it in front of the famished Condemned Man.

The Officer quickly collected himself. "I didn't want to upset you in any way," he said. "I know it is impossible to make someone understand those days now. Besides, the machine still works and operates on its own. It operates on its own even when it is standing alone in this valley. And at the end, the body still keeps falling in that incredibly soft flight into the pit, even if hundreds of people are not gathered like flies around the hole the way they used to be. Back then we had to erect a strong railing around the pit. It was pulled out long ago."

The Traveler wanted to turn his face away from the Officer and looked aimlessly around him. The Officer thought he was looking at the wasteland of the valley. So he grabbed his hands, turned him around in order to catch his gaze, and asked, "Do you see the shame of it?"

But the Traveler said nothing. The Officer left him alone for a while. With his legs apart and his hands on his hips, the Officer stood still and looked at the ground. Then he smiled at the Traveler cheerfully and said, "Yesterday I was nearby when the Commandant invited you. I heard the invitation. I know the Commandant. I understood right away what he intended with his invitation. Although his power might be sufficiently great to take action against me, he doesn't yet dare to. But my guess is that with you he is exposing me to the judgment of a respected foreigner. He calculates things with care. You are now in your second day on the island. You didn't know the Old Commandant and his way of thinking. You are trapped in a European way of seeing things. Perhaps you are fundamentally opposed to the death penalty in general and to this kind of mechanical style of execution in particular. Moreover, you see how the execution is a sad procedure, without any public participation, using a partially damaged machine. Now, if we take all this together (so the Commandant thinks) surely one could easily imagine that you would not consider my procedure proper? And if you didn't consider it right, you wouldn't keep quiet about it—I'm still speaking the mind of the Commandant—for you no doubt have faith that your tried-and-true convictions are correct. It's true that you have seen many peculiar things among many peoples and have learned to respect them. Thus, you will probably not speak out against the procedure with your full power, as you would perhaps in your own homeland. But the Commandant doesn't really need that. A casual word, merely a careless remark, is enough. It doesn't have to match your convictions at all, so long as it corresponds to his wishes. I'm certain he will use all his shrewdness to interrogate you. And his women will sit around in a circle and perk up their ears. You will say something like, 'Among us the judicial procedures are different,' or 'With us the accused is questioned before the verdict,' or 'We had torture only in the Middle Ages.' For you these observations appear as correct as they are self-evident—innocent remarks which do not impugn my procedure. But how will the Commandant take them? I see him, our excellent Commandant—the way he immediately pushes his stool aside and hurries out to the balcony—I see his women, how they stream after him. I hear his voice—the women call it a thunder voice. And now he's speaking: 'A great Western explorer who has been commissioned to inspect judicial procedures in all countries has just said that our process based on old customs is inhumane. After the verdict of such a personality it is, of course, no longer possible for me to tolerate this procedure. So from this day on I am ordering . . . and so forth.' You want to intervene—you didn't say what he is reporting—you didn't call my procedure inhumane; by contrast, in keeping with your deep insight, you consider it most humane and most worthy of human beings. You also admire this machinery. But it is too late. You don't even go onto the balcony, which is already filled with women. You want to attract attention. You want to cry out. But a lady's hand is covering your mouth, and I and the Old Commandant's work are lost."

The Traveler had to suppress a smile. So the work which he had considered so difficult was easy. He said evasively, "You're exaggerating my influence. The Commandant has read my letters of recommendation. He knows that I am no expert in judicial processes. If I were to express an opinion, it would be that of a lay person, no more significant than the opinion of anyone else, and in any case far less significant than the opinion of the Commandant, who, as I understand it, has very extensive powers in this penal colony. If his views of this procedure are as definite as you think they are, then I'm afraid the time has come for this procedure to end, without any need for my humble opinion."

Did the Officer understand by now? No, he did not yet get it. He shook his head vigorously, briefly looked back at the Condemned Man and the Soldier, who both flinched and stopped eating the rice, went up really close up to the Traveler, without looking into his face, but gazing at parts of his jacket, and said more gently than before: "You don't know the Commandant. Where he and all of us are concerned you are—forgive the expression—to a certain extent innocent. Your influence, believe me, cannot be overestimated. In fact, I was blissfully happy when I heard that you were to be present at the execution by yourself. This order of the Commandant was aimed at me, but now I'll turn it to my advantage. Without being distracted by false insinuations and disparaging looks—which could not have been avoided with a greater number of participants at the execution—you have listened to my explanation, looked at the machine, and are now about to view the execution. Your verdict is no doubt already fixed. If some small uncertainties remain, witnessing the execution will remove them. And now I'm asking you—help me with the Commandant!"

The Traveler did not let him go on talking. "How can I do that," he cried. "It's totally impossible. I can help you as little as I can harm you."

"You could do it," said the Officer. With some apprehension the Traveler observed that the Officer was clenching his fists. "You could do it," repeated the Officer, even more emphatically. "I have a plan which must succeed. You think your influence is insufficient. I know it will be enough. But assuming you're right, doesn't saving this whole procedure require one to try even those methods which may be inadequate? So listen to my plan. To carry it out, it's necessary, above all, for you to keep as quiet as possible today in the colony about your verdict on this procedure. Unless someone asks you directly, you should not express any view whatsoever. But what you do say must be short and vague. People should notice that it's difficult for you to speak about the subject, that you feel bitter, that, if you were to speak openly, you'd have to burst out cursing on the spot. I'm not asking you to lie, not at all. You should only give brief answers—something like, 'Yes, I've seen the execution' or 'Yes, I've heard the full explanation.' That's all—nothing further. For that will be enough of an indication for people to observe in you a certain bitterness, even if that's not what the Commandant will think. Naturally, he will completely misunderstand the issue and interpret it in his own way. My plan is based on that. Tomorrow a large meeting of all the higher administrative officials takes place at headquarters under the chairmanship of the Commandant. He, of course, understands how to turn such a meeting into a spectacle. A gallery has been built, which is always full of spectators. I'm compelled to take part in the discussions, though they fill me with disgust. In any case, you will certainly be invited to the meeting. If you follow my plan today and behave accordingly, the invitation will become an emphatic request. But should you for some inexplicable reason still not be invited, you must make sure you request an invitation. Then you'll receive one without question. Now, tomorrow you are sitting with the women in the Commandant's box. With frequent upward glances he reassures himself that you are there. After various trivial and ridiculous agenda items designed for the spectators—mostly harbor construction—always harbor construction—the judicial process comes up for discussion. If it's not raised by the Commandant himself or does not occur soon enough, I'll make sure that it comes up. I'll stand up and report on today's execution. Really briefly—just the report. Such a report is not really customary; however, I'll do it, nonetheless. The Commandant thanks me, as always, with a friendly smile. And now he cannot restrain himself. He seizes this excellent opportunity. 'The report of the execution,' he'll say, or something like that, 'has just been given. I would like to add to this report only the fact that this particular execution was attended by the great explorer whose visit confers such extraordinary honor on our colony, as you all know. Even the significance of our meeting today has been increased by his presence. Should we not now ask this great explorer for his appraisal of the execution based on old customs and of the process which preceded it?' Of course, there is the noise of applause everywhere, universal agreement. And I'm louder than anyone. The Commandant bows before you and says, 'Then in everyone's name, I'm putting the question to you.' And now you step up to the railing. Place your hands where everyone can see them. Otherwise the ladies will grab them and play with your fingers. And now finally come your remarks. I don't know how I'll bear the tension up to then. In your speech you mustn't hold back. Let truth resound. Lean over the railing and shout it out—yes, yes, roar your opinion at the Commandant, your unshakeable opinion. But perhaps you don't want to do that. It doesn't suit your character. Perhaps in your country people behave differently in such situations. That's all right. That's perfectly satisfactory. Don't stand up at all. Just say a couple of words. Whisper them so that only the officials underneath you can just hear them. That's enough. You don't even have to say anything at all about the lack of attendance at the execution or about the squeaky wheel, the torn strap, the disgusting felt. No.

I'll take over all further details, and, believe me, if my speech doesn't chase him out of the room, it will force him to his knees, so he'll have to admit it: 'Old Commandant, I bow down before you.' That's my plan. Do you want to help me carry it out? But, of course, you want to. More than that—you have to."

And the officer gripped the traveler by both arms and looked at him, breathing heavily into his face. He had yelled the last sentences so loudly that even the Soldier and the Condemned Man were paying attention. Although they couldn't understand a thing, they stopped eating and looked over at the Traveler, still chewing.

From the start the Traveler had had no doubts about the answer he must give. He had experienced too much in his life to be able to waver here. Basically he was honest and unafraid. Still, with the Soldier and the Condemned Man looking at him, he hesitated a moment. But finally he said, as he had to, "No." The Officer's eyes blinked several times, but he did not take his eyes off the Traveler. "Would you like an explanation?" asked the Traveler. The Officer nodded dumbly. "I am opposed to this procedure," said the Traveler. "Even before you took me into your confidence—and, of course, I will never abuse your confidence under any circumstances—I was already thinking about whether I was entitled to intervene against this procedure and whether my intervention could have the smallest chance of success. And if that was the case, it was clear to me whom I had to turn to first of all—naturally, to the Commandant. You clarified the issue for me even more, but without reinforcing my decision in any way—quite the reverse. I find your conviction genuinely moving, even if it cannot deter me."

The Officer remained quiet, turned toward the machine, grabbed one of the brass rods, and then, leaning back a little, looked up at the inscriber, as if he was checking that everything was in order. The Soldier and the Condemned Man seemed to have made friends with each other. The Condemned Man was making signs to the Soldier, although, given the tight straps on him, this was difficult for him to do. The Soldier was leaning into him. The Condemned Man whispered something to him, and the Soldier nodded. The Traveler went over to the Officer and said, "You don't yet know what I'll do. Yes, I will tell the Commandant my opinion of the procedure—not in a meeting, but in private. In addition, I won't stay here long enough to be able to get called in to some meeting or other. Early tomorrow morning I leave, or at least I go on board ship." It didn't look as if the Officer had been listening. "So the process has not convinced you," he said to himself, smiling the way an old man smiles over the silliness of a child, concealing his own true thoughts behind that smile.

"Well then, it's time," he said finally and suddenly looked at the Traveler with bright eyes which contained some sort of demand, some appeal for participation. "Time for what?" asked the Traveler uneasily. But there was no answer.

"You are free," the Officer told the Condemned Man in his own language. At first the man did not believe him. "You are free now," said the Officer. For the first time the face of the Condemned Man showed signs of real life. Was it the truth? Was it only the Officer's mood, which could change? Had the foreign Traveler brought him a reprieve? What was it? That's what the man's face seemed to be asking. But not for long. Whatever the case might be, if he could he wanted to be truly free, and he began to shake back and forth, as much as the harrow permitted.

"You're tearing my straps," cried the Officer. "Be still! We'll undo them right away." And, giving a signal to the Soldier, he set to work with him. The Condemned Man said nothing and smiled slightly to himself. He turned his face to the Officer and then to the Soldier and then back again, without ignoring the Traveler.

"Pull him out," the Officer ordered the Soldier. This process required a certain amount of care because of the harrow. The Condemned Man already had a few small wounds on his back, thanks to his own impatience.

From this point on, however, the Officer paid him hardly any attention. He went up to the Traveler, pulled out the small leather folder once more, leafed through it, finally found the sheet he was looking for, and showed it to the Traveler. "Read that," he said. "I can't," said the Traveler. "I've already told you I can't read these pages." "But take a close look at the page," said the Officer, and moved up right next to the Traveler in order to read with him. When that didn't help, he raised his little finger high up over the paper, as if the page must not be touched under any circumstances, so that using this he might make the task of reading easier for the Traveler. The Traveler also made an effort so that at least he could satisfy the Officer, but it was impossible for him. Then the Officer began to spell out the inscription and then read out once again the joined up letters. " 'Be just!' it states," he said. "Now you can read it." The Traveler bent so low over the paper that the Officer, afraid that he might touch it, moved it further away. The Traveler didn't say anything more, but it was clear that he was still unable to read anything. " 'Be just!' it says," the Officer remarked once again.

"That could be," said the Traveler. "I do believe that's written there." "Good," said the Officer, at least partially satisfied. He climbed up the ladder, holding the paper. With great care he set the page in the inscriber and appeared to rotate the gear mechanism completely around. This was very tiring work. It must have required him to deal with extremely small wheels. He had to inspect the gears so closely that sometimes his head disappeared completely into the inscriber.

The Traveler followed this work from below without looking away. His neck grew stiff, and his eyes found the sunlight pouring down from the sky painful. The Soldier and the Condemned Man were keeping each other busy. With the tip of his bayonet the Soldier pulled out the Condemned Man's shirt and trousers which were lying in the hole. The shirt was horribly dirty, and the Condemned Man washed it in the bucket of water. When he was putting on his shirt and trousers, the Soldier and the Condemned Man had to laugh out loud, for the pieces of clothing were cut in two up the back. Perhaps the Condemned Man thought that it was his duty to amuse the Soldier. In his ripped-up clothes he circled around the Soldier, who crouched down on the ground, laughed, and slapped his knees. But they restrained themselves out of consideration for the two gentlemen present.

When the Officer was finally finished up on the machine, with a smile he looked over the whole thing and all its parts one more time, and this time closed the cover of the inscriber, which had been open up to this point. He climbed down, looked into the hole and then at the Condemned Man, observed with satisfaction that he had pulled out his clothes, then went to the bucket of water to wash his hands, recognized too late that it was disgustingly dirty, and was upset that now he couldn't wash his hands. Finally he pushed them into the sand. This option didn't satisfy him, but he had to do what he could in the circumstances. Then he stood up and began to unbutton the coat of his uniform. As he did this, the two lady's handkerchiefs, which he had pushed into the back of his collar, fell into his hands. "Here you have your handkerchiefs," he said and threw them over to the Condemned Man. And to the Traveler he said by way of an explanation, "Presents from the ladies."

In spite of the obvious speed with which he took off the coat of his uniform and then undressed himself completely, he handled each piece of clothing very carefully, even running his fingers over the silver braids on his tunic with special care and shaking a tassel into place. But in great contrast to this care, as soon he was finished handling an article of clothing, he immediately flung it angrily into the hole. The last items he had left were his short sword and its harness. He pulled the sword out of its scabbard, broke it in pieces, gathered up everything—the pieces of the sword, the scabbard, and the harness—and threw them away so forcefully that they rattled against each other down in the pit.

Now he stood there naked. The Traveler bit his lip and said nothing. For he was aware what would happen, but he had no right to hinder the Officer in any way. If the judicial process to which the officer clung was really so close to the point of being canceled—perhaps as a result of the intervention of the Traveler, something to which he for his part felt duty-bound—then the Officer was now acting in a completely correct manner. In his place, the Traveler would not have acted any differently.

The Soldier and the Condemned Man at first didn't understand a thing. To begin with they didn't look, not even once. The Condemned Man was extremely happy to get the handkerchiefs back, but he couldn't enjoy them very long, for the Soldier snatched them from him with a quick grab, which he had not anticipated. The Condemned Man then tried to pull the handkerchiefs out from the Soldier's belt, where he had put them for safe keeping, but the Soldier was too wary. So they were fighting, half in jest. Only when the Officer was fully naked did they start to pay attention. The Condemned Man especially seemed to be struck by a premonition of some sort of significant transformation. What had happened to him was now taking place with the Officer. Perhaps this time the procedure would play itself out to its conclusion. The foreign Traveler had probably given the order. So that was revenge. Without having suffered all the way to the end himself, nonetheless he would be completely revenged. A wide, silent laugh now appeared on his face and did not go away.

The Officer, however, had turned towards the machine. If earlier on it had already become clear that he understood the machine thoroughly, one might well get alarmed now at the way he handled it and how it obeyed. He only had to bring his hand near the harrow for it to rise and sink several times, until it had reached the correct position to make room for him. He only had to grasp the bed by the edges, and it already began to quiver. The stump of felt moved up to his mouth. One could see how the Officer really didn't want to accept it, but his hesitation was only momentary—he immediately submitted and took it in. Everything was ready, except that the straps still hung down on the sides. But they were clearly unnecessary. The Officer did not have to be strapped down. When the Condemned Man saw the loose straps, he thought the execution would be incomplete unless they were fastened. He waved eagerly to the Soldier, and they ran over to strap in the Officer. The latter had already stuck out his foot to kick the crank designed to set the inscriber in motion. Then he saw the two men coming. So he pulled his foot back and let himself be strapped in. But now he could no longer reach the crank. Neither the Soldier nor the Condemned Man would find it, and the Traveler was determined not to touch it. But that was unnecessary. Hardly were the straps attached when the machine already started working. The bed quivered, the needles danced on his skin, and the harrow swung up and down. The Traveler had already been staring for some time before he remembered that a wheel in the inscriber was supposed to squeak. But everything was quiet, without the slightest audible hum.

Because of its silent working, the machine did not really attract attention. The Traveler looked over at the Soldier and the Condemned Man. The Condemned Man was the livelier of the two. Everything in the machine interested him. At times he bent down—at other times he stretched up, all the time pointing with his forefinger in order to show something to the Soldier. For the Traveler it was embarrassing. He was determined to remain here until the end, but he could no longer endure the sight of the two men. "Go home," he said. The Soldier might have been ready to do that, but the Condemned Man took the order as a direct punishment. With his hands folded he begged and pleaded to be allowed to stay there. And when the Traveler shook his head and was unwilling to give in, he even knelt down. Seeing that orders were of no help here, the Traveler wanted to go over and chase the two away.

Then he heard a noise from up in the inscriber. He looked up. So was the gear wheel going out of alignment? But it was something else. The lid on the inscriber was lifting up slowly. Then it fell completely open. The teeth of a cog wheel were exposed and lifted up. Soon the entire wheel appeared. It was as if some huge force was compressing the inscriber, so that there was no longer sufficient room for this wheel. The wheel rolled all the way to the edge of the inscriber, fell down, rolled upright a bit in the sand, and then fell over and lay still. But already up on the inscriber another gear wheel was moving upwards. Several others followed—large ones, small ones, ones hard to distinguish. With each of them the same thing happened. One kept thinking that now the inscriber must surely be empty, but then a new cluster with lots of parts would move up, fall down, roll in the sand, and lie still. With all this going on, the Condemned Man totally forgot the Traveler's order. The gear wheels completely delighted him. He kept wanting to grab one, and at the same time he was urging the Soldier to help him. But he kept pulling his hand back startled, for immediately another wheel followed, which, at least in its initial rolling, surprised him.

The Traveler, by contrast, was very upset. Obviously the machine was breaking up. Its quiet operation had been an illusion. He felt as if he had to look after the Officer, now that the latter could no longer look after himself. But while the falling gear wheels were claiming all his attention, he had neglected to look at the rest of the machine. However, when he now bent over the harrow, once the last gear wheel had left the inscriber, he had a new, even more unpleasant surprise. The harrow was not writing but only stabbing, and the bed was not rolling the body, but lifting it, quivering, up into the needles. The Traveler wanted to reach in to stop the whole thing, if possible. This was not the torture the Officer wished to attain. It was murder, pure and simple. He stretched out his hands. But at that point the harrow was already moving upwards and to the side, with the skewered body—just as it did in other cases, but only in the twelfth hour. Blood flowed out in hundreds of streams, not mixed with water—the water tubes had also failed to work this time. Then one last thing went wrong: the body would not come loose from the needles. Its blood streamed out, but it hung over the pit without falling. The harrow wanted to move back to its original position, but, as if it realized that it could not free itself of its load, it remained over the hole.

"Help," the Traveler yelled out to the Soldier and the Condemned Man and grabbed the Officer's feet. He wanted to push against the feet himself and have the two others grab the Officer's head from the other side, so he could be slowly taken off the needles. But now the two men could not make up their mind whether to come or not. The Condemned Man turned away at once. The Traveler had to go over to him and drag him to the Officer's head by force. At this point, almost against his will, he looked at the face of the corpse. It was as it had been in his life. He could discover no sign of the promised transfiguration. What all the others had found in the machine, the Officer had not. His lips were pressed firmly together, his eyes were open and looked as they had when he was alive, his gaze was calm and convinced. The tip of a large iron needle had gone through his forehead.

* * * * *

As the Traveler, with the Soldier and the Condemned Man behind him, came to the first houses in the colony, the Soldier pointed to one and said, "That's the tea house."

On the ground floor of one of the houses was a deep, low room, like a cave, with smoke-covered walls and ceiling. On the street side it was open along its full width. Although there was little difference between the tea house and the rest of the houses in the colony, which were all very dilapidated, except for the Commandant's palatial structure, the Traveler was struck by the impression of historical memory, and he felt the power of earlier times. Followed by his companions, he walked closer, going between the unoccupied tables, which stood in the street in front of the tea house, and took a breath of the cool, stuffy air which came from inside. "The old man is buried here," said the soldier; "a place in the cemetery was denied him by the chaplain. For a long time people were undecided where they should bury him. Finally they buried him here. Of course, the Officer explained none of that to you, for naturally he was the one most ashamed about it. A few times he even tried to dig up the old man at night, but he was always chased off." "Where is the grave?" asked the Traveler, who could not believe the Soldier. Instantly both men, the Soldier and the Condemned Man, ran in front of him and with hands outstretched pointed to the place where the grave was located. They led the Traveler to the back wall, where guests were sitting at a few tables. They were presumably dock workers, strong men with short, shiny, black beards. None of them wore coats, and their shirts were torn. They were poor, oppressed people. As the Traveler came closer, a few got up, leaned against the wall, and looked at him. A whisper went up around the Traveler—"It's a foreigner. He wants to look at the grave." They pushed one of the tables aside, under which there was a real grave stone. It was a simple stone, low enough for it to remain hidden under a table. It bore an inscription in very small letters. In order to read it the Traveler had to kneel down. It read, "Here rests the Old Commandant. His followers, who are now not permitted to have a name, buried him in this grave and erected this stone. There exists a prophecy that the Commandant will rise again after a certain number of years and from this house will lead his followers to a re-conquest of the colony. Have faith and wait!"

When the Traveler had read it and got up, he saw the men standing around him and smiling, as if they had read the inscription with him, found it ridiculous, and were asking him to share their opinion. The Traveler acted as if he hadn't noticed, distributed some coins among them, waited until the table was pushed back over the grave, left the tea house, and went to the harbor.

In the tea house the Soldier and the Condemned Man had come across some people they knew who detained them. However, they must have broken free of them soon, because by the time the Traveler found himself in the middle of a long staircase which led to the boats, they were already running after him. They probably wanted to force the Traveler at the last minute to take them with him. While the Traveler was haggling at the bottom of the stairs with a sailor about his passage out to the steamer, the two men were racing down the steps in silence, for they didn't dare cry out. But as they reached the bottom, the Traveler was already in the boat, and the sailor at once cast off from shore. They could still have jumped into the boat, but the Traveler picked up a heavy knotted rope from the boat bottom, threatened them with it, and thus prevented them from jumping in.

The Interlopers

Saki

In a forest of mixed growth somewhere on the eastern spurs of the Carpathians, a man stood one winter night watching and listening, as though he waited for some beast of the woods to come within the range of his vision, and, later, of his rifle. But the game for whose presence he kept so keen an outlook was none that figured in the sportsman's calendar as lawful and proper for the chase; Ulrich von Gradwitz patrolled the dark forest in quest of a human enemy.

The forest lands of Gradwitz were of wide extent and well stocked with game; the narrow strip of precipitous woodland that lay on its outskirt was not remarkable for the game it harboured or the shooting it afforded, but it was the most jealously guarded of all its owner's territorial possessions. A famous lawsuit, in the days of his grandfather, had wrested it from the illegal possession of a neighbouring family of petty landowners; the dispossessed party had never acquiesced in the judgment of the Courts, and a long series of poaching affrays and similar scandals had embittered the relationships between the families for three generations. The neighbour feud had grown into a personal one since Ulrich had come to be head of his family; if there was a man in the world whom he detested and wished ill to it was Georg Znaeym, the inheritor of the quarrel and the tireless game-snatcher and raider of the disputed border-forest. The feud might, perhaps, have died down or been compromised if the personal ill-will of the two men had not stood in the way; as boys they had thirsted for one another's blood, as men each prayed that misfortune might fall on the other, and this wind-scourged winter night Ulrich had banded together his foresters to watch the dark forest, not in quest of four-footed quarry, but to keep a look-out for the prowling thieves whom he suspected of being afoot from across the land boundary. The roebuck, which usually kept in the sheltered hollows during a storm-wind, were running like driven things tonight, and there was movement and unrest among the creatures that were wont to sleep through the dark hours. Assuredly there was a disturbing element in the forest, and Ulrich could guess the quarter from whence it came.

He strayed away by himself from the watchers whom he had placed in ambush on the crest of the hill, and wandered far down the steep slopes amid the wild tangle of undergrowth, peering through the tree trunks and listening through the whistling and skirling of the wind and the restless beating of the branches for sight and sound of the marauders. If only on this wild night, in this dark, lone spot, he might come across Georg Znaeym, man to man, with none to witness—that was the wish that was uppermost in his thoughts. And as he stepped round the trunk of a huge beech he came face to face with the man he sought.

The two enemies stood glaring at one another for a long silent moment. Each had a rifle in his hand, each had hate in his heart and murder uppermost in his mind. The chance had come to give full play to the passions of a lifetime. But a man who has been brought up under the code of a restraining civilisation cannot easily nerve himself to shoot down his neighbour in cold blood and without word spoken, except for an offence against his hearth and honour. And before the moment of hesitation had given way to action a deed of Nature's own violence overwhelmed them both. A fierce shriek of the storm had been answered by a splitting crash over their heads, and ere they could leap aside a mass of falling beech tree had thundered down on them. Ulrich von Gradwitz found himself stretched on the ground, one arm numb beneath him and the other held almost as helplessly in a tight tangle of forked branches, while both legs were pinned beneath the fallen mass. His heavy shooting-boots had saved his feet from being crushed to pieces, but if his fractures were not as serious as they might have been, at least it was evident that he could not move from his present position till someone came to release him. The descending twig had slashed the skin of his face, and he had to wink away some drops of blood from his eyelashes before he could take in a general view of the disaster. At his side, so near that under ordinary circumstances he could almost have touched him, lay Georg Znaeym, alive and struggling, but obviously as helplessly pinioned down as himself. All round them lay a thick-strewn wreckage of splintered branches and broken twigs.

Relief at being alive and exasperation at his captive plight brought a strange medley of pious thank-offerings and sharp curses to Ulrich's lips. Georg, who was early blinded with the blood which trickled across his eyes, stopped his struggling for a moment to listen, and then gave a short, snarling laugh.

"So you're not killed, as you ought to be, but you're caught, anyway," he cried; "caught fast. Ho, what a jest, Ulrich von Gradwitz snared in his stolen forest. There's real justice for you!"

And he laughed again, mockingly and savagely.

"I'm caught in my own forest-land," retorted Ulrich. "When my men come to release us you will wish, perhaps, that you were in a better plight than caught poaching on a neighbour's land, shame on you."

Georg was silent for a moment; then he answered quietly:

"Are you sure that your men will find much to release? I have men, too, in the forest tonight, close behind me, and *they* will be here first and do the releasing. When they drag me out from under these damned branches it won't need much clumsiness on their part to roll this mass of trunk right over on the top of you. Your men will find you dead under a fallen beech tree. For form's sake I shall send my condolences to your family."

"It is a useful hint," said Ulrich fiercely. "My men had orders to follow in ten minutes' time, seven of which must have gone by already, and when they get me out—I will remember the hint. Only as you will have met your death poaching on my lands I don't think I can decently send any message of condolence to your family."

"Good," snarled Georg, "good. We fight this quarrel out to the death, you and I and our foresters, with no cursed interlopers to come between us. Death and damnation to you, Ulrich von Gradwitz."

"The same to you, Georg Znaeym, forest-thief, game-snatcher."

Both men spoke with the bitterness of possible defeat before them, for each knew that it might be long before his men would seek him out or find him; it was a bare matter of chance which party would arrive first on the scene.

Both had now given up the useless struggle to free themselves from the mass of wood that held them down; Ulrich limited his endeavours to an effort to bring his one partially free arm near enough to his outer coat-pocket to draw out his wine-flask. Even when he had accomplished that operation it was long before he could manage the unscrewing of the stopper or get any of the liquid down his throat. But what a Heaven-sent draught it seemed! It was an open winter, and little snow had fallen as yet, hence the captives suffered less from the cold than might have been the case at that season of the year; nevertheless, the wine was warming and reviving to the wounded man, and he looked across with something like a throb of pity to where his enemy lay, just keeping the groans of pain and weariness from crossing his lips.

"Could you reach this flask if I threw it over to you?" asked Ulrich suddenly; "there is good wine in it, and one may as well be as comfortable as one can. Let us drink, even if tonight one of us dies."

"No, I can scarcely see anything; there is so much blood caked round my eyes," said Georg, "and in any case I don't drink wine with an enemy."

Ulrich was silent for a few minutes, and lay listening to the weary screeching of the wind. An idea was slowly forming and growing in his brain, an idea that gained strength every time that he looked across at the man who was fighting so grimly against pain and exhaustion. In the pain and languor that Ulrich himself was feeling the old fierce hatred seemed to be dying down.

"Neighbour," he said presently, "do as you please if your men come first. It was a fair compact. But as for me, I've changed my mind. If my men are the first to come you shall be the first to be helped, as though you were my guest. We have quarrelled like devils all our lives over this stupid strip of forest, where the trees can't even stand upright in a breath of wind. Lying here tonight thinking I've come to think we've been rather fools; there are better things in life than getting the better of a boundary dispute. Neighbour, if you will help me to bury the old quarrel I—I will ask you to be my friend."

Georg Znaeym was silent for so long that Ulrich thought, perhaps, he had fainted with the pain of his injuries. Then he spoke slowly and in jerks.

"How the whole region would stare and gabble if we rode into the market-square together. No one living can remember seeing a Znaeym and a von Gradwitz talking to one another in friendship. And what peace there would be among the forester folk if we ended our feud tonight. And if we choose to make peace among our people there is none other to interfere, no interlopers from outside . . . You would come and keep the Sylvester night beneath my roof, and I would come and feast on some high day at your castle . . . I would never fire a shot on your land, save when you invited me as a guest; and you should come and shoot with me down in the marshes where the wildfowl are. In all the countryside there are none that could hinder if we willed to make peace. I never thought to have wanted to do other than hate you all my life, but I think I have changed my mind about things too, this last half-hour. And you offered me your wine-flask . . . Ulrich von Gradwitz, I will be your friend."

For a space both men were silent, turning over in their minds the wonderful changes that this dramatic reconciliation would bring about. In the cold, gloomy forest, with the wind tearing in fitful gusts through the naked branches and whistling round the tree-trunks, they lay and waited for the help that would now bring release and succour to both parties. And each prayed a private prayer that his men might be the first to arrive, so that he might be the first to show honourable attention to the enemy that had become a friend.

Presently, as the wind dropped for a moment, Ulrich broke silence.

"Let's shout for help," he said; "in this lull our voices may carry a little way."

"They won't carry far through the trees and undergrowth," said Georg, "but we can try. Together, then."

The two raised their voices in a prolonged hunting call.

"Together again," said Ulrich a few minutes later, after listening in vain for an answering halloo.

"I heard nothing but the pestilential wind," said Georg hoarsely.

There was silence again for some minutes, and then Ulrich gave a joyful cry.

"I can see figures coming through the wood. They are following in the way I came down the hillside."

Both men raised their voices in as loud a shout as they could muster.

"They hear us! They've stopped. Now they see us. They're running down the hill towards us," cried Ulrich.

"How many of them are there?" asked Georg.

"I can't see distinctly," said Ulrich; "nine or ten."

"Then they are yours," said Georg; "I had only seven out with me."

"They are making all the speed they can, brave lads," said Ulrich gladly.

"Are they your men?" asked Georg. "Are they your men?" he repeated impatiently as Ulrich did not answer.

"No," said Ulrich with a laugh, the idiotic chattering laugh of a man unstrung with hideous fear.

"Who are they?" asked Georg quickly, straining his eyes to see what the other would gladly not have seen.

"Wolves."

The Fall of the House of Usher

Edgar Allan Poe

Son coeur est un luth suspendu;
Sitôt qu'on le touche il résonne.
—De Beranger

During the whole of a dull, dark, and soundless day in the autumn of the year, when the clouds hung oppressively low in the heavens, I had been passing alone, on horseback, through a singularly dreary tract of country; and at length found myself, as the shades of the evening drew on, within view of the melancholy House of Usher. I know not how it was—but, with the first glimpse of the building, a sense of insufferable gloom pervaded my spirit. I say insufferable; for the feeling was unrelieved by any of that half-pleasurable, because poetic, sentiment, with which the mind usually receives even the sternest natural images of the desolate or terrible. I looked upon the scene before me—upon the mere house, and the simple landscape features of the domain—upon the bleak walls—upon the vacant eye-like windows—upon a few rank sedges—and upon a few white trunks of decayed trees—with an utter depression of soul which I can compare to no earthly sensation more properly than to the after-dream of the reveller upon opium—the bitter lapse into everyday life—the hideous dropping off of the veil. There was an iciness, a sinking, a sickening of the heart—an unredeemed dreariness of thought which no goading of the imagination could torture into aught of the sublime. What was it—I paused to think—what was it that so unnerved me in the contemplation of the House of Usher? It was a mystery all insoluble; nor could I grapple with the shadowy fancies that crowded upon me as I pondered. I was forced to fall back upon the unsatisfactory conclusion, that while, beyond doubt, there are combinations of very simple natural objects which have the power of thus affecting us, still the analysis of this power lies among considerations beyond our depth. It was possible, I reflected, that a mere different arrangement of the particulars of the scene, of the details of the picture, would be sufficient to modify, or perhaps to annihilate its capacity for sorrowful impression; and, acting upon this idea, I reined my horse to the precipitous brink of a black and lurid tarn that lay in unruffled lustre by the dwelling, and gazed down—but with a shudder even more thrilling than before—upon the remodelled and inverted images of the gray sedge, and the ghastly tree-stems, and the vacant and eye-like windows.

Nevertheless, in this mansion of gloom I now proposed to myself a sojourn of some weeks. Its proprietor, Roderick Usher, had been one of my boon companions in boyhood; but many years had elapsed since our last meeting. A letter, however, had lately reached me in a distant part of the country—a letter from him—which, in its wildly importunate nature, had admitted of no other than a personal reply. The MS. gave evidence of nervous agitation. The writer spoke of acute bodily illness—of a mental disorder which oppressed him—and of an earnest desire to see me, as his best, and indeed his only personal friend, with a view of attempting, by the cheerfulness of my society, some alleviation of his malady. It was the manner in which all this, and much more, was said—it was the apparent *heart* that went with his request—which allowed me no room for hesitation; and I accordingly obeyed forthwith what I still considered a very singular summons.

Although, as boys, we had been even intimate associates, yet I really knew little of my friend. His reserve had been always excessive and habitual. I was aware, however, that his very ancient family had been noted, time out of mind, for a peculiar sensibility of temperament, displaying itself, through long ages, in many works of exalted art, and manifested, of late, in repeated deeds of munificent yet unobtrusive charity, as well as in a passionate devotion to the intricacies, perhaps even more than to the orthodox and easily recognisable beauties, of musical science. I had learned, too, the very remarkable fact, that the stem of the Usher race, all time-honored as it was, had put forth, at no period, any enduring branch; in other words, that the entire family lay in the direct line of descent, and had always, with very trifling and very temporary variation, so lain. It was this deficiency, I considered, while running over in thought the perfect keeping of the character of the premises with the accredited character of the people, and while speculating upon the possible influence which the one, in the long lapse of centuries, might have exercised upon the other—it was this deficiency, perhaps, of collateral issue, and the consequent undeviating transmission, from sire to son, of the patrimony with the name, which had, at length, so identified the two as to merge the original title of the estate in the quaint and equivocal appellation of the "House of Usher"—an appellation which seemed to include, in the minds of the peasantry who used it, both the family and the family mansion.

I have said that the sole effect of my somewhat childish experiment—that of looking down within the tarn—had been to deepen the first singular impression. There can be no doubt that the consciousness of the rapid increase of my superstition—for why should I not so term it?—served mainly to accelerate the increase itself. Such, I have long known, is the paradoxical law of all sentiments having terror as a basis. And it might have been for this reason only, that, when I again uplifted my eyes to the house itself, from its image in the pool, there grew in my mind a strange fancy—a fancy so ridiculous, indeed, that I but mention it to show the vivid force of the sensations which oppressed me. I had so worked upon my imagination as really to believe that about the whole mansion and domain there hung an atmosphere peculiar to themselves and their immediate vicinity—an atmosphere which had no affinity with the air of heaven, but which had reeked up from the decayed trees, and the gray wall, and the silent tarn—a pestilent and mystic vapor, dull, sluggish, faintly discernible, and leaden-hued.

Shaking off from my spirit what must have been a dream, I scanned more narrowly the real aspect of the building. Its principal feature seemed to be that of an excessive antiquity. The discoloration of ages had been great. Minute fungi overspread the whole exterior, hanging in a fine tangled web-work from the eaves. Yet all this was apart from any extraordinary dilapidation. No portion of the masonry had fallen; and there appeared to be a wild inconsistency between its still perfect adaptation of parts, and the crumbling condition of the individual stones. In this there was much that reminded me of the specious totality of old wood-work which has rotted for long years in some neglected vault, with no disturbance from the breath of the external air. Beyond this indication of extensive decay, however, the fabric gave little token of instability. Perhaps the eye of a scrutinizing observer might have discovered a barely perceptible fissure, which, extending from the roof of the building in front, made its way down the wall in a zigzag direction, until it became lost in the sullen waters of the tarn.

Noticing these things, I rode over a short causeway to the house. A servant in waiting took my horse, and I entered the Gothic archway of the hall. A valet, of stealthy step, thence conducted me, in silence, through many dark and intricate passages in my progress to the studio of his master. Much that I encountered on the way contributed, I know not how, to heighten the vague sentiments of which I have already spoken. While the objects around me—while the carvings of the ceilings, the sombre tapestries of the walls, the ebon blackness of the floors, and the phantasmagoric armorial trophies which rattled as I strode, were but matters to which, or to such as which, I had been accustomed from my infancy—while I hesitated not to acknowledge how familiar was all this—I still wondered to find how unfamiliar were the fancies which ordinary images were stirring up. On one of the staircases, I met the physician of the family. His countenance, I thought, wore a mingled expression of low cunning and perplexity. He accosted me with trepidation and passed on. The valet now threw open a door and ushered me into the presence of his master.

The room in which I found myself was very large and lofty. The windows were long, narrow, and pointed, and at so vast a distance from the black oaken floor as to be altogether inaccessible from within. Feeble gleams of encrimsoned light made their way through the trellissed panes, and served to render sufficiently distinct the more prominent objects around; the eye, however, struggled in vain to reach the remoter angles of the chamber, or the recesses of the vaulted and fretted ceiling. Dark draperies hung upon the walls. The general furniture was profuse, comfortless, antique, and tattered. Many books and musical instruments lay scattered about, but failed to give any vitality to the scene. I felt that I breathed an atmosphere of sorrow. An air of stern, deep, and irredeemable gloom hung over and pervaded all.

Upon my entrance, Usher arose from a sofa on which he had been lying at full length, and greeted me with a vivacious warmth which had much in it, I at first thought, of an overdone cordiality—of the constrained effort of the *ennuye;* man of the world. A glance, however, at his countenance, convinced me of his perfect sincerity. We sat down; and for some moments, while he spoke not, I gazed upon him with a feeling half of pity, half of awe. Surely, man had never before so terribly altered, in so brief a period, as had Roderick Usher! It was with difficulty that I could bring myself to admit the identity of the wan being before me with the companion of my early boyhood. Yet the character of his face had been at all times remarkable. A cadaverousness of complexion; an eye large, liquid, and luminous beyond comparison; lips somewhat thin and very pallid, but of a surpassingly beautiful curve; a nose of a delicate Hebrew model, but with a breadth of nostril unusual in similar formations; a finely moulded chin, speaking, in its want of prominence, of a want of moral energy; hair of a more than web-like softness and tenuity; these features, with an inordinate expansion above the regions of the temple, made up altogether a countenance not easily to be forgotten. And now in the mere exaggeration of the prevailing character of these features, and of the expression they were wont to convey, lay so much of change that I doubted to whom I spoke. The now ghastly pallor of the skin, and the now miraculous lustre of the eye, above all things startled and even awed me. The silken hair, too, had been suffered to grow all unheeded, and as, in its wild gossamer texture, it floated rather than fell about the face, I could not, even with effort, connect its Arabesque expression with any idea of simple humanity.

In the manner of my friend I was at once struck with an incoherence—an inconsistency; and I soon found this to arise from a series of feeble and futile struggles to overcome an habitual trepidancy—an excessive nervous agitation. For something of this nature I had indeed been prepared, no less by his letter, than by reminiscences of certain boyish traits, and by conclusions deduced from his peculiar physical conformation and temperament. His action was alternately vivacious and sullen. His voice varied rapidly from a tremulous indecision (when the animal spirits seemed utterly in abeyance) to that species of energetic concision—that abrupt, weighty, unhurried, and hollow-sounding enunciation—that leaden, self-balanced and perfectly modulated guttural utterance, which may be observed in the lost drunkard, or the irreclaimable eater of opium, during the periods of his most intense excitement.

It was thus that he spoke of the object of my visit, of his earnest desire to see me, and of the solace he expected me to afford him. He entered, at some length, into what he conceived to be the nature of his malady. It was, he said, a constitutional and a family evil, and one for which he despaired to find a remedy—a mere nervous affection, he immediately added, which would undoubtedly soon pass off. It displayed itself in a host of unnatural sensations. Some of these, as he detailed them, interested and bewildered me; although, perhaps, the terms, and the general manner of the narration had their weight. He suffered much from a morbid acuteness of the senses; the most insipid food was alone endurable; he could wear only garments of certain texture; the odors of all flowers were oppressive; his eyes were tortured by even a faint light; and there were but peculiar sounds, and these from stringed instruments, which did not inspire him with horror.

To an anomalous species of terror I found him a bounden slave. "I shall perish," said he, "I *must* perish in this deplorable folly. Thus, thus, and not otherwise, shall I be lost. I dread the events of the future, not in themselves, but in their results. I shudder at the thought of any, even the most trivial, incident, which may operate upon this intolerable agitation of soul. I have, indeed, no abhorrence of danger, except in its absolute effect—in terror. In this unnerved—in this pitiable condition—I feel that the period will sooner or later arrive when I must abandon life and reason together, in some struggle with the grim phantasm, *fear*."

I learned, moreover, at intervals, and through broken and equivocal hints, another singular feature of his mental condition. He was enchained by certain superstitious impressions in regard to the dwelling which he tenanted, and whence, for many years, he had never ventured forth—in regard to an influence whose supposititious force was conveyed in terms too shadowy here to be re-stated—an influence which some peculiarities in the mere form and substance of his family mansion, had, by dint of long sufferance, he said, obtained over his spirit—an effect which the *physique* of the gray walls and turrets, and of the dim tarn into which they all looked down, had, at length, brought about upon the *morale* of his existence.

He admitted, however, although with hesitation, that much of the peculiar gloom which thus afflicted him could be traced to a more natural and far more palpable origin—to the severe and long-continued illness—indeed to the evidently approaching dissolution—of a tenderly beloved sister—his sole companion for long years—his last and only relative on earth. "Her decease," he said, with a bitterness which I can never forget, "would leave him (him the hopeless and the frail) the last of the ancient race of the Ushers." While he spoke, the Lady Madeline (for so was she called) passed slowly through a remote portion of the apartment, and, without having noticed my presence, disappeared. I regarded her with an utter astonishment not unmingled with dread—and yet I found it impossible to account for such feelings. A sensation of stupor oppressed me, as my eyes followed her retreating steps. When a door, at length, closed upon her, my glance sought instinctively and eagerly the countenance of the brother—but he had buried his face in his hands, and I could only perceive that a far more than ordinary wanness had overspread the emaciated fingers through which trickled many passionate tears.

The disease of the Lady Madeline had long baffled the skill of her physicians. A settled apathy, a gradual wasting away of the person, and frequent although transient affections of a partially cataleptical character, were the unusual diagnosis. Hitherto she had steadily borne up against the pressure of her malady, and had not betaken herself finally to bed; but, on the closing in of the evening of my arrival at the house, she succumbed (as her brother told me at night with inexpressible agitation) to the prostrating power of the destroyer; and I learned that the glimpse I had obtained of her person would thus probably be the last I should obtain—that the lady, at least while living, would be seen by me no more.

For several days ensuing, her name was unmentioned by either Usher or myself: and during this period I was busied in earnest endeavors to alleviate the melancholy of my friend. We painted and read together; or I listened, as if in a dream, to the wild improvisations of his speaking guitar. And thus, as a closer and still closer intimacy admitted me more unreservedly into the recesses of his spirit, the more bitterly did I perceive the futility of all attempt at cheering a mind from which darkness, as if an inherent positive quality, poured forth upon all objects of the moral and physical universe, in one unceasing radiation of gloom.

I shall ever bear about me a memory of the many solemn hours I thus spent alone with the master of the House of Usher. Yet I should fail in any attempt to convey an idea of the exact character of the studies, or of the occupations, in which he involved me, or led me the way. An excited and highly distempered ideality threw a sulphureous lustre over all. His long improvised dirges will ring forever in my ears. Among other things, I hold painfully in mind a certain singular perversion and amplification of the wild air of the last waltz of Von Weber. From the paintings over which his elaborate fancy brooded, and which grew, touch by touch, into vaguenesses at which I shuddered the more thrillingly, because I shuddered knowing not why—from these paintings (vivid as their images now are before me) I would in vain endeavor to educe more than a small portion which should lie within the compass of merely written words. By the utter simplicity, by the nakedness of his designs, he arrested and overawed attention. If ever mortal painted an idea, that mortal was Roderick Usher. For me at least—in the circumstances then surrounding me—there arose out of the pure abstractions which the hypochondriac contrived to throw upon his canvass, an intensity of intolerable awe, no shadow of which felt I ever yet in the contemplation of the certainly glowing yet too concrete reveries of Fuseli.

One of the phantasmagoric conceptions of my friend, partaking not so rigidly of the spirit of abstraction, may be shadowed forth, although feebly, in words. A small picture presented the interior of an immensely long and rectangular vault or tunnel, with low walls, smooth, white, and without interruption or device. Certain accessory points of the design served well to convey the idea that this excavation lay at an exceeding depth below the surface of the earth. No outlet was observed in any portion of its vast extent, and no torch, or other artificial source of light was discernible; yet a flood of intense rays rolled throughout, and bathed the whole in a ghastly and inappropriate splendor.

I have just spoken of that morbid condition of the auditory nerve which rendered all music intolerable to the sufferer, with the exception of certain effects of stringed instruments. It was, perhaps, the narrow limits to which he thus confined himself upon the guitar, which gave birth, in great measure, to the fantastic character of his performances. But the fervid *facility* of his *impromptus* could not be so accounted for. They must have been, and were, in the notes, as well as in the words of his wild fantasias (for he not unfrequently accompanied himself with rhymed verbal improvisations), the result of that intense mental collectedness and concentration to which I have previously alluded as observable only in particular moments of the highest artificial excitement. The words of one of these rhapsodies I have easily remembered. I was, perhaps, the more forcibly impressed with it, as he gave it, because, in the under or mystic current of its meaning, I fancied that I perceived, and for the first time, a full consciousness on the part of Usher, of the tottering of his lofty reason upon her throne. The verses, which were entitled "The Haunted Palace," ran very nearly, if not accurately, thus:

I

In the greenest of our valleys,
By good angels tenanted,
Once a fair and stately palace—
Radiant palace—reared its head.
In the monarch Thought's dominion—
It stood there!
Never seraph spread a pinion
Over fabric half so fair.

II

Banners yellow, glorious, golden,
On its roof did float and flow;
(This—all this—was in the olden
Time long ago)
And every gentle air that dallied,
In that sweet day,
Along the ramparts plumed and pallid,
A winged odor went away.

III

Wanderers in that happy valley
Through two luminous windows saw
Spirits moving musically
To a lute's well-tuned law,
Round about a throne, where sitting
(Porphyrogene!)

In state his glory well befitting,
    The ruler of the realm was seen.

IV

And all with pearl and ruby glowing
    Was the fair palace door,
Through which came flowing, flowing, flowing,
    And sparkling evermore,
A troop of Echoes whose sweet duty
    Was but to sing,
In voices of surpassing beauty,
    The wit and wisdom of their king.

V

But evil things, in robes of sorrow,
    Assailed the monarch's high estate;
(Ah, let us mourn, for never morrow
    Shall dawn upon him, desolate!)
And, round about his home, the glory
    That blushed and bloomed
Is but a dim-remembered story
    Of the old time entombed.

VI

And travellers now within that valley,
    Through the red-litten windows, see
Vast forms that move fantastically
    To a discordant melody;
While, like a rapid ghastly river,
    Through the pale door,
A hideous throng rush out forever,
    And laugh—but smile no more.

I well remember that suggestions arising from this ballad, led us into a train of thought wherein there became manifest an opinion of Usher's which I mention not so much on account of its novelty (for other men have thought thus), as on account of the pertinacity with which he maintained it. This opinion, in its general form, was that of the sentience of all vegetable things. But, in his disordered fancy, the idea had assumed a more daring character, and trespassed, under certain conditions, upon the kingdom of inorganization. I lack words to express the full extent, or the earnest abandon of his persuasion. The belief, however, was connected (as I have previously hinted) with the gray stones of the home of his forefathers. The conditions of the sentience had been here, he imagined, fulfilled in the method of collocation of these stones—in the order of their arrangement, as well as in that of the many *fungi* which overspread them, and of the decayed trees which stood around—above all, in the long undisturbed endurance of this arrangement, and in its reduplication in the still waters of the tarn. Its evidence—the evidence of the sentience—was to be seen, he said (and I here started as he spoke), in the gradual yet certain condensation of an atmosphere of their own about the waters and the walls. The result was discoverable, he added, in that silent, yet importunate and terrible influence which for centuries had moulded the destinies of his family, and which made him what I now saw him—what he was. Such opinions need no comment, and I will make none.

Our books—the books which, for years, had formed no small portion of the mental existence of the invalid—were, as might be supposed, in strict keeping with this character of phantasm. We pored together over such works as the Ververt et Chartreuse of Gresset; the Belphegor of Machiavelli; the Heaven and Hell of Swedenborg; the Subterranean Voyage of Nicholas Klimm by Holberg; the Chiromancy of Robert Flud, of Jean D'Indagine, and of De la Chambre; the Journey into the Blue Distance of Tieck; and the City of the Sun of Campanella. One favorite volume was a small octavo edition of the *Directorium Inquisitorium*, by the Dominican Eymeric de Gironne; and there were passages in Pomponius Mela, about the old African Satyrs and Oegipans, over which Usher would sit dreaming for hours. His chief delight, however, was found in the perusal of an exceedingly rare and curious book in quarto Gothic—the manual of a forgotten church—the *Vigiliae Mortuorum secundum Chorum Ecclesiae Maguntinae*.

I could not help thinking of the wild ritual of this work, and of its probable influence upon the hypochondriac, when, one evening, having informed me abruptly that the Lady Madeline was no more, he stated his intention of preserving her corpse for a fortnight (previously to its final interment), in one of the numerous vaults within the main walls of the building. The worldly reason, however, assigned for this singular proceeding, was one which I did not feel at liberty to dispute. The brother had been led to his resolution (so he told me) by consideration of the unusual character of the malady of the deceased, of certain obtrusive and eager inquiries on the part of her medical men, and of the remote and exposed situation of the burial-ground of the family. I will not deny that when I called to mind the sinister countenance of the person whom I met upon the staircase, on the day of my arrival at the house, I had no desire to oppose what I regarded as at best but a harmless, and by no means an unnatural, precaution.

At the request of Usher, I personally aided him in the arrangements for the temporary entombment. The body having been encoffined, we two alone bore it to its rest. The vault in which we placed it (and which had been so long unopened that our torches, half smothered in its oppressive atmosphere, gave us little opportunity for investigation) was small, damp, and entirely without means of admission for light; lying, at great depth, immediately beneath that portion of the building in which was my own sleeping apartment. It had been used, apparently, in remote feudal times, for the worst purposes of a donjon-keep, and, in later days, as a place of deposit for powder, or some other highly combustible substance, as a portion of its floor, and the whole interior of a long archway through which we reached it, were carefully sheathed with copper. The door, of massive iron, had been, also, similarly protected. Its immense weight caused an unusually sharp grating sound, as it moved upon its hinges.

Having deposited our mournful burden upon tressels within this region of horror, we partially turned aside the yet unscrewed lid of the coffin, and looked upon the face of the tenant. A striking similitude between the brother and sister now first arrested my attention; and Usher, divining, perhaps, my thoughts, murmured out some few words from which I learned that the deceased and himself had been twins, and that sympathies of a scarcely intelligible nature had always existed between them. Our glances, however, rested not long upon the dead—for we could not regard her unawed. The disease which had thus entombed the lady in the maturity of youth, had left, as usual in all maladies of a strictly cataleptical character, the mockery of a faint blush upon the bosom and the face, and that suspiciously lingering smile upon the lip which is so terrible in death. We replaced and screwed down the lid, and, having secured the door of iron, made our way, with toil, into the scarcely less gloomy apartments of the upper portion of the house.

And now, some days of bitter grief having elapsed, an observable change came over the features of the mental disorder of my friend. His ordinary manner had vanished. His ordinary occupations were neglected or forgotten. He roamed from chamber to chamber with hurried, unequal, and objectless step. The pallor of his countenance had assumed, if possible, a more ghastly hue—but the luminousness of his eye had utterly gone out. The once occasional huskiness of his tone was heard no more; and a tremulous quaver, as if of extreme terror, habitually characterized his utterance. There were times, indeed, when I thought his unceasingly agitated mind was laboring with some oppressive secret, to divulge which he struggled for the necessary courage. At times, again, I was obliged to resolve all into the mere inexplicable vagaries of madness, for I beheld him gazing upon vacancy for long hours, in an attitude of the profoundest attention, as if listening to some imaginary sound. It was no wonder that his condition terrified—that it infected me. I felt creeping upon me, by slow yet certain degrees, the wild influences of his own fantastic yet impressive superstitions.

It was, especially, upon retiring to bed late in the night of the seventh or eighth day after the placing of the Lady Madeline within the donjon, that I experienced the full power of such feelings. Sleep came not near my couch—while the hours waned and waned away. I struggled to reason off the nervousness which had dominion over me. I endeavored to believe that much, if not all of what I felt, was due to the bewildering influence of the gloomy furniture of the room—of the dark and tattered draperies, which, tortured into motion by the breath of a rising tempest, swayed fitfully to and fro upon the walls, and rustled uneasily about the decorations of the bed. But my efforts were fruitless. An irrepressible tremor gradually pervaded my frame; and, at length, there sat upon my very heart an incubus of utterly causeless alarm. Shaking this off with a gasp and a struggle, I uplifted myself upon the pillows, and, peering earnestly within the intense darkness of the chamber, harkened—I know not why, except that an instinctive spirit prompted me—to certain low and indefinite sounds which came, through the pauses of the storm, at long intervals, I knew not whence. Overpowered by an intense sentiment of horror, unaccountable yet unendurable, I threw on my clothes with haste (for I felt that I should sleep no more during the night), and endeavored to arouse myself from the pitiable condition into which I had fallen, by pacing rapidly to and fro through the apartment.

I had taken but few turns in this manner, when a light step on an adjoining staircase arrested my attention. I presently recognised it as that of Usher. In an instant afterward he rapped, with a gentle touch, at my door, and entered, bearing a lamp. His countenance was, as usual, cadaverously wan—but, moreover, there was a species of mad hilarity in his eyes—an evidently restrained hysteria in his whole demeanor. His air appalled me—but anything was preferable to the solitude which I had so long endured, and I even welcomed his presence as a relief.

"And you have not seen it?" he said abruptly, after having stared about him for some moments in silence—"you have not then seen it?—but, stay! you shall." Thus speaking, and having carefully shaded his lamp, he hurried to one of the casements, and threw it freely open to the storm.

The impetuous fury of the entering gust nearly lifted us from our feet. It was, indeed, a tempestuous yet sternly beautiful night, and one wildly singular in its terror and its beauty. A whirlwind had apparently collected its force in our vicinity; for there were frequent and violent alterations in the direction of the wind; and the exceeding density of the clouds (which hung so low as to press upon the turrets of the house) did not prevent our perceiving the life-like velocity with which they flew careering from all points against each other, without passing away into the distance. I say that even their exceeding density did not prevent our perceiving this—yet we had no glimpse of the moon or stars—nor was there any flashing forth of the lightning. But the under surfaces of the huge masses of agitated vapor, as well as all terrestrial objects immediately around us, were glowing in the unnatural light of a faintly luminous and distinctly visible gaseous exhalation which hung about and enshrouded the mansion.

"You must not—you shall not behold this!" said I, shudderingly, to Usher, as I led him, with a gentle violence, from the window to a seat. "These appearances, which bewilder you, are merely electrical phenomena not uncommon—or it may be that they have their ghastly origin in the rank miasma of the tarn. Let us close this casement—the air is chilling and dangerous to your frame. Here is one of your favorite romances. I will read, and you shall listen—and so we will pass away this terrible night together."

The antique volume which I had taken up was the "Mad Trist" of Sir Launcelot Canning; but I had called it a favorite of Usher's more in sad jest than in earnest; for, in truth, there is little in its uncouth and unimaginative prolixity which could have had interest for the lofty and spiritual ideality of my friend. It was, however, the only book immediately at hand; and I indulged a vague hope that the excitement which now agitated the hypochondriac, might find relief (for the history of mental disorder is full of similar anomalies) even in the extremeness of the folly which I should read. Could I have judged, indeed, by the wild overstrained air of vivacity with which he harkened, or apparently harkened, to the words of the tale, I might well have congratulated myself upon the success of my design.

I had arrived at that well-known portion of the story where Ethelred, the hero of the Trist, having sought in vain for peaceable admission into the dwelling of the hermit, proceeds to make good an entrance by force. Here, it will be remembered, the words of the narrative run thus:

"And Ethelred, who was by nature of a doughty heart, and who was now mighty withal, on account of the powerfulness of the wine which he had drunken, waited no longer to hold parley with the hermit, who, in sooth, was of an obstinate and maliceful turn, but, feeling the rain upon his shoulders, and fearing the rising of the tempest, uplifted his mace outright, and, with blows, made quickly room in the plankings of the door for his gauntleted hand; and now pulling therewith sturdily, he so cracked, and ripped, and tore all asunder, that the noise of the dry and hollow-sounding wood alarummed and reverberated throughout the forest."

At the termination of this sentence I started, and for a moment, paused; for it appeared to me (although I at once concluded that my excited fancy had deceived me)—it appeared to me that, from some very remote portion of the mansion, there came, indistinctly, to my ears, what might have been, in its exact similarity of character, the echo (but a stifled and dull one certainly) of the very cracking and ripping sound which Sir Launcelot had so particularly described. It was, beyond doubt, the coincidence alone which had arrested my attention; for, amid the rattling of the sashes of the casements, and the ordinary commingled noises of the still increasing storm, the sound, in itself, had nothing, surely, which should have interested or disturbed me. I continued the story:

"But the good champion Ethelred, now entering within the door, was sore enraged and amazed to perceive no signal of the maliceful hermit; but, in the stead thereof, a dragon of a scaly and prodigious demeanor, and of a fiery tongue, which sate in guard before a palace of gold, with a floor of silver; and upon the wall there hung a shield of shining brass with this legend enwritten:

Who entereth herein, a conqueror hath bin;
Who slayeth the dragon, the shield he shall win;

And Ethelred uplifted his mace, and struck upon the head of the dragon, which fell before him, and gave up his pesty breath, with a shriek so horrid and harsh, and withal so piercing, that Ethelred had fain to close his ears with his hands against the dreadful noise of it, the like whereof was never before heard."

Here again I paused abruptly, and now with a feeling of wild amazement—for there could be no doubt whatever that, in this instance, I did actually hear (although from what direction it proceeded I found it impossible to say) a low and apparently distant, but harsh, protracted, and most unusual screaming or grating sound—the exact counterpart of what my fancy had already conjured up for the dragon's unnatural shriek as described by the romancer.

Oppressed, as I certainly was, upon the occurrence of this second and most extraordinary coincidence, by a thousand conflicting sensations, in which wonder and extreme terror were predominant, I still retained sufficient presence of mind to avoid exciting, by any observation, the sensitive nervousness of my companion. I was by no means certain that he had noticed the sounds in question; although, assuredly, a strange alteration had, during the last few minutes, taken place in his demeanor. From a position fronting my own, he had gradually brought round his chair, so as to sit with his face to the door of the chamber; and thus I could but partially perceive his features, although I saw that his lips trembled as if he were murmuring inaudibly. His head had dropped upon his breast—yet I knew that he was not asleep, from the wide and rigid opening of the eye as I caught a glance of it in profile. The motion of his body, too, was at variance with this idea—for he rocked from side to side with a gentle yet constant and uniform sway. Having rapidly taken notice of all this, I resumed the narrative of Sir Launcelot, which thus proceeded:

"And now, the champion, having escaped from the terrible fury of the dragon, bethinking himself of the brazen shield, and of the breaking up of the enchantment which was upon it, removed the carcass from out of the way before him, and approached valorously over the silver pavement of the castle to where the shield was upon the wall; which in sooth the feet upon the silver floor, with a mighty great and terrible ringing sound."

No sooner had these syllables passed my lips, than—as if a shield of brass had indeed, at the moment, fallen heavily upon a floor of silver—I became aware of a distinct, hollow, metallic, and clangorous, yet apparently muffled reverberation. Completely unnerved, I leaped to my feet; but the measured rocking movement of Usher was undisturbed. I rushed to the chair in which he sat. His eyes were bent fixedly before him, and throughout his whole countenance there reigned a stony rigidity. But, as I placed my hand upon his shoulder, there came a strong shudder over his whole person; a sickly smile quivered about his lips; and I saw that he spoke in a low, hurried, and gibbering murmur, as if unconscious of my presence. Bending closely over him, I at length drank in the hideous import of his words.

"Not hear it?—yes, I hear it, and have heard it. Long—long—long—many minutes, many hours, many days, have I heard it—yet I dared not—oh, pity me, miserable wretch that I am!—I dared not—I dared not speak!

We have put her living in the tomb! Said I not that my senses were acute? I now tell you that I heard her first feeble movements in the hollow coffin. I heard them—many, many days ago—yet I dared not—*I dared not speak!* And now—tonight—Ethelred—ha! ha!—the breaking of the hermit's door, and the death-cry of the dragon, and the clangor of the shield!—say, rather, the rending of her coffin, and the grating of the iron hinges of her prison, and her struggles within the coppered archway of the vault! Oh whither shall I fly? Will she not be here anon? Is she not hurrying to upbraid me for my haste? Have I not heard her footstep on the stair? Do I not distinguish that heavy and horrible beating of her heart? Madman!"—here he sprang furiously to his feet, and shrieked out his syllables, as if in the effort he were giving up his soul—*"Madman! I tell you that she now stands without the door!"*

As if in the superhuman energy of his utterance there had been found the potency of a spell—the huge antique panels to which the speaker pointed, threw slowly back, upon the instant, their ponderous and ebony jaws. It was the work of the rushing gust—but then without those doors there *did* stand the lofty and enshrouded figure of the Lady Madeline of Usher. There was blood upon her white robes, and the evidence of some bitter struggle upon every portion of her emaciated frame. For a moment she remained trembling and reeling to and fro upon the threshold—then, with a low moaning cry, fell heavily inward upon the person of her brother, and in her violent and now final death-agonies, bore him to the floor a corpse, and a victim to the terrors he had anticipated.

From that chamber, and from that mansion, I fled aghast. The storm was still abroad in all its wrath as I found myself crossing the old causeway. Suddenly there shot along the path a wild light, and I turned to see whence a gleam so unusual could have issued; for the vast house and its shadows were alone behind me. The radiance was that of the full, setting, and blood-red moon, which now shone vividly through that once barely-discernible fissure, of which I have before spoken as extending from the roof of the building, in a zigzag direction, to the base. While I gazed, this fissure rapidly widened—there came a fierce breath of the whirlwind—the entire orb of the satellite burst at once upon my sight—my brain reeled as I saw the mighty walls rushing asunder—there was a long tumultuous shouting sound like the voice of a thousand waters—and the deep and dank tarn at my feet closed sullenly and silently over the fragments of the "House of Usher."

The Japanned Box

Arthur Conan Doyle

It was a curious thing, said the private tutor; one of those grotesque and whimsical incidents which occur to one as one goes through life. I lost the best situation which I am ever likely to have through it. But I am glad that I went to Thorpe Place, for I gained—well, as I tell you the story you will learn what I gained.

I don't know whether you are familiar with that part of the Midlands which is drained by the Avon. It is the most English part of England. Shakespeare, the flower of the whole race, was born right in the middle of it. It is a land of rolling pastures, rising in higher folds to the westwards, until they swell into the Malvern Hills. There are no towns, but numerous villages, each with its grey Norman church. You have left the brick of the southern and eastern counties behind you, and everything is stone—stone for the walls, and lichened slabs of stone for the roofs. It is all grim and solid and massive, as befits the heart of a great nation.

It was in the middle of this country, not very far from Evesham, that Sir John Bollamore lived in the old ancestral home of Thorpe Place, and thither it was that I came to teach his two little sons. Sir John was a widower—his wife had died three years before—and he had been left with these two lads aged eight and ten, and one dear little girl of seven. Miss Witherton, who is now my wife, was governess to this little girl. I was tutor to the two boys. Could there be a more obvious prelude to an engagement? She governs me now, and I tutor two little boys of our own. But, there—I have already revealed what it was which I gained in Thorpe Place!

It was a very, very old house, incredibly old—pre-Norman, some of it—and the Bollamores claimed to have lived in that situation since long before the Conquest. It struck a chill to my heart when first I came there, those enormously thick grey walls, the rude crumbling stones, the smell as from a sick animal which exhaled from the rotting plaster of the aged building. But the modern wing was bright and the garden was well kept. No house could be dismal which had a pretty girl inside it and such a show of roses in front.

Apart from a very complete staff of servants there were only four of us in the household. These were Miss Witherton, who was at that time four-and-twenty and as pretty—well, as pretty as Mrs. Colmore is now—myself, Frank

Colmore, aged thirty, Mrs. Stevens, the housekeeper, a dry, silent woman, and Mr. Richards, a tall military-looking man, who acted as steward to the Bollamore estates. We four always had our meals together, but Sir John had his usually alone in the library. Sometimes he joined us at dinner, but on the whole we were just as glad when he did not.

For he was a very formidable person. Imagine a man six feet three inches in height, majestically built, with a high-nosed, aristocratic face, brindled hair, shaggy eyebrows, a small, pointed Mephistophelian beard, and lines upon his brow and round his eyes as deep as if they had been carved with a penknife. He had grey eyes, weary, hopeless-looking eyes, proud and yet pathetic, eyes which claimed your pity and yet dared you to show it. His back was rounded with study, but otherwise he was as fine a looking man of his age—five-and-fifty perhaps—as any woman would wish to look upon.

But his presence was not a cheerful one. He was always courteous, always refined, but singularly silent and retiring. I have never lived so long with any man and known so little of him. If he were indoors he spent his time either in his own small study in the Eastern Tower, or in the library in the modern wing. So regular was his routine that one could always say at any hour exactly where he would be. Twice in the day he would visit his study, once after breakfast, and once about ten at night. You might set your watch by the slam of the heavy door. For the rest of the day he would be in his library—save that for an hour or two in the afternoon he would take a walk or a ride, which was solitary like the rest of his existence. He loved his children, and was keenly interested in the progress of their studies, but they were a little awed by the silent, shaggy-browed figure, and they avoided him as much as they could. Indeed, we all did that.

It was some time before I came to know anything about the circumstances of Sir John Bollamore's life, for Mrs. Stevens, the housekeeper, and Mr. Richards, the land-steward, were too loyal to talk easily of their employer's affairs. As to the governess, she knew no more than I did, and our common interest was one of the causes which drew us together. At last, however, an incident occurred which led to a closer acquaintance with Mr. Richards and a fuller knowledge of the life of the man whom I served.

The immediate cause of this was no less than the falling of Master Percy, the youngest of my pupils, into the mill-race, with imminent danger both to his life and to mine, since I had to risk myself in order to save him. Dripping and exhausted—for I was far more spent than the child—I was making for my room when Sir John, who had heard the hubbub, opened the door of his little study and asked me what was the matter. I told him of the accident, but assured him that his child was in no danger, while he listened with a rugged, immobile face, which expressed in its intense eyes and tightened lips all the emotion which he tried to conceal.

"One moment! Step in here! Let me have the details!" said he, turning back through the open door.

And so I found myself within that little sanctum, inside which, as I afterwards learned, no other foot had for three years been set save that of the old servant who cleaned it out. It was a round room, conforming to the shape of the tower in which it was situated, with a low ceiling, a single narrow, ivy-wreathed window, and the simplest of furniture. An old carpet, a single chair, a deal table, and a small shelf of books made up the whole contents. On the table stood a full-length photograph of a woman—I took no particular notice of the features, but I remember, that a certain gracious gentleness was the prevailing impression. Beside it were a large black japanned box and one or two bundles of letters or papers fastened together with elastic bands.

Our interview was a short one, for Sir John Bollamore perceived that I was soaked, and that I should change without delay. The incident led, however, to an instructive talk with Richards, the agent, who had never penetrated into the chamber which chance had opened to me. That very afternoon he came to me, all curiosity, and walked up and down the garden path with me, while my two charges played tennis upon the lawn beside us.

"You hardly realize the exception which has been made in your favour," said he. "That room has been kept such a mystery, and Sir John's visits to it have been so regular and consistent, that an almost superstitious feeling has arisen about it in the household. I assure you that if I were to repeat to you the tales which are flying about, tales of mysterious visitors there, and of voices overheard by the servants, you might suspect that Sir John had relapsed into his old ways."

"Why do you say relapsed?" I asked.

He looked at me in surprise.

"Is it possible," said he, "that Sir John Bollamore's previous history is unknown to you?"

"Absolutely."

"You astound me. I thought that every man in England knew something of his antecedents. I should not mention the matter if it were not that you are now one of ourselves, and that the facts might come to your ears in some harsher form if I were silent upon them. I always took it for granted that you knew that you were in the service of 'Devil' Bollamore."

"But why 'Devil'?" I asked.

"Ah, you are young and the world moves fast, but twenty years ago the name of 'Devil' Bollamore was one of the best known in London. He was the leader of the fastest set, bruiser, driver, gambler, drunkard—a survival of the old type, and as bad as the worst of them."

I stared at him in amazement.

"What!" I cried, "that quiet, studious, sad-faced man?"

"The greatest rip and debauchee in England! All between ourselves, Colmore. But you understand now what I mean when I say that a woman's voice in his room might even now give rise to suspicions."

"But what can have changed him so?"

"Little Beryl Clare, when she took the risk of becoming his wife. That was the turning point. He had got so far that his own fast set had thrown him over. There is a world of difference, you know, between a man who drinks and a drunkard. They all drink, but they taboo a drunkard. He had become a slave to it—hopeless and helpless. Then she stepped in, saw the possibilities of a fine man in the wreck, took her chance in marrying him though she might have had the pick of a dozen, and, by devoting her life to it, brought him back to manhood and decency. You have observed that no liquor is ever kept in the house. There never has been any since her foot crossed its threshold. A drop of it would be like blood to a tiger even now."

"Then her influence still holds him?"

"That is the wonder of it. When she died three years ago, we all expected and feared that he would fall back into his old ways. She feared it herself, and the thought gave a terror to death, for she was like a guardian angel to that man, and lived only for the one purpose. By the way, did you see a black japanned box in his room?"

"Yes."

"I fancy it contains her letters. If ever he has occasion to be away, if only for a single night, he invariably takes his black japanned box with him. Well, well, Colmore, perhaps I have told you rather more than I should, but I shall expect you to reciprocate if anything of interest should come to your knowledge."

I could see that the worthy man was consumed with curiosity and just a little piqued that I, the newcomer, should have been the first to penetrate into the untrodden chamber. But the fact raised me in his esteem, and from that time onwards I found myself upon more confidential terms with him.

And now the silent and majestic figure of my employer became an object of greater interest to me. I began to understand that strangely human look in his eyes, those deep lines upon his care-worn face. He was a man who was fighting a ceaseless battle, holding at arm's length, from morning till night, a horrible adversary who was forever trying to close with him—an adversary which would destroy him body and soul could it but fix its claws once more upon him. As I watched the grim, round-backed figure pacing the corridor or walking in the garden, this imminent danger seemed to take bodily shape, and I could almost fancy that I saw this most loathsome and dangerous of all the fiends crouching closely in his very shadow, like a half-cowed beast which slinks beside its keeper, ready at any unguarded moment to spring at his throat. And the dead woman, the woman who had spent her life in warding off this danger, took shape also to my imagination, and I saw her as a shadowy but beautiful presence which intervened for ever with arms uplifted to screen the man whom she loved.

In some subtle way he divined the sympathy which I had for him, and he showed in his own silent fashion that he appreciated it. He even invited me once to share his afternoon walk, and although no word passed between us on this occasion, it was a mark of confidence which he had never shown to anyone before. He asked me also to index his library (it was one of the best private libraries in England), and I spent many hours in the evening in his presence, if not in his society, he reading at his desk and I sitting in a recess by the window reducing to order the chaos which existed among his books. In spite of these close relations I was never again asked to enter the chamber in the turret.

And then came my revulsion of feeling. A single incident changed all my sympathy to loathing, and made me realize that my employer still remained all that he had ever been, with the additional vice of hypocrisy. What happened was as follows.

One evening Miss Witherton had gone down to Broadway, the neighbouring village, to sing at a concert for some charity, and I, according to my promise, had walked over to escort her back. The drive sweeps round under the eastern turret, and I observed as I passed that the light was lit in the circular room. It was a summer evening, and the window, which was a little higher than our heads, was open. We were, as it happened, engrossed in our own conversation at the moment and we had paused upon the lawn which skirts the old turret, when suddenly something broke in upon our talk and turned our thoughts away from our own affairs.

It was a voice—the voice undoubtedly of a woman. It was low—so low that it was only in that still night air that we could have heard it, but, hushed as it was, there was no mistaking its feminine timbre. It spoke hurriedly, gaspingly for a few sentences, and then was silent—a piteous, breathless, imploring sort of voice. Miss Witherton and I stood for an instant staring at each other. Then we walked quickly in the direction of the hall-door.

"It came through the window," I said.

"We must not play the part of eavesdroppers," she answered. "We must forget that we have ever heard it."

There was an absence of surprise in her manner which suggested a new idea to me.

"You have heard it before," I cried.

"I could not help it. My own room is higher up on the same turret. It has happened frequently."

"Who can the woman be?"

"I have no idea. I had rather not discuss it."

Her voice was enough to show me what she thought. But granting that our employer led a double and dubious life, who could she be, this mysterious woman who kept him company in the old tower? I knew from my own inspection how bleak and bare a room it was. She certainly did not live there. But in that case where did she come from? It could not be anyone of the household. They were all under the vigilant eyes of Mrs. Stevens. The visitor must come from without. But how?

And then suddenly I remembered how ancient this building was, and how probable that some mediaeval passage existed in it. There is hardly an old castle without one. The mysterious room was the basement of the turret, so that if there were anything of the sort it would open through the floor. There were numerous cottages in the immediate vicinity. The other end of the secret passage might lie among some tangle of bramble in the neighbouring copse. I said nothing to anyone, but I felt that the secret of my employer lay within my power.

And the more convinced I was of this the more I marvelled at the manner in which he concealed his true nature. Often as I watched his austere figure, I asked myself if it were indeed possible that such a man should be living this double life, and I tried to persuade myself that my suspicions might after all prove to be ill-founded. But there was the female voice, there was the secret nightly rendezvous in the turret-chamber—how could such facts admit of an innocent interpretation. I conceived a horror of the man. I was filled with loathing at his deep, consistent hypocrisy.

Only once during all those months did I ever see him without that sad but impassive mask which he usually presented towards his fellow-man. For an instant I caught a glimpse of those volcanic fires which he had damped down so long. The occasion was an unworthy one, for the object of his wrath was none other than the aged charwoman whom I have already mentioned as being the one person who was allowed within his mysterious chamber. I was passing the corridor which led to the turret—for my own room lay in that direction—when I heard a sudden, startled scream, and merged in it the husky, growling note of a man who is inarticulate with passion. It was the snarl of a furious wild beast. Then I heard his voice thrilling with anger. "You would dare!" he cried. "You would dare to disobey my directions!" An instant later the charwoman passed me, flying down the passage, white-faced and tremulous, while the terrible voice thundered behind her. "Go to Mrs. Stevens for your money! Never set foot in Thorpe Place again!" Consumed with curiosity, I could not help following the woman, and found her round the corner leaning against the wall and palpitating like a frightened rabbit.

"What is the matter, Mrs. Brown?" I asked.

"It's master!" she gasped. "Oh, 'ow 'e frightened me! If you had seen 'is eyes, Mr. Colmore, sir. I thought 'e would 'ave been the death of me."

"But what had you done?"

"Done, sir! Nothing. At least nothing to make so much of. Just laid my 'and on that black box of 'is—'adn't even opened it, when in 'e came and you 'eard the way 'e went on. I've lost my place, and glad I am of it, for I would never trust myself within reach of 'im again."

So it was the japanned box which was the cause of this outburst—the box from which he would never permit himself to be separated. What was the connection, or was there any connection between this and the secret visits of the lady whose voice I had overheard? Sir John Bollamore's wrath was enduring as well as fiery, for from that day Mrs. Brown, the charwoman, vanished from our ken, and Thorpe Place knew her no more.

And now I wish to tell you the singular chance which solved all these strange questions and put my employer's secret in my possession. The story may leave you with some lingering doubts as to whether my curiosity did not get the better of my honour, and whether I did not condescend to play the spy. If you choose to think so I cannot help it, but can only assure you that, improbable as it may appear, the matter came about exactly as I describe it.

The first stage in this denouement was that the small room in the turret became uninhabitable. This occurred through the fall of the worm-eaten oaken beam which supported the ceiling. Rotten with age, it snapped in the middle one morning, and brought down a quantity of plaster with it. Fortunately Sir John was not in the room at the time. His precious box was rescued from amongst the debris and brought into the library, where, henceforward, it was locked within his bureau. Sir John took no steps to repair the damage, and I never had an opportunity of searching for that secret passage, the existence of which I had surmised. As to the lady, I had thought that this would have brought her visits to an end, had I not one evening heard Mr. Richards asking Mrs. Stevens who the woman was whom he had overheard talking to Sir John in the library. I could not catch her reply, but I saw from her manner that it was not the first time that she had had to answer or avoid the same question.

"You've heard the voice, Colmore?" said the agent.

I confessed that I had.

"And what do you think of it?"

I shrugged my shoulders, and remarked that it was no business of mine.

"Come, come, you are just as curious as any of us. Is it a woman or not?"

"It is certainly a woman."

"Which room did you hear it from?"

"From the turret-room, before the ceiling fell."

"But I heard it from the library only last night. I passed the doors as I was going to bed, and I heard something wailing and praying just as plainly as I hear you. It may be a woman—"

"Why, what else *could* it be?"

He looked at me hard.

"There are more things in heaven and earth," said he. "If it is a woman, how does she get there?"

"I don't know."

"No, nor I. But if it is the other thing—but there, for a practical business man at the end of the nineteenth century this is rather a ridiculous line of conversation." He turned away, but I saw that he felt even more than he had said. To all the old ghost stories of Thorpe Place a new one was being added before our very eyes. It may by this time have taken its permanent place, for though an explanation came to me, it never reached the others.

And my explanation came in this way. I had suffered a sleepless night from neuralgia, and about midday I had taken a heavy dose of chlorodyne to alleviate the pain. At that time I was finishing the indexing of Sir John Bollamore's library, and it was my custom to work there from five till seven. On this particular day I struggled against the double effect of my bad night and the narcotic. I have already mentioned that there was a recess in the library, and in this it was my habit to work. I settled down steadily to my task, but my weariness overcame me and, falling back upon the settee, I dropped into a heavy sleep.

How long I slept I do not know, but it was quite dark when I awoke. Confused by the chlorodyne which I had taken, I lay motionless in a semi-conscious state. The great room with its high walls covered with books loomed darkly all round me. A dim radiance from the moonlight came through the farther window, and against this lighter background I saw that Sir John Bollamore was sitting at his study table. His well-set head and clearly cut profile were sharply outlined against the glimmering square behind him. He bent as I watched him, and I heard the sharp turning of a key and the rasping of metal upon metal. As if in a dream I was vaguely conscious that this was the japanned box which stood in front of him, and that he had drawn something out of it, something squat and uncouth, which now lay before him upon the table. I never realized—it never occurred to my bemuddled and torpid brain that I was intruding upon his privacy, that he imagined himself to be alone in the room. And then, just as it rushed upon my horrified perceptions, and I had half risen to announce my presence, I heard a strange, crisp, metallic clicking, and then the voice.

Yes, it was a woman's voice; there could not be a doubt of it. But a voice so charged with entreaty and with yearning love, that it will ring for ever in my ears. It came with a curious faraway tinkle, but every word was clear, though faint—very faint, for they were the last words of a dying woman.

"I am not really gone, John," said the thin, gasping voice. "I am here at your very elbow, and shall be until we meet once more. I die happy to think that morning and night you will hear my voice. Oh, John, be strong, be strong, until we meet again."

I say that I had risen in order to announce my presence, but I could not do so while the voice was sounding. I could only remain half lying, half sitting, paralysed, astounded, listening to those yearning distant musical words. And he—he was so absorbed that even if I had spoken he might not have heard me. But with the silence of the voice came my half articulated apologies and explanations. He sprang across the room, switched on the electric light, and in its white glare I saw him, his eyes gleaming with anger, his face twisted with passion, as the hapless charwoman may have seen him weeks before.

"Mr. Colmore!" he cried. "You here! What is the meaning of this, sir?"

With halting words I explained it all, my neuralgia, the narcotic, my luckless sleep and singular awakening. As he listened the glow of anger faded from his face, and the sad, impassive mask closed once more over his features.

"My secret is yours, Mr. Colmore," said he. "I have only myself to blame for relaxing my precautions. Half confidences are worse than no confidences, and so you may know all since you know so much. The story may go where you will when I have passed away, but until then I rely upon your sense of honour that no human soul shall hear it from your lips. I am proud still—God help me!—or, at least, I am proud enough to resent that pity which this story would draw upon me. I have smiled at envy, and disregarded hatred, but pity is more than I can tolerate.

"You have heard the source from which the voice comes—that voice which has, as I understand, excited so much curiosity in my household. I am aware of the rumours to which it has given rise. These speculations, whether scandalous or superstitious, are such as I can disregard and forgive. What I should never forgive would be a disloyal spying and eavesdropping in order to satisfy an illicit curiosity. But of that, Mr. Colmore, I acquit you.

"When I was a young man, sir, many years younger than you are now, I was launched upon town without a friend or adviser, and with a purse which brought only too many false friends and false advisers to my side. I drank deeply of the wine of life—if there is a man living who has drunk more deeply he is not a man whom I envy. My purse suffered, my character suffered, my constitution suffered, stimulants became a necessity to me, I was a creature from whom my memory recoils. And it was at that time, the time of my blackest degradation, that God sent into my life the gentlest, sweetest spirit that ever descended as a ministering angel from above. She loved me, broken as I was, loved me, and spent her life in making a man once more of that which had degraded itself to the level of the beasts.

"But a fell disease struck her, and she withered away before my eyes. In the hour of her agony it was never of herself, of her own sufferings and her own death that she thought. It was all of me. The one pang which her fate brought to her was the fear that when her influence was removed I should revert to that which I had been. It was in vain that I made oath to her that no drop of wine would ever cross my lips. She knew only too well the hold that the devil had upon me—she who had striven so to loosen it—and it haunted her night and day the thought that my soul might again be within his grip.

"It was from some friend's gossip of the sick room that she heard of this invention—this phonograph—and with the quick insight of a loving woman she saw how she might use it for her ends. She sent me to London to procure the best which money could buy. With her dying breath she gasped into it the words which have held me straight ever since. Lonely and broken, what else have I in all the world to uphold me? But it is enough. Please God, I shall face her without shame when He is pleased to reunite us! That is my secret, Mr. Colmore, and whilst I live I leave it in your keeping."

The Tomb

H. P. Lovecraft

"Sedibus ut saltem placidis in morte quiescam."
—VIRGIL

In relating the circumstances which have led to my confinement within this refuge for the demented, I am aware that my present position will create a natural doubt of the authenticity of my narrative. It is an unfortunate fact that the bulk of humanity is too limited in its mental vision to weigh with patience and intelligence those isolated phenomena, seen and felt only by a psychologically sensitive few, which lie outside its common experience. Men of broader intellect know that there is no sharp distinction betwixt the real and the unreal; that all things appear as they do only by virtue of the delicate individual physical and mental media through which we are made conscious of them; but the prosaic materialism of the majority condemns as madness the flashes of super-sight which penetrate the common veil of obvious empiricism.

My name is Jervas Dudley, and from earliest childhood I have been a dreamer and a visionary. Wealthy beyond the necessity of a commercial life, and temperamentally unfitted for the formal studies and social recreations of my acquaintances, I have dwelt ever in realms apart from the visible world; spending my youth and adolescence in ancient and little-known books, and in roaming the fields and groves of the region near my ancestral home. I do not think that what I read in these books or saw in these fields and groves was exactly what other boys read and saw there; but of this I must say little, since detailed speech would but confirm those cruel slanders upon my intellect which I sometimes overhear from the whispers of the stealthy attendants around me. It is sufficient for me to relate events without analysing causes.

I have said that I dwelt apart from the visible world, but I have not said that I dwelt alone. This no human creature may do; for lacking the fellowship of the living, he inevitably draws upon the companionship of things that are not, or are no longer, living. Close by my home there lies a singular wooded hollow, in whose twilight deeps I spent most of my time; reading, thinking, and dreaming. Down its moss-covered slopes my first steps of infancy were taken, and around its grotesquely gnarled oak trees my first fancies of boyhood were woven. Well did I come to know the presiding dryads of those trees, and often have I watched their wild dances in the struggling beams of a waning moon—but of these things I must not now speak. I will tell only of the lone tomb in the darkest of the hillside thickets; the deserted tomb of the Hydes, an old and exalted family whose last direct descendant had been laid within its black recesses many decades before my birth.

The vault to which I refer is of ancient granite, weathered and discoloured by the mists and dampness of generations. Excavated back into the hillside, the structure is visible only at the entrance. The door, a ponderous and forbidding slab of stone, hangs upon rusted iron hinges, and is fastened ajar in a queerly sinister way by means of heavy iron chains and padlocks, according to a gruesome fashion of half a century ago. The abode of the race whose scions are here inurned had once crowned the declivity which holds the tomb, but had long since fallen victim to the flames which sprang up from a disastrous stroke of lightning. Of the midnight storm which destroyed this gloomy mansion, the older inhabitants of the region sometimes speak in hushed and uneasy voices; alluding to what they call "divine wrath" in a manner that in later years vaguely increased the always strong fascination which I felt for the forest-darkened sepulchre. One man only had perished in the fire. When the last of the Hydes was buried in this place of shade and stillness, the sad urnful of ashes had come from a distant land; to which the family had repaired when the mansion burned down. No one remains to lay flowers before the granite portal, and few care to brave the depressing shadows which seem to linger strangely about the water-worn stones.

I shall never forget the afternoon when first I stumbled upon the half-hidden house of death. It was in mid-summer, when the alchemy of Nature transmutes the sylvan landscape to one vivid and almost homogeneous mass of green; when the senses are well-nigh intoxicated with the surging seas of moist verdure and the subtly indefinable odours of the soil and the vegetation. In such surroundings the mind loses its perspective; time and space become trivial and unreal, and echoes of a forgotten prehistoric past beat insistently upon the enthralled consciousness. All day I had been wandering through the mystic groves of the hollow; thinking thoughts I need not discuss, and conversing with things I need not name. In years a child of ten, I had seen and heard many wonders unknown to the throng; and was oddly aged in certain respects. When, upon forcing my way between two savage clumps of briers, I suddenly encountered the entrance of the vault, I had no knowledge of what I had discovered. The dark blocks of granite, the door so curiously ajar, and the funereal carvings above the arch, aroused in me no associations of mournful or terrible character. Of graves and tombs I knew and imagined much, but had on account of my peculiar temperament been kept from all personal contact with churchyards and cemeteries. The strange stone house on the woodland slope was to me only a source of interest and speculation; and its cold, damp interior, into which I vainly peered through the aperture so tantalisingly left, contained for me no hint of death or decay. But in that instant of curiosity was born the madly unreasoning desire which has brought me to this hell of confinement. Spurred on by a voice which must have come from the hideous soul of the forest, I resolved to enter the beckoning gloom in spite of the ponderous chains which barred my passage. In the waning light of day I alternately rattled the rusty impediments with a view to throwing wide the stone door, and essayed to squeeze my slight form through the space already provided; but neither plan met with success. At first curious, I was now frantic; and when in the thickening twilight I returned to my home, I had sworn to the hundred gods of the grove that at any cost I would some day force an entrance to the black, chilly depths that seemed calling out to me. The physician with the iron-grey beard who comes each day to my room once told a visitor that this decision marked the beginning of a pitiful monomania; but I will leave final judgment to my readers when they shall have learnt all.

The months following my discovery were spent in futile attempts to force the complicated padlock of the slightly open vault, and in carefully guarded inquiries regarding the nature and history of the structure. With the traditionally receptive ears of the small boy, I learned much; though an habitual secretiveness caused me to tell no one of my information or my resolve. It is perhaps worth mentioning that I was not at all surprised or terrified on learning of the nature of the vault. My rather original ideas regarding life and death had caused me to associate the cold clay with the breathing body in a vague fashion; and I felt that the great and sinister family of the burned-down mansion was in some way represented within the stone space I sought to explore. Mumbled tales of the weird rites and godless revels of bygone years in the ancient hall gave to me a new and potent interest in the tomb, before whose door I would sit for hours at a time each day. Once I thrust a candle within the nearly closed entrance, but could see nothing save a flight of damp stone steps leading downward. The odour of the place repelled yet bewitched me. I felt I had known it before, in a past remote beyond all recollection; beyond even my tenancy of the body I now possess.

The year after I first beheld the tomb, I stumbled upon a worm-eaten translation of Plutarch's *Lives* in the book-filled attic of my home. Reading the life of Theseus, I was much impressed by that passage telling of the great stone beneath which the boyish hero was to find his tokens of destiny whenever he should become old enough to lift its enormous weight. This legend had the effect of dispelling my keenest impatience to enter the vault, for it made me feel that the time was not yet ripe. Later, I told myself, I should grow to a strength and ingenuity which might enable me to unfasten the heavily chained door with ease; but until then I would do better by conforming to what seemed the will of Fate.

Accordingly my watches by the dank portal became less persistent, and much of my time was spent in other though equally strange pursuits. I would sometimes rise very quietly in the night, stealing out to walk in those churchyards and places of burial from which I had been kept by my parents. What I did there I may not say, for I am not now sure of the reality of certain things; but I know that on the day after such a nocturnal ramble I would often astonish those about me with my knowledge of topics almost forgotten for many generations. It was after a night like this that I shocked the community with a queer conceit about the burial of the rich and celebrated Squire Brewster, a maker of local history who was interred in 1711, and whose slate headstone, bearing a graven skull and crossbones, was slowly crumbling to powder. In a moment of childish imagination I vowed not only that the undertaker, Goodman Simpson, had stolen the silver-buckled shoes, silken hose, and satin small-clothes of the deceased before burial; but that the Squire himself, not fully inanimate, had turned twice in his mound-covered coffin on the day after interment.

But the idea of entering the tomb never left my thoughts; being indeed stimulated by the unexpected genealogical discovery that my own maternal ancestry possessed at least a slight link with the supposedly extinct family of the Hydes. Last of my paternal race, I was likewise the last of this older and more mysterious line. I began to feel that the tomb was mine, and to look forward with hot eagerness to the time when I might pass within that stone door and down those slimy stone steps in the dark. I now formed the habit of listening very intently at the slightly open portal, choosing my favourite hours of midnight stillness for the odd vigil. By the time I came of age, I had made a small clearing in the thicket before the mould-stained facade of the hillside, allowing the surrounding vegetation to encircle and overhang the space like the walls and roof of a sylvan bower. This bower was my temple, the fastened door my shrine, and here I would lie outstretched on the mossy ground, thinking strange thoughts and dreaming strange dreams.

The night of the first revelation was a sultry one. I must have fallen asleep from fatigue, for it was with a distinct sense of awakening that I heard the voices. Of those tones and accents I hesitate to speak; of their quality I will not speak; but I may say that they presented certain uncanny differences in vocabulary, pronunciation, and mode of utterance. Every shade of New England dialect, from the uncouth syllables of the Puritan colonists to the precise rhetoric of fifty years ago, seemed represented in that shadowy colloquy, though it was only later that I noticed the fact. At the time, indeed, my attention was distracted from this matter by another phenomenon; a phenomenon so fleeting that I could not take oath upon its reality. I barely fancied that as I awoke, a *light* had been hurriedly extinguished within the sunken sepulchre. I do not think I was either astounded or panic-stricken, but I know that I was greatly and permanently changed that night. Upon returning home I went with much directness to a rotting chest in the attic, wherein I found the key which next day unlocked with ease the barrier I had so long stormed in vain.

It was in the soft glow of late afternoon that I first entered the vault on the abandoned slope. A spell was upon me, and my heart leaped with an exultation I can but ill describe. As I closed the door behind me and descended the dripping steps by the light of my lone candle, I seemed to know the way; and though the candle sputtered with the stifling reek of the place, I felt singularly at home in the musty, charnel-house air. Looking about me, I beheld many marble slabs bearing coffins, or the remains of coffins. Some of these were sealed and intact, but others had nearly vanished, leaving the silver handles and plates isolated amidst certain curious heaps of whitish dust. Upon one plate I read the name of Sir Geoffrey Hyde, who had come from Sussex in 1640 and died here a few years later. In a conspicuous alcove was one fairly well-preserved and untenanted casket, adorned with a single name which brought to me both a smile and a shudder. An odd impulse caused me to climb upon the broad slab, extinguish my candle, and lie down within the vacant box.

In the grey light of dawn I staggered from the vault and locked the chain of the door behind me. I was no longer a young man, though but twenty-one winters had chilled my bodily frame. Early-rising villagers who observed my homeward progress looked at me strangely, and marvelled at the signs of ribald revelry which they saw in one whose life was known to be sober and solitary. I did not appear before my parents till after a long and refreshing sleep.

Henceforward I haunted the tomb each night; seeing, hearing, and doing things I must never reveal. My speech, always susceptible to environmental influences, was the first thing to succumb to the change; and my suddenly acquired archaism of diction was soon remarked upon. Later a queer boldness and recklessness came into my demeanour, till I unconsciously grew to possess the bearing of a man of the world despite my lifelong seclusion. My formerly silent tongue waxed voluble with the easy grace of a Chesterfield or the godless cynicism of a Rochester. I displayed a peculiar erudition utterly unlike the fantastic, monkish lore over which I had pored in youth; and covered the flyleaves of my books with facile impromptu epigrams which brought up suggestions of Gay, Prior, and the sprightliest of the Augustan wits and rimesters. One morning at breakfast I came close to disaster by declaiming in palpably liquorish accents an effusion of eighteenth-century Bacchanalian mirth; a bit of Georgian playfulness never recorded in a book, which ran something like this:

Come hither, my lads, with your tankards of ale,
And drink to the present before it shall fail;
Pile each on your platter a mountain of beef,
For 'tis eating and drinking that bring us relief:
  So fill up your glass,
  For life will soon pass;
When you're dead ye'll ne'er drink to your king or your lass!

Anacreon had a red nose, so they say;
But what's a red nose if ye're happy and gay?
Gad split me! I'd rather be red whilst I'm here,
Than white as a lily—and dead half a year!
  So Betty, my miss,
  Come give me a kiss;
In hell there's no innkeeper's daughter like this!

Young Harry, propp'd up just as straight as he's able,
Will soon lose his wig and slip under the table;
But fill up your goblets and pass 'em around—
Better under the table than under the ground!
  So revel and chaff
  As ye thirstily quaff:
Under six feet of dirt 'tis less easy to laugh!

The fiend strike me blue! I'm scarce able to walk,
And damn me if I can stand upright or talk!

Here, landlord, bid Betty to summon a chair;
I'll try home for a while, for my wife is not there!
    So lend me a hand;
    I'm not able to stand,
But I'm gay whilst I linger on top of the land!

About this time I conceived my present fear of fire and thunderstorms. Previously indifferent to such things, I had now an unspeakable horror of them; and would retire to the innermost recesses of the house whenever the heavens threatened an electrical display. A favourite haunt of mine during the day was the ruined cellar of the mansion that had burned down, and in fancy I would picture the structure as it had been in its prime. On one occasion I startled a villager by leading him confidently to a shallow sub-cellar, of whose existence I seemed to know in spite of the fact that it had been unseen and forgotten for many generations.

At last came that which I had long feared. My parents, alarmed at the altered manner and appearance of their only son, commenced to exert over my movements a kindly espionage which threatened to result in disaster. I had told no one of my visits to the tomb, having guarded my secret purpose with religious zeal since childhood; but now I was forced to exercise care in threading the mazes of the wooded hollow, that I might throw off a possible pursuer. My key to the vault I kept suspended from a cord about my neck, its presence known only to me. I never carried out of the sepulchre any of the things I came upon whilst within its walls.

One morning as I emerged from the damp tomb and fastened the chain of the portal with none too steady hand, I beheld in an adjacent thicket the dreaded face of a watcher. Surely the end was near; for my bower was discovered, and the objective of my nocturnal journeys revealed. The man did not accost me, so I hastened home in an effort to overhear what he might report to my careworn father. Were my sojourns beyond the chained door about to be proclaimed to the world? Imagine my delighted astonishment on hearing the spy inform my parent in a cautious whisper *that I had spent the night in the bower outside the tomb;* my sleep-filmed eyes fixed upon the crevice where the padlocked portal stood ajar! By what miracle had the watcher been thus deluded? I was now convinced that a supernatural agency protected me. Made bold by this heaven-sent circumstance, I began to resume perfect openness in going to the vault; confident that no one could witness my entrance. For a week I tasted to the full the joys of that charnel conviviality which I must not describe, when the thing happened, and I was borne away to this accursed abode of sorrow and monotony.

I should not have ventured out that night; for the taint of thunder was in the clouds, and a hellish phosphorescence rose from the rank swamp at the bottom of the hollow. The call of the dead, too, was different. Instead of the hillside tomb, it was the charred cellar on the crest of the slope whose presiding daemon beckoned to me with unseen fingers. As I emerged from an intervening grove upon the plain before the ruin, I beheld in the misty moonlight a thing I had always vaguely expected. The mansion, gone for a century, once more reared its stately height to the raptured vision; every window ablaze with the splendour of many candles. Up the long drive rolled the coaches of the Boston gentry, whilst on foot came a numerous assemblage of powdered exquisites from the neighbouring mansions. With this throng I mingled, though I knew I belonged with the hosts rather than with the guests. Inside the hall were music, laughter, and wine on every hand. Several faces I recognised; though I should have known them better had they been shrivelled or eaten away by death and decomposition. Amidst a wild and reckless throng I was the wildest and most abandoned. Gay blasphemy poured in torrents from my lips, and in my shocking sallies I heeded no law of God, Man, or Nature. Suddenly a peal of thunder, resonant even above the din of the swinish revelry, clave the very roof and laid a hush of fear upon the boisterous company. Red tongues of flame and searing gusts of heat engulfed the house; and the roysterers, struck with terror at the descent of a calamity which seemed to transcend the bounds of unguided Nature, fled shrieking into the night. I alone remained, riveted to my seat by a grovelling fear which I had never felt before. And then a second horror took possession of my soul. Burnt alive to ashes, my body dispersed by the four winds, *I might never lie in the tomb of the Hydes!* Was not my coffin prepared for me? Had I not a right to rest till eternity amongst the descendants of Sir Geoffrey Hyde? Aye! I would claim my heritage of death, even though my soul go seeking through the ages for another corporeal tenement to represent it on that vacant slab in the alcove of the vault. *Jervas Hyde* should never share the sad fate of Palinurus!

As the phantom of the burning house faded, I found myself screaming and struggling madly in the arms of two men, one of whom was the spy who had followed me to the tomb. Rain was pouring down in torrents, and upon the southern horizon were flashes of the lightning that had so lately passed over our heads. My father, his face lined with sorrow, stood by as I shouted my demands to be laid within the tomb; frequently admonishing my captors to treat me as gently as they could. A blackened circle on the floor of the ruined cellar told of a violent stroke from the heavens; and from this spot a group of curious villagers with lanterns were prying a small box of antique workmanship which the thunderbolt had brought to light. Ceasing my futile and now objectless writhing, I watched the spectators as they viewed the treasure-trove, and was permitted to share in their discoveries. The box, whose fastenings were broken by the stroke which had unearthed it, contained many papers and objects of value; but I had eyes for one thing alone. It was the porcelain miniature of a young man in a smartly curled bag-wig, and bore the initials "J. H." The face was such that as I gazed, I might well have been studying my mirror.

On the following day I was brought to this room with the barred windows, but I have been kept informed of certain things through an aged and simple-minded servitor, for whom I bore a fondness in infancy, and who like me loves the churchyard. What I have dared relate of my experiences within the vault has brought me only pitying smiles. My father, who visits me frequently, declares that at no time did I pass the chained portal, and swears that the rusted padlock had not been touched for fifty years when he examined it. He even says that all the village knew of my journeys to the tomb, and that I was often watched as I slept in the bower outside the grim facade, my half-open eyes fixed on the crevice that leads to the interior. Against these assertions I have no tangible proof to offer, since my key to the padlock was lost in the struggle on that night of horrors. The strange things of the past which I learnt during those nocturnal meetings with the dead he dismisses as the fruits of my lifelong and omnivorous browsing amongst the ancient volumes of the family library. Had it not been for my old servant Hiram, I should have by this time become quite convinced of my madness.

But Hiram, loyal to the last, has held faith in me, and has done that which impels me to make public at least a part of my story. A week ago he burst open the lock which chains the door of the tomb perpetually ajar, and descended with a lantern into the murky depths. On a slab in an alcove he found an old but empty coffin whose tarnished plate bears the single word "Jervas." In that coffin and in that vault they have promised me I shall be buried.

Word Cloud Classics

12 Years a Slave

A Christmas Carol and Other Holiday Treasures

Adventures of Huckleberry Finn

The Adventures of Sherlock Holmes

Aesop's Fables

The Age of Innocence

Alice's Adventures in Wonderland and Through the Looking-Glass

Anna Karenina

Anne of Green Gables

The Art of War

The Autobiography of Benjamin Franklin and Other Writings

The Awakening and Other Stories

Black Beauty

The Brothers Grimm 101 Fairy Tales

The Brothers Grimm Volume II: 110 Grimmer Fairy Tales

Bulfinch's Mythology: Stories of Gods and Heroes

The Call of the Wild and Other Stories

Classic Horror Tales

Classic Westerns: Zane Grey

Common Sense and Selected Works of Thomas Paine

The Count of Monte Cristo

Crime and Punishment

Don Quixote

Dracula

Emma

Frankenstein

Great Expectations

Hans Christian Andersen Tales

H. P. Lovecraft Cthulhu Mythos Tales

Inferno

Jane Eyre

The Jungle Book

Lady Chatterley's Lover

Leaves of Grass

The Legend of Sleepy Hollow and Other Tales

Les Misérables

Little Women

Word Cloud Classics

Madame Bovary

Mansfield Park

The Merry Adventures of Robin Hood

Moby-Dick

My Ántonia

Narrative of the Life of Frederick Douglass and Other Works

Northanger Abbey

Odyssey

Persuasion

Peter Pan

The Phantom of the Opera

The Picture of Dorian Gray

The Poetry of Emily Dickinson

Pride and Prejudice

The Prince and Other Writings

The Red Badge of Courage and Other Stories

The Romantic Poets

The Scarlet Letter

The Secret Garden

Selected Works of Alexander Hamilton

Sense and Sensibility

Shakespeare's Sonnets and Other Poems

Strange Case of Dr. Jekyll and Mr. Hyde & Other Stories

Tarzan of the Apes & The Return of Tarzan

The Three Musketeers

Treasure Island

Twenty Thousand Leagues Under the Sea

Uncle Tom's Cabin, or Life Among the Lowly

The U.S. Constitution and Other Key American Writings

Walden and Civil Disobedience

The Wizard of Oz

Wuthering Heights

The Brothers Grimm
101 Fairy Tales

Word Cloud Classics

Adventures of Huckleberry Finn

The Adventures of Sherlock Holmes

Aesop's Fables

Alice's Adventures in Wonderland and Through the Looking-Glass

Anna Karenina

Anne of Green Gables

The Art of War

The Autobiography of Benjamin Franklin and Other Writings

The Awakening and Other Stories

The Brothers Grimm 101 Fairy Tales

The Brothers Grimm Volume II: 110 Grimmer Fairy Tales

Classic Horror Tales

Classic Westerns: Zane Grey

The Count of Monte Cristo

Crime and Punishment

Don Quixote

Frankenstein

Hans Christian Andersen Tales

H. P. Lovecraft Cthulhu Mythos Tales

The Jungle Book

Leaves of Grass

Les Misérables

My Ántonia

Narrative of the Life of Frederick Douglass and Other Works

Odyssey

Peter Pan

The Phantom of the Opera

The Picture of Dorian Gray

Pride and Prejudice

The Romantic Poets

Selected Works of Alexander Hamilton

Sense and Sensibility

Shakespeare's Sonnets and Other Poems

Treasure Island

Twenty Thousand Leagues Under the Sea

Uncle Tom's Cabin, or Life Among the Lowly

The Wizard of Oz

Wuthering Heights

The Brothers Grimm
101 Fairy Tales

Word Cloud Classics
San Diego

Canterbury Classics
An imprint of Printers Row Publishing Group
9717 Pacific Heights Blvd, San Diego, CA 92121
www.canterburyclassicsbooks.com • mail@canterburyclassicsbooks.com

Printers Row Publishing Group is a division of Readerlink Distribution Services, LLC.
Canterbury Classics and Word Cloud Classics are registered trademarks of Readerlink Distribution Services, LLC.

Correspondence concerning the content of this book should be sent to Canterbury Classics, Editorial Department, at the above address.

Publisher: Peter Norton • Associate Publisher: Ana Parker
Art Director: Charles McStravick
Senior Developmental Editor: April Graham
Publishing/Editorial Team: Kathryn C. Dalby, JoAnn Padgett, Melinda Allman, Traci Douglas
Production/Design Team: Jonathan Lopes, Rusty von Dyl, Beno Chan, Julie Greene, Rosemary Rae

Spine art: gio_banfi/DigitalVision Vectors via Getty Images
Endpapers: Pobytov/DigitalVision Vectors via Getty Images

ISBN: 978-1-6672-0317-1

Printed in China
27 26 25 24 23   2 3 4 5 6

MIX
Paper | Supporting responsible forestry
FSC® C144853
FSC www.fsc.org

Editor's Note: These works have been published in their original form to preserve the authors' intent and style.

CONTENTS

1. THE FROG-KING, OR IRON HENRY

In old times when wishing still helped one, there lived a king whose daughters were all beautiful, but the youngest was so beautiful that the sun itself, which has seen so much, was astonished whenever it shone in her face. Close by the King's castle lay a great dark forest, and under an old lime tree in the forest was a well, and when the day was very warm, the King's child went out into the forest and sat down by the side of the cool fountain, and when she was bored she took a golden ball, and threw it up on high and caught it, and this ball was her favorite plaything.

Now it so happened that on one occasion the princess's golden ball did not fall into the little hand which she was holding up for it, but on to the ground beyond, and rolled straight into the water. The King's daughter followed it with her eyes, but it vanished, and the well was deep, so deep that the bottom could not be seen. At this she began to cry, and cried louder and louder, and could not be comforted.

And as she thus lamented someone said to her, "What ails you, King's daughter? Your tears would melt a heart of stone."

She looked round to the side from where the voice came, and saw a frog stretching forth its thick, ugly head from the water. "Ah! Old water-splasher, is it you?" said she; "I am weeping for my golden ball, which has fallen into the well."

"Be quiet, and do not weep," answered the frog, "I can help you, but what will you give me if I bring your plaything up again?"

"Whatever you will have, dear frog," said she—"My clothes, my pearls and jewels, and even the golden crown which I am wearing."

The frog answered, "I do not care for your clothes, your pearls and jewels, or your golden crown, but if you will love me and let me be your companion and playmate, and sit by you at your little table, and eat off your little golden plate, and drink out of your little cup, and sleep in your little bed—if you will promise me this I will go down below, and bring you your golden ball up again."

"Oh yes," said she, "I promise you all you wish, if you will but bring me my ball back again." She, however, thought, "How the silly frog does talk! He lives in the water with the other frogs, and croaks, and can be no companion to any human being!"

But the frog when he had received this promise, put his head into the water and sank down, and in a short while came swimming up again with the ball in his mouth, and threw it on the grass. The King's daughter was delighted to see her pretty plaything once more, and picked it up, and ran away with it.

"Wait, wait," said the frog. "Take me with you. I can't run as you can."

But what did it avail him to scream his *croak*, *croak*, after her, as loudly as he could? She did not listen to it, but ran home and soon forgot the poor frog, who was forced to go back into his well again.

The next day when she had seated herself at table with the King and all the courtiers, and was eating from her little golden plate, something came creeping *splish splash*, *splish splash*, up the marble staircase, and when it had got to the top, it knocked at the door and cried, "Princess, youngest princess, open the door for me."

She ran to see who was outside, but when she opened the door, there sat the frog in front of it. Then she slammed the door, in great haste, sat down to dinner again, and was quite frightened. The King saw plainly that her heart was beating violently, and said, "My child, what are you so afraid of? Is there perchance a giant outside who wants to carry you away?"

"Ah, no," replied she. "It is no giant but a disgusting frog."

"What does a frog want with you?"

"Ah, dear father, yesterday as I was in the forest sitting by the well, playing, my golden ball fell into the water. And because I cried so, the frog brought it out again for me, and because he so insisted, I promised him he should be my companion, but I never thought he would be able to come out of his water! And now he is outside there, and wants to come in to me."

In the meantime it knocked a second time, and cried,

"Princess! Youngest princess!
Open the door for me!
Do you not know what you said to me
Yesterday by the cool waters of the fountain?
Princess, youngest princess!
Open the door for me!"

Then said the King, "That which you have promised you must perform. Go and let him in."

She went and opened the door, and the frog hopped in and followed her, step by step, to her chair. There he sat and cried, "Lift me up beside you." She delayed, until at last the King commanded her to do it. When the frog was once on the chair he wanted to be on the table, and when he was on the table he said, "Now, push your little golden plate nearer to me that we may eat together." She did this, but it was easy to see that she did not do it willingly. The frog enjoyed what he ate, but almost every mouthful she took choked her. At length he said, "I have eaten and am satisfied; now I am tired, carry me into your little room and make your little silken bed ready, and we will both lie down and go to sleep."

The King's daughter began to cry, for she was afraid of the cold frog which she did not like to touch, and which was now to sleep in her pretty, clean little bed. But the King grew angry and said, "He who helped you when you were in trouble ought not be despised by you afterwards."

So she took hold of the frog with two fingers, carried him upstairs, and put him in a corner. But when she was in bed he crept to her and said, "I am tired, I want to sleep as well as you, lift me up or I will tell your father."

Then she was terribly angry, and took him up and threw him with all her might against the wall. "Now, you will be quiet, odious frog," said she.

But when he fell down he was no frog but a King's son with beautiful kind eyes. And it came to pass that, with her father's consent, he became her dear companion and husband. He told her how he had been bewitched by a wicked witch, and how no one could have delivered him from the well but herself, and that tomorrow they would go together into his Kingdom. Then they went to sleep, and next morning when the sun awoke them, a carriage came driving up with eight white horses, which had white ostrich feathers on their heads, and were harnessed with golden chains, and behind stood the young King's servant Faithful Henry. Faithful Henry had been so unhappy when his master was changed into a frog, that he had caused three iron bands to be laid round his heart, lest it should burst with grief and sadness. The carriage was to conduct the young King into his Kingdom. Faithful Henry helped them both in, and placed himself behind again, and was full of joy because of this deliverance. And when they had driven a part of the way the King's son heard a cracking behind him as if something had broken. So he turned round and cried, "Henry, the carriage is breaking."

"No, master, it is not the carriage. It is a band from my heart, which was put there in my great pain when you were a frog and imprisoned in the well." Again and once again while they were on their way something cracked, and each time the King's son thought the carriage was breaking; but it was only the bands which were springing from the heart of faithful Henry because his master was set free and was happy.

2. *CAT AND MOUSE IN PARTNERSHIP*

A certain cat had made the acquaintance of a mouse, and had said so much to her about the great love and friendship she felt for her, that at length the mouse agreed that they should live and keep house together. "But we must make a provision for winter, or else we shall suffer from hunger," said the cat, "and you, little mouse, cannot venture everywhere, or you will be caught in a trap some day." The good advice was followed, and a pot of fat was bought, but they did not know where to put it. At length, after much consideration, the cat said, "I know no place where it will be better stored up than in the church, for no one dares take anything away from there. We will set it beneath the altar, and not touch it until we are really in need of it." So the pot was placed in safety, but it was not long before the cat had a great yearning for it, and said to the mouse, "I want to tell you something, little mouse; my cousin has brought a little son into the world, and has asked me to be godmother; he is white with brown spots, and I am to hold him over the font at the christening. Let me go out today, and you look after the house by yourself."

"Yes, yes," answered the mouse, "by all means go, and if you get anything very good, think of me, I should like a drop of sweet red christening wine, too."

All this, however, was untrue; the cat had no cousin, and had not been asked to be godmother. She went straight to the church, stole to the pot of fat, began to lick at it, and licked the top of the fat off. Then she took a walk upon the roofs of the town, looked out for opportunities, and then stretched herself in the sun, and licked her lips whenever she thought of the pot of fat, and not until it was evening did she return home.

"Well, here you are again," said the mouse, "no doubt you have had a merry day."

"All went off well," answered the cat.

"What name did they give the child?"

"Top off!" said the cat quite coolly.

"Top off!" cried the mouse, "that is a very odd and uncommon name, is it a usual one in your family?"

"What does it matter?" said the cat."It is no worse than Crumb-stealer, as your god-children are called."

Before long the cat was seized by another fit of longing. She said to the mouse, "You must do me a favor, and once more manage the house for a day alone. I am again asked to be godmother, and, as the child has a white ring round its neck, I cannot refuse." The good mouse consented, but the cat crept behind the town walls to the church, and devoured half the pot of fat. "Nothing ever seems so good as what one keeps to oneself," said she, and was quite satisfied with her day's work.

When she went home the mouse inquired, "And what was this child christened?"

"Half-done," answered the cat.

"Half-done! What are you saying? I never heard the name in my life, I'll wager anything it is not in the calendar of saints!"

The cat's mouth soon began to water for some more licking. "All good things go in threes," said she, "I am asked to stand godmother again. The child is quite black, only it has white paws, but with that exception, it has not a single white hair on its whole body; this only happens once every few years, you will let me go, won't you?"

"Top-off! Half-done!" answered the mouse. "They are such odd names, they make me very thoughtful."

"You sit at home," said the cat, "in your dark-grey fur coat and long tail, and are filled with fancies, that's because you do not go out in the daytime." During the cat's absence the mouse cleaned the house, and put it in order but the greedy cat entirely emptied the pot of fat. "When everything is eaten up one has some peace," said she to herself, and well filled and fat she did not return home till night. The mouse at once asked what name had been given to the third child. "It will not please you more than the others," said the cat. "He is called All-gone."

"All-gone," cried the mouse, "that is the most suspicious name of all! I have never seen it in print. All-gone; what can that mean?" and she shook her head, curled herself up, and lay down to sleep.

From this time forth no one invited the cat to be godmother, but when the winter had come and there was no longer anything to be found outside, the mouse thought of their provision, and said, "Come cat, we will go to our pot of fat which we have stored up for ourselves—we shall enjoy that."

"Yes," answered the cat, "you will enjoy it as much as you would enjoy sticking that dainty tongue of yours out of the window." They set out on their way, but when they arrived, the pot of fat certainly was still in its place, but it was empty.

"Alas!" said the mouse. "Now I see what has happened, now it comes to light! You are a true friend! You have devoured all when you were standing godmother. First top off, then half done, then—"

"Will you hold your tongue," cried the cat, "one word more and I will eat you too."

"All gone" was already on the poor mouse's lips; scarcely had she spoken it before the cat sprang on her, seized her, and swallowed her down. And that is the way of the world.

3. OUR LADY'S CHILD

Near a great forest dwelt a woodcutter with his wife, who had an only child, a little girl three years old. They were so poor, however, that they no longer had daily bread, and did not know how to get food for her. One morning the woodcutter went out sorrowfully to his work in the forest, and while he was cutting wood, suddenly there stood before him a tall and beautiful woman with a crown of shining stars on her head, who said to him, "I am the Virgin Mary, mother of the child Jesus. You are poor and needy, bring your child to me, I will take her with me and be her mother, and care for her." The woodcutter obeyed, brought his child, and gave her to the Virgin Mary, who took her up to heaven with her. There the child fared well, ate sugar-cakes, and drank sweet milk, and her clothes were of gold, and the little angels played with her. And when she was fourteen years of age, the Virgin Mary called her one day and said, "Dear child, I am about to make a long journey, so take into your keeping the keys of the thirteen doors of heaven. Twelve of these you may open, and behold the glory which is within them, but the thirteenth, to which this little key belongs, is forbidden. Beware of opening it, or you will bring misery on yourself." The girl promised to be obedient, and when the Virgin Mary was gone, she began to examine the dwellings of the kingdom of heaven. Each day she opened one of them, until she had made the round of the twelve. In each of them sat one of the Apostles in the midst of a great light, and she rejoiced in all the magnificence and splendor, and the little angels who always accompanied her rejoiced with her. Then the forbidden door alone remained, and she felt a great desire to know what could be hidden behind it, and said to the angels, "I will not quite open it, and I will not go inside it, but I will unlock it so that we can just see a little through the opening."

"Oh no," said the little angels, "that would be a sin. The Virgin Mary has forbidden it, and it might easily cause you unhappiness."

Then she was silent, but the desire in her heart was not stilled, but gnawed there and tormented her, and let her have no rest. And once when the angels had all gone out, she thought, "Now I am quite alone, and I could peep in. If I do it, no one will ever know." She sought out the key, and when she had got it in her hand, she put it in the lock, and when she had put it in, she turned it round as well. Then the door sprang open, and she saw there the Trinity sitting in fire and splendor. She stayed there awhile, and looked at everything in amazement; then she touched the light a little with her finger, and her finger became quite golden. Immediately a great fear fell on her. She shut the door violently, and ran away. Her terror too would not quit her, let her do what she might, and her heart beat continually and would not be still; the gold too stayed on her finger, and would not go away, no matter how much she rubbed it and washed it.

It was not long before the Virgin Mary came back from her journey. She called the girl before her, and asked to have the keys of heaven back. When the maiden gave her the bunch, the Virgin looked into her eyes and said, "Have you not opened the thirteenth door also?"

"No," she replied.

Then she laid her hand on the girl's heart, and felt how it beat and beat, and saw right well that she had disobeyed her order and had opened the door. Then she said once again, "Are you certain that you have not done it?"

"Yes," said the girl, for the second time.

Then she perceived the finger which had become golden from touching the fire of heaven, and saw well that the child had sinned, and said for the third time "Have you not done it?"

"No," said the girl for the third time.

Then said the Virgin Mary, "You have not obeyed me, and besides that you have lied; you are no longer worthy to be in heaven."

Then the girl fell into a deep sleep, and when she awoke she lay on the earth below, and in the midst of a wilderness. She wanted to cry out, but she could bring forth no sound. She sprang up and wanted to run away, but wherever she turned herself, she was continually held back by thick hedges of thorns through which she could not break. In the desert in which she was imprisoned, there stood an old hollow tree, and this had to be her dwelling-place. Into this she crept when night came, and here she slept. Here, too, she found a shelter from storm and rain, but it was a miserable life, and bitterly did she weep when she remembered how happy she had been in heaven, and how the angels had played with her. Roots and wild berries were her only food, and for these she searched as far as she could go. In the autumn she picked up the fallen nuts and leaves, and carried them into the hole. The nuts were her food in winter, and when snow and ice came, she crept amongst the leaves like a poor little animal that she might not freeze. Before long her clothes were all torn, and one bit of them after another fell off her. As soon, however, as the sun shone warm again, she went out and sat in front of the tree, and her long hair covered her on all sides like a mantle. Thus she sat year after year, and felt the pain and the misery of the world.

One day, when the trees were once more clothed in fresh green, the King of the country was hunting in the forest, and followed a deer, and as it had fled into the thicket which shut in this part of the forest, he got off his horse, tore the bushes asunder, and cut himself a path with his sword. When he had at last forced his way through, he saw a wonderfully beautiful maiden sitting under the tree; and she sat there and was entirely covered with her golden hair down to her very feet. He stood still and looked at her full of surprise, then he spoke to her and said, "Who are you? Why are you sitting here in the wilderness?" But she gave no answer, for she could not open her mouth. The King continued, "Will you go with me to my castle?" Then she just nodded her head a little. The King took her in his arms, carried her to his horse, and rode home with her, and when he reached the royal castle he caused her to be dressed in beautiful garments, and gave her all things in abundance. Although she could not speak, she was still so beautiful and charming that he began to love her with all his heart, and it was not long before he married her.

After a year or so had passed, the Queen brought a son into the world. Thereupon the Virgin Mary appeared to her in the night when she lay in her bed alone, and said, "If you will tell the truth and confess that you did unlock the forbidden door, I will open your mouth and give you back your speech, but if you persevere in your sin, and deny obstinately, I will take your newborn child away with me."

Then the queen was permitted to answer, but she remained hard, and said, "No, I did not open the forbidden door;" and the Virgin Mary took the newborn child from her arms, and vanished with it. Next morning when the child was not to be found, it was whispered among the people that the Queen was a man-eater, and had killed her own child. She heard all this and could say nothing to the contrary, but the King would not believe it, for he loved her so much.

When a year had gone by the Queen again bore a son, and in the night the Virgin Mary again came to her, and said, "If you will confess that you opened the forbidden door, I will give you your child back and untie your tongue; but if you continue in sin and deny it, I will take away with me this new child also."

Then the Queen again said, "No, I did not open the forbidden door;" and the Virgin took the child out of her arms, and away with her to heaven. Next morning, when this child also had disappeared, the people declared quite loudly that the Queen had devoured it, and the King's councilors demanded that she should be brought to justice. The King, however, loved her so dearly that he would not believe it, and commanded the councilors under pain of death not to say any more about it.

The following year the Queen gave birth to a beautiful little daughter, and for the third time the Virgin Mary appeared to her in the night and said, "Follow me." She took the Queen by the hand and led her to heaven, and showed her there her two eldest children, who smiled at her, and were playing with the ball of the world. When the Queen rejoiced at this, the Virgin Mary said, "Is your heart not yet softened? If you will own that you opened the forbidden door, I will give you back your two little sons."

But for the third time the Queen answered, "No, I did not open the forbidden door." Then the Virgin let her sink down to earth once more, and took from her likewise her third child.

Next morning, when the loss was reported abroad, all the people cried loudly, "The Queen is a man-eater. She must be judged," and the King was no longer able to restrain his councilors.

Thereupon a trial was held, and as she could not answer, and defend herself, she was condemned to be burned alive. The wood was got together, and when she was fast bound to the stake, and the fire began to burn round about her, the hard ice of pride melted, her heart was moved by repentance, and she thought, "If I could but confess before my death that I opened the door." Then her voice came back to her, and she cried out loudly, "Yes, Mary, I did it;" and straight-away rain fell from the sky and extinguished the flames of fire, and a light broke forth above her, and the Virgin Mary descended with the two little sons by her side, and the newborn daughter in her arms.

She spoke kindly to her, and said, "He who repents his sin and acknowledges it, is forgiven." Then she gave her the three children, untied her tongue, and granted her happiness for her whole life.

4. THE STORY OF THE YOUTH WHO WENT FORTH TO LEARN WHAT FEAR WAS

A certain father had two sons, the elder of whom was smart and sensible, and could do everything, but the younger was stupid and could neither learn nor understand anything, and when people saw him they said, "There's a fellow who will give his father some trouble!"

When anything had to be done, it was always the elder who was forced to do it; but if his father asked him to fetch anything when it was late, or in the night-time, and the way led through the churchyard, or any other dismal place, he answered, "Oh, no, father, I'll not go there, it makes me shudder!" for he was afraid. Or when stories were told by the fire at night which made the flesh creep, the listeners sometimes said, "Oh, it makes us shudder!"

The younger sat in a corner and listened with the rest of them, and could not imagine what they could mean. "They are always saying 'it makes me shudder, it makes me shudder!' It does not make me shudder," thought he. "That, too, must be an art of which I understand nothing."

Now it came to pass that his father said to him one day, "Listen to me, you fellow in the corner there, you are growing tall and strong, and you too must learn something by which you can earn your living. Look how your brother works, but you do not even earn your salt."

"Well, father," he replied, "I am quite willing to learn something—indeed, if it could but be managed, I should like to learn how to shudder. I don't understand that at all yet."

The elder brother smiled when he heard that, and thought to himself, "Good God, what a blockhead that brother of mine is! He will never be good for anything as long as he lives. He who wants to be a sickle must bend himself early."

The father sighed, and answered him, "You shall soon learn what it is to shudder, but you will not earn your bread by that."

Soon after this the sexton came to the house on a visit, and the father bewailed his trouble, and told him how his younger son was so backward in every respect that he knew nothing and learned nothing. "Just think," said he, "when I asked him how he was going to earn his bread, he actually wanted to learn to shudder."

"If that be all," replied the sexton, "he can learn that with me. Send him to me, and I will soon polish him."

The father was glad to do it, for he thought, "It will train the boy a little." The sexton therefore took him into his house, and he had to ring the bell. After a day or two, the sexton awoke him at midnight, and bade him arise and go up into the church tower and ring the bell. "You shall soon learn what shuddering is," thought he, and secretly went there before him; and when the boy was at the top of the tower and turned round, and was just going to take hold of the bell rope, he saw a white figure standing on the stairs opposite the sounding hole.

"Who is there?" cried he, but the figure made no reply, and did not move or stir. "Give an answer," cried the boy, "or take yourself off, you have no business here at night."

The sexton, however, remained standing motionless that the boy might think he was a ghost. The boy cried a second time, "What do you want here?—Speak if you are an honest fellow, or I will throw you down the steps!" The sexton thought, "He can't intend to be as bad as his words," uttered no sound and stood as if he were made of stone. Then the boy called to him for the third time, and as that was also to no avail, he ran against him and pushed the ghost down the stairs, so that it fell down ten steps and remained lying there in a corner. Thereupon he rang the bell, went home, and without saying a word went to bed, and fell asleep.

The sexton's wife waited a long time for her husband, but he did not come back. At length she became uneasy, and wakened the boy, and asked, "Do you not know where my husband is? He climbed up the tower before you did."

"No, I don't know," replied the boy, "but someone was standing by the sounding hole on the other side of the steps, and as he would neither give an answer nor go away, I took him for a scoundrel, and threw him downstairs. Just go there and you will see if it was he. I should be sorry if it were." The woman ran away and found her husband, who was lying moaning in the corner, and had broken his leg.

She carried him down, and then with loud screams she hastened to the boy's father. "Your boy," cried she, "has been the cause of a great misfortune! He has thrown my husband down the steps and made him break his leg. Take the good-for-nothing fellow away from our house."

The father was terrified, and ran there and scolded the boy. "What wicked tricks are these?" said he, "The devil must have put this into your head."

"Father," he replied, "do listen to me. I am quite innocent. He was standing there by night like one who is intending to do some evil. I did not know who it was, and I warned him three times either to speak or to go away." "Ah," said the father, "I have nothing but unhappiness with you. Go out of my sight. I will see you no more."

"Yes, father, right willingly, wait only until it is day. Then I will go forth and learn how to shudder, and then I shall, at any rate, understand one art which will support me."

"Learn what you will," said the father, "It is all the same to me. Here are fifty talers for you. Take these and go into the wide world, and tell no one from where you come, and who is your father, for I have reason to be ashamed of you."

"Yes, father, it shall be as you will. If you desire nothing more than that, I can easily keep it in mind."

When day dawned, therefore, the boy put his fifty talers into his pocket, and went forth on the great highway, and continually said to himself, "If I could but shudder! If I could but shudder!"

Then a man approached who heard this conversation which the youth was holding with himself, and when they had walked a little farther to where they could see the gallows, the man said to him, "Look, there is the tree where seven men have married the ropemaker's daughter, and are now learning how to fly. Sit down below it, and wait till night comes, and you will soon learn how to shudder."

"If that is all that is wanted," answered the youth, "it is easily done; but if I learn how to shudder as fast as that, you shall have my fifty talers. Just come back to me early in the morning."

Then the youth went to the gallows, sat down below it, and waited till evening came. And as he was cold, he lighted himself a fire, but at midnight the wind blew so sharply that in spite of his fire, he could not get warm. And as the wind knocked the hanged men against each other, and they moved backwards and forwards, he thought to himself, "You shiver below by the fire, but how those up above must freeze and suffer!" And as he felt pity for them, he raised the ladder, and climbed up, unbound one of them after the other, and brought down all seven. Then he stirred the fire, blew it, and set them all round it to warm themselves. But they sat there and did not stir, and the fire caught their clothes. So he said, "Take care, or I will hang you up again." The dead men, however, did not hear, but were quite silent, and let their rags go on burning.

At this he grew angry, and said, "If you will not take care, I cannot help you, I will not be burnt with you," and he hung them up again each in his turn. Then he sat down by his fire and fell asleep, and the next morning the man came to him and wanted to have the fifty talers, and said, "Well, do you know how to shudder?"

"No," answered he, "how was I to get to know? Those fellows up there did not open their mouths, and were so stupid that they let the few old rags which they had on their bodies get burnt."

Then the man saw that he would not get the fifty talers that day, and went away saying, "One of this kind has never come my way before."

The youth likewise went his way, and once more began to mutter to himself, "Ah, if I could but shudder! Ah, if I could but shudder!"

A waggoner who was striding behind him heard that and asked, "Who are you?"

"I don't know," answered the youth.

Then the waggoner asked, "From where do you come?"

"I know not."

"Who is your father?"

"That I may not tell you."

"What is it that you are always muttering between your teeth?"

"Ah," replied the youth, "I do so wish I could shudder, but no one can teach me how to do it."

"Give up your foolish chatter," said the waggoner. "Come, go with me, I will see about a place for you."

The youth went with the waggoner, and in the evening they arrived at an inn where they wished to pass the night. Then at the entrance of the room the youth again said quite loudly, "If I could but shudder! If I could but shudder!"

The host who heard this laughed and said, "If that is your desire, there ought to be a good opportunity for you here."

"Ah, be silent," said the hostess, "so many inquisitive persons have already lost their lives, it would be a pity and a shame if such beautiful eyes as these should never see the daylight again."

But the youth said, "However difficult it may be, I will learn it and for this purpose I have journeyed forth." He let the host have no rest, until the latter told him that not far from there stood a haunted castle where anyone could very easily learn what shuddering was, if he would but sleep in it for three nights. The King had promised that he who would venture should have his daughter as wife, and she was the most beautiful maiden the sun shone on. Great treasures likewise lay in the castle which were guarded by evil spirits, and these treasures would then be freed, and would make a poor man rich enough. Already many men had gone into the castle, but as yet none had come out again. Then the youth went next morning to the King and said if he were allowed he would watch three nights in the haunted castle.

The King looked at him, and as the youth pleased him, he said, "You may ask for three things to take into the castle with you, but they must be things without life."

Then he answered, "Then I ask for a fire, a turning lathe, and a cuttingboard with the knife." The King had these things carried into the castle for him during the day. When night was drawing near, the youth went up and made himself a bright fire in one of the rooms, placed the cuttingboard and knife beside it, and seated himself by the turning-lathe. "Ah, if I could but shudder!" said he, "but I shall not learn it here either."

Towards midnight he was about to poke his fire, and as he was blowing it, something cried suddenly from one corner, "Au, miau! How cold we are!"

"You simpletons!" cried he, "What are you crying about? If you are cold, come and take a seat by the fire and warm yourselves."

And when he had said that, two great black cats came with one tremendous leap and sat down on each side of him, and looked savagely at him with their fiery eyes. After a short time, when they had warmed themselves, they said, "Comrade, shall we have a game at cards?"

"Why not?" he replied, "But just show me your paws." Then they stretched out their claws. "Oh," said he, "what long nails you have! Wait, I must first cut them for you." Thereupon he seized them by the throats, put them on the cuttingboard and screwed their feet fast. "I have looked at your fingers," said he, "and my fancy for card-playing has gone," and he struck them dead and threw them out into the water. But when he had made away with these two, and was about to sit down again by his fire, out from every hole and corner came black cats and black dogs with red-hot chains, and more and more of them came until he could no longer stir, and they yelled horribly, and got on his fire, pulled it to pieces, and tried to put it out. He watched them for a while quietly, but at last when they were going too far, he seized his cutting-knife, and cried, "Away with ye, vermin," and began to cut them down. Part of them ran away, but the others he killed, and threw out into the fish-pond.

When he came back he fanned the embers of his fire again and warmed himself. And as he thus sat, his eyes would keep open no longer, and he felt a desire to sleep. Then he looked round and saw a great bed in the corner. "That is the very thing for me," said he, and got into it. When he was just going to shut his eyes, however, the bed began to move of its own accord, and went over the whole of the castle.

"That's right," said he, "but go faster." Then the bed rolled on as if six horses were harnessed to it, up and down, over thresholds and steps, but suddenly hop, hop, it turned over upside down, and lay on him like a mountain. But he threw quilts and pillows up in the air, got out and said, "Now anyone who likes, may drive," and lay down by his fire, and slept till it was day.

In the morning the King came, and when he saw him lying there on the ground, he thought the evil spirits had killed him and he was dead. Then said he, "After all it is a pity—he is a handsome man."

The youth heard it, got up, and said, "It has not come to that yet." Then the King was astonished, but very glad, and asked how he had fared. "Very well indeed," answered he; "one night is past, the two others will get over likewise."

Then he went to the innkeeper, who opened his eyes very wide, and said, "I never expected to see you alive again! Have you learned how to shudder yet?"

"No," said he, "it is all in vain. If someone would but tell me."

The second night he again went up into the old castle, sat down by the fire, and once more began his old song, "If I could but shudder." When midnight came, an uproar and noise of tumbling about was heard; at first it was low, but it grew louder and louder. Then it was quiet for awhile, and at length with a loud scream, half a man came down the chimney and fell before him.

"Hollo!" cried he, "Another half belongs to this. This is too little!"

Then the uproar began again, there was a roaring and howling, and the other half fell down likewise.

"Wait," said the youth, "I will just blow up the fire a little for you." When he had done that and looked round again, the two pieces were joined together, and a frightful man was sitting in his place. "That is no part of our bargain," said the youth, "the bench is mine." The man wanted to push him away; the youth, however, would not allow that, but thrust him off with all his strength, and seated himself again in his own place. Then still more men fell down, one after the other; they brought nine dead men's legs and two skulls, and set them up and played at nine-pins with them. The youth also wanted to play and said, "Can I join you?"

"Yes, if you have any money."

"Money enough," replied he, "but your balls are not quite round." Then he took the skulls and put them in the lathe and turned them till they were round. "There, now, they will roll better!" said he. "Hurrah! Now it goes merrily!" He played with them and lost some of his money, but when it struck twelve, everything vanished from his sight. He lay down and quietly fell asleep.

Next morning the King came to inquire after him. "How has it fared with you this time?" asked he.

"I have been playing at nine-pins," he answered, "and have lost a couple of farthings."

"Have you not shuddered then?"

"Eh, what?" said he, "I have made merry. If I did but know what it was to shudder!"

The third night he sat down again on his bench and said quite sadly, "If I could but shudder." When it grew late, six tall men came in and brought a coffin. Then said he, "Ha, ha, that is certainly my little cousin, who died only a few days ago," and he beckoned with his finger, and cried, "Come, little cousin, come." They placed the coffin on the ground, but he went to it and took the lid off, and a dead man lay therein. He felt his face, but it was cold as ice. "Stop," said he, "I will warm you a little," and went to the fire and warmed his hand and laid it on the dead man's face, but he remained cold. Then he took him out, and sat down by the fire and laid him on his breast and rubbed his arms that the blood might circulate again. As this also did no good, he thought to himself, "When two people lie in bed together, they warm each other," and carried him to the bed, covered him over and lay down by him. After a short time the dead man became warm too, and began to move. Then said the youth, "See, little cousin, have I not warmed you?" The dead man, however, got up and cried, "Now I will strangle you."

"What!" said he, "Is that the way you thank me? You shall at once go into your coffin again," and he took him up, threw him into it, and shut the lid. Then came the six men and carried him away again. "I cannot manage to shudder," said he. "I shall never learn it here as long as I live."

Then a man entered who was taller than all others, and looked terrible. He was old, however, and had a long white beard. "You wretch," cried he, "you shall soon learn what it is to shudder, for you shall die."

"Not so fast," replied the youth.

"If I am to die, I shall have to have a say in it."

"I will soon seize you," said the fiend.

"Softly, softly, do not talk so big. I am as strong as you are, and perhaps even stronger."

"We shall see," said the old man. "If you are stronger, I will let you go—come, we will try." Then he led him by dark passages to a smith's forge, took an axe, and with one blow struck an anvil into the ground.

"I can do better than that," said the youth, and went to the other anvil. The old man placed himself near and wanted to look on, and his white beard hung down. Then the youth seized the axe, split the anvil with one blow, and struck the old man's beard in with it. "Now I have you," said the youth. "Now it is you who will have to die." Then he seized an iron bar and beat the old man till he moaned and entreated him to stop, and he would give him great riches. The youth drew out the axe and let him go.

The old man led him back into the castle, and in a cellar showed him three chests full of gold. "Of these," said he, "one part is for the poor, the other for the king, the third is yours."

In the meantime it struck twelve, and the spirit disappeared; the youth, therefore, was left in darkness. "I shall still be able to find my way out," said he, and felt about, found the way into the room, and slept there by his fire.

Next morning the King came and said, "Now you must have learned what shuddering is?"

"No," he answered; "what can it be? My dead cousin was here, and a bearded man came and showed me a great deal of money down below, but no one told me what it was to shudder."

"Then," said the King, "you have delivered the castle from enchantment, and shall marry my daughter."

"That is all very well," said he, "but still I do not know what it is to shudder."

Then the gold was brought up and the wedding celebrated; but however much the young king loved his wife, and however happy he was, he still said always, "If I could but shudder—if I could but shudder." And at last she was angry at this. Her waiting-maid said, "I will find a cure for him; he shall soon learn what it is to shudder." She went out to the stream which flowed through the garden, and had a whole bucketful of gudgeons brought to her. At night when the young king was sleeping, his wife was to draw the clothes off him and empty the bucketful of cold water with the gudgeons in it over him, so that the little fishes would sprawl about him. When this was done, he woke up and cried, "Oh, what makes me shudder so?—What makes me shudder so, dear wife? Ah! Now I know what it is to shudder!"

5. THE WOLF AND THE SEVEN LITTLE KIDS

There was once upon a time an old goat who had seven little kids, and loved them with all the love of a mother for her children. One day she wanted to go into the forest and fetch some food. So she called all seven to her and said, "Dear children, I have to go into the forest, be on your guard against the wolf; if he comes in, he will devour you all—skin, hair, and all. The wretch often disguises himself, but you will know him at once by his rough voice and his black feet."

The kids said, "Dear mother, we will take good care of ourselves; you may go away without any anxiety." Then the old one bleated, and went on her way with an easy mind.

It was not long before someone knocked at the door and called, "Open the door, dear children; your mother is here, and has brought something back with her for each of you."

But the little kids knew that it was the wolf, by the rough voice; "We will not open the door," cried they, "you are not our mother. She has a soft, pleasant voice, but your voice is rough; you are the wolf!"

Then the wolf went away to a shopkeeper and bought himself a great lump of chalk, ate this and made his voice soft with it. The he came back, knocked at the door of the house, and cried, "Open the door, dear children, your mother is here and has brought something back with her for each of you."

But the wolf had laid his black paws against the window, and the children saw them and cried, "We will not open the door, our mother has not black feet like you; you are the wolf."

Then the wolf ran to a baker and said, "I have hurt my feet, rub some dough over them for me." And when the baker had rubbed his feet over, he ran to the miller and said, "Strew some white meal over my feet for me." The miller thought to himself, "The wolf wants to deceive someone," and refused; but the wolf said, "If you will not do it, I will devour you." Then the miller was afraid, and made his paws white for him. Yes, that's how people are.

So now the wretch went for the third time to the door, knocked at it and said, "Open the door for me, children, your dear little mother has come home, and has brought everyone of you something back from the forest with her."

The little kids cried, "First show us your paws that we may know if you are our dear little mother." Then he put his paws in through the window, and when the kids saw that they were white, they believed that all he said was true, and opened the door. But who should come in but the wolf! They were terrified and wanted to hide themselves. One sprang under the table, the second into the bed, the third into the stove, the fourth into the kitchen, the fifth into the cupboard, the sixth under the washing-bowl, and the seventh into the clock-case. But the wolf found them, and used no great ceremony; one after the other he swallowed them down his throat. The youngest, who was in the clock-case, was the only one he did not find. When the wolf had satisfied his appetite he took himself off, laid himself down under a tree in the green meadow outside, and began to sleep.

Soon afterwards the old goat came home again from the forest. Ah! What a sight she saw there! The door stood wide open. The table, chairs, and benches were thrown down, the washing-bowl lay broken to pieces, and the quilts and pillows were pulled off the bed. She sought her children, but they were nowhere to be found. She called them one after another by name, but no one answered. At last, when she came to the youngest, a soft voice cried, "Dear mother, I am in the clock-case." She took the kid out, and it told her that the wolf had come and had eaten all the others. Then you may imagine how she wept over her poor children.

At length in her grief she went out, and the youngest kid ran with her. When they came to the meadow, there the wolf lay by the tree and snored so loud that the branches shook. She looked at him on every side and saw that something was moving and struggling in his gorged belly. "Ah, heavens," said she, "is it possible that my poor children whom he has swallowed down for his supper, can still be alive?" Then the kid had to run home and fetch scissors, and a needle and thread, and the goat cut open the monster's stomach, and hardly had she made one cut, than one little kid thrust its head out, and when she cut farther, all six sprang out one after another, and were all still alive, and had suffered no injury whatever, for in his greediness the monster had swallowed them down whole. What rejoicing there was! They embraced their dear mother, and jumped like a sailor at his wedding. The mother, however, said, "Now go and look for some big stones, and we will fill the wicked beast's stomach with them while he is still asleep." Then the seven kids dragged the stones there with all speed, and put as many of them into his stomach as they could get in; and the mother sewed him up again in the greatest haste, so that he was not aware of anything and never once stirred.

When the wolf at length had had his sleep out, he got on his legs, and as the stones in his stomach made him very thirsty, he wanted to go to a well to drink. But when he began to walk and move about, the stones in his stomach knocked against each other and rattled. Then cried he,

> "What rumbles and tumbles
> Against my poor bones?
> I thought 't was six kids,
> But it's naught but big stones."

And when he got to the well and stooped over the water and was just about to drink, the heavy stones made him fall in, and there was no help, but he had to drown miserably. When the seven kids saw that, they came running to the spot and cried aloud, "The wolf is dead! The wolf is dead!" and danced for joy round about the well with their mother.

6. *FAITHFUL JOHN*

There was once upon a time an old King who was ill, and thought to himself, "I am lying on what must be my deathbed." Then said he, "Tell Faithful John to come to me." Faithful John was his favorite servant, and was so called because he had for his whole life long been so true to him. Therefore when he came beside the bed, the King said to him, "Most faithful John, I feel my end approaching, and have no anxiety except about my son. He is still of tender age, and cannot always know how to guide himself. If you do not promise me to teach him everything that he ought to know, and to be his foster father, I cannot close my eyes in peace."

Then answered Faithful John, "I will not forsake him, and will serve him with fidelity, even if it should cost me my life."

At this, the old King said, "Now I die in comfort and peace." Then he added, "After my death, you shall show him the whole castle: all the chambers, halls, and vaults, and all the treasures which lie therein, but the last chamber in the long gallery, in which is the picture of the princess of the Golden Dwelling, you shall not show. If he sees that picture, he will fall violently in love with her, and will drop down in a swoon, and go through great danger for her sake; therefore you must preserve him from that." And when Faithful John had once more given his promise to the old King about this, the King said no more, but laid his head on his pillow, and died.

When the old King had been carried to his grave, Faithful John told the young King all that he had promised his father on his deathbed, and said, "This I will assuredly perform, and will be faithful to you as I have been faithful to him, even if it should cost me my life." When the mourning was over, Faithful John said to him, "It is now time that you should see your inheritance. I will show you your father's palace." Then he took him about everywhere, up and down, and let him see all the riches, and the magnificent apartments, only there was one room which he did not open, that in which hung the dangerous picture. The picture was, however, so placed that when the door was opened you looked straight on it, and it was so admirably painted that it seemed to breathe and live, and there was nothing more charming or more beautiful in the whole world.

The young King, however, plainly remarked that Faithful John always walked past this one door, and said, "Why do you never open this one for me?"

"There is something within it," he replied, "which would terrify you."

But the King answered, "I have seen all the palace, and I will know what is in this room also," and he went and tried to break open the door by force.

Then Faithful John held him back and said, "I promised your father before his death that you should not see that which is in this chamber, it might bring the greatest misfortune on you and on me."

"Ah, no," replied the young King, "if I do not go in, it will be my certain destruction. I should have no rest day or night until I had seen it with my own eyes. I shall not leave the place now until you have unlocked the door."

Then Faithful John saw that there was no help for it now, and with a heavy heart and many sighs, sought out the key from the great bunch. When he had opened the door, he went in first, and thought by standing before him he could hide the portrait so that the King should not see it in front of him, but to what avail? The King stood on tip-toe and saw it over his shoulder. And when he saw the portrait of the maiden, which was so magnificent and shone with gold and precious stones, he fell fainting to the ground. Faithful John took him up, carried him to his bed, and sorrowfully thought, "The misfortune has befallen us, Lord God, what will be the end of it?" Then he strengthened him with wine, until he came to himself again.

The first words the King said were, "Ah, the beautiful portrait! Whose is it?"

"That is the princess of the Golden Dwelling," answered Faithful John.

Then the King continued, "My love for her is so great, that if all the leaves on all the trees were tongues, they could not declare it. I will give my life to win her. You are my most faithful John, you must help me."

The faithful servant considered within himself for a long time how to set about the matter, for it was difficult even to obtain a sight of the King's daughter. At length he thought of a way, and said to the King, "Everything which she has about her is of gold—tables, chairs, dishes, glasses, bowls, and household furniture. Among your treasures are five tons of gold; let one of the goldsmiths of the Kingdom work these up into all manner of vessels and utensils, into all kinds of birds, wild beasts and strange animals, such as may please her, and we will go there with them and try our luck."

The King ordered all the goldsmiths to be brought to him, and they had to work night and day until at last the most splendid things were prepared. When everything was stowed on board a ship, Faithful John put on the clothing of a merchant, and the King was forced to do the same in order to make himself quite unrecognizable. Then they sailed across the sea, and sailed on until they came to the town where the princess of the Golden Dwelling resided.

Faithful John bade the King stay behind on the ship, and wait for him. "Perhaps I shall bring the princess with me," said he, "therefore see that everything is in order; have the golden vessels set out and the whole ship decorated." Then he gathered together in his apron all kinds of gold things, went on shore and walked straight to the royal palace. When he entered the courtyard of the palace, a beautiful girl was standing there by the well with two golden buckets in her hand, drawing water with them. And when she was just turning round to carry away the sparkling water she saw the stranger, and asked who he was. So he answered, "I am a merchant," and opened his apron, and let her look in.

Then she cried, "Oh, what beautiful gold things!" and put her pails down and looked at the golden wares one after the other. Then said the girl, "The princess must see these, she has such great pleasure in golden things that she will buy all you have." She took him by the hand and led him upstairs, for she was the waiting-maid.

When the King's daughter saw the wares, she was quite delighted and said, "They are so beautifully worked that I will buy them all from you."

But Faithful John said, "I am only the servant of a rich merchant. The things I have here are not to be compared with those my master has in his ship. They are the most beautiful and valuable things that have ever been made in gold." She wanted to have everything brought to her there, but he said, "There are so many of them that it would take a great many days to do that, and so many rooms would be required to exhibit them, that your house is not big enough."

Then her curiosity and longing were still more excited, until at last she said, "Take me to the ship, I will go there myself, and behold the treasures of your master."

On this Faithful John was quite delighted, and led her to the ship, and when the King saw her, he perceived that her beauty was even greater than the picture had represented it to be, and thought no other than that his heart would burst. Then she got into the ship, and the King led her within. Faithful John, however, remained behind with the pilot, and ordered the ship to be pushed off, saying, "Set all sails, till it fly like a bird in air."

Inside, however, the King showed her the golden vessels, everyone of them, and the wild beasts and strange animals. Many hours went by while she was seeing everything, and in her delight she did not observe that the ship was sailing away. After she had looked at the last piece, she thanked the merchant and wanted to go home, but when she came to the side of the ship, she saw that it was on the deep sea far from land, and hurrying onwards with all sails set. "Ah," cried she in her alarm, "I am betrayed! I am carried away and have fallen into the power of a merchant—I would rather die!"

The King, however, seized her hand, and said, "I am not a merchant. I am a king, and of no worse origin than you are, and if I have carried you away with subtlety, that has come to pass because of my exceeding great love for you. The first time that I looked on your portrait, I fell fainting to the ground." When the princess of the Golden Dwelling heard that, she was comforted, and her heart was inclined unto him, so that she willingly consented to be his wife.

It so happened, however, while they were sailing onwards over the deep sea, that Faithful John, who was sitting on the fore part of the vessel, making music, saw three ravens in the air, which came flying towards them. At this he stopped playing and listened to what they were saying to each other, for that he well understood. One cried, "Oh, there he is carrying home the princess of the Golden Dwelling."

"Yes," replied the second, "but he has not got her yet."

Said the third, "But he has got her, she is sitting beside him in the ship."

Then the first began again, and cried, "What good will that do him? When they reach land a chestnut horse will leap forward to meet him, and the prince will want to mount it, but if he does that, it will run away with him, and rise up into the air with him, and he will never see his maiden again."

Said the second, "But is there no escape?"

"Oh, yes, if anyone else gets on it swiftly, and takes out the pistol which must be in its holster, and shoots the horse dead with it, the young King is saved. But who knows that? And whoever does know it, and tells it to him, will be turned to stone from the toe to the knee."

Then said the second, "I know more than that; even if the horse is killed, the young King will still not keep his bride. When they go into the castle together, a wrought bridal garment will be lying there in a dish, and looking as if it were woven of gold and silver; it is, however, nothing but sulfur and pitch, and if he puts it on, it will burn him to the very bone and marrow."

Said the third, "Is there no escape at all?"

"Oh, yes," replied the second, "if anyone with gloves on seizes the garment and throws it into the fire and burns it, the young King will be saved. But what's the good in that? Whoever knows it and tells it to him, half his body will become stone from the knee to the heart."

Then said the third, "I know still more; even if the bridal garment be burnt, the young King will still not have his bride. After the wedding, when the dancing begins and the young queen is dancing, she will suddenly turn pale and fall down as if dead, and if someone does not lift her up and suck three drops of blood from her right breast and spit them out again, she will die. But if anyone who knows that were to declare it, he would become stone from the crown of his head to the sole of his foot."

When the ravens had spoken of this together, they flew onwards, and Faithful John had well understood everything, but from that time forth he became quiet and sad, for if he concealed what he had heard, his master would suffer, and if he revealed it to him, he himself must sacrifice his life. At length, however, he said to himself, "I will save my master, even if it brings destruction on myself."

When therefore they came to shore, all happened as had been foretold by the ravens, and a magnificent chestnut horse sprang forward. "Good," said the King, "he shall carry me to my palace," and was about to mount it when Faithful John got before him, jumped quickly on it, drew the pistol out of the holster, and shot the horse.

Then the other attendants of the King, who after all were not very fond of Faithful John, cried, "How shameful to kill the beautiful animal that was to have carried the King to his palace."

But the King said, "Hold your peace and leave him alone, he is my most faithful John. Who knows what good may come of his actions?" They went into the palace, and in the hall there stood a dish, and inside lay the bridal garment looking no otherwise than as if it were made of gold and silver. The young King went towards it and was about to take hold of it, but Faithful John pushed him away, seized it with gloves on, carried it quickly to the fire and burned it.

The other attendants again began to murmur, and said, "Behold, now he is even burning the King's bridal garment!"

But the young King said, "Who knows what good he may have done. Leave him alone, he is my most faithful John."

And now the wedding was solemnized: the dance began, and the bride also took part in it; then Faithful John was watchful and looked into her face, and suddenly she turned pale and fell to the ground, as if she were dead. At this he ran hastily to her, lifted her up and bore her into a chamber—then he laid her down, and knelt and sucked the three drops of blood from her right breast, and spat them out. Immediately she breathed again and recovered herself, but the young King had seen this, and being ignorant why Faithful John had done it, was angry and cried, "Throw him into a dungeon."

Next morning Faithful John was condemned, and led to the gallows, and when he stood up high, and was about to be executed, he said, "Everyone who has to die is permitted before his end to make one last speech; may I too claim the right?"

"Yes," answered the King, "it shall be granted."

Then said Faithful John, "I am unjustly condemned, and have always been true to you," and he related how he had hearkened to the conversation of the ravens when at sea, and how he had been obliged to do all these things in order to save his master.

Then cried the King, "Oh, my most faithful John. Pardon, pardon—bring him down." But as Faithful John spoke the last word he had fallen down lifeless and become a stone.

At this the King and the Queen suffered great anguish, and the King said, "Ah, how ill I have requited great fidelity!" and ordered the stone figure to be taken up and placed in his bedroom beside his bed. And as often as he looked at it he wept and said, "Ah, if I could bring you to life again, my most faithful John." Some time passed and the Queen bore twins, two sons who grew fast and were her delight. Once when the Queen was at church and the two children were sitting playing beside their father, the latter full of grief again looked at the stone figure, sighed and said, "Ah, if I could but bring you to life again, my most faithful John."

Then the stone began to speak and said, "You can bring me to life again *if* you will *sacrifice* what is dearest to you."

Then cried the King, "I will give everything I have in the world for you."

The stone continued, "If you will cut off the heads of your two children with your own hand, and sprinkle me with their blood, I shall be restored to life."

The King was terrified when he heard that he himself must kill his dearest children, but he thought of Faithful John's great fidelity, and how he had died for him, drew his sword, and with his own hand cut off the children's heads. And when he had smeared the stone with their blood, life returned to it, and Faithful John stood once more safe and healthy before him. He said to the King, "Your fidelity shall not go unrewarded," and took the heads of the children, put them on again, and rubbed the wounds with their blood, at which they became whole again immediately, and jumped about, and went on playing as if nothing had happened.

Then the King was full of joy, and when he saw the Queen coming he hid Faithful John and the two children in a great cupboard. When she entered, he said to her, "Have you been praying in the church?"

"Yes," answered she, "but I have constantly been thinking of Faithful John and what misfortune has befallen him through us."

Then said he, "Dear wife, we can give him his life again, but it will cost us our two little sons, whom we must sacrifice."

The Queen turned pale, and her heart was full of terror, but she said, "We owe it to him, for his great fidelity."

Then the King rejoiced that she thought as he had thought, and went and opened the cupboard, and brought forth Faithful John and the children, and said, "God be praised, he is saved, and we have our little sons again also," and told her how everything had occurred. Then they dwelt together in much happiness until their death.

7. THE GOOD BARGAIN

There was once a peasant who had driven his cow to the fair, and sold her for seven talers. On the way home he had to pass a pond, and already from afar he heard the frogs crying, "Aik, aik, aik, aik."

"Well," said he to himself, "they are talking without rhyme or reason, it is seven that I have received, not eight." When he got to the water, he cried to them, "Stupid animals that you are! Don't you know better than that? It is seven talers and not eight."

The frogs, however, stood to their "aik aik, aik, aik."

"Come, then, if you won't believe it, I can count it out to you." And he took his money out of his pocket and counted out the seven talers, always reckoning twenty-four groschen to a taler. The frogs, however, paid no attention to his reckoning, but still cried, "aik, aik, aik, aik."

"What," cried the peasant, quite angry, "since you are determined to know better than I, count it yourselves," and threw all the money into the water to them. He stood still and wanted to wait until they were done and had brought him his own again, but the frogs maintained their opinion and cried continually, "aik, aik, aik, aik," and besides that, did not throw the money out again. He still waited a long while until evening came and he was forced to go home. Then he abused the frogs and cried, "You water-splashers, you thick-heads, you goggle-eyes, you have great mouths and can screech till you hurt one's ears, but you cannot count seven talers! Do you think I'm going to stand here till you get done?" And with that he went away, but the frogs still cried, "aik, aik, aik, aik," after him till he went home quite angry.

After a while he bought another cow, which he killed, and he made the calculation that if he sold the meat well he might gain as much as the two cows were worth, and still have the hide in the bargain. When he got to the town with the meat, a great troop of dogs were gathered together in front of the gate, with a large greyhound at the head of them, which jumped at the meat, snuffed at it, and barked, "Wow, wow, wow."

As there was no stopping him, the peasant said to him, "Yes, yes, I know quite well that you are saying, 'wow, wow, wow,' because you want some of the meat; but I should fare badly if I were to give it to you."

The dog, however, answered nothing but "wow, wow."

"Will you promise not to devour it all then, and will you vouch for your companions?"

"Wow, wow, wow," said the dog.

"Well, if you insist on it, I will leave it for you. I know you well, and know who your master is, but this I tell you: I must have my money in three days or else it will go badly for you; you must bring it out to me." With that he unloaded the meat and turned back. The dogs fell upon it and loudly barked, "wow, wow."

The countryman, who heard them from afar, said to himself, "Now they all want some, but the big one is responsible to me for it."

When three days had passed, the countryman thought, "Tonight my money will be in my pocket," and was quite delighted. But no one would come and pay it. "There is no trusting anyone now," said he, and at last he lost patience, and went into the town to the butcher and demanded his money. The butcher thought it was a joke, but the peasant said, "Jesting apart, I will have my money! Did not the great dog bring you the meat of the slaughtered cow three days ago?" Then the butcher grew angry, snatched a broomstick and drove him out. "Wait a while," said the peasant, "there is still some justice in the world!" and went to the royal palace and begged for an audience. He was led before the King, who sat there with his daughter, and asked him what injury he had suffered. "Alas!" said he, "the frogs and the dogs have taken from me what is mine, and the butcher has paid me for it with the stick," and he related at full length all that had happened.

At this the King's daughter began to laugh heartily, and the King said to him, "I cannot give you justice in this, but you shall have my daughter to wed for it—in her whole life she has never yet laughed as she has just done at you, and I have promised her to the man who could make her laugh. You may thank God for your good fortune!"

"Oh," answered the peasant, "I will not have her. I have a wife already, and she is one too many for me; when I go home, it is just as bad as if I had a wife standing in every corner."

Then the King grew angry, and said, "You are a boor."

"Ah, lord King," replied the peasant, "what can you expect from a pig, but pork?"

"Stop," answered the King, "you shall have another reward. Be off now, but come back in three days, and then you shall have five hundred counted out in full."

When the peasant went out by the gate, the sentry said, "You have made the King's daughter laugh, so you will certainly receive something good."

"Yes, that is what I think," answered the peasant; "five hundred are to be counted out to me."

"Listen," said the soldier, "give me some of it. What can you do with all that money?"

"Because it is you," said the peasant, "you shall have two hundred; present yourself in three days' time before the King, and let it be paid to you."

A Jew, who was standing by and had heard the conversation, ran after the peasant, held him by the coat, and said, "Oh, wonder! What a lucky man you are! I will change it for you, I will change it for you into small coins. What would you do with the great talers?"

"Jew," said the countryman, "three hundred you can have; give it to me at once in coin. In three days from this, you will be paid for it by the King." The Jew was delighted with the profit, and brought the sum in bad groschen, three of which were worth two good ones. After three days had passed, according to the King's command, the peasant went before the King.

"Pull his coat off," said the latter, "and he shall have his five hundred."

"Ah!" said the peasant, "they no longer belong to me; I presented two hundred of them to the sentinel, and three hundred the Jew has changed for me, so by right nothing at all belongs to me."

In the meantime the soldier and the Jew entered and demanded what they were owed by the peasant, and this conduct angered the King. They received the blows strictly counted out. The soldier bore it patiently and knew already how it felt, but the Jew said sorrowfully, "Alas, alas, are these the hard talers?"

The King could not help laughing at the peasant, and once all his anger was gone, he said, "As you have already lost your reward before it came to you, I will give you something in the place of it. Go into my treasure chamber and get some money for yourself, as much as you will."

The peasant did not need to be told twice, and stuffed into his big pockets whatever would go in. Afterwards he went to an inn and counted out his money. The Jew had crept after him and heard how he muttered to himself, "That rogue of a King has cheated me after all. Why could he not have given me the money himself, and then I should have known what I had? How can I tell now if what I have had the luck to put in my pockets is right or not?"

"Good heavens!" said the Jew to himself, "that man is speaking disrespectfully of our lord the King. I will run and inform, and then I shall get a reward, and he will be punished as well."

When the King heard of the peasant's words he fell into a passion, and commanded the Jew to go and bring the offender to him. The Jew ran to the peasant, "You are to go at once to the lord King in the very clothes you have on."

"I know what's right better than that," answered the peasant, "I shall have a new coat made first. Do you think that a man with so much money in his pocket is to go there in his ragged old coat?"

The Jew, as he saw that the peasant would not stir without another coat, and as he feared that if the King's anger cooled, he himself would lose his reward, and the peasant his punishment, said, "I will out of pure friendship lend you a coat for the short time. What will people not do for love!" The peasant was contented with this, put the Jew's coat on, and went off with him.

The King reproached the countryman because of the evil speaking of which the Jew had informed him. "Ah," said the peasant, "what a Jew says is always false—no true word ever comes out of his mouth! That rascal there is capable of maintaining that I have his coat on."

"What is that?" shrieked the Jew. "Is the coat not mine? Have I not lent it to you out of pure friendship, in order that you might appear before the lord King?"

When the King heard that, he said, "The Jew has assuredly deceived one or the other of us, either myself or the peasant," and again he ordered something to be counted out to him in hard talers.

The peasant, however, went home in the good coat, with the good money in his pocket, and said to himself, "This time I have hit it!"

8. *THE WONDERFUL MUSICIAN*

There was once a wonderful musician, who went quite alone through a forest and thought of all manner of things, and when nothing was left for him to think about, he said to himself, "Time is beginning to pass heavily with me here in the forest, I will fetch a good companion for myself." Then he took his fiddle from his back, and played so that it echoed through the trees. It was not long before a wolf came trotting through the thicket towards him. "Ah, here is a wolf coming! I have no desire for him!" said the musician; but the wolf came nearer and said to him, "Ah, dear musician, how beautifully you do play. I should like to learn that, too."

"It is soon learned," the musician replied, "only you have to do all that I bid you."

"Oh, musician," said the wolf, "I will obey you as a scholar obeys his master." The musician had him follow, and when they had gone part of the way together, they came to an old oak tree which was hollow inside, and cleft in the middle.

"Look," said the musician, "if you will learn to fiddle, put your forepaws into this crevice." The wolf obeyed, but the musician quickly picked up a stone and with one blow wedged his two paws so fast that he was forced to stay there like a prisoner. "Stay there until I come back again," said the musician, and went his way.

After a while he again said to himself, "Time is beginning to pass heavily with me here in the forest, I will fetch another companion," and took his fiddle and again played in the forest. It was not long before a fox came creeping through the trees towards him. "Ah, there's a fox coming!" said the musician. "I have no desire for him."

The fox came up to him and said, "Oh, dear musician, how beautifully you do play! I should like to learn that too."

"That is soon learned," said the musician. "You have only to do everything that I bid you."

"Oh, musician," then said the fox, "I will obey you as a scholar obeys his master."

"Follow me," said the musician; and when they had walked part of the way, they came to a footpath, with high bushes on both sides of it.

There the musician stood still, and from one side bent a young hazel-bush down to the ground, and put his foot on the top of it, then he bent down a young tree from the other side as well, and said, "Now little fox, if you will learn something, give me your left front paw." The fox obeyed, and the musician fastened his paw to the left bough. "Little fox," said he, "now reach me your right paw," and he tied it to the right bough. When he had examined whether they were firm enough, he let go, and the bushes sprang up again, and jerked up the little fox, so that it hung struggling in the air. "Wait there till I come back again," said the musician, and went his way.

Again he said to himself, "Time is beginning to pass heavily with me here in the forest, I will fetch another companion," so he took his fiddle, and the sound echoed through the forest. Then a little hare came springing towards him. "Why, a hare is coming," said the musician, "I do not want him."

"Ah, dear musician," said the hare, "how beautifully you do fiddle; I too, should like to learn that."

"That is soon learned," said the musician, "you have only to do everything that I bid you."

"Oh, musician," replied the little hare, "I will obey you as a scholar obeys his master." They went a part of the way together until they came to an open space in the forest, where stood an aspen tree. The musician tied a long string round the little hare's neck, the other end of which he fastened to the tree.

"Now briskly, little hare, run twenty times round the tree!" cried the musician, and the little hare obeyed, and when it had run round twenty times, it had twisted the string twenty times round the trunk of the tree, and the little hare was caught, and let it pull and tug as it liked, it only made the string cut into its tender neck. "Wait there till I come back," said the musician, and went onwards.

The wolf, in the meantime, had pushed and pulled and bitten at the stone, and had worked so long that he had set his feet free and had drawn them once more out of the cleft. Full of anger and rage he hurried after the musician and wanted to tear him to pieces.

When the fox saw him running, he began to lament, and cried with all his might, "Brother wolf, come to my help, the musician has betrayed me!" The wolf drew down the little tree, bit the cord in two, and freed the fox, who went with him to take revenge on the musician.

They found the tied-up hare, whom likewise they released, and then they all sought the enemy together.

The musician had once more played his fiddle as he went on his way, and this time he had been more fortunate. The sound reached the ears of a poor woodcutter, who instantly, without a thought, gave up his work and came with his hatchet under his arm to listen to the music. "At last comes the right companion," said the musician, "for I was seeking a human being, and no wild beast." And he began and played so beautifully and delightfully that the poor man stood there as if bewitched, and his heart leaped with gladness. And as he thus stood, the wolf, the fox, and the hare came up, and he saw well that they had some evil design. So he raised his glittering axe and placed himself before the musician, as if to say, "Whoever wishes to touch him let him beware, for he will have to deal with me!" Then the beasts were terrified and ran back into the forest. The musician, however, played once more to the man out of gratitude, and then went onwards.

9. THE TWELVE BROTHERS

There were once upon a time a king and a queen who lived happily together and had twelve children, but they were all boys. Then said the King to his wife, "If the thirteenth child which you are about to bring into the world is a girl, the twelve boys shall die, in order that her possessions may be great, and that the kingdom may fall to her alone." He caused likewise twelve coffins to be made, which were already filled with shavings, and in each lay the little pillow for the dead, and he had them taken into a locked-up room, and then he gave the Queen the key of it, and bade her not to speak of this to anyone.

The mother, however, now sat and lamented all day long, until the youngest son, who was always with her, and whom she had named Benjamin, from the Bible, said to her, "Dear mother, why are you so sad?"

"Dearest child," she answered, "I may not tell you." But he let her have no rest until she went and unlocked the room, and showed him the twelve coffins ready filled with shavings. Then she said, "my dearest Benjamin, your father has had these coffins made for you and for your eleven brothers, for if I bring a little girl into the world, you are all to be killed and buried in them."

And as she wept while she was saying this, the son comforted her and said, "Weep not, dear mother, we will save ourselves, and go away."

But she said, "Go forth into the forest with your eleven brothers, and let one sit constantly on the highest tree which can be found, and keep watch, looking towards the tower here in the castle. If I give birth to a little son, I will put up a white flag, and then you may venture to come back, but if I bear a daughter, I will hoist a red flag, and then fly away as quickly as you are able, and may the good God protect you. And every night I will rise up and pray for you—in winter that you may be able to warm yourself at a fire, and in summer that you may not faint away in the heat."

After she had blessed her sons, they went forth into the forest. They each kept watch in turn, and sat on the highest oak and looked towards the tower. When eleven days had passed and the turn came to Benjamin, he saw that a flag was being raised. It was, however, not the white, but the blood-red flag which announced that they were all to die. When the brothers heard that, they were very angry and said, "Are we all to suffer death for the sake of a girl? We swear that we will avenge ourselves! Wherever we find a girl, her red blood shall flow."

Thereupon they went deeper into the forest, and in the midst of it, where it was the darkest, they found a little bewitched hut, which was standing empty. Then said they, "Here we will dwell, and you Benjamin, who are the youngest and weakest, you shall stay at home and keep house, we others will go out and get food." Then they went into the forest and shot hares, wild deer, birds and pigeons, and whatever there was to eat; this they took to Benjamin, who had to dress it for them in order that they might appease their hunger. They lived together ten years in the little hut, and the time did not appear long to them.

The little daughter which their mother the Queen had given birth to, was now grown up; she was good of heart, and fair of face, and had a golden star on her forehead. Once, when a big washing had been done, she saw twelve men's shirts among the things, and asked her mother, "To whom do these twelve shirts belong, for they are far too small for father?"

Then the Queen answered with a heavy heart, "Dear child, these belong to your twelve brothers."

Said the maiden, "Where are my twelve brothers, I have never yet heard of them?"

She replied, "God knows where they are, they are wandering about the world." Then she took the maiden and opened the chamber for her, and showed her the twelve coffins with the shavings, and pillows for the head. "These coffins," said she, "were destined for your brothers, but they went away secretly before you were born," and she related to her how everything had happened; then said the maiden, "Dear mother, weep not, I will go and seek my brothers."

So she took the twelve shirts and went forth, and straight into the great forest. She walked the whole day, and in the evening she came to the bewitched hut. Then she entered it and found a young boy, who asked, "Where do you come from, and where are you bound?" and was astonished that she was so beautiful, and wore royal garments, and had a star on her forehead.

And she answered, "I am a king's daughter, and am seeking my twelve brothers, and I will walk as far as the sky is blue until I find them." She likewise showed him the twelve shirts which belonged to them.

Then Benjamin saw that she was his sister, and said, "I am Benjamin, your youngest brother." And she began to weep for joy, and Benjamin wept also, and they kissed and embraced each other with the greatest love. But after this he said, "Dear sister, there is still one difficulty. We have agreed that every maiden whom we meet shall die, because we have been obliged to leave our kingdom on account of a girl."

Then said she, "I will willingly die, if by so doing I can save my twelve brothers."

"No," answered he, "you shall not die, seat yourself beneath this tub until our eleven brothers come, and then I will soon come to an agreement with them."

She did so, and when it was night the others came from hunting, and their dinner was ready. And as they were sitting at table, and eating, they asked, "What news is there?" Said Benjamin, "Don't you know anything?"

"No," they answered.

He continued, "You have been in the forest and I have stayed at home, and yet I know more than you do."

"Tell us then," they cried.

He answered, "But promise me that the first maiden who meets us shall not be killed."

"Yes," they all cried, "she shall have mercy, only do tell us."

Then said he, "Our sister is here," and he lifted up the tub, and the King's daughter came forth in her royal garments with the golden star on her forehead, and she was beautiful, delicate and fair. Then they were all rejoiced, and hugged, and kissed and loved her with all their hearts.

Now she stayed at home with Benjamin and helped him with the work. The eleven went into the forest and caught game, and deer, and birds, and wood-pigeons that they might have food, and the little sister and Benjamin took care to make it ready for them. She sought for the wood for cooking and herbs for vegetables, and put the pans on the fire so that the dinner was always ready when the eleven came. She likewise kept order in the little house, and put beautifully white clean coverings on the little beds, and the brothers were always contented and lived in great harmony with her.

Once on a time the two at home had prepared a beautiful meal, and when they were all together, they sat down and ate and drank and were full of gladness. There was, however, a little garden belonging to the bewitched house where there were twelve lily flowers, which are likewise called students. She wished to give her brothers pleasure, and plucked the twelve flowers, and thought she would present each brother with one while at dinner. But at the same moment that she plucked the flowers the twelve brothers were changed into twelve ravens, and flew away over the forest, and the house and garden vanished likewise. And now the poor maiden was alone in the wild forest, and when she looked around, an old woman was standing near her who said, "My child, what have you done? Why did you not leave the twelve white flowers growing? They were your brothers, who are now forevermore changed into ravens."

The maiden said, weeping, "Is there no way of saving them?"

"No," said the woman, "there is but one in the whole world, and that is so hard that you will not succeed at it, for you must be dumb for seven years, and may not speak or laugh, and if you speak one single word, and only an hour of the seven years is wanting, all is in vain, and your brothers will be killed by the one word."

Then said the maiden in her heart, "I know with certainty that I shall set my brothers free," and went and sought a high tree and she sat spinning, and she neither spoke nor laughed. Now it so happened that a king was hunting in the forest, who had a great greyhound which ran to the tree on which the maiden was sitting, and sprang about it, whining, and barking at her. Then the King came by and saw the beautiful King's daughter with the golden star on her brow, and was so charmed with her beauty that he called to ask her if she would be his wife. She made no answer, but nodded a little with her head. So he climbed up the tree himself, carried her down, placed her on his horse, and took her home. Then the wedding was solemnized with great magnificence and rejoicing, but the bride neither spoke nor smiled.

When they had lived happily together for a few years, the King's mother, who was a wicked woman, began to slander the young Queen, and said to the King, "This is a common beggar girl whom you have brought back with you. Who knows what impious tricks she practices secretly! Even if she is dumb, and not able to speak, she still might laugh for once; but those who do not laugh have bad consciences." At first the

King would not believe it, but the old woman urged this so long, and accused her of so many evil things, that at last the King let himself be persuaded and sentenced her to death.

And now a great fire was lighted in the courtyard in which she was to be burnt, and the King stood above at the window and looked on with tearful eyes, because he still loved her so much. And when she was bound fast to the stake, and the fire was licking at her clothes with its red tongue, the last instant of the seven years expired. Then a whirring sound was heard in the air, and twelve ravens came flying towards the place, and sank downwards, and when they touched the earth they were her twelve brothers, whom she had saved. They tore the fire asunder, extinguished the flames, set their dear sister free, and kissed and embraced her. And now as she dared to open her mouth and speak, she told the King why she had been dumb, and had never laughed. The King rejoiced when he heard that she was innocent, and they all lived in great unity until their death. The wicked stepmother was taken before the judge, and put into a barrel filled with boiling oil and venomous snakes, and died an evil death.

10. THE PACK OF RAGAMUFFINS

The cock once said to the hen, "It is now the time when our nuts are ripe, so let us go to the hill together and for once eat our fill before the squirrel takes them all away."

"Yes," replied the hen, "come, we will have some pleasure together."

Then they went away to the hill, and because it was a bright day they stayed till evening. Now I do not know whether it was that they had eaten till they were too fat, or whether they had become proud, but they would not go home on foot, and the cock had to build a little carriage of nut shells. When it was ready, the little hen seated herself in it and said to the cock, "You can just harness yourself to it."

"Ha, I like that!" said the cock, "I would rather go home on foot than let myself be harnessed to it; no, that is not our bargain. I do not mind being coachman and sitting on the box, but I will not drag it myself."

As they were thus disputing, a duck quacked at them, "You thieving folks, who told you to go to my nut-hill? Well, you shall suffer for it!" and ran with open beak at the cock.

But the cock also was not idle, and fell boldly on the duck, and at last wounded her so with his spurs that she begged for mercy, and willingly let herself be harnessed to the carriage as a punishment. The little cock now seated himself on the box and was coachman, and thereupon they went off in a gallop, with "Duck, go as fast as you can."

When they had driven a part of the way they met two foot-passengers, a pin and a needle. They cried, "Stop! Stop!" and said that it would soon be as dark as pitch, and then they could not go a step further, and that it was so dirty on the road, and asked if they could not get into the carriage for a while. They had been at the tailor's tavern by the gate, and had stayed too long over the beer. As they were thin and did not take up much room, the cock let them both get in, but they had to promise him and his little hen not to step on their feet. Late in the evening they came to an inn, and as they did not like to go further by night, and as the duck also was not strong on her feet, and fell from one side to the other, they went in. The host at first made many objections, his house was already full, and he thought they could not be very distinguished persons; but at last, as they made pleasant speeches, and told him that he should have the egg which the little hen has laid on the way, and should likewise keep the duck, which laid one every day, he at length said that they might stay the night. And now they had themselves well served, and they feasted and caroused. Early in the morning, when day was breaking, and everyone was asleep, the cock awoke the hen, brought the egg, pecked it open, and they ate it together, but they threw the shell on the hearth. Then they went to the needle which was still asleep, took it by the head and stuck it into the cushion of the landlord's chair, and put the pin in his towel, and at last without more ado they flew away over the heath. The duck, who liked to sleep in the open air and had stayed in the yard, heard them going away, made herself merry and found a stream, down which she swam, which was a much quicker way of traveling than being harnessed to a carriage.

The host did not get out of bed for two hours after this; he washed himself and wanted to dry himself, then the pin went over his face and made a red streak from one ear to the other. After this he went into the kitchen and wanted to light a pipe, but when he came to the hearth the eggshell darted into his eyes. "This morning everything attacks my head," said he, and angrily sat down on his grandfather's chair, but he quickly started up again and cried, "Woe is me," for the needle had pricked him still worse than the pin, and not in the head. Now he was thoroughly angry, and suspected the guests who had come so late the night before, and when he went and looked about for them, they were gone. Then he made a vow to take no more ragamuffins into his house, for they consume much, pay for nothing, and play mischievous tricks as thanks.

11. LITTLE BROTHER AND LITTLE SISTER

Little brother took his little sister by the hand and said, "Since our mother died we have had no happiness; our stepmother beats us every day, and if we come near her she kicks us away with her foot. Our meals are the hard crusts of bread that are left over; and the little dog under the table is better off, for she often throws it a nice bit. May Heaven pity us. If our mother only knew! Come, we will go forth together into the wide world."

They walked the whole day over meadows, fields, and stony places; and when it rained the little sister said, "Heaven and our hearts are weeping together." In the evening they came to a large forest, and they were so weary with sorrow and hunger and the long walk, that they lay down in a hollow tree and fell asleep.

The next day when they awoke, the sun was already high in the sky, and shone down hot into the tree. Then the brother said, "Sister, I am thirsty; if I knew of a little brook I would go and just take a drink; I think I hear one running." The brother got up and took the little sister by the hand, and they set off to find the brook.

But the wicked stepmother was a witch, and had seen how the two children had gone away, and had crept after them stealthily, as witches do creep, and had bewitched all the brooks in the forest.

Now when they found a little brook leaping brightly over the stones, the brother was going to drink out of it, but the sister heard how it said as it ran, "Whoever drinks of me will become a tiger; whoever drinks of me will become a tiger." Then the sister cried, "Pray, dear brother, do not drink, or you will become a wild beast, and tear me to pieces."

The brother did not drink, although he was so thirsty, but said, "I will wait for the next spring."

When they came to the next brook the sister heard this also say, "Whoever drinks of me will become a wolf; whoever drinks of me will become a wolf." Then the sister cried out, "Pray, dear brother, do not drink, or you will become a wolf, and devour me."

The brother did not drink, and said, "I will wait until we come to the next spring, but then I must drink, say what you like; for my thirst is too great."

And when they came to the third brook the sister heard how it said as it ran, "Whoever drinks of me will become a deer; whoever drinks of me will become a deer." The sister said, "Oh, I pray you, dear brother, do not drink, or you will become a deer, and run away from me." But the brother had knelt down at once by the brook, and had bent down and drunk some of the water, and as soon as the first drops touched his lips he lay there a young deer.

And now the sister wept over her poor bewitched brother, and the little deer wept also, and sat sorrowfully near her. But at last the girl said, "Be quiet, dear little fawn, I will never, never leave you."

Then she untied her golden garter and put it round the fawn's neck, and she plucked reeds and wove them into a soft cord. With this she tied the little beast and led it on, and she walked deeper and deeper into the forest.

And when they had gone a very long way they came at last to a little house, and the girl looked in; and as it was empty, she thought, "We can stay here and live." Then she sought for leaves and moss to make a soft bed for the fawn; and every morning she went out and gathered roots and berries and nuts for herself, and brought tender grass for the fawn, who ate out of her hand, and was content and played round about her. In the evening, when the sister was tired, and had said her prayer, she laid her head upon the fawn's back: that was her pillow, and she slept softly on it. And if only the brother had had his human form it would have been a delightful life.

For some time they were alone like this in the wilderness. But it happened that the King of the country held a great hunt in the forest. Then the blasts of the horns, the barking of dogs, and the merry shouts of the huntsmen rang through the trees, and the fawn heard all, and was only too anxious to be there. "Oh," said he, to his sister, "let me be off to the hunt, I cannot bear it any longer," and he begged so much that at last she agreed.

"But," said she to him, "come back to me in the evening; I must shut my door for fear of the rough huntsmen, so knock and say, 'My little sister, let me in!' that I may know you; and if you do not say that, I shall not open the door." Then the young fawn sprang away; so happy was he and so merry in the open air.

The King and the huntsmen saw the pretty creature, and started after him, but they could not catch him, and when they thought that they surely had him, away he sprang through the bushes and could not be seen. When it was dark he ran to the cottage, knocked, and said, "My little sister, let me in." Then the door was opened for him, and he jumped in, and rested himself the whole night through upon his soft bed.

The next day the hunt went on afresh, and when the fawn again heard the bugle-horn, and the Ho! Ho! of the huntsmen, he had no peace, but said, "Sister, let me out, I must be off."

His sister opened the door for him, and said, "But you must be here again in the evening and say your password."

When the King and his huntsmen again saw the young fawn with the golden collar, they all chased him, but he was too quick and nimble for them. This went on for the whole day, but at last by the evening the huntsmen had surrounded him, and one of them wounded him a little in the foot, so that he limped and ran slowly. Then a hunter crept after him to the cottage and heard how he said, "My little sister, let me in," and saw that the door was opened for him, and was shut again at once. The hunter took notice of it all, and went to the King and told him what he had seen and heard. Then the King said, "Tomorrow we will hunt once more."

The little sister, however, was dreadfully frightened when she saw that her fawn was hurt. She washed the blood off him, laid herbs on the wound, and said, "Go to your bed, dear fawn, that you may get well again."

But the wound was so slight that the fawn, next morning, did not feel it any more. And when he again heard the sport outside, he said, "I cannot bear it, I must be there; they shall not find it so easy to catch me."

The sister cried, and said, "This time they will kill you, and here am I alone in the forest and forsaken by all the world. I will not let you out."

"Then you will have me die of grief," answered the fawn; "when I hear the bugle-horns I feel as if I must jump out of my skin." Then the sister could not do otherwise, but opened the door for him with a heavy heart, and the fawn, full of health and joy, bounded into the forest.

When the King saw him, he said to his huntsmen, "Now chase him all day long till nightfall, but take care that no one does him any harm."

As soon as the sun had set, the King said to the hunter, "Now come and show me the cottage in the wood;" and when he was at the door, he knocked and called out, "Dear little sister, let me in." Then the door opened, and the King walked in, and there stood a maiden more lovely than any he had ever seen. The maiden was frightened when she saw, not her little fawn, but a man come in who wore a golden crown upon his head. But the King looked kindly at her, stretched out his hand, and said, "Will you go with me to my palace and be my dear wife?"

"Yes, indeed," answered the maiden, "but the little fawn must go with me, I cannot leave him."

The King said, "It shall stay with you as long as you live, and shall want nothing." Just then he came running in, and the sister again tied him with the cord of reeds, took it in her own hand, and went away with the King from the cottage.

The King took the lovely maiden upon his horse and carried her to his palace, where the wedding was held with great pomp. She was now the Queen, and they lived for a long time happily together; the fawn was tended and cherished, and ran about in the palace garden.

But the wicked stepmother, because of whom the children had gone out into the world, thought all the time that the sister had been torn to pieces by the wild beasts in the wood, and that the brother had been shot for a fawn by the huntsmen. Now when she heard that they were so happy, and so well off, envy and hatred rose in her heart and left her no peace, and she thought of nothing but how she could bring them again to misfortune. Her own daughter, who was ugly as night, and had only one eye, grumbled at her and said, "A Queen! That ought to have been my luck."

"Nevermind," answered the old woman, and comforted her by saying, "when the time comes I shall be ready."

As time went on, the Queen delivered a pretty little boy, and it happened when the King was out hunting. The old witch took the form of the chamber-maid, went into the room where the Queen lay, and said to her, "Come, the bath is ready; it will do you good, and give you fresh strength; make haste before it gets cold."

The daughter also was close by, so they carried the weakly Queen into the bathroom, and put her into the bath; then they shut the door and ran away. But in the bathroom they had made a fire of such deadly heat that the beautiful young Queen was soon suffocated.

When this was done the old woman took her daughter, put a nightcap on her head, and laid her in bed in place of the Queen. She gave her too the shape and the look of the Queen, only she could do nothing for the lost eye. But in order that the King might not see it, she was to lie on the side on which she had no eye.

In the evening when he came home and heard that he had a son he was heartily glad, and was going to the bed of his dear wife to see how she was. But the old woman quickly called out, "For your life leave the curtains closed; the Queen ought not to see the light yet, and must have rest." The King went away, and did not find out that a false Queen was lying in the bed.

But at midnight, when all slept, the nurse, who was sitting in the nursery by the cradle, and who was the only person awake, saw the door open and the true Queen walk in. The Queen took the child out of the cradle, laid it on her arm, and suckled it. Then she shook up its pillow, laid the child down again, and covered it with the little quilt. And she did not forget the fawn, but went into the corner where it lay, and stroked its back. Then she went quite silently out of the door again. The next morning the nurse asked the guards whether anyone had come into the palace during the night, but they answered, "No, we have seen no one."

She came thus many nights and never spoke a word. The nurse always saw her, but she did not dare to tell anyone about it.

When some time had passed in this manner, the Queen began to speak in the night, and said—

"How fares my child, how fares my fawn?
Twice shall I come, then never more."

The nurse did not answer, but when the Queen had gone again, went to the King and told him all. The King said, "Ah, heavens! What is this? Tomorrow night I will watch by the child." In the evening he went into the nursery, and at midnight the Queen again appeared and said—

"How fares my child, how fares my fawn?
Once will I come, then never more."

And she nursed the child as she did before she disappeared. The King dared not speak to her, but on the next night he watched again. Then she said—

"How fares my child, how fares my fawn?
This time I come, then never more."

Then the King could not restrain himself; he sprang towards her, and said, "You can be none other than my dear wife."

She answered, "Yes, I am your dear wife," and at the same moment she received life again, and by God's grace became fresh, rosy, and full of health.

Then she told the King the evil deed which the wicked witch and her daughter had been guilty of towards her. The King ordered both to be led before the judge, and judgment was delivered against them. The daughter was taken into the forest where she was torn to pieces by wild beasts, but the witch was cast into the fire and miserably burnt. And as soon as she was burnt the fawn changed his shape, and received his human form again, so the sister and brother lived happily together all their lives.

12. RAPUNZEL

There were once a man and a woman who had long in vain wished for a child. At length the woman hoped that God was about to grant her desire. These people had a little window at the back of their house from which a splendid garden could be seen, which was full of the most beautiful flowers and herbs. It was, however, surrounded by a high wall, and no one dared to go into it because it belonged to an enchantress named Dame Gothel, who had great power and was dreaded by all the world. One day the woman was standing by this window and looking down into the garden, when she saw a bed which was planted with the most beautiful rampion (rapunzel), and it looked so fresh and green that she longed for it, and had the greatest desire to eat some. This desire increased every day, and as she knew that she could not get any of it, she quite pined away, and looked pale and miserable. Then her husband was alarmed, and asked, "What ails you, dear wife?"

"Ah," she replied, "if I can't get some of the rampion, which is in the garden behind our house, I shall die."

The man, who loved her, thought, "Sooner than let your wife die, bring her some of the rampion yourself, let it cost you what it will." In the twilight of the evening, he clambered down over the wall into the garden of the enchantress, hastily clutched a handful of rampion, and took it to his wife. She at once made herself a salad of it, and ate it with much delight. She, however, liked it so much—so very much, that the next day she longed for it three times as much as before. If he was to have any rest, her husband must once more descend into the garden. In the gloom of evening, therefore, he let himself down again; but when he had clambered down the wall he was terribly afraid, for he saw the enchantress standing before him.

"How can you dare," said she with an angry look, "to descend into my garden and steal my rampion like a thief? You shall suffer for it!"

"Ah," answered he, "let mercy take the place of justice, I only made up my mind to do it out of necessity. My wife saw your rampion from the window, and felt such a longing for it that she would have died if she had not got some to eat."

Then the enchantress allowed her anger to be softened, and said to him, "If the case be as you say, I will allow you to take away with you as much rampion as you will, only I make one condition. You must give me the child which your wife will bring into the world; it shall be well treated, and I will care for it like a mother." The man in his terror consented to everything, and when the woman gave birth, the enchantress appeared at once, gave the child the name of Rapunzel, and took it away with her.

Rapunzel grew into the most beautiful child beneath the sun. When she was twelve years old, the enchantress shut her into a tower, which lay in a forest, and had neither stairs nor door, but quite at the top was a little window. When the enchantress wanted to go in, she placed herself beneath it and cried,

"Rapunzel, Rapunzel,
Let down your hair to me."

Rapunzel had magnificent long hair, fine as spun gold, and when she heard the voice of the enchantress she unfastened her braided tresses, wound them round one of the hooks of the window above, and then the hair fell twenty ells down, and the enchantress climbed up by it.

After a year or two, it came to pass that the King's son rode through the forest and went by the tower. Then he heard a song, which was so charming that he stood still and listened. This was Rapunzel, who in her solitude passed her time in letting her sweet voice resound. The King's son wanted to climb up to her, and looked for the door of the tower, but none was to be found. He rode home, but the singing had so deeply touched his heart, that every day he went out into the forest and listened to it. Once when he was thus standing behind a tree, he saw that an enchantress came there, and he heard how she cried,

"Rapunzel, Rapunzel,
Let down your hair."

Then Rapunzel let down the braids of her hair, and the enchantress climbed up to her. "If that is the ladder by which one mounts, I will at once try my fortune," said he, and the next day when it began to grow dark, he went to the tower and cried,

"Rapunzel, Rapunzel,
Let down your hair."

Immediately the hair fell down and the King's son climbed up.

At first Rapunzel was terribly frightened when a man such as her eyes had never yet beheld, came to her; but the King's son began to talk to her quite like a friend, and told her that his heart had been so stirred that it had let him have no rest, and he had been forced to see her. Then Rapunzel lost her fear, and when he asked her if she would take him for her husband, and she saw that he was young and handsome, she thought, "He will love me more than old Dame Gothel does;" and she said yes, and laid her hand in his. She said, "I will willingly go away with you, but I do not know how to get down. Bring with you a skein of silk every time that you come, and I will weave a ladder with it, and when that is ready I will descend, and you will take me on your horse." They agreed that until that time he should come to her every evening, for the old woman came by day. The enchantress remarked nothing of this, until once Rapunzel said to her, "Tell me, Dame Gothel, how it happens that you are so much heavier for me to draw up than the young King's son—he is with me in hardly a minute."

"Ah! You wicked child," cried the enchantress "What do I hear you say! I thought I had separated you from all the world, and yet you have deceived me." In her anger she clutched Rapunzel's beautiful tresses, wrapped them twice round her left hand, seized a pair of scissors with the right, and snip, snap, they were cut off, and the lovely braids lay on the ground. And she was so pitiless that she took poor Rapunzel into a desert where she had to live in great grief and misery.

On the same day that she cast out Rapunzel, the enchantress fastened the braids of hair which she had kept onto the hook of the window, and in the evening when the King's son came and cried,

"Rapunzel, Rapunzel,
Let down your hair,"

she let the hair down. The King's son ascended, but he did not find his dearest Rapunzel above, but the enchantress, who gazed at him with wicked and venomous looks.

"Aha!" she cried mockingly, "You would fetch your dearest, but the beautiful bird sits no longer singing in the nest; the cat has got it, and will scratch out your eyes as well. Rapunzel is lost to you; you will never see her more." The King's son was beside himself with pain, and in his despair he leapt down from the tower. He escaped with his life, but the thorns into which he fell pierced his eyes. Then he wandered quite blind about the forest, ate nothing but roots and berries, and did nothing but lament and weep over the loss of his dearest wife. Thus he roamed about in misery for some years, and at length came to the desert where Rapunzel, with the twins to which she had given birth, a boy and a girl, lived in wretchedness. He heard a voice, and it seemed so familiar to him that he went towards it, and when he approached, Rapunzel knew him and embraced him and wept. Two of her tears wetted his eyes and they grew clear again, and he could see with them as before. He led her to his Kingdom where he was joyfully received, and they lived for a long time afterwards, happy and contented.

13. THE THREE LITTLE MEN IN THE WOOD

There was once a man whose wife died, and a woman whose husband died, and the man had a daughter, and the woman also had a daughter. The girls were acquainted with each other, and went out walking together, and afterwards came to the woman in her house. Then she said to the man's daughter, "Listen, tell your father that I would like to marry him, and then you shall wash yourself in milk every morning, and drink wine, but my own daughter shall wash herself in water and drink water."

The girl went home, and told her father what the woman had said. The man said, "What shall I do? Marriage is a joy and also a torment." At length as he could come to no decision, he pulled off his boot, and said, "Take this boot, it has a hole in the sole of it. Go with it up to the loft, hang it on the big nail, and then pour water into it. If it holds the water, then I will again take a wife, but if it runs through, I will not." The girl did as she was ordered, but the water drew the hole together, and the boot became full to the top. She informed her father how it had turned out. Then he himself went up, and when he saw that she was right, he went to the widow and wooed her, and the wedding was celebrated.

The next morning, when the two girls got up, there stood before the man's daughter milk for her to wash in and wine for her to drink, but before the woman's daughter stood water to wash herself with and water for drinking. On the second morning, stood milk for washing and wine for drinking before the man's daughter as well as water before the woman's daughter. And on the third morning stood water for washing and water for drinking before the man's daughter, and milk for washing and wine for drinking before the woman's daughter, and so it continued. The woman became bitterly unkind to her stepdaughter, and day by day did her best to treat her still worse. She was also envious because her stepdaughter was beautiful and lovable, and her own daughter ugly and repulsive.

Once, in winter, when everything was frozen as hard as a stone, and hill and vale lay covered with snow, the woman made a frock of paper, called her stepdaughter, and said, "Here, put on this dress and go out into the wood, and fetch me a little basketful of strawberries—I have a fancy for some."

"Good heavens!" said the girl, "No strawberries grow in winter! The ground is frozen, and besides the snow has covered everything. And why am I to go in this paper frock? It is so cold outside that one's very breath freezes! The wind will blow through the frock, and the thorns will tear it off my body."

"Will you contradict me again?" said the stepmother, "See that you go, and do not show your face again until you have the basketful of strawberries!" Then she gave her a little piece of hard bread, and said, "This will last you the day," and thought, "You will die of cold and hunger outside, and will never be seen again by me."

Then the maiden was obedient, and put on the paper frock, and went out with the basket. Far and wide there was nothing but snow, and not a green blade to be seen. When she got into the wood she saw a small house out of which peeped three elves. She wished them good day, and knocked modestly at the door. They cried, "Come in," and she entered the room and seated herself on the bench by the stove, where she began to warm herself and eat her breakfast. The elves said, "Give us, too, some of it."

"Willingly," she said, and divided her bit of bread in two and gave them the half.

They asked, "What are you doing in the forest in the winter time, in your thin dress?"

"Ah," she answered, "I am to look for a basketful of strawberries, and am not to go home until I can take them with me."

When she had eaten her bread, they gave her a broom and said, "Sweep away the snow at the back door with it." But when she was outside, the three little men said to each other, "What shall we give her as she is so good, and has shared her bread with us?" Then said the first, "My gift is, that she shall every day grow more beautiful." The second said, "My gift is, that gold pieces shall fall out of her mouth every time she speaks." The third said, "My gift is, that a king shall come and take her as wife."

The girl, however, did as the little men had bidden her, swept away the snow behind the little house with the broom, and what did she find but real ripe strawberries, which came up quite dark-red out of the snow! In her joy she hastily gathered her basket full, thanked the little men, shook hands with each of them, and ran home to take her stepmother what she had longed for so much. When she went in and said good evening, a piece of gold at once fell from her mouth. Thereupon she related what had happened to her in the wood, but with every word she spoke, gold pieces fell from her mouth, until very soon the whole room was covered with them.

"Now look at her arrogance," cried the stepsister, "to throw about gold in that way!" but she was secretly envious of it, and wanted to go into the forest also to seek strawberries.

The mother said, "No, my dear little daughter, it is too cold, you might die of cold." However, as her daughter let her have no peace, the mother at last yielded, made her a magnificent dress of fur, which she was obliged to put on, and gave her bread-and-butter and cake to take with her.

The girl went into the forest and straight up to the little house. The three little elves peeped out again, but she did not greet them, and without looking round at them and without speaking to them, she went awkwardly into the room, seated herself by the stove, and began to eat her bread-and-butter and cake. "Give us some of it," cried the little men; but she replied, "There is not enough for myself, so how can I give it away to other people?"

When she had finished eating, they said, "There is a broom for you, sweep all clean for us outside by the back door."

"Humph! Sweep for yourselves," she answered, "I am not your servant." When she saw that they were not going to give her anything, she went out by the door.

Then the little men said to each other, "What shall we give her as she is so naughty, and has a wicked envious heart, that will never let her do a good deed for anyone?"

The first said, "I grant that she may grow uglier every day."

The second said, "I grant that at every word she says, a toad shall spring out of her mouth."

The third said, "I grant that she may die a miserable death." The maiden looked for strawberries outside, but as she found none, she went angrily home. And when she opened her mouth, and was about to tell her mother what had happened to her in the wood, with every word she said, a toad sprang out of her mouth, so that everyone was seized with horror of her.

Then the stepmother was still more enraged, and thought of nothing but how to do every possible injury to the man's daughter, whose beauty, however, grew daily greater. At length she took a cauldron, set it on the fire, and boiled yarn in it. When it was boiled, she flung it on the poor girl's shoulder, and gave her an axe in order that she might go on the frozen river, cut a hole in the ice, and rinse the yarn. She was obedient, went and cut a hole in the ice; and while she was in the midst of her cutting, a splendid carriage came driving up, in which sat the King. The carriage stopped, and the King asked, "My child, who are you, and what are you doing here?"

"I am a poor girl, and I am rinsing yarn."

Then the King felt compassion, and when he saw that she was so very beautiful, he said to her, "Will you go away with me?"

"Ah, yes, with all my heart," she answered, for she was glad to get away from the mother and sister.

So she got into the carriage and drove away with the King, and when they arrived at his palace, the wedding was celebrated with great pomp, as the little men had granted to the maiden. When a year was over, the young Queen bore a son, and as the stepmother had heard of her great good fortune, she came with her daughter to the palace and pretended that she wanted to pay her a visit. Once, however, the King had gone out, and no one else was present, the wicked woman seized the Queen by the head, and her daughter seized her by the feet, and they lifted her out of the bed, and threw her out of the window into the stream which flowed by. Then the ugly daughter laid herself in the bed, and the old woman covered her up over her head. When the King came home again and wanted to speak to his wife, the old woman cried, "Hush, hush, that can't be now, she is lying in a violent perspiration; you must let her rest today." The King suspected no evil, and did not come back again till next morning; and as he talked with his wife and she answered him, with every word a toad leaped out, whereas formerly a piece of gold had fallen out. Then he asked what that could be, but the old woman said that she had got that from the violent perspiration, and would soon lose it again. During the night, however, the kitchen boy saw a duck come swimming up the gutter, and it said,

"King, what are you doing?
Are you awake, or slumbering?

And as he returned no answer, it said,

"And my guests, what about them?"

The kitchen boy said,

"They are sleeping soundly, too."

Then it asked again,

"What of my little baby mine?"

He answered,

"Asleep in her cradle."

Then she went upstairs in the form of the Queen, nursed the baby, shook up its little bed, covered it over, and then swam away again down the gutter in the shape of a duck. She came thus for two nights; on the third, she said to the kitchen boy, "Go and tell the King to take his sword and swing it three times over me on the threshold." Then the kitchen boy ran and told this to the King, who came with his sword and swung it thrice over the spirit, and at the third time, his wife stood before him strong, alive, and as healthy as she had been before. At this the King was full of great joy, but he kept the Queen hidden in a chamber until the Sunday when the baby was to be christened. And when it was christened he said, "What does a person deserve who drags another out of bed and throws him in the water?"

"The wretch deserves nothing better," answered the old woman, "than to be taken and put in a barrel stuck full of nails, and rolled downhill into the water."

"Then," said the King, "You have pronounced your own sentence;" and he ordered such a barrel to be brought, and the old woman to be put into it with her daughter, and then the top was hammered on, and the barrel rolled downhill until it went into the river.

14. THE THREE SPINNERS

There was once a girl who was idle and would not spin, and let her mother try as she might, she could not bring her to it. At last the mother was so overcome with anger and impatience, that she beat her, on which the girl began to weep loudly. Now at this very moment the Queen drove by, and when she heard the weeping she stopped her carriage, went into the house and asked the mother why she was beating her daughter so that the cries could be heard out on the road? Then the woman was ashamed to reveal the laziness of her daughter and said, "I cannot get her to quit spinning. She insists on spinning forever and ever, and I am poor, and cannot procure the flax."

Then answered the Queen, "There is nothing that I like better than the sound of spinning, and I am never happier than when the wheels are humming. Let me have your daughter with me in the palace. I have flax enough, and there she shall spin as much as she likes." The mother was heartily satisfied with this, and the Queen took the girl with her. When they had arrived at the palace, she led her up into three rooms which were filled from the bottom to the top with the finest flax. "Now spin me this flax," said she, "and when you have done it, you shall have my eldest son for a husband, even if you are poor. I do not care about that, for you are an industrious worker." The girl was secretly terrified, for she could not have spun the flax, no, not if she had lived till she was three hundred years old, and had sat at it every day from morning till night. When she was alone, she began to weep, and sat thus for three days without moving a finger. On the third day came the Queen, and when she saw that nothing had been spun yet, she was surprised; but the girl excused herself by saying that she had not been able to begin because of her great distress at leaving her mother's house. The queen was satisfied with this, but said when she was going away, "Tomorrow you must begin to work."

When the girl was alone again, she did not know what to do, and in her distress went to the window. Then she saw three women coming towards her, the first of whom had a broad flat foot, the second had such a great underlip that it hung down over her chin, and the third had a broad thumb. They remained standing before the window, looked up, and asked the girl what was amiss with her? She complained of her trouble, and then they offered her their help and said, "If you will invite us to the wedding, not be ashamed of us, and will call us your aunts, and likewise will place us at your table, we will spin up the flax for you, and that in a very short time."

"With all my heart," she replied, "come in and begin the work at once." Then she let in the three strange women, and cleared a place in the first room, where they seated themselves and began their spinning. The one drew the thread and trod the wheel, the other wetted the thread, the third twisted it, and struck the table with her finger, and as often as she struck it, a skein of thread fell to the ground that was spun in the finest manner possible. The girl concealed the three spinners from the Queen, and showed her whenever she came the great quantity of spun thread, until the latter could not praise her enough. When the first room was empty she went to the second, and at last to the third, and that too was quickly cleared.

Then the three women took leave and said to the girl, "Do not forget what you have promised us—it will make your fortune."

When the maiden showed the Queen the empty rooms, and the great heap of yarn, she gave orders for the wedding, and the bridegroom rejoiced that he was to have such a clever and industrious wife, and praised her mightily. "I have three aunts," said the girl, "and as they have been very kind to me, I should not like to forget them in my good fortune; allow me to invite them to the wedding, and let them sit with us at table."

The Queen and the bridegroom said, "Why should we not allow that?"

Therefore when the feast began, the three women entered in strange apparel, and the bride said, "Welcome, dear aunts."

"Ah," said the bridegroom, "how ever did you get such odious friends?" He went to the one with the broad flat foot, and said, "How do you come by such a broad foot?"

"By treading," she answered, "by treading."

Then the bridegroom went to the second, and said, "How do you come by your falling lip?"

"By licking," she answered, "by licking."

Then he asked the third, "How do you come by your broad thumb?"

"By twisting the thread," she answered, "by twisting the thread."

At this the King's son was alarmed and said, "Neither now nor ever shall my beautiful bride touch a spinning wheel." And thus she got rid of the hateful flax-spinning.

15. HANSEL AND GRETEL

Near a great forest dwelt a poor woodcutter with his wife and his two children. The boy was called Hansel and the girl Gretel. He had little to bite and to break, and when great scarcity fell on the land, he could no longer procure daily bread. Now when he thought over this at night in his bed, and tossed about in his anxiety, he groaned and said to his wife, "What is to become of us? How are we to feed our poor children, when we no longer have anything even for ourselves?"

"I'll tell you what, husband," answered the woman, "Early tomorrow morning we will take the children out into the forest where it is the thickest. There we will light a fire for them, and give each of them one piece of bread, and then we will go to our work and leave them alone. They will not find the way home again, and we shall be rid of them."

"No, wife," said the man, "I will not do that; how can I bear to leave my children alone in the forest?—the wild animals would soon come and tear them to pieces."

"O, you fool!" said she, "Then we must all four die of hunger. You may as well plane the planks for our coffins," and she left him no peace until he consented.

"But I feel very sorry for the poor children, all the same," said the man.

The two children had also not been able to sleep for hunger, and had heard what their stepmother had said to their father. Gretel wept bitter tears, and said to Hansel, "Now all is over for us."

"Hush, Gretel," said Hansel, "do not distress yourself, I will soon find a way to help us." And when the old folks had fallen asleep, he got up, put on his little coat, opened the door below, and crept outside. The moon shone brightly, and the white pebbles which lay in front of the house glittered like real silver pennies. Hansel stooped and put as many of them in the little pocket of his coat as he could possibly get in. Then he went back and said to Gretel, "Be comforted, dear little sister, and sleep in peace, God will not forsake us," and he lay down again in his bed.

When day dawned, but before the sun had risen, the woman came and awoke the two children, saying, "Get up, you sluggards! We are going into the forest to fetch wood." She gave each a little piece of bread, and said, "There is something for your dinner, but do not eat it up before then, for you will get nothing else." Gretel took the bread under her apron, as Hansel had the stones in his pocket. Then they all set out together on the way to the forest. When they had walked a short time, Hansel stood still and peeped back at the house, and did so again and again.

His father said, "Hansel, what are you looking at there and staying behind for? Mind yourself, and do not forget how to use your legs."

"Ah, father," said Hansel, "I am looking at my little white cat, which is sitting up on the roof, and wants to say goodbye to me."

The wife said, "Fool, that is not your little cat, that is the morning sun which is shining on the chimneys." Hansel, however, had not been looking back at the cat, but had been constantly throwing one of the white pebble-stones out of his pocket on the road.

When they had reached the middle of the forest, the father said, "Now, children, pile up some wood, and I will light a fire that you may not be cold." Hansel and Gretel gathered brushwood together, as high as a little hill.

The brushwood was lighted, and when the flames were burning very high, the woman said, "Now, children, lay yourselves down by the fire and rest. We will go into the forest and cut some wood. When we have done, we will come back and fetch you away."

Hansel and Gretel sat by the fire, and when noon came, each ate a little piece of bread, and as they heard the strokes of the wood-axe they believed that their father was near. It was not, however, the axe, it was a branch which he had fastened to a withered tree which the wind was blowing backwards and forwards. And as they had been sitting such a long time, their eyes shut with fatigue, and they fell fast asleep. When at last they awoke, it was already dark night. Gretel began to cry and said, "How are we to get out of the forest now?"

But Hansel comforted her and said, "Just wait a little, until the moon has risen, and then we will soon find the way." And when the full moon had risen, Hansel took his little sister by the hand, and followed the pebbles which shone like newly-coined silver pieces, and showed them the way.

They walked the whole night long, and by break of day came once more to their father's house. They knocked at the door, and when the woman opened it and saw that it was Hansel and Gretel, she said, "You naughty children, why have you slept so long in the forest? We thought you were never coming back at all!" The father, however, rejoiced, for it had cut him to the heart to leave them behind alone.

Not long afterwards, there was once more great scarcity in all parts, and the children heard their mother saying at night to their father, "Everything is eaten again, we have one half loaf left, and after that there is no more. The children must go. We will take them farther into the wood, so that they will not find their way out again; there is no other means of saving ourselves!"

The man's heart was heavy, and he thought, "It would be better for you to share the last mouthful with your children." The woman, however, would listen to nothing that he had to say, but scolded and reproached him. He who says A must say B, likewise, and as he had yielded the first time, he had to do so a second time also.

The children were, however, still awake and had heard the conversation. When the old folks were asleep, Hansel again got up, and wanted to go out and pick up pebbles as he had done before, but the woman had locked the door, and Hansel could not get out. Nevertheless he comforted his little sister, and said, "Do not cry, Gretel, go to sleep quietly, the good God will help us."

Early in the morning came the woman, and took the children out of their beds. Their bit of bread was given to them, but it was still smaller than the time before. On the way into the forest Hansel crumbled his in his pocket, and often stood still and threw a morsel on the ground.

"Hansel, why do you stop and look round?" said the father, "Go on."

"I am looking back at my little pigeon which is sitting on the roof, and wants to say goodbye to me," answered Hansel.

"Simpleton!" said the woman, "That is not your little pigeon, that is the morning sun that is shining on the chimney." Hansel, however, little by little, threw all the crumbs on the path.

The woman led the children still deeper into the forest, where they had never in their lives been before. Then a great fire was again made, and the mother said, "Just sit there, you children, and when you are tired you may sleep a little; we are going into the forest to cut wood, and in the evening when we are done, we will come and fetch you away."

When it was noon, Gretel shared her piece of bread with Hansel, who had scattered his by the way. Then they fell asleep and evening came and went, but no one came to the poor children. They did not awake until it was dark night, and Hansel comforted his little sister and said, "Just wait, Gretel, until the moon rises, and then we shall see the crumbs of bread which I have strewn about, they will show us our way home again." When the moon came they set out, but they found no crumbs, for the many thousands of birds which fly about in the woods and fields had picked them all up. Hansel said to Gretel, "We shall soon find the way," but they did not find it. They walked the whole night and all the next day, too, from morning till evening, but they did not get out of the forest, and were very hungry, for they had nothing to eat but two or three berries, which grew on the ground. And as they were so weary that their legs would carry them no longer, they lay down beneath a tree and fell asleep.

It was now three mornings since they had left their father's house. They began to walk again, but they always got deeper into the forest, and if help did not come soon, they would die of hunger and weariness. When it was midday, they saw a beautiful snow-white bird sitting on a bough, which sang so delightfully that they stood still and listened to it. And when it had finished its song, it spread its wings and flew away before them, and they followed it until they reached a little house, on the roof of which it alighted; and when they came quite up to the little house they saw that it was built of bread and covered with cakes, but that the windows were of clear sugar. "We will set to work on that," said Hansel, "and have a good meal. I will eat a bit of the roof, and you, Gretel, can eat some of the window, it will taste sweet." Hansel reached up above, and broke off a little of the roof to try how it tasted, and Gretel leaned against the window and nibbled at the panes. Then a soft voice cried from the room,

"Nibble, nibble, gnaw,
Who is nibbling at my little house?"

The children answered,

"The wind, the wind,
The heaven-born wind,"

and went on eating without disturbing themselves. Hansel, who thought the roof tasted very nice, tore down a great piece of it, and Gretel pushed out the whole of one round windowpane, sat down, and enjoyed herself with it. Suddenly the door opened, and a very, very old woman, who supported herself on crutches, came creeping out. Hansel and Gretel were so terribly frightened that they let fall what they had in their hands. The old woman, however, nodded her head, and said, "Oh, you dear children, who has brought you here? Do come in, and stay with me. No harm shall happen to you." She took them both by the hand, and led them into her little house. Then good food was set before them, milk and pancakes, with sugar, apples, and nuts. Afterwards two pretty little beds were covered with clean white linen, and Hansel and Gretel lay down in them, and thought they were in heaven.

The old woman had only pretended to be so kind; she was in reality a wicked witch, who lay in wait for children, and had only built the little house of bread in order to entice them there. When a child fell into her power, she killed it, cooked and ate it, and that was a feast day with her. Witches have red eyes, and cannot see far, but they have a keen scent like the beasts, and are aware when human beings draw near. When Hansel and Gretel came into her neighborhood, she laughed maliciously, and said mockingly, "I have them, they shall not escape me again!"

Early in the morning before the children were awake, she was already up, and when she saw both of them sleeping and looking so pretty, with their plump red cheeks, she muttered to herself, "That will be a dainty mouthful!"

Then she seized Hansel with her shriveled hand, carried him into a little stable, and shut him in with a grated door. He might scream as he liked, that was of no use. Then she went to Gretel, shook her till she awoke, and cried, "Get up, lazy thing, fetch some water, and cook something good for your brother, he is in the stable outside, and is to be made fat. When he is fat, I will eat him." Gretel began to weep bitterly, but it was all in vain; she was forced to do what the wicked witch ordered her.

And now the best food was cooked for poor Hansel, but Gretel got nothing but crab shells. Every morning the woman crept to the little stable, and cried, "Hansel, stretch out your finger that I may feel if you will soon be fat." Hansel, however, stretched out a little bone to her, and the old woman, who had dim eyes, could not see it, and thought it was Hansel's finger, and was astonished that there was no way of fattening him. When four weeks had gone by, and Hansel still stayed thin, she was seized with impatience and would not wait any longer.

"Now, Gretel," she cried to the girl, "be active, and bring some water. Let Hansel be fat or lean, tomorrow I will kill him, and cook him."

Ah, how the poor little sister did lament when she had to fetch the water, and how her tears did flow down over her cheeks! "Dear God, do help us," she cried. "If the wild beasts in the forest had devoured us, at least we should have died together."

"Just keep your noise to yourself," said the old woman, "all that won't help you at all."

Early in the morning, Gretel had to go out and hang up the cauldron with the water, and light the fire. "We will bake first," said the old woman. "I have already heated the oven, and kneaded the dough." She pushed poor Gretel out to the oven, from which flames of fire were already darting. "Creep in," said the witch, "and see if it is properly heated, so that we can shut the bread in." And once Gretel was inside, she intended to shut the oven and let her bake in it, and then she would eat her, too.

But Gretel saw what she had in her mind, and said, "I do not know how I am to do it; how do you get in?"

"Silly goose," said the old woman, "The door is big enough; just look, I can get in myself!" and she crept up and thrust her head into the oven. Then Gretel gave her a push that drove her far into it, and shut the iron door, and fastened the bolt. Oh! Then she began to howl quite horribly, but Gretel ran away, and the godless witch was miserably burnt to death.

Gretel, however, ran like lightning to Hansel, opened his little stable, and cried, "Hansel, we are saved! The old witch is dead!" Then Hansel sprang out like a bird from its cage when the door is opened for it. How they did rejoice and embrace each other, and dance about and kiss each other! And as they had no longer any need to fear her, they went into the witch's house, and in every corner there stood chests full of pearls and jewels.

"These are far better than pebbles!" said Hansel, and thrust into his pockets whatever could be got in, and Gretel said, "I, too, will take something home with me," and filled her pinafore full. "But now we will go away," said Hansel, "that we may get out of the witch's forest."

When they had walked for two hours, they came to a great body of water. "We cannot get over," said Hansel, "I see no foot-plank, and no bridge."

"And no boat crosses either," answered Gretel, "but a white duck is swimming there; if I ask her, she will help us over." Then she cried,

> "Little duck, little duck, do you see,
> Hansel and Gretel are waiting for you?
> There's never a plank, or bridge in sight,
> Take us across on your back so white."

The duck came to them, and Hansel seated himself on its back, and told his sister to sit by him. "No," replied Gretel, "that will be too heavy for the little duck; she shall take us across, one after the other." The good little duck did so, and when they were safely across and had walked for a short time, the forest seemed to be more and more familiar to them, and at length they saw from afar their father's house. Then they began to run, rushed into the parlor, and threw themselves into their father's arms. The man had not known one happy hour since he had left the children in the forest; the woman, however, was dead. Gretel emptied her pinafore until pearls and precious stones ran about the room, and Hansel threw one handful after another out of his pocket to add to them. Then all anxiety was at an end, and they lived together in perfect happiness. My tale is done, see the mouse run, whoever catches it, may make himself a big fur cap out of it.

16. THE THREE SNAKE-LEAVES

There was once on a time a poor man, who could no longer support his only son. Then said the son, "Dear father, things go so badly with us that I am a burden to you. I would rather go away and see how I can earn my bread." So the father gave him his blessing, and with great sorrow they parted. At this time the King of a mighty empire was at war, and the youth entered his service, and with him went out to fight. And when he came before the enemy, there was a battle, and great danger, and it rained shot until his comrades fell on all sides, and when the leader also was killed, those left were about to take flight, but the youth stepped forth, spoke boldly to them, and cried, "We will not let our fatherland be ruined!" Then the others followed him, and he pressed on and conquered the enemy. When the King heard that he owed the victory to him alone, he raised him above all the others, gave him great treasures, and made him the first in the Kingdom.

The King had a daughter who was very beautiful, but she was also very strange. She had made a vow to take no one as her lord and husband who did not promise to let himself be buried alive with her if she died first. "If he loves me with all his heart," said she, "of what use will life be to him afterwards?" On her side she would do the same, and if he died first, would go down to the grave with him. This strange oath had up to this time frightened away all wooers, but the youth became so charmed with her beauty that he cared for nothing, but asked her father for her.

"But do you know what you must promise?" said the King.

"I must be buried with her," he replied, "if I outlive her, but my love is so great that I do not mind the danger." Then the King consented, and the wedding was solemnized with great splendor.

They lived now for a while happy and contented with each other, and then it befell that the young Queen was attacked by a severe illness, and no physician could save her. And as she lay there dead, the young King remembered what he had been obliged to promise, and was horrified at having to lie down alive in the grave, but there was no escape. The King had placed sentries at all the gates, and it was not possible to avoid his fate. When the day came when the corpse was to be buried, he was taken down into the royal vault with it and then the door was shut and bolted.

Near the coffin stood a table on which were four candles, four loaves of bread, and four bottles of wine, and when this provision came to an end, he would have to die of hunger. And now he sat there full of pain and grief, ate every day only a little piece of bread, drank only a mouthful of wine, and nevertheless saw death daily drawing nearer. While he thus gazed before him, he saw a snake creep out of a corner of the vault and approach the dead body. And as he thought it came to gnaw at it, he drew his sword and said, "As long as I live, you shall not touch her," and hewed the snake in three pieces.

After a time a second snake crept out of the hole, and when it saw the other lying dead and cut in pieces, it went back, but soon came again with three green leaves in its mouth. Then it took the three pieces of the snake, laid them together, as they ought to go, and placed one of the leaves on each wound. Immediately the severed parts joined themselves together, the snake moved, and became alive again, and both of them hastened away together. The leaves were left lying on the ground, and a desire came into the mind of the unhappy man who had been watching all this, to know if the wondrous power of the leaves which had brought the snake to life again, could not likewise be of service to a human being. So he picked up the leaves and laid one of them on the mouth of his dead wife, and the two others on her eyes. And hardly had he done this than the blood stirred in her veins, rose into her pale face, and colored it again. Then she drew breath, opened her eyes, and said, "Ah, God, where am I?"

"You are with me, dear wife," he answered, and told her how everything had happened, and how he had brought her back to life again. Then he gave her some wine and bread, and when she had regained her strength, he raised her up and they went to the door and knocked, and called so loudly that the sentries heard it, and told the King. The King came down himself and opened the door, and there he found both strong and well, and rejoiced with them that now all sorrow was over.

The young King, however, took the three snake-leaves with him, gave them to a servant and said, "Keep them for me carefully, and carry them constantly about you; who knows in what trouble they may yet be of service to us!"

A change had, however, taken place in his wife; after she had been restored to life, it seemed as if all love for her husband had gone out of her heart. After some time, when he wanted to make a voyage over the sea, to visit his old father, and they had gone on board a ship, she forgot the great love and fidelity which he had shown her, and which had been the means of rescuing her from death, and conceived a wicked inclination for the skipper. And once when the young King lay there asleep, she called in the skipper and seized the sleeper by the head, and the skipper took him by the feet, and thus they threw him down into the sea. When the shameful deed was done, she said, "Now let us return home, and say that he died on the way. I will extol and praise you so to my father that he will marry me to you, and make you the heir to his crown." But the faithful servant who had seen all that they did, unseen by them, unfastened a little boat from the ship, got into it, sailed after his master, and let the traitors go on their way. He fished up the dead body, and by the help of the three snake-leaves which he carried about with him, and laid on the eyes and mouth, he fortunately brought the young King back to life.

They both rowed with all their strength day and night, and their little boat flew so swiftly that they reached the old King before the others did. He was astonished when he saw them come alone, and asked what had happened to them. When he learned the wickedness of his daughter he said, "I cannot believe that she has behaved so ill, but the truth will soon come to light," and bade both go into a secret chamber and keep themselves hidden from everyone. Soon afterwards the great ship came sailing in, and the godless woman appeared before her father with a troubled countenance. He said, "Why do you come back alone? Where is your husband?"

"Ah, dear father," she replied, "I come home again in great grief; during the voyage, my husband became suddenly ill and died, and if the good skipper had not given me his help, it would have gone badly for me. He was present at his death, and can tell you all." The King said, "I will make the dead alive again," and opened the chamber, and bade the two come out. When the woman saw her husband, she was thunderstruck, and fell on her knees and begged for mercy.

The King said, "There is no mercy. He was ready to die with you and restored you to life again, but you have murdered him in his sleep, and shall receive the reward that you deserve." Then she was placed with her accomplice in a ship which had been pierced with holes, and sent out to sea, where they soon sank amid the waves.

17. THE WHITE SNAKE

A long time ago there lived a king who was famed for his wisdom through all the land. Nothing was hidden from him, and it seemed as if news of the most secret things was brought to him through the air. But he had a strange custom; every day after dinner, when the table was cleared, and no one else was present, a trusty servant had to bring him one more dish. It was covered, however, and even the servant did not know what was in it, nor did anyone know, for the King never took off the cover to eat until he was quite alone.

This had gone on for a long time, when one day the servant, who took away the dish, was overcome with such curiosity that he could not help carrying the dish into his room. When he had carefully locked the door, he lifted up the cover, and saw a white snake lying on the dish. But when he saw it he could not deny himself the pleasure of tasting it, so he cut off a little bit and put it into his mouth. No sooner had it touched his tongue than he heard a strange whispering of little voices outside his window. He went and listened, and then noticed that it was the sparrows who were chattering together, and telling one another of all kinds of things which they had seen in the fields and woods. Eating the snake had given him power of understanding the language of animals.

Now it so happened that on this very day the Queen lost her most beautiful ring, and suspicion of having stolen it fell upon this trusty servant, who was allowed to go everywhere. The King ordered the man to be brought before him, and threatened with angry words that unless he could before the morrow point out the thief, he himself should be looked upon as guilty and executed. In vain he declared his innocence; he was dismissed with no better answer.

In his trouble and fear he went down into the courtyard and thought about how to help himself out of his trouble. Now some ducks were sitting together quietly by a brook and taking their rest; and, while they were making their feathers smooth with their bills, they were having a confidential conversation together. The servant stood by and listened. They were telling one another of all the places where they had been waddling about all the morning, and what good food they had found, and one said in a pitiful tone, "Something lies heavy in my stomach; as

I was eating in haste I swallowed a ring which lay under the Queen's window."

The servant at once seized her by the neck, carried her to the kitchen, and said to the cook, "Here is a fine duck; pray, kill her."

"Yes," said the cook, and weighed her in his hand; "she has spared no trouble to fatten herself, and has been waiting to be roasted long enough." So he cut off her head, and as she was being dressed for the spit, the Queen's ring was found inside her.

The servant could now easily prove his innocence; and the King, to make amends for the wrong, allowed him to ask a favor, and promised him the best place in the court that he could wish for. The servant refused everything, and only asked for a horse and some money for traveling, as he had a mind to see the world and go about a little.

When his request was granted he set out on his way, and one day came to a pond, where he saw three fishes caught in the reeds and gasping for water. Now, though it is said that fishes are mute, he heard them lamenting that they must perish so miserably, and, as he had a kind heart, he got off his horse and put the three prisoners back into the water. They quivered with delight, put out their heads, and cried to him, "We will remember you and repay you for saving us!"

He rode on, and after a while it seemed to him that he heard a voice in the sand at his feet. He listened, and heard an ant king complain, "Why cannot folks, with their clumsy beasts, keep off our bodies? That stupid horse, with his heavy hoofs, has been treading down my people without mercy!" So the servant turned on to a side path and the ant king cried out to him, "We will remember you—one good turn deserves another!"

The path led him into a wood, and here he saw two old ravens standing by their nest, and throwing out their young ones. "Out with you, you idle, good-for-nothing creatures!" cried they; "we cannot find food for you any longer; you are big enough, and can provide for yourselves."

But the poor young ravens lay upon the ground, flapping their wings, and crying, "Oh, what helpless chicks we are! We must shift for ourselves, and yet we cannot fly! What can we do, but lie here and starve?" So the good young fellow alighted and killed his horse with his sword, and gave it to them for food. Then they came hopping up to it, satisfied their hunger, and cried, "We will remember you—one good turn deserves another!"

And now he had to use his own legs, and when he had walked a long way, he came to a large city. There was a great noise and crowd in the streets, and a man rode up on horseback, crying aloud, "The King's daughter wants a husband; but whoever pursues her hand must perform a hard task, and if he does not succeed he will forfeit his life." Many had already made the attempt, but in vain; nevertheless when the youth saw the King's daughter he was so overcome by her great beauty that he forgot all danger, went before the King, and declared himself a suitor.

So he was led out to the sea, and a gold ring was thrown into it, in his sight; then the King ordered him to fetch this ring up from the bottom of the sea, and added, "If you come up again without it you will be thrown in again and again until you perish amid the waves." All the people grieved for the handsome youth; then they went away, leaving him alone by the sea.

He stood on the shore and considered what he should do, when suddenly he saw three fishes come swimming towards him, and they were the very fishes whose lives he had saved. The one in the middle held a mussel in its mouth, which it laid on the shore at the youth's feet, and when he had taken it up and opened it, there lay the gold ring in the shell. Full of joy he took it to the King, and expected that he would grant him the promised reward.

But when the proud princess perceived that he was not her equal in birth, she scorned him, and required him first to perform another task. She went down into the garden and strewed with her own hands ten sacks full of millet seed on the grass; then she said, "Tomorrow morning before sunrise these must be picked up, with not a single grain missing."

The youth sat down in the garden and considered how it might be possible to perform this task, but he could think of nothing, and there he sat sorrowfully awaiting the break of day, when he should be led to death. But as soon as the first rays of the sun shone into the garden he saw all the ten sacks standing side by side, quite full, and not a single grain was missing. The ant king had come in the night with thousands and thousands of ants, and the grateful creatures had by great industry picked up all the millet seed and gathered them into the sacks.

Presently the King's daughter herself came down into the garden, and was amazed to see that the young man had done the task she had given him. But she could not yet conquer her proud heart, and said,

"Although he has performed both the tasks, he shall not be my husband until he has brought me an apple from the Tree of Life."

The youth did not know where the Tree of Life stood, but he set out, and would have gone on forever, as long as his legs would carry him, though he had no hope of finding it. After he had wandered through three kingdoms, he came one evening to a wood, and lay down under a tree to sleep. But he heard a rustling in the branches, and a golden apple fell into his hand. At the same time three ravens flew down to him, perched themselves upon his knee, and said, "We are the three young ravens whom you saved from starving; when we had grown big, and heard that you were seeking the Golden Apple, we flew over the sea to the end of the world, where the Tree of Life stands, and have brought you the apple." The youth, full of joy, set out homewards, and took the Golden Apple to the King's beautiful daughter, who had no more excuses left to make. They cut the Apple of Life in two and ate it together; and then her heart became full of love for him, and they lived in undisturbed happiness to a great age.

18. THE STRAW, THE COAL, AND THE BEAN

In a village dwelt a poor old woman, who had gathered together a dish of beans and wanted to cook them. So she made a fire on her hearth, and so that it might burn quicker, she lighted it with a handful of straw. When she was emptying the beans into the pan, one dropped without her observing it, and lay on the ground beside a straw, and soon afterwards a burning coal from the fire leapt down to the two. Then the straw began and said, "Dear friends, from where do you come here?"

The coal replied, "I fortunately sprang out of the fire, and if I had not escaped by main force, my death would have been certain—I should have been burnt to ashes."

The bean said, "I too have escaped with a whole skin, but if the old woman had got me into the pan, I should have been made into broth without any mercy, like my comrades."

"And would a better fate have fallen to my lot?" said the straw. "The old woman has destroyed all my brethren in fire and smoke; she seized sixty of them at once, and took their lives. I luckily slipped through her fingers."

"But what are we to do now?" said the coal.

"I think," answered the bean, "that as we have so fortunately escaped death, we should keep together like good companions, and lest a new misfortune should overtake us here, we should go away together, to a foreign country."

The proposition pleased the two others, and they set out on their way in company. Soon, however, they came to a little brook, and as there was no bridge or foot-plank, they did not know how they were to get over it. The straw hit on a good idea, and said, "I will lay myself straight across, and then you can walk over on me as on a bridge." The straw therefore stretched itself from one bank to the other, and the coal, who was of an impetuous disposition, tripped quite boldly on to the newly-built bridge. But when she had reached the middle, and heard the water rushing beneath her, she was, after all, afraid, and stood still, and ventured no farther. The straw, however, began to burn, broke in two pieces, and fell into the stream. The coal slipped after her, hissed when she got into the water, and breathed her last. The bean, who had prudently stayed behind on the shore, could not but laugh at the event, was unable to stop, and laughed so heartily that she burst. It would have been all over for her, likewise, if, by good fortune, a tailor who was traveling in search of work, had not sat down to rest by the brook. As he had a compassionate heart he pulled out his needle and thread, and sewed her together. The bean thanked him most prettily, but as the tailor used black thread, all beans since then have a black seam.

19. THE FISHERMAN AND HIS WIFE

There was once upon a time a fisherman who lived with his wife in a miserable pigsty close by the sea, and every day he went out fishing. And once as he was sitting with his rod, looking at the clear water, his line suddenly went down, far down below, and when he drew it up again he brought out a large flounder. Then the flounder said to him, "Listen, you fisherman, I pray you, let me live, I am no flounder really, but an enchanted prince. What good will it do you to kill me? I should not be good to eat, put me in the water again, and let me go."

"Come," said the fisherman, "there is no need for so many words about it—a fish that can talk I should certainly let go, anyhow." With that he put him back again into the clear water, and the flounder went to the bottom, leaving a long streak of blood behind him. Then the fisherman got up and went home to his wife in the pigsty.

"Husband," said the woman, "have you caught nothing today?"

"No," said the man, "I did catch a flounder, who said he was an enchanted prince, so I let him go again."

"Did you not wish for anything first?" said the woman.

"No," said the man; "what should I wish for?"

"Ah," said the woman, "it is surely hard to have to live always in this dirty pigsty; you might have wished for a small cottage for us. Go back and call him. Tell him we want to have a small cottage, he will certainly give us that."

"Ah," said the man, "why should I go there again?"

"Why," said the woman, "you did catch him, and you let him go again; he is sure to do it. Go at once." The man still did not quite like to go, but did not like to oppose his wife, and went to the sea.

When he got there the sea was all green and yellow, and no longer so smooth; so he stood still and said,

"Flounder, flounder in the sea,
Come, I pray you, here to me;
For my wife, good Isabel,
Has sent me here against my will."

Then the flounder came swimming to him and said, "Well what does she want, then?"

"Ah," said the man, "I did catch you, and my wife says I really ought to have wished for something. She does not like to live in a wretched pigsty any longer. She would like to have a cottage."

"Go, then," said the flounder, "she has it already."

When the man went home, his wife was no longer in the pigsty, but instead of it there stood a small cottage, and she was sitting on a bench before the door. Then she took him by the hand and said to him, "Just come inside, look, now isn't this a great deal better?" So they went in, and there was a small porch, and a pretty little parlor and bedroom, and a kitchen and pantry, with the best of furniture, and fitted up with the most beautiful things made of tin and brass, whatever was wanted. And behind the cottage there was a small yard, with hens and ducks, and a little garden with flowers and fruit. "Look," said the wife, "is not that nice!"

"Yes," said the husband, "and so we must always think it. Now we will live quite contented."

"We will think about that," said the wife. With that they ate something and went to bed.

Everything went well for a week or a fortnight, and then the woman said, "Listen, husband, this cottage is far too small for us, and the garden and yard are little; the flounder might just as well have given us a larger house. I should like to live in a great stone castle; go to the flounder, and tell him to give us a castle."

"Ah, wife," said the man, "the cottage is quite good enough; why should we live in a castle?"

"What!" said the woman; "Just go there, the flounder can always do that."

"No, wife," said the man, "the flounder has just given us the cottage, I do not like to go back so soon, it might make him angry."

"Go," said the woman, "he can do it quite easily, and will be glad to do it; just you go to him."

The man's heart grew heavy, and he did not want to go. He said to himself, "It is not right," and yet he went. And when he came to the sea the water was quite purple and dark blue, and grey and thick, and no longer so green and yellow, but it was still quiet. And he stood there and said—

"Flounder, flounder in the sea,
Come, I pray you, here to me;
For my wife, good Isabel,
Has sent me here against my will."

"Well, what does she want, then?" said the flounder.

"Alas," said the man, half scared, "she wants to live in a great stone castle."

"Go to it, then, she is standing before the door," said the flounder.

Then the man went away, intending to go home, but when he got there, he found a great stone palace, and his wife was just standing on the steps going in, and she took him by the hand and said, "Come in." So he went in with her, and in the castle was a great hall paved with marble, and many servants, who flung the doors wide. And the walls were all bright with beautiful hangings, and in the rooms were chairs and tables of pure gold, and crystal chandeliers hung from the ceiling, and all the rooms and bed-rooms had carpets, and food and wine of the very best were standing on all the tables, so that they nearly broke down beneath it. Behind the house, too, there was a great courtyard, with stables for horses and cows, and the very best of carriages; there was a magnificent large garden, too, with the most beautiful flowers and fruit trees, and a park half a mile long, in which were stags, deer, and hares, and everything that could be desired. "Come," said the woman, "isn't that beautiful?"

"Yes, indeed," said the man, "now let it be; and we will live in this beautiful castle and be content."

"We will consider about that," said the woman, "and sleep upon it." Then they went to bed.

Next morning the wife awoke first, and it was just daybreak, and from her bed she saw the beautiful country lying before her. Her husband was still stretching himself, so she poked him in the side with her elbow, and said, "Get up, husband, and just peep out of the window. Look you, couldn't we be the King over all that land? Go to the flounder, we will be the King."

"Ah, wife," said the man, "why should we be King? I do not want to be King."

"Well," said the wife, "if you won't be King, I will; go to the flounder, for I will be King."

"Ah, wife," said the man, "why do you want to be King? I do not want to say that to him."

"Why not?" said the woman; "Go to him this instant; I must be King!"

So the man went, and was quite unhappy because his wife wished to be King. "It is not right; it is not right," thought he. He did not wish to go, but yet he went.

And when he came to the sea, it was quite dark-grey, and the water heaved up from below, and smelled putrid. Then he went and stood by it, and said,

"Flounder, flounder in the sea,
Come, I pray you, here to me;
For my wife, good Isabel,
Has sent me here against my will."

"Well, what does she want, then?" said the flounder.

"Alas," said the man, "she wants to be King."

"Go to her; she is King already."

So the man went, and when he came to the palace, the castle had become much larger, and had a great tower and magnificent ornaments, and the sentinel was standing before the door, and there were numbers of soldiers with kettle-drums and trumpets. And when he went inside the house, everything was of real marble and gold, with velvet covers and great golden tassels. Then the doors of the hall were opened, and there was the court in all its splendor, and his wife was sitting on a high throne of gold and diamonds, with a great crown of gold on her head, and a scepter of pure gold and jewels in her hand, and on both sides of her stood her maids-in-waiting in a row, each of them always one head shorter than the last.

Then he went and stood before her, and said, "Ah, wife, and now you are King."

"Yes," said the woman, "now I am King." So he stood and looked at her, and when he had looked at her thus for some time, he said, "And now that you are King, let all else be, now we will wish for nothing more."

"Nay, husband," said the woman, quite anxiously, "I find time passes very heavily, I can bear it no longer; go to the flounder—I am King, but I must be Emperor, too."

"Alas, wife, why do you wish to be Emperor?"

"Husband," said she, "go to the flounder. I will be Emperor."

"Alas, wife," said the man, "he cannot make you Emperor; I may not say that to the fish. There is only one Emperor in the land. An Emperor the flounder cannot make you! I assure you he cannot."

"What!" said the woman, "I am the King, and you are nothing but my husband; will you go this moment? Go at once! If he can make a King he can make an emperor. I will be Emperor; go instantly." So he was forced to go.

As the man went, however, he was troubled in mind, and thought to himself, "It will not end well; it will not end well! Emperor is too shameless! The flounder will at last be tired out."

With that he reached the sea, and the sea was quite black and thick, and began to boil up from below, so that it threw up bubbles, and such a sharp wind blew over it that it curdled, and the man was afraid. Then he went and stood by it, and said,

"Flounder, flounder in the sea,
Come, I pray you, here to me;
For my wife, good Isabel,
Has sent me here against my will."

"Well, what does she want, then?" said the flounder. "Alas, flounder," said he, "my wife wants to be Emperor."

"Go to her," said the flounder; "she is Emperor already."

So the man went, and when he got there the whole palace was made of polished marble with alabaster figures and golden ornaments, and soldiers were marching before the door blowing trumpets, and beating cymbals and drums; and in the house, barons, and counts, and dukes were going about as servants. Then they opened the doors to him, which were made of pure gold. And when he entered, there sat his wife on a throne, which was made of one piece of gold, and was at least two miles high; and she wore a great golden crown that was three yards high, and set with diamonds and carbuncles, and in one hand she had the scepter, and in the other the imperial orb; and on both sides of her stood the yeomen of the guard in two rows, each being smaller than the one before him, from the biggest giant, who was two miles high, to the very smallest dwarf, just as big as my little finger. And before it stood a number of princes and dukes.

Then the man went and stood among them, and said, "Wife, are you Emperor now?"

"Yes," said she, "now I am Emperor."

Then he stood and looked at her well, and when he had looked at her for some time, he said, "Ah, wife, be content, now that you are Emperor."

"Husband," said she, "why are you standing there? Now, I am Emperor, but I will be Pope too; go to the flounder."

"Alas, wife," said the man, "what will you not wish for? You cannot be Pope. There is but one in Christendom. He cannot make you Pope."

"Husband," said she, "I will be Pope; go immediately, I must be Pope this very day."

"No, wife," said the man, "I do not want to say that to him; that would not do, it is too much; the flounder can't make you Pope."

"Husband," said she, "what nonsense! If he can make an emperor he can make a pope. Go to him directly. I am Emperor, and you are nothing but my husband; will you go at once?"

Then he was afraid and went; but he was quite faint, and shivered and shook, and his knees and legs trembled. And a high wind blew over the land, and the clouds flew, and towards evening all grew dark, and the leaves fell from the trees, and the water rose and roared as if it were boiling, and splashed upon the shore. And in the distance he saw ships which were firing guns in distress, pitching and tossing on the waves. And yet in the midst of the sky there was still a small bit of blue, though on every side it was as red as in a heavy storm. So, full of despair, he went and stood in much fear and said,

"Flounder, flounder in the sea,
Come, I pray you, here to me;
For my wife, good Isabel,
Has sent me here against my will."

"Well, what does she want, then?" said the flounder.

"Alas," said the man, "she wants to be Pope."

"Go to her then," said the flounder; "she is Pope already."

So he went, and when he got there, he saw what seemed to be a large church surrounded by palaces. He pushed his way through the crowd. Inside, however, everything was lighted up with thousands and thousands of candles, and his wife was clad in gold, and she was sitting on a much higher throne, and had three great golden crowns on, and round about her there was much ecclesiastical splendor; and on both sides of her was a row of candles the largest of which was as tall as the very tallest tower, down to the very smallest kitchen candle, and all the emperors and kings were on their knees before her, kissing her shoe. "Wife," said the man, and looked attentively at her, "are you now Pope?"

"Yes," said she, "I am Pope."

So he stood and looked at her, and it was just as if he was looking at the bright sun. When he had stood looking at her thus for a short time, he said, "Ah, wife, if you are Pope, do let well enough alone!" But she looked as stiff as a post, and did not move or show any signs of life. Then said he, "Wife, now that you are Pope, be satisfied, you cannot become anything greater now."

"I will consider about that," said the woman. At this they both went to bed, but she was not satisfied, and greediness let her have no sleep, for she was continually thinking what there was left for her to be.

The man slept well and soundly, for he had run about a great deal during the day; but the woman could not fall asleep at all, and flung herself from one side to the other the whole night through, thinking always what more was left for her to be, but unable to call to mind anything else. At length the sun began to rise, and when the woman saw the red of dawn, she sat up in bed and looked at it. And when, through the window, she saw the sun thus rising, she said, "Cannot I, too, order the sun and moon to rise?" "Husband," she said, poking him in the ribs with her elbow, "wake up! Go to the flounder, for I wish to be like God is."

The man was still half asleep, but he was so horrified that he fell out of bed. He thought he must have heard wrong, and rubbed his eyes, and said, "Alas, wife, what are you saying?"

"Husband," said she, "if I can't order the sun and moon to rise, and have to look on and see the sun and moon rising, I can't bear it. I shall not know what it is to have another happy hour, unless I can make them rise myself." Then she looked at him so terribly that a shudder ran over him, and said, "Go at once; I wish to be like God."

"Alas, wife," said the man, falling on his knees before her, "the flounder cannot do that; he can make an emperor and a pope; I beseech you, go on as you are, and be Pope."

Then she fell into a rage, and her hair flew wildly about her head, and she cried, "I will not endure this, I'll not bear it any longer; will you go?"

Then he put on his trousers and ran away like a madman. But outside a great storm was raging, and blowing so hard that he could scarcely keep his feet; houses and trees toppled over, the mountains trembled, rocks rolled into the sea, the sky was pitch black, and it thundered and lightened, and the sea came in with black waves as high as church-towers and mountains, and all with crests of white foam at the top. Then he cried, but could not hear his own words,

"Flounder, flounder in the sea,
Come, I pray you, here to me;
For my wife, good Isabel,
Has sent me here against my will."

"Well, what does she want, then?" said the flounder.

"Alas," said he, "she wants to be like God."

"Go to her, and you will find her back again in the dirty pigsty." And there they are living still at this very time.

20. *THE VALIANT LITTLE TAILOR*

One summer's morning a little tailor was sitting on his table by the window; he was in good spirits, and sewed with all his might. Then came a peasant woman down the street crying, "Good jams, cheap! Good jams, cheap!"

This rang pleasantly in the tailor's ears; he stretched his delicate head out of the window, and called, "Come up here, dear woman; here you will get rid of your goods." The woman came up the three steps to the tailor with her heavy basket, and he made her unpack all of the pots for him. He inspected all of them, lifted them up, put his nose to them, and at length said, "The jam seems to me to be good, so weigh me out three ounces, dear woman, and if it comes to a quarter of a pound I will not complain." The woman who had hoped to find a good sale, gave him what he desired, but went away quite angry and grumbling. "Now, God bless this jam," cried the little tailor, "and give me health and strength;" so he brought the bread out of the cupboard, cut himself a piece right across the loaf and spread the jam over it. "This won't taste bitter," said he, "but I will just finish the jacket before I take a bite." He laid the bread near him, sewed on, and in his joy, made bigger and bigger stitches. In the meantime the smell of the sweet jam ascended to the wall, where the flies were sitting in great numbers, that they were attracted and descended on it in hosts. "Ho! Who invited you?" said the little tailor, and drove the unbidden guests away. The flies, however, who understood no words, would not be turned away, but came back again in ever-increasing companies. The little tailor at last lost all patience, and got a bit of cloth from the hole under his worktable, and saying, "Wait, and I will give it to you," struck it mercilessly on them. When he drew it away and counted, there lay before him no fewer than seven, dead and with legs stretched out. "Are you a fellow of that sort?" said he, and could not help admiring his own bravery. "The whole town shall know of this!" And the little tailor hastened to cut himself a girdle, stitched it, and embroidered on it in large letters, "Seven at one stroke!" "What, the town!" he continued, "The whole world shall hear of it!" and his heart wagged with joy like a lamb's tail. The tailor put on the girdle, and resolved to go forth into the world, because he thought his workshop was too small for his valor. Before he went away, he sought about in the house to see if there was anything which he could take with him; however, he found nothing but old cheese, and that he put in his pocket. In front of the door he observed a bird which had caught itself in the thicket. It had to go into his pocket with the cheese. Now he took to the road boldly, and as he was light and nimble, he felt no fatigue. The road led him up a mountain, and when he had reached the highest point of it, there sat a powerful giant looking about him quite comfortably. The little tailor went bravely up, spoke to him, and said, "Good day, comrade, so you are sitting there overlooking the wide-spread world! I am just on my way there, and want to try my luck. Have you any inclination to go with me?"

The giant looked contemptuously at the tailor, and said, "You ragamuffin! You miserable creature!"

"Oh, indeed?" answered the little tailor, and unbuttoned his coat, and showed the giant the girdle, "There you may read what kind of a man I am!"

The giant read, "Seven at one stroke," and thought that they had been men whom the tailor had killed, and began to feel a little respect for the tiny fellow. Nevertheless, he wished to try him first, and took a stone in his hand and squeezed it together so that water dropped out of it. "Do that likewise," said the giant, "if you have strength?"

"Is that all?" said the tailor, "that is child's play with us!" and put his hand into his pocket, brought out the soft cheese, and pressed it until the liquid ran out of it. "Faith," said he, "that was good, wasn't it?"

The giant did not know what to say, and could not believe it of the little man. Then the giant picked up a stone and threw it so high that the eye could scarcely follow it. "Now, little mite of a man, do that likewise."

"Well thrown," said the tailor, "but after all the stone came down to earth again; I will throw you one which shall never come back at all." And he put his hand into his pocket, took out the bird, and threw it into the air. The bird, delighted with its liberty, rose, flew away and did not come back. "How does that shot please you, comrade?" asked the tailor.

"You can certainly throw," said the giant, "but now we will see if you are able to carry anything properly." He took the little tailor to a mighty oak tree which lay there felled on the ground, and said, "If you are strong enough, help me to carry the tree out of the forest."

"Readily," answered the little man; "you take the trunk on your shoulders, and I will raise up the branches and twigs; after all, they are the heaviest." The giant took the trunk on his shoulder, but the tailor seated himself on a branch, and the giant who could not look round, had to carry away the whole tree, and the little tailor to boot. The tailor was quite merry and happy, and whistled the song, "Three tailors rode forth from the gate," as if carrying the tree were child's play.

The giant, after he had dragged the heavy burden part of the way, could go no further, and cried, "Ho, I shall have to let the tree fall!"

The tailor sprang nimbly down, seized the tree with both arms as if he had been carrying it, and said to the giant, "You are such a great fellow, and yet cannot even carry the tree!"

They went on together, and as they passed a cherry tree, the giant laid hold of the top of the tree where the ripest fruit was hanging, bent it down, put it into the tailor's hand, and bade him eat. But the little tailor was much too weak to hold the tree, and when the giant let it go, it sprang back again, and the tailor was hurried into the air with it. When he had fallen down again without injury, the giant said, "What is this? Have you not strength enough to hold the weak twig?"

"There is no lack of strength," answered the little tailor. "Do you think that could be anything to a man who has struck down seven at one blow? I leapt over the tree because the huntsmen are shooting down there in the thicket. Jump as I did, if you can do it." The giant made the attempt, but could not get over the tree, and remained hanging in the branches, so that in this also the tailor kept the upper hand.

The giant said, "If you are such a valiant fellow, come with me into our cavern and spend the night with us." The little tailor was willing, and followed him. When they went into the cave, other giants were sitting there by the fire, and each of them had a roasted sheep in his hand and was eating it. The little tailor looked round and thought, "It is much more spacious here than in my workshop." The giant showed him a bed, and said he was to lie down in it and sleep. The bed, however, was too big for the little tailor; he did not lie down in it, but crept into a corner. When it was midnight, and the giant thought that the little tailor was lying in a sound sleep, he got up, took a great iron bar, cut through the bed with one blow, and thought he had given the runt his finishing stroke. With the earliest dawn the giants went into the forest, and had quite forgotten the little tailor, when all at once he walked up to them quite merrily and boldly. The giants were terrified, they were afraid that he would strike them all dead, and ran away in a great hurry.

The little tailor went onwards, always following his own pointed nose. After he had walked for a long time, he came to the courtyard of a royal palace, and as he felt weary, he lay down on the grass and fell asleep. While he lay there, the people came and inspected him on all sides, and read on his girdle, "Seven at one stroke." "Ah," said they, "Why is the great warrior here in the midst of peace? He must be a mighty lord." They went and announced him to the King, and gave it as their opinion that if war should break out, this would be a weighty and useful man who ought on no account to be allowed to depart. The counsel pleased the King, and he sent one of his courtiers to the little tailor to offer him military service when he awoke. The ambassador remained standing by the sleeper, waited until he stretched his limbs and opened his eyes, and then conveyed to him this proposal.

"For this very reason I have come here," the tailor replied, "I am ready to enter the King's service." He was therefore honorably received and a special dwelling was assigned him.

The soldiers, however, were set against the little tailor, and wished him a thousand miles away. "What is to be the end of this?" they said amongst themselves. "If we quarrel with him, and he strikes about him, seven of us will fall at every blow; not one of us can stand against him." They came therefore to a decision, went to the King, and begged for their dismissal. "We are not prepared," said they, "to stay with a man who kills seven at one stroke."

The King was sorry that for the sake of one he should lose all his faithful servants, wished that he had never set eyes on the tailor, and would willingly get rid of him again. But he did not venture to give him his dismissal, for he dreaded that he should strike him and all his people dead, and place himself on the royal throne. He thought about it for a long time, and at last found good counsel. He sent to the little tailor and had him informed that as he was such a great warrior, the King had one request to make to him. In a forest of his country lived two giants who caused great mischief with their robbing, murdering, ravaging, and burning, and no one could approach them without putting himself in danger of death. If the tailor conquered and killed these two giants, he would give him his only daughter to wed, and half of his kingdom as a dowry, likewise one hundred horsemen should go with him to assist him.

"That would indeed be a fine thing for a man like me!" thought the little tailor. "One is not offered a beautiful princess and half a kingdom every day of one's life!" "Oh, yes," he replied, "I will soon subdue the giants, and do not require the help of the hundred horsemen to do it; he who can hit seven with one blow has no need to be afraid of two."

The little tailor went forth, and the hundred horsemen followed him. When he came to the outskirts of the forest, he said to his followers, "Just stay waiting here, I alone will soon finish off the giants." Then he bounded into the forest and looked about right and left. After a while he perceived both giants. They lay sleeping under a tree, and snored so that the branches waved up and down. The little tailor, not idle, gathered two pocketfuls of stones, and with these climbed up the tree. When he was halfway up, he slipped down by a branch, until he sat just above the sleepers, and then let one stone after another fall on the breast of one of the giants. For a long time the giant felt nothing, but at last he awoke, pushed his comrade, and said, "Why are you knocking me?"

"You must be dreaming," said the other, "I am not knocking you." They laid themselves down to sleep again, and then the tailor threw a stone down on the second. "What is the meaning of this?" cried the other. "Why are you pelting me?"

"I am not pelting you," answered the first, growling. They disputed about it for a time, but as they were weary they let the matter rest, and their eyes closed once more. The little tailor began his game again, picked out the biggest stone, and threw it with all his might on the breast of the first giant. "That is too much!" cried he, and sprang up like a madman, and pushed his companion against the tree until it shook. The other paid him back in the same coin, and they got into such a rage that they tore up trees and belabored each other so long, that at last they both fell down dead on the ground at the same time. Then the little tailor leapt down.

"It is a lucky thing," said he, "that they did not tear up the tree on which I was sitting, or I should have had to spring on to another like a squirrel; but we tailors are nimble." He drew out his sword and gave each of them a couple of thrusts in the breast, and then went out to the horsemen and said, "The work is done; I have given both of them their finishing stroke, but it was hard work! They tore up trees in their sore need, and defended themselves with them, but all that is to no purpose when a man like myself comes, who can kill seven at one blow."

"But are you not wounded?" asked the horsemen.

"You need not concern yourself about that," answered the tailor, "They have not bent one hair of mine." The horsemen would not believe him, and rode into the forest; there they found the giants swimming in their blood, and all round about lay the torn-up trees.

The little tailor demanded of the King the promised reward; he, however, repented of his promise, and again thought of how he could get rid of the hero. "Before you receive my daughter, and the half of my kingdom," said he to him, "you must perform one more heroic deed. In the forest roams a unicorn which does great harm, and you must catch it first."

"I fear one unicorn still less than two giants. Seven at one blow, is my kind of affair." He took a rope and an axe with him, went forth into the forest, and again bade those who were sent with him to wait outside. He had to seek long. The unicorn soon came towards him, and rushed directly at the tailor, as if it would spear him on his horn without more ceremony. "Softly, softly; it can't be done as quickly as that," said he, and stood still and waited until the animal was quite close, and then sprang nimbly behind the tree. The unicorn ran against the tree with all its strength, and struck its horn so fast in the trunk that it had not enough strength to draw it out again, and thus it was caught. "Now, I have got him," said the tailor, and came out from behind the tree and put the rope round its neck, and then with his axe he hewed the horn out of the tree, and when all was ready he led the beast away and took it to the King.

The King still would not give him the promised reward, and made a third demand. Before the wedding the tailor was to catch him a wild boar that made great havoc in the forest, and the huntsmen should give him their help. "Willingly," said the tailor, "that is child's play!" He did not take the huntsmen with him into the forest, and they were well pleased that he did not, for the wild boar had several times received them in such a manner that they had no inclination to lie in wait for him. When the boar perceived the tailor, it ran at him with foaming mouth and whetted tusks, and was about to throw him to the ground, but the active hero sprang into a chapel which was near, and up to the window at once, and in one bound out again. The boar ran in after him, but the tailor ran round outside and shut the door behind it, and then the raging beast, which was much too heavy and awkward to leap out of the window, was caught. The little tailor called the huntsmen there that they might see the prisoner with their own eyes. The hero, went to the King, who was now, whether he liked it or not, obliged to keep his promise, and the King gave him his daughter and the half of his kingdom. Had he known that it was no warlike hero, but a little tailor who was standing before him, it would have made his heart even less happy than it was. The wedding was held with great magnificence and small joy, and out of a tailor a king was made.

After some time the young Queen heard her husband say in his dreams at night, "Boy, make me the doublet, and patch the pantaloons, or else I will rap the yard-measure over your ears." Then she discovered in what state of life the young lord had been born, and next morning complained of her wrongs to her father, and begged him to help her to get rid of her husband, who was nothing else but a tailor. The King comforted her and said, "Leave your bedroom door open this night, and my servants shall stand outside, and when he has fallen asleep shall go in, bind him, and take him on board a ship which shall carry him into the wide world." The woman was satisfied with this; but the King's amour-bearer, who had heard all, was friendly with the young lord, and informed him of the whole plot.

"I'll put a screw into that business," said the little tailor. At night he went to bed with his wife at the usual time, and when she thought that he had fallen asleep, she got up, opened the door, and then lay down again. The little tailor, who was only pretending to be asleep, began to cry out in a clear voice, "Boy, make me the doublet and patch me the pantaloons, or I will rap the yard-measure over your ears. I slayed seven at one blow. I killed two giants, I brought away one unicorn and caught a wild boar, and now I am expected to fear those who are standing outside the room." When these men heard the tailor speaking thus, they were overcome by a great dread, and ran as if the wild hunter were behind them, and none of them would venture anything further against him. So the little tailor was a king and remained one, to the end of his life.

21. CINDERELLA

The wife of a rich man fell sick, and as she felt that her end was drawing near, she called her only daughter to her bedside and said, "Dear child, be good and pious, and then the good God will always protect you, and I will look down on you from heaven and be near you." Then she closed her eyes and departed. Every day the maiden went out to her mother's grave, and wept, and she remained pious and good. When winter came the snow spread a white sheet over the grave, and when the spring sun had drawn it off again, the man had taken another wife.

The woman had brought two daughters into the house with her, who were beautiful and fair of face, but vile and black of heart. Now began a bad time for the poor stepchild. "Is the stupid goose to sit in the parlor with us?" said they. "He who wants to eat bread must earn it; out with the kitchen-wench." They took her pretty clothes away from her, put an old grey bed gown on her, and gave her wooden shoes. "Just look at the proud princess, how decked out she is!" they cried, and laughed, and led her into the kitchen. There she had to do hard work from morning till night, get up before daybreak, carry water, light fires, cook and wash. Besides this, the sisters did her every imaginable injury—they mocked her and emptied her peas and lentils into the ashes, so that she was forced to sit and pick them out again. In the evening when she had worked till she was weary she had no bed to go to, but had to sleep by the fireside in the ashes. And since on that account she always looked dusty and dirty, they called her Cinderella. It happened that the father was once going to the fair, and he asked his two stepdaughters what he should bring back for them.

"Beautiful dresses," said one.

"Pearls and jewels," said the second.

"And you, Cinderella," said he, "what will you have?"

"Father, break off for me the first branch which knocks against your hat on your way home." So he bought beautiful dresses, pearls and jewels for his two stepdaughters, and on his way home, as he was riding through a green thicket, a hazel twig brushed against him and knocked off his hat. Then he broke off the branch and took it with him. When he reached home he gave his stepdaughters the things which they had wished for, and to Cinderella he gave the branch from the hazel-bush. Cinderella thanked him, went to her mother's grave and planted the branch on it, and wept so much that the tears fell down on it and watered it. And it grew, however, and became a handsome tree. Thrice a day Cinderella went and sat beneath it, and wept and prayed, and a little white bird always came on the tree, and if Cinderella expressed a wish, the bird threw down to her what she had wished for.

It happened, however, that the King appointed a festival which was to last three days, and to which all the beautiful young girls in the country were invited, in order that his son might choose himself a bride. When the two stepsisters heard that they too were to appear among the number, they were delighted, called Cinderella and said, "Comb our hair for us, brush our shoes and fasten our buckles, for we are going to the festival at the King's palace." Cinderella obeyed, but wept, because she too would have liked to go with them to the dance, and begged her stepmother to allow her to do so.

"You go, Cinderella!" said she; "You are dusty and dirty and would go to the festival? You have no clothes and shoes, and yet would dance!" As, however, Cinderella went on asking, the stepmother at last said, "I have emptied a dish of lentils into the ashes for you, if you have picked them out again in two hours, you shall go with us."

The maiden went through the back door into the garden, and called, "You tame pigeons, you turtledoves, and all you birds beneath the sky, come and help me to pick

"The good into the pot,
The bad into the crop."

Then two white pigeons came in by the kitchen window, and afterwards the turtledoves, and at last all the birds beneath the sky, came whirring and crowding in, and alighted amongst the ashes. And the pigeons nodded with their heads and began pick, pick, pick, pick, and the rest began also pick, pick, pick, pick, and gathered all the good grains into the dish. Hardly had one hour passed before they had finished, and all flew out again. Then the girl took the dish to her stepmother, and was glad, and believed that now she would be allowed to go with them to the festival. But the stepmother said, "No,

Cinderella, you have no clothes and you cannot dance; you would only be laughed at." And as Cinderella wept at this, the stepmother said, "If you can pick two dishes of lentils out of the ashes for me in one hour, you shall go with us." And she thought to herself, "That she most certainly cannot do." When the stepmother had emptied the two dishes of lentils amongst the ashes, the maiden went through the back door into the garden and cried,

"You tame pigeons,
You turtledoves,
And all you birds under heaven,
Come and help me to pick
The good into the pot,
The bad into the crop."

Then two white pigeons came in by the kitchen window, and afterwards the turtledoves, and at length all the birds beneath the sky, came whirring and crowding in, and alighted amongst the ashes. And the doves nodded with their heads and began pick, pick, pick, pick, and the others began also pick, pick, pick, pick, and gathered all the good seeds into the dishes, and before half an hour was over they had already finished, and all flew out again. Then the maiden carried the dishes to the stepmother and was delighted, and believed that she might now go with them to the festival.

But the stepmother said, "All this will not help you; you can not go with us, for you have no clothes and cannot dance; we should be ashamed of you!" With this she turned her back on Cinderella, and hurried away with her two proud daughters.

As no one was now at home, Cinderella went to her mother's grave beneath the hazel tree, and cried,

"Shiver and quiver, little tree,
Silver and gold throw down over me."

Then the bird threw a gold and silver dress down to her, and slippers embroidered with silk and silver. She put on the dress with all speed, and went to the festival. Her stepsisters and the stepmother however did not know her, and thought she must be a foreign princess, for she looked so beautiful in the golden dress. They never once thought of

Cinderella, and believed that she was sitting at home in the dirt, picking lentils out of the ashes. The prince went to meet her, took her by the hand and danced with her. He would dance with no other maiden, and never let go of her hand, and if anyone else came to invite her, he said, "This is my partner."

She danced till it was evening, and then she wanted to go home. But the King's son said, "I will go with you and bear you company," for he wished to see to whom the beautiful maiden belonged. She escaped from him, however, and sprang into the pigeon-house. The King's son waited until her father came, and then he told him that the strange maiden had leapt into the pigeon-house.

The old man thought, "Can it be Cinderella?" and they had to bring him an axe and a pickaxe that he might hew the pigeon-house to pieces, but no one was inside it. And when they got home Cinderella lay in her dirty clothes among the ashes, and a dim little oillamp was burning on the mantlepiece, for Cinderella had jumped quickly down from the back of the pigeon-house and had run to the little hazel tree, and there she had taken off her beautiful clothes and laid them on the grave, and the bird had taken them away again, and then she had placed herself in the kitchen amongst the ashes in her grey gown.

Next day when the festival began afresh, and her parents and the stepsisters had gone once more, Cinderella went to the hazel tree and said—

"Shiver and quiver, my little tree,
Silver and gold throw down over me."

Then the bird threw down a much more beautiful dress than on the preceding day. And when Cinderella appeared at the festival in this dress, everyone was astonished at her beauty. The King's son had waited until she came, and instantly took her by the hand and danced with no one but her. When others came and invited her, he said, "She is my partner." When evening came she wished to leave, and the King's son followed her and wanted to see into which house she went. But she sprang away from him, and into the garden behind the house. There stood a beautiful tall tree on which hung the most magnificent pears. She clambered so nimbly between the branches like a squirrel that the King's son did not know where she had gone. He waited until her father came, and said to him, "The strange maiden has escaped from me, and

I believe she has climbed up the pear tree." The father thought, "Can it be Cinderella?" and had an axe brought and cut the tree down, but no one was on it. And when they got into the kitchen, Cinderella lay there amongst the ashes, as usual, for she had jumped down on the other side of the tree, had taken the beautiful dress to the bird on the little hazel tree, and put on her grey gown.

On the third day, when the parents and sisters had gone away, Cinderella went once more to her mother's grave and said to the little tree—

> "Shiver and quiver, my little tree,
> Silver and gold throw down over me."

And now the bird threw down to her a dress which was more splendid and magnificent than any she had yet had, and the slippers were golden. And when she went to the festival in the dress, no one knew how to speak for astonishment. The King's son danced with her only, and if anyone invited her to dance, he said, "She is my partner."

When evening came, Cinderella wished to leave, and the King's son was anxious to go with her, but she escaped from him so quickly that he could not follow her. The King's son had, however, used a stratagem, and had caused the whole staircase to be smeared with pitch, and there, when she ran down, had the maiden's left slipper which remained sticking. The King's son picked it up, and it was small and dainty, and all golden. Next morning, he brought it to the father, and said to him, "No one shall be my wife but she whose foot fits this golden slipper."

Then the two sisters were glad, for they had pretty feet. The eldest went with the shoe into her room and wanted to try it on, and her mother stood by. But she could not get her big toe into it, and the shoe was too small for her. Then her mother gave her a knife and said, "Cut the toe off; when you are Queen you will have no more need to go on foot." The maiden cut the toe off, forced the foot into the shoe, swallowed the pain, and went out to the King's son. Then he took her on his horse as his bride and rode away with her.

They were, however, obliged to pass the grave, and there, on the hazel tree, sat the two pigeons and cried,

"Turn and peep, turn and peep,
There's blood within the shoe,
The shoe it is too small for her,
The true bride waits for you."

Then he looked at her foot and saw how the blood was streaming from it. He turned his horse round and took the false bride home again, and said she was not the true one, and that the other sister was to put the shoe on. Then this one went into her chamber and got her toes safely into the shoe, but her heel was too large. So her mother gave her a knife and said, "Cut a bit off your heel; when you are Queen you will have no more need to go on foot." The maiden cut a bit off her heel, forced her foot into the shoe, swallowed the pain, and went out to the King's son.

He took her on his horse as his bride, and rode away with her, but when they passed by the hazel tree, two little pigeons sat on it and cried,

"Turn and peep, turn and peep,
There's blood within the shoe
The shoe it is too small for her,
The true bride waits for you."

He looked down at her foot and saw how the blood was running out of her shoe, and how it had stained her white stocking. Then he turned his horse and took the false bride home again. "This also is not the right one," said he. "Have you no other daughter?"

"No," said the man, "There is still a little stunted kitchen-wench which my late wife left behind, but she cannot possibly be the bride."

The King's son said he was to send her up to him; but the mother answered, "Oh, no, she is much too dirty, she cannot show herself!"

He absolutely insisted on it, and Cinderella had to be called. She first washed her hands and face clean, and then went and bowed down before the King's son, who gave her the golden shoe. Then she seated herself on a stool, drew her foot out of the heavy wooden shoe, and put it into the slipper, which fit like a glove. And when she rose up and the King's son looked at her face he recognized the beautiful maiden who had danced with him and cried, "That is the true bride!" The stepmother and the two sisters were terrified and became pale with rage; he, however, took Cinderella on his horse and rode away with her. As they passed by the hazel tree, the two white doves cried—

"Turn and peep, turn and peep,
No blood is in the shoe,
The shoe is not too small for her,
The true bride rides with you,"

and when they had cried that, the two came flying down and placed themselves on Cinderella's shoulders, one on the right, the other on the left, and remained sitting there.

When the wedding with the King's son was celebrated, the two false sisters came and wanted to get into favor with Cinderella and share her good fortune. When the betrothed couple went to church, the elder was at the right side and the younger at the left, and the pigeons pecked out one eye of each of them. Afterwards as they came back, the elder was at the left, and the younger at the right, and then the pigeons pecked out the other eye of each. And thus, for their wickedness and falsehood, they were punished with blindness as long as they lived.

22. *THE RIDDLE*

There was once a King's son who was seized with a desire to travel about the world, and took no one with him but a faithful servant. One day he came to a great forest, and when darkness overtook him he could find no shelter, and knew not where to pass the night. Then he saw a girl who was going towards a small house, and when he came nearer, he saw that the maiden was young and beautiful. He spoke to her, and said, "Dear child, can I and my servant find shelter for the night in the little house?"

"Oh, yes," said the girl in a sad voice, "that you certainly can, but I do not advise you to venture it. Do not go in."

"Why not?" asked the King's son.

The maiden sighed and said, "My stepmother practices wicked arts; she is ill disposed toward strangers." Then he saw very well that he had come to the house of a witch, but as it was dark, and he could not go farther, and also was not afraid, he entered. The old woman was sitting in an armchair by the fire, and looked at the stranger with her red eyes.

"Good evening," growled she, and pretended to be quite friendly. "Take a seat and rest yourselves." She blew up the fire on which she was cooking something in a small pot. The daughter warned the two to be prudent, to eat nothing, and drink nothing, for the old woman brewed evil drinks. They slept quietly until early morning. When they were readying for their departure, and the King's son was already seated on his horse, the old woman said, "Stop a moment, I will first hand you a parting draught." While she fetched it, the King's son rode away, and the servant who had to buckle his saddle tight, was the only one present when the wicked witch came with the drink. "Take that to your master," said she. But at that instant the glass broke and the poison spurted on the horse, and it was so strong that the animal immediately fell down dead. The servant ran after his master and told him what had happened, but would not leave his saddle behind him, and ran back to fetch it. When, however, he came to the dead horse a raven was already sitting on it devouring it.

"Who knows whether we shall find anything better today?" said the servant; so he killed the raven, and took it with him. And now they journeyed onwards into the forest the whole day, but could not get out of it. By nightfall they found an inn and entered it. The servant gave the raven to the innkeeper to make ready for supper. They had, however, stumbled on a den of murderers, and during the darkness twelve of these came, intending to kill the strangers and rob them. Before they set about this work, they sat down to supper, and the innkeeper and the witch sat down with them, and together they ate a dish of soup in which was cut up the flesh of the raven. Hardly, however, had they swallowed a couple of mouthfuls, before they all fell down dead, for the raven had passed on to them the poison from the horse-flesh. There was no one else left in the house but the innkeeper's daughter, who was honest, and had taken no part in their godless deeds. She opened all doors to the stranger and showed him the heaped-up treasures. But the King's son said she might keep everything, he would have none of it, and rode onwards with his servant.

After they had traveled about for a long time, they came to a town in which was a beautiful but proud princess, who had caused it to be proclaimed that whoever should set her a riddle which she could not guess, that man should be her husband; but if she guessed it, his head must be cut off. She had three days to guess it in, but was so clever that she always found the answer to the riddle given her, before the appointed time. Nine suitors had already perished in this manner, when the King's son arrived, and blinded by her great beauty, was willing to stake his life for it. Then he went to her and laid his riddle before her. "What is this?" said he, "One slew none, and yet slew twelve."

She did not know what that was, she thought and thought, but she could not find out, she opened her riddle books, but it was not in them—in short, her wisdom was at an end. As she did not know how to help herself, she ordered her maid to creep into the lord's sleeping-chamber, and listen to his dreams, and thought that he would perhaps speak in his sleep and discover the riddle. But the clever servant had placed himself in the bed instead of his master, and when the maid came there, he tore off from her the mantle in which she had wrapped herself, and chased her out with rods. The second night the King's daughter sent her maid-in-waiting, who was to see if she could succeed better in listening, but the servant took her mantle also away from her, and hunted her out with rods. Now the master believed himself safe for the third night, and lay down in his own bed. Then came the princess herself, and she had put on a misty-grey mantle, and she seated herself near him. And when she thought that he was asleep and dreaming, she spoke to him, and hoped that he would answer in his sleep, as many do, but he was awake, and understood and heard everything quite well. Then she asked, "One slew none, what is that?"

He replied, "A raven, which ate of a dead and poisoned horse, and died of it."

She inquired further, "And yet slew twelve, what is that?"

He answered, "That means twelve murderers, who ate the raven and died of it."

When she knew the answer to the riddle she wanted to steal away, but he held her mantle so fast that she was forced to leave it behind. Next morning, the King's daughter announced that she had guessed the riddle, and sent for the twelve judges and expounded it before them. But the youth begged for a hearing, and said, "She stole into my room in the night and questioned me, otherwise she could not have discovered it."

The judges said, "Bring us a proof of this."

Then the three mantles were brought by the servant, and when the judges saw the misty-grey one which the King's daughter usually wore, they said, "Let the mantle be embroidered with gold and silver, and then it will be your wedding mantle."

23. THE MOUSE, THE BIRD, AND THE SAUSAGE

Once upon a time a mouse, a bird, and a sausage became companions, kept house together, lived well and happily with each other, and wonderfully increased their possessions. The bird's work was to fly every day into the forest and bring back wood. The mouse had to carry water, light the fire, and lay the table, but the sausage had to cook.

He who is too well off is always longing for something new. One day, therefore, the bird met with another bird on the way, to whom it related its excellent circumstances and boasted of them. The other bird, however, called it a poor simpleton for his hard work, but said that the two at home had good times. For when the mouse had made her fire and carried her water, she went into her little room to rest until they called her to lay the table. The sausage stayed by the pot, saw that the food was cooking well, and, when it was nearly time for dinner, it rolled itself once or twice through the broth or vegetables and then they were buttered, salted, and ready. When the bird came home and laid his burden down, they sat down to dinner, and after they had had their meal, they slept their fill till next morning, and that was a splendid life.

Next day the bird, prompted by the other bird, would go no more into the wood, saying that he had been servant long enough, and had been made a fool of by them, and that they must change about for once, and try to arrange it in another way. And, though the mouse and the sausage also begged most earnestly, the bird would have his way, and said it must be tried. They drew lots about it, and the lot fell on the sausage who was to carry wood, and the mouse became cook, and the bird was to fetch water.

What happened? The little sausage went out towards the wood, the little bird lighted the fire, the mouse stayed by the pot and waited alone until little sausage came home and brought wood for next day. But the little sausage stayed so long on the road that they both feared something was amiss, and the bird flew out a little way in the air to meet it. Not far off, however, it met a dog on the road who had fallen on the poor sausage as lawful booty, and had seized and swallowed it. The bird charged the dog with an act of barefaced robbery, but it was in vain to speak, for the dog said he had found forged letters on the sausage, a capital offense.

The bird sadly took up the wood, flew home, and related what he had seen and heard. They were much troubled, but agreed to do their best and remain together. The bird therefore laid the cloth, and the mouse prepared the food, and wanted to dress it, and to get into the pot as the sausage used to do, and roll and creep amongst the vegetables to mix them; but before she got into the midst of them she was stopped, and lost her skin and hair and life in the attempt.

When the bird came to carry up the dinner, no cook was there. In its distress the bird threw the wood here and there, called and searched, but no cook was to be found! Owing to his carelessness the wood caught fire, so that a conflagration ensued, the bird hastened to fetch water, and then the bucket dropped from his claws into the well, and he fell down with it, and could not recover himself, but had to drown there.

24. MOTHER HOLLE

There was once a widow who had two daughters—one of whom was pretty and industrious, while the other was ugly and idle. But she was much fonder of the ugly and idle one, because she was her own daughter; and the other, who was a stepdaughter, was obliged to do all the work, and be the Cinderella of the house. Every day the poor girl had to sit by a well, on the roadside, and spin and spin till her fingers bled.

Now it happened that one day the shuttle was marked with her blood, so she dipped it in the well, to wash the mark off; but it dropped out of her hand and fell to the bottom. She began to weep, and ran to her stepmother and told her of the mishap. But she scolded her sharply, and was so merciless as to say, "Since you have let the shuttle fall in, you must fetch it out again."

So the girl went back to the well, and did not know what to do; and in the sorrow of her heart she jumped into the well to get the shuttle. She lost her senses; and when she awoke and came to herself again, she was in a lovely meadow where the sun was shining and many thousands of flowers were growing.

Along this meadow she went, and at last came to a baker's oven full of bread, and the bread cried out, "Oh, take me out! Take me out! Or I shall burn; I have been baked a long time!" So she went up to it, and took out all the loaves one after another with the bread-shovel.

After that she went on till she came to a tree covered with apples, which called out to her, "Oh, shake me! Shake me! We apples are all ripe!" So she shook the tree till the apples fell like rain, and went on shaking till they were all down, and when she had gathered them into a heap, she went on her way.

At last she came to a little house, out of which an old woman peeped; but she had such large teeth that the girl was frightened, and was about to run away.

But the old woman called out to her, "What are you afraid of, dear child? Stay with me; if you will do all the work in the house properly, you shall be the better for it. Only you must take care to make my bed well, and shake it thoroughly till the feathers fly—for then it will snow on the earth. I am Mother Holle."

As the old woman spoke so kindly to her, the girl took courage and agreed to enter her service. She attended to everything to the satisfaction of her mistress, and always shook her bed so vigorously that the feathers flew about like snowflakes. So she had a pleasant life with her; never an angry word; and boiled or roast meat every day.

She stayed some time with Mother Holle, and then she became sad. At first she did not know what was the matter with her, but found at length that it was homesickness. Although she was many thousand times better off here than at home, still she had a longing to be there. At last she said to the old woman, "I have a longing for home; and however well off I am down here, I cannot stay any longer; I must go up again to my own people."

Mother Holle said, "I am pleased that you long for your home again, and as you have served me so truly, I myself will take you up again." Then she took her by the hand, and led her to a large door. The door was opened, and just as the maiden was standing beneath the doorway, a heavy shower of golden rain fell, and all the gold stuck to her, so that she was completely covered over with it.

"You shall have that because you have been so industrious," said Mother Holle, and at the same time she gave her back the shuttle which she had let fall into the well. Thereupon the door closed, and the maiden found herself up above upon the earth, not far from her mother's house.

And as she went into the yard the cock was standing by the well-side, and cried—

"Cock-a-doodle-doo!
Your golden girl's come back to you!"

So she went in to her mother, and as she arrived thus covered with gold, she was well received, both by her and her sister.

The girl told all that had happened to her; and as soon as the mother heard how she had come by so much wealth, she was very anxious to obtain the same good luck for the ugly and lazy daughter. She had to seat herself by the well and spin; and in order that her shuttle might be stained with blood, she stuck her hand into a thorn bush and pricked her finger. Then she threw her shuttle into the well, and jumped in after it.

She came, like the other, to the beautiful meadow and walked along the very same path. When she got to the oven the bread again cried,

"Oh, take me out! Take me out! Or I shall burn; I have been baked a long time!"

But the lazy thing answered, "As if I had any wish to make myself dirty!" and on she went.

Soon she came to the apple tree, which cried, "Oh, shake me! Shake me! We apples are all ripe!"

But she answered, "Wouldn't you like that! One of you might fall on my head," and so went on.

When she came to Mother Holle's house she was not afraid, for she had already heard of her big teeth, and she offered work to her immediately.

The first day she forced herself to work diligently, and obeyed Mother Holle when she told her to do anything, for she was thinking of all the gold that she would give her. But on the second day she began to be lazy, and on the third day still more so, and then she would not get up in the morning at all. Nor did she make Mother Holle's bed as she ought, and did not shake it so as to make the feathers fly up. Mother Holle was soon tired of this, and gave her notice to leave. The lazy girl was willing enough to go, and thought that now the golden rain would come. Mother Holle led her also to the great door; but while she was standing beneath it, instead of the gold a big kettleful of pitch was emptied over her. "That is the reward for your service," said Mother Holle, and shut the door.

So the lazy girl went home; but she was quite covered with pitch, and the cock by the well-side, as soon as he saw her, cried out—

"Cock-a-doodle-doo!
Your pitchy girl's come back to you!"

But the pitch stuck fast to her, and could not be got off as long as she lived.

25. THE SEVEN RAVENS

There was once a man who had seven sons, and still he had no daughter, however much he wished for one. At length his wife again gave him hope of a child, and when it came into the world it was a girl. The joy was great, but the child was sickly and small, and had to be privately baptized on account of its weakness. The father sent one of the boys in haste to the spring to fetch water for the baptism. The other six went with him, and as each of them wanted to be first to fill it, the jug fell into the well. There they stood and did not know what to do, and none of them dared to go home. As they still did not return, the father grew impatient, and said, "They have certainly forgotten it for some game, the wicked boys!" He became afraid that the girl would have to die without being baptized, and in his anger cried, "I wish the boys were all turned into ravens." Hardly was the word spoken before he heard a whirring of wings over his head in the air, looked up and saw seven coal-black ravens flying away. The parents could not recall the curse, and however sad they were at the loss of their seven sons, they still to some extent comforted themselves with their dear little daughter, who soon grew strong and every day became more beautiful.

For a long time she did not know that she had had brothers, for her parents were careful not to mention them before her, but one day she accidentally heard some people saying of herself, "that the girl was certainly beautiful, but that in reality she was to blame for the misfortune which had befallen her seven brothers." Then she was much troubled, and went to her father and mother and asked if it was true that she had had brothers, and what had become of them? The parents now dared keep the secret no longer, but said that what had befallen her brothers was the will of Heaven, and that her birth was not to blame. But the maiden took it to heart daily, and thought she must save her brothers. She had no rest or peace until she set out secretly, and went forth into the wide world to find her brothers and set them free, let it cost what it might. She took nothing with her but a little ring belonging to her parents as a keepsake, a loaf of bread against hunger, a little pitcher of water against thirst, and a little chair as a provision against weariness.

And now she went continually onwards, far, far to the very end of the world. Then she came to the sun, but it was too hot and terrible, and devoured little children. Hastily she ran away, and ran to the moon, but it was far too cold, and also awful and malicious, and when it saw the child, it said, "I smell, I smell the flesh of men."

At this she ran swiftly away, and came to the stars, which were kind and good to her, and each of them sat on its own particular little chair. But the morning star arose, and gave her the drumstick of a chicken, and said, "If you have not that drumstick you cannot open the glass mountain, and in the glass mountain are your brothers."

The maiden took the drumstick, wrapped it carefully in a cloth, and went onwards again until she came to the glass mountain. The door was shut, and she thought she would take out the drumstick; but when she undid the cloth, it was empty, and she had lost the good star's present. What was she now to do? She wished to rescue her brothers, and had no key to the glass mountain. The good sister took a knife, cut off one of her little fingers, put it in the door, and succeeded in opening it.

When she had gone inside, a little dwarf came to meet her, who said, "My child, what are you looking for?"

"I am looking for my brothers, the seven ravens," she replied.

The dwarf said, "The lord ravens are not at home, but if you will wait here until they come, step in." Thereupon the little dwarf carried the ravens' dinner in, on seven little plates, and in seven little glasses, and the little sister ate a morsel from each plate, and from each little glass she took a sip, but in the last little glass she dropped the ring which she had brought away with her.

Suddenly she heard a whirring of wings and a rushing through the air, and then the little dwarf said, "Now the lord ravens are flying home."

Then they came, and wanted to eat and drink, and looked for their little plates and glasses. Then said one after the other, "Who has eaten something from my plate? Who has drunk out of my little glass? It was a human mouth."

And when the seventh came to the bottom of the glass, the ring rolled against his mouth. Then he looked at it, and saw that it was a ring belonging to his father and mother, and said, "God grant that our sister may be here, and then we shall be free." When the maiden, who was standing behind the door watching, heard that wish, she came forth, and at this all the ravens were restored to their human form again. And they embraced and kissed each other, and went joyfully home.

26. *LITTLE RED CAP*

Once upon a time there was a dear little girl who was loved by everyone who looked at her, but most of all by her grandmother, and there was nothing that she would not have given to the child. Once she gave her a little cap of red velvet, which suited her so well that she would never wear anything else; so she was always called "Little Red Cap."

One day her mother said to her, "Come, Little Red Cap, here is a piece of cake and a bottle of wine; take them to your grandmother, she is ill and weak, and they will do her good. Set out before it gets hot, and when you are going, walk nicely and quietly and do not run off the path, or you may fall and break the bottle, and then your grandmother will get nothing; and when you go into her room, don't forget to say, 'Good morning,' and don't peep into every corner before you do it."

"I will take great care," said Little Red Cap to her mother, and gave her hand on it.

The grandmother lived out in the wood, half a league from the village, and just as Little Red Cap entered the wood, a wolf met her. Red Cap did not know what a wicked creature he was, and was not at all afraid of him.

"Good day, Little Red Cap," said he.

"Thank you kindly, wolf."

"Where do you go so early, Little Red Cap?"

"To my grandmother's."

"What have you got in your apron?"

"Cake and wine; yesterday was baking day, so poor sick grandmother is to have something good, to make her stronger."

"Where does your grandmother live, Little Red Cap?"

"A good quarter of a league farther on in the wood; her house stands under the three large oak trees, the nut trees are just below; you surely must know it," replied Little Red Cap.

The wolf thought to himself, "What a tender young creature! What a nice plump mouthful—she will be better to eat than the old woman. I must act craftily, so as to catch both." So he walked for a short time by the side of Little Red Cap, and then he said, "See Little Red Cap, how pretty the flowers are about here—why do you not look round? I believe, too, that you do not hear how sweetly the little birds are singing; you walk gravely along as if you were going to school, while everything else out here in the wood is merry."

Little Red Cap raised her eyes, and when she saw the sunbeams dancing here and there through the trees, and pretty flowers growing everywhere, she thought, "Suppose I take grandmother a fresh nosegay; that would please her too. It is so early in the day that I shall still get there in good time," and so she ran from the path into the wood to look for flowers. And whenever she had picked one, she fancied that she saw a still prettier one farther on, and ran after it, and so got deeper and deeper into the wood.

Meanwhile the wolf ran straight to the grandmother's house and knocked at the door.

"Who is there?"

"Little Red Cap," replied the wolf. "She is bringing cake and wine; open the door."

"Lift the latch," called out the grandmother, "I am too weak, and cannot get up."

The wolf lifted the latch, the door flew open, and without saying a word he went straight to the grandmother's bed, and devoured her. Then he put on her clothes, dressed himself in her cap, laid himself in bed and drew the curtains.

Little Red Cap, however, had been running about picking flowers, and when she had gathered so many that she could carry no more, she remembered her grandmother, and set out on the way to her.

She was surprised to find the cottage door standing open, and when she went into the room, she had such a strange feeling that she said to herself, "Oh dear! How uneasy I feel today, and at other times I like being with grandmother so much." She called out, "Good morning," but received no answer; so she went to the bed and drew back the curtains. There lay her grandmother with her cap pulled far over her face, and looking very strange.

"Oh! Grandmother," she said, "what big ears you have!"

"The better to hear you with, my child," was the reply.

"But, grandmother, what big eyes you have!" she said.

"The better to see you with, my dear."

"But, grandmother, what large hands you have!"

"The better to hug you with."

"Oh! But, grandmother, what a terrible big mouth you have!"

"The better to eat you with!"

And scarcely had the wolf said this, than with one bound he was out of bed and swallowed up Red Cap.

When the wolf had appeased his appetite, he lay down again in the bed, fell asleep and began to snore very loud. The hunter was just passing the house, and thought to himself, "How the old woman is snoring! I must just see if she wants anything." So he went into the room, and when he came to the bed, he saw that the wolf was lying in it. "Do I find you here, you old sinner!" said he. "I have long sought you!"

Then just as he was going to fire at him, it occurred to him that the wolf might have devoured the grandmother, and that she might still be saved, so he did not fire, but took a pair of scissors, and began to cut open the stomach of the sleeping wolf. When he had made two snips, he saw the little Red Cap shining, and then he made two snips more, and the little girl sprang out, crying, "Ah, how frightened I have been! How dark it was inside the wolf;" and after that the aged grandmother came out alive also, but scarcely able to breathe. Red Cap, however, quickly fetched great stones with which they filled the wolf's body, and when he awoke, he wanted to run away, but the stones were so heavy that he fell down at once, and fell dead.

Then all three were delighted. The hunter drew off the wolf's skin and went home with it; the grandmother ate the cake and drank the wine which Red Cap had brought, and revived, but Red Cap thought to herself, "As long as I live, I will never by myself leave the path, to run into the wood, when my mother has forbidden me to do so."

*****

It is also related that once when Red Cap was again taking cakes to the old grandmother, another wolf spoke to her, and tried to entice her from the path. Red Cap, however, was on her guard, and went straight forward on her way, and told her grandmother that she had met the wolf, and that he had said "good morning" to her, but with such a wicked look in his eyes, that if they had not been on the public road she was certain he would have eaten her up. "Well," said the grandmother, "we will shut the door, that he may not come in."

Soon afterwards the wolf knocked, and cried, "Open the door, grandmother, I am little Red Cap, and am fetching you some cakes."

But they did not speak, or open the door, so the grey-beard stole twice or thrice round the house, and at last jumped on the roof, intending to wait until Red Cap went home in the evening, and then to steal after her and devour her in the darkness. But the grandmother saw what was in his thoughts. In front of the house was a great stone trough, so she said to the child, "Take the pail, Red Cap; I made some sausages yesterday, so carry the water in which I boiled them to the trough." Red Cap carried until the great trough was quite full. Then the smell of the sausages reached the wolf, and he sniffed and peeped down, and at last stretched out his neck so far that he could no longer keep his footing and began to slip, and slipped down from the roof straight into the great trough, and drowned. But Red Cap went joyously home, and never did anything to harm anyone.

27. *THE BREMEN TOWN-MUSICIANS*

A certain man had a donkey, which had carried the sacks of corn to the mill tirelessly for many long years; but his strength was going, and he was growing more and more unfit for work. Then his master began to consider doing away with him; but the donkey, seeing that trouble was in the air, ran away and set out on the road to Bremen. "There," he thought, "I can surely join the town band." When he had walked some distance, he found a hound lying on the road, gasping like one who had run till he was tired. "Why are you gasping so, you big fellow?" asked the donkey.

"Ah," replied the hound, "as I am old, and daily grow weaker, and no longer can hunt, my master wanted to kill me, so I took to flight; but now how am I to earn my bread?"

"I tell you what," said the donkey, "I am going to Bremen, and shall be town-musician there; go with me and engage yourself also as a musician. I will play the lute, and you shall beat the kettledrum."

The hound agreed, and on they went.

Before long they came to a cat, sitting on the path, with a face like three rainy days. "Now then, old whiskers, what has gone askew with you?" asked the donkey.

"Who can be merry when his neck is in danger?" answered the cat. "Because I am now getting old, and my teeth are worn to stumps, and I prefer to sit by the fire and spin, rather than hunt about after mice, my mistress wanted to drown me, so I ran away. But now good advice is scarce. Where am I to go?"

"Go with us to Bremen. You understand night-serenading, you can be a town-musician."

The cat thought well of it, and went with them. After this the three fugitives came to a farmyard, where the cock was sitting upon the gate, crowing with all his might. "Your crow goes on and on," said the donkey. "What is the matter?"

"I have been foretelling fine weather, because it is the day on which Our Lady washes the Christ Child's little shirts, and wants to dry them," said the cock; "but guests are coming for Sunday, so the housewife has no pity, and has told the cook that she intends to eat me in the soup tomorrow, and this evening I am to have my head cut off. Now I am crowing at full pitch while I can."

"Ah, but red-comb," said the donkey, "you had better come away with us. We are going to Bremen; you can find something better than death everywhere; you have a good voice, and if we make music together it must have some quality!"

The cock agreed to this plan, and all four went on together. They could not, however, reach the city of Bremen in one day, and in the evening they came to a forest where they meant to pass the night. The donkey and the hound laid themselves down under a large tree, the cat settled itself in the branches, and the cock flew right to the top, where he was most safe. Before he went to sleep he looked round on all four sides, and thought he saw in the distance a little spark burning; so he called out to his companions that there must be a house not far off, for he saw a light. The donkey said, "If so, we had better get up and go on, for the shelter here is bad." The hound thought that a few bones with some meat on them would do him good, too.

So they made their way to the place where the light was, and soon saw it shine brighter and grow larger, until they came to a well-lighted robber's house. The donkey, as the biggest, went to the window and looked in.

"What do you see, my grey-horse?" asked the cock.

"What do I see?" answered the donkey; "a table covered with good things to eat and drink, and robbers sitting at it enjoying themselves."

"That would be the sort of thing for us," said the cock.

"Yes, yes; ah, how I wish we were there!" said the donkey.

Then the animals took counsel together how they should manage to drive away the robbers, and at last they thought of a plan. The donkey was to place himself with his forefeet upon the window ledge, the hound was to jump on the donkey's back, the cat was to climb upon the dog, and lastly the cock was to fly up and perch upon the head of the cat.

When this was done, at a given signal, they began to perform their music together: the donkey brayed, the hound barked, the cat mewed, and the cock crowed; then they burst through the window into the room, so that the glass clattered! At this horrible din, the robbers sprang up, thinking that a ghost had come in, and fled in a great fright out into the forest. The four companions now sat down at the table, well content with what was left, and ate as if they were going to fast for a month.

As soon as the four minstrels had done, they put out the light, and each sought for himself a sleeping-place according to his nature and to what suited him. The donkey laid himself down upon some straw in the yard, the hound behind the door, the cat upon the hearth near the warm ashes, and the cock perched himself upon a beam of the roof; and being tired from their long walk, they soon went to sleep.

When it was past midnight, and the robbers saw from afar that the light was no longer burning in their house, and all appeared quiet, the captain said, "We ought not to have let ourselves be frightened out of our wits," and ordered one of them to go and examine the house.

The messenger, finding all still, went into the kitchen to light a candle, and, taking the glistening fiery eyes of the cat for live coals, he held a match to them to light it. But the cat did not think it was funny, and flew in his face, spitting and scratching. He was dreadfully frightened, and ran to the back door, but the dog who lay there sprang up and bit his leg; and as he ran across the yard by the straw heap, the donkey gave him a smart kick with its hind foot. The cock, too, who had been awakened by the noise, and had become lively, cried down from the beam, "Cock-a-doodle-doo!"

Then the robber ran back as fast as he could to his captain, and said, "Ah, there is a horrible witch sitting in the house, who spat on me and scratched my face with her long claws; and by the door stands a man with a knife, who stabbed me in the leg; and in the yard there lies a black monster, who beat me with a wooden club; and above, upon the roof, sits the judge, who called out, 'Bring the rogue here to me!' so I got away as well as I could."

After this the robbers did not trust themselves in the house again; but it suited the four musicians of Bremen so well that they did not care to leave it any more. And the mouth of the man who last told this story is still warm.

28. THE SINGING BONE

In a certain country there was once great lamentation over a wild boar that ravaged the farmer's fields, killed the cattle, and ripped up people's bodies with his tusks. The King promised a large reward to anyone who would free the land from this plague; but the beast was so big and strong that no one dared to go near the forest in which it lived. At last the King gave notice that whoever should capture or kill the wild boar should have his only daughter as wife.

Now there lived in the country two brothers, sons of a poor man, who declared themselves willing to undertake the hazardous enterprise; the elder, who was crafty and shrewd, out of pride; the younger, who was innocent and simple, from a kind heart. The King said, "In order to be sure of finding the beast, you must go into the forest from opposite sides." So the elder went in on the west side, and the younger on the east.

When the younger had gone a short way, a little man stepped up to him. He held in his hand a black spear and said, "I give you this spear because your heart is pure and good; with this you can boldly attack the wild boar, and it will do you no harm."

He thanked the little man, shouldered the spear, and went on fearlessly.

Before long he saw the beast, which rushed at him; but he held the spear towards it, and in its blind fury it ran so swiftly against it that its heart was cut in two. Then he took the monster on his back and went homewards with it to the King.

As he came out at the other side of the wood, there stood at the entrance a house where people were making merry with wine and dancing. His elder brother had gone in here, and, thinking that after all the boar would not run away, was going to drink until he felt brave. But when he saw his young brother coming out of the wood laden with his booty, his envious, evil heart gave him no peace. He called out to him, "Come in, dear brother, rest and refresh yourself with a cup of wine."

The youth, who suspected no evil, went in and told him about the good little man who had given him the spear with which he had slain the boar.

The elder brother kept him there until the evening, and then they went away together, and when in the darkness they came to a bridge over a brook, the elder brother let the other go first; and when he was halfway across he gave him such a blow from behind that he fell down dead. He buried him beneath the bridge, took the boar, and carried it to the King, pretending that he had killed it; whereupon he obtained the King's daughter in marriage. And when his younger brother did not come back he said, "The boar must have killed him," and everyone believed it.

But as nothing remains hidden from God, this black deed was to come to light.

Years afterwards a shepherd was driving his herd across the bridge, and saw lying in the sand beneath, a snow-white little bone. He thought that it would make a good mouthpiece, so he clambered down, picked it up, and cut out of it a mouthpiece for his horn. But when he blew through it for the first time, to his great astonishment, the bone began of its own accord to sing:

"Ah, friend, you blow upon my bone!
Long have I lain beside the water;
My brother slew me for the boar,
And took for his wife the King's young daughter."

"What a wonderful horn!" said the shepherd; "It sings by itself; I must take it to my lord the King." And when he came with it to the King the horn again began to sing its little song. The King understood it all, and ordered the ground below the bridge to be dug up, and then the whole skeleton of the murdered man came to light. The wicked brother could not deny the deed, and was sewn up in a sack and drowned. But the bones of the murdered man were laid to rest in a beautiful tomb in the churchyard.

29. THE DEVIL WITH THE THREE GOLDEN HAIRS

There was once a poor woman who gave birth to a little son; and as he came into the world with a caul on, it was predicted that in his fourteenth year he would have the King's daughter for his wife. It happened that soon afterwards the King came into the village, and no one knew that he was the King, and when he asked the people what news there was, they answered, "A child has just been born with a caul on; whatever he undertakes in life will turn out well. It is prophesied, too, that in his fourteenth year he will have the King's daughter for his wife."

The King, who had a bad heart, and was angry about the prophecy, went to the parents, and, seeming quite friendly, said, "You poor people, let me have your child, and I will take care of it." At first they refused, but when the stranger offered them a large amount of gold for it, and they thought, "It is a luck child, and everything must turn out well for it," they at last consented, and gave him the child.

The King put it in a box and rode away with it until he came to a deep piece of water; then he threw the box into it and thought, "I have freed my daughter from her unlooked-for suitor."

The box, however, did not sink, but floated like a boat, and not a drop of water made its way into it. And it floated to within two miles of the King's chief city, where there was a mill, and it came to a standstill at the mill dam. A miller's boy, who by good luck was standing there, noticed it and pulled it out with a hook, thinking that he had found a great treasure, but when he opened it there lay a pretty boy inside, quite fresh and lively. He took him to the miller and his wife, and as they had no children they were glad, and said, "God has given him to us." They took great care of the foundling, and he grew up in all goodness.

It happened that once in a storm, the King went into the mill, and he asked the miller and his wife if the tall youth was their son. "No," answered they, "he's a foundling. Fourteen years ago he floated down to the mill dam in a box, and the mill boy pulled him out of the water."

Then the King knew that it was none other than the luck child which he had thrown into the water, and he said, "My good people, could not the youth take a letter to the Queen; I will give him two gold pieces as a reward?"

"Just as the King commands," answered they, and they told the boy to get ready.

Then the King wrote a letter to the Queen, in which he said, "As soon as the boy arrives with this letter, let him be killed and buried, and all must be done before I come home."

The boy set out with this letter; but he lost his way, and in the evening came to a large forest. In the darkness he saw a small light; he went towards it and reached a cottage. When he went in, an old woman was sitting by the fire quite alone. She started when she saw the boy, and said, "From where do you come, and where are you going?"

"I come from the mill," he answered, "and wish to go to the Queen, to whom I am taking a letter; but as I have lost my way in the forest I should like to stay here overnight."

"You poor boy," said the woman, "you have come into a den of thieves, and when they come home they will kill you."

"Let them come," said the boy, "I am not afraid; but I am so tired that I cannot go any farther," and he stretched himself upon a bench and fell asleep.

Soon afterwards the robbers came, and angrily asked what strange boy was lying there? "Ah," said the old woman, "it is an innocent child who has lost himself in the forest, and out of pity I have let him come in; he has to take a letter to the Queen." The robbers opened the letter and read it, and in it was written that as soon as he arrived the boy should be put to death. Then the hardhearted robbers felt pity, and their leader tore up the letter and wrote another, saying, that as soon as the boy came, he should be married at once to the King's daughter. Then they let him lie quietly on the bench until the next morning, and when he awoke they gave him the letter, and showed him the right way.

And the Queen, when she had received the letter and read it, did as was written in it, and had a splendid wedding feast prepared, and the King's daughter was married to the luck child, and as the youth was handsome and agreeable she lived with him in joy and contentment.

After some time the King returned to his palace and saw that the prophecy was fulfilled, and the luck child married to his daughter. "How has that come to pass?" said he; "I gave quite another order in my letter."

So the Queen gave him the letter, and said that he might see for himself what was written in it. The King read the letter and saw quite well that it had been exchanged for the other. He asked the youth what had become of the letter entrusted to him, and why he had brought another instead of it.

"I know nothing about it," answered he; "It must have been changed in the night, when I slept in the forest."

The King said in a passion, "You shall not have everything quite so much your own way; whoever marries my daughter must fetch me from Hell three golden hairs from the head of the Devil; bring me what I want, and you shall keep my daughter." In this way the King hoped to be rid of him forever. But the luck child answered, "I will fetch the golden hairs, I am not afraid of the Devil," thereupon he took leave of them and began his journey.

The road led him to a large town, where the watchman by the gates asked him what his trade was, and what he knew. "I know everything," answered the luck child.

"Then you can do us a favor," said the watchman, "if you will tell us why our marketplace's fountain which once flowed with wine has become dry, and no longer gives even water?"

"That you shall know," answered he, "Only wait until I come back."

Then he went farther and came to another town, and there also the gatekeeper asked him what was his trade, and what he knew. "I know everything," answered he.

"Then you can do us a favor and tell us why a tree in our town which once bore golden apples now does not even put forth leaves?"

"You shall know that," answered he, "Only wait until I come back."

Then he went on and came to a wide river over which he must go. The ferryman asked him what his trade was, and what he knew. "I know everything," answered he.

"Then you can do me a favor," said the ferryman, "and tell me why I must always be rowing backwards and forwards, and no one comes to relieve me?"

"You shall know that," answered he, "Only wait until I come back."

When he had crossed the water he found the entrance to Hell. It was black and sooty within, and the Devil was not at home, but his grandmother was sitting in a large armchair. "What do you want?" said she to him, but she did not look so very wicked.

"I should like to have three golden hairs from the Devil's head," answered he, "else I cannot keep my wife."

"That is a good deal to ask for," said she, "If the Devil comes home and finds you, it will cost you your life; but as I pity you, I will see if I cannot help you."

She changed him into an ant and said, "Creep into the folds of my dress, you will be safe there."

"Yes," answered he, "so far, so good; but there are three things besides that I want to know: why a fountain which once flowed with wine has become dry, and no longer gives even water; why a tree which once bore golden apples does not even put forth leaves; and why a ferryman must always be going backwards and forwards, and is never set free?"

"Those are difficult questions," answered she, "but only be silent and quiet and pay attention to what the Devil says when I pull out the three golden hairs."

As evening came, the Devil returned home. No sooner had he entered than he noticed that the air was not pure. "I smell man's flesh," said he, "All is not right here." Then he pried into every corner, and searched, but could not find anything.

His grandmother scolded him. "It has just been swept," said she, "and everything put in order, and now you are upsetting it again; you have always got man's flesh in your nose. Sit down and eat your supper."

When he had eaten and drunk he was tired, and laid his head in his grandmother's lap, and before long he was fast asleep, snoring and breathing heavily. Then the old woman took hold of a golden hair, pulled it out, and laid it down near her. "Oh!" cried the Devil, "What are you doing?"

"I have had a bad dream," answered the grandmother, "so I seized hold of your hair."

"What did you dream then?" said the Devil.

"I dreamed that a fountain in a marketplace from which wine once flowed was dried up, and not even water would flow out of it; what could be the cause of it?"

"Oh, ho! If they did but know it," answered the Devil, "There is a toad sitting under a stone in the well; if they killed it, the wine would flow again."

He went to sleep again and snored until the windows shook. Then she pulled the second hair out. "Ouch! What are you doing?" cried the Devil angrily.

"Do not get angry," said she, "I did it in a dream."

"What have you dreamt this time?" asked he.

"I dreamt that in a certain kingdom there stood an apple tree which had once borne golden apples, but now would not even bear leaves. What do you think was the reason?"

"Oh! If they did but know," answered the Devil. "A mouse is gnawing at the root; if they killed this they would have golden apples again, but if it gnaws much longer the tree will wither altogether. But leave me alone with your dreams; if you disturb me in my sleep again you will get a slap on the ear."

The grandmother spoke gently to him until he fell asleep again and snored. Then she took hold of the third golden hair and pulled it out. The Devil jumped up, roared out, and would have treated her ill if she had not quieted him once more and said, "Who can help bad dreams?"

"What was the dream, then?" asked he, and was quite curious. "I dreamt of a ferryman who complained that he must always ferry from one side to the other, and was never released. What is the cause of it?"

"Ah! The fool," answered the Devil, "When anyone comes and wants to go across he must put the oar in his hand, and the other man will have to ferry and he will be free." As the grandmother had plucked out the three golden hairs, and the three questions were answered, she let the old serpent alone, and he slept until daybreak.

When the Devil had gone out again the old woman took the ant out of the folds of her dress, and gave the luck child his human shape again. "There are the three golden hairs for you," said she. "What the Devil said to your three questions, I suppose you heard?"

"Yes," answered he, "I heard, and will take care to remember."

"You have what you want," said she, "and now you can go your way." He thanked the old woman for helping him in his need, and left hell well content that everything had turned out so fortunately.

When he came to the ferryman he was expected to give the promised answer. "Ferry me across first," said the luck child, "and then I will tell you how you can be set free," and when he reached the opposite shore he gave him the Devil's advice: "Next time anyone comes who wants to be ferried over, just put the oar in his hand."

He went on and came to the town where the unfruitful tree stood, and there too the watchman wanted an answer. So he told him what he had heard from the Devil: "Kill the mouse which is gnawing at its root, and it will again bear golden apples." Then the watchman thanked him, and gave him as a reward two asses laden with gold, which followed him.

At last he came to the town whose well was dry. He told the watchman what the Devil had said: "A toad is in the well beneath a stone; you must find it and kill it, and the well will again give wine in plenty." The watchman thanked him, and also gave him two asses laden with gold.

At last the luck child got home to his wife, who was heartily glad to see him again, and to hear how well he had prospered in everything. To the King he took what he had asked for, the Devil's three golden hairs, and when the King saw the four asses laden with gold he was quite content, and said, "Now all the conditions are fulfilled, and you can keep my daughter. But tell me, dear son-in-law, where did all that gold come from? This is tremendous wealth!"

"I was rowed across a river," answered he, "and got it there; the shore is made of gold instead of sand."

"Can I too fetch some of it?" said the King, and he was quite eager about it.

"As much as you like," answered he. "There is a ferryman on the river; let him ferry you over, and you can fill your sacks on the other side." The greedy King set out in all haste, and when he came to the river he beckoned to the ferryman to put him across. The ferryman came and bade him get in, and when they got to the other shore he put the oar in his hand and sprang out. But from this time forth the King had to ferry, as a punishment for his sins. Perhaps he is ferrying still? If he is, it is because no one has taken the oar from him.

30. THE LOUSE AND THE FLEA

A louse and a flea kept house together and were brewing beer in an eggshell. Then the little louse fell in and burnt herself. At this the little flea began to scream loudly. Then said the little door, "Little flea, why are you screaming?"

"Because the louse has burnt herself."

Then the little door began to creak. At this a little broom in the corner said, "Why are you creaking, little door?"

"Have I not reason to creak?

"The little louse has burnt herself,
The little flea is weeping."

So the little broom began to sweep frantically. Then a little cart passed by and said, "Why are you sweeping, little broom?"

"Have I not reason to sweep?

"The little louse has burnt herself,
The little flea is weeping,
The little door is creaking."

So the little cart said, "Then I will run," and began to run wildly.

Then said the garbage heap by which it ran, "Why are you running so, little cart?"

"Have I not reason to run?

"The little louse has burnt herself,
The little flea is weeping,
The little door is creaking,
The little broom is sweeping."

The garbage heap said, "Then I will burn furiously," and began to burn in clear flames.

A little tree stood near the heap and said, "Garbage heap, why are you burning?"

"Have I not reason to burn?

"The little louse has burnt herself,
The little flea is weeping,
The little door is creaking,
The little broom is sweeping,
The little cart is running."

The little tree said, "Then I will shake myself," and began to shake herself so that all her leaves fell off. A girl who came up with her water pitcher saw that, and said, "Little tree, why are you shaking yourself?"

"Have I not reason to shake myself?

"The little louse has burnt herself,
The little flea is weeping,
The little door is creaking,
The little broom is sweeping,
The little cart is running,
The little heap is burning."

At this the girl said, "Then I will break my little water pitcher," and she broke her little water pitcher.

Then said the little spring from which ran the water, "Girl, why are you breaking your water jug?"

"Have I not reason to break my water jug?

"The little louse has burnt herself,
The little flea is weeping,
The little door is creaking,
The little broom is sweeping,
The little cart is running,
The little heap is burning,
The little tree is shaking itself."

"Oh, ho!" said the spring, "Then I will begin to flow," and began to flow violently. And in the water everything was drowned, the girl, the little tree, the little garbage heap, the little cart, the little broom, the little door, the little flea, the little louse, all together.

31. THE GIRL WITHOUT HANDS

A certain miller had little by little fallen into poverty, and had nothing left but his mill and a large apple tree behind it. Once when he had gone into the forest to fetch wood, an old man stepped up to him whom he had never seen before, and said, "Why do you plague yourself with cutting wood? I will make you rich, if you will promise me what is standing behind your mill."

"What can that be but my apple tree?" thought the miller, and said, "Yes," and gave a written promise to the stranger.

He, however, laughed mockingly and said, "When three years have passed, I will come and carry away what belongs to me," and then he went.

When the miller got home, his wife came to meet him and said, "Tell me, miller, from where comes this sudden wealth into our house? All at once every box and chest was filled; no one brought it in, and I know not how it happened."

He answered, "It comes from a stranger who met me in the forest, and promised me great treasure. I, in return, have promised him what stands behind the mill; we can very well give him the big apple tree for it."

"Ah, husband," said the terrified wife, "that must have been the devil! He did not mean the apple tree, but our daughter, who was standing behind the mill sweeping the yard."

The miller's daughter was a beautiful, God-fearing girl, and lived through the three years in piety and without sin. When therefore the time was over, and the day came when the Evil One was to fetch her, she washed herself clean, and made a circle round herself with chalk. The devil appeared quite early, but he could not come near her. Angrily, he said to the miller, "Take all water away from her, that she may no longer be able to wash herself, for otherwise I have no power over her." The miller was afraid, and did so.

The next morning the devil came again, but she had wept on her hands, and they were quite clean. Again he could not get near her, and furiously said to the miller, "Cut her hands off, or else I cannot get the better of her."

The miller was shocked and answered, "How could I cut off my own child's hands?"

Then the Evil One threatened him and said, "If you do not do it you are mine, and I will take you yourself."

The father became alarmed, and promised to obey him. So he went to the girl and said, "My child, if I do not cut off both your hands, the devil will carry me away, and in my terror I have promised to do it. Help me in my need, and forgive me the harm I do you."

She replied, "Dear father, do with me what you will, I am your child." Thereupon she laid down both her hands, and let them be cut off. The devil came for the third time, but she had wept so long and so much on the stumps, that after all they were quite clean. Then he had to give in, and had lost all right over her.

The miller said to her, "Because of you I have received such great wealth that I will keep you most delicately as long as you live."

But she replied, "Here I cannot stay, I will go forth, compassionate people will give me as much as I require." Thereupon she had her maimed arms bound to her back, and by sunrise she set out on her way, and walked the whole day until night fell. Then she came to a royal garden, and by the shimmering of the moon she saw that trees covered with beautiful fruits grew in it, but she could not enter, for there was much water round about it. And as she had walked the whole day and not eaten one mouthful, and hunger tormented her, she thought, "Ah, if I were but inside, then I might eat the fruit, else I must die of hunger!" Then she knelt down, called on God the Lord, and prayed. And suddenly an angel came towards her, who made a dam in the water, so that the moat became dry and she could walk through it. And now she went into the garden and the angel went with her. She saw a tree covered with beautiful pears, but they were all counted. Then she went to them, and to still her hunger, ate one with her mouth from the tree, but no more. The gardener was watching; but as the angel was standing by, he was afraid and thought the maiden was a spirit, and was silent, neither did he dare to cry out, or to speak to the spirit. When she had eaten the pear, she was satisfied, and went and concealed herself among the bushes. The King to whom the garden belonged, came down to it next morning, and counted, and saw that one of the pears was missing, and asked the gardener what had become of it, as it was not lying beneath the tree, but was gone.

Then answered the gardener, "Last night, a spirit came in, who had no hands, and ate off one of the pears with its mouth."

The King said, "How did the spirit get over the water, and where did it go after it had eaten the pear?"

The gardener answered, "Someone from heaven came in a snow-white garment and made a dam, and kept back the water, that the spirit might walk through the moat. And as it must have been an angel, I was afraid, and asked no questions, and did not cry out. When the spirit had eaten the pear, it went back again."

The King said, "If it is as you say, I will watch with you tonight."

When it grew dark the King came into the garden and brought a priest with him, who was to speak to the spirit. All three seated themselves beneath the tree and watched. At midnight the maiden came creeping out of the thicket, went to the tree, and again ate one pear off it with her mouth, and beside her stood the angel in white garments. Then the priest went out to them and said, "Come you from heaven or from earth? Are you a spirit, or a human being?"

She replied, "I am no spirit, but an unhappy mortal deserted by all but God."

The King said, "Though you are forsaken by all the world, I will not forsake you." He took her with him into his royal palace, and as she was so beautiful and good, he loved her with all his heart, had silver hands made for her, and took her for his wife.

After a year the King had to go to war, so he placed his young Queen in the care of his mother and said, "If she is brought to bed take care of her, nurse her well, and tell me of it at once in a letter." Then she gave birth to a fine boy. So the old mother made haste to write and announce the joyful news to him. But the messenger rested by a brook on the way, and as he was fatigued by the great distance, he fell asleep. Then came the Devil, who was always seeking to injure the good Queen, and exchanged the letter for another, in which was written that the Queen had brought a monster into the world. When the King read the letter he was shocked and much troubled, but he wrote in answer that they were to take great care of the Queen and nurse her well until his arrival. The messenger went back with the letter, but rested at the same place and again fell asleep. Then came the Devil once more, and put a different letter in his pocket, in which it was written that they were to put the Queen and her child to death. The old mother was terribly shocked when she received the letter, and could not believe it. She wrote back again to the King, but received no other answer, because each time the Devil substituted a false letter, and in the last letter it was also written that she was to preserve the Queen's tongue and eyes as a token that she had obeyed.

But the old mother wept to think such innocent blood was to be shed, and had a doe brought by night and cut out her tongue and eyes, and kept them. Then said she to the Queen, "I cannot have you killed as the King commands, but here you may stay no longer. Go forth into the wide world with your child, and never come here again." The poor woman tied her child on her back, and went away with eyes full of tears.

She came into a great wild forest, and then she fell on her knees and prayed to God, and the angel of the Lord appeared to her and led her to a little house on which was a sign with the words, "Here all dwell free." A snow-white maiden came out of the little house and said, "Welcome, Lady Queen," and led her inside. Then they unbound the little boy from her back, and held him to her breast that he might feed, and laid him in a beautifully-made little bed.

Then said the poor woman, "How do you know that I was a queen?"

The white maiden answered, "I am an angel sent by God, to watch over you and your child." The Queen stayed seven years in the little house, and was well cared for, and by God's grace, because of her piety, her hands which had been cut off, grew once more.

At last the King came home again from the war, and his first wish was to see his wife and the child. Then his aged mother began to weep and said, "You wicked man, why did you write to me that I was to take those two innocent lives?" and she showed him the two letters which the Evil One had forged, and then continued, "I did as you bade me," and she showed the tokens, the tongue and eyes. Then the King began to weep for his poor wife and his little son so much more bitterly than she was doing, that the aged mother had compassion on him and said, "Be at peace, she still lives; I secretly had a doe killed, and took these tokens from it; but I bound the child to your wife's back and bade her go forth into the wide world, and made her promise never to come back here again, because you were so angry with her."

Then spoke the King, "I will go as far as the sky is blue, and will neither eat nor drink until I have found again my dear wife and my child, if in the meantime they have not been killed, or died of hunger."

Thereupon the King traveled about for seven long years, and sought her in every cleft of the rocks and in every cave, but he did not find her, and thought she had died of want. During the whole of this time he neither ate nor drank, but God supported him. At length he came into a great forest, and found therein the little house whose sign was, "Here all dwell free." Then forth came the white maiden, took him by the hand, led him in, and said, "Welcome, Lord King," and asked him from where he came.

He answered, "I have traveled about for the space of seven years, and I seek my wife and her child, but cannot find them." The angel offered him meat and drink, but he did not take anything, and only wished to rest a little. Then he lay down to sleep, and put a handkerchief over his face.

Thereupon the angel went into the chamber where the Queen sat with her son, whom she usually called "Sorrowful," and said to her, "Go out with your child, your husband has come."

So she went to the place where he lay, and the handkerchief fell from his face. Then said she, "Sorrowful, pick up your father's handkerchief, and cover his face again." The child picked it up, and put it over his face again. The King in his sleep heard what passed, and had pleasure in letting the handkerchief fall once more.

But the child grew impatient, and said, "Dear mother, how can I cover my father's face when I have no father in this world? I have learnt to say the prayer, 'Our Father, which art in Heaven,' you have told me that my father was in Heaven, and was the good God, and how can I recognize a wild man like this? He is not my father." When the King heard that, he got up, and asked who they were.

Then said she, "I am your wife, and that is your son, Sorrowful."

And he saw her living hands, and said, "My wife had silver hands."

She answered, "The good God has caused my natural hands to grow again;" and the angel went into the inner room, and brought the silver hands, and showed them to him.

Then he knew for a certainty that it was his dear wife and his dear child, and he kissed them, and was glad, and said, "A heavy stone has fallen from off my heart." Then the angel of God gave them one meal with her, and after that they went home to the King's aged mother. There were great rejoicings everywhere, and the King and Queen were married again, and lived contentedly to their happy end.

32. *CLEVER HANS*

The mother of Hans said, "Where away, Hans?"

Hans answered, "To Gretel."

"Behave well, Hans."

"Oh, I'll behave well. Goodbye, mother."

"Goodbye, Hans."

Hans comes to Gretel. "Good day, Gretel."

"Good day, Hans. What do you bring that is good?"

"I bring nothing, I want to have something given to me." Gretel presents Hans with a needle. Hans says, "Goodbye, Gretel."

"Goodbye, Hans."

Hans takes the needle, sticks it into a hay cart, and follows the cart home. "Good evening, mother."

"Good evening, Hans. Where have you been?"

"With Gretel."

"What did you take her?"

"Took nothing; had something given to me."

"What did Gretel give you?"

"Gave me a needle."

"Where is the needle, Hans?"

"Stuck it in the hay cart."

"That was foolish, Hans. You should have stuck the needle in your sleeve."

"Never mind, I'll do better next time."

"Where away, Hans?"

"To Gretel, mother."

"Behave well, Hans."

"Oh, I'll behave well. Goodbye, mother."

"Goodbye, Hans."

Hans comes to Gretel. "Good day, Gretel."

"Good day, Hans. What do you bring that is good?"

"I bring nothing; I want to have something given to me." Gretel presents Hans with a knife. "Goodbye, Gretel."

"Goodbye Hans."

Hans takes the knife, sticks it in his sleeve, and goes home. "Good evening, mother."

"Good evening, Hans. Where have you been?"

"With Gretel."

"What did you take her?"

"Took her nothing, she gave me something."

"What did Gretel give you?"

"Gave me a knife."

"Where is the knife, Hans?"

"Stuck in my sleeve."

"That's foolish, Hans, you should have put the knife in your pocket."

"Never mind, will do better next time."

"Where away, Hans?"

"To Gretel, mother."

"Behave well, Hans."

"Oh, I'll behave well. Goodbye, mother."

"Goodbye, Hans."

Hans comes to Gretel. "Good day, Gretel."

"Good day, Hans. What good thing do you bring?"

"I bring nothing, I want something given to me." Gretel presents Hans with a young goat. "Goodbye, Gretel."

"Goodbye, Hans."

Hans takes the goat, ties its legs, and puts it in his pocket. When he gets home it is suffocated. "Good evening, mother."

"Good evening, Hans. Where have you been?"

"With Gretel."

"What did you take her?"

"Took nothing, she gave me something."

"What did Gretel give you?"

"She gave me a goat."

"Where is the goat, Hans?"

"Put it in my pocket."

"That was foolish, Hans, you should have put a rope round the goat's neck."

"Never mind, will do better next time."

"Where away, Hans?"

"To Gretel, mother."

"Behave well, Hans."

"Oh, I'll behave well. Goodbye, mother."

"Goodbye, Hans."

Hans comes to Gretel. "Good day, Gretel."

"Good day, Hans. What good thing do you bring?"

"I bring nothing, I want something given to me." Gretel presents Hans with a piece of bacon. "Goodbye, Gretel."

"Goodbye, Hans."

Hans takes the bacon, ties it to a rope, and drags it away behind him. The dogs come and devour the bacon. When he gets home, he has the rope in his hand, and there is no longer anything hanging to it. "Good evening, mother."

"Good evening, Hans."

"Where have you been?"

"With Gretel."

"What did you take her?"

"I took her nothing, she gave me something."

"What did Gretel give you?"

"Gave me a bit of bacon."

"Where is the bacon, Hans?"

"I tied it to a rope, brought it home, dogs took it."

"That was foolish, Hans, you should have carried the bacon on your head."

"Never mind, will do better next time."

"Where away, Hans?"

"To Gretel, mother."

"Behave well, Hans."

"I'll behave well. Goodbye, mother."

"Goodbye, Hans."

Hans comes to Gretel. "Good day, Gretel."

"Good day, Hans."

"What good thing do you bring?"

"I bring nothing, but would have something given." Gretel presents Hans with a calf. "Goodbye, Gretel."

"Goodbye, Hans."

Hans takes the calf, puts it on his head, and the calf kicks his face. "Good evening, mother."

"Good evening, Hans. Where have you been?"

"With Gretel."

"What did you take her?"

"I took nothing, but had something given me."

"What did Gretel give you?"

"A calf."

"Where is the calf, Hans?"

"I set it on my head and it kicked my face."

"That was foolish, Hans, you should have led the calf, and put it in the stall."

"Never mind, will do better next time."

"Where away, Hans?"

"To Gretel, mother."

"Behave well, Hans."

"I'll behave well. Goodbye, mother."

"Goodbye, Hans."

Hans comes to Gretel. "Good day, Gretel."

"Good day, Hans. What good thing do you bring?"

"I bring nothing, but would have something given."

Gretel says to Hans, "I will go with you."

Hans takes Gretel, ties her to a rope, leads her to the feed rack and binds her fast. Then Hans goes to his mother. "Good evening, mother."

"Good evening, Hans. Where have you been?"

"With Gretel."

"What did you take her?"

"I took her nothing."

"What did Gretel give you?"

"She gave me nothing, she came with me."

"Where have you left Gretel?"

"I led her by the rope, tied her to the rack, and scattered some grass for her."

"That was foolish, Hans, you should have cast friendly eyes on her."

"Never mind, will do better."

Hans went into the stable, cut out all the calves' and sheep's eyes, and threw them in Gretel's face. Then Gretel became angry, tore herself loose and ran away, and never became the bride of Hans.

33. THE THREE LANGUAGES

An aged count once lived in Switzerland, who had an only son, but he was stupid, and could learn nothing. Then said the father, "Listen, my son, I can get nothing into your head, let me try as I will. You must go from here, I will give you into the care of a celebrated master, who shall see what he can do with you." The youth was sent into a strange town, and remained a whole year with the master. At the end of this time, he came home again, and his father asked, "Now, my son, what have you learnt?"

"Father, I have learnt what the dogs say when they bark."

"Lord have mercy on us!" cried the father, "Is that all you have learnt? I will send you into another town, to another master." The youth was taken there, and stayed a year with this master likewise. When he came back the father again asked, "My son, what have you learnt?"

He answered, "Father, I have learnt what the birds say."

Then the father fell into a rage and said, "Oh, you lost man, you have spent precious time and learnt nothing; are you not ashamed to appear before my eyes? I will send you to a third master, but if you learn nothing this time also, I will no longer be your father." The youth remained a whole year with the third master also, and when he came home again, and his father inquired, "My son, what have you learnt?" he answered, "Dear father, I have this year learnt what the frogs croak."

Then the father fell into the most furious anger, sprang up, called his people over, and said, "This man is no longer my son, I cast him out, and command you to take him out into the forest, and kill him." They took him there, but when they should have killed him, they could not do it for pity, and let him go, and they cut the eyes and the tongue out of a deer that they might carry them to the old man as a token.

The youth wandered on, and after some time came to a fortress where he begged for a night's lodging. "Yes," said the lord of the castle, "if you will pass the night down there in the old tower, go there; but I warn you, it is at the peril of your life, for it is full of wild dogs, which bark and howl without stopping, and at certain hours a man has to be given to them, whom they at once devour." The whole district was in sorrow and dismay because of them, and yet no one could do anything to stop this.

The youth, however, was without fear, and said, "Just let me go down to the barking dogs, and give me something that I can throw to them; they will do nothing to harm me." Since he himself insisted, they gave him some food for the wild animals, and led him down to the tower. When he went inside, the dogs did not bark at him, but wagged their tails quite amicably around him, ate what he set before them, and did not hurt one hair on his head.

Next morning, to the astonishment of everyone, he came out again safe and unharmed, and said to the lord of the castle, "The dogs have revealed to me, in their own language, why they dwell there, and bring evil on the land. They are bewitched, and are obliged to watch over a great treasure which is below in the tower, and they can have no rest until it is taken away, and I have likewise learnt, from their discourse, how that is to be done." Then all who heard this rejoiced, and the lord of the castle said he would adopt him as a son if he accomplished it successfully. He went down again, and as he knew what he had to do, he did it thoroughly, and brought a chest full of gold out with him. The howling of the wild dogs was heard no more; they had disappeared, and the country was freed from the trouble.

After some time he took it into his head that he would travel to Rome. On the way he passed by a marsh, in which a number of frogs were sitting croaking. He listened to them, and when he became aware of what they were saying, he grew very thoughtful and sad. At last he arrived in Rome, where the Pope had just died, and there was great difficulty as to whom they should appoint as his successor. They at length agreed that the person chosen as pope should be distinguished by some divine and miraculous token. And just as that was decided on, the young count entered into the church, and suddenly two snow-white doves flew on his shoulders and remained sitting there. The ecclesiastics recognized that as a token from above, and asked him on the spot if he would be pope. He was undecided, and knew not if he were worthy of this, but the doves counseled him to do it, and at length he said yes. Then was he anointed and consecrated, and thus was fulfilled the prophecy he had heard from the frogs on his way, which had so disturbed him, that he was to be his Holiness the Pope. Then he had to sing a mass, and did not know one word of it, but the two doves sat continually on his shoulders, and said it all in his ear.

34. CLEVER ELSIE

There was once a man who had a daughter who was called Clever Elsie. And when she had grown up her father said, "We will get her married."

"Yes," said the mother; "if only anyone would come who would have her."

At length a man came from a distance and wooed her, who was called Hans; but he stipulated that Clever Elsie should be really wise. "Oh," said the father, "she's sharp enough," and the mother said, "Oh, she can see the wind coming up the street, and hear the flies coughing."

"Well," said Hans, "if she is not really wise, I won't have her."

When they were sitting at dinner and had eaten, the mother said, "Elsie, go into the cellar and fetch some beer." Then Clever Elsie took the pitcher from the wall, went into the cellar, and clapped the lid up and down as she went, to pass the time. When she was below she fetched herself a chair, and set it before the barrel so that she had no need to stoop, and did not hurt her back or do herself any unexpected injury. Then she placed the can before her, and turned the tap, and while the beer was running she would not let her eyes be idle, but looked up at the wall, and after much peering here and there, saw a pickaxe exactly above her, which the masons had accidentally left there.

Then Clever Elsie began to weep, and said, "If I get Hans, and we have a child, and he grows big, and we send him into the cellar here to draw beer, then the pickaxe will fall on his head and kill him." Then she sat and wept and screamed with all the strength of her body, over the misfortune which lay before her.

Those upstairs waited for the drink, but Clever Elsie still did not come. Then the woman said to the servant, "Just go down into the cellar and see where Elsie is." The maid went and found her sitting in front of the barrel, screaming loudly.

"Elsie, why do you weep" asked the maid.

"Ah," she answered, "have I not reason to weep? If I get Hans, and we have a child, and he grows big, and has to draw beer here, the pickaxe will perhaps fall on his head, and kill him."

Then said the maid, "What a clever Elsie we have!" and sat down beside her and began loudly to weep over the misfortune.

After a while, as the maid did not come back, those upstairs were thirsty for the beer, the man said to the boy, "Just go down into the cellar and see where Elsie and the girl are."

The boy went down, and there sat Clever Elsie and the girl both weeping together. Then he asked, "Why are you weeping?"

"Ah," said Elsie, "have I not reason to weep? If I get Hans, and we have a child, and he grows big, and has to draw beer here, the pickaxe will fall on his head and kill him."

Then said the boy, "What a clever Elsie we have!" and sat down by her, and likewise began to howl loudly.

Upstairs they waited for the boy, but as he still did not return, the man said to the woman, "Just go down into the cellar and see where Elsie is!"

The woman went down, and found all three in the midst of their lamentations, and inquired what was the cause; then Elsie told her that her future child was to be killed by the pickaxe, when it grew big and had to draw beer, and the pickaxe fell down. Then said the mother likewise, "What a clever Elsie we have!" and sat down and wept with them.

The man upstairs waited a short time, but as his wife did not come back and his thirst grew ever greater, he said, "I must go into the cellar myself and see where Elsie is." But when he got into the cellar, and they were all sitting together crying, and he heard the reason, and that Elsie's child was the cause, and that Elsie might perhaps bring one into the world some day, and that it might be killed by the pickaxe, if it should happen to be sitting beneath it, drawing beer just at the very time when it fell down, he cried, "Oh, what a clever Elsie!" and sat down, and likewise wept with them.

The bridegroom stayed upstairs alone for a long time; then as no one would come back he thought, "They must be waiting for me below; I too must go there and see what they are about." When he got down, five of them were sitting screaming and lamenting quite piteously, each outdoing the other. "What misfortune has happened then?" he asked.

"Ah, dear Hans," said Elsie, "if we marry each other and have a child, and he is big, and we perhaps send him here to draw something to drink, then the pickaxe which has been left up there might dash his brains out if it were to fall down, so have we not reason to weep?"

"Come," said Hans, "more understanding than that is not needed for my household, as you are such a clever Elsie, I will have you," and he seized her hand, took her upstairs with him, and married her.

After Hans had had her some time, he said, "Wife, I am going out to work and earn some money for us; go into the field and cut the corn that we may have some bread."

"Yes, dear Hans, I will do that." After Hans had gone away, she cooked herself some good broth and took it into the field with her. When she came to the field she said to herself, "What shall I do; shall I shear first, or shall I eat first? Oh, I will eat first." Then she emptied her basin of broth, and when she was fully satisfied, she once more said, "What shall I do? Shall I shear first, or shall I sleep first? I will sleep first." Then she lay down among the corn and fell asleep.

Hans had been at home for a long time, but Elsie did not come; then said he, "What a clever Elsie I have; she is so industrious that she does not even come home to eat." As evening came, however, she still stayed away, and Hans went out to see what she had cut, but nothing was cut, and she was lying among the corn asleep. Then Hans hastened home and brought a fowler's net with little bells and hung it round about her, and she still went on sleeping. Then he ran home, shut the door, and sat down in his chair and worked.

At length, when it was quite dark, Clever Elsie awoke and when she got up there was a jingling all round about her, and the bells rang at each step which she took. Then she was alarmed, and became uncertain whether she really was Clever Elsie or not, and said, "Is it I, or is it not I?" But she did not know the answer to this, and stood for a time in doubt; at length she thought, "I will go home and ask if it is me or not, they will be sure to know." She ran to the door of her own house, but it was shut; then she knocked at the window and cried, "Hans, is Elsie inside?"

"Yes," answered Hans, "she is inside."

At that she was terrified, and said, "Ah, heavens! Then it is not I," and went to another door; but when the people heard the jingling of the bells they would not open it, and she could get in nowhere. Then she ran out of the village, and no one has seen her since.

35. THE TAILOR IN HEAVEN

One very fine day it came to pass that the good God wished to enjoy himself in the heavenly garden, and took all the apostles and saints with him, so that no one stayed in heaven but Saint Peter. The Lord had commanded him to let no one in during his absence, so Peter stood by the door and kept watch. Before long someone knocked. Peter asked who was there, and what he wanted?

"I am a poor, honest tailor who prays for admission," replied a smooth voice.

"Honest indeed," said Peter, "like the thief on the gallows! You have been light-fingered and have stolen snippets of folks' clothes. You will not get into heaven. The Lord has forbidden me to let anyone in while he is out."

"Come, do be merciful," cried the tailor. "Little scraps which fall off the table of their own accord are not stolen, and are not worth speaking about. Look, I am lame, and have blisters on my feet from walking here, I cannot possibly turn back again. Let me in, and I will do all the rough work. I will carry the children, and wash their clothes, and wash and clean the benches on which they have been playing, and patch all their torn clothes." Saint Peter let himself be moved by pity, and opened the door of heaven just wide enough for the lame tailor to slip his lean body in. He was forced to sit down in a corner behind the door, and was to stay quietly and peaceably there, in order that the Lord, when he returned, might not observe him and be angry. The tailor obeyed, but once when Saint Peter went outside the door, he got up, and full of curiosity, went round about into every corner of heaven, and inspected the arrangement of every place. At length he came to a spot where many beautiful and delightful chairs were standing, and in the middle was a seat all of gold which was set with shining jewels. It was much higher than the other chairs, and a footstool of gold was before it. It was, however, the seat on which the Lord sat when he was at home, and from which he could see everything which happened on earth. The tailor stood still, and looked at the seat for a long time, for it pleased him better than all else. At last he could master his curiosity no longer, and climbed up and seated himself in the chair. Then he saw everything which was happening on earth, and observed an ugly old woman who was washing clothes by the side of a stream, secretly laying two veils on the side for herself. The sight of this made the tailor so angry that he laid hold of the golden footstool, and threw it down to earth through heaven, at the old thief. Since, however, he could not bring the stool back again, he slipped quietly out of the chair, seated himself in his place behind the door, and behaved as if he had never stirred from the spot.

When the Lord and master came back again with his heavenly companions, he did not see the tailor behind the door, but when he seated himself on his chair the footstool was missing. He asked Saint Peter what had become of the stool, but he did not know. Then he asked if he had let anyone come in. "I know of no one who has been here," answered Peter, "but a lame tailor, who is still sitting behind the door." Then the Lord had the tailor brought before him, and asked him if he had taken away the stool, and where he had put it?

"Oh, Lord," answered the tailor joyously, "I threw it in my anger down to earth at an old woman whom I saw stealing two veils while washing."

"Oh, you knave," said the Lord, "were I to judge as you judge, how do you think you could have escaped judgment so long? I should have no chairs, benches, seats, nay, not even fire tongs, for I would have thrown everything down at the sinners long ago. Now you can stay no longer in heaven, but must go outside the door again. Then go where you will. No one shall give punishment here, but I alone, the Lord."

Saint Peter was obliged to take the tailor out of heaven again, and as he had torn shoes, and feet covered with blisters, he took a stick in his hand, and went to Wait-a-bit, where the good soldiers sit and make merry.

36. *THE WISHING TABLE, THE GOLD ASS, AND THE CUDGEL IN THE SACK*

There was once upon a time a tailor who had three sons, and only one goat. But as the goat supported the whole of them with her milk, she was obliged to have good food, and to be taken every day to pasture. The sons, therefore, did this, in turn. Once the eldest took her to the churchyard, where the finest herbs were to be found, and let her eat and run about there. At night when it was time to go home he asked, "Goat, have you had enough?" The goat answered,

> "I have eaten so much,
> Not a leaf more I'll touch, meh! Meh!"

"Come home, then," said the youth, and took hold of the cord round her neck, led her into the stable and tied her up securely.

"Well," said the old tailor, "has the goat had as much food as she should?"

"Oh," answered the son, "she has eaten so much, not a leaf more she'll touch."

But the father wished to see for himself, and went down to the stable, stroked the dear animal and asked, "Goat, are you satisfied?" The goat answered,

> "Why should I be satisfied?
> Among the graves I leapt about,
> And found no food, so went without, meh! Meh!"

"What do I hear?" cried the tailor, and ran upstairs and said to the youth, "Hollo, you liar: you said the goat had had enough, and have let her hunger!" and in his anger he took the yard-measure from the wall, and drove him out with blows.

Next day it was the turn of the second son, who looked out for a place along the garden hedge, where nothing but good herbs grew, and the goat cleared them all off. At night when he wanted to go home, he asked, "Goat, are you satisfied?" The goat answered,

"I have eaten so much,
Not a leaf more I'll touch, meh! Meh!"

"Come home, then," said the youth, and led her home, and tied her up in the stable.

"Well," said the old tailor, "has the goat had as much food as she should?"

"Oh," answered the son, "she has eaten so much, not a leaf more she'll touch."

The tailor would not rely on this, but went down to the stable and said, "Goat, have you had enough?" The goat answered,

"Why should I be satisfied?
Among the graves I leapt about,
And found no food, so went without, meh! Meh!"

"The godless wretch!" cried the tailor, "to let such a good animal hunger," and he ran up and drove the youth outside with the yard-measure.

Now came the turn of the third son, who wanted to do the thing well, and sought out some bushes with the finest leaves, and let the goat devour them. In the evening when he wanted to go home, he asked, "Goat, have you had enough?" The goat answered,

"I have eaten so much,
Not a leaf more I'll touch, meh! Meh!"

"Come home, then," said the youth, and led her into the stable, and tied her up.

"Well," said the old tailor, "has the goat had a proper amount of food?"

"She has eaten so much, not a leaf more she'll touch."

The tailor did not trust to that, but went down and asked, "Goat, have you had enough?" The wicked beast answered,

"Why should I be satisfied?
Among the graves I leapt about,
And found no leaves, so went without, meh! Meh!"

"Oh, the brood of liars!" cried the tailor, "each as wicked and forgetful of his duty as the other! You shall no longer make a fool of me," and quite beside himself with anger, he ran upstairs and belabored the poor young fellow so vigorously with the yard-measure that he sprang out of the house.

The old tailor was now alone with his goat. Next morning he went down into the stable, caressed the goat and said, "Come, my dear little animal, I will take you to feed myself." He took her by the rope and led her to green hedges, and amongst milfoil, and whatever else goats like to eat. "There you may for once eat to your heart's content," said he to her, and let her browse till evening. Then he asked, "Goat, are you satisfied?" She replied,

"I have eaten so much,
Not a leaf more I'll touch, meh! Meh!"

"Come home, then," said the tailor, and led her into the stable, and tied her fast. When he was going away, he turned round again and said, "Well, are you satisfied for once?" But the goat did not behave the better to him, and cried,

"Why should I be satisfied?
Among the graves I leapt about,
And found no leaves, so went without, meh! Meh!"

When the tailor heard that, he was shocked, and saw clearly that he had driven away his three sons without cause. "Wait, you ungrateful creature," cried he, "it is not enough to throw you out, I will mark you so that you will no more dare to show yourself amongst honest tailors." In great haste he ran upstairs, fetched his razor, lathered the goat's head, and shaved her as clean as the palm of his hand. And as the yard-measure would have been too good for her, he brought the horsewhip, and gave her such cuts with it that she ran away in violent haste.

When the tailor was thus left quite alone in his house he fell into great grief, and would gladly have had his sons back again, but no one knew where they had gone. The eldest had apprenticed himself to a carpenter, and learnt industriously and indefatigably, and when the time came for him to go traveling, his master presented him with a little table which had no particular appearance, and was made of common wood, but it had one good property; if anyone set it out, and said, "Little table, set yourself," the good little table was at once covered with a clean little cloth, and a plate was there, and a knife and fork beside it, and dishes with boiled meats and roasted meats, as many as there was room for, and a great glass of red wine shone so that it made the heart glad.

The young journeyman thought, "With this you have enough for your whole life," and went joyously about the world and never troubled himself at all whether an inn was good or bad, or if anything was to be found in it or not. When it suited him he did not enter an inn at all, but either on the plain, in a wood, a meadow, or wherever he fancied, he took his little table off his back, set it down before him, and said, "Set yourself," and then everything appeared that his heart desired. At length he took it into his head to go back to his father, whose anger would now be appeased, and who would now willingly receive him with his wishing table. It came to pass that on his way home one evening, he came to an inn which was filled with guests. They bade him welcome, and invited him to sit and eat with them, for otherwise he would have difficulty in getting anything. "No," answered the carpenter, "I will not take the few bites out of your mouths; rather than that, you shall be my guests." They laughed, and thought he was jesting with them; he, however, placed his wooden table in the middle of the room, and said, "Little table, set yourself." Instantly it was covered with food, so good that the host could never have procured it, and the smell of it ascended pleasantly to the nostrils of the guests. "Go ahead, dear friends," said the carpenter; and when the guests saw that he meant it, did not need to be asked twice, but drew near, pulled out their knives and attacked it valiantly. And what surprised them the most was that when a dish became empty, a full one instantly took its place of its own accord.

The innkeeper stood in one corner and watched the affair; he did not at all know what to say, but thought, "You could easily find a use for such a cook as that in your kitchen." The carpenter and his comrades made merry until late into the night; at length they lay down to sleep, and the young apprentice also went to bed, and set his magic table against the wall. The host's thoughts, however, let him have no rest; it occurred to him that there was a little old table in his storeroom which looked just like the apprentice's and he brought it out quite softly, and exchanged it for the wishing table. Next morning, the carpenter paid for his bed, took up his table, never thinking that he had got a false one, and went his way.

At midday he reached his father, who received him with great joy. "Well, my dear son, what have you learnt?" said he.

"Father, I have become a carpenter."

"A good trade," replied the old man, "but what have you brought back with you from your apprenticeship?"

"Father, the best thing which I have brought back with me is this little table."

The tailor inspected it on all sides and said, "You did not make a masterpiece when you made that; it is a bad old table."

"But it is a table which furnishes itself," replied the son. "When I set it out, and tell it to cover itself, the most beautiful dishes stand on it, and a wine also, which gladdens the heart. Just invite all our relations and friends, they shall refresh and enjoy themselves for once, for the table will give them all they require." When the company was assembled, he put his table in the middle of the room and said, "Little table, set yourself," but the little table did not stir itself, and remained just as bare as any other table which did not understand language. Then the poor apprentice became aware that his table had been changed, and was ashamed at having to stand there like a liar. The relations, however, mocked him, and were forced to go home without having eaten or drunk. The father brought out his patches again, and went on tailoring, but the son went to work with a master in the craft.

The second son had gone to a miller and had apprenticed himself to him. When his years were over, the master said, "As you have conducted yourself so well, I give you an ass of a peculiar kind, which neither draws a cart nor carries a sack."

"What use is he, then?" asked the young apprentice.

"He lets gold drop from his mouth," answered the miller. "If you set him on a cloth and say 'Bricklebrit,' the good animal will drop gold pieces for you."

"That is a fine thing," said the apprentice, and thanked the master, and went out into the world. When he had need of gold, he had only to say "Bricklebrit" to his ass, and it rained gold pieces, and he had nothing to do but pick them off the ground. Wherever he went, the best of everything was good enough for him, and the dearer the better, for he always had a full purse. When he had looked about the world for some time, he thought, "You must seek out your father; if you go to him with the gold ass he will forget his anger, and receive you well." It came to pass that he came to the same inn where his brother's table had been exchanged. He led his ass by the bridle, and the host was about to take the animal from him and tie him up, but the young apprentice said, "Don't trouble yourself, I will take my grey horse into the stable, and tie him up myself too, for I must know where he stands." This struck the host as odd, and he thought that a man who was forced to look after his ass himself, could not have much to spend; but when the stranger put his hand in his pocket and brought out two gold pieces, and said he was to buy something good for him, the host opened his eyes wide, and ran and sought out the best fare he could muster. After dinner the guest asked what he owed. The host did not see why he should not double the reckoning, and said the apprentice must give two more gold pieces. He felt in his pocket, but his gold was just at an end. "Wait an instant, sir host," said he, "I will go and fetch some money," but he took the tablecloth with him. The host could not imagine what this could mean, and being curious, stole after him, and as the guest bolted the stable door, he peeped through a hole left by a knot in the wood. The stranger spread out the cloth under the animal and cried, "Bricklebrit," and immediately the beast began to let gold pieces fall, so that it fairly rained down money on the ground.

"Eh, my word," said the host, "ducats are quickly coined there! A purse like that can't be wrong." The guest paid his score, and went to bed, but in the night the host stole down into the stable, led away the master of the mint, and tied up another ass in his place.

Early next morning the apprentice traveled away with his ass, and thought that he had his gold ass. At midday he reached his father, who rejoiced to see him again, and gladly took him in. "What have you made of yourself, my son?" asked the old man.

"A miller, dear father," he answered.

"What have you brought back with you from your travels?"

"Nothing else but an ass."

"There are asses enough here," said the father,

"I would rather have had a good goat."

"Yes," replied the son, "but it is no common ass, but a gold ass, when I say 'Bricklebrit,' the good beast opens its mouth and drops a whole sheetful of gold pieces. Just summon all our relations, and I will make them rich folks."

"That suits me well," said the tailor, "for then I shall have no need to torment myself any longer with the needle," and ran out himself and called the relations together.

As soon as they were assembled, the miller bade them make way, spread out his cloth, and brought the ass into the room. "Now watch," said he, and cried, "Bricklebrit," but no gold pieces fell, and it was clear that the animal knew nothing of the art, for every ass does not attain such perfection. Then the poor miller made a frown, saw that he was betrayed, and begged pardon of the relatives, who went home as poor as they came. There was no help for it, the old man had to take to his needle once more, and the youth hired himself to a miller.

The third brother had apprenticed himself to a turner, and as creating by lathe is skilled labor, he was the longest in learning. His brothers, however, told him in a letter how badly things had gone with them, and how the innkeeper had cheated them of their beautiful wishing gifts on the last evening before they reached home. When the turner had served his time, and had to set out on his travels, as he had conducted himself so well, his master presented him with a sack and said, "There is a cudgel in it."

"I can put on the sack," said he, "and it may be of good service to me, but why should the cudgel be in it? It only makes it heavy."

"I will tell you why," replied the master, "if anyone has done anything to injure you, do but say, 'Out of the sack, Cudgel!' and the cudgel will leap forth among the people, and play such a dance on their backs that they will not be able to stir or move for a week, and it will not leave off until you say, 'Into the sack, Cudgel!'"

The apprentice thanked him, and put the sack on his back, and when anyone came too near him, and wished to attack him, he said, "Out of the sack, Cudgel!" and instantly the cudgel sprang out, and beat the coat or jacket of one after the other right on their backs, and never stopped until it had stripped it off them, and it was done so quickly, that before anyone was aware, it was already his own turn. In the evening the young turner reached the inn where his brothers had been cheated. He laid his sack on the table before him, and began to talk of all the wonderful things which he had seen in the world. "Yes," said he, "people may easily find a table which will cover itself, a gold ass, and things of that kind—extremely good things which I by no means despise—but these are nothing in comparison with the treasure which I have won for myself, and am carrying about with me in my sack there."

The innkeeper pricked up his ears, "What in the world can that be?" thought he; "the sack must be filled with nothing but jewels; I ought to get them cheap too, for all good things go in threes."

When it was time for sleep, the guest stretched himself on the bench, and laid his sack beneath him for a pillow. When the innkeeper thought his guest was lying in a sound sleep, he went to him and pushed and pulled quite gently and carefully at the sack to see if he could possibly draw it away and lay another in its place. The turner had, however, been waiting for this for a long time, and now just as the innkeeper was about to give a hearty tug, he cried, "Out of the sack, Cudgel!" Instantly the little cudgel came forth, and fell on the innkeeper and gave him a sound thrashing.

The host cried for mercy; but the louder he cried, so much more heavily the cudgel beat the time on his back, until at length he fell to the ground exhausted. Then the turner said, "If you do not give back the table which covers itself, and the gold ass, the dance shall begin afresh."

"Oh, no," cried the host, quite humbly, "I will gladly produce everything, only make the accursed goblin creep back into the sack."

Then said the apprentice, "I will let mercy take the place of justice, but beware of getting into mischief again!" So he cried, "Into the sack, Cudgel!" and let him have rest.

Next morning the turner went home to his father with the wishing table, and the gold ass. The tailor rejoiced when he saw him once more, and asked him likewise what he had learned in foreign parts. "Dear father," said he, "I have become a turner."

"A skilled trade," said the father. "What have you brought back with you from your travels?"

"A precious thing, dear father," replied the son, "a cudgel in the sack."

"What!" cried the father, "A cudgel! That's worth your trouble, indeed! From every tree you can cut yourself one."

"But not one like this, dear father. If I say, 'Out of the sack, Cudgel!' the cudgel springs out and leads anyone who means ill with me a weary dance, and never stops until he lies on the ground and prays for fair weather. Look, with this cudgel I have got back the wishing table and the gold ass which the thievish innkeeper took away from my brothers. Now let them both be sent for, and invite all our kinsmen. I will give them food and drink, and will fill their pockets with gold too." The old tailor would not quite believe it, but nevertheless got the relatives together. Then the turner spread a cloth in the room and led in the gold ass, and said to his brother, "Now, dear brother, speak to him."

The miller said, "Bricklebrit," and instantly the gold pieces fell down on the cloth like a thundershower, and the ass did not stop until everyone of them had so much that he could carry no more. (I can see in your face that you also would like to be there.)

Then the turner brought the little table, and said, "Now dear brother, speak to it." And scarcely had the carpenter said, "Table, set yourself," than it was spread and amply covered with the most exquisite dishes. Then such a meal took place as the good tailor had never yet known in his house, and the whole party of kinsmen stayed together till far in the night, and were all merry and glad. The tailor locked away needle and thread, yard-measure and flatiron, in a cupboard, and lived with his three sons in joy and splendor.

*****

(What, however, has become of the goat who was to blame for the tailor driving out his three sons? That I will tell you. She was ashamed that she had a bald head, and ran to a fox's hole and crept into it. When the fox came home, he was met by two great eyes shining out of the darkness, and was terrified and ran away. A bear met him, and as the fox looked quite disturbed, he said, "What is the matter with you, brother Fox, why do you look like that?"

"Ah," answered Redcoat, "a fierce beast is in my cave and stared at me with its fiery eyes."

"We will soon drive him out," said the bear, and went with him to the cave and looked in, but when he saw the fiery eyes, fear seized on him likewise; he would have nothing to do with the furious beast, and took to his heels.

The bee met him, and as she saw that he was ill at ease, she said, "Bear, you are really making a very pitiful face; what has become of all your gaiety?"

"It is all very well for you to talk," replied the bear, "a furious beast with staring eyes is in Redcoat's house, and we can't drive him out."

The bee said, "Bear, I pity you, I am a poor weak creature whom you would not turn aside to look at, but still, I believe, I can help you." She flew into the fox's cave, lighted on the goat's smoothly-shorn head, and stung her so violently, that she sprang up, crying "Meh, meh," and ran forth into the world as if mad, and to this hour no one knows where she has gone.)

37. *THUMBLING*

There was once a poor peasant who sat in the evening by the hearth and poked the fire, and his wife sat spinning. Then said he, "How sad it is that we have no children! With us all is so quiet, and in other houses it is noisy and lively."

"Yes," replied the wife, and sighed, "even if we had only one, and it were quite small, and only as big as a thumb, I should be quite satisfied, and we would still love it with all our hearts." Now it so happened that the woman fell ill, and after seven months gave birth to a child, that was perfect in all its limbs, but no longer than a thumb. Then said they, "It is as we wished it to be, and it shall be our dear child," and because of its size, they called it Thumbling. They fed it plenty of food, and the child did not grow taller, and remained as it had been at the first. Nevertheless it looked sensibly out of its eyes, and soon showed itself to be a wise and nimble creature, for everything it did turned out well.

One day the peasant was getting ready to go into the forest to cut wood, when he said as if to himself, "How I wish that there was anyone who would bring the cart to me!"

"Oh father," cried Thumbling, "I will soon bring the cart, rely on that; it shall be in the forest at the appointed time."

The man smiled and said, "How can that be done, you are far too small to lead the horse by the reins?"

"That's of no consequence, father, if my mother will only harness it, I shall sit in the horse's ear and call out to him how he is to go."

"Well," answered the man, "for once we will try it."

When the time came, the mother harnessed the horse, and placed Thumbling in its ear, and then the little creature cried, "Gee up, gee up!"

Then it went quite properly as if with its master, and the cart went the right way into the forest. It so happened that just as he was turning a corner, and the little one was crying, "Gee up," two strange men came towards him. "My word!" said one of them, "What is this? There is a cart coming, and a driver is calling to the horse and still he is not to be seen!"

"That can't be right," said the other, "we will follow the cart and see where it stops." The cart, however, drove right into the forest, and exactly to the place where the wood had been cut.

When Thumbling saw his father, he cried to him, "See, father, here I am with the cart; now take me down." The father got hold of the horse with his left hand and with the right took his little son out of the ear. Thumbling sat down quite merrily on a straw, but when the two strange men saw him, they did not know what to say for astonishment.

Then one of them took the other aside and said, "Listen, the little fellow would make our fortune if we exhibited him in a large town, for money. We will buy him." They went to the peasant and said, "Sell us the little man. He shall be well treated with us."

"No," replied the father, "he is the apple of my eye, and all the money in the world cannot buy him from me."

Thumbling, however, when he heard of the bargain, had crept up the folds of his father's coat, placed himself on his shoulder, and whispered in his ear, "Father do give me away, I will soon come back again." Then the father sold him to the two men for a handsome bit of money.

"Where will you sit?" they said to him.

"Oh just set me on the rim of your hat, and then I can walk backwards and forwards and look at the country, and still not fall down." They did as he wished, and when Thumbling had taken leave of his father, they went away with him. They walked until it was dusk, and then the little fellow said, "Do take me down, I want to come down." The man took his hat off, and put the little fellow on the ground by the wayside, and he leapt and crept about a little between the sods, and then he suddenly slipped into a mousehole which he had spied. "Good evening, gentlemen, just go home without me," he cried to them, and mocked them. They ran and stuck their sticks into the mousehole, but it was all lost labor. Thumbling crept still farther in, and as it soon became quite dark, they were forced to go home with their vexation and their empty purses.

When Thumbling saw that they were gone, he crept back out of the subterranean passage. "It is so dangerous to walk on the ground in the dark," said he, "how easily a neck or a leg is broken!" Fortunately he knocked against an empty snail shell. "Thank God!" said he. "In that, I can pass the night in safety," and got into it.

Not long afterwards, when he was just going to sleep, he heard two men go by, and one of them was saying, "How shall we contrive to get hold of the rich pastor's silver and gold?"

"I could tell you that," cried Thumbling, interrupting them.

"What was that?" said one of the thieves in fright, "I heard someone speaking."

They stood still listening, and Thumbling spoke again, and said, "Take me with you, and I'll help you."

"But where are you?"

"Just look on the ground, and observe from where my voice comes," he replied.

There the thieves at length found him, and lifted him up. "You little imp, how will you help us?" they said.

"A great deal," said he, "I will creep into the pastor's room through the iron bars, and will hand out to you whatever you want to have."

"Come then," they said, "and we will see what you can do."

When they got to the pastor's house, Thumbling crept into the room, but instantly cried out with all his might, "Do you want to have everything that is here?"

The thieves were alarmed, and said, "But do speak softly, so as not to waken anyone!"

Thumbling however, behaved as if he had not understood this, and cried again, "What do you want? Do you want to have everything that is here?"

The cook, who slept in the next room, heard this and sat up in bed, and listened. The thieves, however, had in their fright run some distance away, but at last they took courage, and thought, "The little rascal wants to mock us." They came back and whispered to him, "Come, be serious, and reach something out to us."

Then Thumbling again cried as loudly as he could, "I really will give you everything, just put your hands in." The maid, who was listening, heard this quite distinctly, and jumped out of bed and rushed to the door. The thieves took flight, and ran as if the Wild Huntsman were behind them, but as the maid could not see anything, she went to light a candle. When she came back with it, Thumbling, unperceived, fled to the barn, and the maid, after she had examined every corner and found nothing, lay down in her bed again, and believed that, after all, she had only been dreaming with open eyes and ears.

Thumbling had climbed up among the hay and found a beautiful place to sleep in; there he intended to rest until day, and then go home again to his parents. But he had other things to go through. Truly, there is much affliction and misery in this world! When day dawned, the maid arose from her bed to feed the cows. Her first walk was into the barn, where she laid hold of an armful of hay, and precisely that very one in which poor Thumbling was lying asleep. He, however, was sleeping so soundly that he was aware of nothing, and did not awake until he was in the mouth of the cow, who had picked him up with the hay. "Ah, heavens!" cried he, "How have I got into the mill?" but he soon discovered where he was. Then it was necessary to be careful not to let himself go between the teeth and be dismembered, but he was nevertheless forced to slip down into the stomach with the hay. "In this little room the windows are forgotten," said he, "and no sun shines in, neither will a candle be brought." His quarters were especially unpleasing to him, and the worst was, more and more hay was always coming in by the door, and the space grew less and less. Then at length in his anguish, he cried as loud as he could, "Bring me no more fodder, bring me no more fodder."

The maid was just milking the cow, and when she heard someone speaking, and saw no one, and perceived that it was the same voice that she had heard in the night, she was so terrified that she slipped off her stool, and spilled the milk. She ran in great haste to her master, and said, "Oh heavens, pastor, the cow has been speaking!"

"You are mad," replied the pastor; but he went himself to the barn to see what was there.

Hardly, however had he set his foot inside when Thumbling again cried, "Bring me no more fodder, bring me no more fodder." Then the pastor himself was alarmed, and thought that an evil spirit had gone into the cow, and ordered her to be killed. She was killed, but the stomach, in which Thumbling was, was thrown on the rubbish pile. Thumbling had great difficulty in working his way to the surface; however, he succeeded, but just as he was going to thrust his head out, a new misfortune occurred. A hungry wolf ran over, and swallowed the whole stomach in one gulp. Thumbling did not lose courage.

"Perhaps," thought he, "the wolf will listen to what I have got to say," and he called to him from his stomach, "Dear wolf, I know of a magnificent feast for you."

"Where is it?" said the wolf.

"In such and such a house; you must creep into it through the kitchen sink, and will find cakes, and bacon, and sausages, and as much of them as you can eat," and he described to him exactly his father's house. The wolf did not need to be told this twice, squeezed himself in at night through the sink, and ate to his heart's content in the larder. When he had eaten his fill, he wanted to go out again, but he had become so big that he could not go out by the same way. Thumbling had reckoned on this, and now began to make a violent noise in the wolf's body, and raged and screamed as loudly as he could.

"Will you be quiet," said the wolf, "you will wake up the people!"

"Nonsense," replied the little fellow, "you have eaten your fill, and I will make merry likewise," and began once more to scream with all his strength. At last his father and mother were aroused by it, and ran to the room and looked in through the opening in the door. When they saw that a wolf was inside, they ran away, and the husband fetched his axe, and the wife the scythe.

"Stay behind," said the man, when they entered the room. "When I have given him a blow, if he is not killed by it, you must cut him down and hew his body to pieces."

Then Thumbling heard his parents' voices and cried, "Dear father, I am here; I am in the wolf's body."

Said the father, full of joy, "Thank God, our dear child has found us again," and bade the woman take away her scythe, that Thumbling might not be hurt with it. After that he raised his arm, and struck the wolf such a blow on his head that he fell down dead, and then they got knives and scissors and cut his body open and drew the little fellow out. "Ah," said the father, "what sorrow we have gone through for your sake."

"Yes father, I have gone about the world a great deal. Thank heaven, I breathe fresh air again!"

"Where have you been, then?"

"Ah, father, I have been in a mouse's hole, in a cow's stomach, and then in a wolf's; now I will stay with you."

"And we will not sell you again, no, not for all the riches in the world," said his parents, and they embraced and kissed their dear Thumbling. They gave him food and drink, and had some new clothes made for him, for his own had been spoiled on his journey.

38. THE WEDDING OF MRS. FOX

FIRST STORY

There was once an old fox with nine tails, who believed that his wife was not faithful to him, and wished to test her. He stretched himself out under the bench, did not move a limb, and behaved as if he were stone dead. Mrs. Fox went up to her room, shut herself in, and her maid, Miss Cat, sat by the fire, and did the cooking. When it became known that the old fox was dead, wooers presented themselves. The maid heard someone standing at the door, knocking. She went and opened it, and it was a young fox, who said,

"What may you be about, Miss Cat?
Do you sleep or do you wake?"

She answered,

"I am not sleeping, I am waking,
Would you know what I am making?
I am boiling warm beer with butter so nice,
Will the gentleman enter and drink some likewise?"

"No, thank you, miss," said the fox. "What is Mrs. Fox doing?" The maid replied,

"She sits all alone,
And makes her moan,
Weeping her little eyes quite red,
Because old Mr. Fox is dead."

"Do just tell her, miss, that a young fox is here, who would like to woo her."

"Certainly, young sir."

The cat goes up the stairs trip, trap,
The door she knocks at tap, tap, tap,
"Mistress Fox, are you inside?"

"Oh yes, my little cat," she cried.
"A wooer he stands at the door out there."
"Tell me what he is like, my dear?"

"But has he nine tails as beautiful as the late Mr. Fox?"

"Oh, no," answered the cat, "he has only one."

"Then I will not have him." Miss Cat went downstairs and sent the wooer away. Soon afterwards there was another knock, and another fox was at the door who wished to woo Mrs. Fox. He had two tails, but he did not fare better than the first. After this still more came, each with one tail more than the other, but they were all turned away, until at last one came who had nine tails, like old Mr. Fox. When the widow heard that, she said joyfully to the cat,

"Now open the gates and doors all wide,
And carry old Mr. Fox outside."

But just as the wedding was going to be solemnized, old Mr. Fox stirred under the bench, and cudgeled all the rabble, and drove them and Mrs. Fox out of the house.

SECOND STORY

When old Mr. Fox was dead, the wolf came as a wooer, and knocked at the door, and the cat who was servant to Mrs. Fox, opened it for him. The wolf greeted her, and said,

"Good day, Mrs. Cat of Kehrewit,
How comes it that alone you sit?
What are you making that's good?"

The cat replied,

"In milk I'm breaking bread so sweet,
Will the gentleman please come in and eat?"

"No, thank you, Mrs. Cat," answered the wolf. "Is Mrs. Fox not at home?"

The cat said,

"She sits upstairs in her room,
Bewailing her sorrowful doom,
Bewailing her trouble so sore,
For old Mr. Fox is no more."

The wolf answered,

"If she's in want of a husband now,
Then will it please her to step below?
The cat runs quickly up the stair,
And lets her tail fly here and there,
Until she comes to the parlor door.
With her five gold rings at the door she knocks,
"Are you within, good Mistress Fox?
If you're in want of a husband now,
Then will it please you to step below?"

Mrs. Fox asked, "Has the gentleman red stockings on, and has he a pointed mouth?"

"No," answered the cat.

"Then he won't do for me."

When the wolf was gone, came a dog, a stag, a hare, a bear, a lion, and all the beasts of the forest, one after the other. But one of the good points which old Mr. Fox had possessed, was always lacking, and the cat had continually to send the wooers away. At length came a young fox. Then Mrs. Fox said, "Has the gentleman red stockings on, and has he a little pointed mouth?"

"Yes," said the cat, "he has."

"Then let him come upstairs," said Mrs. Fox, and ordered the servant to prepare the wedding feast.

"Sweep me the room as clean as you can,
Up with the window, fling out my old man!
For many a fine fat mouse he brought,
Yet of his wife he never thought,
But ate up everyone he caught."

Then the wedding was solemnized with young Mr. Fox, and there was much rejoicing and dancing; and if they have not left off, they are dancing still.

39. *THE ELVES*

FIRST STORY

A shoemaker, by no fault of his own, had become so poor that at last he had nothing left but leather for one pair of shoes. So in the evening, he cut out the shoes which he wished to begin to make the next morning, and as he had a good conscience, he lay down quietly in his bed, commended himself to God, and fell asleep. In the morning, after he had said his prayers, and was just going to sit down to work, the two shoes stood quite finished on his table. He was astounded, and knew not what to say to it. He took the shoes in his hands to observe them closer, and they were so neatly made that there was not one bad stitch in them, just as if they were intended as a masterpiece. Soon after, a buyer came in, and as the shoes pleased him so well, he paid more for them than was customary, and, with the money, the shoemaker was able to purchase leather for two pairs of shoes. He cut them out at night, and next morning was about to set to work with fresh courage; but he had no need to do so, for, when he got up, they were already made, and they found buyers who gave him money enough to buy leather for four pairs of shoes. The following morning, too, he found the four pairs made; and so it went on constantly, what he cut out in the evening was finished by the morning, so that he soon had his honest independence again, and at last became a wealthy man. Now it happened that one evening not long before Christmas, when the man had been cutting out, he said to his wife, before going to bed, "What do you think of staying up tonight to see who it is that lends us this helping hand?" The woman liked the idea, and lighted a candle, and then they hid themselves in a corner of the room, behind some clothes which were hanging up there, and watched. When it was midnight, two pretty little naked men came, sat down by the shoemaker's table, took all the work which was cut out before them and began to stitch, and sew, and hammer so skillfully and so quickly with their little fingers that the shoemaker could not turn away his eyes for astonishment. They did not stop until all was done, and stood finished on the table, and they ran quickly away.

Next morning the woman said, "The little men have made us rich, and we really must show that we are grateful for it. They run about so, and have nothing on, and must be cold. I'll tell you what I'll do: I will make them little shirts, and coats, and vests, and trousers, and knit both of them a pair of stockings, and you, too, make them two little pairs of shoes."

The man said, "I shall be very glad to do it," and one night, when everything was ready, they laid their presents all together on the table instead of the cut-out leather, and then concealed themselves to see how the little men would behave. At midnight they came bounding in, and wanted to get to work at once, but as they did not find any leather cut out, but only the pretty little articles of clothing, they were at first astonished, and then they showed intense delight. They dressed themselves rapidity, putting the pretty clothes on, and singing,

"Now we are boys so fine to see,
We should no longer cobblers be!"

Then they danced and skipped and leapt over chairs and benches. At last they danced out the door. From that time forth they came no more, but as long as the shoemaker lived all went well with him, and all his undertakings prospered.

SECOND STORY

There was once a poor servant girl, who was industrious and cleanly, and swept the house every day, and emptied her sweepings on the great heap in front of the door. One morning when she was just going back to her work, she found a letter on this heap, and as she could not read, she put her broom in the corner, and took the letter to her master and mistress. It was an invitation from the elves, who asked the girl to hold a child for them at its christening and be its godmother. The girl did not know what to do, but at length, after much persuasion, and as they told her that it was not right to refuse an invitation of this kind, she consented. Then three elves came and led her to a hollow mountain, where the little folks lived. Everything there was small, but more elegant and beautiful than can be described. The baby's mother lay in a bed of black ebony ornamented with pearls, the coverlids were embroidered with gold, the cradle was of ivory, the bath of gold. The girl stood as godmother, and then wanted to go home again, but the little elves begged her to stay three days with them. So she stayed, and passed the time in pleasure and gaiety, and the little folks did all they could to make her happy. At last she set out on her way home, after they filled her pockets quite full of money, and led her out of the mountain again. When she got home, she wanted to begin her work, and took the broom, which was still standing in the corner, in her hand and began to sweep. Then some strangers came out of the house, who asked her who she was, and what business she had there? And she had not, as she thought, been gone three days with the little men in the mountains, but seven years, and in the meantime her former masters had died.

THIRD STORY

A certain mother's child had been taken away out of its cradle by the elves, and a changeling with a large head and staring eyes, which would do nothing but eat and drink, laid in its place. In her trouble she went to her neighbor, and asked her advice. The neighbor said that she was to carry the changeling into the kitchen, set it down on the hearth, light a fire, and boil some water in two eggshells, which would make the changeling laugh, and if he laughed, that would be the end of him. The woman did everything that her neighbor bade her. When she put the eggshells with water on the fire, the imp said, "I am as old now as the Wester forest, but never yet have I seen anyone boil anything in an eggshell!" And he began to laugh at it. While he was laughing, suddenly came a host of little elves, who brought the right child, set it down on the hearth, and took the changeling away with them.

40. THE ROBBER BRIDEGROOM

There was once on a time a miller, who had a beautiful daughter, and as she grew up, he wished that she was provided for, and well married. He thought, "If any good suitor comes and asks for her, I will give her to him." Not long afterwards, a suitor came, who appeared to be very rich, and as the miller had no fault to find with him, he promised his daughter to him. The maiden, however, did not like him quite so much as a girl should like the man to whom she is engaged, and had no confidence in him. Whenever she saw, or thought of him, she felt a secret horror. Once he said to her, "You are my betrothed, and yet you have never once paid me a visit."

The maiden replied, "I know not where your house is."

Then said the bridegroom, "My house is out there in the dark forest." She tried to excuse herself and said she could not find the way there. The bridegroom said, "Next Sunday you must come out there to me; I have already invited the guests, and I will strew ashes so that you may find your way through the forest." When Sunday came, and the maiden had to set out on her way, she became very uneasy, she herself knew not exactly why, and to mark her way she filled both her pockets full of peas and lentils. Ashes were strewn at the entrance of the forest, and these she followed, but at every step she threw a couple of peas on the ground. She walked almost the whole day until she reached the middle of the forest, where it was the darkest, and there stood a solitary house, which she did not like, for it looked so dark and dismal. She went inside it, but no one was within, and the most absolute stillness reigned. Suddenly a voice cried,

> "Turn back, turn back, young maiden dear,
> 'Tis a murderer's house you enter here."

The maiden looked up, and saw that the voice came from a bird, which was hanging in a cage on the wall. Again it cried,

> "Turn back, turn back, young maiden dear,
> 'Tis a murderer's house you enter here."

Then the young maiden went on farther from one room to another, and walked through the whole house, but it was entirely empty and not one human being was to be found. At last she came to the cellar, and there sat an extremely aged woman, whose head shook constantly. "Can you not tell me," said the maiden, "if my betrothed lives here?"

"Alas, poor child," replied the old woman, "do you know where you have come? You are in a murderer's den. You think you are a bride soon to be married, but you will wed death at your wedding. Look, I have been forced to put a great kettle on there, with water in it, and when they have you in their power, they will cut you to pieces without mercy, will cook you, and eat you, for they are eaters of human flesh. If I do not have compassion on you, and save you, you are lost."

Thereupon the old woman led her behind a great barrel where she could not be seen. "Be as still as a mouse," said she, "do not make a sound, or move, or all will be over for you. At night, when the robbers are asleep, we will escape; I have long waited for an opportunity." Hardly was this done, than the godless crew came home. They dragged with them another young girl. They were drunk, and paid no heed to her screams and lamentations. They gave her wine to drink, three glasses full, one glass of white wine, one glass of red, and a glass of yellow, and with this her heart burst in two. Thereupon they tore off her delicate raiment, laid her on a table, cut her beautiful body in pieces and strewed salt on it. The poor bride behind the cask trembled and shook, for she saw right well what fate the robbers had destined for her. One of them noticed a gold ring on the little finger of the murdered girl, and as it would not come off at once, he took an axe and cut the finger off, but it sprang up in the air, away over the cask and fell straight into the bride's bosom. The robber took a candle and wanted to look for it, but could not find it. Then another of them said, "Have you looked behind the great barrel?"

But the old woman cried, "Come and get something to eat, and leave off looking till the morning, the finger won't run away from you."

Then the robbers said, "The old woman is right," and gave up their search, and sat down to eat, and the old woman poured a sleeping potion in their wine, so that they soon lay down in the cellar, and slept and snored. When the bride heard that, she came out from behind the barrel, and had to step over the sleepers, for they lay in rows on the ground, and great was her terror lest she should awaken one of them.

But God helped her, and she got safely over. The old woman went up with her, opened the doors, and they hurried out of the murderers' den with all the speed in their power. The wind had blown away the strewn ashes, but the peas and lentils had sprouted and grown up, and showed them the way in the moonlight. They walked the whole night, until in the morning they arrived at the mill, and then the maiden told her father everything exactly as it had happened.

When the day came when the wedding was to be celebrated, the bridegroom appeared, and the miller had invited all his relations and friends. As they sat at table, each was bidden to relate a story. The bride sat still, and said nothing. Then said the bridegroom to the bride, "Come, my darling, do you know nothing? Relate something to us like the rest."

She replied, "Then I will relate a dream. I was walking alone through a wood, and at last I came to a house, in which no living soul was, but on the wall there was a bird in a cage which cried,

"Turn back, turn back, young maiden dear,
'Tis a murderer's house you enter here."

And this it cried once more. My darling, it was only a dream. Then I went through all the rooms, and they were all empty, and there was something so horrible about them! At last I went down into the cellar, and there sat a very, very old woman, whose head shook; I asked her, 'Does my bridegroom live in this house?'

She answered, 'Alas poor child, you have got into a murderer's den, your bridegroom does live here, but he will hew you in pieces, and kill you, and then he will cook you, and eat you.' My darling, it was only a dream. But the old woman hid me behind a great barrel, and, scarcely was I hidden, when the robbers came home, dragging a maiden with them, to whom they gave three kinds of wine to drink, white, red, and yellow, with which her heart broke in two. My darling, it was only a dream. Thereupon they pulled off her pretty clothes, and hewed her fair body in pieces on a table, and sprinkled them with salt. My darling, it was only a dream. And one of the robbers saw that there was still a ring on her little finger, and as it was hard to draw off, he took an axe and cut it off, but the finger sprang up in the air, and sprang behind the great barrel, and fell in my bosom. And there is the finger with the ring!" And with these words she drew it forth, and showed it to those present.

The robber, who had during this story become as pale as ashes, leapt up and wanted to escape, but the guests held him fast, and delivered him over to justice. Then he and his whole troop were executed for their infamous deeds.

41. MR. KORBES

There were once a cock and a hen who wanted to take a journey together. So the cock built a beautiful carriage, which had four red wheels, and harnessed four mice to it. The hen seated herself in it with the cock, and they drove away together. Not long afterwards they met a cat who said, "Where are you going?"

The cock replied, "We are going to the house of Mr. Korbes."

"Take me with you," said the cat.

The cock answered, "Most willingly, get up behind, lest you fall off in front. Take great care not to dirty my little red wheels. And you little wheels, roll on, and you little mice pipe out, as we go forth on our way to the house of Mr. Korbes."

After this came a millstone, then an egg, then a duck, then a pin, and at last a needle, who all seated themselves in the carriage, and drove with them. When, however, they reached the house of Mr. Korbes, Mr. Korbes was not there. The mice drew the carriage into the barn, the hen flew with the cock upon a perch. The cat sat down by the hearth, the duck on the sink. The egg rolled itself into a towel, the pin stuck itself into the chair cushion, the needle jumped onto the bed in the middle of the pillow, and the millstone laid itself over the door. Then Mr. Korbes came home, went to the hearth, and was about to light the fire, when the cat threw a quantity of ashes in his face. He ran into the kitchen in a great hurry to wash it off, and the duck splashed some water in his face. He wanted to dry it with the towel, but the egg rolled up against him, broke, and glued up his eyes. He wanted to rest, and sat down in the chair, and then the pin pricked him. He fell in a passion, and threw himself on his bed, but as soon as he laid his head on the pillow, the needle pricked him, so that he screamed aloud, and was just going to run out into the wide world in his rage, but when he came to the door, the millstone leapt down and struck him dead. Mr. Korbes must have been a very wicked man!

42. THE GODFATHER

A poor man had so many children that he had already asked everyone in the world to be godfather, and when still another child was born, no one else was left whom he could invite. He knew not what to do, and, in his perplexity, he lay down and fell asleep. Then he dreamed that he was to go outside the gate, and ask the first person who met him to be godfather. When he awoke, he was determined to obey his dream, and went outside the gate, and asked the first person who came up to him to be godfather. The stranger presented him with a little glass of water, and said, "This is a wonderful water, with it you can heal the sick, only you must see where Death is standing. If he is standing by the patient's head, give the patient some of the water and he will be healed, but if Death is standing by his feet, all trouble will be in vain, for the sick man must die." From this time forth, the man could always say whether a patient could be saved or not, and became famous for his skill, and earned a great deal of money. Once he was called in to the child of the King, and when he entered, he saw death standing by the child's head and cured it with the water, and he did the same a second time, but the third time Death was standing by its feet, and then he knew the child was meant to die.

Once the man thought he would visit the godfather, and tell him how he had succeeded with the water. But when he entered the house, it was such a strange establishment! On the first flight of stairs, the broom and shovel were disputing, and knocking each other about violently. He asked them, "Where does the godfather live?"

The broom replied, "One flight of stairs higher up."

When he came to the second flight, he saw a heap of dead fingers lying. He asked, "Where does the godfather live?"

One of the fingers replied, "One flight of stairs higher."

On the third flight lay a heap of dead skulls, which again directed him to the flight beyond. On the fourth flight, he saw fishes on the fire, which frizzled in the pans and baked themselves.

They, too, said, "One flight of stairs higher." And when he had ascended the fifth, he came to the door of a room and peeped through the keyhole, and there he saw the godfather who had a pair of long horns. When he opened the door and went in, the godfather got into bed in a great hurry and covered himself up.

Then said the man, "Sir godfather, what a strange household you have! When I came to your first flight of stairs, the shovel and broom were quarreling, and beating each other violently."

"How stupid you are!" said the godfather. "That was the boy and the maid talking to each other."

"But on the second flight I saw dead fingers lying."

"Oh, how silly you are! Those were some roots of scorzonera."

"On the third flight lay a heap of dead men's skulls."

"Foolish man, those were cabbages."

"On the fourth flight, I saw fishes in a pan, which were hissing and baking themselves." When he had said that, the fishes came and served themselves up. "And when I got to the fifth flight, I peeped through the keyhole of a door, and there, godfather, I saw you, and you had long, long horns."

"Oh, that is a lie!" The man became alarmed, and ran out, and if he had not, who knows what the godfather would have done to him.

43. FRAU TRUDE

There was once a little girl who was obstinate and inquisitive, and when her parents told her to do anything, she did not obey them, so how could she fare well? One day she said to her parents, "I have heard so much of Frau Trude, I will go to her some day. People say that everything about her does look so strange, and that there are such odd things in her house, that I have become quite curious!"

Her parents absolutely forbade her, and said, "Frau Trude is a bad woman, who does wicked things, and if you go to her; you are no longer our child."

But the maiden did not let herself be stopped by her parent's prohibition, and still went to Frau Trude. And when she got to her, Frau Trude said, "Why are you so pale?"

"Ah," she replied, and her whole body trembled, "I have been so terrified at what I have seen."

"What have you seen?"

"I saw a black man on your steps."

"That was a collier."

"Then I saw a green man."

"That was a hunter."

"After that I saw a blood-red man."

"That was a butcher."

"Ah, Frau Trude, I was terrified; I looked through the window and saw not you, but, as I verily believe, the devil himself with a head of fire."

"Oho!" said she, "Then you have seen the witch in her proper costume. I have been waiting for you, and wanting you a long time already; you shall give me some light." Then she changed the girl into a block of wood, and threw it into the fire. And when it was in full blaze she sat down close to it, and warmed herself by it, and said, "That shines bright for once."

44. GODFATHER DEATH

A poor man had twelve children and was forced to work night and day to provide them even with bread. When therefore the thirteenth came into the world, he knew not what to do in his trouble, but ran out into the great highway, and resolved to ask the first person whom he met to be godfather. The first to meet him was the good God who already knew what troubled him, and said to him, "Poor man, I pity you. I will hold your child at its christening, and will take charge of it and make it happy on earth."

The man said, "Who are you?"

"I am God."

"Then I do not desire to have you for a godfather," said the man, "You give to the rich, and leave the poor to hunger." Thus spoke the man, for he did not know how wisely God apportions riches and poverty. He turned therefore away from the Lord, and went farther.

Then the Devil came to him and said, "What do you seek? If you will take me as a godfather for your child, I will give him gold in plenty and all the joys of the world as well."

The man asked, "Who are you?"

"I am the Devil."

"Then I do not desire to have you for godfather," said the man, "You deceive men and lead them astray."

He went onwards, and then came Death striding up to him with withered legs, and said, "Take me as godfather."

The man asked, "Who are you?"

"I am Death, and I make all equal."

Then said the man, "You are the right one, you take the rich as well as the poor, without distinction; you shall be godfather."

Death answered, "I will make your child rich and famous, for he who has me for a friend can lack nothing."

The man said, "Next Sunday is the christening; be there at the right time." Death appeared as he had promised, and stood godfather quite in the usual way.

When the boy had grown up, his godfather one day appeared and bade him go with him. He led him forth into a forest, and showed him an herb which grew there, and said, "Now you shall receive your godfather's present. I make you a celebrated physician. When you are called to a patient, I will always appear to you. If I stand by the head of the sick man, you may say with confidence that you will make him well again, and if you give him this herb he will recover; but if I stand by the patient's feet, he is mine, and you must say that all remedies are in vain, and that no physician in the world could save him. But beware of using the herb against my will, or it might fare badly for you."

It was not long before the youth was the most famous physician in the whole world. People said of him: "He had only to look at the patient and he knew his condition at once, and if he would recover, or must die." From far and wide people came to him, sent for him when they had anyone ill, and gave him so much money that he soon became a rich man. Now it so happened that the King became ill, and the physician was summoned, and was to say if recovery were possible. But when he came to the bed, Death was standing by the feet of the sick man, and the herb did not grow which could save him. "If I could but cheat Death for once," thought the physician, "he is sure to be angry if I do, but, as I am his godson, he may shut one eye; I will risk it." He therefore took up the sick man, and laid him the other way, so that now Death was standing by his head. Then he gave the King some of the herb, and he recovered and grew healthy again.

But Death came to the physician, looking very black and angry, threatened him with his finger, and said, "You have overreached me; this time I will pardon it, as you are my godson; but if you venture it again, it will cost you your neck, for I will take *you* away with me."

Soon afterwards the King's daughter fell into a severe illness. She was his only child, and he wept day and night, so that he began to lose the sight of his eyes, and he made it known that whoever rescued her from death should be her husband and inherit the crown. When the physician came to the sick girl's bed, he saw Death by her feet. He ought to have remembered the warning given by his godfather, but he was so infatuated by the great beauty of the King's daughter, and the happiness of becoming her husband, that he flung all thought to the winds. He did not see that Death was casting angry glances on him, that he was raising his hand in the air, and threatening him with his withered fist. He raised up the sick girl, and placed her head where her feet had lain. Then he gave her some of the herb, and instantly her cheeks flushed red, and life stirred afresh in her.

When Death saw that for a second time he was defrauded of his own property, he walked up to the physician with long strides, and said, "All is over for you, and now the lot falls on you," and seized him so firmly with his ice-cold hand, that he could not resist, and led him into a cave below the earth. There he saw how thousands and thousands of candles were burning in countless rows, some large, others half-sized, others small. Every instant some were extinguished, and others again burnt up, so that the flames seemed to leap here and there in perpetual change. "See," said Death, "these are the lights of men's lives. The large ones belong to children, the half-sized ones to married people in their prime, the little ones belong to old people; but children and young folks likewise have often only a tiny candle."

"Show me the light of my life," said the physician, and he thought that it would be very tall.

Death pointed to a little end which was just threatening to go out, and said, "Look, it is there."

"Ah, dear godfather," said the horrified physician, "light a new one for me, do it for love of me, that I may enjoy my life, be King, and the husband of the King's beautiful daughter."

"I cannot," answered Death, "one must go out before a new one is lighted."

"Then place the old one on a new one, that will go on burning when the old one has come to an end," pleaded the physician. Death behaved as if he were going to fulfill his wish, and took hold of a tall new candle; but as he desired revenge, he purposely made a mistake in fixing it, and the little piece fell down and was extinguished. Immediately the physician fell on the ground, and now he himself was in the hands of Death.

45. THUMBLING'S TRAVELS

A certain tailor had a son, who happened to be small, and no bigger than a thumb, and on this account he was always called Thumbling. He had, however, some courage in him, and said to his father, "Father, I must and will go out into the world."

"That's right, my son," said the old man, and took a long darning needle and made a knob of sealing wax on it at the candle, "and there is a sword for you to take with you on the way." Then the little tailor wanted to have one more meal with them, and hopped into the kitchen to see what his mother had cooked for the last time. It was just dished up, and the dish stood on the hearth.

Then he said, "Mother, what is there to eat today?"

"See for yourself," said his mother.

So Thumbling jumped onto the hearth, and peeped into the dish, but as he stretched his neck in too far the steam from the food caught hold of him, and carried him up the chimney. He rode about in the air on the steam for a while, until at length he sank down to the ground again. Now the little tailor was outside in the wide world, and he traveled about, and went to work with a master in his craft, but the food was not good enough for him. "Mistress, if you give us no better food," said Thumbling, "I will go away, and early tomorrow morning I will write with chalk on the door of your house, 'Too many potatoes, too little meat! Farewell, Mr. Potato King.'"

"You wretched, grasshopper!" said the angry mistress, and seized a dishcloth, and was just going to strike him; but my little tailor crept nimbly under a thimble, peeped out from beneath it, and put his tongue out at the mistress. She took up the thimble, and wanted to get hold of him, but little Thumbling hopped into the cloth, and while the mistress was opening it out and looking for him, he got into a crevice in the table.

"Ho, ho, lady mistress," cried he, and thrust his head out, and when she began to strike him he leapt down into the drawer. At last, however, she caught him and drove him out of the house.

The little tailor journeyed on and came to a great forest, and there he fell in with a band of robbers who had a design to steal the King's treasure. When they saw the little tailor, they thought, "A little fellow like that can creep through a keyhole and serve as picklock to us."

"Hollo," cried one of them, "you giant Goliath, will you go to the treasure chamber with us? You can slip yourself in and throw out the money."

Thumbling reflected a while, and at length he said, "yes," and went with them to the treasure chamber. Then he looked at the doors above and below, to see if there was any crack in them. It was not long before he spied one which was broad enough to let him in. He was therefore about to get in at once, but one of the two sentries who stood before the door, observed him, and said to the other, "What an ugly spider is creeping there; I will kill it."

"Leave the poor creature alone," said the other; "it has done you no harm."

Then Thumbling got safely through the crevice into the treasure chamber, opened the window beneath which the robbers were standing, and threw out to them one taler after another. When the little tailor was in the full swing of his work, he heard the King coming to inspect his treasure chamber, and crept hastily into a hiding place.

The King noticed that several solid talers were missing, but could not conceive who could have stolen them, for locks and bolts were in good condition, and all seemed well guarded. Then he went away again, and said to the sentries, "Be on the watch, someone is after the money."

When Thumbling recommenced his labors, they heard the money moving, and a sound of *klink*, *klink*, *klink*. They ran swiftly in to seize the thief, but the little tailor, who heard them coming, was still swifter, and leapt into a corner and covered himself with a taler, so that nothing could be seen of him, and at the same time he mocked the sentries and cried, "Here I am!" The sentries ran over, but as they got there, he had already hopped into another corner under a taler, and was crying, "Ho, ho, here I am!" The watchmen sprang there in haste, but Thumbling had long ago got into a third corner, and was crying, "Ho, ho, here I am!" And thus he made fools of them, and drove them so long round about the treasure chamber that they were weary and went away. Then little by little he threw all the talers out, dispatching the last with all his might, then hopped nimbly upon it, and flew down with it through the window.

The robbers paid him great compliments. "You are a valiant hero," said they, "Will you be our captain?"

Thumbling, however, declined, and said he wanted to see the world first. They now divided the booty, but the little tailor only asked for a kreuzer because he could not carry more.

Then he once more buckled on his sword, bade the robbers goodbye, and took to the road. First, he went to work with some masters, but he had no liking for that, and at last he hired himself as servant in an inn. The maids, however, could not endure him, for he saw all they did secretly, without their seeing him, and he told their master and mistress what they had taken off the plates, and carried away out of the cellar, for themselves. Then said they, "Wait, and we will pay you off!" and arranged with each other to play a trick. Soon afterwards when one of the maids was mowing in the garden, and saw Thumbling jumping about and creeping up and down the plants, she mowed him up quickly with the grass, tied all in a great cloth, and secretly threw it to the cows. Now amongst them there was a great black one, who swallowed him down without hurting him. Down below, however, it did not please him, for it was quite dark, and there was no candle burning. When the cow was being milked he cried,

"Strip, strap, strull,
Will the pail soon be full?"

But the noise of the milking prevented his being understood. After this the master of the house came into the barn and said, "That cow shall be killed tomorrow."

Then Thumbling was so alarmed that he cried out in a clear voice, "Let me out first, for I am shut up inside her."

The master heard that quite well, but did not know from where the voice came. "Where are you?" asked he.

"In the black one," answered Thumbling, but the master did not understand what that meant, and went out.

Next morning the cow was killed. Happily Thumbling did not meet with one blow at the cutting up and chopping; he got among the sausage meat. And when the butcher came in and began his work, he cried out with all his might, "Don't chop too deep, don't chop too deep, I am amongst it." No one heard this because of the noise of the chopping knife. Now poor Thumbling was in trouble, but trouble sharpens the wits, and he sprang out so adroitly between the blows that none of them touched him, and he escaped with a whole skin. But still he could not get away, he could only let himself be thrust into a black pudding with the bits of bacon. His quarters there were rather confined, and besides that he was hung up in the chimney to be smoked, and there time did hang terribly heavy on his hands.

In winter he was taken down again, as the black pudding was to be served to a guest. When the hostess was cutting it in slices, he took care not to stretch out his head too far lest a bit of it should be cut off; at last he saw his opportunity, cleared a passage for himself, and jumped out.

The little tailor, however, would not stay any longer in a house where he fared so badly, so at once set out on his journey again. But his liberty did not last long. In the open country he met with a fox who snapped him up in a fit of absence. "Hollo, Mr. Fox," cried the little tailor, "it is I who am sticking in your throat, set me at liberty again."

"You are right," answered the fox. "You are next to nothing for me, but if you will promise me the fowls in your father's yard I will let you go."

"With all my heart," replied Thumbling. "You shall have all the cocks and hens, that I promise you."

Then the fox let him go, and even carried him home. When the father once more saw his dear son, he willingly gave the fox all the fowls which he had. "For this I likewise bring you a handsome bit of money," said Thumbling, and gave his father the kreuzer which he earned on his travels.

"But why did the fox get the poor chickens to eat?"

"Oh, you goose, *your* father would surely love his child far more than the fowls in the yard!"

46. FOWLER'S FOWL

There was once a wizard who used to take the form of a poor man, and went to houses and begged, and caught pretty girls. No one knew where he carried them, for they were never seen again. One day he appeared before the door of a man who had three pretty daughters; he looked like a poor weak beggar, and carried a basket on his back, as if he meant to collect charitable gifts in it. He begged for a little food, and when the eldest daughter came out and was just handing him a piece of bread, he barely touched her, and she was forced to jump into his basket. Then he hurried away with long strides, and carried her away into a dark forest to his house, which stood in the midst of it. Everything in the house was magnificent; he gave her whatever she could possibly desire, and said, "My darling, you will certainly be happy with me, for you have everything your heart can wish for." This lasted a few days, and then he said, "I must journey forth, and leave you alone for a short time; there are the keys of the house; you may go everywhere and look at everything except in one room, which this little key here opens, and I forbid you to go there on pain of death." He likewise gave her an egg and said, "Preserve the egg carefully for me, and carry it continually about with you, for a great misfortune would arise from the loss of it."

She took the keys and the egg, and promised to obey him in everything. When he was gone, she went all round the house from the bottom to the top, and examined everything. The rooms shone with silver and gold, and she thought she had never seen such great splendor. At length she came to the forbidden door; she wished to pass it by, but curiosity let her have no rest. She examined the key, it looked just like any other; she put it in the keyhole and turned it a little, and the door sprang open. But what did she see when she went in? A great bloody basin stood in the middle of the room, and therein lay human beings, dead and hewn to pieces, and nearby was a block of wood, and a gleaming axe lay upon it. She was so terribly alarmed that the egg which she held in her hand fell into the basin. She got it out and washed the blood off, but in vain, it appeared again in a moment. She washed and scrubbed, but she could not get it out.

It was not long before the man came back from his journey, and the first things which he asked for were the key and the egg. She gave them to him, but she trembled as she did so, and he saw at once by the red spots that she had been in the bloody chamber. "Since you have gone into the room against my will," said he, "you shall go back into it against your own. Your life is ended." He threw her down, dragged her there by her hair, cut her head off on the block, and hewed her in pieces so that her blood ran on the ground. Then he threw her into the basin with the rest.

"Now I will fetch myself the second," said the wizard, and again he went to the house in the shape of a poor man, and begged. Then the second daughter brought him a piece of bread; he caught her like the first, by simply touching her, and carried her away. She did not fare better than her sister. She allowed herself to be led away by her curiosity, opened the door of the bloody chamber, looked in, and had to atone for it with her life on the wizard's return. Then he went and brought the third sister, but she was clever and crafty. When he had given her the keys and the egg, and had left her, she first put the egg away with great care, and then she examined the house, and at last went into the forbidden room. Alas, what did she behold! Both her sisters lay there in the basin, cruelly murdered, and cut in pieces. But she began to gather their limbs together and put them in order, head, body, arms and legs. And when nothing further was wanting the limbs began to move and unite themselves together, and both the maidens opened their eyes and were once more alive. Then they rejoiced and kissed and caressed each other.

On his arrival, the man at once demanded the keys and the egg, and as he could perceive no trace of any blood on it, he said, "You have stood the test, you shall be my bride." Now he no longer had any power over her, and was forced to do whatever she desired.

"Oh, very well," said she, "you shall first take a basketful of gold to my father and mother, and carry it yourself on your back; in the meantime I will prepare for the wedding." Then she ran to her sisters, whom she had hidden in a little chamber, and said, "The moment has come when I can save you. The wretch shall carry you home again, but as soon as you are at home send help to me." She put both of them in a basket and covered them quite over with gold, so that nothing of them was to be seen, then she called in the wizard and said to him, "Now carry the basket away, but I shall look through my little window and watch to see if you stop on the way to stand or to rest."

The wizard raised the basket on his back and went away with it, but it weighed him down so heavily that the perspiration streamed from his face. Then he sat down and wanted to rest awhile, but immediately one of the girls in the basket cried, "I am looking through my little window, and I see that you are resting. Will you go on at once?"

He thought it was his bride who was calling that to him; and got up on his legs again. Once more he was going to sit down, but instantly she cried, "I am looking through my little window, and I see that you are resting. Will you go on directly?"

And whenever he stood still, she cried this, and then he was forced to go onwards, until at last, groaning and out of breath, he took the basket with the gold and the two maidens into their parents' house. At home, however, the bride prepared the marriage feast, and sent invitations to the friends of the wizard. Then she took a skull with grinning teeth, put some ornaments on it and a wreath of flowers, carried it upstairs to the attic window, and let it look out from there. When all was ready, she dipped into a barrel of honey, and then cut the featherbed open and rolled herself in it, until she looked like a wondrous bird, and no one could recognize her. Then she went out of the house, and on her way she met some of the wedding guests, who asked,

"O, Fowler's fowl, how come you here?"
"I come from Fitz the Fowler's house quite near."
"And what may the young bride be doing?"
"From cellar to garret she's swept all clean,
And now from the window she's peeping, I ween."

At last she met the bridegroom, who was coming slowly back. He, like the others, asked,

"O, Fowler's fowl, how come you here?"
"I come from Fitz the Fowler's house quite near."
"And what may the young bride be doing?"
"From cellar to garret she's swept all clean,
And now from the window she's peeping, I ween."

The bridegroom looked up, saw the decked-out skull, thought it was his bride, and nodded to her, greeting her kindly. But when he and his guests had all gone into the house, the brothers and kinsmen of the bride, who had been sent to rescue her, arrived. They locked all the doors of the house, that no one might escape, set fire to it, and the wizard and all his crew had to burn.

47. THE JUNIPER TREE

It is now long ago, at least two thousand years, since there was a rich man who had a beautiful and pious wife, and they loved each other dearly. They had, however, no children, though they wished for them very much, and the woman prayed for them day and night, but still they had none. Now there was a courtyard in front of their house in which was a juniper tree, and one day in winter the woman was standing beneath it, paring herself an apple, and while she was paring herself the apple she cut her finger, and the blood fell on the snow. "Ah," said the woman, and sighed heavily, and looked at the blood before her, and was most unhappy. "Ah, if I had but a child as red as blood and as white as snow!" And while she thus spoke, she became quite happy in her mind, and felt just as if that were going to happen.

Then she went into the house and a month went by and the snow was gone, and two months, and then everything was green, and three months, and then all the flowers came out of the earth, and four months, and then all the trees in the wood grew thicker, and the green branches were all closely entwined, and the birds sang until the wood resounded and the blossoms fell from the trees, then the fifth month passed away and she stood under the juniper-tree, which smelled so sweetly that her heart leapt, and she fell on her knees and was beside herself with joy, and when the sixth month was over the fruit was large and fine, and then she was quite still, and the seventh month she snatched at the juniper berries and ate them greedily, then she grew sick and sorrowful, then the eighth month passed, and she called her husband to her, and wept and said, "If I die then bury me beneath the juniper-tree." Then she was quite comforted and happy until the next month was over, and then she had a child as white as snow and as red as blood, and when she saw it she was so delighted that she died.

Then her husband buried her beneath the juniper-tree, and he began to weep sorely; after some time he was more at ease, and though he still wept he could bear it, and after some time longer he took another wife.

By the second wife he had a daughter named Marlinchen, but the first wife's child was a little son, and he was as red as blood and as white as snow. When the woman looked at her daughter she loved her very much, but then she looked at the little boy and it seemed to cut her to the heart, for the thought came into her mind that he would always stand in her way, and she was forever thinking how she could get all the fortune for her daughter, and the Evil One filled her mind with this till she quite hated the little boy, and slapped him here and cuffed him there, until the unhappy child was in continual terror, for when he came out of school he had no peace in any place.

One day the woman had gone upstairs to her room, and her little daughter went up too, and said, "Mother, give me an apple."

"Yes, my child," said the woman, and gave her a fine apple out of the chest, but the chest had a great heavy lid with a great sharp iron lock.

"Mother," said the little daughter, "is brother not to have one too?"

This made the woman angry, but she said, "Yes, when he comes out of school." And when she saw from the window that he was coming, it was just as if the Devil entered into her, and she snatched at the apple and took it away again from her daughter, and said, "You shall not have one before your brother." Then she threw the apple into the chest, and shut it. Then the little boy came in the door, and the Devil made her say to him kindly, "My son, will you have an apple?" and she looked wickedly at him.

"Mother," said the little boy, "how dreadful you look! Yes, give me an apple."

Then it seemed to her as if she were forced to say to him, "Come with me," and she opened the lid of the chest and said, "Take out an apple for yourself," and while the little boy was stooping inside, the Devil prompted her, and crash! She shut the lid down, and his head flew off and fell among the red apples. Then she was overwhelmed with terror, and thought, "If I could but make them think that it was not done by me!" So she went upstairs to her room to her chest of drawers, and took a white handkerchief out of the top drawer, and set the head on the neck again, and folded the handkerchief so that nothing could be seen, and she set him on a chair in front of the door, and put the apple in his hand.

After this Marlinchen came into the kitchen to her mother, who was standing by the fire with a pan of hot water before her which she was constantly stirring round. "Mother," said Marlinchen, "brother is sitting at the door, and he looks quite white and has an apple in his hand. I asked him to give me the apple, but he did not answer me, and I was quite frightened."

"Go back to him," said her mother, "and if he will not answer you, give him a box on the ear." So Marlinchen went to him and said, "Brother, give me the apple." But he was silent, and she gave him a box on the ear, on which his head fell down. Marlinchen was terrified, and began crying and screaming, and ran to her mother, and said, "Alas, mother, I have knocked my brother's head off!" and she wept and wept and could not be comforted.

"Marlinchen," said the mother, "what have you done? But be quiet and let no one know it; it cannot be helped now, we will make him into black puddings." Then the mother took the little boy and chopped him in pieces, put him into the pan and made him into black puddings; but Marlinchen stood by weeping and weeping, and all her tears fell into the pan and there was no need of any salt.

Then the father came home, and sat down to dinner and said, "But where is my son?" And the mother served up a great dish of black puddings, and Marlinchen wept and could not leave off. Then the father again said, "But where is my son?"

"Ah," said the mother, "he has gone across the country to his mother's great uncle; he will stay there awhile."

"And what is he going to do there? He did not even say goodbye to me."

"Oh, he wanted to go, and asked me if he might stay six weeks, he is well taken care of there."

"Ah," said the man, "I feel so unhappy. It's not right what he's done. He ought to have said goodbye to me." With that he began to eat and said, "Marlinchen, why are you crying? Your brother will certainly come back." Then he said, "Ah, wife, how delicious this food is, give me some more." And the more he ate the more he wanted to have, and he said, "Give me some more, you shall have none of it. It seems to me as if it were all mine." And he ate and ate and threw all the bones under the table, until he had finished the whole. But Marlinchen went away to her chest of drawers, and took her best silk handkerchief out of the bottom drawer, and got all the bones from beneath the table, and tied them up in her silk handkerchief, and carried them outside the door, weeping tears of blood. Then the juniper-tree began to stir itself, and the branches parted, and moved together again, just as if someone was rejoicing and clapping his hands. At the same time a mist seemed to arise from the tree, and in the centre of this mist it burned like a fire, and a beautiful bird flew out of the fire singing magnificently, and he flew high up in the air, and when he was gone, the juniper-tree was just as it had been before, and the handkerchief with the bones was no longer there. Marlinchen, however, was as gay and happy as if her brother were still alive. And she went merrily into the house, and sat down to dinner and ate.

But the bird flew away and lighted on a goldsmith's house, and began to sing,

"My mother she killed me,
My father he ate me,
My sister, little Marlinchen,
Gathered together all my bones,
Tied them in a silken handkerchief,
Laid them beneath the juniper-tree,
Kywitt, kywitt, what a beautiful bird am I!"

The goldsmith was sitting in his workshop making a gold chain, when he heard the bird which was sitting singing on his roof, and very beautiful the song seemed to him. He stood up, but as he crossed the threshold he lost one of his slippers. But he walked right up the middle of the street with one shoe on and one sock; he had his apron on, and in one hand he had the gold chain and in the other his pincers, and the sun was shining brightly on the street. Then he went right over and stood still, and said to the bird, "Bird," said he then, "how beautifully you can sing! Sing me that piece again."

"No," said the bird, "I'll not sing it twice for nothing! Give me the golden chain, and then I will sing it again for you."

"There," said the goldsmith, "there is the golden chain for you, now sing me that song again." Then the bird came and took the golden chain in his right claw, and went and sat in front of the goldsmith, and sang,

"My mother she killed me,
My father he ate me,
My sister, little Marlinchen,
Gathered together all my bones,
Tied them in a silken handkerchief,
Laid them beneath the juniper-tree,
Kywitt, kywitt, what a beautiful bird am I!"

Then the bird flew away to a shoemaker, and lighted on his roof and sang,

> "My mother she killed me,
> My father he ate me,
> My sister, little Marlinchen,
> Gathered together all my bones,
> Tied them in a silken handkerchief,
> Laid them beneath the juniper-tree,
> Kywitt, kywitt, what a beautiful bird am I!"

The shoemaker heard that and ran outside before even putting on a coat, and looked up at his roof, and was forced to hold his hand before his eyes lest the sun should blind him. "Bird," said he, "how beautifully you can sing!" Then he called in at his door, "Wife, just come outside, there is a bird, look at that bird, he can sing so well." Then he called his daughter and children, and apprentices, boys and girls, and they all came up the street and looked at the bird and saw how beautiful he was, and what fine red and green feathers he had, and how like real gold his neck was, and how his eyes shone like stars. "Bird," said the shoemaker, "now sing me that song again."

"Nay," said the bird, "I do not sing twice for nothing; you must give me something."

"Wife," said the man, "go to the garret, on the top shelf there stands a pair of red shoes, bring them down." Then the wife went and brought the shoes. "There, bird," said the man, "now sing me that piece again." Then the bird came and took the shoes in his left claw, and flew back on the roof, and sang,

> "My mother she killed me,
> My father he ate me,
> My sister, little Marlinchen,
> Gathered together all my bones,
> Tied them in a silken handkerchief,
> Laid them beneath the juniper-tree,
> Kywitt, kywitt, what a beautiful bird am I!"

And once he had sung it he flew away. In his right claw he had the chain and the shoes in his left, and he flew far away to a mill, and the mill went, *klipp klapp, klipp klapp, klipp klapp,* and in the mill sat twenty miller's men hewing a stone, and cutting, *hick hack, hick hack, hick hack*, and the mill went *klipp klapp, klipp klapp, klipp klapp*. Then the bird went and sat on a lime tree which stood in front of the mill, and sang,

> "My mother she killed me,"

then one of them stopped working,

> "My father he ate me,"

then two more stopped working and listened to that,

> "My sister, little Marlinchen,"

then four more stopped,

> "Gathered together all my bones,
> Tied them in a silken handkerchief,"

now eight only were hewing,

> "Laid them beneath,"

now only five,

> "The juniper-tree,"

and now only one,

> "Kywitt, kywitt, what a beautiful bird am I!"

Then the last stopped also, and heard the last words. "Bird," said he, "how beautifully you sing! Let me, too, hear that. Sing that once more for me."

"Nay," said the bird, "I will not sing twice for nothing. Give me the millstone, and then I will sing it again."

"Yes," said he, "if it belonged to only me, you should have it."

"Yes," said the others, "if he sings again he shall have it." Then the bird came down, and the twenty millers all set to work with a beam and raised the stone up. And the bird stuck his neck through the hole, and put the stone on as if it were a collar, and flew on to the tree again, and sang,

"My mother she killed me,
My father he ate me,
My sister, little Marlinchen,
Gathered together all my bones,
Tied them in a silken handkerchief,
Laid them beneath the juniper-tree,
Kywitt, kywitt, what a beautiful bird am I!"

And when he was done singing, he spread his wings, and in his right claw he had the chain, and in his left the shoes, and round his neck the millstone, and he flew far away to his father's house.

In the room sat the father, the mother, and Marlinchen at dinner, and the father said, "How lighthearted I feel, how happy I am!"

"Nay," said the mother, "I feel so uneasy, just as if a heavy storm were coming."

Marlinchen, however, sat weeping and weeping, and then came the bird flying, and as it seated itself on the roof the father said, "Ah, I feel so truly happy, and the sun is shining so beautifully outside, I feel just as if I were about to see some old friend again."

"Nay," said the woman, "I feel so anxious, my teeth chatter, and I seem to have fire in my veins." And she tore her bodice open, but Marlinchen sat in a corner crying, and held her apron over her eyes and cried till it was quite wet. Then the bird sat on the juniper tree, and sang,

"My mother she killed me,"

then the mother plugged her ears, and shut her eyes, and would not see or hear, but there was a roaring in her ears like the most violent storm, and her eyes burned and flashed like lightning,

"My father he ate me."

"Ah, mother," says the man, "that is a beautiful bird! He sings so splendidly, and the sun shines so warm, and there is a smell just like cinnamon."

"My sister, little Marlinchen,"

then Marlinchen laid her head on her knees and wept without ceasing, but the man said, "I am going out, I must see the bird quite close."

"Oh, don't go," said the woman, "I feel as if the whole house were shaking and on fire." But the man went out and looked at the bird:

"Gathered together all my bones,
Tied them in a silken handkerchief,
Laid them beneath the juniper tree,
Kywitt, kywitt, what a beautiful bird am I!"

On this the bird let the golden chain fall, and it fell exactly round the man's neck, and so exactly round that it fitted beautifully. Then he went in and said, "Just look what a fine bird that is, and what a handsome gold chain he has given me, and how pretty he is!" But the woman was terrified, and fell down on the floor in the room, and her cap fell off her head. Then sang the bird once more,

"My mother she killed me."

"If only I were a thousand feet beneath the earth so as not to hear that!"

"My father he ate me,"

then the woman fell down again as if dead.

"My sister, little Marlinchen,"

"Ah," said Marlinchen, "I too will go out and see if the bird will give me anything," and she went out.

"Gathered together all my bones,
Tied them in a silken handkerchief,"

then he threw down the shoes to her.

"Laid them beneath the juniper-tree,
Kywitt, kywitt, what a beautiful bird am I!"

Then she was lighthearted and joyous, and she put on the new red shoes, and danced and leaped into the house. "Ah," said she, "I was so sad when I went out and now I am so lighthearted; that is a splendid bird, he has given me a pair of red shoes!"

"Well," said the woman, and sprang to her feet and her hair stood up like flames of fire, "I feel as if the world were coming to an end! I, too, will go out and see if my heart feels lighter." And as she went out the door, crash! the bird threw down the millstone on her head, and she was entirely crushed by it. The father and Marlinchen heard what had happened and went out, and smoke, flames, and fire were rising, and when that was over, there stood the little brother, and he took his father and Marlinchen by the hand, and all three were right glad, and they went into the house for dinner, and ate.

48. OLD SULTAN

A farmer once had a faithful dog called Sultan, who had grown old, and lost all his teeth, so that he could no longer hold anything tight. One day the farmer was standing with his wife before the door, and said, "Tomorrow I intend to shoot Old Sultan, he is no longer of any use."

His wife, who felt pity for the faithful beast, answered, "He has served us so long, and been so faithful, that we might well give him his keep."

"Eh! What?" said the man. "You are not very sharp. He has not a tooth left in his mouth, and not a thief is afraid of him; now he may be off. If he has served us, he has been well fed for it."

The poor dog, who was lying stretched out in the sun not far off, had heard everything, and was sorry that the morrow was to be his last day. He had a good friend, the wolf, and he crept out in the evening into the forest to him, and complained of the fate that awaited him. "Listen, friend," said the wolf, "be of good cheer, I will help you out of your trouble. I have thought of something. Tomorrow, early in the morning, your master is going with his wife to make hay, and they will take their little child with them, and no one will be left behind in the house. While at work they always lay the child under the hedge in the shade; you lay yourself there too, just as if you wished to guard it. Then I will come out of the wood, and carry off the child. You must rush swiftly after me, as if you would rescue it from me. I will let it fall, and you will take it back to its parents, who will think that you have saved it, and will be far too grateful to do you any harm; on the contrary, you will be in high favor, and they will never let you want for anything again."

The plan pleased the dog, and it was carried out just as it was arranged. The father screamed when he saw the wolf running across the field with his child, but when Old Sultan brought it back, then he was full of joy, and stroked him and said, "Not a hair of yours shall be hurt, you shall be well fed as long as you live." And to his wife he said, "Go home at once and make Old Sultan some soup that he will not have to chew, and bring the pillow from my bed, I will give him that to lie upon."

Hereforth Old Sultan was as well off as he could wish to be.

Soon afterwards the wolf visited him, and was pleased that everything had succeeded so well. "But now," said he, "you will just turn a blind eye if, when I have a chance, I carry off one of your master's fat sheep."

"Do not reckon upon that," answered the dog, "I will remain true to my master; I cannot agree to that."

The wolf, who thought that this could not be spoken in earnest, came creeping about in the night and was going to take away the sheep. But the farmer, to whom the faithful Sultan had told the wolf's plan, caught him and beat his hide soundly with the flail. The wolf had to flee, but he cried out to the dog, "Wait a bit, you scoundrel, you shall pay for this."

The next morning the wolf sent the boar to challenge the dog to come out into the forest so that they might settle the affair. Old Sultan could find no one to stand by him but a cat with only three legs, and as they went out together the poor cat limped along, and at the same time stretched out her tail into the air with pain.

The wolf and his friend were already on the spot appointed, but when they saw their enemy coming they thought that he was bringing a saber with him, for they mistook the outstretched tail of the cat for one. And when the poor beast hopped on its three legs, they could only think every time that it was picking up a stone to throw at them. So they were both afraid; the wild boar crept into the thicket and the wolf jumped up a tree.

The dog and the cat, when they came up, wondered that there was no one to be seen. The wild boar, however, had not been able to hide himself altogether; and one of his ears was still to be seen. While the cat was looking carefully about, the boar moved his ear; the cat, who thought it was a mouse moving there, jumped upon it and bit it hard. The boar made a fearful noise and ran away, crying out, "The guilty one is up in the tree." The dog and cat looked up and saw the wolf, who was ashamed of having shown himself so timid, and made friends with the dog again.

49. THE SIX SWANS

Once upon a time, a certain King was hunting in a great forest, and he chased a wild beast so eagerly that none of his attendants could follow him. When evening drew near he stopped and looked around him, and then he saw that he had lost his way. He sought a way out, but could find none. Then he perceived an aged woman with a head which nodded perpetually, who came towards him, but she was a witch. "Good woman," said he to her, "Can you not show me the way through the forest?"

"Oh, yes, Lord King," she answered, "that I certainly can, but on one condition, and if you do not fulfill that, you will never get out of the forest, and will die of hunger in it."

"What kind of condition is it?" asked the King.

"I have a daughter," said the old woman, "who is as beautiful as anyone in the world, and well deserves to be your wife, and if you will make her your Queen, I will show you the way out of the forest." In the anguish of his heart the King consented, and the old woman led him to her little hut, where her daughter was sitting by the fire. She received the King as if she had been expecting him, and he saw that she was very beautiful, but still she did not please him, and he could not look at her without secret horror. After he had taken the maiden up on his horse, the old woman showed him the way, and the King reached his royal palace again, where the wedding was celebrated.

The King had already been married once, and had by his first wife, seven children, six boys and a girl, whom he loved better than anything else in the world. As he now feared that the stepmother might not treat them well, and even do them some injury, he took them to a lonely castle which stood in the middle of a forest. It lay so concealed, and the way was so difficult to find that he himself would not have found it, if a wise woman had not given him a ball of yarn with wonderful properties. When he threw it down before him, it unrolled itself and showed him his path. The King, however, went so frequently away to his dear children that the Queen observed his absence; she was curious and wanted to know what he did when he was quite alone in the forest. She gave a great deal of money to his servants, and they betrayed the secret to her, and told her likewise of the ball which alone could point out the way. And now she knew no rest until she had learnt where the King kept the ball of yarn, and then she made little shirts of white silk, and as she had learnt the art of witchcraft from her mother, she sewed a charm inside them. And when the King had ridden off to hunt, she took the little shirts and went into the forest, and the ball showed her the way. The children, who saw from a distance that someone was approaching, thought that their dear father was coming to them, and full of joy, ran to meet him. Then she threw one of the little shirts over each of them, and no sooner had the shirts touched their bodies than they were changed into swans, and flew away over the forest. The Queen went home quite delighted, and thought she had got rid of her stepchildren, but the girl had not run out with her brothers, and the Queen knew nothing about her.

Next day the King went to visit his children, but he found no one but the little girl. "Where are your brothers?" asked the King.

"Alas, dear father," she answered, "they have gone away and left me alone!" and she told him that she had seen from her little window how her brothers had flown away over the forest in the shape of swans, and she showed him the feathers, which they had let fall in the courtyard, and which she had picked up. The King mourned, but he did not think that the Queen had done this wicked deed, and since he feared that the girl would also be stolen away from him, he wanted to take her away with him. But she was afraid of her stepmother, and begged the King to let her stay just this one night more in the forest castle.

The poor girl thought, "I can no longer stay here. I will go and seek my brothers." And when night came, she ran away, and went straight into the forest. She walked the whole night long, and next day also without stopping, until she could go no farther for weariness. Then she saw a forest hut, and went into it, and found a room with six little beds, but she did not venture to get into one of them, but crept under one, and lay down on the hard ground, intending to pass the night there. Just before sunset, however, she heard a rustling, and saw six swans come flying in at the window. They alighted on the ground and blew at each other, and blew all the feathers off, and their swan's skins stripped off like a shirt. Then the maiden looked at them and recognized her brothers, was glad and crept forth from beneath the bed.

The brothers were not less delighted to see their little sister, but their joy was of short duration. "Here can you not abide," they said to her. "This is a shelter for robbers, if they come home and find you, they will kill you."

"But can you not protect me?" asked the little sister.

"No," they replied, "only for one quarter of an hour each evening can we lay aside our swan's skins and have during that time our human form; after that, we are once more turned into swans."

The little sister wept and said, "Can you not be set free?"

"Alas, no," they answered, "the conditions are too hard! For six years you may neither speak nor laugh, and in that time you must sew together six little shirts of starflowers for us. And if one single word falls from your lips, all your work will be lost." And when the brothers had said this, the quarter of an hour was over, and they flew out of the window again as swans.

The maiden, however, firmly resolved to save her brothers, even if it should cost her her life. She left the hut, went into the middle of the forest, seated herself on a tree, and there passed the night. Next morning she went out and gathered starflowers and began to sew. She could not speak to anyone, and she had no inclination to laugh; she sat there and looked at nothing but her work. When she had already spent a long time there it came to pass that the King of the country was hunting in the forest, and his huntsmen came to the tree on which the maiden was sitting. They called to her and said, "Who are you?" But she made no answer. "Come down to us," said they. "We will not do you any harm." She only shook her head. As they pressed her further with questions she threw her golden necklace down to them, and thought this would satisfy them. They, however, did not cease, and then she threw her girdle down to them, and as this also was to no purpose, her garters, and by degrees everything that she had on that she could do without until she had nothing left but her shift. The huntsmen, however, did not let themselves be put off by that, but climbed the tree and fetched the maiden down and led her before the King.

The King asked, "Who are you? What are you doing on the tree?" But she did not answer. He put the question in every language that he knew, but she remained as mute as a fish. As she was so beautiful, the King's heart was touched, and he was smitten with a great love for her. He put his mantle on her, placed her before him on his horse, and carried her to his castle. Then he had her dressed in rich garments, and she shone in her beauty like bright daylight, but no word could be drawn from her. He placed her by his side at the able, and her modest bearing and courtesy pleased him so much that he said, "She is the one whom I wish to marry, and no other woman in the world." And after some days he united himself to her.

The King, however, had a wicked mother who was dissatisfied with this marriage and spoke ill of the young Queen. "Who knows," said she, "where she comes from? She is not worthy of a king!"

After a year had passed, when the Queen brought her first child into the world, the old woman took it away from her, and smeared her mouth with blood as she slept. Then she went to the King and accused the Queen of being a man-eater. The King would not believe it, and would not allow anyone to do her any injury. She, however, sat continually sewing at the shirts, and cared for nothing else. The next time, when she again bore a beautiful boy, the false stepmother used the same treachery, but the King could not bring himself to give credit to her words. He said, "She is too pious and good to do anything of that kind; if she were not dumb, and could defend herself, her innocence would come to light." But when the old woman stole away the newly-born child for the third time, and accused the Queen, who did not utter one word of defense, the King could do no otherwise than deliver her over to justice, and she was sentenced to suffer death by fire.

When the day came for the sentence to be executed, it was the last day of the six years during which she was not to speak or laugh, and she had delivered her dear brothers from the power of the enchantment. The six shirts were ready, only the left sleeve of the sixth was missing. When, therefore, she was led to the stake, she laid the shirts on her arm, and when she stood up high and the fire was just going to be lighted, she looked around and six swans came flying through the air towards her. Then she saw that she would be saved, and her heart leapt with joy. The swans swept towards her and sank down so that she could throw the shirts over them, and as they were touched by them, their swan's skins fell off, and her brothers stood in their own bodily form before her, and were vigorous and handsome. The youngest only lacked his left arm, and had in the place of it a swan's wing on his shoulder. They embraced and kissed each other, and the Queen went to the King, who was greatly moved, and she began to speak and said, "Dearest husband, now I may speak and declare to you that I am innocent, and falsely accused." And she told him of the treachery of the old woman who had taken away her three children and hidden them. Then to the great joy of the King they were brought there, and as a punishment, the wicked stepmother was bound to the stake, and burnt to ashes. But the King and the Queen with their six brothers lived many years in happiness and peace.

50. THE SLEEPING BEAUTY (BRIAR ROSE)

A long time ago there were a King and Queen who said every day, "Ah, if only we had a child!" but they never had one.

But it happened that once when the Queen was bathing, a frog crept out of the water onto the land, and said to her, "Your wish shall be fulfilled; before a year has gone by, you shall have a daughter."

What the frog had said came true, and the Queen had a little girl who was so pretty that the King could not contain himself for joy, and ordered a great feast. He invited not only his kindred, friends and acquaintance, but also the Wise Women, in order that they might be kind and well-disposed towards the child. There were thirteen of them in his kingdom, but, as he had only twelve golden plates for them to eat out of, one of them had to be left at home.

The feast was held with all manner of splendor and when it came to an end the Wise Women bestowed their magic gifts upon the baby: one gave virtue, another beauty, a third riches, and so on with everything in the world that one can wish for.

When eleven of them had made their promises, suddenly the thirteenth came in. She wished to avenge herself for not having been invited, and without greeting, or even looking at anyone, she cried with a loud voice, "The King's daughter shall in her fifteenth year prick herself with a spindle, and fall down dead." And, without saying a word more, she turned round and left the room.

They were all shocked; but the twelfth, whose good wish still remained unspoken, came forward, and as she could not undo the evil sentence, but only soften it, she said, "It shall not be death, but a deep sleep of a hundred years, into which the princess shall fall."

The King, who wished to keep his dear child from the misfortune, gave orders that every spindle in the whole kingdom should be burned. Meanwhile the gifts of the Wise Women came true for the young girl, for she was so beautiful, modest, good-natured, and wise, that everyone who saw her was bound to love her.

It happened that on the very day she turned fifteen years old, the King and Queen were not at home, and the maiden was left in the palace quite alone. So she went round into all sorts of places, looked into rooms and bedchambers just as she liked, and at last came to an old tower. She climbed up the narrow winding staircase, and reached a little door. A rusty key was in the lock, and when she turned it the door sprang open, and there in a little room sat an old woman with a spindle, busily spinning her flax.

"Good day, old dame," said the King's daughter; "what are you doing there?"

"I am spinning," said the old woman, and nodded her head. "What sort of thing is that, that rattles round so merrily?" said the girl, and she took the spindle and wanted to spin too. But scarcely had she touched the spindle when the magic decree was fulfilled, and she pricked her finger with it.

And, in the very moment when she felt the prick, she fell down upon the bed that stood there, and lay in a deep sleep. And this sleep extended over the whole palace; the King and Queen who had just come home, and had entered the great hall, began to go to sleep, and all of the court too. The horses, too, went to sleep in the stable, the dogs in the yard, the pigeons upon the roof, the flies on the wall; even the fire that was flaming on the hearth became quiet and slept, the roast meat left off frizzling, and the cook, who was just going to pull the hair of the kitchen boy, because he had forgotten something, let him go, and went to sleep. And the wind fell, and on the trees outside the castle not a leaf moved again.

But round about the castle there began to grow a hedge of thorns, which every year became higher, and at last grew close up round the castle and all over it, so that there was nothing of it to be seen, not even the flag upon the roof. But the story of the beautiful sleeping "Briar Rose," for so the princess was named, went about the country, so that from time to time kings' sons came and tried to get through the thorny hedge into the castle.

But they found it impossible, for the thorns held fast together, as if they had hands, and the youths were caught in them, could not get loose again, and died a miserable death.

After long, long years a King's son came again to that country, and heard an old man talking about the briar hedge, and that a castle was said to stand behind it in which a wonderfully beautiful princess, named Briar Rose, had been asleep for a hundred years; and that the King and

Queen and the whole court were asleep likewise. He had heard, too, from his grandfather, that many kings' sons had already come, and had tried to get through the thorny hedge, but they had remained sticking fast in it, and had died a pitiful death. Then the youth said, "I am not afraid, I will go and see the beautiful Briar Rose." The good old man tried to dissuade him, but he did not listen to his words.

But by this time the hundred years had just passed, and the day had come when Briar Rose was to awake again. When the King's son came near to the briar hedge, it was nothing but large and beautiful flowers, which parted from each other of their own accord, and let him pass unhurt, then they closed again behind him like a hedge. In the courtyard he saw the horses and the spotted hounds lying asleep; on the roof sat the pigeons with their heads under their wings. And when he entered the house, the flies were asleep upon the wall, the cook in the kitchen was still holding out his hand to seize the boy, and the maid was sitting by the black hen which she was going to pluck.

He went on farther, and in the great hall he saw the whole of the court lying asleep, and up by the throne lay the King and Queen.

Then he went on still farther, and all was so quiet that a breath could be heard, and at last he came to the tower, and opened the door into the little room where Briar Rose was sleeping. There she lay, so beautiful that he could not turn his eyes away; and he stooped down and gave her a kiss. But as soon as he kissed her, Briar Rose opened her eyes and awoke, and looked at him quite sweetly.

Then they went down together, and the King awoke, and the Queen, and the whole court, and looked at each other in great astonishment. And the horses in the courtyard stood up and shook themselves; the hounds jumped up and wagged their tails; the pigeons on the roof pulled out their heads from under their wings, looked round, and flew into the open country; the flies on the wall crept again; the fire in the kitchen burned up and flickered and cooked the meat; the roast began to turn and frizzle again, and the cook gave the boy such a box on the ear that he screamed, and the maid plucked the fowl ready for the spit.

And then the marriage of the King's son with Briar Rose was celebrated with all splendor, and they lived contented to the end of their days.

51. FUNDEVOGEL (FLEDGLING)

There was once a forester who went into the forest to hunt, and as he entered it he heard a sound of screaming as if a little child were there. He followed the sound, and at last came to a high tree, and at the top of this a little child was sitting, for the mother had fallen asleep under the tree with the child, and a bird of prey had seen it in her arms, had flown down, snatched it away, and set it up high on the tree.

The forester climbed up, brought the child down, and thought to himself, "You will take him home with you, and bring him up with your Lina." He took it home, therefore, and the two children grew up together. The one, however, which he had found on a tree was called Fundevogel, because a bird had carried it away. Fundevogel and Lina loved each other so dearly that when they did not see each other they were sad.

The forester had an old cook, who one evening took two pails and began to fetch water, and did not go once, but many times, out to the spring. Lina saw this and said, "Old Sanna, why are you fetching so much water?"

"If you will never repeat it to anyone, I will tell you why." So Lina said, no, she would never repeat it to anyone, and then the cook said, "Early tomorrow morning, when the forester is out hunting, I will heat the water, and when it is boiling in the kettle, I will throw in Fundevogel, and will boil him in it."

Early next morning the forester got up and went out hunting, and when he was gone the children were still in bed. Then Lina said to Fundevogel, "If you will never leave me, I too will never leave you."

Fundevogel said, "Neither now, nor ever will I leave you."

Then said Lina, "Then I will tell you. Last night, old Sanna carried so many buckets of water into the house that I asked her why she was doing that, and she said that if I would promise not to tell anyone she would tell me, and I said I would be sure not to tell anyone, and she said that early tomorrow morning when father was out hunting, she would set the kettle full of water, throw you into it and boil you; but we will get up quickly, dress ourselves, and go away together."

The two children therefore got up, dressed themselves quickly, and went away. When the water in the kettle was boiling, the cook went into the bedroom to fetch Fundevogel and throw him into it. But when she came in, and went to the beds, both the children were gone. Then she was terribly alarmed, and she said to herself, "What shall I say now when the forester comes home and sees that the children are gone? Quickly, they must be followed and brought back again."

Then the cook sent three servants after them, who were to run and overtake the children. The children, however, were sitting outside the forest, and when they saw from afar the three servants running, Lina said to Fundevogel, "Never leave me, and I will never leave you."

Fundevogel said, "Neither now, nor ever."

Then said Lina, "Do become a rosebush, and I will be the rose upon it."

When the three servants came to the forest, nothing was there but a rosebush and one rose on it, but the children were nowhere. Then said they, "There is nothing to be done here," and they went home and told the cook that they had seen nothing in the forest but a little rosebush with one rose on it.

Then the old cook scolded and said, "You simpletons, you should have cut the rosebush in two, broken off the rose and brought it home with you; go, and do it now." They had therefore to go out and look for the second time. The children, however, saw them coming from a distance.

Then Lina said, "Fundevogel, never leave me, and I will never leave you."

Fundevogel said, "Neither now, nor ever."

Said Lina, "Then you become a church, and I'll be the chandelier in it."

So when the three servants came, nothing was there but a church, with a chandelier in it. They said therefore to each other, "What can we do here, let us go home."

When they got home, the cook asked if they had not found them; so they said no, they had found nothing but a church, and that there was a chandelier in it. And the cook scolded them and said, "You fools! Why did you not pull the church to pieces, and bring the chandelier home with you?" And now the old cook herself got up, and went with the three servants in pursuit of the children. The children, however, saw from afar that the three servants were coming, and the cook waddling after them.

Then said Lina, "Fundevogel, never leave me, and I will never leave you."

Then said Fundevogel, "Neither now, nor ever."

Said Lina, "Be a fishpond, and I will be the duck upon it."

The cook, however, came up to them, and when she saw the pond she lay down by it, and was about to drink it up. But the duck swam quickly to her, seized her head in its beak and drew her into the water, and there the old witch had to drown. Then the children went home together, and were heartily delighted, and if they are not dead, they are living still.

52. KING THRUSHBEARD

A King had a daughter who was beautiful beyond all measure, but so proud and haughty that no suitor was good enough for her. She sent away one after the other, and ridiculed them as well.

Once the King made a great feast and invited there, from far and near, all the young men likely to marry. They were all marshaled in a row according to their rank and standing; first came the kings, then the grand-dukes, then the princes, the earls, the barons, and the gentry. Then the King's daughter was led through the ranks, but to everyone she had some objection to make; one was too fat, "A wine cask," she said. Another was too tall, "Long and thin has little in." The third was too short, "Short and thick is never quick." The fourth was too pale, "As pale as death." The fifth too red, "A fighting cock." The sixth was not straight enough, "A green log dried behind the stove."

So she had something to say against everyone, but she made herself especially merry over a good king who stood quite high up in the row, and whose chin had grown a little crooked. "Well," she cried and laughed, "he has a chin like a thrush's beak!" and from that time he got the name of King Thrushbeard.

But the old King, when he saw that his daughter did nothing but mock the people, and despised all the suitors who were gathered there, was very angry, and swore that she should have for her husband the very first beggar that came to his doors.

A few days afterwards a fiddler came and sang beneath the windows, trying to earn a small alms. When the King heard him he said, "Let him come up." So the fiddler came in, in his dirty, ragged clothes, and sang before the King and his daughter, and when he had ended he asked for a trifling gift. The King said, "Your song has pleased me so well that I will give you my daughter to wed."

The King's daughter shuddered, but the King said, "I have taken an oath to give you to the very first beggar, and I will keep it." All she could say was in vain; the priest was brought, and she had to let herself be wedded to the fiddler on the spot. When that was done the King said, "Now it is not proper for you, a beggar-woman, to stay any longer in my palace, you may just go away with your husband."

The beggar led her out by the hand, and she was obliged to walk away on foot with him. When they came to a large forest she asked, "To whom does that beautiful forest belong?" "It belongs to King Thrushbeard; if you had taken him, it would have been yours." "Ah, unhappy girl that I am, if I had but taken King Thrushbeard!"

Afterwards they came to a meadow, and she asked again, "To whom does this beautiful green meadow belong?"

"It belongs to King Thrushbeard; if you had taken him, it would have been yours."

"Ah, unhappy girl that I am, if I had but taken King Thrushbeard!"

Then they came to a large town, and she asked again, "To whom does this fine large town belong?"

"It belongs to King Thrushbeard; if you had taken him, it would have been yours."

"Ah, unhappy girl that I am, if I had but taken King Thrushbeard!"

"It does not please me," said the fiddler, "to hear you always wishing for another husband; am I not good enough for you?"

At last they came to a very little hut, and she said, "Oh goodness! What a small house; to whom does this miserable, shack belong?"

The fiddler answered, "That is my house and yours, where we shall live together."

She had to stoop in order to enter the low door. "Where are the servants?" said the King's daughter.

"What servants?" answered the beggar, "You must do yourself what you wish to have done. Just make a fire at once, and set on water to cook my supper, I am quite tired."

But the King's daughter knew nothing about lighting fires or cooking, and the beggar had to lend a hand to get anything fairly done. When they had finished their scanty meal they went to bed; but he forced her to get up quite early in the morning in order to look after the house.

For a few days they lived in this way, until they came to the end of all their provisions. Then the man said, "Wife, we cannot go on any longer eating and drinking here and earning nothing. You must weave baskets." He went out, cut some willows, and brought them home. Then she began to weave, but the tough willows wounded her delicate hands.

"I see that this will not do," said the man, "You had better spin, perhaps you can do that better." She sat down and tried to spin, but the hard thread soon cut her soft fingers so that the blood ran down. "See," said the man, "you are fit for no sort of work; I have made a bad bargain with you. Now I will try to make a business with pots and earthenware; you must sit in the marketplace and sell them."

"Alas," thought she, "if any of the people from my father's kingdom come to the market and see me sitting there, selling, how they will mock me!" But it was of no use, she had to yield unless she chose to die of hunger.

For the first time she succeeded, for the people were glad to buy the woman's wares because she was good-looking, and they paid her what she asked; many even gave her the money and left the pots with her as well. So they lived on what she had earned as long as it lasted, then the husband bought a new supply of crockery. With this she sat down at the corner of the marketplace, and set it out around her ready for sale. But suddenly there came a drunken hussar galloping along, and he rode right amongst the pots so that they were all broken into a thousand bits. She began to weep, and did now know what to do for fear. "Alas! what will happen to me?" cried she, "What will my husband say to this?"

She ran home and told him of the misfortune. "Who would seat herself at a corner of the marketplace with crockery?" said the man. "Stop crying, I see very well that you cannot do any ordinary work, so I have been to our King's palace and have asked whether they can find a place for a kitchen maid, and they have promised me to take you; in that way you will get your food for nothing."

The King's daughter was now a kitchen maid, and had to be at the cook's beck and call, and do the dirtiest work. In both her pockets she fastened a little jar, in which she took home her share of the scraps, and upon this they lived.

It happened that the wedding of the King's eldest son was to be celebrated, so the poor woman went up and placed herself by the door of the hall to watch. When all the candles were lit, and people, each more beautiful than the other, entered, and all was full of pomp and splendor, she thought of her fate with a sad heart, and cursed the pride and haughtiness which had humbled her and brought her to so great poverty.

The smell of the delicious dishes which were being taken in and out reached her, and now and then the servants threw her a few morsels of them: these she put in her jars to take home.

Suddenly the King's son entered, clothed in velvet and silk, with gold chains about his neck. And when he saw the beautiful woman standing by the door he seized her by the hand, and would have danced with her; but she refused and shrank with fear, for she saw that it was King Thrushbeard, her suitor whom she had driven away with scorn. Her struggles were of no avail, he pulled her into the hall; but the band to which her pockets were fastened broke, the pots fell down, the soup ran out, and the scraps were scattered all about. And when the people saw it, there arose general laughter and derision, and she was so ashamed that she would rather have been a thousand fathoms below the ground. She sprang to the door and would have run away, but on the stairs a man caught her and brought her back; and when she looked at him it was King Thrushbeard again.

He said to her kindly, "Do not be afraid, I am the fiddler who has been living with you in that wretched pigsty. For love of you I disguised myself so; and I also was the hussar who rode through your crockery. This was all done to humble your proud spirit, and to punish you for the insolence with which you mocked me."

Then she wept bitterly and said, "I have done great wrong, and am not worthy to be your wife."

But he said, "Be comforted, the evil days are past; now we will celebrate our wedding." Then the maids-in-waiting came and dressed her in the most splendid clothing, and her father and his whole court came and wished her happiness in her marriage with King Thrushbeard, and the joy now began in earnest. I wish you and I had been there too.

53. LITTLE SNOW WHITE

Once upon a time in the middle of winter, when the flakes of snow were falling like feathers from the sky, a queen sat at a window sewing, and the frame of the window was made of black ebony. And while she was sewing and looking out of the window at the snow, she pricked her finger with the needle, and three drops of blood fell upon the snow. And the red looked pretty upon the white snow, and she thought to herself, "If only I had a child as white as snow, as red as blood, and as black as the wood of the window frame."

Soon after that she had a little daughter, who was as white as snow, and as red as blood, and her hair was as black as ebony; and she was therefore called Little Snow White. And when the child was born, the Queen died.

After a year had passed the King took another wife. She was a beautiful woman, but proud and haughty, and she could not bear that anyone else should surpass her in beauty. She had a wonderful looking-glass, and when she stood in front of it and looked at herself in it, and said—

"Looking-glass, Looking-glass, on the wall,
Who in this land is the fairest of all?"

The looking-glass answered—

"You, O Queen, are the fairest of all!"

Then she was satisfied, for she knew that the looking-glass spoke the truth.

But Snow White was growing up, and grew more and more beautiful; and when she was seven years old she was as beautiful as the day, and more beautiful than the Queen herself. And once when the Queen asked her looking-glass—

"Looking-glass, Looking-glass, on the wall,
Who in this land is the fairest of all?"

It answered—

> "You are fairer than all who are here, Lady Queen."
> But more beautiful still is Snow White, as I ween."

Then the Queen was shocked, and turned yellow and green with envy. From that time, whenever she looked at Snow White, her heart heaved in her breast, she hated the girl so much.

And envy and pride grew higher and higher in her heart like a weed, so that she had no peace day or night. She called a hunter, and said, "Take the child away into the forest; I will no longer have her in my sight. Kill her, and bring me back her heart as a token." The hunter obeyed, and took her away; but when he had drawn his knife, and was about to pierce Snow White's innocent heart, she began to weep, and said, "Ah dear hunter, spare me my life! I will run away into the wild forest, and never come home again."

And as she was so beautiful the hunter had pity on her and said, "Run away, then, you poor child." "The wild beasts will soon devour you," thought he, and yet it seemed as if a stone had been rolled from his heart since he no longer needed to kill her. And as a young boar just then came running by he stabbed it, and cut out its heart and took it to the Queen as proof that the child was dead. The cook had to salt this, and the wicked Queen ate it, and thought she had eaten the heart of Snow White.

But now the poor child was all alone in the great forest, and so terrified that she looked at every leaf of every tree, and did not know what to do. Then she began to run, and ran over sharp stones and through thorns, and the wild beasts ran past her, but did her no harm.

She ran as far as her feet would go until it was almost evening; then she saw a little cottage and went into it to rest. Everything in the cottage was small, but neater and cleaner than you can imagine. There was a table on which was a white cover, and seven little plates, and on each plate a little spoon; moreover, there were seven little knives and forks, and seven little mugs. Against the wall stood seven little beds side by side, and covered with snow-white bedspreads.

Little Snow White was so hungry and thirsty that she ate some vegetables and bread from each plate and drank a drop of wine out of each mug, for she did not wish to take all from only one. Then, as she was so tired, she laid herself down on each of the little beds, but none of them suited her; one was too long, another too short, but at last she found that the seventh one was right, and so she remained in it, said a prayer and went to sleep.

When it was quite dark the owners of the cottage came back; they were seven dwarfs who dug and delved in the mountains for ore. They lit their seven candles, and now that the cottage was lit they saw that someone had been there, foreverything was not in the same order in which they had left it.

The first said, "Who has been sitting on my chair?"

The second, "Who has been eating off my plate?"

The third, "Who has been taking some of my bread?"

The fourth, "Who has been eating my vegetables?"

The fifth, "Who has been using my fork?"

The sixth, "Who has been cutting with my knife?"

The seventh, "Who has been drinking out of my mug?"

Then the first looked round and saw that there was a little hole on his bed, and he said, "Who has been getting into my bed?" The others came up and each called out, "Somebody has been lying in my bed too." But the seventh when he looked at his bed saw little Snow White, who was lying asleep in it. And he called the others, who came running up, and they cried out with astonishment, and brought their seven little candles and let the light fall on little Snow White. "Oh, heavens! Oh, heavens!" cried they, "What a lovely child!" and they were so glad that they did not wake her up, but let her sleep in the bed. And the seventh dwarf slept with his companions, one hour with each, and so got through the night.

When it was morning little Snow White awoke, and was frightened when she saw the seven dwarfs. But they were friendly and asked her what her name was. "My name is Snow White," she answered.

"How have you come to our house?" said the dwarfs. Then she told them that her stepmother had wished to have her killed, but that the hunter had spared her life, and that she had run for the whole day, until at last she had found their dwelling. The dwarfs said, "If you will take care of our house, cook, make the beds, wash, sew, and knit, and if you will keep everything neat and clean, you can stay with us and you shall want for nothing."

"Yes," said Snow White, "with all my heart," and she stayed with them. She kept the house in order for them; in the mornings they went to the mountains and looked for copper and gold, in the evenings they came back, and then their supper had to be ready.

The girl was alone the whole day, so the good dwarfs warned her and said, "Beware of your stepmother, she will soon know that you are here; be sure to let no one come in."

But the Queen, believing that she had eaten Snow White's heart, was certain that she was again the first and most beautiful of all; and she went to her looking-glass and said—

"Looking-glass, Looking-glass, on the wall,
Who in this land is the fairest of all?"

And the glass answered—

"Oh, Queen, you are fairest of all I see,
But over the hills, where the seven dwarfs dwell,
Snow White is still alive and well,
And none is so fair as she."

Then she was astounded, for she knew that the looking-glass never spoke falsely, and she knew that the hunter had betrayed her, and that little Snow White was still alive.

And so she thought and thought again how she might kill her, for so long as she was not the fairest in the whole land, envy let her have no rest. And when she had at last thought of something to do, she painted her face, and dressed herself like an old peddler, and no one could have known her. In this disguise she went over the seven mountains to the seven dwarfs, and knocked at the door and cried, "Pretty things to sell, very cheap, very cheap."

Little Snow White looked out the window and called out, "Good day my good woman, what have you to sell?"

"Good things, pretty things," she answered; "laces of all colors," and she pulled out one which was woven of bright-colored silk.

"I may let the worthy old woman in," thought Snow White, and she unbolted the door and bought the pretty laces.

"Child," said the old woman, "what a fright you look; come, I will lace you properly for once." Snow White had no suspicion, but stood before her, and let herself be laced with the new laces. But the old woman laced so quickly and so tightly that Snow White lost her breath and fell down as if dead. "Now I am the most beautiful," said the Queen to herself, and ran away.

Not long afterwards, in the evening, the seven dwarfs came home, but were shocked that they saw their dear little Snow White lying on the ground, and that she neither stirred nor moved, and seemed to be dead. They lifted her up, and, as they saw that she was laced too tightly, they cut the laces; then she began to breathe a little, and after a while came to life again. When the dwarfs heard what had happened they said, "The old peddler was none other than the wicked Queen; take care and let no one come in when we are not with you."

But the wicked woman when she had reached home went in front of the glass and asked—

"Looking-glass, Looking-glass, on the wall,
Who in this land is the fairest of all?"

And it answered as before—

"Oh, Queen, you are fairest of all I see,
But over the hills, where the seven dwarfs dwell,
Snow White is still alive and well,
And none is so fair as she."

When she heard that, all her blood rushed to her heart with fear, for she saw plainly that little Snow White was again alive. "But now," she said, "I will think of something that shall put an end to you," and by the help of witchcraft, which she understood, she made a poisonous comb. Then she disguised herself and took the shape of another old woman.

So she went over the seven mountains to the seven dwarfs, knocked at the door, and cried, "Good things to sell, cheap, cheap!"

Little Snow White looked out and said, "Go away; I cannot let anyone come in."

"I suppose you can look," said the old woman, and pulled the poisonous comb out and held it up. It pleased the girl so well that she let herself be fooled, and opened the door. When they had struck a bargain the old woman said, "Now I will comb you properly for once." Poor little Snow White had no suspicion, and let the old woman do as she pleased, but hardly had she put the comb in her hair than the poison in it took effect, and the girl fell down senseless. "You paragon of beauty," said the wicked woman, "you are done for good," and she went away.

But fortunately it was almost evening, when the seven dwarfs came home. When they saw Snow White lying as if dead upon the ground they at once suspected the stepmother, and they looked and found the poisoned comb. Scarcely had they taken it out when Snow White came to, and told them what had happened. Then they warned her once more to be upon her guard and to open the door to no one.

The Queen, at home, went in front of the glass and said—

"Looking-glass, Looking-glass, on the wall,
Who in this land is the fairest of all?"

Then it answered as before—

"Oh, Queen, you are fairest of all I see,
But over the hills, where the seven dwarfs dwell,
Snow White is still alive and well,
And none is so fair as she."

When she heard the glass speak she trembled and shook with rage. "Snow White shall die," she cried, "even if it costs me my life!"

With that she went into a quite secret, lonely room, where no one ever came, and there she made a very poisonous apple. Outside it looked pretty, white with a red cheek, so that everyone who saw it longed for it; but whoever ate a piece of it must surely die.

When the apple was ready she painted her face, and dressed herself up as a country woman, and so she went over the seven mountains to the seven dwarfs. She knocked at the door. Snow White put her head out of the window and said, "I cannot let anyone in; the seven dwarfs have forbidden me."

"It is all the same to me," answered the woman, "I shall soon get rid of my apples. Here, I will give you one."

"No," said Snow White, "I dare not take anything."

"Are you afraid of poison?" said the old woman; "look, I will cut the apple in two pieces; you eat the red cheek, and I will eat the white."

The apple was so cunningly made that only the red cheek was poisoned. Snow White longed for the fine apple, and when she saw that the woman ate part of it she could resist no longer, and stretched out her hand and took the poisonous half. But hardly had she taken a bite than she fell down dead. Then the Queen looked at her with a dreadful look, and laughed aloud and said, "White as snow, red as blood, black as ebony wood! This time the dwarfs cannot wake you up again."

And when she asked the Looking-glass at home—

> "Looking-glass, Looking-glass, on the wall,
> Who in this land is the fairest of all?"

it answered at last—

> "Oh, Queen, in this land you are fairest of all."

Then her envious heart had rest, so far as an envious heart can have rest.

The dwarfs, when they came home in the evening, found Snow White lying upon the ground; she breathed no longer and was dead. They lifted her up, looked to see whether they could find anything poisonous, unlaced her, combed her hair, washed her with water and wine, but it was all of no use; the poor child was dead, and remained dead. They laid her upon a bier, and all seven of them sat round it and wept for her, and wept three days long.

Then they were going to bury her, but she still looked as if she were alive, and still had her pretty red cheeks. They said, "We could not bury her in the dark ground," and they had a transparent coffin of glass made, so that she could be seen from all sides, and they laid her in it, and in golden letters wrote upon it her name, and that she was a king's daughter. Then they put the coffin out upon the mountain, and one of them always stayed by it and watched it. And birds came too, and wept for Snow White; first an owl, then a raven, and last a dove.

And now Snow White lay a long, long time in the coffin, and she did not change, but looked as if she were asleep; for she was as white as snow, as red as blood, and her hair was as black as ebony.

It happened, however, that a king's son came into the forest, and went to the dwarfs' house to spend the night. He saw the coffin on the mountain, and the beautiful Snow White inside it, and read what was written upon it in golden letters. Then he said to the dwarfs, "Let me have the coffin, I will give you whatever you want for it."

But the dwarfs answered, "We will not part with it for all the gold in the world."

Then he said, "Let me have it as a gift, for I cannot live without seeing Snow White. I will honor and prize her as my dearest possession." As he spoke in this way the good dwarfs took pity upon him, and gave him the coffin.

And now the King's son had it carried away by his servants on their shoulders. And it happened that they stumbled over a tree stump, and with the shock the poisonous piece of apple which Snow White had bitten off came out of her throat. And before long she opened her eyes, lifted up the lid of the coffin, sat up, and was once more alive. "Oh, heavens, where am I?" she cried.

The King's son, full of joy, said, "You are with me," and told her what had happened, and said, "I love you more than everything in the world; come with me to my father's palace, you shall be my wife."

And Snow White was willing, and went with him, and their wedding was held with great show and splendor. But Snow White's wicked stepmother was also invited to the feast. When she had dressed herself in beautiful clothes she went before the Looking-glass, and said—

"Looking-glass, Looking-glass, on the wall,
Who in this land is the fairest of all?"

The glass answered—

"Oh, Queen, of all here the fairest is you,
But the young Queen is fairer by far, it is true."

Then the wicked woman uttered a curse, and was so miserable, so utterly miserable, that she knew not what to do. At first she would not go to the wedding at all, but she had no peace, and must go to see the young Queen. And when she went in she knew Snow White; and she stood still with rage and fear, and could not stir. But iron slippers had already been put upon the fire, and they were brought in with tongs, and set before her. Then she was forced to put on the red-hot shoes, and dance until she dropped down dead.

54. THE KNAPSACK, THE HAT, AND THE HORN

There were once three brothers who had fallen deeper and deeper into poverty, and at last their need was so great that they had to endure hunger, and had nothing to eat or drink. Then said they, "We cannot go on this way, we had better go into the world and seek our fortune." They therefore set out, and had already walked over many a long road and many a blade of grass, but had not yet met with good luck. One day they arrived in a great forest, and in the middle of it was a hill, and when they came nearer they saw that the hill was all silver.

Then spoke the eldest, "Now I have found the good luck I wished for, and I desire nothing more." He took as much of the silver as he could possibly carry, and then turned back and went home again.

But the two others said, "We want something more from good luck than mere silver," and did not touch it, but went onwards.

After they had walked for two days longer without stopping, they came to a hill which was all gold. The second brother stopped, thought to himself, and was undecided. "What shall I do?" said he, "Shall I take for myself so much of this gold that I have plenty for all the rest of my life, or shall I go farther?" At length he made a decision, and putting as much into his pockets as would go in, said farewell to his brother, and went home.

But the third said, "Silver and gold do not move me, I will not give up my chance of fortune, perhaps something even better will be given me."

He journeyed onwards, and when he had walked for three days, he got into a forest which was still larger than the one before, and never would come to an end, and as he found nothing to eat or to drink, he was exhausted. Then he climbed up a high tree to find out if up there he could see the end of the forest, but so far as his eye could see he saw nothing but the tops of trees. Then he began to descend the tree again, but hunger tormented him, and he thought to himself, "If I could but eat my fill once more!"

When he got down he saw with astonishment a table beneath the tree richly spread with food, the steam of which rose up to meet him. "This time," said he, "my wish has been fulfilled at the right moment." And without inquiring who had brought the food, or who had cooked it, he approached the table, and ate with enjoyment until he had appeased his hunger.

When he was done, he thought, "It would after all be a pity if the pretty little tablecloth were to be spoiled in the forest here," and folded it up tidily and put it in his pocket. Then he went onwards, and in the evening, when hunger arose again, he wanted to try out his little cloth, and spread it out and said, "I wish you to be covered with good cheer again," and scarcely had the wish crossed his lips than as many dishes with the most exquisite food on them stood on the table as there was room for. "Now I perceive," said he, "in what kitchen my cooking is done. You shall be dearer to me than the mountains of silver and gold." For he saw plainly that it was a wishing cloth. The cloth, however, was still not enough to enable him to return and sit quietly at home; he preferred to wander about the world and pursue his fortune farther.

One night he met, in a lonely wood, a dusty, black charcoal-burner, who was burning charcoal there, and had some potatoes by the fire that he was going to make into a meal. "Good evening, blackbird!" said the youth. "How do you get on in your solitude?"

"One day is like another," replied the charcoal-burner, "and every night potatoes! Have you a mind to have some, and will you be my guest?"

"Many thanks," replied the traveler, "I won't rob you of your supper; you did not reckon on a visitor, but if you will put up with what I have, you shall have an invitation."

"Who is to prepare it for you?" said the charcoal-burner. "I see that you have nothing with you, and there is no one within a two hours' walk who could give you anything."

"And yet there shall be a meal," answered the youth, "and better than any you have ever tasted." Thereupon he brought his cloth out of his knapsack, spread it on the ground, and said, "Little cloth, cover yourself," and instantly boiled meat and baked meat stood there, and as hot as if it had just come out of the kitchen.

The charcoal-burner stared, but did not require much pressing; he fell to, and thrust larger and larger mouthfuls into his black mouth. When they had eaten everything, the charcoal-burner smiled contentedly, and said, "Your tablecloth has my approval; it would be a fine thing for me in this forest, where no one ever cooks me anything good. I will propose an exchange to you; there in the corner hangs a soldier's knapsack, which is certainly old and shabby, but in it wonderful powers lie concealed; but, as I no longer use it, I will give it to you for the tablecloth."

"I must first know what these wonderful powers are," answered the youth.

"That I will tell you," replied the charcoal-burner; "every time you tap it with your hand, a corporal comes with six men armed from head to foot, and they do whatever you command them."

"So far as I am concerned," said the youth, "if nothing else can be done, we will exchange," and he gave the charcoal-burner the cloth, took the knapsack from the hook, put it on, and bade farewell.

When he had walked a while, he wished to make a trial of the magical powers of his knapsack and tapped it. Immediately the seven warriors stepped up to him, and the corporal said, "What does my lord and ruler wish for?"

"March with all speed to the charcoal-burner, and demand my wishing cloth back." They faced to the left, and it was not long before they brought what he required, and had taken it from the charcoal-burner without asking many questions. The young man bade them retire, went onwards, and hoped fortune would shine yet more brightly on him.

By sunset he came to another charcoal-burner, who was making his supper ready by the fire. "If you will eat some potatoes with salt, but with no dripping, come and sit down with me," said the sooty fellow.

"No, he replied, "this time you shall be my guest," and he spread out his cloth, which was instantly covered with the most beautiful dishes. They ate and drank together, and enjoyed themselves heartily.

After the meal was over, the charcoal-burner said, "Up there on that shelf lies a little old worn-out hat which has strange properties: when anyone puts it on, and turns it round on his head, the cannons go off as if twelve were fired all together, and they shoot down everything so that no one can withstand them. The hat is of no use to me, and I will willingly give it for your tablecloth."

"That suits me very well," he answered, took the hat, put it on, and left his tablecloth behind him. Hardly, however, had he walked away than he tapped on his knapsack, and his soldiers had to fetch the cloth back again. "One thing comes on the top of another," thought he, "and I feel as if my luck had not yet come to an end." Nor had his thoughts deceived him.

After he had walked on for the whole of one day, he came to a third charcoal-burner, who like the previous ones, invited him to potatoes without dripping. But he let him too dine with him from his wishing cloth, and the charcoal-burner liked it so well, that at last he offered him a horn for it, which had very different properties from those of the hat. When anyone blew it all the walls and fortifications fell down, and all towns and villages became ruins. He certainly gave the charcoal-burner the cloth for it, but he afterwards sent his soldiers to demand it back again, so that at length he had the knapsack, hat and horn, all three. "Now," said he, "I am a made man, and it is time for me to go home and see how my brothers are getting on."

When he reached home, his brothers had built themselves a handsome house with their silver and gold, and were living in prosperity. He went to see them, but as he came in a ragged coat, with his shabby hat on his head, and his old knapsack on his back, they would not acknowledge him as their brother. They mocked and said, "You claim that you are our brother who despised silver and gold, and craved for something still better for himself. He will come in his carriage in full splendor like a mighty king, not like a beggar," and they drove him out of doors. Then he fell into a rage, and tapped his knapsack until a hundred and fifty men stood before him armed from head to foot. He commanded them to surround his brothers' house, and two of them were to take hazel-rods with them, and beat the two insolent men until they knew who he was. A violent disturbance arose, people ran together, and wanted to lend the two some help in their need, but against the soldiers they could do nothing.

News of this at length came to the King, who was very angry, and ordered a captain to march out with his troop, and drive this disturber of the peace out of the town; but the man with the knapsack soon got a greater body of men together, who repulsed the captain and his men, so that they were forced to retire with bloody noses. The King said, "This vagabond is not brought to order yet," and next day sent a still larger troop against him, but they could do even less.

The youth set still more men against them, and in order to be done even sooner, he turned his hat twice round on his head, and heavy guns began to play, and the king's men were beaten and put to flight. "And now," said he, "I will not make peace until the King gives me his daughter for my wife, and I govern the whole kingdom in his name."

He caused this to be announced to the King, and the latter said to his daughter, "Necessity is a hard nut to crack, what remains for me but to do what he desires? If I want peace and to keep the crown on my head, I must give you away."

So the wedding was celebrated, but the King's daughter was vexed that her husband should be a common man, who wore a shabby hat, and put on an old knapsack. She wished much to get rid of him, and night and day studied how she could accomplish this. Then she thought to herself, "Is it possible that his wonderful powers lie in the knapsack?" and she dissembled and caressed him, and when his heart was softened, she said, "If you would but lay aside that ugly knapsack, it disfigures you so, that I can't help being ashamed of you."

"Dear child," said he, "this knapsack is my greatest treasure; as long as I have it, there is no power on earth that I am afraid of." And he revealed to her the wonderful virtue with which it was endowed. Then she threw herself in his arms as if she were going to kiss him, but dexterously took the knapsack off his shoulders, and ran away with it.

As soon as she was alone she tapped it, and commanded the warriors to seize their former master, and take him out of the royal palace. They obeyed, and the false wife sent still more men after him, who were to drive him quite out of the country. Then he would have been ruined if he had not had the little hat. But his hands were scarcely at liberty before he turned it twice. Immediately the cannon began to thunder, and struck down everything, and the King's daughter herself was forced to come and beg for mercy. As she entreated in such moving terms, and promised to change, he allowed himself to be persuaded and granted her peace. She behaved in a friendly manner to him, and acted as if she loved him very much, and after some time managed to so fool him, that he confided to her that even if someone got the knapsack into his power, he could do nothing against him so long as the old hat was still his. When she knew the secret, she waited until he was asleep, and then she took the hat away from him, and had it thrown out into the street. But the horn still remained to him, and in great anger he blew it with all his strength. Instantly all walls, fortifications, towns, and villages, toppled down, and crushed the King and his daughter to death. And had he not put down the horn and had blown just a little longer, everything would have been in ruins, and not one stone would have been left standing on another. Then no one opposed him any longer, and he made himself King of the whole country.

55. *RUMPELSTILTSKIN*

Once there was a miller who was poor, but who had a beautiful daughter. Now it happened that he had to go and speak to the King, and in order to make himself appear important he said to him, "I have a daughter who can spin straw into gold."

The King said to the miller, "That is an art which pleases me well; if your daughter is as clever as you say, bring her tomorrow to my palace, and I will try what she can do."

And when the girl was brought to him he took her into a room which was quite full of straw, gave her a spinning wheel and a reel, and said, "Now set to work, and if by tomorrow morning early you have not spun this straw into gold during the night, you must die." Thereupon he himself locked up the room, and left her in it alone. So there sat the poor miller's daughter, and for the life of her could not tell what to do; she had no idea how straw could be spun into gold, and she grew more and more miserable, until at last she began to weep.

But all at once the door opened, and in came a little man, and said, "Good evening, Mistress Miller; why are you crying so?"

"Alas!" answered the girl, "I have to spin straw into gold, and I do not know how to do it."

"What will you give me," said the manikin, "if I do it for you?"

"My necklace," said the girl. The little man took the necklace, seated himself in front of the wheel, and "whirr, whirr, whirr," three turns, and the reel was full; then he put another on, and whirr, whirr, whirr, three times round, and the second was full too. And so it went on until the morning, when all the straw was spun, and all the reels were full of gold.

By daybreak the King was already there, and when he saw the gold he was astonished and delighted, but his heart became only more greedy. He had the miller's daughter taken into another room full of straw, which was much larger, and commanded her to spin that also in one night if she valued her life. The girl knew not how to help herself, and was crying, when the door again opened, and the little man appeared, and said, "What will you give me if I spin that straw into gold for you?"

"The ring on my finger," answered the girl. The little man took the ring, again began to turn the wheel, and by morning had spun all the straw into glittering gold.

The King rejoiced beyond measure at the sight, but still he had not enough gold; and he had the miller's daughter taken into a still larger room full of straw, and said, "You must spin this, too, in the course of this night; but if you succeed, you shall be my wife." And he thought, "Even if she be a miller's daughter, I could not find a richer wife in the whole world."

When the girl was alone the manikin came again for the third time, and said, "What will you give me if I spin the straw for you this time also?"

"I have nothing left that I could give," answered the girl.

"Then promise me, if you should become Queen, your first child."

"Who knows whether that will ever happen?" thought the miller's daughter; and, not knowing how else to help herself in this strait, she promised the manikin what he wanted, and for that he once more span the straw into gold.

And when the King came in the morning, and found all as he had wished, he took her in marriage, and the pretty miller's daughter became a Queen.

A year after, she had a beautiful child, and she never gave a thought to the manikin. But suddenly he came into her room, and said, "Now give me what you promised."

The Queen was horror-struck, and offered the manikin all the riches of the kingdom if he would leave her the child. But the manikin said, "No, something that is living is dearer to me than all the treasures in the world." Then the Queen began to weep and cry, so that the manikin pitied her. "I will give you three days' time," said he, "if by that time you find out my name, then you shall keep your child."

So the Queen thought the whole night of all the names that she had ever heard, and she sent a messenger over the country to inquire, far and wide, for any other names that there might be. When the manikin came the next day, she began with Caspar, Melchior, Balthazar, and said all the names she knew, one after another; but to everyone the little man said, "That is not my name."

On the second day she had inquiries made in the neighborhood as to the names of the people there, and she repeated to the manikin the most uncommon and curious. "Perhaps your name is Shortribs, or Sheepshanks, or Laceleg?" but he always answered, "That is not my name."

On the third day the messenger came back again, and said, "I have not been able to find a single new name, but as I came to a high mountain at the end of the forest, where the fox and the hare bid each other good night, there I saw a little house, and before the house a fire was burning, and round about the fire quite a ridiculous little man was jumping: he hopped upon one leg, and shouted—

"Today I bake, tomorrow brew,
The next I'll have the young Queen's child.
Ha! Glad am I that no one knew
That Rumpelstiltskin I am styled."

You may think how glad the Queen was when she heard the name! And when soon afterwards the little man came in, and asked, "Now, Mistress Queen, what is my name?" at first she said, "Is your name Conrad?"

"No."

"Is your name Harry?"

"No."

"Perhaps your name is Rumpelstiltskin?"

"The devil has told you that! The devil has told you that!" cried the little man, and in his anger he plunged his right foot so deep into the earth that his whole leg went in; and then in rage he pulled at his left leg so hard with both hands that he tore himself in two.

56. SWEETHEART ROLAND

There was once on a time a woman who was a real witch and had two daughters, one ugly and wicked, and this one she loved because she was her own daughter, and one beautiful and good, and this one she hated, because she was her stepdaughter. The stepdaughter once had a pretty apron, which the other fancied so much that she became envious, and told her mother that she must and would have that apron. "Be quiet, my child," said the old woman, "and you shall have it. Your stepsister has long deserved death, tonight when she is asleep I will come and cut her head off. Only be careful that you are at the far side of the bed, and push her well to the front." It would have been all over with the poor girl if she had not just then been standing in a corner, and heard everything. All day long she dared not go out of doors, and when bedtime had come, the witch's daughter got into bed first, so as to lie at the far side, but when she was asleep, the other pushed her gently to the front, and took for herself the place at the back, close by the wall. In the night, the old woman came creeping in, she held an axe in her right hand, and felt with her left to see if anyone was lying on the outside, and then she grasped the axe with both hands, and cut her own child's head off.

When she had gone away, the girl got up and went to her sweetheart, who was called Roland, and knocked at his door. When he came out, she said to him, "Hear me, dearest Roland, we must fly in all haste; my stepmother wanted to kill me, but has struck her own child. When daylight comes, and she sees what she has done, we shall be lost."

"But," said Roland, "I counsel you first to take away her magic wand, or we cannot escape if she pursues us."

The maiden fetched the magic wand, and she took the dead girl's head and dropped three drops of blood on the ground, one in front of the bed, one in the kitchen, and one on the stairs. Then she hurried away with her lover. When the old witch got up next morning, she called her daughter, and wanted to give her the apron, but she did not come. Then the witch cried, "Where are you?"

"Here, on the stairs, I am sweeping," answered the first drop of blood.

The old woman went out, but saw no one on the stairs, and cried again, "Where are you?"

"Here in the kitchen, I am warming myself," cried the second drop of blood. She went into the kitchen, but found no one.

Then she cried again, "Where are you?"

"Ah, here in the bed, I am sleeping," cried the third drop of blood. She went into the room to the bed. What did she see there? Her own child, whose head she had cut off, bathed in her blood. The witch fell into a passion, sprang to the window, and as she could look forth quite far into the world, she perceived her stepdaughter hurrying away with her sweetheart Roland.

"That shall not serve you," cried she, "even if you have gone a long way off, you still shall not escape me." She put on her boots, in which she went an hour's walk with every step, and it was not long before she overtook them. The girl, however, when she saw the old woman striding towards her, used her magic wand to change her sweetheart Roland into a lake, and herself into a duck swimming in the middle of it. The witch placed herself on the shore, threw bread crumbs in, and took great pains to entice the duck; but the duck did not let herself be enticed, and the old woman had to go home at night as she had come. At this the girl and her sweetheart Roland resumed their natural shapes again, and they walked on the whole night until daybreak. Then the maiden changed herself into a beautiful flower which stood in the middle of a briar hedge, and her sweetheart Roland into a fiddler.

It was not long before the witch came striding up towards them, and said to the musician, "Dear musician, may I pluck that beautiful flower for myself?"

"Oh, yes," he replied, "I will play to you while you do it." As she was hastily creeping into the hedge and was just going to pluck the flower, for she well knew who the flower was, he began to play, and whether she would like it or not, she was forced to dance, for it was a magical dance. The quicker he played, the more violent springs she was forced to make, and the thorns tore her clothes from her body, and pricked her and wounded her till she bled, and as he did not stop, she had to dance till she lay dead on the ground.

When they were saved, Roland said, "Now I will go to my father and arrange for the wedding."

"Then in the meantime I will stay here and wait for you," said the girl, "and that no one may recognize me, I will change myself into a red milestone."

Then Roland went away, and the girl stood like a red milestone in the field and waited for her beloved. But when Roland got home, he fell into the snares of another, who prevailed on him so far that he forgot the maiden. The poor girl remained there a long time, but at length, as he did not return at all, she was sad, and changed herself into a flower, and thought, "Someone will surely come this way, and trample me down."

It happened, however, that a shepherd kept his sheep in the field, and saw the flower, and as it was so pretty, plucked it, took it with him, and laid it away in his chest. From that time forth, strange things happened in the shepherd's house. When he arose in the morning, all the work was already done, the room was swept, the table and benches cleaned, the fire on the hearth was lighted, and the water was fetched, and at noon, when he came home, the table was laid, and a good dinner served. He could not conceive how this came to pass, for he never saw a human being in his house, and no one could have concealed himself in it. He was certainly pleased with this good attendance, but still at last he was so afraid that he went to a wise woman and asked for her advice. The wise woman said, "There is some enchantment behind it, listen very early some morning if anything is moving in the room, and if you see anything, let it be what it may, throw a white cloth over it, and then the magic will be stopped."

The shepherd did as she bade him, and next morning just as day dawned, he saw the chest open, and the flower come out. Swiftly he sprang towards it, and threw a white cloth over it. Instantly the transformation came to an end, and a beautiful girl stood before him, who told him that she had been the flower, and that up to this time she had attended to his housekeeping. She told him her story, and since she pleased him he asked her if she would marry him, but she answered, "No," for she wanted to remain faithful to her sweetheart Roland, although he had deserted her. However, she promised not to go away, but to go on keeping house for the shepherd.

And now the time drew near when Roland's wedding was to be celebrated, and then, according to an old custom in the country, it was announced that all the girls were to be present at it, and sing in honor of the bridal pair. When the faithful maiden heard of this, she grew so sad that she thought her heart would break, and she would not go, but the other girls came and took her. When her turn came to sing, she stepped back, until at last she was the only one left, and then she could not refuse. But when she began her song, and it reached Roland's ears, he sprang up and cried, "I know the voice, that is the true bride, I will have no other!" Everything he had forgotten, and which had vanished from his mind, had suddenly come home again to his heart. Then the faithful maiden held her wedding with her sweetheart Roland, and grief came to an end and joy began.

57. THE GOLDEN BIRD

In olden times there was a king, who had behind his palace a beautiful garden in which there was a tree that bore golden apples. When the apples were getting ripe they were counted, but on the very next morning one was missing. This was told to the King, and he ordered that a watch should be kept every night beneath the tree.

The King had three sons, the eldest of whom he sent, as soon as night came on, into the garden; but when midnight came he could not keep himself from sleeping, and next morning again an apple was gone.

The following night the second son had to keep watch, it fared no better with him; as soon as twelve o'clock had struck he fell asleep, and in the morning an apple was gone.

Now it came to the turn of the third son to watch; and he was quite ready, but the King had not much trust in him, and thought that he would be of less use even than his brothers; but at last he let him go. The youth lay down beneath the tree, but kept awake, and did not let sleep master him. When it struck twelve, something rustled through the air, and in the moonlight he saw a bird coming whose feathers were all shining with gold. The bird alighted on the tree, and had just plucked off an apple, when the youth shot an arrow at him. The bird flew off, but the arrow had struck his plumage, and one of his golden feathers fell down. The youth picked it up, and the next morning took it to the King and told him what he had seen in the night. The King called his council together, and everyone declared that a feather like this was worth more than the whole kingdom. "If the feather is so precious," declared the King, "one alone will not do for me; I must and will have the whole bird!"

The eldest son set out; he trusted to his cleverness, and thought that he would easily find the Golden Bird. When he had gone some distance he saw a Fox sitting at the edge of a wood, so he cocked his gun and took aim at him. The Fox cried, "Do not shoot me! And in return I will give you some good counsel. You are on the way to the Golden Bird; and this evening you will come to a village in which stand two inns opposite to one another. One of them is lighted up brightly, and all goes on merrily within, but do not go into it; go rather into the other, even though it seems a bad one."

"How can such a silly beast give wise advice?" thought the King's son, and he pulled the trigger. But he missed the Fox, who stretched out his tail and ran quickly into the wood.

So he pursued his way, and by evening came to the village where the two inns were; in one they were singing and dancing; the other had a poor, miserable look. "I should be a fool, indeed," he thought, "if I were to go into the shabby tavern, and pass by the good one." So he went into the cheerful one, lived there in riot and revel, and forgot the bird and his father, and all good counsels.

When some time had passed, and the eldest son for month after month did not come back home, the second set out, wishing to find the Golden Bird. The Fox met him as he had met the eldest, and gave him the good advice of which he took no heed. He came to the two inns, and his brother was standing at the window of the one from which came the music, and called out to him. He could not resist, but went inside and lived only for pleasure.

Again some time passed, and then the King's youngest son wanted to set off and try his luck, but his father would not allow it. "It is of no use," said he, "he will find the Golden Bird no better than his brothers, and if a mishap were to befall him he knows not how to help himself; he is a little wanting at the best." But at last, as he had no peace, he let him go.

Again the Fox was sitting outside the wood, and begged for his life, and offered his good advice. The youth was good-natured, and said, "Be easy, little Fox, I will do you no harm."

"You shall not repent it," answered the Fox, "And that you may get on more quickly, get up behind on my tail." And scarcely had he seated himself when the Fox began to run, and away he went over stock and stone till his hair whistled in the wind. When they came to the village the youth got off; he followed the good advice, and without looking round turned into the little inn, where he spent the night quietly.

The next morning, as soon as he got into the open country, there sat the Fox already, and said, "I will tell you further what you have to do. Go on quite straight, and at last you will come to a castle, in front of which a whole regiment of soldiers is lying, but do not trouble yourself about them, for they will all be asleep and snoring. Go through the midst of them straight into the castle, and go through all the rooms, till at last you will come to a chamber where a Golden Bird is hanging in a wooden cage. Close by, there stands an empty gold cage for show, but beware of taking the bird out of the common cage and putting it into the fine one, or it may go badly for you." With these words the Fox again stretched out his tail, and the King's son seated himself upon it, and away he went over stock and stone till his hair whistled in the wind.

When he came to the castle he found everything as the Fox had said. The King's son went into the chamber where the Golden Bird was shut up in a wooden cage, while a golden one stood nearby; and the three golden apples lay about the room. "But," thought he, "it would be absurd if I were to leave the beautiful bird in the common and ugly cage," so he opened the door, laid hold of it, and put it into the golden cage. But at the same moment the bird uttered a shrill cry. The soldiers awoke, rushed in, and took him off to prison. The next morning he was taken before a court of justice, and as he confessed everything, was sentenced to death.

The King, however, said that he would grant him his life on one condition namely, if he brought him the Golden Horse which ran faster than the wind; and in that case he should receive, over and above, as a reward, the Golden Bird.

The King's son set off, but he sighed and was sorrowful, for how was he to find the Golden Horse? But all at once he saw his old friend the Fox sitting on the road. "Look," said the Fox, "this has happened because you did not give heed to me. However, be of good courage. I will give you my help, and tell you how to get to the Golden Horse. You must go straight on, and you will come to a castle, where in the stable stands the horse. The grooms will be lying in front of the stable; but they will be asleep and snoring, and you can quietly lead out the Golden Horse. But of one thing you must take heed; put on him the common saddle of wood and leather, and not the golden one, which hangs close by, else it will go badly for you." Then the Fox stretched out his tail, the King's son seated himself upon it, and away he went over stock and stone until his hair whistled in the wind.

Everything happened just as the Fox had said; the prince came to the stable in which the Golden Horse was standing, but just as he was going to put the common saddle upon him, he thought, "It will be a shame to such a beautiful beast, if I do not give him the good saddle which belongs to him by right." But scarcely had the golden saddle touched the horse than he began to neigh loudly. The grooms awoke, seized the youth, and threw him into prison. The next morning he was sentenced by the court to death; but the King promised to grant him his life, and the Golden Horse as well, if he could bring back the beautiful princess from the Golden Castle.

With a heavy heart the youth set out; yet luckily for him he soon found the trusty Fox. "I ought only to leave you to your bad luck," said the Fox, "but I pity you, and will help you once more out of your trouble. This road takes you straight to the Golden Castle, you will reach it by evening; and at night when everything is quiet the beautiful princess goes to the bathing-house to bathe. When she enters it, run up to her and give her a kiss, then she will follow you, and you can take her away with you; only do not allow her to take leave of her parents first, or it will go badly for you."

Then the Fox stretched out his tail, the King's son seated himself upon it, and away the Fox went, over stock and stone, till his hair whistled in the wind.

When he reached the Golden Castle it was just as the Fox had said. He waited until midnight, when everything lay in deep sleep, and the beautiful princess was going to the bathing-house. Then he sprang out and gave her a kiss. She said that she would like to go with him, but she asked him pitifully, and with tears, to allow her first to take leave of her parents. At first he withstood her prayer, but when she wept more and more, and fell at his feet, he at last gave in. But no sooner had the maiden reached the bedside of her father than he and all the rest in the castle awoke, and the youth was laid hold of and put into prison.

The next morning the King said to him, "Your life is forfeited, and you can only find mercy if you take away the hill which stands in front of my windows, and prevents my seeing beyond it; and you must finish it all within eight days. If you do that you shall have my daughter as your reward."

The King's son began, and dug and shoveled without leaving off, but when after seven days he saw how little he had done, and how all his work was as good as nothing, he fell into great sorrow and gave up all hope. But on the evening of the seventh day the Fox appeared and said, "You do not deserve that I should take any trouble for you; but just go away and lie down to sleep, and I will do the work for you."

The next morning when he awoke and looked out of the window the hill had gone. The youth ran, full of joy, to the King, and told him that the task was fulfilled, and whether he liked it or not, the King had to hold to his word and give him his daughter.

So the two set forth together, and it was not long before the trusty Fox came up with them. "You have certainly got what is best," said he, "but the Golden Horse also belongs to the maiden of the Golden Castle."

"How shall I get it?" asked the youth.

"That I will tell you," answered the Fox, "first take the beautiful maiden to the King who sent you to the Golden Castle. There will be unheard-of rejoicing; they will gladly give you the Golden Horse, and will bring it out to you. Mount it as soon as possible, and offer your hand to all in farewell; last of all to the beautiful maiden. And as soon as you have taken her hand swing her up onto the horse, and gallop away, and no one will be able to bring you back, for the horse runs faster than the wind."

All was carried out successfully, and the King's son carried off the beautiful princess on the Golden Horse.

The Fox did not remain behind, and he said to the youth, "Now I will help you to get the Golden Bird. When you come near the castle where the Golden Bird is to be found, let the maiden get down, and I will take her into my care. Then ride with the Golden Horse into the castleyard; there will be great rejoicing at the sight, and they will bring out the Golden Bird for you. As soon as you have the cage in your hand gallop back to us, and take the maiden away again."

When the plan had succeeded, and the King's son was about to ride home with his treasures, the Fox said, "Now you shall reward me for my help."

"What do you require for it?" asked the youth.

"When you get into the wood yonder, shoot me dead, and chop off my head and feet."

"That would be fine gratitude," said the King's son. "I cannot possibly do that for you."

The Fox said, "If you will not do it I must leave you, but before I go away I will give you a piece of good advice. Be careful about two things. Buy no gallows'-flesh, and do not sit at the edge of any well." And then he ran into the wood.

The youth thought, "That is a wonderful beast, he has strange whims; who is going to buy gallows'-flesh? and the desire to sit at the edge of a well has never yet seized me."

He rode on with the beautiful maiden, and his road took him again through the village in which his two brothers had remained. There was a great stir and noise, and, when he asked what was going on, he was told that two men were going to be hanged. As he came nearer to the place he saw that they were his brothers, who had been playing all kinds of wicked pranks, and had squandered all their wealth. He inquired whether they could not be set free. "If you will pay for them," answered the people, "but why should you waste your money on wicked men, and buy them free." He did not think twice about it, but paid for them, and when they were set free they all went on their way together.

They came to the wood where the Fox had first met them, and as it was cool and pleasant there, the two brothers said, "Let us rest a little by the well, and eat and drink." He agreed, and while they were talking he forgot himself, and sat down upon the edge of the well without thinking of any evil. But the two brothers threw him backwards into the well, took the maiden, the Horse, and the Bird, and went home to their father. "Here we bring you not only the Golden Bird," said they, "We have won the Golden Horse also, and the maiden from the Golden Castle." Then was there great joy; but the Horse would not eat, the Bird would not sing, and the maiden sat and wept.

But the youngest brother was not dead. By good fortune the well was dry, and he fell upon soft moss without being hurt, but he could not get out again. Even in this strait the faithful Fox did not leave him: it came and leapt down to him, and upbraided him for having forgotten its advice. "But yet I cannot give it up so," he said, "I will help you up again into daylight." He bade him grasp his tail and keep tight hold of it; and then he pulled him up.

"You are not out of all danger yet," said the Fox. "Your brothers were not sure of your death, and have surrounded the wood with watchers, who are to kill you if you let yourself be seen." But a poor man was sitting on the road, with whom the youth changed clothes, and in this way he got to the King's palace.

No one knew him, but the Bird began to sing, the Horse began to eat, and the beautiful maiden left off weeping. The King, astonished, asked, "What does this mean?"

Then the maiden said, "I do not know, but I have been so sorrowful and now I am so happy! I feel as if my true bridegroom has come."

She told him all that had happened, although the other brothers had threatened her with death if she were to betray anything.

The King commanded that all people who were in his castle should be brought before him; and amongst them came the youth in his ragged clothes; but the maiden knew him at once and fell upon his neck. The wicked brothers were seized and put to death, but he was married to the beautiful maiden and declared heir to the King.

But how did it fare with the poor Fox? Long afterwards the King's son was once again walking in the wood, when the Fox met him and said, "You have everything now that you can wish for, but there is never an end to my misery, and yet it is in your power to free me," and again he asked him with tears to shoot him dead and chop off his head and feet. So he did it, and scarcely was it done when the Fox was changed into a man, and was no other than the brother of the beautiful princess, who at last was freed from the magic charm which had been laid upon him. And now they never lacked in happiness as long as they lived.

58. THE DOG AND THE SPARROW

A sheep-dog had not a good master, but, on the contrary, one who let him suffer hunger. As he could stay no longer with him, he went quite sadly away. On the road he met a sparrow who said, "Brother dog, why are you so sad?"

The dog replied, "I am hungry, and have nothing to eat."

Then said the sparrow, "Dear brother, come into the town with me, and I will satisfy your hunger." So they went into the town together, and when they came in front of a butcher's shop the sparrow said to the dog, "Stay there, and I will pick a bit of meat down for you," and he alighted on the stall, looked about him to see that no one was observing him, and pecked and pulled and tore so long at a piece which lay on the edge, that it slipped down. Then the dog seized it, ran into a corner, and devoured it. The sparrow said, "Now come with me to another shop, and then I will get you one more piece that you may be satisfied."

When the dog had devoured the second piece as well, the sparrow asked, "Brother dog, have you now had enough?"

"Yes, I have had meat enough," he answered, "but I have had no bread yet."

Said the sparrow, "You shall have that also, come with me." Then he took him to a baker's shop, and pecked at a couple of little buns till they rolled down, and as the dog wanted still more, he led him to another stall, and again got bread for him. When that was consumed, the sparrow said, "Brother dog, have you now had enough?"

"Yes," he replied, "now we will walk awhile outside the town." Then they both went out onto the highway. It was, however, warm weather, and when they had walked a little way the dog said, "I am tired, and would like to sleep."

"Well, do sleep," answered the sparrow, "and in the meantime I will seat myself on a branch."

So the dog lay down on the road, and fell fast asleep. While he lay sleeping there, a waggoner came driving by, who had a cart with three horses, laden with two barrels of wine. The sparrow, however, saw that he was not going to turn aside, but was staying in the wheel track in which the dog was lying, so it cried, "Waggoner, don't do it, or I will make you poor."

The waggoner, however, growled to himself, "You will not make me poor," and cracked his whip and drove the cart over the dog, and the wheels killed him.

Then the sparrow cried, "You have run over my brother dog and killed him, it shall cost you your cart and horses."

"Cart and horses indeed!" said the waggoner. "What harm can you do me?" and drove onwards. Then the sparrow crept under the cover of the cart, and pecked so long at the bung-hole of one of the casks that he got the bung out, and then all the wine ran out without the driver noticing it. But once when he was looking behind him he saw that the cart was dripping, and looked at the barrels and saw that one of them was empty. "Unfortunate fellow that I am," cried he.

"Not unfortunate enough yet," said the sparrow, and flew onto the head of one of the horses and pecked his eyes out.

When the driver saw that, he drew out his axe and wanted to hit the sparrow, but the sparrow flew into the air, and he hit his horse on the head, and it fell down dead. "Oh, what an unfortunate man I am," cried he.

"Not unfortunate enough yet," said the sparrow, and when the driver drove on with the two horses, the sparrow again crept under the cover, and pecked the bung out of the second cask, so all the wine was spilled.

When the driver became aware of it, he again cried, "Oh, what an unfortunate man I am," but the sparrow replied, "Not unfortunate enough yet," and seated himself on the head of the second horse, and pecked his eyes out. The driver ran up to it and raised his axe to strike, but the sparrow flew into the air and the blow struck the horse, which fell.

"Oh, what an unfortunate man I am."

"Not unfortunate enough yet," said the sparrow, and lighted on the third horse's head, and pecked out his eyes. The driver, in his rage, struck at the sparrow without looking round, and did not hit him but killed his third horse likewise.

"Oh, what an unfortunate man I am," cried he.

"Not unfortunate enough yet," answered the sparrow. "Now will I make you unfortunate in your home," and flew away.

The driver had to leave the wagon standing, and full of anger and vexation went home. "Ah," said he to his wife, "what misfortunes I have had! My wine has run out, and the horses are all three dead!"

"Alas, husband," she answered, "what a malicious bird has come into the house! It has gathered together every bird there is in the world, and they have fallen on our corn up there, and are devouring it." Then he went upstairs, and thousands and thousands of birds were sitting in the loft and had eaten up all the corn, and the sparrow was sitting in the midst of them.

Then the driver cried, "Oh, what an unfortunate man I am."

"Not unfortunate enough yet!" answered the sparrow, "Waggoner, it shall cost you your life as well," and flew out.

Then the waggoner had lost all his property, and he went downstairs into the room, sat down behind the stove and was quite furious and bitter. But the sparrow sat outside in front of the window, and cried, "Waggoner, it shall cost you your life." Then the waggoner snatched the axe and threw it at the sparrow, but it only broke the window, and did not hit the bird. The sparrow now hopped in, placed itself on the stove and cried, "Waggoner, it shall cost you your life." The latter, quite mad and blind with rage, hacked the stove in two, and as the sparrow flew from one place to another, chopped all his household furniture, looking-glass, benches, table, and at last the walls of his house, and yet he could not hit the bird. At length, however, he caught it with his hand.

Then his wife said, "Shall I kill it?"

"No," cried he, "that would be too merciful. It shall die much more cruelly," and he took it and swallowed it whole.

The sparrow, however, began to flutter about in his body, and fluttered up again into the man's mouth; then it stretched out its head, and cried, "Waggoner, it shall still cost you your life."

The driver gave the axe to his wife, and said, "Wife, kill the bird in my mouth for me." The woman struck, but missed her blow, and hit the waggoner right on his head, so that he fell dead. But the sparrow flew up and away.

59. FREDERICK AND CATHERINE

There was once on a time a man who was called Frederick and a woman called Catherine, who had married each other and lived together as young married folks. One day Frederick said, "I will now go and plow, Catherine; when I come back, there must be some roast meat on the table for hunger, and a fresh draught for thirst."

"Just go, Frederick," answered Catherine, "just go, I will have all ready for you." Therefore when dinnertime drew near she got a sausage out of the chimney, put it in the frying pan, added some butter to it, and set it on the fire. The sausage began to fry and to hiss, Catherine stood beside it and held the handle of the pan, and had her own thoughts as she was doing it.

Then it occurred to her, "While the sausage is getting done you could go into the cellar and draw beer." So she set the frying pan safely on the fire, took a can, and went down into the cellar to draw beer.

The beer ran into the can and Catherine watched it, and then she thought, "Oh, dear! The dog upstairs is not fastened up, it might get the sausage out of the pan. Well thought of." And in a trice she was up the cellar steps again, but the dog had the sausage in its mouth already, and trailed it away on the ground. But Catherine, who was not idle, set out after it, and chased it a long way into the field; the dog, however, was swifter than Catherine and did not let the sausage journey easily, but skipped over the furrows with it.

"What's gone is gone!" said Catherine, and turned round, and as she had run till she was weary, she now walked quietly and comfortably, and cooled herself. During this time the beer was still running out of the cask, for Catherine had not turned the tap. And when the can was full and there was no other place for it, it ran into the cellar and did not stop until the whole cask was empty. As soon as Catherine was on the steps she saw the mischance. "Good gracious!" she cried. "What shall I do now to stop Frederick knowing it!"

She thought for a while, and at last she remembered that up in the loft was still standing a sack of the finest wheat flour from the last fair, and she would fetch that down and strew it over the beer. "Yes," said she, "he who saves a thing when he ought, has it afterwards when he needs it," and she climbed up to the loft and carried the sack below, and threw it straight down on the can of beer, which she knocked over, and Frederick's draught swam also in the cellar. "It is all right," said Catherine, "where the one is the other ought to be also," and she strewed the meal over the whole cellar. When it was done she was heartily delighted with her work, and said, "How clean and wholesome it does look here!"

At midday Frederick came home: "Now, wife, what have you ready for me?"

"Ah, Freddy," she answered, "I was frying a sausage for you, but while I was drawing the beer to drink with it, the dog took it away out of the pan, and while I was running after the dog, all the beer ran out, and while I was drying up the beer with the flour, I knocked over the can as well, but be easy, the cellar is quite dry again."

Said Frederick, "Catherine, Catherine, you should not have done that! To let the sausage be carried off and the beer run out of the cask, and throw out all our flour too!"

"Indeed, Frederick, I did not know that, you should have told me."

The man thought, "If my wife is like this, I must look after things more." Now he had got together a good number of talkers which he changed into gold, and said to Catherine, "Look, these are counters for playing games; I will put them in a pot and bury them in the stable under the cow's manger, but mind you keep away from them, or it will be the worse for you."

Said she, "Oh, no, Frederick, I certainly will stay away." And when Frederick was gone some peddlers came into the village who had cheap earthen bowls and pots, and asked the young woman if there was nothing she wanted to bargain in exchange for them?

"Oh, dear people," said Catherine, "I have no money and can buy nothing, but if you have any use for yellow counters I will buy from you."

"Yellow counters, why not? But just let us see them."

"Then go into the stable and dig under the cow's manger, and you will find the yellow counters. I am not allowed to go there." The rogues went there, dug and found pure gold. Then they laid hold of it, ran away, and left their pots and bowls behind in the house. Catherine thought she must use her new things, and as she had no lack in the kitchen already without these, she knocked the bottom out of every pot, and set them all as ornaments on the fence which went round about the house.

When Frederick came and saw the new decorations, he said, "Catherine, what have you been doing?"

"I have bought them, Frederick, for the counters which were under the cow's manger. I did not go there myself, the peddlers had to dig them out for themselves."

"Ah, wife," said Frederick, "what have you done? Those were not counters, but pure gold, and all our wealth; you should not have done that."

"Indeed, Frederick," said she, "I did not know that, you should have forewarned me."

Catherine stood for a while and thought to herself; then she said, "Listen, Frederick, we will soon get the gold back again, we will run after the thieves."

"Come, then," said Frederick, "we will try it; but take with you some butter and cheese that we may have something to eat on the way."

"Yes, Frederick, I will take them." They set out, and as Frederick was the better walker, Catherine followed him. "It is to my advantage," thought she, "when we turn back I shall be a little way in advance." Then she came to a hill where there were deep ruts on both sides of the road.

"There one can see," said Catherine, "how they have torn and skinned and galled the poor earth, it will never be whole again as long as it lives," and in her heart's compassion she took her butter and smeared the ruts right and left, that they might not be so hurt by the wheels, and as she was thus bending down in her charity, one of the cheeses rolled out of her pocket down the hill. Said Catherine, "I have made my way once up here, I will not go down again; another may run and fetch it back." So she took another cheese and rolled it down. But the cheeses did not come back, so she let a third run down, thinking, "Perhaps they are waiting for company, and do not like to walk alone."

As all three stayed away she said, "I do not know what that can mean, but it may perhaps be that the third has not found the way, and has gone wrong, I will just send the fourth to call it." But the fourth did no better than the third. Then Catherine was angry, and threw down the fifth and sixth as well, and these were her last. She remained standing for some time watching for their coming, but when they still did not come, she said, "Oh, you are good folks to send in search of death, you stay a fine long time away! Do you think I will wait any longer for you? I shall go my way, you may run after me; you have younger legs than I."

Catherine went on and found Frederick, who was standing waiting for her because he wanted something to eat. "Now just let us have what you have brought with you," said he. She gave him the dry bread. "Where have you the butter and the cheeses?" asked the man.

"Ah, Freddy," said Catherine, "I smeared the cart-ruts with the butter and the cheeses will come soon; one ran away from me, so I sent the others after to call it."

Said Frederick, "You should not have done that, Catherine, to smear the butter on the road, and let the cheeses run down the hill!"

"Really, Frederick, you should have told me."

Then they ate the dry bread together, and Frederick said, "Catherine, did you make the house safe when you came away?"

"No, Frederick, you should have told me to do it before."

"Then go home again, and make the house safe before we go any farther, and bring with you something else to eat. I will wait here for you."

Catherine went back and thought, "Frederick wants something more to eat, he does not like butter and cheese, so I will take with me a handkerchief full of dried pears and a pitcher of vinegar for him." Then she bolted the upper half of the door fast, but unhinged the lower door, and took it on her back, believing that when she had placed the door in security the house must be well taken care of. Catherine took her time on the way, and thought, "Frederick will rest himself so much the longer."

When she had once reached him she said, "Here is the door for you, Frederick, and now you can take care of the house yourself."

"Oh, heavens," said he, "what a wise wife I have! She takes the under-door off the hinges that everything may run in, and bolts the upper one. It is now too late to go back home again, but since you have brought the door here, you shall just carry it farther."

"I will carry the door, Frederick, but the dried pears and the vinegar-jug will be too heavy for me; I will hang them on the door, it may carry them."

And now they went into the forest, and sought the rogues, but did not find them. At length as it grew dark they climbed into a tree and resolved to spend the night there. Scarcely, however, had they sat down at the top of it than the rascals came to carry away with them what does not want to go, and find things before they are lost. They sat down under the very tree in which Frederick and Catherine were sitting, lighted a fire, and were about to share their booty. Frederick got down on the other side and collected some stones together. Then he climbed up again with them, and wished to throw them at the thieves and kill them. The stones, however, did not hit them, and the knaves cried, "It will soon be morning, the wind is shaking down the fir-apples."

Catherine still had the door on her back, and as it pressed so heavily on her, she thought it was the fault of the dried pears, and said, "Frederick, I must throw the pears down."

"No, Catherine, not now," he replied, "they might betray us."

"Oh, but, Frederick, I must! They weigh me down far too much."

"Do it, then, and be hanged!"

Then the dried pears rolled down between the branches, and the rascals below said, "The leaves are falling."

A short time afterwards, as the door was still heavy, Catherine said, "Ah, Frederick, I must pour out the vinegar."

"No, Catherine, you must not, it might betray us."

"Ah, but, Frederick, I must, it weighs me down far too much."

"Then do it and be hanged!" So she emptied out the vinegar, and it besprinkled the robbers.

They said amongst themselves, "The dew is already falling."

At length Catherine thought, "Can it really be the door which weighs me down so?" and said, "Frederick, I must throw the door down."

"No, not now, Catherine, it might reveal us."

"Oh, but, Frederick, I must. It weighs me down far too much."

"Oh, no, Catherine, do hold it fast."

"Ah, Frederick, I am letting it fall!"

"Let it go, then, in the devil's name."

Then it fell down with a violent clatter, and the rascals below cried, "The devil is coming down the tree!" and they ran away and left everything behind them. Early next morning, when the two came down they found all their gold again, and carried it home.

When they were once more at home, Frederick said, "And now, Catherine, you, too, must be industrious and work."

"Yes, Frederick, I will soon do that, I will go into the field and cut corn."

When Catherine got into the field, she said to herself, "Shall I eat before I cut, or shall I sleep before I cut? Oh, I will eat first." Then Catherine ate and eating made her sleepy, and she began to cut, and half in a dream cut all her clothes to pieces, her apron, her gown, and her shift. When Catherine awoke again after a long sleep she was standing there half-naked, and said to herself, "Is it I, or is it not I? Alas, it is not I."

Soon night came, and Catherine ran into the village, knocked at her husband's window, and cried, "Frederick."

"What is the matter?"

"I should very much like to know if Catherine is in?"

"Yes, yes," replied Frederick, "she must be in and asleep."

Said she, " 'Tis well, then I am certainly at home already," and ran away.

Outside Catherine found some vagabonds who were going to steal. Then she went to them and said, "I will help you to steal." The rascals thought that she knew of a good place and opportunity, and were glad. But Catherine went in front of the houses, and cried, "Good folks, have you anything? We want to steal."

The thieves thought to themselves, "That's a fine way of doing things," and wished themselves once more rid of Catherine. Then they said to her, "Outside the village the pastor has some turnips in the field. Go there and pull up some turnips for us." Catherine went to the ground, and began to pull them up, but was so idle that she did not gather them together.

Then a man came by, saw her, and stood still and thought that it was the devil who was thus rooting amongst the turnips. He ran away into the village to the pastor, and said, "Mr. Pastor, the devil is in your turnip-field, rooting up turnips."

"Ah, heavens," answered the pastor, "I have a lame foot, I cannot go out and drive him away."

Said the man, "Then I will carry you on my back," and he carried him out on his back. And when they came to the ground, Catherine arose and stood up her full height.

"Ah, the devil!" cried the pastor, and both hurried away, and in his great fright the pastor could run better with his lame foot than the man who had carried him on his back could do with his sound one.

60. THE TWO BROTHERS

There were once upon a time two brothers, one rich and the other poor. The rich one was a goldsmith and evil-hearted. The poor one supported himself by making brooms, and was good and honorable. The poor one had two children, who were twin brothers and as like each other as two drops of water. The two boys went backwards and forwards to the rich house, and often got some of the scraps to eat. It happened once when the poor man was going into the forest to fetch brush-wood, that he saw a bird which was quite golden and more beautiful than any he had ever chanced to meet with. He picked up a small stone, threw it at him, and was lucky enough to hit him, but only one golden feather fell down, and the bird flew away.

The man took the feather and carried it to his brother, who looked at it and said, "It is pure gold!" and gave him a great deal of money for it. Next day the man climbed into a birch tree, and was about to cut off a couple of branches when the same bird flew out, and when the man searched he found a nest, and an egg lay inside it, which was of gold. He took the egg home with him, and carried it to his brother, who again said, "It is pure gold," and gave him what it was worth. At last the goldsmith said, "I should indeed like to have the bird itself."

The poor man went into the forest for the third time, and again saw the golden bird sitting on the tree, so he took a stone and knocked it down and carried it to his brother, who gave him a great heap of gold for it. "Now I can get on," thought he, and went contentedly home.

The goldsmith was crafty and cunning, and knew very well what kind of a bird it was. He called his wife and said, "Roast me the gold bird, and take care that none of it is lost. I have a fancy to eat it all myself." The bird, however, was no common one, but of so wondrous a kind that whoever ate its heart and liver found every morning a piece of gold beneath his pillow. The woman made the bird ready, put it on the spit, and let it roast.

Now it happened that while it was on the fire, and the woman was forced to go out of the kitchen on account of some other work, the two children of the poor broom-maker ran in, stood by the spit and turned it round once or twice. And as at that very moment two little bits of the bird fell down into the dripping-tray, one of the boys said, "We will eat these two little bits; I am so hungry, and no one will ever miss them."

Then the two ate the pieces, but the woman came into the kitchen and saw that they were eating something and said, "What have you been eating?"

"Two little morsels which fell out of the bird," answered they.

"That must have been the heart and the liver," said the woman, quite frightened, and so that her husband might not miss them and be angry, she quickly killed a young cock, took out his heart and liver, and put them beside the golden bird. When it was ready, she carried it to the goldsmith, who consumed it all alone, and left none of it. Next morning, however, when he felt beneath his pillow, and expected to bring out the piece of gold, no more gold pieces were there than there had always been.

The two children did not know what a piece of good fortune had fallen to their lot. Next morning when they arose, something fell rattling to the ground, and when they picked it up there were two gold pieces! They took them to their father, who was astonished and said, "How can that have happened?"

When next morning they again found two, and so on daily, he went to his brother and told him the strange story. The goldsmith at once knew how it had come to pass, and that the children had eaten the heart and liver of the golden bird, and in order to avenge himself, and because he was envious and hard-hearted, he said to the father, "Your children are in league with the Evil One, do not take the gold, and do not suffer them to stay any longer in your house, for he has them in his power, and may ruin you likewise." The father feared the Evil One, and painful as it was to him, he nevertheless led the twins forth into the forest, and with a sad heart left them there.

And now the two children ran about the forest, and sought the way home again, but could not find it, and only lost themselves more and more. At length they met with a hunter, who asked, "To whom do you children belong?"

"We are the poor broom-maker's boys," they replied, and they told him that their father would not keep them any longer in the house because a piece of gold lay every morning under their pillows.

"Come," said the hunter, "that is not so very bad, if at the same time you keep honest, and are not idle." As the good man liked the children, and had none of his own, he took them home with him and said, "I will be your father, and bring you up till you are big." They learned huntership from him, and the piece of gold which each of them found when he awoke, was kept for them by him in case they should need it in the future.

When they were grown up, their foster father one day took them into the forest with him, and said, "Today you shall make your trial shot, so that I may release you from your apprenticeship, and make you hunters." They went with him to lie in wait and stayed there a long time, but no game appeared. The hunter, however, looked above him and saw a covey of wild geese flying in the form of a triangle, and said to one of them, "Shoot me down one from each corner." He did it, and thus accomplished his trial shot. Soon after another covey came flying by in the form of the figure two, and the hunter bade the other also bring down one from each corner, and his trial shot was likewise successful.

"Now," said the foster father, "I pronounce you out of your apprenticeship; you are skilled hunters."

Thereupon the two brothers went forth together into the forest, and took counsel with each other and planned something. And in the evening when they had sat down to supper, they said to their foster father, "We will not touch food, or take one mouthful, until you have granted us a request."

Said he, "What, then, is your request?"

They replied, "We have now finished learning, and we must prove ourselves in the world, so allow us to go away and travel."

Then spoke the old man joyfully, "You talk like brave hunters, that which you desire has been my wish; go forth, all will go well with you." Thereupon they ate and drank joyously together.

When the appointed day came, their foster father presented each of them with a good gun and a dog, and let each of them take as many of his saved-up gold pieces as he chose. Then he accompanied them a part of the way, and when taking leave, he gave them a bright knife, and said, "If ever you separate, stick this knife into a tree at the place where you part, and when one of you goes back, he will be able to see how his absent brother is faring, for the side of the knife which is turned in the direction that he went, will rust if he dies, but will remain bright as long as he is alive."

The two brothers went still farther onwards, and came to a forest which was so large that it was impossible for them to get out of it in one day. So they passed the night in it, and ate what they had put in their hunting-pouches, but they walked all the second day likewise, and still did not get out. As they had nothing to eat, one of them said, "We must shoot something for ourselves or we shall suffer from hunger," and loaded his gun, and looked about him. And when an old hare came running up towards them, he laid his gun on his shoulder, but the hare cried,

"Dear hunters, do but let me live,
Two little ones to you I'll give,"

and sprang instantly into the thicket, and brought two young ones. But the little creatures played so merrily, and were so pretty, that the hunters could not find it in their hearts to kill them. They therefore kept them with them, and the little hares followed on foot. Soon after this, a fox crept past; they were just going to shoot it, but the fox cried,

"Dear hunters, do but let me live,
Two little ones I'll also give."

He, too, brought two little foxes, and the hunters did not like to kill them either, but gave them to the hares for company, and they followed behind. It was not long before a wolf strode out of the thicket; the hunters made ready to shoot him, but the wolf cried,

"Dear hunters, do but let me live,
Two little ones I'll likewise give."

The hunters put the two wolves beside the other animals, and they followed behind. Then a bear came who wanted to trot about a little longer, and cried:

"Dear hunters, do but let me live,
Two little ones I, too, will give."

The two young bears were added to the others, and there were already eight of them. At length who came? A lion came, and tossed his mane. But the hunters did not let themselves be frightened and aimed at him likewise, but the lion also said,

"Dear hunters, do but let me live,
Two little ones I, too, will give."

And he brought his little ones to them, and now the hunters had two lions, two bears, two wolves, two foxes, and two hares, who followed them and served them. In the meantime their hunger was not appeased by this, and they said to the foxes, "Listen, cunning fellows, provide us with something to eat. You are crafty and deep."

They replied, "Not far from here lies a village, from which we have already brought many a fowl; we will show you the way there." So they went into the village, bought themselves something to eat, had some food given to their beasts, and then traveled onwards. The foxes, however, knew their way very well about the district and where the henhouses were, and were able to guide the hunters.

Now they traveled about for a while, but could find no suitable place where they could remain together, so they said, "There is nothing else to do, we must part." They divided the animals, so that each of them had a lion, a bear, a wolf, a fox, and a hare, then they took leave of each other, promised to love each other like brothers till their death, and stuck the knife which their foster father had given them, into a tree, after which one went east, and the other went west.

The younger, however, arrived with his beasts in a town which was all hung with black crape. He went into an inn, and asked the host if he could accommodate his animals. The innkeeper gave him a stable, where there was a hole in the wall, and the hare crept out and fetched himself the head of a cabbage, and the fox fetched himself a hen, and when he had devoured that got the cock as well, but the wolf, the bear, and the lion could not get out because they were too big. Then the innkeeper let them be taken to a place where a cow was just then lying on the grass, that they might eat till they were satisfied. And when the hunter had taken care of his animals, he asked the innkeeper why the town was thus hung with black crape? Said the host, "Because our King's only daughter is to die tomorrow."

The hunter inquired if she was "sick unto death?"

"No," answered the host, "she is vigorous and healthy, nevertheless she must die!"

"How is that?" asked the hunter.

"There is a high hill outside the town, where dwells a dragon who every year must have a pure virgin, or he will destroy the whole country, and now all the maidens have already been given to him, and there is no longer anyone left but the King's daughter, yet there is no mercy for her; she must be given up to him, and that is to be done tomorrow."

Said the hunter, "Why is the dragon not killed?"

"Ah," replied the host, "so many knights have tried it, but it has cost all of them their lives. The King has promised that he who conquers the dragon shall have his daughter as wife, and shall likewise govern the kingdom after his own death."

The hunter said nothing more to this, but next morning took his animals, and with them ascended the dragon's hill. A little church stood at the top of it, and on the altar three full cups were standing, with the inscription, "Whoever empties the cups will become the strongest man on earth, and will be able to wield the sword which is buried before the threshold of the door." The hunter did not drink, but went out and sought for the sword in the ground, but was unable to move it from its place. Then he went in and emptied the cups, and now he was strong enough to take up the sword, and his hand could quite easily wield it. When the hour came when the maiden was to be delivered over to the dragon, the King, the marshal, and courtiers accompanied her. From afar she saw the hunter on the dragon's hill, and thought it was the dragon standing there waiting for her, and did not want to go up to him, but at last, because otherwise the whole town would have been destroyed, she was forced to go the miserable journey. The King and courtiers returned home full of grief; the King's marshal, however, was to remain, and see all from a distance.

When the King's daughter got to the top of the hill, it was not the dragon which stood there, but the young hunter, who comforted her, and said he would save her, led her into the church, and locked her in. It was not long before the seven-headed dragon came there with loud roaring. When he perceived the hunter, he was astonished and said, "What business have you here on the hill?"

The hunter answered, "I want to fight with you."

Said the dragon, "Many knights have left their lives here, I shall soon have made an end of you too," and he breathed fire out of seven jaws. The fire was to have lighted the dry grass, and the hunter was to have been suffocated in the heat and smoke, but the animals came running up and trampled out the fire. Then the dragon rushed upon the hunter, but he swung his sword until it sang through the air, and struck off three of his heads. Then the dragon grew right furious, and rose up in the air, and spat out flames of fire over the hunter, and was about to plunge down on him, but the hunter once more drew out his sword, and again cut off three of his heads. The monster became faint and sank down, nevertheless it was just able to rush upon the hunter, but with his last strength he slashed its tail off, and as he could fight no longer, called up his animals who tore it in pieces. When the struggle was over, the hunter unlocked the church, and found the King's daughter lying on the floor, as she had lost her senses with anguish and terror during the contest. He carried her out, and when she came to herself once more, and opened her eyes, he showed her the dragon all cut to pieces, and told her that she was now safe.

She rejoiced and said, "Now you will be my dearest husband, for my father has promised me to whoever kills the dragon." Thereupon she took off her necklace of coral, and divided it amongst the animals in order to reward them, and the lion received the golden clasp. Her pocket handkerchief, which bore her name, she gave to the hunter, who went and cut the tongues out of the dragon's seven heads, wrapped them in the handkerchief, and preserved them carefully.

That done, as he was so faint and weary with the fire and the battle, he said to the maiden, "We are both faint and weary, we will sleep awhile." Then she said, "yes," and they lay down on the ground, and the hunter said to the lion, "You shall keep watch, that no one surprises us in our sleep," and both fell asleep.

The lion lay down beside them to watch, but he also was so weary with the fight, that he called to the bear and said, "Lie down near me, I must sleep a little: if anything comes, wake me."

Then the bear lay down beside him, but he also was tired, and called the wolf and said, "Lie down by me, I must sleep a little, but if anything comes, wake me."

Then the wolf lay down by him, but he was tired likewise, and called the fox and said, "Lie down by me, I must sleep a little; if anything comes, wake me."

Then the fox lay down beside him, but he too was weary, and called the hare and said, "Lie down near me, I must sleep a little, and if anything should come, wake me."

Then the hare sat down by him, but the poor hare was tired too, and had no one whom he could call there to keep watch, and fell asleep. And now the King's daughter, the hunter, the lion, the bear, the wolf, the fox, and the hare, were all sleeping a sound sleep. The marshal, however, who was to look on from a distance, took courage when he did not see the dragon flying away with the maiden, and finding that all the hill had become quiet, ascended it. There lay the dragon hacked and hewn to pieces on the ground, and not far from it were the King's daughter and a hunter with his animals, and all of them were sunk in a sound sleep. And as he was wicked and godless he took his sword, cut off the hunter's head, and seized the maiden in his arms, and carried her down the hill. Then she awoke and was terrified, but the marshal said, "You are in my hands, you shall say that it was I who killed the dragon."

"I cannot do that," she replied, "for it was a hunter with his animals who did it."

Then he drew his sword, and threatened to kill her if she did not obey him, and so compelled her that she promised it. Then he took her to the King, who did not know how to contain himself for joy when he once more saw his dear child alive, whom he had believed to have been torn to pieces by the monster. The marshal said to him, "I have killed the dragon, and delivered the maiden and the whole kingdom as well, therefore I demand her as my wife, as was promised."

The King said to the maiden, "Is what he says true?"

"Ah, yes," she answered, "it must indeed be true, but I will not consent to have the wedding celebrated until after a year and a day," for she thought in that time she should hear something of her dear hunter.

The animals, however, were still lying sleeping beside their dead master on the dragon's hill, and there came a great bumble-bee that alighted on the hare's nose, but the hare wiped it off with his paw, and went on sleeping. The bumble-bee came a second time, but the hare again rubbed it off and slept on. Then it came for the third time, and stung his nose so that he awoke. As soon as the hare was awake, he roused the fox, and the fox, the wolf, and the wolf the bear, and the bear the lion. And when the lion awoke and saw that the maiden was gone, and his master was dead, he began to roar frightfully and cried, "Who has done that? Bear, why did you not wake me?"

The bear asked the wolf, "Why did you not wake me?" and the wolf the fox, "Why did you not wake me?" and the fox the hare, "Why did you not wake me?"

The poor hare alone did not know what answer to make, and the blame rested with him. Then they were just going to fall upon him, but he entreated them and said, "Don't kill me, I will bring our master to life again. I know a mountain on which a root grows which, when placed in the mouth of anyone, cures him of all illness and every wound. But the mountain lies two hundred miles from here."

The lion said, "You have twenty-four hours to run there and come back, and bring the root with you." Then the hare sprang away, and in twenty-four hours he was back, and brought the root with him. The lion put the hunter's head on again, and the hare placed the root in his mouth, and immediately everything united together again, and his heart beat, and life came back.

Then the hunter awoke, and was alarmed when he did not see the maiden, and thought, "She must have gone away while I was sleeping, in order to get rid of me." The lion in his great haste had put his master's head on the wrong way round, but the hunter did not observe it because of his melancholy thoughts about the King's daughter. But at noon, when he was going to eat something, he saw that his head was turned backwards and could not understand it, and asked the animals what had happened to him in his sleep. Then the lion told him that they, too, had all fallen asleep from weariness, and on awaking, had found him dead with his head cut off, that the hare had brought the life-giving root, and that he, in his haste, had laid the head the wrong way, but that he would repair his mistake. Then he tore the hunter's head off again, turned it round, and the hare healed it with the root.

The hunter, however, was sad at heart, and traveled about the world, and made his animals dance before people. It came to pass that precisely at the end of one year he came back to the same town where he had delivered the King's daughter from the dragon, and this time the town was gaily hung with red cloth. Then he said to the host, "What does this mean? Last year the town was all hung with black crape, what means the red cloth today?"

The host answered, "Last year our King's daughter was to have been delivered over to the dragon, but the marshal fought with it and killed it, and so tomorrow their wedding is to be solemnized, and that is why the town was then hung with black crape for mourning, and is today covered with red cloth for joy."

Next day when the wedding was to take place, the hunter said at midday to the innkeeper, "Do you believe, sir host, that while with you here today I shall eat bread from the King's own table?"

"Nay," said the host, "I would bet a hundred pieces of gold that that will not come true."

The hunter accepted the wager, and set against it a purse with just the same number of gold pieces. Then he called the hare and said, "Go, my dear runner, and fetch me some of the bread which the King is eating."

Now the little hare was the lowest of the animals, and could not transfer this order to any of the others, but had to go on foot himself. "Alas!" thought he, "If I bound through the streets thus alone, the butchers' dogs will all be after me." It happened as he expected, and the dogs came after him and wanted to make holes in his good skin. But he sprang away, have you never seen one running? And sheltered himself in a sentry-box without the soldier being aware of it. Then the dogs came and wanted to have him out, but the soldier did not let them pass, and struck them with the butt-end of his gun, till they ran away yelling and howling. As soon as the hare saw that the way was clear, he ran into the palace and straight to the King's daughter, sat down under her chair, and scratched at her foot.

Then she said, "Will you get away?" and thought it was her dog. The hare scratched her foot for the second time, and she again said, "Will you get away?" and thought it was her dog. But the hare did not let itself be turned from its purpose, and scratched her for the third time. Then she peeped down, and knew the hare by her necklace. She took him on her lap, carried him into her chamber, and said, "Dear hare, what do you want?"

He answered, "My master, who killed the dragon, is here, and has sent me to ask for a loaf of bread like that which the King eats." Then she was full of joy and had the baker summoned, and ordered him to bring a loaf such as that eaten by the King. The little hare said, "But the baker must likewise carry it there for me, that the butchers' dogs may do no harm to me." The baker carried if for him as far as the door of the inn, and then the hare got on his hind legs, took the loaf in his front paws, and carried it to his master.

Then said the hunter, "See, sir host, the hundred pieces of gold are mine." The host was astonished, but the hunter went on to say, "Yes, sir host, I have the bread, but now I will likewise have some of the King's roast meat."

The host said, "I should indeed like to see that," but he would make no more wagers.

The hunter called the fox and said, "My little fox, go and fetch me some roast meat, such as the King eats." The red fox knew the byways better, and went by holes and corners without any dog seeing him, seated himself under the chair of the King's daughter, and scratched her foot.

Then she looked down and recognized the fox by its necklace, took him into her chamber with her and said, "Dear fox, what do you want?"

He answered, "My master, who killed the dragon, is here, and has sent me. I am to ask for some roast meat such as the King is eating." Then she made the cook come, who was obliged to prepare a roast, the same as was eaten by the King, and to carry it for the fox as far as the door. Then the fox took the dish, and with his tail waved away the flies which had settled on the meat, and then carried it to his master.

"Look, sir host," said the hunter, "bread and meat are here but now I will also have proper vegetables with it, such as those eaten by the King." Then he called the wolf, and said, "Dear wolf, go there and fetch me vegetables such as the King eats." Then the wolf went straight to the palace, as he feared no one, and when he got to the King's daughter's chamber, he twitched at the back of her dress, so that she was forced to look round.

She recognized him by his necklace, and took him into her chamber with her, and said, "Dear wolf, what do you want?"

He answered, "My master, who killed the dragon, is here, I am to ask for some vegetables, such as the King eats." Then she made the cook come, and he had to make ready a dish of vegetables, such as the King ate, and had to carry it for the wolf as far as the door, and then the wolf took the dish from him, and carried it to his master.

"See, sir host," said the hunter, "now I have bread and meat and vegetables, but I will also have some pastry to eat like that which the King eats." He called the bear, and said, "Dear bear, you are fond of licking anything sweet; go and bring me some confectionery, such as the King eats." Then the bear trotted to the palace, and everyone got out of his way, but when he went to the guard, they presented their muskets, and would not let him go into the royal palace. But he got up on his hind legs, and gave them a few boxes on the ears, right and left, with his paws, so that the whole watch broke up, and then he went straight to the King's daughter, placed himself behind her, and growled a little.

Then she looked behind her, knew the bear, and bade him go into her room with her, and said, "Dear bear, what do you want?"

He answered, "My master, who killed the dragon, is here, and I am to ask for some confectionery, such as the King eats." Then she summoned her confectioner, who had to bake confectionery such as the King ate, and carry it to the door for the bear; then the bear first licked up the sugar drips which had rolled down, and then he stood upright, took the dish, and carried it to his master.

"Behold, sir host," said the hunter, "now I have bread, meat, vegetables and confectionery, but I will drink wine also, and such as the King drinks." He called his lion to him and said, "Dear lion, you yourself like to drink till you are intoxicated, go and fetch me some wine, such as that which is drunk by the King." Then the lion strode through the streets, and the people fled from him, and when he came to the watch, they wanted to bar the way against him, but he did but roar once, and they all ran away. Then the lion went to the royal apartment, and knocked at the door with his tail.

Then the King's daughter came forth, and was almost afraid of the lion, but she knew him by the golden clasp of her necklace, and bade him go with her into her chamber, and said, "Dear lion, what will you have?"

He answered, "My master, who killed the dragon, is here, and I am to ask for some wine such as the King drinks." Then she bade the cup-bearer be called, who was to give the lion some wine like that which was drunk by the King. The lion said, "I will go with him, and see that I get the right wine."

Then he went down with the cup-bearer, and when they were below, the cup-bearer wanted to draw him some of the common wine that was drunk by the King's servants, but the lion said, "Stop, I will taste the wine first," and he drew half a measure, and swallowed it down at one gulp. "No," said he, "that is not right." The cup-bearer glared at him, but went on, and was about to give him some out of another barrel which was for the King's marshal. The lion said, "Stop, let me taste the wine first," and drew half a measure and drank it. "That is better, but still not right," said he.

Then the cup-bearer grew angry and said, "How can a stupid animal like you understand wine?" But the lion gave him a blow behind the ears, which made him fall down by no means gently, and when he had got up again, he conducted the lion quite silently into a separate little cellar, where the King's wine lay, from which no one ever drank.

The lion first drew half a measure and tried the wine, and then he said, "That may possibly be the right sort, and bade the cup-bearer fill six bottles of it. And now they went upstairs again, but when the lion came out of the cellar into the open air, he reeled here and there, and was rather drunk, and the cup-bearer was forced to carry the wine as far as the door for him, and then the lion took the handle of the basket in his mouth, and took it to his master.

The hunter said, "Look, sir host, here have I bread, meat, vegetables, confectionery and wine such as the King has, and now I will dine with my animals," and he sat down and ate and drank, and allowed the hare, the fox, the wolf, the bear, and the lion also to eat and to drink, and was joyful, for he saw that the King's daughter still loved him. And when he had finished his dinner, he said, "Sir host, now have I eaten and drunk, as the King eats and drinks, and now I will go to the King's court and marry the King's daughter."

Said the host, "How can that be, when she already has a betrothed husband, and when the wedding is to be solemnized today?"

Then the hunter drew forth the handkerchief which the King's daughter had given him on the dragon's hill, and in which were folded the monster's seven tongues, and said, "That which I hold in my hand shall help me to do it."

Then the innkeeper looked at the handkerchief, and said, "Whatever I believe, I do not believe that, and I am willing to stake my house and courtyard on it."

The hunter, however, took a bag with a thousand gold pieces, put it on the table, and said, "I stake that on it."

Now the King said to his daughter, at the royal table, "What did all the wild animals want, which have been coming to you, and going in and out of my palace?"

She replied, "I may not tell you, but send and have the master of these animals brought, and you will know."

The King sent a servant to the inn, and invited the stranger, and the servant came just as the hunter had laid his wager with the innkeeper. Then said he, "Now, sir host, the King sends his servant and invites me, but I do not go in this way." And he said to the servant, "I request the Lord King to send me royal clothing, and a carriage with six horses, and servants to attend me."

When the King heard the answer, he said to his daughter, "What shall I do?"

She said, "Have him fetched as he desires to be, and you will do well."

Then the King sent royal apparel, a carriage with six horses, and servants to wait on him. When the hunter saw them coming, he said, "See, sir host, now I am fetched as I desired to be," and he put on the royal garments, took the handkerchief with the dragon's tongues with him, and drove off to the King.

When the King saw him coming, he said to his daughter, "How shall I receive him?"

She answered, "Go to meet him and you will do well."

Then the King went to meet him and led him in, and his animals followed. The King gave him a seat near himself and his daughter, and the marshal, as bridegroom, sat on the other side, but no longer knew the hunter. And now at this very moment, the seven heads of the dragon were brought in as a spectacle, and the King said, "The seven heads were cut off the dragon by the marshal, therefore today I give him my daughter as wife."

The hunter stood up, opened the seven mouths, and said, "Where are the seven tongues of the dragon?"

Then the marshal was terrified, and grew pale and knew not what to answer, and at length in his anguish he said, "Dragons have no tongues."

The hunter said, "Liars ought to have none, but the dragon's tongues are the tokens of the victor," and he unfolded the handkerchief, and there lay all seven inside it. And he put each tongue in the mouth to which it belonged, and it fitted exactly.

Then he took the handkerchief on which the name of the princess was embroidered, and showed it to the maiden, and asked to whom she had given it, and she replied, "To the man who killed the dragon."

And then he called his animals, and took the collar off each of them and the golden clasp from the lion, and showed them to the maiden and asked to whom they belonged. She answered, "The necklace and golden clasp were mine, but I divided them among the animals who helped to conquer the dragon."

Then the hunter said, "When I, tired with the fight, was resting and sleeping, the marshal came and cut off my head. Then he carried away the King's daughter, and pretended that it was he who had killed the dragon, but with the tongues, the handkerchief, and the necklace, I prove that he lied." And then he related how his animals had healed him by means of a wonderful root, and how he had traveled about with them for one year, and had at length again come there and had learnt the treachery of the marshal by the innkeeper's story.

Then the King asked his daughter, "Is it true that this man killed the dragon?"

And she answered, "Yes, it is true. Now I can reveal the wicked deed of the marshal, as it has come to light, for he wrung from me a promise to be silent. For this reason, however, I made the condition that the marriage should not be solemnized for a year and a day."

Then the King bade twelve councilors be summoned who were to pronounce judgment on the marshal, and they sentenced him to be torn to pieces by four bulls. The marshal was therefore executed, but the King gave his daughter to the hunter, and named him his viceroy over the whole kingdom. The wedding was celebrated with great joy, and the young King sent for his father and his foster father, and loaded them with treasures. He sent for the innkeeper too, and said, "Now, sir host, I have married the King's daughter, and your house and yard are mine."

The host said, "Yes, according to justice it is so."

But the young King said, "It shall be done according to mercy," and told him that he should keep his house and yard, and gave him the thousand pieces of gold as well.

And now the young King and Queen were thoroughly happy, and lived in gladness together. He often went out hunting because it was a delight to him, and the faithful animals had to accompany him. In the neighborhood, however, there was a forest of which it was reported that it was haunted, and that whoever entered it did not easily get out again. The young King, however, had a great inclination to hunt in it, and let the old King have no peace until he allowed him to do so. So he rode forth with a great following, and when he came to the forest, he saw a snow-white deer and said to his people, "Wait here until I return, I want to chase that beautiful creature," and he rode into the forest after it, followed only by his animals. The attendants halted and waited until evening, but he did not return, so they rode home, and told the young

Queen that the young King had followed a white deer into the enchanted forest, and had not come back again. Then she had the greatest concern about him. He, however, had still continued to ride on and on after the beautiful wild animal, and had never been able to overtake it; when he thought he was near enough to aim, he instantly saw it bound away into the far distance, and at length it vanished altogether. And now he perceived that he had penetrated deep into the forest, and blew his horn but he received no answer, for his attendants could not hear it. And as night, too, was falling, he saw that he could not get home that day, so he dismounted from his horse, lighted himself a fire near a tree, and resolved to spend the night by it. While he was sitting by the fire, and his animals were lying down beside him, it seemed to him that he heard a human voice. He looked round, but could perceive nothing. Soon afterwards, he again heard a groan as if from above, and then he looked up, and saw an old woman sitting in the tree, who wailed unceasingly, "Oh, oh, oh, how cold I am!"

Said he, "Come down, and warm yourself if you are cold."

But she said, "No, your animals will bite me."

He answered, "They will do you no harm, old mother, do come down."

She, however, was a witch, and said, "I will throw down a wand from the tree, and if you strike them on the back with it, they will do me no harm." Then she threw him a small wand, and he struck them with it, and instantly they lay still and were turned into stone. And when the witch was safe from the animals, she leapt down and touched him also with a wand, and changed him to stone. Thereupon she laughed, and dragged him and the animals into a vault, where many more such stones already lay.

As, however, the young King did not come back at all, the Queen's anguish and care grew constantly greater. And it so happened that at this very time the other brother who had turned to the east when they separated, came into the kingdom. He had sought a home, and had found none, and had then traveled about here and there, and had made his animals dance. Then it came into his mind that he would just go and look at the knife that they had thrust in the trunk of a tree at their parting, that he might learn how his brother was. When he got there his brother's side of the knife was half rusted, and half bright.

Then he was alarmed and thought, "A great misfortune must have befallen my brother, but perhaps I can still save him, for half the knife is still bright." He and his animals traveled towards the west, and when he entered the gate of the town, the guard came to meet him, and asked if he was to announce him to his consort the young Queen, who had for a couple of days been in the greatest sorrow about his staying away, and was afraid he had been killed in the enchanted forest. The sentries, indeed, thought no otherwise than that he was the young King himself, for he looked so like him, and had wild animals running behind him. Then he saw that they were speaking of his brother, and thought, "It will be better if I pass myself off as him, and then I can rescue him more easily." So he allowed himself to be escorted into the castle by the guard, and was received with the greatest joy. The young Queen indeed thought that he was her husband, and asked him why he had stayed away so long.

He answered, "I had lost myself in a forest, and could not find my way out again any sooner." At night he was taken to the royal bed, but he laid a two-edged sword between him and the young Queen; she did not know what that could mean, but did not venture to ask.

He remained in the palace a couple of days, and in the meantime inquired into everything which related to the enchanted forest, and at last he said, "I must hunt there once more." The King and the young Queen wanted to persuade him not to do it, but he held out against them, and went forth with a large following. When he had got into the forest, everything happened with him as with his brother; he saw a white deer and said to his people, "Stay here, and wait until I return, I want to chase the lovely wild beast," and then he rode into the forest and his animals ran after him. But he could not overtake the deer, and got so deep into the forest that he was forced to pass the night there. And when he had lighted a fire, he heard someone wailing above him, "Oh, oh, oh, how cold I am!"

Then he looked up, and the same witch was sitting in the tree.

Said he, "If you are cold, come down, little old mother, and warm yourself."

She answered, "No, your animals will bite me."

But he said, "They will not hurt you."

Then she cried, "I will throw down a wand to you, and if you strike them with it they will do me no harm."

When the hunter heard that, he had no confidence in the old

woman, and said, "I will not strike my animals. Come down, or I will fetch you."

Then she cried, "What do you want? You shall not touch me."

But he replied, "If you do not come, I will shoot you."

Said she, "Shoot away, I do not fear your bullets!" Then he aimed, and fired at her, but the witch was proof against all leaden bullets, and laughed, and yelled and cried, "You shall not hit me."

The hunter knew what to do, tore three silver buttons off his coat, and loaded his gun with them, for against them her arts were useless, and when he fired she fell down at once with a scream. Then he set his foot on her and said, "Old witch, if you do not instantly confess where my brother is, I will seize you with both my hands and throw you into the fire."

She was in a great fright, begged for mercy and said, "He and his animals lie in a vault, turned to stone."

Then he compelled her to go there with him, threatened her, and said, "Old witch, now you shall make my brother and all the human beings lying here, alive again, or you shall go into the fire!" She took a wand and touched the stones, and then his brother with his animals came to life again, and many others, merchants, artisans, and shepherds, arose, thanked him for their deliverance, and went to their homes. But when the twin brothers saw each other again, they kissed each other and rejoiced with all their hearts. Then they seized the witch, bound her and laid her on the fire, and when she was burnt the forest opened of its own accord, and was light and clear, and the King's palace could be seen at about the distance of a three hours walk.

After this the two brothers went home together, and on the way told each other their histories. And when the youngest said that he was ruler of the whole country in the King's stead, the other observed, "That I learned very well, for when I came to the town, and was taken for you, all royal honors were paid me; the young Queen looked at me as her husband, and I had to eat at her side, and sleep in your bed."

When the other heard that, he became so jealous and angry that he drew his sword, and struck off his brother's head. But when he saw him lying there dead, and saw his red blood flowing, he repented most violently: "My brother saved me," cried he, "and I have killed him for it," and he bewailed him aloud. Then his hare came and offered to go and bring some of the root of life, and bounded away and brought it while there was still time, and the dead man was brought to life again, and knew nothing about the wound.

After this they journeyed onwards, and the youngest said, "You look like me, have royal apparel on as I have, and the animals follow you as they do me; we will go in by opposite gates, and arrive at the same time from the two sides in the aged King's presence."

So they separated, and at the same time came the watchmen from the one door and from the other, and announced that the young King and the animals had returned from the chase. The King said, "It is not possible, the gates lie quite a mile apart." In the meantime, however, the two brothers entered the courtyard of the palace from opposite sides, and both mounted the steps. Then the King said to the daughter, "Say which is your husband. Each of them looks exactly like the other, I cannot tell."

Then she was in great distress, and could not tell; but at last she remembered the necklace which she had given to the animals, and she sought for and found her little golden clasp on the lion, and she cried in her delight, "He who is followed by this lion is my true husband."

Then the young King laughed and said, "Yes, he is the right one," and they sat down together, and ate and drank, and were merry.

At night when the young King went to bed, his wife said, "Why have you for these last nights always laid a two-edged sword in our bed? I thought you had a wish to kill me." Then he knew how true his brother had been.

61. THE LITTLE PEASANT

There was a certain village where no one lived but really rich peasants, and just one poor one, whom they called the little peasant. He had not even so much as a cow, and still less money to buy one, and yet he and his wife did so wish to have one. One day he said to her, "Say, I have a good thought, there is our friend the carpenter, he shall make us a wooden calf, and paint it brown, so that it looks like any other, and in time it will certainly get big and be a cow." The woman also liked the idea, and their friend the carpenter cut and planed the calf, and painted it as it ought to be, and made it with its head hanging down as if it were eating.

Next morning when the cows were being driven out, the little peasant called the cowherd and said, "Look, I have a little calf there, but it is still small and has to still be carried."

The cowherd said, "All right," and took it in his arms and carried it to the pasture, and set it among the grass. The little calf always remained standing and seemed to be eating all the time, and the cowherd said, "It will soon be able to run alone, just look how it eats already!"

At night when he was going to drive the herd home again, he said to the calf, "If you can stand there and eat your fill, you can also go on your four legs; I don't care to drag you home again in my arms."

But the little peasant stood at his door, and waited for his little calf, and when the cowherd drove the cows through the village, and the calf was missing, he inquired where it was. The cowherd answered, "It is still standing out there eating. It would not stop and come with us."

But the little peasant said, "Oh, but I must have my beast back again." Then they went back to the meadow together, but someone had stolen the calf, and it was gone.

The cowherd said, "It must have run away."

The peasant, however, said, "Don't tell me that," and brought the cowherd before the mayor, who for his carelessness condemned him to give the peasant a cow for the calf which had run away.

And now the little peasant and his wife had the cow for which they had so long wished, and they were heartily glad, but they had no food for it, and could give it nothing to eat, so it soon had to be killed. They salted the flesh, and the peasant went into the town and wanted to sell the skin there, so that he might buy a new calf with the proceeds. On the way he passed by a mill, and there sat a raven with broken wings, and out of pity he took him and wrapped him in the skin. As, however, the weather grew so bad and there was a storm of rain and wind, he could go no farther, and turned back to the mill and begged for shelter. The miller's wife was alone in the house, and said to the peasant, "Lay yourself on the straw there," and gave him a slice of bread with cheese on it. The peasant ate it, and lay down with his skin beside him, and the woman thought, "He is tired and has gone to sleep."

In the meantime came the parson; the miller's wife received him well, and said, "My husband is out, so we will have a feast." The peasant listened, and when he heard about feasting he was vexed that he had been forced to make do with a slice of bread with cheese on it. Then the woman served up four different things, roast meat, salad, cakes, and wine.

Just as they were about to sit down and eat, there was a knocking outside. The woman said, "Oh, heavens! It is my husband!" She quickly hid the roast meat inside the tiled stove, the wine under the pillow, the salad on the bed, the cakes under it, and the parson in the cupboard in the entrance. Then she opened the door for her husband, and said, "Thank heaven, you are back again! There is such a storm, it looks as if the world were coming to an end."

The miller saw the peasant lying on the straw, and asked, "What is that fellow doing there?"

"Ah," said the wife, "the poor knave came in the storm and rain, and begged for shelter, so I gave him a bit of bread and cheese, and showed him where the straw was."

The man said, "I have no objection, but be quick and get me something to eat."

The woman said, "But I have nothing but bread and cheese."

"I am contented with anything," replied the husband, "so far as I am concerned, bread and cheese will do," and looked at the peasant and said, "Come and eat some more with me."

The peasant did not require to be invited twice, but got up and ate. After this the miller saw the skin in which the raven was wrapped, lying on the ground, and asked, "What have you there?" The peasant answered, "I have a soothsayer inside it."

"Can he foretell anything to me?" said the miller.

"Why not?" answered the peasant, "But he only says four things, and the fifth he keeps to himself."

The miller was curious, and said, "Let him foretell something for once." Then the peasant pinched the raven's head, so that he croaked and made a noise like *krr*, *krr*. The miller said, "What did he say?"

The peasant answered, "In the first place, he says that there is some wine hidden under the pillow."

"Bless me!" cried the miller, and went there and found the wine. "Now go on," said he.

The peasant made the raven croak again, and said, "In the second place, he says that there is some roast meat in the tiled stove."

"Upon my word!" cried the miller, and went there, and found the roast meat.

The peasant made the raven prophesy still more, and said, "Thirdly, he says that there is some salad on the bed."

"That would be a fine thing!" cried the miller, and went there and found the salad.

At last the peasant pinched the raven once more till he croaked, and said, "Fourthly, he says that there are some cakes under the bed."

"That would be a fine thing!" cried the miller, and looked there, and found the cakes.

And now the two sat down to the table together, but the miller's wife was frightened to death, and went to bed and took all the keys with her. The miller would have much liked to know the fifth, but the little peasant said, "First, we will quickly eat the four things, for the fifth is something bad."

So they ate, and after that they bargained how much the miller was to give for the fifth prophesy, until they agreed on three hundred talkers. Then the peasant once more pinched the raven's head till he croaked loudly. The miller asked, "What did he say?"

The peasant replied, "He says that the Devil is hiding there in the cupboard in the entrance."

The miller said, "The Devil must go out," and opened the door; then the woman was forced to give up the keys, and the peasant unlocked the cupboard. The parson ran out as fast as he could, and the miller said, "It was true; I saw the black rascal with my own eyes." The peasant made off next morning by daybreak with the three hundred talkers.

At home the small peasant gradually launched out; he built a beautiful house, and the peasants said, "The small peasant has certainly been to the place where golden snow falls, and people carry the gold home in shovels."

Then the small peasant was brought before the Mayor, and bidden to say from where his wealth came. He answered, "I sold my cow's skin in the town, for three hundred talkers."

When the peasants heard that, they too wished to enjoy this great profit, and ran home, killed all their cows, and stripped off their skins in order to sell them in the town to the greatest advantage. The Mayor, however, said, "But my servant must go first."

When she came to the merchant in the town, he did not give her more than two talkers for a skin, and when the others came, he did not give them so much, and said, "What can I do with all these skins?"

Then the peasants were vexed that the small peasant should have thus deceived them, wanted to take vengeance on him, and accused him of this treachery before the Mayor. The innocent little peasant was unanimously sentenced to death, and was to be rolled into the water, in a barrel pierced full of holes. He was led forth, and a priest was brought who was to say a mass for his soul. The others were all obliged to retire to a distance, and when the peasant looked at the priest, he recognized the man who had been with the miller's wife. He said to him, "I set you free from the cupboard, set me free from the barrel."

At this same moment up came, with a flock of sheep, the very shepherd who the peasant knew had long been wishing to be Mayor, so he cried with all his might, "No, I will not do it; if the whole world insists on it, I will not do it!"

The shepherd hearing that, came up to him, and asked, "What are you about? What is it that you will not do?"

The peasant said, "They want to make me Mayor, if I will but put myself in the barrel, but I will not do it."

The shepherd said, "If nothing more than that is needed in order to be Mayor, I would get into the barrel at once."

The peasant said, "If you will get in, you will be Mayor."

The shepherd was willing, and got in, and the peasant shut the top down on him; then he took the shepherd's flock for himself, and drove it away. The parson went to the crowd, and declared that the mass had been said. Then they came and rolled the barrel towards the water.

When the barrel began to roll, the shepherd cried, "I am quite willing to be Mayor."

They believed that it was the peasant who was saying this, and answered, "That is what we intend, but first you shall go down below and look about you a little," and they rolled the barrel down into the water.

After that the peasants went home, and as they were entering the village, the small peasant also came quietly in, driving a flock of sheep and looking quite contented. Then the peasants were astonished, and said, "Peasant, from where do you come? Have you come out of the water?"

"Yes, truly," replied the peasant, "I sank deep, deep down, until at last I got to the bottom; I pushed the bottom out of the barrel, and crept out, and there were pretty meadows on which a number of lambs were feeding, and from there I brought this flock away with me."

Said the peasants, "Are there any more there?"

"Oh, yes," said he, "more than I could do anything with."

Then the peasants made up their minds that they too would fetch some sheep for themselves, a flock apiece, but the Mayor said, "I come first." So they went to the water together, and just then there were some of the small fleecy clouds in the blue sky, which are called little lambs, and they were reflected in the water, and the peasants cried, "We already see the sheep down below!"

The Mayor pressed forward and said, "I will go down first, and look about me, and if things look promising I'll call you." So he jumped in; *splash*! went the water; he made a sound as if he were calling them, and the whole crowd plunged in after him. Then the entire village was dead, and the small peasant, as sole heir, became a rich man.

62. THE QUEEN BEE

Two kings' sons once went out in search of adventures, and fell into a wild, disorderly way of living, so that they never came home again. The youngest, who was called Simpleton, set out to seek his brothers, but when at length he found them they mocked him for thinking that he could get through the world with his simplicity, when they both could not make their way, and yet were so much cleverer. They all three traveled away together, and came to an anthill. The two eldest wanted to destroy it, to see the little ants creeping about in their terror, and carrying their eggs away, but Simpleton said, "Leave the creatures in peace; I will not allow you to disturb them."

Then they went onwards and came to a lake, on which a great number of ducks were swimming. The two brothers wanted to catch a couple and roast them, but Simpleton would not permit it, and said, "Leave the creatures in peace, I will not allow you to kill them."

At length they came to a bee's nest, in which there was so much honey that it ran out of the trunk of the tree where it was. The two wanted to make a fire beneath the tree, and suffocate the bees in order to take away the honey, but Simpleton again stopped them and said, "Leave the creatures in peace, I will not allow you to burn them."

At length the three brothers arrived at a castle where stone horses were standing in the stables, and no human being was to be seen, and they went through all the halls until, quite at the end, they came to a door in which were three locks. In the middle of the door, however, there was a little pane, through which they could see into the room. There they saw a little grey man, who was sitting at a table. They called him, once, twice, but he did not hear; at last they called him for the third time, when he got up, opened the locks, and came out. He said nothing, however, but conducted them to a handsomely-spread table, and when they had eaten and drunk, he took each of them to a bedroom. Next morning the little grey man came to the eldest, beckoned to him, and conducted him to a stone table, on which were inscribed three tasks, that when performed could deliver the castle from enchantment. The first was that in the forest, beneath the moss, lay the princess's pearls, a thousand in number, which must be picked up, and if by sunset one single pearl was wanting, he who had looked for them would be turned into stone. The eldest went there, and sought the whole day, but when it came to an end, he had only found one hundred, and what was written on the table came to pass, and he was changed into stone. Next day, the second brother undertook the adventure; it did not, however, fare much better with him than with the eldest; he did not find more than two hundred pearls, and was changed to stone. At last the turn came to Simpleton also, who sought in the moss. It was, however, so hard to find the pearls, and he got on so slowly, that he seated himself on a stone, and wept. And while he was thus sitting, the King of the ants whose life he had once saved, came with five thousand ants, and before long the little creatures had got all the pearls together, and laid them in a heap. The second task, however, was to fetch out of the lake the key of the King's daughter's bedchamber. When Simpleton came to the lake, the ducks which he had saved, swam up to him, dived down, and brought the key out of the water. But the third task was the most difficult; from amongst the three sleeping daughters of the King he was to choose the youngest and dearest. They, however, resembled each other exactly, and were only to be distinguished by their having eaten different sweetmeats before they fell asleep; the eldest a bit of sugar; the second a little syrup; and the youngest a spoonful of honey. Then the Queen of the bees, which Simpleton had protected from the fire, came and tasted the lips of all three, and at last she remained sitting on the mouth which had eaten honey, and thus the King's son recognized the right princess. Then the enchantment was at an end; everything was released from sleep, and those who had been turned to stone received once more their natural forms. Simpleton married the youngest and sweetest princess, and after her father's death became King, and his two brothers received the two other sisters.

63. THE THREE FEATHERS

There was once upon a time a King who had three sons, of whom two were clever and wise, but the third did not speak much, and was simple, and was called the Simpleton. When the King had become old and weak, and was thinking of his end, he did not know which of his sons should inherit the kingdom after him. Then he said to them, "Go forth, and he who brings me the most beautiful carpet shall be King after my death." And that there should be no dispute amongst them, he took them outside his castle, blew three feathers in the air, and said, "You shall go as they fly." One feather flew to the east, the other to the west, but the third flew straight up and did not fly far, but soon fell to the ground. And now one brother went to the right, and the other to the left, and they mocked Simpleton, who was forced to stay where the third feather had fallen.

He sat down and was sad, then all at once he saw that there was a trapdoor close by the feather. He raised it up, found some steps, and went down them, and then he came to another door, knocked at it, and heard somebody inside calling,

"Little green maiden small,
Hopping here and there;
Hop to the door,
And quickly see who is there."

The door opened, and he saw a great, fat toad sitting, and round about her a crowd of little toads. The fat toad asked what he wanted? He answered, "I should like to have the prettiest and finest carpet in the world." Then she called a young one and said,

"Little green maiden small,
Hopping here and there,
Hop quickly and bring me
The great box here."

The young toad brought the box, and the fat toad opened it, and gave Simpleton a carpet out of it, so beautiful and so fine, that on the earth above, none could have been woven like it. Then he thanked her, and ascended again.

The two others had, however, looked on their youngest brother as so stupid that they believed he would find and bring nothing at all. "Why should we give ourselves a great deal of trouble to search?" said they, and got some coarse handkerchiefs from the first shepherds' wives whom they met, and carried them home to the King.

At the same time Simpleton also came back, and brought his beautiful carpet, and when the King saw it he was astonished, and said, "If justice be done, the Kingdom belongs to the youngest." But the two others let their father have no peace, and said that it was impossible that Simpleton, who lacked understanding in everything, should be King, and entreated him to make a new agreement with them.

Then the father said, "He who brings me the most beautiful ring shall inherit the kingdom," and led the three brothers out, and blew into the air three feathers, which they were to follow. Those of the two eldest again went east and west, and Simpleton's feather flew straight up, and fell down near the door into the earth. Then he went down again to the fat toad, and told her that he wanted the most beautiful ring. She at once ordered her great box to be brought, and gave him a ring out of it, which sparkled with jewels, and was so beautiful that no goldsmith on earth would have been able to make it.

The two eldest laughed at Simpleton for going to seek a golden ring. They gave themselves no trouble, but knocked the nails out of an old ring from the harness of a carriage horse, and took it to the King; but when Simpleton produced his golden ring, his father again said, "The Kingdom belongs to him."

The two eldest did not cease from tormenting the King until he made a third condition, and declared that the one who brought the most beautiful woman home, should have the Kingdom. He again blew the three feathers into the air, and they flew as before.

Then Simpleton without more ado went down to the fat toad, and said, "I am to take home the most beautiful woman!"

"Oh," answered the toad, "the most beautiful woman! She is not at hand at the moment, but still you shall have her." She gave him a yellow turnip which had been hollowed out, to which six mice were harnessed.

Then Simpleton said quite mournfully, "What am I to do with that?"

The toad answered, "Just put one of my little toads into it." Then he seized one at random out of the circle, and put her into the yellow coach, but hardly was she seated inside it than she turned into a wonderfully beautiful maiden, and the turnip into a coach, and the six mice into horses. So he kissed her, and drove off quickly with the horses, and took her to the King.

His brothers came afterwards; they had given themselves no trouble at all to seek beautiful girls, but had brought with them the first peasant women they chanced to meet. When the King saw them he said, "After my death the kingdom belongs to my youngest son."

But the two eldest deafened the King's ears with their clamor, "We cannot consent to Simpleton's being King," and demanded that the one whose wife could leap through a ring which hung in the center of the hall should have the Kingdom. They thought, "The peasant women can do that easily; they are strong enough, but the delicate maiden will jump herself to death." The aged King agreed to this. Then the two peasant women jumped, and jumped through the ring, but were so stout that they fell, and their coarse arms and legs broke in two. And then the pretty maiden whom Simpleton had brought with him, sprang, and sprang through as lightly as a deer, and all opposition had to cease. So he received the crown, and has ruled wisely for a length of time.

64. THE GOLDEN GOOSE

There was a man who had three sons, the youngest of whom was called Dummling, and was despised, mocked, and put down on every occasion.

It happened that the eldest wanted to go into the forest to hew wood, and before he went his mother gave him a beautiful sweet cake and a bottle of wine so that he might not suffer from hunger or thirst.

When he entered the forest he met a little grey-haired old man who bade him good day, and said, "Do give me a piece of cake out of your pocket, and let me have a drink of your wine; I am so hungry and thirsty."

But the prudent youth answered, "If I give you my cake and wine, I shall have none for myself; be off with you," and he left the little man standing and went on.

But when he began to hew down a tree, it was not long before he made a false stroke, and the axe cut him in the arm, so that he had to go home and have it bound up. And this was the little grey man's doing.

After this the second son went into the forest, and his mother gave him, like the eldest, a cake and a bottle of wine. The little old grey man met him likewise, and asked him for a piece of cake and a drink of wine. But the second son, too, said with much reason, "What I give you will be taken away from myself; be off!" and he left the little man standing and went on. His punishment, however, was not delayed; when he had made a few strokes at the tree he struck himself in the leg, so that he had to be carried home.

Then Dummling said, "Father, do let me go and cut wood."

The father answered, "Your brothers have hurt themselves by it, leave it alone, you do not understand anything about it." But Dummling begged so long that at last he said, "Just go then, you will get wiser by hurting yourself." His mother gave him a cake made with water and baked in the cinders, and with it a bottle of sour beer.

When he came to the forest the little old grey man met him likewise, and greeting him, said, "Give me a piece of your cake and a drink out of your bottle; I am so hungry and thirsty."

Dummling answered, "I have only cinder-cake and sour beer; if that pleases you, we will sit down and eat."

So they sat down, and when Dummling pulled out his cinder-cake, it was a fine sweet cake, and the sour beer had become good wine. So they ate and drank, and after that the little man said, "Since you have a good heart, and are willing to divide what you have, I will give you good luck. There stands an old tree, cut it down, and you will find something at the roots." Then the little man took leave of him.

Dummling went and cut down the tree, and when it fell there was a goose sitting in the roots with feathers of pure gold. He lifted her up, and taking her with him, went to an inn where he thought he would stay the night. Now the host had three daughters, who saw the goose and were curious to know what wonderful kind of bird it might be, and would have liked to have one of its golden feathers.

The eldest thought, "I shall soon find an opportunity of pulling out a feather," and as soon as Dummling had gone out she seized the goose by the wing, but her finger and hand remained sticking fast to it.

The second came soon afterwards, thinking only of how she might get a feather for herself, but she had scarcely touched her sister than she was held fast.

At last the third also came with the same intent, and the others screamed out, "Keep away; for goodness' sake keep away!"

But she did not understand why she was to keep away. "The others are there," she thought, "I may as well be there too," and ran to them; but as soon as she had touched her sister, she remained sticking fast to her. So they had to spend the night with the goose.

The next morning Dummling took the goose under his arm and set out, without troubling himself about the three girls who were hanging onto it. They were obliged to run after him continually, now left, now right, just as he was inclined to go.

In the middle of the fields the parson met them, and when he saw the procession he said, "For shame, you good-for-nothing girls, why are you running across the fields after this young man? Is that seemly?" At the same time he seized the youngest by the hand in order to pull her away, but as soon as he touched her he likewise stuck fast, and was himself obliged to run behind.

Before long the sexton came by and saw his master, the parson, running behind three girls. He was astonished at this and called out,

"Ho, your reverence, where do you go so quickly? Do not forget that we have a christening today!" and running after him he took him by the sleeve, but was also held fast to it.

While the five were trotting one behind the other, two laborers came with their hoes from the fields; the parson called out to them and begged that they would set him and the sexton free. But they had scarcely touched the sexton when they were held fast, and now there were seven of them running behind Dummling and the goose.

Soon afterwards he came to a city, where a king ruled who had a daughter who was so serious that no one could make her laugh. So he had put forth a decree that whoever should be able to make her laugh should marry her. When Dummling heard this, he went with his goose and all her train before the King's daughter, and as soon as she saw the seven people running on and on, one behind the other, she began to laugh quite loudly, and as if she would never leave off. Upon this Dummling asked to have her for his wife, and the wedding was celebrated. After the King's death, Dummling inherited the Kingdom and lived a long time contentedly with his wife.

65. THOUSANDFURS

There was once upon a time a King who had a wife with golden hair, and she was so beautiful that her equal was not to be found on earth. It came to pass that she lay ill, and as she felt that she must soon die, she called the King and said, "If you wish to marry again after my death, she must be as beautiful as I am, and have such golden hair as I have: this you must promise me." And after the King had promised her this she closed her eyes and died.

For a long time the King could not be comforted, and had no thought of taking another wife. At length his councilors said, "There is no helping it, the King must marry again, that we may have a Queen." And now messengers were sent about far and wide, to seek a bride who equaled the late Queen in beauty. In the whole world, however, none was to be found, and even if one had been found, still there would have been no one who had such golden hair. So the messengers came home as they went.

Now the King had a daughter, who was just as beautiful as her dead mother, and had the same golden hair. When she was grown up the King looked at her one day, and saw that in every respect she was like his late wife, and suddenly felt a violent love for her. Then he said to his councilors, "I will marry my daughter, for she is the counterpart of my late wife, otherwise I can find no bride who resembles her."

When the councilors heard that, they were shocked, and said, "God has forbidden a father to marry his daughter, no good can come from such a crime, and the Kingdom will be involved in the ruin."

The daughter was still more shocked when she became aware of her father's resolution, but hoped to change his mind. Then she said to him, "Before I fulfill your wish, I must have three dresses, one as golden as the sun, one as silvery as the moon, and one as bright as the stars; besides this, I wish for a mantle of a thousand different kinds of fur and hair joined together, and one of every kind of animal in your Kingdom must give a piece of his skin for it." But she thought, "To get that will be quite impossible, and thus I shall divert my father from his wicked intentions."

The King, however, did not give it up, and the cleverest maidens in his Kingdom had to weave the three dresses, one as golden as the sun, one as silvery as the moon, and one as bright as the stars, and his hunters had to catch one of every kind of animal in the whole of his kingdom, and take from it a piece of its skin, and out of these was made a mantle of a thousand different kinds of fur. At length, when all was ready, the King had the mantle brought, spread it out before her, and said, "The wedding shall be tomorrow."

When the King's daughter saw that there was no longer any hope of turning her father's heart, she resolved to run away from him. In the night while everyone was asleep, she got up, and took three different things from her treasures, a golden ring, a golden spinning wheel, and a golden reel. The three dresses of the sun, moon, and stars she put into a nutshell, put on her mantle of all kinds of fur, and blackened her face and hands with soot. Then she commended herself to God, and went away, and walked the whole night until she reached a great forest. And as she was tired, she got into a hollow tree, and fell asleep.

The sun rose, and she slept on, and she was still sleeping when it was full day. Then it so happened that the King to whom this forest belonged, was hunting in it. When his dogs came to the tree, they sniffed, and ran barking round about it. The King said to the hunters, "Just see what kind of wild beast has hidden itself in there."

The hunters obeyed his order, and when they came back they said, "A wondrous beast is lying in the hollow tree; we have never before seen one like it. Its skin is fur of a thousand different kinds, but it is lying asleep."

Said the King, "See if you can catch it alive, and then fasten it to the carriage, and we will take it with us."

When the hunters laid hold of the maiden, she awoke full of terror, and cried to them, "I am a poor child, deserted by father and mother; have pity on me, and take me with you."

Then said they, "Thousandfurs, you will be useful in the kitchen, come with us, and you can sweep up the ashes." So they put her in the carriage, and took her home to the royal palace. There they pointed out to her a closet under the stairs, where no daylight entered, and said, "Hairy animal, there you can live and sleep." Then she was sent into the kitchen, and there she carried wood and water, swept the hearth, plucked the fowls, picked the vegetables, raked the ashes, and did all the dirty work.

Thousandfurs lived there for a long time in great wretchedness. Alas, fair princess, what is to become of you now! It happened, however, that one day a feast was held in the palace, and she said to the cook, "May I go upstairs for a while, and look on? I will place myself outside the door."

The cook answered, "Yes, go, but you must be back here in half-an-hour to sweep the hearth."

Then she took her oil lamp, went into her den, took off her fur-dress, and washed the soot off her face and hands, so that her full beauty once more came to light. And she opened the nut, and took out her dress which shone like the sun, and when she had done that she went up to the festival, and everyone made way for her, for no one knew her, and thought no otherwise than that she was a king's daughter.

The King came to meet her, gave his hand to her, and danced with her, and thought in his heart, "My eyes have never yet seen anyone so beautiful!" When the dance was over she curtsied, and when the King looked round again she had vanished, and no one knew where. The guards who stood outside the palace were called and questioned, but no one had seen her.

She had, however, run into her little den, had quickly taken off her dress, made her face and hands black again, put on the fur-mantle, and again was Thousandfurs. And now when she went into the kitchen, and was about to get to her work and sweep up the ashes, the cook said, "Leave that alone till morning, and make me the soup for the King; I, too, will go upstairs awhile, and take a look; but let no hairs fall in, or in future you shall have nothing to eat."

So the cook went away, and Thousandfurs made the soup for the king, and made the bread soup the best she could, and when it was ready she fetched her golden ring from her little den, and put it in the bowl in which the soup was served. When the dancing was over, the King had his soup brought and ate it, and he liked it so much that it seemed to him he had never tasted better. But when he came to the bottom of the bowl, he saw a golden ring, and could not conceive how it could have got there. Then he ordered the cook to appear before him. The cook was terrified when he heard the order, and said to Thousandfurs, "You have certainly let a hair fall into the soup, and if you have, you shall be beaten for it."

When he came before the King the latter asked who had made the soup? The cook replied, "I made it."

But the King said, "That is not true, for it was much better than usual, and cooked differently."

He answered, "I must acknowledge that I did not make it, it was made by the rough animal."

The King said, "Go and bid it come up here."

When Thousandfurs came, the King said, "Who are you?"

"I am a poor girl who no longer has any father or mother."

He asked further, "Of what use are you in my palace?"

She answered, "I am good for nothing but to have boots thrown at my head."

He continued, "Where did you get the ring which was in the soup?"

She answered, "I know nothing about the ring." So the King could learn nothing, and had to send her away again.

After a while, there was another festival, and then, as before, Thousandfurs begged the cook for leave to go and look on. He answered, "Yes, but come back again in half-an-hour, and make the King the bread soup which he so much likes."

Then she ran into her den, washed herself quickly, and took out of the nut the dress which was as silvery as the moon, and put it on. Then she went up and was like a princess, and the King stepped forward to meet her, and rejoiced to see her once more, and as the dance was just beginning they danced it together. But when it ended, she again disappeared so quickly that the King could not observe where she went. She, however, sprang into her den, and once more made herself a hairy animal, and went into the kitchen to prepare the bread soup. When the cook had gone upstairs, she fetched the little golden spinning wheel, and put it in the bowl so that the soup covered it. Then it was taken to the King, who ate it, and liked it as much as before, and had the cook brought, who this time likewise was forced to confess that Thousandfurs had prepared the soup. Thousandfurs again came before the King, but she answered that she was good for nothing else but to have boots thrown at her head, and that she knew nothing at all about the little golden spinning wheel.

When, for the third time, the King held a festival, all happened just as it had done before. The cook said, "Surely, rough-skin, you are a witch, and always put something in the soup which makes it so good that the King likes it better than that which I cook," but as she begged so hard, he let her go up at the appointed time. And now she put on the dress which shone like the stars, and thus entered the hall. Again the King danced with the beautiful maiden, and thought that she had never yet been so beautiful. And while she was dancing, he contrived, without her noticing it, to slip a golden ring on her finger, and he had given orders that the dance should last a very long time. When it ended, he wanted to hold her fast by her hands, but she tore herself loose, and sprang away so quickly through the crowd that she vanished from his sight. She ran as fast as she could into her den beneath the stairs, but as she had been too long, and had stayed more than half-an-hour she could not take off her pretty dress, but only threw over it her fur-mantle, and in her haste she did not make herself quite black, but one finger remained white. Then Thousandfurs ran into the kitchen, and cooked the bread soup for the King, and as the cook was away, put her golden reel into it. When the King found the reel at the bottom of it, he had Thousandfurs summoned, and then he spied the white finger, and saw the ring which he had put on it during the dance. Then he grasped her by the hand, and held her fast, and when she wanted to release herself and run away, her mantle of fur opened a little, and the star-dress shone forth. The King clutched the mantle and tore it off. Then her golden hair shone forth, and she stood there in full splendor, and could no longer hide herself. And when she had washed the soot and ashes from her face, she was more beautiful than anyone who had ever been seen on earth. The King said, "You are my dear bride, and we will never again part from each other." Thereupon the marriage was solemnized, and they lived happily until their death.

66. *THE HARE'S BRIDE*

There was once a woman and her daughter who lived in a pretty garden with cabbages; and a little hare came into it, and during the wintertime ate all the cabbages. Then says the mother to the daughter, "Go into the garden, and chase the hare away."

The girl says to the little hare, "Sh-sh, hare, you are still eating up all our cabbages."

Says the hare, "Come, maiden, and seat yourself on my little hare's tail, and come with me into my little hare's hut." The girl will not do it.

Next day the hare comes again and eats the cabbages, then says the mother to the daughter, "Go into the garden, and drive the hare away."

The girl says to the hare, "Sh-sh, little hare, you are still eating all the cabbages."

The little hare says, "Maiden, seat yourself on my little hare's tail, and come with me into my little hare's hut." The maiden refuses.

The third day the hare comes again, and eats the cabbages. At this the mother says to the daughter, "Go into the garden, and chase the hare away."

Says the maiden, "Sh-sh, little hare, you are still eating all our cabbages."

Says the little hare, "Come, maiden, seat yourself on my little hare's tail, and come with me into my little hare's hut."

The girl seats herself on the little hare's tail, and then the hare takes her far away to his little hut, and says, "Now cook green cabbage and millet seed, and I will invite the wedding guests." Then all the wedding guests assembled. (Who were the wedding guests? That I can tell you as another told it to me. They were all hares, and the crow was there as parson to marry the bride and bridegroom, and the fox as clerk, and the altar was under the rainbow.)

The girl, however, was sad, for she was all alone. The little hare comes and says, "Open the doors, open the doors, the wedding guests are merry." The bride says nothing, but weeps. The little hare goes away. The little hare comes back and says, "Take off the lid, take off the lid, the wedding guests are hungry." The bride again says nothing, and weeps. The little hare goes away. The little hare comes back and says, "Take off the lid, take off the lid, the wedding guests are waiting." Then the bride says nothing, and the hare goes away, but she dresses a straw-doll in her clothes, and gives her a spoon to stir with, and sets her by the pan with the millet seed, and goes back to her mother. The little hare comes once more and says, "Take off the lid, take off the lid," and gets up, and strikes the doll on the head so that her cap falls off.

Then the little hare sees that it is not his bride, and goes away and is sorrowful.

67. *THE TWELVE HUNTERS*

There was once a King's son who was betrothed to a maiden whom he loved very much. And when he was sitting beside her and very happy, news came that his father lay sick and dying, and desired to see him once again before his end. Then he said to his beloved, "I must go now and leave you, I give you a ring as a remembrance of me. When I am King, I will return and fetch you."

So he rode away, and when he reached his father, the latter was dangerously ill, and near his death. He said to him, "Dear son, I wished to see you once again before my end, promise me to marry as I wish," and he named a certain King's daughter who was to be his wife.

The son was so upset that he did not think what he was doing, and said, "Yes, dear father, your will shall be done," and then the King shut his eyes, and died.

When the son had been proclaimed King, and the time of mourning was over, he was forced to keep the promise which he had given his father, and sent to the King's daughter to ask her hand in marriage, and she was promised to him.

His first betrothed heard of this, and fretted so much about his faithlessness that she nearly died. Then her father said to her, "Dearest child, why are you so sad? You shall have whatever you want."

She thought for a moment and said, "Dear father, I wish for eleven girls exactly like myself in face, figure, and size."

The father said, "If it is possible, your desire shall be fulfilled," and he ordered a search to be made of his whole kingdom, until eleven young maidens were found who exactly resembled his daughter in face, figure, and size.

When they came to the King's daughter, she had twelve suits of hunters's clothes made, all alike, and the eleven maidens had to put on the hunters's clothes, and she herself put on the twelfth suit. Then she took leave of her father, and rode away with them, and rode to the court of her former betrothed, whom she loved so dearly. Then she inquired if he required any hunters, and if he would take the whole of them into his service. The King looked at her and did not know her, but as they were such handsome fellows, he said, "Yes," and that he would willingly take them, and now they were the King's twelve hunters.

The King, however, had a lion which was a wondrous animal, for he knew all concealed and secret things. It came to pass that one evening he said to the King, "You think you have twelve hunters?"

"Yes," said the King, "they are twelve hunters."

The lion continued, "You are mistaken, they are twelve girls."

The King said, "That cannot be true! How will you prove that to me?"

"Oh, just let some peas be strewn in your anteroom," answered the lion, "and then you will soon see it. Men have a firm step, and when they walk over the peas none of them stir, but girls trip and skip, and drag their feet, and the peas roll about." The King was well pleased with the counsel, and caused the peas to be strewn.

There was, however, a servant of the King's who favored the hunters, and when he heard that they were going to be put to this test he went to them and repeated everything, and said, "The lion wants to make the King believe that you are girls."

Then the King's daughter thanked him, and said to her maidens, "Have some strength, and step firmly on the peas."

So next morning when the King had the twelve hunters called before him, and they came into the anteroom where the peas were lying, they stepped so firmly on them, and had such a strong, sure walk, that not one of the peas either rolled or stirred. Then they went away again, and the King said to the lion, "You have lied to me, they walk just like men."

The lion said, "They have got to know that they were going to be put to the test, and have assumed some strength. Just let twelve spinning wheels be brought into the anteroom some day, and they will go to them and be pleased with them, and that is what no man would do." The King liked the advice, and had the spinning wheels placed in the anteroom.

But the servant, who was well disposed to the hunters, went to them, and disclosed the project. Then when they were alone the King's daughter said to her eleven girls, "Have some constraint on yourselves, and do not look round at the spinning wheels." And next morning when the King had his twelve hunters summoned, they went through the anteroom, and never once looked at the spinning wheels. Then the King again said to the lion, "You have deceived me, they are men, for they have not looked at the spinning wheels."

The lion replied, "They have learnt that they were going to be put to the test, and have restrained themselves." The King, however, would no longer believe the lion.

The twelve hunters always followed the King to the chase, and his liking for them continually increased. Now it came to pass that once when they were out hunting, news came that the King's betrothed was approaching. When the true bride heard that, it hurt her so much that her heart was almost broken, and she fell fainting to the ground. The King thought something had happened to his dear hunter, ran up to him, wanted to help him, and drew his glove off. Then he saw the ring which he had given to his first bride, and when he looked in her face he recognized her. Then his heart was so touched that he kissed her, and when she opened her eyes he said, "You are mine, and I am your's, and no one in the world can alter that."

He sent a messenger to the other bride, and entreated her to return to her own kingdom, for he had a wife already, and a man who had just found an old dish did not require a new one. Soon the wedding was celebrated, and the lion was again taken into favor, because, after all, he had told the truth.

68. THE THIEF AND HIS MASTER

Hans wished to send his son to learn a trade, so he went into the church and prayed to our Lord God to know which would be most advantageous for him. Then the clerk got behind the altar, and said, "Thieving, thieving."

At this Hans goes back to his son, and tells him he is to learn thieving, and that the Lord God had said so. So he goes with his son to seek a man who is acquainted with thieving. They walk a long time and come into a great forest, where stands a little house with an old woman in it. Hans says, "Do you know of a man who is acquainted with thieving?"

"You can learn that here quite well," says the woman, "my son is a master of it."

So he speaks with the son, and asks if he knows thieving really well? The master-thief says, "I will teach him well. Come back when a year is over, and then if you recognize your son, I will take no payment at all for teaching him; but if you don't know him, you must give me two hundred talkers."

The father goes home again, and the son learns witchcraft and thieving, thoroughly. When the year is over, the father is full of anxiety to know how he is to recognize his son. As he is thus going about in his trouble, he meets a little dwarf, who says, "Man, what ails you, that you are always in such trouble?"

"Oh," says Hans, "a year ago I placed my son with a master-thief who told me I was to come back when the year was over, and that if I did not know my son when I saw him, I was to pay two hundred talkers; but if I did know him I was to pay nothing, and now I am afraid of not knowing him and can't tell where I am to get the money."

Then the dwarf tells him to take a small basket of bread with him, and to stand beneath the chimney. "There on the crossbeam is a basket, out of which a little bird is peeping, and that is your son."

Hans goes there, and throws a little basket full of black bread in front of the basket with the bird in it, and the little bird comes out, and looks up. "Hello, my son, are you here?" says the father, and the son is delighted to see his father, but the master-thief says, "The devil must have prompted you, or how could you have known your son?"

"Father, let us go now," said the youth.

Then the father and son set out homeward. On the way a carriage comes driving by, and the son says to his father, "I will change myself into a large greyhound, and then you can earn a great deal of money by me."

Then the gentleman calls from the carriage, "My man, will you sell your dog?"

"Yes," says the father.

"How much do you want for it?"

"Thirty talkers."

"Eh, man, that is too much, but as it is such a very fine dog I will have it." The gentleman takes it into his carriage, but when they have driven a little farther the dog springs out of the carriage through the window, and goes back to his father, and is no longer a greyhound.

They go home together. Next day there is a fair in the neighboring town, so the youth says to his father, "I will now change myself into a beautiful horse, and you can sell me; but when you have sold me, you must take off my bridle, or I cannot become a man again."

Then the father goes with the horse to the fair, and the master-thief comes and buys the horse for a hundred talkers, but the father forgets, and does not take off the bridle. So the man goes home with the horse, and puts it in the stable.

When the maid crosses the threshold, the horse says, "Take off my bridle, take off my bridle."

Then the maid stands still, and says, "What, can you speak?"

So she goes and takes the bridle off, and the horse becomes a sparrow, and flies out at the door, and the master becomes a sparrow also, and flies after him. Then they come together and cast lots, but the master loses, and changes himself to the water and is a fish. Then the youth also becomes a fish, and they cast lots again, and the master loses. So the master changes himself into a cock, and the youth becomes a fox, and bites the master's head off, and he died and has remained dead to this day.

69. *JORINDA AND JORINGEL*

There was once an old castle in the middle of a large and thick forest, and in it an old woman who was a witch dwelt all alone. In the daytime she changed herself into a cat or a screech-owl, but in the evening she took her proper shape again as a human being. She could lure wild beasts and birds to her, and then she killed and boiled and roasted them. If anyone came within one hundred paces of the castle he was obliged to stand still, and could not stir from the place until she bade him be free. But whenever an innocent maiden came within this circle, she changed her into a bird, and shut her up in a wickerwork cage, and carried the cage into a room in the castle. She had about seven thousand cages of rare birds in the castle.

Now, there was once a maiden who was called Jorinda, who was fairer than all other girls. She and a handsome youth named Joringel had promised to marry each other. They were still in the days of betrothal, and their greatest happiness was being together. One day in order that they might be able to talk together in quiet they went for a walk in the forest. "Take care," said Joringel, "that you do not go too near the castle."

It was a beautiful evening; the sun shone brightly between the trunks of the trees into the dark green of the forest, and the turtledoves sang mournfully upon the young boughs of the birch trees.

Jorinda wept now and then. She sat down in the sunshine and was sorrowful. Joringel was sorrowful too; they were as sad as if they were about to die. Then they looked around them, and were quite at a loss, for they did not know by which way they should go home. The sun was still half above the mountain and half set.

Joringel looked through the bushes, and saw the old walls of the castle close at hand. He was horror-stricken and filled with deadly fear. Jorinda was singing—

"My little bird, with the necklace red,
Sings sorrow, sorrow, sorrow,
He sings that the dove must soon be dead,
Sings sorrow, sor—jug, jug, jug."

Joringel looked for Jorinda. She was changed into a nightingale, and sang, "jug, jug, jug." A screech owl with glowing eyes flew three times round about her, and three times cried, "to-whoo, to-whoo, to-whoo!"

Joringel could not move: he stood there like a stone, and could neither weep nor speak, nor move hand or foot.

The sun had now set. The owl flew into the thicket, and directly afterwards there came out of it a crooked old woman, yellow and lean, with large red eyes and a hooked nose, the point of which reached to her chin. She muttered to herself, caught the nightingale, and took it away in her hand.

Joringel could neither speak nor move from the spot; the nightingale was gone. At last the woman came back, and said in a hollow voice, "Greetings, Zachiel. If the moon shines on the cage, Zachiel, let him loose at once."

Then Joringel was freed. He fell on his knees before the woman and begged that she would give him back his Jorinda, but she said that he should never have her again, and went away. He called, he wept, he lamented, but all in vain, "Ah, what is to become of me?"

Joringel went away, and at last came to a strange village; there he kept sheep for a long time. He often walked round and round the castle, but not too near it. At last he dreamt one night that he found a blood-red flower, in the middle of which was a beautiful large pearl; that he picked the flower and went with it to the castle, and that everything he touched with the flower was freed from enchantment; he also dreamt that by means of it he recovered his Jorinda.

In the morning, when he awoke, he began to seek over hill and dale if he could find such a flower. He sought until the ninth day, and then, early in the morning, he found the blood-red flower. In the middle of it there was a large dewdrop, as big as the finest pearl.

Day and night he journeyed with this flower to the castle. When he was within a hundred paces of it he was not held fast, but walked on to the door. Joringel was full of joy; he touched the door with the flower, and it sprang open. He walked in through the courtyard, and listened for the sound of the birds. At last he heard it. He went on and found the room from which it came, and there the witch was feeding the birds in the seven thousand cages.

When she saw Joringel she was angry, very angry, and scolded and spat poison and gall at him, but she could not come within two paces of him. He did not take any notice of her, but went and looked at the cages with the birds; but there were many hundred nightingales, how was he to find his Jorinda again?

Just then he saw the old woman quietly take away a cage with a bird in it, and go towards the door.

Swiftly he sprang towards her, touched the cage with the flower, and also the old woman. She could now no longer bewitch anyone; and Jorinda was standing there, clasping him round the neck, and she was as beautiful as ever!

70. THE THREE SONS OF FORTUNE

A father once called his three sons before him, and he gave to the first a cock, to the second a scythe, and to the third a cat. "I am already aged," said he, "my death is near, and I have wished to take thought for you before my end; money I have not, and what I now give you seems of little worth, but all depends on your making a sensible use of it. Seek out a country where such things are still unknown, and your fortune is made."

After the father's death the eldest went away with his cock, but wherever he came the cock was already known; in every town he saw from a long distance a cock, sitting upon the steeples and turning round with the wind, and in the villages he heard more than one crowing; no one would show any wonder at the creature, so that it did not look as if he would make his fortune by it.

At last, however, it happened that he came to an island where the people knew nothing about cocks, and did not even understand how to divide their time. They certainly knew when it was morning or evening, but at night, if they did not sleep through it, not one of them knew how to find out the time.

"Look!" said he, "What a proud creature! It has a ruby-red crown upon its head, and wears spurs like a knight; it calls you three times during the night, at fixed hours, and when it calls for the last time, the sun soon rises. But if it crows by broad daylight, then take notice, for there will certainly be a change of weather."

The people were well pleased; for a whole night they did not sleep, and listened with great delight as the cock at two, four, and six o'clock, loudly and clearly proclaimed the time. They asked if the creature were for sale, and how much he wanted for it? "About as much gold as an ass can carry," answered he. "A ridiculously small price for such a precious creature!" they cried unanimously, and willingly gave him what he had asked.

When he came home with his wealth his brothers were astonished, and the second said, "Well, I will go forth and see whether I cannot get rid of my scythe as profitably." But it did not look as if he would, for laborers met him everywhere, and they had scythes upon their shoulders as well as he.

At last, however, he chanced upon an island where the people knew nothing of scythes. When the corn was ripe there, they took cannon out to the fields and shot it down. Now this was rather an uncertain affair; many shot right over it, others hit the ears instead of the stems, and shot them away, whereby much was lost, and besides all this, it made a terrible noise. So the man set to work and mowed it down so quietly and quickly that the people opened their mouths with astonishment. They agreed to give him what he wanted for the scythe, and he received a horse laden with as much gold as it could carry.

And now the third brother wanted to take his cat to the right man. He fared just like the others; so long as he stayed on the mainland there was nothing to be done. Every place had cats, and there were so many of them that newborn kittens were generally drowned in the ponds.

At last he sailed over to an island, and it luckily happened that no cats had ever yet been seen there, and that the mice had got the upper hand so much that they danced upon the tables and benches whether the master were at home or not. The people complained bitterly of the plague; the King himself in his palace did not know how to secure himself against them; mice squeaked in every corner, and gnawed whatever they could lay hold of with their teeth. But now the cat began her chase, and soon cleared a couple of rooms, and the people begged the King to buy the wonderful beast for the country. The King willingly gave what was asked, which was a mule laden with gold and jewels, and the third brother came home with the greatest treasure of all.

The cat made herself merry with the mice in the royal palace, and killed so many that they could not be counted. At last she grew warm with the work and thirsty, so she stood still, lifted up her head and cried, "Mew! Mew!"

When they heard this strange cry, the King and all his people were frightened, and in their terror ran all at once out of the palace. Then the King took counsel what was best to be done; at last it was determined to send a herald to the cat, and demand that she should leave the palace, or if not, she was to expect that force would be used against her. The councilors said, "We would rather let ourselves be plagued with the mice, for to that misfortune we are accustomed, than give up our lives to such a monster as this."

A noble youth, therefore, was sent to ask the cat "whether she would peaceably quit the castle?" But the cat, whose thirst had become still greater, merely answered, "Mew! Mew!"

The youth understood her to say, "Most certainly not! Most certainly not!" and took this answer to the King.

"Then," said the councilors, "she shall yield to force." Cannon were brought out, and the palace was soon in flames. When the fire reached the room where the cat was sitting, she sprang safely out of the window; but the besiegers did not leave off until the whole palace was shot down to the ground.

71. HOW SIX MEN GOT ON IN THE WORLD

There was once a man who understood all kinds of arts; he served in war, and behaved well and bravely, but when the war was over he received his dismissal, and three farthings for his expenses on the way. "Stop," said he, "I shall not be content with this. If I can only meet with the right people, the King will have yet to give me all the treasure of the country."

Then full of anger he went into the forest, and saw a man standing there who had plucked up six trees as if they were blades of corn. He said to him, "Will you be my servant and go with me?"

"Yes," he answered, "but, first, I will take this little bundle of sticks home to my mother," and he took one of the trees, and wrapped it round the five others, lifted the bundle on his back, and carried it away.

Then he returned and went with his master, who said, "We two ought to be able to get through the world very well," and when they had walked on for a short while they found a hunter who was kneeling, had shouldered his gun, and was about to fire. The master said to him, "Hunter, what are you going to shoot?"

He answered, "Two miles from here a fly is sitting on the branch of an oak tree, and I want to shoot its left eye out."

"Oh, come with me," said the man, "if we three are together, we certainly ought to be able to get on in the world!"

The hunter was ready, and went with him, and they came to seven windmills whose sails were turning round with great speed, and yet no wind was blowing either on the right or the left, and no leaf was stirring. Then said the man, "I know not what is driving the windmills, not a breath of air is stirring," and he went onwards with his servants, and when they had walked two miles they saw a man sitting on a tree who was shutting one nostril, and blowing out of the other.

"Good gracious! what are you doing up there?"

He answered, "Two miles from here are seven windmills; look, I am blowing them till they turn round."

"Oh, come with me," said the man. "If we four are together, we shall carry the whole world before us!"

Then the blower came down and went with him, and after a while they saw a man who was standing on one leg and had taken off the other, and laid it beside him. Then the master said, "You have arranged things very comfortably to have a rest."

"I am a runner," he replied, "and to stop myself running far too fast, I have taken off one of my legs, for if I run with both, I go quicker than any bird can fly."

"Oh, go with me. If we five are together, we shall carry the whole world before us."

So he went with them, and it was not long before they met a man who wore a cap, but had put it over just one ear. Then the master said to him, "Gracefully, gracefully, don't stick your cap on one ear, you look just like a tom-fool!"

"I must not wear it otherwise," said he, "for if I set my hat straight, a terrible frost comes on, and all the birds in the air are frozen, and drop dead on the ground."

"Oh, come with me," said the master. "If we six are together, we can carry the whole world before us."

Now the six came to a town where the King had proclaimed that whoever ran a race with his daughter and won the victory, should be her husband, but whoever lost it, must lose his head. Then the man presented himself and said, "I will, however, let my servant run for me."

The King replied, "Then his life also must be staked, so that his head and yours are both set on the victory."

When that was settled and made secure, the man buckled the other leg on the runner, and said to him, "Now be nimble, and help us to win." It was fixed that the one who was first to bring some water from a far distant well was to be the victor. The runner received a pitcher, and the King's daughter one too, and they began to run at the same time, but in an instant, when the King's daughter had got a very little way, the people who were looking on could see no more of the runner, and it was just as if the wind had whistled by. In a short time he reached the well, filled his pitcher with water, and turned back. Halfway home, however, he was overcome with fatigue, and set down his pitcher, lay down, and fell asleep. He had, however, made a pillow of a horse's skull which was lying on the ground, in order that he might lie uncomfortably, and soon wake up again.

In the meantime the King's daughter, who could also run very well, quite as well as any ordinary mortal can, had reached the well, and was hurrying back with her pitcher full of water, and when she saw the runner lying there asleep, she was glad and said, "My rival is delivered over into my hands," emptied his pitcher, and ran on. And now all would have been lost if by good luck the hunter had not been standing at the top of the castle, and had not seen everything with his sharp eyes.

Then said he, "The King's daughter shall still not prevail against us," and he loaded his gun, and shot so cleverly, that he shot the horse's skull away from under the runner's head without hurting him. Then the runner awoke, leapt up, and saw that his pitcher was empty, and that the King's daughter was already far in advance. He did not lose heart, however, but ran back to the well with his pitcher, again drew some water, and was at home again, ten minutes before the King's daughter. "Look!" said he, "I have barely stretched my legs till now, it did not deserve to be called running before."

But it pained the King, and still more his daughter, that she should be carried off by a common disbanded soldier like that; so they took counsel with each other how to get rid of him and his companions. Then said the King to her, "I have thought of a way; don't be afraid, they shall not come back again." And he said to them, "You shall now make merry together, and eat and drink," and he conducted them to a room which had a floor of iron, and the doors also were of iron, and the windows were guarded with iron bars. There was a table in the room covered with delicious food, and the King said to them, "Go in, and enjoy yourselves."

And when they were inside, he ordered the doors to be shut and bolted. Then he sent for the cook, and commanded him to make a fire under the room until the iron became red-hot. This the cook did, and the six who were sitting at the table began to feel quite warm, and they thought the heat was caused by the food; but as it became still greater, and they wanted to get out, and found that the doors and windows were bolted, they became aware that the King must have an evil intention, and wanted to suffocate them.

"He shall not succeed, however," said the one with the cap. "I will cause a frost to come, that shall make the fire feel ashamed, and creep away." Then he put his cap on straight, and immediately there came such a frost that all heat disappeared, and the food on the dishes began to freeze. When an hour or two had passed by, and the King believed that they had perished in the heat, he had the doors opened to see them himself. But when the doors were opened, all six were standing there, alive and well, and said that they should very much like to get out to warm themselves, for the very food was fast frozen to the dishes with the cold.

Then, full of anger, the King went down to the cook, scolded him, and asked why he had not done what he had been ordered to do. But the cook replied, "There is heat enough there, just look yourself." Then the King saw that a fierce fire was burning under the iron room, and perceived that there was no getting the better of the six in this way.

Again the King considered how to get rid of his unpleasant guests, and had their chief brought and said, "If you will take gold and renounce my daughter, you shall have as much as you will."

"Oh, yes, Lord King," he answered, "give me as much as my servant can carry, and I will not ask for your daughter."

At this the King was satisfied, and the other continued, "In fourteen days, I will come and fetch it." Then he summoned together all the tailors in the whole kingdom, and they were to sit for fourteen days and sew a sack. And when it was ready, the strong one who could tear up trees had to take it on his back, and go with it to the King.

Then said the King, "Who can that strong fellow be who is carrying a bundle of linen on his back that is as big as a house?" and he was alarmed and said, "What a lot of gold he can carry away!"

Then he commanded a ton of gold to be brought; it took sixteen of his strongest men to carry it, but the strong one snatched it up in one hand, put it in his sack, and said, "Why don't you bring more at the same time? That hardly covers the bottom!" Then, little by little, the King had all his treasure brought there, and the strong one pushed it into the sack, and still the sack was not half full with it.

"Bring more," cried he, "these few crumbs don't fill it." Then seven thousand carts with gold had to be gathered together in the whole kingdom, and the strong one thrust them into his sack with the oxen still harnessed to them. "I will not look too closely," said he, "but will just take what comes, so long as the sack is full." When all that was inside, there was still room for a great deal more; then he said, "I will just make an end of this; I will tie up the sack even though it is not full." So he took it on his back, and went away with his comrades.

When the King now saw how one single man was carrying away the entire wealth of the country, he became enraged, and bade his horsemen mount and pursue the six, and ordered them to take the sack away from the strong one. Two regiments speedily overtook the six, and called out, "You are prisoners, put down the sack with the gold, or you will all be cut to pieces!"

"What say you?" cried the blower, "That we are prisoners! Rather than that should happen, all of you shall dance about in the air." And he closed one nostril, and with the other blew on the two regiments. Then they were driven away from each other, and carried into the blue sky over all the mountains, one here, the other there.

One sergeant cried for mercy; he had nine wounds, and was a brave fellow who did not deserve ill treatment. The blower stopped a little so that he came down without injury, and then the blower said to him, "Now go home to your King, and tell him he had better send some more horsemen, and I will blow them all into the air."

When the King was informed of this he said, "Let the rascals go. They have the best of it." Then the six carried the riches home, divided it amongst them, and lived in content until their death.

72. THE WOLF AND THE MAN

Once on a time the fox was talking to the wolf about the strength of man; how no animal could withstand him, and how all were obliged to employ cunning in order to preserve themselves from him. Then the wolf answered, "If I had but the chance of seeing a man for once, I would set on him all the same."

"I can help you to do that," said the fox. "Come to me early tomorrow morning, and I will show you one."

The wolf presented himself early, and the fox took him out on the road by which the hunters went daily. First came an old discharged soldier. "Is that a man?" inquired the wolf.

"No," answered the fox, "that *was* one."

Afterwards came a little boy who was going to school. "Is that a man?"

"No, that is going to be one."

At length came a hunter with his double-barreled gun at his back, and knife by his side. Said the fox to the wolf, "Look, there comes a man, you must attack him, but I will take myself off to my hole."

The wolf then rushed on the man. When the hunter saw him he said, "It is a pity that I have not loaded with a bullet," aimed, and fired his small shot in his face. The wolf made a very wry face, but did not let himself be frightened, and attacked him again, on which the hunter gave him the second barrel. The wolf swallowed his pain, and rushed on the hunter, but he drew out his bright knife, and gave him a few cuts with it right and left, so that, bleeding everywhere, he ran howling back to the fox.

"Well, brother wolf," said the fox, "how have you got on with man?"

"Ah!" replied the wolf, "I never imagined the strength of man to be what it is! First, he took a stick from his shoulder, and blew into it, and then something flew into my face which tickled me terribly; then he breathed once more into the stick, and it flew into my nose like lightning and hail; when I was quite close, he drew a white rib out of his side, and he beat me with it till I was all but left lying dead."

"See what a braggart you are!" said the fox. "You have overreached yourself. You throw your hatchet so far that you cannot fetch it back again!"

73. THE WOLF AND THE FOX

The wolf had the fox with him, and whatever the wolf wished, that the fox was compelled to do, for he was weaker, and he would gladly have been rid of his master. It chanced that once as they were going through the forest, the wolf said, "Red fox, get me something to eat, or else I will eat you yourself."

Then the fox answered, "I know a farmyard where there are two young lambs; if you are inclined, we will fetch one of them."

That suited the wolf, and they went there, and the fox stole the little lamb, took it to the wolf, and went away. The wolf devoured it, but was not satisfied with one; he wanted the other as well, and went to get it. Since, however, he did it so awkwardly, the mother of the little lamb heard him, and began to cry out terribly, and to bleat so that the farmer came running there. They found the wolf, and beat him so mercilessly, that he went to the fox limping and howling. "You have misled me finely," said he, "I wanted to fetch the other lamb, and the country folks surprised me, and have beaten me to a jelly."

The fox replied, "Why are you such a glutton?"

Next day they again went into the country, and the greedy wolf once more said, "Red fox, get me something to eat, or I will eat you yourself."

Then answered the fox, "I know a farmhouse where the wife is baking pancakes tonight; we will get some of them for ourselves." They went there, and the fox slipped round the house, and peeped and sniffed about until he discovered where the dish was, and then drew down six pancakes and carried them to the wolf. "There is something for you to eat," said he to him, and then went his way.

The wolf swallowed down the pancakes in an instant, and said, "They make one want more," and went back and tore the whole dish down so that it broke in pieces. This made such a great noise that the woman came out, and when she saw the wolf she called the people, who hurried there, and beat him as long as their sticks would hold together, till with two lame legs, and howling loudly, he got back to the fox in the forest. "How abominably you have misled me!" cried he, "The peasants caught me, and tanned my skin for me."

But the fox replied, "Why are you such a glutton?"

On the third day, when they were out together, and the wolf could only limp along painfully, he again said, "Red fox, get me something to eat, or I will eat you yourself."

The fox answered, "I know a man who has been killing, and the salted meat is lying in a barrel in the cellar; we will get that."

Said the wolf, "I will go when you do, that you may help me if I am not able to get away."

"I am willing," said the fox, and showed him the bypaths and ways by which at length they reached the cellar.

There was meat in abundance, and the wolf attacked it instantly and thought, "There is plenty of time before I need leave off!" The fox liked it also, but looked about everywhere, and often ran to the hole by which they had come in, and tried if his body was still thin enough to slip through it. The wolf said, "Dear fox, tell me why you are running here and there so much, and jumping in and out?"

"I must see that no one is coming," replied the crafty fellow. "Don't eat too much!"

Then said the wolf, "I shall not leave until the barrel is empty." In the meantime the farmer, who had heard the noise of the fox's jumping, came into the cellar. When the fox saw him he was out of the hole in one bound. The wolf wanted to follow him, but he had made himself so fat with eating that he could no longer get through, but stuck fast. Then came the farmer with a cudgel and struck him dead, but the fox bounded into the forest, glad to be rid of the old glutton.

74. THE FOX AND HIS COUSIN

The wolf gave birth to a cub and invited the fox to be godfather. "After all, he is a near relative of ours," said she, "he has a good understanding, and much talent; he can instruct my little son, and help him forward in the world."

The fox, too, appeared quite honest, and said, "Dear cousin, I thank you for the honor which you are doing me; I will, however, conduct myself in such a way that you shall be repaid for it." He enjoyed himself at the feast, and made merry; afterwards he said, "Dear cousin wolf, it is our duty to take care of the child, it must have good food that it may be strong. I know a farm from which we might fetch a nice morsel."

The wolf was pleased with the ditty, and she went out with the fox to the farmyard. He pointed out the barn from afar, and said, "You will be able to creep in there without being seen, and in the meantime I will look about on the other side to see if I can pick up a chicken."

He, however, did not go there, but sat down at the entrance to the forest, stretched his legs and rested. The wolf crept into the stable. A dog was lying there, and it made such a noise that the peasants came running out, caught cousin wolf, and poured a strong burning mixture, which had been prepared for washing, over her skin. At last she escaped, and dragged herself outside. There lay the fox, who pretended to be full of complaints, and said, "Ah, dear cousin wolf, how ill I have fared, the peasants have fallen on me, and have broken every limb I have; if you do not want me to lie where I am and perish, you must carry me away." The wolf herself was only able to go away slowly, but she was in such concern about the fox that she took him on her back, and slowly carried him perfectly safe and sound to her house.

Then the fox cried to her, "Farewell, dear cousin, may the roasting you have had do you good," laughed heartily at her, and bounded off.

75. THE FOX AND THE CAT

It happened that the cat met the fox in a forest, and as she thought to herself, "He is clever and full of experience, and much esteemed in the world," she spoke to him in a friendly way. "Good day, dear Mr. Fox, how are you? How is all with you? How are you getting through this dear season?"

The fox, full of all kinds of arrogance, looked at the cat from head to foot, and for a long time did not know whether he would give any answer or not. At last he said, "Oh, you wretched whisker-cleaner, you piebald fool, you hungry mouse-hunter, what can you be thinking of? Do you venture to ask how I am getting on? What have you learnt? How many arts do you understand?"

"I understand but one," replied the cat, modestly.

"What art is that?" asked the fox.

"When the hounds are following me, I can spring into a tree and save myself."

"Is that all?" said the fox. "I am master of a hundred arts, and also have a sackful of cunning. You make me sorry for you; come with me, I will teach you how people get away from the hounds."

Just then came a hunter with four dogs. The cat sprang nimbly up a tree, and sat down on top of it, where the branches and foliage quite concealed her. "Open your sack of cunning, Mr. Fox, open your sack," cried the cat to him, but the dogs had already seized him, and were holding him fast. "Ah, Mr. Fox," cried the cat. "You with your hundred arts are left in the lurch! Had you been able to climb like me, you would not have lost your life."

76. THE PINK

There was once on a time a Queen to whom God had given no children. Every morning she went into the garden and prayed to God in heaven to bestow on her a son or a daughter. Then an angel from heaven came to her and said, "Be at rest, you shall have a son with the power of wishing, so that whatever in the world he wishes for, that shall he have."

Then she went to the King, and told him the joyful tidings, and when the time came she gave birth to a son, and the King was filled with gladness. Every morning she went with the child to the garden where the wild beasts were kept, and washed herself there in a clear stream. It happened one day when the child was a little older, that it was lying in her arms and she fell asleep. Then came the old cook, who knew that the child had the power of wishing, and stole it away, and he took a hen, and cut it in pieces, and dropped some of its blood on the Queen's apron and on her dress. Then he carried the child away to a secret place, where a nurse was obliged to suckle it, and he ran to the King and accused the Queen of having allowed her child to be taken from her by the wild beasts. When the King saw the blood on her apron, he believed this, fell into such a passion that he ordered a high tower to be built, in which neither sun nor moon could be seen, and had his wife put into it, and walled up. Here she was to stay for seven years without meat or drink, and die of hunger. But God sent two angels from heaven in the shape of white doves, which flew to her twice a day, and carried her food until the seven years were over.

The cook, however, thought to himself, "If the child has the power of wishing, and I am here, he might very easily get me into trouble." So he left the palace and went to the boy, who was already big enough to speak, and said to him, "Wish for a beautiful palace for yourself with a garden, and all else that pertains to it." Scarcely were the words out of the boy's mouth, when everything was there that he had wished for. After a while the cook said to him, "It is not good for you to be so alone, wish for a pretty girl as a companion." Then the King's son wished for one, and she immediately stood before him, and was more beautiful than any painter could have painted her. The two played together, and loved each other with all their hearts, and the old cook went out hunting like a nobleman.

The thought, however, occurred to him that the King's son might someday wish to be with his father, and thus bring him into great peril. So he went out and took the maiden aside, and said, "Tonight when the boy is asleep, go to his bed and plunge this knife into his heart, and bring me his heart and tongue, and if you do not do it, you shall lose your life."

Thereupon he went away, and when he returned next day she had not done it, and said, "Why should I shed the blood of an innocent boy who has never harmed anyone?"

The cook once more said, "If you do not do it, it shall cost you your own life."

When he had gone away, she had a little deer brought to her, and ordered her to be killed, and took her heart and tongue, and laid them on a plate, and when she saw the old man coming, she said to the boy, "Lie down in your bed, and draw the covers over you."

Then the wicked wretch came in and said, "Where are the boy's heart and tongue?"

The girl reached the plate to him, but the King's son threw off the quilt, and said, "You old sinner, why did you want to kill me? Now I will pronounce your sentence. You shall become a black poodle and have a gold collar round your neck, and shall eat burning coals, till the flames burst forth from your throat." And when he had spoken these words, the old man was changed into a poodle dog, and had a gold collar round his neck, and the cooks were ordered to bring up some live coals, and these he ate, until the flames broke forth from his throat.

The King's son remained there a short while longer, and he thought of his mother, and wondered if she were still alive. At length he said to the maiden, "I will go home to my own country; if you will go with me, I will provide for you."

"Ah," she replied, "the way is so long, and what shall I do in a strange land where I am unknown?" As she did not seem quite willing, and as they could not be parted from each other, he wished that she might be changed into a beautiful pink, and took her with him.

Then he went away to his own country, and the poodle had to run after him. He went to the tower in which his mother was confined, and as it was so high, he wished for a ladder which would reach up to the very top. Then he mounted up and looked inside, and cried, "Beloved mother, Lady Queen, are you still alive, or are you dead?"

She answered, "I have just eaten, and am still satisfied," for she thought the angels were there.

Said he, "I am your dear son, whom the wild beasts were said to have torn from your arms; but I am alive still, and will speedily rescue you."

Then he descended again, and went to his father, and had himself announced as a strange hunter, and asked if he could enter his service. The King said yes, if he was skillful and could get game for him, he should come join him, but that deer had never taken up their quarters in any part of the district or country. Then the hunter promised to procure as much game for him as he could possibly use at the royal table. So he summoned all the hunters together, and bade them go out into the forest with him. And he went with them and made them form a great circle, open at one end where he stationed himself, and began to wish. Two hundred deer and more came running inside the circle at once, and the hunters shot them. Then they were all placed on sixty country wagons, and driven home to the King, and for once he was able to deck his table with game, after having had none at all for years.

Now the King felt great joy at this, and commanded that his entire household should eat with him next day, and made a great feast. When they were all assembled together, he said to the hunter, "As you are so clever, you shall sit by me."

He replied, "Lord King, your majesty must excuse me, I am a poor hunter."

But the King insisted on it, and said, "You shall sit by me," until he did it.

While he was sitting there, he thought of his dearest mother, and wished that one of the King's principal servants would begin to speak of her, and would ask how it was faring with the Queen in the tower, and if she were alive still, or had perished. Hardly had he formed the wish than the marshal began, and said, "Your majesty, we live joyously here, but how is the Queen living in the tower? Is she still alive, or has she died?"

But the King replied, "She let my dear son be torn to pieces by wild beasts; I will not have her named."

Then the hunter arose and said, "Gracious lord father, she is alive still, and I am her son, and I was not carried away by wild beasts, but by that wretch the old cook, who tore me from her arms when she was asleep, and sprinkled her apron with the blood of a chicken." Thereupon he took the dog with the golden collar, and said, "That is the wretch!" and caused live coals to be brought, and these the dog was compelled to devour before the sight of all, until flames burst forth from its throat. At this the hunter asked the King if he would like to see the dog in his true shape, and wished him back into the form of the cook, in which he stood immediately, with his white apron, and his knife by his side. When the King saw him he fell into a passion, and ordered him to be cast into the deepest dungeon.

Then the hunter spoke further and said, "Father, will you see the maiden who brought me up so tenderly and who was afterwards to murder me, but did not do it, though her own life depended on it?"

The King replied, "Yes, I would like to see her."

The son said, "Most gracious father, I will show her to you in the form of a beautiful flower," and he thrust his hand into his pocket and brought forth the pink, and placed it on the royal table, and it was so beautiful that the King had never seen one to equal it. Then the son said, "Now I will show her to you in her own form," and wished that she might become a maiden, and she stood there looking so beautiful that no painter could have made her look more so.

And the King sent two waiting-maids and two attendants into the tower, to fetch the Queen and bring her to the royal table. But when she was led in she ate nothing, and said, "The gracious and merciful God who has supported me in the tower, will speedily release me." She lived three days more, and then died happily, and when she was buried, the two white doves which had brought her food to the tower, and were angels of heaven, followed her body and seated themselves on her grave. The aged King ordered the cook to be torn in four pieces, but grief consumed the King's own heart, and he soon died. His son married the beautiful maiden whom he had brought with him as a flower in his pocket, and whether they are still alive or not, is known to God.

77. CLEVER GRETEL

There was once a cook named Gretel, who wore shoes with red heels, and when she walked out with them on, she turned herself this way and that, and thought, "You certainly are a pretty girl!" And when she came home she drank, in her gladness of heart, a gulp of wine, and as wine excites a desire to eat, she tasted the best of whatever she was cooking until she was satisfied, and said, "The cook must know what the food is like."

It came to pass that the master one day said to her, "Gretel, there is a guest coming this evening; prepare me two fowls very daintily."

"I will see to it, master," answered Gretel. She killed two fowls, scalded them, plucked them, put them on the spit, and towards evening set them before the fire, that they might roast. The fowls began to turn brown, and were nearly ready, but the guest had not yet arrived.

Then Gretel called out to her master, "If the guest does not come, I must take the fowls away from the fire, but it will be a sin and a shame if they are not eaten directly, when they are juiciest."

The master said, "I will run myself, and fetch the guest."

When the master had turned his back, Gretel laid the spit with the fowls on one side, and thought, "Standing so long by the fire there, makes one hot and thirsty; who knows when they will come? Meanwhile, I will run into the cellar, and take a drink." She ran down, took a jug, said, "God bless it to your use, Gretel," and took a good drink, and took yet another hearty drink.

Then she went and put the fowls down again to the fire, basted them, and drove the spit merrily round. But as the roast meat smelled so good, Gretel thought, "Something might be wrong, it ought to be tasted!" She touched it with her finger, and said, "Ah! How good fowls are! It certainly is a sin and a shame that they are not eaten directly!" She ran to the window, to see if the master was not coming with his guest, but she saw no one, and went back to the fowls and thought, "One of the wings is burning! I had better take it off and eat it." So she cut it off, ate it, and enjoyed it, and once she had, she thought, "The other must go down too, or else master will observe that something is missing." When the two wings were eaten, she went and looked for her master, and did not see him.

It suddenly occurred to her, "Who knows? They are perhaps not coming at all, and have turned in somewhere." Then she said, "Hallo, Gretel, enjoy yourself, one fowl has been cut into, take another drink, and eat it up entirely; when it is eaten you will have some peace, why should God's good gifts be spoiled?" So she ran into the cellar again, took an enormous drink and ate up the one chicken in great glee. When one of the chickens was swallowed down, and still her master did not come, Gretel looked at the other and said, "Where one is, the other should be likewise, the two go together; what's right for the one is right for the other; I think if I were to take another drink it would do me no harm." So she took another hearty drink, and let the second chicken rejoin the first.

While she was just in the best of the eating, her master came and cried, "Hurry up, Gretel, the guest is coming directly after me!"

"Yes, sir, I will soon serve up," answered Gretel. Meantime the master looked to see that the table was properly laid, and took the great knife, with which he was going to carve the chickens, and sharpened it on the steps. Presently the guest came, and knocked politely and courteously at the door. Gretel ran, and looked to see who was there, and when she saw the guest, she put her finger to her lips and said, "Hush! Hush! Get away as quickly as you can, if my master catches you it will be bad for you; he certainly did ask you to supper, but his intention is to cut off your two ears. Just listen how he is sharpening the knife for it!"

The guest heard the sharpening, and hurried down the steps again as fast as he could. Gretel was not idle; she ran screaming to her master, and cried, "You have invited a fine guest!"

"Eh, why, Gretel? What do you mean by that?"

"Yes," said she, "he has taken the chickens which I was just going to serve up, off the dish, and has run away with them!"

"That's a nice trick!" said her master, and lamented the fine chickens. "If he had but left me one, so that something remained for me to eat." He called to him to stop, but the guest pretended not to hear. Then he ran after him with the knife still in his hand, crying, "Just one, just one," meaning that the guest should leave him just one chicken, and not take both. The guest, however, thought no otherwise than that he was to give up one of his ears, and ran as if fire were burning under him, in order to take them both home with him.

78. THE OLD MAN AND HIS GRANDSON

There was once a very old man, whose eyes had become dim, his ears dull of hearing, his knees trembled, and when he sat at dinner he could hardly hold the spoon, and spilled the broth upon the tablecloth or let it run out of his mouth. His son and his son's wife were disgusted at this, so the old grandfather at last had to sit in the corner behind the stove, and they gave him his food in an earthenware bowl, and not even enough of it. And he used to look towards the table with his eyes full of tears. Once, too, his trembling hands could not hold the bowl, and it fell to the ground and broke. The young wife scolded him, but he said nothing and only sighed. Then they bought him a wooden bowl for a few half-pence, out of which he had to eat.

They were once sitting thus when the little grandson of four years old began to gather together some bits of wood upon the ground. "What are you doing there?" asked the father.

"I am making a little trough," answered the child, "for father and mother to eat out of when I am big."

The man and his wife looked at each other for a while, and presently began to cry. Then they took the old grandfather to the table, and from then on always let him eat with them, and likewise said nothing if he did spill a little of anything.

79. *THE WATER NIXIE*

A little brother and sister were once playing by a well, and while they were thus playing, they both fell in. A water nixie lived down below, who said, "Now I have got you, now you shall work hard for me!" and carried them off with her. She gave the girl dirty tangled flax to spin, and she had to fetch water in a bucket with a hole in it, and the boy had to hew down a tree with a blunt axe, and they got nothing to eat but dumplings as hard as stones. Then at last the children became so impatient, that they waited until one Sunday, when the nixie was at church, and ran away. But when church was over, the nixie saw that the birds had flown, and followed them with great strides. The children saw her from afar, and the girl threw a brush behind her which formed an immense hill of bristles, with thousands and thousands of spikes, over which the nixie was forced to scramble with great difficulty; at last, however, she got over. When the children saw this, the boy threw behind him a comb which made a great hill of combs with a thousand times a thousand teeth, but the nixie managed to keep herself steady on them, and at last crossed over that. Then the girl threw behind her a looking-glass which formed a hill of mirrors, and was so slippery that it was impossible for the nixie to cross it. Then she thought, "I will go home quickly and fetch my axe, and cut the hill of glass in half." Long before she returned, however, and had hewn through the glass, the children had escaped to a great distance, and the water nixie was obliged to retreat to her well again.

80. THE DEATH OF THE LITTLE HEN

Once upon a time the little hen went with the little cock to the nuthill, and they agreed together that whoever of them found a kernel of a nut should share it with the other. Then the hen found a large, large nut, but said nothing about it, intending to eat the kernel herself. The kernel, however, was so large that she could not swallow it, and it remained sticking in her throat, so that she was alarmed lest she should be choked. Then she cried, "Cock, I entreat you to run as fast you can, and fetch me some water, or I shall choke."

The little cock did run as fast as he could to the spring, and said, "Stream, you are to give me some water; the little hen is lying on the nuthill, and she has swallowed a large nut, and is choking."

The well answered, "First run to the bride, and get her to give you some red silk."

The little cock ran to the bride and said, "Bride, you are to give me some red silk; I want to give red silk to the well, the well is to give me some water, I am to take the water to the little hen who is lying on the nuthill and has swallowed a great kernel, and is choking on it."

The bride answered, "First run and bring me my little wreath which is hanging to a willow." So the little cock ran to the willow, and drew the wreath from the branch and took it to the bride, and the bride gave him some water for it. Then the little cock took the water to the hen, but when he got there the hen had choked in the meantime, and lay there dead and motionless. Then the cock was so distressed that he cried aloud, and every animal came to lament the little hen, and six mice built a little carriage to carry her to her grave, and when the carriage was ready they harnessed themselves to it, and the cock drove.

On the way, however, they met the fox, who said, "Where are you going, little cock?"

"I am going to bury my little hen."

"May I drive with you?"

"Yes, but seat yourself at the back of the carriage, for in the front my little horses could not drag you." Then the fox seated himself at the back, and after that the wolf, the bear, the stag, the lion, and all the beasts of the forest did the same. Then the procession went onwards, and they reached the stream.

"How are we to get over?" said the little cock.

A straw was lying by the stream, and it said, "I will lay myself across, and you shall drive over me." But when the six mice came to the bridge, the straw slipped and fell into the water, and the six mice all fell in and were drowned.

Then they were again in difficulty, and a coal came and said, "I am large enough, I will lay myself across and you shall drive over me." So the coal also laid itself across the water, but unfortunately just touched it a little, on which the coal hissed, was extinguished and died.

When a stone saw that, it took pity on the little cock, wished to help him, and laid itself over the water. Then the cock drew the carriage himself, but when he got it over and reached the other shore with the dead hen, and was about to draw over the others who were sitting behind as well, there were too many of them, the carriage ran back, and they all fell into the water together, and were drowned. Then the little cock was left alone with the dead hen, and dug a grave for her and laid her in it, and made a mound above it, on which he sat down and fretted until he died too, and then everyone was dead.

81. BROTHER LUSTIG

There was once a great war, and when it came to an end, many soldiers were discharged. Then Brother Lustig also received his dismissal, and besides that, nothing but a small loaf of bread, and four kreuzers in money, with which he departed. St. Peter had, however, placed himself in his way in the shape of a poor beggar, and when Brother Lustig came up, he begged alms of him. Brother Lustig replied, "Dear beggar, what am I to give you? I have been a soldier, and have received my dismissal, and have nothing but this little loaf of bread, and four kreuzers of money; when that is gone, I shall have to beg as well as you. Still I will give you something." Thereupon he divided the loaf into four parts, and gave the apostle one of them, and a kreuzer likewise. St. Peter thanked him, went onwards, and threw himself again in the soldier's way as a beggar, but in another shape; and when he came up begged a gift of him as before. Brother Lustig spoke as he had done before, and again gave him a quarter of the loaf and one kreuzer. St. Peter thanked him, and went onwards, but for the third time placed himself in another shape as a beggar on the road, and spoke to Brother Lustig. Brother Lustig gave him also the third quarter of bread and the third kreuzer. St. Peter thanked him, and Brother Lustig went onwards, and had but a quarter of the loaf, and one kreuzer. With that he went into an inn, ate the bread, and ordered one kreuzer's worth of beer. When he had had it, he journeyed onwards, and then St. Peter, who had assumed the appearance of a discharged soldier, met and spoke to him thus: "Good day, comrade, can you not give me a bit of bread, and a kreuzer to get a drink?"

"Where am I to procure it?" answered Brother Lustig; "I have been discharged, and I got nothing but a loaf of bread and four kreuzers in money. I met three beggars on the road, and I gave each of them a quarter of my bread, and one kreuzer. The last quarter I ate in the inn, and had a drink with the last kreuzer. Now my pockets are empty, and if you also have nothing we can go a-begging together."

"No," answered St. Peter, "we need not do that. I know a little about medicine, and I will soon earn as much as I require by that."

"Indeed," said Brother Lustig, "I know nothing of that, so I must go and beg alone."

"Just come with me," said St. Peter, "and if I earn anything, you shall have half of it."

"All right," said Brother Lustig, so they went away together.

Then they came to a peasant's house inside which they heard loud lamentations and cries; so they went in, and there the husband was lying sick unto death, and very near his end, and his wife was crying and weeping quite loudly. "Stop that howling and crying," said St. Peter, "I will make the man well again," and he took a salve out of his pocket, and healed the sick man in a moment, so that he could get up, and was in perfect health. In great delight the man and his wife said, "How can we reward you? What shall we give you?"

But St. Peter would take nothing, and the more the peasant folks offered him, the more he refused. Brother Lustig, however, nudged St. Peter, and said, "Take something; sure enough we are in need of it."

At length the woman brought a lamb and said to St. Peter that he really must take that, but he would not. Then Brother Lustig gave him a poke in the side, and said, "Do take it, you stupid fool; we are in great want of it!"

Then St. Peter said at last, "Well, I will take the lamb, but I won't carry it; if you will insist on having it, you must carry it."

"That is nothing," said Brother Lustig. "I will easily carry it," and took it on his shoulder. Then they departed and came to a wood, but Brother Lustig had begun to feel the lamb heavy, and he was hungry, so he said to St. Peter, "Look, that's a good place, we might cook the lamb there, and eat it."

"As you like," answered St. Peter, "but I can't have anything to do with the cooking; if you will cook, there is a kettle for you, and in the meantime I will walk about a little until it is ready. You must, however, not begin to eat until I have come back, I will come at the right time."

"Well, go, then," said Brother Lustig, "I understand cookery, I will manage it." Then St. Peter went away, and Brother Lustig killed the lamb, lighted a fire, threw the meat into the kettle, and boiled it. The lamb was, however, quite ready, and the apostle Peter had not come back, so Brother Lustig took it out of the kettle, cut it up, and found the heart.

"That is said to be the best part," said he, and tasted it, but at last he ate it all up.

At length St. Peter returned and said, "You may eat the whole of the lamb yourself, I will only have the heart, give me that."

Then Brother Lustig took a knife and fork, and pretended to look anxiously about amongst the lamb's flesh, but not to be able to find the heart, and at last he said abruptly, "There is none here."

"But where can it be?" said the apostle.

"I don't know," replied Brother Lustig, "but look, what fools we both are, to seek for the lamb's heart, and neither of us to remember that a lamb has no heart!"

"Oh," said St. Peter, "that is something quite new! Every animal has a heart, why is a lamb to have none?"

"No, be assured, my brother," said Brother Lustig, "that a lamb has no heart; just consider it seriously, and then you will see that it really has none."

"Well, it is all right," said St. Peter, "if there is no heart, then I want none of the lamb; you may eat it alone."

"What I can't eat now, I will carry away in my knapsack," said Brother Lustig, and he ate half the lamb, and put the rest in his knapsack.

They went farther, and then St. Peter caused a great stream of water to flow right across their path, and they were obliged to pass through it. Said St. Peter, "You go first."

"No," answered Brother Lustig, "you must go first," and he thought, "if the water is too deep I will stay behind." Then St. Peter strode through it, and the water just reached to his knee. So Brother Lustig began to go through also, but the water grew deeper and reached to his throat. Then he cried, "Brother, help me!"

St. Peter said, "Then will you confess that you have eaten the lamb's heart?"

"No," said he, "I have not eaten it." Then the water grew deeper still and rose to his mouth. "Help me, brother," cried the soldier.

St. Peter said, "Then will you confess that you have eaten the lamb's heart?"

"No," he replied, "I have not eaten it." St. Peter, however, would not let him be drowned, but made the water sink and helped him through it.

Then they journeyed onwards, and came to a kingdom where they heard that the King's daughter lay sick and dying. "Hollo, brother!" said the soldier to St. Peter, "this is a chance for us; if we can heal her we shall be provided for, for life!" But St. Peter was not half quick enough for him, "Come, lift your legs, my dear brother," said he, "that we may get there in time." But St. Peter walked slower and slower, though Brother Lustig did all he could to drive and push him on, and at last they heard that the princess was dead. "Now we are done for!" said Brother Lustig; "that is what comes of your sleepy way of walking!"

"Just be quiet," answered St. Peter, "I can do more than cure sick people; I can bring dead ones to life again."

"Well, if you can do that," said Brother Lustig, "it's all right, but you should earn at least half the Kingdom for us by doing that." Then they went to the royal palace, where everyone was in great grief, but St. Peter told the King that he would restore his daughter to life.

He was taken to her, and said, "Bring me a kettle and some water," and when that was brought, he bade everyone go out, and allowed no one to remain with him but Brother Lustig. Then he cut off all the dead girl's limbs, and threw them in the water, lighted a fire beneath the kettle, and boiled them. And when the flesh had fallen away from the bones, he took out the beautiful white bones, and laid them on a table, and arranged them together in their natural order. When he had done that, he stepped forward and said three times, "In the name of the holy Trinity, dead woman, arise." And at the third time, the princess arose, living, healthy and beautiful. Then the King was in the greatest joy, and said to St. Peter, "Ask for your reward; even if it were half my kingdom, I would give it you."

But St. Peter said, "I want nothing for it."

"Oh, you tomfool!" thought Brother Lustig to himself, and nudged his comrade's side, and said, "Don't be so stupid! If you have no need of anything, I have." St. Peter, however, would have nothing, but as the King saw that the other would very much like to have something, he ordered his treasurer to fill Brother Lustig's knapsack with gold.

Then they went on their way, and when they came to a forest, St. Peter said to Brother Lustig, "Now, we will divide the gold."

"Yes," he replied, "we will." So St. Peter divided the gold, and divided it into three heaps. Brother Lustig thought to himself, "What craze has he got in his head now? He is making three shares, and there are only two of us!"

But St. Peter said, "I have divided it exactly; there is one share for me, one for you, and one for whoever ate the lamb's heart."

"Oh, I ate that!" replied Brother Lustig, and hastily swept up the gold. "You may trust what I say."

"But how can that be true," said St. Peter, "when a lamb has no heart?"

"Nonsense, brother, what can you be thinking of? Lambs have hearts like other animals, why should only they have none?"

"Well, so be it," said St. Peter, "keep the gold to yourself, but I will stay with you no longer; I will go my way alone."

"As you like, dear brother," answered Brother Lustig. "Farewell."

Then St. Peter went a different road, but Brother Lustig thought, "It is a good thing that he has taken himself off, he is certainly a strange saint, after all." Then he had money enough, but did not know how to manage it, squandered it, gave it away, and when some time had gone by, once more had nothing. Then he arrived in a certain country where he heard that a King's daughter was dead. "Oh, ho!" thought he, "That may be a good thing for me; I will bring her to life again, and see that I am paid as I ought to be."

So he went to the King, and offered to raise the dead girl to life again. Now the King had heard that a discharged soldier was traveling about and bringing dead persons to life again, and thought that Brother Lustig was the man; but as he had no confidence in him, he consulted his councilors first, who said that he might give it a trial as his daughter was already dead. Then Brother Lustig ordered water to be brought to him in a kettle, bade everyone go out, cut the limbs off, threw them in the water and lighted a fire beneath, just as he had seen St. Peter do. The water began to boil, the flesh fell off, and then he took the bones out and laid them on the table, but he did not know the order in which to lay them, and placed them all wrong and in confusion. Then he stood before them and said, "In the name of the most holy Trinity, dead maiden, I bid you arise," and he said this thrice, but the bones did not stir. So he said it thrice more, but also in vain: "Confounded girl that you are, get up!" cried he, "Get up, or it shall be even worse for you!"

When he had said that, St. Peter suddenly appeared in his former shape as a discharged soldier; he entered by the window and said, "Godless man, what are you doing? How can the dead maiden arise, when you have thrown about her bones in such confusion?"

"Dear brother, I have done everything to the best of my ability," he answered.

"This once, I will help you out of your difficulty, but one thing I tell you, and that is that if you ever undertake anything of the kind again, it will be the worse for you, and also that you must neither demand nor accept the smallest thing from the King for this!" Thereupon St. Peter laid the bones in their right order, said to the maiden three times, "In the name of the most holy Trinity, dead maiden, arise," and the King's daughter arose, healthy and beautiful as before.

Then St. Peter went away again by the window, and Brother Lustig was rejoiced to find that all had passed off so well, but was very much vexed to think that after all he was not to take anything for it. "I should just like to know," thought he, "what fancy that fellow has got in his head, for what he gives with one hand he takes away with the other. There is no sense whatsoever in it!" Then the King offered Brother Lustig whatever he wished to have, but he did not dare to take anything; however, by hints and cunning, he contrived to make the King order his knapsack to be filled with gold for him, and with that he departed.

When he got out, St. Peter was standing by the door, and said, "Just look what a man you are; did I not forbid you to take anything, and there you have your knapsack full of gold!"

"How can I help that," answered Brother Lustig, "if people will put it in for me?"

"Well, I tell you this, that if you ever set about anything of this kind again you shall suffer for it!"

"Eh, brother, have no fear, now I have money, why should I trouble myself with washing bones?"

"Faith," said St. Peter, "the gold will not last a long time! In order that after this you may never tread in unlawful paths, I will bestow on your knapsack this property, namely, that whatever you wish to have inside it, shall be there. Farewell, you will now never see me again."

"Good-bye," said Brother Lustig, and thought to himself, "I am very glad that you have taken yourself off, you strange fellow; I shall certainly not follow you." But of the magical power which had been bestowed on his knapsack, he thought no more.

Brother Lustig traveled about with his money, and squandered and wasted what he had as before. When at last he had no more than four kreuzers, he passed by an inn and thought, "The money must go," and ordered three kreuzers' worth of wine and one kreuzer's worth of bread for himself. As he was sitting there drinking, the smell of roast goose made its way to his nose. Brother Lustig looked about and peeped, and saw that the host had two geese standing in the oven. Then he remembered that his comrade had said that whatever he wished to have in his knapsack should be there, so he said, "Oh, ho! I must try that with the geese." So he went out, and when he was outside the door, he said, "I wish those two roasted geese out of the oven and in my knapsack," and when he had said that, he unbuckled it and looked in, and there they were inside it. "Ah, that's right!" said he, "Now I am a made man!" and went away to a meadow and took out the roast meat.

When he was in the middle of his meal, two journeymen came up and looked at the second goose, which was not yet touched, with hungry eyes. Brother Lustig thought to himself, "One is enough for me," and called the two men up and said, "Take the goose, and eat it to my health." They thanked him, and went with it to the inn, ordered themselves a half bottle of wine and a loaf, took out the goose which had been given them, and began to eat. The hostess saw them and said to her husband, "Those two are eating a goose; just look and see if it is not one of ours, out of the oven."

The landlord ran over, and behold the oven was empty! "What!" cried he, "You thievish crew, you want to eat goose as cheap as that? Pay for it this moment; or I will wash you well with green hazel-sap."

The two said, "We are no thieves, a discharged soldier gave us the goose, outside there in the meadow."

"You shall not throw dust in my eyes that way! The soldier was here but he went out by the door, like an honest fellow. I looked after him myself; you are the thieves and shall pay!" But as they could not pay, he took a stick, and cudgeled them out of the house.

Brother Lustig went his way and came to a place where there was a magnificent castle, and not far from it a wretched inn. He went to the inn and asked for a night's lodging, but the landlord turned him away, and said, "There is no more room here, the house is full of noble guests."

"It surprises me that they should come to you and not go to that splendid castle," said Brother Lustig.

"Ah, indeed," replied the host, "but it is no slight matter to sleep there for a night; no one who has tried it so far, has ever come out of it alive."

"If others have tried it," said Brother Lustig, "I will try it too."

"Leave it alone," said the host, "it will cost you your neck."

"It won't kill me at once," said Brother Lustig, "just give me the key, and some good food and wine." So the host gave him the key, and food and wine, and with this Brother Lustig went into the castle, enjoyed his supper, and at length, as he was sleepy, he lay down on the ground, for there was no bed. He soon fell asleep, but during the night was disturbed by a great noise, and when he awoke, he saw nine ugly devils in the room, who had made a circle, and were dancing around him. Brother Lustig said, "Well, dance as long as you like, but none of you must come too close." But the devils pressed continually nearer to him, and almost stepped on his face with their hideous feet.

"Stop, you devils' ghosts," said he, but they behaved still worse. Then Brother Lustig grew angry, and cried, "Ho! But I will soon make it quiet," and got the leg of a chair and struck out into the midst of them with it. But nine devils against one soldier were still too many, and when he struck those in front of him, the others seized him behind by the hair, and tore it unmercifully. "Devils' crew," cried he, "it is getting too bad, but just you wait. Into my knapsack, all nine of you!" In an instant they were in it, and then he buckled it up and threw it into a corner.

After this all was suddenly quiet, and Brother Lustig lay down again, and slept till it was bright day. Then came the innkeeper, and the nobleman to whom the castle belonged, to see how he had fared; but when they perceived that he was merry and well they were astonished, and asked, "Have the spirits done you no harm, then?"

"The reason why they have not," answered Brother Lustig, "is because I have got the whole nine of them in my knapsack! You may once more inhabit your castle quite tranquilly, none of them will ever haunt it again." The nobleman thanked him, gave him rich presents, and begged him to remain in his service, and he would provide for him as long as he lived.

"No," replied Brother Lustig, "I am used to wandering about, I will travel farther." Then he went away, and entered into a smithy, laid the knapsack, which contained the nine devils on the anvil, and asked the smith and his apprentices to strike it. So they struck with their great hammers with all their strength, and the devils uttered howls which were quite pitiable. When he opened the knapsack after this, eight of them were dead, but one which had been lying in a fold of it, was still alive, slipped out, and went back again to hell. Thereupon Brother Lustig traveled a long time about the world, and those who know them can tell many a story about him, but at last he grew old, and thought of his end, so he went to a hermit who was known to be a pious man, and said to him, "I am tired of wandering about, and want to now behave in such a manner that I shall enter into the kingdom of Heaven."

The hermit replied, "There are two roads, one is broad and pleasant, and leads to hell, the other is narrow and rough, and leads to heaven."

"I should be a fool," thought Brother Lustig, "if I were to take the narrow, rough road." So he set out and took the broad and pleasant road, and at length came to a great black door, which was the door of Hell. Brother Lustig knocked, and the gatekeeper peeped out to see who was there. But when he saw Brother Lustig, he was terrified, for he was the very same ninth devil who had been shut up in the knapsack, and had escaped from it with a black eye. So he pushed the bolt in again as quickly as he could, ran to the devil's lieutenant, and said, "There is a fellow outside with a knapsack, who wants to come in, but as you value your lives don't allow him to enter, or he will wish the whole of hell into his knapsack. He once gave me a frightful hammering when I was inside it." So they called out to Brother Lustig that he was to go away, for he should not get in there!

"If they won't have me here," thought he, "I will see if I can find a place for myself in heaven, for I must be somewhere." So he turned about and went onwards until he came to the door of Heaven, where he knocked.

St. Peter was sitting nearby as gatekeeper. Brother Lustig recognized him at once, and thought, "Here I find an old friend, I shall get on better."

But St. Peter said, "I really believe that you want to come into Heaven."

"Let me in, brother; I must get in somewhere; if they would have taken me into Hell, I should not have come here."

"No," said St. Peter, "you shall not enter."

"Then if you will not let me in, take your knapsack back, for I will have nothing at all from you."

"Give it here, then," said St. Peter.

Then Brother Lustig gave him the knapsack into Heaven through the bars, and St. Peter took it, and hung it beside his seat. Then said Brother Lustig, "And now I wish myself inside my knapsack," and in a second he was in it, and in Heaven, and St. Peter was forced to let him stay there.

82. GAMBLING HANSEL

Once upon a time there was a man who did nothing but gamble, and for that reason people never called him anything but Gambling Hansel, and as he never ceased to gamble, he played away his house and all that he had. Now the very day before his creditors were to take his house from him, came the Lord and St. Peter, and asked him to give them shelter for the night. Then Gambling Hansel said, "For my part, you may stay the night, but I cannot give you a bed or anything to eat."

So the Lord said he was just to take them in, and they themselves would buy something to eat, to which Gambling Hansel made no objection. Thereupon St. Peter gave him three groschen, and said he was to go to the baker's and fetch some bread. So Gambling Hansel went, but when he reached the house where the other gambling vagabonds were gathered together, they, although they had won all that he had, greeted him clamorously, and said, "Hansel, do come in."

"Oh," said he, "do you want to win the three groschen too?" At this they would not let him go. So he went in, and played away the three groschen also.

Meanwhile St. Peter and the Lord were waiting, and as he was so long in coming, they set out to meet him. When Gambling Hansel came, however, he pretended that the money had fallen into the gutter, and kept raking about in it all the while to find it, but our Lord already knew that he had lost it in play. St. Peter again gave him three groschen, and now he did not allow himself to be led away once more, but fetched them the loaf. Our Lord then inquired if he had no wine, and he said, "Alack, sir, the casks are all empty!" But the Lord said he was to go down into the cellar, for the best wine was still there.

For a long time he would not believe this, but at length he said, "Well, I will go down, but I know that there is none there." When he turned the tap, however, lo and behold, the best of wine ran out! So he took it to them, and the two passed the night there. Early next day our Lord told Gambling Hansel that he might beg three favors. The Lord expected that he would ask to go to Heaven; but Gambling Hansel asked for a pack of cards with which he could win everything, for dice with which he would win everything, and for a tree on which every kind of fruit would grow, and from which no one who had climbed up, could descend until he bade him do so. The Lord gave him all that he had asked, and departed with St. Peter.

And now Gambling Hansel at once set about gambling in real earnest, and before long he had gained half the world. Upon this St. Peter said to the Lord, "Lord, this thing must not go on, he will win, and you lose, the whole world. We must send Death to him."

When Death appeared, Gambling Hansel had just seated himself at the gaming table, and Death said, "Hansel, come out a while."

But Gambling Hansel said, "Just wait a little until the game is done, and in the meantime get up into that tree out there, and gather a little fruit that we may have something to munch on our way." Thereupon Death climbed up, but when he wanted to come down again, he could not, and Gambling Hansel left him up there for seven years, during which time no one died.

So St. Peter said to the Lord, "Lord, this thing must not go on. People no longer die; we must go ourselves." And they went themselves, and the Lord commanded Hansel to let Death come down. So Hansel went at once to Death and said to him, "Come down," and Death took him directly and put an end to him. They went away together and came to the next world, and then Gambling Hansel made straight for the door of Heaven, and knocked at it.

"Who is there?"

"Gambling Hansel."

"Ah, we will have nothing to do with him! Be gone!"

So he went to the door of Purgatory, and knocked once more.

"Who is there?"

"Gambling Hansel."

"Ah, there is quite enough weeping and wailing here without him. We do not want to gamble, just go away again."

Then he went to the door of Hell, and there they let him in. There was, however, no one at home but old Lucifer and the crooked devils who had just been doing their evil work in the world. And no sooner was Hansel there than he sat down to gamble again. Lucifer, however, had nothing to lose, but his misshapen devils, and Gambling Hansel won them from him, as with his cards he could not fail to do. And now he was off again with his crooked devils, and they went to Hohenfuert and pulled up a hop-pole, and with it went to Heaven and began to thrust the pole against it, and Heaven began to crack. So again St. Peter said, "Lord, this thing cannot go on, we must let him in, or he will throw us down from Heaven."

And they let him in. But Gambling Hansel instantly began to play again, and there was such a noise and confusion that there was no hearing what they themselves were saying. Therefore St. Peter once more said, "Lord, this cannot go on, we must throw him down, or he will make all Heaven rebellious." So they went to him at once, and threw him down, and his soul broke into fragments, and went into the gambling vagabonds who are living this very day.

83. HANS IN LUCK

Hans had served his master for seven years, so he said to him, "Master, my time is up; now I should be glad to go back home to my mother; give me my wages."

The master answered, "You have served me faithfully and honestly; as the service was so the reward shall be," and he gave Hans a piece of gold as big as his head. Hans pulled his handkerchief out of his pocket, wrapped up the lump in it, put it on his shoulder, and set out on the way home.

As he went on, always putting one foot before the other, he saw a horseman trotting quickly and merrily by on a lively horse. "Ah!" said Hans quite loud, "What a fine thing it is to ride! There you sit as on a chair; you stumble over no stones, you save your shoes, and get on one hardly knows how."

The rider, who had heard him, stopped and called out, "Hello! Hans, why do you go on foot, then?"

"I must," answered he, "for I have this lump to carry home; it is true that it is gold, but I cannot hold my head straight for it, and it hurts my shoulder."

"I will tell you what," said the rider, "we will exchange: I will give you my horse, and you can give me your lump."

"With all my heart," said Hans, "but I can tell you, you will have to crawl along with it."

The rider got down, took the gold, and helped Hans up; then gave him the bridle tight in his hands and said, "If you want to go at a really good pace, you must click your tongue and call out, "Jup! Jup!"

Hans was heartily delighted as he sat upon the horse and rode away so bold and free. After a little while he thought that it ought to go faster, and he began to click with his tongue and call out, "Jup! Jup!" The horse put himself into a sharp trot, and before Hans knew where he was, he was thrown off and lying in a ditch which separated the field from the highway. The horse would have gone off too if it had not been stopped by a countryman, who was coming along the road and driving a cow before him.

Hans got his limbs together and stood up on his legs again, but he was vexed, and said to the countryman, "It is a poor joke, this riding, especially when one gets hold of a mare like this, that kicks and throws one off, so that one has a chance of breaking one's neck. Never again will I mount it. Now I like your cow, for one can walk quietly behind her, and have, over and above, one's milk, butter and cheese every day without fail. What would I not give to have such a cow."

"Well," said the countryman, "if it would give you so much pleasure, I do not mind giving the cow for the horse." Hans agreed with the greatest delight; the countryman jumped upon the horse, and rode quickly away.

Hans drove his cow quietly before him, and thought over his lucky bargain. "If only I had a morsel of bread—and that can hardly fail me—I can eat butter and cheese with it as often as I like; if I am thirsty, I can milk my cow and drink the milk. Good heart, what more can I want?"

When he came to an inn he made a halt, and in his great content ate up what he had with him—his dinner and supper—and all he had, and with his last few farthings had half a glass of beer. Then he drove his cow onwards along the road to his mother's village.

As it drew nearer midday, the heat was more oppressive, and Hans found himself upon a moor which it took about an hour to cross. He felt it very hot and his tongue stuck to the roof of his mouth with thirst. "I can find a cure for this," thought Hans; "I will milk the cow now and refresh myself with the milk." He tied her to a withered tree, and as he had no pail he put his leather cap underneath; but try as he would, not a drop of milk came. And as he set himself to work in a clumsy way, the impatient beast at last gave him such a blow on his head with its hind foot, that he fell on the ground, and for a long time could not think where he was.

By good fortune a butcher just then came along the road with a wheelbarrow, in which lay a young pig. "What sort of a trick is this?" cried he, and helped the good Hans up. Hans told him what had happened. The butcher gave him his flask and said, "Take a drink and refresh yourself. The cow will certainly give no milk, it is an old beast; at the best it is only fit for the plow, or for the butcher."

"Well, well," said Hans, as he stroked his hair down on his head, "who would have thought it? Certainly it is a fine thing when one can kill a beast like that at home; what meat one has! But I do not care much for beef, it is not juicy enough for me. A young pig like that now is the thing to have, it tastes quite different; and then there are the sausages!"

"Listen, Hans," said the butcher, "out of love for you I will exchange, and will let you have the pig for the cow."

"Heaven repay you for your kindness!" said Hans as he gave up the cow, while the pig was unbound from the barrow, and the cord by which it was tied was put in his hand.

Hans went on, and thought to himself how everything was going just as he wished; if he did meet with any vexation it was immediately set right. Presently there joined him a lad who was carrying a fine white goose under his arm. They said good morning to each other, and Hans began to tell of his good luck, and how he had always made such good bargains. The boy told him that he was taking the goose to a christening feast. "Just lift her," added he, and laid hold of her by the wings; "how heavy she is—she has been fattened up for the last eight weeks. Whoever has a bit of her when she is roasted will have to wipe the fat from both sides of his mouth."

"Yes," said Hans, as he weighed her in one hand, "she is a good weight, but my pig is no bad one."

Meanwhile the lad looked suspiciously from one side to the other, and shook his head. "Look here," he said at length, "it may not be all right with your pig. In the village through which I passed, the Mayor himself had just had one stolen out of its sty. I fear—I fear that you have got hold of it there. They have sent out some people and it would be a bad business if they caught you with the pig; at the very least, you would be shut up in the dark hole."

The good Hans was terrified. "Goodness!" he said, "Help me out of this fix; you know more about this place than I do, take my pig and leave me your goose."

"I shall risk something at that game," answered the lad, "but I will not be the cause of your getting into trouble." So he took the cord in his hand, and drove away the pig quickly along a bypath.

The good Hans, free from care, went homewards with the goose under his arm. "When I think over it properly," said he to himself, "I have even gained by the exchange; first there is the good roast meat, then the quantity of fat which will drip from it, and which will give me dripping for my bread for a quarter of a year, and lastly the beautiful white feathers; I will have my pillow stuffed with them, and then indeed I shall go to sleep without rocking. How glad my mother will be!"

As he was going through the last village, there stood a scissors grinder with his barrow; as his wheel whirred he sang—

"I sharpen scissors and quickly grind,
My coat blows out in the wind behind."

Hans stood still and looked at him; at last he spoke to him and said, "All's well with you, as you are so merry with your grinding."

"Yes," answered the scissors grinder, "the trade has a golden foundation. A real grinder is a man who as often as he puts his hand into his pocket finds gold in it. But where did you buy that fine goose?"

"I did not buy it, but exchanged my pig for it."

"And the pig?"

"That I got for a cow."

"And the cow?"

"I took that instead of a horse."

"And the horse?"

"For that I gave a lump of gold as big as my head."

"And the gold?"

"Well, that was my wages for seven years' service."

"You have known how to look after yourself each time," said the grinder. "If you can only get on so far as to hear the money jingle in your pocket whenever you stand up, you will have made your fortune."

"How shall I manage that?" said Hans.

"You must be a grinder, as I am; nothing particular is wanted for it but a grindstone, the rest finds itself. I have one here; it is certainly a little worn, but you need not give me anything for it but your goose; will you do it?"

"How can you ask?" answered Hans. "I shall be the luckiest fellow on earth; if I have money whenever I put my hand in my pocket, what need I trouble about any longer?" and he handed him the goose and received the grindstone in exchange.

"Now," said the grinder, as he took up an ordinary heavy stone that lay by him, "here is a strong stone for you into the bargain; you can hammer well upon it, and straighten your old nails. Take it with you and keep it carefully."

Hans loaded himself with the stones, and went on with a contented heart; his eyes shone with joy. "I must have been born under a lucky star," he cried, "everything I want happens to me just as if I were a Sunday's child."

Meanwhile, as he had been on his legs since daybreak, he began to feel tired. Hunger also tormented him, for in his joy at the bargain by which he got the cow he had eaten up all his store of food at once. At last he could only go on with great trouble, and was forced to stop every minute; the stones, too, weighed him down dreadfully. Then he could not help thinking how nice it would be if he did not have to carry them just then.

He crept like a snail to a well in a field, and there he thought that he would rest and refresh himself with a cool drink of water, but in order that he might not injure the stones in sitting down, he laid them carefully by his side on the edge of the well. Then he sat down on it, and was to stoop and drink, when he made a slip, pushed against the stones, and both of them fell into the water. When Hans saw them with his own eyes sinking to the bottom, he jumped for joy, and then knelt down, and with tears in his eyes thanked God for having shown him this favor also, and released him in so good a way, and without his having any need to reproach himself, from those heavy stones which had been the only things that troubled him.

"There is no man under the sun so fortunate as I," he cried out. With a light heart and free from every burden he now ran on until he was with his mother at home.

84. HANS MARRIED

There was once upon a time a young peasant named Hans, whose uncle wanted to find him a rich wife. He therefore seated Hans behind the stove, and had it made very hot. Then he fetched a pot of milk and plenty of white bread, gave him a bright newly-coined farthing in his hand, and said, "Hans, hold that farthing fast, crumble the white bread into the milk, and stay where you are, and do not stir from that spot till I come back."

"Yes," said Hans, "I will do all that."

Then the wooer put on a pair of old patched trousers, went to a rich peasant's daughter in the next village, and said, "Won't you marry my nephew Hans? You will get an honest and sensible man who will suit you."

The covetous father asked, "How is it with regard to his means? Has he bread to break?"

"Dear friend," replied the wooer, "my young nephew has a snug berth, a nice bit of money in hand, and plenty of bread to break, besides he has quite as many patches as I have," (and as he spoke, he slapped the patches on his trousers, but in that district small pieces of land were called patches also). "If you will give yourself the trouble to go home with me, you shall see at once that all is as I have said."

Then the miser did not want to lose this good opportunity, and said, "If that is the case, I have nothing further to say against the marriage."

So the wedding was celebrated on the appointed day, and when the young wife went out of doors to see the bridegroom's property, Hans took off his Sunday coat and put on his patched smock and said, "I might spoil my good coat." Then together they went out and wherever a boundary line came in sight, or fields and meadows were divided from each other, Hans pointed with his finger and then slapped either a large or a small patch on his smock, and said, "That patch is mine, and that too, my dearest, just look at it," meaning that his wife should not stare at the broad land, but look at his garment, which was his own.

"Were you indeed at the wedding?"

"Yes, indeed I was there, and in fulldress. My headdress was of snow; then the sun came out, and it was melted. My coat was of cobwebs, and I had to pass by some thorns which tore it off me, my shoes were of glass, and I pushed against a stone and they said, "Klink," and broke in two.

85. THE GOLD CHILDREN

There was once a poor man and a poor woman who had nothing but a little cottage, and who earned their bread by fishing, and always lived from hand to mouth. But it came to pass one day when the man was sitting by the shore, and casting his net, that he drew out a fish entirely of gold. As he was looking at the fish, full of astonishment, it began to speak and said, "Listen, fisherman, if you will throw me back again into the water, I will change your little hut into a splendid castle."

Then the fisherman answered, "Of what use is a castle to me, if I have nothing to eat?"

The gold fish continued, "That shall be taken care of, there will be a cupboard in the castle in which, when you open it, shall be dishes of the most delicate meats, and as many of them as you can desire."

"If that be true," said the man, "then I can well do you a favor."

"Yes," said the fish, "there is, however, the condition that you shall disclose to no one in the world, whoever he may be, where you get your good luck. If you speak but one single word, all will be over."

Then the man threw the wonderful fish back again into the water, and went home. But where his hut had formerly stood, now stood a great castle. He opened wide his eyes, entered, and saw his wife dressed in beautiful clothes, sitting in a splendid room, and she was quite delighted, and said, "Husband, how has all this come to pass? It suits me very well."

"Yes," said the man, "it suits me too, but I am frightfully hungry, just give me something to eat."

Said the wife, "But I have got nothing and don't know where to find anything in this new house."

"There is no need to know," said the man, "for I see yonder a great cupboard, just unlock it." When she opened it, there stood cakes, meat, fruit, wine, quite a bright prospect.

Then the woman cried joyfully, "What more can you want, my dear?" and they sat down, and ate and drank together. When they had had enough, the woman said, "But husband, where do all these riches come from?"

"Alas," answered he, "do not question me about it, for I dare not tell you anything; if I disclose it to anyone, then all our good fortune will fly."

"Very good," said she, "if I am not to know anything, then I do not want to know anything." However, she was not in earnest; she never rested day or night, and she goaded her husband until in his impatience he revealed that all was owing to a wonderful golden fish which he had caught, and to which in return he had given its liberty. And as soon as the secret was out, the splendid castle with the cupboard immediately disappeared, they were once more in the old fisherman's hut, and the man was obliged to follow his former trade and fish. But fortune would so have it, that he once more drew out the golden fish.

"Listen," said the fish, "if you will throw me back into the water again, I will once more give you the castle with the cupboard full of roast and boiled meats; only be firm, for your life's sake don't reveal from whom you got it, or you will lose it all again!"

"I will take good care," answered the fisherman, and threw the fish back into the water. Now at home everything was once more in its former magnificence, and the wife was overjoyed at their good fortune, but curiosity left her no peace, so that after a couple of days she began to ask again how it had come to pass, and how he had managed to secure it. The man kept silence for a short time, but at last she made him so angry that he broke out, and betrayed the secret. In an instant the castle disappeared, and they were back again in their old hut.

"Now you have got what you want," said he, "and we can gnaw at a bare bone again."

"Ah," said the woman, "I had rather not have riches if I am not to know from whom they come, for then I have no peace."

The man went back to fish, and after a while he chanced to draw out the gold fish for a third time. "Listen," said the fish, "I see very well that I am fated to fall into your hands, take me home and cut me into six pieces; give your wife two of them to eat, two to your horse and bury two of them in the ground, then they will bring you a blessing."

The fisherman took the fish home with him, and did as it had bidden him. It came to pass, however, that from the two pieces that were buried in the ground two golden lilies sprang up, that the horse had two golden foals, and the fisherman's wife bore two children who were made entirely of gold. The children grew up, became tall and handsome, and the lilies and horses grew likewise. Then they said,

"Father, we want to mount our golden steeds and travel out in the world."

But he answered sorrowfully, "How shall I bear it if you go away, and I know not how it fares with you?"

Then they said, "The two golden lilies remain here. By them you can see how it is with us; if they are fresh, then we are in health; if they are withered, we are ill; if they perish, then we are dead."

So they rode forth and came to an inn, in which were many people, and when they perceived the gold children they began to laugh, and jeer. When one of them heard the mocking he felt ashamed and would not go out into the world, but turned back and went home again to his father. But the other rode forward and reached a great forest.

As he was about to enter it, the people said, "It is not safe for you to ride through, the wood is full of robbers who would treat you badly. You will fare ill, and when they see that you are all of gold, and your horse likewise, they will assuredly kill you."

But he would not allow himself to be frightened, and said, "I must and will ride through it." Then he took bearskins and covered himself and his horse with them, so that the gold was no more to be seen, and rode fearlessly into the forest.

When he had ridden onward a little he heard a rustling in the bushes, and heard voices speaking together. From one side came cries of, "There is one," but from the other, "Let him go, 'tis an idle fellow, as poor and bare as a church mouse, what should we gain from him?"

So the gold child rode joyfully through the forest, and no evil befell him. One day he entered a village where he saw a maiden, who was so beautiful that he did not believe that any more beautiful than she existed in the world. And as such a mighty love took possession of him, he went up to her and said, "I love you with my whole heart, will you be my wife?"

He, too, pleased the maiden so much that she agreed and said, "Yes, I will be your wife, and be true to you my whole life long."

Then they were married, and just as they were in the greatest happiness, home came the father of the bride, and when he saw that his daughter's wedding was being celebrated, he was astonished, and said, "Where is the bridegroom?" They showed him the gold child, who, however, still wore his bearskins. Then the father said wrathfully, "A vagabond shall never have my daughter!" and was about to kill him.

Then the bride begged as hard as she could, and said, "He is my husband, and I love him with all my heart!" until at last he allowed himself to be appeased.

Nevertheless the idea never left his thoughts, so that next morning he rose early, wishing to see whether his daughter's husband was a common ragged beggar. But when he peeped in, he saw a magnificent golden man in the bed, and the cast-off bearskins lying on the ground. Then he went back and thought, "What a good thing it was that I restrained my anger! I should have committed a great crime."

But the gold child dreamed that he rode out to hunt a splendid stag, and when he awoke in the morning, he said to his wife, "I must go out hunting."

She was uneasy, and begged him to stay there, and said, "You might easily meet with a great misfortune," but he answered, "I must and will go."

Thereupon he got up, and rode forth into the forest, and it was not long before a fine stag crossed his path exactly according to his dream. He aimed and was about to shoot it, when the stag ran away. He gave chase over hedges and ditches for the whole day without feeling tired, but in the evening the stag vanished from his sight, and when the gold child looked round him, he was standing before a little house, in which was a witch. He knocked, and a little old woman came out and asked, "What are you doing so late in the middle of the great forest?"

"Have you not seen a stag?"

"Yes," answered she, "I know the stag well," and a little dog which had come out of the house with her, barked at the man violently.

"Will you be silent, you odious toad," said he, "or I will shoot you dead."

Then the witch cried out in a passion, "What! Will you slay my little dog?" and immediately transformed him, so that he lay like a stone, and his bride awaited him in vain and thought, "That which I so greatly dreaded, which lay so heavily on my heart, has come upon him!"

But at home the other brother was standing by the gold lilies, when one of them suddenly drooped. "Good heavens!" said he, "My brother has met with some great misfortune! I must go away to see if I can possibly rescue him."

Then the father said, "Stay here, if I lose you also, what shall I do?"

But he answered, "I must and will go forth!"

Then he mounted his golden horse, and rode forth and entered the great forest, where his brother lay turned to stone. The old witch came out of her house and called him, wishing to entrap him also, but he did not go near her, and said, "I will shoot you, if you will not bring my brother to life again." She touched the stone, though very unwillingly, with her forefinger, and he was immediately restored to his human shape.

The two gold children rejoiced when they saw each other again, kissed and caressed each other, and rode away together out of the forest, the one home to his bride, and the other to his father. The father then said, "I knew well that you had rescued your brother, for the golden lily suddenly rose up and blossomed out again." Then they lived happily, and all prospered with them until their death.

86. THE FOX AND THE GEESE

The fox once came to a meadow in which was a flock of fine fat geese, at which he smiled and said, "I come in the nick of time, you are sitting together quite beautifully, so that I can eat you up one after the other." The geese cackled with terror, sprang up, and began to wail and beg piteously for their lives. But the fox would listen to nothing, and said, "There is no mercy to be had! You must die."

At length one of them took heart and said, "If we poor geese are to give up our vigorous young lives, show us the only possible favor and allow us one more prayer, that we may not die in our sins, and then we will place ourselves in a row, so that you can pick yourself out the fattest."

"Yes," said the fox, "that is reasonable, and a pious request. Pray away, I will wait till you are done."

Then the first began a good long prayer, forever saying, "Ga! Ga!" and as she would make no end, the second did not wait until her turn came, but began also, "Ga! Ga!" The third and fourth followed her, and soon they were all cackling together.

When they have done praying, the story shall be continued further, but at present they are still praying without stopping.

87. THE POOR MAN AND THE RICH MAN

In olden times, when the Lord himself still used to walk about on this earth among men, it once happened that he was tired and overtaken by the darkness before he could reach an inn. Now there stood on the road before him two houses facing each other; the one large and beautiful, the other small and poor. The large one belonged to a rich man, and the small one to a poor man.

Then the Lord thought, "I shall be no burden to the rich man, I will stay the night with him." When the rich man heard someone knocking at his door, he opened the window and asked the stranger what he wanted. The Lord answered, "I only ask for a night's lodging."

Then the rich man looked at the traveler from head to foot, and as the Lord was wearing common clothes, and did not look like one who had much money in his pocket, he shook his head, and said, "No, I cannot take you in, my rooms are full of herbs and seeds; and if I were to lodge everyone who knocked at my door, I might very soon go begging myself. Go somewhere else for a lodging," and with this he shut down the window and left the Lord standing there.

So the Lord turned his back on the rich man, and went across to the small house and knocked. He had hardly done so when the poor man opened the little door and bade the traveler come in. "Pass the night with me, it is already dark," said he, "you cannot go any further tonight." This pleased the Lord, and he went in. The poor man's wife shook hands with him, and welcomed him, and said he was to make himself at home and put up with what they had; they had not much to offer him, but what they had they would give him with all their hearts. Then she put the potatoes on the fire, and while they were boiling, she milked the goat, that they might have a little milk with them. When the cloth was laid, the Lord sat down with the man and his wife, and he enjoyed their coarse food, for there were happy faces at the table.

When they had had supper and it was bedtime, the woman called her husband apart and said, "Dear husband, let us make up a bed of straw for ourselves tonight, and then the poor traveler can sleep in our bed and have a good rest, for he has been walking the whole day through, and that makes one weary."

"With all my heart," he answered, "I will go and offer it to him," and he went to the stranger and invited him, if he had no objection, to sleep in their bed and rest his limbs properly. But the Lord was unwilling to take the bed from the two old folks; however, they would not be satisfied, until at length he did it and lay down in the bed, while they themselves lay on some straw on the ground.

Next morning they got up before daybreak, and made as good a breakfast as they could for the guest. When the sun shone in through the little window, and the Lord had got up, he again ate with them, and then prepared to set out on his journey.

But as he was standing at the door he turned round and said, "As you are so kind and good, you may wish three things for yourselves and I will grant them."

Then the man said, "What else should I wish for but eternal happiness, and that we two, as long as we live, may be healthy and have every day our daily bread; for the third wish, I do not know what to have."

And the Lord said to him, "Will you wish for a new house instead of this old one?"

"Oh, yes," said the man; "if I can have that, too, I should like it very much." And the Lord fulfilled his wish, and changed their old house into a new one, again gave them his blessing, and went on.

The sun was high when the rich man got up and leaned out of his window and saw, on the opposite side of the way, a new clean-looking house with red tiles and bright windows where the old hut used to be. He was very much astonished, and called his wife and said to her, "Tell me, what can have happened? Last night there was a miserable little hut standing there, and today there is a beautiful new house. Run over and see how that has come to pass."

So his wife went and asked the poor man, and he said to her, "Yesterday evening a traveler came here and asked for a night's lodging, and this morning when he took leave of us he granted us three wishes—eternal happiness, health during this life and our daily bread as well, and besides this, a beautiful new house instead of our old hut."

When the rich man's wife heard this, she ran back in haste and told her husband how it had happened. The man said, "I could tear myself to pieces! If I had but known that! That traveler came to our house too, and wanted to sleep here, and I sent him away."

"Quick!" said his wife, "Get on your horse. You can still catch the man up, and then you must ask to have three wishes granted to you."

The rich man followed the good counsel and galloped away on his horse, and soon caught up with the Lord. He spoke to him softly and pleasantly, and begged him not to take it amiss that he had not let him in directly; he was looking for the front-door key, and in the meantime the stranger had gone away, if he returned the same way he must come and stay with him. "Yes," said the Lord, "if I ever come back again, I will do so." Then the rich man asked if might not wish for three things too, as his neighbor had done? "Yes," said the Lord, he might, but it would not be to his advantage, and he had better not wish for anything; but the rich man thought that he could easily ask for something which would add to his happiness, if he only knew that it would be granted. So the Lord said to him, "Ride home, then, and three wishes which you shall form, shall be fulfilled."

The rich man had now gained what he wanted, so he rode home, and began to consider what he should wish for. As he was thus thinking he let the bridle fall, and the horse began to caper about, so that he was continually disturbed in his meditations, and could not collect his thoughts at all. He patted its neck, and said, "Gently, Lisa," but the horse only began new tricks. Then at last he was angry, and cried quite impatiently, "I wish your neck was broken!"

As soon as he had said the words, down the horse fell on the ground, and there it lay dead and never moved again. And thus was his first wish fulfilled. As he was miserly by nature, he did not like to leave the harness lying there; so he cut it off, and put it on his back; and now he had to go on foot. "I still have two wishes left," said he, and comforted himself with that thought.

And now as he was walking slowly through the sand, and the sun was burning hot at midday, he grew quite hot-tempered and angry. The saddle hurt his back, and he had not yet any idea what to wish for. "If I were to wish for all the riches and treasures in the world," said he to himself, "I should still think of all kinds of other things later on, I know that, beforehand. But I will manage so that there is nothing at all left for me to wish for afterwards." Then he sighed and said, "Ah, if I were but that Bavarian peasant, who likewise had three wishes granted to him, and knew quite well what to do, and in the first place wished for a great deal of beer, and in the second for as much beer as he was able to drink, and in the third for a barrel of beer into the bargain."

Many a time he thought he had found it, but then it seemed to him to be, after all, too little. Then it came into his mind, what an easy life his wife had, for she stayed at home in a cool room and enjoyed herself. This really did vex him, and before he was aware, he said, "I just wish she was sitting there on this saddle, and could not get off it, instead of my having to drag it along on my back." And as the last word was spoken, the saddle disappeared from his back, and he saw that his second wish had been fulfilled. Then he really did feel warm.

He began to run and wanted to be quite alone in his own room at home, to think of something really large for his last wish. But when he arrived there and opened the parlor door, he saw his wife sitting in the middle of the room on the saddle, crying and complaining, and quite unable to get off it. So he said, "Do bear it, and I will wish for all the riches on earth for you, only stay where you are."

She, however, called him a fool, and said, "What good will all the riches on earth do me, if I am to sit on this saddle? You have wished me on it, so you must help me off."

So whether he liked it or not, he was forced to let his third wish be that she should be free of the saddle, and able to get off it, and immediately the wish was fulfilled. So he got nothing by it but vexation, trouble, abuse, and the loss of his horse; but the poor people lived happily, quietly, and piously until their happy death.

88. THE SINGING, SPRINGING LARK

There was once a man who was about to set out on a long journey, and on parting he asked his three daughters what he should bring back with him for them. The eldest wished for pearls, the second wished for diamonds, but the third said, "Dear father, I should like a singing, soaring lark."

The father said, "Yes, if I can get it, you shall have it," kissed all three, and set out.

Now when the time had come for him to be on his way home again, he had brought pearls and diamonds for the two eldest, but he had sought everywhere in vain for a singing, soaring lark for the youngest, and he was very unhappy about it, for she was his favorite child. Then his road lay through a forest, and in the middle of it was a splendid castle, and near the castle stood a tree, but quite on the top of the tree, he saw a singing, soaring lark.

"Aha, you come just at the right moment!" he said, quite delighted, and called to his servant to climb up and catch the little creature. But as he approached the tree, a lion leapt from beneath it, shook himself, and roared till the leaves on the trees trembled.

"He who tries to steal my singing, soaring lark," he cried, "I will devour."

Then the man said, "I did not know that the bird belonged to you. I will make amends for the wrong I have done and ransom myself with a large sum of money, only spare my life."

The lion said, "Nothing can save you, unless you will promise to give me for my own what first meets you on your return home; and if you will do that, I will grant you your life, and you shall have the bird for your daughter, into the bargain."

But the man hesitated and said, "That might be my youngest daughter, she loves me best, and always runs to meet me on my return home."

The servant, however, was terrified and said, "Why should your daughter be the very one to meet you, it might as easily be a cat, or dog?"

Then the man allowed himself to be persuaded, took the singing, soaring lark, and promised to give the lion whatever should first meet him on his return home.

When he reached home and entered his house, the first who met him was no other than his youngest and dearest daughter, who came running up, kissed and embraced him, and when she saw that he had brought with him a singing, soaring lark, she was beside herself with joy. The father, however, could not rejoice, but began to weep, and said, "My dearest child, I have bought the little bird dear. In return for it, I have been obliged to promise you to a savage lion, and when he has you he will tear you in pieces and devour you," and he told her all, just as it had happened, and begged her not to go there, come what might.

But she consoled him and said, "Dearest father, indeed your promise must be fulfilled. I will go there and soften the lion, so that I may return to you safely." Next morning she had the road pointed out to her, took leave, and went fearlessly out into the forest. The lion, however, was an enchanted prince and was by day a lion, and all his people were lions with him, but in the night they resumed their natural human shapes. On her arrival she was kindly received and led into the castle. When night came, the lion turned into a handsome man, and their wedding was celebrated with great magnificence. They lived happily together, remained awake at night, and slept in the daytime.

One day he came and said, "Tomorrow there is a feast in your father's house, because your eldest sister is to be married, and if you are inclined to go there, my lions shall take you."

She said, "Yes, I should very much like to see my father again," and went there, accompanied by the lions. There was great joy when she arrived, for they had all believed that she had been torn in pieces by the lion, and had long ceased to live. But she told them what a handsome husband she had, and how well off she was, remained with them while the wedding feast lasted, and then went back again to the forest.

When the second daughter was about to be married, and she was again invited to the wedding, she said to the lion, "This time I will not be alone, you must come with me." The lion, however, said that it was too dangerous for him, for if a ray from a burning candle fell on him, he would be changed into a dove, and for seven long years would have to fly about with the doves. She said, "Ah, but do come with me, I will take great care of you, and guard you from all light."

So they went away together, and took with them their little child as well. She had a chamber built there, so strong and thick that no ray could pierce through it; in this he was to shut himself up when the candles were lit for the wedding feast. But the door was made of green wood which warped and left a little crack which no one noticed. The wedding was celebrated with magnificence, but when the procession with all its candles and torches came back from church, and passed by this apartment, a ray about the breadth of a hair fell on the King's son, and when this ray touched him, he was transformed in an instant, and when she came in and looked for him, she did not see him, but a white dove was sitting there.

The dove said to her, "For seven years I must fly about the world, but at every seventh step that you take I will let fall a drop of red blood and a white feather, and these will show you the way, and if you follow the trace you can release me." Thereupon the dove flew out at the door, and she followed him, and at every seventh step a red drop of blood and a little white feather fell down and showed her the way.

So she went continually further and further in the wide world, never looking about her or resting, and the seven years were almost past; then she rejoiced and thought that they would soon be delivered, and yet they were so far from it! Once when they were thus moving onwards, no little feather and no drop of red blood fell, and when she raised her eyes the dove had disappeared. And as she thought to herself, "In this no man can help you," she climbed up to the sun, and said to him, "You shine into every crevice, and over every peak, have you not seen a white dove flying?"

"No," said the sun, "I have seen none, but I present you with a casket, open it when you are in sorest need."

Then she thanked the sun, and went on until evening came and the moon appeared; she then asked her, "You shine the whole night through, and on every field and forest, have you not seen a white dove flying?"

"No," said the moon, "I have seen no dove, but here I give you an egg, break it when you are in great need."

She thanked the moon, and went on until the night wind came up and blew on her, then she said to it, "You blow over every tree and under every leaf, have you not seen a white dove flying?"

"No," said the night wind, "I have seen none, but I will ask the three other winds, perhaps they have seen it."

The east wind and the west wind came, and had seen nothing, but the south wind said, "I have seen the white dove, it has flown to the

Red Sea, where it has become a lion again, for the seven years are over, and the lion is there fighting with a dragon; the dragon, however, is an enchanted princess."

The night wind then said to her, "I will advise you; go to the Red Sea, on the right bank are some tall reeds, count them, break off the eleventh, and strike the dragon with it, then the lion will be able to subdue it, and both will then regain their human form. After that, look round and you will see the griffin which is by the Red Sea; swing yourself, with your beloved, onto his back, and the bird will carry you over the sea to your own home. Here is a nut for you, when you are above the center of the sea, let the nut fall, it will immediately shoot up, and a tall nut tree will grow out of the water on which the griffin may rest; for if he cannot rest, he will not be strong enough to carry you across, and if you forget to throw down the nut, he will let you fall into the sea."

Then she went there, and found everything as the night wind had said. She counted the reeds by the sea, and cut off the eleventh, struck the dragon with it, whereupon the lion overcame it, and immediately both of them regained their human shapes. But when the princess, who had before been the dragon, was delivered from enchantment, she took the youth by the arm, seated herself on the griffin, and carried him off with her.

There stood the poor maiden who had wandered so far and was again forsaken. She sat down and cried, but at last she took courage and said, "Still I will go as far as the wind blows and as long as the cock crows, until I find him," and she went forth by long, long roads, until at last she came to the castle where both of them were living together; there she heard that soon a feast was to be held, in which they would celebrate their wedding, but she said, "God still helps me," and opened the casket that the sun had given her. A dress lay inside as brilliant as the sun itself. So she took it out and put it on, and went up into the castle, and everyone, even the bride herself, looked at her with astonishment. The dress pleased the bride so well that she thought it might do for her wedding dress, and asked if it was for sale.

"Not for money or land," answered she, "but for flesh and blood." The bride asked her what she meant by that, so she said, "Let me sleep a night in the chamber where the bridegroom sleeps." The bride would not, yet wanted very much to have the dress; at last she consented, but the page was to give the prince a sleeping-potion.

When it was night, therefore, and the youth was already asleep, she was led into the chamber; she seated herself on the bed and said, "I have followed after you for seven years. I have been to the sun and the moon, and the four winds, and have inquired for you, and have helped you against the dragon; will you, then, quite forget me?" But the prince slept so soundly that it only seemed to him as if the wind were whistling outside in the fir trees.

When day broke, she was led out again, and had to give up the golden dress. And as even that had been of no avail, she was sad, went out into a meadow, sat down there, and wept. While she was sitting there, she thought of the egg which the moon had given her; she opened it, and there came out a clucking hen with twelve chickens all of gold, and they ran about chirping, and crept again under the old hen's wings; nothing more beautiful was ever seen in the world! Then she arose, and drove them through the meadow before her, until the bride looked out of the window. The little chickens pleased her so much that she immediately came down and asked if they were for sale.

"Not for money or land, but for flesh and blood; let me sleep another night in the chamber where the bridegroom sleeps."

The bride said, "Yes," intending to cheat her as on the former evening. But when the prince went to bed he asked the page what the murmuring and rustling in the night had been. At this the page told all; that he had been forced to give him a sleeping-potion, because a poor girl had slept secretly in the chamber, and that he was to give him another that night. The prince said, "Pour out the potion by the bedside."

At night, she was again led in, and when she began to relate how ill all had fared with her, he immediately recognized his beloved wife by her voice, sprang up and cried, "Now I really am released! I have been as it were in a dream, for the strange princess has bewitched me so that I have been compelled to forget you, but God has delivered me from the spell at the right time." Then they both left the castle secretly in the night, for they feared the father of the princess, who was a sorcerer, and they seated themselves on the griffin which bore them across the Red Sea, and when they were in the middle of it, she let the nut fall. Immediately a tall nut tree grew up, on which the bird rested, and then carried them home, where they found their child, who had grown tall and beautiful, and they lived happily until their death.

89. THE GOOSE GIRL

There was once upon a time an old Queen whose husband had been dead for many years, and she had a beautiful daughter. When the princess grew up she was betrothed to a prince who lived at a great distance. When the time came for her to be married, and she had to journey forth into the distant kingdom, the aged Queen packed up for her many costly vessels of silver and gold, and trinkets also of gold and silver, and cups and jewels; in short, everything which appertained to a royal dowry, for she loved her child with all her heart. She likewise sent her maid in waiting, who was to ride with her, and hand her over to the bridegroom, and each had a horse for the journey, but the horse of the King's daughter was called Falada, and could speak. So when the hour of parting had come, the aged mother went into her bedroom, took a small knife and cut her finger with it until it bled, then she held a white handkerchief to it into which she let three drops of blood fall, gave it to her daughter and said, "Dear child, preserve this carefully, it will be of service to you on your way."

So they took a sorrowful leave of each other; the princess put the piece of cloth in her bosom, mounted her horse, and then went away to her bridegroom. After she had ridden for a while she felt a burning thirst, and said to her waiting-maid, "Dismount, and take my cup which you have brought with you for me, and get me some water from the stream, for I should like to drink."

"If you are thirsty," said the waiting-maid, "get off your horse yourself, and lie down and drink out of the water, I don't choose to be your servant."

So in her great thirst the princess alighted, bent down over the water in the stream and drank, and was not allowed to drink out of the golden cup. Then she said, "Ah, Heaven!" and the three drops of blood answered, "If your mother knew, her heart would break." But the King's daughter was humble, said nothing, and mounted her horse again.

She rode some miles further, but the day was warm, the sun scorched her, and she was thirsty once more, and when they came to a stream of water, she again cried to her waiting-maid, "Dismount, and give me some water in my golden cup," for she had long ago forgotten the girl's ill words.

But the waiting-maid said still more haughtily, "If you wish to drink, drink as you can, I don't choose to be your maid."

Then in her great thirst the King's daughter alighted, bent over the flowing stream, wept and said, "Ah, Heaven!" and the drops of blood again replied, "If your mother knew this, her heart would break." And as she was thus drinking and leaning right over the stream, the handkerchief with the three drops of blood fell out of her bosom, and floated away with the water without her observing it, so great was her trouble.

The waiting-maid, however, had seen it, and she rejoiced to think that she now had power over the bride, for since the princess had lost the drops of blood, she had become weak and powerless. So now when she wanted to mount her horse again, the one that was called Falada, the waiting-maid said, "Falada is more suitable for me, and my nag will do for you" and the princess had to be content with that. Then the waiting-maid, with many hard words, bade the princess exchange her royal apparel for her own shabby clothes; and at length she was compelled to swear by the clear sky above her, that she would not say one word of this to anyone at the royal court, and if she had not taken this oath she would have been killed on the spot. But Falada saw all this, and observed it well.

The waiting-maid now mounted Falada, and the true bride the bad horse, and thus they traveled onwards, until at length they entered the royal palace. There were great rejoicings over her arrival, and the prince sprang forward to meet her, lifted the waiting-maid from her horse, and thought she was his consort. She was conducted upstairs, but the real princess was left standing below. Then the old King looked out of the window and saw her standing in the courtyard, and how dainty and delicate and beautiful she was, and instantly went to the royal apartment, and asked the bride about the girl she had with her who was standing down below in the courtyard, and who she was? "I picked her up on my way for a companion; give the girl something to work at, that she may not stand idle."

But the old King had no work for her, and knew of none, so he said, "I have a little boy who tends the geese, she may help him." The boy was called Conrad, and the true bride had to help him to tend the geese.

Soon afterwards the false bride said to the young King, "Dearest husband, I beg you to do me a favor."

He answered, "I will do so most willingly."

"Then send for the knacker, and have the head of the horse on which I rode here cut off, for it vexed me on the way." In reality, she was afraid that the horse might tell how she had behaved to the King's daughter. Then she succeeded in making the King promise that it should be done, and the faithful Falada was to die; this came to the ears of the real princess, and she secretly promised to pay the knacker a piece of gold if he would perform a small service for her. There was a great dark-looking gateway in the town, through which morning and evening she had to pass with the geese: would he be so good as to nail up Falada's head on it, so that she might see him again, more than once. The knacker promised to do that, and cut off the head, and nailed it fast beneath the dark gateway.

Early in the morning, when she and Conrad drove out their flock beneath this gateway, she said in passing,

"Alas, Falada, hanging there!"

Then the head answered,

"Alas, young Queen, how ill you fare!
If this your tender mother knew,
Her heart would surely break in two."

Then they went still further out of the town, and drove their geese into the country. And when they had come to the meadow, she sat down and unbound her hair which was like pure gold, and Conrad saw it and delighted in its brightness, and wanted to pluck out a few hairs. Then she said,

"Blow, blow, you gentle wind, I say,
Blow Conrad's little hat away,
And make him chase it here and there,
Until I have braided all my hair,
And bound it up again."

And there came such a violent wind that it blew Conrad's hat far away across country, and he was forced to run after it. When he came back she had finished combing her hair and was putting it up again, and he could not get any of it. Then Conrad was angry, and would not speak to her, and thus they watched the geese until the evening, and then they went home.

Next day when they were driving the geese out through the dark gateway, the maiden said,

"Alas, Falada, hanging there!"

Falada answered,

"Alas, young Queen, how ill you fare!
If this your tender mother knew,
Her heart would surely break in two."

And she sat down again in the field and began to comb out her hair, and Conrad ran and tried to clutch it, so she said in haste,

"Blow, blow, you gentle wind, I say,
Blow Conrad's little hat away,
And make him chase it here and there,
Until I have braided all my hair,
And bound it up again."

Then the wind blew, and blew his little hat off his head and far away, and Conrad was forced to run after it, and when he came back, her hair had been put up a long time, and he could get none of it, and so they looked after their geese till evening came.

But in the evening after they had got home, Conrad went to the old King, and said, "I won't tend the geese with that girl any longer!"

"Why not?" inquired the aged King.

"Oh, because she vexes me the whole day long." Then the aged King commanded him to relate what it was that she did to him. And Conrad said, "In the morning when we pass beneath the dark gateway with the flock, there is a sorry horse's head on the wall, and she says to it,

"Alas, Falada, hanging there!"

And the head replies,

"Alas, young Queen how ill you fare!
If this your tender mother knew,
Her heart would surely break in two."

And Conrad went on to relate what happened on the goose pasture, and how when there he had to chase his hat.

The aged King commanded him to drive his flock out again next day, and as soon as morning came, he placed himself behind the dark gateway, and heard how the maiden spoke to the head of Falada, and then he too went into the country, and hid himself in the thicket in the meadow. There he soon saw with his own eyes the goose girl and the goose boy bringing their flock, and how after a while she sat down and unplaited her hair, which shone with radiance. And soon she said,

"Blow, blow, you gentle wind, I say,
Blow Conrad's little hat away,
And make him chase it here and there,
Until I have braided all my hair,
And bound it up again."

Then came a blast of wind and carried off Conrad's hat, so that he had to run far away, while the maiden quietly went on combing and plaiting her hair, all of which the King observed. Then, quite unseen, he went away, and when the goose girl came home in the evening, he called her aside, and asked why she did all these things.

"I may not tell you that, and I dare not lament my sorrows to any human being, for I have sworn not to do so by the heaven which is above me; if I had not done that, I should have lost my life."

He urged her and left her no peace, but he could draw nothing from her. Then said he, "If you will not tell me anything, tell your sorrows to the iron stove there," and he went away.

Then she crept into the iron stove, and began to weep and lament, and emptied her whole heart, and said, "Here I am deserted by the whole world, and yet I am a King's daughter, and a false waiting-maid has by force brought me to such a pass that I have been compelled to put off my royal apparel, and she has taken my place with my bridegroom, and I have to perform menial service as a goose girl. If my mother did but know that, her heart would break."

The aged King, however, was standing outside by the pipe of the stove, and was listening to what she said, and heard it. Then he came back again, and bade her come out of the stove. And royal garments were placed on her, and it was marvelous how beautiful she was! The aged King summoned his son, and revealed to him that he had got the false bride who was only a waiting-maid, but that the true one was standing there, who had been the goose girl. The young King rejoiced with all his heart when he saw her beauty and youth, and a great feast was made ready to which all the people and all good friends were invited. At the head of the table sat the bridegroom with the King's daughter at one side of him, and the waiting-maid on the other, but the waiting-maid was blinded, and did not recognize the princess in her dazzling array. When they had eaten and drunk, and were merry, the aged King asked the waiting-maid as a riddle, what a person deserved who had behaved in such and such a way to her master, and at the same time related the whole story, and asked what sentence such a one merited?

Then the false bride said, "She deserves no better fate than to be stripped entirely naked, and put in a barrel which is studded inside with pointed nails, and two white horses should be harnessed to it, which will drag her along through one street after another, till she is dead."

"It is you," said the aged King, "and you have pronounced your own sentence, and thus shall it be done unto you." And when the sentence had been carried out, the young King married his true bride, and both of them reigned over their kingdom in peace and happiness.

90. THE YOUNG GIANT

Once upon a time a countryman had a son who was as big as a thumb, and did not become any bigger, and during several years did not grow one hair's breadth. Once when the father was going out to plow, the little one said, "Father, I will go out with you."

"You would go out with me?" said the father. "Stay here, you will be of no use out there, besides you might get lost!" Then Thumbling began to cry, and for the sake of peace his father put him in his pocket, and took him with him. When he was outside in the field, he took him out again, and set him in a freshly-cut furrow. While he was there, a great giant came over the hill.

"Do you see that great bogie?" said the father, for he wanted to frighten the little fellow to make him good, "he is coming to fetch you." The giant, however, had scarcely taken two steps with his long legs before he was in the furrow. He took up little Thumbling carefully with two fingers, examined him, and without saying one word went away with him. His father stood by, but could not utter a sound for terror, and he thought nothing else but that his child was lost, and that as long as he lived he should never set eyes on him again.

The giant, however, carried him home, suckled him, and Thumbling grew and became tall and strong after the manner of giants. When two years had passed, the old giant took him into the forest, wanted to try him, and said, "Pull up a stick for yourself." Then the boy was already so strong that he tore up a young tree out of the earth by the roots. But the giant thought, "We must do better than that," took him back again, and suckled him two years longer.

When he tried him, his strength had increased so much that he could tear an old tree out of the ground. That was still not enough for the giant; he again suckled him for two years, and when he then went with him into the forest and said, "Now just tear up a proper stick for me," the boy tore up the strongest oak tree from the earth, so that it split, and that was a mere trifle to him. "Now that will do," said the giant, "you are perfect," and took him back to the field from where he had brought him. His father was there following the plow.

The young giant went up to him, and said, "Does my father see what a fine man his son has grown into?"

The farmer was alarmed, and said, "No, you are not my son; I don't want you—leave me!"

"Truly I am your son; allow me to do your work, I can plow as well as you, nay better."

"No, no, you are not my son; and you cannot plow—go away!" However, as he was afraid of this great man, he let go of the plow, stepped back and stood at one side of the piece of land. Then the youth took the plow, and just pressed it with one hand, but his grasp was so strong that the plow went deep into the earth. The farmer could not bear to see that, and called to him, "If you are determined to plow, you must not press so hard on it, that makes bad work."

The youth, however, unharnessed the horses, and drew the plow himself, saying, "Just go home, father, and bid my mother make ready a large dish of food, and in the meantime I will go over the field." Then the farmer went home, and ordered his wife to prepare the food; but the youth plowed the field which was two acres large, quite alone, and then he harnessed himself to the harrow, and harrowed the whole of the land, using two harrows at once. When he had done it, he went into the forest, and pulled up two oak trees, laid them across his shoulders, and hung on them one harrow behind and one before, and also one horse behind and one before, and carried all as if it had been a bundle of straw, to his parents' house.

When he entered the yard, his mother did not recognize him, and asked, "Who is that horrible tall man?"

The farmer said, "That is our son."

She said, "No that cannot be our son, we never had such a tall one, ours was a little thing." She called to him, "Go away, we do not want you!"

The youth was silent, but led his horses to the stable, gave them some oats and hay, and all that they wanted. When he had done this, he went into the parlor, sat down on the bench and said, "Mother, now I should like something to eat, will it soon be ready?"

Then she said, "Yes," and brought in two immense dishes full of food, which would have been enough to satisfy herself and her husband for a week. The youth, however, ate the whole of it himself, and asked if she had nothing more to set before him. "No," she replied, "that is all we have."

"But that was only a taste, I must have more." She did not dare to oppose him, and went and put a huge caldron full of food on the fire, and when it was ready, carried it in. "At length come a few crumbs," said he, and ate all there was, but it was still not sufficient to appease his hunger. Then said he, "Father, I see well that with you I shall never have food enough; if you will get me an iron staff which is strong, and which I cannot break against my knees, I will go out into the world."

The farmer was glad, put his two horses in his cart, and fetched from the smith a staff so large and thick, that the two horses could only just bring it away. The youth laid it across his knees, and snap! he broke it in two in the middle like a beanstalk, and threw it away. The father then harnessed four horses, and brought a bar which was so long and thick, that the four horses could only just drag it. The son snapped this also in two against his knees, threw it away, and said, "Father, this can be of no use to me, you must harness more horses, and bring a stronger staff." So the father harnessed eight horses, and brought one which was so long and thick, that the eight horses could only just carry it. When the son took it in his hand, he broke off a bit from the top of it also, and said, "Father, I see that you will not be able to procure me any such staff as I want, I will remain no longer with you."

So he went away, and gave out that he was a smith's apprentice. He arrived at a village, where a smith lived who was a greedy fellow, who never did a kindness to anyone, but wanted everything for himself. The youth went into the smithy and asked if he needed a journeyman. "Yes," said the smith, and looked at him, and thought, "That is a strong fellow who will strike out well, and earn his bread." So he asked, "How much wages do you want?"

"I don't want any at all," he replied, "only every fortnight, when the other journeymen are paid, I will give you two blows, and you must bear them." The miser was heartily satisfied, and thought he would thus save much money.

Next morning, the strange journeyman was to begin to work, but when the master brought the glowing bar, and the youth struck his first blow, the iron flew asunder, and the anvil sank so deep into the earth, that there was no bringing it out again. Then the miser grew angry, and said, "Oh, but I can't make any use of you, you strike far too powerfully; what will you have for the one blow?"

Then said he, "I will only give you quite a small blow, that's all."

And he raised his foot, and gave him such a kick that he flew away over four loads of hay. Then he sought out the thickest iron bar in the smithy for himself, took it as a stick in his hand and went onwards.

When he had walked for some time, he came to a small farm, and asked the bailiff if he did not require a head-servant. "Yes," said the bailiff, "I can make use of one; you look a strong fellow who can do something, how much a year do you want as wages?" He again replied that he wanted no wages at all, but that every year he would give him three blows, which he must bear. Then the bailiff was satisfied, for he, too, was a covetous fellow.

Next morning all the servants were to go into the wood, and the others were already up, but the head-servant was still in bed. Then one of them called to him, "Get up, it is time; we are going into the wood, and you must go with us."

"Ah," said he in a rough and surly tone, "you may just go, then; I shall be back again before any of you." Then the others went to the bailiff, and told him that the head-man was still lying in bed, and would not go into the wood with them. The bailiff said they were to awaken him again, and tell him to harness the horses. The head-man, however, said as before, "Just go there, I shall be back again before any of you." And then he stayed in bed two hours longer.

At length he arose from the feathers, but first he got himself two bushels of peas from the loft, made himself some broth with them, ate it at his leisure, and when that was done, went and harnessed the horses, and drove into the wood. Not far from the wood was a ravine through which he had to pass, so he first drove the horses on, and then stopped them, and went behind the cart, took trees and brushwood, and made a great barricade, so that no horse could get through. When he was entering the wood, the others were just driving out of it with their loaded carts to go home; then said he to them, "Drive on, I will still get home before you do." He did not drive far into the wood, but at once tore two of the very largest trees of all out of the earth, threw them on his cart, and turned round. When he came to the barricade, the others were still standing there, not able to get through. "Don't you see," said he, "that if you had stayed with me, you would have got home just as quickly, and would have had another hour's sleep?"

He now wanted to drive on, but his horses could not work their way through, so he unharnessed them, laid them on the top of the cart, took the shafts in his own hands, and pulled it all through, and he did this just as easily as if it had been laden with feathers. When he was over, he said to the others, "There, you see, I have got over quicker than you," and drove on, and the others had to stay where they were.

In the yard, he took a tree in his hand, showed it to the bailiff, and said, "Isn't that a fine bundle of wood?"

Then said the bailiff to his wife, "The servant is a good one, if he does sleep long, he is still home before the others."

So he served the bailiff for a year, and when that was over, and the other servants were getting their wages, he said it was time for him to take his too. The bailiff, however, was afraid of the blows which he was to receive, and earnestly entreated him to excuse him from having them; for rather than that, he himself would be head-servant, and the youth should be bailiff. "No," said he, "I will not be a bailiff, I am head-servant, and will remain so, but I will administer that which we agreed on."

The bailiff was willing to give him whatever he demanded, but it was of no use, the head-servant said no to everything. Then the bailiff did not know what to do, and begged for a fortnight's delay, for he wanted to find some way of escape. The head-servant consented to this delay. The bailiff summoned all his clerks together, and they were to think the matter over, and give him advice. The clerks pondered for a long time, but at last they said that no one was sure of his life with the head-servant, for he could kill a man as easily as a midge, and that the bailiff ought to make him get into the well and clean it, and when he was down below, they would roll up one of the millstones which was lying there, and throw it on his head; and then he would never return to daylight.

The advice pleased the bailiff, and the head-servant was quite willing to go down the well. When he was standing down below at the bottom, they rolled down the largest millstone and thought they had broken his skull, but he cried, "Chase away those hens from the well, they are scratching in the sand up there, and throwing the grains into my eyes, so that I can't see."

So the bailiff cried, "Sh-sh," and pretended to frighten the hens away.

When the head-servant had finished his work, he climbed up and said, "Just look what a beautiful necktie I have on," and behold it was the millstone which he was wearing round his neck. The head-servant now wanted to take his reward, but the bailiff again begged for a fortnight's delay. The clerks met together and advised him to send the head-servant to the haunted mill to grind corn by night, for as yet no man had ever returned from there in the morning alive.

The proposal pleased the bailiff, he called the head-servant that very evening, and ordered him to take eight bushels of corn to the mill, and grind it that night, for it was wanted. So the head-servant went to the loft, and put two bushels in his right pocket, and two in his left, and took four in a wallet, half on his back, and half on his breast, and thus laden went to the haunted mill. The miller told him that he could grind there very well by day, but not by night, for the mill was haunted, and that up to the present time whoever had gone into it at night had been found in the morning lying dead inside. He said, "I will manage it, just you go away to bed." Then he went into the mill, and poured out the corn.

About eleven o'clock he went into the miller's room, and sat down on the bench. When he had sat there a while, a door suddenly opened, and a large table came in, and on the table, wine and roasted meats placed themselves, and much good food besides, but everything came of itself, for no one was there to carry it. After this the chairs pushed themselves up, but no people came, until all at once he saw fingers, which handled knives and forks, and laid food on the plates, but with this exception he saw nothing. As he was hungry, and saw the food, he, too, place himself at the table, ate with those who were eating and enjoyed it. When he had had enough, and the others also had quite emptied their dishes, he distinctly heard all the candles being suddenly snuffed out, and as it was now pitch dark, he felt something like a box on the ear. Then he said, "If anything of that kind comes again, I shall strike out in return." And when he had received a second box on the ear, he, too struck out. And so it continued the whole night. He took nothing without returning it, but repaid everything with interest, and did not lay about him in vain.

At daybreak, however, everything ceased. When the miller had got up, he wanted to look after him, and wondered if he were still alive. Then the youth said, "I have eaten my fill, have received some boxes on the ears, but I have given some in return." The miller rejoiced, and said that the mill was now released from the spell, and wanted to give him much money as a reward. But he said, "Money, I will not have, I have enough of it." So he took his meal on his back, went home, and told the bailiff that he had done what he had been told to do, and would now have the reward agreed on.

When the bailiff heard that, he was seriously alarmed and quite beside himself; he walked backwards and forwards in the room, and drops of perspiration ran down from his forehead. Then he opened the window to get some fresh air, but before he was aware, the head-servant had given him such a kick that he flew through the window out into the air, and so far away that no one ever saw him again. Then said the head-servant to the bailiff's wife, "If he does not come back, you must take the other blow."

She cried, "No, no I cannot bear it," and opened the other window, because drops of perspiration were running down her forehead. Then he gave her such a kick that she, too, flew out, and as she was lighter she went much higher than her husband.

Her husband cried, "Do come to me," but she replied, "Come you to me, I cannot come to you." And they hovered about there in the air, and could not get to each other, and whether they are still hovering about, or not, I do not know, but the young giant took up his iron bar, and went on his way.

91. THE GNOME

There was once upon a time a rich King who had three daughters, who daily went to walk in the palace garden, and the King was a great lover of all kinds of fine trees, but there was one for which he had such an affection, that if anyone gathered an apple from it he wished him a hundred fathoms underground. And when harvest time came, the apples on this tree were all as red as blood. The three daughters went every day beneath the tree, and looked to see if the wind had not blown down an apple, but they never by any chance found one, and the tree was so loaded with them that it was almost breaking, and the branches hung down to the ground. Then the King's youngest child had a great desire for an apple, and said to her sisters, "Our father loves us far too much to wish us underground, it is my belief that he would only do that to people who were strangers." And while she was speaking, the child plucked off quite a large apple, and ran to her sisters, saying, "Just taste, my dear little sisters, for never in my life have I tasted anything so delightful." Then the two other sisters also ate some of the apple, after which all three sank deep down into the earth, where they could hear no cock crow.

When midday came, the King wished to call them to come to dinner, but they were nowhere to be found. He sought them everywhere in the palace and garden, but could not find them. Then he was much troubled, and made known to the whole land that whoever brought his daughters back again should have one of them to wed. Hereupon so many young men went about the country in search, that there was no counting them, for everyone loved the three children because they were so kind to all, and so fair of face. Three young hunters also went out, and when they had traveled about for eight days, they arrived at a great castle, in which were beautiful apartments, and in one room a table was laid on which were delicate dishes which were still so warm that they were smoking, but in the whole of the castle no human being was either to be seen or heard. They waited there for half a day, and the food still remained warm and smoking, and at length they were so hungry that they sat down and ate, and agreed with each other that they would stay and live in that castle, and that one of them, who should be chosen by casting lots, should remain in the house, and the two others seek the King's daughters. They cast lots, and the lot fell on the eldest; so next day the two younger went out to seek, and the eldest had to stay home. At midday came a small, small manikin and begged for a piece of bread, then the hunter took the bread which he had found there, and cut a round off the loaf and was about to give it to him, but while he was giving it to the manikin, the latter let it fall, and asked the hunter to be so good as to give him that piece again. The hunter was about to do so and stooped, on which the manikin took a stick, seized him by the hair, and gave him a good beating. Next day, the second stayed at home, and he fared no better. When the two others returned in the evening, the eldest said, "Well, how have you got on?"

"Oh, very badly," said he, and then they lamented their misfortune together, but they said nothing about it to the youngest, for they did not like him at all, and always called him Stupid Hans, because he did not exactly belong to the forest. On the third day, the youngest stayed at home, and again the little manikin came and begged for a piece of bread. When the youth gave it to him, he let it fall as before, and asked him to be so good as to give him that piece again.

Then said Hans to the little manikin, "What! Can you not pick up that piece yourself? If you will not take as much trouble as that for your daily bread, you do not deserve to have it."

Then the manikin grew very angry and said he was to do it, but the hunter would not, and took my dear manikin, and gave him a thorough beating. Then the manikin screamed terribly, and cried, "Stop, stop, and let me go, and I will tell you where the King's daughters are."

When Hans heard that, he left off beating him and the manikin told him that he was a gnome, and that there were more than a thousand like him, and that if he would go with him he would show him where the King's daughters were. Then he showed him a deep well, but there was no water in it. And the little man said that he knew well that the companions Hans had with him did not intend to deal honorably with him, therefore if he wished to deliver the King's children, he must do it alone. The two other brothers would also be very glad to recover the King's daughters, but they did not want to have any trouble or danger. Hans was therefore to take a large basket, and he must seat himself in it with his knife and a bell, and be let down. Below were three rooms, and in each of them was a princess, with a many-headed dragon, whose heads she was to comb and trim, but he must cut them off. And having said all this, the manikin vanished.

When it was evening the two brothers came and asked how he had got on, and he said, "pretty well so far," and that he had seen no one except at midday when a little manikin had come and begged for a piece of bread, that he had given some to him, but that the manikin had let it fall and had asked him to pick it up again; but as he did not choose to do that, the little man had begun to lose his temper, and that he had done what he ought not, and had given the manikin a beating, after which he had told him where the King's daughters were. Then the two were so angry at this that they grew green and yellow.

Next morning they went to the well together, and drew lots who should first seat himself in the basket, and again the lot fell on the eldest, and he was to seat himself in it, and take the bell with him. Then he said, "If I ring, you must draw me up again immediately."

When he had gone down for a short distance, he rang, and they at once drew him up again. Then the second seated himself in the basket, but he did just the same as the first, and then it was the turn of the youngest, but he let himself be lowered quite to the bottom. When he had got out of the basket, he took his knife, and went and stood outside the first door and listened, and heard the dragon snoring quite loudly. He opened the door slowly, and one of the princesses was sitting there, and had nine dragon's heads lying upon her lap, and was combing them. Then he took his knife and hewed at them, and the nine fell off. The princess sprang up, threw her arms round his neck, embraced and kissed him repeatedly, and took her stomacher, which was made of pure gold, and hung it round his neck. Then he went to the second princess, who had a dragon with five heads to comb, and delivered her also, and to the youngest, who had a dragon with four heads, he went likewise. And they all rejoiced, and embraced him and kissed him without stopping. Then he rang very loud, so that those above heard him, and he placed the princesses one after the other in the basket, and had them all drawn up, but when it came to his own turn he remembered the words of the manikin, who had told him that his comrades did not mean well by him. So he took a great stone which was lying there, and placed it in the basket, and when it was about halfway up, his false brothers above cut the rope, so that the basket with the stone fell to the ground, and they thought that he was dead, and ran away with the three princesses, making them promise to tell their father that it was they who had delivered them, and then they went to the King, and each demanded a princess in marriage.

In the meantime the youngest hunter was wandering about the three chambers in great trouble, fully expecting to have to end his days there, when he saw, hanging on the wall, a flute; then said he, "Why do you hang there, no one can be merry here?" He looked at the dragons' heads likewise and said, "You too cannot help me now." He walked backwards and forwards for such a long time that he made the surface of the ground quite smooth. But at last other thoughts came to his mind, and he took the flute from the wall, and played a few notes on it, and suddenly a number of gnomes appeared, and with every note that he sounded one more came. Then he played until the room was entirely filled. They all asked what he desired, so he said he wished to get above ground back to daylight, on which they seized him by every hair that grew on his head, and thus they flew with him onto the earth again. When he was above ground, he at once went to the King's palace, just as the wedding of one princess was about to be celebrated, and he went to the room where the King and his three daughters were. When the princesses saw him they fainted. At this the King was angry, and ordered him to be put in prison at once, because he thought he must have done some injury to the children. When the princesses came to themselves, however, they entreated the King to set him free again. The King asked why, and they said that they were not allowed to tell that, but their father said that they were to tell it to the stove. And he went out, listened at the door, and heard everything. Then he sentenced the two brothers to be hanged on the gallows, and to the third he gave his youngest daughter, and on that occasion I wore a pair of glass shoes, and I struck them against a stone, and they said, "Klink," and were broken.

92. THE KING OF THE GOLDEN MOUNTAIN

There was a certain merchant who had two children, a boy and a girl; they were both young, and could not walk. And two richly-laden ships of his sailed forth to sea with all his property on board, and just as he was expecting to win much money by them, news came that they had gone to the bottom, and now instead of being a rich man he was a poor one, and had nothing left but one field outside the town. In order to drive his misfortune a little out of his thoughts, he went out to this field, and as he was walking forwards and backwards in it, a little black manikin stood suddenly by his side, and asked why he was so sad, and what he was taking so much to heart. Then said the merchant, "If you could help me I would willingly tell you."

"Who knows?" replied the black dwarf. "Perhaps, I can help you." Then the merchant told him that all he possessed had gone to the bottom of the sea, and that he had nothing left but this field. "Do not trouble yourself," said the dwarf. "If you will promise to give me the first thing that rubs itself against your leg when you are at home again, and to bring it here to this place in twelve years' time, you shall have as much money as you will."

The merchant thought, "What can that be but my dog?" and did not remember his little boy, so he said yes, gave the black man a written and sealed promise, and went home.

When he reached home, his little boy was so delighted that he held by a bench, tottered up to him and seized him fast by the legs. The father was shocked, for he remembered his promise, and now knew what he had pledged himself to do; as however, he still found no money in his chest, he thought the dwarf had only been jesting. A month afterwards he went up to the attic, intending to gather together some old tin and to sell it, and saw a great heap of money lying. Then he was happy again, made purchases, became a greater merchant than before, and felt that this world was well-governed. In the meantime the boy grew tall, and at the same time sharp and clever. But the nearer the twelfth year approached the more anxious the merchant grew, so that his distress might be seen in his face. One day his son asked what ailed him, but the father would not say. The boy, however, persisted so long, that at last he told him that without being aware of what he was doing, he had promised him to a black dwarf, and had received much money for doing so. He said likewise that he had set his hand and seal to this, and that now when twelve years had gone by he would have to give him up.

Then said the son, "Oh, father, do not be uneasy, all will go well. The black man has no power over me." The son had himself blessed by the priest, and when the time came, father and son went together to the field, and the son made a circle and placed himself inside it with his father.

Then came the black dwarf and said to the old man, "Have you brought with you that which you have promised me?"

He was silent, but the son asked, "What do you want here?"

Then said the black dwarf, "I have to speak with your father, and not with you."

The son replied, "You have betrayed and misled my father, give back the writing."

"No," said the black dwarf, "I will not give up my rights." They spoke together for a long time after this, but at last they agreed that the son, as he did not belong to the enemy of mankind, nor did he to his father, should seat himself in a small boat, which should lie on water which was flowing away from them, and that the father should push it off with his own foot, and then the son should remain given up to the water. So he took leave of his father, placed himself in a little boat, and the father had to push it off with his own foot. The boat capsized so that the keel was uppermost, and the father believed his son was lost, and went home and mourned for him.

The boat, however, did not sink, but floated quietly away, and the boy sat safely inside it, and it floated thus for a long time, until at last it stopped by an unknown shore. Then he landed and saw a beautiful castle before him, and set out to go to it. But when he entered it, he found that it was bewitched. He went through every room, but all were empty until he reached the last, where a snake lay coiled in a ring. The snake, however, was an enchanted maiden, who rejoiced to see him, and said, "Have you come, oh, my deliverer? I have already waited twelve years for you; this kingdom is bewitched, and you must set it free."

"How can I do that?" he inquired.

"Tonight come twelve black men, covered with chains who will ask what you are doing here; keep silent; give them no answer, and let them do what they will with you; they will torment you, beat you, stab you; let everything pass, only do not speak; at twelve o'clock, they must go away again. On the second night twelve others will come; on the third, twenty-four, who will cut off your head, but at twelve o'clock their power will be over, and then if you have endured all, and have not spoken the slightest word, I shall be released. I will come to you, and will have, in a bottle, some of the water of life. I will rub you with that, and then you will come to life again, and be as healthy as before."

Then said he, "I will gladly set you free." And everything happened just as she had said; the black men could not force a single word from him, and on the third night the snake became a beautiful princess, who came with the water of life and brought him back to life again. So she threw herself into his arms and kissed him, and there was joy and gladness in the whole castle. After this their marriage was celebrated, and he was King of the Golden Mountain.

They lived very happily together, and the Queen bore a fine boy. Eight years had already gone by, when the King thought of his father; his heart was moved, and he wished to visit him. The Queen, however, would not let him go away, and said, "I know beforehand that it will cause my unhappiness;" but he suffered her to have no rest until she consented. At their parting she gave him a wishing ring, and said, "Take this ring and put it on your finger, and then you will immediately be transported wherever you would be, only you must promise me not to use it in wishing me away from this place and with your father."

That he promised her, put the ring on his finger, and wished himself at home, just outside the town where his father lived. Instantly he found himself there, and made for the town, but when he came to the gate, the sentries would not let him in, because he wore such strange and yet such rich and magnificent clothing. Then he went to a hill where a shepherd was watching his sheep, changed clothes with him, put on his old shepherd's coat, and then entered the town without hindrance. When he came to his father, he made himself known to him, but he did not at all believe that the shepherd was his son, and said he certainly had had a son, but that he was dead long ago; however, as he saw he was a poor, needy shepherd, he would give him something to eat. Then the shepherd said to his parents, "I am verily your son. Do you know of no mark on my body by which you could recognize me?"

"Yes," said his mother, "our son had a raspberry mark under his right arm." He slipped back his shirt, and they saw the raspberry under his right arm, and no longer doubted that he was their son. Then he told them that he was King of the Golden Mountain, and a king's daughter was his wife, and that they had a fine son of seven years old.

Then said the father, "That is certainly not true; it is a fine kind of a king who goes about in a ragged shepherd's coat."

At this the son fell in a passion, and without thinking of his promise, turned his ring round, and wished both his wife and child with him. They were there in a second, but the Queen wept, and reproached him, and said that he had broken his word, and had brought misfortune upon her. He said, "I have done it thoughtlessly, and not with evil intention," and tried to calm her, and she pretended to believe this; but she had mischief in her mind.

Then he led her out of the town into the field, and showed her the stream where the little boat had been pushed off, and then he said, "I am tired; sit down, I will sleep awhile on your lap." And he laid his head on her lap, and fell asleep. When he was asleep, she first drew the ring from his finger, then she drew away the foot which was under him, leaving only the slipper behind her, and she took her child in her arms, and wished herself back in her own kingdom.

When he awoke, there he lay quite deserted, and his wife and child were gone, and so was the ring from his finger, only the slipper was still there as a token. "Home to your parents you cannot return," thought he, "they would say that you were a wizard; you must be off, and walk on until you arrive in your own kingdom." So he went away and came at length to a hill by which three giants were standing, disputing with each other because they did not know how to divide their father's property. When they saw him passing by, they called to him and said little men had quick wits, and that he was to divide their inheritance for them. The inheritance, however, consisted of a sword, which had this property that if anyone took it in his hand, and said, "All heads off but mine," every head would lie on the ground; secondly, of a cloak which made anyone who put it on invisible; thirdly, of a pair of boots which could transport the wearer to any place he wished in a moment.

He said, "Give me the three things that I may see if they are still in good condition." They gave him the cloak, and when he had put it on, he was invisible and changed into a fly. Then he resumed his own form and said, "The cloak is a good one, now give me the sword."

They said, "No, we will not give you that; if you were to say, 'All heads off but mine,' all our heads would be off, and you alone would be left with yours." Nevertheless they gave it to him with the condition that he was only to try it against a tree. This he did, and the sword cut in two the trunk of a tree as if it had been a blade of straw.

Then he wanted to have the boots likewise, but they said, "No, we will not give them; if you had them on your feet and were to wish yourself at the top of the hill, we should be left down here with nothing."

"Oh, no," said he, "I will not do that." So they gave him the boots as well. And now when he had got all these things, he thought of nothing but his wife and his child, and said as though to himself, "Oh, if I were but on the Golden Mountain," and at the same moment he vanished from the sight of the giants, and thus their inheritance was divided.

When he was near his palace, he heard sounds of joy, and fiddles, and flutes, and the people told him that his wife was celebrating her wedding with another. Then he fell into a rage, and said, "False woman, she betrayed and deserted me while I was asleep!" So he put on his cloak, and unseen by all went into the palace. When he entered the dining hall a great table was spread with delicious food, and the guests were eating and drinking, and laughing, and jesting. She sat on a royal seat in the middle of them in splendid apparel, with a crown on her head. He placed himself behind her, and no one saw him. When she put a piece of meat on a plate for herself, he took it away and ate it, and when she poured out a glass of wine for herself, he took it away and drank it. She was always helping herself to something, and yet she never got anything, for plate and glass disappeared immediately.

Then dismayed and ashamed, she arose and went to her chamber and wept, but he followed her there. She said, "Has the devil power over me, or did my deliverer never come?"

Then he struck her in the face, and said, "Did your deliverer never come? It is he who has you in his power, you traitor. Have I deserved this from you?" Then he made himself visible, went into the hall, and cried, "The wedding is at an end, the true King has returned."

The kings, princes, and councilors who were assembled there, ridiculed and mocked him, but he did not trouble to answer them, and said, "Will you go away, or not?" At this they tried to seize him and pressed upon him, but he drew his sword and said, "All heads off but mine," and all the heads rolled on the ground, and he alone was master, and once more King of the Golden Mountain.

93. THE RAVEN

There was once upon a time a Queen who had a little daughter who was still so young that she had to be carried. One day the child was naughty, and the mother might say what she liked, but the child would not be quiet. Then she became impatient, and as the ravens were flying about the palace, she opened the window and said, "I wish you were a raven and would fly away, and then I should have some rest." Scarcely had she spoken the words, before the child was changed into a raven, and flew from her arms out of the window. It flew into a dark forest, and stayed in it a long time, and the parents heard nothing of their child. Then one day a man was on his way through this forest and heard the raven crying, and followed the voice, and when he came nearer, the bird said, "I am a king's daughter by birth, and am bewitched, but you can set me free."

"What am I to do?" asked he.

She said, "Go further into the forest, and you will find a house, wherein sits an aged woman, who will offer you meat and drink, but you must accept nothing, for if you eat and drink anything, you will fall into a sleep, and then you will not be able to deliver me. In the garden behind the house there is a great heap of tan, and on this you shall stand and wait for me. For three days I will come every afternoon at two o'clock in a carriage. On the first day four white horses will be harnessed to it, then four chestnut horses, and lastly four black ones; but if you are not awake, but sleeping, I shall not be set free." The man promised to do everything that she desired, but the raven said, alas, "I know already that you will not deliver me; you will accept something from the woman."

Then the man once more promised that he would certainly not touch anything either to eat or to drink. But when he entered the house the old woman came to him and said, "Poor man, how faint you are; come and refresh yourself; eat and drink."

"No," said the man, "I will not eat or drink."

She, however, let him have no peace, and said, "If you will not eat, take one drink out of the glass; one is nothing." Then he let himself be persuaded, and drank.

Shortly before two o'clock in the afternoon he went into the garden to the tan heap to wait for the raven. As he was standing there, his weariness all at once became so great that he could not struggle against it, and lay down for a short time, but he was determined not to go to sleep. Hardly, however, had he lain down, than his eyes closed of their own accord, and he fell asleep and slept so soundly that nothing in the world could have aroused him.

At two o'clock the raven came driving up with four white horses, but she was already in deep grief and said, "I know he is asleep." And when she came into the garden, he was indeed lying there asleep on the heap of tan. She alighted from the carriage, went to him, shook him, and called him, but he did not awake.

Next day about noon, the old woman came again and brought him food and drink, but he would not take any of it. But she let him have no rest and persuaded him until at length he again took one drink out of the glass. Towards two o'clock he went into the garden to the tan heap to wait for the raven, but all at once felt such a great weariness that his limbs would no longer support him. He could not help himself, and was forced to lie down, and fell into a heavy sleep. When the raven drove up with four brown horses, she was already full of grief, and said, "I know he is asleep." She went to him, but there he lay sleeping, and there was no waking him.

Next day the old woman asked what was the meaning of this? He was neither eating nor drinking anything; did he want to die? He replied, "I am not allowed to eat or drink, and will not do so." But she set a dish with food, and a glass with wine before him, and when he smelled it he could not resist, and swallowed a deep drink. When the time came, he went out into the garden to the heap of tan, and waited for the King's daughter; but he became still more weary than on the day before, and lay down and slept as soundly as if he had been a stone.

At two o'clock the raven came with four black horses, and the coachman and everything else was black. She was already in the deepest grief, and said, "I know that he is asleep and cannot deliver me." When she came to him, there he was lying fast asleep. She shook him and called him, but she could not wake him.

Then she laid a loaf beside him, and after that a piece of meat, and thirdly a bottle of wine, and he might consume as much of all of them as he liked, but they would never grow less. After this she took a gold ring from her finger, and put it on his, and her name was graven on it. Lastly, she laid a letter beside him wherein was written what she had given him, and that none of the things would ever grow less; and in it was also written, "I see right well that here you will never be able to deliver me, but if you are still willing to deliver me, come to the golden castle of Stromberg; it lies in your power, of that I am certain." And when she had given him all these things, she seated herself in her carriage, and drove to the golden castle of Stromberg.

When the man awoke and saw that he had slept, he was sad at heart, and said, "She has certainly driven by, and I have not set her free." Then he perceived the things which were lying beside him, and read the letter wherein was written how everything had happened. So he arose and went away, intending to go to the golden castle of Stromberg, but he did not know where it was. After he had walked about the world for a long time, he entered into a dark forest, and walked for fourteen days, and still could not find his way out. Then it was once more evening, and he was so tired that he lay down in a thicket and fell asleep. Next day he went onwards, and in the evening, as he was again about to lie down beneath some bushes, he heard such a howling and crying that he could not go to sleep. And at the time when people light the candles, he saw one glimmering, and arose and went towards it. Then he came to a house which seemed very small, for in front of it a great giant was standing. He thought to himself, "If I go in, and the giant sees me, it will very likely cost me my life."

At length he ventured it and went in. When the giant saw him, he said, "It is well that you come, for it is long since I have eaten; I will at once eat you for my supper."

"I'd rather you would leave that alone," said the man, "I do not like to be eaten; but if you have any desire to eat, I have quite enough here to satisfy you."

"If that be true," said the giant, "you may be easy, I was only going to devour you because I had nothing else." Then they went, and sat down to the table, and the man took out the bread, wine, and meat which would never come to an end. "This pleases me well," said the giant, and ate to his heart's content.

Then the man said to him, "Can you tell me where the golden castle of Stromberg is?"

The giant said, "I will look at my map; all the towns, and villages, and houses are to be found on it." He brought out the map which he had in the room and looked for the castle, but it was not to be found on it. "It's no matter!" said he, "I have some still larger maps in my cupboard upstairs, and we will look in them." But there, too, it was in vain.

The man now wanted to go onwards, but the giant begged him to wait a few days longer until his brother, who had gone out to bring some provisions, came home. When the brother came home they inquired about the golden castle of Stromberg. He replied, "When I have eaten and have had enough, I will look in the map." Then he went with them up to his chamber, and they searched in his map, but could not find it. Then he brought out still older maps, and they never rested until they found the golden castle of Stromberg, but it was many thousand miles away.

"How am I to get there?" asked the man.

The giant said, "I have two hours' time, during which I will carry you into the neighborhood, but after that I must be at home to suckle the child that we have." So the giant carried the man to about a hundred leagues from the castle, and said, "You can very well walk the rest of the way alone." And he turned back.

The man, however, went onwards day and night, until at length he came to the golden castle of Stromberg. It stood on a glass mountain, and the bewitched maiden drove in her carriage round the castle, and then went inside it. He rejoiced when he saw her and wanted to climb up to her, but when he began to do so he always slipped down the glass again. And when he saw that he could not reach her, he was filled with trouble, and said to himself, "I will stay down here below, and wait for her."

So he built himself a hut and stayed in it for a whole year, and every day saw the King's daughter driving about above, but never could go to her. Then one day he saw from his hut three robbers who were beating each other, and cried to them, "God be with you!" They stopped when they heard the cry, but as they saw no one, they once more began to beat each other, and that too most dangerously. So he again cried, "God be with you!" Again they stopped, looked round about, but as they saw no one they went on beating each other. Then he cried for the third time, "God be with you," and thought, "I must see what these three are about," and went over and asked why they were beating each other so furiously.

One of them said that he found a stick, and that when he struck a door with it, that door would spring open. The next said that he had found a mantle, and that whenever he put it on, he was invisible, but the third said he had found a horse on which a man could ride everywhere, even up the glass mountain. And now they did not know whether they ought to have these things in common, or whether they ought to divide them. Then the man said, "I will give you something in exchange for these three things. Money indeed have I not, but I have other things of more value; but first I must try yours to see if you have told the truth."

Then they put him on the horse, threw the mantle round him, and gave him the stick in his hand, and when he had all these things they were no longer able to see him. So he gave them some vigorous blows and cried, "Now, vagabonds, you have got what you deserve, are you satisfied?" And he rode up the glass mountain, but when he came in front of the castle at the top, it was shut. Then he struck the door with his stick, and it sprang open immediately. He went in and ascended the stairs until he came to the hall where the maiden was sitting with a golden cup full of wine before her. She, however, could not see him because he had the mantle on. And when he came up to her, he drew from his finger the ring which she had given him, and threw it into the cup so that it rang. Then she cried, "That is my ring, so the man who is to set me free must be here."

The courtiers searched the whole castle and did not find him, but he had gone out, and had seated himself on the horse and thrown off the mantle. When they came to the door, they saw him and cried aloud in their delight. Then he alighted and took the King's daughter in his arms, but she kissed him and said, "Now you have set me free, and tomorrow we will celebrate our wedding."

94. THE PEASANT'S WISE DAUGHTER

There was once a poor peasant who had no land, but only a small house, and one daughter. Then said the daughter, "We ought to ask our lord the King for a bit of newly-cleared land." When the King heard of their poverty, he presented them with a piece of land, which she and her father dug up, and intended to sow with a little corn and grain of that kind. When they had dug nearly the whole of the field, they found in the earth a mortar made of pure gold.

"Listen," said the father to the girl, "as our lord the King has been so gracious and presented us with the field, we ought to give him this mortar in return for it."

The daughter, however, would not consent to this, and said, "Father, if we have the mortar without having the pestle as well, we shall have to get the pestle, so you had much better say nothing about it."

He would, however, not obey her, but took the mortar and carried it to the King, said that he had found it in the cleared land, and asked if he would accept it as a present. The King took the mortar, and asked if he had found nothing besides that? "No," answered the countryman.

Then the King said that he must now bring him the pestle. The peasant said they had not found that, but he might just as well have spoken to the wind; he was put in prison, and was to stay there until he produced the pestle. The servants had daily to carry him bread and water, which is what people get in prison, and they heard how the man cried out continually, "Ah! If I had but listened to my daughter! Alas, alas, if I had but listened to my daughter!" and would neither eat nor drink. So he commanded the servants to bring the prisoner before him, and then the King asked the peasant why he was always crying, "Ah! If I had but listened to my daughter!" and what it was that his daughter had said.

"She told me that I ought not to take the mortar to you, for I should have to produce the pestle as well."

"If you have a daughter who is as wise as that, let her come here." She was therefore obliged to appear before the King, who asked her if she really was so wise, and said he would set her a riddle, and if she could guess that, he would marry her. She at once said yes, she would guess it. Then said the King, "Come to me not clothed, not naked, not riding, not walking, not in the road, and not out of the road, and if you can do that I will marry you."

So she went away, put off everything she had on, and then she was not clothed, and took a great fishing net, and seated herself in it and wrapped it entirely round and round her, so that she was not naked, and she hired an ass, and tied the fisherman's net to its tail, so that it was forced to drag her along, and that was neither riding nor walking. The ass had also to drag her in the ruts, so that she only touched the ground with her great toe, and that was neither being in the road nor out of the road. And when she arrived in that fashion, the King said she had guessed the riddle and fulfilled all the conditions. Then he ordered her father to be released from the prison, took her as wife, and gave into her care all the royal possessions.

Now when some years had passed, the King was once drawing up his troops on parade, when it happened that some peasants who had been selling wood stopped with their wagons before the palace; some of them had oxen yoked to them, and some horses. There was one peasant who had three horses, one of which delivered a young foal, and it ran away and lay down between two oxen which were in front of the wagon. When the peasants came together, they began to dispute, to beat each other and make a disturbance, and the peasant with the oxen wanted to keep the foal, and said one of the oxen had given birth to it, and the other said his horse had had it, and that it was his. The quarrel came before the King, and he give the verdict that the foal should stay where it had been found, and so the peasant with the oxen, to whom it did not belong, got it. Then the other went away, and wept and lamented over his foal.

Now he had heard how gracious his lady the Queen was because she herself had sprung from poor peasant folks, so he went to her and begged her to see if she could not help him to get his foal back again. Said she, "Yes, I will tell you what to do, if you will promise me not to betray me. Early tomorrow morning, when the King parades the guard, place yourself there in the middle of the road by which he must pass, take a great fishing net and pretend to be fishing; go on fishing, too, and empty out the net as if you had got it full"—and then she told him also what he was to say if he was questioned by the King.

The next day, therefore, the peasant stood there, and fished on dry ground. When the King passed by, and saw that, he sent his messenger to ask what the stupid man was about? He answered, "I am fishing."

The messenger asked how he could fish when there was no water there? The peasant said, "It is as easy for me to fish on dry land as it is for an ox to have a foal."

The messenger went back and took the answer to the King, who ordered the peasant to be brought to him and told him that this was not his own idea, and he wanted to know whose it was? The peasant must confess this at once. The peasant, however, would not do so, and said always, God forbid he should!—The idea was his own. They laid him, however, on a heap of straw, and beat him and tormented him so long that at last he admitted that he had got the idea from the Queen.

When the King reached home again, he said to his wife, "Why have you behaved so falsely to me? I will not have you any longer for a wife; your time is up, go back to the place from where you came, to your peasant's hut."

One favor, however, he granted her; she might take with her the one thing that was dearest and best in her eyes; and thus she was dismissed. She said, "Yes, my dear husband, if you command this, I will do it," and she embraced him and kissed him, and said she would take leave of him.

Then she ordered a powerful sleeping potion to be brought, to drink farewell to him; the King took a long drink, but she took only a little. He soon fell into a deep sleep, and when she perceived that, she called a servant and took a fair white linen cloth and wrapped the King in it, and the servant was forced to carry him into a carriage that stood before the door, and she drove with him to her own little house. She laid him in her own little bed, and he slept one day and one night without awakening, and when he awoke he looked round and said, "Good God! Where am I?" He called his attendants, but none of them were there.

At length his wife came to his bedside and said, "My dear lord and King, you told me I might bring away with me from the palace that which was dearest and most precious in my eyes. I have nothing more precious and dear than yourself, so I have brought you with me."

Tears rose to the King's eyes and he said, "Dear wife, you shall be mine and I will be yours," and he took her back with him to the royal palace and was married again to her, and at the present time they are very likely still living.

95. OLD HILDEBRAND

Once upon a time lived a peasant and his wife, and the parson of the village had a fancy for the wife, and had wished for a long while to spend a whole day happily with her. The peasant woman, too, was quite willing. One day, therefore, he said to the woman, "Listen, my dear friend, I have now thought of a way by which we can for once spend a whole day happily together. I'll tell you what; on Wednesday, you must take to your bed, and tell your husband you are ill, and if you only complain and act being ill properly, and go on doing so until Sunday when I have to preach, I will then say in my sermon that whoever has at home a sick child, a sick husband, a sick wife, a sick father, a sick mother, a sick brother or whoever else it may be, and makes a pilgrimage to the Göckerli hill in Italy, where you can get a peck of laurel leaves for a kreuzer, the sick child, the sick husband, the sick wife, the sick father, the sick mother, the sick sister, or whoever else it may be, will be restored to health immediately."

"I will manage it," said the woman promptly. Now therefore on the Wednesday, the peasant woman took to her bed, and complained and lamented as agreed on, and her husband did everything for her that he could think of, but nothing did her any good, and when Sunday came the woman said, "I feel as ill as if I were going to die at once, but there is one thing I should like to do before my end. I should like to hear the parson's sermon that he is going to preach today."

At that the peasant said, "Ah, my child, do not do it—you might make yourself worse if you were to get up. Look, I will go to the sermon, and will attend to it very carefully, and will tell you everything the parson says."

"Well," said the woman, "go, then, and pay great attention, and repeat to me all that you hear." So the peasant went to the sermon, and the parson began to preach and said, if anyone had at home a sick child, a sick husband, a sick wife, a sick father a sick mother, a sick sister, brother or anyone else, and would make a pilgrimage to the Göckerli hill in Italy, where a peck of laurel leaves costs a kreuzer, the sick child, sick husband, sick wife, sick father, sick mother, sick sister, brother, or whoever else it might be, would be restored to health instantly, and whoever wished to undertake the journey was to go to him after the service was over, and he would give him the sack for the laurel leaves and the kreuzer.

Then no one was more rejoiced than the peasant, and after the service was over, he went at once to the parson, who gave him the bag for the laurel leaves and the kreuzer. After that he went home, and even at the house door he cried, "Hurrah! Dear wife, it is now almost the same thing as if you were well! The parson has preached today that whoever had at home a sick child, a sick husband, a sick wife, a sick father, a sick mother, a sick sister, brother or whoever it might be, and would make a pilgrimage to the Göckerli hill in Italy, where a peck of laurel leaves costs a kreuzer, the sick child, sick husband, sick wife, sick father, sick mother, sick sister, brother, or whoever else it was, would be cured immediately, and now I have already got the bag and the kreuzer from the parson, and will at once begin my journey so that you may get well the faster," and thereupon he went away. He was, however, hardly gone before the woman got up, and the parson was there directly.

But now we will leave these two for a while, and follow the peasant, who walked on quickly without stopping, in order to get the sooner to the Göckerli hill, and on his way he met his gossip. His gossip was an egg merchant, and was just coming from the market, where he had sold his eggs. "May you be blessed," said the gossip, "where are you off to so fast?"

"To all eternity, my friend," said the peasant, "my wife is ill, and I have been today to hear the parson's sermon, and he preached that if anyone had in his house a sick child, a sick husband, a sick wife, a sick father, a sick mother, a sick sister, brother or anyone else, and made a pilgrimage to the Göckerli hill in Italy, where a peck of laurel leaves costs a kreuzer, the sick child, the sick husband, the sick wife, the sick father, the sick mother, the sick sister, brother or whoever else it was, would be cured immediately, and so I have got the bag for the laurel leaves and the kreuzer from the parson, and now I am beginning my pilgrimage."

"But listen, gossip," said the egg merchant to the peasant, "are you, then, stupid enough to believe such a thing as that? Don't you know what it means? The parson wants to spend a whole day alone with your wife in peace, so he has given you this job to do to get you out of the way."

"My word!" said the peasant. "How I'd like to know if that's true!"

"Come, then," said the gossip, "I'll tell you what to do. Get into my egg basket and I will carry you home, and then you will see for yourself." So that was settled, and the gossip put the peasant into his egg basket and carried him home.

When they got to the house, hurrah! But all was going merry there! The woman had already had nearly everything killed that was in the farmyard, and had made pancakes, and the parson was there, and had brought his fiddle with him. The gossip knocked at the door, and the woman asked who was there. "It is I, gossip," said the egg merchant, "give me shelter this night; I have not sold my eggs at the market, so now I have to carry them home again, and they are so heavy that I shall never be able to do it, for it is dark already."

"Indeed, my friend," said the woman, "you come at a very inconvenient time for me, but as you are here it can't be helped, come in, and take a seat there on the bench by the stove." Then she placed the gossip and the basket which he carried on his back on the bench by the stove. The parson, however, and the woman, were as merry as possible.

At length the parson said, "Listen, my dear friend, you can sing beautifully; sing something to me."

"Oh," said the woman, "I cannot sing now, in my young days indeed I could sing well enough, but that's all over now."

"Come," said the parson once more, "do sing some little song."

At that the woman began and sang,

> "I've sent my husband away from me
> To the Göckerli hill in Italy."

Thereupon the parson sang,

> "I wish 'twas a year before he came back,
> I'd never ask him for the laurel leaf sack.
> Hallelujah."

Then the gossip who was in the background began to sing (but I ought to tell you the peasant was called Hildebrand), so the gossip sang,

"What are you doing, my Hildebrand dear,
There on the bench by the stove so near?
Hallelujah."

And then the peasant sang from his basket,

"All singing I ever shall hate from this day,
And here in this basket no longer I'll stay.
Hallelujah."

And he got out of the basket, and cudgeled the parson out of the house.

96. THE THREE LITTLE BIRDS

About a thousand or more years ago, there were in this country nothing but small kings, and one of them who lived on the Keuterberg was very fond of hunting. Once on a time when he was riding forth from his castle with his hunters, three girls were watching their cows upon the mountain, and when they saw the King with all his followers, the eldest girl pointed to him, and called to the two other girls, "If I do not get that one, I will have none."

Then the second girl answered from the other side of the hill, and pointed to the one who was on the King's right hand, "Hello! Hello! If I do not get him, I will have no one."

These, however, were the two ministers. The King heard all this, and when he had come back from the chase, he had the three girls brought to him, and asked them what they had said yesterday on the mountain. This they would not tell him, so the King asked the eldest if she really would take him for her husband? Then she said, "Yes," and the two ministers married her two sisters, for they were all three fair and beautiful of face, especially the Queen, who had hair like flax.

But the two sisters had no children, and once when the King was obliged to go from home he invited them to come to the Queen in order to cheer her, for she was about to bear a child. She had a little boy who brought a bright red star into the world with him. Then the two sisters said to each other that they would throw the beautiful boy into the water. When they had thrown him in (I believe it was into the Weser) a little bird flew up into the air, which sang,

"To your death are you sped,
Until God's word be said.
In the white lily bloom,
Brave boy, is your tomb."

When the two heard that, they were frightened to death, and ran away in great haste. When the King came home they told him that the Queen had birthed a dog. Then the King said, "What God does, is well done!" But a fisherman who dwelt near the water fished the little boy out again while he was still alive, and as his wife had no children, they reared him. When a year had gone by, the King again went away, and the Queen had another little boy, whom the false sisters likewise took and threw into the water. Then up flew a little bird again and sang,

> "To your death are you sped,
> Until God's word be said.
> In the white lily bloom,
> Brave boy, is your tomb."

And when the King came back, they told him that the Queen had once more given birth to a dog, and he again said, "What God does, is well done." The fisherman, however, fished this one also out of the water, and reared him.

Then the King again journeyed forth, and the Queen had a little girl, whom also the false sisters threw into the water. Then again a little bird flew up on high and sang,

> "To your death are you sped
> Until God's word be said.
> In the white lily bloom,
> Bonny girl, is your tomb."

And when the King came home they told him that the Queen had delivered a cat. Then the King grew angry, and ordered his wife to be cast into prison, and there she was shut up for many long years.

In the meantime the children had grown up. The eldest once went out with some other boys to fish, but the other boys would not have him with them, and said, "Go your way, foundling."

Hereupon he was much troubled, and asked the old fisherman if that was true? The fisherman told him that once when he was fishing he had drawn him out of the water. So the boy said he would go forth and seek his father. The fisherman, however, entreated him to stay, but he would not let himself be hindered, and at last the fisherman consented. Then the boy went on his way and walked for many days, and at last he came to a great body of water by the side of which stood an old woman fishing. "Good day, mother," said the boy.

"Many thanks," said she.

"You will fish long enough before you catch anything."

"And you will seek long enough before you find your father. How will you get over the water?" said the woman.

"God knows."

Then the old woman took him up on her back and carried him through it, and he sought for a long time, but could not find his father.

When a year had gone by, the second boy set out to seek his brother. He came to the water, and all fared with him just as with his brother. And now there was no one at home but the daughter, and she mourned for her brothers so much that at last she also begged the fisherman to let her set forth, for she wished to go in search of her brothers. Then she likewise came to the great body of water, and she said to the old woman, "Good day, mother."

"Many thanks," replied the old woman.

"May God help you with your fishing," said the maiden. When the old woman heard that, she became quite friendly, and carried her over the water, gave her a wand, and said to her, "Go, my daughter, ever onwards by this road, and when you come to a great black dog, you must pass it silently and boldly, without either laughing or looking at it. Then you will come to a great high castle, on the threshold of which you must let the wand fall, and go straight through the castle, and out again on the other side. There you will see an old fountain out of which a large tree has grown, whereon hangs a bird in a cage which you must take down. Take likewise a glass of water out of the fountain, and with these two things go back by the same way. Pick up the wand again from the threshold and take it with you, and when you again pass by the dog, strike him in the face with it, but be sure that you hit him, and then just come back here to me." The maiden found everything exactly as the old woman had said, and on her way back she found her two brothers who had sought each other over half the world. They went together to the place where the black dog was lying on the road; she struck it in the face, and it turned into a handsome prince who went with them to the river. There the old woman was still standing. She rejoiced much to see them again, and carried them all over the water, and then she too went away, for now she was freed. The others, however, went to the old fisherman, and all were glad that they had found each other again, but they hung the bird on the wall.

But the second son could not settle at home, and took his crossbow and went hunting. When he was tired he took his flute, and made music.

The King was hunting too, and heard that and went there, and when he met the youth, he said, "Who has given you leave to hunt here?"

"Oh, no one."

"To whom do you belong, then?"

"I am the fisherman's son."

"But he has no children."

"If you will not believe, come with me."

That the King did, and questioned the fisherman, who told everything to him, and the little bird on the wall began to sing,

"The mother sits alone
There in the prison small,
O King of royal blood,
These are your children all.
The sisters both so false,
They wrought the children woe,
There in the waters deep
Where the fishermen come and go."

Then they were all terrified, and the King took the bird, the fisherman and the three children back with him to the castle, and ordered the prison to be opened and brought his wife out again. She had, however, grown quite ill and weak. Then the daughter gave her some of the water of the fountain to drink, and she became strong and healthy. But the two false sisters were burned, and the daughter married the prince.

97. THE WATER OF LIFE

There was once a King who had an illness, and no one believed that he would come out of it with his life. He had three sons who were much distressed about it, and went down into the palace garden and wept. There they met an old man who inquired as to the cause of their grief. They told him that their father was so ill that he would most certainly die, for nothing seemed to cure him. Then the old man said, "I know of one more remedy, and that is the water of life; if he drinks of it he will become well again; but it is hard to find."

The eldest said, "I will manage to find it," and went to the sick King, and begged to be allowed to go forth in search of the water of life, for that alone could save him.

"No," said the King, "the danger of it is too great. I would rather die." But he begged so long that the King consented.

The prince thought in his heart, "If I bring the water, then I shall be best beloved of my father, and shall inherit the Kingdom."

So he set out, and when he had ridden forth a little distance, a dwarf stood there in the road who called to him and said, "Where away so fast?"

"Silly shrimp," said the prince, very haughtily, "it is nothing to do with you," and rode on. But the little dwarf had grown angry, and had wished an evil wish. Soon after this the prince entered a ravine, and the further he rode the closer the mountains drew together, and at last the road became so narrow that he could not advance a step further; it was impossible either to turn his horse or to dismount from the saddle, and he was shut in there as if in prison. The sick King waited long for him, but he did not come.

Then the second son said, "Father, let me go forth to seek the water," and thought to himself, "If my brother is dead, then the Kingdom will fall to me."

At first the King would not allow him to go either, but at last he yielded, so the prince set out on the same road that his brother had taken, and he too met the dwarf, who stopped him to ask, where was he going in such haste? "Little shrimp," said the prince, "that is nothing to you," and rode on without giving him another look. But the dwarf bewitched him, and he, like the other, rode into a ravine, and could neither go forwards nor backwards. So fare haughty people.

As the second son also remained away, the youngest begged to be allowed to go forth to fetch the water, and at last the King was obliged to let him go. When he met the dwarf and the latter asked him where he was going in such haste, he stopped, gave him an explanation, and said, "I am seeking the water of life, for my father is sick unto death."

"Do you know, then, where that is to be found?"

"No," said the prince.

"As you have borne yourself kindly, and not haughtily like your false brothers, I will give you the information and tell you how you may obtain the water of life. It springs from a fountain in the courtyard of an enchanted castle, but you will not be able to make your way to it, if I do not give you an iron wand and two small loaves of bread. Strike thrice with the wand on the iron door of the castle and it will spring open: inside lie two lions with gaping jaws, but if you throw a loaf to each of them, they will be quieted. Then hasten to fetch some of the water of life before the clock strikes twelve, else the door will shut again, and you will be imprisoned."

The prince thanked him, took the wand and the bread, and set out on his way. When he arrived, everything was as the dwarf had said. The door sprang open at the third stroke of the wand, and when he had appeased the lions with the bread, he entered the castle, and came to a large and splendid hall, wherein sat some enchanted princes whose rings he drew off their fingers. A sword and a loaf of bread were lying there, which he carried away. After this, he entered a chamber, in which was a beautiful maiden who rejoiced when she saw him, kissed him, and told him that he had delivered her, and should have the whole of her kingdom, and that if he would return in a year their wedding should be celebrated; likewise she told him where the spring of the water of life was, and that he was to hasten and draw some of it before the clock struck twelve. Then he went onwards, and at last entered a room where there was a beautiful newly-made bed, and as he was very weary, he felt inclined to rest a little. So he lay down and fell asleep.

When he awoke, it was striking a quarter to twelve. He sprang up in a fright, ran to the spring, drew some water in a cup which stood near, and hastened away. But just as he was passing through the iron door, the clock struck twelve, and the door fell to with such violence that it carried away a piece of his heel. He, however, rejoiced at having obtained the water of life, went homewards, and again passed the dwarf.

When the latter saw the sword and the loaf, he said, "With these you have won great wealth; with the sword you can slay whole armies, and the bread will never come to an end."

But the prince would not go home to his father without his brothers, and said, "Dear dwarf, can you not tell me where my two brothers are? They went out before I did in search of the water of life, and have not returned."

"They are imprisoned between two mountains," said the dwarf. "I have condemned them to stay there, because they were so haughty." Then the prince begged until the dwarf released them; but he warned him, however, and said, "Beware of them, for they have bad hearts."

When his brothers came, he rejoiced, and told them how things had gone with him, that he had found the water of life and had brought a cupful away with him, and had rescued a beautiful princess, who was willing to wait a year for him, and then their wedding was to be celebrated and he would obtain a great kingdom. After that they rode on together, and chanced upon a land where war and famine reigned, and the King already thought he must perish, for the scarcity was so great. Then the prince went to him and gave him the loaf, with which he fed and satisfied the whole of his Kingdom, and then the prince gave him the sword too with which he slew the hosts of his enemies, and could now live in rest and peace. The prince then took back his loaf and his sword, and the three brothers rode on. But after this they entered two more countries where war and famine reigned and each time the prince gave his loaf and his sword to the Kings, and had now delivered three kingdoms, and after that they went on board a ship and sailed over the sea.

During the passage, the two eldest conversed apart and said, "The youngest has found the water of life and not we, for that our father will give him the Kingdom the Kingdom which belongs to us, and he will rob us of all our fortune." They then began to seek revenge, and plotted with each other to destroy him. They waited until they found him fast asleep, then they poured the water of life out of the cup, and took it for themselves, but into the cup they poured salt seawater. Now therefore, when they arrived home, the youngest took his cup to the sick King in order that he might drink out of it, and be cured. But scarcely had he drunk a very little of the salt seawater than he became still worse than before. And as he was lamenting over this, the two eldest brothers came, and accused the youngest of having intended to poison him, and said that they had brought him the true water of life, and handed it to him. He had scarcely tasted it, when he felt his sickness departing, and became strong and healthy as in the days of his youth.

After that they both went to the youngest, mocked him, and said, "You certainly found the water of life, but you have had the pain, and we the gain; you should have been sharper, and should have kept your eyes open. We took it from you while you were asleep at sea, and when a year is over, one of us will go and fetch the beautiful princess. But beware that you do not disclose any of this to our father; indeed he does not trust you, and if you say a single word, you shall lose your life into the bargain, but if you keep silent, you shall have it as a gift."

The old King was angry with his youngest son, and thought he had plotted against his life. So he summoned the court together and had sentence pronounced upon his son, that he should be secretly shot. And once when the prince was riding forth to the chase, suspecting no evil, the King's hunter had to go with him, and when they were quite alone in the forest, the hunter looked so sorrowful that the prince said to him, "Dear hunter, what ails you?"

The hunter said, "I cannot tell you, and yet I ought."

Then the prince said, "Say openly what it is, I will pardon you."

"Alas!" said the hunter, "I am to shoot you dead, the King has ordered me to do it."

Then the prince was shocked, and said, "Dear hunter, let me live; there, I give you my royal garments; give me your common ones in their stead."

The hunter said, "I will willingly do that, indeed I should not have been able to shoot you." Then they exchanged clothes, and the hunter returned home; the prince, however, went further into the forest.

After a time three wagons of gold and precious stones came to the King for his youngest son, which were sent by the three Kings who had slain their enemies with the prince's sword, and maintained their people with his bread, and who wished to show their gratitude for it. The old King then thought, "Can my son have been innocent?" and said to his people, "Would that he were still alive, how it grieves me that I have suffered him to be killed!"

"He still lives," said the hunter, "I could not find it in my heart to carry out your command," and told the King how it had happened. Then a stone fell from the King's heart, and he had it proclaimed in every country that his son might return and be taken into favor again.

The princess, however, had a road made up to her palace which was quite bright and golden, and told her people that whoever came riding straight along it to her, would be the right wooer and was to be admitted, and whoever rode by the side of it, was not the right one, and was not to be admitted. As the time was now close at hand, the eldest thought he would hasten to go to the King's daughter, and give himself out as her deliverer, and thus win her for his bride, and the Kingdom to boot. Therefore he rode forth, and when he arrived in front of the palace, and saw the splendid golden road, he thought, it would be a sin and a shame if he were to ride over that, and turned aside, and rode on the right side of it. But when he came to the door, the servants told him that he was not the right man, and was to go away again. Soon after this the second prince set out, and when he came to the golden road, and his horse had put one foot on it, he thought, it would be a sin and a shame to tread a piece of it off, and he turned aside and rode on the left side of it, and when he reached the door, the attendants told him he was not the right one, and he was to go away again. When at last the year had entirely expired, the third son likewise wished to ride out of the forest to his beloved, and with her forget his sorrows. So he set out and thought of her so incessantly, and wished to be with her so much, that he never noticed the golden road at all. So his horse rode onwards up the middle of it, and when he came to the door, it was opened and the princess received him with joy, and said he was her deliverer, and lord of the kingdom, and their wedding was celebrated with great rejoicing. When it was over she told him that his father invited him to come to him, and had forgiven him. So he rode there, and told him everything; how his brothers had betrayed him, and how he had nevertheless kept silence. The old King wished to punish them, but they had gone to sea, and never came back as long as they lived.

98. *DOCTOR KNOWALL*

There was once on a time a poor peasant called Crabb, who drove with two oxen a load of wood to the town, and sold it to a doctor for two talkers. When the money was being counted out to him, it so happened that the doctor was sitting at table, and when the peasant saw how daintily he ate and drank, his heart desired what he saw, and he would willingly have been a doctor too. So he remained standing a while, and at length inquired if he too could not be a doctor. "Oh, yes," said the doctor, "that is soon managed."

"What must I do?" asked the peasant.

"In the first place buy yourself an ABC book of the kind which has a cock on the frontispiece: in the second, turn your cart and your two oxen into money, and get yourself some clothes, and whatever else pertains to medicine; thirdly, have a sign painted for yourself with the words, "I am Doctor Knowall," and have that nailed up above your door."

The peasant did everything that he had been told to do. When he had doctored people awhile, but not long, a rich and great lord had some money stolen. Then he was told about Doctor Knowall who lived in such and such a village, and must know what had become of the money. So the lord had the horses put in his carriage, drove out to the village, and asked Crabb if he were Doctor Knowall? Yes, he was, he said. Then he was to go with him and bring back the stolen money. "Oh, yes, but Grethe, my wife, must go too." The lord was willing and let both of them have a seat in the carriage, and they all drove away together.

When they came to the nobleman's castle, the table was spread, and Crabb was told to sit down and eat. "Yes, but my wife, Grethe, too," said he, and he seated himself with her at the table. And when the first servant came with a dish of delicate fare, the peasant nudged his wife, and said, "Grethe, that was the first," meaning that was the servant who brought the first dish.

The servant, however, thought he intended by that to say, "That is the first thief," and as he actually was so, he was terrified, and said to his comrade outside, "The doctor knows all: we shall fare ill, he said I was the first."

The second did not want to go in at all, but was forced. So when he went in with his dish, the peasant nudged his wife, and said, "Grethe, that is the second." This servant was just as much alarmed, and he got out. The third did not fare better, for the peasant again said, "Grethe, that is the third." The fourth had to carry in a dish that was covered, and the lord told the doctor that he was to show his skill, and guess what was beneath the cover. The doctor looked at the dish, had no idea what it was, and cried, "Ah, poor Crabb."

When the lord heard that, he cried, "There! He knows it, he knows who has the money!"

On this the servants looked terribly uneasy, and made a sign to the doctor that they wished him to step outside for a moment. When therefore he went out, all four of them confessed to him that they had stolen the money, and said that they would willingly restore it and give him a heavy sum into the bargain, if he would not denounce them, for if he did they would be hanged. They led him to the spot where the money was concealed. With this the doctor was satisfied, and returned to the hall, sat down to the table, and said, "My lord, now I will search in my book where the gold is hidden." The fifth servant, however, crept into the stove to hear if the doctor knew still more. The Doctor, however, sat still and opened his ABC book, turned the pages backwards and forwards, and looked for the cock. As he could not find it immediately he said, "I know you are there, so you had better show yourself."

Then the fellow in the stove thought that the doctor meant him, and full of terror, sprang out, crying, "That man knows everything!" Then Dr. Knowall showed the count where the money was, but did not say who had stolen it, and received from both sides much money in reward, and became a renowned man.

99. *THE SPIRIT IN THE BOTTLE*

There was once a poor woodcutter who toiled from early morning till late night. When at last he had laid by some money he said to his boy, "You are my only child, I will spend the money which I have earned with the sweat of my brow on your education; if you learn some honest trade you can support me in my old age, when my limbs have grown stiff and I am obliged to stay at home." Then the boy went to a high school and learned diligently so that his masters praised him, and he remained there a long time. When he had worked through two classes, but was still not yet perfect in everything, the little pittance which the father had earned was all spent, and the boy was obliged to return home to him.

"Ah," said the father, sorrowfully, "I can give you no more, and in these hard times I cannot earn a farthing more than will suffice for our daily bread."

"Dear father," answered the son, "don't trouble yourself about it, if it is God's will, it will turn to my advantage I shall soon accustom myself to it." When the father wanted to go into the forest to earn money by helping to pile and stack wood and also chop it, the son said, "I will go with you and help you."

"Nay, my son," said the father, "that would be hard for you; you are not accustomed to rough work, and will not be able to bear it, besides I have only one axe and no money left to buy another."

"Just go to the neighbor," answered the son, "he will lend you his axe until I have earned one for myself."

The father then borrowed an axe of the neighbor, and next morning at break of day they went out into the forest together. The son helped his father and was quite merry and brisk about it. But when the sun was right over their heads, the father said, "We will rest, and have our dinner, and then we shall work as well again."

The son took his bread in his hands, and said, "Just you rest, father, I am not tired; I will walk up and down a little in the forest, and look for birds' nests."

"Oh, you fool," said the father, "why should you want to run about there? Afterwards you will be tired, and no longer able to raise your arm; stay here, and sit down beside me."

The son, however, went into the forest, ate his bread, was very merry and peered in among the green branches to see if he could discover a bird's nest anywhere. So he went up and down to see if he could find a bird's nest until at last he came to a great dangerous-looking oak, which certainly was already many hundred years old, and which five men could not have spanned. He stood still and looked at it, and thought, "Many a bird must have built its nest in that."

Then all at once it seemed to him that he heard a voice. He listened and became aware that someone was crying in a very smothered voice, "Let me out, let me out!"

He looked around, but could discover nothing; nevertheless, he fancied that the voice came out of the ground. Then he cried, "Where are you?"

The voice answered, "I am down here among the roots of the oak tree. Let me out! Let me out!"

The scholar began to loosen the earth under the tree, and search among the roots, until at last he found a glass bottle in a little hollow. He lifted it up and held it against the light, and then saw a creature shaped like a frog, springing up and down in it. "Let me out! Let me out!" it cried anew, and the scholar thinking no evil, drew the cork out of the bottle. Immediately a spirit ascended from it, and began to grow, and grew so fast that in a very few moments he stood before the scholar, a terrible fellow as big as half the tree by which he was standing.

"Do you know," he cried in an awful voice, "what your wages are for having let me out?"

"No," replied the scholar fearlessly, "how should I know that?"

"Then I will tell you," cried the spirit; "I must strangle you for it."

"You should have told me that sooner," said the scholar, "for I should then have left you shut up, but my head shall stand fast for all you can do; more persons than one must be consulted about that."

"More persons here, more persons there," said the spirit. "You shall have the wages you have earned. Do you think that I was shut up there for such a long time as a favor? No, it was a punishment for me. I am the mighty Mercurius. Whoever releases me, I must strangle."

"Softly," answered the scholar, "not so fast. I must first know that you really were shut up in that little bottle, and that you are the right spirit. If, indeed, you can get in again, I will believe and then you may do as you will with me."

The spirit said haughtily, "That is a very trifling feat," drew himself together, and made himself as small and slender as he had been at first, so that he crept through the same opening, and right through the neck of the bottle in again. Scarcely was he inside than the scholar thrust the cork he had drawn back into the bottle, and threw it among the roots of the oak into its old place, and the spirit was betrayed.

And now the scholar was about to return to his father, but the spirit cried very piteously, "Ah, do let me out! Ah, do let me out!"

"No," answered the scholar, "not a second time! He who has once tried to take my life shall not be set free by me, now that I have caught him again."

"If you will set me free," said the spirit, "I will give you so much that you will have plenty all the days of your life."

"No," answered the boy, "you would cheat me as you did the first time."

"You are playing away with your own good luck," said the spirit; "I will do you no harm but will reward you richly."

The scholar thought, "I will venture it, perhaps he will keep his word, and anyhow he shall not get the better of me." Then he took out the cork, and the spirit rose up from the bottle as he had done before, stretched himself out and became as big as a giant.

"Now you shall have your reward," said he, and handed the scholar a little bag just like a plaster, and said, "If you spread one end of this over a wound it will heal, and if you rub steel or iron with the other end it will be changed into silver."

"I must just try that," said the scholar, and went to a tree, tore off the bark with his axe, and rubbed it with one end of the plaster. It immediately closed together and was healed. "Now, it is all right," he said to the spirit, "and we can part." The spirit thanked him for his release, and the boy thanked the spirit for his present, and went back to his father.

"Where have you been racing about?" said the father, "Why have you forgotten your work? I said at once that you would never get on with anything."

"Be easy, father, I will make it up."

"Make it up indeed," said the father angrily, "there's no art in that."

"Take care, father, I will soon hew that tree there, so that it will split." Then he took his plaster, rubbed the axe with it, and dealt a mighty blow, but as the iron had changed into silver, the edge turned;

"Hollo, father, just look what a bad axe you've given me, it has become quite crooked."

The father was shocked and said, "Ah, what have you done? Now I shall have to pay for that, and have not the wherewithal, and that is all the good I have got by your work."

"Don't get angry," said the son, "I will soon pay for the axe."

"Oh, you blockhead," cried the father, "with what will you pay for it? You have nothing but what I give you. These are students' tricks that are sticking in your head, but you have no idea of woodcutting."

After a while the scholar said, "Father, I can really work no more, we had better take a holiday."

"Eh, what!" answered he, "Do you think I will sit with my hands lying in my lap like you? I must go on working, but you may take yourself off home."

"Father, I am here in this wood for the first time, I don't know my way alone. Do go with me."

As his anger had now abated, the father at last let himself be persuaded and went home with him. Then he said to the son, "Go and sell your damaged axe, and see what you can get for it, and I must earn the difference, in order to pay the neighbor."

The son took the axe, and carried it into town to a goldsmith, who tested it, laid it in the scales, and said, "It is worth four hundred thalers, I have not so much as that with me."

The son said, "Give me what you have, I will lend you the rest." The goldsmith gave him three hundred thalers, and remained a hundred in his debt. The son thereupon went home and said, "Father, I have got the money, go and ask the neighbor what he wants for the axe."

"I know that already," answered the old man, "one thaler, six groschen."

"Then give him two thalers, twelve groschen, that is double and enough; see, I have money in plenty," and he gave the father a hundred thalers, and said, "You shall never know want, live as comfortably as you like."

"Good heavens!" said the father, "How have you come by these riches?" The scholar then told how all had come to pass, and how he, trusting in his luck, had made such a good hit. But with the money that was left, he went back to the high school and went on learning more, and as he could heal all wounds with his plaster, he became the most famous doctor in the whole world.

100. THE DEVIL'S SOOTY BROTHER

A disbanded soldier had nothing to live on, and did not know how to get on. So he went out into the forest and when he had walked for a short time, he met a little man who was, however, the Devil. The little man said to him, "What ails you, you seem so very sorrowful?"

Then the soldier said, "I am hungry, but have no money."

The Devil said, "If you will hire yourself to me, and be my serving-man, you shall have enough for all your life. You shall serve me for seven years, and after that you shall again be free. But one thing I must tell you, and that is, you must not wash, comb, or trim yourself, or cut your hair or nails, or wipe the water from your eyes."

The soldier said, "All right, if there is no help for it," and went off with the little man, who straightway led him down into hell. Then he told him what he had to do. He was to poke the fire under the kettles wherein the hell-broth was stewing, keep the house clean, drive all the sweepings behind the doors, and see that everything was in order, but if he once peeped into the kettles, it would go ill with him. The soldier said, "Good, I will take care."

And then the old Devil went out again on his wanderings, and the soldier entered upon his new duties, made the fire, and swept the dirt well behind the doors, just as he had been bidden. When the old Devil came back again, he looked to see if all had been done, appeared satisfied, and went forth a second time.

The soldier now took a good look on every side; the kettles were standing all round hell with a mighty fire below them, and inside they were boiling and sputtering. He would have given anything to look inside them, if the Devil had not so particularly forbidden him: at last, he could no longer restrain himself, slightly raised the lid of the first kettle, and peeped in, and there he saw his former corporal shut in. "Aha, old bird!" said he, "Do I meet you here? You once had me in your power, now I have you," and he quickly let the lid fall, poked the fire, and added a fresh log.

After that, he went to the second kettle, raised its lid also a little, and peeped in; his former ensign was in that. "Aha, old bird, so I find you here! You once had me in your power, now I have you." He closed the lid again, and fetched yet another log to make it really hot.

Then he wanted to see who might be sitting up in the third kettle—it was actually a general. "Aha, old bird, do I meet you here? Once you had me in your power, now I have you." And he fetched the bellows and made hell-fire blaze right under him.

So he did his work seven years in hell, did not wash, comb, or trim himself, or cut his hair or nails, or wash the water out of his eyes, and the seven years seemed so short to him that he thought he had only been half a year. Now when the time had fully gone by, the Devil came and said, "Well Hans, what have you done?"

"I poked the fire under the kettles, and I have swept all the dirt well behind the doors."

"But you have peeped into the kettles as well; it is lucky for you that you added fresh logs to them, or else your life would have been forfeited; now that your time is up, will you go home again?"

"Yes," said the soldier, "I should very much like to see what my father is doing at home."

The Devil said, "In order that you may receive the wages you have earned, go and fill your knapsack full of the sweepings, and take it home with you. You must also go unwashed and uncombed, with long hair on your head and beard, and with uncut nails and dim eyes, and when you are asked where you are from, you must say, "From hell," and when you are asked who you are, you are to say, "The Devil's sooty brother, and my King as well."

The soldier held his peace, and did as the Devil bade him, but he was not at all satisfied with his wages. Then as soon as he was up in the forest again, he took his knapsack from his back, to empty it, but on opening it, the sweepings had become pure gold. "I should never have expected that," said he, and was well pleased, and entered the town.

The landlord was standing in front of the inn, and when he saw the soldier approaching, he was terrified, because Hans looked so horrible, worse than a scarecrow. He called to him and asked, "Where do you come from?"

"From hell."

"Who are you?"

"The Devil's sooty brother, and my King as well."

Then the host would not let him enter, but when Hans showed him the gold, he came and unlatched the door himself. Hans then ordered the best room and attendance, ate, and drank his fill, but neither washed nor combed himself as the Devil had bidden him, and at last lay down to sleep. But the knapsack full of gold remained before the eyes of the landlord, and left him no peace, and during the night he crept in and stole it away.

Next morning, however, when Hans got up and wanted to pay the landlord and travel further, his knapsack was gone! But he soon composed himself and thought, "You have been unfortunate from no fault of your own," and straightway went back again to hell, complained of his misfortune to the old Devil, and begged for his help.

The Devil said, "Seat yourself, I will wash, comb, and trim you, cut your hair and nails, and wash your eyes for you," and when he had done with him, he gave him the knapsack back again full of sweepings, and said, "Go and tell the landlord that he must return you your money, or else I will come and fetch him, and he shall poke the fire in your place."

Hans went up and said to the landlord, "You have stolen my money; if you do not return it, you shall go down to hell in my place, and will look as horrible as I." Then the landlord gave him the money, and more besides, only begging him to keep it secret, and Hans was now a rich man.

He set out on his way home to his father, bought himself a shabby smock-frock to wear, and strolled about making music, for he had learned to do that while he was with the Devil in hell. There was however, an old King in that country, before whom he had to play, and the King was so delighted with his playing, that he promised him his eldest daughter in marriage. But when she heard that she was to be married to a common fellow in a smock-frock, she said, "Rather than do that, I would go into the deepest water."

Then the King gave him the youngest, who was quite willing to do it to please her father, and thus the Devil's sooty brother got the King's daughter, and when the aged King died, the whole Kingdom likewise.

101. BEARSKIN

There was once a young fellow who enlisted as a soldier, conducted himself bravely, and was always the foremost when it rained bullets. So long as the war lasted, all went well, but when peace was made, he received his dismissal, and the captain said he might go where he liked. His parents were dead, and he had no longer a home, so he went to his brothers and begged them to take him in, and keep him until war broke out again. The brothers, however, were hardhearted and said, "What can we do with you? You are of no use to us; go and make a living for yourself."

The soldier had nothing left but his gun; he took that on his shoulder, and went forth into the world. He came to a wide heath, on which nothing was to be seen but a circle of trees; under these he sat sorrowfully down, and began to think over his fate. "I have no money," thought he, "I have learned no trade but that of fighting, and now that they have made peace they don't want me any longer; so I see beforehand that I shall have to starve."

All at once he heard a rustling, and when he looked round, a strange man stood before him, who wore a green coat and looked right stately, but had a hideous cloven foot. "I know already what you are in need of," said the man; "gold and possessions you shall have, as much as you can make away with, do what you will, but first I must know if you are fearless, that I may not bestow my money in vain."

"A soldier and fear—how can those two things go together?" he answered; "You can put me to the proof."

"Very well, then," answered the man, "look behind you." The soldier turned round, and saw a large bear, which came growling towards him.

"Oho!" cried the soldier, "I will tickle your nose for you, so that you shall soon lose your fancy for growling," and he aimed at the bear and shot it through the muzzle; it fell down and never stirred again.

"I see quite well," said the stranger, "that you are not wanting in courage, but there is still another condition which you will have to fulfill."

"If it does not endanger my salvation," replied the soldier, who knew very well who was standing by him. "If it does, I'll have nothing to do with it."

"You will look to that for yourself," answered Greencoat; "you shall for the next seven years neither wash yourself, nor comb your beard, nor your hair, nor cut your nails, nor say one paternoster. I will give you a coat and a cloak, which during this time you must wear. If you die during these seven years, you are mine; if you remain alive, you are free, and rich to boot, for all the rest of your life." The soldier thought of the great extremity in which he now found himself, and as he so often had gone to meet death, he resolved to risk it now also, and agreed to the terms. The Devil took off his green coat, gave it to the soldier, and said, "If you have this coat on your back and put your hand into the pocket, you will always find it full of money." Then he pulled the skin off the bear and said, "This shall be your cloak, and your bed also, for on this you shall sleep, and in no other bed shall you lie, and because of this apparel you shall be called Bearskin." After this the Devil vanished.

The soldier put the coat on, felt at once in the pocket, and found that the thing was really true. Then he put on the bearskin and went forth into the world, and enjoyed himself, refraining from nothing that did him good and his money harm. During the first year his appearance was passable, but during the second he began to look like a monster. His hair covered nearly the whole of his face, his beard was like a piece of coarse felt, his fingers had claws, and his face was so covered with dirt that if cress had been sown on it, it would have grown. Whoever saw him, ran away, but as he always gave the poor money to pray that he might not die during the seven years, and as he paid well for everything he still always found shelter. In the fourth year, he entered an inn where the landlord would not receive him, and would not even let him have a place in the stable, because he was afraid the horses would be scared. But as Bearskin thrust his hand into his pocket and pulled out a handful of ducats, the host let himself be persuaded and gave him a room in an outhouse. Bearskin was, however, obliged to promise not to let himself be seen, lest the inn should get a bad name.

As Bearskin was sitting alone in the evening, and wishing from the bottom of his heart that the seven years were over, he heard a loud lamenting in a neighboring room. He had a compassionate heart, so he opened the door, and saw an old man weeping bitterly, and wringing his hands. Bearskin went nearer, but the man sprang to his feet and tried to escape from him. At last when the man perceived that Bearskin's voice was human he let himself be prevailed on, and by kind words bearskin succeeded so far that the old man revealed the cause of his grief. His property had dwindled away by degrees, he and his daughters would have to starve, and he was so poor that he could not pay the innkeeper, and was to be put in prison. "If that is your only trouble," said Bearskin, "I have plenty of money." He had the innkeeper brought there, paid him and put a purse full of gold into the poor old man's pocket besides.

When the old man saw himself set free from all his troubles he did not know how to be grateful enough. "Come with me," said he to Bearskin; "my daughters are all miracles of beauty, choose one of them for yourself as a wife. When she hears what you have done for me, she will not refuse you. You do in truth look a little strange, but she will soon put you to rights again." This pleased Bearskin well, and he went.

When the eldest saw him she was so terribly alarmed at his face that she screamed and ran away. The second stood still and looked at him from head to foot, but then she said, "How can I accept a husband who no longer has a human form? The shaven bear that once was here and passed itself off for a man pleased me far better, for at any rate it wore a hussar's dress and white gloves. If it were nothing but ugliness, I might get used to that."

The youngest, however, said, "Dear father, that must be a good man to have helped you out of your trouble, so if you have promised him a bride for doing it, your promise must be kept."

It was a pity that Bearskin's face was covered with dirt and with hair, for if not they might have seen how delighted he was when he heard these words. He took a ring from his finger, broke it in two, and gave her one half, the other he kept for himself. He wrote his name, however, on her half, and hers on his, and begged her to keep her piece carefully, and then he took his leave and said, "I must still wander about for three years, and if I do not return then, you are free, for I shall be dead. But pray to God to preserve my life."

The poor betrothed bride dressed herself entirely in black, and when she thought of her future bridegroom, tears came into her eyes. Nothing but contempt and mockery fell to her lot from her sisters. "Take care," said the eldest, "if you give him your hand, he will strike his claws into it."

"Beware!" said the second. "Bears like sweet things, and if he takes a fancy to you, he will eat you up."

"You must always do as he likes," began the elder again, "or else he will growl."

And the second continued, "But the wedding will be a merry one, for bears dance well."

The bride was silent, and did not let them vex her. Bearskin, however, traveled about the world from one place to another, did good where he was able, and gave generously to the poor that they might pray for him.

At length, as the last day of the seven years dawned, he went once more out onto the heath, and seated himself beneath the circle of trees. It was not long before the wind whistled, and the Devil stood before him and looked angrily at him; then he threw Bearskin his old coat, and asked for his own green one back. "We have not got so far as that yet," answered Bearskin, "you must first make me clean." Whether the Devil liked it or not, he was forced to fetch water, and wash Bearskin, comb his hair, and cut his nails. After this, he looked like a brave soldier, and was much handsomer than he had ever been before.

When the Devil had gone away, Bearskin was quite lighthearted. He went into the town, put on a magnificent velvet coat, seated himself in a carriage drawn by four white horses, and drove to his bride's house. No one recognized him, the father took him for a distinguished general, and led him into the room where his daughters were sitting. He was forced to place himself between the two eldest, they helped him to wine, gave him the best pieces of meat, and thought that in all the world they had never seen a handsomer man. The bride, however, sat opposite to him in her black dress, and never raised her eyes, nor spoke a word. When at length he asked the father if he would give him one of his daughters to wed, the two eldest jumped up, and ran into their bedrooms to put on splendid dresses, for each of them fancied she was the chosen one. The stranger, as soon as he was alone with his bride, brought out his half of the ring, and threw it in a glass of wine which he reached across the table to her. She took the wine, but when she had drunk it, and found the half ring lying at the bottom, her heart began to beat. She got the other half, which she wore on a ribbon round her neck, joined them, and saw that the two pieces fitted exactly together. Then said he, "I am your betrothed bridegroom, whom you saw as Bearskin, but through God's grace I have again received my human form, and have once more become clean." He went up to her, embraced her, and gave her a kiss.

In the meantime the two sisters came back in full dress, and when they saw that the handsome man had fallen to the share of the youngest, and heard that he was Bearskin, they ran out full of anger and rage. One of them drowned herself in the well, the other hanged herself on a tree. In the evening, someone knocked at the door, and when the bridegroom opened it, it was the Devil in his green coat, who said, "You see, I have now got two souls in the place of your one!"